Timeless Legends

These great stories from Greek, Roman and Norse mythology are the fountainhead of all literature. In them, the figures of antiquity come vividly to life.

Here are the gods of high Olympus—mighty Zeus, all too human, and Hera, prototype of the jealous wife. Here are the famous love stories of Cupid and Psyche, Pyramus and Thisbe, and Pygmalion and Galatea; the thrilling adventures of Jason and the perilous Quest of the Golden Fleece; the Trojan War, and the superhuman achievements of Odysseus and Aeneas. And here too, you'll meet the families whose turbulent histories formed the plots of the famous Greek plays—Agamemnon and his children; tragic Oedipus and heroic Antigone. And from Norse mythology come the stirring legends of Signy and Sigurd—tragic tales of love, death and heroism.

Renowned for her love and understanding of classic literature, Edith Hamilton has retold these great myths for modern readers in a way that preserves the flavor and excitement of the originals.

"Classical mythology has long needed such a popular exposition as Miss Edith Hamilton has given us in this volume, which is at once a reference book and a book which may be read for stimulation and pleasure."—*New York Times*

"Mythology as it should be written . . . She has the rare quality which is able to penetrate into modes of thought not our own and to transcribe the spirit of another age."—*Book-of-the-Month Club News*

MYTHOLOGY

By EDITH HAMILTON

Illustrated
by Steele Savage

A MENTOR BOOK from.
NEW AMERICAN LIBRARY
TIMES MIRROR
New York and Scarborough, Ontario
The New English Library Limited, London

Foreword

A book on Mythology must draw from widely different sources. Twelve hundred years separate the first writers through whom the myths have come down to us from the last, and there are stories as unlike each other as "Cinderella" and "King Lear." To bring them all together in one volume is really somewhat comparable to doing the same for the stories of English literature from Chaucer to the ballads, through Shakespeare and Marlowe and Swift and Defoe and Dryden and Pope and so on, ending with, say, Tennyson and Browning, or even, to make the comparison truer, Kipling and Galsworthy. The English collection would be bigger, but it would not contain more dissimilar material. In point of fact, Chaucer is more like Galsworthy and the ballads like Kipling than Homer is like Lucian or Aeschylus like Ovid.

Faced with this problem, I determined at the outset to dismiss any idea of unifying the tales. That would have meant either writing "King Lear," so to speak, down to the level of "Cinderella"—the vice versa procedure being obviously not possible—or else telling in my own way stories which were in no sense mine and had been told by great writers in ways they thought suited their subjects. I do not mean, of course, that a great writer's style can be reproduced or that I should dream of attempting such a feat. My aim has been nothing more ambitious than to keep distinct for the reader the very different writers from whom our knowledge of the myths comes. For example, Hesiod is a notably simple writer and devout; he is naïve, even childish, sometimes crude, always full of piety. Many of the stories in this book are told only by him. Side by side with them are stories told only by Ovid, subtle, polished, artificial, self-conscious, and the complete skeptic. My effort has been to make the reader see some difference between writers who were so different. After all, when one takes up a book like this one does not ask how entertainingly the author has retold the stories, but how close he has brought the reader to the original.

My hope is that those who do not know the classics will gain in this way not only a knowledge of the myths, but some little idea of what the writers were like who told them—who have been proved, by two thousand years and more, to be immortal.

Contents

Illustrations

Introduction To Classical Mythology

Of old the Hellenic race was marked off from the barbarian as more keen-witted and more free from nonsense.

HERODOTUS I: 60.

Greek and Roman mythology is quite generally supposed to show us the way the human race thought and felt untold ages ago. Through it, according to this view, we can retrace the path from civilized man who lives so far from nature, to man who lived in close companionship with nature; and the real interest of the myths is that they lead us back to a time when the world was young and people had a connection with the earth, with trees and seas and flowers and hills, unlike anything we ourselves can feel. When the stories were being shaped, we are given to understand, little distinction had as yet been made between the real and the unreal. The imagination was vividly alive and not checked by the reason, so that anyone in the woods might see through the trees a fleeing nymph, or bending over a clear pool to drink, behold in the depths a naiad's face.

The prospect of traveling back to this delightful state of things is held out by nearly every writer who touches upon classical mythology, above all by the poets. In that infinitely remote time primitive man could

> Have sight of Proteus rising from the sea;
> Or hear old Triton blow his wreathèd horn.

And we for a moment can catch, through the myths he made, a glimpse of that strangely and beautifully animated world.

But a very brief consideration of the ways of uncivilized peoples everywhere and in all ages is enough to prick that romantic bubble. Nothing is clearer than the fact that primitive man, whether in New Guinea today or eons ago in the prehistoric wilderness, is not and never has been a creature who peoples his world with bright fancies and lovely visions. Horrors lurked in the primeval forest, not nymphs and naiads. Terror lived there, with its close attendant, Magic, and its most common defense, Human Sacrifice. Mankind's chief hope of escaping the wrath of whatever divinities were then abroad lay in some magical rite, senseless but powerful, or in some offering made at the cost of pain and grief.

THE MYTHOLOGY OF THE GREEKS

This dark picture is worlds apart from the stories of classical mythology. The study of the way early man looked at his surroundings does not get much help from the Greeks. How briefly the anthropologists treat the Greek myths is noteworthy.

Of course the Greeks too had their roots in the primeval slime. Of course they too once lived a savage life, ugly and brutal. But what the myths show is how high they had risen above the ancient filth and fierceness by the time we have any knowledge of them. Only a few traces of that time are to be found in the stories.

We do not know when these stories were first told in their present shape; but whenever it was, primitive life had been left far behind. The myths as we have them are the creation of great poets. The first written record of Greece is the *Iliad*. Greek mythology begins with Homer, generally believed to be not earlier than a thousand years before Christ. The *Iliad* is, or contains, the oldest Greek literature; and it is written in a rich and subtle and beautiful language which must have had behind it centuries when men were striving to express themselves with clarity and beauty, an indisputable proof of civilization. The tales of Greek mythology do not throw any clear light upon what early mankind was like. They do throw an abundance of light upon what early Greeks were like—a matter, it would seem, of more importance to us, who are their descendants intellectually, artistically, and politically, too. Nothing we learn about them is alien to ourselves.

People often speak of "the Greek miracle." What the phrase tries to express is the new birth of the world with the awakening of Greece. "Old things are passed away; behold, all things are become new." Something like that happened in Greece.

The Greeks, unlike the Egyptians, made
their gods in their own image

Why it happened, or when, we have no idea at all. We know only that in the earliest Greek poets a new point of view dawned, never dreamed of in the world before them, but never to leave the world after them. With the coming forward of Greece, mankind became the center of the universe, the most important thing in it. This was a revolution in thought. Human beings had counted for little heretofore. In Greece man first realized what mankind was.

The Greeks made their gods in their own image. That had not entered the mind of man before. Until then, gods had had no semblance of reality. They were unlike all living things. In Egypt, a towering colossus, immobile, beyond the power of the imagination to endow with movement, as fixed in the stone as the tremendous temple columns, a representation of the human shape deliberately made unhuman. Or a rigid figure, a woman with a cat's head suggesting inflexible, inhuman cruelty. Or a monstrous mysterious sphinx, aloof from all that lives. In Mesopotamia, bas-reliefs of bestial shapes unlike any beast ever known, men with birds' heads and lions with bulls' heads and both with eagles' wings, creations of artists who were intent upon producing something never seen except in their own minds, the very consummation of unreality.

These and their like were what the pre-Greek world worshiped. One need only place beside them in imagination any Greek statue of a god, so normal and natural with all its beauty, to perceive what a new idea had come into the world. With its coming, the universe became rational.

Saint Paul said the invisible must be understood by the visible. That was not a Hebrew idea, it was Greek. In Greece alone in the ancient world people were preoccupied with the visible; they were finding the satisfaction of their desires in what was actually in the world around them. The sculptor watched the athletes contending in the games and he felt that nothing he could imagine would be as beautiful as those strong young bodies. So he made his statue of Apollo. The storyteller found Hermes among the people he passed in the street. He saw the god "like a young man at the age when youth is loveliest," as Homer says. Greek artists and poets realized how splendid a man could be, straight and swift and strong. He was the fulfillment of their search for beauty. They had no wish to create some fantasy shaped in their own minds. All the art and all the thought of Greece centered in human beings.

Human gods naturally made heaven a pleasantly familiar place. The Greeks felt at home in it. They knew just what the divine inhabitants did there, what they ate and drank and where they banqueted and how they amused themselves. Of course they were to be feared; they were very powerful and very dangerous when angry. Still, with proper care a man could be quite fairly at ease with them. He was even perfectly free to laugh at them. Zeus, trying to hide his love affairs from his wife and invariably shown up, was a capital figure of fun. The Greeks enjoyed him and liked him all the better for it. Hera was that stock character of comedy, the typical jealous wife, and her ingenious tricks to discomfit her husband and punish her rival, far from displeasing the Greeks, entertained them as much as Hera's modern counterpart does us today. Such stories made for a friendly feeling. Laughter in the presence of an Egyptian sphinx or an Assyrian bird-beast was inconceivable; but it was perfectly natural in Olympus, and it made the gods companionable.

On earth, too, the deities were exceedingly and humanly attractive. In the form of lovely youths and maidens they peopled the woodland, the forest, the rivers, the sea, in harmony with the fair earth and the bright waters.

That is the miracle of Greek mythology—a humanized world, men freed from the paralyzing fear of an omnipotent Unknown. The terrifying incomprehensibilities which were worshiped elsewhere, and the fearsome spirits with which earth, air and sea swarmed, were banned from Greece. It may seem odd to say that the men who made the myths disliked the irrational and had a love for facts; but it is true, no matter how wildly fantastic some of the stories are. Anyone who reads them with attention discovers that even the most nonsensical take place in a world which is essentially rational and matter-of-fact. Hercules, whose life was one long combat against preposterous monsters, is always said to have had his home in the city of Thebes. The exact spot where Aphrodite was born of the foam could be visited by any ancient tourist; it was just offshore from the island of Cythera. The winged steed Pegasus, after skimming the air all day, went every night to a comfortable stable in Corinth. A familiar local habitation gave reality to all the mythical beings. If the mixture seems childish, consider how reassuring and how sensible the solid background is as compared with the Genie who comes from nowhere when Aladdin rubs the lamp and, his task accomplished, returns to nowhere.

The terrifying irrational has no place in classical mythology. Magic, so powerful in the world before and after Greece, is almost nonexistent. There are no men and only two women with dreadful, supernatural powers. The demoniac wizards and the hideous old witches who haunted Europe and America, too, up to quite recent years, play no part at all in the stories. Circe and Medea are the only witches and they are young and of surpassing beauty—delightful, not horrible. Astrology, which has flourished from the days of ancient Babylon down to today, is completely absent from classical Greece. There are many stories about the stars, but not a trace of the idea that they influence men's lives. Astronomy is what the Greek mind finally made out of the stars. Not a single story has a magical priest who is terribly to be feared because he knows ways of winning over the gods or alienating them. The priest is rarely seen and is never of importance. In the *Odyssey* when a priest and a poet fall on their knees before Odysseus, praying him to spare their lives, the hero kills the priest without a thought, but saves the poet. Homer says that he felt awe to slay a man who had been taught his divine art by the gods. Not the priest, but the poet, had influence with heaven—and no one was ever afraid of a poet. Ghosts, too, which have played so large and so fearsome a part in other lands, never appear on earth in any Greek story. The Greeks were not afraid of the dead—"the piteous dead," the *Odyssey* calls them.

The world of Greek mythology was not a place of terror for the human spirit. It is true that the gods were disconcertingly incalculable. One could never tell where Zeus's thunderbolt would strike. Nevertheless, the whole divine company, with a very few and for the most part not important exceptions, were entrancingly beautiful with a human beauty, and nothing humanly beautiful is really terrifying. The early Greek mythologists transformed a world full of fear into a world full of beauty.

This bright picture has its dark spots. The change came about slowly and was never quite completed. The gods-become-human were for a long time a very slight improvement upon their worshipers. They were incomparably lovelier and more powerful, and they were of course immortal; but they often acted in a way no decent man or woman would. In the *Iliad* Hector is nobler by far than any of the heavenly beings, and Andromache infinitely to be preferred to Athena or Aphrodite. Hera from first to last is a goddess on a very low level of humanity. Almost every one of the radiant divinities could act cruelly or contemptibly. A very limited sense of right and wrong prevailed in Homer's heaven, and for a long time after.

Other dark spots too stand out. There are traces of a time when there were beast-gods. The satyrs are goat-men and the centaurs are half man, half horse. Hera is often called "cow-faced," as if the adjective had somehow stuck to her through all her changes from a divine cow to the very human queen of heaven. There are also stories which point back clearly to a time when there was human sacrifice. But what is astonishing is not that bits of savage belief were left here and there. The strange thing is that they are so few.

Of course the mythical monster is present in any number of shapes,

> Gorgons and hydras and chimaeras dire,

but they are there only to give the hero his meed of glory. What could a hero do in a world without them? They are always overcome by him. The great hero of mythology, Hercules, might be an allegory of Greece herself. He fought the monsters and freed the earth from them just as Greece freed the earth from the monstrous idea of the unhuman supreme over the human.

Greek mythology is largely made up of stories about gods and goddesses, but it must not be read as a kind of Greek Bible, an account of the Greek religion. According to the most modern idea, a real myth has nothing to do with religion. It is an explanation of something in nature; how, for instance, any and everything in the universe came into existence: men, animals, this or that tree or flower, the sun, the moon, the stars, storms, eruptions, earthquakes, all that is and all that happens. Thunder and lightning are caused when Zeus hurls his thunderbolt. A volcano erupts because a terrible creature is imprisoned in the mountain and every now and then struggles to get free. The Dipper, the constellation called also the Great Bear, does not set below the horizon because a goddess once was angry at it and decreed that it should never sink into the sea. Myths are early science, the result of men's first trying to explain what they saw around them. But there are many so-called myths which explain nothing at all. These tales are pure entertainment, the sort of thing people would tell each other on a long winter's evening. The story of Pygmalion and Galatea is an example; it has no conceivable connection with any event in nature. Neither has the Quest of the Golden Fleece, nor Orpheus and Eurydice, nor many another. This fact is now generally accepted; and we do not have to try to find in every mythological heroine the moon or the dawn and in every hero's life a sun myth. The stories are early literature as well as early science.

But religion is there, too. In the background, to be sure, but nevertheless plain to see. From Homer through the tragedians and even later, there is a deepening realization of what human beings need and what they must have in their gods.

Zeus the Thunderer was, it seems certain, once a rain-god. He was supreme even over the sun, because rocky Greece needed rain more than sunshine and the God of Gods would be the one who could give the precious water of life to his worshipers. But Homer's Zeus is not a fact of nature. He is a person living in a world where civilization has made an entry, and of course he has a standard of right and wrong. It is not very high, certainly, and seems chiefly applicable to others, not to himself; but he does punish men who lie and break their oaths; he is angered by any ill treatment of the dead; and he pities and helps old Priam when he goes as a suppliant to Achilles. In the *Odyssey,* he has reached a higher level. The swineherd there says that the needy and the stranger are from Zeus and he who fails to help them sins against Zeus himself. Hesiod, not much later than the *Odyssey* if at all, says of a man who does evil to the suppliant and the stranger, or who wrongs orphan children, "with that man Zeus is angry."

Then Justice became Zeus's companion. That was a new idea. The buccaneering chieftains in the *Iliad* did not want justice. They wanted to be able to take whatever they chose because they were strong and they wanted a god who was on the side of the strong. But Hesiod, who was a peasant living in a poor man's world, knew that the poor must have a just god. He wrote, "Fishes and beasts and fowls of the air devour one another. But to man, Zeus has given justice. Beside Zeus on his throne Justice has her seat." These passages show that the great and bitter needs of the helpless were reaching up to heaven and changing the god of the strong into the protector of the weak.

So, back of the stories of an amorous Zeus and a cowardly Zeus and a ridiculous Zeus, we can catch sight of another Zeus coming into being, as men grow continually more conscious of what life demanded of them and what human beings needed in the god they worshiped. Gradually this Zeus displaced the others, until he occupied the whole scene. At last he became, in the words of Dio Chrysostom, who wrote during the second century A.D.: "Our Zeus, the giver of every good gift, the common father and saviour and guardian of mankind."

The *Odyssey* speaks of "the divine for which all men long," and hundreds of years later Aristotle wrote, "Excellence, much labored for by the race of mortals." The Greeks from the earliest mythologists on had a perception of the divine and the excellent. Their longing for them was great enough to make them never give up laboring to see them clearly, until at last the thunder and lightning were changed into the Universal Father.

THE GREEK AND ROMAN WRITERS OF MYTHOLOGY

Most of the books about the stories of classical mythology depend chiefly upon the Latin poet Ovid, who wrote during the reign of Augustus. Ovid is a compendium of mythology. No ancient writer can compare with him in this respect. He told almost all the stories and he told them at great length. Occasionally stories familiar to us through literature and art have come down to us only in his pages. In this book I have avoided using him as far as possible. Undoubtedly he was a good poet and a good storyteller and able to appreciate the myths enough to realize what excellent material they offered him; but he was really farther away from them in his point of view than we are today. They were sheer nonsense to him. He wrote,

> I prate of ancient poets' monstrous lies,
> Ne'er seen or now or then by human eyes.

He says in effect to his reader, "Never mind how silly they are. I will dress them up so prettily for you that you will like them." And he does, often very prettily indeed, but in his hands the stories which were factual truth and solemn truth to the early Greek poets Hesiod and Pindar, and vehicles of deep religious truth to the Greek tragedians, become idle tales, sometimes witty and diverting, often sentimental and distressingly rhetorical. The Greek mythologists are not rhetoricians and are notably free from sentimentality.

The list of the chief writers through whom the myths have come down to us is not long. Homer heads it, of course. The *Iliad* and the *Odyssey* are, or rather contain, the oldest Greek writings we have. There is no way to date accurately any part of them. Scholars differ widely, and will no doubt continue to do so. As unobjectionable a date as any is 1000 B.C.— at any rate for the *Iliad*, the older of the two poems.

In all that follows, here and in the rest of the book, the date given is to be understood as before Christ, unless it is otherwise stated.

The second writer on the list is sometimes placed in the ninth century, sometimes in the eighth. Hesiod was a poor farmer whose life was hard and bitter. There cannot be a greater contrast than that between his poem, the *Works and Days*, which tries to show men how to live a good life in a harsh world, and the courtly splendor of the *Iliad* and the *Odyssey*. But Hesiod has much to say about the gods, and a second poem, usually ascribed to him, the *Theogony*, is entirely concerned with mythology. If Hesiod did write it, then a humble peasant, living on a lonely farm far from cities was the first man in Greece to wonder how everything had happened, the world, the sky, the gods, mankind, and to think out an explanation. Homer never wondered about anything. The *Theogony* is an account of the creation of the universe and the generations of the gods, and it is very important for mythology.

Next in order come the Homeric Hymns, poems written to honor various gods. They cannot be definitely dated, but the earliest are considered by most scholars to belong to the end of the eighth century or the beginning of the seventh. The last one of importance—there are thirty-three in all—belongs to fifth-century or possibly fourth-century Athens.

Pindar, the greatest lyric poet of Greece, began to write toward the end of the sixth century. He wrote Odes in honor of the victors in the games at the great national festivals of Greece, and in every one of his poems myths are told or alluded to. Pindar is quite as important for mythology as Hesiod.

Aeschylus, the oldest of the three tragic poets, was a contemporary of Pindar's. The other two, Sophocles and Euripides, were a little younger. Euripides, the youngest, died at the end of the fifth century. Except for Aeschylus' *Persians*, written to celebrate the victory of the Greeks over the Persians at Salamis, all the plays have mythological subjects. With Homer, they are the most important source of our knowledge of the myths.

The great writer of comedy, Aristophanes, who lived in the last part of the fifth century and the beginning of the fourth, refers often to the myths, as do also two great prose writers, Herodotus, the first historian of Europe, who was a contemporary of Euripides, and Plato, the philosopher, who lived less than a generation later.

The Alexandrian poets lived around 250 B.C. They were so called because, when they wrote, the center of Greek literature had moved from Greece to Alexandria in Egypt. Apollonius of Rhodes told at length the Quest of the Golden Fleece, and in connection with the story a number of other myths. He and three other Alexandrians, who also wrote about mythology, the pastoral poets Theocritus, Bion and Moschus, have lost the simplicity of Hesiod's and Pindar's belief in the gods, and are far removed from the depth and gravity of the tragic poets' view of religion; but they are not frivolous like Ovid.

Two late writers, Apuleius, a Latin, and Lucian, a Greek, both of the second century A.D., make an important contribution. The famous story of Cupid and Psyche is told only by Apuleius, who writes very much like Ovid. Lucian writes like no one except himself. He satirized the gods. In his time they had become a joking matter. Nevertheless, he gives by the way a good deal of information about them.

Apollodorus, also a Greek, is, next to Ovid, the most voluminous ancient writer on mythology, but, unlike Ovid, he is very matter-of-fact and very dull. His date has been differently set all the way from the first century B.C. to the ninth century A.D. The English scholar, Sir J. G. Frazer, thinks he probably wrote in either the first or the second century of our era.

The Greek Pausanias, an ardent traveler, the author of the first guidebook ever written, has a good deal to say about the mythological events reported to have happened in the places he visited. He lived as late as the second century A.D., but he does not question any of the stories. He writes about them with complete seriousness.

Of the Roman writers, Virgil stands far ahead. He did not believe in the myths any more than Ovid did, whose contemporary he was, but he found human nature in them and he brought mythological personages to life as no one had done since the Greek tragedians.

Other Roman poets wrote of the myths. Catullus tells several of the stories, and Horace alludes to them often, but neither is important for mythology. To all Romans the stories were infinitely remote, mere shadows. The best guides to a knowledge of Greek mythology are the Greek writers, who believed in what they wrote.

PART ONE

The Gods, The Creation, and the Earliest Heroes

1 The Gods

Strange clouded fragments of an ancient glory,
Late lingerers of the company divine,
They breathe of that far world wherefrom they come,
Lost halls of heaven and Olympian air.

The Greeks did not believe that the gods created the universe. It was the other way about: the universe created the gods. Before there were gods heaven and earth had been formed. They were the first parents. The Titans were their children, and the gods were their grandchildren.

THE TITANS AND THE TWELVE GREAT OLYMPIANS

The Titans, often called the Elder Gods, were for untold ages supreme in the universe. They were of enormous size and of incredible strength. There were many of them, but only a few appear in the stories of mythology. The most important was CRONUS, in Latin SATURN. He ruled over the other Titans until his son Zeus dethroned him and seized the power for himself. The Romans said that when Jupiter, their name for

Zeus, ascended the throne, Saturn fled to Italy and brought in the Golden Age, a time of perfect peace and happiness, which lasted as long as he reigned.

The other notable Titans were OCEAN, the river that was supposed to encircle the earth; his wife TETHYS; HYPERION, the father of the sun, the moon and the dawn; MNEMOSYNE, which means Memory; THEMIS, usually translated by Justice; and IAPETUS, important because of his sons, ATLAS, who bore the world on his shoulders, and PROMETHEUS, who was the savior of mankind. These alone among the older gods were not banished with the coming of Zeus, but they took a lower place.

The twelve great Olympians were supreme among the gods who succeeded to the Titans. They were called the Olympians because Olympus was their home. What Olympus was, however, is not easy to say. There is no doubt that at first it was held to be a mountain top, and generally identified with Greece's highest mountain, Mt. Olympus in Thessaly, in the northeast of Greece. But even in the earliest Greek poem, the *Iliad*, this idea is beginning to give way to the idea of an Olympus in some mysterious region far above all the mountains of the earth. In one passage of the *Iliad* Zeus talks to the gods from "the topmost peak of many-ridged Olympus," clearly a mountain. But only a little further on he says that if he willed he could hang earth and sea from a pinnacle of Olympus, clearly no longer a mountain. Even so, it is not heaven. Homer makes Poseidon say that he rules the sea, Hades the dead, Zeus the heavens, but Olympus is common to all three.

Wherever it was, the entrance to it was a great gate of clouds kept by the Seasons. Within were the gods' dwellings, where they lived and slept and feasted on ambrosia and nectar and listened to Apollo's lyre. It was an abode of perfect blessedness. No wind, Homer says, ever shakes the untroubled peace of Olympus; no rain ever falls there or snow; but the cloudless firmament stretches around it on all sides and the white glory of sunshine is diffused upon its walls.

The twelve Olympians made up a divine family:—

(1) ZEUS (JUPITER), the chief; his two brothers next, (2) POSEIDON (NEPTUNE), and (3) HADES, also called PLUTO; (4) HESTIA (VESTA), their sister; (5) HERA (JUNO), Zeus's wife, and (6) ARES (MARS), their son; Zeus's children: (7) ATHENA (MINERVA), (8) APOLLO, (9) APHRODITE (VENUS), (10) HERMES (MERCURY), and (11) ARTEMIS (DIANA); and Hera's son (12) HEPHAESTUS (VULCAN), sometimes said to be the son of Zeus too.

Olympus

ZEUS (JUPITER)

Zeus and his brothers drew lots for their share of the universe. The sea fell to Poseidon, and the underworld to Hades. Zeus became the supreme ruler. He was Lord of the Sky, the Rain-god and the Cloud-gatherer, who wielded the awful thunderbolt. His power was greater than that of all the other divinities together. In the *Iliad* he tells his family, "I am mightiest of all. Make trial that you may know. Fasten a rope of gold to heaven and lay hold, every god and goddess. You could not drag down Zeus. But if I wished to drag you down, then I would. The rope I would bind to a pinnacle of Olympus and all would hang in air, yes, the very earth and the sea too."

Nevertheless he was not omnipotent or omniscient, either. He could be opposed and deceived. Poseidon dupes him in the *Iliad* and so does Hera. Sometimes, too, the mysterious power, Fate, is spoken of as stronger than he. Homer makes Hera ask him scornfully if he proposes to deliver from death a man Fate has doomed.

He is represented as falling in love with one woman after another and descending to all manner of tricks to hide his infidelity from his wife. The explanation why such actions were ascribed to the most majestic of the gods is, the scholars say, that the Zeus of song and story has been made by combining many gods. When his worship spread to a town where there was already a divine ruler the two were slowly fused into one. The wife of the early god was then transferred to Zeus. The result, however, was unfortunate and the later Greeks did not like these endless love affairs.

Still, even in the earliest records Zeus had grandeur. In the *Iliad* Agamemnon prays: "Zeus, most glorious, most great, God of the storm-cloud, thou that dwellest in the heavens." He demanded, too, not only sacrifices from men, but right action. The Greek Army at Troy is told "Father Zeus never helps liars or those who break their oaths." The two ideas of him, the low and the high, persisted side by side for a long time.

His breastplate was the aegis, awful to behold; his bird was the eagle, his tree the oak. His oracle was Dodona in the land of oak trees. The god's will was revealed by the rustling of the oak leaves which the priests interpreted.

HERA (JUNO)

She was Zeus's wife and sister. The Titans Ocean and Tethys brought her up. She was the protector of marriage, and married women were her peculiar care. There is very little that is attractive in the portrait the poets draw of her. She is called, indeed, in an early poem,

> Golden-throned Hera, among immortals the queen.
> Chief among them in beauty, the glorious lady
> All the blessed in high Olympus revere,
> Honor even as Zeus, the lord of the thunder.

But when any account of her gets down to details, it shows her chiefly engaged in punishing the many women Zeus fell in love with, even when they yielded only because he coerced or tricked them. It made no difference to Hera how reluctant any of them were or how innocent; the goddess treated them all alike. Her implacable anger followed them and their children too. She never forgot an injury. The Trojan War would have ended in an honorable peace, leaving both sides unconquered, if it had not been for her hatred of a Trojan who had judged another goddess lovelier than she. The wrong of her slighted beauty remained with her until Troy fell in ruins.

In one important story, the Quest of the Golden Fleece, she is the gracious protector of heroes and the inspirer of heroic deeds, but not in any other. Nevertheless she was venerated in every home. She was the goddess married women turned to for help. Ilithyia (or Eileithyia), who helped women in childbirth, was her daughter.

The cow and the peacock were sacred to her. Argos was her favorite city.

POSEIDON (NEPTUNE)

He was the ruler of the sea, Zeus's brother and second only to him in eminence. The Greeks on both sides of the Aegean were seamen and the God of the Sea was all-important to them. His wife was Amphitrite, a granddaughter of the Titan, Ocean. Poseidon had a splendid palace beneath the sea, but he was oftener to be found in Olympus.

Besides being Lord of the Sea he gave the first horse to man, and he was honored as much for the one as for the other.

> Lord Poseidon, from you this pride is ours,
> The strong horses, the young horses, and also the rule
> of the deep.

Storm and calm were under his control:—

> He commanded and the storm wind rose
> And the surges of the sea.

But when he drove in his golden car over the waters, the thunder of the waves sank into stillness, and tranquil peace followed his smooth-rolling wheels.

He was commonly called "Earth-shaker" and was always shown carrying his trident, a three-pronged spear, with which he would shake and shatter whatever he pleased.

He had some connection with bulls as well as with horses, but the bull was connected with many other gods too.

HADES (PLUTO)

He was the third brother among the Olympians, who drew for his share the underworld and the rule over the dead. He was also called Pluto, the God of Wealth, of the precious metals hidden in the earth. The Romans as well as the Greeks called him by this name, but often they translated it into *Dis*, the Latin word for rich. He had a far-famed cap or helmet which made whoever wore it invisible. It was rare that he left his dark realm to visit Olympus or the earth, nor was he urged to do so. He was not a welcome visitor. He was unpitying, inexorable, but just; a terrible, not an evil god.

His wife was Persephone (Proserpine) whom he carried away from the earth and made Queen of the Lower World.

He was King of the Dead—not Death himself, whom the Greeks called Thanatos and the Romans, Orcus.

PALLAS ATHENA (MINERVA)

She was the daughter of Zeus alone. No mother bore her. Full-grown and in full armor, she sprang from his head. In the earliest account of her, the *Iliad*, she is a fierce and ruthless battle-goddess, but elsewhere she is warlike only to defend the State and the home from outside enemies. She was pre-eminently the Goddess of the City, the protector of civilized life, of handicrafts and agriculture; the inventor of the bridle, who first tamed horses for men to use.

She was Zeus's favorite child. He trusted her to carry the awful aegis, his buckler, and his devastating weapon, the thunderbolt.

The word oftenest used to describe her is "gray-eyed," or, as it is sometimes translated, "flashing-eyed." Of the three virgin goddesses she was the chief and was called the Maiden, Parthenos, and her temple the Parthenon. In later poetry she is the embodiment of wisdom, reason, purity.

Athens was her special city; the olive created by her was her tree; the owl her bird.

PHOEBUS APOLLO

The son of Zeus and Leto (Latona), born in the little island of Delos. He has been called "the most Greek of all the gods." He is a beautiful figure in Greek poetry, the master musician who delights Olympus as he plays on his golden lyre; the lord too of the silver bow, the Archer-god, far-shooting; the Healer, as well, who first taught men the healing art. Even more than of these good and lovely endowments, he is the God of Light, in whom is no darkness at all, and so he is the God of Truth. No false word ever falls from his lips.

> O Phoebus, from your throne of truth,
> From your dwelling-place at the heart of the world,
> You speak to men.
> By Zeus's decree no lie comes there,
> No shadow to darken the word of truth.
> Zeus sealed by an everlasting right
> Apollo's honour, that all may trust
> With unshaken faith when he speaks.

Delphi under towering Parnassus, where Apollo's oracle was, plays an important part in mythology. Castalia was its sacred spring; Cephissus its river. It was held to be the center of the world, so many pilgrims came to it, from foreign countries as well as Greece. No other shrine rivaled it. The answers to the questions asked by the anxious seekers for Truth were delivered by a priestess who went into a trance before she spoke. The trance was supposed to be caused by a vapor rising from a deep cleft in the rock over which her seat was placed, a three-legged stool, the tripod.

Apollo was called Delian from Delos, the island of his birth, and Pythian from his killing of a serpent, Python, which once lived in the caves of Parnassus. It was a frightful monster and the contest was severe, but in the end the god's unerring arrows won the victory. Another name often given him was "the Lycian," variously explained as meaning Wolf-god, God of Light, and God of Lycia. In the *Iliad* he is called "the Sminthian," the Mouse-god, but whether because he protected mice or destroyed them no one knows. Often he was the Sun-god too. His name Phoebus means "brilliant" or "shining." Accurately, however, the Sun-god was Helios, child of the Titan Hyperion.

Apollo at Delphi was a purely beneficent power, a direct link between gods and men, guiding men to know the divine will, showing them how to make peace with the gods; the purifier, too, able to cleanse even those stained with the blood of their kindred. Nevertheless, there are a few tales told of him which show him pitiless and cruel. Two ideas were fighting in him as in all the gods: a primitive, crude idea and one that was beautiful and poetic. In him only a little of the primitive is left.

The laurel was his tree. Many creatures were sacred to him, chief among them the dolphin and the crow.

ARTEMIS (DIANA)

> Also called Cynthia, from her birthplace, Mount Cynthus in Delos.

Apollo's twin sister, daughter of Zeus and Leto. She was one of the three maiden goddesses of Olympus:—

Golden Aphrodite who stirs with love all creation,
Cannot bend nor ensnare three hearts: the pure maiden Vesta,
Gray-eyed Athena who cares but for war and the arts of the craftsmen,
Artemis, lover of woods and the wild chase over the mountain.

She was the Lady of Wild Things, Huntsman-in-chief to the gods, an odd office for a woman. Like a good huntsman, she was careful to preserve the young; she was "the protectress of dewy youth" everywhere. Nevertheless, with one of those startling contradictions so common in mythology, she kept the Greek Fleet from sailing to Troy until they sacrificed a maiden to her. In many another story, too, she is fierce and revengeful. On the other hand, when women died a swift and painless death, they were held to have been slain by her silver arrows.

As Phoebus was the Sun, she was the Moon, called Phoebe and Selene (Luna in Latin). Neither name originally belonged to her. Phoebe was a Titan, one of the older gods. So too was Selene—a moon-goddess, indeed, but not connected with Apollo. She was the sister of Helios, the sun-god with whom Apollo was confused.

In the later poets, Artemis is identified with Hecate. She is "the goddess with three forms," Selene in the sky, Artemis on earth, Hecate in the lower world and in the world above when it is wrapped in darkness. Hecate was the Goddess of the Dark

of the Moon, the black nights when the moon is hidden. She
was associated with deeds of darkness, the Goddess of the
Crossways, which were held to be ghostly places of evil
magic. An awful divinity,

> Hecate of hell,
> Mighty to shatter every stubborn thing.
> Hark! Hark! her hounds are baying through the town.
> Where three roads meet, there she is standing.

It is a strange transformation from the lovely Huntress flashing through the forest, from the Moon making all beautiful
with her light, from the pure Maiden-Goddess for whom

> Whoso is chaste of spirit utterly
> May gather leaves and fruits and flowers.
> The unchaste never.

In her is shown most vividly the uncertainty between good
and evil which is apparent in every one of the divinities.

The cypress was sacred to her; and all wild animals, but
especially the deer.

APHRODITE (VENUS)

The Goddess of Love and Beauty, who beguiled all, gods and
men alike; the laughter-loving goddess, who laughed sweetly
or mockingly at those her wiles had conquered; the irresistible goddess who stole away even the wits of the wise.

She is the daughter of Zeus and Dione in the *Iliad*, but in
the later poems she is said to have sprung from the foam of
the sea, and her name was explained as meaning "the foam-
risen." *Aphros* is foam in Greek. This sea-birth took place
near Cythera, from where she was wafted to Cyprus. Both
islands were ever after sacred to her, and she was called
Cytherea or the Cyprian as often as by her proper name.

One of the Homeric Hymns, calling her "Beautiful, golden
goddess," says of her:—

> The breath of the west wind bore her
> Over the sounding sea,
> Up from the delicate foam,
> To wave-ringed Cyprus, her isle.
> And the Hours golden-wreathed
> Welcomed her joyously.
> They clad her in raiment immortal,
> And brought her to the gods.
> Wonder seized them all as they saw
> Violet-crowned Cytherea.

The Romans wrote of her in the same way. With her, beauty comes. The winds flee before her and the storm clouds; sweet flowers embroider the earth; the waves of the sea laugh; she moves in radiant light. Without her there is no joy nor loveliness anywhere. This is the picture the poets like best to paint of her.

But she had another side too. It was natural that she should cut a poor figure in the *Iliad,* where the battle of heroes is the theme. She is a soft, weak creature there, whom a mortal need not fear to attack. In later poems she is usually shown as treacherous and malicious, exerting a deadly and destructive power over men.

In most of the stories she is the wife of Hephaestus (Vulcan), the lame and ugly god of the forge.

The myrtle was her tree; the dove her bird—sometimes, too, the sparrow and the swan.

HERMES (MERCURY)

Zeus was his father and Maia, daughter of Atlas, his mother. Because of a very popular statue his appearance is more familiar to us than that of any other god. He was graceful and swift of motion. On his feet were winged sandals; wings were on his low-crowned hat, too, and on his magic wand, the Caduceus. He was Zeus's Messenger, who "flies as fleet as thought to do his bidding."

Of all the gods he was the shrewdest and most cunning; in fact he was the Master Thief, who started upon his career before he was a day old.

> The babe was born at the break of day,
> And ere the night fell he had stolen away
> Apollo's herds.

Zeus made him give them back, and he won Apollo's forgiveness by presenting him with the lyre which he had just invented, making it out of a tortoise's shell. Perhaps there was some connection between that very early story of him and the fact that he was God of Commerce and the Market, protector of traders.

In odd contrast to this idea of him, he was also the solemn guide of the dead, the Divine Herald who led the souls down to their last home.

He appears oftener in the tales of mythology than any other god.

ARES (MARS)

The God of War, son of Zeus and Hera, both of whom, Homer says, detested him. Indeed, he is hateful throughout the *Iliad*, poem of war though it is. Occasionally the heroes "rejoice in the delight of Ares' battle," but far oftener in having escaped "the fury of the ruthless god." Homer calls him murderous, bloodstained, the incarnate curse of mortals; and, strangely, a coward, too, who bellows with pain and runs away when he is wounded. Yet he has a train of attendants on the battlefield which should inspire anyone with confidence. His sister is there, Eris, which means Discord, and Strife, her son. The Goddess of War, Enyo,—in Latin Bellona,—walks beside him, and with her are Terror and Trembling and Panic. As they move, the voice of groaning arises behind them and the earth streams with blood.

The Romans liked Mars better than the Greeks liked Ares. He never was to them the mean whining deity of the *Iliad*, but magnificent in shining armor, redoubtable, invincible. The warriors of the great Latin heroic poem, the *Aeneid*, far from rejoicing to escape from him, rejoice when they see that they are to fall "on Mars' field of renown." They "rush on glorious death" and find it "sweet to die in battle."

Ares figures little in mythology. In one story he is the lover of Aphrodite and held up to the contempt of the Olympians by Aphrodite's husband, Hephaestus; but for the most part he is little more than a symbol of war. He is not a distinct personality, like Hermes or Hera or Apollo.

He had no cities where he was worshiped. The Greeks said vaguely that he came from Thrace, home of a rude, fierce people in the northeast of Greece.

Appropriately, his bird was the vulture. The dog was wronged by being chosen as his animal.

HEPHAESTUS (VULCAN AND MULCIBER)

The God of Fire, sometimes said to be the son of Zeus and Hera, sometimes of Hera alone, who bore him in retaliation for Zeus's having brought forth Athena. Among the perfectly beautiful immortals he only was ugly. He was lame as well. In one place in the *Iliad* he says that his shameless mother, when she saw that he was born deformed, cast him out of heaven; in another place he declares that Zeus did this, angry with him for trying to defend Hera. This second story is the better known, because of Milton's familiar lines: Mulciber was

> Thrown by angry Jove
> Sheer o'er the crystal battlements; from morn
> To noon he fell, from noon to dewy eve,
> A summer's day, and with the setting sun
> Dropt from the zenith like a falling star,
> On Lemnos, the Aegean isle.

These events, however, were supposed to have taken place in the far-distant past. In Homer he is in no danger of being driven from Olympus; he is highly honored there, the workman of the immortals, their armorer and smith, who makes their dwellings and their furnishings as well as their weapons. In his workshop he has handmaidens he has forged out of gold who can move and who help him in his work.

In the later poets his forge is often said to be under this or that volcano, and to cause eruptions.

His wife is one of the three Graces in the *Iliad*, called Aglaia in Hesiod; in the *Odyssey* she is Aphrodite.

He was a kindly, peace-loving god, popular on earth as in heaven. With Athena, he was important in the life of the city. The two were the patrons of handicrafts, the arts which along with agriculture are the support of civilization; he the protector of the smiths as she of the weavers. When children were formally admitted to the city organization, the god of the ceremony was Hephaestus.

HESTIA (VESTA)

She was Zeus's sister, and like Athena and Artemis a virgin goddess. She has no distinct personality and she plays no part in the myths. She was the Goddess of the Hearth, the symbol of the home, around which the newborn child must be carried before it could be received into the family. Every meal began and ended with an offering to her.

> Hestia, in all dwellings of men and immortals
> Yours is the highest honor, the sweet wine offered
> First and last at the feast, poured out to you duly.
> Never without you can gods or mortals hold banquet.

Each city too had a public hearth sacred to Hestia, where the fire was never allowed to go out. If a colony was to be founded, the colonists carried with them coals from the hearth of the mother-city with which to kindle the fire on the new city's hearth.

In Rome her fire was cared for by six virgin priestesses, called Vestals.

THE LESSER GODS OF OLYMPUS

There were other divinities in heaven besides the twelve great Olympians. The most important of them was the God of Love, EROS (Cupid in Latin). Homer knows nothing of him, but to Hesiod he is

> Fairest of the deathless gods.

In the early stories, he is oftenest a beautiful serious youth who gives good gifts to men. This idea the Greeks had of him is best summed up not by a poet, but by a philosopher, Plato: "Love—Eros—makes his home in men's hearts, but not in every heart, for where there is hardness he departs. His greatest glory is that he cannot do wrong nor allow it; force never comes near him. For all men serve him of their own free will. And he whom Love touches not walks in darkness."

In the early accounts Eros was not Aphrodite's son, but merely her occasional companion. In the later poets he was her son and almost invariably a mischievous, naughty boy, or worse.

> Evil his heart, but honey-sweet his tongue.
> No truth in him, the rogue. He is cruel in his play.
> Small are his hands, yet his arrows fly far as death.
> Tiny his shaft, but it carries heaven-high.
> Touch not his treacherous gifts, they are dipped in fire.

He was often represented as blindfolded, because love is often blind. In attendance upon him was ANTEROS, said sometimes to be the avenger of slighted love, sometimes the one who opposes love; also HIMEROS or Longing, and HYMEN, the God of the Wedding Feast.

HEBE was the Goddess of Youth, the daughter of Zeus and Hera. Sometimes she appears as cupbearer to the gods; sometimes that office is held by Ganymede, a beautiful young Trojan prince who was seized and carried up to Olympus by Zeus's eagle. There are no stories about Hebe except that of her marriage to Hercules.

IRIS was the Goddess of the Rainbow and a messenger of the gods, in the *Iliad* the only messenger. Hermes appears first in that capacity in the *Odyssey*, but he does not take Iris' place. Now the one, now the other is called upon by the gods.

There were also in Olympus two bands of lovely sisters, the Muses and the Graces.

THE GRACES were three: Aglaia (Splendor), Euphrosyne (Mirth) and Thalia (Good Cheer). They were the daughters of Zeus and Eurynome, a child of the Titan, Ocean. Except in a story Homer and Hesiod tell, that Aglaia married Hephaestus, they are not treated as separate personalities, but always together, a triple incarnation of grace and beauty. The gods delighted in them when they danced enchantingly to Apollo's lyre, and the man they visited was happy. They "give life its bloom." Together with their companions, the Muses, they were "queens of song," and no banquet without them could please.

THE MUSES were nine in number, the daughters of Zeus and Mnemosyne, Memory. At first, like the Graces, they were not distinguished from each other. "They are all," Hesiod says, "of one mind, their hearts are set upon song and their spirit is free from care. He is happy whom the Muses love. For though a man has sorrow and grief in his soul, yet when the servant of the Muses sings, at once he forgets his dark thoughts and remembers not his troubles. Such is the holy gift of the Muses to men."

In later times each had her own special field. Clio was Muse of history, Urania of astronomy, Melpomene of tragedy, Thalia of comedy, Terpsichore of the dance, Calliope of epic poetry, Erato of love-poetry, Polyhymnia of songs to the gods, Euterpe of lyric poetry.

Hesiod lived near Helicon, one of the Muses' mountains—the other were Pierus in Pieria, where they were born, Parnassus and, of course, Olympus. One day the Nine appeared to him and they told him, "We know how to speak false things that seem true, but we know, when we will, to utter true things." They were companions of Apollo, the God of Truth, as well as of the Graces. Pindar calls the lyre theirs as well as Apollo's, "the golden lyre to which the step, the dancer's step, listens, owned alike by Apollo and the violet-wreathed Muses." The man they inspired was sacred far beyond any priest.

As the idea of Zeus became loftier, two august forms sat beside him in Olympus. THEMIS, which means the Right, or Divine Justice, and DIKE, which is Human Justice. But they never became real personalities. The same was true of two personified emotions esteemed highest of all feelings in Homer and Hesiod: NEMESIS, usually translated as Righteous Anger, and AIDOS, a difficult word to translate, but in common use among the Greeks. It means reverence and the shame that holds men back from wrongdoing, but it also means the feeling a prosperous man should have in the presence of the unfortunate—not compassion, but a sense that the difference between him and those poor wretches is not deserved.

It does not seem, however, that either Nemesis or Aidos had their home with the gods. Hesiod says that only when men have finally become completely wicked will Nemesis and Aidos, their beautiful faces veiled in white raiment, leave the wide-wayed earth and depart to the company of the immortals.

From time to time a few mortals were translated to Olympus, but once they had been brought to heaven they vanished from literature. Their stories will be told later.

THE GODS OF THE WATERS

POSEIDON (Neptune), was the Lord and Ruler of the Sea (the Mediterranean) and the Friendly Sea (the Euxine, now the Black Sea). Underground rivers, too, were his.

OCEAN, a Titan, was Lord of the river Ocean, a great river encircling the earth. His wife, also a Titan, was Tethys. The Oceanids, the nymphs of this great river, were their daughters. The gods of all the rivers on earth were their sons.

PONTUS, which means the Deep Sea, was a son of Mother Earth and the father of NEREUS, a sea-god far more important than he himself was.

NEREUS was called the Old Man of the Sea (the Mediterranean)—"A trusty god and gentle," Hesiod says, "who thinks just and kindly thoughts and never lies." His wife was Doris, a daughter of Ocean. They had fifty lovely daughters, the nymphs of the Sea, called NEREIDS from their father's name, one of whom, THETIS, was the mother of Achilles. Poseidon's wife, AMPHITRITE, was another.

TRITON was the trumpeter of the Sea. His trumpet was a great shell. He was the son of Poseidon and Amphitrite.

PROTEUS was sometimes said to be Poseidon's son, sometimes his attendant. He had the power both of foretelling the future and of changing his shape at will.

THE NAIADS were also water nymphs. They dwelt in brooks and spring and fountains.

LEUCOTHEA and her son PALAEMON, once mortals, became divinities of the sea, as did also GLAUCUS, but all three were unimportant.

THE UNDERWORLD

The kingdom of the dead was ruled by one of the twelve great Olympians, Hades or Pluto, and his Queen, Persephone. It is often called by his name, Hades. It lies, the *Iliad* says, beneath the secret places of the earth. In the *Odyssey*, the way to it leads over the edge of the world across Ocean. In later poets there are various entrances to it from the earth through caverns and beside deep lakes.

Tartarus and Erebus are sometimes two divisions of the underworld, Tartarus the deeper of the two, the prison of the Sons of Earth; Erebus where the dead pass as soon as they die. Often, however, there is no distinction between the two, and either is used, especially Tartarus, as a name for the entire lower region.

In Homer the underworld is vague, a shadowy place inhabited by shadows. Nothing is real there. The ghosts' existence, if it can be called that, is like a miserable dream. The later poets define the world of the dead more and more clearly as the place where the wicked are punished and the good rewarded. In the Roman poet Virgil this idea is presented in great detail as in no Greek poet. All the torments of the one class and the joys of the other are described at length. Virgil too is the only poet who gives clearly the geography of the underworld. The path down to it leads to where Acheron, the river of woe, pours into Cocytus, the river of lamentation. An aged boatman named Charon ferries the souls of the dead across the water to the farther bank, where stands the adamantine gate to Tartarus (the name Virgil prefers). Charon will receive into his boat only the souls of those upon whose lips the passage money was placed when they died and who were duly buried.

On guard before the gate sits CERBERUS, the three-headed, dragon-tailed dog, who permits all spirits to enter, but none to return. On his arrival each one is brought before three judges, Rhadamanthus, Minos, and Aeacus, who pass sentence and send the wicked to everlasting torment and the good to a place of blessedness called the Elysian Fields.

Three other rivers, besides Acheron and Cocytus, separate the underworld from the world above: Phlegethon, the river of fire; Styx, the river of the unbreakable oath by which the gods swear; and Lethe, the river of forgetfulness.

Somewhere in this vast region is Pluto's palace, but beyond saying that it is many-gated and crowded with innumerable guests, no writer describes it. Around it are wide wastes, wan and cold, and meadows of asphodel, presumably strange, pallid, ghostly flowers. We do not know anything more about it. The poets did not care to linger in that gloom-hidden abode.

THE ERINYES (the FURIES), are placed by Virgil in the underworld, where they punish evildoers. The Greek poets thought of them chiefly as pursuing sinners on the earth. They were inexorable, but just. Heraclitus says, "Not even the sun will transgress his orbit but the Erinyes, the ministers of justice, overtake him." They were usually represented as three: Tisiphone, Megaera and Alecto.

SLEEP, and DEATH, his brother, dwelt in the lower world. Dreams too ascended from there to men. They passed through two gates, one of horn through which true dreams went, one of ivory for false dreams.

THE LESSER GODS OF EARTH

Earth herself was called the All-Mother, but she was not really a divinity. She was never separated from the actual earth and personified. The Goddess of the Corn, DEMETER (CERES), a daughter of Cronus and Rhea, and the God of the Vine, DIONYSUS, also called BACCHUS, were the supreme deities of the earth and of great importance in Greek and Roman mythology. Their stories will be found in the next chapter. The other divinities who lived in the world were comparatively unimportant.

PAN was the chief. He was Hermes' son; a noisy, merry god, the Homeric Hymn in his honor calls him; but he was part animal too, with a goat's horns, and goat's hoofs instead of feet. He was the goatherds' god, and the shepherds' god, and also the gay companion of the woodland nymphs when they danced. All wild places were his home, thickets and forests and mountains, but best of all he loved Arcady, where he was born. He was a wonderful musician. Upon his pipes of reed he played melodies as sweet as the nightingale's song. He was always in love with one nymph or another, but always rejected because of his ugliness.

Sounds heard in a wilderness at night by the trembling traveler were supposed to be made by him, so that it is easy to see how the expression "panic" fear arose.

SILENUS was sometimes said to be Pan's son; sometimes his brother, a son of Hermes. He was a jovial fat old man who usually rode an ass because he was too drunk to walk. He is associated with Bacchus as well as with Pan; he taught him when the Wine-god was young, and, as is shown by his perpetual drunkenness, after being his tutor he became his devoted follower.

Besides these gods of the earth there was a very famous and very popular pair of brothers, CASTOR and POLLUX (Polydeuces), who in most of the accounts were said to live half of their time on earth and half in heaven.

They were the sons of LEDA, and are usually represented as being gods, the special protectors of sailors,

> Saviors of swift-going ships when the storm winds rage
> Over the ruthless sea.

They were also powerful to save in battle. They were especially honored in Rome, where they were worshiped as

> The great Twin Brethren to whom all Dorians pray.

But the accounts of them are contradictory. Sometimes Pollux alone is held to be divine, and Castor a mortal who won a kind of half-and-half immortality merely because of his brother's love.

LEDA was the wife of King Tyndareus of Sparta, and the usual story is that she bore two mortal children to him, Castor and Clytemnestra, Agamemnon's wife; and to Zeus, who visited her in the form of a swan, two others who were immortal, Pollux and Helen, the heroine of Troy. Nevertheless, both brothers, Castor and Pollux, were often called "sons of Zeus"; indeed, the Greek name they are best known by, the *Dioscouri*, means "the striplings of Zeus." On the other hand, they were also called "sons of Tyndareus," the *Tyndaridae*.

They are always represented as living just before the Trojan War, at the same time as Theseus and Jason and Atalanta. They took part in the Calydonian boar-hunt; they went on the Quest of the Golden Fleece; and they rescued Helen when Theseus carried her off. But in all the stories they play an unimportant part except in the account of Castor's death, when Pollux proved his brotherly devotion.

The two went, we are not told why, to the land of some cattle owners, Idas and Lynceus. There, Pindar says, Idas, made angry in some way about his oxen, stabbed and killed Castor. Other writers say the cause of the dispute was the two daughters of the king of the country, Leucippus. Pollux stabbed Lynceus, and Zeus struck Idas with his thunderbolt. But Castor was dead and Pollux was inconsolable. He prayed to die also, and Zeus in pity allowed him to share his life with his brother, to live,

> Half of thy time beneath the earth and half
> Within the golden homes of heaven.

According to this version the two were never separated again. One day they dwelt in Hades, the next in Olympus, always together.

The late Greek writer Lucian gives another version, in which their dwelling places are heaven and earth; and when Pollux goes to one, Castor goes to the other, so that they are never with each other. In Lucian's little satire, Apollo asks Hermes: "I say, why do we never see Castor and Pollux at the same time?"

"Well," Hermes replies, "they are so fond of each other that when fate decreed one of them must die and only one be immortal, they decided to share immortality between them."

"Not very wise, Hermes. What proper employment can they engage in, that way? I foretell the future; Aesculapius cures diseases; you are a good messenger—but these two—are they to idle away their whole time?"

"No, surely. They're in Poseidon's service. Their business is to save any ship in distress."

"Ah, now you say something. I'm delighted they're in such a good business."

Two stars were supposed to be theirs: the Gemini, the Twins.

They were always represented as riding splendid snow-white horses, but Homer distinguishes Castor above Pollux for horsemanship. He calls the two

> Castor, tamer of horses, Polydeuces, good as a boxer.

The SILENI were creatures part man and part horse. They walked on two legs, not four, but they often had horses' hoofs instead of feet, sometimes horses' ears, and always horses' tails. There are no stories about them, but they are often seen on Greek vases.

The SATYRS, like Pan, were goat-men, and like him they had their home in the wild places of the earth.

In contrast to these unhuman, ugly gods the goddesses of the woodland were all lovely maiden forms, the OREADS, nymphs of the mountains, and the DRYADS, sometimes called HAMADRYADS, nymphs of trees, whose life was in each case bound up with that of her tree.

AEOLUS, King of the Winds, also lived on the earth. An island, Aeolia, was his home. Accurately he was only regent of the Winds, viceroy of the gods. The four chief Winds were BOREAS, the North Wind, in Latin AQUILO; ZEPHYR, the West Wind, which had a second Latin name, FAVONIUS; NOTUS, the South Wind, also called in Latin AUSTER; and the East Wind, EURUS, the same in both Greek and Latin.

There were some beings, neither human nor divine, who had their home on the earth. Prominent among them were:—

THE CENTAURS. They were half man, half horse, and for the most part they were savage creatures, more like beasts than men. One of them, however, CHIRON, was known everywhere for his goodness and his wisdom.

THE GORGONS were also earth-dwellers. There were three, and two of them were immortal. They were dragonlike creatures with wings, whose look turned men to stone. Phorcys, son of the Sea and the Earth, was their father.

THE GRAIAE were their sisters, three gray women who had but one eye between them. They lived on the farther bank of Ocean.

THE SIRENS lived on an island in the Sea. They had enchanting voices and their singing lured sailors to their death. It was not known what they looked like, for no one who saw them ever returned.

Very important but assigned to no abode whether in heaven or on the earth were THE FATES, *Moirae* in Greek, *Parcae* in Latin, who, Hesiod says, give to men at birth evil and good to have. They were three, Clotho, the Spinner, who spun the thread of life; Lachesis, the Disposer of Lots, who assigned to each man his destiny; Atropos, she who could not be turned, who carried "the abhorrèd shears" and cut the thread at death.

THE ROMAN GODS

The Twelve great Olympians mentioned earlier were turned into Roman gods also. The influence of Greek art and literature became so powerful in Rome that ancient Roman deities were changed to resemble the corresponding Greek gods, and were considered to be the same. Most of them, however, in Rome had Roman names. These were Jupiter (Zeus), Juno (Hera), Neptune (Poseidon), Vesta (Hestia), Mars (Ares),

Minerva (Athena), Venus (Aphrodite), Mercury (Hermes), Diana (Artemis), Vulcan or Mulciber (Hephaestus), Ceres (Demeter).

Two kept their Greek names: Apollo and Pluto; but the latter was never called Hades, as was usual in Greece. Bacchus, never Dionysus, was the name of the wine-god, who had also a Latin name, Liber.

It was a simple matter to adopt the Greek gods because the Romans did not have definitely personified gods of their own. They were a people of deep religious feeling, but they had little imagination. They could never have created the Olympians, each a distinct, vivid personality. Their gods, before they took over from the Greeks, were vague, hardly more than a "those that are above." They were THE NUMINA, which means the Powers or the Wills—the Will-Powers, perhaps.

Until Greek literature and art entered Italy the Romans felt no need for beautiful, poetic gods. They were a practical people and they did not care about "Violet-tressed Muses who inspire song," or "Lyric Apollo making sweet melodies upon his golden lyre," or anything of that sort. They wanted useful gods. An important Power, for example, was One who Guards the Cradle. Another was One Who Presides over Children's Food. No stories were ever told about the Numina. For the most part they were not even distinguished as male or female. The simple acts of everyday life, however, were closely connected with them and gained dignity from them as was not the case with any of the Greek gods except Demeter and Dionysus.

The most prominent and revered of them all were the LARES and PENATES. Every Roman family had a Lar, who was the spirit of an ancestor, and several Penates, gods of the hearth and guardians of the storehouse. They were the family's own gods, belonging only to it, really the most important part of it, the protectors and defenders of the entire household. They were never worshiped in temples, but only in the home, where some of the food at each meal was offered to them. There were also public Lares and Penates, who did for the city what the others did for the family.

There were also many Numina connected with the life of the household, such as TERMINUS, Guardian of Boundaries; PRIAPUS, Cause of Fertility; PALES, Strengthener of Cattle; SYLVANUS, Helper of Plowmen and Woodcutters. A long list could be made. Everything important to the farm was under the care of a beneficient power, never conceived of as having a definite shape.

SATURN was originally one of the Numina, the Protector of the Sowers and the Seed, as his wife OPS was a Harvest Helper. In later days, he was said to be the same as the Greek Cronus and the father of Jupiter, the Roman Zeus. In this way he became a personality and a number of stories were told about him. In memory of the Golden Age, when he reigned in Italy, the great feast of the Saturnalia was held every year during the winter. The idea of it was that the Golden Age returned to the earth during the days it lasted. No war could be then declared; slaves and masters ate at the same table; executions were postponed; it was a season for giving presents; it kept alive in men's minds the idea of equality, of a time when all were on the same level.

JANUS, too, was originally one of the Numina, "the god of good beginnings," which are sure to result in good endings. He became personified to a certain degree. His chief temple in Rome ran east and west, where the day begins and ends, and had two doors, between which stood his statue with two faces, one young and one old. These doors were closed only when Rome was at peace. In the first seven hundred years of the city's life they were closed three times, in the reign of the good king, Numa; after the first Punic War when Carthage was defeated in 241 B.C.; and in the reign of Augustus when, Milton says,

> No war or battle's sound
> Was heard the world around.

Naturally his month, January, began the new year.

FAUNUS was Saturn's grandson. He was a sort of Roman Pan, a rustic god. He was a prophet too, and spoke to men in their dreams.

THE FAUNS were Roman satyrs.

QUIRINUS was the name of the deified Romulus, the founder of Rome.

THE MANES were the spirits of the good dead in Hades. Sometimes they were regarded as divine and worshiped.

THE LEMURES or LARVAE were the spirits of the wicked dead and were greatly feared.

THE CAMENAE began as useful and practical goddesses who cared for springs and wells and cured disease and foretold the future. But when the Greek gods came to Rome, the Camenae were identified with those impractical deities the Muses, who cared only for art and science. Egeria who taught King Numa was said to be a Camena.

LUCINA was sometimes regarded as a Roman EILEITHYIA, the goddess of childbirth, but usually the name is used as an epithet of both Juno and Diana.

POMONA AND VERTUMNUS began as Numina, as Powers Protecting Orchards and Gardens. But they were personified later and a story was told about how they fell in love with each other.

2 The Two Great Gods of Earth

For the most part the immortal gods were of little use to human beings and often they were quite the reverse of useful: Zeus a dangerous lover for mortal maidens and completely incalculable in his use of the terrible thunderbolt; Ares the maker of war and a general pest; Hera with no idea of justice when she was jealous as she perpetually was; Athena also a war maker, and wielding the lightning's sharp lance quite as irresponsibly as Zeus did; Aphrodite using her power chiefly to ensnare and betray. They were a beautiful, radiant company, to be sure, and their adventures made excellent stories; but when they were not positively harmful, they were capricious and undependable and in general mortals got on best without them.

There were two, however, who were altogether different —who were, indeed, mankind's best friends: Demeter, in Latin Ceres, the Goddess of the Corn, a daughter of Cronus and Rhea; and Dionysus, also called Bacchus, the God of Wine. Demeter was the older, as was natural. Corn was sowed long before vines were planted. The first cornfield was the beginning of settled life on earth. Vineyards came later. It was natural, too, that the divine power which brought forth the grain should be thought of as a goddess, not a god. When the business of men was hunting and fighting, the care of the fields belonged to the women, and as they plowed and scattered the seed and reaped the harvest, they felt that a woman divinity could best understand and help woman's work. They could best understand her, too, who was worshiped, not like other gods by the bloody sacrifices men liked, but in every humble act that made the farm fruitful. Through her the field of grain was hallowed. "Demeter's holy grain."

The threshing-floor, too, was under her protection. Both were her temples where at any moment she might be present. "At the sacred threshing-floor, when they are winnowing, she herself, Demeter of the corn-ripe yellow hair, divides the grain and the chaff in the rush of the wind, and the heap of chaff grows white." "May it be mine," the reaper prays, "beside Demeter's altar to dig the great winnowing fan through her heaps of corn, while she stands smiling by with sheaves and poppies in her hand."

Her chief festival, of course, came at the harvest time. In earlier days it must have been a simple reapers' thanksgiving day when the first loaf baked from the new grain was broken and reverently eaten with grateful prayers to the goddess from whom had come this best and most necessary gift for human life. In later years the humble feast grew into a mysterious worship, about which we know little. The great festival, in September, came only every five years, but it lasted for nine days. They were most sacred days, when much of the ordinary business of life was suspended. Processions took place, sacrifices were held with dances and song, there was general rejoicing. All this was public knowledge and has been related by many a writer. But the chief part of the ceremony which took place in the precincts of the temple has never been described. Those who beheld it were bound by a vow of silence and they kept it so well that we know only stray bits of what was done.

The great temple was at Eleusis, a little town near Athens, and the worship was called the Eleusinian Mysteries. Throughout the Greek world and the Roman, too, they were held in especial veneration. Cicero, writing in the century before Christ, says: "Nothing is higher than these mysteries. They have sweetened our characters and softened our customs; they have made us pass from the condition of savages to true humanity. They have not only shown us the way to live joyfully, but they have taught us how to die with a better hope."

And yet even so, holy and awesome though they were, they kept the mark of what they had sprung from. One of the few pieces of information we have about them is that at a very solemn moment the worshipers were shown "an ear of corn which had been reaped in silence."

In some way, no one knows clearly how or when, the God of the Vine, Dionysus, came to take his place, too, at Eleusis, side by side with Demeter.

> Beside Demeter when the cymbals sound
> Enthroned sits Dionysus of the flowing hair.

It was natural that they should be worshiped together, both divinities of the good gifts of earth, both present in the homely daily acts that life depends on, the breaking of bread and the drinking of wine. The harvest was Dionysus' festival, too, when the grapes were brought to the wine-press.

> The joy-god Dionysus, the pure star
> That shines amid the gathering of the fruit.

But he was not always a joy-god, nor was Demeter always the happy goddess of the summertime. Each knew pain as well as joy. In that way, too, they were closely linked together; they were both suffering gods. The other immortals were untouched by lasting grief. "Dwelling in Olympus where the wind never blows and no rain falls ever nor the least white star of snow, they are happy all their days, feasting upon nectar and ambrosia, rejoicing in all-glorious Apollo as he strikes his silver lyre, and the sweet voices of the Muses answer him, while the Graces dance with Hebe and with Aphrodite, and a radiance shines round them all." But the two divinities of Earth knew heart-rending grief.

What happens to the corn plants and the luxuriant branching vines when the grain is harvested, the grapes gathered, and the black frost sets in, killing the fresh green life of the fields? That is what men asked themselves when the first stories were told to explain what was so mysterious, the changes always passing before their eyes, of day and night and the seasons and the stars in their courses. Though Demeter and Dionysus were the happy gods of the harvest, during the winter it was clear that they were altogether different. They sorrowed, and the earth was sad. The men of long ago wondered why this should be, and they told stories to explain the reason.

DEMETER (CERES)

> *This story is told only in a very early poem, one of the earliest of the Homeric Hymns, dating from the eighth or the beginning of the seventh century. The original has the marks of early Greek poetry, great simplicity and directness and delight in the beautiful world.*

Demeter had an only daughter, Persephone (in Latin Proserpine), the maiden of the spring. She lost her and in her terrible grief she withheld her gifts from the earth, which turned into a frozen desert. The green and flowering land was icebound and lifeless because Persephone had disappeared.

The lord of the dark underworld, the king of the multitudinous dead, carried her off when, enticed by the wondrous bloom of the narcissus, she strayed too far from her companions. In his chariot drawn by coal-black steeds he rose up through a chasm in the earth, and grasping the maiden by the wrist set her beside him. He bore her away weeping, down to the underworld. The high hills echoed her cry and the depths of the sea, and her mother heard it. She sped like a bird over sea and land seeking her daughter. But no one would tell her the truth, "no man nor god, nor any sure messenger from the birds." Nine days Demeter wandered, and all that time she would not taste of ambrosia or put sweet nectar to her lips. At last she came to the Sun and he told her all the story: Persephone was down in the world beneath the earth, among the shadowy dead.

Then a still greater grief entered Demeter's heart. She left Olympus; she dwelt on earth, but so disguised that none knew her, and, indeed, the gods are not easily discerned by mortal men. In her desolate wanderings she came to Eleusis and sat by the wayside near a well. She seemed an aged woman, such as in great houses care for the children or guard the storerooms. Four lovely maidens, sisters, coming to draw water from the well, saw her and asked her pityingly what she did there. She answered that she had fled from pirates who had meant to sell her as a slave, and that she knew no one in this strange land to go to for help. They told her that any house in the town would welcome her, but that they would like best to bring her to their own if she would wait there while they went to ask their mother. The goddess bent her head in assent, and the girls, filling their shining pitchers with water, hurried home. Their mother, Metaneira, bade them return at once and invite the stranger to come, and speeding back they found the glorious goddess still sitting there, deeply veiled and covered to her slender feet by her dark robe. She followed them, and as she crossed the threshold to the hall where the mother sat holding her young son, a divine radiance filled the doorway and awe fell upon Metaneira.

She bade Demeter be seated and herself offered her honeysweet wine, but the goddess would not taste it. She asked instead for barley-water flavored with mint, the cooling draught of the reaper at harvest time and also the sacred cup given the worshipers at Eleusis. Thus refreshed she took the child and held him to her fragrant bosom and his mother's heart was glad. So Demeter nursed Demophoön, the son that Metaneira had borne to wise Celeus. And the child grew like a young god, for daily Demeter anointed him with ambrosia

The rape of Persephone (Proserpine)

and at night she would place him in the red heart of the fire. Her purpose was to give him immortal youth.

Something, however, made the mother uneasy, so that one night she kept watch and screamed in terror when she saw the child laid in the fire. The goddess was angered; she seized the boy and cast him on the ground. She had meant to set him free from old age and from death, but that was not to be. Still, he had lain upon her knees and slept in her arms and therefore he should have honor throughout his life.

Then she showed herself the goddess manifest. Beauty breathed about her and a lovely fragrance; light shone from her so that the great house was filled with brightness. She was Demeter, she told the awestruck women. They must build her a great temple near the town and so win back the favor of her heart.

Thus she left them, and Metaneira fell speechless to the earth and all there trembled with fear. In the morning they told Celeus what had happened and he called the people together and revealed to them the command of the goddess. They worked willingly to build her a temple, and when it was finished Demeter came to it and sat there—apart from the gods in Olympus, alone, wasting away with longing for her daughter.

That year was most dreadful and cruel for mankind over all the earth. Nothing grew; no seed sprang up; in vain the oxen drew the plowshare through the furrows. It seemed the whole race of men would die of famine. At last Zeus saw that he must take the matter in hand. He sent the gods to Demeter, one after another, to try to turn her from her anger, but she listened to none of them. Never would she let the earth bear fruit until she had seen her daughter. Then Zeus realized that his brother must give way. He told Hermes to go down to the underworld and to bid the lord of it let his bride go back to Demeter.

Hermes found the two sitting side by side, Persephone shrinking away, reluctant because she longed for her mother. At Hermes' words she sprang up joyfully, eager to go. Her husband knew that he must obey the word of Zeus and send her up to earth away from him, but he prayed her as she left him to have kind thoughts of him and not be so sorrowful that she was the wife of one who was great among the immortals. And he made her eat a pomegranate seed, knowing in his heart that if she did so she must return to him.

He got ready his golden car and Hermes took the reins and drove the black horses straight to the temple where Demeter was. She ran out to meet her daughter as swiftly as a Maenad runs down the mountainside. Persephone sprang into her arms and was held fast there. All day they talked of what had happened to them both, and Demeter grieved when she heard of the pomegranate seed, fearing that she could not keep her daughter with her.

Then Zeus sent another messenger to her, a great personage, none other than his revered mother Rhea, the oldest of the gods. Swiftly she hastened down from the heights of Olympus to the barren, leafless earth, and standing at the door of the temple she spoke to Demeter.

Come, my daughter, for Zeus, far-seeing, loud-thundering, bids you.
Come once again to the halls of the gods where you shall have honor,
Where you will have your desire, your daughter, to comfort your sorrow
As each year is accomplished and bitter winter is ended.
For a third part only the kingdom of darkness shall hold her.
For the rest you will keep her, you and the happy immortals.
Peace now. Give men life which comes alone from your giving.

Demeter did not refuse, poor comfort though it was that she must lose Persephone for four months every year and see her young loveliness go down to the world of the dead. But she was kind; the "Good Goddess," men always called her. She was sorry for the desolation she had brought about. She made the fields once more rich with abundant fruit and the whole world bright with flowers and green leaves. Also she went to the princes of Eleusis who had built her temple and she chose one, Triptolemus, to be her ambassador to men, instructing them how to sow the corn. She taught him and Celeus and the others her sacred rites, "mysteries which no one may utter, for deep awe checks the tongue. Blessed is he who has seen them; his lot will be good in the world to come."

• • •

Queen of fragrant Eleusis,
Giver of earth's good gifts,
Give me your grace, O Demeter.
You, too, Persephone, fairest,
Maiden all lovely, I offer
Song for your favor.

• • •

In the stories of both goddesses, Demeter and Persephone, the idea of sorrow was foremost. Demeter, goddess of the harvest wealth, was still more the divine sorrowing mother who saw her daughter die each year. Persephone was the radiant maiden of the spring and the summertime, whose light step upon the dry, brown hillside was enough to make it fresh and blooming, as Sappho writes,

> I heard the footfall of the flower spring . . .

—Persephone's footfall. But all the while Persephone knew how brief that beauty was; fruits, flowers, leaves, all the fair growth of earth, must end with the coming of the cold and pass like herself into the power of death. After the lord of the dark world below carried her away she was never again the gay young creature who had played in the flowery meadow without a thought of care or trouble. She did indeed rise from the dead every spring, but she brought with her the memory of where she had come from; with all her bright beauty there was something strange and awesome about her. She was often said to be "the maiden whose name may not be spoken."

The Olympians were "the happy gods," "the deathless gods," far removed from suffering mortals destined to die. But in their grief and at the hour of death, men could turn for compassion to the goddess who sorrowed and the goddess who died.

DIONYSUS OR BACCHUS

> *This story is very differently told from the story of Demeter. Dionysus was the last god to enter Olympus. Homer did not admit him. There are no early sources for his story except a few brief allusions in Hesiod, in the eighth or ninth century. A late Homeric Hymn, perhaps even as late as the fourth century, gives the only account of the pirates' ship, and the fate of Pentheus is the subject of the last play of Euripides, in the fifth century, the most modern of all Greek poets.*

Thebes was Dionysus' own city, where he was born, the son of Zeus and the Theban princess Semele. He was the only god whose parents were not both divine.

> At Thebes alone do mortal women bear
> Immortal gods.

Semele was the most unfortunate woman of all those Zeus fell in love with, and in her case too the reason was Hera. Zeus was madly in love with her and told her that anything she asked of him he would do; he swore it by the river Styx, the oath which not even he himself could break. She told him that what she wanted above all else was to see him in his full splendor as King of Heaven and Lord of the Thunderbolt. It was Hera who had put that wish into her heart. Zeus knew that no mortal could behold him thus and live, but he could do nothing. He had sworn by the Styx. He came as she had asked, and before that awful glory of burning light she died. But Zeus snatched from her her child that was near birth, and hid it in his own side away from Hera until the time had come for it to be born. Then Hermes carried it to be cared for by the nymphs of Nysa—the loveliest of earth's valleys, but no man has ever looked upon Nysa or knows where it lies. Some say the nymphs were the Hyades, whom Zeus afterwards placed in the sky as stars, the stars which bring rain when they near the horizon.

So the God of the Vine was born of fire and nursed by rain, the hard burning heat that ripens the grapes and the water that keeps the plant alive.

Grown to manhood, Dionysus wandered far to strange places.

> The lands of Lydia rich in gold,
> Of Phrygia too; the sun-struck plains
> Of Persia; the great walls of Bactria.
> The storm-swept country of the Medes;
> And Araby the Blest.

Everywhere he taught men the culture of the vine and the mysteries of his worship and everywhere they accepted him as a god until he drew near to his own country.

One day over the sea near Greece a pirates' ship came sailing. On a great headland by the shore they saw a beautiful youth. His rich dark hair flowed down over a purple cloak that covered his strong shoulders. He looked like a son of kings, one whose parents could pay a great ransom. Exulting, the sailors sprang ashore and seized him. On board the ship they fetched rude bonds to fetter him with, but to their amazement they were unable to bind him; the ropes would not hold together; they fell apart when they touched his hands or feet. And he sat looking at them with a smile in his dark eyes.

Alone among them the helmsman understood and cried out that this must be a god and should be set free at once or deadly harm would come to them. But the captain mocked him for a silly fool and bade the crew hasten to hoist the sail. The wind filled it and the men drew taut the sheets, but the ship did not move. Then wonder upon wonder happened. Fragrant wine ran in streams down the deck; a vine with many clusters spread out over the sail; a dark green ivy-plant twined around the mast like a garland, with flowers in it and lovely fruits. Terror-stricken, the pirates ordered the helmsman to put in to land. Too late, for as they spoke their captive became a lion, roaring and glaring terribly. At that, they leaped overboard and instantly were changed into dolphins, all except the good helmsman. On him the god had mercy. He held him back and bade him take courage, for he had found favor with one who was indeed a god— Dionysus, whom Semele bore in union with Zeus.

When he passed through Thrace on his way to Greece, the god was insulted by one of the kings there, Lycurgus, who bitterly opposed this new worship. Dionysus retreated before him and even took refuge from him in the depths of the sea. But later he came back, overpowered him and punished him for his wickedness, though mildly, by

> Imprisoning him within a rocky cave
> Until his first fierce maddening rage
> Passed slowly and he learned to know
> The god whom he had mocked.

But the other gods were not mild. Zeus struck Lycurgus blind and he died soon after. None lived long who strove with gods.

Some time during his wanderings, Dionysus came upon the princess of Crete, Ariadne, when she was utterly desolate, having been abandoned on the shore of the island of Naxos by the Athenian prince, Theseus, whose life she had saved. Dionysus had compassion upon her. He rescued her, and in the end loved her. When she died Dionysus took a crown he had given her and placed it among the stars.

The mother whom he had never seen was not forgotten. He longed for her so greatly that at last he dared the terrible descent to the lower world to seek her. When he found her, he defied the power of Death to keep her from him; and Death yielded. Dionysus brought her away, but not to live on earth. He took her up to Olympus, where the gods consented to receive her as one of themselves, a mortal, indeed, but the mother of a god and therefore fit to dwell with immortals.

The God of Wine could be kind and beneficent. He could also be cruel and drive men on to frightful deeds. Often he made them mad. The MAENADS, or the BACCHANTES, as they were also called, were women frenzied with wine. They rushed through woods and over mountains uttering sharp cries, waving pine-cone-tipped wands, swept away in a fierce ecstasy. Nothing could stop them. They would tear to pieces the wild creatures they met and devour the bloody shreds of flesh. They sang,

Oh, sweet upon the mountain
The dancing and the singing,
The maddening rushing flight.
Oh, sweet to sink to earth outworn
When the wild goat has been hunted and caught.
Oh, the joy of the blood and the raw red flesh!

The gods of Olympus loved order and beauty in their sacrifices and their temples. The madwomen, the Maenads, had no temples. They went to the wilderness to worship, to the wildest mountains, the deepest forests, as if they kept to the customs of an ancient time before men had thought of building houses for their gods. They went out of the dusty, crowded city, back to the clean purity of the untrodden hills and woodlands. There Dionysus gave them food and drink: herbs and berries and the milk of the wild goat. Their beds were on the soft meadow grass; under the thick-leaved trees; where the pine needles fall year after year. They woke to a sense of peace and heavenly freshness; they bathed in a clear brook. There was much that was lovely, good, and freeing in this worship under the open sky and the ecstasy of joy it brought in the wild beauty of the world. And yet always present, too, was the horrible bloody feast.

The worship of Dionysus was centered in these two ideas so far apart—of freedom and ecstatic joy and of savage brutality. The God of Wine could give either to his worshipers. Throughout the story of his life he is sometimes man's blessing, sometimes his ruin. Of all the terrible deeds laid to his account the worst was done in Thebes, his mother's city.

Dionysus came to Thebes to establish his worship there. He was accompanied, as was his custom, by a train of women dancing and singing exultant songs, wearing fawn-skins over their robes, waving ivy-wreathed wands. They seemed mad with joy. They sang,

O Bacchanals, come,
Oh, come.
Sing Dionysus,
Sing to the timbrel,
The deep-voiced timbrel.
Joyfully praise him,
Him who brings joy.
Holy, all holy
Music is calling.
To the hills, to the hills,
Fly, O Bacchanal
Swift of foot.
On, O joyful, be fleet.

Pentheus, the King of Thebes, was the son of Semele's sister, but he had no idea that the leader of this band of excited, strange-acting women was his own cousin. He did not know that when Semele died Zeus had saved her child. The wild dancing and the loud joyous singing and the generally queer behavior of these strangers seemed to him highly objectionable, and to be stopped at once. Pentheus ordered his guards to seize and imprison the visitors, especially the leader, "whose face is flushed with wine, a cheating sorcerer from Lydia." But as he said these words he heard behind him a solemn warning: "The man you reject is a new god. He is Semele's child, whom Zeus rescued. He, with divine Demeter, is greatest upon earth for men." The speaker was the old blind prophet Teiresias, the holy man of Thebes who knew as no one else the will of the gods. But as Pentheus turned to answer him he saw that he was tricked out like the wild women: a wreath of ivy on his white hair, his old shoulders covered by a fawn-skin, a queer pine-tipped stick in his trembling hand. Pentheus laughed mockingly as he looked him over and then ordered him with contempt out of his sight. Thus he brought upon himself his doom; he would not hear when the gods spoke to him.

Dionysus was led in before him by a band of his soldiers. They said he had not tried to flee or to resist, but had done all possible to make it easy for them to seize and bring him until they felt ashamed and told him they were acting under orders, not of their own free will. They declared, too, that the maidens they had imprisoned had all escaped to the mountains. The fetters would not keep fastened; the doors unbarred themselves. "This man," they said, "has come to Thebes with many wonders—"

Pentheus by now was blind to everything except his anger and his scorn. He spoke roughly to Dionysus, who answered him with entire gentleness, seeming to try to reach his real self and open his eyes to see that he was face to face with divinity. He warned him that he could not keep him in prison, "for God will set me free."

"God?" Pentheus asked jeeringly.

"Yes," Dionysus answered. "He is here and sees my suffering."

"Not where my eyes can see him," Pentheus said.

"He is where I am," answered Dionysus. "You cannot see him for you are not pure."

Pentheus angrily ordered the soldiers to bind him and take him to the prison and Dionysus went, saying, "The wrongs you do to me are wrongs done to the gods."

But the prison could not hold Dionysus. He came forth,

and going to Pentheus again he tried to persuade him to yield to what these wonders plainly showed was divine, and welcome this new worship of a new and great god. When, however, Pentheus only heaped insults and threats upon him, Dionysus left him to his doom. It was the most horrible that there could be.

Pentheus went to pursue the god's followers among the hills where the maidens had fled when they escaped from prison. Many of the Theban women had joined them; Pentheus' mother and her sisters were there. And there Dionysus showed himself in his most terrible aspect. He made them all mad. The women thought Pentheus a wild beast, a mountain lion, and they rushed to destroy him, his mother first. As they fell upon him he knew at last that he had fought against a god and must pay with his life. They tore him limb from limb, and then, only then, the god restored their senses, and his mother saw what she had done. Looking at her in her agony the maidens, all sobered now, the dancing over and the singing and the wild wand-waving, said to one another.

> In strange ways hard to know gods come to men.
> Many a thing past hope they had fulfilled,
> And what was looked for went another way.
> A path we never thought to tread God found for us.
> So has this come to pass.

* * *

The ideas about Dionysus in these various stories seem at first sight contradictory. In one he is the joy-god—

> He whose locks are bound with gold,
> Ruddy Bacchus,
> Comrade of the Maenads, whose
> Blithe torch blazes.

In another he is the heartless god, savage, brutal—

> He who with a mocking laugh
> Hunts his prey,
> Snares and drags him to his death
> With his Bacchanals.

The truth is, however, that both ideas arose quite simply and reasonably from the fact of his being the god of wine. Wine is bad as well as good. It cheers and warms men's hearts; it also makes them drunk. The Greeks were a people who saw facts very clearly. They could not shut their eyes to the ugly and degrading side of wine-drinking and see only the delightful side. Dionysus was the God of the Vine; therefore he was a power which sometimes made men commit frightful and atrocious crimes. No one could defend them; no one would ever try to defend the fate Pentheus suffered. But, the Greeks said to each other, such things really do happen when people are frenzied with drink. This truth did not blind them to the other truth, that wine was "the merrymaker," lightening men's hearts, bringing careless ease and fun and gaiety.

> The wine of Dionysus,
> When the weary cares of men
> Leave every heart.
> We travel to a land that never was.
> The poor grow rich, the rich grow great of heart.
> All-conquering are the shafts made from the Vine.

The reason that Dionysus was so different at one time from another was because of this double nature of wine and so of the god of wine. He was man's benefactor and he was man's destroyer.

On his beneficent side he was not only the god that makes men merry. His cup was

> Life-giving, healing every ill.

Under his influence courage was quickened and fear banished, at any rate for the moment. He uplifted his worshipers; he made them feel that they could do what they had thought they could not. All this happy freedom and confidence passed away, of course, as they either grew sober or got drunk, but while it lasted it was like being possessed by a power greater than themselves. So people felt about Dionysus as about no other god. He was not only outside of them, he was within them, too. They could be transformed by him into being like him. The momentary sense of exultant power wine-drinking can give was only a sign to show men that they had within them more than they knew; "they could themselves become divine."

To think in this way was far removed from the old idea of worshiping the god by drinking enough to be gay or to be freed from care or to get drunk. There were followers of Dionysus who never drank wine at all. It is not known when the great change took place, lifting the god who freed men for a moment through drunkenness to the god who freed them through inspiration, but one very remarkable result of it made Dionysus for all future ages the most important of the gods of Greece.

The Eleusinian Mysteries, which were always chiefly Demeter's, had indeed great importance. For hundreds of years they helped men, as Cicero said, "to live with joy and to die with hope." But their influence did not last, very likely because nobody was allowed to teach their ideas openly or write about them. In the end only a dim memory of them was left. It was quite otherwise with Dionysus. What was done at his great festival was open to all the world and is a living influence today. No other festival in Greece could compare with it. It took place in the spring when the vine begins to put forth its branches, and it lasted for five days. They were days of perfect peace and enjoyment. All the ordinary business of life stopped. No one could be put in prison; prisoners were even released so that they could share in the general rejoicing. But the place where people gathered to do honor to the god was not a wild wilderness made horrible by savage deeds and a bloody feast; it was not even a temple precinct with ordered sacrifices and priestly ceremonies. It was a theater; and the ceremony was the performance of a play. The greatest poetry in Greece, and among the greatest in the world, was written for Dionysus. The poets who wrote the plays, the actors and singers who took part in them, were all regarded as servants of the god. The performances were sacred; the spectators, too, along with the writers and the performers, were engaged in an act of worship. Dionysus himself was supposed to be present; his priest had the seat of honor.

It is clear, therefore, that the idea of the god of holy inspiration who could fill men with his spirit to write gloriously and to act gloriously became far more important than the earlier ideas of him. The first tragic plays, which are among the best there are, never equaled except by Shakespeare, were produced in the theater of Dionysus. Comedies were produced there, too, but tragedies far outnumbered them, and there was a reason why.

This strange god, the gay reveler, the cruel hunter, the lofty inspirer, was also the sufferer. He, like Demeter, was afflicted, not because of grief for another, as she was, but because of his own pain. He was the vine, which is always pruned as nothing else that bears fruit; every branch cut away, only the bare stock left; through the winter a dead thing to look at, an old gnarled stump seeming incapable of ever putting forth leaves again. Like Persephone Dionysus died with the coming of the cold. Unlike her, his death was terrible: he was torn to pieces, in some stories by the Titans, in others by Hera's orders. He was always brought back to life; he died and rose again. It was his joyful resurrection they celebrated in his theater, but the idea of terrible deeds done to him and done by men under his influence was too closely associated with him ever to be forgotten. He was more than the suffering god. He was the tragic god. There was none other.

He had still another side. He was the assurance that death does not end all. His worshipers believed that his death and resurrection showed that the soul lives on forever after the body dies. This faith was part of the mysteries of Eleusis. At first it centered in Persephone who also rose from the dead every spring. But as queen of the black underworld she kept even in the bright world above a suggestion of something strange and awful: how could she who carried always about her the reminder of death stand for the resurrection, the conquest of death? Dionysus, on the contrary, was never thought of as a power in the kingdom of the dead. There are many stories about Persephone in the lower world; only one about Dionysus—he rescued his mother from it. In his resurrection he was the embodiment of the life that is stronger than death. He and not Persephone became the center of the belief in immortality.

Around the year 80 A.D., a great Greek writer, Plutarch, received news, when he was far from home, that a little daughter of his had died—a child of most gentle nature, he says. In his letter to his wife he writes: "About that which you have heard, dear heart, that the soul once departed from the body vanishes and feels nothing, I know that you give no belief to such assertions because of those sacred and faithful promises given in the mysteries of Bacchus which we who are of that religious brotherhood know. We hold it firmly for an undoubted truth that our soul is incorruptible and immortal. We are to think (of the dead) that they pass into a better place and a happier condition. Let us behave ourselves accordingly, outwardly ordering our lives, while within all should be purer, wiser, incorruptible."

3 How the World and Mankind Were Created

With the exception of the story of Prometheus' punishment, told by Aeschylus in the fifth century, I have taken the material of this chapter chiefly from Hesiod, who lived at least three hundred years earlier. He is the principal authority for the myths about the beginning of everything. Both the crudity of the story of Cronus and the naïveté of the story of Pandora are characteristic of him.

> First there was Chaos, the vast immeasurable abyss,
> Outrageous as a sea, dark, wasteful, wild.

These words are Milton's, but they express with precision what the Greeks thought lay back of the very first beginning of things. Long before the gods appeared, in the dim past, uncounted ages ago, there was only the formless confusion of Chaos brooded over by unbroken darkness. At last, but how no one ever tried to explain, two children were born to this shapeless nothingness. Night was the child of Chaos and so was Erebus, which is the unfathomable depth where death dwells. In the whole universe there was nothing else; all was black, empty, silent, endless.

And then a marvel of marvels came to pass. In some mysterious way, from this horror of blank boundless vacancy the best of all things came into being. A great playwright, the comic poet Aristophanes, describes its coming in words often quoted:—

> . . . Black-winged Night
> Into the bosom of Erebus dark and deep
> Laid a wind-born egg, and as the seasons rolled
> Forth sprang Love, the longed-for, shining, with
> wings of gold.

From darkness and from death Love was born, and with its birth, order and beauty began to banish blind confusion. Love created Light with its companion, radiant Day.

What took place next was the creation of the earth, but this, too, no one ever tried to explain. It just happened. With the coming of love and light it seemed natural that the earth also should appear. The poet Hesiod, the first Greek who tried to explain how things began, wrote,

> Earth, the beautiful, rose up,
> Broad-bosomed, she that is the steadfast base
> Of all things. And fair Earth first bore
> The starry Heaven, equal to herself,
> To cover her on all sides and to be
> A home forever for the blessed gods.

In all this thought about the past no distinction had as yet been made between places and persons. Earth was the solid ground, yet vaguely a personality, too. Heaven was the blue vault on high, but it acted in some ways as a human being would. To the people who told these stories all the universe was alive with the same kind of life they knew in themselves. They were individual persons, so they personified everything which had the obvious marks of life, everything which moved and changed: earth in winter and summer; the sky with its shifting stars; the restless sea, and so on. It was only a dim personification: something vague and immense which with its motion brought about change and therefore was alive.

But when they told of the coming of love and light the early storytellers were setting the scene for the appearance of mankind, and they began to personify more precisely. They gave natural forces distinct shapes. They thought of them as the precursors of men and they defined them far more clearly as individuals than they had earth and heaven. They showed them acting in every way as human beings did; walking, for instance, and eating, as Earth and Heaven obviously did not. These two were set apart. If they were alive, it was in a way peculiar to them alone.

The first creatures who had the appearance of life were the children of Mother Earth and Father Heaven (Gaea and Ouranos). They were monsters. Just as we believe that the earth was once inhabited by strange gigantic creatures, so did the Greeks. They did not, however, think of them as huge lizards and mammoths, but as somewhat like men and yet unhuman. They had the shattering, overwhelming strength of earthquake and hurricane and volcano. In the tales about them they do not seem really alive, but rather to belong to a world where as yet there was no life, only tremendous movements of irresistible forces lifting up the mountains and scooping out the seas. The Greeks apparently had some such feeling because in their stories, although they represent these creatures as living beings, they make them unlike any form of life known to man.

Three of them, monstrously huge and strong, had each a hundred hands and fifty heads. To three others was given the name of *Cyclops* (the Wheel-eyed), because each had only one enormous eye, as round and as big as a wheel, in the middle of the forehead. The Cyclopes, too, were gigantic, towering up like mighty mountain crags and devastating in their power. Last came the Titans. There were a number of these and they were in no way inferior to the others in size and strength, but they were not purely destructive. Several of them were even beneficent. One, indeed, after men had been created, saved them from destruction.

It was natural to think of these fearful creations as the children of Mother Earth, brought forth from her dark depths when the world was young. But it is extremely odd that they were also the children of Heaven. However, that was what the Greeks said, and they made Heaven out to be a very poor father. He hated the things with a hundred hands and fifty heads, even though they were his sons, and as each was born he imprisoned it in a secret place within the earth. The Cyclopes and the Titans he left at large; and Earth, enraged at the maltreatment of her other children, appealed to them to help her. Only one was bold enough, the Titan Cronus. He lay in wait for his father and wounded him terribly. The Giants, the fourth race of monsters, sprang up from his blood. From this same blood, too, the Erinyes (the Furies) were born. Their office was to pursue and punish sinners. They were called "those who walk in darkness," and they were terrible of aspect, with writhing snakes for hair and eyes that wept tears of blood. The other monsters were finally driven from the earth, but not the Erinyes. As long as there was sin in the world they could not be banished.

From that time on for untold ages, Cronus, he whom as we have seen the Romans called Saturn, was lord of the universe, with his sister-queen, Rhea (Ops in Latin). Finally one of their sons, the future ruler of heaven and earth, whose name in Greek is Zeus and in Latin Jupiter, rebelled against him. He had good cause to do so, for Cronus had learned that one of his children was destined some day to dethrone him and he thought to go against fate by swallowing them as soon as they were born. But when Rhea bore Zeus, her sixth child, she succeeded in having him secretly carried off to Crete, while she gave her husband a great stone wrapped in swaddling clothes which he supposed was the baby and swallowed down accordingly. Later, when Zeus was grown, he forced his father with the help of his grandmother, the Earth, to disgorge it along with the five earlier children, and it was set up at Delphi where eons later a great traveler, Pausanias by name, reports that he saw it about 180 A.D.: "A stone of no great size which the priests of Delphi anoint every day with oil."

There followed a terrible war between Cronus, helped by his brother Titans, against Zeus with his five brothers and sisters—a war that almost wrecked the universe.

> A dreadful sound troubled the boundless sea.
> The whole earth uttered a great cry.
> Wide heaven, shaken, groaned.
> From its foundation far Olympus reeled
> Beneath the onrush of the deathless gods,
> And trembling seized upon black Tartarus.

The Titans were conquered, partly because Zeus released from their prison the hundred-handed monsters who fought for him with their irresistible weapons—thunder, lightning, and earthquake—and also because one of the sons of the Titan Iapetus, whose name was Prometheus and who was very wise, took sides with Zeus.

Zeus punished his conquered enemies terribly. They were

> Bound in bitter chains beneath the wide-wayed earth,
> As far below the earth as over earth
> Is heaven, for even so far down lies Tartarus.
> Nine days and nights would a bronze anvil fall
> And on the tenth reach earth from heaven.
> And then again falling nine days and nights,
> Would come to Tartarus, the brazen-fenced.

Prometheus' brother Atlas suffered a still worse fate. He was condemned

> To bear on his back forever
> The cruel strength of the crushing world
> And the vault of the sky.
> Upon his shoulders the great pillar
> That holds apart the earth and heaven,
> A load not easy to be borne.

Bearing this burden he stands forever before the place that is wrapped in clouds and darkness, where Night and Day draw near and greet one another. The house within never holds both Night and Day, but always one, departing, visits the earth, and the other in the house awaits the hour for her journeying hence, one with far-seeing light for those on earth, the other holding in her hands Sleep, the brother of Death.

Even after the Titans were conquered and crushed, Zeus was not completely victorious. Earth gave birth to her last and most frightful offspring, a creature more terrible than any that had gone before. His name was Typhon.

> A flaming monster with a hundred heads,
> Who rose up against all the gods.
> Death whistled from his fearful jaws,
> His eyes flashed glaring fire.

But Zeus had now got the thunder and lightning under his own control. They had become his weapons, used by no one else. He struck Typhon down with

> The bolt that never sleeps,
> Thunder with breath of flame.
> Into his very heart the fire burned.
> His strength was turned to ashes.
> And now he lies a useless thing
> By Aetna, whence sometimes there burst
> Rivers red-hot, consuming with fierce jaws
> The level fields of Sicily,
> Lovely with fruits.
> And that is Typhon's anger boiling up,
> His fire-breathing darts.

Still later, one more attempt was made to unseat Zeus: the Giants rebelled. But by this time the gods were very strong and they were helped, too, by mighty Hercules, a son of Zeus. The Giants were defeated and hurled down to Tartarus; and the victory of the radiant powers of Heaven over the brutal forces of Earth was complete. From then on, Zeus and his brothers and sisters ruled, undisputed lords of all.

As yet there were no human beings; but the world, now cleared of the monsters, was ready for mankind. It was a place where people could live in some comfort and security, without having to fear the sudden appearance of a Titan or a Giant. The earth was believed to be a round disk, divided into two equal parts by the Sea, as the Greeks called it,— which we know as the Mediterranean,—and by what we call the Black Sea. (The Greeks called this first the Axine, which means the Unfriendly Sea, and then, perhaps as people became familiar with it, the Euxine, the Friendly Sea. It is sometimes suggested that they gave it this pleasant name to make it feel pleasantly disposed toward them.) Around the earth flowed the great river, Ocean, never troubled by wind or storm. On the farther bank of Ocean were mysterious people, whom few on earth ever found their way to. The Cimmerians lived there, but whether east, west, north or south, no one knew. It was a land cloud-wrapped and misty, where the light of day was never seen; upon which the shining sun never looked with his splendor, not when he climbed through the starry sky at dawn, nor when at evening he turned toward the earth from the sky. Endless night was spread over its melancholy people.

Except in this one country, all those who lived across Ocean were exceedingly fortunate. In the remotest North, so far away it was at the back of the North Wind, was a blissful land where the Hyperboreans lived. Only a few strangers, great heroes, had ever visited it. Not by ship nor yet on foot might one find the road to the marvelous meeting place of the Hyperboreans. But the Muses lived not far from them, such were their ways. For everywhere the dance of maidens swayed and the clear call of the lyre sounded and the ringing notes of flutes. With golden laurel they bound their hair and they feasted merrily. In that holy race, sickness and deathly old age had no part. Far to the south was the country of the Ethiopians, of whom we know only that the gods held them in such favor they would sit at joyful banquets with them in their halls.

On Ocean's bank, too, was the abode of the blessed dead. In that land, there was no snowfall nor much winter nor any storm of rain; but from Ocean the West Wind sang soft and thrillingly to refresh the souls of men. Here those who kept themselves pure from all wrong came when they left the earth.

> Their boon is life forever freed from toil.
> No more to trouble earth or the sea waters
> With their strong hands,
> Laboring for the food that does not satisfy.
> But with the honored of the gods they live
> A life where there are no more tears.
> Around those blessed isles soft sea winds breathe,
> And flowers of gold are blazing on the trees,
> Upon the waters, too.

By now all was ready for the appearance of mankind. Even the places the good and bad should go to after death had been arranged. It was time for men to be created. There is more than one account of how that came to pass. Some say it was delegated by the gods to Prometheus, the Titan who had sided with Zeus in the war with the Titans, and to his brother, Epimetheus. Prometheus, whose name means forethought, was very wise, wiser even than the gods, but Epimetheus, which means afterthought, was a scatterbrained person who invariably followed his first impulse and then changed his mind. So he did in this case. Before making men he gave all the best gifts to the animals, strength and swiftness and courage and shrewd cunning, fur and feathers and wings and shells and the like—until no good was left for men, no protective covering and no quality to make them a match for the beasts. Too late, as always, he was sorry and asked his brother's help. Prometheus, then, took over the task of creation and thought out a way to make mankind superior. He fashioned them in a nobler shape than the animals, upright like the gods; and then he went to heaven, to the sun, where he lit a torch and brought down fire, a protection to men far better than anything else, whether fur or feathers or strength or swiftness.

> And now, though feeble and short-lived,
> Mankind has flaming fire and therefrom
> Learns many crafts.

According to another story, the gods themselves created men. They made first a golden race. These, although mortal, lived like gods without sorrow of heart, far from toil and pain. The cornland of itself bore fruit abundantly. They were rich also in flocks and beloved of the gods. When the grave covered them they became pure spirits, beneficent, the guardians of mankind.

In this account of the creation the gods seemed bent on experimenting with the various metals, and, oddly enough, proceeding downward from the excellent to the good to the worse and so on. When they had tried gold they went to silver. This second race of silver was very inferior to the first. They had so little intelligence that they could not keep from injuring each other. They too passed away, but, unlike the gold race, their spirits did not live on after them. The next race was of brass. They were terrible men, immensely strong, and such lovers of war and violence that they were completely destroyed by their own hands. This, however, was all to the good, for they were followed by a splendid race of godlike heroes who fought glorious wars and went on great adventures which men have talked and sung of through all the ages since. They departed finally to the isles of the blessed, where they lived in perfect bliss forever.

The fifth race is that which is now upon the earth: the iron race. They live in evil times and their nature too has much of evil, so that they never have rest from toil and sorrow. As the generations pass, they grow worse; sons are always inferior to their fathers. A time will come when they have grown so wicked that they will worship power; might will be right to them, and reverence for the good will cease to be. At last when no man is angry any more at wrongdoing or feels shame in the presence of the miserable, Zeus will destroy them too. And yet even then something might be done, if only the common people would arise and put down rulers that oppress them.

[◉]   [◉]   [◉]

These two stories of the creation,—the story of the five ages, and the story of Prometheus and Epimetheus,—different as they are, agree in one point. For a long time, certainly throughout the happy Golden Age, only men were upon the earth; there were no women. Zeus created these later, in his anger at Prometheus for caring so much for men. Prometheus had not only stolen fire for men; he had also arranged that they should get the best part of any animal sacrificed and the gods the worst. He cut up a great ox and wrapped the good eatable parts in the hide, disguising them further by piling entrails on top. Beside this heap he put another of all the bones, dressed up with cunning and covered with shining fat, and bade Zeus choose between them. Zeus took up the white fat and was angry when he saw the bones craftily tricked out. But he had made his choice and he had to abide by it. Thereafter only fat and bones were burned to the gods upon their altars. Men kept the good meat for themselves.

But the Father of Men and of Gods was not one to put up with this sort of treatment. He swore to be revenged, on mankind first and then on mankind's friend. He made a great evil for men, a sweet and lovely thing to look upon, in the likeness of a shy maiden, and all the gods gave her gifts, silvery raiment and a broidered veil, a wonder to behold, and bright garlands of blooming flowers and a crown of gold—great beauty shone out from it. Because of what they gave her they called her *Pandora*, which means "the gift of all." When this beautiful disaster had been made, Zeus brought her out and wonder took hold of gods and men when they beheld her. From her, the first woman, comes the race of women, who are an evil to men, with a nature to do evil.

Another story about Pandora is that the source of all misfortune was not her wicked nature, but only her curiosity. The gods presented her with a box into which each had put something harmful, and forbade her ever to open it. Then they sent her to Epimetheus, who took her gladly although Prometheus had warned him never to accept anything from Zeus. He took her, and afterward when that dangerous thing, a woman, was his, he understood how good his brother's advice had been. For Pandora, like all women, was possessed of a lively curiosity. She *had* to know what was in the box. One day she lifted the lid—and out flew plagues innumerable, sorrow and mis-

**Pandora lifted the lid and out flew plagues
and sorrows for mankind**

chief for mankind. In terror Pandora clapped the lid down, but too late. One good thing, however, was there—Hope. It was the only good the casket had held among the many evils, and it remains to this day mankind's sole comfort in misfortune. So mortals learned that it is not possible to get the better of Zeus or ever deceive him. The wise and compassionate Prometheus, too, found that out.

When Zeus had punished men by giving them women he turned his attention to the arch-sinner himself. The new ruler of the gods owed Prometheus much for helping him conquer the other Titans, but he forgot his debt. Zeus had his servants, Force and Violence, seize him and take him to the Caucasus, where they bound him

> To a high-piercing, headlong rock
> In adamantine chains that none can break,

and they told him,

> Forever shall the intolerable present grind you down.
> And he who will release you is not born.
> Such fruit you reap for your man-loving ways.
> A god yourself, you did not dread God's anger,
> But gave to mortals honor not their due.
> And therefore you must guard this joyless rock—
> No rest, no sleep, no moment's respite.
> Groans shall your speech be, lamentation your only words.

The reason for inflicting this torture was not only to punish Prometheus, but also to force him to disclose a secret very important to the lord of Olympus. Zeus knew that fate, which brings all things to pass, had decreed that a son should some day be born to him who would dethrone him and drive the gods from their home in heaven, but only Prometheus knew who would be the mother of this son. As he lay bound upon the rock in agony, Zeus sent his messenger, Hermes, to bid him disclose the secret. Prometheus told him:—

> Go and persuade the sea wave not to break.
> You will persuade me no more easily.

Hermes warned him that if he persisted in his stubborn silence, he should suffer still more terrible things.

> An eagle red with blood
> Shall come, a guest unbidden to your banquet.
> All day long he will tear to rags your body,
> Feasting in fury on the blackened liver.

But nothing, no threat, nor torture, could break Prometheus. His body was bound but his spirit was free. He refused to submit to cruelty and tyranny. He knew that he had served Zeus well and that he had done right to pity mortals in their helplessness. His suffering was utterly unjust, and he would not give in to brutal power no matter at what cost. He told Hermes:—

> There is no force which can compel my speech.
> So let Zeus hurl his blazing bolts,
> And with the white wings of the snow,
> With thunder and with earthquake,
> Confound the reeling world.
> None of all this will bend my will.

Hermes, crying out,

> Why, these are ravings you may hear from madmen,

left him to suffer what he must. Generations later we know he was released, but why and how is not told clearly anywhere. There is a strange story that the Centaur, Chiron, though immortal, was willing to die for him and that he was allowed to do so. When Hermes was urging Prometheus to give in to Zeus he spoke of this, but in such a way as to make it seem an incredible sacrifice:—

> Look for no ending to this agony
> Until a god will freely suffer for you,
> Will take on him your pain, and in your stead
> Descend to where the sun is turned to darkness,
> The black depths of death.

But Chiron did do this and Zeus seems to have accepted him as a substitute. We are told, too, that Hercules slew the eagle and delivered Prometheus from his bonds, and that Zeus was willing to have this done. But why Zeus changed his mind and whether Prometheus revealed the secret when he was freed, we do not know. One thing, however, is certain: in whatever way the two were reconciled, it was not Prometheus who yielded. His name has stood through all the centuries, from Greek days to our own, as that of the great rebel against injustice and the authority of power.

:●   ●   ●:

There is still another account of the creation of mankind. In the story of the five ages men are descended from the iron race. In the story of Prometheus, it is uncertain whether the men he saved from destruction belonged to that race or the bronze race. Fire would have been as necessary to the one as to the other. In the third story, men are descended from a race of stone. This story begins with the Deluge.

All over the earth men grew so wicked that finally Zeus determined to destroy them. He decided

> To mingle storm and tempest over boundless earth
> And make an utter end of mortal man.

He sent the flood. He called upon his brother, the God of the Sea, to help him, and together, with torrents of rain from heaven and rivers loosed upon the earth, the two drowned the land.

> The might of water overwhelmed dark earth,

over the summits of the highest mountains. Only towering Parnassus was not quite covered, and the bit of dry land on its very topmost peak was the means by which mankind escaped destruction. After it had rained through nine days and nine nights, there came drifting to that spot what looked to be a great wooden chest, but safe within it were two living human beings, a man and a woman. They were Deucalion and Pyrrha—he Prometheus' son, and she his niece, the daughter of Epimetheus and Pandora. The wisest person in all the universe, Prometheus had well been able to protect his own family. He knew the flood would come, and he had bidden his son build the chest, store it with provisions, and embark in it with his wife.

Fortunately Zeus was not offended, because the two were pious, faithful worshipers of the gods. When the chest came to land and they got out, to see no sign of life anywhere, only a wild waste of waters, Zeus pitied them and drained off the flood. Slowly like the ebbing tide the sea and the rivers drew back and the earth was dry again. Pyrrha and Deucalion came down from Parnassus, the only living creatures in a dead world. They found a temple all slimy and moss-grown, but not quite in ruins, and there they gave thanks for their escape and prayed for help in their dreadful loneliness. They heard a voice. "Veil your heads and cast behind you the bones of your mother." The command struck them with horror. Pyrrha said, "We dare not do such a thing." Deucalion was forced to agree that she was right, but he tried to think out what might lie behind the words and suddenly he saw their meaning. "Earth is the mother of all," he told his wife. "Her bones are the stones. These we may cast behind us without doing wrong." So they did, and as the stones fell they took human shape. They were called the Stone People, and they were a hard, enduring race, as was to be expected and, indeed, as they had need to be, to rescue the earth from the desolation left by the flood.

4 The Earliest Heroes

PROMETHEUS AND IO

The materials for this story are taken from two poets, the Greek Aeschylus and the Roman Ovid, separated from each other by four hundred and fifty years and still more by their gifts and temperaments. They are the best sources for the tale. It is easy to distinguish the parts told by each, Aeschylus grave and direct, Ovid light and amusing. The touch about lovers' lies is characteristic of Ovid, as also the little story about Syrinx.

In those days when Prometheus had just given fire to men and when he was first bound to the rocky peak on Caucasus, he had a strange visitor. A distracted fleeing creature came clambering awkwardly up over the cliffs and crags to where he lay. It looked like a heifer, but talked like a girl who seemed mad with misery. The sight of Prometheus stopped her short. She cried,

> This that I see—
> A form storm-beaten,
> Bound to the rock.
> Did you do wrong?
> Is this your punishment?
> Where am I?
> Speak to a wretched wanderer.
> Enough—I have been tried enough—
> My wandering—long wandering.
> Yet I have found nowhere
> To leave my misery.
> I am a girl who speak to you,
> But horns are on my head.

Prometheus recognized her. He knew her story and he spoke her name.

> I know you, girl, Inachus' daughter, Io.
> You made the god's heart hot with love
> And Hera hates you. She it is
> Who drives you on this flight that never ends.

Wonder checked Io's frenzy. She stood still, all amazed. Her name—spoken by this strange being in this strange, lonely place! She begged,

> Who are you, sufferer, that speak the truth
> To one who suffers?

And he answered,

> You see Prometheus who gave mortals fire.

She knew him, then, and his story.

> You—he who succored the whole race of men?
> You, that Prometheus, the daring, the enduring?

They talked freely to each other. He told her how Zeus had treated him, and she told him that Zeus was the reason why she, once a princess and a happy girl, had been changed into

> A beast, a starving beast,
> That frenzied runs with clumsy leaps and bounds.
> Oh, shame . . .

Zeus's jealous wife, Hera, was the direct cause of her misfortunes, but back of them all was Zeus himself. He fell in love with her, and sent

> Ever to my maiden chamber
> Visions of the night
> Persuading me with gentle words:
> "O happy, happy girl,
> Why are you all too long a maid?
> The arrow of desire has pierced Zeus.
> For you he is on fire.
> With you it is his will to capture love."
> Always, each night, such dreams possessed me.

But still greater than Zeus's love was his fear of Hera's jealousy. He acted, however, with very little wisdom for the Father of Gods and Men when he tried to hide Io and himself by wrapping the earth in a cloud so thick and dark that a sudden night seemed to drive the clear daylight away. Hera knew perfectly well that there was a reason for this odd occurrence, and instantly suspected her husband. When she could not find him anywhere in heaven she glided swiftly down to the earth and ordered the cloud off. But Zeus too had been quick. As she caught sight of him he was standing beside a most lovely white heifer—Io, of course. He swore that he had never seen her until just now when she had sprung forth, newborn, from the earth. And this, Ovid says, shows that the lies lovers tell do not anger the gods. However, it also shows that they are not very useful, for Hera did not believe a word of it. She said the heifer was very pretty and would Zeus please make her a present of it. Sorry as he was, he saw at once that to refuse would give the whole thing away. What excuse could he make? An insignificant little cow . . . He turned Io reluctantly over to his wife and Hera knew very well how to keep her away from him.

She gave her into the charge of Argus, an excellent arrangement for Hera's purpose, since Argus had a hundred eyes. Before such a watchman, who could sleep with some of the eyes and keep on guard with the rest, Zeus seemed helpless. He watched Io's misery, turned into a beast, driven from her home; he dared not come to her help. At last, however, he went to his son Hermes, the messenger of the gods, and told him he must find a way to kill Argus. There was no god cleverer than Hermes. As soon as he had sprung to earth from heaven he laid aside everything that marked him as a god and approached Argus like a country fellow, playing very sweetly upon a pipe of reeds. Argus was pleased at the sound and called to the musician to come nearer. "You might as well sit by me on this rock," he said, "you see it's shady—just right for shepherds." Nothing could have been better for Hermes' plan, and yet nothing happened. He played and then he talked on and on, as drowsily and monotonously as he could; some of the hundred eyes would go to sleep, but some were always awake. At last, however, one story was successful—about the god Pan, how he loved a nymph named Syrinx who fled from him and just as he was about to seize her was turned into a tuft of reeds by her sister nymphs. Pan said, "Still you shall be mine," and he made from what she had become

A shepherd's pipe
Of reeds with beeswax joined.

The little story does not seem especially tiresome, as such stories go, but Argus found it so. All of his eyes went to sleep. Hermes killed him at once, of course, but Hera took the eyes and set them in the tail of the peacock, her favorite bird.

It seemed then that Io was free, but no; Hera at once

turned on her again. She sent a gad-fly to plague her, which stung her to madness. Io told Prometheus,

> He drives me all along the long sea strand.
> I may not stop for food or drink.
> He will not let me sleep.

Prometheus tried to comfort her, but he could point her only to the distant future. What lay immediately before her was still more wandering and in fearsome lands. To be sure, the part of the sea she first ran along in her frenzy would be called Ionian after her, and the Bosphorus, which means the Ford of the Cow, would preserve the memory of when she went through it, but her real consolation must be that at long last she would reach the Nile, where Zeus would restore her to her human form. She would bear him a son named Epaphus, and live forever after happy and honored. And

> Know this, that from your race will spring
> One glorious with the bow, bold-hearted,
> And he shall set me free.

Io's descendant would be Hercules, greatest of heroes, than whom hardly the gods were greater, and to whom Prometheus would owe his freedom.

EUROPA

This story, so like the Renaissance idea of the classical— fantastic, delicately decorated, bright-colored—is taken entirely from a poem of the third-century Alexandrian poet Moschus, by far the best account of it.

Io was not the only girl who gained geographical fame because Zeus fell in love with her. There was another, known far more widely—Europa, the daughter of the King of Sidon. But whereas the wretched Io had to pay dearly for the distinction, Europa was exceedingly fortunate. Except for a few moments of terror when she found herself crossing the deep sea on the back of a bull she did not suffer at all. The story does not say what Hera was about at the time, but it is clear that she was off guard and her husband free to do as he pleased.

Up in heaven one spring morning as he idly watched the earth, Zeus suddenly saw a charming spectacle. Europa had waked early, troubled just as Io had been by a dream, only this time not of a god who loved her but of two Continents who each in the shape of a woman tried to possess her, Asia saying that she had given her birth and therefore owned her, and the other, as yet nameless, declaring that Zeus would give the maiden to her.

Once awake from this strange vision which had come at dawn, the time when true dreams oftenest visit mortals, Europa decided not to try to go to sleep again, but to summon her companions, girls born in the same year as herself and all of noble birth, to go out with her to the lovely blooming meadows near the sea. Here was their favorite meeting place, whether they wanted to dance or bathe their fair bodies at the river mouth or gather flowers.

This time all had brought baskets, knowing that the flowers were now at their perfection. Europa's was of gold, exquisitely chased with figures which showed, oddly enough, the story of Io, her journeys in the shape of a cow, the death of Argus, and Zeus lightly touching her with his divine hand and changing her back into a woman. It was, as may be perceived, a marvel worth gazing upon, and had been made by no less a personage than Hephaestus, the celestial workman of Olympus.

Lovely as the basket was, there were flowers as lovely to fill it with, sweet-smelling narcissus and hyacinths and violets and yellow crocus, and most radiant of all, the crimson splendor of the wild rose. The girls gathered them delightedly, wandering here and there over the meadow, each one a maiden fairest among the fair; yet even so, Europa shone out among them as the Goddess of Love outshines the sister Graces. And it was that very Goddess of Love who brought about what next happened. As Zeus in heaven watched the pretty scene, she who alone can conquer Zeus—along with her son, the mischievous boy Cupid—shot one of her shafts into his heart, and that very instant he fell madly in love with Europa. Even though Hera was away, he thought it well to be cautious, and before appearing to Europa he changed himself into a bull. Not such a one as you might see in a stall or grazing in a field, but one beautiful beyond all bulls that ever were, bright chestnut in color, with a silver circle on his brow and horns like the crescent of the young moon. He seemed so gentle as well as so lovely that the girls were not frightened at his coming, but gathered around to caress him and to breathe the heavenly fragrance that came from him, sweeter even than that of the flowery meadow. It was Europa he drew toward, and as she gently touched him, he lowed so musically, no flute could give forth a more melodious sound.

Then he lay down before her feet and seemed to show her his broad back, and she cried to the others to come with her and mount him.

The rape of Europa

> For surely he will bear us on his back,
> He is so mild and dear and gentle to behold.
> He is not like a bull, but like a good, true man,
> Except he cannot speak.

Smiling she sat down on his back, but the others, quick though they were to follow her, had no chance. The bull leaped up and at full speed rushed to the seashore and then not into, but over, the wide water. As he went the waves grew smooth before him and a whole procession rose up from the deep and accompanied him—the strange sea-gods, Nereids riding upon dolphins, and Tritons blowing their horns, and the mighty Master of the Sea himself, Zeus's own brother.

Europa, frightened equally by the wondrous creatures she saw and the moving waters all around, clung with one hand to the bull's great horn and with the other caught up her purple dress to keep it dry, and the winds

> Swelled out the deep folds even as a sail
> Swells on a ship, and ever gently thus
> They wafted her.

No bull could this be, thought Europa, but most certainly a god; and she spoke pleadingly to him, begging him to pity her and not leave her in some strange place all alone. He spoke to her in answer and showed her she had guessed rightly what he was. She had no cause to fear, he told her. He was Zeus, greatest of gods, and all he was doing was from love of her. He was taking her to Crete, his own island, where his mother had hidden him from Cronus when he was born, and there she would bear him

> Glorious sons whose sceptres shall hold sway
> Over all men on earth.

Everything happened, of course, as Zeus had said. Crete came into sight; they landed, and the Seasons, the gatekeepers of Olympus, arrayed her for her bridal. Her sons were famous men, not only in this world but in the next—where two of them, Minos and Rhadamanthus, were rewarded for their justice upon the earth by being made the judges of the dead. But her own name remains the best known of all.

THE CYCLOPS POLYPHEMUS

The first part of this story goes back to the Odyssey; *the second part is told only by the third-century Alexandrian poet Theocritus; the last part could have been written by no one except the satirist Lucian, in the second century*

A.D. *At least a thousand years separate the beginning from the end. Homer's vigor and power of storytelling, the pretty fancies of Theocritus, the smart cynicism of Lucian, illustrate in their degree the course of Greek literature.*

All the monstrous forms of life which were first created, the hundred-handed creatures, the Giants, and so on, were permanently banished from the earth when they had been conquered, with the single exception of the Cyclopes. They were allowed to come back, and they became finally great favorites of Zeus. They were wonderful workmen and they forged his thunderbolts. At first there had been only three, but later there were many. Zeus gave them a home in a fortunate country where the vineyards and cornlands, unplowed and unsown, bore fruits plenteously. They had great flocks of sheep and goats as well, and they lived at their ease. Their fierceness and savage temper, however, did not grow less; they had no laws or courts of justice, but each one did as he pleased. It was not a good country for strangers.

Ages after Prometheus was punished, when the descendants of the men he helped had grown civilized and had learned to build far-sailing ships, a Greek prince beached his boat on the shore of this dangerous land. His name was Odysseus (Ulysses in Latin) and he was on his way home after the destruction of Troy. In the hardest battle he had fought with the Trojans, he had never come as near to death as he did then.

Not far from the spot where his crew had made the vessel fast was a cave, open toward the sea and very lofty. It looked inhabited; there was a strong fence before the entrance. Odysseus started off to explore it with twelve of his men. They were in need of food and he took with him a goatskin full of very potent and mellow wine to give whoever lived there in return for hospitality. The gate in the fence was not closed and they made their way into the cave. No one was there, but it was clearly the dwelling of some very prosperous person. Along the sides of the cave were many crowded pens of lambs and kids. Also there were racks full of cheeses and pails brimming with milk, delightful to the sea-worn travelers who ate and drank as they waited for the master.

At last he came, hideous and huge, tall as a great mountain crag. Driving his flock before him he entered and closed the cave's mouth with a ponderous slab of stone. Then looking around he caught sight of the strangers, and cried out in a dreadful booming voice, "Who are you who enter unbidden the house of Polyphemus? Traders or thieving pirates?" They were terror-stricken at the sight and sound of him, but Odysseus made swift to answer, and firmly, too: "Shipwrecked warriors from Troy are we, and your suppliants, under the protection of Zeus, the suppliants' god." But Polyphemus roared out that he cared not for Zeus. He was bigger than any god and feared none of them. With that, he stretched out his mighty arms and in each great hand he seized one of the men and dashed his brains out on the ground. Slowly he feasted off them to the last shred, and then, satisfied, stretched himself out across the cavern and slept. He was safe from attack. No one but he could roll back the huge stone before the door, and if the horrified men had been able to summon courage and strength enough to kill him they would have been imprisoned there forever.

During that long terrible night Odysseus faced the awful thing that had happened and would happen to every one of them if he could not think out some way of escape. But by the time day had dawned and the flock gathering at the entrance woke the Cyclops up, no idea at all had come to him. He had to watch two more of his company die, for Polyphemus breakfasted as he had supped. Then he drove out his flock, moving back the big block at the door and pushing it into place again as easily as a man opens and shuts the lid to his quiver. Throughout the day, shut in the cave, Odysseus thought and thought. Four of his men had perished hideously. Must they all go the same dreadful way? At last a plan shaped itself in his mind. An enormous timber lay near the pens, as long and as thick as the mast of a twenty-oared ship. From this he cut off a good piece, and then he and his men sharpened it and hardened the point by turning it round and round in the fire. They had finished and hidden it by the time the Cyclops came back. There followed the same horrible feast as before. When it was over Odysseus filled a cup with his own wine that he had brought with him and offered it to the Cyclops. He emptied it with delight and demanded more, and Odysseus poured for him until finally a drunken sleep overcame him. Then Odysseus and his men drew out the great stake from its hiding-place and heated the point in the fire until it almost burst into flame. Some power from on high breathed a mad courage into them and they drove the red-hot spike right into the Cyclops' eye. With an awful scream he sprang up and wrenched the point out. This way and that he flung around the cavern searching for his tormentors, but, blind as he was, they were able to slip away from him.

At last he pushed aside the stone at the entrance and sat down there, stretching his arms across, thinking thus to catch them when they tried to get away. But Odysseus had made a plan for this, too. He bade each man choose out three thick-fleeced rams and bind them together with strong, pliant strips of bark; then to wait for day, when the flock would be sent out to pasture. At last the dawn came and as the beasts crowding through the entrance passed out Polyphemus felt them over to be sure no one carried a man on his back. He never thought to feel underneath, but that was where the men were, each tucked under the middle ram, holding on to the great fleece. Once out of that fearful place they dropped to the ground and, hurrying to the ship, in no time launched it and were aboard. But Odysseus was too angry to leave in prudent silence. He sent a great shout over the water to the blind giant at the cave's mouth. "So, Cyclops, you were not quite strong enough to eat all of the puny men? You are rightly punished for what you did to those who were guests in your house."

The words stung Polyphemus to the heart. Up he sprang and tore a great crag from the mountain and flung it at the ship. It came within a hair's breadth of crushing the prow, and with the backwash the boat was borne landward. The crew put all their strength into their oars and just succeeded in pulling out to sea. When Odysseus saw that they were safely away, he cried again tauntingly, "Cyclops, Odysseus, wrecker of cities, put out your eye, and do you so tell anyone who asks." But they were too far off by then; the giant could do nothing. He sat blinded on the shore.

This was the only story told about Polyphemus for many years. Centuries passed and he was still the same, a frightful monster, shapeless, huge, his eye put out. But finally he changed, as what is ugly and evil is apt to change and grow milder with time. Perhaps some storyteller saw the helpless, suffering creature Odysseus left behind as a thing to be pitied. At all events, the next story about him shows him in a very pleasing light, not terrifying at all, but a most poor credulous monster, a most ridiculous monster, quite aware of how hideous and uncouth and repulsive he was, and therefore wretched, because he was madly in love with the charming, mocking sea nymph, Galatea. By this time the place where he lived was Sicily and he had somehow got his eye back, perhaps by some miracle of his father who in this story is Poseidon, the great God of the Sea. The lovelorn giant knew Galatea would never have him; his case was hopeless. And yet, whenever his pain made him harden his heart against her and bid himself, "Milk the ewe you have; why pursue what shuns you?", the minx would come softly stealing near him; then suddenly a shower of apples would pelt his flock and her voice would ring in his ears calling him a laggard in love. But no sooner was he up and after her than she would be off, laughing at his slow clumsiness as he tried to follow her. All he could do was again to sit wretched and helpless on the shore, but this time not trying in fury to kill people, only singing mournful love songs to soften the sea nymph's heart.

In a much later story, Galatea turned kind, not because the exquisite, delicate, milk-white maid, as Polyphemus called her in his songs, fell in love with the hideous one-eyed creature (in this tale, too, he has got back his eye), but because she prudently reflected that he was the favored son of the Lord of the Sea and by no means to be despised. So she told her sister nymph, Doris, who had rather hoped to attract the Cyclops herself, and who began the talk by saying scornfully, "A fine lover you've got—that Sicilian shepherd. Everybody's talking about it."

GALATEA: None of your airs, please. He's the son of Poseidon. There!

DORIS: Zeus's, for all I care. One thing's certain—he's an ugly, ill-mannered brute.

GALATEA: Just let me tell you, Doris, there's something very manly about him. Of course it's true he's got only one eye, but he sees as well with it as if he had two.

DORIS: It sounds as if you were in love yourself.

GALATEA: I in love—with Polyphemus! Not I—but of course I can guess why you're talking like this. You know perfectly well he has never noticed you—only me.

DORIS: A shepherd with only one eye thinks you handsome! That's something to be proud of. Anyway, you won't have to cook for him. He can make a very good meal off a traveler, I understand.

But Polyphemus never won Galatea. She fell in love with a beautiful young prince named Acis, whom Polyphemus, furiously jealous, killed. However, Acis was changed into a river-god, so that story ended well. But we are not told that Polyphemus ever loved any maiden except Galatea, or that any maiden ever loved Polyphemus.

FLOWER-MYTHS: NARCISSUS, HYACINTH, ADONIS

The first story about the creation of the narcissus is told only in an early Homeric Hymn of the seventh or eighth century, the second I have taken from Ovid. There is an immense difference between the two poets, who are separated from each other not only by six or seven hundred years, but also by the fundamental difference between the Greek and the Roman. The Hymn is written objectively, simply, without a touch of affectation. The poet is thinking of his subject. Ovid is as always thinking of his audience. But he tells this story well. The bit about

*the ghost trying to look at itself in the river of death is
a subtle touch which is quite characteristic of him and
quite unlike any Greek writer. Euripides gives the best
account of the festival of Hyacinthus; Apollodorus and
Ovid both tell his story. Whenever there is any vividness
in my narrative it may be ascribed securely to Ovid.
Apollodorus never deviates into anything like that.
Adonis I have taken from two third-century poets, Theocritus and Bion. The tale is typical of the Alexandrian
poets, tender, a little soft, but always in exquisite taste.*

In Greece there are most lovely wild flowers. They would be
beautiful anywhere, but Greece is not a rich and fertile country of wide meadows and fruitful fields where flowers seem
at home. It is a land of rocky ways and stony hills and
rugged mountains, and in such places the exquisite vivid
bloom of the wild flowers,

> A profusion of delight,
> Gay, bewilderingly bright,

comes as a startling surprise. Bleak heights are carpeted in
radiant colors; every crack and crevice of a frowning crag
blossoms. The contrast of this laughing, luxuriant beauty
with the clear-cut, austere grandeur all around arrests the
attention sharply. Elsewhere wild flowers may be little noticed—but never in Greece.

That was as true in the days of old as it is now. In the
faraway ages when the tales of Greek mythology were taking
shape men found the brilliant blossoms of the Greek spring a
wonder and a delight. Those people separated from us by
thousands of years, and almost completely unknown to us,
felt as we do before that miracle of loveliness, each flower
so delicate, yet all together covering the land like a rainbow
mantle flung over the hills. The first storytellers in Greece
told story after story about them, how they had been created
and why they were so beautiful.

It was the most natural thing possible to connect them
with the gods. All things in heaven and earth were mysteri-
ously linked with the divine powers, but beautiful things
most of all. Often an especially exquisite flower was held to be
the direct creation of a god for his own purpose. That was
true of the narcissus, which was not like ours of that name,
but a lovely bloom of glowing purple and silver. Zeus called
it into being to help his brother, the lord of the dark underworld, when he wanted to carry away the maiden he had
fallen in love with, Demeter's daughter, Persephone. She was
gathering flowers with her companions in the vale of Enna,

in a meadow of soft grass and roses and crocus and lovely violets and iris and hyacinths. Suddenly she caught sight of something quite new to her, a bloom more beautiful by far than any she had ever seen, a strange glory of a flower, a marvel to all, immortal gods and mortal men. A hundred blossoms grew up from the roots, and the fragrance was very sweet. The broad sky above and the whole earth laughed to see it, and the salt wave of the sea.

Only Persephone among the maidens had spied it. The rest were at the other end of the meadow. She stole toward it, half fearful at being alone, but unable to resist the desire to fill her basket with it, exactly as Zeus had supposed she would feel. Wondering she stretched out her hands to take the lovely plaything, but before she touched it a chasm opened in the earth and out of it coal-black horses sprang, drawing a chariot and driven by one who had a look of dark splendor, majestic and beautiful and terrible. He caught her to him and held her close. The next moment she was being borne away from the radiance of earth in springtime to the world of the dead by the king who rules it.

This was not the only story about the narcissus. There was another, as magical, but quite different. The hero of it was a beautiful lad, whose name was Narcissus. His beauty was so great, all the girls who saw him longed to be his, but he would have none of them. He would pass the loveliest carelessly by, no matter how much she tried to make him look at her. Heartbroken maidens were nothing to him. Even the sad case of the fairest of the nymphs, Echo, did not move him. She was a favorite of Artemis, the goddess of woods and wild creatures, but she came under the displeasure of a still mightier goddess, Hera herself, who was at her usual occupation of trying to discover what Zeus was about. She suspected that he was in love with one of the nymphs and she went to look them over to try to discover which. However, she was immediately diverted from her investigation by Echo's gay chatter. As she listened amused, the others silently stole away and Hera could come to no conclusion as to where Zeus's wandering fancy had alighted. With her usual injustice she turned against Echo. That nymph became another unhappy girl whom Hera punished. The goddess condemned her never to use her tongue again except to repeat what was said to her. "You will always have the last word," Hera said, "but no power to speak first."

This was very hard, but hardest of all when Echo, too, with all the other lovelorn maidens, loved Narcissus. She could follow him, but she could not speak to him. How then could she make a youth who never looked at a girl pay attention to her? One day, however, it seemed her chance had come. He was calling to his companions. "Is anyone here?" and she called back in rapture, "Here—Here." She was still hidden by the trees so that he did not see her, and he shouted, "Come!" —just what she longed to say to him. She answered joyfully, "Come!" and stepped forth from the woods with her arms outstretched. But he turned away in angry disgust. "Not so," he said; "I will die before I give you power over me." All she could say was, humbly, entreatingly, "I give you power over me," but he was gone. She hid her blushes and her shame in a lonely cave, and never could be comforted. Still she lives in places like that, and they say she has so wasted away with longing that only her voice now is left to her.

So Narcissus went on his cruel way, a scorner of love. But at last one of those he wounded prayed a prayer and it was answered by the gods: "May he who loves not others love himself." The great goddess Nemesis, which means righteous anger, undertook to bring this about. As Narcissus bent over a clear pool for a drink and saw there his own reflection, on the moment he fell in love with it. "Now I know," he cried, "what others have suffered from me, for I burn with love of my own self—and yet how can I reach that loveliness I see mirrored in the water? But I cannot leave it. Only death can set me free." And so it happened. He pined away, leaning perpetually over the pool, fixed in one long gaze. Echo was near him, but she could do nothing; only when, dying, he called to his image, "Farewell—farewell," she could repeat the words as a last good-by to him.

They say that when his spirit crossed the river that encircles the world of the dead, it leaned over the boat to catch a final glimpse of itself in the water.

The nymphs he had scorned were kind to him in death and sought his body to give it burial, but they could not find it. Where it had lain there was blooming a new and lovely flower, and they called it by his name, Narcissus.

Another flower that came into being through the death of a beautiful youth was the hyacinth, again not like the flower we call by that name, but lily-shaped and of a deep purple, or, some say, a splendid crimson. That was a tragic death, and each year it was commemorated by

> The festival of Hyacinthus
> That lasts throughout the tranquil night.
> In a contest with Apollo
> He was slain.

Discus throwing they competed,
And the god's swift cast
Sped beyond the goal he aimed at

and struck Hyacinthus full in the forehead a terrible wound.
He had been Apollo's dearest companion. There was no rival-
ry between them when they tried which could throw the discus farthest; they were only playing a game. The god was hor-
ror-struck to see the blood gush forth and the lad, deathly pale,
fall to the ground. He turned as pale himself as he caught
him up in his arms and tried to staunch the wound. But it
was too late. While he held him the boy's head fell back as a
flower does when its stem is broken. He was dead and Apollo
kneeling beside him wept for him, dying so young, so beautiful. He had killed him, although through no fault of his, and
he cried, "Oh, if I could give my life for yours, or die with you."
Even as he spoke, the bloodstained grass turned green again and
there bloomed forth the wondrous flower that was to make the
lad's name known forever. Apollo himself inscribed the petals
—some say with Hyacinth's initial, and others with the two
letters of the Greek word that means "Alas"; either way, a memorial of the god's great sorrow.

There is a story, too, that Zephyr, the West Wind, not
Apollo, was the direct cause of the death, that he also loved
this fairest of youths and in his jealous anger at seeing the
god preferred to him he blew upon the discus and made it
strike Hyacinth.

• • •

Such charming tales of lovely young people who, dying in
the springtime of life, were fittingly changed into spring flowers, have probably a dark background. They give a hint of
black deeds that were done in the far-distant past. Long before there were any stories told in Greece or any poems sung
which have come down to us, perhaps even before there were
storytellers and poets, it might happen, if the fields around a
village were not fruitful, if the corn did not spring up as it
should, that one of the villagers would be killed and his—or
her—blood sprinkled over the barren land. There was no idea
as yet of the radiant gods of Olympus who would have loathed
the hateful sacrifice. Mankind had only a dim feeling that
as their own life depended utterly on seedtime and harvest,
there must be a deep connection between themselves and the
earth and that their blood, which was nourished by the corn,
could in turn nourish it at need. What more natural then, if a
beautiful boy had thus been killed, than to think when later
the ground bloomed with narcissus or hyacinths that the flow-

ers were his very self, changed and yet living again? So they would tell each other it had happened, a lovely miracle which made the cruel death seem less cruel. Then as the ages passed and people no longer believed that the earth needed blood to be fruitful, all that was cruel in the story would be dropped and in the end forgotten. No one would remember that terrible things had once been done. Hyacinthus, they would say, died not slaughtered by his kinsfolk to get food for them, but only because of a sorrowful mistake.

* * *

Of these deaths and flowery resurrections the most famous was that of Adonis. Every year the Greek girls mourned for him and every year they rejoiced when his flower, the blood-red anemone, the windflower, was seen blooming again. Aphrodite loved him; the Goddess of Love, who pierces with her shafts the hearts of gods and men alike, was fated herself to suffer that same piercing pain.

She saw him when he was born and even then loved him and decided he should be hers. She carried him to Persephone to take charge of him for her, but Persephone loved him too and would not give him back to Aphrodite, not even when the goddess went down to the underworld to get him. Neither goddess would yield, and finally Zeus himself had to judge between them. He decided that Adonis should spend half the year with each, the autumn and winter with the Queen of the Dead; the spring and summer with the Goddess of Love and Beauty.

All the time he was with Aphrodite she sought only to please him. He was keen for the chase, and often she would leave her swan-drawn car, in which she was used to glide at her ease through the air, and follow him along rough woodland ways dressed like a huntress. But one sad day she happened not to be with him and he tracked down a mighty boar. With his hunting dogs he brought the beast to bay. He hurled his spear at it, but he only wounded it, and before he could spring away, the boar mad with pain rushed at him and gored him with its great tusks. Aphrodite in her winged car high over the earth heard her lover's groan and flew to him.

He was softly breathing his life away, the dark blood flowing down his skin of snow and his eyes growing heavy and dim. She kissed him, but Adonis knew not that she kissed him as he died. Cruel as his wound was, the wound in her heart was deeper. She spoke to him, although she knew he could not hear her:—

"You die, O thrice desired,
 And my desire has flown like a dream.
 Gone with you is the girdle of my beauty,

But I myself must live who am a goddess
 And may not follow you.
 Kiss me yet once again, the last, long kiss,
 Until I draw your soul within my lips
 And drink down all your love."

The mountains all were calling and the oak trees answering,
 Oh, woe, woe for Adonis. He is dead.
 And Echo cried in answer, Oh, woe, woe for Adonis.
 And all the Loves wept for him and all the Muses too.

But down in the black underworld Adonis could not hear
them, nor see the crimson flower that sprang up where each
drop of his blood had stained the earth.

PART TWO

Stories of Love and Adventure

5 Cupid and Psyche

This story is told only by Apuleius, a Latin writer of the second century A.D. The Latin names of the gods are therefore used. It is a prettily told tale, after the manner of Ovid. The writer is entertained by what he writes; he believes none of it.

There was once a king who had three daughters, all lovely maidens, but the youngest, Psyche, excelled her sisters so greatly that beside them she seemed a very goddess consorting with mere mortals. The fame of her surpassing beauty spread over the earth, and everywhere men journeyed to gaze upon her with wonder and adoration and to do her homage as though she were in truth one of the immortals. They would even say that Venus herself could not equal this mortal. As they thronged in ever-growing numbers to worship her loveliness no one any more gave a thought to Venus herself. Her temples were neglected; her altars foul with cold ashes; her favorite towns deserted and falling in ruins. All the honors once hers were now given to a mere girl destined some day to die.

It may well be believed that the goddess would not put up with this treatment. As always when she was in trouble she turned for help to her son, that beautiful winged youth whom some call Cupid and others Love, against whose arrows there is no defense, neither in heaven nor on the earth. She told him her wrongs and as always he was ready to do her bidding. "Use your power," she said, "and make the hussy fall madly in love with the vilest and most despicable creature there is in the whole world." And so no doubt he would have done, if Venus had not first shown him Psyche, never thinking in her jealous rage what such beauty might do even to the God of Love himself. As he looked upon her it was as if he had shot one of his arrows into his own heart. He said nothing to his mother, indeed he had no power to utter a word, and Venus left him with the happy confidence that he would swiftly bring about Psyche's ruin.

What happened, however, was not what she had counted on. Psyche did not fall in love with a horrible wretch, she did not fall in love at all. Still more strange, no one fell in love with her. Men were content to look and wonder and worship —and then pass on to marry someone else. Both her sisters, inexpressibly inferior to her, were splendidly married, each to a king. Psyche, the all-beautiful, sat sad and solitary, only admired, never loved. It seemed that no man wanted her.

This was, of course, most disturbing to her parents. Her father finally traveled to an oracle of Apollo to ask his advice on how to get her a good husband. The god answered him, but his words were terrible. Cupid had told him the whole story and had begged for his help. Accordingly Apollo said that Psyche, dressed in deepest mourning, must be set on the summit of a rocky hill and left alone, and that there her destined husband, a fearful winged serpent, stronger than the gods themselves, would come to her and make her his wife.

The misery of all when Psyche's father brought back this lamentable news can be imagined. They dressed the maiden as though for her death and carried her to the hill with greater sorrowing than if it had been to her tomb. But Psyche herself kept her courage. "You should have wept for me before," she told them, "because of the beauty that has drawn down upon me the jealousy of Heaven. Now go, knowing that I am glad the end has come." They went in despairing grief, leaving the lovely helpless creature to meet her doom alone, and they shut themselves in their palace to mourn all their days for her.

On the high hilltop in the darkness Psyche sat, waiting for she knew not what terror. There, as she wept and trembled, a soft breath of air came through the stillness to her, the gentle breathing of Zephyr, sweetest and mildest of winds. She felt it lift her up. She was floating away from the rocky hill and down until she lay upon a grassy meadow soft as a bed and fragrant with flowers. It was so peaceful there, all her trouble left her and she slept. She woke beside a bright river; and on its bank was a mansion stately and beautiful as though built for a god, with pillars of gold and walls of silver and floors inlaid with precious stones. No sound was to be heard; the place seemed deserted and Psyche drew near, awestruck at the sight of such splendor. As she hesitated on the threshold, voices sounded in her ear. She could see no one, but the words they spoke came clearly to her. The house was for her, they told her. She must enter without fear and bathe and refresh herself. Then a banquet table would be spread for her. "We are your servants," the voices said, "ready to do whatever you desire."

The bath was the most delightful, the food the most delicious, she had ever enjoyed. While she dined, sweet music breathed around her: a great choir seemed to sing to a harp, but she could only hear, not see, them. Throughout the day, except for the strange companionship of the voices, she was alone, but in some inexplicable way she felt sure that with the coming of the night her husband would be with her. And so it happened. When she felt him beside her and heard his voice softly murmuring in her ear, all her fears left her. She knew without seeing him that here was no monster or shape of terror, but the lover and husband she had longed and waited for.

This half-and-half companionship could not fully content her; still she was happy and the time passed swiftly. One night, however, her dear though unseen husband spoke gravely to her and warned her that danger in the shape of her two sisters was approaching. "They are coming to the hill where you disappeared, to weep for you," he said; "but you must not let them see you or you will bring great sorrow upon me and ruin to yourself." She promised him she would not, but all the next day she passed in weeping, thinking of her sisters and herself unable to comfort them. She was still in tears when her husband came and even his caresses could not check them. At last he yielded sorrowfully to her great desire. "Do what you will," he said, "but you are seeking your own destruction." Then he warned her solemnly not to be persuaded by anyone to try to see him, on pain of being separated from him forever. Psyche cried out that she would never do so. She would die a hundred times over rather than live without him. "But give me this joy," she said: "to see my sisters." Sadly he promised her that it should be so.

The next morning the two came, brought down from the mountain by Zephyr. Happy and excited, Psyche was waiting for them. It was long before the three could speak to each other; their joy was too great to be expressed except by tears and embraces. But when at last they entered the palace and the elder sisters saw its surpassing treasures; when they sat at the rich banquet and heard the marvelous music, bitter envy took possession of them and a devouring curiosity as to who was the lord of all this magnificence and their sister's husband. But Psyche kept faith; she told them only that he was a young man, away now on a hunting expedition. Then filling their hands with gold and jewels, she had Zephyr bear them back to the hill. They went willingly enough, but their hearts were on fire with jealousy. All their own wealth and good fortune seemed to them as nothing compared with Psyche's, and their envious anger so worked in them that they came finally to plotting how to ruin her.

That very night Psyche's husband warned her once more. She would not listen when he begged her not to let them come again. She never could see him, she reminded him. Was she also to be forbidden to see all others, even her sisters so dear to her? He yielded as before, and very soon the two wicked women arrived, with their plot carefully worked out.

Already, because of Psyche's stumbling and contradictory answers when they asked her what her husband looked like, they had become convinced that she had never set eyes on him and did not really know what he was. They did not tell her this, but they reproached her for hiding her terrible state from them, her own sisters. They had learned, they said, and knew for a fact, that her husband was not a man, but the fearful serpent Apollo's oracle had declared he would be. He was kind now, no doubt, but he would certainly turn upon her some night and devour her.

Psyche, aghast, felt terror flooding her heart instead of love. She had wondered so often why he would never let her see him. There must be some dreadful reason. What did she really know about him? If he was not horrible to look at, then he was cruel to forbid her ever to behold him. In extreme misery, faltering and stammering, she gave her sisters to understand that she could not deny what they said, because she had been with him only in the dark. "There must be something very wrong," she sobbed, "for him so to shun the light of day." And she begged them to advise her.

They had their advice all prepared beforehand. That night she must hide a sharp knife and a lamp near her bed. When her husband was fast asleep she must leave the bed, light the lamp, and get the knife. She must steel herself to plunge it swiftly into the body of the frightful being the light would certainly show her. "We will be near," they said, "and carry you away with us when he is dead."

Then they left her torn by doubt and distracted what to do. She loved him; he was her dear husband. No; he was a horrible serpent and she loathed him. She would kill him— She would not. She must have certainty—She did not want certainty. So all day long her thoughts fought with each other. When evening came, however, she had given the struggle up.

One thing she was determined to do: she would see him.

When at last he lay sleeping quietly, she summoned all her courage and lit the lamp. She tiptoed to the bed and holding the light high above her she gazed at what lay there. Oh, the relief and the rapture that filled her heart. No monster was revealed, but the sweetest and fairest of all creatures, at whose sight the very lamp seemed to shine brighter. In her first shame at her folly and lack of faith, Psyche fell on her knees and would have plunged the knife into her own breast if it had not fallen from her trembling hands. But those same unsteady hands that saved her betrayed her, too, for as she hung over him, ravished at the sight of him and unable to deny herself the bliss of filling her eyes with his beauty, some hot oil fell from the lamp upon his shoulder. He started awake: he saw the light and knew her faithlessness, and without a word he fled from her.

She rushed out after him into the night. She could not see him, but she heard his voice speaking to her. He told her who he was, and sadly bade her farewell. "Love cannot live where there is no trust," he said, and flew away. "The God of Love!" she thought. "He was my husband, and I, wretch that I am, could not keep faith with him. Is he gone from me forever? . . . At any rate," she told herself with rising courage, "I can spend the rest of my life searching for him. If he has no more love left for me, at least I can show him how much I love him." And she started on her journey. She had no idea where to go; she knew only that she would never give up looking for him.

He meanwhile had gone to his mother's chamber to have his wound cared for, but when Venus heard his story and learned that it was Psyche whom he had chosen, she left him angrily alone in his pain, and went forth to find the girl of whom he had made her still more jealous. Venus was determined to show Psyche what it meant to draw down the displeasure of a goddess.

Poor Psyche in her despairing wanderings was trying to win the gods over to her side. She offered ardent prayers to them perpetually, but not one of them would do anything to make Venus their enemy. At last she perceived that there was no hope for her, either in heaven or on earth, and she took a desperate resolve. She would go straight to Venus; she would offer herself humbly to her as her servant, and try to soften her anger. "And who knows," she thought, "if he himself is not there in his mother's house." So she set forth to find the goddess who was looking everywhere for her.

When she came into Venus' presence the goddess laughed aloud and asked her scornfully if she was seeking a husband

Psyche gazed at the sleeping Cupid

since the one she had had would have nothing to do with her because he had almost died of the burning wound she had given him. "But really," she said, "you are so plain and ill-favored a girl that you will never be able to get you a lover except by the most diligent and painful service. I will therefore show my good will to you by training you in such ways." With that she took a great quantity of the smallest of the seeds, wheat and poppy and millet and so on, and mixed them all together in a heap. "By nightfall these must all be sorted," she said. "See to it for your own sake." And with that she departed.

Psyche, left alone, sat still and stared at the heap. Her mind was all in a maze because of the cruelty of the command; and, indeed, it was of no use to start a task so manifestly impossible. But at this direful moment she who had awakened no compassion in mortals or immortals was pitied by the tiniest creatures of the field, the little ants, the swift-runners. They cried to each other, "Come, have mercy on this poor maid and help her diligently." At once they came, waves of them, one after another, and they labored separating and dividing, until what had been a confused mass lay all ordered, every seed with its kind. This was what Venus found when she came back, and very angry she was to see it. "Your work is by no means over," she said. Then she gave Psyche a crust of bread and bade her sleep on the ground while she herself went off to her soft, fragrant couch. Surely if she could keep the girl at hard labor and half starve her, too, that hateful beauty of hers would soon be lost. Until then she must see that her son was securely guarded in his chamber where he was still suffering from his wound. Venus was pleased at the way matters were shaping.

The next morning she devised another task for Psyche, this time a dangerous one. "Down there near the riverbank," she said, "where the bushes grow thick, are sheep with fleeces of gold. Go fetch me some of their shining wool." When the worn girl reached the gently flowing stream, a great longing seized her to throw herself into it and end all her pain and despair. But as she was bending over the water she heard a little voice from near her feet, and looking down saw that it came from a green reed. She must not drown herself, it said. Things were not as bad as that. The sheep were indeed very fierce, but if Psyche would wait until they came out of the bushes toward evening to rest beside the river, she could go into the thicket and find plenty of the golden wool hanging on the sharp briars.

So spoke the kind and gentle reed, and Psyche, following the directions, was able to carry back to her cruel mistress a quantity of the shining fleece. Venus received it with an evil smile. "Someone helped you," she said sharply. "Never did you do this by yourself. However, I will give you an opportunity to prove that you really have the stout heart and the singular prudence you make such a show of. Do you see that black water which falls from the hill yonder? It is the source of the terrible river which is called hateful, the river Styx. You are to fill this flask from it." That was the worst task yet, as Psyche saw when she approached the waterfall. Only a winged creature could reach it, so steep and slimy were the rocks on all sides, and so fearful the onrush of the descending waters. But by this time it must be evident to all the readers of this story (as, perhaps, deep in her heart it had become evident to Psyche herself) that although each of her trials seemed impossibly hard, an excellent way out would always be provided for her. This time her savior was an eagle, who poised on his great wings beside her, seized the flask from her with his beak and brought it back to her full of the black water.

But Venus kept on. One cannot but accuse her of some stupidity. The only effect of all that had happened was to make her try again. She gave Psyche a box which she was to carry to the underworld and ask Proserpine to fill with some of her beauty. She was to tell her that Venus really needed it, she was so worn-out from nursing her sick son. Obediently as always Psyche went forth to look for the road to Hades. She found her guide in a tower she passed. It gave her careful directions how to get to Proserpine's palace, first through a great hole in the earth, then down to the river of death, where she must give the ferryman, Charon, a penny to take her across. From there the road led straight to the palace. Cerberus, the three-headed dog, guarded the doors, but if she gave him a cake he would be friendly and let her pass.

All happened, of course, as the tower had foretold. Proserpine was willing to do Venus a service, and Psyche, greatly encouraged, bore back the box, returning far more quickly than she had gone down.

Her next trial she brought upon herself through her curiosity and, still more, her vanity. She felt that she must see what that beauty-charm in the box was; and, perhaps, use a little of it herself. She knew quite as well as Venus did that her looks were not improved by what she had gone through, and always in her mind was the thought that she might suddenly meet Cupid. If only she could make herself more lovely for him! She was unable to resist the temptation; she opened the box. To her sharp disappointment she saw nothing there; it seemed empty. Immediately, however, a deadly languor took possession of her and she fell into a heavy sleep.

At this juncture the God of Love himself stepped forward.

Cupid was healed of his wound by now and longing for Psyche. It is a difficult matter to keep Love imprisoned. Venus had locked the door, but there were the windows. All Cupid had to do was to fly out and start looking for his wife. She was lying almost beside the palace, and he found her at once. In a moment he had wiped the sleep from her eyes and put it back into the box. Then waking her with just a prick from one of his arrows, and scolding her a little for her curiosity, he bade her take Proserpine's box to his mother and he assured her that all thereafter would be well.

While the joyful Psyche hastened on her errand, the god flew up to Olympus. He wanted to make certain that Venus would give them no more trouble, so he went straight to Jupiter himself. The Father of Gods and Men consented at once to all that Cupid asked—"Even though," he said, "you have done me great harm in the past—seriously injured my good name and my dignity by making me change myself into a bull and a swan and so on. . . . However, I cannot refuse you."

Then he called a full assembly of the gods, and announced to all, including Venus, that Cupid and Psyche were formally married, and that he proposed to bestow immortality upon the bride. Mercury brought Psyche into the palace of the gods, and Jupiter himself gave her the ambrosia to taste which made her immortal. This, of course, completely changed the situation. Venus could not object to a goddess for her daughter-in-law; the alliance had become eminently suitable. No doubt she reflected also that Psyche, living up in heaven with a husband and children to care for, could not be much on the earth to turn men's heads and interfere with her own worship.

So all came to a most happy end. Love and the Soul (for that is what Psyche means) had sought and, after sore trials, found each other; and that union could never be broken.

6 Eight Brief Tales of Lovers

PYRAMUS AND THISBE

This story is found only in Ovid. It is quite characteristic of him at his best: well-told; several rhetorical monologues; a little essay on Love by the way.

Once upon a time the deep red berries of the mulberry tree were white as snow. The change in color came about strangely and sadly. The death of two young lovers was the cause.

Pyramus and Thisbe, he the most beautiful youth and she the loveliest maiden of all the East, lived in Babylon, the city of Queen Semiramis, in houses so close together that one wall was common to both. Growing up thus side by side they learned to love each other. They longed to marry, but their parents forbade. Love, however, cannot be forbidden. The more that flame is covered up, the hotter it burns. Also love can always find a way. It was impossible that these two whose hearts were on fire should be kept apart.

In the wall both houses shared there was a little chink. No one before had noticed it, but there is nothing a lover does not notice. Our two young people discovered it and through it they were able to whisper sweetly back and forth. Thisbe on one side, Pyramus on the other. The hateful wall that separated them had become their means of reaching each other. "But for you we could touch, kiss," they would say. "But at least you let us speak together. You give a passage for loving words to reach loving ears. We are not ungrateful." So they would talk, and as night came on and they must part, each would press on the wall kisses that could not go through to the lips on the other side.

Every morning when the dawn had put out the stars, and the sun's rays had dried the hoarfrost on the grass, they would steal to the crack and, standing there, now utter words of burning love and now lament their hard fate, but always in softest whispers. Finally a day came when they could endure no longer. They decided that that very night they would try to slip away and steal out through the city into the open country where at last they could be together in freedom. They agreed to meet at a well-known place, the Tomb of Ninus, under a tree there, a tall mulberry full of snow-white berries, near which a cool spring bubbled up. The plan pleased them and it seemed to them the day would never end.

At last the sun sank into the sea and night arose. In the darkness Thisbe crept out and made her way in all secrecy to the tomb. Pyramus had not come; still she waited for him, her love making her bold. But of a sudden she saw by the light of the moon a lioness. The fierce beast had made a kill; her jaws were bloody and she was coming to slake her thirst in the spring. She was still far enough away for Thisbe to escape, but as she fled she dropped her cloak. The lioness came upon it on her way back to her lair and she mouthed it and tore it before disappearing into the woods. That is what Pyramus saw when he appeared a few minutes later. Before him lay the bloodstained shreds of the cloak and clear in the dust were the tracks of the lioness. The conclusion was inevitable. He never doubted that he knew all. Thisbe was dead. He had let his love, a tender maiden, come alone to a place full of danger, and not been there first to protect her. "It is I who killed you," he said. He lifted up from the trampled dust what was left of the cloak and kissing it again and again carried it to the mulberry tree. "Now," he said, "you shall drink my blood too." He drew his sword and plunged it into his side. The blood spurted up over the berries and dyed them a dark red.

Thisbe, although terrified of the lioness, was still more afraid to fail her lover. She ventured to go back to the tree of the tryst, the mulberry with the shining white fruit. She could not find it. A tree was there, but not one gleam of white was on the branches. As she stared at it, something moved on the ground beneath. She started back shuddering. But in a moment, peering through the shadows, she saw what was there. It was Pyramus, bathed in blood and dying. She flew to him and threw her arms around him. She kissed his cold lips and begged him to look at her, to speak to her. "It is I, your Thisbe, your dearest," she cried to him. At the sound of her name he opened his heavy eyes for one look. Then death closed them.

She saw his sword fallen from his hand and beside it her cloak stained and torn. She understood all. "Your own hand killed you," she said, "and your love for me. I too can be brave. I too can love. Only death would have had the power to separate us. It shall not have that power now." She plunged into her heart the sword that was still wet with his life's blood.

The gods were pitiful at the end, and the lovers' parents too. The deep red fruit of the mulberry is the everlasting memorial of these true lovers, and one urn holds the ashes of the two whom not even death could part.

ORPHEUS AND EURYDICE

> *The account of Orpheus with the Argonauts is told only by Apollonius of Rhodes, a third-century Greek poet. The rest of the story is told best by two Roman poets, Virgil and Ovid, in very much the same style. The Latin names of the gods are therefore used here. Apollonius influenced Virgil a good deal. Indeed, any one of the three might have written the entire story as it stands.*

The very earliest musicians were the gods. Athena was not distinguished in that line, but she invented the flute although she never played upon it. Hermes made the lyre and gave it to Apollo who drew from it sounds so melodious that when he played in Olympus the gods forgot all else. Hermes also made the shepherd-pipe for himself and drew enchanting music from it. Pan made the pipe of reeds which can sing as sweetly as the nightingale in spring. The Muses had no instrument peculiar to them, but their voices were lovely beyond compare.

Next in order came a few mortals so excellent in their art that they almost equaled the divine performers. Of these by far the greatest was Orpheus. On his mother's side he was more than mortal. He was the son of one of the Muses and a Thracian prince. His mother gave him the gift of music and Thrace where he grew up fostered it. The Thracians were the most musical of the peoples of Greece. But Orpheus had no rival there or anywhere except the gods alone. There was no limit to his power when he played and sang. No one and nothing could resist him.

> In the deep still woods upon the Thracian mountains
> Orpheus with his singing lyre led the trees,
> Led the wild beasts of the wilderness.

Everything animate and inanimate followed him. He moved the rocks on the hillside and turned the courses of the rivers.

Little is told about his life before his ill-fated marriage, for which he is even better known than for his music, but he went on one famous expedition and proved himself a most useful member of it. He sailed with Jason on the *Argo*, and when the heroes were weary or the rowing was especially difficult he would strike his lyre and they would be aroused to fresh zeal and their oars would smite the sea together in time to the melody. Or if a quarrel threatened he would play so tenderly and soothingly that the fiercest spirits would grow calm and forget their anger. He saved the heroes, too, from the Sirens. When they heard far over the sea singing so enchantingly sweet that it drove out all other thoughts except a desperate longing to hear more, and they turned the ship to the shore where the Sirens sat, Orpheus snatched up his lyre and played a tune so clear and ringing that it drowned the sound of those lovely fatal voices. The ship was put back on her course and the winds sped her away from the dangerous place. If Orpheus had not been there the Argonauts, too, would have left their bones on the Sirens' island.

Where he first met and how he wooed the maiden he loved, Eurydice, we are not told, but it is clear that no maiden he wanted could have resisted the power of his song. They were married, but their joy was brief. Directly after the wedding, as the bride walked in a meadow with her bridesmaids, a viper stung her and she died. Orpheus' grief was overwhelming. He could not endure it. He determined to go down to the world of death and try to bring Eurydice back. He said to himself,

> With my song
> I will charm Demeter's daughter,
> I will charm the Lord of the Dead,
> Moving their hearts with my melody.
> I will bear her away from Hades.

He dared more than any other man ever dared for his love. He took the fearsome journey to the underworld. There he struck his lyre, and at the sound all that vast multitude were charmed to stillness. The dog Cerberus relaxed his guard; the wheel of Ixion stood motionless; Sisiphus sat at rest upon his stone; Tantalus forgot his thirst; for the first time the faces of the dread goddesses, the Furies, were wet with tears. The ruler of Hades drew near to listen with his queen. Orpheus sang,

> O Gods who rule the dark and silent world,
> To you all born of a woman needs must come.
> All lovely things at last go down to you.
> You are the debtor who is always paid.
> A little while we tarry up on earth.
> Then we are yours forever and forever.
> But I seek one who came to you too soon.

The bud was plucked before the flower bloomed.
I tried to bear my loss. I could not bear it.
Love was too strong a god. O King, you know
If that old tale men tell is true, how once
The flowers saw the rape of Proserpine.
Then weave again for sweet Eurydice
Life's pattern that was taken from the loom
Too quickly. See, I ask a little thing,
Only that you will lend, not give, her to me.
She shall be yours when her years' span is full.

No one under the spell of his voice could refuse him anything. He

Drew iron tears down Pluto's cheek,
And made Hell grant what Love did seek.

They summoned Eurydice and gave her to him, but upon one condition: that he would not look back at her as she followed him, until they had reached the upper world. So the two passed through the great doors of Hades to the path which would take them out of the darkness, climbing up and up. He knew that she must be just behind him, but he longed unutterably to give one glance to make sure. But now they were almost there, the blackness was turning gray; now he had stepped out joyfully into the daylight. Then he turned to her. It was too soon; she was still in the cavern. He saw her in the dim light, and he held out his arms to clasp her; but on the instant she was gone. She had slipped back into the darkness. All he heard was one faint word, "Farewell."

Desperately he tried to rush after her and follow her down, but he was not allowed. The gods would not consent to his entering the world of the dead a second time, while he was still alive. He was forced to return to the earth alone, in utter desolation. Then he forsook the company of men. He wandered through the wild solitudes of Thrace, comfortless except for his lyre, playing, always playing, and the rocks and the rivers and the trees heard him gladly, his only companions. But at last a band of Maenads came upon him. They were as frenzied as those who killed Pentheus so horribly. They slew the gentle musician, tearing him limb from limb, and flung the severed head into the swift river Hebrus. It was borne along past the river's mouth on to the Lesbian shore, nor had it suffered any change from the sea when the Muses found it and buried it in the sanctuary of the island. His limbs they gathered and placed in a tomb at the foot of Mount Olympus, and there to this day the nightingales sing more sweetly than anywhere else.

CEYX AND ALCYONE

Ovid is the best source for this story. The exaggeration of the storm is typically Roman. Sleep's abode with its charming details shows Ovid's power of description. The names of the gods, of course, are Latin.

Ceyx, a king in Thessaly, was the son of Lucifer, the light-bearer, the star that brings in the day, and all his father's bright gladness was in his face. His wife Alcyone was also of high descent; she was the daughter of Aeolus, King of the Winds. The two loved each other devotedly and were never willingly apart. Nevertheless, a time came when he decided he must leave her and make a long journey across the sea. Various matters had happened to disturb him and he wished to consult the oracle, men's refuge in trouble. When Alcyone learned what he was planning she was overwhelmed with grief and terror. She told him with streaming tears and in a voice broken with sobs, that she knew as few others could the power of the winds upon the sea. In her father's palace she had watched them from her childhood, their stormy meetings, the black clouds they summoned and the wild red lightning. "And many a time upon the beach," she said, "I have seen the broken planks of ships tossed up. Oh, do not go. But if I cannot persuade you, at least take me with you. I can endure whatever comes to us together."

Ceyx was deeply moved, for she loved him no better than he loved her, but his purpose held fast. He felt that he must get counsel from the oracle and he would not hear of her sharing the perils of the voyage. She had to yield and let him go alone. Her heart was so heavy when she bade him farewell it was as if she foresaw what was to come. She waited on the shore watching the ship until it sailed out of sight.

That very night a fierce storm broke over the sea. The winds all met in a mad hurricane, and the waves rose up mountain-high. Rain fell in such sheets that the whole heaven seemed falling into the sea and the sea seemed leaping up into the sky. The men on the quivering, battered boat were mad with terror, all except one who thought only of Alcyone and re-joiced that she was in safety. Her name was on his lips when the ship sank and the waters closed over him.

Alcyone was counting off the days. She kept herself busy, weaving a robe for him against his return and another for her-self to be lovely in when he first saw her. And many times each day she prayed to the gods for him, to Juno most of all. The goddess was touched by those prayers for one who had long been dead. She summoned her messenger Iris and ordered her to go to the house of Somnus, God of Sleep, and bid him send a dream to Alcyone to tell her the truth about Ceyx.

The abode of Sleep is near the black country of the Cimmerians, in a deep valley where the sun never shines and dusky twilight wraps all things in shadows. No cock crows there; no watchdog breaks the silence; no branches rustle in the breeze; no clamor of tongues disturbs the peace. The only sound comes from the gently flowing stream of Lethe, the river of forgetfulness, where the waters murmuring entice to sleep. Before the door poppies bloom, and other drowsy herbs. Within, the God of Slumber lies upon a couch downy-soft and black of hue. There came Iris in her cloak of many colors, trailing across the sky in a rainbow curve, and the dark house was lit up with the shining of her garments. Even so, it was hard for her to make the god open his heavy eyes and understand what he was required to do. As soon as she was sure he was really awake and her errand done, Iris sped away, fearful that she too might sink forever into slumber.

The old God of Sleep aroused his son, Morpheus, skilled in assuming the form of any and every human being, and he gave him Juno's orders. On noiseless wings Morpheus flew through the darkness and stood by Alcyone's bed. He had taken on the face and form of Ceyx drowned. Naked and dripping wet he bent over her couch. "Poor wife," he said, "look, your husband is here. Do you know me or is my face changed in death? I am dead, Alcyone. Your name was on my lips when the waters overwhelmed me. There is no hope for me any more. But give me your tears. Let me not go down to the shadowy land unwept." In her sleep Alcyone moaned and stretched her arms out to clasp him. She cried aloud, "Wait for me. I will go with you," and her cry awakened her. She woke to the conviction that her husband was dead, that what she had seen was no dream, but himself. "I saw him, on that very spot," she told herself. "So piteous he looked. He is dead and soon I shall die. Could I stay here when his dear body is tossed about in the waves? I will not leave you, my husband; I will not try to live."

With the first daylight she went to the shore, to the headland where she had stood to watch him sail away. As she gazed seaward, far off on the water she saw something floating. The tide was setting in and the thing came nearer and nearer until she knew it was a dead body. She watched it with pity and horror in her heart as it drifted slowly toward her. And now it was close to the headland, almost beside her. It was he, Ceyx, her husband. She ran and leaped into the water, crying, "Husband, dearest!"—and then oh, wonder, instead of sinking into the waves she was flying over them. She had wings; her body was covered with feathers. She had been changed into a bird. The gods were kind. They did the same to Ceyx. As she flew to the body it was gone, and he, changed into a bird like herself, joined her. But their love was unchanged. They are always seen together, flying or riding the waves.

Every year there are seven days on end when the sea lies still and calm; no breath of wind stirs the waters. These are the days when Alcyone broods over her nest floating on the sea. After the young birds are hatched the charm is broken; but each winter these days of perfect peace come, and they are called after her, Alcyon, or, more commonly, Halcyon days.

> While birds of calm sit brooding on the charmed wave.

PYGMALION AND GALATEA

> *This story is told only by Ovid and the Goddess of Love is therefore Venus. It is an excellent example of Ovid's way of dressing up a myth, for which see the Introduction.*

A gifted young sculptor of Cyprus, named Pygmalion, was a woman-hater.

> Detesting the faults beyond measure which nature
> has given to women,

he resolved never to marry. His art, he told himself, was enough for him. Nevertheless, the statue he made and devoted all his genius to was that of a woman. Either he could not dismiss what he so disapproved of from his mind as easily as from his life, or else he was bent on forming a perfect woman and showing men the deficiencies of the kind they had to put up with.

However that was, he labored long and devotedly on the statue and produced a most exquisite work of art. But lovely as it was he could not rest content. He kept on working at it and daily under his skillful fingers it grew more beautiful. No woman ever born, no statue ever made, could approach it. When nothing could be added to its perfections, a strange fate had befallen its creator: he had fallen in love, deeply, passionately in love, with the thing he had made. It must be said in explanation that the statue did not look like a statue; no one would have thought it was ivory or stone, but warm

Pygmalion and Galatea

human flesh, motionless for a moment only. Such was the wondrous power of this disdainful young man. The supreme achievement of art was his, the art of concealing art.

But from that time on, the sex he scorned had their revenge. No hopeless lover of a living maiden was ever so desperately unhappy as Pygmalion. He kissed those enticing lips—they could not kiss him back; he caressed her hands, her face—they were unresponsive; he took her in his arms—she remained a cold and passive form. For a time he tried to pretend, as children do with their toys. He would dress her in rich robes, trying the effect of one delicate or glowing color after another, and imagine she was pleased. He would bring her the gifts real maidens love, little birds and gay flowers and the shining tears of amber Phaëthon's sisters weep, and then dream that she thanked him with eager affection. He put her to bed at night, and tucked her in all soft and warm, as little girls do their dolls. But he was not a child; he could not keep on pretending. In the end he gave up. He loved a lifeless thing and he was utterly and hopelessly wretched.

This singular passion did not long remain concealed from the Goddess of Passionate Love. Venus was interested in something that seldom came her way, a new kind of lover, and she determined to help a young man who could be enamored and yet original.

The feast day of Venus was, of course, especially honored in Cyprus, the island which first received the goddess after she rose from the foam. Snow-white heifers whose horns had been gilded were offered in numbers to her; the heavenly odor of incense was spread through the island from her many altars; crowds thronged her temples; not an unhappy lover but was there with his gift, praying that his love might turn kind. There too, of course, was Pygmalion. He dared to ask the goddess only that he might find a maiden like his statue, but Venus knew what he really wanted and as a sign that she favored his prayer the flame on the altar he stood before leaped up three times, blazing into the air.

Very thoughtful at this good omen Pygmalion sought his house and his love, the thing he had created and given his heart to. There she stood on her pedestal, entrancingly beautiful. He caressed her and then he started back. Was it self-deception or did she really feel warm to his touch? He kissed her lips, a long lingering kiss, and felt them grow soft beneath his. He touched her arms, her shoulders; their hardness vanished. It was like watching wax soften in the sun. He clasped her wrist; blood was pulsing there. Venus, he thought. This is the goddess's doing. And with unutterable gratitude and joy he put his arms around his love and saw her smile into his eyes and blush.

Venus herself graced their marriage with her presence, but what happened after that we do not know, except that Pygmalion named the maiden Galatea, and that their son, Paphos, gave his name to Venus' favorite city.

BAUCIS AND PHILEMON

> *Ovid is the only source for this story. It shows especially well his love of details and the skillful way he uses them to make a fairy tale seem realistic. The Latin names of the gods are used.*

In the Phrygian hill-country there were once two trees which all the peasants near and far pointed out as a great marvel, and no wonder, for one was an oak and the other a linden, yet they grew from a single trunk. The story of how this came about is a proof of the immeasurable power of the gods, and also of the way they reward the humble and the pious.

Sometimes when Jupiter was tired of eating ambrosia and drinking nectar up in Olympus and even a little weary of listening to Apollo's lyre and watching the Graces dance, he would come down to the earth, disguise himself as a mortal and go looking for adventures. His favorite companion on these tours was Mercury, the most entertaining of all the gods, the shrewdest and the most resourceful. On this particular trip Jupiter had determined to find out how hospitable the people of Phrygia were. Hospitality was, of course, very important to him, since all guests, all who seek shelter in a strange land, were under his especial protection.

The two gods, accordingly, took on the appearance of poor wayfarers and wandered through the land, knocking at each lowly hut or great house they came to and asking for food and a place to rest in. Not one would admit them; every time they were dismissed insolently and the door barred against them. They made trial of hundreds; all treated them in the same way. At last they came upon a little hovel of the humblest sort, poorer than any they had yet found, with a roof made only of reeds. But here, when they knocked, the door was opened wide and a cheerful voice bade them enter. They had to stoop to pass through the low entrance, but once inside they found themselves in a snug and very clean room, where a kindly-faced old man and woman welcomed them in the friendliest fashion and bustled about to make them comfortable.

The old man set a bench near the fire and told them to stretch out on it and rest their tired limbs, and the old woman threw a soft covering over it. Her name was Baucis, she told the strangers, and her husband was called Philemon. They had lived in that cottage all their married life and had always been happy. "We are poor folk," she said, "but poverty isn't so bad when you're willing to own up to it, and a contented spirit is a great help, too." All the while she was talking, she was busy doing things for them. The coals under the ashes on the dark hearth she fanned to life until a cheerful fire was burning. Over this she hung a little kettle full of water and just as it began to boil her husband came in with a fine cabbage he had got from the garden. Into the kettle it went, with a piece of the pork which was hanging from one of the beams. While this cooked Baucis set the table with her trembling old hands. One table-leg was too short, but she propped it up with a bit of broken dish. On the board she placed olives and radishes and several eggs which she had roasted in the ashes. By this time the cabbage and bacon were done, and the old man pushed two rickety couches up to the table and bade his guests recline and eat.

Presently he brought them cups of beechwood and an earthenware mixing bowl which held some wine very like vinegar, plentifully diluted with water. Philemon, however, was clearly proud and happy at being able to add such cheer to the supper and he kept on the watch to refill each cup as soon as it was emptied. The two old folks were so pleased and excited by the success of their hospitality that only very slowly a strange thing dawned upon them. The mixing bowl kept full. No matter how many cups were poured out from it, the level of the wine stayed the same, up to the brim. As they saw this wonder each looked in terror at the other, and dropping their eyes they prayed silently. Then in quavering voices and trembling all over they begged their guests to pardon the poor refreshments they had offered. "We have a goose," the old man said, "which we ought to have given your lordships. But if you will only wait, it shall be done at once." To catch the goose, however, proved beyond their powers. They tried in vain until they were worn out, while Jupiter and Mercury watched them greatly entertained.

But when both Philemon and Baucis had had to give up the chase panting and exhausted, the gods felt that the time had come for them to take action. They were really very kind. "You have been hosts to gods," they said, "and you shall have your reward. This wicked country which despises the poor stranger will be bitterly punished, but not you." They then escorted the two out of the hut and told them to look around them. To their amazement all they saw was water. The whole countryside had disappeared. A great lake surrounded them. Their neighbors had not been good to the old couple; nevertheless standing there they wept for them. But of a sudden their tears were dried by an overwhelming wonder. Before their eyes the tiny, lowly hut which had been their home for so long was turned into a stately pillared temple of whitest marble with a golden roof.

"Good people," Jupiter said, "ask whatever you want and you shall have your wish." The old people exchanged a hurried whisper, then Philemon spoke. "Let us be your priests, guarding this temple for you—and oh, since we have lived so long together, let neither of us ever have to live alone. Grant that we may die together."

The gods assented, well pleased with the two. A long time they served in that grand building, and the story does not say whether they ever missed their little cozy room with its cheerful hearth. But one day standing before the marble and golden magnificence they fell to talking about the former life, which had been so hard and yet so happy. By now both were in extreme old age. Suddenly as they exchanged memories each saw the other putting forth leaves. Then bark was growing around them. They had time only to cry, "Farewell, dear companion." As the words passed their lips they became trees, but still they were together. The linden and the oak grew from one trunk.

From far and wide people came to admire the wonder, and always wreaths of flowers hung on the branches in honor of the pious and faithful pair.

ENDYMION

> *I have taken this story from the third-century poet Theocritus. He tells it in the true Greek manner, simply and with restraint.*

This youth, whose name is so famous, has a very short history. Some of the poets say he was a king, some a hunter, but most of them say he was a shepherd. All agree that he was a youth of surpassing beauty and that this was the cause of his singular fate.

> Endymion the shepherd,
> As his flock he guarded,
> She, the Moon, Selene,
> Saw him, loved him, sought him,

> Coming down from heaven
> To the glade on Latmus,
> Kissed him, lay beside him.
> Blessed is his fortune.
> Evermore he slumbers,
> Tossing not nor turning,
> Endymion the shepherd.

He never woke to see the shining silvery form bending over him. In all the stories about him he sleeps forever, immortal, but never conscious. Wondrously beautiful he lies on the mountainside, motionless and remote as if in death, but warm and living, and night after night the Moon visits him and covers him with her kisses. It is said that this magic slumber was her doing. She lulled him to sleep so that she might always find him and caress him as she pleased. But it is said, too, that her passion brings her only a burden of pain, fraught with many sighs.

DAPHNE

> *Ovid alone tells this story. Only a Roman could have written it. A Greek poet would never have thought of an elegant dress and coiffure for the wood nymph.*

Daphne was another of those independent, love-and-marriage-hating young huntresses who are met with so often in the mythological stories. She is said to have been Apollo's first love. It is not strange that she fled from him. One unfortunate maiden after another beloved of the gods had had to kill her child secretly or be killed herself. The best such a one could expect was exile, and many women thought that worse than death. The ocean nymphs who visited Prometheus on the crag in the Caucasus spoke only the most ordinary common sense when they said to him:—

> May you never, oh, never behold me
> Sharing the couch of a god.
> May none of the dwellers in heaven
> Draw near to me ever.
> Such love as the high gods know,
> From whose eyes none can hide,
> May that never be mine.
> To war with a god-lover is not war,
> It is despair.

Daphne would have agreed completely. But indeed she did not want any mortal lovers either. Her father, the river-god Peneus, was greatly tried because she refused all the handsome and eligible young men who wooed her. He would scold her gently and lament, "Am I never to have a grandson?" But when she threw her arms around him and coaxed him, "Father, dearest, let me be like Diana," he would yield and she would be off to the deep woods, blissful in her freedom.

But at last Apollo saw her, and everything ended for her. She was hunting, her dress short to the knee, her arms bare, her hair in wild disarray. Nevertheless she was enchantingly beautiful. Apollo thought, "What would she not look like properly dressed and with her hair nicely arranged?" The idea made the fire that was devouring his heart blaze up even more fiercely and he started off in pursuit. Daphne fled, and she was an excellent runner. Even Apollo for a few minutes was hard put to it to overtake her; still, of course, he soon gained. As he ran he sent his voice ahead of him, entreating her, persuading her, reassuring her. "Do not fear," he called. "Stop and find out who I am, no rude rustic or shepherd. I am the Lord of Delphi, and I love you."

But Daphne flew on, even more frightened than before. If Apollo was indeed following her, the case was hopeless, but she was determined to struggle to the very end. It had all but come; she felt his breath upon her neck, but there in front of her the trees opened and she saw her father's river. She screamed to him, "Help me! Father, help me!" At the words a dragging numbness came upon her, her feet seemed rooted in the earth she had been so swiftly speeding over. Bark was enclosing her; leaves were sprouting forth. She had been changed into a tree, a laurel.

Apollo watched the transformation with dismay and grief. "O fairest of maidens, you are lost to me," he mourned. "But at least you shall be my tree. With your leaves my victors shall wreathe their brows. You shall have your part in all my triumphs. Apollo and his laurel shall be joined together wherever songs are sung and stories told."

The beautiful shining-leaved tree seemed to nod its waving head as if in happy consent.

ALPHEUS AND ARETHUSA

This story is told in full only by Ovid. There is nothing noteworthy in his treatment of it. The verse at the end is taken from the Alexandrian poet Moschus.

In Ortygia, an island which formed part of Syracuse, the greatest city of Sicily, there is a sacred spring called Arethusa. Once, however, Arethusa was not water or even a water nymph, but a fair young huntress and a follower of Artemis. Like her mistress she would have nothing to do with men; like her she loved hunting and the freedom of the forest.

One day, tired and hot from the chase, she came upon a crystal-clear river deeply shaded by silvery willows. No more delightful place for a bath could be imagined. Arethusa undressed and slipped into the cool delicious water. For a while she swam idly to and fro in utter peace; then she seemed to feel something stir in the depths beneath her. Frightened, she sprang to the bank—and as she did so she heard a voice: "Why such haste, fairest maiden?" Without looking back she fled away from the stream to the woods and ran with all the speed her fear gave her. She was hotly pursued and by one stronger if not swifter than she. The unknown called to her to stop. He told her he was the god of the river, Alpheus, and that he was following her only because he loved her. But she wanted none of him; she had but one thought, to escape. It was a long race, but the issue was never in doubt; he could keep on running longer than she. Worn out at last, Arethusa called to her goddess, and not in vain. Artemis changed her into a spring of water, and cleft the earth so that a tunnel was made under the sea from Greece to Sicily. Arethusa plunged down and emerged in Ortygia, where the place in which her spring bubbles up is holy ground, sacred to Artemis.

But it is said that even so she was not free of Alpheus. The story is that the god, changing back into a river, followed her through the tunnel and that now his water mingles with hers in the fountain. They say that often Greek flowers are seen coming up from the bottom, and that if a wooden cup is thrown into the Alpheus in Greece, it will reappear in Arethusa's well in Sicily.

Alpheus makes his way far under the deep with his waters,
Travels to Arethusa with bridal gifts, fair leaves and flowers.
Teacher of strange ways is Love, that knavish boy, maker of mischief.
With his magical spell he taught a river to dive.

7 The Quest of the Golden Fleece

This is the title of a long poem, very popular in classical days, by the third-century poet Apollonius of Rhodes. He tells the whole story of the Quest except the part about Jason and Pelias which I have taken from Pindar. It is the subject of one of his most famous odes, written in the first half of the fifth century. Apollonius ends his poem with the return of the heroes to Greece. I have added the account of what Jason and Medea did there, taking it from the fifth-century tragic poet Euripides, who made it the subject of one of his best plays.

These three writers are very unlike each other. No prose paraphrase can give any idea of Pindar, except, perhaps, something of his singular power for vivid and minutely detailed description. Readers of the Aeneid *will be reminded of Virgil by Apollonius. The difference between Euripides' Medea and Apollonius' heroine and also Virgil's Dido is in its degree a measure of what Greek tragedy was.*

The first hero in Europe who undertook a great journey was the leader of the Quest of the Golden Fleece. He was supposed to have lived a generation earlier than the most famous Greek traveler, the hero of the *Odyssey*. It was of course a journey by water. Rivers, lakes, and seas, were the only highways; there were no roads. All the same, a voyager had to face perils not only on the deep, but on the land as well. Ships did not sail by night, and any place where sailors put in might harbor a monster or a magician who could work more deadly harm than storm and shipwreck. High courage was necessary to travel, especially outside of Greece.

No story proved this fact better than the account of what the heroes suffered who sailed in the ship *Argo* to find the Golden Fleece. It may be doubted, indeed, if there ever was a voyage on which sailors had to face so many and such varied dangers. However, they were all heroes of renown, some of them the greatest in Greece, and they were quite equal to their adventures.

The tale of the Golden Fleece begins with a Greek king named Athamas, who got tired of his wife, put her away, and married another, the Princess Ino. Nephele, the first wife, was afraid for her two children, especially the boy, Phrixus. She thought the second wife would try to kill him so that her own son could inherit the kingdom, and she was right. This second wife came from a great family. Her father was Cadmus, the excellent King of Thebes; her mother and her three sisters were women of blameless lives. But she herself, Ino, determined to bring about the little boy's death, and she made an elaborate plan how this was to be done. Somehow she got possession of all the seed-corn and parched it before the men went out for the sowing, so that, of course, there was no harvest at all. When the King sent a man to ask the oracle what he should do in this fearful distress, she persuaded or, more probably, bribed the messenger to say that the oracle had declared the corn would not grow again unless they offered up the young Prince as a sacrifice.

The people, threatened with starvation, forced the King to yield and permit the boy's death. To the later Greeks the idea of such a sacrifice was as horrible as it is to us, and when it played a part in a story they almost always changed it into something less shocking. As this tale has come down to us, when the boy had been taken to the altar a wondrous ram, with a fleece of pure gold, snatched him and his sister up and bore them away through the air. Hermes had sent him in answer to their mother's prayer.

While they were crossing the strait which separates Europe and Asia, the girl, whose name was Helle, slipped and fell into the water. She was drowned; and the strait was named for her: the Sea of Helle, the Hellespont. The boy came safely to land, to the country of Colchis on the Unfriendly Sea (the Black Sea, which had not yet become friendly). The Colchians were a fierce people. Nevertheless, they were kind to Phrixus; and their King, Æetes, let him marry one of his daughters. It seems odd that Phrixus sacrificed to Zeus the ram that had saved him, in gratitude for having been saved; but he did so, and he gave the precious Golden Fleece to King Æetes.

Phrixus had an uncle who was by rights a king in Greece, but had had his kingdom taken away from him by his nephew, a man named Pelias. The King's young son, Jason, the rightful heir to the kingdom, had been sent secretly away to a place of safety, and when he was grown he came boldly back to claim the kingdom from his wicked cousin.

The usurper Pelias had been told by an oracle that he would die at the hands of kinsmen, and that he should beware of anyone whom he saw shod with only a single sandal. In due time such a man came to the town. One foot was bare, although in all other ways he was well-clad—a garment fitting close to his splendid limbs, and around his shoulders a leopard's skin to turn the showers. He had not shorn the bright locks of his hair; they ran rippling down his back. He went straight into the town and entered the marketplace fearlessly, at the time when the multitude filled it.

None knew him, but one and another wondered at him and said, "Can he be Apollo? Or Aphrodite's lord? Not one of Poseidon's bold sons, for they are dead." So they questioned each other. But Pelias came in hot haste at the tidings and when he saw the single sandal he was afraid. He hid his terror in his heart, however, and addressed the stranger: "What country is your fatherland? No hateful and defiling lies, I beg you. Tell me the truth." With gentle words the other answered: "I have come to my home to recover the ancient honor of my house, this land no longer ruled aright, which Zeus gave to my father. I am your cousin, and they call me by the name of Jason. You and I must rule ourselves by the law of right—not appeal to brazen swords or spears. Keep all the wealth you have taken, the flocks and the tawny herds of cattle and the fields, but the sovereign scepter and the throne release to me, so that no evil quarrel will arise from them."

Pelias gave him a soft answer. "So shall it be. But one thing must first be done. The dead Phrixus bids us bring back the Golden Fleece and thus bring back his spirit to his home. The oracle has spoken. But for me, already old age is my companion, while the flower of your youth is only now coming into full bloom. Do you go upon this quest, and I swear with Zeus as witness that I will give up the kingdom and the sovereign rule to you." So he spoke, believing in his heart that no one could make the attempt and come back alive.

The idea of the great adventure was delightful to Jason. He agreed, and let it be known everywhere that this would be a voyage indeed. The young men of Greece joyfully met the challenge. They came, all the best and noblest, to join the company. Hercules, the greatest of all heroes, was there; Orpheus, the master musician; Castor with his brother Pollux; Achilles' father, Peleus; and many another. Hera was helping Jason, and it was she who kindled in each one the desire not to be left behind nursing a life without peril by his mother's side, but even at the price of death to drink with his comrades the peerless elixir of valor. They set sail in the ship *Argo*. Jason took in his hands a golden goblet and, pouring a libation of wine into the sea, called upon Zeus whose lance is the lightning to speed them on their way.

Great perils lay before them, and some of them paid with their lives for drinking that peerless elixir. They put in first at Lemnos, a strange island where only women lived. They had risen up against the men and had killed them all, except one, the old king. His daughter, Hypsipyle, a leader among the women, had spared her father and set him afloat on the sea in a hollow chest, which finally carried him to safety. These fierce creatures, however, welcomed the Argonauts, and helped them with good gifts of food and wine and garments before they sailed away.

Soon after they left Lemnos the Argonauts lost Hercules from the company. A lad named Hylas, his armor-bearer, very dear to him, was drawn under the water as he dipped his pitcher in a spring, by a water nymph who saw the rosy flush of his beauty and wished to kiss him. She threw her arms around his neck and drew him down into the depths and he was seen no more. Hercules sought him madly everywhere, shouting his name and plunging deeper and deeper into the forest away from the sea. He had forgotten the Fleece and the *Argo* and his comrades: everything except Hylas. He did not come back, and finally the ship had to sail without him.

Their next adventure was with the Harpies, frightful flying creatures with hooked beaks and claws who always left behind them a loathsome stench, sickening to all living creatures. Where the Argonauts had beached their boat for the night lived a lonely and wretched old man, to whom Apollo, the truth-teller, had given the gift of prophecy. He foretold unerringly what would happen, and this had displeased Zeus, who always liked to wrap in mystery what he would do—and very sensibly, too, in the opinion of all who knew Hera. So he inflicted a terrible punishment upon the old man. Whenever he was about to dine, the Harpies who were called "the hounds of Zeus" swooped down and defiled the food, leaving it so foul that no one could bear to be near it, much less eat it. When the Argonauts saw the poor old creature—his name was Phineus—he was like a lifeless dream, creeping on withered feet, trembling for weakness, and only the skin on his body held his bones together. He welcomed them gladly and begged them to help him. He knew through his gift of prophecy that he could be defended from the Harpies by two men alone, who were among the company on the *Argo*—the sons of Boreas, the great North Wind. All listened to him with pity and the two gave him eagerly their promise to help.

The Harpies and the Argonauts

While the others set forth food for him, Boreas' sons took their stand beside him with drawn swords. He had hardly put a morsel to his lips when the hateful monsters darted down from the sky and in a moment had devoured everything and were flying off, leaving the intolerable odor behind them. But the wind-swift sons of the North Wind followed them; they caught up with them and struck at them with their swords. They would assuredly have cut them to pieces if Iris, the rainbow messenger of the gods, gliding down from heaven, had not checked them. They must forbear to kill the hounds of Zeus, she said, but she swore by the waters of the Styx, the oath that none can break, that they would never again trouble Phineus. So the two returned gladly and comforted the old man, who in his joy sat feasting with the heroes all through the night.

He gave them wise advice, too, about the dangers before them, in especial about the Clashing Rocks, the Symplegades, that rolled perpetually against one another while the sea boiled up around them. The way to pass between them, he said, was first to make trial with a dove. If she passed through safely, then the chances were that they too would get through. But if the dove were crushed, they must turn back and give up all hope of the Golden Fleece.

The next morning they started, with a dove, of course, and were soon in sight of the great rolling rocks. It seemed impossible that there could be a way between them, but they freed the dove and watched her. She flew through and came out safe. Only the tips of her tail-feathers were caught between the rocks as they rolled back together; and those were torn away. The heroes went after her as swiftly as they could. The rocks parted, the rowers put forth all their strength, and they too came through safely. Just in time, however, for as the rocks clashed together again the extreme end of the stern ornament was shorn off. By so little they escaped destruction. But ever since they passed them the rocks have been rooted fast to each other and have never any more brought disaster to sailors.

Not far from there was the country of the warrior women, the Amazons—the daughters, strangely enough, of that most peace-loving nymph, sweet Harmony. But their father was Ares, the terrible god of war, whose ways they followed and not their mother's. The heroes would gladly have halted and closed in battle with them, and it would not have been a battle without bloodshed, for the Amazons were not gentle foes. But the wind was favorable and they hurried on. They caught a glimpse of the Caucasus as they sped past, and of Prometheus on his rock high above them, and they heard the fanning of the eagle's huge wings as it darted down to its bloody feast.

They stopped for nothing, and that same day at sunset they reached Colchis, the country of the Golden Fleece.

They spent the night facing they knew not what and feeling that there was no help for them anywhere except in their own valor. Up in Olympus, however, a consultation was being held about them. Hera, troubled at the danger they were in, went to ask Aphrodite's help. The Goddess of Love was surprised at the visit, for Hera was no friend of hers. Still, when the great Queen of Olympus begged for her aid, she was awed and promised to do all she could. Together they planned that Aphrodite's son Cupid should make the daughter of the Colchian King fall in love with Jason. That was an excellent plan —for Jason. The maiden, who was named Medea, knew how to work very powerful magic, and could undoubtedly save the Argonauts if she would use her dark knowledge for them. So Aphrodite went to Cupid and told him she would give him a lovely plaything, a ball of shining gold and deep blue enamel, if he would do what she wanted. He was delighted, seized his bow and quiver, and swept down from Olympus through the vast expanse of air to Colchis.

Meantime the heroes had started for the city to ask the King for the Golden Fleece. They were safe from any trouble on the way, for Hera wrapped them in a thick mist, so that they reached the palace unseen. It dissolved when they approached the entrance, and the warders, quick to notice the band of splendid young strangers, led them courteously within and sent word to the King of their arrival.

He came at once and bade them welcome. His servants hastened to make all ready, build fires and heat water for the baths and prepare food. Into this busy scene stole the Princess Medea, curious to see the visitors. As her eyes fell upon Jason, Cupid swiftly drew his bow and shot a shaft deep into the maiden's heart. It burned there like a flame and her soul melted with sweet pain, and her face went now white, now red. Amazed and abashed she stole back to her chamber.

Only after the heroes had bathed and refreshed themselves with meat and drink could King Æetes ask them who they were and why they had come. It was accounted great discourtesy to put any question to a guest before his wants had been satisfied. Jason answered that they were all men of noblest birth, sons or grandsons of the gods, who had sailed from Greece in the hope that he would give them the Golden Fleece in return for whatever service he would ask of them. They would conquer his enemies for him, or do anything he wished.

A great anger filled King Æetes' heart as he listened. He did not like foreigners, any more than the Greeks did; he wanted them to keep away from his country, and he said to himself.

"If these strangers had not eaten at my table I would kill them." In silence he pondered what he should do, and a plan came to him.

He told Jason that he bore no grudge against brave men and that if they proved themselves such he would give the Fleece to them. "And the trial of your courage," he said, "shall be only what I myself have done." This was to yoke two bulls he had, whose feet were of bronze and whose breath was flaming fire, and with them to plow a field. Then the teeth of a dragon must be cast into the furrows, like seed-corn—which would spring up at once into a crop of armed men. These must be cut down as they advanced to the attack—a fearful harvesting. "I have done all this myself," he said; "and I will give the Fleece to no man less brave than I." For a time Jason sat speechless. The contest seemed impossible, beyond the strength of anyone. Finally he answered, "I will make the trial, monstrous though it is, even if it is my doom to die." With that he rose up and led his comrades back to the ship for the night, but Medea's thoughts followed after him. All through the long night when he had left the palace she seemed to see him, his beauty and his grace, and to hear the words he had uttered. Her heart was tormented with fear for him. She guessed what her father was planning.

Returned to the ship, the heroes held a council and one and another urged Jason to let him take the trial upon himself; but in vain, Jason would yield to none of them. As they talked there came to them one of the King's grandsons whose life Jason once had saved, and he told them of Medea's magic power. There was nothing she could not do, he said, check the stars, even, and the moon. If she were persuaded to help, she could make Jason able to conquer the bulls and the dragon-teeth men. It seemed the only plan that offered any hope and they urged the prince to go back and try to win Medea over, not knowing that the God of Love had already done that.

She sat alone in her room, weeping and telling herself she was shamed forever because she cared so much for a stranger that she wanted to yield to a mad passion and go against her father. "Far better die," she said. She took in her hand a casket which held herbs for killing, but as she sat there with it, she thought of life and the delightful things that are in the world; and the sun seemed sweeter than ever before. She put the casket away; and no longer wavering she determined to use her power for the man she loved. She had a magic ointment which would make him who rubbed it on his body safe for that day; he could not be harmed by anything. The plant it was made from sprang up first when Prometheus' blood dripped down upon the earth. She put it in her bosom and went to find her nephew, the prince whom Jason had helped. She met him as he was looking for her to beg her to do just what she had already decided on. She agreed at once to all he said and sent him to the ship to tell Jason to meet her without delay in a certain place. As soon as he heard the message Jason started, and as he went Hera shed radiant grace upon him, so that all who saw him marveled at him. When he reached Medea it seemed to her as if her heart left her to go to him; a dark mist clouded her eyes and she had no strength to move. The two stood face to face without a word, as lofty pine trees when the wind is still. Then again when the wind stirs they murmur; so these two also, stirred by the breath of love, were fated to tell out all their tale to each other.

He spoke first and implored her to be kind to him. He could not but have hope, he said, because her loveliness must surely mean that she excelled in gentle courtesy. She did not know how to speak to him; she wanted to pour out all she felt at once. Silently she drew the box of ointment from her bosom and gave it to him. She would have given her soul to him if he had asked her. And now both were fixing their eyes on the ground abashed, and again were throwing glances at each other, smiling with love's desire.

At last Medea spoke and told him how to use the charm and that when it was sprinkled on his weapons it would make them as well as himself invincible for a day. If too many of the dragon-teeth men rushed to attack him, he must throw a stone into their midst, which would make them turn against each other and fight until all were killed. "I must go back to the palace now," she said. "But when you are once more safe at home remember Medea, as I will remember you forever." He answered passionately, "Never by night and never by day will I forget you. If you will come to Greece, you shall be worshiped for what you have done for us, and nothing except death will come between us."

They parted, she to the palace to weep over her treachery to her father, he to the ship to send two of his comrades for the dragon's teeth. Meantime he made trial of the ointment and at the touch of it a terrible, irresistible power entered into him and the heroes all exulted. Yet, even so, when they reached the field where the King and the Colchians were waiting, and the bulls rushed out from their lair breathing forth flames of fire, terror overcame them. But Jason withstood the fearful creatures as a great rock in the sea withstands the waves. He forced first one and then the other down on its knees and fastened the yoke upon them, while all wondered at his mighty prowess. Over the field he drove them, pressing the plow down firmly and casting the dragon's teeth into the furrows. By the time the plowing was done the crop was springing up, men bristling with arms who came rushing to attack him. Jason remembered Medea's words and flung a huge stone into their midst. With that, the warriors turned upon each other and fell beneath their own spears while the furrows ran with blood. So Jason's contest was ended in victory, bitter to King Æetes.

The King went back to the palace planning treachery against the heroes and vowing they should never have the Golden Fleece. But Hera was working for them. She made Medea, all bewildered with love and misery, determine to fly with Jason. That night she stole out of the house and sped along the dark path to the ship, where they were rejoicing in their good fortune with no thought of evil. She fell on her knees before them and begged them to take her with them. They must get the Fleece at once, she told them, and then make all haste away or they would be killed. A terrible serpent guarded the Fleece, but she would lull it to sleep so that it would do them no harm. She spoke in anguish, but Jason rejoiced and raised her gently and embraced her, and promised her she would be his own wedded wife when once they were back in Greece. Then taking her on board they went where she directed and reached the sacred grove where the Fleece hung. The guardian serpent was very terrible, but Medea approached it fearlessly and singing a sweet magical song she charmed it to sleep. Swiftly Jason lifted the golden wonder from the tree it hung on, and hurrying back they reached the ship as dawn was breaking. The strongest were put at the oars and they rowed with all their might down the river to the sea.

By now what had happened was known to the King, and he sent his son in pursuit—Medea's brother, Apsyrtus. He led an army so great that it seemed impossible for the little band of heroes either to conquer it or to escape, but Medea saved them again, this time by a horrible deed. She killed her brother. Some say she sent him word that she was longing to go back to her home and that she had the Fleece for him if he would meet her that night at a certain spot. He came all unsuspecting and Jason struck him down and his dark blood dyed his sister's silvery robe as she shrank away. With its leader dead, the army scattered in disorder and the way to the sea lay open to the heroes.

Others say that Apsyrtus set sail on the *Argo* with Medea, although why he did so is not explained, and that it was the King who pursued them. As his ship gained on them, Medea herself struck her brother down and cutting him limb from limb cast the pieces into the sea. The King stopped to gather them, and the *Argo* was saved.

By then the adventures of the Argonauts were almost over.

One terrible trial they had while passing between the smooth, sheer rock of Scylla and the whirlpool of Charybdis, where the sea forever spouted and roared and the furious waves mounting up touched the very sky. But Hera had seen to it that sea nymphs should be at hand to guide them and send the ship on to safety.

Next came Crete—where they would have landed but for Medea. She told them that Talus lived there, the last man left of the ancient bronze race, a creature made all of bronze except one ankle where alone he was vulnerable. Even as she spoke, he appeared, terrible to behold, and threatened to crush the ship with rocks if they drew nearer. They rested on their oars, and Medea kneeling prayed to the hounds of Hades to come and destroy him. The dread powers of evil heard her. As the bronze man lifted a pointed crag to hurl it at the *Argo* he grazed his ankle and the blood gushed forth until he sank and died. Then the heroes could land and refresh themselves for the voyage still before them.

Upon reaching Greece they disbanded, each hero going to his home, and Jason with Medea took the Golden Fleece to Pelias. But they found that terrible deeds had been done there. Pelias had forced Jason's father to kill himself and his mother had died of grief. Jason, bent upon punishing this wickedness, turned to Medea for the help which had never failed him. She brought about the death of Pelias by a cunning trick. To his daughters she said that she knew a secret, how to make the old young again; and to prove her words she cut up before them a ram worn out with many years, and put the pieces into a pot of boiling water. Then she uttered a charm and in a moment out from the water sprang a lamb and ran frisking away. The maidens were convinced. Medea gave Pelias a potent sleeping-draught and called upon his daughters to cut him into bits. With all their longing to make him young again they could hardly force themselves to do so, but at last the dreadful task was done, the pieces in the water, and they looked to Medea to speak the magic words that would bring him back to them and to his youth. But she was gone—gone from the palace and from the city, and horrified they realized that they were their father's murderers. Jason was revenged, indeed.

There is a story, too, that Medea restored Jason's father to life and made him young again, and that she gave to Jason the secret of perpetual youth. All that she did of evil and of good was done for him alone, and in the end, all the reward she got was that he turned traitor to her.

They came to Corinth after Pelias' death. Two sons were born to them and all seemed well, even to Medea in her exile, lonely as exile must always be. But her great love for Jason made the loss of her family and her country seem to her a little thing. And then Jason showed the meanness that was in him, brilliant hero though he had seemed to be: he engaged himself to marry the daughter of the King of Corinth. It was a splendid marriage and he thought of ambition only, never of love or of gratitude. In the first amazement at his treachery and in the passion of her anguish, Medea let fall words which made the King of Corinth fear she would do harm to his daughter, —he must have been a singularly unsuspicious man not to have thought of that before,—and he sent her word that she and her sons must leave the country at once. That was a doom almost as bad as death. A woman in exile with little helpless children had no protection for herself or them.

As she sat brooding over what she should do and thinking of her wrongs and her wretchedness,—wishing for death to end the life she could no longer bear; sometimes remembering with tears her father and her home; sometimes shuddering at the stain nothing could wash out of her brother's blood, of Pelias', too; conscious above all of the wild passionate devotion that had brought her to this evil and this misery,—as she sat thus, Jason appeared before her. She looked at him; she did not speak. He was there beside her, yet she was far away from him, alone with her outraged love and her ruined life. His feelings had nothing in them to make him silent. He told her coldly that he had always known how uncontrolled her spirit was. If it had not been for her foolish, mischievous talk about his bride she might have stayed on comfortably in Corinth. However, he had done his best for her. It was entirely through his efforts that she was only to be exiled, not killed. He had had a very hard time indeed to persuade the King, but he had spared no pains. He had come to her now because he was not a man to fail a friend, and he would see that she had plenty of gold and everything necessary for her journey.

This was too much. The torrent of Medea's wrongs burst forth. "You come to me?" she said—

To me, of all the race of men?
Yet it is well you came.
For I shall ease the burden of my heart
If I can make your baseness manifest.
I saved you. Every man in Greece knows that.
The bulls, the dragon-men, the serpent warder of the Fleece,
I conquered them. I made you victor.
I held the light that saved you.
Father and home—I left them
For a strange country.
I overthrew your foes,
Contrived for Pelias the worst of deaths.

Now you forsake me.
Where shall I go? Back to my father's house?
To Pelias' daughters? I have become for you
The enemy of all.
Myself, I had no quarrel with them.
Oh, I have had in you
A loyal husband, to be admired of men.
An exile now, O God, O God.
No one to help. I am alone.

His answer was that he had been saved not by her, but by Aphrodite, who had made her fall in love with him, and that she owed him a great deal for bringing her to Greece, a civilized country. Also that he had done very well for her in letting it be known how she had helped the Argonauts, so that people praised her. If only she could have had some common sense, she would have been glad of his marriage, as such a connection would have been profitable for her and the children, too. Her exile was her own fault only.

Whatever else she lacked Medea had plenty of intelligence. She wasted no more words upon him except to refuse his gold. She would take nothing, no help from him. Jason flung away angrily from her. "Your stubborn pride," he told her—

It drives away all those who would be kind.
But you will grieve the more for it.

From that moment Medea set herself to be revenged, as well she knew how.

By death, oh, by death, shall the conflict of life be decided,
Life's little day ended.

She determined to kill Jason's bride, and then—then? But she would not think of what else she saw before her. "Her death first," she said.

She took from a chest a most lovely robe. This she anointed with deadly drugs and placing it in a casket she sent her sons with it to the new bride. They must ask her, she told them, to show that she accepted the gift by wearing it at once. The Princess received them graciously, and agreed. But no sooner had she put it on than a fearful, devouring fire enveloped her. She dropped dead; her very flesh had melted away.

When Medea knew the deed was done she turned her mind to one still more dreadful. There was no protection for her children, no help for them anywhere. A slave's life might be theirs, nothing more. "I will not let them live for strangers to ill-use," she thought—

To die by other hands more merciless than mine.
No; I who gave them life will give them death.
Oh, now no cowardice, no thought how young they are,
How dear they are, how when they first were born—
Not that—I will forget they are my sons
One moment, one short moment—then forever sorrow.

When Jason came full of fury for what she had done to his bride and determined to kill her, the two boys were dead, and Medea on the roof of the house was stepping into a chariot drawn by dragons. They carried her away through the air out of his sight as he cursed her, never himself, for what had come to pass.

8 Four Great Adventures

PHAËTHON

This is one of Ovid's best stories, vividly told, details used not for mere decoration, but to heighten the effect.

The palace of the Sun was a radiant place. It shone with gold and gleamed with ivory and sparkled with jewels. Everything without and within flashed and glowed and glittered. It was always high noon there. Shadowy twilight never dimmed the brightness. Darkness and night were unknown. Few among mortals could have long endured that unchanging brilliancy of light, but few had ever found their way thither.

Nevertheless, one day a youth, mortal on his mother's side, dared to approach. Often he had to pause and clear his dazzled eyes, but the errand which had brought him was so urgent that his purpose held fast and he pressed on, up to the palace, through the burnished doors, and into the throne-room where surrounded by a blinding, blazing splendor the Sun-god sat. There the lad was forced to halt. He could bear no more.

Nothing escapes the eyes of the Sun. He saw the boy instantly and he looked at him very kindly. "What brought you here?" he asked. "I have come," the other answered boldly, "to find out if you are my father or not. My mother said you were, but the boys at school laugh when I tell them I am your son. They will not believe me. I told my mother and she said I had better go and ask you." Smiling, the Sun took off his crown of burning light so that the lad could look at him without distress. "Come here, Phaëthon," he said. "You are my son. Clymene told you the truth. I expect you will not doubt my word too? But I will give you a proof. Ask anything you want of me and you shall have it. I call the Styx to be witness to my promise, the river of the oath of the gods."

No doubt Phaëthon had often watched the Sun riding through the heavens and had told himself with a feeling, half awe, half excitement, "It is my father up there." And then he would wonder what it would be like to be in that chariot, guiding the steeds along that dizzy course, giving light to the world. Now at his father's words this wild dream had become possible. Instantly he cried, "I choose to take your place, Father. That is the only thing I want. Just for a day, a single day, let me have your car to drive."

The Sun realized his own folly. Why had he taken that fatal oath and bound himself to give in to anything that happened to enter a boy's rash young head? "Dear lad," he said, "this is the only thing I would have refused you. I know I cannot refuse. I have sworn by the Styx. I must yield if you persist. But I do not believe you will. Listen while I tell you what this is you want. You are Clymene's son as well as mine. You are mortal and no mortal could drive my chariot. Indeed, no god except myself can do that. The ruler of the gods cannot. Consider the road. It rises up from the sea so steeply that the horses can hardly climb it, fresh though they are in the early morning. In midheaven it is so high that even I do not like to look down. Worst of all is the descent, so precipitous that the Sea-gods waiting to receive me wonder how I can avoid falling headlong. To guide the horses, too, is a perpetual struggle. Their fiery spirits grow hotter as they climb and they scarcely suffer my control. What would they do with you?

"Are you fancying that there are all sorts of wonders up there, cities of the gods full of beautiful things? Nothing of the kind. You will have to pass beasts, fierce beasts of prey, and they are all that you will see. The Bull, the Lion, the Scorpion, the great Crab, each will try to harm you. Be persuaded. Look around you. See all the goods the rich world holds. Choose from them your heart's desire and it shall be yours. If what you want is to be proved my son, my fears for you are proof enough that I am your father."

But none of all this wise talk meant anything to the boy. A glorious prospect opened before him. He saw himself proudly standing in that wondrous car, his hands triumphantly guiding those steeds which Jove himself could not master. He did not give a thought to the dangers his father detailed. He felt not a quiver of fear, not a doubt of his own powers. At last the Sun gave up trying to dissuade him. It was hopeless, as he saw. Besides, there was no time. The moment for starting was at hand.

Already the gates of the east glowed purple, and Dawn had opened her courts full of rosy light. The stars were leaving the sky; even the lingering morning star was dim.

There was need for haste, but all was ready. The seasons, the gatekeepers of Olympus, stood waiting to fling the doors wide. The horses had been bridled and yoked to the car. Proudly and joyously Phaëthon mounted it and they were off. He had made his choice. Whatever came of it he could not change now. Not that he wanted to in that first exhilarating rush through the air, so swift that the East Wind was outstripped and left far behind. The horses' flying feet went through the low-banked clouds near the ocean as through a thin sea mist and then up and up in the clear air, climbing the height of heaven. For a few ecstatic moments Phaëthon felt himself the Lord of the Sky. But suddenly there was a change. The chariot was swinging wildly to and fro; the pace was faster; he had lost control. Not he, but the horses were directing the course. That light weight in the car, those feeble hands clutching the reins, had told them their own driver was not there. They were the masters then. No one else could command them. They left the road and rushed where they chose, up, down, to the right, to the left. They nearly wrecked the chariot against the Scorpion; they brought up short and almost ran into the Crab. By this time the poor charioteer was half fainting with terror, and he let the reins fall.

That was the signal for still more mad and reckless running. The horses soared up to the very top of the sky and then, plunging headlong down, they set the world on fire. The highest mountains were the first to burn, Ida and Helicon, where the Muses dwell, Parnassus, and heaven-piercing Olympus. Down their slopes the flame ran to the low-lying valleys and the dark forest lands, until all things everywhere were ablaze. The springs turned into steam; the rivers shrank. It is said that it was then the Nile fled and hid his head, which still is hidden.

In the car Phaëthon, hardly keeping his place there, was wrapped in thick smoke and heat as if from a fiery furnace. He wanted nothing except to have this torment and terror ended. He would have welcomed death. Mother Earth, too, could bear no more. She uttered a great cry which reached up to the gods. Looking down from Olympus they saw that they must act quickly if the world was to be saved. Jove seized his thunderbolt and hurled it at the rash, repentant driver. It struck him dead, shattered the chariot, and made the maddened horses rush down into the sea.

Phaëthon all on fire fell from the car through the air to the earth. The mysterious river Eridanus, which no mortal eyes have ever seen, received him and put out the flames and cooled the body. The naiads, in pity for him, so bold and so young to die, buried him and carved upon the tomb:—

> Here Phaëthon lies who drove the Sun-god's car.
> Greatly he failed, but he had greatly dared.

His sisters, the Heliades, the daughters of Helios, the Sun, came to his grave to mourn for him. There they were turned into poplar trees, on the bank of the Eridanus,

> Where sorrowing they weep into the stream forever.
> And each tear as it falls shines in the water
> A glistening drop of amber.

PEGASUS AND BELLEROPHON

> *Two of the episodes in this story are taken from the earliest poets. Hesiod in the eighth or ninth century tells about the Chimaera, and Anteia's love and the sad end of Bellerophon are in the* Iliad. *The rest of the story is told first and best by Pindar in the first half of the fifth century.*

In Ephyre, the city later called Corinth, Glaucus was King. He was the son of Sisyphus who in Hades must forever try to roll a stone uphill because he once betrayed a secret of Zeus. Glaucus, too, drew down on himself the displeasure of heaven. He was a great horseman and he fed his horses human flesh to make them fierce in battle. Such monstrous deeds always angered the gods and they served him as he had served others. He was thrown from his chariot and his horses tore him to pieces and devoured him.

In the city a bold and beautiful young man named Bellerophon was generally held to be his son. It was rumored, however, that Bellerophon had a mightier father, Poseidon himself, the Ruler of the Sea, and the youth's surpassing gifts of spirit and body made this account of his birth seem likely. Moreover his mother, Eurynome, although a mortal, had been taught by Athena until in wit and wisdom she was the peer of the gods. It was only to be expected on all scores that Bellerophon should seem less mortal than divine. Great adventures would call to such a one as he and no peril would ever hold him back. And yet the deed for which he is best known needed no courage at all, no effort, even. Indeed, it proved that

> What man would swear cannot be done,—
> Must not be hoped for,—the great Power on high
> Can give into his hand, in easy mastery.

More than anything on earth Bellerophon wanted Pegasus, a marvelous horse which had sprung from the Gorgon's blood when Perseus killed her.* He was

> A winged steed, unwearying of flight,
> Sweeping through air swift as a gale of wind.

Wonders attended him. The spring beloved of poets, Hippocrene, on Helicon, the Muses' mountain, had sprung up where his hoof had struck the earth. Who could catch and tame such a creature? Bellerophon suffered from hopeless longing.

The wise seer of Ephyre (Corinth), Polyidus, to whom he told his desperate desire, advised him to go to Athena's temple and sleep there. The gods often spoke to men in their dreams. So Bellerophon went to the holy place and when he was lying deep in slumber beside the altar he seemed to see the goddess standing before him with some golden thing in her hand. She said to him, "Asleep? Nay, wake. Here is what will charm the steed you covet." He sprang to his feet. No goddess was there, but a marvelous object lay in front of him, a bridle all of gold, such as never had been seen before. Hopeful at last with it in his hand, he hurried out to the fields to find Pegasus. He caught sight of him, drinking from the far-famed spring of Corinth, Pirene; and he drew gently near. The horse looked at him tranquilly, neither startled nor afraid, and suffered himself to be bridled without the least trouble. Athena's charm had worked. Bellerophon was master of the glorious creature.

In his full suit of bronze armor he leaped upon his back and put him through his paces, the horse seeming to delight in the sport as much as he himself. Now he was lord of the air, flying wherever he would, envied of all. As matters turned out, Pegasus was not only a joy, but a help in time of need as well, for hard trials lay before Bellerophon.

In some way, we are not told how except that it was purely through accident, he killed his brother; and he went to Argos where the King, Proetus, purified him. There his trials began and his great deeds as well. Anteia, the wife of Proetus, fell in love with him, and when he turned from her and would have nothing to do with her, in her bitter anger she told her husband that his guest had wronged her and must die. Enraged though he was, Proetus would not kill him. Bellerophon had eaten at his table; he could not bring himself to use violence against him. However, he made a plan which seemed certain to have the same result. He asked the youth to take a letter to the King of Lycia in Asia and Bellerophon easily agreed. Long journeys meant nothing to him on Pegasus' back. The Lycian king

* See Part Three, Chapter 9.

Bellerophon on Pegasus killing the Chimaera

eceived him with antique hospitality and entertained him
plendidly for nine days before he asked to see the letter. Then
ae read that Proetus wanted the young man killed.

He did not care to do so, for the same reason that had made
Proetus unwilling: Zeus's well-known hostility to those who
oroke the bond between host and guest. There could be no
objection, however, to sending the stranger on an adventure,
him and his winged horse. So he asked him to go and slay the
Chimaera, feeling quite assured that he would never come
back. The Chimaera was held to be unconquerable. She was a
most singular portent, a lion in front, a serpent behind, a goat
in between—

> A fearful creature, great and swift of foot and strong,
> Whose breath was flame unquenchable.

But for Bellerophon riding Pegasus there was no need to come
anywhere near the flaming monster. He soared up over her and
shot her with his arrows at no risk to himself.

When he went back to Proetus, the latter had to think out
other ways of disposing of him. He got him to go on an expedition, against the Solymi, mighty warriors; and then when Bellerophon had succeeded in conquering these, on another
against the Amazons, where he did equally well. Finally Proetus was won over by his courage and his good fortune, too; he
became friends with him and gave him his daughter to marry.

He lived happily thus for a long time; then he made the gods
angry. His eager ambition along with his great success led him
to think "thoughts too great for man," the thing of all others
the gods objected to. He tried to ride Pegasus up to Olympus.
He believed he could take his place there with the immortals.
The horse was wiser. He would not try the flight, and he threw
his rider. Thereafter Bellerophon, hated of the gods, wandered
alone, devouring his own soul and avoiding the paths of men
until he died.

Pegasus found shelter in the heavenly stalls of Olympus
where the steeds of Zeus were cared for. Of them all he was
foremost, as was proved by the extraordinary fact the poets
report, that when Zeus wished to use his thunderbolt, it was
Pegasus who brought the thunder and lightning to him.

OTUS AND EPHIALTES

> *This story is alluded to in the* Odyssey *and the* Aeneid,
> *but only Apollodorus tells it in full. He wrote, probably,
> in the first or second century* A.D. *A dull writer, but less
> dull than usual in this tale.*

These twin brothers were Giants, but they did not look like the monsters of old. They were straight of form and noble of face. Homer says they were

Tallest of all that the life-giving earth with her bread ever nourished,
Handsomest too, after peerless Orion alone.

Virgil speaks chiefly of their mad ambition. He says they were

Twins, huge-bodied, who strove with their hands to destroy the high heavens,
Strove to push Jupiter down from his kingdom supernal.

They were the sons of Iphimedia, some say; others, of Canace. At all events, whoever their mother was, their father was certainly Poseidon, although they went generally by the name of the Aloadae, the sons of Aloeus, their mother's husband.

They were still very young when they set about proving that they were the gods' superiors. They imprisoned Ares, bound him with chains of brass and shut him up. The Olympians were reluctant to try to free him by force. They sent the cunning Hermes to his assistance, who contrived stealthily by night to get him out of his prison. Then the two arrogant youths dared still more. They threatened that they would pile Mount Pelion on Mount Ossa and scale the heights of heaven, as the Giants of old had piled Ossa on Pelion. This passed the endurance of the immortals, and Zeus got ready his thunderbolt to strike them. But before he hurled it Poseidon came begging him to spare them and promising to keep them in order. Zeus agreed and Poseidon was as good as his word. The twins stopped warring against heaven and Poseidon felt pleased with himself, but the fact was that the two had turned to other plans which interested them more.

Otus thought it would be an excellent adventure to carry Hera off, and Ephialtes was in love with Artemis, or thought he was. In truth the two brothers cared only for each other. Theirs was a great devotion. They drew lots to decide which should first seize his lady, and fortune favored Ephialtes. They sought Artemis everywhere over the hills and in the woods, but when at last they caught sight of her she was on the seashore, making directly for the sea. She knew their evil purpose and she knew too how she would punish them. They sprang after her, but she kept straight on over the sea. All of Poseidon's sons had the same power: they could run dry-shod on the sea as on the land, so the two followed her with no trouble. She led them to the wooded island of Naxos, and there, when they had all but caught up with her, she disappeared. They saw instead a most lovely milk-white hind springing into the forest. At the sight they forgot the goddess and turned in pursuit of the beautiful creature. They lost her in the thick woods and they separated in order to double the chance of finding her. At the same moment each suddenly saw her standing with ears pricked in an open glade, but neither saw that back in the trees just beyond her was his brother. They threw their javelins and the hind vanished. The weapons sped on across the empty glade into the wood and there found their mark. The towering forms of the young hunters crashed to the ground, each pierced by the spear of the other, each slaying and being slain by the only creature he loved.

Such was the vengeance of Artemis.

DAEDALUS

Both Ovid and Apollodorus tell this story. Apollodorus lived probably more than a hundred years after Ovid. He is a very pedestrian writer and Ovid is far from that. But in this case I have followed Apollodorus. Ovid's account shows him at his worst, sentimental and exclamatory.

Daedalus was the architect who had contrived the Labyrinth for the Minotaur in Crete, and who showed Ariadne how Theseus could escape from it.* When King Minos learned that the Athenians had found their way out, he was convinced that they could have done so only if Daedalus had helped them. Accordingly he imprisoned him and his son Icarus in the Labyrinth, certainly a proof that it was excellently devised since not even the maker of it could discover the exit without a clue. But the great inventor was not at a loss. He told his son,

Escape may be checked by water and land, but the air and the sky are free,

and he made two pairs of wings for them. They put them on and just before they took flight Daedalus warned Icarus to keep a middle course over the sea. If he flew too high the sun might melt the glue and the wings drop off. However, as stories so often show, what elders say youth disregards. As the two flew lightly and without effort away from Crete the delight of

* See Part Three. Chapter 10.

this new and wonderful power went to the boy's head. He soared exultingly up and up, paying no heed to his father's anguished commands. Then he fell. The wings had come off. He dropped into the sea and the waters closed over him. The afflicted father flew safely to Sicily, where he was received kindly by the King.

Minos was enraged at his escape and determined to find him. He made a cunning plan. He had it proclaimed everywhere that a great reward would be given to whoever could pass a thread through an intricately spiraled shell. Daedalus told the Sicilian king that he could do it. He bored a small hole in the closed end of the shell, fastened a thread to an ant, introduced the ant into the hole, and then closed it. When the ant finally came out at the other end, the thread, of course, was running clear through all the twists and turns. "Only Daedalus would think of that," Minos said, and he came to Sicily to seize him. But the King refused to surrender him, and in the contest Minos was slain.

PART THREE

The Great Heroes before the Trojan War

9 Perseus

This story is on the level of the fairy story. Hermes and Athena act like the fairy godmother in Cinderella. The magical wallet and cap belong to the properties fairy tales abound in everywhere. It is the only myth in which magic plays a decisive part, and it seems to have been a great favorite in Greece. Many poets allude to it. The description of Danaë in the wooden chest was the most famous passage of a famous poem by Simonides of Ceos, a great lyric poet who lived in the sixth century. The entire story is told by both Ovid and Apollodorus. The latter, probably a hundred years later than Ovid, is here the superior of the two. His account is simple and straightforward; Ovid's extremely verbose—for instance, he takes a hundred lines to kill the sea serpent. I have followed Apollodorus, but I have added the fragment from Simonides, and short quotations from other poets, notably Hesiod and Pindar.

King Acrisius of Argos had only one child, a daughter, Danaë. She was beautiful above all the other women of the land, but this was small comfort to the King for not having a son. He journeyed to Delphi to ask the god if there was any hope that some day he would be the father of a boy. The priestess told him no, and added what was far worse: that his daughter would have a son who would kill him.

The only sure way to escape that fate was for the King to have Danaë instantly put to death—taking no chances, but seeing to it himself. This Acrisius would not do. His fatherly affection was not strong, as events proved, but his fear of the gods was. They visited with terrible punishment those who shed the blood of kindred. Acrisius did not dare slay his daughter. Instead, he had a house built all of bronze and sunk underground, but with part of the roof open to the sky so that light and air could come through. Here he shut her up and guarded her.

> So Danaë endured, the beautiful,
> To change the glad daylight for brass-bound walls,
> And in that chamber secret as the grave
> She lived a prisoner. Yet to her came
> Zeus in the golden rain.

As she sat there through the long days and hours with nothing to do, nothing to see except the clouds moving by overhead, a mysterious thing happened, a shower of gold fell from the sky and filled her chamber. How it was revealed to her that it was Zeus who had visited her in this shape we are not told, but she knew that the child she bore was his son.

For a time she kept his birth secret from her father, but it became increasingly difficult to do so in the narrow limits of that bronze house and finally one day the little boy—his name was Perseus—was discovered by his grandfather. "Your child!" Acrisius cried in great anger. "Who is his father?" But when Danaë answered proudly, "Zeus," he would not believe her. One thing only he was sure of, that the boy's life was a terrible danger to his own. He was afraid to kill him for the same reason that had kept him from killing her, fear of Zeus and the Furies who pursue such murderers. But if he could not kill them outright, he could put them in the way of tolerably certain death. He had a great chest made, and the two placed in it. Then it was taken out to sea and cast into the water.

In that strange boat Danaë sat with her little son. The daylight faded and she was alone on the sea.

> When in the carven chest the winds and waves
> Struck fear into her heart she put her arms,
> Not without tears, round Perseus tenderly
> She said, "O son, what grief is mine.
> But you sleep softly, little child,
> Sunk deep in rest within your cheerless home,
> Only a box, brass-bound. The night, this darkness visible,
> The scudding waves so near to your soft curls,
> The shrill voice of the wind, you do not heed,
> Nestled in your red cloak, fair little face."

Through the night in the tossing chest she listened to the waters that seemed always about to wash over them. The dawn came, but with no comfort to her for she could not see it. Neither could she see that around them there were islands rising high above the sea, many islands. All she knew was that presently a wave seemed to lift them and carry them swiftly on and then, retreating, leave them on something solid and motionless. They had made land; they were safe from the sea, but they were still in the chest with no way to get out.

Fate willed it—or perhaps Zeus, who up to now had done little for his love and his child—that they should be discovered by a good man, a fisherman named Dictys. He came upon the great box and broke it open and took the pitiful cargo home to his wife who was as kind as he. They had no children and they cared for Danaë and Perseus as if they were their own. The two lived there many years, Danaë content to let her son follow the fisherman's humble trade, out of harm's way. But in the end more trouble came. Polydectes, the ruler of the little island, was the brother of Dictys, but he was a cruel and ruthless man. He seems to have taken no notice of the mother and son for a long time, but at last Danaë attracted his attention. She was still radiantly beautiful even though Perseus by now was full grown, and Polydectes fell in love with her. He wanted her, but he did not want her son, and he set himself to think out a way of getting rid of him.

There were some fearsome monsters called Gorgons who lived on an island and were known far and wide because of their deadly power. Polydectes evidently talked to Perseus about them; he probably told him that he would rather have the head of one of them than anything else in the world. This seems practically certain from the plan he devised for killing Perseus. He announced that he was about to be married and he called his friends together for a celebration, including Perseus in the invitation. Each guest, as was customary, brought a gift for the bride-to-be, except Perseus alone. He had nothing he could give. He was young and proud and keenly mortified. He stood up before them all and did exactly what the King had hoped he would do, declared that he would give him a present better than any there. He would go off and kill Medusa and bring back her head as his gift. Nothing could have suited the King better. No one in his senses would have made such a proposal. Medusa was one of the Gorgons,

> And they are three, the Gorgons, each with wings
> And snaky hair, most horrible to mortals.
> Whom no man shall behold and draw again
> The breath of life,

for the reason that whoever looked at them was turned instantly into stone. It seemed that Perseus had been led by his angry pride into making an empty boast. No man unaided could kill Medusa.

But Perseus was saved from his folly. Two great gods were watching over him. He took ship as soon as he left the King's hall, not daring to see his mother first and tell her what he intended, and he sailed to Greece to learn where the three monsters were to be found. He went to Delphi, but all the priestess would say was to bid him seek the land where men eat not Demeter's golden grain, but only acorns. So he went to Dodona, in the land of oak trees, where the talking oaks were which declared Zeus's will and where the Selli lived who made their bread from acorns. They could tell him, however, no more than this, that he was under the protection of the gods. They did not know where the Gorgons lived.

When and how Hermes and Athena came to his help is not told in any story, but he must have known despair before they did so. At last, however, as he wandered on, he met a strange and beautiful person. We know what he looked like from many a poem, a young man with the first down upon his cheek when youth is loveliest, carrying, as no other young man ever did, a wand of gold with wings at one end, wearing a winged hat, too, and winged sandals. At sight of him hope must have entered Perseus' heart, for he would know that this could be none other than Hermes, the guide and the giver of good.

This radiant personage told him that before he attacked Medusa he must first be properly equipped, and that what he needed was in the possession of the nymphs of the North. To find the nymphs' abode, they must go to the Gray Women who alone could tell them the way. These women dwelt in a land where all was dim and shrouded in twilight. No ray of sun looked ever on that country, nor the moon by night. In that gray place the three women lived, all gray themselves and withered as in extreme old age. They were strange creatures, indeed, most of all because they had but one eye for the three, which it was their custom to take turns with, each removing it from her forehead when she had had it for a time and handing it to another.

All this Hermes told Perseus and then he unfolded his plan. He would himself guide Perseus to them. Once there Perseus must keep hidden until he saw one of them take the eye out of her forehead to pass it on. At that moment, when none of the three could see, he must rush forward and seize the eye and refuse to give it back until they told him how to reach the nymphs of the North.

He himself, Hermes said, would give him a sword to attack Medusa with—which could not be bent or broken by the Gorgon's scales, no matter how hard they were. This was a wonderful gift, no doubt, and yet of what use was a sword when the creature to be struck by it could turn the swordsman into stone before he was within striking distance? But another great deity was at hand to help. Pallas Athena stood beside Perseus. She took off the shield of polished bronze which covered her breast and held it out to him. "Look into this when you attack the Gorgon," she said. "You will be able to see her in it as in a mirror, and so avoid her deadly power."

Now, indeed, Perseus had good reason to hope. The journey to the twilight land was long, over the stream of Ocean and on to the very border of the black country where the Cimmerians dwell, but Hermes was his guide and he could not go astray. They found the Gray Women at last, looking in the wavering light like gray birds, for they had the shape of swans. But their heads were human and beneath their wings they had arms and hands. Perseus did just as Hermes had said, he held back until he saw one of them take the eye out of her forehead. Then before she could give it to her sister, he snatched it out of her hand. It was a moment or two before the three realized they had lost it. Each thought one of the others had it. But Perseus spoke out and told them he had taken it and that it would be theirs again only when they showed him how to find the nymphs of the North. They gave him full directions at once; they would have done anything to get their eye back. He returned it to them and went on the way they had pointed out to him. He was bound, although he did not know it, to the blessed country of the Hyperboreans, at the back of the North Wind, of which it is said: "Neither by ship nor yet by land shall one find the wondrous road to the gathering place of the Hyperboreans." But Perseus had Hermes with him, so that the road lay open to him, and he reached that host of happy people who are always banqueting and holding joyful revelry. They showed him great kindness: they welcomed him to their feast, and the maidens dancing to the sound of flute and lyre paused to get for him the gifts he sought. These were three: winged sandals, a magic wallet which would always become the right size for whatever was to be carried in it, and, most important of all, a cap which made the wearer invisible. With these and Athena's shield and Hermes' sword Perseus was ready for the Gorgons. Hermes knew where they lived, and leaving the happy land the two flew back across Ocean and over the sea to the Terrible Sisters' island.

By great good fortune they were all asleep when Perseus found them. In the mirror of the bright shield he could see them clearly, creatures with great wings and bodies covered with golden scales and hair a mass of twisting snakes. Athena was beside him now as well as Hermes. They told him which one was Medusa and that was important, for she alone of the three could be killed; the other two were immortal. Perseus on his winged sandals hovered above them, looking, however, only at the shield. Then he aimed a stroke down at Medusa's throat and Athena guided his hand. With a single sweep of his sword he cut through her neck and, his eyes still fixed on the shield with never a glance at her, he swooped low enough to seize the head. He dropped it into the wallet which closed around it. He had nothing to fear from it now. But the two other Gorgons had awakened and, horrified at the sight of their sister slain, tried to pursue the slayer. Perseus was safe; he had on the cap of darkness and they could not find him.

> So over the sea rich-haired Danaë's son,
> Perseus, on his winged sandals sped,
> Flying swift as thought.
> In a wallet of silver,
> A wonder to behold,
> He bore the head of the monster,
> While Hermes, the son of Maia,
> The messenger of Zeus,
> Kept ever at his side.

On his way back he came to Ethiopia and alighted there. By this time Hermes had left him. Perseus found, as Hercules was later to find, that a lovely maiden had been given up to be devoured by a horrible sea serpent. Her name was Andromeda and she was the daughter of a silly vain woman,

> That starred Ethiop queen who strove
> To set her beauty's praise above
> The sea-nymphs, and their power offended.

She had boasted that she was more beautiful than the daughters of Nereus, the Sea-god. An absolutely certain way in those days to draw down on one a wretched fate was to claim superiority in anything over any deity; nevertheless people were perpetually doing so. In this case the punishment for the arrogance the gods detested fell not on Queen Cassiopeia, Andromeda's mother, but on her daughter. The Ethiopians were being devoured in numbers by the serpent; and, learning from the oracle that they could be freed from the pest only if Andromeda were offered up to it, they forced Cepheus, her father, to consent. When Perseus arrived the maiden was on a rocky ledge by the sea, chained there to wait for the coming

Perseus holding Medusa's head

of the monster. Perseus saw her and on the instant loved her.
He waited beside her until the great snake came for its prey;
then he cut its head off just as he had the Gorgon's. The
headless body dropped back into the water; Perseus took
Andromeda to her parents and asked for her hand, which they
gladly gave him.

With her he sailed back to the island and his mother, but
in the house where he had lived so long he found no one. The
fisherman Dictys' wife was long since dead, and the two others,
Danaë and the man who had been like a father to Perseus,
had had to fly and hide themselves from Polydectes, who was
furious at Danaë's refusal to marry him. They had taken
refuge in a temple, Perseus was told. He learned also that the
King was holding a banquet in the palace and all the men
who favored him were gathered there. Perseus instantly saw
his opportunity. He went straight to the palace and entered
the hall. As he stood at the entrance, Athena's shining buckler
on his breast, the silver wallet at his side, he drew the eyes
of every man there. Then before any could look away he held
up the Gorgon's head; and at the sight one and all, the cruel
King and his servile courtiers, were turned into stone. There
they sat, a row of statues, each, as it were, frozen stiff in the
attitude he had struck when he first saw Perseus.

When the islanders knew themselves freed from the tyrant
it was easy for Perseus to find Danaë and Dictys. He made
Dictys king of the island, but he and his mother decided that
they would go back with Andromeda to Greece and try to be
reconciled to Acrisius, to see if the many years that had
passed since he had put them in the chest had not softened
him so that he would be glad to receive his daughter and
grandson. When they reached Argos, however, they found that
Acrisius had been driven away from the city, and where he
was no one could say. It happened that soon after their arrival Perseus heard that the King of Larissa, in the North,
was holding a great athletic contest, and he journeyed there
to take part. In the discus-throwing when his turn came and
he hurled the heavy missile, it swerved and fell among the
spectators. Acrisius was there on a visit to the King, and the
discus struck him. The blow was fatal and he died at once.

So Apollo's oracle was again proved true. If Perseus felt
any grief, at least he knew that his grandfather had done his
best to kill him and his mother. With his death their troubles
came to an end. Perseus and Andromeda lived happily ever
after. Their son, Electryon, was the grandfather of Hercules.

Medusa's head was given to Athena, who bore it always
upon the aegis, Zeus's shield, which she carried for him.

10 Theseus

This dearest of heroes to the Athenians engaged the attention of many writers. Ovid, who lived in the Augustan Age, tells his life in detail and so does Apollodorus, in the first or second century A.D. Plutarch, too, toward the end of the first century A.D. He is a prominent character in three of Euripides' plays and in one of Sophocles. There are many allusions to him in prose writers as well as poets. I have followed Apollodorus on the whole, but I have added from Euripides the stories of the appeal of Adrastus, the madness of Hercules, and the fate of Hippolytus; from Sophocles his kindness to Oedipus; from Plutarch the story of his death, to which Apollodorus gives only a sentence.

The great Athenian hero was Theseus. He had so many adventures and took part in so many great enterprises that there grew up a saying in Athens, "Nothing without Theseus."

He was the son of the Athenian King, Aegeus. He spent his youth, however, in his mother's home, a city in southern Greece. Aegeus went back to Athens before the child was born, but first he placed in a hollow a sword and a pair of shoes and covered them with a great stone. He did this with the knowledge of his wife and told her that whenever the boy—if it was a boy—grew strong enough to roll away the stone and get the things beneath it, she could send him to Athens to claim him as his father. The child was a boy and he grew up strong far beyond others, so that when his mother finally took him to the stone he lifted it with no trouble at all. She told him then that the time had come for him to seek his father, and a ship was placed at his disposal by his grandfather. But Theseus refused to go by water, because the voyage was safe and easy. His idea was to become a great hero as quickly as possible, and easy safety was certainly not the way to do that. Hercules,* who was the most magnificent of all the heroes of Greece, was always in his mind, and the determination to be just as magnificent himself. This was quite natural since the two were cousins.

He steadfastly refused, therefore, the ship his mother and grandfather urged on him, telling them that to sail on it would be a contemptible flight from danger, and he set forth to go to Athens by land. The journey was long and very hazardous because of the bandits that beset the road. He killed them all, however; he left not one alive to trouble future travelers. His idea of dealing justice was simple, but effective: what each had done to others, Theseus did to him. Sciron, for instance, who had made those he captured kneel to wash his feet and then kicked them down into the sea, Theseus hurled over a precipice. Sinis, who killed people by fastening them to two pine trees bent down to the ground and letting the trees go, died in that way himself. Procrustes was placed upon the iron bed which he used for his victims, tying them to it and then making them the right length for it by stretching those who were too short and cutting off as much as was necessary from those who were too long. The story does not say which of the two methods was used in his case, but there was not much to choose between them and in one way or the other Procrustes' career ended.

It can be imagined how Greece rang with the praises of the young man who had cleared the land of these banes to travelers. When he reached Athens he was an acknowledged hero and he was invited to a banquet by the King, who of course was unaware that Theseus was his son. In fact he was afraid of the young man's great popularity, thinking that he might win the people over to make him king, and he invited him with the idea of poisoning him. The plan was not his, but Medea's, the heroine of the Quest of the Golden Fleece who knew through her sorcery who Theseus was. She had fled to Athens when she left Corinth in her winged car, and she had acquired great influence over Aegeus, which she did not want disturbed by the appearance of a son. But as she handed him the poisoned cup Theseus, wishing to make himself known at once to his father, drew his sword. The King instantly recognized it and dashed the cup to the ground. Medea escaped as she always did and got safely away to Asia.

Aegeus then proclaimed to the country that Theseus was his son and heir. The new heir apparent soon had an opportunity to endear himself to the Athenians.

Years before his arrival in Athens, a terrible misfortune

---

* See next chapter.

had happened to the city. Minos, the powerful ruler of Crete, had lost his only son, Androgeus, while the young man was visiting the Athenian King. King Aegeus had done what no host should do, he had sent his guest on an expedition full of peril—to kill a dangerous bull. Instead, the bull had killed the youth. Minos invaded the country, captured Athens and declared that he would raze it to the ground unless every nine years the people sent him a tribute of seven maidens and seven youths. A horrible fate awaited these young creatures. When they reached Crete they were given to the Minotaur to devour.

The Minotaur was a monster, half bull, half human, the offspring of Minos' wife Pasiphaë and a wonderfully beautiful bull. Poseidon had given this bull to Minos in order that he should sacrifice it to him, but Minos could not bear to slay it and had kept it for himself. To punish him, Poseidon had made Pasiphaë fall madly in love with it.

When the Minotaur was born Minos did not kill him. He had Daedalus, a great architect and inventor, construct a place of confinement for him from which escape was impossible. Daedalus built the Labyrinth, famous throughout the world. Once inside, one would go endlessly along its twisting paths without ever finding the exit. To this place the young Athenians were each time taken and left to the Minotaur. There was no possible way to escape. In whatever direction they ran they might be running straight to the monster; if they stood still he might at any moment emerge from the maze. Such was the doom which awaited fourteen youths and maidens a few days after Theseus reached Athens. The time had come for the next installment of the tribute.

At once Theseus came forward and offered to be one of the victims. All loved him for his goodness and admired him for his nobility, but they had no idea that he intended to try to kill the Minotaur. He told his father, however, and promised him that if he succeeded, he would have the black sail which the ship with its cargo of misery always carried changed to a white one, so that Aegeus could know long before it came to land that his son was safe.

When the young victims arrived in Crete they were paraded before the inhabitants on their way to the Labyrinth. Minos' daughter Ariadne was among the spectators and she fell in love with Theseus at first sight as he marched past her. She sent for Daedalus and told him he must show her a way to get out of the Labyrinth, and she sent for Theseus and told him she would bring about his escape if he would promise to take her back to Athens and marry her. As may be imagined, he made no difficulty about that, and she gave him the clue she had got from Daedalus, a ball of thread which he was to fasten at one end to the inside of the door and unwind as he went on. This he did and, certain that he could retrace his steps whenever he chose, he walked boldly into the maze looking for the Minotaur. He came upon him asleep and fell upon him, pinning him to the ground; and with his fists—he had no other weapon—he battered the monster to death.

> As an oak tree falls on the hillside
> Crushing all that lies beneath,
> So Theseus. He presses out the life,
> The brute's savage life, and now it lies dead.
> Only the head sways slowly, but the horns are useless now.

When Theseus lifted himself up from that terrific struggle, the ball of thread lay where he had dropped it. With it in his hands, the way out was clear. The others followed and taking Ariadne with them they fled to the ship and over the sea toward Athens.

On the way there they put in at the island of Naxos and what happened then is differently reported. One story says that Theseus deserted Ariadne. She was asleep and he sailed away without her, but Dionysus found her and comforted her. The other story is much more favorable to Theseus. She was extremely seasick, and he set her ashore to recover while he returned to the ship to do some necessary work. A violent wind carried him out to sea and kept him there a long time. On his return he found that Ariadne had died, and he was deeply afflicted.

Both stories agree that when they drew near to Athens he forgot to hoist the white sail. Either his joy at the success of his voyage put every other thought out of his head, or his grief for Ariadne. The black sail was seen by his father, King Aegeus, from the Acropolis, where for days he had watched the sea with straining eyes. It was to him the sign of his son's death and he threw himself down from a rocky height into the sea, and was killed. The sea into which he fell was called the Aegean ever after.

So Theseus became King of Athens, a most wise and disinterested king. He declared to the people that he did not wish to rule over them; he wanted a people's government where all would be equal. He resigned his royal power and organized a commonwealth, building a council hall where the citizens should gather and vote. The only office he kept for himself was that of Commander in Chief. Thus Athens became, of all earth's cities, the happiest and most prosperous, the only true home of liberty, the one place in the world where the

The Minotaur in the Labyrinth

people governed themselves. It was for this reason that in the great War of the Seven against Thebes,* when the victorious Thebans refused burial to those of the enemy who had died, the vanquished turned to Theseus and Athens for help, believing that free men under such a leader would never consent to having the helpless dead wronged. They did not turn in vain. Theseus led his army against Thebes, conquered her and forced her to allow them to be buried. But when he was victor he did not return evil to the Thebans for the evil they had done. He showed himself the perfect knight. He refused to let his army enter and loot the city. He had come not to harm Thebes, but to bury the Argive dead, and that duty done he led his soldiers back to Athens.

In many other stories he shows the same qualities. He received the aged Oedipus whom everyone else had cast out.* He was with him when he died, sustaining and comforting him. He protected his two helpless daughters and sent them safely home after their father's death. When Hercules ** in his madness killed his wife and children and upon his return to sanity determined to kill himself, Theseus alone stood by him. Hercules' other friends fled, fearing to be polluted by the presence of one who had done so horrible a deed, but Theseus gave him his hand, roused his courage, told him to die would be a coward's act, and took him to Athens.

All the cares of state, however, and all the deeds of knight-errantry to defend the wronged and helpless, could not restrain Theseus' love of danger for the sake of danger. He went to the country of the Amazons, the women warriors, some say with Hercules, some say alone, and brought away one of them, whose name is given sometimes as Antiope, sometimes as Hippolyta. It is certain that the son she bore Theseus was named Hippolytus, and also that after his birth the Amazons came to rescue her and invaded Attica, the country around Athens, even making their way into the city. They were finally defeated and no other enemy entered Attica as long as Theseus lived.

But he had many other adventures. He was one of the men who sailed on the *Argo* to find the Golden Fleece. He took part in the great Calydonian Hunt, when the King of Calydon called upon the noblest in Greece to help him kill the terrible boar which was laying waste his country. During the hunt Theseus saved the life of his rash friend Pirithoüs, as he did, indeed, a number of times. Pirithoüs was quite as adventurous as Theseus, but by no means as successful, so that he was perpetually in trouble. Theseus was devoted to him and al-

* See Part Five, Chapter 18.
** See Part Three, Chapter 11.

ways helped him out. The friendship between them came about through an especially rash act on Pirithoüs' part. It occured to him that he would like to see for himself if Theseus was as great a hero as he was said to be, and he forthwith went into Attica and stole some of Theseus' cattle. When he heard that Theseus was pursuing him, instead of hurrying away he turned around and went to meet him, with the intention, of course, of deciding then and there which was the better man. But as the two faced each other Pirithoüs, impulsive as always, suddenly forgot everything in his admiration of the other. He held out his hand to him and cried, "I will submit to any penalty you impose. You be the judge." Theseus, delighted at this warm-hearted action, answered, "All I want is for you to be my friend and brother-in-arms." And they took a solemn oath of friendship.

When Pirithoüs, who was King of the Lapithae, married, Theseus was, of course, one of the guests, and was exceedingly useful there. The marriage feast was perhaps the most unfortunate that ever took place. The Centaurs, creatures who each had the body of a horse and the chest and face of a man, were related to the bride and came to the wedding. They proceeded to get drunk and to seize the women. Theseus leaped to the defense of the bride and struck down the Centaur who was trying to carry her off. A terrible battle followed, but the Lapithae conquered and finally drove the whole race of Centaurs out of the country, Theseus helping them to the end.

But in the last adventure the two undertook he could not save his friend. Quite characteristically, Pirithoüs, after the bride of the disastrous wedding feast was dead, decided that for his second wife he would try to get the most carefully guarded lady in all the universe, none other than Persephone herself. Theseus agreed, of course, to help him, but, stimulated probably by the idea of this magnificently dangerous undertaking, declared that first he would himself carry off Helen, the future heroine of Troy,* then a child, and when she was grown marry her. This, though less hazardous than the rape of Persephone, was perilous enough to satisfy the most ambitious. Helen's brothers were Castor and Pollux, more than a match for any mortal hero. Theseus succeeded in kidnaping the little girl, just how we are not told, but the two brothers marched against the town she had been taken to, and got her back. Luckily for him they did not find Theseus there. He was on his way to the underworld with Pirithoüs.

The details of their journey and arrival there are not known

* See Part Four, Chapters 13 and 14.

beyond the fact that the Lord of Hades was perfectly aware of their intention and amused himself by frustrating it in a novel way. He did not kill them, of course, as they were already in the realm of death, but he invited them as a friendly gesture to sit in his presence. They did so on the seat he pointed them to—and there they stayed. They could not arise from it. It was called the Chair of Forgetfulness. Whoever sat on it forgot everything. His mind became a blank and he did not move. There Pirithoüs sits forever, but Theseus was freed by his cousin. When Hercules came to the underworld he lifted Theseus from the seat and brought him back to earth. He tried to do the same for Pirithoüs, but could not. The King of the Dead knew that it was he who had planned to carry off Persephone, and he held him fast.

In the later years of his life Theseus married Ariadne's sister Phaedra, and thereby drew down terrible misfortunes on her and on himself and on his son Hippolytus, the son the Amazon had borne him. He had sent Hippolytus away while still a young child to be brought up in the southern city where Theseus had spent his own youth. The boy grew to splendid manhood, a great athlete and hunter, despising those who lived in luxurious ease and still more those who were soft enough and silly enough to fall in love. He scorned Aphrodite, he worshiped only Artemis, the huntress chaste and fair. So matters stood when Theseus came to his old home bringing Phaedra with him. A strong affection grew up at once between father and son. They delighted in each other's company. As for Phaedra, her stepson Hippolytus took no notice of her; he never noticed women. But it was far otherwise with her. She fell in love with him, madly and miserably, overwhelmed with shame at such a love, but utterly unable to conquer it. Aphrodite was back of this wretched and ominous state of affairs. She was angry at Hippolytus and determined to punish him to the utmost.

Phaedra, in her anguish, desperate, seeing no help for her anywhere, resolved to die and let no one know why. Theseus at the time was away from home, but her old nurse—completely devoted to her and unable to think anything bad that Phaedra wanted—discovered all, her secret passion, her despair, and her determination to kill herself. With only one thought in her mind, to save her mistress, she went straight to Hippolytus.

"She is dying for love of you," she said. "Give her life. Give her love for love."

Hippolytus drew away from her with loathing. The love of any woman would have disgusted him, but this guilty love sickened and horrified him. He rushed out into the courtyard, she following him and beseeching him. Phaedra was sitting there, but he never saw her. He turned in furious indignation on the old woman.

"You pitiable wretch," he said, "trying to make me betray my father. I feel polluted by merely hearing such words. Oh, women, vile women—every one of them vile. I will never enter this house again except when my father is in it."

He flung away and the nurse, turning, faced Phaedra. She had risen and there was a look on her face which frightened the old woman.

"I'll help you still," she stammered.

"Hush," Phaedra said. "I will settle my own affairs." With that she entered the house and the nurse trembling crept after her.

A few minutes later the voices of men were heard greeting the master of the house on his return and Theseus entered the courtyard. Weeping women met him there. They told him that Phaedra was dead. She had killed herself. They had just found her, quite dead, but in her hand a letter to her husband.

"O dearest and best," Theseus said. "Are your last desires written here? This is your seal—yours who will never more smile up at me."

He opened and read it and read it again. Then he turned to the servants filling the courtyard.

"This letter cries aloud," he said. "The words speak—they have a tongue. Know all of you that my son laid violent hands upon my wife. O Poseidon, God, hear me while I curse him, and fulfill my curse."

The silence that followed was broken by hurrying footsteps. Hippolytus entered.

"What happened?" he cried. "How did she die? Father, tell me yourself. Do not hide your grief from me."

"There ought to be a true yardstick to measure affection by," said Theseus, "some means to know who is to be trusted and who is not. You here, look at my son—proved base by the hand of her who is dead. He offered her violence. Her letter outweighs any words he could speak. Go. You are an exile from this land. Go to your ruin and at once."

"Father," Hippolytus answered, "I have no skill in speaking and there is no witness to my innocence. The only one is dead. All I can do is to swear by Zeus above that I never touched your wife, never desired to, never gave her a thought. May I die in wretchedness if I am guilty."

"Dead she proves her truth," Theseus said. "Go. You are banished from the land."

Hippolytus went, but not into exile; death was waiting close at hand for him too. As he drove along the sea-road away from the home he was leaving forever, his father's curse was fulfilled. A monster came up from the water and his horses, terrified beyond even his firm control, ran away. The chariot was shattered and he was mortally hurt.

Theseus was not spared. Artemis appeared to him and told him the truth.

> I do not come to bring you help, but only pain,
> To show you that your son was honorable.
> Your wife was guilty, mad with love for him,
> And yet she fought her passion and she died.
> But what she wrote was false.

As Theseus listened, overwhelmed by this sum of terrible events, Hippolytus still breathing was carried in.

He gasped out, "I was innocent. Artemis, you? My goddess, your huntsman is dying."

"And no other can take your place, dearest of men to me," she told him.

Hippolytus turned his eyes from her radiance to Theseus brokenhearted.

"Father, dear Father," he said. "It was not your fault."

"If only I could die for you," Theseus cried.

The calm sweet voice of the goddess broke in on their anguish. "Take your son in your arms, Theseus," she said. "It was not you that killed him. It was Aphrodite. Know this, that he will never be forgotten. In song and story men will remember him."

She vanished from sight, but Hippolytus, too, was gone. He had started on the road that leads down to the realm of death.

Theseus' death, also, was wretched. He was at the court of a friend, King Lycomedes, where a few years later Achilles was to hide disguised as a girl. Some say that Theseus had gone there because Athens had banished him. At all events, the King, his friend and his host, killed him, we are not told why.

Even if the Athenians did banish him, very soon after his death they honored him as no other mortal. They built a great tomb for him and decreed that it should be forever a sanctuary for slaves and for all poor and helpless people, in memory of one who through his life had been the protector of the defenseless.

11 Hercules

Ovid gives an account of Hercules' life, but very briefly, quite unlike his usual extremely detailed method. He never cares to dwell on heroic exploits; he loves best a pathetic story. At first sight it seems odd that he passes over Hercules' slaying of his wife and children, but that tale had been told by a master, the fifth-century poet Euripides, and Ovid's reticence was probably due to his intelligence. He has very little to say about any of the myths the Greek tragedians write of. He passes over also one of the most famous tales about Hercules, how he freed Alcestis from death, which was the subject of another of Euripides' plays. Sophocles, Euripides' contemporary, describes how the hero died. His adventure with the snakes when he was a baby is told by Pindar in the fifth century and by Theocritus in the third. In my account I have followed the stories given by the two tragic poets and by Theocritus, rather than Pindar, one of the most difficult of poets to translate or even to paraphrase. For the rest I have followed Apollodorus, a prose writer of the first or second century A.D. who is the only writer except Ovid to tell Hercules' life in full. I have preferred his treatment to Ovid's because, in this instance only, it is more detailed.

The greatest hero of Greece was Hercules. He was a personage of quite another order from the great hero of Athens, Theseus. He was what all Greece except Athens most admired. The Athenians were different from the other Greeks and their hero therefore was different. Theseus was, of course, bravest of the brave as all heroes are, but unlike other heroes he was as compassionate as he was brave and a man of great intellect as well as great bodily strength. It was natural that the Athenians should have such a hero because they valued thought and ideas as no other part of the country did. In Theseus their ideal was embodied. But Hercules embodied what the rest of Greece most valued. His qualities were those the Greeks in general honored and admired. Except for unflinching courage, they were not those that distinguished Theseus.

Hercules was the strongest man on earth and he had the supreme self-confidence magnificent physical strength gives. He considered himself on an equality with the gods—and with some reason. They needed his help to conquer the Giants. In the final victory of the Olympians over the brutish sons of Earth, Hercules' arrows played an important part. He treated the gods accordingly. Once when the priestess at Delphi gave no response to the question he asked, he seized the tripod she sat on and declared that he would carry it off and have an oracle of his own. Apollo, of course, would not put up with this, but Hercules was perfectly willing to fight him and Zeus had to intervene. The quarrel was easily settled, however. Hercules was quite good-natured about it. He did not want to quarrel with Apollo, he only wanted an answer from his oracle. If Apollo would give it the matter was settled as far as he was concerned. Apollo on his side, facing this undaunted person, felt an admiration for his boldness and made his priestess deliver the response.

Throughout his life Hercules had this perfect confidence that no matter who was against him he could never be defeated, and facts bore him out. Whenever he fought with anyone the issue was certain beforehand. He could be overcome only by a supernatural force. Hera used hers against him with terrible effect and in the end he was killed by magic, but nothing that lived in the air, sea, or on land ever defeated him.

Intelligence did not figure largely in anything he did and was often conspicuously absent. Once when he was too hot he pointed an arrow at the sun and threatened to shoot him. Another time when the boat he was in was tossed about by the waves he told the waters that he would punish them if they did not grow calm. His intellect was not strong. His emotions were. They were quickly aroused and apt to get out of control, as when he deserted the *Argo* and forgot all about his comrades and the Quest of the Golden Fleece in his despairing grief at losing his young armor-bearer, Hylas. This power of deep feeling in a man of his tremendous strength was oddly endearing, but it worked immense harm, too. He had sudden outbursts of furious anger which were always fatal to the often innocent objects. When the rage had passed and he had come to himself he would show a most disarming penitence and agree humbly to any punishment it was proposed to inflict on him. Without his consent he could not have been punished by anyone—yet nobody ever endured so many punishments. He spent a large part of his life expiating one unfortunate deed after another and never rebelling against the almost impossible demands made upon him. Sometimes he punished himself when others were inclined to exonerate him.

It would have been ludicrous to put him in command of a kingdom as Theseus was put; he had more than enough to do to command himself. He could never have thought out any new or great idea as the Athenian hero was held to have done. His thinking was limited to devising a way to kill a monster which was threatening to kill him. Nevertheless he had true greatness. Not because he had complete courage based upon overwhelming strength, which is merely a matter of course, but because, by his sorrow for wrongdoing and his willingness to do anything to expiate it, he showed greatness of soul. If only he had had some greatness of mind as well, at least enough to lead him along the ways of reason, he would have been the perfect hero.

He was born in Thebes and for a long time was held to be the son of Amphitryon, a distinguished general. In those earlier years he was called Alcides, or descendant of Alcaeus who was Amphitryon's father. But in reality he was the son of Zeus, who had visited Amphitryon's wife Alcmena in the shape of her husband when the general was away fighting. She bore two children, Hercules to Zeus and Iphicles to Amphitryon. The difference in the boys' descent was clearly shown in the way each acted in face of a great danger which came to them before they were a year old. Hera, as always, was furiously jealous and she determined to kill Hercules.

One evening Alcmena gave both the children their baths and their fill of milk and laid them in their crib, caressing them and saying, "Sleep, my little ones, soul of my soul. Happy be your slumber and happy your awakening." She rocked the cradle and in a moment the babies were asleep. But at darkest midnight when all was silent in the house two great snakes came crawling into the nursery. There was a light in the room and as the two reared up above the crib, with weaving heads and flickering tongues, the children woke. Iphicles screamed and tried to get out of bed, but Hercules sat up and grasped the deadly creatures by the throat. They turned and twisted and wound their coils around his body, but he held them fast. The mother heard Iphicles' screams and, calling to her husband, rushed to the nursery. There sat Hercules laughing, in each hand a long limp body. He gave them gleefully to Amphitryon. They were dead. All knew then that the child was destined to great things. Teiresias, the blind prophet of Thebes, told Alcmena: "I swear that many a Greek woman as she cards the wool at eventide shall sing of this your son and you who bore him. He shall be the hero of all mankind."

Great care was taken with his education, but teaching him what he did not wish to learn was a dangerous business. He seems not to have liked music, which was a most important part of a Greek boy's training, or else he disliked his music master. He flew into a rage with him and brained him with his lute. This was the first time he dealt a fatal blow without intending it. He did not mean to kill the poor musician; he just struck out on the impulse of the moment without thinking, hardly aware of his strength. He was sorry, very sorry, but that did not keep him from doing the same thing again and again. The other subjects he was taught, fencing, wrestling, and driving, he took to more kindly, and his teachers in these branches all survived. By the time he was eighteen he was full-grown and he killed, alone by himself, a great lion which lived in the woods of Cithaeron, the Thespian lion. Ever after he wore its skin as a cloak with the head forming a kind of hood over his own head.

His next exploit was to fight and conquer the Minyans, who had been exacting a burdensome tribute from the Thebans. The grateful citizens gave him as a reward the hand of the Princess Megara. He was devoted to her and to their children and yet this marriage brought upon him the greatest sorrow of his life as well as trials and dangers such as no one ever went through, before or after. When Megara had borne him three sons he went mad. Hera who never forgot a wrong sent the madness upon him. He killed his children and Megara, too, as she tried to protect the youngest. Then his sanity returned. He found himself in his bloodstained hall, the dead bodies of his sons and his wife beside him. He had no idea what had happened, how they had been killed. Only a moment since, as it seemed to him, they had all been talking together. As he stood there in utter bewilderment the terrified people who were watching him from a distance saw that the mad fit was over, and Amphitryon dared to approach him. There was no keeping the truth from Hercules. He had to know how this horror had come to pass and Amphitryon told him. Hercules heard him out; then he said, "And I myself am the murderer of my dearest."

"Yes," Amphitryon answered trembling. "But you were out of your mind."

Hercules paid no attention to the implied excuse.

"Shall I spare my own life then?" he said. "I will avenge upon myself these deaths."

But before he could rush out and kill himself, even as he

started to do so, his desperate purpose was changed and his life was spared. This miracle—it was nothing less—of recalling Hercules, from frenzied feeling and violent action to sober reason and sorrowful acceptance, was not wrought by a god descending from the sky. It was a miracle caused by human friendship. His friend Theseus stood before him and stretched out his hands to clasp those bloodstained hands. Thus according to the common Greek idea he would himself become defiled and have a part in Hercules' guilt.

"Do not start back," he told Hercules. "Do not keep me from sharing all with you. Evil I share with you is not evil to me. And hear me. Men great of soul can bear the blows of heaven and not flinch."

Hercules said, "Do you know what I have done?"

"I know this," Theseus answered. "Your sorrows reach from earth to heaven."

"So I will die," said Hercules.

"No hero spoke those words," Theseus said.

"What can I do but die?" Hercules cried. "Live? A branded man, for all to say, 'Look. There is he who killed his wife and sons!' Everywhere my jailers, the sharp scorpions of the tongue!"

"Even so, suffer and be strong," Theseus answered. "You shall come to Athens with me, share my home and all things with me. And you will give to me and to the city a great return, the glory of having helped you."

A long silence followed. At last Hercules spoke, slow, heavy words. "So let it be," he said, "I will be strong and wait for death."

The two went to Athens, but Hercules did not stay there long. Theseus, the thinker, rejected the idea that a man could be guilty of murder when he had not known what he was doing and that those who helped such a one could be reckoned defiled. The Athenians agreed and welcomed the poor hero. But he himself could not understand such ideas. He could not think the thing out at all; he could only feel. He had killed his family. Therefore he was defiled and a defiler of others. He deserved that all should turn from him with loathing. At Delphi where he went to consult the oracle, the priestess looked at the matter just as he did. He needed to be purified, she told him, and only a terrible penance could do that. She bade him go to his cousin Eurystheus, King of Mycenae (of Tiryns in some stories) and submit to whatever he demanded of him. He went willingly, ready to do anything that could make him clean again. It is plain from the rest of the story that the priestess knew what Eurystheus was like and that he would beyond question purge Hercules thoroughly.

Eurystheus was by no means stupid, but of a very ingenious turn of mind, and when the strongest man on earth came to him humbly prepared to be his slave, he devised a series of penances which from the point of view of difficulty and danger could not have been improved upon. It must be said, however, that he was helped and urged on by Hera. To the end of Hercules' life she never forgave him for being Zeus's son. The tasks Eurystheus gave him to do are called "the Labors of Hercules." There were twelve of them and each one was all but impossible.

The first was to kill the lion of Nemea, a beast no weapons could wound. That difficulty Hercules solved by choking the life out of him. Then he heaved the huge carcass up on his back and carried it into Mycenae. After that, Eurystheus, a cautious man, would not let him inside the city. He gave him his orders from afar.

The second labor was to go to Lerna and kill a creature with nine heads called the Hydra which lived in a swamp there. This was exceedingly hard to do, because one of the heads was immortal and the others almost as bad, inasmuch as when Hercules chopped off one, two grew up instead. However, he was helped by his nephew Iolaus who brought him a burning brand with which he seared the neck as he cut each head off so that it could not sprout again. When all had been chopped off he disposed of the one that was immortal by burying it securely under a great rock.

The third labor was to bring back alive a stag with horns of gold, sacred to Artemis, which lived in the forests of Cerynitia. He could have killed it easily, but to take it alive was another matter and he hunted it a whole year before he succeeded.

The fourth labor was to capture a great boar which had its lair on Mount Erymanthus. He chased the beast from one place to another until it was exhausted; then he drove it into deep snow and trapped it.

The fifth labor was to clean the Augean stables in a single day. Augeas had thousands of cattle and their stalls had not been cleared out for years. Hercules diverted the courses of two rivers and made them flow through the stables in a great flood that washed out the filth in no time at all.

The sixth labor was to drive away the Stymphalian birds, which were a plague to the people of Stymphalus because of their enormous numbers. He was helped by Athena to drive them out of their coverts, and as they flew up he shot them.

The seventh labor was to go to Crete and fetch from there the beautiful savage bull that Poseidon had given Minos. Hercules mastered him, put him in a boat and brought him to Eurystheus.

The eighth labor was to get the man-eating mares of King Diomedes of Thrace. Hercules slew Diomedes first and then drove off the mares unopposed.

The ninth labor was to bring back the girdle of Hippolyta, the Queen of the Amazons. When Hercules arrived she met him kindly and told him she would give him the girdle, but Hera stirred up trouble. She made the Amazons think that Hercules was going to carry off their queen, and they charged down on his ship. Hercules, without a thought of how kind Hippolyta had been, without any thought at all, instantly killed her, taking it for granted that she was responsible for the attack. He was able to fight off the others and get away with the girdle.

The tenth labor was to bring back the cattle of Geryon, who was a monster with three bodies living on Erythia, a western island. On his way there Hercules reached the land at the end of the Mediterranean and he set up as a memorial of his journey two great rocks, called the pillars of Hercules (now Gibraltar and Ceuta). Then he got the oxen and took them to Mycenae.

The eleventh labor was the most difficult of all so far. It was to bring back the Golden Apples of the Hesperides, and he did not know where they were to be found. Atlas, who bore the vault of heaven upon his shoulders, was the father of the Hesperides, so Hercules went to him and asked him to get the apples for him. He offered to take upon himself the burden of the sky while Atlas was away. Atlas, seeing a chance of being relieved forever from his heavy task, gladly agreed. He came back with the apples, but he did not give them to Hercules. He told Hercules he could keep on holding up the sky, for Atlas himself would take the apples to Eurystheus. On this occasion Hercules had only his wits to trust to; he had to give all his strength to supporting that mighty load. He was successful, but because of Atlas' stupidity rather than his own cleverness. He agreed to Atlas' plan, but asked him to take the sky back for just a moment so that Hercules could put a pad on his shoulders to ease the pressure. Atlas did so, and Hercules picked up the apples and went off.

The twelfth labor was the worst of all. It took him down to the lower world, and it was then that he freed Theseus from the Chair of Forgetfulness. His task was to bring Cerberus, the three-headed dog, up from Hades. Pluto gave him permission provided Hercules used no weapons to overcome him. He could use his hands only. Even so, he forced the terrible mon-

Hercules carrying Cerberus

ster to submit to him. He lifted him and carried him all the
way up to the earth and on to Mycenae. Eurystheus very sensibly did not want to keep him and made Hercules carry him
back. This was his last labor.

When all were completed and full expiation made for the
death of his wife and children, he would seem to have earned
ease and tranquillity for the rest of his life. But it was not so.
He was never tranquil and at ease. An exploit quite as difficult
as most of the labors was the conquest of Antaeus, a Giant and
a mighty wrestler who forced strangers to wrestle with him on
condition that if he was victor he should kill them. He was
roofing a temple with the skulls of his victims. As long as he
could touch the earth he was invincible. If thrown to the ground
he sprang up with renewed strength from the contact. Hercules lifted him up and holding him in the air strangled
him.

Story after story is told of his adventures. He fought the
river-god Achelous because Achelous was in love with the girl
Hercules now wanted to marry. Like everyone else by this time,
Achelous had no desire to fight him and he tried to reason
with him. But that never worked with Hercules. It only made
him more angry. He said, "My hand is better than my tongue.
Let me win fighting and you may win talking." Achelous took
the form of a bull and attacked him fiercely, but Hercules
was used to subduing bulls. He conquered him and broke off
one of his horns. The cause of the contest, a young princess
named Deianira, became his wife.

He traveled to many lands and did many other great deeds.
At Troy he rescued a maiden who was in the same plight as
Andromeda, waiting on the shore to be devoured by a sea monster which could be appeased in no other way. She was the
daughter of King Laomedon, who had cheated Apollo and Poseidon of their wages after at Zeus's command they had built
for the King the walls of Troy. In return Apollo sent a pestilence, and Poseidon the sea serpent. Hercules agreed to rescue
the girl if her father would give him the horses Zeus had given
his grandfather. Laomedon promised, but when Hercules had
slain the monster the King refused to pay. Hercules captured
the city, killed the King, and gave the maiden to his friend,
Telamon of Salamis, who had helped him.

On his way to Atlas to ask him about the Golden Apples,
Hercules came to the Caucasus, where he freed Prometheus,
slaying the eagle that preyed on him.

Along with these glorious deeds there were others not glorious. He killed with a careless thrust of his arm a lad who was
serving him by pouring water on his hands before a feast. It
was an accident and the boy's father forgave Hercules, but Her-

cules could not forgive himself and he went into exile for a time. Far worse was his deliberately slaying a good friend in order to avenge an insult offered him by the young man's father, King Eurytus. For this base action Zeus himself punished him: he sent him to Lydia to be a slave to the Queen, Omphale, some say for a year, some for three years. She amused herself with him, making him at times dress up as a woman and do woman's work, weave or spin. He submitted patiently, as always, but he felt himself degraded by this servitude and with complete unreason blamed Eurytus for it and swore he would punish him to the utmost when he was freed.

All the stories told about him are characteristic, but the one which gives the clearest picture of him is the account of a visit he made when he was on his way to get the man-eating mares of Diomedes, one of the twelve labors. The house he had planned to spend a night in, that of his friend Admetus, a king in Thessaly, was a place of deep mourning when he came to it although he did not know. Admetus had just lost his wife in a very strange way.

The cause of her death went back into the past, to the time when Apollo in anger at Zeus for killing his son Aesculapius killed Zeus's workmen, the Cyclopes. He was punished by being forced to serve on earth as a slave for a year and Admetus was the master he chose or Zeus chose for him. During his servitude Apollo made friends with the household, especially with the head of it and his wife Alcestis. When he had an opportunity to prove how strong his friendship was he took it. He learned that the three Fates had spun all of Admetus' thread of life, and were on the point of cutting it. He obtained from them a respite. If someone would die in Admetus' stead, he could live. This news he took to Admetus, who at once set about finding a substitute for himself. He went first quite confidently to his father and mother. They were old and they were devoted to him. Certainly one or the other would consent to take his place in the world of the dead. But to his astonishment he found they would not. They told him, "God's daylight is sweet even to the old. We do not ask you to die for us. We will not die for you." And they were completely unmoved by his angry contempt: "You, standing palsied at the gate of death and yet afraid to die!"

He would not give up, however. He went to his friends begging one after another of them to die and let him live. He evidently thought his life was so valuable that someone would surely save it even at the cost of the supreme sacrifice. But he met with an invariable refusal. At last in despair he went back to his house and there he found a substitute. His wife Alcestis offered to die for him. No one who has read so far will need to be told that he accepted the offer. He felt exceedingly sorry for her and still more for himself in having to lose so good a wife, and he stood weeping beside her as she died. When she was gone he was overwhelmed with grief and decreed that she should have the most magnificent of funerals.

It was at this point that Hercules arrived, to rest and enjoy himself under a friend's roof on his journey north to Diomedes. The way Admetus treated him shows more plainly than any other story we have how high the standards of hospitality were, how much was expected from a host to a guest.

As soon as Admetus was told of Hercules' arrival, he came to meet him with no appearance of mourning except in his dress. His manner was that of one gladly welcoming a friend. To Hercules' question who was dead he answered quietly that a woman of his household, but no relative of his, was to be buried that day. Hercules instantly declared that he would not trouble him with his presence at such a time, but Admetus steadily refused to let him go elsewhere. "I will not have you sleep under another's roof," he told him. To his servants he said that the guest was to be taken to a distant room where he could hear no sounds of grief, and given dinner and lodging there. No one must let him know what had happened.

Hercules dined alone, but he understood that Admetus must as a matter of form attend the funeral and the fact did not stand in the way of his enjoying himself. The servants left at home to attend to him were kept busy satisfying his enormous appetite and, still more, refilling his wine-jug. Hercules became very happy and very drunk and very noisy. He roared out songs at the top of his voice, some of them highly objectionable songs, and behaved himself in a way that was nothing less than indecent at the time of a funeral. When the servants looked their disapproval he shouted at them not to be so solemn. Couldn't they give him a smile now and then like good fellows? Their gloomy faces took away his appetite. "Have a drink with me," he cried, "many drinks."

One of them answered timidly that it was not a time for laughter and drinking.

"Why not?" thundered Hercules. "Because a stranger woman is dead?"

"A stranger—" faltered the servant.

"Well, that's what Admetus told me," Hercules said angrily. "I suppose you won't say he lied to me."

"Oh, no," the servant answered. "Only—he's too hospitable. But please have some more wine. Our trouble is only our own."

He turned to fill the winecup but Hercules seized him—and no one ever disregarded that grasp.

"There's something strange here," he said to the frightened man. "What is wrong?"

"You see for yourself we are in mourning," the other answered.

"But why, man, why?" Hercules cried. "Has my host made a fool of me? Who is dead?"

"Alcestis," the servant whispered. "Our Queen."

There was a long silence. Then Hercules threw down his cup.

"I might have known," he said. "I saw he had been weeping. His eyes were red. But he swore it was a stranger. He made me come in. Oh, good friend and good host. And I—got drunk, made merry, in this house of sorrow. Oh, he should have told me."

Then he did as always, he heaped blame upon himself. He had been a fool, a drunken fool, when the man he cared for was crushed with grief. As always, too, his thoughts turned quickly to find some way of atoning. What could he do to make amends? There was nothing he could not do. He was perfectly sure of that, but what was there which would help his friend? Then light dawned on him. "Of course," he said to himself. "That is the way. I must bring Alcestis back from the dead. Of course. Nothing could be clearer. I'll find that old fellow, Death. He is sure to be near her tomb and I'll wrestle with him. I will crack his body between my arms until he gives her to me. If he is not by the grave I will go down to Hades after him. Oh, I will return good to my friend who has been so good to me." He hurried out exceedingly pleased with himself and enjoying the prospect of what promised to be a very good wrestling match.

When Admetus returned to his empty and desolate house Hercules was there to greet him, and by his side was a woman. "Look at her, Admetus," he said. "Is she like anyone you know?" And when Admetus cried out, "A ghost! Is it a trick— some mockery of the gods?" Hercules answered, "It is your wife. I fought Death for her and I made him give her back."

There is no other story about Hercules which shows so clearly his character as the Greeks saw it: his simplicity and blundering stupidity; his inability not to get roaring drunk in a house where someone was dead; his quick penitence and desire to make amends at no matter what cost; his perfect confidence that not even Death was his match. That is the portrait of Hercules. To be sure, it would have been still more accurate if it had shown him in a fit of rage killing one of the servants who were annoying him with their gloomy faces, but the poet Euripides from whom we get the story kept it clear of everything that did not bear directly on Alcestis' death and return to life. Another death or two, however natural when Hercules was present, would have blurred the picture he wanted to paint.

As Hercules had sworn to do while he was Omphale's slave, no sooner was he free than he started to punish King Eurytus because he himself had been punished by Zeus for killing Eurytus' son. He collected an army, captured the King's city and put him to death. But Eurytus, too, was avenged, for indirectly this victory was the cause of Hercules' own death.

Before he had quite completed the destruction of the city, he sent home—where Deianira, his devoted wife, was waiting for him to come back from Omphale in Lydia—a band of captive maidens, one of them especially beautiful, Iole, the King's daughter. The man who brought them to Deianira told her that Hercules was madly in love with this Princess. This news was not so hard for Deianira as might be expected, because she believed she had a powerful love-charm which she had kept for years against just such an evil, a woman in her own house preferred before her. Directly after her marriage, when Hercules was taking her home, they had reached a river where the Centaur Nessus acted as ferryman, carrying travelers over the water. He took Deianira on his back and in midstream insulted her. She shrieked and Hercules shot the beast as he reached the other bank. Before he died he told Deianira to take some of his blood and use it as a charm for Hercules if ever he loved another woman more than her. When she heard about Iole, it seemed to her the time had come, and she anointed a splendid robe with the blood and sent it to Hercules by the messenger.

As the hero put it on, the effect was the same as that of the robe Medea had sent her rival whom Jason was about to marry. A fearful pain seized him, as though he were in a burning fire. In his first agony he turned on Deianira's messenger, who was, of course, completely innocent, seized him and hurled him down into the sea. He could still slay others, but it seemed that he himself could not die. The anguish he felt hardly weakened him. What had instantly killed the young Princess of Corinth could not kill Hercules. He was in torture, but he lived and they brought him home. Long before, Deianira had heard what her gift had done to him and had killed herself. In the end he did the same. Since death would not come to him, he would go to death. He ordered those around him to build a great pyre on Mount Oeta and carry him to it. When at last he reached it he knew that now he could die and he was glad. "This is rest," he said. "This is the end." And as they lifted him to the pyre he lay down on it as one who at a banquet table lies down upon his couch.

He asked his youthful follower, Philoctetes, to hold the torch to set the wood on fire; and he gave him his bow and arrows, which were to be far-famed in the young man's hands, too, at Troy. Then the flames rushed up and Hercules was seen no more on earth. He was taken to heaven, where he was reconciled to Hera and married her daughter Hebe, and where

> After his mighty labors he has rest.
> His choicest prize eternal peace
> Within the homes of blessedness.

But it is not easy to imagine him contentedly enjoying rest and peace, or allowing the blessed gods to do so, either.

12 Atalanta

*Her story is told in full only by the late writers Ovid
and Apollodorus, but it is an old tale. One of the
poems ascribed to Hesiod, but probably of a somewhat later date, say, the early seventh century, describes the race and the golden apples, and the* Iliad
*gives an account of the Calydonian boar hunt. I have
followed in my account Apollodorus, who probably
wrote in the first or second century* A.D. *Ovid's tale is
good only occasionally. He gives a charming picture
of Atalanta among the hunters which I have put into
my account, but often, as in the description of the
boar, he is so exaggerated, he verges on the ridiculous.
Apollodorus is not picturesque, but he is never absurd.*

Sometimes there are said to have been two heroines of that
name. Certainly two men, Iasus and Schoenius, are each called
the father of Atalanta, but then it often happens in old stories
that different names are given to unimportant persons. If there
were two Atalantas it is certainly remarkable that both wanted
to sail on the *Argo,* both took part in the Calydonian boar hunt,
both married a man who beat them in a foot race, and both
were ultimately changed into lionesses. Since the story of each
is practically the same as that of the other it is simpler to take
it for granted that there was only one. Indeed it would seem
passing the bounds of the probable even in mythological stories
to suppose that there were two maidens living at the same time
who loved adventure as much as the most dauntless hero, and
who could outshoot and outrun and outwrestle, too, the men
of one of the two great ages of heroism.

Atalanta's father, whatever his name was, when a daughter
and not a son was born to him, was, of course, bitterly disap-
pointed. He decided that she was not worth bringing up and
had the tiny creature left on a wild mountainside to die of cold
and hunger. But, as so often happens in stories, animals proved

kinder than humans. A she-bear took charge of her, nursed her and kept her warm, and the baby grew up thus into an active, daring little girl. Kind hunters then found her and took her to live with them. She became in the end more than their equal in all the arduous feats of a hunter's life. Once two Centaurs, swifter and stronger by far than any mortal, caught sight of her when she was alone and pursued her. She did not run from them; that would have been folly. She stood still and fitted an arrow to her bow and shot. A second arrow followed. Both Centaurs fell, mortally wounded.

Then came the famous hunt of the Calydonian boar. This was a terrible creature sent to ravage the country of Calydon by Artemis in order to punish the King, Oeneus, because he forgot her when he was sacrificing the first fruits to the gods at the harvest-time. The brute devastated the land, destroyed the cattle, killed the men who tried to kill it. Finally Oeneus called for help upon the bravest men of Greece, and a splendid band of young heroes assembled, many of whom sailed later on the *Argo*. With them came as a matter of course Atalanta, "The pride of the woods of Arcady." We have a description of how she looked when she walked in on that masculine gathering: "A shining buckle clasped her robe at the neck; her hair was simply dressed, caught up in a knot behind. An ivory quiver hung upon her left shoulder and in her hand was a bow. Thus was she attired. As for her face, it seemed too maidenly to be that of a boy, and too boyish to be that of a maiden." To one man there, however, she looked lovelier and more desirable than any maiden he had ever seen. Oeneus' son, Meleager, fell in love with her at first sight. But, we may be sure, Atalanta treated him as a good comrade, not as a possible lover. She had no liking for men except as companions in the hunt and she was determined never to marry.

Some of the heroes resented her presence and felt it beneath them to go hunting with a woman, but Meleager insisted and they finally gave in to him. It proved well for them that they did, because when they surrounded the boar, the brute rushed upon them so swiftly that it killed two men before the others could come to their help, and, what was equally ominous, a third man fell pierced by a misdirected javelin. In this confusion of dying men and wildly flying weapons Atalanta kept her head and wounded the boar. Her arrow was the first to strike it. Meleager then rushed on the wounded creature and stabbed it to the heart. Technically speaking it was he who killed it, but the honors of the hunt went to Atalanta and Meleager insisted that they should give her the skin.

Strangely enough this was the cause of his own death. When he was just a week old the Fates had appeared to his mother,

Althea, and thrown a log of wood into the fire burning in her chamber. Then spinning as they ever did, twirling the distaff and twisting the thread of destiny, they sang,

> To you, O new-born child, we grant a gift,
> To live until this wood turns into ash.

Althea snatched the brand from the fire, quenched the flame, and hid it in a chest. Her brothers were among those who went to hunt the boar. They felt themselves insulted and were furiously angry at having the prize go to a girl—as, no doubt, was the case with others, but they were Meleager's uncles and did not need to stand on any ceremony with him. They declared that Atalanta should not have the skin and told Meleager he had no more right to give it away than anyone else had. Whereupon Meleager killed them both, taking them completely off their guard.

This news was brought to Althea. Her beloved brothers had been slain by her son because he had made a fool of himself over a shameless hussy who went hunting with men. A passion of rage took possession of her. She rushed to the chest for the brand and threw it into the fire. As it blazed up, Meleager fell to the ground dying, and by the time it was consumed his spirit had slipped away from his body. It is said that Althea, horror-stricken at what she had done, hanged herself. So the Calydonian boar hunt ended in tragedy.

To Atalanta, however, it was only the beginning of her adventures. Some say that she sailed with the Argonauts; others that Jason persuaded her not to do so. She is never mentioned in the story of their exploits and she was certainly not one to hold back when deeds of daring were to be done, so that it seems probable that she did not go. The next time we hear of her is after the Argonauts returned, when Medea had killed Jason's uncle Pelias under the pretext of restoring him to youth. At the funeral games held in his honor Atalanta appeared among the contestants, and in the wrestling match conquered the young man who was to be the father of Achilles, the great hero Peleus.

It was after this achievement that she discovered who her parents were and went to live with them, her father apparently being reconciled to having a daughter who really seemed almost if not quite as good as a son. It seems odd that a number of men wanted to marry her because she could hunt and shoot and wrestle, but it was so; she had a great many suitors. As a way of disposing of them easily and agreeably she declared that she would marry whoever could beat her in a foot race, knowing well that there was no such man alive. She had a delightful

Atalanta and the golden apples

time. Fleet-footed young men were always arriving to race with her and she always outran them.

But at last one came who used his head as well as his heels. He knew he was not as good a runner as she, but he had a plan. By the favor of Aphrodite, always on the lookout to subdue wild young maidens who despised love, this ingenious young man, whose name was either Melanion (Milanion) or Hippomenes, got possession of three wondrous apples, all of pure gold, beautiful as those that grew in the garden of the Hesperides. No one alive could see them and not want them.

On the race course as Atalanta—poised for the starting signal, and a hundredfold more lovely disrobed than with her garments on—looked fiercely around her, wonder at her beauty took hold of all who saw her, but most of all the man who was waiting to run against her. He kept his head, however, and held fast to his golden apples. They started, she flying swift as an arrow, her hair tossed back over her white shoulders, a rosy flush tinging her fair body. She was outstripping him when he rolled one of the apples directly in front of her. It needed but a moment for her to stoop and pick the lovely thing up, but that brief pause brought him abreast of her. A moment more and he threw the second, this time a little to the side. She had to swerve to reach it and he got ahead of her. Almost at once, however, she had caught up with him and the goal was now very near. But then the third golden sphere flashed across her path and rolled far into the grass beside the course. She saw the gleam through the green, she could not resist it. As she picked the apple up, her lover panting and almost winded touched the goal. She was his. Her free days alone in the forest and her athletic victories were over.

The two are said to have been turned into lions because of some affront offered either to Zeus or to Aphrodite. But before that Atalanta had borne a son, Parthenopaeus, who was one of the Seven against Thebes.

PART FOUR

The Heroes of the Trojan War

13 The Trojan War

This story, of course, is taken almost entirely from Homer. The Iliad, *however, begins after the Greeks have reached Troy, when Apollo sends the pestilence upon them. It does not mention the sacrifice of Iphigenia, and makes only a dubious allusion to the Judgment of Paris. I have taken Iphigenia's story from a play by the fifth-century tragic poet Aeschylus, the* Agamemnon, *and the Judgment of Paris from the* Trojan Woman, *a play by his contemporary, Euripides, adding a few details, such as the tale of Oenone, from the prose-writer Apollodorus, who wrote probably in the first or second century* A.D. *He is usually very uninteresting, but in treating the events leading up to the* Iliad *he was apparently inspired by touching so great a subject and he is less dull than in almost any other part of his book.*

More than a thousand years before Christ, near the eastern end of the Mediterranean was a great city very rich and powerful, second to none on earth. The name of it was Troy and even to-day no city is more famous. The cause of this long-lasting fame was a war told of in one of the world's greatest poems, the *Iliad*, and the cause of the war went back to a dispute between three jealous goddesses.

Prologue: THE JUDGMENT OF PARIS

The evil goddess of Discord, Eris, was naturally not popular in Olympus, and when the gods gave a banquet they were apt to leave her out. Resenting this deeply, she determined to make trouble—and she succeeded very well indeed. At an important marriage, that of King Peleus and the sea nymph Thetis, to which she alone of all the divinities was not invited, she threw into the banqueting hall a golden apple marked *For the Fairest*. Of course all the goddesses wanted it, but in the end the choice was narrowed down to three: Aphrodite, Hera and Pallas Athena. They asked Zeus to judge between them, but very wisely he refused to have anything to do with the matter. He told them to go to Mount Ida, near Troy, where the young prince Paris, also called Alexander, was keeping his father's sheep. He was an excellent judge of beauty, Zeus told them. Paris, though a royal prince, was doing shepherd's work because his father Priam, the King of Troy, had been warned that this prince would some day be the ruin of his country, and so had sent him away. At the moment Paris was living with a lovely nymph named Oenone.

His amazement can be imagined when there appeared before him the wondrous forms of the three great goddesses. He was not asked, however, to gaze at the radiant divinities and choose which of them seemed to him the fairest, but only to consider the bribes each offered and choose which seemed to him best worth taking. Nevertheless, the choice was not easy. What men care for most was set before him. Hera promised to make him Lord of Europe and Asia; Athena, that he would lead the Trojans to victory against the Greeks and lay Greece in ruins; Aphrodite, that the fairest woman in all the world should be his. Paris, a weakling and something of a coward, too, as later events showed, chose the last. He gave Aphrodite the golden apple.

That was the Judgment of Paris, famed everywhere as the real reason why the Trojan War was fought.

THE TROJAN WAR

The fairest woman in the world was Helen, the daughter of Zeus and Leda and the sister of Castor and Pollux. Such was the report of her beauty that not a young prince in Greece but wanted to marry her. When her suitors assembled in her home to make a formal proposal for her hand they were so many and from such powerful families that her reputed father, King

The judgment of Paris

Tyndareus, her mother's husband, was afraid to select one among them, fearing that the others would unite against him. He therefore exacted first a solemn oath from all that they would champion the cause of Helen's husband, whoever he might be, if any wrong was done to him through his marriage. It was, after all, to each man's advantage to take the oath, since each was hoping he would be the person chosen, so they all bound themselves to punish to the uttermost anyone who carried or tried to carry Helen away. Then Tyndareus chose Menelaus, the brother of Agamemnon, and made him King of Sparta as well.

So matters stood when Paris gave the golden apple to Aphrodite. The Goddess of Love and Beauty knew very well where the most beautiful woman on earth was to be found. She led the young shepherd, with never a thought of Oenone left forlorn, straight to Sparta, where Menelaus and Helen received him graciously as their guest. The ties between guest and host were strong. Each was bound to help and never harm the other. But Paris broke that sacred bond. Menelaus trusting completely to it left Paris in his home and went off to Crete. Then,

> Paris who coming
> Entered a friend's kind dwelling,
> Shamed the hand there that gave him food,
> Stealing away a woman.

Menelaus got back to find Helen gone, and he called upon all Greece to help him. The chieftains responded, as they were bound to do. They came eager for the great enterprise, to cross the sea and lay mighty Troy in ashes. Two, however, of the first rank, were missing: Odysseus, King of the Island of Ithaca, and Achilles, the son of Peleus and the sea nymph Thetis. Odysseus, who was one of the shrewdest and most sensible men in Greece, did not want to leave his house and family to embark on a romantic adventure overseas for the sake of a faithless woman. He pretended, therefore, that he had gone mad, and when a messenger from the Greek Army arrived, the King was plowing a field and sowing it with salt instead of seed. But the messenger was shrewd too. He seized Odysseus' little son and put him directly in the way of the plow. Instantly the father turned the plow aside, thus proving that he had all his wits about him. However reluctant, he had to join the Army.

Achilles was kept back by his mother. The sea nymph knew that if he went to Troy he was fated to die there. She sent him to the court of Lycomedes, the king who had treacherously killed Theseus, and made him wear women's clothes and hide among the maidens. Odysseus was dispatched by the chieftains to find him out. Disguised as a pedlar he went to the court where the lad was said to be, with gay ornaments in his pack such as women love, and also some fine weapons. While the girls flocked around the trinkets, Achilles fingered the swords and daggers. Odysseus knew him then, and he had no trouble at all in making him disregard what his mother had said and go to the Greek camp with him.

So the great fleet made ready. A thousand ships carried the Greek host. They met at Aulis, a place of strong winds and dangerous tides, impossible to sail from as long as the north wind blew. And it kept on blowing, day after day.

> It broke men's heart,
> Spared not ship nor cable.
> The time dragged,
> Doubling itself in passing.

The Army was desperate. At last the soothsayer, Calchas, declared that the gods had spoken to him: Artemis was angry. One of her beloved wild creatures, a hare, had been slain by the Greeks, together with her young, and the only way to calm the wind and ensure a safe voyage to Troy was to appease her by sacrificing to her a royal maiden, Iphigenia, the eldest daughter of the Commander in Chief, Agamemnon. This was terrible to all, but to her father hardly bearable.

> If I must slay
> The joy of my house, my daughter.
> A father's hands
> Stained with dark streams flowing
> From blood of a girl
> Slaughtered before the altar.

Nevertheless he yielded. His reputation with the Army was at stake, and his ambition to conquer Troy and exalt Greece.

> He dared the deed,
> Slaying his child to help a war.

He sent home for her, writing his wife that he had arranged a great marriage for her, to Achilles, who had already shown himself the best and greatest of all the chieftains. But when she came to her wedding she was carried to the altar to be killed.

> And all her prayers—cries of Father, Father,
> Her maiden life,
> These they held as nothing,
> The savage warriors, battle-mad.

She died and the north wind ceased to blow and the Greek ships sailed out over a quiet sea, but the evil price they had paid was bound some day to bring evil down upon them.

When they reached the mouth of the Simois, one of the rivers of Troy, the first man to leap ashore was Protesilaus. It was a brave deed, for the oracle had said that he who landed first would be the first to die. Therefore when he had fallen by a Trojan spear the Greeks paid him honors as though he were divine and the gods, too, greatly distinguished him. They had Hermes bring him up from the dead to see once again his deeply mourning wife, Laodamia. She would not give him up a second time, however. When he went back to the underworld she went with him; she killed herself.

The thousand ships carried a great host of fighting men and the Greek Army was very strong, but the Trojan City was strong, too. Priam, the King, and his Queen, Hecuba, had many brave sons to lead the attack and to defend the walls, one above all, Hector, than whom no man anywhere was nobler or more brave, and only one a greater warrior, the champion of the Greeks, Achilles. Each knew that he would die before Troy was taken. Achilles had been told by his mother: "Very brief is your lot. Would that you could be free now from tears and troubles, for you shall not long endure, my child, short-lived beyond all men and to be pitied." No divinity had told Hector, but he was equally sure. "I know well in my heart and in my soul," he said to his wife Andromache, "the day shall come when holy Troy will be laid low and Priam and Priam's people." Both heroes fought under the shadow of certain death.

For nine years victory wavered, now to this side, now to that. Neither was ever able to gain any decided advantage. Then a quarrel flared up between two Greeks, Achilles and Agamemnon, and for a time it turned the tide in favor of the Trojans. Again a woman was the reason, Chryseis, daughter of Apollo's priest, whom the Greeks had carried off and given to Agamemnon. Her father came to beg for her release, but Agamemnon would not let her go. Then the priest prayed to the mighty god he served and Phoebus Apollo heard him. From his sun-chariot he shot fiery arrows down upon the Greek Army, and men sickened and died so that the funeral pyres were burning continually.

At last Achilles called an assembly of the chieftains. He told them that they could not hold out against both the pestilence and the Trojans, and that they must either find a way to appease Apollo or else sail home. Then the prophet Calchas stood up and said he knew why the god was angry, but that he was afraid to speak unless Achilles would guarantee his safety. "I do so," Achilles answered, "even if you accuse Agamemnon himself." Every man there understood what that meant; they knew how Apollo's priest had been treated. When Calchas declared that Chryseis must be given back to her father, he had all the chiefs behind him and Agamemnon, greatly angered, was obliged to agree. "But if I lose her who was my prize of honor," he told Achilles, "I will have another in her stead."

Therefore when Chryseis had been returned to her father, Agamemnon sent two of his squires to Achilles' tent to take his prize of honor away from him, the maiden Briseis. Most unwillingly they went and stood before the hero in heavy silence. But he knowing their errand told them it was not they who were wronging him. Let them take the girl without fear for themselves, but hear him first while he swore before gods and men that Agamemnon would pay dearly for the deed.

That night Achilles' mother, silver-footed Thetis the sea nymph, came to him. She was as angry as he. She told him to have nothing more to do with the Greeks, and with that she went up to heaven and asked Zeus to give success to the Trojans. Zeus was very reluctant. The war by now had reached Olympus—the gods were ranged against each other. Aphrodite, of course, was on the side of Paris. Equally, of course, Hera and Athena were against him. Ares, God of War, always took sides with Aphrodite; while Poseidon, Lord of the Sea, favored the Greeks, a sea people, always great sailors. Apollo cared for Hector and for his sake helped the Trojans, and Artemis, as his sister, did so too. Zeus liked the Trojans best, on the whole, but he wanted to be neutral because Hera was so disagreeable whenever he opposed her openly. However, he could not resist Thetis. He had a hard time with Hera, who guessed, as she usually did, what he was about. He was driven finally into telling her that he would lay hands upon her if she did not stop talking. Hera kept silence then, but her thoughts were busy as to how she might help the Greeks and circumvent Zeus.

The plan Zeus made was simple. He knew that the Greeks without Achilles were inferior to the Trojans, and he sent a lying dream to Agamemnon promising him victory if he attacked. While Achilles stayed in his tent a fierce battle followed, the hardest yet fought. Up on the wall of Troy the old King Priam and the other old men, wise in the ways of war, sat watching the contest. To them came Helen, the cause of all that agony and death, yet as they looked at her, they could not feel any blame. "Men must fight for such as she," they said to each other. "For her face was like to that of an immortal spirit." She stayed by them, telling them the names of this and that Greek hero, until to their astonishment the battle ceased. The armies drew back on either side and in the space between, Paris and Menelaus faced each other. It was evident that the sensible decision had been reached to let the two most concerned fight it out alone.

Paris struck first, but Menelaus caught the swift spear on his shield, then hurled his own. It rent Paris' tunic, but did not wound him. Menelaus drew his sword, his only weapon now, but as he did so it fell from his hand broken. Undaunted though unarmed he leaped upon Paris and seizing him by his helmet's crest swung him off his feet. He would have dragged him to the Greeks victoriously if it had not been for Aphrodite. She tore away the strap that kept the helmet on so that it came away in Menelaus' hand. Paris himself, who had not fought at all except to throw his spear, she caught up in a cloud and took back to Troy.

Furiously Menelaus went through the Trojan ranks seeking Paris, and not a man there but would have helped him for they all hated Paris, but he was gone, no one knew how or where. So Agamemnon spoke to both armies, declaring that Menelaus was victor and bidding the Trojans give Helen back. This was just, and the Trojans would have agreed if Athena, at Hera's prompting, had not interfered. Hera was determined that the war should not end until Troy was ruined. Athena, sweeping down to the battlefield, persuaded the foolish heart of Pandarus, a Trojan, to break the truce and shoot an arrow at Menelaus. He did so and wounded him, only slightly, but the Greeks in rage at the treachery turned upon the Trojans and the battle was on again. Terror and Destruction and Strife, whose fury never slackens, all friends of the murderous War-god, were there to urge men on to slaughter each other. Then the voice of groaning was heard and the voice of triumph from slayer and from slain and the earth streamed with blood.

On the Greek side, with Achilles gone, the two greatest champions were Ajax and Diomedes. They fought gloriously that day and many a Trojan lay on his face in the dust before them. The best and bravest next to Hector, the Prince Aeneas, came near to death at Diomedes' hands. He was of more than royal blood; his mother was Aphrodite herself, and when Diomedes wounded him she hastened down to the battlefield to save him. She lifted him in her soft arms, but Diomedes, knowing she was a coward goddess, not one of those who like Athena are masters where warriors fight, leaped toward her and wounded her hand. Crying out she let Aeneas fall, and weeping for pain made her way to Olympus, where Zeus smiling to see the laughter-loving goddess in tears bade her stay away from battle and remember hers were the works of love and not of war. But although his mother failed him Aeneas was not killed. Apollo enveloped him in a cloud and carried him to sacred Pergamos, the holy place of Troy, where Artemis healed him of his wound.

But Diomedes raged on, working havoc in the Trojan ranks until he came face to face with Hector. There to his dismay he saw Ares too. The bloodstained murderous god of war was fighting for Hector. At the sight Diomedes shuddered and cried to the Greeks to fall back, slowly, however, and with their faces toward the Trojans. Then Hera was angry. She urged her horses to Olympus and asked Zeus if she might drive that bane of men, Ares, from the battlefield. Zeus who loved him no more than Hera did even though he was their son, willingly gave her leave. She hastened down to stand beside Diomedes and urge him to smite the terrible god and have no fear. At that, joy filled the hero's heart. He rushed at Ares and hurled his spear at him. Athena drove it home, and it entered Ares' body. The War-god bellowed as loud as ten thousand cry in battle, and at the awful sound trembling seized the whole host, Greeks and Trojans alike.

Ares, really a bully at heart and unable to bear what he brought upon unnumbered multitudes of men, fled up to Zeus in Olympus and complained bitterly of Athena's violence. But Zeus looked at him sternly and told him he was as intolerable as his mother, and bade him cease his whining. With Ares gone, however, the Trojans were forced to fall back. At this crisis a brother of Hector's, wise in discerning the will of the gods, urged Hector to go with all speed to the city and tell the Queen, his mother, to offer to Athena the most beautiful robe she owned and pray her to have mercy. Hector felt the wisdom of the advice and sped through the gates to the palace, where his mother did all as he said. She took a robe so precious that it shone like a star, and laying it on the goddess's knees she besought her: "Lady Athena, spare the city and the wives of the Trojans and the little children." But Pallas Athena denied the prayer.

As Hector went back to the battle he turned aside to see once more, perhaps for the last time, the wife he tenderly loved, Andromache, and his son Astyanax. He met her on the wall where she had gone in terror to watch the fighting when she heard the Trojans were in retreat. With her was a hand-maid carrying the little boy. Hector smiled and looked at them silently, but Andromache took his hand in hers and wept. "My dear lord," she said, "you who are father and mother and brother unto me as well as husband, stay here with us. Do not make me a widow and your child an orphan." He refused her gently. He could not be a coward, he said. It was for him to fight always in the forefront of the battle. Yet she could know that he never forgot what her anguish would be when he died. That was the thought that troubled him above all else, more than his many other cares. He turned to leave her, but first he held out his arms to his son. Terrified the little boy shrank back, afraid of the helmet and its fierce nodding crest. Hector laughed and took the shining helmet from his head. Then holding the child in his arms he caressed him and prayed, "O Zeus, in after years may men say of this my son when he returns from battle, 'Far greater is he than his father was.' "

So he laid the boy in his wife's arms and she took him, smiling, yet with tears. And Hector pitied her and touched her tenderly with his hand and spoke to her: "Dear one, be not so sorrowful. That which is fated must come to pass, but against my fate no man can kill me." Then taking up his helmet he left her and she went to her house, often looking back at him and weeping bitterly.

Once again on the battlefield he was eager for the fight, and better fortune for a time lay before him. Zeus had by now remembered his promise to Thetis to avenge Achilles' wrong. He ordered all the other immortals to stay in Olympus; he himself went down to earth to help the Trojans. Then it went hard with the Greeks. Their great champion was far away. Achilles sat alone in his tent, brooding over his wrongs. The great Trojan champion had never before shown himself so brilliant and so brave. Hector seemed irresistible. Tamer of horses, the Trojans always called him, and he drove his car through the Greek ranks as if the same spirit animated steeds and driver. His glancing helm was everywhere and one gallant warrior after another fell beneath his terrible bronze spear. When evening ended the battle, the Trojans had driven the Greeks back almost to their ships.

There was rejoicing in Troy that night, but grief and despair in the Greek camp. Agamemnon himself was all for giving up and sailing back to Greece. Nestor, however, who was the oldest among the chieftains and therefore the wisest, wiser even than the shrewd Odysseus, spoke out boldly and told Agamemnon that if he had not angered Achilles they would not have been defeated. "Try to find some way of appeasing him," he said, "instead of going home disgraced." All applauded the advice and Agamemnon confessed that he had acted like a fool. He would send Briseis back, he promised them, and with her many other splendid gifts, and he begged Odysseus to take his offer to Achilles.

Odysseus and the two chieftains chosen to accompany him found the hero with his friend Patroclus, who of all men on earth was dearest to him. Achilles welcomed them courteously and set food and drink before them, but when they told him why they had come and all the rich gifts that would be his if he would yield, and begged him to have pity on his hard-pressed countrymen, they received an absolute refusal. Not all the treasures of Egypt could buy him, he told them. He was sailing home and they would be wise to do the same.

But all rejected that counsel when Odysseus brought back the answer. The next day they went into battle with the desperate courage of brave men cornered. Again they were driven back, until they stood fighting on the beach where their ships were drawn up. But help was at hand. Hera had laid her plans. She saw Zeus sitting on Mount Ida watching the Trojans conquer, and she thought how she detested him. But she knew well that she could get the better of him only in one way. She must go to him looking so lovely that he could not resist her. When he took her in his arms she would pour sweet sleep upon him and he would forget the Trojans. So she did. She went to her chamber and used every art she knew to make herself beautiful beyond compare. Last of all she borrowed Aphrodite's girdle wherein were all her enchantments, and with this added charm she appeared before Zeus. As he saw her, love overcame his heart so that he thought no more of his promise to Thetis.

At once the battle turned in favor of the Greeks. Ajax hurled Hector to the ground, although before he could wound him Aeneas lifted him and bore him away. With Hector gone, the Greeks were able to drive the Trojans far back from the ships and Troy might have been sacked that very day if Zeus had not awakened. He leaped up and saw the Trojans in flight and Hector lying gasping on the plain. All was clear to him and he turned fiercely to Hera. This was her doing, he said, her crafty, crooked ways. He was half-minded to give her then and there a beating. When it came to that kind of fighting Hera knew she was helpless. She promptly denied that she had had anything to do with the Trojans' defeat. It was all Poseidon, she said, and indeed the Sea-god had been helping the Greeks contrary to Zeus's orders, but only because she had begged him. However, Zeus was glad enough of an excuse not to lay hands on her. He sent her back to Olympus and summoned Iris, the rainbow messenger, to carry his command to Poseidon to withdraw from the field. Sullenly the Sea-god obeyed and once more the tide of battle turned against the Greeks.

Apollo had revived the fainting Hector and breathed into him surpassing power. Before the two, the god and the hero, the Greeks were like a flock of frightened sheep driven by mountain lions. They fled in confusion to the ships, and the wall they had built to defend them went down like a sand wall children heap up on the shore and then scatter in their play. The Trojans were almost near enough to set the ships on fire. The Greeks, hopeless, thought only of dying bravely.

Patroclus, Achilles' beloved friend, saw the rout with horror. Not even for Achilles' sake could he stay longer away from the battle. "You can keep your wrath while your countrymen go down in ruin," he cried to Achilles. "I cannot. Give me your armor. If they think I am you, the Trojans may pause and the worn-out Greeks have a breathing space. You and I are fresh. We might yet drive back the enemy. But if you will sit nursing your anger, at least let me have the armor." As he spoke one of the Greek ships burst into flame. "That way they can cut off the Army's retreat," Achilles said. "Go. Take my armor, my men too, and defend the ships. I cannot go. I am a man dishonored. For my own ships, if the battle comes near them, I will fight. I will not fight for men who have disgraced me."

So Patroclus put on the splendid armor all the Trojans knew and feared, and led the Myrmidons, Achilles' men, to the battle. At the first onset of this new band of warriors the Trojans wavered; they thought Achilles led them on. And indeed for a time Patroclus fought as gloriously as that great hero himself could have done. But at last he met Hector face to face and his doom was sealed as surely as a boar is doomed when he faces a lion. Hector's spear gave him a mortal wound and his soul fled from his body down to the house of Hades. Then Hector stripped his armor from him and casting his own aside, put it on. It seemed as though he had taken on, too, Achilles' strength, and no man of the Greeks could stand before him.

Evening came that puts an end to battle. Achilles sat by his tent waiting for Patroclus to return. But instead he saw old Nestor's son running toward him, fleet-footed Antilochus. He was weeping hot tears as he ran. "Bitter tidings," he cried out. "Patroclus is fallen and Hector has his armor." Grief took hold of Achilles, so black that those around him feared for his life. Down in the sea caves his mother knew his sorrow and came up to try to comfort him. "I will no longer live among men," he told her, "if I do not make Hector pay with his death for Patroclus dead." Then Thetis weeping bade him remember that he himself was fated to die straightway after Hector. "So may I do," Achilles answered, "I who did not help my comrade in his sore need. I will kill the destroyer of him I loved; then I will accept death when it comes."

Thetis did not attempt to hold him back. "Only wait until morning," she said, "and you will not go unarmed to battle. I will bring you arms fashioned by the divine armorer, the god Hephaestus himself."

Marvelous arms they were when Thetis brought them, worthy of their maker, such as no man on earth had ever borne. The Myrmidons gazed at them with awe and a flame of fierce joy blazed in Achilles' eyes as he put them on. Then at last he left the tent in which he had sat so long, and went down to where the Greeks were gathered, a wretched company, Diomedes grievously wounded, Odysseus, Agamemnon, and many another. He felt shame before them and he told them he saw his own exceeding folly in allowing the loss of a mere girl to make him forget everything else. But that was over; he was ready to lead them as before. Let them prepare at once for the battle. The chieftains applauded joyfully, but Odysseus spoke for all when he said they must first take their fill of food and wine, for fasting men made poor fighters. "Our comrades lie dead on the field and you call to food," Achilles answered scornfully. "Down my throat shall go neither bite nor sup until my dear comrade is avenged." And to himself he said, "O dearest of friends, for want of you I cannot eat, I cannot drink."

When the others had satisfied their hunger he led the attack. This was the last fight between the two great champions, as all the immortals knew. They also knew how it would turn out. Father Zeus hung his golden balances and set in one the lot of Hector's death and in the other that of Achilles. Hector's lot sank down. It was appointed that he should die.

Nevertheless, the victory was long in doubt. The Trojans under Hector fought as brave men fight before the walls of their home. Even the great river of Troy, which the gods call Xanthus and men Scamander, took part and strove to drown Achilles as he crossed its waters. In vain, for nothing could check him as he rushed on slaughtering all in his path and seeking everywhere for Hector. The gods by now were fighting, too, as hotly as the men, and Zeus sitting apart in Olympus laughed pleasantly to himself when he saw god matched against god: Athena felling Ares to the ground; Hera seizing the bow of Artemis from her shoulders and boxing her ears with it this way and that; Poseidon provoking Apollo with taunting words to strike him first. The Sun-god refused the challenge. He knew it was of no use now to fight for Hector.

By this time the gates, the great Scaean gates of Troy, had been flung wide, for the Trojans at last were in full flight and were crowding into the town. Only Hector stood immovable before the wall. From the gates old Priam, his father, and his mother Hecuba cried to him to come within and save himself, but he did not heed. He was thinking, "I led the Trojans. Their defeat is my fault. Then am I to spare myself? And yet—what if I were to lay down shield and spear and go tell Achilles that we will give Helen back and half of Troy's treasures with her? Useless. He would but kill me unarmed as if I were a woman. Better to join battle with him now even if I die."

On came Achilles, glorious as the sun when he rises. Beside him was Athena, but Hector was alone. Apollo had left him to his fate. As the pair drew near he turned and fled. Three times around the wall of Troy pursued and pursuer ran with flying feet. It was Athena who made Hector halt. She appeared beside him in the shape of his brother, Deiphobus, and with this ally as he thought, Hector faced Achilles. He cried out to him, "If I kill you I will give back your body to your friends and do you do the same to me." But Achilles answered, "Madman. There are no covenants between sheep and wolves, nor between you and me." So saying he hurled his spear. It missed its aim, but Athena brought it back. Then Hector struck with a true aim; the spear hit the center of Achilles' shield. But to what good? That armor was magical and could not be pierced. He turned quickly to Deiphobus to get his spear, but he was not there. Then Hector knew the truth. Athena had tricked him and there was no way of escape. "The gods have summoned me to death," he thought. "At least I will not die without a struggle, but in some great deed of arms which men yet to be born will tell each other." He drew his sword, his only weapon now, and rushed upon his enemy. But Achilles had a spear, the one Athena had recovered for him. Before Hector could approach, he who knew well that armor taken by Hector from the dead Patroclus aimed at an opening in it near the throat, and drove the spearpoint in. Hector fell, dying at last. With his last breath he prayed, "Give back my body to my father and my mother." "No prayers from you to me, you dog," Achilles answered. "I would that I could make myself devour raw your flesh for the evil you have brought upon me." Then Hector's soul flew forth from his body and was gone to Hades, bewailing his fate, leaving vigor and youth behind.

Achilles stripped the bloody armor from the corpse while the Greeks ran up to wonder how tall he was as he lay there and how noble to look upon. But Achilles' mind was on other matters. He pierced the feet of the dead man and fastened them with thongs to the back of his chariot, letting the head trail. Then he lashed his horses and round and round the walls of Troy he dragged all that was left of glorious Hector.

At last when his fierce soul was satisfied with vengeance he stood beside the body of Patroclus and said, "Hear me even in the house of Hades. I have dragged Hector behind my chariot and I will give him to the dogs to devour beside your funeral pyre."

Up in Olympus there was dissension. This abuse of the dead displeased all the immortals except Hera and Athena and Poseidon. Especially it displeased Zeus. He sent Iris to Priam, to order him to go without fear to Achilles to redeem Hector's body, bearing a rich ransom. She was to tell him that violent as Achilles was, he was not really evil, but one who would treat properly a suppliant.

Then the aged King heaped a car with splendid treasures, the best in Troy, and went over the plain to the Greek camp. Hermes met him, looking like a Greek youth and offering himself as a guide to Achilles' tent. So accompanied the old man passed the guards and came into the presence of the man who had killed and maltreated his son. He clasped his knees and kissed his hands and as he did so Achilles felt awe and so did all the others there, looking strangely upon one another. "Remember, Achilles," Priam said, "your own father, of like years with me and like me wretched for want of a son. Yet I am by far more to be pitied who have braved what no man on earth ever did before, to stretch out my hand to the slayer of my son."

Grief stirred within Achilles' heart as he listened. Gently he raised the old man. "Sit by me here," he said, "and let our sorrow lie quiet in our hearts. Evil is all men's lot, but yet we must keep courage." Then he bade his servants wash and anoint Hector's body and cover it with a soft robe, so that Priam should not see it, frightfully mangled as it was, and be unable to keep back his wrath. He feared for his own self-control if Priam vexed him. "How many days do you desire to make his funeral?" he asked. "For so long I will keep the Greeks back from battle." Then Priam brought Hector home, mourned in Troy as never another. Even Helen wept. "The other Trojans upbraid me," she said, "but always I had comfort from you through the gentleness of your spirit and your gentle words. You only were my friend."

Nine days they lamented him; then they laid him on a lofty pyre and set fire to it. When all was burned they quenched the flame with wine and gathered the bones into a golden urn, shrouding them in soft purple. They set the urn in a hollow grave and piled great stones over it.

This was the funeral of Hector, tamer of horses.

And with it the *Iliad* ends.

14 The Fall of Troy

The greater part of this story comes from Virgil. The capture of Troy is the subject of the second book of the Aeneid, *and it is one of the best, if not the best, story Virgil ever told—concise, pointed, vivid. The beginning and the end of my account are not in Virgil. I have taken the story of Philoctetes and the death of Ajax from two plays of the fifth-century tragic poet Sophocles. The end, the tale of what happened to the Trojan women when Troy fell, comes from a play by Sophocles' fellow playwright, Euripides. It is a curious contrast to the martial spirit of the* Aeneid. *To Virgil as to all Roman poets, war was the noblest and most glorious of human activities. Four hundred years before Virgil a Greek poet looked at it differently. What was the end of that far-famed war? Euripides seems to ask. Just this, a ruined town, a dead baby, a few wretched women.*

With Hector dead, Achilles knew, as his mother had told him, that his own death was near. One more great feat of arms he did before his fighting ended forever. Prince Memnon of Ethiopia, the son of the Goddess of the Dawn, came to the assistance of Troy with a large army and for a time, even though Hector was gone, the Greeks were hard-pressed and lost many a gallant warrior, including swift-footed Antilochus, old Nestor's son. Finally, Achilles killed Memnon in a glorious combat, the Greek hero's last battle. Then he himself fell beside the Scaean gates. He had driven the Trojans before him up to the wall of Troy. There Paris shot an arrow at him and Apollo guided it so that it struck his foot in the one spot where he could be wounded, his heel. His mother Thetis when he was born had intended to make him invulnerable by dipping him into the

River Styx, but she was careless and did not see to it that the water covered the part of the foot by which she was holding him. He died, and Ajax carried his body out of the battle while Odysseus held the Trojans back. It is said that after he had been burned on the funeral pyre his bones were placed in the same urn that held those of his friend Patroclus.

His arms, those marvelous arms Thetis had brought him from Hephaestus, caused the death of Ajax. It was decided in full assembly that the heroes who best deserved them were Ajax and Odysseus. A secret vote was then taken between the two, and Odysseus got the arms. Such a decision was a very serious matter in those days. It was not only that the man who won was honored; the man who was defeated was held to be dishonored. Ajax saw himself disgraced and in a fit of furious anger he determined to kill Agamemnon and Menelaus. He believed and with reason that they had turned the vote against him. At nightfall he went to find them and he had reached their quarters when Athena struck him with madness. He thought the flocks and herds of the Greeks were the Army, and rushed to kill them, believing that he was slaying now this chieftain, now that. Finally he dragged to his tent a huge ram which to his distracted mind was Odysseus, bound him to the tent-pole and beat him savagely. Then his frenzy left him. He regained his reason and saw that his disgrace in not winning the arms had been but a shadow as compared with the shame his own deeds had drawn down upon him. His rage, his folly, his madness, would be apparent to everyone. The slaughtered animals were lying all over the field. "The poor cattle," he said to himself, "killed to no purpose by my hand! And I stand here alone, hateful to men and to gods. In such a state only a coward clings to life. A man if he cannot live nobly can die nobly." He drew his sword and killed himself. The Greeks would not burn his body; they buried him. They held that a suicide should not be honored with a funeral pyre and urn-burial.

His death following so soon upon Achilles' dismayed the Greeks. Victory seemed as far off as ever. Their prophet Calchas told them that he had no message from the gods for them, but that there was a man among the Trojans who knew the future, the prophet Helenus. If they captured him they could learn from him what they should do. Odysseus succeeded in making him a prisoner, and he told the Greeks Troy would not fall until some one fought against the Trojans with the bow and arrows of Hercules. These had been given when Hercules died to the Prince Philoctetes, the man who had fired his funeral pyre and who later had joined the Greek host when they sailed to Troy. On the voyage the Greeks stopped at an island to offer a sacrifice and Philoctetes was bitten by a serpent, a most frightful wound. It would not heal; it was impossible to carry him to Troy as he was; the Army could not wait. They left him finally at Lemnos, then an uninhabited island although once the heroes of the Quest of the Golden Fleece had found plenty of women there.

It was cruel to desert the helpless sufferer, but they were desperate to get on to Troy, and with his bow and arrows he would at least never lack for food. When Helenus spoke, however, the Greeks knew well that it would be hard to persuade him whom they had so wronged, to give his precious weapons to them. So they sent Odysseus, the master of crafty cunning, to get them by trickery. Some say that Diomedes went with him and others Neoptolemus, also called Pyrrhus, the young son of Achilles. They succeeded in stealing the bow and arrows, but when it came to leaving the poor wretch alone there deprived of them, they could not do it. In the end they persuaded him to go with them. Back at Troy the wise physician of the Greeks healed him, and when at last he went joyfully once again into battle the first man he wounded with his arrows was Paris. As he fell Paris begged to be carried to Oenone, the nymph he had lived with on Mount Ida before the three goddesses came to him. She had told him that she knew a magic drug to cure any ailment. They took him to her and he asked her for his life, but she refused. His desertion of her, his long forgetfulness, could not be forgiven in a moment because of his need. She watched him die; then she went away and killed herself.

Troy did not fall because Paris was dead. He was, indeed, no great loss. At last the Greeks learned that there was a most sacred image of Pallas Athena in the city, called the Palladium, and that as long as the Trojans had it Troy could not be taken. Accordingly, the two greatest of the chieftains left alive by then, Odysseus and Diomedes, determined to try to steal it. Diomedes was the one who bore the image off. In a dark night he climbed the wall with Odysseus' help, found the Palladium and took it to the camp. With this great encouragement the Greeks determined to wait no longer, but devise some way to put an end to the endless war.

They saw clearly by now that unless they could get their Army into the city and take the Trojans by surprise, they would never conquer. Almost ten years had passed since they had first laid siege to the town, and it seemed as strong as ever. The walls stood uninjured. They had never suffered a real attack. The fighting had taken place, for the most part, at a distance from them. The Greeks must find a secret way of entering the city, or accept defeat. The result of this new determination and new vision was the stratagem of the wooden horse. It was, as anyone would guess, the creation of Odysseus' wily mind.

He had a skillful worker in wood make a huge wooden horse which was hollow and so big that it could hold a number of men. Then he persuaded—and had a great deal of difficulty in doing so—certain of the chieftains to hide inside it, along with himself, of course. They were all terror-stricken except Achilles' son Neoptolemus, and indeed what they faced was no slight danger. The idea was that all the other Greeks should strike camp, and apparently put out to sea, but they would really hide beyond the nearest island where they could not be seen by the Trojans. Whatever happened they would be safe; they could sail home if anything went wrong. But in that case the men inside the wooden horse would surely die.

Odysseus, as can be readily believed, had not overlooked this fact. His plan was to leave a single Greek behind in the deserted camp, primed with a tale calculated to make the Trojans draw the horse into the city—and without investigating it. Then, when night was darkest, the Greeks inside were to leave their wooden prison and open the city gates to the Army, which by that time would have sailed back, and be waiting before the wall.

A night came when the plan was carried out. Then the last day of Troy dawned. On the wall the Trojan watchers saw with astonishment two sights, each as startling as the other. In front of the Scaean gates stood an enormous figure of a horse, such a thing as no one had ever seen, an apparition so strange that it was vaguely terrifying, even though there was no sound or movement coming from it. No sound or movement anywhere, indeed. The noisy Greek camp was hushed; nothing was stirring there. And the ships were gone. Only one conclusion seemed possible: The Greeks had given up. They had sailed for Greece; they had accepted defeat. All Troy exulted. Her long warfare was over; her sufferings lay behind her.

The people flocked to the abandoned Greek camp to see the sights: here Achilles had sulked so long; there Agamemnon's tent had stood; this was the quarters of the trickster, Odysseus. What rapture to see the places empty, nothing in them now to fear. At last they drifted back to where that monstrosity, the wooden horse, stood, and they gathered around it, puzzled what to do with it. Then the Greek who had been left behind in the camp discovered himself to them. His name was Sinon, and he was a most plausible speaker. He was seized and dragged to Priam, weeping and protesting that he no longer wished to be a Greek. The story he told was one of Odysseus' master-

The wooden horse

pieces. Pallas Athena had been exceedingly angry, Sinon said, at the theft of the Palladium, and the Greeks in terror had sent to the oracle to ask how they could appease her. The oracle answered: "With blood and with a maiden slain you calmed the winds when first you came to Troy. With blood must your return be sought. With a Greek life make expiation." He himself, Sinon told Priam, was the wretched victim chosen to be sacrificed. All was ready for the awful rite, which was to be carried out just before the Greeks' departure, but in the night he had managed to escape and hidden in a swamp had watched the ships sail away.

It was a good tale and the Trojans never questioned it. They pitied Sinon and assured him that he should henceforth live as one of themselves. So it befell that by false cunning and pretended tears those were conquered whom great Diomedes had never overcome, nor savage Achilles, nor ten years of warfare, nor a thousand ships. For Sinon did not forget the second part of his story. The wooden horse had been made, he said, as a votive offering to Athena, and the reason for its immense size was to discourage the Trojans from taking it into the city. What the Greeks hoped for was that the Trojans would destroy it and so draw down upon them Athena's anger. Placed in the city, it would turn her favor to them and away from the Greeks. The story was clever enough to have had by itself, in all probability, the desired effect; but Poseidon, the most bitter of all the gods against Troy, contrived an addition which made the issue certain. The priest Laocoön, when the horse was first discovered, had been urgent with the Trojans to destroy it. "I fear the Greeks even when they bear gifts," he said. Cassandra, Priam's daughter, had echoed his warning, but no one ever listened to her and she had gone back to the palace before Sinon appeared. Laocoön and his two sons heard his story with suspicion, the only doubters there. As Sinon finished, suddenly over the sea came two fearful serpents swimming to the land. Once there, they glided straight to Laocoön. They wrapped their huge coils around him and the two lads and they crushed the life out of them. Then they disappeared within Athena's temple.

There could be no further hesitation. To the horrified spectators Laocoön had been punished for opposing the entry of the horse which most certainly no one else would now do. All the people cried,

> "Bring the carven image in.
> Bear it to Athena,
> Fit gift for the child of Zeus."

Who of the young but hurried forth?
Who of the old would stay at home?
With song and rejoicing they brought death in,
Treachery and destruction.

They dragged the horse through the gate and up to the temple of Athena. Then, rejoicing in their good fortune, believing the war ended and Athena's favor restored to them, they went to their houses in peace as they had not for ten years.

In the middle of the night the door in the horse opened. One by one the chieftains let themselves down. They stole to the gates and threw them wide, and into the sleeping town marched the Greek Army. What they had first to do could be carried out silently. Fires were started in buildings throughout the city. By the time the Trojans were awake, before they realized what had happened, while they were struggling into their armor, Troy was burning. They rushed out to the street one by one in confusion. Bands of soldiers were waiting there to strike each man down before he could join himself to others. It was not fighting, it was butchery. Very many died without ever a chance of dealing a blow in return. In the more distant parts of the town the Trojans were able to gather together here and there and then it was the Greeks who suffered. They were borne down by desperate men who wanted only to kill before they were killed. They knew that the one safety for the conquered was to hope for no safety. This spirit often turned the victors into the vanquished. The quickest-witted Trojans tore off their own armor and put on that of the dead Greeks, and many and many a Greek thinking he was joining friends discovered too late that they were enemies and paid for his error with his life.

On top of the houses they tore up the roofs and hurled the beams down upon the Greeks. An entire tower standing on the roof of Priam's palace was lifted from its foundations and toppled over. Exulting the defenders saw it fall and annihilate a great band who were forcing the palace doors. But the success brought only a short respite. Others rushed up carrying a huge beam. Over the debris of the tower and the crushed bodies they battered the doors with it. It crashed through and the Greeks were in the palace before the Trojans could leave the roof. In the inner courtyard around the altar were the women and children and one man, the old King. Achilles had spared Priam, but Achilles' son struck him down before the eyes of his wife and daughters.

By now the end was near. The contest from the first had been unequal. Too many Trojans had been slaughtered in the first surprise. The Greeks could not be beaten back anywhere. Slowly the defense ceased. Before morning all the leaders were dead, except one. Aphrodite's son Aeneas alone among the Trojan chiefs escaped. He fought the Greeks as long as he could find a living Trojan to stand with him, but as the slaughter spread and death came near he thought of his home, the helpless people he had left there. He could do nothing more for Troy, but perhaps something could be done for them. He hurried to them, his old father, his little son, his wife, and as he went his mother Aphrodite appeared to him, urging him on and keeping him safe from the flames and from the Greeks. Even with the goddess's help he could not save his wife. When they left the house she got separated from him and was killed. But the other two he brought away, through the enemy, past the city gates, out into the country, his father on his shoulders, his son clinging to his hand. No one but a divinity could have saved them, and Aphrodite was the only one of the gods that day who helped a Trojan.

She helped Helen too. She got her out of the city and took her to Menelaus. He received her gladly, and as he sailed for Greece she was with him.

When morning came what had been the proudest city in Asia was a fiery ruin. All that was left of Troy was a band of helpless captive women, whose husbands were dead, whose children had been taken from them. They were waiting for their masters to carry them overseas to slavery.

Chief among the captives was the old Queen, Hecuba, and her daughter-in-law, Hector's wife Andromache. For Hecuba all was ended. Crouched on the ground, she saw the Greek ships getting ready and she watched the city burn. Troy is no longer, she told herself, and I—who am I? A slave men drive like cattle. An old gray woman that has no home.

> What sorrow is there that is not mine?
> Country lost and husband and children.
> Glory of all my house brought low.

And the women around her answered:—

> We stand at the same point of pain.
> We too are slaves.
> Our children are crying, call to us with tears,
> "Mother, I am all alone.
> To the dark ships now they drive me,
> And I cannot see you, Mother."

One woman still had her child. Andromache held in her arms her son Astyanax, the little boy who had once shrunk back from his father's high-crested helmet. "He is so young," she thought. "They will let me take him with me." But from the Greek camp a herald came to her and spoke faltering words. He told her that she must not hate him for the news he brought to her against his will. Her son . . . She broke in,

> Not that he does not go with me?

He answered,

> The boy must die—be thrown
> Down from the towering wall of Troy.
> Now—now—let it be done. Endure
> Like a brave woman. Think. You are alone.
> One woman and a slave and no help anywhere.

She knew what he said was true. There was no help. She said good-by to her child.

> Weeping, my little one? There, there.
> You cannot know what waits for you.
> —How will it be? Falling down—down—all broken—
> And none to pity.
> Kiss me. Never again. Come closer, closer.
> Your mother who bore you—put your arms around my neck.
> Now kiss me, lips to lips.

The soldiers carried him away. Just before they threw him from the wall they had killed on Achilles' grave a young girl, Hecuba's daughter Polyxena. With the death of Hector's son, Troy's last sacrifice was accomplished. The women waiting for the ships watched the end.

> Troy has perished, the great city.
> Only the red flame now lives there.

> The dust is rising, spreading out like a great wing of smoke,
>   And all is hidden.
> We now are gone, one here, one there.
>   And Troy is gone forever.

> Farewell, dear city.
>   Farewell, my country, where my children lived.
> There below, the Greek ships wait.

15 The Adventures of Odysseus

The only authority for this story is the Odyssey, *ex* *cept for the account of Athena's agreement with Po* *seidon to destroy the Greek Fleet, which is not in* *the* Odyssey *and which I have taken from Euripides'* Trojan Women. *Part of the interest of the* Odyssey, *a distinguished from the* Iliad, *lies in the details, such as are given in the story of Nausicaä and the visit of Telemachus to Menelaus. They are used with admirable skill to enliven the story and make it seem real never to hold it up or divert the reader's attention from the main issue.*

When the victorious Greek Fleet put out to sea after the fall of Troy, many a captain, all unknowing, faced troubles a black as those he had brought down on the Trojans. Athena and Poseidon had been the Greeks' greatest allies among the gods, but when Troy fell all that had changed. They became their bitterest enemies. The Greeks went mad with victor the night they entered the city; they forgot what was due to the gods; and on their voyage home they were terribly punished.

Cassandra, one of Priam's daughters, was a prophetess. Apollo had loved her and given her the power to foretell the future. Later he turned against her because she refused his love and although he could not take back his gift—divine favor once bestowed might not be revoked—he made it of no account: no one ever believed her. She told the Trojans each time what would happen; they would never listen to her. She declared that Greeks were hidden in the wooden horse no one gave her words a thought. It was her fate always to know the disaster that was coming and be unable to avert it. When the Greeks sacked the city she was in Athena's temple clinging to her image, under the goddess's protection. The Greeks found her there and they dared to lay violent hands on her. Ajax—not the great Ajax, of course, who was dead, but a lesser chieftain of the same name—tore her from the altar and dragged her out of the sanctuary. Not one Greek protested against the sacrilege. Athena's wrath was deep. She went to Poseidon and laid her wrongs before him. "Help me to vengeance," she said. "Give the Greeks a bitter homecoming. Stir up your waters with wild whirlwinds when they sail. Let dead men choke the bays and line the shores and reefs."

Poseidon agreed. Troy was a heap of ashes by now. He could afford to lay aside his anger against the Trojans. In the fearful tempest which struck the Greeks after they left for Greece, Agamemnon came near to losing all his ships; Menelaus was blown to Egypt; and the arch-sinner, sacrilegious Ajax, was drowned. At the height of the storm his boat was shattered and sank, but he succeeded in swimming to shore. He would have been saved if in his mad folly he had not cried out that he was one that the sea could not drown. Such arrogance always aroused the anger of the gods. Poseidon broke off the jagged bit of rock to which he was clinging. Ajax fell and the waves swept him away to his death.

Odysseus did not lose his life, but if he did not suffer as much as some of the Greeks, he suffered longer than them all. He wandered for ten years before he saw his home. When he reached it, the little son he had left there was grown to manhood. Twenty years had passed since Odysseus sailed for Troy.

On Ithaca, the island where his home was, things had gone from bad to worse. Everyone by now took it for granted that he was dead, except Penelope, his wife, and his son Telemachus. They almost despaired, but not quite. All the people assumed that Penelope was a widow and could and should marry again. From the islands round about and, of course, from Ithaca, men came swarming to Odysseus' house to woo his wife. She would have none of them; the hope that her husband would return was faint, but it never died. Moreover she detested every one of them and so did Telemachus, and with good reason. They were rude, greedy, overbearing men, who spent their days sitting in the great hall of the house devouring Odysseus' store of provisions, slaughtering his cattle, his sheep, his swine, drinking his wine, burning his wood, giving orders to his servants. They would never leave, they declared, until Penelope consented to marry one of them. Telemachus they treated with amused contempt as if he were a mere boy and quite beneath their notice. It was an intolerable state of things to both mother and son, and yet they were helpless, only two and one of them a woman against a great company.

Penelope had at first hoped to tire them out. She told them that she could not marry until she had woven a very fine and exquisitely wrought shroud for Odysseus' father, the aged Laertes, against the day of his death. They had to give in to so pious a purpose, and they agreed to wait until the work was finished. But it never was, inasmuch as Penelope unwove each night what she had woven during the day. But finally the trick failed. One of her handmaidens told the suitors and they discovered her in the very act. Of course after that they were more insistent and unmanageable than ever. So matters stood when the tenth year of Odysseus' wanderings neared its close.

Because of the wicked way they had treated Cassandra, Athena had been angry at all the Greeks indiscriminately, but before that, during the Trojan War, she had especially favored Odysseus. She delighted in his wily mind, his shrewdness and his cunning; she was always forward to help him. After Troy fell she included him with the others in her wrathful displeasure and he too was caught by the storm when he set sail and driven so completely off his course that he never found it again. Year after year he voyaged, hurried from one perilous adventure to another.

Ten years, however, is a long time for anger to last. The gods had by now grown sorry for Odysseus, with the single exception of Poseidon, and Athena was sorriest of all. Her old feeling for him had returned; she was determined to put an end to his sufferings and bring him home. With these thoughts in her mind, she was delighted to find one day that Poseidon was absent from the gathering in Olympus. He had gone to visit the Ethiopians, who lived on the farther bank of Ocean, to the south, and it was certain he would stay there some time, feasting merrily with them. Instantly she brought the sad case of Odysseus before the others. He was at the moment, she told them, a virtual prisoner on an island ruled over by the nymph Calypso, who loved him and planned never to let him go. In every other way except in giving him his freedom she overwhelmed him with kindness; all that she had was at his disposal. But Odysseus was utterly wretched. He longed for his home, his wife, his son. He spent his days on the seashore, searching the horizon for a sail that never came, sick with longing to see even the smoke curling up from his house.

The Olympians were moved by her words. They felt that Odysseus had deserved better at their hands and Zeus spoke for them all when he said they must put their heads together and contrive a way for him to return. If they were agreed Poseidon could not stand alone against them. For his part,

Zeus said, he would send Hermes to Calypso to tell her that she must start Odysseus on his voyage back. Athena well-pleased left Olympus and glided down to Ithaca. She had already made her plans.

She was exceedingly fond of Telemachus, not only because he was her dear Odysseus' son, but because he was a sober, discreet young man, steady and prudent and dependable. She thought it would do him good to take a journey while Odysseus was sailing home, instead of perpetually watching in silent fury the outrageous behavior of the suitors. Also it would advance him in the opinion of men everywhere if the object of his journey was to seek for some news of his father. They would think him, as indeed, he was, a pious youth with the most admirable filial sentiments. Accordingly, she disguised herself to look like a seafaring man and went to the house. Telemachus saw her waiting by the threshold and was vexed to the heart that a guest should not find instant welcome. He hastened to greet the stranger, take his spear, and seat him on a chair of honor. The attendants also hurried to show the hospitality of the great house, setting food and wine before him and stinting him in nothing. Then the two talked together. Athena began by asking gently was this some sort of drinking-bout she had happened upon? She did not wish to offend, but a well-mannered man might be excused for showing disgust at the way the people around them were acting. Then Telemachus told her all, the fear that Odysseus must surely by now be dead; how every man from far and near had come wooing his mother who could not reject their offers out-and-out, but would not accept any of them, and how the suitors were ruining them, eating up their substance and making havoc of the house. Athena showed great indignation. It was a shameful tale, she said. If once Odysseus got home those evil men would have a short shrift and a bitter end. Then she advised him strongly to try to find out something about his father's fate. The men most likely to be able to give the news, she said, were Nestor and Menelaus. With that she departed, leaving the young man full of ardor and decision, all his former uncertainty and hesitation gone. He felt the change with amazement and the belief took hold of him that his visitor had been divine.

The next day he summoned the assembly and told them what he purposed to do and asked them for a well-built ship and twenty rowers to man her, but he got no answer except jeers and taunts. Let him sit at home and get his news there, the suitors bade him. They would see to it that he went on no voyage. With mocking laughter they swaggered off to Odysseus' palace. Telemachus in despair went far away along the seashore and as he walked he prayed to Athena. She heard him and came. She had put on the appearance of Mentor, whom of all the Ithacans Odysseus had most trusted, and she spoke good words of comfort and courage to him. She promised him that a fast ship should be made ready for him, and that she herself would sail with him. Telemachus of course had no idea except that it was Mentor himself speaking to him, but with this help he was ready to defy the suitors and he hurried home to get all ready for the voyage. He waited prudently until night to leave. Then, when all in the house were asleep, he went down to the ship where Mentor (Athena) was waiting, embarked and put out to sea toward Pylos, old Nestor's home.

They found him and his sons on the shore offering a sacrifice to Poseidon. Nestor made them heartily welcome, but about the object of their coming he could give them little help. He knew nothing of Odysseus; they had not left Troy together and no word of him had reached Nestor since. In his opinion the man most likely to have news would be Menelaus, who had voyaged all the way to Egypt before coming home. If Telemachus wished he would send him to Sparta in a chariot with one of his sons who knew the way, which would be much quicker than by sea. Telemachus accepted gratefully and leaving Mentor in charge of the ship he started the next day for Menelaus' palace with Nestor's son.

They drew rein in Sparta before the lordly dwelling, a house far more splendid than either young man had ever seen. A princely welcome awaited them. The house-maidens led them to the bath place where they bathed them in silver bathtubs and rubbed them with sweet-smelling oil. Then they wrapped them in warm purple mantles over fine tunics, and conducted them to the banquet hall. There a servant hastened to them with water in a golden ewer which she poured over their fingers into a silver bowl. A shining table was set beside them and covered with rich food in profusion, and a golden goblet full of wine was placed for each. Menelaus gave them a courteous greeting and bade them eat their fill. The young men were happy, but a little abashed by all the magnificence. Telemachus whispered to his friend, very softly for fear someone might hear, "Zeus's hall in Olympus must be like this. It takes my breath away." But a moment later he had forgotten his shyness, for Menelaus began to speak of Odysseus—of his greatness and his long sorrows. As the young man listened tears gathered in his eyes and he held his cloak before his face to hide his agitation. But Menelaus had remarked it and he guessed who he must be.

Just then, however, came an interruption which distracted the thoughts of every man there. Helen the beautiful came down from her fragrant chamber attended by her women, one carrying her chair, another a soft carpet for her feet, and a third her silver work-basket filled with violet wool. She recognized Telemachus instantly from his likeness to his father and she called him by name. Nestor's son answered and said that she was right. His friend was Odysseus' son and he had come to them for help and advice. Then Telemachus spoke and told them of the wretchedness at home from which only his father's return could deliver them, and asked Menelaus if he could give him any news about him, whether good or bad.

"It is a long story," answered Menelaus, "but I did learn something about him and in a very strange way. It was in Egypt. I was weather-bound for many days on an island there called Pharos. Our provisions were giving out and I was in despair when a sea-goddess had pity on me. She let me know that her father, the sea-god Proteus, could tell me how to leave the hateful island and get safely home if only I could make him do so. For that I must manage to catch him and hold him until I learned from him what I wanted. The plan she made was an excellent one. Each day Proteus came up from the sea with a number of seals and lay down with them on the sand, always in the same place. There I dug four holes in which I and three of my men hid, each under a sealskin the goddess gave us. When the old god lay down not far from me it was no task at all for us to spring up out of our holes and seize him. But to hold him—that was another matter. He had the power of changing his shape at will, and there in our hands he became a lion and a dragon and many other animals, and finally even a high-branched tree. But we held him firmly throughout, and at last he gave in and told me all I wished to know. Of your father he said that he was on an island, pining away from homesickness, kept there by a nymph, Calypso. Except for that, I know nothing of him since we left Troy, ten years ago." When he finished speaking, silence fell upon the company. They all thought of Troy and what had happened since, and they wept—Telemachus for his father; Nestor's son for his brother, swift-footed Antilochus, dead before the walls of Troy; Menelaus for many a brave comrade fallen on the Trojan plain, and Helen—but who could say for whom Helen's tears fell? Was she thinking of Paris as she sat in her husband's splendid hall?

That night the young men spent in Sparta. Helen ordered her house-maidens to arrange beds for them in the entry porch, soft and warm with thick purple blankets covered by smoothly woven rugs and on top of all woolen cloaks. A servant, torch in hand, showed them out and they slept there in comfort until the dawn appeared.

Meantime Hermes had gone to carry Zeus's command to Calypso. He laced to his feet the sandals of imperishable gold which bore him swift as a breath of air over sea and earth. He took his wand with which he could charm men's eyes to slumber, and springing into the air he flew down to sea-level. Skimming the wave-crests he reached at last the lovely island which had become for Odysseus a hateful prison. He found the divine nymph alone; Odysseus as usual was on the sandy shore letting his salt tears flow while he gazed at the empty sea. Calypso took Zeus's orders in very ill part. She had saved the man's life, she said, when his ship was wrecked near the island, and cared for him ever since. Of course everyone must give in to Zeus, but it was very unfair. And how was she to manage the voyage back? She had no ships and crews at command. But Hermes felt this was not his affair. "Just take care not to make Zeus angry," he said and went gaily off.

Calypso gloomily set about the necessary preparations. She told Odysseus, who was at first inclined to think it all a trick on her part to do something detestable to him,—drown him, very likely,—but she finally convinced him. She would help him build a splendidly strong raft, she promised him, and send him away on it equipped with everything necessary. Never did any man do work more joyfully than Odysseus made his raft. Twenty great trees furnished the wood, all very dry so that they would float high. On the raft Calypso put food and drink in abundance, even a sack of the dainties Odysseus specially liked. The fifth morning after Hermes' visit found Odysseus putting out to sea before a fair wind over quiet waters.

Seventeen days he journeyed without change of weather, always steering, never letting sleep close his eyes. On the eighteenth day a cloudy mountain top arose up across the sea. He believed that he was saved.

At that very moment, however, Poseidon, on his way back from Ethiopia, caught sight of him. He knew at once what the gods had done. "But," he muttered to himself, "I think I can give him even yet a long journey into sorrow before he reaches land." With that he summoned all the violent winds and let them loose, blinding sea and land with storm-clouds. The East Wind fought with the South, and the ill-blowing West with the North, and the waves rose up mightily. Odysseus saw death before him. "Oh, happy the men who fell gloriously on the plain of Troy!" he thought. "For me to die thus ignobly!" It seemed indeed that he could not escape. The raft was tossed as a dried thistle goes rolling over a field in autumn days.

But a kindly goddess was at hand, Ino of the slim ankles, who had once been a Theban princess. She pitied him and rising lightly from the water like a sea-gull she told him his one chance was to abandon the raft and swim to shore. She gave him her veil, which would keep him from harm as long as he was in the sea. Then she disappeared beneath the billows.

Odysseus had no choice but to follow her advice. Poseidon sent a wave of waves to him, a terror of the sea. It tore the logs of the raft apart as a great wind scatters a heap of dried chaff; it flung Odysseus into the wild waters. But, if he had only known it, bad as things seemed the worst was over. Poseidon felt satisfied and went off contentedly to plan some other storm somewhere, and Athena, left free to act, calmed the waves. Even so, Odysseus had to swim for two days and nights before he reached land and could find a safe landing-place. He came out of the surf exhausted and starving and naked. It was evening; not a house, not a living creature, was to be seen. But Odysseus was not only a hero, he was a man of great resourcefulness. He found a place where a few trees grew so thick and close to the ground, no moisture could penetrate them. Beneath were heaps of dry leaves, enough to cover many men. He scooped out a hollow and lying down piled the leaves over him like a thick coverlet. Then, warm and still at last, with the sweet land odors blowing to him, he slept in peace.

He had of course no idea where he was, but Athena had arranged matters well for him. The country belonged to the Phaeacians, a kind people and splendid sailors. Their king, Alcinoüs, was a good, sensible man who knew that his wife Arete was a great deal wiser than he and always let her decide anything important for him. They had a fair daughter as yet unmarried.

Nausicaä, for so the girl was called, never imagined the next morning that she was to play the part of rescuer to a hero. When she woke up she thought only about doing the family washing. She was a princess, indeed, but in those days high-born ladies were expected to be useful, and the household linen was in Nausicaä's charge. Washing clothes was then a very agreeable occupation. She had the servants make ready an easy-running mule-cart and pack it with the soiled clothes. Her mother filled a box for her with all sorts of good things to eat and drink; she gave her too a golden flask of limpid olive oil to use if she and her maids went bathing. Then they started, Nausicaä driving. They were bound for the very place where Odysseus had landed. A lovely river flowed into the sea there which had excellent washing pools with an abundance of clear bubbling water. What the girls did was to lay the clothes in the water and dance on them until all the dirt was worked out. The pools were cool and shadowy; it was very pleasant work. Afterwards they stretched the linen smooth to dry on the shore where the sea had washed it clean.

Then they could take their ease. They bathed and anointed themselves with the sleek oil, and had their lunch, and amused themselves with a ball which they threw to one another, dancing all the while. But at last the setting sun warned them the delightful day was over. They gathered up the linen, yoked in the mules, and were about to start home when they saw a wild-looking naked man suddenly step out of the bushes. Odysseus had been awakened by the girls' voices. In terror they ran away, all except Nausicaä. She faced him fearlessly and he spoke to her as persuasively as his eloquent tongue could. "I am a suppliant at your knees, O Queen," he said. "But whether you are mortal or divine I cannot tell. Never anywhere have I set eyes on such a one. I wonder as I look at you. Be gracious to your suppliant, a shipwrecked man, friendless and helpless, without a rag to cover him."

Nausicaä answered him kindly. She told him where he was and that the people of the country were kind to luckless wanderers. The King, her father, would receive him with all courteous hospitality. She summoned the frightened maids and bade them give the stranger the oil so that he could cleanse himself and find for him a mantle and a tunic. They waited while he bathed and dressed, then all set forth for the city. Before they reached Nausicaä's home, however, that discreet maiden directed Odysseus to fall back and let her and the girls go on alone. "People's tongues are so ill-natured," she said. "If they saw a handsome man like you with me, they would be hinting at all sorts of things. And you can easily find my father's house, it is so much the most splendid. Enter boldly and go straight to my mother, who will be spinning at the hearth. What my mother says my father will do."

Odysseus agreed at once. He admired her good sense, and he followed her directions exactly. Entering the house he strode through the hall to the hearth and sank down before the Queen, clasping her knees and praying her for help. The King quickly raised him and bade him sit at table and take his fill of food and drink without fear. Whoever he was and wherever his home, he could rest assured that they would arrange to send him there in one of their ships. It was now the time for sleep, but in the morning he could tell them his name and how he had made his way to them. So they slept through the night,

Odysseus blissfully, on a couch soft and warm as he had not known since he left Calypso's isle.

The next day in the presence of all the Phaeacian chiefs he told the story of his ten years' wandering. He began with the departure from Troy and the storm that struck the Fleet. He and his ships were driven across the sea for nine days. On the tenth they made the land of the Lotus-eaters and put in there. But weary though they were and in need of refreshment they were forced to leave quickly. The inhabitants met them with kindness and gave them their flower-food to eat, but those who tasted it, only a few fortunately, lost their longing for home. They wanted only to dwell in the Lotus Land, and let the memory of all that had been fade from their minds. Odysseus had to drag them on shipboard and chain them there. They wept, so great was their desire to stay, tasting forever the honey-sweet flowers.

Their next adventure was with the Cyclops Polyphemus, a full account of which is given in Part One, Chapter 4. They lost a number of their comrades at his hands, and what was even worse, made Poseidon, who was Polyphemus' father, so angry that he swore Odysseus should reach his own country again only after long misery and when he had lost all his men. For these ten years his anger had followed him over the sea.

From the Cyclops' island they came to the country of the Winds, ruled over by King Aeolus. Zeus had made him keeper of the Winds, to still them or arouse them at his will. Aeolus received them hospitably and when they left gave Odysseus as a parting gift a leather sack, into which he had put all the Storm Winds. It was so tightly fastened that not the very least puff of any Wind that spells danger for a ship could leak out. In this excellent situation for sailors Odysseus' crew managed to bring them all near to death. They thought the carefully stored bag was probably full of gold; at any rate, they wanted to see what was in it. They opened it, with the result, of course, that all the Winds rushed out at once and swept them away in a terrific tempest. Finally, after days of danger, they saw land, but they had better have stayed on the stormy sea for it was the country of the Laestrygons, a people of gigantic size and cannibals too. These horrible folk destroyed all Odysseus' ships except the one he himself was in—which had not yet entered the harbor when the attack was made.

This was by far the worst disaster yet, and it was with despairing hearts that they put in at the next island they reached. Never would they have landed if they had known what lay before them. They had come to Aeaea, the realm of Circe, a most beautiful and most dangerous witch. Every man who approached her she turned into a beast. Only his reason remained as before: he knew what had happened to him. She enticed into her house the party Odysseus dispatched to spy out the land, and there she changed them into swine. She penned them in a sty and gave them acorns to eat. They ate them; they were swine. Yet inside they were men, aware of their vile state, but completely in her power.

Luckily for Odysseus, one of the party had been too cautious to enter the house. He watched what happened and fled in horror back to the ship. The news drove any thought of caution out of Odysseus. He started off, all alone—not one of the crew would go with him—to try to do something, bring some help to his men. On his way Hermes met him. He seemed a young man, of that age when youth looks its loveliest. He told Odysseus he knew a herb which could save him from Circe's deadly art. With it he could taste anything she gave him and suffer no harm. When he had drunk the cup she offered him, Hermes said, he must threaten to run her through with his sword unless she freed his followers. Odysseus took the herb and went thankfully on his way. All turned out even better than Hermes had predicted. When Circe had used on Odysseus the magic which had always hitherto been successful and to her amazement saw him stand unchanged before her, she so marveled at the man who could resist her enchantment that she loved him. She was ready to do whatever he asked and she turned his companions at once back into men again. She treated them all with such kindness, feasting them sumptuously in her house, that for a whole year they stayed happily with her.

When at last they felt that the time had come to depart she used her magical knowledge for them. She found out what they must do next in order to reach home safely. It was a fearful undertaking she put before them. They must cross the river Ocean and beach the ship on Persephone's shore where there was an entrance to the dark realm of Hades. Odysseus then must go down and find the spirit of the prophet Teiresias who had been the holy man of Thebes. He would tell Odysseus how to get back home. There was only one way to induce his ghost to come to him, by killing sheep and filling a pit with their blood. All ghosts had an irresistible craving to drink blood. Every one of them would come rushing to the pit, but Odysseus must draw his sword and keep them away until Teiresias spoke to him.

This was bad news, indeed, and all were weeping when they left Circe's isle and turned their prow toward Erebus where Hades rules with awesome Persephone. It was terrible indeed when the trench was dug and filled with blood and the spirits

Odysseus and Circe

of the dead flocked to it. But Odysseus kept his courage. He held them off with his sharp weapon until he saw the ghost of Teiresias. He let him approach and drink of the black blood, then put his question to him. The seer was ready with his answer. The chief danger that threatened them, he said, was that they might do some injury to the oxen of the Sun when they reached the island where they lived. The doom of all who harmed them was certain. They were the most beautiful oxen in the world and very much prized by the Sun. But in any event Odysseus himself would reach home and although he would find trouble waiting for him, in the end he would prevail.

After the prophet ceased speaking, a long procession of the dead came up to drink the blood and speak to Odysseus and pass on, great heroes and fair women of old; warriors, too, who had fallen at Troy. Achilles came and Ajax, still wrathful because of the armor of Achilles which the Greek captains had given to Odysseus and not to him. Many others came, all eager to speak to him. Too many, in the end. Terror at the thronging numbers took hold of Odysseus. He hastened back to the ship and bade his crew set sail.

From Circe he had learned that they must pass the island of the Sirens. These were marvelous singers whose voices would make a man forget all else, and at last their song would steal his life away. Moldering skeletons of those they had lured to their death lay banked high up around them where they sat singing on the shore. Odysseus told his men about them and that the only way to pass them safely was for each man to stop his ears with wax. He himself, however, was determined to hear them, and he proposed that the crew should tie him to the mast so strongly that he could not get away however much he tried. This they did and drew near the island, all except Odysseus deaf to the enchanting song. He heard it and the words were even more enticing than the melody, at least to a Greek. They would give knowledge to each man who came to them, they said, ripe wisdom and a quickening of the spirit. "We know all things which shall be hereafter upon the earth." So rang their song in lovely cadences, and Odysseus' heart ached with longing.

But the ropes held him and that danger was safely passed. A sea peril next awaited them—the passage between Scylla and Charybdis. The Argonauts had got through it; Aeneas, who just about that time had sailed for Italy, had been able to avoid it because of a prophet's warning; of course Odysseus with Athena looking after him succeeded in passing it. But it was a frightful ordeal and six of the crew lost their lives there. However, they would not in any case have lived much longer, for at their next stopping place, the Island of the Sun, the men acted with incredible folly. They were hungry and they killed the sacred oxen. Odysseus was away. He had gone into the island alone by himself to pray. He was in despair when he returned, but the beasts had been roasted and eaten and nothing could be done. The vengeance of the Sun was swift. As soon as the men left the island a thunderbolt shattered the ship. All were drowned except Odysseus. He clung to the keel and was able to ride out the storm. Then he drifted for days, until finally he was cast ashore on Calypso's island, where he had to stay for many years. At last he started home, but a tempest shipwrecked him and only after many and great dangers had he succeeded in reaching the Phaeacian land, a helpless, destitute man.

The long story was ended, but the audience sat silent, entranced by the tale. At last the King spoke. His troubles were over, he assured Odysseus. They would send him home that very day and every man present would give him a parting gift to enrich him. All agreed. The ship was made ready, the presents were stowed within, and Odysseus embarked after taking a grateful leave of his kind hosts. He stretched himself on the deck and a sweet sleep closed his eyes. When he woke he was on dry land, lying on a beach. The sailors had set him ashore just as he was, ranged his belongings beside him, and departed. He started up and stood staring around him. He did not recognize his own country. A young man approached him, seemingly a shepherd lad, but fine and well-mannered like the sons of kings when they tend sheep. So he seemed to Odysseus, but really it was Athena in his semblance. She answered his eager question and told him he was in Ithaca. Even in his joy at the news Odysseus kept his caution. He spun her a long tale about who he was and why he had come, with not a word of truth in it, at the end of which the goddess smiled and patted him. Then she appeared in her own form, divinely tall and beautiful. "You crooked, shifty rogue!" she laughed. "Anyone who would keep pace with your craftiness must be a canny dealer." Odysseus greeted her with rapture, but she bade him remember how much there was to do and the two settled down to work out a plan. Athena told him how things were in his house and promised she would help him clear it of the suitors. For the present she would change him into an old beggar so that he could go everywhere unrecognized. That night he must spend with his swineherd, Eumaeus, a man faithful and trustworthy beyond praise. When they had hidden the treasures in a near-by cave they separated, she to summon Telemachus home, he, whom her art had turned into a shambling ragged old man, to seek the swineherd. Eumaeus welcomed the poor stranger, fed him well and lodged him for the night, giving him his own thick mantle to cover him.

Meanwhile, at Pallas Athena's prompting, Telemachus took leave of Helen and Menelaus, and as soon as he reached his ship embarked, eager to get home with all speed. He planned—and again Athena had put the thought in his mind—not to go directly to the house on landing, but first to the swineherd to learn if anything had happened in his absence. Odysseus was helping prepare breakfast when the young man appeared at the door. Eumaeus greeted him with tears of joy and begged him to sit and eat. Before he would do so, however, he dispatched the swineherd to inform Penelope of his return. Then father and son were alone together. At that moment Odysseus perceived Athena just beyond the door beckoning to him. He went out to her and in a flash she turned him back into his own form and bade him tell Telemachus who he was. That young man had noticed nothing until instead of the old beggar a majestic-looking person returned to him. He started up amazed, believing he saw a god. "I am your father," Odysseus said, and the two embraced each other and wept. But the time was short and there was much to plan. An anxious talk followed. Odysseus was determined to drive the suitors away by force, but how could two men take on a whole company? At last it was decided that the next morning they should go to the house, Odysseus disguised, of course, and that Telemachus should hide all the weapons of war, leaving only enough for the two of them where they could easily get at them. Athena was quick to aid. When Eumaeus came back he found the old beggar he had left.

Next day Telemachus went on alone, leaving the other two to follow. They reached the town, they came to the palace, and at last after twenty years Odysseus entered his dear dwelling. As he did so an old dog lying there lifted his head and pricked his ears. It was Argos, whom Odysseus had bred before he went to Troy. Yet the moment his master appeared he knew him and wagged his tail, but he had no strength to drag himself even a little toward him. Odysseus knew him too and brushed away a tear. He dared not go to him for fear of arousing suspicion in the swineherd, and as he turned away that moment the old dog died.

Within the hall the suitors, idly loafing after their meal, were in a mood to make fun of the miserable old beggar who entered, and Odysseus listened to all their mocking words with submissive patience. At last one of them, an evil-tempered man, became irritated and gave him a blow. He dared to strike a stranger who was asking for hospitality. Penelope heard of the outrage and declared that she would herself speak with the ill-treated man, but she decided first to pay a visit to the banqueting hall. She wanted to see Telemachus and also it seemed wise to her to show herself to the suitors. She was as prudent as her son. If Odysseus was dead, it would certainly be well for her to marry the richest of these men and the most liberal. She must not discourage them too much. Besides, she had an idea which seemed to promise very well. So she went down from her room into the hall, attended by two maids and holding a veil before her face, looking so lovely her courtiers trembled to see her. One and another arose to compliment her, but the discreet lady answered she knew very well that she had lost all her looks by now, what with her grieving and her many cares. Her purpose in coming to speak to them was a serious one. No doubt her husband would never come back. Why then did they not court her in the proper way for a lady of family and fortune by giving her costly gifts? The suggestion was acted upon at once. All had their pages bring and present her with most lovely things, robes and jewels and golden chains. Her maids carried them upstairs and demure Penelope retired with great contentment in her heart.

Then she sent for the stranger who had been ill-used. She spoke graciously to him and Odysseus told her a tale of meeting her husband on his way to Troy which made her weep until he pitied her. Still he did not reveal himself, but kept his face hard as iron. By and by Penelope remembered her duties as hostess. She summoned an old nurse, Eurycleia, who had cared for Odysseus from babyhood, and bade her wash the stranger's feet. Odysseus was frightened, for on one foot was a scar made in boyhood days by a wild boar he had hunted, and he thought she would recognize it. She did, and she let the foot fall so that the tub was upset. Odysseus caught her hand and muttered, "Dear nurse, you know. But not a word to another soul." She whispered her promise, and Odysseus took his leave. He found a bed in the entrance hall, but he could not sleep for wondering how he could overcome so many shameless fellows. At last he reminded himself that his state in the Cyclops' cave had been still worse and that with Athena's help he could hope here too to be successful, and then he slept.

Morning brought the suitors back, more insolent even than before. Carelessly and at ease they sat down to the rich feast spread for them, not knowing that the goddess and the much-enduring Odysseus were preparing a ghastly banquet for them.

Penelope all unknowing forwarded their plan. During the night she had made one of her own. When morning came she went to her store-chamber where among many treasures was a great bow and a quiver full of arrows. They belonged to Odysseus and no hand but his had ever strung the bow or used it.

Carrying them herself she descended to where the suitors were gathered. "Hear me, my lords," she said. "I set before you the bow of godlike Odysseus. He who strings the bow and shoots an arrow straight through twelve rings in a line, I will take as my husband." Telemachus instantly saw how this could be turned to their advantage and he was quick to play up to her. "Come on, suitors all," he cried. "No holding back or excuses. But stay. I will try first and see if I am man enough to bear my father's arms." With this he set the rings in order, placing them exactly in line. Then he took the bow and did his utmost to string it. Perhaps he might in the end have succeeded if Odysseus had not signed to him to give up. After him the others, one by one, took their turn, but the bow was too stiff; the strongest could not bend it even a little.

Certain that no one would be successful Odysseus left the contest and stepped out into the courtyard where the swineherd was talking to the keeper of the cattle, a fellow as trustworthy as himself. He needed their help and he told them who he was. As proof he showed them the scar on his foot which in other years they had both seen many a time. They recognized it and burst out weeping for joy. But Odysseus hushed them quickly. "None of that now," he said. "Listen to what I want of you. Do you, Eumaeus, find some way to put the bow and arrows into my hands; then see that the women's quarters are closed so that no one can enter. And you, O herder of cattle, must shut and bar the gates of the court here." He turned back to the hall, the two following him. When they entered the last suitor to make the trial had just failed. Odysseus said, "Pass me the bow and let me see if the strength I once had is still mine." An angry clamor broke out at the words. A beggarly foreigner should never touch the bow, they cried. But Telemachus spoke sternly to them. It was for him, not them, to say who should handle the bow, and he bade Eumaeus give it to Odysseus.

All watched intently as he took it and examined it. Then, with effortless ease, as a skilled musician fits a bit of catgut to his lyre, he bent the bow and strung it. He notched an arrow to the string and drew, and not moving from his seat he sent it straight through the twelve rings. The next instant with one leap he was at the door and Telemachus was beside him. "At last, at last," he cried in a great voice and he shot an arrow. It found its mark; one of the suitors fell dying to the floor. The others sprang up in horror. Their weapons—where were they? None were to be seen. And Odysseus was shooting steadily. As each arrow whistled through the hall a man fell dead. Telemachus on guard with his long spear kept the crowd back so that they could not rush out through the door either to escape or to attack Odysseus from the rear. They made an easy target, gathered there together, and as long as the supply of arrows held out they were slaughtered without a chance to defend themselves. Even with the arrows gone they fared little better, for Athena had now come to take a part in the great deeds being done and she made each attempt to reach Odysseus miscarry. But his flashing spear never missed its stroke and the dreadful sound of cracking skulls was heard and the floor flowed with blood.

At last only two of that roistering, impudent band were left, the priest of the suitors and their bard. Both of them cried for mercy, but the priest, clasping Odysseus' knees in his agony of supplication, met with none. The hero's sword ran him through and he died in the midst of his prayer. The bard was fortunate. Odysseus shrank from killing such a man, taught by the gods to sing divinely, and he spared him for further song.

The battle—slaughter, rather—was ended. The old nurse Eurycleia and her maids were summoned to cleanse the place and restore all to order. They surrounded Odysseus, weeping and laughing and welcoming him home until they stirred within his own heart the desire to weep. At last they set to work, but Eurycleia climbed the stairs to her mistress's chamber. She stood by her bed. "Awake, my dear," she said, "for Odysseus has come home and all the suitors are dead." "O crazy old woman," Penelope complained. "And I was sleeping so sweetly. Off with you and be glad you are not smartly slapped as anyone else would have been who waked me." But Eurycleia persisted, "Indeed, indeed Odysseus is here. He showed me the scar. It is his very self." Still Penelope could not believe her. She hurried down to the hall to see with her own eyes.

A man tall and princely-looking was sitting by the hearth where the firelight fell full on him. She sat down opposite him and looked at him in silence. She was bewildered. At one moment she seemed to recognize him, the next, he was a stranger to her. Telemachus cried out at her: "Mother, Mother, oh, cruel! What other woman would hold herself aloof when her man came home after twenty years?" "My son," she answered, "I have no strength to move. If this is in truth Odysseus, then we two have ways of knowing each other." At this Odysseus smiled and bade Telemachus leave her alone. "We will find each other out presently," he said.

Then the well-ordered hall was filled with rejoicing. The minstrel drew sweet sounds from his lyre and waked in all the longing for the dance. Gaily they trod a measure, men and fair-robed women, till the great house around them rang with their footfalls. For Odysseus at last after long wandering had come home and every heart was glad.

16 The Adventures of Aeneas

The Aeneid, *the greatest of Latin poems, is the chief authority for this story. It was written when Augustus had taken over the bankrupt Roman world after the chaos that followed Caesar's assassination. His strong hand ended the furious civil wars and brought about the Pax Augusta, which lasted for nearly half a century. Virgil and all his generation were fired with enthusiasm for the new order, and the* Aeneid *was written to exalt the Empire, to provide a great national hero and a founder for "the race destined to hold the world beneath its rule." Virgil's patriotic purpose is probably responsible for the change from the human Aeneas of the first books to the unhuman prodigy of the last. The poet was finally carried away into the purely fantastic by his determination to create a hero for Rome that would make all other heroes seem insignificant. A tendency to exaggeration was a Roman trait. The Latin names of the gods are, of course, used; and the Latin forms in the case of any personage who has a Latin as well as a Greek name. Ulysses, for instance, is Latin for Odysseus.*

Part One: FROM TROY TO ITALY

Aeneas, the son of Venus, was among the most famous of the heroes who fought the Trojan War. On the Trojan side he was second only to Hector. When the Greeks captured Troy, he was able with his mother's help to escape from the city with his father and his little son, and to sail away to a new home.

After long wanderings and many trials on land and sea he reached Italy, where he defeated those who opposed his entering the country, married the daughter of a powerful king and founded a city. He was always held to be the real founder of Rome because Romulus and Remus, the actual founders, were born in the city his son built, in Alba Longa.

When he set sail from Troy many Trojans had joined him. All were eager to find somewhere to settle, but no one had any clear idea where that should be. Several times they started to build a city, but they were always driven away by misfortunes or bad omens. At last Aeneas was told in a dream that the place destined for them was a country far away to the west, Italy— in those days called Hesperia, the Western Country. They were then on the island of Crete, and although the promised land was distant by a long voyage over unknown seas they were thankful for the assurance that they would some day have their own home and they started at once on the journey. Before they reached their desired haven, however, a long time passed, and much happened which if they had known beforehand might have checked their eagerness.

Although the Argonauts had sailed east from Greece and Aeneas' company were westward bound from Crete, the Trojans came upon the Harpies just as Jason and his men had done. The Greek heroes had been bolder, however, or else better swordsmen. They were on the point of killing the horrid creatures when Iris intervened, but the Trojans were driven away by them, and forced to put out to sea to escape them.

At their next landing place they met to their amazement Hector's wife Andromache. When Troy fell she had been given to Neoptolemus, sometimes called Pyrrhus, Achilles' son, the man who had killed old Priam at the altar. He soon abandoned her for Hermione, Helen's daughter, but he did not long survive this marriage and after his death Andromache married the Trojan prophet Helenus. They were now ruling the country and of course were rejoiced to welcome Aeneas and his men. They entertained them with the utmost hospitality and before they bade them farewell Helenus gave them useful advice about their journey. They must not land on the nearest coast of Italy, the east coast, he told them, because it was full of Greeks. Their destined home was on the west coast, somewhat to the north, but they must by no means take the shortest way and go up between Sicily and Italy. In those waters was that most perilous strait guarded by Scylla and Charybdis, which the Argonauts had succeeded in passing only because Thetis helped them and where Ulysses had lost six of his men. It is not clear how the Argonauts on their way from Asia to Greece got to the west coast of Italy, nor for that matter how Ulysses did, either, but at any rate there was no doubt in Helenus' mind exactly where the strait was and he gave Aeneas careful directions how to avoid those pests to mariners—by making a long circuit southward around Sicily, and reaching Italy far to the north of the whirlpool of implacable Charybdis and the black cavern into which Scylla sucked whole ships.

When the Trojans had taken leave of their kind hosts and had successfully rounded the eastern tip of Italy, they kept on sailing southwestward around Sicily with all confidence in their prophetic guide. Apparently, however, for all his mysterious powers Helenus was not aware that Sicily, at least the southern part, was now occupied by the Cyclopes, for he did not warn the Trojans against landing there. They reached the island after sunset and made camp on the shore with no hesitation at all. Probably they would all have been captured and eaten if very early the next morning, before any of the monsters were astir, a poor wretch of a man had not come running to where Aeneas was lying. He threw himself upon his knees, but indeed his obvious misery was enough of an appeal, his pallor like that of one half dead from starvation, his clothes held together only by thorns, his face squalid in the extreme with a thick growth of hair. He was one of Ulysses' sailors, he told them, who had been left behind unintentionally in Polyphemus' cave and had ever since lived in the woods on whatever he could find there, terrified perpetually lest one of the Cyclopes should come upon him. There were a hundred of them, he said, all as big and as frightful as Polyphemus. "Fly," he urged them. "Up and away with all speed. Break the ropes that hold the boats to the shore." They did as he said, cutting the cables, making breathless haste, all as silently as possible. But they had only launched the ships when the blind giant was seen slowly making his way down to the shore to wash the cavity where his eye had been, which still flowed with blood. He heard the splashing of the oars and he rushed toward the sound out into the sea. The Trojans, however, had got enough of a start. Before he could reach them the water had deepened too much even for his towering height.

They escaped that peril, but only to meet another as great. While rounding Sicily they were struck by a storm such as there never was before or since: the waves were so high that their crests licked the stars, and the gulfs between them so deep that the floor of the ocean was disclosed. It was clearly something more than a mere mortal storm and in point of fact Juno was back of it.

She hated all Trojans, of course; she never forgot the judgment of Paris and she had been Troy's bitterest enemy during the war, but she felt an especial hatred for Aeneas. She knew that Rome, which was to be founded by men of Trojan blood, although generations after Aeneas, was destined by the Fates to conquer Carthage some day, and Carthage was her pet city, beloved by her beyond all other places on earth. It is not known whether she really thought she could go against the decrees of the Fates, which Jupiter himself could not do, but certainly she did her best to drown Aeneas. She went to Aeolus, the King of the Winds, who had tried to help Ulysses, and asked him to sink the Trojan ships, promising him in return her loveliest nymph for his wife. The stupendous storm was the result. It would undoubtedly have done all that Juno wished if it had not been for Neptune. As Juno's brother he was quite aware of her way of doing things and it did not suit him to have her interfere with his sea. He was as cautious, however, in dealing with her as Jupiter always was. He said not a word to her, but contented himself with sending a stern reprimand to Aeolus. Then he calmed the sea, and made it possible for the Trojans to get to land. The north coast of Africa was where they finally beached their ships. They had been blown all the way down there from Sicily. As it happened, the place they came ashore was quite near to Carthage and Juno began at once to consider how she could turn this arrival to their disadvantage and the advantage of the Carthaginians.

Carthage had been founded by a woman, Dido, who was still its ruler and under whom it was growing into a great and splendid city. She was beautiful and a widow; Aeneas had lost his wife on the night he left Troy. Juno's plan was to have the two fall in love with each other and so divert Aeneas from Italy and induce him to settle down with Dido. It would have been a good plan if it had not been for Venus. She suspected what was in Juno's mind, and was determined to block it. She had her own plan. She was quite willing to have Dido fall in love with Aeneas, so that no harm could come to him in Carthage; but she intended to see to it that his feeling for Dido should be no more than an entire willingness to take anything she wanted to give; by no means such as to interfere in the least with his sailing away to Italy whenever that seemed best. At this juncture she went up to Olympus to talk to Jupiter. She reproached him and her lovely eyes filled with tears. Her dear son Aeneas was all but ruined, she said. And he, the King of Gods and Men, had sworn to her that Aeneas should be the ancestor of a race who would some day rule the world. Jupiter laughed and kissed away her tears. He told her that what he had promised would surely come to pass. Aeneas' descendants would be the Romans, to whom the Fates had decreed a boundless and endless empire.

Venus took her leave greatly comforted, but to make matters still more sure she turned for help to her son Cupid. Dido, she thought, could be trusted to make unaided the necessary impression upon Aeneas, but she was not at all certain that Aeneas by himself could get Dido to fall in love with him. She was known to be not susceptible. All the kings of the country round about had tried to persuade her to marry them with no success. So Venus summoned Cupid, who promised that he would set Dido's heart on fire with love as soon as she laid eyes on Aeneas. It was a simple matter for Venus to bring about a meeting between the two.

The morning after they landed, Aeneas with his friend, the faithful Achates, left his wretched shipwrecked followers to try to find out what part of the world they were in. He spoke cheering words to them before he started.

Comrades, you and I have had long acquaintance with sorrow.
Evils still worse we have known. These also will end. Call back
    courage.
Send away gloomy fear. Perhaps some day to remember
This trouble too will bring pleasure. . . .

As the two heroes explored the strange country, Venus disguised as a huntress appeared to them. She told them where they were and advised them to go straight to Carthage whose Queen would surely help them. Greatly reassured they took the path Venus pointed out, protected, although they did not know it, by a thick mist she wrapped around them. So they reached the city without interference and walked unnoticed through the busy streets. Before a great temple they paused wondering how they could get to the Queen, and there new hope came to them. As they gazed at the splendid building they saw marvelously carved upon the walls the battles around Troy in which they themselves had taken part. They saw the likenesses of their foes and their friends: the sons of Atreus, old Priam stretching out his hand to Achilles, the dead Hector. "I take courage," Aeneas said. "Here too there are tears for things, and hearts are touched by the fate of all that is mortal."

At that moment Dido, lovely as Diana herself, approached with a great train of attendants. Forthwith the mist around Aeneas dissolved and he stood forth beautiful as Apollo. When he told her who he was the Queen received him with the utmost graciousness and welcomed him and his company to her city. She knew how these desolate homeless men felt, for she herself had come to Africa with a few friends fleeing from her brother who wanted to murder her. "Not ignorant of suffering, I have learned how to help the unfortunate," she said.

She gave a splendid banquet for the strangers that night at which Aeneas told their story, the fall of Troy first and then their long journeying. He spoke admirably and eloquently, and perhaps Dido would have succumbed to such heroism and such beautiful language even if there had been no god in the case, but as it was, Cupid was there and she had no choice.

For a time she was happy. Aeneas seemed devoted to her, and she for her part lavished everything she had on him. She gave him to understand that her city was his as well as she herself. He, a poor shipwrecked man, had equal honor with her. She made the Carthaginians treat him as if he too were their ruler. His companions as well were distinguished by her favor. She could not do enough for them. In all this she wanted only to give; she asked nothing for herself except Aeneas' love. On his side he received what her generosity bestowed with great contentment. He lived at his ease with a beautiful woman and a powerful Queen to love him and provide everything for him and arrange hunting parties for his amusement and not only permit him, but beg him, to tell over and over again the tale of his adventures.

It is small wonder that the idea of setting sail for an unknown land grew less and less attractive to him. Juno was very well satisfied with the way things were going, but even so Venus was quite undisturbed. She understood Jupiter better than his wife did. She was sure that he would make Aeneas in the end go to Italy and that this little interlude with Dido would not be in the least to her son's discredit. She was quite right. Jupiter was very effective when he once roused himself. He dispatched Mercury to Carthage with a stinging message for Aeneas. The god found the hero walking about dressed to admiration, with a superb sword at his side studded with jasper and over his shoulders a beautiful cloak of purple inwrought with thread of gold, both Dido's presents, of course, the latter, indeed, the work of her own hands. Suddenly this elegant gentleman was startled out of his state of indolent contentment. Stern words sounded in his ear. "How long are you going to waste time here in idle luxury?" a severe voice asked. He turned and Mercury, visibly the god, stood before him. "The ruler of heaven himself has sent me to you," he said. "He bids you depart and seek the kingdom which is your destiny." With that he vanished as a wreath of mist dissolves into the air, leaving Aeneas awed and excited, indeed, and determined to obey, but chiefly wretchedly conscious how very difficult it was going to be with Dido.

He called his men together and ordered them to fit out a fleet and prepare for immediate departure, but to do all secretly. Nevertheless Dido learned and she sent for him. She was very gentle with him at first. She could not believe that he really meant to leave her. "Is it from me you would fly?" she asked. "Let these tears plead for me, this hand I gave to you. If I have in any way deserved well of you, if anything of mine was ever sweet to you—"

He answered that he was not the man to deny that she had done well by him and that he would never forget her. But she on her side must remember that he had not married her and was free to leave her whenever he chose. Jupiter had ordered him to go and he must obey. "Cease these complaints," he begged her, "which only trouble us both."

Then she told him what she thought. How he had come to her cast away, starving, in need of everything, and how she had given herself and her kingdom to him. But before his complete impassivity her passion was helpless. In the midst of her burning words her voice broke. She fled from him and hid herself where no one could see her.

The Trojans sailed that same night, very wisely. One word from the Queen and their departure would have been forever impossible. On shipboard looking back at the walls of Carthage Aeneas saw them illumined by a great fire. He watched the flames leap up and slowly die down and he wondered what was the cause. All unknowing he was looking at the glow of Dido's funeral pyre. When she saw that he was gone she killed herself.

Part Two: THE DESCENT INTO THE LOWER WORLD

The journey from Carthage to the west coast of Italy was easy as compared with what had gone before. A great loss, however, was the death of the trusty pilot Palinurus who was drowned as they neared the end of their perils by sea.

Aeneas had been told by the prophet Helenus as soon as he reached the Italian land to seek the cave of the Sibyl of Cumae, a woman of deep wisdom, who could foretell the future and would advise him what to do. He found her and she told him she would guide him to the underworld where he would learn all he needed to know from his father Anchises, who had died just before the great storm. She warned him, however, that it was no light undertaking:—

Trojan, Anchises' son, the descent of Avernus is easy.
All night long, all day, the doors of dark Hades stand open.
But to retrace the path, to come up to the sweet air of heaven,
That is labor indeed.

Nevertheless, if he was determined she would go with him. First he must find in the forest a golden bough growing on a tree, which he must break off and take with him. Only with this in his hand would he be admitted to Hades. He started at once to look for it, accompanied by the ever-faithful Achates.

They went almost hopelessly into the great wilderness of trees where it seemed impossible to find anything. But suddenly they caught sight of two doves, the birds of Venus. The men followed as they flew slowly on until they were close to Lake Avernus, a dark foul-smelling sheet of water where the Sibyl had told Aeneas was the cavern from which the road led down to the underworld. Here the doves soared up to a tree through whose foliage came a bright yellow gleam. It was the golden bough. Aeneas plucked it joyfully and took it to the Sibyl. Then, together, prophetess and hero started on their journey.

Other heroes had taken it before Aeneas and not found it especially terrifying. The crowding ghosts had, to be sure, finally frightened Ulysses, but Theseus, Hercules, Orpheus, Pollux, had apparently encountered no great difficulty on the way. Indeed, the timid Psyche had gone there all alone to get the beauty charm for Venus from Proserpine and had seen nothing worse than the three-headed dog Cerberus, who had been easily mollified by a bit of cake. But the Roman hero found horrors piled upon horrors. The way the Sibyl thought it necessary to start was calculated to frighten any but the boldest. At dead of night in front of the dark cavern on the bank of the somber lake she slaughtered four coal-black bullocks to Hecate, the dread Goddess of Night. As she placed the sacrificial parts upon a blazing altar, the earth rumbled and quaked beneath their feet and from afar dogs howled through the darkness. With a cry to Aeneas, "Now will you need all your courage," she rushed into the cave, and undaunted he followed her. They found themselves soon on a road wrapped in shadows which yet permitted them to see frightful forms on either side, pale Disease and avenging Care, and Hunger that persuades to crime, and so on, a great company of terrors. Death-dealing War was there and mad Discord with snaky, bloodstained hair, and many another curse to mortals. They passed unmolested through them and finally reached a place where an old man was rowing a boat over a stretch of water. There they saw a pitiful sight, spirits on the shore innumerable as the leaves which fall in the forest at the first cold of winter, all stretching out their hands and praying the ferryman to carry them across to the farther bank. But the gloomy old man made his own choice among them; some he admitted to his skiff, others he pushed away. As Aeneas stared in wonder the Sibyl told him they had reached the junction of two great rivers of the underworld, the Cocytus, named of lamentation loud, and the Acheron. The ferryman was Charon and those he would not admit to his boat were the unfortunates who had not been duly buried. They were doomed to wander aimlessly for a hundred years, with never a place to rest in.

Charon was inclined to refuse Aeneas and his guide when they came down to the boat. He bade them halt and told them he did not ferry the living, only the dead. At sight of the golden bough, however, he yielded and took them across. The dog Cerberus was there on the other bank to dispute the way, but they followed Psyche's example. The Sibyl, too, had some cake for him and he gave them no trouble. As they went on they came to the solemn place in which Minos, Europa's son, the inflexible judge of the dead, was passing the final sentence on the souls before him. They hastened away from that inexorable presence and found themselves in the Fields of Mourning, where the unhappy lovers dwelt who had been driven by their misery to kill themselves. In that sorrowful but lovely spot, shaded with groves of myrtle, Aeneas caught sight of Dido. He wept as he greeted her. "Was I the cause of your death?" he asked her. "I swear I left you against my will." She neither looked at him nor answered him. A piece of marble could not have seemed less moved. He himself, however, was a good deal shaken, and he continued to shed tears for some time after he lost sight of her.

At last they reached a spot where the road divided. From the left branch came horrid sounds, groans and savage blows and the clanking of chains. Aeneas halted in terror. The Sibyl, however, bade him have no fear, but fasten boldly the golden bough on the wall that faced the crossroads. The regions to the left, she said, were ruled over by stern Rhadamanthus, also a son of Europa, who punished the wicked for their misdeeds. But the road to the right led to the Elysian Fields where Aeneas would find his father. There when they arrived everything was delightful, soft green meadows, lovely groves, a delicious life-giving air, sunlight that glowed softly purple, an abode of peace and blessedness. Here dwelt the great and good dead, heroes, poets, priests, and all who had made men remember them by helping others. Among them Aeneas soon came upon Anchises, who greeted him with incredulous joy. Father and son alike shed happy tears at this strange meeting between the dead and the living whose love had been strong enough to bring him down to the world of death.

They had much, of course, to say to each other. Anchises led Aeneas to Lethe, the river of forgetfulness, of which the souls on their way to live again in the world above must all drink. "A draught of long oblivion," Anchises said. And he showed his son those who were to be their descendants, his own and Aeneas', now waiting by the river for their time to drink and lose the memory of what in former lives they had done and suffered. A magnificent company they were—the future Romans, the masters of the world. One by one Anchises pointed

Aeneas and the Sibyl enter Charon's boat

them out, and told of the deeds they would do which men would never through all time forget. Finally, he gave his son instructions how he would best establish his home in Italy and how he could avoid or endure all the hardships that lay before him.

Then they took leave of each other, but calmly, knowing that they were parting only for a time. Aeneas and the Sibyl made their way back to the earth and Aeneas returned to his ships. Next day the Trojans sailed up the coast of Italy looking for their promised home.

Part Three: THE WAR IN ITALY

Terrible trials awaited the little band of adventurers. Juno was again the cause of the trouble. She made the most powerful peoples of the country, the Latins and the Rutulians, fiercely opposed to the Trojans settling there. If it had not been for her, matters would have gone well. The aged Latinus, a great-grandson of Saturn and King of the City of Latium, had been warned by the spirit of his father, Faunus, not to marry his daughter Lavinia, his only child, to any man of the country, but to a stranger who was soon to arrive. From that union would be born a race destined to hold the entire world under their sway. Therefore, when an embassy arrived from Aeneas asking for a narrow resting place upon the coast and the common liberty of air and water, Latinus received them with great good will. He felt convinced that Aeneas was the son-in-law Faunus had predicted, and he said as much to the envoys. They would never lack a friend while he lived, he told them. To Aeneas he sent this message, that he had a daughter forbidden by heaven to wed with any except a foreigner, and that he believed the Trojan chief was this man of destiny.

But here Juno stepped in. She summoned Alecto, one of the Furies, from Hades and bade her loose bitter war over the land. She obeyed gladly. First she inflamed the heart of Queen Amata, wife of Latinus, to oppose violently a marriage between her daughter and Aeneas. Then she flew to the King of the Rutulians, Turnus, who up to now had been the most favored among the many suitors for Lavinia's hand. Her visit to arouse him against the Trojans was hardly necessary. The idea of anyone except himself marrying Lavinia was enough to drive Turnus to frenzy. As soon as he heard of the Trojan embassy to the King he started with his army to march to Latium and prevent by force any treaty between the Latins and the strangers.

Alecto's third effort was cleverly devised. There was a pet stag belonging to a Latin farmer, a beautiful creature, so tame that it would run free by day, but at nightfall always come to the well-known door. The farmer's daughter tended it with loving care; she would comb its coat and wreathe its horns with garlands. All the farmers far and near knew it and protected it. Anyone, even of their own number, who had harmed it would have been severely punished. But for a foreigner to dare such a deed was to enrage the whole countryside. And that is what Aeneas' young son did under the guiding hand of Alecto. Ascanius was out hunting and he and his hounds were directed by the Fury to where the stag was lying in the forest. He shot at it and wounded it mortally, but it succeeded in reaching its home and its mistress before it died. Alecto took care that the news should spread quickly, and fighting started at once, the furious farmers bent upon killing Ascanius and the Trojans defending him.

This news reached Latium just after Turnus had arrived. The fact that his people were already in arms and the still more ominous fact that the Rutulian Army had encamped before his gates were too much for King Latinus. His furious Queen, too, undoubtedly played a part in his final decision. He shut himself up in his palace and let matters go as they would. If Lavinia was to be won Aeneas could not count on any help from his future father-in-law.

There was a custom in the city that when war was determined upon, the two folding-gates of the temple of the god Janus, always kept closed in time of peace, should be unbarred by the King while trumpets blared and warriors shouted. But Latinus, locked in his palace, was not available for the sacred rite. As the citizens hesitated as to what to do, Juno herself swept down from heaven, smote with her own hand the bars and flung wide the doors. Joy filled the city, joy in the battle-array, the shining armor and spirited chargers and proud standards, joy at facing a war to the death.

A formidable army, Latins and Rutulians together, were now opposed to the little band of Trojans. Their leader, Turnus, was a brave and skilled warrior; another able ally was Mezentius, an excellent soldier, but so cruel that his subjects, the great Etruscan people, had rebelled against him and he had fled to Turnus. A third ally was a woman, the maiden Camilla, who had been reared by her father in a remote wilderness, and as a baby, with a sling or a bow in her tiny hand, had learned to bring down the swift-flying crane or the wild swan, herself hardly less swift of foot than they of wing. She was mistress of all the ways of warfare, unexcelled with the javelin and the two-edged ax as well as with the bow. Marriage she disdained. She loved the chase and the battle and her freedom. A band of warriors followed her, among them a number of maidens.

In this perilous situation for the Trojans, Father Tiber, the god of the great river they were encamped near, visited Aeneas in a dream. He bade him go swiftly upstream to where Evander dwelt, a King of a poor little town which was destined to become in future ages the proudest of earth's cities, whence the towers of Rome should soar up to the skies. Here, the river-god promised, Aeneas would get the help he needed. At dawn he started with a chosen few and for the first time a boat filled with armed men floated on the Tiber. When they reached Evander's home a warm welcome was given them by the King and his young son, Pallas. As they led their guests to the rude building which served as palace they pointed out the sights: the great Tarpeian rock; near it a hill sacred to Jove, now rough with brambles, where some day the golden, glittering Capitol would rise; a meadow filled with lowing cattle, which would be the gathering place of the world, the Roman Forum. "Once fauns and nymphs lived here," the King said, "and a savage race of men. But Saturn came to the country, a homeless exile fleeing from his son Jupiter. Everything then was changed. Men forsook their rude and lawless ways. He ruled with such justice and in such peace that ever since his reign has been called 'the Golden Age.' But in later times other customs prevailed; peace and justice fled before the greed for gold and the frenzy for war. Tyrants ruled the land until fate brought me here, an exile from Greece, from my dear home in Arcady."

As the old man ended his story they reached the simple hut where he lived and there Aeneas spent the night on a couch of leaves with a bear's skin to cover him. Next morning, awakened by the dawn and the call of birds, they all arose. The King went forth with two great dogs following him, his sole retinue and bodyguard. After they had broken their fast he gave Aeneas the advice he had come to seek. Arcady—he had called his new country after his old—was a feeble state, he said, and could do little to help the Trojans. But on the farther bank of the river lived the rich and powerful Etruscans, whose fugitive king, Mezentius, was helping Turnus. This fact alone would make the nation choose Aeneas' side in the war, so intense was the hatred felt for their former ruler. He had shown himself a monster of cruelty; he delighted in inflicting suffering. He had devised a way of killing people more horrible than any other known to man: he would link dead and living together, coupling hand with hand and face with face, and leave the slow poison of that sickening embrace to bring about a lingering death.

All Etruria had finally risen against him, but he had succeeded in escaping. They were determined, however, to get him back and punish him as he deserved. Aeneas would find them willing and powerful allies. For himself, the old king said, he would send Pallas who was his only son, to enter the service of the War-god under the Trojan hero's guidance, and with him a band of youths, the flower of the Arcadian chivalry. Also he gave each of his guests a gallant steed, to enable them to reach quickly the Etruscan Army and enlist their help.

Meantime the Trojan camp, fortified only by earthworks and deprived of its leader and its best warriors, was hard-pressed. Turnus attacked it in force. Throughout the first day the Trojans defended themselves successfully, following the strict orders which Aeneas at his departure had given them on no account to undertake an offensive. But they were greatly outnumbered; the prospect was dark unless they could get word to Aeneas what was happening. The question was whether this was possible, with the Rutulians completely surrounding the fort. However, there were two men in that little band who scorned to weigh the chances of success or failure, to whom the extreme peril of the attempt was a reason for making it. These two resolved to try to pass through the enemy under the cover of the night and reach Aeneas.

Nisus and Euryalus were their names, the first a valiant and experienced soldier, the other only a stripling, but equally brave and full of generous ardor for heroic deeds. It was their habit to fight side by side. Wherever one was, whether on guard or in the field, there the other would always be found. The idea of the great enterprise came first to Nisus as he looked over the ramparts at the enemy and observed how few and dim the lights were and how deep a silence reigned as of men fast asleep. He told his plan to his friend, but with no thought of his going too. When the lad cried out that he would never be left behind, that he scorned life in comparison with death in so glorious an attempt, Nisus felt only grief and dismay. "Let me go alone," he begged. "If by chance something goes amiss— and in such a venture as this there are a thousand chances— you will be here to ransom me or to give me the rites of burial. Remember too that you are young; life is all before you." "Idle words," Euryalus answered. "Let us start and with no delay." Nisus saw the impossibility of persuading him and sorrowfully yielded.

They found the Trojan leaders holding a council, and they put their plan before them. It was instantly accepted and the princes with choked voices and falling tears thanked them and promised them rich rewards. "I want only one," said Euryalus. "My mother is here in the camp. She would not stay behind with the other women. She would follow me. I am all she has. If I die—" "She will be my mother," Ascanius broke in. "She shall have the place of the mother I lost that last night in Troy.

I swear it to you. And take this with you, my own sword. It will not fail you."

Then the two started, through the trench and on to the enemy's camp. All around lay sleeping men. Nisus whispered, "I am going to clear a path for us. Do you keep watch." With that he killed man after man, so skillfully that not one uttered a sound as he died. Not a groan gave the alarm. Euryalus soon joined in the bloody work. When they reached the end of the camp they had cleared as it were a great highway through it, where only dead men were lying. But they had been wrong to delay. Daylight was dawning; a troop of horses coming from Latium caught sight of the shining helmet of Euryalus and challenged him. When he pushed on through the trees without answering they knew he was an enemy and they surrounded the wood. In their haste the two friends got separated and Euryalus took the wrong path. Nisus wild with anxiety turned back to find him. Unseen himself he saw him in the hands of the troopers. How could he rescue him? He was all alone. It was hopeless and yet he knew it was better to make the attempt and die than leave him. He fought them, one man against a whole company, and his flying spear struck down warrior after warrior. The leader, not knowing from what quarter this deadly attack was coming, turned upon Euryalus shouting, "You shall pay for this!" Before his lifted sword could strike him, Nisus rushed forward. "Kill me, me," he cried. "The deed is all mine. He only followed me." But with the words still on his lips, the sword was thrust into the lad's breast. As he fell dying, Nisus cut down the man who had killed him; then pierced with many darts he too fell dead beside his friend.

The rest of the Trojans' adventures were all on the battlefield. Aeneas came back with a large army of Etruscans in time to save the camp, and furious war raged. From then on, the story turns into little more than an account of men slaughtering each other. Battle follows battle, but they are all alike. Countless heroes are always slain, rivers of blood drench the earth, the brazen throats of trumpets blare, arrows plenteous as hail fly from sharp-springing bows, hoofs of fiery steeds spurting gory dew trample on the dead. Long before the end, the horrors have ceased to horrify. All the Trojans' enemies are killed, of course. Camilla falls after giving a very good account of herself; the wicked Mezentius meets the fate he so richly deserves, but only after his brave young son is killed defending him. Many good allies die, too, Evander's son Pallas among them.

Finally Turnus and Aeneas meet in single combat. By this time Aeneas, who in the earlier part of the story seemed as human as Hector or Achilles, has changed into something strange and portentous; he is not a human being. Once he carried tenderly his old father out of burning Troy and encouraged his little son to run beside him; when he came to Carthage he felt what it meant to meet with compassion, to reach a place where "There are tears for things"; he was very human too when he strutted about Dido's palace in his fine clothes. But on the Latin battlefields he is not a man, but a fearful prodigy. He is "vast as Mount Athos, vast as Father Apennine himself when he shakes his mighty oaks and lifts his snow-topped peak to the sky"; like "Aegaeon who had a hundred arms and a hundred hands and flashed fire through fifty mouths, thundering on fifty strong shields and drawing fifty sharp swords—even so Aeneas slakes his victorious fury the whole field over." When he faces Turnus in the last combat there is no interest in the outcome. It is as futile for Turnus to fight Aeneas as to fight the lightning or an earthquake.

Virgil's poem ends with Turnus' death. Aeneas, we are given to understand, married Lavinia and founded the Roman race —who, Virgil said, "left to other nations such things as art and science, and ever remembered that they were destined to bring under their empire the peoples of earth, to impose the rule of submissive nonresistance, to spare the humbled and to crush the proud."

PART FIVE

The Great Families of Mythology

17 The House of Atreus

The chief importance of the story of Atreus and his descendants is that the fifth-century tragic poet Aeschylus took it for the subject of his greatest drama, the Oresteia, *which is made up of three plays, the* Agamemnon, *the* Libation Bearers, *the* Eumenides. *It has no rival in Greek tragedy except the four plays of Sophocles about Oedipus and his children. Pindar in the early fifth century tells the current tale about the feast Tantalus made the gods and protests that it is not true. The punishment of Tantalus is described often, first in the* Odyssey, *from which I have taken it. Amphion's story, and Niobe's, I have taken from Ovid, who alone tells them in full. For Pelops' winning the chariot race I have preferred Apollodorus, of the first or second century A.D., who gives the fullest account that has come down to us. The story of Atreus' and Thyestes' crimes and all that followed them is taken from Aeschylus'* Oresteia.

The House of Atreus is one of the most famous families in mythology. Agamemnon, who led the Greeks against Troy, belonged to it. All of his immediate family, his wife Clytemnestra, his children, Iphigenia, Orestes and Electra, were as well known as he was. His brother Menelaus was the husband of Helen, for whose sake the Trojan War was fought.

It was an ill-fated house. The cause of all the misfortunes was held to be an ancestor, a King of Lydia named Tantalus, who brought upon himself a most terrible punishment by a most wicked deed. That was not the end of the matter. The evil he started went on after his death. His descendants also did wickedly and were punished. A curse seemed to hang over the family, making men sin in spite of themselves and bringing suffering and death down upon the innocent as well as the guilty.

TANTALUS AND NIOBE

Tantalus was the son of Zeus and honored by the gods beyond all the mortal children of Zeus. They allowed him to eat at their table, to taste the nectar and ambrosia which except for him alone none but the immortals could partake of. They did more; they came to a banquet in his palace; they condescended to dine with him. In return for their favor he acted so atrociously that no poet ever tried to explain his conduct. He had his only son Pelops killed, boiled in a great cauldron, and served to the gods. Apparently he was driven by a passion of hatred against them which made him willing to sacrifice his son in order to bring upon them the horror of being cannibals. It may be, too, that he wanted to show in the most startling and shocking way possible how easy it was to deceive the awful, venerated, humbly adored divinities. In his scorn of the gods and his measureless self-confidence he never dreamed that his guests would realize what manner of food he had set before them.

He was a fool. The Olympians knew. They drew back from the horrible banquet and they turned upon the criminal who had contrived it. He should be so punished, they declared, that no man to come, hearing what this man had suffered, would dare ever again to insult them. They set the arch-sinner in a pool in Hades, but whenever in his tormenting thirst he stooped to drink he could not reach the water. It disappeared, drained into the ground as he bent down. When he stood up it was there again. Over the pool fruit trees hung heavy laden with pears, pomegranates, rosy apples, sweet figs. Each time he stretched out his hand to grasp them the wind tossed them high away out of reach. Thus he stood forever, his undying throat always athirst, his hunger in the midst of plenty never satisfied.

His son Pelops was restored to life by the gods, but they had to fashion a shoulder for him out of ivory. One of the goddesses, some say Demeter, some Thetis, inadvertently had eaten of the loathsome dish and when the boy's limbs were reassembled one shoulder was wanting. This ugly story seems to have come down in its early brutal form quite unsoftened. The latter Greeks did not like it and protested against it. The poet Pindar called it

A tale decked out with glittering lies against the word of truth. Let a man not speak of cannibal deeds among the blessed gods.

However that might be, the rest of Pelops' life was successful. He was the only one of Tantalus' descendants not marked out by misfortune. He was happy in his marriage, although he wooed a dangerous lady who had been the cause of many deaths, the Princess Hippodamia. The reason men died for her was not her own fault, but her father's. This King had a wonderful pair of horses Ares had given him—superior, of course, to all mortal horses. He did not want his daughter to marry, and whenever a suitor came for her hand the youth was told he could race with her father for her. If the suitor's horses won, she would be his; if her father's won, the suitor must pay with his life for his defeat. In this way a number of rash young men met their death. Even so, Pelops dared. He had horses he could trust, a present from Poseidon. He won the race; but there is a story that Hippodamia had more to do with the victory than Poseidon's horses. Either she fell in love with Pelops or she felt the time had come to put a stop to that sort of racing. She bribed her father's charioteer, a man named Myrtilus, to help her. He pulled out the bolts that held the wheels of the King's chariot, and the victory was Pelops' with no trouble at all. Later, Myrtilus was killed by Pelops, cursing him as he died, and some said that this was the cause of the misfortunes that afterward followed the family. But most writers said, and certainly with better reason, that it was the wickedness of Tantalus which doomed his descendants.

None of them suffered a worse doom than his daughter Niobe. And yet it seemed at first that the gods had chosen her out for good fortune as they had her brother Pelops. She was happy in her marriage. Her husband was Amphion, a son of Zeus and an incomparable musician. He and his twin brother Zethus undertook once to fortify Thebes, building a lofty wall around it. Zethus was a man of great physical strength who despised his brother's neglect of manly sports and his devotion to his art. Yet when it came to the heavy task of getting enough rocks for the wall, the gentle musician outdid the strong athlete: he drew such entrancing sounds from his lyre that the very stones were moved and followed him to Thebes.

There he and Niobe ruled in entire content until she showed that the mad arrogance of Tantalus lived on in her. She held herself raised by her great prosperity above all that ordinary mortals fear and reverence. She was rich and nobly born and powerful. Seven sons had been born to her, brave and beautiful young men, and seven daughters, the fairest of the fair. She thought herself strong enough not only to deceive the gods as her father had tried to do, but to defy them openly.

She called upon the people of Thebes to worship her. "You burn incense to Leto," she said, "and what is she as compared with me? She had but two children, Apollo and Artemis. I have seven times as many. I am a queen. She was a homeless wanderer until tiny Delos alone of all places on earth consented to receive her. I am happy, strong, great—too great for any, men or gods, to do me harm. Make your sacrifices to me in Leto's temple, mine now, not hers."

Insolent words uttered in the arrogant consciousness of power were always heard in heaven and always punished. Apollo and Artemis glided swiftly to Thebes from Olympus, the archer god and the divine huntress, and shooting with deadly aim they struck down all of Niobe's sons and daughters. She saw them die with anguish too great for expression. Beside those bodies so lately young and strong, she sank down motionless in stony grief, dumb as a stone and her heart like a stone within her. Only her tears flowed and could not stop. She was changed into a stone which forever, night and day, was wet with tears.

To Pelops two sons were born, Atreus and Thyestes. The inheritance of evil descended to them in full force. Thyestes fell in love with his brother's wife and succeeded in making her false to her marriage vows. Atreus found out and swore that Thyestes should pay as no man ever had. He killed his brother's two little children, had them cut limb from limb, boiled, and served up to their father. When he had eaten—

> Poor wretch, when he had learned the deed abhorrent,
> He cried a great cry, falling back—spewed out
> That flesh, called down upon that house a doom
> Intolerable, the banquet board sent crashing.

Atreus was King. Thyestes had no power. The atrocious crime was not avenged in Atreus' lifetime, but his children and his children's children suffered.

AGAMEMNON AND HIS CHILDREN

On Olympus the gods were met in full assembly. The father of Gods and Men began first to speak. Zeus was sorely vexed at the mean way men perpetually acted toward the gods, blaming the divine powers for what their own wickedness brought about, and that too even when the Olympians had tried to hold them back. "You all know about Aegisthus, whom Agamemnon's son Orestes has slain," Zeus said, "how he loved the wife of Agamemnon and killed him on his return from Troy. Certainly no blame attaches to us from that. We warned him by the mouth of Hermes. 'The death of the son of Atreus will be avenged by Orestes.' Those were Hermes' very words, but not even such friendly advice could restrain Aegisthus, who now pays the final penalty."

This passage in the *Iliad* is the first mention of the House of Atreus. In the *Odyssey* when Odysseus reached the land of the Phaeacians and was telling them about his descent to Hades and the ghosts he encountered, he said that, of them all, the spirit of Agamemnon had most moved him to pity. He had begged him to say how he died and the chief told him that he was killed ingloriously as he sat at table, struck down as one butchers an ox. "It was Aegisthus," he said, "with the aid of my accursed wife. He invited me to his house and as I feasted he killed me. My men too. You have seen many die in single combat or in battle, but never one who died as we did, by the wine bowl and the loaded tables in a hall where the floor flowed with blood. Cassandra's death-shriek rang in my ears as she fell. Clytemnestra slew her over my body. I tried to lift up my hands for her, but they fell back. I was dying then."

That was the way the story was first told: Agamemnon had been killed by his wife's lover. It was a sordid tale. How long it held the stage we do not know, but the next account we have, centuries later, written by Aeschylus about 450 B.C., is very different. It is a great story now of implacable vengeance and tragic passions and inevitable doom. The motive for Agamemnon's death is no longer the guilty love of a man and a woman, but a mother's love for a daughter killed by her own father, and a wife's determination to avenge that death by killing her husband. Aegisthus fades; he is hardly in the picture. The wife of Agamemnon, Clytemnestra, has all the foreground to herself.

The two sons of Atreus, Agamemnon, the commander of the Greek forces at Troy, and Menelaus, the husband of Helen, ended their lives very differently. Menelaus, at first the less successful, was notably prosperous in his later years. He lost his wife for a time, but after the fall of Troy he got her back. His ship was driven all the way to Egypt by the storm Athena sent to the Greek Fleet, but finally he reached home safely and lived happily with Helen ever after. It was far otherwise with his brother.

When Troy fell, Agamemnon was the most fortunate of the victorious chieftains. His ship came safely through the storm which wrecked or drove to distant countries so many others. He entered his city not only safe after peril by land and sea, but triumphant, the proud conqueror of Troy. His home was expecting him. Word had been sent that he had landed, and the townspeople joined in a great welcome to him. It seemed that he was of all men the most gloriously successful, after a brilliant victory back with his own again, peace and prosperity before him.

But in the crowd that greeted him with thanksgiving for his return there were anxious faces, and words of dark foreboding passed from one man to another. "He will find evil happenings," they muttered. "Things once were right there in the palace, but no more. That house could tell a tale if it could speak."

Before the palace the elders of the city were gathered to ao their king honor, but they too were in distress, with a still heavier anxiety, a darker foreboding, than that which weighed upon the doubtful crowd. As they waited they talked in low tones of the past. They were old and it was almost more real to them than the present. They recalled the sacrifice of Iphigenia, lovely, innocent young thing, trusting her father utterly, and then confronted with the altar, the cruel knives, and only pitiless faces around her. As the old men spoke, it was like a vivid memory to them, as if they themselves had been there, as if they had heard with her the father she loved telling men to lift her and hold her over the altar to slay her. He had killed her, not willingly, but driven by the Army impatient for good winds to sail to Troy. And yet the matter was not as simple as that. He yielded to the Army because the old wickedness in generation after generation of his race was bound to work out in evil for him too. The elders knew the curse that hung over the house.

> . . . The thirst for blood—
> It is in their flesh. Before the old wound
> Can be healed, there is fresh blood flowing.

Ten years had passed since Iphigenia died, but the results of her death reached through to the present. The elders were wise. They had learned that every sin causes fresh sin; every wrong brings another in its train. A menace from the dead girl hung over her father in this hour of triumph. And yet perhaps, they said to each other, perhaps it would not take actual shape for a time. So they tried to find some bit of hope, but at the bottom of their hearts they knew and dared not say aloud that vengeance was already there in the palace waiting for Agamemnon.

It had waited ever since the Queen, Clytemnestra, had come back from Aulis, where she had seen her daughter die. She did not keep faith with her husband who had killed her child and his; she took a lover and all the people knew it. They knew too that she had not sent him away when the news of Agamemnon's return reached her. He was still there with her. What was being planned behind the palace doors? As they wondered and feared, a tumult of noise reached them, chariots rolling, voices shouting. Into the courtyard swept the royal car with the King and beside him a girl, very beautiful, but very strange-looking. Attendants and townspeople were following them and as they came to a halt the doors of the great house swung open and the Queen appeared.

The King dismounted, praying aloud, "O Victory now mine, be mine forever." His wife advanced to meet him. Her face was radiant, her head high. She knew that every man there except Agamemnon was aware of her infidelity, but she faced them all and told them with smiling lips that even in their presence she must at such a moment speak out the great love she bore her husband and the agonizing grief she had suffered in his absence. Then in words of exultant joy she bade him welcome. "You are our safety," she told him, "our sure defense. The sight of you is dear as land after storm to the sailor, as a gushing stream to a thirsty wayfarer."

He answered her, but with reserve, and he turned to go into the palace. First he pointed to the girl in the chariot. She was Cassandra, Priam's daughter, he told his wife—the Army's gift to him, the flower of all the captive women. Let Clytemnestra see to her and treat her well. With that he entered the house and the doors closed behind the husband and the wife. They would never open again for both of them.

The crowd had gone. Only the old men still waited uneasily before the silent building and the blank doors. The captive princess caught their attention and they looked curiously at her. They had heard of her strange fame as a prophetess whom no one ever believed and yet whose prophecies were always proved true by the event. She turned a terrified face to them. Where had she been brought, she asked them wildly—What house was this? They answered soothingly that it was where the son of Atreus lived. She cried out, "No! It is a house God hates, where men are killed and the floor is red with blood."

The old men stole frightened glances at each other. Blood, men killed, that was what they too were thinking of, the dark past with its promise of more darkness. How could she, a stranger and a foreigner, know that past? "I hear children crying," she wailed,

> . . . Crying for wounds that bleed.
> A father feasted—and the flesh his children.

Thyestes and his sons . . . Where had she heard of that? More wild words poured from her lips. It seemed as if she had seen what had happened in that house through the years, as if she had stood by while death followed death, each a crime and all working together to produce more crime. Then from the past she turned to the future. She cried out that on that very day two more deaths would be added to the list, one her own. "I will endure to die," she said, as she turned away and moved toward the palace. They tried to hold her back from that ominous house, but she would not have it; she entered and the doors closed forever on her, too. The silence that followed when she had gone was suddenly and terribly broken. A cry rang out, the voice of a man in agony: "God! I am struck! My death blow—" and silence again. The old men, terrified, bewildered, huddled together. That was the King's voice. What should they do? "Break into the palace? Quick, be quick," they urged each other. "We must know." But there was no need now of any violence. The doors opened and on the threshold stood the Queen.

Dark red stains were on her dress, her hands, her face, yet she herself looked unshaken, strongly sure of herself. She proclaimed for all to hear what had been done. "Here lies my husband dead, struck down justly by my hand," she said. It was his blood that stained her dress and face and she was glad.

> He fell and as he gasped, his blood
> Spouted and splashed me with dark spray, a dew
> Of death, sweet to me as heaven's sweet raindrops
> When the corn-land buds.

She saw no reason to explain her act or excuse it. She was not a murderer in her own eyes, she was an executioner. She had punished a murderer, the murderer of his own child,

> Who cared no more than if a beast should die
> When flocks are plenty in the fleecy fold,
> But slew his daughter—slew her for a charm
> Against the Thracian winds.

Her lover followed her and stood beside her—Aegisthus, the youngest child of Thyestes, born after that horrible feast. He had no quarrel with Agamemnon himself, but Atreus, who had had the children slaughtered and placed on the banquet table for their father, was dead and vengeance could not reach him. Therefore his son must pay the penalty.

The two, the Queen and her lover, had reason to know that wickedness cannot be ended by wickedness. The dead body of the man they had just killed was a proof. But in their triumph they did not stop to think that this death, too, like all the others, would surely bring evil in its train. "No more blood for you and me," Clytemnestra said to Aegisthus. "We are lords here now. We two will order all things well." It was a baseless hope.

Iphigenia had been one of three children. The other two were a girl and a boy, Electra and Orestes. Aegisthus would certainly have killed the boy if Orestes had been there, but he had been sent away to a trusted friend. The girl Aegisthus disdained to kill; he only made her utterly wretched in every way possible until her whole life was concentrated in one hope, that Orestes would come back and avenge their father. That vengeance—what would it be? Over and over she asked herself this. Aegisthus, of course, must die, but to kill him alone would never satisfy justice. His crime was less black than another's. What then? Could it be justice that a son should take a mother's life to avenge a father's death? So she brooded through the bitter days of the long years that followed, while Clytemnestra and Aegisthus ruled the land.

As the boy grew to manhood he saw even more clearly than she the terrible situation. It was a son's duty to kill his father's murderers, a duty that came before all others. But a son who killed his mother was abhorrent to gods and to men. A most sacred obligation was bound up with a most atrocious crime. He who wanted only to do right was so placed that he must choose between two hideous wrongs. He must be a traitor to his father or he must be the murderer of his mother.

In this agony of doubt he journeyed to Delphi to ask the oracle to help him, and Apollo spoke to him in clear words bidding him,

> Slay the two who slew.
> Atone for death by death.
> Shed blood for old blood shed.

And Orestes knew that he must work out the curse of his house, exact vengeance and pay with his own ruin. He went to the home he had not seen since he was a little boy, and with him went his cousin and friend Pylades. The two had grown up together and were devoted in a way far beyond usual friendship. Electra, with no idea that they were actually arriving, was yet on the watch. Her life was spent in watching for the brother who would bring her the only thing life held for her.

One day at her father's tomb she made an offering to the dead and prayed, "O Father, guide Orestes to his home." Suddenly he was beside her, claiming her as his sister, showing her as proof the cloak he wore, the work of her hands, which she had wrapped him in when he went away. But she did not need a proof. She cried, "Your face is my father's face." And she poured out to him all the love no one had wanted from her through the wretched years:—

> All, all is yours,
> The love I owed my father who is dead,
> The love I might have given to my mother,
> And my poor sister cruelly doomed to die.
> All yours now, only yours.

He was too sunk in his own thought, too intent upon the thing he faced, to answer her or even to listen. He broke in upon her words to tell her what filled his mind so that nothing else could reach it: the terrible words of the oracle of Apollo. Orestes spoke with horror:—

> He told me to appease the angry dead.
> That who hears not when his dead cry to him,
> For such there is no home, no refuge anywhere.
> No altarfire burns for him, no friend greets him.
> He dies alone and vile. O God, shall I believe
> Such oracles? But yet—but yet
> The deed is to be done and I must do it.

The three made their plans. Orestes and Pylades were to go to the palace claiming to be the bearers of a message that Orestes had died. It would be joyful news to Clytemnestra and Aegisthus who had always feared what he might do, and they would certainly want to see the messengers. Once in the palace the brother and his friend could trust to their own swords and the complete surprise of their attack.

They were admitted and Electra waited. That had been her bitter part all through her life. Then the doors opened slowly and a woman came out and stood tranquilly on the steps. It was Clytemnestra. She had been there only a moment or so when a slave rushed out screaming, "Treason! Our master! Treason!" He saw Clytemnestra and gasped, "Orestes—alive—here." She knew then. Everything was clear to her, what had happened and what was still to come. Sternly she bade the slave bring her a battle-ax. She was resolved to fight for her life, but the weapon was no sooner in her hand than she changed her mind. A man came through the doors, his sword red with blood, whose blood she knew as she knew too who held the sword. Instantly she saw a surer way to defend herself than with an ax. She was the mother of the man before her. "Stop, my son," she said. "Look—my breast. Your heavy head dropped on it and you slept, oh, many a time. Your baby mouth, where never a tooth was, sucked the milk, and so you grew—" Orestes cried, "O Pylades, she is my mother. May I spare—" His friend told him solemnly: No. Apollo had commanded. The gods must be obeyed. "I will obey," Orestes said. "You—follow me." Clytemnestra knew that she had lost. She said calmly, "It seems, my son, that you will kill your mother." He motioned her into the house. She went and he followed her.

When he came out again those waiting in the courtyard did not need to be told what he had done. Asking no question they watched him, their master now, with compassion. He seemed not to see them; he was looking at a horror beyond them. Stammering words came from his lips: "The man is dead. I am not guilty there. An adulterer. He had to die. But she—Did she do it or did she not? O you, my friends. I say I killed my mother—yet not without reason—she was vile and she killed my father and God hated her."

His eyes were fixed always on that unseen horror. He screamed, "Look! Look! Women there. Black, all black, and long hair like snakes." They told him eagerly there were no women. "It is only your fancy. Oh, do not fear." "You do not see them?" he cried. "No fancy. I—I see them. My mother has sent them. They crowd around me and their eyes drip blood. Oh, let me go." He rushed away, alone except for those invisible companions.

When next he came to his country, years had passed. He had been a wanderer in many lands, always pursued by the same terrible shapes. He was worn with suffering, but in his loss of everything men prize there was a gain too. "I have been taught by misery," he said. He had learned that no crime was beyond atonement, that even he, defiled by a mother's murder, could be made clean again. He traveled to Athens, sent there by Apollo to plead his case before Athena. He had come to beg for help; nevertheless, in his heart there was confidence. Those who desire to be purified cannot be refused and the black stain of his guilt had grown fainter and fainter through his years of lonely wandering and pain. He believed that by now it had faded away. "I can speak to Athena with pure lips," he said.

Clytemnestra and Orestes

The goddess listened to his plea. Apollo was beside him. "It is I who am answerable for what he did," he said. "He killed at my command." The dread forms of his pursuers, the Erinyes, the Furies, were arrayed against him, but Orestes listened calmly to their demand for vengeance. "I, not Apollo, was guilty of my mother's murder," he said, "but I have been cleansed of my guilt." These were words never spoken before by any of the House of Atreus. The killers of that race had never suffered from their guilt and sought to be made clean. Athena accepted the plea. She persuaded the avenging goddesses also to accept it, and with this new law of mercy established they themselves were changed. From the Furies of frightful aspect they became the Benignant Ones, the Eumenides, protectors of the suppliant. They acquitted Orestes, and with the words of acquittal the spirit of evil which had haunted his house for so long was banished. Orestes went forth from Athena's tribunal a free man. Neither he nor any descendant of his would ever again be driven into evil by the irresistible power of the past. The curse of the House of Atreus was ended.

IPHIGENIA AMONG THE TAURIANS

I have taken this story entirely from two plays of Euripides, the fifth-century tragic poet. No other writer tells the story in full. The happy end brought about by a divinity, the deus ex machina, *is a common device with Euripides alone of the three tragic poets. According to our ideas it is a weakness; and certainly it is unnecessary in this case, where the same end could have been secured by merely omitting the head-wind. Athena's appearance, in point of fact, harms a good plot. A possible reason for this lapse on the part of one of the greatest poets the world has known is that the Athenians, who were suffering greatly at the time from the war with Sparta, were eager for miracles and that Euripides chose to humor them.*

The Greeks, as has been said, did not like stories in which human beings were offered up, whether to appease angry gods or to make Mother Earth bear a good harvest or to bring about anything whatsoever. They thought about such sacrifices as we do. They were abominable. Any deity who demanded them was thereby proved to be evil, and, as the poet Euripides said, "If gods do evil then they are not gods." It was inevitable therefore that another story should grow up about the sacrifice of Iphigenia at Aulis. According to the old account, she was killed because one of the wild animals Artemis loved had been slain by the Greeks and the guilty hunters could win back the goddess's favor only by the death of a young girl. But to the later Greeks this was to slander Artemis. Never would such a demand have been made by the lovely lady of the woodland and the forest, who was especially the protector of little helpless creatures.

> So gentle is she, Artemis the holy,
> To dewy youth, to tender nurslings,
> The young of all that roam the meadow,
> Of all who live within the forest.

So another ending was given to the story. When the Greek soldiers at Aulis came to get Iphigenia where she was waiting for the summons to death, her mother beside her, she forbade Clytemnestra to go with her to the altar. "It is better so for me as well as for you," she said. The mother was left alone. At last she saw a man approaching. He was running and she wondered why anyone should hasten to bring her the tidings he must bear. But he cried out to her, "Wonderful news!" Her daughter had not been sacrificed, he said. That was certain, but exactly what had happened to her no one knew. As the priest was about to strike her, anguish troubled every man there and all bowed their heads. But a cry came from the priest and they looked up to see a marvel hardly to be believed. The girl had vanished, but on the ground beside the altar lay a deer, its throat cut. "This is Artemis' doing," the priest proclaimed. "She will not have her altar stained with human blood. She has herself furnished the victim and she receives the sacrifice." "I tell you, O Queen," the messenger said, "I was there and the thing happened thus. Clearly your child has been borne away to the gods."

But Iphigenia had not been carried to heaven. Artemis had taken her to the land of the Taurians (today the Crimea) on the shore of the Unfriendly Sea—a fierce people whose savage custom it was to sacrifice to the goddess any Greek found in the country. Artemis took care that Iphigenia should be safe; she made her priestess of her temple. But as such it was her terrible task to conduct the sacrifices, not actually herself kill her countrymen, but consecrate them by long-established rites and deliver them over to those who would kill them.

She had been serving the goddess thus for many years when a Greek galley put in at the inhospitable shore, not under stern necessity, storm-driven, but voluntarily. And yet it was known everywhere what the Taurians did to the Greeks they captured. An overwhelmingly strong motive made the ship anchor there. From it in the early dawn two young men came and stealthily found their way to the temple. Both were clearly of exalted birth; they looked like the sons of kings, but the face of one was deeply marked with lines of pain. It was he who whispered to his friend, "Don't you think this is the temple, Pylades?" "Yes, Orestes," the other answered. "It must be that bloodstained spot."

Orestes here and his faithful friend? What were they doing in a country so perilous to Greeks? Did this happen before or after Orestes had been absolved of the guilt of his mother's murder? It was some time after. Although Athena had pronounced him clear of guilt, in this story all the Erinyes had not accepted the verdict. Some of them continued to pursue him, or else Orestes thought that they did. Even the acquittal pronounced by Athena had not restored to him his peace of mind. His pursuers were fewer, but they were still with him.

In his despair he went to Delphi. If he could not find help there, in the holiest place of Greece, he could find it nowhere. Apollo's oracle gave him hope, but only at the risk of his life. He must go to the Taurian country, the Delphic priestess said, and bring away the sacred image of Artemis from her temple. When he had set it up in Athens he would at last be healed and at peace. He would never again see terrible forms haunting him. It was a most perilous enterprise, but everything for him depended on it. At whatever cost he was bound to make the attempt and Pylades would not let him make it alone.

When the two reached the temple they saw at once that they must wait for the night before doing anything. There was no chance by day of getting into the place unseen. They retreated to keep under cover in some dark lonely spot.

Iphigenia, sorrowful as always, was going through her round of duties to the goddess when she was interrupted by a messenger who told her that two young men, Greeks, had been taken prisoners and were to be sacrificed at once. He had been sent on to bid her make all ready for the sacred rites. The horror which she had felt so often seized her again. She shuddered at the thought, terribly familiar though it was, of the hideous bloodshed, of the agony of the victims. But this time a new thought came as well. She asked herself, "Would a goddess command such things? Would she take pleasure in sacrificial murder? I do not believe it," she told herself. "It is the men of this land who are bloodthirsty and they lay their own guilt on the gods."

As she stood thus, deep in meditation, the captives were led in. She sent the attendants into the temple to make ready for them, and when the three were alone together she spoke to the young men. Where was their home, she asked, the home which they would never see again? She could not keep her tears back and they wondered to see her so compassionate. Orestes told her gently not to grieve for them. When they came to the land they had faced what might befall them. But she continued questioning. Were they brothers? Yes, in love, Orestes replied, but not by birth. What were their names? "Why ask that of a man about to die?" Orestes said.

"Will you not even tell me what your city is?" she asked.

"I come from Mycenae," Orestes answered, "that city once so prosperous."

"The King of it was certainly prosperous," Iphigenia said. "His name was Agamemnon."

"I do not know about him," Orestes said abruptly. "Let us end this talk."

"No—no. Tell me of him," she begged.

"Dead," said Orestes. "His own wife killed him. Ask me no more."

"One thing more," she cried. "Is she—the wife—alive?"

"No," Orestes told her. "Her son killed her."

The three looked at each other in silence.

"It was just," Iphigenia whispered shuddering; "just—yet evil, horrible." She tried to collect herself. Then she asked, "Do they ever speak of the daughter who was sacrificed?"

"Only as one speaks of the dead," Orestes said. Iphigenia's face changed. She looked eager, alert.

"I have thought of a plan to help both you and me," she said. "Would you be willing to carry a letter to my friends in Mycenae if I can save you?"

"No, not I," Orestes said. "But my friend will. He came here only for my sake. Give him your letter and kill me."

"So be it," Iphigenia answered. "Wait while I fetch the letter." She hurried away and Pylades turned to Orestes.

"I will not leave you here to die alone," he told him. "All will call me a coward if I do so. No. I love you—and I fear what men may say."

"I gave my sister to you to protect," Orestes said. "Electra is your wife. You cannot abandon her. As for me—it is no misfortune for me to die." As they spoke to each other in hurried whispers, Iphigenia entered with a letter in her hand. "I will persuade the King. He will let my messenger go, I am sure. But first—" she turned to Pylades—"I will tell you what is in the letter so that even if through some mischance you lose your belongings, you will carry my message in your memory and bear it to my friends."

"A good plan," Pylades said. "To whom am I to bear it?"

"To Orestes," Iphigenia said. "Agamemnon's son."

She was looking away, her thoughts were in Mycenae. She did not see the startled gaze the two men fixed on her.

"You must say to him," she went on, "that she who was sacrificed at Aulis sends this message. She is not dead—"

"Can the dead return to life?" Orestes cried.

"Be still," Iphigenia said with anger. "The time is short. Say to him, 'Brother, bring me back home. Free me from this murderous priesthood, this barbarous land.' Mark well, young man, the name is Orestes."

"O God, God," Orestes groaned. "It is not credible."

"I am speaking to you, not to him," Iphigenia said to Pylades. "You will remember the name?"

"Yes," Pylades answered, "but it will not take me long to deliver your message. Orestes, here is a letter. I bring it from your sister."

"And I accept it," Orestes said, "with a happiness words cannot utter."

The next moment he held Iphigenia in his arms. But she freed herself.

"I do not know," she cried. "How can I know? What proof is there?"

"Do you remember the last bit of embroidery you did before you went to Aulis?" Orestes asked. "I will describe it to you. Do you remember your chamber in the palace? I will tell you what was there."

He convinced her and she threw herself into his arms. She sobbed out, "Dearest! You are my dearest, my darling, my dear one. A baby, a little baby, when I left you. More than marvelous is this thing that has come to me."

"Poor girl," Orestes said, "mated to sorrow, as I have been. And you might have killed your own brother."

"Oh, horrible," Iphigenia cried. "But I have brought myself to do horrible things. These hands might have slain you. And even now—how can I save you? What god, what man, will help us?" Pylades had been waiting in silence, sympathetic, but impatient. He thought the hour for action had emphatically arrived. "We can talk," he reminded the brother and sister, "when once we are out of this dreadful place."

"Suppose we kill the King," Orestes proposed eagerly, but Iphigenia rejected the idea with indignation. King Thoas had been kind to her. She would not harm him. At that moment a plan flashed into her mind, perfect, down to the last detail. Hurriedly she explained it and the young men agreed at once. All three then entered the temple.

After a few moments Iphigenia came out bearing an image in her arms. A man was just stepping across the threshold of the temple enclosure. Iphigenia cried out, "O King, halt. Stay where you are." In astonishment he asked her what was happening. She told him that the two men he had sent her for the goddess were not pure. They were tainted, vile; they had killed their mother, and Artemis was angry.

"I am taking the image to the seashore to purify it," she said. "And there too I will cleanse the men from their pollution. Only after that can the sacrifice be made. All that I do must be done in solitude. Let the captives be brought forth and proclaim to the city that no one may draw near to me."

"Do as you wish," Thoas answered, "and take all the time you need." He watched the procession move off, Iphigenia leading with the image, Orestes and Pylades following, and attendants carrying vessels for the purifying rite. Iphigenia was praying aloud: "Maiden and Queen, daughter of Zeus and Leto, you shall dwell where purity is, and we shall be happy." They passed out of sight on their way to the inlet where Orestes' ship lay. It seemed as if Iphigenia's plan could not fail.

And yet it did. She was able indeed to make the attendants leave her alone with her brother and Pylades before they reached the sea. They stood in awe of her and they did just what she bade them. Then the three made all haste and boarded the ship and the crew pushed it off. But at the mouth of the harbor where it opened out to the sea a heavy wind blowing landward struck them and they could make no headway against it. They were driven back in spite of all they could do. The vessel seemed rushing on the rocks. The men of the country by now were aroused to what was being done. Some watched to seize the ship when it was stranded; others ran with the news to King Thoas. Furious with anger, he was hurrying from the temple to capture and put to death the impious strangers and the treacherous priestess, when suddenly above him in the air a radiant form appeared—manifestly a goddess. The King started back and awe checked his steps.

"Stop, O King," the Presence said. "I am Athena. This is my word to you. Let the ship go. Even now Poseidon is calming the winds and waves to give it a safe passage. Iphigenia and the others are acting under divine guidance. Dismiss your anger."

Thoas answered submissively, "Whatever is your pleasure, Goddess, shall be done." And the watchers on the shore saw the wind shift, the waves subside, and the Greek ship leave the harbor, flying under full sail to the sea beyond.

18 The Royal House of Thebes

The story of the Theban family rivals that of the House of Atreus in fame and for the same reason. Just as the greatest plays of Aeschylus, in the fifth century, are about Atreus' descendants, so the greatest plays of his contemporary Sophocles are about Oedipus and his children.

CADMUS AND HIS CHILDREN

The tale of Cadmus and his daughters is only a prologue to the greater story. It was popular in classical days, and several writers told it in whole or part. I have preferred the account of Apollodorus, who wrote in the first or second century A.D. He tells it simply and clearly.

When Europa was carried away by the bull, her father sent her brothers to search for her, bidding them not to return until they had found her. One of them, Cadmus, instead of looking vaguely here and there, went very sensibly to Delphi to ask Apollo where she was. The god told him not to trouble further about her or his father's determination not to receive him without her, but to found a city of his own. He would come upon a heifer when he left Delphi, Apollo said; he was to follow her and build his city at the spot where she lay down to rest. In this way Thebes was founded and the country round about got the name of the heifer's land, Boeotia. First, however, Cadmus had to fight and kill a terrible dragon which guarded a spring near by and slew all his companions when they went to get water. Alone he could never have built the city, but when the dragon was dead Athena appeared to him and told him to sow the earth with the dragon's teeth. He obeyed with no idea what was to happen, and to his terror saw armed men spring up from the furrows. However, they paid no attention to him, but turned upon each other until all were killed except five whom Cadmus induced to become his helpers.

With the aid of the five Cadmus made Thebes a glorious city and ruled over it in great prosperity and with great wisdom. Herodotus says that he introduced the alphabet into Greece. His wife was Harmonia, the daughter of Ares and Aphrodite. The gods graced their marriage with their presence and Aphrodite gave Harmonia a wondrous necklace which had been made by Hephaestus, the workman of Olympus, but which for all its divine origin was to bring disaster in a later generation.

They had four daughters and one son, and they learned through their children that the wind of the gods' favor never blows steadily for long. All of their daughters were visited by great misfortunes. One of them was Semele, mother of Dionysus, who perished before the unveiled glory of Zeus. Ino was another. She was the wicked stepmother of Phrixus, the boy who was saved from death by the ram of the Golden Fleece. Her husband was struck with madness and killed their son, Melicertes. With his dead body in her arms she leaped into the sea. The gods saved them both, however. She became a sea-goddess, the one who saved Odysseus from drowning when his raft was shattered, and her son became a sea-god. In the *Odyssey* she is still called Ino, but later her name was changed to Leucothea and her son was called Palaemon. Like her sister Semele she was fortunate in the end. The two others were not. Both suffered through their sons. Agave was the most wretched of all mothers, driven mad by Dionysus so that she believed her son Pentheus was a lion and killed him with her own hands. Autonoe's son was Actaeon, a great hunter. Autonoe was less wretched than Agave, in that she did not herself kill her son, but she had to endure his dying a terrible death in the strength of his young manhood, a death, too, completely undeserved; he had done no wrong.

He was out hunting and hot and thirsty entered a grotto where a little stream widened into a pool. He wanted only to cool himself in the crystal water. But all unknowing he had chanced upon the favorite bathing place of Artemis—and at the very moment when the goddess had let fall her garments and stood in her naked beauty on the water's edge. The offended divinity gave not a thought to whether the youth had purposely insulted her or had come there in all innocence. She flung into his face drops from her wet hand and as they fell upon him he was changed into a stag. Not only outwardly. His heart became a deer's heart and he who had never known fear before was afraid and fled. His dogs saw him running and chased him. Even his agony of terror could not make him swift enough to outstrip the keen-scented pack. They fell upon him, his own faithful hounds, and killed him.

Thus great sorrows for their children and grandchildren came upon Cadmus and Harmonia in old age after great prosperity. After Pentheus died they fled from Thebes as if trying to flee also from misfortune. But misfortune followed them. When they reached far-distant Illyria the gods changed them into serpents, not as a punishment, for they had done no wrong. Their fate indeed was a proof that suffering was not a punishment for wrongdoing; the innocent suffered as often as the guilty.

Of all that unfortunate race no one was more innocent of wrongdoing than Oedipus, a great-great-grandson of Cadmus, and no one suffered so greatly.

OEDIPUS

> *I have taken this story entirely from Sophocles' play of that name except for the riddle of the Sphinx which Sophocles merely alludes to. It is given by many writers, always in substantially the same form.*

King Laius of Thebes was the third in descent from Cadmus. He married a distant cousin, Jocasta. With their reign Apollo's oracle at Delphi began to play a leading part in the family's fortunes.

Apollo was the God of Truth. Whatever the priestess at Delphi said would happen infallibly came to pass. To attempt to act in such a way that the prophecy would be made void was as futile as to set oneself against the decrees of fate. Nevertheless, when the oracle warned Laius that he would die at the hands of his son he determined that this should not be. When the child was born he bound its feet together and had it exposed on a lonely mountain where it must soon die. He felt no more fear; he was sure that on this point he could foretell the future better than the god. His folly was not brought home to him. He was killed, indeed, but he thought the man who attacked him was a stranger. He never knew that in his death he had proved Apollo's truth.

When he died he was away from home and many years had passed since the baby had been left on the mountain. It was reported that a band of robbers had slain him together with his attendants, all except one, who brought the news home. The matter was not carefully investigated because Thebes was in sore straits at the time. The country around was beset by a frightful monster, the Sphinx, a creature shaped like a winged lion, but with the breast and face of a woman. She lay in wait for the wayfarers along the roads to the city and whomever she seized she put a riddle to, telling him if he could answer it, she would let him go. No one could, and the horrible creature devoured man after man until the city was in a state of siege. The seven great gates which were the Thebans' pride remained closed, and famine drew near to the citizens.

So matters stood when there came into the stricken country a stranger, a man of great courage and great intelligence, whose name was Oedipus. He had left his home, Corinth, where he was held to be the son of the King, Polybus, and the reason for his self-exile was another Delphic oracle. Apollo had declared that he was fated to kill his father. He, too, like Laius, thought to make it impossible for the oracle to come true; he resolved never to see Polybus again. In his lonely wanderings he came into the country around Thebes and he heard what was happening there. He was a homeless, friendless man to whom life meant little and he determined to seek the Sphinx out and try to solve the riddle. "What creature," the Sphinx asked him, "goes on four feet in the morning, on two at noonday, on three in the evening?" "Man," answered Oedipus. "In childhood he creeps on hands and feet; in manhood he walks erect; in old age he helps himself with a staff." It was the right answer. The Sphinx, inexplicably, but most fortunately, killed herself; the Thebans were saved. Oedipus gained all and more than he had left. The grateful citizens made him their King and he married the dead King's wife, Jocasta. For many years they lived happily. It seemed that in this case Apollo's words had been proved to be false.

But when their two sons had grown to manhood Thebes was visited by a terrible plague. A blight fell upon everything. Not only were men dying throughout the country, the flocks and herds and the fruits of the field were blasted as well. Those who were spared death by disease faced death by famine. No one suffered more than Oedipus. He regarded himself as the father of the whole state; the people in it were his children; the misery of each one was his too. He dispatched Jocasta's brother Creon to Delphi to implore the god's help.

Creon returned with good news. Apollo had declared that the plague would be stayed upon one condition: whoever

Oedipus and the Sphinx

had murdered King Laius must be punished. Oedipus was enormously relieved. Surely the men or the man could be found even after all these years, and they would know well how to punish him. He proclaimed to the people gathered to hear the message Creon brought back:—

> . . . Let no one of this land
> Give shelter to him. Bar him from your homes,
> As one defiled, companioned by pollution.
> And solemnly I pray, may he who killed
> Wear out his life in evil, being evil.

Oedipus took the matter in hand with energy. He sent for Teiresias, the old blind prophet, the most revered of Thebans. Had he any means of finding out, he asked him, who the guilty were? To his amazement and indignation the seer at first refused to answer. "For the love of God," Oedipus implored him. "If you have knowledge—" "Fools," Teiresias said. "Fools all of you. I will not answer." But when Oedipus went so far as to accuse him of keeping silence because he had himself taken part in the murder, the prophet in his turn was angered and words he had meant never to speak fell heavily from his lips: "You are yourself the murderer you seek." To Oedipus the old man's mind was wandering; what he said was sheer madness. He ordered him out of his sight and never again to appear before him.

Jocasta too treated the assertion with scorn. "Neither prophets nor oracles have any sure knowledge," she said. She told her husband how the priestess at Delphi had prophesied that Laius should die at the hand of his son and how he and she together had seen to it that this should not happen by having the child killed. "And Laius was murdered by robbers, where three roads meet on the way to Delphi," she concluded triumphantly. Oedipus gave her a strange look. "When did this happen?" he asked slowly. "Just before you came to Thebes," she said.

"How many were with him?" Oedipus asked. "They were five in all," Jocasta spoke quickly, "all killed but one." "I must see that man," he told her. "Send for him." "I will," she said. "At once. But I have a right to know what is in your mind." "You shall know all that I know," he answered. "I went to Delphi just before I came here because a man had flung it in my face that I was not the son of Polybus. I went to ask the god. He did not answer me, but he told me horrible things— that I should kill my father, marry my mother, and have children men would shudder to look upon. I never went back to Corinth. On my way from Delphi, at a place where three roads met, I came upon a man with four attendants. He tried to force me from the path; he struck me with his stick. Angered I fell upon them and I killed them. Could it be the leader was Laius?" "The one man left alive brought back a tale of robbers," Jocasta said, "Laius was killed by robbers, not by his son—the poor innocent who died upon the mountain."

As they talked a further proof seemed given them that Apollo could speak falsely. A messenger came from Corinth to announce to Oedipus the death of Polybus. "O oracle of the god," Jocasta cried, "where are you now? The man died, but not by his son's hand." The messenger smiled wisely. "Did the fear of killing your father drive you from Corinth?" he asked. "Ah, King, you were in error. You never had reason to fear—for you were not the son of Polybus. He brought you up as though you were his, but he took you from my hands." "Where did you get me?" Oedipus asked. "Who were my father and mother?" "I know nothing of them," the messenger said. "A wandering shepherd gave you to me, a servant of Laius."

Jocasta turned white; a look of horror was on her face. "Why waste a thought upon what such a fellow says?" she cried. "Nothing he says can matter." She spoke hurriedly, yet fiercely. Oedipus could not understand her. "My birth does not matter?" he asked. "For God's sake, go no further," she said. "My misery is enough." She broke away and rushed into the palace.

At that moment an old man entered. He and the messenger eyed each other curiously. "The very man, O King," the messenger cried. "The shepherd who gave you to me." "And you," Oedipus asked the other, "do you know him as he knows you?" The old man did not answer, but the messenger insisted. "You must remember. You gave me once a little child you had found—and the King here is that child." "Curse you," the other muttered. "Hold your tongue." "What!" Oedipus said angrily. "You would conspire with him to hide from me what I desire to know? There are ways, be sure, to make you speak."

The old man wailed, "Oh, do not hurt me. I did give him the child, but do not ask more, master, for the love of God." "If I have to order you a second time to tell me where you got him, you are lost," Oedipus said. "Ask your lady," the old man cried. "She can tell you best." "She gave him to you?" asked Oedipus. "Oh, yes, oh, yes," the other groaned. "I was to kill the child. There was a prophecy—" "A prophecy!" Oedipus repeated. "That he should kill his father?" "Yes," the old man whispered.

A cry of agony came from the King. At last he understood.

"All true! Now shall my light be changed to darkness. I am accursed." He had murdered his father, he had married his father's wife, his own mother. There was no help for him, for her, for their children. All were accursed.

Within the palace Oedipus wildly sought for his wife that was his mother. He found her in her chamber. She was dead. When the truth broke upon her she had killed herself. Standing beside her he too turned his hand against himself, but not to end his life. He changed his light to darkness. He put out his eyes. The black world of blindness was a refuge; better to be there than to see with strange shamed eyes the old world that had been so bright.

ANTIGONE

> *I have taken this story from the* Antigone *and the* Oedipus at Colonus, *two of Sophocles' plays, with the exception of the death of Menoeceus, which is told in a play of Euripides,* The Suppliants.

After Jocasta's death and all the evils that came with it, Oedipus lived on in Thebes while his children were growing up. He had two sons, Polyneices and Eteocles, and two daughters, Antigone and Ismene. They were very unfortunate young people, but they were far from being monsters all would shudder to look at, as the oracle had told Oedipus. The two lads were well liked by the Thebans and the two girls were as good daughters as a man could have.

Oedipus of course resigned the throne. Polyneices, the elder son, did the same. The Thebans felt that this was wise because of the terrible position of the family, and they accepted Creon, Jocasta's brother, as the regent. For many years they treated Oedipus with kindness, but at last they decided to expel him from the city. What induced them to do this is not known, but Creon urged it and Oedipus' sons consented to it. The only friends Oedipus had were his daughters. Through all his misfortunes they were faithful to him. When he was driven out of the city Antigone went with him to guide him in his blindness and care for him, and Ismene stayed in Thebes to look out for his interests and keep him informed of whatever happened that touched him.

After he had gone his two sons asserted their right to the throne, and each tried to be made king. Eteocles succeeded although he was the younger, and he expelled his brother from Thebes. Polyneices took refuge in Argos and did all he could to arouse enmity against Thebes. His intention was to collect an army to march against the city.

In the course of their desolate wanderings Oedipus and Antigone came to Colonus, a lovely spot near Athens, where the one-time Erinyes, the Furies, now the Benignant Goddesses, had a place sacred to them and therefore a refuge for suppliants. The blind old man and his daughter felt safe there, and there Oedipus died. Most unhappy in much of his life, he was happy at the end. The oracle which once had spoken terrible words to him comforted him when he was dying. Apollo promised that he, the disgraced, the homeless wanderer, would bring to the place where his grave should be a mysterious blessing from the gods. Theseus, the King of Athens, received him with all honor, and the old man died rejoicing that he was no longer hateful to men, but welcomed as a benefactor to the land that harbored him.

Ismene, who had come to tell her father the good news of this oracle, was with her sister when he died and afterward they were both sent safely home by Theseus. They arrived to find one brother marching against their city, resolved to capture it, and the other determined to defend it to the end. Polyneices, the one who attacked it, had the better right to it, but the younger, Eteocles, was fighting for Thebes, to save her from capture. It was impossible for the two sisters to take sides against either brother.

Polyneices had been joined by six chieftains, one of them the King of Argos, Adrastus, and another Adrastus' brother-in-law, Amphiaraus. This last joined the enterprise most unwillingly because he was a prophet and he knew that none of the seven would come back alive except Adrastus. However, he was under oath to let his wife Eriphyle decide whenever there was a dispute between him and her brother. He had sworn this once when he and Adrastus had quarreled and Eriphyle had reconciled them. Polyneices won her over to his side by bribing her with the wonderful necklace that had been the wedding gift of his ancestress Harmonia, and she made her husband go to the war.

There were seven champions to attack the seven gates of Thebes, and seven others within as bold to defend them. Eteocles defended the gate which Polyneices attacked, and Antigone and Ismene within the palace waited to hear which had killed the other. But before any decisive combat had taken place, a youth in Thebes not yet grown to manhood had died for his country and in his death had shown himself the noblest of all. This was Creon's younger son, Menoeceus.

Teiresias, the prophet who had brought so many distressful prophecies to the royal family, came to bring still another. He told Creon that Thebes would be saved only if Menoeceus was killed. The father utterly refused to bring this about. He would be willing to die himself, he said—"But not even for my own city will I slay my son." He bade the boy, who was present when Teiresias spoke, "Up, my child, and fly with all speed from the land before the city learns." "Where, Father?" asked the lad. "What city seek—what friend?" "Far, far away," the father answered. "I will find means—I will find gold." "Go get it then," said Menoeceus, but when Creon had hurried away he spoke other words:—

> My father—he would rob our town of hope,
> Make me a coward. Ah well—he is old
> And so to be forgiven. But I am young.
> If I betray Thebes there is no forgiveness.
> How can he think I will not save the city
> And for her sake go forth to meet my death?
> What would my life be if I fled away
> When I can free my country?

He went to join the battle and, all unskilled in warfare, he was killed at once.

Neither the besiegers nor the besieged could gain any real advantage and finally both sides agreed to let the matter be decided by a combat between the brothers. If Eteocles was the victor, the Argive Army would withdraw; if Eteocles was conquered, Polyneices should be king. Neither was victor; they killed each other, Eteocles dying looked upon his brother and wept; he had no strength to speak. Polyneices could murmur a few words: "My brother, my enemy, but loved, always loved. Bury me in my homeland—to have so much at least of my city."

The combat had decided nothing and the battle was renewed. But Menoeceus had not died in vain; in the end the Thebans prevailed and of the seven champions all were killed except Adrastus only. He fled with the broken Army to Athens. In Thebes, Creon was in control and he proclaimed that none of those who had fought against the city should be given burial. Eteocles should be honored with every rite that the noblest received at death, but Polyneices should be left for beasts and birds to tear and devour. This was to carry vengeance beyond the ordinance of the gods, beyond the law of right; it was to punish the dead. The souls of the unburied might not pass the river that encircles the kingdom of death, but must wander in desolation, with no abiding-place, no rest ever for their weariness. To bury the dead was a most sacred duty, not only to bury one's own, but any stranger one might come upon. But this duty, Creon's proclamation said, was changed in the case of Polyneices to a crime. He who buried him would be put to death.

Antigone and Ismene heard with horror what Creon had decided. To Ismene, shocking as it was, overwhelming her with anguish for the pitiful dead body and the lonely, home-less soul, it seemed, nevertheless, that nothing could be done except to acquiesce. She and Antigone were utterly alone. All Thebes was exulting that the man who had brought war upon them should be thus terribly punished. "We are women," she told her sister. "We must obey. We have no strength to defy the State." "Choose your own part," Antigone said. "I go to bury the brother I love." "You are not strong enough," Ismene cried. "Why, then when my strength fails," Antigone an-swered, "I will give up." She left her sister; Ismene dared not follow her.

Some hours later, Creon in the palace was startled by a shout, "Against your orders Polyneices has been buried." He hurried out to be confronted with the guards he had set on the dead body and with Antigone. "This girl buried him," they cried. "We saw her. A thick dust-storm gave her her chance. When it cleared, the body had been buried and the girl was making an offering to the dead." "You knew my edict?" Creon asked. "Yes," Antigone replied. "And you transgressed the law?" "Your law, but not the law of Justice who dwells with the gods," Antigone said. "The unwritten laws of heaven are not of today nor yesterday, but from all time."

Ismene weeping came from the palace to stand with her sis-ter. "I helped do it," she said. But Antigone would not have that. "She had no share in it," she told Creon. And she bade her sister say no more. "Your choice was to live," she said, "mine to die."

As she was led away to death, she spoke to the bystand-ers:—

> ... Behold me, what I suffer
> Because I have upheld that which is high.

Ismene disappears. There is no story, no poem, about her. The House of Oedipus, the last of the royal family of Thebes, was known no more.

THE SEVEN AGAINST THEBES

> *Two great writers told this story. It is the subject of one of Aeschylus' plays and one of Euripides'. I have chosen Euripides' version which, as so often with him, reflects remarkably our own point of view. Aeschylus tells the tale splendidly, but in his hands it is a stirring martial poem. Euripides' play,* The Suppliants, *shows his mod-ern mind better than any of his other plays.*

Polyneices had been given burial at the price of his sister's life; his soul was free to be ferried across the river and find a home among the dead. But five of the chieftains who had marched with him to Thebes lay unburied, and according to Creon's decree would be left so forever.

Adrastus, the only one alive of the seven who had started the war, came to Theseus, King of Athens, to beseech him to induce the Thebans to allow the bodies to be buried. With him were the mothers and the sons of the dead men. "All we seek," he told Theseus, "is burial for our dead. We come to you for help, because Athens of all cities is compassionate."

"I will not be your ally," Theseus answered. "You led your people against Thebes. The war was of your doing, not hers."

But Aethra, Theseus' mother, to whom those other sorrowing mothers had first turned, was bold to interrupt the two Kings. "My son," she said, "may I speak for your honor and for Athens?"

"Yes, speak," he answered and listened intently while she told him what was in her mind.

"You are bound to defend all who are wronged," she said. "These men of violence who refuse the dead their right of burial, you are bound to compel them to obey the law. It is sacred through all Greece. What holds our states together and all states everywhere, except this, that each one honors the great laws of right?"

"Mother," Theseus cried, "these are true words. Yet of myself I cannot decide the matter. For I have made this land a free state with an equal vote for all. If the citizens consent, then I will go to Thebes."

The poor women waited, Aethra with them, while he went to summon the assembly which would decide the misery or happiness of their dead children. They prayed: "O city of Athena, help us, so that the laws of justice shall not be defiled and through all lands the helpless and oppressed shall be delivered." When Theseus returned he brought good news. The assembly had voted to tell the Thebans that Athens wished to be a good neighbor, but that she could not stand by and see a great wrong done. "Yield to our request," they would ask Thebes. "We want only what is right. But if you will not, then you choose war, for we must fight to defend those who are defenseless."

Before he finished speaking a herald entered. He asked, "Who is the master here, the lord of Athens? I bring a message to him from the master of Thebes."

"You seek one who does not exist," Theseus answered. "There is no master here. Athens is free. Her people rule."

"That is well for Thebes," the herald cried. "Our city is not governed by a mob which twists this way and that, but by one man. How can the ignorant crowd wisely direct a nation's course?"

"We in Athens," Theseus said, "write our own laws and then are ruled by them. We hold there is no worse enemy to a state than he who keeps the law in his own hands. This great advantage then is ours, that our land rejoices in all her sons who are strong and powerful by reason of their wisdom and just dealing. But to a tyrant such are hateful. He kills them, fearing they will shake his power.

"Go back to Thebes and tell her we know how much better peace is for men than war. Fools rush on war to make a weaker country their slave. We would not harm your state. We seek the dead only, to return to earth the body, of which no man is the owner, but only for a brief moment the guest. Dust must return to dust again."

Creon would not listen to Theseus' plea, and the Athenians marched against Thebes. They conquered. The panic-stricken people in the town thought only that they would be killed or enslaved and their city ruined. But although the way lay clear to the victorious Athenian Army, Theseus held them back. "We came not to destroy the town," he said, "but only to reclaim the dead." "And our King," said the messenger who brought the news to the anxiously waiting people of Athens, "Theseus himself, made ready for the grave those five poor bodies, washed them and covered them and set them on a bier."

Some measure of comfort came to the sorrowful mothers as their sons were laid upon the funeral pyre with all reverence and honor. Adrastus spoke the last words for each: "Capaneus lies here, a mighty man of wealth, yet humble as a poor man always and a true friend to all. He knew no guile; upon his lips were kind words only. Eteocles is next, poor in everything save honor. There he was rich indeed. When men would give him gold he would not take it. He would not be a slave to wealth. Beside him Hippomedon lies. He was a man who suffered hardship gladly, a hunter and a soldier. From boyhood he disdained an easy life. Atalanta's son is next, Parthenopaeus, of many a man, of many a woman loved, and one who never did a wrong to any man. His joy was in his country's good, his grief when it went ill with her. The last is Tydeus, a silent man. He could best reason with his sword and shield. His soul was lofty; deeds, not words, revealed how high it soared."

As the pyre was kindled, on a rocky height above it a woman appeared. It was Evadne, the wife of Capaneus. She cried,

I have found the light of your pyre, your tomb.
I will end there the grief and the anguish of life.
Oh, sweet death to die with the dear dead I love.

She leaped down to the blazing pyre and went with her husband to the world below.

Peace came to the mothers, with the knowledge that at last their children's spirits were at rest. Not so to the young sons of the dead men. They vowed as they watched the pyre burn that when they were grown they would take vengeance upon Thebes. "Our fathers sleep in the tomb, but the wrong done to them can never sleep," they said. Ten years later they marched to Thebes. They were victorious; the conquered Thebans fled and their city was leveled to the ground. Teiresias the prophet perished during the flight. All that was left of the old Thebes was Harmonia's necklace, which was taken to Delphi and for hundreds of years shown to the pilgrims there. The sons of the seven champions, although they succeeded where their fathers failed, were always called the Epigoni, "the After-Born," as if they had come into the world too late, after all great deeds had been done. But when Thebes fell, the Greek ships had not yet sailed to the Trojan land; and the son of Tydeus, Diomedes, was to be famed as one of the most glorious of the warriors who fought before the walls of Troy.

19 The Royal House of Athens

I have taken the Procne and Philomela story from Ovid. He tells it better than anyone else, but even so he is sometimes inconceivably bad. He describes in fifteen long lines (which I omit) exactly how Philomela's tongue was cut out and what it looked like as it lay "palpitating" on the earth where Tereus had flung it. The Greek poets were not given to such details, but the Latin had no manner of objection to them. I have followed Ovid, too, for the most part in the stories of Procris and Orithyia, taking a few details from Apollodorus. The tale of Creüsa and Ion is the subject of a play of Euripides, one of the many plays in which he tried to show the Athenians what the gods of the myths really were when judged by the ordinary human standards of mercy, honor, self-control. Greek mythology was full of stories such as that of the rape of Europa, in which never a suggestion was allowed that the deity in question had acted somewhat less than divinely. In his version of the story of Creüsa Euripides said to his audience, "Look at your Apollo, the sun-bright Lord of the Lyre, the pure God of Truth. This is what he did. He brutally forced a helpless young girl and then he abandoned her." The end of Greek mythology was at hand when such plays drew full houses in Athens.

This family was especially marked, even among the other remarkable mythological families, by the very peculiar happenings which visited its members. There is nothing stranger told in any story than some of the events in their lives.

CECROPS

The first King of Attica was named Cecrops. He had no human ancestor and he was himself only half human.

> Cecrops, lord and hero,
> Born of a dragon,
> Dragon-shaped below.

He was the person usually held to be responsible for Athena's becoming the protector of Athens. Poseidon, too, wanted the city, and to show how great a benefactor he could be, he struck open the rock of the Acropolis with his trident so that salt water leaped forth from the cleft and subsided into a deep well. But Athena did still better. She made an olive tree grow there, the most prized of all the trees of Greece.

> The gray-gleaming olive
> Athena showed to men,
> The glory of shining Athens,
> Her crown from on high.

In return for this good gift Cecrops, who had been made arbiter, decided that Athens was hers. Poseidon was greatly angered and punished the people by sending a disastrous flood.

In one story of this contest between the two deities, woman's suffrage plays a part. In those early days, we are told, women voted as well as men. All the women voted for the goddess, and all the men for the god. There was one more woman than there were men, so Athena won. But the men, along with Poseidon, were greatly chagrined at this female triumph; and while Poseidon proceeded to flood the land the men decided to take the vote away from the women. Nevertheless, Athena kept Athens.

Most writers say that these events happened before the Deluge, and that the Cecrops who belonged to the famous Athenian family was not the ancient half-dragon, half-human creature but an ordinary man, important only because of his relatives. He was the son of a distinguished king, a nephew of two well-known mythological heroines, and the brother of three. Above all, he was the great-grandfather of Athens' hero, Theseus.

His father, King Erechtheus of Athens, was usually said to be the king in whose reign Demeter came to Eleusis and agriculture began. He had two sisters, Procne and Philomela, noted for their misfortunes. Their story was tragic in the extreme.

PROCNE AND PHILOMELA

Procne, the elder of the two, was married to Tereus of Thrace, a son of Ares, who proved to have inherited all his father's detestable qualities. The two had a son, Itys, and when he was five years old Procne, who had all this while been living in Thrace separated from her family, begged Tereus to let her invite her sister Philomela to visit her. He agreed, and said he would go to Athens himself and escort her. But as soon as he set eyes on the girl he fell in love with her. She was beautiful as a nymph or a naiad. He easily persuaded her father to allow her to go back with him, and she herself was happy beyond words at the prospect. All went well on the voyage, but when they disembarked and started overland for the palace, Tereus told Philomela that he had received news of Procne's death and he forced her into a pretended marriage. Within a very short time, however, she learned the truth, and she was ill-advised enough to threaten him. She would surely find means to let the world know what he had done, she told him, and he would be an outcast among men. She aroused both his fury and his fear. He seized her and cut out her tongue. Then he left her in a strongly guarded place and went to Procne with a story that Philomela had died on the journey.

Philomela's case looked hopeless. She was shut up; she could not speak; in those days there was no writing. It seemed that Tereus was safe. However, although people then could not write, they could tell a story without speaking because they were marvelous craftsmen, such as have never been known since. A smith could make a shield which showed on its surface a lion-hunt, two lions devouring a bull while herdsmen urged their dogs on to attack them. Or he could depict a harvest scene, a field with reapers and sheaf-binders, and a vineyard teeming with clusters of grapes which youths and maidens gathered into baskets while one of them played on a shepherd's pipe to cheer their labors. The women were equally remarkable in their kind of work. They could weave, into the lovely stuffs they made, forms so lifelike anyone could see what tale they illustrated. Philomela accordingly turned to her loom. She had a greater motive to make clear the story she wove than any artist ever had. With infinite pains and surpassing skill she produced a wondrous tapestry on which the whole account of her wrongs was unfolded. She gave it to the old woman who attended her and signified that it was for the Queen.

Proud of bearing so beautiful a gift the aged creature carried it to Procne, who was still wearing deep mourning for her sister and whose spirit was as mournful as her garments.

She unrolled the web. There she saw Philomela, her very face and form, and Tereus equally unmistakable. With horror she read what had happened, all as plain to her as if in print. Her deep sense of outrage helped her to self-control. Here was no room for tears or for words, either. She bent her whole mind to delivering her sister and devising a fit punishment for her husband. First, she made her way to Philomela, doubtless through the old woman messenger, and when she had told her, who could not speak in return, that she knew all, she took her back to the palace. There while Philomela wept, Procne thought. "Let us weep hereafter," she told her sister. "I am prepared for any deed that will make Tereus pay for what he has done to you." At this moment her little son, Itys, ran into the room and suddenly as she looked at him it seemed to her that she hated him. "How like your father you are," she said slowly, and with the words her plan was clear to her. She killed the child with one stroke of a dagger. She cut the little dead body up, put the limbs in a kettle over the fire, and served them to Tereus that night for supper. She watched him as he ate; then she told him what he had feasted on.

In his first sickening horror he could not move, and the two sisters were able to flee. Near Daulis, however, he overtook them, and was about to kill them when suddenly the gods turned them into birds, Procne into a nightingale and Philomela into a swallow, which, because her tongue was cut out, only twitters and can never sing. Procne,

> The bird with wings of brown,
> Musical nightingale,
> Mourns forever; O Itys, child,
> Lost to me, lost.

Of all the birds her song is sweetest because it is saddest. She never forgets the son she killed.

The wretched Tereus too was changed into a bird, an ugly bird with a huge beak, said sometimes to be a hawk.

The Roman writers who told the story somehow got the sisters confused and said that the tongueless Philomela was the nightingale, which was obviously absurd. But so she is always called in English poetry.

PROCRIS AND CEPHALUS

The niece of these unfortunate women was Procris, and she was almost as unfortunate as they. She was married very happily to Cephalus, a grandson of the King of the Winds, Aeolus; but they had been married only a few weeks when Cephalus was carried off by no less a personage than Aurora herself, the Goddess of the Dawn. He was a lover of the chase and used to rise early to track the deer. So it happened that many a time as the day broke Dawn saw the young hunter, and finally she fell in love with him. But Cephalus loved Procris. Not even the radiant goddess could make him faithless. Procris alone was in his heart. Enraged at this obstinate devotion which none of her wiles could weaken, Aurora at last dismissed him and told him to go back to his wife, but to make sure that she had been as true to him during his absence as he to her.

This malicious suggestion drove Cephalus mad with jealousy. He had been so long away and Procris was so beautiful. . . . He decided that he could never rest satisfied unless he proved to himself beyond all doubt that she loved him alone and would not yield to any other lover. Accordingly, he disguised himself. Some say that Aurora helped him, but at all events, the disguise was so good that when he went back to his home no one recognized him. It was comforting to see that the whole household was longing for his return, but his purpose held firm. When he was admitted to Procris' presence, however, her manifest grief, her sad face and subdued manner, came near to making him give up the test he had planned. He did not do so, however; he could not forget Aurora's mocking words. He began at once to try to get Procris to fall in love with him, a stranger, as she supposed him to be. He made passionate love to her, always reminding her, too, that her husband had forsaken her. Nevertheless for a long time he could not move her. To all his pleas she made the same answer, "I belong to him. Wherever he is I keep my love for him."

But one day when he was pouring out petitions, persuasions, promises, she hesitated. She did not give in; she only did not firmly oppose him, but that was enough for Cephalus. He cried out, "O false and shameless woman, I am your husband. By my own witness you are a traitor." Procris looked at him. Then she turned and without a word left him and the house, too. Her love for him seemed turned into hate; she loathed the whole race of men and she went to the mountains to live alone. Cephalus, however, had quickly come to his senses and realized the poor part he had played. He searched everywhere for her until he found her. Then he humbly begged her forgiveness.

She could not give it to him at once, she had resented too deeply the deception he had practised upon her. In the end, however, he won her back and they spent some happy years together. Then one day they went hunting, as they often did. Procris had given Cephalus a javelin that never failed to strike what it was aimed at. The husband and wife, reaching the woods, separated in search of game. Cephalus looking keenly around saw something move in the thicket ahead and threw the javelin. It found the mark. Procris was there and she sank to the ground dead, pierced to the heart.

ORITHYIA AND BOREAS

One of the sisters of Procris was Orithyia. Boreas, the North Wind, fell in love with her, but her father, Erechtheus, and the people of Athens, too, were opposed to his suit. Because of Procne's and Philomela's sad fate and the fact that the wicked Tereus came from the North, they had conceived a hatred for all who lived there and they refused to give the maiden to Boreas. But they were foolish to think they could keep what the great North Wind wanted. One day when Orithyia was playing with her sisters on the bank of a river, Boreas swept down in a great gust and carried her away. The two sons she bore him, Zetes and Calais, went on the Quest of the Golden Fleece with Jason.

Once Socrates, the great Athenian teacher, who lived hundreds of years, thousands, perhaps, after the mythological stories were first told, went on a walk with a young man he was fond of named Phaedrus. They talked as they wandered idly on and Phaedrus asked, "Is not the place somewhere near here where Boreas is said to have carried off Orithyia from the banks of the Ilissus?"

"That is the story," Socrates answered.

"Do you suppose this is the exact spot?" Phaedrus wondered. "The little stream is delightfully clear and bright. I can fancy that there might be maidens playing near."

"I believe," replied Socrates, "the spot is about a quarter of a mile lower down, and there is, I think, some sort of altar to Boreas there."

"Tell me, Socrates," said Phaedrus. "Do you believe the story?"

"The wise are doubtful," Socrates returned, "and I should not be singular if I too doubted."

This conversation took place in the last part of the fifth century B.C. The old stories had begun by then to lose their hold on men's minds.

CREÜSA AND ION

Creüsa was the sister of Procris and Orithyia, and she too was an unfortunate woman. One day when she was hardly more than a child she was gathering crocuses on a cliff where there was a deep cave. Her veil, which she had used for a basket, was full of the yellow blooms and she had turned to go home when she was caught up in the arms of a man who had appeared from nowhere, as if the invisible had suddenly become visible. He was divinely beautiful, but in her agony of terror she never noticed what he was like. She screamed for her mother, but there was no help for her. Her abductor was Apollo himself. He carried her off to the dark cave.

God though he was she hated him, especially when the time came for her child to be born and he showed her no sign, gave her no aid. She did not dare tell her parents. The fact that the lover was a god and could not be resisted was, as many stories show, not accepted as an excuse. A girl ran every risk of being killed if she confessed.

When Creüsa's time had come she went all alone to that same dark cave, and there her son was born. There, too, she left him to die. Later, driven by an agony of longing to know what had happened to him, she went back. The cave was empty and no bloodstains could be seen anywhere. The child had certainly not been killed by a wild animal. Also, what was very strange, the soft things she had wrapped him in, her veil and a cloak woven by her own hands, were gone. She wondered fearfully if a great eagle or vulture had entered and had carried all away in its cruel talons, the clothing with the baby. It seemed the only possible explanation.

After a time she was married. King Erechtheus, her father, rewarded with her hand a foreigner who had helped him in a war. This man, Xuthus by name, was a Greek, to be sure, but he did not belong to Athens or to Attica, and he was considered a stranger and an alien, and as such was so looked down on that when he and Creüsa had no children the Athenians did not think it a misfortune. Xuthus did, however. He more than Creüsa passionately desired a son. They went accordingly to Delphi, the Greeks' refuge in time of trouble, to ask the god if they could hope for a child.

Creüsa, leaving her husband in the town with one of the priests, went on up to the sanctuary by herself. She found in the outer court a beautiful lad in priestly attire intent on purifying the sacred place with water from a golden vessel, singing as he worked a hymn of praise to the god. He looked at the lovely stately lady with kindness and she at him, and they began to talk. He told her that he could see that she was highly born and blessed by good fortune. She answered bitterly, "Good fortune! Say, rather, sorrow that makes life insupportable." All her misery was in the words, her terror and her pain of long ago, her grief for her child, the burden of the secret she had carried through the years. But at the wonder in the boy's eyes she collected herself and asked him who he was, so young and yet seemingly so dedicated to this high service in Greece's holy of holies. He told her that his name was Ion, but that he did not know where he had come from. The Pythoness, Apollo's priestess and prophetess, had found him one morning, a little baby, lying on the temple stairway, and had brought him up as tenderly as a mother. Always he had been happy, working joyfully in the temple, proud to serve not men, but gods.

He ventured then to question her. Why, he asked her gently, was she so sad, her eyes wet with tears? That was not the way pilgrims to Delphi came, but rejoicing to approach the pure shrine of Apollo, the God of Truth.

"Apollo!" Creüsa said. "No! I do not so approach him." Then, in answer to Ion's startled reproachful look, she told him that she had come on a secret errand to Delphi. Her husband was here to ask if he might hope for a son, but her purpose was to find out what had been the fate of a child who was the son of . . . She faltered, and was silent. Then she spoke quickly, ". . . of a friend of mine, a wretched woman whom this Delphic holy god of yours wronged. And when the child was born that he forced her to bear, she abandoned it. It must be dead. Years ago it happened. But she longs to be sure, and to know how it died. So I am here to ask Apollo for her."

Ion was horrified at the accusation she brought against his lord and master. "It is not true," he said hotly. "It was some man, and she excused her shame by putting it on the god."

"No," Creüsa said positively. "It was Apollo."

Ion was silent. Then he shook his head. "Even if it were true," he said, "what you would do is folly. You must not approach the god's altar to try to prove him a villain."

Creüsa felt her purpose grow weak and ebb away while the strange boy spoke. "I will not," she said submissively. "I will do as you say."

Feelings she did not understand were stirring within her. As the two stood looking at each other Xuthus entered, triumph in his face and bearing. He held out his arms to Ion, who stepped back in cold distaste. But Xuthus managed to enfold him, to his great discomfort.

"You are my son," he cried. "Apollo has declared it."

A sense of bitter antagonism stirred in Creüsa's heart. "Your son?" she questioned clearly. "Who is his mother?"

"I don't know." Xuthus was confused. "I think he is my son, but perhaps the god gave him to me. Either way he is mine."

To this group, Ion icily remote, Xuthus bewildered but happy, Creüsa feeling that she hated men and that she would not put up with having the son of some unknown, low woman foisted on her, there entered the aged priestess, Apollo's prophetess. In her hands she carried two things that made Creüsa, in all her preoccupation, start and look sharply at them. One was a veil and the other a maiden's cloak. The holy woman told Xuthus that the priest wished to speak to him, and when he was gone she held out to Ion what she was carrying.

"Dear lad," she said, "you must take these with you when you go to Athens with your new-found father. They are the clothes you were wrapped in when I found you."

"Oh," Ion cried, "my mother must have put them around me. They are a clue to my mother. I will seek her everywhere —through Europe and through Asia."

But Creüsa had stolen up to him and, before he could draw back offended a second time, she had thrown her arms around his neck; and weeping and pressing her face to his she was calling him, "My son—my son!"

This was too much for Ion. "She must be mad," he cried.

"No, no," Creüsa said. "That veil, that cloak, they are mine. I covered you with them when I left you. See. That friend I told you of. . . . It was no friend, but my own self. Apollo is your father. Oh, do not turn away. I can prove it. Unfold these wrappings. I will tell you all the embroideries on them. I made them with these hands. And look. You will find two little serpents of gold fastened to the cloak. I put them there."

Ion found the jewels and looked from them to her. "My mother," he said wonderingly. "But then is the God of Truth false? He said I was Xuthus' son. O Mother, I am troubled."

"Apollo did not say you were Xuthus' own son. He gave you to him as a gift," Creüsa cried, but she was trembling, too.

A sudden radiance from on high fell on the two and made them look up. Then all their distress was forgotten in awe and wonder. A divine form stood above them, beautiful and majestic beyond compare.

"I am Pallas Athena," the vision said. "Apollo has sent me to you to tell you that Ion is his son and yours. He had him brought here from the cave where you left him. Take him with you to Athens, Creüsa. He is worthy to rule over my land and city."

She vanished. The mother and son looked at each other, Ion with perfect joy. But Creüsa? Did Apollo's late reparation make up to her for all that she had suffered? We can only guess; the story does not say.

Athena appears to Creüsa and Ion

PART SIX

The Less Important Myths

20 Midas—and Others

The story of Midas is told best by Ovid from whom I have taken it. Pindar is my authority for Aesculapius, whose life he tells in full. The Danaïds are the subject of one of the plays of Aeschylus. Glaucus and Scylla, Pomona and Vertumnus, Erysichthon, all come from Ovid.

Midas, whose name has become a synonym for a rich man, had very little profit from his riches. The experience of possessing them lasted for less than a day and it threatened him with speedy death. He was an example of folly being as fatal as sin, for he meant no harm; he merely did not use any intelligence. His story suggests that he had none to use.

He was King of Phrygia, the land of roses, and he had great rose gardens near his palace. Into them once strayed old Silenus, who, intoxicated as always, had wandered off from Bacchus' train where he belonged and lost his way. The fat old drunkard was found asleep in a bower of roses by some of the servants of the palace. They bound him with rosy garlands, set a flowering wreath on his head, woke him up, and bore him in this ridiculous guise to Midas as a great joke. Midas welcomed him and entertained him for ten days. Then he led him to Bacchus, who, delighted to get him back, told Midas whatever wish he made would come true. Without giving a thought to the inevitable result Midas wished that whatever he touched would turn into gold. Of course Bacchus in granting the favor foresaw what would happen at the next meal, but Midas saw nothing until the food he lifted to his lips became a lump of metal. Dismayed and very hungry and thirsty, he was forced to hurry off to the god and implore him to take his favor back. Bacchus told him to go wash in the source of the river Pactolus and he would lose the fatal gift. He did so, and that was said to be the reason why gold was found in the sands of the river.

Later on, Apollo changed Midas' ears into those of an ass; but again the punishment was for stupidity, not for any wrong-doing. He was chosen as one of the umpires in a musical contest between Apollo and Pan. The rustic god could play very pleasing tunes on his pipes of reed, but when Apollo struck his silver lyre there was no sound on earth or in heaven that could equal the melody except only the choir of the Muses. Nevertheless, although the umpire, the mountain-god Tmolus, gave the palm to Apollo, Midas, no more intelligent musically than in any other way, honestly preferred Pan. Of course, this was double stupidity on his part. Ordinary prudence would have reminded him that it was dangerous to side against Apollo with Pan, infinitely the less powerful. And so he got his asses' ears. Apollo said that he was merely giving to ears so dull and dense the proper shape. Midas hid them under a cap especially made for that purpose, but the servant who cut his hair was obliged to see them. He swore a solemn oath never to tell, but the secrecy so weighed upon the man that he finally went and dug a hole in a field and spoke softly into it, "King Midas has asses' ears." Then he felt relieved and filled the hole up. But in the spring reeds grew up there, and when stirred by the wind they whispered those buried words—and revealed to men not only the truth of what had happened to the poor, stupid King, but also that when gods are contestants the only safe course is to side with the strongest.

AESCULAPIUS

There was a maiden in Thessaly named Coronis, of beauty so surpassing that Apollo loved her. But strangely enough she did not care long for her divine lover; she preferred a mere mortal. She did not reflect that Apollo, the God of Truth, who never deceived, could not himself be deceived.

> The Pythian Lord of Delphi,
> He has a comrade he can trust,
> Straightforward, never wandering astray.

It is his mind which knows all things,
Which never touches falsehood, which no one
Or god or mortal can outwit. He sees,
Whether the deed is done, or only planned.

Coronis was foolish indeed to hope that he would not learn of her faithlessness. It is said that the news was brought to him by his bird, the raven, then pure white with beautiful snowy plumage, and that Apollo in a fit of furious anger, and with the complete injustice the gods usually showed when they were angry, punished the faithful messenger by turning his feathers black. Of course Coronis was killed. Some say that the god did it himself, others that he got Artemis to shoot one of her unerring arrows at her.

In spite of his ruthlessness, he felt a pang of grief as he watched the maiden placed on the funeral pyre and the wild flames roar up. "At least I will save my child," he said to himself; and just as Zeus had done when Semele perished, he snatched away the babe which was very near birth. He took it to Chiron, the wise and kindly old Centaur, to bring up in his cave on Mount Pelion, and told him to call the child Aesculapius. Many notables had given Chiron their sons to rear, but of all his pupils the child of dead Coronis was dearest to him. He was not like other lads, forever running about and bent on sport; he wanted most of all to learn whatever his foster-father could teach him about the art of healing. And that was not a little. Chiron was learned in the use of herbs and gentle incantations and cooling potions. But his pupil surpassed him. He was able to give aid in all manner of maladies. Whoever came to him suffering, whether from wounded limbs or bodies wasting away with disease, even those who were sick unto death, he delivered from their torment.

A gentle craftsman who drove pain away,
Soother of cruel pangs, a joy to men,
Bringing them golden health.

He was a universal benefactor. And yet he too drew down on himself the anger of the gods and by the sin the gods never forgave. He thought "thoughts too great for man." He was once given a large fee to raise one from the dead, and he did so. It is said by many that the man called back to life was Hippolytus. Theseus' son who died so unjustly, and that he never again fell under the power of death, but lived in Italy, immortal forever, where he was called Virbius and worshiped as a god.

However, the great physician who had delivered him from Hades had no such happy fate. Zeus would not allow a mortal to have power over the dead and he struck Aesculapius with his thunderbolt and slew him. Apollo, in great anger at his son's death, went to Etna, where the Cyclopes forged the thunderbolts; and killed with his arrows, some say the Cyclopes themselves, some say their sons. Zeus, greatly angered in his turn, condemned Apollo to serve King Admetus as a slave—for a period which is differently given as one or nine years. It was this Admetus whose wife, Alcestis, Hercules rescued from Hades.

But Aesculapius, even though he had so displeased the King of Gods and Men, was honored on earth as no other mortal. For hundreds of years after his death the sick and the maimed and the blind came for healing to his temples. There they would pray and sacrifice, and after that go to sleep. Then in their dreams the good physician would reveal to them how they could be cured. Snakes played some part in the cure, just what is not known, but they were held to be the sacred servants of Aesculapius.

It is certain that thousands upon thousands of sick people through the centuries believed that he had freed them from their pain and restored them to health.

THE DANAÏDS

These maidens are famous—far more so than anyone reading their story would expect. They are often referred to by the poets and they are among the most prominent sufferers in the hell of mythology, where they must forever try to carry water in leaking jars. Yet except for one of them, Hypermnestra, they did only what the Argonauts found the women of Lemnos had done: they killed their husbands. Nevertheless, the Lemnians are hardly ever mentioned, while everyone who knows even a little about mythology has heard of the Danaïds.

There were fifty of them, all of them daughters of Danaüs, one of Io's descendants, who dwelt by the Nile. Their fifty cousins, sons of Danaüs' brother Aegyptus, wanted to marry them, which for some unexplained reason they were absolutely opposed to doing. They fled with their father by ship to Argos, where they found sanctuary. The Argives voted unanimously to maintain the right of the suppliant. When the sons of Aegyptus arrived ready to fight to gain their brides, the city repulsed them. They would allow no woman to be forced to marry against her will they told the newcomers, nor would they surrender any suppliant, no matter how feeble, and no matter how powerful the pursuer.

At this point there is a break in the story. When it is resumed, in the next chapter, so to speak, the maidens are being married to their cousins and their father is presiding at the marriage feast. There is no explanation of how this came about, but at once it is clear that it was not through any change of mind in either Danaüs or his daughters, because at the feast he is represented as giving each girl a dagger. As the event shows, all of them had been told what to do and had agreed. After the marriage, in the dead of night, they killed their bridegrooms—everyone except Hypermnestra. She alone was moved by pity. She looked at the strong young man lying motionless in sleep beside her, and she could not strike with her dagger to change that glowing vigor into cold death. Her promise to her father and her sisters was forgotten. She was, the Latin poet Horace says, splendidly false. She woke the youth,—his name was Lynceus,—told him all, and helped him to flee.

Her father threw her into prison for her treachery to him. One story says that she and Lynceus came together again and lived at last in happiness, and that their son was Abas, the great-grandfather of Perseus. The other stories end with the fatal wedding night and her imprisonment.

All of them, however, tell of the unending futility of the task the forty-nine Danaïds were compelled to pursue in the lower world as a punishment for murdering their husbands. At the river's edge they filled forever jars riddled with holes, so that the water poured away and they must return to fill them again, and again see them drained dry.

GLAUCUS AND SCYLLA

Glaucus was a fisherman who was fishing one day from a green meadow which sloped down to the sea. He had spread his catch out on the grass and was counting the fish when he saw them all begin to stir and then, moving toward the water, slip into it and swim away. He was utterly amazed. Had a god done this or was there some strange power in the grass? He picked a handful and ate it. At once an irresistible longing for the sea took possession of him. There was no denying it. He ran and leaped into the waves. The sea-gods received him kindly and called on Ocean and Tethys to purge his mortal nature away and make him one of them. A hundred rivers were summoned to pour their waters upon him. He lost consciousness in the rushing flood. When he recovered he was a sea-god with hair green like the sea and a body ending in a fish's tail, to the dwellers in the water a fine and familiar form, but strange and repellent to the dwellers on earth. So he seemed to the lovely nymph Scylla when she was bathing in a little bay and caught sight of him rising from the sea. She fled from him until she

Glaucus and Scylla

stood on a lofty promontory where she could safely watch him, wondering at the half-man, half-fish. Glaucus called up to her, "Maiden, I am no monster. I am a god with power over the waters—and I love you." But Scylla turned from him and hastening inland was lost to his sight.

Glaucus was in despair, for he was madly in love; and he determined to go to Circe, the enchantress, and beg her for a love-potion to melt Scylla's hard heart. But as he told her his tale of love and implored her help Circe fell in love with him. She wooed him with her sweetest words and looks, but Glaucus would have none of her. "Trees will cover the sea bottom and seaweed the mountain tops before I cease to love Scylla," he told her. Circe was furiously angry, but with Scylla, not Glaucus. She prepared a vial of very powerful poison and, going to the bay where Scylla bathed, she poured into it the baleful liquid. As soon as Scylla entered the water she was changed into a frightful monster. Out from her body grew serpents' and fierce dogs' heads. The beastly forms were part of her; she could not fly from them or push them away. She stood there rooted to a rock, in her unutterable misery hating and destroying everything that came within her reach, a peril to all sailors who passed near her, as Jason and Odysseus and Aeneas found out.

ERYSICHTHON

One woman had power given her to assume different shapes, power as great as Proteus had. She used it, strangely enough, to procure food for her starving father. Her story is the only one in which the good goddess, Ceres, appears cruel and vindictive. Erysichthon had the wicked audacity to cut down the tallest oak in a grove sacred to Ceres. His servants shrank from the sacrilege when he ordered them to fell it; whereupon he seized an ax himself and attacked the mighty trunk around which the dryads used to hold their dances. Blood flowed from the tree when he struck it and a voice came from within warning him that Ceres would surely punish his crime. But these marvels did not check his fury; he struck again and again until the great oak crashed to the ground. The dryads hastened to Ceres to tell her what had happened, and the goddess, deeply offended, told them she would punish the criminal in a way never known before. She sent one of them in her car to the bleak region where Famine dwells to order her to take possession of Erysichthon. "Bid her see to it," Ceres said, "that no abundance shall ever satisfy him. He shall starve in the very act of devouring food."

Famine obeyed the command. She entered Erysichthon's room where he slept and she wrapped her skinny arms around him. Holding him in her foul embrace she filled him with herself and planted hunger within him. He woke with a raging desire for food and called for something to eat. But the more he ate the more he wanted. Even as he crammed meat down his throat he starved. He spent all his wealth on vast supplies of food which never gave him a moment's satisfaction. At last he had nothing left except his daughter. He sold her too. On the seashore, where her owner's ship lay, she prayed to Poseidon to save her from slavery and the god heard her prayer. He changed her into a fisherman. Her master, who had been but a little behind her, saw on the long stretch of beach only the figure of a man busy with his fishing lines. He called to him, "Where has that girl gone who was here a moment ago? Here are her footprints and they suddenly stop." The supposed fisherman answered, "I swear by the God of the Sea that no man except myself has come to this shore, and no woman either." When the other, completely bewildered, had gone off in his boat, the girl returned to her own shape. She went back to her father and delighted him by telling him what had happened. He saw an endless opportunity of making money by her. He sold her again and again. Each time Poseidon changed her, now into a mare, now into a bird, and so on. Each time she escaped from her owner and came back to her father. But at last, when the money she thus earned for him was not enough for his needs, he turned upon his own body and devoured it until he killed himself.

POMONA AND VERTUMNUS

These two were Roman divinities, not Greek. Pomona was the only nymph who did not love the wild woodland. She cared for fruits and orchards and that was all she cared for. Her delight was in pruning and grafting and everything that belongs to the gardener's art. She shut herself away from men, alone with her beloved trees, and let no wooer come near her. Of all that sought her Vertumnus was the most ardent, but he could make no headway. Often he was able to enter her presence in disguise, now as a rude reaper bringing her a basket of barley-ears, now as a clumsy herdsman, or a vine-pruner. At such times he had the joy of looking at her, but also the wretchedness of knowing she would never look at such a one as he seemed to be. At last, however, he made a better plan. He came to her disguised as a very old woman, so that it did not seem strange to Pomona when after admiring her fruit he said to her, "But you are far more beautiful," and kissed her. Still, he kept on kissing her as no old woman would have done, and Pomona was startled. Perceiving this he let her go and sat down opposite an elm tree over which grew a vine loaded with purple grapes. He said softly, "How lovely they are together, and how different they would be apart, the tree useless and the vine flat on the ground unable to bear fruit. Are not you like such a vine? You turn from all who desire you. You will try to stand alone. And yet there is one—listen to an old woman who loves you more than you know—you would do well not to reject, Vertumnus. You are his first love and will be his last. And he too cares for the orchard and the garden. He would work by your side." Then, speaking with great seriousness, he pointed out to her how Venus had shown many a time that she hated hard-hearted maidens; and he told her the sad story of Anaxarete, who had disdained her suitor Iphis, until in despair he hanged himself from her gatepost, whereupon Venus turned the heartless girl into a stone image. "Be warned," he begged, "and yield to your true lover." With this, he dropped his disguise and stood before her a radiant youth. Pomona yielded to such beauty joined to such eloquence, and henceforward her orchards had two gardeners.

21—Brief Myths Arranged
Alphabetically

AMALTHEA

According to one story she was a goat on whose milk the infant Zeus was fed. According to another she was a nymph who owned the goat. She was said to have a horn which was always full of whatever food or drink anyone wanted, the Horn of Plenty (in Latin *Cornu copiae*—also known as "the Cornucopia" in Latin mythology). But the Latins said the Cornucopia was the horn of Achelous which Hercules broke off when he conquered that river-god, who had taken the form of a bull to fight him. It was always magically full of fruits and flowers.

THE AMAZONS

Aeschylus calls them "The warring Amazons, men-haters." They were a nation of women, all warriors. They were supposed to live around the Caucasus and their chief city was Themiscyra. Curiously enough, they inspired artists to make statues and pictures of them far more than poets to write of them. Familiar though they are to us there are few stories about them. They invaded Lycia and were repulsed by Bellerophon. They invaded Phrygia when Priam was young, and Attica when Theseus was King. He had carried off their Queen and they tried to rescue her, but Theseus defeated them. In the Trojan War they fought the Greeks under their Queen, Penthesilea, according to a story not in the *Iliad*, told by Pausanias. He says that she was killed by Achilles, who mourned for her as she lay dead, so young and so beautiful.

AMYMONE

She was one of the Danaïds. Her father sent her to draw water and a satyr saw her and pursued her. Poseidon heard her cry for help, loved her and saved her from the satyr. With his trident he made in her honor the spring which bears her name.

ANTIOPE

A princess of Thebes, Antiope, bore two sons to Zeus, Zethus and Amphion. Fearing her father's anger she left the children on a lonely mountain as soon as they were born, but they were discovered by a herdsman and brought up by him. The man then ruling Thebes, Lycus, and his wife Dirce, treated Antiope with great cruelty until she determined to hide herself from them. Finally she came to the cottage where her sons lived. Somehow they recognized her or she them, and gathering a band of their friends they went to the palace to avenge her. They killed Lycus and brought a terrible death upon Dirce, tying her by her hair to a bull. The brothers threw her body into the spring which was ever after called by her name.

ARACHNE

(This story is told only by the Latin poet, Ovid. Therefore the Latin names of the gods are given.)

The fate of this maiden was another example of the danger of claiming equality with the gods in anything whatsoever. Minerva was the weaver among the Olympians as Vulcan was the smith. Quite naturally she considered the stuffs she wove unapproachable for fineness and beauty, and she was outraged when she heard that a simple peasant girl named Arachne declared her own work to be superior. The goddess went forthwith to the hut where the maiden lived and challenged her to a contest. Arachne accepted. Both set up their looms and stretched the warp upon them. Then they went to work. Heaps of skeins of beautiful threads colored like the rainbow lay beside each, and threads of gold and silver too. Minerva did her best and the result was a marvel, but Arachne's work, finished at the same moment, was in no way inferior. The goddess in a fury of anger slit the web from top to bottom and beat the girl around the head with her shuttle. Arachne, disgraced and mortified and furiously angry, hanged herself. Then a little repentance entered Minerva's heart. She lifted the body from the noose and sprinkled it with a magic liquid. Arachne was changed into a spider, and her skill in weaving was left to her.

ARION

He seems to have been a real person, a poet who lived about 700 B.C., but none of his poems have come down to us, and all that is actually known of him is the story of his escape from death, which is quite like a mythological story. He had gone from Corinth to Sicily to take part in a music contest. He was a master of the lyre and he won the prize. On the voyage home the sailors coveted the prize and planned to kill him. Apollo told him in a dream of his danger and how to save his life. When the sailors attacked him he begged them as a last favor to let him play and sing, before he died. At the end of the song he flung himself into the sea, where dolphins, who had been drawn to the ship by the enchanting music, bore him up as he sank and carried him to land.

ARISTAEUS

He was a keeper of bees, the son of Apollo and a water nymph, Cyrene. When his bees all died from some unknown cause he went for help to his mother. She told him that Proteus, the wise old god of the sea, could show him how to prevent another such disaster, but that he would do so only if compelled. Aristaeus must seize him and chain him, a very difficult task, as Menelaus on his way home from Troy found. Proteus had the power to change himself into any number of different forms. However, if his captor was resolute enough to hold him fast through all the changes, he would finally give in and answer what he was asked. Aristaeus followed directions. He went to the favorite haunt of Proteus, the island of Pharos, or some say Carpathos. There he seized Proteus and did not let him go, in spite of the terrible forms he assumed, until the god was discouraged and returned to his own shape. Then he told Aristaeus to sacrifice to the gods and leave the carcasses of the animals in the place of sacrifice. Nine days later he must go back and examine the bodies. Again Aristaeus did as he was bid, and on the ninth day he found a marvel, a great swarm of bees in one of the carcasses. He never again was troubled by any blight or disease among them.

AURORA AND TITHONUS

The story of these two is alluded to in the *Iliad:*—

Now from her couch where she lay beside high-born Tithonus, the goddess
Dawn, rosy-fingered, arose to bring light to the gods and to mortals.

This Tithonus, the husband of Aurora, the Goddess of the Dawn, was the father of her son, the dark-skinned prince Memnon of Ethiopia who was killed at Troy, fighting for the Trojans. Tithonus himself had a strange fate. Aurora asked Zeus to make him immortal and he agreed, but she had not thought to ask also that he should remain young. So it came to pass that he grew old, but could not die. Helpless at last, unable to move hand or foot, he prayed for death, but there was no release for him. He must live on forever, with old age forever pressing upon him more and more. At last in pity the goddess laid him in a room and left him, shutting the door. There he babbled endlessly, words with no meaning. His mind had gone with his strength of body. He was only the dry husk of a man.

There is a story too that he shrank and shrank in size until at last Aurora with a feeling for the natural fitness of things turned him into the skinny and noisy grasshopper.

To Memnon, his son, a great statue was erected in Egypt at Thebes, and it was said that when the first rays of the dawn fell upon it a sound came from it like the twanging of a harp-string.

BITON AND CLEOBIS were the sons of Cydippe, a priest-ess of Hera. She longed to see a most beautiful statue of the goddess of Argos, made by the great sculptor Polyclitus the Elder, who was said to be as great as his younger contempo-rary, Phidias. Argos was too far away for her to walk there and they had no horses or oxen to draw her. But her two sons determined that she should have her wish. They yoked them-selves to a car and drew her all the long way through dust and heat. Everyone admired their filial piety when they ar-rived, and the proud and happy mother standing before the statue prayed that Hera would reward them by giving them the best gift in her power. As she finished her prayer the two lads sank to the ground. They were smiling, and they looked as if they were peacefully asleep; but they were dead.

CALLISTO

She was the daughter of Lycaon, a king of Arcadia who had been changed into a wolf because of his wickedness. He had set human flesh on the table for Zeus when the god was his guest. His punishment was deserved, but his daughter suffered as terribly as he and she was innocent of all wrong. Zeus saw her hunting in the train of Artemis and fell in love with her.

Hera, furiously angry, turned the maiden into a bear after her son was born. When the boy was grown and out hunting, the goddess brought Callisto before him, intending to have him shoot his mother, in ignorance, of course. But Zeus snatched the bear away and placed her among the stars, where she is called the Great Bear. Later, her son Arcas was placed beside her and called the Lesser Bear. Hera, enraged at this honor to her rival, persuaded the God of the Sea to forbid the Bears to descend into the ocean like the other stars. They alone of the constellations never set below the horizon.

CHIRON

He was one of the Centaurs, but unlike the others who were violent fierce creatures, he was known everywhere for his goodness and wisdom, so much so that the young sons of heroes were entrusted to him to train and teach. Achilles was his pupil and Aesculapius, the great physician; the famous hunter Actaeon, too, and many another. He alone among the Centaurs was immortal and yet in the end he died and went to the lower world. Indirectly and unintentionally Hercules was the cause of his dying. He had stopped in to see a Centaur who was a friend of his, Pholus, and being very thirsty he persuaded him to open a jar of wine which was the common property of all the Centaurs. The aroma of the wonderful liquor informed the others what had happened and they rushed down to take vengeance on the offender. But Hercules was more than a match for them all. He fought them off, but in the fight he accidentally wounded Chiron, who had taken no part in the attack. The wound proved to be incurable and finally Zeus permitted Chiron to die rather than live forever in pain.

CLYTIE

Her story is unique, for instead of a god in love with an unwilling maiden, a maiden is in love with an unwilling god. Clytie loved the Sun-god and he found nothing to love in her. She pined away sitting on the ground out-of-doors where she could watch him, turning her face and following him with her eyes as he journeyed over the sky. So gazing she was changed into a flower, the sunflower, which ever turns toward the sun.

DRYOPE

Her story, like a number of others, shows how strongly the ancient Greeks disapproved of destroying or injuring a tree.

With her sister Iole she went one day to a pool intending to make garlands for the nymphs. She was carrying her little son, and seeing near the water a lotus tree full of bright blossoms she plucked some of them to please the baby. To her horror she saw drops of blood flowing down the stem. The tree was really the nymph, Lotis, who fleeing from a pursuer had taken refuge in this form. When Dryope, terrified at the ominous sight, tried to hurry away, her feet would not move; they seemed rooted in the ground. Iole watching her helplessly saw bark begin to grow upward covering her body. It had reached her face when her husband came to the spot with her father. Iole cried out what had happened and the two, rushing to the tree, embraced the still warm trunk and watered it with their tears. Dryope had time only to declare that she had done no wrong intentionally and to beg them to bring the child often to the tree to play in its shade, and some day to tell him her story so that he would think whenever he saw the spot: "Here in this tree-trunk my mother is hidden." "Tell him too," she said, "never to pluck flowers, and to think every bush may be a goddess in disguise." Then she could speak no more; the bark closed over her face. She was gone forever.

EPIMENIDES

A figure of mythology only because of the story of his long sleep. He lived around 600 B.C. and is said as a boy when looking for a lost sheep to have been overcome by a slumber which lasted for fifty-seven years. On waking he continued the search for the sheep unaware of what had happened, and found everything changed. He was sent by the oracle at Delphi to purify Athens of a plague. When the grateful Athenians would have given him a large sum of money he refused and asked only that there should be friendship between Athens and his own home, Cnossus in Crete.

ERICTHONIUS

He is the same as Erechtheus. Homer knew only one man of that name. Plato speaks of two. He was the son of Hephaestus, reared by Athena, half man, half serpent. Athena gave a chest in which she had put the infant to the three daughters of Cecrops, forbidding them to open it. They did open it, however, and saw in it the serpent-like creature. Athena drove them mad as a punishment, and they killed themselves, jumping from the Acropolis. When Ericthonius grew up he became King of Athens. His grandson was called by his name, and was the father of the second Cecrops, Procris, Creüsa, and Orithyia.

HERO AND LEANDER

Leander was a youth of Abydus, a town on the Hellespont, and Hero was Priestess of Aphrodite in Sestus on the opposite shore. Every night Leander swam across to her, guided by the light, some say of the lighthouse in Sestus, some of a torch Hero always set blazing on the top of a tower. One very stormy night the light was blown out by the wind and Leander perished. His body was washed up on the shore and Hero, finding it, killed herself.

THE HYADES were daughters of Atlas and half sisters of the Pleiades. They were the rainy stars, supposed to bring rain because the time of their evening and morning setting, which comes in early May and November, is usually rainy. They were six in number. Dionysus as a baby was entrusted to them by Zeus, and to reward them for their care he set them among the stars.

IBYCUS AND THE CRANES

He is not a mythological character, but a poet who lived about 550 B.C. Only a very few fragments of his poems have come down to us. All that is known of him is the dramatic story of his death. He was attacked by robbers near Corinth and mortally wounded. A flock of cranes flew by overhead, and he called on them to avenge him. Soon after, over the open theater in Corinth where a play was being performed to a full house, a flock of cranes appeared, hovering above the crowd. Suddenly a man's voice was heard. He cried out as if panic-stricken, "The cranes of Ibycus, the avengers!" The audience in turn shouted, "The murderer has informed against himself." The man was seized, the other robbers discovered, and all put to death.

LETO (*LATONA*)

She was the daughter of the Titans Phoebe and Coeus. Zeus loved her, but when she was about to bear a child he abandoned her, afraid of Hera. All countries and islands, afraid for the same reason, refused to receive her and give her a place where her child could be born. On and on she wandered in desperation until she reached a bit of land which was floating on the sea. It had no foundation, but was tossed hither and thither by waves and winds. It was called Delos and besides being of all islands the most insecure it was rocky and barren. But when Leto set foot on it and asked for refuge, the little isle welcomed her gladly, and at that moment four lofty pillars rose from the bottom of the sea and held it firmly anchored forever. There Leto's children were born, Artemis and Phoebus Apollo; and in after years Apollo's glorious temple stood there, visited by men from all over the world. The barren rock was called "the heaven-built isle," and from being the most despised it became the most renowned of islands.

LINUS

In the *Iliad* a vineyard is described with youths and maidens singing, as they gather the fruit, "a sweet Linus song." This was probably a lament for the young son of Apollo and Psamathe—Linus, who was deserted by his mother, brought up by shepherds, and before he was full-grown torn to pieces by dogs. This Linus was, like Adonis and Hyacinthus, a type of all lovely young life that dies or is withered before it has borne fruit. The Greek word *ailinon!*, meaning "woe for Linus!" grew to mean no more than the English "alas!" and was used in any lament. There was another Linus, the son of Apollo and a Muse, who taught Orpheus and tried to teach Hercules, but was killed by him.

MARPESSA

She was more fortunate than other maidens beloved of the gods. Idas, one of the heroes of the Calydonian Hunt and also one of the Argonauts, carried her off from her father with her consent. They would have lived happily ever after, but Apollo fell in love with her. Idas refused to give her up; he even dared to fight with Apollo for her. Zeus parted them and told Marpessa to choose which she would have. She chose the mortal, fearing, certainly not without reason, that the god would not be faithful to her.

MARSYAS

The flute was invented by Athena, but she threw it away because in order to play it she had to puff out her cheeks and disfigure her face. Marsyas, a satyr, found it and played so enchantingly upon it that he dared to challenge Apollo to a contest. The god won, of course, and punished Marsyas by flaying him.

MELAMPUS

He saved and reared two little snakes when his servants killed the parent snakes, and as pets they repaid him well. Once when he was asleep they crept upon his couch and licked his ears. He started up in a great fright, but he found that he understood what two birds on his window sill were saying to each other. The snakes had made him able to understand the language of all flying and all creeping creatures. He learned in this way the art of divination as no one ever had, and he became a famous soothsayer. He saved himself, too, by his knowledge. His enemies once captured him and kept him a prisoner in a little cell. While there, he heard the worms saying that the roof-beam had been almost gnawed through so that it would soon fall and crush all beneath it. At once he told his captors and asked to be moved elsewhere. They did as he said and directly afterward the roof fell in. Then they saw how great a diviner he was and they freed and rewarded him.

MEROPE

Her husband, Cresphontes, a son of Hercules, and king of Messenia, was killed in a rebellion together with two of his sons. The man who succeeded him, Polyphontes, took her as his wife. But her third son, Aepytus, had been hidden by her in Arcadia. He returned years later pretending to be a man who had slain Aepytus and was kindly received therefore by Polyphontes. His mother, however, not knowing who he was, planned to kill her son's murderer, as she thought him. However, in the end she found out who he was and the two together brought about Polyphontes' death. Aepytus became king.

THE MYRMIDONS

These were men created from ants on the island of Aegina, in the reign of Aeacus, Achilles' grandfather, and they were Achilles' followers in the Trojan War. Not only were they thrifty and industrious, as one would suppose from their origin, but they were also brave. They were changed into men from ants because of one of Hera's attacks of jealousy. She was angry because Zeus loved Aegina, the maiden for whom the island was named, and whose son, Aeacus, became its king. Hera sent a fearful pestilence which destroyed the people by thousands. It seemed that no one would be left alive. Aeacus climbed to the lofty temple of Zeus and prayed to him, reminding him that he was his son and the son of a woman the god had loved. As he spoke he saw a troop of busy ants. "O Father," he cried, "make of these creatures a people for me, as numerous as they, and fill my empty city." A peal of thunder seemed to answer him and that night he dreamed that he saw the ants being transformed into human shape. At daybreak his son Telamon woke him saying that a great host of men was approaching the palace. He went out and saw a multitude, as many as the ants in number, all crying out that they were his faithful subjects. So Aegina was repopulated from an ant hill and its people were called Myrmidons after the ant (*myrmex*) from which they had sprung.

NISUS AND SCYLLA

Nisus, King of Megara, had on his head, a purple lock of hair which he had been warned never to cut. The safety of his throne depended upon his preserving it. Minos of Crete laid siege to his city, but Nisus knew that no harm would come to it as long as he had the purple lock. His daughter, Scylla, used to watch Minos from the city wall and she fell madly in love with him. She could think of no way to make him care for her except by taking her father's lock of hair to him and enabling him to conquer the town. She did this; she cut it from her father's head in his sleep and carrying it to Minos she confessed what she had done. He shrank from her in horror and drove her out of his sight. When the city had been conquered and the Cretans launched their ships to sail home, she came rushing to the shore, mad with passion, and leaping into the water seized the rudder of the boat that carried Minos. But at this moment a great eagle swooped down upon her. It was her father, whom the gods had saved by changing him into a bird. In terror she let go her hold, and would have fallen into the water, but suddenly she too became a bird. Some god had pity on her, traitor though she was, because she had sinned through love.

ORION

He was a young man of gigantic stature and great beauty, and a mighty hunter. He fell in love with the daughter of the King of Chios, and for love of her he cleared the island of wild beasts. The spoils of the chase he brought always home to his beloved, whose name is sometimes said to be Aero, sometimes Merope. Her father, Oenopion, agreed to give her to Orion, but he kept putting the marriage off. One day when Orion was drunk he insulted the maiden, and Oenopion appealed to Dionysus to punish him. The god threw him into a deep sleep and Oenopion blinded him. An oracle told him, however, that he would be able to see again if he went to the east and let the rays of the rising sun fall on his eyes. He went as far east as Lemnos and there he recovered his sight. Instantly he started back to Chios to take vengeance on the king, but he had fled and Orion could not find him. He went on to Crete, and lived there as Artemis' huntsman. Nevertheless in the end the goddess killed him. Some say that Dawn, also called Aurora, loved him and that Artemis in jealous anger shot him. Others say that he made Apollo angry and that the god by a trick got his sister to slay him. After his death he was placed in heaven as a constellation, which shows him with a girdle, sword, club and lion's skin.

THE PLEIADES

They were the daughters of Atlas, seven in number. Their names were Electra, Maia, Taygete, Alcyone, Merope, Celaeno, Sterope. Orion pursued them but they fled before him and he could never seize any of them. Still he continued to follow them until Zeus, pitying them, placed them in the heavens as stars. But it was said that even there Orion continued his pursuit, always unsuccessful, yet persistent. While they lived on earth one of them, Maia, was the mother of Hermes. Another, Electra, was the mother of Dardanus, the founder of the Trojan race. Although it is agreed that there were seven of them, only six stars are clearly visible. The seventh is invisible except to those who have specially keen sight.

RHOECUS seeing an oak about to fall propped it up. The dryad who would have perished with it told him to ask anything he desired and she would give it. He answered that he wanted only her love and she consented. She bade him keep on the alert for she would send him a messenger, a bee, to tell him her wishes. But Rhoecus met some companions and forgot all about the bee, so much so that when he heard one buzzing he drove it away and hurt it. Returning to the tree he was blinded by the dryad, who was angry at the disregard of her words and the injury to her messenger.

SALMONEUS

This man was another illustration of how fatal it was for mortals to try to emulate the gods. What he did was so foolish, however, that in later years it was often said that he had gone mad. He pretended that he was Zeus. He had a chariot made in such a way that there was a loud clanging of brass when it moved. On the day of Zeus's festival he drove it furiously through the town, scattering at the same time fire-brands and shouting to the people to worship him because he was Zeus the Thunderer. But instantly there came a crash of actual thunder and a flash of lightning. Salmoneus fell from his chariot dead.

The story is often explained as pointing back to a time when weather-magic was practised. Salmoneus, according to this view, was a magician trying to bring on a rainstorm by imitating it, a common magical method.

SISYPHUS was King of Corinth. One day he chanced to see a mighty eagle, greater and more splendid than any mortal bird, bearing a maiden to an island not far away. When the river-god Asopus came to him to tell him that his daughter Aegina had been carried off, he strongly suspected by Zeus, and to ask his help in finding her, Sisyphus told him what he had seen. Thereby he drew down on himself the relentless wrath of Zeus. In Hades he was punished by having to try forever to roll a rock uphill which forever rolled back upon him. Nor did he help Asopus. The river-god went to the island but Zeus drove him away with his thunderbolt. The name of the island was changed to Aegina in honor of the maiden, and her son Aeacus was the grandfather of Achilles, who was called sometimes Aeacides, descendant of Aeacus.

TYRO was the daughter of Salmoneus. She bore twin sons to Poseidon—but fearing her father's displeasure if he learned of the children's birth, she abandoned them. They were found by the keeper of Salmoneus' horses, and brought up by him and his wife, who called one Pelias and the other Neleus. Tyro's husband Cretheus discovered, years later, what her relations with Poseidon had been. In great anger he put her away and married one of her maids, Sidero, who ill-treated her. When Cretheus died the twins were told by their foster-mother who their real parents were. They went at once to seek out Tyro and discover themselves to her. They found her living in great misery and so they looked for Sidero, to punish her. She had heard of their arrival and she had taken refuge in Hera's temple. Nevertheless Pelias slew her, defying the goddess's anger. Hera revenged herself, but only after many years. Pelias' half-brother, the son of Tyro and Cretheus, was the father of Jason, whom Pelias tried to kill by sending him after the Golden Fleece. Instead, Jason was indirectly the cause of his death. He was killed by his daughters under the direction of Medea, Jason's wife.

PART SEVEN
The Mythology of the Norsemen

Introduction to Norse Mythology

The world of Norse mythology is a strange world. Asgard, the home of the gods, is unlike any other heaven men have dreamed of. No radiancy of joy is in it, no assurance of bliss. It is a grave and solemn place, over which hangs the threat of an inevitable doom. The gods know that a day will come when they will be destroyed. Sometime they will meet their enemies and go down beneath them to defeat and death. Asgard will fall in ruins. The cause the forces of good are fighting to defend against the forces of evil is hopeless. Nevertheless, the gods will fight for it to the end.

Necessarily the same is true of humanity. If the gods are finally helpless before evil, men and women must be more so. The heroes and heroines of the early stories face disaster. They know that they cannot save themselves, not by any courage or endurance or great deed. Even so, they do not yield. They die resisting. A brave death entitles them—at least the heroes—to a seat in Valhalla, one of the halls in Asgard, but there too they must look forward to final defeat and destruction. In the last battle between good and evil they will fight on the side of the gods and die with them.

This is the conception of life which underlies the Norse religion, as somber a conception as the mind of man has ever given birth to. The only sustaining support possible for the human spirit, the one pure unsullied good men can hope to attain, is heroism; and heroism depends on lost causes. The hero can prove what he is only by dying. The power of good is shown not by triumphantly conquering evil, but by continuing to resist evil while facing certain defeat.

Such an attitude toward life seems at first sight fatalistic, but actually the decrees of an inexorable fate played no more part in the Norseman's scheme of existence than predestination did in St. Paul's or in that of his militant Protestant followers, and for precisely the same reason. Although the Norse hero was doomed if he did not yield, he could choose between yielding or dying. The decision was in his own hands. Even more than that. A heroic death, like a martyr's death, is not a defeat, but a triumph. The hero in one of the Norse stories who laughs aloud while his foes cut his heart out of his living flesh shows himself superior to his conquerors. He says to them, in effect, You can do nothing to me because I do not care what you do. They kill him, but he dies undefeated.

This is stern stuff for humanity to live by, as stern in its totally different way as the Sermon on the Mount, but the easy way has never in the long run commanded the allegiance of mankind. Like the early Christians, the Norsemen measured their life by heroic standards. The Christian, however, looked forward to a heaven of eternal joy. The Norseman did not. But it would appear that for unknown centuries, until the Christian missionaries came, heroism was enough.

The poets of the Norse mythology, who saw that victory was possible in death and that courage was never defeated, are the only spokesmen for the belief of the whole great Teutonic race—of which England is a part, and ourselves through the first settlers in America. Everywhere else in northwestern Europe the early records, the traditions, the songs and stories, were obliterated by the priests of Christianity, who felt a bitter hatred for the paganism they had come to destroy. It is extraordinary how clean a sweep they were able to make. A few bits survived: *Beowulf* in England, the *Nibelungenlied* in Germany, and some stray fragments here and there. But if it were not for the two Icelandic Eddas we should know practically nothing of the religion which molded the race to which we belong. In Iceland, naturally by its position the last northern country to be Christianized, the missionaries seem to have been gentler, or, perhaps, they had less influence. Latin did not drive Norse out as the literary tongue. The people still told the old stories in the common speech, and some of them were written down, although by whom or when we do not know. The oldest manuscript of the *Elder Edda* is dated at about 1300, three hundred years after the Christians arrived, but the poems it is made up of are purely pagan and adjudged by all scholars to be very old. The *Younger Edda*, in prose, was written down by one Snorri Sturluson in the last part of the twelfth century. The chief part of it is a technical treatise on how to write poetry, but it also contains some prehistoric mythological material which is not in the *Elder Edda*.

The *Elder Edda* is much the more important of the two. It is made up of separate poems, often about the same story, but never connected with each other. The material for a great epic is there, as great as the *Iliad*, perhaps even greater, but no poet came to work it over as Homer did the early stories which preceded the *Iliad*. There was no man of genius in the Northland to weld the poems into a whole and make it a thing of beauty and power; no one even to discard the crude and the commonplace and cut out the childish and wearisome repetitions. There are lists of names in the *Edda* which sometimes run on unbroken for pages. Nevertheless the somber grandeur of the stories comes through in spite of the style. Perhaps no one should speak of "the style" who cannot read ancient Norse; but all the translations are so alike in being singularly awkward and involved that one cannot but suspect the original of being responsible, at least in part. The poets of the *Elder Edda* seem to have had conceptions greater than their skill to put them into words. Many of the stories are splendid. There are none to equal them in Greek mythology, except those retold by the tragic poets. All the best Northern tales are tragic, about men and women who go steadfastly forward to meet death, often deliberately choose it, even plan it long beforehand. The only light in the darkness is heroism.

22 The Stories of Signy and Sigurd

*I have selected these two stories to tell because they
seem to me to present better than any other the Norse
character and the Norse point of view. Sigurd is the
most famous of Norse heroes; his story is largely
that of the hero of the* Nibelungenlied, *Siegfried. He
plays the chief part in the* Volsungasaga, *the Norse
version of the German tale which Wagner's operas
have made familiar. I have not gone to it, however,
for my story, but to the* Elder Edda, *where the love
and death of Sigurd and Brynhild and Gudrun are the
subject of a number of the poems. The sagas, all prose
tales, are of later date. Signy's story is told only in
the* Volsungasaga.

Signy was the daughter of Volsung and the sister of Sigmund.
Her husband slew Volsung by treachery and captured his sons.
One by one he chained them at night to where the wolves
would find them and devour them. When the last, who was
Sigmund, was brought out and chained, Signy had devised a
way to save him. She freed him and the two took a vow to
avenge their father and brothers. Signy determined that Sigmund should have one of their own blood to help him and
she visited him in disguise and spent three nights with him. He
never knew who she was. When the boy who was born of their
union was of an age to leave her, she sent him to Sigmund and
the two lived together until the lad—his name was Sinfiotli—
was grown to manhood. All this time Signy was living with her
husband, bearing him children, showing him nothing of the
one burning desire in her heart, to take vengeance upon him.
The day for it came at last. Sigmund and Sinfiotli surprised
the household. They killed Signy's other children; they shut
her husband in the house and set fire to it. Signy watched them

with never a word. When all was done she told them that they had gloriously avenged the dead, and with that she entered the burning dwelling and died there. Through the years while she had waited she had planned when she killed her husband to die with him. Clytemnestra would fade beside her if there had been a Norse Aeschylus to write her story.

The story of Siegfried is so familiar that that of his Norse prototype, Sigurd, can be briefly told. Brynhild, a Valkyrie, has disobeyed Odin and is punished by being put to sleep until some man shall wake her. She begs that he who comes to her shall be one whose heart knows no fear, and Odin surrounds her couch with flaming fire which only a hero would brave. Sigurd, the son of Sigmund, does the deed. He forces his horse through the flames and wakens Brynhild, who gives herself to him joyfully because he has proved his valor in reaching her. Some days later he leaves her in the same fire-ringed place.

Sigurd goes to the home of the Giukungs where he swears brotherhood with the king, Gunnar. Griemhild, Gunnar's mother, wants Sigurd for her daughter Gudrun, and gives him a magic potion which makes him forget Brynhild. He marries Gudrun; then, assuming through Griemhild's magical power the appearance of Gunnar, he rides through the flames again to win Brynhild for Gunnar, who is not hero enough to do this himself. Sigurd spends three nights there with her, but he places his sword between them in the bed. Brynhild goes with him to the Giukungs, where Sigurd takes his own shape again, but without Brynhild's knowledge. She marries Gunnar, believing that Sigurd was faithless to her and that Gunnar had ridden through the flames for her. In a quarrel with Gudrun she learns the truth and she plans her revenge. She tells Gunnar that Sigurd broke his oath to him, that he really possessed her those three nights when he declared that his sword lay between them, and that unless Gunnar kills Sigurd she will leave him. Gunnar himself cannot kill Sigurd because of the oath of brotherhood he has sworn, but he persuades his younger brother to slay Sigurd in his sleep, and Gudrun wakes to find her husband's blood flowing over her.

> Then Brynhild laughed,
> Only once, with all her heart,
> When she heard the wail of Gudrun.

But although, or because, she brought about his death, she will not live when Sigurd is dead. She says to her husband:—

> One alone of all I loved.
> I never had a changing heart.

Sigurd riding through the fire to Brynhild

She tells him that Sigurd had not been false to his oath when he rode through the fiery ring to win her for Gunnar.

> In one bed together we slept
> As if he had been my brother.
> Ever with grief and all too long
> Are men and women born in the world—

She kills herself, praying that her body shall be laid on the funeral pyre with Sigurd's.

Beside his body Gudrun sits in silence. She cannot speak; she cannot weep. They fear that her heart will break unless she can find relief, and one by one the women tell her of their own grief,

> The bitterest pain each had ever borne.

Husband, daughters, sisters, brothers,—one says,—all were taken from me, and still I live.

> Yet for her grief Gudrun could not weep.
> So hard was her heart by the hero's body.

My seven sons fell in the southern land, another says, and my husband too, all eight in battle. I decked with my own hands the bodies for the grave. One half-year brought me this to bear. And no one came to comfort me.

> Yet for her grief Gudrun could not weep.
> So hard was her heart by the hero's body.

Then one wiser than the rest lifts the shroud from the dead.

> . . . She laid
> His well-loved head on the knees of his wife.
> "Look on him thou loved and press thy lips
> To his as if he still were living."
> Only once did Gudrun look.
> She saw his hair all clotted with blood,
> His blinded eyes that had been so bright,
> Then she bent and bowed her head,
> And her tears ran down like drops of rain.

• • •

Such are the early Norse stories. Man is born to sorrow as the sparks fly upward. To live is to suffer and the only solution of the problem of life is to suffer with courage. Sigurd, on his way to Brynhild the first time, meets a wise man and asks him what his fate shall be,

> Hide nothing from me however hard.

The wise man answers:—

> Thou knowest that I will not lie.
> Never shalt thou be stained by baseness.
> Yet a day of doom shall come upon thee,
> A day of wrath and a day of anguish.
> But ever remember, ruler of men,
> That fortune lies in the hero's life.
> And a nobler man shall never live
> Beneath the sun than Sigurd.

23 The Norse Gods

No god of Greece could be heroic. All the Olympians were immortal and invincible. They could never feel the glow of courage; they could never defy danger. When they fought they were sure of victory and no harm could ever come near them. It was different in Asgard. The Giants, whose city was Jötunheim, were the active, persistent enemies of the Aesir, as the gods were called, and they not only were an ever-present danger, but knew that in the end complete victory was assured to them.

This knowledge was heavy on the hearts of all the dwellers in Asgard, but it weighed heaviest on their chief and ruler, ODIN. Like Zeus, Odin was the sky-father,

> Clad in a cloud-gray kirtle and a hood as blue as the sky.

But there the resemblance ends. It would be hard to conceive anything less like the Zeus of Homer than Odin. He is a strange and solemn figure, always aloof. Even when he sits at the feasts of the gods in his golden palace, Gladsheim, or with the heroes in Valhalla, he eats nothing. The food set before him he gives to the two wolves who crouch at his feet. On his shoulders perch two ravens, who fly each day through the world and bring him back news of all that men do. The name of the one is Thought (Hugin) and of the other Memory (Munin).

While the other gods feasted, Odin pondered on what Thought and Memory taught him.

He had the responsibility more than all the other gods together of postponing as long as possible the day of doom, Ragnarok, when heaven and earth would be destroyed. He was the All-father, supreme among gods and men, yet even so he constantly sought for more wisdom. He went down to the Well of Wisdom guarded by Mimir the wise, to beg for a draught from it, and when Mimir answered that he must pay for it with one of his eyes, he consented to lose the eye. He won the knowledge of the Runes, too, by suffering. The Runes were magical inscriptions, immensely powerful for him who could inscribe them on anything—wood, metal, stone. Odin learned them at the cost of mysterious pain. He says in the *Elder Edda* that he hung

> Nine whole nights on a wind-rocked tree,
> Wounded with a spear.
> I was offered to Odin, myself to myself,
> On that tree of which no man knows.

He passed the hard-won knowledge on to men. They too were able to use the Runes to protect themselves. He imperiled his life again to take away from the Giants the skaldic mead, which made anyone who tasted it a poet. This good gift he bestowed upon men as well as upon the gods. In all ways he was mankind's benefactor.

Maidens were his attendants, the VALKYRIES. They waited on the table in Asgard and kept the drinking horns full, but their chief task was to go to the battlefield and decide at Odin's bidding who should win and who should die, and carry the brave dead to Odin. *Val* means "slain," and the Valkyries were the Choosers of the Slain; and the place to which they brought the heroes was the Hall of the Slain, Valhalla. In battle, the hero doomed to die would see

> Maidens excellent in beauty,
> Riding their steeds in shining armor,
> Solemn and deep in thought,
> With their white hands beckoning.

Wednesday is of course Odin's day. The Southern form of his name was Woden.

Of the other gods, only five were important: BALDER, THOR, FREYR, HEIMDALL, and TYR.

BALDER was the most beloved of the gods, on earth as in heaven. His death was the first of the disasters which fell upon the gods. One night he was troubled with dreams which seemed to foretell some great danger to him. When his mother, FRIGGA, the wife of Odin, heard this she determined to protect him from the least chance of danger. She went through the world and exacted an oath from everything, all things with life and without life, never to do him harm. But Odin still feared. He rode down to NIFLHEIM, the world of the dead, where he found the dwelling of HELA, or HEL, the Goddess of the Dead, all decked out in festal array. A Wise Woman told him for whom the house had been made ready:—

> The mead has been brewed for Balder.
> The hope of the high gods has gone.

Odin knew then that Balder must die, but the other gods believed that Frigga had made him safe. They played a game accordingly which gave them much pleasure. They would try to hit Balder, to throw a stone at him or hurl a dart or shoot an arrow or strike him with a sword, but always the weapons fell short of him or rolled harmlessly away. Nothing would hurt Balder. He seemed raised above them by this strange exemption and all honored him for it, except one only, LOKI. He was not a god, but the son of a Giant, and wherever he came trouble followed. He continually involved the gods in difficulties and dangers, but he was allowed to come freely to Asgard because for some reason never explained Odin had sworn brotherhood with him. He always hated the good, and he was jealous of Balder. He determined to do his best to find some way of injuring him. He went to Frigga disguised as a woman and entered into talk with her. Frigga told him of her journey to ensure Balder's safety and how everything had sworn to do him no harm. Except for one little shrub, she said, the mistletoe, so insignificant she had passed it by.

That was enough for Loki. He got the mistletoe and went with it to where the gods were amusing themselves. HODER, Balder's brother, who was blind, sat apart. "Why not join in the game?" asked Loki. "Blind as I am?" said Hoder. "And with nothing to throw at Balder, either?" "Oh, do your part," Loki said. "Here is a twig. Throw it and I will direct your aim." Hoder took the mistletoe and hurled it with all his strength. Under Loki's guidance it sped to Balder and pierced his heart. Balder fell to the ground dead.

His mother refused even then to give up hope. Frigga cried out to the gods for a volunteer to go down to Hela and try to ransom Balder. Hermod, one of her sons, offered himself. Odin gave him his horse Sleipnir and he sped down to Niflheim.

The others prepared the funeral. They built a lofty pyre on a great ship, and there they laid Balder's body. Nanna, his wife, went to look at it for the last time; her heart broke and she fell to the deck dead. Her body was placed beside his. Then the pyre was kindled and the ship pushed from the shore. As it sailed out to sea, the flames leaped up and wrapped it in fire.

When Hermod reached Hela with the gods' petition, she answered that she would give Balder back if it were proved to her that all everywhere mourned for him. But if one thing or one living creature refused to weep for him she would keep him. The gods dispatched messengers everywhere to ask all creation to shed tears so that Balder could be redeemed from death. They met with no refusal. Heaven and earth and everything therein wept willingly for the beloved god. The messengers rejoicing started back to carry the news to the gods. Then, almost at the end of their journey, they came upon a Giantess —and all the sorrow of the world was turned to futility, for she refused to weep. "Only dry tears will you get from me," she said mockingly. "I had no good from Balder, nor will I give him good." So Hela kept her dead.

Loki was punished. The gods seized him and bound him in a deep cavern. Above his head a serpent was placed so that its venom fell upon his face, causing him unutterable pain. But his wife, Sigyn, came to help him. She took her place at his side and caught the venom in a cup. Even so, whenever she had to empty the cup and the poison fell on him, though but for a moment, his agony was so intense that his convulsions shook the earth.

Of the three other great gods, THOR was the Thunder-god, for whom Thursday is named, the strongest of the Aesir; FREYR cared for the fruits of the earth; HEIMDALL was the warder of Bifröst, the rainbow bridge which led to Asgard; TYR was the God of War, for whom Tuesday, once Tyr's day, was named.

In Asgard goddesses were not as important as they were in Olympus. No one among the Norse goddesses is comparable to Athena, and only two are really notable. Frigga, Odin's wife, for whom some say Friday is named, was reputed to be very wise, but she was also very silent and she told no one, not even Odin, what she knew. She is a vague figure, oftenest depicted at her spinning-wheel, where the threads she spins are of gold, but what she spins them for is a secret.

FREYA was the Goddess of Love and Beauty, but, strangely to our ideas, half of those slain in battle were hers. Odin's Valkyries could carry only half to Valhalla. Freya herself rode to the battlefield and claimed her share of the dead, and to the Norse poets that was a natural and fitting office for the Goddess of Love. Friday is generally held to have been named for her.

But there was one realm which was handed over to the sole rule of a goddess. The Kingdom of Death was Hela's. No god had any authority there, not Odin, even. Asgard the Golden belonged to the gods; glorious Valhalla to the heroes; Midgard was the battlefield for men, not the business of women. Gudrun, in the *Elder Edda*, says,

> The fierceness of men rules the fate of women.

The cold pale world of the shadowy dead was woman's sphere in Norse mythology.

THE CREATION

In the *Elder Edda* a Wise Woman says:—

> Of old there was nothing,
> Nor sand, nor sea, nor cool waves.
> No earth, no heaven above.
> Only the yawning chasm.
> The sun knew not her dwelling,
> Nor the moon his realm.
> The stars had not their places.

But the chasm, tremendous though it was, did not extend everywhere. Far to the north was Niflheim, the cold realm of death, and far to the south was MUSPELHEIM, the land of fire. From Niflheim twelve rivers poured which flowed into the chasm and freezing there filled it slowly up with ice. From Muspelheim came fiery clouds that turned the ice to mist. Drops of water fell from the mist and out of them there were formed the frost maidens and YMIR, the first Giant. His son was Odin's father, whose mother and wife were frost maidens.

Odin and his two brothers killed Ymir. They made the earth and sky from him, the sea from his blood, the earth from his body, the heavens from his skull. They took sparks from Muspelheim and placed them in the sky as the sun, moon, and stars. The earth was round and encircled by the sea. A great wall which the gods built out of Ymir's eyebrows defended the place where mankind was to live. The space within was called Midgard. Here the first man and woman were created from trees, the man from an ash, the woman from an elm. They were the parents of all mankind. In the world were also DWARFS—ugly creatures, but masterly craftsmen, who lived under the earth; and ELVES, lovely sprites, who tended the flowers and streams.

A wondrous ash-tree, YGGDRASIL, supported the universe. It struck its roots through the worlds.

> Three roots there are to Yggdrasil
> Hel lives beneath the first.
> Beneath the second the frost-giants,
> And men beneath the third.

It is also said that "one of the roots goes up to Asgard." Beside this root was a well of white water, URDA'S WELL, so holy that none might drink of it. The three NORNS guarded it, who

> Allot their lives to the sons of men,
> And assign to them their fate.

The three were URDA (the Past), VERDANDI (the Present), and SKULD (the Future). Here each day the gods came, passing over the quivering rainbow bridge to sit beside the well and pass judgment on the deeds of men. Another well beneath another root was the WELL OF KNOWLEDGE, guarded by MIMIR the Wise.

Over Yggdrasil, as over Asgard, hung the threat of destruction. Like the gods it was doomed to die. A serpent and his brood gnawed continually at the root beside Niflheim, Hel's home. Some day they would succeed in killing the tree, and the universe would come crashing down.

The Frost Giants and the Mountain Giants who lived in Jötunheim were the enemies of all that is good. They were the brutal powers of earth, and in the inevitable contest between them and the divine powers of heaven, brute force would conquer.

> The gods are doomed and the end is death.

But such a belief is contrary to the deepest conviction of the human spirit, that good is stronger than evil. Even these sternly hopeless Norsemen, whose daily life in their icy land through the black winters was a perpetual challenge to heroism, saw a far-away light break through the darkness. There is a prophecy in the *Elder Edda*, singularly like the Book of Revelation, that after the defeat of the gods,—when

> The sun turns black, earth sinks in the sea,
> The hot stars fall from the sky,
> And fire leaps high about heaven itself,

—there would be a new heaven and a new earth,

> In wondrous beauty once again.
> The dwellings roofed with gold.
> The fields unsowed bear ripened fruit
> In happiness forevermore.

Then would come the reign of One who was higher even than Odin and beyond the reach of evil—

> A greater than all.
> But I dare not ever to speak his name.
> And there are few who can see beyond
> The moment when Odin falls.

This vision of a happiness infinitely remote seems a thin sustenance against despair, but it was the only hope the Eddas afforded.

THE NORSE WISDOM

Another view of the Norse character, oddly unlike its heroic aspect, is also given prominence in the *Elder Edda*. There are several collections of wise sayings which not only do not reflect heroism at all, but give a view of life which dispenses with it. This Norse wisdom-literature is far less profound than the Hebrew Book of Proverbs; indeed it rarely deserves to have the great word "wisdom" applied to it, but the Norsemen who created it had at any rate a large store of good sense, a striking contrast to the uncompromising spirit of the hero. Like the writers of Proverbs the authors seem old; they are men of experience who have meditated on human affairs. Once, no doubt, they were heroes, but now they have retired from battlefields and they see things from a different point of view. Sometimes they even look at life with a touch of humor:—

> There lies less good than most believe
> In ale for mortal men.

> A man knows nothing if he knows not
> That wealth oft begets an ape.

> A coward thinks he will live forever
> If only he can shun warfare.

> Tell one your thoughts, but beware of two.
> All know what is known to three.

> A silly man lies awake all night,
> Thinking of many things.
> When the morning comes he is worn with care,
> And his trouble is just as it was.

Some show a shrewd knowledge of human nature:—

> A paltry man and poor of mind
> Is he who mocks at all things.

> Brave men can live well anywhere.
> A coward dreads all things.

Now and then they are cheerful, almost light-hearted:—

> I once was young and traveled alone.
> I met another and thought myself rich.
> Man is the joy of man.

Be a friend to your friend.
Give him laughter for laughter.

To a good friend's house
The path is straight
Though he is far away.

A surprisingly tolerant spirit appears occasionally:—

No man has nothing but misery, let him be never so sick.
To this one his sons are a joy, and to that
His kin, to another his wealth.
And to yet another the good he has done.

In a maiden's words let no man place faith,
Nor in what a woman says.
But I know men and women both.
Men's minds are unstable toward women.

None so good that he has no faults,
None so wicked that he is worth naught.

There is real depth of insight sometimes:—

Moderately wise each one should be,
Not overwise, for a wise man's heart
Is seldom glad.

Cattle die and kindred die. We also die.
But I know one thing that never dies,
Judgment on each one dead.

Two lines near the end of the most important of the collections show wisdom:—

The mind knows only
What lies near the heart.

• • •

Along with their truly awe-inspiring heroism, these men of the North had delightful common sense. The combination seems impossible, but the poems are here to prove it. By race we are connected with the Norse; our culture goes back to the Greeks. Norse mythology and Greek mythology together give a clear picture of what the people were like from whom comes a major part of our spiritual and intellectual inheritance.

The Principal Gods

(Heaven) Uranus = Gaea (Earth)

Cronus = Rhea   Coeus = Phoebe   Ocean = Tethys

Iapetus

Prometheus   Atlas   Epimetheus

Zeus = Maia   Zeus = Dione

Hermes   Aphrodite (usually said to be born of the sea foam)

Leto = Zeus

Apollo   Artemis

Hestia   Pluto   Poseidon   Zeus = Hera   Demeter = Zeus

Persephone

Ares   Hebe   Athena   Hephaestus (often said to be only Hera's son)

Descendants of Prometheus

Ancestors of Perseus and Hercules

Ancestors of Achilles

Ocean = Tethys
|
Asopus (a river-god)
|
Aegina = Zeus
|
Aeacus
|
Peleus = Thetis
|
ACHILLES

The House of Troy

Teucer
Dardanus = Batea
Erichthonius
Tros

Ilus — Assaracus

Laomedon — Capys

Priam = Hecuba — Anchises = Aphrodite

HECTOR Deiphobus Paris — AENEAS

The Family of Helen of Troy

Aeolus

Perieres — Deion

Tyndareus = Leda = Zeus — Icarius Cephalus = Procris

CLYTEMNESTRA CASTOR HELEN POLLUX — Arcesius

Laertes

PENELOPE = ODYSSEUS

Telemachus

The Royal House of Thebes and the Atreidae

The House of Atreus

The House of Athens

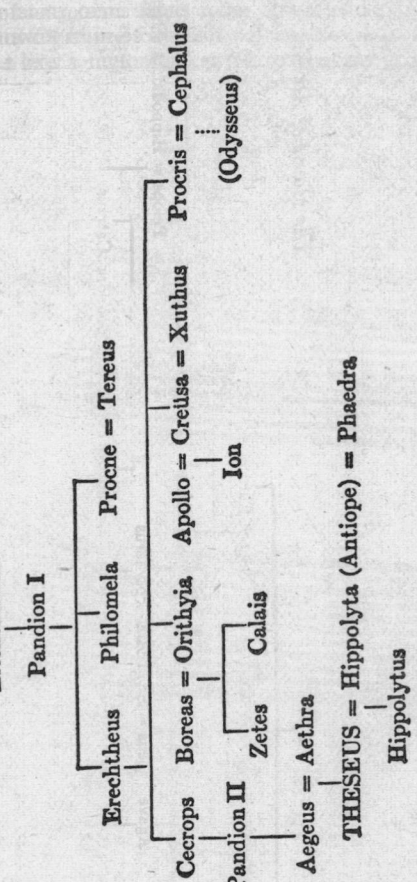

Index

The names without page numbers
do not appear in the book.

MENTOR Books of Related Interest

☐ **THE MEDIEVAL MYTHS by Norma Lorre Goodrich.** A brilliant re-creation of the great myths of the medieval world, from Beowulf to the Cid; their historical backgrounds and development into masterpieces of world literature. (#MY1364—$1.25)

☐ **GOD, HEROES, AND MEN OF ANCIENT GREECE by W. H. D. Rouse.** A retelling of the ancient Greek legends in a lively narrative for readers of all ages. (#MY1299—$1.25)

☐ **MYTHS OF THE GREEKS AND ROMANS by Michael Grant.** Taking full advantage of contemporary scholarship, Dr. Grant presents the ancient myths in engrossing fashion. He is also the author of the Mentor book, **The World of Rome.** (#ME1506—$2.25)

☐ **BULFINCH'S MYTHOLOGY: VOLUME I—THE AGE OF FABLE.** A retelling of the myths of ancient Greece and Rome, with introduction by Palmer Bovie. (#MW1482—$1.50)

☐ **BULFINCH'S MYTHOLOGY: VOLUMES II AND III—THE AGE OF CHIVALRY AND THE LEGENDS OF CHARLE-MAGNE.** The great legends of the Middle Ages with an Introduction by Palmer Bovie. (#ME1458—$1.75)

Master the *NEC*® with support tools from the source!

NEC®2005
HANDBOOK

NFPA 70: National Electrical Code®
International Electrical Code® Series

nec

Mark W. Earley   Joseph V. Sheehan

Jeffery S. Sargent   John M. Caloggo

International Codes ...anization

NFPA®
Your source
for the new
2005 *NEC*®.

NFPA 70

National Electrical Code®

2005 Edition

This edition of NFPA 70, *National Electrical Code*, was prepared by the National Electrical Code Committee and acted on by NFPA at its May Association Technical Meeting held May 23–26, 2004, in Salt Lake City, UT. It was issued by the Standards Council on July 16, 2004, with an effective date of August 5, 2004, and supersedes all previous editions.

A tentative interim amendment (TIA) to Section 604.6(A)(1) was issued on July 15, 2004. For further information on tentative interim amendments see Section 5 of the NFPA Regulations Governing Committee Projects available at:

http://www.nfpa.org/Codes/NFPADirectory.asp#Regs&Procedures

This edition of NFPA 70 was approved as an American National Standard on August 5, 2004.

History and Development of the *National Electrical Code*®

The National Fire Protection Association has acted as sponsor of the *National Electrical Code* since 1911. The original *Code* document was developed in 1897 as a result of the united efforts of various insurance, electrical, architectural, and allied interests.

In accordance with the provisions of the NFPA Regulations Governing Committee Projects, a National Electrical Code Committee Report on Proposals containing proposed amendments to the 2002 *National Electrical Code* was published by NFPA in July 2003. This report recorded the actions of the various Code-Making Panels and the Correlating Committee of the National Electrical Code Committee on each proposal that had been made to revise the 2002 *Code*. The report was circulated to all members of the National Electrical Code Committee and was made available to other interested NFPA members and to the public for review and comment. Following the close of the public comment period, the Code-Making Panels met, acted on each comment, and reported their action to the Correlating Committee. NFPA published the National Electrical Code Committee Report on Comments in April 2004, which recorded the actions of the Code-Making Panels and the Correlating Committee on each public comment to the National Electrical Code Committee Report on Proposals. The National Electrical Code Committee Report on Proposals and the National Electrical Code Committee Report on Comments were presented to the 2004 May Association Technical Meeting for adoption.

NFPA has an Electrical Section that provides particular opportunity for NFPA members interested in electrical safety to become better informed and to contribute to the development of the *National Electrical Code* and other NFPA electrical standards. Each of the Code-Making Panels and the Chairman of the Correlating Committee reported their recommendations to meetings of the Electrical Section at the 2004 NFPA World Safety Conference and Exposition. The Electrical Section thus had opportunity to discuss and review the report of the National Electrical Code Committee prior to the adoption of this edition of the *Code* by the Association at its 2004 May Technical Session.

This 2005 edition supersedes all other previous editions, supplements, and printings dated 1897, 1899, 1901, 1903, 1904, 1905, 1907, 1909, 1911, 1913, 1915, 1918, 1920, 1923, 1925, 1926, 1928, 1930, 1931, 1933, 1935, 1937, 1940, 1942, 1943, 1947, 1949, 1951, 1953, 1954, 1955, 1956, 1957, 1958, 1959, 1962, 1965, 1968, 1971, 1975, 1978, 1981, 1984, 1987, 1990, 1993, 1996, 1999, and 2002. The 2005 edition marks the 50th edition of the *National Electrical Code*.

Changes other than editorial are indicated by a vertical rule beside the paragraph, table, or figure in which the change occurred. These rules are included as an aid to the user in identifying changes from the previous edition. Where one or more complete paragraphs have been deleted, the deletion is indicated by a bullet (•) between the paragraphs that remain.

This *Code* is purely advisory as far as NFPA is concerned. It is made available for a wide variety of both public and private uses in the interest of life and property protection. These include both use in law and for regulatory purposes, and use in private self-regulation and standardization activities as insurance underwriting, building and facilities construction and management, and product testing and certification.

Contents

ARTICLE 366

Chapter 4 Equipment for General Use

CONTENTS

Chapter 7 Special Conditions

NATIONAL ELECTRICAL CODE COMMITTEE

These lists represent the membership at the time the Committee was balloted on the final text of this edition. Since that time, changes in the membership may have occurred. A key to classifications is found at the back of this document.

Technical Correlating Committee

James W. Carpenter, *Chair*
International Association of Electrical Inspectors, TX [E]
Rep. International Association of Electrical Inspectors

Mark W. Earley, *Secretary*
NFPA, MA
(nonvoting)

Jean A. O'Connor, *Recording Secretary*
NFPA, MA
(nonvoting)

James E. Brunssen, Telcordia, NJ [UT]
Rep. Alliance for Telecommunications Industry Solutions
Michael I. Callanan, National Joint Apprentice & Training Committee, MD [L]
Rep. International Brotherhood of Electrical Workers
William R. Drake, Marinco, CA [M]
John R. Kovacik, Underwriters Laboratories Incorporated, IL [RT]
James T. Pauley, Square D Company, KY [M]
Rep. National Electrical Manufacturers Association
Michael D. Toman, MEGA Power Electrical Services, Incorporated, MD [IM]
Rep. National Electrical Contractors Association
John W. Troglia, Edison Electric Institute, WI [UT]
Rep. Electric Light & Power Group/EEI
Craig M. Wellman, DuPont Engineering, DE [U]
Rep. American Chemistry Council

James M. Daly, General Cable, NJ [M]
Rep. National Electrical Manufacturers Association
(Alt. to J. T. Pauley)
Stanley J. Folz, Folz Electric, Incorporated, IL [IM]
Rep. National Electrical Contractors Association
(Alt. to M. D. Toman)
Palmer L. Hickman, National Joint Apprentice & Training Committee, MD [L]
Rep. International Brotherhood of Electrical Workers
(Alt. to M. I. Callanan)
Neil F. LaBrake, Jr., Niagara Mohawk, a National Grid Company, NY [UT]
Rep. Electric Light & Power Group/EEI
(Alt. to J. W. Troglia)
William M. Lewis, Eli Lilly & Company, IN [U]
Rep. American Chemistry Council
(Alt. to C. M. Wellman)
Mark C. Ode, Underwriters Laboratories Incorporated, NC [RT]
(Alt. to J. R. Kovacik)

Alternates

Jeffrey Boksiner, Telcordia Technologies, Incorporated, NJ [UT]
Rep. Alliance for Telecommunications Industry Solutions
(Alt. to J. E. Brunssen)
Philip H. Cox, Bigelow, AR [E]
Rep. International Association of Electrical Inspectors
(Alt. to J. W. Carpenter)

Nonvoting

Richard G. Biermann, Biermann Electric Company, Incorporated, IA [IM]
D. Harold Ware, Libra Electric Company, OK [IM]

CODE–MAKING PANEL NO. 1
Articles 90, 100, 110, Annex A, Annex G

John D. Minick, *Chair*
National Electrical Manufacturers Association, TX [M]
Rep. National Electrical Manufacturers Association

Michael A. Anthony, University of Michigan, MI [U]
Rep. The Association of Higher Education Facilities Officers
Louis A. Barrios, Jr., Shell Global Solutions, TX [U]
Rep. American Chemistry Council
David A. Dini, Underwriters Laboratories Incorporated, IL [RT]
William T. Fiske, Intertek Testing Services NA, Incorporated, NY [RT]

H. Landis Floyd II, The DuPont Company, DE [U]
Rep. Institute of Electrical & Electronics Engineers, Incorporated
Palmer L. Hickman, National Joint Apprentice & Training Committee, MD [L]
Rep. International Brotherhood of Electrical Workers
David L. Hittinger, IEC of Greater Cincinnati, OH [IM]
Rep. Independent Electrical Contractors, Incorporated

Randall R. McCarver, Telcordia Technologies, Incorporated, NJ [U]
    Rep. Alliance for Telecommunications Industry Solutions
Lanny G. McMahill, City of Phoenix, AZ [E]
    Rep. International Association of Electrical Inspectors
H. Brooke Stauffer, National Electrical Contractors Association, MD [IM]
    Rep. National Electrical Contractors Association
John W. Troglia, Edison Electric Institute, WI [UT]
    Rep. Electric Light & Power Group/EEI

Alternates

Lawrence S. Ayer, Biz Com Electric, Incorporated, OH [IM]
    Rep. Independent Electrical Contractors, Incorporated
    (Alt. to D. L. Hittinger)
Kenneth P. Boyce, Underwriters Laboratories Incorporated, IL [RT]
    (Alt. to D. A. Dini)
Ernest J. Gallo, Telcordia Technologies, Incorporated, NJ [U]
    Rep. Alliance for Telecommunications Industry Solutions
    (Alt. to R. R. McCarver)
Russell J. Helmick, Jr., City of Irvine, CA [E]
    Rep. International Association of Electrical Inspectors
    (Alt. to L. G. McMahill)

Neil F. LaBrake, Jr., Niagara Mohawk, a National Grid Company, NY [UT]
    Rep. Electric Light & Power Group/EEI
    (Alt. to J. W. Troglia)
Donald H. McCullough, II, Westinghouse Savannah River Company, SC [U]
    Rep. Institute of Electrical & Electronics Engineers, Incorporated
    (Alt. to H. L. Floyd II)
Gil Moniz, National Electrical Manufacturers Association, MA [M]
    Rep. National Electrical Manufacturers Association
    (Alt. to J. D. Minick)
Rick Munch, Frischhertz Electric Company, LA [L]
    Rep. International Brotherhood of Electrical Workers
    (Alt. to P. L. Hickman)

Nonvoting

Ark Tsisserev, City of Vancouver, BC, Canada
    Rep. Canadian Standards Association International

CODE–MAKING PANEL NO. 2
Articles 210, 215, 220, Annex D, Examples 1 through 6

Raymond W. Weber, *Chair*
State of Wisconsin, WI [E]
Rep. International Association of Electrical Inspectors

Richard W. Becker, Engineered Electrical Systems, Incorporated, WA [U]
    Rep. Institute of Electrical & Electronics Engineers, Incorporated
Frank Coluccio, New York City Department of Buildings, NY [E]
Matthew D. Dobson, National Association of Home Builders, DC [U]
    Rep. National Association of Home Builders
Thomas L. Harman, University of Houston/Clear Lake, TX [SE]
Donald M. King, IBEW Local Union 313, DE [L]
    Rep. International Brotherhood of Electrical Workers
Christopher P. O'Neil, National Grid USA Service Company, MA
    Rep. Electric Light & Power Group/EEI, MA
James T. Pauley, Square D Company, KY [M]
    Rep. National Electrical Manufacturers Association
Susan W. Porter, Underwriters Laboratories Incorporated, NY [RT]
Joseph Patterson Roché, Celanese Acetate, SC [U]
    Rep. American Chemistry Council
Albert F. Sidhom, U.S. Army Corps of Engineers, CA [U]
Michael D. Toman, MEGA Power Electrical Services, Incorporated, MD [IM]
    Rep. National Electrical Contractors Association
Robert G. Wilkinson, Independent Electrical Contractors of Texas Gulf Coast, TX [IM]
    Rep. Independent Electrical Contractors, Incorporated

Alternates

Kevin J. Brooks, IBEW Local Union 16, IN [L]
    Rep. International Brotherhood of Electrical Workers
    (Alt. to D. M King)

Ernest S. Broome, City of Knoxville, TN [E]
    Rep. International Association of Electrical Inspectors
    (Alt. to R. W. Weber)
James R. Jones, University of Alabama at Birmingham, AL [U]
    Rep. Institute of Electrical & Electronics Engineers, Incorporated
    (Alt. to R. W. Becker)
Daniel J. Kissane, Pass & Seymour/Legrand, NY [M]
    Rep. National Electrical Manufacturers Association
    (Alt. to J. T. Pauley)
Brian J. Nenninger, The Dow Chemical Company, TX [U]
    Rep. American Chemistry Council
    (Alt. to J. P. Roché)
Clifford L. Rediger, Independent Electrical Contractors Training Fund, CO [IM]
    Rep. Independent Electrical Contractors, Incorporated
    (Alt. to R. G. Wilkinson)
Richard V. Wagner, Underwriters Laboratories Incorporated, NY [RT]
    (Alt. to S. W. Porter)
Joseph E. Wiehagen, National Association of Home Builders, MD [U]
    Rep. National Association of Home Builders
    (Alt. to M. D. Dobson)

Nonvoting

Douglas A. Lee, U.S. Consumer Product Safety Commission, MD [C]
Andrew M. Trotta, U.S. Consumer Product Safety Commission, MD [C]
    (Alt. to D. A. Lee)

CODE–MAKING PANEL NO. 3

Articles 300, 590, 720, 725, 727, 760, Chapter 9, Tables 11(a) and (b), and Tables 12(a) and (b)

Richard P. Owen, *Chair*
City of St. Paul, MN [E]
Rep. International Association of Electrical Inspectors

Lawrence S. Ayer, Biz Com Electric, Incorporated, OH [IM]
    Rep. Independent Electrical Contracians, Incorporated
Paul J. Casparro, Scranton Electricians JATC, PA [L]
    Rep. International Brotherhood of Electrical Workers
Les Easter, Allied Tube and Conduit, IL [M]
    Rep. National Electrical Manufacturers Association
Sanford E. Egesdal, Egesdal Associates PLC, MN [M]
    Rep. Automatic Fire Alarm Association, Incorporated
Thomas J. Guida, Underwriters Laboratories, Inc., NY [RT]
Dennis B. Horman, PacifiCorp, UT [UT]
    Rep. Electric Light & Power Group/EEI
Ray R. Keden, ERICO, Incorporated, CA [M]
    Rep. Building Industry Consulting Services International
Ronald E. Maassen, Lemberg Electric Company, Incorporated, WI [IM]
    Rep. National Electrical Contractors Association
Steven J. Owen, Steven J. Owen, Incorporated, AL [IM]
    Rep. Associated Builders and Contractors, Incorporated
David A. Pace, Olin Corporation, AL [U]
    Rep. American Chemistry Council
Melvin K. Sanders, Things Electrical Company, Incorporated (TECo., Incorporated), IA [U]
    Rep. Institute of Electrical & Electronics Engineers, Incorporated
John E. Sleights, Travelers Insurance, CT [I]

Adam D. Corbin, Corbin Electrical Services, Incorporated, NJ [IM]
    Rep. Independent Electrical Contractors, Inc.
    (Alt. to L. S. Ayer)
John C. Hudak, Old Forge, PA [E]
    Rep. International Association of Electrical Inspectors
    (Alt. to R. P. Owen)
Danny Liggett, DuPont Engineering, DE [U]
    Rep. American Chemistry Council
    (Alt. to D. A. Pace)
Juan C. Menendez, Southern California Edison Company, CA [UT]
    Rep. Electric Light & Power Group/EEI
    (Alt. to D. B. Horman)
T. David Mills, Bechtel Savannah River, Incorporated, SC [U]
    Rep. Institute of Electrical & Electronics Engineers, Incorporated
    (Alt. to M. K. Sanders)
Mark C. Ode, Underwriters Laboratories Incorporated, NC [RT]
    (Alt. to T. J. Guida)
Lorena Orbanic, Carlon, Lamson & Sessions, OH [M]
    Rep. Building Industry Consulting Services International
    (Alt. to R. R. Keden)
Roger S. Passmore, Davis Electrical Constructors, Incorporated, SC [IM]
    Rep. Associated Builders and Contractors, Incorporated
    (Alt. to S. J. Owen)
George A. Straniero, AFC Cable Systems, Incorporated, NJ [M]
    Rep. National Electrical Manufacturers Association
    (Alt. to L. Easter)

Alternates

Mark E Christian, Chattanooga Electrical JATC, TN [L]
    Rep. International Brotherhood of Electrical Workers
    (Alt. to P. J. Casparro)
Dr. Shane M. Clary, Bay Alarm Company, Incorporated, CA [M]
    Rep. Automatic Fire Alarm Association, Incorporated
    (Alt. to S. E. Egesdal)

CODE–MAKING PANEL NO. 4

Articles 225, 230

James M. Naughton, *Chair*
IBEW Local Union 103, MA [L]
Rep. International Brotherhood of Electrical Workers

Malcolm Allison, Ferraz Shawmut, MA [M]
C. John Beck, Pacific Gas and Electric Company, CA [UT]
    Rep. Electric Light & Power Group/EEI
Robert J. Deaton, The Dow Chemical Company, TX [U]
    Rep. Institute of Electrical & Electronics Engineers, Incorporated
Howard D. Hughes, Hughes Electric Company Incorporated, AR [IM]
    Rep. National Electrical Contractors Association
William M. Lewis, Eli Lilly & Company, IN [U]
    Rep. American Chemistry Council
Mark C. Ode, Underwriters Laboratories Incorporated, NC [RT]
James J. Rogers, Towns of Oak Bluffs, Tisbury, West Tisbury, MA [E]
    Rep. International Association of Electrical Inspectors

John W. Young, Siemens Energy & Automation, Incorporated, GA [M]
    Rep. National Electrical Manufacturers Association
Vincent Zinnante, Advantage Electric, Incorporated, TX [IM]
    Rep. Independent Electrical Contractors, Incorporated

Alternates

Thomas L. Adams, Exelon Corporation, IL [UT]
    Rep. Electric Light & Power Group/EEI
    (Alt. to C. J. Beck)
Ronald Breschini, Underwriters Laboratories Incorporated, CA [RT]
    (Alt. to M. C. Ode)
Terry D. Cole, Hamer Electric, WA [IM]
    Rep. Independent Electrical Contractors, Incorporated
    (Alt. to V. Zinnante)

Mark R. Hilbert, State of New Hampshire, NH [E]
Rep. International Association of Electrical Inspectors
(Alt. to J. J. Rogers)

Philip M. Piqueira, General Electric Company, CT [M]
Rep. National Electrical Manufacturers Association
(Alt. to J. W. Young)

Francis E. Rose, Jr., W. S. Nelson and Company,
Incorporated, LA [U]
Rep. Institute of Electrical & Electronics Engineers,
Incorporated
(Alt. to R. J. Deaton)

John Sigmund, PPG Industries, Incorporated,
LA [U]
Rep. American Chemistry Council
(Alt. to W. M. Lewis)

Mark H. Sumrall, IBEW Local Union 527, TX [L]
Rep. International Brotherhood of Electrical
Workers
(Alt. to J. M. Naughton)

Kent Walker, Ferraz Shawmut, MA [M]
(Alt. to M. Allison)

CODE-MAKING PANEL NO. 5
Articles 200, 250, 280, 285

Ronald J. Toomer, *Chair*
Toomer Electrical Company Incorporated, LA [IM]
Rep. National Electrical Contractors Association

Jeffrey Boksiner, Telcordia Technologies, Incorporated,
NJ [UT]
Rep. Alliance for Telecommunications Industry
Solutions

David T. Brender, Copper Development Association,
Incorporated, NY [M]
Rep. Copper Development Association, Incorporated

Martin J. Brett, Jr., Wheatland Tube Company,
NJ [M]
Rep. American Iron and Steel Institute

Elio L. Checca, U.S. Department of Labor, VA [E]

Paul Dobrowsky, Eastman Kodak Company, NY [U]
Rep. American Chemistry Council

Gerald L. Hadeen, Tehachapi, CA [M]
Rep. The Aluminum Association

Dan Hammel, IBEW Local Union 704, IA [L]
Rep. International Brotherhood of Electrical Workers

Michael J. Johnston, International Association of Electrical
Inspectors, TX [E]
Rep. International Association of Electrical Inspectors

Charles Mello, Electro-Test, Incorporated, OR [IM]
Rep. InterNational Electrical Testing Association
Incorporated

Elliot Rappaport, Electro Technology Consultants,
Incorporated, FL [U]
Rep. Institute of Electrical & Electronics Engineers,
Incorporated

Ted G. Robertson, Robertson Electric, Incorporated,
TX [IM]
Rep. Independent Electrical Contractors, Incorporated

Walter Skuggevig, Underwriters Laboratories Incorporated,
NY [RT]

Gregory J. Steinman, Thomas & Betts Corporation,
TN [M]
Rep. National Electrical Manufacturers Association

Robert G. Stoll, Thomas Associates, Incorporated,
OH [M]
Rep. Power Tool Institute, Incorporated

C. Douglas White, CenterPoint Energy, Incorporated,
TX [UT]
Rep. Electric Light & Power Group/EEI

Alternates

Martin D. Adams, Adams Electric, Incorporated, CO [IM]
Rep. National Electrical Contractors Association
(Alt. to R. J. Toomer)

David A. Dini, Underwriters Laboratories Incorporated, IL
[RT]
(Alt. to W. Skuggevig)

Timothy Edwards, Alcan Cable Company, GA [M]
Rep. The Aluminum Association
(Alt. to G. L. Hadeen)

Robert Figlia, New York Board of Fire Underwriters, NY
[E]
Rep. International Association of Electrical Inspectors
(Alt. to M. J. Johnston)

G. Scott Harding, F. B. Harding, Incorporated, MD [IM]
Rep. Independent Electrical Contractors, Incorporated
(Alt. to T. G. Robertson)

William J. Helfrich, U.S. Department of Labor, PA [E]
(Alt. to E. L. Checca)

Ronald Lai, FCI Electrical, NH [M]
Rep. National Electrical Manufacturers Association
(Alt. to G. J. Steinman)

Paul J. LeVasseur, Bay City JEATC, MI [L]
Rep. International Brotherhood of Electrical Workers
(Alt. to D. Hammel)

Richard E. Loyd, R & N Associates, AZ [M]
Rep. American Iron and Steel Institute
(Alt. to M. J. Brett, Jr.)

Daleep C. Mohla, DCM Electrical Consulting Services,
Incorporated, TX [U]
Rep. Institute of Electrical & Electronics Engineers,
Incorporated
(Alt. to E. Rappaport)

David Peot, Ryobi, SC [M]
Rep. Power Tool Institute, Incorporated
(Alt. to R. G. Stoll)

J. Philip Simmons, Simmons Electrical Services, WA [M]
Rep. Copper Development Association, Incorporated
(Alt. to D. T. Brender)

James S. Simpson, Southern Company Services, AL [UT]
Rep. Electric Light & Power Group/EEI
(Alt. to C. D.White)

CODE-MAKING PANEL NO. 6
Articles 310, 400, 402, Chapter 9 Tables 5 through 9, Annex B

Stephen J. Thorwegen, Jr., *Chair*
Fisk Electric Company, TX [IM]
Rep. National Electrical Contractors Association

Robert Edwards, Alcan Aluminum Corporation, ON, Canada [M]
Rep. The Aluminum Association
Samuel B. Friedman, BICC General Cable Corporation, RI [M]
Rep. National Electrical Manufacturers Association
G. W. "Jerry" Kent, Kent Electric & Plumbing Systems, TX [IM]
Rep. Independent Electrical Contractors, Incorporated
David G. Komassa, WE Energies, WI [UT]
Rep. Electric Light & Power Group/EEI
William F. Laidler, South Shore VoTech/IBEW 223, MA [L]
Rep. International Brotherhood of Electrical Workers
Danny P. Liggett, DuPont Engineering, TX [U]
Rep. American Chemistry Council
L. Bruce McClung, Electrical Safety Consulting Services, Incorporated, WV [U]
Rep. Institute of Electrical & Electronics Engineers, Incorporated
Oran P. Post, City of Cuyahoga Falls, OH [E]
Rep. International Association of Electrical Inspectors
Austin D. Wetherell, Underwriters Laboratories Incorporated, NY [RT]
Joseph S. Zimnoch, The Okonite Company, NJ [M]
Rep. Copper Development Association, Incorporated

James M. Daly, General Cable, NJ [M]
Rep. Copper Development Association, Incorporated
(Alt. to J. S. Zimnoch)
Robert L. Huddleston, Jr., Eastman Chemical Company, TN [U]
Rep. American Chemistry Council
(Alt. to D. P. Liggett)
Philip T. Laudicini, Underwriters Laboratories Incorporated, NY [RT]
(Alt. to A. D. Wetherell)
Lowell S. Lisker, American Insulated Wire Corporation, RI [M]
Rep. National Electrical Manufacturers Association
(Alt. to S. B. Friedman)
Paul R. Picard, AFC Cable Systems, Incorporated, MA [M]
Rep. The Aluminum Association
(Alt. to R. Edwards)
Harry J. Sassaman, Forest Electric Corporation, NJ [IM]
Rep. National Electrical Contractors Association
(Alt. to S. J. Thorwegen, Jr.)
John Stacey, City of St. Louis, MO [E]
Rep. International Association of Electrical Inspectors
(Alt. to O. P. Post)
Donald A. Voltz, Mustang Engineering, Incorporated, TX [U]
Rep. Institute of Electrical & Electronics Engineers, Incorporated
(Alt. to L. B. McClung)
David R. Wellington, Toledo Electrical JATC, OH [L]
Rep. International Brotherhood of Electrical Workers
(Alt. to W. F. Laidler)

Alternates

Peter E. Bowers, Satellite Electric Company, Incorporated, MD [IM]
Rep. Independent Electrical Contractors, Incorporated
(Alt. to G. W. Kent)

CODE-MAKING PANEL NO. 7
Articles 320, 322, 324, 326, 328, 330, 332, 334, 336, 338, 340, 382, 394, 396, 398

Gaylen D. Rogers, *Chair*
State of Utah, UT [E]
Rep. International Association of Electrical Inspectors

James J. Anastasi, Intertek/ETL Semko, NY [RT]
Harry C. Brown, IBEW Local Union 606, FL [L]
Rep. International Brotherhood of Electrical Workers
John J. Cangemi, Underwriters Laboratories Incorporated, NY [RT]
James M. Daly, General Cable, NJ [M]
Rep. National Electrical Manufacturers Association
Chris J. Fahrenthold, Encompass Electrical Technologies, TX [IM]
Rep. Independent Electrical Contractors, Incorporated
Robert L. Gotham, Rose City Electric Company, Incorporated, OR [IM]
Rep. National Electrical Contractors Association
Herman J. Hall, Austin, TX [M]
Rep. Society of the Plastics Industry Incorporated
Ronald G. Nickson, National Multi Housing Council, DC [U]
Rep. National Multi Housing Council
Bruce W. Nutt, Oncor, TX [UT]
Rep. Electric Light & Power Group/EEI

Gregory L. Runyon, Eli Lilly and Company, IN [U]
Rep. American Chemistry Council
David E. Schumacher, All County Electric Company, IA [IM]
Rep. Associated Builders and Contractors, Incorporated
H. R. Stewart, HRS Consulting, TX [U]
Rep. Institute of Electrical & Electronics Engineers, Incorporated
George A. Straniero, AFC Cable Systems, Incorporated, NJ [M]
Rep. Copper Development Association, Incorporated
Richard Temblador, Alflex Corporation, CA [M]
Rep. The Aluminum Association

Alternates

William B. Crist, Houston Stafford Electric Company, TX [IM]
Rep. Independent Electrical Contractors, Incorporated
(Alt. to C. J. Fahrenthold)
James D. Erwin, Celanese, Limited, TX [U]
Rep. American Chemistry Council
(Alt. to G. L. Runyon)

James K. Hinrichs, State of Washington, WA [E]
Rep. International Association of Electrical Inspectors
(Alt. to G. D. Rogers)

Samuel R. LaDart, City of Memphis, TN [L]
Rep. International Brotherhood of Electrical Workers
(Alt. to H. C. Brown)

C. David Mercier, Southwire Company, GA [M]
Rep. National Electrical Manufacturers Association
(Alt. to J. M. Daly)

Dennis A. Nielsen, Lawrence Berkeley National Laboratory, CA [U]
Rep. Institute of Electrical & Electronics Engineers, Incorporated
(Alt. to H. R. Stewart)

Paul A. Orr, Underwriters Laboratories Incorporated, NY [RT]
(Alt. to J. J. Cangemi)

John W. "Wes" Ray, Duke Energy Corporation, NC [UT]
Rep. Electric Light & Power Group/EEI
(Alt. to B. W. Nutt)

David K. Smith, Encore Wire Limited, TX [M]
Rep. Copper Development Association, Incorporated
(Alt. to G. A. Straniero)

John Thomas Thompson, ABC Marathon Electrical Company, Incorporated, AL [IM]
Rep. Associated Builders and Contractors, Incorporated
(Alt. to D. E. Schumacher)

Larry G. Watkins, Alcan Aluminum Corporation, GA [M]
Rep. The Aluminum Association
(Alt. to R. Temblador)

Thomas H. Wood, Cecil B. Wood Incorporated, IL [IM]
Rep. National Electrical Contractors Association
(Alt. to R. L. Gotham)

CODE-MAKING PANEL NO. 8

Articles 342, 344, 348, 350, 352, 353, 354, 356, 358, 360, 362, 366, 368, 370, 372, 374, 376, 378, 380, 384, 386, 388, 390, 392, Chapter 9 Tables 1 through 4, Annex C

Julian R. Burns, *Chair*
Burns Electrical/Quality Power Solutions, Incorporated, NC [IM]
Rep. Independent Electrical Contractors, Incorporated

John S. Corry, Corry Electric Incorporated, CA [IM]
Rep. Associated Builders and Contractors, Incorporated

Joseph G. Dabe, City of St. Paul, MN [L]
Rep. International Brotherhood of Electrical Workers

George R. Dauberger, Thomas & Betts Corporation, TN [M]
Rep. National Electrical Manufacturers Association

James C. Dollins, AFC Cable Systems, MA [M]
Rep. The Aluminum Association

Ronald E. Duren, PacifiCorp, WA [UT]
Rep. Electric Light & Power Group/EEI

M. Shan Griffith, Kelloff, Brown & Root, Incorporated, TX [U]
Rep. Institute of Electrical & Electronics Engineers, Incorporated

David H. Kendall, Carlon, Lamson & Sessions, OH [M]
Rep. Society of the Plastics Industry Incorporated

Wayne A. Lilly, City of Harrisonburg, VA [E]
Rep. International Association of Electrical Inspectors

Richard E. Loyd, R & N Associates, AZ [M]
Rep. American Iron and Steel Institute

Stephen P. Poholski, Newkirk Electric Associates, Incorporated, MI [IM]
Rep. National Electrical Contractors Association

Dennis L. Rowe, New York Board of Fire Underwriters, NY [E]
Rep. New York Board of Fire Underwriters

George F. Walbrecht, Underwriters Laboratories Incorporated, IL [RT]

Charles W. Forsberg, Shaker Heights, OH [M]
Rep. Society of the Plastics Industry Incorporated
(Alt. to D. H. Kendall)

Dr. Jack A. Gruber, Wheatland Tube Company, PA [M]
Rep. American Iron and Steel Institute
(Alt. to R. E. Loyd)

James M. Imlah, City of Hillsboro, OR [E]
Rep. International Association of Electrical Inspectors
(Alt. to W. A. Lilly)

Alan Manche, Schneider Electric/Square D Company, KY [M]
Rep. National Electrical Manufacturers Association
(Alt. to G. R. Dauberger)

Jamie McNamara, City of St. Paul, MN [L]
Rep. International Brotherhood of Electrical Workers
(Alt. to J. G. Dabe)

C. Ernest Reynolds, Hatfield-Reynolds Electric Company, AZ [IM]
Rep. Independent Electrical Contractors, Incorporated
(Alt. to J. R. Burns)

Richard Temblador, Alflex Corporation, CA [M]
Rep. The Aluminum Association
(Alt. to J. C. Dollins)

Ronald J. Toomer, Toomer Electrical Company Incorporated, LA [IM]
Rep. National Electrical Contractors Association
(Alt. to S. P. Poholski)

James Van Den Heuvel, West Electric Incorporated, WI [IM]
Rep. Associated Builders and Contractors, Incorporated
(Alt. to J. S. Corry)

Leslie R. Zielke, South Carolina Electric & Gas Company, SC [UT]
Rep. Electric Light & Power Group/EEI
(Alt. to R. E. Duren)

Alternates

Richard Berman, Underwriters Laboratories Incorporated, IL [RT]
(Alt. to G. F. Walbrecht)

Duane A. Carlson, PRS Consulting Engineers, WA [U]
Rep. Institute of Electrical & Electronics Engineers, Incorporated
(Alt. to M. S. Griffith)

CODE-MAKING PANEL NO. 9
Articles 312, 314, 404, 408, 450, 490

Timothy M. Croushore, *Chair*
Allegheny Power, PA [UT]
Rep. Electric Light & Power Group/EEI

Jeffery Bernson, IBEW Local Union 701, IL [L]
Rep. International Brotherhood of Electrical Workers
Hector R. de Vega, Fluor Daniel, TX [U]
Rep. Associated Builders and Contractors, Incorporated
Frederic P. Hartwell, Hartwell Electrical Services, MA [SE]
Robert J. Kaemmerlen, Kaemmerlen Electric Company,
MO [IM]
Rep. National Electrical Contractors Association
Jacob Killinger, Underwriters Laboratories Incorporated,
IL [RT]
Thomas J. LeMay, LeMay Electric, Incorporated, GA [IM]
Rep. Independent Electrical Contractors, Incorporated
Donald R. Offerdahl, North Dakota State Electrical Board,
ND [E]
Rep. International Association of Electrical Inspectors
Bradford D. Rupp, Allied Moulded Products, Incorporated,
OH [M]
Rep. National Electrical Manufacturers Association
Sukanta Sengupta, FMC Corporation, NJ [U]
Rep. Institute of Electrical & Electronics Engineers,
Incorporated
Ralph H. Young, Eastman Chemical Company, TN [U]
Rep. American Chemistry Council

Joseph M. Bolesina, Pinellas County Building Inspections,
FL [E]
Rep. International Association of Electrical Inspectors
(Alt. to D. R. Offerdahl)
Julian R. Burns, Burns Electrical/Quality Power Solutions,
Incorporated, NC [IM]
Rep. Independent Electrical Contractors, Incorporated
(Alt. to T. J. LeMay)
James C. Carroll, Square D Company, TN [M]
Rep. National Electrical Manufacturers Association
(Alt. to B. D. Rupp)
Richard P. Fogarty, Consolidated Edison Company of NY,
Incorporated, NY [UT]
Rep. Electric Light & Power Group/EEI
(Alt. to T. M. Croushore)
Robert D. Osborne, Underwriters Laboratories Incorporated,
NC [RT]
(Alt. to J. Killinger)
Jerome W. Seigel, West Hartford, CT [U]
Rep. Institute of Electrical & Electronics Engineers,
Incorporated
(Alt. to S. Sengupta)
Monte Szendre, Wilson Construction Company, OR [IM]
Rep. National Electrical Contractors Association
(Alt. to R. J. Kaemmerlen)

Alternates

Rodney D. Belisle, NECA-IBEW Training Center, WA [L]
Rep. International Brotherhood of Electrical Workers
(Alt. to L. Bernson)

CODE-MAKING PANEL NO. 10
Articles 240, 780

James T. Dollard, Jr., *Chair*
IBEW Local Union 98, PA [L]
Rep. International Brotherhood of Electrical Workers

Charles K. Blizard, American Electrical Testing Company,
Incorporated, MA [IM]
Rep. InterNational Electrical Testing Association
Incorporated
Madeline Borthick, IEC of Houston, Incorporated, TX [IM]
Rep. Independent Electrical Contractors, Incorporated
Scott Cline, McMurtrey Electric, Incorporated, CA [IM]
Rep. National Electrical Contractors Association
Dennis M. Darling, Ayres, Lewis, Norris & May,
Incorporated, MI [U]
Rep. Institute of Electrical & Electronics Engineers,
Incorporated
Charles K. Eldridge, Indianapolis Power & Light Company,
IN [UT]
Rep. Electric Light & Power Group/EEI
Carl J. Fredericks, The Dow Chemical Company, TX [U]
Rep. American Chemistry Council
C. W. Kimblin, Cutler-Hammer, Incorporated, PA [M]
Rep. National Electrical Manufacturers Association
Arden L. Munson, Hussmann Corporation, MO [M]
Rep. Air-Conditioning and Refrigeration Institute
George J. Ockuly, Chesterfield, MO [M]
Gerald W. Williams, County of Ventura, California, CA [E]
Rep. International Association of Electrical Inspectors

John A. Zaplatosch, Underwriters Laboratories
Incorporated, IL [RT]

Alternates

Robert R. Gage, Niagara Mohawk, A National Grid
Company, NY [UT]
Rep. Electric Light & Power Group/EEI
(Alt. to C. K. Eldridge)
George D. Gregory, Square D Company, IA [M]
Rep. National Electrical Manufacturers Association
(Alt. to C. W. Kimblin)
Roderic L. Hageman, PRIT Service, Incorporated, IL [IM]
Rep. InterNational Electrical Testing Association
Incorporated
(Alt. to C. K. Blizard)
Charles D. Hughes, Westinghouse Savannah River
Company, SC [U]
Rep. Institute of Electrical & Electronics Engineers,
Incorporated
(Alt. to D. M. Darling)
Robert J. Kauer, Middle Department Inspection Agency,
Incorporated, PA [E]
Rep. International Association of Electrical Inspectors
(Alt. to G. W. Williams)

Richard E. Lofton, II, IBEW Local Union 280, OR [L]
Rep. International Brotherhood of Electrical Workers
(Alt. to J. T. Dollard, Jr.)
Robert W. Mount, Jr., Hussmann Corporation, MO [M]
Rep. Air-Conditioning and Refrigeration Institute
(Alt. to A. L. Munson)
Paul J. Notarian, Underwriters Laboratories Incorporated,
NY [RT]
(Alt. to J. A. Zaplatosch)
Vincent J. Saporita, Cooper Bussmann, MO [M]
(Alt. to G. J. Ockuly)

James R. Sicard, Shell Oil Company, TX [U]
Rep. American Chemistry Council
(Alt. to C. J. Fredericks)
Steve A. Struble, Freeman's Electric Service, Incorporated,
SD [IM]
Rep. Independent Electrical Contractors, Incorporated
(Alt. to M. Borthick)

Nonvoting

Rick C. Gilmour, Canadian Standards Association (CSA),
ON, Canada

CODE-MAKING PANEL NO. 11
Articles 409, 430, 440, 460, 470, Annex D, Example D8

Wayne Brinkmeyer, *Chair*
Biddle Electric Corporation, TX [IM]
Rep. National Electrical Contractors Association

Frederick Bried, Spring, TX [U]
Rep. American Petroleum Institute
Rick L. Bunch, Tecumseh Products Company, MI [M]
Rep. Air-Conditioning and Refrigeration Institute
Joe David Cox, Eastman Chemical Company, TN [U]
Rep. American Chemistry Council
Michael A. D'Amico, IBEW Local Union 488, CT [L]
Rep. International Brotherhood of Electrical Workers
Thomas J. Garvey, State of Wisconsin, WI [E]
Rep. International Association of Electrical Inspectors
Charles A. Goetz, Underwriters Laboratories Incorporated,
IL [RT]
Rep. Associated Builders and Contractors, Incorporated
Paul E. Guidry, Fluor Enterprises, Incorporated, TX [U]
Rep. Associated Builders & Contractors, Incorporated
Leo H. Haas, Jr., CenterPoint Energy, Incorporated,
TX, [UT]
Rep. Electric Light & Power Group/EEI
Vincent J. Saporita, Cooper Bussmann, MO [M]
Lynn F. Saunders, General Motors WFG-Utilities Services,
MI [U]
Rep. Institute of Electrical & Electronics Engineers,
Incorporated
Lawrence E. Todd, Intertek Testing Services NA,
Incorporated, OR [RT]
Ron Widup, Shermco Industries, Incorporated, TX [IM]
Rep. InterNational Electrical Testing Association
Incorporated
James R. Wright, Siemens Energy & Automation,
Incorporated, IL [M]
Rep. National Electrical Manufacturers Association

Alternates

Elwood J. Dodge, Addison Products Company, FL [M]
Rep. Air-Conditioning and Refrigeration Institute
(Alt. to R. L. Bunch)

Ralph M. Esemplare, Consolidated Edison Company of
New York, NY [UT]
Rep. Electric Light & Power Group/EEI
(Alt. to L. H. Haas, Jr.)
James M. Fahey, IBEW Local Union 103, MA [L]
Rep. International Brotherhood of Electrical Workers
(Alt. to M. A. D'Amico)
Stanley J. Folz, Folz Electric, Incorporated, IL [IM]
Rep. National Electrical Contractors Association
(Alt. to W. Brinkmeyer)
William D. Glover, PPG Industries, Incorporated, WV [U]
Rep. American Chemistry Council
(Alt. to J. D. Cox)
Paul S. Hamer, ChevronTexaco Corporation, CA [U]
Rep. American Petroleum Institute
(Alt. to F. Bried)
Robert J. Keough, Emerson Motor Company, MO [M]
Rep. National Electrical Manufacturers Association
(Alt. to J. R. Wright)
Thomas E. Moore, Stark County Building Department,
OH [E]
Rep. International Association of Electrical Inspectors
(Alt. to T. J. Garvey)
George J. Ockuly, Chesterfield, MO [M]
(Alt. to V. J. Saporita)
Frederic A. Salzman, Underwriters Laboratories
Incorporated, IL [RT]
(Alt. to C. A. Goetz)
Arthur J. Smith, III, Waldemar S. Nelson & Company,
Incorporated, LA [U]
Rep. Institute of Electrical & Electronics Engineers,
Incorporated
(Alt. to L. F. Saunders)

Nonvoting

Nino Mancini, CSA International, ON, Canada

CODE-MAKING PANEL NO. 12

Articles 610, 620, 625, 630, 640, 645, 647, 650, 660, 665, 668, 669, 670, 685, Annex D, Examples D9 and D10

Charles M. Trout, *Chair*
Maron Electric Company, FL [IM]
Rep. National Electrical Contractors Association

Thomas M. Burke, Underwriters Laboratories Incorporated, CA [RT]

Kent B. Givens, Aluminum Company of America, TX [M]
Rep. The Aluminum Association
(VL to 610, 625, 630, 645, 660, 665, 668, 669, 685)

Ron L. Janikowski, City of Wausau, Wisconsin, WI [E]
Rep. International Association of Electrical Inspectors

Robert E. Johnson, ITE Safety, MA [U]
Rep. Information Technology Industry Council
(VL to 640, 645, 647, 685)

Robert A. Jones, Independent Electrical Contractors, Incorporated, TX [IM]
Rep. Independent Electrical Contractors, Incorporated

Andy Juhasz, Kone Incorporated, IL [M]
Rep. National Elevator Industry Incorporated
(VL to 610, 620, 630)

Sam Marcovici, New York City Department of Buildings, NY [E]

John H. Mortimer, Inductotherm Corporation, NJ [M]
(VL to 665)

Ralph C. Prichard, Hercules Incorporated, DE [U]
Rep. Institute of Electrical & Electronics Engineers, Incorporated

Ronald L. Purvis, Georgia Power Company, GA [UT]
Rep. Electric Light & Power Group/EEI

David R. Quave, IBEW Local Union 903, MS [L]
Rep. International Brotherhood of Electrical Workers

Robert H. Reuss, Morris Material Handling, LLC, WI [M]
Rep. Crane Manufacturers Association of America Incorporated
(VL to 610)

Arthur E. Schlueter, Jr., A. E. Schlueter Pipe Organ Company, GA [M]
Rep. American Institute of Organ Builders
(VL to 640, 650)

Kenneth P. White, Olin Corporation, TN [U]
Rep. American Chemistry Council

James E. Winfrey, Square D Company, NC [M]
Rep. National Electrical Manufacturers Association

Alternates

William E. Anderson, The Procter & Gamble Company, OH [U]
Rep. Institute of Electrical & Electronics Engineers, Incorporated
(Alt. to R. C. Prichard)

Jeffrey W. Blain, Schindler Elevator Corporation, NJ [M]
Rep. National Elevator Industry Incorporated
(Alt. to A. Juhasz)
(VL to 610, 620, 630)

William A. Brunner, IBEW Local Union 714, ND [L]
Rep. International Brotherhood of Electrical Workers
(Alt. to D. R. Quave)

Scott Cline, McMurtrey Electric, Incorporated, CA [IM]
Rep. National Electrical Contractors Association
(Alt. to C. M. Trout)

Robert Michael Forister, City of Sheridan, Wyoming, WY [E]
Rep. International Association of Electrical Inspectors
(Alt. to R. L. Janikowski)

Barry G. Karnes, Underwriters Laboratories Incorporated, CA [RT]
(Alt. to T. M. Burke)

Todd F. Lottmann, Cooper Bussmann, MO [M]
Rep. National Electrical Manufacturers Association
(Alt. to J. E. Winfrey)

Roger D. McDaniel, Georgia Power Company, GA [UT]
Rep. Electric Light & Power Group/EEI
(Alt. to R. L. Purvis)

George S. Tidden, George's Electrical Service Incorporated, TX [IM]
Rep. Independent Electrical Contractors, Incorporated
(Alt. to R. A. Jones)

Robert C. Turner, Inductotherm Corporation, NJ [M]
(Alt. to J. H. Mortimer)
(VL to 665)

CODE-MAKING PANEL NO. 13

Articles 445, 455, 480, 690, 692, 695, 700, 701, 702, 705

Thomas H. Wood, *Chair*
Cecil B. Wood Incorporated, IL [IM]
Rep. National Electrical Contractors Association

Tarry L. Baker, Broward County Board of Rules & Appeals, FL [E]
Rep. International Association of Electrical Inspectors

Ward I. Bower, Sandia National Laboratories, NM [U]
Rep. Solar Energy Industries Association
(VL to 690, 692, 705)

Douglas L. Elkins, ExxonMobil Chemical Company, TX [U]
Rep. American Chemistry Council

George W. Flach, George W. Flach Consultant, Incorporated, LA [SE]

Ernest J. Gallo, Telcordia Technologies, Incorporated, NJ [U]
Rep. Alliance for Telecommunications Industry Solutions
(VL to 445, 480, 690, 692)

Michael V. Glenn, Longview Fibre Company, WA [U]
Rep. Institute of Electrical & Electronics Engineers, Incorporated

Banks Hattaway, Hattaway Brothers, Incorporated, AL [IM]
Rep. Associated Builders and Contractors, Incorporated

Timothy D. Holleman, AC Corporation, NC [IM]
Rep. Independent Electrical Contractors, Incorporated

Barry N. Hornberger, PECO Energy Company, PA [UT]
Rep. Electric Light & Power Group/EEI
John R. Kovacik, Underwriters Laboratories Incorporated, IL [RT]
Kenneth Krastins, Plug Power, Incorporated, NY [M]
Rep. U.S. Fuel Cell Council
(VL to 690, 692, 705)
James S. Nasby, Master Control Systems, Inc., IL [M]
Rep. National Electrical Manufacturers Association
Steven H. Pasternack, Intertek Testing Services NA, Incorporated, NY [RT]
Todd W. Stafford, National Joint Apprentice & Training Committee, IBEW-NJATC, TN [L]
Rep. International Brotherhood of Electrical Workers
LaVerne E. Stetson, Lincoln, NE [U]
Rep. American Society of Agricultural Engineers
Herbert V. Whittall, Electrical Generating Systems Association, FL [M]
Rep. Electrical Generating Systems Association

Alternates

Daniel Batta, Jr., Constellation Generation Group, LLC, MD [UT]
Rep. Electric Light & Power Group/EEI
(Alt. to B. N. Hornberger)
Sonya M. Bird, Underwriters Laboratories Incorporated, NC [RT]
(Alt. to J. R. Kovacik)

Ron B. Chilton, North Carolina Department of Insurance, NC [E]
Rep. International Association of Electrical Inspectors
(Alt. to T. L. Baker)
Brian L. Crise, NIETC, OR [L]
Rep. International Brotherhood of Electrical Workers
(Alt. to T. W. Stafford)
Steven J. Fredette, UTC Cells, LLC, CT [M]
Rep. U.S. Fuel Cell Council
(Alt. to K. Krastins)
(VL to 690, 692, 705)
Ronald H. Minter, Thomas & Betts, TN [M]
Rep. National Electrical Manufacturers Association
(Alt. to J. S. Nasby)
Duke W. Schamel, Copperhead Electric Inc, CA [IM]
Rep. Independent Electrical Contractors, Incorporated
(Alt. to T. D. Holleman)
Robert L. Simpson, Simpson Electrical Engineering Company, GA [U]
Rep. Institute of Electrical & Electronics Engineers, Incorporated
(Alt. to M. V. Glenn)
Richard Sobel, Quantum Electric Corporation, NY [IM]
Rep. National Electrical Contractors Association
(Alt. to T. H. Wood)
Dale A. Triffo, Shell Oil Products US, TX [U]
Rep. American Chemistry Council
(Alt. to D. L. Elkins)

CODE-MAKING PANEL NO. 14

Articles 500, 501, 502, 503, 504, 505, 506, 510, 511, 513, 514, 515, 516

Donald R. Cook, *Chair*
Shelby County Building Inspections, AL [E]
Rep. International Association of Electrical Inspectors

Troy Beall, B & D Electric Company, Incorporated, NM [IM]
Rep. National Electrical Contractors Association
Edward M. Briesch, Underwriters Laboratories Incorporated, IL [RT]
Al Engler, EGS Electrical Group, IL [M]
Rep. International Society for Measurement and Control
Mark Goodman, Jacobs Engineering Group, CA [U]
Rep. American Petroleum Institute
Gregory D. Hall, Better-Way Electric, Incorporated, CO [IM]
Rep. Independent Electrical Contractors, Incorporated
John Katunar, III, GE Global Asset Protection Services, MO [I]
Rep. GE Global Asset Protection Services
Joseph H. Kuczka, Killark Electric Manufacturing Company, MO [M]
Rep. National Electrical Manufacturers Association
William G. Lawrence, Jr., FM Global, MA [I]
Rep. FM Global/FM Research
Jeremy Neagle, Intertek Testing Services NA, Incorporated, NY [RT]
Mike O'Meara, Arizona Public Service Company, AZ [UT]
Rep. Electric Light & Power Group/EEI
David B. Wechsler, The Dow Chemical Company, TX [U]
Rep. American Chemistry Council
James A. Weldon, IBEW Local Union 728, FL [L]
Rep. International Brotherhood of Electrical Workers
Mark C. Wirfs, R & W Engineering Incorporated, OR [U]
Rep. Grain Elevator and Processing Society
Donald W. Zipse, Zipse Electrical Engineering Incorporated, PA [U]
Rep. Institute of Electrical & Electronics Engineers, Incorporated

Alternates

A. W. Ballard, Crouse-Hinds, NY [M]
Rep. National Electrical Manufacturers Association
(Alt. to J. H. Kuczka)
Marc J. Bernsen, Southwestern Idaho Electrical JATC, ID [L]
Rep. International Brotherhood of Electrical Workers
(Alt. to J. A. Weldon)
Mark W. Bonk, Cargill Incorporated, MN [U]
Rep. Grain Elevator and Processing Society
(Alt. to M. C. Wirfs)
Giovanni Hummel Borges, Underwriters Laboratories Incorporated, Brasil [RT]
(Alt. to E. M. Briesch)
James D. Cospolich, Waldemar S. Nelson & Company Incorporated, LA [U]
Rep. Institute of Electrical & Electronics Engineers, Incorporated
(Alt. to D. W. Zipse)
Larry E. Fuhrman, City of Titusville, FL [E]
Rep. International Association of Electrical Inspectors
(Alt. to D. R. Cook)
Nicholas P. Ludlam, FM Global, MA [I]
Rep. FM Global/FM Research
(Alt. to W. G. Lawrence, Jr.)
Michael E. McNeil, FMC Corporation/Bio Polymer, ME [U]
Rep. American Chemistry Council
(Alt. to D. B. Wechsler)
Ted H. Schnaare, Rosemount Incorporated, MN [M]
Rep. International Society for Measurement and Control
(Alt. to A. Engler)

Francis M. Stone, Jr., Shell Exploration and Production
Company, TX [U]
  Rep. American Petroleum Institute
  (Alt. to M. Goodman)

Nonvoting

Eduardo N. Solano, Estudio Ingeniero Solano S.A.,
Argentina [SE]
Fred K. Walker, U.S. Air Force, FL [U]
  Rep. TC on Airport Facilities

CODE-MAKING PANEL NO. 15
Articles 517, 518, 520, 525, 530, 540

Donald J. Talka, *Chair*
Underwriters Laboratories Incorporated, NY [RT]

James R. Duncan, Sparling Electrical Engineering, WA [U]
  Rep. Institute of Electrical & Electronics Engineers,
  Incorporated
Tom Dunn, Butler Amusements, CA [U]
  Rep. Outdoor Amusement Business Association,
  Incorporated
  (VL to 525)
Douglas S. Erickson, American Society for Healthcare
Engineering, Virgin Islands [U]
  Rep. American Society for Healthcare Engineering
Michael B. Klein, Metropolitan Engineering, Incorporated,
DC [IM]
  Rep. Illuminating Engineering Society of North America
  (VL to 518, 520, 525, 530, 540)
Edwin S. Kramer, Radio City Music Hall, NY [L]
  Rep. International Alliance of Theatrical Stage Employees
  (VL to 518, 520, 525, 530, 540)
Larry Lau, U.S. Department of Veterans Affairs, DC [U]
  (VL to 517, 518)
Dennis W. Marshall, TAG Electric Companies, TX [IM]
  Rep. Independent Electrical Contractors, Incorporated
Eugene E. Morgan, County of Clackamas, Oregon, OR [E]
  Rep. International Association of Electrical Inspectors
Hugh O. Nash, Jr., Nash Lipsey Burch, LLC, TN [SE]
  Rep. TC on Electrical Systems
Bruce D. Shelly, Shelly Electric Company, Inc., PA [IM]
  Rep. National Electrical Contractors Association
Donald J. Sherratt, Intertek Testing Services NA,
Incorporated, MA [RT]
Michael D. Skinner, CBS Studio Center, CA [U]
  Rep. Alliance of Motion Picture and Television Producers
  (VL to 518, 520, 525, 530, 540)
Richard H. Smith, OG&E Electric Services, OK [UT]
  Rep. Electric Light & Power Group/EEI
Kenneth E. Vannice, Leviton Manufacturing Company
Incorporated, OR [M]
  Rep. U.S. Institute for Theatre Technology
  (VL to 518, 520, 525, 530, 540)
Michael Velvikis, High Voltage Maintenance Corporation,
WI [IM]
  Rep. InterNational Electrical Testing Association
  Incorporated

Andrew White, IBEW Local Union 3, NY [L]
  Rep. International Brotherhood of Electrical Workers
James L. Wiseman, Square D Company, TN [M]
  Rep. National Electrical Manufacturers Association

Alternates
James R. Cook, IBEW Local Union 364, IL [L]
  Rep. International Brotherhood of Electrical Workers
  (Alt. to A. White)
Matthew B. Dozier, IDesign Services, TN [U]
  Rep. Institute of Electrical & Electronics Engineers,
  Incorporated
  (Alt. to J. R. Duncan)
Samuel B. Friedman, BICC General Cable Corporation,
RI [M]
  Rep. National Electrical Manufacturers Association
  (Alt. to J. L. Wiseman)
Dale A. Hallerberg, Underwriters Laboratories Incorporated,
IL [RT]
  (Alt. to D. J. Talka)
Mitchell K. Hefter, Entertainment Technology, TX [IM]
  Rep. Illuminating Engineering Society of North America
  (Alt. to M. B. Klein)
  (VL to 518, 520, 525, 530, 540))
Stanley D. Kahn, Tri-City Electric Company, Incorporated,
CA [IM]
  Rep. National Electrical Contractors Association
  (Alt. to B. D. Shelly)
Malinda Joyce Sampson, Minnesota Electricity Board,
MN [E]
  Rep. International Association of Electrical Inspectors
  (Alt. to E. E. Morgan)
James C. Seabury, III, Enterprise Electric, LLC, TN [IM]
  Rep. Independent Electrical Contractors, Incorporated
  (Alt. to D. W. Marshall)
Steven R. Terry, Electronic Theatre Controls Incorporated,
NY [M]
  Rep. U.S. Institute for Theatre Technology
  (Alt. to K. E. Vannice)
  (VL to 518, 520, 525, 530, 540)
Rodney M. Young, Detroit Edison Company, MI [UT]
  Rep. Electric Light & Power Group/EEI
  (Alt. to R. H. Smith)

CODE-MAKING PANEL NO. 16
Articles 770, 800, 810, 820, 830

Stanley D. Kahn, *Chair*
Tri-City Electric Company, Incorporated, CA [IM]
Rep. National Electrical Contractors Association

J. Robert Boyer, Edwards Systems Technology, Incorporated, NJ [M]
Rep. National Electrical Manufacturers Association
James E. Brunssen, Telcordia, NJ [U]
Rep. Alliance for Telecommunications Industry Solutions
Larry Chan, City of New Orleans, LA [E]
Rep. International Association of Electrical Inspectors
Gerald Lee Dorna, Belden Wire & Cable, IN [M]
Rep. Insulated Cable Engineers Association Incorporated
Roland W. Gubisch, Intertek Testing Services NA, Incorporated, MA [RT]
Robert L. Hughes, The DuPont Company, TN [U]
Rep. American Chemistry Council
Robert W. Jensen, dbi-Telecommunication Infrastructure Design, TX [M]
Rep. Building Industry Consulting Services International
Steven C. Johnson, Time Warner Cable, NC [UT]
Rep. National Cable & Telecommunications Association
Ronald G. Jones, Ronald G. Jones, P.E., TX [U]
Rep. Institute of Electrical & Electronics Engineers, Incorporated
Barrett (Barry) Kalian, Underwriters Laboratories of Canada, ON, Canada [RT]
Harold C. Ohde, IBEW/NECA Technical Institute, IL [L]
Rep. International Brotherhood of Electrical Workers
Joseph W. Rao, R.A.O. Electric Company, FL [IM]
Rep. Independent Electrical Contractors, Incorporated
James W. Romlein, MV Labs LLC, WI [M]
Rep. Telecommunications Industry Association
Kyle E. Todd, Entergy Corporation, TX [UT]
Rep. Electric Light & Power Group/EEI

Alternates

Alan Amato, Times Fiber Communications, Incorporated, CT [UT]
Rep. National Cable & Telecommunications Association
(Alt. to S. C. Johnson)
Donna Ballast, University of Texas at Austin, TX [M]
Rep. Building Industry Consulting Services International
(Alt. to R. W. Jensen)

Chrysanthos Chrysanthou, Telcordia Technologies/SAIC, NJ [U]
Rep. Alliance for Telecommunications Industry Solutions
(Alt. to J. E. Brunssen)
Terry C. Coleman, National Joint Apprentice & Training Committee, TN [L]
Rep. International Brotherhood of Electrical Workers
(Alt. to H. C. Ohde)
William K. Hopple, Tyco/SimplexGrinnell, CA [M]
Rep. National Electrical Manufacturers Association
(Alt. to J. R. Boyer)
Dr. Stanley Kaufman, CableSafe/OFS, GA [M]
Rep. Insulated Cable Engineers Association Incorporated
(Alt. to G. L. Dorna)
Robert W. McCourt, Public Service Electric and Gas Company, NJ [UT]
Rep. Electric Light & Power Group/EEI
(Alt. to K. E. Todd)
William J. McCoy, Verizon Wireless, TX [U]
Rep. Institute of Electrical & Electronics Engineers, Incorporated
(Alt. to R. G. Jones)
Robert P. McGann, City of Cambridge, MA [E]
Rep. International Association of Electrical Inspectors
(Alt. to L. Chan)
W. Douglas Pirkle, Pirkle Electric Company, Incorporated, GA [IM]
Rep. National Electrical Contractors Association
(Alt. to S. D. Kahn)
Luigi G. Prezioso, M. C. Dean, Incorporated, VA [IM]
Rep. Independent Electrical Contractors, Incorporated
(Alt. to J. W. Rao)
Bradley C. Rowe, Underwriters Laboratories Incorporated, IL [RT]
(Alt. to B. Kalian)

Nonvoting

Irving Mande, Westport, CT [M]

CODE-MAKING PANEL NO. 17
Articles 422, 424, 426, 427, 680, 682

Don W. Jhonson, *Chair*
Interior Electric, Incorporated, FL [IM]
Rep. National Electrical Contractors Association

Richard J. Cripps, Association of Home Appliance Manufacturers, DC [M]
Rep. Association of Home Appliance Manufacturers
(VL to 422, 424)
Bill Hanthorn, Tyco Thermal Controls, ON, Canada [M]
Rep. Copper Development Association, Incorporated
Bruce R. Hirsch, Baltimore Gas & Electric Company, MD [UT]
Rep. Electric Light & Power Group/EEI
Christopher T. Hutchings, Underwriters Laboratories Incorporated, CA [RT]

Walter Koessel, Intertek Testing Services NA, Incorporated, MO [RT]
Robert M. Milatovich, Clark County Building Department, NV [E]
Rep. International Association of Electrical Inspectors
Marcos Ramirez, Hatfield-Reynolds Electric Company, AZ [IM]
Rep. Independent Electrical Contractors, Incorporated
Brian E. Rock, Hubbell Incorporated, CT [M]
Rep. National Electrical Manufacturers Association

Anthony P. Sardina, UTC Carrier Corporation, NY [M]
Rep. Air-Conditioning and Refrigeration Institute
(VL to 422, 424)

Lee L. West, Balboa Instruments, Incorporated, CA [M]
Rep. National Spa and Pool Institute
(VL to 680)

Randy J. Yasenchak, IBEW Local Union 607, PA [L]
Rep. International Brotherhood of Electrical Workers

Robert M. Yurkanin, Electran Process International
Incorporated, NJ [U]
Rep. Institute of Electrical & Electronics Engineers,
Incorporated

Alternates

Dennis L. Baker, Springs & Sons Electrical Contractors
Incorporated, AZ [IM]
Rep. Independent Electrical Contractors, Incorporated
(Alt. to M. Ramirez)

Mark R. Berner, PPL Electric Utilities Corporation,
PA [UT]
Rep. Electric Light & Power Group/EEI
(Alt. to B. R. Hirsch)

J. Ron Caccamese, Nathan Electric Company, LTD., TX [L]
Rep. International Brotherhood of Electrical Workers
(Alt. to R. J. Yasenchak)

Aaron B. Chase, Leviton Manufacturing Company,
Incorporated, NY [M]
Rep. National Electrical Manufacturers Association
(Alt. to B. E. Rock)

Paul Crivell, Kennedy Jenks Consultants, WA [U]
Rep. Institute of Electrical & Electronics Engineers,
Incorporated
(Alt. to R. M. Yurkanin)

James E. Maldonado, City of Tempe, AZ [E]
Rep. International Association of Electrical Inspectors
(Alt. to R. M. Milatovich)

Cannon Sun, Underwriters Laboratories Incorporated,
Taiwan [RT]
(Alt. to C. T. Hutchings)

D. Harold Ware, Libra Electric Company, OK [IM]
Rep. National Electrical Contractors Association
(Alt. to D. W. Jhonson)

Robert E. Wisenburg, Coates Heater Company,
Incorporated, WA [M]
Rep. National Spa and Pool Institute
(Alt. to L. L. West)
(VL to 680)

Nonvoting

William H. King, Jr., U.S. Consumer Product Safety
Commission, MD [C]
(Alt. to A. M. Trotta)

Andrew M. Trotta, U.S. Consumer Product Safety
Commission, MD [C]

CODE-MAKING PANEL NO. 18
Articles 406, 410, 411, 600, 605

Michael N. Ber, *Chair*
IEC, Houston, TX [IM]
Rep. Independent Electrical Contractors, Incorporated

Paul Costello, NECA and IBEW Local 90 JATC, CT [L]
Rep. International Brotherhood of Electrical Workers

Kenneth A. Fetzer, Underwriters Laboratories Incorporated,
NC [RT]

Stephen G. Kieffer, Kieffer & Company, Incorporated,
WI [M]
Rep. International Sign Association
(VL to 600)

Steven A. Larson, BWXT Y-12, LLC, TN [U]
Rep. Institute of Electrical & Electronics Engineers,
Incorporated

Michael S. O'Boyle, Genlyte Thomas Group, MA [M]
Rep. American Lighting Association
(VL to 410, 411)

Timothy S. Owens, City of San Diego, CA [E]
Rep. International Association of Electrical Inspectors

Jim F. Pierce, Intertek Testing Services NA, Incorporated,
OR [RT]

Saul Rosenbaum, Leviton Manufacturing Company
Incorporated, NY [M]
Rep. National Electrical Manufacturers Association

Michael W. Smith, Guarantee Electrical Company,
MO [IM]
Rep. National Electrical Contractors Association

Carl Tim Wall, Alabama Power Company, AL [UT]
Rep. Electric Light & Power Group/EEI

Jack Wells, Pass & Seymour/Legrand, NY [M]

Alternates

Robert T. Carlock, R. T. Carlock Company, TN [IM]
Rep. Independent Electrical Contractors, Incorporated
(Alt. to M. N. Ber)

Frederick L. Carpenter, Lithonia Lighting, GA [M]
Rep. National Electrical Manufacturers Association
(Alt. to S. Rosenbaum)

Amos D. Lowrance, Jr., City of Chattanooga, Tennessee,
TN [E]
Rep. International Association of Electrical Inspectors
(Alt. to T. S. Owens)

Ronald Michaelis, South Bend Vicinity Electrical JATC,
IN [L]
Rep. International Brotherhood of Electrical Workers
(Alt. to P. Costello)

Christopher P. O'Neil, National Grid USA Service
Company, MA [UT]
Rep. Electric Light & Power Group/EEI
(Alt. to C. T. Wall)

Alan M. Smith, France/Scott Fetzer Company, TN [M]
Rep. International Sign Association
(Alt. to S. G. Kieffer)
(VL to 600)

Rachna Stegall, Underwriters Laboratories Incorporated,
IL [RT]
(Alt. to K. A. Fetzer)

Charles M. Trout, Maron Electric Company, FL [IM]
Rep. National Electrical Contractors Association
(Alt. to M. W. Smith)

CODE-MAKING PANEL NO. 19

Articles 545, 547, 550, 551, 552, 553, 555, 604, 675, Annex D, Examples D11 and D12

Robert A. McCullough, *Chair*
Ocean County Construction Inspection Department, NJ [E]
Rep. International Association of Electrical Inspectors

Barry Bauman, Alliant Energy, WI [U]
Rep. American Society of Agricultural Engineers
James W. Finch, Kampgrounds of America, Incorporated, MT [U]
(VL to 550, 551, 552, 555)
Bruce A. Hopkins, Recreation Vehicle Industry Association, VA [M]
Rep. Recreation Vehicle Industry Association
(VL to 550, 551, 552)
Robert L. La Rocca, Underwriters Laboratories Incorporated, NY [RT]
Timothy P. McNeive, Thomas & Betts Corporation, TN [M]
Rep. National Electrical Manufacturers Association
John Mikel, Skyline Corporation, IN [M]
Rep. Manufactured Housing Institute
(VL to 550, 551, 552)
Tug L. Miller, National Association of RV Parks & Campgrounds, CA [U]
Rep. National Association of RV Parks & Campgrounds
(VL to 550, 551, 552)
Leslie Sabin-Mercado, San Diego Gas & Electric Company, CA [UT]
Rep. Electric Light & Power Group/EEI
William J. Tipton, IBEW Local Union 575, OH [L]
Rep. International Brotherhood of Electrical Workers
Kenneth Weakley, Mountain Electric, Incorporated, CA [IM]
Rep. National Electrical Contractors Association
William A. Zanicchi, AAA Certified Electric Incorporated, FL [IM]
Rep. Independent Electrical Contractors, Incorporated
Michael L. Zieman, RADCO, CA [RT]
(VL to 545, 550, 551, 552)

Steven J. Blais, EGS Electrical Group, IL [M]
Rep. National Electrical Manufacturers Association
(Alt. to T. P. McNeive)
Monte R. Ewing, Wisconsin Department of Commerce, WI [E]
Rep. International Association of Electrical Inspectors
(Alt. to R. A. McCullough)
Thomas R. Lichtenstein, Underwriters Laboratories Incorporated, IL [RT]
(Alt. to R. L. La Rocca)
Linda J. Little, IBEW Local Union 1, MO [L]
Rep. International Brotherhood of Electrical Workers
(Alt. to W. J. Tipton)
Suzanne Mark, National Association of RV Parks & Campgrounds, VA [U]
Rep. National Association of RV Parks & Campgrounds
(Alt. to T. L. Miller)
(VL to 550, 551, 552)
N. Kent Morgan, AC Corporation, NC [IM]
Rep. Independent Electrical Contractors, Incorporated
(Alt. to W. A. Zanicchi)
Kent Perkins, Recreation Vehicle Industry Association, VA [M]
Rep. Recreation Vehicle Industry Association
(Alt. to B. A. Hopkins)
(VL to 550, 551, 552)
John G. Sims, NTA Incorporated, IN [M]
Rep. Manufactured Housing Institute
(Alt. to J. Mikel)
(VL to 550, 551, 552)
Keith G. Tinsey, Michigan State University, MI [U]
Rep. American Society of Agricultural Engineers
(Alt. to B. Bauman)
Raymond F. Tucker, Consulting Professional Engineer, CA [RT]
(Alt. to M. L. Zieman)
(VL to 545, 550, 551, 552)

Alternates

Glenn H. Ankenbrand, Conectiv Power, MD [UT]
Rep. Electric Light & Power Group/EEI
(Alt. to L. Sabin-Mercado)

NFPA Electrical Engineering Division Technical Staff

Mark W. Earley, Assistant Vice President/Chief Electrical Engineer
Kenneth G. Mastrullo, Senior Electrical Specialist
Jean A. O'Connor, Electrical Project Specialist/Support Supervisor

Lee F. Richardson, Senior Electrical Engineer
Richard J. Roux, Senior Electrical Specialist
Jeffrey S. Sargent, Senior Electrical Specialist
Joseph V. Sheehan, Principal Electrical Engineer
Donald W. Shields, Senior Electrical Specialist

NFPA Staff Editor
Joyce G. Grandy, Senior Project Editor

Note: Membership on a committee shall not in and of itself constitute an endorsement of the Association or any document developed by the Committee on which the member serves.

Committee Scope: This Committee shall have primary responsibility for documents on minimizing the risk of electricity as a source of electric shock and as a potential ignition source of fires and explosions. It shall also be responsible for text to minimize the propagation of fire and explosions due to electrical installations.

NFPA 70

National Electrical Code®

2005 Edition

IMPORTANT NOTE: This NFPA document is made available for use subject to important notices and legal disclaimers. These notices and disclaimers appear in all publications containing this document and may be found under the heading "Important Notices and Disclaimers Concerning NFPA Documents." They can also be obtained on request from NFPA or viewed at www.nfpa.org/disclaimers.

ARTICLE 90
Introduction

90.1 Purpose.

(A) Practical Safeguarding. The purpose of this *Code* is the practical safeguarding of persons and property from hazards arising from the use of electricity.

(B) Adequacy. This *Code* contains provisions that are considered necessary for safety. Compliance therewith and proper maintenance results in an installation that is essentially free from hazard but not necessarily efficient, convenient, or adequate for good service or future expansion of electrical use.

> FPN: Hazards often occur because of overloading of wiring systems by methods or usage not in conformity with this *Code*. This occurs because initial wiring did not provide for increases in the use of electricity. An initial adequate installation and reasonable provisions for system changes provide for future increases in the use of electricity.

(C) Intention. This *Code* is not intended as a design specification or an instruction manual for untrained persons.

(D) Relation to Other International Standards. The requirements in this *Code* address the fundamental principles of protection for safety contained in Section 131 of International Electrotechnical Commission Standard 60364-1, *Electrical Installations of Buildings*.

> FPN: IEC 60364-1, Section 131, contains fundamental principles of protection for safety that encompass protection against electric shock, protection against thermal effects, protection against overcurrent, protection against fault currents, and protection against overvoltage. All of these potential hazards are addressed by the requirements in this *Code*.

90.2 Scope.

(A) Covered. This *Code* covers the installation of electrical conductors, equipment, and raceways; signaling and communications conductors, equipment, and raceways; and optical fiber cables and raceways for the following:

(1) Public and private premises, including buildings, structures, mobile homes, recreational vehicles, and floating buildings

(2) Yards, lots, parking lots, carnivals, and industrial substations

> FPN to (2): For additional information concerning such installations in an industrial or multibuilding complex, see ANSI C2-2002, *National Electrical Safety Code*.

(3) Installations of conductors and equipment that connect to the supply of electricity

(4) Installations used by the electric utility, such as office buildings, warehouses, garages, machine shops, and recreational buildings, that are not an integral part of a generating plant, substation, or control center.

(B) Not Covered. This *Code* does not cover the following:

(1) Installations in ships, watercraft other than floating buildings, railway rolling stock, aircraft, or automotive vehicles other than mobile homes and recreational vehicles

> FPN: Although the scope of this *Code* indicates that the *Code* does not cover installations in ships, portions of this *Code* are incorporated by reference into Title 46, *Code of Federal Regulations*, Parts 110–113.

(2) Installations underground in mines and self-propelled mobile surface mining machinery and its attendant electrical trailing cable

(3) Installations of railways for generation, transformation, transmission, or distribution of power used exclusively for operation of rolling stock or installations used exclusively for signaling and communications purposes

(4) Installations of communications equipment under the exclusive control of communications utilities located outdoors or in building spaces used exclusively for such installations

(5) Installations under the exclusive control of an electric utility where such installations

  a. Consist of service drops or service laterals, and associated metering, or

  b. Are located in legally established easements, rights-of-way, or by other agreements either designated by or recognized by public service commissions, utility commissions, or other regulatory agencies having jurisdiction for such installations, or

  c. Are on property owned or leased by the electric utility for the purpose of communications, metering, generation, control, transformation, transmission, or distribution of electric energy.

FPN to (4) and (5): Examples of utilities may include those entities that are typically designated or recognized by governmental law or regulation by public service/utility commissions and that install, operate, and maintain electric supply (such as generation, transmission, or distribution systems) or communication systems (such as telephone, CATV, Internet, satellite, or data services). Utilities may be subject to compliance with codes and standards covering their regulated activities as adopted under governmental law or regulation. Additional information can be found through consultation with the appropriate governmental bodies, such as state regulatory commissions, Federal Energy Regulatory Commission, and Federal Communications Commission.

(C) Special Permission. The authority having jurisdiction for enforcing this *Code* may grant exception for the installation of conductors and equipment that are not under the exclusive control of the electric utilities and are used to connect the electric utility supply system to the service-entrance conductors of the premises served, provided such installations are outside a building or terminate immediately inside a building wall.

90.3 Code Arrangement. This *Code* is divided into the introduction and nine chapters, as shown in Figure 90.3. Chapters 1, 2, 3, and 4 apply generally; Chapters 5, 6, and 7 apply to special occupancies, special equipment, or other special conditions. These latter chapters supplement or modify the general rules. Chapters 1 through 4 apply except as amended by Chapters 5, 6, and 7 for the particular conditions.

Chapter 8 covers communications systems and is not subject to the requirements of Chapters 1 through 7 except where the requirements are specifically referenced in Chapter 8.

Chapter 9 consists of tables.

Annexes are not part of the requirements of this *Code* but are included for informational purposes only.

90.4 Enforcement. This *Code* is intended to be suitable for mandatory application by governmental bodies that exercise legal jurisdiction over electrical installations, including signaling and communications systems, and for use by insurance inspectors. The authority having jurisdiction for enforcement of the *Code* has the responsibility for making interpretations of the rules, for deciding on the approval of equipment and materials, and for granting the special permission contemplated in a number of the rules.

By special permission, the authority having jurisdiction may waive specific requirements in this *Code* or permit alternative methods where it is assured that equivalent objectives can be achieved by establishing and maintaining effective safety.

This *Code* may require new products, constructions, or materials that may not yet be available at the time the *Code* is adopted. In such event, the authority having jurisdiction may permit the use of the products, constructions, or materials that comply with the most recent previous edition of this *Code* adopted by the jurisdiction.

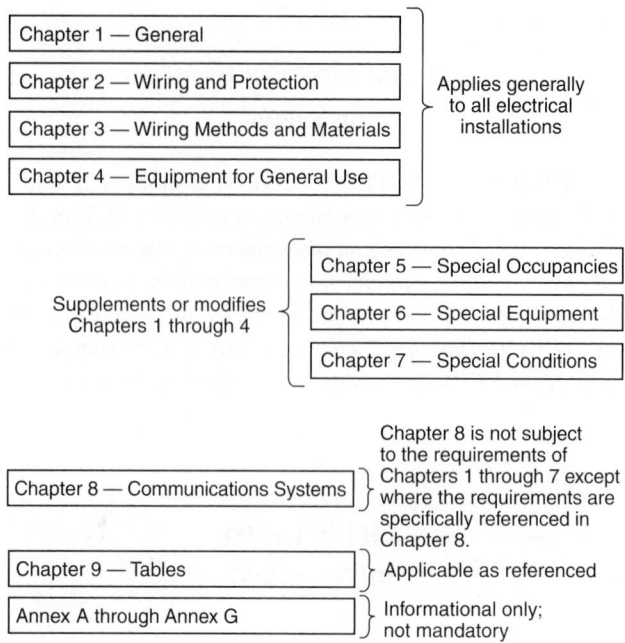

Figure 90.3 Code Arrangement.

90.5 Mandatory Rules, Permissive Rules, and Explanatory Material.

(A) Mandatory Rules. Mandatory rules of this *Code* are those that identify actions that are specifically required or prohibited and are characterized by the use of the terms *shall* or *shall not*.

(B) Permissive Rules. Permissive rules of this *Code* are those that identify actions that are allowed but not required, are normally used to describe options or alternative methods, and are characterized by the use of the terms *shall be permitted* or *shall not be required*.

(C) Explanatory Material. Explanatory material, such as references to other standards, references to related sections of this *Code,* or information related to a *Code* rule, is included in this *Code* in the form of fine print notes (FPNs). Fine print notes are informational only and are not enforceable as requirements of this *Code*.

Brackets containing section references to another NFPA document are for informational purposes only and are provided as a guide to indicate the source of the extracted text. These bracketed references immediately follow the extracted text.

FPN: The format and language used in this *Code* follows guidelines established by NFPA and published in the *NEC Style Manual.* Copies of this manual can be obtained from NFPA.

90.6 Formal Interpretations. To promote uniformity of interpretation and application of the provisions of this *Code,* formal interpretation procedures have been established and are found in the NFPA Regulations Governing Committee Projects.

90.7 Examination of Equipment for Safety. For specific items of equipment and materials referred to in this *Code,* examinations for safety made under standard conditions provide a basis for approval where the record is made generally available through promulgation by organizations properly equipped and qualified for experimental testing, inspections of the run of goods at factories, and service-value determination through field inspections. This avoids the necessity for repetition of examinations by different examiners, frequently with inadequate facilities for such work, and the confusion that would result from conflicting reports on the suitability of devices and materials examined for a given purpose.

It is the intent of this *Code* that factory-installed internal wiring or the construction of equipment need not be inspected at the time of installation of the equipment, except to detect alterations or damage, if the equipment has been listed by a qualified electrical testing laboratory that is recognized as having the facilities described in the preceding paragraph and that requires suitability for installation in accordance with this *Code.*

FPN No. 1: See requirements in 110.3.

FPN No. 2: *Listed* is defined in Article 100.

FPN No. 3: Annex A contains an informative list of product safety standards for electrical equipment.

90.8 Wiring Planning.

(A) Future Expansion and Convenience. Plans and specifications that provide ample space in raceways, spare raceways, and additional spaces allow for future increases in electric power and communication circuits. Distribution centers located in readily accessible locations provide convenience and safety of operation.

(B) Number of Circuits in Enclosures. It is elsewhere provided in this *Code* that the number of wires and circuits confined in a single enclosure be varyingly restricted. Limiting the number of circuits in a single enclosure minimizes the effects from a short circuit or ground fault in one circuit.

90.9 Units of Measurement.

(A) Measurement System of Preference. For the purpose of this *Code,* metric units of measurement are in accordance with the modernized metric system known as the International System of Units (SI).

(B) Dual System of Units. SI units shall appear first, and inch-pound units shall immediately follow in parentheses. Conversion from inch-pound units to SI units shall be based on hard conversion except as provided in 90.9(C).

(C) Permitted Uses of Soft Conversion. The cases given in 90.9(C)(1) through (C)(4) shall not be required to use hard conversion and shall be permitted to use soft conversion.

(1) Trade Sizes. Where the actual measured size of a product is not the same as the nominal size, trade size designators shall be used rather than dimensions. Trade practices shall be followed in all cases.

(2) Extracted Material. Where material is extracted from another standard, the context of the original material shall not be compromised or violated. Any editing of the extracted text shall be confined to making the style consistent with that of the *NEC.*

(3) Industry Practice. Where industry practice is to express units in inch-pound units, the inclusion of SI units shall not be required.

(4) Safety. Where a negative impact on safety would result, soft conversion shall be used.

(D) Compliance. Conversion from inch-pound units to SI units shall be permitted to be an approximate conversion. Compliance with the numbers shown in either the SI system or the inch-pound system shall constitute compliance with this *Code.*

FPN No. 1: Hard conversion is considered a change in dimensions or properties of an item into new sizes that might or might not be interchangeable with the sizes used in the original measurement. Soft conversion is considered a direct mathematical conversion and involves a change in the description of an existing measurement but not in the actual dimension.

FPN No. 2: SI conversions are based on IEEE/ASTM SI 10-1997, *Standard for the Use of the International System of Units (SI): The Modern Metric System.*

Chapter 1 General

ARTICLE 100
Definitions

Scope. This article contains only those definitions essential to the proper application of this *Code*. It is not intended to include commonly defined general terms or commonly defined technical terms from related codes and standards. In general, only those terms that are used in two or more articles are defined in Article 100. Other definitions are included in the article in which they are used but may be referenced in Article 100.

Part I of this article contains definitions intended to apply wherever the terms are used throughout this *Code*. Part II contains definitions applicable only to the parts of articles specifically covering installations and equipment operating at over 600 volts, nominal.

I. General

Accessible (as applied to equipment). Admitting close approach; not guarded by locked doors, elevation, or other effective means.

Accessible (as applied to wiring methods). Capable of being removed or exposed without damaging the building structure or finish or not permanently closed in by the structure or finish of the building.

Accessible, Readily (Readily Accessible). Capable of being reached quickly for operation, renewal, or inspections without requiring those to whom ready access is requisite to climb over or remove obstacles or to resort to portable ladders, and so forth.

Ampacity. The current, in amperes, that a conductor can carry continuously under the conditions of use without exceeding its temperature rating.

Appliance. Utilization equipment, generally other than industrial, that is normally built in standardized sizes or types and is installed or connected as a unit to perform one or more functions such as clothes washing, air conditioning, food mixing, deep frying, and so forth.

Approved. Acceptable to the authority having jurisdiction.

Askarel. A generic term for a group of nonflammable synthetic chlorinated hydrocarbons used as electrical insulating media. Askarels of various compositional types are used. Under arcing conditions, the gases produced, while consisting predominantly of noncombustible hydrogen chloride, can include varying amounts of combustible gases, depending on the askarel type.

Attachment Plug (Plug Cap) (Plug). A device that, by insertion in a receptacle, establishes a connection between the conductors of the attached flexible cord and the conductors connected permanently to the receptacle.

Authority Having Jurisdiction (AHJ). The organization, office, or individual responsible for approving equipment, materials, an installation, or a procedure.

> FPN: The phrase "authority having jurisdiction" is used in NFPA documents in a broad manner, since jurisdictions and approval agencies vary, as do their responsibilities. Where public safety is primary, the AHJ may be a federal, state, local, or other regional department or individual such as a fire chief; fire marshal; chief of a fire prevention bureau, labor department, or health department; building official; electrical inspector; or others having statutory authority. For insurance purposes, an insurance inspection department, rating bureau, or other insurance company representative may be the AHJ. In many circumstances, the property owner or his or her designated agent assumes the role of the AHJ; at government installations, the commanding officer or departmental official may be the AHJ.

Automatic. Self-acting, operating by its own mechanism when actuated by some impersonal influence, as, for example, a change in current, pressure, temperature, or mechanical configuration.

Bathroom. An area including a basin with one or more of the following: a toilet, a tub, or a shower.

Bonding (Bonded). The permanent joining of metallic parts to form an electrically conductive path that ensures electrical continuity and the capacity to conduct safely any current likely to be imposed.

Bonding Jumper. A reliable conductor to ensure the required electrical conductivity between metal parts required to be electrically connected.

Bonding Jumper, Equipment. The connection between two or more portions of the equipment grounding conductor.

Bonding Jumper, Main. The connection between the grounded circuit conductor and the equipment grounding conductor at the service.

Bonding Jumper, System. The connection between the grounded circuit conductor and the equipment grounding conductor at a separately derived system.

Branch Circuit. The circuit conductors between the final overcurrent device protecting the circuit and the outlet(s).

Branch Circuit, Appliance. A branch circuit that supplies energy to one or more outlets to which appliances are to be connected and that has no permanently connected luminaires (lighting fixtures) that are not a part of an appliance.

Branch Circuit, General-Purpose. A branch circuit that supplies two or more receptacles or outlets for lighting and appliances.

Branch Circuit, Individual. A branch circuit that supplies only one utilization equipment.

Branch Circuit, Multiwire. A branch circuit that consists of two or more ungrounded conductors that have a voltage between them, and a grounded conductor that has equal voltage between it and each ungrounded conductor of the circuit and that is connected to the neutral or grounded conductor of the system.

Building. A structure that stands alone or that is cut off from adjoining structures by fire walls with all openings therein protected by approved fire doors.

Cabinet. An enclosure that is designed for either surface mounting or flush mounting and is provided with a frame, mat, or trim in which a swinging door or doors are or can be hung.

Circuit Breaker. A device designed to open and close a circuit by nonautomatic means and to open the circuit automatically on a predetermined overcurrent without damage to itself when properly applied within its rating.

> FPN: The automatic opening means can be integral, direct acting with the circuit breaker, or remote from the circuit breaker.

Adjustable (as applied to circuit breakers). A qualifying term indicating that the circuit breaker can be set to trip at various values of current, time, or both, within a predetermined range.

Instantaneous Trip (as applied to circuit breakers). A qualifying term indicating that no delay is purposely introduced in the tripping action of the circuit breaker.

Inverse Time (as applied to circuit breakers). A qualifying term indicating that there is purposely introduced a delay in the tripping action of the circuit breaker, which delay decreases as the magnitude of the current increases.

Nonadjustable (as applied to circuit breakers). A qualifying term indicating that the circuit breaker does not have any adjustment to alter the value of current at which it will trip or the time required for its operation.

Setting (of circuit breakers). The value of current, time, or both, at which an adjustable circuit breaker is set to trip.

Concealed. Rendered inaccessible by the structure or finish of the building. Wires in concealed raceways are considered concealed, even though they may become accessible by withdrawing them.

Conductor, Bare. A conductor having no covering or electrical insulation whatsoever.

Conductor, Covered. A conductor encased within material of composition or thickness that is not recognized by this *Code* as electrical insulation.

Conductor, Insulated. A conductor encased within material of composition and thickness that is recognized by this *Code* as electrical insulation.

Conduit Body. A separate portion of a conduit or tubing system that provides access through a removable cover(s) to the interior of the system at a junction of two or more sections of the system or at a terminal point of the system.

Boxes such as FS and FD or larger cast or sheet metal boxes are not classified as conduit bodies.

Connector, Pressure (Solderless). A device that establishes a connection between two or more conductors or between one or more conductors and a terminal by means of mechanical pressure and without the use of solder.

Continuous Load. A load where the maximum current is expected to continue for 3 hours or more.

Controller. A device or group of devices that serves to govern, in some predetermined manner, the electric power delivered to the apparatus to which it is connected.

Cooking Unit, Counter-Mounted. A cooking appliance designed for mounting in or on a counter and consisting of one or more heating elements, internal wiring, and built-in or mountable controls.

Coordination (Selective). Localization of an overcurrent condition to restrict outages to the circuit or equipment affected, accomplished by the choice of overcurrent protective devices and their ratings or settings.

Copper-Clad Aluminum Conductors. Conductors drawn from a copper-clad aluminum rod with the copper metallurgically bonded to an aluminum core. The copper forms a minimum of 10 percent of the cross-sectional area of a solid conductor or each strand of a stranded conductor.

Cutout Box. An enclosure designed for surface mounting that has swinging doors or covers secured directly to and telescoping with the walls of the box proper.

Dead Front. Without live parts exposed to a person on the operating side of the equipment.

Demand Factor. The ratio of the maximum demand of a system, or part of a system, to the total connected load of a system or the part of the system under consideration.

Device. A unit of an electrical system that is intended to carry or control but not utilize electric energy.

Disconnecting Means. A device, or group of devices, or other means by which the conductors of a circuit can be disconnected from their source of supply.

Dusttight. Constructed so that dust will not enter the enclosing case under specified test conditions.

Duty, Continuous. Operation at a substantially constant load for an indefinitely long time.

Duty, Intermittent. Operation for alternate intervals of (1) load and no load; or (2) load and rest; or (3) load, no load, and rest.

Duty, Periodic. Intermittent operation in which the load conditions are regularly recurrent.

Duty, Short-Time. Operation at a substantially constant load for a short and definite, specified time.

Duty, Varying. Operation at loads, and for intervals of time, both of which may be subject to wide variation.

Dwelling Unit. A single unit, providing complete and independent living facilities for one or more persons, including permanent provisions for living, sleeping, cooking, and sanitation.

Dwelling, One-Family. A building that consists solely of one dwelling unit.

Dwelling, Two-Family. A building that consists solely of two dwelling units.

Dwelling, Multifamily. A building that contains three or more dwelling units.

Electric Sign. A fixed, stationary, or portable self-contained, electrically illuminated utilization equipment with words or symbols designed to convey information or attract attention.

Enclosed. Surrounded by a case, housing, fence, or wall(s) that prevents persons from accidentally contacting energized parts.

Enclosure. The case or housing of apparatus, or the fence or walls surrounding an installation to prevent personnel from accidentally contacting energized parts or to protect the equipment from physical damage.

FPN: See Table 430.91 for examples of enclosure types.

Energized. Electrically connected to, or is, a source of voltage.

Equipment. A general term including material, fittings, devices, appliances, luminaires (fixtures), apparatus, and the like used as a part of, or in connection with, an electrical installation.

Explosionproof Apparatus. Apparatus enclosed in a case that is capable of withstanding an explosion of a specified gas or vapor that may occur within it and of preventing the ignition of a specified gas or vapor surrounding the enclosure by sparks, flashes, or explosion of the gas or vapor within, and that operates at such an external temperature that a surrounding flammable atmosphere will not be ignited thereby.

FPN: For further information, see ANSI/UL 1203-1999, *Explosion-Proof and Dust-Ignition-Proof Electrical Equipment for Use in Hazardous (Classified) Locations.*

Exposed (as applied to live parts). Capable of being inadvertently touched or approached nearer than a safe distance by a person. It is applied to parts that are not suitably guarded, isolated, or insulated.

Exposed (as applied to wiring methods). On or attached to the surface or behind panels designed to allow access.

Externally Operable. Capable of being operated without exposing the operator to contact with live parts.

Feeder. All circuit conductors between the service equipment, the source of a separately derived system, or other power supply source and the final branch-circuit overcurrent device.

Festoon Lighting. A string of outdoor lights that is suspended between two points.

Fitting. An accessory such as a locknut, bushing, or other part of a wiring system that is intended primarily to perform a mechanical rather than an electrical function.

Garage. A building or portion of a building in which one or more self-propelled vehicles can be kept for use, sale, storage, rental, repair, exhibition, or demonstration purposes.

FPN: For commercial garages, repair and storage, see Article 511.

Ground. A conducting connection, whether intentional or accidental, between an electrical circuit or equipment and the earth or to some conducting body that serves in place of the earth.

Grounded. Connected to earth or to some conducting body that serves in place of the earth.

Grounded, Effectively. Intentionally connected to earth through a ground connection or connections of sufficiently low impedance and having sufficient current-carrying capacity to prevent the buildup of voltages that may result in undue hazards to connected equipment or to persons.

Grounded, Solidly. Connected to ground without inserting any resistor or impedance device.

Grounded Conductor. A system or circuit conductor that is intentionally grounded.

Ground-Fault Circuit Interrupter (GFCI). A device intended for the protection of personnel that functions to de-energize a circuit or portion thereof within an established period of time when a current to ground exceeds the values established for a Class A device.

> FPN: Class A ground-fault circuit interrupters trip when the current to ground has a value in the range of 4 mA to 6 mA. For further information, see UL 943, *Standard for Ground-Fault Circuit Interrupters.*

Ground-Fault Protection of Equipment. A system intended to provide protection of equipment from damaging line-to-ground fault currents by operating to cause a disconnecting means to open all ungrounded conductors of the faulted circuit. This protection is provided at current levels less than those required to protect conductors from damage through the operation of a supply circuit overcurrent device.

Grounding Conductor. A conductor used to connect equipment or the grounded circuit of a wiring system to a grounding electrode or electrodes.

Grounding Conductor, Equipment. The conductor used to connect the non–current-carrying metal parts of equipment, raceways, and other enclosures to the system grounded conductor, the grounding electrode conductor, or both, at the service equipment or at the source of a separately derived system.

Grounding Electrode. A device that establishes an electrical connection to the earth.

Grounding Electrode Conductor. The conductor used to connect the grounding electrode(s) to the equipment grounding conductor, to the grounded conductor, or to both, at the service, at each building or structure where supplied by a feeder(s) or branch circuit(s), or at the source of a separately derived system.

Guarded. Covered, shielded, fenced, enclosed, or otherwise protected by means of suitable covers, casings, barriers, rails, screens, mats, or platforms to remove the likelihood of approach or contact by persons or objects to a point of danger.

Guest Room. An accommodation combining living, sleeping, sanitary, and storage facilities within a compartment.

Guest Suite. An accommodation with two or more contiguous rooms comprising a compartment, with or without doors between such rooms, that provides living, sleeping, sanitary, and storage facilities.

Handhole Enclosure. An enclosure identified for use in underground systems, provided with an open or closed bottom, and sized to allow personnel to reach into, but not enter, for the purpose of installing, operating, or maintaining equipment or wiring or both.

Hoistway. Any shaftway, hatchway, well hole, or other vertical opening or space in which an elevator or dumbwaiter is designed to operate.

Identified (as applied to equipment). Recognizable as suitable for the specific purpose, function, use, environment, application, and so forth, where described in a particular *Code* requirement.

> FPN: Some examples of ways to determine suitability of equipment for a specific purpose, environment, or application include investigations by a qualified testing laboratory (listing and labeling), an inspection agency, or other organizations concerned with product evaluation.

In Sight From (Within Sight From, Within Sight). Where this *Code* specifies that one equipment shall be "in sight from," "within sight from," or "within sight," and so forth, of another equipment, the specified equipment is to be visible and not more than 15 m (50 ft) distant from the other.

Interrupting Rating. The highest current at rated voltage that a device is intended to interrupt under standard test conditions.

> FPN: Equipment intended to interrupt current at other than fault levels may have its interrupting rating implied in other ratings, such as horsepower or locked rotor current.

Isolated (as applied to location). Not readily accessible to persons unless special means for access are used.

Labeled. Equipment or materials to which has been attached a label, symbol, or other identifying mark of an organization that is acceptable to the authority having jurisdiction and concerned with product evaluation, that maintains periodic inspection of production of labeled equipment or materials, and by whose labeling the manufacturer indicates compliance with appropriate standards or performance in a specified manner.

Lighting Outlet. An outlet intended for the direct connection of a lampholder, a luminaire (lighting fixture), or a pendant cord terminating in a lampholder.

Listed. Equipment, materials, or services included in a list published by an organization that is acceptable to the authority having jurisdiction and concerned with evaluation of products or services, that maintains periodic inspection of production of listed equipment or materials or periodic evaluation of services, and whose listing states that the equipment, material, or services either meets appropriate designated standards or has been tested and found suitable for a specified purpose.

> FPN: The means for identifying listed equipment may vary for each organization concerned with product evaluation, some of which do not recognize equipment as listed unless it is also labeled. Use of the system employed by the listing organization allows the authority having jurisdiction to identify a listed product.

Live Parts. Energized conductive components.

Location, Damp. Locations protected from weather and not subject to saturation with water or other liquids but subject to moderate degrees of moisture. Examples of such locations include partially protected locations under canopies, marquees, roofed open porches, and like locations, and interior locations subject to moderate degrees of moisture, such as some basements, some barns, and some cold-storage warehouses.

Location, Dry. A location not normally subject to dampness or wetness. A location classified as dry may be temporarily subject to dampness or wetness, as in the case of a building under construction.

Location, Wet. Installations under ground or in concrete slabs or masonry in direct contact with the earth; in locations subject to saturation with water or other liquids, such as vehicle washing areas; and in unprotected locations exposed to weather.

Luminaire. A complete lighting unit consisting of a lamp or lamps together with the parts designed to distribute the light, to position and protect the lamps and ballast (where applicable), and to connect the lamps to the power supply.

Metal-Enclosed Power Switchgear. A switchgear assembly completely enclosed on all sides and top with sheet metal (except for ventilating openings and inspection windows) containing primary power circuit switching, interrupting devices, or both, with buses and connections. The assembly may include control and auxiliary devices. Access to the interior of the enclosure is provided by doors, removable covers, or both.

Motor Control Center. An assembly of one or more enclosed sections having a common power bus and principally containing motor control units.

Multioutlet Assembly. A type of surface, flush, or freestanding raceway designed to hold conductors and receptacles, assembled in the field or at the factory.

Nonautomatic. Action requiring personal intervention for its control. As applied to an electric controller, nonautomatic control does not necessarily imply a manual controller, but only that personal intervention is necessary.

Nonlinear Load. A load where the wave shape of the steady-state current does not follow the wave shape of the applied voltage.

> FPN: Electronic equipment, electronic/electric-discharge lighting, adjustable-speed drive systems, and similar equipment may be nonlinear loads.

Outlet. A point on the wiring system at which current is taken to supply utilization equipment.

Outline Lighting. An arrangement of incandescent lamps, electric discharge lighting, or other electrically powered light sources to outline or call attention to certain features such as the shape of a building or the decoration of a window.

Overcurrent. Any current in excess of the rated current of equipment or the ampacity of a conductor. It may result from overload, short circuit, or ground fault.

> FPN: A current in excess of rating may be accommodated by certain equipment and conductors for a given set of conditions. Therefore, the rules for overcurrent protection are specific for particular situations.

Overload. Operation of equipment in excess of normal, full-load rating, or of a conductor in excess of rated ampacity that, when it persists for a sufficient length of time, would cause damage or dangerous overheating. A fault, such as a short circuit or ground fault, is not an overload.

Panelboard. A single panel or group of panel units designed for assembly in the form of a single panel, including buses and automatic overcurrent devices, and equipped with or without switches for the control of light, heat, or power circuits; designed to be placed in a cabinet or cutout box placed in or against a wall, partition, or other support; and accessible only from the front.

Plenum. A compartment or chamber to which one or more air ducts are connected and that forms part of the air distribution system.

Power Outlet. An enclosed assembly that may include receptacles, circuit breakers, fuseholders, fused switches, buses, and watt-hour meter mounting means; intended to supply and control power to mobile homes, recreational vehicles, park trailers, or boats or to serve as a means for distributing power required to operate mobile or temporarily installed equipment.

Premises Wiring (System). That interior and exterior wiring, including power, lighting, control, and signal circuit wiring together with all their associated hardware, fittings, and wiring devices, both permanently and temporarily installed, that extends from the service point or source of power, such as a battery, a solar photovoltaic system, or a generator, transformer, or converter windings, to the outlet(s). Such wiring does not include wiring internal to appliances, luminaires (fixtures), motors, controllers, motor control centers, and similar equipment.

Qualified Person. One who has skills and knowledge related to the construction and operation of the electrical equipment and installations and has received safety training on the hazards involved.

> FPN: Refer to NFPA 70E-2004, *Standard for Electrical Safety in the Workplace*, for electrical safety training requirements.

Raceway. An enclosed channel of metal or nonmetallic materials designed expressly for holding wires, cables, or busbars, with additional functions as permitted in this *Code*. Raceways include, but are not limited to, rigid metal conduit, rigid nonmetallic conduit, intermediate metal conduit, liquidtight flexible conduit, flexible metallic tubing, flexible metal conduit, electrical nonmetallic tubing, electrical metallic tubing, underfloor raceways, cellular concrete floor raceways, cellular metal floor raceways, surface raceways, wireways, and busways.

Rainproof. Constructed, protected, or treated so as to prevent rain from interfering with the successful operation of the apparatus under specified test conditions.

Raintight. Constructed or protected so that exposure to a beating rain will not result in the entrance of water under specified test conditions.

Receptacle. A receptacle is a contact device installed at the outlet for the connection of an attachment plug. A single receptacle is a single contact device with no other contact device on the same yoke. A multiple receptacle is two or more contact devices on the same yoke.

Receptacle Outlet. An outlet where one or more receptacles are installed.

Remote-Control Circuit. Any electric circuit that controls any other circuit through a relay or an equivalent device.

Sealable Equipment. Equipment enclosed in a case or cabinet that is provided with a means of sealing or locking so that live parts cannot be made accessible without opening the enclosure. The equipment may or may not be operable without opening the enclosure.

Separately Derived System. A premises wiring system whose power is derived from a source of electric energy or equipment other than a service. Such systems have no direct electrical connection, including a solidly connected grounded circuit conductor, to supply conductors originating in another system.

Service. The conductors and equipment for delivering electric energy from the serving utility to the wiring system of the premises served.

Service Cable. Service conductors made up in the form of a cable.

Service Conductors. The conductors from the service point to the service disconnecting means.

Service Drop. The overhead service conductors from the last pole or other aerial support to and including the splices, if any, connecting to the service-entrance conductors at the building or other structure.

Service-Entrance Conductors, Overhead System. The service conductors between the terminals of the service equip-

ment and a point usually outside the building, clear of building walls, where joined by tap or splice to the service drop.

Service-Entrance Conductors, Underground System. The service conductors between the terminals of the service equipment and the point of connection to the service lateral.

> FPN: Where service equipment is located outside the building walls, there may be no service-entrance conductors or they may be entirely outside the building.

Service Equipment. The necessary equipment, usually consisting of a circuit breaker(s) or switch(es) and fuse(s) and their accessories, connected to the load end of service conductors to a building or other structure, or an otherwise designated area, and intended to constitute the main control and cutoff of the supply.

Service Lateral. The underground service conductors between the street main, including any risers at a pole or other structure or from transformers, and the first point of connection to the service-entrance conductors in a terminal box or meter or other enclosure, inside or outside the building wall. Where there is no terminal box, meter, or other enclosure, the point of connection is considered to be the point of entrance of the service conductors into the building.

Service Point. The point of connection between the facilities of the serving utility and the premises wiring.

Show Window. Any window used or designed to be used for the display of goods or advertising material, whether it is fully or partly enclosed or entirely open at the rear and whether or not it has a platform raised higher than the street floor level.

Signaling Circuit. Any electric circuit that energizes signaling equipment.

Solar Photovoltaic System. The total components and subsystems that, in combination, convert solar energy into electrical energy suitable for connection to a utilization load.

Special Permission. The written consent of the authority having jurisdiction.

Structure. That which is built or constructed.

Supplementary Overcurrent Protective Device. A device intended to provide limited overcurrent protection for specific applications and utilization equipment such as luminaires (lighting fixtures) and appliances. This limited protection is in addition to the protection provided in the required branch circuit by the branch circuit overcurrent protective device.

Switch, Bypass Isolation. A manually operated device used in conjunction with a transfer switch to provide a means of directly connecting load conductors to a power source and of disconnecting the transfer switch.

Switch, General-Use. A switch intended for use in general distribution and branch circuits. It is rated in amperes, and it is capable of interrupting its rated current at its rated voltage.

Switch, General-Use Snap. A form of general-use switch constructed so that it can be installed in device boxes or on box covers, or otherwise used in conjunction with wiring systems recognized by this *Code.*

Switch, Isolating. A switch intended for isolating an electric circuit from the source of power. It has no interrupting rating, and it is intended to be operated only after the circuit has been opened by some other means.

Switch, Motor-Circuit. A switch rated in horsepower that is capable of interrupting the maximum operating overload current of a motor of the same horsepower rating as the switch at the rated voltage.

Switch, Transfer. An automatic or nonautomatic device for transferring one or more load conductor connections from one power source to another.

Switchboard. A large single panel, frame, or assembly of panels on which are mounted on the face, back, or both, switches, overcurrent and other protective devices, buses, and usually instruments. Switchboards are generally accessible from the rear as well as from the front and are not intended to be installed in cabinets.

Thermally Protected (as applied to motors). The words *Thermally Protected* appearing on the nameplate of a motor or motor-compressor indicate that the motor is provided with a thermal protector.

Thermal Protector (as applied to motors). A protective device for assembly as an integral part of a motor or motor-compressor that, when properly applied, protects the motor against dangerous overheating due to overload and failure to start.

FPN: The thermal protector may consist of one or more sensing elements integral with the motor or motor-compressor and an external control device.

Utilization Equipment. Equipment that utilizes electric energy for electronic, electromechanical, chemical, heating, lighting, or similar purposes.

Ventilated. Provided with a means to permit circulation of air sufficient to remove an excess of heat, fumes, or vapors.

Volatile Flammable Liquid. A flammable liquid having a flash point below 38°C (100°F), or a flammable liquid whose temperature is above its flash point, or a Class II combustible liquid that has a vapor pressure not exceeding 276 kPa (40 psia) at 38°C (100°F) and whose temperature is above its flash point.

Voltage (of a circuit). The greatest root-mean-square (rms) (effective) difference of potential between any two conductors of the circuit concerned.

FPN: Some systems, such as 3-phase 4-wire, single-phase 3-wire, and 3-wire direct current, may have various circuits of various voltages.

Voltage, Nominal. A nominal value assigned to a circuit or system for the purpose of conveniently designating its voltage class (e.g., 120/240 volts, 480Y/277 volts, 600 volts). The actual voltage at which a circuit operates can vary from the nominal within a range that permits satisfactory operation of equipment.

FPN: See ANSI C84.1-1995, *Voltage Ratings for Electric Power Systems and Equipment (60 Hz).*

Voltage to Ground. For grounded circuits, the voltage between the given conductor and that point or conductor of the circuit that is grounded; for ungrounded circuits, the greatest voltage between the given conductor and any other conductor of the circuit.

Watertight. Constructed so that moisture will not enter the enclosure under specified test conditions.

Weatherproof. Constructed or protected so that exposure to the weather will not interfere with successful operation.

FPN: Rainproof, raintight, or watertight equipment can fulfill the requirements for weatherproof where varying weather conditions other than wetness, such as snow, ice, dust, or temperature extremes, are not a factor.

II. Over 600 Volts, Nominal

Whereas the preceding definitions are intended to apply wherever the terms are used throughout this *Code,* the following definitions are applicable only to parts of the article specifically covering installations and equipment operating at over 600 volts, nominal.

Electronically Actuated Fuse. An overcurrent protective device that generally consists of a control module that provides current sensing, electronically derived time–current characteristics, energy to initiate tripping, and an interrupting module that interrupts current when an overcurrent occurs. Electronically actuated fuses may or may not operate in a current-limiting fashion, depending on the type of control selected.

Fuse. An overcurrent protective device with a circuit-opening fusible part that is heated and severed by the passage of overcurrent through it.

FPN: A fuse comprises all the parts that form a unit capable of performing the prescribed functions. It may or may not be the complete device necessary to connect it into an electrical circuit.

Controlled Vented Power Fuse. A fuse with provision for controlling discharge circuit interruption such that no solid material may be exhausted into the surrounding atmosphere.

> FPN: The fuse is designed so that discharged gases will not ignite or damage insulation in the path of the discharge or propagate a flashover to or between grounded members or conduction members in the path of the discharge where the distance between the vent and such insulation or conduction members conforms to manufacturer's recommendations.

Expulsion Fuse Unit (Expulsion Fuse). A vented fuse unit in which the expulsion effect of gases produced by the arc and lining of the fuseholder, either alone or aided by a spring, extinguishes the arc.

Nonvented Power Fuse. A fuse without intentional provision for the escape of arc gases, liquids, or solid particles to the atmosphere during circuit interruption.

Power Fuse Unit. A vented, nonvented, or controlled vented fuse unit in which the arc is extinguished by being drawn through solid material, granular material, or liquid, either alone or aided by a spring.

Vented Power Fuse. A fuse with provision for the escape of arc gases, liquids, or solid particles to the surrounding atmosphere during circuit interruption.

Multiple Fuse. An assembly of two or more single-pole fuses.

Switching Device. A device designed to close, open, or both, one or more electric circuits.

Circuit Breaker. A switching device capable of making, carrying, and interrupting currents under normal circuit conditions, and also of making, carrying for a specified time, and interrupting currents under specified abnormal circuit conditions, such as those of short circuit.

Cutout. An assembly of a fuse support with either a fuseholder, fuse carrier, or disconnecting blade. The fuseholder or fuse carrier may include a conducting element (fuse link) or may act as the disconnecting blade by the inclusion of a nonfusible member.

Disconnecting (or Isolating) Switch (Disconnector, Isolator). A mechanical switching device used for isolating a circuit or equipment from a source of power.

Disconnecting Means. A device, group of devices, or other means whereby the conductors of a circuit can be disconnected from their source of supply.

Interrupter Switch. A switch capable of making, carrying, and interrupting specified currents.

Oil Cutout (Oil-Filled Cutout). A cutout in which all or part of the fuse support and its fuse link or disconnecting blade is mounted in oil with complete immersion of the contacts and the fusible portion of the conducting element (fuse link) so that arc interruption by severing of the fuse link or by opening of the contacts will occur under oil.

Oil Switch. A switch having contacts that operate under oil (or askarel or other suitable liquid).

Regulator Bypass Switch. A specific device or combination of devices designed to bypass a regulator.

ARTICLE 110
Requirements for Electrical Installations

I. General

110.1 Scope. This article covers general requirements for the examination and approval, installation and use, access to and spaces about electrical conductors and equipment; enclosures intended for personnel entry; and tunnel installations.

110.2 Approval. The conductors and equipment required or permitted by this *Code* shall be acceptable only if approved.

> FPN: See 90.7, Examination of Equipment for Safety, and 110.3, Examination, Identification, Installation, and Use of Equipment. See definitions of *Approved, Identified, Labeled,* and *Listed.*

110.3 Examination, Identification, Installation, and Use of Equipment.

(A) Examination. In judging equipment, considerations such as the following shall be evaluated:

(1) Suitability for installation and use in conformity with the provisions of this *Code*

> FPN: Suitability of equipment use may be identified by a description marked on or provided with a product to identify the suitability of the product for a specific purpose, environment, or application. Suitability of equipment may be evidenced by listing or labeling.

(2) Mechanical strength and durability, including, for parts designed to enclose and protect other equipment, the adequacy of the protection thus provided

(3) Wire-bending and connection space

(4) Electrical insulation

(5) Heating effects under normal conditions of use and also under abnormal conditions likely to arise in service

(6) Arcing effects

(7) Classification by type, size, voltage, current capacity, and specific use

(8) Other factors that contribute to the practical safeguarding of persons using or likely to come in contact with the equipment

(B) Installation and Use. Listed or labeled equipment shall be installed and used in accordance with any instructions included in the listing or labeling.

110.4 Voltages. Throughout this *Code*, the voltage considered shall be that at which the circuit operates. The voltage rating of electrical equipment shall not be less than the nominal voltage of a circuit to which it is connected.

110.5 Conductors. Conductors normally used to carry current shall be of copper unless otherwise provided in this *Code*. Where the conductor material is not specified, the material and the sizes given in this *Code* shall apply to copper conductors. Where other materials are used, the size shall be changed accordingly.

> FPN: For aluminum and copper-clad aluminum conductors, see 310.15.

110.6 Conductor Sizes. Conductor sizes are expressed in American Wire Gage (AWG) or in circular mils.

110.7 Insulation Integrity. Completed wiring installations shall be free from short circuits and from grounds other than as required or permitted in Article 250.

110.8 Wiring Methods. Only wiring methods recognized as suitable are included in this *Code*. The recognized methods of wiring shall be permitted to be installed in any type of building or occupancy, except as otherwise provided in this *Code*.

110.9 Interrupting Rating. Equipment intended to interrupt current at fault levels shall have an interrupting rating sufficient for the nominal circuit voltage and the current that is available at the line terminals of the equipment.

Equipment intended to interrupt current at other than fault levels shall have an interrupting rating at nominal circuit voltage sufficient for the current that must be interrupted.

110.10 Circuit Impedance and Other Characteristics. The overcurrent protective devices, the total impedance, the component short-circuit current ratings, and other characteristics of the circuit to be protected shall be selected and coordinated to permit the circuit-protective devices used to clear a fault to do so without extensive damage to the electrical components of the circuit. This fault shall be assumed to be either between two or more of the circuit conductors or between any circuit conductor and the grounding conductor or enclosing metal raceway. Listed products applied in accordance with their listing shall be considered to meet the requirements of this section.

110.11 Deteriorating Agents. Unless identified for use in the operating environment, no conductors or equipment shall be located in damp or wet locations; where exposed to gases, fumes, vapors, liquids, or other agents that have a deteriorating effect on the conductors or equipment; or where exposed to excessive temperatures.

> FPN No. 1: See 300.6 for protection against corrosion.
>
> FPN No. 2: Some cleaning and lubricating compounds can cause severe deterioration of many plastic materials used for insulating and structural applications in equipment.

Equipment identified only as "dry locations," "Type 1," or "indoor use only" shall be protected against permanent damage from the weather during building construction.

110.12 Mechanical Execution of Work. Electrical equipment shall be installed in a neat and workmanlike manner.

> FPN: Accepted industry practices are described in ANSI/NECA 1-2000, *Standard Practices for Good Workmanship in Electrical Contracting,* and other ANSI-approved installation standards.

(A) Unused Openings. Unused cable or raceway openings in boxes, raceways, auxiliary gutters, cabinets, cutout boxes, meter socket enclosures, equipment cases, or housings shall be effectively closed to afford protection substantially equivalent to the wall of the equipment. Where metallic plugs or plates are used with nonmetallic enclosures, they shall be recessed at least 6 mm (¼ in.) from the outer surface of the enclosure.

(B) Subsurface Enclosures. Conductors shall be racked to provide ready and safe access in underground and subsurface enclosures into which persons enter for installation and maintenance.

(C) Integrity of Electrical Equipment and Connections. Internal parts of electrical equipment, including busbars, wiring terminals, insulators, and other surfaces, shall not be damaged or contaminated by foreign materials such as paint, plaster, cleaners, abrasives, or corrosive residues. There shall be no damaged parts that may adversely affect safe operation or mechanical strength of the equipment such as parts that are broken; bent; cut; or deteriorated by corrosion, chemical action, or overheating.

110.13 Mounting and Cooling of Equipment.

(A) Mounting. Electrical equipment shall be firmly secured to the surface on which it is mounted. Wooden plugs driven into holes in masonry, concrete, plaster, or similar materials shall not be used.

(B) Cooling. Electrical equipment that depends on the natural circulation of air and convection principles for cooling of exposed surfaces shall be installed so that room airflow over such surfaces is not prevented by walls or by adjacent installed equipment. For equipment designed for floor mounting, clearance between top surfaces and adjacent surfaces shall be provided to dissipate rising warm air.

Electrical equipment provided with ventilating openings shall be installed so that walls or other obstructions do not prevent the free circulation of air through the equipment.

110.14 Electrical Connections. Because of different characteristics of dissimilar metals, devices such as pressure terminal or pressure splicing connectors and soldering lugs shall be identified for the material of the conductor and shall be properly installed and used. Conductors of dissimilar metals shall not be intermixed in a terminal or splicing connector where physical contact occurs between dissimilar conductors (such as copper and aluminum, copper and copper-clad aluminum, or aluminum and copper-clad aluminum), unless the device is identified for the purpose and conditions of use. Materials such as solder, fluxes, inhibitors, and compounds, where employed, shall be suitable for the use and shall be of a type that will not adversely affect the conductors, installation, or equipment.

> FPN: Many terminations and equipment are marked with a tightening torque.

(A) Terminals. Connection of conductors to terminal parts shall ensure a thoroughly good connection without damaging the conductors and shall be made by means of pressure connectors (including set-screw type), solder lugs, or splices to flexible leads. Connection by means of wire-binding screws or studs and nuts that have upturned lugs or the equivalent shall be permitted for 10 AWG or smaller conductors.

Terminals for more than one conductor and terminals used to connect aluminum shall be so identified.

(B) Splices. Conductors shall be spliced or joined with splicing devices identified for the use or by brazing, welding, or soldering with a fusible metal or alloy. Soldered splices shall first be spliced or joined so as to be mechanically and electrically secure without solder and then be soldered. All splices and joints and the free ends of conductors shall be covered with an insulation equivalent to that of the conductors or with an insulating device identified for the purpose.

Wire connectors or splicing means installed on conductors for direct burial shall be listed for such use.

(C) Temperature Limitations. The temperature rating associated with the ampacity of a conductor shall be selected and coordinated so as not to exceed the lowest temperature rating of any connected termination, conductor, or device. Conductors with temperature ratings higher than specified for terminations shall be permitted to be used for ampacity adjustment, correction, or both.

(1) Equipment Provisions. The determination of termination provisions of equipment shall be based on 110.14(C)(1)(a) or (C)(1)(b). Unless the equipment is listed and marked otherwise, conductor ampacities used in determining equipment termination provisions shall be based on Table 310.16 as appropriately modified by 310.15(B)(6).

(a) Termination provisions of equipment for circuits rated 100 amperes or less, or marked for 14 AWG through 1 AWG conductors, shall be used only for one of the following:
(1) Conductors rated 60°C (140°F).
(2) Conductors with higher temperature ratings, provided the ampacity of such conductors is determined based on the 60°C (140°F) ampacity of the conductor size used.
(3) Conductors with higher temperature ratings if the equipment is listed and identified for use with such conductors.
(4) For motors marked with design letters B, C, or D, conductors having an insulation rating of 75°C (167°F) or higher shall be permitted to be used, provided the ampacity of such conductors does not exceed the 75°C (167°F) ampacity.

(b) Termination provisions of equipment for circuits rated over 100 amperes, or marked for conductors larger than 1 AWG, shall be used only for one of the following:
(1) Conductors rated 75°C (167°F)
(2) Conductors with higher temperature ratings, provided the ampacity of such conductors does not exceed the 75°C (167°F) ampacity of the conductor size used, or up to their ampacity if the equipment is listed and identified for use with such conductors

(2) Separate Connector Provisions. Separately installed pressure connectors shall be used with conductors at the ampacities not exceeding the ampacity at the listed and identified temperature rating of the connector.

> FPN: With respect to 110.14(C)(1) and (C)(2), equipment markings or listing information may additionally restrict the sizing and temperature ratings of connected conductors.

110.15 High-Leg Marking. On a 4-wire, delta-connected system where the midpoint of one phase winding is grounded, only the conductor or busbar having the higher phase voltage to ground shall be durably and permanently marked by an outer finish that is orange in color or by other effective means. Such identification shall be placed at each point on the system where a connection is made if the grounded conductor is also present.

110.16 Flash Protection. Switchboards, panelboards, industrial control panels, meter socket enclosures, and motor control centers that are in other than dwelling occupancies and are likely to require examination, adjustment, servicing, or maintenance while energized shall be field marked to warn qualified persons of potential electric arc flash hazards. The marking shall be located so as to be clearly visible to qualified persons before examination, adjustment, servicing, or maintenance of the equipment.

FPN No. 1: NFPA 70E-2004, *Standard for Electrical Safety in the Workplace*, provides assistance in determining severity of potential exposure, planning safe work practices, and selecting personal protective equipment.

FPN No. 2: ANSI Z535.4-1998, *Product Safety Signs and Labels*, provides guidelines for the design of safety signs and labels for application to products.

110.18 Arcing Parts. Parts of electric equipment that in ordinary operation produce arcs, sparks, flames, or molten metal shall be enclosed or separated and isolated from all combustible material.

FPN: For hazardous (classified) locations, see Articles 500 through 517. For motors, see 430.14.

110.19 Light and Power from Railway Conductors. Circuits for lighting and power shall not be connected to any system that contains trolley wires with a ground return.

Exception: Such circuit connections shall be permitted in car houses, power houses, or passenger and freight stations operated in connection with electric railways.

110.21 Marking. The manufacturer's name, trademark, or other descriptive marking by which the organization responsible for the product can be identified shall be placed on all electric equipment. Other markings that indicate voltage, current, wattage, or other ratings shall be provided as specified elsewhere in this *Code*. The marking shall be of sufficient durability to withstand the environment involved.

110.22 Identification of Disconnecting Means. Each disconnecting means shall be legibly marked to indicate its purpose unless located and arranged so the purpose is evident. The marking shall be of sufficient durability to withstand the environment involved.

Where circuit breakers or fuses are applied in compliance with the series combination ratings marked on the equipment by the manufacturer, the equipment enclosure(s) shall be legibly marked in the field to indicate the equipment has been applied with a series combination rating. The marking shall be readily visible and state the following:

CAUTION — SERIES COMBINATION SYSTEM RATED _____ AMPERES. IDENTIFIED REPLACEMENT COMPONENTS REQUIRED.

FPN: See 240.86(B) for interrupting rating marking for end-use equipment.

110.23 Current Transformers. Unused current transformers associated with potentially energized circuits shall be short-circuited.

II. 600 Volts, Nominal, or Less

110.26 Spaces About Electrical Equipment. Sufficient access and working space shall be provided and maintained about all electric equipment to permit ready and safe operation and maintenance of such equipment. Enclosures housing electrical apparatus that are controlled by a lock(s) shall be considered accessible to qualified persons.

(A) Working Space. Working space for equipment operating at 600 volts, nominal, or less to ground and likely to require examination, adjustment, servicing, or maintenance while energized shall comply with the dimensions of 110.26(A)(1), (A)(2), and (A)(3) or as required or permitted elsewhere in this *Code*.

(1) Depth of Working Space. The depth of the working space in the direction of live parts shall not be less than that specified in Table 110.26(A)(1) unless the requirements of 110.26(A)(1)(a), (A)(1)(b), or (A)(1)(c) are met. Distances shall be measured from the exposed live parts or from the enclosure or opening if the live parts are enclosed.

Table 110.26(A)(1) Working Spaces

Nominal Voltage to Ground	Minimum Clear Distance		
	Condition 1	Condition 2	Condition 3
0–150	900 mm (3 ft)	900 mm (3 ft)	900 mm (3 ft)
151–600	900 mm (3 ft)	1.1 m (3½ ft)	1.2 m (4 ft)

Note: Where the conditions are as follows:
Condition 1 — Exposed live parts on one side of the working space and no live or grounded parts on the other side of the working space, or exposed live parts on both sides of the working space that are effectively guarded by insulating materials.
Condition 2 — Exposed live parts on one side of the working space and grounded parts on the other side of the working space. Concrete, brick, or tile walls shall be considered as grounded.
Condition 3 — Exposed live parts on both sides of the working space.

(a) Dead-Front Assemblies. Working space shall not be required in the back or sides of assemblies, such as dead-front switchboards or motor control centers, where all connections and all renewable or adjustable parts, such as fuses or switches, are accessible from locations other than the back or sides. Where rear access is required to work on nonelectrical parts on the back of enclosed equipment, a minimum horizontal working space of 762 mm (30 in.) shall be provided.

(b) Low Voltage. By special permission, smaller working spaces shall be permitted where all exposed live parts operate at not greater than 30 volts rms, 42 volts peak, or 60 volts dc.

(c) Existing Buildings. In existing buildings where electrical equipment is being replaced, Condition 2 working clearance shall be permitted between dead-front switchboards, panelboards, or motor control centers located across the aisle from each other where conditions of maintenance and supervision ensure that written procedures have been adopted to prohibit equipment on both sides of the aisle from being open at the same time and qualified persons who are authorized will service the installation.

(2) Width of Working Space. The width of the working space in front of the electric equipment shall be the width of the equipment or 750 mm (30 in.), whichever is greater. In all cases, the work space shall permit at least a 90 degree opening of equipment doors or hinged panels.

(3) Height of Working Space. The work space shall be clear and extend from the grade, floor, or platform to the height required by 110.26(E). Within the height requirements of this section, other equipment that is associated with the electrical installation and is located above or below the electrical equipment shall be permitted to extend not more than 150 mm (6 in.) beyond the front of the electrical equipment.

(B) Clear Spaces. Working space required by this section shall not be used for storage. When normally enclosed live parts are exposed for inspection or servicing, the working space, if in a passageway or general open space, shall be suitably guarded.

(C) Entrance to Working Space.

(1) Minimum Required. At least one entrance of sufficient area shall be provided to give access to working space about electrical equipment.

(2) Large Equipment. For equipment rated 1200 amperes or more that contains overcurrent devices, switching devices, or control devices, there shall be one entrance to the required working space not less than 610 mm (24 in.) wide and 2.0 m (6½ ft) high at each end of the working space. Where the entrance has a personnel door(s), the door(s) shall open in the direction of egress and be equipped with panic bars, pressure plates, or other devices that are normally latched but open under simple pressure.

A single entrance to the required working space shall be permitted where either of the conditions in 110.26(C)(2)(a) or (C)(2)(b) is met.

(a) Unobstructed Exit. Where the location permits a continuous and unobstructed way of exit travel, a single entrance to the working space shall be permitted.

(b) Extra Working Space. Where the depth of the working space is twice that required by 110.26(A)(1), a single entrance shall be permitted. It shall be located so that the distance from the equipment to the nearest edge of the entrance is not less than the minimum clear distance specified in Table 110.26(A)(1) for equipment operating at that voltage and in that condition.

(D) Illumination. Illumination shall be provided for all working spaces about service equipment, switchboards, panelboards, or motor control centers installed indoors. Additional lighting outlets shall not be required where the work space is illuminated by an adjacent light source or as permitted by 210.70(A)(1), Exception No. 1, for switched receptacles. In electrical equipment rooms, the illumination shall not be controlled by automatic means only.

(E) Headroom. The minimum headroom of working spaces about service equipment, switchboards, panelboards, or motor control centers shall be 2.0 m (6½ ft). Where the electrical equipment exceeds 2.0 m (6½ ft) in height, the minimum headroom shall not be less than the height of the equipment.

Exception: In existing dwelling units, service equipment or panelboards that do not exceed 200 amperes shall be permitted in spaces where the headroom is less than 2.0 m (6½ ft).

(F) Dedicated Equipment Space. All switchboards, panelboards, distribution boards, and motor control centers shall be located in dedicated spaces and protected from damage.

Exception: Control equipment that by its very nature or because of other rules of the Code must be adjacent to or within sight of its operating machinery shall be permitted in those locations.

(1) Indoor. Indoor installations shall comply with 110.26(F)(1)(a) through (F)(1)(d).

(a) Dedicated Electrical Space. The space equal to the width and depth of the equipment and extending from the floor to a height of 1.8 m (6 ft) above the equipment or to the structural ceiling, whichever is lower, shall be dedicated to the electrical installation. No piping, ducts, leak protection apparatus, or other equipment foreign to the electrical installation shall be located in this zone.

Exception: Suspended ceilings with removable panels shall be permitted within the 1.8-m (6-ft) zone.

(b) Foreign Systems. The area above the dedicated space required by 110.26(F)(1)(a) shall be permitted to contain foreign systems, provided protection is installed to avoid damage to the electrical equipment from condensation, leaks, or breaks in such foreign systems.

(c) Sprinkler Protection. Sprinkler protection shall be permitted for the dedicated space where the piping complies with this section.

(d) Suspended Ceilings. A dropped, suspended, or similar ceiling that does not add strength to the building structure shall not be considered a structural ceiling.

(2) Outdoor. Outdoor electrical equipment shall be installed in suitable enclosures and shall be protected from accidental contact by unauthorized personnel, or by vehicular traffic, or by accidental spillage or leakage from piping systems. The working clearance space shall include the zone described in 110.26(A). No architectural appurtenance or other equipment shall be located in this zone.

110.27 Guarding of Live Parts.

(A) Live Parts Guarded Against Accidental Contact. Except as elsewhere required or permitted by this *Code,* live parts of electrical equipment operating at 50 volts or more shall be guarded against accidental contact by approved enclosures or by any of the following means:

(1) By location in a room, vault, or similar enclosure that is accessible only to qualified persons.

(2) By suitable permanent, substantial partitions or screens arranged so that only qualified persons have access to the space within reach of the live parts. Any openings in such partitions or screens shall be sized and located so that persons are not likely to come into accidental contact with the live parts or to bring conducting objects into contact with them.

(3) By location on a suitable balcony, gallery, or platform elevated and arranged so as to exclude unqualified persons.

(4) By elevation of 2.5 m (8 ft) or more above the floor or other working surface.

(B) Prevent Physical Damage. In locations where electric equipment is likely to be exposed to physical damage, enclosures or guards shall be so arranged and of such strength as to prevent such damage.

(C) Warning Signs. Entrances to rooms and other guarded locations that contain exposed live parts shall be marked with conspicuous warning signs forbidding unqualified persons to enter.

> FPN: For motors, see 430.232 and 430.233. For over 600 volts, see 110.34.

III. Over 600 Volts, Nominal

110.30 General. Conductors and equipment used on circuits over 600 volts, nominal, shall comply with Part I of this article and with the following sections, which supplement or modify Part I. In no case shall the provisions of this part apply to equipment on the supply side of the service point.

110.31 Enclosure for Electrical Installations. Electrical installations in a vault, room, or closet or in an area surrounded by a wall, screen, or fence, access to which is controlled by a lock(s) or other approved means, shall be considered to be accessible to qualified persons only. The type of enclosure used in a given case shall be designed and constructed according to the nature and degree of the hazard(s) associated with the installation.

For installations other than equipment as described in 110.31(D), a wall, screen, or fence shall be used to enclose an outdoor electrical installation to deter access by persons who are not qualified. A fence shall not be less than 2.1 m (7 ft) in height or a combination of 1.8 m (6 ft) or more of fence fabric and a 300-mm (1-ft) or more extension utilizing three or more strands of barbed wire or equivalent. The distance from the fence to live parts shall be not less than given in Table 110.31.

Table 110.31 Minimum Distance from Fence to Live Parts

Nominal Voltage	Minimum Distance to Live Parts	
	m	ft
601 – 13,799	3.05	10
13,800 – 230,000	4.57	15
Over 230,000	5.49	18

Note: For clearances of conductors for specific system voltages and typical BIL ratings, see ANSI C2-2002, *National Electrical Safety Code.*

> FPN: See Article 450 for construction requirements for transformer vaults.

(A) Fire Resistivity of Electrical Vaults. The walls, roof, floors, and doorways of vaults containing conductors and equipment over 600 volts, nominal, shall be constructed of materials that have adequate structural strength for the conditions, with a minimum fire rating of 3 hours. The floors of vaults in contact with the earth shall be of concrete that is not less than 4 in. (102 mm) thick, but where the vault is constructed with a vacant space or other stories below it, the floor shall have adequate structural strength for the load imposed on it and a minimum fire resistance of 3 hours. For the purpose of this section, studs and wallboards shall not be considered acceptable.

(B) Indoor Installations.

(1) In Places Accessible to Unqualified Persons. Indoor electrical installations that are accessible to unqualified persons shall be made with metal-enclosed equipment. Metal-enclosed switchgear, unit substations, transformers, pull boxes, connection boxes, and other similar associated equipment shall be marked with appropriate caution signs. Openings in ventilated dry-type transformers or similar openings in other equipment shall be designed so that foreign objects inserted through these openings are deflected from energized parts.

(2) In Places Accessible to Qualified Persons Only. Indoor electrical installations considered accessible only to qualified persons in accordance with this section shall comply with 110.34, 110.36, and 490.24.

(C) Outdoor Installations.

(1) In Places Accessible to Unqualified Persons. Outdoor electrical installations that are open to unqualified persons shall comply with Parts I, II, and III of Article 225.

> FPN: For clearances of conductors for system voltages over 600 volts, nominal, see ANSI C2-2002, *National Electrical Safety Code.*

(2) In Places Accessible to Qualified Persons Only. Outdoor electrical installations that have exposed live parts shall be accessible to qualified persons only in accordance with the first paragraph of this section and shall comply with 110.34, 110.36, and 490.24.

(D) Enclosed Equipment Accessible to Unqualified Persons. Ventilating or similar openings in equipment shall be designed such that foreign objects inserted through these openings are deflected from energized parts. Where exposed to physical damage from vehicular traffic, suitable guards shall be provided. Nonmetallic or metal-enclosed equipment located outdoors and accessible to the general public shall be designed such that exposed nuts or bolts cannot be readily removed, permitting access to live parts. Where nonmetallic or metal-enclosed equipment is accessible to the general public and the bottom of the enclosure is less than 2.5 m (8 ft) above the floor or grade level, the enclosure door or hinged cover shall be kept locked. Doors and covers of enclosures used solely as pull boxes, splice boxes, or junction boxes shall be locked, bolted, or screwed on. Underground box covers that weigh over 45.4 kg (100 lb) shall be considered as meeting this requirement.

110.32 Work Space About Equipment. Sufficient space shall be provided and maintained about electric equipment to permit ready and safe operation and maintenance of such equipment. Where energized parts are exposed, the minimum clear work space shall not be less than 2.0 m (6½ ft) high (measured vertically from the floor or platform) or less than 900 mm (3 ft) wide (measured parallel to the equipment). The depth shall be as required in 110.34(A). In all cases, the work space shall permit at least a 90 degree opening of doors or hinged panels.

110.33 Entrance and Access to Work Space.

(A) Entrance. At least one entrance not less than 610 mm (24 in.) wide and 2.0 m (6½ ft) high shall be provided to give access to the working space about electric equipment. Where the entrance has a personnel door(s), the door(s) shall open in the direction of egress and be equipped with panic bars, pressure plates, or other devices that are normally latched but open under simple pressure.

(1) Large Equipment. On switchboard and control panels exceeding 1.8 m (6 ft) in width, there shall be one entrance at each end of the equipment. A single entrance to the required working space shall be permitted where either of the conditions in 110.33(A)(1)(a) or (A)(1)(b) is met.

  (a) Unobstructed Exit. Where the location permits a continuous and unobstructed way of exit travel, a single entrance to the working space shall be permitted.

  (b) Extra Working Space. Where the depth of the working space is twice that required by 110.34(A), a single entrance shall be permitted. It shall be located so that the distance from the equipment to the nearest edge of the entrance is not less than the minimum clear distance specified in Table 110.34(A) for equipment operating at that voltage and in that condition.

(2) Guarding. Where bare energized parts at any voltage or insulated energized parts above 600 volts, nominal, to ground are located adjacent to such entrance, they shall be suitably guarded.

(B) Access. Permanent ladders or stairways shall be provided to give safe access to the working space around electric equipment installed on platforms, balconies, or mezzanine floors or in attic or roof rooms or spaces.

110.34 Work Space and Guarding.

(A) Working Space. Except as elsewhere required or permitted in this *Code*, the minimum clear working space in the direction of access to live parts of electrical equipment shall not be less than specified in Table 110.34(A). Distances shall be measured from the live parts, if such are exposed, or from the enclosure front or opening if such are enclosed.

Exception: Working space shall not be required in back of equipment such as dead-front switchboards or control assemblies where there are no renewable or adjustable parts (such as fuses or switches) on the back and where all connections are accessible from locations other than the back. Where rear access is required to work on de-energized parts on the back of enclosed equipment, a minimum working space of 750 mm (30 in.) horizontally shall be provided.

(B) Separation from Low-Voltage Equipment. Where switches, cutouts, or other equipment operating at 600 volts, nominal, or less are installed in a vault, room, or enclosure where there are exposed live parts or exposed wiring operating at over 600 volts, nominal, the high-voltage equipment shall be effectively separated from the space occupied by the low-voltage equipment by a suitable partition, fence, or screen.

Table 110.34(A) Minimum Depth of Clear Working Space at Electrical Equipment

Nominal Voltage to Ground	Minimum Clear Distance		
	Condition 1	Condition 2	Condition 3
601–2500 V	900 mm (3 ft)	1.2 m (4 ft)	1.5 m (5 ft)
2501–9000 V	1.2 m (4 ft)	1.5 m (5 ft)	1.8 m (6 ft)
9001–25,000 V	1.5 m (5 ft)	1.8 m (6 ft)	2.8 m (9 ft)
25,001V–75 kV	1.8 m (6 ft)	2.5 m (8 ft)	3.0 m (10 ft)
Above 75 kV	2.5 m (8 ft)	3.0 m (10 ft)	3.7 m (12 ft)

Note: Where the conditions are as follows:

Condition 1 — Exposed live parts on one side of the working space and no live or grounded parts on the other side of the working space, or exposed live parts on both sides of the working space that are effectively guarded by insulating materials.

Condition 2 — Exposed live parts on one side of the working space and grounded parts on the other side of the working space. Concrete, brick, or tile walls shall be considered as grounded.

Condition 3 — Exposed live parts on both sides of the working space.

Exception: Switches or other equipment operating at 600 volts, nominal, or less and serving only equipment within the high-voltage vault, room, or enclosure shall be permitted to be installed in the high-voltage vault, room or enclosure without a partition, fence, or screen if accessible to qualified persons only.

(C) Locked Rooms or Enclosures. The entrance to all buildings, vaults, rooms, or enclosures containing exposed live parts or exposed conductors operating at over 600 volts, nominal, shall be kept locked unless such entrances are under the observation of a qualified person at all times.

Where the voltage exceeds 600 volts, nominal, permanent and conspicuous warning signs shall be provided, reading as follows:

DANGER — HIGH VOLTAGE — KEEP OUT

(D) Illumination. Illumination shall be provided for all working spaces about electrical equipment. The lighting outlets shall be arranged so that persons changing lamps or making repairs on the lighting system are not endangered by live parts or other equipment.

The points of control shall be located so that persons are not likely to come in contact with any live part or moving part of the equipment while turning on the lights.

(E) Elevation of Unguarded Live Parts. Unguarded live parts above working space shall be maintained at elevations not less than required by Table 110.34(E).

(F) Protection of Service Equipment, Metal-Enclosed Power Switchgear, and Industrial Control Assemblies. Pipes or ducts foreign to the electrical installation and requiring periodic maintenance or whose malfunction would endanger the operation of the electrical system

Table 110.34(E) Elevation of Unguarded Live Parts Above Working Space

Nominal Voltage Between Phases	Elevation	
	m	ft
601–7500 V	2.8	9
7501–35,000 V	2.9	9½
Over 35 kV	2.9 m + 9.5 mm/kV above 35	9½ ft + 0.37 in./kV above 35

shall not be located in the vicinity of the service equipment, metal-enclosed power switchgear, or industrial control assemblies. Protection shall be provided where necessary to avoid damage from condensation leaks and breaks in such foreign systems. Piping and other facilities shall not be considered foreign if provided for fire protection of the electrical installation.

110.36 Circuit Conductors. Circuit conductors shall be permitted to be installed in raceways; in cable trays; as metal-clad cable, as bare wire, cable, and busbars; or as Type MV cables or conductors as provided in 300.37, 300.39, 300.40, and 300.50. Bare live conductors shall conform with 490.24.

Insulators, together with their mounting and conductor attachments, where used as supports for wires, single-conductor cables, or busbars, shall be capable of safely withstanding the maximum magnetic forces that would prevail when two or more conductors of a circuit were subjected to short-circuit current.

Exposed runs of insulated wires and cables that have a bare lead sheath or a braided outer covering shall be supported in a manner designed to prevent physical damage to the braid or sheath. Supports for lead-covered cables shall be designed to prevent electrolysis of the sheath.

110.40 Temperature Limitations at Terminations. Conductors shall be permitted to be terminated based on the 90°C (194°F) temperature rating and ampacity as given in Table 310.67 through Table 310.86, unless otherwise identified.

IV. Tunnel Installations over 600 Volts, Nominal

110.51 General.

(A) Covered. The provisions of this part shall apply to the installation and use of high-voltage power distribution and utilization equipment that is portable, mobile, or both, such as substations, trailers, cars, mobile shovels, draglines, hoists, drills, dredges, compressors, pumps, conveyors, underground excavators, and the like.

(B) Other Articles. The requirements of this part shall be additional to, or amendatory of, those prescribed in Articles 100 through 490 of this *Code*. Special attention shall be paid to Article 250.

(C) Protection Against Physical Damage. Conductors and cables in tunnels shall be located above the tunnel floor and so placed or guarded to protect them from physical damage.

110.52 Overcurrent Protection. Motor-operated equipment shall be protected from overcurrent in accordance with Parts III, IV, and V of Article 430. Transformers shall be protected from overcurrent in accordance with 450.3.

110.53 Conductors. High-voltage conductors in tunnels shall be installed in metal conduit or other metal raceway, Type MC cable, or other approved multiconductor cable. Multiconductor portable cable shall be permitted to supply mobile equipment.

110.54 Bonding and Equipment Grounding Conductors.

(A) Grounded and Bonded. All non–current-carrying metal parts of electric equipment and all metal raceways and cable sheaths shall be effectively grounded and bonded to all metal pipes and rails at the portal and at intervals not exceeding 300 m (1000 ft) throughout the tunnel.

(B) Equipment Grounding Conductors. An equipment grounding conductor shall be run with circuit conductors inside the metal raceway or inside the multiconductor cable jacket. The equipment grounding conductor shall be permitted to be insulated or bare.

110.55 Transformers, Switches, and Electrical Equipment. All transformers, switches, motor controllers, motors, rectifiers, and other equipment installed below ground shall be protected from physical damage by location or guarding.

110.56 Energized Parts. Bare terminals of transformers, switches, motor controllers, and other equipment shall be enclosed to prevent accidental contact with energized parts.

110.57 Ventilation System Controls. Electrical controls for the ventilation system shall be arranged so that the airflow can be reversed.

110.58 Disconnecting Means. A switch or circuit breaker that simultaneously opens all ungrounded conductors of the circuit shall be installed within sight of each transformer or motor location for disconnecting the transformer or motor. The switch or circuit breaker for a transformer shall have an ampere rating not less than the ampacity of the transformer supply conductors. The switch or circuit breaker for a motor shall comply with the applicable requirements of Article 430.

110.59 Enclosures. Enclosures for use in tunnels shall be dripproof, weatherproof, or submersible as required by the environmental conditions. Switch or contactor enclosures shall not be used as junction boxes or as raceways for conductors feeding through or tapping off to other switches, unless the enclosures comply with 312.8.

V. Manholes and Other Electric Enclosures Intended for Personnel Entry, All Voltages

110.70 General. Electric enclosures intended for personnel entry and specifically fabricated for this purpose shall be of sufficient size to provide safe work space about electric equipment with live parts that is likely to require examination, adjustment, servicing, or maintenance while energized. Such enclosures shall have sufficient size to permit ready installation or withdrawal of the conductors employed without damage to the conductors or to their insulation. They shall comply with the provisions of this part.

Exception: Where electric enclosures covered by Part V of this article are part of an industrial wiring system operating under conditions of maintenance and supervision that ensure that only qualified persons monitor and supervise the system, they shall be permitted to be designed and installed in accordance with appropriate engineering practice. If required by the authority having jurisdiction, design documentation shall be provided.

110.71 Strength. Manholes, vaults, and their means of access shall be designed under qualified engineering supervision and shall withstand all loads likely to be imposed on the structures.

> FPN: See ANSI C2-2002, *National Electrical Safety Code,* for additional information on the loading that can be expected to bear on underground enclosures.

110.72 Cabling Work Space. A clear work space not less than 900 mm (3 ft) wide shall be provided where cables are located on both sides, and not less than 750 mm (2½ ft) where cables are only on one side. The vertical headroom shall not be less than 1.8 m (6 ft) unless the opening is within 300 mm (1 ft), measured horizontally, of the adjacent interior side wall of the enclosure.

Exception: A manhole containing only one or more of the following shall be permitted to have one of the horizontal work space dimensions reduced to 600 mm (2 ft) where the other horizontal clear work space is increased so the sum of the two dimensions is not less than 1.8 m (6 ft):

(1) Optical fiber cables as covered in Article 770

(2) Power-limited fire alarm circuits supplied in accordance with 760.41(A)

(3) Class 2 or Class 3 remote-control and signaling circuits, or both, supplied in accordance with 725.41

110.73 Equipment Work Space. Where electric equipment with live parts that is likely to require examination, adjustment, servicing, or maintenance while energized is installed in a manhole, vault, or other enclosure designed for personnel access, the work space and associated requirements in 110.26 shall be met for installations operating at 600 volts or less. Where the installation is over 600 volts, the work space and associated requirements in 110.34 shall be met. A manhole access cover that weighs over 45 kg (100 lb) shall be considered as meeting the requirements of 110.34(C).

110.74 Bending Space for Conductors. Bending space for conductors operating at 600 volts or below shall be provided in accordance with the requirements of 314.28. Conductors operating over 600 volts shall be provided with bending space in accordance with 314.71(A) and 314.71(B), as applicable. All conductors shall be cabled, racked up, or arranged in an approved manner that provides ready and safe access for persons to enter for installation and maintenance.

Exception: Where 314.71(B) applies, each row or column of ducts on one wall of the enclosure shall be calculated individually, and the single row or column that provides the maximum distance shall be used.

110.75 Access to Manholes.

(A) Dimensions. Rectangular access openings shall not be less than 650 mm × 550 mm (26 in. × 22 in.). Round access openings in a manhole shall not be less than 650 mm (26 in.) in diameter.

Exception: A manhole that has a fixed ladder that does not obstruct the opening or that contains only one or more of the following shall be permitted to reduce the minimum cover diameter to 600 mm (2 ft):

(1) Optical fiber cables as covered in Article 770

(2) Power-limited fire alarm circuits supplied in accordance with 760.41

(3) Class 2 or Class 3 remote-control and signaling circuits, or both, supplied in accordance with 725.41

(B) Obstructions. Manhole openings shall be free of protrusions that could injure personnel or prevent ready egress.

(C) Location. Manhole openings for personnel shall be located where they are not directly above electric equipment or conductors in the enclosure. Where this is not practicable, either a protective barrier or a fixed ladder shall be provided.

(D) Covers. Covers shall be over 45 kg (100 lb) or otherwise designed to require the use of tools to open. They shall be designed or restrained so they cannot fall into the manhole or protrude sufficiently to contact electrical conductors or equipment within the manhole.

(E) Marking. Manhole covers shall have an identifying mark or logo that prominently indicates their function, such as "electric."

110.76 Access to Vaults and Tunnels.

(A) Location. Access openings for personnel shall be located where they are not directly above electric equipment or conductors in the enclosure. Other openings shall be permitted over equipment to facilitate installation, maintenance, or replacement of equipment.

(B) Locks. In addition to compliance with the requirements of 110.34, if applicable, access openings for personnel shall be arranged such that a person on the inside can exit when the access door is locked from the outside, or in the case of normally locking by padlock, the locking arrangement shall be such that the padlock can be closed on the locking system to prevent locking from the outside.

110.77 Ventilation. Where manholes, tunnels, and vaults have communicating openings into enclosed areas used by the public, ventilation to open air shall be provided wherever practicable.

110.78 Guarding. Where conductors or equipment, or both, could be contacted by objects falling or being pushed through a ventilating grating, both conductors and live parts shall be protected in accordance with the requirements of 110.27(A)(2) or 110.31(B)(1), depending on the voltage.

110.79 Fixed Ladders. Fixed ladders shall be corrosion resistant.

Chapter 2 Wiring and Protection

ARTICLE 200
Use and Identification of Grounded Conductors

200.1 Scope. This article provides requirements for the following:

(1) Identification of terminals
(2) Grounded conductors in premises wiring systems
(3) Identification of grounded conductors

> FPN: See Article 100 for definitions of *Grounded Conductor* and *Grounding Conductor*.

200.2 General. All premises wiring systems, other than circuits and systems exempted or prohibited by 210.10, 215.7, 250.21, 250.22, 250.162, 503.155, 517.63, 668.11, 668.21, and 690.41 Exception, shall have a grounded conductor that is identified in accordance with 200.6.

The grounded conductor, where insulated, shall have insulation that is (1) suitable, other than color, for any ungrounded conductor of the same circuit on circuits of less than 1000 volts or impedance grounded neutral systems of 1 kV and over, or (2) rated not less than 600 volts for solidly grounded neutral systems of 1 kV and over as described in 250.184(A).

200.3 Connection to Grounded System. Premises wiring shall not be electrically connected to a supply system unless the latter contains, for any grounded conductor of the interior system, a corresponding conductor that is grounded. For the purpose of this section, *electrically connected* shall mean connected so as to be capable of carrying current, as distinguished from connection through electromagnetic induction.

200.6 Means of Identifying Grounded Conductors.

(A) Sizes 6 AWG or Smaller. An insulated grounded conductor of 6 AWG or smaller shall be identified by a continuous white or gray outer finish or by three continuous white stripes on other than green insulation along its entire length. Wires that have their outer covering finished to show a white or gray color but have colored tracer threads in the braid identifying the source of manufacture shall be considered as meeting the provisions of this section. Insulated grounded conductors shall also be permitted to be identified as follows:

(1) The grounded conductor of a mineral-insulated, metal-sheathed cable shall be identified at the time of installation by distinctive marking at its terminations.

(2) A single-conductor, sunlight-resistant, outdoor-rated cable used as a grounded conductor in photovoltaic power systems as permitted by 690.31 shall be identified at the time of installation by distinctive white marking at all terminations.

(3) Fixture wire shall comply with the requirements for grounded conductor identification as specified in 402.8.

(4) For aerial cable, the identification shall be as above, or by means of a ridge located on the exterior of the cable so as to identify it.

(B) Sizes Larger Than 6 AWG. An insulated grounded conductor larger than 6 AWG shall be identified by one of the following means:

(1) By a continuous white or gray outer finish.

(2) By three continuous white stripes along its entire length on other than green insulation.

(3) At the time of installation, by a distinctive white or gray marking at its terminations. This marking shall encircle the conductor or insulation.

(C) Flexible Cords. An insulated conductor that is intended for use as a grounded conductor, where contained within a flexible cord, shall be identified by a white or gray outer finish or by methods permitted by 400.22.

(D) Grounded Conductors of Different Systems. Where grounded conductors of different systems are installed in the same raceway, cable, box, auxiliary gutter, or other type of enclosure, each grounded conductor shall be identified by system. Identification that distinguishes each system grounded conductor shall be permitted by one of the following means:

(1) One system grounded conductor shall have an outer covering conforming to 200.6(A) or 200.6(B).

(2) The grounded conductor(s) of other systems shall have a different outer covering conforming to 200.6(A) or 200.6(B) or by an outer covering of white or gray with a readily distinguishable colored stripe other than green running along the insulation.

(3) Other and different means of identification as allowed by 200.6(A) or 200.6(B) that will distinguish each system grounded conductor.

This means of identification shall be permanently posted at each branch-circuit panelboard.

(E) Grounded Conductors of Multiconductor Cables. The insulated grounded conductors in a multiconductor cable shall be identified by a continuous white or gray outer finish or by three continuous white stripes on other than green insulation along its entire length. Multiconductor flat cable 4 AWG or larger shall be permitted to employ an external ridge on the grounded conductor.

Exception No. 1: Where the conditions of maintenance and supervision ensure that only qualified persons service the installation, grounded conductors in multiconductor cables shall be permitted to be permanently identified at their terminations at the time of installation by a distinctive white marking or other equally effective means.

Exception No. 2: The grounded conductor of a multiconductor varnished-cloth-insulated cable shall be permitted to be identified at its terminations at the time of installation by a distinctive white marking or other equally effective means.

> FPN: The color gray may have been used in the past as an ungrounded conductor. Care should be taken when working on existing systems.

200.7 Use of Insulation of a White or Gray Color or with Three Continuous White Stripes.

(A) General. The following shall be used only for the grounded circuit conductor, unless otherwise permitted in 200.7(B) and 200.7(C):

(1) A conductor with continuous white or gray covering

(2) A conductor with three continuous white stripes on other than green insulation

(3) A marking of white or gray color at the termination

(B) Circuits of Less Than 50 Volts. A conductor with white or gray color insulation or three continuous white stripes or having a marking of white or gray at the termination for circuits of less than 50 volts shall be required to be grounded only as required by 250.20(A).

(C) Circuits of 50 Volts or More. The use of insulation that is white or gray or that has three continuous white stripes for other than a grounded conductor for circuits of 50 volts or more shall be permitted only as in (1) through (3).

(1) If part of a cable assembly and where the insulation is permanently reidentified to indicate its use as an un-grounded conductor, by painting or other effective means at its termination, and at each location where the conductor is visible and accessible. Identification shall encircle the insulation and shall be a color other than white, gray, or green.

(2) Where a cable assembly contains an insulated conductor for single-pole, 3-way or 4-way switch loops and the conductor with white or gray insulation or a marking of three continuous white stripes is used for the supply to the switch but not as a return conductor from the switch to the switched outlet. In these applications, the conductor with white or gray insulation or with three continuous white stripes shall be permanently re-identified to indicate its use by painting or other effec-

tive means at its terminations and at each location where the conductor is visible and accessible.

(3) Where a flexible cord, having one conductor identified by a white or gray outer finish or three continuous white stripes or by any other means permitted by 400.22, is used for connecting an appliance or equipment permitted by 400.7. This shall apply to flexible cords connected to outlets whether or not the outlet is supplied by a circuit that has a grounded conductor.

> FPN: The color gray may have been used in the past as an ungrounded conductor. Care should be taken when working on existing systems.

200.9 Means of Identification of Terminals.
The identification of terminals to which a grounded conductor is to be connected shall be substantially white in color. The identification of other terminals shall be of a readily distinguishable different color.

Exception: Where the conditions of maintenance and supervision ensure that only qualified persons service the installations, terminals for grounded conductors shall be permitted to be permanently identified at the time of installation by a distinctive white marking or other equally effective means.

200.10 Identification of Terminals.

(A) Device Terminals. All devices, excluding panelboards, provided with terminals for the attachment of conductors and intended for connection to more than one side of the circuit shall have terminals properly marked for identification, unless the electrical connection of the terminal intended to be connected to the grounded conductor is clearly evident.

Exception: Terminal identification shall not be required for devices that have a normal current rating of over 30 amperes, other than polarized attachment plugs and polarized receptacles for attachment plugs as required in 200.10(B).

(B) Receptacles, Plugs, and Connectors. Receptacles, polarized attachment plugs, and cord connectors for plugs and polarized plugs shall have the terminal intended for connection to the grounded conductor identified as follows:

(1) Identification shall be by a metal or metal coating that is substantially white in color or by the word *white* or the letter *W* located adjacent to the identified terminal.

(2) If the terminal is not visible, the conductor entrance hole for the connection shall be colored white or marked with the word *white* or the letter *W*.

> FPN: See 250.126 for identification of wiring device equipment grounding conductor terminals.

(C) Screw Shells. For devices with screw shells, the terminal for the grounded conductor shall be the one connected to the screw shell.

(D) Screw Shell Devices with Leads. For screw shell devices with attached leads, the conductor attached to the screw shell shall have a white or gray finish. The outer finish of the other conductor shall be of a solid color that will not be confused with the white or gray finish used to identify the grounded conductor.

> FPN: The color gray may have been used in the past as an ungrounded conductor. Care should be taken when working on existing systems.

(E) Appliances. Appliances that have a single-pole switch or a single-pole overcurrent device in the line or any line-connected screw shell lampholders, and that are to be connected by (1) a permanent wiring method or (2) field-installed attachment plugs and cords with three or more wires (including the equipment grounding conductor), shall have means to identify the terminal for the grounded circuit conductor (if any).

200.11 Polarity of Connections. No grounded conductor shall be attached to any terminal or lead so as to reverse the designated polarity.

ARTICLE 210
Branch Circuits

I. General Provisions

210.1 Scope. This article covers branch circuits except for branch circuits that supply only motor loads, which are covered in Article 430. Provisions of this article and Article 430 apply to branch circuits with combination loads.

210.2 Other Articles for Specific-Purpose Branch Circuits. Branch circuits shall comply with this article and also with the applicable provisions of other articles of this *Code*. The provisions for branch circuits supplying equipment listed in Table 210.2 amend or supplement the provisions in this article and shall apply to branch circuits referred to therein.

210.3 Rating. Branch circuits recognized by this article shall be rated in accordance with the maximum permitted ampere rating or setting of the overcurrent device. The rating for other than individual branch circuits shall be 15, 20, 30, 40, and 50 amperes. Where conductors of higher ampacity are used for any reason, the ampere rating or setting of the specified overcurrent device shall determine the circuit rating.

Exception: Multioutlet branch circuits greater than 50 amperes shall be permitted to supply nonlighting outlet loads on industrial premises where conditions of maintenance and supervision ensure that only qualified persons service the equipment.

Table 210.2 Specific-Purpose Branch Circuits

Equipment	Article	Section
Air-conditioning and refrigerating equipment		440.6, 440.31, 440.32
Audio signal processing, amplification, and reproduction equipment		640.8
Busways		368.17
Circuits and equipment operating at less than 50 volts	720	
Central heating equipment other than fixed electric space-heating equipment		422.12
Class 1, Class 2, and Class 3 remote-control, signaling, and power-limited circuits	725	
Closed-loop and programmed power distribution	780	
Cranes and hoists		610.42
Electric signs and outline lighting		600.6
Electric welders	630	
Elevators, dumbwaiters, escalators, moving walks, wheelchair lifts, and stairway chair lifts		620.61
Fire alarm systems	760	
Fixed electric heating equipment for pipelines and vessels		427.4
Fixed electric space-heating equipment		424.3
Fixed outdoor electric deicing and snow-melting equipment		426.4
Information technology equipment		645.5
Infrared lamp industrial heating equipment		422.48, 424.3
Induction and dielectric heating equipment	665	
Marinas and boatyards		555.19
Mobile homes, manufactured homes, and mobile home parks	550	
Motion picture and television studios and similar locations	530	
Motors, motor circuits, and controllers	430	
Pipe organs		650.7
Recreational vehicles and recreational vehicle parks	551	
Switchboards and panelboards		408.52
Theaters, audience areas of motion picture and television studios, and similar locations		520.41, 520.52, 520.62
X-ray equipment		660.2, 517.73

210.4 Multiwire Branch Circuits.

(A) General. Branch circuits recognized by this article shall be permitted as multiwire circuits. A multiwire circuit shall be permitted to be considered as multiple circuits. All conductors shall originate from the same panelboard or similar distribution equipment.

> FPN: A 3-phase, 4-wire, wye-connected power system used to supply power to nonlinear loads may necessitate that the power system design allow for the possibility of high harmonic neutral currents.

(B) Devices or Equipment. Where a multiwire branch circuit supplies more than one device or equipment on the same yoke, a means shall be provided to disconnect simultaneously all ungrounded conductors supplying those devices or equipment at the point where the branch circuit originates.

(C) Line-to-Neutral Loads. Multiwire branch circuits shall supply only line-to-neutral loads.

Exception No. 1: A multiwire branch circuit that supplies only one utilization equipment.

Exception No. 2: Where all ungrounded conductors of the multiwire branch circuit are opened simultaneously by the branch-circuit overcurrent device.

> FPN: See 300.13(B) for continuity of grounded conductor on multiwire circuits.

210.5 Identification for Branch Circuits.

(A) Grounded Conductor. The grounded conductor of a branch circuit shall be identified in accordance with 200.6.

(B) Equipment Grounding Conductor. The equipment grounding conductor shall be identified in accordance with 250.119.

(C) Ungrounded Conductors. Where the premises wiring system has branch circuits supplied from more than one nominal voltage system, each ungrounded conductor of a branch circuit, where accessible, shall be identified by system. The means of identification shall be permitted to be by separate color coding, marking tape, tagging, or other approved means and shall be permanently posted at each branch-circuit panelboard or similar branch-circuit distribution equipment.

210.6 Branch-Circuit Voltage Limitations.
The nominal voltage of branch circuits shall not exceed the values permitted by 210.6(A) through 210.6(E).

(A) Occupancy Limitation. In dwelling units and guest rooms or guest suites of hotels, motels, and similar occupancies, the voltage shall not exceed 120 volts, nominal, between conductors that supply the terminals of the following:

(1) Luminaires (lighting fixtures)

(2) Cord-and-plug-connected loads 1440 volt-amperes, nominal, or less or less than ¼ hp

(B) 120 Volts Between Conductors. Circuits not exceeding 120 volts, nominal, between conductors shall be permitted to supply the following:

(1) The terminals of lampholders applied within their voltage ratings

(2) Auxiliary equipment of electric-discharge lamps

(3) Cord-and-plug-connected or permanently connected utilization equipment

(C) 277 Volts to Ground. Circuits exceeding 120 volts, nominal, between conductors and not exceeding 277 volts, nominal, to ground shall be permitted to supply the following:

(1) Listed electric-discharge luminaires (lighting fixtures)

(2) Listed incandescent luminaires (lighting fixtures), where supplied at 120 volts or less from the output of a step-down autotransformer that is an integral component of the luminaire (fixture) and the outer shell terminal is electrically connected to a grounded conductor of the branch circuit

(3) Luminaires (lighting fixtures) equipped with mogul-base screw shell lampholders

(4) Lampholders, other than the screw shell type, applied within their voltage ratings

(5) Auxiliary equipment of electric-discharge lamps

(6) Cord-and-plug-connected or permanently connected utilization equipment

(D) 600 Volts Between Conductors. Circuits exceeding 277 volts, nominal, to ground and not exceeding 600 volts, nominal, between conductors shall be permitted to supply the following:

(1) The auxiliary equipment of electric-discharge lamps mounted in permanently installed luminaires (fixtures) where the luminaires (fixtures) are mounted in accordance with one of the following:

a. Not less than a height of 6.7 m (22 ft) on poles or similar structures for the illumination of outdoor areas such as highways, roads, bridges, athletic fields, or parking lots

b. Not less than a height of 5.5 m (18 ft) on other structures such as tunnels

(2) Cord-and-plug-connected or permanently connected utilization equipment other than luminaires (fixtures)

> FPN: See 410.78 for auxiliary equipment limitations.

Exception No. 1 to (B), (C), and (D): For lampholders of infrared industrial heating appliances as provided in 422.14.

Exception No. 2 to (B), (C), and (D): For railway properties as described in 110.19.

(E) Over 600 Volts Between Conductors. Circuits exceeding 600 volts, nominal, between conductors shall be permitted to supply utilization equipment in installations where conditions of maintenance and supervision ensure that only qualified persons service the installation.

210.7 Branch Circuit Receptacle Requirements.

(A) Receptacle Outlet Location. Receptacle outlets shall be located in branch circuits in accordance with Part III of Article 210.

(B) Multiple Branch Circuits. Where two or more branch circuits supply devices or equipment on the same yoke, a means to simultaneously disconnect the ungrounded conductors supplying those devices shall be provided at the point at which the branch circuits originate.

210.8 Ground-Fault Circuit-Interrupter Protection for Personnel.

FPN: See 215.9 for ground-fault circuit-interrupter protection for personnel on feeders.

(A) Dwelling Units. All 125-volt, single-phase, 15- and 20-ampere receptacles installed in the locations specified in (1) through (8) shall have ground-fault circuit-interrupter protection for personnel.

(1) Bathrooms

(2) Garages, and also accessory buildings that have a floor located at or below grade level not intended as habitable rooms and limited to storage areas, work areas, and areas of similar use

Exception No. 1 to (2): Receptacles that are not readily accessible.

Exception No. 2 to (2): A single receptacle or a duplex receptacle for two appliances located within dedicated space for each appliance that, in normal use, is not easily moved from one place to another and that is cord-and-plug connected in accordance with 400.7(A)(6), (A)(7), or (A)(8).

Receptacles installed under the exceptions to 210.8(A)(2) shall not be considered as meeting the requirements of 210.52(G)

(3) Outdoors

Exception to (3): Receptacles that are not readily accessible and are supplied by a dedicated branch circuit for electric snow-melting or deicing equipment shall be permitted to be installed in accordance with 426.28.

(4) Crawl spaces — at or below grade level

(5) Unfinished basements — for purposes of this section, unfinished basements are defined as portions or areas of the basement not intended as habitable rooms and limited to storage areas, work areas, and the like

Exception No. 1 to (5): Receptacles that are not readily accessible.

Exception No. 2 to (5): A single receptacle or a duplex receptacle for two appliances located within dedicated space for each appliance that, in normal use, is not easily moved from one place to another and that is cord-and-plug connected in accordance with 400.7(A)(6), (A)(7), or (A)(8).

Exception No. 3 to (5): A receptacle supplying only a permanently installed fire alarm or burglar alarm system shall not be required to have ground-fault circuit-interrupter protection.

Receptacles installed under the exceptions to 210.8(A)(5) shall not be considered as meeting the requirements of 210.52(G).

(6) Kitchens — where the receptacles are installed to serve the countertop surfaces

(7) Laundry, utility, and wet bar sinks — where the receptacles are installed within 1.8 m (6 ft) of the outside edge of the sink

(8) Boathouses

(B) Other Than Dwelling Units. All 125-volt, single-phase, 15- and 20-ampere receptacles installed in the locations specified in (1) through (5) shall have ground-fault circuit-interrupter protection for personnel:

(1) Bathrooms

(2) Commercial and institutional kitchens — for the purposes of this section, a kitchen is an area with a sink and permanent facilities for food preparation and cooking

(3) Rooftops

(4) Outdoors in public spaces—for the purpose of this section a public space is defined as any space that is for use by, or is accessible to, the public

Exception to (3) and (4): Receptacles that are not readily accessible and are supplied from a dedicated branch circuit for electric snow-melting or deicing equipment shall be permitted to be installed in accordance with the applicable provisions of Article 426.

(5) Outdoors, where installed to comply with 210.63

(C) Boat Hoists. Ground-fault circuit-interrupter protection for personnel shall be provided for outlets that supply boat hoists installed in dwelling unit locations and supplied by 125-volt, 15- and 20-ampere branch circuits.

210.9 Circuits Derived from Autotransformers. Branch circuits shall not be derived from autotransformers unless the circuit supplied has a grounded conductor that is electrically connected to a grounded conductor of the system supplying the autotransformer.

Exception No. 1: An autotransformer shall be permitted without the connection to a grounded conductor where transforming from a nominal 208 volts to a nominal 240-volt supply or similarly from 240 volts to 208 volts.

Exception No. 2: In industrial occupancies, where conditions of maintenance and supervision ensure that only qualified persons service the installation, autotransformers shall be permitted to supply nominal 600-volt loads from nominal 480-volt systems, and 480-volt loads from nominal 600-volt systems, without the connection to a similar grounded conductor.

210.10 Ungrounded Conductors Tapped from Grounded Systems. Two-wire dc circuits and ac circuits of two or more ungrounded conductors shall be permitted to be tapped from the ungrounded conductors of circuits that have a grounded neutral conductor. Switching devices in each tapped circuit shall have a pole in each ungrounded conductor. All poles of multipole switching devices shall manually switch together where such switching devices also serve as a disconnecting means as required by the following:

(1) 410.48 for double-pole switched lampholders

(2) 410.54(B) for electric-discharge lamp auxiliary equipment switching devices

(3) 422.31(B) for an appliance

(4) 424.20 for a fixed electric space-heating unit

(5) 426.51 for electric deicing and snow-melting equipment

(6) 430.85 for a motor controller

(7) 430.103 for a motor

210.11 Branch Circuits Required. Branch circuits for lighting and for appliances, including motor-operated appliances, shall be provided to supply the loads calculated in accordance with 220.10. In addition, branch circuits shall be provided for specific loads not covered by 220.10 where required elsewhere in this *Code* and for dwelling unit loads as specified in 210.11(C).

(A) Number of Branch Circuits. The minimum number of branch circuits shall be determined from the total calculated load and the size or rating of the circuits used. In all installations, the number of circuits shall be sufficient to supply the load served. In no case shall the load on any circuit exceed the maximum specified by 220.18.

(B) Load Evenly Proportioned Among Branch Circuits. Where the load is calculated on the basis of volt-amperes per square meter or per square foot, the wiring system up to and including the branch-circuit panelboard(s) shall be provided to serve not less than the calculated load. This load shall be evenly proportioned among multioutlet branch circuits within the panelboard(s). Branch-circuit overcurrent devices and circuits shall only be required to be installed to serve the connected load.

(C) Dwelling Units.

(1) Small-Appliance Branch Circuits. In addition to the number of branch circuits required by other parts of this section, two or more 20-ampere small-appliance branch circuits shall be provided for all receptacle outlets specified by 210.52(B).

(2) Laundry Branch Circuits. In addition to the number of branch circuits required by other parts of this section, at least one additional 20-ampere branch circuit shall be provided to supply the laundry receptacle outlet(s) required by 210.52(F). This circuit shall have no other outlets.

(3) Bathroom Branch Circuits. In addition to the number of branch circuits required by other parts of this section, at least one 20-ampere branch circuit shall be provided to supply bathroom receptacle outlet(s). Such circuits shall have no other outlets.

Exception: Where the 20-ampere circuit supplies a single bathroom, outlets for other equipment within the same bathroom shall be permitted to be supplied in accordance with 210.23(A)(1) and (A)(2).

FPN: See Examples D1(a), D1(b), D2(b), and D4(a) in Annex D.

210.12 Arc-Fault Circuit-Interrupter Protection.

(A) Definition: Arc-Fault Circuit Interrupter. An arc-fault circuit interrupter is a device intended to provide protection from the effects of arc faults by recognizing characteristics unique to arcing and by functioning to de-energize the circuit when an arc fault is detected.

(B) Dwelling Unit Bedrooms. All 120-volt, single phase, 15- and 20-ampere branch circuits supplying outlets installed in dwelling unit bedrooms shall be protected by a listed arc-fault circuit interrupter, combination type installed to provide protection of the branch circuit.

Branch/feeder AFCIs shall be permitted to be used to meet the requirements of 210.12(B) until January 1, 2008.

FPN: For information on types of arc-fault circuit interrupters, see UL 1699-1999, *Standard for Arc-Fault Circuit Interrupters.*

Exception: The location of the arc-fault circuit interrupter shall be permitted to be at other than the origination of the branch circuit in compliance with (a) and (b):

(a) The arc-fault circuit interrupter installed within 1.8 m (6 ft) of the branch circuit overcurrent device as measured along the branch circuit conductors.

(b) The circuit conductors between the branch circuit overcurrent device and the arc-fault circuit interrupter shall be installed in a metal raceway or a cable with a metallic sheath.

210.18 Guest Rooms and Guest Suites. Guest rooms and guest suites that are provided with permanent provisions for cooking shall have branch circuits and outlets installed to meet the rules for dwelling units.

II. Branch-Circuit Ratings

210.19 Conductors — Minimum Ampacity and Size.

(A) Branch Circuits Not More Than 600 Volts.

(1) General. Branch-circuit conductors shall have an ampacity not less than the maximum load to be served. Where a branch circuit supplies continuous loads or any combination of continuous and noncontinuous loads, the minimum branch-circuit conductor size, before the application of any adjustment or correction factors, shall have an allowable ampacity not less than the noncontinuous load plus 125 percent of the continuous load.

Exception: Where the assembly, including the overcurrent devices protecting the branch circuit(s), is listed for operation at 100 percent of its rating, the allowable ampacity of the branch circuit conductors shall be permitted to be not less than the sum of the continuous load plus the noncontinuous load.

> FPN No. 1: See 310.15 for ampacity ratings of conductors.
>
> FPN No. 2: See Part II of Article 430 for minimum rating of motor branch-circuit conductors.
>
> FPN No. 3: See 310.10 for temperature limitation of conductors.
>
> FPN No. 4: Conductors for branch circuits as defined in Article 100, sized to prevent a voltage drop exceeding 3 percent at the farthest outlet of power, heating, and lighting loads, or combinations of such loads, and where the maximum total voltage drop on both feeders and branch circuits to the farthest outlet does not exceed 5 percent, provide reasonable efficiency of operation. See FPN No. 2 of 215.2(A)(3) for voltage drop on feeder conductors.

(2) Multioutlet Branch Circuits. Conductors of branch circuits supplying more than one receptacle for cord-and-plug-connected portable loads shall have an ampacity of not less than the rating of the branch circuit.

(3) Household Ranges and Cooking Appliances. Branch-circuit conductors supplying household ranges, wall-mounted ovens, counter-mounted cooking units, and other household cooking appliances shall have an ampacity not less than the rating of the branch circuit and not less than the maximum load to be served. For ranges of 8¾ kW or more rating, the minimum branch-circuit rating shall be 40 amperes.

Exception No. 1: Tap conductors supplying electric ranges, wall-mounted electric ovens, and counter-mounted electric cooking units from a 50-ampere branch circuit shall have an ampacity of not less than 20 and shall be

sufficient for the load to be served. These tap conductors include any conductors that are a part of the leads supplied with the appliance that are smaller than the branch circuit conductors. The taps shall not be longer than necessary for servicing the appliance.

Exception No. 2: The neutral conductor of a 3-wire branch circuit supplying a household electric range, a wall-mounted oven, or a counter-mounted cooking unit shall be permitted to be smaller than the ungrounded conductors where the maximum demand of a range of 8¾ kW or more rating has been calculated according to Column C of Table 220.55, but such conductor shall have an ampacity of not less than 70 percent of the branch-circuit rating and shall not be smaller than 10 AWG.

(4) Other Loads. Branch-circuit conductors that supply loads other than those specified in 210.2 and other than cooking appliances as covered in 210.19(A)(3) shall have an ampacity sufficient for the loads served and shall not be smaller than 14 AWG.

Exception No. 1: Tap conductors shall have an ampacity sufficient for the load served. In addition, they shall have an ampacity of not less than 15 for circuits rated less than 40 amperes and not less than 20 for circuits rated at 40 or 50 amperes and only where these tap conductors supply any of the following loads:

(a) Individual lampholders or luminaires (fixtures) with taps extending not longer than 450 mm (18 in.) beyond any portion of the lampholder or luminaire (fixture).

(b) A fixture having tap conductors as provided in 410.67.

(c) Individual outlets, other than receptacle outlets, with taps not over 450 mm (18 in.) long.

(d) Infrared lamp industrial heating appliances.

(e) Nonheating leads of deicing and snow-melting cables and mats.

Exception No. 2: Fixture wires and flexible cords shall be permitted to be smaller than 14 AWG as permitted by 240.5.

(B) Branch Circuits Over 600 Volts. The ampacity of conductors shall be in accordance with 310.15 and 310.60, as applicable. Branch-circuit conductors over 600 volts shall be sized in accordance with 210.19(B)(1) or (B)(2).

(1) General. The ampacity of branch-circuit conductors shall not be less than 125 percent of the designed potential load of utilization equipment that will be operated simultaneously.

(2) Supervised Installations. For supervised installations, branch-circuit conductor sizing shall be permitted to be determined by qualified persons under engineering supervision. Supervised installations are defined as those portions of a facility where both of the following conditions are met:

(1) Conditions of design and installation are provided under engineering supervision.

(2) Qualified persons with documented training and experience in over 600-volt systems provide maintenance, monitoring, and servicing of the system.

210.20 Overcurrent Protection. Branch-circuit conductors and equipment shall be protected by overcurrent protective devices that have a rating or setting that complies with 210.20(A) through (D).

(A) Continuous and Noncontinuous Loads. Where a branch circuit supplies continuous loads or any combination of continuous and noncontinuous loads, the rating of the overcurrent device shall not be less than the noncontinuous load plus 125 percent of the continuous load.

Exception: Where the assembly, including the overcurrent devices protecting the branch circuit(s), is listed for operation at 100 percent of its rating, the ampere rating of the overcurrent device shall be permitted to be not less than the sum of the continuous load plus the noncontinuous load.

(B) Conductor Protection. Conductors shall be protected in accordance with 240.4. Flexible cords and fixture wires shall be protected in accordance with 240.5.

(C) Equipment. The rating or setting of the overcurrent protective device shall not exceed that specified in the applicable articles referenced in Table 240.3 for equipment.

(D) Outlet Devices. The rating or setting shall not exceed that specified in 210.21 for outlet devices.

210.21 Outlet Devices. Outlet devices shall have an ampere rating that is not less than the load to be served and shall comply with 210.21(A) and (B).

(A) Lampholders. Where connected to a branch circuit having a rating in excess of 20 amperes, lampholders shall be of the heavy-duty type. A heavy-duty lampholder shall have a rating of not less than 660 watts if of the admedium type, or not less than 750 watts if of any other type.

(B) Receptacles.

(1) Single Receptacle on an Individual Branch Circuit. A single receptacle installed on an individual branch circuit shall have an ampere rating not less than that of the branch circuit.

Exception No. 1: A receptacle installed in accordance with 430.81(B).

Exception No. 2: A receptacle installed exclusively for the use of a cord-and-plug-connected arc welder shall be permitted to have an ampere rating not less than the minimum branch-circuit conductor ampacity determined by 630.11(A) for arc welders.

FPN: See the definition of *receptacle* in Article 100.

(2) Total Cord-and-Plug-Connected Load. Where connected to a branch circuit supplying two or more receptacles or outlets, a receptacle shall not supply a total cord-and-plug-connected load in excess of the maximum specified in Table 210.21(B)(2).

Table 210.21(B)(2) Maximum Cord-and-Plug-Connected Load to Receptacle

Circuit Rating (Amperes)	Receptacle Rating (Amperes)	Maximum Load (Amperes)
15 or 20	15	12
20	20	16
30	30	24

(3) Receptacle Ratings. Where connected to a branch circuit supplying two or more receptacles or outlets, receptacle ratings shall conform to the values listed in Table 210.21(B)(3), or where larger than 50 amperes, the receptacle rating shall not be less than the branch-circuit rating.

Exception No. 1: Receptacles for one or more cord-and-plug-connected arc welders shall be permitted to have ampere ratings not less than the minimum branch-circuit conductor ampacity permitted by 630.11(A) or (B) as applicable for arc welders.

Exception No. 2: The ampere rating of a receptacle installed for electric discharge lighting shall be permitted to be based on 410.30(C).

Table 210.21(B)(3) Receptacle Ratings for Various Size Circuits

Circuit Rating (Amperes)	Receptacle Rating (Amperes)
15	Not over 15
20	15 or 20
30	30
40	40 or 50
50	50

(4) Range Receptacle Rating. The ampere rating of a range receptacle shall be permitted to be based on a single range demand load as specified in Table 220.55.

210.23 Permissible Loads. In no case shall the load exceed the branch-circuit ampere rating. An individual branch circuit shall be permitted to supply any load for which it is rated. A branch circuit supplying two or more outlets or receptacles shall supply only the loads specified according to its size as specified in 210.23(A) through (D) and as summarized in 210.24 and Table 210.24.

(A) 15- and 20-Ampere Branch Circuits. A 15- or 20-ampere branch circuit shall be permitted to supply lighting units or other utilization equipment, or a combination of both, and shall comply with 210.23(A)(1) and (A)(2).

Exception: The small appliance branch circuits, laundry branch circuits, and bathroom branch circuits required in a dwelling unit(s) by 210.11(C)(1), (C)(2), and (C)(3) shall supply only the receptacle outlets specified in that section.

(1) Cord-and-Plug-Connected Equipment Not Fastened in Place. The rating of any one cord-and-plug-connected utilization equipment not fastened in place shall not exceed 80 percent of the branch-circuit ampere rating.

(2) Utilization Equipment Fastened in Place. The total rating of utilization equipment fastened in place, other than luminaires (lighting fixtures), shall not exceed 50 percent of the branch-circuit ampere rating where lighting units, cord-and-plug-connected utilization equipment not fastened in place, or both, are also supplied.

(B) 30-Ampere Branch Circuits. A 30-ampere branch circuit shall be permitted to supply fixed lighting units with heavy-duty lampholders in other than a dwelling unit(s) or utilization equipment in any occupancy. A rating of any one cord-and-plug-connected utilization equipment shall not exceed 80 percent of the branch-circuit ampere rating.

(C) 40- and 50-Ampere Branch Circuits. A 40- or 50-ampere branch circuit shall be permitted to supply cooking appliances that are fastened in place in any occupancy. In other than dwelling units, such circuits shall be permitted to supply fixed lighting units with heavy-duty lampholders, infrared heating units, or other utilization equipment.

(D) Branch Circuits Larger Than 50 Amperes. Branch circuits larger than 50 amperes shall supply only nonlighting outlet loads.

210.24 Branch-Circuit Requirements — Summary. The requirements for circuits that have two or more outlets or receptacles, other than the receptacle circuits of 210.11(C)(1) and (C)(2), are summarized in Table 210.24. This table provides only a summary of minimum requirements. See 210.19, 210.20, and 210.21 for the specific requirements applying to branch circuits.

210.25 Common Area Branch Circuits. Branch circuits in dwelling units shall supply only loads within that dwelling unit or loads associated only with that dwelling unit. Branch circuits required for the purpose of lighting, central alarm, signal, communications, or other needs for public or common areas of a two-family or multifamily dwelling shall not be supplied from equipment that supplies an individual dwelling unit.

III. Required Outlets

210.50 General. Receptacle outlets shall be installed as specified in 210.52 through 210.63.

(A) Cord Pendants. A cord connector that is supplied by a permanently connected cord pendant shall be considered a receptacle outlet.

(B) Cord Connections. A receptacle outlet shall be installed wherever flexible cords with attachment plugs are used. Where flexible cords are permitted to be permanently connected, receptacles shall be permitted to be omitted for such cords.

Table 210.24 Summary of Branch-Circuit Requirements

Circuit Rating	15 A	20 A	30 A	40 A	50 A
Conductors (min. size):					
Circuit wires[1]	14	12	10	8	6
Taps	14	14	14	12	12
Fixture wires and cords — see 240.5					
Overcurrent Protection	**15 A**	**20 A**	**30 A**	**40 A**	**50 A**
Outlet devices:					
Lampholders permitted	Any type	Any type	Heavy duty	Heavy duty	Heavy duty
Receptacle rating[2]	15 max. A	15 or 20 A	30 A	40 or 50 A	50 A
Maximum Load	**15 A**	**20 A**	**30 A**	**40 A**	**50 A**
Permissible load	See 210.23(A)	See 210.23(A)	See 210.23(B)	See 210.23(C)	See 210.23(C)

[1]These gauges are for copper conductors.
[2]For receptacle rating of cord-connected electric-discharge luminaires (lighting fixtures), see 410.30(C).

(C) Appliance Outlets. Appliance receptacle outlets installed in a dwelling unit for specific appliances, such as laundry equipment, shall be installed within 1.8 m (6 ft) of the intended location of the appliance.

210.52 Dwelling Unit Receptacle Outlets. This section provides requirements for 125-volt, 15- and 20-ampere receptacle outlets. Receptacle outlets required by this section shall be in addition to any receptacle that is part of a luminaire (lighting fixture) or appliance, located within cabinets or cupboards, or located more than 1.7 m (5½ ft) above the floor.

Permanently installed electric baseboard heaters equipped with factory-installed receptacle outlets or outlets provided as a separate assembly by the manufacturer shall be permitted as the required outlet or outlets for the wall space utilized by such permanently installed heaters. Such receptacle outlets shall not be connected to the heater circuits.

> FPN: Listed baseboard heaters include instructions that may not permit their installation below receptacle outlets.

(A) General Provisions. In every kitchen, family room, dining room, living room, parlor, library, den, sunroom, bedroom, recreation room, or similar room or area of dwelling units, receptacle outlets shall be installed in accordance with the general provisions specified in 210.52(A)(1) through (A)(3).

(1) Spacing. Receptacles shall be installed so that no point measured horizontally along the floor line in any wall space is more than 1.8 m (6 ft) from a receptacle outlet.

(2) Wall Space. As used in this section, a wall space shall include the following:

(1) Any space 600 mm (2 ft) or more in width (including space measured around corners) and unbroken along the floor line by doorways, fireplaces, and similar openings

(2) The space occupied by fixed panels in exterior walls, excluding sliding panels

(3) The space afforded by fixed room dividers such as free-standing bar-type counters or railings

(3) Floor Receptacles. Receptacle outlets in floors shall not be counted as part of the required number of receptacle outlets unless located within 450 mm (18 in.) of the wall.

(B) Small Appliances.

(1) Receptacle Outlets Served. In the kitchen, pantry, breakfast room, dining room, or similar area of a dwelling unit, the two or more 20-ampere small-appliance branch circuits required by 210.11(C)(1) shall serve all wall and floor receptacle outlets covered by 210.52(A), all countertop outlets covered by 210.52(C), and receptacle outlets for refrigeration equipment.

Exception No. 1: In addition to the required receptacles specified by 210.52, switched receptacles supplied from a general-purpose branch circuit as defined in 210.70(A)(1), Exception No. 1, shall be permitted.

Exception No. 2: The receptacle outlet for refrigeration equipment shall be permitted to be supplied from an individual branch circuit rated 15 amperes or greater.

(2) No Other Outlets. The two or more small-appliance branch circuits specified in 210.52(B)(1) shall have no other outlets.

Exception No. 1: A receptacle installed solely for the electrical supply to and support of an electric clock in any of the rooms specified in 210.52(B)(1).

Exception No. 2: Receptacles installed to provide power for supplemental equipment and lighting on gas-fired ranges, ovens, or counter-mounted cooking units.

(3) Kitchen Receptacle Requirements. Receptacles installed in a kitchen to serve countertop surfaces shall be supplied by not fewer than two small-appliance branch circuits, either or both of which shall also be permitted to supply receptacle outlets in the same kitchen and in other rooms specified in 210.52(B)(1). Additional small-appliance branch circuits shall be permitted to supply receptacle outlets in the kitchen and other rooms specified in 210.52(B)(1). No small-appliance branch circuit shall serve more than one kitchen.

(C) Countertops. In kitchens and dining rooms of dwelling units, receptacle outlets for counter spaces shall be installed in accordance with 210.52(C)(1) through (C)(5).

(1) Wall Counter Spaces. A receptacle outlet shall be installed at each wall counter space that is 300 mm (12 in.) or wider. Receptacle outlets shall be installed so that no point along the wall line is more than 600 mm (24 in.) measured horizontally from a receptacle outlet in that space.

Exception: Receptacle outlets shall not be required on a wall directly behind a range or sink in the installation described in Figure 210.52.

(2) Island Counter Spaces. At least one receptacle shall be installed at each island counter space with a long dimension of 600 mm (24 in.) or greater and a short dimension of 300 mm (12 in.) or greater. Where a rangetop or sink is installed in an island counter and the width of the counter behind the rangetop or sink is less than 300 mm (12 in.), the rangetop or sink is considered to divide the island into two separate countertop spaces as defined in 210.52(C)(4).

(3) Peninsular Counter Spaces. At least one receptacle outlet shall be installed at each peninsular counter space with a long dimension of 600 mm (24 in.) or greater and a short dimension of 300 mm (12 in.) or greater. A peninsular countertop is measured from the connecting edge.

Sink or range extending from face of counter

Sink or range mounted in corner

Figure 210.52 Determination of Area Behind Sink or Range.

(4) Separate Spaces. Countertop spaces separated by rangetops, refrigerators, or sinks shall be considered as separate countertop spaces in applying the requirements of 210.52(C)(1), (C)(2), and (C)(3).

(5) Receptacle Outlet Location. Receptacle outlets shall be located above, but not more than 500 mm (20 in.) above, the countertop. Receptacle outlets rendered not readily accessible by appliances fastened in place, appliance garages, sinks, or rangetops as covered in 210.52(C)(1), Exception, or appliances occupying dedicated space shall not be considered as these required outlets.

Exception to (5): To comply with the conditions specified in (1) or (2), receptacle outlets shall be permitted to be mounted not more than 300 mm (12 in.) below the countertop. Receptacles mounted below a countertop in accordance with this exception shall not be located where the countertop extends more than 150 mm (6 in.) beyond its support base.

(1) Construction for the physically impaired

(2) On island and peninsular countertops where the countertop is flat across its entire surface (no backsplashes, dividers, etc.) and there are no means to mount a receptacle within 500 mm (20 in.) above the countertop, such as an overhead cabinet

(D) Bathrooms. In dwelling units, at least one receptacle outlet shall be installed in bathrooms within 900 mm (3 ft) of the outside edge of each basin. The receptacle outlet shall be located on a wall or partition that is adjacent to the basin or basin countertop.

Exception: The receptacle shall not be required to be mounted in the wall or partition where it is installed on the side or face of the basin cabinet not more than 300 mm (12 in.) below the countertop.

(E) Outdoor Outlets. For a one-family dwelling and each unit of a two-family dwelling that is at grade level, at least one receptacle outlet accessible at grade level and not more than 2.0 m (6½ ft) above grade shall be installed at the front and back of the dwelling.

For each dwelling unit of a multifamily dwelling where the dwelling unit is located at grade level and provided with individual exterior entrance/egress, at least one receptacle outlet accessible from grade level and not more than 2.0 m (6½ ft) above grade shall be installed. See 210.8(A)(3).

(F) Laundry Areas. In dwelling units, at least one receptacle outlet shall be installed for the laundry.

Exception No. 1: In a dwelling unit that is an apartment or living area in a multifamily building where laundry facilities are provided on the premises and are available to all building occupants, a laundry receptacle shall not be required.

Exception No. 2: In other than one-family dwellings where laundry facilities are not to be installed or permitted, a laundry receptacle shall not be required.

(G) Basements and Garages. For a one-family dwelling, at least one receptacle outlet, in addition to any provided for laundry equipment, shall be installed in each basement and in each attached garage, and in each detached garage with electric power. See 210.8(A)(2) and (A)(5). Where a portion of the basement is finished into one or more habitable rooms, each separate unfinished portion shall have a receptacle outlet installed in accordance with this section.

(H) Hallways. In dwelling units, hallways of 3.0 m (10 ft) or more in length shall have at least one receptacle outlet.

As used in this subsection, the hall length shall be considered the length along the centerline of the hall without passing through a doorway.

210.60 Guest Rooms or Guest Suites.

(A) General. Guest rooms or guest suites in hotels, motels, and similar occupancies shall have receptacle outlets installed in accordance with 210.52(A) and 210.52(D). Guest rooms or guest suites provided with permanent provisions for cooking shall have receptacle outlets installed in accordance with all of the applicable rules in 210.52.

(B) Receptacle Placement. In applying the provisions of 210.52(A), the total number of receptacle outlets shall not be less than the minimum number that would comply with the provisions of that section. These receptacle outlets shall be permitted to be located conveniently for permanent furniture layout. At least two receptacle outlets shall be readily accessible. Where receptacles are installed behind the bed, the receptacle shall be located to prevent the bed from contacting any attachment plug that may be installed or the receptacle shall be provided with a suitable guard.

210.62 Show Windows. At least one receptacle outlet shall be installed directly above a show window for each 3.7 linear m (12 linear ft) or major fraction thereof of show window area measured horizontally at its maximum width.

210.63 Heating, Air-Conditioning, and Refrigeration Equipment Outlet. A 125-volt, single-phase, 15- or 20-ampere-rated receptacle outlet shall be installed at an accessible location for the servicing of heating, air-conditioning, and refrigeration equipment. The receptacle shall be located on the same level and within 7.5 m (25 ft) of the heating, air-conditioning, and refrigeration equipment. The receptacle outlet shall not be connected to the load side of the equipment disconnecting means.

Exception: A receptacle outlet shall not be required at one- and two-family dwellings for the service of evaporative coolers.

> FPN: See 210.8 for ground-fault circuit-interrupter requirements.

210.70 Lighting Outlets Required. Lighting outlets shall be installed where specified in 210.70(A), (B), and (C).

(A) Dwelling Units. In dwelling units, lighting outlets shall be installed in accordance with 210.70(A)(1), (A)(2), and (A)(3).

(1) Habitable Rooms. At least one wall switch-controlled lighting outlet shall be installed in every habitable room and bathroom.

Exception No. 1: In other than kitchens and bathrooms, one or more receptacles controlled by a wall switch shall be permitted in lieu of lighting outlets.

Exception No. 2: Lighting outlets shall be permitted to be controlled by occupancy sensors that are (1) in addition to

wall switches or (2) located at a customary wall switch location and equipped with a manual override that will allow the sensor to function as a wall switch.

(2) Additional Locations. Additional lighting outlets shall be installed in accordance with (A)(2)(a), (A)(2)(b), and (A)(2)(c).

 (a) At least one wall switch-controlled lighting outlet shall be installed in hallways, stairways, attached garages, and detached garages with electric power.

 (b) For dwelling units, attached garages, and detached garages with electric power, at least one wall switch–controlled lighting outlet shall be installed to provide illumination on the exterior side of outdoor entrances or exits with grade level access. A vehicle door in a garage shall not be considered as an outdoor entrance or exit.

 (c) Where one or more lighting outlet(s) are installed for interior stairways, there shall be a wall switch at each floor level, and landing level that includes an entryway, to control the lighting outlet(s) where the stairway between floor levels has six risers or more.

Exception to (A)(2)(a), (A)(2)(b), and (A)(2)(c): In hallways, stairways, and at outdoor entrances, remote, central, or automatic control of lighting shall be permitted.

(3) Storage or Equipment Spaces. For attics, underfloor spaces, utility rooms, and basements, at least one lighting outlet containing a switch or controlled by a wall switch shall be installed where these spaces are used for storage or contain equipment requiring servicing. At least one point of control shall be at the usual point of entry to these spaces. The lighting outlet shall be provided at or near the equipment requiring servicing.

(B) Guest Rooms or Guest Suites. In hotels, motels, or similar occupancies, guest rooms or guest suites shall have at least one wall switch–controlled lighting outlet installed in every habitable room and bathroom.

Exception No. 1: In other than bathrooms and kitchens where provided, one or more receptacles controlled by a wall switch shall be permitted in lieu of lighting outlets.

Exception No. 2: Lighting outlets shall be permitted to be controlled by occupancy sensors that are (1) in addition to wall switches or (2) located at a customary wall switch location and equipped with a manual override that will allow the sensor to function as a wall switch.

(C) Other Than Dwelling Units. For attics and underfloor spaces containing equipment requiring servicing, such as heating, air-conditioning, and refrigeration equipment, at least one lighting outlet containing a switch or controlled by a wall switch shall be installed in such spaces. At least one point of control shall be at the usual point of entry to these spaces. The lighting outlet shall be provided at or near the equipment requiring servicing.

ARTICLE 215
Feeders

215.1 Scope. This article covers the installation requirements, overcurrent protection requirements, minimum size, and ampacity of conductors for feeders supplying branch-circuit loads.

Exception: Feeders for electrolytic cells as covered in 668.3(C)(1) and (C)(4).

215.2 Minimum Rating and Size.

(A) Feeders Not More Than 600 Volts.

(1) General. Feeder conductors shall have an ampacity not less than required to supply the load as calculated in Parts III, IV, and V of Article 220. The minimum feeder-circuit conductor size, before the application of any adjustment or correction factors, shall have an allowable ampacity not less than the noncontinuous load plus 125 percent of the continuous load.

Exception: Where the assembly, including the overcurrent devices protecting the feeder(s), is listed for operation at 100 percent of its rating, the allowable ampacity of the feeder conductors shall be permitted to be not less than the sum of the continuous load plus the noncontinuous load.

The size of the feeder circuit grounded conductor shall not be smaller than that required by 250.122, except that 250.122(F) shall not apply where grounded conductors are run in parallel.

Additional minimum sizes shall be as specified in 215.2(A)(2) and (A)(3) under the conditions stipulated.

(2) Ampacity Relative to Service Conductors. The feeder conductor ampacity shall not be less than that of the service conductors where the feeder conductors carry the total load supplied by service conductors with an ampacity of 55 amperes or less.

(3) Individual Dwelling Unit or Mobile Home Conductors. Feeder conductors for individual dwelling units or mobile homes need not be larger than service conductors. Paragraph 310.15(B)(6) shall be permitted to be used for conductor size.

> FPN No. 1: See Examples D1 through D11 in Annex D.
>
> FPN No. 2: Conductors for feeders as defined in Article 100, sized to prevent a voltage drop exceeding 3 percent at the farthest outlet of power, heating, and lighting loads, or combinations of such loads, and where the maximum total voltage drop on both feeders and branch circuits to the farthest outlet does not exceed 5 percent, will provide reasonable efficiency of operation.
>
> FPN No. 3: See 210.19(A), FPN No. 4, for voltage drop for branch circuits.

(B) Feeders Over 600 Volts. The ampacity of conductors shall be in accordance with 310.15 and 310.60 as applicable. Where installed, the size of the feeder circuit grounded conductor shall not be smaller than that required by 250.122, except that 250.122(F) shall not apply where grounded conductors are run in parallel. Feeder conductors over 600 volts shall be sized in accordance with 215.2(B)(1), (B)(2), or (B)(3).

(1) Feeders Supplying Transformers. The ampacity of feeder conductors shall not be less than the sum of the nameplate ratings of the transformers supplied when only transformers are supplied.

(2) Feeders Supplying Transformers and Utilization Equipment. The ampacity of feeders supplying a combination of transformers and utilization equipment shall not be less than the sum of the nameplate ratings of the transformers and 125 percent of the designed potential load of the utilization equipment that will be operated simultaneously.

(3) Supervised Installations. For supervised installations, feeder conductor sizing shall be permitted to be determined by qualified persons under engineering supervision. Supervised installations are defined as those portions of a facility where all of the following conditions are met:

(1) Conditions of design and installation are provided under engineering supervision.
(2) Qualified persons with documented training and experience in over 600-volt systems provide maintenance, monitoring, and servicing of the system.

215.3 Overcurrent Protection. Feeders shall be protected against overcurrent in accordance with the provisions of Part I of Article 240. Where a feeder supplies continuous loads or any combination of continuous and noncontinuous loads, the rating of the overcurrent device shall not be less than the noncontinuous load plus 125 percent of the continuous load.

Exception No. 1: Where the assembly, including the overcurrent devices protecting the feeder(s), is listed for operation at 100 percent of its rating, the ampere rating of the overcurrent device shall be permitted to be not less than the sum of the continuous load plus the noncontinuous load.

Exception No. 2: Overcurrent protection for feeders over 600 volts, nominal, shall comply with Part XI of Article 240.

215.4 Feeders with Common Neutral.

(A) Feeders with Common Neutral. Two or three sets of 3-wire feeders or two sets of 4-wire or 5-wire feeders shall be permitted to utilize a common neutral.

(B) In Metal Raceway or Enclosure. Where installed in a metal raceway or other metal enclosure, all conductors of all feeders using a common neutral shall be enclosed within the same raceway or other enclosure as required in 300.20.

215.5 Diagrams of Feeders. If required by the authority having jurisdiction, a diagram showing feeder details shall be provided prior to the installation of the feeders. Such a diagram shall show the area in square feet of the building or other structure supplied by each feeder, the total calculated load before applying demand factors, the demand factors used, the calculated load after applying demand factors, and the size and type of conductors to be used.

215.6 Feeder Conductor Grounding Means. Where a feeder supplies branch circuits in which equipment grounding conductors are required, the feeder shall include or provide a grounding means, in accordance with the provisions of 250.134, to which the equipment grounding conductors of the branch circuits shall be connected.

215.7 Ungrounded Conductors Tapped from Grounded Systems. Two-wire dc circuits and ac circuits of two or more ungrounded conductors shall be permitted to be tapped from the ungrounded conductors of circuits having a grounded neutral conductor. Switching devices in each tapped circuit shall have a pole in each ungrounded conductor.

215.9 Ground-Fault Circuit-Interrupter Protection for Personnel. Feeders supplying 15- and 20-ampere receptacle branch circuits shall be permitted to be protected by a ground-fault circuit interrupter in lieu of the provisions for such interrupters as specified in 210.8 and 590.6(A).

215.10 Ground-Fault Protection of Equipment. Each feeder disconnect rated 1000 amperes or more and installed on solidly grounded wye electrical systems of more than 150 volts to ground, but not exceeding 600 volts phase-to-phase, shall be provided with ground-fault protection of equipment in accordance with the provisions of 230.95.

> FPN: For buildings that contain healthcare occupancies, see the requirements of 517.17.

Exception No. 1: The provisions of this section shall not apply to a disconnecting means for a continuous industrial process where a nonorderly shutdown will introduce additional or increased hazards.

Exception No. 2: The provisions of this section shall not apply to fire pumps.

Exception No. 3: The provisions of this section shall not apply if ground-fault protection of equipment is provided on the supply side of the feeder.

215.11 Circuits Derived from Autotransformers. Feeders shall not be derived from autotransformers unless the system supplied has a grounded conductor that is electrically connected to a grounded conductor of the system supplying the autotransformer.

Exception No. 1: An autotransformer shall be permitted without the connection to a grounded conductor where transforming from a nominal 208 volts to a nominal 240-volt supply or similarly from 240 volts to 208 volts.

Exception No. 2: In industrial occupancies, where conditions of maintenance and supervision ensure that only qualified persons service the installation, autotransformers shall be permitted to supply nominal 600-volt loads from nominal 480-volt systems, and 480-volt loads from nominal 600-volt systems, without the connection to a similar grounded conductor.

215.12 Identification for Feeders.

(A) Grounded Conductor. The grounded conductor of a feeder shall be identified in accordance with 200.6.

(B) Equipment Grounding Conductor. The equipment grounding conductor shall be identified in accordance with 250.119.

(C) Ungrounded Conductors. Where the premises wiring system has feeders supplied from more than one nominal voltage system, each ungrounded conductor of a feeder, where accessible, shall be identified by system. The means of identification shall be permitted to be by separate color coding, marking tape, tagging, or other approved means and shall be permanently posted at each feeder panelboard or similar feeder distribution equipment.

ARTICLE 220
Branch-Circuit, Feeder, and Service Calculations

I. General

220.1 Scope. This article provides requirements for calculating branch-circuit, feeder, and service loads. Part I provides for general requirements for calculation methods. Part II provides calculation methods for branch circuit loads. Parts III and IV provide calculation methods for feeders and services. Part V provides calculation methods for farms.

> FPN: See Figure 220.1 for information on the organization of Article 220.

220.3 Application of Other Articles. In other articles applying to the calculation of loads in specialized applications, there are requirements provided in Table 220.3 that are in addition to, or modifications of, those within this article.

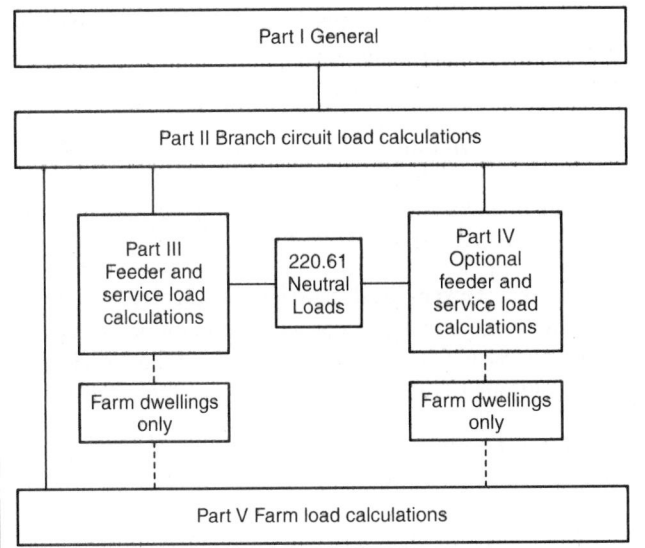

Figure 220.1 Branch-Circuit, Feeder, and Service Calculation Methods.

220.5 Calculations.

(A) Voltages. Unless other voltages are specified, for purposes of calculating branch-circuit and feeder loads, nominal system voltages of 120, 120/240, 208Y/120, 240, 347, 480Y/277, 480, 600Y/347, and 600 volts shall be used.

(B) Fractions of an Ampere. Where calculations result in a fraction of an ampere that is less than 0.5, such fractions shall be permitted to be dropped.

II. Branch Circuit Load Calculations

220.10 General. Branch-circuit loads shall be calculated as shown in 220.12, 220.14, and 220.16.

220.12 Lighting Load for Specified Occupancies. A unit load of not less than that specified in Table 220.12 for occupancies specified therein shall constitute the minimum

Table 220.3 Additional Load Calculation References

Calculation	Article	Section (or Part)
Air-Conditioning and Refrigerating Equipment, Branch-Circuit Conductor Sizing	440	Part IV
Cranes and Hoists, Rating and Size of Conductors	610	610.14
Electric Welders, ampacity calculations	630	630.11, 630.31
Electrically Driven or Controlled Irrigation Machines	675	675.7(A), 675.22(A)
Electrolytic Cell Lines	668	668.3(C)
Electroplating, Branch-Circuit Conductor Sizing	669	669.5
Elevator Feeder Demand Factors	620	620.14
Fire Pumps, Voltage Drop (mandatory calculation)	695	695.7
Fixed Electric Heating Equipment for Pipelines and Vessels, Branch-Circuit Sizing	427	427.4
Fixed Electric Space Heating Equipment, Branch-Circuit Sizing	424	424.3
Fixed Outdoor Electric Deicing and Snow-Melting Equipment, Branch-Circuit Sizing	426	426.4
Industrial Machinery, Supply Conductor Sizing	670	670.4(A)
Marinas and Boatyards, Feeder and Service Load Calculations	555	555.12
Mobile Homes, Manufactured Homes, and Mobile Home Parks, Total Load for Determining Power Supply	550	550.18(B)
Mobile Homes, Manufactured Homes, and Mobile Home Parks, Allowable Demand Factors for Park Electrical Wiring Systems	550	550.31
Motion Picture and Television Studios and Similar Locations – Sizing of Feeder Conductors for Television Studio Sets	530	530.19
Motors, Feeder Demand Factor	430	430.26
Motors, Multimotor and Combination-Load Equipment	430	430.25
Motors, Several Motors or a Motor(s) and Other Load(s)	430	430.24
Over 600 Volt Branch Circuit Calculations	210	210.19(B)
Over 600 Volt Feeder Calculations	215	215.2(B)
Phase Converters, Conductors	455	455.6
Recreational Vehicle Parks, Basis of Calculations	551	551.73(A)
Sensitive Electrical Equipment, Voltage Drop (mandatory calculation)	647	647.4(D)
Solar Photovoltaic Systems, Circuit Sizing and Current	690	690.8
Storage-Type Water Heaters	422	422.11(E)
Theaters, Stage Switchboard Feeders	520	520.27

lighting load. The floor area for each floor shall be calculated from the outside dimensions of the building, dwelling unit, or other area involved. For dwelling units, the calculated floor area shall not include open porches, garages, or unused or unfinished spaces not adaptable for future use.

FPN: The unit values herein are based on minimum load conditions and 100 percent power factor and may not provide sufficient capacity for the installation contemplated.

Table 220.12 General Lighting Loads by Occupancy

	Unit Load	
Type of Occupancy	Volt-Amperes per Square Meter	Volt-Amperes per Square Foot
Armories and auditoriums	11	1
Banks	39[b]	3½[b]
Barber shops and beauty parlors	33	3
Churches	11	1
Clubs	22	2
Court rooms	22	2
Dwelling units[a]	33	3
Garages — commercial (storage)	6	½
Hospitals	22	2
Hotels and motels, including apartment houses without provision for cooking by tenants[a]	22	2
Industrial commercial (loft) buildings	22	2
Lodge rooms	17	1½
Office buildings	39[b]	3½[b]
Restaurants	22	2
Schools	33	3
Stores	33	3
Warehouses (storage)	3	¼
In any of the preceding occupancies except one-family dwellings and individual dwelling units of two-family and multifamily dwellings:		
Assembly halls and auditoriums	11	1
Halls, corridors, closets, stairways	6	½
Storage spaces	3	¼

[a]See 220.14(J).
[b]See 220.14(K).

220.14 Other Loads — All Occupancies. In all occupancies, the minimum load for each outlet for general-use receptacles and outlets not used for general illumination shall not be less than that calculated in 220.14(A) through (L), the loads shown being based on nominal branch-circuit voltages.

Exception: The loads of outlets serving switchboards and switching frames in telephone exchanges shall be waived from the calculations.

(A) Specific Appliances or Loads. An outlet for a specific appliance or other load not covered in 220.14(B) through (L) shall be calculated based on the ampere rating of the appliance or load served.

(B) Electric Dryers and Household Electric Cooking Appliances. Load calculations shall be permitted as specified in 220.54 for electric dryers and in 220.55 for electric ranges and other cooking appliances.

(C) Motor Loads. Outlets for motor loads shall be calculated in accordance with the requirements in 430.22, 430.24, and 440.6.

(D) Luminaires (Lighting Fixtures). An outlet supplying luminaire(s) [lighting fixture(s)] shall be calculated based on the maximum volt-ampere rating of the equipment and lamps for which the luminaire(s) [fixture(s)] is rated.

(E) Heavy-Duty Lampholders. Outlets for heavy-duty lampholders shall be calculated at a minimum of 600 volt-amperes.

(F) Sign and Outline Lighting. Sign and outline lighting outlets shall be calculated at a minimum of 1200 volt-amperes for each required branch circuit specified in 600.5(A).

(G) Show Windows. Show windows shall be calculated in accordance with either of the following:

(1) The unit load per outlet as required in other provisions of this section

(2) At 200 volt-amperes per 300 mm (1 ft) of show window

(H) Fixed Multioutlet Assemblies. Fixed multioutlet assemblies used in other than dwelling units or the guest rooms or guest suites of hotels or motels shall be calculated in accordance with (H)(1) or (H)(2). For the purposes of this section, the calculation shall be permitted to be based on the portion that contains receptacle outlets.

(1) Where appliances are unlikely to be used simultaneously, each 1.5 m (5 ft) or fraction thereof of each separate and continuous length shall be considered as one outlet of not less than 180 volt-amperes.

(2) Where appliances are likely to be used simultaneously, each 300 mm (1 ft) or fraction thereof shall be considered as an outlet of not less than 180 volt-amperes.

(I) Receptacle Outlets. Except as covered in 220.14(J) and (K), receptacle outlets shall be calculated at not less than 180 volt-amperes for each single or for each multiple receptacle on one yoke. A single piece of equipment consisting of a multiple receptacle comprised of four or more receptacles shall be calculated at not less than 90 volt-amperes per receptacle. This provision shall not be applicable to the receptacle outlets specified in 210.11(C)(1) and (C)(2).

(J) Dwelling Occupancies. In one-family, two-family, and multifamily dwellings and in guest rooms or guest suites of hotels and motels, the outlets specified in (J)(1), (J)(2), and (J)(3) are included in the general lighting load calculations of 220.12. No additional load calculations shall be required for such outlets.

(1) All general-use receptacle outlets of 20-ampere rating or less, including receptacles connected to the circuits in 210.11(C)(3)

(2) The receptacle outlets specified in 210.52(E) and (G)

(3) The lighting outlets specified in 210.70(A) and (B)

(K) Banks and Office Buildings. In banks or office buildings, the receptacle loads shall be calculated to be the larger of (1) or (2):

(1) The computed load from 220.14(I)

(2) 11 volt-amperes/m^2 or 1 volt-ampere/ft^2

(L) Other Outlets. Other outlets not covered in 220.14(A) through (K) shall be calculated based on 180 volt-amperes per outlet.

220.16 Loads for Additions to Existing Installations.

(A) Dwelling Units. Loads added to an existing dwelling unit(s) shall comply with the following as applicable:

(1) Loads for structural additions to an existing dwelling unit or for a previously unwired portion of an existing dwelling unit, either of which exceeds 46.5 m^2 (500 ft^2), shall be calculated in accordance with 220.12 and 220.14.

(2) Loads for new circuits or extended circuits in previously wired dwelling units shall be calculated in accordance with either 220.12 or 220.14, as applicable.

(B) Other Than Dwelling Units. Loads for new circuits or extended circuits in other than dwelling units shall be calculated in accordance with either 220.12 or 220.14, as applicable.

220.18 Maximum Loads. The total load shall not exceed the rating of the branch circuit, and it shall not exceed the maximum loads specified in 220.18(A) through (C) under the conditions specified therein.

(A) Motor-Operated and Combination Loads. Where a circuit supplies only motor-operated loads, Article 430 shall apply. Where a circuit supplies only air-conditioning equipment, refrigerating equipment, or both, Article 440 shall apply. For circuits supplying loads consisting of motor-operated uti-

lization equipment that is fastened in place and has a motor larger than ⅛ hp in combination with other loads, the total calculated load shall be based on 125 percent of the largest motor load plus the sum of the other loads.

(B) Inductive Lighting Loads. For circuits supplying lighting units that have ballasts, transformers, or autotransformers, the calculated load shall be based on the total ampere ratings of such units and not on the total watts of the lamps.

(C) Range Loads. It shall be permissible to apply demand factors for range loads in accordance with Table 220.55, including Note 4.

III. Feeder and Service Load Calculations

220.40 General. The calculated load of a feeder or service shall not be less than the sum of the loads on the branch circuits supplied, as determined by Part II of this article, after any applicable demand factors permitted by Parts III or IV or required by Part V have been applied.

FPN: See Examples D1(a) through D10 in Annex D. See 220.18(B) for the maximum load in amperes permitted for lighting units operating at less than 100 percent power factor.

220.42 General Lighting. The demand factors specified in Table 220.42 shall apply to that portion of the total branch-circuit load calculated for general illumination. They shall not be applied in determining the number of branch circuits for general illumination.

220.43 Show-Window and Track Lighting.

(A) Show Windows. For show-window lighting, a load of not less than 660 volt-amperes/linear meter or 200 volt-amperes/linear foot shall be included for a show window, measured horizontally along its base.

FPN: See 220.14(G) for branch circuits supplying show windows.

(B) Track Lighting. For track lighting in other than dwelling units or guest rooms or guest suites of hotels or motels, an additional load of 150 volt-amperes shall be included for every 600 mm (2 ft) of lighting track or fraction thereof. Where multicircuit track is installed, the load shall be considered to be divided equally between the track circuits.

220.44 Receptacle Loads — Other Than Dwelling Units. Receptacle loads calculated in accordance with 220.14(H) and (I) shall be permitted to be made subject to the demand factors given in Table 220.42 or Table 220.44.

220.50 Motors. Motor loads shall be calculated in accordance with 430.24, 430.25, and 430.26 and with 440.6 for hermetic refrigerant motor compressors.

Table 220.42 Lighting Load Demand Factors

Type of Occupancy	Portion of Lighting Load to Which Demand Factor Applies (Volt-Amperes)	Demand Factor (Percent)
Dwelling units	First 3000 or less at	100
	From 3001 to 120,000 at	35
	Remainder over 120,000 at	25
Hospitals*	First 50,000 or less at	40
	Remainder over 50,000 at	20
Hotels and motels, including apartment houses without provision for cooking by tenants*	First 20,000 or less at	50
	From 20,001 to 100,000 at	40
	Remainder over 100,000 at	30
Warehouses (storage)	First 12,500 or less at	100
	Remainder over 12,500 at	50
All others	Total volt-amperes	100

*The demand factors of this table shall not apply to the calculated load of feeders or services supplying areas in hospitals, hotels, and motels where the entire lighting is likely to be used at one time, as in operating rooms, ballrooms, or dining rooms.

Table 220.44 Demand Factors for Non-dwelling Receptacle Loads

Portion of Receptacle Load to Which Demand Factor Applies (Volt-Amperes)	Demand Factor (Percent)
First 10 kVA or less at	100
Remainder over 10 kVA at	50

220.51 Fixed Electric Space Heating. Fixed electric space heating loads shall be calculated at 100 percent of the total connected load. However, in no case shall a feeder or service load current rating be less than the rating of the largest branch circuit supplied.

Exception: Where reduced loading of the conductors results from units operating on duty-cycle, intermittently, or from all units not operating at the same time, the authority having jurisdiction may grant permission for feeder and service conductors to have an ampacity less than 100 percent, provided the conductors have an ampacity for the load so determined.

220.52 Small Appliance and Laundry Loads — Dwelling Unit.

(A) Small Appliance Circuit Load. In each dwelling unit, the load shall be calculated at 1500 volt-amperes for each 2-wire small-appliance branch circuit required by 210.11(C)(1). Where the load is subdivided through two or more feeders, the calculated load for each shall include not less than 1500 volt-amperes for each 2-wire small-appliance branch circuit. These loads shall be permitted to be included with the general lighting load and subjected to the demand factors provided in Table 220.42.

Exception: The individual branch circuit permitted by 210.52(B)(1), Exception No. 2, shall be permitted to be excluded from the calculation required by 220.52.

(B) Laundry Circuit Load. A load of not less than 1500 volt-amperes shall be included for each 2-wire laundry branch circuit installed as required by 210.11(C)(2). This load shall be permitted to be included with the general lighting load and subjected to the demand factors provided in Table 220.42.

220.53 Appliance Load — Dwelling Unit(s). It shall be permissible to apply a demand factor of 75 percent to the nameplate rating load of four or more appliances fastened in place, other than electric ranges, clothes dryers, space-heating equipment, or air-conditioning equipment, that are served by the same feeder or service in a one-family, two-family, or multifamily dwelling.

220.54 Electric Clothes Dryers — Dwelling Unit(s). The load for household electric clothes dryers in a dwelling unit(s) shall be either 5000 watts (volt-amperes) or the nameplate rating, whichever is larger, for each dryer served. The use of the demand factors in Table 220.54 shall be permitted. Where two or more single-phase dryers are supplied by a 3-phase, 4-wire feeder or service, the total load shall be calculated on the basis of twice the maximum number connected between any two phases.

220.55 Electric Ranges and Other Cooking Appliances — Dwelling Unit(s). The load for household electric ranges, wall-mounted ovens, counter-mounted cooking units, and other household cooking appliances individually rated in excess of 1¾ kW shall be permitted to be calculated in accordance with Table 220.55. Kilovolt-amperes (kVA) shall be considered equivalent to kilowatts (kW) for loads calculated under this section.

Where two or more single-phase ranges are supplied by a 3-phase, 4-wire feeder or service, the total load shall be calculated on the basis of twice the maximum number connected between any two phases.

Table 220.54 Demand Factors for Household Electric Clothes Dryers

Number of Dryers	Demand Factor (Percent)
1–4	100%
5	85%
6	75%
7	65%
8	60%
9	55%
10	50%
11	47%
12–22	% = 47 – (number of dryers – 11)
23	35%
24–42	% = 35 – [0.5 × (number of dryers – 23)]
43 and over	25%

FPN No. 1: See Example D5(A) in Annex D.

FPN No. 2: See Table 220.56 for commercial cooking equipment.

FPN No. 3: See the examples in Annex D.

220.56 Kitchen Equipment — Other Than Dwelling Unit(s). It shall be permissible to calculate the load for commercial electric cooking equipment, dishwasher booster heaters, water heaters, and other kitchen equipment in accordance with Table 220.56. These demand factors shall be applied to all equipment that has either thermostatic control or intermittent use as kitchen equipment. These demand factors shall not apply to space-heating, ventilating, or air-conditioning equipment.

However, in no case shall the feeder or service calculated load be less than the sum of the largest two kitchen equipment loads.

Table 220.56 Demand Factors for Kitchen Equipment — Other Than Dwelling Unit(s)

Number of Units of Equipment	Demand Factor (Percent)
1	100
2	100
3	90
4	80
5	70
6 and over	65

220.60 Noncoincident Loads. Where it is unlikely that two or more noncoincident loads will be in use simultaneously, it shall be permissible to use only the largest load(s) that will be used at one time for calculating the total load of a feeder or service.

220.61 Feeder or Service Neutral Load.

(A) Basic Calculation. The feeder or service neutral load shall be the maximum unbalance of the load determined by this article. The maximum unbalanced load shall be the maximum net calculated load between the neutral and any one ungrounded conductor.

Exception: For 3-wire, 2-phase or 5-wire, 2-phase systems, the maximum unbalanced load shall be the maximum net calculated load between the neutral and any one ungrounded conductor multiplied by 140 percent.

(B) Permitted Reductions. A service or feeder supplying the following loads shall be permitted to have an additional demand factor of 70 percent applied to the amount in 220.61(B)(1) or portion of the amount in 220.61(B)(2) determined by the basic calculation:

(1) A feeder or service supplying household electric ranges, wall-mounted ovens, counter-mounted cooking units, and electric dryers, where the maximum unbalanced load has been determined in accordance with Table 220.55 for ranges and Table 220.54 for dryers

(2) That portion of the unbalanced load in excess of 200 amperes where the feeder or service is supplied from a 3-wire dc or single-phase ac system, or a 4-wire, 3-phase; 3-wire, 2-phase system, or a 5-wire, 2-phase system

(C) Prohibited Reductions. There shall be no reduction of the neutral or grounded conductor capacity applied to the amount in 220.61(C)(1), or portion of the amount in (C)(2), from that determined by the basic calculation:

(1) Any portion of a 3-wire circuit consisting of 2-phase wires and the neutral of a 4-wire, 3-phase, wye-connected system

(2) That portion consisting of nonlinear loads supplied from a 4-wire, wye-connected, 3-phase system

FPN No. 1: See Examples D1(a), D1(b), D2(b), D4(a), and D5(a) in Annex D.

FPN No. 2: A 3-phase, 4-wire, wye-connected power system used to supply power to nonlinear loads may necessitate that the power system design allow for the possibility of high harmonic neutral currents.

IV. Optional Feeder and Service Load Calculations

220.80 General. Optional feeder and service load calculations shall be permitted in accordance with Part IV.

Table 220.55 Demand Factors and Loads for Household Electric Ranges, Wall-Mounted Ovens, Counter-Mounted Cooking Units, and Other Household Cooking Appliances over 1¾ kW Rating (Column C to be used in all cases except as otherwise permitted in Note 3.)

Number of Appliances	Demand Factor (Percent) (See Notes)		Column C Maximum Demand (kW) (See Notes) (Not over 12 kW Rating)
	Column A (Less than 3½ kW Rating)	Column B (3½ kW to 8¾ kW Rating)	
1	80	80	8
2	75	65	11
3	70	55	14
4	66	50	17
5	62	45	20
6	59	43	21
7	56	40	22
8	53	36	23
9	51	35	24
10	49	34	25
11	47	32	26
12	45	32	27
13	43	32	28
14	41	32	29
15	40	32	30
16	39	28	31
17	38	28	32
18	37	28	33
19	36	28	34
20	35	28	35
21	34	26	36
22	33	26	37
23	32	26	38
24	31	26	39
25	30	26	40
26–30	30	24	15 kW + 1 kW for each range
31–40	30	22	
41–50	30	20	25 kW + ¾ kW for each range
51–60	30	18	
61 and over	30	16	

1. Over 12 kW through 27 kW ranges all of same rating. For ranges individually rated more than 12 kW but not more than 27 kW, the maximum demand in Column C shall be increased 5 percent for each additional kilowatt of rating or major fraction thereof by which the rating of individual ranges exceeds 12 kW.

2. Over 8¾ kW through 27 kW ranges of unequal ratings. For ranges individually rated more than 8¾ kW and of different ratings, but none exceeding 27 kW, an average value of rating shall be calculated by adding together the ratings of all ranges to obtain the total connected load (using 12 kW for any range rated less than 12 kW) and dividing by the total number of ranges. Then the maximum demand in Column C shall be increased 5 percent for each kilowatt or major fraction thereof by which this average value exceeds 12 kW.

3. Over 1¾ kW through 8¾ kW. In lieu of the method provided in Column C, it shall be permissible to add the nameplate ratings of all household cooking appliances rated more than 1¾ kW but not more than 8¾ kW and multiply the sum by the demand factors specified in Column A or B for the given number of appliances. Where the rating of cooking appliances falls under both Column A and Column B, the demand factors for each column shall be applied to the appliances for that column, and the results added together.

4. Branch-Circuit Load. It shall be permissible to calculate the branch-circuit load for one range in accordance with Table 220.55. The branch-circuit load for one wall-mounted oven or one counter-mounted cooking unit shall be the nameplate rating of the appliance. The branch-circuit load for a counter-mounted cooking unit and not more than two wall-mounted ovens, all supplied from a single branch circuit and located in the same room, shall be calculated by adding the nameplate rating of the individual appliances and treating this total as equivalent to one range.

5. This table also applies to household cooking appliances rated over 1¾ kW and used in instructional programs.

220.82 Dwelling Unit.

(A) Feeder and Service Load. This section applies to a dwelling unit having the total connected load served by a single 120/240-volt or 208Y/120-volt set of 3-wire service or feeder conductors with an ampacity of 100 or greater. It shall be permissible to calculate the feeder and service loads in accordance with this section instead of the method specified in Part III of this article. The calculated load shall be the result of adding the loads from 220.82(B) and (C). Feeder and service-entrance conductors whose calculated load is determined by this optional calculation shall be permitted to have the neutral load determined by 220.61.

(B) General Loads. The general calculated load shall be not less than 100 percent of the first 10 kVA plus 40 percent of the remainder of the following loads:

(1) 33 volt-amperes/m^2 or 3 volt-amperes/ft^2 for general lighting and general-use receptacles. The floor area for each floor shall be calculated from the outside dimensions of the dwelling unit. The calculated floor area shall not include open porches, garages, or unused or unfinished spaces not adaptable for future use.

(2) 1500 volt-amperes for each 2-wire, 20-ampere small-appliance branch circuit and each laundry branch circuit specified in 220.52.

(3) The nameplate rating of all appliances that are fastened in place, permanently connected, or located to be on a specific circuit, ranges, wall-mounted ovens, counter-mounted cooking units, clothes dryers, and water heaters.

(4) The nameplate ampere or kVA rating of all motors and of all low-power-factor loads.

(C) Heating and Air-Conditioning Load. The largest of the following six selections (load in kVA) shall be included:

(1) 100 percent of the nameplate rating(s) of the air conditioning and cooling.

(2) 100 percent of the nameplate rating(s) of the heating when a heat pump is used without any supplemental electric heating.

(3) 100 percent of the nameplate ratings of electric thermal storage and other heating systems where the usual load is expected to be continuous at the full nameplate value. Systems qualifying under this selection shall not be calculated under any other selection in 220.82(C).

(4) 100 percent of the nameplate rating(s) of the heat pump compressor and 65 percent of the supplemental electric heating for central electric space heating systems. If the heat pump compressor is prevented from operating at the same time as the supplementary heat, it does not need to be added to the supplementary heat for the total central space heating load.

(5) 65 percent of the nameplate rating(s) of electric space heating if less than four separately controlled units.

(6) 40 percent of the nameplate rating(s) of electric space heating if four or more separately controlled units.

220.83 Existing Dwelling Unit.

This section shall be permitted to be used to determine if the existing service or feeder is of sufficient capacity to serve additional loads. Where the dwelling unit is served by a 120/240-volt or 208Y/120-volt, 3-wire service, it shall be permissible to calculate the total load in accordance with 220.83(A) or (B).

(A) Where Additional Air-Conditioning Equipment or Electric Space-Heating Equipment Is Not to Be Installed. The following formula shall be used for existing and additional new loads.

Load (kVA)	Percent of Load
First 8 kVA of load at	100
Remainder of load at	40

Load calculations shall include the following:

(1) General lighting and general-use receptacles at 33 volt-amperes/m^2 or 3 volt-amperes/ft^2 as determined by 220.12

(2) 1500 volt-amperes for each 2-wire, 20-ampere small-appliance branch circuit and each laundry branch circuit specified in 220.52

(3) Household range(s), wall-mounted oven(s), and counter-mounted cooking unit(s)

(4) All other appliances that are permanently connected, fastened in place, or connected to a dedicated circuit, at nameplate rating

(B) Where Additional Air-Conditioning Equipment or Electric Space-Heating Equipment Is to Be Installed. The following formula shall be used for existing and additional new loads. The larger connected load of air-conditioning or space-heating, but not both, shall be used.

Load	Percent of Load
Air-conditioning equipment	100
Central electric space heating	100
Less than four separately controlled space-heating units	100
First 8 kVA of all other loads	100
Remainder of all other loads	40

Other loads shall include the following:

(1) General lighting and general-use receptacles at 33 volt-amperes/m^2 or 3 volt-amperes/ft^2 as determined by 220.12

(2) 1500 volt-amperes for each 2-wire, 20-ampere small-appliance branch circuit and each laundry branch circuit specified in 220.52

(3) Household range(s), wall-mounted oven(s), and counter-mounted cooking unit(s)

(4) All other appliances that are permanently connected, fastened in place, or connected to a dedicated circuit, including four or more separately controlled space-heating units, at nameplate rating

220.84 Multifamily Dwelling.

(A) Feeder or Service Load. It shall be permissible to calculate the load of a feeder or service that supplies three or more dwelling units of a multifamily dwelling in accordance with Table 220.84 instead of Part III of this article if all the following conditions are met:

(1) No dwelling unit is supplied by more than one feeder.

(2) Each dwelling unit is equipped with electric cooking equipment.

Exception: When the calculated load for multifamily dwellings without electric cooking in Part III of this article exceeds that calculated under Part IV for the identical load plus electric cooking (based on 8 kW per unit), the lesser of the two loads shall be permitted to be used.

(3) Each dwelling unit is equipped with either electric space heating or air conditioning, or both. Feeders and service conductors whose calculated load is determined by this optional calculation shall be permitted to have the neutral load determined by 220.61.

(B) House Loads. House loads shall be calculated in accordance with Part III of this article and shall be in addition to the dwelling unit loads calculated in accordance with Table 220.84.

(C) Connected Loads. The calculated load to which the demand factors of Table 220.84 apply shall include the following:

(1) 33 volt-amperes/m² or 3 volt-amperes/ft² for general lighting and general-use receptacles.

(2) 1500 volt-amperes for each 2-wire, 20-ampere small-appliance branch circuit and each laundry branch circuit specified in 220.52.

(3) The nameplate rating of all appliances that are fastened in place, permanently connected or located to be on a specific circuit, ranges, wall-mounted ovens, counter-mounted cooking units, clothes dryers, water heaters, and space heaters. If water heater elements are interlocked so that all elements cannot be used at the same time, the maximum possible load shall be considered the nameplate load.

(4) The nameplate ampere or kilovolt-ampere rating of all motors and of all low-power-factor loads.

(5) The larger of the air-conditioning load or the space-heating load.

Table 220.84 Optional Calculations — Demand Factors for Three or More Multifamily Dwelling Units

Number of Dwelling Units	Demand Factor (Percent)
3–5	45
6–7	44
8–10	43
11	42
12–13	41
14–15	40
16–17	39
18–20	38
21	37
22–23	36
24–25	35
26–27	34
28–30	33
31	32
32–33	31
34–36	30
37–38	29
39–42	28
43–45	27
46–50	26
51–55	25
56–61	24
62 and over	23

220.85 Two Dwelling Units. Where two dwelling units are supplied by a single feeder and the calculated load under Part III of this article exceeds that for three identical units calculated under 220.84, the lesser of the two loads shall be permitted to be used.

220.86 Schools. The calculation of a feeder or service load for schools shall be permitted in accordance with Table 220.86 in lieu of Part III of this article where equipped with electric space heating, air conditioning, or both. The connected load to which the demand factors of Table 220.86 apply shall include all of the interior and exterior lighting, power, water heating, cooking, other loads, and the larger of the air-conditioning load or space-heating load within the building or structure.

Feeders and service-entrance conductors whose calculated load is determined by this optional calculation shall be permitted to have the neutral load determined by 220.61. Where the building or structure load is calculated by this optional method, feeders within the building or structure shall have ampacity as permitted in Part III of this article; however, the ampacity of an individual feeder shall not be required to be larger than the ampacity for the entire building.

This section shall not apply to portable classroom buildings.

Table 220.86 Optional Method — Demand Factors for Feeders and Service-Entrance Conductors for Schools

Connected Load		Demand Factor (Percent)
First 33 VA/m^2 Plus,	(3 VA/ft^2) at	100
Over 33 to 220 VA/m^2 Plus,	(3 to 20 VA/ft^2) at	75
Remainder over 220 VA/m^2	(20 VA/ft^2) at	25

220.87 Determining Existing Loads. The calculation of a feeder or service load for existing installations shall be permitted to use actual maximum demand to determine the existing load under all of the following conditions:

(1) The maximum demand data is available for a 1-year period.

Exception: If the maximum demand data for a 1-year period is not available, the calculated load shall be permitted to be based on the maximum demand (measure of average power demand over a 15-minute period) continuously recorded over a minimum 30-day period using a recording ammeter or power meter connected to the highest loaded phase of the feeder or service, based on the initial loading at the start of the recording. The recording shall reflect the maximum demand of the feeder or service by being taken when the building or space is occupied and shall include by measurement or calculation the larger of the heating or cooling equipment load, and other loads that may be periodic in nature due to seasonal or similar conditions.

(2) The maximum demand at 125 percent plus the new load does not exceed the ampacity of the feeder or rating of the service.

(3) The feeder has overcurrent protection in accordance with 240.4, and the service has overload protection in accordance with 230.90.

220.88 New Restaurants. Calculation of a service or feeder load, where the feeder serves the total load, for a new restaurant shall be permitted in accordance with Table 220.88 in lieu of Part III of this article.

The overload protection of the service conductors shall be in accordance with 230.90 and 240.4.

Feeder conductors shall not be required to be of greater ampacity than the service conductors.

Service or feeder conductors whose calculated load is determined by this optional calculation shall be permitted to have the neutral load determined by 220.61.

V. Farm Load Calculation

220.100 General. Farm loads shall be calculated in accordance with Part V.

220.102 Farm Loads — Buildings and Other Loads.

(A) Dwelling Unit. The feeder or service load of a farm dwelling unit shall be calculated in accordance with the provisions for dwellings in Part III or IV of this article. Where the dwelling has electric heat and the farm has electric grain-drying systems, Part IV of this article shall not be used to calculate the dwelling load where the dwelling and farm load are supplied by a common service.

(B) Other Than Dwelling Unit. Where a feeder or service supplies a farm building or other load having two or more separate branch circuits, the load for feeders, service conductors, and service equipment shall be calculated in accordance with demand factors not less than indicated in Table 220.102.

220.103 Farm Loads — Total. Where supplied by a common service, the total load of the farm for service conductors and service equipment shall be calculated in accordance with the farm dwelling unit load and demand factors specified in Table 220.103. Where there is equipment in two or more farm equipment buildings or for loads having the same function, such loads shall be calculated in accordance with Table 220.102 and shall be permitted to be combined as a single load in Table 220.103 for calculating the total load.

Table 220.88 Optional Method — Permitted Load Calculations for Service and Feeder Conductors for New Restaurants

Total Connected Load (kVA)	All Electric Restaurant Calculated Loads (kVA)	Not All Electric Restaurant Calculated Loads (kVA)
0–200	80%	100%
201–325	10% (amount over 200) + 160.0	50% (amount over 200) + 200.0
326–800	50% (amount over 325) + 172.5	45% (amount over 325) + 262.5
Over 800	50% (amount over 800) + 410.0	20% (amount over 800) + 476.3

Note: Add all electrical loads, including both heating and cooling loads, to calculate the total connected load. Select the one demand factor that applies from the table, then multiply the total connected load by this single demand factor.

Table 220.102 Method for Calculating Farm Loads for Other Than Dwelling Unit

Ampere Load at 240 Volts Maximum	Demand Factor (Percent)
Loads expected to operate simultaneously, but not less than 125 percent full-load current of the largest motor and not less than the first 60 amperes of load	100
Next 60 amperes of all other loads	50
Remainder of other load	25

Table 220.103 Method for Calculating Total Farm Load

Individual Loads Calculated in Accordance with Table 220.102	Demand Factor (Percent)
Largest load	100
Second largest load	75
Third largest load	65
Remaining loads	50

Note: To this total load, add the load of the farm dwelling unit calculated in accordance with Part III or IV of this article. Where the dwelling has electric heat and the farm has electric grain-drying systems, Part IV of this article shall not be used to calculate the dwelling load.

ARTICLE 225
Outside Branch Circuits and Feeders

225.1 Scope. This article covers requirements for outside branch circuits and feeders run on or between buildings, structures, or poles on the premises; and electric equipment and wiring for the supply of utilization equipment that is located on or attached to the outside of buildings, structures, or poles.

> FPN: For additional information on wiring over 600 volts, see ANSI C2-2002, *National Electrical Safety Code*.

225.2 Other Articles. Application of other articles, including additional requirements to specific cases of equipment and conductors, is shown in Table 225.2.

I. General

225.3 Calculation of Loads 600 Volts, Nominal, or Less.

(A) Branch Circuits. The load on outdoor branch circuits shall be as determined by 220.10.

(B) Feeders. The load on outdoor feeders shall be as determined by Part III of Article 220.

Table 225.2 Other Articles

Equipment/Conductors	Article
Branch circuits	210
Class 1, Class 2, and Class 3 remote-control, signaling, and power-limited circuits	725
Communications circuits	800
Community antenna television and radio distribution systems	820
Conductors for general wiring	310
Electrically driven or controlled irrigation machines	675
Electric signs and outline lighting	600
Feeders	215
Fire alarm systems	760
Fixed outdoor electric deicing and snow-melting equipment	426
Floating buildings	553
Grounding	250
Hazardous (classified) locations	500
Hazardous (classified) locations — specific	510
Marinas and boatyards	555
Messenger supported wiring	396
Mobile homes, manufactured homes, and mobile home parks	550
Open wiring on insulators	398
Over 600 volts, general	490
Overcurrent protection	240
Radio and television equipment	810
Services	230
Solar photovoltaic systems	690
Swimming pools, fountains, and similar installations	680
Use and identification of grounded conductors	200

225.4 Conductor Covering. Where within 3.0 m (10 ft) of any building or structure other than supporting poles or towers, open individual (aerial) overhead conductors shall be insulated or covered. Conductors in cables or raceways, except Type MI cable, shall be of the rubber-covered type or thermoplastic type and, in wet locations, shall comply with 310.8. Conductors for festoon lighting shall be of the rubber-covered or thermoplastic type.

Exception: Equipment grounding conductors and grounded circuit conductors shall be permitted to be bare or covered as specifically permitted elsewhere in this Code.

225.5 Size of Conductors 600 Volts, Nominal, or Less. The ampacity of outdoor branch-circuit and feeder conductors shall be in accordance with 310.15 based on loads as determined under 220.10 and Part III of Article 220.

225.6 Conductor Size and Support.

(A) Overhead Spans. Open individual conductors shall not be smaller than the following:

(1) For 600 volts, nominal, or less, 10 AWG copper or 8 AWG aluminum for spans up to 15 m (50 ft) in length, and 8 AWG copper or 6 AWG aluminum for a longer span unless supported by a messenger wire

(2) For over 600 volts, nominal, 6 AWG copper or 4 AWG aluminum where open individual conductors, and 8 AWG copper or 6 AWG aluminum where in cable

(B) Festoon Lighting. Overhead conductors for festoon lighting shall not be smaller than 12 AWG unless the conductors are supported by messenger wires. In all spans exceeding 12 m (40 ft), the conductors shall be supported by messenger wire. The messenger wire shall be supported by strain insulators. Conductors or messenger wires shall not be attached to any fire escape, downspout, or plumbing equipment.

225.7 Lighting Equipment Installed Outdoors.

(A) General. For the supply of lighting equipment installed outdoors, the branch circuits shall comply with Article 210 and 225.7(B) through (D).

(B) Common Neutral. The ampacity of the neutral conductor shall not be less than the maximum net computed load current between the neutral and all ungrounded conductors connected to any one phase of the circuit.

(C) 277 Volts to Ground. Circuits exceeding 120 volts, nominal, between conductors and not exceeding 277 volts, nominal, to ground shall be permitted to supply luminaires (lighting fixtures) for illumination of outdoor areas of industrial establishments, office buildings, schools, stores, and other commercial or public buildings where the luminaires (fixtures) are not less than 900 mm (3 ft) from windows, platforms, fire escapes, and the like.

(D) 600 Volts Between Conductors. Circuits exceeding 277 volts, nominal, to ground and not exceeding 600 volts, nominal, between conductors shall be permitted to supply the auxiliary equipment of electric-discharge lamps in accordance with 210.6(D)(1).

225.10 Wiring on Buildings. The installation of outside wiring on surfaces of buildings shall be permitted for circuits of not over 600 volts, nominal, as open wiring on insulators, as multiconductor cable, as Type MC cable, as Type MI cable, as messenger supported wiring, in rigid metal conduit, in intermediate metal conduit, in rigid nonmetallic conduit, in cable trays, as cablebus, in wireways, in auxiliary gutters, in electrical metallic tubing, in flexible metal conduit, in liquidtight flexible metal conduit, in liquidtight flexible nonmetallic conduit, and in busways. Circuits of over 600 volts, nominal, shall be installed as provided in 300.37.

225.11 Circuit Exits and Entrances. Where outside branch and feeder circuits leave or enter a building, the requirements of 230.52 and 230.54 shall apply.

225.12 Open-Conductor Supports. Open conductors shall be supported on glass or porcelain knobs, racks, brackets, or strain insulators.

225.14 Open-Conductor Spacings.

(A) 600 Volts, Nominal, or Less. Conductors of 600 volts, nominal, or less, shall comply with the spacings provided in Table 230.51(C).

(B) Over 600 Volts, Nominal. Conductors of over 600 volts, nominal, shall comply with the spacings provided in 110.36 and 490.24.

(C) Separation from Other Circuits. Open conductors shall be separated from open conductors of other circuits or systems by not less than 100 mm (4 in.).

(D) Conductors on Poles. Conductors on poles shall have a separation of not less than 300 mm (1 ft) where not placed on racks or brackets. Conductors supported on poles shall provide a horizontal climbing space not less than the following:

(1) Power conductors below communications conductors — 750 mm (30 in.)
(2) Power conductors alone or above communications conductors:
    a. 300 volts or less — 600 mm (24 in.)
    b. Over 300 volts — 750 mm (30 in.)
(3) Communications conductors below power conductors — same as power conductors
(4) Communications conductors alone — no requirement

225.15 Supports over Buildings. Supports over a building shall be in accordance with 230.29.

225.16 Attachment to Buildings.

(A) Point of Attachment. The point of attachment to a building shall be in accordance with 230.26.

(B) Means of Attachment. The means of attachment to a building shall be in accordance with 230.27.

225.17 Masts as Supports. Where a mast is used for the support of final spans of feeders or branch circuits, it shall be of adequate strength or be supported by braces or guys to withstand safely the strain imposed by the overhead drop. Where raceway-type masts are used, all raceway fittings shall be identified for use with masts. Only the feeder or branch circuit conductors specified within this section shall be permitted to be attached to the feeder and/or branch circuit mast.

225.18 Clearance from Ground. Overhead spans of open conductors and open multiconductor cables of not over 600 volts, nominal, shall have a clearance of not less than the following:

(1) 3.0 m (10 ft) — above finished grade, sidewalks, or from any platform or projection from which they might be reached where the voltage does not exceed 150 volts to ground and accessible to pedestrians only

(2) 3.7 m (12 ft) — over residential property and driveways, and those commercial areas not subject to truck traffic where the voltage does not exceed 300 volts to ground

(3) 4.5 m (15 ft) — for those areas listed in the 3.7-m (12-ft) classification where the voltage exceeds 300 volts to ground

(4) 5.5 m (18 ft) — over public streets, alleys, roads, parking areas subject to truck traffic, driveways on other than residential property, and other land traversed by vehicles, such as cultivated, grazing, forest, and orchard

225.19 Clearances from Buildings for Conductors of Not Over 600 Volts, Nominal.

(A) Above Roofs. Overhead spans of open conductors and open multiconductor cables shall have a vertical clearance of not less than 2.5 m (8 ft) above the roof surface. The vertical clearance above the roof level shall be maintained for a distance not less than 900 mm (3 ft) in all directions from the edge of the roof.

Exception No. 1: The area above a roof surface subject to pedestrian or vehicular traffic shall have a vertical clearance from the roof surface in accordance with the clearance requirements of 225.18.

Exception No. 2: Where the voltage between conductors does not exceed 300, and the roof has a slope of 100 mm in 300 mm (4 in. in 12 in.) or greater, a reduction in clearance to 900 mm (3 ft) shall be permitted.

Exception No. 3: Where the voltage between conductors does not exceed 300, a reduction in clearance above only the overhanging portion of the roof to not less than 450 mm (18 in.) shall be permitted if (1) not more than 1.8 m (6 ft) of the conductors, 1.2 m (4 ft) horizontally, pass above the roof overhang and (2) they are terminated at a through-the-roof raceway or approved support.

Exception No. 4: The requirement for maintaining the vertical clearance 900 mm (3 ft) from the edge of the roof shall not apply to the final conductor span where the conductors are attached to the side of a building.

(B) From Nonbuilding or Nonbridge Structures. From signs, chimneys, radio and television antennas, tanks, and other nonbuilding or nonbridge structures, clearances —

vertical, diagonal, and horizontal — shall not be less than 900 mm (3 ft).

(C) Horizontal Clearances. Clearances shall not be less than 900 mm (3 ft).

(D) Final Spans. Final spans of feeders or branch circuits shall comply with 225.19(D)(1), (D)(2), and (D)(3).

(1) Clearance from Windows. Final spans to the building they supply, or from which they are fed, shall be permitted to be attached to the building, but they shall be kept not less than 900 mm (3 ft) from windows that are designed to be opened, and from doors, porches, balconies, ladders, stairs, fire escapes, or similar locations.

Exception: Conductors run above the top level of a window shall be permitted to be less than the 900-mm (3-ft) requirement.

(2) Vertical Clearance. The vertical clearance of final spans above, or within 900 mm (3 ft) measured horizontally of, platforms, projections, or surfaces from which they might be reached shall be maintained in accordance with 225.18.

(3) Building Openings. The overhead branch-circuit and feeder conductors shall not be installed beneath openings through which materials may be moved, such as openings in farm and commercial buildings, and shall not be installed where they obstruct entrance to these buildings' openings.

(E) Zone for Fire Ladders. Where buildings exceed three stories or 15 m (50 ft) in height, overhead lines shall be arranged, where practicable, so that a clear space (or zone) at least 1.8 m (6 ft) wide will be left either adjacent to the buildings or beginning not over 2.5 m (8 ft) from them to facilitate the raising of ladders when necessary for fire fighting.

225.20 Mechanical Protection of Conductors. Mechanical protection of conductors on buildings, structures, or poles shall be as provided for services in 230.50.

225.21 Multiconductor Cables on Exterior Surfaces of Buildings. Supports for multiconductor cables on exterior surfaces of buildings shall be as provided in 230.51.

225.22 Raceways on Exterior Surfaces of Buildings or Other Structures. Raceways on exteriors of buildings or other structures shall be arranged to drain and shall be raintight in wet locations.

Exception: Flexible metal conduit, where permitted in 348.12(1), shall not be required to be raintight.

225.24 Outdoor Lampholders. Where outdoor lampholders are attached as pendants, the connections to the circuit wires shall be staggered. Where such lampholders have terminals of a type that puncture the insulation and make contact with the conductors, they shall be attached only to conductors of the stranded type.

225.25 Location of Outdoor Lamps. Locations of lamps for outdoor lighting shall be below all energized conductors, transformers, or other electric utilization equipment, unless either of the following apply:

(1) Clearances or other safeguards are provided for relamping operations.

(2) Equipment is controlled by a disconnecting means that can be locked in the open position.

225.26 Vegetation as Support. Vegetation such as trees shall not be used for support of overhead conductor spans.

II. More Than One Building or Other Structure

225.30 Number of Supplies. Where more than one building or other structure is on the same property and under single management, each additional building or other structure that is served by a branch circuit or feeder on the load side of the service disconnecting means shall be supplied by only one feeder or branch circuit unless permitted in 225.30(A) through (E). For the purpose of this section, a multiwire branch circuit shall be considered a single circuit.

(A) Special Conditions. Additional feeders or branch circuits shall be permitted to supply the following:

(1) Fire pumps

(2) Emergency systems

(3) Legally required standby systems

(4) Optional standby systems

(5) Parallel power production systems

(6) Systems designed for connection to multiple sources of supply for the purpose of enhanced reliability

(B) Special Occupancies. By special permission, additional feeders or branch circuits shall be permitted for either of the following:

(1) Multiple-occupancy buildings where there is no space available for supply equipment accessible to all occupants

(2) A single building or other structure sufficiently large to make two or more supplies necessary

(C) Capacity Requirements. Additional feeders or branch circuits shall be permitted where the capacity requirements are in excess of 2000 amperes at a supply voltage of 600 volts or less.

(D) Different Characteristics. Additional feeders or branch circuits shall be permitted for different voltages, frequencies, or phases or for different uses, such as control of outside lighting from multiple locations.

(E) Documented Switching Procedures. Additional feeders or branch circuits shall be permitted to supply installations under single management where documented safe switching procedures are established and maintained for disconnection.

225.31 Disconnecting Means. Means shall be provided for disconnecting all ungrounded conductors that supply or pass through the building or structure.

225.32 Location. The disconnecting means shall be installed either inside or outside of the building or structure served or where the conductors pass through the building or structure. The disconnecting means shall be at a readily accessible location nearest the point of entrance of the conductors. For the purposes of this section, the requirements in 230.6 shall be utilized.

Exception No. 1: For installations under single management, where documented safe switching procedures are established and maintained for disconnection, and where the installation is monitored by qualified individuals, the disconnecting means shall be permitted to be located elsewhere on the premises.

Exception No. 2: For buildings or other structures qualifying under the provisions of Article 685, the disconnecting means shall be permitted to be located elsewhere on the premises.

Exception No. 3: For towers or poles used as lighting standards, the disconnecting means shall be permitted to be located elsewhere on the premises.

Exception No. 4: For poles or similar structures used only for support of signs installed in accordance with Article 600, the disconnecting means shall be permitted to be located elsewhere on the premises.

225.33 Maximum Number of Disconnects.

(A) General. The disconnecting means for each supply permitted by 225.30 shall consist of not more than six switches or six circuit breakers mounted in a single enclosure, in a group of separate enclosures, or in or on a switchboard. There shall be no more than six disconnects per supply grouped in any one location.

Exception: For the purposes of this section, disconnecting means used solely for the control circuit of the ground-fault protection system, or the control circuit of the power-operated supply disconnecting means, installed as part of the listed equipment, shall not be considered a supply disconnecting means.

(B) Single-Pole Units. Two or three single-pole switches or breakers capable of individual operation shall be permitted on multiwire circuits, one pole for each ungrounded conductor, as one multipole disconnect, provided they are equipped with handle ties or a master handle to disconnect all ungrounded conductors with no more than six operations of the hand.

225.34 Grouping of Disconnects.

(A) General. The two to six disconnects as permitted in 225.33 shall be grouped. Each disconnect shall be marked to indicate the load served.

Exception: One of the two to six disconnecting means permitted in 225.33, where used only for a water pump also intended to provide fire protection, shall be permitted to be located remote from the other disconnecting means.

(B) Additional Disconnecting Means. The one or more additional disconnecting means for fire pumps or for emergency, legally required standby or optional standby system permitted by 225.30 shall be installed sufficiently remote from the one to six disconnecting means for normal supply to minimize the possibility of simultaneous interruption of supply.

225.35 Access to Occupants. In a multiple-occupancy building, each occupant shall have access to the occupant's supply disconnecting means.

Exception: In a multiple-occupancy building where electric supply and electrical maintenance are provided by the building management and where these are under continuous building management supervision, the supply disconnecting means supplying more than one occupancy shall be permitted to be accessible to authorized management personnel only.

225.36 Suitable for Service Equipment. The disconnecting means specified in 225.31 shall be suitable for use as service equipment.

Exception: For garages and outbuildings on residential property, a snap switch or a set of 3-way or 4-way snap switches shall be permitted as the disconnecting means.

225.37 Identification. Where a building or structure has any combination of feeders, branch circuits, or services passing through it or supplying it, a permanent plaque or directory shall be installed at each feeder and branch-circuit disconnect location denoting all other services, feeders, or branch circuits supplying that building or structure or passing through that building or structure and the area served by each.

Exception No. 1: A plaque or directory shall not be required for large-capacity multibuilding industrial installations under single management, where it is ensured that disconnection can be accomplished by establishing and maintaining safe switching procedures.

Exception No. 2: This identification shall not be required for branch circuits installed from a dwelling unit to a second building or structure.

225.38 Disconnect Construction. Disconnecting means shall meet the requirements of 225.38(A) through (D).

Exception: For garages and outbuildings on residential property, snap switches or sets of 3-way or 4-way snap switches shall be permitted as the disconnecting means.

(A) Manually or Power Operable. The disconnecting means shall consist of either (1) a manually operable switch or a circuit breaker equipped with a handle or other suitable operating means or (2) a power-operable switch or circuit breaker, provided the switch or circuit breaker can be opened by hand in the event of a power failure.

(B) Simultaneous Opening of Poles. Each building or structure disconnecting means shall simultaneously disconnect all ungrounded supply conductors that it controls from the building or structure wiring system.

(C) Disconnection of Grounded Conductor. Where the building or structure disconnecting means does not disconnect the grounded conductor from the grounded conductors in the building or structure wiring, other means shall be provided for this purpose at the location of disconnecting means. A terminal or bus to which all grounded conductors can be attached by means of pressure connectors shall be permitted for this purpose.

In a multisection switchboard, disconnects for the grounded conductor shall be permitted to be in any of the switchboard, provided any such switchboard is marked.

(D) Indicating. The building or structure disconnecting means shall plainly indicate whether it is in the open or closed position.

225.39 Rating of Disconnect. The feeder or branch-circuit disconnecting means shall have a rating of not less than the load to be supplied, determined in accordance with Parts I and II of Article 220 for branch circuits, Parts III or IV of Article 220 for feeders, or Part V of Article 220 for farm loads. In no case shall the rating be lower than specified in 225.39(A), (B), (C), or (D).

(A) One-Circuit Installation. For installations to supply only limited loads of a single branch circuit, the branch circuit disconnecting means shall have a rating of not less than 15 amperes.

(B) Two-Circuit Installations. For installations consisting of not more than two 2-wire branch circuits, the feeder or branch-circuit disconnecting means shall have a rating of not less than 30 amperes.

(C) One-Family Dwelling. For a one-family dwelling, the feeder disconnecting means shall have a rating of not less than 100 amperes, 3-wire.

(D) All Others. For all other installations, the feeder or branch-circuit disconnecting means shall have a rating of not less than 60 amperes.

225.40 Access to Overcurrent Protective Devices. Where a feeder overcurrent device is not readily accessible, branch-circuit overcurrent devices shall be installed on the load side, shall be mounted in a readily accessible location, and shall be of a lower ampere rating than the feeder overcurrent device.

III. Over 600 Volts

225.50 Sizing of Conductors. The sizing of conductors over 600 volts shall be in accordance with 210.19(B) for branch circuits and 215.2(B) for feeders.

225.51 Isolating Switches. Where oil switches or air, oil, vacuum, or sulfur hexafluoride circuit breakers constitute a building disconnecting means, an isolating switch with visible break contacts and meeting the requirements of 230.204(B), (C), and (D) shall be installed on the supply side of the disconnecting means and all associated equipment.

Exception: The isolating switch shall not be required where the disconnecting means is mounted on removable truck panels or metal-enclosed switchgear units that cannot be opened unless the circuit is disconnected and that, when removed from the normal operating position, automatically disconnect the circuit breaker or switch from all energized parts.

225.52 Location. A building or structure disconnecting means shall be located in accordance with 225.32, or it shall be electrically operated by a similarly located remote-control device.

225.53 Type. Each building or structure disconnect shall simultaneously disconnect all ungrounded supply conductors it controls and shall have a fault-closing rating not less than the maximum available short-circuit current available at its supply terminals.

Where fused switches or separately mounted fuses are installed, the fuse characteristics shall be permitted to contribute to the fault closing rating of the disconnecting means.

225.60 Clearances over Roadways, Walkways, Rail, Water, and Open Land.

(A) 22 kV Nominal to Ground or Less. The clearances over roadways, walkways, rail, water, and open land for conductors and live parts up to 22 kV nominal to ground or less shall be not less than the values shown in Table 225.60.

(B) Over 22 kV Nominal to Ground. Clearances for the categories shown in Table 225.60 shall be increased by 10 mm (0.4 in.) per kV above 22,000 volts.

(C) Special Cases. For special cases, such as where crossings will be made over lakes, rivers, or areas using large vehicles such as mining operations, specific designs shall be engineered considering the special circumstances and shall be approved by the authority having jurisdiction.

FPN: For additional information, see ANSI C2-2002, *National Electrical Safety Code.*

Table 225.60 Clearances over Roadways, Walkways, Rail, Water, and Open Land

Location	Clearance	
	m	ft
Open land subject to vehicles, cultivation, or grazing	5.6	18.5
Roadways, driveways, parking lots, and alleys	5.6	18.5
Walkways	4.1	13.5
Rails	8.1	26.5
Spaces and ways for pedestrians and restricted traffic	4.4	14.5
Water areas not suitable for boating	5.2	17

225.61 Clearances over Buildings and Other Structures.

(A) 22 kV Nominal to Ground or Less. The clearances over buildings and other structures for conductors and live parts up to 22 kV, nominal, to ground or less shall be not less than the values shown in Table 225.61.

(B) Over 22 kV Nominal to Ground. Clearances for the categories shown in Table 225.61 shall be increased by 10 mm (0.4 in.) per kV above 22,000 volts.

FPN: For additional information, see ANSI C2-2002, *National Electrical Safety Code.*

Table 225.61 Clearances over Buildings and Other Structures

Clearance from Conductors or Live Parts from:	Horizontal		Vertical	
	m	ft	m	ft
Building walls, projections, and windows	2.3	7.5	—	—
Balconies, catwalks, and similar areas accessible to people	2.3	7.5	4.1	13.5
Over or under roofs or projections not readily accessible to people	—	—	3.8	12.5
Over roofs accessible to vehicles but not trucks	—	—	4.1	13.5
Over roofs accessible to trucks	—	—	5.6	18.5
Other structures	2.3	7.5	—	—

ARTICLE 230
Services

230.1 Scope. This article covers service conductors and equipment for control and protection of services and their installation requirements.

FPN: See Figure 230.1.

General	Part I
Overhead Service-Drop Conductors	Part II
Underground Service-Lateral Conductors	Part III
Service-Entrance Conductors	Part IV
Service Equipment—General	Part V
Service Equipment—Disconnecting Means	Part VI
Service Equipment—Overcurrent Protection	Part VII
Services Exceeding 600 Volts, Nominal	Part VIII

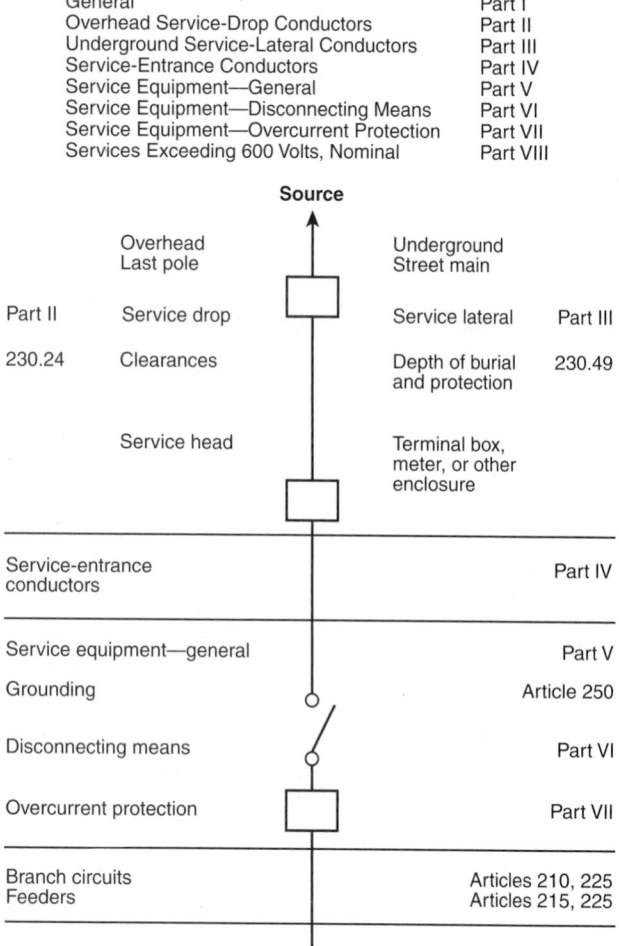

Figure 230.1 Services.

I. General

230.2 Number of Services. A building or other structure served shall be supplied by only one service unless permitted in 230.2(A) through (D). For the purpose of 230.40, Exception No. 2 only, underground sets of conductors, 1/0 AWG and larger, running to the same location and connected together at their supply end but not connected together at their load end shall be considered to be supplying one service.

(A) Special Conditions. Additional services shall be permitted to supply the following:

(1) Fire pumps

(2) Emergency systems

(3) Legally required standby systems

(4) Optional standby systems

(5) Parallel power production systems

(6) Systems designed for connection to multiple sources of supply for the purpose of enhanced reliability

(B) Special Occupancies. By special permission, additional services shall be permitted for either of the following:

(1) Multiple-occupancy buildings where there is no available space for service equipment accessible to all occupants

(2) A single building or other structure sufficiently large to make two or more services necessary

(C) Capacity Requirements. Additional services shall be permitted under any of the following:

(1) Where the capacity requirements are in excess of 2000 amperes at a supply voltage of 600 volts or less

(2) Where the load requirements of a single-phase installation are greater than the serving agency normally supplies through one service

(3) By special permission

(D) Different Characteristics. Additional services shall be permitted for different voltages, frequencies, or phases, or for different uses, such as for different rate schedules.

(E) Identification. Where a building or structure is supplied by more than one service, or any combination of branch circuits, feeders, and services, a permanent plaque or directory shall be installed at each service disconnect location denoting all other services, feeders, and branch circuits supplying that building or structure and the area served by each. See 225.37.

230.3 One Building or Other Structure Not to Be Supplied Through Another. Service conductors supplying a building or other structure shall not pass through the interior of another building or other structure.

230.6 Conductors Considered Outside the Building. Conductors shall be considered outside of a building or other structure under any of the following conditions:

(1) Where installed under not less than 50 mm (2 in.) of concrete beneath a building or other structure

(2) Where installed within a building or other structure in a raceway that is encased in concrete or brick not less than 50 mm (2 in.) thick

(3) Where installed in any vault that meets the construction requirements of Article 450, Part III

(4) Where installed in conduit and under not less than 450 mm (18 in.) of earth beneath a building or other structure

230.7 Other Conductors in Raceway or Cable. Conductors other than service conductors shall not be installed in the same service raceway or service cable.

Exception No. 1: Grounding conductors and bonding jumpers.

Exception No. 2: Load management control conductors having overcurrent protection.

230.8 Raceway Seal. Where a service raceway enters a building or structure from an underground distribution system, it shall be sealed in accordance with 300.5(G). Spare or unused raceways shall also be sealed. Sealants shall be identified for use with the cable insulation, shield, or other components.

230.9 Clearances on Buildings. Service conductors and final spans shall comply with 230.9(A), (B), and (C).

(A) Clearances. Service conductors installed as open conductors or multiconductor cable without an overall outer jacket shall have a clearance of not less than 900 mm (3 ft) from windows that are designed to be opened, doors, porches, balconies, ladders, stairs, fire escapes, or similar locations.

Exception: Conductors run above the top level of a window shall be permitted to be less than the 900-mm (3-ft) requirement.

(B) Vertical Clearance. The vertical clearance of final spans above, or within 900 mm (3 ft) measured horizontally of, platforms, projections, or surfaces from which they might be reached shall be maintained in accordance with 230.24(B).

(C) Building Openings. Overhead service conductors shall not be installed beneath openings through which materials may be moved, such as openings in farm and commercial buildings, and shall not be installed where they obstruct entrance to these building openings.

230.10 Vegetation as Support. Vegetation such as trees shall not be used for support of overhead service conductors.

II. Overhead Service-Drop Conductors

230.22 Insulation or Covering. Individual conductors shall be insulated or covered.

Exception: The grounded conductor of a multiconductor cable shall be permitted to be bare.

230.23 Size and Rating.

(A) General. Conductors shall have sufficient ampacity to carry the current for the load as calculated in accordance with Article 220 and shall have adequate mechanical strength.

(B) Minimum Size. The conductors shall not be smaller than 8 AWG copper or 6 AWG aluminum or copper-clad aluminum.

Exception: Conductors supplying only limited loads of a single branch circuit — such as small polyphase power, controlled water heaters, and similar loads — shall not be smaller than 12 AWG hard-drawn copper or equivalent.

(C) Grounded Conductors. The grounded conductor shall not be less than the minimum size as required by 250.24(C).

230.24 Clearances. Service-drop conductors shall not be readily accessible and shall comply with 230.24(A) through (D) for services not over 600 volts, nominal.

(A) Above Roofs. Conductors shall have a vertical clearance of not less than 2.5 m (8 ft) above the roof surface. The vertical clearance above the roof level shall be maintained for a distance of not less than 900 mm (3 ft) in all directions from the edge of the roof.

Exception No. 1: The area above a roof surface subject to pedestrian or vehicular traffic shall have a vertical clearance from the roof surface in accordance with the clearance requirements of 230.24(B).

Exception No. 2: Where the voltage between conductors does not exceed 300 and the roof has a slope of 100 mm in 300 mm (4 in. in 12 in.) or greater, a reduction in clearance to 900 mm (3 ft) shall be permitted.

Exception No. 3: Where the voltage between conductors does not exceed 300, a reduction in clearance above only the overhanging portion of the roof to not less than 450 mm (18 in.) shall be permitted if (1) not more than 1.8 m (6 ft) of service-drop conductors, 1.2 m (4 ft) horizontally, pass above the roof overhang, and (2) they are terminated at a through-the-roof raceway or approved support.

FPN: See 230.28 for mast supports.

Exception No. 4: The requirement for maintaining the vertical clearance 900 mm (3 ft) from the edge of the roof shall not apply to the final conductor span where the service drop is attached to the side of a building.

(B) Vertical Clearance from Ground. Service-drop conductors, where not in excess of 600 volts, nominal, shall have the following minimum clearance from final grade:

(1) 3.0 m (10 ft) — at the electric service entrance to buildings, also at the lowest point of the drip loop of the building electric entrance, and above areas or sidewalks accessible only to pedestrians, measured from final grade or other accessible surface only for service-drop cables supported on and cabled together with a grounded bare messenger where the voltage does not exceed 150 volts to ground

(2) 3.7 m (12 ft) — over residential property and driveways, and those commercial areas not subject to truck traffic where the voltage does not exceed 300 volts to ground

(3) 4.5 m (15 ft) — for those areas listed in the 3.7-m (12-ft) classification where the voltage exceeds 300 volts to ground

(4) 5.5 m (18 ft) — over public streets, alleys, roads, parking areas subject to truck traffic, driveways on other than residential property, and other land such as cultivated, grazing, forest, and orchard

(C) Clearance from Building Openings. See 230.9.

(D) Clearance from Swimming Pools. See 680.8.

230.26 Point of Attachment. The point of attachment of the service-drop conductors to a building or other structure shall provide the minimum clearances as specified in 230.9 and 230.24. In no case shall this point of attachment be less than 3.0 m (10 ft) above finished grade.

230.27 Means of Attachment. Multiconductor cables used for service drops shall be attached to buildings or other structures by fittings identified for use with service conductors. Open conductors shall be attached to fittings identified for use with service conductors or to noncombustible, nonabsorbent insulators securely attached to the building or other structure.

230.28 Service Masts as Supports. Where a service mast is used for the support of service-drop conductors, it shall be of adequate strength or be supported by braces or guys to withstand safely the strain imposed by the service drop. Where raceway-type service masts are used, all raceway fittings shall be identified for use with service masts. Only power service-drop conductors shall be permitted to be attached to a service mast.

230.29 Supports over Buildings. Service-drop conductors passing over a roof shall be securely supported by substantial structures. Where practicable, such supports shall be independent of the building.

III. Underground Service-Lateral Conductors

230.30 Insulation. Service-lateral conductors shall be insulated for the applied voltage.

Exception: A grounded conductor shall be permitted to be uninsulated as follows:

(1) Bare copper used in a raceway.

(2) Bare copper for direct burial where bare copper is judged to be suitable for the soil conditions.

(3) Bare copper for direct burial without regard to soil conditions where part of a cable assembly identified for underground use.

(4) Aluminum or copper-clad aluminum without individual insulation or covering where part of a cable assembly identified for underground use in a raceway or for direct burial.

230.31 Size and Rating.

(A) General. Service-lateral conductors shall have sufficient ampacity to carry the current for the load as calculated in accordance with Article 220 and shall have adequate mechanical strength.

(B) Minimum Size. The conductors shall not be smaller than 8 AWG copper or 6 AWG aluminum or copper-clad aluminum.

Exception: Conductors supplying only limited loads of a single branch circuit — such as small polyphase power, controlled water heaters, and similar loads — shall not be smaller than 12 AWG copper or 10 AWG aluminum or copper-clad aluminum.

(C) Grounded Conductors. The grounded conductor shall not be less than the minimum size required by 250.24(C).

230.32 Protection Against Damage. Underground service-lateral conductors shall be protected against damage in accordance with 300.5. Service-lateral conductors entering a building shall be installed in accordance with 230.6 or protected by a raceway wiring method identified in 230.43.

230.33 Spliced Conductors. Service-lateral conductors shall be permitted to be spliced or tapped in accordance with 110.14, 300.5(E), 300.13, and 300.15.

IV. Service-Entrance Conductors

230.40 Number of Service-Entrance Conductor Sets. Each service drop or lateral shall supply only one set of service-entrance conductors.

Exception No. 1: A building shall be permitted to have one set of service-entrance conductors for each service, as defined in 230.2, run to each occupancy or group of occupancies.

Exception No. 2: Where two to six service disconnecting means in separate enclosures are grouped at one location and supply separate loads from one service drop or lateral, one set of service-entrance conductors shall be permitted to supply each or several such service equipment enclosures.

Exception No. 3: A single-family dwelling unit and a separate structure shall be permitted to have one set of service-entrance conductors run to each from a single service drop or lateral.

Exception No. 4: A two-family dwelling or a multifamily dwelling shall be permitted to have one set of service-entrance conductors installed to supply the circuits covered in 210.25.

Exception No. 5: One set of service-entrance conductors connected to the supply side of the normal service disconnecting means shall be permitted to supply each or several systems covered by 230.82(5) or 230.82(6).

230.41 Insulation of Service-Entrance Conductors. Service-entrance conductors entering or on the exterior of buildings or other structures shall be insulated.

Exception: A grounded conductor shall be permitted to be uninsulated as follows:

(1) Bare copper used in a raceway or part of a service cable assembly.

(2) Bare copper for direct burial where bare copper is judged to be suitable for the soil conditions.

(3) Bare copper for direct burial without regard to soil conditions where part of a cable assembly identified for underground use.

(4) Aluminum or copper-clad aluminum without individual insulation or covering where part of a cable assembly or identified for underground use in a raceway, or for direct burial.

(5) Bare conductors used in an auxiliary gutter.

230.42 Minimum Size and Rating.

(A) General. The ampacity of the service-entrance conductors before the application of any adjustment or correction factors shall not be less than either (A)(1) or (A)(2). Loads shall be determined in accordance with Article 220. Ampacity shall be determined from 310.15. The maximum allowable current of busways shall be that value for which the busway has been listed or labeled.

(1) The sum of the noncontinuous loads plus 125 percent of continuous loads

(2) The sum of the noncontinuous load plus the continuous load if the service-entrance conductors terminate in an overcurrent device where both the overcurrent device and its assembly are listed for operation at 100 percent of their rating

(B) Specific Installations. In addition to the requirements of 230.42(A), the minimum ampacity for ungrounded conductors for specific installations shall not be less than the rating of the service disconnecting means specified in 230.79(A) through (D).

(C) Grounded Conductors. The grounded conductor shall not be less than the minimum size as required by 250.24(C).

230.43 Wiring Methods for 600 Volts, Nominal, or Less. Service-entrance conductors shall be installed in accordance with the applicable requirements of this *Code* covering the type of wiring method used and shall be limited to the following methods:

(1) Open wiring on insulators

(2) Type IGS cable

(3) Rigid metal conduit

(4) Intermediate metal conduit

(5) Electrical metallic tubing

(6) Electrical nonmetallic tubing (ENT)

(7) Service-entrance cables

(8) Wireways

(9) Busways

(10) Auxiliary gutters

(11) Rigid nonmetallic conduit

(12) Cablebus

(13) Type MC cable

(14) Mineral-insulated, metal-sheathed cable

(15) Flexible metal conduit not over 1.8 m (6 ft) long or liquidtight flexible metal conduit not over 1.8 m (6 ft) long between raceways, or between raceway and service equipment, with equipment bonding jumper routed with the flexible metal conduit or the liquidtight flexible metal conduit according to the provisions of 250.102(A), (B), (C), and (E)

(16) Liquidtight flexible nonmetallic conduit

230.44 Cable Trays. Cable tray systems shall be permitted to support service-entrance conductors. Cable trays used to support service-entrance conductors shall contain only service-entrance conductors.

Exception: Conductors other than service-entrance conductors shall be permitted to be installed in a cable tray with service-entrance conductors, provided a solid fixed barrier of a material compatible with the cable tray is installed to separate the service-entrance conductors from other conductors installed in the cable tray.

230.46 Spliced Conductors. Service-entrance conductors shall be permitted to be spliced or tapped in accordance with 110.14, 300.5(E), 300.13, and 300.15.

230.49 Protection Against Physical Damage — Underground. Underground service-entrance conductors shall be protected against physical damage in accordance with 300.5.

230.50 Protection of Open Conductors and Cables Against Damage — Above Ground. Service-entrance conductors installed above ground shall be protected against physical damage as specified in 230.50(A) or (B).

(A) Service Cables. Service cables, where subject to physical damage, shall be protected by any of the following:

(1) Rigid metal conduit

(2) Intermediate metal conduit

(3) Schedule 80 rigid nonmetallic conduit

(4) Electrical metallic tubing

(5) Other approved means

(B) Other Than Service Cable. Individual open conductors and cables other than service cables shall not be installed within 3.0 m (10 ft) of grade level or where exposed to physical damage.

Exception: Type MI and Type MC cable shall be permitted within 3.0 m (10 ft) of grade level where not exposed to physical damage or where protected in accordance with 300.5(D).

230.51 Mounting Supports. Cables or individual open service conductors shall be supported as specified in 230.51(A), (B), or (C).

(A) Service Cables. Service cables shall be supported by straps or other approved means within 300 mm (12 in.) of every service head, gooseneck, or connection to a raceway or enclosure and at intervals not exceeding 750 mm (30 in.).

(B) Other Cables. Cables that are not approved for mounting in contact with a building or other structure shall be mounted on insulating supports installed at intervals not exceeding 4.5 m (15 ft) and in a manner that maintains a clearance of not less than 50 mm (2 in.) from the surface over which they pass.

(C) Individual Open Conductors. Individual open conductors shall be installed in accordance with Table 230.51(C). Where exposed to the weather, the conductors shall be mounted on insulators or on insulating supports attached to racks, brackets, or other approved means. Where not exposed to the weather, the conductors shall be mounted on glass or porcelain knobs.

230.52 Individual Conductors Entering Buildings or Other Structures. Where individual open conductors enter a building or other structure, they shall enter through roof bushings or through the wall in an upward slant through individual, noncombustible, nonabsorbent insulating tubes. Drip loops shall be formed on the conductors before they enter the tubes.

230.53 Raceways to Drain. Where exposed to the weather, raceways enclosing service-entrance conductors shall be raintight and arranged to drain. Where embedded in masonry, raceways shall be arranged to drain.

Exception: As permitted in 348.12(1).

230.54 Overhead Service Locations.

(A) Raintight Service Head. Service raceways shall be equipped with a raintight service head at the point of connection to service-drop conductors.

(B) Service Cable Equipped with Raintight Service Head or Gooseneck. Service cables shall be equipped with a raintight service head.

Exception: Type SE cable shall be permitted to be formed in a gooseneck and taped with a self-sealing weather-resistant thermoplastic.

(C) Service Heads and Goosenecks Above Service-Drop Attachment. Service heads and goosenecks in service-entrance cables shall be located above the point of attachment of the service-drop conductors to the building or other structure.

Exception: Where it is impracticable to locate the service head or gooseneck above the point of attachment, the service head or gooseneck location shall be permitted not farther than 600 mm (24 in.) from the point of attachment.

(D) Secured. Service cables shall be held securely in place.

(E) Separately Bushed Openings. Service heads shall have conductors of different potential brought out through separately bushed openings.

Table 230.51(C) Supports

Maximum Volts	Maximum Distance Between Supports		Minimum Clearance			
			Between Conductors		From Surface	
	m	ft	mm	in.	mm	in.
600	2.7	9	150	6	50	2
600	4.5	15	300	12	50	2
300	1.4	4½	75	3	50	2
600*	1.4*	4½*	65*	2½*	25*	1*

*Where not exposed to weather.

Exception: For jacketed multiconductor service cable without splice.

(F) Drip Loops. Drip loops shall be formed on individual conductors. To prevent the entrance of moisture, service-entrance conductors shall be connected to the service-drop conductors either (1) below the level of the service head or (2) below the level of the termination of the service-entrance cable sheath.

(G) Arranged That Water Will Not Enter Service Raceway or Equipment. Service-drop conductors and service-entrance conductors shall be arranged so that water will not enter service raceway or equipment.

230.56 Service Conductor with the Higher Voltage to Ground. On a 4-wire, delta-connected service where the midpoint of one phase winding is grounded, the service conductor having the higher phase voltage to ground shall be durably and permanently marked by an outer finish that is orange in color, or by other effective means, at each termination or junction point.

V. Service Equipment — General

230.62 Service Equipment — Enclosed or Guarded. Energized parts of service equipment shall be enclosed as specified in 230.62(A) or guarded as specified in 230.62(B).

(A) Enclosed. Energized parts shall be enclosed so that they will not be exposed to accidental contact or shall be guarded as in 230.62(B).

(B) Guarded. Energized parts that are not enclosed shall be installed on a switchboard, panelboard, or control board and guarded in accordance with 110.18 and 110.27. Where energized parts are guarded as provided in 110.27(A)(1) and (A)(2), a means for locking or sealing doors providing access to energized parts shall be provided.

230.66 Marking. Service equipment rated at 600 volts or less shall be marked to identify it as being suitable for use as service equipment. Individual meter socket enclosures shall not be considered service equipment.

VI. Service Equipment — Disconnecting Means

230.70 General. Means shall be provided to disconnect all conductors in a building or other structure from the service-entrance conductors.

(A) Location. The service disconnecting means shall be installed in accordance with 230.70(A)(1), (A)(2), and (A)(3).

(1) Readily Accessible Location. The service disconnecting means shall be installed at a readily accessible location either outside of a building or structure or inside nearest the point of entrance of the service conductors.

(2) Bathrooms. Service disconnecting means shall not be installed in bathrooms.

(3) Remote Control. Where a remote control device(s) is used to actuate the service disconnecting means, the service disconnecting means shall be located in accordance with 230.70(A)(1).

(B) Marking. Each service disconnect shall be permanently marked to identify it as a service disconnect.

(C) Suitable for Use. Each service disconnecting means shall be suitable for the prevailing conditions. Service equipment installed in hazardous (classified) locations shall comply with the requirements of Articles 500 through 517.

230.71 Maximum Number of Disconnects.

(A) General. The service disconnecting means for each service permitted by 230.2, or for each set of service-entrance conductors permitted by 230.40, Exception Nos. 1, 3, 4, or 5, shall consist of not more than six switches or sets of circuit breakers, or a combination of not more than six switches and sets of circuit breakers, mounted in a single enclosure, in a group of separate enclosures, or in or on a switchboard. There shall be not more than six sets of disconnects per service grouped in any one location. For the purpose of this section, disconnecting means used solely for power monitoring equipment, transient voltage surge suppressors, or the control circuit of the ground-fault protection system or power-operable service disconnecting means, installed as part of the listed equipment, shall not be considered a service disconnecting means.

(B) Single-Pole Units. Two or three single-pole switches or breakers, capable of individual operation, shall be permitted on multiwire circuits, one pole for each ungrounded conductor, as one multipole disconnect, provided they are equipped with handle ties or a master handle to disconnect all conductors of the service with no more than six operations of the hand.

FPN: See 408.36(A) for service equipment in panelboards, and see 430.95 for service equipment in motor control centers.

230.72 Grouping of Disconnects.

(A) General. The two to six disconnects as permitted in 230.71 shall be grouped. Each disconnect shall be marked to indicate the load served.

Exception: One of the two to six service disconnecting means permitted in 230.71, where used only for a water pump also intended to provide fire protection, shall be permitted to be located remote from the other disconnecting means.

(B)) Additional Service Disconnecting Means. The one or more additional service disconnecting means for fire pumps, emergency systems, legally required standby, or optional standby services permitted by 230.2 shall be installed remote from the one to six service disconnecting means for normal service to minimize the possibility of simultaneous interruption of supply.

(C) Access to Occupants. In a multiple-occupancy building, each occupant shall have access to the occupant's service disconnecting means.

Exception: In a multiple-occupancy building where electric service and electrical maintenance are provided by the building management and where these are under continuous building management supervision, the service disconnecting means supplying more than one occupancy shall be permitted to be accessible to authorized management personnel only.

230.74 Simultaneous Opening of Poles. Each service disconnect shall simultaneously disconnect all ungrounded service conductors that it controls from the premises wiring system.

230.75 Disconnection of Grounded Conductor. Where the service disconnecting means does not disconnect the grounded conductor from the premises wiring, other means shall be provided for this purpose in the service equipment. A terminal or bus to which all grounded conductors can be attached by means of pressure connectors shall be permitted for this purpose. In a multisection switchboard, disconnects for the grounded conductor shall be permitted to be in any section of the switchboard, provided any such switchboard section is marked.

230.76 Manually or Power Operable. The service disconnecting means for ungrounded service conductors shall consist of one of the following:

(1) A manually operable switch or circuit breaker equipped with a handle or other suitable operating means

(2) A power-operated switch or circuit breaker, provided the switch or circuit breaker can be opened by hand in the event of a power supply failure

230.77 Indicating. The service disconnecting means shall plainly indicate whether it is in the open or closed position.

230.79 Rating of Service Disconnecting Means. The service disconnecting means shall have a rating not less than the load to be carried, determined in accordance with Article 220. In no case shall the rating be lower than specified in 230.79(A), (B), (C), or (D).

(A) One-Circuit Installation. For installations to supply only limited loads of a single branch circuit, the service disconnecting means shall have a rating of not less than 15 amperes.

(B) Two-Circuit Installations. For installations consisting of not more than two 2-wire branch circuits, the service disconnecting means shall have a rating of not less than 30 amperes.

(C) One-Family Dwelling. For a one-family dwelling, the service disconnecting means shall have a rating of not less than 100 amperes, 3-wire.

(D) All Others. For all other installations, the service disconnecting means shall have a rating of not less than 60 amperes.

230.80 Combined Rating of Disconnects. Where the service disconnecting means consists of more than one switch or circuit breaker, as permitted by 230.71, the combined ratings of all the switches or circuit breakers used shall not be less than the rating required by 230.79.

230.81 Connection to Terminals. The service conductors shall be connected to the service disconnecting means by pressure connectors, clamps, or other approved means. Connections that depend on solder shall not be used.

230.82 Equipment Connected to the Supply Side of Service Disconnect. Only the following equipment shall be permitted to be connected to the supply side of the service disconnecting means:

(1) Cable limiters or other current-limiting devices

(2) Meters and meter sockets nominally rated not in excess of 600 volts, provided all metal housings and service enclosures are grounded

(3) Meter disconnect switches nominally rated not in excess of 600 volts that have a short-circuit current rating equal to or greater than the available short circuit current, provided all metal housings and service enclosures are grounded

(4) Instrument transformers (current and voltage), impedance shunts, load management devices, and arresters

(5) Taps used only to supply load management devices, circuits for standby power systems, fire pump equipment, and fire and sprinkler alarms, if provided with service equipment and installed in accordance with requirements for service-entrance conductors

(6) Solar photovoltaic systems, fuel cell systems, or interconnected electric power production sources

(7) Control circuits for power-operable service disconnecting means, if suitable overcurrent protection and disconnecting means are provided

(8) Ground-fault protection systems or transient voltage surge suppressors, where installed as part of listed equipment, if suitable overcurrent protection and disconnecting means are provided

VII. Service Equipment — Overcurrent Protection

230.90 Where Required. Each ungrounded service conductor shall have overload protection.

(A) Ungrounded Conductor. Such protection shall be provided by an overcurrent device in series with each ungrounded service conductor that has a rating or setting not higher than the allowable ampacity of the conductor. A set of fuses shall be considered all the fuses required to protect all the ungrounded conductors of a circuit. Single-pole circuit breakers, grouped in accordance with 230.71(B), shall be considered as one protective device.

Exception No. 1: For motor-starting currents, ratings that conform with 430.52, 430.62, and 430.63 shall be permitted.

Exception No. 2: Fuses and circuit breakers with a rating or setting that conforms with 240.4(B) or (C) and 240.6 shall be permitted.

Exception No. 3: Two to six circuit breakers or sets of fuses shall be permitted as the overcurrent device to provide the overload protection. The sum of the ratings of the circuit breakers or fuses shall be permitted to exceed the ampacity of the service conductors, provided the calculated load does not exceed the ampacity of the service conductors.

Exception No. 4: Overload protection for fire pump supply conductors shall conform with 695.4(B)(1).

Exception No. 5: Overload protection for 120/240-volt, 3-wire, single-phase dwelling services shall be permitted in accordance with the requirements of 310.15(B)(6).

(B) Not in Grounded Conductor. No overcurrent device shall be inserted in a grounded service conductor except a circuit breaker that simultaneously opens all conductors of the circuit.

230.91 Location. The service overcurrent device shall be an integral part of the service disconnecting means or shall be located immediately adjacent thereto.

230.92 Locked Service Overcurrent Devices. Where the service overcurrent devices are locked or sealed or are not readily accessible to the occupant, branch-circuit overcurrent devices shall be installed on the load side, shall be mounted in a readily accessible location, and shall be of lower ampere rating than the service overcurrent device.

230.93 Protection of Specific Circuits. Where necessary to prevent tampering, an automatic overcurrent device that protects service conductors supplying only a specific load, such as a water heater, shall be permitted to be locked or sealed where located so as to be accessible.

230.94 Relative Location of Overcurrent Device and Other Service Equipment. The overcurrent device shall protect all circuits and devices.

Exception No. 1: The service switch shall be permitted on the supply side.

Exception No. 2: High-impedance shunt circuits, surge arresters, surge-protective capacitors, and instrument transformers (current and voltage) shall be permitted to be connected and installed on the supply side of the service disconnecting means as permitted in 230.82.

Exception No. 3: Circuits for load management devices shall be permitted to be connected on the supply side of the service overcurrent device where separately provided with overcurrent protection.

Exception No. 4: Circuits used only for the operation of fire alarm, other protective signaling systems, or the supply to fire pump equipment shall be permitted to be connected on the supply side of the service overcurrent device where separately provided with overcurrent protection.

Exception No. 5: Meters nominally rated not in excess of 600 volts shall be permitted, provided all metal housings and service enclosures are grounded.

Exception No. 6: Where service equipment is power operable, the control circuit shall be permitted to be connected ahead of the service equipment if suitable overcurrent protection and disconnecting means are provided.

230.95 Ground-Fault Protection of Equipment. Ground-fault protection of equipment shall be provided for solidly grounded wye electrical services of more than 150 volts to ground but not exceeding 600 volts phase-to-phase for each service disconnect rated 1000 amperes or more. The grounded conductor for the solidly grounded wye system shall be connected directly to ground without inserting any resistor or impedance device.

The rating of the service disconnect shall be considered to be the rating of the largest fuse that can be installed or the highest continuous current trip setting for which the actual overcurrent device installed in a circuit breaker is rated or can be adjusted.

Exception No. 1: The ground-fault protection provisions of this section shall not apply to a service disconnect for a continuous industrial process where a nonorderly shutdown will introduce additional or increased hazards.

Exception No. 2: The ground-fault protection provisions of this section shall not apply to fire pumps.

(A) Setting. The ground-fault protection system shall operate to cause the service disconnect to open all ungrounded conductors of the faulted circuit. The maximum setting of the ground-fault protection shall be 1200 amperes, and the maximum time delay shall be one second for ground-fault currents equal to or greater than 3000 amperes.

(B) Fuses. If a switch and fuse combination is used, the fuses employed shall be capable of interrupting any current higher than the interrupting capacity of the switch during a time that the ground-fault protective system will not cause the switch to open.

(C) Performance Testing. The ground-fault protection system shall be performance tested when first installed on site. The test shall be conducted in accordance with instructions that shall be provided with the equipment. A written record of this test shall be made and shall be available to the authority having jurisdiction.

> FPN No. 1: Ground-fault protection that functions to open the service disconnect affords no protection from faults on the line side of the protective element. It serves only to limit damage to conductors and equipment on the load side in the event of an arcing ground fault on the load side of the protective element.

> FPN No. 2: This added protective equipment at the service equipment may make it necessary to review the overall wiring system for proper selective overcurrent protection coordination. Additional installations of ground-fault protective equipment may be needed on feeders and branch circuits where maximum continuity of electrical service is necessary.

> FPN No. 3: Where ground-fault protection is provided for the service disconnect and interconnection is made with another supply system by a transfer device, means or devices may be needed to ensure proper ground-fault sensing by the ground-fault protection equipment.

> FPN No. 4: See 517.17(A) for information on where an additional step of ground fault protection is required for hospitals and other buildings with critical areas or life support equipment.

VIII. Services Exceeding 600 Volts, Nominal

230.200 General. Service conductors and equipment used on circuits exceeding 600 volts, nominal, shall comply with all the applicable provisions of the preceding sections of this article and with the following sections that supplement or modify the preceding sections. In no case shall the provisions of Part VIII apply to equipment on the supply side of the service point.

> FPN: For clearances of conductors of over 600 volts, nominal, see ANSI C2-2002, *National Electrical Safety Code*.

230.202 Service-Entrance Conductors. Service-entrance conductors to buildings or enclosures shall be installed to conform to 230.202(A) and (B).

(A) Conductor Size. Service-entrance conductors shall not be smaller than 6 AWG unless in multiconductor cable. Multiconductor cable shall not be smaller than 8 AWG.

(B) Wiring Methods. Service-entrance conductors shall be installed by one of the wiring methods covered in 300.37 and 300.50.

230.204 Isolating Switches.

(A) Where Required. Where oil switches or air, oil, vacuum, or sulfur hexafluoride circuit breakers constitute the service disconnecting means, an isolating switch with visible break contacts shall be installed on the supply side of the disconnecting means and all associated service equipment.

Exception: An isolating switch shall not be required where the circuit breaker or switch is mounted on removable truck panels or metal-enclosed switchgear units where both of the following conditions apply:

(1) Cannot be opened unless the circuit is disconnected.
(2) Where all energized parts are automatically disconnected when the circuit breaker or switch is removed from the normal operating position.

(B) Fuses as Isolating Switch. Where fuses are of the type that can be operated as a disconnecting switch, a set of such fuses shall be permitted as the isolating switch.

(C) Accessible to Qualified Persons Only. The isolating switch shall be accessible to qualified persons only.

(D) Grounding Connection. Isolating switches shall be provided with a means for readily connecting the load side conductors to ground when disconnected from the source of supply.

A means for grounding the load side conductors shall not be required for any duplicate isolating switch installed and maintained by the electric supply company.

230.205 Disconnecting Means.

(A) Location. The service disconnecting means shall be located in accordance with 230.70.

(B) Type. Each service disconnect shall simultaneously disconnect all ungrounded service conductors that it controls and shall have a fault-closing rating that is not less than the maximum short-circuit current available at its supply terminals.

Where fused switches or separately mounted fuses are installed, the fuse characteristics shall be permitted to contribute to the fault-closing rating of the disconnecting means.

(C) Remote Control. For multibuilding, industrial installations under single management, the service disconnecting means shall be permitted to be located at a separate building or structure. In such cases, the service disconnecting means shall be permitted to be electrically operated by a readily accessible, remote-control device.

230.206 Overcurrent Devices as Disconnecting Means. Where the circuit breaker or alternative for it, as specified in 230.208 for service overcurrent devices, meets the requirements specified in 230.205, they shall constitute the service disconnecting means.

230.208 Protection Requirements. A short-circuit protective device shall be provided on the load side of, or as an integral part of, the service disconnect, and shall protect all ungrounded conductors that it supplies. The protective device shall be capable of detecting and interrupting all values of current, in excess of its trip setting or melting point, that can occur at its location. A fuse rated in continuous amperes not to exceed three times the ampacity of the conductor, or a circuit breaker with a trip setting of not more than six times the ampacity of the conductors, shall be considered as providing the required short-circuit protection.

FPN: See Table 310.67 through Table 310.86 for ampacities of conductors rated 2001 volts and above.

Overcurrent devices shall conform to 230.208(A) and (B).

(A) Equipment Type. Equipment used to protect service-entrance conductors shall meet the requirements of Article 490, Part II.

(B) Enclosed Overcurrent Devices. The restriction to 80 percent of the rating for an enclosed overcurrent device for continuous loads shall not apply to overcurrent devices installed in systems operating at over 600 volts.

230.209 Surge Arresters (Lightning Arresters). Surge arresters installed in accordance with the requirements of Article 280 shall be permitted on each ungrounded overhead service conductor.

230.210 Service Equipment — General Provisions. Service equipment, including instrument transformers, shall conform to Article 490, Part I.

230.211 Metal-Enclosed Switchgear. Metal-enclosed switchgear shall consist of a substantial metal structure and a sheet metal enclosure. Where installed over a combustible floor, suitable protection thereto shall be provided.

230.212 Over 35,000 Volts. Where the voltage exceeds 35,000 volts between conductors that enter a building, they shall terminate in a metal-enclosed switchgear compartment or a vault conforming to the requirements of 450.41 through 450.48.

ARTICLE 240
Overcurrent Protection

I. General

240.1 Scope. Parts I through VII of this article provide the general requirements for overcurrent protection and overcurrent protective devices not more than 600 volts, nominal. Part VIII covers overcurrent protection for those portions of supervised industrial installations operating at voltages of not more than 600 volts, nominal. Part IX covers overcurrent protection over 600 volts, nominal.

FPN: Overcurrent protection for conductors and equipment is provided to open the circuit if the current reaches a value that will cause an excessive or dangerous temperature in conductors or conductor insulation. See also 110.9 for requirements for interrupting ratings and 110.10 for requirements for protection against fault currents.

240.2 Definitions.

Current-Limiting Overcurrent Protective Device. A device that, when interrupting currents in its current-limiting range, reduces the current flowing in the faulted circuit to a magnitude substantially less than that obtainable in the same circuit if the device were replaced with a solid conductor having comparable impedance.

Supervised Industrial Installation. For the purposes of Part VIII, the industrial portions of a facility where all of the following conditions are met:

(1) Conditions of maintenance and engineering supervision ensure that only qualified persons monitor and service the system.

(2) The premises wiring system has 2500 kVA or greater of load used in industrial process(es), manufacturing activities, or both, as calculated in accordance with Article 220.

(3) The premises has at least one service or feeder that is more than 150 volts to ground and more than 300 volts phase-to-phase.

This definition excludes installations in buildings used by the industrial facility for offices, warehouses, garages, machine shops, and recreational facilities that are not an integral part of the industrial plant, substation, or control center.

Tap Conductors. As used in this article, a tap conductor is defined as a conductor, other than a service conductor, that has overcurrent protection ahead of its point of supply that exceeds the value permitted for similar conductors that are protected as described elsewhere in 240.4.

240.3 Other Articles. Equipment shall be protected against overcurrent in accordance with the article in this *Code* that covers the type of equipment specified in Table 240.3.

Table 240.3 Other Articles

Equipment	Article
Air-conditioning and refrigerating equipment	440
Appliances	422
Assembly occupancies	518
Audio signal processing, amplification, and reproduction equipment	640
Branch circuits	210
Busways	368
Capacitors	460
Class 1, Class 2, and Class 3 remote-control, signaling, and power-limited circuits	725
Closed-loop and programmed power distribution	780
Cranes and hoists	610
Electric signs and outline lighting	600
Electric welders	630
Electrolytic cells	668
Elevators, dumbwaiters, escalators, moving walks, wheelchair lifts, and stairway chair lifts	620
Emergency systems	700
Fire alarm systems	760
Fire pumps	695
Fixed electric heating equipment for pipelines and vessels	427
Fixed electric space-heating equipment	424
Fixed outdoor electric deicing and snow-melting equipment	426
Generators	445
Health care facilities	517
Induction and dielectric heating equipment	665
Industrial machinery	670
Luminaires (lighting fixtures), lampholders, and lamps	410
Motion picture and television studios and similar locations	530
Motors, motor circuits, and controllers	430
Phase converters	455
Pipe organs	650
Receptacles	406
Services	230
Solar photovoltaic systems	690
Switchboards and panelboards	408
Theaters, audience areas of motion picture and television studios, and similar locations	520
Transformers and transformer vaults	450
X-ray equipment	660

240.4 Protection of Conductors. Conductors, other than flexible cords, flexible cables, and fixture wires, shall be protected against overcurrent in accordance with their ampacities specified in 310.15, unless otherwise permitted or required in 240.4(A) through (G).

(A) Power Loss Hazard. Conductor overload protection shall not be required where the interruption of the circuit would create a hazard, such as in a material-handling magnet circuit or fire pump circuit. Short-circuit protection shall be provided.

FPN: See NFPA 20-2003, *Standard for the Installation of Stationary Pumps for Fire Protection.*

(B) Devices Rated 800 Amperes or Less. The next higher standard overcurrent device rating (above the ampacity of the conductors being protected) shall be permitted to be used, provided all of the following conditions are met:

(1) The conductors being protected are not part of a multioutlet branch circuit supplying receptacles for cord-and-plug-connected portable loads.

(2) The ampacity of the conductors does not correspond with the standard ampere rating of a fuse or a circuit breaker without overload trip adjustments above its rating (but that shall be permitted to have other trip or rating adjustments).

(3) The next higher standard rating selected does not exceed 800 amperes.

(C) Devices Rated Over 800 Amperes. Where the overcurrent device is rated over 800 amperes, the ampacity of the conductors it protects shall be equal to or greater than the rating of the overcurrent device defined in 240.6.

(D) Small Conductors. Unless specifically permitted in 240.4(E) or 240.4(G), the overcurrent protection shall not exceed 15 amperes for 14 AWG, 20 amperes for 12 AWG, and 30 amperes for 10 AWG copper; or 15 amperes for 12 AWG and 25 amperes for 10 AWG aluminum and copper-clad aluminum after any correction factors for ambient temperature and number of conductors have been applied.

(E) Tap Conductors. Tap conductors shall be permitted to be protected against overcurrent in accordance with the following:

(1) 210.19(A)(3) and (A)(4) Household Ranges and Cooking Appliances and Other Loads

(2) 240.5(B)(2) Fixture Wire

(3) 240.21 Location in Circuit

(4) 368.17(B) Reduction in Ampacity Size of Busway

(5) 368.17(C) Feeder or Branch Circuits (busway taps)

(6) 430.53(D) Single Motor Taps

(F) Transformer Secondary Conductors. Single-phase (other than 2-wire) and multiphase (other than delta-delta, 3-wire) transformer secondary conductors shall not be considered to be protected by the primary overcurrent protective device. Conductors supplied by the secondary side of a single-phase transformer having a 2-wire (single-voltage) secondary, or a three-phase, delta-delta connected transformer having a 3-wire (single-voltage) secondary, shall be permitted to be protected by overcurrent protection provided on the primary (supply) side of the transformer, provided this protection is in accordance with 450.3 and does not exceed the value determined by multiplying the secondary conductor ampacity by the secondary to primary transformer voltage ratio.

(G) Overcurrent Protection for Specific Conductor Applications. Overcurrent protection for the specific conductors shall be permitted to be provided as referenced in Table 240.4(G).

Table 240.4(G) Specific Conductor Applications

Conductor	Article	Section
Air-conditioning and refrigeration equipment circuit conductors	440, Parts III, VI	
Capacitor circuit conductors	460	460.8(B) and 460.25(A)–(D)
Control and instrumentation circuit conductors (Type ITC)	727	727.9
Electric welder circuit conductors	630	630.12 and 630.32
Fire alarm system circuit conductors	760	760.23, 760.24, 760.41, and Chapter 9, Tables 12(A) and 12(B)
Motor-operated appliance circuit conductors	422, Part II	
Motor and motor-control circuit conductors	430, Parts III, IV, V, VI, VII	
Phase converter supply conductors	455	455.7
Remote-control, signaling, and power-limited circuit conductors	725	725.23, 725.24, 725.41, and Chapter 9, Tables 11(A) and 11(B)
Secondary tie conductors	450	450.6

240.5 Protection of Flexible Cords, Flexible Cables, and Fixture Wires. Flexible cord and flexible cable, including tinsel cord and extension cords, and fixture wires shall be protected against overcurrent by either 240.5(A) or (B).

(A) Ampacities. Flexible cord and flexible cable shall be protected by an overcurrent device in accordance with their ampacity as specified in Table 400.5(A) and Table 400.5(B). Fixture wire shall be protected against overcurrent in accordance with its ampacity as specified in Table 402.5.

Supplementary overcurrent protection, as in 240.10, shall be permitted to be an acceptable means for providing this protection.

(B) Branch Circuit Overcurrent Device. Flexible cord shall be protected where supplied by a branch circuit in accordance with one of the methods described in 240.5(B)(1), (B)(2), (B)(3), or (B)(4).

(1) Supply Cord of Listed Appliance or Portable Lamps. Where flexible cord or tinsel cord is approved for and used with a specific listed appliance or portable lamp, it shall be considered to be protected when applied within the appliance or portable lamp listing requirements.

(2) Fixture Wire. Fixture wire shall be permitted to be tapped to the branch circuit conductor of a branch circuit in accordance with the following:

(1) 20-ampere circuits — 18 AWG, up to 15 m (50 ft) of run length

(2) 20-ampere circuits — 16 AWG, up to 30 m (100 ft) of run length

(3) 20-ampere circuits — 14 AWG and larger

(4) 30-ampere circuits — 14 AWG and larger

(5) 40-ampere circuits — 12 AWG and larger

(6) 50-ampere circuits — 12 AWG and larger

(3) Extension Cord Sets. Flexible cord used in listed extension cord sets shall be considered to be protected when applied within the extension cord listing requirements.

(4) Field Assembled Extension Cord Sets. Flexible cord used in extension cords made with separately listed and installed components shall be permitted to be supplied by a branch circuit in accordance with the following:

20-ampere circuits — 16 AWG and larger

240.6 Standard Ampere Ratings.

(A) Fuses and Fixed-Trip Circuit Breakers. The standard ampere ratings for fuses and inverse time circuit breakers shall be considered 15, 20, 25, 30, 35, 40, 45, 50, 60, 70, 80, 90, 100, 110, 125, 150, 175, 200, 225, 250, 300, 350, 400, 450, 500, 600, 700, 800, 1000, 1200, 1600, 2000, 2500, 3000, 4000, 5000, and 6000 amperes. Additional standard ampere ratings for fuses shall be 1, 3, 6, 10, and 601. The use of fuses and inverse time circuit breakers with nonstandard ampere ratings shall be permitted.

(B) Adjustable-Trip Circuit Breakers. The rating of adjustable-trip circuit breakers having external means for adjusting the current setting (long-time pickup setting), not meeting the requirements of 240.6(C), shall be the maximum setting possible.

(C) Restricted Access Adjustable-Trip Circuit Breakers. A circuit breaker(s) that has restricted access to the adjusting means shall be permitted to have an ampere rating(s) that is equal to the adjusted current setting (long-time pickup setting). Restricted access shall be defined as located behind one of the following:

(1) Removable and sealable covers over the adjusting means

(2) Bolted equipment enclosure doors

(3) Locked doors accessible only to qualified personnel

240.8 Fuses or Circuit Breakers in Parallel. Fuses and circuit breakers shall be permitted to be connected in parallel where they are factory assembled in parallel and listed as a unit. Individual fuses, circuit breakers, or combinations thereof shall not otherwise be connected in parallel.

240.9 Thermal Devices. Thermal relays and other devices not designed to open short circuits or ground faults shall not be used for the protection of conductors against overcurrent due to short circuits or ground faults, but the use of such devices shall be permitted to protect motor branch-circuit conductors from overload if protected in accordance with 430.40.

240.10 Supplementary Overcurrent Protection. Where supplementary overcurrent protection is used for luminaires (lighting fixtures), appliances, and other equipment or for internal circuits and components of equipment, it shall not be used as a substitute for required branch-circuit overcurrent devices or in place of the required branch-circuit protection. Supplementary overcurrent devices shall not be required to be readily accessible.

240.12 Electrical System Coordination. Where an orderly shutdown is required to minimize the hazard(s) to personnel and equipment, a system of coordination based on the following two conditions shall be permitted:

(1) Coordinated short-circuit protection

(2) Overload indication based on monitoring systems or devices

> FPN: The monitoring system may cause the condition to go to alarm, allowing corrective action or an orderly shutdown, thereby minimizing personnel hazard and equipment damage.

240.13 Ground-Fault Protection of Equipment. Ground-fault protection of equipment shall be provided in accordance with the provisions of 230.95 for solidly grounded wye electrical systems of more than 150 volts to ground but not exceeding 600 volts phase-to-phase for each individual device used as a building or structure main disconnecting means rated 1000 amperes or more.

The provisions of this section shall not apply to the disconnecting means for the following:

(1) Continuous industrial processes where a nonorderly shutdown will introduce additional or increased hazards

(2) Installations where ground-fault protection is provided by other requirements for services or feeders

(3) Fire pumps

II. Location

240.20 Ungrounded Conductors.

(A) Overcurrent Device Required. A fuse or an overcurrent trip unit of a circuit breaker shall be connected in series with each ungrounded conductor. A combination of a current transformer and overcurrent relay shall be considered equivalent to an overcurrent trip unit.

> FPN: For motor circuits, see Parts III, IV, V, and XI of Article 430.

(B) Circuit Breaker as Overcurrent Device. Circuit breakers shall open all ungrounded conductors of the circuit both manually and automatically unless otherwise permitted in 240.20(B)(1), (B)(2), and (B)(3).

(1) Multiwire Branch Circuit. Except where limited by 210.4(B), individual single-pole circuit breakers, with or without identified handle ties, shall be permitted as the protection for each ungrounded conductor of multiwire branch circuits that serve only single-phase line-to-neutral loads.

(2) Grounded Single-Phase and 3-Wire dc Circuits. In grounded systems, individual single-pole circuit breakers with identified handle ties shall be permitted as the protection for each ungrounded conductor for line-to-line connected loads for single-phase circuits or 3-wire, direct-current circuits.

(3) 3-Phase and 2-Phase Systems. For line-to-line loads in 4-wire, 3-phase systems or 5-wire, 2-phase systems having a grounded neutral and no conductor operating at a voltage greater than permitted in 210.6, individual single-pole circuit breakers with identified handle ties shall be permitted as the protection for each ungrounded conductor.

(C) Closed-Loop Power Distribution Systems. Listed devices that provide equivalent overcurrent protection in closed-loop power distribution systems shall be permitted as a substitute for fuses or circuit breakers.

240.21 Location in Circuit. Overcurrent protection shall be provided in each ungrounded circuit conductor and shall be located at the point where the conductors receive their supply except as specified in 240.21(A) through (G). No conductor supplied under the provisions of 240.21(A) through (G) shall supply another conductor under those provisions, except through an overcurrent protective device meeting the requirements of 240.4.

(A) Branch-Circuit Conductors. Branch-circuit tap conductors meeting the requirements specified in 210.19 shall be permitted to have overcurrent protection located as specified in that section.

(B) Feeder Taps. Conductors shall be permitted to be tapped, without overcurrent protection at the tap, to a feeder as specified in 240.21(B)(1) through (B)(5). The provisions of 240.4(B) shall not be permitted for tap conductors.

(1) Taps Not Over 3 m (10 ft) Long. Where the length of the tap conductors does not exceed 3 m (10 ft) and the tap conductors comply with all of the following:

(1) The ampacity of the tap conductors is

   a. Not less than the combined calculated loads on the circuits supplied by the tap conductors, and

   b. Not less than the rating of the device supplied by the tap conductors or not less than the rating of the overcurrent-protective device at the termination of the tap conductors.

(2) The tap conductors do not extend beyond the switchboard, panelboard, disconnecting means, or control devices they supply.

(3) Except at the point of connection to the feeder, the tap conductors are enclosed in a raceway, which shall extend from the tap to the enclosure of an enclosed switchboard, panelboard, or control devices, or to the back of an open switchboard.

(4) For field installations where the tap conductors leave the enclosure or vault in which the tap is made, the rating of the overcurrent device on the line side of the tap conductors shall not exceed 10 times the ampacity of the tap conductor.

FPN: For overcurrent protection requirements for lighting and appliance branch-circuit panelboards and certain power panelboards, see 408.36(A), (B), and (E).

(2) Taps Not Over 7.5 m (25 ft) Long. Where the length of the tap conductors does not exceed 7.5 m (25 ft) and the tap conductors comply with all the following:

(1) The ampacity of the tap conductors is not less than one-third of the rating of the overcurrent device protecting the feeder conductors.

(2) The tap conductors terminate in a single circuit breaker or a single set of fuses that will limit the load to the ampacity of the tap conductors. This device shall be permitted to supply any number of additional overcurrent devices on its load side.

(3) The tap conductors are protected from physical damage by being enclosed in an approved raceway or by other approved means.

(3) Taps Supplying a Transformer [Primary Plus Secondary Not Over 7.5 m (25 ft) Long]. Where the tap conductors supply a transformer and comply with all the following conditions:

(1) The conductors supplying the primary of a transformer have an ampacity at least one-third the rating of the overcurrent device protecting the feeder conductors.

(2) The conductors supplied by the secondary of the transformer shall have an ampacity that is not less than the value of the primary-to-secondary voltage ratio multiplied by one-third of the rating of the overcurrent device protecting the feeder conductors.

(3) The total length of one primary plus one secondary conductor, excluding any portion of the primary conductor that is protected at its ampacity, is not over 7.5 m (25 ft).

(4) The primary and secondary conductors are protected from physical damage by being enclosed in an approved raceway or by other approved means.

(5) The secondary conductors terminate in a single circuit breaker or set of fuses that limit the load current to not more than the conductor ampacity that is permitted by 310.15.

(4) Taps Over 7.5 m (25 ft) Long. Where the feeder is in a high bay manufacturing building over 11 m (35 ft) high at walls and the installation complies with all the following conditions:

(1) Conditions of maintenance and supervision ensure that only qualified persons service the systems.

(2) The tap conductors are not over 7.5 m (25 ft) long horizontally and not over 30 m (100 ft) total length.

(3) The ampacity of the tap conductors is not less than one-third the rating of the overcurrent device protecting the feeder conductors.

(4) The tap conductors terminate at a single circuit breaker or a single set of fuses that limit the load to the ampacity of the tap conductors. This single overcurrent device shall be permitted to supply any number of additional overcurrent devices on its load side.

(5) The tap conductors are protected from physical damage by being enclosed in an approved raceway or by other approved means.

(6) The tap conductors are continuous from end-to-end and contain no splices.

(7) The tap conductors are sized 6 AWG copper or 4 AWG aluminum or larger.

(8) The tap conductors do not penetrate walls, floors, or ceilings.

(9) The tap is made no less than 9 m (30 ft) from the floor.

(5) Outside Taps of Unlimited Length. Where the conductors are located outdoors of a building or structure, except at the point of load termination, and comply with all of the following conditions:

(1) The conductors are protected from physical damage in an approved manner.

(2) The conductors terminate at a single circuit breaker or a single set of fuses that limit the load to the ampacity of the conductors. This single overcurrent device shall be permitted to supply any number of additional overcurrent devices on its load side.

(3) The overcurrent device for the conductors is an integral part of a disconnecting means or shall be located immediately adjacent thereto.

(4) The disconnecting means for the conductors is installed at a readily accessible location complying with one of the following:

a. Outside of a building or structure

b. Inside, nearest the point of entrance of the conductors

c. Where installed in accordance with 230.6, nearest the point of entrance of the conductors

(C) Transformer Secondary Conductors. Each set of conductors feeding separate loads shall be permitted to be connected to a transformer secondary, without overcurrent protection at the secondary, as specified in 240.21(C)(1) through (C)(6). The provisions of 240.4(B) shall not be permitted for transformer secondary conductors.

FPN: For overcurrent protection requirements for transformers, see 450.3.

(1) Protection by Primary Overcurrent Device. Conductors supplied by the secondary side of a single-phase transformer having a 2-wire (single-voltage) secondary, or a three-phase, delta-delta connected transformer having a 3-wire (single-voltage) secondary, shall be permitted to be protected by overcurrent protection provided on the primary (supply) side of the transformer, provided this protection is in accordance with 450.3 and does not exceed the value determined by multiplying the secondary conductor ampacity by the secondary to primary transformer voltage ratio.

Single-phase (other than 2-wire) and multiphase (other than delta-delta, 3-wire) transformer secondary conductors are not considered to be protected by the primary overcurrent protective device.

(2) Transformer Secondary Conductors Not Over 3 m (10 ft) Long. Where the length of secondary conductor does not exceed 3 m (10 ft) and complies with all of the following:

(1) The ampacity of the secondary conductors is

a. Not less than the combined calculated loads on the circuits supplied by the secondary conductors, and

b. Not less than the rating of the device supplied by the secondary conductors or not less than the rating of the overcurrent-protective device at the termination of the secondary conductors, and

c. Not less than one-tenth of the rating of the overcurrent device protecting the primary of the transformer, multiplied by the primary to secondary transformer voltage ratio

(2) The secondary conductors do not extend beyond the switchboard, panelboard, disconnecting means, or control devices they supply.

(3) The secondary conductors are enclosed in a raceway, which shall extend from the transformer to the enclosure of an enclosed switchboard, panelboard, or control devices or to the back of an open switchboard.

FPN: For overcurrent protection requirements for lighting and appliance branch-circuit panelboards and certain power panelboards, see 408.36(A), (B), and (E).

(3) Industrial Installation Secondary Conductors Not Over 7.5 m (25 ft) Long. For industrial installations only, where the length of the secondary conductors does not exceed 7.5 m (25 ft) and complies with all of the following:

(1) The ampacity of the secondary conductors is not less than the secondary current rating of the transformer, and the sum of the ratings of the overcurrent devices does not exceed the ampacity of the secondary conductors.

(2) All overcurrent devices are grouped.

(3) The secondary conductors are protected from physical damage by being enclosed in an approved raceway or by other approved means.

(4) Outside Secondary Conductors. Where the conductors are located outdoors of a building or structure, except at the point of load termination, and comply with all of the following conditions:

(1) The conductors are protected from physical damage in an approved manner.

(2) The conductors terminate at a single circuit breaker or a single set of fuses that limit the load to the ampacity of the conductors. This single overcurrent device shall be permitted to supply any number of additional overcurrent devices on its load side.

(3) The overcurrent device for the conductors is an integral part of a disconnecting means or shall be located immediately adjacent thereto.

(4) The disconnecting means for the conductors is installed at a readily accessible location complying with one of the following:

a. Outside of a building or structure

b. Inside, nearest the point of entrance of the conductors

c. Where installed in accordance with 230.6, nearest the point of entrance of the conductors

(5) Secondary Conductors from a Feeder Tapped Transformer. Transformer secondary conductors installed in accordance with 240.21(B)(3) shall be permitted to have overcurrent protection as specified in that section.

(6) Secondary Conductors Not Over 7.5 m (25 ft) Long. Where the length of secondary conductor does not exceed 7.5 m (25 ft) and complies with all of the following:

(1) The secondary conductors shall have an ampacity that is not less than the value of the primary-to-secondary voltage ratio multiplied by one-third of the rating of the overcurrent device protecting the primary of the transformer.

(2) The secondary conductors terminate in a single circuit breaker or set of fuses that limit the load current to not more than the conductor ampacity that is permitted by 310.15.

(3) The secondary conductors are protected from physical damage by being enclosed in an approved raceway or by other approved means.

(D) Service Conductors. Service-entrance conductors shall be permitted to be protected by overcurrent devices in accordance with 230.91.

(E) Busway Taps. Busways and busway taps shall be permitted to be protected against overcurrent in accordance with 368.17.

(F) Motor Circuit Taps. Motor-feeder and branch-circuit conductors shall be permitted to be protected against overcurrent in accordance with 430.28 and 430.53, respectively.

(G) Conductors from Generator Terminals. Conductors from generator terminals that meet the size requirement in 445.13 shall be permitted to be protected against overload by the generator overload protective device(s) required by 445.12.

240.22 Grounded Conductor. No overcurrent device shall be connected in series with any conductor that is intentionally grounded, unless one of the following two conditions is met:

(1) The overcurrent device opens all conductors of the circuit, including the grounded conductor, and is designed so that no pole can operate independently.

(2) Where required by 430.36 or 430.37 for motor overload protection.

240.23 Change in Size of Grounded Conductor. Where a change occurs in the size of the ungrounded conductor, a similar change shall be permitted to be made in the size of the grounded conductor.

240.24 Location in or on Premises.

(A) Accessibility. Overcurrent devices shall be readily accessible and shall be installed so that the center of the grip of the operating handle of the switch or circuit breaker, when in its highest position, is not more than 2.0 m (6 ft 7 in.) above the floor or working platform unless one of the following applies:

(1) For busways, as provided in 368.17(C).

(2) For supplementary overcurrent protection, as described in 240.10.

(3) For overcurrent devices, as described in 225.40 and 230.92.

(4) For overcurrent devices adjacent to utilization equipment that they supply, access shall be permitted to be by portable means.

(B) Occupancy. Each occupant shall have ready access to all overcurrent devices protecting the conductors supplying that occupancy.

Exception No. 1: Where electric service and electrical maintenance are provided by the building management and where these are under continuous building management supervision, the service overcurrent devices and feeder overcurrent devices supplying more than one occupancy shall be permitted to be accessible to only authorized management personnel in the following:

(1) Multiple-occupancy buildings

(2) Guest rooms or guest suites of hotels and motels that are intended for transient occupancy

Exception No. 2: Where electric service and electrical maintenance are provided by the building management and where these are under continuous building management supervision, the branch circuit overcurrent devices supplying any guest rooms or guest suites shall be permitted to be accessible to only authorized management personnel for guest rooms of hotels and motels that are intended for transient occupancy.

(C) Not Exposed to Physical Damage. Overcurrent devices shall be located where they will not be exposed to physical damage.

FPN: See 110.11, Deteriorating Agents.

(D) Not in Vicinity of Easily Ignitible Material. Overcurrent devices shall not be located in the vicinity of easily ignitible material, such as in clothes closets.

(E) Not Located in Bathrooms. In dwelling units and guest rooms or guest suites of hotels and motels, overcurrent devices, other than supplementary overcurrent protection, shall not be located in bathrooms.

III. Enclosures

240.30 General.

(A) Protection from Physical Damage. Overcurrent devices shall be protected from physical damage by one of the following:

(1) Installation in enclosures, cabinets, cutout boxes, or equipment assemblies

(2) Mounting on open-type switchboards, panelboards, or control boards that are in rooms or enclosures free from dampness and easily ignitible material and are accessible only to qualified personnel

(B) Operating Handle. The operating handle of a circuit breaker shall be permitted to be accessible without opening a door or cover.

240.32 Damp or Wet Locations. Enclosures for overcurrent devices in damp or wet locations shall comply with 312.2(A).

240.33 Vertical Position. Enclosures for overcurrent devices shall be mounted in a vertical position unless that is shown to be impracticable. Circuit breaker enclosures shall be permitted to be installed horizontally where the circuit breaker is installed in accordance with 240.81. Listed busway plug-in units shall be permitted to be mounted in orientations corresponding to the busway mounting position.

IV. Disconnecting and Guarding

240.40 Disconnecting Means for Fuses. Cartridge fuses in circuits of any voltage where accessible to other than qualified persons, and all fuses in circuits over 150 volts to ground, shall be provided with a disconnecting means on their supply side so that each circuit containing fuses can be independently disconnected from the source of power. A current-limiting device without a disconnecting means shall be permitted on the supply side of the service disconnecting means as permitted by 230.82. A single disconnecting means shall be permitted on the supply side of more than one set of fuses as permitted by 430.112, Exception, for group operation of motors and 424.22(C) for fixed electric space-heating equipment.

240.41 Arcing or Suddenly Moving Parts. Arcing or suddenly moving parts shall comply with 240.41(A) and (B).

(A) Location. Fuses and circuit breakers shall be located or shielded so that persons will not be burned or otherwise injured by their operation.

(B) Suddenly Moving Parts. Handles or levers of circuit breakers, and similar parts that may move suddenly in such a way that persons in the vicinity are likely to be injured by being struck by them, shall be guarded or isolated.

V. Plug Fuses, Fuseholders, and Adapters

240.50 General.

(A) Maximum Voltage. Plug fuses shall be permitted to be used in the following circuits:

(1) Circuits not exceeding 125 volts between conductors

(2) Circuits supplied by a system having a grounded neutral where the line-to-neutral voltage does not exceed 150 volts

(B) Marking. Each fuse, fuseholder, and adapter shall be marked with its ampere rating.

(C) Hexagonal Configuration. Plug fuses of 15-ampere and lower rating shall be identified by a hexagonal configuration of the window, cap, or other prominent part to distinguish them from fuses of higher ampere ratings.

(D) No Energized Parts. Plug fuses, fuseholders, and adapters shall have no exposed energized parts after fuses or fuses and adapters have been installed.

(E) Screw Shell. The screw shell of a plug-type fuseholder shall be connected to the load side of the circuit.

240.51 Edison-Base Fuses.

(A) Classification. Plug fuses of the Edison-base type shall be classified at not over 125 volts and 30 amperes and below.

(B) Replacement Only. Plug fuses of the Edison-base type shall be used only for replacements in existing installations where there is no evidence of overfusing or tampering.

240.52 Edison-Base Fuseholders. Fuseholders of the Edison-base type shall be installed only where they are made to accept Type S fuses by the use of adapters.

240.53 Type S Fuses. Type S fuses shall be of the plug type and shall comply with 240.53(A) and (B).

(A) Classification. Type S fuses shall be classified at not over 125 volts and 0 to 15 amperes, 16 to 20 amperes, and 21 to 30 amperes.

(B) Noninterchangeable. Type S fuses of an ampere classification as specified in 240.53(A) shall not be interchangeable with a lower ampere classification. They shall be designed so that they cannot be used in any fuseholder other than a Type S fuseholder or a fuseholder with a Type S adapter inserted.

240.54 Type S Fuses, Adapters, and Fuseholders.

(A) To Fit Edison-Base Fuseholders. Type S adapters shall fit Edison-base fuseholders.

(B) To Fit Type S Fuses Only. Type S fuseholders and adapters shall be designed so that either the fuseholder itself or the fuseholder with a Type S adapter inserted cannot be used for any fuse other than a Type S fuse.

(C) Nonremovable. Type S adapters shall be designed so that once inserted in a fuseholder, they cannot be removed.

(D) Nontamperable. Type S fuses, fuseholders, and adapters shall be designed so that tampering or shunting (bridging) would be difficult.

(E) Interchangeability. Dimensions of Type S fuses, fuseholders, and adapters shall be standardized to permit interchangeability regardless of the manufacturer.

VI. Cartridge Fuses and Fuseholders

240.60 General.

(A) Maximum Voltage — 300-Volt Type. Cartridge fuses and fuseholders of the 300-volt type shall be permitted to be used in the following circuits:

(1) Circuits not exceeding 300 volts between conductors

(2) Single-phase line-to-neutral circuits supplied from a 3-phase, 4-wire, solidly grounded neutral source where the line-to-neutral voltage does not exceed 300 volts

(B) Noninterchangeable — 0–6000-Ampere Cartridge Fuseholders. Fuseholders shall be designed so that it will be difficult to put a fuse of any given class into a fuseholder that is designed for a current lower, or voltage higher, than that of the class to which the fuse belongs. Fuseholders for current-limiting fuses shall not permit insertion of fuses that are not current-limiting.

(C) Marking. Fuses shall be plainly marked, either by printing on the fuse barrel or by a label attached to the barrel showing the following:

(1) Ampere rating

(2) Voltage rating

(3) Interrupting rating where other than 10,000 amperes

(4) Current limiting where applicable

(5) The name or trademark of the manufacturer

The interrupting rating shall not be required to be marked on fuses used for supplementary protection.

(D) Renewable Fuses. Class H cartridge fuses of the renewable type shall only be permitted to be used for replacement in existing installations where there is no evidence of overfusing or tampering.

240.61 Classification. Cartridge fuses and fuseholders shall be classified according to voltage and amperage ranges. Fuses rated 600 volts, nominal, or less shall be permitted to be used for voltages at or below their ratings.

VII. Circuit Breakers

240.80 Method of Operation. Circuit breakers shall be trip free and capable of being closed and opened by manual operation. Their normal method of operation by other than manual means, such as electrical or pneumatic, shall be permitted if means for manual operation are also provided.

240.81 Indicating. Circuit breakers shall clearly indicate whether they are in the open "off" or closed "on" position.

Where circuit breaker handles are operated vertically rather than rotationally or horizontally, the "up" position of the handle shall be the "on" position.

240.82 Nontamperable. A circuit breaker shall be of such design that any alteration of its trip point (calibration) or the time required for its operation requires dismantling of the device or breaking of a seal for other than intended adjustments.

240.83 Marking.

(A) Durable and Visible. Circuit breakers shall be marked with their ampere rating in a manner that will be durable and visible after installation. Such marking shall be permitted to be made visible by removal of a trim or cover.

(B) Location. Circuit breakers rated at 100 amperes or less and 600 volts or less shall have the ampere rating molded, stamped, etched, or similarly marked into their handles or escutcheon areas.

(C) Interrupting Rating. Every circuit breaker having an interrupting rating other than 5000 amperes shall have its interrupting rating shown on the circuit breaker. The interrupting rating shall not be required to be marked on circuit breakers used for supplementary protection.

(D) Used as Switches. Circuit breakers used as switches in 120-volt and 277-volt fluorescent lighting circuits shall be listed and shall be marked SWD or HID. Circuit breakers used as switches in high-intensity discharge lighting circuits shall be listed and shall be marked as HID.

(E) Voltage Marking. Circuit breakers shall be marked with a voltage rating not less than the nominal system voltage that is indicative of their capability to interrupt fault currents between phases or phase to ground.

240.85 Applications. A circuit breaker with a straight voltage rating, such as 240V or 480V, shall be permitted to be applied in a circuit in which the nominal voltage between any two conductors does not exceed the circuit breaker's voltage rating. A two-pole circuit breaker shall not be used for protecting a 3-phase, corner-grounded delta circuit unless the circuit breaker is marked 1ϕ–3ϕ to indicate such suitability.

A circuit breaker with a slash rating, such as 120/240V or 480Y/277V, shall be permitted to be applied in a solidly grounded circuit where the nominal voltage of any conductor to ground does not exceed the lower of the two values of the circuit breaker's voltage rating and the nominal voltage between any two conductors does not exceed the higher value of the circuit breaker's voltage rating.

FPN: Proper application of molded case circuit breakers on 3-phase systems, other than solidly grounded wye, particularly on corner grounded delta systems, considers the circuit breakers' individual pole-interrupting capability.

240.86 Series Ratings. Where a circuit breaker is used on a circuit having an available fault current higher than the marked interrupting rating by being connected on the load side of an acceptable overcurrent protective device having a higher rating, the circuit breaker shall meet the requirements specified in (A) or (B), and (C).

(A) Selected Under Engineering Supervision in Existing Installations. The series rated combination devices shall be selected by a licensed professional engineer engaged primarily in the design or maintenance of electrical installations. The selection shall be documented and stamped by the professional engineer. This documentation shall be available to those authorized to design, install, inspect, maintain, and operate the system. This series combination rating, including identification of the upstream device, shall be field marked on the end use equipment.

(B) Tested Combinations. The combination of line-side overcurrent device and load-side circuit breaker(s) is tested and marked on the end use equipment, such as switchboards and panelboards.

(C) Motor Contribution. Series ratings shall not be used where

(1) Motors are connected on the load side of the higher-rated overcurrent device and on the line side of the lower-rated overcurrent device, and

(2) The sum of the motor full-load currents exceeds 1 percent of the interrupting rating of the lower-rated circuit breaker.

VIII. Supervised Industrial Installations

240.90 General. Overcurrent protection in areas of supervised industrial installations shall comply with all of the other applicable provisions of this article, except as provided in Part VIII. The provisions of Part VIII shall be permitted only to apply to those portions of the electrical system in the supervised industrial installation used exclusively for manufacturing or process control activities.

240.92 Location in Circuit. An overcurrent device shall be connected in each ungrounded circuit conductor as required in 240.92(A) through (D).

(A) Feeder and Branch-Circuit Conductors. Feeder and branch-circuit conductors shall be protected at the point the conductors receive their supply as permitted in 240.21 or as otherwise permitted in 240.92(B), (C), or (D).

(B) Transformer Secondary Conductors of Separately Derived Systems. Conductors shall be permitted to be connected to a transformer secondary of a separately derived system, without overcurrent protection at the connection, where the conditions of 240.92(B)(1), (B)(2), and (B)(3) are met.

(1) Short-Circuit and Ground-Fault Protection. The conductors shall be protected from short-circuit and ground-fault conditions by complying with one of the following conditions:

(1) The length of the secondary conductors does not exceed 30 m (100 ft) and the transformer primary overcurrent device has a rating or setting that does not exceed 150 percent of the value determined by multiplying the secondary conductor ampacity by the secondary-to-primary transformer voltage ratio.

(2) The conductors are protected by a differential relay with a trip setting equal to or less than the conductor ampacity.

FPN: A differential relay is connected to be sensitive only to short-circuit or fault currents within the protected zone and is normally set much lower than the conductor ampacity. The differential relay is connected to trip protective devices that will de-energize the protected conductors if a short-circuit condition occurs.

(3) The conductors shall be considered to be protected if calculations, made under engineering supervision, determine that the system overcurrent devices will protect the conductors within recognized time vs. current limits for all short-circuit and ground-fault conditions.

(2) Overload Protection. The conductors shall be protected against overload conditions by complying with one of the following:

(1) The conductors terminate in a single overcurrent device that will limit the load to the conductor ampacity.

(2) The sum of the overcurrent devices at the conductor termination limits the load to the conductor ampacity. The overcurrent devices shall consist of not more than six circuit breakers or sets of fuses, mounted

in a single enclosure, in a group of separate enclosures, or in or on a switchboard. There shall be no more than six overcurrent devices grouped in any one location.

(3) Overcurrent relaying is connected [with a current transformer(s), if needed] to sense all of the secondary conductor current and limit the load to the conductor ampacity by opening upstream or downstream devices.

(4) Conductors shall be considered to be protected if calculations, made under engineering supervision, determine that the system overcurrent devices will protect the conductors from overload conditions.

(3) Physical Protection. The secondary conductors are protected from physical damage by being enclosed in an approved raceway or by other approved means.

(C) Outside Feeder Taps. Outside conductors shall be permitted to be tapped to a feeder or to be connected at a transformer secondary, without overcurrent protection at the tap or connection, where all the following conditions are met:

(1) The conductors are protected from physical damage in an approved manner.

(2) The sum of the overcurrent devices at the conductor termination limits the load to the conductor ampacity. The overcurrent devices shall consist of not more than six circuit breakers or sets of fuses mounted in a single enclosure, in a group of separate enclosures, or in or on a switchboard. There shall be no more than six overcurrent devices grouped in any one location.

(3) The tap conductors are installed outdoors of a building or structure except at the point of load termination.

(4) The overcurrent device for the conductors is an integral part of a disconnecting means or shall be located immediately adjacent thereto.

(5) The disconnecting means for the conductors are installed at a readily accessible location complying with one of the following:

   a. Outside of a building or structure

   b. Inside, nearest the point of entrance of the conductors

   c. Where installed in accordance with 230.6, nearest the point of entrance of the conductors

(D) Protection by Primary Overcurrent Device. Conductors supplied by the secondary side of a transformer shall be permitted to be protected by overcurrent protection provided on the primary (supply) side of the transformer,

provided the primary device time–current protection characteristic, multiplied by the maximum effective primary-to-secondary transformer voltage ratio, effectively protects the secondary conductors.

IX. Overcurrent Protection Over 600 Volts, Nominal

240.100 Feeders and Branch Circuits.

(A) Location and Type of Protection. Feeder and branch-circuit conductors shall have overcurrent protection in each ungrounded conductor located at the point where the conductor receives its supply or at an alternative location in the circuit when designed under engineering supervision that includes but is not limited to considering the appropriate fault studies and time–current coordination analysis of the protective devices and the conductor damage curves. The overcurrent protection shall be permitted to be provided by either 240.100(A)(1) or (A)(2).

(1) Overcurrent Relays and Current Transformers. Circuit breakers used for overcurrent protection of 3-phase circuits shall have a minimum of three overcurrent relay elements operated from three current transformers. The separate overcurrent relay elements (or protective functions) shall be permitted to be part of a single electronic protective relay unit.

On 3-phase, 3-wire circuits, an overcurrent relay element in the residual circuit of the current transformers shall be permitted to replace one of the phase relay elements.

An overcurrent relay element, operated from a current transformer that links all phases of a 3-phase, 3-wire circuit, shall be permitted to replace the residual relay element and one of the phase-conductor current transformers. Where the neutral is not regrounded on the load side of the circuit as permitted in 250.184(B), the current transformer shall be permitted to link all 3-phase conductors and the grounded circuit conductor (neutral).

(2) Fuses. A fuse shall be connected in series with each ungrounded conductor.

(B) Protective Devices. The protective device(s) shall be capable of detecting and interrupting all values of current that can occur at their location in excess of their trip-setting or melting point.

(C) Conductor Protection. The operating time of the protective device, the available short-circuit current, and the conductor used shall be coordinated to prevent damaging or dangerous temperatures in conductors or conductor insulation under short-circuit conditions.

240.101 Additional Requirements for Feeders.

(A) Rating or Setting of Overcurrent Protective Devices. The continuous ampere rating of a fuse shall not exceed three times the ampacity of the conductors. The long-time trip element setting of a breaker or the minimum trip setting of an electronically actuated fuse shall not exceed six times the ampacity of the conductor. For fire pumps, conductors shall be permitted to be protected for overcurrent in accordance with 695.4(B).

(B) Feeder Taps. Conductors tapped to a feeder shall be permitted to be protected by the feeder overcurrent device where that overcurrent device also protects the tap conductor.

ARTICLE 250
Grounding and Bonding

I. General

250.1 Scope. This article covers general requirements for grounding and bonding of electrical installations, and specific requirements in (1) through (6).

(1) Systems, circuits, and equipment required, permitted, or not permitted to be grounded

(2) Circuit conductor to be grounded on grounded systems

(3) Location of grounding connections

(4) Types and sizes of grounding and bonding conductors and electrodes

(5) Methods of grounding and bonding

(6) Conditions under which guards, isolation, or insulation may be substituted for grounding

250.2 Definitions.

Effective Ground-Fault Current Path. An intentionally constructed, permanent, low-impedance electrically conductive path designed and intended to carry current under ground-fault conditions from the point of a ground fault on a wiring system to the electrical supply source and that facilitates the operation of the overcurrent protective device or ground fault detectors on high-impedance grounded systems.

Ground Fault. An unintentional, electrically conducting connection between an ungrounded conductor of an electrical circuit and the normally non–current-carrying conductors, metallic enclosures, metallic raceways, metallic equipment, or earth.

Ground-Fault Current Path. An electrically conductive path from the point of a ground fault on a wiring system through normally non–current-carrying conductors, equipment, or the earth to the electrical supply source.

FPN: Examples of ground-fault current paths could consist of any combination of equipment grounding conductors, metallic raceways, metallic cable sheaths, electrical equipment, and any other electrically conductive material such as metal water and gas piping, steel framing members, stucco mesh, metal ducting, reinforcing steel, shields of communications cables, and the earth itself.

250.3 Application of Other Articles. In other articles applying to particular cases of installation of conductors and equipment, requirements are identified in Table 250.3 that are in addition to, or modifications of, those of this article.

250.4 General Requirements for Grounding and Bonding. The following general requirements identify what grounding and bonding of electrical systems are required to accomplish. The prescriptive methods contained in Article 250 shall be followed to comply with the performance requirements of this section.

(A) Grounded Systems.

(1) Electrical System Grounding. Electrical systems that are grounded shall be connected to earth in a manner that will limit the voltage imposed by lightning, line surges, or unintentional contact with higher-voltage lines and that will stabilize the voltage to earth during normal operation.

(2) Grounding of Electrical Equipment. Non–current-carrying conductive materials enclosing electrical conductors or equipment, or forming part of such equipment, shall be connected to earth so as to limit the voltage to ground on these materials.

(3) Bonding of Electrical Equipment. Non–current-carrying conductive materials enclosing electrical conductors or equipment, or forming part of such equipment, shall be connected together and to the electrical supply source in a manner that establishes an effective ground-fault current path.

(4) Bonding of Electrically Conductive Materials and Other Equipment. Electrically conductive materials that are likely to become energized shall be connected together and to the electrical supply source in a manner that establishes an effective ground-fault current path.

(5) Effective Ground-Fault Current Path. Electrical equipment and wiring and other electrically conductive material likely to become energized shall be installed in a manner that creates a permanent, low-impedance circuit facilitating the operation of the overcurrent device or ground detector for high-impedance grounded systems. It shall be capable of safely carrying the maximum ground-fault current likely to be imposed on it from any point on the wiring system where a ground fault may occur to the electrical supply source. The earth shall not be considered as an effective ground-fault current path.

Table 250.3 Additional Grounding Requirements

Conductor/Equipment	Article	Section
Agricultural buildings		547.9 and 547.10
Audio signal processing, amplification, and reproduction equipment		640.7
Branch circuits		210.5, 210.6, 406.3
Cablebus		370.9
Cable trays	392	392.3(C), 392.7
Capacitors		460.10, 460.27
Circuits and equipment operating at less than 50 volts	720	
Closed-loop and programmed power distribution		780.3
Communications circuits	800	
Community antenna television and radio distribution systems		820.93, 820.100, 820.103
Conductors for general wiring	310	
Cranes and hoists	610	
Electrically driven or controlled irrigation machines		675.11(C), 675.12, 675.13, 675.14, 675.15
Electric signs and outline lighting	600	
Electrolytic cells	668	
Elevators, dumbwaiters, escalators, moving walks, wheelchair lifts, and stairway chair lifts	620	
Fire alarm systems		760.9
Fixed electric heating equipment for pipelines and vessels		427.29, 427.48
Fixed outdoor electric deicing and snow-melting equipment		426.27
Flexible cords and cables		400.22, 400.23
Floating buildings		553.8, 553.10, 553.11
Grounding-type receptacles, adapters, cord connectors, and attachment plugs		406.9
Hazardous (classified) locations	500–517	
Health care facilities	517	
Induction and dielectric heating equipment	665	
Industrial machinery	670	
Information technology equipment		645.15
Intrinsically safe systems		504.50
Luminaires (lighting fixtures) and lighting equipment		410.17, 410.18, 410.20, 410.21, 410.105(B)
Luminaires (fixtures), lampholders, and lamps	410	
Marinas and boatyards		555.15
Mobile homes and mobile home park	550	
Motion picture and television studios and similar locations		530.20, 530.64(B)
Motors, motor circuits, and controllers	430	
Outlet, device, pull, and junction boxes; conduit bodies; and fittings		314.4, 314.25
Over 600 volts, nominal, underground wiring methods		300.50(B)
Panelboards		408.40
Pipe organs	650	
Radio and television equipment	810	
Receptacles and cord connectors		406.3
Recreational vehicles and recreational vehicle parks	551	
Services	230	
Solar photovoltaic systems		690.41, 690.42, 690.43, 690.45, 690.47
Swimming pools, fountains, and similar installations	680	
Switchboards and panelboards		408.3(D)
Switches		404.12
Theaters, audience areas of motion picture and television studios, and similar locations		520.81
Transformers and transformer vaults		450.10
Use and identification of grounded conductors	200	
X-ray equipment	660	517.78

(B) Ungrounded Systems.

(1) Grounding Electrical Equipment. Non–current-carrying conductive materials enclosing electrical conductors or equipment, or forming part of such equipment, shall be connected to earth in a manner that will limit the voltage imposed by lightning or unintentional contact with higher-voltage lines and limit the voltage to ground on these materials.

(2) Bonding of Electrical Equipment. Non–current-carrying conductive materials enclosing electrical conductors or equipment, or forming part of such equipment, shall be connected together and to the supply system grounded equipment in a manner that creates a permanent, low-impedance path for ground-fault current that is capable of carrying the maximum fault current likely to be imposed on it.

(3) Bonding of Electrically Conductive Materials and Other Equipment. Electrically conductive materials that are likely to become energized shall be connected together and to the supply system grounded equipment in a manner that creates a permanent, low-impedance path for ground-fault current that is capable of carrying the maximum fault current likely to be imposed on it.

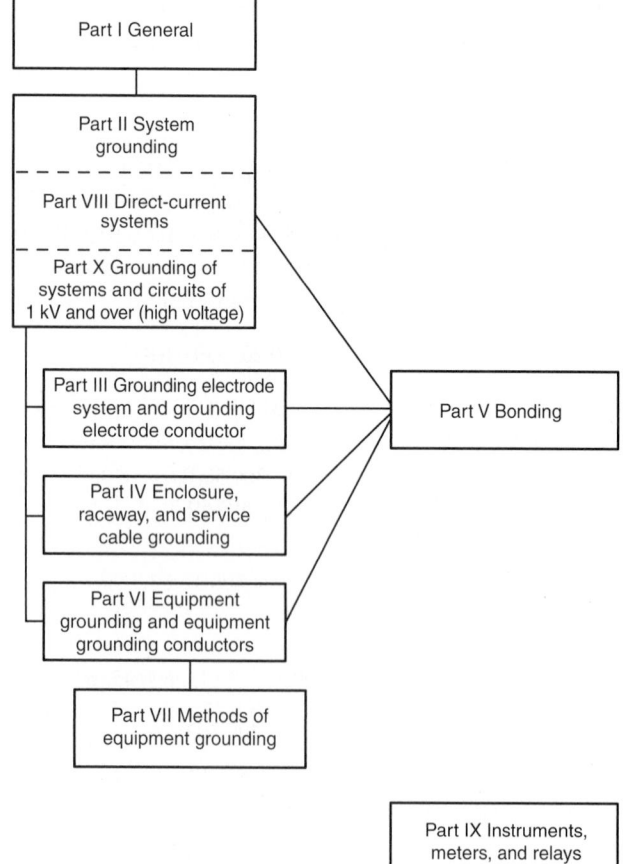

Figure 250.4 Grounding.

(4) Path for Fault Current. Electrical equipment, wiring, and other electrically conductive material likely to become energized shall be installed in a manner that creates a permanent, low-impedance circuit from any point on the wiring system to the electrical supply source to facilitate the operation of overcurrent devices should a second fault occur on the wiring system. The earth shall not be considered as an effective fault-current path.

> FPN No. 1: A second fault that occurs through the equipment enclosures and bonding is considered a ground fault.

> FPN No. 2: See Figure 250.4 for information on the organization of Article 250.

250.6 Objectionable Current over Grounding Conductors.

(A) Arrangement to Prevent Objectionable Current. The grounding of electrical systems, circuit conductors, surge arresters, and conductive non–current-carrying materials and equipment shall be installed and arranged in a manner that will prevent objectionable current over the grounding conductors or grounding paths.

(B) Alterations to Stop Objectionable Current. If the use of multiple grounding connections results in objectionable current, one or more of the following alterations shall be permitted to be made, provided that the requirements of 250.4(A)(5) or (B)(4) are met:

(1) Discontinue one or more but not all of such grounding connections.

(2) Change the locations of the grounding connections.

(3) Interrupt the continuity of the conductor or conductive path interconnecting the grounding connections.

(4) Take other suitable remedial and approved action.

(C) Temporary Currents Not Classified as Objectionable Currents. Temporary currents resulting from accidental conditions, such as ground-fault currents, that occur only while the grounding conductors are performing their intended protective functions shall not be classified as objectionable current for the purposes specified in 250.6(A) and (B).

(D) Limitations to Permissible Alterations. The provisions of this section shall not be considered as permitting electronic equipment from being operated on ac systems or branch circuits that are not grounded as required by this article. Currents that introduce noise or data errors in electronic equipment shall not be considered the objectionable currents addressed in this section.

(E) Isolation of Objectionable Direct-Current Ground Currents. Where isolation of objectionable dc ground currents from cathodic protection systems is required, a listed ac coupling/dc isolating device shall be permitted in the equipment grounding path to provide an effective return path for ac ground-fault current while blocking dc current.

250.8 Connection of Grounding and Bonding Equipment. Grounding conductors and bonding jumpers shall be connected by exothermic welding, listed pressure connectors, listed clamps, or other listed means. Connection devices or fittings that depend solely on solder shall not be used. Sheet metal screws shall not be used to connect grounding conductors or connection devices to enclosures.

250.10 Protection of Ground Clamps and Fittings. Ground clamps or other fittings shall be approved for general use without protection or shall be protected from physical damage as indicated in (1) or (2) as follows:

(1) In installations where they are not likely to be damaged

(2) Where enclosed in metal, wood, or equivalent protective covering

250.12 Clean Surfaces. Nonconductive coatings (such as paint, lacquer, and enamel) on equipment to be grounded shall be removed from threads and other contact surfaces to ensure good electrical continuity or be connected by means of fittings designed so as to make such removal unnecessary.

II. System Grounding

250.20 Alternating-Current Systems to Be Grounded. Alternating-current systems shall be grounded as provided for in 250.20(A), (B), (C), or (D). Other systems shall be permitted to be grounded. If such systems are grounded, they shall comply with the applicable provisions of this article.

> FPN: An example of a system permitted to be grounded is a corner-grounded delta transformer connection. See 250.26(4) for conductor to be grounded.

(A) Alternating-Current Systems of Less Than 50 Volts. Alternating-current systems of less than 50 volts shall be grounded under any of the following conditions:

(1) Where supplied by transformers, if the transformer supply system exceeds 150 volts to ground

(2) Where supplied by transformers, if the transformer supply system is ungrounded

(3) Where installed as overhead conductors outside of buildings

(B) Alternating-Current Systems of 50 Volts to 1000 Volts. Alternating-current systems of 50 volts to 1000 volts that supply premises wiring and premises wiring systems shall be grounded under any of the following conditions:

(1) Where the system can be grounded so that the maximum voltage to ground on the ungrounded conductors does not exceed 150 volts

(2) Where the system is 3-phase, 4-wire, wye connected in which the neutral is used as a circuit conductor

(3) Where the system is 3-phase, 4-wire, delta connected in which the midpoint of one phase winding is used as a circuit conductor

(C) Alternating-Current Systems of 1 kV and Over. Alternating-current systems supplying mobile or portable equipment shall be grounded as specified in 250.188. Where supplying other than mobile or portable equipment, such systems shall be permitted to be grounded.

(D) Separately Derived Systems. Separately derived systems, as covered in 250.20(A) or (B), shall be grounded as specified in 250.30.

> FPN No. 1: An alternate ac power source such as an on-site generator is not a separately derived system if the neutral is solidly interconnected to a service-supplied system neutral.

> FPN No. 2: For systems that are not separately derived and are not required to be grounded as specified in 250.30, see 445.13 for minimum size of conductors that must carry fault current.

(E) Impedance Grounded Neutral Systems. Impedance grounded neutral systems shall be grounded in accordance with 250.36 or 250.186.

250.21 Alternating-Current Systems of 50 Volts to 1000 Volts Not Required to Be Grounded. The following ac systems of 50 volts to 1000 volts shall be permitted to be grounded but shall not be required to be grounded:

(1) Electric systems used exclusively to supply industrial electric furnaces for melting, refining, tempering, and the like

(2) Separately derived systems used exclusively for rectifiers that supply only adjustable-speed industrial drives

(3) Separately derived systems supplied by transformers that have a primary voltage rating less than 1000 volts, provided that all the following conditions are met:

    a. The system is used exclusively for control circuits.

    b. The conditions of maintenance and supervision ensure that only qualified persons service the installation.

    c. Continuity of control power is required.

    d. Ground detectors are installed on the control system.

(4) Other systems that are not required to be grounded in accordance with the requirements of 250.20(B).

Where an alternating-current system is not grounded as permitted in 250.21(1) through (4), ground detectors shall be installed on the system.

Exception: Systems of less than 120 volts to ground as permitted by this Code shall not be required to have ground detectors.

250.22 Circuits Not to Be Grounded. The following circuits shall not be grounded:

(1) Circuits for electric cranes operating over combustible fibers in Class III locations, as provided in 503.155

(2) Circuits in health care facilities as provided in 517.61 and 517.160

(3) Circuits for equipment within electrolytic cell working zone as provided in Article 668

(4) Secondary circuits of lighting systems as provided in 411.5(A)

250.24 Grounding Service-Supplied Alternating-Current Systems.

(A) System Grounding Connections. A premises wiring system supplied by a grounded ac service shall have a grounding electrode conductor connected to the grounded service conductor, at each service, in accordance with 250.24(A)(1) through (A)(5).

(1) General. The connection shall be made at any accessible point from the load end of the service drop or service lateral to and including the terminal or bus to which the grounded service conductor is connected at the service disconnecting means.

FPN: See definitions of *Service Drop* and *Service Lateral* in Article 100.

(2) Outdoor Transformer. Where the transformer supplying the service is located outside the building, at least one additional grounding connection shall be made from the grounded service conductor to a grounding electrode, either at the transformer or elsewhere outside the building.

Exception: The additional grounding connection shall not be made on high-impedance grounded neutral systems. The system shall meet the requirements of 250.36.

(3) Dual Fed Services. For services that are dual fed (double ended) in a common enclosure or grouped together in separate enclosures and employing a secondary tie, a single grounding electrode connection to the tie point of the grounded conductor(s) from each power source shall be permitted.

(4) Main Bonding Jumper as Wire or Busbar. Where the main bonding jumper specified in 250.28 is a wire or busbar and is installed from the grounded conductor terminal bar or bus to the equipment grounding terminal bar or bus in the service equipment, the grounding electrode conductor shall be permitted to be connected to the equipment grounding terminal, bar, or bus to which the main bonding jumper is connected.

(5) Load-Side Grounding Connections. A grounding connection shall not be made to any grounded conductor on the load side of the service disconnecting means except as otherwise permitted in this article.

FPN: See 250.30(A) for separately derived systems, 250.32 for connections at separate buildings or structures, and 250.142 for use of the grounded circuit conductor for grounding equipment.

(B) Main Bonding Jumper. For a grounded system, an unspliced main bonding jumper shall be used to connect the equipment grounding conductor(s) and the service-disconnect enclosure to the grounded conductor within the enclosure for each service disconnect in accordance with 250.28.

Exception No. 1: Where more than one service disconnecting means is located in an assembly listed for use as service equipment, an unspliced main bonding jumper shall bond the grounded conductor(s) to the assembly enclosure.

Exception No. 2: Impedance grounded neutral systems shall be permitted to be connected as provided in 250.36 and 250.186.

(C) Grounded Conductor Brought to Service Equipment. Where an ac system operating at less than 1000 volts is grounded at any point, the grounded conductor(s) shall be run to each service disconnecting means and shall be bonded to each disconnecting means enclosure. The grounded conductor(s) shall be installed in accordance with 250.24(C)(1) through (C)(3).

Exception: Where more than one service disconnecting means are located in an assembly listed for use as service equipment, it shall be permitted to run the grounded conductor(s) to the assembly, and the conductor(s) shall be bonded to the assembly enclosure.

(1) Routing and Sizing. This conductor shall be routed with the phase conductors and shall not be smaller than the required grounding electrode conductor specified in Table 250.66 but shall not be required to be larger than the largest ungrounded service-entrance phase conductor. In addition, for service-entrance phase conductors larger than 1100 kcmil copper or 1750 kcmil aluminum, the grounded conductor shall not be smaller than 12½ percent of the area of the largest service-entrance phase conductor. The grounded conductor of a 3-phase, 3-wire delta service shall have an ampacity not less than that of the ungrounded conductors.

(2) Parallel Conductors. Where the service-entrance phase conductors are installed in parallel, the size of the grounded conductor shall be based on the total circular mil area of the parallel conductors as indicated in this section. Where installed in two or more raceways, the size of the grounded conductor in each raceway shall be based on the size of the ungrounded service-entrance conductor in the raceway but not smaller than 1/0 AWG.

FPN: See 310.4 for grounded conductors connected in parallel.

(3) High Impedance. The grounded conductor on a high-impedance grounded neutral system shall be grounded in accordance with 250.36.

(D) Grounding Electrode Conductor. A grounding electrode conductor shall be used to connect the equipment grounding conductors, the service-equipment enclosures, and, where the system is grounded, the grounded service conductor to the grounding electrode(s) required by Part III of this article.

High-impedance grounded neutral system connections shall be made as covered in 250.36.

FPN: See 250.24(A) for ac system grounding connections.

(E) Ungrounded System Grounding Connections. A premises wiring system that is supplied by an ac service that is ungrounded shall have, at each service, a grounding electrode conductor connected to the grounding electrode(s) required by Part III of this article. The grounding electrode conductor shall be connected to a metal enclosure of the service conductors at any accessible point from the load end of the service drop or service lateral to the service disconnecting means.

250.26 Conductor to Be Grounded — Alternating-Current Systems. For ac premises wiring systems, the conductor to be grounded shall be as specified in the following:

(1) Single-phase, 2-wire — one conductor

(2) Single-phase, 3-wire — the neutral conductor

(3) Multiphase systems having one wire common to all phases — the common conductor

(4) Multiphase systems where one phase is grounded — one phase conductor

(5) Multiphase systems in which one phase is used as in (2) — the neutral conductor

250.28 Main Bonding Jumper and System Bonding Jumper. For a grounded system, main bonding jumpers and system bonding jumpers shall be installed as follows:

(A) Material. Main bonding jumpers and system bonding jumpers shall be of copper or other corrosion-resistant material. A main bonding jumper and a system bonding jumper shall be a wire, bus, screw, or similar suitable conductor.

(B) Construction. Where a main bonding jumper or a system bonding jumper is a screw only, the screw shall be identified with a green finish that shall be visible with the screw installed.

(C) Attachment. Main bonding jumpers and system bonding jumpers shall be attached in the manner specified by the applicable provisions of 250.8.

(D) Size. Main bonding jumpers and system bonding jumpers shall not be smaller than the sizes shown in Table 250.66. Where the supply conductors are larger than 1100 kcmil copper or 1750 kcmil aluminum, the bonding jumper shall have an area that is not less than 12½ percent of the area of the largest phase conductor except that, where the phase conductors and the bonding jumper are of different materials (copper or aluminum), the minimum size of the bonding jumper shall be based on the assumed use of phase conductors of the same material as the bonding jumper and with an ampacity equivalent to that of the installed phase conductors.

250.30 Grounding Separately Derived Alternating-Current Systems.

(A) Grounded Systems. A separately derived ac system that is grounded shall comply with 250.30(A)(1) through (A)(8). A grounding connection shall not be made to any grounded circuit conductor on the load side of the point of grounding of the separately derived system except as otherwise permitted in this article.

FPN: See 250.32 for connections at separate buildings or structures, and 250.142 for use of the grounded circuit conductor for grounding equipment.

Exception: Impedance grounded neutral system grounding connections shall be made as specified in 250.36 or 250.186.

(1) System Bonding Jumper. An unspliced system bonding jumper in compliance with 250.28(A) through (D) that is sized based on the derived phase conductors shall be used to connect the equipment grounding conductors of the separately derived system to the grounded conductor. This connection shall be made at any single point on the separately derived system from the source to the first system disconnecting means or overcurrent device, or it shall be made at the source of a separately derived system that has no disconnecting means or overcurrent devices.

Exception No. 1: For separately derived systems that are dual fed (double ended) in a common enclosure or grouped together in separate enclosures and employing a secondary tie, a single system bonding jumper connection to the tie point of the grounded circuit conductors from each power source shall be permitted.

Exception No. 2: A system bonding jumper at both the source and the first disconnecting means shall be permitted where doing so does not establish a parallel path for the grounded conductor. Where a grounded conductor is used in this manner, it shall not be smaller than the size specified for the system bonding jumper but shall not be required to be larger than the ungrounded conductor(s). For the purposes of this exception, connection through the earth shall not be considered as providing a parallel path.

Exception No. 3: The size of the system bonding jumper for a system that supplies a Class 1, Class 2, or Class 3 circuit, and is derived from a transformer rated not more than 1000 volt-amperes, shall not be smaller than the derived phase conductors and shall not be smaller than 14 AWG copper or 12 AWG aluminum.

(2) Equipment Bonding Jumper Size. Where a bonding jumper of the wire type is run with the derived phase conductors from the source of a separately derived system to the first disconnecting means, it shall be sized in accordance with 250.102(C), based on the size of the derived phase conductors.

(3) Grounding Electrode Conductor, Single Separately Derived System. A grounding electrode conductor for a single separately derived system shall be sized in accordance with 250.66 for the derived phase conductors and shall be used to connect the grounded conductor of the derived system to the grounding electrode as specified in 250.30(A)(7). This connection shall be made at the same point on the separately derived system where the system bonding jumper is installed.

Exception No. 1: Where the system bonding jumper specified in 250.30(A)(1) is a wire or busbar, it shall be permitted to connect the grounding electrode conductor to the equipment grounding terminal, bar, or bus, provided the equipment grounding terminal, bar, or bus is of sufficient size for the separately derived system.

Exception No. 2: Where a separately derived system originates in listed equipment suitable as service equipment, the grounding electrode conductor from the service or feeder equipment to the grounding electrode shall be permitted as the grounding electrode conductor for the separately derived system, provided the grounding electrode conductor is of sufficient size for the separately derived system. Where the equipment ground bus internal to the equipment is not smaller than the required grounding electrode conductor for the separately derived system, the grounding electrode connection for the separately derived system shall be permitted to be made to the bus.

Exception No. 3: A grounding electrode conductor shall not be required for a system that supplies a Class 1, Class 2, or Class 3 circuit and is derived from a transformer rated not more than 1000 volt-amperes, provided the grounded conductor is bonded to the transformer frame or enclosure by a jumper sized in accordance with 250.30(A)(1), Exception No. 3, and the transformer frame or enclosure is grounded by one of the means specified in 250.134.

(4) Grounding Electrode Conductor, Multiple Separately Derived Systems. Where more than one separately derived system is installed, it shall be permissible to connect a tap from each separately derived system to a common grounding electrode conductor. Each tap conductor shall connect the grounded conductor of the separately derived system to the common grounding electrode conductor. The grounding electrode conductors and taps shall comply with 250.30(A)(4)(a) through (A)(4)(c).

Exception No. 1: Where the system bonding jumper specified in 250.30(A)(1) is a wire or busbar, it shall be permitted to connect the grounding electrode conductor to the equipment grounding terminal, bar, or bus, provided the equipment grounding terminal, bar, or bus is of sufficient size for the separately derived system.

Exception No. 2: A grounding electrode conductor shall not be required for a system that supplies a Class 1, Class 2, or Class 3 circuit and is derived from a transformer rated not more than 1000 volt-amperes, provided the system grounded conductor is bonded to the transformer frame or enclosure by a jumper sized in accordance with 250.30(A)(1), Exception No. 3 and the transformer frame or enclosure is grounded by one of the means specified in 250.134.

    (a)   Common Grounding Electrode Conductor Size. The common grounding electrode conductor shall not be smaller than 3/0 AWG copper or 250 kcmil aluminum.

    (b)   Tap Conductor Size. Each tap conductor shall be sized in accordance with 250.66 based on the derived phase conductors of the separately derived system it serves.

Exception: Where a separately derived system originates in listed equipment suitable as service equipment, the grounding electrode conductor from the service or feeder equipment to the grounding electrode shall be permitted as the grounding electrode conductor for the separately derived system, provided the grounding electrode conductor is of sufficient size for the separately derived system. Where the equipment ground bus internal to the equipment is not smaller than the required grounding electrode conductor for the separately derived system, the grounding electrode connection for the separately derived system shall be permitted to be made to the bus.

    (c)   Connections. All tap connections to the common grounding electrode conductor shall be made at an accessible location by one of the following methods:

(1) A listed connector.
(2) Listed connections to aluminum or copper busbars not less than 6 mm × 50 mm (¼ in. × 2 in.). Where aluminum busbars are used, the installation shall comply with 250.64(A).
(3) By the exothermic welding process.

    Tap conductors shall be connected to the common grounding electrode conductor in such a manner that the common grounding electrode conductor remains without a splice or joint.

(5) Installation. The installation of all grounding electrode conductors shall comply with 250.64(A), (B), (C), and (E).

(6) Bonding. Structural steel and metal piping shall be bonded in accordance with 250.104(D).

(7) Grounding Electrode. The grounding electrode shall be as near as practicable to and preferably in the same area as the grounding electrode conductor connection to the system. The grounding electrode shall be the nearest one of the following:

(1) Metal water pipe grounding electrode as specified in 250.52(A)(1)

(2) Structural metal grounding electrode as specified in 250.52(A)(2)

Exception No. 1: Any of the other electrodes identified in 250.52(A) shall be used where the electrodes specified by 250.30(A)(7) are not available.

Exception No. 2 to (1) and (2): Where a separately derived system originates in listed equipment suitable for use as service equipment, the grounding electrode used for the service or feeder equipment shall be permitted as the grounding electrode for the separately derived system.

> FPN: See 250.104(D) for bonding requirements of interior metal water piping in the area served by separately derived systems.

(8) Grounded Conductor. Where a grounded conductor is installed and the system bonding jumper is not located at the source of the separately derived system, 250.30(A)(8)(a), (A)(8)(b), and (A)(8)(c) shall apply.

(a) Routing and Sizing. This conductor shall be routed with the derived phase conductors and shall not be smaller than the required grounding electrode conductor specified in Table 250.66 but shall not be required to be larger than the largest ungrounded derived phase conductor. In addition, for phase conductors larger than 1100 kcmil copper or 1750 kcmil aluminum, the grounded conductor shall not be smaller than 12½ percent of the area of the largest derived phase conductor. The grounded conductor of a 3-phase, 3-wire delta system shall have an ampacity not less than that of the ungrounded conductors.

(b) Parallel Conductors. Where the derived phase conductors are installed in parallel, the size of the grounded conductor shall be based on the total circular mil area of the parallel conductors, as indicated in this section. Where installed in two or more raceways, the size of the grounded conductor in each raceway shall be based on the size of the ungrounded conductors in the raceway but not smaller than 1/0 AWG.

> FPN: See 310.4 for grounded conductors connected in parallel.

(c) Impedance Grounded System. The grounded conductor of an impedance grounded neutral system shall be installed in accordance with 250.36 or 250.186.

(B) Ungrounded Systems. The equipment of an ungrounded separately derived system shall be grounded as specified in 250.30(B)(1) and (B)(2).

(1) Grounding Electrode Conductor. A grounding electrode conductor, sized in accordance with 250.66 for the derived phase conductors, shall be used to connect the metal enclosures of the derived system to the grounding electrode as specified in 250.30(B)(2). This connection shall be made at any point on the separately derived system from the source to the first system disconnecting means.

(2) Grounding Electrode. Except as permitted by 250.34 for portable and vehicle-mounted generators, the grounding electrode shall comply with 250.30(A)(7).

250.32 Buildings or Structures Supplied by Feeder(s) or Branch Circuit(s).

(A) Grounding Electrode. Building(s) or structure(s) supplied by feeder(s) or branch circuit(s) shall have a grounding electrode or grounding electrode system installed in accordance with 250.50. The grounding electrode conductor(s) shall be connected in accordance with 250.32(B) or (C). Where there is no existing grounding electrode, the grounding electrode(s) required in 250.50 shall be installed.

Exception: A grounding electrode shall not be required where only a single branch circuit supplies the building or structure and the branch circuit includes an equipment grounding conductor for grounding the conductive non–current-carrying parts of equipment. For the purpose of this section, a multiwire branch circuit shall be considered as a single branch circuit.

(B) Grounded Systems. For a grounded system at the separate building or structure, the connection to the grounding electrode and grounding or bonding of equipment, structures, or frames required to be grounded or bonded shall comply with either 250.32(B)(1) or (B)(2).

(1) Equipment Grounding Conductor. An equipment grounding conductor as described in 250.118 shall be run with the supply conductors and connected to the building or structure disconnecting means and to the grounding electrode(s). The equipment grounding conductor shall be used for grounding or bonding of equipment, structures, or frames required to be grounded or bonded. The equipment grounding conductor shall be sized in accordance with 250.122. Any installed grounded conductor shall not be connected to the equipment grounding conductor or to the grounding electrode(s).

(2) Grounded Conductor. Where (1) an equipment grounding conductor is not run with the supply to the building or structure, (2) there are no continuous metallic paths bonded to the grounding system in each building or structure involved, and (3) ground-fault protection of equipment has not been installed on the supply side of the feeder(s), the grounded conductor run with the supply to the building or structure shall be connected to the building or structure disconnecting means and to the grounding electrode(s) and shall be used for grounding or bonding of equipment, structures, or frames required to be grounded or bonded. The size of the grounded conductor shall not be smaller than the larger of either of the following:

(1) That required by 220.61

(2) That required by 250.122

(C) Ungrounded Systems. The grounding electrode(s) shall be connected to the building or structure disconnecting means.

(D) Disconnecting Means Located in Separate Building or Structure on the Same Premises. Where one or more disconnecting means supply one or more additional buildings or structures under single management, and where these disconnecting means are located remote from those buildings or structures in accordance with the provisions of 225.32, Exception Nos. 1 and 2, all of the following conditions shall be met:

(1) The connection of the grounded conductor to the grounding electrode at a separate building or structure shall not be made.

(2) An equipment grounding conductor for grounding any non–current-carrying equipment, interior metal piping systems, and building or structural metal frames is run with the circuit conductors to a separate building or structure and bonded to existing grounding electrode(s) required in Part III of this article, or, where there are no existing electrodes, the grounding electrode(s) required in Part III of this article shall be installed where a separate building or structure is supplied by more than one branch circuit.

(3) Bonding the equipment grounding conductor to the grounding electrode at a separate building or structure shall be made in a junction box, panelboard, or similar enclosure located immediately inside or outside the separate building or structure.

(E) Grounding Electrode Conductor. The size of the grounding electrode conductor to the grounding electrode(s) shall not be smaller than given in 250.66, based on the largest ungrounded supply conductor. The installation shall comply with Part III of this article.

250.34 Portable and Vehicle-Mounted Generators.

(A) Portable Generators. The frame of a portable generator shall not be required to be connected to a grounding electrode as defined in 250.52 for a system supplied by the generator under the following conditions:

(1) The generator supplies only equipment mounted on the generator, cord-and-plug-connected equipment through receptacles mounted on the generator, or both, and

(2) The non–current-carrying metal parts of equipment and the equipment grounding conductor terminals of the receptacles are bonded to the generator frame.

(B) Vehicle-Mounted Generators. The frame of a vehicle shall not be required to be connected to a grounding electrode as defined in 250.52 for a system supplied by a generator located on this vehicle under the following conditions:

(1) The frame of the generator is bonded to the vehicle frame, and

(2) The generator supplies only equipment located on the vehicle or cord-and-plug-connected equipment through receptacles mounted on the vehicle, or both equipment located on the vehicle and cord-and-plug-connected equipment through receptacles mounted on the vehicle or on the generator, and

(3) The non–current-carrying metal parts of equipment and the equipment grounding conductor terminals of the receptacles are bonded to the generator frame.

(C) Grounded Conductor Bonding. A system conductor that is required to be grounded by 250.26 shall be bonded to the generator frame where the generator is a component of a separately derived system.

FPN: For grounding portable generators supplying fixed wiring systems, see 250.20(D).

250.36 High-Impedance Grounded Neutral Systems. High-impedance grounded neutral systems in which a grounding impedance, usually a resistor, limits the ground-fault current to a low value shall be permitted for 3-phase ac systems of 480 volts to 1000 volts where all the following conditions are met:

(1) The conditions of maintenance and supervision ensure that only qualified persons service the installation.

(2) Continuity of power is required.

(3) Ground detectors are installed on the system.

(4) Line-to-neutral loads are not served.

High-impedance grounded neutral systems shall comply with the provisions of 250.36(A) through (G).

(A) Grounding Impedance Location. The grounding impedance shall be installed between the grounding electrode conductor and the system neutral. Where a neutral is not available, the grounding impedance shall be installed between the grounding electrode conductor and the neutral derived from a grounding transformer.

(B) Neutral Conductor. The neutral conductor from the neutral point of the transformer or generator to its connection point to the grounding impedance shall be fully insulated.

The neutral conductor shall have an ampacity of not less than the maximum current rating of the grounding impedance. In no case shall the neutral conductor be smaller than 8 AWG copper or 6 AWG aluminum or copper-clad aluminum.

(C) System Neutral Connection. The system neutral conductor shall not be connected to ground except through the grounding impedance.

> FPN: The impedance is normally selected to limit the ground-fault current to a value slightly greater than or equal to the capacitive charging current of the system. This value of impedance will also limit transient overvoltages to safe values. For guidance, refer to criteria for limiting transient overvoltages in ANSI/IEEE 142-1991, *Recommended Practice for Grounding of Industrial and Commercial Power Systems.*

(D) Neutral Conductor Routing. The conductor connecting the neutral point of the transformer or generator to the grounding impedance shall be permitted to be installed in a separate raceway. It shall not be required to run this conductor with the phase conductors to the first system disconnecting means or overcurrent device.

(E) Equipment Bonding Jumper. The equipment bonding jumper (the connection between the equipment grounding conductors and the grounding impedance) shall be an unspliced conductor run from the first system disconnecting means or overcurrent device to the grounded side of the grounding impedance.

(F) Grounding Electrode Conductor Location. The grounding electrode conductor shall be attached at any point from the grounded side of the grounding impedance to the equipment grounding connection at the service equipment or first system disconnecting means.

(G) Equipment Bonding Jumper Size. The equipment bonding jumper shall be sized in accordance with (1) or (2) as follows:

(1) Where the grounding electrode conductor connection is made at the grounding impedance, the equipment bonding jumper shall be sized in accordance with 250.66, based on the size of the service entrance conductors for a service or the derived phase conductors for a separately derived system.

(2) Where the grounding electrode conductor is connected at the first system disconnecting means or overcurrent device, the equipment bonding jumper shall be sized the same as the neutral conductor in 250.36(B).

III. Grounding Electrode System and Grounding Electrode Conductor

250.50 Grounding Electrode System. All grounding electrodes as described in 250.52(A)(1) through (A)(6) that are present at each building or structure served shall be bonded together to form the grounding electrode system. Where none of these grounding electrodes exist, one or more of the grounding electrodes specified in 250.52(A)(4) through (A)(7) shall be installed and used.

Exception: Concrete-encased electrodes of existing buildings or structures shall not be required to be part of the grounding electrode system where the steel reinforcing bars or rods are not accessible for use without disturbing the concrete.

250.52 Grounding Electrodes.

(A) Electrodes Permitted for Grounding.

(1) Metal Underground Water Pipe. A metal underground water pipe in direct contact with the earth for 3.0 m (10 ft) or more (including any metal well casing effectively bonded to the pipe) and electrically continuous (or made electrically continuous by bonding around insulating joints or insulating pipe) to the points of connection of the grounding electrode conductor and the bonding conductors. Interior metal water piping located more than 1.52 m (5 ft) from the point of entrance to the building shall not be used as a part of the grounding electrode system or as a conductor to interconnect electrodes that are part of the grounding electrode system.

Exception: In industrial and commercial buildings or structures where conditions of maintenance and supervision ensure that only qualified persons service the installation, interior metal water piping located more than 1.52 m (5 ft) from the point of entrance to the building shall be permitted as a part of the grounding electrode system or as a conductor to interconnect electrodes that are part of the grounding electrode system, provided that the entire length, other than short sections passing perpendicular through walls, floors, or ceilings, of the interior metal water pipe that is being used for the conductor is exposed.

(2) Metal Frame of the Building or Structure. The metal frame of the building or structure, where any of the following methods are used to make an earth connection:

(1) 3.0 m (10 ft) or more of a single structural metal member in direct contact with the earth or encased in concrete that is in direct contact with the earth

(2) The structural metal frame is bonded to one or more of the grounding electrodes as defined in 250.52(A)(1), (A)(3), or (A)(4)

(3) The structural metal frame is bonded to one or more of the grounding electrodes as defined in 250.52(A)(5) or (A)(6) that comply with 250.56, or

(4) Other approved means of establishing a connection to earth.

(3) Concrete-Encased Electrode. An electrode encased by at least 50 mm (2 in.) of concrete, located within and near the bottom of a concrete foundation or footing that is in direct contact with the earth, consisting of at least 6.0 m (20 ft) of one or more bare or zinc galvanized or other electrically conductive coated steel reinforcing bars or rods of not less than 13 mm (½ in.) in diameter, or consisting of at least 6.0 m (20 ft) of bare copper conductor not smaller than 4 AWG. Reinforcing bars shall be permitted to be bonded together by the usual steel tie wires or other effective means.

(4) Ground Ring. A ground ring encircling the building or structure, in direct contact with the earth, consisting of at least 6.0 m (20 ft) of bare copper conductor not smaller than 2 AWG.

(5) Rod and Pipe Electrodes. Rod and pipe electrodes shall not be less than 2.5 m (8 ft) in length and shall consist of the following materials.

(a) Electrodes of pipe or conduit shall not be smaller than metric designator 21 (trade size ¾) and, where of iron or steel, shall have the outer surface galvanized or otherwise metal-coated for corrosion protection.

(b) Electrodes of rods of iron or steel shall be at least 15.87 mm (⅝ in.) in diameter. Stainless steel rods less than 16 mm (⅝ in.) in diameter, nonferrous rods, or their equivalent shall be listed and shall not be less than 13 mm (½ in.) in diameter.

(6) Plate Electrodes. Each plate electrode shall expose not less than 0.186 m² (2 ft²) of surface to exterior soil. Electrodes of iron or steel plates shall be at least 6.4 mm (¼ in.) in thickness. Electrodes of nonferrous metal shall be at least 1.5 mm (0.06 in.) in thickness.

(7) Other Local Metal Underground Systems or Structures. Other local metal underground systems or structures such as piping systems, underground tanks, and underground metal well casings that are not effectively bonded to a metal water pipe.

(B) Electrodes Not Permitted for Grounding. The following shall not be used as grounding electrodes:

(1) Metal underground gas piping system

(2) Aluminum electrodes

FPN: See 250.104(B) for bonding requirements of gas piping.

250.53 Grounding Electrode System Installation.

FPN: See 547.9 and 547.10 for special grounding and bonding requirements for agricultural buildings.

(A) Rod, Pipe, and Plate Electrodes. Where practicable, rod, pipe, and plate electrodes shall be embedded below permanent moisture level. Rod, pipe, and plate electrodes shall be free from nonconductive coatings such as paint or enamel.

(B) Electrode Spacing. Where more than one of the electrodes of the type specified in 250.52(A)(5) or (A)(6) are used, each electrode of one grounding system (including that used for air terminals) shall not be less than 1.83 m (6 ft) from any other electrode of another grounding system. Two or more grounding electrodes that are effectively bonded together shall be considered a single grounding electrode system.

(C) Bonding Jumper. The bonding jumper(s) used to connect the grounding electrodes together to form the grounding electrode system shall be installed in accordance with 250.64(A), (B), and (E), shall be sized in accordance with 250.66, and shall be connected in the manner specified in 250.70.

(D) Metal Underground Water Pipe. Where used as a grounding electrode, metal underground water pipe shall meet the requirements of 250.53(D)(1) and (D)(2).

(1) Continuity. Continuity of the grounding path or the bonding connection to interior piping shall not rely on water meters or filtering devices and similar equipment.

(2) Supplemental Electrode Required. A metal underground water pipe shall be supplemented by an additional electrode of a type specified in 250.52(A)(2) through (A)(7). Where the supplemental electrode is a rod, pipe, or plate type, it shall comply with 250.56. The supplemental electrode shall be permitted to be bonded to the grounding electrode conductor, the grounded service-entrance conductor, the nonflexible grounded service raceway, or any grounded service enclosure.

Exception: The supplemental electrode shall be permitted to be bonded to the interior metal water piping at any convenient point as covered in 250.52(A)(1), Exception.

(E) Supplemental Electrode Bonding Connection Size. Where the supplemental electrode is a rod, pipe, or plate electrode, that portion of the bonding jumper that is the sole connection to the supplemental grounding electrode shall not be required to be larger than 6 AWG copper wire or 4 AWG aluminum wire.

(F) Ground Ring. The ground ring shall be buried at a depth below the earth's surface of not less than 750 mm (30 in.).

(G) Rod and Pipe Electrodes. The electrode shall be installed such that at least 2.44 m (8 ft) of length is in contact with the soil. It shall be driven to a depth of not less than

2.44 m (8 ft) except that, where rock bottom is encountered, the electrode shall be driven at an oblique angle not to exceed 45 degrees from the vertical or, where rock bottom is encountered at an angle up to 45 degrees, the electrode shall be permitted to be buried in a trench that is at least 750 mm (30 in.) deep. The upper end of the electrode shall be flush with or below ground level unless the aboveground end and the grounding electrode conductor attachment are protected against physical damage as specified in 250.10.

(H) Plate Electrode. Plate electrodes shall be installed not less than 750 mm (30 in.) below the surface of the earth.

250.54 Supplementary Grounding Electrodes. Supplementary grounding electrodes shall be permitted to be connected to the equipment grounding conductors specified in 250.118 and shall not be required to comply with the electrode bonding requirements of 250.50 or 250.53(C) or the resistance requirements of 250.56, but the earth shall not be used as an effective ground-fault current path as specified in 250.4(A)(5) and 250.4(B)(4).

250.56 Resistance of Rod, Pipe, and Plate Electrodes. A single electrode consisting of a rod, pipe, or plate that does not have a resistance to ground of 25 ohms or less shall be augmented by one additional electrode of any of the types specified by 250.52(A)(2) through (A)(7). Where multiple rod, pipe, or plate electrodes are installed to meet the requirements of this section, they shall not be less than 1.8 m (6 ft) apart.

> FPN: The paralleling efficiency of rods longer than 2.5 m (8 ft) is improved by spacing greater than 1.8 m (6 ft).

250.58 Common Grounding Electrode. Where an ac system is connected to a grounding electrode in or at a building or structure, the same electrode shall be used to ground conductor enclosures and equipment in or on that building or structure. Where separate services, feeders, or branch circuits supply a building and are required to be connected to a grounding electrode(s), the same grounding electrode(s) shall be used.

Two or more grounding electrodes that are effectively bonded together shall be considered as a single grounding electrode system in this sense.

250.60 Use of Air Terminals. Air terminal conductors and driven pipes, rods, or plate electrodes used for grounding air terminals shall not be used in lieu of the grounding electrodes required by 250.50 for grounding wiring systems and equipment. This provision shall not prohibit the required bonding together of grounding electrodes of different systems.

> FPN No. 1: See 250.106 for spacing from air terminals. See 800.100(D), 810.21(J), and 820.100(D) for bonding of electrodes.

> FPN No. 2: Bonding together of all separate grounding electrodes will limit potential differences between them and between their associated wiring systems.

250.62 Grounding Electrode Conductor Material. The grounding electrode conductor shall be of copper, aluminum, or copper-clad aluminum. The material selected shall be resistant to any corrosive condition existing at the installation or shall be suitably protected against corrosion. The conductor shall be solid or stranded, insulated, covered, or bare.

250.64 Grounding Electrode Conductor Installation. Grounding electrode conductors shall be installed as specified in 250.64(A) through (F).

(A) Aluminum or Copper-Clad Aluminum Conductors. Bare aluminum or copper-clad aluminum grounding conductors shall not be used where in direct contact with masonry or the earth or where subject to corrosive conditions. Where used outside, aluminum or copper-clad aluminum grounding conductors shall not be terminated within 450 mm (18 in.) of the earth.

(B) Securing and Protection Against Physical Damage. Where exposed, a grounding electrode conductor or its enclosure shall be securely fastened to the surface on which it is carried. A 4 AWG or larger copper or aluminum grounding electrode conductor shall be protected where exposed to physical damage. A 6 AWG grounding electrode conductor that is free from exposure to physical damage shall be permitted to be run along the surface of the building construction without metal covering or protection where it is securely fastened to the construction; otherwise, it shall be in rigid metal conduit, intermediate metal conduit, rigid nonmetallic conduit, electrical metallic tubing, or cable armor. Grounding electrode conductors smaller than 6 AWG shall be in rigid metal conduit, intermediate metal conduit, rigid nonmetallic conduit, electrical metallic tubing, or cable armor.

(C) Continuous. Grounding electrode conductor(s) shall be installed in one continuous length without a splice or joint except as permitted in (1) through (4):

(1) Splicing shall be permitted only by irreversible compression-type connectors listed as grounding and bonding equipment or by the exothermic welding process.

(2) Sections of busbars shall be permitted to be connected together to form a grounding electrode conductor.

(3) Bonding jumper(s) from grounding electrode(s) and grounding electrode conductor(s) shall be permitted to be connected to an aluminum or copper busbar not less than 6 mm × 50 mm (¼ in. × 2 in.). The busbar shall be securely fastened and shall be installed in an accessible location. Connections shall be made by a listed connector or by the exothermic welding process.

(4) Where aluminum busbars are used, the installation shall comply with 250.64(A).

(D) Grounding Electrode Conductor Taps. Where a service consists of more than a single enclosure as permitted in 230.71(A), it shall be permitted to connect taps to the common grounding electrode conductor. Each such tap conductor shall extend to the inside of each such enclosure. The common grounding electrode conductor shall be sized in accordance with 250.66, based on the sum of the circular mil area of the largest ungrounded service entrance conductors. Where more than one set of service entrance conductors as permitted by 230.40, Exception No. 2 connect directly to a service drop or lateral, the common grounding electrode conductor shall be sized in accordance with Table 250.66 Note 1. The tap conductors shall be permitted to be sized in accordance with the grounding electrode conductors specified in 250.66 for the largest conductor serving the respective enclosures. The tap conductors shall be connected to the common grounding electrode conductor in such a manner that the common grounding electrode conductor remains without a splice or joint.

(E) Enclosures for Grounding Electrode Conductors. Ferrous metal enclosures for grounding electrode conductors shall be electrically continuous from the point of attachment to cabinets or equipment to the grounding electrode and shall be securely fastened to the ground clamp or fitting. Nonferrous metal enclosures shall not be required to be electrically continuous. Ferrous metal enclosures that are not physically continuous from cabinets or equipment to the grounding electrode shall be made electrically continuous by bonding each end of the raceway or enclosure to the grounding electrode conductor. Bonding shall apply at each end and to all intervening ferrous raceways, boxes, and enclosures between the service equipment and the grounding electrode. The bonding jumper for a grounding electrode conductor raceway or cable armor shall be the same size as, or larger than, the required enclosed grounding electrode conductor. Where a raceway is used as protection for a grounding electrode conductor, the installation shall comply with the requirements of the appropriate raceway article.

(F) To Electrode(s). A grounding electrode conductor shall be permitted to be run to any convenient grounding electrode available in the grounding electrode system, or to one or more grounding electrode(s) individually, or to the aluminum or copper busbar as permitted in 250.64(C). The grounding electrode conductor shall be sized for the largest grounding electrode conductor required among all the electrodes connected to it.

250.66 Size of Alternating-Current Grounding Electrode Conductor. The size of the grounding electrode conductor of a grounded or ungrounded ac system shall not be less than given in Table 250.66, except as permitted in 250.66(A) through (C).

> FPN: See 250.24(C) for size of ac system conductor brought to service equipment.

Table 250.66 Grounding Electrode Conductor for Alternating-Current Systems

Size of Largest Ungrounded Service-Entrance Conductor or Equivalent Area for Parallel Conductors[a] (AWG/kcmil)		Size of Grounding Electrode Conductor (AWG/kcmil)	
Copper	Aluminum or Copper-Clad Aluminum	Copper	Aluminum or Copper-Clad Aluminum[b]
2 or smaller	1/0 or smaller	8	6
1 or 1/0	2/0 or 3/0	6	4
2/0 or 3/0	4/0 or 250	4	2
Over 3/0 through 350	Over 250 through 500	2	1/0
Over 350 through 600	Over 500 through 900	1/0	3/0
Over 600 through 1100	Over 900 through 1750	2/0	4/0
Over 1100	Over 1750	3/0	250

Notes:
1. Where multiple sets of service-entrance conductors are used as permitted in 230.40, Exception No. 2, the equivalent size of the largest service-entrance conductor shall be determined by the largest sum of the areas of the corresponding conductors of each set.
2. Where there are no service-entrance conductors, the grounding electrode conductor size shall be determined by the equivalent size of the largest service-entrance conductor required for the load to be served.
[a]This table also applies to the derived conductors of separately derived ac systems.
[b]See installation restrictions in 250.64(A).

(A) Connections to Rod, Pipe, or Plate Electrodes. Where the grounding electrode conductor is connected to rod, pipe, or plate electrodes as permitted in 250.52(A)(5) or (A)(6), that portion of the conductor that is the sole connection to the grounding electrode shall not be required to be larger than 6 AWG copper wire or 4 AWG aluminum wire.

(B) Connections to Concrete-Encased Electrodes. Where the grounding electrode conductor is connected to a concrete-encased electrode as permitted in 250.52(A)(3), that portion of the conductor that is the sole connection to the grounding electrode shall not be required to be larger than 4 AWG copper wire.

(C) Connections to Ground Rings. Where the grounding electrode conductor is connected to a ground ring as permitted in 250.52(A)(4), that portion of the conductor that is the sole connection to the grounding electrode shall not be required to be larger than the conductor used for the ground ring.

250.68 Grounding Electrode Conductor and Bonding Jumper Connection to Grounding Electrodes.

(A) Accessibility. The connection of a grounding electrode conductor or bonding jumper to a grounding electrode shall be accessible.

Exception No. 1: An encased or buried connection to a concrete-encased, driven, or buried grounding electrode shall not be required to be accessible.

Exception No. 2: An exothermic or irreversible compression connection to fire-proofed structural metal shall not be required to be accessible.

(B) Effective Grounding Path. The connection of a grounding electrode conductor or bonding jumper to a grounding electrode shall be made in a manner that will ensure a permanent and effective grounding path. Where necessary to ensure the grounding path for a metal piping system used as a grounding electrode, effective bonding shall be provided around insulated joints and around any equipment likely to be disconnected for repairs or replacement. Bonding conductors shall be of sufficient length to permit removal of such equipment while retaining the integrity of the bond.

250.70 Methods of Grounding and Bonding Conductor Connection to Electrodes. The grounding or bonding conductor shall be connected to the grounding electrode by exothermic welding, listed lugs, listed pressure connectors, listed clamps, or other listed means. Connections depending on solder shall not be used. Ground clamps shall be listed for the materials of the grounding electrode and the grounding electrode conductor and, where used on pipe, rod, or other buried electrodes, shall also be listed for direct soil burial or concrete encasement. Not more than one conductor shall be connected to the grounding electrode by a single clamp or fitting unless the clamp or fitting is listed for multiple conductors. One of the following methods shall be used:

(1) A pipe fitting, pipe plug, or other approved device screwed into a pipe or pipe fitting

(2) A listed bolted clamp of cast bronze or brass, or plain or malleable iron

(3) For indoor telecommunications purposes only, a listed sheet metal strap-type ground clamp having a rigid metal base that seats on the electrode and having a strap of such material and dimensions that it is not likely to stretch during or after installation

(4) An equally substantial approved means

IV. Enclosure, Raceway, and Service Cable Grounding

250.80 Service Raceways and Enclosures. Metal enclosures and raceways for service conductors and equipment shall be grounded.

Exception: A metal elbow that is installed in an underground installation of rigid nonmetallic conduit and is isolated from possible contact by a minimum cover of 450 mm (18 in.) to any part of the elbow shall not be required to be grounded.

250.84 Underground Service Cable or Raceway.

(A) Underground Service Cable. The sheath or armor of a continuous underground metal-sheathed or armored service cable system that is bonded to the grounded underground system shall not be required to be grounded at the building or structure. The sheath or armor shall be permitted to be insulated from the interior metal raceway conduit or piping.

(B) Underground Service Raceway Containing Cable. An underground metal service raceway that contains a metal-sheathed or armored cable bonded to the grounded underground system shall not be required to be grounded at the building or structure. The sheath or armor shall be permitted to be insulated from the interior metal raceway or piping.

250.86 Other Conductor Enclosures and Raceways. Except as permitted by 250.112(I), metal enclosures and raceways for other than service conductors shall be grounded.

Exception No. 1: Metal enclosures and raceways for conductors added to existing installations of open wire, knob and tube wiring, and nonmetallic-sheathed cable shall not be required to be grounded where these enclosures or wiring methods comply with (1) through (4) as follows:

(1) Do not provide an equipment ground

(2) Are in runs of less than 7.5 m (25 ft)

(3) Are free from probable contact with ground, grounded metal, metal lath, or other conductive material

(4) Are guarded against contact by persons

Exception No. 2: Short sections of metal enclosures or raceways used to provide support or protection of cable assemblies from physical damage shall not be required to be grounded.

Exception No. 3: A metal elbow shall not be required to be grounded where it is installed in a nonmetallic raceway and is isolated from possible contact by a minimum cover of 450 mm (18 in.) to any part of the elbow or is encased in not less than 50 mm (2 in.) of concrete.

V. Bonding

250.90 General. Bonding shall be provided where necessary to ensure electrical continuity and the capacity to conduct safely any fault current likely to be imposed.

250.92 Services.

(A) Bonding of Services. The non–current-carrying metal parts of equipment indicated in 250.92(A)(1), (A)(2), and (A)(3) shall be effectively bonded together.

(1) The service raceways, cable trays, cablebus framework, auxiliary gutters, or service cable armor or sheath except as permitted in 250.84.

(2) All service enclosures containing service conductors, including meter fittings, boxes, or the like, interposed in the service raceway or armor.

(3) Any metallic raceway or armor enclosing a grounding electrode conductor as specified in 250.64(B). Bonding shall apply at each end and to all intervening raceways, boxes, and enclosures between the service equipment and the grounding electrode.

(B) Method of Bonding at the Service. Electrical continuity at service equipment, service raceways, and service conductor enclosures shall be ensured by one of the following methods:

(1) Bonding equipment to the grounded service conductor in a manner provided in 250.8

(2) Connections utilizing threaded couplings or threaded bosses on enclosures where made up wrenchtight

(3) Threadless couplings and connectors where made up tight for metal raceways and metal-clad cables

(4) Other listed devices, such as bonding-type locknuts, bushings, or bushings with bonding jumpers

Bonding jumpers meeting the other requirements of this article shall be used around concentric or eccentric knockouts that are punched or otherwise formed so as to impair the electrical connection to ground. Standard locknuts or bushings shall not be the sole means for the bonding required by this section.

250.94 Bonding for Other Systems.
An accessible means external to enclosures for connecting intersystem bonding and grounding electrode conductors shall be provided at the service equipment and at the disconnecting means for any additional buildings or structures by at least one of the following means:

(1) Exposed nonflexible metallic raceways

(2) Exposed grounding electrode conductor

(3) Approved means for the external connection of a copper or other corrosion-resistant bonding or grounding conductor to the grounded raceway or equipment

FPN No. 1: A 6 AWG copper conductor with one end bonded to the grounded nonflexible metallic raceway or equipment and with 150 mm (6 in.) or more of the other end made accessible on the outside wall is an example of the approved means covered in 250.94(3).

FPN No. 2: See 800.100, 810.21, and 820.100 for bonding and grounding requirements for communications circuits, radio and television equipment, and CATV circuits.

250.96 Bonding Other Enclosures.

(A) General. Metal raceways, cable trays, cable armor, cable sheath, enclosures, frames, fittings, and other metal non–current-carrying parts that are to serve as grounding conductors, with or without the use of supplementary equipment grounding conductors, shall be effectively bonded where necessary to ensure electrical continuity and the capacity to conduct safely any fault current likely to be imposed on them. Any nonconductive paint, enamel, or similar coating shall be removed at threads, contact points, and contact surfaces or be connected by means of fittings designed so as to make such removal unnecessary.

(B) Isolated Grounding Circuits. Where required for the reduction of electrical noise (electromagnetic interference) on the grounding circuit, an equipment enclosure supplied by a branch circuit shall be permitted to be isolated from a raceway containing circuits supplying only that equipment by one or more listed nonmetallic raceway fittings located at the point of attachment of the raceway to the equipment enclosure. The metal raceway shall comply with provisions of this article and shall be supplemented by an internal insulated equipment grounding conductor installed in accordance with 250.146(D) to ground the equipment enclosure.

FPN: Use of an isolated equipment grounding conductor does not relieve the requirement for grounding the raceway system.

250.97 Bonding for Over 250 Volts.
For circuits of over 250 volts to ground, the electrical continuity of metal raceways and cables with metal sheaths that contain any conductor other than service conductors shall be ensured by one or more of the methods specified for services in 250.92(B), except for (B)(1).

Exception: Where oversized, concentric, or eccentric knockouts are not encountered, or where a box or enclosure with concentric or eccentric knockouts is listed to provide a permanent, reliable electrical bond, the following methods shall be permitted:

(1) *Threadless couplings and connectors for cables with metal sheaths*

(2) *Two locknuts, on rigid metal conduit or intermediate metal conduit, one inside and one outside of boxes and cabinets*

(3) *Fittings with shoulders that seat firmly against the box or cabinet, such as electrical metallic tubing connectors, flexible metal conduit connectors, and cable connectors, with one locknut on the inside of boxes and cabinets*

(4) *Listed fittings*

250.98 Bonding Loosely Jointed Metal Raceways. Expansion fittings and telescoping sections of metal raceways shall be made electrically continuous by equipment bonding jumpers or other means.

250.100 Bonding in Hazardous (Classified) Locations. Regardless of the voltage of the electrical system, the electrical continuity of non–current-carrying metal parts of equipment, raceways, and other enclosures in any hazardous (classified) location as defined in Article 500 shall be ensured by any of the methods specified in 250.92(B)(2) through (B)(4) that are approved for the wiring method used. One or more of these bonding methods shall be used whether or not supplementary equipment grounding conductors are installed.

250.102 Equipment Bonding Jumpers.

(A) Material. Equipment bonding jumpers shall be of copper or other corrosion-resistant material. A bonding jumper shall be a wire, bus, screw, or similar suitable conductor.

(B) Attachment. Equipment bonding jumpers shall be attached in the manner specified by the applicable provisions of 250.8 for circuits and equipment and by 250.70 for grounding electrodes.

(C) Size — Equipment Bonding Jumper on Supply Side of Service. The bonding jumper shall not be smaller than the sizes shown in Table 250.66 for grounding electrode conductors. Where the service-entrance phase conductors are larger than 1100 kcmil copper or 1750 kcmil aluminum, the bonding jumper shall have an area not less than 12½ percent of the area of the largest phase conductor except that, where the phase conductors and the bonding jumper are of different materials (copper or aluminum), the minimum size of the bonding jumper shall be based on the assumed use of phase conductors of the same material as the bonding jumper and with an ampacity equivalent to that of the installed phase conductors. Where the service-entrance conductors are paralleled in two or more raceways or cables, the equipment bonding jumper, where routed with the raceways or cables, shall be run in parallel. The size of the bonding jumper for each raceway or cable shall be based on the size of the service-entrance conductors in each raceway or cable.

(D) Size — Equipment Bonding Jumper on Load Side of Service. The equipment bonding jumper on the load side of the service overcurrent devices shall be sized, as a minimum, in accordance with the sizes listed in Table 250.122, but shall not be required to be larger than the largest ungrounded circuit conductors supplying the equipment and shall not be smaller than 14 AWG.

A single common continuous equipment bonding jumper shall be permitted to bond two or more raceways or cables where the bonding jumper is sized in accordance with Table 250.122 for the largest overcurrent device supplying circuits therein.

(E) Installation. The equipment bonding jumper shall be permitted to be installed inside or outside of a raceway or enclosure. Where installed on the outside, the length of the equipment bonding jumper shall not exceed 1.8 m (6 ft) and shall be routed with the raceway or enclosure. Where installed inside of a raceway, the equipment bonding jumper shall comply with the requirements of 250.119 and 250.148.

Exception: An equipment bonding jumper longer than 1.8 m (6 ft) shall be permitted at outside pole locations for the purpose of bonding or grounding isolated sections of metal raceways or elbows installed in exposed risers of metal conduit or other metal raceway.

250.104 Bonding of Piping Systems and Exposed Structural Steel.

(A) Metal Water Piping. The metal water piping system shall be bonded as required in (A)(1), (A)(2), or (A)(3) of this section. The bonding jumper(s) shall be installed in accordance with 250.64(A), (B), and (E). The points of attachment of the bonding jumper(s) shall be accessible.

(1) General. Metal water piping system(s) installed in or attached to a building or structure shall be bonded to the service equipment enclosure, the grounded conductor at the service, the grounding electrode conductor where of sufficient size, or to the one or more grounding electrodes used. The bonding jumper(s) shall be sized in accordance with Table 250.66 except as permitted in 250.104(A)(2) and (A)(3).

(2) Buildings of Multiple Occupancy. In buildings of multiple occupancy where the metal water piping system(s) installed in or attached to a building or structure for the individual occupancies is metallically isolated from all other occupancies by use of nonmetallic water piping, the metal water piping system(s) for each occupancy shall be permitted to be bonded to the equipment grounding terminal of the panelboard or switchboard enclosure (other than service equipment) supplying that occupancy. The bonding jumper shall be sized in accordance with Table 250.122.

(3) Multiple Buildings or Structures Supplied by a Feeder(s) or Branch Circuit(s). The metal water piping system(s) installed in or attached to a building or structure shall be bonded to the building or structure disconnecting means enclosure where located at the building or structure, to the equipment grounding conductor run with the supply conductors, or to the one or more grounding electrodes used. The bonding jumper(s) shall be sized in accordance with 250.66, based on the size of the feeder or branch circuit conductors that supply the building. The bonding jumper shall not be required to be larger than the largest ungrounded feeder or branch circuit conductor supplying the building.

(B) Other Metal Piping. Where installed in or attached to a building or structure, metal piping system(s), including gas piping, that is likely to become energized shall be bonded to the service equipment enclosure, the grounded conductor at the service, the grounding electrode conductor where of sufficient size, or to the one or more grounding electrodes used. The bonding jumper(s) shall be sized in accordance with 250.122, using the rating of the circuit that is likely to energize the piping system(s). The equipment grounding conductor for the circuit that is likely to energize the piping shall be permitted to serve as the bonding means. The points of attachment of the bonding jumper(s) shall be accessible.

> FPN: Bonding all piping and metal air ducts within the premises will provide additional safety.

(C) Structural Metal. Exposed structural metal that is interconnected to form a metal building frame and is not intentionally grounded and is likely to become energized shall be bonded to the service equipment enclosure, the grounded conductor at the service, the grounding electrode conductor where of sufficient size, or the one or more grounding electrodes used. The bonding jumper(s) shall be sized in accordance with Table 250.66 and installed in accordance with 250.64(A), (B), and (E). The points of attachment of the bonding jumper(s) shall be accessible.

(D) Separately Derived Systems. Metal water piping systems and structural metal that is interconnected to form a building frame shall be bonded to separately derived systems in accordance with (D)(1) through (D)(3).

(1) Metal Water Piping System(s). The grounded conductor of each separately derived system shall be bonded to the nearest available point of the metal water piping system(s) in the area served by each separately derived system. This connection shall be made at the same point on the separately derived system where the grounding electrode conductor is connected. Each bonding jumper shall be sized in accordance with Table 250.66 based on the largest ungrounded conductor of the separately derived system.

Exception No. 1: A separate bonding jumper to the metal water piping system shall not be required where the metal water piping system is used as the grounding electrode for the separately derived system.

Exception No. 2: A separate water piping bonding jumper shall not be required where the metal frame of a building or structure is used as the grounding electrode for a separately derived system and is bonded to the metal water piping in the area served by the separately derived system.

(2) Structural Metal. Where exposed structural metal that is interconnected to form the building frame exists in the area served by the separately derived system, it shall be bonded to the grounded conductor of each separately derived system.

This connection shall be made at the same point on the separately derived system where the grounding electrode conductor is connected. Each bonding jumper shall be sized in accordance with Table 250.66 based on the largest ungrounded conductor of the separately derived system.

Exception No. 1: A separate bonding jumper to the building structural metal shall not be required where the metal frame of a building or structure is used as the grounding electrode for the separately derived system.

Exception No. 2: A separate bonding jumper to the building structural metal shall not be required where the water piping of a building or structure is used as the grounding electrode for a separately derived system and is bonded to the building structural metal in the area served by the separately derived system.

(3) Common Grounding Electrode Conductor. Where a common grounding electrode conductor is installed for multiple separately derived systems as permitted by 250.30(A)(4), and exposed structural metal that is interconnected to form the building frame or interior metal piping exists in the area served by the separately derived system, the metal piping and the structural metal member shall be bonded to the common grounding electrode conductor.

Exception: A separate bonding jumper from each derived system to metal water piping and to structural metal members shall not be required where the metal water piping and the structural metal members in the area served by the separately derived system are bonded to the common grounding electrode conductor.

250.106 Lightning Protection Systems. The lightning protection system ground terminals shall be bonded to the building or structure grounding electrode system.

> FPN No. 1: See 250.60 for use of air terminals. For further information, see NFPA 780-2004, *Standard for the Installation of Lightning Protection Systems*, which contains detailed information on grounding, bonding, and spacing from lightning protection systems.

> FPN No. 2: Metal raceways, enclosures, frames, and other non–current-carrying metal parts of electric equipment installed on a building equipped with a lightning protection system may require bonding or spacing from the lightning protection conductors in accordance with NFPA 780-2004, *Standard for the Installation of Lightning Protection Systems*. Separation from lightning protection conductors is typically 1.8 m (6 ft) through air or 900 mm (3 ft) through dense materials such as concrete, brick, or wood.

VI. Equipment Grounding and Equipment Grounding Conductors

250.110 Equipment Fastened in Place or Connected by Permanent Wiring Methods (Fixed). Exposed non–current-carrying metal parts of fixed equipment likely to become energized shall be grounded under any of the following conditions:

(1) Where within 2.5 m (8 ft) vertically or 1.5 m (5 ft) horizontally of ground or grounded metal objects and subject to contact by persons

(2) Where located in a wet or damp location and not isolated

(3) Where in electrical contact with metal

(4) Where in a hazardous (classified) location as covered by Articles 500 through 517

(5) Where supplied by a metal-clad, metal-sheathed, metal-raceway, or other wiring method that provides an equipment ground, except as permitted by 250.86, Exception No. 2, for short sections of metal enclosures

(6) Where equipment operates with any terminal at over 150 volts to ground

Exception No. 1: Metal frames of electrically heated appliances, exempted by special permission, in which case the frames shall be permanently and effectively insulated from ground.

Exception No. 2: Distribution apparatus, such as transformer and capacitor cases, mounted on wooden poles, at a height exceeding 2.5 m (8 ft) above ground or grade level.

Exception No. 3: Listed equipment protected by a system of double insulation, or its equivalent, shall not be required to be grounded. Where such a system is employed, the equipment shall be distinctively marked.

250.112 Fastened in Place or Connected by Permanent Wiring Methods (Fixed) — Specific. Exposed, non–current-carrying metal parts of the kinds of equipment described in 250.112(A) through (K), and non–current-carrying metal parts of equipment and enclosures described in 250.112(L) and (M), shall be grounded regardless of voltage.

(A) Switchboard Frames and Structures. Switchboard frames and structures supporting switching equipment, except frames of 2-wire dc switchboards where effectively insulated from ground.

(B) Pipe Organs. Generator and motor frames in an electrically operated pipe organ, unless effectively insulated from ground and the motor driving it.

(C) Motor Frames. Motor frames, as provided by 430.242.

(D) Enclosures for Motor Controllers. Enclosures for motor controllers unless attached to ungrounded portable equipment.

(E) Elevators and Cranes. Electric equipment for elevators and cranes.

(F) Garages, Theaters, and Motion Picture Studios. Electric equipment in commercial garages, theaters, and motion picture studios, except pendant lampholders supplied by circuits not over 150 volts to ground.

(G) Electric Signs. Electric signs, outline lighting, and associated equipment as provided in Article 600.

(H) Motion Picture Projection Equipment. Motion picture projection equipment.

(I) Power-Limited Remote-Control, Signaling, and Fire Alarm Circuits. Equipment supplied by Class 1 power-limited circuits and Class 1, Class 2, and Class 3 remote-control and signaling circuits, and by fire alarm circuits, shall be grounded where system grounding is required by Part II or Part VIII of this article.

(J) Luminaires (Lighting Fixtures). Luminaires (lighting fixtures) as provided in Part V of Article 410.

(K) Skid Mounted Equipment. Permanently mounted electrical equipment and skids shall be grounded with an equipment bonding jumper sized as required by 250.122.

(L) Motor-Operated Water Pumps. Motor-operated water pumps, including the submersible type.

(M) Metal Well Casings. Where a submersible pump is used in a metal well casing, the well casing shall be bonded to the pump circuit equipment grounding conductor.

250.114 Equipment Connected by Cord and Plug. Under any of the conditions described in 250.114(1) through (4), exposed non–current-carrying metal parts of cord-and-plug-connected equipment likely to become energized shall be grounded.

Exception: Listed tools, listed appliances, and listed equipment covered in 250.114(2) through (4) shall not be required to be grounded where protected by a system of double insulation or its equivalent. Double insulated equipment shall be distinctively marked.

(1) In hazardous (classified) locations (see Articles 500 through 517)

(2) Where operated at over 150 volts to ground

Exception No. 1: Motors, where guarded, shall not be required to be grounded.

Exception No. 2: Metal frames of electrically heated appliances, exempted by special permission, shall not be required to be grounded, in which case the frames shall be permanently and effectively insulated from ground.

(3) In residential occupancies:

   a. Refrigerators, freezers, and air conditioners

   b. Clothes-washing, clothes-drying, dish-washing machines; kitchen waste disposers; information technology equipment; sump pumps and electrical aquarium equipment

c. Hand-held motor-operated tools, stationary and fixed motor-operated tools, light industrial motor-operated tools

d. Motor-operated appliances of the following types: hedge clippers, lawn mowers, snow blowers, and wet scrubbers

e. Portable handlamps

(4) In other than residential occupancies:

a. Refrigerators, freezers, and air conditioners

b. Clothes-washing, clothes-drying, dish-washing machines; information technology equipment; sump pumps and electrical aquarium equipment

c. Hand-held motor-operated tools, stationary and fixed motor-operated tools, light industrial motor-operated tools

d. Motor-operated appliances of the following types: hedge clippers, lawn mowers, snow blowers, and wet scrubbers

e. Portable handlamps

f. Cord-and-plug-connected appliances used in damp or wet locations or by persons standing on the ground or on metal floors or working inside of metal tanks or boilers

g. Tools likely to be used in wet or conductive locations

Exception: Tools and portable handlamps likely to be used in wet or conductive locations shall not be required to be grounded where supplied through an isolating transformer with an ungrounded secondary of not over 50 volts.

250.116 Nonelectric Equipment. The metal parts of nonelectric equipment described in this section shall be grounded.

(1) Frames and tracks of electrically operated cranes and hoists

(2) Frames of nonelectrically driven elevator cars to which electric conductors are attached

(3) Hand-operated metal shifting ropes or cables of electric elevators

FPN: Where extensive metal in or on buildings may become energized and is subject to personal contact, adequate bonding and grounding will provide additional safety.

250.118 Types of Equipment Grounding Conductors. The equipment grounding conductor run with or enclosing the circuit conductors shall be one or more or a combination of the following:

(1) A copper, aluminum, or copper-clad aluminum conductor. This conductor shall be solid or stranded; insulated, covered, or bare; and in the form of a wire or a busbar of any shape.

(2) Rigid metal conduit.

(3) Intermediate metal conduit.

(4) Electrical metallic tubing.

(5) Listed flexible metal conduit meeting all the following conditions:

a. The conduit is terminated in fittings listed for grounding.

b. The circuit conductors contained in the conduit are protected by overcurrent devices rated at 20 amperes or less.

c. The combined length of flexible metal conduit and flexible metallic tubing and liquidtight flexible metal conduit in the same ground return path does not exceed 1.8 m (6 ft).

d. Where used to connect equipment where flexibility is necessary after installation, an equipment grounding conductor shall be installed.

(6) Listed liquidtight flexible metal conduit meeting all the following conditions:

a. The conduit is terminated in fittings listed for grounding.

b. For metric designators 12 through 16 (trade sizes ⅜ through ½), the circuit conductors contained in the conduit are protected by overcurrent devices rated at 20 amperes or less.

c. For metric designators 21 through 35 (trade sizes ¾ through 1¼), the circuit conductors contained in the conduit are protected by overcurrent devices rated not more than 60 amperes and there is no flexible metal conduit, flexible metallic tubing, or liquidtight flexible metal conduit in trade sizes metric designators 12 through 16 (trade sizes ⅜ through ½) in the grounding path.

d. The combined length of flexible metal conduit and flexible metallic tubing and liquidtight flexible metal conduit in the same ground return path does not exceed 1.8 m (6 ft).

e. Where used to connect equipment where flexibility is necessary after installation, an equipment grounding conductor shall be installed.

(7) Flexible metallic tubing where the tubing is terminated in fittings listed for grounding and meeting the following conditions:

a. The circuit conductors contained in the tubing are protected by overcurrent devices rated at 20 amperes or less.

b. The combined length of flexible metal conduit and flexible metallic tubing and liquidtight flexible metal conduit in the same ground return path does not exceed 1.8 m (6 ft).

(8) Armor of Type AC cable as provided in 320.108.

(9) The copper sheath of mineral-insulated, metal-sheathed cable.

(10) Type MC cable where listed and identified for grounding in accordance with the following:

   a. The combined metallic sheath and grounding conductor of interlocked metal tape–type MC cable

   b. The metallic sheath or the combined metallic sheath and grounding conductors of the smooth or corrugated tube type MC cable

(11) Cable trays as permitted in 392.3(C) and 392.7.

(12) Cablebus framework as permitted in 370.3.

(13) Other listed electrically continuous metal raceways and listed auxiliary gutters.

(14) Surface metal raceways listed for grounding.

250.119 Identification of Equipment Grounding Conductors.

Unless required elsewhere in this *Code,* equipment grounding conductors shall be permitted to be bare, covered, or insulated. Individually covered or insulated equipment grounding conductors shall have a continuous outer finish that is either green or green with one or more yellow stripes except as permitted in this section. Conductors with insulation or individual covering that is green, green with one or more yellow stripes, or otherwise identified as permitted by this section shall not be used for ungrounded or grounded circuit conductors.

(A) Conductors Larger Than 6 AWG. Equipment grounding conductors larger than 6 AWG shall comply with 250.119(A)(1) and (A)(2).

(1) An insulated or covered conductor larger than 6 AWG shall be permitted, at the time of installation, to be permanently identified as an equipment grounding conductor at each end and at every point where the conductor is accessible.

Exception: Conductors larger than 6 AWG shall not be required to be marked in conduit bodies that contain no splices or unused hubs.

(2) Identification shall encircle the conductor and shall be accomplished by one of the following:

   a. Stripping the insulation or covering from the entire exposed length

   b. Coloring the exposed insulation or covering green

   c. Marking the exposed insulation or covering with green tape or green adhesive labels

(B) Multiconductor Cable. Where the conditions of maintenance and supervision ensure that only qualified persons service the installation, one or more insulated conductors in a multiconductor cable, at the time of installation, shall be permitted to be permanently identified as equipment grounding conductors at each end and at every point where the conductors are accessible by one of the following means:

(1) Stripping the insulation from the entire exposed length

(2) Coloring the exposed insulation green

(3) Marking the exposed insulation with green tape or green adhesive labels

(C) Flexible Cord. An uninsulated equipment grounding conductor shall be permitted, but, if individually covered, the covering shall have a continuous outer finish that is either green or green with one or more yellow stripes.

250.120 Equipment Grounding Conductor Installation.

An equipment grounding conductor shall be installed in accordance with 250.120(A), (B), and (C).

(A) Raceway, Cable Trays, Cable Armor, Cablebus, or Cable Sheaths. Where it consists of a raceway, cable tray, cable armor, cablebus framework, or cable sheath or where it is a wire within a raceway or cable, it shall be installed in accordance with the applicable provisions in this *Code* using fittings for joints and terminations approved for use with the type raceway or cable used. All connections, joints, and fittings shall be made tight using suitable tools.

(B) Aluminum and Copper-Clad Aluminum Conductors. Equipment grounding conductors of bare or insulated aluminum or copper-clad aluminum shall be permitted. Bare conductors shall not come in direct contact with masonry or the earth or where subject to corrosive conditions. Aluminum or copper-clad aluminum conductors shall not be terminated within 450 mm (18 in.) of the earth.

(C) Equipment Grounding Conductors Smaller Than 6 AWG. Equipment grounding conductors smaller than 6 AWG shall be protected from physical damage by a raceway or cable armor except where run in hollow spaces of walls or partitions, where not subject to physical damage, or where protected from physical damage.

250.122 Size of Equipment Grounding Conductors.

(A) General. Copper, aluminum, or copper-clad aluminum equipment grounding conductors of the wire type shall not be smaller than shown in Table 250.122 but shall not be required to be larger than the circuit conductors supplying the equipment. Where a raceway or a cable armor or sheath is used as the equipment grounding conductor, as provided in 250.118 and 250.134(A), it shall comply with 250.4(A)(5) or (B)(4).

(B) Increased in Size. Where ungrounded conductors are increased in size, equipment grounding conductors, where installed, shall be increased in size proportionately according to circular mil area of the ungrounded conductors.

(C) Multiple Circuits. Where a single equipment grounding conductor is run with multiple circuits in the same raceway or cable, it shall be sized for the largest overcurrent device protecting conductors in the raceway or cable.

(D) Motor Circuits. Where the overcurrent device consists of an instantaneous trip circuit breaker or a motor short-circuit protector, as allowed in 430.52, the equipment grounding conductor size shall be permitted to be based on the rating of the motor overload protective device but shall not be less than the size shown in Table 250.122.

(E) Flexible Cord and Fixture Wire. The equipment grounding conductor in a flexible cord with the largest circuit conductor 10 AWG or smaller, and the equipment grounding conductor used with fixture wires of any size in accordance with 240.5, shall not be smaller than 18 AWG copper and shall not be smaller than the circuit conductors. The equipment grounding conductor in a flexible cord with a circuit conductor larger than 10 AWG shall be sized in accordance with Table 250.122.

(F) Conductors in Parallel. Where conductors are run in parallel in multiple raceways or cables as permitted in 310.4, the equipment grounding conductors, where used, shall be run in parallel in each raceway or cable. One of the methods in 250.122(F)(1) or (F)(2) shall be used to ensure the equipment grounding conductors are protected.

(1) Based on Rating of Overcurrent Protective Device. Each parallel equipment grounding conductor shall be sized on the basis of the ampere rating of the overcurrent device protecting the circuit conductors in the raceway or cable in accordance with Table 250.122.

(2) Ground-Fault Protection of Equipment Installed. Where ground-fault protection of equipment is installed, each parallel equipment grounding conductor in a multiconductor cable shall be permitted to be sized in accordance with Table 250.122 on the basis of the trip rating of the ground-fault protection where the following conditions are met:

(1) Conditions of maintenance and supervision ensure that only qualified persons will service the installation.

(2) The ground-fault protection equipment is set to trip at not more than the ampacity of a single ungrounded conductor of one of the cables in parallel.

(3) The ground-fault protection is listed for the purpose of protecting the equipment grounding conductor.

(G) Feeder Taps. Equipment grounding conductors run with feeder taps shall not be smaller than shown in Table 250.122 based on the rating of the overcurrent device ahead of the feeder but shall not be required to be larger than the tap conductors.

250.124 Equipment Grounding Conductor Continuity.

(A) Separable Connections. Separable connections such as those provided in drawout equipment or attachment plugs and mating connectors and receptacles shall provide

Table 250.122 Minimum Size Equipment Grounding Conductors for Grounding Raceway and Equipment

Rating or Setting of Automatic Overcurrent Device in Circuit Ahead of Equipment, Conduit, etc., Not Exceeding (Amperes)	Size (AWG or kcmil)	
	Copper	Aluminum or Copper-Clad Aluminum*
15	14	12
20	12	10
30	10	8
40	10	8
60	10	8
100	8	6
200	6	4
300	4	2
400	3	1
500	2	1/0
600	1	2/0
800	1/0	3/0
1000	2/0	4/0
1200	3/0	250
1600	4/0	350
2000	250	400
2500	350	600
3000	400	600
4000	500	800
5000	700	1200
6000	800	1200

Note: Where necessary to comply with 250.4(A)(5) or (B)(4), the equipment grounding conductor shall be sized larger than given in this table.

*See installation restrictions in 250.120.

for first-make, last-break of the equipment grounding conductor. First-make, last-break shall not be required where interlocked equipment, plugs, receptacles, and connectors preclude energization without grounding continuity.

(B) Switches. No automatic cutout or switch shall be placed in the equipment grounding conductor of a premises wiring system unless the opening of the cutout or switch disconnects all sources of energy.

250.126 Identification of Wiring Device Terminals.
The terminal for the connection of the equipment grounding conductor shall be identified by one of the following:

(1) A green, not readily removable terminal screw with a hexagonal head.

(2) A green, hexagonal, not readily removable terminal nut.

(3) A green pressure wire connector. If the terminal for the grounding conductor is not visible, the conductor entrance hole shall be marked with the word *green* or *ground*, the letters *G* or *GR*, a grounding symbol, or otherwise identified by a distinctive green color. If the terminal for the equipment grounding conductor is readily removable, the area adjacent to the terminal shall be similarly marked.

FPN: See FPN Figure 250.126.

FPN Figure 250.126 One Example of a Symbol Used to Identify the Grounding Termination Point for an Equipment Grounding Conductor.

VII. Methods of Equipment Grounding

250.130 Equipment Grounding Conductor Connections. Equipment grounding conductor connections at the source of separately derived systems shall be made in accordance with 250.30(A)(1). Equipment grounding conductor connections at service equipment shall be made as indicated in 250.130(A) or (B). For replacement of non–grounding-type receptacles with grounding-type receptacles and for branch-circuit extensions only in existing installations that do not have an equipment grounding conductor in the branch circuit, connections shall be permitted as indicated in 250.130(C).

(A) For Grounded Systems. The connection shall be made by bonding the equipment grounding conductor to the grounded service conductor and the grounding electrode conductor.

(B) For Ungrounded Systems. The connection shall be made by bonding the equipment grounding conductor to the grounding electrode conductor.

(C) Nongrounding Receptacle Replacement or Branch Circuit Extensions. The equipment grounding conductor of a grounding-type receptacle or a branch-circuit extension shall be permitted to be connected to any of the following:

(1) Any accessible point on the grounding electrode system as described in 250.50
(2) Any accessible point on the grounding electrode conductor
(3) The equipment grounding terminal bar within the enclosure where the branch circuit for the receptacle or branch circuit originates
(4) For grounded systems, the grounded service conductor within the service equipment enclosure
(5) For ungrounded systems, the grounding terminal bar within the service equipment enclosure

FPN: See 406.3(D) for the use of a ground-fault circuit-interrupting type of receptacle.

250.132 Short Sections of Raceway. Isolated sections of metal raceway or cable armor, where required to be grounded, shall be grounded in accordance with 250.134.

250.134 Equipment Fastened in Place or Connected by Permanent Wiring Methods (Fixed) — Grounding. Unless grounded by connection to the grounded circuit conductor as permitted by 250.32, 250.140, and 250.142, non–current-carrying metal parts of equipment, raceways, and other enclosures, if grounded, shall be grounded by one of the following methods.

(A) Equipment Grounding Conductor Types. By any of the equipment grounding conductors permitted by 250.118.

(B) With Circuit Conductors. By an equipment grounding conductor contained within the same raceway, cable, or otherwise run with the circuit conductors.

Exception No. 1: As provided in 250.130(C), the equipment grounding conductor shall be permitted to be run separately from the circuit conductors.

Exception No. 2: For dc circuits, the equipment grounding conductor shall be permitted to be run separately from the circuit conductors.

FPN No. 1: See 250.102 and 250.168 for equipment bonding jumper requirements.

FPN No. 2: See 400.7 for use of cords for fixed equipment.

250.136 Equipment Considered Effectively Grounded. Under the conditions specified in 250.136(A) and (B), the non–current-carrying metal parts of the equipment shall be considered effectively grounded.

(A) Equipment Secured to Grounded Metal Supports. Electrical equipment secured to and in electrical contact with a metal rack or structure provided for its support and grounded by one of the means indicated in 250.134. The structural metal frame of a building shall not be used as the required equipment grounding conductor for ac equipment.

(B) Metal Car Frames. Metal car frames supported by metal hoisting cables attached to or running over metal sheaves or drums of elevator machines that are grounded by one of the methods indicated in 250.134.

250.138 Cord-and-Plug-Connected Equipment. Non–current-carrying metal parts of cord-and-plug-connected equipment, if grounded, shall be grounded by one of the methods in 250.138(A) or (B).

(A) By Means of an Equipment Grounding Conductor. By means of an equipment grounding conductor run with the power supply conductors in a cable assembly or flexible cord properly terminated in a grounding-type attachment plug with one fixed grounding contact.

Exception: The grounding contacting pole of grounding-type plug-in ground-fault circuit interrupters shall be permitted to be of the movable, self-restoring type on circuits operating at not over 150 volts between any two conductors or over 150 volts between any conductor and ground.

(B) By Means of a Separate Flexible Wire or Strap. By means of a separate flexible wire or strap, insulated or bare, protected as well as practicable against physical damage, where part of equipment.

250.140 Frames of Ranges and Clothes Dryers. Frames of electric ranges, wall-mounted ovens, counter-mounted cooking units, clothes dryers, and outlet or junction boxes that are part of the circuit for these appliances shall be grounded in the manner specified by 250.134 or 250.138.

Exception: For existing branch circuit installations only where an equipment grounding conductor is not present in the outlet or junction box, the frames of electric ranges, wall-mounted ovens, counter-mounted cooking units, clothes dryers, and outlet or junction boxes that are part of the circuit for these appliances shall be permitted to be grounded to the grounded circuit conductor if all the following conditions are met.

(1) The supply circuit is 120/240-volt, single-phase, 3-wire; or 208Y/120-volt derived from a 3-phase, 4-wire, wye-connected system.

(2) The grounded conductor is not smaller than 10 AWG copper or 8 AWG aluminum.

(3) The grounded conductor is insulated, or the grounded conductor is uninsulated and part of a Type SE service-entrance cable and the branch circuit originates at the service equipment.

(4) Grounding contacts of receptacles furnished as part of the equipment are bonded to the equipment.

250.142 Use of Grounded Circuit Conductor for Grounding Equipment.

(A) Supply-Side Equipment. A grounded circuit conductor shall be permitted to ground non–current-carrying metal parts of equipment, raceways, and other enclosures at any of the following locations:

(1) On the supply side or within the enclosure of the ac service-disconnecting means

(2) On the supply side or within the enclosure of the main disconnecting means for separate buildings as provided in 250.32(B)

(3) On the supply side or within the enclosure of the main disconnecting means or overcurrent devices of a separately derived system where permitted by 250.30(A)(1)

(B) Load-Side Equipment. Except as permitted in 250.30(A)(1) and 250.32(B), a grounded circuit conductor shall not be used for grounding non–current-carrying metal parts of equipment on the load side of the service disconnecting means or on the load side of a separately derived system disconnecting means or the overcurrent devices for a separately derived system not having a main disconnecting means.

Exception No. 1: The frames of ranges, wall-mounted ovens, counter-mounted cooking units, and clothes dryers under the conditions permitted for existing installations by 250.140 shall be permitted to be grounded by a grounded circuit conductor.

Exception No. 2: It shall be permissible to ground meter enclosures by connection to the grounded circuit conductor on the load side of the service disconnect where all of the following conditions apply:

(1) No service ground-fault protection is installed.

(2) All meter socket enclosures are located immediately adjacent to the service disconnecting means.

(3) The size of the grounded circuit conductor is not smaller than the size specified in Table 250.122 for equipment grounding conductors.

Exception No. 3: Direct-current systems shall be permitted to be grounded on the load side of the disconnecting means or overcurrent device in accordance with 250.164.

Exception No. 4: Electrode-type boilers operating at over 600 volts shall be grounded as required in 490.72(E)(1) and 490.74.

250.144 Multiple Circuit Connections. Where equipment is required to be grounded and is supplied by separate connection to more than one circuit or grounded premises wiring system, a means for grounding shall be provided for each such connection as specified in 250.134 and 250.138.

250.146 Connecting Receptacle Grounding Terminal to Box. An equipment bonding jumper shall be used to connect the grounding terminal of a grounding-type receptacle to a grounded box unless grounded as in 250.146(A) through (D).

(A) Surface Mounted Box. Where the box is mounted on the surface, direct metal-to-metal contact between the device yoke and the box or a contact yoke or device that complies with 250.146(B) shall be permitted to ground the receptacle to the box. At least one of the insulating washers shall be removed from receptacles that do not have a contact yoke or device that complies with 250.146(B) to ensure direct metal-to-metal contact. This provision shall not apply to cover-mounted receptacles unless the box and cover combination are listed as providing satisfactory ground continuity between the box and the receptacle.

(B) Contact Devices or Yokes. Contact devices or yokes designed and listed as self-grounding shall be permitted in conjunction with the supporting screws to establish the grounding circuit between the device yoke and flush-type boxes.

(C) Floor Boxes. Floor boxes designed for and listed as providing satisfactory ground continuity between the box and the device shall be permitted.

(D) Isolated Receptacles. Where required for the reduction of electrical noise (electromagnetic interference) on the grounding circuit, a receptacle in which the grounding terminal is purposely insulated from the receptacle mounting means shall be permitted. The receptacle grounding terminal shall be grounded by an insulated equipment grounding conductor run with the circuit conductors. This grounding conductor shall be permitted to pass through one or more panelboards without connection to the panelboard grounding terminal as permitted in 408.40, Exception, so as to terminate within the same building or structure directly at an equipment grounding conductor terminal of the applicable derived system or service.

> FPN: Use of an isolated equipment grounding conductor does not relieve the requirement for grounding the raceway system and outlet box.

250.148 Continuity and Attachment of Equipment Grounding Conductors to Boxes. Where circuit conductors are spliced within a box, or terminated on equipment within or supported by a box, any equipment grounding conductor(s) associated with those circuit conductors shall be spliced or joined within the box or to the box with devices suitable for the use in accordance with 250.148(A) through (E).

Exception: The equipment grounding conductor permitted in 250.146(D) shall not be required to be connected to the other equipment grounding conductors or to the box.

(A) Connections. Connections and splices shall be made in accordance with 110.14(B) except that insulation shall not be required.

(B) Grounding Continuity. The arrangement of grounding connections shall be such that the disconnection or the removal of a receptacle, luminaire (fixture), or other device fed from the box does not interfere with or interrupt the grounding continuity.

(C) Metal Boxes. A connection shall be made between the one or more equipment grounding conductors and a metal box by means of a grounding screw that shall be used for no other purpose or a listed grounding device.

(D) Nonmetallic Boxes. One or more equipment grounding conductors brought into a nonmetallic outlet box shall be arranged such that a connection can be made to any fitting or device in that box requiring grounding.

(E) Solder. Connections depending solely on solder shall not be used.

VIII. Direct-Current Systems

250.160 General. Direct-current systems shall comply with Part VIII and other sections of Article 250 not specifically intended for ac systems.

250.162 Direct-Current Circuits and Systems to Be Grounded. Direct-current circuits and systems shall be grounded as provided for in 250.162(A) and (B).

(A) Two-Wire, Direct-Current Systems. A 2-wire, dc system supplying premises wiring and operating at greater than 50 volts but not greater than 300 volts shall be grounded.

Exception No. 1: A system equipped with a ground detector and supplying only industrial equipment in limited areas shall not be required to be grounded.

Exception No. 2: A rectifier-derived dc system supplied from an ac system complying with 250.20 shall not be required to be grounded.

Exception No. 3: Direct-current fire alarm circuits having a maximum current of 0.030 amperes as specified in Article 760, Part III, shall not be required to be grounded.

(B) Three-Wire, Direct-Current Systems. The neutral conductor of all 3-wire, dc systems supplying premises wiring shall be grounded.

250.164 Point of Connection for Direct-Current Systems.

(A) Off-Premises Source. Direct-current systems to be grounded and supplied from an off-premises source shall have the grounding connection made at one or more supply stations. A grounding connection shall not be made at individual services or at any point on the premises wiring.

(B) On-Premises Source. Where the dc system source is located on the premises, a grounding connection shall be made at one of the following:

(1) The source
(2) The first system disconnection means or overcurrent device
(3) By other means that accomplish equivalent system protection and that utilize equipment listed and identified for the use

250.166 Size of Direct-Current Grounding Electrode Conductor.
The size of the grounding electrode conductor for a dc system shall be as specified in 250.166(A) through (E).

(A) Not Smaller Than the Neutral Conductor. Where the dc system consists of a 3-wire balancer set or a balancer winding with overcurrent protection as provided in 445.12(D), the grounding electrode conductor shall not be smaller than the neutral conductor and not smaller than 8 AWG copper or 6 AWG aluminum.

(B) Not Smaller Than the Largest Conductor. Where the dc system is other than as in 250.166(A), the grounding electrode conductor shall not be smaller than the largest conductor supplied by the system, and not smaller than 8 AWG copper or 6 AWG aluminum.

(C) Connected to Rod, Pipe, or Plate Electrodes. Where connected to rod, pipe, or plate electrodes as in 250.52(A)(5) or 250.52(A)(6), that portion of the grounding electrode conductor that is the sole connection to the grounding electrode shall not be required to be larger than 6 AWG copper wire or 4 AWG aluminum wire.

(D) Connected to a Concrete-Encased Electrode. Where connected to a concrete-encased electrode as in 250.52(A)(3), that portion of the grounding electrode conductor that is the sole connection to the grounding electrode shall not be required to be larger than 4 AWG copper wire.

(E) Connected to a Ground Ring. Where connected to a ground ring as in 250.52(A)(4), that portion of the grounding electrode conductor that is the sole connection to the grounding electrode shall not be required to be larger than the conductor used for the ground ring.

250.168 Direct-Current Bonding Jumper.
For dc systems, the size of the bonding jumper shall not be smaller than the system grounding electrode conductor specified in 250.166.

250.169 Ungrounded Direct-Current Separately Derived Systems.
Except as otherwise permitted in 250.34 for portable and vehicle-mounted generators, an ungrounded dc separately derived system supplied from a stand-alone power source (such as an engine–generator set) shall have a grounding electrode conductor connected to an electrode that complies with Part III to provide for grounding of metal enclosures, raceways, cables, and exposed non–current-carrying metal parts of equipment. The grounding electrode conductor connection shall be to the metal enclosure at any point on the separately derived system from the source to the first system disconnecting means or overcurrent device, or it shall be made at the source of a separately derived system that has no disconnecting means or overcurrent devices.

The size of the grounding electrode conductor shall be in accordance with 250.166.

IX. Instruments, Meters, and Relays

250.170 Instrument Transformer Circuits.
Secondary circuits of current and potential instrument transformers shall be grounded where the primary windings are connected to circuits of 300 volts or more to ground and, where on switchboards, shall be grounded irrespective of voltage.

Exception: Circuits where the primary windings are connected to circuits of less than 1000 volts with no live parts or wiring exposed or accessible to other than qualified persons.

250.172 Instrument Transformer Cases.
Cases or frames of instrument transformers shall be grounded where accessible to other than qualified persons.

Exception: Cases or frames of current transformers, the primaries of which are not over 150 volts to ground and that are used exclusively to supply current to meters.

250.174 Cases of Instruments, Meters, and Relays Operating at Less Than 1000 Volts.
Instruments, meters, and relays operating with windings or working parts at less than 1000 volts shall be grounded as specified in 250.174(A), (B), or (C).

(A) Not on Switchboards. Instruments, meters, and relays not located on switchboards, operating with windings or working parts at 300 volts or more to ground, and accessible to other than qualified persons, shall have the cases and other exposed metal parts grounded.

(B) On Dead-Front Switchboards. Instruments, meters, and relays (whether operated from current and potential transformers or connected directly in the circuit) on switchboards having no live parts on the front of the panels shall have the cases grounded.

(C) On Live-Front Switchboards. Instruments, meters, and relays (whether operated from current and potential transformers or connected directly in the circuit) on switchboards having exposed live parts on the front of panels shall not have their cases grounded. Mats of insulating rubber or other suitable floor insulation shall be provided for the operator where the voltage to ground exceeds 150.

250.176 Cases of Instruments, Meters, and Relays — Operating Voltage 1 kV and Over. Where instruments, meters, and relays have current-carrying parts of 1 kV and over to ground, they shall be isolated by elevation or protected by suitable barriers, grounded metal, or insulating covers or guards. Their cases shall not be grounded.

Exception: Cases of electrostatic ground detectors where the internal ground segments of the instrument are connected to the instrument case and grounded and the ground detector is isolated by elevation.

250.178 Instrument Grounding Conductor. The grounding conductor for secondary circuits of instrument transformers and for instrument cases shall not be smaller than 12 AWG copper or 10 AWG aluminum. Cases of instrument transformers, instruments, meters, and relays that are mounted directly on grounded metal surfaces of enclosures or grounded metal switchboard panels shall be considered to be grounded, and no additional grounding conductor shall be required.

X. Grounding of Systems and Circuits of 1 kV and Over (High Voltage)

250.180 General. Where high-voltage systems are grounded, they shall comply with all applicable provisions of the preceding sections of this article and with 250.182 through 250.190, which supplement and modify the preceding sections.

250.182 Derived Neutral Systems. A system neutral derived from a grounding transformer shall be permitted to be used for grounding high-voltage systems.

250.184 Solidly Grounded Neutral Systems. Solidly grounded neutral systems shall be permitted to be either single point grounded or multigrounded neutral.

(A) Neutral Conductor.

(1) Insulation Level. The minimum insulation level for neutral conductors of solidly grounded systems shall be 600 volts.

Exception No. 1: Bare copper conductors shall be permitted to be used for the neutral of service entrances and the neutral of direct-buried portions of feeders.

Exception No. 2: Bare conductors shall be permitted for the neutral of overhead portions installed outdoors.

Exception No. 3: The neutral grounded conductor shall be permitted to be a bare conductor if isolated from phase conductors and protected from physical damage.

FPN: See 225.4 for conductor covering where within 3.0 m (10 ft) of any building or other structure.

(2) Ampacity. The neutral conductor shall be of sufficient ampacity for the load imposed on the conductor but not less than 33⅓ percent of the ampacity of the phase conductors.

Exception: In industrial and commercial premises under engineering supervision, it shall be permissible to size the ampacity of the neutral conductor to not less than 20 percent of the ampacity of the phase conductor.

(B) Single Point Grounded System. Where a single point grounded neutral system is used, the following shall apply:

(1) A single point grounded system shall be permitted to be supplied from (a) or (b):

  a. A separately derived system

  b. A multigrounded neutral system with an equipment grounding conductor connected to the multigrounded neutral at the source of the single point grounded system

(2) A grounding electrode shall be provided for the system.

(3) A grounding electrode conductor shall connect the grounding electrode to the system neutral.

(4) A bonding jumper shall connect the equipment grounding conductor to the grounding electrode conductor.

(5) An equipment bonding conductor shall be provided to each building, structure, and equipment enclosure.

(6) A neutral shall only be required where phase to neutral loads are supplied.

(7) The neutral, where provided, shall be insulated and isolated from earth except at one location.

(8) An equipment grounding conductor shall be run with the phase conductors and shall comply with (a), (b), and (c):

  a. Shall not carry continuous load

  b. May be bare or insulated

  c. Shall have sufficient ampacity for fault current duty

(C) Multigrounded Neutral Systems. Where a multi-grounded neutral system is used, the following shall apply:

(1) The neutral of a solidly grounded neutral system shall be permitted to be grounded at more than one point. Grounding shall be permitted at one or more of the following locations:

    a. Transformers supplying conductors to a building or other structure

    b. Underground circuits where the neutral is exposed

    c. Overhead circuits installed outdoors

(2) The multigrounded neutral conductor shall be grounded at each transformer and at other additional locations by connection to a made or existing electrode.

(3) At least one grounding electrode shall be installed and connected to the multigrounded neutral circuit conductor every 400 m (1300 ft).

(4) The maximum distance between any two adjacent electrodes shall not be more than 400 m (1300 ft).

(5) In a multigrounded shielded cable system, the shielding shall be grounded at each cable joint that is exposed to personnel contact.

250.186 Impedance Grounded Neutral Systems. Impedance grounded neutral systems in which a grounding impedance, usually a resistor, limits the ground-fault current, shall be permitted where all of the following conditions are met:

(1) The conditions of maintenance and supervision ensure that only qualified persons will service the installation.

(2) Ground detectors are installed on the system.

(3) Line-to-neutral loads are not served.

Impedance grounded neutral systems shall comply with the provisions of 250.186(A) through (D).

(A) Location. The grounding impedance shall be inserted in the grounding conductor between the grounding electrode of the supply system and the neutral point of the supply transformer or generator.

(B) Identified and Insulated. The neutral conductor of an impedance grounded neutral system shall be identified, as well as fully insulated with the same insulation as the phase conductors.

(C) System Neutral Connection. The system neutral shall not be connected to ground, except through the neutral grounding impedance.

(D) Equipment Grounding Conductors. Equipment grounding conductors shall be permitted to be bare and shall be electrically connected to the ground bus and grounding electrode conductor.

250.188 Grounding of Systems Supplying Portable or Mobile Equipment. Systems supplying portable or mobile high-voltage equipment, other than substations installed on a temporary basis, shall comply with 250.188(A) through (F).

(A) Portable or Mobile Equipment. Portable or mobile high-voltage equipment shall be supplied from a system having its neutral grounded through an impedance. Where a delta-connected high-voltage system is used to supply portable or mobile equipment, a system neutral shall be derived.

(B) Exposed Non–Current-Carrying Metal Parts. Exposed non–current-carrying metal parts of portable or mobile equipment shall be connected by an equipment grounding conductor to the point at which the system neutral impedance is grounded.

(C) Ground-Fault Current. The voltage developed between the portable or mobile equipment frame and ground by the flow of maximum ground-fault current shall not exceed 100 volts.

(D) Ground-Fault Detection and Relaying. Ground-fault detection and relaying shall be provided to automatically de-energize any high-voltage system component that has developed a ground fault. The continuity of the equipment grounding conductor shall be continuously monitored so as to de-energize automatically the high-voltage circuit to the portable or mobile equipment upon loss of continuity of the equipment grounding conductor.

(E) Isolation. The grounding electrode to which the portable or mobile equipment system neutral impedance is connected shall be isolated from and separated in the ground by at least 6.0 m (20 ft) from any other system or equipment grounding electrode, and there shall be no direct connection between the grounding electrodes, such as buried pipe and fence, and so forth.

(F) Trailing Cable and Couplers. High-voltage trailing cable and couplers for interconnection of portable or mobile equipment shall meet the requirements of Part III of Article 400 for cables and 490.55 for couplers.

250.190 Grounding of Equipment. All non–current-carrying metal parts of fixed, portable, and mobile equipment and associated fences, housings, enclosures, and supporting structures shall be grounded.

Exception: Where isolated from ground and located so as to prevent any person who can make contact with ground from contacting such metal parts when the equipment is energized.

Grounding conductors not an integral part of a cable assembly shall not be smaller than 6 AWG copper or 4 AWG aluminum.

FPN: See 250.110, Exception No. 2, for pole-mounted distribution apparatus.

ARTICLE 280
Surge Arresters

I. General

280.1 Scope. This article covers general requirements, installation requirements, and connection requirements for surge arresters installed on premises wiring systems.

280.2 Definition.

Surge Arrester. A protective device for limiting surge voltages by discharging or bypassing surge current, and it also prevents continued flow of follow current while remaining capable of repeating these functions.

280.3 Number Required. Where used at a point on a circuit, a surge arrester shall be connected to each ungrounded conductor. A single installation of such surge arresters shall be permitted to protect a number of interconnected circuits, provided that no circuit is exposed to surges while disconnected from the surge arresters.

280.4 Surge Arrester Selection.

(A) Circuits of Less Than 1000 Volts. Surge arresters installed on a circuit of less than 1000 volts shall comply with all of the following:

(1) The rating of the surge arrester shall be equal to or greater than the maximum continuous phase-to-ground power frequency voltage available at the point of application.

(2) Surge arresters installed on circuits of less than 1000 volts shall be listed.

(3) Surge arresters shall be marked with a short circuit current rating and shall not be installed at a point on the system where the available fault current is in excess of that rating.

(4) Surge arresters shall not be installed on ungrounded systems, impedance grounded systems, or corner grounded delta systems unless listed specifically for use on these systems.

(B) Circuits of 1 kV and Over — Silicon Carbide Types. The rating of a silicon carbide-type surge arrester shall be not less than 125 percent of the maximum continuous phase-to-ground voltage available at the point of application.

FPN No. 1: For further information on surge arresters, see ANSI/IEEE C62.1-1989, *Standard for Gapped Silicon-Carbide Surge Arresters for AC Power Circuits*; ANSI/IEEE C62.2-1987, *Guide for the Application of Gapped Silicon-Carbide Surge Arresters for Alternating-Current Systems*; ANSI/IEEE C62.11-1993, *Standard for Metal-Oxide Surge Arresters for Alternating-Current Power Circuits*; and ANSI/IEEE C62.22-1991, *Guide for the Application of Metal-Oxide Surge Arresters for Alternating-Current Systems*.

FPN No. 2: The selection of a properly rated metal oxide arrester is based on considerations of maximum continuous operating voltage and the magnitude and duration of overvoltages at the arrester location as affected by phase-to-ground faults, system grounding techniques, switching surges, and other causes. See the manufacturer's application rules for selection of the specific arrester to be used at a particular location.

II. Installation

280.11 Location. Surge arresters shall be permitted to be located indoors or outdoors. Surge arresters shall be made inaccessible to unqualified persons, unless listed for installation in accessible locations.

280.12 Routing of Surge Arrester Connections. The conductor used to connect the surge arrester to line or bus and to ground shall not be any longer than necessary and shall avoid unnecessary bends.

III. Connecting Surge Arresters

280.21 Installed at Services of Less Than 1000 Volts. Line and ground connecting conductors shall not be smaller than 14 AWG copper or 12 AWG aluminum. The arrester grounding conductor shall be connected to one of the following:

(1) Grounded service conductor

(2) Grounding electrode conductor

(3) Grounding electrode for the service

(4) Equipment grounding terminal in the service equipment

280.22 Installed on the Load Side Services of Less Than 1000 Volts. Line and ground connecting conductors shall not be smaller than 14 AWG copper or 12 AWG aluminum. A surge arrester shall be permitted to be connected between any two conductors — ungrounded conductor(s), grounded conductor, grounding conductor. The grounded conductor and the grounding conductor shall be interconnected only by the normal operation of the surge arrester during a surge.

280.23 Circuits of 1 kV and Over — Surge-Arrester Conductors. The conductor between the surge arrester and the line and the surge arrester and the grounding connection shall not be smaller than 6 AWG copper or aluminum.

280.24 Circuits of 1 kV and Over — Interconnections. The grounding conductor of a surge arrester protecting a transformer that supplies a secondary distribution system shall be interconnected as specified in 280.24(A), (B), or (C).

(A) Metallic Interconnections. A metallic interconnection shall be made to the secondary grounded circuit conductor or the secondary circuit grounding conductor provided that, in addition to the direct grounding connection at the surge arrester, the following occurs:

(1) The grounded conductor of the secondary has elsewhere a grounding connection to a continuous metal underground water piping system. However, in urban water-pipe areas where there are at least four water-pipe connections on the neutral and not fewer than four such connections in each mile of neutral, the metallic interconnection shall be permitted to be made to the secondary neutral with omission of the direct grounding connection at the surge arrester.

(2) The grounded conductor of the secondary system is a part of a multiground neutral system or static wire of which the primary neutral or static wire has at least four ground connections in each mile of line in addition to a ground at each service.

(B) Through Spark Gap or Device. Where the surge arrester grounding conductor is not connected as in 280.24(A) or where the secondary is not grounded as in 280.24(A) but is otherwise grounded as in 250.52, an interconnection shall be made through a spark gap or listed device as follows:

(1) For ungrounded or unigrounded primary systems, the spark gap or listed device shall have a 60-Hz breakdown voltage of at least twice the primary circuit voltage but not necessarily more than 10 kV, and there shall be at least one other ground on the grounded conductor of the secondary that is not less than 6.0 m (20 ft) distant from the surge arrester grounding electrode.

(2) For multigrounded neutral primary systems, the spark gap or listed device shall have a 60-Hz breakdown of not more than 3 kV, and there shall be at least one other ground on the grounded conductor of the secondary that is not less than 6.0 m (20 ft) distant from the surge arrester grounding electrode.

(C) By Special Permission. An interconnection of the surge arrester ground and the secondary neutral, other than as provided in 280.24(A) or (B), shall be permitted to be made only by special permission.

280.25 Grounding. Except as indicated in this article, surge arrester grounding connections shall be made as specified in Article 250. Grounding conductors shall not be run in metal enclosures unless bonded to both ends of such enclosure.

ARTICLE 285
Transient Voltage Surge Suppressors: TVSSs

I. General

285.1 Scope. This article covers general requirements, installation requirements, and connection requirements for transient voltage surge suppressors (TVSSs) permanently installed on premises wiring systems.

285.2 Definition.

Transient Voltage Surge Suppressor (TVSS). A protective device for limiting transient voltages by diverting or limiting surge current; it also prevents continued flow of follow current while remaining capable of repeating these functions.

285.3 Uses Not Permitted. A TVSS device shall not be installed in the following:

(1) Circuits exceeding 600 volts

(2) On ungrounded systems, impedance grounded systems, or corner grounded delta systems unless listed specifically for use on these systems.

(3) Where the rating of the TVSS is less than the maximum continuous phase-to-ground power frequency voltage available at the point of application

FPN: For further information on TVSSs, see NEMA LS 1-1992, *Standard for Low Voltage Surge Suppression Devices.* The selection of a properly rated TVSS is based on criteria such as maximum continuous operating voltage, the magnitude and duration of overvoltages at the suppressor location as affected by phase-to-ground faults, system grounding techniques, and switching surges.

285.4 Number Required. Where used at a point on a circuit, the TVSS shall be connected to each ungrounded conductor.

285.5 Listing. A TVSS shall be a listed device.

285.6 Short Circuit Current Rating. The TVSS shall be marked with a short circuit current rating and shall not be installed at a point on the system where the available fault current is in excess of that rating. This marking requirement shall not apply to receptacles.

II. Installation

285.11 Location. TVSSs shall be permitted to be located indoors or outdoors and shall be made inaccessible to unqualified persons, unless listed for installation in accessible locations.

285.12 Routing of Connections. The conductors used to connect the TVSS to the line or bus and to ground shall not be any longer than necessary and shall avoid unnecessary bends.

III. Connecting Transient Voltage Surge Suppressors

285.21 Connection. Where a TVSS is installed, it shall comply with 285.21(A) through (C).

(A) Location.

(1) Service Supplied Building or Structure. The transient voltage surge suppressor shall be connected on the load side of a service disconnect overcurrent device required in 230.91, unless installed in accordance with 230.82(8).

(2) Feeder Supplied Building or Structure. The transient voltage surge suppressor shall be connected on the load side of the first overcurrent device at the building or structure.

Exception to (1) and (2): Where the TVSS is also listed as a surge arrester, the connection shall be as permitted by Article 280.

(3) Separately Derived System. The TVSS shall be connected on the load side of the first overcurrent device in a separately derived system.

(B) Conductor Size. Line and ground connecting conductors shall not be smaller than 14 AWG copper or 12 AWG aluminum.

(C) Connection Between Conductors. A TVSS shall be permitted to be connected between any two conductors — ungrounded conductor(s), grounded conductor, grounding conductor. The grounded conductor and the grounding conductor shall be interconnected only by the normal operation of the TVSS during a surge.

285.25 Grounding. Grounding conductors shall not be run in metal enclosures unless bonded to both ends of such enclosure.

Chapter 3   Wiring Methods and Materials

ARTICLE 300
Wiring Methods

I. General Requirements

300.1 Scope.

(A) All Wiring Installations. This article covers wiring methods for all wiring installations unless modified by other articles.

(B) Integral Parts of Equipment. The provisions of this article are not intended to apply to the conductors that form an integral part of equipment, such as motors, controllers, motor control centers, or factory assembled control equipment or listed utilization equipment.

(C) Metric Designators and Trade Sizes. Metric designators and trade sizes for conduit, tubing, and associated fittings and accessories shall be as designated in Table 300.1(C).

Table 300.1(C) Metric Designator and Trade Sizes

Metric Designator	Trade Size
12	⅜
16	½
21	¾
27	1
35	1¼
41	1½
53	2
63	2½
78	3
91	3½
103	4
129	5
155	6

Note: The metric designators and trade sizes are for identification purposes only and are not actual dimensions.

300.2 Limitations.

(A) Voltage. Wiring methods specified in Chapter 3 shall be used for 600 volts, nominal, or less where not specifically limited in some section of Chapter 3. They shall be permitted for over 600 volts, nominal, where specifically permitted elsewhere in this *Code*.

(B) Temperature. Temperature limitation of conductors shall be in accordance with 310.10.

300.3 Conductors.

(A) Single Conductors. Single conductors specified in Table 310.13 shall only be installed where part of a recognized wiring method of Chapter 3.

Exception: Individual conductors shall be permitted where installed as separate overhead conductors in accordance with 225.6.

(B) Conductors of the Same Circuit. All conductors of the same circuit and, where used, the grounded conductor and all equipment grounding conductors and bonding conductors shall be contained within the same raceway, auxiliary gutter, cable tray, cablebus assembly, trench, cable, or cord, unless otherwise permitted in accordance with 300.3(B)(1) through (B)(4).

(1) Paralleled Installations. Conductors shall be permitted to be run in parallel in accordance with the provisions of 310.4. The requirement to run all circuit conductors within the same raceway, auxiliary gutter, cable tray, trench, cable, or cord shall apply separately to each portion of the paralleled installation, and the equipment grounding conductors shall comply with the provisions of 250.122. Parallel runs in cable tray shall comply with the provisions of 392.8(D).

Exception: Conductors installed in nonmetallic raceways run underground shall be permitted to be arranged as isolated phase installations. The raceways shall be installed in close proximity, and the conductors shall comply with the provisions of 300.20(B).

(2) Grounding and Bonding Conductors. Equipment grounding conductors shall be permitted to be installed outside a raceway or cable assembly where in accordance with the provisions of 250.130(C) for certain existing installations or in accordance with 250.134(B), Exception No. 2, for dc circuits. Equipment bonding conductors shall be permitted to be installed on the outside of raceways in accordance with 250.102(E).

(3) Nonferrous Wiring Methods. Conductors in wiring methods with a nonmetallic or other nonmagnetic sheath, where run in different raceways, auxiliary gutters, cable trays, trenches, cables, or cords, shall comply with the provisions of 300.20(B). Conductors in single-conductor Type MI cable with a nonmagnetic sheath shall comply with the provisions of 332.31. Conductors of single-conductor Type MC cable with a nonmagnetic sheath shall comply with the provisions of 330.31, 330.116, and 300.20(B).

(4) Enclosures. Where an auxiliary gutter runs between a column-width panelboard and a pull box, and the pull box includes neutral terminations, the neutral conductors of circuits supplied from the panelboard shall be permitted to originate in the pull box.

(C) Conductors of Different Systems.

(1) 600 Volts, Nominal, or Less. Conductors of circuits rated 600 volts, nominal, or less, ac circuits, and dc circuits shall be permitted to occupy the same equipment wiring enclosure, cable, or raceway. All conductors shall have an insulation rating equal to at least the maximum circuit voltage applied to any conductor within the enclosure, cable, or raceway.

Exception: For solar photovoltaic systems in accordance with 690.4(B).

> FPN: See 725.55(A) for Class 2 and Class 3 circuit conductors.

(2) Over 600 Volts, Nominal. Conductors of circuits rated over 600 volts, nominal, shall not occupy the same equipment wiring enclosure, cable, or raceway with conductors of circuits rated 600 volts, nominal, or less unless otherwise permitted in (C)(2)(a) through (C)(2)(e).

(a) Secondary wiring to electric-discharge lamps of 1000 volts or less, if insulated for the secondary voltage involved, shall be permitted to occupy the same luminaire (fixture), sign, or outline lighting enclosure as the branch-circuit conductors.

(b) Primary leads of electric-discharge lamp ballasts insulated for the primary voltage of the ballast, where contained within the individual wiring enclosure, shall be permitted to occupy the same luminaire (fixture), sign, or outline lighting enclosure as the branch-circuit conductors.

(c) Excitation, control, relay, and ammeter conductors used in connection with any individual motor or starter shall be permitted to occupy the same enclosure as the motor-circuit conductors.

(d) In motors, switchgear and control assemblies, and similar equipment, conductors of different voltage ratings shall be permitted.

(e) In manholes, if the conductors of each system are permanently and effectively separated from the conductors of the other systems and securely fastened to racks, insulators, or other approved supports, conductors of different voltage ratings shall be permitted.

Conductors having nonshielded insulation and operating at different voltage levels shall not occupy the same enclosure, cable, or raceway.

300.4 Protection Against Physical Damage. Where subject to physical damage, conductors shall be protected.

(A) Cables and Raceways Through Wood Members.

(1) Bored Holes. In both exposed and concealed locations, where a cable- or raceway-type wiring method is installed through bored holes in joists, rafters, or wood members, holes shall be bored so that the edge of the hole is not less than 32 mm (1¼ in.) from the nearest edge of the wood member. Where this distance cannot be maintained, the cable or raceway shall be protected from penetration by screws or nails by a steel plate or bushing, at least 1.6 mm (¹⁄₁₆ in.) thick, and of appropriate length and width installed to cover the area of the wiring.

Exception No. 1: Steel plates shall not be required to protect rigid metal conduit, intermediate metal conduit, rigid nonmetallic conduit, or electrical metallic tubing.

Exception No. 2: A listed and marked steel plate less than 1.6 mm (¹⁄₁₆ in.) thick that provides equal or better protection against nail or screw penetration shall be permitted.

(2) Notches in Wood. Where there is no objection because of weakening the building structure, in both exposed and concealed locations, cables or raceways shall be permitted to be laid in notches in wood studs, joists, rafters, or other wood members where the cable or raceway at those points is protected against nails or screws by a steel plate at least 1.6 mm (¹⁄₁₆ in.) thick, and of appropriate length and width, installed to cover the area of the wiring. The steel plate shall be installed before the building finish is applied.

Exception No. 1: Steel plates shall not be required to protect rigid metal conduit, intermediate metal conduit, rigid nonmetallic conduit, or electrical metallic tubing.

Exception No. 2: A listed and marked steel plate less than 1.6 mm (¹⁄₁₆ in.) thick that provides equal or better protection against nail or screw penetration shall be permitted.

(B) Nonmetallic-Sheathed Cables and Electrical Nonmetallic Tubing Through Metal Framing Members.

(1) Nonmetallic-Sheathed Cable. In both exposed and concealed locations where nonmetallic-sheathed cables pass through either factory or field punched, cut, or drilled slots or holes in metal members, the cable shall be protected by listed bushings or listed grommets covering all metal edges that are securely fastened in the opening prior to installation of the cable.

(2) Nonmetallic-Sheathed Cable and Electrical Nonmetallic Tubing. Where nails or screws are likely to penetrate nonmetallic-sheathed cable or electrical nonmetallic tubing, a steel sleeve, steel plate, or steel clip not less than 1.6 mm (¹⁄₁₆ in.) in thickness shall be used to protect the cable or tubing.

Exception: A listed and marked steel plate less than 1.6 mm (¹⁄₁₆ in.) thick that provides equal or better protection against nail or screw penetration shall be permitted.

(C) Cables Through Spaces Behind Panels Designed to Allow Access. Cables or raceway-type wiring methods, installed behind panels designed to allow access, shall be supported according to their applicable articles.

(D) Cables and Raceways Parallel to Framing Members and Furring Strips. In both exposed and concealed locations, where a cable- or raceway-type wiring method is installed parallel to framing members, such as joists, rafters, or studs, or is installed parallel to furring strips, the cable or raceway shall be installed and supported so that the nearest outside surface of the cable or raceway is not less than 32 mm (1¼ in.) from the nearest edge of the framing member or furring strips where nails or screws are likely to penetrate. Where this distance cannot be maintained, the cable or raceway shall be protected from penetration by nails or screws by a steel plate, sleeve, or equivalent at least 1.6 mm (¹⁄₁₆ in.) thick.

Exception No. 1: Steel plates, sleeves, or the equivalent shall not be required to protect rigid metal conduit, intermediate metal conduit, rigid nonmetallic conduit, or electrical metallic tubing.

Exception No. 2: For concealed work in finished buildings, or finished panels for prefabricated buildings where such supporting is impracticable, it shall be permissible to fish the cables between access points.

Exception No. 3: A listed and marked steel plate less than 1.6 mm (¹⁄₁₆ in.) thick that provides equal or better protection against nail or screw penetration shall be permitted.

(E) Cables and Raceways Installed in Shallow Grooves. Cable- or raceway-type wiring methods installed in a groove, to be covered by wallboard, siding, paneling, carpeting, or similar finish, shall be protected by 1.6 mm (¹⁄₁₆ in.) thick steel plate, sleeve, or equivalent or by not less than 32-mm (1¼-in.) free space for the full length of the groove in which the cable or raceway is installed.

Exception No. 1: Steel plates, sleeves, or the equivalent shall not be required to protect rigid metal conduit, intermediate metal conduit, rigid nonmetallic conduit, or electrical metallic tubing.

Exception No. 2: A listed and marked steel plate less than 1.6 mm (¹⁄₁₆ in.) thick that provides equal or better protection against nail or screw penetration shall be permitted.

(F) Insulated Fittings. Where raceways containing ungrounded conductors 4 AWG or larger enter a cabinet, box enclosure, or raceway, the conductors shall be protected by a substantial fitting providing a smoothly rounded insulating surface, unless the conductors are separated from the fitting or raceway by substantial insulating material that is securely fastened in place.

Exception: Where threaded hubs or bosses that are an integral part of a cabinet, box enclosure, or raceway provide a smoothly rounded or flared entry for conductors.

Conduit bushings constructed wholly of insulating material shall not be used to secure a fitting or raceway. The insulating fitting or insulating material shall have a temperature rating not less than the insulation temperature rating of the installed conductors.

300.5 Underground Installations.

(A) Minimum Cover Requirements. Direct-buried cable or conduit or other raceways shall be installed to meet the minimum cover requirements of Table 300.5.

(B) Listing. Cables and insulated conductors installed in enclosures or raceways in underground installations shall be listed for use in wet locations.

(C) Underground Cables Under Buildings. Underground cable installed under a building shall be in a raceway that is extended beyond the outside walls of the building.

(D) Protection from Damage. Direct-buried conductors and cables shall be protected from damage in accordance with 300.5(D)(1) through (D)(4).

(1) Emerging from Grade. Direct-buried conductors and enclosures emerging from grade shall be protected by enclosures or raceways extending from the minimum cover distance below grade required by 300.5(A) to a point at least 2.5 m (8 ft) above finished grade. In no case shall the protection be required to exceed 450 mm (18 in.) below finished grade.

(2) Conductors Entering Buildings. Conductors entering a building shall be protected to the point of entrance.

(3) Service Conductors. Underground service conductors that are not encased in concrete and that are buried 450 mm (18 in.) or more below grade shall have their location identified by a warning ribbon that is placed in the trench at least 300 mm (12 in.) above the underground installation.

(4) Enclosure or Raceway Damage. Where the enclosure or raceway is subject to physical damage, the conductors shall be installed in rigid metal conduit, intermediate metal conduit, Schedule 80 rigid nonmetallic conduit, or equivalent.

(E) Splices and Taps. Direct-buried conductors or cables shall be permitted to be spliced or tapped without the use of splice boxes. The splices or taps shall be made in accordance with 110.14(B).

(F) Backfill. Backfill that contains large rocks, paving materials, cinders, large or sharply angular substances, or corrosive material shall not be placed in an excavation where materials may damage raceways, cables, or other substructures or prevent adequate compaction of fill or contribute to corrosion of raceways, cables, or other substructures.

Table 300.5 Minimum Cover Requirements, 0 to 600 Volts, Nominal, Burial in Millimeters (Inches)

Location of Wiring Method or Circuit	Type of Wiring Method or Circuit									
	Column 1 Direct Burial Cables or Conductors		Column 2 Rigid Metal Conduit or Intermediate Metal Conduit		Column 3 Nonmetallic Raceways Listed for Direct Burial Without Concrete Encasement or Other Approved Raceways		Column 4 Residential Branch Circuits Rated 120 Volts or Less with GFCI Protection and Maximum Overcurrent Protection of 20 Amperes		Column 5 Circuits for Control of Irrigation and Landscape Lighting Limited to Not More Than 30 Volts and Installed with Type UF or in Other Identified Cable or Raceway	
	mm	in.	mm	in.	mm	in.	mm	in.	mm	in.
All locations not specified below	600	24	150	6	450	18	300	12	150	6
In trench below 50-mm (2-in.) thick concrete or equivalent	450	18	150	6	300	12	150	6	150	6
Under a building	0 (in raceway only)	0	0	0	0	0	0 (in raceway only)	0	0 (in raceway only)	0
Under minimum of 102-mm (4-in.) thick concrete exterior slab with no vehicular traffic and the slab extending not less than 152 mm (6 in.) beyond the underground installation	450	18	100	4	100	4	150 (direct burial) 100 (in raceway)	6 / 4	150 (direct burial) 100 (in raceway)	6 / 4
Under streets, highways, roads, alleys, driveways, and parking lots	600	24	600	24	600	24	600	24	600	24
One- and two-family dwelling driveways and outdoor parking areas, and used only for dwelling-related purposes	450	18	450	18	450	18	300	12	450	18
In or under airport runways, including adjacent areas where trespassing prohibited	450	18	450	18	450	18	450	18	450	18

Notes:

1. Cover is defined as the shortest distance in millimeters (inches) measured between a point on the top surface of any direct-buried conductor, cable, conduit, or other raceway and the top surface of finished grade, concrete, or similar cover.

2. Raceways approved for burial only where concrete encased shall require concrete envelope not less than 50 mm (2 in.) thick.

3. Lesser depths shall be permitted where cables and conductors rise for terminations or splices or where access is otherwise required.

4. Where one of the wiring method types listed in Columns 1–3 is used for one of the circuit types in Columns 4 and 5, the shallowest depth of burial shall be permitted.

5. Where solid rock prevents compliance with the cover depths specified in this table, the wiring shall be installed in metal or nonmetallic raceway permitted for direct burial. The raceways shall be covered by a minimum of 50 mm (2 in.) of concrete extending down to rock.

Where necessary to prevent physical damage to the raceway or cable, protection shall be provided in the form of granular or selected material, suitable running boards, suitable sleeves, or other approved means.

(G) Raceway Seals. Conduits or raceways through which moisture may contact live parts shall be sealed or plugged at either or both ends.

FPN: Presence of hazardous gases or vapors may also necessitate sealing of underground conduits or raceways entering buildings.

(H) Bushing. A bushing, or terminal fitting, with an integral bushed opening shall be used at the end of a conduit or other raceway that terminates underground where the conductors or cables emerge as a direct burial wiring method. A seal incorporating the physical protection characteristics of a bushing shall be permitted to be used in lieu of a bushing.

(I) Conductors of the Same Circuit. All conductors of the same circuit and, where used, the grounded conductor and all equipment grounding conductors shall be installed in the same raceway or cable or shall be installed in close proximity in the same trench.

Exception No. 1: Conductors in parallel in raceways or cables shall be permitted, but each raceway or cable shall contain all conductors of the same circuit including grounding conductors.

Exception No. 2: Isolated phase, polarity, grounded conductor, and equipment grounding and bonding conductor installations shall be permitted in nonmetallic raceways or cables with a nonmetallic covering or nonmagnetic sheath in close proximity where conductors are paralleled as permitted in 310.4, and where the conditions of 300.20(B) are met.

(J) Ground Movement. Where direct-buried conductors, raceways, or cables are subject to movement by settlement or frost, direct-buried conductors, raceways, or cables shall be arranged so as to prevent damage to the enclosed conductors or to equipment connected to the raceways.

FPN: This section recognizes "S" loops in underground direct burial to raceway transitions, expansion fittings in raceway risers to fixed equipment, and, generally, the provision of flexible connections to equipment subject to settlement or frost heaves.

(K) Directional Boring. Cables or raceways installed using directional boring equipment shall be approved for the purpose.

300.6 Protection Against Corrosion and Deterioration. Raceways, cable trays, cablebus, auxiliary gutters, cable armor, boxes, cable sheathing, cabinets, elbows, couplings, fittings, supports, and support hardware shall be of materials suitable for the environment in which they are to be installed.

(A) Ferrous Metal Equipment. Ferrous metal raceways, cable trays, cablebus, auxiliary gutters, cable armor, boxes, cable sheathing, cabinets, metal elbows, couplings, nipples, fittings, supports, and support hardware shall be suitably protected against corrosion inside and outside (except threads at joints) by a coating of approved corrosion-resistant material. Where corrosion protection is necessary and the conduit is threaded in the field, the threads shall be coated with an approved electrically conductive, corrosion-resistant compound.

Exception: Stainless steel shall not be required to have protective coatings.

(1) Protected from Corrosion Solely by Enamel. Where protected from corrosion solely by enamel, ferrous metal raceways, cable trays, cablebus, auxiliary gutters, cable armor, boxes, cable sheathing, cabinets, metal elbows, couplings, nipples, fittings, supports, and support hardware shall not be used outdoors or in wet locations as described in 300.6(D).

(2) Organic Coatings on Boxes or Cabinets. Where boxes or cabinets have an approved system of organic coatings and are marked "Raintight," "Rainproof," or "Outdoor Type," they shall be permitted outdoors.

(3) In Concrete or in Direct Contact with the Earth. Ferrous metal raceways, cable armor, boxes, cable sheathing, cabinets, elbows, couplings, nipples, fittings, supports, and support hardware shall be permitted to be installed in concrete or in direct contact with the earth, or in areas subject to severe corrosive influences where made of material approved for the condition, or where provided with corrosion protection approved for the condition.

(B) Non-Ferrous Metal Equipment. Non-ferrous raceways, cable trays, cablebus, auxiliary gutters, cable armor, boxes, cable sheathing, cabinets, elbows, couplings, nipples, fittings, supports, and support hardware embedded or encased in concrete or in direct contact with the earth shall be provided with supplementary corrosion protection.

(C) Nonmetallic Equipment. Nonmetallic raceways, cable trays, cablebus, auxiliary gutters, boxes, cables with a nonmetallic outer jacket and internal metal armor or jacket, cable sheathing, cabinets, elbows, couplings, nipples, fittings, supports, and support hardware shall be made of material approved for the condition and shall comply with (C)(1) and (C)(2) as applicable to the specific installation.

(1) Exposed to Sunlight. Where exposed to sunlight, the materials shall be listed as sunlight resistant or shall be identified as sunlight resistant.

(2) Chemical Exposure. Where subject to exposure to chemical solvents, vapors, splashing, or immersion, materials or coatings shall either be inherently resistant to chemicals based on its listing or be identified for the specific chemical reagent.

(D) Indoor Wet Locations. In portions of dairy processing facilities, laundries, canneries, and other indoor wet locations, and in locations where walls are frequently washed or where there are surfaces of absorbent materials, such as damp paper or wood, the entire wiring system, where installed exposed, including all boxes, fittings, raceways, and cable used therewith, shall be mounted so that there is at least a 6-mm (¼-in.) airspace between it and the wall or supporting surface.

Exception: Nonmetallic raceways, boxes, and fittings shall be permitted to be installed without the airspace on a concrete, masonry, tile, or similar surface.

> FPN: In general, areas where acids and alkali chemicals are handled and stored may present such corrosive conditions, particularly when wet or damp. Severe corrosive conditions may also be present in portions of meatpacking plants, tanneries, glue houses, and some stables; in installations immediately adjacent to a seashore and swimming pool areas; in areas where chemical deicers are used; and in storage cellars or rooms for hides, casings, fertilizer, salt, and bulk chemicals.

300.7 Raceways Exposed to Different Temperatures.

(A) Sealing. Where portions of a cable raceway or sleeve are known to be subjected to different temperatures and where condensation is known to be a problem, as in cold storage areas of buildings or where passing from the interior to the exterior of a building, the raceway or sleeve shall be filled with an approved material to prevent the circulation of warm air to a colder section of the raceway or sleeve. An explosionproof seal shall not be required for this purpose.

(B) Expansion Fittings. Raceways shall be provided with expansion fittings where necessary to compensate for thermal expansion and contraction.

> FPN: Table 352.44(A) provides the expansion information for polyvinyl chloride (PVC). A nominal number for steel conduit can be determined by multiplying the expansion length in this table by 0.20. The coefficient of expansion for steel electrical metallic tubing, intermediate metal conduit, and rigid conduit is 11.70×10^{-6} (0.0000117 mm per mm of conduit for each °C in temperature change) [6.50×10^{-6} (0.0000065 in. per inch of conduit for each °F in temperature change)].

300.8 Installation of Conductors with Other Systems. Raceways or cable trays containing electric conductors shall not contain any pipe, tube, or equal for steam, water, air, gas, drainage, or any service other than electrical.

300.10 Electrical Continuity of Metal Raceways and Enclosures. Metal raceways, cable armor, and other metal enclosures for conductors shall be metallically joined together into a continuous electric conductor and shall be connected to all boxes, fittings, and cabinets so as to provide effective electrical continuity. Unless specifically permitted elsewhere in this *Code*, raceways and cable assemblies shall be mechanically secured to boxes, fittings, cabinets, and other enclosures.

Exception No. 1: Short sections of raceways used to provide support or protection of cable assemblies from physical damage shall not be required to be made electrically continuous.

Exception No. 2: Equipment enclosures to be isolated, as permitted by 250.96(B), shall not be required to be metallically joined to the metal raceway.

300.11 Securing and Supporting.

(A) Secured in Place. Raceways, cable assemblies, boxes, cabinets, and fittings shall be securely fastened in place. Support wires that do not provide secure support shall not be permitted as the sole support. Support wires and associated fittings that provide secure support and that are installed in addition to the ceiling grid support wires shall be permitted as the sole support. Where independent support wires are used, they shall be secured at both ends. Cables and raceways shall not be supported by ceiling grids.

(1) Fire-Rated Assemblies. Wiring located within the cavity of a fire-rated floor–ceiling or roof–ceiling assembly shall not be secured to, or supported by, the ceiling assembly, including the ceiling support wires. An independent means of secure support shall be provided and shall be permitted to be attached to the assembly. Where independent support wires are used, they shall be distinguishable by color, tagging, or other effective means from those that are part of the fire-rated design.

Exception: The ceiling support system shall be permitted to support wiring and equipment that have been tested as part of the fire-rated assembly.

> FPN: One method of determining fire rating is testing in accordance with NFPA 251-1999, *Standard Methods of Tests of Fire Endurance of Building Construction and Materials.*

(2) Non–Fire-Rated Assemblies. Wiring located within the cavity of a non–fire-rated floor–ceiling or roof–ceiling assembly shall not be secured to, or supported by, the ceiling assembly, including the ceiling support wires. An independent means of secure support shall be provided.

Exception: The ceiling support system shall be permitted to support branch-circuit wiring and associated equipment where installed in accordance with the ceiling system manufacturer's instructions.

(B) Raceways Used as Means of Support. Raceways shall be used only as a means of support for other raceways, cables, or nonelectric equipment under any of the following conditions:

(1) Where the raceway or means of support is identified for the purpose

(2) Where the raceway contains power supply conductors for electrically controlled equipment and is used to support Class 2 circuit conductors or cables that are solely for the purpose of connection to the equipment control circuits

(3) Where the raceway is used to support boxes or conduit bodies in accordance with 314.23 or to support luminaires (fixtures) in accordance with 410.16(F)

(C) Cables Not Used as Means of Support. Cable wiring methods shall not be used as a means of support for other cables, raceways, or nonelectrical equipment.

300.12 Mechanical Continuity — Raceways and Cables. Metal or nonmetallic raceways, cable armors, and cable sheaths shall be continuous between cabinets, boxes, fittings, or other enclosures or outlets.

Exception: Short sections of raceways used to provide support or protection of cable assemblies from physical damage shall not be required to be mechanically continuous.

300.13 Mechanical and Electrical Continuity — Conductors.

(A) General. Conductors in raceways shall be continuous between outlets, boxes, devices, and so forth. There shall be no splice or tap within a raceway unless permitted by 300.15; 368.56(A); 376.56; 378.56; 384.56; 386.56; 388.56; or 390.6.

(B) Device Removal. In multiwire branch circuits, the continuity of a grounded conductor shall not depend on device connections such as lampholders, receptacles, and so forth, where the removal of such devices would interrupt the continuity.

300.14 Length of Free Conductors at Outlets, Junctions, and Switch Points. At least 150 mm (6 in.) of free conductor, measured from the point in the box where it emerges from its raceway or cable sheath, shall be left at each outlet, junction, and switch point for splices or the connection of luminaires (fixtures) or devices. Where the opening to an outlet, junction, or switch point is less than 200 mm (8 in.) in any dimension, each conductor shall be long enough to extend at least 75 mm (3 in.) outside the opening.

Exception: Conductors that are not spliced or terminated at the outlet, junction, or switch point shall not be required to comply with 300.14.

300.15 Boxes, Conduit Bodies, or Fittings — Where Required. A box shall be installed at each outlet and switch point for concealed knob-and-tube wiring.

Fittings and connectors shall be used only with the specific wiring methods for which they are designed and listed.

Where the wiring method is conduit, tubing, Type AC cable, Type MC cable, Type MI cable, nonmetallic-sheathed cable, or other cables, a box or conduit body shall be installed at each conductor splice point, outlet point, switch point, junction point, termination point, or pull point, unless otherwise permitted in 300.15(A) through (M).

(A) Wiring Methods with Interior Access. A box or conduit body shall not be required for each splice, junction, switch, pull, termination, or outlet points in wiring methods with removable covers, such as wireways, multioutlet assemblies, auxiliary gutters, and surface raceways. The covers shall be accessible after installation.

(B) Equipment. An integral junction box or wiring compartment as part of approved equipment shall be permitted in lieu of a box.

(C) Protection. A box or conduit body shall not be required where cables enter or exit from conduit or tubing that is used to provide cable support or protection against physical damage. A fitting shall be provided on the end(s) of the conduit or tubing to protect the cable from abrasion.

(D) Type MI Cable. A box or conduit body shall not be required where accessible fittings are used for straight-through splices in mineral-insulated metal-sheathed cable.

(E) Integral Enclosure. A wiring device with integral enclosure identified for the use, having brackets that securely fasten the device to walls or ceilings of conventional on-site frame construction, for use with nonmetallic-sheathed cable, shall be permitted in lieu of a box or conduit body.

FPN: See 334.30(C); 545.10; 550.15(I); 551.47(E), Exception No. 1; and 552.48(E), Exception No. 1.

(F) Fitting. A fitting identified for the use shall be permitted in lieu of a box or conduit body where conductors are not spliced or terminated within the fitting. The fitting shall be accessible after installation.

(G) Direct-Buried Conductors. As permitted in 300.5(E), a box or conduit body shall not be required for splices and taps in direct-buried conductors and cables.

(H) Insulated Devices. As permitted in 334.40(B), a box or conduit body shall not be required for insulated devices supplied by nonmetallic-sheathed cable.

(I) Enclosures. A box or conduit body shall not be required where a splice, switch, terminal, or pull point is in a cabinet or cutout box, in an enclosure for a switch or overcurrent device as permitted in 312.8, in a motor controller as permitted in 430.10(A), or in a motor control center.

(J) Luminaires (Fixtures). A box or conduit body shall not be required where a luminaire (fixture) is used as a raceway as permitted in 410.31 and 410.32.

(K) Embedded. A box or conduit body shall not be required for splices where conductors are embedded as permitted in 424.40, 424.41(D), 426.22(B), 426.24(A), and 427.19(A).

(L) Manholes and Handhole Enclosures. Where accessible only to qualified persons, a box or conduit body shall not be required for conductors in manholes or handhole enclosures, except where connecting to electrical equipment. The installation shall comply with the provisions of Part V of Article 110 for manholes, and 314.30 for handhole enclosures.

(M) Closed Loop. A box shall not be required with a closed-loop power distribution system where a device identified and listed as suitable for installation without a box is used.

300.16 Raceway or Cable to Open or Concealed Wiring.

(A) Box or Fitting. A box or terminal fitting having a separately bushed hole for each conductor shall be used wherever a change is made from conduit, electrical metallic tubing, electrical nonmetallic tubing, nonmetallic-sheathed cable, Type AC cable, Type MC cable, or mineral-insulated, metal-sheathed cable and surface raceway wiring to open wiring or to concealed knob-and-tube wiring. A fitting used for this purpose shall contain no taps or splices and shall not be used at luminaire (fixture) outlets.

(B) Bushing. A bushing shall be permitted in lieu of a box or terminal where the conductors emerge from a raceway and enter or terminate at equipment, such as open switchboards, unenclosed control equipment, or similar equipment. The bushing shall be of the insulating type for other than lead-sheathed conductors.

300.17 Number and Size of Conductors in Raceway. The number and size of conductors in any raceway shall not be more than will permit dissipation of the heat and ready installation or withdrawal of the conductors without damage to the conductors or to their insulation.

> FPN: See the following sections of this *Code*: intermediate metal conduit, 342.22; rigid metal conduit, 344.22; flexible metal conduit, 348.22; liquidtight flexible metal conduit, 350.22; rigid nonmetallic conduit, 352.22; liquidtight nonmetallic flexible conduit, 356.22; electrical metallic tubing, 358.22; flexible metallic tubing, 360.22; electrical nonmetallic tubing, 362.22; cellular concrete floor raceways, 372.11; cellular metal floor raceways, 374.5; metal wireways, 376.22; nonmetallic wireways, 378.22; surface metal raceways, 386.22; surface nonmetallic raceways, 388.22; underfloor raceways, 390.5; fixture wire, 402.7; theaters,

520.6; signs, 600.31(C); elevators, 620.33; audio signal processing, amplification, and reproduction equipment, 640.23(A) and 640.24; Class 1, Class 2, and Class 3 circuits, Article 725; fire alarm circuits, Article 760; and optical fiber cables and raceways, Article 770.

300.18 Raceway Installations.

(A) Complete Runs. Raceways, other than busways or exposed raceways having hinged or removable covers, shall be installed complete between outlet, junction, or splicing points prior to the installation of conductors. Where required to facilitate the installation of utilization equipment, the raceway shall be permitted to be initially installed without a terminating connection at the equipment. Prewired raceway assemblies shall be permitted only where specifically permitted in this *Code* for the applicable wiring method.

Exception: Short sections of raceways used to contain conductors or cable assemblies for protection from physical damage shall not be required to be installed complete between outlet, junction, or splicing points.

(B) Welding. Metal raceways shall not be supported, terminated, or connected by welding to the raceway unless specifically designed to be or otherwise specifically permitted to be in this *Code*.

300.19 Supporting Conductors in Vertical Raceways.

(A) Spacing Intervals — Maximum. Conductors in vertical raceways shall be supported if the vertical rise exceeds the values in Table 300.19(A). One cable support shall be provided at the top of the vertical raceway or as close to the top as practical. Intermediate supports shall be provided as necessary to limit supported conductor lengths to not greater than those values specified in Table 300.19(A).

Exception: Steel wire armor cable shall be supported at the top of the riser with a cable support that clamps the steel wire armor. A safety device shall be permitted at the lower end of the riser to hold the cable in the event there is slippage of the cable in the wire-armored cable support. Additional wedge-type supports shall be permitted to relieve the strain on the equipment terminals caused by expansion of the cable under load.

(B) Support Methods. One of the following methods of support shall be used.

(1) By clamping devices constructed of or employing insulating wedges inserted in the ends of the raceways. Where clamping of insulation does not adequately support the cable, the conductor also shall be clamped.

(2) By inserting boxes at the required intervals in which insulating supports are installed and secured in a satisfactory manner to withstand the weight of the conductors attached thereto, the boxes being provided with covers.

Table 300.19(A) Spacings for Conductor Supports

Size of Wire	Support of Conductors in Vertical Raceways	Conductors			
		Aluminum or Copper-Clad Aluminum		Copper	
		m	ft	m	ft
18 AWG through 8 AWG	Not greater than	30	100	30	100
6 AWG through 1/0 AWG	Not greater than	60	200	30	100
2/0 AWG through 4/0 AWG	Not greater than	55	180	25	80
Over 4/0 AWG through 350 kcmil	Not greater than	41	135	18	60
Over 350 kcmil through 500 kcmil	Not greater than	36	120	15	50
Over 500 kcmil through 750 kcmil	Not greater than	28	95	12	40
Over 750 kcmil	Not greater than	26	85	11	35

(3) In junction boxes, by deflecting the cables not less than 90 degrees and carrying them horizontally to a distance not less than twice the diameter of the cable, the cables being carried on two or more insulating supports and additionally secured thereto by tie wires if desired. Where this method is used, cables shall be supported at intervals not greater than 20 percent of those mentioned in the preceding tabulation.

(4) By a method of equal effectiveness.

300.20 Induced Currents in Metal Enclosures or Metal Raceways.

(A) Conductors Grouped Together. Where conductors carrying alternating current are installed in metal enclosures or metal raceways, they shall be arranged so as to avoid heating the surrounding metal by induction. To accomplish this, all phase conductors and, where used, the grounded conductor and all equipment grounding conductors shall be grouped together.

Exception No. 1: Equipment grounding conductors for certain existing installations shall be permitted to be installed separate from their associated circuit conductors where run in accordance with the provisions of 250.130(C).

Exception No. 2: A single conductor shall be permitted to be installed in a ferromagnetic enclosure and used for skin-effect heating in accordance with the provisions of 426.42 and 427.47.

(B) Individual Conductors. Where a single conductor carrying alternating current passes through metal with magnetic properties, the inductive effect shall be minimized by (1) cutting slots in the metal between the individual holes through which the individual conductors pass or (2) passing all the conductors in the circuit through an insulating wall sufficiently large for all of the conductors of the circuit.

Exception: In the case of circuits supplying vacuum or electric-discharge lighting systems or signs or X-ray appara-tus, the currents carried by the conductors are so small that the inductive heating effect can be ignored where these conductors are placed in metal enclosures or pass through metal.

FPN: Because aluminum is not a magnetic metal, there will be no heating due to hysteresis; however, induced currents will be present. They will not be of sufficient magnitude to require grouping of conductors or special treatment in passing conductors through aluminum wall sections.

300.21 Spread of Fire or Products of Combustion. Electrical installations in hollow spaces, vertical shafts, and ventilation or air-handling ducts shall be made so that the possible spread of fire or products of combustion will not be substantially increased. Openings around electrical penetrations through fire-resistant–rated walls, partitions, floors, or ceilings shall be firestopped using approved methods to maintain the fire resistance rating.

FPN: Directories of electrical construction materials published by qualified testing laboratories contain many listing installation restrictions necessary to maintain the fire-resistive rating of assemblies where penetrations or openings are made. Building codes also contain restrictions on membrane penetrations on opposite sides of a fire-resistance–rated wall assembly. An example is the 600-mm (24-in.) minimum horizontal separation that usually applies between boxes installed on opposite sides of the wall. Assistance in complying with 300.21 can be found in building codes, fire resistance directories, and product listings.

300.22 Wiring in Ducts, Plenums, and Other Air-Handling Spaces. The provisions of this section apply to the installation and uses of electric wiring and equipment in ducts, plenums, and other air-handling spaces.

FPN: See Article 424, Part VI, for duct heaters.

(A) Ducts for Dust, Loose Stock, or Vapor Removal. No wiring systems of any type shall be installed in ducts used to transport dust, loose stock, or flammable vapors. No wiring system of any type shall be installed in any duct, or shaft containing only such ducts, used for vapor removal or for ventilation of commercial-type cooking equipment.

(B) Ducts or Plenums Used for Environmental Air. Only wiring methods consisting of Type MI cable, Type MC cable employing a smooth or corrugated impervious metal sheath without an overall nonmetallic covering, electrical metallic tubing, flexible metallic tubing, intermediate metal conduit, or rigid metal conduit without an overall nonmetallic covering shall be installed in ducts or plenums specifically fabricated to transport environmental air. Flexible metal conduit shall be permitted, in lengths not to exceed 1.2 m (4 ft), to connect physically adjustable equipment and devices permitted to be in these ducts and plenum chambers. The connectors used with flexible metal conduit shall effectively close any openings in the connection. Equipment and devices shall be permitted within such ducts or plenum chambers only if necessary for their direct action upon, or sensing of, the contained air. Where equipment or devices are installed and illumination is necessary to facilitate maintenance and repair, enclosed gasketed-type luminaires (fixtures) shall be permitted.

(C) Other Space Used for Environmental Air. This section applies to space used for environmental air-handling purposes other than ducts and plenums as specified in 300.22(A) and (B). It does not include habitable rooms or areas of buildings, the prime purpose of which is not air handling.

FPN: The space over a hung ceiling used for environmental air-handling purposes is an example of the type of other space to which this section applies.

Exception: This section shall not apply to the joist or stud spaces of dwelling units where the wiring passes through such spaces perpendicular to the long dimension of such spaces.

(1) Wiring Methods. The wiring methods for such other space shall be limited to totally enclosed, nonventilated, insulated busway having no provisions for plug-in connections, Type MI cable, Type MC cable without an overall nonmetallic covering, Type AC cable, or other factory-assembled multiconductor control or power cable that is specifically listed for the use, or listed prefabricated cable assemblies of metallic manufactured wiring systems without nonmetallic sheath. Other types of cables and conductors shall be installed in electrical metallic tubing, flexible metallic tubing, intermediate metal conduit, rigid metal conduit without an overall nonmetallic covering, flexible metal conduit, or, where accessible, surface metal raceway or metal wireway with metal covers or solid bottom metal cable tray with solid metal covers.

(2) Equipment. Electrical equipment with a metal enclosure, or with a nonmetallic enclosure listed for the use and having adequate fire-resistant and low-smoke-producing characteristics, and associated wiring material suitable for the ambient temperature shall be permitted to be installed in such other space unless prohibited elsewhere in this *Code.*

Exception: Integral fan systems shall be permitted where specifically identified for such use.

(D) Information Technology Equipment. Electric wiring in air-handling areas beneath raised floors for information technology equipment shall be permitted in accordance with Article 645.

300.23 Panels Designed to Allow Access. Cables, raceways, and equipment installed behind panels designed to allow access, including suspended ceiling panels, shall be arranged and secured so as to allow the removal of panels and access to the equipment.

II. Requirements for Over 600 Volts, Nominal

300.31 Covers Required. Suitable covers shall be installed on all boxes, fittings, and similar enclosures to prevent accidental contact with energized parts or physical damage to parts or insulation.

300.32 Conductors of Different Systems. See 300.3(C)(2).

300.34 Conductor Bending Radius. The conductor shall not be bent to a radius less than 8 times the overall diameter for nonshielded conductors or 12 times the overall diameter for shielded or lead-covered conductors during or after installation. For multiconductor or multiplexed single conductor cables having individually shielded conductors, the minimum bending radius is 12 times the diameter of the individually shielded conductors or 7 times the overall diameter, whichever is greater.

300.35 Protection Against Induction Heating. Metallic raceways and associated conductors shall be arranged so as to avoid heating of the raceway in accordance with the applicable provisions of 300.20.

300.37 Aboveground Wiring Methods. Aboveground conductors shall be installed in rigid metal conduit, in intermediate metal conduit, in electrical metallic tubing, in rigid nonmetallic conduit, in cable trays, as busways, as cablebus, in other identified raceways, or as exposed runs of metal-clad cable suitable for the use and purpose. In locations accessible to qualified persons only, exposed runs of Type MV cables, bare conductors, and bare busbars shall also be permitted. Busbars shall be permitted to be either copper or aluminum.

300.39 Braid-Covered Insulated Conductors — Exposed Installation. Exposed runs of braid-covered insulated conductors shall have a flame-retardant braid. If the conductors used do not have this protection, a flame-retardant saturant shall be applied to the braid covering after installation. This treated braid covering shall be stripped back a safe distance at conductor terminals, according to the operating voltage. Where practicable, this distance shall not be less than 25 mm (1 in.) for each kilovolt of the conductor-to-ground voltage of the circuit.

300.40 Insulation Shielding. Metallic and semiconducting insulation shielding components of shielded cables shall be removed for a distance dependent on the circuit voltage and insulation. Stress reduction means shall be provided at all terminations of factory-applied shielding.

Metallic shielding components such as tapes, wires, or braids, or combinations thereof, and their associated conducting or semiconducting components shall be grounded.

300.42 Moisture or Mechanical Protection for Metal-Sheathed Cables. Where cable conductors emerge from a metal sheath and where protection against moisture or physical damage is necessary, the insulation of the conductors shall be protected by a cable sheath terminating device.

300.50 Underground Installations.

(A) General. Underground conductors shall be identified for the voltage and conditions under which they are installed. Direct burial cables shall comply with the provisions of 310.7. Underground cables shall be installed in accordance with 300.50(A)(1) or (A)(2), and the installation shall meet the depth requirements of Table 300.50.

(1) Shielded Cables and Nonshielded Cables in Metal-Sheathed Cable Assemblies. Underground cables, including nonshielded, Type MC and moisture-impervious metal sheath cables, shall have those sheaths grounded through an effective grounding path meeting the requirements of 250.4(A)(5) or (B)(4). They shall be direct buried or installed in raceways identified for the use.

(2) Other Nonshielded Cables. Other nonshielded cables not covered in 300.50(A)(1) shall be installed in rigid metal conduit, intermediate metal conduit, or rigid nonmetallic conduit encased in not less than 75 mm (3 in.) of concrete.

(B) Protection from Damage. Conductors emerging from the ground shall be enclosed in listed raceways. Raceways installed on poles shall be of rigid metal conduit, intermediate

Table 300.50 Minimum Cover[1] Requirements

Circuit Voltage	General Conditions (not otherwise specified)						Special Conditions (use if applicable)					
	(1) Direct-Buried Cables		(2) Rigid Nonmetallic Conduit[2]		(3) Rigid Metal Conduit and Intermediate Metal Conduit		(4) Raceways under buildings or exterior concrete slabs, 100 mm (4 in.) minimum thickness[3]		(5) Cables in airport runways or adjacent areas where trespass is prohibited		(6) Areas subject to vehicular traffic, such as thoroughfares and commercial parking areas	
	mm	in.	mm	in.	mm	in.	mm	in.	mm	in.	mm	in.
Over 600 V through 22 kV	750	30	450	18	150	6	100	4	450	18	600	24
Over 22 kV through 40 kV	900	36	600	24	150	6	100	4	450	18	600	24
Over 40 kV	1000	42	750	30	150	6	100	4	450	18	600	24

Notes:

1. Lesser depths shall be permitted where cables and conductors rise for terminations or splices or where access is otherwise required.

2. Where solid rock prevents compliance with the cover depths specified in this table, the wiring shall be installed in a metal or nonmetallic raceway permitted for direct burial. The raceways shall be covered by a minimum of 50 mm (2 in.) of concrete extending down to rock.

[1] Cover is defined as the shortest distance in millimeters (inches) measured between a point on the top surface of any direct-buried conductor, cable, conduit, or other raceway and the top surface of finished grade, concrete, or similar cover.

[2] Listed by a qualified testing agency as suitable for direct burial without encasement. All other nonmetallic systems shall require 50 mm (2 in.) of concrete or equivalent above conduit in addition to the table depth.

[3] The slab shall extend a minimum of 150 mm (6 in.) beyond the underground installation, and a warning ribbon or other effective means suitable for the conditions shall be placed above the underground installation.

metal conduit, PVC Schedule 80, or equivalent, extending from the minimum cover depth specified in Table 300.50 to a point 2.5 m (8 ft) above finished grade. Conductors entering a building shall be protected by an approved enclosure or raceway from the minimum cover depth to the point of entrance. Where direct-buried conductors, raceways, or cables are subject to movement by settlement or frost, they shall be installed to prevent damage to the enclosed conductors or to the equipment connected to the raceways. Metallic enclosures shall be grounded.

(C) Splices. Direct burial cables shall be permitted to be spliced or tapped without the use of splice boxes, provided they are installed using materials suitable for the application. The taps and splices shall be watertight and protected from mechanical damage. Where cables are shielded, the shielding shall be continuous across the splice or tap.

Exception: At splices of an engineered cabling system, metallic shields of direct-buried single-conductor cables with maintained spacing between phases shall be permitted to be interrupted and overlapped. Where shields are interrupted and overlapped, each shield section shall be grounded at one point.

(D) Backfill. Backfill containing large rocks, paving materials, cinders, large or sharply angular substances, or corrosive materials shall not be placed in an excavation where materials can damage or contribute to the corrosion of raceways, cables, or other substructures or where it may prevent adequate compaction of fill.

Protection in the form of granular or selected material or suitable sleeves shall be provided to prevent physical damage to the raceway or cable.

(E) Raceway Seal. Where a raceway enters from an underground system, the end within the building shall be sealed with an identified compound so as to prevent the entrance of moisture or gases, or it shall be so arranged to prevent moisture from contacting live parts.

ARTICLE 310
Conductors for General Wiring

310.1 Scope. This article covers general requirements for conductors and their type designations, insulations, markings, mechanical strengths, ampacity ratings, and uses. These requirements do not apply to conductors that form an integral part of equipment, such as motors, motor controllers, and similar equipment, or to conductors specifically provided for elsewhere in this *Code*.

FPN: For flexible cords and cables, see Article 400. For fixture wires, see Article 402.

310.2 Conductors.

(A) Insulated. Conductors shall be insulated.

Exception: Where covered or bare conductors are specifically permitted elsewhere in this Code.

FPN: See 250.184 for insulation of neutral conductors of a solidly grounded high-voltage system.

(B) Conductor Material. Conductors in this article shall be of aluminum, copper-clad aluminum, or copper unless otherwise specified.

310.3 Stranded Conductors. Where installed in raceways, conductors of size 8 AWG and larger shall be stranded.

Exception: As permitted or required elsewhere in this Code.

310.4 Conductors in Parallel. Aluminum, copper-clad aluminum, or copper conductors of size 1/0 AWG and larger, comprising each phase, polarity, neutral, or grounded circuit conductor, shall be permitted to be connected in parallel (electrically joined at both ends).

Exception No. 1: As permitted in 620.12(A)(1).

Exception No. 2: Conductors in sizes smaller than 1/0 AWG shall be permitted to be run in parallel to supply control power to indicating instruments, contactors, relays, solenoids, and similar control devices, provided all of the following apply:

(a) They are contained within the same raceway or cable.

(b) The ampacity of each individual conductor is sufficient to carry the entire load current shared by the parallel conductors.

(c) The overcurrent protection is such that the ampacity of each individual conductor will not be exceeded if one or more of the parallel conductors become inadvertently disconnected.

Exception No. 3: Conductors in sizes smaller than 1/0 AWG shall be permitted to be run in parallel for frequencies of 360 Hz and higher where conditions (a), (b), and (c) of Exception No. 2 are met.

Exception No. 4: Under engineering supervision, grounded neutral conductors in sizes 2 AWG and larger shall be permitted to be run in parallel for existing installations.

FPN: Exception No. 4 can be used to alleviate overheating of neutral conductors in existing installations due to high content of triplen harmonic currents.

The paralleled conductors in each phase, polarity, neutral, or grounded circuit conductor shall comply with all of the following:

(1) Be the same length

(2) Have the same conductor material

(3) Be the same size in circular mil area

(4) Have the same insulation type

(5) Be terminated in the same manner

Where run in separate raceways or cables, the raceways or cables shall have the same physical characteristics. Where conductors are in separate raceways or cables, the same number of conductors shall be used in each raceway or cable. Conductors of one phase, polarity, neutral, or grounded circuit conductor shall not be required to have the same physical characteristics as those of another phase, polarity, neutral, or grounded circuit conductor to achieve balance.

> FPN: Differences in inductive reactance and unequal division of current can be minimized by choice of materials, methods of construction, and orientation of conductors.

Where equipment grounding conductors are used with conductors in parallel, they shall comply with the requirements of this section except that they shall be sized in accordance with 250.122.

Conductors installed in parallel shall comply with the provisions of 310.15(B)(2)(a).

310.5 Minimum Size of Conductors. The minimum size of conductors shall be as shown in Table 310.5, except as permitted elsewhere in this *Code*.

Table 310.5 Minimum Size of Conductors

Conductor Voltage Rating (Volts)	Minimum Conductor Size (AWG)	
	Copper	Aluminum or Copper-Clad Aluminum
0–2000	14	12
2001–8000	8	8
8001–15,000	2	2
15,001–28,000	1	1
28,001–35,000	1/0	1/0

310.6 Shielding. Solid dielectric insulated conductors operated above 2000 volts in permanent installations shall have ozone-resistant insulation and shall be shielded. All metallic insulation shields shall be grounded through an effective grounding path meeting the requirements of 250.4(A)(5) or 250.4(B)(4). Shielding shall be for the purpose of confining the voltage stresses to the insulation.

Exception: Nonshielded insulated conductors listed by a qualified testing laboratory shall be permitted for use up to 2400 volts under the following conditions:

(a) Conductors shall have insulation resistant to electric discharge and surface tracking, or the insulated con-

ductor(s) shall be covered with a material resistant to ozone, electric discharge, and surface tracking.

(b) Where used in wet locations, the insulated conductor(s) shall have an overall nonmetallic jacket or a continuous metallic sheath.

(c) Insulation and jacket thicknesses shall be in accordance with Table 310.63.

310.7 Direct Burial Conductors. Conductors used for direct burial applications shall be of a type identified for such use.

Cables rated above 2000 volts shall be shielded.

Exception: Nonshielded multiconductor cables rated 2001–5000 volts shall be permitted if the cable has an overall metallic sheath or armor.

The metallic shield, sheath, or armor shall be grounded through an effective grounding path meeting the requirements of 250.4(A)(5) or (B)(4).

> FPN No. 1: See 300.5 for installation requirements for conductors rated 600 volts or less.

> FPN No. 2: See 300.50 for installation requirements for conductors rated over 600 volts.

310.8 Locations.

(A) Dry Locations. Insulated conductors and cables used in dry locations shall be any of the types identified in this *Code*.

(B) Dry and Damp Locations. Insulated conductors and cables used in dry and damp locations shall be Types FEP, FEPB, MTW, PFA, RHH, RHW, RHW-2, SA, THHN, THW, THW-2, THHW, THHW-2, THWN, THWN-2, TW, XHH, XHHW, XHHW-2, Z, or ZW.

(C) Wet Locations. Insulated conductors and cables used in wet locations shall be

(1) Moisture-impervious metal-sheathed;

(2) Types MTW, RHW, RHW-2, TW, THW, THW-2, THHW, THHW-2, THWN, THWN-2, XHHW, XHHW-2, ZW; or

(3) Of a type listed for use in wet locations.

(D) Locations Exposed to Direct Sunlight. Insulated conductors or cables used where exposed to direct rays of the sun shall comply with one of the following:

(1) Cables listed, or listed and marked, as being sunlight resistant

(2) Conductors listed, or listed and marked, as being sunlight resistant

(3) Covered with insulating material, such as tape or sleeving, that is listed, or listed and marked, as being sunlight resistant

310.9 Corrosive Conditions. Conductors exposed to oils, greases, vapors, gases, fumes, liquids, or other substances having a deleterious effect on the conductor or insulation shall be of a type suitable for the application.

310.10 Temperature Limitation of Conductors. No conductor shall be used in such a manner that its operating temperature exceeds that designated for the type of insulated conductor involved. In no case shall conductors be associated together in such a way, with respect to type of circuit, the wiring method employed, or the number of conductors, that the limiting temperature of any conductor is exceeded.

> FPN No. 1: The temperature rating of a conductor (see Table 310.13 and Table 310.61) is the maximum temperature, at any location along its length, that the conductor can withstand over a prolonged time period without serious degradation. The allowable ampacity tables, the ampacity tables of Article 310 and the ampacity tables of Annex B, the correction factors at the bottom of these tables, and the notes to the tables provide guidance for coordinating conductor sizes, types, allowable ampacities, ampacities, ambient temperatures, and number of associated conductors.
>
> The principal determinants of operating temperature are as follows:
>
> (1) Ambient temperature — ambient temperature may vary along the conductor length as well as from time to time.
> (2) Heat generated internally in the conductor as the result of load current flow, including fundamental and harmonic currents.
> (3) The rate at which generated heat dissipates into the ambient medium. Thermal insulation that covers or surrounds conductors affects the rate of heat dissipation.
> (4) Adjacent load-carrying conductors — adjacent conductors have the dual effect of raising the ambient temperature and impeding heat dissipation.
>
> FPN No. 2: Conductors installed in conduit exposed to direct sunlight in close proximity to rooftops have been shown, under certain conditions, to experience a temperature rise of 17°C (30°F) above ambient temperature on which the ampacity is based.

310.11 Marking.

(A) Required Information. All conductors and cables shall be marked to indicate the following information, using the applicable method described in 310.11(B):

(1) The maximum rated voltage
(2) The proper type letter or letters for the type of wire or cable as specified elsewhere in this *Code*
(3) The manufacturer's name, trademark, or other distinctive marking by which the organization responsible for the product can be readily identified
(4) The AWG size or circular mil area

> FPN: See Conductor Properties, Table 8 of Chapter 9, for conductor area expressed in SI units for conductor sizes specified in AWG or circular mil area.

(5) Cable assemblies where the neutral conductor is smaller than the ungrounded conductors shall be so marked

(B) Method of Marking.

(1) Surface Marking. The following conductors and cables shall be durably marked on the surface. The AWG size or circular mil area shall be repeated at intervals not exceeding 610 mm (24 in.). All other markings shall be repeated at intervals not exceeding 1.0 m (40 in.).

(1) Single-conductor and multiconductor rubber- and thermoplastic-insulated wire and cable
(2) Nonmetallic-sheathed cable
(3) Service-entrance cable
(4) Underground feeder and branch-circuit cable
(5) Tray cable
(6) Irrigation cable
(7) Power-limited tray cable
(8) Instrumentation tray cable

(2) Marker Tape. Metal-covered multiconductor cables shall employ a marker tape located within the cable and running for its complete length.

Exception No. 1: Mineral-insulated, metal-sheathed cable.

Exception No. 2: Type AC cable.

Exception No. 3: The information required in 310.11(A) shall be permitted to be durably marked on the outer nonmetallic covering of Type MC, Type ITC, or Type PLTC cables at intervals not exceeding 1.0 m (40 in.).

Exception No. 4: The information required in 310.11(A) shall be permitted to be durably marked on a nonmetallic covering under the metallic sheath of Type ITC or Type PLTC cable at intervals not exceeding 1.0 m (40 in.).

> FPN: Included in the group of metal-covered cables are Type AC cable (Article 320), Type MC cable (Article 330), and lead-sheathed cable.

(3) Tag Marking. The following conductors and cables shall be marked by means of a printed tag attached to the coil, reel, or carton:

(1) Mineral-insulated, metal-sheathed cable
(2) Switchboard wires
(3) Metal-covered, single-conductor cables
(4) Type AC cable

(4) Optional Marking of Wire Size. The information required in 310.11(A)(4) shall be permitted to be marked on the surface of the individual insulated conductors for the following multiconductor cables:

(1) Type MC cable
(2) Tray cable
(3) Irrigation cable

(4) Power-limited tray cable

(5) Power-limited fire alarm cable

(6) Instrumentation tray cable

(C) Suffixes to Designate Number of Conductors. A type letter or letters used alone shall indicate a single insulated conductor. The letter suffixes shall be indicated as follows:

(1) D — For two insulated conductors laid parallel within an outer nonmetallic covering

(2) M — For an assembly of two or more insulated conductors twisted spirally within an outer nonmetallic covering

(D) Optional Markings. All conductors and cables contained in Chapter 3 shall be permitted to be surface marked to indicate special characteristics of the cable materials. These markings include, but are not limited to, markings for limited smoke, sunlight resistant, and so forth.

310.12 Conductor Identification.

(A) Grounded Conductors. Insulated or covered grounded conductors shall be identified in accordance with 200.6.

(B) Equipment Grounding Conductors. Equipment grounding conductors shall be in accordance with 250.119.

(C) Ungrounded Conductors. Conductors that are intended for use as ungrounded conductors, whether used as a single conductor or in multiconductor cables, shall be finished to be clearly distinguishable from grounded and grounding conductors. Distinguishing markings shall not conflict in any manner with the surface markings required by 310.11(B)(1). Branch-circuit ungrounded conductors shall be identified in accordance with 210.5(C). Feeders shall be identified in accordance with 215.12.

Exception: Conductor identification shall be permitted in accordance with 200.7.

310.13 Conductor Constructions and Applications. In-

sulated conductors shall comply with the applicable provisions of one or more of the following: Table 310.13, Table 310.61, Table 310.62, Table 310.63, and Table 310.64.

These conductors shall be permitted for use in any of the wiring methods recognized in Chapter 3 and as specified in their respective tables or as permitted elsewhere in this *Code.*

FPN: Thermoplastic insulation may stiffen at temperatures lower than −10°C (+14°F). Thermoplastic insulation may also be deformed at normal temperatures where subjected to pressure, such as at points of support. Thermoplastic insulation, where used on dc circuits in wet locations, may result in electroendosmosis between conductor and insulation.

310.14 Aluminum Conductor Material. Solid aluminum

conductors 8, 10, and 12 AWG shall be made of an AA-8000 series electrical grade aluminum alloy conductor material.

Stranded aluminum conductors 8 AWG through 1000 kcmil marked as Type RHH, RHW, XHHW, THW, THHW, THWN, THHN, service-entrance Type SE Style U and SE Style R shall be made of an AA-8000 series electrical grade aluminum alloy conductor material.

310.15 Ampacities for Conductors Rated 0–2000 Volts.

(A) General.

(1) Tables or Engineering Supervision. Ampacities for conductors shall be permitted to be determined by tables as provided in 310.15(B) or under engineering supervision, as provided in 310.15(C).

FPN No. 1: Ampacities provided by this section do not take voltage drop into consideration. See 210.19(A), FPN No. 4, for branch circuits and 215.2(A), FPN No. 2, for feeders.

FPN No. 2: For the allowable ampacities of Type MTW wire, see Table 13.5.1 in NFPA 79-2002, *Electrical Standard for Industrial Machinery.*

(2) Selection of Ampacity. Where more than one calculated or tabulated ampacity could apply for a given circuit length, the lowest value shall be used.

Exception: Where two different ampacities apply to adjacent portions of a circuit, the higher ampacity shall be permitted to be used beyond the point of transition, a distance equal to 3.0 m (10 ft) or 10 percent of the circuit length figured at the higher ampacity, whichever is less.

FPN: See 110.14(C) for conductor temperature limitations due to termination provisions.

(B) Tables. Ampacities for conductors rated 0 to 2000 volts shall be as specified in the Allowable Ampacity Table 310.16 through Table 310.19, and Ampacity Table 310.20 and Table 310.21 as modified by (B)(1) through (B)(6).

FPN: Table 310.16 through Table 310.19 are application tables for use in determining conductor sizes on loads calculated in accordance with Article 220. Allowable ampacities result from consideration of one or more of the following:

(1) Temperature compatibility with connected equipment, especially the connection points.
(2) Coordination with circuit and system overcurrent protection.
(3) Compliance with the requirements of product listings or certifications. See 110.3(B).
(4) Preservation of the safety benefits of established industry practices and standardized procedures.

(1) General. For explanation of type letters used in tables and for recognized sizes of conductors for the various conductor insulations, see 310.13. For installation requirements, see 310.1 through 310.10 and the various articles of this *Code.* For flexible cords, see Table 400.4, Table 400.5(A), and Table 400.5(B).

Table 310.13 Conductor Application and Insulations

Trade Name	Type Letter	Maximum Operating Temperature	Application Provisions	Insulation	Thickness of Insulation				Outer Covering[1]
					AWG or kcmil	mm		mils	
Fluorinated ethylene propylene	FEP or FEPB	90°C 194°F	Dry and damp locations	Fluorinated ethylene propylene	14–10 8–2	0.51 0.76		20 30	None
		200°C 392°F	Dry locations — special applications[2]	Fluorinated ethylene propylene	14–8	0.36		14	Glass braid
					6–2	0.36		14	Glass or other suitable braid material
Mineral insulation (metal sheathed)	MI	90°C 194°F	Dry and wet locations	Magnesium oxide	18–16[3] 16–10	0.58 0.91		23 36	Copper or alloy steel
		250°C 482°F	For special applications[2]		9–4 3–500	1.27 1.40		50 55	
Moisture-, heat-, and oil-resistant thermoplastic	MTW	60°C 140°F	Machine tool wiring in wet locations	Flame-retardant moisture-, heat-, and oil-resistant thermoplastic		(A) (B)		(A) (B)	(A) None (B) Nylon jacket or equivalent
		90°C 194°F	Machine tool wiring in dry locations. FPN: See NFPA 79.		22–12 10 8 6 4–2 1–4/0 213–500 501–1000	0.76 0.38 0.76 0.51 1.14 0.76 1.52 0.76 1.52 1.02 2.03 1.27 2.41 1.52 2.79 1.78		30 15 30 20 45 30 60 30 60 40 80 50 95 60 110 70	
Paper		85°C 185°F	For underground service conductors, or by special permission	Paper					Lead sheath
Perfluoro-alkoxy	PFA	90°C 194°F	Dry and damp locations	Perfluoro-alkoxy	14–10 8–2 1–4/0	0.51 0.76 1.14		20 30 45	None
		200°C 392°F	Dry locations — special applications[2]						
Perfluoro-alkoxy	PFAH	250°C 482°F	Dry locations only. Only for leads within apparatus or within raceways connected to apparatus (nickel or nickel-coated copper only)	Perfluoro-alkoxy	14–10 8–2 1–4/0	0.51 0.76 1.14		20 30 45	None
Thermoset	RHH	90°C 194°F	Dry and damp locations		14–10 8–2 1–4/0 213–500 501–1000 1001–2000 For 601–2000 see Table 310.62.	1.14 1.52 2.03 2.41 2.79 3.18		45 60 80 95 110 125	Moisture-resistant, flame-retardant, nonmetallic covering[1]
Moisture-resistant thermoset	RHW[4]	75°C 167°F	Dry and wet locations	Flame-retardant, moisture-resistant thermoset	14–10 8–2 1–4/0 213–500 501–1000 1001–2000 For 601–2000, see Table 310.62.	1.14 1.52 2.03 2.41 2.79 3.18		45 60 80 95 110 125	Moisture-resistant, flame-retardant, nonmetallic covering[5]
Moisture-resistant thermoset	RHW-2	90°C 194°F	Dry and wet locations	Flame-retardant moisture-resistant thermoset	14–10 8–2 1-4/0 213–500 501–1000 1001–2000 For 601–2000, see Table 310.62.	1.14 1.52 2.03 2.41 2.79 3.18		45 60 80 95 110 125	Moisture-resistant, flame-retardant, nonmetallic covering[5]

(Continues)

Table 310.13 *Continued*

Trade Name	Type Letter	Maximum Operating Temperature	Application Provisions	Insulation	Thickness of Insulation			Outer Covering[1]
					AWG or kcmil	mm	mils	
Silicone	SA	90°C 194°F 200°C 392°F	Dry and damp locations For special application[2]	Silicone rubber	14–10 8–2 1–4/0 213–500 501–1000 1001–2000	1.14 1.52 2.03 2.41 2.79 3.18	45 60 80 95 110 125	Glass or other suitable braid material
Thermoset	SIS	90°C 194°F	Switchboard wiring only	Flame-retardant thermoset	14–10 8–2 1–4/0	0.76 1.14 2.41	30 45 95	None
Thermoplastic and fibrous outer braid	TBS	90°C 194°F	Switchboard wiring only	Thermoplastic	14–10 8 6–2 1–4/0	0.76 1.14 1.52 2.03	30 45 60 80	Flame-retardant, nonmetallic covering
Extended polytetra-fluoro-ethylene	TFE	250°C 482°F	Dry locations only. Only for leads within apparatus or within raceways connected to apparatus, or as open wiring (nickel or nickel-coated copper only)	Extruded polytetra-fluoro-ethylene	14–10 8–2 1–4/0	0.51 0.76 1.14	20 30 45	None
Heat-resistant thermoplastic	THHN	90°C 194°F	Dry and damp locations	Flame-retardant, heat-resistant thermoplastic	14–12 10 8–6 4–2 1–4/0 250–500 501–1000	0.38 0.51 0.76 1.02 1.27 1.52 1.78	15 20 30 40 50 60 70	Nylon jacket or equivalent
Moisture- and heat-resistant thermoplastic	THHW	75°C 167°F 90°C 194°F	Wet location Dry location	Flame-retardant, moisture- and heat-resistant thermoplastic	14–10 8 6–2 1–4/0 213–500 501–1000	0.76 1.14 1.52 2.03 2.41 2.79	30 45 60 80 95 110	None
Moisture- and heat-resistant thermoplastic	THW[4]	75°C 167°F 90°C 194°F	Dry and wet locations Special applications within electric discharge lighting equipment. Limited to 1000 open-circuit volts or less. (size 14-8 only as permitted in 410.33)	Flame-retardant, moisture- and heat-resistant thermoplastic	14–10 8 6–2 1–4/0 213–500 501–1000 1001–2000	0.76 1.14 1.52 2.03 2.41 2.79 3.18	30 45 60 80 95 110 125	None
Moisture- and heat-resistant thermoplastic	THWN[4]	75°C 167°F	Dry and wet locations	Flame-retardant, moisture- and heat-resistant thermoplastic	14–12 10 8–6 4–2 1–4/0 250–500 501–1000	0.38 0.51 0.76 1.02 1.27 1.52 1.78	15 20 30 40 50 60 70	Nylon jacket or equivalent
Moisture-resistant thermoplastic	TW	60°C 140°F	Dry and wet locations	Flame-retardant, moisture- resistant thermoplastic	14–10 8 6–2 1–4/0 213–500 501–1000 1001–2000	0.76 1.14 1.52 2.03 2.41 2.79 3.18	30 45 60 80 95 110 125	None

Table 310.13 *Continued*

Trade Name	Type Letter	Maximum Operating Temperature	Application Provisions	Insulation	Thickness of Insulation			Outer Covering[1]
					AWG or kcmil	mm	mils	
Underground feeder and branch-circuit cable — single conductor (for Type UF cable employing more than one conductor, see Article 340.)	UF	60°C 140°F 75°C 167°F[7]	See Article 340.	Moisture-resistant Moisture- and heat-resistant	14–10 8–2 1–4/0	1.52 2.03 2.41	60[6] 80[6] 95[6]	Integral with insulation
Underground service-entrance cable — single conductor (for Type USE cable employing more than one conductor, see Article 338.)	USE[4]	75°C 167°F	See Article 338.	Heat- and moisture-resistant	14–10 8–2 1–4/0 213–500 501–1000 1001–2000	1.14 1.52 2.03 2.41 2.79 3.18	45 60 80 95[8] 110 125	Moisture-resistant nonmetallic covering (See 338.2.)
Thermoset	XHH	90°C 194°F	Dry and damp locations	Flame-retardant thermoset	14–10 8–2 1–4/0 213–500 501–1000 1001–2000	0.76 1.14 1.40 1.65 2.03 2.41	30 45 55 65 80 95	None
Moisture-resistant thermoset	XHHW[4]	90°C 194°F 75°C 167°F	Dry and damp locations Wet locations	Flame-retardant, moisture-resistant thermoset	14–10 8–2 1–4/0 213–500 501–1000 1001–2000	0.76 1.14 1.40 1.65 2.03 2.41	30 45 55 65 80 95	None
Moisture-resistant thermoset	XHHW-2	90°C 194°F	Dry and wet locations	Flame-retardant, moisture-resistant thermoset	14–10 8–2 1–4/0 213–500 501–1000 1001–2000	0.76 1.14 1.40 1.65 2.03 2.41	30 45 55 65 80 95	None
Modified ethylene tetrafluoro-ethylene	Z	90°C 194°F 150°C 302°F	Dry and damp locations Dry locations — special applications[2]	Modified ethylene tetrafluoro- ethylene	14–12 10 8–4 3–1 1/0–4/0	0.38 0.51 0.64 0.89 1.14	15 20 25 35 45	None
Modified ethylene tetrafluoro-ethylene	ZW[4]	75°C 167°F 90°C 194°F 150°C 302°F	Wet locations Dry and damp locations Dry locations — special applications[2]	Modified ethylene tetrafluoro-ethylene	14–10 8–2	0.76 1.14	30 45	None

[1] Some insulations do not require an outer covering.

[2] Where design conditions require maximum conductor operating temperatures above 90°C (194°F).

[3] For signaling circuits permitting 300-volt insulation.

[4] Listed wire types designated with the suffix "2," such as RHW-2, shall be permitted to be used at a continuous 90°C (194°F) operating temperature, wet or dry.

[5] Some rubber insulations do not require an outer covering.

[6] Includes integral jacket.

[7] For ampacity limitation, see 340.80.

[8] Insulation thickness shall be permitted to be 2.03 mm (80 mils) for listed Type USE conductors that have been subjected to special investigations. The nonmetallic covering over individual rubber-covered conductors of aluminum-sheathed cable and of lead-sheathed or multiconductor cable shall not be required to be flame retardant. For Type MC cable, see 330.104. For nonmetallic-sheathed cable, see Article 334, Part III. For Type UF cable, see Article 340, Part III.

(2) Adjustment Factors.

(a)   More Than Three Current-Carrying Conductors in a Raceway or Cable. Where the number of current-carrying conductors in a raceway or cable exceeds three, or where single conductors or multiconductor cables are stacked or bundled longer than 600 mm (24 in.) without maintaining spacing and are not installed in raceways, the allowable ampacity of each conductor shall be reduced as shown in Table 310.15(B)(2)(a). Each current-carrying conductor of a paralleled set of conductors shall be counted as a current-carrying conductor.

> FPN No. 1: See Annex B, Table B.310.11, for adjustment factors for more than three current-carrying conductors in a raceway or cable with load diversity.

> FPN No. 2: See 366.23(A) for correction factors for conductors in sheet metal auxiliary gutters and 376.22 for correction factors for conductors in metal wireways.

Exception No. 1: Where conductors of different systems, as provided in 300.3, are installed in a common raceway or cable, the derating factors shown in Table 310.15(B)(2)(a) shall apply only to the number of power and lighting conductors (Articles 210, 215, 220, and 230).

Exception No. 2: For conductors installed in cable trays, the provisions of 392.11 shall apply.

Exception No. 3: Derating factors shall not apply to conductors in nipples having a length not exceeding 600 mm (24 in.).

Exception No. 4: Derating factors shall not apply to underground conductors entering or leaving an outdoor trench if those conductors have physical protection in the form of rigid metal conduit, intermediate metal conduit, or rigid nonmetallic conduit having a length not exceeding 3.05 m (10 ft) and if the number of conductors does not exceed four.

Exception No. 5: Adjustment factors shall not apply to Type AC cable or to Type MC cable without an overall outer jacket under the following conditions:

(1) Each cable has not more than three current-carrying conductors.

(2) The conductors are 12 AWG copper.

(3) Not more than 20 current-carrying conductors are bundled, stacked, or supported on "bridle rings."

A 60 percent adjustment factor shall be applied where the current-carrying conductors in these cables that are stacked or bundled longer than 600 mm (24 in.) without maintaining spacing exceeds 20.

(b)   More Than One Conduit, Tube, or Raceway. Spacing between conduits, tubing, or raceways shall be maintained.

Table 310.15(B)(2)(a) Adjustment Factors for More Than Three Current-Carrying Conductors in a Raceway or Cable

Number of Current-Carrying Conductors	Percent of Values in Tables 310.16 through 310.19 as Adjusted for Ambient Temperature if Necessary
4–6	80
7–9	70
10–20	50
21–30	45
31–40	40
41 and above	35

(3) Bare or Covered Conductors. Where bare or covered conductors are used with insulated conductors, their allowable ampacities shall be limited to those permitted for the adjacent insulated conductors.

(4) Neutral Conductor.

(a)   A neutral conductor that carries only the unbalanced current from other conductors of the same circuit shall not be required to be counted when applying the provisions of 310.15(B)(2)(a).

(b)   In a 3-wire circuit consisting of two phase wires and the neutral of a 4-wire, 3-phase, wye-connected system, a common conductor carries approximately the same current as the line-to-neutral load currents of the other conductors and shall be counted when applying the provisions of 310.15(B)(2)(a).

(c)   On a 4-wire, 3-phase wye circuit where the major portion of the load consists of nonlinear loads, harmonic currents are present in the neutral conductor; the neutral shall therefore be considered a current-carrying conductor.

(5) Grounding or Bonding Conductor. A grounding or bonding conductor shall not be counted when applying the provisions of 310.15(B)(2)(a).

(6) 120/240-Volt, 3-Wire, Single-Phase Dwelling Services and Feeders. For individual dwelling units of one family, two-family, and multifamily dwellings, conductors, as listed in Table 310.15(B)(6), shall be permitted as 120/240-volt, 3-wire, single-phase service-entrance conductors, service lateral conductors, and feeder conductors that serve as the main power feeder to each dwelling unit and are installed in raceway or cable with or without an equipment grounding conductor. For application of this section, the main power feeder shall be the feeder(s) between the main disconnect and the lighting and appliance branch-circuit panelboards(s). The feeder conductors to a dwelling unit shall not be required to have an allowable ampacity rating greater than their service-entrance conductors. The grounded conductor shall be permitted to be smaller than the ungrounded conductors, provided the requirements of 215.2, 220.61, and 230.42 are met.

Table 310.15(B)(6) Conductor Types and Sizes for 120/240-Volt, 3-Wire, Single-Phase Dwelling Services and Feeders. Conductor Types RHH, RHW, RHW-2, THHN, THHW, THW, THW-2, THWN, THWN-2, XHHW, XHHW-2, SE, USE, USE-2

Conductor (AWG or kcmil)		Service or Feeder Rating (Amperes)
Copper	Aluminum or Copper-Clad Aluminum	
4	2	100
3	1	110
2	1/0	125
1	2/0	150
1/0	3/0	175
2/0	4/0	200
3/0	250	225
4/0	300	250
250	350	300
350	500	350
400	600	400

(C) Engineering Supervision. Under engineering supervision, conductor ampacities shall be permitted to be calculated by means of the following general formula:

$$I = \sqrt{\frac{TC - (TA + \Delta TD)}{RDC(1 + YC)RCA}}$$

where:

TC = conductor temperature in degrees Celsius (°C)

TA = ambient temperature in degrees Celsius (°C)

ΔTD = dielectric loss temperature rise

RDC = dc resistance of conductor at temperature TC

YC = component ac resistance resulting from skin effect and proximity effect

RCA = effective thermal resistance between conductor and surrounding ambient

FPN: See Annex B for examples of formula applications.

310.60 Conductors Rated 2001 to 35,000 Volts.

(A) Definitions.

Electrical Ducts. As used in Article 310, electrical ducts shall include any of the electrical conduits recognized in Chapter 3 as suitable for use underground; other raceways round in cross section, listed for underground use, and embedded in earth or concrete.

Thermal Resistivity. As used in this *Code*, the heat transfer capability through a substance by conduction. It is the reciprocal of thermal conductivity and is designated Rho and expressed in the units °C-cm/watt.

(B) Ampacities of Conductors Rated 2001 to 35,000 Volts. Ampacities for solid dielectric-insulated conductors shall be permitted to be determined by tables or under engineering supervision, as provided in 310.60(C) and (D).

(1) Selection of Ampacity. Where more than one calculated or tabulated ampacity could apply for a given circuit length, the lowest value shall be used.

Exception: Where two different ampacities apply to adjacent portions of a circuit, the higher ampacity shall be permitted to be used beyond the point of transition, a distance equal to 3.0 m (10 ft) or 10 percent of the circuit length figured at the higher ampacity, whichever is less.

FPN: See 110.40 for conductor temperature limitations due to termination provisions.

Table 310.16 Allowable Ampacities of Insulated Conductors Rated 0 Through 2000 Volts, 60°C Through 90°C (140°F Through 194°F), Not More Than Three Current-Carrying Conductors in Raceway, Cable, or Earth (Directly Buried), Based on Ambient Temperature of 30°C (86°F)

Size AWG or kcmil	Temperature Rating of Conductor (See Table 310.13.)						Size AWG or kcmil
	60°C (140°F)	75°C (167°F)	90°C (194°F)	60°C (140°F)	75°C (167°F)	90°C (194°F)	
	Types TW, UF	Types RHW, THHW, THW, THWN, XHHW, USE, ZW	Types TBS, SA, SIS, FEP, FEPB, MI, RHH, RHW-2, THHN, THHW, THW-2, THWN-2, USE-2, XHH, XHHW, XHHW-2, ZW-2	Types TW, UF	Types RHW, THHW, THW, THWN, XHHW, USE	Types TBS, SA, SIS, THHN, THHW, THW-2, THWN-2, RHH, RHW-2, USE-2, XHH, XHHW, XHHW-2, ZW-2	
	COPPER			ALUMINUM OR COPPER-CLAD ALUMINUM			
18	—	—	14	—	—	—	—
16	—	—	18	—	—	—	—
14*	20	20	25	—	—	—	—
12*	25	25	30	20	20	25	12*
10*	30	35	40	25	30	35	10*
8	40	50	55	30	40	45	8
6	55	65	75	40	50	60	6
4	70	85	95	55	65	75	4
3	85	100	110	65	75	85	3
2	95	115	130	75	90	100	2
1	110	130	150	85	100	115	1
1/0	125	150	170	100	120	135	1/0
2/0	145	175	195	115	135	150	2/0
3/0	165	200	225	130	155	175	3/0
4/0	195	230	260	150	180	205	4/0
250	215	255	290	170	205	230	250
300	240	285	320	190	230	255	300
350	260	310	350	210	250	280	350
400	280	335	380	225	270	305	400
500	320	380	430	260	310	350	500
600	355	420	475	285	340	385	600
700	385	460	520	310	375	420	700
750	400	475	535	320	385	435	750
800	410	490	555	330	395	450	800
900	435	520	585	355	425	480	900
1000	455	545	615	375	445	500	1000
1250	495	590	665	405	485	545	1250
1500	520	625	705	435	520	585	1500
1750	545	650	735	455	545	615	1750
2000	560	665	750	470	560	630	2000

CORRECTION FACTORS

Ambient Temp. (°C)	For ambient temperatures other than 30°C (86°F), multiply the allowable ampacities shown above by the appropriate factor shown below.						Ambient Temp. (°F)
21–25	1.08	1.05	1.04	1.08	1.05	1.04	70–77
26–30	1.00	1.00	1.00	1.00	1.00	1.00	78–86
31–35	0.91	0.94	0.96	0.91	0.94	0.96	87–95
36–40	0.82	0.88	0.91	0.82	0.88	0.91	96–104
41–45	0.71	0.82	0.87	0.71	0.82	0.87	105–113
46–50	0.58	0.75	0.82	0.58	0.75	0.82	114–122
51–55	0.41	0.67	0.76	0.41	0.67	0.76	123–131
56–60	—	0.58	0.71	—	0.58	0.71	132–140
61–70	—	0.33	0.58	—	0.33	0.58	141–158
71–80	—	—	0.41	—	—	0.41	159–176

* See 240.4(D).

Table 310.17 Allowable Ampacities of Single-Insulated Conductors Rated 0 Through 2000 Volts in Free Air, Based on Ambient Air Temperature of 30°C (86°F)

	Temperature Rating of Conductor (See Table 310.13.)						
	60°C (140°F)	75°C (167°F)	90°C (194°F)	60°C (140°F)	75°C (167°F)	90°C (194°F)	
Size AWG or kcmil	Types TW, UF	Types RHW, THHW, THW, THWN, XHHW, ZW	Types TBS, SA, SIS, FEP, FEPB, MI, RHH, RHW-2, THHN, THHW, THW-2, THWN-2, USE-2, XHH, XHHW, XHHW-2, ZW-2	Types TW, UF	Types RHW, THHW, THW, THWN, XHHW	Types TBS, SA, SIS, THHN, THHW, THW-2, THWN-2, RHH, RHW-2, USE-2, XHH, XHHW, XHHW-2, ZW-2	Size AWG or kcmil
	COPPER			ALUMINUM OR COPPER-CLAD ALUMINUM			
18	—	—	18	—	—	—	—
16	—	—	24	—	—	—	—
14*	25	30	35	—	—	—	—
12*	30	35	40	25	30	35	12*
10*	40	50	55	35	40	40	10*
8	60	70	80	45	55	60	8
6	80	95	105	60	75	80	6
4	105	125	140	80	100	110	4
3	120	145	165	95	115	130	3
2	140	170	190	110	135	150	2
1	165	195	220	130	155	175	1
1/0	195	230	260	150	180	205	1/0
2/0	225	265	300	175	210	235	2/0
3/0	260	310	350	200	240	275	3/0
4/0	300	360	405	235	280	315	4/0
250	340	405	455	265	315	355	250
300	375	445	505	290	350	395	300
350	420	505	570	330	395	445	350
400	455	545	615	355	425	480	400
500	515	620	700	405	485	545	500
600	575	690	780	455	540	615	600
700	630	755	855	500	595	675	700
750	655	785	885	515	620	700	750
800	680	815	920	535	645	725	800
900	730	870	985	580	700	785	900
1000	780	935	1055	625	750	845	1000
1250	890	1065	1200	710	855	960	1250
1500	980	1175	1325	795	950	1075	1500
1750	1070	1280	1445	875	1050	1185	1750
2000	1155	1385	1560	960	1150	1335	2000

CORRECTION FACTORS

Ambient Temp. (°C)	For ambient temperatures other than 30°C (86°F), multiply the allowable ampacities shown above by the appropriate factor shown below.						Ambient Temp. (°F)
21–25	1.08	1.05	1.04	1.08	1.05	1.04	70–77
26–30	1.00	1.00	1.00	1.00	1.00	1.00	78–86
31–35	0.91	0.94	0.96	0.91	0.94	0.96	87–95
36–40	0.82	0.88	0.91	0.82	0.88	0.91	96–104
41–45	0.71	0.82	0.87	0.71	0.82	0.87	105–113
46–50	0.58	0.75	0.82	0.58	0.75	0.82	114–122
51–55	0.41	0.67	0.76	0.41	0.67	0.76	123–131
56–60	—	0.58	0.71	—	0.58	0.71	132–140
61–70	—	0.33	0.58	—	0.33	0.58	141–158
71–80	—	—	0.41	—	—	0.41	159–176

* See 240.4(D).

Table 310.18 Allowable Ampacities of Insulated Conductors Rated 0 Through 2000 Volts, 150°C Through 250°C (302°F Through 482°F). Not More Than Three Current-Carrying Conductors in Raceway or Cable, Based on Ambient Air Temperature of 40°C (104°F)

Size AWG or kcmil	Temperature Rating of Conductor (See Table 310.13.)				Size AWG or kcmil
	150°C (302°F)	200°C (392°F)	250°C (482°F)	150°C (302°F)	
	Type Z	Types FEP, FEPB, PFA, SA	Types PFAH, TFE	Type Z	
			NICKEL OR NICKEL-COATED COPPER	ALUMINUM OR COPPER-CLAD ALUMINUM	
	COPPER				
14	34	36	39	—	14
12	43	45	54	30	12
10	55	60	73	44	10
8	76	83	93	57	8
6	96	110	117	75	6
4	120	125	148	94	4
3	143	152	166	109	3
2	160	171	191	124	2
1	186	197	215	145	1
1/0	215	229	244	169	1/0
2/0	251	260	273	198	2/0
3/0	288	297	308	227	3/0
4/0	332	346	361	260	4/0

CORRECTION FACTORS

Ambient Temp. (°C)	For ambient temperatures other than 40°C (104°F), multiply the allowable ampacities shown above by the appropriate factor shown below.				Ambient Temp. (°F)
41–50	0.95	0.97	0.98	0.95	105–122
51–60	0.90	0.94	0.95	0.90	123–140
61–70	0.85	0.90	0.93	0.85	141–158
71–80	0.80	0.87	0.90	0.80	159–176
81–90	0.74	0.83	0.87	0.74	177–194
91–100	0.67	0.79	0.85	0.67	195–212
101–120	0.52	0.71	0.79	0.52	213–248
121–140	0.30	0.61	0.72	0.30	249–284
141–160	—	0.50	0.65	—	285–320
161–180	—	0.35	0.58	—	321–356
181–200	—	—	0.49	—	357–392
201–225	—	—	0.35	—	393–437

Table 310.19 Allowable Ampacities of Single-Insulated Conductors, Rated 0 Through 2000 Volts, 150°C Through 250°C (302°F Through 482°F), in Free Air, Based on Ambient Air Temperature of 40°C (104°F)

Size AWG or kcmil	Temperature Rating of Conductor (See Table 310.13.)				Size AWG or kcmil
	150°C (302°F)	200°C (392°F)	250°C (482°F)	150°C (302°F)	
	Type Z	Types FEP, FEPB, PFA, SA	Types PFAH, TFE	Type Z	
	COPPER		NICKEL, OR NICKEL-COATED COPPER	ALUMINUM OR COPPER-CLAD ALUMINUM	
14	46	54	59	—	14
12	60	68	78	47	12
10	80	90	107	63	10
8	106	124	142	83	8
6	155	165	205	112	6
4	190	220	278	148	4
3	214	252	327	170	3
2	255	293	381	198	2
1	293	344	440	228	1
1/0	339	399	532	263	1/0
2/0	390	467	591	305	2/0
3/0	451	546	708	351	3/0
4/0	529	629	830	411	4/0

CORRECTION FACTORS

Ambient Temp. (°C)	For ambient temperatures other than 40°C (104°F), multiply the allowable ampacities shown above by the appropriate factor shown below.				Ambient Temp. (°F)
41–50	0.95	0.97	0.98	0.95	105–122
51–60	0.90	0.94	0.95	0.90	123–140
61–70	0.85	0.90	0.93	0.85	141–158
71–80	0.80	0.87	0.90	0.80	159–176
81–90	0.74	0.83	0.87	0.74	177–194
91–100	0.67	0.79	0.85	0.67	195–212
101–120	0.52	0.71	0.79	0.52	213–248
121–140	0.30	0.61	0.72	0.30	249–284
141–160	—	0.50	0.65	—	285–320
161–180	—	0.35	0.58	—	321–356
181–200	—	—	0.49	—	357–392
201–225	—	—	0.35	—	393–437

Table 310.20 Ampacities of Not More Than Three Single Insulated Conductors, Rated 0 Through 2000 Volts, Supported on a Messenger, Based on Ambient Air Temperature of 40°C (104°F)

Size AWG or kcmil	Temperature Rating of Conductor (See Table 310.13.)				Size AWG or kcmil
	75°C (167°F)	90°C (194°F)	75°C (167°F)	90°C (194°F)	
	Types RHW, THHW, THW, THWN, XHHW, ZW	Types MI, THHN, THHW, THW-2, THWN-2, RHH, RHW-2, USE-2, XHHW, XHHW-2, ZW-2	Types RHW, THW, THWN, THHW, XHHW	Types THHN, THHW, RHH, XHHW, RHW-2, XHHW-2, THW-2, THWN-2, USE-2, ZW-2	
	COPPER		ALUMINUM OR COPPER-CLAD ALUMINUM		
8	57	66	44	51	8
6	76	89	59	69	6
4	101	117	78	91	4
3	118	138	92	107	3
2	135	158	106	123	2
1	158	185	123	144	1
1/0	183	214	143	167	1/0
2/0	212	247	165	193	2/0
3/0	245	287	192	224	3/0
4/0	287	335	224	262	4/0
250	320	374	251	292	250
300	359	419	282	328	300
350	397	464	312	364	350
400	430	503	339	395	400
500	496	580	392	458	500
600	553	647	440	514	600
700	610	714	488	570	700
750	638	747	512	598	750
800	660	773	532	622	800
900	704	826	572	669	900
1000	748	879	612	716	1000

CORRECTION FACTORS

Ambient Temp. (°C)	For ambient temperatures other than 40°C (104°F), multiply the allowable ampacities shown above by the appropriate factor shown below.				Ambient Temp. (°F)
21–25	1.20	1.14	1.20	1.14	70–77
26–30	1.13	1.10	1.13	1.10	79–86
31–35	1.07	1.05	1.07	1.05	88–95
36–40	1.00	1.00	1.00	1.00	97–104
41–45	0.93	0.95	0.93	0.95	106–113
46–50	0.85	0.89	0.85	0.89	115–122
51–55	0.76	0.84	0.76	0.84	124–131
56–60	0.65	0.77	0.65	0.77	133–140
61–70	0.38	0.63	0.38	0.63	142–158
71–80	—	0.45	—	0.45	160–176

Table 310.21 Ampacities of Bare or Covered Conductors in Free Air, Based on 40°C (104°F) Ambient, 80°C (176°F) Total Conductor Temperature, 610 mm/sec (2 ft/sec) Wind Velocity

Copper Conductors				AAC Aluminum Conductors			
Bare		Covered		Bare		Covered	
AWG or kcmil	Amperes	AWG or kcmil	Amperes	AWG or kcmil	Amperes	AWG or kcmil	Amperes
8	98	8	103	8	76	8	80
6	124	6	130	6	96	6	101
4	155	4	163	4	121	4	127
2	209	2	219	2	163	2	171
1/0	282	1/0	297	1/0	220	1/0	231
2/0	329	2/0	344	2/0	255	2/0	268
3/0	382	3/0	401	3/0	297	3/0	312
4/0	444	4/0	466	4/0	346	4/0	364
250	494	250	519	266.8	403	266.8	423
300	556	300	584	336.4	468	336.4	492
500	773	500	812	397.5	522	397.5	548
750	1000	750	1050	477.0	588	477.0	617
1000	1193	1000	1253	556.5	650	556.5	682
—	—	—	—	636.0	709	636.0	744
—	—	—	—	795.0	819	795.0	860
—	—	—	—	954.0	920	—	—
—	—	—	—	1033.5	968	1033.5	1017
—	—	—	—	1272	1103	1272	1201
—	—	—	—	1590	1267	1590	1381
—	—	—	—	2000	1454	2000	1527

(C) Tables. Ampacities for conductors rated 2001 to 35,000 volts shall be as specified in the Ampacity Table 310.67 through Table 310.86. Ampacities at ambient temperatures other than those shown in the tables shall be determined by the formula in 310.60(C)(4).

FPN No. 1: For ampacities calculated in accordance with 310.60(B), reference IEEE 835-1994 (IPCEA Pub. No. P-46-426), *Standard Power Cable Ampacity Tables,* and the references therein for availability of all factors and constants.

FPN No. 2: Ampacities provided by this section do not take voltage drop into consideration. See 210.19(A), FPN No. 4, for branch circuits and 215.2(A), FPN No. 2, for feeders.

(1) Grounded Shields. Ampacities shown in Table 310.69, Table 310.70, Table 310.81, and Table 310.82 are for cable with shields grounded at one point only. Where shields are grounded at more than one point, ampacities shall be adjusted to take into consideration the heating due to shield currents.

(2) Burial Depth of Underground Circuits. Where the burial depth of direct burial or electrical duct bank circuits is modified from the values shown in a figure or table, ampacities shall be permitted to be modified as indicated in (C)(a) and (C)(b).

(a) Where burial depths are increased in part(s) of an electrical duct run, no decrease in ampacity of the conductors is needed, provided the total length of parts of the duct run increased in depth is less than 25 percent of the total run length.

(b) Where burial depths are deeper than shown in a specific underground ampacity table or figure, an ampacity derating factor of 6 percent per 300-mm (1-ft) increase in depth for all values of rho shall be permitted.

No rating change is needed where the burial depth is decreased.

(3) Electrical Ducts in Figure 310.60. At locations where electrical ducts enter equipment enclosures from under ground, spacing between such ducts, as shown in Figure 310.60, shall be permitted to be reduced without requiring the ampacity of conductors therein to be reduced.

(4) Ambients Not in Tables. Ampacities at ambient temperatures other than those shown in the tables shall be determined by means of the following formula:

$$I_2 = I_1 \sqrt{\frac{TC - TA_2 - \Delta TD}{TC - TA_1 - \Delta TD}}$$

where:

I_1 = ampacity from tables at ambient TA_1

I_2 = ampacity at desired ambient TA_2

TC = conductor temperature in degrees Celsius (°C)

TA_1 = surrounding ambient from tables in degrees Celsius (°C)

TA_2 = desired ambient in degrees Celsius (°C)

ΔTD = dielectric loss temperature rise

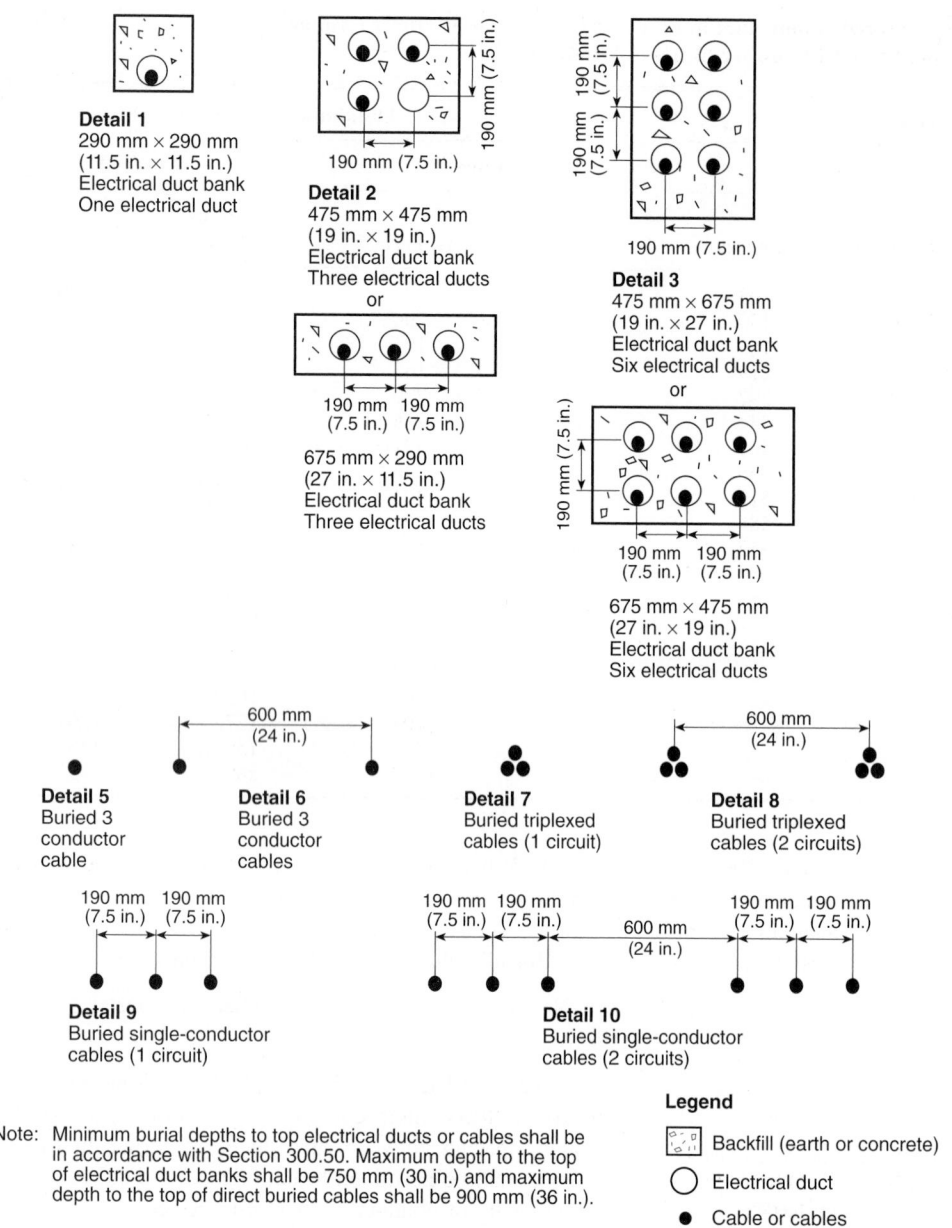

Figure 310.60 Cable Installation Dimensions for Use with Table 310.77 Through Table 310.86.

(D) Engineering Supervision. Under engineering supervision, conductor ampacities shall be permitted to be calculated by means of the following general formula:

$$I = \sqrt{\frac{TC - (TA + \Delta TD)}{RDC(1 + YC)RCA}}$$

where:

TC = conductor temperature in °C

TA = ambient temperature in °C

ΔTD = dielectric loss temperature rise

RDC = dc resistance of conductor at temperature TC

YC = component ac resistance resulting from skin effect and proximity effect

RCA = effective thermal resistance between conductor and surrounding ambient

FPN: See Annex B for examples of formula applications.

Table 310.61 Conductor Application and Insulation

Trade Name	Type Letter	Maximum Operating Temperature	Application Provision	Insulation	Outer Covering
Medium voltage solid dielectric	MV-90 MV-105*	90°C 105°C	Dry or wet locations rated 2001 volts and higher	Thermoplastic or thermosetting	Jacket, sheath, or armor

*Where design conditions require maximum conductor temperatures above 90°C.

Table 310.62 Thickness of Insulation for 601- to 2000-Volt Nonshielded Types RHH and RHW

Conductor Size (AWG or kcmil)	Column A[1]		Column B[2]	
	mm	mils	mm	mils
14–10	2.03	80	1.52	60
8	2.03	80	1.78	70
6–2	2.41	95	1.78	70
1–2/0	2.79	110	2.29	90
3/0–4/0	2.79	110	2.29	90
213–500	3.18	125	2.67	105
501–1000	3.56	140	3.05	120
1001–2000	3.56	140	3.56	140

[1]Column A insulations are limited to natural, SBR, and butyl rubbers.
[2]Column B insulations are materials such as cross-linked polyethylene, ethylene propylene rubber, and composites thereof.

Table 310.63 Thickness of Insulated Conductors Rated 2400 Volts and Jacket for Nonshielded Solid Dielectric Insulation

Conductor Size (AWG or kcmil)	Dry Locations, Single Conductor						Wet or Dry Locations					
	Without Jacket Insulation		With Jacket				Single Conductor				Multiconductor Insulation*	
			Insulation		Jacket		Insulation		Jacket			
	mm	mils	mm	mils	mm	mils	mm	mils	mm	mils	mm	mils
8	2.79	110	2.29	90	0.76	30	3.18	125	2.03	80	2.29	90
6	2.79	110	2.29	90	0.76	30	3.18	125	2.03	80	2.29	90
4–2	2.79	110	2.29	90	1.14	45	3.18	125	2.03	80	2.29	90
1–2/0	2.79	110	2.29	90	1.14	45	3.18	125	2.03	80	2.29	90
3/0–4/0	2.79	110	2.29	90	1.65	65	3.18	125	2.41	95	2.29	90
213–500	3.05	120	2.29	90	1.65	65	3.56	140	2.79	110	2.29	90
501–750	3.30	130	2.29	90	1.65	65	3.94	155	3.18	125	2.29	90
751–1000	3.30	130	2.29	90	1.65	65	3.94	155	3.18	125	2.29	90

*Under a common overall covering such as a jacket, sheath, or armor.

Table 310.64 Thickness of Insulation for Shielded Solid Dielectric Insulated Conductors Rated 2001 to 35,000 Volts

Conductor Size (AWG or kcmil)	2001–5000 Volts		5001–8000 volts						8001–15,000 volts						15,001–25,000 volts					
			100 Percent Insulation Level [1]		133 Percent Insulation Level [2]		173 Percent Insulation Level[3]		100 Percent Insulation Level[1]		133 Percent Insulation Level[2]		173 Percent Insulation Level[3]		100 Percent Insulation Level[1]		133 Percent Insulation Level[2]		173 Percent Insulation Level[3]	
	mm	mils	mm	mils	mm	mils	mm	mils	mm	mils	mm	mils	mm	mils	mm	mils	mm	mils	mm	mils
8	2.29	90	—	—	—	—	—	—	—	—	—	—	—	—	—	—	—	—	—	—
6–4	2.29	90	2.92	115	3.56	140	4.45	175	—	—	—	—	—	—	—	—	—	—	—	—
2	2.29	90	2.92	115	3.56	140	4.45	175	4.45	175	5.59	220	6.60	260	—	—	—	—	—	—
1	2.29	90	2.92	115	3.56	140	4.45	175	4.45	175	5.59	220	6.60	260	6.60	260	8.13	320	10.67	420
1/0–2000	2.29	90	2.92	115	3.56	140	4.45	175	4.45	175	5.59	220	6.60	260	6.60	260	8.13	320	10.67	420

(continues)

Table 310.64 *Continued*

Conductor Size (AWG or kcmil)	25,001–28000 volts						28,001–35,000 volts					
	100 Percent Insulation Level[1]		133 Percent Insulation Level[2]		173 Percent Insulation Level[3]		100 Percent Insulation Level[1]		133 Percent Insulation Level[2]		173 Percent Insulation Level[3]	
	mm	mils	mm	mils	mm	mils	mm	mils	mm	mils	mm	mils
1	7.11	280	8.76	345	11..30	445	—	—	—	—	—	—
1/0–2000	7.11	280	8.76	345	11.30	445	8.76	345	10.67	420	14.73	580

Notes:

[1]**100 Percent Insulation Level.** Cables in this category shall be permitted to be applied where the system is provided with relay protection such that ground faults will be cleared as rapidly as possible but, in any case, within 1 minute. While these cables are applicable to the great majority of cable installations that are on grounded systems, they shall be permitted to be used also on other systems for which the application of cables is acceptable, provided the above clearing requirements are met in completely de-energizing the faulted section.

[2]**133 Percent Insulation Level.** This insulation level corresponds to that formerly designated for ungrounded systems. Cables in this category shall be permitted to be applied in situations where the clearing time requirements of the 100 percent level category cannot be met and yet there is adequate assurance that the faulted section will be de-energized in a time not exceeding 1 hour. Also, they shall be permitted to be used in 100 percent insulation level applications where additional insulation is desirable.

[3]**173 Percent Insulation Level.** Cables in this category shall be permitted to be applied under all of the following conditions:

(1) In industrial establishments where the conditions of maintenance and supervision ensure that only qualified persons service the installation

(2) Where the fault clearing time requirements of the 133 percent level category cannot be met

(3) Where an orderly shutdown is essential to protect equipment and personnel

(4) There is adequate assurance that the faulted section will be de-energized in an orderly shutdown

Also, cables with this insulation thickness shall be permitted to be used in 100 or 133 percent insulation level applications where additional insulation strength is desirable.

Table 310.67 Ampacities of Insulated Single Copper Conductor Cables Triplexed in Air Based on Conductor Temperatures of 90°C (194°F) and 105°C (221°F) and Ambient Air Temperature of 40°C (104°F)

Conductor Size (AWG or kcmil)	Temperature Rating of Conductor (See Table 310.61.)			
	2001–5000 Volts Ampacity		5001–35,000 Volts Ampacity	
	90°C (194°F) Type MV-90	105°C (221°F) Type MV-105	90°C (194°F) Type MV-90	105°C (221°F) Type MV-105
8	65	74	—	—
6	90	99	100	110
4	120	130	130	140
2	160	175	170	195
1	185	205	195	225
1/0	215	240	225	255
2/0	250	275	260	295
3/0	290	320	300	340
4/0	335	375	345	390
250	375	415	380	430
350	465	515	470	525
500	580	645	580	650
750	750	835	730	820
1000	880	980	850	950

Table 310.68 Ampacities of Insulated Single Aluminum Conductor Cables Triplexed in Air Based on Conductor Temperatures of 90°C (194°F) and 105°C (221°F) and Ambient Air Temperature of 40°C (104°F)

Conductor Size (AWG or kcmil)	Temperature Rating of Conductor (See Table 310.61.)			
	2001–5000 Volts Ampacity		5001–35,000 Volts Ampacity	
	90°C (194°F) Type MV-90	105°C (221°F) Type MV-105	90°C (194°F) Type MV-90	105°C (221°F) Type MV-105
8	50	57	—	—
6	70	77	75	84
4	90	100	100	110
2	125	135	130	150
1	145	160	150	175
1/0	170	185	175	200
2/0	195	215	200	230
3/0	225	250	230	265
4/0	265	290	270	305
250	295	325	300	335
350	365	405	370	415
500	460	510	460	515
750	600	665	590	660
1000	715	800	700	780

Table 310.69 Ampacities of Insulated Single Copper Conductor Isolated in Air Based on Conductor Temperatures of 90°C (194°F) and 105°C (221°F) and Ambient Air Temperature of 40°C (104°F)

| | Temperature Rating of Conductor (See Table 310.61.) | | | | | |
| | 2001–5000 Volts Ampacity | | 5001–15,000 Volts Ampacity | | 15,001–35,000 Volts Ampacity | |
Conductor Size (AWG or kcmil)	90°C (194°F) Type MV-90	105°C (221°F) Type MV-105	90°C (194°F) Type MV-90	105°C (221°F) Type MV-105	90°C (194°F) Type MV-90	105°C (221°F) Type MV-105
8	83	93	—	—	—	—
6	110	120	110	125	—	—
4	145	160	150	165	—	—
2	190	215	195	215	—	—
1	225	250	225	250	225	250
1/0	260	290	260	290	260	290
2/0	300	330	300	335	300	330
3/0	345	385	345	385	345	380
4/0	400	445	400	445	395	445
250	445	495	445	495	440	490
350	550	615	550	610	545	605
500	695	775	685	765	680	755
750	900	1000	885	990	870	970
1000	1075	1200	1060	1185	1040	1160
1250	1230	1370	1210	1350	1185	1320
1500	1365	1525	1345	1500	1315	1465
1750	1495	1665	1470	1640	1430	1595
2000	1605	1790	1575	1755	1535	1710

Table 310.70 Ampacities of Insulated Single Aluminum Conductor Isolated in Air Based on Conductor Temperatures of 90°C (194°F) and 105°C (221°F) and Ambient Air Temperature of 40°C (104°F)

| | Temperature Rating of Conductor (See Table 310.61.) | | | | | |
| | 2001–5000 Volts Ampacity | | 5001–15,000 Volts Ampacity | | 15,001–35,000 Volts Ampacity | |
Conductor Size (AWG or kcmil)	90°C (194°F) Type MV-90	105°C (221°F) Type MV-105	90°C (194°F) Type MV-90	105°C (221°F) Type MV-105	90°C (194°F) Type MV-90	105°C (221°F) Type MV-105
8	64	71	—	—	—	—
6	85	95	87	97	—	—
4	115	125	115	130	—	—
2	150	165	150	170	—	—
1	175	195	175	195	175	195
1/0	200	225	200	225	200	225
2/0	230	260	235	260	230	260
3/0	270	300	270	300	270	300
4/0	310	350	310	350	310	345
250	345	385	345	385	345	380
350	430	480	430	480	430	475
500	545	605	535	600	530	590
750	710	790	700	780	685	765
1000	855	950	840	940	825	920
1250	980	1095	970	1080	950	1055
1500	1105	1230	1085	1215	1060	1180
1750	1215	1355	1195	1335	1165	1300
2000	1320	1475	1295	1445	1265	1410

Table 310.71 Ampacities of an Insulated Three-Conductor Copper Cable Isolated in Air Based on Conductor Temperatures of 90°C (194°F) and 105°C (221°F) and Ambient Air Temperature of 40°C (104°F)

| | Temperature Rating of Conductor (See Table 310.61.) | | | |
| | 2001–5000 Volts Ampacity | | 5001–35,000 Volts Ampacity | |
Conductor Size (AWG or kcmil)	90°C (194°F) Type MV-90	105°C (221°F) Type MV-105	90°C (194°F) Type MV-90	105°C (221°F) Type MV-105
8	59	66	—	—
6	79	88	93	105
4	105	115	120	135
2	140	154	165	185
1	160	180	185	210
1/0	185	205	215	240
2/0	215	240	245	275
3/0	250	280	285	315
4/0	285	320	325	360
250	320	355	360	400
350	395	440	435	490
500	485	545	535	600
750	615	685	670	745
1000	705	790	770	860

Table 310.72 Ampacities of an Insulated Three-Conductor Aluminum Cable Isolated in Air Based on Conductor Temperatures of 90°C (194°F) and 105°C (221°F) and Ambient Air Temperature of 40°C (104°F)

| | Temperature Rating of Conductor (See Table 310.61.) | | | |
| | 2001–5000 Volts Ampacity | | 5001–35,000 Volts Ampacity | |
Conductor Size (AWG or kcmil)	90°C (194°F) Type MV-90	105°C (221°F) Type MV-105	90°C (194°F) Type MV-90	105°C (221°F) Type MV-105
8	46	51	—	—
6	61	68	72	80
4	81	90	95	105
2	110	120	125	145
1	125	140	145	165
1/0	145	160	170	185
2/0	170	185	190	215
3/0	195	215	220	245
4/0	225	250	255	285
250	250	280	280	315
350	310	345	345	385
500	385	430	425	475
750	495	550	540	600
1000	585	650	635	705

Table 310.73 Ampacities of an Insulated Triplexed or Three Single-Conductor Copper Cables in Isolated Conduit in Air Based on Conductor Temperatures of 90°C (194°F) and 105°C (221°F) and Ambient Air Temperature of 40°C (104°F)

	Temperature Rating of Conductor (See Table 310.61.)			
	2001–5000 Volts Ampacity		5001–35,000 Volts Ampacity	
Conductor Size (AWG or kcmil)	90°C (194°F) Type MV-90	105°C (221°F) Type MV-105	90°C (194°F) Type MV-90	105°C (221°F) Type MV-105
8	55	61	—	—
6	75	84	83	93
4	97	110	110	120
2	130	145	150	165
1	155	175	170	190
1/0	180	200	195	215
2/0	205	225	225	255
3/0	240	270	260	290
4/0	280	305	295	330
250	315	355	330	365
350	385	430	395	440
500	475	530	480	535
750	600	665	585	655
1000	690	770	675	755

Table 310.74 Ampacities of an Insulated Triplexed or Three Single-Conductor Aluminum Cables in Isolated Conduit in Air Based on Conductor Temperatures of 90°C (194°F) and 105°C (221°F) and Ambient Air Temperature of 40°C (104°F)

	Temperature Rating of Conductor (See Table 310.61.)			
	2001–5000 Volts Ampacity		5001–35,000 Volts Ampacity	
Conductor Size (AWG or kcmil)	90°C (194°F) Type MV-90	105°C (221°F) Type MV-105	90°C (194°F) Type MV-90	105°C (221°F) Type MV-105
8	43	48	—	—
6	58	65	65	72
4	76	85	84	94
2	100	115	115	130
1	120	135	130	150
1/0	140	155	150	170
2/0	160	175	175	200
3/0	190	210	200	225
4/0	215	240	230	260
250	250	280	255	290
350	305	340	310	350
500	380	425	385	430
750	490	545	485	540
1000	580	645	565	640

Table 310.75 Ampacities of an Insulated Three-Conductor Copper Cable in Isolated Conduit in Air Based on Conductor Temperatures of 90°C (194°F) and 105°C (221°F) and Ambient Air Temperature of 40°C (104°F)

	Temperature Rating of Conductor (See Table 310.61.)			
	2001–5000 Volts Ampacity		5001–35,000 Volts Ampacity	
Conductor Size (AWG or kcmil)	90°C (194°F) Type MV-90	105°C (221°F) Type MV-105	90°C (194°F) Type MV-90	105°C (221°F) Type MV-105
8	52	58	—	—
6	69	77	83	92
4	91	100	105	120
2	125	135	145	165
1	140	155	165	185
1/0	165	185	195	215
2/0	190	210	220	245
3/0	220	245	250	280
4/0	255	285	290	320
250	280	315	315	350
350	350	390	385	430
500	425	475	470	525
750	525	585	570	635
1000	590	660	650	725

Table 310.76 Ampacities of an Insulated Three-Conductor Aluminum Cable in Isolated Conduit in Air Based on Conductor Temperatures of 90°C (194°F) and 105°C (221°F) and Ambient Air Temperature of 40°C (104°F)

	Temperature Rating of Conductor (See Table 310.61.)			
	2001–5000 Volts Ampacity		5001–35,000 Volts Ampacity	
Conductor Size (AWG or kcmil)	90°C (194°F) Type MV-90	105°C (221°F) Type MV-105	90°C (194°F) Type MV-90	105°C (221°F) Type MV-105
8	41	46	—	—
6	53	59	64	71
4	71	79	84	94
2	96	105	115	125
1	110	125	130	145
1/0	130	145	150	170
2/0	150	165	170	190
3/0	170	190	195	220
4/0	200	225	225	255
250	220	245	250	280
350	275	305	305	340
500	340	380	380	425
750	430	480	470	520
1000	505	560	550	615

Table 310.77 Ampacities of Three Single-Insulated Copper Conductors in Underground Electrical Ducts (Three Conductors per Electrical Duct) Based on Ambient Earth Temperature of 20°C (68°F), Electrical Duct Arrangement per Figure 310.60, 100 Percent Load Factor, Thermal Resistance (RHO) of 90, Conductor Temperatures of 90°C (194°F) and 105°C (221°F)

| Conductor Size (AWG or kcmil) | Temperature Rating of Conductor (See Table 310.61.) | | | |
| | 2001–5000 Volts Ampacity | | 5001–35,000 Volts Ampacity | |
	90°C (194°F) Type MV-90	105°C (221°F) Type MV-105	90°C (194°F) Type MV-90	105°C (221°F) Type MV-105
One Circuit (See Figure 310.60, Detail 1.)				
8	64	69	—	—
6	85	92	90	97
4	110	120	115	125
2	145	155	155	165
1	170	180	175	185
1/0	195	210	200	215
2/0	220	235	230	245
3/0	250	270	260	275
4/0	290	310	295	315
250	320	345	325	345
350	385	415	390	415
500	470	505	465	500
750	585	630	565	610
1000	670	720	640	690
Three Circuits (See Figure 310.60, Detail 2.)				
8	56	60	—	—
6	73	79	77	83
4	95	100	99	105
2	125	130	130	135
1	140	150	145	155
1/0	160	175	165	175
2/0	185	195	185	200
3/0	210	225	210	225
4/0	235	255	240	255
250	260	280	260	280
350	315	335	310	330
500	375	405	370	395
750	460	495	440	475
1000	525	565	495	535
Six Circuits (See Figure 310.60, Detail 3.)				
8	48	52	—	—
6	62	67	64	68
4	80	86	82	88
2	105	110	105	115
1	115	125	120	125
1/0	135	145	135	145
2/0	150	160	150	165
3/0	170	185	170	185
4/0	195	210	190	205
250	210	225	210	225
350	250	270	245	265
500	300	325	290	310
750	365	395	350	375
1000	410	445	390	415

Table 310.78 Ampacities of Three Single-Insulated Aluminum Conductors in Underground Electrical Ducts (Three Conductors per Electrical Duct) Based on Ambient Earth Temperature of 20°C (68°F), Electrical Duct Arrangement per Figure 310.60, 100 Percent Load Factor, Thermal Resistance (RHO) of 90, Conductor Temperatures of 90°C (194°F) and 105°C (221°F)

| Conductor Size (AWG or kcmil) | Temperature Rating of Conductor (See Table 310.61.) | | | |
| | 2001–5000 Volts Ampacity | | 5001–35,000 Volts Ampacity | |
	90°C (194°F) Type MV-90	105°C (221°F) Type MV-105	90°C (194°F) Type MV-90	105°C (221°F) Type MV-105
One Circuit (See Figure 310.60, Detail 1.)				
8	50	54	—	—
6	66	71	70	75
4	86	93	91	98
2	115	125	120	130
1	130	140	135	145
1/0	150	160	155	165
2/0	170	185	175	190
3/0	195	210	200	215
4/0	225	245	230	245
250	250	270	250	270
350	305	325	305	330
500	370	400	370	400
750	470	505	455	490
1000	545	590	525	565
Three Circuits (See Figure 310.60, Detail 2.)				
8	44	47	—	—
6	57	61	60	65
4	74	80	77	83
2	96	105	100	105
1	110	120	110	120
1/0	125	135	125	140
2/0	145	155	145	155
3/0	160	175	165	175
4/0	185	200	185	200
250	205	220	200	220
350	245	265	245	260
500	295	320	290	315
750	370	395	355	385
1000	425	460	405	440
Six Circuits (See Figure 310.60, Detail 3.)				
8	38	41	—	—
6	48	52	50	54
4	62	67	64	69
2	80	86	80	88
1	91	98	90	99
1/0	105	110	105	110
2/0	115	125	115	125
3/0	135	145	130	145
4/0	150	165	150	160
250	165	180	165	175
350	195	210	195	210
500	240	255	230	250
750	290	315	280	305
1000	335	360	320	345

Table 310.79 Ampacities of Three Insulated Copper Conductors Cabled Within an Overall Covering (Three-Conductor Cable) in Underground Electrical Ducts (One Cable per Electrical Duct) Based on Ambient Earth Temperature of 20°C (68°F), Electrical Duct Arrangement per Figure 310.60, 100 Percent Load Factor, Thermal Resistance (RHO) of 90, Conductor Temperatures of 90°C (194°F) and 105°C (221°C)

| Conductor Size (AWG or kcmil) | Temperature Rating of Conductor (See Table 310.61.) | | | |
| | 2001–5000 Volts Ampacity | | 5001–35,000 Volts Ampacity | |
	90°C (194°F) Type MV-90	105°C (221°F) Type MV-105	90°C (194°F) Type MV-90	105°C (221°F) Type MV-105
One Circuit (See Figure 310.60, Detail 1.)				
8	59	64	—	—
6	78	84	88	95
4	100	110	115	125
2	135	145	150	160
1	155	165	170	185
1/0	175	190	195	210
2/0	200	220	220	235
3/0	230	250	250	270
4/0	265	285	285	305
250	290	315	310	335
350	355	380	375	400
500	430	460	450	485
750	530	570	545	585
1000	600	645	615	660
Three Circuits (See Figure 310.60, Detail 2.)				
8	53	57	—	—
6	69	74	75	81
4	89	96	97	105
2	115	125	125	135
1	135	145	140	155
1/0	150	165	160	175
2/0	170	185	185	195
3/0	195	210	205	220
4/0	225	240	230	250
250	245	265	255	270
350	295	315	305	325
500	355	380	360	385
750	430	465	430	465
1000	485	520	485	515
Six Circuits (See Figure 310.60, Detail 3.)				
8	46	50	—	—
6	60	65	63	68
4	77	83	81	87
2	98	105	105	110
1	110	120	115	125
1/0	125	135	130	145
2/0	145	155	150	160
3/0	165	175	170	180
4/0	185	200	190	200
250	200	220	205	220
350	240	270	245	275
500	290	310	290	305
750	350	375	340	365
1000	390	420	380	405

Table 310.80 Ampacities of Three Insulated Aluminum Conductors Cabled Within an Overall Covering (Three-Conductor Cable) in Underground Electrical Ducts (One Cable per Electrical Duct) Based on Ambient Earth Temperature of 20°C (68°F), Electrical Duct Arrangement per Figure 310.60, 100 Percent Load Factor, Thermal Resistance (RHO) of 90, Conductor Temperatures of 90°C (194°F) and 105°C (221°C)

| Conductor Size (AWG or kcmil) | Temperature Rating of Conductor (See Table 310.61.) | | | |
| | 2001–5000 Volts Ampacity | | 5001–35,000 Volts Ampacity | |
	90°C (194°F) Type MV-90	105°C (221°F) Type MV-105	90°C (194°F) Type MV-90	105°C (221°F) Type MV-105
One Circuit (See Figure 310.60, Detail 1.)				
8	46	50	—	—
6	61	66	69	74
4	80	86	89	96
2	105	110	115	125
1	120	130	135	145
1/0	140	150	150	165
2/0	160	170	170	185
3/0	180	195	195	210
4/0	205	220	220	240
250	230	245	245	265
350	280	310	295	315
500	340	365	355	385
750	425	460	440	475
1000	495	535	510	545
Three Circuits (See Figure 310.60, Detail 2.)				
8	41	44	—	—
6	54	58	59	64
4	70	75	75	81
2	90	97	100	105
1	105	110	110	120
1/0	120	125	125	135
2/0	135	145	140	155
3/0	155	165	160	175
4/0	175	185	180	195
250	190	205	200	215
350	230	250	240	255
500	280	300	285	305
750	345	375	350	375
1000	400	430	400	430
Six Circuits (See Figure 310.60, Detail 3.)				
8	36	39	—	—
6	46	50	49	53
4	60	65	63	68
2	77	83	80	86
1	87	94	90	98
1/0	99	105	105	110
2/0	110	120	115	125
3/0	130	140	130	140
4/0	145	155	150	160
250	160	170	160	170
350	190	205	190	205
500	230	245	230	245
750	280	305	275	295
1000	320	345	315	335

Table 310.81 Ampacities of Single Insulated Copper Conductors Directly Buried in Earth Based on Ambient Earth Temperature of 20°C (68°F), Arrangement per Figure 310.60, 100 Percent Load Factor, Thermal Resistance (RHO) of 90, Conductor Temperatures of 90°C (194°F) and 105°C (221°C)

| Conductor Size (AWG or kcmil) | Temperature Rating of Conductor (See Table 310.61.) | | | |
| | 2001–5000 Volts Ampacity | | 5001–35,000 Volts Ampacity | |
	90°C (194°F) Type MV-90	105°C (221°F) Type MV-105	90°C (194°F) Type MV-90	105°C (221°F) Type MV-105
One Circuit, Three Conductors (See Figure 310.60, Detail 9.)				
8	110	115	—	—
6	140	150	130	140
4	180	195	170	180
2	230	250	210	225
1	260	280	240	260
1/0	295	320	275	295
2/0	335	365	310	335
3/0	385	415	355	380
4/0	435	465	405	435
250	470	510	440	475
350	570	615	535	575
500	690	745	650	700
750	845	910	805	865
1000	980	1055	930	1005
Two Circuits, Six Conductors (See Figure 310.60, Detail 10.)				
8	100	110	—	—
6	130	140	120	130
4	165	180	160	170
2	215	230	195	210
1	240	260	225	240
1/0	275	295	255	275
2/0	310	335	290	315
3/0	355	380	330	355
4/0	400	430	375	405
250	435	470	410	440
350	520	560	495	530
500	630	680	600	645
750	775	835	740	795
1000	890	960	855	920

Table 310.82 Ampacities of Single Insulated Aluminum Conductors Directly Buried in Earth Based on Ambient Earth Temperature of 20°C (68°F), Arrangement per Figure 310.60, 100 Percent Load Factor, Thermal Resistance (RHO) of 90, Conductor Temperatures of 90°C (194°F) and 105°C (221°F)

| Conductor Size (AWG or kcmil) | Temperature Rating of Conductor (See Table 310.61) | | | |
| | 2001–5000 Volts Ampacity | | 5001–35,000 Volts Ampacity | |
	90°C (194°F) Type MV-90	105°C (221°F) Type MV-105	90°C (194°F) Type MV-90	105°C (221°F) Type MV-105
One Circuit, Three Conductors (See Figure 310.60, Detail 9.)				
8	85	90	—	—
6	110	115	100	110
4	140	150	130	140
2	180	195	165	175
1	205	220	185	200
1/0	230	250	215	230
2/0	265	285	245	260
3/0	300	320	275	295
4/0	340	365	315	340
250	370	395	345	370
350	445	480	415	450
500	540	580	510	545
750	665	720	635	680
1000	780	840	740	795
Two Circuits, Six Conductors (See Figure 310.60, Detail 10.)				
8	80	85	—	—
6	100	110	95	100
4	130	140	125	130
2	165	180	155	165
1	190	200	175	190
1/0	215	230	200	215
2/0	245	260	225	245
3/0	275	295	255	275
4/0	310	335	290	315
250	340	365	320	345
350	410	440	385	415
500	495	530	470	505
750	610	655	580	625
1000	710	765	680	730

Table 310.83 Ampacities of Three Insulated Copper Conductors Cabled Within an Overall Covering (Three-Conductor Cable), Directly Buried in Earth Based on Ambient Earth Temperature of 20°C (68°F), Arrangement per Figure 310.60, 100 Percent Load Factor, Thermal Resistance (RHO) of 90, Conductor Temperatures of 90°C (194°F) and 105°C (221°F)

| Conductor Size (AWG or kcmil) | Temperature Rating of Conductor (See Table 310.61.) | | | |
| | 2001–5000 Volts Ampacity | | 5001–35,000 Volts Ampacity | |
	90°C (194°F) Type MV-90	105°C (221°F) Type MV-105	90°C (194°F) Type MV-90	105°C (221°F) Type MV-105
One Circuit (See Figure 310.60, Detail 5.)				
8	85	89	—	—
6	105	115	115	120
4	135	150	145	155
2	180	190	185	200
1	200	215	210	225
1/0	230	245	240	255
2/0	260	280	270	290
3/0	295	320	305	330
4/0	335	360	350	375
250	365	395	380	410
350	440	475	460	495
500	530	570	550	590
750	650	700	665	720
1000	730	785	750	810
Two Circuits (See Figure 310.60, Detail 6.)				
8	80	84	—	—
6	100	105	105	115
4	130	140	135	145
2	165	180	170	185
1	185	200	195	210
1/0	215	230	220	235
2/0	240	260	250	270
3/0	275	295	280	305
4/0	310	335	320	345
250	340	365	350	375
350	410	440	420	450
500	490	525	500	535
750	595	640	605	650
1000	665	715	675	730

Table 310.84 Ampacities of Three Insulated Aluminum Conductors Cabled Within an Overall Covering (Three-Conductor Cable), Directly Buried in Earth Based on Ambient Earth Temperature of 20°C (68°F), Arrangement per Figure 310.60, 100 Percent Load Factor, Thermal Resistance (RHO) of 90, Conductor Temperatures of 90°C (194°F) and 105°C (221°F)

| Conductor Size (AWG or kcmil) | Temperature Rating of Conductor (See Table 310.61.) | | | |
| | 2001–5000 Volts Ampacity | | 5001–35,000 Volts Ampacity | |
	90°C (194°F) Type MV-90	105°C (221°F) Type MV-105	90°C (194°F) Type MV-90	105°C (221°F) Type MV-105
One Circuit (See Figure 310.60, Detail 5.)				
8	65	70	—	—
6	80	88	90	95
4	105	115	115	125
2	140	150	145	155
1	155	170	165	175
1/0	180	190	185	200
2/0	205	220	210	225
3/0	230	250	240	260
4/0	260	280	270	295
250	285	310	300	320
350	345	375	360	390
500	420	450	435	470
750	520	560	540	580
1000	600	650	620	665
Two Circuits (See Figure 310.60, Detail 6.)				
8	60	66	—	—
6	75	83	80	95
4	100	110	105	115
2	130	140	135	145
1	145	155	150	165
1/0	165	180	170	185
2/0	190	205	195	210
3/0	215	230	220	240
4/0	245	260	250	270
250	265	285	275	295
350	320	345	330	355
500	385	415	395	425
750	480	515	485	525
1000	550	590	560	600

Table 310.85 Ampacities of Three Triplexed Single Insulated Copper Conductors Directly Buried in Earth Based on Ambient Earth Temperature of 20°C (68°F), Arrangement per Figure 310.60, 100 Percent Load Factor, Thermal Resistance (RHO) of 90, Conductor Temperatures 90°C (194°F) and 105°C (221°F)

	Temperature Rating of Conductor (See Table 310.61.)			
	2001–5000 Volts Ampacity		5001–35,000 Volts Ampacity	
Conductor Size (AWG or kcmil)	90°C (194°F) Type MV-90	105°C (221°F) Type MV-105	90°C (194°F) Type MV-90	105°C (221°F) Type MV-105
One Circuit, Three Conductors (See Figure 310.60, Detail 7.)				
8	90	95	—	—
6	120	130	115	120
4	150	165	150	160
2	195	205	190	205
1	225	240	215	230
1/0	255	270	245	260
2/0	290	310	275	295
3/0	330	360	315	340
4/0	375	405	360	385
250	410	445	390	410
350	490	580	470	505
500	590	635	565	605
750	725	780	685	740
1000	825	885	770	830
Two Circuits, Six Conductors (See Figure 310.60, Detail 8.)				
8	85	90	—	—
6	110	115	105	115
4	140	150	140	150
2	180	195	175	190
1	205	220	200	215
1/0	235	250	225	240
2/0	265	285	255	275
3/0	300	320	290	315
4/0	340	365	325	350
250	370	395	355	380
350	445	480	425	455
500	535	575	510	545
750	650	700	615	660
1000	740	795	690	745

Table 310.86 Ampacities of Three Triplexed Single Insulated Aluminum Conductors Directly Buried in Earth Based on Ambient Earth Temperature of 20°C (68°F), Arrangement per Figure 310.60, 100 Percent Load Factor, Thermal Resistance (RHO) of 90, Conductor Temperatures 90°C (194°F) and 105°C (221°F)

	Temperature Rating of Conductor (See Table 310.61.)			
	2001–5000 Volts Ampacity		5001–35,000 Volts Ampacity	
Conductor Size (AWG or kcmil)	90°C (194°F) Type MV-90	105°C (221°F) Type MV-105	90°C (194°F) Type MV-90	105°C (221°F) Type MV-105
One Circuit, Three Conductors (See Figure 310.60, Detail 7.)				
8	70	75	—	—
6	90	100	90	95
4	120	130	115	125
2	155	165	145	155
1	175	190	165	175
1/0	200	210	190	205
2/0	225	240	215	230
3/0	255	275	245	265
4/0	290	310	280	305
250	320	350	305	325
350	385	420	370	400
500	465	500	445	480
750	580	625	550	590
1000	670	725	635	680
Two Circuits, Six Conductors (See Figure 310.60, Detail 8.)				
8	65	70	—	—
6	85	95	85	90
4	110	120	105	115
2	140	150	135	145
1	160	170	155	170
1/0	180	195	175	190
2/0	205	220	200	215
3/0	235	250	225	245
4/0	265	285	255	275
250	290	310	280	300
350	350	375	335	360
500	420	455	405	435
750	520	560	485	525
1000	600	645	565	605

ARTICLE 312
Cabinets, Cutout Boxes, and Meter Socket Enclosures

312.1 Scope. This article covers the installation and construction specifications of cabinets, cutout boxes, and meter socket enclosures.

I. Installation

312.2 Damp, Wet, or Hazardous (Classified) Locations.

(A) Damp and Wet Locations. In damp or wet locations, surface-type enclosures within the scope of this article shall be placed or equipped so as to prevent moisture or water from entering and accumulating within the cabinet or cutout box, and shall be mounted so there is at least 6-mm (¼-in.) airspace between the enclosure and the wall or other supporting surface. Enclosures installed in wet locations shall be weatherproof. For enclosures in wet locations, raceways or cables entering above the level of uninsulated live parts shall use fittings listed for wet locations.

Exception: Nonmetallic enclosures shall be permitted to be installed without the airspace on a concrete, masonry, tile, or similar surface.

    FPN: For protection against corrosion, see 300.6.

(B) Hazardous (Classified) Locations. Installations in hazardous (classified) locations shall conform to Articles 500 through 517.

312.3 Position in Wall. In walls of concrete, tile, or other noncombustible material, cabinets shall be installed so that the front edge of the cabinet is not set back of the finished surface more than 6 mm (¼ in.). In walls constructed of wood or other combustible material, cabinets shall be flush with the finished surface or project therefrom.

312.4 Repairing Plaster and Drywall or Plasterboard. Plaster, drywall, or plasterboard surfaces that are broken or incomplete shall be repaired so there will be no gaps or open spaces greater than 3 mm (⅛ in.) at the edge of the cabinet or cutout box employing a flush-type cover.

312.5 Cabinets, Cutout Boxes, and Meter Socket Enclosures. Conductors entering enclosures within the scope of this article shall be protected from abrasion and shall comply with 312.5(A) through (C).

(A) Openings to Be Closed. Openings through which conductors enter shall be adequately closed.

(B) Metal Cabinets, Cutout Boxes, and Meter Socket Enclosures. Where metal enclosures within the scope of this article are installed with messenger supported wiring, open wiring on insulators, or concealed knob-and-tube wiring, conductors shall enter through insulating bushings or, in dry locations, through flexible tubing extending from the last insulating support and firmly secured to the enclosure.

(C) Cables. Where cable is used, each cable shall be secured to the cabinet, cutout box, or meter socket enclosure.

Exception: Cables with entirely nonmetallic sheaths shall be permitted to enter the top of a surface-mounted enclosure through one or more nonflexible raceways not less than 450 mm (18 in.) and not more than 3.0 m (10 ft) in length, provided all of the following conditions are met:

    (a) Each cable is fastened within 300 mm (12 in.), measured along the sheath, of the outer end of the raceway.

    (b) The raceway extends directly above the enclosure and does not penetrate a structural ceiling.

    (c) A fitting is provided on each end of the raceway to protect the cable(s) from abrasion and the fittings remain accessible after installation.

    (d) The raceway is sealed or plugged at the outer end using approved means so as to prevent access to the enclosure through the raceway.

    (e) The cable sheath is continuous through the raceway and extends into the enclosure beyond the fitting not less than 6 mm (¼ in.).

    (f) The raceway is fastened at its outer end and at other points in accordance with the applicable article.

    (g) Where installed as conduit or tubing, the allowable cable fill does not exceed that permitted for complete conduit or tubing systems by Table 1 of Chapter 9 of this Code and all applicable notes thereto.

    FPN: See Table 1 in Chapter 9, including Note 9, for allowable cable fill in circular raceways. See 310.15(B)(2)(a) for required ampacity reductions for multiple cables installed in a common raceway.

312.6 Deflection of Conductors. Conductors at terminals or conductors entering or leaving cabinets or cutout boxes and the like shall comply with 312.6(A) through (C).

Exception: Wire-bending space in enclosures for motor controllers with provisions for one or two wires per terminal shall comply with 430.10(B).

(A) Width of Wiring Gutters. Conductors shall not be deflected within a cabinet or cutout box unless a gutter having a width in accordance with Table 312.6(A) is provided. Conductors in parallel in accordance with 310.4 shall be judged on the basis of the number of conductors in parallel.

Table 312.6(A) Minimum Wire-Bending Space at Terminals and Minimum Width of Wiring Gutters

Wire Size (AWG or kcmil)	Wires per Terminal									
	1		2		3		4		5	
	mm	in.	mm	in.	mm	in.	mm	in.	mm	in.
14–10	Not specified		—	—	—	—	—	—	—	—
8–6	38.1	1½	—	—	—	—	—	—	—	—
4–3	50.8	2	—	—	—	—	—	—	—	—
2	63.5	2½	—	—	—	—	—	—	—	—
1	76.2	3	—	—	—	—	—	—	—	—
1/0–2/0	88.9	3½	127	5	178	7	—	—	—	—
3/0–4/0	102	4	152	6	203	8	—	—	—	—
250	114	4½	152	6	203	8	254	10	—	—
300–350	127	5	203	8	254	10	305	12	—	—
400–500	152	6	203	8	254	10	305	12	356	14
600–700	203	8	254	10	305	12	356	14	406	16
750–900	203	8	305	12	356	14	406	16	457	18
1000–1250	254	10	—	—	—	—	—	—	—	—
1500–2000	305	12	—	—	—	—	—	—	—	—

Note: Bending space at terminals shall be measured in a straight line from the end of the lug or wire connector (in the direction that the wire leaves the terminal) to the wall, barrier, or obstruction.

(B) Wire-Bending Space at Terminals. Wire-bending space at each terminal shall be provided in accordance with 312.6(B)(1) or (B)(2).

(1) Conductors Not Entering or Leaving Opposite Wall. Table 312.6(A) shall apply where the conductor does not enter or leave the enclosure through the wall opposite its terminal.

(2) Conductors Entering or Leaving Opposite Wall. Table 312.6(B) shall apply where the conductor does enter or leave the enclosure through the wall opposite its terminal.

Exception No. 1: Where the distance between the wall and its terminal is in accordance with Table 312.6(A), a conductor shall be permitted to enter or leave an enclosure through the wall opposite its terminal, provided the conductor enters or leaves the enclosure where the gutter joins an adjacent gutter that has a width that conforms to Table 312.6(B) for the conductor.

Exception No. 2: A conductor not larger than 350 kcmil shall be permitted to enter or leave an enclosure containing only a meter socket(s) through the wall opposite its terminal, provided the distance between the terminal and the opposite wall is not less than that specified in Table 312.6(A) and the terminal is a lay-in type, where the terminal is either of the following:

(a) Directed toward the opening in the enclosure and within a 45 degree angle of directly facing the enclosure wall

(b) Directly facing the enclosure wall and offset not greater than 50 percent of the bending space specified in Table 312.6(A)

FPN: *Offset* is the distance measured along the enclosure wall from the axis of the centerline of the terminal to a line passing through the center of the opening in the enclosure.

(C) Conductors 4 AWG or Larger. Installation shall comply with 300.4(F).

312.7 Space in Enclosures. Cabinets and cutout boxes shall have sufficient space to accommodate all conductors installed in them without crowding.

312.8 Enclosures for Switches or Overcurrent Devices. Enclosures for switches or overcurrent devices shall not be used as junction boxes, auxiliary gutters, or raceways for conductors feeding through or tapping off to other switches or overcurrent devices, unless adequate space for this purpose is provided. The conductors shall not fill the wiring space at any cross section to more than 40 percent of the cross-sectional area of the space, and the conductors, splices, and taps shall not fill the wiring space at any cross section to more than 75 percent of the cross-sectional area of that space.

312.9 Side or Back Wiring Spaces or Gutters. Cabinets and cutout boxes shall be provided with back-wiring spaces, gutters, or wiring compartments as required by 312.11(C) and (D).

Table 312.6(B) Minimum Wire-Bending Space at Terminals

Wire Size (AWG or kcmil)		Wires per Terminal							
		1		2		3		4 or More	
All Other Conductors	Compact Stranded AA-8000 Aluminum Alloy Conductors (See Note 3.)	mm	in.	mm	in.	mm	in.	mm	in.
14–10	12–8	Not specified		—	—	—	—	—	—
8	6	38.1	1½	—	—	—	—	—	—
6	4	50.8	2	—	—	—	—	—	—
4	2	76.2	3	—	—	—	—	—	—
3	1	76.2	3	—	—	—	—	—	—
2	1/0	88.9	3½	—	—	—	—	—	—
1	2/0	114	4½	—	—	—	—	—	—
1/0	3/0	140	5½	140	5½	178	7	—	—
2/0	4/0	152	6	152	6	190	7½	—	—
3/0	250	165[a]	6½[a]	165[a]	6½[a]	203	8	—	—
4/0	300	178[b]	7[b]	190[c]	7½[c]	216[a]	8½[a]	—	—
250	350	216[d]	8½[d]	229[d]	8½[d]	254[b]	9[b]	254	10
300	400	254[e]	10[e]	254[d]	10[d]	279[b]	11[b]	305	12
350	500	305[e]	12[e]	305[e]	12[e]	330[e]	13[e]	356[d]	14[d]
400	600	330[e]	13[e]	330[e]	13[e]	356[e]	14[e]	381[e]	15[e]
500	700–750	356[e]	14[e]	356[e]	14[e]	381[e]	15[e]	406[e]	16[e]
600	800–900	381[e]	15[e]	406[e]	16[e]	457[e]	18[e]	483[e]	19[e]
700	1000	406[e]	16[e]	457[e]	18[e]	508[e]	20[e]	559[e]	22[e]
750	—	432[e]	17[e]	483[e]	19[e]	559[e]	22[e]	610[e]	24[e]
800	—	457	18	508	20	559	22	610	24
900	—	483	19	559	22	610	24	610	24
1000	—	508	20	—	—	—	—	—	
1250	—	559	22	—		—		—	
1500	—	610	24	—		—		—	
1750	—	610	24	—		—		—	
2000	—	610	24	—		—		—	

1. Bending space at terminals shall be measured in a straight line from the end of the lug or wire connector in a direction perpendicular to the enclosure wall.

2. For removable and lay-in wire terminals intended for only one wire, bending space shall be permitted to be reduced by the following number of millimeters (inches):

   [a] 12.7 mm (½ in.)   [d] 50.8 mm (2 in.)
   [b] 25.4 mm (1 in.)   [e] 76.2 mm (3 in.)
   [c] 38.1 mm (1½ in.)

3. This column shall be permitted to determine the required wire-bending space for compact stranded aluminum conductors in sizes up to 1000 kcmil and manufactured using AA-8000 series electrical grade aluminum alloy conductor material in accordance with 310.14.

II. Construction Specifications

312.10 Material. Cabinets, cutout boxes, and meter socket enclosures shall comply with 312.10(A) through (C).

(A) Metal Cabinets and Cutout Boxes. Metal enclosures within the scope of this article shall be protected both inside and outside against corrosion.

FPN: For information on protection against corrosion, see 300.6.

(B) Strength. The design and construction of enclosures within the scope of this article shall be such as to secure ample strength and rigidity. If constructed of sheet steel, the metal thickness shall not be less than 1.35 mm (0.053 in.) uncoated.

(C) Nonmetallic Cabinets. Nonmetallic cabinets shall be listed, or they shall be submitted for approval prior to installation.

312.11 Spacing. The spacing within cabinets and cutout boxes shall comply with 312.11(A) through (D).

(A) General. Spacing within cabinets and cutout boxes shall be sufficient to provide ample room for the distribution of wires and cables placed in them and for a separation between metal parts of devices and apparatus mounted within them as follows.

(1) Base. Other than at points of support, there shall be an airspace of at least 1.59 mm (0.0625 in.) between the base of the device and the wall of any metal cabinet or cutout box in which the device is mounted.

(2) Doors. There shall be an airspace of at least 25.4 mm (1.00 in.) between any live metal part, including live metal parts of enclosed fuses, and the door.

Exception: Where the door is lined with an approved insulating material or is of a thickness of metal not less than 2.36 mm (0.093 in.) uncoated, the airspace shall not be less than 12.7 mm (0.500 in.).

(3) Live Parts. There shall be an airspace of at least 12.7 mm (0.500 in.) between the walls, back, gutter partition, if of metal, or door of any cabinet or cutout box and the nearest exposed current-carrying part of devices mounted within the cabinet where the voltage does not exceed 250. This spacing shall be increased to at least 25.4 mm (1.00 in.) for voltages of 251 to 600, nominal.

Exception: Where the conditions in 312.11(A)(2), Exception, are met, the airspace for nominal voltages from 251 to 600 shall be permitted to be not less than 12.7 mm (0.500 in.).

(B) Switch Clearance. Cabinets and cutout boxes shall be deep enough to allow the closing of the doors when 30-ampere branch-circuit panelboard switches are in any position, when combination cutout switches are in any position, or when other single-throw switches are opened as far as their construction permits.

(C) Wiring Space. Cabinets and cutout boxes that contain devices or apparatus connected within the cabinet or box to more than eight conductors, including those of branch circuits, meter loops, feeder circuits, power circuits, and similar circuits, but not including the supply circuit or a continuation thereof, shall have back-wiring spaces or one or more side-wiring spaces, side gutters, or wiring compartments.

(D) Wiring Space — Enclosure. Side-wiring spaces, side gutters, or side-wiring compartments of cabinets and cutout boxes shall be made tight enclosures by means of covers, barriers, or partitions extending from the bases of the devices contained in the cabinet, to the door, frame, or sides of the cabinet.

Exception: Side-wiring spaces, side gutters, and side-wiring compartments of cabinets shall not be required to be made tight enclosures where those side spaces contain only conductors that enter the cabinet directly opposite to the devices where they terminate.

Partially enclosed back-wiring spaces shall be provided with covers to complete the enclosure. Wiring spaces that are required by 312.11(C) and are exposed when doors are open shall be provided with covers to complete the enclosure. Where adequate space is provided for feed-through conductors and for splices as required in 312.8, additional barriers shall not be required.

ARTICLE 314
Outlet, Device, Pull, and Junction Boxes; Conduit Bodies; Fittings; and Handhole Enclosures

I. Scope and General

314.1 Scope. This article covers the installation and use of all boxes and conduit bodies used as outlet, device, junction, or pull boxes, depending on their use, and handhole enclosures. Cast, sheet metal, nonmetallic, and other boxes such as FS, FD, and larger boxes are not classified as conduit bodies. This article also includes installation requirements for fittings used to join raceways and to connect raceways and cables to boxes and conduit bodies.

314.2 Round Boxes. Round boxes shall not be used where conduits or connectors requiring the use of locknuts or bushings are to be connected to the side of the box.

314.3 Nonmetallic Boxes. Nonmetallic boxes shall be permitted only with open wiring on insulators, concealed knob-and-tube wiring, cabled wiring methods with entirely nonmetallic sheaths, flexible cords, and nonmetallic raceways.

Exception No. 1: Where internal bonding means are provided between all entries, nonmetallic boxes shall be permitted to be used with metal raceways or metal-armored cables.

Exception No. 2: Where integral bonding means with a provision for attaching an equipment bonding jumper inside the box are provided between all threaded entries in nonmetallic boxes listed for the purpose, nonmetallic boxes shall be permitted to be used with metal raceways or metal-armored cables.

314.4 Metal Boxes. All metal boxes shall be grounded in accordance with the provisions of Article 250.

314.5 Short-Radius Conduit Bodies. Conduit bodies such as capped elbows and service-entrance elbows that enclose conductors 6 AWG or smaller, and are only intended to enable the installation of the raceway and the contained conductors, shall not contain splices, taps, or devices and shall be of sufficient size to provide free space for all conductors enclosed in the conduit body.

II. Installation

314.15 Damp, Wet, or Hazardous (Classified) Locations.

(A) Damp or Wet Locations. In damp or wet locations, boxes, conduit bodies, and fittings shall be placed or equipped so as to prevent moisture from entering or accumulating within the box, conduit body, or fitting. Boxes, conduit bodies, and fittings installed in wet locations shall be listed for use in wet locations.

FPN No. 1: For boxes in floors, see 314.27(C).

FPN No. 2: For protection against corrosion, see 300.6.

(B) Hazardous (Classified) Locations. Installations in hazardous (classified) locations shall conform to Articles 500 through 517.

314.16 Number of Conductors in Outlet, Device, and Junction Boxes, and Conduit Bodies. Boxes and conduit bodies shall be of sufficient size to provide free space for all enclosed conductors. In no case shall the volume of the box, as calculated in 314.16(A), be less than the fill calculation as calculated in 314.16(B). The minimum volume for conduit bodies shall be as calculated in 314.16(C).

The provisions of this section shall not apply to terminal housings supplied with motors.

FPN: For volume requirements of motor terminal housings, see 430.12.

Boxes and conduit bodies enclosing conductors 4 AWG or larger shall also comply with the provisions of 314.28.

(A) Box Volume Calculations. The volume of a wiring enclosure (box) shall be the total volume of the assembled sections and, where used, the space provided by plaster rings, domed covers, extension rings, and so forth, that are marked with their volume or are made from boxes the dimensions of which are listed in Table 314.16(A).

(1) Standard Boxes. The volumes of standard boxes that are not marked with their volume shall be as given in Table 314.16(A).

(2) Other Boxes. Boxes 1650 cm³ (100 in.³) or less, other than those described in Table 314.16(A), and nonmetallic

boxes shall be durably and legibly marked by the manufacturer with their volume. Boxes described in Table 314.16(A) that have a volume larger than is designated in the table shall be permitted to have their volume marked as required by this section.

(B) Box Fill Calculations. The volumes in paragraphs 314.16(B)(1) through (B)(5), as applicable, shall be added together. No allowance shall be required for small fittings such as locknuts and bushings.

(1) Conductor Fill. Each conductor that originates outside the box and terminates or is spliced within the box shall be counted once, and each conductor that passes through the box without splice or termination shall be counted once. A looped, unbroken conductor not less than twice the minimum length required for free conductors in 300.14 shall be counted twice. The conductor fill shall be calculated using Table 314.16(B). A conductor, no part of which leaves the box, shall not be counted.

Exception: An equipment grounding conductor or conductors or not over four fixture wires smaller than 14 AWG, or both, shall be permitted to be omitted from the calculations where they enter a box from a domed luminaire (fixture) or similar canopy and terminate within that box.

(2) Clamp Fill. Where one or more internal cable clamps, whether factory or field supplied, are present in the box, a single volume allowance in accordance with Table 314.16(B) shall be made based on the largest conductor present in the box. No allowance shall be required for a cable connector with its clamping mechanism outside the box.

(3) Support Fittings Fill. Where one or more luminaire (fixture) studs or hickeys are present in the box, a single volume allowance in accordance with Table 314.16(B) shall be made for each type of fitting based on the largest conductor present in the box.

(4) Device or Equipment Fill. For each yoke or strap containing one or more devices or equipment, a double volume allowance in accordance with Table 314.16(B) shall be made for each yoke or strap based on the largest conductor connected to a device(s) or equipment supported by that yoke or strap.

(5) Equipment Grounding Conductor Fill. Where one or more equipment grounding conductors or equipment bonding jumpers enter a box, a single volume allowance in accordance with Table 314.16(B) shall be made based on the largest equipment grounding conductor or equipment bonding jumper present in the box. Where an additional set of equipment grounding conductors, as permitted by 250.146(D), is present in the box, an additional volume allowance shall be made based on the largest equipment grounding conductor in the additional set.

Table 314.16(A) Metal Boxes

Box Trade Size			Minimum Volume		Maximum Number of Conductors*						
mm	in.		cm³	in.³	18	16	14	12	10	8	6
100 × 32	(4 × 1¼)	round/octagonal	205	12.5	8	7	6	5	5	5	2
100 × 38	(4 × 1½)	round/octagonal	254	15.5	10	8	7	6	6	5	3
100 × 54	(4 × 2⅛)	round/octagonal	353	21.5	14	12	10	9	8	7	4
100 × 32	(4 × 1¼)	square	295	18.0	12	10	9	8	7	6	3
100 × 38	(4 × 1½)	square	344	21.0	14	12	10	9	8	7	4
100 × 54	(4 × 2⅛)	square	497	30.3	20	17	15	13	12	10	6
120 × 32	(4¹¹⁄₁₆ × 1¼)	square	418	25.5	17	14	12	11	10	8	5
120 × 38	(4¹¹⁄₁₆ × 1½)	square	484	29.5	19	16	14	13	11	9	5
120 × 54	(4¹¹⁄₁₆ × 2⅛)	square	689	42.0	28	24	21	18	16	14	8
75 × 50 × 38	(3 × 2 × 1½)	device	123	7.5	5	4	3	3	3	2	1
75 × 50 × 50	(3 × 2 × 2)	device	164	10.0	6	5	5	4	4	3	2
75 × 50 × 57	(3 × 2 × 2¼)	device	172	10.5	7	6	5	4	4	3	2
75 × 50 × 65	(3 × 2 × 2½)	device	205	12.5	8	7	6	5	5	4	2
75 × 50 × 70	(3 × 2 × 2¾)	device	230	14.0	9	8	7	6	5	4	2
75 × 50 × 90	(3 × 2 × 3½)	device	295	18.0	12	10	9	8	7	6	3
100 × 54 × 38	(4 × 2⅛ × 1½)	device	169	10.3	6	5	5	4	4	3	2
100 × 54 × 48	(4 × 2⅛ × 1⅞)	device	213	13.0	8	7	6	5	5	4	2
100 × 54 × 54	(4 × 2⅛ × 2⅛)	device	238	14.5	9	8	7	6	5	4	2
95 × 50 × 65	(3¾ × 2 × 2½)	masonry box/gang	230	14.0	9	8	7	6	5	4	2
95 × 50 × 90	(3¾ × 2 × 3½)	masonry box/gang	344	21.0	14	12	10	9	8	7	4
min. 44.5 depth	FS — single cover/gang (1¾)		221	13.5	9	7	6	6	5	4	2
min. 60.3 depth	FD — single cover/gang (2⅜)		295	18.0	12	10	9	8	7	6	3
min. 44.5 depth	FS — multiple cover/gang (1¾)		295	18.0	12	10	9	8	7	6	3
min. 60.3 depth	FD — multiple cover/gang (2⅜)		395	24.0	16	13	12	10	9	8	4

*Where no volume allowances are required by 314.16(B)(2) through (B)(5).

Table 314.16(B) Volume Allowance Required per Conductor

Size of Conductor (AWG)	Free Space Within Box for Each Conductor	
	cm³	in.³
18	24.6	1.50
16	28.7	1.75
14	32.8	2.00
12	36.9	2.25
10	41.0	2.50
8	49.2	3.00
6	81.9	5.00

(C) Conduit Bodies.

(1) General. Conduit bodies enclosing 6 AWG conductors or smaller, other than short-radius conduit bodies as described in 314.5, shall have a cross-sectional area not less than twice the cross-sectional area of the largest conduit or tubing to which it is attached. The maximum number of conductors permitted shall be the maximum number permitted by Table 1 of Chapter 9 for the conduit or tubing to which it is attached.

(2) With Splices, Taps, or Devices. Only those conduit bodies that are durably and legibly marked by the manufacturer with their volume shall be permitted to contain splices, taps, or devices. The maximum number of conductors shall be calculated in accordance with 314.16(B). Conduit bodies shall be supported in a rigid and secure manner.

314.17 Conductors Entering Boxes, Conduit Bodies, or Fittings. Conductors entering boxes, conduit bodies, or fittings shall be protected from abrasion and shall comply with 314.17(A) through (D).

(A) Openings to Be Closed. Openings through which conductors enter shall be adequately closed.

(B) Metal Boxes and Conduit Bodies. Where metal boxes or conduit bodies are installed with messenger supported wiring, open wiring on insulators, or concealed knob-and-tube wiring, conductors shall enter through insulating bushings or, in dry locations, through flexible tubing extending from the last insulating support to not less than 6 mm (¼ in.) inside the box and beyond any cable clamps. Except as provided in 300.15(C), the wiring shall be firmly secured to the box or conduit body. Where raceway or cable is installed with metal boxes or conduit bodies, the raceway or cable shall be secured to such boxes and conduit bodies.

(C) Nonmetallic Boxes and Conduit Bodies. Nonmetallic boxes and conduit bodies shall be suitable for the lowest temperature-rated conductor entering the box. Where nonmetallic boxes and conduit bodies are used with messenger supported wiring, open wiring on insulators, or concealed knob-and-tube wiring, the conductors shall enter the box through individual holes. Where flexible tubing is used to enclose the conductors, the tubing shall extend from the last insulating support to not less than 6 mm (¼ in.) inside the box and beyond any cable clamp. Where nonmetallic-sheathed cable or multiconductor Type UF cable is used, the sheath shall extend not less than 6 mm (¼ in.) inside the box and beyond any cable clamp. In all instances, all permitted wiring methods shall be secured to the boxes.

Exception: Where nonmetallic-sheathed cable or multiconductor Type UF cable is used with single gang boxes not larger than a nominal size 57 mm × 100 mm (2 ¼ in. × 4 in.) mounted in walls or ceilings, and where the cable is fastened within 200 mm (8 in.) of the box measured along the sheath and where the sheath extends through a cable knockout not less than 6 mm (¼ in.), securing the cable to the box shall not be required. Multiple cable entries shall be permitted in a single cable knockout opening.

(D) Conductors 4 AWG or Larger. Installation shall comply with 300.4(F).

> FPN: See 110.12(A) for requirements on closing unused cable and raceway knockout openings.

314.19 Boxes Enclosing Flush Devices. Boxes used to enclose flush devices shall be of such design that the devices will be completely enclosed on back and sides and substantial support for the devices will be provided. Screws for supporting the box shall not be used in attachment of the device contained therein.

314.20 In Wall or Ceiling. In walls or ceilings with a surface of concrete, tile, gypsum, plaster, or other noncombustible material, boxes employing a flush-type cover or faceplate shall be installed so that the front edge of the box, plaster ring, extension ring, or listed extender will not be set back of the finished surface more than 6 mm (¼ in.).

In walls and ceilings constructed of wood or other combustible surface material, boxes, plaster rings, extension rings, or listed extenders shall be flush with the finished surface or project therefrom.

314.21 Repairing Plaster and Drywall or Plasterboard. Plaster, drywall, or plasterboard surfaces that are broken or incomplete around boxes employing a flush-type cover or faceplate shall be repaired so there will be no gaps or open spaces greater than 3 mm (⅛ in.) at the edge of the box.

314.22 Exposed Surface Extensions. Surface extensions from a flush-mounted box shall be made by mounting and mechanically securing an extension ring over the flush box. Equipment grounding and bonding shall be in accordance with Article 250.

Exception: A surface extension shall be permitted to be made from the cover of a flush-mounted box where the cover is designed so it is unlikely to fall off or be removed if its securing means becomes loose. The wiring method shall be flexible for a length sufficient to permit removal of the cover and provide access to the box interior, and arranged so that any bonding or grounding continuity is independent of the connection between the box and cover.

314.23 Supports. Enclosures within the scope of this article shall be supported in accordance with one or more of the provisions in 314.23(A) through (H).

(A) Surface Mounting. An enclosure mounted on a building or other surface shall be rigidly and securely fastened in place. If the surface does not provide rigid and secure support, additional support in accordance with other provisions of this section shall be provided.

(B) Structural Mounting. An enclosure supported from a structural member of a building or from grade shall be rigidly supported either directly or by using a metal, polymeric, or wood brace.

(1) Nails and Screws. Nails and screws, where used as a fastening means, shall be attached by using brackets on the outside of the enclosure, or they shall pass through the interior within 6 mm (¼ in.) of the back or ends of the enclosure. Screws shall not be permitted to pass through the box unless exposed threads in the box are protected using approved means to avoid abrasion of conductor insulation.

(2) Braces. Metal braces shall be protected against corrosion and formed from metal that is not less than 0.51 mm (0.020 in.) thick uncoated. Wood braces shall have a cross section not less than nominal 25 mm × 50 mm (1 in. × 2 in.). Wood braces in wet locations shall be treated for the conditions. Polymeric braces shall be identified as being suitable for the use.

(C) Mounting in Finished Surfaces. An enclosure mounted in a finished surface shall be rigidly secured thereto by clamps, anchors, or fittings identified for the application.

(D) Suspended Ceilings. An enclosure mounted to structural or supporting elements of a suspended ceiling shall be not more than 1650 cm³ (100 in.³) in size and shall be securely fastened in place in accordance with either (D)(1) or (D)(2).

(1) Framing Members. An enclosure shall be fastened to the framing members by mechanical means such as bolts, screws, or rivets, or by the use of clips or other securing means identified for use with the type of ceiling framing member(s) and enclosure(s) employed. The framing members shall be adequately supported and securely fastened to each other and to the building structure.

(2) Support Wires. The installation shall comply with the provisions of 300.11(A). The enclosure shall be secured, using methods identified for the purpose, to ceiling support wire(s), including any additional support wire(s) installed for that purpose. Support wire(s) used for enclosure support shall be fastened at each end so as to be taut within the ceiling cavity.

(E) Raceway Supported Enclosure, Without Devices, Luminaires (Fixtures), or Lampholders. An enclosure that does not contain a device(s) other than splicing devices or support a luminaire(s) [fixture(s)], lampholder, or other equipment and is supported by entering raceways shall not exceed 1650 cm³ (100 in.³) in size. It shall have threaded entries or have hubs identified for the purpose. It shall be supported by two or more conduits threaded wrenchtight into the enclosure or hubs. Each conduit shall be secured within 900 mm (3 ft) of the enclosure, or within 450 mm (18 in.) of the enclosure if all conduit entries are on the same side.

Exception: Rigid metal, intermediate metal, or rigid nonmetallic conduit or electrical metallic tubing shall be permitted to support a conduit body of any size, including a conduit body constructed with only one conduit entry, provided the trade size of the conduit body is not larger than the largest trade size of the conduit or electrical metallic tubing.

(F) Raceway Supported Enclosures, with Devices, Luminaires (Fixtures), or Lampholders. An enclosure that contains a device(s), other than splicing devices, or supports a luminaire(s) [fixture(s)], lampholder, or other equipment and is supported by entering raceways shall not exceed 1650 cm³ (100 in.³) in size. It shall have threaded entries or have hubs identified for the purpose. It shall be supported by two or more conduits threaded wrenchtight into the enclosure or hubs. Each conduit shall be secured within 450 mm (18 in.) of the enclosure.

Exception No. 1: Rigid metal or intermediate metal conduit shall be permitted to support a conduit body of any

size, including a conduit body constructed with only one conduit entry, provided the trade size of the conduit body is not larger than the largest trade size of the conduit.

Exception No. 2: An unbroken length(s) of rigid or intermediate metal conduit shall be permitted to support a box used for luminaire (fixture) or lampholder support, or to support a wiring enclosure that is an integral part of a luminaire (fixture) and used in lieu of a box in accordance with 300.15(B), where all of the following conditions are met:

(a) The conduit is securely fastened at a point so that the length of conduit beyond the last point of conduit support does not exceed 900 mm (3 ft).

(b) The unbroken conduit length before the last point of conduit support is 300 mm (12 in.) or greater, and that portion of the conduit is securely fastened at some point not less than 300 mm (12 in.) from its last point of support.

(c) Where accessible to unqualified persons, the luminaire (fixture) or lampholder, measured to its lowest point, is at least 2.5 m (8 ft) above grade or standing area and at least 900 mm (3 ft) measured horizontally to the 2.5 m (8 ft) elevation from windows, doors, porches, fire escapes, or similar locations.

(d) A luminaire (fixture) supported by a single conduit does not exceed 300 mm (12 in.) in any direction from the point of conduit entry.

(e) The weight supported by any single conduit does not exceed 9 kg (20 lb).

(f) At the luminaire (fixture) or lampholder end, the conduit(s) is threaded wrenchtight into the box, conduit body, or integral wiring enclosure, or into hubs identified for the purpose. Where a box or conduit body is used for support, the luminaire (fixture) shall be secured directly to the box or conduit body, or through a threaded conduit nipple not over 75 mm (3 in.) long.

(G) Enclosures in Concrete or Masonry. An enclosure supported by embedment shall be identified as suitably protected from corrosion and securely embedded in concrete or masonry.

(H) Pendant Boxes. An enclosure supported by a pendant shall comply with 314.23(H)(1) or (H)(2).

(1) Flexible Cord. A box shall be supported from a multiconductor cord or cable in an approved manner that protects the conductors against strain, such as a strain-relief connector threaded into a box with a hub.

(2) Conduit. A box supporting lampholders or luminaires (lighting fixtures), or wiring enclosures within luminaires (fixtures) used in lieu of boxes in accordance with 300.15(B), shall be supported by rigid or intermediate metal conduit stems. For stems longer than 450 mm (18 in.), the stems shall be connected to the wiring system with flexible fittings suitable for the location. At the luminaire (fixture) end, the conduit(s) shall be threaded wrenchtight into the box or wiring enclosure, or into hubs identified for the purpose.

Where supported by only a single conduit, the threaded joints shall be prevented from loosening by the use of setscrews or other effective means, or the luminaire (fixture), at any point, shall be at least 2.5 m (8 ft) above grade or standing area and at least 900 mm (3 ft) measured horizontally to the 2.5 m (8 ft) elevation from windows, doors, porches, fire escapes, or similar locations. A luminaire (fixture) supported by a single conduit shall not exceed 300 mm (12 in.) in any horizontal direction from the point of conduit entry.

314.24 Depth of Outlet Boxes. No box shall have an internal depth of less than 12.7 mm (½ in.). Boxes intended to enclose flush devices shall have an internal depth of not less than 23.8 mm ($^{15}/_{16}$ in.).

314.25 Covers and Canopies. In completed installations, each box shall have a cover, faceplate, lampholder, or luminaire (fixture) canopy, except where the installation complies with 410.14(B).

(A) Nonmetallic or Metal Covers and Plates. Nonmetallic or metal covers and plates shall be permitted. Where metal covers or plates are used, they shall comply with the grounding requirements of 250.110.

> FPN: For additional grounding requirements, see 410.18(A) for metal luminaire (fixture) canopies, and 404.12 and 406.5(B) for metal faceplates.

(B) Exposed Combustible Wall or Ceiling Finish. Where a luminaire (fixture) canopy or pan is used, any combustible wall or ceiling finish exposed between the edge of the canopy or pan and the outlet box shall be covered with noncombustible material.

(C) Flexible Cord Pendants. Covers of outlet boxes and conduit bodies having holes through which flexible cord pendants pass shall be provided with bushings designed for the purpose or shall have smooth, well-rounded surfaces on which the cords may bear. So-called hard rubber or composition bushings shall not be used.

314.27 Outlet Boxes.

(A) Boxes at Luminaire (Lighting Fixture) Outlets. Boxes used at luminaire (lighting fixture) or lampholder outlets shall be designed for the purpose. At every outlet used exclusively for lighting, the box shall be designed or installed so that a luminaire (lighting fixture) may be attached.

Exception: A wall-mounted luminaire (fixture) weighing not more than 3 kg (6 lb) shall be permitted to be supported

on other boxes or plaster rings that are secured to other boxes, provided the luminaire (fixture) or its supporting yoke is secured to the box with no fewer than two No. 6 or larger screws.

(B) Maximum Luminaire (Fixture) Weight. Outlet boxes or fittings installed as required by 314.23 shall be permitted to support luminaires (lighting fixtures) weighing 23 kg (50 lb) or less. A luminaire (lighting fixture) that weighs more than 23 kg (50 lb) shall be supported independently of the outlet box unless the outlet box is listed for the weight to be supported.

(C) Floor Boxes. Boxes listed specifically for this application shall be used for receptacles located in the floor.

Exception: Where the authority having jurisdiction judges them free from likely exposure to physical damage, moisture, and dirt, boxes located in elevated floors of show windows and similar locations shall be permitted to be other than those listed for floor applications. Receptacles and covers shall be listed as an assembly for this type of location.

(D) Boxes at Ceiling-Suspended (Paddle) Fan Outlets. Outlet boxes or outlet box systems used as the sole support of a ceiling-suspended (paddle) fan shall be listed, shall be marked by their manufacturer as suitable for this purpose, and shall not support ceiling-suspended (paddle) fans that weigh more than 32 kg (70 lb). For outlet boxes or outlet box systems designed to support ceiling-suspended (paddle) fans that weigh more than 16 kg (35 lb), the required marking shall include the maximum weight to be supported.

314.28 Pull and Junction Boxes and Conduit Bodies. Boxes and conduit bodies used as pull or junction boxes shall comply with 314.28(A) through (D).

Exception: Terminal housings supplied with motors shall comply with the provisions of 430.12.

(A) Minimum Size. For raceways containing conductors of 4 AWG or larger, and for cables containing conductors of 4 AWG or larger, the minimum dimensions of pull or junction boxes installed in a raceway or cable run shall comply with (A)(1) through (A)(3). Where an enclosure dimension is to be calculated based on the diameter of entering raceways, the diameter shall be the metric designator (trade size) expressed in the units of measurement employed.

(1) Straight Pulls. In straight pulls, the length of the box shall not be less than eight times the metric designator (trade size) of the largest raceway.

(2) Angle or U Pulls. Where splices or where angle or U pulls are made, the distance between each raceway entry inside the box and the opposite wall of the box shall not be less than six times the metric designator (trade size) of the largest raceway in a row. This distance shall be increased for additional entries by the amount of the sum of the diameters of all other raceway entries in the same row on the same wall of the box. Each row shall be calculated individually, and the single row that provides the maximum distance shall be used.

Exception: Where a raceway or cable entry is in the wall of a box or conduit body opposite a removable cover, the distance from that wall to the cover shall be permitted to comply with the distance required for one wire per terminal in Table 312.6(A).

The distance between raceway entries enclosing the same conductor shall not be less than six times the metric designator (trade size) of the larger raceway.

When transposing cable size into raceway size in 314.28(A)(1) and (A)(2), the minimum metric designator (trade size) raceway required for the number and size of conductors in the cable shall be used.

(3) Smaller Dimensions. Boxes or conduit bodies of dimensions less than those required in 314.28(A)(1) and (A)(2) shall be permitted for installations of combinations of conductors that are less than the maximum conduit or tubing fill (of conduits or tubing being used) permitted by Table 1 of Chapter 9, provided the box or conduit body has been listed for, and is permanently marked with, the maximum number and maximum size of conductors permitted.

(B) Conductors in Pull or Junction Boxes. In pull boxes or junction boxes having any dimension over 1.8 m (6 ft), all conductors shall be cabled or racked up in an approved manner.

(C) Covers. All pull boxes, junction boxes, and conduit bodies shall be provided with covers compatible with the box or conduit body construction and suitable for the conditions of use. Where used, metal covers shall comply with the grounding requirements of 250.110. An extension from the cover of an exposed box shall comply with 314.22, Exception.

(D) Permanent Barriers. Where permanent barriers are installed in a box, each section shall be considered as a separate box.

314.29 Boxes, Conduit Bodies, and Handhole Enclosures to Be Accessible. Boxes, conduit bodies, and handhole enclosures shall be installed so that the wiring contained in them can be rendered accessible without removing any part of the building or, in underground circuits, without excavating sidewalks, paving, earth, or other substance that is to be used to establish the finished grade.

Exception: Listed boxes and handhole enclosures shall be permitted where covered by gravel, light aggregate, or noncohesive granulated soil if their location is effectively identified and accessible for excavation.

314.30 Handhole Enclosures. Handhole enclosures shall be designed and installed to withstand all loads likely to be imposed.

> FPN: See ANSI/SCTE 77-2002, *Specification for Underground Enclosure Integrity*, for additional information on deliberate and nondeliberate traffic loading that can be expected to bear on underground enclosures.

(A) Size. Handhole enclosures shall be sized in accordance with 314.28(A) for conductors operating at 600 volts or below, and in accordance with 314.71 for conductors operating at over 600 volts. For handhole enclosures without bottoms where the provisions of 314.28(A)(2), Exception, or 314.71(B)(1), Exception No. 1, apply, the measurement to the removable cover shall be taken from the end of the conduit or cable assembly.

(B) Wiring Entries. Underground raceways and cable assemblies entering a handhole enclosure shall extend into the enclosure, but they shall not be required to be mechanically connected to the enclosure.

(C) Handhole Enclosures Without Bottoms. Where handhole enclosures without bottoms are installed, all enclosed conductors and any splices or terminations, if present, shall be listed as suitable for wet locations.

(D) Covers. Handhole enclosure covers shall have an identifying mark or logo that prominently identifies the function of the enclosure, such as "electric." Handhole enclosure covers shall require the use of tools to open, or they shall weigh over 45 kg (100 lb). Metal covers and other exposed conductive surfaces shall be bonded in accordance with 250.96(A).

III. Construction Specifications

314.40 Metal Boxes, Conduit Bodies, and Fittings.

(A) Corrosion Resistant. Metal boxes, conduit bodies, and fittings shall be corrosion resistant or shall be well-galvanized, enameled, or otherwise properly coated inside and out to prevent corrosion.

> FPN: See 300.6 for limitation in the use of boxes and fittings protected from corrosion solely by enamel.

(B) Thickness of Metal. Sheet steel boxes not over 1650 cm^3 (100 in.^{3}) in size shall be made from steel not less than 1.59 mm (0.0625 in.) thick. The wall of a malleable iron box or conduit body and a die-cast or permanent-mold cast aluminum, brass, bronze, or zinc box or conduit body shall not be less than 2.38 mm ($\frac{3}{32}$ in.) thick. Other cast metal boxes or conduit bodies shall have a wall thickness not less than 3.17 mm ($\frac{1}{8}$ in.).

Exception No. 1: Listed boxes and conduit bodies shown to have equivalent strength and characteristics shall be permitted to be made of thinner or other metals.

Exception No. 2: The walls of listed short radius conduit bodies, as covered in 314.5, shall be permitted to be made of thinner metal.

(C) Metal Boxes Over 1650 cm³ (100 in.³). Metal boxes over 1650 cm³ (100 in.³) in size shall be constructed so as to be of ample strength and rigidity. If of sheet steel, the metal thickness shall not be less than 1.35 mm (0.053 in.) uncoated.

(D) Grounding Provisions. A means shall be provided in each metal box for the connection of an equipment grounding conductor. The means shall be permitted to be a tapped hole or equivalent.

314.41 Covers. Metal covers shall be of the same material as the box or conduit body with which they are used, or they shall be lined with firmly attached insulating material that is not less than 0.79 mm ($\frac{1}{32}$ in.) thick, or they shall be listed for the purpose. Metal covers shall be the same thickness as the boxes or conduit body for which they are used, or they shall be listed for the purpose. Covers of porcelain or other approved insulating materials shall be permitted if of such form and thickness as to afford the required protection and strength.

314.42 Bushings. Covers of outlet boxes and conduit bodies having holes through which flexible cord pendants may pass shall be provided with approved bushings or shall have smooth, well-rounded surfaces on which the cord may bear. Where individual conductors pass through a metal cover, a separate hole equipped with a bushing of suitable insulating material shall be provided for each conductor. Such separate holes shall be connected by a slot as required by 300.20.

314.43 Nonmetallic Boxes. Provisions for supports or other mounting means for nonmetallic boxes shall be outside of the box, or the box shall be constructed so as to prevent contact between the conductors in the box and the supporting screws.

314.44 Marking. All boxes and conduit bodies, covers, extension rings, plaster rings, and the like shall be durably and legibly marked with the manufacturer's name or trademark.

IV. Pull and Junction Boxes for Use on Systems Over 600 Volts, Nominal

314.70 General. Where pull and junction boxes are used on systems over 600 volts, the installation shall comply with the provisions of Part IV and also with the following general provisions of this article:

(1) Part I, 314.2, 314.3, and 314.4

(2) Part II, 314.15; 314.17; 314.20; 314.23(A), (B), or (G); 314.28(B); and 314.29

(3) Part III, 314.40(A) and (C) and 314.41

314.71 Size of Pull and Junction Boxes. Pull and junction boxes shall provide adequate space and dimensions for the installation of conductors, and they shall comply with the specific requirements of this section.

Exception: Terminal housings supplied with motors shall comply with the provisions of 430.12.

(A) For Straight Pulls. The length of the box shall not be less than 48 times the outside diameter, over sheath, of the largest shielded or lead-covered conductor or cable entering the box. The length shall not be less than 32 times the outside diameter of the largest nonshielded conductor or cable.

(B) For Angle or U Pulls.

(1) Distance to Opposite Wall. The distance between each cable or conductor entry inside the box and the opposite wall of the box shall not be less than 36 times the outside diameter, over sheath, of the largest cable or conductor. This distance shall be increased for additional entries by the amount of the sum of the outside diameters, over sheath, of all other cables or conductor entries through the same wall of the box.

Exception No. 1: Where a conductor or cable entry is in the wall of a box opposite a removable cover, the distance from that wall to the cover shall be permitted to be not less than the bending radius for the conductors as provided in 300.34.

Exception No. 2: Where cables are nonshielded and not lead covered, the distance of 36 times the outside diameter shall be permitted to be reduced to 24 times the outside diameter.

(2) Distance Between Entry and Exit. The distance between a cable or conductor entry and its exit from the box shall not be less than 36 times the outside diameter, over sheath, of that cable or conductor.

Exception: Where cables are nonshielded and not lead covered, the distance of 36 times the outside diameter shall be permitted to be reduced to 24 times the outside diameter.

(C) Removable Sides. One or more sides of any pull box shall be removable.

314.72 Construction and Installation Requirements.

(A) Corrosion Protection. Boxes shall be made of material inherently resistant to corrosion or shall be suitably protected, both internally and externally, by enameling, galvanizing, plating, or other means.

(B) Passing Through Partitions. Suitable bushings, shields, or fittings having smooth, rounded edges shall be provided where conductors or cables pass through partitions and at other locations where necessary.

(C) Complete Enclosure. Boxes shall provide a complete enclosure for the contained conductors or cables.

(D) Wiring Is Accessible. Boxes shall be installed so that the wiring is accessible without removing any part of the building. Working space shall be provided in accordance with 110.34.

(E) Suitable Covers. Boxes shall be closed by suitable covers securely fastened in place. Underground box covers that weigh over 45 kg (100 lb) shall be considered meeting this requirement. Covers for boxes shall be permanently marked "DANGER — HIGH VOLTAGE — KEEP OUT." The marking shall be on the outside of the box cover and shall be readily visible. Letters shall be block type and at least 13 mm (½ in.) in height.

(F) Suitable for Expected Handling. Boxes and their covers shall be capable of withstanding the handling to which they are likely to be subjected.

ARTICLE 320
Armored Cable: Type AC

I. General

320.1 Scope. This article covers the use, installation, and construction specifications for armored cable, Type AC.

320.2 Definition.

Armored Cable, Type AC. A fabricated assembly of insulated conductors in a flexible metallic enclosure. See 320.100.

II. Installation

320.10 Uses Permitted. Type AC cable shall be permitted as follows:

(1) In both exposed and concealed work

(2) In cable trays

(3) In dry locations

(4) Embedded in plaster finish on brick or other masonry, except in damp or wet locations

(5) To be run or fished in the air voids of masonry block or tile walls where such walls are not exposed or subject to excessive moisture or dampness

   FPN: The "Uses Permitted" is not an all-inclusive list.

320.12 Uses Not Permitted. Type AC cable shall not be used as follows:

(1) Where subject to physical damage

(2) In damp or wet locations

(3) In air voids of masonry block or tile walls where such walls are exposed or subject to excessive moisture or dampness

(4) Where exposed to corrosive fumes or vapors

(5) Embedded in plaster finish on brick or other masonry in damp or wet locations

320.15 Exposed Work. Exposed runs of cable, except as provided in 300.11(A), shall closely follow the surface of the building finish or of running boards. Exposed runs shall also be permitted to be installed on the underside of joists where supported at each joist and located so as not to be subject to physical damage.

320.17 Through or Parallel to Framing Members. Type AC cable shall be protected in accordance with 300.4(A), (C), and (D) where installed through or parallel to framing members.

320.23 In Accessible Attics. Type AC cables in accessible attics or roof spaces shall be installed as specified in 320.23(A) and (B).

(A) Where Run Across the Top of Floor Joists. Where run across the top of floor joists, or within 2.1 m (7 ft) of floor or floor joists across the face of rafters or studding, in attics and roof spaces that are accessible, the cable shall be protected by substantial guard strips that are at least as high as the cable. Where this space is not accessible by permanent stairs or ladders, protection shall only be required within 1.8 m (6 ft) of the nearest edge of the scuttle hole or attic entrance.

(B) Cable Installed Parallel to Framing Members. Where the cable is installed parallel to the sides of rafters, studs, or floor joists, neither guard strips nor running boards shall be required, and the installation shall also comply with 300.4(D).

320.24 Bending Radius. Bends in Type AC cable shall be made such that the cable is not damaged. The radius of the curve of the inner edge of any bend shall not be less than five times the diameter of the Type AC cable.

320.30 Securing and Supporting.

(A) General. Type AC cable shall be supported and secured by staples, cable ties, straps, hangers, or similar fittings, designed and installed so as not to damage the cable.

(B) Securing. Unless otherwise provided, Type AC cable shall be secured within 300 mm (12 in.) of every outlet box, junction box, cabinet, or fitting and at intervals not exceeding 1.4 m (4½ ft) where installed on or across framing members.

(C) Supporting. Unless otherwise provided, Type AC cable shall be supported at intervals not exceeding 1.4 m (4½ ft).

Horizontal runs of Type AC cable installed in wooden or metal framing members or similar supporting means shall be considered supported where such support does not exceed 1.4-m (4½-ft) intervals.

(D) Unsupported Cables. Type AC cable shall be permitted to be unsupported where the cable complies with any of the following:

(1) Is fished between access points through concealed spaces in finished buildings or structures and supporting is impracticable

(2) Is not more than 600 mm (2 ft) in length at terminals where flexibility is necessary

(3) Is not more than 1.8 m (6 ft) in length from the last point of cable support to the point of connection to a luminaire(s) [lighting fixture(s)] or other electrical equipment and the cable and point of connection are within an accessible ceiling. For the purposes of this section, Type AC cable fittings shall be permitted as a means of cable support.

320.40 Boxes and Fittings. At all points where the armor of AC cable terminates, a fitting shall be provided to protect wires from abrasion, unless the design of the outlet boxes or fittings is such as to afford equivalent protection, and, in addition, an insulating bushing or its equivalent protection shall be provided between the conductors and the armor. The connector or clamp by which the Type AC cable is fastened to boxes or cabinets shall be of such design that the insulating bushing or its equivalent will be visible for inspection. Where change is made from Type AC cable to other cable or raceway wiring methods, a box, fitting, or conduit body shall be installed at junction points as required in 300.15.

320.80 Ampacity. The ampacity shall be determined by 310.15.

(A) Thermal Insulation. Armored cable installed in thermal insulation shall have conductors rated at 90°C (194°F). The ampacity of cable installed in these applications shall be that of 60°C (140°F) conductors. The 90°C (194°F) rating shall be permitted to be used for ampacity derating purposes, provided the final derated ampacity does not exceed that for a 60°C (140°F) rated conductor.

(B) Cable Tray. The ampacity of Type AC cable installed in cable tray shall be determined in accordance with 392.11.

III. Construction Specifications

320.100 Construction. Type AC cable shall have an armor of flexible metal tape and shall have an internal bonding strip of copper or aluminum in intimate contact with the armor for its entire length.

320.104 Conductors. Insulated conductors shall be of a type listed in Table 310.13 or those identified for use in this cable. In addition, the conductors shall have an overall moisture-resistant and fire-retardant fibrous covering. For Type ACT, a moisture-resistant fibrous covering shall be required only on the individual conductors.

320.108 Equipment Grounding. Type AC cable shall provide an adequate path for equipment grounding as required by 250.4(A)(5) or 250.4(B)(4).

320.120 Marking. The cable shall be marked in accordance with 310.11, except that Type AC shall have ready identification of the manufacturer by distinctive external markings on the cable sheath throughout its entire length.

ARTICLE 322
Flat Cable Assemblies: Type FC

I. General

322.1 Scope. This article covers the use, installation, and construction specifications for flat cable assemblies, Type FC.

322.2 Definition.

Flat Cable Assembly, Type FC. An assembly of parallel conductors formed integrally with an insulating material web specifically designed for field installation in surface metal raceway.

II. Installation

322.10 Uses Permitted. Flat cable assemblies shall be permitted only as follows:

(1) As branch circuits to supply suitable tap devices for lighting, small appliances, or small power loads. The rating of the branch circuit shall not exceed 30 amperes.

(2) Where installed for exposed work.

(3) In locations where they will not be subjected to physical damage. Where a flat cable assembly is installed less than 2.5 m (8 ft) above the floor or fixed working platform, it shall be protected by a cover identified for the use.

(4) In surface metal raceways identified for the use. The channel portion of the surface metal raceway systems shall be installed as complete systems before the flat cable assemblies are pulled into the raceways.

322.12 Uses Not Permitted. Flat cable assemblies shall not be used as follows:

(1) Where subject to corrosive vapors unless suitable for the application

(2) In hoistways or on elevators or escalators

(3) In any hazardous (classified) location

(4) Outdoors or in wet or damp locations unless identified for the use

322.30 Securing and Supporting. The flat cable assemblies shall be supported by means of their special design features, within the surface metal raceways.

The surface metal raceways shall be supported as required for the specific raceway to be installed.

322.40 Boxes and Fittings.

(A) Dead Ends. Each flat cable assembly dead end shall be terminated in an end-cap device identified for the use.

The dead-end fitting for the enclosing surface metal raceway shall be identified for the use.

(B) Luminaire (Fixture) Hangers. Luminaire (fixture) hangers installed with the flat cable assemblies shall be identified for the use.

(C) Fittings. Fittings to be installed with flat cable assemblies shall be designed and installed to prevent physical damage to the cable assemblies.

(D) Extensions. All extensions from flat cable assemblies shall be made by approved wiring methods, within the junction boxes, installed at either end of the flat cable assembly runs.

322.56 Splices and Taps.

(A) Splices. Splices shall be made in listed junction boxes.

(B) Taps. Taps shall be made between any phase conductor and the grounded conductor or any other phase conductor by means of devices and fittings identified for the use. Tap devices shall be rated at not less than 15 amperes, or more than 300 volts to ground, and shall be color-coded in accordance with the requirements of 322.120(C).

III. Construction

322.100 Construction. Flat cable assemblies shall consist of two, three, four, or five conductors.

322.104 Conductors. Flat cable assemblies shall have conductors of 10 AWG special stranded copper wires.

322.112 Insulation. The entire flat cable assembly shall be formed to provide a suitable insulation covering all the conductors and using one of the materials recognized in Table 310.13 for general branch-circuit wiring.

322.120 Marking.

(A) Temperature Rating. In addition to the provisions of 310.11, Type FC cable shall have the temperature rating durably marked on the surface at intervals not exceeding 600 mm (24 in.).

(B) Identification of Grounded Conductor. The grounded conductor shall be identified throughout its length by means of a distinctive and durable white or gray marking.

> FPN: The color gray may have been used in the past as an ungrounded conductor. Care should be taken when working on existing systems.

(C) Terminal Block Identification. Terminal blocks identified for the use shall have distinctive and durable markings for color or word coding. The grounded conductor section shall have a white marking or other suitable designation. The next adjacent section of the terminal block shall have a black marking or other suitable designation. The next section shall have a red marking or other suitable designation. The final or outer section, opposite the grounded conductor section of the terminal block, shall have a blue marking or other suitable designation.

ARTICLE 324
Flat Conductor Cable: Type FCC

I. General

324.1 Scope. This article covers a field-installed wiring system for branch circuits incorporating Type FCC cable and associated accessories as defined by the article. The wiring system is designed for installation under carpet squares.

324.2 Definitions.

Bottom Shield. A protective layer that is installed between the floor and Type FCC flat conductor cable to protect the cable from physical damage and may or may not be incorporated as an integral part of the cable.

Cable Connector. A connector designed to join Type FCC cables without using a junction box.

FCC System. A complete wiring system for branch circuits that is designed for installation under carpet squares. The FCC system includes Type FCC cable and associated shielding, connectors, terminators, adapters, boxes, and receptacles.

Insulating End. An insulator designed to electrically insulate the end of a Type FCC cable.

Metal Shield Connections. Means of connection designed to electrically and mechanically connect a metal shield to another metal shield, to a receptacle housing or self-contained device, or to a transition assembly.

Top Shield. A grounded metal shield covering under-carpet components of the FCC system for the purposes of providing protection against physical damage.

Transition Assembly. An assembly to facilitate connection of the FCC system to other wiring systems, incorporating (1) a means of electrical interconnection and (2) a suitable box or covering for providing electrical safety and protection against physical damage.

Type FCC Cable. Three or more flat copper conductors placed edge-to-edge and separated and enclosed within an insulating assembly.

324.6 Listing Requirements. Type FCC cable and associated fittings shall be listed.

II. Installation

324.10 Uses Permitted.

(A) Branch Circuits. Use of FCC systems shall be permitted both for general-purpose and appliance branch circuits and for individual branch circuits.

(B) Branch-Circuit Ratings.

(1) Voltage. Voltage between ungrounded conductors shall not exceed 300 volts. Voltage between ungrounded conductors and the grounded conductor shall not exceed 150 volts.

(2) Current. General-purpose and appliance branch circuits shall have ratings not exceeding 20 amperes. Individual branch circuits shall have ratings not exceeding 30 amperes.

(C) Floors. Use of FCC systems shall be permitted on hard, sound, smooth, continuous floor surfaces made of concrete, ceramic, or composition flooring, wood, and similar materials.

(D) Walls. Use of FCC systems shall be permitted on wall surfaces in surface metal raceways.

(E) Damp Locations. Use of FCC systems in damp locations shall be permitted.

(F) Heated Floors. Materials used for floors heated in excess of 30°C (86°F) shall be identified as suitable for use at these temperatures.

(G) System Height. Any portion of an FCC system with a height above floor level exceeding 2.3 mm (0.090 in.) shall be tapered or feathered at the edges to floor level.

(H) Coverings. Floor-mounted Type FCC cable, cable connectors, and insulating ends shall be covered with carpet squares not larger than 914 mm (36 in.) square. Carpet squares that are adhered to the floor shall be attached with release-type adhesives.

(I) Corrosion Resistance. Metal components of the system shall be either corrosion resistant, coated with corrosion-resistant materials, or insulated from contact with corrosive substances.

(J) Metal-Shield Connectors. Metal shields shall be connected to each other and to boxes, receptacle housings, self-contained devices, and transition assemblies using metal-shield connectors.

324.12 Uses Not Permitted. FCC systems shall not be used in the following locations:

(1) Outdoors or in wet locations

(2) Where subject to corrosive vapors

(3) In any hazardous (classified) location

(4) In residential, school, and hospital buildings

324.18 Crossings. Crossings of more than two Type FCC cable runs shall not be permitted at any one point. Crossings of a Type FCC cable over or under a flat communications or signal cable shall be permitted. In each case, a grounded layer of metal shielding shall separate the two cables, and crossings of more than two flat cables shall not be permitted at any one point.

324.30 Securing and Supporting. All FCC system components shall be firmly anchored to the floor or wall using an adhesive or mechanical anchoring system identified for this use. Floors shall be prepared to ensure adherence of the FCC system to the floor until the carpet squares are placed.

324.40 Boxes and Fittings.

(A) Cable Connections and Insulating Ends. All Type FCC cable connections shall use connectors identified for their use, installed such that electrical continuity, insulation, and sealing against dampness and liquid spillage are provided. All bare cable ends shall be insulated and sealed against dampness and liquid spillage using listed insulating ends.

(B) Polarization of Connections. All receptacles and connections shall be constructed and installed so as to maintain proper polarization of the system.

(C) Shields.

(1) Top Shield. A metal top shield shall be installed over all floor-mounted Type FCC cable, connectors, and insulating ends. The top shield shall completely cover all cable runs, corners, connectors, and ends.

(2) Bottom Shield. A bottom shield shall be installed beneath all Type FCC cable, connectors, and insulating ends.

(D) Connection to Other Systems. Power feed, grounding connection, and shield system connection between the FCC system and other wiring systems shall be accomplished in a transition assembly identified for this use.

(E) Metal-Shield Connectors. Metal shields shall be connected to each other and to boxes, receptacle housings, self-contained devices, and transition assemblies using metal-shield connectors.

324.41 Floor Coverings. Floor-mounted Type FCC cable, cable connectors, and insulating ends shall be covered with carpet squares not larger than 914 mm (36 in.) square. Carpet squares that are adhered to the floor shall be attached with release-type adhesives.

324.42 Devices.

(A) Receptacles. All receptacles, receptacle housings, and self-contained devices used with the FCC system shall be identified for this use and shall be connected to the Type FCC cable and metal shields. Connection from any grounding conductor of the Type FCC cable shall be made to the shield system at each receptacle.

(B) Receptacles and Housings. Receptacle housings and self-contained devices designed either for floor mounting or for in-wall or on-wall mounting shall be permitted for use with the FCC system. Receptacle housings and self-contained devices shall incorporate means for facilitating entry and termination of Type FCC cable and for electrically connecting the housing or device with the metal shield. Receptacles and self-contained devices shall comply with 406.3. Power and communications outlets installed together in common housing shall be permitted in accordance with 800.133(A)(1)(c), Exception No. 2.

324.56 Splices and Taps.

(A) FCC Systems Alterations. Alterations to FCC systems shall be permitted. New cable connectors shall be used at new connection points to make alterations. It shall be permitted to leave unused cable runs and associated cable connectors in place and energized. All cable ends shall be covered with insulating ends.

(B) Transition Assemblies. All transition assemblies shall be identified for their use. Each assembly shall incorporate means for facilitating entry of the Type FCC cable into the assembly, for connecting the Type FCC cable to grounded conductors, and for electrically connecting the assembly to the metal cable shields and to equipment grounding conductors.

324.60 Grounding. All metal shields, boxes, receptacle housings, and self-contained devices shall be electrically continuous to the equipment grounding conductor of the supplying branch circuit. All such electrical connections shall be made with connectors identified for this use. The electrical resistivity of such shield system shall not be more than that of one conductor of the Type FCC cable used in the installation.

III. Construction

324.100 Construction.

(A) Type FCC Cable. Type FCC cable shall be listed for use with the FCC system and shall consist of three, four, or five flat copper conductors, one of which shall be an equipment grounding conductor.

(B) Shields.

(1) Materials and Dimensions. All top and bottom shields shall be of designs and materials identified for their use. Top shields shall be metal. Both metallic and nonmetallic materials shall be permitted for bottom shields.

(2) Resistivity. Metal shields shall have cross-sectional areas that provide for electrical resistivity of not more than that of one conductor of the Type FCC cable used in the installation.

324.101 Corrosion Resistance. Metal components of the system shall be either corrosion resistant, coated with corrosion-resistant materials, or insulated from contact with corrosive substances.

324.112 Insulation. The insulating material of the cable shall be moisture resistant and flame retardant. All insulating materials in the FCC systems shall be identified for their use.

324.120 Markings.

(A) Cable Marking. Type FCC cable shall be clearly and durably marked on both sides at intervals of not more than 610 mm (24 in.) with the information required by 310.11(A) and with the following additional information:
(1) Material of conductors
(2) Maximum temperature rating
(3) Ampacity

(B) Conductor Identification. Conductors shall be clearly and durably identified on both sides throughout their length as specified in 310.12.

ARTICLE 326
Integrated Gas Spacer Cable: Type IGS

I. General

326.1 Scope. This article covers the use, installation, and construction specifications for integrated gas spacer cable, Type IGS.

326.2 Definition.

Integrated Gas Spacer Cable, Type IGS. A factory assembly of one or more conductors, each individually insulated and enclosed in a loose fit, nonmetallic flexible conduit as an integrated gas spacer cable rated 0 through 600 volts.

II. Installation

326.10 Uses Permitted. Type IGS cable shall be permitted for use under ground, including direct burial in the earth, as the following:

(1) Service-entrance conductors

(2) Feeder or branch-circuit conductors

326.12 Uses Not Permitted. Type IGS cable shall not be used as interior wiring or be exposed in contact with buildings.

326.24 Bending Radius. Where the coilable nonmetallic conduit and cable is bent for installation purposes or is flexed or bent during shipment or installation, the radii of bends measured to the inside of the bend shall not be less than specified in Table 326.24.

Table 326.24 Minimum Radii of Bends

Conduit Size		Minimum Radii	
Metric Designator	Trade Size	mm	in.
53	2	600	24
78	3	900	35
103	4	1150	45

326.26 Bends. A run of Type IGS cable between pull boxes or terminations shall not contain more than the equivalent of four quarter bends (360 degrees total), including those bends located immediately at the pull box or terminations.

326.40 Fittings. Terminations and splices for Type IGS cable shall be identified as a type that is suitable for maintaining the gas pressure within the conduit. A valve and cap shall be provided for each length of the cable and conduit to check the gas pressure or to inject gas into the conduit.

326.80 Ampacity. The ampacity of Type IGS cable shall not exceed the values shown in Table 326.80.

Table 326.80 Ampacity of Type IGS Cable

Size (kcmil)	Amperes	Size (kcmil)	Amperes
250	119	2500	376
500	168	3000	412
750	206	3250	429
1000	238	3500	445
1250	266	3750	461
1500	292	4000	476
1750	315	4250	491
2000	336	4500	505
2250	357	4750	519

III. Construction Specifications

326.104 Conductors. The conductors shall be solid aluminum rods, laid parallel, consisting of one to nineteen 12.7 mm ($\frac{1}{2}$ in.) diameter rods. The minimum conductor size shall be 250 kcmil, and the maximum size shall be 4750 kcmil.

326.112 Insulation. The insulation shall be dry kraft paper tapes and a pressurized sulfur hexafluoride gas (SF_6), both approved for electrical use. The nominal gas pressure shall be 138 kPa gauge (20 pounds per square inch gauge). The thickness of the paper spacer shall be as specified in Table 326.112.

Table 326.112 Paper Spacer Thickness

Size (kcmil)	Thickness	
	mm	in.
250–1000	1.02	0.040
1250–4750	1.52	0.060

326.116 Conduit. The conduit shall be a medium density polyethylene identified as suitable for use with natural gas rated pipe in metric designator 53, 78, or 103 (trade size 2, 3, or 4). The percent fill dimensions for the conduit are shown in Table 326.116.

The size of the conduit permitted for each conductor size shall be calculated for a percent fill not to exceed those found in Table 1, Chapter 9.

326.120 Marking. The cable shall be marked in accordance with 310.11(A), 310.11(B)(1), and 310.11(D).

Table 326.116 Conduit Dimensions

Conduit Size		Actual Outside Diameter		Actual Inside Diameter	
Metric Designator	Trade Size	mm	in.	mm	in.
53	2	60	2.375	49.46	1.947
78	3	89	3.500	73.30	2.886
103	4	114	4.500	94.23	3.710

ARTICLE 328
Medium Voltage Cable: Type MV

I. General

328.1 Scope. This article covers the use, installation, and construction specifications for medium voltage cable, Type MV.

328.2 Definition.

Medium Voltage Cable, Type MV. A single or multiconductor solid dielectric insulated cable rated 2001 volts or higher.

II. Installation

328.10 Uses Permitted. Type MV cable shall be permitted for use on power systems rated up to 35,000 volts nominal as follows:

(1) In wet or dry locations

(2) In raceways

(3) In cable trays as specified in 392.3(B)(2)

(4) Direct buried in accordance with 300.50

(5) In messenger-supported wiring

FPN: The "Uses Permitted" is not an all-inclusive list.

328.12 Uses Not Permitted. Unless identified for the use, Type MV cable shall not be used as follows:

(1) Where exposed to direct sunlight

(2) In cable trays, unless specified in 392.3(B)(2)

(3) Direct buried, unless in accordance with 300.50

328.80 Ampacity. The ampacity of Type MV cable shall be determined in accordance with 310.60. The ampacity of Type MV cable installed in cable tray shall be determined in accordance with 392.13.

III. Construction Specifications

328.100 Construction. Type MV cables shall have copper, aluminum, or copper-clad aluminum conductors and shall comply with Table 310.61 and Table 310.63 or Table 310.64.

328.120 Marking. Medium voltage cable shall be marked as required by 310.11.

ARTICLE 330
Metal-Clad Cable: Type MC

I. General

330.1 Scope. This article covers the use, installation, and construction specifications of metal-clad cable, Type MC.

330.2 Definition.

Metal Clad Cable, Type MC. A factory assembly of one or more insulated circuit conductors with or without optical fiber members enclosed in an armor of interlocking metal tape, or a smooth or corrugated metallic sheath.

II. Installation

330.10 Uses Permitted.

(A) General Uses. Type MC cable shall be permitted as follows:

(1) For services, feeders, and branch circuits

(2) For power, lighting, control, and signal circuits

(3) Indoors or outdoors

(4) Exposed or concealed

(5) To be direct buried where identified for such use

(6) In cable tray where identified for such use

(7) In any raceway

(8) As aerial cable on a messenger

(9) In hazardous (classified) locations as permitted

(10) In dry locations and embedded in plaster finish on brick or other masonry except in damp or wet locations

(11) In wet locations where any of the following conditions are met:

    a. The metallic covering is impervious to moisture.

    b. A lead sheath or moisture-impervious jacket is provided under the metal covering.

    c. The insulated conductors under the metallic covering are listed for use in wet locations.

(12) Where single-conductor cables are used, all phase conductors and, where used, the neutral conductor shall be grouped together to minimize induced voltage on the sheath.

(B) Specific Uses. Type MC cable shall be permitted to be installed in compliance with Parts II and III of Article 725 and 770.133 as applicable and in accordance with 330.10(B)(1) through (B)(4).

(1) Cable Tray. Type MC cable installed in cable tray shall comply with 392.3, 392.4, 392.6, and 392.8 through 392.13.

(2) Direct Buried. Direct-buried cable shall comply with 300.5 or 300.50, as appropriate.

(3) Installed as Service-Entrance Cable. Type MC cable installed as service-entrance cable shall be permitted in accordance with 230.43.

(4) Installed Outside of Buildings or as Aerial Cable. Type MC cable installed outside of buildings or as aerial cable shall comply with 225.10, 396.10, and 396.12.

FPN: The "Uses Permitted" is not an all-inclusive list.

330.12 Uses Not Permitted. Type MC cable shall not be used where exposed to the following destructive corrosive conditions, unless the metallic sheath is suitable for the conditions or is protected by material suitable for the conditions:

(1) Where subject to physical damage
(2) Direct burial in the earth
(3) In concrete

FPN to (3): MC cable that is identified for direct burial applications is suitable for installation in concrete.

(4) Where subject to cinder fills, strong chlorides, caustic alkalis, or vapors of chlorine or of hydrochloric acids

330.17 Through or Parallel to Framing Members. Type MC cable shall be protected in accordance with 300.4(A), (C), and (D) where installed through or parallel to framing members.

330.23 In Accessible Attics. The installation of Type MC cable in accessible attics or roof spaces shall also comply with 320.23.

330.24 Bending Radius. Bends in Type MC cable shall be so made that the cable will not be damaged. The radius of the curve of the inner edge of any bend shall not be less than required in 330.24(A) through (C).

(A) Smooth Sheath.
(1) Ten times the external diameter of the metallic sheath for cable not more than 19 mm (¾ in.) in external diameter
(2) Twelve times the external diameter of the metallic sheath for cable more than 19 mm (¾ in.) but not more than 38 mm (1½ in.) in external diameter
(3) Fifteen times the external diameter of the metallic sheath for cable more than 38 mm (1½ in.) in external diameter

(B) Interlocked-Type Armor or Corrugated Sheath. Seven times the external diameter of the metallic sheath.

(C) Shielded Conductors. Twelve times the overall diameter of one of the individual conductors or seven times the overall diameter of the multiconductor cable, whichever is greater.

330.30 Securing and Supporting.

(A) General. Type MC cable shall be supported and secured by staples, cable ties, straps, hangers, or similar fittings or other approved means designed and installed so as not to damage the cable.

(B) Securing. Unless otherwise provided, cables shall be secured at intervals not exceeding 1.8 m (6 ft). Cables containing four or fewer conductors sized no larger than 10 AWG shall be secured within 300 mm (12 in.) of every box, cabinet, fitting, or other cable termination.

(C) Supporting. Unless otherwise provided, cables shall be supported at intervals not exceeding 1.8-m (6-ft).

Horizontal runs of Type MC cable installed in wooden or metal framing members or similar supporting means shall be considered supported and secured where such support does not exceed 1.8-m (6-ft) intervals.

(D) Unsupported Cables. Type MC cable shall be permitted to be unsupported where the cable:
(1) Is fished between access points through concealed spaces in finished buildings or structures and supporting is impractical; or
(2) Is not more than 1.8 m (6 ft) in length from the last point of cable support to the point of connection to a luminaire (lighting fixture) or other piece of electrical equipment and the cable and point of connection are within an accessible ceiling. For the purpose of this section, Type MC cable fittings shall be permitted as a means of cable support.

330.31 Single Conductors. Where single-conductor cables with a nonferrous armor or sheath are used, the installation shall comply with 300.20.

330.40 Boxes and Fitting. Fittings used for connecting Type MC cable to boxes, cabinets, or other equipment shall be listed and identified for such use.

330.80 Ampacity. The ampacity of Type MC cable shall be determined in accordance with 310.15 or 310.60 for 14 AWG and larger conductors and in accordance with Table 402.5 for 18 AWG and 16 AWG conductors. The installation shall not exceed the temperature ratings of terminations and equipment.

(A) Type MC Cable Installed in Cable Tray. The ampacities for Type MC cable installed in cable tray shall be determined in accordance with 392.11 and 392.13.

(B) Single Type MC Conductors Grouped Together. Where single Type MC conductors are grouped together in a triangular or square configuration and installed on a messenger or exposed with a maintained free airspace of not less than 2.15 times one conductor diameter (2.15 × O.D.) of the largest conductor contained within the configuration and adjacent conductor configurations or cables, the ampacity of the conductors shall not exceed the allowable ampacities in the following tables:

(1) Table 310.20 for conductors rated 0 through 2000 volts
(2) Table 310.67 and Table 310.68 for conductors rated over 2000 volts

III. Construction Specifications

330.104 Conductors. The conductors shall be of copper, aluminum, or copper-clad aluminum, solid or stranded. The minimum conductor size shall be 18 AWG copper and 12 AWG aluminum or copper-clad aluminum.

330.108 Equipment Grounding. Where Type MC cable is used for equipment grounding, it shall comply with 250.118(10) and 250.122.

330.112 Insulation. Insulated conductors shall comply with 330.112(A) or (B).

(A) 600 Volts. Insulated conductors in sizes 18 AWG and 16 AWG shall be of a type listed in Table 402.3, with a maximum operating temperature not less than 90°C (194°F) and as permitted by 725.27. Conductors larger than 16 AWG shall be of a type listed in Table 310.13 or of a type identified for use in Type MC cable.

(B) Over 600 Volts. Insulated conductors shall be of a type listed in Table 310.61 through Table 310.64.

330.116 Sheath. Metallic covering shall be one of the following types: smooth metallic sheath, corrugated metallic sheath, interlocking metal tape armor. The metallic sheath shall be continuous and close fitting. A nonmagnetic sheath or armor shall be used on single conductor Type MC. Supplemental protection of an outer covering of corrosion-resistant material shall be permitted and shall be required where such protection is needed. The sheath shall not be used as a current-carrying conductor.

FPN: See 300.6 for protection against corrosion.

ARTICLE 332
Mineral-Insulated, Metal-Sheathed Cable: Type MI

I. General

332.1 Scope. This article covers the use, installation, and construction specifications for mineral-insulated, metal-sheathed cable, Type MI.

332.2 Definition.

Mineral-Insulated, Metal-Sheathed Cable, Type MI. A factory assembly of one or more conductors insulated with a highly compressed refractory mineral insulation and enclosed in a liquidtight and gastight continuous copper or alloy steel sheath.

II. Installation

332.10 Uses Permitted. Type MI cable shall be permitted as follows:

(1) For services, feeders, and branch circuits
(2) For power, lighting, control, and signal circuits
(3) In dry, wet, or continuously moist locations
(4) Indoors or outdoors
(5) Where exposed or concealed
(6) Where embedded in plaster, concrete, fill, or other masonry, whether above or below grade
(7) In any hazardous (classified) location
(8) Where exposed to oil and gasoline
(9) Where exposed to corrosive conditions not deteriorating to its sheath
(10) In underground runs where suitably protected against physical damage and corrosive conditions
(11) In or attached to cable tray

FPN: The "Uses Permitted" is not an all-inclusive list.

332.12 Uses Not Permitted. Type MI cable shall not be used under the following conditions or in the following locations:

(1) In underground runs unless protected from physical damage, where necessary
(2) Where exposed to conditions that are destructive and corrosive to the metallic sheath, unless additional protection is provided

332.17 Through or Parallel to Framing Members. Type MI cable shall be protected in accordance with 300.4 where installed through or parallel to framing members.

332.24 Bending Radius. Bends in Type MI cable shall be so made that the cable will not be damaged. The radius of the inner edge of any bend shall not be less than required as follows:

(1) Five times the external diameter of the metallic sheath for cable not more than 19 mm (¾ in.) in external diameter

(2) Ten times the external diameter of the metallic sheath for cable greater than 19 mm (¾ in.) but not more than 25 mm (1 in.) in external diameter

332.30 Securing and Supporting. Type MI cable shall be supported and secured by staples, straps, hangers, or similar fittings, designed and installed so as not to damage the cable, at intervals not exceeding 1.8 m (6 ft).

(A) Horizontal Runs Through Holes and Notches. In other than vertical runs, cables installed in accordance with 300.4 shall be considered supported and secured where such support does not exceed 1.8 m (6 ft) intervals.

(B) Unsupported Cable. Type MI cable shall be permitted to be unsupported where the cable is fished between access points through concealed spaces in finished buildings or structures and supporting is impracticable.

(C) Cable Trays. All MI cable installed in cable trays shall comply with 392.8(B).

332.31 Single Conductors. Where single-conductor cables are used, all phase conductors and, where used, the neutral conductor shall be grouped together to minimize induced voltage on the sheath.

332.40 Boxes and Fittings.

(A) Fittings. Fittings used for connecting Type MI cable to boxes, cabinets, or other equipment shall be identified for such use.

(B) Terminal Seals. Where Type MI cable terminates, an end seal fitting shall be installed immediately after stripping to prevent the entrance of moisture into the insulation. The conductors extending beyond the sheath shall be individually provided with an insulating material.

332.80 Ampacity. The ampacity of Type MI cable shall be determined in accordance with 310.15. The conductor temperature at the end seal fitting shall not exceed the temperature rating of the listed end seal fitting, and the installation shall not exceed the temperature ratings of terminations or equipment.

(A) Type MI Cable Installed in Cable Tray. The ampacities for Type MI cable installed in cable tray shall be determined in accordance with 392.11.

(B) Single Type MI Conductors Grouped Together. Where single Type MI conductors are grouped together in a triangular or square configuration, as required by 332.31,

and installed on a messenger or exposed with a maintained free air space of not less than 2.15 times one conductor diameter (2.15 × O.D.) of the largest conductor contained within the configuration and adjacent conductor configurations or cables, the ampacity of the conductors shall not exceed the allowable ampacities of Table 310.17.

III. Construction Specifications

332.104 Conductors. Type MI cable conductors shall be of solid copper, nickel, or nickel-coated copper with a resistance corresponding to standard AWG and kcmil sizes.

332.108 Equipment Grounding. Where the outer sheath is made of copper, it shall provide an adequate path for equipment grounding purposes. Where made of steel, an equipment grounding conductor shall be provided.

332.112 Insulation. The conductor insulation in Type MI cable shall be a highly compressed refractory mineral that provides proper spacing for all conductors.

332.116 Sheath. The outer sheath shall be of a continuous construction to provide mechanical protection and moisture seal.

ARTICLE 334
Nonmetallic-Sheathed Cable: Types NM, NMC, and NMS

I. General

334.1 Scope. This article covers the use, installation, and construction specifications of nonmetallic-sheathed cable.

334.2 Definitions.

Nonmetallic-Sheathed Cable. A factory assembly of two or more insulated conductors enclosed within an overall nonmetallic jacket.

Type NM. Insulated conductors enclosed within an overall nonmetallic jacket.

Type NMC. Insulated conductors enclosed within an overall, corrosion resistant, nonmetallic jacket.

Type NMS. Insulated power or control conductors with signaling, data, and communications conductors within an overall nonmetallic jacket.

334.6 Listed. Type NM, Type NMC, and Type NMS cables shall be listed.

II. Installation

334.10 Uses Permitted. Type NM, Type NMC, and Type NMS cables shall be permitted to be used in the following:

(1) One- and two-family dwellings.

(2) Multifamily dwellings permitted to be of Types III, IV, and V construction except as prohibited in 334.12.

(3) Other structures permitted to be of Types III, IV, and V construction except as prohibited in 334.12. Cables shall be concealed within walls, floors, or ceilings that provide a thermal barrier of material that has at least a 15-minute finish rating as identified in listings of fire-rated assemblies.

> FPN No. 1: Types of building construction and occupancy classifications are defined in NFPA 220-1999, *Standard on Types of Building Construction*, or the applicable building code, or both.

> FPN No. 2: See Annex E for determination of building types [NFPA 220, Table 3-1].

(4) Cable trays in structures permitted to be Types III, IV, or V where the cables are identified for the use.

> FPN: See 310.10 for temperature limitation of conductors.

(A) Type NM. Type NM cable shall be permitted as follows:

(1) For both exposed and concealed work in normally dry locations except as prohibited in 334.10(3)

(2) To be installed or fished in air voids in masonry block or tile walls

(B) Type NMC. Type NMC cable shall be permitted as follows:

(1) For both exposed and concealed work in dry, moist, damp, or corrosive locations, except as prohibited by 334.10(3)

(2) In outside and inside walls of masonry block or tile

(3) In a shallow chase in masonry, concrete, or adobe protected against nails or screws by a steel plate at least 1.59 mm (1/16 in.) thick and covered with plaster, adobe, or similar finish

(C) Type NMS. Type NMS cable shall be permitted as follows:

(1) For both exposed and concealed work in normally dry locations except as prohibited by 334.10(3)

(2) To be installed or fished in air voids in masonry block or tile walls

334.12 Uses Not Permitted.

(A) Types NM, NMC, and NMS. Types NM, NMC, and NMS cables shall not be permitted as follows:

(1) In any dwelling or structure not specifically permitted in 334.10(1), (2), and (3)

(2) Exposed in dropped or suspended ceilings in other than one- and two-family and multifamily dwellings

(3) As service-entrance cable

(4) In commercial garages having hazardous (classified) locations as defined in 511.3

(5) In theaters and similar locations, except where permitted in 518.4(B)

(6) In motion picture studios

(7) In storage battery rooms

(8) In hoistways or on elevators or escalators

(9) Embedded in poured cement, concrete, or aggregate

(10) In hazardous (classified) locations, except where permitted by the following:

    a. 501.10(B)(3)

    b. 502.10(B)(3)

    c. 504.20

(B) Types NM and NMS. Types NM and NMS cables shall not be used under the following conditions or in the following locations:

(1) Where exposed to corrosive fumes or vapors

(2) Where embedded in masonry, concrete, adobe, fill, or plaster

(3) In a shallow chase in masonry, concrete, or adobe and covered with plaster, adobe, or similar finish

(4) Where exposed or subject to excessive moisture or dampness

334.15 Exposed Work. In exposed work, except as provided in 300.11(A), cable shall be installed as specified in 334.15(A) through (C).

(A) To Follow Surface. Cable shall closely follow the surface of the building finish or of running boards.

(B) Protection from Physical Damage. Cable shall be protected from physical damage where necessary by rigid metal conduit, intermediate metal conduit, electrical metallic tubing, Schedule 80 PVC rigid nonmetallic conduit, or other approved means. Where passing through a floor, the cable shall be enclosed in rigid metal conduit, intermediate metal conduit, electrical metallic tubing, Schedule 80 PVC rigid nonmetallic conduit, or other approved means extending at least 150 mm (6 in.) above the floor.

Where Type NMC cable is installed in shallow chases in masonry, concrete, or adobe, the cable shall be protected against nails or screws by a steel plate at least 1.59 mm (1/16 in.) thick and covered with plaster, adobe, or similar finish.

(C) In Unfinished Basements. Where cable is run at angles with joists in unfinished basements, it shall be permissible to secure cables not smaller than two 6 AWG or three 8 AWG conductors directly to the lower edges of the joists. Smaller cables shall be run either through bored holes in joists or on running boards. NM cable used on a wall of an unfinished basement shall be permitted to be installed in a listed conduit or tubing. Conduit or tubing shall utilize a nonmetallic bushing or adapter at the point the cable enters the raceway. Metal conduit and tubings and metal outlet boxes shall be grounded.

334.17 Through or Parallel to Framing Members. Types NM, NMC, or NMS cable shall be protected in accordance with 300.4 where installed through or parallel to framing members. Grommets used as required in 300.4(B)(1) shall remain in place and be listed for the purpose of cable protection.

334.23 In Accessible Attics. The installation of cable in accessible attics or roof spaces shall also comply with 320.23.

334.24 Bending Radius. Bends in Types NM, NMC, and NMS cable shall be so made that the cable will not be damaged. The radius of the curve of the inner edge of any bend during or after installation shall not be less than five times the diameter of the cable.

334.30 Securing and Supporting. Nonmetallic-sheathed cable shall be supported and secured by staples, cable ties, straps, hangers, or similar fittings designed and installed so as not to damage the cable, at intervals not exceeding 1.4 m (4½ ft) and within 300 mm (12 in.) of every outlet box, junction box, cabinet, or fitting. Flat cables shall not be stapled on edge.

Sections of cable protected from physical damage by raceway shall not be required to be secured within the raceway.

(A) Horizontal Runs Through Holes and Notches. In other than vertical runs, cables installed in accordance with 300.4 shall be considered to be supported and secured where such support does not exceed 1.4-m (4½-ft) intervals and the nonmetallic-sheathed cable is securely fastened in place by an approved means within 300 mm (12 in.) of each box, cabinet, conduit body, or other nonmetallic-sheathed cable termination.

FPN: See 314.17(C) for support where nonmetallic boxes are used.

(B) Unsupported Cables. Nonmetallic-sheathed cable shall be permitted to be unsupported where the cable:

(1) Is fished between access points through concealed spaces in finished buildings or structures and supporting is impractical.

(2) Is not more than 1.4 m (4½ ft) from the last point of cable support to the point of connection to a luminaire (lighting fixture) or other piece of electrical equipment and the cable and point of connection are within an accessible ceiling.

(C) Wiring Device Without a Separate Outlet Box. A wiring device identified for the use, without a separate outlet box, and incorporating an integral cable clamp shall be permitted where the cable is secured in place at intervals not exceeding 1.4 m (4½ ft) and within 300 mm (12 in.) from the wiring device wall opening, and there shall be at least a 300 mm (12 in.) loop of unbroken cable or 150 mm (6 in.) of a cable end available on the interior side of the finished wall to permit replacement.

334.40 Boxes and Fittings.

(A) Boxes of Insulating Material. Nonmetallic outlet boxes shall be permitted as provided by 314.3.

(B) Devices of Insulating Material. Switch, outlet, and tap devices of insulating material shall be permitted to be used without boxes in exposed cable wiring and for rewiring in existing buildings where the cable is concealed and fished. Openings in such devices shall form a close fit around the outer covering of the cable, and the device shall fully enclose the part of the cable from which any part of the covering has been removed. Where connections to conductors are by binding-screw terminals, there shall be available as many terminals as conductors.

(C) Devices with Integral Enclosures. Wiring devices with integral enclosures identified for such use shall be permitted as provided by 300.15(E).

334.80 Ampacity. The ampacity of Types NM, NMC, and NMS cable shall be determined in accordance with 310.15. The ampacity shall be in accordance with the 60°C (140°F) conductor temperature rating. The 90°C (194°F) rating shall be permitted to be used for ampacity derating purposes, provided the final derated ampacity does not exceed that for a 60°C (140°F) rated conductor. The ampacity of Types NM, NMC, and NMS cable installed in cable tray shall be determined in accordance with 392.11.

Where more than two NM cables containing two or more current-carrying conductors are bundled together and pass through wood framing that is to be fire- or draft-stopped using thermal insulation or sealing foam, the allowable ampacity of each conductor shall be adjusted in accordance with Table 310.15(B)(2)(a).

III. Construction Specifications

334.100 Construction. The outer cable sheath of nonmetallic-sheathed cable shall be a nonmetallic material.

334.104 Conductors. The 600 volt insulated conductors shall be sizes 14 AWG through 2 AWG copper conductors or sizes 12 AWG through 2 AWG aluminum or copper-clad aluminum conductors. The signaling conductors shall comply with 780.5. The communication conductors shall comply with Part V of Article 800.

334.108 Equipment Grounding. In addition to the insulated conductors, the cable shall have an insulated or bare conductor for equipment grounding purposes only.

334.112 Insulation. The insulated power conductors shall be one of the types listed in Table 310.13 that are suitable for branch circuit wiring or one that is identified for use in these cables. Conductor insulation shall be rated at 90°C (194°F).

FPN: Types NM, NMC, and NMS cable identified by the markings NM-B, NMC-B, and NMS-B meet this requirement.

334.116 Sheath. The outer sheath of nonmetallic-sheathed cable shall comply with 334.116(A), (B), and (C).

(A) Type NM. The overall covering shall be flame retardant and moisture resistant.

(B) Type NMC. The overall covering shall be flame retardant, moisture resistant, fungus resistant, and corrosion resistant.

(C) Type NMS. The overall covering shall be flame retardant and moisture resistant. The sheath shall be applied so as to separate the power conductors from the communications and signaling conductors. The signaling conductors shall be permitted to be shielded. An optional outer jacket shall be permitted.

FPN: For composite optical cable, see 770.9 and 770.133.

ARTICLE 336
Power and Control Tray Cable: Type TC

I. General

336.1 Scope. This article covers the use, installation, and construction specifications for power and control tray cable, Type TC.

336.2 Definition.

Power and Control Tray Cable, Type TC. A factory assembly of two or more insulated conductors, with or without associated bare or covered grounding conductors, under a nonmetallic jacket.

II. Installation

336.10 Uses Permitted. Type TC cable shall be permitted to be used as follows:

(1) For power, lighting, control, and signal circuits.
(2) In cable trays.
(3) In raceways.
(4) In outdoor locations supported by a messenger wire.

(5) For Class 1 circuits as permitted in Parts II and III of Article 725.
(6) For non–power-limited fire alarm circuits if conductors comply with the requirements of 760.27.
(7) In industrial establishments where the conditions of maintenance and supervision ensure that only qualified persons service the installation, and where the cable is continuously supported and protected against physical damage using mechanical protection, such as struts, angles, or channels, Type TC tray cable that complies with the crush and impact requirements of Type MC cable and is identified for such use with the marking Type TC–ER shall be permitted between a cable tray and the utilization equipment or device. The cable shall be secured at intervals not exceeding 1.8 m (6 ft). Equipment grounding for the utilization equipment shall be provided by an equipment grounding conductor within the cable. In cables containing conductors sized 6 AWG or smaller, the equipment grounding conductor shall be provided within the cable or, at the time of installation, one or more insulated conductors shall be permanently identified as an equipment grounding conductor in accordance with 250.119(B).
(8) Where installed in wet locations, Type TC cable shall also be resistant to moisture and corrosive agents.

FPN: See 310.10 for temperature limitation of conductors.

336.12 Uses Not Permitted. Type TC tray cable shall not be installed or used as follows:

(1) Installed where it will be exposed to physical damage
(2) Installed outside a raceway or cable tray system, except as permitted in 336.10(7)
(3) Used where exposed to direct rays of the sun, unless identified as sunlight resistant
(4) Direct buried, unless identified for such use

336.24 Bending Radius. Bends in Type TC cable shall be made so as not to damage the cable. For Type TC cable without metal shielding, the minimum bending radius shall be as follows:

(1) Four times the overall diameter for cables 25 mm (1 in.) or less in diameter
(2) Five times the overall diameter for cables larger than 25 mm (1 in.) but not more than 50 mm (2 in.) in diameter
(3) Six times the overall diameter for cables larger than 50 mm (2 in.) in diameter

Type TC cables with metallic shielding shall have a minimum bending radius of not less than 12 times the cable overall diameter.

336.80 Ampacity. The ampacity of Type TC tray cable shall be determined in accordance with 392.11 for 14 AWG and larger conductors, in accordance with 402.5 for 18 AWG through 16 AWG conductors where installed in cable tray, and in accordance with 310.15 where installed in a raceway or as messenger supported wiring.

III. Construction Specifications

336.100 Construction. A metallic sheath or armor as defined in 330.116 shall not be permitted either under or over the nonmetallic jacket. Metallic shield(s) shall be permitted over groups of conductors, under the outer jacket, or both.

336.104 Conductors. The insulated conductors of Type TC tray cable shall be in sizes 18 AWG through 1000 kcmil copper and sizes 12 AWG through 1000 kcmil aluminum or copper-clad aluminum. Insulated conductors of sizes 14 AWG and larger copper and sizes 12 AWG and larger aluminum or copper-clad aluminum shall be one of the types listed in Table 310.13 or Table 310.62 that is suitable for branch circuit and feeder circuits or one that is identified for such use.

(A) Fire Alarm Systems. Where used for fire alarm systems, conductors shall also be in accordance with 760.27.

(B) Thermocouple Circuits. Conductors in Type TC cable used for thermocouple circuits in accordance with Part III of Article 725 shall also be permitted to be any of the materials used for thermocouple extension wire.

(C) Class 1 Circuit Conductors. Insulated conductors of 18 AWG and 16 AWG copper shall also be in accordance with 725.27.

336.116 Jacket. The outer jacket shall be a flame-retardant, nonmetallic material.

336.120 Marking. There shall be no voltage marking on a Type TC cable employing thermocouple extension wire.

ARTICLE 338
Service-Entrance Cable: Types SE and USE

I. General

338.1 Scope. This article covers the use, installation, and construction specifications of service-entrance cable.

338.2 Definitions.

Service-Entrance Cable. A single conductor or multiconductor assembly provided with or without an overall covering, primarily used for services, and of the following types:

Type SE. Service-entrance cable having a flame-retardant, moisture-resistant covering.

Type USE. Service-entrance cable, identified for underground use, having a moisture-resistant covering, but not required to have a flame-retardant covering.

II. Installation

338.10 Uses Permitted.

(A) Service-Entrance Conductors. Service-entrance cable shall be permitted to be used as service-entrance conductors and shall be installed in accordance with 230.6, 230.7, and Parts II, III, and IV of Article 230.

Type USE used for service laterals shall be permitted to emerge from the ground outside at terminations in meter bases or other enclosures where protected in accordance with 300.5(D).

(B) Branch Circuits or Feeders.

(1) Grounded Conductor Insulated. Type SE service-entrance cables shall be permitted in wiring systems where all of the circuit conductors of the cable are of the rubber-covered or thermoplastic type.

(2) Grounded Conductor Not Insulated. Type SE service-entrance cable shall be permitted for use where the insulated conductors are used for circuit wiring and the uninsulated conductor is used only for equipment grounding purposes.

Exception: Uninsulated conductors shall be permitted as a grounded conductor in accordance with 250.140, 250.32, and 225.30 through 225.40.

(3) Temperature Limitations. Type SE service-entrance cable used to supply appliances shall not be subject to conductor temperatures in excess of the temperature specified for the type of insulation involved.

(4) Installation Methods for Branch Circuits and Feeders.

(a) *Interior Installations.* In addition to the provisions of this article, Type SE service-entrance cable used for interior wiring shall comply with the installation requirements of Parts I and II of Article 334, excluding 334.80.

FPN: See 310.10 for temperature limitation of conductors.

(b) *Exterior Installations.* In addition to the provisions of this article, service-entrance cable used for feeders or branch circuits, where installed as exterior wiring, shall be installed in accordance with Part I of Article 225. The cable shall be supported in accordance with 334.30, unless used as messenger-supported wiring as permitted in Part II of Article 396. Type USE cable installed as underground feeder and branch circuit cable shall comply with Part II of

Article 340. Where Type USE cable emerges from the ground at terminations, it shall be protected in accordance with 300.5(D). Multiconductor service-entrance cable shall be permitted to be installed as messenger-supported wiring in accordance with 225.10 and Part II of Article 396.

338.24 Bending Radius. Bends in Types USE and SE cable shall be so made that the cable will not be damaged. The radius of the curve of the inner edge of any bend, during or after installation, shall not be less than five times the diameter of the cable.

III. Construction

338.100 Construction. Cabled, single-conductor, Type USE constructions recognized for underground use shall be permitted to have a bare copper conductor cabled with the assembly. Type USE single, parallel, or cabled conductor assemblies recognized for underground use shall be permitted to have a bare copper concentric conductor applied. These constructions shall not require an outer overall covering.

> FPN: See 230.41, Exception, item (2), for directly buried, uninsulated service-entrance conductors.

Type SE or USE cable containing two or more conductors shall be permitted to have one conductor uninsulated.

338.120 Marking. Service-entrance cable shall be marked as required in 310.11. Cable with the neutral conductor smaller than the ungrounded conductors shall be so marked.

ARTICLE 340
Underground Feeder and Branch-Circuit Cable: Type UF

I. General

340.1 Scope. This article covers the use, installation, and construction specifications for underground feeder and branch-circuit cable, Type UF.

340.2 Definition.

Underground Feeder and Branch-Circuit Cable, Type UF. A factory assembly of one or more insulated conductors with an integral or an overall covering of nonmetallic material suitable for direct burial in the earth.

340.6 Listing Requirements. Type UF cable shall be listed.

II. Installation

340.10 Uses Permitted. Type UF cable shall be permitted as follows:

(1) For use underground, including direct burial in the earth. For underground requirements, see 300.5.

(2) As single-conductor cables. Where installed as single-conductor cables, all conductors of the feeder grounded conductor or branch circuit, including the grounded conductor and equipment grounding conductor, if any, shall be installed in accordance with 300.3.

(3) For wiring in wet, dry, or corrosive locations under the recognized wiring methods of this *Code*.

(4) Installed as nonmetallic-sheathed cable. Where so installed, the installation and conductor requirements shall comply with Parts II and III of Article 334 and shall be of the multiconductor type.

(5) For solar photovoltaic systems in accordance with 690.31.

(6) As single-conductor cables as the nonheating leads for heating cables as provided in 424.43.

(7) Supported by cable trays. Type UF cable supported by cable trays shall be of the multiconductor type.

> FPN: See 310.10 for temperature limitation of conductors.

340.12 Uses Not Permitted. Type UF cable shall not be used as follows:

(1) As service-entrance cable

(2) In commercial garages

(3) In theaters and similar locations

(4) In motion picture studios

(5) In storage battery rooms

(6) In hoistways or on elevators or escalators

(7) In hazardous (classified) locations

(8) Embedded in poured cement, concrete, or aggregate, except where embedded in plaster as nonheating leads where permitted in 424.43

(9) Where exposed to direct rays of the sun, unless identified as sunlight resistant

(10) Where subject to physical damage

(11) As overhead cable, except where installed as messenger-supported wiring in accordance with Part II of Article 396

340.24 Bending Radius. Bends in Type UF cable shall be so made that the cable is not damaged. The radius of the curve of the inner edge of any bend shall not be less than five times the diameter of the cable.

340.80 Ampacity. The ampacity of Type UF cable shall be that of 60°C (140°F) conductors in accordance with 310.15.

III. Construction Specifications

340.104 Conductors. The conductors shall be sizes 14 AWG copper or 12 AWG aluminum or copper-clad aluminum through 4/0 AWG.

340.108 Equipment Grounding. In addition to the insulated conductors, the cable shall be permitted to have an insulated or bare conductor for equipment grounding purposes only.

340.112 Insulation. The conductors of Type UF shall be one of the moisture-resistant types listed in Table 310.13 that is suitable for branch-circuit wiring or one that is identified for such use. Where installed as a substitute wiring method for NM cable, the conductor insulation shall be rated 90°C (194°F).

340.116 Sheath. The overall covering shall be flame retardant; moisture, fungus, and corrosion resistant; and suitable for direct burial in the earth.

ARTICLE 342
Intermediate Metal Conduit: Type IMC

I. General

342.1 Scope. This article covers the use, installation, and construction specifications for intermediate metal conduit (IMC) and associated fittings.

342.2 Definition.

Intermediate Metal Conduit (IMC). A steel threadable raceway of circular cross section designed for the physical protection and routing of conductors and cables and for use as an equipment grounding conductor when installed with its integral or associated coupling and appropriate fittings.

342.6 Listing Requirements. IMC, factory elbows and couplings, and associated fittings shall be listed.

II. Installation

342.10 Uses Permitted.

(A) All Atmospheric Conditions and Occupancies. Use of IMC shall be permitted under all atmospheric conditions and occupancies.

(B) Corrosion Environments. IMC, elbows, couplings, and fittings shall be permitted to be installed in concrete, in direct contact with the earth, or in areas subject to severe corrosive influences where protected by corrosion protection and judged suitable for the condition.

(C) Cinder Fill. IMC shall be permitted to be installed in or under cinder fill where subject to permanent moisture where protected on all sides by a layer of noncinder concrete not less than 50 mm (2 in.) thick; where the conduit is not less than 450 mm (18 in.) under the fill; or where protected by corrosion protection and judged suitable for the condition.

(D) Wet Locations. All supports, bolts, straps, screws, and so forth, shall be of corrosion-resistant materials or protected against corrosion by corrosion-resistant materials.

FPN: See 300.6 for protection against corrosion.

342.14 Dissimilar Metals. Where practicable, dissimilar metals in contact anywhere in the system shall be avoided to eliminate the possibility of galvanic action.

Aluminum fittings and enclosures shall be permitted to be used with IMC.

342.20 Size.

(A) Minimum. IMC smaller than metric designator 16 (trade size ½) shall not be used.

(B) Maximum. IMC larger than metric designator 103 (trade size 4) shall not be used.

FPN: See 300.1(C) for the metric designators and trade sizes. These are for identification purposes only and do not relate to actual dimensions.

342.22 Number of Conductors. The number of conductors shall not exceed that permitted by the percentage fill specified in Table 1, Chapter 9.

Cables shall be permitted to be installed where such use is not prohibited by the respective cable articles. The number of cables shall not exceed the allowable percentage fill specified in Table 1, Chapter 9.

342.24 Bends — How Made. Bends of IMC shall be so made that the conduit will not be damaged and the internal diameter of the conduit will not be effectively reduced. The radius of the curve of any field bend to the centerline of the conduit shall not be less than indicated in Table 2, Chapter 9.

342.26 Bends — Number in One Run. There shall not be more than the equivalent of four quarter bends (360 degrees total) between pull points, for example, conduit bodies and boxes.

342.28 Reaming and Threading. All cut ends shall be reamed or otherwise finished to remove rough edges. Where conduit is threaded in the field, a standard cutting die with a taper of 1 in 16 (¾ in. taper per foot) shall be used.

FPN: See ANSI/ASME B.1.20.1-1983, *Standard for Pipe Threads, General Purpose (Inch).*

342.30 Securing and Supporting. IMC shall be installed as a complete system in accordance with 300.18 and shall be securely fastened in place and supported in accordance with 342.30(A) and (B).

(A) Securely Fastened. Each IMC shall be securely fastened within 900 mm (3 ft) of each outlet box, junction box, device box, cabinet, conduit body, or other conduit termination. Fastening shall be permitted to be increased to a distance of 1.5 m (5 ft) where structural members do not readily permit fastening within 900 mm (3 ft). Where approved, conduit shall not be required to be securely fastened within 900 mm (3 ft) of the service head for above-the-roof termination of a mast.

(B) Supports. IMC shall be supported in accordance with one of the following:

(1) Conduit shall be supported at intervals not exceeding 3 m (10 ft).

(2) The distance between supports for straight runs of conduit shall be permitted in accordance with Table 344.30(B)(2), provided the conduit is made up with threaded couplings and such supports prevent transmission of stresses to termination where conduit is deflected between supports.

(3) Exposed vertical risers from industrial machinery or fixed equipment shall be permitted to be supported at intervals not exceeding 6 m (20 ft) if the conduit is made up with threaded couplings, the conduit is supported and securely fastened at the top and bottom of the riser, and no other means of intermediate support is readily available.

(4) Horizontal runs of IMC supported by openings through framing members at intervals not exceeding 3 m (10 ft) and securely fastened within 900 mm (3 ft) of termination points shall be permitted.

342.42 Couplings and Connectors.

(A) Threadless. Threadless couplings and connectors used with conduit shall be made tight. Where buried in masonry or concrete, they shall be the concretetight type. Where installed in wet locations, they shall comply with 314.15(A). Threadless couplings and connectors shall not be used on threaded conduit ends unless listed for the purpose.

(B) Running Threads. Running threads shall not be used on conduit for connection at couplings.

342.46 Bushings. Where a conduit enters a box, fitting, or other enclosure, a bushing shall be provided to protect the wire from abrasion unless the design of the box, fitting, or enclosure is such as to afford equivalent protection.

FPN: See 300.4(F) for the protection of conductors 4 AWG and larger at bushings.

342.56 Splices and Taps. Splices and taps shall be made in accordance with 300.15.

342.60 Grounding. IMC shall be permitted as an equipment grounding conductor.

III. Construction Specifications

342.120 Marking. Each length shall be clearly and durably marked at least every 1.5 m (5 ft) with the letters IMC. Each length shall be marked as required in 110.21.

342.130 Standard Lengths. The standard length of IMC shall be 3.05 m (10 ft), including an attached coupling, and each end shall be threaded. Longer or shorter lengths with or without coupling and threaded or unthreaded shall be permitted.

ARTICLE 344
Rigid Metal Conduit: Type RMC

I. General

344.1 Scope. This article covers the use, installation, and construction specifications for rigid metal conduit (RMC) and associated fittings.

344.2 Definition.

Rigid Metal Conduit (RMC). A threadable raceway of circular cross section designed for the physical protection and routing of conductors and cables and for use as an equipment grounding conductor when installed with its integral or associated coupling and appropriate fittings. RMC is generally made of steel (ferrous) with protective coatings or aluminum (nonferrous). Special use types are silicon bronze and stainless steel.

344.6 Listing Requirements. RMC, factory elbows and couplings, and associated fittings shall be listed.

II. Installation

344.10 Uses Permitted.

(A) All Atmospheric Conditions and Occupancies. Use of RMC shall be permitted under all atmospheric conditions and occupancies. Ferrous raceways and fittings protected from corrosion solely by enamel shall be permitted only indoors and in occupancies not subject to severe corrosive influences.

(B) Corrosion Environments. RMC, elbows, couplings, and fittings shall be permitted to be installed in concrete, in direct contact with the earth, or in areas subject to severe corrosive influences where protected by corrosion protection and judged suitable for the condition.

(C) Cinder Fill. RMC shall be permitted to be installed in or under cinder fill where subject to permanent moisture where protected on all sides by a layer of noncinder concrete not less than 50 mm (2 in.) thick; where the conduit is not less than 450 mm (18 in.) under the fill; or where protected by corrosion protection and judged suitable for the condition.

(D) Wet Locations. All supports, bolts, straps, screws, and so forth, shall be of corrosion-resistant materials or protected against corrosion by corrosion-resistant materials.

FPN: See 300.6 for protection against corrosion.

344.14 Dissimilar Metals. Where practicable, dissimilar metals in contact anywhere in the system shall be avoided to eliminate the possibility of galvanic action. Aluminum fittings and enclosures shall be permitted to be used with steel RMC, and steel fittings and enclosures shall be permitted to be used with aluminum RMC where not subject to severe corrosive influences.

344.20 Size.

(A) Minimum. RMC smaller than metric designator 16 (trade size ½) shall not be used.

Exception: For enclosing the leads of motors as permitted in 430.245(B).

(B) Maximum. RMC larger than metric designator 155 (trade size 6) shall not be used.

FPN: See 300.1(C) for the metric designators and trade sizes. These are for identification purposes only and do not relate to actual dimensions.

344.22 Number of Conductors. The number of conductors shall not exceed that permitted by the percentage fill specified in Table 1, Chapter 9.

Cables shall be permitted to be installed where such use is not prohibited by the respective cable articles. The number of cables shall not exceed the allowable percentage fill specified in Table 1, Chapter 9.

344.24 Bends — How Made. Bends of RMC shall be so made that the conduit will not be damaged and so that the internal diameter of the conduit will not be effectively reduced. The radius of the curve of any field bend to the centerline of the conduit shall not be less than indicated in Table 2, Chapter 9.

344.26 Bends — Number in One Run. There shall not be more than the equivalent of four quarter bends (360 degrees total) between pull points, for example, conduit bodies and boxes.

344.28 Reaming and Threading. All cut ends shall be reamed or otherwise finished to remove rough edges. Where conduit is threaded in the field, a standard cutting die with a 1 in 16 taper (¾-in. taper per foot) shall be used.

FPN: See ANSI/ASME B.1.20.1-1983, *Standard for Pipe Threads, General Purpose (Inch)*.

344.30 Securing and Supporting. RMC shall be installed as a complete system in accordance with 300.18 and shall be securely fastened in place and supported in accordance with 344.30(A) and (B).

(A) Securely Fastened. RMC shall be securely fastened within 900 mm (3 ft) of each outlet box, junction box, device box, cabinet, conduit body, or other conduit termination. Fastening shall be permitted to be increased to a distance of 1.5 m (5 ft) where structural members do not readily permit fastening within 900 mm (3 ft). Where approved, conduit shall not be required to be securely fastened within 900 mm (3 ft) of the service head for above-the-roof termination of a mast.

(B) Supports. RMC shall be supported in accordance with one of the following:

(1) Conduit shall be supported at intervals not exceeding 3 m (10 ft).

(2) The distance between supports for straight runs of conduit shall be permitted in accordance with Table 344.30(B)(2), provided the conduit is made up with threaded couplings, and such supports prevent transmission of stresses to termination where conduit is deflected between supports.

(3) Exposed vertical risers from industrial machinery or fixed equipment shall be permitted to be supported at intervals not exceeding 6 m (20 ft) if the conduit is made up with threaded couplings, the conduit is supported and securely fastened at the top and bottom of the riser, and no other means of intermediate support is readily available.

(4) Horizontal runs of RMC supported by openings through framing members at intervals not exceeding 3 m (10 ft) and securely fastened within 900 mm (3 ft) of termination points shall be permitted.

344.42 Couplings and Connectors.

(A) Threadless. Threadless couplings and connectors used with conduit shall be made tight. Where buried in masonry or concrete, they shall be the concretetight type. Where installed in wet locations, they shall comply with 314.15(A). Threadless couplings and connectors shall not be used on threaded conduit ends unless listed for the purpose.

Table 344.30(B)(2) Supports for Rigid Metal Conduit

Conduit Size		Maximum Distance Between Rigid Metal Conduit Supports	
Metric Designator	Trade Size	m	ft
16–21	½–¾	3.0	10
27	1	3.7	12
35–41	1¼–1½	4.3	14
53–63	2–2½	4.9	16
78 and larger	3 and larger	6.1	20

(B) Running Threads. Running threads shall not be used on conduit for connection at couplings.

344.46 Bushings. Where a conduit enters a box, fitting, or other enclosure, a bushing shall be provided to protect the wire from abrasion unless the design of the box, fitting, or enclosure is such as to afford equivalent protection.

> FPN: See 300.4(F) for the protection of conductors sizes 4 AWG and larger at bushings.

344.56 Splices and Taps. Splices and taps shall be made in accordance with 300.15.

344.60 Grounding. RMC shall be permitted as an equipment grounding conductor.

III. Construction Specifications

344.120 Marking. Each length shall be clearly and durably identified in every 3 m (10 ft) as required in the first sentence of 110.21. Nonferrous conduit of corrosion-resistant material shall have suitable markings.

344.130 Standard Lengths. The standard length of RMC shall be 3.05 m (10 ft), including an attached coupling, and each end shall be threaded. Longer or shorter lengths with or without coupling and threaded or unthreaded shall be permitted.

ARTICLE 348
Flexible Metal Conduit: Type FMC

I. General

348.1 Scope. This article covers the use, installation, and construction specifications for flexible metal conduit (FMC) and associated fittings.

348.2 Definition.

Flexible Metal Conduit (FMC). A raceway of circular cross section made of helically wound, formed, interlocked metal strip.

348.6 Listing Requirements. FMC and associated fittings shall be listed.

II. Installation

348.10 Uses Permitted. FMC shall be permitted to be used in exposed and concealed locations.

348.12 Uses Not Permitted. FMC shall not be used in the following:

(1) In wet locations unless the conductors are approved for the specific conditions and the installation is such that liquid is not likely to enter raceways or enclosures to which the conduit is connected

(2) In hoistways, other than as permitted in 620.21(A)(1)

(3) In storage battery rooms

(4) In any hazardous (classified) location other than as permitted in 501.10(B) and 504.20

(5) Where exposed to materials having a deteriorating effect on the installed conductors, such as oil or gasoline

(6) Underground or embedded in poured concrete or aggregate

(7) Where subject to physical damage

348.20 Size.

(A) Minimum. FMC less than metric designator 16 (trade size ½) shall not be used unless permitted in 348.20(A)(1) through (A)(5) for metric designator 12 (trade size ⅜).

(1) For enclosing the leads of motors as permitted in 430.245(B)

(2) In lengths not in excess of 1.8 m (6 ft) for any of the following uses:

    a. For utilization equipment

    b. As part of a listed assembly

    c. For tap connections to luminaires (lighting fixtures) as permitted in 410.67(C)

(3) For manufactured wiring systems as permitted in 604.6(A)

(4) In hoistways as permitted in 620.21(A)(1)

(5) As part of a listed assembly to connect wired luminaire (fixture) sections as permitted in 410.77(C)

(B) Maximum. FMC larger than metric designator 103 (trade size 4) shall not be used.

> FPN: See 300.1(C) for the metric designators and trade sizes. These are for identification purposes only and do not relate to actual dimensions.

348.22 Number of Conductors. The number of conductors shall not exceed that permitted by the percentage fill specified in Table 1, Chapter 9, or as permitted in Table 348.22, or for metric designator 12 (trade size ⅜).

Cables shall be permitted to be installed where such use is not prohibited by the respective cable articles. The number of cables shall not exceed the allowable percentage fill specified in Table 1, Chapter 9.

348.24 Bends — How Made. Bends in conduit shall be made so that the conduit is not damaged and the internal diameter of the conduit is not effectively reduced. Bends shall be permitted to be made manually without auxiliary equipment. The radius of the curve to the centerline of any bend shall not be less than shown in Table 2, Chapter 9 using the column "Other Bends."

348.26 Bends — Number in One Run. There shall not be more than the equivalent of four quarter bends (360 degrees total) between pull points, for example, conduit bodies and boxes.

348.28 Trimming. All cut ends shall be trimmed or otherwise finished to remove rough edges, except where fittings that thread into the convolutions are used.

348.30 Securing and Supporting. FMC shall be securely fastened in place and supported in accordance with 348.30(A) and (B).

(A) Securely Fastened. FMC shall be securely fastened in place by an approved means within 300 mm (12 in.) of each box, cabinet, conduit body, or other conduit termination and shall be supported and secured at intervals not to exceed 1.4 m (4½ ft).

Exception No. 1:   Where FMC is fished.

Exception No. 2:   At terminals where flexibility is required, lengths shall not exceed the following:

(1) 900 mm (3 ft) for metric designators 16 through 35 (trade sizes ½ through 1¼)

(2) 1200 mm (4 ft) for metric designators 41 through 53 (trade sizes 1½ through 2)

(3) 1500 mm (5 ft) for metric designators 63 (trade size 2½) and larger

Exception No. 3:   Lengths not exceeding 1.8 m (6 ft) from a luminaire (fixture) terminal connection for tap connections to luminaires (light fixtures) as permitted in 410.67(C).

Exception No. 4:   Lengths not exceeding 1.8 m (6 ft) from the last point where the raceway is securely fastened for connections within an accessible ceiling to luminaire(s) [lighting fixture(s)] or other equipment.

(B) Supports. Horizontal runs of FMC supported by openings through framing members at intervals not greater than 1.4 m (4½ ft) and securely fastened within 300 mm (12 in.) of termination points shall be permitted.

348.42 Couplings and Connectors. Angle connectors shall not be used for concealed raceway installations.

348.56 Splices and Taps. Splices and taps shall be made in accordance with 300.15.

348.60 Grounding and Bonding. Where used to connect equipment where flexibility is required, an equipment grounding conductor shall be installed.

Where flexibility is not required, FMC shall be permitted to be used as an equipment grounding conductor when installed in accordance with 250.118(5) .

Where required or installed, equipment grounding conductors shall be installed in accordance with 250.134(B).

Where required or installed, equipment bonding jumpers shall be installed in accordance with 250.102.

Table 348.22 Maximum Number of Insulated Conductors in Metric Designator 12 (Trade Size ⅜) Flexible Metal Conduit*

Size (AWG)	Types RFH-2, SF-2		Types TF, XHHW, TW		Types TFN, THHN, THWN		Types FEP, FEBP, PF, PGF	
	Fittings Inside Conduit	Fittings Outside Conduit	Fittings Inside Conduit	Fittings Outside Conduit	Fittings Inside Conduit	Fittings Outside Conduit	Fittings Inside Conduit	Fittings Outside Conduit
18	2	3	3	5	5	8	5	8
16	1	2	3	4	4	6	4	6
14	1	2	2	3	3	4	3	4
12	—	—	1	2	2	3	2	3
10	—	—	1	1	1	1	1	2

*In addition, one covered or bare equipment grounding conductor of the same size shall be permitted.

ARTICLE 350
Liquidtight Flexible Metal Conduit: Type LFMC

I. General

350.1 Scope. This article covers the use, installation, and construction specifications for liquidtight flexible metal conduit (LFMC) and associated fittings.

350.2 Definition.

Liquidtight Flexible Metal Conduit (LFMC). A raceway of circular cross section having an outer liquidtight, non-metallic, sunlight-resistant jacket over an inner flexible metal core with associated couplings, connectors, and fittings for the installation of electric conductors.

350.6 Listing Requirements. LFMC and associated fittings shall be listed.

II. Installation

350.10 Uses Permitted. LFMC shall be permitted to be used in exposed or concealed locations as follows:

(1) Where conditions of installation, operation, or maintenance require flexibility or protection from liquids, vapors, or solids

(2) As permitted by 501.10(B), 502.10, 503.10, and 504.20 and in other hazardous (classified) locations where specifically approved, and by 553.7(B)

(3) For direct burial where listed and marked for the purpose

350.12 Uses Not Permitted. LFMC shall not be used as follows:

(1) Where subject to physical damage

(2) Where any combination of ambient and conductor temperature produces an operating temperature in excess of that for which the material is approved

350.20 Size.

(A) Minimum. LFMC smaller than metric designator 16 (trade size ½) shall not be used.

Exception: LFMC of metric designator 12 (trade size ⅜) shall be permitted as covered in 348.20(A).

(B) Maximum. The maximum size of LFMC shall be metric designator 103 (trade size 4).

FPN: See 300.1(C) for the metric designators and trade sizes. These are for identification purposes only and do not relate to actual dimensions.

350.22 Number of Conductors or Cables.

(A) Metric Designators 16 through 103 (Trade Sizes ½ through 4). The number of conductors shall not exceed that permitted by the percentage fill specified in Table 1, Chapter 9.

Cables shall be permitted to be installed where such use is not prohibited by the respective cable articles. The number of cables shall not exceed the allowable percentage fill specified in Table 1, Chapter 9.

(B) Metric Designator 12 (Trade Size ⅜). The number of conductors shall not exceed that permitted in Table 348.22, "Fittings Outside Conduit" columns.

350.24 Bends — How Made. Bends in conduit shall be so made that the conduit will not be damaged and the internal diameter of the conduit will not be effectively reduced. Bends shall be permitted to be made manually without auxiliary equipment. The radius of the curve to the centerline of any bend shall not be less than required in Table 2, Chapter 9 using the column "Other Bends."

350.26 Bends — Number in One Run. There shall not be more than the equivalent of four quarter bends (360 degrees total) between pull points, for example, conduit bodies and boxes.

350.30 Securing and Supporting. LFMC shall be securely fastened in place and supported in accordance with 350.30(A) and (B).

(A) Securely Fastened. LFMC shall be securely fastened in place by an approved means within 300 mm (12 in.) of each box, cabinet, conduit body, or other conduit termination and shall be supported and secured at intervals not to exceed 1.4 m (4½ ft).

Exception No. 1: Where LFMC is fished.

Exception No. 2: Lengths not exceeding 900 mm (3 ft) at terminals where flexibility is necessary.

Exception No. 3: Lengths not exceeding 1.8 m (6 ft) from a luminaire (fixture) terminal connection for tap conductors to luminaires (lighting fixtures), as permitted in 410.67(C).

Exception No. 4: Lengths not exceeding 1.8 m (6 ft) from the last point where the raceway is securely fastened for connections within an accessible ceiling to luminaire(s) [lighting fixture(s)] or other equipment.

(B) Supports. Horizontal runs of LFMC supported by openings through framing members at intervals not greater than 1.4 m (4½ ft) and securely fastened within 300 mm (12 in.) of termination points shall be permitted.

350.42 Couplings and Connectors. Angle connectors shall not be used for concealed raceway installations.

350.56 Splices and Taps. Splices and taps shall be made in accordance with 300.15.

350.60 Grounding and Bonding. Where used to connect equipment where flexibility is required, an equipment grounding conductor shall be installed.

Where flexibility is not required, LFMC shall be permitted to be used as an equipment grounding conductor when installed in accordance with 250.118(6).

Where required or installed, equipment grounding conductors shall be installed in accordance with 250.134(B).

Where required or installed, equipment bonding jumpers shall be installed in accordance with 250.102.

FPN: See 501.30(B), 502.30(B), and 503.30(B) for types of equipment grounding conductors.

III. Construction Specifications

350.120 Marking. LFMC shall be marked according to 110.21. The trade size and other information required by the listing shall also be marked on the conduit. Conduit suitable for direct burial shall be so marked.

ARTICLE 352
Rigid Nonmetallic Conduit: Type RNC

I. General

352.1 Scope. This article covers the use, installation, and construction specifications for rigid nonmetallic conduit (RNC) and associated fittings.

352.2 Definition.

Rigid Nonmetallic Conduit (RNC). A nonmetallic raceway of circular cross section, with integral or associated couplings, connectors, and fittings for the installation of electrical conductors and cables.

352.6 Listing Requirements. RNC, factory elbows, and associated fittings shall be listed.

II. Installation

352.10 Uses Permitted. The use of RNC shall be permitted in accordance with 352.10(A) through (H).

FPN: Extreme cold may cause some nonmetallic conduits to become brittle and therefore more susceptible to damage from physical contact.

(A) Concealed. RNC shall be permitted in walls, floors, and ceilings.

(B) Corrosive Influences. RNC shall be permitted in locations subject to severe corrosive influences as covered in 300.6 and where subject to chemicals for which the materials are specifically approved.

(C) Cinders. RNC shall be permitted in cinder fill.

(D) Wet Locations. RNC shall be permitted in portions of dairies, laundries, canneries, or other wet locations and in locations where walls are frequently washed, the entire conduit system including boxes and fittings used therewith shall be installed and equipped so as to prevent water from entering the conduit. All supports, bolts, straps, screws, and so forth, shall be of corrosion-resistant materials or be protected against corrosion by approved corrosion-resistant materials.

(E) Dry and Damp Locations. RNC shall be permitted for use in dry and damp locations not prohibited by 352.12.

(F) Exposed. RNC shall be permitted for exposed work where not subject to physical damage if identified for such use.

(G) Underground Installations. For underground installations, see 300.5 and 300.50.

FPN: Refer to Article 353 for High Density Polyethylene Conduit: Type HDPE.

(H) Support of Conduit Bodies. Rigid nonmetallic conduit shall be permitted to support nonmetallic conduit bodies not larger than the largest trade size of an entering raceway. These conduit bodies shall not support luminaires (fixtures) or other equipment and shall not contain devices other than splicing devices as permitted by 110.14(B) and 314.16(C)(2).

352.12 Uses Not Permitted. RNC shall not be used under the following conditions.

(A) Hazardous (Classified) Locations.

(1) In hazardous (classified) locations, except as permitted in 503.10(A), 504.20, 514.8 Exception No. 2, and 515.8

(2) In Class I, Division 2 locations, except as permitted in 501.10(B)(3)

(B) Support of Luminaires (Fixtures). For the support of luminaires (fixtures) or other equipment not described in 352.10(H).

(C) Physical Damage. Where subject to physical damage unless identified for such use.

(D) Ambient Temperatures. Where subject to ambient temperatures in excess of 50°C (122°F) unless listed otherwise.

(E) Insulation Temperature Limitations. For conductors or cables operating at a temperature higher than the RNC listed operating temperature rating.

Exception: Conductors or cables rated at a temperature higher than the RNC listed temperature rating shall be permitted to be installed in RNC, provided they are not operated at a temperature higher than the RNC listed temperature rating.

(F) Theaters and Similar Locations. In theaters and similar locations, except as provided in 518.4 and 520.5.

352.20 Size.

(A) Minimum. RNC smaller than metric designator 16 (trade size ½) shall not be used.

(B) Maximum. RNC larger than metric designator 155 (trade size 6) shall not be used.

> FPN: The trade sizes and metric designators are for identification purposes only and do not relate to actual dimensions. See 300.1(C).

352.22 Number of Conductors. The number of conductors shall not exceed that permitted by the percentage fill specified in Table 1, Chapter 9.

Cables shall be permitted to be installed where such use is not prohibited by the respective cable articles. The number of cables shall not exceed the allowable percentage fill specified in Table 1, Chapter 9.

352.24 Bends — How Made. Bends shall be so made that the conduit will not be damaged and the internal diameter of the conduit will not be effectively reduced. Field bends shall be made only with bending equipment identified for the purpose. The radius of the curve to the centerline of such bends shall not be less than shown in Table 2, Chapter 9.

352.26 Bends — Number in One Run. There shall not be more than the equivalent of four quarter bends (360 degrees total) between pull points, for example, conduit bodies and boxes.

352.28 Trimming. All cut ends shall be trimmed inside and outside to remove rough edges.

352.30 Securing and Supporting. RNC shall be installed as a complete system as provided in 300.18 and shall be fastened so that movement from thermal expansion or contraction is permitted. RNC shall be securely fastened and supported in accordance with 352.30(A) and (B).

(A) Securely Fastened. RNC shall be securely fastened within 900 mm (3 ft) of each outlet box, junction box, device box, conduit body, or other conduit termination. Conduit listed for securing at other than 900 mm (3 ft) shall be permitted to be installed in accordance with the listing.

(B) Supports. RNC shall be supported as required in Table 352.30(B). Conduit listed for support at spacings other than as shown in Table 352.30(B) shall be permitted to be installed in accordance with the listing. Horizontal runs of RNC supported by openings through framing members at intervals not exceeding those in Table 352.30(B) and securely fastened within 900 mm (3 ft) of termination points shall be permitted.

Table 352.30(B) Support of Rigid Nonmetallic Conduit (RNC)

Conduit Size		Maximum Spacing Between Supports	
Metric Designator	Trade Size	mm or m	ft
16–27	½–1	900 mm	3
35–53	1¼–2	1.5 m	5
63–78	2½–3	1.8 m	6
91–129	3½–5	2.1 m	7
155	6	2.5 m	8

352.44 Expansion Fittings. Expansion fittings for RNC shall be provided to compensate for thermal expansion and contraction where the length change, in accordance with Table 352.44(A) or Table 352.44(B), is expected to be 6 mm (¼ in.) or greater in a straight run between securely mounted items such as boxes, cabinets, elbows, or other conduit terminations.

352.46 Bushings. Where a conduit enters a box, fitting, or other enclosure, a bushing or adapter shall be provided to protect the wire from abrasion unless the box, fitting, or enclosure design provides equivalent protection.

> FPN: See 300.4(F) for the protection of conductors 4 AWG and larger at bushings.

352.48 Joints. All joints between lengths of conduit, and between conduit and couplings, fittings, and boxes, shall be made by an approved method.

352.56 Splices and Taps. Splices and taps shall be made in accordance with 300.15.

352.60 Grounding. Where equipment grounding is required, a separate equipment grounding conductor shall be installed in the conduit.

Exception No. 1: As permitted in 250.134(B), Exception No. 2, for dc circuits and 250.134(B), Exception No. 1, for separately run equipment grounding conductors.

Exception No. 2: Where the grounded conductor is used to ground equipment as permitted in 250.142.

Table 352.44(A) Expansion Characteristics of PVC Rigid Nonmetallic Conduit Coefficient of Thermal Expansion = 6.084×10^{-5} mm/mm/°C (3.38×10^{-5} in./in./°F)

Temperature Change (°C)	Length Change of PVC Conduit (mm/m)	Temperature Change (°F)	Length Change of PVC Conduit (in./100 ft)	Temperature Change (°F)	Length Change of PVC Conduit (in./100 ft)
5	0.30	5	0.20	105	4.26
10	0.61	10	0.41	110	4.46
15	0.91	15	0.61	115	4.66
20	1.22	20	0.81	120	4.87
25	1.52	25	1.01	125	5.07
30	1.83	30	1.22	130	5.27
35	2.13	35	1.42	135	5.48
40	2.43	40	1.62	140	5.68
45	2.74	45	1.83	145	5.88
50	3.04	50	2.03	150	6.08
55	3.35	55	2.23	155	6.29
60	3.65	60	2.43	160	6.49
65	3.95	65	2.64	165	6.69
70	4.26	70	2.84	170	6.90
75	4.56	75	3.04	175	7.10
80	4.87	80	3.24	180	7.30
85	5.17	85	3.45	185	7.50
90	5.48	90	3.65	190	7.71
95	5.78	95	3.85	195	7.91
100	6.08	100	4.06	200	8.11

Table 352.44(B) Expansion Characteristics of Reinforced Thermosetting Resin Conduit (RTRC) Coefficient of Thermal Expansion = 2.7×10^{-5} mm/mm/°C (1.5×10^{-5} in./in./°F)

Temperature Change (°C)	Length Change of RTRC Conduit (mm/m)	Temperature Change (°F)	Length Change of RTRC Conduit (in./100 ft)	Temperature Change (°F)	Length Change of RTRC Conduit (in./100 ft)
5	0.14	5	0.09	105	1.89
10	0.27	10	0.18	110	1.98
15	0.41	15	0.27	115	2.07
20	0.54	20	0.36	120	2.16
25	0.68	25	0.45	125	2.25
30	0.81	30	0.54	130	2.34
35	0.95	35	0.63	135	2.43
40	1.08	40	0.72	140	2.52
45	1.22	45	0.81	145	2.61
50	1.35	50	0.90	150	2.70
55	1.49	55	0.99	155	2.79
60	1.62	60	1.08	160	2.88
65	1.76	65	1.17	165	2.97
70	1.89	70	1.26	170	3.06
75	2.03	75	1.35	175	3.15
80	2.16	80	1.44	180	3.24
85	2.30	85	1.53	185	3.33
90	2.43	90	1.62	190	3.42
95	2.57	95	1.71	195	3.51
100	2.70	100	1.80	200	3.60

III. Construction Specifications

352.100 Construction. RNC and fittings shall be composed of suitable nonmetallic material that is resistant to moisture and chemical atmospheres. For use above ground, it shall also be flame retardant, resistant to impact and crushing, resistant to distortion from heat under conditions likely to be encountered in service, and resistant to low temperature and sunlight effects. For use underground, the material shall be acceptably resistant to moisture and corrosive agents and shall be of sufficient strength to withstand abuse, such as by impact and crushing, in handling and during installation. Where intended for direct burial, without encasement in concrete, the material shall also be capable of withstanding continued loading that is likely to be encountered after installation.

352.120 Marking. Each length of RNC shall be clearly and durably marked at least every 3 m (10 ft) as required in the first sentence of 110.21. The type of material shall also be included in the marking unless it is visually identifiable. For conduit recognized for use above ground, these markings shall be permanent. For conduit limited to underground use only, these markings shall be sufficiently durable to remain legible until the material is installed. Conduit shall be permitted to be surface marked to indicate special characteristics of the material.

FPN: Examples of these markings include but are not limited to "limited smoke" and "sunlight resistant."

ARTICLE 353
High Density Polyethylene Conduit: Type HDPE Conduit

I. General

353.1 Scope. This article covers the use, installation, and construction specifications for high density polyethylene (HDPE) conduit and associated fittings.

353.2 Definition.

High Density Polyethylene (HDPE) Conduit. A nonmetallic raceway of circular cross section, with associated couplings, connectors, and fittings for the installation of electrical conductors.

353.6 Listing Requirements. HDPE conduit and associated fittings shall be listed.

II. Installation

353.10 Uses Permitted. The use of HDPE conduit shall be permitted under the following conditions:

(1) In discrete lengths or in continuous lengths from a reel

(2) In locations subject to severe corrosive influences as covered in 300.6 and where subject to chemicals for which the conduit is listed

(3) In cinder fill

(4) In direct burial installations in earth or concrete

    FPN to (4): Refer to 300.5 and 300.50 for underground installations.

353.12 Uses Not Permitted. HDPE conduit shall not be used under the following conditions:

(1) Where exposed

(2) Within a building

(3) In hazardous (classified) locations, except as permitted in 504.20

(4) Where subject to ambient temperatures in excess of 50°C (122°F) unless listed otherwise

(5) For conductors or cables operating at a temperature higher than the HDPE conduit listed operating temperature rating

Exception: Conductors or cables rated at a temperature higher than the HDPE conduit listed temperature rating shall be permitted to be installed in HDPE conduit, provided they are not operated at a temperature higher than the HDPE conduit listed temperature rating.

353.20 Size.

(A) Minimum. HDPE conduit smaller than metric designator 16 (trade size ½) shall not be used.

(B) Maximum. HDPE conduit larger than metric designator 103 (trade size 4) shall not be used.

    FPN: The trade sizes and metric designators are for identification purposes only and do not relate to actual dimensions. See 300.1(C).

353.22 Number of Conductors. The number of conductors shall not exceed that permitted by the percentage fill specified in Table 1, Chapter 9.

Cables shall be permitted to be installed where such use is not prohibited by the respective cable articles. The number of cables shall not exceed the allowable percentage fill specified in Table 1, Chapter 9.

353.24 Bends — How Made. Bends shall be so made that the conduit will not be damaged and the internal diameter of the conduit will not be effectively reduced. Bends shall be permitted to be made manually without auxiliary equipment, and the radius of the curve to the centerline of such bends shall not be less than shown in Table 354.24.

353.26 Bends — Number in One Run. There shall not be more than the equivalent of four quarter bends (360 degrees total) between pull points, for example, conduit bodies and boxes.

353.28 Trimming. All cut ends shall be trimmed inside and outside to remove rough edges.

353.46 Bushings. Where a conduit enters a box, fitting, or other enclosure, a bushing or adapter shall be provided to protect the wire from abrasion unless the box, fitting, or enclosure design provides equivalent protection.

> FPN: See 300.4(F) for the protection of conductors 4 AWG and larger at bushings.

353.48 Joints. All joints between lengths of conduit, and between conduit and couplings, fittings, and boxes, shall be made by an approved method.

353.56 Splices and Taps. Splices and taps shall be made in accordance with 300.15.

353.60 Grounding. Where equipment grounding is required, a separate equipment grounding conductor shall be installed in the conduit.

Exception No. 1:   The equipment grounding conductor shall be permitted to be run separately from the conduit where used for grounding dc circuits as permitted in 250.134, Exception No. 2.

Exception No. 2:   The equipment grounding conductor shall not be required where the grounded conductor is used to ground equipment as permitted in 250.142.

III. Construction Specifications

353.100 Construction. HDPE conduit shall be composed of high density polyethylene that is resistant to moisture and chemical atmospheres. The material shall be resistant to moisture and corrosive agents and shall be of sufficient strength to withstand abuse, such as by impact and crushing, in handling and during installation. Where intended for direct burial, without encasement in concrete, the material shall also be capable of withstanding continued loading that is likely to be encountered after installation.

353.120 Marking. Each length of HDPE shall be clearly and durably marked at least every 3 m (10 ft) as required in 110.21. The type of material shall also be included in the marking.

ARTICLE 354
Nonmetallic Underground Conduit with Conductors: Type NUCC

I. General

354.1 Scope. This article covers the use, installation, and construction specifications for nonmetallic underground conduit with conductors (NUCC).

354.2 Definition.

Nonmetallic Underground Conduit with Conductors (NUCC). A factory assembly of conductors or cables inside a nonmetallic, smooth wall conduit with a circular cross section.

354.6 Listing Requirements. NUCC and associated fittings shall be listed.

II. Installation

354.10 Uses Permitted. The use of NUCC and fittings shall be permitted in the following:

(1) For direct burial underground installation (For minimum cover requirements, see Table 300.5 and Table 300.50 under Rigid Nonmetallic Conduit.)
(2) Encased or embedded in concrete
(3) In cinder fill
(4) In underground locations subject to severe corrosive influences as covered in 300.6 and where subject to chemicals for which the assembly is specifically approved

354.12 Uses Not Permitted. NUCC shall not be used in the following:

(1) In exposed locations
(2) Inside buildings

Exception: The conductor or the cable portion of the assembly, where suitable, shall be permitted to extend within the building for termination purposes in accordance with 300.3.

(3) In hazardous (classified) locations except as permitted by 503.10(A), 504.20, 514.8, and 515.8, and in Class I, Division 2 locations as permitted in 501.10(B)(3)

354.20 Size.

(A) Minimum. NUCC smaller than metric designator 16 (trade size ½) shall not be used.

(B) Maximum. NUCC larger than metric designator 103 (trade size 4) shall not be used.

> FPN: See 300.1(C) for the metric designators and trade sizes. These are for identification purposes only and do not relate to actual dimensions.

354.22 Number of Conductors. The number of conductors or cables shall not exceed that permitted by the percentage fill in Table 1, Chapter 9.

354.24 Bends — How Made. Bends shall be manually made so that the conduit will not be damaged and the internal diameter of the conduit will not be effectively reduced. The radius of the curve of the centerline of such bends shall not be less than shown in Table 354.24.

Table 354.24 Minimum Bending Radius for Nonmetallic Underground Conduit with Conductors (NUCC)

Conduit Size		Minimum Bending Radius	
Metric Designator	Trade Size	mm	in.
16	$^1/_2$	250	10
21	$^3/_4$	300	12
27	1	350	14
35	1¼	450	18
41	1½	500	20
53	2	650	26
63	2½	900	36
78	3	1200	48
103	4	1500	60

354.26 Bends — Number in One Run. There shall not be more than the equivalent of four quarter bends (360 degrees total) between termination points.

354.28 Trimming. For termination, the conduit shall be trimmed away from the conductors or cables using an approved method that will not damage the conductor or cable insulation or jacket. All conduit ends shall be trimmed inside and out to remove rough edges.

354.46 Bushings. Where the NUCC enters a box, fitting, or other enclosure, a bushing or adapter shall be provided to protect the conductor or cable from abrasion unless the design of the box, fitting, or enclosure provides equivalent protection.

> FPN: See 300.4(F) for the protection of conductors size 4 AWG or larger.

354.48 Joints. All joints between conduit, fittings, and boxes shall be made by an approved method.

354.50 Conductor Terminations. All terminations between the conductors or cables and equipment shall be made by an approved method for that type of conductor or cable.

354.56 Splices and Taps. Splices and taps shall be made in junction boxes or other enclosures.

354.60 Grounding. Where equipment grounding is required, an assembly containing a separate equipment grounding conductor shall be used.

III. Construction Specifications

354.100 Construction.

(A) General. NUCC is an assembly that is provided in continuous lengths shipped in a coil, reel, or carton.

(B) Nonmetallic Underground Conduit. The nonmetallic underground conduit shall be listed and composed of a material that is resistant to moisture and corrosive agents. It shall also be capable of being supplied on reels without damage or distortion and shall be of sufficient strength to withstand abuse, such as impact or crushing, in handling and during installation without damage to conduit or conductors.

(C) Conductors and Cables. Conductors and cables used in NUCC shall be listed and shall comply with 310.8(C). Conductors of different systems shall be installed in accordance with 300.3(C).

(D) Conductor Fill. The maximum number of conductors or cables in NUCC shall not exceed that permitted by the percentage fill in Table 1, Chapter 9.

354.120 Marking. NUCC shall be clearly and durably marked at least every 3.05 m (10 ft) as required by 110.21. The type of conduit material shall also be included in the marking.

Identification of conductors or cables used in the assembly shall be provided on a tag attached to each end of the assembly or to the side of a reel. Enclosed conductors or cables shall be marked in accordance with 310.11.

ARTICLE 356
Liquidtight Flexible Nonmetallic Conduit: Type LFNC

I. General

356.1 Scope. This article covers the use, installation, and construction specifications for liquidtight flexible nonmetallic conduit (LFNC) and associated fittings.

356.2 Definition.

Liquidtight Flexible Nonmetallic Conduit (LFNC). A raceway of circular cross section of various types as follows:

(1) A smooth seamless inner core and cover bonded together and having one or more reinforcement layers between the core and covers, designated as Type LFNC-A

(2) A smooth inner surface with integral reinforcement within the conduit wall, designated as Type LFNC-B

(3) A corrugated internal and external surface without integral reinforcement within the conduit wall, designated as LFNC-C

LFNC is flame resistant and with fittings and is approved for the installation of electrical conductors.

FPN: FNMC is an alternative designation for LFNC.

356.6 Listing Requirements. LFNC and associated fittings shall be listed.

II. Installation

356.10 Uses Permitted. LFNC shall be permitted to be used in exposed or concealed locations for the following purposes:

FPN: Extreme cold may cause some types of nonmetallic conduits to become brittle and therefore more susceptible to damage from physical contact.

(1) Where flexibility is required for installation, operation, or maintenance

(2) Where protection of the contained conductors is required from vapors, liquids, or solids

(3) For outdoor locations where listed and marked as suitable for the purpose

(4) For direct burial where listed and marked for the purpose

(5) Type LFNC-B shall be permitted to be installed in lengths longer than 1.8 m (6 ft) where secured in accordance with 356.30

(6) Type LFNC-B as a listed manufactured prewired assembly, metric designator 16 through 27 (trade size ½ through 1) conduit

356.12 Uses Not Permitted. LFNC shall not be used as follows:

(1) Where subject to physical damage

(2) Where any combination of ambient and conductor temperatures is in excess of that for which the LFNC is approved

(3) In lengths longer than 1.8 m (6 ft), except as permitted by 356.10(5) or where a longer length is approved as essential for a required degree of flexibility

(4) Where the operating voltage of the contained conductors is in excess of 600 volts, nominal, except as permitted in 600.32(A)

(5) In any hazardous (classified) location other than as permitted in 501.10(B), 502.10(A) and (B), 503.10(A), and 504.20

356.20 Size.

(A) Minimum. LFNC smaller than metric designator 16 (trade size ½) shall not be used unless permitted in 356.20(A)(1) through (A)(3) for metric designator 12 (trade size ⅜).

(1) For enclosing the leads of motors as permitted in 430.245(B)

(2) In lengths not exceeding 1.8 m (6 ft) as part of a listed assembly for tap connections to luminaires (lighting fixtures) as required in 410.67(C), or for utilization equipment

(3) For electric sign conductors in accordance with 600.32(A)

(B) Maximum. LFNC larger than metric designator 103 (trade size 4) shall not be used.

FPN: See 300.1(C) for the metric designators and trade sizes. These are for identification purposes only and do not relate to actual dimensions.

356.22 Number of Conductors. The number of conductors shall not exceed that permitted by the percentage fill specified in Table 1, Chapter 9.

Cables shall be permitted to be installed where such use is not prohibited by the respective cable articles. The number of cables shall not exceed the allowable percentage fill specified in Table 1, Chapter 9.

356.24 Bends — How Made. Bends in conduit shall be so made that the conduit is not damaged and the internal diameter of the conduit is not effectively reduced. Bends shall be permitted to be made manually without auxiliary equipment. The radius of the curve to the centerline of any bend shall not be less than shown in Table 2, Chapter 9 using the column "Other Bends."

356.26 Bends — Number in One Run. There shall not be more than the equivalent of four quarter bends (360 degrees total) between pull points, for example, conduit bodies and boxes.

356.28 Trimming. All cut ends of conduit shall be trimmed inside and outside to remove rough edges.

356.30 Securing and Supporting. Type LFNC-B shall be securely fastened and supported in accordance with one of the following:

(1) Where installed in lengths exceeding 1.8 m (6 ft), the conduit shall be securely fastened at intervals not exceeding 900 mm (3 ft) and within 300 mm (12 in.) on each side of every outlet box, junction box, cabinet, or fitting.

(2) Securing or supporting of the conduit shall not be required where it is fished, installed in lengths not exceeding 900 mm (3 ft) at terminals where flexibility is required, or installed in lengths not exceeding 1.8 m (6 ft) from a luminaire (fixture) terminal connection for tap conductors to luminaires (lighting fixtures) permitted in 410.67(C).

(3) Horizontal runs of LFNC supported by openings through framing members at intervals not exceeding 900 mm (3 ft) and securely fastened within 300 mm (12 in.) of termination points shall be permitted.

(4) Securing or supporting of LFNC-B shall not be required where installed in lengths not exceeding 1.8 m (6 ft) from the last point where the raceway is securely fastened for connections within an accessible ceiling to luminaire(s) [lighting fixture(s)] or other equipment.

356.42 Couplings and Connectors. Only fittings listed for use with LFNC shall be used. Angle connectors shall not be used for concealed raceway installations. Straight LFNC fittings are permitted for direct burial or encasement in concrete.

356.56 Splices and Taps. Splices and taps shall be made in accordance with 300.15.

356.60 Grounding and Bonding. Where used to connect equipment where flexibility is required, an equipment grounding conductor shall be installed.

Where required or installed, equipment grounding conductors shall be installed in accordance with 250.134(B).

Where required or installed, equipment bonding jumpers shall be installed in accordance with 250.102.

III. Construction Specifications

356.100 Construction. LFNC-B as a prewired manufactured assembly shall be provided in continuous lengths capable of being shipped in a coil, reel, or carton without damage.

356.120 Marking. LFNC shall be marked at least every 600 mm (2 ft) in accordance with 110.21. The marking shall include a type designation in accordance with 356.2 and the trade size. Conduit that is intended for outdoor use or direct burial shall be marked.

The type, size, and quantity of conductors used in prewired manufactured assemblies shall be identified by means of a printed tag or label attached to each end of the manufactured assembly and either the carton, coil, or reel. The enclosed conductors shall be marked in accordance with 310.11.

ARTICLE 358
Electrical Metallic Tubing: Type EMT

I. General

358.1 Scope. This article covers the use, installation, and construction specifications for electrical metallic tubing (EMT) and associated fittings.

358.2 Definition.

Electrical Metallic Tubing (EMT). An unthreaded thin-wall raceway of circular cross section designed for the physical protection and routing of conductors and cables and for use as an equipment grounding conductor when installed utilizing appropriate fittings. EMT is generally made of steel (ferrous) with protective coatings or aluminum (nonferrous).

358.6 Listing Requirements. EMT, factory elbows, and associated fittings shall be listed.

II. Installation

358.10 Uses Permitted.

(A) Exposed and Concealed. The use of EMT shall be permitted for both exposed and concealed work.

(B) Corrosion Protection. Ferrous or nonferrous EMT, elbows, couplings, and fittings shall be permitted to be installed in concrete, in direct contact with the earth, or in areas subject to severe corrosive influences where protected by corrosion protection and judged suitable for the condition.

(C) Wet Locations. All supports, bolts, straps, screws, and so forth shall be of corrosion-resistant materials or protected against corrosion by corrosion-resistant materials.

FPN: See 300.6 for protection against corrosion.

358.12 Uses Not Permitted. EMT shall not be used under the following conditions:

(1) Where, during installation or afterward, it will be subject to severe physical damage

(2) Where protected from corrosion solely by enamel

(3) In cinder concrete or cinder fill where subject to permanent moisture unless protected on all sides by a layer of noncinder concrete at least 50 mm (2 in.) thick or unless the tubing is at least 450 mm (18 in.) under the fill

(4) In any hazardous (classified) location except as permitted by 502.10, 503.10, and 504.20

(5) For the support of luminaires (fixtures) or other equipment except conduit bodies no larger than the largest trade size of the tubing

(6) Where practicable, dissimilar metals in contact anywhere in the system shall be avoided to eliminate the possibility of galvanic action

Exception: Aluminum fittings and enclosures shall be permitted to be used with steel EMT where not subject to severe corrosive influences.

358.20 Size.

(A) Minimum. EMT smaller than metric designator 16 (trade size ½) shall not be used.

Exception: For enclosing the leads of motors as permitted in 430.245(B).

(B) Maximum. The maximum size of EMT shall be metric designator 103 (trade size 4).

FPN: See 300.1(C) for the metric designators and trade sizes. These are for identification purposes only and do not relate to actual dimensions.

358.22 Number of Conductors. The number of conductors shall not exceed that permitted by the percentage fill specified in Table 1, Chapter 9.

Cables shall be permitted to be installed where such use is not prohibited by the respective cable articles. The number of cables shall not exceed the allowable percentage fill specified in Table 1, Chapter 9.

358.24 Bends — How Made. Bends shall be made so that the tubing is not damaged and the internal diameter of the tubing is not effectively reduced. The radius of the curve of any field bend to the centerline of the tubing shall not be less than shown in Table 2, Chapter 9 for one-shot and full shoe benders.

358.26 Bends — Number in One Run. There shall not be more than the equivalent of four quarter bends (360 degrees total) between pull points, for example, conduit bodies and boxes.

358.28 Reaming and Threading.

(A) Reaming. All cut ends of EMT shall be reamed or otherwise finished to remove rough edges.

(B) Threading. EMT shall not be threaded.

Exception: EMT with factory threaded integral couplings complying with 358.100.

358.30 Securing and Supporting. EMT shall be installed as a complete system in accordance with 300.18 and shall be securely fastened in place and supported in accordance with 358.30(A) and (B).

(A) Securely Fastened. EMT shall be securely fastened in place at least every 3 m (10 ft). In addition, each EMT run between termination points shall be securely fastened within 900 mm (3 ft) of each outlet box, junction box, device box, cabinet, conduit body, or other tubing termination.

Exception No. 1: Fastening of unbroken lengths shall be permitted to be increased to a distance of 1.5 m (5 ft) where structural members do not readily permit fastening within 900 mm (3 ft).

Exception No. 2: For concealed work in finished buildings or prefinished wall panels where such securing is impracticable, unbroken lengths (without coupling) of EMT shall be permitted to be fished.

(B) Supports. Horizontal runs of EMT supported by openings through framing members at intervals not greater than 3 m (10 ft) and securely fastened within 900 mm (3 ft) of termination points shall be permitted.

358.42 Couplings and Connectors. Couplings and connectors used with EMT shall be made up tight. Where buried in masonry or concrete, they shall be concretetight type. Where installed in wet locations, they shall comply with 314.15(A).

358.56 Splices and Taps. Splices and taps shall be made in accordance with 300.15.

358.60 Grounding. EMT shall be permitted as an equipment grounding conductor.

III. Construction Specifications

358.100 Construction. Factory-threaded integral couplings shall be permitted. Where EMT with a threaded integral coupling is used, threads for both the tubing and coupling shall be factory-made. The coupling and EMT threads shall be designed so as to prevent bending of the tubing at any part of the thread.

358.120 Marking. EMT shall be clearly and durably marked at least every 3 m (10 ft) as required in the first sentence of 110.21.

ARTICLE 360
Flexible Metallic Tubing: Type FMT

I. General

360.1 Scope. This article covers the use, installation, and construction specifications for flexible metallic tubing (FMT) and associated fittings.

360.2 Definition.

Flexible Metallic Tubing (FMT). A raceway that is circular in cross section, flexible, metallic, and liquidtight without a nonmetallic jacket.

360.6 Listing Requirements. FMT and associated fittings shall be listed.

II. Installation

360.10 Uses Permitted. FMT shall be permitted to be used for branch circuits as follows:

(1) In dry locations

(2) Where concealed

(3) In accessible locations

(4) For system voltages of 1000 volts maximum

360.12 Uses Not Permitted. FMT shall not be used as follows:

(1) In hoistways

(2) In storage battery rooms

(3) In hazardous (classified) locations unless otherwise permitted under other articles in this *Code*

(4) Under ground for direct earth burial, or embedded in poured concrete or aggregate

(5) Where subject to physical damage

(6) In lengths over 1.8 m (6 ft)

360.20 Size.

(A) Minimum. FMT smaller than metric designator 16 (trade size ½) shall not be used.

Exception No. 1: FMT of metric designator 12 (trade size ⅜) shall be permitted to be installed in accordance with 300.22(B) and (C).

Exception No. 2: FMT of metric designator 12 (trade size ⅜) shall be permitted in lengths not in excess of 1.8 m (6 ft) as part of an approved assembly or for luminaires (lighting fixtures). See 410.67(C).

(B) Maximum. The maximum size of FMT shall be metric designator 21 (trade size ¾).

FPN: See 300.1(C) for the metric designators and trade sizes. These are for identification purposes only and do not relate to actual dimensions.

360.22 Number of Conductors.

(A) FMT — Metric Designators 16 and 21 (Trade Sizes ½ and ¾). The number of conductors in metric designators 16 (trade size ½) and 21 (trade size ¾) shall not exceed that permitted by the percentage fill specified in Table 1, Chapter 9.

Cables shall be permitted to be installed where such use is not prohibited by the respective cable articles. The number of cables shall not exceed the allowable percentage fill specified in Table 1, Chapter 9.

(B) FMT — Metric Designator 12 (Trade Size ⅜). The number of conductors in metric designator 12 (trade size ⅜) shall not exceed that permitted in Table 348.22.

360.24 Bends.

(A) Infrequent Flexing Use. Where FMT may be infrequently flexed in service after installation, the radii of bends measured to the inside of the bend shall not be less than specified in Table 360.24(A).

Table 360.24(A) Minimum Radii for Flexing Use

Metric Designator	Trade Size	Minimum Radii for Flexing Use	
		mm	in.
12	⅜	25.4	10
16	½	317.5	12½
21	¾	444.5	17½

(B) Fixed Bends. Where FMT is bent for installation purposes and is not flexed or bent as required by use after installation, the radii of bends measured to the inside of the bend shall not be less than specified in Table 360.24(B).

Table 360.24(B) Minimum Radii for Fixed Bends

Metric Designator	Trade Size	Minimum Radii for Fixed Bends	
		mm	in.
12	⅜	88.9	3½
16	½	101.6	4
21	¾	127.0	5

360.40 Boxes and Fittings. Fittings shall effectively close any openings in the connection.

360.56 Splices and Taps. Splices and taps shall be made in accordance with 300.15.

360.60 Grounding. FMT shall be permitted as an equipment grounding conductor where installed in accordance with 250.118(7).

III. Construction Specifications

360.120 Marking. FMT shall be marked according to 110.21.

ARTICLE 362
Electrical Nonmetallic Tubing: Type ENT

I. General

362.1 Scope. This article covers the use, installation, and construction specifications for electrical nonmetallic tubing (ENT) and associated fittings.

362.2 Definition.

Electrical Nonmetallic Tubing (ENT). A nonmetallic pliable corrugated raceway of circular cross section with integral or associated couplings, connectors, and fittings for the installation of electric conductors. ENT is composed of a material that is resistant to moisture and chemical atmospheres and is flame retardant.

A pliable raceway is a raceway that can be bent by hand with a reasonable force but without other assistance.

362.6 Listing Requirements. ENT and associated fittings shall be listed.

II. Installation

362.10 Uses Permitted. For the purpose of this article, the first floor of a building shall be that floor that has 50 percent or more of the exterior wall surface area level with or above finished grade. One additional level that is the first level and not designed for human habitation and used only for vehicle parking, storage, or similar use shall be permitted. The use of ENT and fittings shall be permitted in the following:

(1) In any building not exceeding three floors above grade as follows:

     a. For exposed work, where not prohibited by 362.12
     b. Concealed within walls, floors, and ceilings

(2) In any building exceeding three floors above grade, ENT shall be concealed within walls, floors, and ceilings where the walls, floors, and ceilings provide a thermal barrier of material that has at least a 15-minute finish rating as identified in listings of fire-rated assemblies. The 15-minute-finish-rated thermal barrier shall be permitted to be used for combustible or noncombustible walls, floors, and ceilings.

Exception to (2): Where a fire sprinkler system(s) is installed in accordance with NFPA 13-2002, Standard for the Installation of Sprinkler Systems, on all floors, ENT shall be permitted to be used within walls, floors, and ceilings, exposed or concealed, in buildings exceeding three floors above grade.

FPN: A finish rating is established for assemblies containing combustible (wood) supports. The finish rating is defined as the time at which the wood stud or wood joist reaches an average temperature rise of 121°C (250°F) or an individual temperature of 163°C (325°F) as measured on the plane of the wood nearest the fire. A finish rating is not intended to represent a rating for a membrane ceiling.

(3) In locations subject to severe corrosive influences as covered in 300.6 and where subject to chemicals for which the materials are specifically approved.

(4) In concealed, dry, and damp locations not prohibited by 362.12.

(5) Above suspended ceilings where the suspended ceilings provide a thermal barrier of material that has at least a 15-minute finish rating as identified in listings of fire-rated assemblies, except as permitted in 362.10(1)(a).

Exception to (5): ENT shall be permitted to be used above suspended ceilings in buildings exceeding three floors above grade where the building is protected throughout by a fire sprinkler system installed in accordance with NFPA 13-2002, Standard for the Installation of Sprinkler Systems.

(6) Encased in poured concrete, or embedded in a concrete slab on grade where ENT is placed on sand or approved screenings, provided fittings identified for this purpose are used for connections.

(7) For wet locations indoors as permitted in this section or in a concrete slab on or below grade, with fittings listed for the purpose.

(8) Metric designator 16 through 27 (trade size ½ through 1) as listed manufactured prewired assembly.

FPN: Extreme cold may cause some types of nonmetallic conduits to become brittle and therefore more susceptible to damage from physical contact.

362.12 Uses Not Permitted. ENT shall not be used in the following:

(1) In hazardous (classified) locations, except as permitted by 504.20 and 505.15(A)(1)

(2) For the support of luminaires (fixtures) and other equipment

(3) Where subject to ambient temperatures in excess of 50°C (122°F) unless listed otherwise

(4) For conductors or cables operating at a temperature higher than the ENT listed temperature rating

Exception to (4): Conductors or cables rated at a temperature higher than the ENT listed temperature rating shall be permitted to be installed in ENT, provided they are not operated at a temperature higher than the ENT listed temperature rating.

(5) For direct earth burial

(6) Where the voltage is over 600 volts

(7) In exposed locations, except as permitted by 362.10(1), 362.10(5), and 362.10(7)

(8) In theaters and similar locations, except as provided in 518.4 and 520.5

(9) Where exposed to the direct rays of the sun, unless identified as sunlight resistant

(10) Where subject to physical damage

362.20 Size.

(A) Minimum. ENT smaller than metric designator 16 (trade size ½) shall not be used.

(B) Maximum. ENT larger than metric designator 53 (trade size 2) shall not be used.

> FPN: See 300.1(C) for the metric designators and trade sizes. These are for identification purposes only and do not relate to actual dimensions.

362.22 Number of Conductors. The number of conductors shall not exceed that permitted by the percentage fill in Table 1, Chapter 9.

Cables shall be permitted to be installed where such use is not prohibited by the respective cable articles. The number of cables shall not exceed the allowable percentage fill specified in Table 1, Chapter 9.

362.24 Bends — How Made. Bends shall be so made that the tubing will not be damaged and the internal diameter of the tubing will not be effectively reduced. Bends shall be permitted to be made manually without auxiliary equipment, and the radius of the curve to the centerline of such bends shall not be less than shown in Table 2, Chapter 9 using the column "Other Bends."

362.26 Bends — Number in One Run. There shall not be more than the equivalent of four quarter bends (360 degrees total) between pull points, for example, conduit bodies and boxes.

362.28 Trimming. All cut ends shall be trimmed inside and outside to remove rough edges.

362.30 Securing and Supporting. ENT shall be installed as a complete system in accordance with 300.18 and shall be securely fastened in place and supported in accordance with 362.30(A) and (B).

(A) Securely Fastened. ENT shall be securely fastened at intervals not exceeding 900 mm (3 ft). In addition, ENT shall be securely fastened in place within 900 mm (3 ft) of each outlet box, device box, junction box, cabinet, or fitting where it terminates.

Exception No. 1: Lengths not exceeding a distance of 1.8 m (6 ft) from a luminaire (fixture) terminal connection for tap connections to lighting luminaires (fixtures) shall be permitted without being secured.

Exception No. 2: Lengths not exceeding 1.8 m (6 ft) from the last point where the raceway is securely fastened for connections within an accessible ceiling to luminaire(s) [lighting fixture(s)] or other equipment.

(B) Supports. Horizontal runs of ENT supported by openings in framing members at intervals not exceeding 900 mm (3 ft) and securely fastened within 900 mm (3 ft) of termination points shall be permitted.

362.46 Bushings. Where a tubing enters a box, fitting, or other enclosure, a bushing or adapter shall be provided to protect the wire from abrasion unless the box, fitting, or enclosure design provides equivalent protection.

> FPN: See 300.4(F) for the protection of conductors size 4 AWG or larger.

362.48 Joints. All joints between lengths of tubing and between tubing and couplings, fittings, and boxes shall be by an approved method.

362.56 Splices and Taps. Splices and taps shall be made only in accordance with 300.15.

> FPN: See Article 314 for rules on the installation and use of boxes and conduit bodies.

362.60 Grounding. Where equipment grounding is required, a separate equipment grounding conductor shall be installed in the raceway.

III. Construction Specifications

362.100 Construction. ENT shall be made of material that does not exceed the ignitibility, flammability, smoke generation, and toxicity characteristics of rigid (nonplasticized) polyvinyl chloride.

ENT, as a prewired manufactured assembly, shall be provided in continuous lengths capable of being shipped in a coil, reel, or carton without damage.

362.120 Marking. ENT shall be clearly and durably marked at least every 3 m (10 ft) as required in the first sentence of 110.21. The type of material shall also be included in the marking. Marking for limited smoke shall be permitted on the tubing that has limited smoke-producing characteristics.

The type, size, and quantity of conductors used in prewired manufactured assemblies shall be identified by means of a printed tag or label attached to each end of the manufactured assembly and either the carton, coil, or reel. The enclosed conductors shall be marked in accordance with 310.11.

ARTICLE 366
Auxiliary Gutters

I. General

366.1 Scope. This article covers the use, installation, and construction requirements of metal auxiliary gutters and nonmetallic auxiliary gutters and associated fittings.

366.2 Definitions.

Metallic Auxiliary Gutters. Sheet metal enclosures with hinged or removable covers for housing and protecting electric wires, cable, and busbars in which conductors are laid in place after the wireway has been installed as a complete system.

Nonmetallic Auxiliary Gutters. Flame retardant, nonmetallic enclosures with removable covers for housing and protecting electric wires, cable, and busbars in which conductors are laid in place after the wireway has been installed as a complete system.

366.6 Listing Requirements.

(A) Outdoors. Nonmetallic auxiliary gutters installed outdoors shall comply with the following:

(1) Be listed as suitable for exposure to sunlight

(2) Be listed as suitable for use in wet locations

(3) Be listed for maximum ambient temperature of the installation

(B) Indoors. Nonmetallic auxiliary gutters installed indoors shall be listed for the maximum ambient temperature of the installation.

II. Installation

366.10 Uses Permitted. Auxiliary gutters shall be permitted to supplement wiring spaces at meter centers, distribution centers, switchboards, and similar points of wiring systems and may enclose conductors or busbars.

(A) Sheet Metal Auxiliary Gutters.

(1) Indoor and Outdoor Use. Sheet metal auxiliary gutters shall be permitted for indoor and outdoor use.

(2) Wet Locations. Sheet metal auxiliary gutters installed in wet locations shall be suitable for such locations.

(B) Nonmetallic Auxiliary Gutters. Nonmetallic auxiliary gutters shall be listed for the maximum ambient temperature of the installation and marked for the installed conductor insulation temperature rating.

(1) Outdoors. Nonmetallic auxiliary gutters shall be permitted to be installed outdoors where listed and marked as suitable for the purpose.

> FPN: Extreme cold may cause nonmetallic auxiliary gutter to become brittle and therefore more susceptible to damage from physical contact.

(2) Indoors. Nonmetallic auxiliary gutters shall be permitted to be installed indoors.

366.12 Uses Not Permitted. Auxiliary gutters shall not be used under the following conditions:

(1) To enclose switches, overcurrent devices, appliances, or other similar equipment.

(2) To extend a greater distance than 9 m (30 ft) beyond the equipment that it supplements.

Exception: As permitted in 620.35 for elevators, an auxiliary gutter shall be permitted to extend a distance greater than 9 m (30 ft) beyond the equipment it supplements.

> FPN: For wireways, see Articles 376 and 378. For busways, see Article 368.

366.22 Number of Conductors.

(A) Sheet Metal Auxiliary Gutters. The sum of the cross-sectional areas of all contained conductors at any cross section of a sheet metal auxiliary gutter shall not exceed 20 percent of the interior cross-sectional area of the sheet metal auxiliary gutter. The derating factors in 310.15(B)(2)(a) shall be applied only where the number of current-carrying conductors, including neutral conductors classified as current-carrying under the provisions of 310.15(B)(4), exceeds 30. Conductors for signaling circuits or controller conductors between a motor and its starter and used only for starting duty shall not be considered as current-carrying conductors.

(B) Nonmetallic Auxiliary Gutters. The sum of cross-sectional areas of all contained conductors at any cross section of the nonmetallic auxiliary gutter shall not exceed 20 percent of the interior cross-sectional area of the nonmetallic auxiliary gutter.

366.23 Ampacity of Conductors.

(A) Sheet Metal Auxiliary Gutters. Where the number of current-carrying conductors contained in the sheet metal auxiliary gutter is 30 or less, the correction factors specified in 310.15(B)(2)(a) shall not apply. The current carried continuously in bare copper bars in sheet metal auxiliary gutters shall not exceed 1.55 amperes/mm^2 (1000 amperes/in.^{2}) of cross section of the conductor. For aluminum bars, the current carried continuously shall not exceed 1.09 amperes/mm^2 (700 amperes/in.^{2}) of cross section of the conductor.

(B) Nonmetallic Auxiliary Gutters. The derating factors specified in 310.15(B)(2)(a) shall be applicable to the current-carrying conductors in the nonmetallic auxiliary gutter.

366.30 Securing and Supporting.

(A) Sheet Metal Auxiliary Gutters. Sheet metal auxiliary gutters shall be supported throughout their entire length at intervals not exceeding 1.5 m (5 ft).

(B) Nonmetallic Auxiliary Gutters. Nonmetallic auxiliary gutters shall be supported at intervals not to exceed 900 mm (3 ft) and at each end or joint, unless listed for other support intervals. In no case shall the distance between supports exceed 3 m (10 ft).

366.44 Expansion Fittings. Expansion fittings shall be installed where expected length change, due to expansion and contraction due to temperature change, is more than 6 mm (0.25 in.).

366.56 Splices and Taps. Splices and taps shall comply with 366.56(A) through (D).

(A) Within Gutters. Splices or taps shall be permitted within gutters where they are accessible by means of removable covers or doors. The conductors, including splices and taps, shall not fill the gutter to more than 75 percent of its area.

(B) Bare Conductors. Taps from bare conductors shall leave the gutter opposite their terminal connections, and conductors shall not be brought in contact with uninsulated current-carrying parts of different potential.

(C) Suitably Identified. All taps shall be suitably identified at the gutter as to the circuit or equipment that they supply.

(D) Overcurrent Protection. Tap connections from conductors in auxiliary gutters shall be provided with overcurrent protection as required in 240.21.

366.58 Insulated Conductors.

(A) Deflected Insulated Conductors. Where insulated conductors are deflected within an auxiliary gutter, either at the ends or where conduits, fittings, or other raceways or cables enter or leave the gutter, or where the direction of the gutter is deflected greater than 30 degrees, dimensions corresponding to one wire per terminal in Table 312.6(A) shall apply.

(B) Auxiliary Gutters Used as Pullboxes. Where insulated conductors 4 AWG or larger are pulled through an auxiliary gutter, the distance between raceway and cable entries enclosing the same conductor shall not be less

than that required in 314.28(A)(1) for straight pulls and 314.28(A)(2) for angle pulls.

366.60 Grounding. Metal auxiliary gutters shall be grounded.

III. Construction Specifications

366.100 Construction.

(A) Electrical and Mechanical Continuity. Gutters shall be constructed and installed so that adequate electrical and mechanical continuity of the complete system is secured.

(B) Substantial Construction. Gutters shall be of substantial construction and shall provide a complete enclosure for the contained conductors. All surfaces, both interior and exterior, shall be suitably protected from corrosion. Corner joints shall be made tight, and where the assembly is held together by rivets, bolts, or screws, such fasteners shall be spaced not more than 300 mm (12 in.) apart.

(C) Smooth Rounded Edges. Suitable bushings, shields, or fittings having smooth, rounded edges shall be provided where conductors pass between gutters, through partitions, around bends, between gutters and cabinets or junction boxes, and at other locations where necessary to prevent abrasion of the insulation of the conductors.

(D) Covers. Covers shall be securely fastened to the gutter.

(E) Clearance of Bare Live Parts. Bare conductors shall be securely and rigidly supported so that the minimum clearance between bare current-carrying metal parts of different potential mounted on the same surface will not be less than 50 mm (2 in.), nor less than 25 mm (1 in.) for parts that are held free in the air. A clearance not less than 25 mm (1 in.) shall be secured between bare current-carrying metal parts and any metal surface. Adequate provisions shall be made for the expansion and contraction of busbars.

366.120 Marking.

(A) Outdoors. Nonmetallic auxiliary gutters installed outdoors shall have the following markings:
(1) Suitable for exposure to sunlight
(2) Suitable for use in wet locations
(3) Installed conductor insulation temperature rating

(B) Indoors. Nonmetallic auxiliary gutters installed indoors shall have the following markings:
(1) Installed conductor insulation temperature rating

ARTICLE 368
Busways

I. General Requirements

368.1 Scope. This article covers service-entrance, feeder, and branch-circuit busways and associated fittings.

368.2 Definition.

Busway. A grounded metal enclosure containing factory-mounted, bare or insulated conductors, which are usually copper or aluminum bars, rods, or tubes.

FPN: For cablebus, refer to Article 370.

II. Installation

368.10 Uses Permitted. Busways shall be permitted to be installed where they are located in accordance with 368.10(A) through (C).

(A) Exposed. Busways shall be permitted to be located in the open where visible, except as permitted in 368.10(C).

(B) Concealed. Busways shall be permitted to be installed behind access panels, provided the busways are totally enclosed, of nonventilating-type construction, and installed so that the joints between sections and at fittings are accessible for maintenance purposes. Where installed behind access panels, means of access shall be provided, and either of the following conditions shall be met:

(1) The space behind the access panels shall not be used for air-handling purposes.
(2) Where the space behind the access panels is used for environmental air, other than ducts and plenums, there shall be no provisions for plug-in connections, and the conductors shall be insulated.

(C) Through Walls and Floors. Busways shall be permitted to be installed through walls or floors in accordance with (C)(1) and (C)(2).

(1) Walls. Unbroken lengths of busway shall be permitted to be extended through dry walls.

(2) Floors. Floor penetrations shall comply with (a) and (b):

(a) Busways shall be permitted to be extended vertically through dry floors if totally enclosed (unventilated) where passing through and for a minimum distance of 1.8 m (6 ft) above the floor to provide adequate protection from physical damage.

(b) In other than industrial establishments, where a vertical riser penetrates two or more dry floors, a minimum 100-mm (4-in.) high curb shall be installed around all floor openings for riser busways to prevent liquids from entering the opening. The curb shall be installed within 300 mm (12 in.) of the floor opening. Electrical equipment shall be located so that it will not be damaged by liquids that are retained by the curb.

FPN: See 300.21 for information concerning the spread of fire or products of combustion.

368.12 Uses Not Permitted.

(A) Physical Damage. Busways shall not be installed where subject to severe physical damage or corrosive vapors.

(B) Hoistways. Busways shall not be installed in hoistways.

(C) Hazardous Locations. Busways shall not be installed in any hazardous (classified) location, unless specifically approved for such use.

FPN: See 501.10(B).

(D) Wet Locations. Busways shall not be installed outdoors or in wet or damp locations unless identified for such use.

(E) Working Platform. Lighting busway and trolley busway shall not be installed less than 2.5 m (8 ft) above the floor or working platform unless provided with a cover identified for the purpose.

368.17 Overcurrent Protection. Overcurrent protection shall be provided in accordance with 368.17(A) through (D).

(A) Rating of Overcurrent Protection — Feeders. A busway shall be protected against overcurrent in accordance with the allowable current rating of the busway.

Exception No. 1: The applicable provisions of 240.4 shall be permitted.

Exception No. 2: Where used as transformer secondary ties, the provisions of 450.6(A)(3) shall be permitted.

(B) Reduction in Ampacity Size of Busway. Overcurrent protection shall be required where busways are reduced in ampacity.

Exception: For industrial establishments only, omission of overcurrent protection shall be permitted at points where busways are reduced in ampacity, provided that the length of the busway having the smaller ampacity does not exceed 15 m (50 ft) and has an ampacity at least equal to one-third the rating or setting of the overcurrent device next back on the line, and provided that such busway is free from contact with combustible material.

(C) Feeder or Branch Circuits. Where a busway is used as a feeder, devices or plug-in connections for tapping off feeder or branch circuits from the busway shall contain the overcurrent devices required for the protection of the feeder or branch circuits. The plug-in device shall consist of an externally operable circuit breaker or an externally operable fusible switch. Where such devices are mounted out of reach and contain disconnecting means, suitable means such as ropes, chains, or sticks shall be provided for operating the disconnecting means from the floor.

Exception No. 1: As permitted in 240.21.

Exception No. 2: For fixed or semifixed luminaires (lighting fixtures), where the branch-circuit overcurrent device is part of the luminaire (fixture) cord plug on cord-connected luminaires (fixtures).

Exception No. 3: Where luminaires (fixtures) without cords are plugged directly into the busway and the overcurrent device is mounted on the luminaire (fixture).

(D) Rating of Overcurrent Protection — Branch Circuits. A busway used as a branch circuit shall be protected against overcurrent in accordance with 210.20.

368.30 Support. Busways shall be securely supported at intervals not exceeding 1.5 m (5 ft) unless otherwise designed and marked.

368.56 Branches from Busways. Branches from busways shall be permitted to be made in accordance with 368.56(A), (B), and (C).

(A) General. Branches from busways shall be permitted to use any of the following wiring methods:

(1) Type AC armored cable
(2) Type MC metal-clad cable
(3) Type MI mineral-insulated, metal-sheathed cable
(4) Type IMC intermediate metal conduit
(5) Type RMC rigid metal conduit
(6) Type FMC flexible metal conduit
(7) Type LFMC liquidtight flexible metal conduit
(8) Type RNC rigid nonmetallic conduit
(9) Type LFNC liquidtight flexible nonmetal conduit
(10) Type EMT electrical metallic tubing
(11) Type ENT electrical nonmetallic tubing
(12) Busways
(13) Strut-type channel raceway
(14) Surface metal raceways
(15) Surface nonmetallic raceways

Where a separate equipment grounding conductor is used, connection of the equipment grounding conductor to the busway shall comply with 250.8 and 250.12.

(B) Cord and Cable Assemblies. Suitable cord and cable assemblies approved for extra-hard usage or hard usage, and listed bus drop cable shall be permitted as branches from busways for the connection of portable equipment or the connection of stationary equipment to facilitate their interchange in accordance with 400.7 and 400.8 and the following conditions:

(1) The cord or cable shall be attached to the building by an approved means.
(2) The length of the cord or cable from a busway plug-in device to a suitable tension take-up support device shall not exceed 1.8 m (6 ft).
(3) The cord and cable shall be installed as a vertical riser from the tension take-up support device to the equipment served.
(4) Strain relief cable grips shall be provided for the cord or cable at the busway plug-in device and equipment terminations.

Exception to (B)(2): In industrial establishments only, where the conditions of maintenance and supervision ensure that only qualified persons service the installation, lengths exceeding 1.8 m (6 ft) shall be permitted between the busway plug-in device and the tension take-up support device where the cord or cable is supported at intervals not exceeding 2.5 m (8 ft).

(C) Branches from Trolley-Type Busways. Suitable cord and cable assemblies approved for extra-hard usage or hard usage and listed bus drop cable shall be permitted as branches from trolley-type busways for the connection of movable equipment in accordance with 400.7 and 400.8.

368.58 Dead Ends. A dead end of a busway shall be closed.

368.60 Grounding. Busway shall be grounded.

III. Construction

368.120 Marking. Busways shall be marked with the voltage and current rating for which they are designed, and with the manufacturer's name or trademark in such a manner as to be visible after installation.

IV. Requirements for Over 600 Volts, Nominal

368.214 Adjacent and Supporting Structures. Metal-enclosed busways shall be installed so that temperature rise from induced circulating currents in any adjacent metallic parts will not be hazardous to personnel or constitute a fire hazard.

368.234 Barriers and Seals.

(A) Vapor Seals. Busway runs that have sections located both inside and outside of buildings shall have a vapor seal at the building wall to prevent interchange of air between indoor and outdoor sections.

Exception: Vapor seals shall not be required in forced-cooled bus.

(B) Fire Barriers. Fire barriers shall be provided where fire walls, floors, or ceilings are penetrated.

FPN: See 300.21 for information concerning the spread of fire or products of combustion.

368.236 Drain Facilities.
Drain plugs, filter drains, or similar methods shall be provided to remove condensed moisture from low points in busway run.

368.237 Ventilated Bus Enclosures.
Ventilated busway enclosures shall be installed in accordance with Article 110, Part III, and 490.24.

368.238 Terminations and Connections.
Where bus enclosures terminate at machines cooled by flammable gas, seal-off bushings, baffles, or other means shall be provided to prevent accumulation of flammable gas in the busway enclosures.

All conductor termination and connection hardware shall be accessible for installation, connection, and maintenance.

368.239 Switches.
Switching devices or disconnecting links provided in the busway run shall have the same momentary rating as the busway. Disconnecting links shall be plainly marked to be removable only when bus is de-energized. Switching devices that are not load-break shall be interlocked to prevent operation under load, and disconnecting link enclosures shall be interlocked to prevent access to energized parts.

368.240 Wiring 600 Volts or Less, Nominal.
Secondary control devices and wiring that are provided as part of the metal-enclosed bus run shall be insulated by fire-retardant barriers from all primary circuit elements with the exception of short lengths of wire, such as at instrument transformer terminals.

368.244 Expansion Fittings.
Flexible or expansion connections shall be provided in long, straight runs of bus to allow for temperature expansion or contraction, or where the busway run crosses building vibration insulation joints.

368.258 Neutral.
Neutral bus, where required, shall be sized to carry all neutral load current, including harmonic currents, and shall have adequate momentary and short-circuit rating consistent with system requirements.

368.260 Grounding.
Metal-enclosed busway shall be grounded.

368.320 Marking.
Each busway run shall be provided with a permanent nameplate on which the following information shall be provided:

(1) Rated voltage.
(2) Rated continuous current; if bus is forced-cooled, both the normal forced-cooled rating and the self-cooled (not forced-cooled) rating for the same temperature rise shall be given.
(3) Rated frequency.
(4) Rated impulse withstand voltage.
(5) Rated 60-Hz withstand voltage (dry).
(6) Rated momentary current.
(7) Manufacturer's name or trademark.

FPN: See ANSI C37.23-1987 (R1991), *Guide for Metal-Enclosed Bus and Calculating Losses in Isolated-Phase Bus*, for construction and testing requirements for metal-enclosed buses.

ARTICLE 370
Cablebus

370.1 Scope. This article covers the use and installation requirements of cablebus and associated fittings.

370.2 Definition.

Cablebus. An assembly of insulated conductors with fittings and conductor terminations in a completely enclosed, ventilated protective metal housing. Cablebus is ordinarily assembled at the point of installation from the components furnished or specified by the manufacturer in accordance with instructions for the specific job. This assembly is designed to carry fault current and to withstand the magnetic forces of such current.

370.3 Use. Approved cablebus shall be permitted at any voltage or current for which spaced conductors are rated and shall be installed only for exposed work, except as permitted in 370.6. Cablebus installed outdoors or in corrosive, wet, or damp locations shall be identified for such use. Cablebus shall not be installed in hoistways or hazardous (classified) locations unless specifically approved for such use. Cablebus shall be permitted to be used for branch circuits, feeders, and services.

Cablebus framework, where bonded, shall be permitted to be used as the equipment grounding conductor for branch circuits and feeders.

370.4 Conductors.

(A) Types of Conductors. The current-carrying conductors in cablebus shall have an insulation rating of 75°C (167°F) or higher and be an approved type suitable for the application.

(B) Ampacity of Conductors. The ampacity of conductors in cablebus shall be in accordance with Table 310.17 and Table 310.19, or with Table 310.69 and Table 310.70 for installations over 600 volts.

(C) Size and Number of Conductors. The size and number of conductors shall be that for which the cablebus is designed, and in no case smaller than 1/0 AWG.

(D) Conductor Supports. The insulated conductors shall be supported on blocks or other mounting means designed for the purpose.

The individual conductors in a cablebus shall be supported at intervals not greater than 900 mm (3 ft) for horizontal runs and 450 mm (1½ ft) for vertical runs. Vertical and horizontal spacing between supported conductors shall not be less than one conductor diameter at the points of support.

370.5 Overcurrent Protection.
Cablebus shall be protected against overcurrent in accordance with the allowable ampacity of the cablebus conductors in accordance with 240.4.

Exception: Overcurrent protection shall be permitted in accordance with 240.100 and 240.101 for over 600 volts, nominal.

370.6 Support and Extension Through Walls and Floors.

(A) Support. Cablebus shall be securely supported at intervals not exceeding 3.7 m (12 ft).

Exception: Where spans longer than 3.7 m (12 ft) are required, the structure shall be specifically designed for the required span length.

(B) Transversely Routed. Cablebus shall be permitted to extend transversely through partitions or walls, other than fire walls, provided the section within the wall is continuous, protected against physical damage, and unventilated.

(C) Through Dry Floors and Platforms. Except where firestops are required, cablebus shall be permitted to extend vertically through dry floors and platforms, provided the cablebus is totally enclosed at the point where it passes through the floor or platform and for a distance of 1.8 m (6 ft) above the floor or platform.

(D) Through Floors and Platforms in Wet Locations. Except where firestops are required, cablebus shall be permitted to extend vertically through floors and platforms in wet locations where (1) there are curbs or other suitable means to prevent waterflow through the floor or platform opening, and (2) where the cablebus is totally enclosed at the point where it passes through the floor or platform and for a distance of 1.8 m (6 ft) above the floor or platform.

370.7 Fittings.
A cablebus system shall include approved fittings for the following:

(1) Changes in horizontal or vertical direction of the run
(2) Dead ends
(3) Terminations in or on connected apparatus or equipment or the enclosures for such equipment
(4) Additional physical protection where required, such as guards where subject to severe physical damage

370.8 Conductor Terminations.
Approved terminating means shall be used for connections to cablebus conductors.

370.9 Grounding.
A cablebus installation shall be grounded and bonded in accordance with Article 250, excluding 250.86, Exception No. 2.

370.10 Marking.
Each section of cablebus shall be marked with the manufacturer's name or trade designation and the maximum diameter, number, voltage rating, and ampacity of the conductors to be installed. Markings shall be located so as to be visible after installation.

ARTICLE 372
Cellular Concrete Floor Raceways

372.1 Scope.
This article covers cellular concrete floor raceways, the hollow spaces in floors constructed of precast cellular concrete slabs, together with suitable metal fittings designed to provide access to the floor cells.

372.2 Definitions.

Cell. A single, enclosed tubular space in a floor made of precast cellular concrete slabs, the direction of the cell being parallel to the direction of the floor member.

Header. Transverse metal raceways for electric conductors, providing access to predetermined cells of a precast cellular concrete floor, thereby permitting the installation of electric conductors from a distribution center to the floor cells.

372.4 Uses Not Permitted. Conductors shall not be installed in precast cellular concrete floor raceways as follows:

(1) Where subject to corrosive vapor

(2) In any hazardous (classified) locations except as permitted by 504.20, and in Class I, Division 2 locations as permitted in 501.10(B)(3)

(3) In commercial garages, other than for supplying ceiling outlets or extensions to the area below the floor but not above

FPN: See 300.8 for installation of conductors with other systems.

372.5 Header. The header shall be installed in a straight line at right angles to the cells. The header shall be mechanically secured to the top of the precast cellular concrete floor. The end joints shall be closed by a metal closure fitting and sealed against the entrance of concrete. The header shall be electrically continuous throughout its entire length and shall be electrically bonded to the enclosure of the distribution center.

372.6 Connection to Cabinets and Other Enclosures. Connections from headers to cabinets and other enclosures shall be made by means of listed metal raceways and listed fittings.

372.7 Junction Boxes. Junction boxes shall be leveled to the floor grade and sealed against the free entrance of water or concrete. Junction boxes shall be of metal and shall be mechanically and electrically continuous with the header.

372.8 Markers. A suitable number of markers shall be installed for the future location of cells.

372.9 Inserts. Inserts shall be leveled and sealed against the entrance of concrete. Inserts shall be of metal and shall be fitted with grounded-type receptacles. A grounding conductor shall connect the insert receptacles to a positive ground connection provided on the header. Where cutting through the cell wall for setting inserts or other purposes (such as providing access openings between header and cells), chips and other dirt shall not be allowed to remain in the raceway, and the tool used shall be designed so as to prevent the tool from entering the cell and damaging the conductors.

372.10 Size of Conductors. No conductor larger than 1/0 AWG shall be installed, except by special permission.

372.11 Maximum Number of Conductors. The combined cross-sectional area of all conductors or cables shall not exceed 40 percent of the cross-sectional area of the cell or header.

372.12 Splices and Taps. Splices and taps shall be made only in header access units or junction boxes.

For the purposes of this section, so-called loop wiring (continuous unbroken conductor connecting the individual outlets) shall not be considered to be a splice or tap.

372.13 Discontinued Outlets. When an outlet is abandoned, discontinued, or removed, the sections of circuit conductors supplying the outlet shall be removed from the raceway. No splices or reinsulated conductors, such as would be the case of abandoned outlets on loop wiring, shall be allowed in raceways.

372.17 Ampacity of Conductors. The ampacity adjustment factors, provided in 310.15(B)(2), shall apply to conductors installed in cellular concrete floor raceways.

ARTICLE 374
Cellular Metal Floor Raceways

374.1 Scope. This article covers the use and installation requirements for cellular metal floor raceways.

374.2 Definitions.

Cellular Metal Floor Raceway. The hollow spaces of cellular metal floors, together with suitable fittings, that may be approved as enclosures for electric conductors.

Cell. A single enclosed tubular space in a cellular metal floor member, the axis of the cell being parallel to the axis of the metal floor member.

Header. A transverse raceway for electric conductors, providing access to predetermined cells of a cellular metal floor, thereby permitting the installation of electric conductors from a distribution center to the cells.

374.3 Uses Not Permitted. Conductors shall not be installed in cellular metal floor raceways as follows:

(1) Where subject to corrosive vapor

(2) In any hazardous (classified) location except as permitted by 504.20, and in Class I, Division 2 locations as permitted by 501.10(B)(3)

(3) In commercial garages, other than for supplying ceiling outlets or extensions to the area below the floor but not above

FPN: See 300.8 for installation of conductors with other systems.

I. Installation

374.4 Size of Conductors. No conductor larger than 1/0 AWG shall be installed, except by special permission.

374.5 Maximum Number of Conductors in Raceway. The combined cross-sectional area of all conductors or cables shall not exceed 40 percent of the interior cross-sectional area of the cell or header.

374.6 Splices and Taps. Splices and taps shall be made only in header access units or junction boxes.

For the purposes of this section, so-called loop wiring (continuous unbroken conductor connecting the individual outlets) shall not be considered to be a splice or tap.

374.7 Discontinued Outlets. When an outlet is abandoned, discontinued, or removed, the sections of circuit conductors supplying the outlet shall be removed from the raceway. No splices or reinsulated conductors, such as would be the case with abandoned outlets on loop wiring, shall be allowed in raceways.

374.8 Markers. A suitable number of markers shall be installed for locating cells in the future.

374.9 Junction Boxes. Junction boxes shall be leveled to the floor grade and sealed against the free entrance of water or concrete. Junction boxes used with these raceways shall be of metal and shall be electrically continuous with the raceway.

374.10 Inserts. Inserts shall be leveled to the floor grade and sealed against the entrance of concrete. Inserts shall be of metal and shall be electrically continuous with the raceway. In cutting through the cell wall and setting inserts, chips and other dirt shall not be allowed to remain in the raceway, and tools shall be used that are designed to prevent the tool from entering the cell and damaging the conductors.

374.11 Connection to Cabinets and Extensions from Cells. Connections between raceways and distribution centers and wall outlets shall be made by means of liquidtight flexible metal conduit, flexible metal conduit where not installed in concrete, rigid metal conduit, intermediate metal conduit, electrical metallic tubing, or approved fittings. Where there are provisions for the termination of an equipment grounding conductor, nonmetallic conduit, electrical nonmetallic tubing, or liquidtight flexible nonmetallic conduit shall be permitted. Where installed in concrete, liquidtight flexible nonmetallic conduit shall be listed and marked for direct burial.

> FPN: Liquidtight flexible metal conduit and liquidtight flexible nonmetallic conduit that is suitable for installation in concrete is listed and marked for direct burial.

374.17 Ampacity of Conductors. The ampacity adjustment factors in 310.15(B)(2) shall apply to conductors installed in cellular metal floor raceways.

II. Construction Specifications

374.100 General. Cellular metal floor raceways shall be constructed so that adequate electrical and mechanical continuity of the complete system will be secured. They shall provide a complete enclosure for the conductors. The interior surfaces shall be free from burrs and sharp edges, and surfaces over which conductors are drawn shall be smooth. Suitable bushings or fittings having smooth rounded edges shall be provided where conductors pass.

ARTICLE 376
Metal Wireways

I. General

376.1 Scope. This article covers the use, installation, and construction specifications for metal wireways and associated fittings.

376.2 Definition.

Metal Wireways. Sheet metal troughs with hinged or removable covers for housing and protecting electric wires and cable and in which conductors are laid in place after the wireway has been installed as a complete system.

II. Installation

376.10 Uses Permitted. The use of metal wireways shall be permitted in the following:

(1) For exposed work

(2) In concealed spaces as permitted in 376.10(4)

(3) In hazardous (classified) locations as permitted by 501.10(B) for Class I, Division 2 locations; 502.10(B) for Class II, Division 2 locations; and 504.20 for intrinsically safe wiring. Where installed in wet locations, wireways shall be listed for the purpose.

(4) As extensions to pass transversely through walls if the length passing through the wall is unbroken. Access to the conductors shall be maintained on both sides of the wall.

376.12 Uses Not Permitted. Metal wireways shall not be used in the following:

(1) Where subject to severe physical damage

(2) Where subject to severe corrosive environments

376.21 Size of Conductors. No conductor larger than that for which the wireway is designed shall be installed in any wireway.

376.22 Number of Conductors. The sum of the cross-sectional areas of all contained conductors at any cross section of a wireway shall not exceed 20 percent of the interior cross-sectional area of the wireway. The derating factors in 310.15(B)(2)(a) shall be applied only where the number of current-carrying conductors, including neutral conductors classified as current-carrying under the provisions of 310.15(B)(4), exceeds 30. Conductors for signaling circuits or controller conductors between a motor and its starter and used only for starting duty shall not be considered as current-carrying conductors.

376.23 Insulated Conductors. Insulated conductors installed in a metallic wireway shall comply with 376.23(A) and (B).

(A) Deflected Insulated Conductors. Where insulated conductors are deflected within a metallic wireway, either at the ends or where conduits, fittings, or other raceways or cables enter or leave the metallic wireway, or where the direction of the metallic wireway is deflected greater than 30 degrees, dimensions corresponding to one wire per terminal in Table 312.6(A) shall apply.

(B) Metallic Wireways Used as Pull Boxes. Where insulated conductors 4 AWG or larger are pulled through a wireway, the distance between raceway and cable entries enclosing the same conductor shall not be less than that required by 314.28(A)(1) for straight pulls and 314.28(A)(2) for angle pulls. When transposing cable size into raceway size, the minimum metric designator (trade size) raceway required for the number and size of conductors in the cable shall be used.

376.30 Securing and Supporting. Metal wireways shall be supported in accordance with 376.30(A) and (B).

(A) Horizontal Support. Wireways shall be supported where run horizontally at each end and at intervals not to exceed 1.5 m (5 ft) or for individual lengths longer than 1.5 m (5 ft) at each end or joint, unless listed for other support intervals. The distance between supports shall not exceed 3 m (10 ft).

(B) Vertical Support. Vertical runs of wireways shall be securely supported at intervals not exceeding 4.5 m (15 ft) and shall not have more than one joint between supports. Adjoining wireway sections shall be securely fastened together to provide a rigid joint.

376.56 Splices, Taps, and Power Distribution Blocks.

(A) Splices and Taps. Splices and taps shall be permitted within a wireway, provided they are accessible. The conductors, including splices and taps, shall not fill the wireway to more than 75 percent of its area at that point.

(B) Power Distribution Blocks.

(1) Installation. Power distribution blocks installed in metal wireways shall be listed.

(2) Size of Enclosure. In addition to the wiring space requirement in 376.56(A), the power distribution block shall be installed in a wireway with dimensions not smaller than specified in the installation instructions of the power distribution block.

(3) Wire Bending Space. Wire bending space at the terminals of power distribution blocks shall comply with 312.6(B).

(4) Live Parts. Power distribution blocks shall not have exposed live parts in the wireway after installation.

376.58 Dead Ends. Dead ends of metal wireways shall be closed.

376.70 Extensions from Metal Wireways. Extensions from wireways shall be made with cord pendants installed in accordance with 400.10 or with any wiring method in Chapter 3 that includes a means for equipment grounding. Where a separate equipment grounding conductor is employed, connection of the equipment grounding conductors in the wiring method to the wireway shall comply with 250.8 and 250.12.

III. Construction Specifications

376.120 Marking. Metal wireways shall be so marked that their manufacturer's name or trademark will be visible after installation.

ARTICLE 378
Nonmetallic Wireways

I. General

378.1 Scope. This article covers the use, installation, and construction specifications for nonmetallic wireways and associated fittings.

378.2 Definition.

Nonmetallic Wireways. Flame retardant, nonmetallic troughs with removable covers for housing and protecting electric wires and cables in which conductors are laid in place after the wireway has been installed as a complete system.

378.6 Listing Requirements. Nonmetallic wireways and associated fittings shall be listed.

II. Installation

378.10 Uses Permitted. The use of nonmetallic wireways shall be permitted in the following:

(1) Only for exposed work, except as permitted in 378.10(4).

(2) Where subject to corrosive environments where identified for the use.

(3) In wet locations where listed for the purpose.

> FPN: Extreme cold may cause nonmetallic wireways to become brittle and therefore more susceptible to damage from physical contact.

(4) As extensions to pass transversely through walls if the length passing through the wall is unbroken. Access to the conductors shall be maintained on both sides of the wall.

378.12 Uses Not Permitted. Nonmetallic wireways shall not be used in the following:

(1) Where subject to physical damage

(2) In any hazardous (classified) location, except as permitted in 504.20

(3) Where exposed to sunlight unless listed and marked as suitable for the purpose

(4) Where subject to ambient temperatures other than those for which nonmetallic wireway is listed

(5) For conductors whose insulation temperature limitations would exceed those for which the nonmetallic wireway is listed

378.21 Size of Conductors. No conductor larger than that for which the nonmetallic wireway is designed shall be installed in any nonmetallic wireway.

378.22 Number of Conductors. The sum of cross-sectional areas of all contained conductors at any cross section of the nonmetallic wireway shall not exceed 20 percent of the interior cross-sectional area of the nonmetallic wireway. Conductors for signaling circuits or controller conductors between a motor and its starter and used only for starting duty shall not be considered as current-carrying conductors.

The derating factors specified in 310.15(B)(2)(a) shall be applicable to the current-carrying conductors up to and including the 20 percent fill specified above.

378.23 Insulated Conductors. Insulated conductors installed in a nonmetallic wireway shall comply with 378.23(A) and (B).

(A) Deflected Insulated Conductors. Where insulated conductors are deflected within a nonmetallic wireway, either at the ends or where conduits, fittings, or other raceways or cables enter or leave the nonmetallic wireway, or where the direction of the nonmetallic wireway is deflected greater than 30 degrees, dimensions corresponding to one wire per terminal in Table 312.6(A) shall apply.

(B) Nonmetallic Wireways Used as Pull Boxes. Where insulated conductors 4 AWG or larger are pulled through a wireway, the distance between raceway and cable entries enclosing the same conductor shall not be less than that required in 314.28(A)(1) for straight pulls and in 314.28(A)(2) for angle pulls. When transposing cable size into raceway size, the minimum metric designator (trade size) raceway required for the number and size of conductors in the cable shall be used.

378.30 Securing and Supporting. Nonmetallic wireway shall be supported in accordance with 378.30(A) and (B).

(A) Horizontal Support. Nonmetallic wireways shall be supported where run horizontally at intervals not to exceed 900 mm (3 ft), and at each end or joint, unless listed for other support intervals. In no case shall the distance between supports exceed 3 m (10 ft).

(B) Vertical Support. Vertical runs of nonmetallic wireway shall be securely supported at intervals not exceeding 1.2 m (4 ft), unless listed for other support intervals, and shall not have more than one joint between supports. Adjoining nonmetallic wireway sections shall be securely fastened together to provide a rigid joint.

378.44 Expansion Fittings. Expansion fittings for nonmetallic wireway shall be provided to compensate for thermal expansion and contraction where the length change is expected to be 6 mm (0.25 in.) or greater in a straight run.

> FPN: See Table 352.44(A) for expansion characteristics of PVC rigid nonmetallic conduit. The expansion characteristics of PVC nonmetallic wireway are identical.

378.56 Splices and Taps. Splices and taps shall be permitted within a nonmetallic wireway, provided they are accessible. The conductors, including splices and taps, shall not fill the nonmetallic wireway to more than 75 percent of its area at that point.

378.58 Dead Ends. Dead ends of nonmetallic wireway shall be closed using listed fittings.

378.60 Grounding. Where equipment grounding is required, a separate equipment grounding conductor shall be installed in the nonmetallic wireway. A separate equipment grounding conductor shall not be required where the grounded conductor is used to ground equipment as permitted in 250.142.

378.70 Extensions from Nonmetallic Wireways. Extensions from nonmetallic wireway shall be made with cord pendants or any wiring method of Chapter 3. A separate equipment grounding conductor shall be installed in, or an equipment grounding connection shall be made to, any of the wiring methods used for the extension.

III. Construction Specifications

378.120 Marking. Nonmetallic wireways shall be marked so that the manufacturer's name or trademark and interior cross-sectional area in square inches shall be visible after installation. Marking for limited smoke shall be permitted on the nonmetallic wireways that have limited smoke-producing characteristics.

ARTICLE 380
Multioutlet Assembly

380.1 Scope. This article covers the use and installation requirements for multioutlet assemblies.

380.2 Use.

(A) Permitted. The use of a multioutlet assembly shall be permitted in dry locations.

(B) Not Permitted. A multioutlet assembly shall not be installed as follows:

(1) Where concealed, except that it shall be permissible to surround the back and sides of a metal multioutlet assembly by the building finish or recess a nonmetallic multioutlet assembly in a baseboard

(2) Where subject to severe physical damage

(3) Where the voltage is 300 volts or more between conductors unless the assembly is of metal having a thickness of not less than 1.02 mm (0.040 in.)

(4) Where subject to corrosive vapors

(5) In hoistways

(6) In any hazardous (classified) locations except Class I, Division 2 locations as permitted in 501.10(B)(3)

380.3 Metal Multioutlet Assembly Through Dry Partitions. It shall be permissible to extend a metal multioutlet assembly through (not run within) dry partitions if arrangements are made for removing the cap or cover on all exposed portions and no outlet is located within the partitions.

ARTICLE 382
Nonmetallic Extensions

I. General

382.1 Scope. This article covers the use, installation, and construction specifications for nonmetallic extensions.

382.2 Definition.

Nonmetallic Extension. An assembly of two insulated conductors within a nonmetallic jacket or an extruded thermoplastic covering. The classification includes surface extensions intended for mounting directly on the surface of walls or ceilings.

II. Installation

382.10 Uses Permitted. Nonmetallic extensions shall be permitted only in accordance with 382.10(A), (B), and (C).

(A) From an Existing Outlet. The extension shall be from an existing outlet on a 15- or 20-ampere branch circuit.

(B) Exposed and in a Dry Location. The extension shall be run exposed and in a dry location.

(C) Residential or Offices. For nonmetallic surface extensions mounted directly on the surface of walls or ceilings, the building shall be occupied for residential or office purposes and shall not exceed three floors above grade.

    FPN No. 1: See 310.10 for temperature limitation of conductors.

    FPN No. 2: See 362.10 for definition of *first floor*.

382.12 Uses Not Permitted. Nonmetallic extensions shall not be used as follows:

(1) In unfinished basements, attics, or roof spaces

(2) Where the voltage between conductors exceeds 150 volts for nonmetallic surface extension and 300 volts for aerial cable

(3) Where subject to corrosive vapors

(4) Where run through a floor or partition, or outside the room in which it originates

382.15 Exposed. One or more extensions shall be permitted to be run in any direction from an existing outlet, but not on the floor or within 50 mm (2 in.) from the floor.

382.26 Bends. A bend that reduces the normal spacing between the conductors shall be covered with a cap to protect the assembly from physical damage.

382.30 Securing and Supporting. Nonmetallic surface extensions shall be secured in place by approved means at intervals not exceeding 200 mm (8 in.), with an allowance for 300 mm (12 in.) to the first fastening where the connection to the supplying outlet is by means of an attachment plug. There shall be at least one fastening between each two adjacent outlets supplied. An extension shall be attached to only woodwork or plaster finish and shall not be in contact with any metal work or other conductive material other than with metal plates on receptacles.

382.40 Boxes and Fittings. Each run shall terminate in a fitting that covers the end of the assembly. All fittings and devices shall be of a type identified for the use.

382.56 Splices and Taps. Extensions shall consist of a continuous unbroken length of the assembly, without splices, and without exposed conductors between fittings. Taps shall be permitted where approved fittings completely covering the tap connections are used. Aerial cable and its tap connectors shall be provided with an approved means for polarization. Receptacle-type tap connectors shall be of the locking type.

ARTICLE 384
Strut-Type Channel Raceway

I. General

384.1 Scope. This article covers the use, installation, and construction specifications of strut-type channel raceway.

384.2 Definition.

Strut-Type Channel Raceway. A metallic raceway that is intended to be mounted to the surface of or suspended from a structure, with associated accessories for the installation of electrical conductors and cables.

384.6 Listing Requirements. Strut-type channel raceways, closure strips, and accessories shall be listed and identified for such use.

II. Installation

384.10 Uses Permitted. The use of strut-type channel raceways shall be permitted in the following:

(1) Where exposed.

(2) In dry locations.

(3) In locations subject to corrosive vapors where protected by finishes judged suitable for the condition.

(4) Where the voltage is 600 volts or less.

(5) As power poles.

(6) In Class I, Division 2 hazardous (classified) locations as permitted in 501.10(B)(3).

(7) As extensions of unbroken lengths through walls, partitions, and floors where closure strips are removable from either side and the portion within the wall, partition, or floor remains covered.

(8) Ferrous channel raceways and fittings protected from corrosion solely by enamel shall be permitted only indoors.

384.12 Uses Not Permitted. Strut type channel raceways shall not be used as follows:

(1) Where concealed.

(2) Ferrous channel raceways and fittings protected from corrosion solely by enamel shall not be permitted where subject to severe corrosive influences.

384.21 Size of Conductors. No conductor larger than that for which the raceway is listed shall be installed in strut-type channel raceways.

384.22 Number of Conductors. The number of conductors permitted in strut-type channel raceways shall not exceed the percentage fill using Table 384.22 and applicable outside diameter (O.D.) dimensions of specific types and sizes of wire given in the tables in Chapter 9.

The derating factors of 310.15(B)(2)(a) shall not apply to conductors installed in strut-type channel raceways where all of the following conditions are met:

(1) The cross-sectional area of the raceway exceeds 2500 mm^2 (4 in.^{2}).

(2) The current-carrying conductors do not exceed 30 in number.

(3) The sum of the cross-sectional areas of all contained conductors does not exceed 20 percent of the interior cross-sectional area of the strut-type channel raceways, calculated in accordance with the following formula for wire fill:

$$n = \frac{ca}{wa}$$

where:

n = number of wires

ca = channel area in square inches

wa = wire area

384.30 Securing and Supporting.

(A) Surface Mount. A surface mount strut-type channel raceway shall be secured to the mounting surface with retention straps external to the channel at intervals not exceeding 3 m (10 ft) and within 900 mm (3 ft) of each outlet box, cabinet, junction box, or other channel raceway termination.

Table 384.22 Channel Size and Inside Diameter Area

Size Channel	Area		40% Area*		25% Area**	
	in.²	mm²	in.²	mm²	in.²	mm²
1⅝ × ¹³⁄₁₆	0.887	572	0.355	229	0.222	143
1⅝ × 1	1.151	743	0.460	297	0.288	186
1⅝ × 1⅜	1.677	1076	0.671	433	0.419	270
1⅝ × 1⅝	2.028	1308	0.811	523	0.507	327
1⅝ × 2⁷⁄₁₆	3.169	2045	1.267	817	0.792	511
1⅝ × 3¼	4.308	2780	1.723	1112	1.077	695
1½ × ¾	0.849	548	0.340	219	0.212	137
1½ × 1½	1.828	1179	0.731	472	0.457	295
1½ × 1⅞	2.301	1485	0.920	594	0.575	371
1½ × 3	3.854	2487	1.542	995	0.964	622

*Raceways with external joiners shall use a 40 percent wire fill calculation to determine the number of conductors permitted.

**Raceways with internal joiners shall use a 25 percent wire fill calculation to determine the number of conductors permitted.

(B) Suspension Mount. Strut-type channel raceways shall be permitted to be suspension mounted in air with approved appropriate methods designed for the purpose at intervals not to exceed 3 m (10 ft) and within 900 mm (3 ft) of channel raceway terminations and ends.

384.56 Splices and Taps. Splices and taps shall be permitted in raceways that are accessible after installation by having a removable cover. The conductors, including splices and taps, shall not fill the raceway to more than 75 percent of its area at that point. All splices and taps shall be made by approved methods.

384.60 Grounding. Strut-type channel raceway enclosures providing a transition to or from other wiring methods shall have a means for connecting an equipment grounding conductor. Strut-type channel raceways shall be permitted as an equipment grounding conductor in accordance with 250.118(14). Where a snap-fit metal cover for strut-type channel raceways is used to achieve electrical continuity in accordance with the listing, this cover shall not be permitted as the means for providing electrical continuity for a receptacle mounted in the cover.

III. Construction Specifications

384.100 Construction. Strut-type channel raceways and their accessories shall be of a construction that distinguishes them from other raceways. Raceways and their elbows, couplings, and other fittings shall be designed such that the sections can be electrically and mechanically coupled together and installed without subjecting the wires to abrasion. They shall comply with 384.100(A), (B), and (C).

(A) Material. Raceways and accessories shall be formed of steel, stainless steel, or aluminum.

(B) Corrosion Protection. Steel raceways and accessories shall be protected against corrosion by galvanizing or by an organic coating.

FPN: Enamel and PVC coatings are examples of organic coatings that provide corrosion protection.

(C) Cover. Covers of strut-type channel raceways shall be either metallic or nonmetallic.

384.120 Marking. Each length of strut-type channel raceways shall be clearly and durably identified as required in the first sentence of 110.21.

ARTICLE 386
Surface Metal Raceways

I. General

386.1 Scope. This article covers the use, installation, and construction specifications for surface metal raceways and associated fittings.

386.2 Definition.

Surface Metal Raceway. A metallic raceway that is intended to be mounted to the surface of a structure, with associated couplings, connectors, boxes, and fittings for the installation of electrical conductors.

386.6 Listing Requirements. Surface metal raceway and associated fittings shall be listed.

II. Installation

386.10 Uses Permitted. The use of surface metal raceways shall be permitted in the following:

(1) In dry locations.

(2) In Class I, Division 2 hazardous (classified) locations as permitted in 501.10(B)(3).

(3) Under raised floors, as permitted in 645.5(D)(2).

(4) Extension through walls and floors. Surface metal raceway shall be permitted to pass transversely through dry walls, dry partitions, and dry floors if the length passing through is unbroken. Access to the conductors shall be maintained on both sides of the wall, partition, or floor.

386.12 Uses Not Permitted. Surface metal raceways shall not be used in the following:

(1) Where subject to severe physical damage, unless otherwise approved

(2) Where the voltage is 300 volts or more between conductors, unless the metal has a thickness of not less than 1.02 mm (0.040 in.) nominal

(3) Where subject to corrosive vapors

(4) In hoistways

(5) Where concealed, except as permitted in 386.10

386.21 Size of Conductors. No conductor larger than that for which the raceway is designed shall be installed in surface metal raceway.

386.22 Number of Conductors or Cables. The number of conductors or cables installed in surface metal raceway shall not be greater than the number for which the raceway is designed. Cables shall be permitted to be installed where such use is not prohibited by the respective cable articles.

The derating factors of 310.15(B)(2)(a) shall not apply to conductors installed in surface metal raceways where all of the following conditions are met:

(1) The cross-sectional area of the raceway exceeds 2500 mm^2 (4 in.^{2})

(2) The current-carrying conductors do not exceed 30 in number

(3) The sum of the cross-sectional areas of all contained conductors does not exceed 20 percent of the interior cross-sectional area of the surface metal raceway

386.30 Securing and Supporting. Surface metal raceways shall be supported at intervals in accordance with the manufacturer's installation instructions.

386.56 Splices and Taps. Splices and taps shall be permitted in surface metal raceways having a removable cover that is accessible after installation. The conductors, including splices and taps, shall not fill the raceway to more than 75 percent of its area at that point. Splices and taps in surface metal raceways without removable covers shall be made only in boxes. All splices and taps shall be made by approved methods.

Taps of Type FC cable installed in surface metal raceway shall be made in accordance with 322.56(B).

386.60 Grounding. Surface metal raceway enclosures providing a transition from other wiring methods shall have a means for connecting an equipment grounding conductor.

386.70 Combination Raceways. When combination surface metallic raceways are used for both signaling and for lighting and power circuits, the different systems shall be run in separate compartments identified by stamping, imprinting, or color coding of the interior finish.

III. Construction Specifications

386.100 Construction. Surface metal raceways shall be of such construction as will distinguish them from other raceways. Surface metal raceways and their elbows, couplings, and similar fittings shall be designed so that the sections can be electrically and mechanically coupled together and installed without subjecting the wires to abrasion.

Where covers and accessories of nonmetallic materials are used on surface metal raceways, they shall be identified for such use.

ARTICLE 388
Surface Nonmetallic Raceways

I. General

388.1 Scope. This article covers the use, installation, and construction specifications for surface nonmetallic raceways and associated fittings.

388.2 Definition.

Surface Nonmetallic Raceway. A nonmetallic raceway that is intended to be mounted to the surface of a structure, with associated couplings, connectors, boxes, and fittings for the installation of electrical conductors.

388.6 Listing Requirements. Surface nonmetallic raceway and associated fittings shall be listed.

II. Installation

388.10 Uses Permitted. Surface nonmetallic raceway shall be permitted as follows:

(1) The use of surface nonmetallic raceways shall be permitted in dry locations.

(2) Extension through walls and floors shall be permitted. Surface nonmetallic raceway shall be permitted to pass transversely through dry walls, dry partitions, and dry floors if the length passing through is unbroken. Access to the conductors shall be maintained on both sides of the wall, partition, or floor.

388.12 Uses Not Permitted. Surface nonmetallic raceways shall not be used in the following:

(1) Where concealed, except as permitted in 388.10(2)

(2) Where subject to severe physical damage

(3) Where the voltage is 300 volts or more between conductors, unless listed for higher voltage

(4) In hoistways

(5) In any hazardous (classified) location except Class I, Division 2 locations as permitted in 501.10(B)(3)

(6) Where subject to ambient temperatures exceeding those for which the nonmetallic raceway is listed

(7) For conductors whose insulation temperature limitations would exceed those for which the nonmetallic raceway is listed

388.21 Size of Conductors. No conductor larger than that for which the raceway is designed shall be installed in surface nonmetallic raceway.

388.22 Number of Conductors or Cables. The number of conductors or cables installed in surface nonmetallic raceway shall not be greater than the number for which the raceway is designed. Cables shall be permitted to be installed where such use is not prohibited by the respective cable articles.

388.56 Splices and Taps. Splices and taps shall be permitted in surface nonmetallic raceways having a removable cover that is accessible after installation. The conductors, including splices and taps, shall not fill the raceway to more than 75 percent of its area at that point. Splices and taps in surface nonmetallic raceways without removable covers shall be made only in boxes. All splices and taps shall be made by approved methods.

388.60 Grounding. Where equipment grounding is required, a separate equipment grounding conductor shall be installed in the raceway.

388.70 Combination Raceways. When combination surface nonmetallic raceways are used both for signaling and for lighting and power circuits, the different systems shall be run in separate compartments identified by stamping, imprinting, or color coding of the interior finish.

III. Construction Specifications

388.100 Construction. Surface nonmetallic raceways shall be of such construction as will distinguish them from other raceways. Surface nonmetallic raceways and their elbows, couplings, and similar fittings shall be designed so that the sections can be mechanically coupled together and installed without subjecting the wires to abrasion.

Surface nonmetallic raceways and fittings are made of suitable nonmetallic material that is resistant to moisture and chemical atmospheres. It shall also be flame retardant, resistant to impact and crushing, resistant to distortion from heat under conditions likely to be encountered in service, and resistant to low-temperature effects.

388.120 Marking. Surface nonmetallic raceways that have limited smoke-producing characteristics shall be permitted to be so identified.

ARTICLE 390
Underfloor Raceways

390.1 Scope. This article covers the use and installation requirements for underfloor raceways.

390.2 Use.

(A) Permitted. The installation of underfloor raceways shall be permitted beneath the surface of concrete or other flooring material or in office occupancies where laid flush with the concrete floor and covered with linoleum or equivalent floor covering.

(B) Not Permitted. Underfloor raceways shall not be installed (1) where subject to corrosive vapors or (2) in any hazardous (classified) locations, except as permitted by 504.20 and in Class I, Division 2 locations as permitted in 501.10(B)(3). Unless made of a material judged suitable for the condition or unless corrosion protection approved for the condition is provided, ferrous or nonferrous metal underfloor raceways, junction boxes, and fittings shall not be installed in concrete or in areas subject to severe corrosive influences.

390.3 Covering. Raceway coverings shall comply with 390.3(A) through (D).

(A) Raceways Not Over 100 mm (4 in.) Wide. Half-round and flat-top raceways not over 100 mm (4 in.) in width shall have not less than 20 mm (¾ in.) of concrete or wood above the raceway.

Exception: As permitted in 390.3(C) and (D) for flat-top raceways.

(B) Raceways Over 100 mm (4 in.) Wide But Not Over 200 mm (8 in.) Wide. Flat-top raceways over 100 mm (4 in.) but not over 200 mm (8 in.) wide with a minimum of 25 mm (1 in.) spacing between raceways shall be covered with concrete to a depth of not less than 25 mm (1 in.). Raceways spaced less than 25 mm (1 in.) apart shall be covered with concrete to a depth of 38 mm (1½ in.).

(C) Trench-Type Raceways Flush with Concrete. Trench-type flush raceways with removable covers shall be permitted to be laid flush with the floor surface. Such approved raceways shall be designed so that the cover plates provide adequate mechanical protection and rigidity equivalent to junction box covers.

(D) Other Raceways Flush with Concrete. In office occupancies, approved metal flat-top raceways, if not over 100 mm (4 in.) in width, shall be permitted to be laid flush with the concrete floor surface, provided they are covered with substantial linoleum that is not less than 1.6 mm ($\frac{1}{16}$ in.) thick or with equivalent floor covering. Where more than one and not more than three single raceways are each installed flush with the concrete, they shall be contiguous with each other and joined to form a rigid assembly.

390.4 Size of Conductors. No conductor larger than that for which the raceway is designed shall be installed in underfloor raceways.

390.5 Maximum Number of Conductors in Raceway. The combined cross-sectional area of all conductors or cables shall not exceed 40 percent of the interior cross-sectional area of the raceway.

390.6 Splices and Taps. Splices and taps shall be made only in junction boxes.

For the purposes of this section, so-called loop wiring (continuous, unbroken conductor connecting the individual outlets) shall not be considered to be a splice or tap.

Exception: Splices and taps shall be permitted in trench-type flush raceway having a removable cover that is accessible after installation. The conductors, including splices and taps, shall not fill more than 75 percent of the raceway area at that point.

390.7 Discontinued Outlets. When an outlet is abandoned, discontinued, or removed, the sections of circuit conductors supplying the outlet shall be removed from the raceway. No splices or reinsulated conductors, such as would be the case with abandoned outlets on loop wiring, shall be allowed in raceways.

390.8 Laid in Straight Lines. Underfloor raceways shall be laid so that a straight line from the center of one junction box to the center of the next junction box coincides with the centerline of the raceway system. Raceways shall be firmly held in place to prevent disturbing this alignment during construction.

390.9 Markers at Ends. A suitable marker shall be installed at or near each end of each straight run of raceways to locate the last insert.

390.10 Dead Ends. Dead ends of raceways shall be closed.

390.13 Junction Boxes. Junction boxes shall be leveled to the floor grade and sealed to prevent the free entrance of water or concrete. Junction boxes used with metal raceways shall be metal and shall be electrically continuous with the raceways.

390.14 Inserts. Inserts shall be leveled and sealed to prevent the entrance of concrete. Inserts used with metal raceways shall be metal and shall be electrically continuous with the

raceway. Inserts set in or on fiber raceways before the floor is laid shall be mechanically secured to the raceway. Inserts set in fiber raceways after the floor is laid shall be screwed into the raceway. When cutting through the raceway wall and setting inserts, chips and other dirt shall not be allowed to remain in the raceway, and tools shall be used that are designed so as to prevent the tool from entering the raceway and damaging conductors that may be in place.

390.15 Connections to Cabinets and Wall Outlets. Connections from underfloor raceways to distribution centers and wall outlets shall be made by approved fittings or by any of the wiring methods in Chapter 3, where installed in accordance with the provisions of the respective articles.

390.17 Ampacity of Conductors. The ampacity adjustment factors, in 310.15(B)(2), shall apply to conductors installed in underfloor raceways.

ARTICLE 392
Cable Trays

392.1 Scope. This article covers cable tray systems, including ladder, ventilated trough, ventilated channel, solid bottom, and other similar structures.

FPN: For further information on cable trays, see ANSI/NEMA–VE 1-1998, *Metal Cable Tray Systems*; NEMA–VE 2-1996, *Metal Cable Tray Installation Guidelines*; and NEMA–FG-1998, *Nonmetallic Cable Tray Systems*.

392.2 Definition.

Cable Tray System. A unit or assembly of units or sections and associated fittings forming a structural system used to securely fasten or support cables and raceways.

392.3 Uses Permitted. Cable tray shall be permitted to be used as a support system for service conductors, feeders, branch circuits, communications circuits, control circuits, and signaling circuits. Cable tray installations shall not be limited to industrial establishments. Where exposed to direct rays of the sun, insulated conductors and jacketed cables shall be identified as being sunlight resistant. Cable trays and their associated fittings shall be identified for the intended use.

(A) Wiring Methods. The wiring methods in Table 392.3(A) shall be permitted to be installed in cable tray systems under the conditions described in their respective articles and sections.

Table 392.3(A) Wiring Methods

Wiring Method	Article	Section
Armored cable	320	
Communication raceways	800	
Electrical metallic tubing	358	
Electrical nonmetallic tubing	362	
Fire alarm cables	760	
Flexible metal conduit	348	
Flexible metallic tubing	360	
Instrumentation tray cable	727	
Intermediate metal conduit	342	
Liquidtight flexible metal conduit	350	
Liquidtight flexible nonmetallic conduit	356	
Metal-clad cable	330	
Mineral-insulated, metal-sheathed cable	332	
Multiconductor service-entrance cable	338	
Multiconductor underground feeder and branch-circuit cable	340	
Multipurpose and communications cables	800	
Nonmetallic-sheathed cable	334	
Power and control tray cable	336	
Power-limited tray cable		725.61(C) and 725.82(E)
Optical fiber cables	770	
Optical fiber raceways	770	
Other factory-assembled, multiconductor control, signal, or power cables that are specifically approved for installation in cable trays		
Rigid metal conduit	344	
Rigid nonmetallic conduit	352	

(B) In Industrial Establishments. The wiring methods in Table 392.3(A) shall be permitted to be used in any industrial establishment under the conditions described in their respective articles. In industrial establishments only, where conditions of maintenance and supervision ensure that only qualified persons service the installed cable tray system, any of the cables in 392.3(B)(1) and (B)(2) shall be permitted to be installed in ladder, ventilated trough, solid bottom, or ventilated channel cable trays.

(1) Single Conductors. Single-conductor cables shall be permitted to be installed in accordance with (B)(1)(a) through (B)(1)(c).

(a) Single-conductor cable shall be 1/0 AWG or larger and shall be of a type listed and marked on the surface for use in cable trays. Where 1/0 AWG through 4/0 AWG single-conductor cables are installed in ladder cable tray, the maximum allowable rung spacing for the ladder cable tray shall be 225 mm (9 in.).

(b) Welding cables shall comply with the provisions of Article 630, Part IV.

(c) Single conductors used as equipment grounding conductors shall be insulated, covered, or bare, and they shall be 4 AWG or larger.

(2) Medium Voltage. Single- and multiconductor medium voltage cables shall be Type MV cable. Single conductors shall be installed in accordance with 392.3(B)(1).

(C) Equipment Grounding Conductors. Metallic cable trays shall be permitted to be used as equipment grounding conductors where continuous maintenance and supervision ensure that qualified persons service the installed cable tray system and the cable tray complies with provisions of 392.7.

(D) Hazardous (Classified) Locations. Cable trays in hazardous (classified) locations shall contain only the cable types permitted in 501.10, 502.10, 503.10, 504.20, and 505.15.

(E) Nonmetallic Cable Tray. In addition to the uses permitted elsewhere in 392.3, nonmetallic cable tray shall be permitted in corrosive areas and in areas requiring voltage isolation.

392.4 Uses Not Permitted. Cable tray systems shall not be used in hoistways or where subject to severe physical damage. Cable tray systems shall not be used in ducts, plenums, and other air-handling spaces, except as permitted in 300.22, to support wiring methods recognized for use in such spaces.

392.5 Construction Specifications.

(A) Strength and Rigidity. Cable trays shall have suitable strength and rigidity to provide adequate support for all contained wiring.

(B) Smooth Edges. Cable trays shall not have sharp edges, burrs, or projections that could damage the insulation or jackets of the wiring.

(C) Corrosion Protection. Cable tray systems shall be corrosion resistant. If made of ferrous material, the system shall be protected from corrosion as required by 300.6.

(D) Side Rails. Cable trays shall have side rails or equivalent structural members.

(E) Fittings. Cable trays shall include fittings or other suitable means for changes in direction and elevation of runs.

(F) Nonmetallic Cable Tray. Nonmetallic cable trays shall be made of flame-retardant material.

392.6 Installation.

(A) Complete System. Cable trays shall be installed as a complete system. Field bends or modifications shall be so made that the electrical continuity of the cable tray system and support for the cables is maintained. Cable tray systems shall be permitted to have mechanically discontinuous segments between cable tray runs or between cable tray runs and equipment. The system shall provide for the support of the cables in accordance with their corresponding articles.

Where cable trays support individual conductors and where the conductors pass from one cable tray to another, or from a cable tray to raceway(s) or from a cable tray to equipment where the conductors are terminated, the distance between cable trays or between the cable tray and the raceway(s) or the equipment shall not exceed 1.8 m (6 ft). The conductors shall be secured to the cable tray(s) at the transition, and they shall be protected, by guarding or by location, from physical damage.

A bonding jumper sized in accordance with 250.102 shall connect the two sections of cable tray, or the cable tray and the raceway or equipment. Bonding shall be in accordance with 250.96.

(B) Completed Before Installation. Each run of cable tray shall be completed before the installation of cables.

(C) Supports. Supports shall be provided to prevent stress on cables where they enter raceways or other enclosures from cable tray systems.

Cable trays shall be supported at intervals in accordance with the installation instructions.

(D) Covers. In portions of runs where additional protection is required, covers or enclosures providing the required protection shall be of a material that is compatible with the cable tray.

(E) Multiconductor Cables Rated 600 Volts or Less. Multiconductor cables rated 600 volts or less shall be permitted to be installed in the same cable tray.

(F) Cables Rated Over 600 Volts. Cables rated over 600 volts and those rated 600 volts or less installed in the same cable tray shall comply with either of the following:
(1) The cables rated over 600 volts are Type MC.
(2) The cables rated over 600 volts are separated from the cables rated 600 volts or less by a solid fixed barrier of a material compatible with the cable tray.

(G) Through Partitions and Walls. Cable trays shall be permitted to extend transversely through partitions and walls or vertically through platforms and floors in wet or dry locations where the installations, complete with installed cables, are made in accordance with the requirements of 300.21.

(H) Exposed and Accessible. Cable trays shall be exposed and accessible except as permitted by 392.6(G).

(I) Adequate Access. Sufficient space shall be provided and maintained about cable trays to permit adequate access for installing and maintaining the cables.

(J) Raceways, Cables, Boxes, and Conduit Bodies Supported from Cable Tray Systems. In industrial facilities where conditions of maintenance and supervision ensure that only qualified persons service the installation and where the cable tray systems are designed and installed to support the load, such systems shall be permitted to support raceways and cables, and boxes and conduit bodies covered in 314.1. For raceways terminating at the tray, a listed cable tray clamp or adapter shall be used to securely fasten the raceway to the cable tray system. Additional supporting and securing of the raceway shall be in accordance with the requirements of the appropriate raceway article.

For raceways or cables running parallel to and attached to the bottom or side of a cable tray system, fastening and supporting shall be in accordance with the requirements of the appropriate raceway or cable article.

For boxes and conduit bodies attached to the bottom or side of a cable tray system, fastening and supporting shall be in accordance with the requirements of 314.23.

392.7 Grounding.

(A) Metallic Cable Trays. Metallic cable trays that support electrical conductors shall be grounded as required for conductor enclosures in accordance with 250.96.

(B) Steel or Aluminum Cable Tray Systems. Steel or aluminum cable tray systems shall be permitted to be used as equipment grounding conductors, provided that all the following requirements are met:
(1) The cable tray sections and fittings shall be identified for grounding purposes.
(2) The minimum cross-sectional area of cable trays shall conform to the requirements in Table 392.7(B).
(3) All cable tray sections and fittings shall be legibly and durably marked to show the cross-sectional area of metal in channel cable trays, or cable trays of one-piece construction, and the total cross-sectional area of both side rails for ladder or trough cable trays.
(4) Cable tray sections, fittings, and connected raceways shall be bonded in accordance with 250.96, using bolted mechanical connectors or bonding jumpers sized and installed in accordance with 250.102.

392.8 Cable Installation.

(A) Cable Splices. Cable splices made and insulated by approved methods shall be permitted to be located within a cable tray, provided they are accessible and do not project above the side rails.

Table 392.7(B) Metal Area Requirements for Cable Trays Used as Equipment Grounding Conductor

Maximum Fuse Ampere Rating, Circuit Breaker Ampere Trip Setting, or Circuit Breaker Protective Relay Ampere Trip Setting for Ground-Fault Protection of Any Cable Circuit in the Cable Tray System	Minimum Cross-Sectional Area of Metal[a]			
	Steel Cable Trays		Aluminum Cable Trays	
	mm²	in.²	mm²	in.²
60	129	0.20	129	0.20
100	258	0.40	129	0.20
200	451.5	0.70	129	0.20
400	645	1.00	258	0.40
600	967.5	1.50[b]	258	0.40
1000	—	—	387	0.60
1200	—	—	645	1.00
1600	—	—	967.5	1.50
2000	—	—	1290	2.00[b]

[a]Total cross-sectional area of both side rails for ladder or trough cable trays; or the minimum cross-sectional area of metal in channel cable trays or cable trays of one-piece construction.

[b]Steel cable trays shall not be used as equipment grounding conductors for circuits with ground-fault protection above 600 amperes. Aluminum cable trays shall not be used as equipment grounding conductors for circuits with ground-fault protection above 2000 amperes.

(B) Fastened Securely. In other than horizontal runs, the cables shall be fastened securely to transverse members of the cable trays.

(C) Bushed Conduit and Tubing. A box shall not be required where cables or conductors are installed in bushed conduit and tubing used for support or for protection against physical damage.

(D) Connected in Parallel. Where single conductor cables comprising each phase, neutral, or grounded conductor of an alternating-current circuit are connected in parallel as permitted in 310.4, the conductors shall be installed in groups consisting of not more than one conductor per phase, neutral, or grounded conductor to prevent current imbalance in the paralleled conductors due to inductive reactance.

Single conductors shall be securely bound in circuit groups to prevent excessive movement due to fault-current magnetic forces unless single conductors are cabled together, such as triplexed assemblies.

(E) Single Conductors. Where any of the single conductors installed in ladder or ventilated trough cable trays are 1/0 through 4/0 AWG, all single conductors shall be installed in a single layer. Conductors that are bound together to comprise each circuit group shall be permitted to be installed in other than a single layer.

392.9 Number of Multiconductor Cables, Rated 2000 Volts or Less, in Cable Trays. The number of multiconductor cables, rated 2000 volts or less, permitted in a single cable tray shall not exceed the requirements of this section. The conductor sizes herein apply to both aluminum and copper conductors.

(A) Any Mixture of Cables. Where ladder or ventilated trough cable trays contain multiconductor power or lighting cables, or any mixture of multiconductor power, lighting, control, and signal cables, the maximum number of cables shall conform to the following:

(1) Where all of the cables are 4/0 AWG or larger, the sum of the diameters of all cables shall not exceed the cable tray width, and the cables shall be installed in a single layer.

(2) Where all of the cables are smaller than 4/0 AWG, the sum of the cross-sectional areas of all cables shall not exceed the maximum allowable cable fill area in Column 1 of Table 392.9 for the appropriate cable tray width.

(3) Where 4/0 AWG or larger cables are installed in the same cable tray with cables smaller than 4/0 AWG, the sum of the cross-sectional areas of all cables smaller than 4/0 AWG shall not exceed the maximum allowable fill area resulting from the calculation in Column 2 of Table 392.9 for the appropriate cable tray width. The 4/0 AWG and larger cables shall be installed in a single layer, and no other cables shall be placed on them.

(B) Multiconductor Control and/or Signal Cables Only. Where a ladder or ventilated trough cable tray having a usable inside depth of 150 mm (6 in.) or less contains multiconductor control and/or signal cables only, the sum of the cross-sectional areas of all cables at any cross section shall not exceed 50 percent of the interior cross-sectional area of the cable tray. A depth of 150 mm (6 in.) shall be used to calculate the allowable interior cross-sectional area of any cable tray that has a usable inside depth of more than 150 mm (6 in.).

(C) Solid Bottom Cable Trays Containing Any Mixture. Where solid bottom cable trays contain multiconductor power or lighting cables, or any mixture of multiconductor power, lighting, control, and signal cables, the maximum number of cables shall conform to the following:

(1) Where all of the cables are 4/0 AWG or larger, the sum of the diameters of all cables shall not exceed 90 percent of the cable tray width, and the cables shall be installed in a single layer.

(2) Where all of the cables are smaller than 4/0 AWG, the sum of the cross-sectional areas of all cables shall not exceed the maximum allowable cable fill area in Column 3 of Table 392.9 for the appropriate cable tray width.

Table 392.9 Allowable Cable Fill Area for Multiconductor Cables in Ladder, Ventilated Trough, or Solid Bottom Cable Trays for Cables Rated 2000 Volts or Less

Inside Width of Cable Tray		Maximum Allowable Fill Area for Multiconductor Cables						
		Ladder or Ventilated Trough Cable Trays, 392.9(A)				Solid Bottom Cable Trays, 392.9(C)		
		Column 1 Applicable for 392.9(A)(2) Only		Column 2[a] Applicable for 392.9(A)(3) Only		Column 3 Applicable for 392.9(C)(2) Only		Column 4[a] Applicable for 392.9(C)(3) Only	
mm	in.	mm²	in.²	mm²	in.²	mm²	in.²	mm²	in.²
150	6.0	4,500	7.0	$4{,}500 - (30\ Sd)^b$	$7 - (1.2\ Sd)^b$	3,500	5.5	$3{,}500 - (25\ Sd^b)$	$5.5 - Sd^b$
225	9.0	6,800	10.5	$6{,}800 - (30\ Sd)$	$10.5 - (1.2\ Sd)$	5,100	8.0	$5{,}100 - (25\ Sd)$	$8.0 - Sd$
300	12.0	9,000	14.0	$9{,}000 - (30\ Sd)$	$14 - (1.2\ Sd)$	7,100	11.0	$7{,}100 - (25\ Sd)$	$11.0 - Sd$
450	18.0	13,500	21.0	$13{,}500 - (30\ Sd)$	$21 - (1.2\ Sd)$	10,600	16.5	$10{,}600 - (25\ Sd)$	$16.5 - Sd$
600	24.0	18,000	28.0	$18{,}000 - (30\ Sd)$	$28 - (1.2\ Sd)$	14,200	22.0	$14{,}200 - (25\ Sd)$	$22.0 - Sd$
750	30.0	22,500	35.0	$22{,}500 - (30\ Sd)$	$35 - (1.2\ Sd)$	17,700	27.5	$17{,}700 - (25\ Sd)$	$27.5 - Sd$
900	36.0	27,000	42.0	$27{,}000 - (30\ Sd)$	$42 - (1.2\ Sd)$	21,300	33.0	$21{,}300 - (25\ Sd)$	$33.0 - Sd$

[a]The maximum allowable fill areas in Columns 2 and 4 shall be calculated. For example, the maximum allowable fill in mm² for a 150-mm wide cable tray in Column 2 shall be 4500 minus (30 multiplied by Sd) [the maximum allowable fill, in square inches, for a 6-in. wide cable tray in Column 2 shall be 7 minus (1.2 multiplied by Sd)].

[b]The term *Sd* in Columns 2 and 4 is equal to the sum of the diameters, in mm, of all cables 107.2 mm (in inches, of all 4/0 AWG) and larger multiconductor cables in the same cable tray with smaller cables.

(3) Where 4/0 AWG or larger cables are installed in the same cable tray with cables smaller than 4/0 AWG, the sum of the cross-sectional areas of all cables smaller than 4/0 AWG shall not exceed the maximum allowable fill area resulting from the computation in Column 4 of Table 392.9 for the appropriate cable tray width. The 4/0 AWG and larger cables shall be installed in a single layer, and no other cables shall be placed on them.

(D) Solid Bottom Cable Tray — Multiconductor Control and/or Signal Cables Only. Where a solid bottom cable tray having a usable inside depth of 150 mm (6 in.) or less contains multiconductor control and/or signal cables only, the sum of the cross-sectional areas of all cables at any cross section shall not exceed 40 percent of the interior cross-sectional area of the cable tray. A depth of 150 mm (6 in.) shall be used to calculate the allowable interior cross-sectional area of any cable tray that has a usable inside depth of more than 150 mm (6 in.).

(E) Ventilated Channel Cable Trays. Where ventilated channel cable trays contain multiconductor cables of any type, the following shall apply:

(1) Where only one multiconductor cable is installed, the cross-sectional area shall not exceed the value specified in Column 1 of Table 392.9(E).

(2) Where more than one multiconductor cable is installed, the sum of the cross-sectional area of all cables shall not exceed the value specified in Column 2 of Table 392.9(E).

Table 392.9(E) Allowable Cable Fill Area for Multiconductor Cables in Ventilated Channel Cable Trays for Cables Rated 2000 Volts or Less

Inside Width of Cable Tray		Maximum Allowable Fill Area for Multiconductor Cables			
		Column 1 One Cable		Column 2 More Than One Cable	
mm	in.	mm²	in.²	mm²	in.²
75	3	1500	2.3	850	1.3
100	4	2900	4.5	1600	2.5
150	6	4500	7.0	2450	3.8

(F) Solid Channel Cable Trays. Where solid channel cable trays contain multiconductor cables of any type, the following shall apply:

(1) Where only one multiconductor cable is installed, the cross-sectional area of the cable shall not exceed the value specified in Column 1 of Table 392.9(F).

(2) Where more than one multiconductor cable is installed, the sum of the cross-sectional area of all cable shall not exceed the value specified in Column 2 of Table 392.9(F).

Table 392.9(F) Allowable Cable Fill Area for Multiconductor Cables in Solid Channel Cable Trays for Cables Rated 2000 Volts or Less

Inside Width of Cable Tray		Column 1 One Cable		Column 2 More Than One Cable	
mm	in.	mm²	in.²	mm²	in.²
50	2	850	1.3	500	0.8
75	3	1300	2.0	700	1.1
100	4	2400	3.7	1400	2.1
150	6	3600	5.5	2100	3.2

392.10 Number of Single-Conductor Cables, Rated 2000 Volts or Less, in Cable Trays. The number of single-conductor cables, rated 2000 volts or less, permitted in a single cable tray section shall not exceed the requirements of this section. The single conductors, or conductor assemblies, shall be evenly distributed across the cable tray. The conductor sizes herein apply to both aluminum and copper conductors.

(A) Ladder or Ventilated Trough Cable Trays. Where ladder or ventilated trough cable trays contain single-conductor cables, the maximum number of single conductors shall conform to the following:

(1) Where all of the cables are 1000 kcmil or larger, the sum of the diameters of all single conductor cables shall not exceed cable tray width, and the cables shall be installed in a single layer. Conductors that are bound together to comprise each circuit group shall be permitted to be installed in other than a single layer.

(2) Where all of the cables are from 250 kcmil up to 1000 kcmil, the sum of the cross-sectional areas of all single-conductor cables shall not exceed the maximum allowable cable fill area in Column 1 of Table 392.10(A) for the appropriate cable tray width.

(3) Where 1000 kcmil or larger single-conductor cables are installed in the same cable tray with single-conductor cables smaller than 1000 kcmil, the sum of the cross-sectional areas of all cables smaller than 1000 kcmil shall not exceed the maximum allowable fill area resulting from the computation in Column 2 of Table 392.10(A) for the appropriate cable tray width.

(4) Where any of the single conductor cables are 1/0 through 4/0 AWG, the sum of the diameters of all single conductor cables shall not exceed the cable tray width.

(B) Ventilated Channel Cable Trays. Where 50 mm (2 in.), 75 mm (3 in.), 100 mm (4 in.), or 150 mm (6 in.) wide ventilated channel cable trays contain single-conductor cables, the sum of the diameters of all single conductors shall not exceed the inside width of the channel.

392.11 Ampacity of Cables, Rated 2000 Volts or Less, in Cable Trays.

(A) Multiconductor Cables. The allowable ampacity of multiconductor cables, nominally rated 2000 volts or less, installed according to the requirements of 392.9 shall be as given in Table 310.16 and Table 310.18, subject to the provisions of (1), (2), (3), and 310.15(A)(2).

Table 392.10(A) Allowable Cable Fill Area for Single-Conductor Cables in Ladder or Ventilated Trough Cable Trays for Cables Rated 2000 Volts or Less

Inside Width of Cable Tray		Maximum Allowable Fill Area for Single-Conductor Cables in Ladder or Ventilated Trough Cable Trays			
		Column 1 Applicable for 392.10(A)(2) Only		Column 2[a] Applicable for 392.10(A)(3) Only	
mm	in.	mm²	in.²	mm²	in.²
150	6	4,200	6.5	4,200 − (28 Sd)[b]	6.5 − (1.1 Sd)[b]
225	9	6,100	9.5	6,100 − (28 Sd)	9.5 − (1.1 Sd)
300	12	8,400	13.0	8,400 − (28 Sd)	13.0 − (1.1 Sd)
450	18	12,600	19.5	12,600 − (28 Sd)	19.5 − (1.1 Sd)
600	24	16,800	26.0	16,800 − (28 Sd)	26.0 − (1.1 Sd)
750	30	21,000	32.5	21,000 − (28 Sd)	32.5 − (1.1 Sd)
900	36	25,200	39.0	25,200 − (28 Sd)	39.0 − (1.1 Sd)

[a]The maximum allowable fill areas in Column 2 shall be calculated. For example, the maximum allowable fill, in mm², for a 150 mm wide cable tray in Column 2 shall be 4200 minus (28 multiplied by Sd) [the maximum allowable fill, in square inches, for a 6-in. wide cable tray in Column 2 shall be 6.5 minus (1.1 multiplied by Sd)].
[b]The term Sd in Column 2 is equal to the sum of the diameters, in mm, of all cables 507 mm² (in inches, of all 1000 kcmil) and larger single-conductor cables in the same ladder or ventilated trough cable tray with small cables.

(1) The derating factors of 310.15(B)(2)(a) shall apply only to multiconductor cables with more than three current-carrying conductors. Derating shall be limited to the number of current-carrying conductors in the cable and not to the number of conductors in the cable tray.

(2) Where cable trays are continuously covered for more than 1.8 m (6 ft) with solid unventilated covers, not over 95 percent of the allowable ampacities of Table 310.16 and Table 310.18 shall be permitted for multiconductor cables.

(3) Where multiconductor cables are installed in a single layer in uncovered trays, with a maintained spacing of not less than one cable diameter between cables, the ampacity shall not exceed the allowable ambient temperature-corrected ampacities of multiconductor cables, with not more than three insulated conductors rated 0 through 2000 volts in free air, in accordance with 310.15(C).

FPN: See Table B.310.3.

(B) Single-Conductor Cables. The allowable ampacity of single-conductor cables shall be as permitted by 310.15(A)(2). The derating factors of 310.15(B)(2)(a) shall not apply to the ampacity of cables in cable trays. The ampacity of single-conductor cables, or single conductors cabled together (triplexed, quadruplexed, etc.), nominally rated 2000 volts or less, shall comply with the following:

(1) Where installed according to the requirements of 392.10, the ampacities for 600 kcmil and larger single-conductor cables in uncovered cable trays shall not exceed 75 percent of the allowable ampacities in Table 310.17 and Table 310.19. Where cable trays are continuously covered for more than 1.8 m (6 ft) with solid unventilated covers, the ampacities for 600 kcmil and larger cables shall not exceed 70 percent of the allowable ampacities in Table 310.17 and Table 310.19.

(2) Where installed according to the requirements of 392.10, the ampacities for 1/0 AWG through 500 kcmil single-conductor cables in uncovered cable trays shall not exceed 65 percent of the allowable ampacities in Table 310.17 and Table 310.19. Where cable trays are continuously covered for more than 1.8 m (6 ft) with solid unventilated covers, the ampacities for 1/0 AWG through 500 kcmil cables shall not exceed 60 percent of the allowable ampacities in Table 310.17 and Table 310.19.

(3) Where single conductors are installed in a single layer in uncovered cable trays, with a maintained space of not less than one cable diameter between individual conductors, the ampacity of 1/0 AWG and larger cables shall not exceed the allowable ampacities in Table 310.17 and Table 310.19.

Exception to (B)(3): For solid bottom cable trays the ampacity of single conductor cables shall be determined by 310.15(C).

(4) Where single conductors are installed in a triangular or square configuration in uncovered cable trays, with a maintained free airspace of not less than 2.15 times one conductor diameter (2.15 × O.D.) of the largest conductor contained within the configuration and adjacent conductor configurations or cables, the ampacity of 1/0 AWG and larger cables shall not exceed the allowable ampacities of two or three single insulated conductors rated 0 through 2000 volts supported on a messenger in accordance with 310.15(B).

FPN: See Table 310.20.

392.12 Number of Type MV and Type MC Cables (2001 Volts or Over) in Cable Trays. The number of cables rated 2001 volts or over permitted in a single cable tray shall not exceed the requirements of this section.

The sum of the diameters of single-conductor and multiconductor cables shall not exceed the cable tray width, and the cables shall be installed in a single layer. Where single conductor cables are triplexed, quadruplexed, or bound together in circuit groups, the sum of the diameters of the single conductors shall not exceed the cable tray width, and these groups shall be installed in single layer arrangement.

392.13 Ampacity of Type MV and Type MC Cables (2001 Volts or Over) in Cable Trays. The ampacity of cables, rated 2001 volts, nominal, or over, installed according to 392.12 shall not exceed the requirements of this section.

(A) Multiconductor Cables (2001 Volts or Over). The allowable ampacity of multiconductor cables shall be as given in Table 310.75 and Table 310.76, subject to the following provisions:

(1) Where cable trays are continuously covered for more than 1.8 m (6 ft) with solid unventilated covers, not more than 95 percent of the allowable ampacities of Table 310.75 and Table 310.76 shall be permitted for multiconductor cables.

(2) Where multiconductor cables are installed in a single layer in uncovered cable trays, with maintained spacing of not less than one cable diameter between cables, the ampacity shall not exceed the allowable ampacities of Table 310.71 and Table 310.72.

(B) Single-Conductor Cables (2001 Volts or Over). The ampacity of single-conductor cables, or single conductors cabled together (triplexed, quadruplexed, etc.), shall comply with the following:

(1) The ampacities for 1/0 AWG and larger single-conductor cables in uncovered cable trays shall not exceed 75 percent of the allowable ampacities in Table 310.69 and Table 310.70. Where the cable trays are covered for more

than 1.8 m (6 ft) with solid unventilated covers, the ampacities for 1/0 AWG and larger single-conductor cables shall not exceed 70 percent of the allowable ampacities in Table 310.69 and Table 310.70.

(2) Where single-conductor cables are installed in a single layer in uncovered cable trays, with a maintained space of not less than one cable diameter between individual conductors, the ampacity of 1/0 AWG and larger cables shall not exceed the allowable ampacities in Table 310.69 and Table 310.70.

(3) Where single conductors are installed in a triangular or square configuration in uncovered cable trays, with a maintained free air space of not less than 2.15 times the diameter (2.15 × O.D.) of the largest conductor contained within the configuration and adjacent conductor configurations or cables, the ampacity of 1/0 AWG and larger cables shall not exceed the allowable ampacities in Table 310.67 and Table 310.68.

ARTICLE 394
Concealed Knob-and-Tube Wiring

I. General

394.1 Scope. This article covers the use, installation, and construction specifications of concealed knob-and-tube wiring.

394.2. Definition.

Concealed Knob-and-Tube Wiring. A wiring method using knobs, tubes, and flexible nonmetallic tubing for the protection and support of single insulated conductors.

II. Installation

394.10 Uses Permitted. Concealed knob-and-tube wiring shall be permitted to be installed in the hollow spaces of walls and ceilings or in unfinished attics and roof spaces as provided by 394.23 only as follows:

(1) For extensions of existing installations

(2) Elsewhere by special permission

394.12 Uses Not Permitted. Concealed knob-and-tube wiring shall not be used in the following:

(1) Commercial garages

(2) Theaters and similar locations

(3) Motion picture studios

(4) Hazardous (classified) locations

(5) Hollow spaces of walls, ceilings, and attics where such spaces are insulated by loose, rolled, or foamed-in-place insulating material that envelops the conductors

394.17 Through or Parallel to Framing Members. Conductors shall comply with 398.17 where passing through holes in structural members. Where passing through wood cross members in plastered partitions, conductors shall be protected by noncombustible, nonabsorbent, insulating tubes extending not less than 75 mm (3 in.) beyond the wood member.

394.19 Clearances.

(A) General. A clearance of not less than 75 mm (3 in.) shall be maintained between conductors and a clearance of not less than 25 mm (1 in.) between the conductor and the surface over which it passes.

(B) Limited Conductor Space. Where space is too limited to provide these minimum clearances, such as at meters, panelboards, outlets, and switch points, the individual conductors shall be enclosed in flexible nonmetallic tubing, which shall be continuous in length between the last support and the enclosure or terminal point.

(C) Clearance from Piping, Exposed Conductors, and So Forth. Conductors shall comply with 398.19 for clearances from other exposed conductors, piping, and so forth.

394.23 In Accessible Attics. Conductors in unfinished attics and roof spaces shall comply with 394.23(A) or (B).

FPN: See 310.10 for temperature limitation of conductors.

(A) Accessible by Stairway or Permanent Ladder. Conductors shall be installed along the side of or through bored holes in floor joists, studs, or rafters. Where run through bored holes, conductors in the joists and in studs or rafters to a height of not less than 2.1 m (7 ft) above the floor or floor joists shall be protected by substantial running boards extending not less than 25 mm (1 in.) on each side of the conductors. Running boards shall be securely fastened in place. Running boards and guard strips shall not be required where conductors are installed along the sides of joists, studs, or rafters.

(B) Not Accessible by Stairway or Permanent Ladder. Conductors shall be installed along the sides of or through bored holes in floor joists, studs, or rafters.

Exception: In buildings completed before the wiring is installed, attic and roof spaces that are not accessible by stairway or permanent ladder and have headroom at all points less than 900 mm (3 ft), the wiring shall be permitted to be installed on the edges of rafters or joists facing the attic or roof space.

394.30 Securing and Supporting.

(A) Supporting. Conductors shall be rigidly supported on noncombustible, nonabsorbent insulating materials and shall not contact any other objects. Supports shall be installed as follows:

(1) Within 150 mm (6 in.) of each side of each tap or splice, and

(2) At intervals not exceeding 1.4 m (4½ ft).

Where it is impracticable to provide supports, conductors shall be permitted to be fished through hollow spaces in dry locations, provided each conductor is individually enclosed in flexible nonmetallic tubing that is in continuous lengths between supports, between boxes, or between a support and a box.

(B) Securing. Where solid knobs are used, conductors shall be securely tied thereto by tie wires having insulation equivalent to that of the conductor.

394.42 Devices. Switches shall comply with 404.4 and 404.10(B).

394.56 Splices and Taps. Splices shall be soldered unless approved splicing devices are used. In-line or strain splices shall not be used.

III. Construction Specifications

394.104 Conductors. Conductors shall be of a type specified by Article 310.

ARTICLE 396
Messenger Supported Wiring

I. General

396.1 Scope. This article covers the use, installation, and construction specifications for messenger supported wiring.

396.2 Definition.

Messenger Supported Wiring. An exposed wiring support system using a messenger wire to support insulated conductors by any one of the following:

(1) A messenger with rings and saddles for conductor support

(2) A messenger with a field-installed lashing material for conductor support

(3) Factory-assembled aerial cable

(4) Multiplex cables utilizing a bare conductor, factory assembled and twisted with one or more insulated conductors, such as duplex, triplex, or quadruplex type of construction

II. Installation

396.10 Uses Permitted.

(A) Cable Types. The cable types in Table 396.10(A) shall be permitted to be installed in messenger supported wiring under the conditions described in the article or section referenced for each.

Table 396.10(A) Cable Types

Cable Type	Section	Article
Metal-clad cable		330
Mineral-insulated, metal-sheathed cable		332
Multiconductor service-entrance cable		338
Multiconductor underground feeder and branch-circuit cable		340
Other factory-assembled, multiconductor control, signal, or power cables that are identified for the use		
Power and control tray cable		336
Power-limited tray cable	725.61(C) and 725.82(E)	

(B) In Industrial Establishments. In industrial establishments only, where conditions of maintenance and supervision ensure that only qualified persons service the installed messenger supported wiring, the following shall be permitted:

(1) Any of the conductor types shown in Table 310.13 or Table 310.62

(2) MV cable

Where exposed to weather, conductors shall be listed for use in wet locations. Where exposed to direct rays of the sun, conductors or cables shall be sunlight resistant.

(C) Hazardous (Classified) Locations. Messenger supported wiring shall be permitted to be used in hazardous (classified) locations where the contained cables are permitted for such use in 501.10, 502.10, 503.10, and 504.20.

396.12 Uses Not Permitted. Messenger supported wiring shall not be used in hoistways or where subject to physical damage.

396.30 Messenger Support. The messenger shall be supported at dead ends and at intermediate locations so as to eliminate tension on the conductors. The conductors shall not be permitted to come into contact with the messenger supports or any structural members, walls, or pipes.

396.56 Conductor Splices and Taps. Conductor splices and taps made and insulated by approved methods shall be permitted in messenger supported wiring.

396.60 Grounding. The messenger shall be grounded as required by 250.80 and 250.86 for enclosure grounding.

ARTICLE 398
Open Wiring on Insulators

I. General

398.1 Scope. This article covers the use, installation, and construction specifications of open wiring on insulators.

398.2 Definition.

Open Wiring on Insulators. An exposed wiring method using cleats, knobs, tubes, and flexible tubing for the protection and support of single insulated conductors run in or on buildings.

II. Installation

398.10 Uses Permitted. Open wiring on insulators shall be permitted only for industrial or agricultural establishments on systems of 600 volts, nominal, or less, as follows:

(1) Indoors or outdoors

(2) In wet or dry locations

(3) Where subject to corrosive vapors

(4) For services

398.12 Uses Not Permitted. Open wiring on insulators shall not be installed where concealed by the building structure.

398.15 Exposed Work.

(A) Dry Locations. In dry locations, where not exposed to physical damage, conductors shall be permitted to be separately enclosed in flexible nonmetallic tubing. The tubing shall be in continuous lengths not exceeding 4.5 m (15 ft) and secured to the surface by straps at intervals not exceeding 1.4 m (4½ ft).

(B) Entering Spaces Subject to Dampness, Wetness, or Corrosive Vapors. Conductors entering or leaving locations subject to dampness, wetness, or corrosive vapors shall have drip loops formed on them and shall then pass upward and inward from the outside of the buildings, or from the damp, wet, or corrosive location, through noncombustible, nonabsorbent insulating tubes.

FPN: See 230.52 for individual conductors entering buildings or other structures.

(C) Exposed to Physical Damage. Conductors within 2.1 m (7 ft) from the floor shall be considered exposed to physical damage. Where open conductors cross ceiling joists and wall studs and are exposed to physical damage, they shall be protected by one of the following methods:

(1) Guard strips not less than 25 mm (1 in.) nominal in thickness and at least as high as the insulating supports, placed on each side of and close to the wiring.

(2) A substantial running board at least 13 mm (½ in.) thick in back of the conductors with side protections. Running boards shall extend at least 25 mm (1 in.) outside the conductors, but not more than 50 mm (2 in.), and the protecting sides shall be at least 50 mm (2 in.) high and at least 25 mm (1 in.) nominal in thickness.

(3) Boxing made in accordance with 398.15(C)(1) or (C)(2) and furnished with a cover kept at least 25 mm (1 in.) away from the conductors within. Where protecting vertical conductors on side walls, the boxing shall be closed at the top and the holes through which the conductors pass shall be bushed.

(4) Rigid metal conduit, intermediate metal conduit, rigid nonmetallic conduit, or electrical metallic tubing. When installed in metal piping, the conductors shall be encased in continuous lengths of approved flexible tubing.

398.17 Through or Parallel to Framing Members. Open conductors shall be separated from contact with walls, floors, wood cross members, or partitions through which they pass by tubes or bushings of noncombustible, nonabsorbent insulating material. Where the bushing is shorter than the hole, a waterproof sleeve of noninductive material shall be inserted in the hole and an insulating bushing slipped into the sleeve at each end in such a manner as to keep the conductors absolutely out of contact with the sleeve. Each conductor shall be carried through a separate tube or sleeve.

FPN: See 310.10 for temperature limitation of conductors.

398.19 Clearances. Open conductors shall be separated at least 50 mm (2 in.) from metal raceways, piping, or other conducting material, and from any exposed lighting, power, or signaling conductor, or shall be separated therefrom by a continuous and firmly fixed nonconductor in addition to the insulation of the conductor. Where any insulating tube is used, it shall be secured at the ends. Where practicable, conductors shall pass over rather than under any piping subject to leakage or accumulations of moisture.

398.23 In Accessible Attics. Conductors in unfinished attics and roof spaces shall comply with 398.23(A) or (B).

(A) Accessible by Stairway or Permanent Ladder. Conductors shall be installed along the side of or through bored holes in floor joists, studs, or rafters. Where run through bored holes, conductors in the joists and in studs or rafters to a height of not less than 2.1 m (7 ft) above the floor or floor joists shall be protected by substantial running boards extending not less than 25 mm (1 in.) on each side of the conductors. Running boards shall be securely fastened in place. Running boards and guard strips shall not be required for conductors installed along the sides of joists, studs, or rafters.

(B) Not Accessible by Stairway or Permanent Ladder. Conductors shall be installed along the sides of or through bored holes in floor joists, studs, or rafters.

Exception: In buildings completed before the wiring is installed, in attic and roof spaces that are not accessible by stairway or permanent ladder and have headroom at all points less than 900 mm (3 ft), the wiring shall be permitted to be installed on the edges of rafters or joists facing the attic or roof space.

398.30 Securing and Supporting.

(A) Conductor Sizes Smaller Than 8 AWG. Conductors smaller than 8 AWG shall be rigidly supported on noncombustible, nonabsorbent insulating materials and shall not contact any other objects. Supports shall be installed as follows:

(1) Within 150 mm (6 in.) from a tap or splice

(2) Within 300 mm (12 in.) of a dead-end connection to a lampholder or receptacle

(3) At intervals not exceeding 1.4 m (4½ ft) and at closer intervals sufficient to provide adequate support where likely to be disturbed

(B) Conductor Sizes 8 AWG and Larger. Supports for conductors 8 AWG or larger installed across open spaces shall be permitted up to 4.5 m (15 ft) apart if noncombustible, nonabsorbent insulating spacers are used at least every 1.4 m (4½ ft) to maintain at least 65 mm (2½ in.) between conductors.

Where not likely to be disturbed in buildings of mill construction, 8 AWG and larger conductors shall be permitted to be run across open spaces if supported from each wood cross member on approved insulators maintaining 150 mm (6 in.) between conductors.

(C) Industrial Establishments. In industrial establishments only, where conditions of maintenance and supervision ensure that only qualified persons service the system, conductors of sizes 250 kcmil and larger shall be permitted to be run across open spaces where supported at intervals up to 9.0 m (30 ft) apart.

(D) Mounting of Conductor Supports. Where nails are used to mount knobs, they shall not be smaller than tenpenny. Where screws are used to mount knobs, or where nails or screws are used to mount cleats, they shall be of a length sufficient to penetrate the wood to a depth equal to at least one-half the height of the knob and the full thickness of the cleat. Cushion washers shall be used with nails.

(E) Tie Wires. 8 AWG or larger conductors supported on solid knobs shall be securely tied thereto by tie wires having an insulation equivalent to that of the conductor.

398.42 Devices. Surface-type snap switches shall be mounted in accordance with 404.10(A), and boxes shall not be required. Other type switches shall be installed in accordance with 404.4.

III. Construction Specifications

398.104 Conductors. Conductors shall be of a type specified by Article 310.

Chapter 4 Equipment for General Use

ARTICLE 400
Flexible Cords and Cables

I. General

400.1 Scope. This article covers general requirements, applications, and construction specifications for flexible cords and flexible cables.

400.2 Other Articles. Flexible cords and flexible cables shall comply with this article and with the applicable provisions of other articles of this *Code*.

400.3 Suitability. Flexible cords and cables and their associated fittings shall be suitable for the conditions of use and location.

400.4 Types. Flexible cords and flexible cables shall conform to the description in Table 400.4. Types of flexible cords and flexible cables other than those listed in the table shall be the subject of special investigation.

Table 400.4 Flexible Cords and Cables *(See 400.4.)*

Trade Name	Type Letter	Voltage	AWG or kcmil	Number of Conductors	Insulation	Nominal Insulation Thickness[1]			Braid on Each Conductor	Outer Covering	Use		
						AWG or kcmil	mm	mils					
Lamp cord	C	300 600	18–16 14–10	2 or more	Thermoset or thermoplastic	18–16 14–10	0.76 1.14	30 45	Cotton	None	Pendant or portable	Dry locations	Not hard usage
Elevator cable	E See Note 5. See Note 9. See Note 10.	300 or 600	20–2	2 or more	Thermoset	20–16 14–12 12–10 8–2	0.51 0.76 1.14 1.52	20 30 45 60	Cotton	Three cotton, Outer one flame-retardant & moisture-resistant. See Note 3.	Elevator lighting and control	Unclassified locations	
						20–16 14–12 12–10 8–2	0.51 0.76 1.14 1.52	20 30 45 60	Flexible nylon jacket				
Elevator cable	EO See Note 5. See Note 10.	300 or 600	20–2	2 or more	Thermoset	20–16 14–12 12–10 8–2	0.51 0.76 1.14 1.52	20 30 45 60	Cotton	Outer one Three cotton, flame-retardant & moisture-resistant. See Note 3.	Elevator lighting and control	Unclassified locations	
										One cotton and a neoprene jacket. See Note 3.		Hazardous (classified) locations	
Elevator cable	ETP See Note 5. See Note 10.	300 or 600							Rayon	Thermoplastic	Hazardous (classified) locations		
	ETT See Note 5. See Note 10.	300 or 600							None	One cotton or equivalent and a thermoplastic jacket			

Table 400.4 *Continued*

Trade Name	Type Letter	Voltage	AWG or kcmil	Number of Conductors	Insulation	Nominal Insulation Thickness[1]			Braid on Each Conductor	Outer Covering	Use		
						AWG or kcmil	mm	mils					
Electric vehicle cable	EV	600	18–500 See Note 11.	2 or more plus grounding conductor(s), plus optional hybrid data, signal communications, and optical fiber cables	Thermoset with optional nylon See Note 12.	18–16 14–10 8–2 1–4/0 250–500	0.76 (0.51) 1.14 (0.76) 1.52 (1.14) 2.03 (1.52) 2.41 (1.90)	30 (20) 45 (30) 60 (45) 80 (60) 95 (75) See Note 12.	Optional	Thermoset	Electric vehicle charging	Wet locations	Extra hard usage
	EVJ	300	18–12 See Note 11.			18–12	0.76(0.51)	30 (20) See Note 12.					Hard usage
	EVE	600	18–500 See Note 11.	2 or more plus grounding conductor(s), plus optional hybrid data, signal communications, and optical fiber cables	Thermoplastic elastomer with optional nylon See Note 12.	18–16 14–10 8–2 1–4/0 250–500	0.76 (0.51) 1.14 (0.76) 1.52 (1.14) 2.03 (1.52) 2.41 (1.90)	30 (20) 45 (30) 60 (45) 80 (60) 95 (75) See Note 12.		Thermoplastic elastomer			Extra hard usage
	EVJE	300	18–12 See Note 11.			18–12	0.76 (0.51)	30 (20) See Note 12.					Hard usage
	EVT	600	18–500 See Note 11.	2 or more plus grounding conductor(s), plus optional hybrid data, signal communications, and optical fiber cables	Thermoplastic with optional nylon See Note 12.	18–16 14–10 8–2 1–4/0 250–500	0.76 (0.51) 1.14 (0.76) 1.52 (1.14) 2.03 (1.52) 2.41 (1.90)	30 (20) 45 (30) 60 (45) 80 (60) 95 (75) See Note 12.	Optional	Thermoplastic	Electric vehicle charging	Wet Locations	Extra hard usage
	EVJT	300	18–12 See Note 11.			18–12	0.76 (0.51)	30 (20) See Note 12.					Hard usage
Portable power cable	G	2000	12–500	2–6 plus grounding conductor(s)	Thermoset	12–2 1–4/0 250–500	1.52 2.03 2.41	60 80 95		Oil-resistant thermoset	Portable and extra hard usage		
	G-GC	2000	12–500	3–6 plus grounding conductors and 1 ground check conductor	Thermoset	12–2 1–4/0 250–500	1.52 2.03 2.41	60 80 95		Oil-resistant thermoset			
Heater cord	HPD	300	18–12	2, 3, or 4	Thermoset	18–16 14–12	0.38 0.76	15 30	None	Cotton or rayon	Portable heaters	Dry locations	Not hard usage
Parallel heater cord	HPN See Note 6.	300	18–12	2 or 3	Oil-resistant thermoset	18–16 14–12	1.14 1.52 2.41	45 60 95	None	Oil-resistant thermoset	Portable	Damp locations	Not hard usage

(Continues)

Table 400.4 *Continued*

Trade Name	Type Letter	Voltage	AWG or kcmil	Number of Conductors	Insulation	Nominal Insulation Thickness[1] AWG or kcmil	mm	mils	Braid on Each Conductor	Outer Covering	Use		
Thermoset jacketed heater cords	HSJ	300	18–12	2, 3, or 4	Thermoset	18–16	0.76	30	None	Cotton and Thermoset	Portable or portable heater	Damp locations	Hard usage
	HSJO	300	18–12		Oil-resistant thermoset	14–12	1.14	45		Cotton and oil-resistant thermoset			
	HSJOO	300	18–12										
Non-integral parallel cords	NISP-1 See Note 6.	300	20–18	2 or 3	Thermoset	20–18	0.38	15	None	Thermoset	Pendant or portable	Damp locations	Not hard usage
	NISP-2 See Note 6.	300	18–16			18–16	0.76	30					
	NISPE-1 See Note 6.	300	20–18		Thermoplastic elastomer	20–18	0.38	15		Thermoplastic elastomer			
	NISPE-2 See Note 6.	300	18–16			18–16	0.76	30					
	NISPT-1 See Note 6.	300	20–18		Thermoplastic	20–18	0.38	15		Thermoplastic			
	NISPT-2 See Note 6.	300	18–16			18–16	0.76	30					
Twisted portable cord	PD	300 600	18–16 14–10	2 or more	Thermoset or thermoplastic	18–16 14–10	0.76 1.14	30 45	Cotton	Cotton or rayon	Pendant or portable	Dry locations	Not hard usage
Portable power cable	PPE	2000	12–500	1–6 plus optional grounding conductor(s)	Thermoplastic elastomer	12–2 1–4/0 250–500	1.52 2.03 2.41	60 80 95		Oil-resistant thermoplastic elastomer	Portable, extra hard usage		
Hard service cord	S See Note 4.	600	18–12	2 or more	Thermoset	18–16 14–10 8–2	0.76 1.14 1.52	30 45 60	None	Thermoset	Pendant or portable	Damp locations	Extra hard usage
Flexible stage and lighting power cable	SC	600	8–250	1 or more		8–2 1–4/0 250	1.52 2.03 2.41	60 80 95		Thermoset[2]	Portable, extra hard usage		
	SCE	600			Thermoplastic elastomer					Thermoplastic elastomer[2]			
	SCT	600			Thermoplastic					Thermoplastic[2]			
Hard service cord	SE See Note 4.	600	18–2	2 or more	Thermoplastic elastomer	18–16 14–10 8–2	0.76 1.14 1.52	30 45 60	None	Thermoplastic elastomer	Pendant or portable	Damp locations	Extra hard usage
	SEW See Note 4. See Note 13.	600										Damp and wet locations	
	SEO See Note 4.	600								Oil-resistant thermoplastic elastomer		Damp locations	
	SEOW See Note 4. See Note 13.	600										Damp and wet locations	

Table 400.4 Continued

Trade Name	Type Letter	Voltage	AWG or kcmil	Number of Conductors	Insulation	Nominal Insulation Thickness[1]			Braid on Each Conductor	Outer Covering	Use		
						AWG or kcmil	mm	mils					
	SEOO See Note 4.	600	18–2	2 or more	Oil-resistant thermoplastic elastomer	18–16 14–10 8–2	0.76 1.14 1.52	30 45 60	None	Oil-resistant thermoplastic elastomer	Pendant or portable	Damp locations	Extra hard usage
	SEOOW See Note 4. See Note 13.	600										Damp and wet locations	
Junior hard service cord	SJ	300	18–10	2–6	Thermoset	18–12	0.76	30	None	Thermoset	Pendant or portable	Damp locations	Hard usage
	SJE	300			Thermoplastic elastomer					Thermoplastic elastomer			
	SJEW See Note 13.	300										Damp and wet locations	
	SJEO	300								Oil-resistant thermoplastic elastomer		Damp locations	
	SJEOW See Note 13.	300										Damp and wet locations	
	SJEOO	300			Oil-resistant thermoplastic elastomer							Damp locations	
	SJEOOW See Note 13.	300										Damp and wet locations	
	SJO	300			Thermoset					Oil-resistant thermoset		Damp locations	
	SJOW See Note 13.	300										Damp and wet locations	
	SJOO	300			Oil-resistant thermoset							Damp locations	
	SJOOW See Note 13.	300										Damp and wet locations	
	SJT	300			Thermoplastic	10	1.14	45		Thermoplastic		Damp locations	
	SJTW See Note 13.	300										Damp and wet locations	
	SJTO	300				18–12	0.76	30		Oil-resistant thermoplastic		Damp locations	
	SJTOW See Note 13.	300										Damp and wet locations	
	SJTOO	300			Oil-resistant thermoplastic							Damp locations	
	SJTOOW See Note 13.	300										Damp and wet locations	

(Continues)

Table 400.4 *Continued*

Trade Name	Type Letter	Voltage	AWG or kcmil	Number of Conductors	Insulation	Nominal Insulation Thickness[1]			Braid on Each Conductor	Outer Covering	Use		
						AWG or kcmil	mm	mils					
Hard service cord	SO See Note 4.	600	18–2	2 or more	Thermoset	18–16	0.76	30	None	Oil-resistant thermoset	Pendant or portable	Damp locations	Extra hard usage
	SOW See Note 4. See Note 13.	600										Damp and wet locations	
	SOO See Note 4.	600			Oil-resistant thermoset	14–10 8–2	1.14 1.52	45 60				Damp locations	
	SOOW See Note 4. See Note 13.	600										Damp and wet locations	
All thermoset parallel cord	SP-1 See Note 6.	300	20–18	2 or 3	Thermoset	20–18	0.76	30	None	None	Pendant or portable	Damp locations	Not hard usage
	SP-2 See Note 6.	300	18–16			18–16	1.14	45					
	SP-3 See Note 6.	300	18–10			18–16 14 12 10	1.52 2.03 2.41 2.80	60 80 95 110			Refrigerators, room air conditioners, and as permitted in 422.16(B)		
All elastomer (thermoplastic) parallel cord	SPE-1 See Note 6.	300	20–18	2 or 3	Thermoplastic elastomer	20–18	0.76	30	None	None	Pendant or portable	Damp locations	Not Hard usage
	SPE-2 See Note 6.	300	18–16			18–16	1.14	45					
	SPE-3 See Note 6.	300	18–10			18–16 14 12 10	1.52 2.03 2.41 2.80	60 80 95 110			Refrigerators, room air conditioners, and as permitted in 422.16(B)		
All plastic parallel cord	SPT-1 See Note 6.	300	20–18	2 or 3	Thermoplastic	20–18	0.76	30	None	None	Pendant or portable	Damp locations	Not hard usage
	SPT-1W See Note 6. See Note 13.	300										Damp and wet locations	
	SPT-2 See Note 6.	300	18–16			18–16	1.14	45				Damp locations	
	SPT-2W See Note 6. See Note 13.	300										Damp and wet locations	
	SPT-3 See Note 6.	300	18–10			18–16 14 12 10	1.52 2.03 2.41 2.80	60 80 95 110			Refrigerators, room air conditioners, and as permitted in 422.16(B)	Damp locations	Not hard usage

Table 400.4 *Continued*

Trade Name	Type Letter	Voltage	AWG or kcmil	Number of Conductors	Insulation	Nominal Insulation Thickness[1]			Braid on Each Conductor	Outer Covering	Use		
						AWG or kcmil	mm	mils					
Range, dryer cable	SRD	300	10–4	3 or 4	Thermoset	10–4	1.14	45	None	Thermoset	Portable	Damp locations	Ranges, dryers
	SRDE	300	10–4	3 or 4	Thermoplastic elastomer				None	Thermoplastic elastomer			
	SRDT	300	10–4	3 or 4	Thermoplastic				None	Thermoplastic			
Hard service cord	ST See Note 4.	600	18–2	2 or more	Thermoplastic	18–16 14–10 8–2	0.76 1.14 1.52	30 45 60	None	Thermoplastic	Pendant or portable	Damp locations	Extra hard usage
	STW See Note 4. See Note 13.	600										Damp and wet locations	
	STO See Note 4.	600								Oil-resistant thermoplastic		Damp locations	
	STOW See Note 4. See Note 13.	600										Damp and wet locations	
	STOO See Note 4.	600				Oil-resistant thermoplastic						Damp locations	
	STOOW See Note 4.	600										Damp and wet locations	
Vacuum cleaner cord	SV See Note 6.	300	18–16	2 or 3	Thermoset	18–16	0.38	15	None	Thermoset	Pendant or portable	Damp locations	Not hard usage
	SVE See Note 6.	300			Thermoplastic elastomer					Thermoplastic elastomer			
	SVEO See Note 6.	300								Oil-resistant termoplastic elastomer			
	SVEOO See Note 6.	300			Oil-resistant thermoplastic elastomer								
	SVO	300			Thermoset					Oil-resistant thermoset			
	SVOO	300			Oil-resistant thermoset					Oil-resistant thermoset			
	SVT See Note 6.	300			Thermoplastic					Thermoplastic			
	SVTO See Note 6.	300			Thermoplastic					Oil-resistant thermoplastic			
	SVTOO	300			Oil-resistant thermoplastic								
Parallel tinsel cord	TPT See Note 2.	300	27	2	Thermoplastic	27	0.76	N30	None	Thermoplastic	Attached to an appliance	Damp locations	Not hard usage

(Continues)

Table 400.4   *Continued*

Trade Name	Type Letter	Voltage	AWG or kcmil	Number of Conductors	Insulation	Nominal Insulation Thickness[1]			Braid on Each Conductor	Outer Covering	Use		
						AWG or kcmil	mm	mils					
Jacketed tinsel cord	TST See Note 2.	300	27	2	Thermo-plastic	27	0.38	N15	None	Thermoplastic	Attached to an appliance	Damp locations	Not hard usage
Portable power-cable	W	2000	12–500 501–1000	1–6 1	Thermoset	12–2 1–4/0 250–500 501–1000	1.52 2.03 2.41 2.80	N60 N80 N95 110		Oil-resistant thermoset	Portable, extra hard usage		

*See Note 8.

**The required outer covering on some single conductor cables may be integral with the insulation.

Notes:

1. All types listed in Table 400.4 shall have individual conductors twisted together except for Types HPN, SP-1, SP-2, SP-3, SPE-1, SPE-2, SPE-3, SPT-1, SPT-2, SPT-3, TPT, NISP-1, NISP-2, NISPT-1, NISPT-2, NISPE-1, NISPE-2, and three-conductor parallel versions of SRD, SRDE, and SRDT.

2. Types TPT and TST shall be permitted in lengths not exceeding 2.5 m (8 ft) where attached directly, or by means of a special type of plug, to a portable appliance rated at 50 watts or less and of such nature that extreme flexibility of the cord is essential.

3. Rubber-filled or varnished cambric tapes shall be permitted as a substitute for the inner braids.

4. Types G, G-GC, S, SC, SCE, SCT, SE, SEO, SEOO, SO, SOO, ST, STO, STOO, PPE, and W shall be permitted for use on theater stages, in garages, and elsewhere where flexible cords are permitted by this *Code*.

5. Elevator traveling cables for operating control and signal circuits shall contain nonmetallic fillers as necessary to maintain concentricity. Cables shall have steel supporting members as required for suspension by 620.41. In locations subject to excessive moisture or corrosive vapors or gases, supporting members of other materials shall be permitted. Where steel supporting members are used, they shall run straight through the center of the cable assembly and shall not be cabled with the copper strands of any conductor.

In addition to conductors used for control and signaling circuits, Types E, EO, ETP, and ETT elevator cables shall be permitted to incorporate in the construction one or more 20 AWG telephone conductor pairs, one or more coaxial cables, or one or more optical fibers. The 20 AWG conductor pairs shall be permitted to be covered with suitable shielding for telephone, audio, or higher frequency communications circuits; the coaxial cables consist of a center conductor, insulation, and shield for use in video or other radio frequency communications circuits. The optical fiber shall be suitably covered with flame-retardant thermoplastic. The insulation of the conductors shall be rubber or thermoplastic of thickness not less than specified for the other conductors of the particular type of cable. Metallic shields shall have their own protective covering. Where used, these components shall be permitted to be incorporated in any layer of the cable assembly but shall not run straight through the center.

6. The third conductor in these cables shall be used for equipment grounding purpose only. The insulation of the grounding conductor for Types SPE-1, SPE-2, SPE-3, SPT-1, SPT-2, SPT-3, NISPT-1, NISPT-2, NISPE-1, and NISPE-2 shall be permitted to be thermoset polymer.

7. The individual conductors of all cords, except those of heat-resistant cords, shall have a thermoset or thermoplastic insulation, except that the equipment grounding conductor where used shall be in accordance with 400.23(B).

8. Where the voltage between any two conductors exceeds 300, but does not exceed 600, flexible cord of 10 AWG and smaller shall have thermoset or thermoplastic insulation on the individual conductors at least 1.14 mm (45 mils) in thickness, unless Type S, SE, SEO, SEOO, SO, SOO, ST, STO, or STOO cord is used.

9. Insulations and outer coverings that meet the requirements as flame retardant, limited smoke, and are so listed, shall be permitted to be marked for limited smoke after the code type designation.

10. Elevator cables in sizes 20 AWG through 14 AWG are rated 300 volts, and sizes 10 through 2 are rated 600 volts. 12 AWG is rated 300 volts with a 0.76-mm (30-mil) insulation thickness and 600 volts with a 1.14-mm (45-mil) insulation thickness.

11. Conductor size for Types EV, EVJ, EVE, EVJE, EVT, and EVJT cables apply to nonpower-limited circuits only. Conductors of power-limited (data, signal, or communications) circuits may extend beyond the stated AWG size range. All conductors shall be insulated for the same cable voltage rating.

12. Insulation thickness for Types EV, EVJ, EVEJE, EVT, and EVJT cables of nylon construction is indicated in parentheses.

13. Cords that comply with the requirements for outdoor cords and are so listed shall be permitted to be designated as weather and water resistant with the suffix "W" after the code type designation. Cords with the "W" suffix are suitable for use in wet locations.

400.5 Ampacities for Flexible Cords and Cables.

(A) Ampacity Tables. Table 400.5(A) provides the allowable ampacities, and Table 400.5(B) provides the ampacities for flexible cords and cables with not more than three current-carrying conductors. These tables shall be used in conjunction with applicable end-use product standards to ensure selection of the proper size and type. Where cords are used in ambient temperatures exceeding 30°C (86°F), the temperature correction factors from Table 310.16 that correspond to the temperature rating of the cord shall be applied to the ampacity from Table 400.5(B). Where the number of current-carrying conductors exceeds three, the allowable ampacity or the ampacity of each conductor shall be reduced from the 3-conductor rating as shown in Table 400.5.

Table 400.5 Adjustment Factors for More Than Three Current-Carrying Conductors in a Flexible Cord or Cable

Number of Conductors	Percent of Value in Tables 400.5(A) and 400.5(B)
4 – 6	80
7 – 9	70
10 – 20	50
21 – 30	45
31 – 40	40
41 and above	35

(B) Ultimate Insulation Temperature. In no case shall conductors be associated together in such a way with respect to the kind of circuit, the wiring method used, or the number of conductors such that the limiting temperature of the conductors is exceeded.

A neutral conductor that carries only the unbalanced current from other conductors of the same circuit shall not be required to meet the requirements of a current-carrying conductor.

In a 3-wire circuit consisting of two phase wires and the neutral of a 4-wire, 3-phase, wye-connected system, a common conductor carries approximately the same current as the line-to-neutral currents of the other conductors and shall be considered to be a current-carrying conductor.

On a 4-wire, 3-phase, wye circuit where the major portion of the load consists of nonlinear loads, there are harmonic currents present in the neutral conductor and the neutral shall be considered to be a current-carrying conductor.

An equipment grounding conductor shall not be considered a current-carrying conductor.

Where a single conductor is used for both equipment grounding and to carry unbalanced current from other conductors, as provided for in 250.140 for electric ranges and electric clothes dryers, it shall not be considered as a current-carrying conductor.

Exception: For other loading conditions, adjustment factors shall be permitted to be calculated under 310.15(C).

FPN: See Annex B, Table B.310.11, for adjustment factors for more than three current-carrying conductors in a raceway or cable with load diversity.

400.6 Markings.

(A) Standard Markings. Flexible cords and cables shall be marked by means of a printed tag attached to the coil reel or carton. The tag shall contain the information required in 310.11(A). Types S, SC, SCE, SCT, SE, SEO, SEOO, SJ, SJE, SJEO, SJEOO, SJO, SJT, SJTO, SJTOO, SO, SOO, ST, STO, STOO, SEW, SEOW, SEOOW, SJEW, SJEOW, SJEOOW, SJOW, SJTW, SJTOW, SJTOOW, SOW, SOOW, STW, STOW, and STOOW flexible cords and G, G-GC, PPE, and W flexible cables shall be durably marked on the surface at intervals not exceeding 610 mm (24 in.) with the type designation, size, and number of conductors.

(B) Optional Markings. Flexible cords and cable types listed in Table 400.4 shall be permitted to be surface marked to indicate special characteristics of the cable materials. These markings include, but are not limited to, markings for limited smoke, sunlight resistance, and so forth.

400.7 Uses Permitted.

(A) Uses. Flexible cords and cables shall be used only for the following:

(1) Pendants

(2) Wiring of luminaires (fixtures)

(3) Connection of portable lamps, portable and mobile signs, or appliances

(4) Elevator cables

(5) Wiring of cranes and hoists

(6) Connection of utilization equipment to facilitate frequent interchange

(7) Prevention of the transmission of noise or vibration

(8) Appliances where the fastening means and mechanical connections are specifically designed to permit ready removal for maintenance and repair, and the appliance is intended or identified for flexible cord connection

(9) Connection of moving parts

(10) Where specifically permitted elsewhere in this *Code*

(B) Attachment Plugs. Where used as permitted in 400.7(A)(3), (A)(6), and (A)(8), each flexible cord shall be equipped with an attachment plug and shall be energized from a receptacle outlet.

Exception: As permitted in 368.56.

400.8 Uses Not Permitted.
Unless specifically permitted in 400.7, flexible cords and cables shall not be used for the following:

(1) As a substitute for the fixed wiring of a structure

Table 400.5(A) Allowable Ampacity for Flexible Cords and Cables [Based on Ambient Temperature of 30°C (86°F). See 400.13 and Table 400.4.]

Size (AWG)	Thermoplastic Types TPT, TST	Thermoset Types C, E, EO, PD, S, SJ, SJO, SJOW, SJOO, SJOOW, SO, SOW, SOO, SOOW, SP-1, SP-2, SP-3, SRD, SV, SVO, SVOO / Thermoplastic Types ET, ETLB, ETP, ETT, SE, SEW, SEO, SEOW, SEOOW, SJE, SJEW, SJEO, SJEOW, SJEOOW, SJT, SJTW, SJTO, SJTOW, SJTOO, SJTOOW, SPE-1, SPE-2, SPE-3, SPT-1, SPT-1W, SPT-2, SPT-2W, SPT-3, ST, SRDE, SRDT, STO, STOW, STOO, STOOW, SVE, SVEO, SVT, SVTO, SVTOO		Types HPD, HPN, HSJ, HSJO, HSJOO
		A⁺	B⁺	
27*	0.5	—	—	—
20	—	5**	***	—
18	—	7	10	10
17	—	—	12	13
16	—	10	13	15
15	—	—	—	17
14	—	15	18	20
12	—	20	25	30
10	—	25	30	35
8	—	35	40	—
6	—	45	55	—
4	—	60	70	—
2	—	80	95	—

*Tinsel cord.

**Elevator cables only.

***7 amperes for elevator cables only; 2 amperes for other types.

+The allowable currents under Column A apply to 3-conductor cords and other multiconductor cords connected to utilization equipment so that only 3 conductors are current-carrying. The allowable currents under Column B apply to 2-conductor cords and other multiconductor cords connected to utilization equipment so that only 2 conductors are current carrying.

(2) Where run through holes in walls, structural ceilings, suspended ceilings, dropped ceilings, or floors

(3) Where run through doorways, windows, or similar openings

(4) Where attached to building surfaces

Exception to (4): Flexible cord and cable shall be permitted to be attached to building surfaces in accordance with the provisions of 368.56(B)

(5) Where concealed by walls, floors, or ceilings or located above suspended or dropped ceilings

(6) Where installed in raceways, except as otherwise permitted in this *Code*

(7) Where subject to physical damage

400.9 Splices. Flexible cord shall be used only in continuous lengths without splice or tap where initially installed in appli-

cations permitted by 400.7(A). The repair of hard-service cord and junior hard-service cord (see Trade Name column in Table 400.4) 14 AWG and larger shall be permitted if conductors are spliced in accordance with 110.14(B) and the completed splice retains the insulation, outer sheath properties, and usage characteristics of the cord being spliced.

400.10 Pull at Joints and Terminals. Flexible cords and cables shall be connected to devices and to fittings so that tension is not transmitted to joints or terminals.

Exception: Listed portable single-pole devices that are intended to accommodate such tension at their terminals shall be permitted to be used with single-conductor flexible cable.

FPN: Some methods of preventing pull on a cord from being transmitted to joints or terminals are knotting the cord, winding with tape, and fittings designed for the purpose.

Table 400.5(B) Ampacity of Cable Types SC, SCE, SCT, PPE, G, G-GC, and W. [Based on Ambient Temperature of 30°C (86°F). See Table 400.4.]

Size (AWG or kcmil)	60°C (140°F)			75°C (167°F)			90°C (194°F)		
	D[1]	E[2]	F[3]	D[1]	E[2]	F[3]	D[1]	E[2]	F[3]
12	—	31	26	—	37	31	—	42	35
10	—	44	37	—	52	43	—	59	49
8	60	55	48	70	65	57	80	74	65
6	80	72	63	95	88	77	105	99	87
4	105	96	84	125	115	101	140	130	114
3	120	113	99	145	135	118	165	152	133
2	140	128	112	170	152	133	190	174	152
1	165	150	131	195	178	156	220	202	177
1/0	195	173	151	230	207	181	260	234	205
2/0	225	199	174	265	238	208	300	271	237
3/0	260	230	201	310	275	241	350	313	274
4/0	300	265	232	360	317	277	405	361	316
250	340	296	259	405	354	310	455	402	352
300	375	330	289	445	395	346	505	449	393
350	420	363	318	505	435	381	570	495	433
400	455	392	343	545	469	410	615	535	468
500	515	448	392	620	537	470	700	613	536
600	575	—	—	690	—	—	780	—	—
700	630	—	—	755	—	—	855	—	—
750	655	—	—	785	—	—	885	—	—
800	680	—	—	815	—	—	920	—	—
900	730	—	—	870	—	—	985	—	—
1000	780	—	—	935	—	—	1055	—	—

[1]The ampacities under subheading D shall be permitted for single-conductor Types SC, SCE, SCT, PPE, and W cable only where the individual conductors are not installed in raceways and are not in physical contact with each other except in lengths not to exceed 600 mm (24 in.) where passing through the wall of an enclosure.

[2]The ampacities under subheading E apply to two-conductor cables and other multiconductor cables connected to utilization equipment so that only two conductors are current carrying.

[3]The ampacities under subheading F apply to three-conductor cables and other multiconductor cables connected to utilization equipment so that only three conductors are current carrying.

400.11 In Show Windows and Show Cases. Flexible cords used in show windows and show cases shall be Type S, SE, SEO, SEOO, SJ, SJE, SJEO, SJEOO, SJO, SJOO, SJT, SJTO, SJTOO, SO, SOO, ST, STO, STOO, SEW, SEOW, SEOOW, SJEW, SJEOW, SJEOOW, SJOW, SJOOW, SJTW, SJTOW, SJTOOW, SOW, SOOW, STW, STOW, or STOOW.

Exception No. 1: For the wiring of chain-supported luminaires (lighting fixtures).

Exception No. 2: As supply cords for portable lamps and other merchandise being displayed or exhibited.

400.12 Minimum Size. The individual conductors of a flexible cord or cable shall not be smaller than the sizes in Table 400.4.

Exception: The size of the insulated ground-check conductor of Type G-GC cables shall be not smaller than 10 AWG.

400.13 Overcurrent Protection. Flexible cords not smaller than 18 AWG, and tinsel cords or cords having equivalent characteristics of smaller size approved for use with specific appliances, shall be considered as protected against overcurrent by the overcurrent devices described in 240.5.

400.14 Protection from Damage. Flexible cords and cables shall be protected by bushings or fittings where passing through holes in covers, outlet boxes, or similar enclosures.

In industrial establishments where the conditions of maintenance and supervision ensure that only qualified persons service the installation, flexible cords and cables shall be permitted to be installed in aboveground raceways that are no longer than 15 m (50 ft) to protect the flexible cord or cable from physical damage. Where more than three current-carrying conductors are installed within the raceway, the allowable ampacity shall be reduced in accordance with Table 400.5.

II. Construction Specifications

400.20 Labels. Flexible cords shall be examined and tested at the factory and labeled before shipment.

400.21 Nominal Insulation Thickness. The nominal thickness of insulation for conductors of flexible cords and cables shall not be less than specified in Table 400.4.

Exception: The nominal insulation thickness for the ground-check conductors of Type G-GC cables shall not be less than 1.14 mm (45 mils) for 8 AWG and not less than 0.76 mm (30 mils) for 10 AWG.

400.22 Grounded-Conductor Identification. One conductor of flexible cords that is intended to be used as a grounded circuit conductor shall have a continuous marker that readily distinguishes it from the other conductor or conductors. The identification shall consist of one of the methods indicated in 400.22(A) through 400.22(F).

(A) Colored Braid. A braid finished to show a white or gray color and the braid on the other conductor or conductors finished to show a readily distinguishable solid color or colors.

(B) Tracer in Braid. A tracer in a braid of any color contrasting with that of the braid and no tracer in the braid of the other conductor or conductors. No tracer shall be used in the braid of any conductor of a flexible cord that contains a conductor having a braid finished to show white or gray.

Exception: In the case of Types C and PD and cords having the braids on the individual conductors finished to show white or gray. In such cords, the identifying marker shall be permitted to consist of the solid white or gray finish on one conductor, provided there is a colored tracer in the braid of each other conductor.

(C) Colored Insulation. A white or gray insulation on one conductor and insulation of a readily distinguishable color or colors on the other conductor or conductors for cords having no braids on the individual conductors.

For jacketed cords furnished with appliances, one conductor having its insulation colored light blue, with the other conductors having their insulation of a readily distinguishable color other than white or gray.

Exception: Cords that have insulation on the individual conductors integral with the jacket.

The insulation shall be permitted to be covered with an outer finish to provide the desired color.

(D) Colored Separator. A white or gray separator on one conductor and a separator of a readily distinguishable solid color on the other conductor or conductors of cords

having insulation on the individual conductors integral with the jacket.

(E) Tinned Conductors. One conductor having the individual strands tinned and the other conductor or conductors having the individual strands untinned for cords having insulation on the individual conductors integral with the jacket.

(F) Surface Marking. One or more ridges, grooves, or white stripes located on the exterior of the cord so as to identify one conductor for cords having insulation on the individual conductors integral with the jacket.

400.23 Equipment Grounding Conductor Identification. A conductor intended to be used as an equipment grounding conductor shall have a continuous identifying marker readily distinguishing it from the other conductor or conductors. Conductors having a continuous green color or a continuous green color with one or more yellow stripes shall not be used for other than equipment grounding purposes. The identifying marker shall consist of one of the methods in 400.23(A) or 400.23(B).

(A) Colored Braid. A braid finished to show a continuous green color or a continuous green color with one or more yellow stripes.

(B) Colored Insulation or Covering. For cords having no braids on the individual conductors, an insulation of a continuous green color or a continuous green color with one or more yellow stripes.

400.24 Attachment Plugs. Where a flexible cord is provided with an equipment grounding conductor and equipped with an attachment plug, the attachment plug shall comply with 250.138(A) and 250.138(B).

III. Portable Cables Over 600 Volts, Nominal

400.30 Scope. This part applies to multiconductor portable cables used to connect mobile equipment and machinery.

400.31 Construction.

(A) Conductors. The conductors shall be 8 AWG copper or larger and shall employ flexible stranding.

Exception: The size of the insulated ground-check conductor of Type G-GC cables shall be not smaller than 10 AWG.

(B) Shields. Cables operated at over 2000 volts shall be shielded. Shielding shall be for the purpose of confining the voltage stresses to the insulation.

(C) Equipment Grounding Conductor(s). An equipment grounding conductor(s) shall be provided. The total area shall not be less than that of the size of the equipment grounding conductor required in 250.122.

400.32 Shielding. All shields shall be grounded.

400.33 Grounding. Grounding conductors shall be connected in accordance with Part V of Article 250.

400.34 Minimum Bending Radii. The minimum bending radii for portable cables during installation and handling in service shall be adequate to prevent damage to the cable.

400.35 Fittings. Connectors used to connect lengths of cable in a run shall be of a type that lock firmly together. Provisions shall be made to prevent opening or closing these connectors while energized. Suitable means shall be used to eliminate tension at connectors and terminations.

400.36 Splices and Terminations. Portable cables shall not contain splices unless the splices are of the permanent molded, vulcanized types in accordance with 110.14(B). Terminations on portable cables rated over 600 volts, nominal, shall be accessible only to authorized and qualified personnel.

ARTICLE 402
Fixture Wires

402.1 Scope. This article covers general requirements and construction specifications for fixture wires.

402.2 Other Articles. Fixture wires shall comply with this article and also with the applicable provisions of other articles of this *Code*.

> FPN: For application in luminaires (lighting fixtures), see Article 410.

402.3 Types. Fixture wires shall be of a type listed in Table 402.3, and they shall comply with all requirements of that table. The fixture wires listed in Table 402.3 are all suitable for service at 600 volts, nominal, unless otherwise specified.

> FPN: Thermoplastic insulation may stiffen at temperatures colder than −10°C (+14°F), requiring that care be exercised during installation at such temperatures. Thermoplastic insulation may also be deformed at normal temperatures where subjected to pressure, requiring that care be exercised during installation and at points of support.

Table 402.3 Fixture Wires

Name	Type Letter	Insulation	Thickness of Insulation			Outer Covering	Maximum Operating Temperature	Application Provisions
			AWG	mm	mils			
Heat-resistant rubber-covered fixture wire — flexible stranding	FFH-2	Heat-resistant rubber Cross-linked synthetic polymer	18–16 18–16	0.76 0.76	30 30	Nonmetallic covering	75°C 167°F	Fixture wiring
ECTFE — solid or 7-strand	HF	Ethylene chlorotrifluoroethylene	18–14	0.38	15	None	150°C 302°F	Fixture wiring
ECTFE — flexible stranding	HFF	Ethylene chlorotrifluoroethylene	18–14	0.38	15	None	150°C 302°F	Fixture wiring
Tape insulated fixture wire — solid or 7-strand	KF-1	Aromatic polyimide tape	18–10	0.14	5.5	None	200°C 392°F	Fixture wiring — limited to 300 volts
	KF-2	Aromatic polyimide tape	18–10	0.21	8.4	None	200°C 392°F	Fixture wiring
Tape insulated fixture wire — flexible stranding	KFF-1	Aromatic polyimide tape	18–10	0.14	5.5	None	200°C 392°F	Fixture wiring — limited to 300 volts
	KFF-2	Aromatic polyimide tape	18–10	0.21	8.4	None	200°C 392°F	Fixture wiring

(Continues)

Table 402.3 *Continued*

Name	Type Letter	Insulation	Thickness of Insulation			Outer Covering	Maximum Operating Temperature	Application Provisions
			AWG	mm	mils			
Perfluoro- alkoxy — solid or 7- strand (nickel or nickel-coated copper)	PAF	Perfluoro-alkoxy	18–14	0.51	20	None	250°C 482°F	Fixture wiring (nickel or nickel-coated copper)
Perfluoro-alkoxy — flexible stranding	PAFF	Perfluoro-alkoxy	18–14	0.51	20	None	150°C 302°F	Fixture wiring
Fluorinated ethylene propylene fixture wire — solid or 7-strand	PF	Fluorinated ethylene propylene	18–14	0.51	20	None	200°C 392°F	Fixture wiring
Fluorinated ethylene propylene fixture wire — flexible stranding	PFF	Fluorinated ethylene propylene	18–14	0.51	20	None	150°C 302°F	Fixture wiring
Fluorinated ethylene propylene fixture wire — solid or 7-strand	PGF	Fluorinated ethylene propylene	18–14	0.36	14	Glass braid	200°C 392°F	Fixture wiring
Fluorinated ethylene propylene fixture wire — flexible stranding	PGFF	Fluorinated ethylene propylene	18–14	0.36	14	Glass braid	150°C 302°F	Fixture wiring
Extruded polytetraflu-oroethylene — solid or 7-strand (nickel or nickel-coated copper)	PTF	Extruded polytetraflu-oroethylene	18–14	0.51	20	None	250°C 482°F	Fixture wiring (nickel or nickel-coated copper)
Extruded polytetraflu-oroethylene — flexible stranding 26-36 (AWG silver or nickel- coated copper)	PTFF	Extruded polytetraflu-oroethylene	18–14	0.51	20	None	150°C 302°F	Fixture wiring (silver or nickel-coated copper)
Heat-resistant rubber-covered fixture wire — solid or 7-strand	RFH-1	Heat-resistant rubber	18	0.38	15	Nonmetallic covering	75°C 167°F	Fixture wiring — limited to 300 volts
	RFH-2	Heat-resistant rubber Cross-linked synthetic polymer	18–16	0.76	30	None or nonmetallic covering	75°C 167°F	Fixture wiring
Heat-resistant cross-linked synthetic polymer-insulated fixture wire — solid or 7- strand	RFHH-2*	Cross-linked synthetic polymer	18–16	0.76	30	None or nonmetallic covering	90°C 194°F	Fixture wiring —
	RFHH-3*		18–16	1.14	45			

Table 402.3 *Continued*

Name	Type Letter	Insulation	Thickness of Insulation			Outer Covering	Maximum Operating Temperature	Application Provisions
			AWG	mm	mils			
Silicone insulated fixture wire — solid or 7-strand	SF-1	Silicone rubber	18	0.38	15	Nonmetallic covering	200°C 392°F	Fixture wiring — limited to 300 volts
	SF-2	Silicone rubber	18–12 10	0.76 1.14	30 45	Nonmetallic covering	200°C 392°F	Fixture wiring
Silicone insulated fixture wire — flexible stranding	SFF-1	Silicone rubber	18	0.38	15	Nonmetallic covering	150°C 302°F	Fixture wiring — limited to 300 volts
	SFF-2	Silicone rubber	18–12 10	0.76 1.14	30 45	Nonmetallic covering	150°C 302°F	Fixture wiring
Thermoplastic covered fixture wire — solid or 7-strand	TF*	Thermoplastic	18–16	0.76	30	None	60°C 140°F	Fixture wiring
Thermoplastic covered fixture wire — flexible stranding	TFF*	Thermoplastic	18–16	0.76	30	None	60°C 140°F	Fixture wiring
Heat-resistant thermo plastic covered fixture wire — solid or 7-strand	TFN*	Thermoplastic	18–16	0.38	15	Nylon-jacketed or equivalent	90°C 194°F	Fixture wiring
Heat-resistant thermo plastic covered fixture wire — flexible stranded	TFFN*	Thermoplastic	18–16	0.38	15	Nylon-jacketed or equivalent	90°C 194°F	Fixture wiring
Cross-linked polyolefin insulated fixture wire — solid or 7-strand	XF*	Cross-linked polyolefin	18–14 12–10	0.76 1.14	30 45	None	150°C 302°F	Fixture wiring — limited to 300 volts
Cross-linked polyolefin insulated fixture wire — flexible stranded	XFF*	Cross-linked polyolefin	18–14 12–10	0.76 1.14	30 45	None	150°C 302°F	Fixture wiring — limited to 300 volts
Modified ETFE — solid or 7- strand	ZF	Modified ethylene tetrafluoro-ethylene	18–14	0.38	15	None	150°C 302°F	Fixture wiring
Flexible stranding	ZFF	Modified ethylene tetrafluoro-ethylene	18–14	0.38	15	None	150°C 302°F	Fixture wiring
High temp. modified ETFE — solid or 7- strand	ZHF	Modified ethylene tetrafluoro-ethylene	18–14	0.38	15	None	200°C 392°F	Fixture wiring

*Insulations and outer coverings that meet the requirements of flame retardant, limited smoke, and are so listed shall be permitted to be marked for limited smoke after the *Code* type designation.

402.5 Allowable Ampacities for Fixture Wires. The allowable ampacity of fixture wire shall be as specified in Table 402.5.

No conductor shall be used under such conditions that its operating temperature exceeds the temperature specified in Table 402.3 for the type of insulation involved.

FPN: See 310.10 for temperature limitation of conductors.

Table 402.5 Allowable Ampacity for Fixture Wires

Size (AWG)	Allowable Ampacity
18	6
16	8
14	17
12	23
10	28

402.6 Minimum Size. Fixture wires shall not be smaller than 18 AWG.

402.7 Number of Conductors in Conduit or Tubing. The number of fixture wires permitted in a single conduit or tubing shall not exceed the percentage fill specified in Table 1, Chapter 9.

402.8 Grounded Conductor Identification. Fixture wires that are intended to be used as grounded conductors shall be identified by one or more continuous white stripes on other than green insulation or by the means described in 400.22(A) through 400.22(E).

402.9 Marking.

(A) Method of Marking. Thermoplastic insulated fixture wire shall be durably marked on the surface at intervals not exceeding 610 mm (24 in.). All other fixture wire shall be marked by means of a printed tag attached to the coil, reel, or carton.

(B) Optional Marking. Fixture wire types listed in Table 402.3 shall be permitted to be surface marked to indicate special characteristics of the cable materials. These markings include, but are not limited to, markings for limited smoke, sunlight resistance, and so forth.

402.10 Uses Permitted. Fixture wires shall be permitted (1) for installation in luminaires (lighting fixtures) and in similar equipment where enclosed or protected and not subject to bending or twisting in use, or (2) for connecting luminaires (lighting fixtures) to the branch-circuit conductors supplying the luminaires (fixtures).

402.11 Uses Not Permitted. Fixture wires shall not be used as branch-circuit conductors.

402.12 Overcurrent Protection. Overcurrent protection for fixture wires shall be as specified in 240.5.

ARTICLE 404
Switches

I. Installation

404.1 Scope. The provisions of this article shall apply to all switches, switching devices, and circuit breakers where used as switches.

404.2 Switch Connections.

(A) Three-Way and Four-Way Switches. Three-way and four-way switches shall be wired so that all switching is done only in the ungrounded circuit conductor. Where in metal raceways or metal-armored cables, wiring between switches and outlets shall be in accordance with 300.20(A).

Exception: Switch loops shall not require a grounded conductor.

(B) Grounded Conductors. Switches or circuit breakers shall not disconnect the grounded conductor of a circuit.

Exception: A switch or circuit breaker shall be permitted to disconnect a grounded circuit conductor where all circuit conductors are disconnected simultaneously, or where the device is arranged so that the grounded conductor cannot be disconnected until all the ungrounded conductors of the circuit have been disconnected.

404.3 Enclosure.

(A) General. Switches and circuit breakers shall be of the externally operable type mounted in an enclosure listed for the intended use. The minimum wire-bending space at terminals and minimum gutter space provided in switch enclosures shall be as required in 312.6.

Exception No. 1: Pendant- and surface-type snap switches and knife switches mounted on an open-face switchboard or panelboard shall be permitted without enclosures.

Exception No. 2: Switches and circuit breakers installed in accordance with 110.27(A)(1), (A)(2), (A)(3), or (A)(4) shall be permitted without enclosures.

(B) Used as a Raceway. Enclosures shall not be used as junction boxes, auxiliary gutters, or raceways for conductors feeding through or tapping off to other switches or overcurrent devices, unless the enclosure complies with 312.8.

404.4 Wet Locations. A switch or circuit breaker in a wet location or outside of a building shall be enclosed in a weatherproof enclosure or cabinet that shall comply with 312.2(A). Switches shall not be installed within wet locations in tub or shower spaces unless installed as part of a listed tub or shower assembly.

404.5 Time Switches, Flashers, and Similar Devices. Time switches, flashers, and similar devices shall be of the enclosed type or shall be mounted in cabinets or boxes or equipment enclosures. Energized parts shall be barriered to prevent operator exposure when making manual adjustments or switching.

Exception: Devices mounted so they are accessible only to qualified persons shall be permitted without barriers, provided they are located within an enclosure such that any energized parts within 152 mm (6.0 in.) of the manual adjustment or switch are covered by suitable barriers.

404.6 Position and Connection of Switches.

(A) Single-Throw Knife Switches. Single-throw knife switches shall be placed so that gravity will not tend to close them. Single-throw knife switches, approved for use in the inverted position, shall be provided with an integral mechanical means that ensures that the blades remain in the open position when so set.

(B) Double-Throw Knife Switches. Double-throw knife switches shall be permitted to be mounted so that the throw is either vertical or horizontal. Where the throw is vertical, integral mechanical means shall be provided to hold the blades in the open position when so set.

(C) Connection of Switches. Single-throw knife switches and switches with butt contacts shall be connected such that their blades are de-energized when the switch is in the open position. Bolted pressure contact switches shall have barriers that prevent inadvertent contact with energized blades. Single-throw knife switches, bolted pressure contact switches, molded case switches, switches with butt contacts, and circuit breakers used as switches shall be connected so that the terminals supplying the load are de-energized when the switch is in the open position.

Exception: The blades and terminals supplying the load of a switch shall be permitted to be energized when the switch is in the open position where the switch is connected to circuits or equipment inherently capable of providing a backfeed source of power. For such installations, a permanent sign shall be installed on the switch enclosure or immediately adjacent to open switches with the following words or equivalent: WARNING — LOAD SIDE TERMINALS MAY BE ENERGIZED BY BACKFEED.

404.7 Indicating. General-use and motor-circuit switches, circuit breakers, and molded case switches, where mounted

in an enclosure as described in 404.3, shall clearly indicate whether they are in the open (off) or closed (on) position.

Where these switch or circuit breaker handles are operated vertically rather than rotationally or horizontally, the up position of the handle shall be the (on) position.

Exception No. 1: Vertically operated double-throw switches shall be permitted to be in the closed (on) position with the handle in either the up or down position.

Exception No. 2: On busway installations, tap switches employing a center-pivoting handle shall be permitted to be open or closed with either end of the handle in the up or down position. The switch position shall be clearly indicating and shall be visible from the floor or from the usual point of operation.

404.8 Accessibility and Grouping.

(A) Location. All switches and circuit breakers used as switches shall be located so that they may be operated from a readily accessible place. They shall be installed such that the center of the grip of the operating handle of the switch or circuit breaker, when in its highest position, is not more than 2.0 m (6 ft 7 in.) above the floor or working platform.

Exception No. 1: On busway installations, fused switches and circuit breakers shall be permitted to be located at the same level as the busway. Suitable means shall be provided to operate the handle of the device from the floor.

Exception No. 2: Switches and circuit breakers installed adjacent to motors, appliances, or other equipment that they supply shall be permitted to be located higher than 2.0 m (6 ft 7 in.) and to be accessible by portable means.

Exception No. 3: Hookstick operable isolating switches shall be permitted at greater heights.

(B) Voltage Between Adjacent Devices. A snap switch shall not be grouped or ganged in enclosures with other snap switches, receptacles, or similar devices, unless they are arranged so that the voltage between adjacent devices does not exceed 300 volts, or unless they are installed in enclosures equipped with identified, securely installed barriers between adjacent devices.

404.9 Provisions for General-Use Snap Switches.

(A) Faceplates. Faceplates provided for snap switches mounted in boxes and other enclosures shall be installed so as to completely cover the opening and, where the switch is flush mounted, seat against the finished surface.

(B) Grounding. Snap switches, including dimmer and similar control switches, shall be effectively grounded and shall provide a means to ground metal faceplates, whether or not a metal faceplate is installed. Snap switches shall be considered effectively grounded if either of the following conditions is met:

(1) The switch is mounted with metal screws to a metal box or to a nonmetallic box with integral means for grounding devices.

(2) An equipment grounding conductor or equipment bonding jumper is connected to an equipment grounding termination of the snap switch.

Exception to (B): Where no grounding means exists within the snap-switch enclosure or where the wiring method does not include or provide an equipment ground, a snap switch without a grounding connection shall be permitted for replacement purposes only. A snap switch wired under the provisions of this exception and located within reach of earth, grade, conducting floors, or other conducting surfaces shall be provided with a faceplate of nonconducting, noncombustible material or shall be protected by a ground-fault circuit interrupter.

(C) Construction. Metal faceplates shall be of ferrous metal not less than 0.76 mm (0.030 in.) in thickness or of nonferrous metal not less than 1.02 mm (0.040 in.) in thickness. Faceplates of insulating material shall be noncombustible and not less than 2.54 mm (0.010 in.) in thickness, but they shall be permitted to be less than 2.54 mm (0.010 in.) in thickness if formed or reinforced to provide adequate mechanical strength.

404.10 Mounting of Snap Switches.

(A) Surface-Type. Snap switches used with open wiring on insulators shall be mounted on insulating material that separates the conductors at least 13 mm (½ in.) from the surface wired over.

(B) Box Mounted. Flush-type snap switches mounted in boxes that are set back of the finished surface as permitted in 314.20 shall be installed so that the extension plaster ears are seated against the surface. Flush-type snap switches mounted in boxes that are flush with the finished surface or project from it shall be installed so that the mounting yoke or strap of the switch is seated against the box.

404.11 Circuit Breakers as Switches. A hand-operable circuit breaker equipped with a lever or handle, or a power-operated circuit breaker capable of being opened by hand in the event of a power failure, shall be permitted to serve as a switch if it has the required number of poles.

FPN: See the provisions contained in 240.81 and 240.83.

404.12 Grounding of Enclosures. Metal enclosures for switches or circuit breakers shall be grounded as specified in Article 250. Where nonmetallic enclosures are used with metal raceways or metal-armored cables, provision shall be made for grounding continuity.

Except as covered in 404.9(B), Exception, nonmetallic boxes for switches shall be installed with a wiring method that provides or includes an equipment ground.

404.13 Knife Switches.

(A) Isolating Switches. Knife switches rated at over 1200 amperes at 250 volts or less, and at over 600 amperes at 251 to 600 volts, shall be used only as isolating switches and shall not be opened under load.

(B) To Interrupt Currents. To interrupt currents over 1200 amperes at 250 volts, nominal, or less, or over 600 amperes at 251 to 600 volts, nominal, a circuit breaker or a switch of special design listed for such purpose shall be used.

(C) General-Use Switches. Knife switches of ratings less than specified in 404.13(A) and 404.13(B) shall be considered general-use switches.

FPN: See the definition of *General-Use Switch* in Article 100.

(D) Motor-Circuit Switches. Motor-circuit switches shall be permitted to be of the knife-switch type.

FPN: See the definition of a *Motor-Circuit Switch* in Article 100.

404.14 Rating and Use of Snap Switches. Snap switches shall be used within their ratings and as indicated in 404.14(A) through 404.14(E).

FPN No. 1: For switches on signs and outline lighting, see 600.6.

FPN No. 2: For switches controlling motors, see 430.83, 430.109, and 430.110.

(A) Alternating Current General-Use Snap Switch. A form of general-use snap switch suitable only for use on ac circuits for controlling the following:

(1) Resistive and inductive loads, including electric-discharge lamps, not exceeding the ampere rating of the switch at the voltage involved

(2) Tungsten-filament lamp loads not exceeding the ampere rating of the switch at 120 volts

(3) Motor loads not exceeding 80 percent of the ampere rating of the switch at its rated voltage

(B) Alternating-Current or Direct-Current General-Use Snap Switch. A form of general-use snap switch suitable for use on either ac or dc circuits for controlling the following:

(1) Resistive loads not exceeding the ampere rating of the switch at the voltage applied.

(2) Inductive loads not exceeding 50 percent of the ampere rating of the switch at the applied voltage. Switches rated in horsepower are suitable for controlling motor loads within their rating at the voltage applied.

(3) Tungsten-filament lamp loads not exceeding the ampere rating of the switch at the applied voltage if T-rated.

(C) CO/ALR Snap Switches. Snap switches rated 20 amperes or less directly connected to aluminum conductors shall be listed and marked CO/ALR.

(D) Alternating-Current Specific-Use Snap Switches Rated for 347 Volts. Snap switches rated 347 volts ac shall be listed and shall be used only for controlling the loads permitted by (D)(1) and (D)(2).

(1) Noninductive Loads. Noninductive loads other than tungsten-filament lamps not exceeding the ampere and voltage ratings of the switch.

(2) Inductive Loads. Inductive loads not exceeding the ampere and voltage ratings of the switch. Where particular load characteristics or limitations are specified as a condition of the listing, those restrictions shall be observed regardless of the ampere rating of the load.

The ampere rating of the switch shall not be less than 15 amperes at a voltage rating of 347 volts ac. Flush-type snap switches rated 347 volts ac shall not be readily interchangeable in box mounting with switches identified in 404.14(A) and 404.14(B).

(E) Dimmer Switches. General-use dimmer switches shall be used only to control permanently installed incandescent luminaires (lighting fixtures) unless listed for the control of other loads and installed accordingly.

II. Construction Specifications

404.15 Marking.

(A) Ratings. Switches shall be marked with the current voltage, and, if horsepower rated, the maximum rating for which they are designed.

(B) Off Indication. Where in the off position, a switching device with a marked OFF position shall completely disconnect all ungrounded conductors to the load it controls.

404.16 600-Volt Knife Switches. Auxiliary contacts of a renewable or quick-break type or the equivalent shall be provided on all knife switches rated 600 volts and designed for use in breaking current over 200 amperes.

404.17 Fused Switches. A fused switch shall not have fuses in parallel except as permitted in 240.8.

404.18 Wire-Bending Space. The wire-bending space required by 404.3 shall meet Table 312.6(B) spacings to the enclosure wall opposite the line and load terminals.

ARTICLE 406
Receptacles, Cord Connectors, and Attachment Plugs (Caps)

406.1 Scope. This article covers the rating, type, and installation of receptacles, cord connectors, and attachment plugs (cord caps).

406.2 Receptacle Rating and Type.

(A) Receptacles. Receptacles shall be listed and marked with the manufacturer's name or identification and voltage and ampere ratings.

(B) Rating. Receptacles and cord connectors shall be rated not less than 15 amperes, 125 volts, or 15 amperes, 250 volts, and shall be of a type not suitable for use as lampholders.

FPN: See 210.21(B) for receptacle ratings where installed on branch circuits.

(C) Receptacles for Aluminum Conductors. Receptacles rated 20 amperes or less and designed for the direct connection of aluminum conductors shall be marked CO/ALR.

(D) Isolated Ground Receptacles. Receptacles incorporating an isolated grounding connection intended for the reduction of electrical noise (electromagnetic interference) as permitted in 250.146(D) shall be identified by an orange triangle located on the face of the receptacle.

(1) Isolated Equipment Grounding Conductor Required. Receptacles so identified shall be used only with grounding conductors that are isolated in accordance with 250.146(D).

(2) Installation in Nonmetallic Boxes. Isolated ground receptacles installed in nonmetallic boxes shall be covered with a nonmetallic faceplate.

Exception: Where an isolated ground receptacle is installed in a nonmetallic box, a metal faceplate shall be permitted if the box contains a feature or accessory that permits the effective grounding of the faceplate.

406.3 General Installation Requirements. Receptacle outlets shall be located in branch circuits in accordance with Part III of Article 210. General installation requirements shall be in accordance with 406.3(A) through 406.3(F).

(A) Grounding Type. Receptacles installed on 15- and 20-ampere branch circuits shall be of the grounding type. Grounding-type receptacles shall be installed only on circuits of the voltage class and current for which they are rated, except as provided in Table 210.21(B)(2) and Table 210.21(B)(3).

Exception: Nongrounding-type receptacles installed in accordance with 406.3(D).

(B) To Be Grounded. Receptacles and cord connectors that have grounding contacts shall have those contacts effectively grounded.

Exception No. 1: Receptacles mounted on portable and vehicle-mounted generators in accordance with 250.34.

Exception No. 2: Replacement receptacles as permitted by 406.3(D).

(C) Methods of Grounding. The grounding contacts of receptacles and cord connectors shall be grounded by connection to the equipment grounding conductor of the circuit supplying the receptacle or cord connector.

> FPN: For installation requirements for the reduction of electrical noise, see 250.146(D).

The branch-circuit wiring method shall include or provide an equipment-grounding conductor to which the grounding contacts of the receptacle or cord connector are connected.

> FPN No. 1: See 250.118 for acceptable grounding means.
>
> FPN No. 2: For extensions of existing branch circuits, see 250.130.

(D) Replacements. Replacement of receptacles shall comply with 406.3(D)(1), (D)(2), and (D)(3) as applicable.

(1) Grounding-Type Receptacles. Where a grounding means exists in the receptacle enclosure or a grounding conductor is installed in accordance with 250.130(C), grounding-type receptacles shall be used and shall be connected to the grounding conductor in accordance with 406.3(C) or 250.130(C).

(2) Ground-Fault Circuit Interrupters. Ground-fault circuit-interrupter protected receptacles shall be provided where replacements are made at receptacle outlets that are required to be so protected elsewhere in this *Code.*

(3) Non–grounding-Type Receptacles. Where grounding means does not exist in the receptacle enclosure, the installation shall comply with (D)(3)(a), (D)(3)(b), or (D)(3)(c).

(a) A non–grounding-type receptacle(s) shall be permitted to be replaced with another non–grounding-type receptacle(s).

(b) A non–grounding-type receptacle(s) shall be permitted to be replaced with a ground-fault circuit interrupter-type of receptacle(s). These receptacles shall be marked "No Equipment Ground." An equipment grounding conductor shall not be connected from the ground-fault circuit-interrupter-type receptacle to any outlet supplied from the ground-fault circuit-interrupter receptacle.

(c) A non–grounding-type receptacle(s) shall be permitted to be replaced with a grounding-type receptacle(s) where supplied through a ground-fault circuit interrupter. Grounding-type receptacles supplied through the ground-fault circuit interrupter shall be marked "GFCI Protected" and "No Equipment Ground." An equipment grounding conductor shall not be connected between the grounding-type receptacles.

(E) Cord-and-Plug-Connected Equipment. The installation of grounding-type receptacles shall not be used as a requirement that all cord-and-plug-connected equipment be of the grounded type.

> FPN: See 250.114 for types of cord-and-plug-connected equipment to be grounded.

(F) Noninterchangeable Types. Receptacles connected to circuits that have different voltages, frequencies, or types of current (ac or dc) on the same premises shall be of such design that the attachment plugs used on these circuits are not interchangeable.

406.4 Receptacle Mounting. Receptacles shall be mounted in boxes or assemblies designed for the purpose, and such boxes or assemblies shall be securely fastened in place unless otherwise permitted elsewhere in this *Code.*

(A) Boxes That Are Set Back. Receptacles mounted in boxes that are set back from the finished surface as permitted in 314.20 shall be installed such that the mounting yoke or strap of the receptacle is held rigidly at the finished surface.

(B) Boxes That Are Flush. Receptacles mounted in boxes that are flush with the finished surface or project therefrom shall be installed such that the mounting yoke or strap of the receptacle is held rigidly against the box or box cover.

(C) Receptacles Mounted on Covers. Receptacles mounted to and supported by a cover shall be held rigidly against the cover by more than one screw or shall be a device assembly or box cover listed and identified for securing by a single screw.

(D) Position of Receptacle Faces. After installation, receptacle faces shall be flush with or project from faceplates of insulating material and shall project a minimum of 0.4 mm (0.015 in.) from metal faceplates.

Exception No. 1: Listed kits or assemblies encompassing receptacles and nonmetallic faceplates that cover the receptacle face, where the plate cannot be installed on any other receptacle, shall be permitted.

Exception No. 2: Listed nonmetallic faceplates that cover the receptacle face to a maximum thickness of 1 mm (0.040 in.) shall be permitted.

(E) Receptacles in Countertops and Similar Work Surfaces in Dwelling Units. Receptacles shall not be installed in a face-up position in countertops or similar work surfaces.

(F) Exposed Terminals. Receptacles shall be enclosed so that live wiring terminals are not exposed to contact.

406.5 Receptacle Faceplates (Cover Plates). Receptacle faceplates shall be installed so as to completely cover the opening and seat against the mounting surface.

(A) Thickness of Metal Faceplates. Metal faceplates shall be of ferrous metal not less than 0.76 mm (0.030 in.) in thickness or of nonferrous metal not less than 1.02 mm (0.040 in.) in thickness.

(B) Grounding. Metal faceplates shall be grounded.

(C) Faceplates of Insulating Material. Faceplates of insulating material shall be noncombustible and not less than 2.54 mm (0.10 in.) in thickness but shall be permitted to be less than 2.54 mm (0.10 in.) in thickness if formed or reinforced to provide adequate mechanical strength.

406.6 Attachment Plugs, Cord Connectors, and Flanged Surface Devices. All attachment plugs, cord connectors, and flanged surface devices (inlets and outlets) shall be listed and marked with the manufacturer's name or identification and voltage and ampere ratings.

(A) Construction of Attachment Plugs and Cord Connectors. Attachment plugs and cord connectors shall be constructed so that there are no exposed current-carrying parts except the prongs, blades, or pins. The cover for wire terminations shall be a part that is essential for the operation of an attachment plug or connector (dead-front construction).

(B) Connection of Attachment Plugs. Attachment plugs shall be installed so that their prongs, blades, or pins are not energized unless inserted into an energized receptacle. No receptacle shall be installed so as to require the insertion of an energized attachment plug as its source of supply.

(C) Attachment Plug Ejector Mechanisms. Attachment plug ejector mechanisms shall not adversely affect engagement of the blades of the attachment plug with the contacts of the receptacle.

(D) Flanged Surface Inlet. A flanged surface inlet shall be installed such that the prongs, blades, or pins are not energized unless an energized cord connector is inserted into it.

406.7 Noninterchangeability. Receptacles, cord connectors, and attachment plugs shall be constructed such that receptacle or cord connectors do not accept an attachment plug with a different voltage or current rating from that for which the device is intended. However, a 20-ampere T-slot receptacle or cord connector shall be permitted to accept a 15-ampere attachment plug of the same voltage rating. Non–grounding-type receptacles and connectors shall not accept grounding-type attachment plugs.

406.8 Receptacles in Damp or Wet Locations.

(A) Damp Locations. A receptacle installed outdoors in a location protected from the weather or in other damp locations shall have an enclosure for the receptacle that is weatherproof when the receptacle is covered (attachment plug cap not inserted and receptacle covers closed).

An installation suitable for wet locations shall also be considered suitable for damp locations.

A receptacle shall be considered to be in a location protected from the weather where located under roofed open porches, canopies, marquees, and the like, and will not be subjected to a beating rain or water runoff.

(B) Wet Locations.

(1) 15- and 20-Ampere Receptacles in a Wet Location. 15- and 20-ampere, 125- and 250-volt receptacles installed in a wet location shall have an enclosure that is weatherproof whether or not the attachment plug cap is inserted.

(2) Other Receptacles. All other receptacles installed in a wet location shall comply with (B)(2)(a) or (B)(2)(b).

   (a) A receptacle installed in a wet location, where the product intended to be plugged into it is not attended while in use, shall have an enclosure that is weatherproof with the attachment plug cap inserted or removed.

   (b) A receptacle installed in a wet location where the product intended to be plugged into it will be attended while in use (e.g., portable tools) shall have an enclosure that is weatherproof when the attachment plug is removed.

(C) Bathtub and Shower Space. Receptacles shall not be installed within or directly over a bathtub or shower stall.

(D) Protection for Floor Receptacles. Standpipes of floor receptacles shall allow floor-cleaning equipment to be operated without damage to receptacles.

(E) Flush Mounting with Faceplate. The enclosure for a receptacle installed in an outlet box flush-mounted in a finished surface shall be made weatherproof by means of a weatherproof faceplate assembly that provides a watertight connection between the plate and the finished surface.

406.9 Grounding-Type Receptacles, Adapters, Cord Connectors, and Attachment Plugs.

(A) Grounding Poles. Grounding-type receptacles, cord connectors, and attachment plugs shall be provided with one fixed grounding pole in addition to the circuit poles. The grounding contacting pole of grounding-type plug-in ground-fault circuit interrupters shall be permitted to be of the movable, self-restoring type on circuits operating at not over 150 volts between any two conductors or any conductor and ground.

(B) Grounding-Pole Identification. Grounding-type receptacles, adapters, cord connections, and attachment plugs shall have a means for connection of a grounding conductor to the grounding pole.

A terminal for connection to the grounding pole shall be designated by one of the following:

(1) A green-colored hexagonal-headed or -shaped terminal screw or nut, not readily removable.

(2) A green-colored pressure wire connector body (a wire barrel).

(3) A similar green-colored connection device, in the case of adapters. The grounding terminal of a grounding adapter shall be a green-colored rigid ear, lug, or similar device. The grounding connection shall be so designed that it cannot make contact with current-carrying parts of the receptacle, adapter, or attachment plug. The adapter shall be polarized.

(4) If the terminal for the grounding conductor is not visible, the conductor entrance hole shall be marked with the word *green* or *ground*, the letters *G* or *GR*, a grounding symbol, or otherwise identified by a distinctive green color. If the terminal for the equipment grounding conductor is readily removable, the area adjacent to the terminal shall be similarly marked.

FPN: See FPN Figure 406.9(B)(4).

FPN Figure 406.9(B)(4) One Example of a Symbol Used to Identify the Termination Point for an Equipment Grounding Conductor.

(C) Grounding Terminal Use. A grounding terminal or grounding-type device shall not be used for purposes other than grounding.

(D) Grounding-Pole Requirements. Grounding-type attachment plugs and mating cord connectors and receptacles shall be designed such that the grounding connection is made before the current-carrying connections. Grounding-type devices shall be so designed that grounding poles of attachment plugs cannot be brought into contact with current-carrying parts of receptacles or cord connectors.

(E) Use. Grounding-type attachment plugs shall be used only with a cord having an equipment grounding conductor.

FPN: See 200.10(B) for identification of grounded conductor terminals.

406.10 Connecting Receptacle Grounding Terminal to Box. The connection of the receptacle grounding terminal shall comply with 250.146.

ARTICLE 408
Switchboards and Panelboards

I. General

408.1 Scope. This article covers the following:

(1) All switchboards, panelboards, and distribution boards installed for the control of light and power circuits

(2) Battery-charging panels supplied from light or power circuits

408.2 Other Articles. Switches, circuit breakers, and overcurrent devices used on switchboards, panelboards, and distribution boards, and their enclosures shall comply with this article and also with the requirements of Articles 240, 250, 312, 314, 404, and other articles that apply. Switchboards and panelboards in hazardous (classified) locations shall comply with the requirements of Articles 500 through 517.

408.3 Support and Arrangement of Busbars and Conductors.

(A) Conductors and Busbars on a Switchboard or Panelboard. Conductors and busbars on a switchboard or panelboard shall comply with 408.3(A)(1), (A)(2), and (A)(3) as applicable.

(1) Location. Conductors and busbars shall be located so as to be free from physical damage and shall be held firmly in place.

(2) Service Switchboards. Barriers shall be placed in all service switchboards such that no uninsulated, ungrounded service busbar or service terminal is exposed to inadvertent contact by persons or maintenance equipment while servicing load terminations.

(3) Same Vertical Section. Other than the required interconnections and control wiring, only those conductors that are intended for termination in a vertical section of a switchboard shall be located in that section.

Exception: Conductors shall be permitted to travel horizontally through vertical sections of switchboards where such conductors are isolated from busbars by a barrier.

(B) Overheating and Inductive Effects. The arrangement of busbars and conductors shall be such as to avoid overheating due to inductive effects.

(C) Used as Service Equipment. Each switchboard or panelboard, if used as service equipment, shall be provided with a main bonding jumper sized in accordance with 250.28(D) or the equivalent placed within the panelboard or one of the sections of the switchboard for connecting the grounded service conductor on its supply side to the switchboard or panelboard frame. All sections of a switchboard shall be bonded together using an equipment bonding conductor sized in accordance with Table 250.122 or Table 250.66 as appropriate.

Exception: Switchboards and panelboards used as service equipment on high-impedance grounded-neutral systems in accordance with 250.36 shall not be required to be provided with a main bonding jumper.

(D) Terminals. In switchboards and panelboards, load terminals for field wiring, including grounded circuit conductor load terminals and connections to the ground bus for load equipment grounding conductors, shall be so located that it is not necessary to reach across or beyond an uninsulated ungrounded line bus in order to make connections.

(E) Phase Arrangement. The phase arrangement on 3-phase buses shall be A, B, C from front to back, top to bottom, or left to right, as viewed from the front of the switchboard or panelboard. The B phase shall be that phase having the higher voltage to ground on 3-phase, 4-wire, delta-connected systems. Other busbar arrangements shall be permitted for additions to existing installations and shall be marked.

Exception: Equipment within the same single section or multisection switchboard or panelboard as the meter on 3-phase, 4-wire, delta-connected systems shall be permitted to have the same phase configuration as the metering equipment.

> FPN: See 110.15 for requirements on marking the busbar or phase conductor having the higher voltage to ground where supplied from a 4-wire, delta-connected system.

(F) Minimum Wire-Bending Space. The minimum wire-bending space at terminals and minimum gutter space provided in panelboards and switchboards shall be as required in 312.6.

408.4 Circuit Directory or Circuit Identification. Every circuit and circuit modification shall be legibly identified as to its clear, evident, and specific purpose or use. The identification shall include sufficient detail to allow each circuit to be distinguished from all others. The identification shall be included in a circuit directory that is located on the face or inside of the panel door in the case of a panelboard, and located at each switch on a switchboard.

408.5 Clearance for Conductor Entering Bus Enclosures. Where conduits or other raceways enter a switchboard, floor-standing panelboard, or similar enclosure at the bottom, sufficient space shall be provided to permit installation of conductors in the enclosure. The wiring space shall not be less than shown in Table 408.5 where the conduit or raceways enter or leave the enclosure below the busbars, their supports, or other obstructions. The conduit or raceways, including their end fittings, shall not rise more than 75 mm (3 in.) above the bottom of the enclosure.

Table 408.5 Clearance for Conductors Entering Bus Enclosures

	Minimum Spacing Between Bottom of Enclosure and Busbars, Their Supports, or Other Obstructions	
Conductor	mm	in.
Insulated busbars, their supports, or other obstructions	200	8
Noninsulated busbars	250	10

408.7 Unused Openings. Unused openings for circuit breakers and switches shall be closed using identified closures, or other approved means that provide protection substantially equivalent to the wall of the enclosure.

II. Switchboards

408.16 Switchboards in Damp or Wet Locations. Switchboards in damp or wet locations shall be installed in accordance with 312.2(A).

408.17 Location Relative to Easily Ignitible Material. Switchboards shall be placed so as to reduce to a minimum the probability of communicating fire to adjacent combustible materials. Where installed over a combustible floor, suitable protection thereto shall be provided.

408.18 Clearances.

(A) From Ceiling. For other than a totally enclosed switchboard, a space not less than 900 mm (3 ft) shall be provided between the top of the switchboard and any combustible ceiling, unless a noncombustible shield is provided between the switchboard and the ceiling.

(B) Around Switchboards. Clearances around switchboards shall comply with the provisions of 110.26.

408.19 Conductor Insulation. An insulated conductor used within a switchboard shall be listed, shall be flame retardant, and shall be rated not less than the voltage applied to it and not less than the voltage applied to other conductors or busbars with which it may come in contact.

408.20 Location of Switchboards. Switchboards that have any exposed live parts shall be located in permanently dry locations and then only where under competent supervision and accessible only to qualified persons. Switchboards shall be located such that the probability of damage from equipment or processes is reduced to a minimum.

408.22 Grounding of Instruments, Relays, Meters, and Instrument Transformers on Switchboards. Instruments, relays, meters, and instrument transformers located on switchboards shall be grounded as specified in 250.170 through 250.178.

III. Panelboards

408.30 General. All panelboards shall have a rating not less than the minimum feeder capacity required for the load calculated in accordance with Article 220. Panelboards shall be durably marked by the manufacturer with the voltage and the current rating and the number of phases for which they are designed and with the manufacturer's name or trademark in such a manner so as to be visible after installation, without disturbing the interior parts or wiring.

FPN: See 110.22 for additional requirements.

408.34 Classification of Panelboards. Panelboards shall be classified for the purposes of this article as either lighting and appliance branch-circuit panelboards or power panelboards, based on their content. A lighting and appliance branch circuit is a branch circuit that has a connection to the neutral of the panelboard and that has overcurrent protection of 30 amperes or less in one or more conductors.

(A) Lighting and Appliance Branch-Circuit Panelboard. A lighting and appliance branch-circuit panelboard is one having more than 10 percent of its overcurrent devices protecting lighting and appliance branch circuits.

(B) Power Panelboard. A power panelboard is one having 10 percent or fewer of its overcurrent devices protecting lighting and appliance branch circuits.

408.35 Number of Overcurrent Devices on One Panelboard. Not more than 42 overcurrent devices (other than those provided for in the mains) of a lighting and appliance branch-circuit panelboard shall be installed in any one cabinet or cutout box.

A lighting and appliance branch-circuit panelboard shall be provided with physical means to prevent the installation of more overcurrent devices than that number for which the panelboard was designed, rated, and approved.

For the purposes of this article, a 2-pole circuit breaker shall be considered two overcurrent devices; a 3-pole circuit breaker shall be considered three overcurrent devices.

408.36 Overcurrent Protection.

(A) Lighting and Appliance Branch-Circuit Panelboard Individually Protected. Each lighting and appliance branch-circuit panelboard shall be individually protected on the supply side by not more than two main circuit breakers or two sets of fuses having a combined rating not greater than that of the panelboard.

Exception No. 1: Individual protection for a lighting and appliance panelboard shall not be required if the panelboard feeder has overcurrent protection not greater than the rating of the panelboard.

Exception No. 2: For existing installations, individual protection for lighting and appliance branch-circuit panelboards shall not be required where such panelboards are used as service equipment in supplying an individual residential occupancy.

(B) Power Panelboard Protection. In addition to the requirements of 408.30, a power panelboard with supply conductors that include a neutral, and having more than 10 percent of its overcurrent devices protecting branch circuits rated 30 amperes or less, shall be protected by an overcurrent protective device having a rating not greater than that of the panelboard. This overcurrent protective device shall be located within or at any point on the supply side of the panelboard.

Exception: This individual protection shall not be required for a power panelboard used as service equipment with multiple disconnecting means in accordance with 230.71.

(C) Snap Switches Rated at 30 Amperes or Less. Panelboards equipped with snap switches rated at 30 amperes or less shall have overcurrent protection of 200 amperes or less.

(D) Supplied Through a Transformer. Where a panelboard is supplied through a transformer, the overcurrent protection required by 408.36(A), (B), and (C) shall be located on the secondary side of the transformer.

Exception: A panelboard supplied by the secondary side of a transformer shall be considered as protected by the overcurrent protection provided on the primary side of the transformer where that protection is in accordance with 240.21(C)(1).

(E) Delta Breakers. A 3-phase disconnect or overcurrent device shall not be connected to the bus of any panelboard that has less than 3-phase buses. Delta breakers shall not be installed in panelboards.

(F) Back-Fed Devices. Plug-in-type overcurrent protection devices or plug-in type main lug assemblies that are backfed and used to terminate field-installed ungrounded supply conductors shall be secured in place by an additional fastener that requires other than a pull to release the device from the mounting means on the panel.

408.37 Panelboards in Damp or Wet Locations. Panelboards in damp or wet locations shall be installed to comply with 312.2(A).

408.38 Enclosure. Panelboards shall be mounted in cabinets, cutout boxes, or enclosures designed for the purpose and shall be dead-front.

Exception: Panelboards other than of the dead-front, externally operable type shall be permitted where accessible only to qualified persons.

408.39 Relative Arrangement of Switches and Fuses. In panelboards, fuses of any type shall be installed on the load side of any switches.

Exception: Fuses installed as part of service equipment in accordance with the provisions of 230.94 shall be permitted on the line side of the service switch.

408.40 Grounding of Panelboards. Panelboard cabinets and panelboard frames, if of metal, shall be in physical contact with each other and shall be grounded. Where the panelboard is used with nonmetallic raceway or cable or where separate grounding conductors are provided, a terminal bar for the grounding conductors shall be secured inside the cabinet. The terminal bar shall be bonded to the cabinet and panelboard frame, if of metal; otherwise it shall be connected to the grounding conductor that is run with the conductors feeding the panelboard.

Exception: Where an isolated equipment grounding conductor is provided as permitted by 250.146(D), the insulated equipment grounding conductor that is run with the circuit conductors shall be permitted to pass through the panelboard without being connected to the panelboard's equipment grounding terminal bar.

Grounding conductors shall not be connected to a terminal bar provided for grounded conductors (may be a neutral) unless the bar is identified for the purpose and is located where interconnection between equipment grounding conductors and grounded circuit conductors is permitted or required by Article 250.

408.41 Grounded Conductor Terminations. Each grounded conductor shall terminate within the panelboard in an individual terminal that is not also used for another conductor.

Exception: Grounded conductors of circuits with parallel conductors shall be permitted to terminate in a single terminal if the terminal is identified for connection of more than one conductor.

IV. Construction Specifications

408.50 Panels. The panels of switchboards shall be made of moisture-resistant, noncombustible material.

408.51 Busbars. Insulated or bare busbars shall be rigidly mounted.

408.52 Protection of Instrument Circuits. Instruments, pilot lights, potential transformers, and other switchboard devices with potential coils shall be supplied by a circuit that is protected by standard overcurrent devices rated 15 amperes or less.

Exception No. 1: Overcurrent devices rated more than 15 amperes shall be permitted where the interruption of the circuit could create a hazard. Short-circuit protection shall be provided.

Exception No. 2: For ratings of 2 amperes or less, special types of enclosed fuses shall be permitted.

408.53 Component Parts. Switches, fuses, and fuseholders used on panelboards shall comply with the applicable requirements of Articles 240 and 404.

408.55 Wire-Bending Space in Panelboards. The enclosure for a panelboard shall have the top and bottom wire-bending space sized in accordance with Table 312.6(B) for the largest conductor entering or leaving the enclosure. Side wire-bending space shall be in accordance with Table 312.6(A) for the largest conductor to be terminated in that space.

Exception No. 1: Either the top or bottom wire-bending space shall be permitted to be sized in accordance with Table 312.6(A) for a lighting and appliance branch-circuit panelboard rated 225 amperes or less.

Exception No. 2: Either the top or bottom wire-bending space for any panelboard shall be permitted to be sized in accordance with Table 312.6(A) where at least one side wire-bending space is sized in accordance with Table 312.6(B) for the largest conductor to be terminated in any side wire-bending space.

Exception No. 3: The top and bottom wire-bending space shall be permitted to be sized in accordance with Table 312.6(A) spacings if the panelboard is designed and constructed for wiring using only one single 90 degree bend for each conductor, including the grounded circuit conductor, and the wiring diagram shows and specifies the method of wiring that shall be used.

Exception No. 4: Either the top or the bottom wire-bending space, but not both, shall be permitted to be sized in accordance with Table 312.6(A) where there are no conductors terminated in that space.

408.56 Minimum Spacings. The distance between bare metal parts, busbars, and so forth shall not be less than specified in Table 408.56.

Where close proximity does not cause excessive heating, parts of the same polarity at switches, enclosed fuses, and so forth shall be permitted to be placed as close together as convenience in handling will allow.

Exception: The distance shall be permitted to be less than that specified in Table 408.56 at circuit breakers and switches and in listed components installed in switchboards and panelboards.

Table 408.56 Minimum Spacings Between Bare Metal Parts

Voltage	Opposite Polarity Where Mounted on the Same Surface		Opposite Polarity Where Held Free in Air		Live Parts to Ground*	
	mm	in.	mm	in.	mm	in.
Not over 125 volts, nominal	19.1	¾	12.7	½	12.7	½
Not over 250 volts, nominal	31.8	1¼	19.1	¾	12.7	½
Not over 600 volts, nominal	50.8	2	25.4	1	25.4	1

*For spacing between live parts and doors of cabinets, see 312.11(A)(1), (2), and (3).

ARTICLE 409
Industrial Control Panels

I. General

409.1 Scope. This article covers industrial control panels intended for general use and operating at 600 volts or less.

     FPN: UL 508A is a safety standard for industrial control panels.

409.2 Definition.

Industrial Control Panel. An assembly of a systematic and standard arrangement of two or more components such as motor controllers, overload relays, fused disconnect switches, and circuit breakers and related control devices such as pushbutton stations, selector switches, timers, switches, control relays, and the like with associated wiring, terminal blocks, pilot lights, and similar components. The industrial control panel does not include the controlled equipment.

409.3 Other Articles. In addition to the requirements of Article 409, industrial control panels that contain branch circuits for specific loads or components, or are for control of specific types of equipment addressed in other articles of this *Code*, shall be constructed and installed in accordance with the applicable requirements from the specific articles in Table 409.3.

Table 409.3 Other Articles

Equipment/Occupancy	Article	Section
Branch circuits	210	
Luminaires	410	
Motors, motor circuits, and controllers	430	
Air-conditioning and refrigerating equipment	440	
Capacitors		460.8, 460.9
Hazardous (classified) locations	500, 501, 502, 503, 504, 505	
Commercial garages; aircraft hangars; motor fuel dispensing facilities; bulk storage plants; spray application, dipping, and coating processes; and inhalation anesthetizing locations	511, 513, 514, 515, 516, and 517 Part IV	
Cranes and hoists	610	
Electrically driven or controlled irrigation machines	675	
Elevators, dumbwaiters, escalators, moving walks, wheelchair lifts, and stairway chair lifts	620	
Industrial machinery	670	
Resistors and reactors	470	
Transformers	450	
Class 1, Class 2, and Class 3 remote-control, signaling, and power-limited circuits	725	

II. Installation

409.20 Conductor — Minimum Size and Ampacity. The size of the industrial control panel supply conductor shall have an ampacity not less than 125 percent of the full-load current rating of all resistance heating loads plus 125 percent of the full-load current rating of the highest rated motor plus the sum of the full-load current ratings of all other connected motors and apparatus based on their duty cycle that may be in operation at the same time.

409.21 Overcurrent Protection.

(A) General. Industrial control panels shall be provided with overcurrent protection in accordance with Parts I, II, and IX of Article 240.

(B) Location. This protection shall be provided by either of the following:

(1) An overcurrent protective device located ahead of the industrial control panel.

(2) A single main overcurrent protective device located within the industrial control panel. Where overcurrent protection is provided as part of the industrial control panel, the supply conductors shall be considered as either feeders or taps as covered by 240.21.

(C) Rating. The rating or setting of the overcurrent protective device for the circuit supplying the industrial control panel shall not be greater than the sum of the largest rating or setting of the branch-circuit short-circuit and ground-fault protective device provided with the industrial control panel, plus 125 percent of the full-load current rating of all resistance heating loads, plus the sum of the full-load currents of all other motors and apparatus that could be in operation at the same time.

Exception: Where one or more instantaneous trip circuit breakers or motor short-circuit protectors are used for motor branch-circuit short-circuit and ground-fault protection as permitted by 430.52(C), the procedure specified above for determining the maximum rating of the protective device for the circuit supplying the industrial control panel shall apply with the following provision: For the purpose of the calculation, each instantaneous trip circuit breaker or motor short-circuit protector shall be assumed to have a rating not exceeding the maximum percentage of motor full-load current permitted by Table 430.52 for the type of control panel supply circuit protective device employed.

Where no branch-circuit short-circuit and ground-fault protective device is provided with the industrial control panel for motor or combination of motor and non-motor loads, the rating or setting of the overcurrent protective device shall be based on 430.52 and 430.53, as applicable.

409.30 Disconnecting Means. Disconnecting means that supply motor loads shall comply with Part IX of Article 430.

409.60 Grounding. Multisection industrial control panels shall be bonded together with an equipment grounding conductor or an equivalent grounding bus sized in accordance with Table 250.122. Equipment grounding conductors shall terminate on this grounding bus or to a grounding termination point provided in a single-section industrial control panel.

III. Construction Specifications

409.100 Enclosures. Table 430.91 shall be used as the basis for selecting industrial control panel enclosures for use in specific locations other than hazardous (classified) locations. The enclosures are not intended to protect against conditions such as condensation, icing, corrosion, or contamination that may occur within the enclosure or enter via the conduit or unsealed openings.

409.102 Busbars and Conductors. Industrial control panels utilizing busbars shall comply with 409.102(A) and 409.102(B).

(A) Support and Arrangement. Busbars shall be protected from physical damage and be held firmly in place.

(B) Phase Arrangement. The phase arrangement on 3-phase horizontal common power and vertical buses shall be A, B, C from front to back, top to bottom, or left to right, as viewed from the front of the industrial control panel. The B phase shall be that phase having the higher voltage to ground on 3-phase, 4-wire, delta-connected systems. Other busbar arrangements shall be permitted for additions to existing installations and shall be marked.

409.104 Wiring Space in Industrial Control Panels.

(A) General. Industrial control panel enclosures shall not be used as junction boxes, auxiliary gutters, or raceways for conductors feeding through or tapping off to other switches or overcurrent devices, unless adequate space for this purpose is provided. The conductors shall not fill the wiring space at any cross section to more than 40 percent of the cross-sectional area of the space, and the conductors, splices, and taps shall not fill the wiring space at any cross section to more than 75 percent of the cross-sectional area of that space.

(B) Wire Bending Space. Wire bending space for the main supply terminals shall be in accordance with the requirements in 312.6. Wire bending space for other terminals shall be in accordance with the requirements in 430.10(B). The gutter space shall comply with 312.8.

409.108 Service-Entrance Equipment. Where used as service equipment, each industrial control panel shall be of the type that is suitable for use as service equipment.

Where a grounded conductor is provided, the industrial control panel shall be provided with a main bonding jumper, sized in accordance with 250.28(D), for connecting the grounded conductor, on its supply side, to the industrial control panel equipment ground bus or terminal.

409.110 Marking. An industrial control panel shall be marked with the following information that is plainly visible after installation:

(1) Manufacturer's name, trademark, or other descriptive marking by which the organization responsible for the product can be identified.

(2) Supply voltage, phase, frequency, and full-load current.

(3) Short-circuit current rating of the industrial control panel based on one of the following:

   a. Short-circuit current rating of a listed and labeled assembly

   b. Short-circuit current rating established utilizing an approved method

   FPN: UL 508A-2001, Supplement SB, is an example of an approved method.

(4) If the industrial control panel is intended as service equipment, it shall be marked to identify it as being suitable for use as service equipment.

(5) Electrical wiring diagram or the number of the index to the electrical drawings showing the electrical wiring diagram.

(6) An enclosure type number shall be marked on the industrial control panel enclosure.

ARTICLE 410
Luminaires (Lighting Fixtures), Lampholders, and Lamps

I. General

410.1 Scope. This article covers luminaires (lighting fixtures), lampholders, pendants, incandescent filament lamps, arc lamps, electric-discharge lamps, decorative lighting products, lighting accessories for temporary seasonal and holiday use, portable flexible lighting products, and the wiring and equipment forming part of such products and lighting installations.

410.2 Application of Other Articles. Equipment for use in hazardous (classified) locations shall conform to Articles 500 through 517. Lighting systems operating at 30 volts or less shall conform to Article 411. Arc lamps used in theaters shall comply with 520.61, and arc lamps used in projection machines shall comply with 540.20. Arc lamps used on constant-current systems shall comply with the general requirements of Article 490.

410.3 Live Parts. Luminaires (fixtures), lampholders, and lamps shall have no live parts normally exposed to contact. Exposed accessible terminals in lampholders and switches shall not be installed in metal luminaire (fixture) canopies or in open bases of portable table or floor lamps.

Exception: Cleat-type lampholders located at least 2.5 m (8 ft) above the floor shall be permitted to have exposed terminals.

II. Luminaire (Fixture) Locations

410.4 Luminaires (Fixtures) in Specific Locations.

(A) Wet and Damp Locations. Luminaires (fixtures) installed in wet or damp locations shall be installed so that water cannot enter or accumulate in wiring compartments, lampholders, or other electrical parts. All luminaires (fixtures) installed in wet locations shall be marked, "Suitable for Wet Locations." All luminaires (fixtures) installed in damp locations shall be marked, "Suitable for Wet Locations" or "Suitable for Damp Locations."

(B) Corrosive Locations. Luminaires (fixtures) installed in corrosive locations shall be of a type suitable for such locations.

(C) In Ducts or Hoods. Luminaires (fixtures) shall be permitted to be installed in commercial cooking hoods where all of the following conditions are met:

(1) The luminaire (fixture) shall be identified for use within commercial cooking hoods and installed such that the temperature limits of the materials used are not exceeded.

(2) The luminaire (fixture) shall be constructed so that all exhaust vapors, grease, oil, or cooking vapors are excluded from the lamp and wiring compartment. Diffusers shall be resistant to thermal shock.

(3) Parts of the luminaire (fixture) exposed within the hood shall be corrosion resistant or protected against corrosion, and the surface shall be smooth so as not to collect deposits and to facilitate cleaning.

(4) Wiring methods and materials supplying the luminaire(s) [fixture(s)] shall not be exposed within the cooking hood.

   FPN: See 110.11 for conductors and equipment exposed to deteriorating agents.

(D) Bathtub and Shower Areas. No parts of cord-connected luminaires (fixtures), chain-, cable-, or cord-suspended-luminaires (fixtures), lighting track, pendants, or ceiling-suspended (paddle) fans shall be located within a zone measured 900 mm (3 ft) horizontally and 2.5 m (8 ft) vertically from the top of the bathtub rim or shower stall threshold. This zone is all encompassing and includes the zone directly over the tub or shower stall. Luminaires (lighting fixtures) located in this zone shall be listed for damp locations, or listed for wet locations where subject to shower spray.

(E) Luminaires (Fixtures) in Indoor Sports, Mixed-Use, and All-Purpose Facilities. Luminaires (fixtures) subject to physical damage, using a mercury vapor or metal halide lamp, installed in playing and spectator seating areas of indoor sports, mixed-use, or all-purpose facilities shall be of the type that protects the lamp with a glass or plastic lens. Such luminaires (fixtures) shall be permitted to have an additional guard.

410.5 Luminaires (Fixtures) Near Combustible Material. Luminaires (fixtures) shall be constructed, installed, or equipped with shades or guards so that combustible material is not subjected to temperatures in excess of 90°C (194°F).

410.6 Luminaires (Fixtures) Over Combustible Material. Lampholders installed over highly combustible material shall be of the unswitched type. Unless an individual switch is provided for each luminaire (fixture), lampholders shall be located at least 2.5 m (8 ft) above the floor or shall be located or guarded so that the lamps cannot be readily removed or damaged.

410.7 Luminaires (Fixtures) in Show Windows. Chain-supported luminaires (fixtures) used in a show window shall be permitted to be externally wired. No other externally wired luminaires (fixtures) shall be used.

410.8 Luminaires (Fixtures) in Clothes Closets.

(A) Definition.

Storage Space. The volume bounded by the sides and back closet walls and planes extending from the closet floor vertically to a height of 1.8 m (6 ft) or to the highest clothes-hanging rod and parallel to the walls at a horizontal distance of 600 mm (24 in.) from the sides and back of the closet walls, respectively, and continuing vertically to the closet ceiling parallel to the walls at a horizontal distance of 300 mm (12 in.) or the width of the shelf, whichever is greater; for a closet that permits access to both sides of a hanging rod, this space includes the volume below the highest rod extending 300 mm (12 in.) on either side of the rod on a plane horizontal to the floor extending the entire length of the rod.

> FPN: See Figure 410.8.

(B) Luminaire (Fixture) Types Permitted. Listed luminaires (fixtures) of the following types shall be permitted to be installed in a closet:

(1) A surface-mounted or recessed incandescent luminaire (fixture) with a completely enclosed lamp

(2) A surface-mounted or recessed fluorescent luminaire (fixture)

(C) Luminaire (Fixture) Types Not Permitted. Incandescent luminaires (fixtures) with open or partially enclosed lamps and pendant luminaires (fixtures) or lampholders shall not be permitted.

Figure 410.8 Closet Storage Space.

(D) Location. Luminaires (fixtures) in clothes closets shall be permitted to be installed as follows:

(1) Surface-mounted incandescent luminaires (fixtures) installed on the wall above the door or on the ceiling, provided there is a minimum clearance of 300 mm (12 in.) between the luminaire (fixture) and the nearest point of a storage space

(2) Surface-mounted fluorescent luminaires (fixtures) installed on the wall above the door or on the ceiling, provided there is a minimum clearance of 150 mm (6 in.) between the luminaire (fixture) and the nearest point of a storage space

(3) Recessed incandescent luminaires (fixtures) with a completely enclosed lamp installed in the wall or the ceiling, provided there is a minimum clearance of 150 mm (6 in.) between the luminaire (fixture) and the nearest point of a storage space

(4) Recessed fluorescent luminaires (fixtures) installed in the wall or the ceiling, provided there is a minimum clearance of 150 mm (6 in.) between the luminaire (fixture) and the nearest point of a storage space

410.9 Space for Cove Lighting. Coves shall have adequate space and shall be located so that lamps and equipment can be properly installed and maintained.

III. Provisions at Luminaire (Fixture) Outlet Boxes, Canopies, and Pans

410.10 Space for Conductors. Canopies and outlet boxes taken together shall provide adequate space so that luminaire (fixture) conductors and their connecting devices can be properly installed.

410.11 Temperature Limit of Conductors in Outlet Boxes. Luminaires (fixtures) shall be of such construction or installed so that the conductors in outlet boxes shall not be subjected to temperatures greater than that for which the conductors are rated.

Branch-circuit wiring, other than 2-wire or multiwire branch circuits supplying power to luminaires (fixtures) connected together, shall not be passed through an outlet box that is an integral part of a luminaire (fixture) unless the luminaire (fixture) is identified for through-wiring.

FPN: See 410.32 for wiring supplying power to fixtures connected together.

410.12 Outlet Boxes to Be Covered. In a completed installation, each outlet box shall be provided with a cover unless covered by means of a luminaire (fixture) canopy, lampholder, receptacle, or similar device.

410.13 Covering of Combustible Material at Outlet Boxes. Any combustible wall or ceiling finish exposed between the edge of a luminaire (fixture) canopy or pan and an outlet box shall be covered with noncombustible material.

410.14 Connection of Electric-Discharge Luminaires (Lighting Fixtures).

(A) Independent of the Outlet Box. Electric-discharge luminaires (lighting fixtures) supported independently of the outlet box shall be connected to the branch circuit through metal raceway, nonmetallic raceway, Type MC cable, Type AC cable, Type MI cable, nonmetallic sheathed cable, or by flexible cord as permitted in 410.30(B) or 410.30(C).

(B) Access to Boxes. Electric-discharge luminaires (fixtures) surface mounted over concealed outlet, pull, or junction boxes and designed not to be supported solely by the outlet box shall be provided with suitable openings in the back of the luminaire (fixture) to provide access to the wiring in the box.

IV. Luminaire (Fixture) Supports

410.15 Supports.

(A) General. Luminaires (fixtures) and lampholders shall be securely supported. A luminaire (fixture) that weighs more than 3 kg (6 lb) or exceeds 400 mm (16 in.) in any dimension shall not be supported by the screw shell of a lampholder.

(B) Metal or Nonmetallic Poles Supporting Luminaires (Lighting Fixtures). Metal or nonmetallic poles shall be permitted to be used to support luminaires (lighting fixtures) and as a raceway to enclose supply conductors, provided the following conditions are met:

(1) A pole shall have a handhole not less than 50 mm × 100 mm (2 in. × 4 in.) with a raintight cover to provide access to the supply terminations within the pole or pole base.

Exception No. 1: No handhole shall be required in a pole 2.5 m (8 ft) or less in height above grade where the supply wiring method continues without splice or pull point, and where the interior of the pole and any splices are accessible by removing the luminaire (fixture).

Exception No. 2: No handhole shall be required in a pole 6.0 m (20 ft) or less in height above grade that is provided with a hinged base.

(2) Where raceway risers or cable is not installed within the pole, a threaded fitting or nipple shall be brazed, welded, or attached to the pole opposite the handhole for the supply connection.

(3) A metal pole shall be provided with a grounding terminal as follows:
   a. A pole with a handhole shall have the grounding terminal accessible from the handhole.
   b. A pole with a hinged base shall have the grounding terminal accessible within the base.

Exception to (3): No grounding terminal shall be required in a pole 2.5 m (8 ft) or less in height above grade where the supply wiring method continues without splice or pull, and where the interior of the pole and any splices are accessible by removing the luminaire (fixture).

(4) A metal pole with a hinged base shall have the hinged base and pole bonded together.

(5) Metal raceways or other equipment grounding conductors shall be bonded to the metal pole with an equipment grounding conductor recognized by 250.118 and sized in accordance with 250.122.

(6) Conductors in vertical poles used as raceway shall be supported as provided in 300.19.

410.16 Means of Support.

(A) Outlet Boxes. Outlet boxes or fittings installed as required by 314.23 and complying with the provisions of 314.27(A) and 314.27(B) shall be permitted to support luminaires (fixtures).

(B) Inspection. Luminaires (fixtures) shall be installed such that the connections between the luminaire (fixture) conductors and the circuit conductors can be inspected without requiring the disconnection of any part of the wiring unless the luminaires (fixtures) are connected by attachment plugs and receptacles.

(C) Suspended Ceilings. Framing members of suspended ceiling systems used to support luminaires (fixtures) shall be securely fastened to each other and shall be securely attached to the building structure at appropriate intervals. Luminaires (fixtures) shall be securely fastened to the ceiling framing member by mechanical means such as bolts, screws, or rivets. Listed clips identified for use with the type of ceiling framing member(s) and luminaire(s) [fixture(s)] shall also be permitted.

(D) Luminaire (Fixture) Studs. Luminaire (fixture) studs that are not a part of outlet boxes, hickeys, tripods, and crowfeet shall be made of steel, malleable iron, or other material suitable for the application.

(E) Insulating Joints. Insulating joints that are not designed to be mounted with screws or bolts shall have an exterior metal casing, insulated from both screw connections.

(F) Raceway Fittings. Raceway fittings used to support a luminaire(s) [lighting fixture(s)] shall be capable of supporting the weight of the complete fixture assembly and lamp(s).

(G) Busways. Luminaires (fixtures) shall be permitted to be connected to busways in accordance with 368.17(C).

(H) Trees. Outdoor luminaires (lighting fixtures) and associated equipment shall be permitted to be supported by trees.

> FPN No. 1: See 225.26 for restrictions for support of overhead conductors.

> FPN No. 2: See 300.5(D) for protection of conductors.

V. Grounding

410.17 General. Luminaires (fixtures) and lighting equipment shall be grounded as required in Article 250 and Part V of this article.

410.18 Exposed Luminaire (Fixture) Parts.

(A) Exposed Conductive Parts. Exposed metal parts shall be grounded or insulated from ground and other conducting surfaces or be inaccessible to unqualified personnel. Lamp tie wires, mounting screws, clips, and decorative bands on glass spaced at least 38 mm (1½ in.) from lamp terminals shall not be required to be grounded.

(B) Made of Insulating Material. Luminaires (fixtures) directly wired or attached to outlets supplied by a wiring method that does not provide a ready means for grounding shall be made of insulating material and shall have no exposed conductive parts.

Exception No. 1: Replacement luminaires (fixtures) shall be permitted to connect an equipment grounding conductor from the outlet in compliance with 250.130(C). The luminaire (fixture) shall then be grounded in accordance with 410.18(A).

Exception No. 2: Where no equipment grounding conductor exists at the outlet, replacement luminaires (fixtures) that are GFCI protected shall not be required to be connected to an equipment grounding conductor.

410.20 Equipment Grounding Conductor Attachment. Luminaires (fixtures) with exposed metal parts shall be provided with a means for connecting an equipment grounding conductor for such luminaires (fixtures).

410.21 Methods of Grounding. Luminaires (fixtures) and equipment shall be considered grounded where mechanically connected to an equipment grounding conductor as specified in 250.118 and sized in accordance with 250.122.

VI. Wiring of Luminaires (Fixtures)

410.22 Luminaire (Fixture) Wiring — General. Wiring on or within fixtures shall be neatly arranged and shall not be exposed to physical damage. Excess wiring shall be avoided. Conductors shall be arranged so that they are not subjected to temperatures above those for which they are rated.

410.23 Polarization of Luminaires (Fixtures). Luminaires (fixtures) shall be wired so that the screw shells of lampholders are connected to the same luminaire (fixture) or circuit conductor or terminal. The grounded conductor, where connected to a screw-shell lampholder, shall be connected to the screw shell.

410.24 Conductor Insulation. Luminaires (fixtures) shall be wired with conductors having insulation suitable for the environmental conditions, current, voltage, and temperature to which the conductors will be subjected.

> FPN: For ampacity of luminaire (fixture) wire, maximum operating temperature, voltage limitations, minimum wire size, and so forth, see Article 402.

410.27 Pendant Conductors for Incandescent Filament Lamps.

(A) Support. Pendant lampholders with permanently attached leads, where used for other than festoon wiring, shall be hung from separate stranded rubber-covered conductors that are soldered directly to the circuit conductors but supported independently thereof.

(B) Size. Unless part of listed decorative lighting assemblies, pendant conductors shall not be smaller than 14 AWG for mogul-base or medium-base screw-shell lampholders or smaller than 18 AWG for intermediate or candelabra-base lampholders.

(C) Twisted or Cabled. Pendant conductors longer than 900 mm (3 ft) shall be twisted together where not cabled in a listed assembly.

410.28 Protection of Conductors and Insulation.

(A) Properly Secured. Conductors shall be secured in a manner that does not tend to cut or abrade the insulation.

(B) Protection Through Metal. Conductor insulation shall be protected from abrasion where it passes through metal.

(C) Luminaire (Fixture) Stems. Splices and taps shall not be located within luminaire (fixture) arms or stems.

(D) Splices and Taps. No unnecessary splices or taps shall be made within or on a luminaire (fixture).

> FPN: For approved means of making connections, see 110.14.

(E) Stranding. Stranded conductors shall be used for wiring on luminaire (fixture) chains and on other movable or flexible parts.

(F) Tension. Conductors shall be arranged so that the weight of the luminaire (fixture) or movable parts does not put tension on the conductors.

410.29 Cord-Connected Showcases. Individual showcases, other than fixed, shall be permitted to be connected by flexible cord to permanently installed receptacles, and groups of not more than six such showcases shall be permitted to be coupled together by flexible cord and separable locking-type connectors with one of the group connected by flexible cord to a permanently installed receptacle.

The installation shall comply with 410.29(A) through 410.29(E).

(A) Cord Requirements. Flexible cord shall be of the hard-service type, having conductors not smaller than the branch-circuit conductors, having ampacity at least equal to the branch-circuit overcurrent device, and having an equipment grounding conductor.

> FPN: See Table 250.122 for size of equipment grounding conductor.

(B) Receptacles, Connectors, and Attachment Plugs. Receptacles, connectors, and attachment plugs shall be of a listed grounding type rated 15 or 20 amperes.

(C) Support. Flexible cords shall be secured to the undersides of showcases such that all of the following conditions are ensured:

(1) The wiring is not exposed to mechanical damage.
(2) The separation between cases is not in excess of 50 mm (2 in.), or more than 300 mm (12 in.) between the first case and the supply receptacle.
(3) The free lead at the end of a group of showcases has a female fitting not extending beyond the case.

(D) No Other Equipment. Equipment other than showcases shall not be electrically connected to showcases.

(E) Secondary Circuit(s). Where showcases are cord-connected, the secondary circuit(s) of each electric-discharge lighting ballast shall be limited to one showcase.

410.30 Cord-Connected Lampholders and Luminaires (Fixtures).

(A) Lampholders. Where a metal lampholder is attached to a flexible cord, the inlet shall be equipped with an insulating bushing that, if threaded, is not smaller than metric designator 12 (trade size ⅜) pipe size. The cord hole shall be of a size appropriate for the cord, and all burrs and fins shall be removed in order to provide a smooth bearing surface for the cord.

Bushing having holes 7 mm (9/32 in.) in diameter shall be permitted for use with plain pendant cord and holes 11 mm (13/32 in.) in diameter with reinforced cord.

(B) Adjustable Luminaires (Fixtures). Luminaires (fixtures) that require adjusting or aiming after installation shall not be required to be equipped with an attachment plug or cord connector, provided the exposed cord is of the hard-usage or extra-hard-usage type and is not longer than that required for maximum adjustment. The cord shall not be subject to strain or physical damage.

(C) Electric-Discharge Luminaires (Fixtures).

(1) Cord Connected Installation. A listed luminaire (fixture) or a listed assembly shall be permitted to be cord connected if the following conditions apply:

(1) The luminaire (fixture) is located directly below the outlet or busway.
(2) The flexible cord meets all the following:
   a. Is visible for its entire length outside the luminaire (fixture)
   b. Is not subject to strain or physical damage
   c. Is terminated in a grounding-type attachment plug cap or busway plug, or is a part of a listed assembly incorporating a manufactured wiring system connector in accordance with 604.6(C), or has a luminaire (fixture) assembly with a strain relief and canopy

(2) Provided with Mogul-Base, Screw-Shell Lampholders. Electric-discharge luminaires (lighting fixtures) provided with mogul-base, screw-shell lampholders shall be permitted to be connected to branch circuits of 50 amperes or less by cords complying with 240.5. Receptacles and attachment plugs shall be permitted to be of a lower ampere rating than the branch circuit but not less than 125 percent of the luminaire (fixture) full-load current.

(3) Equipped with Flanged Surface Inlet. Electric-discharge luminaires (lighting fixtures) equipped with a flanged surface inlet shall be permitted to be supplied by cord pendants equipped with cord connectors. Inlets and connectors shall be permitted to be of a lower ampere rating than the branch circuit but not less than 125 percent of the luminaire (fixture) load current.

410.31 Luminaires (Fixtures) as Raceways. Luminaires (fixtures) shall not be used as a raceway for circuit conductors unless listed and marked for use as a raceway.

410.32 Wiring Supplying Luminaires (Fixtures) Connected Together. Luminaires (fixtures) designed for end-to-end connection to form a continuous assembly, or luminaires (fixtures) connected together by recognized wiring methods, shall be permitted to contain the conductors of a 2-wire branch circuit, or one multiwire branch circuit, supplying the connected luminaires (fixtures) and need not be listed as a raceway. One additional 2-wire branch circuit separately supplying one or more of the connected luminaires (fixtures) shall also be permitted.

> FPN: See Article 100 for the definition of *Multiwire Branch Circuit.*

410.33 Branch Circuit Conductors and Ballasts. Branch-circuit conductors within 75 mm (3 in.) of a ballast shall have an insulation temperature rating not lower than 90°C (194°F) unless supplying a luminaire (fixture) listed and marked as suitable for a different insulation temperature.

VII. Construction of Luminaires (Fixtures)

410.34 Combustible Shades and Enclosures. Adequate airspace shall be provided between lamps and shades or other enclosures of combustible material.

410.35 Luminaire (Fixture) Rating.

(A) Marking. All luminaires (fixtures) shall be marked with the maximum lamp wattage or electrical rating, manufacturer's name, trademark, or other suitable means of identification. A luminaire (fixture) requiring supply wire rated higher than 60°C (140°F) shall be marked in letters not smaller than 6 mm (¼ in.) high, prominently displayed on the luminaire (fixture) and shipping carton or equivalent.

(B) Electrical Rating. The electrical rating shall include the voltage and frequency and shall indicate the current rating of the unit, including the ballast, transformer, or autotransformer.

410.36 Design and Material. Luminaires (fixtures) shall be constructed of metal, wood, or other material suitable for the application and shall be designed and assembled so as to secure requisite mechanical strength and rigidity. Wiring compartments, including their entrances, shall be designed and constructed to permit conductors to be drawn in and withdrawn without physical damage.

410.37 Nonmetallic Luminaires (Fixtures). When luminaire (fixture) wiring compartments are constructed from combustible material, armored or lead-covered conductors with suitable fittings shall be used or the wiring compartment shall be lined with metal.

410.38 Mechanical Strength.

(A) Tubing for Arms. Tubing used for arms and stems where provided with cut threads shall not be less than 1.02 mm (0.040 in.) in thickness and, where provided with rolled (pressed) threads, shall not be less than 0.64 mm (0.025 in.) in thickness. Arms and other parts shall be fastened to prevent turning.

(B) Metal Canopies. Metal canopies supporting lampholders, shades, and so forth exceeding 4 kg (8 lb), or incorporating attachment-plug receptacles, shall not be less than 0.51 mm (0.020 in.) in thickness. Other canopies shall not be less than 0.41 mm (0.016 in.) if made of steel and not less than 0.51 mm (0.020 in.) if of other metals.

(C) Canopy Switches. Pull-type canopy switches shall not be inserted in the rims of metal canopies that are less than 0.64 mm (0.025 in.) in thickness, unless the rims are reinforced by the turning of a bead or the equivalent. Pull-type canopy switches, whether mounted in the rims or elsewhere in sheet metal canopies, shall not be located more than 90 mm (3½ in.) from the center of the canopy. Double set-screws, double canopy rings, a screw ring, or equal method shall be used where the canopy supports a pull-type switch or pendant receptacle.

The thickness requirements in the preceding paragraph shall apply to measurements made on finished (formed) canopies.

410.39 Wiring Space. Bodies of luminaires (fixtures), including portable lamps, shall provide ample space for splices and taps and for the installation of devices, if any. Splice compartments shall be of nonabsorbent, noncombustible material.

410.42 Portable Lamps.

(A) General. Portable lamps shall be wired with flexible cord recognized by 400.4 and an attachment plug of the polarized or grounding type. Where used with Edison-base lampholders, the grounded conductor shall be identified and attached to the screw shell and the identified blade of the attachment plug.

(B) Portable Handlamps. In addition to the provisions of 410.42(A), portable handlamps shall comply with the following:

(1) Metal shell, paper-lined lampholders shall not be used.

(2) Handlamps shall be equipped with a handle of molded composition or other insulating material.

(3) Handlamps shall be equipped with a substantial guard attached to the lampholder or handle.

(4) Metallic guards shall be grounded by means of an equipment grounding conductor run with circuit conductors within the power-supply cord.

(5) Portable handlamps shall not be required to be grounded where supplied through an isolating transformer with an ungrounded secondary of not over 50 volts.

410.44 Cord Bushings. A bushing or the equivalent shall be provided where flexible cord enters the base or stem of a portable lamp. The bushing shall be of insulating material unless a jacketed type of cord is used.

410.45 Tests. All wiring shall be free from short circuits and grounds and shall be tested for these defects prior to being connected to the circuit.

410.46 Live Parts. Exposed live parts within porcelain luminaires (fixtures) shall be suitably recessed and located so as to make it improbable that wires come in contact with them. There shall be a spacing of at least 13 mm (½ in.) between live parts and the mounting plane of the luminaire (fixture).

VIII. Installation of Lampholders

410.47 Screw-Shell Type. Lampholders of the screw-shell type shall be installed for use as lampholders only. Where supplied by a circuit having a grounded conductor, the grounded conductor shall be connected to the screw shell.

410.48 Double-Pole Switched Lampholders. Where supplied by the ungrounded conductors of a circuit, the switching device of lampholders of the switched type shall simultaneously disconnect both conductors of the circuit.

410.49 Lampholders in Wet or Damp Locations. Lampholders installed in wet or damp locations shall be of the weatherproof type.

IX. Construction of Lampholders

410.50 Insulation. The outer metal shell and the cap shall be lined with insulating material that prevents the shell and cap from becoming a part of the circuit. The lining shall not extend beyond the metal shell more than 3 mm (⅛ in.) but shall prevent any current-carrying part of the lamp base from being exposed when a lamp is in the lampholding device.

410.52 Switched Lampholders. Switched lampholders shall be of such construction that the switching mechanism interrupts the electrical connection to the center contact. The switching mechanism shall also be permitted to interrupt the electrical connection to the screw shell if the connection to the center contact is simultaneously interrupted.

X. Lamps and Auxiliary Equipment

410.53 Bases, Incandescent Lamps. An incandescent lamp for general use on lighting branch circuits shall not be equipped with a medium base if rated over 300 watts, or with a mogul base if rated over 1500 watts. Special bases or other devices shall be used for over 1500 watts.

410.54 Electric-Discharge Lamp Auxiliary Equipment.

(A) Enclosures. Auxiliary equipment for electric-discharge lamps shall be enclosed in noncombustible cases and treated as sources of heat.

(B) Switching. Where supplied by the ungrounded conductors of a circuit, the switching device of auxiliary equipment shall simultaneously disconnect all conductors.

XI. Special Provisions for Flush and Recessed Luminaires (Fixtures)

410.64 General. Luminaires (fixtures) installed in recessed cavities in walls or ceilings shall comply with 410.65 through 410.72.

410.65 Temperature.

(A) Combustible Material. Luminaires (fixtures) shall be installed so that adjacent combustible material will not be subjected to temperatures in excess of 90°C (194°F).

(B) Fire-Resistant Construction. Where a luminaire (fixture) is recessed in fire-resistant material in a building of fire-resistant construction, a temperature higher than 90°C (194°F) but not higher than 150°C (302°F) shall be considered acceptable if the luminaire (fixture) is plainly marked that it is listed for that service.

(C) Recessed Incandescent Luminaires (Fixtures). Incandescent luminaires (fixtures) shall have thermal protection and shall be identified as thermally protected.

Exception No. 1: Thermal protection shall not be required in a recessed luminaire (fixture) identified for use and installed in poured concrete.

Exception No. 2: Thermal protection shall not be required in a recessed luminaire (fixture) whose design, construction, and thermal performance characteristics are equivalent to a thermally protected luminaire (fixture) and are identified as inherently protected.

410.66 Clearance and Installation.

(A) Clearance.

(1) Non-Type IC. A recessed luminaire (fixture) that is not identified for contact with insulation shall have all recessed parts spaced not less than 13 mm (½ in.) from combustible materials. The points of support and the trim finishing off the opening in the ceiling or wall surface shall be permitted to be in contact with combustible materials.

(2) Type IC. A recessed luminaire (fixture) that is identified for contact with insulation, Type IC, shall be permitted to be in contact with combustible materials at recessed parts, points of support, and portions passing through or finishing off the opening in the building structure.

(B) Installation. Thermal insulation shall not be installed above a recessed luminaire (fixture) or with 75 mm (3 in.) of the recessed luminaire's (fixture's) enclosure, wiring compartment, or ballast unless it is identified for contact with insulation, Type IC.

410.67 Wiring.

(A) General. Conductors that have insulation suitable for the temperature encountered shall be used.

(B) Circuit Conductors. Branch-circuit conductors that have an insulation suitable for the temperature encountered shall be permitted to terminate in the luminaire (fixture).

(C) Tap Conductors. Tap conductors of a type suitable for the temperature encountered shall be permitted to run from the luminaire (fixture) terminal connection to an outlet box placed at least 300 mm (1 ft) from the luminaire (fixture). Such tap conductors shall be in suitable raceway or Type AC or MC cable of at least 450 mm (18 in.) but not more than 1.8 m (6 ft) in length.

XII. Construction of Flush and Recessed Luminaires (Fixtures)

410.68 Temperature. Luminaires (fixtures) shall be constructed such that adjacent combustible material is not subject to temperatures in excess of 90°C (194°F).

410.70 Lamp Wattage Marking. Incandescent lamp luminaires (fixtures) shall be marked to indicate the maximum allowable wattage of lamps. The markings shall be permanently installed, in letters at least 6 mm (¼ in.) high, and shall be located where visible during relamping.

410.71 Solder Prohibited. No solder shall be used in the construction of a luminaire (fixture) box.

410.72 Lampholders. Lampholders of the screw-shell type shall be of porcelain or other suitable insulating materials. Where used, cements shall be of the high-heat type.

XIII. Special Provisions for Electric-Discharge Lighting Systems of 1000 Volts or Less

410.73 General.

(A) Open-Circuit Voltage of 1000 Volts or Less. Equipment for use with electric-discharge lighting systems and designed for an open-circuit voltage of 1000 volts or less shall be of a type intended for such service.

(B) Considered as Energized. The terminals of an electric-discharge lamp shall be considered as energized where any lamp terminal is connected to a circuit of over 300 volts.

(C) Transformers of the Oil-Filled Type. Transformers of the oil-filled type shall not be used.

(D) Additional Requirements. In addition to complying with the general requirements for luminaires (lighting fixtures), such equipment shall comply with Part XIII of this article.

(E) Thermal Protection — Fluorescent Luminaires (Fixtures).

(1) Integral Thermal Protection. The ballast of a fluorescent luminaire (fixture) installed indoors shall have integral thermal protection. Replacement ballasts shall also have thermal protection integral with the ballast.

(2) Simple Reactance Ballasts. A simple reactance ballast in a fluorescent luminaire (fixture) with straight tubular lamps shall not be required to be thermally protected.

(3) Exit Fixtures. A ballast in a fluorescent exit luminaire (fixture) shall not have thermal protection.

(4) Egress Luminaires (Fixtures). A ballast in a fluorescent luminaire (fixture) that is used for egress lighting and energized only during a failure of the normal supply shall not have thermal protection.

(F) High-Intensity Discharge Luminaires (Fixtures).

(1) Recessed. Recessed high-intensity luminaires (fixtures) designed to be installed in wall or ceiling cavities shall have thermal protection and be identified as thermally protected.

(2) Inherently Protected. Thermal protection shall not be required in a recessed high-intensity luminaire (fixture) whose design, construction, and thermal performance characteristics are equivalent to a thermally protected luminaire (fixture) and are identified as inherently protected.

(3) Installed in Poured Concrete. Thermal protection shall not be required in a recessed high-intensity discharge luminaire (fixture) identified for use and installed in poured concrete.

(4) Recessed Remote Ballasts. A recessed remote ballast for a high-intensity discharge luminaire (fixture) shall have thermal protection that is integral with the ballast and be identified as thermally protected.

(5) Metal Halide Lamp Containment. Luminaires (fixtures) that use a metal halide lamp other than a thick-glass parabolic reflector lamp (PAR) shall be provided with a containment barrier that encloses the lamp, or shall be provided with a physical means that only allows the use of a lamp that is Type O.

> FPN: See ANSI Standard C78.387, *American National Standard for Electric Lamps — Metal Halide Lamps, Methods of Measuring Characteristics.*

(G) Disconnecting Means. In indoor locations, other than dwellings and associated accessory structures, fluorescent luminaires (fixtures) that utilize double-ended lamps and contain ballast(s) that can be serviced in place or ballasted luminaires that are supplied from multiwire branch circuits and contain ballast(s) that can be serviced in place shall have a disconnecting means either internal or external to each luminaire (fixture), to disconnect simultaneously from the source of supply all conductors of the ballast, including the grounded conductor if any. The line side terminals of the disconnecting means shall be guarded. The disconnecting means shall be located so as to be accessible to qualified persons before servicing or maintaining the ballast. This requirement shall become effective January 1, 2008.

Exception No. 1: A disconnecting means shall not be required for luminaires (fixtures) installed in hazardous (classified) location(s).

Exception No. 2: A disconnecting means shall not be required for emergency illumination required in 700.16.

Exception No. 3: For cord-and-plug-connected luminaires, an accessible separable connector or an accessible plug and receptacle shall be permitted to serve as the disconnecting means.

Exception No. 4: A disconnecting means shall not be required in industrial establishments with restricted public access where conditions of maintenance and supervision ensure that only qualified persons service the installation by written procedures.

Exception No. 5: Where more than one luminaire is installed and supplied by other than a multiwire branch circuit, a disconnecting means shall not be required for every luminaire when the design of the installation includes locally accessible disconnects, such that the illuminated space cannot be left in total darkness.

410.74 Direct-Current Equipment. Luminaires (fixtures) installed on dc circuits shall be equipped with auxiliary equipment and resistors designed for dc operation. The luminaires (fixtures) shall be marked for dc operation.

410.75 Open-Circuit Voltage Exceeding 300 Volts. Equipment having an open-circuit voltage exceeding 300 volts shall not be installed in dwelling occupancies unless such equipment is designed so that there will be no exposed live parts when lamps are being inserted, are in place, or are being removed.

410.76 Luminaire (Fixture) Mounting.

(A) Exposed Ballasts. Luminaires (fixtures) that have exposed ballasts or transformers shall be installed so that such ballasts or transformers will not be in contact with combustible material.

(B) Combustible Low-Density Cellulose Fiberboard. Where a surface-mounted luminaire (fixture) containing a ballast is to be installed on combustible low-density cellulose fiberboard, it shall be listed for this condition or shall be spaced not less than 38 mm (1½ in.) from the surface of the fiberboard. Where such luminaires (fixtures) are partially or wholly recessed, the provisions of 410.64 through 410.72 shall apply.

> FPN: Combustible low-density cellulose fiberboard includes sheets, panels, and tiles that have a density of 320 kg/m³ (20 lb/ft³) or less and that are formed of bonded plant fiber material but does not include solid or laminated wood or fiberboard that has a density in excess of 320 kg/m³ (20 lb/ft³) or is a material that has been integrally treated with fire-retarding chemicals to the degree that the flame spread in any plane of the material will not exceed 25, determined in accordance with tests for surface burning characteristics of building materials. See ANSI/ASTM E84-1997, *Test Method for Surface Burning Characteristics of Building Materials.*

410.77 Equipment Not Integral with Luminaire (Fixture).

(A) Metal Cabinets. Auxiliary equipment, including reactors, capacitors, resistors, and similar equipment, where not installed as part of a luminaire (lighting fixture) assembly, shall be enclosed in accessible, permanently installed metal cabinets.

(B) Separate Mounting. Separately mounted ballasts that are intended for direct connection to a wiring system shall not be required to be separately enclosed.

(C) Wired Luminaire (Fixture) Sections. Wired luminaire (fixture) sections are paired, with a ballast(s) supplying a lamp or lamps in both. For interconnection between paired units, it shall be permissible to use metric designator 12 (trade size ⅜) flexible metal conduit in lengths not exceeding 7.5 m (25 ft), in conformance with Article 348. Luminaire (fixture) wire operating at line voltage, supplying only the ballast(s) of one of the paired luminaires (fixtures), shall be permitted in the same raceway as the lamp supply wires of the paired luminaires (fixtures).

410.78 Autotransformers. An autotransformer that is used to raise the voltage to more than 300 volts, as part of a ballast for supplying lighting units, shall be supplied only by a grounded system.

410.79 Switches. Snap switches shall comply with 404.14.

XIV. Special Provisions for Electric-Discharge Lighting Systems of More Than 1000 Volts

410.80 General.

(A) Listing. Electric-discharge lighting systems with an open-circuit voltage exceeding 1000 volts shall be listed and installed in conformance with that listing.

(B) Dwelling Occupancies. Equipment that has an open-circuit voltage exceeding 1000 volts shall not be installed in or on dwelling occupancies.

(C) Live Parts. The terminal of an electric-discharge lamp shall be considered as a live part.

(D) Additional Requirements. In addition to complying with the general requirements for luminaires (lighting fixtures), such equipment shall comply with Part XIV of this article.

FPN: For signs and outline lighting, see Article 600.

410.81 Control.

(A) Disconnection. Luminaires (fixtures) or lamp installation shall be controlled either singly or in groups by an externally operable switch or circuit breaker that opens all ungrounded primary conductors.

(B) Within Sight or Locked Type. The switch or circuit breaker shall be located within sight from the luminaires (fixtures) or lamps, or it shall be permitted elsewhere if it is provided with a means for locking in the open position.

410.82 Lamp Terminals and Lampholders. Parts that must be removed for lamp replacement shall be hinged or held captive. Lamps or lampholders shall be designed so that there are no exposed live parts when lamps are being inserted or removed.

410.83 Transformers.

(A) Type. Transformers shall be enclosed, identified for the use, and listed.

(B) Voltage. The secondary-circuit voltage shall not exceed 15,000 volts, nominal, under any load condition. The voltage to ground of any output terminals of the secondary circuit shall not exceed 7500 volts, under any load conditions.

(C) Rating. Transformers shall have a secondary short-circuit current rating of not more than 150 mA if the open-circuit voltage is over 7500 volts, and not more than 300 mA if the open-circuit voltage rating is 7500 volts or less.

(D) Secondary Connections. Secondary circuit outputs shall not be connected in parallel or in series.

410.84 Transformer Locations.

(A) Accessible. Transformers shall be accessible after installation.

(B) Secondary Conductors. Transformers shall be installed as near to the lamps as practicable to keep the secondary conductors as short as possible.

(C) Adjacent to Combustible Materials. Transformers shall be located so that adjacent combustible materials are not subjected to temperatures in excess of 90°C (194°F).

410.85 Exposure to Damage. Lamps shall not be located where normally exposed to physical damage.

410.86 Marking. Each luminaire (fixture) or each secondary circuit of tubing having an open-circuit voltage of over 1000 volts shall have a clearly legible marking in letters not less than 6 mm (¼ in.) high reading "Caution ____ volts." The voltage indicated shall be the rated open-circuit voltage.

410.87 Switches. Snap switches shall comply with 404.4.

XV. Lighting Track

410.100 Definition.

Lighting Track. A manufactured assembly designed to support and energize luminaires (lighting fixtures) that are capable of being readily repositioned on the track. Its length can be altered by the addition or subtraction of sections of track.

410.101 Installation.

(A) Lighting Track. Lighting track shall be permanently installed and permanently connected to a branch circuit. Only lighting track fittings shall be installed on lighting track. Lighting track fittings shall not be equipped with general-purpose receptacles.

(B) Connected Load. The connected load on lighting track shall not exceed the rating of the track. Lighting track shall be supplied by a branch circuit having a rating not more than that of the track.

(C) Locations Not Permitted. Lighting track shall not be installed in the following locations:

(1) Where likely to be subjected to physical damage

(2) In wet or damp locations

(3) Where subject to corrosive vapors

(4) In storage battery rooms

(5) In hazardous (classified) locations

(6) Where concealed

(7) Where extended through walls or partitions

(8) Less than 1.5 m (5 ft) above the finished floor except where protected from physical damage or track operating at less than 30 volts rms open-circuit voltage

(9) Where prohibited by 410.4(D)

(D) Support. Fittings identified for use on lighting track shall be designed specifically for the track on which they are to be installed. They shall be securely fastened to the track, shall maintain polarization and grounding, and shall be designed to be suspended directly from the track.

410.103 Heavy-Duty Lighting Track. Heavy-duty lighting track is lighting track identified for use exceeding 20 amperes. Each fitting attached to a heavy-duty lighting track shall have individual overcurrent protection.

410.104 Fastening. Lighting track shall be securely mounted so that each fastening is suitable for supporting the maximum weight of luminaires (fixtures) that can be installed. Unless identified for supports at greater intervals, a single section 1.2 m (4 ft) or shorter in length shall have two supports, and, where installed in a continuous row, each individual section of not more than 1.2 m (4 ft) in length shall have one additional support.

410.105 Construction Requirements.

(A) Construction. The housing for the lighting track system shall be of substantial construction to maintain rigidity. The conductors shall be installed within the track housing, permitting insertion of a luminaire (fixture), and designed to prevent tampering and accidental contact with live parts. Components of lighting track systems of different voltages shall not be interchangeable. The track conductors shall be a minimum 12 AWG or equal and shall be copper. The track system ends shall be insulated and capped.

(B) Grounding. Lighting track shall be grounded in accordance with Article 250, and the track sections shall be securely coupled to maintain continuity of the circuitry, polarization, and grounding throughout.

XVI. Decorative Lighting and Similar Accessories

410.110 Listing of Decorative Lighting. Decorative lighting and similar accessories used for holiday lighting and similar purposes, in accordance with 590.3(B), shall be listed.

ARTICLE 411
Lighting Systems Operating at 30 Volts or Less

411.1 Scope. This article covers lighting systems operating at 30 volts or less and their associated components.

411.2 Definition.

Lighting Systems Operating at 30 Volts or Less. A lighting system consisting of an isolating power supply operating at 30 volts (42.4 volts peak) or less under any load condition, with one or more secondary circuits, each limited to 25 amperes maximum, supplying luminaires (lighting fixtures) and associated equipment identified for the use.

411.3 Listing Required. Lighting systems operating at 30 volts or less shall be listed.

411.4 Locations Not Permitted. Lighting systems operating at 30 volts or less shall not be installed in the locations described in 411.4(A) and 411.4(B).

(A) Where concealed or extended through a building wall unless permitted in (1) or (2):

(1) Installed using any of the wiring methods specified in Chapter 3

(2) Installed using wiring supplied by a listed Class 2 power source and installed in accordance with 725.52

(B) Where installed within 3.0 m (10 ft) of pools, spas, fountains, or similar locations, unless permitted by Article 680.

411.5 Secondary Circuits.

(A) Grounding. Secondary circuits shall not be grounded.

(B) Isolation. The secondary circuit shall be insulated from the branch circuit by an isolating transformer.

(C) Bare Conductors. Exposed bare conductors and current-carrying parts shall be permitted for indoor installations only. Bare conductors shall not be installed less than 2.1 m (7 ft) above the finished floor, unless specifically listed for a lower installation height.

411.6 Branch Circuit. Lighting systems operating at 30 volts or less shall be supplied from a maximum 20-ampere branch circuit.

411.7 Hazardous (Classified) Locations. Where installed in hazardous (classified) locations, these systems shall conform with Articles 500 through 517 in addition to this article.

ARTICLE 422
Appliances

I. General

422.1 Scope. This article covers electric appliances used in any occupancy.

422.3 Other Articles. The requirements of Article 430 shall apply to the installation of motor-operated appliances, and the requirements of Article 440 shall apply to the installation of appliances containing a hermetic refrigerant motor-compressor(s), except as specifically amended in this article.

422.4 Live Parts. Appliances shall have no live parts normally exposed to contact other than those parts functioning as open-resistance heating elements, such as the heating element of a toaster, which are necessarily exposed.

II. Installation

422.10 Branch-Circuit Rating. This section specifies the ratings of branch circuits capable of carrying appliance current without overheating under the conditions specified.

(A) Individual Circuits. The rating of an individual branch circuit shall not be less than the marked rating of the appliance or the marked rating of an appliance having combined loads as provided in 422.62.

The rating of an individual branch circuit for motor-operated appliances not having a marked rating shall be in accordance with Part II of Article 430.

The branch-circuit rating for an appliance that is continuously loaded, other than a motor-operated appliance, shall be not less than 125 percent of the marked rating, or not less than 100 percent of the marked rating if the branch-circuit device and its assembly are listed for continuous loading at 100 percent of its rating.

Branch circuits for household cooking appliances shall be permitted to be in accordance with Table 220.55.

(B) Circuits Supplying Two or More Loads. For branch circuits supplying appliance and other loads, the rating shall be determined in accordance with 210.23.

422.11 Overcurrent Protection. Appliances shall be protected against overcurrent in accordance with 422.11(A) through 422.11(G) and 422.10.

(A) Branch-Circuit Overcurrent Protection. Branch circuits shall be protected in accordance with 240.4.

If a protective device rating is marked on an appliance, the branch-circuit overcurrent device rating shall not exceed the protective device rating marked on the appliance.

(B) Household-Type Appliances with Surface Heating Elements. Household-type appliances with surface heating elements having a maximum demand of more than 60 amperes calculated in accordance with Table 220.55 shall have its power supply subdivided into two or more circuits, each of which shall be provided with overcurrent protection rated at not over 50 amperes.

(C) Infrared Lamp Commercial and Industrial Heating Appliances. Infrared lamp commercial and industrial heating appliances shall have overcurrent protection not exceeding 50 amperes.

(D) Open-Coil or Exposed Sheathed-Coil Types of Surface Heating Elements in Commercial-Type Heating Appliances. Open-coil or exposed sheathed-coil types of surface heating elements in commercial-type heating appliances shall be protected by overcurrent protective devices rated at not over 50 amperes.

(E) Single Non–motor-Operated Appliance. If the branch circuit supplies a single non–motor-operated appliance, the rating of overcurrent protection shall:

(1) Not exceed that marked on the appliance.

(2) Not exceed 20 amperes if the overcurrent protection rating is not marked and the appliance is rated 13.3 amperes or less; or

(3) Not exceed 150 percent of the appliance rated current if the overcurrent protection rating is not marked and the appliance is rated over 13.3 amperes. Where 150 percent of the appliance rating does not correspond to a standard overcurrent device ampere rating, the next higher standard rating shall be permitted.

(F) Electric Heating Appliances Employing Resistance-Type Heating Elements Rated More Than 48 Amperes.

(1) Electric Heating Appliances. Electric heating appliances employing resistance-type heating elements rated more than 48 amperes, other than household appliances with surface heating elements covered by 422.11(B), and commercial-type heating appliances covered by 422.11(D), shall have the heating elements subdivided. Each subdivided load shall not exceed 48 amperes and shall be protected at not more than 60 amperes.

These supplementary overcurrent protective devices shall be (1) factory-installed within or on the heater enclosure or provided as a separate assembly by the heater manufacturer; (2) accessible; and (3) suitable for branch-circuit protection.

The main conductors supplying these overcurrent protective devices shall be considered branch-circuit conductors.

(2) Commercial Kitchen and Cooking Appliances. Commercial kitchen and cooking appliances using sheathed-type heating elements not covered in 422.11(D) shall be permitted to be subdivided into circuits not exceeding 120 amperes and protected at not more than 150 amperes where one of the following is met:

(1) Elements are integral with and enclosed within a cooking surface.

(2) Elements are completely contained within an enclosure identified as suitable for this use.

(3) Elements are contained within an ASME-rated and stamped vessel.

(3) Water Heaters and Steam Boilers. Water heaters and steam boilers employing resistance-type immersion electric heating elements contained in an ASME-rated and stamped vessel or listed instantaneous water heaters shall be permitted to be subdivided into circuits not exceeding 120 amperes and protected at not more than 150 amperes.

(G) Motor-Operated Appliances. Motors of motor-operated appliances shall be provided with overload protection in accordance with Part III of Article 430. Hermetic refrigerant motor-compressors in air-conditioning or refrigerating equipment shall be provided with overload protection in accordance with Part VI of Article 440. Where appliance overcurrent protective devices that are separate from the appliance are required, data for selection of these devices shall be marked on the appliance. The minimum marking shall be that specified in 430.7 and 440.4.

422.12 Central Heating Equipment. Central heating equipment other than fixed electric space-heating equipment shall be supplied by an individual branch circuit.

Exception No. 1: Auxiliary equipment, such as a pump, valve, humidifier, or electrostatic air cleaner directly associated with the heating equipment, shall be permitted to be connected to the same branch circuit.

Exception No. 2: Permanently connected air-conditioning equipment shall be permitted to be connected to the same branch circuit.

422.13 Storage-Type Water Heaters. A fixed storage-type water heater that has a capacity of 450 L (120 gal) or less shall be considered a continuous load.

FPN: For branch-circuit rating, see 422.10.

422.14 Infrared Lamp Industrial Heating Appliances. In industrial occupancies, infrared heating appliance lampholders shall be permitted to be operated in series on circuits of over 150 volts to ground, provided the voltage rating of the lampholders is not less than the circuit voltage.

Each section, panel, or strip carrying a number of infrared lampholders (including the internal wiring of such section, panel, or strip) shall be considered an appliance. The terminal connection block of each such assembly shall be considered an individual outlet.

422.15 Central Vacuum Outlet Assemblies.

(A) Listed central vacuum outlet assemblies shall be permitted to be connected to a branch circuit in accordance with 210.23(A).

(B) The ampacity of the connecting conductors shall not be less than the ampacity of the branch circuit conductors to which they are connected.

(C) An equipment grounding conductor shall be used where the central vacuum outlet assembly has accessible non–current-carrying metal parts.

422.16 Flexible Cords.

(A) General. Flexible cord shall be permitted (1) for the connection of appliances to facilitate their frequent interchange or to prevent the transmission of noise or vibration or (2) to facilitate the removal or disconnection of appliances that are fastened in place, where the fastening means and mechanical connections are specifically designed to permit ready removal for maintenance or repair and the appliance is intended or identified for flexible cord connection.

(B) Specific Appliances.

(1) Electrically Operated Kitchen Waste Disposers. Electrically operated kitchen waste disposers shall be permitted to be cord-and-plug connected with a flexible cord identified as suitable for the purpose in the installation instructions of the appliance manufacturer, where all of the following conditions are met.

(1) The flexible cord shall be terminated with a grounding-type attachment plug.

Exception: A listed kitchen waste disposer distinctly marked to identify it as protected by a system of double insulation, or its equivalent, shall not be required to be terminated with a grounding-type attachment plug.

(2) The length of the cord shall not be less than 450 mm (18 in.) and not over 900 mm (36 in.).

(3) Receptacles shall be located to avoid physical damage to the flexible cord.

(4) The receptacle shall be accessible.

(2) Built-in Dishwashers and Trash Compactors. Built-in dishwashers and trash compactors shall be permitted to be cord-and-plug connected with a flexible cord identified as suitable for the purpose in the installation instructions of the appliance manufacturer where all of the following conditions are met.

(1) The flexible cord shall be terminated with a grounding-type attachment plug.

Exception: A listed dishwasher or trash compactor distinctly marked to identify it as protected by a system of double insulation, or its equivalent, shall not be required to be terminated with a grounding-type attachment plug.

(2) The length of the cord shall be 0.9 m to 1.2 m (3 ft to 4 ft) measured from the face of the attachment plug to the plane of the rear of the appliance.

(3) Receptacles shall be located to avoid physical damage to the flexible cord.

(4) The receptacle shall be located in the space occupied by the appliance or adjacent thereto.

(5) The receptacle shall be accessible.

(3) Wall-Mounted Ovens and Counter-Mounted Cooking Units. Wall-mounted ovens and counter-mounted cooking units complete with provisions for mounting and for making electrical connections shall be permitted to be permanently connected or, only for ease in servicing or for installation, cord-and-plug connected.

A separable connector or a plug and receptacle combination in the supply line to an oven or cooking unit shall be approved for the temperature of the space in which it is located.

(4) Range Hoods. Range hoods shall be permitted to be cord-and-plug connected with a flexible cord identified as suitable for use on range hoods in the installation instructions of the appliance manufacturer, where all of the following conditions are met:

(1) The flexible cord is terminated with a grounding-type attachment plug.

Exception: A listed range hood distinctly marked to identify it as protected by a system of double insulation, or its equivalent, shall not be required to be terminated with a grounding-type attachment plug.

(2) The length of the cord is not less than 450 mm (18 in.) and not over 900 mm (36 in.).

(3) Receptacles are located to avoid physical damage to the flexible cord.

(4) The receptacle is accessible.

(5) The receptacle is supplied by an individual branch circuit.

422.17 Protection of Combustible Material. Each electrically heated appliance that is intended by size, weight, and service to be located in a fixed position shall be placed so as to provide ample protection between the appliance and adjacent combustible material.

422.18 Support of Ceiling-Suspended (Paddle) Fans. Ceiling-suspended (paddle) fans shall be supported independently of an outlet box or by listed outlet box or outlet box systems identified for the use and installed in accordance with 314.27(D).

422.20 Other Installation Methods. Appliances employing methods of installation other than covered by this article shall be permitted to be used only by special permission.

III. Disconnecting Means

422.30 General. A means shall be provided to disconnect each appliance from all ungrounded conductors in accordance with the following sections of Part III. If an appliance is supplied by more than one source, the disconnecting means shall be grouped and identified.

422.31 Disconnection of Permanently Connected Appliances.

(A) Rated at Not Over 300 Volt-Amperes or ⅛ Horsepower. For permanently connected appliances rated at not over 300 volt-amperes or ⅛ hp, the branch-circuit overcurrent device shall be permitted to serve as the disconnecting means.

(B) Appliances Rated Over 300 Volt-Amperes or ⅛ Horsepower. For permanently connected appliances rated over 300 volt-amperes or ⅛ hp, the branch-circuit switch or circuit breaker shall be permitted to serve as the disconnecting means where the switch or circuit breaker is within sight from the appliance or is capable of being locked in the open position. The provision for locking or adding a lock to the disconnecting means shall be installed on or at the switch or circuit breaker used as the disconnecting means and shall remain in place with or without the lock installed.

FPN: For appliances employing unit switches, see 422.34.

422.32 Disconnecting Means for Motor-Driven Appliance. If a switch or circuit breaker serves as the disconnecting means for a permanently connected motor-driven appliance of more than ⅛ hp, it shall be located within sight from the motor controller and shall comply with Part IX of Article 430.

Exception: If a motor-driven appliance of more than ⅛ hp is provided with a unit switch that complies with 422.34(A), (B), (C), or (D), the switch or circuit breaker serving as the other disconnecting means shall be permitted to be out of sight from the motor controller.

422.33 Disconnection of Cord-and-Plug-Connected Appliances.

(A) Separable Connector or an Attachment Plug and Receptacle. For cord-and-plug-connected appliances, an accessible separable connector or an accessible plug and receptacle shall be permitted to serve as the disconnecting means. Where the separable connector or plug and receptacle are not accessible, cord-and-plug-connected appliances shall be provided with disconnecting means in accordance with 422.31.

(B) Connection at the Rear Base of a Range. For cord-and-plug-connected household electric ranges, an attachment plug and receptacle connection at the rear base of a range, if it is accessible from the front by removal of a drawer, shall be considered as meeting the intent of 422.33(A).

(C) Rating. The rating of a receptacle or of a separable connector shall not be less than the rating of any appliance connected thereto.

Exception: Demand factors authorized elsewhere in this Code shall be permitted to be applied to the rating of a receptacle or of a separable connector.

422.34 Unit Switch(es) as Disconnecting Means. A unit switch(es) with a marked-off position that is a part of an appliance and disconnects all ungrounded conductors shall be permitted as the disconnecting means required by this article where other means for disconnection are provided in occupancies specified in 422.34(A) through 422.34(D).

(A) Multifamily Dwellings. In multifamily dwellings, the other disconnecting means shall be within the dwelling unit, or on the same floor as the dwelling unit in which the appliance is installed, and shall be permitted to control lamps and other appliances.

(B) Two-Family Dwellings. In two-family dwellings, the other disconnecting means shall be permitted either inside or outside of the dwelling unit in which the appliance is installed. In this case, an individual switch or circuit breaker for the dwelling unit shall be permitted and shall also be permitted to control lamps and other appliances.

(C) One-Family Dwellings. In one-family dwellings, the service disconnecting means shall be permitted to be the other disconnecting means.

(D) Other Occupancies. In other occupancies, the branch-circuit switch or circuit breaker, where readily accessible for servicing of the appliance, shall be permitted as the other disconnecting means.

422.35 Switch and Circuit Breaker to Be Indicating. Switches and circuit breakers used as disconnecting means shall be of the indicating type.

IV. Construction

422.40 Polarity in Cord-and-Plug-Connected Appliances. If the appliance is provided with a manually operated, line-connected, single-pole switch for appliance on–off operation, an Edison-base lampholder, or a 15- or 20-ampere receptacle, the attachment plug shall be of the polarized or grounding type.

A 2-wire, nonpolarized attachment plug shall be permitted to be used on a listed double-insulated shaver.

FPN: For polarity of Edison-base lampholders, see 410.42(A).

422.41 Cord-and-Plug-Connected Appliances Subject to Immersion. Cord-and-plug-connected portable, freestanding hydromassage units and hand-held hair dryers shall be constructed to provide protection for personnel against electrocution when immersed while in the "on" or "off" position.

422.42 Signals for Heated Appliances. In other than dwelling-type occupancies, each electrically heated appliance or group of appliances intended to be applied to combustible material shall be provided with a signal or an integral temperature-limiting device.

422.43 Flexible Cords.

(A) Heater Cords. All cord-and-plug-connected smoothing irons and electrically heated appliances that are rated at more than 50 watts and produce temperatures in excess of 121°C (250°F) on surfaces with which the cord is likely to be in contact shall be provided with one of the types of approved heater cords listed in Table 400.4.

(B) Other Heating Appliances. All other cord-and-plug-connected electrically heated appliances shall be connected with one of the approved types of cord listed in Table 400.4, selected in accordance with the usage specified in that table.

422.44 Cord-and-Plug-Connected Immersion Heaters. Electric heaters of the cord-and-plug-connected immersion type shall be constructed and installed so that current-carrying parts are effectively insulated from electrical contact with the substance in which they are immersed.

422.45 Stands for Cord-and-Plug-Connected Appliances. Each smoothing iron and other cord-and-plug-connected electrically heated appliance intended to be applied to combustible material shall be equipped with an approved stand, which shall be permitted to be a separate piece of equipment or a part of the appliance.

422.46 Flatirons. Electrically heated smoothing irons shall be equipped with an identified temperature-limiting means.

422.47 Water Heater Controls. All storage or instantaneous-type water heaters shall be equipped with a temperature-limiting means in addition to its control thermostat to disconnect all ungrounded conductors. Such means shall comply with both of the following:

(1) Installed to sense maximum water temperature.

(2) Be either a trip-free, manually reset type or a type having a replacement element. Such water heaters shall be marked to require the installation of a temperature and pressure relief valve.

Exception No. 1: Storage water heaters that are identified as being suitable for use with supply water temperature of 82°C (180°F) or above and a capacity of 60 kW or above.

Exception No. 2: Instantaneous-type water heaters that are identified as being suitable for such use, with a capacity of 4 L (1 gal) or less.

FPN: See ANSI Z21.22-1999/CSA 4.4-M99, *Relief Valves for Hot Water Supply Systems.*

422.48 Infrared Lamp Industrial Heating Appliances.

(A) 300 Watts or Less. Infrared heating lamps rated at 300 watts or less shall be permitted with lampholders of the medium-base, unswitched porcelain type or other types identified as suitable for use with infrared heating lamps rated 300 watts or less.

(B) Over 300 Watts. Screw-shell lampholders shall not be used with infrared lamps rated over 300 watts, unless the lampholders are identified as being suitable for use with infrared heating lamps rated over 300 watts.

422.49 High-Pressure Spray Washers. All single-phase cord-and-plug-connected high-pressure spray washing machines rated at 250 volts or less shall be provided with factory-installed ground-fault circuit-interrupter protection for personnel. The ground-fault circuit interrupter shall be an integral part of the attachment plug or shall be located in the supply cord within 300 mm (12 in.) of the attachment plug.

422.50 Cord-and-Plug-Connected Pipe Heating Assemblies. Cord-and-plug-connected pipe heating assemblies intended to prevent freezing of piping shall be listed.

422.51 Cord-and-Plug-Connected Vending Machines. Cord-and-plug-connected vending machines manufactured or re-manufactured on or after January 1, 2005, shall include a ground-fault circuit-interrupter as an integral part of the attachment plug or located in the power supply cord within 300 mm (12 in.) of the attachment plug. Cord-and-plug-connected vending machines not incorporating integral GFCI protection shall be connected to a GFCI protected outlet.

V. Marking

422.60 Nameplate.

(A) Nameplate Marking. Each electric appliance shall be provided with a nameplate giving the identifying name and the rating in volts and amperes, or in volts and watts. If the appliance is to be used on a specific frequency or frequencies, it shall be so marked.

Where motor overload protection external to the appliance is required, the appliance shall be so marked.

FPN: See 422.11 for overcurrent protection requirements.

(B) To Be Visible. Marking shall be located so as to be visible or easily accessible after installation.

422.61 Marking of Heating Elements. All heating elements that are rated over one ampere, replaceable in the field, and a part of an appliance shall be legibly marked with the ratings in volts and amperes, or in volts and watts, or with the manufacturer's part number.

422.62 Appliances Consisting of Motors and Other Loads.

(A) Nameplate Horsepower Markings. Where a motor-operated appliance nameplate includes a horsepower rating, that rating shall not be less than the horsepower rating on the motor nameplate. Where an appliance consists of multiple motors, or one or more motors and other loads, the nameplate value shall not be less than the equivalent horsepower of the combined loads, calculated in accordance with 430.110(C)(1).

(B) Additional Nameplate Markings. Appliances, other than those factory-equipped with cords and attachment plugs and with nameplates in compliance with 422.60, shall be marked in accordance with 422.62(B)(1) or (B)(2).

(1) Marking. In addition to the marking required in 422.60, the marking on an appliance consisting of a motor with other load(s) or motors with or without other load(s) shall specify the minimum supply circuit conductor ampacity and the maximum rating of the circuit overcurrent protective device. This requirement shall not apply to an appliance with a nameplate in compliance with 422.60 where both the minimum supply circuit conductor ampacity and maximum rating of the circuit overcurrent protective device are not more than 15 amperes.

(2) Alternate Marking Method. An alternative marking method shall be permitted to specify the rating of the largest motor in volts and amperes, and the additional load(s) in volts and amperes, or volts and watts in addition to the marking required in 422.60. The ampere rating of a motor $1/8$ horsepower or less or a nonmotor load 1 ampere or less shall be permitted to be omitted unless such loads constitute the principal load.

ARTICLE 424
Fixed Electric Space-Heating Equipment

I. General

424.1 Scope. This article covers fixed electric equipment used for space heating. For the purpose of this article, heating equipment shall include heating cable, unit heaters, boilers, central systems, or other approved fixed electric space-heating equipment. This article shall not apply to process heating and room air conditioning.

424.2 Other Articles. Fixed electric space-heating equipment incorporating a hermetic refrigerant motor-compressor shall also comply with Article 440.

424.3 Branch Circuits.

(A) Branch-Circuit Requirements. Individual branch circuits shall be permitted to supply any size fixed electric space-heating equipment.

Branch circuits supplying two or more outlets for fixed electric space-heating equipment shall be rated 15, 20, 25, or 30 amperes. In nondwelling occupancies, fixed infrared heating equipment shall be permitted to be supplied from branch circuits rated not over 50 amperes.

(B) Branch-Circuit Sizing. Fixed electric space heating equipment shall be considered continuous load.

424.6 Listed Equipment. Electric baseboard heaters, heating cables, duct heaters, and radiant heating systems shall be listed and labeled.

II. Installation

424.9 General. All fixed electric space-heating equipment shall be installed in an approved manner.

Permanently installed electric baseboard heaters equipped with factory-installed receptacle outlets, or outlets provided as a separate listed assembly, shall be permitted in lieu of a receptacle outlet(s) that is required by 210.50(B). Such receptacle outlets shall not be connected to the heater circuits.

FPN: Listed baseboard heaters include instructions that may not permit their installation below receptacle outlets.

424.10 Special Permission. Fixed electric space-heating equipment and systems installed by methods other than covered by this article shall be permitted only by special permission.

424.11 Supply Conductors. Fixed electric space-heating equipment requiring supply conductors with over 60°C insulation shall be clearly and permanently marked. This marking shall be plainly visible after installation and shall be permitted to be adjacent to the field connection box.

424.12 Locations.

(A) Exposed to Physical Damage. Where subject to physical damage, fixed electric space-heating equipment shall be protected in an approved manner.

(B) Damp or Wet Locations. Heaters and related equipment installed in damp or wet locations shall be listed for such locations and shall be constructed and installed so that water or other liquids cannot enter or accumulate in or on wired sections, electrical components, or ductwork.

FPN No. 1: See 110.11 for equipment exposed to deteriorating agents.

FPN No. 2: See 680.27(C) for pool deck areas.

424.13 Spacing from Combustible Materials. Fixed electric space-heating equipment shall be installed to provide the required spacing between the equipment and adjacent combustible material, unless it is listed to be installed in direct contact with combustible material.

III. Control and Protection of Fixed Electric Space-Heating Equipment

424.19 Disconnecting Means. Means shall be provided to disconnect the heater, motor controller(s), and supplementary overcurrent protective device(s) of all fixed electric space-heating equipment from all ungrounded conductors. Where heating equipment is supplied by more than one source, the disconnecting means shall be grouped and marked.

(A) Heating Equipment with Supplementary Overcurrent Protection. The disconnecting means for fixed electric space-heating equipment with supplementary overcurrent protection shall be within sight from the supplementary overcurrent protective device(s), on the supply side of these devices, if fuses, and, in addition, shall comply with either 424.19(A)(1) or (A)(2).

(1) Heater Containing No Motor Rated Over ⅛ Horsepower. The above disconnecting means or unit switches complying with 424.19(C) shall be permitted to serve as the required disconnecting means for both the motor controller(s) and heater under either of the following conditions:

(1) The disconnecting means provided is also within sight from the motor controller(s) and the heater.

(2) The disconnecting means provided is capable of being locked in the open position.

(2) Heater Containing a Motor(s) Rated Over ⅛ Horsepower. The above disconnecting means shall be permitted to serve as the required disconnecting means for both the motor controller(s) and heater by one of the following means:

(1) Where the disconnecting means is also in sight from the motor controller(s) and the heater.

(2) Where the disconnecting means is not within sight from the heater, a separate disconnecting means shall be installed, or the disconnecting means shall be capable of being locked in the open position, or unit switches complying with 424.19(C) shall be permitted.

(3) Where the disconnecting means is not within sight from the motor controller location, a disconnecting means complying with 430.102 shall be provided.

(4) Where the motor is not in sight from the motor controller location, 430.102(B) shall apply.

(B) Heating Equipment Without Supplementary Overcurrent Protection.

(1) Without Motor or with Motor Not Over ⅛ Horsepower. For fixed electric space-heating equipment without a motor rated over ⅛ hp, the branch-circuit switch or circuit breaker shall be permitted to serve as the disconnecting means where the switch or circuit breaker is within sight from the heater or is capable of being locked in the open position.

(2) Over ⅛ Horsepower. For motor-driven electric space-heating equipment with a motor rated over ⅛ hp, a disconnecting means shall be located within sight from the motor controller or shall be permitted to comply with the requirements in 424.19(A)(2).

(C) Unit Switch(es) as Disconnecting Means. A unit switch(es) with a marked "off" position that is part of a fixed heater and disconnects all ungrounded conductors shall be permitted as the disconnecting means required by this article where other means for disconnection are provided in the types of occupancies in 424.19(C)(1) through (C)(4).

(1) Multifamily Dwellings. In multifamily dwellings, the other disconnecting means shall be within the dwelling unit, or on the same floor as the dwelling unit in which the fixed heater is installed, and shall also be permitted to control lamps and appliances.

(2) Two-Family Dwellings. In two-family dwellings, the other disconnecting means shall be permitted either inside or outside of the dwelling unit in which the fixed heater is installed. In this case, an individual switch or circuit breaker for the dwelling unit shall be permitted and shall also be permitted to control lamps and appliances.

(3) One-Family Dwellings. In one-family dwellings, the service disconnecting means shall be permitted to be the other disconnecting means.

(4) Other Occupancies. In other occupancies, the branch-circuit switch or circuit breaker, where readily accessible for servicing of the fixed heater, shall be permitted as the other disconnecting means.

424.20 Thermostatically Controlled Switching Devices.

(A) Serving as Both Controllers and Disconnecting Means. Thermostatically controlled switching devices and combination thermostats and manually controlled switches shall be permitted to serve as both controllers and disconnecting means, provided all of the following conditions are met:

(1) Provided with a marked "off" position

(2) Directly open all ungrounded conductors when manually placed in the "off" position

(3) Designed so that the circuit cannot be energized automatically after the device has been manually placed in the "off" position

(4) Located as specified in 424.19

(B) Thermostats That Do Not Directly Interrupt All Ungrounded Conductors. Thermostats that do not directly interrupt all ungrounded conductors and thermostats that operate remote-control circuits shall not be required to meet the requirements of 424.20(A). These devices shall not be permitted as the disconnecting means.

424.21 Switch and Circuit Breaker to Be Indicating. Switches and circuit breakers used as disconnecting means shall be of the indicating type.

424.22 Overcurrent Protection.

(A) Branch-Circuit Devices. Electric space-heating equipment, other than such motor-operated equipment as required by Article 430 and Article 440 to have additional overcurrent protection, shall be permitted to be protected against overcurrent where supplied by one of the branch circuits in Article 210.

(B) Resistance Elements. Resistance-type heating elements in electric space-heating equipment shall be protected at not more than 60 amperes. Equipment rated more than 48 amperes and employing such elements shall have the heating elements subdivided, and each subdivided load shall not exceed 48 amperes. Where a subdivided load is less than 48 amperes, the rating of the supplementary overcurrent protective device shall comply with 424.3(B). A boiler employing resistance-type immersion heating elements contained in an ASME rated and stamped vessel shall be permitted to comply with 424.72(A).

(C) Overcurrent Protective Devices. The supplementary overcurrent protective devices for the subdivided loads specified in 424.22(B) shall be (1) factory-installed within or on the heater enclosure or supplied for use with the heater as a separate assembly by the heater manufacturer; (2) accessible, but shall not be required to be readily accessible; and (3) suitable for branch-circuit protection.

FPN: See 240.10.

Where cartridge fuses are used to provide this overcurrent protection, a single disconnecting means shall be permitted to be used for the several subdivided loads.

FPN No. 1: For supplementary overcurrent protection, see 240.10.

FPN No. 2: For disconnecting means for cartridge fuses in circuits of any voltage, see 240.40.

(D) Branch-Circuit Conductors. The conductors supplying the supplementary overcurrent protective devices shall be considered branch-circuit conductors.

Where the heaters are rated 50 kW or more, the conductors supplying the supplementary overcurrent protective devices specified in 424.22(C) shall be permitted to be sized at not less than 100 percent of the nameplate rating of the heater, provided all of the following conditions are met:

(1) The heater is marked with a minimum conductor size.

(2) The conductors are not smaller than the marked minimum size.

(3) A temperature-actuated device controls the cyclic operation of the equipment.

(E) Conductors for Subdivided Loads. Field-wired conductors between the heater and the supplementary overcurrent protective devices shall be sized at not less than 125 percent of the load served. The supplementary overcurrent protective devices specified in 424.22(C) shall protect these conductors in accordance with 240.4.

Where the heaters are rated 50 kW or more, the ampacity of field-wired conductors between the heater and the supplementary overcurrent protective devices shall be permitted to be not less than 100 percent of the load of their respective subdivided circuits, provided all of the following conditions are met:

(1) The heater is marked with a minimum conductor size.

(2) The conductors are not smaller than the marked minimum size.

(3) A temperature-activated device controls the cyclic operation of the equipment.

IV. Marking of Heating Equipment

424.28 Nameplate.

(A) Marking Required. Each unit of fixed electric space-heating equipment shall be provided with a nameplate giving the identifying name and the normal rating in volts and watts or in volts and amperes.

Electric space-heating equipment intended for use on alternating current only or direct current only shall be marked to so indicate. The marking of equipment consisting of motors over ⅛ hp and other loads shall specify the rating of the motor in volts, amperes, and frequency, and the heating load in volts and watts or in volts and amperes.

(B) Location. This nameplate shall be located so as to be visible or easily accessible after installation.

424.29 Marking of Heating Elements. All heating elements that are replaceable in the field and are part of an electric heater shall be legibly marked with the ratings in volts and watts or in volts and amperes.

V. Electric Space-Heating Cables

424.34 Heating Cable Construction. Heating cables shall be furnished complete with factory-assembled nonheating leads at least 2.1 m (7 ft) in length.

424.35 Marking of Heating Cables. Each unit shall be marked with the identifying name or identification symbol, catalog number, and ratings in volts and watts or in volts and amperes.

Each unit length of heating cable shall have a permanent legible marking on each nonheating lead located within 75 mm (3 in.) of the terminal end. The lead wire shall have the following color identification to indicate the circuit voltage on which it is to be used:

(1) 120 volt, nominal — yellow

(2) 208 volt, nominal — blue

(3) 240 volt, nominal — red

(4) 277 volt, nominal — brown

(5) 480 volt, nominal — orange

424.36 Clearances of Wiring in Ceilings. Wiring located above heated ceilings shall be spaced not less than 50 mm (2 in.) above the heated ceiling and shall be considered as operating at an ambient temperature of 50°C (122°F). The ampacity of conductors shall be calculated on the basis of the correction factors shown in the 0–2000 volt ampacity tables of Article 310. If this wiring is located above thermal insulation having a minimum thickness of 50 mm (2 in.), the wiring shall not require correction for temperature.

424.38 Area Restrictions.

(A) Shall Not Extend Beyond the Room or Area. Heating cables shall not extend beyond the room or area in which they originate.

(B) Uses Prohibited. Heating cables shall not be installed in the following:

(1) In closets

(2) Over walls

(3) Over partitions that extend to the ceiling, unless they are isolated single runs of embedded cable

(4) Over cabinets whose clearance from the ceiling is less than the minimum horizontal dimension of the cabinet to the nearest cabinet edge that is open to the room or area

(C) In Closet Ceilings as Low-Temperature Heat Sources to Control Relative Humidity. The provisions of 424.38(B) shall not prevent the use of cable in closet ceilings as low-temperature heat sources to control relative humidity, provided they are used only in those portions of the ceiling that are unobstructed to the floor by shelves or other permanent luminaires (fixtures).

424.39 Clearance from Other Objects and Openings. Heating elements of cables shall be separated at least 200 mm (8 in.) from the edge of outlet boxes and junction boxes that are to be used for mounting surface luminaires (lighting fixtures). A clearance of not less than 50 mm (2 in.) shall be provided from recessed luminaires (fixtures) and their trims, ventilating openings, and other such openings in room surfaces. Sufficient area shall be provided to ensure that no heating cable is covered by any surface-mounted units.

424.40 Splices. Embedded cables shall be spliced only where necessary and only by approved means, and in no case shall the length of the heating cable be altered.

424.41 Installation of Heating Cables on Dry Board, in Plaster, and on Concrete Ceilings.

(A) In Walls. Cables shall not be installed in walls unless it is necessary for an isolated single run of cable to be installed down a vertical surface to reach a dropped ceiling.

(B) Adjacent Runs. Adjacent runs of cable not exceeding 9 watts/m (2¾ watts/ft) shall not be installed less than 38 mm (1½ in.) on centers.

(C) Surfaces to Be Applied. Heating cables shall be applied only to gypsum board, plaster lath, or other fire-resistant material. With metal lath or other electrically conductive surfaces, a coat of plaster shall be applied to completely separate the metal lath or conductive surface from the cable.

FPN: See also 424.41(F).

(D) Splices. All heating cables, the splice between the heating cable and nonheating leads, and 75-mm (3-in.) minimum of the nonheating lead at the splice shall be embedded in plaster or dry board in the same manner as the heating cable.

(E) Ceiling Surface. The entire ceiling surface shall have a finish of thermally noninsulating sand plaster that has a nominal thickness of 13 mm (½ in.), or other noninsulating material identified as suitable for this use and applied according to specified thickness and directions.

(F) Secured. Cables shall be secured by means of approved stapling, tape, plaster, nonmetallic spreaders, or other approved means either at intervals not exceeding 400 mm (16 in.) or at intervals not exceeding 1.8 m (6 ft) for cables identified for such use. Staples or metal fasteners that straddle the cable shall not be used with metal lath or other electrically conductive surfaces.

(G) Dry Board Installations. In dry board installations, the entire ceiling below the heating cable shall be covered with gypsum board not exceeding 13 mm (½ in.) thickness. The void between the upper layer of gypsum board, plaster lath, or other fire-resistant material and the surface layer of gypsum board shall be completely filled with thermally conductive, nonshrinking plaster or other approved material or equivalent thermal conductivity.

(H) Free from Contact with Conductive Surfaces. Cables shall be kept free from contact with metal or other electrically conductive surfaces.

(I) Joists. In dry board applications, cable shall be installed parallel to the joist, leaving a clear space centered under the joist of 65 mm (2½ in.) (width) between centers of adjacent runs of cable. A surface layer of gypsum board shall be mounted so that the nails or other fasteners do not pierce the heating cable.

(J) Crossing Joists. Cables shall cross joists only at the ends of the room unless the cable is required to cross joists elsewhere in order to satisfy the manufacturer's instructions that the installer avoid placing the cable too close to ceiling penetrations and luminaires (lighting fixtures).

424.42 Finished Ceilings. Finished ceilings shall not be covered with decorative panels or beams constructed of materials that have thermal insulating properties, such as wood, fiber, or plastic. Finished ceilings shall be permitted to be covered with paint, wallpaper, or other approved surface finishes.

424.43 Installation of Nonheating Leads of Cables.

(A) Free Nonheating Leads. Free nonheating leads of cables shall be installed in accordance with approved wiring methods from the junction box to a location within the ceiling. Such installations shall be permitted to be single conductors in approved raceways, single or multiconductor Type UF, Type NMC, Type MI, or other approved conductors.

(B) Leads in Junction Box. Not less than 150 mm (6 in.) of free nonheating lead shall be within the junction box. The marking of the leads shall be visible in the junction box.

(C) Excess Leads. Excess leads of heating cables shall not be cut but shall be secured to the underside of the ceiling and embedded in plaster or other approved material, leaving only a length sufficient to reach the junction box with not less than 150 mm (6 in.) of free lead within the box.

424.44 Installation of Cables in Concrete or Poured Masonry Floors.

(A) Watts per Linear Foot. Constant wattage heating cables shall not exceed 54 watts/linear meter (16½ watts/linear foot) of cable.

(B) Spacing Between Adjacent Runs. The spacing between adjacent runs of cable shall not be less than 25 mm (1 in.) on centers.

(C) Secured in Place. Cables shall be secured in place by nonmetallic frames or spreaders or other approved means while the concrete or other finish is applied.

Cables shall not be installed where they bridge expansion joints unless protected from expansion and contraction.

(D) Spacings Between Heating Cable and Metal Embedded in the Floor. Spacings shall be maintained between the heating cable and metal embedded in the floor, unless the cable is a grounded metal-clad cable.

(E) Leads Protected. Leads shall be protected where they leave the floor by rigid metal conduit, intermediate metal conduit, rigid nonmetallic conduit, electrical metallic tubing, or by other approved means.

(F) Bushings or Approved Fittings. Bushings or approved fittings shall be used where the leads emerge within the floor slab.

(G) Ground-Fault Circuit-Interrupter Protection. Ground-fault circuit-interrupter protection for personnel shall be provided for cables installed in electrically heated floors of bathrooms and in hydromassage bathtub locations.

424.45 Inspection and Tests. Cable installations shall be made with due care to prevent damage to the cable assembly and shall be inspected and approved before cables are covered or concealed.

VI. Duct Heaters

424.57 General. Part VI shall apply to any heater mounted in the airstream of a forced-air system where the air-moving unit is not provided as an integral part of the equipment.

424.58 Identification. Heaters installed in an air duct shall be identified as suitable for the installation.

424.59 Airflow. Means shall be provided to ensure uniform and adequate airflow over the face of the heater in accordance with the manufacturer's instructions.

FPN: Heaters installed within 1.2 m (4 ft) of the outlet of an air-moving device, heat pump, air conditioner, elbows, baffle plates, or other obstructions in ductwork may require turning vanes, pressure plates, or other devices on the inlet side of the duct heater to ensure an even distribution of air over the face of the heater.

424.60 Elevated Inlet Temperature. Duct heaters intended for use with elevated inlet air temperature shall be identified as suitable for use at the elevated temperatures.

424.61 Installation of Duct Heaters with Heat Pumps and Air Conditioners. Heat pumps and air conditioners having duct heaters closer than 1.2 m (4 ft) to the heat pump or air conditioner shall have both the duct heater and heat pump or air conditioner identified as suitable for such installation and so marked.

424.62 Condensation. Duct heaters used with air conditioners or other air-cooling equipment that could result in condensation of moisture shall be identified as suitable for use with air conditioners.

424.63 Fan Circuit Interlock. Means shall be provided to ensure that the fan circuit is energized when any heater circuit is energized. However, time- or temperature-controlled delay in energizing the fan motor shall be permitted.

424.64 Limit Controls. Each duct heater shall be provided with an approved, integral, automatic-reset temperature-limiting control or controllers to de-energize the circuit or circuits.

In addition, an integral independent supplementary control or controllers shall be provided in each duct heater that disconnects a sufficient number of conductors to interrupt current flow. This device shall be manually resettable or replaceable.

424.65 Location of Disconnecting Means. Duct heater controller equipment shall be either accessible with the disconnecting means installed at or within sight from the controller or as permitted by 424.19(A).

424.66 Installation. Duct heaters shall be installed in accordance with the manufacturer's instructions in such a manner that operation does not create a hazard to persons or property. Furthermore, duct heaters shall be located with respect to building construction and other equipment so as to permit access to the heater. Sufficient clearance shall be maintained to permit replacement of controls and heating elements and for adjusting and cleaning of controls and other parts requiring such attention. See 110.26.

FPN: For additional installation information, see NFPA 90A-2002, *Standard for the Installation of Air-Conditioning and Ventilating Systems*, and NFPA 90B-2002, *Standard for the Installation of Warm Air Heating and Air-Conditioning Systems*.

VII. Resistance-Type Boilers

424.70 Scope. The provisions in Part VII of this article shall apply to boilers employing resistance-type heating elements. Electrode-type boilers shall not be considered as employing resistance-type heating elements. See Part VIII of this article.

424.71 Identification. Resistance-type boilers shall be identified as suitable for the installation.

424.72 Overcurrent Protection.

(A) Boiler Employing Resistance-Type Immersion Heating Elements in an ASME Rated and Stamped Vessel. A boiler employing resistance-type immersion heating elements contained in an ASME rated and stamped vessel shall have the heating elements protected at not more than 150 amperes. Such a boiler rated more than 120 amperes shall have the heating elements subdivided into loads not exceeding 120 amperes.

Where a subdivided load is less than 120 amperes, the rating of the overcurrent protective device shall comply with 424.3(B).

(B) Boiler Employing Resistance-Type Heating Elements Rated More Than 48 Amperes and Not Contained in an ASME Rated and Stamped Vessel. A boiler employing resistance-type heating elements not contained in an ASME rated and stamped vessel shall have the heating elements protected at not more than 60 amperes. Such a boiler rated more than 48 amperes shall have the heating elements subdivided into loads not exceeding 48 amperes.

Where a subdivided load is less than 48 amperes, the rating of the overcurrent protective device shall comply with 424.3(B).

(C) Supplementary Overcurrent Protective Devices. The supplementary overcurrent protective devices for the subdivided loads as required by 424.72(A) and 424.72(B) shall be as follows:

(1) Factory-installed within or on the boiler enclosure or provided as a separate assembly by the boiler manufacturer

(2) Accessible, but need not be readily accessible

(3) Suitable for branch-circuit protection

Where cartridge fuses are used to provide this overcurrent protection, a single disconnecting means shall be permitted for the several subdivided circuits. See 240.40.

(D) Conductors Supplying Supplementary Overcurrent Protective Devices. The conductors supplying these supplementary overcurrent protective devices shall be considered branch-circuit conductors.

Where the heaters are rated 50 kW or more, the conductors supplying the overcurrent protective device specified in 424.72(C) shall be permitted to be sized at not less than 100 percent of the nameplate rating of the heater, provided all of the following conditions are met:

(1) The heater is marked with a minimum conductor size.

(2) The conductors are not smaller than the marked minimum size.

(3) A temperature- or pressure-actuated device controls the cyclic operation of the equipment.

(E) Conductors for Subdivided Loads. Field-wired conductors between the heater and the supplementary overcurrent protective devices shall be sized at not less than 125 percent of the load served. The supplementary overcurrent protective devices specified in 424.72(C) shall protect these conductors in accordance with 240.4.

Where the heaters are rated 50 kW or more, the ampacity of field-wired conductors between the heater and the supplementary overcurrent protective devices shall be permitted to be not less than 100 percent of the load of their respective subdivided circuits, provided all of the following conditions are met:

(1) The heater is marked with a minimum conductor size.

(2) The conductors are not smaller than the marked minimum size.

(3) A temperature-activated device controls the cyclic operation of the equipment.

424.73 Overtemperature Limit Control. Each boiler designed so that in normal operation there is no change in state of the heat transfer medium shall be equipped with a temperature-sensitive limiting means. It shall be installed to limit maximum liquid temperature and shall directly or indirectly disconnect all ungrounded conductors to the heating elements. Such means shall be in addition to a temperature regulating system and other devices protecting the tank against excessive pressure.

424.74 Overpressure Limit Control. Each boiler designed so that in normal operation there is a change in state of the heat transfer medium from liquid to vapor shall be equipped with a pressure-sensitive limiting means. It shall be installed to limit maximum pressure and shall directly or indirectly disconnect all ungrounded conductors to the heating elements. Such means shall be in addition to a pressure regulating system and other devices protecting the tank against excessive pressure.

VIII. Electrode-Type Boilers

424.80 Scope. The provisions in Part VIII of this article shall apply to boilers for operation at 600 volts, nominal, or less, in which heat is generated by the passage of current between electrodes through the liquid being heated.

FPN: For over 600 volts, see Part V of Article 490.

424.81 Identification. Electrode-type boilers shall be identified as suitable for the installation.

424.82 Branch-Circuit Requirements. The size of branch-circuit conductors and overcurrent protective devices shall be calculated on the basis of 125 percent of the total load (motors not included). A contactor, relay, or other device, approved for continuous operation at 100 percent of its rating, shall be permitted to supply its full-rated load. See 210.19(A), Exception. The provisions of this section shall not apply to conductors that form an integral part of an approved boiler.

Where an electrode boiler is rated 50 kW or more, the conductors supplying the boiler electrode(s) shall be permitted to be sized at not less than 100 percent of the nameplate rating of the electrode boiler, provided all the following conditions are met:

(1) The electrode boiler is marked with a minimum conductor size.

(2) The conductors are not smaller than the marked minimum size.

(3) A temperature- or pressure-actuated device controls the cyclic operation of the equipment.

424.83 Overtemperature Limit Control. Each boiler, designed so that in normal operation there is no change in state of the heat transfer medium, shall be equipped with a temperature-sensitive limiting means. It shall be installed to limit maximum liquid temperature and shall directly or indirectly interrupt all current flow through the electrodes. Such means shall be in addition to the temperature regulating system and other devices protecting the tank against excessive pressure.

424.84 Overpressure Limit Control. Each boiler, designed so that in normal operation there is a change in state of the heat transfer medium from liquid to vapor, shall be equipped with a pressure-sensitive limiting means. It shall be installed to limit maximum pressure and shall directly or indirectly interrupt all current flow through the electrodes. Such means shall be in addition to a pressure regulating system and other devices protecting the tank against excessive pressure.

424.85 Grounding. For those boilers designed such that fault currents do not pass through the pressure vessel, and the pressure vessel is electrically isolated from the electrodes, all exposed non–current-carrying metal parts, including the pressure vessel, supply, and return connecting piping, shall be grounded in accordance with Article 250.

For all other designs, the pressure vessel containing the electrodes shall be isolated and electrically insulated from ground.

424.86 Markings. All electrode-type boilers shall be marked to show the following:

(1) The manufacturer's name

(2) The normal rating in volts, amperes, and kilowatts

(3) The electrical supply required specifying frequency, number of phases, and number of wires

(4) The marking "Electrode-Type Boiler"

(5) A warning marking, "All Power Supplies Shall Be Disconnected Before Servicing, Including Servicing the Pressure Vessel"

The nameplate shall be located so as to be visible after installation.

IX. Electric Radiant Heating Panels and Heating Panel Sets

424.90 Scope. The provisions of Part IX of this article shall apply to radiant heating panels and heating panel sets.

424.91 Definitions.

Heating Panel. A complete assembly provided with a junction box or a length of flexible conduit for connection to a branch circuit.

Heating Panel Set. A rigid or nonrigid assembly provided with nonheating leads or a terminal junction assembly identified as being suitable for connection to a wiring system.

424.92 Markings.

(A) Location. Markings shall be permanent and in a location that is visible prior to application of panel finish.

(B) Identified as Suitable. Each unit shall be identified as suitable for the installation.

(C) Required Markings. Each unit shall be marked with the identifying name or identification symbol, catalog number, and rating in volts and watts or in volts and amperes.

(D) Labels Provided by Manufacturer. The manufacturers of heating panels or heating panel sets shall provide marking labels that indicate that the space-heating installation incorporates heating panels or heating panel sets and instructions that the labels shall be affixed to the panelboards to identify which branch circuits supply the circuits to those space-heating installations. If the heating panels and heating panel set installations are visible and distinguishable after installation, the labels shall not be required to be provided and affixed to the panelboards.

424.93 Installation.

(A) General.

(1) Manufacturer's Instructions. Heating panels and heating panel sets shall be installed in accordance with the manufacturer's instructions.

(2) Locations Not Permitted. The heating portion shall not be installed as follows:

(1) In or behind surfaces where subject to physical damage

(2) Run through or above walls, partitions, cupboards, or similar portions of structures that extend to the ceiling.

(3) Run in or through thermal insulation, but shall be permitted to be in contact with the surface of thermal insulation.

(3) Separation from Outlets for Luminaires (Lighting Fixtures). Edges of panels and panel sets shall be separated by not less than 200 mm (8 in.) from the edges of any outlet boxes and junction boxes that are to be used for mounting surface luminaires (lighting fixtures). A clearance of not less than 50 mm (2 in.) shall be provided from recessed luminaires (fixtures) and their trims, ventilating openings, and other such openings in room surfaces, unless the heating panels and panel sets are listed and marked for lesser clearances, in which case they shall be permitted to be installed at the marked clearances. Sufficient area shall be provided to ensure that no heating panel or heating panel set is to be covered by any surface-mounted units.

(4) Surfaces Covering Heating Panels. After the heating panels or heating panel sets are installed and inspected, it shall be permitted to install a surface that has been identified by the manufacturer's instructions as being suitable for the installation. The surface shall be secured so that the nails or other fastenings do not pierce the heating panels or heating panel sets.

(5) Surface Coverings. Surfaces permitted by 424.93(A)(4) shall be permitted to be covered with paint, wallpaper, or other approved surfaces identified in the manufacturer's instructions as being suitable.

(B) Heating Panel Sets.

(1) Mounting Location. Heating panel sets shall be permitted to be secured to the lower face of joists or mounted in between joists, headers, or nailing strips.

(2) Parallel to Joists or Nailing Strips. Heating panel sets shall be installed parallel to joists or nailing strips.

(3) Installation of Nails, Staples, or Other Fasteners. Nailing or stapling of heating panel sets shall be done only through the unheated portions provided for this purpose. Heating panel sets shall not be cut through or nailed through any point closer than 6 mm (¼ in.) to the element. Nails, staples, or other fasteners shall not be used where they penetrate current-carrying parts.

(4) Installed as Complete Unit. Heating panel sets shall be installed as complete units unless identified as suitable for field cutting in an approved manner.

424.94 Clearances of Wiring in Ceilings. Wiring located above heated ceilings shall be spaced not less than 50 mm (2 in.) above the heated ceiling and shall be considered as operating at an ambient of 50°C (122°F). The ampacity shall be calculated on the basis of the correction factors given in the 0–2000 volt ampacity tables of Article 310. If this wiring is located above thermal insulations having a minimum thickness of 50 mm (2 in.), the wiring shall not require correction for temperature.

424.95 Location of Branch-Circuit and Feeder Wiring in Walls.

(A) Exterior Walls. Wiring methods shall comply with Article 300 and 310.10.

(B) Interior Walls. Any wiring behind heating panels or heating panel sets located in interior walls or partitions shall be considered as operating at an ambient temperature of 40°C (104°F), and the ampacity shall be calculated on the basis of the correction factors given in the 0–2000 volt ampacity tables of Article 310.

424.96 Connection to Branch-Circuit Conductors.

(A) General. Heating panels or heating panel sets assembled together in the field to form a heating installation in one room or area shall be connected in accordance with the manufacturer's instructions.

(B) Heating Panels. Heating panels shall be connected to branch-circuit wiring by an approved wiring method.

(C) Heating Panel Sets.

(1) Connection to Branch Circuit Wiring. Heating panel sets shall be connected to branch-circuit wiring by a method identified as being suitable for the purpose.

(2) Panel Sets with Terminal Junction Assembly. A heating panel set provided with terminal junction assembly shall be permitted to have the nonheating leads attached at the time of installation in accordance with the manufacturer's instructions.

424.97 Nonheating Leads. Excess nonheating leads of heating panels or heating panel sets shall be permitted to be cut to the required length. They shall meet the installation requirements of the wiring method employed in accordance with 424.96. Nonheating leads shall be an integral part of a heating panel and a heating panel set and shall not be subjected to the ampacity requirements of 424.3(B) for branch circuits.

424.98 Installation in Concrete or Poured Masonry.

(A) Maximum Heated Area. Heating panels or heating panel sets shall not exceed 355 watts/m² (33 watts/ft²) of heated area.

(B) Secured in Place and Identified as Suitable. Heating panels or heating panel sets shall be secured in place by means specified in the manufacturer's instructions and identified as suitable for the installation.

(C) Expansion Joints. Heating panels or heating panel sets shall not be installed where they bridge expansion joints unless provision is made for expansion and contraction.

(D) Spacings. Spacings shall be maintained between heating panels or heating panel sets and metal embedded in the floor. Grounded metal-clad heating panels shall be permitted to be in contact with metal embedded in the floor.

(E) Protection of Leads. Leads shall be protected where they leave the floor by rigid metal conduit, intermediate metal conduit, rigid nonmetallic conduit, or electrical metallic tubing, or by other approved means.

(F) Bushings or Fittings Required. Bushings or approved fittings shall be used where the leads emerge within the floor slabs.

424.99 Installation Under Floor Covering.

(A) Identification. Heating panels or heating panel sets for installation under floor covering shall be identified as suitable for installation under floor covering.

(B) Maximum Heated Area. Heating panels or panel sets installed under floor covering shall not exceed 160 watts/m^2 (15 watts/ft^2) of heated area.

(C) Installation. Listed heating panels or panel sets, if installed under floor covering, shall be installed on floor surfaces that are smooth and flat in accordance with the manufacturer's instructions and shall also comply with 424.99(C)(1) through (C)(5).

(1) Expansion Joints. Heating panels or heating panel sets shall not be installed where they bridge expansion joints unless protected from expansion and contraction.

(2) Connection to Conductors. Heating panels and heating panel sets shall be connected to branch-circuit and supply wiring by wiring methods recognized in Chapter 3.

(3) Anchoring. Heating panels and heating panel sets shall be firmly anchored to the floor using an adhesive or anchoring system identified for this use.

(4) Coverings. After heating panels or heating panel sets are installed and inspected, they shall be permitted to be covered by a floor covering that has been identified by the manufacturer as being suitable for the installation. The covering shall be secured to the heating panel or heating panel sets with release-type adhesives or by means identified for this use.

(5) Fault Protection. A device to open all ungrounded conductors supplying the heating panels or heating panel sets, provided by the manufacturer, shall function when a low- or high-resistance line-to-line, line-to-grounded conductor, or line-to-ground fault occurs, such as the result of a penetration of the element or element assembly.

> FPN: An integral grounding shield may be required to provide this protection.

ARTICLE 426
Fixed Outdoor Electric Deicing and Snow-Melting Equipment

I. General

426.1 Scope. The requirements of this article shall apply to electrically energized heating systems and the installation of these systems.

(A) Embedded. Embedded in driveways, walks, steps, and other areas.

(B) Exposed. Exposed on drainage systems, bridge structures, roofs, and other structures.

426.2 Definitions.

Heating System. A complete system consisting of components such as heating elements, fastening devices, nonheating circuit wiring, leads, temperature controllers, safety signs, junction boxes, raceways, and fittings.

Impedance Heating System. A system in which heat is generated in a pipe or rod, or combination of pipes and rods, by causing current to flow through the pipe or rod by direct connection to an ac voltage source from a dual-winding transformer. The pipe or rod shall be permitted to be embedded in the surface to be heated, or constitute the exposed components to be heated.

Resistance Heating Element. A specific separate element to generate heat that is embedded in or fastened to the surface to be heated.

> FPN: Tubular heaters, strip heaters, heating cable, heating tape, and heating panels are examples of resistance heaters.

Skin-Effect Heating System. A system in which heat is generated on the inner surface of a ferromagnetic envelope embedded in or fastened to the surface to be heated.

> FPN: Typically, an electrically insulated conductor is routed through and connected to the envelope at the other end. The envelope and the electrically insulated conductor are connected to an ac voltage source from a dual-winding transformer.

426.3 Application of Other Articles. Cord-and-plug-connected fixed outdoor electric deicing and snow-melting equipment intended for specific use and identified as suitable for this use shall be installed according to Article 422.

426.4 Continuous Load. Fixed outdoor electric deicing and snow-melting equipment shall be considered as a continuous load.

II. Installation

426.10 General. Equipment for outdoor electric deicing and snow melting shall be identified as being suitable for the following:

(1) The chemical, thermal, and physical environment

(2) Installation in accordance with the manufacturer's drawings and instructions

426.11 Use. Electrical heating equipment shall be installed in such a manner as to be afforded protection from physical damage.

426.12 Thermal Protection. External surfaces of outdoor electric deicing and snow-melting equipment that operate at temperatures exceeding 60°C (140°F) shall be physically guarded, isolated, or thermally insulated to protect against contact by personnel in the area.

426.13 Identification. The presence of outdoor electric deicing and snow-melting equipment shall be evident by the posting of appropriate caution signs or markings where clearly visible.

426.14 Special Permission. Fixed outdoor deicing and snow-melting equipment employing methods of construction or installation other than covered by this article shall be permitted only by special permission.

III. Resistance Heating Elements

426.20 Embedded Deicing and Snow-Melting Equipment.

(A) Watt Density. Panels or units shall not exceed 1300 watts/m² (120 watts/ft²) of heated area.

(B) Spacing. The spacing between adjacent cable runs is dependent upon the rating of the cable and shall be not less than 25 mm (1 in.) on centers.

(C) Cover. Units, panels, or cables shall be installed as follows:

(1) On a substantial asphalt or masonry base at least 50 mm (2 in.) thick and have at least 38 mm (1½ in.) of asphalt or masonry applied over the units, panels, or cables; or

(2) They shall be permitted to be installed over other approved bases and embedded within 90 mm (3½ in.) of masonry or asphalt but not less than 38 mm (1½ in.) from the top surface; or

(3) Equipment that has been specially investigated for other forms of installation shall be installed only in the manner for which it has been investigated.

(D) Secured. Cables, units, and panels shall be secured in place by frames or spreaders or other approved means while the masonry or asphalt finish is applied.

(E) Expansion and Contraction. Cables, units, and panels shall not be installed where they bridge expansion joints unless provision is made for expansion and contraction.

426.21 Exposed Deicing and Snow-Melting Equipment.

(A) Secured. Heating element assemblies shall be secured to the surface being heated by approved means.

(B) Overtemperature. Where the heating element is not in direct contact with the surface being heated, the design of the heater assembly shall be such that its temperature limitations shall not be exceeded.

(C) Expansion and Contraction. Heating elements and assemblies shall not be installed where they bridge expansion joints unless provision is made for expansion and contraction.

(D) Flexural Capability. Where installed on flexible structures, the heating elements and assemblies shall have a flexural capability that is compatible with the structure.

426.22 Installation of Nonheating Leads for Embedded Equipment.

(A) Grounding Sheath or Braid. Nonheating leads having a grounding sheath or braid shall be permitted to be embedded in the masonry or asphalt in the same manner as the heating cable without additional physical protection.

(B) Raceways. All but 25 mm to 150 mm (1 in. to 6 in.) of nonheating leads of Type TW and other approved types not having a grounding sheath shall be enclosed in a rigid conduit, electrical metallic tubing, intermediate metal conduit, or other raceways within asphalt or masonry; and the distance from the factory splice to raceway shall be not less than 25 mm (1 in.) or more than 150 mm (6 in.).

(C) Bushings. Insulating bushings shall be used in the asphalt or masonry where leads enter conduit or tubing.

(D) Expansion and Contraction. Leads shall be protected in expansion joints and where they emerge from masonry or asphalt by rigid conduit, electrical metallic tubing, intermediate metal conduit, other raceways, or other approved means.

(E) Leads in Junction Boxes. Not less than 150 mm (6 in.) of free nonheating lead shall be within the junction box.

426.23 Installation of Nonheating Leads for Exposed Equipment.

(A) Nonheating Leads. Power supply nonheating leads (cold leads) for resistance elements shall be suitable for the temperature encountered. Not less than 150 mm (6 in.) of nonheating leads shall be provided within the junction box. Preassembled factory supplied and field assembled nonheating leads on approved heaters shall be permitted to be shortened if the markings specified in 426.25 are retained.

(B) Protection. Nonheating power supply leads shall be enclosed in a rigid conduit, intermediate metal conduit, electrical metallic tubing, or other approved means.

426.24 Electrical Connection.

(A) Heating Element Connections. Electrical connections, other than factory connections of heating elements to nonheating elements embedded in masonry or asphalt or on exposed surfaces, shall be made with insulated connectors identified for the use.

(B) Circuit Connections. Splices and terminations at the end of the nonheating leads, other than the heating element end, shall be installed in a box or fitting in accordance with 110.14 and 300.15.

426.25 Marking. Each factory-assembled heating unit shall be legibly marked within 75 mm (3 in.) of each end of the nonheating leads with the permanent identification symbol, catalog number, and ratings in volts and watts or in volts and amperes.

426.26 Corrosion Protection. Ferrous and nonferrous metal raceways, cable armor, cable sheaths, boxes, fittings, supports, and support hardware shall be permitted to be installed in concrete or in direct contact with the earth, or in areas subject to severe corrosive influences, where made of material suitable for the condition, or where provided with corrosion protection identified as suitable for the condition.

426.27 Grounding Braid or Sheath. Grounding means, such as copper braid, metal sheath, or other approved means, shall be provided as part of the heated section of the cable, panel, or unit.

426.28 Equipment Protection. Ground-fault protection of equipment shall be provided for fixed outdoor electric deicing and snow-melting equipment, except for equipment that employs mineral-insulated, metal-sheathed cable embedded in a noncombustible medium.

IV. Impedance Heating

426.30 Personnel Protection. Exposed elements of impedance heating systems shall be physically guarded, isolated, or thermally insulated with a weatherproof jacket to protect against contact by personnel in the area.

426.31 Isolation Transformer. A dual-winding transformer with a grounded shield between the primary and secondary windings shall be used to isolate the distribution system from the heating system.

426.32 Voltage Limitations. Unless protected by ground-fault circuit-interrupter protection for personnel, the secondary winding of the isolation transformer connected to the impedance heating elements shall not have an output voltage greater than 30 volts ac.

Where ground-fault circuit-interrupter protection for personnel is provided, the voltage shall be permitted to be greater than 30 but not more than 80 volts.

426.33 Induced Currents. All current-carrying components shall be installed in accordance with 300.20.

426.34 Grounding. An impedance heating system that is operating at a voltage greater than 30 but not more than 80 shall be grounded at a designated point(s).

V. Skin-Effect Heating

426.40 Conductor Ampacity. The current through the electrically insulated conductor inside the ferromagnetic envelope shall be permitted to exceed the ampacity values shown in Article 310, provided it is identified as suitable for this use.

426.41 Pull Boxes. Where pull boxes are used, they shall be accessible without excavation by location in suitable vaults or above grade. Outdoor pull boxes shall be of watertight construction.

426.42 Single Conductor in Enclosure. The provisions of 300.20 shall not apply to the installation of a single conductor in a ferromagnetic envelope (metal enclosure).

426.43 Corrosion Protection. Ferromagnetic envelopes, ferrous or nonferrous metal raceways, boxes, fittings, supports, and support hardware shall be permitted to be installed in concrete or in direct contact with the earth, or in areas subjected to severe corrosive influences, where made of material suitable for the condition, or where provided with corrosion protection identified as suitable for the condition. Corrosion protection shall maintain the original wall thickness of the ferromagnetic envelope.

426.44 Grounding. The ferromagnetic envelope shall be grounded at both ends; and, in addition, it shall be permitted to be grounded at intermediate points as required by its design.

The provisions of 250.30 shall not apply to the installation of skin-effect heating systems.

FPN: For grounding methods, see Article 250.

VI. Control and Protection

426.50 Disconnecting Means.

(A) Disconnection. All fixed outdoor deicing and snow-melting equipment shall be provided with a means for disconnection from all ungrounded conductors. Where readily accessible to the user of the equipment, the branch-circuit switch or circuit breaker shall be permitted to serve as the disconnecting means. The disconnecting means shall be of the indicating type and be provided with a positive lockout in the "off" position.

(B) Cord-and-Plug-Connected Equipment. The factory-installed attachment plug of cord-and-plug-connected equipment rated 20 amperes or less and 150 volts or less to ground shall be permitted to be the disconnecting means.

426.51 Controllers.

(A) Temperature Controller with "Off" Position. Temperature controlled switching devices that indicate an "off" position and that interrupt line current shall open all ungrounded conductors when the control device is in the "off" position. These devices shall not be permitted to serve as the disconnecting means unless provided with a positive lockout in the "off" position.

(B) Temperature Controller Without "Off" Position. Temperature controlled switching devices that do not have an "off" position shall not be required to open all ungrounded conductors and shall not be permitted to serve as the disconnecting means.

(C) Remote Temperature Controller. Remote controlled temperature-actuated devices shall not be required to meet the requirements of 426.51(A). These devices shall not be permitted to serve as the disconnecting means.

(D) Combined Switching Devices. Switching devices consisting of combined temperature-actuated devices and manually controlled switches that serve both as the controller and the disconnecting means shall comply with all of the following conditions:

(1) Open all ungrounded conductors when manually placed in the "off" position

(2) Be so designed that the circuit cannot be energized automatically if the device has been manually placed in the "off" position

(3) Be provided with a positive lockout in the "off" position

426.52 Overcurrent Protection.
Fixed outdoor electric deicing and snow-melting equipment shall be permitted to be protected against overcurrent where supplied by a branch circuit as specified in 426.4.

426.54 Cord-and-Plug-Connected Deicing and Snow-Melting Equipment.
Cord-and-plug-connected deicing and snow-melting equipment shall be listed.

ARTICLE 427
Fixed Electric Heating Equipment for Pipelines and Vessels

I. General

427.1 Scope. The requirements of this article shall apply to electrically energized heating systems and the installation of these systems used with pipelines or vessels or both.

> FPN: For further information, see ANSI/IEEE Std. 515-1997, *Standard for the Testing, Design, Installation and Maintenance of Electrical Resistance Heat Tracing for Industrial Applications*, and ANSI/IEEE Std. 844-2000, *Recommended Practice for Electrical Impedance, Induction, and Skin Effect Heating of Pipelines and Vessels*.

427.2 Definitions.

Impedance Heating System. A system in which heat is generated in a pipeline or vessel wall by causing current to flow through the pipeline or vessel wall by direct connection to an ac voltage source from a dual-winding transformer.

Induction Heating System. A system in which heat is generated in a pipeline or vessel wall by inducing current and hysteresis effect in the pipeline or vessel wall from an external isolated ac field source.

Integrated Heating System. A complete system consisting of components such as pipelines, vessels, heating elements, heat transfer medium, thermal insulation, moisture barrier, nonheating leads, temperature controllers, safety signs, junction boxes, raceways, and fittings.

Pipeline. A length of pipe including pumps, valves, flanges, control devices, strainers, and/or similar equipment for conveying fluids.

Resistance Heating Element. A specific separate element to generate heat that is applied to the pipeline or vessel externally or internally.

> FPN: Tubular heaters, strip heaters, heating cable, heating tape, heating blankets, and immersion heaters are examples of resistance heaters.

Skin-Effect Heating System. A system in which heat is generated on the inner surface of a ferromagnetic envelope attached to a pipeline or vessel, or both.

> FPN: Typically, an electrically insulated conductor is routed through and connected to the envelope at the other end. The envelope and the electrically insulated conductor are connected to an ac voltage source from a dual-winding transformer.

Vessel. A container such as a barrel, drum, or tank for holding fluids or other material.

427.3 Application of Other Articles. Cord-connected pipe heating assemblies intended for specific use and identified as suitable for this use shall be installed according to Article 422.

427.4 Continuous Load. Fixed electric heating equipment for pipelines and vessels shall be considered continuous load.

II. Installation

427.10 General. Equipment for pipeline and vessel electrical heating shall be identified as being suitable for (1) the chemical, thermal, and physical environment and (2) installation in accordance with the manufacturer's drawings and instructions.

427.11 Use. Electrical heating equipment shall be installed in such a manner as to be afforded protection from physical damage.

427.12 Thermal Protection. External surfaces of pipeline and vessel heating equipment that operate at temperatures exceeding 60°C (140°F) shall be physically guarded, isolated, or thermally insulated to protect against contact by personnel in the area.

427.13 Identification. The presence of electrically heated pipelines, vessels, or both, shall be evident by the posting of appropriate caution signs or markings at frequent intervals along the pipeline or vessel.

III. Resistance Heating Elements

427.14 Secured. Heating element assemblies shall be secured to the surface being heated by means other than the thermal insulation.

427.15 Not in Direct Contact. Where the heating element is not in direct contact with the pipeline or vessel being heated, means shall be provided to prevent overtemperature of the heating element unless the design of the heater assembly is such that its temperature limitations will not be exceeded.

427.16 Expansion and Contraction. Heating elements and assemblies shall not be installed where they bridge expansion joints unless provisions are made for expansion and contraction.

427.17 Flexural Capability. Where installed on flexible pipelines, the heating elements and assemblies shall have a flexural capability that is compatible with the pipeline.

427.18 Power Supply Leads.

(A) Nonheating Leads. Power supply nonheating leads (cold leads) for resistance elements shall be suitable for the temperature encountered. Not less than 150 mm (6 in.) of

nonheating leads shall be provided within the junction box. Preassembled factory supplied and field assembled nonheating leads on approved heaters shall be permitted to be shortened if the markings specified in 427.20 are retained.

(B) Power Supply Leads Protection. Nonheating power supply leads shall be protected where they emerge from electrically heated pipeline or vessel heating units by rigid metal conduit, intermediate metal conduit, electrical metallic tubing, or other raceways identified as suitable for the application.

(C) Interconnecting Leads. Interconnecting nonheating leads connecting portions of the heating system shall be permitted to be covered by thermal insulation in the same manner as the heaters.

427.19 Electrical Connections.

(A) Nonheating Interconnections. Nonheating interconnections, where required under thermal insulation, shall be made with insulated connectors identified as suitable for this use.

(B) Circuit Connections. Splices and terminations outside the thermal insulation shall be installed in a box or fitting in accordance with 110.14 and 300.15.

427.20 Marking. Each factory-assembled heating unit shall be legibly marked within 75 mm (3 in.) of each end of the nonheating leads with the permanent identification symbol, catalog number, and ratings in volts and watts or in volts and amperes.

427.22 Equipment Protection. Ground-fault protection of equipment shall be provided for electric heat tracing and heating panels. This requirement shall not apply in industrial establishments where there is alarm indication of ground faults and the following conditions apply:

(1) Conditions of maintenance and supervision ensure that only qualified persons service the installed systems.

(2) Continued circuit operation is necessary for safe operation of equipment or processes.

427.23 Grounded Conductive Covering. Electric heating equipment shall be listed and have a grounded conductive covering in accordance with 427.23(A) or 427.23(B). The conductive covering shall provide an effective ground path for equipment protection.

(A) Heating Wires or Cables. Heating wires or cables shall have a grounded conductive covering that surrounds the heating element and bus wires, if any, and their electrical insulation.

(B) Heating Panels. Heating panels shall have a grounded conductive covering over the heating element and its electrical insulation on the side opposite the side attached to the surface to be heated.

IV. Impedance Heating

427.25 Personnel Protection. All accessible external surfaces of the pipeline, vessel, or both, being heated shall be physically guarded, isolated, or thermally insulated (with a weatherproof jacket for outside installations) to protect against contact by personnel in the area.

427.26 Isolation Transformer. A dual-winding transformer with a grounded shield between the primary and secondary windings shall be used to isolate the distribution system from the heating system.

427.27 Voltage Limitations. Unless protected by ground-fault circuit-interrupter protection for personnel, the secondary winding of the isolation transformer connected to the pipeline or vessel being heated shall not have an output voltage greater than 30 volts ac.

Where ground-fault circuit-interrupter protection for personnel is provided, the voltage shall be permitted to be greater than 30 but not more than 80 volts.

Exception: In industrial establishments, the isolation transformer connected to the pipeline or vessel being heated shall be permitted to have an output voltage not greater than 132 volts ac to ground where all of the following conditions apply:

(1) Conditions of maintenance and supervision ensure that only qualified persons service the installed systems.

(2) Ground fault protection of equipment is provided.

(3) The pipeline or vessel being heated is completely enclosed in a grounded metal enclosure.

(4) The transformer secondary connections to the pipeline or vessel being heated are completely enclosed in a grounded metal mesh or metal enclosure.

427.28 Induced Currents. All current-carrying components shall be installed in accordance with 300.20.

427.29 Grounding. The pipeline, vessel, or both, that is being heated and operating at a voltage greater than 30 but not more than 80 shall be grounded at designated points.

427.30 Secondary Conductor Sizing. The ampacity of the conductors connected to the secondary of the transformer shall be at least 100 percent of the total load of the heater.

V. Induction Heating

427.35 Scope. This part covers the installation of line frequency induction heating equipment and accessories for pipelines and vessels.

FPN: See Article 665 for other applications.

427.36 Personnel Protection. Induction coils that operate or may operate at a voltage greater than 30 volts ac shall be enclosed in a nonmetallic or split metallic enclosure, isolated, or made inaccessible by location to protect personnel in the area.

427.37 Induced Current. Induction coils shall be prevented from inducing circulating currents in surrounding metallic equipment, supports, or structures by shielding, isolation, or insulation of the current paths. Stray current paths shall be bonded to prevent arcing.

VI. Skin-Effect Heating

427.45 Conductor Ampacity. The ampacity of the electrically insulated conductor inside the ferromagnetic envelope shall be permitted to exceed the values given in Article 310, provided it is identified as suitable for this use.

427.46 Pull Boxes. Pull boxes for pulling the electrically insulated conductor in the ferromagnetic envelope shall be permitted to be buried under the thermal insulation, provided their locations are indicated by permanent markings on the insulation jacket surface and on drawings. For outdoor installations, pull boxes shall be of watertight construction.

427.47 Single Conductor in Enclosure. The provisions of 300.20 shall not apply to the installation of a single conductor in a ferromagnetic envelope (metal enclosure).

427.48 Grounding. The ferromagnetic envelope shall be grounded at both ends, and, in addition, it shall be permitted to be grounded at intermediate points as required by its design. The ferromagnetic envelope shall be bonded at all joints to ensure electrical continuity.

The provisions of 250.30 shall not apply to the installation of skin-effect heating systems.

FPN: See Article 250 for grounding methods.

VII. Control and Protection

427.55 Disconnecting Means.

(A) Switch or Circuit Breaker. Means shall be provided to disconnect all fixed electric pipeline or vessel heating equipment from all ungrounded conductors. The branch-circuit switch or circuit breaker, where readily accessible to the user of the equipment, shall be permitted to serve as the disconnecting means. The disconnecting means shall be of the indicating type and shall be provided with a positive lockout in the "off" position.

(B) Cord-and-Plug-Connected Equipment. The factory-installed attachment plug of cord-and-plug-connected equipment rated 20 amperes or less and 150 volts or less to ground shall be permitted to be the disconnecting means.

427.56 Controls.

(A) Temperature Control with "Off" Position. Temperature controlled switching devices that indicate an "off" position and that interrupt line current shall open all ungrounded conductors when the control device is in this "off" position. These devices shall not be permitted to serve as the disconnecting means unless provided with a positive lockout in the "off" position.

(B) Temperature Control Without "Off" Position. Temperature controlled switching devices that do not have an "off" position shall not be required to open all ungrounded conductors and shall not be permitted to serve as the disconnecting means.

(C) Remote Temperature Controller. Remote controlled temperature-actuated devices shall not be required to meet the requirements of 427.56(A) and 427.56(B). These devices shall not be permitted to serve as the disconnecting means.

(D) Combined Switching Devices. Switching devices consisting of combined temperature-actuated devices and manually controlled switches that serve both as the controllers and the disconnecting means shall comply with all the following conditions:

(1) Open all ungrounded conductors when manually placed in the "off" position

(2) Be designed so that the circuit cannot be energized automatically if the device has been manually placed in the "off" position

(3) Be provided with a positive lockout in the "off" position

427.57 Overcurrent Protection. Heating equipment shall be considered as protected against overcurrent where supplied by a branch circuit as specified in 210.3 and 210.23.

ARTICLE 430
Motors, Motor Circuits, and Controllers

I. General

430.1 Scope. This article covers motors, motor branch-circuit and feeder conductors and their protection, motor overload protection, motor control circuits, motor controllers, and motor control centers.

General, 430.1 through 430.18	Part I
Motor Circuit Conductors, 430.21 through 430.29	Part II
Motor and Branch-Circuit Overload Protection, 430.31 through 430.44	Part III
Motor Branch-Circuit Short-Circuit and Ground-Fault Protection, 430.51 through 430.58	Part IV
Motor Feeder Short-Circuit and Ground-Fault Protection, 430.61 through 430.63	Part V
Motor Control Circuits, 430.71 through 430.74	Part VI
Motor Controllers, 430.81 through 430.91	Part VII
Motor Control Centers, 430.92 through 430.98	Part VIII
Disconnecting Means, 430.101 through 430.113	Part IX
Adjustable Speed Drive Systems, 430.120 through 430.128	Part X
Over 600 Volts, Nominal, 430.221 through 430.227	Part XI
Protection of Live Parts—All Voltages, 430.231 through 430.233	Part XII
Grounding—All Voltages, 430.241 through 430.245	Part XIII
Tables, Tables 430.247 through 430.251(B)	Part XIV

Figure 430.1 Article 430 Contents.

FPN No. 1: Installation requirements for motor control centers are covered in 110.26(F). Air conditioning and refrigerating equipment are covered in Article 440.

FPN No. 2: Figure 430.1 is for information only.

430.2 Definitions.

Adjustable Speed Drive. A combination of the power converter, motor, and motor mounted auxiliary devices such as encoders, tachometers, thermal switches and detectors, air blowers, heaters, and vibration sensors.

Adjustable-Speed Drive System. An interconnected combination of equipment that provides a means of adjusting the speed of a mechanical load coupled to a motor. A drive system typically consists of an adjustable speed drive and auxiliary electrical apparatus.

Controller. For the purpose of this article, a controller is any switch or device that is normally used to start and stop a motor by making and breaking the motor circuit current.

Motor Control Circuit. The circuit of a control apparatus or system that carries the electric signals directing the performance of the controller but does not carry the main power current.

System Isolation Equipment. A redundantly monitored, remotely operated contactor-isolating system, packaged to provide the disconnection/isolation function, capable of verifiable operation from multiple remote locations by means of lockout switches, each having the capability of being padlocked in the "off" (open) position.

430.4 Part-Winding Motors. A part-winding start induction or synchronous motor is one that is arranged for starting by first energizing part of its primary (armature) winding and, subsequently, energizing the remainder of this winding in one or more steps. A standard part-winding start induction motor is arranged so that one-half of its primary winding can be energized initially, and, subsequently, the remaining half can be energized, both halves then carrying equal current. A hermetic refrigerant compressor motor shall not be considered a standard part-winding start induction motor.

Where separate overload devices are used with a standard part-winding start induction motor, each half of the motor winding shall be individually protected in accordance with 430.32 and 430.37 with a trip current one-half that specified.

Each motor-winding connection shall have branch-circuit short-circuit and ground-fault protection rated at not more than one-half that specified by 430.52.

Exception: A short-circuit and ground-fault protective device shall be permitted for both windings if the device will allow the motor to start. Where time-delay (dual-element) fuses are used, they shall be permitted to have a rating not exceeding 150 percent of the motor full-load current.

430.5 Other Articles. Motors and controllers shall also comply with the applicable provisions of Table 430.5.

430.6 Ampacity and Motor Rating Determination. The size of conductors supplying equipment covered by Article 430 shall be selected from the allowable ampacity tables in accordance with 310.15(B) or shall be calculated in accordance with 310.15(C). Where flexible cord is used, the size of the conductor shall be selected in accordance with 400.5. The required ampacity and motor ratings shall be determined as specified in 430.6(A), (B), and (C).

(A) General Motor Applications. For general motor applications, current ratings shall be determined based on (A)(1) and (A)(2).

Table 430.5 Other Articles

Equipment/Occupancy	Article	Section
Air-conditioning and refrigerating equipment	440	
Capacitors		460.8, 460.9
Commercial garages; aircraft hangars; motor fuel dispensing facilities; bulk storage plants; spray application, dipping, and coating processes; and inhalation anesthetizing locations	511, 513, 514, 515, 516, and 517 Part IV	
Cranes and hoists	610	
Electrically driven or controlled irrigation machines	675	
Elevators, dumbwaiters, escalators, moving walks, wheelchair lifts, and stairway chair lifts	620	
Fire pumps	695	
Hazardous (classified) locations	500–503 and 505	
Industrial machinery	670	
Motion picture projectors		540.11 and 540.20
Motion picture and television studios and similar locations	530	
Resistors and reactors	470	
Theaters, audience areas of motion picture and television studios, and similar locations		520.48
Transformers and transformer vaults	450	

(1) Table Values. Other than for motors built for low speeds (less than 1200 RPM) or high torques, and for multispeed motors, the values given in Table 430.247, Table 430.248, Table 430.249, and Table 430.250 shall be used to determine the ampacity of conductors or ampere ratings of switches, branch-circuit short-circuit and ground-fault protection, instead of the actual current rating marked on the motor nameplate. Where a motor is marked in amperes, but not horsepower, the horsepower rating shall be assumed to be that corresponding to the value given in Table 430.247, Table 430.248, Table 430.249, and Table 430.250, interpolated if necessary. Motors built for low speeds (less than 1200 RPM) or high torques may have higher full-load currents, and multispeed motors will have full-load current varying with speed, in which case the nameplate current ratings shall be used.

Exception No. 1: Multispeed motors shall be in accordance with 430.22(A) and 430.52.

Exception No. 2: For equipment that employs a shaded-pole or permanent-split capacitor-type fan or blower motor that is marked with the motor type, the full load current for such motor marked on the nameplate of the equipment in which the fan or blower motor is employed shall be used instead of the horsepower rating to determine the ampacity or rating of the disconnecting means, the branch-circuit conductors, the controller, the branch-circuit short-circuit and ground-fault protection, and the separate overload protection. This marking on the equipment nameplate shall not be less than the current marked on the fan or blower motor nameplate.

Exception No. 3: For a listed motor-operated appliance that is marked with both motor horsepower and full-load current, the motor full-load current marked on the nameplate of the appliance shall be used instead of the horsepower rating on the appliance nameplate to determine the ampacity or rating of the disconnecting means, the branch-circuit conductors, the controller, the branch-circuit short-circuit and ground-fault protection, and any separate overload protection.

(2) Nameplate Values. Separate motor overload protection shall be based on the motor nameplate current rating.

(B) Torque Motors. For torque motors, the rated current shall be locked-rotor current, and this nameplate current shall be used to determine the ampacity of the branch-circuit conductors covered in 430.22 and 430.24, the ampere rating of the motor overload protection, and the ampere rating of motor branch-circuit short-circuit and ground-fault protection in accordance with 430.52(B).

FPN: For motor controllers and disconnecting means, see 430.83(D) and 430.110.

(C) Alternating-Current Adjustable Voltage Motors. For motors used in alternating-current, adjustable voltage, variable torque drive systems, the ampacity of conductors, or ampere ratings of switches, branch-circuit short-circuit and ground-fault protection, and so forth, shall be based on the maximum operating current marked on the motor or control nameplate, or both. If the maximum operating current does not appear on the nameplate, the ampacity determination shall be based on 150 percent of the values given in Table 430.249 and Table 430.250.

430.7 Marking on Motors and Multimotor Equipment.

(A) Usual Motor Applications. A motor shall be marked with the following information.

(1) Manufacturer's name.

(2) Rated volts and full-load current. For a multispeed motor, full-load current for each speed, except shaded-pole and permanent-split capacitor motors where amperes are required only for maximum speed.

(3) Rated frequency and number of phases if an ac motor.

(4) Rated full-load speed.

(5) Rated temperature rise or the insulation system class and rated ambient temperature.

(6) Time rating. The time rating shall be 5, 15, 30, or 60 minutes, or continuous.

(7) Rated horsepower if ⅛ hp or more. For a multispeed motor ⅛ hp or more, rated horsepower for each speed, except shaded-pole and permanent-split capacitor motors ⅛ hp or more where rated horsepower is required only for maximum speed. Motors of arc welders are not required to be marked with the horsepower rating.

(8) Code letter or locked-rotor amperes if an alternating-current motor rated ½ hp or more. On polyphase wound-rotor motors, the code letter shall be omitted.

FPN: See 430.7(B).

(9) Design letter for design B, C, or D motors.

FPN: Motor design letter definitions are found in ANSI/NEMA MG 1-1993, *Motors and Generators, Part 1, Definitions,* and in IEEE 100-1996, *Standard Dictionary of Electrical and Electronic Terms.*

(10) Secondary volts and full-load current if a wound-rotor induction motor.

(11) Field current and voltage for dc excited synchronous motors.

(12) Winding — straight shunt, stabilized shunt, compound, or series, if a dc motor. Fractional horsepower dc motors 175 mm (7 in.) or less in diameter shall not be required to be marked.

(13) A motor provided with a thermal protector complying with 430.32(A)(2) or (B)(2) shall be marked "Thermally Protected." Thermally protected motors rated 100 watts or less and complying with 430.32(B)(2) shall be permitted to use the abbreviated marking "T.P."

(14) A motor complying with 430.32(B)(4) shall be marked "Impedance Protected." Impedance protected motors rated 100 watts or less and complying with 430.32(B)(4) shall be permitted to use the abbreviated marking "Z.P."

(15) Motors equipped with electrically powered condensation prevention heaters shall be marked with the rated heater voltage, number of phases, and the rated power in watts.

(B) Locked-Rotor Indicating Code Letters. Code letters marked on motor nameplates to show motor input with locked rotor shall be in accordance with Table 430.7(B).

The code letter indicating motor input with locked rotor shall be in an individual block on the nameplate, properly designated.

Table 430.7(B) Locked-Rotor Indicating Code Letters

Code Letter	Kilovolt-Amperes per Horsepower with Locked Rotor
A	0–3.14
B	3.15–3.54
C	3.55–3.99
D	4.0–4.49
E	4.5–4.99
F	5.0–5.59
G	5.6–6.29
H	6.3–7.09
J	7.1–7.99
K	8.0–8.99
L	9.0–9.99
M	10.0–11.19
N	11.2–12.49
P	12.5–13.99
R	14.0–15.99
S	16.0–17.99
T	18.0–19.99
U	20.0–22.39
V	22.4 and up

(1) Multispeed Motors. Multispeed motors shall be marked with the code letter designating the locked-rotor kilovolt-ampere (kVA) per horsepower for the highest speed at which the motor can be started.

Exception: Constant horsepower multispeed motors shall be marked with the code letter giving the highest locked-rotor kilovolt-ampere (kVA) per horsepower.

(2) Single-Speed Motors. Single-speed motors starting on wye connection and running on delta connections shall be marked with a code letter corresponding to the locked-rotor kilovolt-ampere (kVA) per horsepower for the wye connection.

(3) Dual-Voltage Motors. Dual-voltage motors that have a different locked-rotor kilovolt-ampere (kVA) per horsepower on the two voltages shall be marked with the code letter for the voltage giving the highest locked-rotor kilovolt-ampere (kVA) per horsepower.

(4) 50/60 Hz Motors. Motors with 50- and 60-Hz ratings shall be marked with a code letter designating the locked-rotor kilovolt-ampere (kVA) per horsepower on 60 Hz.

(5) Part Winding Motors. Part-winding start motors shall be marked with a code letter designating the locked-rotor kilovolt-ampere (kVA) per horsepower that is based on the locked-rotor current for the full winding of the motor.

(C) Torque Motors. Torque motors are rated for operation at standstill and shall be marked in accordance with 430.7(A), except that locked-rotor torque shall replace horsepower.

(D) Multimotor and Combination-Load Equipment.

(1) Factory-Wired. Multimotor and combination-load equipment shall be provided with a visible nameplate marked with the manufacturer's name, the rating in volts, frequency, number of phases, minimum supply circuit conductor ampacity, and the maximum ampere rating of the circuit short-circuit and ground-fault protective device. The conductor ampacity shall be calculated in accordance with 430.24 and counting all of the motors and other loads that will be operated at the same time. The short-circuit and ground-fault protective device rating shall not exceed the value calculated in accordance with 430.53. Multimotor equipment for use on two or more circuits shall be marked with the preceding information for each circuit.

(2) Not Factory-Wired. Where the equipment is not factory-wired and the individual nameplates of motors and other loads are visible after assembly of the equipment, the individual nameplates shall be permitted to serve as the required marking.

430.8 Marking on Controllers. A controller shall be marked with the manufacturer's name or identification, the voltage, the current or horsepower rating, the short-circuit current rating, and such other necessary data to properly indicate the applications for which it is suitable.

Exception No. 1: The short-circuit current rating is not required for controllers applied in accordance with 430.81(A) or (B).

Exception No. 2: The short-circuit rating is not required to be marked on the controller when the short-circuit current rating of the controller is marked elsewhere on the assembly.

Exception No. 3: The short-circuit rating is not required to be marked on the controller when the assembly into which it is installed has a marked short-circuit current rating.

Exception No. 4: Short-circuit ratings are not required for controllers rated less than 2 hp at 300 V or less and listed exclusively for general-purpose branch circuits.

A controller that includes motor overload protection suitable for group motor application shall be marked with the motor overload protection and the maximum branch-circuit short-circuit and ground-fault protection for such applications.

Combination controllers that employ adjustable instantaneous trip circuit breakers shall be clearly marked to indicate the ampere settings of the adjustable trip element.

Where a controller is built-in as an integral part of a motor or of a motor-generator set, individual marking of the controller shall not be required if the necessary data are on the nameplate. For controllers that are an integral part of equipment approved as a unit, the above marking shall be permitted on the equipment nameplate.

FPN: See 110.10 for information on circuit impedance and other characteristics.

430.9 Terminals.

(A) Markings. Terminals of motors and controllers shall be suitably marked or colored where necessary to indicate the proper connections.

(B) Conductors. Motor controllers and terminals of control circuit devices shall be connected with copper conductors unless identified for use with a different conductor.

(C) Torque Requirements. Control circuit devices with screw-type pressure terminals used with 14 AWG or smaller copper conductors shall be torqued to a minimum of 0.8 N·m (7 lb-in.) unless identified for a different torque value.

430.10 Wiring Space in Enclosures.

(A) General. Enclosures for motor controllers and disconnecting means shall not be used as junction boxes, auxiliary gutters, or raceways for conductors feeding through or tapping off to the other apparatus unless designs are employed that provide adequate space for this purpose.

FPN: See 312.8 for switch and overcurrent-device enclosures.

(B) Wire-Bending Space in Enclosures. Minimum wire-bending space within the enclosures for motor controllers shall be in accordance with Table 430.10(B) where measured in a straight line from the end of the lug or wire connector (in the direction the wire leaves the terminal) to the wall or barrier. Where alternate wire termination means are substituted for that supplied by the manufacturer of the controller, they shall be of a type identified by the manufacturer for use with the controller and shall not reduce the minimum wire-bending space.

430.11 Protection Against Liquids.
Suitable guards or enclosures shall be provided to protect exposed current-carrying parts of motors and the insulation of motor leads where installed directly under equipment, or in other locations where dripping or spraying oil, water, or other injurious liquid may occur, unless the motor is designed for the existing conditions.

430.12 Motor Terminal Housings.

(A) Material. Where motors are provided with terminal housings, the housings shall be of metal and of substantial construction.

Exception: In other than hazardous (classified) locations, substantial, nonmetallic, nonburning housings shall be permitted, provided an internal grounding means between the motor frame and the equipment grounding connection is incorporated within the housing.

(B) Dimensions and Space — Wire-to-Wire Connections. Where these terminal housings enclose wire-to-wire connections, they shall have minimum dimensions and usable volumes in accordance with Table 430.12(B).

Table 430.10(B) Minimum Wire-Bending Space at the Terminals of Enclosed Motor Controllers

| Size of Wire (AWG or kcmil) | Wires per Terminal* | | | |
| | 1 | | 2 | |
	mm	in.	mm	in.
14–10	Not specified		—	—
8–6	38	1½	—	—
4–3	50	2	—	—
2	65	2½	—	—
1	75	3	—	—
1/0	125	5	125	5
2/0	150	6	150	6
3/0–4/0	175	7	175	7
250	200	8	200	8
300	250	10	250	10
350–500	300	12	300	12
600–700	350	14	400	16
750–900	450	18	475	19

*Where provision for three or more wires per terminal exists, the minimum wire-bending space shall be in accordance with the requirements of Article 312.

Table 430.12(B) Terminal Housings — Wire-to-Wire Connections

Motors 275 mm (11 in.) in Diameter or Less

| Horsepower | Cover Opening Minimum Dimension | | Usable Volume Minimum | |
	mm	in.	cm³	in.³
1 and smaller[a]	41	1⅝	170	10.5
1½, 2, and 3[b]	45	1¾	275	16.8
5 and 7½	50	2	365	22.4
10 and 15	65	2½	595	36.4

Motors Over 275 mm (11 in.) in Diameter — Alternating-Current Motors

| Maximum Full Load Current for 3-Phase Motors with Maximum of 12 Leads (Amperes) | Terminal Box Cover Opening Minimum Dimension | | Usable Volume Minimum | | Typical Maximum Horsepower 3-Phase | |
| | | | | | 230 Volt | 460 Volt |
	mm	in.	cm³	in.³		
45	65	2.5	595	36.4	15	30
70	84	3.3	1,265	77	25	50
110	100	4.0	2,295	140	40	75
160	125	5.0	4,135	252	60	125
250	150	6.0	7,380	450	100	200
400	175	7.0	13,775	840	150	300
600	200	8.0	25,255	1540	250	500

Table 430.12(B) *Continued*

Direct-Current Motors				
Maximum Full-Load Current for Motors with Maximum of 6 Leads (Amperes)	Terminal Box Minimum Dimensions		Usable Volume Minimum	
	mm	in.	cm³	in.³
68	65	2.5	425	26
105	84	3.3	900	55
165	100	4.0	1,640	100
240	125	5.0	2,950	180
375	150	6.0	5,410	330
600	175	7.0	9,840	600
900	200	8.0	18,040	1,100

Note: Auxiliary leads for such items as brakes, thermostats, space heaters, and exciting fields shall be permitted to be neglected if their current-carrying area does not exceed 25 percent of the current-carrying area of the machine power leads.

[a]For motors rated 1 hp and smaller and with the terminal housing partially or wholly integral with the frame or end shield, the volume of the terminal housing shall not be less than 18.0 cm³ (1.1 in.³) per wire-to-wire connection. The minimum cover opening dimension is not specified.

[b]For motors rated 1½, 2, and 3 hp and with the terminal housing partially or wholly integral with the frame or end shield, the volume of the terminal housing shall not be less than 23.0 cm³ (1.4 in.³) per wire-to-wire connection. The minimum cover opening dimension is not specified.

(C) Dimensions and Space — Fixed Terminal Connections. Where these terminal housings enclose rigidly mounted motor terminals, the terminal housing shall be of sufficient size to provide minimum terminal spacings and usable volumes in accordance with Table 430.12(C)(1) and Table 430.12(C)(2).

Table 430.12(C)(1) Terminal Spacings — Fixed Terminals

	Minimum Spacing			
Nominal Volts	Between Line Terminals		Between Line Terminals and Other Uninsulated Metal Parts	
	mm	in.	mm	in.
240 or less	6	¼	6	¼
Over 250 – 600	10	⅜	10	⅜

(D) Large Wire or Factory Connections. For motors with larger ratings, greater number of leads, or larger wire sizes, or where motors are installed as a part of factory-wired equipment, without additional connection being required at the motor terminal housing during equipment installation, the terminal housing shall be of ample size to make connections, but the foregoing provisions for the volumes of terminal housings shall not be considered applicable.

Table 430.12(C)(2) Usable Volumes — Fixed Terminals

Power-Supply Conductor Size (AWG)	Minimum Usable Volume per Power-Supply Conductor	
	cm³	in.³
14	16	1
12 and 10	20	1¼
8 and 6	37	2¼

(E) Equipment Grounding Connections. A means for attachment of an equipment grounding conductor termination in accordance with 250.8 shall be provided at motor terminal housings for wire-to-wire connections or fixed terminal connections. The means for such connections shall be permitted to be located either inside or outside the motor terminal housing.

Exception: Where a motor is installed as a part of factory-wired equipment that is required to be grounded and without additional connection being required at the motor terminal housing during equipment installation, a separate means for motor grounding at the motor terminal housing shall not be required.

430.13 Bushing. Where wires pass through an opening in an enclosure, conduit box, or barrier, a bushing shall be used to protect the conductors from the edges of openings having sharp edges. The bushing shall have smooth, well-rounded surfaces where it may be in contact with the conductors. If used where oils, greases, or other contaminants may be present, the bushing shall be made of material not deleteriously affected.

FPN: For conductors exposed to deteriorating agents, see 310.9.

430.14 Location of Motors.

(A) Ventilation and Maintenance. Motors shall be located so that adequate ventilation is provided and so that maintenance, such as lubrication of bearings and replacing of brushes, can be readily accomplished.

Exception: Ventilation shall not be required for submersible types of motors.

(B) Open Motors. Open motors that have commutators or collector rings shall be located or protected so that sparks cannot reach adjacent combustible material.

Exception: Installation of these motors on wooden floors or supports shall be permitted.

430.16 Exposure to Dust Accumulations. In locations where dust or flying material collects on or in motors in such quantities as to seriously interfere with the ventilation or cooling of motors and thereby cause dangerous temperatures, suitable types of enclosed motors that do not overheat under the prevailing conditions shall be used.

FPN: Especially severe conditions may require the use of enclosed pipe-ventilated motors, or enclosure in separate dusttight rooms, properly ventilated from a source of clean air.

430.17 Highest Rated or Smallest Rated Motor. In determining compliance with 430.24, 430.53(B), and 430.53(C), the highest rated or smallest rated motor shall be based on the rated full-load current as selected from Table 430.247, Table 430.248, Table 430.249, and Table 430.250.

430.18 Nominal Voltage of Rectifier Systems. The nominal value of the ac voltage being rectified shall be used to determine the voltage of a rectifier derived system.

Exception: The nominal dc voltage of the rectifier shall be used if it exceeds the peak value of the ac voltage being rectified.

II. Motor Circuit Conductors

430.21 General. Part II specifies ampacities of conductors that are capable of carrying the motor current without overheating under the conditions specified.

The provisions of Part II shall not apply to motor circuits rated over 600 volts, nominal.

The provisions of Articles 250, 300, and 310 shall not apply to conductors that form an integral part of equipment, such as motors, motor controllers, motor control centers, or other factory-assembled control equipment.

FPN No. 1: See 300.1(B) and 310.1 for similar requirements.

FPN No. 2: See 110.14(C) and 430.9(B) for equipment device terminal requirements.

FPN No. 3: For over 600 volts, nominal, see Part XI.

430.22 Single Motor.

(A) General. Conductors that supply a single motor used in a continuous duty application shall have an ampacity of not less than 125 percent of the motor's full-load current rating as determined by 430.6(A)(1).

Exception: For dc motors operating from a rectified single-phase power supply, the conductors between the field wiring terminals of the rectifier and the motor shall have an ampacity of not less than the following percent of the motor full-load current rating:

(a) Where a rectifier bridge of the single-phase half-wave type is used, 190 percent.

(b) Where a rectifier bridge of the single-phase full-wave type is used, 150 percent.

(B) Multispeed Motor. For a multispeed motor, the selection of branch-circuit conductors on the line side of the controller shall be based on the highest of the full-load current ratings shown on the motor nameplate. The selection of branch-circuit conductors between the controller and the motor shall be based on the current rating of the winding(s) that the conductors energize.

(C) Wye-Start, Delta-Run Motor. For a wye-start, delta-run connected motor, the selection of branch-circuit conductors on the line side of the controller shall be based on the motor full-load current. The selection of conductors between the controller and the motor shall be based on 58 percent of the motor full-load current.

(D) Part-Winding Motor. For a part-winding connected motor, the selection of branch-circuit conductors on the line side of the controller shall be based on the motor full-load current. The selection of conductors between the controller and the motor shall be based on 50 percent of the motor full-load current.

(E) Other Than Continuous Duty. Conductors for a motor used in a short-time, intermittent, periodic, or varying duty application shall have an ampacity of not less than the percentage of the motor nameplate current rating shown in Table 430.22(E), unless the authority having jurisdiction grants special permission for conductors of lower ampacity.

Table 430.22(E) Duty-Cycle Service

	Nameplate Current Rating Percentages			
Classification of Service	**5-Minute Rated Motor**	**15-Minute Rated Motor**	**30- & 60-Minute Rated Motor**	**Continuous Rated Motor**
Short-time duty operating valves, raising or lowering rolls, etc.	110	120	150	—
Intermittent duty freight and passenger elevators, tool heads, pumps, drawbridges, turntables, etc. (for arc welders, see 630.11)	85	85	90	140
Periodic duty rolls, ore- and coal-handling machines, etc.	85	90	95	140
Varying duty	110	120	150	200

Note: Any motor application shall be considered as continuous duty unless the nature of the apparatus it drives is such that the motor will not operate continuously with load under any condition of use.

(F) Separate Terminal Enclosure. The conductors between a stationary motor rated 1 hp or less and the separate terminal enclosure permitted in 430.245(B) shall be permitted to be smaller than 14 AWG but not smaller than 18 AWG, provided they have an ampacity as specified in 430.22(A).

430.23 Wound-Rotor Secondary.

(A) Continuous Duty. For continuous duty, the conductors connecting the secondary of a wound-rotor ac motor to its controller shall have an ampacity not less than 125 percent of the full-load secondary current of the motor.

(B) Other Than Continuous Duty. For other than continuous duty, these conductors shall have an ampacity, in percent of full-load secondary current, not less than that specified in Table 430.22(E).

(C) Resistor Separate from Controller. Where the secondary resistor is separate from the controller, the ampacity of the conductors between controller and resistor shall not be less than that shown in Table 430.23(C).

Table 430.23(C) Secondary Conductor

Resistor Duty Classification	Ampacity of Conductor in Percent of Full-Load Secondary Current
Light starting duty	35
Heavy starting duty	45
Extra-heavy starting duty	55
Light intermittent duty	65
Medium intermittent duty	75
Heavy intermittent duty	85
Continuous duty	110

430.24 Several Motors or a Motor(s) and Other Load(s). Conductors supplying several motors, or a motor(s) and other load(s), shall have an ampacity not less than 125 percent of the full-load current rating of the highest rated motor plus the sum of the full-load current ratings of all the other motors in the group, as determined by 430.6(A), plus the ampacity required for the other loads.

    FPN: See Annex D, Example No. D8.

Exception No. 1: Where one or more of the motors of the group are used for short-time, intermittent, periodic, or varying duty, the ampere rating of such motors to be used in the summation shall be determined in accordance with 430.22(E). For the highest rated motor, the greater of either the ampere rating from 430.22(E) or the largest continuous duty motor full-load current multiplied by 1.25 shall be used in the summation.

Exception No. 2: The ampacity of conductors supplying motor-operated fixed electric space-heating equipment shall conform with 424.3(B).

Exception No. 3: Where the circuitry is interlocked so as to prevent operation of selected motors or other loads at the same time, the conductor ampacity shall be permitted to be based on the summation of the currents of the motors and other loads to be operated at the same time that results in the highest total current.

430.25 Multimotor and Combination-Load Equipment. The ampacity of the conductors supplying multimotor and combination-load equipment shall not be less than the minimum circuit ampacity marked on the equipment in accordance with 430.7(D). Where the equipment is not factory-wired and the individual nameplates are visible in accordance with 430.7(D)(2), the conductor ampacity shall be determined in accordance with 430.24.

430.26 Feeder Demand Factor. Where reduced heating of the conductors results from motors operating on duty-cycle, intermittently, or from all motors not operating at one time, the authority having jurisdiction may grant permission for feeder conductors to have an ampacity less than specified in 430.24, provided the conductors have sufficient ampacity for the maximum load determined in accordance with the sizes and number of motors supplied and the character of their loads and duties.

    FPN: Demand factors determined in the design of new facilities can often be validated against actual historical experience from similar installations. Refer to ANSI/IEEE Std. 141, *IEEE Recommended Practice for Electric Power Distribution for Industrial Plants*, and ANSI/IEEE Std. 241, *Recommended Practice for Electric Power Systems in Commercial Buildings*, for information on the calculation of loads and demand factor.

430.27 Capacitors with Motors. Where capacitors are installed in motor circuits, conductors shall comply with 460.8 and 460.9.

430.28 Feeder Taps. Feeder tap conductors shall have an ampacity not less than that required by Part II, shall terminate in a branch-circuit protective device, and, in addition, shall meet one of the following requirements:

(1) Be enclosed either by an enclosed controller or by a raceway, be not more than 3.0 m (10 ft) in length, and, for field installation, be protected by an overcurrent device on the line side of the tap conductor, the rating or setting of which shall not exceed 1000 percent of the tap conductor ampacity

(2) Have an ampacity of at least one-third that of the feeder conductors, be suitably protected from physical damage or enclosed in a raceway, and be not more than 7.5 m (25 ft) in length

(3) Have an ampacity not less than the feeder conductors

Exception: Feeder taps over 7.5 m (25 ft) long. In high-bay manufacturing buildings [over 11 m (35 ft) high at walls], where conditions of maintenance and supervision ensure that only qualified persons service the systems, conductors tapped to a feeder shall be permitted to be not over 7.5 m (25 ft) long horizontally and not over 30.0 m (100 ft) in total length where all of the following conditions are met:

(a)   The ampacity of the tap conductors is not less than one-third that of the feeder conductors.

(b)   The tap conductors terminate with a single circuit breaker or a single set of fuses conforming with (1) Part IV, where the load-side conductors are a branch circuit, or (2) Part V, where the load-side conductors are a feeder.

(c)   The tap conductors are suitably protected from physical damage and are installed in raceways.

(d)   The tap conductors are continuous from end-to-end and contain no splices.

(e)   The tap conductors shall be 6 AWG copper or 4 AWG aluminum or larger.

(f)   The tap conductors shall not penetrate walls, floors, or ceilings.

(g)   The tap shall not be made less than 9.0 m (30 ft) from the floor.

430.29 Constant Voltage Direct-Current Motors — Power Resistors.
Conductors connecting the motor controller to separately mounted power accelerating and dynamic braking resistors in the armature circuit shall have an ampacity not less than the value calculated from Table 430.29 using motor full-load current. If an armature shunt resistor is used, the power accelerating resistor conductor ampacity shall be calculated using the total of motor full-load current and armature shunt resistor current.

Armature shunt resistor conductors shall have an ampacity of not less than that calculated from Table 430.29 using rated shunt resistor current as full-load current.

Table 430.29 Conductor Rating Factors for Power Resistors

Time in Seconds		Ampacity of Conductor in Percent of Full-Load Current
On	**Off**	
5	75	35
10	70	45
15	75	55
15	45	65
15	30	75
15	15	85
Continuous Duty		110

III. Motor and Branch-Circuit Overload Protection

430.31 General.
Part III specifies overload devices intended to protect motors, motor-control apparatus, and motor branch-circuit conductors against excessive heating due to motor overloads and failure to start.

Overload in electrical apparatus is an operating overcurrent that, when it persists for a sufficient length of time, would cause damage or dangerous overheating of the apparatus. It does not include short circuits or ground faults.

These provisions shall not be interpreted as requiring overload protection where it might introduce additional or increased hazards, as in the case of fire pumps.

FPN: For protection of fire pump supply conductors, see 695.6.

The provisions of Part III shall not apply to motor circuits rated over 600 volts, nominal.

FPN No. 1:   For over 600 volts, nominal, see Part XI.

FPN No. 2:   See Annex D, Example No. D8.

430.32 Continuous-Duty Motors.

(A) More Than 1 Horsepower. Each motor used in a continuous duty application and rated more than 1 hp shall be protected against overload by one of the means in 430.32(A)(1) through (A)(4).

(1) Separate Overload Device. A separate overload device that is responsive to motor current. This device shall be selected to trip or shall be rated at no more than the following percent of the motor nameplate full-load current rating:

Motors with a marked service factor 1.15 or greater	125%
Motors with a marked temperature rise 40°C or less	125%
All other motors	115%

Modification of this value shall be permitted as provided in 430.32(C). For a multispeed motor, each winding connection shall be considered separately.

Where a separate motor overload device is connected so that it does not carry the total current designated on the motor nameplate, such as for wye-delta starting, the proper percentage of nameplate current applying to the selection or setting of the overload device shall be clearly designated on the equipment, or the manufacturer's selection table shall take this into account.

FPN: Where power factor correction capacitors are installed on the load side of the motor overload device, see 460.9.

(2) Thermal Protector. A thermal protector integral with the motor, approved for use with the motor it protects on the basis that it will prevent dangerous overheating of the motor due to overload and failure to start. The ultimate trip current of a thermally protected motor shall not exceed the following percentage of motor full-load current given in Table 430.248, Table 430.249, and Table 430.250:

Motor full-load current 9 amperes or less	170%
Motor full-load current from 9.1 to, and including, 20 amperes	156%
Motor full-load current greater than 20 amperes	140%

If the motor current-interrupting device is separate from the motor and its control circuit is operated by a protective device integral with the motor, it shall be arranged so that the opening of the control circuit will result in interruption of current to the motor.

(3) Integral with Motor. A protective device integral with a motor that will protect the motor against damage due to failure to start shall be permitted if the motor is part of an approved assembly that does not normally subject the motor to overloads.

(4) Larger Than 1500 Horsepower. For motors larger than 1500 hp, a protective device having embedded temperature detectors that cause current to the motor to be interrupted when the motor attains a temperature rise greater than marked on the nameplate in an ambient temperature of 40°C.

(B) One Horsepower or Less, Automatically Started. Any motor of 1 hp or less that is started automatically shall be protected against overload by one of the following means.

(1) Separate Overload Device. By a separate overload device following the requirements of 430.32(A)(1).

For a multispeed motor, each winding connection shall be considered separately. Modification of this value shall be permitted as provided in 430.32(C).

(2) Thermal Protector. A thermal protector integral with the motor, approved for use with the motor that it protects on the basis that it will prevent dangerous overheating of the motor due to overload and failure to start. Where the motor current-interrupting device is separate from the motor and its control circuit is operated by a protective device integral with the motor, it shall be arranged so that the opening of the control circuit results in interruption of current to the motor.

(3) Integral with Motor. A protective device integral with a motor that protects the motor against damage due to failure to start shall be permitted (1) if the motor is part of an approved assembly that does not subject the motor to overloads, or (2) if the assembly is also equipped with other safety controls (such

as the safety combustion controls on a domestic oil burner) that protect the motor against damage due to failure to start. Where the assembly has safety controls that protect the motor, it shall be so indicated on the nameplate of the assembly where it will be visible after installation.

(4) Impedance-Protected. If the impedance of the motor windings is sufficient to prevent overheating due to failure to start, the motor shall be permitted to be protected as specified in 430.32(D)(2)(a) for manually started motors if the motor is part of an approved assembly in which the motor will limit itself so that it will not be dangerously overheated.

> FPN: Many ac motors of less than 1/20 hp, such as clock motors, series motors, and so forth, and also some larger motors such as torque motors, come within this classification. It does not include split-phase motors having automatic switches that disconnect the starting windings.

(C) Selection of Overload Relay. Where the sensing element or setting of the overload relay selected in accordance with 430.32(A)(1) and 430.32(B)(1) is not sufficient to start the motor or to carry the load, higher size sensing elements or incremental settings shall be permitted to be used, provided the trip current of the overload relay does not exceed the following percentage of motor nameplate full-load current rating:

Motors with marked service factor 1.15 or greater	140%
Motors with a marked temperature rise 40°C or less	140%
All other motors	130%

If not shunted during the starting period of the motor as provided in 430.35, the overload device shall have sufficient time delay to permit the motor to start and accelerate its load.

> FPN: A Class 20 or Class 30 overload relay will provide a longer motor acceleration time than a Class 10 or Class 20, respectively. Use of a higher class overload relay may preclude the need for selection of a higher trip current.

(D) One Horsepower or Less, Nonautomatically Started.

(1) Permanently Installed. Overload protection shall be in accordance with 430.32(B).

(2) Not Permanently Installed.

(a) Within Sight from Controller. Overload protection shall be permitted to be furnished by the branch circuit short-circuit and ground-fault protective device; such device, however, shall not be larger than that specified in Part IV of Article 430.

Exception: Any such motor shall be permitted on a nominal 120 volt branch circuit protected at not over 20 amperes.

(b) Not Within Sight from Controller. Overload protection shall be in accordance with 430.32(B).

(E) Wound-Rotor Secondaries. The secondary circuits of wound-rotor ac motors, including conductors, controllers, resistors, and so forth, shall be permitted to be protected against overload by the motor-overload device.

430.33 Intermittent and Similar Duty. A motor used for a condition of service that is inherently short-time, intermittent, periodic, or varying duty, as illustrated by Table 430.22(E), shall be permitted to be protected against overload by the branch-circuit short-circuit and ground-fault protective device, provided the protective device rating or setting does not exceed that specified in Table 430.52.

Any motor application shall be considered to be for continuous duty unless the nature of the apparatus it drives is such that the motor cannot operate continuously with load under any condition of use.

430.35 Shunting During Starting Period.

(A) Nonautomatically Started. For a nonautomatically started motor, the overload protection shall be permitted to be shunted or cut out of the circuit during the starting period of the motor if the device by which the overload protection is shunted or cut out cannot be left in the starting position and if fuses or inverse time circuit breakers rated or set at not over 400 percent of the full-load current of the motor are located in the circuit so as to be operative during the starting period of the motor.

(B) Automatically Started. The motor overload protection shall not be shunted or cut out during the starting period if the motor is automatically started.

Exception: The motor overload protection shall be permitted to be shunted or cut out during the starting period on an automatically started motor where the following apply:

(a) The motor starting period exceeds the time delay of available motor overload protective devices, and

(b) Listed means are provided to perform the following:

(1) *Sense motor rotation and automatically prevent the shunting or cutout in the event that the motor fails to start, and*

(2) *Limit the time of overload protection shunting or cutout to less than the locked rotor time rating of the protected motor, and*

(3) *Provide for shutdown and manual restart if motor running condition is not reached.*

430.36 Fuses — In Which Conductor. Where fuses are used for motor overload protection, a fuse shall be inserted in each ungrounded conductor and also in the grounded conductor if the supply system is 3-wire, 3-phase ac with one conductor grounded.

430.37 Devices Other Than Fuses — In Which Conductor. Where devices other than fuses are used for motor overload protection, Table 430.37 shall govern the minimum allowable number and location of overload units such as trip coils or relays.

Table 430.37 Overload Units

Kind of Motor	Supply System	Number and Location of Overload Units, Such as Trip Coils or Relays
1-phase ac or dc	2-wire, 1-phase ac or dc ungrounded	1 in either conductor
1-phase ac or dc	2-wire, 1-phase ac or dc, one conductor grounded	1 in ungrounded conductor
1-phase ac or dc	3-wire, 1-phase ac or dc, grounded neutral	1 in either ungrounded conductor
1-phase ac	Any 3-phase	1 in ungrounded conductor
2-phase ac	3-wire, 2-phase ac, ungrounded	2, one in each phase
2-phase ac	3-wire, 2-phase ac, one conductor grounded	2 in ungrounded conductors
2-phase ac	4-wire, 2-phase ac, grounded or ungrounded	2, one per phase in ungrounded conductors
2-phase ac	Grounded neutral or 5-wire, 2-phase ac, ungrounded	2, one per phase in any ungrounded phase wire
3-phase ac	Any 3-phase	3, one in each phase*

Exception: An overload unit in each phase shall not be required where overload protection is provided by other approved means.

430.38 Number of Conductors Opened by Overload Device. Motor overload devices, other than fuses or thermal protectors, shall simultaneously open a sufficient number of ungrounded conductors to interrupt current flow to the motor.

430.39 Motor Controller as Overload Protection. A motor controller shall also be permitted to serve as an overload device if the number of overload units complies with Table 430.37 and if these units are operative in both the starting and running position in the case of a dc motor, and in the running position in the case of an ac motor.

430.40 Overload Relays. Overload relays and other devices for motor overload protection that are not capable of opening short circuits or ground faults shall be protected by fuses or circuit breakers with ratings or settings in accordance with 430.52 or by a motor short-circuit protector in accordance with 430.52.

Exception: Where approved for group installation and marked to indicate the maximum size of fuse or inverse time circuit breaker by which they must be protected, the overload devices shall be protected in accordance with this marking.

> FPN: For instantaneous trip circuit breakers or motor short-circuit protectors, see 430.52.

430.42 Motors on General-Purpose Branch Circuits. Overload protection for motors used on general-purpose branch circuits as permitted in Article 210 shall be provided as specified in 430.42(A), (B), (C), or (D).

(A) Not Over 1 Horsepower. One or more motors without individual overload protection shall be permitted to be connected to a general-purpose branch circuit only where the installation complies with the limiting conditions specified in 430.32(B) and 430.32(D) and 430.53(A)(1) and (A)(2).

(B) Over 1 Horsepower. Motors of ratings larger than specified in 430.53(A) shall be permitted to be connected to general-purpose branch circuits only where each motor is protected by overload protection selected to protect the motor as specified in 430.32. Both the controller and the motor overload device shall be approved for group installation with the short-circuit and ground-fault protective device selected in accordance with 430.53.

(C) Cord-and-Plug Connected. Where a motor is connected to a branch circuit by means of an attachment plug and receptacle and individual overload protection is omitted as provided in 430.42(A), the rating of the attachment plug and receptacle shall not exceed 15 amperes at 125 volts or 250 volts. Where individual overload protection is required as provided in 430.42(B) for a motor or motor-operated appliance that is attached to the branch circuit through an attachment plug and receptacle, the overload device shall be an integral part of the motor or of the appliance. The rating of the attachment plug and receptacle shall determine the rating of the circuit to which the motor may be connected, as provided in Article 210.

(D) Time Delay. The branch-circuit short-circuit and ground-fault protective device protecting a circuit to which a motor or motor-operated appliance is connected shall have sufficient time delay to permit the motor to start and accelerate its load.

430.43 Automatic Restarting. A motor overload device that can restart a motor automatically after overload tripping shall not be installed unless approved for use with the motor it protects. A motor overload device that can restart a motor automatically after overload tripping shall not be installed if automatic restarting of the motor can result in injury to persons.

430.44 Orderly Shutdown. If immediate automatic shutdown of a motor by a motor overload protective device(s) would introduce additional or increased hazard(s) to a person(s) and continued motor operation is necessary for safe shutdown of equipment or process, a motor overload sensing device(s) conforming with the provisions of Part III of this article shall be permitted to be connected to a supervised alarm instead of causing immediate interruption of the motor circuit, so that corrective action or an orderly shutdown can be initiated.

IV. Motor Branch-Circuit Short-Circuit and Ground-Fault Protection

430.51 General. Part IV specifies devices intended to protect the motor branch-circuit conductors, the motor control apparatus, and the motors against overcurrent due to short circuits or grounds. These rules add to or amend the provisions of Article 240. The devices specified in Part IV do not include the types of devices required by 210.8, 230.95, and 590.6.

The provisions of Part IV shall not apply to motor circuits rated over 600 volts, nominal.

> FPN No. 1: For over 600 volts, nominal, see Part XI.
>
> FPN No. 2: See Annex D, Example D8.

430.52 Rating or Setting for Individual Motor Circuit.

(A) General. The motor branch-circuit short-circuit and ground-fault protective device shall comply with 430.52(B) and either 430.52(C) or 430.52(D), as applicable.

(B) All Motors. The motor branch-circuit short-circuit and ground-fault protective device shall be capable of carrying the starting current of the motor.

(C) Rating or Setting.

(1) In Accordance with Table 430.52. A protective device that has a rating or setting not exceeding the value calculated according to the values given in Table 430.52 shall be used.

Exception No. 1: Where the values for branch-circuit short-circuit and ground-fault protective devices determined by Table 430.52 do not correspond to the standard sizes or ratings of fuses, nonadjustable circuit breakers, thermal protective devices, or possible settings of adjustable circuit breakers, a higher size, rating, or possible setting that does not exceed the next higher standard ampere rating shall be permitted.

Table 430.52 Maximum Rating or Setting of Motor Branch-Circuit Short-Circuit and Ground-Fault Protective Devices

Type of Motor	Percentage of Full-Load Current			
	Nontime Delay Fuse[1]	Dual Element (Time-Delay) Fuse[1]	Instantaneous Trip Breaker	Inverse Time Breaker[2]
Single-phase motors	300	175	800	250
AC polyphase motors other than wound-rotor				
Squirrel cage — other than Design B energy-efficient	300	175	800	250
Design B energy-efficient	300	175	1100	250
Synchronous[3]	300	175	800	250
Wound rotor	150	150	800	150
Direct current (constant voltage)	150	150	250	150

Note: For certain exceptions to the values specified, see 430.54.

[1]The values in the Nontime Delay Fuse column apply to Time-Delay Class CC fuses.

[2]The values given in the last column also cover the ratings of nonadjustable inverse time types of circuit breakers that may be modified as in 430.52(C), Exception No. 1 and No. 2.

[3]Synchronous motors of the low-torque, low-speed type (usually 450 rpm or lower), such as are used to drive reciprocating compressors, pumps, and so forth, that start unloaded, do not require a fuse rating or circuit-breaker setting in excess of 200 percent of full-load current.

Exception No. 2: Where the rating specified in Table 430.52, as modified by Exception No. 1, is not sufficient for the starting current of the motor:

(a) The rating of a nontime-delay fuse not exceeding 600 amperes or a time-delay Class CC fuse shall be permitted to be increased but shall in no case exceed 400 percent of the full-load current.

(b) The rating of a time-delay (dual-element) fuse shall be permitted to be increased but shall in no case exceed 225 percent of the full-load current.

(c) The rating of an inverse time circuit breaker shall be permitted to be increased but shall in no case exceed 400 percent for full-load currents of 100 amperes or less or 300 percent for full-load currents greater than 100 amperes.

(d) The rating of a fuse of 601–6000 ampere classification shall be permitted to be increased but shall in no case exceed 300 percent of the full-load current.

FPN: See Annex D, Example D8, and Figure 430.1.

(2) Overload Relay Table. Where maximum branch-circuit short-circuit and ground-fault protective device ratings are shown in the manufacturer's overload relay table for use with a motor controller or are otherwise marked on the equipment, they shall not be exceeded even if higher values are allowed as shown above.

(3) Instantaneous Trip Circuit Breaker. An instantaneous trip circuit breaker shall be used only if adjustable and if part of a listed combination motor controller having coordinated motor overload and short-circuit and ground-fault protection in each conductor, and the setting is adjusted to no more than the value specified in Table 430.52.

FPN: For the purpose of this article, instantaneous trip circuit breakers may include a damping means to accommodate a transient motor inrush current without nuisance tripping of the circuit breaker.

Exception No. 1: Where the setting specified in Table 430.52 is not sufficient for the starting current of the motor, the setting of an instantaneous trip circuit breaker shall be permitted to be increased but shall in no case exceed 1300 percent of the motor full-load current for other than Design B energy-efficient motors and no more than 1700 percent of full-load motor current for Design B energy-efficient motors. Trip settings above 800 percent for other than Design B energy-efficient motors and above 1100 percent for Design B energy-efficient motors shall be permitted where the need has been demonstrated by engineering evaluation. In such cases, it shall not be necessary to first apply an instantaneous-trip circuit breaker at 800 percent or 1100 percent.

FPN: For additional information on the requirements for a motor to be classified "energy efficient," see NEMA Standards Publication No. MG1-1993, Revision, *Motors and Generators*, Part 12.59.

Exception No. 2: Where the motor full-load current is 8 amperes or less, the setting of the instantaneous-trip circuit breaker with a continuous current rating of 15 amperes or less in a listed combination motor controller that provides coordinated motor branch-circuit overload and short-circuit and ground-fault protection shall be permitted to be increased to the value marked on the controller.

(4) Multispeed Motor. For a multispeed motor, a single short-circuit and ground-fault protective device shall be permitted for two or more windings of the motor, provided the rating of the protective device does not exceed the above applicable percentage of the nameplate rating of the smallest winding protected.

Exception: For a multispeed motor, a single short-circuit and ground-fault protective device shall be permitted to be used and sized according to the full-load current of the highest current winding, where all of the following conditions are met:

(a) Each winding is equipped with individual overload protection sized according to its full-load current.

(b) The branch-circuit conductors supplying each winding are sized according to the full-load current of the highest full-load current winding.

(c) The controller for each winding has a horsepower rating not less than that required for the winding having the highest horsepower rating.

(5) Power Electronic Devices. Suitable fuses shall be permitted in lieu of devices listed in Table 430.52 for power electronic devices in a solid state motor controller system, provided that the marking for replacement fuses is provided adjacent to the fuses.

(6) Self-Protected Combination Controller. A listed self-protected combination controller shall be permitted in lieu of the devices specified in Table 430.52. Adjustable instantaneous-trip settings shall not exceed 1300 percent of full-load motor current for other than Design B energy-efficient motors and not more than 1700 percent of full-load motor current for Design B energy-efficient motors.

> FPN: Proper application of self-protected combination controllers on 3-phase systems, other than solidly grounded wye, particularly on corner grounded delta systems, considers the self-protected combination controllers' individual pole-interrupting capability.

(7) Motor Short-Circuit Protector. A motor short-circuit protector shall be permitted in lieu of devices listed in Table 430.52 if the motor short-circuit protector is part of a listed combination motor controller having coordinated motor overload protection and short-circuit and ground-fault protection in each conductor and it will open the circuit at currents exceeding 1300 percent of motor full-load current for other than Design B energy-efficient motors and 1700 percent of motor full-load motor current for Design B energy-efficient motors.

(D) Torque Motors. Torque motor branch circuits shall be protected at the motor nameplate current rating in accordance with 240.4(B).

430.53 Several Motors or Loads on One Branch Circuit. Two or more motors or one or more motors and other loads shall be permitted to be connected to the same branch circuit under conditions specified in 430.53(D) and in 430.53(A), (B), or (C).

(A) Not Over 1 Horsepower. Several motors, each not exceeding 1 hp in rating, shall be permitted on a nominal 120-volt branch circuit protected at not over 20 amperes or a branch circuit of 600 volts, nominal, or less, protected at not over 15 amperes, if all of the following conditions are met:

(1) The full-load rating of each motor does not exceed 6 amperes.

(2) The rating of the branch-circuit short-circuit and ground-fault protective device marked on any of the controllers is not exceeded.

(3) Individual overload protection conforms to 430.32.

(B) If Smallest Rated Motor Protected. If the branch-circuit short-circuit and ground-fault protective device is selected not to exceed that allowed by 430.52 for the smallest rated motor, two or more motors or one or more motors and other load(s), with each motor having individual overload protection, shall be permitted to be connected to a branch circuit where it can be determined that the branch-circuit short-circuit and ground-fault protective device will not open under the most severe normal conditions of service that might be encountered.

(C) Other Group Installations. Two or more motors of any rating or one or more motors and other load(s), with each motor having individual overload protection, shall be permitted to be connected to one branch circuit where the motor controller(s) and overload device(s) are (1) installed as a listed factory assembly and the motor branch-circuit short-circuit and ground-fault protective device either is provided as part of the assembly or is specified by a marking on the assembly, or (2) the motor branch-circuit short-circuit and ground-fault protective device, the motor controller(s), and overload device(s) are field-installed as separate assemblies listed for such use and provided with manufacturers' instructions for use with each other, and (3) all of the following conditions are complied with:

(1) Each motor overload device is listed for group installation with a specified maximum rating of fuse, inverse time circuit breaker, or both.

(2) Each motor controller is listed for group installation with a specified maximum rating of fuse, circuit breaker, or both.

(3) Each circuit breaker is listed and is of the inverse time type.

(4) The branch circuit shall be protected by fuses or inverse time circuit breakers having a rating not exceeding that specified in 430.52 for the highest rated motor connected to the branch circuit plus an amount equal to the sum of the full-load current ratings of all other motors and the ratings of other loads connected to the circuit. Where this calculation results in a rating less than the ampacity of the supply conductors, it shall be permitted to increase the maximum rating of the fuses or circuit breaker to a value not exceeding that permitted by 240.4(B).

(5) The branch-circuit fuses or inverse time circuit breakers are not larger than allowed by 430.40 for the overload relay protecting the smallest rated motor of the group.

(6) Overcurrent protection for loads other than motor loads shall be in accordance with Parts I through VII of Article 240.

> FPN: See 110.10 for circuit impedance and other characteristics.

(D) Single Motor Taps. For group installations described above, the conductors of any tap supplying a single motor shall not be required to have an individual branch-circuit short-circuit and ground-fault protective device, provided they comply with one of the following:

(1) No conductor to the motor shall have an ampacity less than that of the branch-circuit conductors.

(2) No conductor to the motor shall have an ampacity less than one-third that of the branch-circuit conductors, with a minimum in accordance with 430.22, the conductors to the motor overload device being not more than 7.5 m (25 ft) long and being protected from physical damage.

(3) Conductors from the branch-circuit short-circuit and ground-fault protective device to a listed manual motor controller additionally marked "Suitable for Tap Conductor Protection in Group Installations" shall be permitted to have an ampacity not less than ¹⁄₁₀ the rating or setting of the branch-circuit short-circuit and ground-fault protective device. The conductors from the controller to the motor shall have an ampacity in accordance with 430.22. The conductors from the branch-circuit short-circuit and ground-fault protective device to the controller shall (1) be suitably protected from physical damage and enclosed either by an enclosed controller or by a raceway and shall be not more than 3 m (10 ft) long or (2) shall have an ampacity not less than that of the branch circuit conductors.

430.54 Multimotor and Combination-Load Equipment. The rating of the branch-circuit short-circuit and ground-fault protective device for multimotor and combination-load equipment shall not exceed the rating marked on the equipment in accordance with 430.7(D).

430.55 Combined Overcurrent Protection. Motor branch-circuit short-circuit and ground-fault protection and motor overload protection shall be permitted to be combined in a single protective device where the rating or setting of the device provides the overload protection specified in 430.32.

430.56 Branch-Circuit Protective Devices — In Which Conductor. Branch-circuit protective devices shall comply with the provisions of 240.20.

430.57 Size of Fuseholder. Where fuses are used for motor branch-circuit short-circuit and ground-fault protection, the fuseholders shall not be of a smaller size than required to accommodate the fuses specified by Table 430.52.

Exception: Where fuses having time delay appropriate for the starting characteristics of the motor are used, it shall be permitted to use fuseholders sized to fit the fuses that are used.

430.58 Rating of Circuit Breaker. A circuit breaker for motor branch-circuit short-circuit and ground-fault protection shall have a current rating in accordance with 430.52 and 430.110.

V. Motor Feeder Short-Circuit and Ground-Fault Protection

430.61 General. Part V specifies protective devices intended to protect feeder conductors supplying motors against overcurrents due to short circuits or grounds.

FPN: See Annex D, Example D8.

430.62 Rating or Setting — Motor Load.

(A) Specific Load. A feeder supplying a specific fixed motor load(s) and consisting of conductor sizes based on 430.24 shall be provided with a protective device having a rating or setting not greater than the largest rating or setting of the branch-circuit short-circuit and ground-fault protective device for any motor supplied by the feeder [based on the maximum permitted value for the specific type of a protective device in accordance with 430.52, or 440.22(A) for hermetic refrigerant motor-compressors], plus the sum of the full-load currents of the other motors of the group.

Where the same rating or setting of the branch-circuit short-circuit and ground-fault protective device is used on two or more of the branch circuits supplied by the feeder, one of the protective devices shall be considered the largest for the above calculations.

Exception No. 1: Where one or more instantaneous trip circuit breakers or motor short-circuit protectors are used for motor branch-circuit short-circuit and ground-fault protection as permitted in 430.52(C), the procedure provided above for determining the maximum rating of the feeder protective device shall apply with the following provision: For the purpose of the calculation, each instantaneous trip circuit breaker or motor short-circuit protector shall be assumed to have a rating not exceeding the maximum percentage of motor full-load current permitted by Table 430.52 for the type of feeder protective device employed.

Exception No. 2: Where the feeder overcurrent protective device also provides overcurrent protection for a motor control center, the provisions of 430.94 shall apply.

FPN: See Annex D, Example D8.

(B) Other Installations. Where feeder conductors have an ampacity greater than required by 430.24, the rating or setting of the feeder overcurrent protective device shall be permitted to be based on the ampacity of the feeder conductors.

430.63 Rating or Setting — Power and Lighting Loads. Where a feeder supplies a motor load and, in addition, a lighting or a lighting and appliance load, the feeder protective device shall have a rating sufficient to carry the lighting or lighting and appliance load, plus the following:

(1) For a single motor, the rating permitted by 430.52

(2) For a single hermetic refrigerant motor-compressor, the rating permitted by 440.22

(3) For two or more motors, the rating permitted by 430.62

Exception: Where the feeder overcurrent device provides the overcurrent protection for a motor control center, the provisions of 430.94 shall apply.

VI. Motor Control Circuits

430.71 General. Part VI contains modifications of the general requirements and applies to the particular conditions of motor control circuits.

    FPN: See 430.9(B) for equipment device terminal requirements.

430.72 Overcurrent Protection.

(A) General. A motor control circuit tapped from the load side of a motor branch-circuit short-circuit and ground-fault protective device(s) and functioning to control the motor(s) connected to that branch circuit shall be protected against overcurrent in accordance with 430.72. Such a tapped control circuit shall not be considered to be a branch circuit and shall be permitted to be protected by either a supplementary or branch-circuit overcurrent protective device(s). A motor control circuit other than such a tapped control circuit shall be protected against overcurrent in accordance with 725.23 or the notes to Table 11(A) and Table 11(B) in Chapter 9, as applicable.

(B) Conductor Protection. The overcurrent protection for conductors shall be provided as specified in 430.72(B)(1) or (B)(2).

Exception No. 1: Where the opening of the control circuit would create a hazard as, for example, the control circuit of a fire pump motor, and the like, conductors of control circuits shall require only short-circuit and ground-fault protection and shall be permitted to be protected by the motor branch-circuit short-circuit and ground-fault protective device(s).

Exception No. 2: Conductors supplied by the secondary side of a single-phase transformer having only a two-wire (single-voltage) secondary shall be permitted to be protected by overcurrent protection provided on the primary (supply) side of the transformer, provided this protection does not exceed the value determined by multiplying the appropriate maximum rating of the overcurrent device for the secondary conductor from Table 430.72(B) by the secondary-to-primary voltage ratio. Transformer secondary conductors (other than two-wire) shall not be considered to be protected by the primary overcurrent protection.

(1) Separate Overcurrent Protection. Where the motor branch-circuit short-circuit and ground-fault protective device does not provide protection in accordance with 430.72(B)(2), separate overcurrent protection shall be provided. The overcurrent protection shall not exceed the values specified in Column A of Table 430.72(B).

(2) Branch-Circuit Overcurrent Protective Device. Conductors shall be permitted to be protected by the motor branch-circuit short-circuit and ground-fault protective device and shall require only short-circuit and ground-fault protection. Where the conductors do not extend beyond the motor control equipment enclosure, the rating of the protective device(s) shall not exceed the value specified in Column B of Table 430.72(B). Where the conductors extend beyond the motor control equipment enclosure, the rating of the protective device(s) shall not exceed the value specified in Column C of Table 430.72(B).

Table 430.72(B) Maximum Rating of Overcurrent Protective Device in Amperes

| | Column A Separate Protection Provided | | Protection Provided by Motor Branch-Circuit Protective Device(s) | | | |
| | | | Column B Conductors Within Enclosure | | Column C Conductors Extend Beyond Enclosure | |
Control Circuit Conductor Size (AWG)	Copper	Aluminum or Copper-Clad Aluminum	Copper	Aluminum or Copper-Clad Aluminum	Copper	Aluminum or Copper-Clad Aluminum
18	7	—	25	—	7	—
16	10	—	40	—	10	—
14	(Note 1)	—	100	—	45	—
12	(Note 1)	(Note 1)	120	100	60	45
10	(Note 1)	(Note 1)	160	140	90	75
Larger than 10	(Note 1)	(Note 1)	(Note 2)	(Note 2)	(Note 3)	(Note 3)

Notes:
1. Value specified in 310.15 as applicable.
2. 400 percent of value specified in Table 310.17 for 60°C conductors.
3. 300 percent of value specified in Table 310.16 for 60°C conductors.

(C) Control Circuit Transformer. Where a motor control circuit transformer is provided, the transformer shall be protected in accordance with 430.72(C)(1), (C)(2), (C)(3), (C)(4), or (C)(5).

Exception: Overcurrent protection shall be omitted where the opening of the control circuit would create a hazard as, for example, the control circuit of a fire pump motor and the like.

(1) Compliance with Article 725. Where the transformer supplies a Class 1 power-limited circuit, Class 2, or Class 3 remote-control circuit conforming with the requirements of Article 725, protection shall comply with Article 725.

(2) Compliance with Article 450. Protection shall be permitted to be provided in accordance with 450.3.

(3) Less Than 50 Volt-Amperes. Control circuit transformers rated less than 50 volt-amperes (VA) and that are an integral part of the motor controller and located within the motor controller enclosure shall be permitted to be protected by primary overcurrent devices, impedance limiting means, or other inherent protective means.

(4) Primary Less Than 2 Amperes. Where the control circuit transformer rated primary current is less than 2 amperes, an overcurrent device rated or set at not more than 500 percent of the rated primary current shall be permitted in the primary circuit.

(5) Other Means. Protection shall be permitted to be provided by other approved means.

430.73 Mechanical Protection of Conductor. Where damage to a motor control circuit would constitute a hazard, all conductors of such a remote motor control circuit that are outside the control device itself shall be installed in a raceway or be otherwise suitably protected from physical damage.

Where one side of the motor control circuit is grounded, the motor control circuit shall be arranged so that an accidental ground in the control circuit remote from the motor controller will (1) not start the motor and (2) not bypass manually operated shutdown devices or automatic safety shutdown devices.

430.74 Disconnection.

(A) General. Motor control circuits shall be arranged so that they will be disconnected from all sources of supply when the disconnecting means is in the open position. The disconnecting means shall be permitted to consist of two or more separate devices, one of which disconnects the motor and the controller from the source(s) of power supply for the motor, and the other(s), the motor control circuit(s) from its power supply. Where separate devices are used, they shall be located immediately adjacent to each other.

Exception No. 1: Where more than 12 motor control circuit conductors are required to be disconnected, the disconnecting means shall be permitted to be located other than immediately adjacent to each other where all of the following conditions are complied with:

(a) Access to energized parts is limited to qualified persons in accordance with Part XI of this article.

(b) A warning sign is permanently located on the outside of each equipment enclosure door or cover permitting access to the live parts in the motor control circuit(s), warning that motor control circuit disconnecting means are remotely located and specifying the location and identification of each disconnect. Where energized parts are not in an equipment enclosure as permitted by 430.232 and 430.233, an additional warning sign(s) shall be located where visible to persons who may be working in the area of the energized parts.

Exception No. 2: The motor control circuit disconnecting means shall be permitted to be remote from the motor controller power supply disconnecting means where the opening of one or more motor control circuit disconnect means may result in potentially unsafe conditions for personnel or property and the conditions of items (a) and (b) of Exception No. 1 are complied with.

(B) Control Transformer in Controller Enclosure. Where a transformer or other device is used to obtain a reduced voltage for the motor control circuit and is located in the controller enclosure, such transformer or other device shall be connected to the load side of the disconnecting means for the motor control circuit.

VII. Motor Controllers

430.81 General. Part VII is intended to require suitable controllers for all motors.

(A) Stationary Motor of ⅛ Horsepower or Less. For a stationary motor rated at ⅛ hp or less that is normally left running and is constructed so that it cannot be damaged by overload or failure to start, such as clock motors and the like, the branch-circuit protective device shall be permitted to serve as the controller.

(B) Portable Motor of ⅓ Horsepower or Less. For a portable motor rated at ⅓ hp or less, the controller shall be permitted to be an attachment plug and receptacle.

430.82 Controller Design.

(A) Starting and Stopping. Each controller shall be capable of starting and stopping the motor it controls and shall be capable of interrupting the locked-rotor current of the motor.

(B) Autotransformer. An autotransformer starter shall provide an "off" position, a running position, and at least one starting position. It shall be designed so that it cannot rest in the starting position or in any position that will render the overload device in the circuit inoperative.

(C) Rheostats. Rheostats shall be in compliance with the following:

(1) Motor-starting rheostats shall be designed so that the contact arm cannot be left on intermediate segments. The point or plate on which the arm rests when in the starting position shall have no electrical connection with the resistor.

(2) Motor-starting rheostats for dc motors operated from a constant voltage supply shall be equipped with automatic devices that will interrupt the supply before the speed of the motor has fallen to less than one-third its normal rate.

430.83 Ratings. The controller shall have a rating as specified in 430.83(A), unless otherwise permitted in 430.83(B) or 430.83(C), or as specified in 430.83(D), under the conditions specified.

(A) General.

(1) Horsepower Ratings. Controllers, other than inverse time circuit breakers and molded case switches, shall have horsepower ratings at the application voltage not lower than the horsepower rating of the motor.

(2) Circuit Breaker. A branch-circuit inverse time circuit breaker rated in amperes shall be permitted as a controller for all motors. Where this circuit breaker is also used for overload protection, it shall conform to the appropriate provisions of this article governing overload protection.

(3) Molded Case Switch. A molded case switch rated in amperes shall be permitted as a controller for all motors.

(B) Small Motors. Devices as specified in 430.81(A) and 430.81(B) shall be permitted as a controller.

(C) Stationary Motors of 2 Horsepower or Less. For stationary motors rated at 2 hp or less and 300 volts or less, the controller shall be permitted to be either of the following:

(1) A general-use switch having an ampere rating not less than twice the full-load current rating of the motor

(2) On ac circuits, a general-use snap switch suitable only for use on ac (not general-use ac–dc snap switches) where the motor full-load current rating is not more than 80 percent of the ampere rating of the switch

(D) Torque Motors. For torque motors, the controller shall have a continuous-duty, full-load current rating not less than the nameplate current rating of the motor. For a motor controller rated in horsepower but not marked with the foregoing

current rating, the equivalent current rating shall be determined from the horsepower rating by using Table 430.247, Table 430.248, Table 430.249, or Table 430.250.

(E) Voltage Rating. A controller with a straight voltage rating, for example, 240 volts or 480 volts, shall be permitted to be applied in a circuit in which the nominal voltage between any two conductors does not exceed the controller's voltage rating. A controller with a slash rating, for example, 240/120 volts or 480Y/277 volts, shall only be applied in a solidly grounded circuit in which the nominal voltage to ground from any conductor does not exceed the lower of the two values of the controller's voltage rating and the nominal voltage between any two conductors does not exceed the higher value of the controller's voltage rating.

430.84 Need Not Open All Conductors. The controller shall not be required to open all conductors to the motor.

Exception: Where the controller serves also as a disconnecting means, it shall open all ungrounded conductors to the motor as provided in 430.111.

430.85 In Grounded Conductors. One pole of the controller shall be permitted to be placed in a permanently grounded conductor, provided the controller is designed so that the pole in the grounded conductor cannot be opened without simultaneously opening all conductors of the circuit.

430.87 Number of Motors Served by Each Controller. Each motor shall be provided with an individual controller.

Exception: For motors rated 600 volts or less, a single controller rated at not less than the equivalent horsepower, as determined in accordance with 430.110(C)(1), of all the motors in the group shall be permitted to serve the group under any of the following conditions:

(a) Where a number of motors drive several parts of a single machine or piece of apparatus, such as metal and woodworking machines, cranes, hoists, and similar apparatus

(b) Where a group of motors is under the protection of one overcurrent device as permitted in 430.53(A)

(c) Where a group of motors is located in a single room within sight from the controller location

430.88 Adjustable-Speed Motors. Adjustable-speed motors that are controlled by means of field regulation shall be equipped and connected so that they cannot be started under a weakened field.

Exception: Starting under a weakened field shall be permitted where the motor is designed for such starting.

430.89 Speed Limitation. Machines of the following types shall be provided with speed-limiting devices or other speed-limiting means:

(1) Separately excited dc motors

(2) Series motors

(3) Motor-generators and converters that can be driven at excessive speed from the dc end, as by a reversal of current or decrease in load

Exception: Separate speed-limiting devices or means shall not be required under either of the following conditions:

(1) Where the inherent characteristics of the machines, the system, or the load and the mechanical connection thereto are such as to safely limit the speed

(2) Where the machine is always under the manual control of a qualified operator

430.90 Combination Fuseholder and Switch as Controller. The rating of a combination fuseholder and switch used as a motor controller shall be such that the fuseholder will accommodate the size of the fuse specified in Part III of this article for motor overload protection.

Exception: Where fuses having time delay appropriate for the starting characteristics of the motor are used, fuseholders of smaller size than specified in Part III of this article shall be permitted.

430.91 Motor Controller Enclosure Types. Table 430.91 provides the basis for selecting enclosures for use in specific locations other than hazardous (classified) locations. The enclosures are not intended to protect against conditions such as condensation, icing, corrosion, or contamination that may occur within the enclosure or enter via the conduit or unsealed openings. These internal conditions shall require special consideration by the installer and user.

VIII. Motor Control Centers

430.92 General. Part VIII covers motor control centers installed for the control of motors, lighting, and power circuits.

430.94 Overcurrent Protection. Motor control centers shall be provided with overcurrent protection in accordance with Parts I, II, and IX of Article 240. The ampere rating or setting of the overcurrent protective device shall not exceed the rating of the common power bus. This protection shall be provided by (1) an overcurrent protective device located ahead of the motor control center or (2) a main overcurrent protective device located within the motor control center.

430.95 Service-Entrance Equipment. Where used as service equipment, each motor control center shall be provided with a single main disconnecting means to disconnect all ungrounded service conductors.

Exception: A second service disconnect shall be permitted to supply additional equipment.

Where a grounded conductor is provided, the motor control center shall be provided with a main bonding jumper, sized in accordance with 250.28(D), within one of the sections for connecting the grounded conductor, on its supply side, to the motor control center equipment ground bus.

Exception: High-impedance grounded neutral systems shall be permitted to be connected as provided in 250.36.

430.96 Grounding. Multisection motor control centers shall be bonded together with an equipment grounding conductor or an equivalent grounding bus sized in accordance with Table 250.122. Equipment grounding conductors shall terminate on this grounding bus or to a grounding termination point provided in a single-section motor control center.

430.97 Busbars and Conductors.

(A) Support and Arrangement. Busbars shall be protected from physical damage and be held firmly in place. Other than for required interconnections and control wiring, only those conductors that are intended for termination in a vertical section shall be located in that section.

Exception: Conductors shall be permitted to travel horizontally through vertical sections where such conductors are isolated from the busbars by a barrier.

(B) Phase Arrangement. The phase arrangement on 3-phase horizontal common power and vertical buses shall be A, B, C from front to back, top to bottom, or left to right, as viewed from the front of the motor control center. The B phase shall be that phase having the higher voltage to ground on 3-phase, 4-wire, delta-connected systems. Other busbar arrangements shall be permitted for additions to existing installations and shall be marked.

Exception: Rear-mounted units connected to a vertical bus that is common to front-mounted units shall be permitted to have a C, B, A phase arrangement where properly identified.

(C) Minimum Wire-Bending Space. The minimum wire-bending space at the motor control center terminals and minimum gutter space shall be as required in Article 312.

(D) Spacings. Spacings between motor control center bus terminals and other bare metal parts shall not be less than specified in Table 430.97.

(E) Barriers. Barriers shall be placed in all service-entrance motor control centers to isolate service busbars and terminals from the remainder of the motor control center.

430.98 Marking.

(A) Motor Control Centers. Motor control centers shall be marked according to 110.21, and such marking shall be plainly visible after installation. Marking shall also include common power bus current rating and motor control center short-circuit rating.

Table 430.91 Motor Controller Enclosure Selection

For Outdoor Use

Provides a Degree of Protection Against the Following Environmental Conditions	Enclosure Type Number[1]									
	3	3R	3S	3X	3RX	3SX	4	4X	6	6P
Incidental contact with the enclosed equipment	X	X	X	X	X	X	X	X	X	X
Rain, snow, and sleet	X	X	X	X	X	X	X	X	X	X
Sleet[2]	—	—	X	—	—	X	—	—	—	—
Windblown dust	X	—	X	X	—	X	X	X	X	X
Hosedown	—	—	—	—	—	—	X	X	X	X
Corrosive agents	—	—	—	X	X	X	—	X	—	X
Temporary submersion	—	—	—	—	—	—	—	—	X	X
Prolonged submersion	—	—	—	—	—	—	—	—	—	X

For Indoor Use

Provides a Degree of Protection Against the Following Environmental Conditions	Enclosure Type Number[1]									
	1	2	4	4X	5	6	6P	12	12K	13
Incidental contact with the enclosed equipment	X	X	X	X	X	X	X	X	X	X
Falling dirt	X	X	X	X	X	X	X	X	X	X
Falling liquids and light splashing	—	X	X	X	X	X	X	X	X	X
Circulating dust, lint, fibers, and flyings	—	—	X	X	—	X	X	X	X	X
Settling airborne dust, lint, fibers, and flyings	—	—	X	X	X	X	X	X	X	X
Hosedown and splashing water	—	—	X	X	—	X	X	—	—	—
Oil and coolant seepage	—	—	—	—	—	—	—	X	X	X
Oil or coolant spraying and splashing	—	—	—	—	—	—	—	—	—	X
Corrosive agents	—	—	—	X	—	—	X	—	—	—
Temporary submersion	—	—	—	—	—	X	X	—	—	—
Prolonged submersion	—	—	—	—	—	—	X	—	—	—

[1]Enclosure type number shall be marked on the motor controller enclosure.

[2]Mechanism shall be operable when ice covered.

FPN: The term *raintight* is typically used in conjunction with Enclosure Types 3, 3S, 3SX, 3X, 4, 4X, 6, 6P. The term *rainproof* is typically used in conjunction with Enclosure Type 3R, 3RX. The term *watertight* is typically used in conjunction with Enclosure Types 4, 4X, 6, 6P. The term *driptight* is typically used in conjunction with Enclosure Types 2, 5, 12, 12K, 13. The term *dusttight* is typically used in conjunction with Enclosure Types 3, 3S, 3SX, 3X, 5, 12, 12K, 13.

Table 430.97 Minimum Spacing Between Bare Metal Parts

Nominal Voltage	Opposite Polarity Where Mounted on the Same Surface		Opposite Polarity Where Held Free in Air		Live Parts to Ground	
	mm	in.	mm	in.	mm	in.
Not over 125 volts, nominal	19.1	¾	12.7	½	12.7	½
Not over 250 volts, nominal	31.8	1¼	19.1	¾	12.7	½
Not over 600 volts, nominal	50.8	2	25.4	1	25.4	1

(B) Motor Control Units. Motor control units in a motor control center shall comply with 430.8.

IX. Disconnecting Means

430.101 General. Part IX is intended to require disconnecting means capable of disconnecting motors and controllers from the circuit.

> FPN No. 1: See Figure 430.1.

> FPN No. 2: See 110.22 for identification of disconnecting means.

430.102 Location.

(A) Controller. An individual disconnecting means shall be provided for each controller and shall disconnect the controller. The disconnecting means shall be located in sight from the controller location.

Exception No. 1: For motor circuits over 600 volts, nominal, a controller disconnecting means capable of being locked in the open position shall be permitted to be out of sight of the controller, provided the controller is marked with a warning label giving the location of the disconnecting means.

Exception No. 2: A single disconnecting means shall be permitted for a group of coordinated controllers that drive several parts of a single machine or piece of apparatus. The disconnecting means shall be located in sight from the controllers, and both the disconnecting means and the controllers shall be located in sight from the machine or apparatus.

(B) Motor. A disconnecting means shall be located in sight from the motor location and the driven machinery location.

Exception: The disconnecting means shall not be required to be in sight from the motor and the driven machinery location under either condition (a) or (b), provided the disconnecting means required in accordance with 430.102(A) is individually capable of being locked in the open position. The provision for locking or adding a lock to the disconnecting means shall be installed on or at the switch or circuit breaker used as the disconnecting means and shall remain in place with or without the lock installed.

(a) Where such a location of the disconnecting means is impracticable or introduces additional or increased hazards to persons or property

(b) In industrial installations, with written safety procedures, where conditions of maintenance and supervision ensure that only qualified persons service the equipment

> FPN No. 1: Some examples of increased or additional hazards include, but are not limited to, motors rated in excess of 100 hp, multimotor equipment, submersible motors, motors associated with adjustable speed drives, and motors located in hazardous (classified) locations.

> FPN No. 2: For information on lockout/tagout procedures, see NFPA 70E-2004, *Standard for Electrical Safety in the Workplace.*

The disconnecting means required in accordance with 430.102(A) shall be permitted to serve as the disconnecting means for the motor if it is located in sight from the motor location and the driven machinery location.

430.103 Operation. The disconnecting means shall open all ungrounded supply conductors and shall be designed so that no pole can be operated independently. The disconnecting means shall be permitted in the same enclosure with the controller.

> FPN: See 430.113 for equipment receiving energy from more than one source.

430.104 To Be Indicating. The disconnecting means shall plainly indicate whether it is in the open (off) or closed (on) position.

430.105 Grounded Conductors. One pole of the disconnecting means shall be permitted to disconnect a permanently grounded conductor, provided the disconnecting means is designed so that the pole in the grounded conductor cannot be opened without simultaneously disconnecting all conductors of the circuit.

430.107 Readily Accessible. At least one of the disconnecting means shall be readily accessible.

430.108 Every Disconnecting Means. Every disconnecting means in the motor circuit between the point of attachment to the feeder and the point of connection to the motor shall comply with the requirements of 430.109 and 430.110.

430.109 Type. The disconnecting means shall be a type specified in 430.109(A), unless otherwise permitted in 430.109(B) through 430.109(G), under the conditions specified.

(A) General.

(1) Motor Circuit Switch. A listed motor-circuit switch rated in horsepower.

(2) Molded Case Circuit Breaker. A listed molded case circuit breaker.

(3) Molded Case Switch. A listed molded case switch.

(4) Instantaneous Trip Circuit Breaker. An instantaneous trip circuit breaker that is part of a listed combination motor controller.

(5) Self-Protected Combination Controller. Listed self-protected combination controller.

(6) Manual Motor Controller. Listed manual motor controllers additionally marked "Suitable as Motor Disconnect" shall be permitted as a disconnecting means where installed between the final motor branch-circuit short-circuit protective device and the motor. Listed manual motor controllers additionally marked "Suitable as Motor Disconnect" shall be permitted as disconnecting means on the line side of the fuses permitted in 430.52(C)(5). In this case, the fuses permitted in 430.52(C)(5) shall be considered supplementary fuses, and suitable branch-circuit short-circuit and ground-fault protective devices shall be installed on the line side of the manual motor controller additionally marked "Suitable as Motor Disconnect."

(7) System Isolation Equipment. System isolation equipment shall be listed for disconnection purposes. System isolation equipment shall be installed on the load side of the overcurrent protection and its disconnecting means. The disconnecting means shall be one of the types permitted by 430.109(A)(1) through (A)(3).

(B) Stationary Motors of ⅛ Horsepower or Less. For stationary motors of ⅛ hp or less, the branch-circuit overcurrent device shall be permitted to serve as the disconnecting means.

(C) Stationary Motors of 2 Horsepower or Less. For stationary motors rated at 2 hp or less and 300 volts or less, the disconnecting means shall be permitted to be one of the devices specified in (1), (2), or (3):

(1) A general-use switch having an ampere rating not less than twice the full-load current rating of the motor

(2) On ac circuits, a general-use snap switch suitable only for use on ac (not general-use ac–dc snap switches) where the motor full-load current rating is not more than 80 percent of the ampere rating of the switch

(3) A listed manual motor controller having a horsepower rating not less than the rating of the motor and marked "Suitable as Motor Disconnect"

(D) Autotransformer-Type Controlled Motors. For motors of over 2 hp to and including 100 hp, the separate disconnecting means required for a motor with an autotransformer-type controller shall be permitted to be a general-use switch where all of the following provisions are met:

(1) The motor drives a generator that is provided with overload protection.

(2) The controller is capable of interrupting the locked-rotor current of the motors, is provided with a no voltage release, and is provided with running overload protection not exceeding 125 percent of the motor full-load current rating.

(3) Separate fuses or an inverse time circuit breaker rated or set at not more than 150 percent of the motor full-load current are provided in the motor branch circuit.

(E) Isolating Switches. For stationary motors rated at more than 40 hp dc or 100 hp ac, the disconnecting means shall be permitted to be a general-use or isolating switch where plainly marked "Do not operate under load."

(F) Cord-and-Plug-Connected Motors. For a cord-and-plug-connected motor, a horsepower-rated attachment plug and receptacle having ratings no less than the motor ratings shall be permitted to serve as the disconnecting means. A horsepower-rated attachment plug and receptacle shall not be required for a cord-and-plug-connected appliance in accordance with 422.32, a room air conditioner in accordance with 440.63, or a portable motor rated ⅓ hp or less.

(G) Torque Motors. For torque motors, the disconnecting means shall be permitted to be a general-use switch.

430.110 Ampere Rating and Interrupting Capacity.

(A) General. The disconnecting means for motor circuits rated 600 volts, nominal, or less shall have an ampere rating not less than 115 percent of the full-load current rating of the motor.

Exception: A listed nonfused motor-circuit switch having a horsepower rating not less than the motor horsepower shall be permitted to have an ampere rating less than 115 percent of the full-load current rating of the motor.

(B) For Torque Motors. Disconnecting means for a torque motor shall have an ampere rating of at least 115 percent of the motor nameplate current.

(C) For Combination Loads. Where two or more motors are used together or where one or more motors are used in combination with other loads, such as resistance heaters, and where the combined load may be simultaneous on a single disconnecting means, the ampere and horsepower ratings of the combined load shall be determined as follows.

(1) Horsepower Rating. The rating of the disconnecting means shall be determined from the sum of all currents, including resistance loads, at the full-load condition and also at the locked-rotor condition. The combined full-load current and the combined locked-rotor current so obtained shall be considered as a single motor for the purpose of this requirement as follows.

The full-load current equivalent to the horsepower rating of each motor shall be selected from Table 430.247, Table 430.248, Table 430.249, or Table 430.250. These full-load currents shall be added to the rating in amperes of other loads to obtain an equivalent full-load current for the combined load.

The locked-rotor current equivalent to the horsepower rating of each motor shall be selected from Table 430.251(A) or Table 430.251(B). The locked-rotor currents shall be added to the rating in amperes of other loads to obtain an equivalent locked-rotor current for the combined load. Where two or more motors or other loads cannot be started simultaneously, the largest sum of locked rotor currents of a motor or group of motors that can be started simultaneously and the full load currents of other concurrent loads shall be permitted to be used to determine the equivalent locked-rotor current for the simultaneous combined loads.

Exception: Where part of the concurrent load is resistance load, and where the disconnecting means is a switch rated in horsepower and amperes, the switch used shall be permitted to have a horsepower rating that is not less than the combined load of the motor(s), if the ampere rating of the switch is not less than the locked-rotor current of the motor(s) plus the resistance load.

(2) Ampere Rating. The ampere rating of the disconnecting means shall not be less than 115 percent of the sum of all currents at the full-load condition determined in accordance with 430.110(C)(1).

Exception: A listed nonfused motor-circuit switch having a horsepower rating equal to or greater than the equivalent horsepower of the combined loads, determined in accordance with 430.110(C)(1), shall be permitted to have an ampere rating less than 115 percent of the sum of all currents at the full-load condition.

(3) Small Motors. For small motors not covered by Table 430.247, Table 430.248, Table 430.249, or Table 430.250,

the locked-rotor current shall be assumed to be six times the full-load current.

430.111 Switch or Circuit Breaker as Both Controller and Disconnecting Means. A switch or circuit breaker shall be permitted to be used as both the controller and disconnecting means if it complies with 430.111(A) and is one of the types specified in 430.111(B).

(A) General. The switch or circuit breaker complies with the requirements for controllers specified in 430.83, opens all ungrounded conductors to the motor, and is protected by an overcurrent device in each ungrounded conductor (which shall be permitted to be the branch-circuit fuses). The overcurrent device protecting the controller shall be permitted to be part of the controller assembly or shall be permitted to be separate. An autotransformer-type controller shall be provided with a separate disconnecting means.

(B) Type. The device shall be one of the types specified in 430.111(B)(1), (B)(2), or (B)(3).

(1) Air-Break Switch. An air-break switch, operable directly by applying the hand to a lever or handle.

(2) Inverse Time Circuit Breaker. An inverse time circuit breaker operable directly by applying the hand to a lever or handle. The circuit breaker shall be permitted to be both power and manually operable.

(3) Oil Switch. An oil switch used on a circuit whose rating does not exceed 600 volts or 100 amperes, or by special permission on a circuit exceeding this capacity where under expert supervision. The oil switch shall be permitted to be both power and manually operable.

430.112 Motors Served by Single Disconnecting Means. Each motor shall be provided with an individual disconnecting means.

Exception: A single disconnecting means shall be permitted to serve a group of motors under any one of the conditions of (a), (b), and (c). The single disconnecting means shall be rated in accordance with 430.110(C).

   (a) Where a number of motors drive several parts of a single machine or piece of apparatus, such as metal- and woodworking machines, cranes, and hoists.

   (b) Where a group of motors is under the protection of one set of branch-circuit protective devices as permitted by 430.53(A).

   (c) Where a group of motors is in a single room within sight from the location of the disconnecting means.

430.113 Energy from More Than One Source. Motor and motor-operated equipment receiving electrical energy from more than one source shall be provided with disconnecting means from each source of electrical energy immediately adjacent to the equipment served. Each source shall be permitted to have a separate disconnecting means. Where multiple disconnecting means are provided, a permanent warning sign shall be provided on or adjacent to each disconnecting means.

Exception No. 1: Where a motor receives electrical energy from more than one source, the disconnecting means for the main power supply to the motor shall not be required to be immediately adjacent to the motor, provided the controller disconnecting means is capable of being locked in the open position.

Exception No. 2: A separate disconnecting means shall not be required for a Class 2 remote-control circuit conforming with Article 725, rated not more than 30 volts, and isolated and ungrounded.

X. Adjustable-Speed Drive Systems

430.120 General. The installation provisions of Part I through Part IX are applicable unless modified or supplemented by Part X.

FPN: Electrical resonance can result from the interaction of the nonsinusoidal currents from this type of load with power factor correction capacitors.

430.122 Conductors — Minimum Size and Ampacity.

(A) Branch/Feeder Circuit Conductors. Circuit conductors supplying power conversion equipment included as part of an adjustable-speed drive system shall have an ampacity not less than 125 percent of the rated input to the power conversion equipment.

(B) Bypass Device. For an adjustable speed drive system that utilizes a bypass device, the conductor ampacity shall not be less than required by 430.6. The ampacity of circuit conductors supplying power conversion equipment included as part of an adjustable-speed drive system that utilizes a bypass device shall be the larger of either of the following:

(1) 125 percent of the rated input to the power conversion equipment

(2) 125 percent of the motor full-load current rating as determined by 430.6

430.124 Overload Protection. Overload protection of the motor shall be provided.

(A) Included in Power Conversion Equipment. Where the power conversion equipment is marked to indicate that motor overload protection is included, additional overload protection shall not be required.

(B) Bypass Circuits. For adjustable speed drive systems that utilize a bypass device to allow motor operation at rated full load speed, motor overload protection as described in Article 430, Part III, shall be provided in the bypass circuit.

(C) Multiple Motor Applications. For multiple motor application, individual motor overload protection shall be provided in accordance with Article 430, Part III.

430.126 Motor Overtemperature Protection.

(A) General. Adjustable speed drive systems shall protect against motor overtemperature conditions. Overtemperature protection is in addition to the conductor protection required in 430.32. Protection shall be provided by one of the following means.

(1) Motor thermal protector in accordance with 430.32

(2) Adjustable speed drive controller with load and speed-sensitive overload protection and thermal memory retention upon shutdown or power loss

(3) Overtemperature protection relay utilizing thermal sensors embedded in the motor and meeting the requirements of 430.32(A)(2) or (B)(2)

(4) Thermal sensor embedded in the motor that is received and acted upon by an adjustable speed drive

(B) Motors with Cooling Systems. Motors that utilize external forced air or liquid cooling systems shall be provided with protection that shall be continuously enabled or enabled automatically if the cooling system fails.

FPN: Protection against cooling system failure can take many forms. Some examples of protection against inoperative or failed cooling systems are direct sensing of the motor temperature as described in 430.32(A)(1), (A)(3), and (A)(4) or sensing of the presence or absence of the cooling media (flow or pressure sensing).

(C) Multiple Motor Applications. For multiple motor application, individual motor overtemperature protection shall be provided.

FPN: The relationship between motor current and motor temperature changes when the motor is operated by an adjustable speed drive. When operated at reduced speed, overheating of motors may occur at current levels less than or equal to a motor's rated full load current. This is the result of reduced motor cooling when its shaft-mounted fan is operating less than rated nameplate RPM.

(D) Automatic Restarting and Orderly Shutdown. The provisions of 430.43 and 430.44 shall apply to the motor overtemperature protection means.

430.128 Disconnecting Means. The disconnecting means shall be permitted to be in the incoming line to the conversion equipment and shall have a rating not less than 115 percent of the rated input current of the conversion unit.

XI. Over 600 Volts, Nominal

430.221 General. Part XI recognizes the additional hazard due to the use of higher voltages. It adds to or amends the other provisions of this article.

430.222 Marking on Controllers. In addition to the marking required by 430.8, a controller shall be marked with the control voltage.

430.223 Conductor Enclosures Adjacent to Motors. Flexible metal conduit or liquidtight flexible metal conduit not exceeding 1.8 m (6 ft) in length shall be permitted to be employed for raceway connection to a motor terminal enclosure.

430.224 Size of Conductors. Conductors supplying motors shall have an ampacity not less than the current at which the motor overload protective device(s) is selected to trip.

430.225 Motor-Circuit Overcurrent Protection.

(A) General. Each motor circuit shall include coordinated protection to automatically interrupt overload and fault currents in the motor, the motor-circuit conductors, and the motor control apparatus.

Exception: Where a motor is vital to operation of the plant and the motor should operate to failure if necessary to prevent a greater hazard to persons, the sensing device(s) shall be permitted to be connected to a supervised annunciator or alarm instead of interrupting the motor circuit.

(B) Overload Protection.

(1) Type of Overload Device. Each motor shall be protected against dangerous heating due to motor overloads and failure to start by a thermal protector integral with the motor or external current-sensing devices, or both.

(2) Wound-Rotor AC Motors. The secondary circuits of wound-rotor ac motors, including conductors, controllers, and resistors rated for the application, shall be considered as protected against overcurrent by the motor overload protection means.

(3) Operation. Operation of the overload interrupting device shall simultaneously disconnect all ungrounded conductors.

(4) Automatic Reset. Overload sensing devices shall not automatically reset after trip unless resetting of the overload sensing device does not cause automatic restarting of the motor or there is no hazard to persons created by automatic restarting of the motor and its connected machinery.

(C) Fault-Current Protection.

(1) Type of Protection. Fault-current protection shall be provided in each motor circuit by one of the following means.

(a) A circuit breaker of suitable type and rating arranged so that it can be serviced without hazard. The circuit breaker shall simultaneously disconnect all ungrounded conductors. The circuit breaker shall be permitted to sense the fault current by means of integral or external sensing elements.

(b) Fuses of a suitable type and rating placed in each ungrounded conductor. Fuses shall be used with suitable disconnecting means, or they shall be of a type that can also serve as the disconnecting means. They shall be arranged so that they cannot be serviced while they are energized.

(2) Reclosing. Fault-current interrupting devices shall not automatically reclose the circuit.

Exception: Automatic reclosing of a circuit shall be permitted where the circuit is exposed to transient faults and where such automatic reclosing does not create a hazard to persons.

(3) Combination Protection. Overload protection and fault-current protection shall be permitted to be provided by the same device.

430.226 Rating of Motor Control Apparatus. The ultimate trip current of overcurrent (overload) relays or other motor-protective devices used shall not exceed 115 percent of the controller's continuous current rating. Where the motor branch-circuit disconnecting means is separate from the controller, the disconnecting means current rating shall not be less than the ultimate trip setting of the overcurrent relays in the circuit.

430.227 Disconnecting Means. The controller disconnecting means shall be capable of being locked in the open position.

XII. Protection of Live Parts — All Voltages

430.231 General. Part XII specifies that live parts shall be protected in a manner judged adequate for the hazard involved.

430.232 Where Required. Exposed live parts of motors and controllers operating at 50 volts or more between terminals shall be guarded against accidental contact by enclosure or by location as follows:

(1) By installation in a room or enclosure that is accessible only to qualified persons

(2) By installation on a suitable balcony, gallery, or platform, elevated and arranged so as to exclude unqualified persons

(3) By elevation 2.5 m (8 ft) or more above the floor

Exception: Live parts of motors operating at more than 50 volts between terminals shall not require additional guarding for stationary motors that have commutators, collectors, and brush rigging located inside of motor-end brackets and not conductively connected to supply circuits operating at more than 150 volts to ground.

430.233 Guards for Attendants. Where live parts of motors or controllers operating at over 150 volts to ground are guarded against accidental contact only by location as specified in 430.232, and where adjustment or other attendance may be necessary during the operation of the apparatus, suitable insulating mats or platforms shall be provided so that the attendant cannot readily touch live parts unless standing on the mats or platforms.

FPN: For working space, see 110.26 and 110.34.

XIII. Grounding — All Voltages

430.241 General. Part XIII specifies the grounding of exposed non–current-carrying metal parts, likely to become energized, of motor and controller frames to prevent a voltage above ground in the event of accidental contact between energized parts and frames. Insulation, isolation, or guarding are suitable alternatives to grounding of motors under certain conditions.

430.242 Stationary Motors. The frames of stationary motors shall be grounded under any of the following conditions:

(1) Where supplied by metal-enclosed wiring

(2) Where in a wet location and not isolated or guarded

(3) If in a hazardous (classified) location as covered in Articles 500 through 517

(4) If the motor operates with any terminal at over 150 volts to ground

Where the frame of the motor is not grounded, it shall be permanently and effectively insulated from the ground.

430.243 Portable Motors. The frames of portable motors that operate at over 150 volts to ground shall be guarded or grounded.

FPN No. 1: See 250.114(4) for grounding of portable appliances in other than residential occupancies.

FPN No. 2: See 250.119(C) for color of equipment grounding conductor.

430.244 Controllers. Controller enclosures shall be grounded regardless of voltage. Controller enclosures shall have means for attachment of an equipment grounding conductor termination in accordance with 250.8.

Exception: Enclosures attached to ungrounded portable equipment shall not be required to be grounded.

430.245 Method of Grounding. Where required, grounding shall be done in the manner specified in Part VI of Article 250.

(A) Grounding Through Terminal Housings. Where the wiring to fixed motors is metal-enclosed cable or in metal raceways, junction boxes to house motor terminals shall be provided, and the armor of the cable or the metal raceways shall be connected to them in the manner specified in Article 250.

FPN: See 430.12(E) for equipment grounding connection means required at motor terminal housings.

(B) Separation of Junction Box from Motor. The junction box required by 430.245(A) shall be permitted to be separated from the motor by not more than 1.8 m (6 ft), provided the leads to the motor are stranded conductors within Type AC cable, interlocked metal tape Type MC cable where listed and identified in accordance with 250.118(10)(a), or armored cord or are stranded leads enclosed in liquidtight flexible metal conduit, flexible metal conduit, intermediate metal conduit, rigid metal conduit, or electrical metallic tubing not smaller than metric designator 12 (trade size ⅜), the armor or raceway being connected both to the motor and to the box.

Liquidtight flexible nonmetallic conduit and rigid nonmetallic conduit shall be permitted to enclose the leads to the motor, provided the leads are stranded and the required equipment grounding conductor is connected to both the motor and to the box.

Where stranded leads are used, protected as specified above, each strand within the conductor shall be not larger than 10 AWG and shall comply with other requirements of this *Code* for conductors to be used in raceways.

(C) Grounding of Controller-Mounted Devices. Instrument transformer secondaries and exposed non–current-carrying metal or other conductive parts or cases of instrument transformers, meters, instruments, and relays shall be grounded as specified in 250.170 through 250.178.

TABLE 430.247   ARTICLE 430 — MOTORS, MOTOR CIRCUITS, AND CONTROLLERS

XIV. Tables

Table 430.247 Full-Load Current in Amperes, Direct-Current Motors
The following values of full-load currents[*] are for motors running at base speed.

| Horsepower | Armature Voltage Rating[*] | | | | | |
	90 Volts	120 Volts	180 Volts	240 Volts	500 Volts	550 Volts
¼	4.0	3.1	2.0	1.6	—	—
⅓	5.2	4.1	2.6	2.0	—	—
½	6.8	5.4	3.4	2.7	—	—
¾	9.6	7.6	4.8	3.8	—	—
1	12.2	9.5	6.1	4.7	—	—
1½	—	13.2	8.3	6.6	—	—
2	—	17	10.8	8.5	—	—
3	—	25	16	12.2	—	—
5	—	40	27	20	—	—
7½	—	58	—	29	13.6	12.2
10	—	76	—	38	18	16
15	—	—	—	55	27	24
20	—	—	—	72	34	31
25	—	—	—	89	43	38
30	—	—	—	106	51	46
40	—	—	—	140	67	61
50	—	—	—	173	83	75
60	—	—	—	206	99	90
75	—	—	—	255	123	111
100	—	—	—	341	164	148
125	—	—	—	425	205	185
150	—	—	—	506	246	222
200	—	—	—	675	330	294

*These are average dc quantities.

Table 430.248 Full-Load Currents in Amperes, Single-Phase Alternating-Current Motors
The following values of full-load currents are for motors running at usual speeds and motors with normal torque characteristics. The voltages listed are rated motor voltages. The currents listed shall be permitted for system voltage ranges of 110 to 120 and 220 to 240 volts.

Horsepower	115 Volts	200 Volts	208 Volts	230 Volts
⅙	4.4	2.5	2.4	2.2
¼	5.8	3.3	3.2	2.9
⅓	7.2	4.1	4.0	3.6
½	9.8	5.6	5.4	4.9
¾	13.8	7.9	7.6	6.9
1	16	9.2	8.8	8.0
1½	20	11.5	11.0	10
2	24	13.8	13.2	12
3	34	19.6	18.7	17
5	56	32.2	30.8	28
7½	80	46.0	44.0	40
10	100	57.5	55.0	50

Table 430.249 Full-Load Current, Two-Phase Alternating-Current Motors (4-Wire)

The following values of full-load current are for motors running at speeds usual for belted motors and motors with normal torque characteristics. Current in the common conductor of a 2-phase, 3-wire system will be 1.41 times the value given. The voltages listed are rated motor voltages. The currents listed shall be permitted for system voltage ranges of 110 to 120, 220 to 240, 440 to 480, and 550 to 600 volts.

	Induction-Type Squirrel Cage and Wound Rotor (Amperes)				
Horsepower	115 Volts	230 Volts	460 Volts	575 Volts	2300 Volts
½	4.0	2.0	1.0	0.8	—
¾	4.8	2.4	1.2	1.0	—
1	6.4	3.2	1.6	1.3	—
1½	9.0	4.5	2.3	1.8	—
2	11.8	5.9	3.0	2.4	—
3	—	8.3	4.2	3.3	—
5	—	13.2	6.6	5.3	—
7½	—	19	9.0	8.0	—

Table 430.249 *Continued*

	Induction-Type Squirrel Cage and Wound Rotor (Amperes)				
Horsepower	115 Volts	230 Volts	460 Volts	575 Volts	2300 Volts
10	—	24	12	10	—
15	—	36	18	14	—
20	—	47	23	19	—
25	—	59	29	24	—
30	—	69	35	28	—
40	—	90	45	36	—
50	—	113	56	45	—
60	—	133	67	53	14
75	—	166	83	66	18
100	—	218	109	87	23
125	—	270	135	108	28
150	—	312	156	125	32
200	—	416	208	167	43

Table 430.250 Full-Load Current, Three-Phase Alternating-Current Motors

The following values of full-load currents are typical for motors running at speeds usual for belted motors and motors with normal torque characteristics.

The voltages listed are rated motor voltages. The currents listed shall be permitted for system voltage ranges of 110 to 120, 220 to 240, 440 to 480, and 550 to 600 volts.

	Induction-Type Squirrel Cage and Wound Rotor (Amperes)							Synchronous-Type Unity Power Factor* (Amperes)			
Horsepower	115 Volts	200 Volts	208 Volts	230 Volts	460 Volts	575 Volts	2300 Volts	230 Volts	460 Volts	575 Volts	2300 Volts
½	4.4	2.5	2.4	2.2	1.1	0.9	—	—	—	—	—
¾	6.4	3.7	3.5	3.2	1.6	1.3	—	—	—	—	—
1	8.4	4.8	4.6	4.2	2.1	1.7	—	—	—	—	—
1½	12.0	6.9	6.6	6.0	3.0	2.4	—	—	—	—	—
2	13.6	7.8	7.5	6.8	3.4	2.7	—	—	—	—	—
3	—	11.0	10.6	9.6	4.8	3.9	—	—	—	—	—
5	—	17.5	16.7	15.2	7.6	6.1	—	—	—	—	—
7½	—	25.3	24.2	22	11	9	—	—	—	—	—
10	—	32.2	30.8	28	14	11	—	—	—	—	—
15	—	48.3	46.2	42	21	17	—	—	—	—	—
20	—	62.1	59.4	54	27	22	—	—	—	—	—
25	—	78.2	74.8	68	34	27	—	53	26	21	—
30	—	92	88	80	40	32	—	63	32	26	—
40	—	120	114	104	52	41	—	83	41	33	—
50	—	150	143	130	65	52	—	104	52	42	—
60	—	177	169	154	77	62	16	123	61	49	12
75	—	221	211	192	96	77	20	155	78	62	15
100	—	285	273	248	124	99	26	202	101	81	20
125	—	359	343	312	156	125	31	253	126	101	25
150	—	414	396	360	180	144	37	302	151	121	30
200	—	552	528	480	240	192	49	400	201	161	40
250	—	—	—	—	302	242	60	—	—	—	—
300	—	—	—	—	361	289	72	—	—	—	—
350	—	—	—	—	414	336	83	—	—	—	—
400	—	—	—	—	477	382	95	—	—	—	—
450	—	—	—	—	515	412	103	—	—	—	—
500	—	—	—	—	590	472	118	—	—	—	—

*For 90 and 80 percent power factor, the figures shall be multiplied by 1.1 and 1.25, respectively.

TABLE 430.251   ARTICLE 430 — MOTORS, MOTOR CIRCUITS, AND CONTROLLERS

Table 430.251(A) Conversion Table of Single-Phase Locked-Rotor Currents for Selection of Disconnecting Means and Controllers as Determined from Horsepower and Voltage Rating

For use only with 430.110, 440.12, 440.41, and 455.8(C).

Rated Horsepower	Maximum Locked-Rotor Current in Amperes, Single Phase		
	115 Volts	208 Volts	230 Volts
½	58.8	32.5	29.4
¾	82.8	45.8	41.4
1	96	53	48
1½	120	66	60
2	144	80	72
3	204	113	102
5	336	186	168
7½	480	265	240
10	600	332	300

Table 430.251(B) Conversion Table of Polyphase Design B, C, and D Maximum Locked-Rotor Currents for Selection of Disconnecting Means and Controllers as Determined from Horsepower and Voltage Rating and Design Letter

For use only with 430.110, 440.12, 440.41 and 455.8(C).

Rated Horsepower	Maximum Motor Locked-Rotor Current in Amperes, Two- and Three-Phase, Design B, C, and D*					
	115 Volts	200 Volts	208 Volts	230 Volts	460 Volts	575 Volts
	B, C, D	B, C, D	B, C, D	B, C, D	B, C, D	B, C, D
½	40	23	22.1	20	10	8
¾	50	28.8	27.6	25	12.5	10
1	60	34.5	33	30	15	12
1½	80	46	44	40	20	16
2	100	57.5	55	50	25	20
3	—	73.6	71	64	32	25.6
5	—	105.8	102	92	46	36.8
7½	—	146	140	127	63.5	50.8
10	—	186.3	179	162	81	64.8
15	—	267	257	232	116	93
20	—	334	321	290	145	116
25	—	420	404	365	183	146
30	—	500	481	435	218	174
40	—	667	641	580	290	232
50	—	834	802	725	363	290
60	—	1001	962	870	435	348
75	—	1248	1200	1085	543	434
100	—	1668	1603	1450	725	580
125	—	2087	2007	1815	908	726
150	—	2496	2400	2170	1085	868
200	—	3335	3207	2900	1450	1160
250	—	—	—	—	1825	1460
300	—	—	—	—	2200	1760
350	—	—	—	—	2550	2040
400	—	—	—	—	2900	2320
450	—	—	—	—	3250	2600
500	—	—	—	—	3625	2900

*Design A motors are not limited to a maximum starting current or locked rotor current.

ARTICLE 440
Air-Conditioning and Refrigerating Equipment

I. General

440.1 Scope. The provisions of this article apply to electric motor-driven air-conditioning and refrigerating equipment and to the branch circuits and controllers for such equipment. It provides for the special considerations necessary for circuits supplying hermetic refrigerant motor-compressors and for any air-conditioning or refrigerating equipment that is supplied from a branch circuit that supplies a hermetic refrigerant motor-compressor.

440.2 Definitions.

Branch-Circuit Selection Current. The value in amperes to be used instead of the rated-load current in determining the ratings of motor branch-circuit conductors, disconnecting means, controllers, and branch-circuit short-circuit and ground-fault protective devices wherever the running overload protective device permits a sustained current greater than the specified percentage of the rated-load current. The value of branch-circuit selection current will always be equal to or greater than the marked rated-load current.

Hermetic Refrigerant Motor-Compressor. A combination consisting of a compressor and motor, both of which are enclosed in the same housing, with no external shaft or shaft seals, the motor operating in the refrigerant.

Leakage Current Detection and Interruption (LCDI) Protection. A device provided in a power supply cord or cord set that senses leakage current flowing between or from the cord conductors and interrupts the circuit at a predetermined level of leakage current.

Rated-Load Current. The rated-load current for a hermetic refrigerant motor-compressor is the current resulting when the motor-compressor is operated at the rated load, rated voltage, and rated frequency of the equipment it serves.

440.3 Other Articles.

(A) Article 430. These provisions are in addition to, or amendatory of, the provisions of Article 430 and other articles in this *Code*, which apply except as modified in this article.

(B) Articles 422, 424, or 430. The rules of Articles 422, 424, or 430, as applicable, shall apply to air-conditioning and refrigerating equipment that does not incorporate a hermetic refrigerant motor-compressor. This equipment includes devices that employ refrigeration compressors driven by conventional motors, furnaces with air-conditioning evaporator coils installed, fan-coil units, remote forced air-cooled condensers, remote commercial refrigerators, and so forth.

(C) Article 422. Equipment such as room air conditioners, household refrigerators and freezers, drinking water coolers, and beverage dispensers shall be considered appliances, and the provisions of Article 422 shall also apply.

(D) Other Applicable Articles. Hermetic refrigerant motor-compressors, circuits, controllers, and equipment shall also comply with the applicable provisions of Table 440.3(D).

Table 440.3(D) Other Articles

Equipment/Occupancy	Article	Section
Capacitors		460.9
Commercial garages, aircraft hangars, motor fuel dispensing facilities, bulk storage plants, spray application, dipping, and coating processes, and inhalation anesthetizing locations	511, 513, 514, 515, 516, and 517 Part IV	
Hazardous (classified) locations	500–503 and 505	
Motion picture and television studios and similar locations	530	
Resistors and reactors	470	

440.4 Marking on Hermetic Refrigerant Motor-Compressors and Equipment.

(A) Hermetic Refrigerant Motor-Compressor Nameplate. A hermetic refrigerant motor-compressor shall be provided with a nameplate that shall indicate the manufacturer's name, trademark, or symbol; identifying designation; phase; voltage; and frequency. The rated-load current in amperes of the motor-compressor shall be marked by the equipment manufacturer on either or both the motor-compressor nameplate and the nameplate of the equipment in which the motor-compressor is used. The locked-rotor current of each single-phase motor-compressor having a rated-load current of more than 9 amperes at 115 volts, or more than 4.5 amperes at 230 volts, and each polyphase motor-compressor shall be marked on the motor-compressor nameplate. Where a thermal protector complying with 440.52(A)(2) and (B)(2) is used, the motor-compressor nameplate or the equipment nameplate shall be marked with the words "thermally protected." Where a protective system complying with 440.52(A)(4) and (B)(4) is used and is furnished with the equipment, the equipment nameplate shall be marked with the words, "thermally protected system." Where a protective system complying with

440.52(A)(4) and (B)(4) is specified, the equipment nameplate shall be appropriately marked.

(B) Multimotor and Combination-Load Equipment.
Multimotor and combination-load equipment shall be provided with a visible nameplate marked with the maker's name, the rating in volts, frequency and number of phases, minimum supply circuit conductor ampacity, the maximum rating of the branch-circuit short-circuit and ground-fault protective device, and the short-circuit current rating of the motor controllers or industrial control panel. The ampacity shall be calculated by using Part IV and counting all the motors and other loads that will be operated at the same time. The branch-circuit short-circuit and ground-fault protective device rating shall not exceed the value calculated by using Part III. Multimotor or combination-load equipment for use on two or more circuits shall be marked with the above information for each circuit.

Exception No. 1: Multimotor and combination-load equipment that is suitable under the provisions of this article for connection to a single 15- or 20-ampere, 120-volt, or a 15-ampere, 208- or 240-volt, single-phase branch circuit shall be permitted to be marked as a single load.

Exception No. 2: The minimum supply circuit conductor ampacity and the maximum rating of the branch-circuit short-circuit and ground-fault protective device shall not be required to be marked on a room air conditioner conforming with 440.62(A).

Exception No. 3: Multimotor and combination-load equipment used in one- and two-family dwellings, cord-and-attachment-plug-connected equipment, or equipment supplied from a branch circuit protected at 60 A or less shall not be required to be marked with a short-circuit current rating.

(C) Branch-Circuit Selection Current. A hermetic refrigerant motor-compressor, or equipment containing such a compressor, having a protection system that is approved for use with the motor-compressor that it protects and that permits continuous current in excess of the specified percentage of nameplate rated-load current given in 440.52(B)(2) or (B)(4) shall also be marked with a branch-circuit selection current that complies with 440.52(B)(2) or (B)(4). This marking shall be provided by the equipment manufacturer and shall be on the nameplate(s) where the rated-load current(s) appears.

440.5 Marking on Controllers. A controller shall be marked with the manufacturer's name, trademark, or symbol; identifying designation; voltage; phase; full-load and locked-rotor current (or horsepower) rating; and such other data as may be needed to properly indicate the motor-compressor for which it is suitable.

440.6 Ampacity and Rating. The size of conductors for equipment covered by this article shall be selected from Table 310.16 through Table 310.19 or calculated in accordance with 310.15 as applicable. The required ampacity of conductors and rating of equipment shall be determined according to 440.6(A) and 440.6(B).

(A) Hermetic Refrigerant Motor-Compressor. For a hermetic refrigerant motor-compressor, the rated-load current marked on the nameplate of the equipment in which the motor-compressor is employed shall be used in determining the rating or ampacity of the disconnecting means, the branch-circuit conductors, the controller, the branch-circuit short-circuit and ground-fault protection, and the separate motor overload protection. Where no rated-load current is shown on the equipment nameplate, the rated-load current shown on the compressor nameplate shall be used.

Exception No. 1: Where so marked, the branch-circuit selection current shall be used instead of the rated-load current to determine the rating or ampacity of the disconnecting means, the branch-circuit conductors, the controller, and the branch-circuit short-circuit and ground-fault protection.

Exception No. 2: For cord-and-plug-connected equipment, the nameplate marking shall be used in accordance with 440.22(B), Exception No. 2.

> FPN: For disconnecting means and controllers, see 440.12 and 440.41.

(B) Multimotor Equipment. For multimotor equipment employing a shaded-pole or permanent split-capacitor-type fan or blower motor, the full-load current for such motor marked on the nameplate of the equipment in which the fan or blower motor is employed shall be used instead of the horsepower rating to determine the ampacity or rating of the disconnecting means, the branch-circuit conductors, the controller, the branch-circuit short-circuit and ground-fault protection, and the separate overload protection. This marking on the equipment nameplate shall not be less than the current marked on the fan or blower motor nameplate.

440.7 Highest Rated (Largest) Motor. In determining compliance with this article and with 430.24, 430.53(B) and 430.53(C), and 430.62(A), the highest rated (largest) motor shall be considered to be the motor that has the highest rated-load current. Where two or more motors have the same highest rated-load current, only one of them shall be considered as the highest rated (largest) motor. For other than hermetic refrigerant motor-compressors, and fan or blower motors as covered in 440.6(B), the full-load current used to determine the highest rated motor shall be the equivalent value corresponding to the motor horsepower rating selected from Table 430.248, Table 430.249, or Table 430.250.

Exception: Where so marked, the branch-circuit selection current shall be used instead of the rated-load current in determining the highest rated (largest) motor-compressor.

440.8 Single Machine. An air-conditioning or refrigerating system shall be considered to be a single machine under the provisions of 430.87, Exception, and 430.112, Exception. The motors shall be permitted to be located remotely from each other.

II. Disconnecting Means

440.11 General. The provisions of Part II are intended to require disconnecting means capable of disconnecting air-conditioning and refrigerating equipment, including motor-compressors and controllers from the circuit conductors.

440.12 Rating and Interrupting Capacity.

(A) Hermetic Refrigerant Motor-Compressor. A disconnecting means serving a hermetic refrigerant motor-compressor shall be selected on the basis of the nameplate rated-load current or branch-circuit selection current, whichever is greater, and locked-rotor current, respectively, of the motor-compressor as follows.

(1) Ampere Rating. The ampere rating shall be at least 115 percent of the nameplate rated-load current or branch-circuit selection current, whichever is greater.

Exception: A listed nonfused motor circuit switch having a horsepower rating not less than the equivalent horsepower determined in accordance with 440.12(A)(2) shall be permitted to have an ampere rating less than 115 percent of the specified current.

(2) Equivalent Horsepower. To determine the equivalent horsepower in complying with the requirements of 430.109, the horsepower rating shall be selected from Table 430.248, Table 430.249, or Table 430.250 corresponding to the rated-load current or branch-circuit selection current, whichever is greater, and also the horsepower rating from Table 430.251(A) or Table 430.251(B) corresponding to the locked-rotor current. In case the nameplate rated-load current or branch-circuit selection current and locked-rotor current do not correspond to the currents shown in Table 430.248, Table 430.249, Table 430.250, Table 430.251(A), or Table 430.251(B), the horsepower rating corresponding to the next higher value shall be selected. In case different horsepower ratings are obtained when applying these tables, a horsepower rating at least equal to the larger of the values obtained shall be selected.

(B) Combination Loads. Where the combined load of two or more hermetic refrigerant motor-compressors or one or more hermetic refrigerant motor-compressor with other motors or loads may be simultaneous on a single discon-

necting means, the rating for the disconnecting means shall be determined in accordance with 440.12(B)(1) and (B)(2).

(1) Horsepower Rating. The horsepower rating of the disconnecting means shall be determined from the sum of all currents, including resistance loads, at the rated-load condition and also at the locked-rotor condition. The combined rated-load current and the combined locked-rotor current so obtained shall be considered as a single motor for the purpose of this requirement as follows.

(a) The full-load current equivalent to the horsepower rating of each motor, other than a hermetic refrigerant motor-compressor, and fan or blower motors as covered in 440.6(B) shall be selected from Table 430.248, Table 430.249, or Table 430.250. These full-load currents shall be added to the motor-compressor rated-load current(s) or branch-circuit selection current(s), whichever is greater, and to the rating in amperes of other loads to obtain an equivalent full-load current for the combined load.

(b) The locked-rotor current equivalent to the horsepower rating of each motor, other than a hermetic refrigerant motor-compressor, shall be selected from Table 430.251(A) or Table 430.251(B), and, for fan and blower motors of the shaded-pole or permanent split-capacitor type marked with the locked-rotor current, the marked value shall be used. The locked-rotor currents shall be added to the motor-compressor locked-rotor current(s) and to the rating in amperes of other loads to obtain an equivalent locked-rotor current for the combined load. Where two or more motors or other loads such as resistance heaters, or both, cannot be started simultaneously, appropriate combinations of locked-rotor and rated-load current or branch-circuit selection current, whichever is greater, shall be an acceptable means of determining the equivalent locked-rotor current for the simultaneous combined load.

Exception: Where part of the concurrent load is a resistance load and the disconnecting means is a switch rated in horsepower and amperes, the switch used shall be permitted to have a horsepower rating not less than the combined load to the motor-compressor(s) and other motor(s) at the locked-rotor condition, if the ampere rating of the switch is not less than this locked-rotor load plus the resistance load.

(2) Full-Load Current Equivalent. The ampere rating of the disconnecting means shall be at least 115 percent of the sum of all currents at the rated-load condition determined in accordance with 440.12(B)(1).

Exception: A listed nonfused motor circuit switch having a horsepower rating not less than the equivalent horsepower determined by 440.12(B)(1) shall be permitted to have an ampere rating less than 115 percent of the sum of all currents.

(C) Small Motor-Compressors. For small motor-compressors not having the locked-rotor current marked on the nameplate, or for small motors not covered by

Table 430.247, Table 430.248, Table 430.249, or Table 430.250, the locked-rotor current shall be assumed to be six times the rated-load current.

(D) Disconnecting Means. Every disconnecting means in the refrigerant motor-compressor circuit between the point of attachment to the feeder and the point of connection to the refrigerant motor-compressor shall comply with the requirements of 440.12.

(E) Disconnecting Means Rated in Excess of 100 Horsepower. Where the rated-load or locked-rotor current as determined above would indicate a disconnecting means rated in excess of 100 hp, the provisions of 430.109(E) shall apply.

440.13 Cord-Connected Equipment. For cord-connected equipment such as room air conditioners, household refrigerators and freezers, drinking water coolers, and beverage dispensers, a separable connector or an attachment plug and receptacle shall be permitted to serve as the disconnecting means.

FPN: For room air conditioners, see 440.63.

440.14 Location. Disconnecting means shall be located within sight from and readily accessible from the air-conditioning or refrigerating equipment. The disconnecting means shall be permitted to be installed on or within the air-conditioning or refrigerating equipment.

The disconnecting means shall not be located on panels that are designed to allow access to the air-conditioning or refrigeration equipment.

Exception No. 1: Where the disconnecting means provided in accordance with 430.102(A) is capable of being locked in the open position, and the refrigerating or air-conditioning equipment is essential to an industrial process in a facility with written safety procedures, and where the conditions of maintenance and supervision ensure that only qualified persons service the equipment, a disconnecting means within sight from the equipment shall not be required. The provision for locking or adding a lock to the disconnecting means shall be permanently installed on or at the switch or circuit breaker used as the disconnecting means.

Exception No. 2: Where an attachment plug and receptacle serve as the disconnecting means in accordance with 440.13, their location shall be accessible but shall not be required to be readily accessible.

FPN: See Parts VII and IX of Article 430 for additional requirements.

III. Branch-Circuit Short-Circuit and Ground-Fault Protection

440.21 General. The provisions of Part III specify devices intended to protect the branch-circuit conductors, control

apparatus, and motors in circuits supplying hermetic refrigerant motor-compressors against overcurrent due to short circuits and grounds. They are in addition to or amendatory of the provisions of Article 240.

440.22 Application and Selection.

(A) Rating or Setting for Individual Motor-Compressor. The motor-compressor branch-circuit short-circuit and ground-fault protective device shall be capable of carrying the starting current of the motor. A protective device having a rating or setting not exceeding 175 percent of the motor-compressor rated-load current or branch-circuit selection current, whichever is greater, shall be permitted, provided that, where the protection specified is not sufficient for the starting current of the motor, the rating or setting shall be permitted to be increased but shall not exceed 225 percent of the motor rated-load current or branch-circuit selection current, whichever is greater.

Exception: The rating of the branch-circuit short-circuit and ground-fault protective device shall not be required to be less than 15 amperes.

(B) Rating or Setting for Equipment. The equipment branch-circuit short-circuit and ground-fault protective device shall be capable of carrying the starting current of the equipment. Where the hermetic refrigerant motor-compressor is the only load on the circuit, the protection shall conform with 440.22(A). Where the equipment incorporates more than one hermetic refrigerant motor-compressor or a hermetic refrigerant motor-compressor and other motors or other loads, the equipment short-circuit and ground-fault protection shall conform with 430.53 and 440.22(B)(1) and (B)(2).

(1) Motor-Compressor Largest Load. Where a hermetic refrigerant motor-compressor is the largest load connected to the circuit, the rating or setting of the branch-circuit short-circuit and ground-fault protective device shall not exceed the value specified in 440.22(A) for the largest motor-compressor plus the sum of the rated-load current or branch-circuit selection current, whichever is greater, of the other motor-compressor(s) and the ratings of the other loads supplied.

(2) Motor-Compressor Not Largest Load. Where a hermetic refrigerant motor-compressor is not the largest load connected to the circuit, the rating or setting of the branch-circuit short-circuit and ground-fault protective device shall not exceed a value equal to the sum of the rated-load current or branch-circuit selection current, whichever is greater, rating(s) for the motor-compressor(s) plus the value specified in 430.53(C)(4) where other motor loads are supplied, or the value specified in 240.4 where only nonmotor loads are supplied in addition to the motor-compressor(s).

Exception No. 1: Equipment that starts and operates on a 15- or 20-ampere 120-volt, or 15-ampere 208- or 240-volt single-phase branch circuit, shall be permitted to be protected by the 15- or 20-ampere overcurrent device protecting the branch circuit, but if the maximum branch-circuit short-circuit and ground-fault protective device rating marked on the equipment is less than these values, the circuit protective device shall not exceed the value marked on the equipment nameplate.

Exception No. 2:   The nameplate marking of cord-and-plug-connected equipment rated not greater than 250 volts, single-phase, such as household refrigerators and freezers, drinking water coolers, and beverage dispensers, shall be used in determining the branch-circuit requirements, and each unit shall be considered as a single motor unless the nameplate is marked otherwise.

(C) Protective Device Rating Not to Exceed the Manufacturer's Values. Where maximum protective device ratings shown on a manufacturer's overload relay table for use with a motor controller are less than the rating or setting selected in accordance with 440.22(A) and 440.22(B), the protective device rating shall not exceed the manufacturer's values marked on the equipment.

IV. Branch-Circuit Conductors

440.31 General. The provisions of Part IV and Article 310 specify ampacities of conductors required to carry the motor current without overheating under the conditions specified, except as modified in 440.6(A), Exception No. 1.

The provisions of these articles shall not apply to integral conductors of motors, motor controllers and the like, or to conductors that form an integral part of approved equipment.

FPN: See 300.1(B) and 310.1 for similar requirements.

440.32 Single Motor-Compressor. Branch-circuit conductors supplying a single motor-compressor shall have an ampacity not less than 125 percent of either the motor-compressor rated-load current or the branch-circuit selection current, whichever is greater.

For a wye-start, delta-run connected motor-compressor, the selection of branch-circuit conductors between the controller and the motor-compressor shall be permitted to be based on 72 percent of either the motor-compressor rated-load current or the branch-circuit selection current, whichever is greater.

FPN: The individual motor circuit conductors of wye-start, delta-run connected motor-compressors carry 58 percent of the rated load current. The multiplier of 72 percent is obtained by multiplying 58 percent by 1.25.

440.33 Motor-Compressor(s) With or Without Additional Motor Loads. Conductors supplying one or more motor-compressor(s) with or without an additional load(s) shall have an ampacity not less than the sum of the rated-load or branch-circuit selection current ratings, whichever

is larger, of all the motor-compressors plus the full-load currents of the other motors, plus 25 percent of the highest motor or motor-compressor rating in the group.

Exception No. 1:   Where the circuitry is interlocked so as to prevent the starting and running of a second motor-compressor or group of motor-compressors, the conductor size shall be determined from the largest motor-compressor or group of motor-compressors that is to be operated at a given time.

Exception No. 2:   The branch circuit conductors for room air conditioners shall be in accordance with Part VII of Article 440.

440.34 Combination Load. Conductors supplying a motor-compressor load in addition to a lighting or appliance load as calculated from Article 220 and other applicable articles shall have an ampacity sufficient for the lighting or appliance load plus the required ampacity for the motor-compressor load determined in accordance with 440.33 or, for a single motor-compressor, in accordance with 440.32.

Exception: Where the circuitry is interlocked so as to prevent simultaneous operation of the motor-compressor(s) and all other loads connected, the conductor size shall be determined from the largest size required for the motor-compressor(s) and other loads to be operated at a given time.

440.35 Multimotor and Combination-Load Equipment. The ampacity of the conductors supplying multimotor and combination-load equipment shall not be less than the minimum circuit ampacity marked on the equipment in accordance with 440.4(B).

V. Controllers for Motor-Compressors

440.41 Rating.

(A) Motor-Compressor Controller. A motor-compressor controller shall have both a continuous-duty full-load current rating and a locked-rotor current rating not less than the nameplate rated-load current or branch-circuit selection current, whichever is greater, and locked-rotor current, respectively, of the compressor. In case the motor controller is rated in horsepower but is without one or both of the foregoing current ratings, equivalent currents shall be determined from the ratings as follows. Table 430.248, Table 430.249, and Table 430.250 shall be used to determine the equivalent full-load current rating. Table 430.251(A) and Table 430.251(B) shall be used to determine the equivalent locked-rotor current ratings.

(B) Controller Serving More Than One Load. A controller serving more than one motor-compressor or a motor-compressor and other loads shall have a continuous-duty full-load current rating and a locked-rotor current rating not less than the combined load as determined in accordance with 440.12(B).

VI. Motor-Compressor and Branch-Circuit Overload Protection

440.51 General. The provisions of Part VI specify devices intended to protect the motor-compressor, the motor-control apparatus, and the branch-circuit conductors against excessive heating due to motor overload and failure to start.

FPN: See 240.4(G) for application of Parts III and VI of Article 440.

440.52 Application and Selection.

(A) Protection of Motor-Compressor. Each motor-compressor shall be protected against overload and failure to start by one of the following means:

(1) A separate overload relay that is responsive to motor-compressor current. This device shall be selected to trip at not more than 140 percent of the motor-compressor rated-load current.

(2) A thermal protector integral with the motor-compressor, approved for use with the motor-compressor that it protects on the basis that it will prevent dangerous overheating of the motor-compressor due to overload and failure to start. If the current-interrupting device is separate from the motor-compressor and its control circuit is operated by a protective device integral with the motor-compressor, it shall be arranged so that the opening of the control circuit will result in interruption of current to the motor-compressor.

(3) A fuse or inverse time circuit breaker responsive to motor current, which shall also be permitted to serve as the branch-circuit short-circuit and ground-fault protective device. This device shall be rated at not more than 125 percent of the motor-compressor rated-load current. It shall have sufficient time delay to permit the motor-compressor to start and accelerate its load. The equipment or the motor-compressor shall be marked with this maximum branch-circuit fuse or inverse time circuit breaker rating.

(4) A protective system, furnished or specified and approved for use with the motor-compressor that it protects on the basis that it will prevent dangerous overheating of the motor-compressor due to overload and failure to start. If the current-interrupting device is separate from the motor-compressor and its control circuit is operated by a protective device that is not integral with the current-interrupting device, it shall be arranged so that the opening of the control circuit will result in interruption of current to the motor-compressor.

(B) Protection of Motor-Compressor Control Apparatus and Branch-Circuit Conductors. The motor-compressor controller(s), the disconnecting means, and the branch-circuit conductors shall be protected against overcurrent due to motor overload and failure to start by one of the following means, which shall be permitted to be the same device or system protecting the motor-compressor in accordance with 440.52(A):

Exception: Overload protection of motor-compressors and equipment on 15- and 20-ampere, single-phase, branch circuits shall be permitted to be in accordance with 440.54 and 440.55.

(1) An overload relay selected in accordance with 440.52(A)(1)

(2) A thermal protector applied in accordance with 440.52(A)(2), that will not permit a continuous current in excess of 156 percent of the marked rated-load current or branch-circuit selection current

(3) A fuse or inverse time circuit breaker selected in accordance with 440.52(A)(3)

(4) A protective system, in accordance with 440.52(A)(4), that will not permit a continuous current in excess of 156 percent of the marked rated-load current or branch-circuit selection current

440.53 Overload Relays. Overload relays and other devices for motor overload protection that are not capable of opening short circuits shall be protected by fuses or inverse time circuit breakers with ratings or settings in accordance with Part III unless approved for group installation or for part-winding motors and marked to indicate the maximum size of fuse or inverse time circuit breaker by which they shall be protected.

Exception: The fuse or inverse time circuit breaker size marking shall be permitted on the nameplate of approved equipment in which the overload relay or other overload device is used.

440.54 Motor-Compressors and Equipment on 15- or 20-Ampere Branch Circuits — Not Cord-and-Attachment-Plug-Connected. Overload protection for motor-compressors and equipment used on 15- or 20-ampere 120-volt, or 15-ampere 208- or 240-volt single-phase branch circuits as permitted in Article 210 shall be permitted as indicated in 440.54(A) and 440.54(B).

(A) Overload Protection. The motor-compressor shall be provided with overload protection selected as specified in 440.52(A). Both the controller and motor overload protective device shall be approved for installation with the short-circuit and ground-fault protective device for the branch circuit to which the equipment is connected.

(B) Time Delay. The short-circuit and ground-fault protective device protecting the branch circuit shall have sufficient time delay to permit the motor-compressor and other motors to start and accelerate their loads.

440.55 Cord-and-Attachment-Plug-Connected Motor-Compressors and Equipment on 15- or 20-Ampere Branch Circuits. Overload protection for motor-compressors and equipment that are cord-and-attachment-plug-connected and used on 15- or 20-ampere 120-volt, or 15-ampere 208- or 240-volt, single-phase branch circuits as permitted in Article 210 shall be permitted as indicated in 440.55(A), (B), and (C).

(A) Overload Protection. The motor-compressor shall be provided with overload protection as specified in 440.52(A). Both the controller and the motor overload protective device shall be approved for installation with the short-circuit and ground-fault protective device for the branch circuit to which the equipment is connected.

(B) Attachment Plug and Receptacle Rating. The rating of the attachment plug and receptacle shall not exceed 20 amperes at 125 volts or 15 amperes at 250 volts.

(C) Time Delay. The short-circuit and ground-fault protective device protecting the branch circuit shall have sufficient time delay to permit the motor-compressor and other motors to start and accelerate their loads.

VII. Provisions for Room Air Conditioners

440.60 General. The provisions of Part VII shall apply to electrically energized room air conditioners that control temperature and humidity. For the purpose of Part VII, a room air conditioner (with or without provisions for heating) shall be considered as an ac appliance of the air-cooled window, console, or in-wall type that is installed in the conditioned room and that incorporates a hermetic refrigerant motor-compressor(s). The provisions of Part VII cover equipment rated not over 250 volts, single phase, and such equipment shall be permitted to be cord-and-attachment-plug-connected.

A room air conditioner that is rated three phase or rated over 250 volts shall be directly connected to a wiring method recognized in Chapter 3, and provisions of Part VII shall not apply.

440.61 Grounding. Room air conditioners shall be grounded in accordance with 250.110, 250.112, and 250.114.

440.62 Branch-Circuit Requirements.

(A) Room Air Conditioner as a Single Motor Unit. A room air conditioner shall be considered as a single motor unit in determining its branch-circuit requirements where all the following conditions are met:

(1) It is cord-and-attachment-plug-connected.

(2) Its rating is not more than 40 amperes and 250 volts, single phase.

(3) Total rated-load current is shown on the room air-conditioner nameplate rather than individual motor currents.

(4) The rating of the branch-circuit short-circuit and ground-fault protective device does not exceed the ampacity of the branch-circuit conductors or the rating of the receptacle, whichever is less.

(B) Where No Other Loads Are Supplied. The total marked rating of a cord-and-attachment-plug-connected room air conditioner shall not exceed 80 percent of the rating of a branch circuit where no other loads are supplied.

(C) Where Lighting Units or Other Appliances Are Also Supplied. The total marked rating of a cord-and-attachment-plug-connected room air conditioner shall not exceed 50 percent of the rating of a branch circuit where lighting outlets, other appliances, or general-use receptacles are also supplied. Where the circuitry is interlocked to prevent simultaneous operation of the room air conditioner and energization of other outlets on the same branch circuit, a cord-and-attachment-plug-connected room air conditioner shall not exceed 80 percent of the branch-circuit rating.

440.63 Disconnecting Means. An attachment plug and receptacle shall be permitted to serve as the disconnecting means for a single-phase room air conditioner rated 250 volts or less if (1) the manual controls on the room air conditioner are readily accessible and located within 1.8 m (6 ft) of the floor or (2) an approved manually operable disconnecting means is installed in a readily accessible location within sight from the room air conditioner.

440.64 Supply Cords. Where a flexible cord is used to supply a room air conditioner, the length of such cord shall not exceed 3.0 m (10 ft) for a nominal, 120-volt rating or 1.8 m (6 ft) for a nominal, 208- or 240-volt rating.

440.65 Leakage Current Detection and Interruption (LCDI) and Arc Fault Circuit Interrupter (AFCI). Single-phase cord-and-plug-connected room air conditioners shall be provided with factory-installed LCDI or AFCI protection. The LCDI or AFCI protection shall be an integral part of the attachment plug or be located in the power supply cord within 300 mm (12 in.) of the attachment plug.

ARTICLE 445
Generators

445.1 Scope. This article covers the installation of generators.

445.10 Location. Generators shall be of a type suitable for the locations in which they are installed. They shall also meet the requirements for motors in 430.14.

445.11 Marking. Each generator shall be provided with a nameplate giving the manufacturer's name, the rated frequency, power factor, number of phases if of alternating current, the subtransient and transient impedances, the rating in kilowatts or kilovolt amperes, the normal volts and amperes corresponding to the rating, rated revolutions per minute, insulation system class and rated ambient temperature or rated temperature rise, and time rating.

445.12 Overcurrent Protection.

(A) Constant-Voltage Generators. Constant-voltage generators, except ac generator exciters, shall be protected from overloads by inherent design, circuit breakers, fuses, or other acceptable overcurrent protective means suitable for the conditions of use.

(B) Two-Wire Generators. Two-wire, dc generators shall be permitted to have overcurrent protection in one conductor only if the overcurrent device is actuated by the entire current generated other than the current in the shunt field. The overcurrent device shall not open the shunt field.

(C) 65 Volts or Less. Generators operating at 65 volts or less and driven by individual motors shall be considered as protected by the overcurrent device protecting the motor if these devices will operate when the generators are delivering not more than 150 percent of their full-load rated current.

(D) Balancer Sets. Two-wire, dc generators used in conjunction with balancer sets to obtain neutrals for 3-wire systems shall be equipped with overcurrent devices that disconnect the 3-wire system in case of excessive unbalancing of voltages or currents.

(E) Three-Wire, Direct-Current Generators. Three-wire, dc generators, whether compound or shunt wound, shall be equipped with overcurrent devices, one in each armature lead, and connected so as to be actuated by the entire current from the armature. Such overcurrent devices shall consist either of a double-pole, double-coil circuit breaker or of a 4-pole circuit breaker connected in the main and equalizer leads and tripped by two overcurrent devices, one in each armature lead. Such protective devices shall be interlocked so that no one pole can be opened without simultaneously disconnecting both leads of the armature from the system.

Exception to (A) through (E): Where deemed by the authority having jurisdiction, a generator is vital to the operation of an electrical system and the generator should operate to failure to prevent a greater hazard to persons. The overload sensing device(s) shall be permitted to be connected to an annunciator or alarm supervised by authorized personnel instead of interrupting the generator circuit.

445.13 Ampacity of Conductors. The ampacity of the conductors from the generator terminals to the first distribution device(s) containing overcurrent protection shall not be less than 115 percent of the nameplate current rating of the generator. It shall be permitted to size the neutral conductors in accordance with 220.61. Conductors that must carry ground-fault currents shall not be smaller than required by 250.24(C). Neutral conductors of dc generators that must carry ground-fault currents shall not be smaller than the minimum required size of the largest conductor.

Exception: Where the design and operation of the generator prevent overloading, the ampacity of the conductors shall not be less than 100 percent of the nameplate current rating of the generator.

445.14 Protection of Live Parts. Live parts of generators operated at more than 50 volts to ground shall not be exposed to accidental contact where accessible to unqualified persons.

445.15 Guards for Attendants. Where necessary for the safety of attendants, the requirements of 430.233 shall apply.

445.16 Bushings. Where wires pass through an opening in an enclosure, conduit box, or barrier, a bushing shall be used to protect the conductors from the edges of an opening having sharp edges. The bushing shall have smooth, well-rounded surfaces where it may be in contact with the conductors. If used where oils, grease, or other contaminants may be present, the bushing shall be made of a material not deleteriously affected.

445.17 Generator Terminal Housings. Generator terminal housings shall comply with 430.12. Where a horsepower rating is required to determine the required minimum size of the generator terminal housing, the full-load current of the generator shall be compared with comparable motors in Table 430.247 through Table 430.250. The higher horsepower rating of Table 430.247 and Table 430.250 shall be used whenever the generator selection is between two ratings.

445.18 Disconnecting Means Required for Generators. Generators shall be equipped with disconnect(s) by means of which the generator and all protective devices and control apparatus are able to be disconnected entirely from the circuits supplied by the generator except where both of the following conditions apply:

(1) The driving means for the generator can be readily shut down.

(2) The generator is not arranged to operate in parallel with another generator or other source of voltage.

ARTICLE 450
Transformers and Transformer Vaults
(Including Secondary Ties)

450.1 Scope. This article covers the installation of all transformers.

Exception No. 1:   Current transformers.

Exception No. 2:   Dry-type transformers that constitute a component part of other apparatus and comply with the requirements for such apparatus.

Exception No. 3:   Transformers that are an integral part of an X-ray, high-frequency, or electrostatic-coating apparatus.

Exception No. 4:   Transformers used with Class 2 and Class 3 circuits that comply with Article 725.

Exception No. 5:   Transformers for sign and outline lighting that comply with Article 600.

Exception No. 6:   Transformers for electric-discharge lighting that comply with Article 410.

Exception No. 7:   Transformers used for power-limited fire alarm circuits that comply with Part III of Article 760.

Exception No. 8:   Transformers used for research, development, or testing, where effective arrangements are provided to safeguard persons from contacting energized parts.

This article covers the installation of transformers dedicated to supplying power to a fire pump installation as modified by Article 695.

This article also covers the installation of transformers in hazardous (classified) locations as modified by Articles 501 through 504.

I. General Provisions

450.2 Definition. For the purpose of this article, the following definition shall apply.

Transformer. An individual transformer, single- or polyphase, identified by a single nameplate, unless otherwise indicated in this article.

450.3 Overcurrent Protection. Overcurrent protection of transformers shall comply with 450.3(A), (B), or (C). As used in this section, the word *transformer* shall mean a transformer or polyphase bank of two or more single-phase transformers operating as a unit.

  FPN No. 1: See 240.4, 240.21, 240.100, and 240.101 for overcurrent protection of conductors.

  FPN No. 2: Nonlinear loads can increase heat in a transformer without operating its overcurrent protective device.

(A) Transformers Over 600 Volts, Nominal. Overcurrent protection shall be provided in accordance with Table 450.3(A).

(B) Transformers 600 Volts, Nominal, or Less. Overcurrent protection shall be provided in accordance with Table 450.3(B).

Exception: Where the transformer is installed as a motor-control circuit transformer in accordance with 430.72(C)(1) through (C)(5).

(C) Voltage Transformers. Voltage transformers installed indoors or enclosed shall be protected with primary fuses.

  FPN: For protection of instrument circuits including voltage transformers, see 408.52.

450.4 Autotransformers 600 Volts, Nominal, or Less.

(A) Overcurrent Protection. Each autotransformer 600 volts, nominal, or less shall be protected by an individual overcurrent device installed in series with each ungrounded input conductor. Such overcurrent device shall be rated or set at not more than 125 percent of the rated full-load input current of the autotransformer. Where this calculation does not correspond to a standard rating of a fuse or nonadjustable circuit breaker and the rated input current is 9 amperes or more, the next higher standard rating described in 240.6 shall be permitted. An overcurrent device shall not be installed in series with the shunt winding (the winding common to both the input and the output circuits) of the autotransformer between Points A and B as shown in Figure 450.4.

Figure 450.4 Autotransformer.

Exception: Where the rated input current of the autotransformer is less than 9 amperes, an overcurrent device rated or set at not more than 167 percent of the input current shall be permitted.

(B) Transformer Field-Connected as an Autotransformer. A transformer field-connected as an autotransformer shall be identified for use at elevated voltage.

  FPN: For information on permitted uses of autotransformers, see 210.9 and 215.11.

Table 450.3(A) Maximum Rating or Setting of Overcurrent Protection for Transformers Over 600 Volts (as a Percentage of Transformer-Rated Current)

Location Limitations	Transformer Rated Impedance	Primary Protection Over 600 Volts		Secondary Protection (See Note 2.)			
				Over 600 Volts		600 Volts or Less	
		Circuit Breaker (See Note 4.)	Fuse Rating	Circuit Breaker (See Note 4.)	Fuse Rating	Circuit Breaker or Fuse Rating	
Any location	Not more than 6%	600% (See Note 1.)	300% (See Note 1.)	300% (See Note 1.)	250% (See Note 1.)	125% (See Note 1.)	
	More than 6% and not more than 10%	400% (See Note 1.)	300% (See Note 1.)	250% (See Note 1.)	225% (See Note 1.)	125% (See Note 1.)	
Supervised locations only (See Note 3.)	Any	300% (See Note 1.)	250% (See Note 1.)	Not required	Not required	Not required	
	Not more than 6%	600%	300%	300% (See Note 5.)	250% (See Note 5.)	250% (See Note 5.)	
	More than 6% and not more than 10%	400%	300%	250% (See Note 5.)	225% (See Note 5.)	250% (See Note 5.)	

Notes:

1. Where the required fuse rating or circuit breaker setting does not correspond to a standard rating or setting, a higher rating or setting that does not exceed the next higher standard rating or setting shall be permitted.

2. Where secondary overcurrent protection is required, the secondary overcurrent device shall be permitted to consist of not more than six circuit breakers or six sets of fuses grouped in one location. Where multiple overcurrent devices are utilized, the total of all the device ratings shall not exceed the allowed value of a single overcurrent device. If both circuit breakers and fuses are used as the overcurrent device, the total of the device ratings shall not exceed that allowed for fuses.

3. A supervised location is a location where conditions of maintenance and supervision ensure that only qualified persons monitor and service the transformer installation.

4. Electronically actuated fuses that may be set to open at a specific current shall be set in accordance with settings for circuit breakers.

5. A transformer equipped with a coordinated thermal overload protection by the manufacturer shall be permitted to have separate secondary protection omitted.

450.5 Grounding Autotransformers. Grounding autotransformers covered in this section are zigzag or T-connected transformers connected to 3-phase, 3-wire ungrounded systems for the purpose of creating a 3-phase, 4-wire distribution system or providing a neutral reference for grounding purposes. Such transformers shall have a continuous per-phase current rating and a continuous neutral current rating. Zig-zag connected transformers shall not be installed on the load side of any system grounding connection, including those made in accordance with 250.24(B), 250.30(A)(1), or 250.32(B)(2).

FPN: The phase current in a grounding autotransformer is one-third the neutral current.

(A) Three-Phase, 4-Wire System. A grounding autotransformer used to create a 3-phase, 4-wire distribution system from a 3-phase, 3-wire ungrounded system shall conform to 450.5(A)(1) through (A)(4).

(1) Connections. The transformer shall be directly connected to the ungrounded phase conductors and shall not be switched or provided with overcurrent protection that is independent of the main switch and common-trip overcurrent protection for the 3-phase, 4-wire system.

(2) Overcurrent Protection. An overcurrent sensing device shall be provided that will cause the main switch or common-trip overcurrent protection referred to in 450.5(A)(1) to open if the load on the autotransformer reaches or exceeds 125 percent of its continuous current per-phase or neutral rating. Delayed tripping for temporary overcurrents sensed at the autotransformer overcurrent device shall be permitted for the purpose of allowing proper operation of branch or feeder protective devices on the 4-wire system.

(3) Transformer Fault Sensing. A fault-sensing system that causes the opening of a main switch or common-trip

Table 450.3(B) Maximum Rating or Setting of Overcurrent Protection for Transformers 600 Volts and Less (as a Percentage of Transformer-Rated Current)

Protection Method	Primary Protection			Secondary Protection (See Note 2.)	
	Currents of 9 Amperes or More	Currents Less Than 9 Amperes	Currents Less Than 2 Amperes	Currents of 9 Amperes or More	Currents Less Than 9 Amperes
Primary only protection	125% (See Note 1.)	167%	300%	Not required	Not required
Primary and secondary protection	250% (See Note 3.)	250% (See Note 3.)	250% (See Note 3.)	125% (See Note 1.)	167%

Notes:

1. Where 125 percent of this current does not correspond to a standard rating of a fuse or nonadjustable circuit breaker, a higher rating that does not exceed the next higher standard rating shall be permitted.

2. Where secondary overcurrent protection is required, the secondary overcurrent device shall be permitted to consist of not more than six circuit breakers or six sets of fuses grouped in one location. Where multiple overcurrent devices are utilized, the total of all the device ratings shall not exceed the allowed value of a single overcurrent device. If both breakers and fuses are utilized as the overcurrent device, the total of the device ratings shall not exceed that allowed for fuses.

3. A transformer equipped with coordinated thermal overload protection by the manufacturer and arranged to interrupt the primary current shall be permitted to have primary overcurrent protection rated or set at a current value that is not more than six times the rated current of the transformer for transformers having not more than 6 percent impedance and not more than four times the rated current of the transformer for transformers having more than 6 percent but not more than 10 percent impedance.

overcurrent device for the 3-phase, 4-wire system shall be provided to guard against single-phasing or internal faults.

> FPN: This can be accomplished by the use of two subtractive-connected donut-type current transformers installed to sense and signal when an unbalance occurs in the line current to the autotransformer of 50 percent or more of rated current.

(4) Rating. The autotransformer shall have a continuous neutral-current rating that is sufficient to handle the maximum possible neutral unbalanced load current of the 4-wire system.

(B) Ground Reference for Fault Protection Devices. A grounding autotransformer used to make available a specified magnitude of ground-fault current for operation of a ground-responsive protective device on a 3-phase, 3-wire ungrounded system shall conform to 450.5(B)(1) and (B)(2).

(1) Rating. The autotransformer shall have a continuous neutral-current rating sufficient for the specified ground-fault current.

(2) Overcurrent Protection. An overcurrent protective device of adequate short-circuit rating that will open simultaneously all ungrounded conductors when it operates shall be applied in the grounding autotransformer branch circuit and shall be rated or set at a current not exceeding 125 percent of the autotransformer continuous per-phase current rating or 42 percent of the continuous-current rating of any series connected devices in the autotransformer neutral connection. Delayed tripping for temporary overcurrents to permit the proper operation of ground-responsive tripping devices on the main system shall be permitted but shall not exceed values that would be more than the short-time current rating of the grounding autotransformer or any series connected devices in the neutral connection thereto.

(C) Ground Reference for Damping Transitory Overvoltages. A grounding autotransformer used to limit transitory overvoltages shall be of suitable rating and connected in accordance with 450.5(A)(1).

450.6 Secondary Ties. As used in this article, a secondary tie is a circuit operating at 600 volts, nominal, or less between phases that connects two power sources or power supply points, such as the secondaries of two transformers. The tie shall be permitted to consist of one or more conductors per phase or neutral. Conductors connecting the secondaries of transformers in accordance with 450.7 shall not be considered secondary ties.

As used in this section, the word *transformer* means a transformer or a bank of transformers operating as a unit.

(A) Tie Circuits. Tie circuits shall be provided with overcurrent protection at each end as required in Parts I, II, and VIII of Article 240.

Under the conditions described in 450.6(A)(1) and 450.6(A)(2), the overcurrent protection shall be permitted to be in accordance with 450.6(A)(3).

(1) Loads at Transformer Supply Points Only. Where all loads are connected at the transformer supply points at each end of the tie and overcurrent protection is not provided in accordance with Parts I, II, and VIII of Article 240, the rated ampacity of the tie shall not be less than 67 percent of the rated secondary current of the highest rated transformer supplying the secondary tie system.

(2) Loads Connected Between Transformer Supply Points. Where load is connected to the tie at any point between transformer supply points and overcurrent protection is not provided in accordance with Parts I, II, and VIII of Article 240, the rated ampacity of the tie shall not be less than 100 percent of the rated secondary current of the highest rated transformer supplying the secondary tie system.

Exception: Tie circuits comprised of multiple conductors per phase shall be permitted to be sized and protected in accordance with 450.6(A)(4).

(3) Tie Circuit Protection. Under the conditions described in 450.6(A)(1) and (A)(2), both supply ends of each ungrounded tie conductor shall be equipped with a protective device that opens at a predetermined temperature of the tie conductor under short-circuit conditions. This protection shall consist of one of the following: (1) a fusible link cable connector, terminal, or lug, commonly known as a limiter, each being of a size corresponding with that of the conductor and of construction and characteristics according to the operating voltage and the type of insulation on the tie conductors or (2) automatic circuit breakers actuated by devices having comparable time-current characteristics.

(4) Interconnection of Phase Conductors Between Transformer Supply Points. Where the tie consists of more than one conductor per phase or neutral, the conductors of each phase or neutral shall comply with one of the following provisions.

(a) *Interconnected.* The conductors shall be interconnected in order to establish a load supply point, and the protective device specified in 450.6(A)(3) shall be provided in each ungrounded tie conductor at this point on both sides of the interconnection. The means of interconnection shall have an ampacity not less than the load to be served.

(b) *Not Interconnected.* The loads shall be connected to one or more individual conductors of a paralleled conductor tie without interconnecting the conductors of each phase or neutral and without the protection specified in 450.6(A)(3) at load connection points. Where this is done, the tie conductors of each phase or neutral shall have a combined capacity ampacity of not less than 133 percent of the rated secondary current of the highest rated transformer supplying the secondary tie system, the total load of such taps shall not exceed the rated secondary current of the highest rated transformer, and the loads shall be equally divided on each phase and on the individual conductors of each phase as far as practicable.

(5) Tie Circuit Control. Where the operating voltage exceeds 150 volts to ground, secondary ties provided with limiters shall have a switch at each end that, when open, de-energizes the associated tie conductors and limiters. The current rating of the switch shall not be less than the rated current ampacity of the conductors connected to the switch. It shall be capable of interrupting its rated current, and it shall be constructed so that it will not open under the magnetic forces resulting from short-circuit current.

(B) Overcurrent Protection for Secondary Connections. Where secondary ties are used, an overcurrent device rated or set at not more than 250 percent of the rated secondary current of the transformers shall be provided in the secondary connections of each transformer supplying the tie system. In addition, an automatic circuit breaker actuated by a reverse-current relay set to open the circuit at not more than the rated secondary current of the transformer shall be provided in the secondary connection of each transformer.

(C) Grounding. Where the secondary tie system is grounded, each transformer secondary supplying the tie system shall be grounded in accordance with the requirements of 250.30 for separately derived systems.

450.7 Parallel Operation. Transformers shall be permitted to be operated in parallel and switched as a unit, provided the overcurrent protection for each transformer meets the requirements of 450.3(A) for primary and secondary protective devices over 600 volts, or 450.3(B) for primary and secondary protective devices 600 volts or less.

450.8 Guarding. Transformers shall be guarded as specified in 450.8(A) through 450.8(D).

(A) Mechanical Protection. Appropriate provisions shall be made to minimize the possibility of damage to transformers from external causes where the transformers are exposed to physical damage.

(B) Case or Enclosure. Dry-type transformers shall be provided with a noncombustible moisture-resistant case or enclosure that provides protection against the accidental insertion of foreign objects.

(C) Exposed Energized Parts. Switches or other equipment operating at 600 volts, nominal, or less and serving only equipment within a transformer enclosure shall be permitted to be installed in the transformer enclosure if accessible to qualified persons only. All energized parts shall be guarded in accordance with 110.27 and 110.34.

(D) Voltage Warning. The operating voltage of exposed live parts of transformer installations shall be indicated by signs or visible markings on the equipment or structures.

450.9 Ventilation. The ventilation shall be adequate to dispose of the transformer full-load losses without creating a temperature rise that is in excess of the transformer rating.

> FPN No. 1: See ANSI/IEEE C57.12.00-1993, *General Requirements for Liquid-Immersed Distribution, Power, and Regulating Transformers*, and ANSI/IEEE C57.12.01-1989, *General Requirements for Dry-Type Distribution and Power Transformers*.

> FPN No. 2: Additional losses may occur in some transformers where nonsinusoidal currents are present, resulting in increased heat in the transformer above its rating. See ANSI/IEEE C57.110-1993, *Recommended Practice for Establishing Transformer Capability When Supplying Nonsinusoidal Load Currents*, where transformers are utilized with nonlinear loads.

Transformers with ventilating openings shall be installed so that the ventilating openings are not blocked by walls or other obstructions. The required clearances shall be clearly marked on the transformer.

450.10 Grounding. Exposed non–current-carrying metal parts of transformer installations, including fences, guards, and so forth, shall be grounded where required under the conditions and in the manner specified for electric equipment and other exposed metal parts in Article 250.

450.11 Marking. Each transformer shall be provided with a nameplate giving the name of the manufacturer, rated kilovolt-amperes, frequency, primary and secondary voltage, impedance of transformers 25 kVA and larger, required clearances for transformers with ventilating openings, and the amount and kind of insulating liquid where used. In addition, the nameplate of each dry-type transformer shall include the temperature class for the insulation system.

450.12 Terminal Wiring Space. The minimum wire-bending space at fixed, 600-volt and below terminals of transformer line and load connections shall be as required in 312.6. Wiring space for pigtail connections shall conform to Table 314.16(B).

450.13 Accessibility. All transformers and transformer vaults shall be readily accessible to qualified personnel for inspection and maintenance or shall meet the requirements of 450.13(A) or 450.13(B).

(A) Open Installations. Dry-type transformers 600 volts, nominal, or less, located in the open on walls, columns, or structures, shall not be required to be readily accessible.

(B) Hollow Space Installations. Dry-type transformers 600 volts, nominal, or less and not exceeding 50 kVA shall be permitted in hollow spaces of buildings not permanently closed in by structure, provided they meet the ventilation

requirements of 450.9 and separation from combustible materials requirements of 450.21(A). Transformers so installed shall not be required to be readily accessible.

II. Specific Provisions Applicable to Different Types of Transformers

450.21 Dry-Type Transformers Installed Indoors.

(A) Not Over 112½ kVA. Dry-type transformers installed indoors and rated 112½ kVA or less shall have a separation of at least 305 mm (12 in.) from combustible material unless separated from the combustible material by a fire-resistant, heat-insulated barrier.

Exception: This rule shall not apply to transformers rated for 600 volts, nominal, or less that are completely enclosed, with or without ventilating openings.

(B) Over 112½ kVA. Individual dry-type transformers of more than 112½ kVA rating shall be installed in a transformer room of fire-resistant construction. Unless specified otherwise in this article, the term *fire resistant* means a construction having a minimum fire rating of 1 hour.

Exception No. 1: Transformers with Class 155 or higher insulation systems and separated from combustible material by a fire-resistant, heat-insulating barrier or by not less than 1.83 m (6 ft) horizontally and 3.7 m (12 ft) vertically.

Exception No. 2: Transformers with Class 155 or higher insulation systems and completely enclosed except for ventilating openings.

> FPN: See ANSI/ASTM E119-1995, *Method for Fire Tests of Building Construction and Materials*, and NFPA 251-1999, *Standard Methods of Tests of Fire Endurance of Building Construction and Materials*.

(C) Over 35,000 Volts. Dry-type transformers rated over 35,000 volts shall be installed in a vault complying with Part III of this article.

450.22 Dry-Type Transformers Installed Outdoors. Dry-type transformers installed outdoors shall have a weatherproof enclosure.

Transformers exceeding 112½ kVA shall not be located within 305 mm (12 in.) of combustible materials of buildings unless the transformer has Class 155 insulation systems or higher and is completely enclosed except for ventilating openings.

450.23 Less-Flammable Liquid-Insulated Transformers. Transformers insulated with listed less-flammable liquids that have a fire point of not less than 300°C shall be permitted to be installed in accordance with 450.23(A) or 450.23(B).

(A) Indoor Installations. Indoor installations shall be permitted in accordance with one of the following:

(1) In Type I or Type II buildings, in areas where all of the following requirements are met:

    a. The transformer is rated 35,000 volts or less.

    b. No combustible materials are stored.

    c. A liquid confinement area is provided.

    d. The installation complies with all restrictions provided for in the listing of the liquid.

(2) With an automatic fire extinguishing system and a liquid confinement area, provided the transformer is rated 35,000 volts or less

(3) In accordance with 450.26

(B) Outdoor Installations. Less-flammable liquid-filled transformers shall be permitted to be installed outdoors, attached to, adjacent to, or on the roof of buildings, where installed in accordance with (1) or (2):

(1) For Type I and Type II buildings, the installation shall comply with all restrictions provided for in the listing of the liquid.

    FPN: Installations adjacent to combustible material, fire escapes, or door and window openings may require additional safeguards such as those listed in 450.27.

(2) In accordance with 450.27.

    FPN No. 1: As used in this section, *Type I and Type II buildings* refers to Type I and Type II building construction as defined in NFPA 220-1999, *Standard on Types of Building Construction. Combustible materials* refers to those materials not classified as noncombustible or limited-combustible as defined in NFPA 220-1999, *Standard on Types of Building Construction.*

    FPN No. 2: See definition of *Listed* in Article 100.

450.24 Nonflammable Fluid-Insulated Transformers.

Transformers insulated with a dielectric fluid identified as nonflammable shall be permitted to be installed indoors or outdoors. Such transformers installed indoors and rated over 35,000 volts shall be installed in a vault. Such transformers installed indoors shall be furnished with a liquid confinement area and a pressure-relief vent. The transformers shall be furnished with a means for absorbing any gases generated by arcing inside the tank, or the pressure-relief vent shall be connected to a chimney or flue that will carry such gases to an environmentally safe area.

    FPN: Safety may be increased if fire hazard analyses are performed for such transformer installations.

For the purposes of this section, a nonflammable dielectric fluid is one that does not have a flash point or fire point and is not flammable in air.

450.25 Askarel-Insulated Transformers Installed Indoors.

Askarel-insulated transformers installed indoors and rated over 25 kVA shall be furnished with a pressure-relief vent. Where installed in a poorly ventilated place, they shall be furnished with a means for absorbing any gases generated by arcing inside the case, or the pressure-relief vent shall be connected to a chimney or flue that carries such gases outside the building. Askarel-insulated transformers rated over 35,000 volts shall be installed in a vault.

450.26 Oil-Insulated Transformers Installed Indoors.

Oil-insulated transformers installed indoors shall be installed in a vault constructed as specified in Part III of this article.

Exception No. 1: Where the total capacity does not exceed 112½ kVA, the vault specified in Part III of this article shall be permitted to be constructed of reinforced concrete that is not less than 100 mm (4 in.) thick.

Exception No. 2: Where the nominal voltage does not exceed 600, a vault shall not be required if suitable arrangements are made to prevent a transformer oil fire from igniting other materials and the total capacity in one location does not exceed 10 kVA in a section of the building classified as combustible or 75 kVA where the surrounding structure is classified as fire-resistant construction.

Exception No. 3: Electric furnace transformers that have a total rating not exceeding 75 kVA shall be permitted to be installed without a vault in a building or room of fire-resistant construction, provided suitable arrangements are made to prevent a transformer oil fire from spreading to other combustible material.

Exception No. 4: A transformer that has a total rating not exceeding 75 kVA and a supply voltage of 600 volts or less that is an integral part of charged-particle-accelerating equipment shall be permitted to be installed without a vault in a building or room of noncombustible or fire-resistant construction, provided suitable arrangements are made to prevent a transformer oil fire from spreading to other combustible material.

Exception No. 5: Transformers shall be permitted to be installed in a detached building that does not comply with Part III of this article if neither the building nor its contents present a fire hazard to any other building or property, and if the building is used only in supplying electric service and the interior is accessible only to qualified persons.

Exception No. 6: Oil-insulated transformers shall be permitted to be used without a vault in portable and mobile surface mining equipment (such as electric excavators) if each of the following conditions is met:

(a) *Provision is made for draining leaking fluid to the ground.*

(b) *Safe egress is provided for personnel.*

(c) *A minimum 6-mm (¼-in.) steel barrier is provided for personnel protection.*

450.27 Oil-Insulated Transformers Installed Outdoors. Combustible material, combustible buildings, and parts of buildings, fire escapes, and door and window openings shall be safeguarded from fires originating in oil-insulated transformers installed on roofs, attached to or adjacent to a building or combustible material.

In cases where the transformer installation presents a fire hazard, one or more of the following safeguards shall be applied according to the degree of hazard involved:

(1) Space separations
(2) Fire-resistant barriers
(3) Automatic fire suppression systems
(4) Enclosures that confine the oil of a ruptured transformer tank

Oil enclosures shall be permitted to consist of fire-resistant dikes, curbed areas or basins, or trenches filled with coarse, crushed stone. Oil enclosures shall be provided with trapped drains where the exposure and the quantity of oil involved are such that removal of oil is important.

> FPN: For additional information on transformers installed on poles or structures or under ground, see ANSI C2-2002, *National Electrical Safety Code.*

450.28 Modification of Transformers. When modifications are made to a transformer in an existing installation that change the type of the transformer with respect to Part II of this article, such transformer shall be marked to show the type of insulating liquid installed, and the modified transformer installation shall comply with the applicable requirements for that type of transformer.

III. Transformer Vaults

450.41 Location. Vaults shall be located where they can be ventilated to the outside air without using flues or ducts wherever such an arrangement is practicable.

450.42 Walls, Roofs, and Floors. The walls and roofs of vaults shall be constructed of materials that have adequate structural strength for the conditions with a minimum fire resistance of 3 hours. The floors of vaults in contact with the earth shall be of concrete that is not less than 100 mm (4 in.) thick, but where the vault is constructed with a vacant space or other stories below it, the floor shall have adequate structural strength for the load imposed thereon and a minimum fire resistance of 3 hours. For the purposes of this section, studs and wallboard construction shall not be acceptable.

Exception: Where transformers are protected with automatic sprinkler, water spray, carbon dioxide, or halon, construction of 1-hour rating shall be permitted.

> FPN No. 1: For additional information, see ANSI/ASTM E119-1995, *Method for Fire Tests of Building Construction*

and Materials, and NFPA 251-1999, *Standard Methods of Tests of Fire Endurance of Building Construction and Materials.*

> FPN No. 2: A typical 3-hour construction is 150 mm (6 in.) thick reinforced concrete.

450.43 Doorways. Vault doorways shall be protected in accordance with 450.43(A), (B), and (C).

(A) Type of Door. Each doorway leading into a vault from the building interior shall be provided with a tight-fitting door that has a minimum fire rating of 3 hours. The authority having jurisdiction shall be permitted to require such a door for an exterior wall opening where conditions warrant.

Exception: Where transformers are protected with automatic sprinkler, water spray, carbon dioxide, or halon, construction of 1-hour rating shall be permitted.

> FPN: For additional information, see NFPA 80-1999, *Standard for Fire Doors and Fire Windows.*

(B) Sills. A door sill or curb that is of sufficient height to confine the oil from the largest transformer within the vault shall be provided, and in no case shall the height be less than 100 mm (4 in.).

(C) Locks. Doors shall be equipped with locks, and doors shall be kept locked, access being allowed only to qualified persons. Personnel doors shall swing out and be equipped with panic bars, pressure plates, or other devices that are normally latched but open under simple pressure.

450.45 Ventilation Openings. Where required by 450.9, openings for ventilation shall be provided in accordance with 450.45(A) through 450.45(F).

(A) Location. Ventilation openings shall be located as far as possible from doors, windows, fire escapes, and combustible material.

(B) Arrangement. A vault ventilated by natural circulation of air shall be permitted to have roughly half of the total area of openings required for ventilation in one or more openings near the floor and the remainder in one or more openings in the roof or in the sidewalls near the roof, or all of the area required for ventilation shall be permitted in one or more openings in or near the roof.

(C) Size. For a vault ventilated by natural circulation of air to an outdoor area, the combined net area of all ventilating openings, after deducting the area occupied by screens, gratings, or louvers, shall not be less than 1900 mm^2 (3 in.^{2}) per kVA of transformer capacity in service, and in no case shall the net area be less than 0.1 m^2 (1 ft^2) for any capacity under 50 kVA.

(D) Covering. Ventilation openings shall be covered with durable gratings, screens, or louvers, according to the treatment required in order to avoid unsafe conditions.

(E) Dampers. All ventilation openings to the indoors shall be provided with automatic closing fire dampers that operate in response to a vault fire. Such dampers shall possess a standard fire rating of not less than 1½ hours.

FPN: See ANSI/UL 555-1995, *Standard for Fire Dampers.*

(F) Ducts. Ventilating ducts shall be constructed of fire-resistant material.

450.46 Drainage. Where practicable, vaults containing more than 100 kVA transformer capacity shall be provided with a drain or other means that will carry off any accumulation of oil or water in the vault unless local conditions make this impracticable. The floor shall be pitched to the drain where provided.

450.47 Water Pipes and Accessories. Any pipe or duct system foreign to the electrical installation shall not enter or pass through a transformer vault. Piping or other facilities provided for vault fire protection, or for transformer cooling, shall not be considered foreign to the electrical installation.

450.48 Storage in Vaults. Materials shall not be stored in transformer vaults.

ARTICLE 455
Phase Converters

I. General

455.1 Scope. This article covers the installation and use of phase converters.

455.2 Definitions.

Manufactured Phase. The manufactured or derived phase originates at the phase converter and is not solidly connected to either of the single-phase input conductors.

Phase Converter. An electrical device that converts single-phase power to 3-phase electrical power.

FPN: Phase converters have characteristics that modify the starting torque and locked-rotor current of motors served, and consideration is required in selecting a phase converter for a specific load.

Rotary-Phase Converter. A device that consists of a rotary transformer and capacitor panel(s) that permits the operation of 3-phase loads from a single-phase supply.

Static-Phase Converter. A device without rotating parts, sized for a given 3-phase load to permit operation from a single-phase supply.

455.3 Other Articles. All applicable requirements of this *Code* shall apply to phase converters except as amended by this article.

455.4 Marking. Each phase converter shall be provided with a permanent nameplate indicating the following:

(1) Manufacturer's name
(2) Rated input and output voltages
(3) Frequency
(4) Rated single-phase input full-load amperes
(5) Rated minimum and maximum single load in kilovolt-amperes (kVA) or horsepower
(6) Maximum total load in kilovolt-amperes (kVA) or horsepower
(7) For a rotary-phase converter, 3-phase amperes at full load

455.5 Equipment Grounding Connection. A means for attachment of an equipment grounding conductor termination in accordance with 250.8 shall be provided.

455.6 Conductors.

(A) Ampacity. The ampacity of the single-phase supply conductors shall be determined by 455.6(A)(1) or (A)(2).

FPN: Single-phase conductors sized to prevent a voltage drop not exceeding 3 percent from the source of supply to the phase converter may help ensure proper starting and operation of motor loads.

(1) Variable Loads. Where the loads to be supplied are variable, the conductor ampacity shall not be less than 125 percent of the phase converter nameplate single-phase input full-load amperes.

(2) Fixed Loads. Where the phase converter supplies specific fixed loads, and the conductor ampacity is less than 125 percent of the phase converter nameplate single-phase input full-load amperes, the conductors shall have an ampacity not less than 250 percent of the sum of the full-load, 3-phase current rating of the motors and other loads served where the input and output voltages of the phase converter are identical. Where the input and output voltages of the phase converter are different, the current as determined by this section shall be multiplied by the ratio of output to input voltage.

(B) Manufactured Phase Marking. The manufactured phase conductors shall be identified in all accessible locations with a distinctive marking. The marking shall be consistent throughout the system and premises.

455.7 Overcurrent Protection. The single-phase supply conductors and phase converter shall be protected from overcurrent by 455.7(A) or 455.7(B). Where the required fuse or nonadjustable circuit breaker rating or settings of adjustable circuit breakers do not correspond to a standard rating or setting, a higher rating or setting that does not exceed the next higher standard rating shall be permitted.

(A) Variable Loads. Where the loads to be supplied are variable, overcurrent protection shall be set at not more than 125 percent of the phase converter nameplate single-phase input full-load amperes.

(B) Fixed Loads. Where the phase converter supplies specific fixed loads and the conductors are sized in accordance with 455.6(A)(2), the conductors shall be protected in accordance with their ampacity. The overcurrent protection determined from this section shall not exceed 125 percent of the phase converter nameplate single-phase input amperes.

455.8 Disconnecting Means. Means shall be provided to disconnect simultaneously all ungrounded single-phase supply conductors to the phase converter.

(A) Location. The disconnecting means shall be readily accessible and located in sight from the phase converter.

(B) Type. The disconnecting means shall be a switch rated in horsepower, a circuit breaker, or a molded-case switch. Where only nonmotor loads are served, an ampere-rated switch shall be permitted.

(C) Rating. The ampere rating of the disconnecting means shall not be less than 115 percent of the rated maximum single-phase input full-load amperes or, for specific fixed loads, shall be permitted to be selected from 455.8(C)(1) or (C)(2).

(1) Current Rated Disconnect. The disconnecting means shall be a circuit breaker or molded-case switch with an ampere rating not less than 250 percent of the sum of the following:

(1) Full-load, 3-phase current ratings of the motors

(2) Other loads served

(2) Horsepower Rated Disconnect. The disconnecting means shall be a switch with a horsepower rating. The equivalent locked rotor current of the horsepower rating of the switch shall not be less than 200 percent of the sum of the following:

(1) Nonmotor loads

(2) The 3-phase, locked-rotor current of the largest motor as determined from Table 430.251(B)

(3) The full-load current of all other 3-phase motors operating at the same time

(D) Voltage Ratios. The calculations in 455.8(C) shall apply directly where the input and output voltages of the phase converter are identical. Where the input and output voltages of the phase converter are different, the current shall be multiplied by the ratio of the output to input voltage.

455.9 Connection of Single-Phase Loads. Where single-phase loads are connected on the load side of a phase converter, they shall not be connected to the manufactured phase.

455.10 Terminal Housings. A terminal housing in accordance with the provisions of 430.12 shall be provided on a phase converter.

II. Specific Provisions Applicable to Different Types of Phase Converters

455.20 Disconnecting Means. The single-phase disconnecting means for the input of a static phase converter shall be permitted to serve as the disconnecting means for the phase converter and a single load if the load is within sight of the disconnecting means.

455.21 Start-Up. Power to the utilization equipment shall not be supplied until the rotary-phase converter has been started.

455.22 Power Interruption. Utilization equipment supplied by a rotary-phase converter shall be controlled in such a manner that power to the equipment will be disconnected in the event of a power interruption.

FPN: Magnetic motor starters, magnetic contactors, and similar devices, with manual or time delay restarting for the load, provide restarting after power interruption.

455.23 Capacitors. Capacitors that are not an integral part of the rotary-phase conversion system but are installed for a motor load shall be connected to the line side of that motor overload protective device.

ARTICLE 460
Capacitors

460.1 Scope. This article covers the installation of capacitors on electric circuits.

Surge capacitors or capacitors included as a component part of other apparatus and conforming with the requirements of such apparatus are excluded from these requirements.

This article also covers the installation of capacitors in hazardous (classified) locations as modified by Articles 501 through 503.

460.2 Enclosing and Guarding.

(A) Containing More Than 11 L (3 gal) of Flammable Liquid. Capacitors containing more than 11 L (3 gal) of flammable liquid shall be enclosed in vaults or outdoor fenced enclosures complying with Article 110, Part III. This limit shall apply to any single unit in an installation of capacitors.

(B) Accidental Contact. Where capacitors are accessible to unauthorized and unqualified persons, they shall be enclosed, located, or guarded so that persons cannot come into accidental contact or bring conducting materials into accidental contact with exposed energized parts, terminals, or buses associated with them. However, no additional guarding is required for enclosures accessible only to authorized and qualified persons.

I. 600 Volts, Nominal, and Under

460.6 Discharge of Stored Energy. Capacitors shall be provided with a means of discharging stored energy.

(A) Time of Discharge. The residual voltage of a capacitor shall be reduced to 50 volts, nominal, or less within 1 minute after the capacitor is disconnected from the source of supply.

(B) Means of Discharge. The discharge circuit shall be either permanently connected to the terminals of the capacitor or capacitor bank or provided with automatic means of connecting it to the terminals of the capacitor bank on removal of voltage from the line. Manual means of switching or connecting the discharge circuit shall not be used.

460.8 Conductors.

(A) Ampacity. The ampacity of capacitor circuit conductors shall not be less than 135 percent of the rated current of the capacitor. The ampacity of conductors that connect a capacitor to the terminals of a motor or to motor circuit conductors shall not be less than one-third the ampacity of the motor circuit conductors and in no case less than 135 percent of the rated current of the capacitor.

(B) Overcurrent Protection. An overcurrent device shall be provided in each ungrounded conductor for each capacitor bank. The rating or setting of the overcurrent device shall be as low as practicable.

Exception: A separate overcurrent device shall not be required for a capacitor connected on the load side of a motor overload protective device.

(C) Disconnecting Means. A disconnecting means shall be provided in each ungrounded conductor for each capacitor bank and shall meet the following requirements:

(1) The disconnecting means shall open all ungrounded conductors simultaneously.

(2) The disconnecting means shall be permitted to disconnect the capacitor from the line as a regular operating procedure.

(3) The rating of the disconnecting means shall not be less than 135 percent of the rated current of the capacitor.

Exception: A separate disconnecting means shall not be required where a capacitor is connected on the load side of a motor controller.

460.9 Rating or Setting of Motor Overload Device. Where a motor installation includes a capacitor connected on the load side of the motor overload device, the rating or setting of the motor overload device shall be based on the improved power factor of the motor circuit.

The effect of the capacitor shall be disregarded in determining the motor circuit conductor rating in accordance with 430.22.

460.10 Grounding. Capacitor cases shall be grounded in accordance with Article 250.

Exception: Capacitor cases shall not be grounded where the capacitor units are supported on a structure designed to operate at other than ground potential.

460.12 Marking. Each capacitor shall be provided with a nameplate giving the name of the manufacturer, rated voltage, frequency, kilovar or amperes, number of phases, and, if filled with a combustible liquid, the volume of liquid. Where filled with a nonflammable liquid, the nameplate shall so state. The nameplate shall also indicate whether a capacitor has a discharge device inside the case.

II. Over 600 Volts, Nominal

460.24 Switching.

(A) Load Current. Group-operated switches shall be used for capacitor switching and shall be capable of the following:

(1) Carrying continuously not less than 135 percent of the rated current of the capacitor installation

(2) Interrupting the maximum continuous load current of each capacitor, capacitor bank, or capacitor installation that will be switched as a unit

(3) Withstanding the maximum inrush current, including contributions from adjacent capacitor installations

(4) Carrying currents due to faults on capacitor side of switch

(B) Isolation.

(1) General. A means shall be installed to isolate from all sources of voltage each capacitor, capacitor bank, or capacitor installation that will be removed from service as a unit. The isolating means shall provide a visible gap in the electrical circuit adequate for the operating voltage.

(2) Isolating or Disconnecting Switches with No Interrupting Rating. Isolating or disconnecting switches (with no interrupting rating) shall be interlocked with the load-interrupting device or shall be provided with prominently displayed caution signs in accordance with 490.22 to prevent switching load current.

(C) Additional Requirements for Series Capacitors. The proper switching sequence shall be ensured by use of one of the following:

(1) Mechanically sequenced isolating and bypass switches

(2) Interlocks

(3) Switching procedure prominently displayed at the switching location

460.25 Overcurrent Protection.

(A) Provided to Detect and Interrupt Fault Current. A means shall be provided to detect and interrupt fault current likely to cause dangerous pressure within an individual capacitor.

(B) Single Pole or Multipole Devices. Single-pole or multipole devices shall be permitted for this purpose.

(C) Protected Individually or in Groups. Capacitors shall be permitted to be protected individually or in groups.

(D) Protective Devices Rated or Adjusted. Protective devices for capacitors or capacitor equipment shall be rated or adjusted to operate within the limits of the safe zone for individual capacitors. If the protective devices are rated or adjusted to operate within the limits for Zone 1 or Zone 2, the capacitors shall be enclosed or isolated.

In no event shall the rating or adjustment of the protective devices exceed the maximum limit of Zone 2.

FPN: For definitions of *Safe Zone, Zone 1,* and *Zone 2,* see ANSI/IEEE 18-1992, *Shunt Power Capacitors.*

460.26 Identification. Each capacitor shall be provided with a permanent nameplate giving the manufacturer's name, rated voltage, frequency, kilovar or amperes, number

of phases, and the volume of liquid identified as flammable, if such is the case.

460.27 Grounding. Capacitor neutrals and cases, if grounded, shall be grounded in accordance with Article 250.

Exception: Where the capacitor units are supported on a structure that is designed to operate at other than ground potential.

460.28 Means for Discharge.

(A) Means to Reduce the Residual Voltage. A means shall be provided to reduce the residual voltage of a capacitor to 50 volts or less within 5 minutes after the capacitor is disconnected from the source of supply.

(B) Connection to Terminals. A discharge circuit shall be either permanently connected to the terminals of the capacitor or provided with automatic means of connecting it to the terminals of the capacitor bank after disconnection of the capacitor from the source of supply. The windings of motors, transformers, or other equipment directly connected to capacitors without a switch or overcurrent device interposed shall meet the requirements of 460.28(A).

ARTICLE 470
Resistors and Reactors

I. 600 Volts, Nominal, and Under

470.1 Scope. This article covers the installation of separate resistors and reactors on electric circuits.

Exception: Resistors and reactors that are component parts of other apparatus.

This article also covers the installation of resistors and reactors in hazardous (classified) locations as modified by Articles 501 through 504.

470.2 Location. Resistors and reactors shall not be placed where exposed to physical damage.

470.3 Space Separation. A thermal barrier shall be required if the space between the resistors and reactors and any combustible material is less than 305 mm (12 in.).

470.4 Conductor Insulation. Insulated conductors used for connections between resistance elements and controllers shall be suitable for an operating temperature of not less than 90°C (194°F).

Exception: Other conductor insulations shall be permitted for motor starting service.

II. Over 600 Volts, Nominal

470.18 General.

(A) Protected Against Physical Damage. Resistors and reactors shall be protected against physical damage.

(B) Isolated by Enclosure or Elevation. Resistors and reactors shall be isolated by enclosure or elevation to protect personnel from accidental contact with energized parts.

(C) Combustible Materials. Resistors and reactors shall not be installed in close enough proximity to combustible materials to constitute a fire hazard and shall have a clearance of not less than 305 mm (12 in.) from combustible materials.

(D) Clearances. Clearances from resistors and reactors to grounded surfaces shall be adequate for the voltage involved.

FPN: See Article 490.

(E) Temperature Rise from Induced Circulating Currents. Metallic enclosures of reactors and adjacent metal parts shall be installed so that the temperature rise from induced circulating currents is not hazardous to personnel or does not constitute a fire hazard.

470.19 Grounding. Resistor and reactor cases or enclosures shall be grounded in accordance with Article 250.

Exception: Resistor or reactor cases or enclosures supported on a structure designed to operate at other than ground potential shall not be grounded.

470.20 Oil-Filled Reactors. Installation of oil-filled reactors, in addition to the above requirements, shall comply with applicable requirements of Article 450.

ARTICLE 480
Storage Batteries

480.1 Scope. The provisions of this article shall apply to all stationary installations of storage batteries.

480.2 Definitions.

Nominal Battery Voltage. The voltage calculated on the basis of 2 volts per cell for the lead-acid type and 1.2 volts per cell for the alkali type.

Sealed Cell or Battery. A sealed cell or battery is one that has no provision for the addition of water or electrolyte or for external measurement of electrolyte specific gravity.

The individual cells shall be permitted to contain a venting arrangement as described in 480.10(B).

Storage Battery. A battery comprised of one or more rechargeable cells of the lead-acid, nickel-cadmium, or other rechargeable electrochemical types.

480.3 Wiring and Equipment Supplied from Batteries.
Wiring and equipment supplied from storage batteries shall be subject to the requirements of this *Code* applying to wiring and equipment operating at the same voltage, unless otherwise permitted by 480.4.

480.4 Overcurrent Protection for Prime Movers. Overcurrent protection shall not be required for conductors from a battery rated less than 50 volts if the battery provides power for starting, ignition, or control of prime movers. Section 300.3 shall not apply to these conductors.

480.6 Insulation of Batteries Not Over 250 Volts. This section shall apply to storage batteries having cells connected so as to operate at a nominal battery voltage of not over 250 volts.

(A) Vented Lead-Acid Batteries. Cells and multicompartment batteries with covers sealed to containers of nonconductive, heat-resistant material shall not require additional insulating support.

(B) Vented Alkaline-Type Batteries. Cells with covers sealed to jars of nonconductive, heat-resistant material shall require no additional insulation support. Cells in jars of conductive material shall be installed in trays of nonconductive material with not more than 20 cells (24 volts, nominal) in the series circuit in any one tray.

(C) Rubber Jars. Cells in rubber or composition containers shall require no additional insulating support where the total nominal voltage of all cells in series does not exceed 150 volts. Where the total voltage exceeds 150 volts, batteries shall be sectionalized into groups of 150 volts or less, and each group shall have the individual cells installed in trays or on racks.

(D) Sealed Cells or Batteries. Sealed cells and multicompartment sealed batteries constructed of nonconductive, heat-resistant material shall not require additional insulating support. Batteries constructed of a conducting container shall have insulating support if a voltage is present between the container and ground.

480.7 Insulation of Batteries of Over 250 Volts. The provisions of 480.6 shall apply to storage batteries having the cells connected so as to operate at a nominal voltage exceeding 250 volts, and, in addition, the provisions of this

section shall also apply to such batteries. Cells shall be installed in groups having a total nominal voltage of not over 250 volts. Insulation, which can be air, shall be provided between groups and shall have a minimum separation between live battery parts of opposite polarity of 50 mm (2 in.) for battery voltages not exceeding 600 volts.

480.8 Racks and Trays. Racks and trays shall comply with 480.8(A) and 480.8(B).

(A) Racks. Racks, as required in this article, are rigid frames designed to support cells or trays. They shall be substantial and be made of one of the following:

(1) Metal, treated so as to be resistant to deteriorating action by the electrolyte and provided with nonconducting members directly supporting the cells or with continuous insulating material other than paint on conducting members

(2) Other construction such as fiberglass or other suitable nonconductive materials

(B) Trays. Trays are frames, such as crates or shallow boxes usually of wood or other nonconductive material, constructed or treated so as to be resistant to deteriorating action by the electrolyte.

480.9 Battery Locations. Battery locations shall conform to 480.9(A), (B), and (C).

(A) Ventilation. Provisions shall be made for sufficient diffusion and ventilation of the gases from the battery to prevent the accumulation of an explosive mixture.

(B) Live Parts. Guarding of live parts shall comply with 110.27.

(C) Working Space. Working space about the battery systems shall comply with 110.26. Working clearance shall be measured from the edge of the battery rack.

480.10 Vents.

(A) Vented Cells. Each vented cell shall be equipped with a flame arrester that is designed to prevent destruction of the cell due to ignition of gases within the cell by an external spark or flame under normal operating conditions.

(B) Sealed Cells. Sealed battery or cells shall be equipped with a pressure-release vent to prevent excessive accumulation of gas pressure, or the battery or cell shall be designed to prevent scatter of cell parts in event of a cell explosion.

ARTICLE 490
Equipment, Over 600 Volts, Nominal

I. General

490.1 Scope. This article covers the general requirements for equipment operating at more than 600 volts, nominal.

> FPN No. 1: See NFPA 70E-2004, *Standard for Electrical Safety in the Workplace*, for electrical safety requirements for employee workplaces.

> FPN No. 2: For further information on hazard signs and labels, see ANSI Z535-4, *Product Signs and Safety Labels*.

490.2 Definition.

High Voltage. For the purposes of this article, more than 600 volts, nominal.

490.3 Oil-Filled Equipment. Installation of electrical equipment, other than transformers covered in Article 450, containing more than 38 L (10 gal) of flammable oil per unit shall meet the requirements of Parts II and III of Article 450.

II. Equipment — Specific Provisions

490.21 Circuit-Interrupting Devices.

(A) Circuit Breakers.

(1) Location.

(a) Circuit breakers installed indoors shall be mounted either in metal-enclosed units or fire-resistant cell-mounted units, or they shall be permitted to be open-mounted in locations accessible to qualified persons only.

(b) Circuit breakers used to control oil-filled transformers shall either be located outside the transformer vault or be capable of operation from outside the vault.

(c) Oil circuit breakers shall be arranged or located so that adjacent readily combustible structures or materials are safeguarded in an approved manner.

(2) Operating Characteristics. Circuit breakers shall have the following equipment or operating characteristics:

(1) An accessible mechanical or other approved means for manual tripping, independent of control power.

(2) Be release free (trip free).

(3) If capable of being opened or closed manually while energized, main contacts that operate independently of the speed of the manual operation.

(4) A mechanical position indicator at the circuit breaker to show the open or closed position of the main contacts.

(5) A means of indicating the open and closed position of the breaker at the point(s) from which they may be operated.

(3) Nameplate. A circuit breaker shall have a permanent and legible nameplate showing manufacturer's name or trademark, manufacturer's type or identification number, continuous current rating, interrupting rating in megavolt-amperes (MVA) or amperes, and maximum voltage rating. Modification of a circuit breaker affecting its rating(s) shall be accompanied by an appropriate change of nameplate information.

(4) Rating. Circuit breakers shall have the following ratings:

(1) The continuous current rating of a circuit breaker shall not be less than the maximum continuous current through the circuit breaker.

(2) The interrupting rating of a circuit breaker shall not be less than the maximum fault current the circuit breaker will be required to interrupt, including contributions from all connected sources of energy.

(3) The closing rating of a circuit breaker shall not be less than the maximum asymmetrical fault current into which the circuit breaker can be closed.

(4) The momentary rating of a circuit breaker shall not be less than the maximum asymmetrical fault current at the point of installation.

(5) The rated maximum voltage of a circuit breaker shall not be less than the maximum circuit voltage.

(B) Power Fuses and Fuseholders.

(1) Use. Where fuses are used to protect conductors and equipment, a fuse shall be placed in each ungrounded conductor. Two power fuses shall be permitted to be used in parallel to protect the same load if both fuses have identical ratings and both fuses are installed in an identified common mounting with electrical connections that divide the current equally. Power fuses of the vented type shall not be used indoors, under ground, or in metal enclosures unless identified for the use.

(2) Interrupting Rating. The interrupting rating of power fuses shall not be less than the maximum fault current the fuse is required to interrupt, including contributions from all connected sources of energy.

(3) Voltage Rating. The maximum voltage rating of power fuses shall not be less than the maximum circuit voltage. Fuses having a minimum recommended operating voltage shall not be applied below this voltage.

(4) Identification of Fuse Mountings and Fuse Units. Fuse mountings and fuse units shall have permanent and legible nameplates showing the manufacturer's type or designation, continuous current rating, interrupting current rating, and maximum voltage rating.

(5) Fuses. Fuses that expel flame in opening the circuit shall be designed or arranged so that they function properly without hazard to persons or property.

(6) Fuseholders. Fuseholders shall be designed or installed so that they are de-energized while a fuse is being replaced.

Exception: Fuses and fuseholders designed to permit fuse replacement by qualified persons using equipment designed for the purpose without de-energizing the fuseholder shall be permitted.

(7) High-Voltage Fuses. Metal-enclosed switchgear and substations that utilize high-voltage fuses shall be provided with a gang-operated disconnecting switch. Isolation of the fuses from the circuit shall be provided by either connecting a switch between the source and the fuses or providing roll-out switch and fuse-type construction. The switch shall be of the load-interrupter type, unless mechanically or electrically interlocked with a load-interrupting device arranged to reduce the load to the interrupting capability of the switch.

Exception: More than one switch shall be permitted as the disconnecting means for one set of fuses where the switches are installed to provide connection to more than one set of supply conductors. The switches shall be mechanically or electrically interlocked to permit access to the fuses only when all switches are open. A conspicuous sign shall be placed at the fuses identifying the presence of more than one source.

(C) Distribution Cutouts and Fuse Links — Expulsion Type.

(1) Installation. Cutouts shall be located so that they may be readily and safely operated and re-fused, and so that the exhaust of the fuses does not endanger persons. Distribution cutouts shall not be used indoors, underground, or in metal enclosures.

(2) Operation. Where fused cutouts are not suitable to interrupt the circuit manually while carrying full load, an approved means shall be installed to interrupt the entire load. Unless the fused cutouts are interlocked with the switch to prevent opening of the cutouts under load, a conspicuous sign shall be placed at such cutouts identifying that they shall not be operated under load.

(3) Interrupting Rating. The interrupting rating of distribution cutouts shall not be less than the maximum fault current the cutout is required to interrupt, including contributions from all connected sources of energy.

(4) Voltage Rating. The maximum voltage rating of cutouts shall not be less than the maximum circuit voltage.

(5) Identification. Distribution cutouts shall have on their body, door, or fuse tube a permanent and legible nameplate or identification showing the manufacturer's type or designation, continuous current rating, maximum voltage rating, and interrupting rating.

(6) Fuse Links. Fuse links shall have a permanent and legible identification showing continuous current rating and type.

(7) Structure Mounted Outdoors. The height of cutouts mounted outdoors on structures shall provide safe clearance between lowest energized parts (open or closed position) and standing surfaces, in accordance with 110.34(E).

(D) Oil-Filled Cutouts.

(1) Continuous Current Rating. The continuous current rating of oil-filled cutouts shall not be less than the maximum continuous current through the cutout.

(2) Interrupting Rating. The interrupting rating of oil-filled cutouts shall not be less than the maximum fault current the oil-filled cutout is required to interrupt, including contributions from all connected sources of energy.

(3) Voltage Rating. The maximum voltage rating of oil-filled cutouts shall not be less than the maximum circuit voltage.

(4) Fault Closing Rating. Oil-filled cutouts shall have a fault closing rating not less than the maximum asymmetrical fault current that can occur at the cutout location, unless suitable interlocks or operating procedures preclude the possibility of closing into a fault.

(5) Identification. Oil-filled cutouts shall have a permanent and legible nameplate showing the rated continuous current, rated maximum voltage, and rated interrupting current.

(6) Fuse Links. Fuse links shall have a permanent and legible identification showing the rated continuous current.

(7) Location. Cutouts shall be located so that they are readily and safely accessible for re-fusing, with the top of the cutout not over 1.5 m (5 ft) above the floor or platform.

(8) Enclosure. Suitable barriers or enclosures shall be provided to prevent contact with nonshielded cables or energized parts of oil-filled cutouts.

(E) Load Interrupters. Load-interrupter switches shall be permitted if suitable fuses or circuit breakers are used in conjunction with these devices to interrupt fault currents. Where these devices are used in combination, they shall be coordinated electrically so that they will safely withstand the effects of closing, carrying, or interrupting all possible currents up to the assigned maximum short-circuit rating.

Where more than one switch is installed with interconnected load terminals to provide for alternate connection to different supply conductors, each switch shall be provided with a conspicuous sign identifying this hazard.

(1) Continuous Current Rating. The continuous current rating of interrupter switches shall equal or exceed the maximum continuous current at the point of installation.

(2) Voltage Rating. The maximum voltage rating of interrupter switches shall equal or exceed the maximum circuit voltage.

(3) Identification. Interrupter switches shall have a permanent and legible nameplate including the following information: manufacturer's type or designation, continuous current rating, interrupting current rating, fault closing rating, maximum voltage rating.

(4) Switching of Conductors. The switching mechanism shall be arranged to be operated from a location where the operator is not exposed to energized parts and shall be arranged to open all ungrounded conductors of the circuit simultaneously with one operation. Switches shall be arranged to be locked in the open position. Metal-enclosed switches shall be operable from outside the enclosure.

(5) Stored Energy for Opening. The stored-energy operator shall be permitted to be left in the uncharged position after the switch has been closed if a single movement of the operating handle charges the operator and opens the switch.

(6) Supply Terminals. The supply terminals of fused interrupter switches shall be installed at the top of the switch enclosure, or, if the terminals are located elsewhere, the equipment shall have barriers installed so as to prevent persons from accidentally contacting energized parts or dropping tools or fuses into energized parts.

490.22 Isolating Means. Means shall be provided to completely isolate an item of equipment. The use of isolating switches shall not be required where there are other ways of de-energizing the equipment for inspection and repairs, such as draw-out-type metal-enclosed switchgear units and removable truck panels.

Isolating switches not interlocked with an approved circuit-interrupting device shall be provided with a sign warning against opening them under load.

A fuseholder and fuse, designed for the purpose, shall be permitted as an isolating switch.

490.23 Voltage Regulators. Proper switching sequence for regulators shall be ensured by use of one of the following:

(1) Mechanically sequenced regulator bypass switch(es)

(2) Mechanical interlocks

(3) Switching procedure prominently displayed at the switching location

490.24 Minimum Space Separation. In field-fabricated installations, the minimum air separation between bare live conductors and between such conductors and adjacent grounded surfaces shall not be less than the values given in Table 490.24. These values shall not apply to interior portions or exterior terminals of equipment designed, manufactured, and tested in accordance with accepted national standards.

Table 490.24 Minimum Clearance of Live Parts*

Nominal Voltage Rating (kV)	Impulse Withstand, B.I.L (kV)		Minimum Clearance of Live Parts							
			Phase-to-Phase				Phase-to-Ground			
	Indoors	Outdoors	Indoors		Outdoors		Indoors		Outdoors	
			mm	in.	mm	in.	mm	in.	mm	in.
2.4–4.16	60	95	115	4.5	180	7	80	3.0	155	6
7.2	75	95	140	5.5	180	7	105	4.0	155	6
13.8	95	110	195	7.5	305	12	130	5.0	180	7
14.4	110	110	230	9.0	305	12	170	6.5	180	7
23	125	150	270	10.5	385	15	190	7.5	255	10
34.5	150	150	320	12.5	385	15	245	9.5	255	10
	200	200	460	18.0	460	18	335	13.0	335	13
46	—	200	—	—	460	18	—	—	335	13
	—	250	—	—	535	21	—	—	435	17
69	—	250	—	—	535	21	—	—	435	17
	—	350	—	—	790	31	—	—	635	25
115	—	550	—	—	1350	53	—	—	1070	42
138	—	550	—	—	1350	53	—	—	1070	42
	—	650	—	—	1605	63	—	—	1270	50
161	—	650	—	—	1605	63	—	—	1270	50
	—	750	—	—	1830	72	—	—	1475	58
230	—	750	—	—	1830	72	—	—	1475	58
	—	900	—	—	2265	89	—	—	1805	71
	—	1050	—	—	2670	105	—	—	2110	83

*The values given are the minimum clearance for rigid parts and bare conductors under favorable service conditions. They shall be increased for conductor movement or under unfavorable service conditions or wherever space limitations permit. The selection of the associated impulse withstand voltage for a particular system voltage is determined by the characteristics of the surge protective equipment.

III. Equipment — Metal-Enclosed Power Switchgear and Industrial Control Assemblies

490.30 General. This part covers assemblies of metal-enclosed power switchgear and industrial control, including but not limited to switches, interrupting devices and their control, metering, protection and regulating equipment, where an integral part of the assembly, with associated interconnections and supporting structures. This part also includes metal-enclosed power switchgear assemblies that form a part of unit substations, power centers, or similar equipment.

490.31 Arrangement of Devices in Assemblies. Arrangement of devices in assemblies shall be such that individual components can safely perform their intended function without adversely affecting the safe operation of other components in the assembly.

490.32 Guarding of High-Voltage Energized Parts Within a Compartment. Where access for other than visual inspection is required to a compartment that contains energized high-voltage parts, barriers shall be provided to prevent accidental contact by persons, tools, or other equipment with energized parts. Exposed live parts shall only be permitted in compartments accessible to qualified persons. Fuses and fuseholders designed to enable future replacement without de-energizing the fuse holder shall only be permitted for use by qualified persons.

490.33 Guarding of Low-Voltage Energized Parts Within a Compartment. Energized bare parts mounted on doors shall be guarded where the door must be opened for maintenance of equipment or removal of draw-out equipment.

490.34 Clearance for Cable Conductors Entering Enclosure. The unobstructed space opposite terminals or opposite raceways or cables entering a switchgear or control assembly shall be adequate for the type of conductor and method of termination.

490.35 Accessibility of Energized Parts.

(A) High-Voltage Equipment. Doors that would provide unqualified persons access to high-voltage energized parts shall be locked.

(B) Low-Voltage Control Equipment. Low-voltage control equipment, relays, motors, and the like shall not be

necdigest™
a publication of NFPA

FREE *necdigest*™ **Subscription Reservation Card**

Please provide the following information completely, along with your signature and date of request, to quality for a subscription to *necdigest*™. Remember you must complete this form to receive *necdigest*™.

1 Please begin my free subscription to *necdigest*™: ☐ Yes ☐ No

SIGNATURE (required) _____ DATE (required) _____

NAME (please print) _____

TITLE _____

COMPANY _____

STREET _____

CITY _____ STATE _____ ZIP _____

PHONE _____ FAX _____

E-MAIL _____

2 Which of the following best describes your primary job title (please check only one)?
- ☐ A. Owner, partner, president, general manager, vice president
- ☐ B. Electrical engineer
- ☐ C. Consulting electrical engineer
- ☐ D. Project engineer
- ☐ E. Systems engineer
- ☐ F. Safety engineer
- ☐ G. Designer, architect
- ☐ H. Plant electrical engineer, plant engineer, chief engineer, facilities manager, maintenance engineer
- ☐ J. Project manager, job superintendent, general foreman, electrical foreman, project supervisor
- ☐ K. Electrician, electrical technician, electrical journeyman, installer
- ☐ L. Inspector
- ☐ M. Purchaser, buyer
- ☐ N. Estimator
- ☐ Z. Other (please specify)

3 Which of these best describes your company or organization and its activities (please check only one):
- ☐ 01. Engineering firm, consulting, design-construct, architecture
- ☐ 02. Electrical contracting
- ☐ 03. Communications/low-voltage contracting
- ☐ 04. General contracting
- ☐ 05. Manufacturing, warehousing
- ☐ 06. Commercial (e.g., office, hotel, financial, retail)
- ☐ 07. Oil, gas, mining
- ☐ 08. Utility
- ☐ 09. Healthcare
- ☐ 10. Institutional
- ☐ 11. Transportation services
- ☐ 99. Other (please specify)

4 What is the number of employees at your company (all locations)?
- ☐ A. 500 or more
- ☐ B. 250-499
- ☐ C. 100-249
- ☐ D. 51-99
- ☐ E. 50 or less

5 What is the approximate value of the electrical equipment or services you specify, purchase, or recommend on an annual basis?
- ☐ 1. $1,000,000 or more
- ☐ 2. $500,000-$999,999
- ☐ 3. $250,000-$499,999
- ☐ 4. $100,000-$249,999
- ☐ 5. Less than $100,000

6 Of the following, which products or services will you recommend, purchase, or specify in the next 12 months (mark all applicable)?
- ☐ 01. Alarm and signal systems
- ☐ 02. Boxes, conduit bodies, and enclosures
- ☐ 03. Circuit protection
- ☐ 04. Computer hardware and software systems
- ☐ 05. Construction equipment, vehicles
- ☐ 06. Contractor services
- ☐ 07. Grounding equipment
- ☐ 08. Electronics
- ☐ 09. Energy management equipment
- ☐ 10. Fire stop systems
- ☐ 11. Instruments and test equipment
- ☐ 12. Insurance
- ☐ 13. Lighting and fixtures
- ☐ 14. Motors and motor controls, sensors
- ☐ 15. Power sources, transformers, and control systems
- ☐ 16. Raceways/cable trays
- ☐ 17. Telecommunications
- ☐ 18. Tools
- ☐ 19. Transmission and power distribution equipment
- ☐ 20. Voice and Data networks
- ☐ 21. Wiring and cable
- ☐ 22. Wiring/cable connectors and devices
- ☐ 40. None of the above

7 Please indicate all the facility types and settings in which you will work during the coming 12 months (check all applicable):
- ☐ 01. Industrial/Plant
- ☐ 02. Commercial
- ☐ 03. Institutional
- ☐ 04. Healthcare
- ☐ 05. Utility
- ☐ 06. Transportation
- ☐ 07. Petroleum, mining
- ☐ 08. Government/Military
- ☐ 09. Municipal facilities
- ☐ 10. Residential
- ☐ 20. None of the above

8 Where and how, during the coming 12 months, will your company purchase equipment (please check all applicable)?
- ☐ 01. Direct from manufacturer, manufacturer's rep
- ☐ 02. Electrical distributor
- ☐ 03. Industrial or other trade distributor
- ☐ 04. Home center or hardware center
- ☐ 20. None of the above

9 Are you a member of NFPA?
- ☐ Yes ☐ No

nec05A

necdigest™

Mail this postpaid card today, or for faster service visit our website at www.necdigest.org.

BUSINESS REPLY MAIL
FIRST-CLASS MAIL   PERMIT NO. 1099   SKOKIE IL

POSTAGE WILL BE PAID BY ADDRESSEE

NECDIGEST™
PO BOX 2131
SKOKIE IL 60076-9231

FOLD HERE AND TAPE FOR MAILING.

MAKE SURE THAT YOU HAVE ANSWERED ALL QUALIFICATION QUESTIONS BEFORE MAILING.

TAPE HERE FOR MAILING.

necdigest™

Mail this postpaid card today, or for faster service visit our website at www.necdigest.org.

The publisher reserves the right to serve on a controlled basis only individuals who meet the publication qualifications. Paid subscriptions are available to others. Incomplete forms cannot be processed.

SUBSCRIBE AT NO COST!

- Use this card to subscribe and you'll receive *necdigest* – NFPA's Official NEC® Magazine – at no cost. *necdigest* is published bimonthly. Complete and mail this form to qualify, or visit www.necdigest.org to complete the online form.

- *All* questions must be answered to process your subscription request.

necdigest™

installed in compartments with exposed high-voltage energized parts or high-voltage wiring unless either of the following conditions is met:

(1) The access means is interlocked with the high-voltage switch or disconnecting means to prevent the access means from being opened or removed.

(2) The high-voltage switch or disconnecting means is in the isolating position.

(C) High-Voltage Instruments or Control Transformers and Space Heaters. High-voltage instrument or control transformers and space heaters shall be permitted to be installed in the high-voltage compartment without access restrictions beyond those that apply to the high-voltage compartment generally.

490.36 Grounding. Frames of switchgear and control assemblies shall be grounded.

490.37 Grounding of Devices. Devices with metal cases or frames, or both, such as instruments, relays, meters, and instrument and control transformers, located in or on switchgear or control, shall have the frame or case grounded.

490.38 Door Stops and Cover Plates. External hinged doors or covers shall be provided with stops to hold them in the open position. Cover plates intended to be removed for inspection of energized parts or wiring shall be equipped with lifting handles and shall not exceed 1.1 m² (12 ft²) in area or 27 kg (60 lb) in weight, unless they are hinged and bolted or locked.

490.39 Gas Discharge from Interrupting Devices. Gas discharged during operating of interrupting devices shall be directed so as not to endanger personnel.

490.40 Inspection Windows. Windows intended for inspection of disconnecting switches or other devices shall be of suitable transparent material.

490.41 Location of Devices.

(A) Control and Instrument Transfer Switch Handles or Pushbuttons. Control and instrument transfer switch handles or pushbuttons other than those covered in 490.41(B) shall be in a readily accessible location at an elevation of not over 2.0 m (78 in.).

Exception: Operating handles requiring more than 23 kg (50 lb) of force shall be located no higher than 1.7 m (66 in.) in either the open or closed position.

(B) Infrequently Operated Devices. Operating handles for infrequently operated devices, such as drawout fuses, fused potential or control transformers and their primary disconnects, and bus transfer switches, shall be permitted to be located where they are safely operable and serviceable from a portable platform.

490.42 Interlocks — Interrupter Switches. Interrupter switches equipped with stored energy mechanisms shall have mechanical interlocks to prevent access to the switch compartment unless the stored energy mechanism is in the discharged or blocked position.

490.43 Stored Energy for Opening. The stored energy operator shall be permitted to be left in the uncharged position after the switch has been closed if a single movement of the operating handle charges the operator and opens the switch.

490.44 Fused Interrupter Switches.

(A) Supply Terminals. The supply terminals of fused interrupter switches shall be installed at the top of the switch enclosure or, if the terminals are located elsewhere, the equipment shall have barriers installed so as to prevent persons from accidentally contacting energized parts or dropping tools or fuses into energized parts.

(B) Backfeed. Where fuses can be energized by backfeed, a sign shall be placed on the enclosure door identifying this hazard.

(C) Switching Mechanism. The switching mechanism shall be arranged to be operated from a location outside the enclosure where the operator is not exposed to energized parts and shall be arranged to open all ungrounded conductors of the circuit simultaneously with one operation. Switches shall be capable of being locked in the open position.

490.45 Circuit Breakers — Interlocks.

(A) Circuit Breakers. Circuit breakers equipped with stored energy mechanisms shall be designed to prevent the release of the stored energy unless the mechanism has been fully charged.

(B) Mechanical Interlocks. Mechanical interlocks shall be provided in the housing to prevent the complete withdrawal of the circuit breaker from the housing when the stored energy mechanism is in the fully charged position, unless a suitable device is provided to block the closing function of the circuit breaker before complete withdrawal.

490.46 Metal Enclosed and Metal Clad Service Equipment. Metal enclosed and metal clad switchgear installed as high-voltage service equipment shall include a ground bus for the connection of service cable shields and to facilitate the attachment of safety grounds for personnel protection. This bus shall be extended into the compartment where the service conductors are terminated.

IV. Mobile and Portable Equipment

490.51 General.

(A) Covered. The provisions of this part shall apply to installations and use of high-voltage power distribution and utilization equipment that is portable, mobile, or both, such as substations and switch houses mounted on skids, trailers, or cars; mobile shovels; draglines; cranes; hoists; drills; dredges; compressors; pumps; conveyors; underground excavators; and the like.

(B) Other Requirements. The requirements of this part shall be additional to, or amendatory of, those prescribed in Articles 100 through 725 of this *Code*. Special attention shall be paid to Article 250.

(C) Protection. Adequate enclosures, guarding, or both, shall be provided to protect portable and mobile equipment from physical damage.

(D) Disconnecting Means. Disconnecting means shall be installed for mobile and portable high-voltage equipment according to the requirements of Part VIII of Article 230 and shall disconnect all ungrounded conductors.

490.52 Overcurrent Protection.
Motors driving single or multiple dc generators supplying a system operating on a cyclic load basis do not require overload protection, provided that the thermal rating of the ac drive motor cannot be exceeded under any operating condition. The branch-circuit protective device(s) shall provide short-circuit and locked-rotor protection and shall be permitted to be external to the equipment.

490.53 Enclosures.
All energized switching and control parts shall be enclosed in effectively grounded metal cabinets or enclosures. These cabinets or enclosures shall be marked "DANGER — HIGH VOLTAGE — KEEP OUT" and shall be locked so that only authorized and qualified persons can enter. Circuit breakers and protective equipment shall have the operating means projecting through the metal cabinet or enclosure so these units can be reset without opening locked doors. With doors closed, reasonable safe access for normal operation of these units shall be provided.

490.54 Collector Rings.
The collector ring assemblies on revolving-type machines (shovels, draglines, etc.) shall be guarded to prevent accidental contact with energized parts by personnel on or off the machine.

490.55 Power Cable Connections to Mobile Machines.
A metallic enclosure shall be provided on the mobile machine for enclosing the terminals of the power cable. The enclosure shall include provisions for a solid connection for the ground wire(s) terminal to effectively ground the machine frame. Ungrounded conductors shall be attached to insulators or be terminated in approved high-voltage cable couplers (which include ground wire connectors) of proper voltage and ampere rating. The method of cable termination used shall prevent any strain or pull on the cable from stressing the electrical connections. The enclosure shall have provision for locking so only authorized and qualified persons may open it and shall be marked

DANGER — HIGH VOLTAGE — KEEP OUT.

490.56 High-Voltage Portable Cable for Main Power Supply.
Flexible high-voltage cable supplying power to portable or mobile equipment shall comply with Article 250 and Article 400, Part III.

V. Electrode-Type Boilers

490.70 General.
The provisions of this part shall apply to boilers operating over 600 volts, nominal, in which heat is generated by the passage of current between electrodes through the liquid being heated.

490.71 Electric Supply System.
Electrode-type boilers shall be supplied only from a 3-phase, 4-wire solidly grounded wye system, or from isolating transformers arranged to provide such a system. Control circuit voltages shall not exceed 150 volts, shall be supplied from a grounded system, and shall have the controls in the ungrounded conductor.

490.72 Branch-Circuit Requirements.

(A) Rating. Each boiler shall be supplied from an individual branch circuit rated not less than 100 percent of the total load.

(B) Common-Trip Fault-Interrupting Device. The circuit shall be protected by a 3-phase, common-trip fault-interrupting device, which shall be permitted to automatically reclose the circuit upon removal of an overload condition but shall not reclose after a fault condition.

(C) Phase-Fault Protection. Phase-fault protection shall be provided in each phase, consisting of a separate phase-overcurrent relay connected to a separate current transformer in the phase.

(D) Ground Current Detection. Means shall be provided for detection of the sum of the neutral and ground currents and shall trip the circuit-interrupting device if the sum of those currents exceeds the greater of 5 amperes or 7½ percent of the boiler full-load current for 10 seconds or exceeds an instantaneous value of 25 percent of the boiler full-load current.

(E) Grounded Neutral Conductor. The grounded neutral conductor shall be as follows:

(1) Connected to the pressure vessel containing the electrodes

(2) Insulated for not less than 600 volts

(3) Have not less than the ampacity of the largest ungrounded branch-circuit conductor

(4) Installed with the ungrounded conductors in the same raceway, cable, or cable tray, or, where installed as open conductors, in close proximity to the ungrounded conductors

(5) Not used for any other circuit

490.73 Pressure and Temperature Limit Control. Each boiler shall be equipped with a means to limit the maximum temperature, pressure, or both, by directly or indirectly interrupting all current flow through the electrodes. Such means shall be in addition to the temperature, pressure, or both, regulating systems and pressure relief or safety valves.

490.74 Grounding. All exposed non–current-carrying metal parts of the boiler and associated exposed grounded structures or equipment shall be bonded to the pressure vessel or to the neutral conductor to which the vessel is connected in accordance with 250.102, except the ampacity of the bonding jumper shall not be less than the ampacity of the neutral conductor.

Chapter 5 Special Occupancies

ARTICLE 500
Hazardous (Classified) Locations, Classes I, II, and III, Divisions 1 and 2

FPN: Rules that are followed by a reference in brackets contain text that has been extracted from NFPA 497, *Recommended Practice for the Classification of Flammable Liquids, Gases, or Vapors and of Hazardous (Classified) Locations for Electrical Installations in Chemical Process Areas,* 2004 edition, and NFPA 499, *Recommended Practice for the Classification of Combustible Dusts and of Hazardous (Classified) Locations for Electrical Installation in Chemical Process Areas,* 2004 edition. Only editorial changes were made to the extracted text to make it consistent with this *Code.*

500.1 Scope — Articles 500 Through 504. Articles 500 through 504 cover the requirements for electrical and electronic equipment and wiring for all voltages in Class I, Divisions 1 and 2; Class II, Divisions 1 and 2; and Class III, Divisions 1 and 2 locations where fire or explosion hazards may exist due to flammable gases or vapors, flammable liquids, combustible dust, or ignitible fibers or flyings.

FPN No. 1: The unique hazards associated with explosives, pyrotechnics, and blasting agents are not addressed in this article.

FPN No. 2: For the requirements for electrical and electronic equipment and wiring for all voltages in Class I, Zone 0, Zone 1, and Zone 2 hazardous (classified) locations where fire or explosion hazards may exist due to flammable gases or vapors or flammable liquids, refer to Article 505.

FPN No. 3: For the requirements for electrical and electronic equipment and wiring for all voltages in Zone 20, Zone 21, and Zone 22 hazardous (classified) locations where fire or explosion hazards may exist due to combustible dusts or ignitible fibers or flyings, refer to Article 506.

500.2 Definitions. For purposes of Articles 500 through 504 and Articles 510 through 516, the following definitions apply.

Associated Nonincendive Field Wiring Apparatus. Apparatus in which the circuits are not necessarily nonincendive themselves but that affect the energy in nonincendive field wiring circuits and are relied upon to maintain nonincendive energy levels. Associated nonincendive field wiring apparatus may be either of the following:

(1) Electrical apparatus that has an alternative type of protection for use in the appropriate hazardous (classified) location

(2) Electrical apparatus not so protected that shall not be used in a hazardous (classified) location

FPN: Associated nonincendive field wiring apparatus has designated associated nonincendive field wiring apparatus connections for nonincendive field wiring apparatus and may also have connections for other electrical apparatus.

Combustible Gas Detection System. A protection technique utilizing stationary gas detectors in industrial establishments.

Control Drawing. A drawing or other document provided by the manufacturer of the intrinsically safe or associated apparatus, or of the nonincendive field wiring apparatus or associated nonincendive field wiring apparatus, that details the allowed interconnections between the intrinsically safe and associated apparatus or between the nonincendive field wiring apparatus or associated nonincendive field wiring apparatus.

Dust-Ignitionproof. Equipment enclosed in a manner that excludes dusts and does not permit arcs, sparks, or heat otherwise generated or liberated inside of the enclosure to cause ignition of exterior accumulations or atmospheric suspensions of a specified dust on or in the vicinity of the enclosure.

FPN: For further information on dust-ignitionproof enclosures, see Type 9 enclosure in ANSI/NEMA 250-1991, *Enclosures for Electrical Equipment,* and ANSI/UL 1203-1994, *Explosionproof and Dust-Ignitionproof Electrical Equipment for Hazardous (Classified) Locations.*

Dusttight. Enclosures constructed so that dust will not enter under specified test conditions.

FPN: See ANSI/ISA 12.12.01-2000, *Nonincendive Electrical Equipment for Use in Class I and II, Division 2, and Class III, Divisions 1 and 2 Hazardous (Classified) Locations,* and UL 1604-1994, *Electrical Equipment for Use in Class I and II, Division 2 and Class III Hazardous (Classified) Locations.*

Electrical and Electronic Equipment. Materials, fittings, devices, appliances, and the like that are part of, or in connection with, an electrical installation.

FPN: Portable or transportable equipment having self-contained power supplies, such as battery-operated equipment, could potentially become an ignition source in hazardous (classified) locations. See ISA-RP12.12.03-2002, *Portable Electronic Products Suitable for Use in Class I and II, Division 2, Class I Zone 2 and Class III, Division 1 and 2 Hazardous (Classified) Locations.*

Explosionproof Apparatus. Apparatus enclosed in a case that is capable of withstanding an explosion of a specified gas or vapor that may occur within it and of preventing the ignition of a specified gas or vapor surrounding the enclosure by sparks, flashes, or explosion of the gas or vapor within, and that operates at such an external temperature that a surrounding flammable atmosphere will not be ignited thereby.

FPN: For further information, see ANSI/UL 1203-1994, *Explosion-Proof and Dust-Ignition-Proof Electrical Equipment for Use in Hazardous (Classified) Locations.*

Hermetically Sealed. Equipment sealed against the entrance of an external atmosphere where the seal is made by fusion, for example, soldering, brazing, welding, or the fusion of glass to metal.

FPN: For further information, see ANSI/ISA 12.12.01-2000, *Nonincendive Electrical Equipment for Use in Class I and II, Division 2, and Class III, Division 1 and 2 Hazardous (Classified) Locations.*

Nonincendive Circuit. A circuit, other than field wiring, in which any arc or thermal effect produced under intended operating conditions of the equipment is not capable, under specified test conditions, of igniting the flammable gas–air, vapor–air, or dust–air mixture.

FPN: Conditions are described in ANSI/ISA 12.12.01-2000, *Nonincendive Electrical Equipment for Use in Class I and II, Division 2, and Class III, Divisions 1 and 2 Hazardous (Classified) Locations.*

Nonincendive Component. A component having contacts for making or breaking an incendive circuit and the contacting mechanism is constructed so that the component is incapable of igniting the specified flammable gas–air or vapor–air mixture. The housing of a nonincendive component is not intended to exclude the flammable atmosphere or contain an explosion.

FPN: For further information, see UL 1604-1994, *Electrical Equipment for Use in Class I and II, Division 2, and Class III Hazardous (Classified) Locations.*

Nonincendive Equipment. Equipment having electrical/electronic circuitry that is incapable, under normal operating conditions, of causing ignition of a specified flammable gas–air, vapor–air, or dust–air mixture due to arcing or thermal means.

FPN: For further information, see ANSI/ISA 12.12.01-2000, *Nonincendive Electrical Equipment for Use in Class I and II, Division 2, and Class III, Divisions 1 and 2 Hazardous (Classified) Locations.*

Nonincendive Field Wiring. Wiring that enters or leaves an equipment enclosure and, under normal operating conditions of the equipment, is not capable, due to arcing or thermal effects, of igniting the flammable gas–air, vapor–air, or dust–air mixture. Normal operation includes opening, shorting, or grounding the field wiring.

Nonincendive Field Wiring Apparatus. Apparatus intended to be connected to nonincendive field wiring.

FPN: For further information see ANSI/ISA 12.12.01-2000, *Nonincendive Electrical Equipment for Use in Class I and II, Division 2, and Class III, Divisions 1 and 2 Hazardous (Classified) Locations.*

Oil Immersion. Electrical equipment immersed in a protective liquid in such a way that an explosive atmosphere that may be above the liquid or outside the enclosure cannot be ignited.

FPN: For further information, see ANSI/UL 698-1995, *Industrial Control Equipment for Use in Hazardous (Classified) Locations.*

Purged and Pressurized. The process of (1) purging, supplying an enclosure with a protective gas at a sufficient flow and positive pressure to reduce the concentration of any flammable gas or vapor initially present to an acceptable level; and (2) pressurization, supplying an enclosure with a protective gas with or without continuous flow at sufficient pressure to prevent the entrance of a flammable gas or vapor, a combustible dust, or an ignitible fiber.

FPN: For further information, see ANSI/ NFPA 496-2003, *Purged and Pressurized Enclosures for Electrical Equipment.*

Unclassified Locations. Locations determined to be neither Class I, Division 1; Class I, Division 2; Class I, Zone 0; Class I, Zone 1; Class I, Zone 2; Class II, Division 1; Class II, Division 2; Class III, Division 1; Class III, Division 2; or any combination thereof.

500.3 Other Articles. Except as modified in Articles 500 through 504, all other applicable rules contained in this *Code* shall apply to electrical equipment and wiring installed in hazardous (classified) locations.

500.4 General.

(A) Documentation. All areas designated as hazardous (classified) locations shall be properly documented. This documentation shall be available to those authorized to design, install, inspect, maintain, or operate electrical equipment at the location.

(B) Reference Standards. Important information relating to topics covered in Chapter 5 may be found in other publications.

FPN No. 1: It is important that the authority having jurisdiction be familiar with recorded industrial experience as well as with the standards of the National Fire Protection Association (NFPA), the American Petroleum Institute (API), and the Instrumentation, Systems, and Automation Society (ISA) that may be of use in the classification of various locations, the determination of adequate ventilation, and the protection against static electricity and lightning hazards.

FPN No. 2: For further information on the classification of locations, see NFPA 30-2003, *Flammable and Combustible Liquids Code*; NFPA 32-2004, *Standard for Drycleaning Plants*; NFPA 33-2003, *Standard for Spray Application Using Flammable or Combustible Materials*; NFPA 34-2003, *Standard for Dipping and Coating Processes Using Flammable or Combustible Liquids*; NFPA 35-1999, *Standard for the Manufacture of Organic Coatings*; NFPA 36-2004, *Standard for Solvent Extraction Plants*; NFPA 45-2004, *Standard on Fire Protection for Laboratories Using Chemicals*; NFPA 50A-1999, *Standard for Gaseous Hydrogen Systems at Consumer Sites*; NFPA 50B-1999, *Standard for Liquefied Hydrogen Systems at Consumer Sites*; NFPA 58-2004, *Liquefied Petroleum Gas Code*; NFPA 59-2004, *Utility LP-Gas Plant Code*; NFPA 497-2004, *Recommended Practice for the Classification of Flammable Liquids, Gases, or Vapors and of Hazardous (Classified) Locations for Electrical Installations in Chemical Process Areas*; NFPA 499-2004, *Recommended Practice for the Classification of Combustible Dusts and of Hazardous (Classified) Locations for Electrical Installations in Chemical Process Areas*; NFPA 820-2003, *Standard for Fire Protection in Wastewater Treatment and Collection Facilities*; ANSI/API RP500-1997, *Recommended Practice for Classification of Locations of Electrical Installations at Petroleum Facilities Classified as Class I, Division 1 and Division 2*; ISA 12.10-1988, *Area Classification in Hazardous (Classified) Dust Locations*.

FPN No. 3: For further information on protection against static electricity and lightning hazards in hazardous (classified) locations, see NFPA 77-2000, *Recommended Practice on Static Electricity*; NFPA 780-2004, *Standard for the Installation of Lightning Protection Systems*; and API RP 2003-1998, *Protection Against Ignitions Arising Out of Static Lightning and Stray Currents*.

FPN No. 4: For further information on ventilation, see NFPA 30-2003, *Flammable and Combustible Liquids Code*; and API RP 500-1997, *Recommended Practice for Classification of Locations for Electrical Installations at Petroleum Facilities Classified as Class I, Division 1 and Division 2*.

FPN No. 5: For further information on electrical systems for hazardous (classified) locations on offshore oil- and gas-producing platforms, see ANSI/API RP 14F-1999, *Recommended Practice for Design and Installation of Electrical Systems for Fixed and Floating Offshore Petroleum Facilities for Unclassified and Class I, Division 1 and Division 2 Locations*.

500.5 Classifications of Locations.

(A) Classifications of Locations. Locations shall be classified depending on the properties of the flammable vapors, liquids, or gases, or combustible dusts or fibers that may be present, and the likelihood that a flammable or combustible concentration or quantity is present. Where pyrophoric materials are the only materials used or handled, these locations shall not be classified. Each room, section, or area shall be considered individually in determining its classification.

FPN: Through the exercise of ingenuity in the layout of electrical installations for hazardous (classified) locations, it is frequently possible to locate much of the equipment in a reduced level of classification or in an unclassified location and, thus, to reduce the amount of special equipment required.

Rooms and areas containing ammonia refrigeration systems that are equipped with adequate mechanical ventilation may be classified as "unclassified" locations.

FPN: For further information regarding classification and ventilation of areas involving ammonia, see ANSI/ASHRAE 15-1994, *Safety Code for Mechanical Refrigeration*, and ANSI/CGA G2.1-1989, *Safety Requirements for the Storage and Handling of Anhydrous Ammonia*.

(B) Class I Locations. Class I locations are those in which flammable gases or vapors are or may be present in the air in quantities sufficient to produce explosive or ignitible mixtures. Class I locations shall include those specified in 500.5(B)(1) and (B)(2).

(1) Class I, Division 1. A Class I, Division 1 location is a location

(1) In which ignitible concentrations of flammable gases or vapors can exist under normal operating conditions, or

(2) In which ignitible concentrations of such gases or vapors may exist frequently because of repair or maintenance operations or because of leakage, or

(3) In which breakdown or faulty operation of equipment or processes might release ignitible concentrations of flammable gases or vapors and might also cause simultaneous failure of electrical equipment in such a way as to directly cause the electrical equipment to become a source of ignition.

FPN No. 1: This classification usually includes the following locations:

(1) Where volatile flammable liquids or liquefied flammable gases are transferred from one container to another

(2) Interiors of spray booths and areas in the vicinity of spraying and painting operations where volatile flammable solvents are used

(3) Locations containing open tanks or vats of volatile flammable liquids

(4) Drying rooms or compartments for the evaporation of flammable solvents

(5) Locations containing fat- and oil-extraction equipment using volatile flammable solvents

(6) Portions of cleaning and dyeing plants where flammable liquids are used

(7) Gas generator rooms and other portions of gas manufacturing plants where flammable gas may escape

(8) Inadequately ventilated pump rooms for flammable gas or for volatile flammable liquids

(9) The interiors of refrigerators and freezers in which volatile flammable materials are stored in open, lightly stoppered, or easily ruptured containers

(10) All other locations where ignitible concentrations of flammable vapors or gases are likely to occur in the course of normal operations

FPN No. 2: In some Division 1 locations, ignitible concentrations of flammable gases or vapors may be present continuously or for long periods of time. Examples include the following:

(1) The inside of inadequately vented enclosures containing instruments normally venting flammable gases or vapors to the interior of the enclosure

(2) The inside of vented tanks containing volatile flammable liquids

(3) The area between the inner and outer roof sections of a floating roof tank containing volatile flammable fluids

(4) Inadequately ventilated areas within spraying or coating operations using volatile flammable fluids

(5) The interior of an exhaust duct that is used to vent ignitible concentrations of gases or vapors

Experience has demonstrated the prudence of avoiding the installation of instrumentation or other electric equipment in these particular areas altogether or where it cannot be avoided because it is essential to the process and other locations are not feasible [see 500.5(A), FPN] using electric equipment or instrumentation approved for the specific application or consisting of intrinsically safe systems as described in Article 504.

(2) Class I, Division 2. A Class I, Division 2 location is a location

(1) In which volatile flammable liquids or flammable gases are handled, processed, or used, but in which the liquids, vapors, or gases will normally be confined within closed containers or closed systems from which they can escape only in case of accidental rupture or breakdown of such containers or systems or in case of abnormal operation of equipment, or

(2) In which ignitible concentrations of gases or vapors are normally prevented by positive mechanical ventilation and which might become hazardous through failure or abnormal operation of the ventilating equipment, or

(3) That is adjacent to a Class I, Division 1 location, and to which ignitible concentrations of gases or vapors might occasionally be communicated unless such communication is prevented by adequate positive-pressure ventilation from a source of clean air and effective safeguards against ventilation failure are provided.

FPN No. 1: This classification usually includes locations where volatile flammable liquids or flammable gases or vapors are used but that, in the judgment of the authority having jurisdiction, would become hazardous only in case of an accident or of some unusual operating condition. The quantity of flammable material that might escape in case of accident, the adequacy of ventilating equipment, the total area involved, and the record of the industry or business with respect to explosions or fires are all factors that merit consideration in determining the classification and extent of each location.

FPN No. 2: Piping without valves, checks, meters, and similar devices would not ordinarily introduce a hazardous condition even though used for flammable liquids or gases. Depending on factors such as the quantity and size of the containers and ventilation, locations used for the storage of flammable liquids or liquefied or compressed gases in sealed containers may be considered either hazardous (classified) or unclassified locations. See NFPA 30-2003, *Flammable and Combustible Liquids Code*, and NFPA 58-2004, *Liquefied Petroleum Gas Code*.

(C) Class II Locations. Class II locations are those that are hazardous because of the presence of combustible dust. Class II locations shall include those specified in 500.5(C)(1) and (C)(2).

(1) Class II, Division 1. A Class II, Division 1 location is a location

(1) In which combustible dust is in the air under normal operating conditions in quantities sufficient to produce explosive or ignitible mixtures, or

(2) Where mechanical failure or abnormal operation of machinery or equipment might cause such explosive or ignitible mixtures to be produced, and might also provide a source of ignition through simultaneous failure of electric equipment, through operation of protection devices, or from other causes, or

(3) In which Group E combustible dusts may be present in quantities sufficient to be hazardous.

FPN: Dusts containing magnesium or aluminum are particularly hazardous, and the use of extreme precaution is necessary to avoid ignition and explosion.

(2) Class II, Division 2. A Class II, Division 2 location is a location

(1) In which combustible dust due to abnormal operations may be present in the air in quantities sufficient to produce explosive or ignitible mixtures; or

(2) Where combustible dust accumulations are present but are normally insufficient to interfere with the normal operation of electrical equipment or other apparatus, but could as a result of infrequent malfunctioning of handling or processing equipment become suspended in the air; or

(3) In which combustible dust accumulations on, in, or in the vicinity of the electrical equipment could be sufficient to interfere with the safe dissipation of heat from electrical equipment, or could be ignitible by abnormal operation or failure of electrical equipment.

FPN No. 1: The quantity of combustible dust that may be present and the adequacy of dust removal systems are factors that merit consideration in determining the classification and may result in an unclassified area.

FPN No. 2: Where products such as seed are handled in a manner that produces low quantities of dust, the amount of dust deposited may not warrant classification.

(D) Class III Locations. Class III locations are those that are hazardous because of the presence of easily ignitible fibers or flyings, but in which such fibers or flyings are not likely to be in suspension in the air in quantities sufficient to produce ignitible mixtures. Class III locations shall include those specified in 500.5(D)(1) and (D)(2).

(1) Class III, Division 1. A Class III, Division 1 location is a location in which easily ignitible fibers or materials producing combustible flyings are handled, manufactured, or used.

> FPN No. 1: Such locations usually include some parts of rayon, cotton, and other textile mills; combustible fiber manufacturing and processing plants; cotton gins and cotton-seed mills; flax-processing plants; clothing manufacturing plants; woodworking plants; and establishments and industries involving similar hazardous processes or conditions.

> FPN No. 2: Easily ignitible fibers and flyings include rayon, cotton (including cotton linters and cotton waste), sisal or henequen, istle, jute, hemp, tow, cocoa fiber, oakum, baled waste kapok, Spanish moss, excelsior, and other materials of similar nature.

(2) Class III, Division 2. A Class III, Division 2 location is a location in which easily ignitible fibers are stored or handled other than in the process of manufacture.

500.6 Material Groups. For purposes of testing, approval, and area classification, various air mixtures (not oxygen-enriched) shall be grouped in accordance with 500.6(A) and 500.6(B).

Exception: Equipment identified for a specific gas, vapor, or dust.

> FPN: This grouping is based on the characteristics of the materials. Facilities are available for testing and identifying equipment for use in the various atmospheric groups.

(A) Class I Group Classifications. Class I groups shall be according to 500.6(A)(1) through (A)(4).

> FPN No. 1: FPN Nos. 2 and 3 apply to 500.6(A).

> FPN No. 2: The explosion characteristics of air mixtures of gases or vapors vary with the specific material involved. For Class I locations, Groups A, B, C, and D, the classification involves determinations of maximum explosion pressure and maximum safe clearance between parts of a clamped joint in an enclosure. It is necessary, therefore, that equipment be identified not only for class but also for the specific group of the gas or vapor that will be present.

> FPN No. 3: Certain chemical atmospheres may have characteristics that require safeguards beyond those required for any of the Class I groups. Carbon disulfide is one of these chemicals because of its low ignition temperature [100°C (212°F)] and the small joint clearance permitted to arrest its flame.

(1) Group A. Acetylene. [NFPA 497:3.3]

(2) Group B. Flammable gas, flammable liquid–produced vapor, or combustible liquid–produced vapor mixed with air that may burn or explode, having either a maximum

experimental safe gap (MESG) value less than or equal to 0.45 mm or a minimum igniting current ratio (MIC ratio) less than or equal to 0.40. [NFPA 497:3.3]

> FPN: A typical Class I, Group B material is hydrogen.

Exception No. 1: Group D equipment shall be permitted to be used for atmospheres containing butadiene, provided all conduit runs into explosionproof equipment are provided with explosionproof seals installed within 450 mm (18 in.) of the enclosure.

Exception No. 2: Group C equipment shall be permitted to be used for atmospheres containing allyl glycidyl ether, n-butyl glycidyl ether, ethylene oxide, propylene oxide, and acrolein, provided all conduit runs into explosionproof equipment are provided with explosionproof seals installed within 450 mm (18 in.) of the enclosure.

(3) Group C. Flammable gas, flammable liquid–produced vapor, or combustible liquid–produced vapor mixed with air that may burn or explode, having either a maximum experimental safe gap (MESG) value greater than 0.45 mm and less than or equal to 0.75 mm, or a minimum igniting current ratio (MIC ratio) greater than 0.40 and less than or equal to 0.80. [NFPA 497:3.3]

> FPN: A typical Class I, Group C material is ethylene.

(4) Group D. Flammable gas, flammable liquid–produced vapor, or combustible liquid–produced vapor mixed with air that may burn or explode, having either a maximum experimental safe gap (MESG) value greater than 0.75 mm or a minimum igniting current ratio (MIC ratio) greater than 0.80. [NFPA 497:3.3]

> FPN No. 1: A typical Class I, Group D material is propane.

> FPN No. 2: For classification of areas involving ammonia atmospheres, see ANSI/ASHRAE 15-1994, *Safety Code for Mechanical Refrigeration*, and ANSI/CGA G2.1-1989, *Safety Requirements for the Storage and Handling of Anhydrous Ammonia*.

(B) Class II Group Classifications. Class II groups shall be in accordance with 500.6(B)(1) through (B)(3).

(1) Group E. Atmospheres containing combustible metal dusts, including aluminum, magnesium, and their commercial alloys, or other combustible dusts whose particle size, abrasiveness, and conductivity present similar hazards in the use of electrical equipment. [NFPA 499:3.3]

> FPN: Certain metal dusts may have characteristics that require safeguards beyond those required for atmospheres containing the dusts of aluminum, magnesium, and their commercial alloys. For example, zirconium, thorium, and uranium dusts have extremely low ignition temperatures [as low as 20°C (68°F)] and minimum ignition energies lower than any material classified in any of the Class I or Class II groups.

(2) Group F. Atmospheres containing combustible carbonaceous dusts that have more than 8 percent total entrapped volatiles (see ASTM D 3175-89, *Standard Test Method for Volatile Material in the Analysis Sample for Coal and Coke*, for coal and coke dusts) or that have been sensitized by other materials so that they present an explosion hazard. Coal, carbon black, charcoal, and coke dusts are examples of carbonaceous dusts. [NFPA 499:3.3]

(3) Group G. Atmospheres containing combustible dusts not included in Group E or F, including flour, grain, wood, plastic, and chemicals.

FPN No. 1: For additional information on group classification of Class II materials, see NFPA 499-2004, *Recommended Practice for the Classification of Combustible Dusts and of Hazardous (Classified) Locations for Electrical Installations in Chemical Process Areas.*

FPN No. 2: The explosion characteristics of air mixtures of dust vary with the materials involved. For Class II locations, Groups E, F, and G, the classification involves the tightness of the joints of assembly and shaft openings to prevent the entrance of dust in the dust-ignitionproof enclosure, the blanketing effect of layers of dust on the equipment that may cause overheating, and the ignition temperature of the dust. It is necessary, therefore, that equipment be identified not only for the class, but also for the specific group of dust that will be present.

FPN No. 3: Certain dusts may require additional precautions due to chemical phenomena that can result in the generation of ignitible gases. See ANSI C2-2002, *National Electrical Safety Code*, Section 127A, Coal Handling Areas.

500.7 Protection Techniques. Section 500.7(A) through 500.7(L) shall be acceptable protection techniques for electrical and electronic equipment in hazardous (classified) locations.

(A) Explosionproof Apparatus. This protection technique shall be permitted for equipment in Class I, Division 1 or 2 locations.

(B) Dust Ignitionproof. This protection technique shall be permitted for equipment in Class II, Division 1 or 2 locations.

(C) Dusttight. This protection technique shall be permitted for equipment in Class II, Division 2 or Class III, Division 1 or 2 locations.

(D) Purged and Pressurized. This protection technique shall be permitted for equipment in any hazardous (classified) location for which it is identified.

(E) Intrinsic Safety. This protection technique shall be permitted for equipment in Class I, Division 1 or 2; or Class II, Division 1 or 2; or Class III, Division 1 or 2 locations. The provisions of Articles 501 through 503 and Articles 510 through 516 shall not be considered applicable to such installations, except as required by Article 504, and

installation of intrinsically safe apparatus and wiring shall be in accordance with the requirements of Article 504.

(F) Nonincendive Circuit. This protection technique shall be permitted for equipment in Class I, Division 2; Class II, Division 2; or Class III, Division 1 or 2 locations.

(G) Nonincendive Equipment. This protection technique shall be permitted for equipment in Class I, Division 2; Class II, Division 2; or Class III, Division 1 or 2 locations.

(H) Nonincendive Component. This protection technique shall be permitted for equipment in Class I, Division 2; Class II, Division 2; or Class III, Division 1 or 2 locations.

(I) Oil Immersion. This protection technique shall be permitted for current-interrupting contacts in Class I, Division 2 locations as described in 501.115(B)(1)(2).

(J) Hermetically Sealed. This protection technique shall be permitted for equipment in Class I, Division 2; Class II, Division 2; or Class III, Division 1 or 2 locations.

(K) Combustible Gas Detection System. A combustible gas detection system shall be permitted as a means of protection in industrial establishments with restricted public access and where the conditions of maintenance and supervision ensure that only qualified persons service the installation. Gas detection equipment shall be listed for detection of the specific gas or vapor to be encountered. Where such a system is installed, equipment specified in 500.7(K)(1), (K)(2), or (K)(3) shall be permitted.

The type of detection equipment, its listing, installation location(s), alarm and shutdown criteria, and calibration frequency shall be documented when combustible gas detectors are used as a protection technique.

FPN No. 1: For further information, see ANSI/ISA-12.13.01, *Performance Requirements, Combustible Gas Detectors.*

FPN No. 2: For further information, see ANSI/API RP 500, *Recommended Practice for Classification of Locations for Electrical Installations at Petroleum Facilities Classified as Class I, Division I or Division 2.*

FPN No. 3: For further information, see ISA-RP12.13.02, *Installation, Operation, and Maintenance of Combustible Gas Detection Instruments.*

(1) Inadequate Ventilation. In a Class I, Division 1 location that is so classified due to inadequate ventilation, electrical equipment suitable for Class I, Division 2 locations shall be permitted.

(2) Interior of a Building. In a building located in, or with an opening into, a Class I, Division 2 location where the interior does not contain a source of flammable gas or vapor, electrical equipment for unclassified locations shall be permitted.

(3) Interior of a Control Panel. In the interior of a control panel containing instrumentation utilizing or measuring flammable liquids, gases, or vapors, electrical equipment suitable for Class I, Division 2 locations shall be permitted.

(L) Other Protection Techniques. Other protection techniques used in equipment identified for use in hazardous (classified) locations.

500.8 Equipment. Articles 500 through 504 require equipment construction and installation that ensure safe performance under conditions of proper use and maintenance.

> FPN No. 1: It is important that inspection authorities and users exercise more than ordinary care with regard to installation and maintenance.
>
> FPN No. 2: Since there is no consistent relationship between explosion properties and ignition temperature, the two are independent requirements.
>
> FPN No. 3: Low ambient conditions require special consideration. Explosionproof or dust-ignitionproof equipment may not be suitable for use at temperatures lower than −25°C (−13°F) unless they are identified for low-temperature service. However, at low ambient temperatures, flammable concentrations of vapors may not exist in a location classified as Class I, Division 1 at normal ambient temperature.

(A) Approval for Class and Properties.

(1) Equipment shall be identified not only for the class of location but also for the explosive, combustible, or ignitible properties of the specific gas, vapor, dust, fiber, or flyings that will be present. In addition, Class I equipment shall not have any exposed surface that operates at a temperature in excess of the ignition temperature of the specific gas or vapor. Class II equipment shall not have an external temperature higher than that specified in 500.8(C)(2). Class III equipment shall not exceed the maximum surface temperatures specified in 503.5.

> FPN: Luminaires (lighting fixtures) and other heat-producing apparatus, switches, circuit breakers, and plugs and receptacles are potential sources of ignition and are investigated for suitability in classified locations. Such types of equipment, as well as cable terminations for entry into explosionproof enclosures, are available as listed for Class I, Division 2 locations. Fixed wiring, however, may utilize wiring methods that are not evaluated with respect to classified locations. Wiring products such as cable, raceways, boxes, and fittings, therefore, are not marked as being suitable for Class I, Division 2 locations. Also see 500.8(B)(6)(a).

Suitability of identified equipment shall be determined by any of the following:

(1) Equipment listing or labeling

(2) Evidence of equipment evaluation from a qualified testing laboratory or inspection agency concerned with product evaluation

(3) Evidence acceptable to the authority having jurisdiction such as a manufacturer's self-evaluation or an owner's engineering judgment

(2) Equipment that has been identified for a Division 1 location shall be permitted in a Division 2 location of the same class, group, and temperature class and shall comply with (a) or (b) as applicable.

    (a) Intrinsically safe apparatus having a control drawing requiring the installation of associated apparatus for a Division 1 installation shall be permitted to be installed in a Division 2 location if the same associated apparatus is used for the Division 2 installation.

    (b) Equipment that is required to be explosionproof shall incorporate seals per 501.15(A) or 501.15(D) when the wiring methods of 501.10(B) are employed.

(3) Where specifically permitted in Articles 501 through 503, general-purpose equipment or equipment in general-purpose enclosures shall be permitted to be installed in Division 2 locations if the equipment does not constitute a source of ignition under normal operating conditions.

(4) Equipment that depends on a single compression seal, diaphragm, or tube to prevent flammable or combustible fluids from entering the equipment shall be identified for a Class I, Division 2 location even if installed in an unclassified location. Equipment installed in a Class I, Division 1 location shall be identified for the Class I, Division 1 location.

> FPN: Equipment used for flow measurement is an example of equipment having a single compression seal, diaphragm, or tube.

(5) Unless otherwise specified, normal operating conditions for motors shall be assumed to be rated full-load steady conditions.

(6) Where flammable gases or combustible dusts are or may be present at the same time, the simultaneous presence of both shall be considered when determining the safe operating temperature of the electrical equipment.

> FPN: The characteristics of various atmospheric mixtures of gases, vapors, and dusts depend on the specific material involved.

(B) Marking. Equipment shall be marked to show the environment for which it has been evaluated. Unless otherwise specified or allowed in (B)(6), the marking shall include the information specified in (B)(1) through (B)(5).

(1) Class. The marking shall specify the class(es) for which the equipment is suitable.

(2) Division. The marking shall specify the division if the equipment is suitable for Division 2 only. Equipment suitable for Division 1 shall be permitted to omit the division marking.

FPN: Equipment not marked to indicate a division, or marked "Division 1" or "Div. 1," is suitable for both Division 1 and 2 locations; see 500.8(A)(2). Equipment marked "Division 2" or "Div. 2" is suitable for Division 2 locations only.

(3) Material Classification Group. The marking shall specify the applicable material classification group(s) in accordance with 500.6.

Exception: Fixed luminaires (lighting fixtures) marked for use only in Class I, Division 2 or Class II, Division 2 locations shall not be required to indicate the group.

(4) Equipment Temperature. The marking shall specify the temperature class or operating temperature at a 40°C ambient temperature, or at the higher ambient temperature if the equipment is rated and marked for an ambient temperature of greater than 40°C. The temperature class, if provided, shall be indicated using the temperature class (T Codes) shown in Table 500.8(B). Equipment for Class I and Class II shall be marked with the maximum safe operating temperature, as determined by simultaneous exposure to the combinations of Class I and Class II conditions.

Table 500.8(B) Classification of Maximum Surface Temperature

Maximum Temperature		Temperature Class (T Code)
°C	°F	
450	842	T1
300	572	T2
280	536	T2A
260	500	T2B
230	446	T2C
215	419	T2D
200	392	T3
180	356	T3A
165	329	T3B
160	320	T3C
135	275	T4
120	248	T4A
100	212	T5
85	185	T6

Exception: Equipment of the non–heat-producing type, such as junction boxes, conduit, and fittings, and equipment of the heat-producing type having a maximum temperature not more than 100°C shall not be required to have a marked operating temperature or temperature class.

FPN: More than one marked temperature class or operating temperature, for gases and vapors, dusts, and different ambient temperatures, may appear.

(5) Ambient Temperature Range. For equipment rated for a temperature range other than –25°C to +40°C, the marking shall specify the special range of ambient temperatures. The marking shall include either the symbol "Ta" or "Tamb."

FPN: As an example, such a marking might be "–30°C ≤ Ta ≤ +40°C."

(6) Special Allowances.

(a) General Purpose Equipment. Fixed general-purpose equipment in Class I locations, other than fixed luminaires (lighting fixtures), that is acceptable for use in Class I, Division 2 locations shall not be required to be marked with the class, division, group, temperature class, or ambient temperature range.

(b) Dusttight Equipment. Fixed dusttight equipment, other than fixed luminaires (lighting fixtures), that is acceptable for use in Class II, Division 2 and Class III locations shall not be required to be marked with the class, division, group, temperature class, or ambient temperature range.

(c) Associated Apparatus. Associated intrinsically safe apparatus and associated nonincendive field wiring apparatus that are not protected by an alternative type of protection shall not be marked with the class, division, group, or temperature class. Associated intrinsically safe apparatus and associated nonincendive field wiring apparatus shall be marked with the class, division, and group of the apparatus to which it is to be connected.

(d) Simple Apparatus. "Simple apparatus" as defined in Article 504, shall not be required to be marked with class, division, group, temperature class, or ambient temperature range.

(C) Temperature.

(1) Class I Temperature. The temperature marking specified in 500.8(B) shall not exceed the ignition temperature of the specific gas or vapor to be encountered.

FPN: For information regarding ignition temperatures of gases and vapors, see NFPA 497-2004, *Recommended Practice for the Classification of Flammable Liquids, Gases, or Vapors, and of Hazardous (Classified) Locations for Electrical Installations in Chemical Process Areas.*

(2) Class II Temperature. The temperature marking specified in 500.8(B) shall be less than the ignition temperature of the specific dust to be encountered. For organic dusts that may dehydrate or carbonize, the temperature marking shall not exceed the lower of either the ignition temperature or 165°C (329°F).

FPN: See NFPA 499-2004, *Recommended Practice for the Classification of Combustible Dusts and of Hazardous (Classified) Locations for Electrical Installations in Chemical Process Areas,* for minimum ignition temperatures of specific dusts.

The ignition temperature for which equipment was approved prior to this requirement shall be assumed to be as shown in Table 500.8(C)(2).

Table 500.8(C)(2) Class II Temperatures

| Class II Group | Equipment Not Subject to Overloading | | Equipment (Such as Motors or Power Transformers) That May Be Overloaded | | | |
| | | | Normal Operation | | Abnormal Operation | |
	°C	°F	°C	°F	°C	°F
E	200	392	200	392	200	392
F	200	392	150	302	200	392
G	165	329	120	248	165	329

(D) Threading. All NPT threaded conduit and fittings referred to herein shall be threaded with a National (American) Standard Pipe Taper (NPT) thread that provides a taper of 1 in 16 (¾-in. taper per foot). Conduit and fittings shall be made wrenchtight to prevent sparking when fault current flows through the conduit system, and to ensure the explosionproof integrity of the conduit system where applicable. Equipment provided with threaded entries for field wiring connections shall be installed in accordance with 500.8(D)(1) or (D)(2). Threaded entries into explosionproof equipment shall be made up with at least five threads fully engaged.

Exception: For listed explosionproof equipment, factory threaded NPT entries shall be made up with at least 4½ threads fully engaged.

(1) Equipment Provided with Threaded Entries for NPT Threaded Conduit or Fittings. For equipment provided with threaded entries for NPT threaded conduit or fittings, listed conduit, conduit fittings, or cable fittings shall be used.

FPN: Thread form specifications for NPT threads are located in ANSI/ASME B1.20.1-1983, *Pipe Threads, General Purpose (Inch)*.

(2) Equipment Provided with Threaded Entries for Metric Threaded Conduit or Fittings. For equipment with metric threaded entries, such entries shall be identified as being metric, or listed adapters to permit connection to conduit or NPT-threaded fittings shall be provided with the equipment. Adapters shall be used for connection to conduit or NPT-threaded fittings. Listed cable fittings that have metric threads shall be permitted to be used.

FPN: Threading specifications for metric threaded entries are located in ISO 965/1-1980, *Metric Screw Threads*, and ISO 965/3-1980, *Metric Screw Threads*.

(E) Fiber Optic Cable Assembly. Where a fiber optic cable assembly contains conductors that are capable of carrying current, the fiber optic cable assembly shall be installed in accordance with the requirements of Articles 500, 501, 502, or 503, as applicable.

500.9 Specific Occupancies. Articles 510 through 517 cover garages, aircraft hangars, motor fuel dispensing facilities, bulk storage plants, spray application, dipping and coating processes, and health care facilities.

ARTICLE 501
Class I Locations

I. General

501.1 Scope. Article 501 covers the requirements for electrical and electronic equipment and wiring for all voltages in Class I, Division 1 and 2 locations where fire or explosion hazards may exist due to flammable gases or vapors or flammable liquids.

FPN: For the requirements for electrical and electronic equipment and wiring for all voltages in Class I, Zone 0, Zone 1, or Zone 2 hazardous (classified) locations where fire or explosion hazards may exist due to flammable gases or vapors or flammable liquids, refer to Article 505.

501.5 General. The general rules of this *Code* shall apply to the electric wiring and equipment in locations classified as Class I in 500.5.

Exception: As modified by this article.

Equipment listed and marked in accordance with 505.9(C)(2) for use in Class I, Zone 0, 1, or 2 locations shall be permitted in Class I, Division 2 locations for the same gas and with a suitable temperature class. Equipment listed and marked in accordance with 505.9(C)(2) for use in Class I, Zone 0 locations shall be permitted in Class I, Division 1 or Division 2 locations for the same gas and with a suitable temperature class.

II. Wiring

501.10 Wiring Methods. Wiring methods shall comply with 501.10(A) or 501.10(B).

(A) Class I, Division 1.

(1) General. In Class I, Division 1 locations, the wiring methods in (a) through (d) shall be permitted.

    (a) Threaded rigid metal conduit or threaded steel intermediate metal conduit.

Exception: Rigid nonmetallic conduit complying with Article 352 shall be permitted where encased in a concrete envelope a minimum of 50 mm (2 in.) thick and provided with not less than 600 mm (24 in.) of cover measured from the top of the conduit to grade. The concrete encasement shall be permitted to be omitted where subject to the pro-

visions of 514.8, Exception No. 2; and 515.8(A). Threaded rigid metal conduit or threaded steel intermediate metal conduit shall be used for the last 600 mm (24 in.) of the underground run to emergence or to the point of connection to the aboveground raceway. An equipment grounding conductor shall be included to provide for electrical continuity of the raceway system and for grounding of non–current-carrying metal parts.

(b) Type MI cable with termination fittings listed for the location. Type MI cable shall be installed and supported in a manner to avoid tensile stress at the termination fittings.

(c) In industrial establishments with restricted public access, where the conditions of maintenance and supervision ensure that only qualified persons service the installation, Type MC-HL cable, listed for use in Class I, Division 1 locations, with a gas/vaportight continuous corrugated metallic sheath, an overall jacket of suitable polymeric material, separate grounding conductors in accordance with 250.122, and provided with termination fittings listed for the application.

FPN: See 330.12 for restrictions on use of Type MC cable.

(d) In industrial establishments with restricted public access, where the conditions of maintenance and supervision ensure that only qualified persons service the installation, Type ITC-HL cable, listed for use in Class I, Division 1 locations, with a gas/vaportight continuous corrugated metallic sheath, an overall jacket of suitable polymeric material and provided with termination fittings listed for the application.

(2) Flexible Connections. Where necessary to employ flexible connections, as at motor terminals, flexible fittings listed for Class I, Division 1 locations or flexible cord in accordance with the provisions of 501.140 shall be permitted.

(3) Boxes and Fittings. All boxes and fittings shall be approved for Class I, Division 1.

(B) Class I, Division 2.

(1) General. In Class I, Division 2 locations, the following wiring methods shall be permitted:

(1) All wiring methods permitted in Article 501.10(A).

(2) Threaded rigid metal conduit, threaded steel intermediate metal conduit.

(3) Enclosed gasketed busways, enclosed gasketed wireways.

(4) Type PLTC cable in accordance with the provisions of Article 725, or in cable tray systems. PLTC shall be installed in a manner to avoid tensile stress at the termination fittings.

(5) Type ITC cable as permitted in 727.4.

(6) Type MI, MC, MV, or TC cable with termination fittings, or in cable tray systems and installed in a manner

to avoid tensile stress at the termination fittings. Single conductor Type MV cables shall be shielded or metallic armored.

(2) Flexible Connections. Where provision must be made for limited flexibility, one or more of the following shall also be permitted:

(1) Flexible metal fittings

(2) Flexible metal conduit with listed fittings

(3) Liquidtight flexible metal conduit with listed fittings

(4) Liquidtight flexible nonmetallic conduit with listed fittings

(5) Flexible cord listed for extra-hard usage and provided with listed bushed fittings. An additional conductor for grounding shall be included in the flexible cord.

FPN: See 501.30(B) for grounding requirements where flexible conduit is used.

(3) Nonincendive Field Wiring. Nonincendive field wiring shall be permitted using any of the wiring methods permitted for unclassified locations. Nonincendive field wiring systems shall be installed in accordance with the control drawing(s). Simple apparatus, not shown on the control drawing, shall be permitted in a nonincendive field wiring circuit, provided the simple apparatus does not interconnect the nonincendive field wiring circuit to any other circuit.

FPN: Simple apparatus is defined in 504.2.

Separate nonincendive field wiring circuits shall be installed in accordance with one of the following:

(1) In separate cables

(2) In multiconductor cables where the conductors of each circuit are within a grounded metal shield

(3) In multiconductor cables, where the conductors of each circuit have insulation with a minimum thickness of 0.25 mm (0.01 in.)

(4) Boxes and Fittings. Boxes and fittings shall not be required to be explosionproof except as required by 501.105(B)(1), 501.115(B)(1), and 501.150(B)(1).

501.15 Sealing and Drainage. Seals in conduit and cable systems shall comply with 501.15(A) through 501.15(F). Sealing compound shall be used in Type MI cable termination fittings to exclude moisture and other fluids from the cable insulation.

FPN No. 1: Seals are provided in conduit and cable systems to minimize the passage of gases and vapors and prevent the passage of flames from one portion of the electrical installation to another through the conduit. Such communication through Type MI cable is inherently prevented by construction of the cable. Unless specifically designed and tested for the purpose, conduit and cable seals are not intended to prevent the passage of liquids, gases, or vapors at a continuous pressure differential across the seal. Even at differences in pressure across the seal equivalent to a few inches of water, there may be a slow passage of gas or vapor through a seal and through conductors passing through the seal. See 501.15(E)(2). Temperature extremes and highly corrosive liquids and vapors can affect the ability of seals to perform their intended function. See 501.15(C)(2).

FPN No. 2: Gas or vapor leakage and propagation of flames may occur through the interstices between the strands of standard stranded conductors larger than 2 AWG. Special conductor constructions, for example, compacted strands or sealing of the individual strands, are means of reducing leakage and preventing the propagation of flames.

(A) Conduit Seals, Class I, Division 1. In Class I, Division 1 locations, conduit seals shall be located in accordance with 501.15(A)(1) through (A)(4).

(1) Entering Enclosures. In each conduit entry into an explosionproof enclosure where either of the following apply:

(1) The enclosure contains apparatus, such as switches, circuit breakers, fuses, relays, or resistors, that may produce arcs, sparks, or high temperatures that are considered to be an ignition source in normal operation.

(2) The entry is metric designator 53 (trade size 2) or larger and the enclosure contains terminals, splices, or taps.

For the purposes of this section, high temperatures shall be considered to be any temperatures exceeding 80 percent of the autoignition temperature in degrees Celsius of the gas or vapor involved.

Exception to 501.15(A)(1)(1): Seals shall not be required for conduit entering an enclosure where such switches, circuit breakers, fuses, relays, or resistors comply with one of the following:

(1) Are enclosed within a chamber hermetically sealed against the entrance of gases or vapors

(2) Are immersed in oil in accordance with 501.115(B)(1)(2)

(3) Are enclosed within a factory-sealed explosionproof chamber located within the enclosure, identified for the location, and marked "factory sealed" or equivalent, unless the enclosure entry is metric designator 53 (trade size 2) or larger

(4) Are in nonincendive circuits

Factory-sealed enclosures shall not be considered to serve as a seal for another adjacent explosionproof enclosure that is required to have a conduit seal.

Conduit seals shall be installed within 450 mm (18 in.) from the enclosure. Only explosionproof unions, couplings, reducers, elbows, capped elbows, and conduit bodies similar to L, T, and Cross types that are not larger than the trade size of the conduit shall be permitted between the sealing fitting and the explosionproof enclosure.

(2) Pressurized Enclosures. In each conduit entry into a pressurized enclosure where the conduit is not pressurized as part of the protection system. Conduit seals shall be installed within 450 mm (18 in.) from the pressurized enclosure.

FPN No. 1: Installing the seal as close as possible to the enclosure will reduce problems with purging the dead air-space in the pressurized conduit.

FPN No. 2: For further information, see NFPA 496-2003, *Standard for Purged and Pressurized Enclosures for Electrical Equipment.*

(3) Two or More Explosionproof Enclosures. Where two or more explosionproof enclosures for which conduit seals are required under 501.15(A)(1) are connected by nipples or by runs of conduit not more than 900 mm (36 in.) long, a single conduit seal in each such nipple connection or run of conduit shall be considered sufficient if located not more than 450 mm (18 in.) from either enclosure.

(4) Class I, Division 1 Boundary. In each conduit run leaving a Class I, Division 1 location. The sealing fitting shall be permitted on either side of the boundary of such location within 3.05 m (10 ft) of the boundary and shall be designed and installed so as to minimize the amount of gas or vapor within the Division 1 portion of the conduit from being communicated to the conduit beyond the seal. Except for listed explosionproof reducers at the conduit seal, there shall be no union, coupling, box, or fitting between the conduit seal and the point at which the conduit leaves the Division 1 location.

Exception No. 1: Metal conduit that contains no unions, couplings, boxes, or fittings, and passes completely through a Class I, Division 1 location with no fittings less than 300 mm (12 in.) beyond each boundary, shall not require a conduit seal if the termination points of the unbroken conduit are in unclassified locations.

Exception No. 2: For underground conduit installed in accordance with 300.5 where the boundary is beneath the ground, the sealing fitting shall be permitted to be installed after the conduit leaves the ground, but there shall be no union, coupling, box, or fitting, other than listed explosionproof reducers at the sealing fitting, in the conduit between the sealing fitting and the point at which the conduit leaves the ground.

(B) Conduit Seals, Class I, Division 2. In Class I, Division 2 locations, conduit seals shall be located in accordance with 501.15(B)(1) and (B)(2).

(1) Entering Enclosures. For connections to enclosures that are required to be explosionproof, a conduit seal shall be provided in accordance with 501.15(A)(1) and (A)(3). All portions of the conduit run or nipple between the seal and such enclosure shall comply with 501.10(A).

(2) Class I, Division 2 Boundary. In each conduit run passing from a Class I, Division 2 location into an unclassified location. The sealing fitting shall be permitted on either side of the boundary of such location within 3.05 m (10 ft) of the boundary. Rigid metal conduit or threaded steel intermediate metal conduit shall be used between the sealing fitting and the point at which the conduit leaves the Division 2 location, and a threaded connection shall be used at the sealing fitting. Except for listed reducers at the conduit seal, there shall be no union, coupling, box, or fitting between the conduit seal and the point at which the conduit leaves the Division 2 location. Conduits shall be sealed to minimize the amount of gas or vapor within the Division 2 portion of the conduit from being communicated to the conduit beyond the seal. Such seals shall not be required to be explosionproof but shall be identified for the purpose of minimizing passage of gases under normal operating conditions and shall be accessible.

Exception No. 1: Metal conduit that contains no unions, couplings, boxes, or fittings, and passes completely through a Class I, Division 2 location with no fittings less than 300 mm (12 in.) beyond each boundary, shall not be required to be sealed if the termination points of the unbroken conduit are in unclassified locations.

Exception No. 2: Conduit systems terminating at an unclassified location where a wiring method transition is made to cable tray, cablebus, ventilated busway, Type MI cable, or cable not installed in any cable tray or raceway system, shall not be required to be sealed where passing from the Class I, Division 2 location into the unclassified location. The unclassified location shall be outdoors or, if the conduit system is all in one room, it shall be permitted to be indoors. The conduits shall not terminate at an enclosure containing an ignition source in normal operation.

Exception No. 3: Conduit systems passing from an enclosure or room that is unclassified as a result of pressurization into a Class I, Division 2 location shall not require a seal at the boundary.

    FPN: For further information, refer to NFPA 496-2003, *Standard for Purged and Pressurized Enclosures for Electrical Equipment.*

Exception No. 4: Segments of aboveground conduit systems shall not be required to be sealed where passing from a Class I, Division 2 location into an unclassified location if all of the following conditions are met:

(1) No part of the conduit system segment passes through a Class I, Division 1 location where the conduit contains unions, couplings, boxes, or fittings within 300 mm (12 in.) of the Class I, Division 1 location.

(2) The conduit system segment is located entirely in outdoor locations.

(3) The conduit system segment is not directly connected to canned pumps, process or service connections for flow, pressure, or analysis measurement, and so forth, that depend on a single compression seal, diaphragm, or tube to prevent flammable or combustible fluids from entering the conduit system.

(4) The conduit system segment contains only threaded metal conduit, unions, couplings, conduit bodies, and fittings in the unclassified location.

(5) The conduit system segment is sealed at its entry to each enclosure or fitting housing terminals, splices, or taps in Class I, Division 2 locations.

(C) Class I, Divisions 1 and 2. Seals installed in Class I, Division 1 and Division 2 locations shall comply with 501.15(C)(1) through (C)(6).

Exception: Seals not required to be explosionproof by 501.15(B)(2) or 504.70.

(1) Fittings. Enclosures for connections or equipment shall be provided with an integral means for sealing, or sealing fittings listed for the location shall be used. Sealing fittings shall be listed for use with one or more specific compounds and shall be accessible.

(2) Compound. The compound shall provide a seal against passage of gas or vapors through the seal fitting, shall not be affected by the surrounding atmosphere or liquids, and shall not have a melting point of less than 93°C (200°F).

(3) Thickness of Compounds. Except for listed cable sealing fittings, the thickness of the sealing compound in a completed seal shall not be less than the metric designator (trade size) of the sealing fitting expressed in the units of measurement employed, and in no case less than 16 mm (⅝ in.).

(4) Splices and Taps. Splices and taps shall not be made in fittings intended only for sealing with compound, nor shall other fittings in which splices or taps are made be filled with compound.

(5) Assemblies. In an assembly where equipment that may produce arcs, sparks, or high temperatures is located in a compartment separate from the compartment containing splices or taps, and an integral seal is provided where conductors pass from one compartment to the other, the entire assembly shall be identified for the location. Seals in conduit connections to the compartment containing splices or taps shall be provided in Class I, Division 1 locations where required by 501.15(A)(1)(2).

(6) Conductor Fill. The cross-sectional area of the conductors permitted in a seal shall not exceed 25 percent of the cross-sectional area of a rigid metal conduit of the same trade size unless it is specifically identified for a higher percentage of fill.

(D) Cable Seals, Class I, Division 1. In Class I, Division 1 locations, cable seals shall be located according to 501.15(D)(1) through (D)(3).

(1) At Terminations. Cable shall be sealed at all terminations. The sealing fitting shall comply with 501.15(C). Multiconductor Type MC-HL cables with a gas/vaportight continuous corrugated metallic sheath and an overall jacket of suitable polymeric material shall be sealed with a listed fitting after removing the jacket and any other covering so that the sealing compound surrounds each individual insulated conductor in such a manner as to minimize the passage of gases and vapors.

Exception: Shielded cables and twisted pair cables shall not require the removal of the shielding material or separation of the twisted pairs, provided the termination is by an approved means to minimize the entrance of gases or vapors and prevent propagation of flame into the cable core.

(2) Cables Capable of Transmitting Gases or Vapors. Cables in conduit with a gas/vaportight continuous sheath capable of transmitting gases or vapors through the cable core shall be sealed in the Division 1 location after removing the jacket and any other coverings so that the sealing compound will surround each individual insulated conductor and the outer jacket.

Exception: Multiconductor cables with a gas/vaportight continuous sheath capable of transmitting gases or vapors through the cable core shall be permitted to be considered as a single conductor by sealing the cable in the conduit within 450 mm (18 in.) of the enclosure and the cable end within the enclosure by an approved means to minimize the entrance of gases or vapors and prevent the propagation of flame into the cable core, or by other approved methods. For shielded cables and twisted pair cables, it shall not be required to remove the shielding material or separate the twisted pair.

(3) Cables Incapable of Transmitting Gases or Vapors. Each multiconductor cable in conduit shall be considered as a single conductor if the cable is incapable of transmitting gases or vapors through the cable core. These cables shall be sealed in accordance with 501.15(A).

(E) Cable Seals, Class I, Division 2. In Class I, Division 2 locations, cable seals shall be located in accordance with 501.15(E)(1) through (E)(4).

(1) Terminations. Cables entering enclosures that are required to be explosionproof shall be sealed at the point of entrance. The sealing fitting shall comply with 501.15(B)(1). Multiconductor cables with a gas/vaportight continuous sheath capable of transmitting gases or vapors through the cable core shall be sealed in a listed fitting in the Division 2 location after removing the jacket and any other coverings so that the sealing compound surrounds each individual insulated conductor

in such a manner as to minimize the passage of gases and vapors. Multiconductor cables in conduit shall be sealed as described in 501.15(D).

Exception No. 1: Cables passing from an enclosure or room that is unclassified as a result of Type Z pressurization into a Class I, Division 2 location shall not require a seal at the boundary.

Exception No. 2: Shielded cables and twisted pair cables shall not require the removal of the shielding material or separation of the twisted pairs, provided the termination is by an approved means to minimize the entrance of gases or vapors and prevent propagation of flame into the cable core.

(2) Cables That Do Not Transmit Gases or Vapors. Cables that have a gas/vaportight continuous sheath and do not transmit gases or vapors through the cable core in excess of the quantity permitted for seal fittings shall not be required to be sealed except as required in 501.15(E)(1). The minimum length of such cable run shall not be less than that length that limits gas or vapor flow through the cable core to the rate permitted for seal fittings [200 cm³/hr (0.007 ft³/hr) of air at a pressure of 1500 pascals (6 in. of water)].

> FPN No. 1: See ANSI/UL 886-1994, *Outlet Boxes and Fittings for Use in Hazardous (Classified) Locations.*

> FPN No. 2: The cable core does not include the interstices of the conductor strands.

(3) Cables Capable of Transmitting Gases or Vapors. Cables with a gas/vaportight continuous sheath capable of transmitting gases or vapors through the cable core shall not be required to be sealed except as required in 501.15(E)(1), unless the cable is attached to process equipment or devices that may cause a pressure in excess of 1500 pascals (6 in. of water) to be exerted at a cable end, in which case a seal, barrier, or other means shall be provided to prevent migration of flammables into an unclassified location.

Exception: Cables with an unbroken gas/vaportight continuous sheath shall be permitted to pass through a Class I, Division 2 location without seals.

(4) Cables Without Gas/Vaportight Sheath. Cables that do not have gas/vaportight continuous sheath shall be sealed at the boundary of the Division 2 and unclassified location in such a manner as to minimize the passage of gases or vapors into an unclassified location.

(F) Drainage.

(1) Control Equipment. Where there is a probability that liquid or other condensed vapor may be trapped within enclosures for control equipment or at any point in the raceway system, approved means shall be provided to prevent accumulation or to permit periodic draining of such liquid or condensed vapor.

(2) Motors and Generators. Where the authority having jurisdiction judges that there is a probability that liquid or condensed vapor may accumulate within motors or generators, joints and conduit systems shall be arranged to minimize the entrance of liquid. If means to prevent accumulation or to permit periodic draining are judged necessary, such means shall be provided at the time of manufacture and shall be considered an integral part of the machine.

(3) Canned Pumps, Process, or Service Connections, etc. For canned pumps, process, or service connections for flow, pressure, or analysis measurement, and so forth, that depend on a single compression seal, diaphragm, or tube to prevent flammable or combustible fluids from entering the electrical raceway or cable system capable of transmitting fluids, an additional approved seal, barrier, or other means shall be provided to prevent the flammable or combustible fluid from entering the raceway or cable system capable of transmitting fluids beyond the additional devices or means, if the primary seal fails. The additional approved seal or barrier and the interconnecting enclosure shall meet the temperature and pressure conditions to which they will be subjected upon failure of the primary seal, unless other approved means are provided to accomplish this purpose. Drains, vents, or other devices shall be provided so that primary seal leakage will be obvious.

FPN: See also the fine print notes to 501.15.

Process-connected equipment that is listed and marked "Dual Seal" shall not require additional process sealing when used within the manufacturer's ratings.

FPN: For construction and testing requirements for dual seal process connected equipment, refer to ISA 12.27.01, *Requirements for Process Sealing Between Electrical Systems and Potentially Flammable or Combustible Process Fluids.*

501.20 Conductor Insulation, Class I, Divisions 1 and 2. Where condensed vapors or liquids may collect on, or come in contact with, the insulation on conductors, such insulation shall be of a type identified for use under such conditions; or the insulation shall be protected by a sheath of lead or by other approved means.

501.25 Uninsulated Exposed Parts, Class I, Divisions 1 and 2. There shall be no uninsulated exposed parts, such as electric conductors, buses, terminals, or components, that operate at more than 30 volts (15 volts in wet locations). These parts shall additionally be protected by a protection technique according to 500.7(E), 500.7(F), or 500.7(G) that is suitable for the location.

501.30 Grounding and Bonding, Class I, Divisions 1 and 2. Wiring and equipment in Class I, Division 1 and 2 locations shall be grounded as specified in Article 250 and with the requirements in 501.30(A) and 501.30(B).

(A) Bonding. The locknut-bushing and double-locknut types of contacts shall not be depended on for bonding purposes, but bonding jumpers with proper fittings or other approved means of bonding shall be used. Such means of bonding shall apply to all intervening raceways, fittings, boxes, enclosures, and so forth between Class I locations and the point of grounding for service equipment or point of grounding of a separately derived system.

Exception: The specific bonding means shall be required only to the nearest point where the grounded circuit conductor and the grounding electrode are connected together on the line side of the building or structure disconnecting means as specified in 250.32(A), (B), and (C), provided the branch-circuit overcurrent protection is located on the load side of the disconnecting means.

FPN: See 250.100 for additional bonding requirements in hazardous (classified) locations.

(B) Types of Equipment Grounding Conductors. Where flexible metal conduit or liquidtight flexible metal conduit is used as permitted in 501.10(B) and is to be relied on to complete a sole equipment grounding path, it shall be installed with internal or external bonding jumpers in parallel with each conduit and complying with 250.102.

Exception: In Class I, Division 2 locations, the bonding jumper shall be permitted to be deleted where all of the following conditions are met:

(1) Listed liquidtight flexible metal conduit 1.8 m (6 ft) or less in length, with fittings listed for grounding, is used.

(2) Overcurrent protection in the circuit is limited to 10 amperes or less.

(3) The load is not a power utilization load.

501.35 Surge Protection.

(A) Class I, Division 1. Surge arresters, transient voltage surge suppressors (TVSS), and capacitors shall be installed in enclosures identified for Class I, Division 1 locations. Surge-protective capacitors shall be of a type designed for specific duty.

(B) Class I, Division 2. Surge arresters and TVSS shall be nonarcing, such as metal-oxide varistor (MOV) sealed type, and surge-protective capacitors shall be of a type designed for specific duty. Enclosures shall be permitted to be of the general-purpose type. Surge protection of types other than described in this paragraph shall be installed in enclosures identified for Class I, Division 1 locations.

501.40 Multiwire Branch Circuits. In a Class I, Division 1 location, a multiwire branch circuit shall not be permitted.

Exception: Where the disconnect device(s) for the circuit opens all ungrounded conductors of the multiwire circuit simultaneously.

III. Equipment

501.100 Transformers and Capacitors.

(A) Class I, Division 1. In Class I, Division 1 locations, transformers and capacitors shall comply with 501.100(A)(1) and (A)(2).

(1) Containing Liquid That Will Burn. Transformers and capacitors containing a liquid that will burn shall be installed only in vaults that comply with 450.41 through 450.48 and with (1) through (4) as follows:

(1) There shall be no door or other communicating opening between the vault and the Division 1 location.

(2) Ample ventilation shall be provided for the continuous removal of flammable gases or vapors.

(3) Vent openings or ducts shall lead to a safe location outside of buildings.

(4) Vent ducts and openings shall be of sufficient area to relieve explosion pressures within the vault, and all portions of vent ducts within the buildings shall be of reinforced concrete construction.

(2) Not Containing Liquid That Will Burn. Transformers and capacitors that do not contain a liquid that will burn shall be installed in vaults complying with 501.100(A)(1) or be approved for Class I locations.

(B) Class I, Division 2. In Class I, Division 2 locations, transformers and capacitors shall comply with 450.21 through 450.27.

501.105 Meters, Instruments, and Relays.

(A) Class I, Division 1. In Class I, Division 1 locations, meters, instruments, and relays, including kilowatt-hour meters, instrument transformers, resistors, rectifiers, and thermionic tubes, shall be provided with enclosures identified for Class I, Division 1 locations. Enclosures for Class I, Division 1 locations include explosionproof enclosures and purged and pressurized enclosures.

> FPN: See NFPA 496-2003, *Standard for Purged and Pressurized Enclosures for Electrical Equipment.*

(B) Class I, Division 2. In Class I, Division 2 locations, meters, instruments, and relays shall comply with 501.105(B)(1) through (B)(6).

(1) Contacts. Switches, circuit breakers, and make-and-break contacts of pushbuttons, relays, alarm bells, and horns shall have enclosures identified for Class I, Division 1 locations in accordance with 501.105(A).

Exception: General-purpose enclosures shall be permitted if current-interrupting contacts comply with one of the following:

(1) Are immersed in oil

(2) Are enclosed within a chamber that is hermetically sealed against the entrance of gases or vapors

(3) Are in nonincendive circuits

(4) Are listed for Division 2

(2) Resistors and Similar Equipment. Resistors, resistance devices, thermionic tubes, rectifiers, and similar equipment that are used in or in connection with meters, instruments, and relays shall comply with 501.105(A).

Exception: General-purpose-type enclosures shall be permitted if such equipment is without make-and-break or sliding contacts [other than as provided in 501.105(B)(1)] and if the maximum operating temperature of any exposed surface will not exceed 80 percent of the ignition temperature in degrees Celsius of the gas or vapor involved or has been tested and found incapable of igniting the gas or vapor. This exception shall not apply to thermionic tubes.

(3) Without Make-or-Break Contacts. Transformer windings, impedance coils, solenoids, and other windings that do not incorporate sliding or make-or-break contacts shall be provided with enclosures. General-purpose-type enclosures shall be permitted.

(4) General-Purpose Assemblies. Where an assembly is made up of components for which general-purpose enclosures are acceptable as provided in 501.105(B)(1), (B)(2), and (B)(3), a single general-purpose enclosure shall be acceptable for the assembly. Where such an assembly includes any of the equipment described in 501.105(B)(2), the maximum obtainable surface temperature of any component of the assembly shall be clearly and permanently indicated on the outside of the enclosure. Alternatively, equipment shall be permitted to be marked to indicate the temperature class for which it is suitable, using the temperature class (T Code) of Table 500.8(B).

(5) Fuses. Where general-purpose enclosures are permitted in 501.105(B)(1) through (B)(4), fuses for overcurrent protection of instrument circuits not subject to overloading in normal use shall be permitted to be mounted in general-purpose enclosures if each such fuse is preceded by a switch complying with 501.105(B)(1).

(6) Connections. To facilitate replacements, process control instruments shall be permitted to be connected through flexible cord, attachment plug, and receptacle, provided all of the following conditions apply:

(1) A switch complying with 501.105(B)(1) is provided so that the attachment plug is not depended on to interrupt current.

(2) The current does not exceed 3 amperes at 120 volts, nominal.

(3) The power-supply cord does not exceed 900 mm (3 ft), is of a type listed for extra-hard usage or for hard usage if protected by location, and is supplied through an attachment plug and receptacle of the locking and grounding type.

(4) Only necessary receptacles are provided.

(5) The receptacle carries a label warning against unplugging under load.

501.115 Switches, Circuit Breakers, Motor Controllers, and Fuses.

(A) Class I, Division 1. In Class I, Division 1 locations, switches, circuit breakers, motor controllers, and fuses, including pushbuttons, relays, and similar devices, shall be provided with enclosures, and the enclosure in each case, together with the enclosed apparatus, shall be identified as a complete assembly for use in Class I locations.

(B) Class I, Division 2. Switches, circuit breakers, motor controllers, and fuses in Class I, Division 2 locations shall comply with 501.115(B)(1) through (B)(4).

(1) Type Required. Circuit breakers, motor controllers, and switches intended to interrupt current in the normal performance of the function for which they are installed shall be provided with enclosures identified for Class I, Division 1 locations in accordance with 501.105(A), unless general-purpose enclosures are provided and any of the following apply:

(1) The interruption of current occurs within a chamber hermetically sealed against the entrance of gases and vapors.

(2) The current make-and-break contacts are oil-immersed and of the general-purpose type having a 50-mm (2-in.) minimum immersion for power contacts and a 25-mm (1-in.) minimum immersion for control contacts.

(3) The interruption of current occurs within a factory-sealed explosionproof chamber.

(4) The device is a solid state, switching control without contacts, where the surface temperature does not exceed 80 percent of the ignition temperature in degrees Celsius of the gas or vapor involved.

(2) Isolating Switches. Fused or unfused disconnect and isolating switches for transformers or capacitor banks that are not intended to interrupt current in the normal performance of the function for which they are installed shall be permitted to be installed in general-purpose enclosures.

(3) Fuses. For the protection of motors, appliances, and lamps, other than as provided in 501.115(B)(4), standard plug or cartridge fuses shall be permitted, provided they are placed within enclosures identified for the location; or fuses shall be permitted if they are within general-purpose enclosures, and if they are of a type in which the operating element is immersed in oil or other approved liquid, or the operating element is enclosed within a chamber hermetically sealed against the entrance of gases and vapors, or the fuse is a nonindicating, filled, current-limiting type.

(4) Fuses Internal to Luminaires (Lighting Fixtures). Listed cartridge fuses shall be permitted as supplementary protection within luminaires (lighting fixtures).

501.120 Control Transformers and Resistors. Transformers, impedance coils, and resistors used as, or in conjunction with, control equipment for motors, generators, and appliances shall comply with 501.120(A) and 501.120(B).

(A) Class I, Division 1. In Class I, Division 1 locations, transformers, impedance coils, and resistors, together with any switching mechanism associated with them, shall be provided with enclosures identified for Class I, Division 1 locations in accordance with 501.105(A).

(B) Class I, Division 2. In Class I, Division 2 locations, control transformers and resistors shall comply with 501.120(B)(1) through (B)(3).

(1) Switching Mechanisms. Switching mechanisms used in conjunction with transformers, impedance coils, and resistors shall comply with 501.115(B).

(2) Coils and Windings. Enclosures for windings of transformers, solenoids, or impedance coils shall be permitted to be of the general-purpose type.

(3) Resistors. Resistors shall be provided with enclosures; and the assembly shall be identified for Class I locations, unless resistance is nonvariable and maximum operating temperature, in degrees Celsius, will not exceed 80 percent of the ignition temperature of the gas or vapor involved or has been tested and found incapable of igniting the gas or vapor.

501.125 Motors and Generators.

(A) Class I, Division 1. In Class I, Division 1 locations, motors, generators, and other rotating electric machinery shall be one of the following:

(1) Identified for Class I, Division 1 locations

(2) Of the totally enclosed type supplied with positive-pressure ventilation from a source of clean air with discharge to a safe area, so arranged to prevent energizing of the machine until ventilation has been established and the enclosure has been purged with at least

10 volumes of air, and also arranged to automatically de-energize the equipment when the air supply fails

(3) Of the totally enclosed inert gas-filled type supplied with a suitable reliable source of inert gas for pressurizing the enclosure, with devices provided to ensure a positive pressure in the enclosure and arranged to automatically de-energize the equipment when the gas supply fails

(4) Of a type designed to be submerged in a liquid that is flammable only when vaporized and mixed with air, or in a gas or vapor at a pressure greater than atmospheric and that is flammable only when mixed with air; and the machine is arranged so to prevent energizing it until it has been purged with the liquid or gas to exclude air, and also arranged to automatically de-energize the equipment when the supply of liquid or gas or vapor fails or the pressure is reduced to atmospheric

Totally enclosed motors of the types specified in 501.125(A)(2) or 501.125(A)(3) shall have no external surface with an operating temperature in degrees Celsius in excess of 80 percent of the ignition temperature of the gas or vapor involved. Appropriate devices shall be provided to detect and automatically de-energize the motor or provide an adequate alarm if there is any increase in temperature of the motor beyond designed limits. Auxiliary equipment shall be of a type identified for the location in which it is installed.

FPN: See D 2155-69, *ASTM Test Procedure.*

(B) Class I, Division 2. In Class I, Division 2 locations, motors, generators, and other rotating electric machinery in which are employed sliding contacts, centrifugal or other types of switching mechanism (including motor overcurrent, overloading, and overtemperature devices), or integral resistance devices, either while starting or while running, shall be identified for Class I, Division 1 locations, unless such sliding contacts, switching mechanisms, and resistance devices are provided with enclosures identified for Class I, Division 2 locations in accordance with 501.105(B). The exposed surface of space heaters used to prevent condensation of moisture during shutdown periods shall not exceed 80 percent of the ignition temperature in degrees Celsius of the gas or vapor involved when operated at rated voltage, and the maximum surface temperature [based on a 40°C (104°F) ambient] shall be permanently marked on a visible nameplate mounted on the motor. Otherwise, space heaters shall be identified for Class I, Division 2 locations. In Class I, Division 2 locations, the installation of open or nonexplosionproof enclosed motors, such as squirrel-cage induction motors without brushes, switching mechanisms, or similar arc-producing devices that are not identified for use in a Class I, Division 2 location, shall be permitted.

FPN No. 1: It is important to consider the temperature of internal and external surfaces that may be exposed to the flammable atmosphere.

FPN No. 2: It is important to consider the risk of ignition due to currents arcing across discontinuities and overheating of parts in multisection enclosures of large motors and generators. Such motors and generators may need equipotential bonding jumpers across joints in the enclosure and from enclosure to ground. Where the presence of ignitible gases or vapors is suspected, clean-air purging may be needed immediately prior to and during start-up periods.

FPN No. 3: For further information on the application of electric motors in Class I, Division 2 hazardous (classified) locations, see IEEE Std. 1349-2001, *IEEE Guide for the Application of Electric Motors in Class I, Division 2 Hazardous (Classified) Locations.*

501.130 Luminaires (Lighting Fixtures). Luminaires (lighting fixtures) shall comply with 501.130(A) or (B).

(A) Class I, Division 1. In Class I, Division 1 locations, luminaires (lighting fixtures) shall comply with 501.130(A)(1) through (A)(4).

(1) Luminaires (Lighting Fixtures). Each luminaire (lighting fixture) shall be identified as a complete assembly for the Class I, Division 1 location and shall be clearly marked to indicate the maximum wattage of lamps for which it is identified. Luminaires (lighting fixtures) intended for portable use shall be specifically listed as a complete assembly for that use.

(2) Physical Damage. Each luminaire (lighting fixture) shall be protected against physical damage by a suitable guard or by location.

(3) Pendant Luminaires (Lighting Fixtures). Pendant luminaires (lighting fixtures) shall be suspended by and supplied through threaded rigid metal conduit stems or threaded steel intermediate conduit stems, and threaded joints shall be provided with set-screws or other effective means to prevent loosening. For stems longer than 300 mm (12 in.), permanent and effective bracing against lateral displacement shall be provided at a level not more than 300 mm (12 in.) above the lower end of the stem, or flexibility in the form of a fitting or flexible connector identified for the Class I, Division 1 location shall be provided not more than 300 mm (12 in.) from the point of attachment to the supporting box or fitting.

(4) Supports. Boxes, box assemblies, or fittings used for the support of luminaires (lighting fixtures) shall be identified for Class I locations.

(B) Class I, Division 2. In Class I, Division 2 locations, luminaires (lighting fixtures) shall comply with 501.130(B)(1) through 501.130(B)(6).

(1) Luminaires (Lighting Fixtures). Where lamps are of a size or type that may, under normal operating conditions, reach surface temperatures exceeding 80 percent of the ignition temperature in degrees Celsius of the gas or vapor involved, fixtures shall comply with 501.130(A)(1) or shall be of a type that has been tested in order to determine the marked operating temperature or temperature class (T Code).

(2) Physical Damage. Luminaires (lighting fixtures) shall be protected from physical damage by suitable guards or by location. Where there is danger that falling sparks or hot metal from lamps or fixtures might ignite localized concentrations of flammable vapors or gases, suitable enclosures or other effective protective means shall be provided.

(3) Pendant Luminaires (Fixtures). Pendant luminaires (lighting fixtures) shall be suspended by threaded rigid metal conduit stems, threaded steel intermediate metal conduit stems, or other approved means. For rigid stems longer than 300 mm (12 in.), permanent and effective bracing against lateral displacement shall be provided at a level not more than 300 mm (12 in.) above the lower end of the stem, or flexibility in the form of an identified fitting or flexible connector shall be provided not more than 300 mm (12 in.) from the point of attachment to the supporting box or fitting.

(4) Portable Lighting Equipment. Portable lighting equipment shall comply with 501.130(A)(1).

Exception: Where portable lighting equipment is mounted on movable stands and is connected by flexible cords, as covered in 501.140, it shall be permitted, where mounted in any position, if it conforms to 501.130(B)(2).

(5) Switches. Switches that are a part of an assembled fixture or of an individual lampholder shall comply with 501.115(B)(1).

(6) Starting Equipment. Starting and control equipment for electric-discharge lamps shall comply with 501.120(B).

Exception: A thermal protector potted into a thermally protected fluorescent lamp ballast if the luminaire (lighting fixture) is identified for the location.

501.135 Utilization Equipment.

(A) Class I, Division 1. In Class I, Division 1 locations, all utilization equipment shall be identified for Class I, Division 1 locations.

(B) Class I, Division 2. In Class I, Division 2 locations, all utilization equipment shall comply with 501.135(B)(1) through (B)(3).

(1) Heaters. Electrically heated utilization equipment shall conform with either item (1) or (2):

(1) The heater shall not exceed 80 percent of the ignition temperature in degrees Celsius of the gas or vapor involved on any surface that is exposed to the gas or vapor when continuously energized at the maximum rated ambient temperature. If a temperature controller is not provided, these conditions shall apply when the heater is operated at 120 percent of rated voltage.

Exception No. 1: For motor-mounted anticondensation space heaters, see 501.125.

Exception No. 2: Where a current-limiting device is applied to the circuit serving the heater to limit the current in the heater to a value less than that required to raise the heater surface temperature to 80 percent of the ignition temperature.

(2) The heater shall be identified for Class I, Division 1 locations.

Exception: Electrical resistance heat tracing identified for Class I, Division 2 locations.

(2) Motors. Motors of motor-driven utilization equipment shall comply with 501.125(B).

(3) Switches, Circuit Breakers, and Fuses. Switches, circuit breakers, and fuses shall comply with 501.115(B).

501.140 Flexible Cords, Class I, Divisions 1 and 2.

(A) Permitted Uses. Flexible cord shall be permitted:

(1) For connection between portable lighting equipment or other portable utilization equipment and the fixed portion of their supply circuit.

(2) For that portion of the circuit where the fixed wiring methods of 501.10(A) cannot provide the necessary degree of movement for fixed and mobile electrical utilization equipment, and the flexible cord is protected by location or by a suitable guard from damage and only in an industrial establishment where conditions of maintenance and engineering supervision ensure that only qualified persons install and service the installation.

(3) For electric submersible pumps with means for removal without entering the wet-pit. The extension of the flexible cord within a suitable raceway between the wet-pit and the power source shall be permitted.

(4) For electric mixers intended for travel into and out of open-type mixing tanks or vats.

(B) Installation. Where flexible cords are used, the cords shall comply with all of the following:

(1) Be of a type listed for extra-hard usage

(2) Contain, in addition to the conductors of the circuit, a grounding conductor complying with 400.23

(3) Be connected to terminals or to supply conductors in an approved manner

(4) Be supported by clamps or by other suitable means in such a manner that there is no tension on the terminal connections

(5) Be provided with suitable seals where the flexible cord enters boxes, fittings, or enclosures of the explosion-proof type

Exception to (5): Seals shall not be required as provided in 501.10(B) and 501.105(B)(6).

(6) Be of continuous length.

> FPN: See 501.20 for flexible cords exposed to liquids having a deleterious effect on the conductor insulation.

501.145 Receptacles and Attachment Plugs, Class I, Divisions 1 and 2. Receptacles and attachment plugs shall be of the type providing for connection to the grounding conductor of a flexible cord and shall be identified for the location.

Exception: As provided in 501.105(B)(6).

501.150 Signaling, Alarm, Remote-Control, and Communications Systems.

(A) Class I, Division 1. In Class I, Division 1 locations, all apparatus and equipment of signaling, alarm, remote-control, and communications systems, regardless of voltage, shall be identified for Class I, Division 1 locations, and all wiring shall comply with 501.10(A), 501.15(A), and 501.15(C).

(B) Class I, Division 2. In Class I, Division 2 locations, signaling, alarm, remote-control, and communications systems shall comply with 501.150(B)(1) through (B)(4).

(1) Contacts. Switches, circuit breakers, and make-and-break contacts of pushbuttons, relays, alarm bells, and horns shall have enclosures identified for Class I, Division 1 locations in accordance with 501.105(A).

Exception: General-purpose enclosures shall be permitted if current-interrupting contacts are one of the following:

(1) Immersed in oil

(2) Enclosed within a chamber hermetically sealed against the entrance of gases or vapors

(3) In nonincendive circuits

(4) Part of a listed nonincendive component

(2) Resistors and Similar Equipment. Resistors, resistance devices, thermionic tubes, rectifiers, and similar equipment shall comply with 501.105(B)(2).

(3) Protectors. Enclosures shall be provided for lightning protective devices and for fuses. Such enclosures shall be permitted to be of the general-purpose type.

(4) Wiring and Sealing. All wiring shall comply with 501.10(B), 501.15(B), and 501.15(C).

ARTICLE 502
Class II Locations

I. General

502.1 Scope. Article 502 covers the requirements for electrical and electronic equipment and wiring for all voltages in Class II, Division 1 and 2 locations where fire or explosion hazards may exist due to combustible dust.

502.5 General. The general rules of this *Code* shall apply to the electric wiring and equipment in locations classified as Class II locations in 500.5(C).

Exception: As modified by this article.

Equipment installed in Class II locations shall be able to function at full rating without developing surface temperatures high enough to cause excessive dehydration or gradual carbonization of any organic dust deposits that may occur.

> FPN: Dust that is carbonized or excessively dry is highly susceptible to spontaneous ignition.

Explosionproof equipment and wiring shall not be required and shall not be acceptable in Class II locations unless identified for such locations.

II. Wiring

502.10 Wiring Methods. Wiring methods shall comply with 502.10(A) or 502.10(B).

(A) Class II, Division 1.

(1) General. In Class II, Division 1 locations, the wiring methods in (1) through (4) shall be permitted.

(1) Threaded rigid metal conduit, or threaded steel intermediate metal conduit.

(2) Type MI cable with termination fittings listed for the location. Type MI cable shall be installed and supported in a manner to avoid tensile stress at the termination fittings.

(3) In industrial establishments with limited public access, where the conditions of maintenance and supervision ensure that only qualified persons service the installation, Type MC cable, listed for use in Class II, Division 1 locations, with a gas/vaportight continuous corrugated metallic sheath, an overall jacket of suitable polymeric material, separate grounding conductors in accordance with 250.122, and provided with termination fittings listed for the application, shall be permitted.

(4) Fittings and boxes shall be provided with threaded bosses for connection to conduit or cable terminations and shall be dusttight. Fittings and boxes in which taps, joints, or terminal connections are made, or that are used in Group E locations, shall be identified for Class II locations.

(2) Flexible Connections. Where necessary to employ flexible connections, one or more of the following shall also be permitted:

(1) Dusttight flexible connectors

(2) Liquidtight flexible metal conduit with listed fittings

(3) Liquidtight flexible nonmetallic conduit with listed fittings

(4) Interlocked armor Type MC cable having an overall jacket of suitable polymeric material and provided with termination fittings listed for Class II, Division 1 locations.

(5) Flexible cord listed for extra-hard usage and provided with bushed fittings. Where flexible cords are used, they shall comply with 502.140.

FPN: See 502.30(B) for grounding requirements where flexible conduit is used.

(B) Class II, Division 2.

(1) General. In Class II, Division 2 locations, the following wiring methods shall be permitted:

(1) All wiring methods permitted in 502.10(A).

(2) Rigid metal conduit, intermediate metal conduit, electrical metallic tubing, dusttight wireways.

(3) Type MC or MI cable with listed termination fittings.

(4) Type PLTC in cable trays.

(5) Type ITC in cable trays.

(6) Type MC, MI, or TC cable installed in ladder, ventilated trough, or ventilated channel cable trays in a single layer, with a space not less than the larger cable diameter between the two adjacent cables, shall be the wiring method employed.

Exception to (6): Type MC cable listed for use in Class II, Division 1 locations shall be permitted to be installed without the spacings required by (6).

(2) Flexible Connections. Where provision must be made for flexibility, 502.10(A)(2) shall apply.

(3) Nonincendive Field Wiring. Nonincendive field wiring shall be permitted using any of the wiring methods permitted for unclassified locations. Nonincendive field wiring systems shall be installed in accordance with the control drawing(s). Simple apparatus, not shown on the control drawing, shall be permitted in a nonincendive field wiring circuit, provided the simple apparatus does not in-terconnect the nonincendive field wiring circuit to any other circuit.

FPN: Simple apparatus is defined in 504.2.

Separate nonincendive field wiring circuits shall be installed in accordance with one of the following:

(1) In separate cables

(2) In multiconductor cables where the conductors of each circuit are within a grounded metal shield

(3) In multiconductor cables where the conductors of each circuit have insulation with a minimum thickness of 0.25 mm (0.01 in.)

(4) Boxes and Fittings. All boxes and fittings shall be dusttight.

502.15 Sealing, Class II, Divisions 1 and 2. Where a raceway provides communication between an enclosure that is required to be dust-ignitionproof and one that is not, suitable means shall be provided to prevent the entrance of dust into the dust-ignitionproof enclosure through the raceway. One of the following means shall be permitted:

(1) A permanent and effective seal

(2) A horizontal raceway not less than 3.05 m (10 ft) long

(3) A vertical raceway not less than 1.5 m (5 ft) long and extending downward from the dust-ignitionproof enclosure

(4) A raceway installed in a manner equivalent to (2) or (3) that extends only horizontally and downward from the dust-ignition proof enclosures.

Where a raceway provides communication between an enclosure that is required to be dust-ignitionproof and an enclosure in an unclassified location, seals shall not be required.

Sealing fittings shall be accessible.

Seals shall not be required to be explosionproof.

FPN: Electrical sealing putty is a method of sealing.

502.25 Uninsulated Exposed Parts, Class II, Divisions 1 and 2. There shall be no uninsulated exposed parts, such as electric conductors, buses, terminals, or components, that operate at more than 30 volts (15 volts in wet locations). These parts shall additionally be protected by a protection technique according to 500.7(E), 500.7(F), or 500.7(G) that is suitable for the location.

502.30 Grounding and Bonding, Class II, Divisions 1 and 2. Wiring and equipment in Class II, Division 1 and 2 locations shall be grounded as specified in Article 250 and with the requirements in 502.30(A) and 502.30(B).

(A) Bonding. The locknut-bushing and double-locknut types of contact shall not be depended on for bonding purposes, but bonding jumpers with proper fittings or other approved means of bonding shall be used. Such means of bonding shall apply to all intervening raceways, fittings, boxes, enclosures, and so forth, between Class II locations and the point of grounding for service equipment or point of grounding of a separately derived system.

Exception: The specific bonding means shall only be required to the nearest point where the grounded circuit conductor and the grounding electrode conductor are connected together on the line side of the building or structure disconnecting means as specified in 250.32(A), (B), and (C), if the branch-circuit overcurrent protection is located on the load side of the disconnecting means.

FPN: See 250.100 for additional bonding requirements in hazardous (classified) locations.

(B) Types of Equipment Grounding Conductors. Where flexible conduit is used as permitted in 502.10, it shall be installed with internal or external bonding jumpers in parallel with each conduit and complying with 250.102.

Exception: In Class II, Division 2 locations, the bonding jumper shall be permitted to be deleted where all of the following conditions are met:

(1) Listed liquidtight flexible metal conduit 1.8 m (6 ft) or less in length, with fittings listed for grounding, is used.

(2) Overcurrent protection in the circuit is limited to 10 amperes or less.

(3) The load is not a power utilization load.

502.35 Surge Protection — Class II, Divisions 1 and 2. Surge arresters and transient voltage surge suppressors (TVSS) installed in a Class II, Division 1 location shall be in suitable enclosures. Surge-protective capacitors shall be of a type designed for specific duty.

502.40 Multiwire Branch Circuits. In a Class II, Division 1 location, a multiwire branch circuit shall not be permitted.

Exception: Where the disconnect device(s) for the circuit opens all ungrounded conductors of the multiwire circuit simultaneously.

III. Equipment

502.100 Transformers and Capacitors.

(A) Class II, Division 1. In Class II, Division 1 locations, transformers and capacitors shall comply with 502.100(A)(1) through (A)(3).

(1) Containing Liquid That Will Burn. Transformers and capacitors containing a liquid that will burn shall be installed only in vaults complying with 450.41 through 450.48, and, in addition, (1), (2), and (3) shall apply.

(1) Doors or other openings communicating with the Division 1 location shall have self-closing fire doors on both sides of the wall, and the doors shall be carefully fitted and provided with suitable seals (such as weather stripping) to minimize the entrance of dust into the vault.

(2) Vent openings and ducts shall communicate only with the outside air.

(3) Suitable pressure-relief openings communicating with the outside air shall be provided.

(2) Not Containing Liquid That Will Burn. Transformers and capacitors that do not contain a liquid that will burn shall be installed in vaults complying with 450.41 through 450.48 or be identified as a complete assembly, including terminal connections for Class II locations.

(3) Metal Dusts. No transformer or capacitor shall be installed in a location where dust from magnesium, aluminum, aluminum bronze powders, or other metals of similarly hazardous characteristics may be present.

(B) Class II, Division 2. In Class II, Division 2 locations, transformers and capacitors shall comply with 502.100(B)(1) through (B)(3).

(1) Containing Liquid That Will Burn. Transformers and capacitors containing a liquid that will burn shall be installed in vaults that comply with 450.41 through 450.48.

(2) Containing Askarel. Transformers containing askarel and rated in excess of 25 kVA shall be as follows:

(1) Provided with pressure-relief vents

(2) Provided with a means for absorbing any gases generated by arcing inside the case, or the pressure-relief vents shall be connected to a chimney or flue that will carry such gases outside the building

(3) Have an airspace of not less than 150 mm (6 in.) between the transformer cases and any adjacent combustible material

(3) Dry-Type Transformers. Dry-type transformers shall be installed in vaults or shall have their windings and terminal connections enclosed in tight metal housings without ventilating or other openings and shall operate at not over 600 volts, nominal.

502.115 Switches, Circuit Breakers, Motor Controllers, and Fuses.

(A) Class II, Division 1. In Class II, Division 1 locations, switches, circuit breakers, motor controllers, and fuses shall comply with 502.115(A)(1) through (A)(3).

(1) Type Required. Switches, circuit breakers, motor controllers, and fuses, including pushbuttons, relays, and similar devices that are intended to interrupt current during normal operation or that are installed where combustible dusts of an electrically conductive nature may be present, shall be provided with identified dust-ignitionproof enclosures.

(2) Isolating Switches. Disconnecting and isolating switches containing no fuses and not intended to interrupt current and not installed where dusts may be of an electrically conductive nature shall be provided with tight metal enclosures that shall be designed to minimize the entrance of dust and that shall (1) be equipped with telescoping or close-fitting covers or with other effective means to prevent the escape of sparks or burning material and (2) have no openings (such as holes for attachment screws) through which, after installation, sparks or burning material might escape or through which exterior accumulations of dust or adjacent combustible material might be ignited.

(3) Metal Dusts. In locations where dust from magnesium, aluminum, aluminum bronze powders, or other metals of similarly hazardous characteristics may be present, fuses, switches, motor controllers, and circuit breakers shall have enclosures identified for such locations.

(B) Class II, Division 2. In Class II, Division 2 locations, enclosures for fuses, switches, circuit breakers, and motor controllers, including pushbuttons, relays, and similar devices, shall be dusttight.

502.120 Control Transformers and Resistors.

(A) Class II, Division 1. In Class II, Division 1 locations, control transformers, solenoids, impedance coils, resistors, and any overcurrent devices or switching mechanisms associated with them shall have dust-ignitionproof enclosures identified for Class II locations. No control transformer, impedance coil, or resistor shall be installed in a location where dust from magnesium, aluminum, aluminum bronze powders, or other metals of similarly hazardous characteristics may be present unless provided with an enclosure identified for the specific location.

(B) Class II, Division 2. . In Class II, Division 2 locations, transformers and resistors shall comply with 502.120(B)(1) through (B)(3).

(1) Switching Mechanisms. Switching mechanisms (including overcurrent devices) associated with control transformers, solenoids, impedance coils, and resistors shall be provided with dusttight enclosures.

(2) Coils and Windings. Where not located in the same enclosure with switching mechanisms, control transformers, solenoids, and impedance coils shall be provided with tight metal housings without ventilating openings.

(3) Resistors. Resistors and resistance devices shall have dust-ignitionproof enclosures identified for Class II locations.

Exception: Where the maximum normal operating temperature of the resistor will not exceed 120°C (248°F), nonadjustable resistors or resistors that are part of an automatically timed starting sequence shall be permitted to have enclosures complying with 502.120(B)(2).

502.125 Motors and Generators.

(A) Class II, Division 1. In Class II, Division 1 locations, motors, generators, and other rotating electrical machinery shall be in conformance with either of the following:

(1) Identified for Class II, Division 1 locations

(2) Totally enclosed pipe-ventilated, meeting temperature limitations in 502.5

(B) Class II, Division 2. In Class II, Division 2 locations, motors, generators, and other rotating electrical equipment shall be totally enclosed nonventilated, totally enclosed pipe-ventilated, totally enclosed water-air-cooled, totally enclosed fan-cooled or dust-ignitionproof for which maximum full-load external temperature shall be in accordance with 500.8(C)(2) for normal operation when operating in free air (not dust blanketed) and shall have no external openings.

Exception: If the authority having jurisdiction believes accumulations of nonconductive, nonabrasive dust will be moderate and if machines can be easily reached for routine cleaning and maintenance, the following shall be permitted to be installed:

(1) Standard open-type machines without sliding contacts, centrifugal or other types of switching mechanism (including motor overcurrent, overloading, and overtemperature devices), or integral resistance devices

(2) Standard open-type machines with such contacts, switching mechanisms, or resistance devices enclosed within dusttight housings without ventilating or other openings

(3) Self-cleaning textile motors of the squirrel-cage type

502.128 Ventilating Piping. Ventilating pipes for motors, generators, or other rotating electric machinery, or for enclosures for electric equipment, shall be of metal not less than 0.53 mm (0.021 in.) in thickness or of equally substantial noncombustible material and shall comply with all of the following:

(1) Lead directly to a source of clean air outside of buildings

(2) Be screened at the outer ends to prevent the entrance of small animals or birds

(3) Be protected against physical damage and against rusting or other corrosive influences

Ventilating pipes shall also comply with 502.128(A) and 502.128(B).

(A) Class II, Division 1. In Class II, Division 1 locations, ventilating pipes, including their connections to motors or to the dust-ignitionproof enclosures for other equipment, shall be dusttight throughout their length. For metal pipes, seams and joints shall comply with one of the following:

(1) Be riveted and soldered

(2) Be bolted and soldered

(3) Be welded

(4) Be rendered dusttight by some other equally effective means

(B) Class II, Division 2. In Class II, Division 2 locations, ventilating pipes and their connections shall be sufficiently tight to prevent the entrance of appreciable quantities of dust into the ventilated equipment or enclosure and to prevent the escape of sparks, flame, or burning material that might ignite dust accumulations or combustible material in the vicinity. For metal pipes, lock seams and riveted or welded joints shall be permitted; and tight-fitting slip joints shall be permitted where some flexibility is necessary, as at connections to motors.

502.130 Luminaires (Lighting Fixtures). Luminaires (lighting fixtures) shall comply with 502.130(A) and 502.130(B).

(A) Class II, Division 1. In Class II, Division 1 locations, luminaires (lighting fixtures) for fixed and portable lighting shall comply with 502.130(A)(1) through (A)(4).

(1) Fixtures. Each luminaire (fixture) shall be identified for Class II locations and shall be clearly marked to indicate the maximum wattage of the lamp for which it is designed. In locations where dust from magnesium, aluminum, aluminum bronze powders, or other metals of similarly hazardous characteristics may be present, luminaires (fixtures) for fixed or portable lighting and all auxiliary equipment shall be identified for the specific location.

(2) Physical Damage. Each luminaire (fixture) shall be protected against physical damage by a suitable guard or by location.

(3) Pendant Luminaires (Fixtures). Pendant luminaires (fixtures) shall be suspended by threaded rigid metal conduit stems, threaded steel intermediate metal conduit stems, by chains with approved fittings, or by other approved means. For rigid stems longer than 300 mm (12 in.), permanent and effective bracing against lateral displacement shall be provided at a level not more than 300 mm (12 in.) above the lower end of the stem, or flexibility in the form of a fitting or a flexible connector listed for the location shall be provided not more than 300 mm (12 in.) from the point of attachment to the supporting box or fitting. Threaded joints shall be provided with set-screws or other effective means to prevent loosening. Where wiring between an outlet box or fitting and a pendant luminaire (fix-

ture) is not enclosed in conduit, flexible cord listed for hard usage shall be used, and suitable seals shall be provided where the cord enters the luminaire (fixture) and the outlet box or fitting. Flexible cord shall not serve as the supporting means for a fixture.

(4) Supports. Boxes, box assemblies, or fittings used for the support of luminaires (lighting fixtures) shall be identified for Class II locations.

(B) Class II, Division 2. In Class II, Division 2 locations, luminaires (lighting fixtures) shall comply with 502.130(B)(1) through (B)(5).

(1) Portable Lighting Equipment. Portable lighting equipment shall be identified for Class II locations. They shall be clearly marked to indicate the maximum wattage of lamps for which they are designed.

(2) Fixed Lighting. Luminaires (lighting fixtures) for fixed lighting, where not of a type identified for Class II locations, shall provide enclosures for lamps and lampholders that shall be designed to minimize the deposit of dust on lamps and to prevent the escape of sparks, burning material, or hot metal. Each fixture shall be clearly marked to indicate the maximum wattage of the lamp that shall be permitted without exceeding an exposed surface temperature in accordance with 500.8(C)(2) under normal conditions of use.

(3) Physical Damage. Luminaires (lighting fixtures) for fixed lighting shall be protected from physical damage by suitable guards or by location.

(4) Pendant Luminaires (Fixtures). Pendant luminaires (fixtures) shall be suspended by threaded rigid metal conduit stems, threaded steel intermediate metal conduit stems, by chains with approved fittings, or by other approved means. For rigid stems longer than 300 mm (12 in.), permanent and effective bracing against lateral displacement shall be provided at a level not more than 300 mm (12 in.) above the lower end of the stem, or flexibility in the form of an identified fitting or a flexible connector shall be provided not more than 300 mm (12 in.) from the point of attachment to the supporting box or fitting. Where wiring between an outlet box or fitting and a pendant luminaire (fixture) is not enclosed in conduit, flexible cord listed for hard usage shall be used. Flexible cord shall not serve as the supporting means for a fixture.

(5) Electric-Discharge Lamps. Starting and control equipment for electric-discharge lamps shall comply with the requirements of 502.120(B).

502.135 Utilization Equipment.

(A) Class II, Division 1. In Class II, Division 1 locations, all utilization equipment shall be identified for Class II locations. Where dust from magnesium, aluminum, aluminum bronze powders, or other metals of similarly hazardous characteristics may be present, such equipment shall be identified for the specific location.

(B) Class II, Division 2. In Class II, Division 2 locations, all utilization equipment shall comply with 502.135(B)(1) through (B)(4).

(1) Heaters. Electrically heated utilization equipment shall be identified for Class II locations.

Exception: Metal-enclosed radiant heating panel equipment shall be dusttight and marked in accordance with 500.8(B).

(2) Motors. Motors of motor-driven utilization equipment shall comply with 502.125(B).

(3) Switches, Circuit Breakers, and Fuses. Enclosures for switches, circuit breakers, and fuses shall be dusttight.

(4) Transformers, Solenoids, Impedance Coils, and Resistors. Transformers, solenoids, impedance coils, and resistors shall comply with 502.120(B).

502.140 Flexible Cords — Class II, Divisions 1 and 2. Flexible cords used in Class II locations shall comply with all of the following:

(1) Be of a type listed for extra-hard usage

Exception: Flexible cord listed for hard usage as permitted by 502.130(A)(3) and (B)(4).

(2) Contain, in addition to the conductors of the circuit, a grounding conductor complying with 400.23

(3) Be connected to terminals or to supply conductors in an approved manner

(4) Be supported by clamps or by other suitable means in such a manner that there will be no tension on the terminal connections

(5) Be provided with suitable seals to prevent the entrance of dust where the flexible cord enters boxes or fittings that are required to be dust-ignitionproof

502.145 Receptacles and Attachment Plugs.

(A) Class II, Division 1. In Class II, Division 1 locations, receptacles and attachment plugs shall be of the type providing for connection to the grounding conductor of the flexible cord and shall be identified for Class II locations.

(B) Class II, Division 2. In Class II, Division 2 locations, receptacles and attachment plugs shall be of the type that provides for connection to the grounding conductor of the flexible cord and shall be designed so that connection to the supply circuit cannot be made or broken while live parts are exposed.

502.150 Signaling, Alarm, Remote-Control, and Communications Systems; and Meters, Instruments, and Relays.

FPN: See Article 800 for rules governing the installation of communications circuits.

(A) Class II, Division 1. In Class II, Division 1 locations, signaling, alarm, remote-control, and communications systems; and meters, instruments, and relays shall comply with 502.150(A)(1) through (A)(6).

(1) Wiring Methods. The wiring method shall comply with 502.10(A).

(2) Contacts. Switches, circuit breakers, relays, contactors, fuses and current-breaking contacts for bells, horns, howlers, sirens, and other devices in which sparks or arcs may be produced shall be provided with enclosures identified for a Class II location.

Exception: Where current-breaking contacts are immersed in oil or where the interruption of current occurs within a chamber sealed against the entrance of dust, enclosures shall be permitted to be of the general-purpose type.

(3) Resistors and Similar Equipment. Resistors, transformers, choke coils, rectifiers, thermionic tubes, and other heat-generating equipment shall be provided with enclosures identified for Class II locations.

Exception: Where resistors or similar equipment are immersed in oil or enclosed in a chamber sealed against the entrance of dust, enclosures shall be permitted to be of the general-purpose type.

(4) Rotating Machinery. Motors, generators, and other rotating electric machinery shall comply with 502.125(A).

(5) Combustible, Electrically Conductive Dusts. Where dusts are of a combustible, electrically conductive nature, all wiring and equipment shall be identified for Class II locations.

(6) Metal Dusts. Where dust from magnesium, aluminum, aluminum bronze powders, or other metals of similarly hazardous characteristics may be present, all apparatus and equipment shall be identified for the specific conditions.

(B) Class II, Division 2. In Class II, Division 2 locations, signaling, alarm, remote-control, and communications systems; and meters, instruments, and relays shall comply with 502.150(B)(1) through (B)(5).

(1) Contacts. Enclosures shall comply with 502.150(A)(2), or contacts shall have tight metal enclosures designed to minimize the entrance of dust and shall have telescoping or tight-fitting covers and no openings through which, after installation, sparks or burning material might escape.

Exception: In nonincendive circuits, enclosures shall be permitted to be of the general-purpose type.

(2) Transformers and Similar Equipment. The windings and terminal connections of transformers, choke coils, and similar equipment shall be provided with tight metal enclosures without ventilating openings.

(3) Resistors and Similar Equipment. Resistors, resistance devices, thermionic tubes, rectifiers, and similar equipment shall comply with 502.130(A)(3).

Exception: Enclosures for thermionic tubes, nonadjustable resistors, or rectifiers for which maximum operating temperature will not exceed 120°C (248°F) shall be permitted to be of the general-purpose type.

(4) Rotating Machinery. Motors, generators, and other rotating electric machinery shall comply with 502.125(B).

(5) Wiring Methods. The wiring method shall comply with 502.10(B).

ARTICLE 503
Class III Locations

I. General

503.1 Scope. Article 503 covers the requirements for electrical and electronic equipment and wiring for all voltages in Class III, Division 1 and 2 locations where fire or explosion hazards may exist due to ignitible fibers or flyings.

503.5 General. The general rules of this *Code* shall apply to electric wiring and equipment in locations classified as Class III locations in 500.5(D).

Exception: As modified by this article.

Equipment installed in Class III locations shall be able to function at full rating without developing surface temperatures high enough to cause excessive dehydration or gradual carbonization of accumulated fibers or flyings. Organic material that is carbonized or excessively dry is highly susceptible to spontaneous ignition. The maximum surface temperatures under operating conditions shall not exceed 165°C (329°F) for equipment that is not subject to overloading, and 120°C (248°F) for equipment (such as motors or power transformers) that may be overloaded.

FPN: For electric trucks, see NFPA 505-2002, *Fire Safety Standard for Powered Industrial Trucks Including Type Designations, Areas of Use, Conversions, Maintenance, and Operation.*

II. Wiring

503.10 Wiring Methods. Wiring methods shall comply with 503.10(A) or 503.10(B).

(A) Class III, Division 1. In Class III, Division 1 locations, the wiring method shall be rigid metal conduit, rigid nonmetallic conduit, intermediate metal conduit, electrical metallic tubing, dusttight wireways, or Type MC or MI cable with listed termination fittings.

(1) Boxes and Fittings. All boxes and fittings shall be dusttight.

(2) Flexible Connections. Where necessary to employ flexible connections, dusttight flexible connectors, liquidtight flexible metal conduit with listed fittings, liquidtight flexible nonmetallic conduit with listed fittings, or flexible cord in conformance with 503.140 shall be used.

FPN: See 503.30(B) for grounding requirements where flexible conduit is used.

(3) Nonincendive Field Wiring. Nonincendive field wiring shall be permitted using any of the wiring methods permitted for unclassified locations. Nonincendive field wiring systems shall be installed in accordance with the control drawing(s). Simple apparatus, not shown on the control drawing, shall be permitted in a nonincendive field wiring circuit, provided the simple apparatus does not interconnect the nonincendive field wiring circuit to any other circuit.

FPN: Simple apparatus is defined in 504.2.

Separate nonincendive field wiring circuits shall be installed in accordance with one of the following:
(1) In separate cables
(2) In multiconductor cables where the conductors of each circuit are within a grounded metal shield
(3) In multiconductor cables where the conductors of each circuit have insulation with a minimum thickness of 0.25 mm (0.01 in.)

(B) Class III, Division 2. In Class III, Division 2 locations, the wiring method shall comply with 503.10(A).

Exception: In sections, compartments, or areas used solely for storage and containing no machinery, open wiring on insulators shall be permitted where installed in accordance with Article 398, but only on condition that protection as required by 398.15(C) be provided where conductors are not run in roof spaces and are well out of reach of sources of physical damage.

503.25 Uninsulated Exposed Parts, Class III, Divisions 1 and 2. There shall be no uninsulated exposed parts, such as electric conductors, buses, terminals, or components, that operate at more than 30 volts (15 volts in wet locations). These parts shall additionally be protected by a protection technique according to 500.7(E), 500.7(F), or 500.7(G) that is suitable for the location.

Exception: As provided in 503.155.

503.30 Grounding and Bonding — Class III, Divisions 1 and 2. Wiring and equipment in Class III, Division 1 and 2 locations shall be grounded as specified in Article 250 and with the following additional requirements in 503.30(A) and 503.30(B).

(A) Bonding. The locknut-bushing and double-locknut types of contacts shall not be depended on for bonding purposes, but bonding jumpers with proper fittings or other approved means of bonding shall be used. Such means of bonding shall apply to all intervening raceways, fittings, boxes, enclosures, and so forth, between Class III locations and the point of grounding for service equipment or point of grounding of a separately derived system.

Exception: The specific bonding means shall only be required to the nearest point where the grounded circuit conductor and the grounding electrode conductor are connected together on the line side of the building or structure disconnecting means as specified in 250.32(A), (B), and (C), if the branch-circuit overcurrent protection is located on the load side of the disconnecting means.

> FPN: See 250.100 for additional bonding requirements in hazardous (classified) locations.

(B) Types of Equipment Grounding Conductors. Where flexible conduit is used as permitted in 503.10, it shall be installed with internal or external bonding jumpers in parallel with each conduit and complying with 250.102.

Exception: In Class III, Division 1 and 2 locations, the bonding jumper shall be permitted to be deleted where all of the following conditions are met:

(1) Listed liquidtight flexible metal 1.8 m (6 ft) or less in length, with fittings listed for grounding, is used.

(2) Overcurrent protection in the circuit is limited to 10 amperes or less.

(3) The load is not a power utilization load.

III. Equipment

503.100 Transformers and Capacitors — Class III, Divisions 1 and 2. Transformers and capacitors shall comply with 502.100(B).

503.115 Switches, Circuit Breakers, Motor Controllers, and Fuses — Class III, Divisions 1 and 2. Switches, circuit breakers, motor controllers, and fuses, including pushbuttons, relays, and similar devices, shall be provided with dusttight enclosures.

503.120 Control Transformers and Resistors — Class III, Divisions 1 and 2. Transformers, impedance coils, and resistors used as or in conjunction with control equipment for motors, generators, and appliances shall be provided with dusttight enclosures complying with the temperature limitations in 503.5.

503.125 Motors and Generators — Class III, Divisions 1 and 2. In Class III, Divisions 1 and 2 locations, motors, generators, and other rotating machinery shall be totally enclosed nonventilated, totally enclosed pipe ventilated, or totally enclosed fan cooled.

Exception: In locations where, in the judgment of the authority having jurisdiction, only moderate accumulations of lint or flyings are likely to collect on, in, or in the vicinity of a rotating electric machine and where such machine is readily accessible for routine cleaning and maintenance, one of the following shall be permitted:

(1) Self-cleaning textile motors of the squirrel-cage type

(2) Standard open-type machines without sliding contacts, centrifugal or other types of switching mechanisms, including motor overload devices

(3) Standard open-type machines having such contacts, switching mechanisms, or resistance devices enclosed within tight housings without ventilating or other openings

503.128 Ventilating Piping — Class III, Divisions 1 and 2. Ventilating pipes for motors, generators, or other rotating electric machinery, or for enclosures for electric equipment, shall be of metal not less than 0.53 mm (0.021 in.) in thickness, or of equally substantial noncombustible material, and shall comply with the following:

(1) Lead directly to a source of clean air outside of buildings

(2) Be screened at the outer ends to prevent the entrance of small animals or birds

(3) Be protected against physical damage and against rusting or other corrosive influences

Ventilating pipes shall be sufficiently tight, including their connections, to prevent the entrance of appreciable quantities of fibers or flyings into the ventilated equipment or enclosure and to prevent the escape of sparks, flame, or burning material that might ignite accumulations of fibers or flyings or combustible material in the vicinity. For metal pipes, lock seams and riveted or welded joints shall be permitted; and tight-fitting slip joints shall be permitted where some flexibility is necessary, as at connections to motors.

503.130 Luminaires (Lighting Fixtures) — Class III, Divisions 1 and 2.

(A) Fixed Lighting. Luminaires (lighting fixtures) for fixed lighting shall provide enclosures for lamps and lampholders that are designed to minimize entrance of fibers and flyings and to prevent the escape of sparks, burning material, or hot metal. Each luminaire (fixture) shall be clearly marked to show the maximum wattage of the lamps that shall be permitted without exceeding an exposed surface temperature of 165°C (329°F) under normal conditions of use.

(B) Physical Damage. A luminaire (fixture) that may be exposed to physical damage shall be protected by a suitable guard.

(C) Pendant Luminaires (Fixtures). Pendant luminaires (fixtures) shall be suspended by stems of threaded rigid metal conduit, threaded intermediate metal conduit, threaded metal tubing of equivalent thickness, or by chains with approved fittings. For stems longer than 300 mm (12 in.), permanent and effective bracing against lateral displacement shall be provided at a level not more than 300 mm (12 in.) above the lower end of the stem, or flexibility in the form of an identified fitting or a flexible connector shall be provided not more than 300 mm (12 in.) from the point of attachment to the supporting box or fitting.

(D) Portable Lighting Equipment. Portable lighting equipment shall be equipped with handles and protected with substantial guards. Lampholders shall be of the un-switched type with no provision for receiving attachment plugs. There shall be no exposed current-carrying metal parts, and all exposed non–current-carrying metal parts shall be grounded. In all other respects, portable lighting equipment shall comply with 503.130(A).

503.135 Utilization Equipment — Class III, Divisions 1 and 2.

(A) Heaters. Electrically heated utilization equipment shall be identified for Class III locations.

(B) Motors. Motors of motor-driven utilization equipment shall comply with 503.125.

(C) Switches, Circuit Breakers, Motor Controllers, and Fuses. Switches, circuit breakers, motor controllers, and fuses shall comply with 503.115.

503.140 Flexible Cords — Class III, Divisions 1 and 2. Flexible cords shall comply with the following:

(1) Be of a type listed for extra-hard usage
(2) Contain, in addition to the conductors of the circuit, a grounding conductor complying with 400.23
(3) Be connected to terminals or to supply conductors in an approved manner
(4) Be supported by clamps or other suitable means in such a manner that there will be no tension on the terminal connections
(5) Be provided with suitable means to prevent the entrance of fibers or flyings where the cord enters boxes or fittings

503.145 Receptacles and Attachment Plugs — Class III, Divisions 1 and 2. Receptacles and attachment plugs shall be of the grounding type and shall be designed so as to minimize the accumulation or the entry of fibers or flyings, and shall prevent the escape of sparks or molten particles.

Exception: In locations where, in the judgment of the authority having jurisdiction, only moderate accumulations of lint or flyings will be likely to collect in the vicinity of a receptacle, and where such receptacle is readily accessible for routine cleaning, general-purpose grounding-type receptacles mounted so as to minimize the entry of fibers or flyings shall be permitted.

503.150 Signaling, Alarm, Remote-Control, and Local Loudspeaker Intercommunications Systems — Class III, Divisions 1 and 2. Signaling, alarm, remote-control, and local loudspeaker intercommunications systems shall comply with the requirements of Article 503 regarding wiring methods, switches, transformers, resistors, motors, luminaires (lighting fixtures), and related components.

503.155 Electric Cranes, Hoists, and Similar Equipment — Class III, Divisions 1 and 2. Where installed for operation over combustible fibers or accumulations of flyings, traveling cranes and hoists for material handling, traveling cleaners for textile machinery, and similar equipment shall comply with 503.155(A) through (D).

(A) Power Supply. Power supply to contact conductors shall be electrically isolated from all other systems, ungrounded, and shall be equipped with an acceptable ground detector that gives an alarm and automatically de-energizes the contact conductors in case of a fault to ground or gives a visual and audible alarm as long as power is supplied to the contact conductors and the ground fault remains.

(B) Contact Conductors. Contact conductors shall be located or guarded so as to be inaccessible to other than authorized persons and shall be protected against accidental contact with foreign objects.

(C) Current Collectors. Current collectors shall be arranged or guarded so as to confine normal sparking and prevent escape of sparks or hot particles. To reduce sparking, two or more separate surfaces of contact shall be provided for each contact conductor. Reliable means shall be provided to keep contact conductors and current collectors free of accumulations of lint or flyings.

(D) Control Equipment. Control equipment shall comply with 503.115 and 503.120.

503.160 Storage Battery Charging Equipment — Class III, Divisions 1 and 2. Storage battery charging equipment shall be located in separate rooms built or lined with substantial noncombustible materials. The rooms shall be constructed to prevent the entrance of ignitible amounts of flyings or lint and shall be well ventilated.

ARTICLE 504
Intrinsically Safe Systems

504.1 Scope. This article covers the installation of intrinsically safe (I.S.) apparatus, wiring, and systems for Class I, II, and III locations.

> FPN: For further information, see ANSI/ISA RP 12.06.01-2002, *Wiring Methods for Hazardous (Classified) Locations Instrumentation — Part 1: Intrinsic Safety.*

504.2 Definitions.

Associated Apparatus. Apparatus in which the circuits are not necessarily intrinsically safe themselves but that affect the energy in the intrinsically safe circuits and are relied on to maintain intrinsic safety. Associated apparatus may be either of the following:

(1) Electrical apparatus that has an alternative-type protection for use in the appropriate hazardous (classified) location

(2) Electrical apparatus not so protected that shall not be used within a hazardous (classified) location

> FPN No. 1: Associated apparatus has identified intrinsically safe connections for intrinsically safe apparatus and also may have connections for nonintrinsically safe apparatus.

> FPN No. 2: An example of associated apparatus is an intrinsic safety barrier, which is a network designed to limit the energy (voltage and current) available to the protected circuit in the hazardous (classified) location, under specified fault conditions.

Control Drawing. See definition in 500.2.

Different Intrinsically Safe Circuits. Intrinsically safe circuits in which the possible interconnections have not been evaluated and identified as intrinsically safe.

Intrinsically Safe Apparatus. Apparatus in which all the circuits are intrinsically safe.

Intrinsically Safe Circuit. A circuit in which any spark or thermal effect is incapable of causing ignition of a mixture of flammable or combustible material in air under prescribed test conditions.

> FPN: Test conditions are described in ANSI/UL 913-1997, *Standard for Safety, Intrinsically Safe Apparatus and Associated Apparatus for Use in Class I, II, and III, Division 1, Hazardous (Classified) Locations.*

Intrinsically Safe System. An assembly of interconnected intrinsically safe apparatus, associated apparatus, and interconnecting cables in that those parts of the system that may be used in hazardous (classified) locations are intrinsically safe circuits.

> FPN: An intrinsically safe system may include more than one intrinsically safe circuit.

Simple Apparatus. An electrical component or combination of components of simple construction with well-defined electrical parameters that does not generate more than 1.5 volts, 100 milliamps, and 25 milliwatts, or a passive component that does not dissipate more than 1.3 watts and is compatible with the intrinsic safety of the circuit in which it is used.

> FPN: The following apparatus are examples of simple apparatus:
>
> (a) Passive components, for example, switches, junction boxes, resistance temperature devices, and simple semiconductor devices such as LEDs
> (b) Sources of generated energy, for example, thermocouples and photocells, which do not generate more than 1.5 V, 100 mA, and 25 mW

504.3 Application of Other Articles. Except as modified by this article, all applicable articles of this *Code* shall apply.

504.4 Equipment. All intrinsically safe apparatus and associated apparatus shall be listed.

Exception: Simple apparatus, as described on the control drawing, shall not be required to be listed.

504.10 Equipment Installation.

(A) Control Drawing. Intrinsically safe apparatus, associated apparatus, and other equipment shall be installed in accordance with the control drawing(s).

Exception: A simple apparatus that does not interconnect intrinsically safe circuits.

> FPN: The control drawing identification is marked on the apparatus.

(B) Location. Intrinsically safe apparatus shall be permitted to be installed in any hazardous (classified) location for which it has been identified. General-purpose enclosures shall be permitted for intrinsically safe apparatus.

Associated apparatus shall be permitted to be installed in any hazardous (classified) location for which it has been identified or, if protected by other means, permitted by Articles 501 through 503 and Article 505.

Simple apparatus shall be permitted to be installed in any hazardous (classified) location in which the maximum surface temperature of the simple apparatus does not exceed the ignition temperature of the flammable gases or vapors, flammable liquids, combustible dusts, or ignitible fibers or flyings present.

For simple apparatus, the maximum surface temperature can be determined from the values of the output power from the associated apparatus or apparatus to which it is connected to obtain the temperature class. The temperature class can be determined by:

(1) Reference to Table 504.10(B)

(2) Calculation using the formula:

$$T = P_o R_{th} + T_{amb}$$

where:

T is the surface temperature

P_o is the output power marked on the associated apparatus or intrinsically safe apparatus

R_{th} is the thermal resistance of the simple apparatus

T_{amb} is the ambient temperature (normally 40°C) and reference Table 500.8(B)

In addition, components with a surface area smaller than 10 cm^2 (excluding lead wires) may be classified as T5 if their surface temperature does not exceed 150°C.

Table 504.10(B) Assessment for T4 Classification According to Component Size and Temperature

Total Surface Area Excluding Lead Wires	Requirement for T4 Classification (Based on 40°C Ambient Temperature)
<20 mm^2	Surface temperature ≤275°C
≥20 mm^2 ≤10 cm^2	Surface temperature ≤200°C
≥20 mm^2	Power not exceeding 1.3 W*

*Reduce to 1.2 W with an ambient of 60°C or 1.0 W with 80°C ambient temperature.

FPN: The following apparatus are examples of simple apparatus:

(1) Passive components, for example, switches, junction boxes, resistance temperature devices, and simple semiconductor devices such as LEDs

(2) Sources of generated energy, for example, thermocouples and photocells, which do not generate more than 1.5 V, 100 mA, and 25 mW

504.20 Wiring Methods. Intrinsically safe apparatus and wiring shall be permitted to be installed using any of the wiring methods suitable for unclassified locations, including Chapter 7 and Chapter 8. Sealing shall be as provided in 504.70, and separation shall be as provided in 504.30.

504.30 Separation of Intrinsically Safe Conductors.

(A) From Nonintrinsically Safe Circuit Conductors.

(1) In Raceways, Cable Trays, and Cables. Conductors of intrinsically safe circuits shall not be placed in any raceway, cable tray, or cable with conductors of any nonintrinsically safe circuit.

Exception No. 1: Where conductors of intrinsically safe circuits are separated from conductors of nonintrinsically safe circuits by a distance of at least 50 mm (2 in.) and secured, or by a grounded metal partition or an approved insulating partition.

FPN: No. 20 gauge sheet metal partitions 0.91 mm (0.0359 in.) or thicker are generally considered acceptable.

Exception No. 2: Where either (1) all of the intrinsically safe circuit conductors or (2) all of the nonintrinsically safe circuit conductors are in grounded metal-sheathed or metal-clad cables where the sheathing or cladding is capable of carrying fault current to ground.

FPN: Cables meeting the requirements of Articles 330 and 332 are typical of those considered acceptable.

(2) Within Enclosures.

(1) Conductors of intrinsically safe circuits shall be separated at least 50 mm (2 in.) from conductors of any nonintrinsically safe circuits, or as specified in 504.30(A).

(2) All conductors shall be secured so that any conductor that might come loose from a terminal cannot come in contact with another terminal.

FPN No. 1: The use of separate wiring compartments for the intrinsically safe and nonintrinsically safe terminals is the preferred method of complying with this requirement.

FPN No. 2: Physical barriers such as grounded metal partitions or approved insulating partitions or approved restricted access wiring ducts separated from other such ducts by at least 19 mm (¾ in.) can be used to help ensure the required separation of the wiring.

(3) Other (Not in Raceway or Cable Tray Systems). Conductors and cables of intrinsically safe circuits run in other than raceway or cable tray systems shall be separated by at least 50 mm (2 in.) and secured from conductors and cables of any nonintrinsically safe circuits.

Exception: Where either (1) all of the intrinsically safe circuit conductors are in Type MI or MC cables or (2) all of the nonintrinsically safe circuit conductors are in raceways or Type MI or MC cables where the sheathing or cladding is capable of carrying fault current to ground.

(B) From Different Intrinsically Safe Circuit Conductors. Different intrinsically safe circuits shall be in separate cables or shall be separated from each other by one of the following means:

(1) The conductors of each circuit are within a grounded metal shield.

(2) The conductors of each circuit have insulation with a minimum thickness of 0.25 mm (0.01 in.).

Exception: Unless otherwise identified.

(3) The clearance between two terminals for connection of field wiring of different intrinsically safe circuits shall be at least 6 mm (0.25 in.) unless this clearance is permitted to be reduced by the control drawing.

504.50 Grounding.

(A) Intrinsically Safe Apparatus, Associated Apparatus, and Raceways. Intrinsically safe apparatus, associated apparatus, cable shields, enclosures, and raceways, if of metal, shall be grounded.

FPN: Supplementary bonding to the grounding electrode may be needed for some associated apparatus, for example, zener diode barriers, if specified in the control drawing. See ANSI/ISA RP 12.06.01-2002, *Wiring Methods for Hazardous (Classified) Locations Instrumentation Part 1: Intrinsic Safety.*

(B) Connection to Grounding Electrodes. Where connection to a grounding electrode is required, the grounding electrode shall be as specified in 250.52(A)(1), (A)(2), (A)(3), and (A)(4) and shall comply with 250.30(A)(7). Section 250.52(A)(5), (A)(6), and (A)(7) shall not be used if electrodes specified in 250.52(A)(1), (A)(2), (A)(3), or (A)(4) are available.

(C) Shields. Where shielded conductors or cables are used, shields shall be grounded.

Exception: Where a shield is part of an intrinsically safe circuit.

504.60 Bonding.

(A) Hazardous Locations. In hazardous (classified) locations, intrinsically safe apparatus shall be bonded in the hazardous (classified) location in accordance with 250.100.

(B) Unclassified. In unclassified or nonhazardous locations, where metal raceways are used for intrinsically safe system wiring in hazardous (classified) locations, associated apparatus shall be bonded in accordance with 501.30(A), 502.30(A), 503.30(A), or 505.25, as applicable.

504.70 Sealing. Conduits and cables that are required to be sealed by 501.15, 502.15, and 505.16 shall be sealed to minimize the passage of gases, vapors, or dusts. Such seals shall not be required to be explosionproof or flameproof.

Exception: Seals shall not be required for enclosures that contain only intrinsically safe apparatus, except as required by 501.15(F)(3).

504.80 Identification. Labels required by this section shall be suitable for the environment where they are installed with consideration given to exposure to chemicals and sunlight.

(A) Terminals. Intrinsically safe circuits shall be identified at terminal and junction locations in a manner that will prevent unintentional interference with the circuits during testing and servicing.

(B) Wiring. Raceways, cable trays, and other wiring methods for intrinsically safe system wiring shall be identified with permanently affixed labels with the wording "Intrinsic Safety Wiring" or equivalent. The labels shall be located so as to be visible after installation and placed so that they may be readily traced through the entire length of the installation. Intrinsic safety circuit labels shall appear in every section of the wiring system that is separated by enclosures, walls, partitions, or floors. Spacing between labels shall not be more than 7.5 m (25 ft).

Exception: Circuits run underground shall be permitted to be identified where they become accessible after emergence from the ground.

FPN No. 1: Wiring methods permitted in unclassified locations may be used for intrinsically safe systems in hazardous (classified) locations. Without labels to identify the application of the wiring, enforcement authorities cannot determine that an installation is in compliance with this *Code.*

FPN No. 2: In unclassified locations, identification is necessary to ensure that nonintrinsically safe wire will not be inadvertently added to existing raceways at a later date.

(C) Color Coding. Color coding shall be permitted to identify intrinsically safe conductors where they are colored light blue and where no other conductors colored light blue are used. Likewise, color coding shall be permitted to identify raceways, cable trays, and junction boxes where they are colored light blue and contain only intrinsically safe wiring.

ARTICLE 505
Class I, Zone 0, 1, and 2 Locations

FPN: Rules that are followed by a reference in brackets contain text that has been extracted from NFPA 497-2004, *Recommended Practice for the Classification of Flammable Liquids, Gases, or Vapors and of Hazardous (Classified) Locations for Electrical Installations in Chemical Process Areas.* Only editorial changes were made to the extracted text to make it consistent with this *Code.*

505.1 Scope. This article covers the requirements for the zone classification system as an alternative to the division classification system covered in Article 500 for electrical and electronic equipment and wiring for all voltages in Class I, Zone 0, Zone 1, and Zone 2 hazardous (classified) locations where fire or explosion hazards may exist due to flammable gases, vapors, or liquids.

FPN: For the requirements for electrical and electronic equipment and wiring for all voltages in Class I, Division 1 or Division 2; Class II, Division 1 or Division 2; and Class III, Division 1 or Division 2 hazardous (classified) locations where fire or explosion hazards may exist due to flammable gases or vapors, flammable liquids, or combustible dusts or fibers, refer to Articles 500 through 504.

505.2 Definitions. For purposes of this article, the following definitions apply.

Combustible Gas Detection System. A protection technique utilizing stationary gas detectors in industrial establishments.

Electrical and Electronic Equipment. Materials, fittings, devices, appliances, and the like that are part of, or in connection with, an electrical installation.

> FPN: Portable or transportable equipment having self-contained power supplies, such as battery-operated equipment, could potentially become an ignition source in hazardous (classified) locations.

Encapsulation "m." Type of protection where electrical parts that could ignite an explosive atmosphere by either sparking or heating are enclosed in a compound in such a way that this explosive atmosphere cannot be ignited.

> FPN: See ANSI/ISA 12.23.01-2002, *Electrical Apparatus for Use in Class I, Zone 1 Hazardous (Classified) Locations, Type of Protection — Encapsulation "m"*; and ANSI/UL 60079–18, *Electrical apparatus for explosive gas atmospheres — Part 18: Encapsulation "m."*

Flameproof "d." Type of protection where the enclosure will withstand an internal explosion of a flammable mixture that has penetrated into the interior, without suffering damage and without causing ignition, through any joints or structural openings in the enclosure, of an external explosive gas atmosphere consisting of one or more of the gases or vapors for which it is designed.

> FPN: See ANSI/ISA 12.22.01-2002, *Electrical Apparatus for Use in Class I, Zone 1 and 2 Hazardous (Classified) Locations, Type of Protection — Flameproof "d"*; and ANSI/UL 60079–1, *Electrical apparatus for explosive gas atmospheres — Part 1: Flameproof enclosures "d."*

Increased Safety "e." Type of protection applied to electrical equipment that does not produce arcs or sparks in normal service and under specified abnormal conditions, in which additional measures are applied so as to give increased security against the possibility of excessive temperatures and of the occurrence of arcs and sparks.

> FPN: See ANSI/ISA — 12.16.01-2002, *Electrical Apparatus for Use in Class I, Zone 1 Hazardous (Classified) Locations, Type of Protection — Increased Safety "e"*; and ANSI/UL 60079-7, *Electrical apparatus for explosive gas atmospheres — Part 7: Increased Safety "e."*

Intrinsic Safety "i." Type of protection where any spark or thermal effect is incapable of causing ignition of a mixture of flammable or combustible material in air under prescribed test conditions.

> FPN No. 1: See ANSI/UL 913-1997, *Intrinsically Safe Apparatus and Associated Apparatus for Use in Class I, II, and III, Hazardous Locations*; ISA 12.02.01-1999, *Electrical Apparatus for Use in Class I, Zones 0, 1 and 2 Hazardous (Classified) Locations — Intrinsic Safety "i"*; and ANSI/UL 60079-11, *Electrical apparatus for explosive gas atmospheres — Part II: Intrinsic safety "i."*

> FPN No. 2: Intrinsic safety is designated type of protection "ia" for use in Zone 0 locations. Intrinsic safety is designated type of protection "ib" for use in Zone 1 locations.

> FPN No. 3: Intrinsically safe associated apparatus, designated by [ia] or [ib], is connected to intrinsically safe apparatus ("ia" or "ib," respectively) but is located outside the hazardous (classified) location unless also protected by another type of protection (such as flameproof).

Oil Immersion "o." Type of protection where electrical equipment is immersed in a protective liquid in such a way that an explosive atmosphere that may be above the liquid or outside the enclosure cannot be ignited.

> FPN: See ISA 12.26.01-1998, *Electrical Apparatus for Use in Class I, Zone 1 Hazardous (Classified) Locations, Type of Protection — Oil-Immersion "o"*; and ANSI/UL 60079-6, *Electrical apparatus for explosive gas atmospheres — Part 6: Oil-immersion "o."*

Powder Filling "q." Type of protection where electrical parts capable of igniting an explosive atmosphere are fixed in position and completely surrounded by filling material (glass or quartz powder) to prevent the ignition of an external explosive atmosphere.

> FPN: See ANSI/ISA-12.25.01-2002, *Electrical Apparatus for Use in Class I, Zone 1 Hazardous (Classified) Locations Type of Protection — Powder Filling "q"*; and ANSI/UL 60079-5, *Electrical apparatus for explosive gas atmospheres — Part 5: Powder filling "q."*

Purged and Pressurized. Type of protection for electrical equipment that uses the technique of guarding against the ingress of the external atmosphere, which may be explosive, into an enclosure by maintaining a protective gas therein at a pressure above that of the external atmosphere.

> FPN No. 1: See NFPA 496-2003, *Standard for Purged and Pressurized Enclosures for Electrical Equipment*.

> FPN No. 2: See IEC 60079-2-2000, *Electrical Apparatus for Explosive Gas Atmospheres — Part 2: Electrical Apparatus, Type of Protection "p"*; and IEC 60079-13-1982, *Electrical Apparatus for Explosive Gas Atmospheres — Part 13: Construction and Use of Rooms or Buildings Protected by Pressurization*.

Type of Protection "n." Type of protection where electrical equipment, in normal operation, is not capable of igniting a surrounding explosive gas atmosphere and a fault capable of causing ignition is not likely to occur.

> FPN: See ANSI/UL 60079-15-2002, *Electrical apparatus for explosive gas atmospheres — Part 15: Type of protection "n"*; and ANSI/ISA 12.12.02-2003, *Electrical apparatus for use in Class I, Zone 2 Hazardous (Classified) Locations: Type of protection "n."*

Unclassified Locations. Locations determined to be neither Class I, Division 1; Class I, Division 2; Class I, Zone 0; Class I, Zone 1; Class I, Zone 2; Class II, Division 1; Class II, Division 2; Class III, Division 1; Class III, Division 2; or any combination thereof.

505.3 Other Articles. All other applicable rules contained in this *Code* shall apply to electrical equipment and wiring installed in hazardous (classified) locations.

Exception: As modified by Article 504 and this article.

505.4 General.

(A) Documentation for Industrial Occupancies. All areas in industrial occupancies designated as hazardous (classified) locations shall be properly documented. This documentation shall be available to those authorized to design, install, inspect, maintain, or operate electrical equipment at the location.

FPN: For examples of area classification drawings, see ANSI/API RP 505-1997, *Recommended Practice for Classification of Locations for Electrical Installations at Petroleum Facilities Classified as Class I, Zone 0, Zone 1, or Zone 2;* ISA RP12.24.01-1998, *Recommended Practice for Classification of Locations for Electrical Installations Classified as Class I, Zone 0, Zone 1, or Zone 2;* IEC 60079-10-1995, *Electrical Apparatus for Explosive Gas Atmospheres, Classification of Hazardous Areas;* and *Model Code of Safe Practice in the Petroleum Industry, Part 15: Area Classification Code for Petroleum Installations,* IP 15, The Institute of Petroleum, London.

(B) Reference Standards. Important information relating to topics covered in Chapter 5 may be found in other publications.

FPN No. 1: It is important that the authority having jurisdiction be familiar with recorded industrial experience as well as with standards of the National Fire Protection Association (NFPA), the American Petroleum Institute (API), the Instrumentation, Systems, and Automation Society (ISA), and the International Electrotechnical Commission (IEC) that may be of use in the classification of various locations, the determination of adequate ventilation, and the protection against static electricity and lightning hazards.

FPN No. 2: For further information on the classification of locations, see ANSI/API RP 505-1997, *Recommended Practice for Classification of Locations for Electrical Installations at Petroleum Facilities Classified as Class I, Zone 0, Zone 1, or Zone 2;* ISA RP 12.24.01-1998, *Recommended Practice for Classification of Locations for Electrical Installations Classified as Class I, Zone 0, Zone 1, or Zone 2;* IEC 60079-10-1995, *Electrical Apparatus for Explosive Gas Atmospheres, Classification of Hazardous Areas;* and *Model Code of Safe Practice in the Petroleum Industry, Part 15: Area Classification Code for Petroleum Installations,* IP 15, The Institute of Petroleum, London.

FPN No. 3: For further information on protection against static electricity and lightning hazards in hazardous (classified) locations, see NFPA 77-2000, *Recommended Practice on Static Electricity;* NFPA 780-2004, *Standard for the Installation of Lightning Protection Systems;* and API RP 2003-1998, *Protection Against Ignitions Arising Out of Static Lightning and Stray Currents.*

FPN No. 4: For further information on ventilation, see NFPA 30-2003, *Flammable and Combustible Liquids Code,* and ANSI/API RP 505-1997, *Recommended Practice for Classification of Locations for Electrical Installations at Petroleum Facilities Classified as Class I, Zone 0, Zone 1, or Zone 2.*

FPN No. 5: For further information on electrical systems for hazardous (classified) locations on offshore oil and gas producing platforms, see ANSI/API RP 14FZ-2000, *Recommended Practice for Design and Installation of Electrical Systems for Fixed and Floating Offshore Petroleum Facilities for Unclassified and Class I, Zone 0, Zone 1, and Zone 2 Locations.*

FPN No. 6: For further information on the installation of electrical equipment in hazardous (classified) locations in general, see IEC 60079-14-1996, *Electrical Apparatus for Explosive Gas Atmospheres — Part 14: Electrical Installations in Explosive Gas Atmospheres (Other Than Mines),* and IEC 60079-16-1990, *Electrical Apparatus for Explosive Gas Atmospheres — Part 16: Artificial Ventilation for the Protection of Analyzer(s) Houses.*

FPN No. 7: For further information on application of electrical equipment in hazardous (classified) locations in general, see ANSI/ISA 12.00.01-2002, *Electrical Apparatus for Use in Class I, Zones 0 and 1, Hazardous (Classified) Locations: General Requirements;* ISA 12.01.01-1999, *Definitions and Information Pertaining to Electrical Apparatus in Hazardous (Classified) Locations;* and ANSI/UL 60079-0, *Electrical apparatus for explosive gas atmospheres — Part 0: General requirements.*

505.5 Classifications of Locations.

(A) Classification of Locations. Locations shall be classified depending on the properties of the flammable vapors, liquids, or gases that may be present and the likelihood that a flammable or combustible concentration or quantity is present. Where pyrophoric materials are the only materials used or handled, these locations shall not be classified. Each room, section, or area shall be considered individually in determining its classification.

FPN No. 1: See 505.7 for restrictions on area classification.

FPN No. 2: Through the exercise of ingenuity in the layout of electrical installations for hazardous (classified) locations, it is frequently possible to locate much of the equipment in reduced level of classification or in an unclassified location and, thus, to reduce the amount of special equipment required.

Rooms and areas containing ammonia refrigeration systems that are equipped with adequate mechanical ventilation may be classified as "unclassified" locations.

FPN: For further information regarding classification and ventilation of areas involving ammonia, see ANSI/ASHRAE 15-1994, *Safety Code for Mechanical Refrigeration;* and ANSI/CGA G2.1-1989 (14-39), *Safety Requirements for the Storage and Handling of Anhydrous Ammonia.*

(B) Class I, Zone 0, 1, and 2 Locations. Class I, Zone 0, 1, and 2 locations are those in which flammable gases or vapors are or may be present in the air in quantities sufficient to produce explosive or ignitible mixtures. Class I, Zone 0, 1, and 2 locations shall include those specified in 505(B)(1), (B)(2), and (B)(3).

(1) Class I, Zone 0. A Class I, Zone 0 location is a location in which

(1) Ignitible concentrations of flammable gases or vapors are present continuously, or

(2) Ignitible concentrations of flammable gases or vapors are present for long periods of time.

FPN No. 1: As a guide in determining when flammable gases or vapors are present continuously or for long periods of time, refer to ANSI/API RP 505-1997, *Recommended Practice for Classification of Locations for Electrical Installations of Petroleum Facilities Classified as Class I, Zone 0, Zone 1 or Zone 2*; ISA 12.24.01-1998, *Recommended Practice for Classification of Locations for Electrical Installations Classified as Class I, Zone 0, Zone 1, or Zone 2*; IEC 60079-10-1995, *Electrical Apparatus for Explosive Gas Atmospheres, Classifications of Hazardous Areas*; and *Area Classification Code for Petroleum Installations, Model Code, Part 15*, Institute of Petroleum.

FPN No. 2: This classification includes locations inside vented tanks or vessels that contain volatile flammable liquids; inside inadequately vented spraying or coating enclosures, where volatile flammable solvents are used; between the inner and outer roof sections of a floating roof tank containing volatile flammable liquids; inside open vessels, tanks and pits containing volatile flammable liquids; the interior of an exhaust duct that is used to vent ignitible concentrations of gases or vapors; and inside inadequately ventilated enclosures that contain normally venting instruments utilizing or analyzing flammable fluids and venting to the inside of the enclosures.

FPN No. 3: It is not good practice to install electrical equipment in Zone 0 locations except when the equipment is essential to the process or when other locations are not feasible. [See 505.5(A) FPN No. 2.] If it is necessary to install electrical systems in a Zone 0 location, it is good practice to install intrinsically safe systems as described by Article 504.

(2) Class I, Zone 1. A Class I, Zone 1 location is a location

(1) In which ignitible concentrations of flammable gases or vapors are likely to exist under normal operating conditions; or

(2) In which ignitible concentrations of flammable gases or vapors may exist frequently because of repair or maintenance operations or because of leakage; or

(3) In which equipment is operated or processes are carried on, of such a nature that equipment breakdown or faulty operations could result in the release of ignitible concentrations of flammable gases or vapors and also cause simultaneous failure of electrical equipment in a mode to cause the electrical equipment to become a source of ignition; or

(4) That is adjacent to a Class I, Zone 0 location from which ignitible concentrations of vapors could be communicated, unless communication is prevented by adequate positive pressure ventilation from a source of clean air and effective safeguards against ventilation failure are provided.

FPN No. 1: Normal operation is considered the situation when plant equipment is operating within its design parameters. Minor releases of flammable material may be part of normal operations. Minor releases include the releases from mechanical packings on pumps. Failures that involve repair or shutdown (such as the breakdown of pump seals and flange gaskets, and spillage caused by accidents) are not considered normal operation.

FPN No. 2: This classification usually includes locations where volatile flammable liquids or liquefied flammable gases are transferred from one container to another. In areas in the vicinity of spraying and painting operations where flammable solvents are used; adequately ventilated drying rooms or compartments for evaporation of flammable solvents; adequately ventilated locations containing fat and oil extraction equipment using volatile flammable solvents; portions of cleaning and dyeing plants where volatile flammable liquids are used; adequately ventilated gas generator rooms and other portions of gas manufacturing plants where flammable gas may escape; inadequately ventilated pump rooms for flammable gas or for volatile flammable liquids; the interiors of refrigerators and freezers in which volatile flammable materials are stored in the open, lightly stoppered, or in easily ruptured containers; and other locations where ignitible concentrations of flammable vapors or gases are likely to occur in the course of normal operation but not classified Zone 0.

(3) Class I, Zone 2. A Class I, Zone 2 location is a location

(1) In which ignitible concentrations of flammable gases or vapors are not likely to occur in normal operation and, if they do occur, will exist only for a short period; or

(2) In which volatile flammable liquids, flammable gases, or flammable vapors are handled, processed, or used but in which the liquids, gases, or vapors normally are confined within closed containers of closed systems from which they can escape, only as a result of accidental rupture or breakdown of the containers or system, or as a result of the abnormal operation of the equipment with which the liquids or gases are handled, processed, or used; or

(3) In which ignitible concentrations of flammable gases or vapors normally are prevented by positive mechanical ventilation but which may become hazardous as a result of failure or abnormal operation of the ventilation equipment; or

(4) That is adjacent to a Class I, Zone 1 location, from which ignitible concentrations of flammable gases or vapors could be communicated, unless such communication is prevented by adequate positive-pressure ventilation from a source of clean air and effective safeguards against ventilation failure are provided.

FPN: The Zone 2 classification usually includes locations where volatile flammable liquids or flammable gases or vapors are used but which would become hazardous only in case of an accident or of some unusual operating condition.

505.6 Material Groups. For purposes of testing, approval, and area classification, various air mixtures (not oxygen enriched) shall be grouped as required in 505.6(A), (B), and (C).

FPN: Group I is intended for use in describing atmospheres that contain firedamp (a mixture of gases, composed mostly of methane, found underground, usually in mines). This *Code* does not apply to installations underground in mines. See 90.2(B).

Group II shall be subdivided into IIC, IIB, and IIA, as noted in 505.6(A), (B), and (C), according to the nature of the gas or vapor, for protection techniques "d," "ia," "ib," "[ia]," and "[ib]," and, where applicable, "n" and "o."

FPN No. 1: The gas and vapor subdivision as described above is based on the maximum experimental safe gap (MESG), minimum igniting current (MIC), or both. Test equipment for determining the MESG is described in IEC 60079-1A-1975, Amendment No. 1 (1993), *Construction and Verification Tests of Flameproof Enclosures of Electrical Apparatus*; and *UL Technical Report No. 58* (1993). The test equipment for determining MIC is described in IEC 60079-11-1999, *Electrical Apparatus for Explosive Gas Atmospheres — Part 11: Intrinsic Safety "i."* The classification of gases or vapors according to their maximum experimental safe gaps and minimum igniting currents is described in IEC 60079-12-1978, *Classification of Mixtures of Gases or Vapours with Air According to Their Maximum Experimental Safe Gaps and Minimum Igniting Currents.*

FPN No. 2: Verification of electrical equipment utilizing protection techniques "e," "m," "p," and "q," due to design technique, does not require tests involving MESG or MIC. Therefore, Group II is not required to be subdivided for these protection techniques.

FPN No. 3: It is necessary that the meanings of the different equipment markings and Group II classifications be carefully observed to avoid confusion with Class I, Divisions 1 and 2, Groups A, B, C, and D.

Class I, Zone 0, 1, and 2, groups shall be as follows:

(A) Group IIC. Atmospheres containing acetylene, hydrogen, or flammable gas, flammable liquid-produced vapor, or combustible liquid-produced vapor mixed with air that may burn or explode, having either a maximum experimental safe gap (MESG) value less than or equal to 0.50 mm or minimum igniting current ratio (MIC ratio) less than or equal to 0.45. [NFPA 497:3.3]

FPN: Group IIC is equivalent to a combination of Class I, Group A, and Class I, Group B, as described in 500.6(A)(1) and 500.6(A)(2).

(B) Group IIB. Atmospheres containing acetaldehyde, ethylene, or flammable gas, flammable liquid-produced vapor, or combustible liquid-produced vapor mixed with air that may burn or explode, having either maximum experimental safe gap (MESG) values greater than 0.50 mm and less than or equal to 0.90 mm or minimum igniting current ratio (MIC ratio) greater than 0.45 and less than or equal to 0.80. [NFPA 497:3.3]

FPN: Group IIB is equivalent to Class I, Group C, as described in 500.6(A)(3).

(C) Group IIA. Atmospheres containing acetone, ammonia, ethyl alcohol, gasoline, methane, propane, or flammable gas, flammable liquid-produced vapor, or combustible liquid-produced vapor mixed with air that may burn or explode, having either a maximum experiment safe gap (MESG) value greater than 0.90 mm or minimum igniting current ratio (MIC ratio) greater than 0.80. [NFPA 497:3.3]

FPN: Group IIA is equivalent to Class I, Group D as described in 500.6(A)(4).

505.7 Special Precaution. Article 505 requires equipment construction and installation that ensures safe performance under conditions of proper use and maintenance.

FPN No. 1: It is important that inspection authorities and users exercise more than ordinary care with regard to the installation and maintenance of electrical equipment in hazardous (classified) locations.

FPN No. 2: Low ambient conditions require special consideration. Electrical equipment depending on the protection techniques described by 505.8(A) may not be suitable for use at temperatures lower than −20°C (−4°F) unless they are identified for use at lower temperatures. However, at low ambient temperatures, flammable concentrations of vapors may not exist in a location classified Class I, Zones 0, 1, or 2 at normal ambient temperature.

(A) Supervision of Work. Classification of areas and selection of equipment and wiring methods shall be under the supervision of a qualified Registered Professional Engineer.

(B) Dual Classification. In instances of areas within the same facility classified separately, Class I, Zone 2 locations shall be permitted to abut, but not overlap, Class I, Division 2 locations. Class I, Zone 0 or Zone 1 locations shall not abut Class I, Division 1 or Division 2 locations.

(C) Reclassification Permitted. A Class I, Division 1 or Division 2 location shall be permitted to be reclassified as a Class I, Zone 0, Zone 1, or Zone 2 location, provided all of the space that is classified because of a single flammable gas or vapor source is reclassified under the requirements of this article.

(D) Solid Obstacles. Flameproof equipment with flanged joints shall not be installed such that the flange openings are closer than the distances shown in Table 505.7(D) to any solid obstacle that is not a part of the equipment (such as steelworks, walls, weather guards, mounting brackets, pipes, or other electrical equipment) unless the equipment is listed for a smaller distance of separation.

Table 505.7(D) Minimum Distance of Obstructions from Flameproof "d" Flange Openings

	Minimum Distance	
Gas Group	mm	in.
IIC	40	1 37/64
IIB	30	1 3/16
IIA	10	25/64

505.8 Protection Techniques. Acceptable protection techniques for electrical and electronic equipment in hazardous (classified) locations shall be as described in 505.8(A) through 505.8(I).

FPN: For additional information, see ANSI/ISA 12.00.01-2002, *Electrical Apparatus for Use in Class I, Zones 0 and 1 Hazardous (Classified) Locations, General Requirements*; ANSI/ISA 12.01.01-2002, *Definitions and Information Pertaining to Electrical Apparatus in Hazardous (Classified) Locations*; and ANSI/UL 60079–0, *Electrical apparatus for explosive gas atmospheres — Part 0: General requirements.*

(A) Flameproof "d." This protection technique shall be permitted for equipment in Class I, Zone 1 or Zone 2 locations.

(B) Purged and Pressurized. This protection technique shall be permitted for equipment in those Class I, Zone 1 or Zone 2 locations for which it is identified.

(C) Intrinsic Safety. This protection technique shall be permitted for apparatus and associated apparatus in Class I, Zone 0, Zone 1, or Zone 2 locations for which it is listed.

(D) Type of Protection "n." This protection technique shall be permitted for equipment in Class I, Zone 2 locations. Type of protection "n" is further subdivided into nA, nC, and nR.

FPN: See Table 505.9(C)(2)(4) for the descriptions of subdivisions for type of protection "n."

(E) Oil Immersion "o." This protection technique shall be permitted for equipment in Class I, Zone 1 or Zone 2 locations.

(F) Increased Safety "e." This protection technique shall be permitted for equipment in Class I, Zone 1 or Zone 2 locations.

(G) Encapsulation "m." This protection technique shall be permitted for equipment in Class I, Zone 1 or Zone 2 locations.

(H) Powder Filling "q." This protection technique shall be permitted for equipment in Class I, Zone 1 or Zone 2 locations.

(I) Combustible Gas Detection System. A combustible gas detection system shall be permitted as a means of protection in industrial establishments with restricted public access and where the conditions of maintenance and supervision ensure that only qualified persons service the installation. Gas detection equipment shall be listed for detection of the specific gas or vapor to be encountered. Where such a system is installed, equipment specified in 505.8(I)(1), I(2), or I(3) shall be permitted. The type of detection equipment, its listing, installation location(s), alarm and shutdown criteria, and calibration frequency shall be documented when combustible gas detectors are used as a protection technique.

FPN No. 1: For further information, see ANSI/ISA-12.13.01, *Performance Requirements, Combustible Gas Detectors.*

FPN No. 2: For further information, see ANSI/API RP 505, *Recommended Practice for Classification of Locations for Electrical Installations at Petroleum Facilities Classified as Class I, Zone 0, Zone 1, and Zone 2.*

FPN No. 3: For further information, see ISA-RP12.13.02, *Installation, Operation, and Maintenance of Combustible Gas Detection Instruments.*

(1) Inadequate Ventilation. In a Class I, Zone 1 location that is so classified due to inadequate ventilation, electrical equipment suitable for Class I, Zone 2 locations shall be permitted.

(2) Interior of a Building. In a building located in, or with an opening into, a Class I, Zone 2 location where the interior does not contain a source of flammable gas or vapor, electrical equipment for unclassified locations shall be permitted.

(3) Interior of a Control Panel. In the interior of a control panel containing instrumentation utilizing or measuring flammable liquids, gases, or vapors, electrical equipment suitable for Class I, Zone 2 locations shall be permitted.

505.9 Equipment.

(A) Suitability. Suitability of identified equipment shall be determined by one of the following:

(1) Equipment listing or labeling

(2) Evidence of equipment evaluation from a qualified testing laboratory or inspection agency concerned with product evaluation

(3) Evidence acceptable to the authority having jurisdiction such as a manufacturer's self-evaluation or an owner's engineering judgment

(B) Listing.

(1) Equipment that is listed for a Zone 0 location shall be permitted in a Zone 1 or Zone 2 location of the same gas or vapor, provided that it is installed in accordance with the requirements for the marked type of protection. Equipment that is listed for a Zone 1 location shall be permitted in a Zone 2 location of the same gas or vapor, provided that it is installed in accordance with the requirements for the marked type of protection.

(2) Equipment shall be permitted to be listed for a specific gas or vapor, specific mixtures of gases or vapors, or any specific combination of gases or vapors.

FPN: One common example is equipment marked for "IIB. + H2."

(C) Marking. Equipment shall be marked in accordance with 505.9(C)(1) or (C)(2).

(1) Division Equipment. Equipment identified for Class I, Division 1 or Class I, Division 2 shall, in addition to being marked in accordance with 500.8(B), be permitted to be marked with all of the following:

(1) Class I, Zone 1 or Class I, Zone 2 (as applicable)

(2) Applicable gas classification group(s) in accordance with Table 505.9(C)

(3) Temperature classification in accordance with 505.9(D)(1)

Table 505.9(C) Gas Classification Groups

Gas Group	Comment
IIC	See 505.6(A)(1)
IIB	See 505.6(A)(2)
IIA	See 505.6(A)(3)

(2) Zone Equipment. Equipment meeting one or more of the protection techniques described in 505.8 shall be marked with all of the following in the order shown:

(1) Class

(2) Zone

(3) Symbol "AEx"

(4) Protection technique(s) in accordance with Table 505.9(C)(2)(4)

(5) Applicable gas classification group(s) in accordance with Table 505.9(C)

(6) Temperature classification in accordance with 505.9(D)(1)

Exception No. 1: Associated apparatus NOT suitable for installation in a hazardous (classified) locations shall be required to be marked only with (3), (4), and (5), but BOTH the symbol AEx (3) and the symbol for the type of protection (4) shall be enclosed within the same square brackets, for example, [AEx ia] IIC.

Exception No. 2: Simple apparatus as defined in 504.2 shall not be required to have a marked operating temperature or temperature class.

Electrical equipment of types of protection "e," "m," "p," or "q" shall be marked Group II. Electrical equipment of types of protection "d," "ia," "ib," "[ia]," or "[ib]" shall be marked Group IIA, IIB, or IIC, or for a specific gas or vapor. Electrical equipment of types of protection "n" shall

Table 505.9(C)(2)(4) Types of Protection Designation

Designation	Technique	Zone*
d	Flameproof enclosure	1
e	Increased safety	1
ia	Intrinsic safety	0
ib	Intrinsic safety	1
[ia]	Associated apparatus	Unclassified
[ib]	Associated apparatus	Unclassified
m	Encapsulation	1
nA	Nonsparking equipment	2
nC	Sparking equipment in which the contacts are suitably protected other than by restricted breathing enclosure	2
nR	Restricted breathing enclosure	2
o	Oil immersion	1
p	Purged and pressurized	1 or 2
q	Powder filled	1

*Does not address use where a combination of techniques is used.

be marked Group II unless it contains enclosed-break devices, nonincendive components, or energy-limited equipment or circuits, in which case it shall be marked Group IIA, IIB, or IIC, or a specific gas or vapor. Electrical equipment of other types of protection shall be marked Group II unless the type of protection utilized by the equipment requires that it be marked Group IIA, IIB, or IIC, or a specific gas or vapor.

FPN No. 1: An example of the required marking for intrinsically safe apparatus for installation in Class I, Zone 0 is "Class I, Zone 0, AEx ia IIC T6." An explanation of the marking that is required is shown in FPN Figure 505.9(C)(2).

FPN No. 2: An example of the required marking for intrinsically safe associated apparatus mounted in a flameproof enclosure for installation in Class I, Zone 1 is "Class I, Zone 1 AEx d[ia] IIC T4."

FPN No. 3: An example of the required marking for intrinsically safe associated apparatus NOT for installation in a hazardous (classified) location is "[AEx ia] IIC."

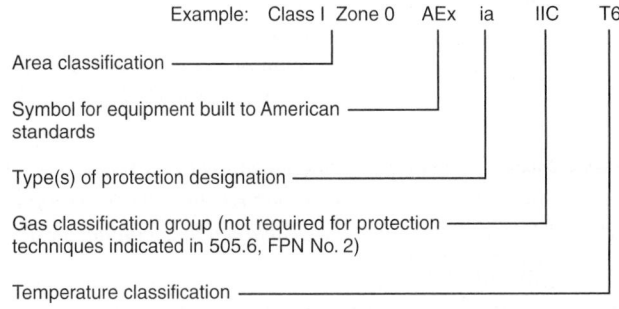

FPN Figure 505.9(C)(2) Zone Equipment Marking.

(D) Class I Temperature. The temperature marking specified below shall not exceed the ignition temperature of the specific gas or vapor to be encountered.

FPN: For information regarding ignition temperatures of gases and vapors, see NFPA 497-2004, *Recommended Practice for the Classification of Flammable Liquids, Gases, or Vapors and of Hazardous (Classified) Locations for Electrical Installations in Chemical Process Areas*; and IEC 60079-20-1996, *Electrical Apparatus for Explosive Gas Atmospheres, Data for Flammable Gases and Vapours, Relating to the Use of Electrical Apparatus*.

(1) Temperature Classifications. Equipment shall be marked to show the operating temperature or temperature class referenced to a 40°C (104°F) ambient. The temperature class, if provided, shall be indicated using the temperature class (T Code) shown in Table 505.9(D)(1).

Table 505.9(D)(1) Classification of Maximum Surface Temperature for Group II Electrical Equipment

Temperature Class (T Code)	Maximum Surface Temperature (°C)
T1	≤450
T2	≤300
T3	≤200
T4	≤135
T5	≤100
T6	≤85

Electrical equipment designed for use in the ambient temperature range between −20°C and +40°C shall require no additional ambient temperature marking.

Electrical equipment that is designed for use in a range of ambient temperatures other than −20°C and +40°C is considered to be special; and the ambient temperature range shall then be marked on the equipment, including either the symbol "Ta" or "Tamb" together with the special range of ambient temperatures. As an example, such a marking might be "−30°C ≤ Ta ≤ + 40°C."

Electrical equipment suitable for ambient temperatures exceeding 40°C (104°F) shall be marked with both the maximum ambient temperature and the operating temperature or temperature class at that ambient temperature.

Exception No. 1: Equipment of the non–heat-producing type, such as conduit fittings, and equipment of the heat-producing type having a maximum temperature of not more than 100°C (212°F) shall not be required to have a marked operating temperature or temperature class.

Exception No. 2: Equipment identified for Class I, Division 1 or Division 2 locations as permitted by 505.20(B) and 505.20(D) shall be permitted to be marked in accordance with 500.8(B) and Table 500.8(B).

(E) Threading. All NPT threaded conduit and fittings referred to herein shall be threaded with a National (American) Standard Pipe Taper (NPT) thread that provides a taper of 1 in 16 (¾-in. taper per foot). Conduit and fittings shall be made wrenchtight to prevent sparking when fault current flows through the conduit system, and to ensure the explosionproof or flameproof integrity of the conduit system where applicable. Equipment provided with threaded entries for field wiring connections shall be installed in accordance with 505.9(E)(1) or 505.9(E)(2). Threaded entries into explosionproof or flameproof equipment shall be made up with at least five threads fully engaged.

Exception: For listed explosionproof or flameproof equipment, factory threaded NPT entries shall be made up with at least 4½ threads fully engaged.

(1) Equipment Provided with Threaded Entries for NPT Threaded Conduit or Fittings. For equipment provided with threaded entries for NPT threaded conduit or fittings, listed conduit fittings or cable fittings shall be used.

FPN: Thread form specifications for NPT threads are located in ANSI/ASME B1.20.1-1983, *Pipe Threads, General Purpose (Inch).*

(2) Equipment Provided with Threaded Entries for Metric Threaded Conduit or Fittings. For equipment with metric threaded entries, such entries shall be identified as being metric, or listed adapters to permit connection to conduit or NPT-threaded fittings shall be provided with the equipment. Adapters shall be used for connection to conduit or NPT-threaded fittings. Listed cable fittings that have metric threads shall be permitted to be used.

FPN: Threading specifications for metric threaded entries are located in ISO 965/1-1980, *Metric Screw Threads*; and ISO 965/3-1980, *Metric Screw Threads.*

505.15 Wiring Methods. Wiring methods shall maintain the integrity of protection techniques and shall comply with 505.15(A) through 505.15(C).

(A) Class I, Zone 0. In Class I, Zone 0 locations, only intrinsically safe wiring methods in accordance with Article 504 shall be permitted.

FPN: Article 504 only includes protection technique "ia."

(B) Class I, Zone 1.

(1) General. In Class I, Zone 1 locations, the wiring methods in (B)(1)(a) through (B)(1)(f) shall be permitted.

(a) All wiring methods permitted by 505.15(A).

(b) In industrial establishments with restricted public access, where the conditions of maintenance and supervision ensure that only qualified persons service the installation, and where the cable is not subject to physical damage,

Type MC-HL cable listed for use in Class I, Zone 1 or Division 1 locations, with a gas/vaportight continuous corrugated metallic sheath, an overall jacket of suitable polymeric material, separate grounding conductors in accordance with 250.122, and provided with termination fittings listed for the application.

FPN: See 330.12 for restrictions on use of Type MC cable.

(c) In industrial establishments with restricted public access, where the conditions of maintenance and supervision ensure that only qualified persons service the installation, and where the cable is not subject to physical damage, Type ITC-HL cable, listed for use in Class I, Zone 1 or Division 1 locations, with a gas/vaportight continuous corrugated metallic sheath, an overall jacket of suitable polymeric material and provided with termination fittings listed for the application.

(d) Type MI cable with termination fittings listed for Class I, Zone 1 or Division 1 locations. Type MI cable shall be installed and supported in a manner to avoid tensile stress at the termination fittings.

(e) Threaded rigid metal conduit, or threaded steel intermediate metal conduit.

(f) Rigid nonmetallic conduit complying with Article 352 shall be permitted where encased in a concrete envelope a minimum of 50 mm (2 in.) thick and provided with not less than 600 mm (24 in.) of cover measured from the top of the conduit to grade. Threaded rigid metal conduit or threaded steel intermediate metal conduit shall be used for the last 600 mm (24 in.) of the underground run to emergence or to the point of connection to the aboveground raceway. An equipment grounding conductor shall be included to provide for electrical continuity of the raceway system and for grounding of non–current-carrying metal parts.

(2) Flexible Connections. Where necessary to employ flexible connections, flexible fittings listed for Class I, Zone 1 or Division 1 locations or flexible cord in accordance with the provisions of 505.17 shall be permitted.

(C) Class I, Zone 2.

(1) General. In Class I, Zone 2 locations, the wiring methods in (C)(1)(a) through (C)(1)(g) shall be permitted.

(a) All wiring methods permitted by 505.15(B).

(b) Types MI, MC, MV, or TC cable with termination fittings, or in cable tray systems and installed in a manner to avoid tensile stress at the termination fittings. Single conductor Type MV cables shall be shielded or metallic-armored.

(c) Type ITC cable as permitted in 727.4.

(d) Type PLTC cable in accordance with the provisions of Article 725, or in cable tray systems. PLTC shall be installed in a manner to avoid tensile stress at the termination fittings.

(e) Enclosed gasketed busways, enclosed gasketed wireways.

(f) Threaded rigid metal conduit, threaded steel intermediate metal conduit.

(g) Nonincendive field wiring shall be permitted using any of the wiring methods permitted for unclassified locations. Nonincendive field wiring systems shall be installed in accordance with the control drawing(s). Simple apparatus, not shown on the control drawing, shall be permitted in a nonincendive field wiring circuit, provided the simple apparatus does not interconnect the nonincendive field wiring circuit to any other circuit.

FPN: Simple apparatus is defined in 504.2.

Separate nonincendive field wiring circuits shall be installed in accordance with one of the following:

(1) In separate cables

(2) In multiconductor cables where the conductors of each circuit are within a grounded metal shield

(3) In multiconductor cables where the conductors of each circuit have insulation with a minimum thickness of 0.25 mm (0.01 in.)

(2) Flexible Connections. Where provision must be made for limited flexibility, flexible metal fittings, flexible metal conduit with listed fittings, liquidtight flexible metal conduit with listed fittings, liquidtight flexible nonmetallic conduit with listed fittings, or flexible cord in accordance with the provisions of 505.17 shall be permitted.

FPN: See 505.25(B) for grounding requirements where flexible conduit is used.

505.16 Sealing and Drainage. Seals in conduit and cable systems shall comply with 505.16(A) through 505.16(E). Sealing compound shall be used in Type MI cable termination fittings to exclude moisture and other fluids from the cable insulation.

FPN No. 1: Seals are provided in conduit and cable systems to minimize the passage of gases and vapors and prevent the passage of flames from one portion of the electrical installation to another through the conduit. Such communication through Type MI cable is inherently prevented by construction of the cable. Unless specifically designed and tested for the purpose, conduit and cable seals are not intended to prevent the passage of liquids, gases, or vapors at a continuous pressure differential across the seal. Even at differences in pressure across the seal equivalent to a few inches of water, there may be a slow passage of gas or vapor through a seal and through conductors passing through the seal. See 505.16(C)(2)(b). Temperature extremes and highly corrosive liquids and vapors can affect the ability of seals to perform their intended function. See 505.16(D)(2).

FPN No. 2: Gas or vapor leakage and propagation of flames may occur through the interstices between the strands of standard stranded conductors larger than 2 AWG. Special conductor constructions, for example, compacted strands or sealing of the individual strands, are means of reducing leakage and preventing the propagation of flames.

(A) Zone 0. In Class I, Zone 0 locations, seals shall be located according to 505.16(A)(1), (A)(2), and (A)(3).

(1) Conduit Seals. Seals shall be provided within 3.05 m (10 ft) of where a conduit leaves a Zone 0 location. There shall be no unions, couplings, boxes, or fittings, except listed reducers at the seal, in the conduit run between the seal and the point at which the conduit leaves the location.

Exception: A rigid unbroken conduit that passes completely through the Zone 0 location with no fittings less than 300 mm (12 in.) beyond each boundary shall not be required to be sealed if the termination points of the unbroken conduit are in unclassified locations.

(2) Cable Seals. Seals shall be provided on cables at the first point of termination after entry into the Zone 0 location.

(3) Not Required to Be Explosionproof or Flameproof. Seals shall not be required to be explosionproof or flameproof.

(B) Zone 1. In Class I, Zone 1 locations, seals shall be located in accordance with 505.16(B)(1) through (B)(8).

(1) Type of Protection "d" or "e" Enclosures. Conduit seals shall be provided within 50 mm (2 in.) for each conduit entering enclosures having type of protection "d" or "e."

Exception No. 1: Where the enclosure having type of protection "d" is marked to indicate that a seal is not required.

Exception No. 2: For type of protection "e," conduit and fittings employing only NPT to NPT raceway joints or fittings listed for type of protection "e" shall be permitted between the enclosure and the seal, and the seal shall not be required to be within 50 mm (2 in.) of the entry.

> FPN: Examples of fittings employing other than NPT threads include conduit couplings, capped elbows, unions, and breather drains.

Exception No. 3: For conduit installed between type of protection "e" enclosures employing only NPT to NPT raceway joints or conduit fittings listed for type of protection "e," a seal shall not be required.

(2) Explosionproof Equipment. Conduit seals shall be provided for each conduit entering explosionproof equipment according to (B)(2)(a), (B)(2)(b), and (B)(2)(c).

    (a) In each conduit entry into an explosionproof enclosure where either (1) the enclosure contains apparatus, such as switches, circuit breakers, fuses, relays, or resistors, that may produce arcs, sparks, or high temperatures that are considered to be an ignition source in normal operation, or (2) the entry is metric designator 53 (trade size 2) or larger and the enclosure contains terminals, splices, or taps. For the purposes of this section, high temperatures shall be considered to be any temperatures exceeding 80 percent of the autoignition temperature in degrees Celsius of the gas or vapor involved.

Exception: Conduit entering an enclosure where such switches, circuit breakers, fuses, relays, or resistors comply with one of the following:

(1) Are enclosed within a chamber hermetically sealed against the entrance of gases or vapors.

(2) Are immersed in oil.

(3) Are enclosed within a factory-sealed explosionproof chamber located within the enclosure, identified for the location, and marked "factory sealed" or equivalent, unless the entry is metric designator 53 (trade size 2) or larger. Factory-sealed enclosures shall not be considered to serve as a seal for another adjacent explosionproof enclosure that is required to have a conduit seal.

    (b) Conduit seals shall be installed within 450 mm (18 in.) from the enclosure. Only explosionproof unions, couplings, reducers, elbows, capped elbows, and conduit bodies similar to L, T, and cross types that are not larger than the trade size of the conduit shall be permitted between the sealing fitting and the explosionproof enclosure.

    (c) Where two or more explosionproof enclosures for which conduit seals are required under 505.16(B)(2) are connected by nipples or by runs of conduit not more than 900 mm (36 in.) long, a single conduit seal in each such nipple connection or run of conduit shall be considered sufficient if located not more than 450 mm (18 in.) from either enclosure.

(3) Pressurized Enclosures. Conduit seals shall be provided in each conduit entry into a pressurized enclosure where the conduit is not pressurized as part of the protection system. Conduit seals shall be installed within 450 mm (18 in.) from the pressurized enclosure.

> FPN No. 1: Installing the seal as close as possible to the enclosure reduces problems with purging the dead airspace in the pressurized conduit.

> FPN No. 2: For further information, see NFPA 496-2003, *Standard for Purged and Pressurized Enclosures for Electrical Equipment.*

(4) Class I, Zone 1 Boundary. Conduit seals shall be provided in each conduit run leaving a Class I, Zone 1 location. The sealing fitting shall be permitted on either side of the boundary of such location within 3.05 m (10 ft) of the boundary and shall be designed and installed so as to minimize the amount of gas or vapor within the Zone 1 portion of the conduit from being communicated to the conduit beyond the seal. Except for listed explosionproof reducers at the conduit seal, there shall be no union, coupling, box, or fitting between the conduit seal and the point at which the conduit leaves the Zone 1 location.

Exception: Metal conduit containing no unions, couplings, boxes, or fittings and passing completely through a Class I, Zone 1 location with no fittings less than 300 mm (12 in.)

beyond each boundary shall not require a conduit seal if the termination points of the unbroken conduit are in unclassified locations.

(5) Cables Capable of Transmitting Gases or Vapors. Conduits containing cables with a gas/vaportight continuous sheath capable of transmitting gases or vapors through the cable core shall be sealed in the Zone 1 location after removing the jacket and any other coverings so that the sealing compound surrounds each individual insulated conductor and the outer jacket.

Exception: Multiconductor cables with a gas/vaportight continuous sheath capable of transmitting gases or vapors through the cable core shall be permitted to be considered as a single conductor by sealing the cable in the conduit within 450 mm (18 in.) of the enclosure and the cable end within the enclosure by an approved means to minimize the entrance of gases or vapors and prevent the propagation of flame into the cable core, or by other approved methods. For shielded cables and twisted pair cables, it shall not be required to remove the shielding material or separate the twisted pair.

(6) Cables Incapable of Transmitting Gases or Vapors. Each multiconductor cable in conduit shall be considered as a single conductor if the cable is incapable of transmitting gases or vapors through the cable core. These cables shall be sealed in accordance with 505.16(D).

(7) Cables Entering Enclosures. Cable seals shall be provided for each cable entering flameproof or explosionproof enclosures. The seal shall comply with 505.16(D).

(8) Class I, Zone 1 Boundary. Cables shall be sealed at the point at which they leave the Zone 1 location.

Exception: Where cable is sealed at the termination point.

(C) Zone 2. In Class I, Zone 2 locations, seals shall be located in accordance with 505.16(C)(1) and (C)(2).

(1) Conduit Seals. Conduit seals shall be located in accordance with (C)(1)(a) and (C)(1)(b).

(a) For connections to enclosures that are required to be flameproof or explosionproof, a conduit seal shall be provided in accordance with 505.16(B)(1) and 505.16(B)(2). All portions of the conduit run or nipple between the seal and such enclosure shall comply with 505.16(B).

(b) In each conduit run passing from a Class I, Zone 2 location into an unclassified location. The sealing fitting shall be permitted on either side of the boundary of such location within 3.05 m (10 ft) of the boundary and shall be designed and installed so as to minimize the amount of gas or vapor within the Zone 2 portion of the conduit from being communicated to the conduit beyond the seal. Rigid metal conduit or threaded steel intermediate metal conduit shall be used between the sealing fitting and the point at which the conduit

leaves the Zone 2 location, and a threaded connection shall be used at the sealing fitting. Except for listed explosionproof reducers at the conduit seal, there shall be no union, coupling, box, or fitting between the conduit seal and the point at which the conduit leaves the Zone 2 location.

Exception No. 1: Metal conduit containing no unions, couplings, boxes, or fittings and passing completely through a Class I, Zone 2 location with no fittings less than 300 mm (12 in.) beyond each boundary shall not be required to be sealed if the termination points of the unbroken conduit are in unclassified locations.

Exception No. 2: Conduit systems terminating at an unclassified location where a wiring method transition is made to cable tray, cablebus, ventilated busway, Type MI cable, or cable that is not installed in a raceway or cable tray system shall not be required to be sealed where passing from the Class I, Zone 2 location into the unclassified location. The unclassified location shall be outdoors or, if the conduit system is all in one room, it shall be permitted to be indoors. The conduits shall not terminate at an enclosure containing an ignition source in normal operation.

Exception No. 3: Conduit systems passing from an enclosure or room that is unclassified as a result of pressurization into a Class I, Zone 2 location shall not require a seal at the boundary.

FPN: For further information, refer to NFPA 496-2003, *Standard for Purged and Pressurized Enclosures for Electrical Equipment.*

Exception No. 4: Segments of aboveground conduit systems shall not be required to be sealed where passing from a Class I, Zone 2 location into an unclassified location if all the following conditions are met:

(1) No part of the conduit system segment passes through a Class I, Zone 0 or Class I, Zone 1 location where the conduit contains unions, couplings, boxes, or fittings within 300 mm (12 in.) of the Class I, Zone 0 or Class I, Zone 1 location.

(2) The conduit system segment is located entirely in outdoor locations.

(3) The conduit system segment is not directly connected to canned pumps, process or service connections for flow, pressure, or analysis measurement, and so forth, that depend on a single compression seal, diaphragm, or tube to prevent flammable or combustible fluids from entering the conduit system.

(4) The conduit system segment contains only threaded metal conduit, unions, couplings, conduit bodies, and fittings in the unclassified location.

(5) The conduit system segment is sealed at its entry to each enclosure or fitting housing terminals, splices, or taps in Class I, Zone 2 locations.

(2) Cable Seals. Cable seals shall be located in accordance with (C)(2)(a), (C)(2)(b), and (C)(2)(c).

(a) Explosionproof and Flameproof Enclosures. Cables entering enclosures required to be flameproof or explosion-proof shall be sealed at the point of entrance. The seal shall comply with 505.16(D). Multiconductor cables with a gas/vaportight continuous sheath capable of transmitting gases or vapors through the cable core shall be sealed in the Zone 2 location after removing the jacket and any other coverings so that the sealing compound surrounds each individual insulated conductor in such a manner as to minimize the passage of gases and vapors. Multiconductor cables in conduit shall be sealed as described in 505.16(B)(4).

Exception No. 1: Cables passing from an enclosure or room that is unclassified as a result of Type Z pressurization into a Class I, Zone 2 location shall not require a seal at the boundary.

Exception No. 2: Shielded cables and twisted pair cables shall not require the removal of the shielding material or separation of the twisted pairs, provided the termination is by an approved means to minimize the entrance of gases or vapors and prevent propagation of flame into the cable core.

(b) Cables That Will Not Transmit Gases or Vapors. Cables with a gas/vaportight continuous sheath and that will not transmit gases or vapors through the cable core in excess of the quantity permitted for seal fittings shall not be required to be sealed except as required in 505.16(C)(2)(a). The minimum length of such cable run shall not be less than the length that limits gas or vapor flow through the cable core to the rate permitted for seal fittings [200 cm^3/hr (0.007 ft^3/hr) of air at a pressure of 1500 pascals (6 in. of water)].

FPN No. 1: See ANSI/UL 886-1994, *Outlet Boxes and Fittings for Use in Hazardous (Classified) Locations.*

FPN No. 2: The cable core does not include the interstices of the conductor strands.

(c) Cables Capable of Transmitting Gases or Vapors. Cables with a gas/vaportight continuous sheath capable of transmitting gases or vapors through the cable core shall not be required to be sealed except as required in 505.16(C)(2)(a), unless the cable is attached to process equipment or devices that may cause a pressure in excess of 1500 pascals (6 in. of water) to be exerted at a cable end, in which case a seal, barrier, or other means shall be provided to prevent migration of flammables into an unclassified area.

Exception: Cables with an unbroken gas/vaportight continuous sheath shall be permitted to pass through a Class I, Zone 2 location without seals.

(d) Cables Without Gas/Vaportight Continuous Sheath. Cables that do not have gas/vaportight continuous sheath shall be sealed at the boundary of the Zone 2 and unclassified location in such a manner as to minimize the passage of gases or vapors into an unclassified location.

FPN: The cable sheath may be either metal or a nonmetallic material.

(D) Class I, Zones 0, 1, and 2. Where required, seals in Class I, Zones 0, 1, and 2 locations shall comply with 505.16(D)(1) through (D)(5).

(1) Fittings. Enclosures for connections or equipment shall be provided with an integral means for sealing, or sealing fittings listed for the location shall be used. Sealing fittings shall be listed for use with one or more specific compounds and shall be accessible.

(2) Compound. The compound shall provide a seal against passage of gas or vapors through the seal fitting, shall not be affected by the surrounding atmosphere or liquids, and shall not have a melting point less than 93°C (200°F).

(3) Thickness of Compounds. In a completed seal, the minimum thickness of the sealing compound shall not be less than the trade size of the sealing fitting and, in no case, less than 16 mm (⅝ in.).

Exception: Listed cable sealing fittings shall not be required to have a minimum thickness equal to the trade size of the fitting.

(4) Splices and Taps. Splices and taps shall not be made in fittings intended only for sealing with compound, nor shall other fittings in which splices or taps are made be filled with compound.

(5) Conductor Fill. The cross-sectional area of the conductors permitted in a seal shall not exceed 25 percent of the cross-sectional area of a rigid metal conduit of the same trade size unless it is specifically listed for a higher percentage of fill.

(E) Drainage.

(1) Control Equipment. Where there is a probability that liquid or other condensed vapor may be trapped within enclosures for control equipment or at any point in the raceway system, approved means shall be provided to prevent accumulation or to permit periodic draining of such liquid or condensed vapor.

(2) Motors and Generators. Where the authority having jurisdiction judges that there is a probability that liquid or condensed vapor may accumulate within motors or generators, joints and conduit systems shall be arranged to minimize entrance of liquid. If means to prevent accumulation or to permit periodic draining are judged necessary, such means shall be provided at the time of manufacture and shall be considered an integral part of the machine.

(3) Canned Pumps, Process, or Service Connections, and So Forth. For canned pumps, process, or service connections for flow, pressure, or analysis measurement, and so forth, that depend on a single compression seal, diaphragm, or tube to prevent flammable or combustible fluids from entering the electrical conduit system, an additional approved seal, barrier, or other means shall be provided to prevent the flammable or combustible fluid from entering the conduit system beyond the additional devices or means if the primary seal fails.

The additional approved seal or barrier and the interconnecting enclosure shall meet the temperature and pressure conditions to which they will be subjected upon failure of the primary seal, unless other approved means are provided to accomplish the purpose in the preceding paragraph.

Drains, vents, or other devices shall be provided so that primary seal leakage is obvious.

FPN: See also the fine print notes to 505.16.

Process-connected equipment that is listed and marked "Dual Seal" shall not require additional process sealing when used within the manufacturer's ratings.

FPN: For construction and testing requirements for dual seal process, connected equipment, refer to ISA 12.27.01, *Requirements for Process Sealing Between Electrical Systems and Potentially Flammable or Combustible Process Fluids.*

505.17 Flexible Cords, Class I, Zones 1 and 2. A flexible cord shall be permitted for connection between portable lighting equipment or other portable utilization equipment and the fixed portion of their supply circuit. Flexible cord shall also be permitted for that portion of the circuit where the fixed wiring methods of 505.15(B) cannot provide the necessary degree of movement for fixed and mobile electrical utilization equipment, in an industrial establishment where conditions of maintenance and engineering supervision ensure that only qualified persons install and service the installation, and the flexible cord is protected by location or by a suitable guard from damage. The length of the flexible cord shall be continuous. Where flexible cords are used, the cords shall comply with all of the following:

(1) Be of a type listed for extra-hard usage

(2) Contain, in addition to the conductors of the circuit, a grounding conductor complying with 400.23

(3) Be connected to terminals or to supply conductors in an approved manner

(4) Be supported by clamps or by other suitable means in such a manner that there will be no tension on the terminal connections

(5) Be provided with listed seals where the flexible cord enters boxes, fittings, or enclosures that are required to be explosionproof or flameproof

Exception: As provided in 505.16.

Electric submersible pumps with means for removal without entering the wet-pit shall be considered portable utilization equipment. The extension of the flexible cord within a suitable raceway between the wet-pit and the power source shall be permitted.

Electric mixers intended for travel into and out of open-type mixing tanks or vats shall be considered portable utilization equipment.

FPN: See 505.18 for flexible cords exposed to liquids having a deleterious effect on the conductor insulation.

505.18 Conductors and Conductor Insulation.

(A) Conductors. For type of protection "e," field wiring conductors shall be copper. Every conductor (including spares) that enters Type "e" equipment shall be terminated at a Type "e" terminal.

(B) Conductor Insulation. Where condensed vapors or liquids may collect on, or come in contact with, the insulation on conductors, such insulation shall be of a type identified for use under such conditions, or the insulation shall be protected by a sheath of lead or by other approved means.

505.19 Uninsulated Exposed Parts. There shall be no uninsulated exposed parts, such as electric conductors, buses, terminals, or components that operate at more than 30 volts (15 volts in wet locations). These parts shall additionally be protected by type of protection ia, ib, or nA that is suitable for the location.

505.20 Equipment Requirements.

(A) Zone 0. In Class I, Zone 0 locations, only equipment specifically listed and marked as suitable for the location shall be permitted.

Exception: Intrinsically safe apparatus listed for use in Class I, Division 1 locations for the same gas, or as permitted by 505.9(B)(2), and with a suitable temperature class shall be permitted.

(B) Zone 1. In Class I, Zone 1 locations, only equipment specifically listed and marked as suitable for the location shall be permitted.

Exception No. 1: Equipment identified for use in Class I, Division 1 or listed for use in Class I, Zone 0 locations for the same gas, or as permitted by 505.9(B)(2), and with a suitable temperature class shall be permitted.

Exception No. 2: Equipment identified for Class I, Zone 1, or Zone 2 type of protection "p" shall be permitted.

(C) Zone 2. In Class I, Zone 2 locations, only equipment specifically listed and marked as suitable for the location shall be permitted.

Exception No. 1:   Equipment listed for use in Class I, Zone 0 or Zone 1 locations for the same gas, or as permitted by 505.9(B)(2), and with a suitable temperature class, shall be permitted.

Exception No. 2:   Equipment identified for Class I, Zone 1 or Zone 2 type of protection "p" shall be permitted.

Exception No. 3:   Equipment identified for use in Class I, Division 1 or Division 2 locations for the same gas, or as permitted by 505.9(B)(2), and with a suitable temperature class shall be permitted.

Exception No. 4:   In Class I, Zone 2 locations, the installation of open or nonexplosionproof or nonflameproof enclosed motors, such as squirrel-cage induction motors without brushes, switching mechanisms, or similar arc-producing devices that are not identified for use in a Class I, Zone 2 location shall be permitted.

> FPN No. 1:   It is important to consider the temperature of internal and external surfaces that may be exposed to the flammable atmosphere.
>
> FPN No. 2:   It is important to consider the risk of ignition due to currents arcing across discontinuities and overheating of parts in multisection enclosures of large motors and generators. Such motors and generators may need equipotential bonding jumpers across joints in the enclosure and from enclosure to ground. Where the presence of ignitible gases or vapors is suspected, clean air purging may be needed immediately prior to and during start-up periods.

(D) Manufacturer's Instructions. Electrical equipment installed in hazardous (classified) locations shall be installed in accordance with the instructions (if any) provided by the manufacturer.

505.21 Multiwire Branch Circuits. In a Class I, Zone 1 location, a multiwire branch circuit shall not be permitted.

Exception: Where the disconnect device(s) for the circuit opens all ungrounded conductors of the multiwire circuit simultaneously.

505.22 Increased Safety "e" Motors and Generators. In Class I, Zone 1 locations, Increased Safety "e" motors and generators of all voltage ratings shall be listed for Class I, Zone 1 locations, and shall comply with all of the following:

(1) Motors shall be marked with the current ratio, I_A/I_N, and time, t_E.

(2) Motors shall have controllers marked with the model or identification number, output rating (horsepower or kilowatt), full-load amperes, starting current ratio (I_A/I_N), and time (t_E) of the motors that they are intended to protect; the controller marking shall also include the specific overload protection type (and setting, if applicable) that is listed with the motor or generator.

(3) Connections shall be made with the specific terminals listed with the motor or generator.

(4) Terminal housings shall be permitted to be of substantial, nonmetallic, nonburning material, provided an internal grounding means between the motor frame and the equipment grounding connection is incorporated within the housing.

(5) The provisions of Part III of Article 430 shall apply regardless of the voltage rating of the motor.

(6) The motors shall be protected against overload by a separate overload device that is responsive to motor current. This device shall be selected to trip or shall be rated in accordance with the listing of the motor and its overload protection.

(7) Sections 430.32(C) and 430.44 shall not apply to such motors.

(8) The motor overload protection shall not be shunted or cut out during the starting period.

505.25 Grounding and Bonding. Grounding and bonding shall comply with Article 250 and the requirements in 505.25(A) and 505.25(B).

(A) Bonding. The locknut-bushing and double-locknut types of contacts shall not be depended on for bonding purposes, but bonding jumpers with proper fittings or other approved means of bonding shall be used. Such means of bonding shall apply to all intervening raceways, fittings, boxes, enclosures, and so forth, between Class I locations and the point of grounding for service equipment or point of grounding of a separately derived system.

Exception: The specific bonding means shall be required only to the nearest point where the grounded circuit conductor and the grounding electrode are connected together on the line side of the building or structure disconnecting means as specified in 250.32(A), (B), and (C), provided the branch-circuit overcurrent protection is located on the load side of the disconnecting means.

> FPN: See 250.100 for additional bonding requirements in hazardous (classified) locations.

(B) Types of Equipment Grounding Conductors. Where flexible metal conduit or liquidtight flexible metal conduit is used as permitted in 505.15(C) and is to be relied on to complete a sole equipment grounding path, it shall be installed with internal or external bonding jumpers in parallel with each conduit and complying with 250.102.

Exception: In Class I, Zone 2 locations, the bonding jumper shall be permitted to be deleted where all of the following conditions are met:

(a)   Listed liquidtight flexible metal conduit 1.8 m (6 ft) or less in length, with fittings listed for grounding, is used.

(b)   Overcurrent protection in the circuit is limited to 10 amperes or less.

(c)   The load is not a power utilization load.

ARTICLE 506
Zone 20, 21, and 22 Locations for Combustible Dusts, Fibers, and Flyings

506.1 Scope. This article covers the requirements for the zone classification system as an alternative to the division classification system covered in Article 500, Article 502, and Article 503 for electrical and electronic equipment and wiring for all voltages in Zone 20, Zone 21, and Zone 22 hazardous (classified) locations where fire and explosion hazards may exist due to combustible dusts, or ignitible fibers or flyings. Combustible metallic dusts are not covered by the requirements of this article.

FPN No. 1: For the requirements for electrical and electronic equipment and wiring for all voltages in Class I, Division 1 or Division 2; Class II, Division 1 or Division 2; Class III, Division 1 or Division 2; and Class I, Zone 0 or Zone 1 or Zone 2 hazardous (classified) locations where fire or explosion hazards may exist due to flammable gases or vapors, flammable liquids, or combustible dusts or fibers, refer to Articles 500 through 505.

FPN No. 2: Zone 20, Zone 21, and Zone 22 area classifications are based on the modified IEC area classification system as defined in ISA 12.10.05, *Electrical Apparatus for Use in Zone 20, Zone 21, and Zone 22 Hazardous (Classified) Locations — Classification of Zone 20, Zone 21, and Zone 22 Hazardous (Classified) Locations (IEC61241-10 Mod).*

FPN No. 3: The unique hazards associated with explosives, pyrotechnics, and blasting agents are not addressed in this article.

506.2 Definitions. For purposes of this article, the following definitions apply.

Associated Nonincendive Field Wiring Apparatus. Apparatus in which the circuits are not necessarily nonincendive themselves but that affect the energy in nonincendive field wiring circuits and are relied upon to maintain nonincendive energy levels. Associated nonincendive field wiring apparatus may be either of the following:

(1) Electrical apparatus that has an alternative type of protection for use in the appropriate hazardous (classified) location

(2) Electrical apparatus not so protected that shall not be used in a hazardous (classified) location

FPN: Associated nonincendive field wiring apparatus has designated associated nonincendive field wiring apparatus connections for nonincendive field wiring apparatus and may also have connections for other electrical apparatus.

Dust-Ignitionproof. Equipment enclosed in a manner that excludes dusts and does not permit arcs, sparks, or heat otherwise generated or liberated inside of the enclosure to cause ignition of exterior accumulations or atmospheric suspensions of a specified dust on or in the vicinity of the enclosure.

FPN: For further information on dust-ignitionproof enclosures, see Type 9 enclosure in ANSI/NEMA 250-1991, *Enclosures for Electrical Equipment*, and ANSI/UL 1203-1994, *Explosionproof and Dust-Ignitionproof Electrical Equipment for Hazardous (Classified) Locations.*

Dusttight. Enclosures constructed so that dust will not enter under specified test conditions.

FPN: See ANSI/ISA 12.12.01-2000, *Nonincendive Electrical Equipment for Use in Class I and II, Division 2, and Class III, Divisions 1 and 2 Hazardous (Classified) Locations*, and UL 1604-1994, *Electrical Equipment for Use in Class I and II, Division 2 and Class III Hazardous (Classified) Locations.*

Nonincendive Circuit. A circuit, other than field wiring, in which any arc or thermal effect produced under intended operating conditions of the equipment is not capable, under specified test conditions, of igniting the flammable gas–air, vapor–air, or dust–air mixture.

FPN: Conditions are described in ANSI/ISA 12.12.01-2000, *Nonincendive Electrical Equipment for Use in Class I and II, Division 2, and Class III, Divisions 1 and 2 Hazardous (Classified) Locations.*

Nonincendive Equipment. Equipment having electrical/electronic circuitry that is incapable, under normal operating conditions, of causing ignition of a specified flammable gas–air, vapor–air, or dust–air mixture due to arcing or thermal means.

FPN: Conditions are described in ANSI/ISA 12.12.01-2000, *Nonincendive Electrical Equipment for Use in Class I and II, Division 2, and Class III, Divisions 1 and 2 Hazardous (Classified) Locations.*

Nonincendive Field Wiring. Wiring that enters or leaves an equipment enclosure and, under normal operating conditions of the equipment, is not capable, due to arcing or thermal effects, of igniting the flammable gas–air, vapor–air, or dust–air mixture. Normal operation includes opening, shorting, or grounding the field wiring.

Nonincendive Field Wiring Apparatus. Apparatus intended to be connected to nonincendive field wiring.

FPN: Conditions are described in ANSI/ISA 12.12.01-2000, *Nonincendive Electrical Equipment for Use in Class I and II, Division 2, and Class III, Divisions 1 and 2 Hazardous (Classified) Locations.*

Pressurized. The process of supplying an enclosure with a protective gas with or without continuous flow at sufficient pressure to prevent the entrance of combustible dust, or an ignitible fiber or flying.

FPN: For further information, see ANSI/ NFPA 496-2003, *Purged and Pressurized Enclosures for Electrical Equipment.*

Zone 20 Hazardous (Classified) Location. An area where combustible dust or ignitible fibers and flyings are present continuously or for long periods of time in quantities sufficient to be hazardous, as classified by 506.5(B)(1).

Zone 21 Hazardous (Classified) Location. An area where combustible dust or ignitible fibers and flyings are likely to exist occasionally under normal operation in quantities sufficient to be hazardous, as classified by 506.5(B)(2).

Zone 22 Hazardous (Classified) Location. An area where combustible dust or ignitible fibers and flyings are not likely to occur under normal operation in quantities sufficient to be hazardous, as classified by 506.5(B)(3).

506.4 General.

(A) Documentation for Industrial Occupancies. Areas designated as hazardous (classified) locations shall be properly documented. This documentation shall be available to those authorized to design, install, inspect, maintain or operate electrical equipment.

(B) Reference Standards. Important information relating to topics covered in Chapter 5 are found in other publications.

> FPN: It is important that the authority having jurisdiction be familiar with the recorded industrial experience as well as with standards of the National Fire Protection Association (NFPA), the ISA, International Society for Measurement and Control, and the International Electrotechnical Commission (IEC) that may be of use in the classification of various locations, the determination of adequate ventilation, and the protection against static electricity and lightning hazards.

506.5 Classification of Locations.

(A) Classifications of Locations. Locations shall be classified on the basis of the properties of the combustible dust, ignitible fibers or flyings that may be present, and the likelihood that a combustible or combustible concentration or quantity is present. Each room, section, or area shall be considered individually in determining its classification. Where pyrophoric materials are the only materials used or handled, these locations are outside of the scope of this article.

(B) Zone 20, Zone 21, and Zone 22 Locations. Zone 20, Zone 21, and Zone 22 locations are those in which combustible dust, ignitible fibers, or flyings are or may be present in the air or in layers, in quantities sufficient to produce explosive or ignitible mixtures. Zone 20, Zone 21, and Zone 22 locations shall include those specified in 506.5(B)(1), (B)(2), and (B)(3).

> FPN: Through the exercise of ingenuity in the layout of electrical installations for hazardous (classified) locations, it is frequently possible to locate much of the equipment in a reduced level of classification, and, thus, to reduce the amount of special equipment required.

(1) Zone 20. A Zone 20 location is a location in which

(a) Ignitible concentrations of combustible dust or ignitible fibers or flyings are present continuously.

(b) Ignitible concentrations of combustible dust or ignitible fibers or flyings are present for long periods of time.

> FPN No. 1: As a guide to classification of Zone 20 locations, refer to ISA 12.10.05, *Electrical Apparatus for Use in Zone 20, Zone 21, and Zone 22 Hazardous (Classified) Locations — Classification of Zone 20, Zone 21, and Zone 22 Hazardous (Classified) Locations (IEC61241-10 Mod)*.

> FPN No. 2: Zone 20 classification includes locations inside dust containment systems; hoppers, silos, etc., cyclones and filters, dust transport systems, except some parts of belt and chain conveyors, etc.; blenders, mills, dryers, bagging equipment, etc.

(2) Zone 21. A Zone 21 location is a location

(a) In which ignitible concentrations of combustible dust or ignitible fibers or flyings are likely to exist occasionally under normal operating conditions; or

(b) In which ignitible concentrations of combustible dust or ignitible fibers or flyings may exist frequently because of repair or maintenance operations or because of leakage; or

(c) In which equipment is operated or processes are carried on, of such a nature that equipment breakdown or faulty operations could result in the release of ignitible concentrations of combustible dust, or ignitible fibers or flyings and also cause simultaneous failure of electrical equipment in a mode to cause the electrical equipment to become a source of ignition; or

(d) That is adjacent to a Zone 20 location from which ignitible concentrations of dust or ignitible fibers or flyings could be communicated, unless communication is prevented by adequate positive pressure ventilation from a source of clean air and effective safeguards against ventilation failure are provided.

> FPN No. 1: As a guide to classification of Zone 21 locations, refer to ISA 12.10.05, *Electrical Apparatus for Use In Zone 20, Zone 21, and Zone 22 Hazardous (Classified) Locations — Classification of Zone 20, Zone 21, and Zone 22 Hazardous (Classified) Locations (IEC61241-10 Mod)*.

> FPN No. 2: This classification usually includes locations outside dust containment and in the immediate vicinity of access doors subject to frequent removal or opening for operation purposes when internal combustible mixtures are present; locations outside dust containment in the proximity of filling and emptying points, feed belts, sampling points, truck dump stations, belt dump over points, etc. where no measures are employed to prevent the formation of combustible mixtures; locations outside dust containment where dust accumulates and where due to process operations the dust layer is likely to be disturbed and form combustible mixtures; locations inside dust containment where explosive dust clouds are likely to occur (but neither continuously, nor for long periods, nor frequently) as, for example, silos (if filled and/or emptied only occasionally) and the dirty side of filters if large self-cleaning intervals are occurring.

(3) Zone 22. A Zone 22 location is a location

(a) In which ignitible concentrations of combustible dust or ignitible fibers or flyings are not likely to occur in normal operation, and if they do occur, will only persist for a short period; or

(b) In which combustible dust, or fibers, or flyings are handled, processed, or used but in which the dust, fibers, or flyings are normally confined within closed containers of closed systems from which they can escape only as a result of the abnormal operation of the equipment with which the dust, or fibers, or flyings are handled, processed, or used; or

(c) That is adjacent to a Zone 21 location, from which ignitible concentrations of dust or fibers or flyings could be communicated, unless such communication is prevented by adequate positive pressure ventilation from a source of clean air and effective safeguards against ventilation failure are provided.

FPN No. 1: As a guide to classification of Zone 22 locations, refer to ISA 12.10.05, *Electrical Apparatus for Use in Zone 20, Zone 21, and Zone 22 Hazardous (Classified) Locations — Classification of Zone 20, Zone 21, and Zone 22 Hazardous (Classified) Locations (IEC61241-10 Mod).*

FPN No. 2: Zone 22 locations usually include outlets from bag filter vents, because in the event of a malfunction there can be emission of combustible mixtures; locations near equipment that has to be opened at infrequent intervals or equipment that from experience can easily form leaks where, due to pressure above atmospheric, dust will blow out; pneumatic equipment, flexible connections that can become damaged, etc.; storage locations for bags containing dusty product, since failure of bags can occur during handling, causing dust leakage; and locations where controllable dust layers are formed that are likely to be raised into explosive dust/air mixtures. Only if the layer is removed by cleaning before hazardous dust–air mixtures can be formed is the area designated non-hazardous.

FPN No. 3: Locations that normally are classified as Zone 21 can fall into Zone 22 when measures are employed to prevent the formation of explosive dust–air mixtures. Such measures include exhaust ventilation. The measures should be used in the vicinity of (bag) filling and emptying points, feed belts, sampling points, truck dump stations, belt dump over points, etc.

506.6 Special Precaution. Article 506 requires equipment construction and installation that ensures safe performance under conditions of proper use and maintenance.

FPN: It is important that inspection authorities and users exercise more than ordinary care with regard to the installation and maintenance of electrical equipment in hazardous (classified) locations.

(A) Implementation of Zone Classification System. Classification of areas, engineering and design, selection of equipment and wiring methods, installation, and inspection shall be performed by qualified persons.

(B) Dual Classification. In instances of areas within the same facility classified separately, Zone 22 locations shall be permitted to abut, but not overlap, Class II or Class III, Division 2 locations. Zone 20 or Zone 21 locations shall not abut Class II or Class III, Division 1 or Division 2 locations.

(C) Reclassification Permitted. A Class II or Class III, Division 1 or Division 2 location shall be permitted to be reclassified as a Zone 20, Zone 21, or Zone 22 location, provided that all of the space that is classified because of a single combustible dust or ignitible fiber or flying source is reclassified under the requirements of this article.

(D) Simultaneous Presence of Flammable Gases and Combustible Dusts, Fibers, or Flyings. Where flammable gases or combustible dusts, fibers, or flyings are or may be present at the same time, the simultaneous presence shall be considered during the selection and installation of the electrical equipment and the wiring methods, including the determination of the safe operating temperature of the electrical equipment.

506.8 Protection Techniques. Acceptable protection techniques for electrical and electronic equipment in hazardous (classified) locations shall be as described in 506.8(A) through 506.8(F).

(A) Dust Ignitionproof. This protection technique shall be permitted for equipment in Zone 20, Zone 21, and Zone 22 locations for which it is identified.

(B) Pressurized. This protection technique shall be permitted for equipment in Zone 21, and Zone 22 locations for which it is identified.

(C) Intrinsic Safety. This protection technique shall be permitted for equipment in Zone 20, Zone 21, and Zone 22 locations for which it is identified. Installation of intrinsically safe apparatus and wiring shall be in accordance with the requirements of Article 504.

(D) Dusttight. This protection technique shall be permitted for equipment in Zone 22 locations for which it is identified.

(E) Nonincendive Circuit. This protection technique shall be permitted for equipment in Zone 22 locations for which it is identified.

(F) Nonincendive Equipment. This protection technique shall be permitted for equipment in Zone 22 locations for which it is identified.

506.9 Equipment Requirements.

(A) Suitability. Suitability of identified equipment shall be determined by one of the following:

(1) Equipment listing or labeling

(2) Evidence of equipment evaluation from a qualified testing laboratory or inspection agency concerned with product evaluation

(3) Evidence acceptable to the authority having jurisdiction such as a manufacturer's self-evaluation or an owner's engineering judgment

(B) Listing.

(1) Equipment that is listed for Zone 20 shall be permitted in a Zone 21 or Zone 22 location of the same dust, or ignitible fiber, or flying. Equipment that is listed for Zone 21 may be used in a Zone 22 location of the same dust, fiber, or flying.

(2) Equipment shall be permitted to be listed for a specific dust, or ignitible fiber or flying, or any specific combination of dusts, fibers, or flyings.

(C) Marking. Equipment identified for Class II, Division 1 or Class II, Division 2 shall, in addition to being marked in accordance with 500.8(B), be permitted to be marked with both of the following:

(1) Zone 20, 21, or 22 (as applicable)

(2) Temperature classification in accordance with 506.9(D)

(D) Temperature Classifications. Equipment shall be marked to show the operating temperature referenced to a 40°C (104°F) ambient. Electrical equipment designed for use in the ambient temperature range between −20°C and +40°C shall require no additional ambient temperature marking. Electrical equipment that is designed for use in a range of ambient temperatures other than −20°C and +40°C is considered to be special; and the ambient temperature range shall then be marked on the equipment, including either the symbol "Ta" or "Tamb" together with the special range of ambient temperatures. As an example, such a marking might be "−30°C ≤ Ta ≤ +40°C." Electrical equipment suitable for ambient temperatures exceeding 40°C (104°F) shall be marked with both the maximum ambient temperature and the operating temperature at that ambient temperature.

Exception No. 1: Equipment of the non–heat-producing type, such as conduit fittings, shall not be required to have a marked operating temperature.

Exception No. 2: Equipment identified for Class II, Division 1 or Class II, Division 2 locations as permitted by 506.20(B) and 506.20(C) shall be permitted to be marked in accordance with 500.8(B) and Table 500.8(B).

(E) Threading. All NPT threads referred to herein shall be threaded with a National (American) Standard Pipe Taper (NPT) thread that provides a taper of 1 in 16 (¾-in. taper per foot). Conduit and fittings shall be made wrenchtight to prevent sparking when the fault current flows through the conduit system, and to ensure the integrity of the conduit

system. Equipment provided with threaded entries for field wiring connections shall be installed in accordance with 506.9(E)(1) or (E)(2).

(1) Equipment Provided with Threaded Entries for NPT Threaded Conduit or Fittings. For equipment provided with threaded entries for NPT threaded conduit or fittings, listed conduit fittings, or cable fittings shall be used.

(2) Equipment Provided with Threaded Entries for Metric Threaded Conduit or Fittings. For equipment with metric threaded entries, such entries shall be identified as being metric, or listed adapters to permit connection to conduit or NPT-threaded fittings shall be provided with the equipment. Adapters shall be used for connection to conduit or NPT-threaded fittings. Listed cable fittings that have metric threads shall be permitted to be used.

506.15 Wiring Methods. Wiring methods shall maintain the integrity of the protection techniques and shall comply with 506.15(A), (B), or (C).

(A) Zone 20. In Zone 20 locations, the wiring methods in (1) through (5) shall be permitted.

(1) Threaded rigid metal conduit, or threaded steel intermediate metal conduit.

(2) Type MI cable with termination fittings listed for the location. Type MI cable shall be installed and supported in a manner to avoid tensile stress at the termination fittings.

Exception: MI cable and fittings listed for Class II, Division 1 locations are permitted to be used.

(3) In industrial establishments with limited public access, where the conditions of maintenance and supervision ensure that only qualified persons service the installation, Type MC cable, listed for continuous use in Zone 20 locations, with a gas/vaportight continuous corrugated metallic sheath, and overall jacket of suitable polymeric material, separate grounding conductors in accordance with 250.122, and provided with termination fittings listed for the application, shall be permitted.

Exception: MC cable and fittings listed for Class II, Division 1 locations are permitted to be used.

(4) Fittings and boxes shall be identified for use in Zone 20 locations.

Exception: Boxes and fittings listed for Class II, Division 1 locations are permitted to be used.

(5) Where necessary to employ flexible connections, liquidtight flexible metal conduit with listed fittings, liquidtight flexible nonmetallic conduit with listed fittings, or flexible cord listed for extra-hard usage and provided

with listed fittings shall be used. Where flexible cords are used, they shall also comply with 506.17. Where flexible connections are subject to oil or other corrosive conditions, the insulation of the conductors shall be of a type listed for the condition or shall be protected by means of a suitable sheath.

Exception: Flexible conduit and flexible conduit and cord fittings listed for Class II, Division 1 locations are permitted to be used.

FPN: See 506.25 for grounding requirements where flexible conduit is used.

(B) Zone 21. In Zone 21 locations, the wiring methods in (B)(1) and (B)(2) shall be permitted.

(1) All wiring methods permitted in 506.15(A)

(2) Fittings and boxes that are dusttight, provided with threaded bosses for connection to conduit, in which taps, joints, or terminal connections are not made, and are not used in locations where metal dust is present, may be used

(C) Zone 22. In Zone 22 locations, the wiring methods in (1) through (8) shall be permitted.

(1) All wiring methods permitted in 506.15(B).

(2) Rigid metal conduit, intermediate metal conduit, electrical metallic tubing, dusttight wireways.

(3) Type MC or MI cable with listed termination fittings.

(4) Type PLTC in cable trays.

(5) Type ITC in cable trays.

(6) Type MC, MI, MV, or TC cable installed in ladder, ventilated trough, or ventilated channel cable trays in a single layer, with a space not less than the larger cable diameter between two adjacent cables, shall be the wiring method employed. Single conductor Type MV cables shall be shielded or metallic armored.

(7) Nonincendive field wiring shall be permitted using any of the wiring methods permitted for unclassified locations. Nonincendive field wiring systems shall be installed in accordance with the control drawing(s).
Simple apparatus, not shown on the control drawing, shall be permitted in a nonincendive field wiring circuit, provided the simple apparatus does not interconnect the nonincendive field wiring circuit to any other circuit.

FPN: *Simple apparatus* is defined in 504.2.

Separation of nonincendive field wiring circuits shall be in accordance with one of the following:

a. Be in separate cables
b. Be in multiconductor cables where the conductors of each circuit are within a grounded metal shield
c. Be in multiconductor cables where the conductors have insulation with a minimum thickness of 0.25 mm (0.01 in.)

(8) Boxes and fittings shall be dusttight.

506.16 Sealing. Where necessary to protect the ingress of combustible dust, or ignitible fibers, or flyings, or to maintain the type of protection, seals shall be provided. The seal shall be identified as capable of preventing the ingress of combustible dust or ignitible fibers or flyings and maintaining the type of protection but need not be explosionproof or flameproof.

506.17 Flexible Cords. Flexible cords used in Zone 20, Zone 21, and Zone 22 locations shall comply with all of the following:

(1) Be of a type listed for extra-hard usage

(2) Contain, in addition to the conductors of the circuit, a grounding conductor in complying with 400.23

(3) Be connected to terminals or to supply conductors in an approved manner

(4) Be supported by clamps or by other suitable means in such a manner to minimize tension on the terminal connections

(5) Be provided with suitable seals to prevent the entrance of combustible dust, or ignitible fibers, or flyings where the flexible cord enters boxes or fittings

506.20 Equipment Installation.

(A) Zone 20. In Zone 20 locations, only equipment listed and marked as suitable for the location shall be permitted.

Exception: Intrinsically safe apparatus listed for use in Class II, Division 1 locations with a suitable temperature class shall be permitted.

(B) Zone 21. In Zone 21 locations, only equipment listed and marked as suitable for the location shall be permitted.

Exception No. 1: Apparatus listed for use in Class II, Division 1 locations with a suitable temperature class shall be permitted.

Exception No. 2: Pressurized equipment identified for Class II, Division 1 shall be permitted.

(C) Zone 22. In Zone 22 locations, only equipment listed and marked as suitable for the location shall be permitted.

Exception No. 1: Apparatus listed for use in Class II, Division 1 or Class II, Division 2 locations with a suitable temperature class shall be permitted.

Exception No. 2: Pressurized equipment identified for Class II, Division 1 or Division 2 shall be permitted.

(D) Manufacturer's Instructions. Electrical equipment installed in hazardous (classified) locations shall be installed in accordance with the instructions (if any) provided by the manufacturer.

(E) Temperature. The temperature marking specified in 506.9(C)(2)(5) shall comply with (E)(1) or (E)(2).

(1) For combustible dusts, less than the lower of either the layer or cloud ignition temperature of the specific combustible dust. For organic dusts that may dehydrate or carbonize, the temperature marking shall not exceed the lower of either the ignition temperature or 165°C (329°F).

(2) For ignitible fibers or flyings, less than 165°C (329°F) for equipment that is not subject to overloading, or 120°C (248°F) for equipment (such as motors or power transformers) that may be overloaded.

FPN: See NFPA 499-2004, *Recommended Practice for the Classification of Combustible Dusts and of Hazardous (Classified) Locations for Electrical Installations in Chemical Processing Areas,* for minimum ignition temperatures of specific dusts.

506.21 Multiwire Branch Circuits. In Zone 20 and Zone 21 locations, a multiwire branch circuit shall not be permitted.

Exception: Where the disconnect device(s) for the circuit opens all ungrounded conductors of the multiwire circuit simultaneously.

506.25 Grounding and Bonding. Grounding and bonding shall comply with Article 250 and the requirements in 506.25(A) and 506.25(B).

(A) Bonding. The locknut-bushing and double-locknut types of contacts shall not be depended on for bonding purposes, but bonding jumpers with proper fittings or other approved means of bonding shall be used. Such means of bonding shall apply to all intervening raceways, fittings, boxes, enclosures, and so forth, between Zone 20, Zone 21, and Zone 22 locations and the point of grounding for service equipment or point of grounding of a separately derived system.

Exception: The specific bonding means shall be required only to the nearest point where the grounded circuit conductor and the grounding electrode conductor are connected together on the line side of the building or structure disconnecting means as specified in 250.32(A), (B), and (C), if the branch side overcurrent protection is located on the load side of the disconnecting means.

FPN: See 250.100 for additional bonding requirements in hazardous (classified) locations.

(B) Types of Equipment Grounding Conductors. Where flexible conduit is used as permitted in 506.15, it shall be installed with internal or external bonding jumpers in parallel with each conduit and complying with 250.102.

Exception: In Zone 22 locations, the bonding jumper shall be permitted to be deleted where all of the following conditions are met:

(1) Listed liquidtight flexible metal conduit 1.8 m (6 ft) or less in length, with fittings listed for grounding, is used.

(2) Overcurrent protection in the circuit is limited to 10 amperes or less.

(3) The load is not a power utilization load.

ARTICLE 510
Hazardous (Classified) Locations — Specific

510.1 Scope. Articles 511 through 517 cover occupancies or parts of occupancies that are or may be hazardous because of atmospheric concentrations of flammable liquids, gases, or vapors, or because of deposits or accumulations of materials that may be readily ignitible.

510.2 General. The general rules of this *Code* and the provisions of Articles 500 through 504 shall apply to electric wiring and equipment in occupancies within the scope of Articles 511 through 517, except as such rules are modified in Articles 511 through 517. Where unusual conditions exist in a specific occupancy, the authority having jurisdiction shall judge with respect to the application of specific rules.

ARTICLE 511
Commercial Garages, Repair and Storage

FPN: Rules that are followed by a reference in brackets contain text that has been extracted from NFPA 30A-2003, *Code for Motor Fuel Dispensing Facilities and Repair Garages.* Only editorial changes were made to the extracted text to make it consistent with this *Code.*

511.1 Scope. These occupancies shall include locations used for service and repair operations in connection with self-propelled vehicles (including, but not limited to, passenger automobiles, buses, trucks, and tractors) in which volatile flammable liquids or flammable gases are used for fuel or power.

511.3 Classifications of Locations.

(A) Unclassified Locations.

(1) Parking and Repair Garages. Parking garages used for parking or storage shall be permitted to be unclassified. Repair garages shall be permitted to be unclassified when designed in accordance with 511.3(A)(2) through 511.3(A)(7).

FPN: For further information, see NFPA 88A-2002, *Standard for Parking Structures*, and NFPA 30A-2003, *Code for Motor Fuel Dispensing Facilities and Repair Garages.*

(2) Alcohol-Based Windshield Washer Fluid. The storage, handling, or dispensing into motor vehicles of alcohol-based windshield washer fluid in areas used for the service and repair operations of the vehicles shall not cause such areas to be classified as hazardous (classified) locations.

FPN: For further information, see 8.3.5, Exception, of NFPA 30A-2003, *Code for Motor Fuel Dispensing Facilities and Repair Garages.*

(3) Specific Areas Adjacent to Classified Locations. Areas adjacent to classified locations in which flammable vapors are not likely to be released, such as stock rooms, switchboard rooms, and other similar locations, shall not be classified where mechanically ventilated at a rate of four or more air changes per hour, or designed with positive air pressure, or where effectively cut off by walls or partitions.

(4) Pits in Lubrication or Service Room Where Class I Liquids Are Not Transferred. Any pit, belowgrade work area, or subfloor work area that is provided with exhaust ventilation at a rate of not less than 0.3 m³/min/m² (1 cfm/ft²) of floor area at all times that the building is occupied or when vehicles are parked in or over this area and where exhaust air is taken from a point within 300 mm (12 in.) of the floor of the pit, belowgrade work area, or subfloor work area is unclassified. [NFPA 30A:7.4.5.4 and Table 8.3.1]

(5) Up to a Level of 450 mm (18 in.) Above the Floor in Lubrication or Service Rooms Where Class I Liquids Are Transferred. For each floor, the entire area up to a level of 450 mm (18 in.) above the floor shall be considered unclassified where there is mechanical ventilation providing a minimum of four air changes per hour or one cubic foot per minute of exchanged air for each square foot of floor area. Ventilation shall provide for air exchange across the entire floor area, and exhaust air shall be taken at a point within 0.3 m (12 in.) of the floor.

(6) Flammable Liquids Having Flash Points Below 38°C (100°F). Where flammable liquids having a flash point below 38°C (100°F) (such as gasoline) or gaseous fuels (such as natural gas, hydrogen, or LPG) will not be transferred, such location shall be considered to be unclassified. unless the location is required to be classified in accordance with 511.3(B)(2) or (B)(4).

(7) Within 450 mm (18 in.) of the Ceiling. In major repair garages, where lighter-than-air gaseous fuels (such as natural gas or hydrogen) vehicles are repaired or stored, the area within 450 mm (18 in.) of the ceiling shall be considered unclassified where ventilation of at least 1 cfm/sq ft of ceiling area taken from a point within 450 mm (18 in.) of the highest point in the ceiling is provided.

FPN: For further information on the definition of *major repair garage*, see 3.3.12.1 of NFPA 30A-2003, *Code for Motor Fuel Dispensing Facilities and Repair Garages.*

(B) Classified Locations.

(1) Flammable Fuel Dispensing Areas. Areas in which flammable fuel is dispensed into vehicle fuel tanks shall conform to Article 514.

(2) Lubrication or Service Room Where Class I Liquids or Gaseous Fuels (Such as Natural Gas, Hydrogen, or LPG) Are Not Transferred. The following spaces that are not designed in accordance with 511.3(A)(4) shall be classified as Class I, Division 2:

(1) Entire area within any unventilated pit, belowgrade work area, or subfloor area.

(2) Area up to 450 mm (18 in.) above any such unventilated pit, belowgrade work area, or subfloor work area and extending a distance of 900 mm (3 ft) horizontally from the edge of any such pit, belowgrade work area, or subfloor work area.

(3) Lubrication or Service Room Where Class I Liquids or Gaseous Fuels (Such as Natural Gas, Hydrogen, or LPG) Are Transferred. The following spaces that are not designed in accordance with 511.3(A)(5) shall be classified as follows:

(1) Up to a Level of 450 mm (18 in.) Above the Floor. For each floor, the entire area up to a level of 450 mm (18 in.) above the floor shall be a Class I, Division 2 location.

(2) Any Unventilated Pit or Depression Below Floor Level. Any unventilated pit or depression below floor level shall be a Class I, Division 1 location and shall extend up to said floor level.

(3) Any Ventilated Pit or Depression Below Floor Level. Any ventilated pit or depression in which six air changes per hour are exhausted from a point within 300 mm (12 in.) of the floor level of the pit shall be a Class I, Division 2 location.

(4) Space Above an Unventilated Pit or Depression Below Floor Level. Above a pit, or depression below floor level, the space up to 450 mm (18 in.) above the floor or grade level and 900 mm (3 ft) horizontally from a lubrication pit shall be a Class I, Division 2 location.

(5) Dispenser for Class I Liquids, Other Than Fuels. Within 900 mm (3 ft) of any fill or dispensing point, extending in all directions shall be a Class I, Division 2 location. See also 511.3(B)(1).

(4) Within 450 mm (18 in.) of the Ceiling. In major repair garages where lighter-than-air gaseous fuel (such as natural gas or hydrogen) vehicles are repaired or stored, ceiling spaces that are not designed in accordance with 511.3(A)(7) shall be classified as Class I, Division 2.

FPN: For further information on the definition of *major repair garage*, see 3.3.12.1 of NFPA 30A, 2003, *Code for Motor Fuel Dispensing Facilities and Repair Garages.*

511.4 Wiring and Equipment in Class I Locations.

(A) Wiring Located in Class I Locations. Within Class I locations as classified in 511.3, wiring shall conform to applicable provisions of Article 501.

(B) Equipment Located in Class I Locations. Within Class I locations as defined in 511.3, equipment shall conform to applicable provisions of Article 501.

(1) Fuel-Dispensing Units. Where fuel-dispensing units (other than liquid petroleum gas, which is prohibited) are located within buildings, the requirements of Article 514 shall govern.

Where mechanical ventilation is provided in the dispensing area, the control shall be interlocked so that the dispenser cannot operate without ventilation, as prescribed in 500.5(B)(2).

(2) Portable Lighting Equipment. Portable lighting equipment shall be equipped with handle, lampholder, hook, and substantial guard attached to the lampholder or handle. All exterior surfaces that might come in contact with battery terminals, wiring terminals, or other objects shall be of nonconducting material or shall be effectively protected with insulation. Lampholders shall be of an unswitched type and shall not provide means for plug-in of attachment plugs. The outer shell shall be of molded composition or other suitable material. Unless the lamp and its cord are supported or arranged in such a manner that they cannot be used in the locations classified in 511.3, they shall be of a type identified for Class I, Division 1 locations.

511.7 Wiring and Equipment Installed Above Class I Locations.

(A) Wiring in Spaces Above Class I Locations.

(1) Fixed Wiring Above Class I Locations. All fixed wiring above Class I locations shall be in metal raceways, rigid nonmetallic conduit, electrical nonmetallic tubing, flexible metal conduit, liquidtight flexible metal conduit, or liquidtight flexible nonmetallic conduit, or shall be Type MC, AC, MI, manufactured wiring systems, or PLTC cable in accordance with Article 725, or Type TC cable or Type ITC cable in accordance with Article 727. Cellular metal floor raceways or cellular concrete floor raceways shall be permitted to be used only for supplying ceiling outlets or extensions to the area below the floor, but such raceways shall have no connections leading into or through any Class I location above the floor.

(2) Pendant. For pendants, flexible cord suitable for the type of service and listed for hard usage shall be used.

(B) Electrical Equipment Installed Above Class I Locations.

(1) Fixed Electrical Equipment. Electrical equipment in a fixed position shall be located above the level of any defined Class I location or shall be identified for the location.

(a) Arcing Equipment. Equipment that is less than 3.7 m (12 ft) above the floor level and that may produce arcs, sparks, or particles of hot metal, such as cutouts, switches, charging panels, generators, motors, or other equipment (excluding receptacles, lamps, and lampholders) having make-and-break or sliding contacts, shall be of the totally enclosed type or constructed so as to prevent the escape of sparks or hot metal particles.

(b) Fixed Lighting. Lamps and lampholders for fixed lighting that is located over lanes through which vehicles are commonly driven or that may otherwise be exposed to physical damage shall be located not less than 3.7 m (12 ft) above floor level, unless of the totally enclosed type or constructed so as to prevent escape of sparks or hot metal particles.

511.9 Sealing. Seals conforming to the requirements of 501.15 and 501.15(B)(2) shall be provided and shall apply to horizontal as well as vertical boundaries of the defined Class I locations.

511.10 Special Equipment.

(A) Battery Charging Equipment. Battery chargers and their control equipment, and batteries being charged, shall not be located within locations classified in 511.3.

(B) Electric Vehicle Charging Equipment.

(1) General. All electrical equipment and wiring shall be installed in accordance with Article 625, except as noted in 511.10(B)(2) and (B)(3). Flexible cords shall be of a type identified for extra-hard usage.

(2) Connector Location. No connector shall be located within a Class I location as defined in 511.3.

(3) Plug Connections to Vehicles. Where the cord is suspended from overhead, it shall be arranged so that the lowest point of sag is at least 150 mm (6 in.) above the floor. Where an automatic arrangement is provided to pull both cord and plug beyond the range of physical damage, no additional connector shall be required in the cable or at the outlet.

511.12 Ground-Fault Circuit-Interrupter Protection for Personnel. All 125-volt, single-phase, 15- and 20-ampere receptacles installed in areas where electrical diagnostic equipment, electrical hand tools, or portable lighting equipment are to be used shall have ground-fault circuit-interrupter protection for personnel.

511.16 Grounded and Grounding Requirements.

(A) General Grounding Requirements. All metal raceways, the metal armor or metallic sheath on cables, and all non–current-carrying metal parts of fixed or portable electrical equipment, regardless of voltage, shall be grounded as provided in Article 250.

(B) Supplying Circuits with Grounded and Grounding Conductors in Class I Locations. Grounding in Class I locations shall comply with 501.30.

(1) Circuits Supplying Portable Equipment or Pendants. Where a circuit supplies portables or pendants and includes a grounded conductor as provided in Article 200, receptacles, attachment plugs, connectors, and similar devices shall be of the grounding type, and the grounded conductor of the flexible cord shall be connected to the screw shell of any lampholder or to the grounded terminal of any utilization equipment supplied.

(2) Approved Means. Approved means shall be provided for maintaining continuity of the grounding conductor between the fixed wiring system and the non–current-carrying metal portions of pendant luminaires (fixtures), portable lamps, and portable utilization equipment.

ARTICLE 513
Aircraft Hangars

513.1 Scope. This article shall apply to buildings or structures in any part of which aircraft containing Class I (flammable) liquids or Class II (combustible) liquids whose temperatures are above their flash points are housed or stored and in which aircraft might undergo service, repairs, or alterations. It shall not apply to locations used exclusively for aircraft that have never contained fuel or unfueled aircraft.

FPN No. 1: For definitions of aircraft hangar and unfueled aircraft, see NFPA 409-2004, *Standard on Aircraft Hangars.*

FPN No. 2: For further information on fuel classification see NFPA 30-2003, *Flammable and Combustible Liquids Code.*

513.2 Definitions. For the purpose of this article, the following definitions shall apply.

Mobile Equipment. Equipment with electric components suitable to be moved only with mechanical aids or is provided with wheels for movement by person(s) or powered devices.

Portable Equipment. Equipment with electric components suitable to be moved by a single person without mechanical aids.

513.3 Classification of Locations.

(A) Below Floor Level. Any pit or depression below the level of the hangar floor shall be classified as a Class I, Division 1 or Zone 1 location that shall extend up to said floor level.

(B) Areas Not Cut Off or Ventilated. The entire area of the hangar, including any adjacent and communicating areas not suitably cut off from the hangar, shall be classified as a Class I, Division 2 or Zone 2 location up to a level 450 mm (18 in.) above the floor.

(C) Vicinity of Aircraft. The area within 1.5 m (5 ft) horizontally from aircraft power plants or aircraft fuel tanks shall be classified as a Class I, Division 2 or Zone 2 location that shall extend upward from the floor to a level 1.5 m (5 ft) above the upper surface of wings and of engine enclosures.

(D) Areas Suitably Cut Off and Ventilated. Adjacent areas in which flammable liquids or vapors are not likely to be released, such as stock rooms, electrical control rooms, and other similar locations, shall not be classified where adequately ventilated and where effectively cut off from the hangar itself by walls or partitions.

513.4 Wiring and Equipment in Class I Locations.

(A) General. All wiring and equipment that is or may be installed or operated within any of the Class I locations defined in 513.3 shall comply with the applicable provisions of Article 501 or Article 505 for the division or zone in which they are used.

Attachment plugs and receptacles in Class I locations shall be identified for Class I locations or shall be designed such that they cannot be energized while the connections are being made or broken.

(B) Stanchions, Rostrums, and Docks. Electric wiring, outlets, and equipment (including lamps) on or attached to stanchions, rostrums, or docks that are located or likely to be located in a Class I location, as defined in 513.3(C), shall comply with the applicable provisions of Article 501 or Article 505 for the division or zone in which they are used.

513.7 Wiring and Equipment Not Installed in Class I Locations.

(A) Fixed Wiring. All fixed wiring in a hangar but not installed in a Class I location as classified in 513.3 shall be installed in metal raceways or shall be Type MI, TC, or MC cable.

Exception: Wiring in unclassified locations, as described in 513.3(D), shall be permitted to be any suitable type wiring method recognized in Chapter 3.

(B) Pendants. For pendants, flexible cord suitable for the type of service and identified for hard usage or extra-hard usage shall be used. Each such cord shall include a separate equipment grounding conductor.

(C) Arcing Equipment. In locations above those described in 513.3, equipment that is less than 3.0 m (10 ft) above wings and engine enclosures of aircraft and that may produce arcs, sparks, or particles of hot metal, such as lamps and lampholders for fixed lighting, cutouts, switches, receptacles, charging panels, generators, motors, or other equipment having make-and-break or sliding contacts, shall be of the totally enclosed type or constructed so as to prevent the escape of sparks or hot metal particles.

Exception: Equipment in areas described in 513.3(D) shall be permitted to be of the general-purpose type.

(D) Lampholders. Lampholders of metal-shell, fiber-lined types shall not be used for fixed incandescent lighting.

(E) Stanchions, Rostrums, or Docks. Where stanchions, rostrums, or docks are not located or likely to be located in a Class I location, as defined in 513.3(C), wiring and equipment shall comply with 513.7, except that such wiring and equipment not more than 457 mm (18 in.) above the floor in any position shall comply with 513.4(B). Receptacles and attachment plugs shall be of a locking type that will not readily disconnect.

(F) Mobile Stanchions. Mobile stanchions with electric equipment complying with 513.7(E) shall carry at least one permanently affixed warning sign with the following words or equivalent:

WARNING
KEEP 5 FT CLEAR OF AIRCRAFT
ENGINES AND FUEL TANK AREAS

or

WARNING
KEEP 1.5 METERS CLEAR OF AIRCRAFT
ENGINES AND FUEL TANK AREAS

513.8 Underground Wiring.

(A) Wiring and Equipment Embedded, Under Slab, or Under Ground. All wiring installed in or under the hangar floor shall comply with the requirements for Class I, Division 1 locations. Where such wiring is located in vaults, pits, or ducts, adequate drainage shall be provided.

(B) Uninterrupted Raceways, Embedded, Under Slab, or Underground. Uninterrupted raceways that are embedded in a hangar floor or buried beneath the hangar floor shall be considered to be within the Class I location above

the floor, regardless of the point at which the raceway descends below or rises above the floor.

513.9 Sealing. Seals shall be provided in accordance with 501.15 or 505.16, as applicable. Sealing requirements specified shall apply to horizontal as well as to vertical boundaries of the defined Class I locations.

513.10 Special Equipment.

(A) Aircraft Electrical Systems.

(1) De-energizing Aircraft Electrical Systems. Aircraft electrical systems shall be de-energized when the aircraft is stored in a hangar and, whenever possible, while the aircraft is undergoing maintenance.

(2) Aircraft Batteries. Aircraft batteries shall not be charged where installed in an aircraft located inside or partially inside a hangar.

(B) Aircraft Battery Charging and Equipment. Battery chargers and their control equipment shall not be located or operated within any of the Class I locations defined in 513.3 and shall preferably be located in a separate building or in an area such as defined in 513.3(D). Mobile chargers shall carry at least one permanently affixed warning sign with the following words or equivalent:

WARNING
KEEP 5 FT CLEAR OF AIRCRAFT ENGINES
AND FUEL TANK AREAS

or

WARNING
KEEP 1.5 METERS CLEAR OF AIRCRAFT
ENGINES AND FUEL TANK AREAS

Tables, racks, trays, and wiring shall not be located within a Class I location and, in addition, shall comply with Article 480.

(C) External Power Sources for Energizing Aircraft.

(1) Not Less Than 450 mm (18 in.) Above Floor. Aircraft energizers shall be designed and mounted such that all electric equipment and fixed wiring will be at least 450 mm (18 in.) above floor level and shall not be operated in a Class I location as defined in 513.3(C).

(2) Marking for Mobile Units. Mobile energizers shall carry at least one permanently affixed warning sign with the following words or equivalent:

WARNING
KEEP 5 FT CLEAR OF AIRCRAFT
ENGINES AND FUEL TANK AREAS

or

WARNING
KEEP 1.5 METERS CLEAR OF AIRCRAFT
ENGINES AND FUEL TANK AREAS

(3) Cords. Flexible cords for aircraft energizers and ground support equipment shall be identified for the type of service and extra-hard usage and shall include an equipment grounding conductor.

(D) Mobile Servicing Equipment with Electric Components.

(1) General. Mobile servicing equipment (such as vacuum cleaners, air compressors, air movers) having electric wiring and equipment not suitable for Class I, Division 2 or Zone 2 locations shall be so designed and mounted that all such fixed wiring and equipment will be at least 450 mm (18 in.) above the floor. Such mobile equipment shall not be operated within the Class I location defined in 513.3(C) and shall carry at least one permanently affixed warning sign with the following words or equivalent:

WARNING
KEEP 5 FT CLEAR OF AIRCRAFT ENGINES
AND FUEL TANK AREAS

or

WARNING
KEEP 1.5 METERS CLEAR OF AIRCRAFT ENGINES
AND FUEL TANK AREAS

(2) Cords and Connectors. Flexible cords for mobile equipment shall be suitable for the type of service and identified for extra-hard usage and shall include an equipment grounding conductor. Attachment plugs and receptacles shall be identified for the location in which they are installed and shall provide for connection of the equipment grounding conductor.

(3) Restricted Use. Equipment that is not identified as suitable for Class I, Division 2 locations shall not be operated in locations where maintenance operations likely to release flammable liquids or vapors are in progress.

(E) Portable Equipment.

(1) Portable Lighting Equipment. Portable lighting equipment that is used within a hangar shall be identified for the location in which they are used. For portable lamps, flexible cord suitable for the type of service and identified for extra-hard usage shall be used. Each such cord shall include a separate equipment grounding conductor.

(2) Portable Utilization Equipment. Portable utilization equipment that is or may be used within a hangar shall be of a type suitable for use in Class I, Division 2 or Zone 2 locations. For portable utilization equipment, flexible cord suitable for the type of service and approved for extra-hard usage shall be used. Each such cord shall include a separate equipment grounding conductor.

513.12 Ground-Fault Circuit-Interrupter Protection for Personnel. All 125-volt, 50/60 Hz, single phase, 15– and 20-ampere receptacles installed in areas where electrical diagnostic equipment, electrical hand tools, or portable lighting equipment are to be used shall have ground-fault circuit-interrupter protection for personnel.

513.16 Grounded and Grounding Requirements.

(A) General Grounding Requirements. All metal raceways, the metal armor or metallic sheath on cables, and all non–current-carrying metal parts of fixed or portable electrical equipment, regardless of voltage, shall be grounded as provided in Article 250. Grounding in Class I locations shall comply with 501.30 for Class I, Division 1 and 2 locations and 505.25 for Class I, Zone 0, 1, and 2 locations.

(B) Supplying Circuits with Grounded and Grounding Conductors in Class I Locations.

(1) Circuits Supplying Portable Equipment or Pendants. Where a circuit supplies portables or pendants and includes a grounded conductor as provided in Article 200, receptacles, attachment plugs, connectors, and similar devices shall be of the grounding type, and the grounded conductor of the flexible cord shall be connected to the screw shell of any lampholder or to the grounded terminal of any utilization equipment supplied.

(2) Approved Means. Approved means shall be provided for maintaining continuity of the grounding conductor between the fixed wiring system and the non–current-carrying metal portions of pendant luminaires (fixtures), portable lamps, and portable utilization equipment.

ARTICLE 514
Motor Fuel Dispensing Facilities

FPN: Rules that are followed by a reference in brackets contain text that has been extracted from NFPA 30A-2003, *Code for Motor Fuel Dispensing Facilities and Repair Garages.* Only editorial changes were made to the extracted text to make it consistent with this *Code.*

514.1 Scope. This article shall apply to motor fuel dispensing facilities, marine/motor fuel dispensing facilities, motor fuel dispensing facilities located inside buildings, and fleet vehicle motor fuel dispensing facilities.

FPN: For further information regarding safeguards for motor fuel dispensing facilities, see NFPA 30A-2003, *Code for Motor Fuel Dispensing Facilities and Repair Garages.*

514.2 Definition.

Motor Fuel Dispensing Facility. That portion of a property where motor fuels are stored and dispensed from fixed equipment into the fuel tanks of motor vehicles or marine craft or into approved containers, including all equipment used in connection therewith. [NFPA 30A:3.3.11]

> FPN: Refer to Articles 510 and 511 with respect to electric wiring and equipment for other areas used as lubritoriums, service rooms, repair rooms, offices, salesrooms, compressor rooms, and similar locations.

514.3 Classification of Locations.

(A) Unclassified Locations. Where the authority having jurisdiction can satisfactorily determine that flammable liquids having a flash point below 38°C (100°F), such as gasoline, will not be handled, such location shall not be required to be classified.

(B) Classified Locations.

(1) Class I Locations. Table 514.3(B)(1) shall be applied where Class I liquids are stored, handled, or dispensed and shall be used to delineate and classify motor fuel dispensing facilities and commercial garages as defined in Article 511. Table 515.3 shall be used for the purpose of delineating and classifying aboveground tanks. A Class I location shall not extend beyond an unpierced wall, roof, or other solid partition. [NFPA 30A:8.1, 8.3]

(2) Compressed Natural Gas, Liquefied Natural Gas, and Liquefied Petroleum Gas Areas. Table 514.3(B)(2) shall be used to delineate and classify areas where compressed natural gas (CNG), liquefied natural gas (LNG), or liquefied petroleum gas (LPG) are stored, handled, or dispensed. Where CNG or LNG dispensers are installed beneath a canopy or enclosure, either the canopy or the enclosure shall be designed to prevent accumulation or entrapment of ignitible vapors, or all electrical equipment installed beneath the canopy or enclosure shall be suitable for Class I, Division 2 hazardous (classified) locations. Dispensing devices for liquefied petroleum gas shall be located not less than 1.5 m (5 ft) from any dispensing device for Class I liquids. [NFPA 30A:12.1, 12.4, 12.5]

> FPN No. 1: For information on area classification where liquefied petroleum gases are dispensed, see NFPA 58-2004, *Liquefied Petroleum Gas Code.*
>
> FPN No. 2: For information on classified areas pertaining to LP-Gas systems other than residential or commercial, see NFPA 58-2004, *Liquefied Petroleum Gas Code,* and NFPA 59-2004, *Utility LP-Gas Plant Code.*
>
> FPN No. 3: See 555.21 for motor fuel dispensing stations in marinas and boatyards.

514.4 Wiring and Equipment Installed in Class I Locations.
All electrical equipment and wiring installed in Class I locations as classified in 514.3 shall comply with the applicable provisions of Article 501.

Exception: As permitted in 514.8.

Figure 514.3 Classified Areas Adjacent to Dispensers as Detailed in Table 514.3(B)(1). [NFPA 30A:Figure 8.3.1]

> FPN: For special requirements for conductor insulation, see 501.20.

514.7 Wiring and Equipment Above Class I Locations.
Wiring and equipment above the Class I locations as classified in 514.3 shall comply with 511.7.

514.8 Underground Wiring.
Underground wiring shall be installed in threaded rigid metal conduit or threaded steel intermediate metal conduit. Any portion of electrical wiring that is below the surface of a Class I, Division 1, or a Class I, Division 2, location [as classified in Table 514.3(B)(1) and Table 514.3(B)(2)] shall be sealed within 3.05 m (10 ft) of the point of emergence above grade. Except for listed explosion-proof reducers at the conduit seal, there shall be no union, coupling, box, or fitting between the conduit seal and the point of emergence above grade. Refer to Table 300.5.

Exception No. 1: Type MI cable shall be permitted where it is installed in accordance with Article 332.

Exception No. 2: Rigid nonmetallic conduit shall be permitted where buried under not less than 600 mm (2 ft) of cover. Where rigid nonmetallic conduit is used, threaded rigid metal conduit or threaded steel intermediate metal conduit shall be used for the last 600 mm (2 ft) of the underground run to emergence or to the point of connection to the aboveground raceway, and an equipment grounding conductor shall be included to provide electrical continuity of the raceway system and for grounding of non–current-carrying metal parts.

| Table 514.3(B)(1) Class I Locations — Motor Fuel Dispensing Facilities

Location	Class I, Group D Division	Extent of Classified Location[1]
Underground Tank		
Fill opening	1	Any pit or box below grade level, any part of which is within the Division 1 or Division 2, Zone 1 or Zone 2 classified location
	2	Up to 450 mm (18 in.) above grade level within a horizontal radius of 3.0 m (10 ft) from a loose fill connection and within a horizontal radius of 1.5 m (5 ft) from a tight fill connection
Vent — discharging upward	1	Within 900 mm (3 ft) of open end of vent, extending in all directions
	2	Space between 900 mm (3 ft) and 1.5 m (5 ft) of open end of vent, extending in all directions
Dispensing Device[2,5] (except overhead type)[3]		
Pits	1	Any pit or box below grade level, any part of which is within the Division 1 or Division 2, Zone 1 or Zone 2 classified location
Dispenser		FPN: Space classification inside the dispenser enclosure is covered in ANSI/UL 87-1995, *Power Operated Dispensing Devices for Petroleum Products.*
	2	Within 450 mm (18 in.) horizontally in all directions extending to grade from the dispenser enclosure or that portion of the dispenser enclosure containing liquid-handling components FPN: Space classification inside the dispenser enclosure is covered in ANSI/UL 87-1995, *Power Operated Dispensing Devices for Petroleum Products.*
Outdoor	2	Up to 450 mm (18 in.) above grade level within 6.0 m (20 ft) horizontally of any edge of enclosure.
Indoor with mechanical ventilation	2	Up to 450 mm (18 in.) above grade or floor level within 6.0 m (20 ft) horizontally of any edge of enclosure
with gravity ventilation	2	Up to 450 mm (18 in.) above grade or floor level within 7.5 m (25 ft) horizontally of any edge of enclosure
Dispensing Device[5]		
Overhead type[3]	1	The space within the dispenser enclosure, and all electrical equipment integral with the dispensing hose or nozzle
	2	A space extending 450 mm (18 in.) horizontally in all directions beyond the enclosure and extending to grade
	2	Up to 450 mm (18 in.) above grade level within 6.0 m (20 ft) horizontally measured from a point vertically below the edge of any dispenser enclosure
Remote Pump — Outdoor	1	Any pit or box below grade level if any part is within a horizontal distance of 3.0 m (10 ft) from any edge of pump
	2	Within 900 mm (3 ft) of any edge of pump, extending in all directions. Also up to 450 mm (18 in.) above grade level within 3.0 m (10 ft) horizontally from any edge of pump
Remote Pump — Indoor	1	Entire space within any pit
	2	Within 1.5 m (5 ft) of any edge of pump, extending in all directions. Also up to 900 mm (3 ft) above grade level within 7.5 m (25 ft) horizontally from any edge of pump

(Continues)

Table 514.3(B)(1) *Continued*

Location	Class I, Group D Division	Extent of Classified Location[1]
Lubrication or Service Room — **Without Dispensing**	2	Entire area within any pit used for lubrication or similar services where Class I liquids may be released
	2	Area up to 450 mm (18 in.) above any such pit and extending a distance of 900 mm (3 ft) horizontally from any edge of the pit
	2	Entire unventilated area within any pit, belowgrade area, or subfloor area
	2	Area up to 450 mm (18 in.) above any such unventilated pit, belowgrade work area, or subfloor work area and extending a distance of 900 mm (3 ft) horizontally from the edge of any such pit, belowgrade work area, or subfloor work area
	Unclassified	Any pit, belowgrade work area, or subfloor work area that is provided with exhaust ventilation at a rate of not less than 0.3 m^3/min/m^2 (1 cfm/ft^2) of floor area at all times that the building is occupied or when vehicles are parked in or over this area and where exhaust air is taken from a point within 300 mm (12 in.) of the floor of the pit, belowgrade work area, or subfloor work area
Special Enclosure Inside Building[4]	1	Entire enclosure
Sales, Storage, and Rest Rooms	Unclassified	If there is any opening to these rooms within the extent of a Division 1 location, the entire room shall be classified as Division 1
Vapor Processing Systems Pits	1	Any pit or box below grade level, any part of which is within a Division 1 or Division 2 classified location or that houses any equipment used to transport or process vapors
Vapor Processing Equipment Located Within Protective Enclosures FPN: See 10.1.7 of NFPA 30A-2003, *Code for Motor Fuel Dispensing Facilities and Repair Garages.*	2	Within any protective enclosure housing vapor processing equipment
Vapor Processing Equipment Not Within Protective Enclosures (excluding piping and combustion devices)	2	The space within 450 mm (18 in.) in all directions of equipment containing flammable vapor or liquid extending to grade level. Up to 450 mm (18 in.) above grade level within 3.0 m (10 ft) horizontally of the vapor processing equipment
Equipment Enclosures	1	Any space within the enclosure where vapor or liquid is present under normal operating conditions
Vacuum-Assist Blowers	2	The space within 450 mm (18 in.) in all directions extending to grade level. Up to 450 mm (18 in.) above grade level within 3.0 m (10 ft) horizontally

[1]For marine application, *grade level* means the surface of a pier extending down to water level.
[2]Refer to Figure 514.3 for an illustration of classified location around dispensing devices.
[3]Ceiling mounted hose reel.
[4]FPN: See 4.3.9 of NFPA 30A-2003, *Code for Motor Fuel Dispensing Facilities and Repair Garages.*
[5]FPN: Area classification inside the dispenser enclosure is covered in ANSI/UL 87-1995, *Power-Operated Dispensing Devices for Petroleum Products.* [NFPA 30A:Table 8.3.1]

Table 514.3(B)(2) Electrical Equipment Classified Areas for Dispensing Devices

Dispensing Device	Extent of Classified Area	
	Class I, Division 1	Class I, Division 2
Compressed natural gas	Entire space within the dispenser enclosure	1.5 m (5 ft) in all directions from dispenser enclosure
Liquefied natural gas	Entire space within the dispenser enclosure and 1.5 m (5 ft) in all directions from the dispenser enclosure	From 1.5 m to 3.0 m (5 ft to 10 ft) in all directions from the dispenser enclosure
Liquefied petroleum gas	Entire space within the dispenser enclosure; 450 mm (18 in.) from the exterior surface of the dispenser enclosure to an elevation of 1.2 m (4 ft) above the base of the dispenser; the entire pit or open space beneath the dispenser and within 6.0 m (20 ft) horizontally from any edge of the dispenser when the pit or trench is not mechanically ventilated.	Up to 450 mm (18 in.) aboveground and within 6.0 m (20 ft) horizontally from any edge of the dispenser enclosure, including pits or trenches within this area when provided with adequate mechanical ventilation

[NFPA 30A:Table 12.6.2]

514.9 Sealing.

(A) At Dispenser. A listed seal shall be provided in each conduit run entering or leaving a dispenser or any cavities or enclosures in direct communication therewith. The sealing fitting shall be the first fitting after the conduit emerges from the earth or concrete.

(B) At Boundary. Additional seals shall be provided in accordance with 501.15. Sections 501.15(A)(4) and (B)(2) shall apply to horizontal as well as to vertical boundaries of the defined Class I locations.

514.11 Circuit Disconnects.

(A) General. Each circuit leading to or through dispensing equipment, including equipment for remote pumping systems, shall be provided with a clearly identified and readily accessible switch or other acceptable means, located remote from the dispensing devices, to disconnect simultaneously from the source of supply, all conductors of the circuits, including the grounded conductor, if any.

Single-pole breakers utilizing handle ties shall not be permitted.

(B) Attended Self-Service Motor Fuel Dispensing Facilities. Emergency controls as specified in 514.11(A) shall be installed at a location acceptable to the authority having jurisdiction, but controls shall not be more than 30 m (100 ft) from dispensers. [NFPA 30A:6.7.1]

(C) Unattended Self-Service Motor Fuel Dispensing Facilities. Emergency controls as specified in 514.11(A) shall be installed at a location acceptable to the authority having jurisdiction, but the control shall be more than 6 m (20 ft) but less than 30 m (100 ft) from the dispensers. Additional emergency controls shall be installed on each group of dispensers or the outdoor equipment used to control the dispensers. Emergency controls shall shut off all power to all dispensing equipment at the station. Controls shall be manually reset only in a manner approved by the authority having jurisdiction. [NFPA 30A:6.7.2]

> FPN: For additional information, see 6.7.1 and 6.7.2 of NFPA 30A-2003, *Code for Motor Fuel Dispensing Facilities and Repair Garages.*

514.13 Provisions for Maintenance and Service of Dispensing Equipment.
Each dispensing device shall be provided with a means to remove all external voltage sources, including feedback, during periods of maintenance and service of the dispensing equipment. The location of this means shall be permitted to be other than inside or adjacent to the dispensing device. The means shall be capable of being locked in the open position.

514.16 Grounding.
All metal raceways, the metal armor or metallic sheath on cables, and all non–current-carrying metal parts of fixed portable electrical equipment, regardless of voltage, shall be grounded as provided in Article 250. Grounding in Class I locations shall comply with 501.30.

ARTICLE 515
Bulk Storage Plants

> FPN: Rules that are followed by a reference in brackets contain text that has been extracted from NFPA 30-2003, *Flammable and Combustible Liquids Code.* Only editorial changes were made to the extracted text to make it consistent with this *Code.*

515.1 Scope.
This article covers a property or portion of a property where flammable liquids are received by tank vessel, pipelines, tank car, or tank vehicle and are stored or blended in bulk for the purpose of distributing such liquids by tank vessel, pipeline, tank car, tank vehicle, portable tank, or container.

515.2 Definition.

Bulk Plant or Terminal. That portion of a property where liquids are received by tank vessel, pipelines, tank car, or tank vehicle and are stored or blended in bulk for the purpose of distributing such liquids by tank vessel, pipeline, tank car, tank vehicle, portable tank, or container. [NFPA 30:3.3.32.1]

FPN: For further information, see NFPA 30-2003, *Flammable and Combustible Liquids Code.*

515.3 Class I Locations.
Table 515.3 shall be applied where Class I liquids are stored, handled, or dispensed and shall be used to delineate and classify bulk storage plants. The class location shall not extend beyond a floor, wall, roof, or other solid partition that has no communicating openings. [NFPA 30:8.1, 8.2.2]

FPN No. 1: The area classifications listed in Table 515.3 are based on the premise that the installation meets the applicable requirements of NFPA 30-2003, *Flammable and Combustible Liquids Code*, Chapter 5, in all respects. Should this not be the case, the authority having jurisdiction has the authority to classify the extent of the classified space.

FPN No. 2: See 555.21 for gasoline dispensing stations in marinas and boatyards.

Table 515.3 Electrical Area Classifications

Location	NEC Class I Division	Zone	Extent of Classified Area
Indoor equipment installed in accordance with Section 5.3 of NFPA 30 where flammable vapor–air mixtures can exist under normal operation	1	0	The entire area associated with such equipment where flammable gases or vapors are present continuously or for long periods of time
	1	1	Area within 1.5 m (5 ft) of any edge of such equipment, extending in all directions
	2	2	Area between 1.5 m and 2.5 m (5 ft and 8 ft) of any edge of such equipment, extending in all directions; also, space up to 900 mm (3 ft) above floor or grade level within 1.5 m to 7.5 m (5 ft to 25 ft) horizontally from any edge of such equipment[1]
Outdoor equipment of the type covered in Section 5.3 of NFPA 30 where flammable vapor–air mixtures may exist under normal operation	1	0	The entire area associated with such equipment where flammable gases or vapors are present continuously or for long periods of time
	1	1	Area within 900 mm (3 ft) of any edge of such equipment, extending in all directions
	2	2	Area between 900 mm (3 ft) and 2.5 m (8 ft) of any edge of such equipment, extending in all directions; also, space up to 900 mm (3 ft) above floor or grade level within 900 mm to 3.0 m (3 ft to 10 ft) horizontally from any edge of such equipment
Tank storage installations inside buildings	1	1	All equipment located below grade level
	2	2	Any equipment located at or above grade level
Tank – aboveground	1	0	Inside fixed roof tank
	1	1	Area inside dike where dike height is greater than the distance from the tank to the dike for more than 50 percent of the tank circumference
Shell, ends, or roof and dike area	2	2	Within 3.0 m (10 ft) from shell, ends, or roof of tank; also, area inside dike to level of top of tank
Vent	1	0	Area inside of vent piping or opening
	1	1	Within 1.5 m (5 ft) of open end of vent, extending in all directions
	2	2	Area between 1.5 m and 3.0 m (5 ft and 10 ft) from open end of vent, extending in all directions
Floating roof with fixed outer roof	1	0	Area between the floating and fixed roof sections and within the shell
Floating roof with no fixed outer roof	1	1	Area above the floating roof and within the shell

Table 515.3 *Continued*

Location	NEC Class I Division	Zone	Extent of Classified Area
Underground tank fill opening	1	1	Any pit, or space below grade level, if any part is within a Division 1 or 2, or Zone 1 or 2, classified location
	2	2	Up to 450 mm (18 in.) above grade level within a horizontal radius of 3.0 m (10 ft) from a loose fill connection, and within a horizontal radius of 1.5 m (5 ft) from a tight fill connection
Vent – discharging upward	1	0	Area inside of vent piping or opening
	1	1	Within 900 mm (3 ft) of open end of vent, extending in all directions
	2	2	Area between 900 mm and 1.5 m (3 ft and 5 ft) of open end of vent, extending in all directions
Drum and container filling – outdoors or indoors	1	0	Area inside the drum or container
	1	1	Within 900 mm (3 ft) of vent and fill openings, extending in all directions
	2	2	Area between 900 mm and 1.5 m (3 ft and 5 ft) from vent or fill opening, extending in all directions; also, up to 450 mm (18 in.) above floor or grade level within a horizontal radius of 3.0 m (10 ft) from vent or fill opening
Pumps, bleeders, withdrawal fittings, Indoors	2	2	Within 1.5 m (5 ft) of any edge of such devices, extending in all directions; also, up to 900 mm (3 ft) above floor or grade level within 7.5 m (25 ft) horizontally from any edge of such devices
Outdoors	2	2	Within 900 mm (3 ft) of any edge of such devices, extending in all directions. Also, up to 450 mm (18 in.) above grade level within 3.0 m (10 ft) horizontally from any edge of such devices
Pits and sumps Without mechanical ventilation	1	1	Entire area within a pit or sump if any part is within a Division 1 or 2, or Zone 1 or 2, classified location
With adequate mechanical ventilation	2	2	Entire area within a pit or sump if any part is within a Division 1 or 2, or Zone 1 or 2, classified location
Containing valves, fittings, or piping, and not within a Division 1 or 2, or Zone 1 or 2, classified location	2	2	Entire pit or sump
Drainage ditches, separators, impounding basins Outdoors	2	2	Area up to 450 mm (18 in.) above ditch, separator, or basin; also, area up to 450 mm (18 in.) above grade within 4.5 m (15 ft) horizontally from any edge
Indoors			Same classified area as pits
Tank vehicle and tank car[2] loading through open dome	1	0	Area inside of the tank
	1	1	Within 900 mm (3 ft) of edge of dome, extending in all directions
	2	2	Area between 900 mm and 4.5 m (3 ft and 15 ft) from edge of dome, extending in all directions

(Continues)

Table 515.3 *Continued*

Location	NEC Class I Division	Zone	Extent of Classified Area
Loading through bottom connections with atmospheric venting	1	0	Area inside of the tank
	1	1	Within 900 mm (3 ft) of point of venting to atmosphere, extending in all directions
	2	2	Area between 900 mm and 4.5 m (3 ft and 15 ft) from point of venting to atmosphere, extending in all directions; also, up to 450 mm (18 in.) above grade within a horizontal radius of 3.0 m (10 ft) from point of loading connection
Office and rest rooms	Ordinary		If there is any opening to these rooms within the extent of an indoor classified location, the room shall be classified the same as if the wall, curb, or partition did not exist.
Loading through closed dome with atmospheric venting	1	1	Within 900 mm (3 ft) of open end of vent, extending in all directions
	2	2	Area between 900 mm and 4.5 m (3 ft and 15 ft) from open end of vent, extending in all directions; also, within 900 mm (3 ft) of edge of dome, extending in all directions
Loading through closed dome with vapor control	2	2	Within 900 mm (3 ft) of point of connection of both fill and vapor lines extending in all directions
Bottom loading with vapor control or any bottom unloading	2	2	Within 900 mm (3 ft) of point of connections, extending in all directions; also up to 450 mm (18 in.) above grade within a horizontal radius of 3.0 m (10 ft) from point of connections
Storage and repair garage for tank vehicles	1	1	All pits or spaces below floor level
	2	2	Area up to 450 mm (18 in.) above floor or grade level for entire storage or repair garage
Garages for other than tank vehicles	Ordinary		If there is any opening to these rooms within the extent of an outdoor classified location, the entire room shall be classified the same as the area classification at the point of the opening.
Outdoor drum storage	Ordinary		
Inside rooms or storage lockers used for the storage of Class I liquids	2	2	Entire room
Indoor warehousing where there is no flammable liquid transfer	Ordinary		If there is any opening to these rooms within the extent of an indoor classified location, the room shall be classified the same as if the wall, curb, or partition did not exist.
Piers and wharves			See Figure 515.3.

[1]The release of Class I liquids may generate vapors to the extent that the entire building, and possibly an area surrounding it, should be considered a Class I, Division 2 or Zone 2 location.

[2]When classifying extent of area, consideration shall be given to fact that tank cars or tank vehicles may be spotted at varying points. Therefore, the extremities of the loading or unloading positions shall be used. [NFPA 30:Table 8.2.2]

Division 1   Division 2   Unclassified

Notes:
(1) The "source of vapor" shall be the operating envelope and stored position of the outboard flange connection of the loading arm (or hose).
(2) The berth area adjacent to tanker and barge cargo tanks is to be Division 2 to the following extent:
  a. 7.6 m (25 ft) horizontally in all directions on the pier side from that portion of the hull containing cargo tanks
  b. From the water level to 7.6 m (25 ft) above the cargo tanks at their highest position
(3) Additional locations may have to be classified as required by the presence of other sources of flammable liquids on the berth, by Coast Guard, or other regulations.

Figure 515.3 Marine Terminal Handling Flammable Liquids. [NFPA 30:Figure 7.7.16]

515.4 Wiring and Equipment Located in Class I Locations.
All electrical wiring and equipment within the Class I locations defined in 515.3 shall comply with the applicable provisions of Article 501 or Article 505 for the division or zone in which they are used.

Exception: As permitted in 515.8.

515.7 Wiring and Equipment Above Class I Locations.

(A) Fixed Wiring. All fixed wiring above Class I locations shall be in metal raceways or PVC Schedule 80 rigid nonmetallic conduit, or equivalent, or be Type MI, TC, or MC cable.

(B) Fixed Equipment. Fixed equipment that may produce arcs, sparks, or particles of hot metal, such as lamps and lampholders for fixed lighting, cutouts, switches, receptacles, motors, or other equipment having make-and-break or sliding contacts, shall be of the totally enclosed type or be constructed so as to prevent the escape of sparks or hot metal particles.

(C) Portable Lamps or Other Utilization Equipment. Portable lamps or other utilization equipment and their flexible cords shall comply with the provisions of Article 501 or Article 505 for the class of location above which they are connected or used.

515.8 Underground Wiring.

(A) Wiring Method. Underground wiring shall be installed in threaded rigid metal conduit or threaded steel intermediate metal conduit or, where buried under not less than 600 mm (2 ft) of cover, shall be permitted in rigid nonmetallic conduit or a listed cable. Where rigid nonmetallic conduit is used, threaded rigid metal conduit or threaded steel intermediate metal conduit shall be used for the last 600 mm (2 ft) of the conduit run to emergence or to the point of connection to the aboveground raceway. Where cable is used, it shall be enclosed in threaded rigid metal conduit or threaded steel intermediate metal conduit from the point of lowest buried cable level to the point of connection to the aboveground raceway.

(B) Insulation. Conductor insulation shall comply with 501.20.

(C) Nonmetallic Wiring. Where rigid nonmetallic conduit or cable with a nonmetallic sheath is used, an equipment grounding conductor shall be included to provide for electrical continuity of the raceway system and for grounding of non–current-carrying metal parts.

515.9 Sealing. Sealing requirements shall apply to horizontal as well as to vertical boundaries of the defined Class I locations. Buried raceways and cables under defined Class I locations shall be considered to be within a Class I, Division 1 or Zone 1 location.

515.10 Special Equipment — Gasoline Dispensers. Where gasoline or other volatile flammable liquids or liquefied flammable gases are dispensed at bulk stations, the applicable provisions of Article 514 shall apply.

515.16 Grounding. All metal raceways, the metal armor or metallic sheath on cables, and all non–current-carrying metal parts of fixed or portable electrical equipment, regardless of voltage, shall be grounded as provided in Article 250. Grounding in Class I locations shall comply with 501.30 for Class I, Division 1 and 2 locations and 505.25 for Class I, Zone 0, 1, and 2 locations.

> FPN: For information on grounding for static protection, see 4.5.3.4 and 4.5.3.5 of NFPA 30-2003, *Flammable and Combustible Liquids Code.*

ARTICLE 516
Spray Application, Dipping, and Coating Processes

> FPN: Rules that are followed by a reference in brackets contain text that has been extracted from NFPA 33-2003, *Standard for Spray Application Using Flammable and Combustible Materials*, or NFPA 34-2003, *Standard for Dipping and Coating Processes Using Flammable or Combustible Liquids.* Only editorial changes were made to the extracted text to make it consistent with this *Code.*

516.1 Scope. This article covers the regular or frequent application of flammable liquids, combustible liquids, and combustible powders by spray operations and the application of flammable liquids, or combustible liquids at temperatures above their flashpoint, by dipping, coating, or other means.

> FPN: For further information regarding safeguards for these processes, such as fire protection, posting of warning signs, and maintenance, see NFPA 33-2003, *Standard for*

Spray Application Using Flammable and Combustible Materials, and NFPA 34-2003, *Standard for Dipping and Coating Processes Using Flammable or Combustible Liquids.* For additional information regarding ventilation, see NFPA 91-2004, *Standard for Exhaust Systems for Air Conveying of Vapors, Gases, Mists, and Noncombustible Particulate Solids.*

516.2 Definitions. For the purpose of this article, the following definitions shall apply.

Spray Area. Normally, locations outside of buildings or localized operations within a larger room or space. Such are normally provided with some local vapor extraction/ventilation system. In automated operations, the area limits shall be the maximum area in the direct path of spray operations. In manual operations, the area limits shall be the maximum area of spray when aimed at 180 degrees to the application surface.

Spray Booth. An enclosure or insert within a larger room used for spray/coating/dipping applications. A spray booth may be fully enclosed or have open front or face and may include separate conveyor entrance and exit. The spray booth is provided with a dedicated ventilation exhaust but may draw supply air from the larger room or have a dedicated air supply.

Spray Room. A purposefully enclosed room built for spray/coating/dipping applications provided with dedicated ventilation supply and exhaust. Normally the room is configured to house the item to be painted, providing reasonable access around the item/process. Depending on the size of the item being painted, such rooms may actually be the entire building or the major portion thereof.

516.3 Classification of Locations. Classification is based on dangerous quantities of flammable vapors, combustible mists, residues, dusts, or deposits.

(A) Class I, Division 1 or Class I, Zone 0 Locations. The following spaces shall be considered Class I, Division 1, or Class I, Zone 0, as applicable:

(1) The interior of any open or closed container of a flammable liquid

(2) The interior of any dip tank or coating tank

> FPN: For additional guidance and explanatory diagrams, see 4.3.5 of NFPA 33-2003, *Standard for Spray Application Using Flammable or Combustible Materials*, and Sections 4.2, 4.3, and 4.4 of NFPA 34-2003, *Standard for Dipping and Coating Processes Using Flammable or Combustible Liquids.*

(B) Class I or Class II, Division 1 Locations. The following spaces shall be considered Class I, Division 1, or Class I, Zone 1, or Class II, Division 1 locations, as applicable:

(1) The interior of spray booths and rooms except as specifically provided in 516.3(D).

(2) The interior of exhaust ducts.

(3) Any area in the direct path of spray operations.

(4) For open dipping and coating operations, all space within a 1.5-m (5-ft) radial distance from the vapor sources extending from these surfaces to the floor. The vapor source shall be the liquid exposed in the process and the drainboard, and any dipped or coated object from which it is possible to measure vapor concentrations exceeding 25 percent of the lower flammable limit at a distance of 300 mm (1 ft), in any direction, from the object.

(5) Sumps, pits, or belowgrade channels within 7.5 m (25 ft) horizontally of a vapor source. If the sump, pit, or channel extends beyond 7.5 m (25 ft) from the vapor source, it shall be provided with a vapor stop or it shall be classified as Class I, Division 1 for its entire length.

(6) All space in all directions outside of but within 900 mm (3 ft) of open containers, supply containers, spray gun cleaners, and solvent distillation units containing flammable liquids.

(C) Class I or Class II, Division 2 Locations. The following spaces shall be considered Class I, Division 2 or Class I, Zone 2, or Class II, Division 2 as applicable.

(1) Open Spraying. For open spraying, all space outside of but within 6 m (20 ft) horizontally and 3 m (10 ft) vertically of the Class I, Division 1 or Class I, Zone 1 location as defined in 516.3(A), and not separated from it by partitions. See Figure 516.3(B)(1) . [NFPA 33:6.5.1]

(2) Closed-Top, Open-Face, and Open-Front Spraying. If spray application operations are conducted within a closed-top, open-face, or open-front booth or room, any electrical wiring or utilization equipment located outside of the booth or room but within the boundaries designated as Division 2 or Zone 2 in Figure 516.3(B)(2) shall be suitable for Class I, Division 2, Class I, Zone 2, or Class II, Division 2 locations, whichever is applicable. The Class I, Division 2, Class I, Zone 2, or Class II, Division 2 locations shown in Figure 516.3(B)(2) shall extend from the edges of the open face or open front of the booth or room in accordance with the following:

(a) If the exhaust ventilation system is interlocked with the spray application equipment, the Division 2 or Zone 2 location shall extend 1.5 m (5 ft) horizontally and 900 mm (3 ft) vertically from the open face or open front of the booth or room, as shown in Figure 516.3(B)(2), top.

(b) If the exhaust ventilation system is not interlocked with the spray application equipment, the Division 2 or Zone 2 location shall extend 3 m (10 ft) horizontally and 900 mm (3 ft) vertically from the open face or open front of the booth or room, as shown in Figure 516.3(B)(2), bottom.

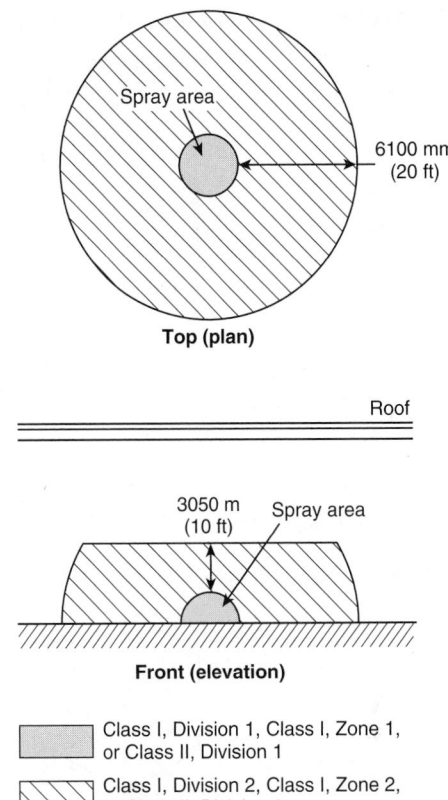

Figure 516.3(B)(1) Electrical Area Classification for Open Spray Areas. [NFPA 33:Figure 6.5.1]

For the purposes of this subsection, *interlocked* shall mean that the spray application equipment cannot be operated unless the exhaust ventilation system is operating and functioning properly and spray application is automatically stopped if the exhaust ventilation system fails. [NFPA 33:6.5.2]

(3) Open-Top Spraying. For spraying operations conducted within an open top spray booth, the space 900 mm (3 ft) vertically above the booth and within 900 mm (3 ft) of other booth openings shall be considered Class I, Division 2, Class I, Zone 2, or Class II, Division 2. [NFPA 33:6.5.3]

(4) Enclosed Booths and Rooms. For spraying operations confined to an enclosed spray booth or room, the space within 900 mm (3 ft) in all directions from any openings shall be considered Class I, Division 2, Class I, or Zone 2, or Class II, Division 2 as shown in Figure 516.3(B)(4) . [NFPA 33:6.5.4]

(5) Dip Tanks and Drain Boards — Surrounding Space. For dip tanks and drain boards, the 914-mm (3-ft) space surrounding the Class I, Division 1 or Class I, Zone 1 location as defined in 516.3(A)(4) and as shown in Figure 516.3(B)(5). [NFPA 34:6.4.3]

Figure 516.3(B)(2) Class I, Division 2, Class I, Zone 2, or Class II, Division 2 Locations Adjacent to a Closed Top, Open Face, or Open Front Spray Booth or Room. [NFPA 33:Figures 6.5.2(a) and 6.5.2(b)]

Figure 516.3(B)(4) Class I, Division 2, Class I, Zone 2, or Class II, Division 2 Locations Adjacent to an Enclosed Spray Booth or Spray Room. [NFPA 33:Figure 6.5.4]

Figure 516.3(B)(5) Electrical Area Classification for Open Processes Without Vapor Containment or Ventilation. [NFPA 34:Figure 6.4(a)]

(6) Dip Tanks and Drain Boards — Space Above Floor. For dip tanks and drain boards, the space 900 mm (3 ft) above the floor and extending 6 m (20 ft) horizontally in all directions from the Class I, Division 1 or Class I, Zone 1 location.

Exception: This space shall not be required to be considered a hazardous (classified) location where the vapor source area is 0.46 m² (5 ft²) or less and where the contents of the open tank trough or container do not exceed 19 L (5 gal). In addition, the vapor concentration during operation and shutdown periods shall not exceed 25 percent of the lower flammable limit outside the Class I location specified in 516.3(A)(4). [NFPA 34:6.4.4]

(7) Open Containers. All space in all directions within 600 mm (2 ft) of the Division 1 or Zone 1 area surrounding open containers, supply containers, spray gun cleaners, and solvent distillation units containing flammable liquids, as well as the area extending 1.5 m (5 ft) beyond the Division 1 or Zone 1 area up to a height of 460 mm (18 in.) above the floor or grade level. [NFPA 33:6.5.5.1(2)]

(D) Enclosed Coating and Dipping Operations. The space adjacent to an enclosed dipping or coating process or apparatus shall be considered unclassified. [NFPA 34:6.5.2]

Exception: The space within 900 mm (3 ft) in all directions from any opening in the enclosures shall be classified as Class I, Division 2 or Class I, Zone 2, as applicable. [NFPA 34:6.5.3]

(E) Adjacent Locations. Adjacent locations that are cut off from the defined Class I or Class II locations by tight partitions without communicating openings, and within which flammable vapors or combustible powders are not likely to be released, shall be unclassified.

(F) Unclassified Locations. Locations using drying, curing, or fusion apparatus and provided with positive mechanical ventilation adequate to prevent accumulation of flammable concentrations of vapors, and provided with effective interlocks to de-energize all electrical equipment (other than equipment identified for Class I locations) in case the ventilating equipment is inoperative, shall be permitted to be unclassified where the authority having jurisdiction so judges.

> FPN: For further information regarding safeguards, see NFPA 86-2003, *Standard for Ovens and Furnaces.*

516.4 Wiring and Equipment in Class I Locations.

(A) Wiring and Equipment — Vapors. All electric wiring and equipment within the Class I location (containing vapor only — not residues) defined in 516.3 shall comply with the applicable provisions of Article 501 or Article 505, as applicable.

(B) Wiring and Equipment — Vapors and Residues. Unless specifically listed for locations containing deposits of dangerous quantities of flammable or combustible vapors, mists, residues, dusts, or deposits (as applicable), there shall be no electrical equipment in any spray area as herein defined whereon deposits of combustible residue may readily accumulate, except wiring in rigid metal conduit, intermediate metal conduit, Type MI cable, or in metal boxes or fittings containing no taps, splices, or terminal connections. [NFPA 33:6.4.2]

(C) Illumination. Illumination of readily ignitible areas through panels of glass or other transparent or translucent material shall be permitted only if it complies with the following:

(1) Fixed lighting units are used as the source of illumination.

(2) The panel effectively isolates the Class I location from the area in which the lighting unit is located.

(3) The lighting unit is identified for its specific location.

(4) The panel is of a material or is protected so that breakage is unlikely.

(5) The arrangement is such that normal accumulations of hazardous residue on the surface of the panel will not be raised to a dangerous temperature by radiation or conduction from the source of illumination.

(D) Portable Equipment. Portable electric lamps or other utilization equipment shall not be used in a spray area during spray operations.

Exception No. 1: Where portable electric lamps are required for operations in spaces not readily illuminated by fixed lighting within the spraying area, they shall be of the type identified for Class I, Division 1 or Class 1, Zone 1 locations where readily ignitible residues may be present. [NFPA 33:6.9]

Exception No. 2: Where portable electric drying apparatus is used in automobile refinishing spray booths and the following requirements are met.

(a) The apparatus and its electrical connections are not located within the spray enclosure during spray operations.

(b) Electrical equipment within 450 mm (18 in.) of the floor is identified for Class I, Division 2 or Class I, Zone 2 locations.

(c) All metallic parts of the drying apparatus are electrically bonded and grounded.

(d) Interlocks are provided to prevent the operation of spray equipment while drying apparatus is within the spray enclosure, to allow for a 3-minute purge of the enclosure before energizing the drying apparatus and to shut off drying apparatus on failure of ventilation system.

(E) Electrostatic Equipment. Electrostatic spraying or detearing equipment shall be installed and used only as provided in 516.10.

> FPN: For further information, see NFPA 33-2003, *Standard for Spray Application Using Flammable or Combustible Materials.*

516.7 Wiring and Equipment Not Within Class I and II Locations.

(A) Wiring. All fixed wiring above the Class I and II locations shall be in metal raceways, rigid nonmetallic conduit, or electrical nonmetallic tubing, or shall be Type MI, TC, or MC cable. Cellular metal floor raceways shall be permitted only for supplying ceiling outlets or extensions to the area below the floor of a Class I or II location, but such raceways shall have no connections leading into or through the Class I or II location above the floor unless suitable seals are provided.

(B) Equipment. Equipment that may produce arcs, sparks, or particles of hot metal, such as lamps and lampholders for fixed lighting, cutouts, switches, receptacles, motors, or other equipment having make-and-break or sliding contacts, where installed above a Class I or II location or above a location where freshly finished goods are handled, shall be of the totally enclosed type or be constructed so as to prevent the escape of sparks or hot metal particles.

516.10 Special Equipment.

(A) Fixed Electrostatic Equipment. This section shall apply to any equipment using electrostatically charged elements for the atomization, charging, and/or precipitation of hazardous materials for coatings on articles or for other similar purposes in which the charging or atomizing device is attached to a mechanical support or manipulator. This shall include robotic devices. This section shall not apply to devices that are held or manipulated by hand. Where robot or programming procedures involve manual manipulation of the robot arm while spraying with the high voltage on, the provisions of 516.10(B) shall apply. The installation of electrostatic spraying equipment shall comply with 516.10(A)(1) through (A)(10). Spray equipment shall be listed. All automatic electrostatic equipment systems shall comply with 516.4(A)(1) through (A)(9).

(1) Power and Control Equipment. Transformers, high-voltage supplies, control apparatus, and all other electric portions of the equipment shall be installed outside of the Class I location as defined in 516.3 or be of a type identified for the location.

Exception: High-voltage grids, electrodes, electrostatic atomizing heads, and their connections shall be permitted within the Class I location.

(2) Electrostatic Equipment. Electrodes and electrostatic atomizing heads shall be adequately supported in permanent locations and shall be effectively insulated from ground. Electrodes and electrostatic atomizing heads that are permanently attached to their bases, supports, reciprocators, or robots shall be deemed to comply with this section.

(3) High-Voltage Leads. High-voltage leads shall be properly insulated and protected from mechanical damage or exposure to destructive chemicals. Any exposed element at high voltage shall be effectively and permanently supported on suitable insulators and shall be effectively guarded against accidental contact or grounding.

(4) Support of Goods. Goods being coated using this process shall be supported on conveyors or hangers. The conveyors or hangers shall be arranged (1) to ensure that the parts being coated are electrically connected to ground with a resistance of 1 megohm or less and (2) to prevent parts from swinging.

(5) Automatic Controls. Electrostatic apparatus shall be equipped with automatic means that will rapidly de-energize the high-voltage elements under any of the following conditions:

(1) Stoppage of ventilating fans or failure of ventilating equipment from any cause
(2) Stoppage of the conveyor carrying goods through the high-voltage field unless stoppage is required by the spray process
(3) Occurrence of excessive current leakage at any point in the high-voltage system
(4) De-energizing the primary voltage input to the power supply

(6) Grounding. All electrically conductive objects in the spray area, except those objects required by the process to be at high voltage, shall be adequately grounded. This requirement shall apply to paint containers, wash cans, guards, hose connectors, brackets, and any other electrically conductive objects or devices in the area.

(7) Isolation. Safeguards such as adequate booths, fencing, railings, interlocks, or other means shall be placed about the equipment or incorporated therein so that they, either by their location, character, or both, ensure that a safe separation of the process is maintained.

(8) Signs. Signs shall be conspicuously posted to convey the following:

(1) Designate the process zone as dangerous with regard to fire and accident
(2) Identify the grounding requirements for all electrically conductive objects in the spray area
(3) Restrict access to qualified personnel only

(9) Insulators. All insulators shall be kept clean and dry.

(10) Other Than Nonincendive Equipment. Spray equipment that cannot be classified as nonincendive shall comply with (A)(10)(a) and (A)(10)(b).

(a) Conveyors or hangers shall be arranged so as to maintain a safe distance of at least twice the sparking distance between goods being painted and electrodes, electrostatic atomizing heads, or charged conductors. Warnings defining this safe distance shall be posted.

(b) The equipment shall provide an automatic means of rapidly de-energizing the high-voltage elements in the event the distance between the goods being painted and the electrodes or electrostatic atomizing heads falls below that specified in (a). [NFPA 33:Chapter 11]

(B) Electrostatic Hand-Spraying Equipment. This section shall apply to any equipment using electrostatically charged elements for the atomization, charging, and/or precipitation of materials for coatings on articles, or for other similar purposes in which the atomizing device is hand-held or manipulated during the spraying operation. Electrostatic hand-spraying equipment and devices used in connection with paint-spraying operations shall be of listed types and shall comply with 516.10(B)(1) through (B)(5).

(1) General. The high-voltage circuits shall be designed so as not to produce a spark of sufficient intensity to ignite the most readily ignitible of those vapor–air mixtures likely to be encountered, or result in appreciable shock hazard upon coming in contact with a grounded object under all normal operating conditions. The electrostatically charged exposed elements of the handgun shall be capable of being energized only by an actuator that also controls the coating material supply.

(2) Power Equipment. Transformers, power packs, control apparatus, and all other electric portions of the equipment shall be located outside of the Class I location or be identified for the location.

Exception: The handgun itself and its connections to the power supply shall be permitted within the Class I location.

(3) Handle. The handle of the spraying gun shall be electrically connected to ground by a metallic connection and be constructed so that the operator in normal operating position is in intimate electrical contact with the grounded handle to prevent buildup of a static charge on the operator's body. Signs indicating the necessity for grounding other persons entering the spray area shall be conspicuously posted.

(4) Electrostatic Equipment. All electrically conductive objects in the spraying area shall be adequately grounded. This requirement shall apply to paint containers, wash cans, and any other electrical conductive objects or devices in the area.

The equipment shall carry a prominent, permanently installed warning regarding the necessity for this grounding feature.

(5) Support of Objects. Objects being painted shall be maintained in metallic contact with the conveyor or other grounded support. Hooks shall be regularly cleaned to ensure adequate grounding of 1 megohm or less. Areas of contact shall be sharp points or knife edges where possible. Points of support of the object shall be concealed from random spray where feasible; and, where the objects being sprayed are supported from a conveyor, the point of attachment to the conveyor shall be located so as to not collect spray material during normal operation. [NFPA 33:Chapter 12]

(C) Powder Coating. This section shall apply to processes in which combustible dry powders are applied. The hazards associated with combustible dusts are present in such a process to a degree, depending on the chemical composition of the material, particle size, shape, and distribution.

(1) Electric Equipment and Sources of Ignition. Electric equipment and other sources of ignition shall comply with the requirements of Article 502. Portable electric lamps and other utilization equipment shall not be used within a Class II location during operation of the finishing processes. Where such lamps or utilization equipment are used during cleaning or repairing operations, they shall be of a type identified for Class II, Division 1 locations, and all exposed metal parts shall be effectively grounded.

Exception: Where portable electric lamps are required for operations in spaces not readily illuminated by fixed lighting within the spraying area, they shall be of the type listed for Class II, Division 1 locations where readily ignitible residues may be present.

(2) Fixed Electrostatic Spraying Equipment. The provisions of 516.10(A) and 516.10(C)(1) shall apply to fixed electrostatic spraying equipment.

(3) Electrostatic Hand-Spraying Equipment. The provisions of 516.10(B) and 516.10(C)(1) shall apply to electrostatic hand-spraying equipment.

(4) Electrostatic Fluidized Beds. Electrostatic fluidized beds and associated equipment shall be of identified types. The high-voltage circuits shall be designed so that any discharge produced when the charging electrodes of the bed are approached or contacted by a grounded object shall not be of sufficient intensity to ignite any powder–air mixture likely to be encountered or to result in an appreciable shock hazard.

(a) Transformers, power packs, control apparatus, and all other electric portions of the equipment shall be located outside the powder-coating area or shall otherwise comply with the requirements of 516.10(C)(1).

Exception: The charging electrodes and their connections to the power supply shall be permitted within the powder-coating area.

(b)   All electrically conductive objects within the powder-coating area shall be adequately grounded. The powder-coating equipment shall carry a prominent, permanently installed warning regarding the necessity for grounding these objects.

(c)   Objects being coated shall be maintained in electrical contact (less than 1 megohm) with the conveyor or other support in order to ensure proper grounding. Hangers shall be regularly cleaned to ensure effective electrical contact. Areas of electrical contact shall be sharp points or knife edges where possible.

(d)   The electric equipment and compressed air supplies shall be interlocked with a ventilation system so that the equipment cannot be operated unless the ventilating fans are in operation. [NFPA 33:Chapter 15]

516.16 Grounding. All metal raceways, the metal armors or metallic sheath on cables, and all non–current-carrying metal parts of fixed or portable electrical equipment, regardless of voltage, shall be grounded as provided in Article 250. Grounding shall comply with 501.30, 502.30, or 505.25, as applicable.

ARTICLE 517
Health Care Facilities

FPN: Rules that are followed by a reference in brackets contain text that has been extracted from NFPA 99-2002, *Standard for Health Care Facilities*. Only editorial changes were made to the extracted text to make it consistent with this *Code*.

I. General

517.1 Scope. The provisions of this article shall apply to electrical construction and installation criteria in health care facilities that provide services to human beings.

The requirements in Parts II and III not only apply to single-function buildings but are also intended to be individually applied to their respective forms of occupancy within a multifunction building (e.g., a doctor's examining room located within a limited care facility would be required to meet the provisions of 517.10).

FPN: For information concerning performance, maintenance, and testing criteria, refer to the appropriate health care facilities documents.

517.2 Definitions.

Alternate Power Source. One or more generator sets, or battery systems where permitted, intended to provide power during the interruption of the normal electrical services or the public utility electrical service intended to provide power during interruption of service normally provided by the generating facilities on the premises.

Ambulatory Health Care Facility. A building or part thereof used to provide services or treatment to four or more patients at the same time and meeting either (1) or (2).

(1) Those facilities that provide, on an outpatient basis, treatment for patients that would render them incapable of taking action for self-preservation under emergency conditions without assistance from others, such as hemodialysis units or freestanding emergency medical units.

(2) Those facilities that provide, on an outpatient basis, surgical treatment requiring general anesthesia.

Anesthetizing Location. Any area of a facility that has been designated to be used for the administration of any flammable or nonflammable inhalation anesthetic agent in the course of examination or treatment, including the use of such agents for relative analgesia.

Critical Branch. A subsystem of the emergency system consisting of feeders and branch circuits supplying energy to task illumination, special power circuits, and selected receptacles serving areas and functions related to patient care, and which are connected to alternate power sources by one or more transfer switches during interruption of the normal power source.

Electrical Life-Support Equipment. Electrically powered equipment whose continuous operation is necessary to maintain a patient's life.

Emergency System. A system of circuits and equipment intended to supply alternate power to a limited number of prescribed functions vital to the protection of life and safety.

Equipment System. A system of circuits and equipment arranged for delayed, automatic, or manual connection to the alternate power source and that serves primarily 3-phase power equipment.

Essential Electrical System. A system comprised of alternate sources of power and all connected distribution systems and ancillary equipment, designed to ensure continuity of electrical power to designated areas and functions of a health care facility during disruption of normal power sources, and also designed to minimize disruption within the internal wiring system.

Exposed Conductive Surfaces. Those surfaces that are capable of carrying electric current and that are unprotected, unenclosed, or unguarded, permitting personal contact. Paint, anodizing, and similar coatings are not considered suitable insulation, unless they are listed for such use.

Fault Hazard Current. See *Hazard Current*.

Flammable Anesthetics. Gases or vapors, such as fluroxene, cyclopropane, divinyl ether, ethyl chloride, ethyl ether, and ethylene, which may form flammable or explosive mixtures with air, oxygen, or reducing gases such as nitrous oxide.

Flammable Anesthetizing Location. Any area of the facility that has been designated to be used for the administration of any flammable inhalation anesthetic agents in the normal course of examination or treatment.

Hazard Current. For a given set of connections in an isolated power system, the total current that would flow through a low impedance if it were connected between either isolated conductor and ground.

Fault Hazard Current. The hazard current of a given isolated system with all devices connected except the line isolation monitor.

Monitor Hazard Current. The hazard current of the line isolation monitor alone.

Total Hazard Current. The hazard current of a given isolated system with all devices, including the line isolation monitor, connected.

Health Care Facilities. Buildings or portions of buildings in which medical, dental, psychiatric, nursing, obstetrical, or surgical care are provided. Health care facilities include, but are not limited to, hospitals, nursing homes, limited care facilities, clinics, medical and dental offices, and ambulatory care centers, whether permanent or movable.

Hospital. A building or part thereof used for the medical, psychiatric, obstetrical, or surgical care, on a 24-hour basis, of four or more inpatients. *Hospital,* wherever used in this *Code,* shall include general hospitals, mental hospitals, tuberculosis hospitals, children's hospitals, and any such facilities providing inpatient care.

Isolated Power System. A system comprising an isolating transformer or its equivalent, a line isolation monitor, and its ungrounded circuit conductors.

Isolation Transformer. A transformer of the multiple-winding type, with the primary and secondary windings physically separated, which inductively couples its secondary winding to the grounded feeder systems that energize its primary winding.

Life Safety Branch. A subsystem of the emergency system consisting of feeders and branch circuits, meeting the requirements of Article 700 and intended to provide adequate power needs to ensure safety to patients and personnel, and which are automatically connected to alternate power sources during interruption of the normal power source.

Limited Care Facility. A building or part thereof used on a 24-hour basis for the housing of four or more persons who are incapable of self-preservation because of age, physical limitation due to accident or illness, or mental limitations, such as mental retardation/developmental disability, mental illness, or chemical dependency.

Line Isolation Monitor. A test instrument designed to continually check the balanced and unbalanced impedance from each line of an isolated circuit to ground and equipped with a built-in test circuit to exercise the alarm without adding to the leakage current hazard.

Monitor Hazard Current. See *Hazard Current.*

Nurses' Stations. Areas intended to provide a center of nursing activity for a group of nurses serving bed patients, where the patient calls are received, nurses are dispatched, nurses' notes written, inpatient charts prepared, and medications prepared for distribution to patients. Where such activities are carried on in more than one location within a nursing unit, all such separate areas are considered a part of the nurses' station.

Nursing Home. A building or part thereof used for the lodging, boarding, and nursing care, on a 24-hour basis, of four or more persons who, because of mental or physical incapacity, may be unable to provide for their own needs and safety without the assistance of another person. *Nursing home,* wherever used in this *Code,* shall include nursing and convalescent homes, skilled nursing facilities, intermediate care facilities, and infirmaries of homes for the aged.

Patient Bed Location. The location of an inpatient sleeping bed; or the bed or procedure table used in a critical patient care area.

Patient Care Area. Any portion of a health care facility wherein patients are intended to be examined or treated. Areas of a health care facility in which patient care is administered are classified as general care areas or critical care areas, either of which may be classified as a wet location. The governing body of the facility designates these areas in accordance with the type of patient care anticipated and with the following definitions of the area classification.

FPN: Business offices, corridors, lounges, day rooms, dining rooms, or similar areas typically are not classified as patient care areas.

General Care Areas. Patient bedrooms, examining rooms, treatment rooms, clinics, and similar areas in which it is intended that the patient will come in contact with ordinary appliances such as a nurse call system, electrical beds, examining lamps, telephone, and entertainment devices. In such areas, it may also be intended that patients be connected to electromedical devices (such as heating pads, electrocardiographs, drainage pumps, monitors, otoscopes, ophthalmoscopes, intravenous lines, etc.).

Critical Care Areas. Those special care units, intensive care units, coronary care units, angiography laboratories, cardiac catheterization laboratories, delivery rooms, operating rooms, and similar areas in which patients are intended to be subjected to invasive procedures and connected to line-operated, electromedical devices.

Wet Locations. Those patient care areas that are normally subject to wet conditions while patients are present. These include standing fluids on the floor or drenching of the work area, either of which condition is intimate to the patient or staff. Routine housekeeping procedures and incidental spillage of liquids do not define a wet location.

Patient Equipment Grounding Point. A jack or terminal bus that serves as the collection point for redundant grounding of electric appliances serving a patient vicinity or for grounding other items in order to eliminate electromagnetic interference problems.

Patient Vicinity. In an area in which patients are normally cared for, the *patient vicinity* is the space with surfaces likely to be contacted by the patient or an attendant who can touch the patient. Typically in a patient room, this encloses a space within the room not less than 1.8 m (6 ft) beyond the perimeter of the bed in its nominal location, and extending vertically not less than 2.3 m (7½ ft) above the floor.

Psychiatric Hospital. A building used exclusively for the psychiatric care, on a 24-hour basis, of four or more inpatients.

Reference Grounding Point. The ground bus of the panelboard or isolated power system panel supplying the patient care area.

Relative Analgesia. A state of sedation and partial block of pain perception produced in a patient by the inhalation of concentrations of nitrous oxide insufficient to produce loss of consciousness (conscious sedation).

Selected Receptacles. A minimum number of electric receptacles to accommodate appliances ordinarily required for local tasks or likely to be used in patient care emergencies.

Task Illumination. Provision for the minimum lighting required to carry out necessary tasks in the described areas, including safe access to supplies and equipment, and access to exits.

Therapeutic High Frequency Diathermy Equipment. Therapeutic high-frequency diathermy equipment is therapeutic induction and dielectric heating equipment.

Total Hazard Current. See *Hazard Current*.

X-Ray Installations, Long-Time Rating. A rating based on an operating interval of 5 minutes or longer.

X-Ray Installations, Mobile. X-ray equipment mounted on a permanent base with wheels, casters, or a combination of both to facilitate moving the equipment while completely assembled.

X-Ray Installations, Momentary Rating. A rating based on an operating interval that does not exceed 5 seconds.

X-Ray Installations, Portable. X-ray equipment designed to be hand carried.

X-Ray Installations, Transportable. X-ray equipment to be installed in a vehicle or that may be readily disassembled for transport in a vehicle.

II. Wiring and Protection

517.10 Applicability.

(A) Applicability. Part II shall apply to patient care areas of all health care facilities.

(B) Not Covered. Part II shall not apply to the following:

(1) Business offices, corridors, waiting rooms, and the like in clinics, medical and dental offices, and outpatient facilities

(2) Areas of nursing homes and limited care facilities wired in accordance with Chapters 1 through 4 of this *Code* where these areas are used exclusively as patient sleeping rooms

FPN: See NFPA *101*®-2003, *Life Safety Code*®.

517.11 General Installation — Construction Criteria.

The purpose of this article is to specify the installation criteria and wiring methods that minimize electrical hazards by the maintenance of adequately low potential differences only between exposed conductive surfaces that are likely to become energized and could be contacted by a patient.

FPN: In a health care facility, it is difficult to prevent the occurrence of a conductive or capacitive path from the patient's body to some grounded object, because that path may be established accidentally or through instrumentation directly connected to the patient. Other electrically conductive surfaces that may make an additional contact with the patient, or instruments that may be connected to the patient, then become possible sources of electric currents that can traverse the patient's body. The hazard is increased as more apparatus is associated with the patient, and, therefore, more intensive precautions are needed. Control of electric shock hazard requires the limitation of electric current that might flow in an electric circuit involving the patient's body by raising the resistance of the conductive circuit that includes the patient, or by insulating exposed surfaces that might become energized, in addition to reducing the potential difference that can appear between exposed conductive surfaces in the patient vicinity, or by combinations of these methods. A special problem is presented by the patient with an externalized direct conductive path to the heart muscle. The patient may be electrocuted at current levels so low that additional protection in the design of appliances, insulation of the catheter, and control of medical practice is required.

517.12 Wiring Methods.

Except as modified in this article, wiring methods shall comply with the applicable requirements of Chapters 1 through 4 of this *Code*.

517.13 Grounding of Receptacles and Fixed Electric Equipment in Patient Care Areas. Wiring in patient care areas shall comply with 517.13(A) and 517.13(B).

(A) Wiring Methods. All branch circuits serving patient care areas shall be provided with a ground path for fault current by installation in a metal raceway system, or a cable having a metallic armor or sheath assembly. The metal raceway system, or metallic cable armor, or sheath assembly shall itself qualify as an equipment grounding return path in accordance with 250.118.

(B) Insulated Equipment Grounding Conductor. The grounding terminals of all receptacles and all non–current-carrying conductive surfaces of fixed electric equipment likely to become energized that are subject to personal contact, operating at over 100 volts, shall be grounded by an insulated copper conductor. The equipment grounding conductor shall be sized in accordance with Table 250.122 and installed in metal raceways or as a part of listed cables having a metallic armor or sheath assembly with the branch-circuit conductors supplying these receptacles or fixed equipment.

Exception No. 1: Metal faceplates shall be permitted to be grounded by means of a metal mounting screw(s) securing the faceplate to a grounded outlet box or grounded wiring device.

Exception No. 2: Luminaires (light fixtures) more than 2.3 m (7½ ft) above the floor and switches located outside of the patient vicinity shall not be required to be grounded by an insulated equipment grounding conductor.

517.14 Panelboard Bonding. The equipment grounding terminal buses of the normal and essential branch-circuit panelboards serving the same individual patient vicinity shall be bonded together with an insulated continuous copper conductor not smaller than 10 AWG. Where two or more panelboards serving the same individual patient vicinity are served from separate transfer switches on the emergency system, the equipment grounding terminal buses of those panelboards shall be bonded together with an insulated continuous copper conductor not smaller than 10 AWG. This conductor shall be permitted to be broken in order to terminate on the equipment grounding terminal bus in each panelboard.

517.16 Receptacles with Insulated Grounding Terminals. Receptacles with insulated grounding terminals, as permitted in 250.146(D), shall be identified; such identification shall be visible after installation.

FPN: Caution is important in specifying such a system with receptacles having insulated grounding terminals, since the grounding impedance is controlled only by the equipment grounding conductors and does not benefit functionally from any parallel grounding paths. This type of installation is typically used where a reduction of electrical noise (electromagnetic interference) is necessary and parallel grounding paths are to be avoided.

517.17 Ground-Fault Protection.

(A) Applicability. The requirements of 517.17 shall apply to hospitals and other buildings (including multiple occupancy buildings) with critical care areas or utilizing electrical life support equipment, and buildings that provide the required essential utilities or services for the operation of critical care areas or electrical life support equipment.

(B) Feeders. Where ground-fault protection is provided for operation of the service disconnecting means or feeder disconnecting means as specified by 230.95 or 215.10, an additional step of ground-fault protection shall be provided in all next level feeder disconnecting means downstream toward the load. Such protection shall consist of overcurrent devices and current transformers or other equivalent protective equipment that shall cause the feeder disconnecting means to open.

The additional levels of ground-fault protection shall not be installed as follows:

(1) On the load side of an essential electrical system transfer switch

(2) Between the on-site generating unit(s) described in 517.35(B) and the essential electrical system transfer switch(es)

(3) On electrical systems that are not solidly grounded wye systems with greater than 150 volts to ground but not exceeding 600 volts phase-to-phase

(C) Selectivity. Ground-fault protection for operation of the service and feeder disconnecting means shall be fully selective such that the feeder device, but not the service device, shall open on ground faults on the load side of the feeder device. A six-cycle minimum separation between the service and feeder ground-fault tripping bands shall be provided. Operating time of the disconnecting devices shall be considered in selecting the time spread between these two bands to achieve 100 percent selectivity.

FPN: See 230.95, fine print note, for transfer of alternate source where ground-fault protection is applied.

(D) Testing. When equipment ground-fault protection is first installed, each level shall be performance tested to ensure compliance with 517.17(C).

517.18 General Care Areas.

(A) Patient Bed Location. Each patient bed location shall be supplied by at least two branch circuits, one from the emergency system and one from the normal system. All branch circuits from the normal system shall originate in the same panelboard.

Exception No. 1: Branch circuits serving only special-purpose outlets or receptacles, such as portable X-ray outlets, shall not be required to be served from the same distribution panel or panels.

Exception No. 2: Requirements of 517.18(A) shall not apply to patient bed locations in clinics, medical and dental offices, and outpatient facilities; psychiatric, substance abuse, and rehabilitation hospitals; sleeping rooms of nursing homes and limited care facilities meeting the requirements of 517.10(B)(2).

Exception No. 3: A general care patient bed location served from two separate transfer switches on the emergency system shall not be required to have circuits from the normal system.

(B) Patient Bed Location Receptacles. Each patient bed location shall be provided with a minimum of four receptacles. They shall be permitted to be of the single or duplex types or a combination of both. All receptacles, whether four or more, shall be listed "hospital grade" and so identified. Each receptacle shall be grounded by means of an insulated copper conductor sized in accordance with Table 250.122.

Exception No. 1: Requirements of 517.18(B) shall not apply to psychiatric, substance abuse, and rehabilitation hospitals meeting the requirements of 517.10(B)(2).

Exception No. 2: Psychiatric security rooms shall not be required to have receptacle outlets installed in the room.

FPN: It is not intended that there be a total, immediate replacement of existing non–hospital grade receptacles. It is intended, however, that non–hospital grade receptacles be replaced with hospital grade receptacles upon modification of use, renovation, or as existing receptacles need replacement.

(C) Pediatric Locations. Receptacles located within the rooms, bathrooms, playrooms, activity rooms, and patient care areas of pediatric wards shall be listed tamper resistant or shall employ a listed tamper resistant cover.

517.19 Critical Care Areas.

(A) Patient Bed Location Branch Circuits. Each patient bed location shall be supplied by at least two branch circuits, one or more from the emergency system and one or more circuits from the normal system. At least one branch circuit from the emergency system shall supply an outlet(s) only at that bed location. All branch circuits from the normal system shall be from a single panelboard. Emergency system receptacles shall be identified and shall also indicate the panelboard and circuit number supplying them.

Exception No. 1: Branch circuits serving only special-purpose receptacles or equipment in critical care areas shall be permitted to be served by other panelboards.

Exception No. 2: Critical care locations served from two separate transfer switches on the emergency system shall not be required to have circuits from the normal system.

(B) Patient Bed Location Receptacles.

(1) Minimum Number and Supply. Each patient bed location shall be provided with a minimum of six receptacles, at least one of which shall be connected to either of the following:

(1) The normal system branch circuit required in 517.19(A)

(2) An emergency system branch circuit supplied by a different transfer switch than the other receptacles at the same location

(2) Receptacle Requirements. The receptacles required in 517.19(B)(1) shall be permitted to be of the single or duplex types or a combination of both. All receptacles, whether six or more, shall be listed "hospital grade" and so identified. Each receptacle shall be grounded to the reference grounding point by means of an insulated copper equipment grounding conductor.

(C) Patient Vicinity Grounding and Bonding (Optional). A patient vicinity shall be permitted to have a patient equipment grounding point. The patient equipment grounding point, where supplied, shall be permitted to contain one or more listed grounding and bonding jacks. An equipment bonding jumper not smaller than 10 AWG shall be used to connect the grounding terminal of all grounding-type receptacles to the patient equipment grounding point. The bonding conductor shall be permitted to be arranged centrically or looped as convenient.

FPN: Where there is no patient equipment grounding point, it is important that the distance between the reference grounding point and the patient vicinity be as short as possible to minimize any potential differences.

(D) Panelboard Grounding. Where a grounded electrical distribution system is used and metal feeder raceway or Type MC or MI cable is installed, grounding of a panelboard or switchboard shall be ensured by one of the following means at each termination or junction point of the raceway or Type MC or MI cable:

(1) A grounding bushing and a continuous copper bonding jumper, sized in accordance with 250.122, with the bonding jumper connected to the junction enclosure or the ground bus of the panel

(2) Connection of feeder raceways or Type MC or MI cable to threaded hubs or bosses on terminating enclosures

(3) Other approved devices such as bonding-type locknuts or bushings

(E) Additional Protective Techniques in Critical Care Areas (Optional). Isolated power systems shall be permitted to be used for critical care areas, and, if used, the isolated power system equipment shall be listed as isolated power equipment. The isolated power system shall be designed and installed in accordance with 517.160.

Exception: The audible and visual indicators of the line isolation monitor shall be permitted to be located at the nursing station for the area being served.

(F) Isolated Power System Grounding. Where an isolated ungrounded power source is used and limits the first-fault current to a low magnitude, the grounding conductor associated with the secondary circuit shall be permitted to be run outside of the enclosure of the power conductors in the same circuit.

> FPN: Although it is permitted to run the grounding conductor outside of the conduit, it is safer to run it with the power conductors to provide better protection in case of a second ground fault.

(G) Special-Purpose Receptacle Grounding. The equipment grounding conductor for special-purpose receptacles, such as the operation of mobile X-ray equipment, shall be extended to the reference grounding points of branch circuits for all locations likely to be served from such receptacles. Where such a circuit is served from an isolated ungrounded system, the grounding conductor shall not be required to be run with the power conductors; however, the equipment grounding terminal of the special-purpose receptacle shall be connected to the reference grounding point.

517.20 Wet Locations.

(A) Receptacles and Fixed Equipment. All receptacles and fixed equipment within the area of the wet location shall have ground-fault circuit-interrupter protection for personnel if interruption of power under fault conditions can be tolerated, or be served by an isolated power system if such interruption cannot be tolerated.

Exception: Branch circuits supplying only listed, fixed, therapeutic and diagnostic equipment shall be permitted to be supplied from a normal grounded service, single- or 3-phase system, provided that

(a) Wiring for grounded and isolated circuits does not occupy the same raceway, and
(b) All conductive surfaces of the equipment are grounded.

(B) Isolated Power Systems. Where an isolated power system is utilized, the isolated power equipment shall be listed as isolated power equipment, and the isolated power system shall be designed and installed in accordance with 517.160.

> FPN: For requirements for installation of therapeutic pools and tubs, see Part VI of Article 680.

517.21 Ground-Fault Circuit-Interrupter Protection for Personnel. Ground-fault circuit-interrupter protection for personnel shall not be required for receptacles installed in those critical care areas where the toilet and basin are installed within the patient room.

III. Essential Electrical System

517.25 Scope. The essential electrical system for these facilities shall comprise a system capable of supplying a limited amount of lighting and power service, which is considered essential for life safety and orderly cessation of procedures during the time normal electrical service is interrupted for any reason. This includes clinics, medical and dental offices, outpatient facilities, nursing homes, limited care facilities, hospitals, and other health care facilities serving patients.

> FPN: For information on the need for an essential electrical system, see NFPA 99-2002, *Standard for Health Care Facilities.*

517.26 Application of Other Articles. The essential electrical system shall meet the requirements of Article 700, except as amended by Article 517.

517.30 Essential Electrical Systems for Hospitals.

(A) Applicability. The requirements of Part III, 517.30 through 517.35, shall apply to hospitals where an essential electrical system is required.

> FPN No. 1: For performance, maintenance, and testing requirements of essential electrical systems in hospitals, see NFPA 99-2002, *Standard for Health Care Facilities.* For installation of centrifugal fire pumps, see NFPA 20-2002, *Standard for the Installation of Stationary Fire Pumps for Fire Protection.*

> FPN No. 2: For additional information, see NFPA 99-2002, *Standard for Health Care Facilities.*

(B) General.

(1) Separate Systems. Essential electrical systems for hospitals shall be comprised of two separate systems capable of supplying a limited amount of lighting and power service, which is considered essential for life safety and effective hospital operation during the time the normal electrical service is interrupted for any reason. These two systems shall be the emergency system and the equipment system.

(2) Emergency Systems. The emergency system shall be limited to circuits essential to life safety and critical patient care. These are designated the life safety branch and the critical branch.

(3) Equipment System. The equipment system shall supply major electrical equipment necessary for patient care and basic hospital operation.

(4) Transfer Switches. The number of transfer switches to be used shall be based on reliability, design, and load considerations. Each branch of the emergency system and each equipment system shall have one or more transfer switches. One transfer switch shall be permitted to serve one or more branches or systems in a facility with a maximum demand on the essential electrical system of 150 kVA.

> FPN No. 1: See NFPA 99-2002, *Standard for Health Care Facilities*: 4.4.3.2, Transfer Switch Operation Type I; 4.4.2.1.4, Automatic Transfer Switch Features; and 4.4.2.1.6, Nonautomatic Transfer Device Features.
>
> FPN No. 2: See FPN Figure 517.30, No. 1.
>
> FPN No. 3: See FPN Figure 517.30, No. 2.

FPN Figure 517.30, No. 1 Hospital — Minimum Requirement for Transfer Switch Arrangement.

(5) Other Loads. Loads served by the generating equipment not specifically named in Article 517 shall be served by their own transfer switches such that the following conditions apply:

(1) These loads shall not be transferred if the transfer will overload the generating equipment.

(2) These loads shall be automatically shed upon generating equipment overloading.

(6) Contiguous Facilities. Hospital power sources and alternate power sources shall be permitted to serve the essential electrical systems of contiguous or same site facilities. [NFPA 99:13.3.4.3]

(C) Wiring Requirements.

(1) Separation from Other Circuits. The life safety branch and critical branch of the emergency system shall be kept entirely independent of all other wiring and equipment and shall not enter the same raceways, boxes, or cabinets with each other or other wiring.

FPN Figure 517.30, No. 2 Hospital — Minimum Requirement (150 kVA or less) for Transfer Switch Arrangement.

Wiring of the life safety branch and the critical branch shall be permitted to occupy the same raceways, boxes, or cabinets of other circuits not part of the branch where such wiring complies with one of the following:

(1) Is in transfer equipment enclosures

(2) Is in exit or emergency luminaires (lighting fixtures) supplied from two sources

(3) Is in a common junction box attached to exit or emergency luminaires (lighting fixtures) supplied from two sources

(4) Is for two or more emergency circuits supplied from the same branch

The wiring of the equipment system shall be permitted to occupy the same raceways, boxes, or cabinets of other circuits that are not part of the emergency system.

(2) Isolated Power Systems. Where isolated power systems are installed in any of the areas in 517.33(A)(1) and (A)(2), each system shall be supplied by an individual circuit serving no other load.

(3) Mechanical Protection of the Emergency System. The wiring of the emergency system in hospitals shall be mechanically protected. Where installed as branch circuits in patient care areas, the installation shall comply with the requirements of 517.13(A) and 517.13(B). The following wiring methods shall be permitted:

(1) Nonflexible metal raceways, Type MI cable, or Schedule 80 rigid nonmetallic conduit. Nonmetallic raceways shall not be used for branch circuits that supply patient care areas.

(2) Where encased in not less than 50 mm (2 in.) of concrete, Schedule 40 rigid nonmetallic conduit, flexible nonmetallic or jacketed metallic raceways, or jacketed metallic cable assemblies listed for installation in concrete. Nonmetallic raceways shall not be used for branch circuits that supply patient care areas.

(3) Listed flexible metal raceways and listed metal sheathed cable assemblies in any of the following:

   a. Where used in listed prefabricated medical headwalls

   b. In listed office furnishings

   c. Where fished into existing walls or ceilings, not otherwise accessible and not subject to physical damage

   d. Where necessary for flexible connection to equipment

(4) Flexible power cords of appliances or other utilization equipment connected to the emergency system.

(5) Secondary circuits of Class 2 or Class 3 communication or signaling systems

   FPN: See 517.13 for additional grounding requirements in patient care areas.

(D) Capacity of Systems. The essential electrical system shall have adequate capacity to meet the demand for the operation of all functions and equipment to be served by each system and branch.

Feeders shall be sized in accordance with Articles 215 and 220. The generator set(s) shall have sufficient capacity and proper rating to meet the demand produced by the load of the essential electrical system(s) at any given time.

Demand calculations for sizing of the generator set(s) shall be based on any of the following:

(1) Prudent demand factors and historical data

(2) Connected load

(3) Feeder calculation procedures described in Article 220

(4) Any combination of the above

The sizing requirements in 700.5 and 701.6 shall not apply to hospital generator set(s).

(E) Receptacle Identification. The cover plates for the electrical receptacles or the electrical receptacles themselves supplied from the emergency system shall have a distinctive color or marking so as to be readily identifiable. [NFPA 99:4.4.2.2.4.2(B)]

517.31 Emergency System. Those functions of patient care depending on lighting or appliances that are connected to the emergency system shall be divided into two mandatory branches: the life safety branch and the critical branch, described in 517.32 and 517.33.

The branches of the emergency system shall be installed and connected to the alternate power source so that all functions specified herein for the emergency system shall be automatically restored to operation within 10 seconds after interruption of the normal source. [NFPA 99:4.4.2.2.2.1, 4.4.3.1]

517.32 Life Safety Branch. No function other than those listed in 517.32(A) through 517.32(G) shall be connected to the life safety branch. The life safety branch of the emergency system shall supply power for the following lighting, receptacles, and equipment.

(A) Illumination of Means of Egress. Illumination of means of egress, such as lighting required for corridors, passageways, stairways, and landings at exit doors, and all necessary ways of approach to exits. Switching arrangements to transfer patient corridor lighting in hospitals from general illumination circuits to night illumination circuits shall be permitted, provided only one of two circuits can be selected and both circuits cannot be extinguished at the same time.

   FPN: See NFPA *101*-2003, *Life Safety Code*, Sections 7.8 and 7.9.

(B) Exit Signs. Exit signs and exit directional signs.

   FPN: See NFPA *101*-2003, *Life Safety Code*, Section 7.10.

(C) Alarm and Alerting Systems. Alarm and alerting systems including the following:

(1) Fire alarms

   FPN: See NFPA *101*-2003, *Life Safety Code*, Section 9.6 and 18.3.4.

(2) Alarms required for systems used for the piping of nonflammable medical gases

   FPN: See NFPA 99-2002, *Standard for Health Care Facilities*, 4.4.2.2.2.2(3).

(D) Communications Systems. Hospital communications systems, where used for issuing instructions during emergency conditions.

(E) Generator Set Location. Task illumination battery charger for emergency battery-powered lighting unit(s) and selected receptacles at the generator set location.

(F) Elevators. Elevator cab lighting, control, communications, and signal systems.

(G) Automatic Doors. Automatically operated doors used for building egress. [NFPA 99:4.4.2.2.2.2]

517.33 Critical Branch.

(A) Task Illumination and Selected Receptacles. The critical branch of the emergency system shall supply power for task illumination, fixed equipment, selected receptacles, and special power circuits serving the following areas and functions related to patient care:

(1) Critical care areas that utilize anesthetizing gases — task illumination, selected receptacles, and fixed equipment

(2) The isolated power systems in special environments

(3) Patient care areas — task illumination and selected receptacles in the following:

   a. Infant nurseries

   b. Medication preparation areas

   c. Pharmacy dispensing areas

   d. Selected acute nursing areas

   e. Psychiatric bed areas (omit receptacles)

   f. Ward treatment rooms

   g. Nurses' stations (unless adequately lighted by corridor luminaires)

(4) Additional specialized patient care task illumination and receptacles, where needed

(5) Nurse call systems

(6) Blood, bone, and tissue banks

(7) Telephone equipment rooms and closets

(8) Task illumination, selected receptacles, and selected power circuits for the following:

   a. General care beds (at least one duplex receptacle per patient bedroom)

   b. Angiographic labs

   c. Cardiac catheterization labs

   d. Coronary care units

   e. Hemodialysis rooms or areas

   f. Emergency room treatment areas (selected)

   g. Human physiology labs

   h. Intensive care units

   i. Postoperative recovery rooms (selected)

(9) Additional task illumination, receptacles, and selected power circuits needed for effective hospital operation. Single-phase fractional horsepower motors shall be permitted to be connected to the critical branch. [NFPA 99:4.4.2.2.2.3(9)]

(B) Subdivision of the Critical Branch. It shall be permitted to subdivide the critical branch into two or more branches.

> FPN: It is important to analyze the consequences of supplying an area with only critical care branch power when failure occurs between the area and the transfer switch. Some proportion of normal and critical power or critical power from separate transfer switches may be appropriate.

517.34 Equipment System Connection to Alternate Power Source. The equipment system shall be installed and connected to the alternate power source such that the equipment described in 517.34(A) is automatically restored to operation at appropriate time-lag intervals following the energizing of the emergency system. Its arrangement shall also provide for the subsequent connection of equipment described in 517.34(B). [NFPA 99:4.4.2.2.3.2]

Exception: For essential electrical systems under 150 kVA, deletion of the time-lag intervals feature for delayed automatic connection to the equipment system shall be permitted.

(A) Equipment for Delayed Automatic Connection. The following equipment shall be arranged for delayed automatic connection to the alternate power source:

(1) Central suction systems serving medical and surgical functions, including controls. Such suction systems shall be permitted on the critical branch.

(2) Sump pumps and other equipment required to operate for the safety of major apparatus, including associated control systems and alarms.

(3) Compressed air systems serving medical and surgical functions, including controls. Such air systems shall be permitted on the critical branch.

(4) Smoke control and stair pressurization systems, or both.

(5) Kitchen hood supply or exhaust systems, or both, if required to operate during a fire in or under the hood. [NFPA 99:4.4.2.2.3.4(5)]

(6) Supply, return, and exhaust ventilating systems for airborne infectious/isolation rooms, protective environment rooms, exhaust fans for laboratory fume hoods, nuclear medicine areas where radioactive material is used, ethylene oxide evacuation and anesthesia evacuation. Where delayed automatic connection is not appropriate, such ventilation systems shall be permitted to be placed on the critical branch. [NFPA 99:4.4.2.2.3.4(6)]

Exception: Sequential delayed automatic connection to the alternate power source to prevent overloading the generator shall be permitted where engineering studies indicate it is necessary.

(B) Equipment for Delayed Automatic or Manual Connection. The following equipment shall be arranged for either delayed automatic or manual connection to the alternate power source:

(1) Heating equipment to provide heating for operating, delivery, labor, recovery, intensive care, coronary care, nurseries, infection/isolation rooms, emergency treatment spaces, and general patient rooms and pressure maintenance (jockey or make-up) pump(s) for water-based fire protection systems.

Exception: eating of general patient rooms and infection/isolation rooms during disruption of the normal source shall not be required under any of the following conditions:

(1) The outside design temperature is higher than −6.7°C (20°F).

(2) The outside design temperature is lower than −6.7°C (20°F), and where a selected room(s) is provided for the needs of all confined patients, only such room(s) need be heated.

(3) The facility is served by a dual source of normal power.

FPN No. 1: The design temperature is based on the 97½ percent design value as shown in Chapter 24 of the ASHRAE *Handbook of Fundamentals* (1997).

FPN No. 2: For a description of a dual source of normal power, see 517.35(C), FPN.

(2) An elevator(s) selected to provide service to patient, surgical, obstetrical, and ground floors during interruption of normal power. In instances where interruption of normal power would result in other elevators stopping between floors, throw-over facilities shall be provided to allow the temporary operation of any elevator for the release of patients or other persons who may be confined between floors.

(3) Hyperbaric facilities.

(4) Hypobaric facilities.

(5) Automatically operated doors.

(6) Minimal electrically heated autoclaving equipment shall be permitted to be arranged for either automatic or manual connection to the alternate source.

(7) Controls for equipment listed in 517.34.

(8) Other selected equipment shall be permitted to be served by the equipment system. [NFPA 99:4.4.2.2.3.5(9)]

(C) AC Equipment for Nondelayed Automatic Connection. Generator accessories, including but not limited to, the transfer fuel pump, electrically operated louvers, and other generator accessories essential for generator operation, shall be arranged for automatic connection to the alternate power source. [NFPA 99:4.4.2.2.3.3]

517.35 Sources of Power.

(A) Two Independent Sources of Power. Essential electrical systems shall have a minimum of two independent sources of power: a normal source generally supplying the entire electrical system and one or more alternate sources for use when the normal source is interrupted. [NFPA 99:4.4.1.1.4]

(B) Alternate Source of Power. The alternate source of power shall be one of the following:

(1) Generator(s) driven by some form of prime mover(s) and located on the premises

(2) Another generating unit(s) where the normal source consists of a generating unit(s) located on the premises

(3) An external utility service when the normal source consists of a generating unit(s) located on the premises

(4) A battery system located on the premises [NFPA 99:4.4.1.2]

(C) Location of Essential Electrical System Components. Careful consideration shall be given to the location of the spaces housing the components of the essential electrical system to minimize interruptions caused by natural forces common to the area (e.g., storms, floods, earthquakes, or hazards created by adjoining structures or activities). Consideration shall also be given to the possible interruption of normal electrical services resulting from similar causes as well as possible disruption of normal electrical service due to internal wiring and equipment failures.

FPN: Facilities in which the normal source of power is supplied by two or more separate central station-fed services experience greater than normal electrical service reliability than those with only a single feed. Such a dual source of normal power consists of two or more electrical services fed from separate generator sets or a utility distribution network that has multiple power input sources and is arranged to provide mechanical and electrical separation so that a fault between the facility and the generating sources is not likely to cause an interruption of more than one of the facility service feeders.

517.40 Essential Electrical Systems for Nursing Homes and Limited Care Facilities.

(A) Applicability. The requirements of Part III, 517.40(C) through 517.44, shall apply to nursing homes and limited care facilities.

Exception: The requirements of Part III, 517.40(C) through 517.44, shall not apply to freestanding buildings used as nursing homes and limited care facilities, provided that the following apply:

    (a) Admitting and discharge policies are maintained that preclude the provision of care for any patient or resident who may need to be sustained by electrical life-support equipment.

    (b) No surgical treatment requiring general anesthesia is offered.

    (c) An automatic battery-operated system(s) or equipment is provided that shall be effective for at least 1½ hours and is otherwise in accordance with 700.12 and that shall be capable of supplying lighting for exit lights, exit corridors, stairways, nursing stations, medical preparation areas, boiler rooms, and communications areas. This system shall also supply power to operate all alarm systems. [NFPA 99:17.3.4.1.2(3), 18.3.4.1.2(3)]

FPN: See NFPA *101*-2003, *Life Safety Code.*

(B) Inpatient Hospital Care Facilities. Nursing homes and limited care facilities that provide inpatient hospital care shall comply with the requirements of Part III, 517.30 through 517.35.

(C) Facilities Contiguous or Located on the Same Site with Hospitals. Nursing homes and limited care facilities that are contiguous or located on the same site with a hospital shall be permitted to have their essential electrical systems supplied by that of the hospital.

FPN: For performance, maintenance, and testing requirements of essential electrical systems in nursing homes and limited care facilities, see NFPA 99-2002, *Standard for Health Care Facilities.*

517.41 Essential Electrical Systems.

(A) General. Essential electrical systems for nursing homes and limited care facilities shall be comprised of two separate branches capable of supplying a limited amount of lighting and power service, which is considered essential for the protection of life safety and effective operation of the institution during the time normal electrical service is interrupted for any reason. These two separate branches shall be the life safety branch and the critical branch. [NFPA 99:Annex A, 4.5.2.2.1]

(B) Transfer Switches. The number of transfer switches to be used shall be based on reliability, design, and load considerations. Each branch of the essential electrical system shall be served by one or more transfer switches. One transfer switch shall be permitted to serve one or more branches or systems in a facility with a maximum demand on the essential electrical system of 150 kVA. [NFPA 99:4.5.2.2.1]

> FPN No. 1: See NFPA 99-2002, *Standard for Health Care Facilities*, 4.5.3.2, Transfer Switch Operation Type II; 4.4.2.1.4, Automatic Transfer Switch Features; and 4.4.2.1.6, Nonautomatic Transfer Device Features.
>
> FPN No. 2: See FPN Figure 517.41, No. 1.
>
> FPN No. 3: See FPN Figure 517.41, No. 2.

FPN Figure 517.41, No. 1 Nursing Home and Limited Health Care Facilities — Minimum Requirement for Transfer Switch Arrangement.

(C) Capacity of System. The essential electrical system shall have adequate capacity to meet the demand for the operation of all functions and equipment to be served by each branch at one time.

(D) Separation from Other Circuits. The life safety branch shall be kept entirely independent of all other wiring and equipment and shall not enter the same raceways, boxes, or cabinets with other wiring except as follows:

(1) In transfer switches

FPN Figure 517.41, No. 2 Nursing Home and Limited Health Care Facilities — Minimum Requirement (150 kVA or less) for Transfer Switch Arrangement.

(2) In exit or emergency luminaires (lighting fixtures) supplied from two sources

(3) In a common junction box attached to exit or emergency luminaires (lighting fixtures) supplied from two sources

The wiring of the critical branch shall be permitted to occupy the same raceways, boxes, or cabinets of other circuits that are not part of the life safety branch.

(E) Receptacle Identification. The cover plates for the electrical receptacles or the electrical receptacles themselves supplied from the emergency system shall have a distinctive color or marking so as to be readily identifiable. [NFPA 99: 4.5.2.2.4.2]

517.42 Automatic Connection to Life Safety Branch.
The life safety branch shall be installed and connected to the alternate source of power so that all functions specified herein shall be automatically restored to operation within 10 seconds after the interruption of the normal source. No functions other than those listed in 517.42(A) through 517.42(G) shall be connected to the life safety branch. The life safety branch shall supply power for the following lighting, receptacles, and equipment.

> FPN: The life safety branch is called the emergency system in NFPA 99-2002, *Standard for Health Care Facilities*.

(A) Illumination of Means of Egress. Illumination of means of egress as is necessary for corridors, passageways, stairways, landings, and exit doors and all ways of approach to exits. Switching arrangement to transfer patient corridor lighting from general illumination circuits shall be permitted, providing only one of two circuits can be selected and both circuits cannot be extinguished at the same time.

FPN: See NFPA *101*-2003, *Life Safety Code*, Sections 7.8 and 7.9.

(B) Exit Signs. Exit signs and exit directional signs.

FPN: See NFPA *101*-2003, *Life Safety Code*, Section 7.10.

(C) Alarm and Alerting Systems. Alarm and alerting systems, including the following:

(1) Fire alarms

FPN: See NFPA *101*-2003, *Life Safety Code*, Sections 9.6 and 18.3.4.

(2) Alarms required for systems used for the piping of nonflammable medical gases

FPN: See NFPA 99-2002, *Standard for Health Care Facilities*, 4.4.2.2.2.2(3).

(D) Communications Systems. Communications systems, where used for issuing instructions during emergency conditions.

(E) Dining and Recreation Areas. Sufficient lighting in dining and recreation areas to provide illumination to exit ways.

(F) Generator Set Location. Task illumination and selected receptacles in the generator set location.

(G) Elevators. Elevator cab lighting, control, communications, and signal systems. [NFPA 99:4.4.2.2.2.2(6), 4.5.2.2.2(7)]

517.43 Connection to Critical Branch. The critical branch shall be installed and connected to the alternate power source so that the equipment listed in 517.43(A) shall be automatically restored to operation at appropriate time-lag intervals following the restoration of the life safety branch to operation. Its arrangement shall also provide for the additional connection of equipment listed in 517.43(B) by either delayed automatic or manual operation.

Exception: For essential electrical systems under 150 kVA, deletion of the time-lag intervals feature for delayed automatic connection to the equipment system shall be permitted.

(A) Delayed Automatic Connection. The following equipment shall be connected to the critical branch and shall be arranged for delayed automatic connection to the alternate power source:

(1) Patient care areas — task illumination and selected receptacles in the following:

   a. Medication preparation areas

   b. Pharmacy dispensing areas

   c. Nurses' stations (unless adequately lighted by corridor luminaires)

(2) Sump pumps and other equipment required to operate for the safety of major apparatus and associated control systems and alarms

(3) Smoke control and stair pressurization systems

(4) Kitchen hood supply and/or exhaust systems, if required to operate during a fire in or under the hood

(5) Supply, return, and exhaust ventilating systems for airborne infectious isolation rooms

(B) Delayed Automatic or Manual Connection. The following equipment shall be connected to the critical branch and shall be arranged for either delayed automatic or manual connection to the alternate power source.

(1) Heating equipment to provide heating for patient rooms.

Exception: Heating of general patient rooms during disruption of the normal source shall not be required under any of the following conditions:

   (1) The outside design temperature is higher than −6.7°C (20°F).

   (2) The outside design temperature is lower than −6.7°C (20°F) and where a selected room(s) is provided for the needs of all confined patients, only such room(s) need be heated.

   (3) The facility is served by a dual source of normal power as described in 517.44(C), FPN.

> FPN: The outside design temperature is based on the 97½ percent design values as shown in Chapter 24 of the ASHRAE *Handbook of Fundamentals* (1997).

(2) Elevator service — in instances where disruption of power would result in elevators stopping between floors, throw-over facilities shall be provided to allow the temporary operation of any elevator for the release of passengers. For elevator cab lighting, control, and signal system requirements, see 517.42(G).

(3) Additional illumination, receptacles, and equipment shall be permitted to be connected only to the critical branch. [NFPA 99:4.5.2.2.3.3(C)]

517.44 Sources of Power.

(A) Two Independent Sources of Power. Essential electrical systems shall have a minimum of two independent sources of power: a normal source generally supplying the entire electrical system and one or more alternate sources for use when the normal source is interrupted. [NFPA 99:4.4.1.1.4]

(B) Alternate Source of Power. The alternate source of power shall be a generator(s) driven by some form of prime mover(s) and located on the premises.

Exception No. 1: Where the normal source consists of generating units on the premises, the alternate source shall be either another generator set or an external utility service.

Exception No. 2: Nursing homes or limited care facilities meeting the requirements of 517.40(A), Exception, shall be permitted to use a battery system or self-contained battery integral with the equipment. [NFPA 99:17.3.4.1.3, 18.3.4.1.1]

(C) Location of Essential Electrical System Components. Careful consideration shall be given to the location of the spaces housing the components of the essential electrical system to minimize interruptions caused by natural forces common to the area (e.g., storms, floods, earthquakes, or hazards created by adjoining structures or activities). Consideration shall also be given to the possible interruption of normal electrical services resulting from similar causes as well as possible disruption of normal electrical service due to internal wiring and equipment failures.

FPN: Facilities in which the normal source of power is supplied by two or more separate central station-fed services experience greater than normal electrical service reliability than those with only a single feed. Such a dual source of normal power consists of two or more electrical services fed from separate generator sets or a utility distribution network that has multiple power input sources and is arranged to provide mechanical and electrical separation so that a fault between the facility and the generating sources will not likely cause an interruption of more than one of the facility service feeders.

517.45 Essential Electrical Systems for Other Health Care Facilities.

(A) Essential Electrical Distribution. The essential electrical distribution system shall be a battery or generator system.

FPN: See NFPA 99–2002, *Standard for Health Care Facilities.*

(B) Electrical Life Support Equipment. Where electrical life support equipment is required, the essential electrical distribution system shall be as described in 517.30 through 517.35. [NFPA 99:14.3.4.2.1]

(C) Critical Care Areas. Where critical care areas are present, the essential electrical distribution system shall be as described in 517.30 through 517.35. [NFPA 99:14.3.4.2.2]

(D) Power Systems. Battery systems shall be installed in accordance with the requirements of Article 700, and generator systems shall be as described in 517.30 through 517.35.

IV. Inhalation Anesthetizing Locations

FPN: For further information regarding safeguards for anesthetizing locations, see NFPA 99-2002, *Standard for Health Care Facilities.*

517.60 Anesthetizing Location Classification.

FPN: If either of the anesthetizing locations in 517.60(A) or 517.60(B) is designated a wet location, refer to 517.20.

(A) Hazardous (Classified) Location.

(1) Use Location. In a location where flammable anesthetics are employed, the entire area shall be considered to be a Class I, Division 1 location that extends upward to a level 1.52 m (5 ft) above the floor. The remaining volume up to the structural ceiling is considered to be above a hazardous (classified) location. [NFPA 99:Annex E, E.1, and E.2]

(2) Storage Location. Any room or location in which flammable anesthetics or volatile flammable disinfecting agents are stored shall be considered to be a Class I, Division 1 location from floor to ceiling.

(B) Other-Than-Hazardous (Classified) Location. Any inhalation anesthetizing location designated for the exclusive use of nonflammable anesthetizing agents shall be considered to be an other-than-hazardous (classified) location.

517.61 Wiring and Equipment.

(A) Within Hazardous (Classified) Anesthetizing Locations.

(1) Isolation. Except as permitted in 517.160, each power circuit within, or partially within, a flammable anesthetizing location as referred to in 517.60 shall be isolated from any distribution system by the use of an isolated power system. [NFPA 99:Annex E, E.6.6.2]

(2) Design and Installation. Where an isolated power system is utilized, the isolated power equipment shall be listed as isolated power equipment, and the isolated power system shall be designed and installed in accordance with 517.160.

(3) Equipment Operating at More Than 10 Volts. In hazardous (classified) locations referred to in 517.60, all fixed wiring and equipment and all portable equipment, including lamps and other utilization equipment, operating at more than 10 volts between conductors shall comply with the requirements of 501.1 through 501.25, and 501.100 through 501.150, and 501.30(A) and 501.30(B) for Class I, Division 1 locations. All such equipment shall be specifically approved for the hazardous atmospheres involved. [NFPA 99:Annex E, E.2.1, E.4.5, E.4.6, and E.4.7]

(4) Extent of Location. Where a box, fitting, or enclosure is partially, but not entirely, within a hazardous (classified) location(s), the hazardous (classified) location(s) shall be considered to be extended to include the entire box, fitting, or enclosure.

(5) Receptacles and Attachment Plugs. Receptacles and attachment plugs in a hazardous (classified) location(s) shall be listed for use in Class I, Group C hazardous (classified) locations and shall have provision for the connection of a grounding conductor.

(6) Flexible Cord Type. Flexible cords used in hazardous (classified) locations for connection to portable utilization equipment, including lamps operating at more than 8 volts between conductors, shall be of a type approved for extra-hard usage in accordance with Table 400.4 and shall include an additional conductor for grounding.

(7) Flexible Cord Storage. A storage device for the flexible cord shall be provided and shall not subject the cord to bending at a radius of less than 75 mm (3 in.).

(B) Above Hazardous (Classified) Anesthetizing Locations.

(1) Wiring Methods. Wiring above a hazardous (classified) location referred to in 517.60 shall be installed in rigid metal conduit, electrical metallic tubing, intermediate metal conduit, Type MI cable, or Type MC cable that employs a continuous, gas/vaportight metal sheath.

(2) Equipment Enclosure. Installed equipment that may produce arcs, sparks, or particles of hot metal, such as lamps and lampholders for fixed lighting, cutouts, switches, generators, motors, or other equipment having make-and-break or sliding contacts, shall be of the totally enclosed type or be constructed so as to prevent escape of sparks or hot metal particles.

Exception: Wall-mounted receptacles installed above the hazardous (classified) location in flammable anesthetizing locations shall not be required to be totally enclosed or have openings guarded or screened to prevent dispersion of particles.

(3) Luminaires (Lighting Fixtures). Surgical and other luminaires (lighting fixtures) shall conform to 501.130(B).

Exception No. 1: The surface temperature limitations set forth in 501.130(B)(1) shall not apply.

Exception No. 2: Integral or pendant switches that are located above and cannot be lowered into the hazardous (classified) location(s) shall not be required to be explosionproof.

(4) Seals. Approved seals shall be provided in conformance with 501.15, and 501.15(A)(4) shall apply to horizontal as well as to vertical boundaries of the defined hazardous (classified) locations.

(5) Receptacles and Attachment Plugs. Receptacles and attachment plugs located above hazardous (classified) anesthetizing locations shall be listed for hospital use for services of prescribed voltage, frequency, rating, and number of conductors with provision for the connection of the grounding conductor. This requirement shall apply to attachment plugs and receptacles of the 2-pole, 3-wire grounding type for single-phase, 120-volt, nominal, ac service.

(6) 250-Volt Receptacles and Attachment Plugs Rated 50 and 60 Amperes. Receptacles and attachment plugs rated 250 volts, for connection of 50-ampere and 60-ampere ac medical equipment for use above hazardous (classified) locations, shall be arranged so that the 60-ampere receptacle will accept either the 50-ampere or the 60-ampere plug. Fifty-

ampere receptacles shall be designed so as not to accept the 60-ampere attachment plug. The attachment plugs shall be of the 2-pole, 3-wire design with a third contact connecting to the insulated (green or green with yellow stripe) equipment grounding conductor of the electrical system.

(C) Other-Than-Hazardous (Classified) Anesthetizing Locations.

(1) Wiring Methods. Wiring serving other-than-hazardous (classified) locations, as defined in 517.60, shall be installed in a metal raceway system or cable assembly. The metal raceway system or cable armor or sheath assembly shall qualify as an equipment grounding return path in accordance with 250.118. Type MC and Type MI cable shall have an outer metal armor or sheath that is identified as an acceptable grounding return path.

Exception: Pendant receptacle constructions that employ at least Type SJO or equivalent flexible cords suspended not less than 1.8 m (6 ft) from the floor shall not be required to be installed in a metal raceway or cable assembly.

(2) Receptacles and Attachment Plugs. Receptacles and attachment plugs installed and used in other-than-hazardous (classified) locations shall be listed for hospital use for services of prescribed voltage, frequency, rating, and number of conductors with provision for connection of the grounding conductor. This requirement shall apply to 2-pole, 3-wire grounding type for single-phase, 120-, 208-, or 240-volt, nominal, ac service.

(3) 250-Volt Receptacles and Attachment Plugs Rated 50 Amperes and 60 Amperes. Receptacles and attachment plugs rated 250 volts, for connection of 50-ampere and 60-ampere ac medical equipment for use in other-than-hazardous (classified) locations, shall be arranged so that the 60-ampere receptacle will accept either the 50-ampere or the 60-ampere plug. Fifty-ampere receptacles shall be designed so as not to accept the 60-ampere attachment plug. The attachment plugs shall be of the 2-pole, 3-wire design with a third contact connecting to the insulated (green or green with yellow stripe) equipment grounding conductor of the electrical system.

517.62 Grounding. In any anesthetizing area, all metal raceways and metal-sheathed cables and all non–current-carrying conductive portions of fixed electric equipment shall be grounded. Grounding in Class I locations shall comply with 501.30.

Exception: Equipment operating at not more than 10 volts between conductors shall not be required to be grounded.

517.63 Grounded Power Systems in Anesthetizing Locations.

(A) Battery-Powered Emergency Lighting Units. One or more battery-powered emergency lighting units shall be provided in accordance with 700.12(F).

(B) Branch-Circuit Wiring. Branch circuits supplying only listed, fixed, therapeutic and diagnostic equipment, permanently installed above the hazardous (classified) location and in other-than-hazardous (classified) locations, shall be permitted to be supplied from a normal grounded service, single- or three-phase system, provided the following apply:

(1) Wiring for grounded and isolated circuits does not occupy the same raceway or cable.

(2) All conductive surfaces of the equipment are grounded.

(3) Equipment (except enclosed X-ray tubes and the leads to the tubes) are located at least 2.5 m (8 ft) above the floor or outside the anesthetizing location.

(4) Switches for the grounded branch circuit are located outside the hazardous (classified) location.

Exception: Sections 517.63(B)(3) and (B)(4) shall not apply in other-than-hazardous (classified) locations.

(C) Fixed Lighting Branch Circuits. Branch circuits supplying only fixed lighting shall be permitted to be supplied by a normal grounded service, provided the following apply:

(1) Such luminaires (fixtures) are located at least 2.5 m (8 ft) above the floor.

(2) All conductive surfaces of luminaires (fixtures) are grounded.

(3) Wiring for circuits supplying power to luminaires (fixtures) does not occupy the same raceway or cable for circuits supplying isolated power.

(4) Switches are wall-mounted and located above hazardous (classified) locations.

Exception: Sections 517.63(C)(1) and (C)(4) shall not apply in other-than-hazardous (classified) locations.

(D) Remote-Control Stations. Wall-mounted remote-control stations for remote-control switches operating at 24 volts or less shall be permitted to be installed in any anesthetizing location.

(E) Location of Isolated Power Systems. Where an isolated power system is utilized, the isolated power equipment shall be listed as isolated power equipment. Isolated power equipment and its grounded primary feeder shall be permitted to be located in an anesthetizing location, provided it is installed above a hazardous (classified) location or in an other-than-hazardous (classified) location.

(F) Circuits in Anesthetizing Locations. Except as permitted above, each power circuit within, or partially within, a flammable anesthetizing location as referred to in 517.60 shall be isolated from any distribution system supplying other-than-anesthetizing locations.

517.64 Low-Voltage Equipment and Instruments.

(A) Equipment Requirements. Low-voltage equipment that is frequently in contact with the bodies of persons or has exposed current-carrying elements shall comply with one of the following:

(1) Operate on an electrical potential of 10 volts or less

(2) Approved as intrinsically safe or double-insulated equipment

(3) Be moisture resistant

(B) Power Supplies. Power shall be supplied to low-voltage equipment from one of the following:

(1) An individual portable isolating transformer (autotransformers shall not be used) connected to an isolated power circuit receptacle by means of an appropriate cord and attachment plug

(2) A common low-voltage isolating transformer installed in an other-than-hazardous (classified) location

(3) Individual dry-cell batteries

(4) Common batteries made up of storage cells located in an other-than-hazardous (classified) location

(C) Isolated Circuits. Isolating-type transformers for supplying low-voltage circuits shall have both of the following:

(1) Approved means for insulating the secondary circuit from the primary circuit

(2) The core and case grounded

(D) Controls. Resistance or impedance devices shall be permitted to control low-voltage equipment but shall not be used to limit the maximum available voltage to the equipment.

(E) Battery-Powered Appliances. Battery-powered appliances shall not be capable of being charged while in operation unless their charging circuitry incorporates an integral isolating-type transformer.

(F) Receptacles or Attachment Plugs. Any receptacle or attachment plug used on low-voltage circuits shall be of a type that does not permit interchangeable connection with circuits of higher voltage.

> FPN: Any interruption of the circuit, even circuits as low as 10 volts, either by any switch or loose or defective connections anywhere in the circuit, may produce a spark that is sufficient to ignite flammable anesthetic agents.

V. X-Ray Installations

Nothing in this part shall be construed as specifying safeguards against the useful beam or stray X-ray radiation.

> FPN No. 1: Radiation safety and performance requirements of several classes of X-ray equipment are regulated under Public Law 90-602 and are enforced by the Department of Health and Human Services.

> FPN No. 2: In addition, information on radiation protection by the National Council on Radiation Protection and Measurements is published as *Reports of the National Council on Radiation Protection and Measurement*. These reports are obtainable from NCRP Publications, P.O. Box 30175, Washington, DC 20014.

517.71 Connection to Supply Circuit.

(A) Fixed and Stationary Equipment. Fixed and stationary X-ray equipment shall be connected to the power supply by means of a wiring method that meets the general requirements of this *Code*.

Exception: Equipment properly supplied by a branch circuit rated at not over 30 amperes shall be permitted to be supplied through a suitable attachment plug and hard-service cable or cord.

(B) Portable, Mobile, and Transportable Equipment. Individual branch circuits shall not be required for portable, mobile, and transportable medical X-ray equipment requiring a capacity of not over 60 amperes.

(C) Over 600-Volt Supply. Circuits and equipment operated on a supply circuit of over 600 volts shall comply with Article 490.

517.72 Disconnecting Means.

(A) Capacity. A disconnecting means of adequate capacity for at least 50 percent of the input required for the momentary rating or 100 percent of the input required for the long-time rating of the X-ray equipment, whichever is greater, shall be provided in the supply circuit.

(B) Location. The disconnecting means shall be operable from a location readily accessible from the X-ray control.

(C) Portable Equipment. For equipment connected to a 120-volt branch circuit of 30 amperes or less, a grounding-type attachment plug and receptacle of proper rating shall be permitted to serve as a disconnecting means.

517.73 Rating of Supply Conductors and Overcurrent Protection.

(A) Diagnostic Equipment.

(1) Branch Circuits. The ampacity of supply branch-circuit conductors and the current rating of overcurrent protective devices shall not be less than 50 percent of the momentary rating or 100 percent of the long-time rating, whichever is greater.

(2) Feeders. The ampacity of supply feeders and the current rating of overcurrent protective devices supplying two or more branch circuits supplying X-ray units shall not be less than 50 percent of the momentary demand rating of the largest unit plus 25 percent of the momentary demand rating of the next largest unit plus 10 percent of the momentary demand rating of each additional unit. Where simultaneous biplane examinations are undertaken with the X-ray units, the supply conductors and overcurrent protective devices shall be 100 percent of the momentary demand rating of each X-ray unit.

FPN: The minimum conductor size for branch and feeder circuits is also governed by voltage regulation requirements. For a specific installation, the manufacturer usually specifies minimum distribution transformer and conductor sizes, rating of disconnecting means, and overcurrent protection.

(B) Therapeutic Equipment. The ampacity of conductors and rating of overcurrent protective devices shall not be less than 100 percent of the current rating of medical X-ray therapy equipment.

FPN: The ampacity of the branch-circuit conductors and the ratings of disconnecting means and overcurrent protection for X-ray equipment are usually designated by the manufacturer for the specific installation.

517.74 Control Circuit Conductors.

(A) Number of Conductors in Raceway. The number of control circuit conductors installed in a raceway shall be determined in accordance with 300.17.

(B) Minimum Size of Conductors. Size 18 AWG or 16 AWG fixture wires as specified in 725.27 and flexible cords shall be permitted for the control and operating circuits of X-ray and auxiliary equipment where protected by not larger than 20-ampere overcurrent devices.

517.75 Equipment Installations. All equipment for new X-ray installations and all used or reconditioned X-ray equipment moved to and reinstalled at a new location shall be of an approved type.

517.76 Transformers and Capacitors. Transformers and capacitors that are part of X-ray equipment shall not be required to comply with Articles 450 and 460.

Capacitors shall be mounted within enclosures of insulating material or grounded metal.

517.77 Installation of High-Tension X-Ray Cables. Cables with grounded shields connecting X-ray tubes and image intensifiers shall be permitted to be installed in cable trays or cable troughs along with X-ray equipment control and power supply conductors without the need for barriers to separate the wiring.

517.78 Guarding and Grounding.

(A) High-Voltage Parts. All high-voltage parts, including X-ray tubes, shall be mounted within grounded enclosures. Air, oil, gas, or other suitable insulating media shall be used to insulate the high-voltage from the grounded enclosure. The connection from the high-voltage equipment to X-ray tubes and other high-voltage components shall be made with high-voltage shielded cables.

(B) Low-Voltage Cables. Low-voltage cables connecting to oil-filled units that are not completely sealed, such as transformers, condensers, oil coolers, and high-voltage switches, shall have insulation of the oil-resistant type.

(C) Noncurrent–Carrying Metal Parts. Noncurrent-carrying metal parts of X-ray and associated equipment (controls, tables, X-ray tube supports, transformer tanks, shielded cables, X-ray tube heads, etc.) shall be grounded in the manner specified in Article 250, as modified by 517.13(A) and 517.13(B).

VI. Communications, Signaling Systems, Data Systems, Fire Alarm Systems, and Systems Less Than 120 Volts, Nominal

517.80 Patient Care Areas. Equivalent insulation and isolation to that required for the electrical distribution systems in patient care areas shall be provided for communications, signaling systems, data system circuits, fire alarm systems, and systems less than 120 volts, nominal.

> FPN: An acceptable alternate means of providing isolation for patient/nurse call systems is by the use of nonelectrified signaling, communications, or control devices held by the patient or within reach of the patient.

517.81 Other-Than-Patient-Care Areas. In other-than-patient-care areas, installations shall be in accordance with the appropriate provisions of Articles 640, 725, 760, and 800.

517.82 Signal Transmission Between Appliances.

(A) General. Permanently installed signal cabling from an appliance in a patient location to remote appliances shall employ a signal transmission system that prevents hazardous grounding interconnection of the appliances.

> FPN: See 517.13(A) for additional grounding requirements in patient care areas.

(B) Common Signal Grounding Wire. Common signal grounding wires (i.e., the chassis ground for single-ended transmission) shall be permitted to be used between appliances all located within the patient vicinity, provided the appliances are served from the same reference grounding point.

VII. Isolated Power Systems

517.160 Isolated Power Systems.

(A) Installations.

(1) Isolated Power Circuits. Each isolated power circuit shall be controlled by a switch that has a disconnecting pole in each isolated circuit conductor to simultaneously disconnect all power. Such isolation shall be accomplished by means of one or more transformers having no electrical connection between primary and secondary windings, by

means of motor generator sets, or by means of suitably isolated batteries.

(2) Circuit Characteristics. Circuits supplying primaries of isolating transformers shall operate at not more than 600 volts between conductors and shall be provided with proper over-current protection. The secondary voltage of such transformers shall not exceed 600 volts between conductors of each circuit. All circuits supplied from such secondaries shall be ungrounded and shall have an approved overcurrent device of proper ratings in each conductor. Circuits supplied directly from batteries or from motor generator sets shall be ungrounded and shall be protected against overcurrent in the same manner as transformer-fed secondary circuits. If an electrostatic shield is present, it shall be connected to the reference grounding point. [NFPA 99:4.3.2.6.1]

(3) Equipment Location. The isolating transformers, motor generator sets, batteries and battery chargers, and associated primary or secondary overcurrent devices shall not be installed in hazardous (classified) locations. The isolated secondary circuit wiring extending into a hazardous anesthetizing location shall be installed in accordance with 501.10.

(4) Isolation Transformers. An isolation transformer shall not serve more than one operating room except as covered in (A)(4)(a) and (A)(4)(b).

For purposes of this section, anesthetic induction rooms are considered part of the operating room or rooms served by the induction rooms.

   (a) Induction Rooms. Where an induction room serves more than one operating room, the isolated circuits of the induction room shall be permitted to be supplied from the isolation transformer of any one of the operating rooms served by that induction room.

   (b) Higher Voltages. Isolation transformers shall be permitted to serve single receptacles in several patient areas where the following apply:

(1) The receptacles are reserved for supplying power to equipment requiring 150 volts or higher, such as portable X-ray units.
(2) The receptacles and mating plugs are not interchangeable with the receptacles on the local isolated power system. [NFPA 99:13.4.1.2.6.6]

(5) Conductor Identification. The isolated circuit conductors shall be identified as follows:

(1) Isolated Conductor No. 1 — Orange
(2) Isolated Conductor No. 2 — Brown

For 3-phase systems, the third conductor shall be identified as yellow. Where isolated circuit conductors supply 125-volt, single-phase, 15- and 20-ampere receptacles, the orange conductor(s) shall be connected to the terminal(s) on the receptacles that are identified in accordance with 200.10(B) for connection to the grounded circuit conductor.

(6) Wire-Pulling Compounds. Wire-pulling compounds that increase the dielectric constant shall not be used on the secondary conductors of the isolated power supply.

> FPN No. 1: It is desirable to limit the size of the isolation transformer to 10 kVA or less and to use conductor insulation with low leakage to meet impedance requirements.

> FPN No. 2: Minimizing the length of branch-circuit conductors and using conductor insulations with a dielectric constant less than 3.5 and insulation resistance constant greater than 6100 megohm-meters (20,000 megohm-feet) at 16°C (60°F) reduces leakage from line to ground, reducing the hazard current.

(B) Line Isolation Monitor.

(1) Characteristics. In addition to the usual control and overcurrent protective devices, each isolated power system shall be provided with a continually operating line isolation monitor that indicates total hazard current. The monitor shall be designed such that a green signal lamp, conspicuously visible to persons in each area served by the isolated power system, remains lighted when the system is adequately isolated from ground. An adjacent red signal lamp and an audible warning signal (remote if desired) shall be energized when the total hazard current (consisting of possible resistive and capacitive leakage currents) from either isolated conductor to ground reaches a threshold value of 5 mA under nominal line voltage conditions. The line monitor shall not alarm for a fault hazard of less than 3.7 mA or for a total hazard current of less than 5 mA.

Exception: A system shall be permitted to be designed to operate at a lower threshold value of total hazard current. A line isolation monitor for such a system shall be permitted to be approved with the provision that the fault hazard current shall be permitted to be reduced but not to less than 35 percent of the corresponding threshold value of the total hazard current, and the monitor hazard current is to be correspondingly reduced to not more than 50 percent of the alarm threshold value of the total hazard current.

(2) Impedance. The line isolation monitor shall be designed to have sufficient internal impedance such that, when properly connected to the isolated system, the maximum internal current that can flow through the line isolation monitor, when any point of the isolated system is grounded, shall be 1 mA.

Exception: The line isolation monitor shall be permitted to be of the low-impedance type such that the current through the line isolation monitor, when any point of the isolated system is grounded, will not exceed twice the alarm threshold value for a period not exceeding 5 milliseconds.

> FPN: Reduction of the monitor hazard current, provided this reduction results in an increased "not alarm" threshold value for the fault hazard current, will increase circuit capacity.

(3) Ammeter. An ammeter calibrated in the total hazard current of the system (contribution of the fault hazard current plus monitor hazard current) shall be mounted in a plainly visible place on the line isolation monitor with the "alarm on" zone at approximately the center of the scale.

Exception: The line isolation monitor shall be permitted to be a composite unit, with a sensing section cabled to a separate display panel section on which the alarm or test functions are located.

> FPN: It is desirable to locate the ammeter so that it is conspicuously visible to persons in the anesthetizing location.

ARTICLE 518
Assembly Occupancies

518.1 Scope. Except for the assembly occupancies explicitly covered by 520.1, this article covers all buildings or portions of buildings or structures designed or intended for the gathering together of 100 or more persons for such purposes as deliberation, worship, entertainment, eating, drinking, amusement, awaiting transportation, or similar purposes.

518.2 General Classification.

(A) Examples. Assembly occupancies shall include, but not be limited to, the following:

Armories	Exhibition halls
Assembly halls	Gymnasiums
Auditoriums	Mortuary chapels
Bowling lanes	Multipurpose rooms
Club rooms	Museums
Conference rooms	Places of awaiting transportation
Courtrooms	Places of religious worship
Dance halls	Pool rooms
Dining and drinking facilities	Restaurants
	Skating rinks

(B) Multiple Occupancies. Where an assembly occupancy forms a portion of a building containing other occupancies, Article 518 applies only to that portion of the building considered an assembly occupancy. Occupancy of any room or space for assembly purposes by less than 100 persons in a building of other occupancy, and incidental to such other occupancy, shall be classified as part of the other occupancy and subject to the provisions applicable thereto.

(C) Theatrical Areas. Where any such building structure, or portion thereof, contains a projection booth or stage platform or area for the presentation of theatrical or musical productions, either fixed or portable, the wiring for that area, including associated audience seating areas, and all equipment that is used in the referenced area, and portable equipment and wiring for use in the production that will not be connected to permanently installed wiring, shall comply with Article 520.

FPN: For methods of determining population capacity, see local building code or, in its absence, NFPA *101*-2003, *Life Safety Code.*

518.3 Other Articles.

(A) Hazardous (Classified) Areas. Electrical installations in hazardous (classified) areas located in assembly occupancies shall comply with Article 500.

(B) Temporary Wiring. In exhibition halls used for display booths, as in trade shows, the temporary wiring shall be installed in accordance with Article 590. Flexible cables and cords approved for hard or extra-hard usage shall be permitted to be laid on floors where protected from contact by the general public. The ground-fault circuit-interrupter requirements of 590.6 shall not apply.

Exception: Where conditions of supervision and maintenance ensure that only qualified persons will service the installation, flexible cords or cables identified in Table 400.4 for hard usage or extra-hard usage shall be permitted in cable trays used only for temporary wiring. All cords or cables shall be installed in a single layer. A permanent sign shall be attached to the cable tray at intervals not to exceed 7.5 m (25 ft). The sign shall read

CABLE TRAY FOR TEMPORARY WIRING ONLY

(C) Emergency Systems. Control of emergency systems shall comply with Article 700.

518.4 Wiring Methods.

(A) General. The fixed wiring methods shall be metal raceways, flexible metal raceways, nonmetallic raceways encased in not less than 50 mm (2 in.) of concrete, Type MI, MC, or AC cable containing an insulated equipment grounding conductor sized in accordance with Table 250.122.

Exception: Fixed wiring methods shall be as provided in

(a) Audio signal processing, amplification, and reproduction equipment — Article 640

(b) Communications circuits — Article 800

(c) Class 2 and Class 3 remote-control and signaling circuits — Article 725

(d) Fire alarm circuits — Article 760

(B) Nonrated Construction. In addition to the wiring methods of 518.4(A), nonmetallic-sheathed cable, Type AC cable, electrical nonmetallic tubing, and rigid nonmetallic conduit shall be permitted to be installed in those buildings or portions thereof that are not required to be of fire-rated construction by the applicable building code.

FPN: Fire-rated construction is the fire-resistive classification used in building codes.

(C) Spaces with Finish Rating. Electrical nonmetallic tubing and rigid nonmetallic conduit shall be permitted to be installed in club rooms, conference and meeting rooms in hotels or motels, courtrooms, dining facilities, restaurants, mortuary chapels, museums, libraries, and places of religious worship where the following apply:

(1) The electrical nonmetallic tubing or rigid nonmetallic conduit is installed concealed within walls, floors, and ceilings where the walls, floors, and ceilings provide a thermal barrier of material that has at least a 15-minute finish rating as identified in listings of fire-rated assemblies.

(2) The electrical nonmetallic tubing or rigid nonmetallic conduit is installed above suspended ceilings where the suspended ceilings provide a thermal barrier of material that has at least a 15-minute finish rating as identified in listings of fire-rated assemblies.

Electrical nonmetallic tubing and rigid nonmetallic conduit are not recognized for use in other space used for environmental air in accordance with 300.22(C).

FPN: A finish rating is established for assemblies containing combustible (wood) supports. The finish rating is defined as the time at which the wood stud or wood joist reaches an average temperature rise of 121°C (250°F) or an individual temperature rise of 163°C (325°F) as measured on the plane of the wood nearest the fire. A finish rating is not intended to represent a rating for a membrane ceiling.

518.5 Supply. Portable switchboards and portable power distribution equipment shall be supplied only from listed power outlets of sufficient voltage and ampere rating. Such power outlets shall be protected by overcurrent devices. Such overcurrent devices and power outlets shall not be accessible to the general public. Provisions for connection of an equipment grounding conductor shall be provided. The neutral of feeders supplying solid-state, 3-phase, 4-wire dimmer systems shall be considered a current-carrying conductor.

ARTICLE 520
Theaters, Audience Areas of Motion Picture and Television Studios, Performance Areas, and Similar Locations

I. General

520.1 Scope. This article covers all buildings or that part of a building or structure, indoor or outdoor, designed or used for presentation, dramatic, musical, motion picture projection, or similar purposes and to specific audience seating areas within motion picture or television studios.

520.2 Definitions.

Border Light. A permanently installed overhead strip light.

Breakout Assembly. An adapter used to connect a multi-pole connector containing two or more branch circuits to multiple individual branch-circuit connectors.

Bundled. Cables or conductors that are physically tied, wrapped, taped or otherwise periodically bound together.

Connector Strip. A metal wireway containing pendant or flush receptacles.

Drop Box. A box containing pendant- or flush-mounted receptacles attached to a multiconductor cable via strain relief or a multipole connector.

Footlight. A border light installed on or in the stage.

Grouped. Cables or conductors positioned adjacent to one another but not in continuous contact with each other.

Performance Area. The stage and audience seating area associated with a temporary stage structure, whether indoors or outdoors, constructed of scaffolding, truss, platforms, or similar devices, that is used for the presentation of theatrical or musical productions or for public presentations.

Portable Equipment. Equipment fed with portable cords or cables intended to be moved from one place to another.

Portable Power Distribution Unit. A power distribution box containing receptacles and overcurrent devices.

Proscenium. The wall and arch that separates the stage from the auditorium (house).

Stand Lamp (Work Light). A portable stand that contains a general-purpose luminaire (lighting fixture) or lampholder with guard for the purpose of providing general illumination on the stage or in the auditorium.

Strip Light. A luminaire (lighting fixture) with multiple lamps arranged in a row.

Two-Fer. An adapter cable containing one male plug and two female cord connectors used to connect two loads to one branch circuit.

520.3 Motion Picture Projectors. Motion picture equipment and its installation and use shall comply with Article 540.

520.4 Audio Signal Processing, Amplification, and Reproduction Equipment. Audio signal processing, amplification, and reproduction equipment and its installation shall comply with Article 640.

520.5 Wiring Methods.

(A) General. The fixed wiring method shall be metal raceways, nonmetallic raceways encased in at least 50 mm (2 in.) of concrete, Type MI cable, MC cable, or AC cable containing an insulated equipment grounding conductor sized in accordance with Table 250.122.

Exception: Fixed wiring methods shall be as provided in Article 640 for audio signal processing, amplification, and reproduction equipment, in Article 800 for communication circuits, in Article 725 for Class 2 and Class 3 remote-control and signaling circuits, and in Article 760 for fire alarm circuits.

(B) Portable Equipment. The wiring for portable switchboards, stage set lighting, stage effects, and other wiring not fixed as to location shall be permitted with approved flexible cords and cables as provided elsewhere in Article 520. Fastening such cables and cords by uninsulated staples or nailing shall not be permitted.

(C) Nonrated Construction. Nonmetallic-sheathed cable, Type AC cable, electrical nonmetallic tubing, and rigid nonmetallic conduit shall be permitted to be installed in those buildings or portions thereof that are not required to be of fire-rated construction by the applicable building code.

520.6 Number of Conductors in Raceway. The number of conductors permitted in any metal conduit, rigid nonmetallic conduit as permitted in this article, or electrical metallic tubing for border or stage pocket circuits or for remote-control conductors shall not exceed the percentage fill shown in Table 1 of Chapter 9. Where contained within an auxiliary gutter or a wireway, the sum of the cross-sectional areas of all contained conductors at any cross section shall not exceed 20 percent of the interior cross-sectional area of the auxiliary gutter or wireway. The 30-conductor limitation of 366.22 and 376.22 shall not apply.

520.7 Enclosing and Guarding Live Parts. Live parts shall be enclosed or guarded to prevent accidental contact by persons and objects. All switches shall be of the externally operable type. Dimmers, including rheostats, shall be placed in cases or cabinets that enclose all live parts.

520.8 Emergency Systems. Control of emergency systems shall comply with Article 700.

520.9 Branch Circuits. A branch circuit of any size supplying one or more receptacles shall be permitted to supply stage set lighting. The voltage rating of the receptacles shall not be less than the circuit voltage. Receptacle ampere ratings and branch-circuit conductor ampacity shall not be less than the branch-circuit overcurrent device ampere rating. Table 210.21(B)(2) shall not apply.

520.10 Portable Equipment. Portable stage and studio lighting equipment and portable power distribution equipment shall be permitted for temporary use outdoors, provided the equipment is supervised by qualified personnel while energized and barriered from the general public.

II. Fixed Stage Switchboards

520.21 Dead Front. Stage switchboards shall be of the dead-front type and shall comply with Part IV of Article 408 unless approved based on suitability as a stage switchboard as determined by a qualified testing laboratory and recognized test standards and principles.

520.22 Guarding Back of Switchboard. Stage switchboards having exposed live parts on the back of such boards shall be enclosed by the building walls, wire mesh grilles, or by other approved methods. The entrance to this enclosure shall be by means of a self-closing door.

520.23 Control and Overcurrent Protection of Receptacle Circuits. Means shall be provided at a stage-lighting switchboard to which load circuits are connected for overcurrent protection of stage-lighting branch circuits, including branch circuits supplying stage and auditorium receptacles used for cord- and plug-connected stage equipment. Where the stage switchboard contains dimmers to control nonstage lighting, the locating of the overcurrent protective devices for these branch circuits at the stage switchboard shall be permitted.

520.24 Metal Hood. A stage switchboard that is not completely enclosed dead-front and dead-rear or recessed into a wall shall be provided with a metal hood extending the full length of the board to protect all equipment on the board from falling objects.

520.25 Dimmers. Dimmers shall comply with 520.25(A) through (D).

(A) Disconnection and Overcurrent Protection. Where dimmers are installed in ungrounded conductors, each dimmer shall have overcurrent protection not greater than 125 percent of the dimmer rating and shall be disconnected from all ungrounded conductors when the master or individual switch or circuit breaker supplying such dimmer is in the open position.

(B) Resistance- or Reactor-Type Dimmers. Resistance- or series reactor-type dimmers shall be permitted to be placed in either the grounded or the ungrounded conductor of the circuit. Where designed to open either the supply circuit to the dimmer or the circuit controlled by it, the dimmer shall then comply with 404.2(B). Resistance- or reactor-type dimmers placed in the grounded neutral conductor of the circuit shall not open the circuit.

(C) Autotransformer-Type Dimmers. The circuit supplying an autotransformer-type dimmer shall not exceed 150 volts between conductors. The grounded conductor shall be common to the input and output circuits.

FPN: See 210.9 for circuits derived from autotransformers.

(D) Solid-State-Type Dimmers. The circuit supplying a solid-state dimmer shall not exceed 150 volts between conductors unless the dimmer is listed specifically for higher voltage operation. Where a grounded conductor supplies a dimmer, it shall be common to the input and output circuits. Dimmer chassis shall be connected to the equipment grounding conductor.

520.26 Type of Switchboard. A stage switchboard shall be either one or a combination of the types specified in 520.26(A), (B), and (C).

(A) Manual. Dimmers and switches are operated by handles mechanically linked to the control devices.

(B) Remotely Controlled. Devices are operated electrically from a pilot-type control console or panel. Pilot control panels either shall be part of the switchboard or shall be permitted to be at another location.

(C) Intermediate. A stage switchboard with circuit interconnections is a secondary switchboard (patch panel) or panelboard remote to the primary stage switchboard. It shall contain overcurrent protection. Where the required branch-circuit overcurrent protection is provided in the dimmer panel, it shall be permitted to be omitted from the intermediate switchboard.

520.27 Stage Switchboard Feeders.

(A) Type of Feeder. Feeders supplying stage switchboards shall be one of the types in 520.27(A)(1) through (A)(3).

(1) Single Feeder. A single feeder disconnected by a single disconnect device.

(2) Multiple Feeders to Intermediate Stage Switchboard (Patch Panel). Multiple feeders of unlimited quantity shall be permitted, provided that all multiple feeders are part of a single system. Where combined, neutral conductors in a given raceway shall be of sufficient ampacity to carry the maximum unbalanced current supplied by multiple feeder conductors in the same raceway, but they need not be greater than the ampacity of the neutral supplying the primary stage switchboard. Parallel neutral conductors shall comply with 310.4.

(3) Separate Feeders to Single Primary Stage Switchboard (Dimmer Bank). Installations with separate feeders to a single primary stage switchboard shall have a disconnecting means for each feeder. The primary stage switchboard shall have a permanent and obvious label stating the number and location of disconnecting means. If the disconnecting means are located in more than one distribution switchboard, the primary stage switchboard shall be provided with barriers to correspond with these multiple locations.

(B) Neutral. The neutral of feeders supplying solid-state, 3-phase, 4-wire dimming systems shall be considered a current-carrying conductor.

(C) Supply Capacity. For the purposes of calculating supply capacity to switchboards, it shall be permissible to consider the maximum load that the switchboard is intended to control in a given installation, provided that the following apply:

(1) All feeders supplying the switchboard shall be protected by an overcurrent device with a rating not greater than the ampacity of the feeder.

(2) The opening of the overcurrent device shall not affect the proper operation of the egress or emergency lighting systems.

FPN: For calculation of stage switchboard feeder loads, see 220.40.

III. Fixed Stage Equipment Other Than Switchboards

520.41 Circuit Loads.

(A) Circuits Rated 20 Amperes or Less. Footlights, border lights, and proscenium sidelights shall be arranged so that no branch circuit supplying such equipment carries a load exceeding 20 amperes.

(B) Circuits Rated Greater Than 20 Amperes. Where only heavy-duty lampholders are used, such circuits shall be permitted to comply with Article 210 for circuits supplying heavy-duty lampholders.

520.42 Conductor Insulation. Foot, border, proscenium, or portable strip lights and connector strips shall be wired with conductors that have insulation suitable for the temperature at which the conductors are operated, but not less than 125°C (257°F). The ampacity of the 125°C (257°F) conductors shall be that of 60°C (140°F) conductors. All drops from connector strips shall be 90°C (194°F) wire sized to the ampacity of 60°C (140°F) cords and cables with no more than 150 mm (6 in.) of conductor extending into the connector strip. Section 310.15(B)(2)(a) shall not apply.

FPN: See Table 310.13 for conductor types.

520.43 Footlights.

(A) Metal Trough Construction. Where metal trough construction is employed for footlights, the trough containing the circuit conductors shall be made of sheet metal not lighter than 0.81 mm (0.032 in.) and treated to prevent oxidation. Lampholder terminals shall be kept at least 13 mm (½ in.) from the metal of the trough. The circuit conductors shall be soldered to the lampholder terminals.

(B) Other-Than-Metal Trough Construction. Where the metal trough construction specified in 520.43(A) is not used, footlights shall consist of individual outlets with lampholders wired with rigid metal conduit, intermediate metal conduit, or flexible metal conduit, Type MC cable, or mineral-insulated, metal-sheathed cable. The circuit conductors shall be soldered to the lampholder terminals.

(C) Disappearing Footlights. Disappearing footlights shall be arranged so that the current supply is automatically disconnected when the footlights are replaced in the storage recesses designed for them.

520.44 Borders and Proscenium Sidelights.

(A) General. Borders and proscenium sidelights shall be as follows:

(1) Constructed as specified in 520.43

(2) Suitably stayed and supported

(3) Designed so that the flanges of the reflectors or other adequate guards protect the lamps from mechanical damage and from accidental contact with scenery or other combustible material

(B) Cords and Cables for Border Lights.

(1) General. Cords and cables for supply to border lights shall be listed for extra-hard usage. The cords and cables shall be suitably supported. Such cords and cables shall be employed only where flexible conductors are necessary. Ampacity of the conductors shall be as provided in 400.5.

(2) Cords and Cables Not in Contact with Heat-Producing Equipment. Listed multiconductor extra-hard-usage-type cords and cables not in direct contact with equipment containing heat-producing elements shall be permitted to have their ampacity determined by Table 520.44. Maximum load current in any conductor with an ampacity determined by Table 520.44 shall not exceed the values in Table 520.44.

Table 520.44 Ampacity of Listed Extra-Hard-Usage Cords and Cables with Temperature Ratings of 75°C (167°F) and 90°C (194°F)* [Based on Ambient Temperature of 30°C (86°F)]

Size (AWG)	Temperature Rating of Cords and Cables		Maximum Rating of Overcurrent Device
	75°C (167°F)	90°C (194°F)	
14	24	28	15
12	32	35	20
10	41	47	25
8	57	65	35
6	77	87	45
4	101	114	60
2	133	152	80

* Ampacity shown is the ampacity for multiconductor cords and cables where only three copper conductors are current-carrying as described in 400.5. If the number of current-carrying conductors in a cord or cable exceeds three and the load diversity factor is a minimum of 50 percent, the ampacity of each conductor shall be reduced as shown in the following table.

Number of Conductors	Percent of Ampacity
4–6	80
7–24	70
25–42	60
43 and above	50

Note: Ultimate insulation temperature. In no case shall conductors be associated together in such a way with respect to the kind of circuit, the wiring method used, or the number of conductors such that the temperature limit of the conductors is exceeded.

A neutral conductor that carries only the unbalanced current from other conductors of the same circuit need not be considered as a current-carrying conductor.

In a 3-wire circuit consisting of two phase wires and the neutral of a 4-wire, 3-phase, wye-connected system, a common conductor carries approximately the same current as the line-to-neutral currents of the other conductors and shall be considered to be a current-carrying conductor.

On a 4-wire, 3-phase, wye circuit where the major portion of the load consists of nonlinear loads such as electric-discharge lighting, electronic computer/data processing, or similar equipment, there are harmonic currents present in the neutral conductor, and the neutral shall be considered to be a current-carrying conductor.

520.45 Receptacles. Receptacles for electrical equipment on stages shall be rated in amperes. Conductors supplying receptacles shall be in accordance with Articles 310 and 400.

520.46 Connector Strips, Drop Boxes, Floor Pockets, and Other Outlet Enclosures. Receptacles for the connection of portable stage-lighting equipment shall be pendant or mounted in suitable pockets or enclosures and shall comply with 520.45. Supply cables for connector strips and drop boxes shall be as specified in 520.44(B).

520.47 Backstage Lamps (Bare Bulbs). Lamps (bare bulbs) installed in backstage and ancillary areas where they can come in contact with scenery shall be located and guarded so as to be free from physical damage and shall provide an air space of not less than 50 mm (2 in.) between such lamps and any combustible material.

Exception: Decorative lamps installed in scenery shall not be considered to be backstage lamps for the purpose of this section.

520.48 Curtain Machines. Curtain machines shall be listed.

520.49 Smoke Ventilator Control. Where stage smoke ventilators are released by an electrical device, the circuit operating the device shall be normally closed and shall be controlled by at least two externally operable switches, one switch being placed at a readily accessible location on stage and the other where designated by the authority having jurisdiction. The device shall be designed for the full voltage of the circuit to which it is connected, no resistance being inserted. The device shall be located in the loft above the scenery and shall be enclosed in a suitable metal box having a tight, self-closing door.

IV. Portable Switchboards on Stage

520.50 Road Show Connection Panel (A Type of Patch Panel). A panel designed to allow for road show connection of portable stage switchboards to fixed lighting outlets by means of permanently installed supplementary circuits. The panel, supplementary circuits, and outlets shall comply with 520.50(A) through (D).

(A) Load Circuits. Circuits shall terminate in grounding-type polarized inlets of current and voltage rating that match the fixed-load receptacle.

(B) Circuit Transfer. Circuits that are transferred between fixed and portable switchboards shall have all circuit conductors transferred simultaneously.

(C) Overcurrent Protection. The supply devices of these supplementary circuits shall be protected by branch-circuit overcurrent protective devices. The individual supplementary circuit, within the road show connection panel and theater, shall be protected by branch-circuit overcurrent protective devices of suitable ampacity installed within the road show connection panel.

(D) Enclosure. Panel construction shall be in accordance with Article 408.

520.51 Supply. Portable switchboards shall be supplied only from power outlets of sufficient voltage and ampere rating. Such power outlets shall include only externally operable, enclosed fused switches or circuit breakers mounted on stage or at the permanent switchboard in locations readily accessible from the stage floor. Provisions for connection of an equipment grounding conductor shall be provided. The neutral of feeders supplying solid-state, 3-phase, 4-wire dimmer systems shall be considered a current-carrying conductor.

520.52 Overcurrent Protection. Circuits from portable switchboards directly supplying equipment containing incandescent lamps of not over 300 watts shall be protected by overcurrent protective devices having a rating or setting of not over 20 amperes. Circuits for lampholders over 300 watts shall be permitted where overcurrent protection complies with Article 210.

520.53 Construction and Feeders. Portable switchboards and feeders for use on stages shall comply with 520.53(A) through (P).

(A) Enclosure. Portable switchboards shall be placed within an enclosure of substantial construction, which shall be permitted to be arranged so that the enclosure is open during operation. Enclosures of wood shall be completely lined with sheet metal of not less than 0.51 mm (0.020 in.) and shall be well galvanized, enameled, or otherwise properly coated to prevent corrosion or be of a corrosion-resistant material.

(B) Energized Parts. There shall not be exposed energized parts within the enclosure.

(C) Switches and Circuit Breakers. All switches and circuit breakers shall be of the externally operable, enclosed type.

(D) Circuit Protection. Overcurrent devices shall be provided in each ungrounded conductor of every circuit supplied through the switchboard. Enclosures shall be provided for all overcurrent devices in addition to the switchboard enclosure.

(E) Dimmers. The terminals of dimmers shall be provided with enclosures, and dimmer faceplates shall be arranged so that accidental contact cannot be readily made with the faceplate contacts.

(F) Interior Conductors.

(1) Type. All conductors other than busbars within the switchboard enclosure shall be stranded. Conductors shall be approved for an operating temperature at least equal to the approved operating temperature of the dimming devices used in the switchboard and in no case less than the following:

(1) Resistance-type dimmers — 200°C (392°F); or
(2) Reactor-type, autotransformer, and solid-state dimmers — 125°C (257°F)

All control wiring shall comply with Article 725.

(2) Protection. Each conductor shall have an ampacity not less than the rating of the circuit breaker, switch, or fuse that it supplies. Circuit interrupting and bus bracing shall be in accordance with 110.9 and 110.10. The short-circuit current rating shall be marked on the switchboard.

Conductors shall be enclosed in metal wireways or shall be securely fastened in position and shall be bushed where they pass through metal.

(G) Pilot Light. A pilot light shall be provided within the enclosure and shall be connected to the circuit supplying the board so that the opening of the master switch does not cut off the supply to the lamp. This lamp shall be on an individual branch circuit having overcurrent protection rated or set at not over 15 amperes.

(H) Supply Conductors.

(1) General. The supply to a portable switchboard shall be by means of listed extra-hard usage cords or cables. The supply cords or cable shall terminate within the switchboard enclosure, in an externally operable fused master switch or circuit breaker or in a connector assembly identified for the purpose. The supply cords or cable (and connector assembly) shall have sufficient ampacity to carry the total load connected to the switchboard and shall be protected by overcurrent devices.

(2) Single-Conductor Cables. Single-conductor portable supply cable sets shall not be smaller than 2 AWG conductors. The equipment grounding conductor shall not be smaller than 6 AWG conductor. Single-conductor grounded neutral cables for a supply shall be sized in accordance with 520.53(O)(2). Where single conductors are paralleled for increased ampacity, the paralleled conductors shall be of the same length and size. Single-conductor supply cables shall be grouped together but not bundled. The equipment grounding conductor shall be permitted to be of a different type, provided it meets the other requirements of this section, and it shall be permitted to be reduced in size as permitted by 250.122. Grounded (neutral) and equipment grounding conductors shall be identified in accordance with 200.6, 250.119, and 310.12. Grounded conductors shall be permitted to be identified by marking at least the first

150 mm (6 in.) from both ends of each length of conductor with white or gray. Equipment grounding conductors shall be permitted to be identified by marking at least the first 150 mm (6 in.) from both ends of each length of conductor with green or green with yellow stripes. Where more than one nominal voltage exists within the same premises, each ungrounded conductor shall be identified by system.

(3) Supply Conductors Not Over 3.0 m (10 ft) Long. Where supply conductors do not exceed 3.0 m (10 ft) in length between supply and switchboard or supply and a subsequent overcurrent device, the supply conductors shall be permitted to be reduced in size where all of the following conditions are met:

(1) The ampacity of the supply conductors shall be at least one-quarter of the ampacity of the supply overcurrent protection device.

(2) The supply conductors shall terminate in a single overcurrent protection device that will limit the load to the ampacity of the supply conductors. This single overcurrent device shall be permitted to supply additional overcurrent devices on its load side.

(3) The supply conductors shall not penetrate walls, floors, or ceilings or be run through doors or traffic areas. The supply conductors shall be adequately protected from physical damage.

(4) The supply conductors shall be suitably terminated in an approved manner.

(5) Conductors shall be continuous without splices or connectors.

(6) Conductors shall not be bundled.

(7) Conductors shall be supported above the floor in an approved manner.

(4) Supply Conductors Not Over 6.0 m (20 ft) Long. Where supply conductors do not exceed 6.0 m (20 ft) in length between supply and switchboard or supply and a subsequent overcurrent protection device, the supply conductors shall be permitted to be reduced in size where all of the following conditions are met:

(1) The ampacity of the supply conductors shall be at least one-half of the ampacity of the supply overcurrent protection device.

(2) The supply conductors shall terminate in a single overcurrent protection device that limits the load to the ampacity of the supply conductors. This single overcurrent device shall be permitted to supply additional overcurrent devices on its load side.

(3) The supply conductors shall not penetrate walls, floors, or ceilings or be run through doors or traffic areas. The supply conductors shall be adequately protected from physical damage.

(4) The supply conductors shall be suitably terminated in an approved manner.

(5) The supply conductors shall be supported in an approved manner at least 2.1 m (7 ft) above the floor except at terminations.

(6) The supply conductors shall not be bundled.

(7) Tap conductors shall be in unbroken lengths.

(5) Supply Conductors Not Reduced in Size. Supply conductors not reduced in size under provisions of 520.53(H)(3) or 520.53(H)(4) shall be permitted to pass through holes in walls specifically designed for the purpose. If penetration is through the fire-resistant–rated wall, it shall be in accordance with 300.21.

(I) Cable Arrangement. Cables shall be protected by bushings where they pass through enclosures and shall be arranged so that tension on the cable is not transmitted to the connections. Where power conductors pass through metal, the requirements of 300.20 shall apply.

(J) Number of Supply Interconnections. Where connectors are used in a supply conductor, there shall be a maximum number of three interconnections (mated connector pairs) where the total length from supply to switchboard does not exceed 30 m (100 ft). In cases where the total length from supply to switchboard exceeds 30 m (100 ft), one additional interconnection shall be permitted for each additional 30 m (100 ft) of supply conductor.

(K) Single-Pole Separable Connectors. Where single-pole portable cable connectors are used, they shall be listed and of the locking type. Sections 400.10, 406.6, and 406.7 shall not apply to listed single-pole separable connectors and single-conductor cable assemblies utilizing listed single-pole separable connectors. Where paralleled sets of current-carrying, single-pole separable connectors are provided as input devices, they shall be prominently labeled with a warning indicating the presence of internal parallel connections. The use of single-pole separable connectors shall comply with at least one of the following conditions:

(1) Connection and disconnection of connectors are only possible where the supply connectors are interlocked to the source, and it is not possible to connect or disconnect connectors when the supply is energized.

(2) Line connectors are of the listed sequential-interlocking type so that load connectors shall be connected in the following sequence:

a. Equipment grounding conductor connection
b. Grounded circuit conductor connection, if provided
c. Ungrounded conductor connection, and that disconnection shall be in the reverse order

(3) A caution notice shall be provided adjacent to the line connectors indicating that plug connection shall be in the following order:

a. Equipment grounding conductor connectors
b. Grounded circuit conductor connectors, if provided
c. Ungrounded conductor connectors, and that disconnection shall be in the reverse order

(L) Protection of Supply Conductors and Connectors. All supply conductors and connectors shall be protected against physical damage by an approved means. This protection shall not be required to be raceways.

(M) Flanged Surface Inlets. Flanged surface inlets (recessed plugs) that are used to accept the power shall be rated in amperes.

(N) Terminals. Terminals to which stage cables are connected shall be located so as to permit convenient access to the terminals.

(O) Neutral.

(1) Neutral Terminal. In portable switchboard equipment designed for use with 3-phase, 4-wire with ground supply, the supply neutral terminal, its associated busbar, or equivalent wiring, or both, shall have an ampacity equal to at least twice the ampacity of the largest ungrounded supply terminal.

Exception: Where portable switchboard equipment is specifically constructed and identified to be internally converted in the field, in an approved manner, from use with a balanced 3-phase, 4-wire with ground supply to a balanced single-phase, 3-wire with ground supply, the supply neutral terminal and its associated busbar, equivalent wiring, or both, shall have an ampacity equal to at least that of the largest ungrounded single-phase supply terminal.

(2) Supply Neutral. The power supply conductors for portable switchboards shall be sized considering the neutral as a current-carrying conductor. Where single-conductor feeder cables, not installed in raceways, are used on multiphase circuits, the grounded neutral conductor shall have an ampacity of at least 130 percent of the ungrounded circuit conductors feeding the portable switchboard.

(P) Qualified Personnel. The routing of portable supply conductors, the making and breaking of supply connectors and other supply connections, and the energization and de-energization of supply services shall be performed by qualified personnel, and portable switchboards shall be so marked, indicating this requirement in a permanent and conspicuous manner.

Exception: A portable switchboard shall be permitted to be connected to a permanently installed supply receptacle by other than qualified personnel, provided that the supply receptacle is protected for its rated ampacity by an overcurrent device of not greater than 150 amperes, and where

the receptacle, interconnection, and switchboard comply with all of the following:

(a) Employ listed multipole connectors suitable for the purpose for every supply interconnection

(b) Prevent access to all supply connections by the general public

(c) Employ listed extra-hard usage multiconductor cords or cables with an ampacity suitable for the type of load and not less than the ampere rating of the connectors.

V. Portable Stage Equipment Other Than Switchboards

520.61 Arc Lamps. Arc lamps, including enclosed arc lamps and associated ballasts, shall be listed. Interconnecting cord sets and interconnecting cords and cables shall be extra-hard usage type and listed.

520.62 Portable Power Distribution Units. Portable power distribution units shall comply with 520.62(A) through (E).

(A) Enclosure. The construction shall be such that no current-carrying part will be exposed.

(B) Receptacles and Overcurrent Protection. Receptacles shall comply with 520.45 and shall have branch-circuit overcurrent protection in the box. Fuses and circuit breakers shall be protected against physical damage. Cords or cables supplying pendant receptacles shall be listed for extra-hard usage.

(C) Busbars and Terminals. Busbars shall have an ampacity equal to the sum of the ampere ratings of all the circuits connected to the busbar. Lugs shall be provided for the connection of the master cable.

(D) Flanged Surface Inlets. Flanged surface inlets (recessed plugs) that are used to accept the power shall be rated in amperes.

(E) Cable Arrangement. Cables shall be adequately protected where they pass through enclosures and be arranged so that tension on the cable is not transmitted to the terminations.

520.63 Bracket Fixture Wiring.

(A) Bracket Wiring. Brackets for use on scenery shall be wired internally, and the fixture stem shall be carried through to the back of the scenery where a bushing shall be placed on the end of the stem. Externally wired brackets or other fixtures shall be permitted where wired with cords designed for hard usage that extend through scenery and without joint or splice in canopy of fixture back and terminate in an approved-type stage connector located, where practical, within 450 mm (18 in.) of the fixture.

(B) Mounting. Fixtures shall be securely fastened in place.

520.64 Portable Strips. Portable strips shall be constructed in accordance with the requirements for border lights and proscenium sidelights in 520.44(A). The supply cable shall be protected by bushings where it passes through metal and shall be arranged so that tension on the cable will not be transmitted to the connections.

FPN No. 1:   See 520.42 for wiring of portable strips.

FPN No. 2:   See 520.68(A)(3) for insulation types required on single conductors.

520.65 Festoons. Joints in festoon wiring shall be staggered. Lamps enclosed in lanterns or similar devices of combustible material shall be equipped with guards.

520.66 Special Effects. Electrical devices used for simulating lightning, waterfalls, and the like shall be constructed and located so that flames, sparks, or hot particles cannot come in contact with combustible material.

520.67 Multipole Branch-Circuit Cable Connectors. Multipole branch-circuit cable connectors, male and female, for flexible conductors shall be constructed so that tension on the cord or cable is not transmitted to the connections. The female half shall be attached to the load end of the power supply cord or cable. The connector shall be rated in amperes and designed so that differently rated devices cannot be connected together; however, a 20-ampere T-slot receptacle shall be permitted to accept a 15-ampere attachment plug of the same voltage rating. Alternating-current multipole connectors shall be polarized and comply with 406.6 and 406.9.

FPN: See 400.10 for pull at terminals.

520.68 Conductors for Portables.

(A) Conductor Type.

(1) General. Flexible conductors, including cable extensions, used to supply portable stage equipment shall be listed extra-hard usage cords or cables.

(2) Stand Lamps. Listed, hard usage cord shall be permitted to supply stand lamps where the cord is not subject to physical damage and is protected by an overcurrent device rated at not over 20 amperes.

(3) High-Temperature Applications. A special assembly of conductors in sleeving not longer than 1.0 m (3.3 ft) shall be permitted to be employed in lieu of flexible cord if the individual wires are stranded and rated not less than 125°C (257°F) and the outer sleeve is glass fiber with a wall thickness of at least 0.635 mm (0.025 in.).

Portable stage equipment requiring flexible supply conductors with a higher temperature rating where one end is permanently attached to the equipment shall be permitted to employ alternate, suitable conductors as determined by a qualified testing laboratory and recognized test standards.

(4) Breakouts. Listed, hard usage (junior hard service) cords shall be permitted in breakout assemblies where all of the following conditions are met:

(1) The cords are utilized to connect between a single multipole connector containing two or more branch circuits and multiple 2-pole, 3-wire connectors.

(2) The longest cord in the breakout assembly does not exceed 6.0 m (20 ft).

(3) The breakout assembly is protected from physical damage by attachment over its entire length to a pipe, truss, tower, scaffold, or other substantial support structure.

(4) All branch circuits feeding the breakout assembly are protected by overcurrent devices rated at not over 20 amperes.

(B) Conductor Ampacity. The ampacity of conductors shall be as given in 400.5, except multiconductor, listed, extra-hard usage portable cords that are not in direct contact with equipment containing heat-producing elements shall be permitted to have their ampacity determined by Table 520.44. Maximum load current in any conductor with an ampacity determined by Table 520.44 shall not exceed the values in Table 520.44.

Exception: Where alternate conductors are allowed in 520.68(A)(3), their ampacity shall be as given in the appropriate table in this Code for the types of conductors employed.

520.69 Adapters. Adapters, two-fers, and other single- and multiple-circuit outlet devices shall comply with 520.69(A), (B), and (C).

(A) No Reduction in Current Rating. Each receptacle and its corresponding cable shall have the same current and voltage rating as the plug supplying it. It shall not be utilized in a stage circuit with a greater current rating.

(B) Connectors. All connectors shall be wired in accordance with 520.67.

(C) Conductor Type. Conductors for adapters and two-fers shall be listed, extra-hard usage or listed, hard usage (junior hard service) cord. Hard usage (junior hard service) cord shall be restricted in overall length to 1.0 m (3.3 ft).

VI. Dressing Rooms

520.71 Pendant Lampholders. Pendant lampholders shall not be installed in dressing rooms.

520.72 Lamp Guards. All exposed incandescent lamps in dressing rooms, where less than 2.5 m (8 ft) from the floor, shall be equipped with open-end guards riveted to the outlet box cover or otherwise sealed or locked in place.

520.73 Switches Required. All lights and any receptacles adjacent to the mirror(s) and above the dressing table counter(s) installed in dressing rooms shall be controlled by wall switches installed in the dressing room(s). Each switch controlling receptacles adjacent to the mirror(s) and above the dressing table counter(s) shall be provided with a pilot light located outside the dressing room, adjacent to the door to indicate when the receptacles are energized. Other outlets installed in the dressing room shall not be required to be switched.

VII. Grounding

520.81 Grounding. All metal raceways and metal-sheathed cables shall be grounded. The metal frames and enclosures of all equipment, including border lights and portable luminaires (lighting fixtures), shall be grounded. Grounding, where used, shall be in accordance with Article 250.

ARTICLE 525
Carnivals, Circuses, Fairs, and Similar Events

I. General Requirements

525.1 Scope. This article covers the installation of portable wiring and equipment for carnivals, circuses, fairs, and similar functions, including wiring in or on all structures.

525.3 Other Articles.

(A) Portable Wiring and Equipment. Wherever the requirements of other articles of this *Code* and Article 525 differ, the requirements of Article 525 shall apply to the portable wiring and equipment.

(B) Permanent Structures. Articles 518 and 520 shall apply to wiring in permanent structures.

(C) Audio Signal Processing, Amplification, and Reproduction Equipment. Article 640 shall apply to the wiring and installation of audio signal processing, amplification, and reproduction equipment.

(D) Attractions Utilizing Pools, Fountains, and Similar Installations with Contained Volumes of Water. This equipment shall be installed to comply with the applicable requirements of Article 680.

525.5 Overhead Conductor Clearances.

(A) Vertical Clearances. Conductors shall have a vertical clearance to ground in accordance with 225.18. These clearances shall apply only to wiring installed outside of tents and concessions.

(B) Clearance to Rides and Attractions. Amusement rides and amusement attractions shall be maintained not less than 4.5 m (15 ft) in any direction from overhead conductors operating at 600 volts or less, except for the conductors supplying the amusement ride or attraction. Amusement rides or attractions shall not be located under or within 4.5 m (15 ft) horizontally of conductors operating in excess of 600 volts.

525.6 Protection of Electrical Equipment. Electrical equipment and wiring methods in or on rides, concessions, or other units shall be provided with mechanical protection where such equipment or wiring methods are subject to physical damage.

II. Power Sources

525.10 Services. Services shall comply with 525.10(A) and 525.10(B).

(A) Guarding. Service equipment shall not be installed in a location that is accessible to unqualified persons, unless the equipment is lockable.

(B) Mounting and Location. Service equipment shall be mounted on solid backing and be installed so as to be protected from the weather, unless of weatherproof construction.

525.11 Multiple Sources of Supply. Where multiple services or separately derived systems or both supply rides, attractions, and other structures, all sources of supply that serve rides, attractions, or other structures separated by less than 3.7 m (12 ft) shall be bonded to the same grounding electrode system.

III. Wiring Methods

525.20 Wiring Methods.

(A) Type. Where flexible cords or cables are used, they shall be listed for extra hard usage. Where flexible cords or cables are used and are not subject to physical damage, they shall be permitted to be listed for hard usage. Where used outdoors, flexible cords and cables shall also be listed for wet locations and shall be sunlight resistant. Extra-hard usage flexible cords or cables shall be permitted for use as permanent wiring on portable amusement rides and attractions where not subject to physical damage.

(B) Single-Conductor. Single-conductor cable shall be permitted only in sizes 2 AWG or larger.

(C) Open Conductors. Open conductors are prohibited except as part of a listed assembly or festoon lighting installed in accordance with Article 225.

(D) Splices. Flexible cords or cables shall be continuous without splice or tap between boxes or fittings.

(E) Cord Connectors. Cord connectors shall not be laid on the ground unless listed for wet locations. Connectors and cable connections shall not be placed in audience traffic paths or within areas accessible to the public unless guarded.

(F) Support. Wiring for an amusement ride, attraction, tent, or similar structure shall not be supported by any other ride or structure unless specifically designed for the purpose.

(G) Protection. Flexible cords or cables accessible to the public shall be arranged to minimize the tripping hazard and shall be permitted to be covered with nonconductive matting, provided that the matting does not constitute a greater tripping hazard than the uncovered cables. It shall be permitted to bury cables. The requirements of 300.5 shall not apply.

(H) Boxes and Fittings. A box or fitting shall be installed at each connection point, outlet, switchpoint, or junction point.

525.21 Rides, Tents and Concessions.

(A) Disconnecting Means. Each ride and concession shall be provided with a fused disconnect switch or circuit breaker located within sight and within 1.8 m (6 ft) of the operator's station. The disconnecting means shall be readily accessible to the operator, including when the ride is in operation. Where accessible to unqualified persons, the enclosure for the switch or circuit breaker shall be of the lockable type. A shunt trip device that opens the fused disconnect or circuit breaker when a switch located in the ride operator's console is closed shall be a permissible method of opening the circuit.

(B) Portable Wiring Inside Tents and Concessions. Electrical wiring for lighting, where installed inside of tents and concessions, shall be securely installed and, where subject to physical damage, shall be provided with mechanical protection. All lamps for general illumination shall be protected from accidental breakage by a suitable fixture or lampholder with a guard.

525.22 Portable Distribution or Termination Boxes. Portable distribution or termination boxes shall comply with 525.22(A) through 525.22(D).

(A) Construction. Boxes shall be designed so that no live parts are exposed to accidental contact. Where installed outdoors, the box shall be of weatherproof construction and mounted so that the bottom of the enclosure is not less than 150 mm (6 in.) above the ground.

(B) Busbars and Terminals. Busbars shall have an ampere rating not less than the overcurrent device supplying the feeder supplying the box. Where conductors terminate directly on busbars, busbar connectors shall be provided.

(C) Receptacles and Overcurrent Protection. Receptacles shall have overcurrent protection installed within the box. The overcurrent protection shall not exceed the ampere rating of the receptacle, except as permitted in Article 430 for motor loads.

(D) Single-Pole Connectors. Where single-pole connectors are used, they shall comply with 530.22.

525.23 Ground-Fault Circuit-Interrupter (GFCI) Protection.

(A) Where GFCI Protection Is Required. The ground-fault circuit interrupter shall be permitted to be an integral part of the attachment plug or located in the power-supply cord, within 300 mm (12 in.) of the attachment plug. Listed cord sets incorporating ground-fault circuit-interrupter for personnel shall be permitted.

(1) 125-volt, single-phase, 15- and 20-ampere non-locking type receptacles used for disassembly and reassembly or readily accessible to the general public.

(2) Equipment that is readily accessible to the general public and supplied from a 125-volt, single-phase, 15- or 20-ampere branch circuit.

(B) Where GFCI Protection Is Not Required. Receptacles that only facilitate quick disconnecting and reconnecting of electrical equipment shall not be required to be provided with GFCI protection. These receptacles shall be of the locking type.

(C) Where GFCI Protection Is Not Permitted. Egress lighting shall not be protected by a GFCI.

IV. Grounding and Bonding

525.30 Equipment Bonding. The following equipment connected to the same source shall be bonded:

(1) Metal raceways and metal-sheathed cable

(2) Metal enclosures of electric equipment

(3) Metal frames and metal parts of rides, concessions, tents, trailers, trucks, or other equipment that contain or support electrical equipment

525.31 Equipment Grounding. All equipment requiring grounding shall be grounded by an equipment grounding conductor of a type and size recognized by 250.118 and installed in accordance with Article 250. The equipment grounding conductor shall be bonded to the system grounded conductor at the service disconnecting means or, in the case of a separately derived system such as a generator, at the generator or first disconnecting means supplied by the generator. The grounded circuit conductor shall not be connected to the equipment grounding conductor on the load side of the service disconnecting means or on the load side of a separately derived system disconnecting means.

525.32 Grounding Conductor Continuity Assurance. The continuity of the grounding conductor system used to reduce electrical shock hazards as required by 250.114, 250.138, 406.3(C), and 590.4(D) shall be verified each time that portable electrical equipment is connected.

ARTICLE 530
Motion Picture and Television Studios and Similar Locations

I. General

530.1 Scope. The requirements of this article shall apply to television studios and motion picture studios using either film or electronic cameras, except as provided in 520.1, and exchanges, factories, laboratories, stages, or a portion of the building in which film or tape more than 22 mm (⅞ in.) in width is exposed, developed, printed, cut, edited, rewound, repaired, or stored.

> FPN: For methods of protecting against cellulose nitrate film hazards, see NFPA 40-2001, *Standard for the Storage and Handling of Cellulose Nitrate Motion Picture Film.*

530.2 Definitions.

Alternating-Current Power Distribution Box (Alternating-Current Plugging Box, Scatter Box). An ac distribution center or box that contains one or more grounding-type polarized receptacles that may contain overcurrent protection devices.

Bull Switch. An externally operated wall-mounted safety switch that may or may not contain overcurrent protection and is designed for the connection of portable cables and cords.

Location (Shooting Location). A place outside a motion picture studio where a production or part of it is filmed or recorded.

Location Board (Deuce Board). Portable equipment containing a lighting contactor or contactors and overcurrent protection designed for remote control of stage lighting.

Motion Picture Studio (Lot). A building or group of buildings and other structures designed, constructed, or permanently altered for use by the entertainment industry for the purpose of motion picture or television production.

Plugging Box. A dc device consisting of one or more 2-pole, 2-wire, nonpolarized, nongrounding-type receptacles intended to be used on dc circuits only.

Portable Equipment. Equipment intended to be moved from one place to another.

Single-Pole Separable Connector. A device that is installed at the ends of portable, flexible, single-conductor cable that is used to establish connection or disconnection between two cables or one cable and a single-pole, panel-mounted separable connector.

Spider (Cable Splicing Block). A device that contains busbars that are insulated from each other for the purpose of splicing or distributing power to portable cables and cords that are terminated with single-pole busbar connectors.

Stage Effect (Special Effect). An electrical or electromechanical piece of equipment used to simulate a distinctive visual or audible effect such as wind machines, lightning simulators, sunset projectors, and the like.

Stage Property. An article or object used as a visual element in a motion picture or television production, except painted backgrounds (scenery) and costumes.

Stage Set. A specific area set up with temporary scenery and properties designed and arranged for a particular scene in a motion picture or television production.

Stand Lamp (Work Light). A portable stand that contains a general-purpose luminaire (lighting fixture) or lampholder with guard for the purpose of providing general illumination in the studio or stage.

Television Studio or Motion Picture Stage (Sound Stage). A building or portion of a building usually insulated from the outside noise and natural light for use by the entertainment industry for the purpose of motion picture, television, or commercial production.

530.6 Portable Equipment. Portable stage and studio lighting equipment and portable power distribution equipment shall be permitted for temporary use outdoors if the equipment is supervised by qualified personnel while energized and barriered from the general public.

II. Stage or Set

530.11 Permanent Wiring. The permanent wiring shall be Type MC cable, Type AC cable containing an insulated equipment grounding conductor sized in accordance with Table 250.122, Type MI cable, or in approved raceways.

Exception: Communications circuits; audio signal processing, amplification, and reproduction circuits; Class 1, Class 2, and Class 3 remote-control or signaling circuits and power-limited fire alarm circuits shall be permitted to be wired in accordance with Articles 640, 725, 760, and 800.

530.12 Portable Wiring.

(A) Stage Set Wiring. The wiring for stage set lighting and other supply wiring not fixed as to location shall be done with listed hard usage flexible cords and cables. Where subject to physical damage, such wiring shall be listed extra-hard usage flexible cords and cables. Splices or taps in cables shall be permitted if the total connected load does not exceed the maximum ampacity of the cable.

(B) Stage Effects and Electrical Equipment Used as Stage Properties. The wiring for stage effects and electrical equipment used as stage properties shall be permitted to be wired with single- or multiconductor listed flexible cords or cables if the conductors are protected from physical damage and secured to the scenery by approved cable ties or by insulated staples. Splices or taps shall be permitted where such are made with listed devices and the circuit is protected at not more than 20 amperes.

(C) Other Electrical Equipment. Cords and cables other than extra-hard usage, where supplied as a part of a listed assembly, shall be permitted.

530.13 Stage Lighting and Effects Control. Switches used for studio stage set lighting and effects (on the stages and lots and on location) shall be of the externally operable type. Where contactors are used as the disconnecting means for fuses, an individual externally operable switch, such as a tumbler switch, for the control of each contactor shall be located at a distance of not more than 1.8 m (6 ft) from the contactor, in addition to remote-control switches. A single externally operable switch shall be permitted to simultaneously disconnect all the contactors on any one location board, where located at a distance of not more than 1.8 m (6 ft) from the location board.

530.14 Plugging Boxes. Each receptacle of dc plugging boxes shall be rated at not less than 30 amperes.

530.15 Enclosing and Guarding Live Parts.

(A) Live Parts. Live parts shall be enclosed or guarded to prevent accidental contact by persons and objects.

(B) Switches. All switches shall be of the externally operable type.

(C) Rheostats. Rheostats shall be placed in approved cases or cabinets that enclose all live parts, having only the operating handles exposed.

(D) Current-Carrying Parts. Current-carrying parts of bull switches, location boards, spiders, and plugging boxes shall be enclosed, guarded, or located so that persons cannot accidentally come into contact with them or bring conductive material into contact with them.

530.16 Portable Lamps. Portable lamps and work lights shall be equipped with flexible cords, composition or metal-sheathed porcelain sockets, and substantial guards.

Exception: Portable lamps used as properties in a motion picture set or television stage set, on a studio stage or lot, or on location shall not be considered to be portable lamps for the purpose of this section.

530.17 Portable Arc Lamps.

(A) Portable Carbon Arc Lamps. Portable carbon arc lamps shall be substantially constructed. The arc shall be provided with an enclosure designed to retain sparks and carbons and to prevent persons or materials from coming into contact with the arc or bare live parts. The enclosures shall be ventilated. All switches shall be of the externally operable type.

(B) Portable Noncarbon Arc Electric-Discharge Lamps. Portable noncarbon arc lamps, including enclosed arc lamps, and associated ballasts shall be listed. Interconnecting cord sets and interconnecting cords and cables shall be extra-hard usage type and listed.

530.18 Overcurrent Protection — General. Automatic overcurrent protective devices (circuit breakers or fuses) for motion picture studio stage set lighting and the stage cables for such stage set lighting shall be as given in 530.18(A) through (G). The maximum ampacity allowed on a given conductor, cable, or cord size shall be as given in the applicable tables of Articles 310 and 400.

(A) Stage Cables. Stage cables for stage set lighting shall be protected by means of overcurrent devices set at not more than 400 percent of the ampacity given in the applicable tables of Articles 310 and 400.

(B) Feeders. In buildings used primarily for motion picture production, the feeders from the substations to the stages shall be protected by means of overcurrent devices (generally located in the substation) having a suitable ampere rating. The overcurrent devices shall be permitted to be multipole or single-pole gang operated. No pole shall be required in the neutral conductor. The overcurrent device setting for each feeder shall not exceed 400 percent of the ampacity of the feeder, as given in the applicable tables of Article 310.

(C) Cable Protection. Cables shall be protected by bushings where they pass through enclosures and shall be arranged so that tension on the cable is not transmitted to the connections. Where power conductors pass through metal, the requirements of 300.20 shall apply.

Portable feeder cables shall be permitted to temporarily penetrate fire-rated walls, floors, or ceilings provided that all of the following apply:

(1) The opening is of noncombustible material.

(2) When in use, the penetration is sealed with a temporary seal of a listed firestop material.

(3) When not in use, the opening shall be capped with a material of equivalent fire rating.

(D) Location Boards. Overcurrent protection (fuses or circuit breakers) shall be provided at the location boards. Fuses in the location boards shall have an ampere rating of not over 400 percent of the ampacity of the cables between the location boards and the plugging boxes.

(E) Plugging Boxes. Cables and cords supplied through plugging boxes shall be of copper. Cables and cords smaller than 8 AWG shall be attached to the plugging box by means of a plug containing two cartridge fuses or a 2-pole circuit breaker. The rating of the fuses or the setting of the circuit breaker shall not be over 400 percent of the rated ampacity of the cables or cords as given in the applicable tables of Articles 310 and 400. Plugging boxes shall not be permitted on ac systems.

(F) Alternating-Current Power Distribution Boxes. Alternating-current power distribution boxes used on sound stages and shooting locations shall contain connection receptacles of a polarized, grounding type.

(G) Lighting. Work lights, stand lamps, and luminaires (fixtures) rated 1000 watts or less and connected to dc plugging boxes shall be by means of plugs containing two cartridge fuses not larger than 20 amperes, or they shall be permitted to be connected to special outlets on circuits protected by fuses or circuit breakers rated at not over 20 amperes. Plug fuses shall not be used unless they are on the load side of the fuse or circuit breakers on the location boards.

530.19 Sizing of Feeder Conductors for Television Studio Sets.

(A) General. It shall be permissible to apply the demand factors listed in Table 530.19(A) to that portion of the maximum possible connected load for studio or stage set lighting for all permanently installed feeders between substations and stages and to all permanently installed feeders between the main stage switchboard and stage distribution centers or location boards.

(B) Portable Feeders. A demand factor of 50 percent of maximum possible connected load shall be permitted for all portable feeders.

Table 530.19(A) Demand Factors for Stage Set Lighting

Portion of Stage Set Lighting Load to Which Demand Factor Applied (volt-amperes)	Feeder Demand Factor
First 50,000 or less at	100%
From 50,001 to 100,000 at	75%
From 100,001 to 200,000 at	60%
Remaining over 200,000 at	50%

530.20 Grounding. Type MC cable, Type MI cable, metal raceways, and all non–current-carrying metal parts of appliances, devices, and equipment shall be grounded as specified in Article 250. This shall not apply to pendant and portable lamps, to stage lighting and stage sound equipment, or to other portable and special stage equipment operating at not over 150 volts dc to ground.

530.21 Plugs and Receptacles.

(A) Rating. Plugs and receptacles shall be rated in amperes. The voltage rating of the plugs and receptacles shall not be less than the circuit voltage. Plug and receptacle ampere ratings for ac circuits shall not be less than the feeder or branch-circuit overcurrent device ampere rating. Table 210.21(B)(2) shall not apply.

(B) Interchangeability. Plugs and receptacles used in portable professional motion picture and television equipment shall be permitted to be interchangeable for ac or dc use on the same premises, provided they are listed for ac/dc use and marked in a suitable manner to identify the system to which they are connected.

530.22 Single-Pole Separable Connectors.

(A) General. Where ac single-pole portable cable connectors are used, they shall be listed and of the locking type. Sections 400.10, 406.6, and 406.7 shall not apply to listed single-pole separable connections and single-conductor cable assemblies utilizing listed single-pole separable connectors. Where paralleled sets of current-carrying single-pole separable connectors are provided as input devices, they shall be prominently labeled with a warning indicating the presence of internal parallel connections. The use of single-pole separable connectors shall comply with at least one of the following conditions:

(1) Connection and disconnection of connectors are only possible where the supply connectors are interlocked to the source and it is not possible to connect or disconnect connectors when the supply is energized.

(2) Line connectors are of the listed sequential-interlocking type so that load connectors shall be connected in the following sequence:

    a. Equipment grounding conductor connection

    b. Grounded circuit conductor connection, if provided

    c. Ungrounded conductor connection, and that disconnection shall be in the reverse order

(3) A caution notice shall be provided adjacent to the line connectors, indicating that plug connection shall be in the following order:

    a. Equipment grounding conductor connectors

    b. Grounded circuit-conductor connectors, if provided

    c. Ungrounded conductor connectors, and that disconnection shall be in the reverse order

(B) Interchangeability. Single-pole separable connectors used in portable professional motion picture and television equipment shall be permitted to be interchangeable for ac or dc use or for different current ratings on the same premises, provided they are listed for ac/dc use and marked in a suitable manner to identify the system to which they are connected.

530.23 Branch Circuits. A branch circuit of any size supplying one or more receptacles shall be permitted to supply stage set lighting loads.

III. Dressing Rooms

530.31 Dressing Rooms. Fixed wiring in dressing rooms shall be installed in accordance with the wiring methods covered in Chapter 3. Wiring for portable dressing rooms shall be approved.

IV. Viewing, Cutting, and Patching Tables

530.41 Lamps at Tables. Only composition or metal-sheathed, porcelain, keyless lampholders equipped with suitable means to guard lamps from physical damage and from film and film scrap shall be used at patching, viewing, and cutting tables.

V. Cellulose Nitrate Film Storage Vaults

530.51 Lamps in Cellulose Nitrate Film Storage Vaults. Lamps in cellulose nitrate film storage vaults shall be installed in rigid fixtures of the glass-enclosed and gasketed type. Lamps shall be controlled by a switch having a pole in each ungrounded conductor. This switch shall be located outside of the vault and provided with a pilot light to indicate whether the switch is on or off. This switch shall disconnect from all sources of supply all ungrounded conductors terminating in any outlet in the vault.

530.52 Electrical Equipment in Cellulose Nitrate Film Storage Vaults. Except as permitted in 530.51, no receptacles, outlets, heaters, portable lights, or other portable electric equipment shall be located in cellulose nitrate film storage vaults. Electric motors shall be permitted, provided they are listed for the application and comply with Article 500, Class I, Division 2.

VI. Substations

530.61 Substations. Wiring and equipment of over 600 volts, nominal, shall comply with Article 490.

530.62 Portable Substations. Wiring and equipment in portable substations shall conform to the sections applying to installations in permanently fixed substations, but, due to the limited space available, the working spaces shall be permitted to be reduced, provided that the equipment shall be arranged so that the operator can work safely and so that other persons in the vicinity cannot accidentally come into contact with current-carrying parts or bring conducting objects into contact with them while they are energized.

530.63 Overcurrent Protection of Direct-Current Generators. Three-wire generators shall have overcurrent protection in accordance with 445.12(E).

530.64 Direct-Current Switchboards.

(A) General. Switchboards of not over 250 volts dc between conductors, where located in substations or switchboard rooms accessible to qualified persons only, shall not be required to be dead-front.

(B) Circuit Breaker Frames. Frames of dc circuit breakers installed on switchboards shall not be required to be grounded.

ARTICLE 540
Motion Picture Projection Rooms

I. General

540.1 Scope. The provisions of this article apply to motion picture projection rooms, motion picture projectors, and associated equipment of the professional and nonprofessional types using incandescent, carbon arc, xenon, or other light source equipment that develops hazardous gases, dust, or radiation.

    FPN: For further information, see NFPA 40-2001, *Standard for the Storage and Handling of Cellulose Nitrate Motion Picture Film.*

540.2 Definitions.

Nonprofessional Projector. Nonprofessional projectors are those types other than as described in 540.2.

Professional Projector. A type of projector using 35- or 70-mm film that has a minimum width of 35 mm (1⅜ in.) and has on each edge 212 perforations per meter (5.4 perforations per inch), or a type using carbon arc, xenon, or other light source equipment that develops hazardous gases, dust, or radiation.

II. Equipment and Projectors of the Professional Type

540.10 Motion Picture Projection Room Required. Every professional-type projector shall be located within a projection room. Every projection room shall be of permanent construction, approved for the type of building in which the projection room is located. All projection ports, spotlight ports, viewing ports, and similar openings shall be provided with glass or other approved material so as to completely close the opening. Such rooms shall not be considered as hazardous (classified) locations as defined in Article 500.

> FPN: For further information on protecting openings in projection rooms handling cellulose nitrate motion picture film, see NFPA *101-2003, Life Safety Code.*

540.11 Location of Associated Electrical Equipment.

(A) Motor Generator Sets, Transformers, Rectifiers, Rheostats, and Similar Equipment. Motor generator sets, transformers, rectifiers, rheostats, and similar equipment for the supply or control of current to projection or spotlight equipment shall, where nitrate film is used, be located in a separate room. Where placed in the projection room, they shall be located or guarded so that arcs or sparks cannot come in contact with film, and the commutator end or ends of motor generator sets shall comply with one of the conditions in 540.11(A)(1) through (A)(6).

(1) Types. Be of the totally enclosed, enclosed fan-cooled, or enclosed pipe-ventilated type.

(2) Separate Rooms or Housings. Be enclosed in separate rooms or housings built of noncombustible material constructed so as to exclude flyings or lint, and properly ventilated from a source of clean air.

(3) Solid Metal Covers. Have the brush or sliding-contact end of motor-generator enclosed by solid metal covers.

(4) Tight Metal Housings. Have brushes or sliding contacts enclosed in substantial, tight metal housings.

(5) Upper and Lower Half Enclosures. Have the upper half of the brush or sliding-contact end of the motor-generator enclosed by a wire screen or perforated metal and the lower half enclosed by solid metal covers.

(6) Wire Screens or Perforated Metal. Have wire screens or perforated metal placed at the commutator of brush ends. No dimension of any opening in the wire screen or perforated metal shall exceed 1.27 mm (0.05 in.), regardless of the shape of the opening and of the material used.

(B) Switches, Overcurrent Devices, or Other Equipment. Switches, overcurrent devices, or other equipment not normally required or used for projectors, sound reproduction, flood or other special effect lamps, or other equipment shall not be installed in projection rooms.

Exception No. 1: In projection rooms approved for use only with cellulose acetate (safety) film, the installation of appurtenant electrical equipment used in conjunction with the operation of the projection equipment and the control of lights, curtains, and audio equipment, and so forth, shall be permitted. In such projection rooms, a sign reading "Safety Film Only Permitted in This Room" shall be posted on the outside of each projection room door and within the projection room itself in a conspicuous location.

Exception No. 2: Remote-control switches for the control of auditorium lights or switches for the control of motors operating curtains and masking of the motion picture screen shall be permitted to be installed in projection rooms.

(C) Emergency Systems. Control of emergency systems shall comply with Article 700.

540.12 Work Space. Each motion picture projector, floodlight, spotlight, or similar equipment shall have clear working space not less than 750 mm (30 in.) wide on each side and at the rear thereof.

Exception: One such space shall be permitted between adjacent pieces of equipment.

540.13 Conductor Size. Conductors supplying outlets for arc and xenon projectors of the professional type shall not be smaller than 8 AWG and shall be of sufficient size for the projector employed. Conductors for incandescent-type projectors shall conform to normal wiring standards as provided in 210.24.

540.14 Conductors on Lamps and Hot Equipment. Insulated conductors having a rated operating temperature of not less than 200°C (392°F) shall be used on all lamps or other equipment where the ambient temperature at the conductors as installed will exceed 50°C (122°F).

540.15 Flexible Cords. Cords approved for hard usage, as provided in Table 400.4, shall be used on portable equipment.

540.20 Approval. Projectors and enclosures for arc, xenon and incandescent lamps and rectifiers, transformers, rheostats, and similar equipment shall be listed.

540.21 Marking. Projectors and other equipment shall be marked with the manufacturer's name or trademark and with the voltage and current for which they are designed in accordance with 110.21.

III. Nonprofessional Projectors

540.31 Motion Picture Projection Room Not Required. Projectors of the nonprofessional or miniature type, where employing cellulose acetate (safety) film, shall be permitted to be operated without a projection room.

540.32 Approval. Projection equipment shall be listed.

IV. Audio Signal Processing, Amplification, and Reproduction Equipment

540.50 Audio Signal Processing, Amplification, and Reproduction Equipment. Audio signal processing, amplification, and reproduction equipment shall be installed as provided in Article 640.

ARTICLE 545
Manufactured Buildings

545.1 Scope. This article covers requirements for a manufactured building and building components as herein defined.

545.2 Definitions.

Building Component. Any subsystem, subassembly, or other system designed for use in or integral with or as part of a structure, which can include structural, electrical, mechanical, plumbing, and fire protection systems, and other systems affecting health and safety.

Building System. Plans, specifications, and documentation for a system of manufactured building or for a type or a system of building components, which can include structural, electrical, mechanical, plumbing, and fire protection systems, and other systems affecting health and safety, and including such variations thereof as are specifically permitted by regulation, and which variations are submitted as part of the building system or amendment thereto.

Closed Construction. Any building, building component, assembly, or system manufactured in such a manner that all concealed parts of processes of manufacture cannot be in-

spected before installation at the building site without disassembly, damage, or destruction.

Manufactured Building. Any building that is of closed construction and is made or assembled in manufacturing facilities on or off the building site for installation, or for assembly and installation on the building site, other than manufactured homes, mobile homes, park trailers, or recreational vehicles.

545.4 Wiring Methods.

(A) Methods Permitted. All raceway and cable wiring methods included in this *Code* and such other wiring systems specifically intended and listed for use in manufactured buildings shall be permitted with listed fittings and with fittings listed and identified for manufactured buildings.

(B) Securing Cables. In closed construction, cables shall be permitted to be secured only at cabinets, boxes, or fittings where 10 AWG or smaller conductors are used and protection against physical damage is provided.

545.5 Supply Conductors. Provisions shall be made to route the service-entrance, service-lateral, feeder, or branch-circuit supply to the service or building disconnecting means conductors.

545.6 Installation of Service-Entrance Conductors. Service-entrance conductors shall be installed after erection at the building site.

Exception: Where point of attachment is known prior to manufacture.

545.7 Service Equipment. Service equipment shall be installed in accordance with 230.70.

545.8 Protection of Conductors and Equipment. Protection shall be provided for exposed conductors and equipment during processes of manufacturing, packaging, in transit, and erection at the building site.

545.9 Boxes.

(A) Other Dimensions. Boxes of dimensions other than those required in Table 314.16(A) shall be permitted to be installed where tested, identified, and listed to applicable standards.

(B) Not Over 1650 cm³ (100 in.³). Any box not over 1650 cm³ (100 in.³) in size, intended for mounting in closed construction, shall be affixed with anchors or clamps so as to provide a rigid and secure installation.

545.10 Receptacle or Switch with Integral Enclosure. A receptacle or switch with integral enclosure and mounting means, where tested, identified, and listed to applicable standards, shall be permitted to be installed.

545.11 Bonding and Grounding. Prewired panels and building components shall provide for the bonding, or bonding and grounding, of all exposed metals likely to become energized, in accordance with Article 250, Parts V, VI, and VII.

545.12 Grounding Electrode Conductor. Provisions shall be made to route a grounding electrode conductor from the service, feeder, or branch-circuit supply to the point of attachment to the grounding electrode.

545.13 Component Interconnections. Fittings and connectors that are intended to be concealed at the time of on-site assembly, where tested, identified, and listed to applicable standards, shall be permitted for on-site interconnection of modules or other building components. Such fittings and connectors shall be equal to the wiring method employed in insulation, temperature rise, and fault-current withstand and shall be capable of enduring the vibration and minor relative motions occurring in the components of manufactured building.

ARTICLE 547
Agricultural Buildings

547.1 Scope. The provisions of this article shall apply to the following agricultural buildings or that part of a building or adjacent areas of similar or like nature as specified in 547.1(A) and 547.1(B).

(A) Excessive Dust and Dust with Water. Agricultural buildings where excessive dust and dust with water may accumulate, including all areas of poultry, livestock, and fish confinement systems, where litter dust or feed dust, including mineral feed particles, may accumulate.

(B) Corrosive Atmosphere. Agricultural buildings where a corrosive atmosphere exists. Such buildings include areas where the following conditions exist:

(1) Poultry and animal excrement may cause corrosive vapors.

(2) Corrosive particles may combine with water.

(3) The area is damp and wet by reason of periodic washing for cleaning and sanitizing with water and cleansing agents.

(4) Similar conditions exist.

547.2 Definitions.

Distribution Point. An electrical supply point from which service drops, service laterals, feeders, or branch circuits to agricultural buildings, associated farm dwelling(s), and associated buildings under single management are supplied.

> FPN No. 1: Distribution points are also known as the center yard pole, meterpole, or the common distribution point.

> FPN No. 2: The service point as defined in Article 100 is typically at the distribution point.

Equipotential Plane. An area where wire mesh or other conductive elements are embedded in or placed under concrete, bonded to all metal structures and fixed nonelectrical equipment that may become energized, and connected to the electrical grounding system to prevent a difference in voltage from developing within the plane.

Site-Isolating Device. A disconnecting means installed at the distribution point for the purposes of isolation, system maintenance, emergency disconnection, or connection of optional standby systems.

547.3 Other Articles. For agricultural buildings not having conditions as specified in 547.1, the electrical installations shall be made in accordance with the applicable articles in this *Code*.

547.4 Surface Temperatures. Electrical equipment or devices installed in accordance with the provisions of this article shall be installed in a manner such that they will function at full rating without developing surface temperatures in excess of the specified normal safe operating range of the equipment or device.

547.5 Wiring Methods.

(A) Wiring Systems. Types UF, NMC, copper SE cables, jacketed Type MC cable, rigid nonmetallic conduit, liquidtight flexible nonmetallic conduit, or other cables or raceways suitable for the location, with approved termination fittings, shall be the wiring methods employed. The wiring methods of Article 502, Part II, shall be permitted for areas described in 547.1(A).

> FPN: See 300.7 and 352.44 for installation of raceway systems exposed to widely different temperatures.

(B) Mounting. All cables shall be secured within 200 mm (8 in.) of each cabinet, box, or fitting. The 6-mm (¼-in.) airspace required for nonmetallic boxes, fittings, conduit, and cables in 300.6(C) shall not be required in buildings covered by this article.

(C) Equipment Enclosures, Boxes, Conduit Bodies, and Fittings.

(1) Excessive Dust. Equipment enclosures, boxes, conduit bodies, and fittings installed in areas of buildings where excessive dust may be present shall be designed to minimize the entrance of dust and shall have no openings (such as holes for attachment screws) through which dust could enter the enclosure.

(2) Damp or Wet Locations. In damp or wet locations, equipment enclosures, boxes, conduit bodies, and fittings shall be placed or equipped so as to prevent moisture from entering or accumulating within the enclosure, box, conduit body, or fitting. In wet locations, including normally dry or damp locations where surfaces are periodically washed or sprayed with water, boxes, conduit bodies, and fittings shall be listed for use in wet locations and equipment enclosures shall be weatherproof.

(3) Corrosive Atmosphere. Where wet dust, excessive moisture, corrosive gases or vapors, or other corrosive conditions may be present, equipment enclosures, boxes, conduit bodies, and fittings shall have corrosion resistance properties suitable for the conditions.

> FPN No. 1: See Table 430.91 for appropriate enclosure type designations.

> FPN No. 2: Aluminum and magnetic ferrous materials may corrode in agricultural environments.

(D) Flexible Connections. Where necessary to employ flexible connections, dusttight flexible connectors, liquidtight flexible conduit, or flexible cord listed and identified for hard usage shall be used. All connectors and fittings used shall be listed and identified for the purpose.

(E) Physical Protection. All electrical wiring and equipment subject to physical damage shall be protected.

(F) Separate Equipment Grounding Conductor. Non–current-carrying metal parts of equipment, raceways, and other enclosures, where required to be grounded, shall be grounded by a copper equipment grounding conductor installed between the equipment and the building disconnecting means. If installed underground, the equipment grounding conductor shall be insulated or covered.

(G) Receptacles. All 125-volt, single-phase, 15- and 20-ampere general-purpose receptacles installed in the following locations shall have ground-fault circuit-interrupter protection for personnel:

(1) In areas having an equipotential plane

(2) Outdoors

(3) Damp or wet locations

(4) Dirt confinement areas for livestock

547.6 Switches, Receptacles, Circuit Breakers, Controllers, and Fuses. Switches, including pushbuttons, relays, and similar devices, receptacles, circuit breakers, control-

lers, and fuses, shall be provided with enclosures as specified in 547.5(C).

547.7 Motors. Motors and other rotating electrical machinery shall be totally enclosed or designed so as to minimize the entrance of dust, moisture, or corrosive particles.

547.8 Luminaires (Lighting Fixtures). Luminaires (lighting fixtures) shall comply with 547.8(A) through 547.8(C).

(A) Minimize the Entrance of Dust. Luminaires (lighting fixtures) shall be installed to minimize the entrance of dust, foreign matter, moisture, and corrosive material.

(B) Exposed to Physical Damage. Any luminaire (lighting fixture) that may be exposed to physical damage shall be protected by a suitable guard.

(C) Exposed to Water. A luminaire (fixture) that may be exposed to water from condensation, building cleansing water, or solution shall be watertight.

547.9 Electrical Supply to Building(s) or Structure(s) from a Distribution Point. Overhead electrical supply shall comply with 547.9(A) and 547.9(B), or with 547.9(C). Underground electrical supply shall comply with 547.9(C) and 547.9(D).

(A) Site-Isolating Device. Site-isolating devices shall comply with 547.9(A)(1) through (A)(9).

(1) Where Required. A site-isolating device shall be installed at the distribution point where two or more agricultural buildings, structures, associated farm dwelling(s), or other buildings are supplied from the distribution point.

(2) Location. The site-isolating device shall be pole-mounted and shall meet the clearance requirements of 230.24.

(3) Operation. The site-isolating device shall simultaneously disconnect all ungrounded service conductors from the premises wiring.

(4) Bonding Provisions. The site-isolating device enclosure shall be bonded to the grounded circuit conductor and the grounding electrode system.

(5) Grounding. At the site-isolating device, the system grounded conductor shall be connected to a grounding electrode system via a grounding electrode conductor.

(6) Rating. The site-isolating device shall be rated for the calculated load as determined by Part V of Article 220.

(7) Overcurrent Protection. The site-isolating device shall not be required to provide overcurrent protection.

(8) Accessibility. Where the site-isolating device is not readily accessible, it shall be capable of being remotely operated by an operating handle installed at a readily accessible location. The operating handle of the site-isolating device, when in its highest position, shall not be more than 2.0 m (6 ft 7 in.) above grade or a working platform.

(9) Series Devices. An additional site-isolating device for the premises wiring system shall not be required where a site-isolating device meeting all applicable requirements of this section is provided by the serving utility as part of their service requirements.

(B) Service Disconnecting Means and Overcurrent Protection at the Building(s) or Structure(s). Where the service disconnecting means and overcurrent protection are located at the building(s) or structure(s), the requirements of 547.9(B)(1) through (B)(3) shall apply.

(1) Conductor Sizing. The supply conductors shall be sized in accordance with Part V of Article 220.

(2) Conductor Installation. The supply conductors shall be installed in accordance with the requirements of Part II of Article 225.

(3) Grounding and Bonding. For each building or structure, the conditions in either (B)(3)(a) or (B)(3)(b) shall be permitted.

(a) System with grounded neutral conductor. The grounded circuit conductor shall be connected to the building disconnecting means and to the grounding electrode system of that building or structure where all the requirements of 250.32(B)(2) are met.

FPN: A system with a grounded neutral conductor is commonly referred to as a "3-wire system" in single-phase applications.

(b) System with separate equipment grounding conductor. A separate equipment-grounding conductor shall be run with the supply conductors to the building(s) or structure(s), and the following conditions shall be met:

FPN: A system with a separate equipment grounding conductor is commonly referred to as a "4-wire system" in single-phase applications.

(1) The equipment grounding conductor shall be the same size as the largest supply conductor if of the same material, or adjusted in size in accordance with the equivalent size columns of Table 250.122 if of different materials.

(2) The equipment grounding conductor is bonded to the grounded circuit conductor and the site-isolating device at the distribution point.

(3) A grounding electrode system is provided in accordance with Part III of Article 250 and connected to the equipment-grounding conductor at the building(s) or structure(s) disconnecting means.

(4) The grounded circuit conductor is not connected to a grounding electrode or to any equipment-grounding conductor on the load side of the distribution point.

(C) Service Disconnecting Means and Overcurrent Protection at the Distribution Point. Where the service disconnecting means and overcurrent protection for each set of feeder conductors are located at the distribution point, feeders to building(s) or structure(s) shall meet the requirements of 250.32 and Article 225, Parts I and II.

FPN: Methods to reduce neutral-to-earth voltages in livestock facilities include supplying buildings or structures with 4-wire single-phase services, sizing 3-wire single-phase service and feeder conductors to limit voltage drop to 2 percent, and connecting loads line-to-line.

(D) Direct-Buried Equipment Grounding Conductors. Where livestock is housed, any portion of a direct-buried equipment grounding conductor run to the building or structure shall be insulated or covered copper.

547.10 Equipotential Planes and Bonding of Equipotential Planes. The installation and bonding of equipotential planes shall comply with 547.10(A) and 547.10(B). For the purposes of this section, the term *livestock* shall not include poultry.

(A) Where Required. Equipotential planes shall be installed in all concrete floor confinement areas in livestock buildings, and in all outdoor confinement areas such as feedlots, containing metallic equipment that may become energized and is accessible to livestock. The equipotential plane shall encompass the area where the livestock stands while accessing metallic equipment that may become energized.

(B) Bonding. Equipotential planes shall be bonded to the electrical grounding system. The bonding conductor shall be copper, insulated, covered or bare, and not smaller than 8 AWG. The means of bonding to wire mesh or conductive elements shall be by pressure connectors or clamps of brass, copper, copper alloy, or an equally substantial approved means. Slatted floors that are supported by structures that are a part of an equipotential plane shall not require bonding.

FPN No. 1: Methods to establish equipotential planes are described in American Society of Agricultural Engineers (ASAE) EP473-2001, *Equipotential Planes in Animal Containment Areas.*

FPN No. 2: Low grounding electrode system resistances may reduce potential differences in livestock facilities.

I. General

550.1 Scope. The provisions of this article cover the electrical conductors and equipment installed within or on mobile and manufactured homes, the conductors that connect mobile and manufactured homes to a supply of electricity, and the installation of electrical wiring, luminaires (fixtures), equipment, and appurtenances related to electrical installations within a mobile home park up to the mobile home service-entrance conductors or, if none, the mobile home service equipment.

FPN: For additional information on manufactured housing see NFPA 501-2003, *Standard on Manufactured Housing*, and Part 3280, *Manufactured Home Construction and Safety Standards*, of the Federal Department of Housing and Urban Development.

550.2 Definitions.

Appliance, Fixed. An appliance that is fastened or otherwise secured at a specific location.

Appliance, Portable. An appliance that is actually moved or can easily be moved from one place to another in normal use.

FPN: For the purpose of this article, the following major appliances, other than built-in, are considered portable if cord connected: refrigerators, range equipment, clothes washers, dishwashers without booster heaters, or other similar appliances.

Appliance, Stationary. An appliance that is not easily moved from one place to another in normal use.

Distribution Panelboard. See definition of panelboard in Article 100.

Feeder Assembly. The overhead or under-chassis feeder conductors, including the grounding conductor, together with the necessary fittings and equipment or a power-supply cord listed for mobile home use, designed for the purpose of delivering energy from the source of electrical supply to the distribution panelboard within the mobile home.

Laundry Area. An area containing or designed to contain a laundry tray, clothes washer, or a clothes dryer.

Manufactured Home. A structure, transportable in one or more sections, that is 2.5 m (8 body ft) or more in width or 12 m (40 body ft) or more in length in the traveling mode or, when erected on site, is 30 m² (320 ft²) or more; which

is built on a chassis and designed to be used as a dwelling, with or without a permanent foundation, when connected to the required utilities, including the plumbing, heating, air conditioning, and electrical systems contained therein. Calculations used to determine the number of square meters (square feet) in a structure will be based on the structure's exterior dimensions, measured at the largest horizontal projections when erected on site. These dimensions include all expandable rooms, cabinets, and other projections containing interior space but do not include inside bay windows.

For the purpose of this *Code* and unless otherwise indicated, the term *mobile home* includes manufactured homes.

FPN No. 1: See the applicable building code for definition of the term *permanent foundation*.

FPN No. 2: See Part 3280, *Manufactured Home Construction and Safety Standards*, of the Federal Department of Housing and Urban Development, for additional information on the definition.

Mobile Home. A factory-assembled structure or structures transportable in one or more sections that is built on a permanent chassis and designed to be used as a dwelling without a permanent foundation where connected to the required utilities and that includes the plumbing, heating, air-conditioning, and electric systems contained therein.

For the purpose of this *Code* and unless otherwise indicated, the term *mobile home* includes manufactured homes.

Mobile Home Accessory Building or Structure. Any awning, cabana, ramada, storage cabinet, carport, fence, windbreak, or porch established for the use of the occupant of the mobile home on a mobile home lot.

Mobile Home Lot. A designated portion of a mobile home park designed for the accommodation of one mobile home and its accessory buildings or structures for the exclusive use of its occupants.

Mobile Home Park. A contiguous parcel of land that is used for the accommodation of occupied mobile homes.

Mobile Home Service Equipment. The equipment containing the disconnecting means, overcurrent protective devices, and receptacles or other means for connecting a mobile home feeder assembly.

Park Electrical Wiring Systems. All of the electrical wiring, luminaires (fixtures), equipment, and appurtenances related to electrical installations within a mobile home park, including the mobile home service equipment.

550.4 General Requirements.

(A) Mobile Home Not Intended as a Dwelling Unit. A mobile home not intended as a dwelling unit — for example, those equipped for sleeping purposes only, contractor's on-site offices, construction job dormitories, mobile studio dressing rooms, banks, clinics, mobile stores, or intended for the display or demonstration of merchandise or machinery — shall not be required to meet the provisions of this article pertaining to the number or capacity of circuits required. It shall, however, meet all other applicable requirements of this article if provided with an electrical installation intended to be energized from a 120-volt or 120/240-volt ac power supply system. Where different voltage is required by either design or available power supply system, adjustment shall be made in accordance with other articles and sections for the voltage used.

(B) In Other Than Mobile Home Parks. Mobile homes installed in other than mobile home parks shall comply with the provisions of this article.

(C) Connection to Wiring System. The provisions of this article shall apply to mobile homes intended for connection to a wiring system rated 120/240 volts, nominal, 3-wire ac, with grounded neutral.

(D) Listed or Labeled. All electrical materials, devices, appliances, fittings, and other equipment shall be listed or labeled by a qualified testing agency and shall be connected in an approved manner when installed.

II. Mobile and Manufactured Homes

550.10 Power Supply.

(A) Feeder. The power supply to the mobile home shall be a feeder assembly consisting of not more than one listed 50-ampere mobile home power-supply cord with an integrally molded or securely attached plug cap or a permanently installed feeder.

Exception No. 1:   A mobile home that is factory equipped with gas or oil-fired central heating equipment and cooking appliances shall be permitted to be provided with a listed mobile home power-supply cord rated 40 amperes.

Exception No. 2:   A feeder assembly shall not be required for manufactured homes constructed in accordance with 550.32(B).

(B) Power-Supply Cord. If the mobile home has a power-supply cord, it shall be permanently attached to the distribution panelboard or to a junction box permanently connected to the distribution panelboard, with the free end terminating in an attachment plug cap.

Cords with adapters and pigtail ends, extension cords, and similar items shall not be attached to, or shipped with, a mobile home.

A suitable clamp or the equivalent shall be provided at the distribution panelboard knockout to afford strain relief for the cord to prevent strain from being transmitted to the terminals when the power-supply cord is handled in its intended manner.

The cord shall be a listed type with four conductors, one of which shall be identified by a continuous green color or a continuous green color with one or more yellow stripes for use as the grounding conductor.

(C) Attachment Plug Cap. The attachment plug cap shall be a 3-pole, 4-wire, grounding type, rated 50 amperes, 125/250 volts with a configuration as shown in Figure 550.10(C) and intended for use with the 50-ampere, 125/250-volt receptacle configuration shown in Figure 550.10(C). It shall be listed, by itself or as part of a power-supply cord assembly, for the purpose and shall be molded to or installed on the flexible cord so that it is secured tightly to the cord at the point where the cord enters the attachment plug cap. If a right-angle cap is used, the configuration shall be oriented so that the grounding member is farthest from the cord.

FPN: Complete details of the 50-ampere plug and receptacle configuration can be found in the National Electrical Manufacturers Association *Standard for Dimensions of Attachment Plugs and Receptacles*, ANSI/NEMA WD 6-1989, Figure 14-50.

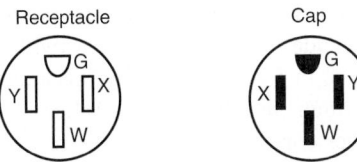

125/250-V, 50-A, 3-pole, 4-wire, grounding type

Figure 550.10(C) 50-Ampere, 125/250-Volt Receptacle and Attachment Plug Cap Configurations, 3-Pole, 4-Wire, Grounding-Types, Used for Mobile Home Supply Cords and Mobile Home Parks.

(D) Overall Length of a Power-Supply Cord. The overall length of a power-supply cord, measured from the end of the cord, including bared leads, to the face of the attachment plug cap shall not be less than 6.4 m (21 ft) and shall not exceed 11 m (36½ ft). The length of the cord from the face of the attachment plug cap to the point where the cord enters the mobile home shall not be less than 6.0 m (20 ft).

(E) Marking. The power-supply cord shall bear the following marking:

FOR USE WITH MOBILE HOMES — 40 AMPERES.

or

FOR USE WITH MOBILE HOMES — 50 AMPERES.

(F) Point of Entrance. The point of entrance of the feeder assembly to the mobile home shall be in the exterior wall, floor, or roof.

(G) Protected. Where the cord passes through walls or floors, it shall be protected by means of conduits and bushings or equivalent. The cord shall be permitted to be installed within the mobile home walls, provided a continuous raceway having a maximum size of 32 mm (1¼ in.) is installed from the branch-circuit panelboard to the underside of the mobile home floor.

(H) Protection Against Corrosion and Mechanical Damage. Permanent provisions shall be made for the protection of the attachment plug cap of the power-supply cord and any connector cord assembly or receptacle against corrosion and mechanical damage if such devices are in an exterior location while the mobile home is in transit.

(I) Mast Weatherhead or Raceway. Where the calculated load exceeds 50 amperes or where a permanent feeder is used, the supply shall be by means of either of the following:

(1) One mast weatherhead installation, installed in accordance with Article 230, containing four continuous, insulated, color-coded feeder conductors, one of which shall be an equipment grounding conductor

(2) A metal raceway or rigid nonmetallic conduit from the disconnecting means in the mobile home to the underside of the mobile home, with provisions for the attachment to a suitable junction box or fitting to the raceway on the underside of the mobile home [with or without conductors as in 550.10(I)(1)]. The manufacturer shall provide written installation instructions stating the proper feeder conductor sizes for the raceway and the size of the junction box to be used.

550.11 Disconnecting Means and Branch-Circuit Protective Equipment. The branch-circuit equipment shall be permitted to be combined with the disconnecting means as a single assembly. Such a combination shall be permitted to be designated as a distribution panelboard. If a fused distribution panelboard is used, the maximum fuse size for the mains shall be plainly marked with lettering at least 6 mm (¼ in.) high and visible when fuses are changed.

Where plug fuses and fuseholders are used, they shall be tamper-resistant Type S, enclosed in dead-front fuse panelboards. Electrical distribution panelboards containing circuit breakers shall also be dead-front type.

FPN: See 110.22 concerning identification of each disconnecting means and each service, feeder, or branch circuit at the point where it originated and the type marking needed.

(A) Disconnecting Means. A single disconnecting means shall be provided in each mobile home consisting of a circuit breaker, or a switch and fuses and its accessories installed in a readily accessible location near the point of entrance of the supply cord or conductors into the mobile home. The main circuit breakers or fuses shall be plainly marked "Main." This equipment shall contain a solderless type of grounding connector or bar for the purposes of grounding, with sufficient terminals for all grounding conductors. The neutral bar termination of the grounded circuit conductors shall be insulated in accordance with 550.16(A). The disconnecting equipment shall have a rating not less than the calculated load. The distribution equipment, either circuit breaker or fused type, shall be located a minimum of 600 mm (24 in.) from the bottom of such equipment to the floor level of the mobile home.

FPN: See 550.20(B) for information on disconnecting means for branch circuits designed to energize heating or air-conditioning equipment, or both, located outside the mobile home, other than room air conditioners.

A distribution panelboard shall be rated not less than 50 amperes and employ a 2-pole circuit breaker rated 40 amperes for a 40-ampere supply cord, or 50 amperes for a 50-ampere supply cord. A distribution panelboard employing a disconnect switch and fuses shall be rated 60 amperes and shall employ a single 2-pole, 60-ampere fuseholder with 40- or 50-ampere main fuses for 40- or 50-ampere supply cords, respectively. The outside of the distribution panelboard shall be plainly marked with the fuse size.

The distribution panelboard shall be located in an accessible location but shall not be located in a bathroom or a clothes closet. A clear working space at least 750 mm (30 in.) wide and 750 mm (30 in.) in front of the distribution panelboard shall be provided. This space shall extend from the floor to the top of the distribution panelboard.

(B) Branch-Circuit Protective Equipment. Branch-circuit distribution equipment shall be installed in each mobile home and shall include overcurrent protection for each branch circuit consisting of either circuit breakers or fuses.

The branch-circuit overcurrent devices shall be rated as follows:

(1) Not more than the circuit conductors; and

(2) Not more than 150 percent of the rating of a single appliance rated 13.3 amperes or more that is supplied by an individual branch circuit; but

(3) Not more than the overcurrent protection size and of the type marked on the air conditioner or other motor-operated appliance.

(C) Two-Pole Circuit Breakers. Where circuit breakers are provided for branch-circuit protection, 240-volt circuits shall be protected by a 2-pole common or companion trip, or handle-tied paired circuit breakers.

(D) Electrical Nameplates. A metal nameplate on the outside adjacent to the feeder assembly entrance shall read:

THIS CONNECTION FOR 120/240-VOLT,
3-POLE, 4-WIRE, 60-HERTZ,
_____ AMPERE SUPPLY

The correct ampere rating shall be marked in the blank space.

Exception: For manufactured homes, the manufacturer shall provide in its written installation instructions or in the data plate the minimum ampere rating of the feeder assembly or, where provided, the service entrance conductors intended for connection to the manufactured home. The rating provided shall not be less than the minimum load calculated in accordance with 550.18.

550.12 Branch Circuits. The number of branch circuits required shall be determined in accordance with 550.12(A) through (E).

(A) Lighting. The number of branch circuits shall be based on 33 volt-amperes/m² (3 VA/ft²) times outside dimensions of the mobile home (coupler excluded) divided by 120 volts to determine the number of 15- or 20-ampere lighting area circuits, for example,

$$\frac{3 \times \text{length} \times \text{width}}{120 \times 15 \text{ (or 20)}}$$

= No. of 15− (or 20−) ampere circuits

(B) Small Appliances. In kitchens, pantries, dining rooms, and breakfast rooms, two or more 20-ampere small-appliance circuits, in addition to the number of circuits required elsewhere in this section, shall be provided for all receptacle outlets required by 550.13(D) in these rooms. Such circuits shall have no other outlets.

Exception No. 1: Receptacle outlets installed solely for the electrical supply and support of an electric clock in any the rooms specified in 550.12(B) shall be permitted.

Exception No. 2: Receptacle outlets installed to provide power for supplemental equipment and lighting on gas-fired ranges, ovens, or counter-mounted cooking units shall be permitted.

Exception No. 3: A single receptacle for refrigeration equipment shall be permitted to be supplied from an individual branch circuit rated 15 amperes or greater.

Countertop receptacle outlets installed in the kitchen shall be supplied by not less than two small-appliance circuit branch circuits, either or both of which shall be permitted to supply receptacle outlets in the kitchen and other locations specified in 550.12(B).

(C) Laundry Area. Where a laundry area is provided, a 20-ampere branch circuit shall be provided to supply the laundry receptacle outlet(s). This circuit shall have no other outlets.

(D) General Appliances. (Including furnace, water heater, range, and central or room air conditioner, etc.). There shall

be one or more circuits of adequate rating in accordance with the following:

FPN: For central air conditioning, see Article 440.

(1) The ampere rating of fixed appliances shall not be over 50 percent of the circuit rating if lighting outlets (receptacles, other than kitchen, dining area, and laundry, considered as lighting outlets) are on the same circuit.

(2) For fixed appliances on a circuit without lighting outlets, the sum of rated amperes shall not exceed the branch-circuit rating. Motor loads or continuous loads shall not exceed 80 percent of the branch-circuit rating.

(3) The rating of a single cord-and-plug-connected appliance on a circuit having no other outlets shall not exceed 80 percent of the circuit rating.

(4) The rating of a range branch circuit shall be based on the range demand as specified for ranges in 550.18(B)(5).

(E) Bathrooms. Bathroom receptacle outlets shall be supplied by at least one 20-ampere branch circuit. Such circuits shall have no other outlets other than as provided for in 550.13(E)(2).

550.13 Receptacle Outlets.

(A) Grounding-Type Receptacle Outlets. All receptacle outlets shall comply with the following:

(1) Be of grounding type

(2) Be installed according to 406.3

(3) Except where supplying specific appliances, be 15- or 20-ampere, 125-volt, either single or multiple type, and accept parallel-blade attachment plugs

(B) Ground-Fault Circuit Interrupters (GFCI). All 125-volt, single-phase, 15- and 20-ampere receptacle outlets installed outdoors, in compartments accessible from outside the unit, or in bathrooms, including receptacles in luminaires (light fixtures), shall have GFCI protection. GFCI protection shall be provided for receptacle outlets serving countertops in kitchens, and receptacle outlets located within 1.8 m (6 ft) of a wet bar sink.

Exception: Receptacles installed for appliances in dedicated spaces, such as for dishwashers, disposals, refrigerators, freezers, and laundry equipment.

Feeders supplying branch circuits shall be permitted to be protected by a ground-fault circuit-interrupter in lieu of the provision for such interrupters specified herein.

(C) Cord-Connected Fixed Appliance. A grounding-type receptacle outlet shall be provided for each cord-connected fixed appliance installed.

(D) Receptacle Outlets Required. Except in the bath, closet, and hall areas, receptacle outlets shall be installed at wall spaces 600 mm (2 ft) wide or more so that no point along the floor line is more than 1.8 m (6 ft) measured horizontally from an outlet in that space. In addition, a receptacle outlet shall be installed in the following locations:

(1) Over or adjacent to countertops in the kitchen [at least one on each side of the sink if countertops are on each side and are 300 mm (12 in.) or over in width].

(2) Adjacent to the refrigerator and freestanding gas-range space. A duplex receptacle shall be permitted to serve as the outlet for a countertop and a refrigerator.

(3) At countertop spaces for built-in vanities.

(4) At countertop spaces under wall-mounted cabinets.

(5) In the wall at the nearest point to where a bar-type counter attaches to the wall.

(6) In the wall at the nearest point to where a fixed room divider attaches to the wall.

(7) In laundry areas within 1.8 m (6 ft) of the intended location of the laundry appliance(s).

(8) At least one receptacle outlet located outdoors and accessible at grade level and not more than 2.0 m (6½ ft) above grade. A receptacle outlet located in a compartment accessible from the outside of the unit shall be considered an outdoor receptacle.

(9) At least one receptacle outlet shall be installed in bathrooms within 900 mm (36 in.) of the outside edge of each basin. The receptacle outlet shall be located above or adjacent to the basin location. This receptacle shall be in addition to any receptacle that is a part of a luminaire (fixture) or appliance. The receptacle shall not be enclosed within a bathroom cabinet or vanity.

(E) Pipe Heating Cable(s) Outlet. For the connection of pipe heating cable(s), a receptacle outlet shall be located on the underside of the unit as follows:

(1) Within 600 mm (2 ft) of the cold water inlet.

(2) Connected to an interior branch circuit, other than a small appliance branch circuit. It shall be permitted to use a bathroom receptacle circuit for this purpose.

(3) On a circuit where all of the outlets are on the load side of the ground-fault circuit-interrupter.

(4) This outlet shall not be considered as the receptacle required by 550.13(D)(8).

(F) Receptacle Outlets Not Permitted. Receptacle outlets shall not be permitted in the following locations:

(1) Receptacle outlets shall not be installed within a bathtub or shower space.

(2) A receptacle shall not be installed in a face-up position in any countertop.

(3) Receptacle outlets shall not be installed above electric baseboard heaters, unless provided for in the listing or manufacturer's instructions.

(G) Receptacle Outlets Not Required. Receptacle outlets shall not be required in the following locations:

(1) In the wall space occupied by built-in kitchen or wardrobe cabinets

(2) In the wall space behind doors that can be opened fully against a wall surface

(3) In room dividers of the lattice type that are less than 2.5 m (8 ft) long, not solid, and within 150 mm (6 in.) of the floor

(4) In the wall space afforded by bar-type counters

550.14 Luminaires (Fixtures) and Appliances.

(A) Fasten Appliances in Transit. Means shall be provided to securely fasten appliances when the mobile home is in transit. (See 550.16 for provisions on grounding.)

(B) Accessibility. Every appliance shall be accessible for inspection, service, repair, or replacement without removal of permanent construction.

(C) Pendants. Listed pendant-type luminaires (fixtures) or pendant cords shall be permitted.

(D) Bathtub and Shower Luminaires (Fixtures). Where a luminaire (lighting fixture) is installed over a bathtub or in a shower stall, it shall be of the enclosed and gasketed type listed for wet locations.

550.15 Wiring Methods and Materials. Except as specifically limited in this section, the wiring methods and materials included in this *Code* shall be used in mobile homes. Aluminum conductors, aluminum alloy conductors, and aluminum core conductors such as copper-clad aluminum shall not be acceptable for use as branch-circuit wiring.

(A) Nonmetallic Boxes. Nonmetallic boxes shall be permitted only with nonmetallic cable or nonmetallic raceways.

(B) Nonmetallic Cable Protection. Nonmetallic cable located 380 mm (15 in.) or less above the floor, if exposed, shall be protected from physical damage by covering boards, guard strips, or raceways. Cable likely to be damaged by stowage shall be so protected in all cases.

(C) Metal-Covered and Nonmetallic Cable Protection. Metal-covered and nonmetallic cables shall be permitted to pass through the centers of the wide side of 2 by 4 studs. However, they shall be protected where they pass through 2 by 2 studs or at other studs or frames where the cable or armor would be less than 32 mm (1¼ in.) from the inside or outside surface of the studs where the wall covering materials are in contact with the studs. Steel plates on each side of the cable, or a tube, with not less than 1.35 mm (0.053 in.) wall thickness shall be required to protect the cable. These plates or tubes shall be securely held in place.

(D) Metal Faceplates. Where metal faceplates are used, they shall be effectively grounded.

(E) Installation Requirements. If a range, clothes dryer, or similar appliance is connected by metal-covered cable or flexible metal conduit, a length of not less than 900 mm (3 ft) of free cable or conduit shall be provided to permit moving the appliance. The cable or flexible metal conduit shall be secured to the wall. Type NM or Type SE cable shall not be used to connect a range or dryer. This shall not prohibit the use of Type NM or Type SE cable between the branch-circuit overcurrent-protective device and a junction box or range or dryer receptacle.

(F) Raceways. Where rigid metal conduit or intermediate metal conduit is terminated at an enclosure with a locknut and bushing connection, two locknuts shall be provided, one inside and one outside of the enclosure. Rigid nonmetallic conduit, electrical nonmetallic tubing, or surface raceway shall be permitted. All cut ends of conduit and tubing shall be reamed or otherwise finished to remove rough edges.

(G) Switches. Switches shall be rated as follows:

(1) For lighting circuits, switches shall be rated not less than 10 amperes, 120 to 125 volts, and in no case less than the connected load.

(2) Switches for motor or other loads shall comply with the provisions of 404.14.

(H) Under-Chassis Wiring (Exposed to Weather). Where outdoor or under-chassis line-voltage (120 volts, nominal, or higher) wiring is exposed to moisture or physical damage, it shall be protected by rigid metal conduit or intermediate metal conduit. The conductors shall be suitable for wet locations.

Exception: Type MI cable, electrical metallic tubing, or rigid nonmetallic conduit shall be permitted where closely routed against frames and equipment enclosures.

(I) Boxes, Fittings, and Cabinets. Boxes, fittings, and cabinets shall be securely fastened in place and shall be supported from a structural member of the home, either directly or by using a substantial brace.

Exception: Snap-in-type boxes. Boxes provided with special wall or ceiling brackets and wiring devices with integral enclosures that securely fasten to walls or ceilings and are identified for the use shall be permitted without support from a structural member or brace. The testing and approval shall include the wall and ceiling construction systems for which the boxes and devices are intended to be used.

(J) Appliance Terminal Connections. Appliances having branch-circuit terminal connections that operate at temperatures higher than 60°C (140°F) shall have circuit conductors as described in the following:

(1) Branch-circuit conductors having an insulation suitable for the temperature encountered shall be permitted to be run directly to the appliance.

(2) Conductors having an insulation suitable for the temperature encountered shall be run from the appliance terminal connection to a readily accessible outlet box placed at least 300 mm (1 ft) from the appliance. These conductors shall be in a suitable raceway or Type AC or MC cable of at least 450 mm (18 in.) but not more than 1.8 m (6 ft) in length.

(K) Component Interconnections. Fittings and connectors that are intended to be concealed at the time of assembly shall be listed and identified for the interconnection of building components. Such fittings and connectors shall be equal to the wiring method employed in insulation, temperature rise, and fault-current withstanding and shall be capable of enduring the vibration and shock occurring in mobile home transportation.

FPN: See 550.19 for interconnection of multiple section units.

550.16 Grounding. Grounding of both electrical and non-electrical metal parts in a mobile home shall be through connection to a grounding bus in the mobile home distribution panelboard. The grounding bus shall be grounded through the green-colored insulated conductor in the supply cord or the feeder wiring to the service ground in the service-entrance equipment located adjacent to the mobile home location. Neither the frame of the mobile home nor the frame of any appliance shall be connected to the grounded circuit conductor (neutral) in the mobile home. Where the distribution panelboard is the service equipment as permitted by 550.32(B), the neutral conductors and the equipment grounding bus shall be connected.

(A) Grounded (Neutral) Conductor.

(1) Insulated. The grounded circuit conductor (neutral) shall be insulated from the grounding conductors and from equipment enclosures and other grounded parts. The grounded (neutral) circuit terminals in the distribution panelboard and in ranges, clothes dryers, counter-mounted cooking units, and wall-mounted ovens shall be insulated from the equipment enclosure. Bonding screws, straps, or buses in the distribution panelboard or in appliances shall be removed and discarded. Where the distribution panelboard is the service equipment as permitted by 550.32(B), the neutral conductors and the equipment grounding bus shall be connected.

(2) Connections of Ranges and Clothes Dryers. Connections of ranges and clothes dryers with 120/240-volt, 3-wire ratings shall be made with 4-conductor cord and 3-pole, 4-wire, grounding-type plugs or by Type AC cable, Type MC cable, or conductors enclosed in flexible metal conduit.

(B) Equipment Grounding Means.

(1) Supply Cord or Permanent Feeder. The green-colored insulated grounding wire in the supply cord or permanent feeder wiring shall be connected to the grounding bus in the distribution panelboard or disconnecting means.

(2) Electrical System. In the electrical system, all exposed metal parts, enclosures, frames, lamp fixture canopies, and so forth shall be effectively bonded to the grounding terminal or enclosure of the distribution panelboard.

(3) Cord-Connected Appliances. Cord-connected appliances, such as washing machines, clothes dryers, and refrigerators, and the electrical system of gas ranges and so forth, shall be grounded by means of a cord with grounding conductor and grounding-type attachment plug.

(C) Bonding of Non–Current-Carrying Metal Parts.

(1) Exposed Non–Current-Carrying Metal Parts. All exposed non–current-carrying metal parts that may become energized shall be effectively bonded to the grounding terminal or enclosure of the distribution panelboard. A bonding conductor shall be connected between the distribution panelboard and accessible terminal on the chassis.

(2) Grounding Terminals. Grounding terminals shall be of the solderless type and listed as pressure-terminal connectors recognized for the wire size used. The bonding conductor shall be solid or stranded, insulated or bare, and shall be 8 AWG copper minimum, or equivalent. The bonding conductor shall be routed so as not to be exposed to physical damage.

(3) Metallic Piping and Ducts. Metallic gas, water, and waste pipes and metallic air-circulating ducts shall be considered bonded if they are connected to the terminal on the chassis [see 550.16(C)(1)] by clamps, solderless connectors, or by suitable grounding-type straps.

(4) Metallic Roof and Exterior Coverings. Any metallic roof and exterior covering shall be considered bonded if the following conditions are met:

(1) The metal panels overlap one another and are securely attached to the wood or metal frame parts by metallic fasteners.

(2) The lower panel of the metallic exterior covering is secured by metallic fasteners at a cross member of the chassis by two metal straps per mobile home unit or section at opposite ends.

The bonding strap material shall be a minimum of 100 mm (4 in.) in width of material equivalent to the skin or a material of equal or better electrical conductivity. The straps shall be fastened with paint-penetrating fittings such as screws and starwashers or equivalent.

550.17 Testing.

(A) Dielectric Strength Test. The wiring of each mobile home shall be subjected to a 1-minute, 900-volt, dielectric strength test (with all switches closed) between live parts (including neutral) and the mobile home ground. Alternatively, the test shall be permitted to be performed at 1080 volts for 1 second. This test shall be performed after branch circuits are complete and after luminaires (fixtures) or appliances are installed.

Exception: Listed luminaires (fixtures) or appliances shall not be required to withstand the dielectric strength test.

(B) Continuity and Operational Tests and Polarity Checks. Each mobile home shall be subjected to all of the following:

(1) An electrical continuity test to ensure that all exposed electrically conductive parts are properly bonded

(2) An electrical operational test to demonstrate that all equipment, except water heaters and electric furnaces, is connected and in working order

(3) Electrical polarity checks of permanently wired equipment and receptacle outlets to determine that connections have been properly made

550.18 Calculations. The following method shall be employed in calculating the supply-cord and distribution-panelboard load for each feeder assembly for each mobile home in lieu of the procedure shown in Article 220 and shall be based on a 3-wire, 120/240-volt supply with 120-volt loads balanced between the two legs of the 3-wire system.

(A) Lighting, Small Appliance, and Laundry Load.

(1) Lighting Volt-Amperes. Length times width of mobile home floor (outside dimensions) times 33 volt-amperes/m² (3 VA/ft²), for example, length × width × 3 = lighting volt-amperes.

(2) Small Appliance Volt-Amperes. Number of circuits times 1500 volt-amperes for each 20-ampere appliance receptacle circuit (see definition of Appliance, Portable, with note in 550.2), for example, number of circuits × 1500 = small appliance volt-amperes.

(3) Laundry Area Circuit Volt-Amperes. 1500 volt-amperes.

(4) Total Volt-Amperes. Lighting volt-amperes plus small appliance volt-amperes plus laundry area volt-amperes equals total volt-amperes.

(5) Net Volt-Amperes. First 3000 total volt-amperes at 100 percent plus remainder at 35 percent equals volt-amperes to be divided by 240 volts to obtain current (amperes) per leg.

(B) Total Load for Determining Power Supply. Total load for determining power supply is the sum of the following:

(1) Lighting and small appliance load as calculated in 550.18(A)(5).

(2) Nameplate amperes for motors and heater loads (exhaust fans, air conditioners, electric, gas, or oil heating). Omit smaller of the heating and cooling loads, except include blower motor if used as air-conditioner evaporator motor. Where an air conditioner is not installed and a 40-ampere power-supply cord is provided, allow 15 amperes per leg for air conditioning.

(3) Twenty-five percent of current of largest motor in (2).

(4) Total of nameplate amperes for waste disposer, dishwasher, water heater, clothes dryer, wall-mounted oven, cooking units. Where the number of these appliances exceeds three, use 75 percent of total.

(5) Derive amperes for freestanding range (as distinguished from separate ovens and cooking units) by dividing the following values by 240 volts:

Nameplate Rating (watts)	Use (volt-amperes)
0 – 10,000	80 percent of rating
Over 10,000 – 12,500	8,000
Over 12,500 – 13,500	8,400
Over 13,500 – 14,500	8,800
Over 14,500 – 15,500	9,200
Over 15,500 – 16,500	9,600
Over 16,500 – 17,500	10,000

(6) If outlets or circuits are provided for other than factory-installed appliances, include the anticipated load.

FPN: Refer to Annex D, Example D11, for an illustration of the application of this calculation.

(C) Optional Method of Calculation for Lighting and Appliance Load. The optional method for calculating lighting and appliance load shown in 220.82 shall be permitted.

550.19 Interconnection of Multiple-Section Mobile or Manufactured Home Units.

(A) Wiring Methods. Approved and listed fixed-type wiring methods shall be used to join portions of a circuit that must be electrically joined and are located in adjacent sections after the home is installed on its support foundation. The circuit's junction shall be accessible for disassembly when the home is prepared for relocation.

FPN: See 550.15(K) for component interconnections.

(B) Disconnecting Means. Expandable or multi-unit manufactured homes not having permanently installed feeders that are to be moved from one location to another shall be permitted to have disconnecting means with branch-circuit protective equipment in each unit when so located that after assembly or joining together of units, the requirements of 550.10 will be met.

550.20 Outdoor Outlets, Luminaires (Fixtures), Air-Cooling Equipment, and So Forth.

(A) Listed for Outdoor Use. Outdoor luminaires (fixtures) and equipment shall be listed for outdoor use. Outdoor receptacle or convenience outlets shall be of a gasketed-cover type for use in wet locations. Where located on the underside of the home or located under roof extensions or similarly protected locations, outdoor luminaires (fixtures) and equipment shall be listed for use in damp locations.

(B) Outside Heating Equipment, Air-Conditioning Equipment, or Both. A mobile home provided with a branch circuit designed to energize outside heating equipment, air-conditioning equipment, or both, located outside the mobile home, other than room air conditioners, shall have such branch-circuit conductors terminate in a listed outlet box, or disconnecting means, located on the outside of the mobile home. A label shall be permanently affixed adjacent to the outlet box and shall contain the following information:

> THIS CONNECTION IS FOR HEATING AND/OR AIR-CONDITIONING EQUIPMENT. THE BRANCH CIRCUIT IS RATED AT NOT MORE THAN _____ AMPERES, AT _____ VOLTS, 60 HERTZ, _____ CONDUCTOR AMPACITY. A DISCONNECTING MEANS SHALL BE LOCATED WITHIN SIGHT OF THE EQUIPMENT.

The correct voltage and ampere rating shall be given. The tag shall be not less than 0.51 mm (0.020 in.) thick etched brass, stainless steel, anodized or alclad aluminum, or equivalent. The tag shall not be less than 75 mm by 45 mm (3 in. by 1¾ in.) minimum size.

550.25 Arc-Fault Circuit-Interrupter Protection.

(A) Definition. Arc-fault circuit interrupters are defined in Article 210.12(A).

(B) Bedrooms of Mobile Homes and Manufactured Homes. All branch circuits that supply 125-volt, single-phase, 15- and 20-ampere outlets installed in bedrooms of mobile homes and manufactured homes shall be protected by arc-fault circuit interrupter(s).

III. Services and Feeders

550.30 Distribution System. The mobile home park secondary electrical distribution system to mobile home lots shall be single-phase, 120/240 volts, nominal. For the purpose of Part III, where the park service exceeds 240 volts, nominal, transformers and secondary distribution panelboards shall be treated as services.

550.31 Allowable Demand Factors. Park electrical wiring systems shall be calculated (at 120/240 volts) on the larger of the following:

(1) 16,000 volt-amperes for each mobile home lot

(2) The load calculated in accordance with 550.18 for the largest typical mobile home that each lot will accept

It shall be permissible to calculate the feeder or service load in accordance with Table 550.31. No demand factor shall be allowed for any other load, except as provided in this *Code*.

Service and feeder conductors to a mobile home in compliance with 310.15(B)(6) shall be permitted.

Table 550.31 Demand Factors for Services and Feeders

Number of Mobile Homes	Demand Factor (percent)
1	100
2	55
3	44
4	39
5	33
6	29
7–9	28
10–12	27
13–15	26
16–21	25
22–40	24
41–60	23
61 and over	22

550.32 Service Equipment.

(A) Mobile Home Service Equipment. The mobile home service equipment shall be located adjacent to the mobile home and not mounted in or on the mobile home. The service equipment shall be located in sight from and not more than 9.0 m (30 ft) from the exterior wall of the mobile home it serves. The service equipment shall be permitted to be located elsewhere on the premises, provided that a disconnecting means suitable for use as service equipment is located within sight from and not more than 9.0 m (30 ft) from the exterior wall of the mobile home it serves and is rated not less than that required for service equipment per 550.32(C). Grounding at the disconnecting means shall be in accordance with 250.32.

(B) Manufactured Home Service Equipment. The manufactured home service equipment shall be permitted to be installed in or on a manufactured home, provided that all of the following conditions are met:

(1) The manufacturer shall include in its written installation instructions information indicating that the home shall be secured in place by an anchoring system or installed on and secured to a permanent foundation.

(2) The installation of the service equipment shall comply with Article 230.

(3) Means shall be provided for the connection of a grounding electrode conductor to the service equipment and routing it outside the structure.

(4) Bonding and grounding of the service shall be in accordance with Article 250.

(5) The manufacturer shall include in its written installation instructions one method of grounding the service equipment at the installation site. The instructions shall clearly state that other methods of grounding are found in Article 250.

(6) The minimum size grounding electrode conductor shall be specified in the instructions.

(7) A red warning label shall be mounted on or adjacent to the service equipment. The label shall state the following:

WARNING
DO NOT PROVIDE ELECTRICAL POWER
UNTIL THE GROUNDING ELECTRODE(S)
IS INSTALLED AND CONNECTED
(SEE INSTALLATION INSTRUCTIONS).

Where the service equipment is not installed in or on the unit, the installation shall comply with the other provisions of this section.

(C) Rating. Mobile home service equipment shall be rated at not less than 100 amperes at 120/240 volts, and provisions shall be made for connecting a mobile home feeder assembly by a permanent wiring method. Power outlets used as mobile home service equipment shall also be permitted to contain receptacles rated up to 50 amperes with appropriate overcurrent protection. Fifty-ampere receptacles shall conform to the configuration shown in Figure 550.10(C).

> FPN: Complete details of the 50-ampere plug and receptacle configuration can be found in ANSI/NEMA WD 6-1989, National Electrical Manufacturers Association *Standard for Wiring Devices — Dimensional Requirements*, Figure 14-50.

(D) Additional Outside Electrical Equipment. Means for connecting a mobile home accessory building or structure or additional electrical equipment located outside a mobile home by a fixed wiring method shall be provided in either the mobile home service equipment or the local external disconnecting means permitted in 550.32(A).

(E) Additional Receptacles. Additional receptacles shall be permitted for connection of electrical equipment located outside the mobile home, and all such 125-volt, single-phase, 15- and 20-ampere receptacles shall be protected by a listed ground-fault circuit interrupter.

(F) Mounting Height. Outdoor mobile home disconnecting means shall be installed so the bottom of the enclosure containing the disconnecting means is not less than 600 mm (2 ft) above finished grade or working platform. The disconnecting means shall be installed so that the center of the grip of the operating handle, when in the highest position, is not more than 2.0 m (6 ft 7 in.) above the finished grade or working platform.

(G) Marking. Where a 125/250-volt receptacle is used in mobile home service equipment, the service equipment shall be marked as follows:

TURN DISCONNECTING SWITCH OR CIRCUIT BREAKER OFF BEFORE INSERTING OR REMOVING PLUG. PLUG MUST BE FULLY INSERTED OR REMOVED.

The marking shall be located on the service equipment adjacent to the receptacle outlet.

550.33 Feeder.

(A) Feeder Conductors. Feeder conductors shall consist of either a listed cord, factory installed in accordance with 550.10(B), or a permanently installed feeder consisting of four insulated, color-coded conductors that shall be identified by the factory or field marking of the conductors in compliance with 310.12. Equipment grounding conductors shall not be identified by stripping the insulation.

Exception: Where a feeder is installed between service equipment and a disconnecting means as covered in 550.32(A), it shall be permitted to omit the equipment grounding conductor where the grounded circuit conductor is grounded at the disconnecting means as required in 250.32(B).

(B) Feeder Capacity. Mobile home and manufactured home lot feeder circuit conductors shall have a capacity not less than the loads supplied and shall be rated at not less than 100 amperes at 120/240 volts.

ARTICLE 551
Recreational Vehicles and Recreational Vehicle Parks

I. General

551.1 Scope. The provisions of this article cover the electrical conductors and equipment other than low-voltage and automotive vehicle circuits or extensions thereof, installed within or on recreational vehicles, the conductors that connect recreational vehicles to a supply of electricity, and the installation of equipment and devices related to electrical installations within a recreational vehicle park.

FPN: For information on low-voltage systems, see NFPA 1192-2002, *Standard for Recreational Vehicles*, and ANSI/RVIA 12V, *Low Voltage Systems in Conversion and Recreational Vehicles*, 2002 edition.

551.2 Definitions. (See Article 100 for additional definitions.)

Air-Conditioning or Comfort-Cooling Equipment. All of that equipment intended or installed for the purpose of processing the treatment of air so as to control simultaneously its temperature, humidity, cleanliness, and distribution to meet the requirements of the conditioned space.

Appliance, Fixed. An appliance that is fastened or otherwise secured at a specific location.

Appliance, Portable. An appliance that is actually moved or can easily be moved from one place to another in normal use.

FPN: For the purpose of this article, the following major appliances, other than built-in, are considered portable if cord connected: refrigerators, range equipment, clothes washers, dishwashers without booster heaters, or other similar appliances.

Appliance, Stationary. An appliance that is not easily moved from one place to another in normal use.

Camping Trailer. A vehicular portable unit mounted on wheels and constructed with collapsible partial side walls that fold for towing by another vehicle and unfold at the campsite to provide temporary living quarters for recreational, camping, or travel use. *(See Recreational Vehicle.)*

Converter. A device that changes electrical energy from one form to another, as from alternating current to direct current.

Dead Front (as applied to switches, circuit breakers, switchboards, and distribution panelboards). Designed, constructed, and installed so that no current-carrying parts are normally exposed on the front.

Disconnecting Means. The necessary equipment usually consisting of a circuit breaker or switch and fuses, and their accessories, located near the point of entrance of supply conductors in a recreational vehicle and intended to constitute the means of cutoff for the supply to that recreational vehicle.

Distribution Panelboard. A single panel or group of panel units designed for assembly in the form of a single panel, including buses, and with or without switches and/or automatic overcurrent-protective devices for the control of light, heat, or power circuits of small individual as well as aggregate capacity; designed to be placed in a cabinet or cutout box placed in or against a wall or partition and accessible only from the front.

Frame. Chassis rail and any welded addition thereto of metal thickness of 1.35 mm (0.053 in.) or greater.

Low Voltage. An electromotive force rated 24 volts, nominal, or less, supplied from a transformer, converter, or battery.

Motor Home. A vehicular unit designed to provide temporary living quarters for recreational, camping, or travel use built on or permanently attached to a self-propelled motor vehicle chassis or on a chassis cab or van that is an integral part of the completed vehicle. *(See Recreational Vehicle.)*

Power-Supply Assembly. The conductors, including ungrounded, grounded, and equipment grounding conductors, the connectors, attachment plug caps, and all other fittings, grommets, or devices installed for the purpose of delivering energy from the source of electrical supply to the distribution panel within the recreational vehicle.

Recreational Vehicle. A vehicular-type unit primarily designed as temporary living quarters for recreational, camping, or travel use, which either has its own motive power or is mounted on or drawn by another vehicle. The basic entities are travel trailer, camping trailer, truck camper, and motor home.

Recreational Vehicle Park. A plot of land upon which two or more recreational vehicle sites are located, established, or maintained for occupancy by recreational vehicles of the general public as temporary living quarters for recreation or vacation purposes.

Recreational Vehicle Site. A plot of ground within a recreational vehicle park set aside for the accommodation of a recreational vehicle on a temporary basis. It can be used as either a recreational vehicle site or as a camping unit site.

Recreational Vehicle Site Feeder Circuit Conductors. The conductors from the park service equipment to the recreational vehicle site supply equipment.

Recreational Vehicle Site Supply Equipment. The necessary equipment, usually a power outlet, consisting of a circuit breaker or switch and fuse and their accessories, located near the point of entrance of supply conductors to a recreational vehicle site and intended to constitute the disconnecting means for the supply to that site.

Recreational Vehicle Stand. That area of a recreational vehicle site intended for the placement of a recreational vehicle.

Transformer. A device that, when used, raises or lowers the voltage of alternating current of the original source.

Travel Trailer. A vehicular unit, mounted on wheels, designed to provide temporary living quarters for recreational, camping, or travel use, of such size or weight as not to require special highway movement permits when towed by a motorized vehicle, and of gross trailer area less than 30 m² (320 ft²). *(See Recreational Vehicle.)*

Truck Camper. A portable unit constructed to provide temporary living quarters for recreational, travel, or camping use, consisting of a roof, floor, and sides, designed to be loaded onto and unloaded from the bed of a pick-up truck. *(See Recreational Vehicle.)*

551.4 General Requirements.

(A) Not Covered. A recreational vehicle not used for the purposes as defined in 551.2 shall not be required to meet the provisions of Part I pertaining to the number or capacity of circuits required. It shall, however, meet all other applicable requirements of this article if the recreational vehicle is provided with an electrical installation intended to be energized from a 120- or 120/240-volt, nominal, ac power-supply system.

(B) Systems. This article covers combination electrical systems, generator installations, and 120- or 120/240-volt, nominal, systems.

> FPN: For information on low-voltage systems, refer to NFPA 1192-2002, *Standard on Recreational Vehicles*, and ANSI/RVIA 12V-2002, *Standard for Low-Voltage Systems in Conversion and Recreational Vehicles.*

II. Combination Electrical Systems

551.20 Combination Electrical Systems.

(A) General. Vehicle wiring suitable for connection to a battery or dc supply source shall be permitted to be connected to a 120-volt source, provided the entire wiring system and equipment are rated and installed in full conformity with Parts I, II, III, IV, and V requirements of this article covering 120-volt electrical systems. Circuits fed from ac transformers shall not supply dc appliances.

(B) Voltage Converters (120-Volt Alternating Current to Low-Voltage Direct Current). The 120-volt ac side of the voltage converter shall be wired in full conformity with Parts I, II, III, IV, and V requirements of this article for 120-volt electrical systems.

Exception: *Converters supplied as an integral part of a listed appliance shall not be subject to 551.20(B).*

All converters and transformers shall be listed for use in recreation vehicles and designed or equipped to provide over-temperature protection. To determine the converter rating, the following formula shall be applied to the total connected load, including average battery charging rate, of all 12-volt equipment:

The first 20 amperes of load at 100 percent, plus
The second 20 amperes of load at 50 percent, plus
All load above 40 amperes at 25 percent

Exception: *A low-voltage appliance that is controlled by a momentary switch (normally open) that has no means for holding in the closed position or refrigerators with a 120-volt function shall not be considered as a connected load when determining the required converter rating. Momentarily energized appliances shall be limited to those used to prepare the vehicle for occupancy or travel.*

(C) Bonding Voltage Converter Enclosures. The non–current-carrying metal enclosure of the voltage converter shall be bonded to the frame of the vehicle with a minimum 8 AWG copper conductor. The voltage converter shall be provided with a separate chassis bonding conductor that shall not be used as a current-carrying conductor.

(D) Dual-Voltage Fixtures, Including Luminaires or Appliances. Fixtures, including luminaires, or appliances having both 120-volt and low-voltage connections shall be listed for dual voltage.

(E) Autotransformers. Autotransformers shall not be used.

(F) Receptacles and Plug Caps. Where a recreational vehicle is equipped with a 120-volt or 120/240-volt ac system, a low-voltage system, or both, receptacles and plug caps of the low-voltage system shall differ in configuration from those of the 120- or 120/240-volt system. Where a vehicle equipped with a battery or other low-voltage system has an external connection for low-voltage power, the connector shall have a configuration that will not accept 120-volt power.

III. Other Power Sources

551.30 Generator Installations.

(A) Mounting. Generators shall be mounted in such a manner as to be effectively bonded to the recreational vehicle chassis.

(B) Generator Protection. Equipment shall be installed to ensure that the current-carrying conductors from the engine generator and from an outside source are not connected to a vehicle circuit at the same time.

Receptacles used as disconnecting means shall be accessible (as applied to wiring methods) and capable of interrupting their rated current without hazard to the operator.

(C) Installation of Storage Batteries and Generators. Storage batteries and internal-combustion-driven generator units (subject to the provisions of this *Code*) shall be secured in place to avoid displacement from vibration and road shock.

(D) Ventilation of Generator Compartments. Compartments accommodating internal-combustion-driven generator units shall be provided with ventilation in accordance with instructions provided by the manufacturer of the generator unit.

FPN: For generator compartment construction requirements, see NFPA 1192-2002, *Standard on Recreational Vehicles.*

(E) Supply Conductors. The supply conductors from the engine generator to the first termination on the vehicle shall be of the stranded type and be installed in listed flexible conduit or listed liquidtight flexible conduit. The point of first termination shall be in one of the following:

(1) Panelboard

(2) Junction box with a blank cover

(3) Junction box with a receptacle

(4) Enclosed transfer switch

(5) Receptacle assembly listed in conjunction with the generator

The panelboard or junction box with a receptacle shall be installed within the vehicle's interior and within 450 mm (18 in.) of the compartment wall but not inside the compartment. If the generator is below the floor level and not in a compartment, the panelboard or junction box with receptacle shall be installed within the vehicle interior within 450 mm (18 in.) of the point of entry into the vehicle. A junction box with a blank cover shall be mounted on the compartment wall and shall be permitted inside or outside the compartment. A receptacle assembly listed in conjunction with the generator shall be mounted in accordance with its listing. If the generator is below floor level and not in a compartment, the junction box with blank cover shall be mounted either to any part of the generator supporting structure (but not to the generator) or to the vehicle floor within 450 mm (18 in.) of any point directly above the generator on either the inside or outside of the floor surface. Overcurrent protection in accordance with 240.4 shall be provided for supply conductors as an integral part of a listed generator or shall be located within 450 mm (18 in.) of their point of entry into the vehicle.

551.31 Multiple Supply Source.

(A) Multiple Supply Sources. Where a multiple supply system consisting of an alternate power source and a power-supply cord is installed, the feeder from the alternate power source shall be protected by an overcurrent-protective device. Installation shall be in accordance with 551.30(A), 551.30(B), and 551.40.

(B) Multiple Supply Sources Capacity. The multiple supply sources shall not be required to be of the same capacity.

(C) Alternate Power Sources Exceeding 30 Amperes. If an alternate power source exceeds 30 amperes, 120 volts, nominal, it shall be permissible to wire it as a 120-volt, nominal, system or a 120/240-volt, nominal, system, provided an overcurrent-protective device of the proper rating is installed in the feeder.

(D) Power-Supply Assembly Not Less Than 30 Amperes. The external power-supply assembly shall be permitted to be less than the calculated load but not less than 30 amperes and shall have overcurrent protection not greater than the capacity of the external power-supply assembly.

551.32 Other Sources. Other sources of ac power, such as inverters, motor generators, or engine generators, shall be listed for use in recreational vehicles and shall be installed in accordance with the terms of the listing. Other sources of ac power shall be wired in full conformity with the requirements in Parts I, II, III, IV, and V of this article covering 120-volt electrical systems.

551.33 Alternate Source Restriction. Transfer equipment, if not integral with the listed power source, shall be installed to ensure that the current-carrying conductors from other sources of ac power and from an outside source are not connected to the vehicle circuit at the same time.

IV. Nominal 120-Volt or 120/240-Volt Systems

551.40 120-Volt or 120/240-Volt, Nominal, Systems.

(A) General Requirements. The electrical equipment and material of recreational vehicles indicated for connection to a wiring system rated 120 volts, nominal, 2-wire with ground, or a wiring system rated 120/240 volts, nominal, 3-wire with ground, shall be listed and installed in accordance with the requirements of Parts I, II, III, IV, and V of this article. Electrical equipment connected line-to-line shall have a voltage rating of 208–230 volts.

(B) Materials and Equipment. Electrical materials, devices, appliances, fittings, and other equipment installed in, intended for use in, or attached to the recreational vehicle shall be listed. All products shall be used only in the manner in which they have been tested and found suitable for the intended use.

(C) Ground-Fault Circuit-Interrupter Protection. The internal wiring of a recreational vehicle having only one 15- or 20-ampere branch circuit as permitted in 551.42(A) and 551.42(B) shall have ground-fault circuit-interrupter protection for personnel. The ground-fault circuit interrupter shall be installed at the point where the power supply assembly terminates within the recreational vehicle. Where a separable cord set is not employed, the ground-fault circuit interrupter shall be permitted to be an integral part of the attachment plug of the power supply assembly. The ground-fault circuit interrupter shall provide protection also under the conditions of an open grounded circuit conductor, interchanged circuit conductors, or both.

551.41 Receptacle Outlets Required.

(A) Spacing. Receptacle outlets shall be installed at wall spaces 600 mm (2 ft) wide or more so that no point along the floor line is more than 1.8 m (6 ft), measured horizontally, from an outlet in that space.

Exception No. 1: Bath and hall areas.

Exception No. 2: Wall spaces occupied by kitchen cabinets, wardrobe cabinets, built-in furniture, behind doors that may open fully against a wall surface, or similar facilities.

(B) Location. Receptacle outlets shall be installed as follows:

(1) Adjacent to countertops in the kitchen [at least one on each side of the sink if countertops are on each side and are 300 mm (12 in.) or over in width]

(2) Adjacent to the refrigerator and gas range space, except where a gas-fired refrigerator or cooking appliance, requiring no external electrical connection, is factory installed

(3) Adjacent to countertop spaces of 300 mm (12 in.) or more in width that cannot be reached from a receptacle required in 551.41(B)(1) by a cord of 1.8 m (6 ft) without crossing a traffic area, cooking appliance, or sink

(C) Ground-Fault Circuit-Interrupter Protection. Where provided, each 125-volt, single-phase, 15- or 20-ampere receptacle outlet shall have ground-fault circuit-interrupter protection for personnel in the following locations:

(1) Adjacent to a bathroom lavatory

(2) Where the receptacles are installed to serve the countertop surfaces and are within 1.8 m (6 ft) of any lavatory or sink

Exception No. 1: Receptacles installed for appliances in dedicated spaces, such as for dishwashers, disposals, refrigerators, freezers, and laundry equipment.

Exception No. 2: Single receptacles for interior connections of expandable room sections.

Exception No. 3: De-energized receptacles that are within 1.8 m (6 ft) of any sink or lavatory due to the retraction of the expandable room section.

(3) In the area occupied by a toilet, shower, tub, or any combination thereof

(4) On the exterior of the vehicle

Exception: Receptacles that are located inside of an access panel that is installed on the exterior of the vehicle to supply power for an installed appliance shall not be required to have ground-fault circuit-interrupter protection.

The receptacle outlet shall be permitted in a listed luminaire (lighting fixture). A receptacle outlet shall not be installed in a tub or combination tub–shower compartment.

(D) Face-Up Position. A receptacle shall not be installed in a face-up position in any countertop or similar horizontal surfaces within the living area.

551.42 Branch Circuits Required. Each recreational vehicle containing a 120-volt electrical system shall contain one of the following.

(A) One 15-Ampere Circuit. One 15-ampere circuit to supply lights, receptacle outlets, and fixed appliances. Such recreational vehicles shall be equipped with one 15-ampere switch and fuse or one 15-ampere circuit breaker.

(B) One 20-Ampere Circuit. One 20-ampere circuit to supply lights, receptacle outlets, and fixed appliances. Such recreational vehicles shall be equipped with one 20-ampere switch and fuse or one 20-ampere circuit breaker.

(C) Two to Five 15- or 20-Ampere Circuits. A maximum of five 15- or 20-ampere circuits to supply lights, receptacle outlets, and fixed appliances shall be permitted. Such recreational vehicles shall be equipped with a distribution panelboard rated at 120 volts maximum with a 30-ampere rated main power supply assembly. Not more than two 120-volt thermostatically controlled appliances (i.e., air conditioner and water heater) shall be installed in such systems unless appliance isolation switching, energy management systems, or similar methods are used.

Exception: Additional 15- or 20-ampere circuits shall be permitted where a listed energy management system rated at 30-ampere maximum is employed within the system.

FPN: See 210.23(A) for permissible loads. See 551.45(C) for main disconnect and overcurrent protection requirements.

(D) More Than Five Circuits Without a Listed Energy Management System. A 50-ampere, 120/240-volt power-supply assembly shall be used where six or more circuits

are employed. The load distribution shall ensure a reasonable current balance between phases.

551.43 Branch-Circuit Protection.

(A) Rating. The branch-circuit overcurrent devices shall be rated as follows:

(1) Not more than the circuit conductors, and

(2) Not more than 150 percent of the rating of a single appliance rated 13.3 amperes or more and supplied by an individual branch circuit, but

(3) Not more than the overcurrent protection size marked on an air conditioner or other motor-operated appliances

(B) Protection for Smaller Conductors. A 20-ampere fuse or circuit breaker shall be permitted for protection for fixtures, including luminaires, leads, cords, or small appliances, and 14 AWG tap conductors, not over 1.8 m (6 ft) long for recessed luminaires (lighting fixtures).

(C) Fifteen-Ampere Receptacle Considered Protected by 20 Amperes. If more than one receptacle or load is on a branch circuit, a 15-ampere receptacle shall be permitted to be protected by a 20-ampere fuse or circuit breaker.

551.44 Power-Supply Assembly. Each recreational vehicle shall have only one of the following main power-supply assemblies.

(A) Fifteen-Ampere Main Power-Supply Assembly. Recreational vehicles wired in accordance with 551.42(A) shall use a listed 15-ampere or larger main power-supply assembly.

(B) Twenty-Ampere Main Power-Supply Assembly. Recreational vehicles wired in accordance with 551.42(B) shall use a listed 20-ampere or larger main power-supply assembly.

(C) Thirty-Ampere Main Power-Supply Assembly. Recreational vehicles wired in accordance with 551.42(C) shall use a listed 30-ampere or larger main power-supply assembly.

(D) Fifty-Ampere Power-Supply Assembly. Recreational vehicles wired in accordance with 551.42(D) shall use a listed 50-ampere, 120/240-volt main power-supply assembly.

551.45 Distribution Panelboard.

(A) Listed and Appropriately Rated. A listed and appropriately rated distribution panelboard or other equipment specifically listed for this purpose shall be used. The grounded conductor termination bar shall be insulated from the enclosure as provided in 551.54(C). An equipment grounding terminal bar shall be attached inside the metal enclosure of the panelboard.

(B) Location. The distribution panelboard shall be installed in a readily accessible location. Working clearance for the panelboard shall be not less than 600 mm (24 in.) wide and 750 mm (30 in.) deep.

Exception No. 1: Where the panelboard cover is exposed to the inside aisle space, one of the working clearance dimensions shall be permitted to be reduced to a minimum of 550 mm (22 in.). A panelboard is considered exposed where the panelboard cover is within 50 mm (2 in.) of the aisle's finished surface.

Exception No. 2: Compartment doors used for access to a generator shall be permitted to be equipped with a locking system.

(C) Dead-Front Type. The distribution panelboard shall be of the dead-front type and shall consist of one or more circuit breakers or Type S fuseholders. A main disconnecting means shall be provided where fuses are used or where more than two circuit breakers are employed. A main overcurrent protective device not exceeding the power-supply assembly rating shall be provided where more than two branch circuits are employed.

551.46 Means for Connecting to Power Supply.

(A) Assembly. The power-supply assembly or assemblies shall be factory supplied or factory installed and be of one of the types specified herein.

(1) Separable. Where a separable power-supply assembly consisting of a cord with a female connector and molded attachment plug cap is provided, the vehicle shall be equipped with a permanently mounted, flanged surface inlet (male, recessed-type motor-base attachment plug) wired directly to the distribution panelboard by an approved wiring method. The attachment plug cap shall be of a listed type.

(2) Permanently Connected. Each power-supply assembly shall be connected directly to the terminals of the distribution panelboard or conductors within a junction box and provided with means to prevent strain from being transmitted to the terminals. The ampacity of the conductors between each junction box and the terminals of each distribution panelboard shall be at least equal to the ampacity of the power-supply cord. The supply end of the assembly shall be equipped with an attachment plug of the type described in 551.46(C). Where the cord passes through the walls or floors, it shall be protected by means of conduit and bushings or equivalent. The cord assembly shall have permanent provisions for protection against corrosion and mechanical damage while the vehicle is in transit.

(B) Cord. The cord exposed usable length shall be measured from the point of entrance to the recreational vehicle or the face of the flanged surface inlet (motor-base attachment plug) to the face of the attachment plug at the supply end.

The cord exposed usable length, measured to the point of entry on the vehicle exterior, shall be a minimum of 7.5 m (25 ft) where the point of entrance is at the side of the vehicle or shall be a minimum 9.0 m (30 ft) where the point of entrance is at the rear of the vehicle.

Where the cord entrance into the vehicle is more than 900 mm (3 ft) above the ground, the minimum cord lengths above shall be increased by the vertical distance of the cord entrance heights above 900 mm (3 ft).

FPN: See 551.46(E).

(C) Attachment Plugs.

(1) Units with One 15-Ampere Branch Circuit. Recreational vehicles having only one 15-ampere branch circuit as permitted by 551.42(A) shall have an attachment plug that shall be 2-pole, 3-wire grounding type, rated 15 amperes, 125 volts, conforming to the configuration shown in Figure 551.46(C) .

FPN: Complete details of this configuration can be found in National Electrical Manufacturers Association's ANSI/NEMA WD 6-1989, *Standard for Dimensions of Attachment Plugs and Receptacle*, Figure 5.15.

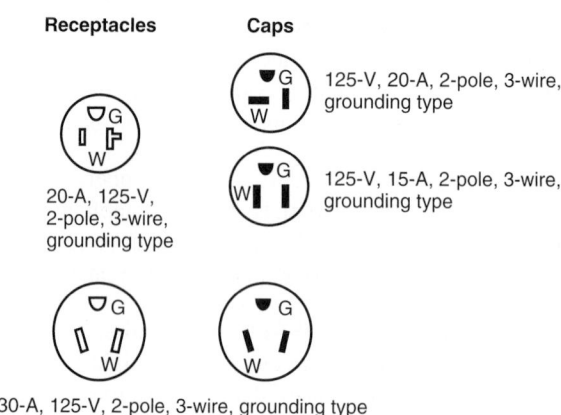

Receptacles   Caps

125-V, 20-A, 2-pole, 3-wire, grounding type

125-V, 15-A, 2-pole, 3-wire, grounding type

20-A, 125-V, 2-pole, 3-wire, grounding type

30-A, 125-V, 2-pole, 3-wire, grounding type

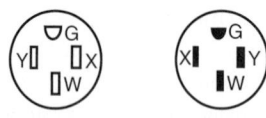

50-A, 125/250-V, 3-pole, 4-wire, grounding type

Figure 551.46(C) Configurations for Grounding-Type Receptacles and Attachment Plug Caps Used for Recreational Vehicle Supply Cords and Recreational Vehicle Lots.

(2) Units with One 20-Ampere Branch Circuit. Recreational vehicles having only one 20-ampere branch circuit as permitted in 551.42(B) shall have an attachment plug that shall be 2-pole, 3-wire grounding type, rated 20 amperes, 125 volts, conforming to the configuration shown in Figure 551.46(C) .

FPN: Complete details of this configuration can be found in ANSI/NEMA WD 6-1989, National Electrical Manufacturers Association's *Standard for Dimensions of Attachment Plugs and Receptacles*, Figure 5.20.

(3) Units with Two to Five 15- or 20-Ampere Branch Circuits. Recreational vehicles wired in accordance with 551.42(C) shall have an attachment plug that shall be 2-pole, 3-wire grounding type, rated 30 amperes, 125 volts, conforming to the configuration shown in Figure 551.46(C), intended for use with units rated at 30 amperes, 125 volts.

FPN: Complete details of this configuration can be found in ANSI/NEMA WD 6-1989, National Electrical Manufacturers Association's *Standard for Dimensions of Attachment Plugs and Receptacles*, Figure TT.

(4) Units with 50-Ampere Power Supply Assembly. Recreational vehicles having a power-supply assembly rated 50 amperes as permitted by 551.42(D) shall have a 3-pole, 4-wire grounding-type attachment plug rated 50 amperes, 125/250 volts, conforming to the configuration shown in Figure 551.46(C) .

FPN: Complete details of this configuration can be found in ANSI/NEMA WD 6-1989, National Electrical Manufacturers Association's *Standard for Dimensions of Attachment Plugs and Receptacles*, Figure 14.50.

(D) Labeling at Electrical Entrance. Each recreational vehicle shall have permanently affixed to the exterior skin, at or near the point of entrance of the power-supply cord(s), a label 75 mm × 45 mm (3 in. × 1¾ in.) minimum size, made of etched, metal-stamped, or embossed brass, stainless steel, or anodized or alclad aluminum not less than 0.51 mm (0.020 in.) thick, or other suitable material [e.g., 0.13 mm (0.005 in.) thick plastic laminate] that reads, as appropriate, either

> THIS CONNECTION IS FOR 110–125-VOLT AC, 60 HZ, _____ AMPERE SUPPLY.

or

> THIS CONNECTION IS FOR 120/240-VOLT AC, 3-POLE, 4-WIRE, 60 HZ, _____ AMPERE SUPPLY.

The correct ampere rating shall be marked in the blank space.

(E) Location. The point of entrance of a power-supply assembly shall be located within 4.5 m (15 ft) of the rear, on the left (road) side or at the rear, left of the longitudinal center of the vehicle, within 450 mm (18 in.) of the outside wall.

Exception No. 1: A recreational vehicle equipped with only a listed flexible drain system or a side-vent drain system shall be permitted to have the electrical point of entrance located on either side, provided the drain(s) for the plumbing system is (are) located on the same side.

Exception No. 2: A recreational vehicle shall be permitted to have the electrical point of entrance located more than 4.5 m (15 ft) from the rear. Where this occurs, the distance beyond the 4.5-m (15-ft) dimension shall be added to the cord's minimum length as specified in 551.46(B).

Exception No. 3: Recreational vehicles designed for transporting livestock shall be permitted to have the electrical point of entrance located on either side or the front.

551.47 Wiring Methods.

(A) Wiring Systems. Cables and raceways installed in accordance with Articles 320, 322, 330 through 340, 342 through 362, 386, and 388 shall be permitted in accordance with their applicable article, except as otherwise specified in this article. An equipment grounding means shall be provided in accordance with 250.118.

(B) Conduit and Tubing. Where rigid metal conduit or intermediate metal conduit is terminated at an enclosure with a locknut and bushing connection, two locknuts shall be provided, one inside and one outside of the enclosure. All cut ends of conduit and tubing shall be reamed or otherwise finished to remove rough edges.

(C) Nonmetallic Boxes. Nonmetallic boxes shall be acceptable only with nonmetallic-sheathed cable or nonmetallic raceways.

(D) Boxes. In walls and ceilings constructed of wood or other combustible material, boxes and fittings shall be flush with the finished surface or project therefrom.

(E) Mounting. Wall and ceiling boxes shall be mounted in accordance with Article 314.

Exception No. 1: Snap-in-type boxes or boxes provided with special wall or ceiling brackets that securely fasten boxes in walls or ceilings shall be permitted.

Exception No. 2: A wooden plate providing a 38-mm (1½-in.) minimum width backing around the box and of a thickness of 13 mm (½ in.) or greater (actual) attached directly to the wall panel shall be considered as approved means for mounting outlet boxes.

(F) Raceway and Cable Continuity. Raceways and cable sheaths shall be continuous between boxes and other enclosures.

(G) Protected. Metal-clad, Type AC, or nonmetallic-sheathed cables and electrical nonmetallic tubing shall be permitted to pass through the centers of the wide side of 2 by 4 wood studs. However, they shall be protected where they pass through 2 by 2 wood studs or at other wood studs or frames where the cable or tubing would be less than 32 mm (1¼ in.) from the inside or outside surface. Steel plates on each side of the cable or tubing or a steel tube, with not less than 1.35 mm (0.053 in.) wall thickness, shall be installed to protect the cable or tubing. These plates or tubes shall be securely held in place. Where nonmetallic-sheathed cables pass through punched, cut, or drilled slots or holes in metal members, the cable shall be protected by bushings or grommets securely fastened in the opening prior to installation of the cable.

(H) Bends. No bend shall have a radius of less than five times the cable diameter.

(I) Cable Supports. Where connected with cable connectors or clamps, cables shall be supported within 300 mm (12 in.) of outlet boxes, distribution panelboards, and splice boxes on appliances. Supports shall be provided every 1.4 m (4½ ft) at other places.

(J) Nonmetallic Box Without Cable Clamps. Nonmetallic-sheathed cables shall be supported within 200 mm (8 in.) of a nonmetallic outlet box without cable clamps. Where wiring devices with integral enclosures are employed with a loop of extra cable to permit future replacement of the device, the cable loop shall be considered as an integral portion of the device.

(K) Physical Damage. Where subject to physical damage, exposed nonmetallic cable shall be protected by covering boards, guard strips, raceways, or other means.

(L) Metal Faceplates. Metal faceplates shall be of ferrous metal not less than 0.76 mm (0.030 in.) in thickness or of nonferrous metal not less than 1.0 mm (0.040 in.) in thickness. Nonmetallic faceplates shall be listed.

(M) Metal Faceplates Effectively Grounded. Where metal faceplates are used, they shall be effectively grounded.

(N) Moisture or Physical Damage. Where outdoor or under-chassis wiring is 120 volts, nominal, or over and is exposed to moisture or physical damage, the wiring shall be protected by rigid metal conduit, by intermediate metal conduit, or by electrical metallic tubing, rigid nonmetallic conduit, or Type MI cable, that is closely routed against frames and equipment enclosures or other raceway or cable identified for the application.

(O) Component Interconnections. Fittings and connectors that are intended to be concealed at the time of assembly shall be listed and identified for the interconnection of building components. Such fittings and connectors shall be equal to the wiring method employed in insulation, temperature rise, and fault-current withstanding and shall be capable of enduring the vibration and shock occurring in recreational vehicles.

(P) Method of Connecting Expandable Units. The method of connecting expandable units to the main body of the vehicle shall comply with 551.47(P)(1) or (P)(2):

(1) Cord-and-Plug Connected. Cord and plug connections shall comply with (a) through (d).

     a. That portion of a branch circuit that is installed in an expandable unit shall be permitted to be connected to the portion of the branch circuit in the main body of the vehicle by means of an attachment plug and cord listed for hard usage. The cord and its connections shall conform to all provisions of Article 400 and shall be considered as a permitted use under 400.7. Where the attachment plug and cord are located within the vehicle's interior, use of plastic thermoset or elastomer parallel cord Type SPT-3, SP-3, or SPE shall be permitted.

     b. Where the receptacle provided for connection of the cord to the main circuit is located on the outside of the vehicle, it shall be protected with a ground-fault circuit interrupter for personnel and be listed for wet locations. A cord located on the outside of a vehicle shall be identified for outdoor use.

     c. Unless removable or stored within the vehicle interior, the cord assembly shall have permanent provisions for protection against corrosion and mechanical damage while the vehicle is in transit.

     d. The attachment plug and cord shall be installed so as not to permit exposed live attachment plug pins.

(2) Direct Wired. That portion of a branch circuit that is installed in an expandable unit shall be permitted to be connected to the portion of the branch circuit in the main body of the vehicle by means of flexible cord in accordance with 551.47(P)(2)(a) through (P)(2)(d).

     a. The flexible cord shall be listed for hard usage and for use in wet locations.

     b. The flexible cord shall be permitted to pass through the interior of a wall or through a floor in lengths not to exceed 600 mm (24 in.) before terminating at an outlet.

     c. The flexible cord shall be installed in a nonflexible conduit or tubing that runs continuously from the outlet box inside the recreational vehicle to a strain relief connector listed for use in wet locations that is located on the underside of the recreational vehicle.

     d. The outer jacket of the flexible cord shall not be removed for that portion that is installed in the conduit or tubing.

(Q) Prewiring for Air-Conditioning Installation. Prewiring installed for the purpose of facilitating future air-conditioning installation shall conform to the applicable portions of this article and the following:

(1) An overcurrent protective device with a rating compatible with the circuit conductors shall be installed in the distribution panelboard and wiring connections completed.

(2) The load end of the circuit shall terminate in a junction box with a blank cover or other listed enclosure. Where a junction box with a blank cover is used, the free ends of the conductors shall be adequately capped or taped.

(3) A label conforming to 551.46(D) shall be placed on or adjacent to the junction box and shall read

AIR-CONDITIONING CIRCUIT.
THIS CONNECTION IS FOR AIR CONDITIONERS
RATED 110–125-VOLT AC,
60 HZ, ___ AMPERES MAXIMUM.
DO NOT EXCEED CIRCUIT RATING.

An ampere rating, not to exceed 80 percent of the circuit rating, shall be legibly marked in the blank space.

(4) The circuit shall serve no other purpose.

(R) Prewiring for Generator Installation. Prewiring installed for the purpose of facilitating future generator installation shall conform to the other applicable portions of this article and the following:

(1) Circuit conductors shall be appropriately sized in relation to the anticipated load and shall be protected by an overcurrent device in accordance with their ampacities.

(2) Where junction boxes are utilized at either of the circuit originating or terminus points, free ends of the conductors shall be adequately capped or taped.

(3) Where devices such as receptacle outlet, transfer switch, and so forth, are installed, the installation shall be complete, including circuit conductor connections. All devices shall be listed and appropriately rated.

(4) A label conforming to 551.46(D) shall be placed on the cover of each junction box containing incomplete circuitry and shall read, as appropriate, either

GENERATOR CIRCUIT. THIS CONNECTION
IS FOR GENERATORS RATED 110–125-VOLT AC,
60 HZ, _____ AMPERES MAXIMUM.

or

GENERATOR CIRCUIT. THIS CONNECTION
IS FOR GENERATORS RATED 120/240-VOLT AC,
60 HZ, _____ AMPERES MAXIMUM.

The correct ampere rating shall be legibly marked in the blank space.

551.48 Conductors and Boxes. The maximum number of conductors permitted in boxes shall be in accordance with 314.16.

551.49 Grounded Conductors. The identification of grounded conductors shall be in accordance with 200.6.

551.50 Connection of Terminals and Splices. Conductor splices and connections at terminals shall be in accordance with 110.14.

551.51 Switches.

(A) Rating. Switches shall be rated in accordance with 551.51(A)(1) and (A)(2).

(1) Lighting Circuits. For lighting circuits, switches shall be rated not less than 10 amperes, 120–125 volts and in no case less than the connected load.

(2) Motors or Other Loads. Switches for motor or other loads shall comply with the provisions of 404.14.

(B) Location. Switches shall not be installed within wet locations in tub or shower spaces unless installed as part of a listed tub or shower assembly.

551.52 Receptacles. All receptacle outlets shall be of the grounding type and installed in accordance with 406.3 and 210.21.

551.53 Luminaires (Lighting Fixtures).

(A) General. Any combustible wall or ceiling finish exposed between the edge of a luminaire (fixture) canopy, or pan and the outlet box, shall be covered with noncombustible material or a material identified for the purpose.

(B) Shower Luminaires (Fixtures). If a luminaire (lighting fixture) is provided over a bathtub or in a shower stall, it shall be of the enclosed and gasketed type and listed for the type of installation, and it shall be ground-fault circuit-interrupter protected.

(C) Outdoor Outlets, Luminaires (Fixtures), Air-Cooling Equipment, and So On. Outdoor luminaires (fixtures) and other equipment shall be listed for outdoor use.

551.54 Grounding. (See also 551.56 on bonding of non–current-carrying metal parts.)

(A) Power-Supply Grounding. The grounding conductor in the supply cord or feeder shall be connected to the grounding bus or other approved grounding means in the distribution panelboard.

(B) Distribution Panelboard. The distribution panelboard shall have a grounding bus with sufficient terminals for all grounding conductors or other approved grounding means.

(C) Insulated Neutral. The grounded circuit conductor (neutral) shall be insulated from the equipment grounding conductors and from equipment enclosures and other grounded parts. The grounded (neutral) circuit terminals in the distribution panelboard and in ranges, clothes dryers, counter-mounted cooking units, and wall-mounted ovens shall be insulated from the equipment enclosure. Bonding screws, straps, or buses in the distribution panelboard or in appliances shall be removed and discarded. Connection of electric ranges and electric clothes dryers utilizing a grounded (neutral) conductor, if cord-connected, shall be made with 4-conductor cord and 3-pole, 4-wire grounding-type plug caps and receptacles.

551.55 Interior Equipment Grounding.

(A) Exposed Metal Parts. In the electrical system, all exposed metal parts, enclosures, frames, luminaire (lighting fixture) canopies, and so forth, shall be effectively bonded to the grounding terminals or enclosure of the distribution panelboard.

(B) Equipment Grounding and Bonding Conductors. Bare wires, insulated wire with an outer finish that is green or green with one or more yellow stripes, shall be used for equipment grounding or bonding conductors only.

(C) Grounding of Electrical Equipment. Grounding of electrical equipment shall be accomplished by one or more of the following methods:

(1) Connection of metal raceway, the sheath of Type MC and Type MI cable where the sheath is identified for grounding, or the armor of Type AC cable to metal enclosures.

(2) A connection between the one or more equipment grounding conductors and a metal enclosure by means of a grounding screw, which shall be used for no other purpose, or a listed grounding device.

(3) The equipment grounding conductor in nonmetallic-sheathed cable shall be permitted to be secured under a screw threaded into the luminaire (fixture) canopy other than a mounting screw or cover screw, or attached to a listed grounding means (plate) in a nonmetallic outlet box for luminaire (fixture) mounting. [Grounding means shall also be permitted for luminaire (fixture) attachment screws.]

(D) Grounding Connection in Nonmetallic Box. A connection between the one or more grounding conductors brought into a nonmetallic outlet box shall be so arranged that a connection can be made to any fitting or device in that box that requires grounding.

(E) Grounding Continuity. Where more than one equipment grounding or bonding conductor of a branch circuit enters a box, all such conductors shall be in good electrical contact with each other, and the arrangement shall be such that the disconnection or removal of a receptacle, luminaire (fixture), or other device fed from the box will not interfere with or interrupt the grounding continuity.

(F) Cord-Connected Appliances. Cord-connected appliances, such as washing machines, clothes dryers, refrigerators, and the electrical system of gas ranges, and so forth, shall be grounded by means of an approved cord with equipment grounding conductor and grounding-type attachment plug.

551.56 Bonding of Non–Current-Carrying Metal Parts.

(A) Required Bonding. All exposed non–current-carrying metal parts that may become energized shall be effectively bonded to the grounding terminal or enclosure of the distribution panelboard.

(B) Bonding Chassis. A bonding conductor shall be connected between any distribution panelboard and an accessible terminal on the chassis. Aluminum or copper-clad aluminum conductors shall not be used for bonding if such conductors or their terminals are exposed to corrosive elements.

Exception: Any recreational vehicle that employs a unitized metal chassis-frame construction to which the distribution panelboard is securely fastened with a bolt(s) and nut(s) or by welding or riveting shall be considered to be bonded.

(C) Bonding Conductor Requirements. Grounding terminals shall be of the solderless type and listed as pressure terminal connectors recognized for the wire size used. The bonding conductor shall be solid or stranded, insulated or bare, and shall be 8 AWG copper minimum, or equal.

(D) Metallic Roof and Exterior Bonding. The metal roof and exterior covering shall be considered bonded where both of the following conditions apply:

(1) The metal panels overlap one another and are securely attached to the wood or metal frame parts by metal fasteners.

(2) The lower panel of the metal exterior covering is secured by metal fasteners at each cross member of the chassis, or the lower panel is bonded to the chassis by a metal strap.

(E) Gas, Water, and Waste Pipe Bonding. The gas, water, and waste pipes shall be considered grounded if they are bonded to the chassis.

(F) Furnace and Metal Air Duct Bonding. Furnace and metal circulating air ducts shall be bonded.

551.57 Appliance Accessibility and Fastening. Every appliance shall be accessible for inspection, service, repair, and replacement without removal of permanent construction. Means shall be provided to securely fasten appliances in place when the recreational vehicle is in transit.

V. Factory Tests

551.60 Factory Tests (Electrical). Each recreational vehicle designed with a 120-volt or a 120/240-volt electrical system shall withstand the applied potential without electrical breakdown of a 1-minute, 900-volt dielectric strength test, or a 1-second, 1080-volt dielectric strength test, with all switches closed, between ungrounded and grounded conductors and the recreational vehicle ground. During the test, all switches and other controls shall be in the "on" position. Fixtures, including luminaires and permanently installed appliances, shall not be required to withstand this test. The test shall be performed after branch circuits are complete prior to energizing the system and again after all outer coverings and cabinetry have been secured.

Each recreational vehicle shall be subjected to all of the following:

(1) A continuity test to ensure that all metal parts are properly bonded

(2) Operational tests to demonstrate that all equipment is properly connected and in working order

(3) Polarity checks to determine that connections have been properly made

VI. Recreational Vehicle Parks

551.71 Type Receptacles Provided. Every recreational vehicle site with electrical supply shall be equipped with at least one 20-ampere, 125-volt receptacle. A minimum of 20 percent of all recreational vehicle sites, with electrical supply, shall each be equipped with a 50-ampere, 125/250-volt receptacle conforming to the configuration as identified in Figure 551.46(C) . These electrical supplies shall be permitted to include additional receptacles that have configurations in accordance with 551.81. A minimum of 70 percent of all recreational vehicle sites with electrical supply shall each be equipped with a 30-ampere, 125-volt receptacle conforming to Figure 551.46(C) . This supply shall be permitted to include additional receptacle configurations conforming to 551.81. The remainder of all recreational vehicle sites with electrical supply shall be equipped with one or more of the receptacle configurations conforming to 551.81. Dedicated tent sites with a 15- or 20-ampere electrical supply shall be permitted to be excluded when determining the percentage of recreational vehicle sites with 30- or 50-ampere receptacles.

Additional receptacles shall be permitted for the connection of electrical equipment outside the recreational vehicle within the recreational vehicle park.

All 125-volt, single-phase, 15- and 20-ampere receptacles shall have listed ground-fault circuit-interrupter protection for personnel.

FPN: The percentage of 50 ampere sites required by 551.71 may be inadequate for seasonal recreational vehicle sites serving a higher percentage of recreational vehicles with 50 ampere electrical systems. In that type of recreational vehicle park, the percentage of 50 ampere sites could approach 100 percent.

551.72 Distribution System. Receptacles rated at 50 amperes shall be supplied from a branch circuit of the voltage

class and rating of the receptacle. Other recreational vehicle sites with 125-volt, 20- and 30-ampere receptacles shall be permitted to be derived from any grounded distribution system that supplies 120-volt single-phase power. The neutral conductors shall not be reduced in size below the size of the ungrounded conductors for the site distribution. The neutral conductors shall be permitted to be reduced in size below the minimum required size of the ungrounded conductors for 240-volt, line-to-line, permanently connected loads only.

551.73 Calculated Load.

(A) Basis of Calculations. Electrical service and feeders shall be calculated on the basis of not less than 9600 volt-amperes per site equipped with 50-ampere, 120/240-volt supply facilities; 3600 volt-amperes per site equipped with both 20-ampere and 30-ampere supply facilities; 2400 volt-amperes per site equipped with only 20-ampere supply facilities; and 600 volt-amperes per site equipped with only 20-ampere supply facilities that are dedicated to tent sites. The demand factors set forth in Table 551.73 shall be the minimum allowable demand factors that shall be permitted in calculating load for service and feeders. Where the electrical supply for a recreational vehicle site has more than one receptacle, the calculated load shall only be calculated for the highest rated receptacle.

Where the electrical supply is in a location that serves two recreational vehicles, the equipment for both sites must comply with 551.77 and the calculated load shall only be computed for the two receptacles with the highest rating.

(B) Transformers and Secondary Distribution Panelboards. For the purpose of this *Code*, where the park service exceeds 240 volts, transformers and secondary distribution panelboards shall be treated as services.

(C) Demand Factors. The demand factor for a given number of sites shall apply to all sites indicated. For example, 20 sites calculated at 45 percent of 3600 volt-amperes results in a permissible demand of 1620 volt-amperes per site or a total of 32,400 volt-amperes for 20 sites.

FPN: These demand factors may be inadequate in areas of extreme hot or cold temperature with loaded circuits for heating or air conditioning.

(D) Feeder-Circuit Capacity. Recreational vehicle site feeder-circuit conductors shall have adequate ampacity for the loads supplied and shall be rated at not less than 30 amperes. The grounded conductors shall have the same ampacity as the ungrounded conductors.

FPN: Due to the long circuit lengths typical in most recreational vehicle parks, feeder conductor sizes found in the ampacity tables of Article 310 may be inadequate to maintain the voltage regulation suggested in the fine print note to 210.19. Total circuit voltage drop is a sum of the voltage drops of each serial circuit segment, where the load for each segment is calculated using the load that segment sees and the demand factors of 551.73(A).

Table 551.73 Demand Factors for Site Feeders and Service-Entrance Conductors for Park Sites

Number of Recreational Vehicle Sites	Demand Factor (percent)
1	100
2	90
3	80
4	75
5	65
6	60
7–9	55
10–12	50
13–15	48
16–18	47
19–21	45
22–24	43
25–35	42
36 plus	41

Loads for other amenities such as, but not limited to, service buildings, recreational buildings, and swimming pools shall be sized separately and then be added to the value calculated for the recreational vehicle sites where they are all supplied by one service.

551.74 Overcurrent Protection. Overcurrent protection shall be provided in accordance with Article 240.

551.75 Grounding. All electrical equipment and installations in recreational vehicle parks shall be grounded as required by Article 250.

551.76 Grounding — Recreational Vehicle Site Supply Equipment.

(A) Exposed Non–Current-Carrying Metal Parts. Exposed non–current-carrying metal parts of fixed equipment, metal boxes, cabinets, and fittings that are not electrically connected to grounded equipment shall be grounded by a continuous equipment grounding conductor run with the circuit conductors from the service equipment or from the transformer of a secondary distribution system. Equipment grounding conductors shall be sized in accordance with 250.122 and shall be permitted to be spliced by listed means.

The arrangement of equipment grounding connections shall be such that the disconnection or removal of a receptacle or other device will not interfere with, or interrupt, the grounding continuity.

(B) Secondary Distribution System. Each secondary distribution system shall be grounded at the transformer.

(C) Neutral Conductor Not to Be Used as an Equipment Ground. The neutral conductor shall not be used as an equipment ground for recreational vehicles or equipment within the recreational vehicle park.

(D) No Connection on the Load Side. No connection to a grounding electrode shall be made to the neutral conductor on the load side of the service disconnecting means except as covered in 250.30(A) for separately derived systems and 250.32(B)(2) for separate buildings.

551.77 Recreational Vehicle Site Supply Equipment.

(A) Location. Where provided on back-in sites, the recreational vehicle site electrical supply equipment shall be located on the left (road) side of the parked vehicle, on a line that is 1.5 m to 2.1 m (5 ft to 7 ft) from the left edge (driver's side of the parked RV) of the stand and shall be located at any point on this line from the rear of the stand to 4.5 m (15 ft) forward of the rear of the stand.

For pull-through sites, the electrical supply equipment shall be permitted to be located at any point along the line that is 1.5 m to 2.1 m (5 ft to 7 ft) from the left edge (driver's side of the parked RV) from 4.9 m (16 ft) forward of the rear of the stand to the center point between the two roads that gives access to and egress from the pull-through sites.

The left edge (driver's side of the parked RV) of the stand shall be marked.

(B) Disconnecting Means. A disconnecting switch or circuit breaker shall be provided in the site supply equipment for disconnecting the power supply to the recreational vehicle.

(C) Access. All site supply equipment shall be accessible by an unobstructed entrance or passageway not less than 600 mm (2 ft) wide and 2.0 m (6 ft 6 in.) high.

(D) Mounting Height. Site supply equipment shall be located not less than 600 mm (2 ft) or more than 2.0 m (6 ft 6 in.) above the ground.

(E) Working Space. Sufficient space shall be provided and maintained about all electrical equipment to permit ready and safe operation, in accordance with 110.26.

(F) Marking. Where the site supply equipment contains a 125/250-volt receptacle, the equipment shall be marked as follows: "Turn disconnecting switch or circuit breaker off before inserting or removing plug. Plug must be fully inserted or removed." The marking shall be located on the equipment adjacent to the receptacle outlet.

551.78 Protection of Outdoor Equipment.

(A) Wet Locations. All switches, circuit breakers, receptacles, control equipment, and metering devices located in wet locations or outside of a building shall be rainproof equipment.

(B) Meters. If secondary meters are installed, meter sockets without meters installed shall be blanked off with an approved blanking plate.

551.79 Clearance for Overhead Conductors. Open conductors of not over 600 volts, nominal, shall have a vertical clearance of not less than 5.5 m (18 ft) and a horizontal clearance of not less than 900 mm (3 ft) in all areas subject to recreational vehicle movement. In all other areas, clearances shall conform to 225.18 and 225.19.

FPN: For clearances of conductors over 600 volts, nominal, see 225.60 and 225.61.

551.80 Underground Service, Feeder, Branch-Circuit, and Recreational Vehicle Site Feeder-Circuit Conductors.

(A) General. All direct-burial conductors, including the equipment grounding conductor if of aluminum, shall be insulated and identified for the use. All conductors shall be continuous from equipment to equipment. All splices and taps shall be made in approved junction boxes or by use of material listed and identified for the purpose.

(B) Protection Against Physical Damage. Direct-buried conductors and cables entering or leaving a trench shall be protected by rigid metal conduit, intermediate metal conduit, electrical metallic tubing with supplementary corrosion protection, rigid nonmetallic conduit, liquidtight flexible nonmetallic conduit, liquidtight flexible metal conduit, or other approved raceways or enclosures. Where subject to physical damage, the conductors or cables shall be protected by rigid metal conduit, intermediate metal conduit, or Schedule 80 rigid nonmetallic conduit. All such protection shall extend at least 450 mm (18 in.) into the trench from finished grade.

FPN: See 300.5 and Article 340 for conductors or Type UF cable used underground or in direct burial in earth.

551.81 Receptacles. A receptacle to supply electric power to a recreational vehicle shall be one of the configurations shown in Figure 551.46(C) in the following ratings.

(1) 50-ampere — 125/250-volt, 50-ampere, 3-pole, 4-wire grounding type for 120/240-volt systems

(2) 30-ampere — 125-volt, 30-ampere, 2-pole, 3-wire grounding type for 120-volt systems

(3) 20-ampere — 125-volt, 20-ampere, 2-pole, 3-wire grounding type for 120-volt systems

FPN: Complete details of these configurations can be found in ANSI/NEMA WD 6-1989, National Electrical Manufacturers Association's *Standard for Dimensions of Attachment Plugs and Receptacles*, Figures 14-50, TT, and 5-20.

ARTICLE 552
Park Trailers

I. General

552.1 Scope. The provisions of this article cover the electrical conductors and equipment installed within or on park trailers not covered fully under Articles 550 and 551.

552.2 Definition. (See Articles 100, 550, and 551 for additional definitions.)

Park Trailer. A unit that is built on a single chassis mounted on wheels and has a gross trailer area not exceeding 37 m² (400 ft²) in the set-up mode.

552.3 Other Articles. Wherever the provisions of other articles and Article 552 differ, the provisions of Article 552 shall apply.

552.4 General Requirements. A park trailer as specified in 552.2 is intended for seasonal use. It is not intended as a permanent dwelling unit or for commercial uses such as banks, clinics, offices, or similar.

II. Low-Voltage Systems

552.10 Low-Voltage Systems.

(A) Low-Voltage Circuits. Low-voltage circuits furnished and installed by the park trailer manufacturer, other than those related to braking, are subject to this *Code*. Circuits supplying lights subject to federal or state regulations shall comply with applicable government regulations and this *Code*.

(B) Low-Voltage Wiring.

(1) Material. Copper conductors shall be used for low-voltage circuits.

Exception: A metal chassis or frame shall be permitted as the return path to the source of supply.

(2) Conductor Types. Conductors shall conform to the requirements for Type GXL, HDT, SGT, SGR, or Type SXL or shall have insulation in accordance with Table 310.13 or the equivalent. Conductor sizes 6 AWG through 18 AWG or SAE shall be listed. Single-wire, low-voltage conductors shall be of the stranded type.

FPN: See SAE Standard J1128-1995 for Types GXL, HDT, and SXL and SAE Standard J1127-1995 for Types SGT and SGR.

(3) Marking. All insulated low-voltage conductors shall be surface marked at intervals not greater than 1.2 m (4 ft) as follows:

(1) Listed conductors shall be marked as required by the listing agency.

(2) SAE conductors shall be marked with the name or logo of the manufacturer, specification designation, and wire gauge.

(3) Other conductors shall be marked with the name or logo of the manufacturer, temperature rating, wire gauge, conductor material, and insulation thickness.

(C) Low-Voltage Wiring Methods.

(1) Physical Protection. Conductors shall be protected against physical damage and shall be secured. Where insulated conductors are clamped to the structure, the conductor insulation shall be supplemented by an additional wrap or layer of equivalent material, except that jacketed cables shall not be required to be so protected. Wiring shall be routed away from sharp edges, moving parts, or heat sources.

(2) Splices. Conductors shall be spliced or joined with splicing devices that provide a secure connection or by brazing, welding, or soldering with a fusible metal or alloy. Soldered splices shall first be spliced or joined to be mechanically and electrically secure without solder, and then soldered. All splices, joints, and free ends of conductors shall be covered with an insulation equivalent to that on the conductors.

(3) Separation. Battery and other low-voltage circuits shall be physically separated by at least a 13-mm (½-in.) gap or other approved means from circuits of a different power source. Acceptable methods shall be by clamping, routing, or equivalent means that ensure permanent total separation. Where circuits of different power sources cross, the external jacket of the nonmetallic-sheathed cables shall be deemed adequate separation.

(4) Ground Connections. Ground connections to the chassis or frame shall be made in an accessible location and shall be mechanically secure. Ground connections shall be by means of copper conductors and copper or copper-alloy terminals of the solderless type identified for the size of wire used. The surface on which ground terminals make contact shall be cleaned and be free from oxide or paint or shall be electrically connected through the use of a cadmium, tin, or zinc-plated internal/external-toothed lockwasher or locking terminals. Ground terminal attaching screws, rivets or bolts, nuts, and lockwashers shall be cadmium, tin, or zinc-plated except rivets shall be permitted to be unanodized aluminum where attaching to aluminum structures.

The chassis-grounding terminal of the battery shall be bonded to the unit chassis with a minimum 8 AWG copper conductor. In the event the power lead from the battery exceeds 8 AWG, the bonding conductor shall be of an equal size.

(D) Battery Installations. Storage batteries subject to the provisions of this *Code* shall be securely attached to the unit and installed in an area vaportight to the interior and ventilated directly to the exterior of the unit. Where batteries are installed in a compartment, the compartment shall be ventilated with openings having a minimum area of 1100 mm^2 (1.7 in.^{2}) at both the top and at the bottom. Where compartment doors are equipped for ventilation, the openings shall be within 50 mm (2 in.) of the top and bottom. Batteries shall not be installed in a compartment containing spark- or flame-producing equipment.

(E) Overcurrent Protection.

(1) Rating. Low-voltage circuit wiring shall be protected by overcurrent protective devices rated not in excess of the ampacity of copper conductors, in accordance with Table 552.10(E)(1).

Table 552.10(E)(1) Low-Voltage Overcurrent Protection

Wire Size (AWG)	Ampacity	Wire Type
18	6	Stranded only
16	8	Stranded only
14	15	Stranded or solid
12	20	Stranded or solid
10	30	Stranded or solid

(2) Type. Circuit breakers or fuses shall be of an approved type, including automotive types. Fuseholders shall be clearly marked with maximum fuse size and shall be protected against shorting and physical damage by a cover or equivalent means.

FPN: For further information, see ANSI/SAE J554-1987, *Standard for Electric Fuses (Cartridge Type)*; SAE J1284-1988, *Standard for Blade Type Electric Fuses*; and UL 275-1993, *Standard for Automotive Glass Tube Fuses.*

(3) Appliances. Appliances such as pumps, compressors, heater blowers, and similar motor-driven appliances shall be installed in accordance with the manufacturer's instructions.

Motors that are controlled by automatic switching or by latching-type manual switches shall be protected in accordance with 430.32(B).

(4) Location. The overcurrent protective device shall be installed in an accessible location on the unit within 450 mm (18 in.) of the point where the power supply connects to the unit circuits. If located outside the park trailer, the device shall be protected against weather and physical damage.

Exception: External low-voltage supply shall be permitted to have the overcurrent protective device within 450 mm (18 in.) after entering the unit or after leaving a metal raceway.

(F) Switches. Switches shall have a dc rating not less than the connected load.

(G) Luminaires (Lighting Fixtures). All low-voltage interior luminaires (lighting fixtures) rated more than 4 watts, employing lamps rated more than 1.2 watts, shall be listed.

III. Combination Electrical Systems

552.20 Combination Electrical Systems.

(A) General. Unit wiring suitable for connection to a battery or other low-voltage supply source shall be permitted to be connected to a 120-volt source, provided that the entire wiring system and equipment are rated and installed in full conformity with Parts I, III, IV, and V requirements of this article covering 120-volt electrical systems. Circuits fed from ac transformers shall not supply dc appliances.

(B) Voltage Converters (120-Volt Alternating Current to Low-Voltage Direct Current). The 120-volt ac side of the voltage converter shall be wired in full conformity with Parts I, III, IV, and V requirements of this article for 120-volt electrical systems.

Exception: Converters supplied as an integral part of a listed appliance shall not be subject to 552.20(B).

All converters and transformers shall be listed for use in recreation units and designed or equipped to provide overtemperature protection. To determine the converter rating, the following formula shall be applied to the total connected load, including average battery charging rate, of all 12-volt equipment:

The first 20 amperes of load at 100 percent; plus
The second 20 amperes of load at 50 percent; plus
All load above 40 amperes at 25 percent

Exception: A low-voltage appliance that is controlled by a momentary switch (normally open) that has no means for holding in the closed position shall not be considered as a connected load when determining the required converter rating. Momentarily energized appliances shall be limited to those used to prepare the unit for occupancy or travel.

(C) Bonding Voltage Converter Enclosures. The non–current-carrying metal enclosure of the voltage converter shall be bonded to the frame of the unit with an 8 AWG copper conductor minimum. The grounding conductor for the battery and the metal enclosure shall be permitted to be the same conductor.

(D) Dual-Voltage Fixtures Including Luminaires or Appliances. Fixtures, including luminaires, or appliances having both 120-volt and low-voltage connections shall be listed for dual voltage.

(E) Autotransformers. Autotransformers shall not be used.

(F) Receptacles and Plug Caps. Where a park trailer is equipped with a 120-volt or 120/240-volt ac system, a low-voltage system, or both, receptacles and plug caps of the low-voltage system shall differ in configuration from those of the 120-volt or 120/240-volt system. Where a unit equipped with a battery or dc system has an external connection for low-voltage power, the connector shall have a configuration that will not accept 120-volt power.

IV. Nominal 120-Volt or 120/240-Volt Systems

552.40 120-Volt or 120/240-Volt, Nominal, Systems.

(A) General Requirements. The electrical equipment and material of park trailers indicated for connection to a wiring system rated 120 volts, nominal, 2-wire with ground, or a wiring system rated 120/240 volts, nominal, 3-wire with ground, shall be listed and installed in accordance with the requirements of Parts I, III, IV, and V of this article.

(B) Materials and Equipment. Electrical materials, devices, appliances, fittings, and other equipment installed, intended for use in, or attached to the park trailer shall be listed. All products shall be used only in the manner in which they have been tested and found suitable for the intended use.

552.41 Receptacle Outlets Required.

(A) Spacing. Receptacle outlets shall be installed at wall spaces 600 mm (2 ft) wide or more so that no point along the floor line is more than 1.8 m (6 ft), measured horizontally, from an outlet in that space.

Exception No. 1: Bath and hall areas.

Exception No. 2: Wall spaces occupied by kitchen cabinets, wardrobe cabinets, built-in furniture; behind doors that may open fully against a wall surface; or similar facilities.

(B) Location. Receptacle outlets shall be installed as follows:

(1) Adjacent to countertops in the kitchen [at least one on each side of the sink if countertops are on each side and are 300 mm (12 in.) or over in width]

(2) Adjacent to the refrigerator and gas range space, except where a gas-fired refrigerator or cooking appliance, requiring no external electrical connection, is factory-installed

(3) Adjacent to countertop spaces of 300 mm (12 in.) or more in width that cannot be reached from a receptacle required in 552.41(B)(1) by a cord of 1.8 m (6 ft) without crossing a traffic area, cooking appliance, or sink

(C) Ground-Fault Circuit-Interrupter Protection. Each 125-volt, single-phase, 15- or 20-ampere receptacle shall have ground-fault circuit-interrupter protection for personnel in the following locations:

(1) Where the receptacles are installed to serve kitchen countertop surfaces

(2) Within 1.8 m (6 ft) of any lavatory or sink

Exception: Receptacles installed for appliances in dedicated spaces, such as for dishwashers, disposals, refrigerators, freezers, and laundry equipment.

(3) In the area occupied by a toilet, shower, tub, or any combination thereof

(4) On the exterior of the unit

Exception: Receptacles that are located inside of an access panel that is installed on the exterior of the unit to supply power for an installed appliance shall not be required to have ground-fault circuit-interrupter protection.

The receptacle outlet shall be permitted in a listed luminaire (lighting fixture). A receptacle outlet shall not be installed in a tub or combination tub–shower compartment.

(D) Pipe Heating Cable Outlet. Where a pipe heating cable outlet is installed, the outlet shall be as follows:

(1) Located within 600 mm (2 ft) of the cold water inlet

(2) Connected to an interior branch circuit, other than a small appliance branch circuit

(3) On a circuit where all of the outlets are on the load side of the ground-fault circuit-interrupter protection for personnel

(4) Mounted on the underside of the park trailer and shall not be considered to be the outdoor receptacle outlet required in 552.41(E)

(E) Outdoor Receptacle Outlets. At least one receptacle outlet shall be installed outdoors. A receptacle outlet located in a compartment accessible from the outside of the park trailer shall be considered an outdoor receptacle. Outdoor receptacle outlets shall be protected as required in 552.41(C)(4).

(F) Receptacle Outlets Not Permitted.

(1) Shower or Bathtub Space. Receptacle outlets shall not be installed in or within reach [750 mm (30 in.)] of a shower or bathtub space.

(2) Face-Up Position. A receptacle shall not be installed in a face-up position in any countertop.

552.43 Power Supply.

(A) Feeder. The power supply to the park trailer shall be a feeder assembly consisting of not more than one listed 30-ampere or 50-ampere park trailer power-supply cord with an integrally molded or securely attached cap, or a permanently installed feeder.

(B) Power-Supply Cord. If the park trailer has a power-supply cord, it shall be permanently attached to the distribution panelboard or to a junction box permanently connected to the distribution panelboard, with the free end terminating in a molded-on attachment plug cap.

Cords with adapters and pigtail ends, extension cords, and similar items shall not be attached to, or shipped with, a park trailer.

A suitable clamp or the equivalent shall be provided at the distribution panelboard knockout to afford strain relief for the cord to prevent strain from being transmitted to the terminals when the power-supply cord is handled in its intended manner.

The cord shall be a listed type with 3-wire, 120-volt or 4-wire, 120/240-volt conductors, one of which shall be identified by a continuous green color or a continuous green color with one or more yellow stripes for use as the grounding conductor.

(C) Mast Weatherhead or Raceway. Where the calculated load exceeds 50 amperes or where a permanent feeder is used, the supply shall be by means of one of the following:

(1) One mast weatherhead installation, installed in accordance with Article 230, containing four continuous, insulated, color-coded feeder conductors, one of which shall be an equipment grounding conductor

(2) A metal raceway, rigid nonmetallic conduit, or liquidtight flexible nonmetallic conduit from the disconnecting means in the park trailer to the underside of the park trailer, with provisions for the attachment to a suitable junction box or fitting to the raceway on the underside of the park trailer [with or without conductors as in 550.10(I)(1)]

552.44 Cord.

(A) Permanently Connected. Each power-supply assembly shall be factory supplied or factory installed and connected directly to the terminals of the distribution panelboard or conductors within a junction box and provided with means to prevent strain from being transmitted to the terminals. The ampacity of the conductors between each junction box and the terminals of each distribution panelboard shall be at least equal to the ampacity of the power-supply cord. The supply end of the assembly shall be equipped with an attachment plug of the type described in 552.44(C). Where the cord passes through the walls or floors, it shall be protected by means of conduit and bushings or equivalent. The cord assembly shall have permanent provisions for protection against corrosion and mechanical damage while the unit is in transit.

(B) Cord Length. The cord-exposed usable length shall be measured from the point of entrance to the park trailer or the face of the flanged surface inlet (motor-base attachment plug) to the face of the attachment plug at the supply end.

The cord-exposed usable length, measured to the point of entry on the unit exterior, shall be a minimum of 7.0 m (23 ft) where the point of entrance is at the side of the unit, or shall be a minimum 8.5 m (28 ft) where the point of entrance is at the rear of the unit. The maximum length shall not exceed 11 m (36½ ft).

Where the cord entrance into the unit is more than 900 mm (3 ft) above the ground, the minimum cord lengths above shall be increased by the vertical distance of the cord entrance heights above 900 mm (3 ft).

(C) Attachment Plugs.

(1) Units with Two to Five 15- or 20-Ampere Branch Circuits. Park trailers wired in accordance with 552.46(A) shall have an attachment plug that shall be 2-pole, 3-wire grounding-type, rated 30 amperes, 125 volts, conforming to the configuration shown in Figure 552.44(C) intended for use with units rated at 30 amperes, 125 volts.

> FPN: Complete details of this configuration can be found in ANSI/NEMA WD 6-1989, National Electrical Manufacturers Association's *Standard for Dimensions of Attachment Plugs and Receptacles*, Figure TT.

(2) Units with 50-Ampere Power Supply Assembly. Park trailers having a power-supply assembly rated 50 amperes as permitted by 552.43(B) shall have a 3-pole, 4-wire grounding-type attachment plug rated 50 amperes, 125/250 volts, conforming to the configuration shown in Figure 552.44(C).

> FPN: Complete details of this configuration can be found in ANSI/NEMA WD 6-1989, National Electrical Manufacturers Association *Standard for Dimensions of Attachment Plugs and Receptacles*, Figure 14-50.

30-A,125-V, 2-pole, 3-wire, grounding type

50-A,125/250-V, 3-pole, 4-wire, grounding type

Figure 552.44(C) Attachment Cap and Receptacle Configurations.

(D) Labeling at Electrical Entrance. Each park trailer shall have permanently affixed to the exterior skin, at or near the point of entrance of the power-supply assembly, a label 75 mm × 45 mm (3 in. × 1¾ in.) minimum size, made of etched, metal-stamped, or embossed brass, stainless steel, or anodized or alclad aluminum not less than 0.51 mm (0.020 in.) thick, or other suitable material [e.g., 0.13 mm (0.005 in.) thick plastic laminate], that reads, as appropriate, either

> THIS CONNECTION IS FOR 110–125-VOLT AC, 60 HZ, 30 AMPERE SUPPLY

or

> THIS CONNECTION IS FOR 120/240-VOLT AC, 3-POLE, 4-WIRE, 60 HZ, _____ AMPERE SUPPLY.

The correct ampere rating shall be marked in the blank space.

(E) Location. The point of entrance of a power-supply assembly shall be located within 4.5 m (15 ft) of the rear, on the left (road) side or at the rear, left of the longitudinal center of the unit, within 450 mm (18 in.) of the outside wall.

Exception: A park trailer shall be permitted to have the electrical point of entrance located more than 4.5 m (15 ft) from the rear. Where this occurs, the distance beyond the 4.5-m (15-ft) dimension shall be added to the cord's minimum length as specified in 551.46(B).

552.45 Distribution Panelboard.

(A) Listed and Appropriately Rated. A listed and appropriately rated distribution panelboard shall be used. The grounded conductor termination bar shall be insulated from the enclosure as provided in 552.55(C). An equipment grounding terminal bar shall be attached inside the metal enclosure of the panelboard.

(B) Location. The distribution panelboard shall be installed in a readily accessible location. Working clearance for the panelboard shall be not less than 600 mm (24 in.) wide and 750 mm (30 in.) deep.

Exception: Where the panelboard cover is exposed to the inside aisle space, one of the working clearance dimensions shall be permitted to be reduced to a minimum of 550 mm (22 in.). A panelboard shall be considered exposed where the panelboard cover is within 50 mm (2 in.) of the aisle's finished surface.

(C) Dead-Front Type. The distribution panelboard shall be of the dead-front type. A main disconnecting means shall be provided where fuses are used or where more than two circuit breakers are employed. A main overcurrent protective device not exceeding the power-supply assembly rating shall be provided where more than two branch circuits are employed.

552.46 Branch Circuits. Branch circuits shall be determined in accordance with 552.46(A) and 552.46(B).

(A) Two to Five 15- or 20-Ampere Circuits. Two to five 15- or 20-ampere circuits to supply lights, receptacle outlets, and fixed appliances shall be permitted. Such park trailers shall be equipped with a distribution panelboard rated at 120 volts maximum with a 30-ampere rated main power supply assembly. Not more than two 120-volt thermostatically controlled appliances (e.g., air conditioner and water heater) shall be installed in such systems unless appliance isolation switching, energy management systems, or similar methods are used.

Exception: Additional 15- or 20-ampere circuits shall be permitted where a listed energy management system rated at 30 amperes maximum is employed within the system.

(B) More Than Five Circuits. Where more than five circuits are needed, they shall be determined in accordance with 552.46(B)(1), (B)(2), and (B)(3).

(1) Lighting. Based on 33 volt-amperes/m² (3 VA/ft²) multiplied by the outside dimensions of the park trailer (coupler excluded) divided by 120 volts to determine the number of 15- or 20-ampere lighting area circuits, for example,

$$\frac{3 \times \text{length} \times \text{width}}{120 \times 15 \text{ (or 20)}}$$
$$= \text{No. of 15- (or 20-) ampere circuits}$$

The lighting circuits shall be permitted to serve built-in gas ovens with electric service only for lights, clocks or timers, or listed cord-connected garbage disposal units.

(2) Small Appliances. Small appliance branch circuits shall be installed in accordance with 210.11(C)(1).

(3) General Appliances. (including furnace, water heater, space heater, range, and central or room air conditioner, etc.) An individual branch circuit shall be permitted to supply any load for which it is rated. There shall be one or more circuits of adequate rating in accordance with (a) through (d).

FPN No. 1: For the laundry branch circuit, see 210.11(C)(2).

FPN No. 2: For central air conditioning, see Article 440.

(a) The total rating of fixed appliances shall not exceed 50 percent of the circuit rating if lighting outlets, general-use receptacles, or both, are also supplied.

(b) For fixed appliances with a motor(s) larger than ⅛ horsepower, the total calculated load shall be based on 125 percent of the largest motor plus the sum of the other loads. Where a branch circuit supplies continuous load(s) or any combination of continuous and noncontinuous loads, the branch-circuit conductor size shall be in accordance with 210.19(A).

(c) The rating of a single cord- and plug-connected appliance supplied by other than an individual branch circuit shall not exceed 80 percent of the circuit rating.

(d) The rating of a range branch circuit shall be based on the range demand as specified for ranges in 552.47(B)(5).

552.47 Calculations. The following method shall be employed in computing the supply-cord and distribution-panelboard load for each feeder assembly for each park trailer in lieu of the procedure shown in Article 220 and shall be based on a 3-wire, 120/240-volt supply with 120-volt loads balanced between the two phases of the 3-wire system.

(A) Lighting and Small Appliance Load. Lighting Volt-Amperes: Length times width of park trailer floor (outside dimensions) times 33 volt-amperes/m² (3 VA/ft²). For example,

$$\text{Length} \times \text{width} \times 3 = \text{lighting volt-amperes}$$

Small Appliance Volt-Amperes: Number of circuits times 1500 volt-amperes for each 20-ampere appliance receptacle circuit (see definition of *Appliance, Portable* with note) including 1500 volt-amperes for laundry circuit. For example,

$$\text{No. of circuits} \times 1500 = \text{small appliance volt-amperes}$$

Total: Lighting volt-amperes plus small appliance volt-amperes = total volt-amperes

First 3000 total volt-amperes at 100 percent plus remainder at 35 percent = volt-amperes to be divided by 240 volts to obtain current (amperes) per leg.

(B) Total Load for Determining Power Supply. Total load for determining power supply is the sum of the following:

(1) Lighting and small appliance load as calculated in 552.47(A).

(2) Nameplate amperes for motors and heater loads (exhaust fans, air conditioners, electric, gas, or oil heating). Omit smaller of the heating and cooling loads, except include blower motor if used as air-conditioner evaporator motor. Where an air conditioner is not installed and a 50-ampere power-supply cord is provided, allow 15 amperes per phase for air conditioning.

(3) Twenty-five percent of current of largest motor in (B)(2).

(4) Total of nameplate amperes for disposal, dishwasher, water heater, clothes dryer, wall-mounted oven, cooking units. Where the number of these appliances exceeds three, use 75 percent of total.

(5) Derive amperes for freestanding range (as distinguished from separate ovens and cooking units) by dividing the following values by 240 volts:

Nameplate Rating (watts)	Use (volt-amperes)
0–10,000	80 percent of rating
Over 10,000–12,500	8,000
Over 12,500–13,500	8,400
Over 13,500–14,500	8,800
Over 14,500–15,500	9,200
Over 15,500–16,500	9,600
Over 16,500–17,500	10,000

(6) If outlets or circuits are provided for other than factory-installed appliances, include the anticipated load.

FPN: Refer to Annex D, Example D12, for an illustration of the application of this calculation.

(C) Optional Method of Calculation for Lighting and Appliance Load. For park trailers, the optional method for calculating lighting and appliance load shown in 220.82 shall be permitted.

552.48 Wiring Methods.

(A) Wiring Systems. Cables and raceways installed in accordance with Articles 320, 322, 330 through 340, 342 through 362, 386, and 388 shall be permitted in accordance with their applicable article, except as otherwise specified in this article. An equipment grounding means shall be provided in accordance with 250.118.

(B) Conduit and Tubing. Where rigid metal conduit or intermediate metal conduit is terminated at an enclosure with a locknut and bushing connection, two locknuts shall be provided, one inside and one outside of the enclosure. All cut ends of conduit and tubing shall be reamed or otherwise finished to remove rough edges.

(C) Nonmetallic Boxes. Nonmetallic boxes shall be acceptable only with nonmetallic-sheathed cable or nonmetallic raceways.

(D) Boxes. In walls and ceilings constructed of wood or other combustible material, boxes and fittings shall be flush with the finished surface or project therefrom.

(E) Mounting. Wall and ceiling boxes shall be mounted in accordance with Article 314.

Exception No. 1: Snap-in-type boxes or boxes provided with special wall or ceiling brackets that securely fasten boxes in walls or ceilings shall be permitted.

Exception No. 2: A wooden plate providing a 38-mm (1½-in.) minimum width backing around the box and of a thickness of 13 mm (½ in.) or greater (actual) attached directly to the wall panel shall be considered as approved means for mounting outlet boxes.

(F) Sheath Armor. The sheath of nonmetallic-sheathed cable, metal-clad cable, and Type AC cable shall be continuous between outlet boxes and other enclosures.

(G) Protected. Metal-clad, Type AC, or nonmetallic-sheathed cables and electrical nonmetallic tubing shall be permitted to pass through the centers of the wide side of 2 by 4 wood studs. However, they shall be protected where they pass through 2 by 2 wood studs or at other wood studs or frames where the cable or tubing would be less than 32 mm (1¼ in.) from the inside or outside surface. Steel plates on each side of the cable or tubing, or a steel tube, with not less than 1.35 mm (0.053 in.) wall thickness, shall be installed to protect the cable or tubing. These plates or tubes shall be securely held in place. Where nonmetallic-sheathed cables pass through punched, cut, or drilled slots or holes in metal members, the cable shall be protected by bushings or grommets securely fastened in the opening prior to installation of the cable.

(H) Cable Supports. Where connected with cable connectors or clamps, cables shall be supported within 300 mm (12 in.) of outlet boxes, distribution panelboards, and splice boxes on appliances. Supports shall be provided every 1.4 m (4½ ft) at other places.

(I) Nonmetallic Box Without Cable Clamps. Nonmetallic-sheathed cables shall be supported within 200 mm (8 in.) of a nonmetallic outlet box without cable clamps.

Exception: Where wiring devices with integral enclosures are employed with a loop of extra cable to permit future replacement of the device, the cable loop shall be considered as an integral portion of the device.

(J) Physical Damage. Where subject to physical damage, exposed nonmetallic cable shall be protected by covering boards, guard strips, raceways, or other means.

(K) Metal Faceplates. Metal faceplates shall be of ferrous metal not less than 0.76 mm (0.030 in.) in thickness or of nonferrous metal not less than 1.0 mm (0.040 in.) in thickness. Nonmetallic faceplates shall be listed.

(L) Metal Faceplates Effectively Grounded. Where metal faceplates are used, they shall be effectively grounded.

(M) Moisture or Physical Damage. Where outdoor or under-chassis wiring is 120 volts, nominal, or over and is exposed to moisture or physical damage, the wiring shall be protected by rigid metal conduit, by intermediate metal conduit, or by electrical metallic tubing or rigid nonmetallic conduit that is closely routed against frames and equipment enclosures or other raceway or cable identified for the application.

(N) Component Interconnections. Fittings and connectors that are intended to be concealed at the time of assembly shall be listed and identified for the interconnection of building components. Such fittings and connectors shall be equal to the wiring method employed in insulation, temperature rise, and fault-current withstanding, and shall be capable of enduring the vibration and shock occurring in park trailers.

(O) Method of Connecting Expandable Units. The method of connecting expandable units to the main body of the vehicle shall comply with the following as applicable:

(1) That portion of a branch circuit that is installed in an expandable unit shall be permitted to be connected to the branch circuit in the main body of the vehicle by means of a flexible cord or attachment plug and cord listed for hard usage. The cord and its connections shall conform to all provisions of Article 400 and shall be considered as a permitted use under 400.7.

(2) If the receptacle provided for connection of the cord to the main circuit is located on the outside of the unit, it shall be protected with a ground-fault circuit interrupter for personnel and be listed for wet locations. A cord located on the outside of a unit shall be identified for outdoor use.

(3) Unless removable or stored within the unit interior, the cord assembly shall have permanent provisions for protection against corrosion and mechanical damage while the unit is in transit.

(4) If an attachment plug and cord is used, it shall be installed so as not to permit exposed live attachment plug pins.

(P) Prewiring for Air-Conditioning Installation. Prewiring installed for the purpose of facilitating future air-conditioning installation shall conform to the applicable portions of this article and the following:

(1) An overcurrent protective device with a rating compatible with the circuit conductors shall be installed in the distribution panelboard and wiring connections completed.

(2) The load end of the circuit shall terminate in a junction box with a blank cover or other listed enclosure. Where a junction box with a blank cover is used, the free ends of the conductors shall be adequately capped or taped.

(3) A label conforming to 552.44(D) shall be placed on or adjacent to the junction box and shall read

AIR-CONDITIONING CIRCUIT.
THIS CONNECTION IS FOR AIR CONDITIONERS
RATED 110–125-VOLT AC, 60 HZ,
_____ AMPERES MAXIMUM.
DO NOT EXCEED CIRCUIT RATING.

An ampere rating, not to exceed 80 percent of the circuit rating, shall be legibly marked in the blank space.

(4) The circuit shall serve no other purpose.

552.49 Maximum Number of Conductors in Boxes. The maximum number of conductors permitted in boxes shall be in accordance with 314.16.

552.50 Grounded Conductors. The identification of grounded conductors shall be in accordance with 200.6.

552.51 Connection of Terminals and Splices. Conductor splices and connections at terminals shall be in accordance with 110.14.

552.52 Switches. Switches shall be rated as required by 552.52(A) and 552.52(B).

(A) Lighting Circuits. For lighting circuits, switches shall be rated not less than 10 amperes, 120/125 volts, and in no case less than the connected load.

(B) Motors or Other Loads. For motors or other loads, switches shall have ampere or horsepower ratings, or both, adequate for loads controlled. (An ac general-use snap switch shall be permitted to control a motor 2 hp or less with full-load current not over 80 percent of the switch ampere rating.)

552.53 Receptacles. All receptacle outlets shall be of the grounding type and installed in accordance with 210.21 and 406.3.

552.54 Luminaires (Lighting Fixtures).

(A) General. Any combustible wall or ceiling finish exposed between the edge of a luminaire (fixture) canopy or pan and the outlet box shall be covered with noncombustible material or a material identified for the purpose.

(B) Shower Luminaires (Fixtures). If a luminaire (lighting fixture) is provided over a bathtub or in a shower stall, it shall be of the enclosed and gasketed type and listed for the type of installation, and it shall be ground-fault circuit-interrupter protected.

The switch for shower luminaires (lighting fixtures) and exhaust fans, located over a tub or in a shower stall, shall be located outside the tub or shower space.

(C) Outdoor Outlets, Luminaires (Fixtures), Air-Cooling Equipment, and So On. Outdoor luminaires (fixtures) and other equipment shall be listed for outdoor use.

552.55 Grounding. (See also 552.57 on bonding of non–current-carrying metal parts.)

(A) Power-Supply Grounding. The grounding conductor in the supply cord or feeder shall be connected to the grounding bus or other approved grounding means in the distribution panelboard.

(B) Distribution Panelboard. The distribution panelboard shall have a grounding bus with sufficient terminals for all grounding conductors or other approved grounding means.

(C) Insulated Neutral. The grounded circuit conductor (neutral) shall be insulated from the equipment grounding conductors and from equipment enclosures and other grounded parts. The grounded (neutral) circuit terminals in the distribution panelboard and in ranges, clothes dryers, counter-mounted cooking units, and wall-mounted ovens shall be insulated from the equipment enclosure. Bonding screws, straps, or buses in the distribution panelboard or in appliances shall be removed and discarded. Connection of electric ranges and electric clothes dryers utilizing a grounded (neutral) conductor, if cord-connected, shall be made with 4-conductor cord and 3-pole, 4-wire, grounding-type plug caps and receptacles.

552.56 Interior Equipment Grounding.

(A) Exposed Metal Parts. In the electrical system, all exposed metal parts, enclosures, frames, luminaire (lighting fixture) canopies, and so forth, shall be effectively bonded to the grounding terminals or enclosure of the distribution panelboard.

(B) Equipment Grounding Conductors. Bare wires, green-colored wires, or green wires with a yellow stripe(s) shall be used for equipment grounding conductors only.

(C) Grounding of Electrical Equipment. Where grounding of electrical equipment is specified, it shall be permitted as follows:

(1) Connection of metal raceway (conduit or electrical metallic tubing), the sheath of Type MC and Type MI cable where the sheath is identified for grounding, or the armor of Type AC cable to metal enclosures.

(2) A connection between the one or more equipment grounding conductors and a metal box by means of a grounding screw, which shall be used for no other purpose, or a listed grounding device.

(3) The equipment grounding conductor in nonmetallic-sheathed cable shall be permitted to be secured under a screw threaded into the luminaire (fixture) canopy other than a mounting screw or cover screw or attached to a listed grounding means (plate) in a nonmetallic outlet box for luminaire (fixture) mounting [grounding means shall also be permitted for luminaire (fixture) attachment screws].

(D) Grounding Connection in Nonmetallic Box. A connection between the one or more grounding conductors brought into a nonmetallic outlet box shall be arranged so that a connection can be made to any fitting or device in that box that requires grounding.

(E) Grounding Continuity. Where more than one equipment grounding conductor of a branch circuit enters a box, all such conductors shall be in good electrical contact with each other, and the arrangement shall be such that the disconnection or removal of a receptacle, fixture, including a luminaire, or other device fed from the box will not interfere with or interrupt the grounding continuity.

(F) Cord-Connected Appliances. Cord-connected appliances, such as washing machines, clothes dryers, refrigerators, and the electrical system of gas ranges, and so on, shall be grounded by means of an approved cord with equipment grounding conductor and grounding-type attachment plug.

552.57 Bonding of Non–Current-Carrying Metal Parts.

(A) Required Bonding. All exposed non–current-carrying metal parts that may become energized shall be effectively bonded to the grounding terminal or enclosure of the distribution panelboard.

(B) Bonding Chassis. A bonding conductor shall be connected between any distribution panelboard and an accessible terminal on the chassis. Aluminum or copper-clad aluminum conductors shall not be used for bonding if such conductors or their terminals are exposed to corrosive elements.

Exception: Any park trailer that employs a unitized metal chassis-frame construction to which the distribution panelboard is securely fastened with a bolt(s) and nut(s) or by welding or riveting shall be considered to be bonded.

(C) Bonding Conductor Requirements. Grounding terminals shall be of the solderless type and listed as pressure terminal connectors recognized for the wire size used. The bonding conductor shall be solid or stranded, insulated or bare, and shall be 8 AWG copper minimum or equivalent.

(D) Metallic Roof and Exterior Bonding. The metal roof and exterior covering shall be considered bonded where both of the following conditions apply:

(1) The metal panels overlap one another and are securely attached to the wood or metal frame parts by metal fasteners.

(2) The lower panel of the metal exterior covering is secured by metal fasteners at each cross member of the chassis, or the lower panel is bonded to the chassis by a metal strap.

(E) Gas, Water, and Waste Pipe Bonding. The gas, water, and waste pipes shall be considered grounded if they are bonded to the chassis.

(F) Furnace and Metal Air Duct Bonding. Furnace and metal circulating air ducts shall be bonded.

552.58 Appliance Accessibility and Fastening. Every appliance shall be accessible for inspection, service, repair, and replacement without removal of permanent construction. Means shall be provided to securely fasten appliances in place when the park trailer is in transit.

552.59 Outdoor Outlets, Fixtures, Including Luminaires, Air-Cooling Equipment, and So On.

(A) Listed for Outdoor Use. Outdoor fixtures, including luminaires, and equipment shall be listed for outdoor use. Outdoor receptacle or convenience outlets shall be of a gasketed-cover type for use in wet locations.

(B) Outside Heating Equipment, Air-Conditioning Equipment, or Both. A park trailer provided with a branch circuit designed to energize outside heating equipment or air-conditioning equipment, or both, located outside the park trailer, other than room air conditioners, shall have such branch-circuit conductors terminate in a listed outlet box or disconnecting means located on the outside of the park trailer. A label shall be permanently affixed within 150 mm (6 in.) from the listed box or disconnecting means, and shall contain the following information:

> THIS CONNECTION IS FOR HEATING
> AND/OR AIR-CONDITIONING EQUIPMENT.
> THE BRANCH CIRCUIT IS RATED AT NOT MORE
> THAN _____ AMPERES, AT _____ VOLTS,
> 60 HZ, _____ CONDUCTOR AMPACITY.
> A DISCONNECTING MEANS SHALL BE
> LOCATED WITHIN SIGHT OF THE EQUIPMENT.

The correct voltage and ampere rating shall be given. The tag shall not be less than 0.51 mm (0.020 in.) thick etched brass, stainless steel, anodized or alclad aluminum, or equivalent. The tag shall not be less than 75 mm × 45 mm (3 in. × 1¾ in.) minimum size.

V. Factory Tests

552.60 Factory Tests (Electrical). Each park trailer shall be subjected to the tests required by 552.60(A) and 552.60(B).

(A) Circuits of 120 Volts or 120/240 Volts. Each park trailer designed with a 120-volt or a 120/240-volt electrical system shall withstand the applied potential without electrical breakdown of a 1-minute, 900-volt dielectric strength test, or a 1-second, 1080-volt dielectric strength test, with all switches closed, between ungrounded and grounded conductors and the park trailer ground. During the test, all switches and other controls shall be in the on position. Fixtures, including luminaires, and permanently installed appliances shall not be required to withstand this test.

Each park trailer shall be subjected to the following:

(1) A continuity test to ensure that all metal parts are properly bonded

(2) Operational tests to demonstrate that all equipment is properly connected and in working order

(3) Polarity checks to determine that connections have been properly made

(4) Receptacles requiring GFCI protection shall be tested for correct function by the use of a GFCI testing device

(B) Low-Voltage Circuits. Low-voltage circuit conductors in each park trailer shall withstand the applied potential without electrical breakdown of a 1-minute, 500-volt or a 1-second, 600-volt dielectric strength test. The potential shall be applied between ungrounded and grounded conductors.

The test shall be permitted on running light circuits before the lights are installed, provided the unit's outer covering and interior cabinetry have been secured. The braking circuit shall be permitted to be tested before being connected to the brakes, provided the wiring has been completely secured.

ARTICLE 553
Floating Buildings

I. General

553.1 Scope. This article covers wiring, services, feeders, and grounding for floating buildings.

553.2 Definition.

Floating Building. A building unit as defined in Article 100 that floats on water, is moored in a permanent location, and has a premises wiring system served through connection by permanent wiring to an electricity supply system not located on the premises.

553.3 Application of Other Articles. Wiring for floating buildings shall comply with the applicable provisions of other articles of this *Code*, except as modified by this article.

II. Services and Feeders

553.4 Location of Service Equipment. The service equipment for a floating building shall be located adjacent to, but not in or on, the building or any floating structure.

553.5 Service Conductors. One set of service conductors shall be permitted to serve more than one set of service equipment.

553.6 Feeder Conductors. Each floating building shall be supplied by a single set of feeder conductors from its service equipment.

Exception: Where the floating building has multiple occupancy, each occupant shall be permitted to be supplied by a single set of feeder conductors extended from the occupant's service equipment to the occupant's panelboard.

553.7 Installation of Services and Feeders.

(A) Flexibility. Flexibility of the wiring system shall be maintained between floating buildings and the supply conductors. All wiring shall be installed so that motion of the water surface and changes in the water level will not result in unsafe conditions.

(B) Wiring Methods. Liquidtight flexible metal conduit or liquidtight flexible nonmetallic conduit with approved fittings shall be permitted for feeders and where flexible connections are required for services. Extra-hard usage portable power cable listed for both wet locations and sunlight resistance shall be permitted for a feeder to a floating building where flexibility is required. Other raceways suitable for the location shall be permitted to be installed where flexibility is not required.

FPN: See 555.1 and 555.13.

III. Grounding

553.8 General Requirements. Grounding at floating buildings shall comply with 553.8(A) through (D).

(A) Grounding of Electrical and Nonelectrical Parts. Grounding of both electrical and nonelectrical parts in a floating building shall be through connection to a grounding bus in the building panelboard.

(B) Installation and Connection of Equipment Grounding Conductor. The equipment grounding conductor shall be installed with the feeder conductors and connected to a grounding terminal in the service equipment.

(C) Identification of Equipment Grounding Conductor. The equipment grounding conductor shall be an insulated copper conductor with a continuous outer finish that is either green or green with one or more yellow stripes. For conductors larger than 6 AWG, or where multiconductor cables are used, re-identification of conductors as allowed in 250.119(A)(2)(b) and (A)(2)(c) or 250.119(B)(2) and (B)(3) shall be permitted.

(D) Grounding Electrode Conductor Connection. The grounding terminal in the service equipment shall be grounded by connection through an insulated grounding electrode conductor to a grounding electrode on shore.

553.9 Insulated Neutral. The grounded circuit conductor (neutral) shall be an insulated conductor identified in conformance with 200.6. The neutral conductor shall be connected to the equipment grounding terminal in the service equipment, and, except for that connection, it shall be insulated from the equipment grounding conductors, equipment enclosures, and all other grounded parts. The neutral circuit terminals in the panelboard and in ranges, clothes dryers, counter-mounted cooking units, and the like shall be insulated from the enclosures.

553.10 Equipment Grounding.

(A) Electrical Systems. All enclosures and exposed metal parts of electrical systems shall be bonded to the grounding bus.

(B) Cord-Connected Appliances. Where required to be grounded, cord-connected appliances shall be grounded by means of an equipment grounding conductor in the cord and a grounding-type attachment plug.

553.11 Bonding of Non–Current-Carrying Metal Parts. All metal parts in contact with the water, all metal piping, and all non–current-carrying metal parts that may become energized shall be bonded to the grounding bus in the panelboard.

ARTICLE 555
Marinas and Boatyards

555.1 Scope. This article covers the installation of wiring and equipment in the areas comprising fixed or floating piers, wharves, docks, and other areas in marinas, boatyards, boat basins, boathouses, yacht clubs, boat condominiums, docking facilities associated with residential condominiums, any multiple docking facility, or similar occupancies, and facilities that are used, or intended for use, for the purpose of repair, berthing, launching, storage, or fueling of small craft and the moorage of floating buildings.

Private, noncommercial docking facilities constructed or occupied for the use of the owner or residents of the associated single-family dwelling are not covered by this article.

FPN: See NFPA 303-2000, *Fire Protection Standard for Marinas and Boatyards*, for additional information.

555.2 Definitions.

Electrical Datum Plane. The electrical datum plane is defined as follows:

(1) In land areas subject to tidal fluctuation, the electrical datum plane is a horizontal plane 606 mm (2 ft) above

the highest tide level for the area occurring under normal circumstances, that is, highest high tide.

(2) In land areas not subject to tidal fluctuation, the electrical datum plane is a horizontal plane 606 mm (2 ft) above the highest water level for the area occurring under normal circumstances.

(3) The electrical datum plane for floating piers and landing stages that are (a) installed to permit rise and fall response to water level, without lateral movement, and (b) that are so equipped that they can rise to the datum plane established for (1) or (2), is a horizontal plane 762 mm (30 in.) above the water level at the floating pier or landing stage and a minimum of 305 mm (12 in.) above the level of the deck.

Marine Power Outlet. An enclosed assembly that can include receptacles, circuit breakers, fused switches, fuses, watt-hour meter(s), and monitoring means approved for marine use.

555.4 Distribution System. Yard and pier distribution systems shall not exceed 600 volts phase to phase.

555.5 Transformers. Transformers and enclosures shall be specifically approved for the intended location. The bottom of enclosures for transformers shall not be located below the electrical datum plane.

555.7 Location of Service Equipment. The service equipment for floating docks or marinas shall be located adjacent to, but not on or in, the floating structure.

555.9 Electrical Connections. All electrical connections shall be located at least 305 mm (12 in.) above the deck of a floating pier. All electrical connections shall be located at least 305 mm (12 in.) above the deck of a fixed pier but not below the electrical datum plane.

555.10 Electrical Equipment Enclosures.

(A) Securing and Supporting. Electrical equipment enclosures installed on piers above deck level shall be securely and substantially supported by structural members, independent of any conduit connected to them. If enclosures are not attached to mounting surfaces by means of external ears or lugs, the internal screw heads shall be sealed to prevent seepage of water through mounting holes.

(B) Location. Electrical equipment enclosures on piers shall be located so as not to interfere with mooring lines.

555.11 Circuit Breakers, Switches, Panelboards, and Marine Power Outlets. Circuit breakers and switches installed in gasketed enclosures shall be arranged to permit required manual operation without exposing the interior of the enclosure. All such enclosures shall be arranged with a weep hole to discharge condensation.

555.12 Load Calculations for Service and Feeder Conductors. General lighting and other loads shall be calculated in accordance with Article 220, and, in addition, the demand factors set forth in Table 555.12 shall be permitted for each service and/or feeder circuit supplying receptacles that provide shore power for boats. These calculations shall be permitted to be modified as indicated in notes (1) and (2) to Table 555.12.

Table 555.12 Demand Factors

Number of Receptacles	Sum of the Rating of the Receptacles (percent)
1–4	100
5–8	90
9–14	80
15–30	70
31–40	60
41–50	50
51–70	40
71-plus	30

Notes:

1. Where shore power accommodations provide two receptacles specifically for an individual boat slip and these receptacles have different voltages (for example, one 30 ampere, 125 volt and one 50 ampere, 125/250 volt), only the receptacle with the larger kilowatt demand shall be required to be calculated.

2. If the facility being installed includes individual kilowatt-hour submeters for each slip and is being calculated using the criteria listed in Table 555.12, the total demand amperes may be multiplied by 0.9 to achieve the final demand amperes.

> FPN: These demand factors may be inadequate in areas of extreme hot or cold temperatures with loaded circuits for heating, air-conditioning, or refrigerating equipment.

555.13 Wiring Methods and Installation.

(A) Wiring Methods.

(1) General. Wiring methods of Chapter 3 shall be permitted where identified for use in wet locations.

(2) Portable Power Cables. Extra-hard usage portable power cables rated not less than 167°F (75°C), 600 volts; listed for both wet locations and sunlight resistance; and having an outer jacket rated to be resistant to temperature extremes, oil, gasoline, ozone, abrasion, acids, and chemicals shall be permitted as follows:

(1) As permanent wiring on the underside of piers (floating or fixed)

(2) Where flexibility is necessary as on piers composed of floating sections

(3) Temporary Wiring. Temporary wiring, except as permitted by Article 590, shall not be used to supply power to boats.

(B) Installation.

(1) Overhead Wiring. Overhead wiring shall be installed to avoid possible contact with masts and other parts of boats being moved in the yard.

Conductors and cables shall be routed to avoid wiring closer than 6.0 m (20 ft) from the outer edge or any portion of the yard that can be used for moving vessels or stepping or unstepping masts.

(2) Outside Branch Circuits and Feeders. Outside branch circuits and feeders shall comply with Article 225 except that clearances for overhead wiring in portions of the yard other than those described in 555.13(B)(1) shall not be less than 5.49 m (18 ft) above grade.

(3) Wiring Over and Under Navigable Water. Wiring over and under navigable water shall be subject to approval by the authority having jurisdiction.

FPN: See NFPA 303-2000, *Fire Protection Standard for Marinas and Boatyards*, for warning sign requirements.

(4) Portable Power Cables.

(a) Where portable power cables are permitted by 555.13(A)(2), the installation shall comply with the following:
(1) Cables shall be properly supported.
(2) Cables shall be located on the underside of the pier.
(3) Cables shall be securely fastened by nonmetallic clips to structural members other than the deck planking.
(4) Cables shall not be installed where subject to physical damage.
(5) Where cables pass through structural members, they shall be protected against chafing by a permanently installed oversized sleeve of nonmetallic material.

(b) Where portable power cables are used as permitted in 555.13(A)(2)(2), there shall be an approved junction box of corrosion-resistant construction with permanently installed terminal blocks on each pier section to which the feeder and feeder extensions are to be connected. Metal junction boxes and their covers, and metal screws and parts that are exposed externally to the boxes, shall be of corrosion-resistant materials or protected by material resistant to corrosion.

(5) Protection. Rigid metal or nonmetallic conduit suitable for the location shall be installed to protect wiring above decks of piers and landing stages and below the enclosure that it serves. The conduit shall be connected to the enclosure by full standard threads. The use of special fittings of nonmetallic material to provide a threaded connection into enclosures on rigid nonmetallic conduit, employing joint design as recommended by the conduit manufacturer, for

attachment of the fitting to the conduit shall be acceptable, provided the equipment and method of attachment are approved and the assembly meets the requirements of installation in damp or wet locations as applicable.

555.15 Grounding. Wiring and equipment within the scope of this article shall be grounded as specified in Article 250 and as required by 555.15(A) through 555.15(E).

(A) Equipment to Be Grounded. The following items shall be connected to an equipment grounding conductor run with the circuit conductors in the same raceway, cable, or trench:
(1) Metal boxes, metal cabinets, and all other metal enclosures
(2) Metal frames of utilization equipment
(3) Grounding terminals of grounding-type receptacles

(B) Type of Equipment Grounding Conductor. The equipment grounding conductor shall be an insulated copper conductor with a continuous outer finish that is either green or green with one or more yellow stripes. The equipment grounding conductor of Type MI cable shall be permitted to be identified at terminations. For conductors larger than 6 AWG, or where multiconductor cables are used, re-identification of conductors as allowed in 250.119(A)(2)(b) and (A)(2)(c) or 250.119(B)(2) and (B)(3) shall be permitted.

(C) Size of Equipment Grounding Conductor. The insulated copper equipment grounding conductor shall be sized in accordance with 250.122 but not smaller than 12 AWG.

(D) Branch-Circuit Equipment Grounding Conductor. The insulated equipment grounding conductor for branch circuits shall terminate at a grounding terminal in a remote panelboard or the grounding terminal in the main service equipment.

(E) Feeder Equipment Grounding Conductors. Where a feeder supplies a remote panelboard, an insulated equipment grounding conductor shall extend from a grounding terminal in the service equipment to a grounding terminal in the remote panelboard.

555.17 Disconnecting Means for Shore Power Connection(s). Disconnecting means shall be provided to isolate each boat from its supply connection(s).

(A) Type. The disconnecting means shall be permitted to consist of a circuit breaker, switch, or both, and shall be properly identified as to which receptacle it controls.

(B) Location. The disconnecting means shall be readily accessible, located not more than 762 mm (30 in.) from the receptacle it controls, and shall be located in the supply circuit ahead of the receptacle. Circuit breakers or switches located in marine power outlets complying with this section shall be permitted as the disconnecting means.

555.19 Receptacles. Receptacles shall be mounted not less than 305 mm (12 in.) above the deck surface of the pier and not below the electrical datum plane on a fixed pier.

(A) Shore Power Receptacles.

(1) Enclosures. Receptacles intended to supply shore power to boats shall be housed in marine power outlets listed as marina power outlets or listed for set locations, or shall be installed in listed enclosures protected from the weather or in listed weatherproof enclosures. The integrity of the assembly shall not be affected when the receptacles are in use with any type of booted or nonbooted attachment plug/cap inserted.

(2) Strain Relief. Means shall be provided where necessary to reduce the strain on the plug and receptacle caused by the weight and catenary angle of the shore power cord.

(3) Branch Circuits. Each single receptacle that supplies shore power to boats shall be supplied from a marine power outlet or panelboard by an individual branch circuit of the voltage class and rating corresponding to the rating of the receptacle.

> FPN: Supplying receptacles at voltages other than the voltages marked on the receptacle may cause overheating or malfunctioning of connected equipment, for example, supplying single-phase, 120/240-volt, 3-wire loads from a 208Y/120-volt, 3-wire source.

(4) Ratings. Shore power for boats shall be provided by single receptacles rated not less than 30 amperes.

> FPN: For locking- and grounding-type receptacles for auxiliary power to boats, see NFPA 303-2000, *Fire Protection Standard for Marinas and Boatyards.*

   (a) Receptacles rated not less than 30 amperes or more than 50 amperes shall be of the locking and grounding type.

> FPN: For various configurations and ratings of locking and grounding-type receptacles and caps, see ANSI/NEMA 18WD 6-1989, National Electrical Manufacturers Association's *Standard for Dimensions of Attachment Plugs and Receptacles.*

   (b) Receptacles rated for 60 amperes or 100 amperes shall be of the pin and sleeve type.

> FPN: For various configurations and ratings of pin and sleeve receptacles, see ANSI/UL 1686, *UL Standard for Safety Pin and Sleeve Configurations.*

(B) Other Than Shore Power.

(1) Ground-Fault Circuit-Interrupter (GFCI) Protection for Personnel. Fifteen- and 20-ampere, single-phase, 125-volt receptacles installed outdoors, in boathouses, in buildings used for storage, maintenance, or repair where portable electrical hand tools, electrical diagnostic equipment, or portable lighting equipment are to be used shall be provided with GFCI protection for personnel. Receptacles in other locations shall be protected in accordance with 210.8(B).

(2) Marking. Receptacles other than those supplying shore power to boats shall be permitted to be housed in marine power outlets with the receptacles that provide shore power to boats, provided they are marked to clearly indicate that they are not to be used to supply power to boats.

555.21 Motor Fuel Dispensing Stations — Hazardous (Classified) Locations. Electrical wiring and equipment located at or serving motor fuel dispensing stations shall comply with Article 514 in addition to the requirements of this article. All electrical wiring for power and lighting shall be installed on the side of the wharf, pier, or dock opposite from the liquid piping system.

> FPN: For additional information, see NFPA 303-2000, *Fire Protection Standard for Marinas and Boatyards,* and NFPA 30A-2003, *Motor Fuel Dispensing Facilities and Repair Garages.*

555.22 Repair Facilities — Hazardous (Classified) Locations. Electrical wiring and equipment located at facilities for the repair of marine craft containing flammable or combustible liquids or gases shall comply with Article 511 in addition to the requirements of this article.

555.23 Marine Hoists, Railways, Cranes, and Monorails. Motors and controls for marine hoists, railways, cranes, and monorails shall not be located below the electrical datum plane. Where it is necessary to provide electric power to a mobile crane or hoist in the yard and a trailing cable is utilized, it shall be a listed portable power cable rated for the conditions of use and be provided with an outer jacket of distinctive color for safety.

ARTICLE 590
Temporary Installations

590.1 Scope. The provisions of this article apply to temporary electrical power and lighting installations.

590.2 All Wiring Installations.

(A) Other Articles. Except as specifically modified in this article, all other requirements of this *Code* for permanent wiring shall apply to temporary wiring installations.

(B) Approval. Temporary wiring methods shall be acceptable only if approved based on the conditions of use and any special requirements of the temporary installation.

590.3 Time Constraints.

(A) During the Period of Construction. Temporary electrical power and lighting installations shall be permitted during the period of construction, remodeling, maintenance, repair, or demolition of buildings, structures, equipment, or similar activities.

(B) 90 Days. Temporary electrical power and lighting installations shall be permitted for a period not to exceed 90 days for holiday decorative lighting and similar purposes.

(C) Emergencies and Tests. Temporary electrical power and lighting installations shall be permitted during emergencies and for tests, experiments, and developmental work.

(D) Removal. Temporary wiring shall be removed immediately upon completion of construction or purpose for which the wiring was installed.

590.4 General.

(A) Services. Services shall be installed in conformance with Article 230.

(B) Feeders. Overcurrent protection shall be provided in accordance with 240.4, 240.5, 240.100, and 240.101. They shall originate in an approved distribution center. Conductors shall be permitted within cable assemblies or within multiconductor cords or cables of a type identified in Table 400.4 for hard usage or extra-hard usage. For the purpose of this section, Type NM and Type NMC cables shall be permitted to be used in any dwelling, building, or structure without any height limitation or limitation by building construction type and without concealment within walls, floors, or ceilings.

Exception: Single insulated conductors shall be permitted where installed for the purpose(s) specified in 590.3(C), where accessible only to qualified persons.

(C) Branch Circuits. All branch circuits shall originate in an approved power outlet or panelboard. Conductors shall be permitted within cable assemblies or within multiconductor cord or cable of a type identified in Table 400.4 for hard usage or extra-hard usage. Conductors shall be protected from overcurrent as provided in 240.4, 240.5, and 240.100. For the purposes of this section, Type NM and Type NMC cables shall be permitted to be used in any dwelling, building, or structure without any height limitation or limitation by building construction type and without concealment within walls, floors, or ceilings.

Exception: Branch circuits installed for the purposes specified in 590.3(B) or 590.3(C) shall be permitted to be run as single insulated conductors. Where the wiring is installed in accordance with 590.3(B), the voltage to ground shall not exceed 150 volts, the wiring shall not be subject to physical damage, and the conductors shall be supported on insulators at intervals of not more than 3.0 m (10 ft); or, for festoon lighting, the conductors shall be so arranged that excessive strain is not transmitted to the lampholders.

(D) Receptacles. All receptacles shall be of the grounding type. Unless installed in a continuous grounded metal raceway or metal-covered cable, all branch circuits shall contain a separate equipment grounding conductor, and all receptacles shall be electrically connected to the equipment grounding conductors. Receptacles on construction sites shall not be installed on branch circuits that supply temporary lighting. Receptacles shall not be connected to the same ungrounded conductor of multiwire circuits that supply temporary lighting.

(E) Disconnecting Means. Suitable disconnecting switches or plug connectors shall be installed to permit the disconnection of all ungrounded conductors of each temporary circuit. Multiwire branch circuits shall be provided with a means to disconnect simultaneously all ungrounded conductors at the power outlet or panelboard where the branch circuit originated. Approved handle ties shall be permitted.

(F) Lamp Protection. All lamps for general illumination shall be protected from accidental contact or breakage by a suitable fixture or lampholder with a guard.

Brass shell, paper-lined sockets, or other metal-cased sockets shall not be used unless the shell is grounded.

(G) Splices. On construction sites, a box shall not be required for splices or junction connections where the circuit conductors are multiconductor cord or cable assemblies, provided that the equipment grounding continuity is maintained with or without the box. See 110.14(B) and 400.9. A box, conduit body, or terminal fitting having a separately bushed hole for each conductor shall be used wherever a change is made to a conduit or tubing system or a metal-sheathed cable system.

(H) Protection from Accidental Damage. Flexible cords and cables shall be protected from accidental damage. Sharp corners and projections shall be avoided. Where passing through doorways or other pinch points, protection shall be provided to avoid damage.

(I) Termination(s) at Devices. Flexible cords and cables entering enclosures containing devices requiring termination shall be secured to the box with fittings designed for the purpose.

(J) Support. Cable assemblies and flexible cords and cables shall be supported in place at intervals that ensure that they will be protected from physical damage. Support shall be in the form of staples, cable ties, straps, or similar type fittings installed so as not to cause damage. Vegetation shall not be used for support of overhead spans of branch circuits or feeders.

Exception: For holiday lighting in accordance with 590.3(B), where the conductors or cables are arranged with proper strain relief devices, tension take-up devices, or other approved means to avoid damage from the movement of the live vegetation, trees shall be permitted to be used for support of overhead spans of branch circuit conductors or cables.

590.5 Listing of Decorative Lighting. Decorative lighting used for holiday lighting and similar purposes, in accordance with 590.3(B), shall be listed.

590.6 Ground-Fault Protection for Personnel. Ground-fault protection for personnel for all temporary wiring installations shall be provided to comply with 590.6(A) and 590.6(B). This section shall apply only to temporary wiring installations used to supply temporary power to equipment used by personnel during construction, remodeling, maintenance, repair, or demolition of buildings, structures, equipment, or similar activities.

(A) Receptacle Outlets. All 125-volt, single-phase, 15-, 20-, and 30-ampere receptacle outlets that are not a part of the permanent wiring of the building or structure and that are in use by personnel shall have ground-fault circuit interrupter protection for personnel. If a receptacle(s) is installed or exists as part of the permanent wiring of the building or structure and is used for temporary electric power, ground-fault circuit-interrupter protection for personnel shall be provided. For the purposes of this section, cord sets or devices incorporating listed ground-fault circuit interrupter protection for personnel identified for portable use shall be permitted.

Exception: In industrial establishments only, where conditions of maintenance and supervision ensure that only qualified personnel are involved, an assured equipment grounding conductor program as specified in 590.6(B)(2) shall be permitted for only those receptacle outlets used to supply equipment that would create a greater hazard if power was interrupted or having a design that is not compatible with GFCI protection.

(B) Use of Other Outlets. Receptacles other than 125-volt, single-phase, 15-, 20-, and 30-ampere receptacles shall have protection in accordance with (B)(1) or the assured equipment grounding conductor program in accordance with (B)(2).

(1) GFCI Protection. Ground-fault circuit interrupter protection for personnel.

(2) Assured Equipment Grounding Conductor Program. A written assured equipment grounding conductor program continuously enforced at the site by one or more designated persons to ensure that equipment grounding conductors for all cord sets, receptacles that are not a part of the permanent wiring of the building or structure, and equipment connected by cord and plug are installed and maintained in accordance with the applicable requirements of 250.114, 250.138, 406.3(C), and 590.4(D).

(a) The following tests shall be performed on all cord sets, receptacles that are not part of the permanent wiring of the building or structure, and cord-and-plug-connected equipment required to be grounded:

(1) All equipment grounding conductors shall be tested for continuity and shall be electrically continuous.
(2) Each receptacle and attachment plug shall be tested for correct attachment of the equipment grounding conductor. The equipment grounding conductor shall be connected to its proper terminal.
(3) All required tests shall be performed as follows:

    a. Before first use on site
    b. When there is evidence of damage
    c. Before equipment is returned to service following any repairs
    d. At intervals not exceeding 3 months

(b) The tests required in item (2)(a) shall be recorded and made available to the authority having jurisdiction.

590.7 Guarding. For wiring over 600 volts, nominal, suitable fencing, barriers, or other effective means shall be provided to limit access only to authorized and qualified personnel.

Chapter 6 Special Equipment

ARTICLE 600
Electric Signs and Outline Lighting

I. General

600.1 Scope. This article covers the installation of conductors and equipment for electric signs and outline lighting. All installations and equipment using neon tubing, such as signs, decorative elements, skeleton tubing, or art forms, are covered by this article.

600.2 Definitions.

Electric-Discharge Lighting. Systems of illumination utilizing fluorescent lamps, high-intensity discharge (HID) lamps, or neon tubing.

Neon Tubing. Electric-discharge tubing manufactured into shapes that form letters, parts of letters, skeleton tubing, outline lighting, other decorative elements, or art forms, and filled with various inert gases.

Section Sign. A sign or outline lighting system, shipped as subassemblies, that requires field-installed wiring between the subassemblies to complete the overall sign.

Sign Body. A portion of a sign that may provide protection from the weather but is not an electrical enclosure.

Skeleton Tubing. Neon tubing that is itself the sign or outline lighting and not attached to an enclosure or sign body.

600.3 Listing. Electric signs, section signs, and outline lighting — fixed, mobile, or portable — shall be listed and installed in conformance with that listing, unless otherwise approved by special permission.

(A) Field-Installed Skeleton Tubing. Field-installed skeleton tubing shall not be required to be listed where installed in conformance with this *Code*.

(B) Outline Lighting. Outline lighting shall not be required to be listed as a system when it consists of listed luminaires (lighting fixtures) wired in accordance with Chapter 3.

600.4 Markings.

(A) Signs and Outline Lighting Systems. Signs and outline lighting systems shall be marked with the manufacturer's name, trademark, or other means of identification; and input voltage and current rating.

(B) With Incandescent Lamp Holders. Signs and outline lighting systems with incandescent lamp holders shall be marked to indicate the maximum allowable wattage of lamps. The markings shall be permanently installed, in letters at least 6 mm (¼ in.) high, and shall be located where visible during relamping.

600.5 Branch Circuits.

(A) Required Branch Circuit. Each commercial building and each commercial occupancy accessible to pedestrians shall be provided with at least one outlet in an accessible location at each entrance to each tenant space for sign or outline lighting system use. The outlet(s) shall be supplied by a branch circuit rated at least 20 amperes that supplies no other load. Service hallways or corridors shall not be considered accessible to pedestrians.

(B) Rating. Branch circuits that supply signs shall be rated in accordance with 600.5(B)(1) or (B)(2).

(1) Incandescent and Fluorescent. Branch circuits that supply signs and outline lighting systems containing incandescent and fluorescent forms of illumination shall be rated not to exceed 20 amperes.

(2) Neon. Branch circuits that supply neon tubing installations shall not be rated in excess of 30 amperes.

(C) Wiring Methods. Wiring methods used to supply signs shall comply with 600.5(C)(1), (C)(2), and (C)(3).

(1) Supply. The wiring method used to supply signs and outline lighting systems shall terminate within a sign, an outline lighting system enclosure, a suitable box, or a conduit body.

(2) Enclosures as Pull Boxes. Signs and transformer enclosures shall be permitted to be used as pull or junction boxes for conductors supplying other adjacent signs, outline lighting systems, or floodlights that are part of a sign and shall be permitted to contain both branch and secondary circuit conductors.

(3) Metal Poles. Metal poles used to support signs shall be permitted to enclose supply conductors, provided the poles and conductors are installed in accordance with 410.15(B).

600.6 Disconnects. Each sign and outline lighting system, or feeder circuit or branch circuit supplying a sign or outline lighting system, shall be controlled by an externally operable switch or circuit breaker that will open all ungrounded conductors. Signs and outline lighting systems located within fountains shall have the disconnect located in accordance with 680.12.

Exception No. 1: A disconnecting means shall not be required for an exit directional sign located within a building.

Exception No. 2: A disconnecting means shall not be required for cord-connected signs with an attachment plug.

(A) Location.

(1) Within Sight of the Sign. The disconnecting means shall be within sight of the sign or outline lighting system that it controls. Where the disconnecting means is out of the line of sight from any section that is able to be energized, the disconnecting means shall be capable of being locked in the open position.

(2) Within Sight of the Controller. The following shall apply for signs or outline lighting systems operated by electronic or electromechanical controllers located external to the sign or outline lighting system:

(1) The disconnecting means shall be permitted to be located within sight of the controller or in the same enclosure with the controller.

(2) The disconnecting means shall disconnect the sign or outline lighting system and the controller from all ungrounded supply conductors.

(3) The disconnecting means shall be designed such that no pole can be operated independently and shall be capable of being locked in the open position.

(B) Control Switch Rating. Switches, flashers, and similar devices controlling transformers and electronic power supplies shall be rated for controlling inductive loads or have a current rating not less than twice the current rating of the transformer.

FPN: See 404.14 for rating of snap switches.

600.7 Grounding. Signs and metal equipment of outline lighting systems shall be grounded.

(A) Flexible Metal Conduit Length. Listed flexible metal conduit or listed liquidtight flexible metal conduit that encloses the secondary circuit conductor from a transformer or power supply for use with electric discharge tubing shall be permitted as a bonding means if the total accumulative length of the conduit in the secondary circuit does not exceed 30 m (100 ft).

(B) Small Metal Parts. Small metal parts not exceeding 50 mm (2 in.) in any dimension, not likely to be energized, and spaced at least 19 mm (¾ in.) from neon tubing shall not require bonding.

(C) Nonmetallic Conduit. Where listed nonmetallic conduit is used to enclose the secondary circuit conductor from a transformer or power supply and a bonding conductor is required, the bonding conductor shall be installed separate and remote from the nonmetallic conduit and be spaced at least 38 mm (1½ in.) from the conduit when the circuit is

operated at 100 Hz or less or 45 mm (1¾ in.) when the circuit is operated at over 100 Hz.

(D) Bonding Conductors. Bonding conductors shall be copper and not smaller than 14 AWG.

(E) Metal Building Parts. Metal parts of a building shall not be permitted as a secondary return conductor or an equipment grounding conductor.

(F) Signs in Fountains. Signs or outline lighting installed inside a fountain shall have all metal parts and equipment grounding conductors bonded to the equipment grounding conductor for the fountain recirculating system. The bonding connection shall be as near as practicable to the fountain and shall be permitted to be made to metal piping systems that are bonded in accordance with 680.53.

FPN: Refer to 600.32(J) for restrictions on length of high-voltage secondary conductors.

600.8 Enclosures. Live parts, other than lamps, and neon tubing shall be enclosed. Transformers and power supplies provided with an integral enclosure, including a primary and secondary circuit splice enclosure, shall not require an additional enclosure.

(A) Strength. Enclosures shall have ample structural strength and rigidity.

(B) Material. Sign and outline lighting system enclosures shall be constructed of metal or shall be listed.

(C) Minimum Thickness of Enclosure Metal. Sheet copper or aluminum shall be at least 0.51 mm (0.020 in.) thick. Sheet steel shall be at least 0.41 mm (0.016 in.) thick.

(D) Protection of Metal. Metal parts of equipment shall be protected from corrosion.

600.9 Location.

(A) Vehicles. Sign or outline lighting system equipment shall be at least 4.3 m (14 ft) above areas accessible to vehicles unless protected from physical damage.

(B) Pedestrians. Neon tubing, other than dry-location portable signs, accessible to pedestrians shall be protected from physical damage.

(C) Adjacent to Combustible Materials. Signs and outline lighting systems shall be installed so that adjacent combustible materials are not subjected to temperatures in excess of 90°C (194°F).

The spacing between wood or other combustible materials and an incandescent or HID lamp or lampholder shall not be less than 50 mm (2 in.).

(D) Wet Location. Signs and outline lighting system equipment for wet location use, other than listed watertight type, shall be weatherproof and have drain holes, as necessary, in accordance with the following:

(1) Drain holes shall not be larger than 13 mm (½ in.) or smaller than 6 mm (¼ in.).

(2) Every low point or isolated section of the equipment shall have at least one drain hole.

(3) Drain holes shall be positioned such that there will be no external obstructions.

600.10 Portable or Mobile Signs.

(A) Support. Portable or mobile signs shall be adequately supported and readily movable without the use of tools.

(B) Attachment Plug. An attachment plug shall be provided for each portable or mobile sign.

(C) Wet or Damp Location. Portable or mobile signs in wet or damp locations shall comply with 600.10(C)(1) and (C)(2).

(1) Cords. All cords shall be junior hard service or hard service types as designated in Table 400.4 and have an equipment grounding conductor.

(2) Ground-Fault Circuit Interrupter. Portable or mobile signs shall be provided with factory-installed ground-fault circuit-interrupter protection for personnel. The ground-fault circuit interrupter shall be an integral part of the attachment plug or shall be located in the power-supply cord within 300 mm (12 in.) of the attachment plug.

(D) Dry Location. Portable or mobile signs in dry locations shall meet the following:

(1) Cords shall be SP-2, SPE-2, SPT-2, or heavier, as designated in Table 400.4.

(2) The cord shall not exceed 4.5 m (15 ft) in length.

600.12 Field-Installed Secondary Wiring. The field-installed secondary circuit wiring of section signs shall comply with 600.31 if 1000 volts or less, or with 600.32 if over 1000 volts.

600.21 Ballasts, Transformers, and Electronic Power Supplies.

(A) Accessibility. Ballasts, transformers, and electronic power supplies shall be located where accessible and shall be securely fastened in place.

(B) Location. Ballasts, transformers, and electronic power supplies shall be installed as near to the lamps or neon tubing as practicable to keep the secondary conductors as short as possible.

(C) Wet Location. Ballasts, transformers, and electronic power supplies used in wet locations shall be of the weatherproof type or be of the outdoor type and protected from the weather by placement in a sign body or separate enclosure.

(D) Working Space. A working space at least 900 mm (3 ft) high, 900 mm (3 ft) wide, by 900 mm (3 ft) deep shall be provided at each ballast, transformer, and electronic power supply or at its enclosure where not installed in a sign.

(E) Attic and Soffit Locations. Ballasts, transformers, and electronic power supplies shall be permitted to be located in attics and soffits, provided there is an access door at least 900 mm by 600 mm (3 ft by 2 ft) and a passageway of at least 900 mm (3 ft) high by 600 mm (2 ft) wide with a suitable permanent walkway at least 300 mm (12 in.) wide extending from the point of entry to each component.

(F) Suspended Ceilings. Ballasts, transformers, and electronic power supplies shall be permitted to be located above suspended ceilings, provided their enclosures are securely fastened in place and not dependent on the suspended ceiling grid for support. Ballasts, transformers, and electronic power supplies installed in suspended ceilings shall not be connected to the branch circuit by flexible cord.

600.22 Ballasts.

(A) Type. Ballasts shall be identified for the use and shall be listed.

(B) Thermal Protection. Ballasts shall be thermally protected.

600.23 Transformers and Electronic Power Supplies.

(A) Type. Transformers and electronic power supplies shall be identified for the use and shall be listed.

(B) Secondary-Circuit Ground-Fault Protection. Transformers and electronic power supplies other than the following shall have secondary-circuit ground-fault protection:

(1) Transformers with isolated ungrounded secondaries and with a maximum open circuit voltage of 7500 volts or less

(2) Transformers with integral porcelain or glass secondary housing for the neon tubing and requiring no field wiring of the secondary circuit

(C) Voltage. Secondary-circuit voltage shall not exceed 15,000 volts, nominal, under any load condition. The voltage to ground of any output terminals of the secondary circuit shall not exceed 7500 volts, under any load condition.

(D) Rating. Transformers and electronic power supplies shall have a secondary-circuit current rating of not more than 300 mA.

(E) Secondary Connections. Secondary circuit outputs shall not be connected in parallel or in series.

(F) Marking. A transformer or power supply shall be marked to indicate that it has secondary-circuit ground-fault protection.

600.24 Class 2 Power Sources. In addition to the requirements of Article 600, signs and outline lighting systems supplied by Class 2 transformers, power supplies, and power sources shall comply with 725.41.

II. Field-Installed Skeleton Tubing

600.30 Applicability. Part II of this article shall apply to field-installed skeleton tubing. These requirements are in addition to the requirements of Part I.

600.31 Neon Secondary-Circuit Conductors, 1000 Volts or Less, Nominal.

(A) Wiring Method. Conductors shall be installed using any wiring method included in Chapter 3 suitable for the conditions.

(B) Insulation and Size. Conductors shall be listed, insulated, and not smaller than 18 AWG.

(C) Number of Conductors in Raceway. The number of conductors in a raceway shall be in accordance with Table 1 of Chapter 9.

(D) Installation. Conductors shall be installed so they are not subject to physical damage.

(E) Protection of Leads. Bushings shall be used to protect wires passing through an opening in metal.

600.32 Neon Secondary Circuit Conductors, Over 1000 Volts, Nominal.

(A) Wiring Methods.

(1) Installation. Conductors shall be installed on insulators, in rigid metal conduit, intermediate metal conduit, rigid nonmetallic conduit, liquidtight flexible nonmetallic conduit, flexible metal conduit, liquidtight flexible metal conduit, electrical metallic tubing, metal enclosures, or other equipment listed for

the purpose and shall be installed in accordance with the requirements of Chapter 3.

(2) Number of Conductors. Conduit or tubing shall contain only one conductor.

(3) Size. Conduit or tubing shall be a minimum of metric designator 16 (trade size ½).

(4) Spacing from Ground. Other than at the location of connection to a metal enclosure or sign body, nonmetallic conduit or flexible nonmetallic conduit shall be spaced no less than 38 mm (1½ in.) from grounded or bonded parts when the conduit contains a conductor operating at 100 Hz or less, and shall be spaced no less than 45 mm (1¾ in.) from grounded or bonded parts when the conduit contains a conductor operating at more than 100 Hz.

(5) Metal Building Parts. Metal parts of a building shall not be permitted as a secondary return conductor or an equipment grounding conductor.

(B) Insulation and Size. Conductors shall be insulated, listed as gas tube sign and ignition cable type GTO, rated for 5, 10, or 15 kV, not smaller than 18 AWG, and have a minimum temperature rating of 105°C (221°F).

(C) Installation. Conductors shall be so installed that they are not subject to physical damage.

(D) Bends in Conductors. Sharp bends in insulated conductors shall be avoided.

(E) Spacing. Secondary conductors shall be separated from each other and from all objects other than insulators or neon tubing by a spacing of not less than 38 mm (1½ in.). GTO cable installed in metal conduit or tubing requires no spacing between the cable insulation and the conduit or tubing.

(F) Insulators and Bushings. Insulators and bushings for conductors shall be listed for the purpose.

(G) Conductors in Raceways.

(1) Damp or Wet Locations. In damp or wet locations, the insulation on all conductors shall extend not less than 100 mm (4 in.) beyond the metal conduit or tubing.

(2) Dry Locations. In dry locations, the insulation on all conductors shall extend not less than 65 mm (2½ in.) beyond the metal conduit or tubing.

(H) Between Neon Tubing and Midpoint Return. Conductors shall be permitted to run between the ends of neon tubing or to the secondary circuit midpoint return of listed transformers or listed electronic power supplies and provided with terminals or leads at the midpoint.

(I) Dwelling Occupancies. Equipment having an open circuit voltage exceeding 1000 volts shall not be installed in or on dwelling occupancies.

(J) Length of Secondary Circuit Conductors.

(1) Secondary Conductor to the First Electrode. The length of secondary circuit conductors from a high-voltage terminal or lead of a transformer or electronic power supply to the first neon tube electrode shall not exceed the following:

(1) 6 m (20 ft) where installed in metal conduit or tubing

(2) 15 m (50 ft) where installed in nonmetallic conduit

(2) Other Secondary Circuit Conductors. All other sections of secondary circuit conductor in a neon tube circuit shall be as short as practicable.

600.41 Neon Tubing.

(A) Design. The length and design of the tubing shall not cause a continuous overcurrent beyond the design loading of the transformer or electronic power supply.

(B) Support. Tubing shall be supported by listed tube supports.

(C) Spacing. A spacing of not less than 6 mm (¼ in.) shall be maintained between the tubing and the nearest surface, other than its support.

600.42 Electrode Connections.

(A) Accessibility. Terminals of the electrode shall not be accessible to unqualified persons.

(B) Electrode Connections. Connections shall be made by use of a connection device, twisting of the wires together, or use of an electrode receptacle. Connections shall be electrically and mechanically secure and shall be in an enclosure listed for the purpose.

(C) Support. The neon tubing and conductor shall be supported not more than 150 mm (6 in.) from the electrode connection.

(D) Receptacles. Electrode receptacles shall be listed.

(E) Bushings. Where electrodes penetrate an enclosure, bushings listed for the purpose shall be used unless receptacles are provided.

(F) Wet Locations. A listed cap shall be used to close the opening between neon tubing and a receptacle where the receptacle penetrates a building. Where a bushing or neon tubing penetrates a building, the opening between neon tubing and the bushing shall be sealed.

(G) Electrode Enclosures. Electrode enclosures shall be listed.

ARTICLE 604
Manufactured Wiring Systems

604.1 Scope. The provisions of this article apply to field-installed wiring using off-site manufactured subassemblies for branch circuits, remote-control circuits, signaling circuits, and communications circuits in accessible areas.

604.2 Definition.

Manufactured Wiring System. A system containing component parts that are assembled in the process of manufacture and cannot be inspected at the building site without damage or destruction to the assembly.

604.3 Other Articles. Except as modified by the requirements of this article, all other applicable articles of this *Code* shall apply.

604.4 Uses Permitted. Manufactured wiring systems shall be permitted in accessible and dry locations and in ducts, plenums, and other air-handling spaces where listed for this application and installed in accordance with 300.22.

Exception No. 1: In concealed spaces, one end of tapped cable shall be permitted to extend into hollow walls for direct termination at switch and outlet points.

Exception No. 2: Manufactured wiring system assemblies installed outdoors shall be listed for use in outdoor locations.

604.5 Uses Not Permitted. Manufactured wiring system types shall not be permitted where limited by the applicable article in Chapter 3 for the wiring method used in its construction.

604.6 Construction.

(A) Cable or Conduit Types.

(1) Cables. Cable shall be listed Type AC cable or listed Type MC cable containing nominal 600-volt, 8 to 12 AWG insulated copper conductors with a bare or insulated copper equipment grounding conductor equivalent in size to the ungrounded conductor.

Other cables as listed in 725.61, 800.113, 820.113, and 830.179 shall be permitted in manufactured wiring systems for wiring of equipment within the scope of their respective articles.

The text of 604.6(A)(1) has been revised by a tentative interim amendment (TIA). See page 1.

(2) Conduits. Conduit shall be listed flexible metal conduit or listed liquidtight flexible conduit containing nominal 600-volt, 8 to 12 AWG insulated copper conductors with a bare or insulated copper equipment grounding conductor equivalent in size to the ungrounded conductor.

Exception No. 1 to (1) and (2): A luminaire (fixture) tap, no longer than 1.8 m (6 ft) and intended for connection to a single luminaire (fixture), shall be permitted to contain conductors smaller than 12 AWG but not smaller than 18 AWG.

Exception No. 2 to (1) and (2): Listed manufactured wiring assemblies containing conductors smaller than 12 AWG shall be permitted for remote-control, signaling, or communication circuits.

(3) Flexible Cord. Flexible cord suitable for hard usage, with minimum 12 AWG conductors, shall be permitted as part of a listed factory-made assembly not exceeding 1.8 m (6 ft) in length when making a transition between components of a manufactured wiring system and utilization equipment, other than luminaires (fixtures), not permanently secured to the building structure. The cord shall be visible for its entire length and shall not be subject to strain or physical damage.

(B) Marking. Each section shall be marked to identify the type of cable, flexible cord, or conduit.

(C) Receptacles and Connectors. Receptacles and connectors shall be of the locking type, uniquely polarized and identified for the purpose, and shall be part of a listed assembly for the appropriate system.

(D) Other Component Parts. Other component parts shall be listed for the appropriate system.

(E) Securing and Supporting. Manufactured wiring systems shall be secured and supported in accordance with the applicable cable or conduit article for the cable or conduit type employed.

(F) Luminaires (Fixtures). Installation of listed electric-discharge luminaires (fixtures) complying with 410.30(C) shall be permitted.

604.7 Unused Outlets. All unused outlets shall be capped to effectively close the connector openings.

ARTICLE 605
Office Furnishings (Consisting of Lighting Accessories and Wired Partitions)

605.1 Scope. This article covers electrical equipment, lighting accessories, and wiring systems used to connect, or contained within, or installed on relocatable wired partitions.

605.2 General. Wiring systems shall be identified as suitable for providing power for lighting accessories and appliances in wired partitions. These partitions shall not extend from floor to ceiling.

Exception: Where permitted by the authority having jurisdiction, these relocatable wired partitions shall be permitted to extend to, but shall not penetrate, the ceiling.

(A) Use. These assemblies shall be installed and used only as provided for by this article.

(B) Other Articles. Except as modified by the requirements of this article, all other articles of this *Code* shall apply.

(C) Hazardous (Classified) Locations. Where used in hazardous (classified) locations, these assemblies shall conform with Articles 500 through 517 in addition to this article.

605.3 Wireways. All conductors and connections shall be contained within wiring channels of metal or other material identified as suitable for the conditions of use. Wiring channels shall be free of projections or other conditions that may damage conductor insulation.

605.4 Partition Interconnections. The electrical connection between partitions shall be a flexible assembly identified for use with wired partitions or shall be permitted to be installed using flexible cord, provided all the following conditions are met:

(1) The cord is extra-hard usage type with 12 AWG or larger conductors, with an insulated grounding conductor.
(2) The partitions are mechanically contiguous.
(3) The cord is not longer than necessary for maximum positioning of the partitions but is in no case to exceed 600 mm (2 ft).
(4) The cord is terminated at an attachment plug and cord connector with strain relief.

605.5 Lighting Accessories. Lighting equipment listed and identified for use with wired partitions shall comply with 605.5(A), (B), and (C).

(A) Support. A means for secure attachment or support shall be provided.

(B) Connection. Where cord and plug connection is provided, the cord length shall be suitable for the intended application but shall not exceed 2.7 m (9 ft) in length. The cord shall not be smaller than 18 AWG, shall contain an equipment grounding conductor, and shall be of the hard usage type. Connection by other means shall be identified as suitable for the condition of use.

(C) Receptacle Outlet. Convenience receptacles shall not be permitted in lighting accessories.

605.6 Fixed-Type Partitions. Wired partitions that are fixed (secured to building surfaces) shall be permanently connected to the building electrical system by one of the wiring methods of Chapter 3. Multiwire branch circuits supplying power to the partition shall be provided with a means to disconnect simultaneously all ungrounded conductors at the panelboard where the branch circuit originates.

605.7 Freestanding-Type Partitions. Partitions of the freestanding type (not fixed) shall be permitted to be connected to the building electrical system by one of the wiring methods of Chapter 3. Multiwire branch circuits supplying power to permanently connected freestanding partitions shall be provided with a means to disconnect simultaneously all ungrounded conductors at the panelboard where the branch circuit originates.

605.8 Freestanding-Type Partitions, Cord-and-Plug-Connected. Individual partitions of the freestanding type, or groups of individual partitions that are electrically connected, are mechanically contiguous, and do not exceed 9.0 m (30 ft) when assembled, shall be permitted to be connected to the building electrical system by a single flexible cord and plug, provided all of the conditions of 605.8(A) through 605.8(D) are met.

(A) Flexible Power-Supply Cord. The flexible power-supply cord shall be extra-hard usage type with 12 AWG or larger conductors with an insulated equipment grounding conductor and shall not exceed 600 mm (2 ft) in length.

(B) Receptacle Supplying Power. The receptacle(s) supplying power shall be on a separate circuit serving only panels and no other loads and shall be located not more than 300 mm (12 in.) from the partition that is connected to it.

(C) Receptacle Outlets, Maximum. Individual partitions or groups of interconnected individual partitions shall not contain more than thirteen 15-ampere, 125-volt receptacle outlets.

(D) Multiwire Circuits, Not Permitted. Individual partitions or groups of interconnected individual partitions shall not contain multiwire circuits.

> FPN: See 210.4 for circuits supplying partitions in 605.6 and 605.7.

ARTICLE 610
Cranes and Hoists

I. General

610.1 Scope. This article covers the installation of electrical equipment and wiring used in connection with cranes, monorail hoists, hoists, and all runways.

> FPN: For further information, see ANSI B30, *Safety Code for Cranes, Derricks, Hoists, Jacks, and Slings.*

610.3 Special Requirements for Particular Locations.

(A) Hazardous (Classified) Locations. All equipment that operates in a hazardous (classified) location shall conform to Article 500.

(1) Class I Locations. Equipment used in locations that are hazardous because of the presence of flammable gases or vapors shall conform to Article 501.

(2) Class II Locations. Equipment used in locations that are hazardous because of combustible dust shall conform to Article 502.

(3) Class III Locations. Equipment used in locations that are hazardous because of the presence of easily ignitible fibers or flyings shall conform to Article 503.

(B) Combustible Materials. Where a crane, hoist, or monorail hoist operates over readily combustible material, the resistors shall be located as permitted in the following:

(1) A well-ventilated cabinet composed of noncombustible material constructed so that it does not emit flames or molten metal

(2) A cage or cab constructed of noncombustible material that encloses the sides of the cage or cab from the floor to a point at least 150 mm (6 in.) above the top of the resistors

(C) Electrolytic Cell Lines. See 668.32.

II. Wiring

610.11 Wiring Method. Conductors shall be enclosed in raceways or be Type AC cable with insulated grounding conductor, Type MC cable, or Type MI cable unless otherwise permitted or required in 610.11(A) through 610.11(E).

(A) Contact Conductor. Contact conductors shall not be required to be enclosed in raceways.

(B) Exposed Conductors. Short lengths of exposed conductors at resistors, collectors, and other equipment shall not be required to be enclosed in raceways.

(C) Flexible Connections to Motors and Similar Equipment. Where flexible connections are necessary, flexible stranded conductors shall be used. Conductors shall be in flexible metal conduit, liquidtight flexible metal conduit, liquidtight flexible nonmetallic conduit, multiconductor cable, or an approved nonmetallic flexible raceway.

(D) Pushbutton Stations Multiconductor Cable. Where multiconductor cable is used with a suspended pushbutton station, the station shall be supported in some satisfactory manner that protects the electric conductors against strain.

(E) Flexibility to Moving Parts. Where flexibility is required for power or control to moving parts, a cord suitable for the purpose shall be permitted, provided the following apply:

(1) Suitable strain relief and protection from physical damage is provided.

(2) In Class I, Division 2 locations, the cord is approved for extra-hard usage.

610.12 Raceway or Cable Terminal Fittings. Conductors leaving raceways or cables shall comply with either 610.12(A) or 610.12(B).

(A) Separately Bushed Hole. A box or terminal fitting that has a separately bushed hole for each conductor shall be used wherever a change is made from a raceway or cable to exposed wiring. A fitting used for this purpose shall not contain taps or splices and shall not be used at luminaire (fixture) outlets.

(B) Bushing in Lieu of a Box. A bushing shall be permitted to be used in lieu of a box at the end of a rigid metal conduit, intermediate metal conduit, or electrical metallic tubing where the raceway terminates at unenclosed controls or similar equipment, including contact conductors, collectors, resistors, brakes, power-circuit limit switches, and dc split-frame motors.

610.13 Types of Conductors. Conductors shall comply with Table 310.13 unless otherwise permitted in 610.13(A) through 610.13(D).

(A) Exposed to External Heat or Connected to Resistors. A conductor(s) exposed to external heat or connected to resistors shall have a flame-resistant outer covering or be covered with flame-resistant tape individually or as a group.

(B) Contact Conductors. Contact conductors along runways, crane bridges, and monorails shall be permitted to be bare and shall be copper, aluminum, steel, or other alloys or combinations thereof in the form of hard-drawn wire, tees, angles, tee rails, or other stiff shapes.

(C) Flexibility. Where flexibility is required, flexible cord or cable shall be permitted to be used and, where necessary, cable reels or take-up devices shall be used.

(D) Class 1, Class 2, and Class 3 Circuits. Conductors for Class 1, Class 2, and Class 3 remote-control, signaling, and power-limited circuits, installed in accordance with Article 725, shall be permitted.

610.14 Rating and Size of Conductors.

(A) Ampacity. The allowable ampacities of conductors shall be as shown in Table 610.14(A).

FPN: For the ampacities of conductors between controllers and resistors, see 430.23.

(B) Secondary Resistor Conductors. Where the secondary resistor is separate from the controller, the minimum size of the conductors between controller and resistor shall be calculated by multiplying the motor secondary current by the appropriate factor from Table 610.14(B) and selecting a wire from Table 610.14(A).

Table 610.14(B) Secondary Conductor Rating Factors

Time in Seconds		Ampacity of Wire in Percent of Full-Load Secondary Current
On	**Off**	
5	75	35
10	70	45
15	75	55
15	45	65
15	30	75
15	15	85
Continuous Duty		110

(C) Minimum Size. Conductors external to motors and controls shall not be smaller than 16 AWG unless otherwise permitted in (1) or (2):

(1) 18 AWG wire in multiconductor cord shall be permitted for control circuits not exceeding 7 amperes.

(2) Wires not smaller than 20 AWG shall be permitted for electronic circuits.

(D) Contact Conductors. Contact wires shall have an ampacity not less than that required by Table 610.14(A) for 75°C (167°F) wire, and in no case shall they be smaller than as shown in Table 610.14(D).

Table 610.14(D) Contact Conductor Supports

Distance Between End Strain Insulators or Clamp-Type Intermediate Supports	Size of Wire (AWG)
Less than 9.0 m (30 ft)	6
9.0 m–18 m (30 ft–60 ft)	4
Over 18 m (60 ft)	2

(E) Calculation of Motor Load.

(1) Single Motor. For one motor, 100 percent of motor nameplate full-load ampere rating shall be used.

(2) Multiple Motors on Single Crane or Hoist. For multiple motors on a single crane or hoist, the minimum ampacity of the power supply conductors shall be the nameplate full-load ampere rating of the largest motor or group of motors for any single crane motion, plus 50 percent of the nameplate full-load ampere rating of the next largest motor or group of motors, using that column of Table 610.14(A) that applies to the longest time-rated motor.

Table 610.14(A) Ampacities of Insulated Copper Conductors Used with Short-Time Rated Crane and Hoist Motors. Based on Ambient Temperature of 30°C (86°F).

Maximum Operating Temperature	Up to Four Conductors in Raceway or Cable[1]				Up to Three ac[2] or Four dc[1] Conductors in Raceway or Cable		Maximum Operating Temperature
	75°C (167°F)		90°C (194°F)		125°C (257°F)		
Size (AWG or kcmil)	Types MTW, RHW, THW, THWN, XHHW, USE, ZW		Types TA, TBS, SA, SIS, PFA, FEP, FEPB, RHH, THHN, XHHW, Z, ZW		Types FEP, FEPB, PFA, PFAH, SA, TFE, Z, ZW		Size (AWG or kcmil)
	60 Min	30 Min	60 Min	30 Min	60 Min	30 Min	
16	10	12	—	—	—	—	16
14	25	26	31	32	38	40	14
12	30	33	36	40	45	50	12
10	40	43	49	52	60	65	10
8	55	60	63	69	73	80	8
6	76	86	83	94	101	119	6
5	85	95	95	106	115	134	5
4	100	117	111	130	133	157	4
3	120	141	131	153	153	183	3
2	137	160	148	173	178	214	2
1	143	175	158	192	210	253	1
1/0	190	233	211	259	253	304	1/0
2/0	222	267	245	294	303	369	2/0
3/0	280	341	305	372	370	452	3/0
4/0	300	369	319	399	451	555	4/0
250	364	420	400	461	510	635	250
300	455	582	497	636	587	737	300
350	486	646	542	716	663	837	350
400	538	688	593	760	742	941	400
450	600	765	660	836	818	1042	450
500	660	847	726	914	896	1143	500

AMPACITY CORRECTION FACTORS

Ambient Temperature (°C)	For ambient temperatures other than 30°C (86°F), multiply the ampacities shown above by the appropriate factor shown below.						Ambient Temperature (°F)
21–25	1.05	1.05	1.04	1.04	1.02	1.02	70–77
26–30	1.00	1.00	1.00	1.00	1.00	1.00	79–86
31–35	0.94	0.94	0.96	0.96	0.97	0.97	88–95
36–40	0.88	0.88	0.91	0.91	0.95	0.95	97–104
41–45	0.82	0.82	0.87	0.87	0.92	0.92	106–113
46–50	0.75	0.75	0.82	0.82	0.89	0.89	115–122
51–55	0.67	0.67	0.76	0.76	0.86	0.86	124–131
56–60	0.58	0.58	0.71	0.71	0.83	0.83	133–140
61–70	0.33	0.33	0.58	0.58	0.76	0.76	142–158
71–80	—	—	0.41	0.41	0.69	0.69	160–176
81–90	—	—	—	—	0.61	0.61	177–194
91–100	—	—	—	—	0.51	0.51	195–212
101–120	—	—	—	—	0.40	0.40	213–248

Note: Other insulations shown in Table 310.13 and approved for the temperature and location shall be permitted to be substituted for those shown in Table 610.14(A). The allowable ampacities of conductors used with 15-minute motors shall be the 30-minute ratings increased by 12 percent.

[1] For 5 to 8 simultaneously energized power conductors in raceway or cable, the ampacity of each power conductor shall be reduced to a value of 80 percent of that shown in this table.

[2] For 4 to 6 simultaneously energized 125°C (257°F) ac power conductors in raceway or cable, the ampacity of each power conductor shall be reduced to a value of 80 percent of that shown in this table.

(3) Multiple Cranes or Hoists on a Common Conductor System. For multiple cranes, hoists, or both, supplied by a common conductor system, calculate the motor minimum ampacity for each crane as defined in 610.14(E), add them together, and multiply the sum by the appropriate demand factor from Table 610.14(E).

Table 610.14(E) Demand Factors

Number of Cranes or Hoists	Demand Factor
2	0.95
3	0.91
4	0.87
5	0.84
6	0.81
7	0.78

(F) Other Loads. Additional loads, such as heating, lighting, and air conditioning, shall be provided for by application of the appropriate sections of this *Code*.

(G) Nameplate. Each crane, monorail, or hoist shall be provided with a visible nameplate marked with the manufacturer's name, rating in volts, frequency, number of phases, and circuit amperes as calculated in 610.14(E) and 610.14(F).

610.15 Common Return. Where a crane or hoist is operated by more than one motor, a common-return conductor of proper ampacity shall be permitted.

III. Contact Conductors

610.21 Installation of Contact Conductors. Contact conductors shall comply with 610.21(A) through 610.21(H).

(A) Locating or Guarding Contact Conductors. Runway contact conductors shall be guarded, and bridge contact conductors shall be located or guarded in such a manner that persons cannot inadvertently touch energized current-carrying parts.

(B) Contact Wires. Wires that are used as contact conductors shall be secured at the ends by means of approved strain insulators and shall be mounted on approved insulators so that the extreme limit of displacement of the wire does not bring the latter within less than 38 mm (1½ in.) from the surface wired over.

(C) Supports Along Runways. Main contact conductors carried along runways shall be supported on insulating supports placed at intervals not exceeding 6.0 m (20 ft) unless otherwise permitted in 610.21(F).

Such conductors shall be separated at not less than 150 mm (6 in.), other than for monorail hoists where a spacing of not less than 75 mm (3 in.) shall be permitted. Where

necessary, intervals between insulating supports shall be permitted to be increased up to 12 m (40 ft), the separation between conductors being increased proportionately.

(D) Supports on Bridges. Bridge wire contact conductors shall be kept at least 65 mm (2½ in.) apart, and, where the span exceeds 25 m (80 ft), insulating saddles shall be placed at intervals not exceeding 15 m (50 ft).

(E) Supports for Rigid Conductors. Conductors along runways and crane bridges, that are of the rigid type specified in 610.13(B) and not contained within an approved enclosed assembly, shall be carried on insulating supports spaced at intervals of not more than 80 times the vertical dimension of the conductor, but in no case greater than 4.5 m (15 ft), and spaced apart sufficiently to give a clear electrical separation of conductors or adjacent collectors of not less than 25 mm (1 in.).

(F) Track as Circuit Conductor. Monorail, tram rail, or crane runway tracks shall be permitted as a conductor of current for one phase of a 3-phase, ac system furnishing power to the carrier, crane, or trolley, provided all of the following conditions are met:

(1) The conductors supplying the other two phases of the power supply are insulated.
(2) The power for all phases is obtained from an insulating transformer.
(3) The voltage does not exceed 300 volts.
(4) The rail serving as a conductor is effectively grounded at the transformer and also shall be permitted to be grounded by the fittings used for the suspension or attachment of the rail to a building or structure.

(G) Electrical Continuity of Contact Conductors. All sections of contact conductors shall be mechanically joined to provide a continuous electrical connection.

(H) Not to Supply Other Equipment. Contact conductors shall not be used as feeders for any equipment other than the crane(s) or hoist(s) that they are primarily designed to serve.

610.22 Collectors. Collectors shall be designed so as to reduce to a minimum sparking between them and the contact conductor; and, where operated in rooms used for the storage of easily ignitible combustible fibers and materials, they shall comply with 503.155.

IV. Disconnecting Means

610.31 Runway Conductor Disconnecting Means. A disconnecting means that has a continuous ampere rating not less than that calculated in 610.14(E) and 610.14(F) shall be provided between the runway contact conductors and the power supply. Such disconnecting means shall consist of a motor-circuit switch, circuit breaker, or molded case switch. This disconnecting means shall be as follows:

(1) Readily accessible and operable from the ground or floor level

(2) Capable of being locked in the open position

(3) Open all ungrounded conductors simultaneously

(4) Placed within view of the runway contact conductors

610.32 Disconnecting Means for Cranes and Monorail Hoists.
A motor-circuit switch, molded-case switch, or circuit breaker shall be provided in the leads from the runway contact conductors or other power supply on all cranes and monorail hoists. The disconnecting means shall be capable of being locked in the open position.

Where a monorail hoist or hand-propelled crane bridge installation meets all of the following, the disconnecting means shall be permitted to be omitted:

(1) The unit is controlled from the ground or floor level.

(2) The unit is within view of the power supply disconnecting means.

(3) No fixed work platform has been provided for servicing the unit.

Where the disconnecting means is not readily accessible from the crane or monorail hoist operating station, means shall be provided at the operating station to open the power circuit to all motors of the crane or monorail hoist.

610.33 Rating of Disconnecting Means.
The continuous ampere rating of the switch or circuit breaker required by 610.32 shall not be less than 50 percent of the combined short-time ampere rating of the motors or less than 75 percent of the sum of the short-time ampere rating of the motors required for any single motion.

V. Overcurrent Protection

610.41 Feeders, Runway Conductors.

(A) Single Feeder. The runway supply conductors and main contact conductors of a crane or monorail shall be protected by an overcurrent device(s) that shall not be greater than the largest rating or setting of any branch-circuit protective device plus the sum of the nameplate ratings of all the other loads with application of the demand factors from Table 610.14(E).

(B) More Than One Feeder Circuit. Where more than one feeder circuit is installed to supply runway conductors, each feeder circuit shall be sized and protected in compliance with 610.41(A).

610.42 Branch-Circuit Short-Circuit and Ground-Fault Protection.
Branch circuits shall be protected in accordance with 610.42(A). Branch-circuit taps, where made, shall comply with 610.42(B).

(A) Fuse or Circuit Breaker Rating. Crane, hoist, and monorail hoist motor branch circuits shall be protected by fuses or inverse-time circuit breakers that have a rating in accordance with Table 430.52. Where two or more motors operate a single motion, the sum of their nameplate current ratings shall be considered as that of a single motor.

(B) Taps.

(1) Multiple Motors. Where two or more motors are connected to the same branch circuit, each tap conductor to an individual motor shall have an ampacity not less than one-third that of the branch circuit. Each motor shall be protected from overload according to 610.43.

(2) Control Circuits. Where taps to control circuits originate on the load side of a branch-circuit protective device, each tap and piece of equipment shall be protected in accordance with 430.72.

(3) Brake Coils. Taps without separate overcurrent protection shall be permitted to brake coils.

610.43 Overload Protection.

(A) Motor and Branch-Circuit Overload Protection. Each motor, motor controller, and branch-circuit conductor shall be protected from overload by one of the following means:

(1) A single motor shall be considered as protected where the branch-circuit overcurrent device meets the rating requirements of 610.42.

(2) Overload relay elements in each ungrounded circuit conductor, with all relay elements protected from short circuit by the branch-circuit protection.

(3) Thermal sensing devices, sensitive to motor temperature or to temperature and current, that are thermally in contact with the motor winding(s). A hoist or trolley shall be considered to be protected if the sensing device is connected in the hoist's upper limit switch circuit so as to prevent further hoisting during an overload condition of either motor.

(B) Manually Controlled Motor. If the motor is manually controlled, with spring return controls, the overload protective device shall not be required to protect the motor against stalled rotor conditions.

(C) Multimotor. Where two or more motors drive a single trolley, truck, or bridge and are controlled as a unit and protected by a single set of overload devices with a rating equal to the sum of their rated full-load currents, a hoist or trolley shall be considered to be protected if the sensing device is connected in the hoist's upper limit switch circuit so as to prevent further hoisting during an overtemperature condition of either motor.

(D) Hoists and Monorail Hoists. Hoists and monorail hoists and their trolleys that are not used as part of an overhead traveling crane shall not require individual motor overload protection, provided the largest motor does not exceed 7½ hp and all motors are under manual control of the operator.

VI. Control

610.51 Separate Controllers. Each motor shall be provided with an individual controller unless otherwise permitted in 610.51(A) or 610.51(B).

(A) Motions with More Than One Motor. Where two or more motors drive a single hoist, carriage, truck, or bridge, they shall be permitted to be controlled by a single controller.

(B) Multiple Motion Controller. One controller shall be permitted to be switched between motors, under the following conditions:

(1) The controller has a horsepower rating that is not lower than the horsepower rating of the largest motor.

(2) Only one motor is operated at one time.

610.53 Overcurrent Protection. Conductors of control circuits shall be protected against overcurrent. Control circuits shall be considered as protected by overcurrent devices that are rated or set at not more than 300 percent of the ampacity of the control conductors, unless otherwise permitted in 610.53(A) or 610.53(B).

(A) Taps to Control Transformers. Taps to control transformers shall be considered as protected where the secondary circuit is protected by a device rated or set at not more than 200 percent of the rated secondary current of the transformer and not more than 200 percent of the ampacity of the control circuit conductors.

(B) Continuity of Power. Where the opening of the control circuit would create a hazard, as for example, the control circuit of a hot metal crane, the control circuit conductors shall be considered as being properly protected by the branch-circuit overcurrent devices.

610.55 Limit Switch. A limit switch or other device shall be provided to prevent the load block from passing the safe upper limit of travel of all hoisting mechanisms.

610.57 Clearance. The dimension of the working space in the direction of access to live parts that are likely to require examination, adjustment, servicing, or maintenance while energized shall be a minimum of 750 mm (2½ ft). Where controls are enclosed in cabinets, the door(s) shall either open at least 90 degrees or be removable.

VII. Grounding

610.61 Grounding. All exposed non–current-carrying metal parts of cranes, monorail hoists, hoists, and accessories, including pendant controls, shall be metallically joined together into a continuous electrical conductor so that the entire crane or hoist will be grounded in accordance with Article 250. Moving parts, other than removable accessories, or attachments that have metal-to-metal bearing surfaces, shall be considered to be electrically connected to each other through bearing surfaces for grounding purposes. The trolley frame and bridge frame shall not be considered as electrically grounded through the bridge and trolley wheels and its respective tracks. A separate bonding conductor shall be provided.

ARTICLE 620
Elevators, Dumbwaiters, Escalators, Moving Walks, Wheelchair Lifts, and Stairway Chair Lifts

I. General

620.1 Scope. This article covers the installation of electrical equipment and wiring used in connection with elevators, dumbwaiters, escalators, moving walks, wheelchair lifts, and stairway chair lifts.

> FPN No. 1: For further information, see ASME/ANSI A17.1-2000, *Safety Code for Elevators and Escalators.*

> FPN No. 2: For further information, see ASME/ANSI A17.5-1996 (CSA B44.1-1996), *Elevator and Escalator Electrical Equipment Certification Standard.*

620.2 Definitions.

Control Room (for Elevator, Dumbwaiter). An enclosed control space outside the hoistway, intended for full bodily entry, that contains the elevator motor controller. The room could also contain electrical and/or mechanical equipment used directly in connection with the elevator or dumbwaiter but not the electric driving machine or the hydraulic machine.

Control Space (for Elevator, Dumbwaiter). A space inside or outside the hoistway, intended to be accessed with or without full bodily entry, that contains the elevator motor controller. This space could also contain electrical and/or mechanical equipment used directly in connection with the elevator or dumbwaiter but not the electric driving machine or the hydraulic machine.

Control System. The overall system governing the starting, stopping, direction of motion, acceleration, speed, and retardation of the moving member.

Controller, Motion. The electric device(s) for that part of the control system that governs the acceleration, speed, retardation, and stopping of the moving member.

Controller, Motor. The operative units of the control system comprised of the starter device(s) and power conversion equipment used to drive an electric motor, or the pumping unit used to power hydraulic control equipment.

Controller, Operation. The electric device(s) for that part of the control system that initiates the starting, stopping, and direction of motion in response to a signal from an operating device.

Machine Room (for Elevator, Dumbwaiter). An enclosed machinery space outside the hoistway, intended for full bodily entry, that contains the electrical driving machine or the hydraulic machine. The room could also contain electrical and/or mechanical equipment used directly in connection with the elevator or dumbwaiter.

Machinery Space (for Elevator, Dumbwaiter). A space inside or outside the hoistway, intended to be accessed with or without full bodily entry, that contains elevator or dumbwaiter mechanical equipment, and could also contain electrical equipment used directly in connection with the elevator or dumbwaiter. This space could also contain the electric driving machine or the hydraulic machine.

Operating Device. The car switch, pushbuttons, key or toggle switch(s), or other devices used to activate the operation controller.

Signal Equipment. Includes audible and visual equipment such as chimes, gongs, lights, and displays that convey information to the user.

> FPN No. 1: The motor controller, motion controller, and operation controller may be located in a single enclosure or a combination of enclosures.
>
> FPN No. 2: FPN Figure 620.2 is for information only.

620.3 Voltage Limitations. The supply voltage shall not exceed 300 volts between conductors unless otherwise permitted in 620.3(A) through 620.3(C).

(A) Power Circuits. Branch circuits to door operator controllers and door motors and branch circuits and feeders to motor controllers, driving machine motors, machine brakes, and motor-generator sets shall not have a circuit voltage in excess of 600 volts. Internal voltages of power conversion and functionally associated equipment, including the interconnecting wiring, shall be permitted to have higher voltages, provided that all such equipment and wiring shall be listed for the higher voltages. Where the voltage exceeds 600 volts, warning labels or signs that read "DANGER — HIGH VOLTAGE" shall be attached to the equipment and shall be plainly visible.

(B) Lighting Circuits. Lighting circuits shall comply with the requirements of Article 410.

(C) Heating and Air-Conditioning Circuits. Branch circuits for heating and air-conditioning equipment located on the elevator car shall not have a circuit voltage in excess of 600 volts.

FPN Figure 620.2 Control System.

620.4 Live Parts Enclosed. All live parts of electrical apparatus in the hoistways, at the landings, in or on the cars of elevators and dumbwaiters, in the wellways or the landings of escalators or moving walks, or in the runways and machinery spaces of wheelchair lifts and stairway chairlifts shall be enclosed to protect against accidental contact.

FPN: See 110.27 for guarding of live parts (600 volts, nominal, or less).

620.5 Working Clearances. Working space shall be provided about controllers, disconnecting means, and other electrical equipment. The minimum working space shall not be less than that specified in 110.26(A).

Where conditions of maintenance and supervision ensure that only qualified persons examine, adjust, service, and maintain the equipment, the clearance requirements of 110.26(A) shall be waived as permitted in 620.5(A) through 620.5(D).

(A) Flexible Connections to Equipment. Electrical equipment in (A)(1) through (A)(4) shall be permitted to be provided with flexible leads to all external connections so that it can be repositioned to meet the clear working space requirements of 110.26(A):

(1) Controllers and disconnecting means for dumbwaiters, escalators, moving walks, wheelchair lifts, and stairway chairlifts installed in the same space with the driving machine

(2) Controllers and disconnecting means for elevators installed in the hoistway or on the car

(3) Controllers for door operators

(4) Other electrical equipment installed in the hoistway or on the car

(B) Guards. Live parts of the electrical equipment are suitably guarded, isolated, or insulated, and the equipment can be examined, adjusted, serviced, or maintained while energized without removal of this protection.

FPN: See definition of *Exposed* in Article 100.

(C) Examination, Adjusting, and Servicing. Electrical equipment is not required to be examined, adjusted, serviced, or maintained while energized.

(D) Low Voltage. Uninsulated parts are at a voltage not greater than 30 volts rms, 42 volts peak, or 60 volts dc.

II. Conductors

620.11 Insulation of Conductors. The insulation of conductors shall comply with 620.11(A) through 620.11(D).

FPN: One method of determining that conductors are flame retardant is by testing the conductors to the VW-1 (Vertical-Wire) Flame Test in ANSI/UL 1581-1991, *Reference Standard for Electrical Wires, Cables, and Flexible Cords.*

(A) Hoistway Door Interlock Wiring. The conductors to the hoistway door interlocks from the hoistway riser shall be flame retardant and suitable for a temperature of not less than 200°C (392°F). Conductors shall be Type SF or equivalent.

(B) Traveling Cables. Traveling cables used as flexible connections between the elevator or dumbwaiter car or counterweight and the raceway shall be of the types of elevator cable listed in Table 400.4 or other approved types.

(C) Other Wiring. All conductors in raceways shall have flame-retardant insulation.

Conductors shall be Type MTW, TF, TFF, TFN, TFFN, THHN, THW, THWN, TW, XHHW, hoistway cable, or any other conductor with insulation designated as flame retardant. Shielded conductors shall be permitted if such conductors are insulated for the maximum nominal circuit voltage applied to any conductor within the cable or raceway system.

(D) Insulation. All conductors shall have an insulation voltage rating equal to at least the maximum nominal circuit voltage applied to any conductor within the enclosure, cable, or raceway. Insulations and outer coverings that are marked for limited smoke and are so listed shall be permitted.

620.12 Minimum Size of Conductors. The minimum size of conductors, other than conductors that form an integral part of control equipment, shall be in accordance with 620.12(A) and 620.12(B).

(A) Traveling Cables.

(1) Lighting Circuits. For lighting circuits, 14 AWG copper. 20 AWG copper or larger conductors shall be permitted in parallel, provided the ampacity is equivalent to at least that of 14 AWG copper.

(2) Other Circuits. For other circuits, 20 AWG copper.

(B) Other Wiring. 24 AWG copper. Smaller size listed conductors shall be permitted.

620.13 Feeder and Branch-Circuit Conductors. Conductors shall have an ampacity in accordance with 620.13(A) through 620.13(D). With generator field control, the conductor ampacity shall be based on the nameplate current rating of the driving motor of the motor-generator set that supplies power to the elevator motor.

FPN No. 1: The heating of conductors depends on root-mean-square current values, which, with generator field control, are reflected by the nameplate current rating of the motor-generator driving motor rather than by the rating of the elevator motor, which represents actual but short-time and intermittent full-load current values.

FPN No. 2: See Figure 620.13.

	To supply	
Common feeder		620.13
Feeder demand factor		620.14
Motor feeder short-circuit and ground-fault protection		620.61(C)
Disconnecting means		620.51
Motor branch-circuit short-circuit and ground-fault protection		620.61(D)
Branch-circuit conductors		620.13
External transformer (optional)		Article 450
Motor controller		620.13, 620.15
Motor control circuits		620.61(A)
Motor overload protection		620.61(B)
Motor conductors		620.13
Motor		Article 430, Part I
Thermal protection		Article 430, Part III

Figure 620.13 Single-Line Diagram.

(A) Conductors Supplying Single Motor. Conductors supplying a single motor shall have an ampacity not less than the percentage of motor nameplate current determined from 430.22(A) and 430.22(E).

> FPN: Elevator motor currents, or those of similar functions, may exceed the nameplate value, but because they are inherently intermittent duty and the heating of the motor and conductors is dependent on the root-mean-square (rms) current value, conductors are sized for duty cycle service as shown in Table 430.22(E).

(B) Conductors Supplying a Single Motor Controller. Conductors supplying a single motor controller shall have an ampacity not less than the motor controller nameplate current rating, plus all other connected loads.

> FPN: Motor controller nameplate current rating may be derived based on the rms value of the motor current using an intermittent duty cycle and other control system loads, if applicable.

(C) Conductors Supplying a Single Power Transformer. Conductors supplying a single power transformer shall have an ampacity not less than the nameplate current rating of the power transformer plus all other connected loads.

> FPN No. 1: The nameplate current rating of a power transformer supplying a motor controller reflects the nameplate current rating of the motor controller at line voltage (transformer primary).
>
> FPN No. 2: See Annex D, Example No. D10.

(D) Conductors Supplying More Than One Motor, Motor Controller, or Power Transformer. Conductors supplying more than one motor, motor controller, or power transformer shall have an ampacity not less than the sum of the nameplate current ratings of the equipment plus all other connected loads. The ampere ratings of motors to be used in the summation shall be determined from Table 430.22(E), and 430.24 and 430.24, Exception No. 1.

> FPN: See Annex D, Example Nos. D9 and D10.

620.14 Feeder Demand Factor. Feeder conductors of less ampacity than required by 620.13 shall be permitted, subject to the requirements of Table 620.14.

Table 620.14 Feeder Demand Factors for Elevators

Number of Elevators on a Single Feeder	Demand Factor
1	1.00
2	0.95
3	0.90
4	0.85
5	0.82
6	0.79
7	0.77
8	0.75
9	0.73
10 or more	0.72

> FPN: Demand factors are based on 50 percent duty cycle (i.e., half time on and half time off).

620.15 Motor Controller Rating. The motor controller rating shall comply with 430.83. The rating shall be permitted to be less than the nominal rating of the elevator motor, when the controller inherently limits the available power to the motor and is marked as power limited.

> FPN: For controller markings, see 430.8.

III. Wiring

620.21 Wiring Methods. Conductors and optical fibers located in hoistways, in escalator and moving walk wellways, in wheelchair lifts, stairway chairlift runways, machinery spaces, control spaces, in or on cars, in machine rooms and control rooms, not including the traveling cables connecting the car or counterweight and hoistway wiring, shall be installed in rigid metal conduit, intermediate metal conduit, electrical metallic tubing, rigid nonmetallic conduit, or wireways, or shall be Type MC, MI, or AC cable unless otherwise permitted in 620.21(A) through 620.21(C).

(A) Elevators.

(1) Hoistways.

(a) Flexible metal conduit, liquidtight flexible metal conduit, or liquidtight flexible nonmetallic conduit shall be permitted in hoistways between risers and limit switches, interlocks, operating buttons, and similar devices.

(b) Cables used in Class 2 power-limited circuits shall be permitted to be installed between risers and signal equipment and operating devices, provided the cables are supported and protected from physical damage and are of a jacketed and flame-retardant type.

(c) Flexible cords and cables that are components of listed equipment and used in circuits operating at 30 volts rms or less or 42 volts dc or less shall be permitted in lengths not to exceed 1.8 m (6 ft), provided the cords and cables are supported and protected from physical damage and are of a jacketed and flame-retardant type.

(d) Flexible metal conduit, liquidtight flexible metal conduit, liquidtight flexible nonmetallic conduit or flexible cords and cables, or conductors grouped together and taped or corded that are part of listed equipment, a driving machine, or a driving machine brake shall be permitted in the hoistway, in lengths not to exceed 1.8 m (6 ft), without being installed in a raceway and where located to be protected from physical damage and are of a flame-retardant type.

(2) Cars.

(a) Flexible metal conduit, liquidtight flexible metal conduit, or liquidtight flexible nonmetallic conduit of metric designator 12 (trade size 3/8), or larger, not exceeding 1.8 m (6 ft) in length, shall be permitted on cars where so located as to be free from oil and if securely fastened in place.

Exception: Liquidtight flexible nonmetallic conduit of metric designator 12 (trade size 3/8), or larger, as defined by 356.2(2), shall be permitted in lengths in excess of 1.8 m (6 ft).

(b) Hard-service cords and junior hard-service cords that conform to the requirements of Article 400 (Table 400.4) shall be permitted as flexible connections between the fixed wiring on the car and devices on the car doors or gates. Hard-service cords only shall be permitted as flexible connections for the top-of-car operating device or the car-top work light. Devices or luminaires (fixtures) shall be grounded by means of an equipment grounding conductor run with the circuit conductors. Cables with smaller conductors and other types and thicknesses of insulation and jackets shall be permitted as flexible connections between the fixed wiring on the car and devices on the car doors or gates, if listed for this use.

(c) Flexible cords and cables that are components of listed equipment and used in circuits operating at 30 volts rms or less or 42 volts dc or less shall be permitted in lengths not to exceed 1.8 m (6 ft), provided the cords and

cables are supported and protected from physical damage and are of a jacketed and flame-retardant type.

(d) Flexible metal conduit, liquidtight flexible metal conduit, liquidtight flexible nonmetallic conduit or flexible cords and cables, or conductors grouped together and taped or corded that are part of listed equipment, a driving machine, or a driving machine brake shall be permitted on the car assembly, in lengths not to exceed 1.8 m (6 ft) without being installed in a raceway and where located to be protected from physical damage and are of a flame-retardant type.

(3) Within Machine Rooms, Control Rooms, and Machinery Spaces and Control Spaces.

(a) Flexible metal conduit, liquidtight flexible metal conduit, or liquidtight flexible nonmetallic conduit of metric designator 12 (trade size 3/8), or larger, not exceeding 1.8 m (6 ft) in length, shall be permitted between control panels and machine motors, machine brakes, motor-generator sets, disconnecting means, and pumping unit motors and valves.

Exception: Liquidtight flexible nonmetallic conduit metric designator 12 (trade size 3/8) or larger, as defined in 356.2(2), shall be permitted to be installed in lengths in excess of 1.8 m (6 ft).

(b) Where motor-generators, machine motors, or pumping unit motors and valves are located adjacent to or underneath control equipment and are provided with extra-length terminal leads not exceeding 1.8 m (6 ft) in length, such leads shall be permitted to be extended to connect directly to controller terminal studs without regard to the carrying-capacity requirements of Articles 430 and 445. Auxiliary gutters shall be permitted in machine and control rooms between controllers, starters, and similar apparatus.

(c) Flexible cords and cables that are components of listed equipment and used in circuits operating at 30 volts rms or less or 42 volts dc or less shall be permitted in lengths not to exceed 1.8 m (6 ft), provided the cords and cables are supported and protected from physical damage and are of a jacketed and flame-retardant type.

(d) On existing or listed equipment, conductors shall also be permitted to be grouped together and taped or corded without being installed in a raceway. Such cable groups shall be supported at intervals not over 900 mm (3 ft) and located so as to be protected from physical damage.

(4) Counterweight. Flexible metal conduit, liquidtight flexible metal conduit, liquidtight flexible nonmetallic conduit or flexible cords and cables, or conductors grouped together and taped or corded that are part of listed equipment, a driving machine, or a driving machine brake shall be permitted on the counterweight assembly, in lengths not to exceed 1.8 m (6 ft) without being installed in a raceway and where located to be protected from physical damage and are of a flame-retardant type.

(B) Escalators.

(1) Wiring Methods. Flexible metal conduit, liquidtight flexible metal conduit, or liquidtight flexible nonmetallic conduit shall be permitted in escalator and moving walk wellways. Flexible metal conduit or liquidtight flexible conduit of metric designator 12 (trade size ⅜) shall be permitted in lengths not in excess of 1.8 m (6 ft).

Exception: Metric designator 12 (trade size ⅜), nominal, or larger liquidtight flexible nonmetallic conduit, as defined in 356.2(2), shall be permitted to be installed in lengths in excess of 1.8 m (6 ft).

(2) Class 2 Circuit Cables. Cables used in Class 2 power-limited circuits shall be permitted to be installed within escalators and moving walkways, provided the cables are supported and protected from physical damage and are of a jacketed and flame-retardant type.

(3) Flexible Cords. Hard-service cords that conform to the requirements of Article 400 (Table 400.4) shall be permitted as flexible connections on escalators and moving walk control panels and disconnecting means where the entire control panel and disconnecting means are arranged for removal from machine spaces as permitted in 620.5.

(C) Wheelchair Lifts and Stairway Chairlift Raceways.

(1) Wiring Methods. Flexible metal conduit or liquidtight flexible metal conduit shall be permitted in wheelchair lifts and stairway chairlift runways and machinery spaces. Flexible metal conduit or liquidtight flexible conduit of metric designator 12 (trade size ⅜) shall be permitted in lengths not in excess of 1.8 m (6 ft).

Exception: Metric designator 12 (trade size ⅜) or larger liquidtight flexible nonmetallic conduit, as defined in 356.2(2), shall be permitted to be installed in lengths in excess of 1.8 m (6 ft).

(2) Class 2 Circuit Cables. Cables used in Class 2 power-limited circuits shall be permitted to be installed within wheelchair lifts and stairway chairlift runways and machinery spaces, provided the cables are supported and protected from physical damage and are of a jacketed and flame-retardant type.

620.22 Branch Circuits for Car Lighting, Receptacle(s), Ventilation, Heating, and Air Conditioning.

(A) Car Light Source. A separate branch circuit shall supply the car lights, receptacle(s), auxiliary lighting power source, and ventilation on each elevator car. The overcurrent device protecting the branch circuit shall be located in the elevator machine room or control room/machinery space or control space.

Required lighting shall not be connected to the load side of a ground-fault circuit interrupter.

(B) Air-Conditioning and Heating Source. A dedicated branch circuit shall supply the air-conditioning and heating units on each elevator car. The overcurrent device protecting the branch circuit shall be located in the elevator machine room or control room/machinery space or control space.

620.23 Branch Circuits for Machine Room or Control Room/Machinery Space or Control Space Lighting and Receptacle(s).

(A) Separate Branch Circuit. A separate branch circuit shall supply the machine room or control room/machinery space or control space lighting and receptacle(s).

Required lighting shall not be connected to the load side of a ground-fault circuit interrupter.

(B) Lighting Switch. The machine room or control room/machinery space or control space lighting switch shall be located at the point of entry.

(C) Duplex Receptacle. At least one 125-volt, single-phase, duplex receptacle shall be provided in each machine room or control room and machinery space or control space.

> FPN: See ANSI/ASME A17.1-2000, *Safety Code for Elevators and Escalators*, for illumination levels.

620.24 Branch Circuit for Hoistway Pit Lighting and Receptacle(s).

(A) Separate Branch Circuit. A separate branch circuit shall supply the hoistway pit lighting and receptacle(s).

Required lighting shall not be connected to the load side of a ground-fault circuit interrupter.

(B) Lighting Switch. The lighting switch shall be so located as to be readily accessible from the pit access door.

(C) Duplex Receptacle. At least one 125-volt, single-phase, duplex receptacle shall be provided in the hoistway pit.

> FPN: See ANSI/ASME A17.1-2000, *Safety Code for Elevators and Escalators*, for illumination levels.

620.25 Branch Circuits for Other Utilization Equipment.

(A) Additional Branch Circuits. Additional branch circuit(s) shall supply utilization equipment not identified in 620.22, 620.23, and 620.24. Other utilization equipment shall be restricted to that equipment identified in 620.1.

(B) Overcurrent Devices. The overcurrent devices protecting the branch circuit(s) shall be located in the elevator machinery room or control room/machinery space or control space.

IV. Installation of Conductors

620.32 Metal Wireways and Nonmetallic Wireways.
The sum of the cross-sectional area of the individual conductors in a wireway shall not be more than 50 percent of the interior cross-sectional area of the wireway.

Vertical runs of wireways shall be securely supported at intervals not exceeding 4.5 m (15 ft) and shall have not more than one joint between supports. Adjoining wireway sections shall be securely fastened together to provide a rigid joint.

620.33 Number of Conductors in Raceways. The sum of the cross-sectional area of the individual conductors in raceways shall not exceed 40 percent of the interior cross-sectional area of the raceway, except as permitted in 620.32 for wireways.

620.34 Supports. Supports for cables or raceways in a hoistway or in an escalator or moving walk wellway or wheelchair lift and stairway chairlift runway shall be securely fastened to the guide rail; escalator or moving walk truss; or to the hoistway, wellway, or runway construction.

620.35 Auxiliary Gutters. Auxiliary gutters shall not be subject to the restrictions of 366.12(2) covering length or of 366.22 covering number of conductors.

620.36 Different Systems in One Raceway or Traveling Cable. Optical fiber cables and conductors for operating devices, operation and motion control, power, signaling, fire alarm, lighting, heating, and air-conditioning circuits of 600 volts or less shall be permitted to be run in the same traveling cable or raceway system if all conductors are insulated for the maximum voltage applied to any conductor within the cables or raceway system and if all live parts of the equipment are insulated from ground for this maximum voltage. Such a traveling cable or raceway shall also be permitted to include shielded conductors and/or one or more coaxial cables, if such conductors are insulated for the maximum voltage applied to any conductor within the cable or raceway system. Conductors shall be permitted to be covered with suitable shielding for telephone, audio, video, or higher frequency communications circuits.

620.37 Wiring in Hoistways, Machine Rooms, Control Rooms, Machinery Spaces, and Control Spaces.

(A) Uses Permitted. Only such electric wiring, raceways, and cables used directly in connection with the elevator or dumbwaiter, including wiring for signals, for communication with the car, for lighting, heating, air conditioning, and ventilating the elevator car, for fire detecting systems, for pit sump pumps, and for heating, lighting, and ventilating the hoistway, shall be permitted inside the hoistway, machine rooms, control rooms, machinery spaces, and control spaces.

(B) Lightning Protection. Bonding of elevator rails (car and/or counterweight) to a lightning protection system grounding down conductor(s) shall be permitted. The lightning protection system grounding down conductor(s) shall not be located within the hoistway. Elevator rails or other hoistway equipment shall not be used as the grounding down conductor for lightning protection systems.

> FPN: See 250.106 for bonding requirements. For further information, see NFPA 780-2004, *Standard for the Installation of Lightning Protection Systems.*

(C) Main Feeders. Main feeders for supplying power to elevators and dumbwaiters shall be installed outside the hoistway unless as follows:

(1) By special permission, feeders for elevators shall be permitted within an existing hoistway if no conductors are spliced within the hoistway.

(2) Feeders shall be permitted inside the hoistway for elevators with driving machine motors located in the hoistway or on the car or counterweight.

620.38 Electrical Equipment in Garages and Similar Occupancies. Electrical equipment and wiring used for elevators, dumbwaiters, escalators, moving walks, and wheelchair lifts and stairway chairlifts in garages shall comply with the requirements of Article 511.

> FPN: Garages used for parking or storage and where no repair work is done in accordance with 511.3 are not classified.

V. Traveling Cables

620.41 Suspension of Traveling Cables. Traveling cables shall be suspended at the car and hoistways' ends, or counterweight end where applicable, so as to reduce the strain on the individual copper conductors to a minimum.

Traveling cables shall be supported by one of the following means:

(1) By their steel supporting member(s)

(2) By looping the cables around supports for unsupported lengths less than 30 m (100 ft)

(3) By suspending from the supports by a means that automatically tightens around the cable when tension is increased for unsupported lengths up to 60 m (200 ft)

> FPN: Unsupported length for the hoistway suspension means is that length of cable as measured from the point of suspension in the hoistway to the bottom of the loop, with the elevator car located at the bottom landing. Unsupported length for the car suspension means is that length of cable as measured from the point of suspension on the car to the bottom of the loop, with the elevator car located at the top landing.

620.42 Hazardous (Classified) Locations. In hazardous (classified) locations, traveling cables shall be of a type approved for hazardous (classified) locations and shall comply with 501.140, 502.140, or 503.140, as applicable.

620.43 Location of and Protection for Cables. Traveling cable supports shall be located so as to reduce to a minimum the possibility of damage due to the cables coming in contact with the hoistway construction or equipment in the hoistway. Where necessary, suitable guards shall be provided to protect the cables against damage.

620.44 Installation of Traveling Cables. Traveling cable shall be permitted to be run without the use of a raceway for a distance not exceeding 1.8 m (6 ft) in length as measured from the first point of support on the elevator car or hoistway wall, or counterweight where applicable, provided the conductors are grouped together and taped or corded, or in the original sheath.

Traveling cables shall be permitted to be continued as fixed wiring to elevator controller enclosures and to elevator car and machine room, control room, machinery space, and control space connections, provided they are suitably supported and protected from physical damage.

VI. Disconnecting Means and Control

620.51 Disconnecting Means. A single means for disconnecting all ungrounded main power supply conductors for each unit shall be provided and be designed so that no pole can be operated independently. Where multiple driving machines are connected to a single elevator, escalator, moving walk, or pumping unit, there shall be one disconnecting means to disconnect the motor(s) and control valve operating magnets.

The disconnecting means for the main power supply conductors shall not disconnect the branch circuit required in 620.22, 620.23, and 620.24.

(A) Type. The disconnecting means shall be an enclosed externally operable fused motor circuit switch or circuit breaker capable of being locked in the open position. The disconnecting means shall be a listed device.

FPN: For additional information, see ASME/ANSI A17.1-2000, *Safety Code for Elevators and Escalators.*

Exception: Where an individual branch circuit supplies a wheelchair lift, the disconnecting means required by 620.51(C)(4) shall be permitted to comply with 430.109(C). This disconnecting means shall be listed and shall be capable of being locked in the open position.

(B) Operation. No provision shall be made to open or close this disconnecting means from any other part of the premises. If sprinklers are installed in hoistways, machine rooms, control rooms, machinery spaces, or control spaces, the disconnecting means shall be permitted to automatically open the power supply to the affected elevator(s) prior to the application of water. No provision shall be made to automatically close this disconnecting means. Power shall only be restored by manual means.

FPN: To reduce hazards associated with water on live elevator electrical equipment.

(C) Location. The disconnecting means shall be located where it is readily accessible to qualified persons.

(1) On Elevators Without Generator Field Control. On elevators without generator field control, the disconnecting means shall be located within sight of the motor controller. Driving machines or motion and operation controllers not within sight of the disconnecting means shall be provided with a manually operated switch installed in the control circuit to prevent starting. The manually operated switch(es) shall be installed adjacent to this equipment.

Where the driving machine of an electric elevator or the hydraulic machine of a hydraulic elevator is located in a remote machine room or remote machinery space, a single means for disconnecting all ungrounded main power supply conductors shall be provided and be capable of being locked in the open position.

(2) On Elevators with Generator Field Control. On elevators with generator field control, the disconnecting means shall be located within sight of the motor controller for the driving motor of the motor-generator set. Driving machines, motor-generator sets, or motion and operation controllers not within sight of the disconnecting means shall be provided with a manually operated switch installed in the control circuit to prevent starting. The manually operated switch(es) shall be installed adjacent to this equipment.

Where the driving machine or the motor-generator set is located in a remote machine room or remote machinery space, a single means for disconnecting all ungrounded main power supply conductors shall be provided and be capable of being locked in the open position.

(3) On Escalators and Moving Walks. On escalators and moving walks, the disconnecting means shall be installed in the space where the controller is located.

(4) On Wheelchair Lifts and Stairway Chairlifts. On wheelchair lifts and stairway chairlifts, the disconnecting means shall be located within sight of the motor controller.

(D) Identification and Signs. Where there is more than one driving machine in a machine room, the disconnecting means shall be numbered to correspond to the identifying number of the driving machine that they control.

The disconnecting means shall be provided with a sign to identify the location of the supply side overcurrent protective device.

620.52 Power from More Than One Source.

(A) Single-Car and Multicar Installations. On single-car and multicar installations, equipment receiving electrical power from more than one source shall be provided with a disconnecting means for each source of electrical power. The disconnecting means shall be within sight of the equipment served.

(B) Warning Sign for Multiple Disconnecting Means. Where multiple disconnecting means are used and parts of the controllers remain energized from a source other than the one disconnected, a warning sign shall be mounted on or next to the disconnecting means. The sign shall be clearly legible and shall read as follows:

WARNING
PARTS OF THE CONTROLLER ARE NOT
DE-ENERGIZED BY THIS SWITCH.

(C) Interconnection Multicar Controllers. Where interconnections between controllers are necessary for the operation of the system on multicar installations that remain energized from a source other than the one disconnected, a warning sign in accordance with 620.52(B) shall be mounted on or next to the disconnecting means.

620.53 Car Light, Receptacle(s), and Ventilation Disconnecting Means.
Elevators shall have a single means for disconnecting all ungrounded car light, receptacle(s), and ventilation power-supply conductors for that elevator car.

The disconnecting means shall be an enclosed externally operable fused motor circuit switch or circuit breaker capable of being locked in the open position and shall be located in the machine room or control room for that elevator car. Where there is no machine room or control room, the disconnecting means shall be located in the same space as the disconnecting means required by 620.51.

Disconnecting means shall be numbered to correspond to the identifying number of the elevator car whose light source they control.

The disconnecting means shall be provided with a sign to identify the location of the supply side overcurrent protective device.

620.54 Heating and Air-Conditioning Disconnecting Means.
Elevators shall have a single means for disconnecting all ungrounded car heating and air-conditioning power-supply conductors for that elevator car.

The disconnecting means shall be an enclosed externally operable fused motor circuit switch or circuit breaker capable of being locked in the open position and shall be located in the machine room or control room for that elevator car. Where there is no machine room or control room, the disconnecting means shall be located in the same space as the disconnecting means required by 620.51.

Where there is equipment for more than one elevator car in the machine room, the disconnecting means shall be numbered to correspond to the identifying number of the elevator car whose heating and air-conditioning source they control.

The disconnecting means shall be provided with a sign to identify the location of the supply side overcurrent protective device.

620.55 Utilization Equipment Disconnecting Means.
Each branch circuit for other utilization equipment shall have a single means for disconnecting all ungrounded conductors. The disconnecting means shall be capable of being locked in the open position and shall be located in the machine room or control room/machine space or control space. Where there is more than one branch circuit for other utilization equipment, the disconnecting means shall be numbered to correspond to the identifying number of the equipment served. The disconnecting means shall be provided with a sign to identify the location of the supply side overcurrent protective device.

VII. Overcurrent Protection

620.61 Overcurrent Protection. Overcurrent protection shall be provided in accordance with 620.61(A) through 620.61(D).

(A) Operating Devices and Control and Signaling Circuits. Operating devices and control and signaling circuits shall be protected against overcurrent in accordance with the requirements of 725.23 and 725.24.

Class 2 power-limited circuits shall be protected against overcurrent in accordance with the requirements of Chapter 9, Notes to Tables 11(A) and 11(B).

(B) Overload Protection for Motors. Motor and branch-circuit overload protection shall conform to Article 430, Part III, and the following:

(1) Duty Rating on Elevator, Dumbwaiter, and Motor-Generator Sets Driving Motors. Duty on elevator and dumbwaiter driving machine motors and driving motors of motor-generators used with generator field control shall be rated as intermittent. Such motors shall be permitted to be protected against overload in accordance with 430.33.

(2) Duty Rating on Escalator Motors. Duty on escalator and moving walk driving machine motors shall be rated as continuous. Such motors shall be protected against overload in accordance with 430.32.

(3) Overload Protection. Escalator and moving walk driving machine motors and driving motors of motor-generator sets shall be protected against running overload as provided in Table 430.37.

(4) Duty Rating and Overload Protection on Wheelchair and Stairway Chairlift Motors. Duty on wheelchair lift and stairway chairlift driving machine motors shall be rated as intermittent. Such motors shall be permitted to be protected against overload in accordance with 430.33.

> FPN: For further information, see 430.44 for orderly shutdown.

(C) Motor Feeder Short-Circuit and Ground-Fault Protection. Motor feeder short-circuit and ground-fault protection shall be as required in Article 430, Part V.

(D) Motor Branch-Circuit Short-Circuit and Ground-Fault Protection. Motor branch-circuit short-circuit and ground-fault protection shall be as required in Article 430, Part IV.

620.62 Selective Coordination. Where more than one driving machine disconnecting means is supplied by a single feeder, the overcurrent protective devices in each disconnecting means shall be selectively coordinated with any other supply side overcurrent protective devices.

VIII. Machine Rooms, Control Rooms, Machinery Spaces, and Control Spaces

620.71 Guarding Equipment. Elevator, dumbwaiter, escalator, and moving walk driving machines; motor-generator sets; motor controllers; and disconnecting means shall be installed in a room or space set aside for that purpose unless otherwise permitted in 620.71(A) or 620.71(B). The room or space shall be secured against unauthorized access.

(A) Motor Controllers. Motor controllers shall be permitted outside the spaces herein specified, provided they are in enclosures with doors or removable panels that are capable of being locked in the closed position and the disconnecting means is located adjacent to or is an integral part of the motor controller. Motor controller enclosures for escalator or moving walks shall be permitted in the balustrade on the side located away from the moving steps or moving treadway. If the disconnecting means is an integral part of the motor controller, it shall be operable without opening the enclosure.

(B) Driving Machines. Elevators with driving machines located on the car, on the counterweight, or in the hoistway, and driving machines for dumbwaiters, wheelchair lifts, and stairway lifts shall be permitted outside the spaces herein specified.

IX. Grounding

620.81 Metal Raceways Attached to Cars. Metal raceways, Type MC cable, Type MI cable, or Type AC cable attached to elevator cars shall be bonded to grounded metal parts of the car that they contact.

620.82 Electric Elevators. For electric elevators, the frames of all motors, elevator machines, controllers, and the metal enclosures for all electrical equipment in or on the car or in the hoistway shall be grounded in accordance with Article 250.

620.83 Nonelectric Elevators. For elevators other than electric having any electric conductors attached to the car, the metal frame of the car, where normally accessible to persons, shall be grounded in accordance with Article 250.

620.84 Escalators, Moving Walks, Wheelchair Lifts, and Stairway Chairlifts. Escalators, moving walks, wheelchair lifts, and stairway chairlifts shall comply with Article 250.

620.85 Ground-Fault Circuit-Interrupter Protection for Personnel. Each 125-volt, single-phase, 15- and 20-ampere receptacle installed in pits, in hoistways, on elevator car tops, and in escalator and moving walk wellways shall be of the ground-fault circuit-interrupter type.

All 125-volt, single-phase, 15- and 20-ampere receptacles installed in machine rooms and machinery spaces shall have ground-fault circuit-interrupter protection for personnel.

A single receptacle supplying a permanently installed sump pump shall not require ground-fault circuit-interrupter protection.

X. Emergency and Standby Power Systems

620.91 Emergency and Standby Power Systems. An elevator(s) shall be permitted to be powered by an emergency or standby power system.

> FPN: See ASME/ANSI A17.1-2000, *Rule 2.27.2*, and CAN/CSA-B44-1994, *Clause 3.12.13*, for additional information.

(A) Regenerative Power. For elevator systems that regenerate power back into the power source that is unable to absorb the regenerative power under overhauling elevator load conditions, a means shall be provided to absorb this power.

(B) Other Building Loads. Other building loads, such as power and lighting, shall be permitted as the energy absorption means required in 620.91(A), provided that such loads are automatically connected to the emergency or standby power system operating the elevators and are large enough to absorb the elevator regenerative power.

(C) Disconnecting Means. The disconnecting means required by 620.51 shall disconnect the elevator from both the emergency or standby power system and the normal power system.

Where an additional power source is connected to the load side of the disconnecting means, the disconnecting means required in 620.51 shall be provided with an auxiliary contact that is positively opened mechanically, and the opening shall not be solely dependent on springs. This contact shall cause the additional power source to be disconnected from its load when the disconnecting means is in the open position.

ARTICLE 625
Electric Vehicle Charging System

I. General

625.1 Scope. The provisions of this article cover the electrical conductors and equipment external to an electric vehicle that connect an electric vehicle to a supply of electricity by conductive or inductive means, and the installation of equipment and devices related to electric vehicle charging.

FPN: For industrial trucks, see NFPA 505-2002, *Fire Safety Standard for Powered Industrial Trucks Including Type Designations, Areas of Use, Conversions, Maintenance, and Operation.*

625.2 Definitions.

Electric Vehicle. An automotive-type vehicle for highway use, such as passenger automobiles, buses, trucks, vans, neighborhood electric vehicles, and the like, primarily powered by an electric motor that draws current from a rechargeable storage battery, fuel cell, photovoltaic array, or other source of electric current. For the purpose of this article, electric motorcycles and similar type vehicles and off-road self-propelled electric vehicles, such as industrial trucks, hoists, lifts, transports, golf carts, airline ground support equipment, tractors, boats, and the like, are not included.

Electric Vehicle Connector. A device that, by insertion into an electric vehicle inlet, establishes an electrical connection to the electric vehicle for the purpose of charging and information exchange. This device is part of the electric vehicle coupler.

Electric Vehicle Coupler. A mating electric vehicle inlet and electric vehicle connector set.

Electric Vehicle Inlet. The device on the electric vehicle into which the electric vehicle connector is inserted for charging and information exchange. This device is part of the electric vehicle coupler. For the purposes of this *Code*, the electric vehicle inlet is considered to be part of the electric vehicle and not part of the electric vehicle supply equipment.

Electric Vehicle Nonvented Storage Battery. A hermetically sealed battery comprised of one or more rechargeable electrochemical cells that has no provision for the release of excessive gas pressure, or for the addition of water or electrolyte, or for external measurements of electrolyte specific gravity.

Electric Vehicle Supply Equipment. The conductors, including the ungrounded, grounded, and equipment grounding conductors and the electric vehicle connectors, attachment plugs, and all other fittings, devices, power outlets, or apparatus installed specifically for the purpose of delivering energy from the premises wiring to the electric vehicle.

Personnel Protection System. A system of personnel protection devices and constructional features that when used together provide protection against electric shock of personnel.

625.3 Other Articles. Wherever the requirements of other articles of this *Code* and Article 625 differ, the requirements of Article 625 shall apply.

625.4 Voltages. Unless other voltages are specified, the nominal ac system voltages of 120, 120/240, 208Y/120, 240, 480Y/277, 480, 600Y/347, and 600 volts shall be used to supply equipment covered by this article.

625.5 Listed or Labeled. All electrical materials, devices, fittings, and associated equipment shall be listed or labeled.

II. Wiring Methods

625.9 Electric Vehicle Coupler. The electric vehicle coupler shall comply with 625.9(A) through 625.9(F).

(A) Polarization. The electric vehicle coupler shall be polarized unless part of a system identified and listed as suitable for the purpose.

(B) Noninterchangeability. The electric vehicle coupler shall have a configuration that is noninterchangeable with wiring devices in other electrical systems. Nongrounding-type electric vehicle couplers shall not be interchangeable with grounding-type electric vehicle couplers.

(C) Construction and Installation. The electric vehicle coupler shall be constructed and installed so as to guard against inadvertent contact by persons with parts made live from the electric vehicle supply equipment or the electric vehicle battery.

(D) Unintentional Disconnection. The electric vehicle coupler shall be provided with a positive means to prevent unintentional disconnection.

(E) Grounding Pole. The electric vehicle coupler shall be provided with a grounding pole, unless part of a system identified and listed as suitable for the purpose in accordance with Article 250.

(F) Grounding Pole Requirements. If a grounding pole is provided, the electric vehicle coupler shall be so designed that the grounding pole connection is the first to make and the last to break contact.

III. Equipment Construction

625.13 Electric Vehicle Supply Equipment. Electric vehicle supply equipment rated at 125 volts, single phase, 15 or 20 amperes or part of a system identified and listed as suitable for the purpose and meeting the requirements of 625.18, 625.19, and 625.29 shall be permitted to be cord-and-plug connected. All other electric vehicle supply equipment shall be permanently connected and fastened in place. This equipment shall have no exposed live parts.

625.14 Rating. Electric vehicle supply equipment shall have sufficient rating to supply the load served. For the purposes of this article, electric vehicle charging loads shall be considered to be continuous loads.

625.15 Markings. The electric vehicle supply equipment shall comply with 625.15(A) through 625.15(C).

(A) General. All electric vehicle supply equipment shall be marked by the manufacturer as follows:

FOR USE WITH ELECTRIC VEHICLES

(B) Ventilation Not Required. Where marking is required by 625.29(C), the electric vehicle supply equipment shall be clearly marked by the manufacturer as follows:

VENTILATION NOT REQUIRED

The marking shall be located so as to be clearly visible after installation.

(C) Ventilation Required. Where marking is required by 625.29(D), the electric vehicle supply equipment shall be clearly marked by the manufacturer "Ventilation Required." The marking shall be located so as to be clearly visible after installation.

625.16 Means of Coupling. The means of coupling to the electric vehicle shall be either conductive or inductive. Attachment plugs, electric vehicle connectors, and electric vehicle inlets shall be listed or labeled for the purpose.

625.17 Cable. The electric vehicle supply equipment cable shall be Type EV, EVJ, EVE, EVJE, EVT, or EVJT flexible cable as specified in Article 400 and Table 400.4. Ampacities shall be as specified in Table 400.5(A) for 10 AWG and smaller, and in Table 400.5(B) for 8 AWG and larger. The overall length of the cable shall not exceed 7.5 m (25 ft) unless equipped with a cable management system that is listed as suitable for the purpose. Other cable types and assemblies listed as being suitable for the purpose, including optional hybrid communications, signal, and optical fiber cables, shall be permitted.

625.18 Interlock. Electric vehicle supply equipment shall be provided with an interlock that de-energizes the electric vehicle connector and its cable whenever the electric connector is uncoupled from the electric vehicle. An interlock shall not be required for portable cord-and-plug-connected electric vehicle supply equipment intended for connection to receptacle outlets rated at 125 volts, single phase, 15 and 20 amperes.

625.19 Automatic De-Energization of Cable. The electric vehicle supply equipment or the cable-connector combination of the equipment shall be provided with an automatic means to de-energize the cable conductors and electric vehicle connector upon exposure to strain that could result in either cable rupture or separation of the cable from the electric connector and exposure of live parts. Automatic means to de-energize the cable conductors and electric vehicle connector shall not be required for portable cord-and-plug-connected electric vehicle supply equipment intended for connection to receptacle outlets rated at 125 volts, single phase, 15 and 20 amperes.

IV. Control and Protection

625.21 Overcurrent Protection. Overcurrent protection for feeders and branch circuits supplying electric vehicle supply equipment shall be sized for continuous duty and shall have a rating of not less than 125 percent of the maximum load of the electric vehicle supply equipment. Where noncontinuous loads are supplied from the same feeder or branch circuit, the overcurrent device shall have a rating of not less than the sum of the noncontinuous loads plus 125 percent of the continuous loads.

625.22 Personnel Protection System. The electric vehicle supply equipment shall have a listed system of protection against electric shock of personnel. The personnel protection system shall be composed of listed personnel protection devices and constructional features. Where cord-and-plug-connected electric vehicle supply equipment is used, the interrupting device of a listed personnel protection system shall be provided and shall be an integral part of the attachment plug or shall be located in the power supply cable not more than 300 mm (12 in.) from the attachment plug.

625.23 Disconnecting Means. For electric vehicle supply equipment rated more than 60 amperes or more than 150 volts to ground, the disconnecting means shall be provided and installed in a readily accessible location. The disconnecting means shall be capable of being locked in the open position.

625.25 Loss of Primary Source. Means shall be provided such that, upon loss of voltage from the utility or other electric system(s), energy cannot be back fed through the electric vehicle and the supply equipment to the premises wiring system unless permitted by 625.26.

625.26 Interactive Systems. Electric vehicle supply equipment and other parts of a system, either on-board or off-board the vehicle, that are identified for and intended to be interconnected to a vehicle and also serve as an optional standby system or an electric power production source or provide for bi-directional power feed shall be listed as suitable for that purpose. When used as an optional standby system, the requirements of Article 702 shall apply, and when used as an electric power production source, the requirements of Article 705 shall apply.

V. Electric Vehicle Supply Equipment Locations

625.28 Hazardous (Classified) Locations. Where electric vehicle supply equipment or wiring is installed in a hazardous (classified) location, the requirements of Articles 500 through 516 shall apply.

625.29 Indoor Sites. Indoor sites shall include, but not be limited to, integral, attached, and detached residential garages; enclosed and underground parking structures; repair and non-repair commercial garages; and agricultural buildings.

(A) Location. The electric vehicle supply equipment shall be located to permit direct connection to the electric vehicle.

(B) Height. Unless specifically listed for the purpose and location, the coupling means of the electric vehicle supply equipment shall be stored or located at a height of not less than 450 mm (18 in.) and not more than 1.2 m (4 ft) above the floor level.

(C) Ventilation Not Required. Where electric vehicle nonvented storage batteries are used or where the electric vehicle supply equipment is listed or labeled as suitable for charging electric vehicles indoors without ventilation and marked in accordance with 625.15(B), mechanical ventilation shall not be required.

(D) Ventilation Required. Where the electric vehicle supply equipment is listed or labeled as suitable for charging electric vehicles that require ventilation for indoor charging, and is marked in accordance with 625.15(C), mechanical ventilation, such as a fan, shall be provided. The ventilation shall include both supply and exhaust equipment and shall be permanently installed and located to intake from, and vent directly to, the outdoors. Positive pressure ventilation systems shall be permitted only in buildings or areas that have been specifically designed and approved for that application. Mechanical ventilation requirements shall be

determined by one of the methods specified in 625.29(D)(1) through (D)(4).

(1) Table Values. For supply voltages and currents specified in Table 625.29(D)(1) or Table 625.29(D)(2), the minimum ventilation requirements shall be as specified in Table 625.29(D)(1) or Table 625.29(D)(2) for each of the total number of electric vehicles that can be charged at one time.

(2) Other Values. For supply voltages and currents other than specified in Table 625.29(D)(1) or Table 625.29(D)(2), the minimum ventilation requirements shall be calculated by means of the following general formulas as applicable:

(1) Single phase: Ventilation $_{\text{single phase}}$ in cubic meters per minute (m^3/min) =

$$\frac{(\text{volts})(\text{amperes})}{1718}$$

Ventilation$_{\text{single phase}}$ in cubic feet per minute (cfm) =

$$\frac{(\text{volts})(\text{amperes})}{48.7}$$

(2) Three phase: Ventilation$_{\text{three phase}}$ in cubic meters per minute (m^3/min) =

$$\frac{1.732(\text{volts})(\text{amperes})}{1718}$$

Ventilation$_{\text{three phase}}$ in cubic feet per minute (cfm) =

$$\frac{1.732(\text{volts})(\text{amperes})}{48.7}$$

(3) Engineered Systems. For an electric vehicle supply equipment ventilation system designed by a person qualified to perform such calculations as an integral part of a building's total ventilation system, the minimum ventilation requirements shall be permitted to be determined per calculations specified in the engineering study.

(4) Supply Circuits. The supply circuit to the mechanical ventilation equipment shall be electrically interlocked with the electric vehicle supply equipment and shall remain energized during the entire electric vehicle charging cycle. Electric vehicle supply equipment shall be marked in accordance with 625.15. Electric vehicle supply equipment receptacles rated at 125 volts, single phase, 15 and 20 amperes shall be marked in accordance with 625.15(C) and shall be switched, and the mechanical ventilation system shall be electrically interlocked through the switch supply power to the receptacle.

Table 625.29(D)(1) Minimum Ventilation Required in Cubic Meters per Minute (m³/min) for Each of the Total Number of Electric Vehicles That Can Be Charged at One Time

Branch-Circuit Ampere Rating	Branch-Circuit Voltage						
	Single Phase			3 Phase			
	120 V	208 V	240 V or 120/240 V	208 V or 208Y/120 V	240 V	480 V or 480Y/277 V	600 V or 600Y/347 V
15	1.1	1.8	2.1	—	—	—	—
20	1.4	2.4	2.8	4.2	4.8	9.7	12
30	2.1	3.6	4.2	6.3	7.2	15	18
40	2.8	4.8	5.6	8.4	9.7	19	24
50	3.5	6.1	7.0	10	12	24	30
60	4.2	7.3	8.4	13	15	29	36
100	7.0	12	14	21	24	48	60
150	—	—	—	31	36	73	91
200	—	—	—	42	48	97	120
250	—	—	—	52	60	120	150
300	—	—	—	63	73	145	180
350	—	—	—	73	85	170	210
400	—	—	—	84	97	195	240

Table 625.29(D)(2) Minimum Ventilation Required in Cubic Feet per Minute (cfm) for Each of the Total Number of Electric Vehicles That Can Be Charged at One Time

Branch-Circuit Ampere Rating	Branch-Circuit Voltage						
	Single Phase			3 Phase			
	120 V	208 V	240 V or 120/240 V	208 V or 208Y/120 V	240 V	480 V or 480Y/277 V	600 V or 600Y/347 V
15	37	64	74	—	—	—	—
20	49	85	99	148	171	342	427
30	74	128	148	222	256	512	641
40	99	171	197	296	342	683	854
50	123	214	246	370	427	854	1066
60	148	256	296	444	512	1025	1281
100	246	427	493	740	854	1708	2135
150	—	—	—	1110	1281	2562	3203
200	—	—	—	1480	1708	3416	4270
250	—	—	—	1850	2135	4270	5338
300	—	—	—	2221	2562	5125	6406
350	—	—	—	2591	2989	5979	7473
400	—	—	—	2961	3416	6832	8541

625.30 Outdoor Sites. Outdoor sites shall include but not be limited to residential carports and driveways, curbside, open parking structures, parking lots, and commercial charging facilities.

(A) Location. The electric vehicle supply equipment shall be located to permit direct connection to the electric vehicle.

(B) Height. Unless specifically listed for the purpose and location, the coupling means of electric vehicle supply equipment shall be stored or located at a height of not less than 600 mm (24 in.) and not more than 1.2 m (4 ft) above the parking surface.

ARTICLE 630
Electric Welders

I. General

630.1 Scope. This article covers apparatus for electric arc welding, resistance welding, plasma cutting, and other similar welding and cutting process equipment that is connected to an electric supply system.

II. Arc Welders

630.11 Ampacity of Supply Conductors. The ampacity of conductors for arc welders shall be in accordance with 630.11(A) and 630.11(B).

(A) Individual Welders. The ampacity of the supply conductors shall not be less than the I_{1eff} value on the rating plate. Alternatively, if the I_{1eff} is not given, the ampacity of the supply conductors shall not be less than the current value determined by multiplying the rated primary current in amperes given on the welder rating plate by the factor shown in Table 630.11(A) based on the duty cycle of the welder.

Table 630.11(A) Duty Cycle Multiplication Factors for Arc Welders

	Multiplier for Arc Welders	
Duty Cycle	Nonmotor Generator	Motor Generator
100	1.00	1.00
90	0.95	0.96
80	0.89	0.91
70	0.84	0.86
60	0.78	0.81
50	0.71	0.75
40	0.63	0.69
30	0.55	0.62
20 or less	0.45	0.55

(B) Group of Welders. Minimum conductor ampacity shall be based on the individual currents determined in 630.11(A) as the sum of 100 percent of the two largest welders, plus 85 percent of the third largest welder, plus 70 percent of the fourth largest welder, plus 60 percent of all remaining welders.

Exception: Percentage values lower than those given in 630.11(B) shall be permitted in cases where the work is such that a high-operating duty cycle for individual welders is impossible.

FPN: Duty cycle considers welder loading based on the use to be made of each welder and the number of welders supplied by the conductors that will be in use at the same time. The load value used for each welder considers both the magnitude and the duration of the load while the welder is in use.

630.12 Overcurrent Protection. Overcurrent protection for arc welders shall be as provided in 630.12(A) and 630.12(B). Where the values as determined by this section do not correspond with the standard ampere ratings provided in 240.6 or the rating or setting specified results in unnecessary opening of the overcurrent device, the next higher standard rating or setting shall be permitted.

(A) For Welders. Each welder shall have overcurrent protection rated or set at not more than 200 percent of I_{1max}. Alternatively, if the I_{1max} is not given, the overcurrent protection shall be rated or set at not more than 200 percent of the rated primary current of the welder.

An overcurrent device shall not be required for a welder that has supply conductors protected by an overcurrent device rated or set at not more than 200 percent of I_{1max} or at the rated primary current of the welder.

If the supply conductors for a welder are protected by an overcurrent device rated or set at not more than 200 percent of I_{1max} or at the rated primary current of the welder, a separate overcurrent device shall not be required.

(B) For Conductors. Conductors that supply one or more welders shall be protected by an overcurrent device rated or set at not more than 200 percent of the conductor ampacity.

FPN: I_{1max} is the maximum value of the rated supply current at maximum rated output. I_{1eff} is the maximum value of the effective supply current, calculated from the rated supply current (I_1), the corresponding duty cycle (duty factor) (X), and the supply current at no-load (I_0) by the following formula:

$$I_{1eff} = \sqrt{I_1^2 X + I_0^2 (1 - X)}$$

630.13 Disconnecting Means. A disconnecting means shall be provided in the supply circuit for each arc welder that is not equipped with a disconnect mounted as an integral part of the welder.

The disconnecting means shall be a switch or circuit breaker, and its rating shall not be less than that necessary to accommodate overcurrent protection as specified under 630.12.

630.14 Marking. A rating plate shall be provided for arc welders giving the following information:

(1) Name of manufacturer

(2) Frequency

(3) Number of phases

(4) Primary voltage

(5) I_{1max} and I_{1eff}, or rated primary current

(6) Maximum open-circuit voltage

(7) Rated secondary current and

(8) Basis of rating, such as the duty cycle

630.15 Grounding of Welder Secondary Circuit. The secondary circuit conductors of an arc welder, consisting of the electrode conductor and the work conductor, shall not be considered as premises wiring for the purpose of applying Article 250.

FPN: Connecting welder secondary circuits to grounded objects can create parallel paths and can cause objectionable current over equipment grounding conductors.

III. Resistance Welders

630.31 Ampacity of Supply Conductors. The ampacity of the supply conductors for resistance welders necessary to limit the voltage drop to a value permissible for the satisfactory performance of the welder is usually greater than that required to prevent overheating as covered in 630.31(A) and 630.31(B).

(A) Individual Welders. The rated ampacity for conductors for individual welders shall comply with the following:

(1) The ampacity of the supply conductors for a welder that may be operated at different times at different values of primary current or duty cycle shall not be less than 70 percent of the rated primary current for seam and automatically fed welders, and 50 percent of the rated primary current for manually operated nonautomatic welders.

(2) The ampacity of the supply conductors for a welder wired for a specific operation for which the actual primary current and duty cycle are known and remain unchanged shall not be less than the product of the actual primary current and the multiplier specified in Table 630.31(A)(2) for the duty cycle at which the welder will be operated.

Table 630.31(A)(2) Duty Cycle Multiplication Factors for Resistance Welders

Duty Cycle (percent)	Multiplier
50	0.71
40	0.63
30	0.55
25	0.50
20	0.45
15	0.39
10	0.32
7.5	0.27
5 or less	0.22

(B) Groups of Welders. The ampacity of conductors that supply two or more welders shall not be less than the sum of the value obtained in accordance with 630.31(A) for the largest welder supplied and 60 percent of the values obtained for all the other welders supplied.

FPN: **Explanation of Terms**

(1) The *rated primary current* is the rated kilovolt-amperes (kVA) multiplied by 1000 and divided by the rated primary voltage, using values given on the nameplate.

(2) The *actual primary current* is the current drawn from the supply circuit during each welder operation at the particular heat tap and control setting used.

(3) The *duty cycle* is the percentage of the time during which the welder is loaded. For instance, a spot welder supplied by a 60-Hz system (216,000 cycles per hour) and making four hundred 15-cycle welds per hour would have a duty cycle of 2.8 percent (400 multiplied by 15, divided by 216,000, multiplied by 100). A seam welder operating 2 cycles "on" and 2 cycles "off" would have a duty cycle of 50 percent.

630.32 Overcurrent Protection. Overcurrent protection for resistance welders shall be as provided in 630.32(A) and 630.32(B). Where the values as determined by this section do not correspond with the standard ampere ratings provided in 240.6 or where the rating or setting specified results in unnecessary opening of the overcurrent device, a higher rating or setting that does not exceed the next higher standard ampere rating shall be permitted.

(A) For Welders. Each welder shall have an overcurrent device rated or set at not more than 300 percent of the rated primary current of the welder. If the supply conductors for a welder are protected by an overcurrent device rated or set at not more than 200 percent of the rated primary current of the welder, a separate overcurrent device shall not be required.

(B) For Conductors. Conductors that supply one or more welders shall be protected by an overcurrent device rated or set at not more than 300 percent of the conductor rating.

630.33 Disconnecting Means. A switch or circuit breaker shall be provided by which each resistance welder and its control equipment can be disconnected from the supply circuit. The ampere rating of this disconnecting means shall not be less than the supply conductor ampacity determined in accordance with 630.31. The supply circuit switch shall be permitted as the welder disconnecting means where the circuit supplies only one welder.

630.34 Marking. A nameplate shall be provided for each resistance welder, giving the following information:

(1) Name of manufacturer
(2) Frequency
(3) Primary voltage
(4) Rated kilovolt-amperes (kVA) at 50 percent duty cycle
(5) Maximum and minimum open-circuit secondary voltage
(6) Short-circuit secondary current at maximum secondary voltage
(7) Specified throat and gap setting

IV. Welding Cable

630.41 Conductors. Insulation of conductors intended for use in the secondary circuit of electric welders shall be flame retardant.

630.42 Installation. Cables shall be permitted to be installed in a dedicated cable tray as provided in 630.42(A), (B), and (C).

(A) Cable Support. The cable tray shall provide support at not greater than 150-mm (6-in.) intervals.

(B) Spread of Fire and Products of Combustion. The installation shall comply with 300.21.

(C) Signs. A permanent sign shall be attached to the cable tray at intervals not greater than 6.0 m (20 ft). The sign shall read as follows:

CABLE TRAY FOR WELDING CABLES ONLY

ARTICLE 640
Audio Signal Processing, Amplification, and Reproduction Equipment

I. General

640.1 Scope. This article covers equipment and wiring for audio signal generation, recording, processing, amplification and reproduction; distribution of sound; public address; speech input systems; temporary audio system installations; and electronic organs or other electronic musical instruments. This also includes audio systems subject to Article 517, Part VI, and Articles 518, 520, 525, and 530.

FPN No. 1: Examples of permanently installed distributed audio system locations include, but are not limited to, restaurant, hotel, business office, commercial and retail sales environments, churches, and schools. Both portable and permanently installed equipment locations include, but are not limited to, residences, auditoriums, theaters, stadiums, and movie and television studios. Temporary installations include, but are not limited to, auditoriums, theaters, stadiums (which use both temporary and permanently installed systems), and outdoor events such as fairs, festivals, circuses, public events, and concerts.

FPN No. 2: Fire and burglary alarm signaling devices are specifically not encompassed by this article.

640.2 Definitions. For purposes of this article, the following definitions apply.

Abandoned Audio Distribution Cable. Installed audio distribution cable that is not terminated at equipment and not identified for future use with a tag.

Audio Amplifier or Pre-Amplifier. Electronic equipment that increases the current or voltage, or both, potential of an audio signal intended for use by another piece of audio equipment. *Amplifier* is the term used to denote an audio amplifier within this article.

Audio Autotransformer. A transformer with a single winding and multiple taps intended for use with an amplifier loudspeaker signal output.

Audio Signal Processing Equipment. Electrically operated equipment that produces, processes, or both, electronic signals that, when appropriately amplified and reproduced by a loudspeaker, produce an acoustic signal within the range of normal human hearing (typically 20–20 kHz). Within this article, the terms *equipment* and *audio equipment* are assumed to be equivalent to audio signal processing equipment.

FPN: This equipment includes, but is not limited to, loudspeakers; headphones; pre-amplifiers; microphones and their power supplies; mixers; MIDI (musical instrument digital interface) equipment or other digital control systems; equalizers, compressors, and other audio signal processing equipment; and audio media recording and playback equipment, including turntables, tape decks and disk players (audio and multimedia), synthesizers, tone generators, and electronic organs. Electronic organs and synthesizers may have integral or separate amplification and loudspeakers. With the exception of amplifier outputs, virtually all such equipment is used to process signals (utilizing analog or digital techniques) that have nonhazardous levels of voltage or current potential.

Audio System. Within this article, the totality of all equipment and interconnecting wiring used to fabricate a fully functional audio signal processing, amplification, and reproduction system.

Audio Transformer. A transformer with two or more electrically isolated windings and multiple taps intended for use with an amplifier loudspeaker signal output.

Equipment Rack. A framework for the support, enclosure, or both, of equipment; may be portable or stationary. See ANSI/EIA/310-D-1992, *Cabinets, Racks, Panels and Associated Equipment.*

Loudspeaker. Equipment that converts an ac electric signal into an acoustic signal. The term *speaker* is commonly used to mean *loudspeaker.*

Maximum Output Power. The maximum output power delivered by an amplifier into its rated load as determined under specified test conditions. This may exceed the manufacturer's rated output power for the same amplifier.

Mixer. Equipment used to combine and level match a multiplicity of electronic signals, such as from microphones, electronic instruments, and recorded audio.

Mixer–Amplifier. Equipment that combines the functions of a mixer and amplifier within a single enclosure.

Portable Equipment. Equipment fed with portable cords or cables intended to be moved from one place to another.

Powered Loudspeaker. Equipment that consists of a loudspeaker and amplifier within the same enclosure. Other signal processing may also be included.

Rated Load Impedance. The amplifier manufacturer's stated or marked speaker impedance into which an amplifier will deliver its rated output power. 2Ω, 4Ω, and 8Ω are typical ratings.

Rated Output Power. The amplifier manufacturer's stated or marked output power capability into its rated load.

Rated Output Voltage. For audio amplifiers of the constant-voltage type, the nominal output voltage when the amplifier is delivering full rated power. Rated output voltage is used for determining approximate acoustic output in distributed speaker systems that typically employ impedance matching transformers. Typical ratings are 25 volts, 70.7 volts, and 100 volts.

Technical Power System. An electrical distribution system with grounding in accordance with 250.146(D), where the equipment grounding conductor is isolated from the premises grounded conductor except at a single grounded termination point within a branch-circuit panelboard, at the originating (main breaker) branch-circuit panelboard, or at the premises grounding electrode.

Temporary Equipment. Portable wiring and equipment intended for use with events of a transient or temporary nature where all equipment is presumed to be removed at the conclusion of the event.

640.3 Locations and Other Articles. Circuits and equipment shall comply with 640.3(A) through 640.3(L), as applicable.

(A) Spread of Fire or Products of Combustion. The accessible portion of abandoned audio distribution cables shall be removed. See 300.21.

(B) Ducts, Plenums, and Other Air-Handling Spaces. See 300.22 for circuits and equipment installed in ducts or plenums or other space used for environmental air.

> FPN: NFPA 90A-2002, *Standard for the Installation of Air Conditioning and Ventilation Systems*, Section 4.3.10.2.6.5, permits loudspeakers, loudspeaker assemblies, and their accessories listed in accordance with UL 2043-1996, *Fire Test for Heat and Visible Smoke Release for Discrete Products and Their Accessories Installed in Air-Handling Spaces*, to be installed in other spaces used for environmental air (ceiling cavity plenums).

(C) Cable Trays. Cable trays shall be used in accordance with Article 392.

> FPN: See 725.61(C) for the use of Class 2, Class 3, and Type PLTC cable in cable trays.

(D) Hazardous (Classified) Locations. Equipment used in hazardous (classified) locations shall comply with the applicable requirements of Chapter 5.

(E) Assembly Occupancies. Equipment used in assembly occupancies shall comply with Article 518.

(F) Theaters, Audience Areas of Motion Picture and Television Studios, and Similar Locations. Equipment used in theaters, audience areas of motion picture and television studios, and similar locations shall comply with Article 520.

(G) Carnivals, Circuses, Fairs, and Similar Events. Equipment used in carnivals, circuses, fairs, and similar events shall comply with Article 525.

(H) Motion Picture and Television Studios. Equipment used in motion picture and television studios shall comply with Article 530.

(I) Swimming Pools, Fountains, and Similar Locations. Audio equipment used in or near swimming pools, fountains, and similar locations shall comply with Article 680.

(J) Combination Systems. Where the authority having jurisdiction permits audio systems for paging or music, or both, to be combined with fire alarm systems, the wiring shall comply with Article 760.

> FPN: For installation requirements for such combination systems, refer to *NFPA 72®*-2002, *National Fire Alarm Code®*, and NFPA *101®*-2003, *Life Safety Code®*.

(K) Antennas. Equipment used in audio systems that contain an audio or video tuner and an antenna input shall comply with Article 810. Wiring other than antenna wiring that connects such equipment to other audio equipment shall comply with this article.

(L) Generators. Generators shall be installed in accordance with 445.10 through 445.12, 445.14 through 445.16, and 445.18. Grounding of portable and vehicle-mounted generators shall be in accordance with 250.34.

640.4 Protection of Electrical Equipment. Amplifiers, loudspeakers, and other equipment shall be so located or protected as to guard against environmental exposure or physical damage, such as might result in fire, shock, or personal hazard.

640.5 Access to Electrical Equipment Behind Panels Designed to Allow Access. Access to equipment shall not be denied by an accumulation of wires and cables that prevents removal of panels, including suspended ceiling panels.

640.6 Mechanical Execution of Work. Equipment and cables shall be installed in a neat workmanlike manner. Cables installed exposed on the surface of ceilings and sidewalls shall be supported in such a manner that the cables will not be damaged by normal building use. Such cables shall be supported by straps, staples, hangers, or similar fittings designed and installed so as not to damage the cable. The installation shall conform to 300.4(D) and 300.11.

> FPN: Accepted industry practices are described in ANSI/NECA/BICSI 568-2001, *Standard for Installing Commercial Building Telecommunications Cabling*, and other ANSI-approved installation standards.

640.7 Grounding.

(A) General. Wireways and auxiliary gutters shall be grounded and bonded in accordance with the requirements of Article 250. Where the wireway or auxiliary gutter does not contain power-supply wires, the equipment grounding conductor shall not be required to be larger than 14 AWG copper or its equivalent. Where the wireway or auxiliary gutter contains power-supply wires, the equipment grounding conductor shall not be smaller than specified in 250.122.

(B) Separately Derived Systems with 60 Volts to Ground. Grounding of separately derived systems with 60 volts to ground shall be in accordance with 647.6.

(C) Isolated Ground Receptacles. Isolated grounding-type receptacles shall be permitted as described in 250.146(D), and for the implementation of other technical power systems in compliance with Article 250. For separately derived systems with 60 volts to ground, the branch-circuit equipment grounding conductor shall be terminated as required in 647.6(B).

> FPN: See 406.2(D) for grounding-type receptacles and required identification.

640.8 Grouping of Conductors.
Insulated conductors of different systems grouped or bundled so as to be in close physical contact with each other in the same raceway or other enclosure, or in portable cords or cables, shall comply with 300.3(C)(1).

640.9 Wiring Methods.

(A) Wiring to and Between Audio Equipment.

(1) Power Wiring. Wiring and equipment from source of power to and between devices connected to the premises wiring systems shall comply with the requirements of Chapters 1 through 4, except as modified by this article.

(2) Separately Derived Power Systems. Separately derived systems shall comply with the applicable articles of this *Code*, except as modified by this article. Separately derived systems with 60 volts to ground shall be permitted for use in audio system installations as specified in Article 647.

(3) Other Wiring. All wiring not connected to the premises wiring system or to a wiring system separately derived from the premises wiring system shall comply with Article 725.

(B) Auxiliary Power Supply Wiring. Equipment that has a separate input for an auxiliary power supply shall be wired in compliance with Article 725. Battery installation shall be in accordance with Article 480.

> FPN No. 1: This section does not apply to the use of uninterruptible power supply (UPS) equipment, or other sources of supply, that are intended to act as a direct replacement for the primary circuit power source and are connected to the primary circuit input.

> FPN No. 2: Refer to *NFPA 72-2002, National Fire Alarm Code*, where equipment is used for a fire alarm system.

(C) Output Wiring and Listing of Amplifiers. Amplifiers with output circuits carrying audio program signals shall be permitted to employ Class 1, Class 2, or Class 3 wiring where the amplifier is listed and marked for use with the specific class of wiring method. Such listing shall ensure the energy output is equivalent to the shock and fire risk of the same class as stated in Article 725. Overcurrent protection shall be provided and shall be permitted to be inherent in the amplifier.

Audio amplifier output circuits wired using Class 1 wiring methods shall be considered equivalent to Class 1 circuits and shall be installed in accordance with 725.25, where applicable.

Audio amplifier output circuits wired using Class 2 or Class 3 wiring methods shall be considered equivalent to Class 2 or Class 3 circuits, respectively. They shall use conductors insulated at not less than the requirements of 725.82 and shall be installed in accordance with 725.54 and 725.61.

> FPN No. 1: ANSI/UL 1711-1994, *Amplifiers for Fire Protective Signaling Systems*, contains requirements for the listing of amplifiers used for fire alarm systems in compliance with *NFPA 72-2002, National Fire Alarm Code*.

> FPN No. 2: Examples of requirements for listing amplifiers used in residential, commercial, and professional use are found in ANSI/UL 813-1996, *Commercial Audio Equipment*; ANSI/UL 1419-1997, *Professional Video and Audio Equipment*; ANSI/UL 1492-1996, *Audio-Video Products and Accessories*; and ANSI/UL 6500-1996, *Audio/Video and Musical Instrument Apparatus for Household, Commercial, and Similar Use*.

(D) Use of Audio Transformers and Autotransformers. Audio transformers and autotransformers shall be used only for audio signals in a manner so as not to exceed the manufacturer's stated input or output voltage, impedance, or power limitations. The input or output wires of an audio transformer or autotransformer shall be allowed to connect directly to the amplifier or loudspeaker terminals. No electrical terminal or lead shall be required to be grounded or bonded.

640.10 Audio Systems Near Bodies of Water.
Audio systems near bodies of water, either natural or artificial, shall be subject to the restrictions specified in 640.10(A) and 640.10(B).

Exception: This section does not include audio systems intended for use on boats, yachts, or other forms of land or water transportation used near bodies of water, whether or not supplied by branch-circuit power.

> FPN: See 680.27(A) for installation of underwater audio equipment.

(A) Equipment Supplied by Branch-Circuit Power. Audio system equipment supplied by branch-circuit power shall not be placed laterally within 1.5 m (5 ft) of the inside wall of a pool, spa, hot tub, or fountain, or within 1.5 m (5 ft) of the prevailing or tidal high water mark. The equipment shall be provided with branch-circuit power protected by a ground-fault circuit interrupter where required by other articles.

(B) Equipment Not Supplied by Branch-Circuit Power. Audio system equipment powered by a listed Class 2 power supply or by the output of an amplifier listed as permitting the use of Class 2 wiring shall be restricted in placement only by the manufacturer's recommendations.

FPN: Placement of the power supply or amplifier, if supplied by branch-circuit power, is still subject to 640.10(A).

II. Permanent Audio System Installations

640.21 Use of Flexible Cords and Cables.

(A) Between Equipment and Branch-Circuit Power. Power supply cords for audio equipment shall be suitable for the use and shall be permitted to be used where the interchange, maintenance, or repair of such equipment is facilitated through the use of a power supply cord.

(B) Between Loudspeakers and Amplifiers or Between Loudspeakers. Cables used to connect loudspeakers to each other or to an amplifier shall comply with Article 725. Other listed cable types and assemblies, including optional hybrid communications, signal, and optical fiber cables, shall be permitted.

(C) Between Equipment. Cables used for the distribution of audio signals between equipment shall comply with Article 725. Other listed cable types and assemblies, including optional hybrid communications, signal, and optical fiber cables, shall be permitted. Other cable types and assemblies specified by the equipment manufacturer as acceptable for the use shall be permitted in accordance with 110.3(B).

(D) Between Equipment and Power Supplies Other Than Branch-Circuit Power. The following power supplies, other than branch-circuit power supplies, shall be installed and wired between equipment in accordance with the requirements of this *Code* for the voltage and power delivered:

(1) Storage batteries
(2) Transformers
(3) Transformer rectifiers
(4) Other ac or dc power supplies

FPN: For some equipment, these sources such as in items (1) and (2) serve as the only source of power. These could, in turn, be supplied with intermittent or continuous branch-circuit power.

(E) Between Equipment Racks and Premises Wiring System. Flexible cords and cables shall be permitted for the electrical connection of permanently installed equipment racks to the premises wiring system to facilitate access to equipment or for the purpose of isolating the technical power system of the rack from the premises ground. Connection shall be made either by using approved plugs and receptacles or by direct connection within an approved enclosure. Flexible cords and cables shall not be subjected to physical manipulation or abuse while the rack is in use.

640.22 Wiring of Equipment Racks and Enclosures.
Metal equipment racks and enclosures shall be grounded. Bonding shall not be required if the rack is connected to a technical power ground.

Equipment racks shall be wired in a neat and workmanlike manner. Wires, cables, structural components, or other equipment shall not be placed in such a manner as to prevent reasonable access to equipment power switches and resettable or replaceable circuit overcurrent protection devices.

Supply cords or cables, if used, shall terminate within the equipment rack enclosure in an identified connector assembly. The supply cords or cable (and connector assembly, if used) shall have sufficient ampacity to carry the total load connected to the equipment rack and shall be protected by overcurrent devices.

640.23 Conduit or Tubing.

(A) Number of Conductors. The number of conductors permitted in a single conduit or tubing shall not exceed the percentage fill specified in Table 1, Chapter 9.

(B) Nonmetallic Conduit or Tubing and Insulating Bushings. The use of nonmetallic conduit or tubing and insulating bushings shall be permitted where a technical power system is employed and shall comply with applicable articles.

640.24 Wireways, Gutters, and Auxiliary Gutters.
The use of metallic and nonmetallic wireways, gutters, and auxiliary gutters shall be permitted for use with audio signal conductors and shall comply with applicable articles with respect to permitted locations, construction, and fill.

640.25 Loudspeaker Installation in Fire Resistance-Rated Partitions, Walls, and Ceilings.
Loudspeakers installed in a fire resistance-rated partition, wall, or ceiling shall be listed for that purpose or installed in an enclosure or recess that maintains the fire resistance rating.

FPN: Fire-rated construction is the fire-resistive classification used in building codes. One method of determining fire rating is testing in accordance with NFPA 251-1999, *Standard Methods of Tests of Fire Endurance of Building Construction and Materials.*

III. Portable and Temporary Audio System Installations

640.41 Multipole Branch-Circuit Cable Connectors.
Multipole branch-circuit cable connectors, male and female, for power supply cords and cables shall be so constructed that tension on the cord or cable is not transmitted to the connections. The female half shall be attached to the load end of the power supply cord or cable. The connector shall be rated in amperes and designed so that differently rated devices cannot be connected together. Alternating-current multipole connectors shall be polarized and comply with 406.6(A) and 406.6(B) and 406.9. Alternating-current or direct-current multipole connectors utilized for connection between loudspeakers and amplifiers, or between loudspeakers, shall not be compatible with nonlocking 15- or 20-ampere rated connectors intended for branch-circuit power or with connectors rated 250 volts or greater and of either the locking or nonlocking type. Signal cabling not intended for such loudspeaker and amplifier interconnection shall not be permitted to be compatible with multipole branch-circuit cable connectors of any accepted configuration.

FPN: See 400.10 for pull at terminals.

640.42 Use of Flexible Cords and Cables.

(A) Between Equipment and Branch-Circuit Power. Power supply cords for audio equipment shall be listed and shall be permitted to be used where the interchange, maintenance, or repair of such equipment is facilitated through the use of a power supply cord.

(B) Between Loudspeakers and Amplifiers, or Between Loudspeakers. Flexible cords and cables used to connect loudspeakers to each other or to an amplifier shall comply with Article 400 and Article 725, respectively. Cords and cables listed for portable use, either hard or extra-hard usage as defined by Article 400, shall also be permitted. Other listed cable types and assemblies, including optional hybrid communications, signal, and optical fiber cables, shall be permitted.

(C) Between Equipment and/or Between Equipment Racks. Flexible cords and cables used for the distribution of audio signals between equipment shall comply with Article 400 and Article 725, respectively. Cords and cables listed for portable use, either hard or extra-hard service as defined by Article 400, shall also be permitted. Other listed cable types and assemblies, including optional hybrid communications, signal, and optical fiber cables, shall be permitted.

(D) Between Equipment, Equipment Racks, and Power Supplies Other Than Branch-Circuit Power. Wiring between the following power supplies, other than branch-circuit power supplies, shall be installed, connected, or wired in accordance with the requirements of this *Code* for the voltage and power required:

(1) Storage batteries
(2) Transformers
(3) Transformer rectifiers
(4) Other ac or dc power supplies

(E) Between Equipment Racks and Branch-Circuit Power. The supply to a portable equipment rack shall be by means of listed extra-hard usage cords or cables, as defined in Table 400.4. For outdoor portable or temporary use, the cords or cables shall be further listed as being suitable for wet locations and sunlight resistant. Sections 520.5, 520.10, and 525.3 shall apply as appropriate when the following conditions exist:

(1) Where equipment racks include audio and lighting and/or power equipment
(2) When using or constructing cable extensions, adapters, and breakout assemblies

640.43 Wiring of Equipment Racks.
Equipment racks fabricated of metal shall be grounded. Nonmetallic racks with covers (if provided) removed shall not allow access to Class 1, Class 3, or primary circuit power without the removal of covers over terminals or the use of tools.

Equipment racks shall be wired in a neat and workmanlike manner. Wires, cables, structural components, or other equipment shall not be placed in such a manner as to prevent reasonable access to equipment power switches and resettable or replaceable circuit overcurrent protection devices.

Wiring that exits the equipment rack for connection to other equipment or to a power supply shall be relieved of strain or otherwise suitably terminated such that a pull on the flexible cord or cable shall not increase the risk of damage to the cable or connected equipment such as to cause an unreasonable risk of fire or electric shock.

640.44 Environmental Protection of Equipment.
Portable equipment not listed for outdoor use shall be permitted only where appropriate protection of such equipment from adverse weather conditions is provided to prevent risk of fire or electrical shock. Where the system is intended to remain operable during adverse weather, arrangements shall be made for maintaining operation and ventilation of heat-dissipating equipment.

640.45 Protection of Wiring.
Where accessible to the public, flexible cords and cables laid or run on the ground or on the floor shall be covered with approved nonconductive mats. Cables and mats shall be arranged so as not to present a tripping hazard.

640.46 Equipment Access.
Equipment likely to present a risk of fire, electrical shock, or physical injury to the public shall be protected by barriers or supervised by qualified personnel so as to prevent public access.

ARTICLE 645
Information Technology Equipment

645.1 Scope. This article covers equipment, power-supply wiring, equipment interconnecting wiring, and grounding of information technology equipment and systems, including terminal units, in an information technology equipment room.

FPN: For further information, see NFPA 75-2003, *Standard for the Protection of Information Technology Equipment.*

645.4 Special Requirements for Information Technology Equipment Room. This article shall apply, provided all of the following conditions are met:

(1) Disconnecting means complying with 645.10 are provided.

(2) A separate heating/ventilating/air-conditioning (HVAC) system is provided that is dedicated for information technology equipment use and is separated from other areas of occupancy. Any HVAC system that serves other occupancies shall be permitted to also serve the information technology equipment room if fire/smoke dampers are provided at the point of penetration of the room boundary. Such dampers shall operate on activation of smoke detectors and also by operation of the disconnecting means required by 645.10.

FPN: For further information, see NFPA 75-2003, *Standard for the Protection of Information Technology Equipment*, Chapter 10, 10.1, 10.1.1, 10.1.2, and 10.1.3.

(3) Listed information technology equipment is installed.

(4) The room is occupied only by those personnel needed for the maintenance and functional operation of the installed information technology equipment.

(5) The room is separated from other occupancies by fire-resistant-rated walls, floors, and ceilings with protected openings.

FPN: For further information on room construction requirements, see NFPA 75-2003, *Standard for the Protection of Information Technology Equipment*, Chapter 5.

645.5 Supply Circuits and Interconnecting Cables.

(A) Branch-Circuit Conductors. The branch-circuit conductors supplying one or more units of a data processing system shall have an ampacity not less than 125 percent of the total connected load.

(B) Cord-and-Plug Connections. The data processing system shall be permitted to be connected to a branch circuit by any of the following listed means:

(1) Flexible cord and attachment plug cap not to exceed 4.5 m (15 ft).

(2) Cord set assembly. Where run on the surface of the floor, they shall be protected against physical damage.

(C) Interconnecting Cables. Separate data processing units shall be permitted to be interconnected by means of listed cables and cable assemblies. Where exposed to physical damage, the installation shall be protected by approved means.

(D) Under Raised Floors. Power cables, communications cables, connecting cables, interconnecting cables, and receptacles associated with the information technology equipment shall be permitted under a raised floor, provided the following conditions are met:

(1) The raised floor is of suitable construction, and the area under the floor is accessible.

(2) The branch-circuit supply conductors to receptacles or field-wired equipment are in rigid metal conduit, rigid nonmetallic conduit, intermediate metal conduit, electrical metallic tubing, electrical nonmetallic tubing, metal wireway, nonmetallic wireway, surface metal raceway with metal cover, nonmetallic surface raceway, flexible metal conduit, liquidtight flexible metal conduit, or liquidtight flexible nonmetallic conduit, Type MI cable, Type MC cable, or Type AC cable. These supply conductors shall be installed in accordance with the requirements of 300.11.

(3) Ventilation in the underfloor area is used for the information technology equipment room only, except as provided in 645.4(2). The ventilation system shall be so arranged, with approved smoke detection devices, that upon the detection of fire or products of combustion in the underfloor space the circulation of air will cease.

(4) Openings in raised floors for cables protect cables against abrasions and minimize the entrance of debris beneath the floor.

(5) Cables, other than those covered in (D)(2) and those complying with (D)(5)(a), (D)(5)(b), or (D)(5)(c), shall be listed as Type DP cable having adequate fire-resistant characteristics suitable for use under raised floors of an information technology equipment room.

  a. Interconnecting cables enclosed in a raceway.

  b. Interconnecting cables listed with equipment manufactured prior to July 1, 1994, being installed with that equipment.

  c. Cable type designations Type TC (Article 336); Types CL2, CL3, and PLTC (Article 725); Type ITC (Article 727); Types NPLF and FPL (Article 760); Types OFC and OFN (Article 770); Type CM (Article 800); and Type CATV (Article 820). These designations shall be permitted to have an additional letter P or R or G. Green, or green with one or more yellow stripes, insulated single conductor cables, 4 AWG and larger, marked "for use in cable trays" or "for CT use" shall be permitted for equipment grounding.

FPN: One method of defining fire resistance is by establishing that the cables do not spread fire to the top of the tray in the "Vertical Tray Flame Test" referenced in ANSI/UL 1581-2001, *Standard for Electrical Wires, Cables, and Flexible Cords.* Another method of defining fire resistance is for the damage (char length) not to exceed 1.5 m (4 ft 11 in.) when performing the CSA "Vertical Flame Test — Cables in Cable Trays," as described in CSA C22.2 No. 0.3-M-2001, *Test Methods for Electrical Wires and Cables.*

(6) Abandoned cables shall be removed unless contained in metal raceways.

(E) Securing in Place. Power cables; communications cables; connecting cables; interconnecting cables; and associated boxes, connectors, plugs, and receptacles that are listed as part of, or for, information technology equipment shall not be required to be secured in place.

645.6 Cables Not in Information Technology Equipment Room. Cables extending beyond the information technology equipment room shall be subject to the applicable requirements of this *Code.*

FPN: For signaling circuits, refer to Article 725; for fiber optic circuits, refer to Article 770; and for communications circuits, refer to Article 800. For fire alarm systems, refer to Article 760.

645.7 Penetrations. Penetrations of the fire-resistant room boundary shall be in accordance with 300.21.

645.10 Disconnecting Means. A means shall be provided to disconnect power to all electronic equipment in the information technology equipment room. There shall also be a similar means to disconnect the power to all dedicated HVAC systems serving the room and cause all required fire/smoke dampers to close. The control for these disconnecting means shall be grouped and identified and shall be readily accessible at the principal exit doors. A single means to control both the electronic equipment and HVAC systems shall be permitted. Where a pushbutton is used as a means to disconnect power, pushing the button in shall disconnect the power.

Exception: Installations qualifying under the provisions of Article 685.

645.11 Uninterruptible Power Supplies (UPS). Except for installations and constructions covered in 645.11(1) or 645.11(2), UPS systems installed within the information technology equipment room, and their supply and output circuits, shall comply with 645.10. The disconnecting means shall also disconnect the battery from its load.

(1) Installations qualifying under the provisions of Article 685

(2) Power sources limited to 750 volt-amperes or less derived either from UPS equipment or from battery circuits integral to electronic equipment

645.15 Grounding. All exposed non–current-carrying metal parts of an information technology system shall be grounded in accordance with Article 250 or shall be double insulated. Power systems derived within listed information technology equipment that supply information technology systems through receptacles or cable assemblies supplied as part of this equipment shall not be considered separately derived for the purpose of applying 250.20(D). Where signal reference structures are installed, they shall be bonded to the equipment grounding system provided for the information technology equipment.

FPN No. 1: The bonding and grounding requirements in the product standards governing this listed equipment ensure that it complies with Article 250.

FPN No. 2: Where isolated grounding-type receptacles are used, see 250.146(D) and 406.2(D).

645.16 Marking. Each unit of an information technology system supplied by a branch circuit shall be provided with a manufacturer's nameplate, which shall also include the input power requirements for voltage, frequency, and maximum rated load in amperes.

645.17 Power Distribution Units. Power distribution units that are used for information technology equipment shall be permitted to have multiple panelboards within a single cabinet, provided that each panelboard has no more than 42 overcurrent devices and the power distribution unit is utilization equipment listed for information technology application.

ARTICLE 647
Sensitive Electronic Equipment

647.1 Scope. This article covers the installation and wiring of separately derived systems operating at 120 volts line-to-line and 60 volts to ground for sensitive electronic equipment.

647.3 General. Use of a separately derived 120-volt single-phase 3-wire system with 60 volts on each of two ungrounded conductors to a grounded neutral conductor shall be permitted for the purpose of reducing objectionable noise in sensitive electronic equipment locations, provided that the following conditions apply:

(1) The system is installed only in commercial or industrial occupancies.

(2) The system's use is restricted to areas under close supervision by qualified personnel.

(3) All of the requirements in 647.4 through 647.8 are met.

647.4 Wiring Methods.

(A) Panelboards and Overcurrent Protection. Use of standard single-phase panelboards and distribution equipment with a higher voltage rating shall be permitted. The system shall be clearly marked on the face of the panel or on the inside of the panel doors. Common trip two-pole circuit breakers or a combination two-pole fused disconnecting means that are identified for use at the system voltage shall be provided for both ungrounded conductors in all feeders and branch circuits. Branch circuits and feeders shall be provided with a means to simultaneously disconnect all ungrounded conductors.

(B) Junction Boxes. All junction box covers shall be clearly marked to indicate the distribution panel and the system voltage.

(C) Color Coding. All feeders and branch-circuit conductors installed under this section shall be identified as to system at all splices and terminations by color, marking, tagging, or equally effective means. The means of identification shall be posted at each branch-circuit panelboard and at the disconnecting means for the building.

(D) Voltage Drop. The voltage drop on any branch circuit shall not exceed 1.5 percent. The combined voltage drop of feeder and branch-circuit conductors shall not exceed 2.5 percent.

(1) Fixed Equipment. The voltage drop on branch circuits supplying equipment connected using wiring methods in Chapter 3 shall not exceed 1.5 percent. The combined voltage drop of feeder and branch-circuit conductors shall not exceed 2.5 percent.

(2) Cord-Connected Equipment. The voltage drop on branch circuits supplying receptacles shall not exceed 1 percent. For the purposes of making this calculation, the load connected to the receptacle outlet shall be considered to be 50 percent of the branch-circuit rating. The combined voltage drop of feeder and branch-circuit conductors shall not exceed 2.0 percent.

> FPN: The purpose of this provision is to limit voltage drop to 1.5 percent where portable cords may be used as a means of connecting equipment.

647.5 Three-Phase Systems.
Where 3-phase power is supplied, a separately derived 6-phase "wye" system with 60 volts to ground installed under this article shall be configured as three separately derived 120-volt single-phase systems having a combined total of no more than six main disconnects.

647.6 Grounding.

(A) General. The system shall be grounded as provided in 250.30 as a separately derived single-phase 3-wire system.

(B) Grounding Conductors Required. Permanently wired utilization equipment and receptacles shall be grounded by means of an equipment grounding conductor run with the circuit conductors to an equipment grounding bus prominently marked "Technical Equipment Ground" in the originating branch-circuit panelboard. The grounding bus shall be connected to the grounded conductor on the line side of the separately derived system's disconnecting means. The grounding conductor shall not be smaller than that specified in Table 250.122 and run with the feeder conductors. The technical equipment grounding bus need not be bonded to the panelboard enclosure. Other grounding methods authorized elsewhere in this *Code* shall be permitted where the impedance of the grounding return path does not exceed the impedance of equipment grounding conductors sized and installed in accordance with this article.

> FPN No. 1: See 250.122 for equipment grounding conductor sizing requirements where circuit conductors are adjusted in size to compensate for voltage drop.

> FPN No. 2: These requirements limit the impedance of the ground fault path where only 60 volts apply to a fault condition instead of the usual 120 volts.

647.7 Receptacles.

(A) General. Where receptacles are used as a means of connecting equipment, the following conditions shall be met:

(1) All 15- and 20-ampere receptacles shall be GFCI protected.

(2) All outlet strips, adapters, receptacle covers, and faceplates shall be marked with the following words or equivalent:

> WARNING — TECHNICAL POWER
> Do not connect to lighting equipment.
> For electronic equipment use only.
> 60/120 V. 1ϕac
> GFCI protected

(3) A 125-volt, single-phase, 15- or 20-ampere-rated receptacle outlet having one of its current-carrying poles connected to a grounded circuit conductor shall be located within 1.8 m (6 ft) of all permanently installed 15- or 20-ampere-rated 60/120-volt technical power-system receptacles.

(4) All 125-volt receptacles used for 60/120-volt technical power shall have a unique configuration and be identified for use with this class of system. All 125-volt, single-phase, 15- or 20-ampere-rated receptacle outlets and attachment plugs that are identified for use with grounded circuit conductors shall be permitted in machine rooms, control rooms, equipment rooms, equipment racks, and other similar locations that are restricted to use by qualified personnel.

(B) Isolated Ground Receptacles. Isolated ground receptacles shall be permitted as described in 250.146(D); however, the branch circuit equipment grounding conductor shall be terminated as required in 647.6(B).

647.8 Lighting Equipment. Lighting equipment installed under this article for the purpose of reducing electrical noise originating from lighting equipment shall meet the conditions of 647.8(A) through 647.8(C).

(A) Disconnecting Means. All luminaires (lighting fixtures) connected to separately derived systems operating at 60 volts to ground, and associated control equipment if provided, shall have a disconnecting means that simultaneously opens all ungrounded conductors. The disconnecting means shall be located within sight of the luminaire (lighting fixture) or be capable of being locked in the open position.

(B) Luminaires (Lighting Fixtures). All luminaires (lighting fixtures) shall be permanently installed and listed for connection to a separately derived system at 120 volts line-to-line and 60 volts to ground.

(C) Screw-Shell. Luminaires installed under this section shall not have an exposed lamp screw-shell.

ARTICLE 650
Pipe Organs

650.1 Scope. This article covers those electrical circuits and parts of electrically operated pipe organs that are employed for the control of the sounding apparatus and keyboards.

650.3 Other Articles. Electronic organs shall comply with the appropriate provisions of Article 640.

650.4 Source of Energy. The source of power shall be a transformer-type rectifier, the dc potential of which shall not exceed 30 volts dc.

650.5 Grounding. The rectifier shall be grounded according to the provisions in 250.112(B).

650.6 Conductors. Conductors shall comply with 650.6(A) through 650.6(D).

(A) Size. Conductors shall be not less than 28 AWG for electronic signal circuits and not less than 26 AWG for electromagnetic valve supply and the like. A main common-return conductor in the electromagnetic supply shall not be less than 14 AWG.

(B) Insulation. Conductors shall have thermoplastic or thermosetting insulation.

(C) Conductors to Be Cabled. Except for the common-return conductor and conductors inside the organ proper, the organ sections and the organ console conductors shall be cabled. The common-return conductors shall be permitted under an additional covering enclosing both cable and return conductor, or they shall be permitted as a separate conductor and shall be permitted to be in contact with the cable.

(D) Cable Covering. Each cable shall be provided with an outer covering, either overall or on each of any subassemblies of grouped conductors. Tape shall be permitted in place of a covering. Where not installed in metal raceway, the covering shall be resistant to flame spread, or the cable or each cable subassembly shall be covered with a closely wound listed fireproof tape.

> FPN: One method of determining that cable is resistant to flame spread is by testing the cable to the VW-1 (vertical-wire) flame test in the ANSI/UL 1581-1991, *Reference Standard for Electrical Wires, Cables and Flexible Cords.*

650.7 Installation of Conductors. Cables shall be securely fastened in place and shall be permitted to be attached directly to the organ structure without insulating supports. Cables shall not be placed in contact with other conductors.

650.8 Overcurrent Protection. Circuits shall be so arranged that 26 AWG and 28 AWG conductors shall be protected by an overcurrent device rated at not more than 6 amperes. Other conductor sizes shall be protected in accordance with their ampacity. A common return conductor shall not require overcurrent protection.

ARTICLE 660
X-Ray Equipment

I. General

660.1 Scope. This article covers all X-ray equipment operating at any frequency or voltage for industrial or other nonmedical or nondental use.

> FPN: See Article 517, Part V, for X-ray installations in health care facilities.

Nothing in this article shall be construed as specifying safeguards against the useful beam or stray X-ray radiation.

> FPN No. 1: Radiation safety and performance requirements of several classes of X-ray equipment are regulated under Public Law 90-602 and are enforced by the Department of Health and Human Services.

FPN No. 2: In addition, information on radiation protection by the National Council on Radiation Protection and Measurements is published as *Reports of the National Council on Radiation Protection and Measurement*. These reports can be obtained from NCRP Publications, 7910 Woodmont Ave., Suite 1016, Bethesda, MD 20814.

660.2 Definitions.

Long-Time Rating. A rating based on an operating interval of 5 minutes or longer.

Mobile. X-ray equipment mounted on a permanent base with wheels and/or casters for moving while completely assembled.

Momentary Rating. A rating based on an operating interval that does not exceed 5 seconds.

Portable. X-ray equipment designed to be hand-carried.

Transportable. X-ray equipment that is to be installed in a vehicle or that may be readily disassembled for transport in a vehicle.

660.3 Hazardous (Classified) Locations. Unless approved for the location, X-ray and related equipment shall not be installed or operated in hazardous (classified) locations.

FPN: See Article 517, Part IV.

660.4 Connection to Supply Circuit.

(A) Fixed and Stationary Equipment. Fixed and stationary X-ray equipment shall be connected to the power supply by means of a wiring method meeting the general requirements of this *Code*. Equipment properly supplied by a branch circuit rated at not over 30 amperes shall be permitted to be supplied through a suitable attachment plug cap and hard-service cable or cord.

(B) Portable, Mobile, and Transportable Equipment. Individual branch circuits shall not be required for portable, mobile, and transportable X-ray equipment requiring a capacity of not over 60 amperes. Portable and mobile types of X-ray equipment of any capacity shall be supplied through a suitable hard-service cable or cord. Transportable X-ray equipment of any capacity shall be permitted to be connected to its power supply by suitable connections and hard-service cable or cord.

(C) Over 600 Volts, Nominal. Circuits and equipment operated at more than 600 volts, nominal, shall comply with Article 490.

660.5 Disconnecting Means. A disconnecting means of adequate capacity for at least 50 percent of the input required for the momentary rating or 100 percent of the input required for the long-time rating of the X-ray equipment, whichever is greater, shall be provided in the supply circuit.

The disconnecting means shall be operable from a location readily accessible from the X-ray control. For equipment connected to a 120-volt, nominal, branch circuit of 30 amperes or less, a grounding-type attachment plug cap and receptacle of proper rating shall be permitted to serve as a disconnecting means.

660.6 Rating of Supply Conductors and Overcurrent Protection.

(A) Branch-Circuit Conductors. The ampacity of supply branch-circuit conductors and the overcurrent protective devices shall not be less than 50 percent of the momentary rating or 100 percent of the long-time rating, whichever is greater.

(B) Feeder Conductors. The rated ampacity of conductors and overcurrent devices of a feeder for two or more branch circuits supplying X-ray units shall not be less than 100 percent of the momentary demand rating [as determined by 660.6(A)] of the two largest X-ray apparatus plus 20 percent of the momentary ratings of other X-ray apparatus.

FPN: The minimum conductor size for branch and feeder circuits is also governed by voltage regulation requirements. For a specific installation, the manufacturer usually specifies minimum distribution transformer and conductor sizes, rating of disconnect means, and overcurrent protection.

660.7 Wiring Terminals. X-ray equipment not provided with a permanently attached cord or cord set shall be provided with suitable wiring terminals or leads for the connection of power-supply conductors of the size required by the rating of the branch circuit for the equipment.

660.8 Number of Conductors in Raceway. The number of control circuit conductors installed in a raceway shall be determined in accordance with 300.17.

660.9 Minimum Size of Conductors. Size 18 AWG or 16 AWG fixture wires, as specified in 725.27, and flexible cords shall be permitted for the control and operating circuits of X-ray and auxiliary equipment where protected by not larger than 20-ampere overcurrent devices.

660.10 Equipment Installations. All equipment for new X-ray installations and all used or reconditioned X-ray equipment moved to and reinstalled at a new location shall be of an approved type.

II. Control

660.20 Fixed and Stationary Equipment.

(A) Separate Control Device. A separate control device, in addition to the disconnecting means, shall be incorporated in the X-ray control supply or in the primary circuit to the high-voltage transformer. This device shall be a part of the X-ray equipment but shall be permitted in a separate enclosure immediately adjacent to the X-ray control unit.

(B) Protective Device. A protective device, which shall be permitted to be incorporated into the separate control device, shall be provided to control the load resulting from failures in the high-voltage circuit.

660.21 Portable and Mobile Equipment. Portable and mobile equipment shall comply with 660.20, but the manually controlled device shall be located in or on the equipment.

660.23 Industrial and Commercial Laboratory Equipment.

(A) Radiographic and Fluoroscopic Types. All radiographic- and fluoroscopic-type equipment shall be effectively enclosed or shall have interlocks that de-energize the equipment automatically to prevent ready access to live current-carrying parts.

(B) Diffraction and Irradiation Types. Diffraction- and irradiation-type equipment or installations not effectively enclosed or not provided with interlocks to prevent access to live current-carrying parts during operation shall be provided with a positive means to indicate when they are energized. The indicator shall be a pilot light, readable meter deflection, or equivalent means.

660.24 Independent Control. Where more than one piece of equipment is operated from the same high-voltage circuit, each piece or each group of equipment as a unit shall be provided with a high-voltage switch or equivalent disconnecting means. This disconnecting means shall be constructed, enclosed, or located so as to avoid contact by persons with its live parts.

III. Transformers and Capacitors

660.35 General. Transformers and capacitors that are part of an X-ray equipment shall not be required to comply with Articles 450 and 460.

660.36 Capacitors. Capacitors shall be mounted within enclosures of insulating material or grounded metal.

IV. Guarding and Grounding

660.47 General.

(A) High-Voltage Parts. All high-voltage parts, including X-ray tubes, shall be mounted within grounded enclosures. Air, oil, gas, or other suitable insulating media shall be used to insulate the high voltage from the grounded enclosure. The connection from the high-voltage equipment to X-ray

tubes and other high-voltage components shall be made with high-voltage shielded cables.

(B) Low-Voltage Cables. Low-voltage cables connecting to oil-filled units that are not completely sealed, such as transformers, condensers, oil coolers, and high-voltage switches, shall have insulation of the oil-resistant type.

660.48 Grounding. Non–current-carrying metal parts of X-ray and associated equipment (controls, tables, X-ray tube supports, transformer tanks, shielded cables, X-ray tube heads, and so forth) shall be grounded in the manner specified in Article 250. Portable and mobile equipment shall be provided with an approved grounding-type attachment plug cap.

Exception: Battery-operated equipment.

ARTICLE 665
Induction and Dielectric Heating Equipment

I. General

665.1 Scope. This article covers the construction and installation of dielectric heating, induction heating, induction melting, and induction welding equipment and accessories for industrial and scientific applications. Medical or dental applications, appliances, or line frequency pipeline and vessel heating are not covered in this article.

> FPN: See Article 427, Part V, for line frequency induction heating of pipelines and vessels.

665.2 Definitions.

Converting Device. That part of the heating equipment that converts input mechanical or electrical energy to the voltage, current, and frequency suitable for the heating applicator. A converting device shall consist of equipment using mains frequency, all static multipliers, oscillator-type units using vacuum tubes, inverters using solid state devices, or motor generator equipment.

Dielectric Heating. Heating of a nominally insulating material due to its own dielectric losses when the material is placed in a varying electric field.

Heating Equipment. As used in this article, any equipment that is used for heating purposes and whose heat is generated by induction or dielectric methods.

Heating Equipment Applicator. The device used to transfer energy between the output circuit and the object or mass to be heated.

Induction Heating, Melting, and Welding. The heating, melting, or welding of a nominally conductive material due to its own I^2R losses when the material is placed in a varying electromagnetic field.

665.3 Other Articles. Unless specifically amended by this article, wiring from the source of power to the heating equipment shall comply with Chapters 1 through 4.

665.4 Hazardous (Classified) Locations. Heating equipment shall not be installed in hazardous (classified) locations as defined in Article 500 unless the equipment and wiring are designed and approved for the hazardous (classified) locations.

665.5 Output Circuit. The output circuit shall include all output components external to the converting device, including contactors, switches, bus bars, and other conductors. The current flow from the output circuit to ground under operating and ground-fault conditions shall be limited to a value that does not cause 50 volts or more to ground to appear on any accessible part of the heating equipment and its load. The output circuit shall be permitted to be isolated from ground.

665.7 Remote Control.

(A) Multiple Control Points. Where multiple control points are used for applicator energization, a means shall be provided and interlocked so that the applicator can be energized from only one control point at a time. A means for de-energizing the applicator shall be provided at each control point.

(B) Foot Switches. Switches operated by foot pressure shall be provided with a shield over the contact button to avoid accidental closing of a foot switch.

665.10 Ampacity of Supply Conductors. The ampacity of supply conductors shall be determined by 665.10(A) or 665.10(B).

(A) Nameplate Rating. The ampacity of conductors supplying one or more pieces of equipment shall not be less than the sum of the nameplate ratings for the largest group of machines capable of simultaneous operation, plus 100 percent of the standby currents of the remaining machines. Where standby currents are not given on the nameplate, the nameplate rating shall be used as the standby current.

(B) Motor-Generator Equipment. The ampacity of supply conductors for motor generator equipment shall be determined in accordance with Article 430, Part II.

665.11 Overcurrent Protection. Overcurrent protection for the heating equipment shall be provided as specified in Article 240. This overcurrent protection shall be permitted to be provided separately or as a part of the equipment.

665.12 Disconnecting Means. A readily accessible disconnecting means shall be provided to disconnect each heating equipment from its supply circuit. The disconnecting means shall be located within sight from the controller or be capable of being locked in the open position. The rating of this disconnecting means shall not be less than the nameplate rating of the heating equipment. Motor-generator equipment shall comply with Article 430, Part IX. The supply circuit disconnecting means shall be permitted to serve as the heating equipment disconnecting means where only one heating equipment is supplied.

II. Guarding, Grounding, and Labeling

665.19 Component Interconnection. The interconnection components required for a complete heating equipment installation shall be guarded.

665.20 Enclosures. The converting device (excluding the component interconnections) shall be completely contained within an enclosure(s) of noncombustible material.

665.21 Control Panels. All control panels shall be of dead-front construction.

665.22 Access to Internal Equipment. Access doors or detachable access panels shall be employed for internal access to heating equipment. Access doors to internal compartments containing equipment employing voltages from 150 volts to 1000 volts ac or dc shall be capable of being locked closed or shall be interlocked to prevent the supply circuit from being energized while the door(s) is open. Access doors to internal compartments containing equipment employing voltages exceeding 1000 volts ac or dc shall be provided with a disconnecting means equipped with mechanical lockouts to prevent access while the heating equipment is energized, or the access doors shall be capable of being locked closed and interlocked to prevent the supply circuit from being energized while the door(s) is open. Detachable panels not normally used for access to such parts shall be fastened in a manner that makes them inconvenient to remove.

665.23 Warning Labels or Signs. Warning labels or signs that read "DANGER — HIGH VOLTAGE — KEEP OUT" shall be attached to the equipment and shall be plainly visible where persons might come in contact with energized parts when doors are open or closed or when panels are removed from compartments containing over 150 volts ac or dc.

665.24 Capacitors. The time and means of discharge shall be in accordance with 460.6 for capacitors rated 600 volts, nominal, and under. The time and means of discharge shall be in accordance with 460.28 for capacitors rated over 600 volts, nominal. Capacitor internal pressure switches connected to a circuit-interrupter device shall be permitted for capacitor overcurrent protection.

665.25 Dielectric Heating Applicator Shielding. Protective cages or adequate shielding shall be used to guard dielectric heating applicators. Interlock switches shall be used on all hinged access doors, sliding panels, or other easy means of access to the applicator. All interlock switches shall be connected in such a manner as to remove all power from the applicator when any one of the access doors or panels is open.

665.26 Grounding and Bonding. Grounding or inter-unit bonding, or both, shall be used wherever required for circuit operation, for limiting to a safe value radio frequency voltages between all exposed non–current-carrying parts of the equipment and earth ground, between all equipment parts and surrounding objects, and between such objects and earth ground. Such grounding and bonding shall be installed in accordance with Article 250, Parts II and V.

> FPN:　Under certain conditions, contact between the object being heated and the applicator results in an unsafe condition, such as eruption of heated materials. This unsafe condition may be prevented by grounding of the object being heated and ground detection.

665.27 Marking. Each heating equipment shall be provided with a nameplate giving the manufacturer's name and model identification and the following input data: line volts, frequency, number of phases, maximum current, full-load kilovolt-amperes (kVA), and full-load power factor. Additional data shall be permitted.

ARTICLE 668
Electrolytic Cells

668.1 Scope. The provisions of this article apply to the installation of the electrical components and accessory equipment of electrolytic cells, electrolytic cell lines, and process power supply for the production of aluminum, cadmium, chlorine, copper, fluorine, hydrogen peroxide, magnesium, sodium, sodium chlorate, and zinc.

Not covered by this article are cells used as a source of electric energy and for electroplating processes and cells used for the production of hydrogen.

> FPN No. 1:　In general, any cell line or group of cell lines operated as a unit for the production of a particular metal, gas, or chemical compound may differ from any other cell lines producing the same product because of variations in the particular raw materials used, output capacity, use of proprietary methods or process practices, or other modifying factors to the extent that detailed *Code* requirements become overly restrictive and do not accomplish the stated purpose of this *Code*.

> FPN No. 2:　For further information, see IEEE 463-1993, *Standard for Electrical Safety Practices in Electrolytic Cell Line Working Zones.*

668.2 Definitions.

Cell Line. An assembly of electrically interconnected electrolytic cells supplied by a source of direct-current power.

Cell Line Attachments and Auxiliary Equipment. As applied to this article, a term that includes, but is not limited to, auxiliary tanks; process piping; ductwork; structural supports; exposed cell line conductors; conduits and other raceways; pumps, positioning equipment, and cell cutout or bypass electrical devices. Auxiliary equipment includes tools, welding machines, crucibles, and other portable equipment used for operation and maintenance within the electrolytic cell line working zone.

In the cell line working zone, auxiliary equipment includes the exposed conductive surfaces of ungrounded cranes and crane-mounted cell-servicing equipment.

Electrically Connected. A connection capable of carrying current as distinguished from connection through electromagnetic induction.

Electrolytic Cell. A tank or vat in which electrochemical reactions are caused by applying electrical energy for the purpose of refining or producing usable materials.

Electrolytic Cell Line Working Zone. The space envelope wherein operation or maintenance is normally performed on or in the vicinity of exposed energized surfaces of electrolytic cell lines or their attachments.

668.3 Other Articles.

(A) Lighting, Ventilating, Material Handling. Chapters 1 through 4 shall apply to services, feeders, branch circuits, and apparatus for supplying lighting, ventilating, material handling, and the like that are outside the electrolytic cell line working zone.

(B) Systems Not Electrically Connected. Those elements of a cell line power-supply system that are not electrically connected to the cell supply system, such as the primary winding of a two-winding transformer, the motor of a motor-generator set, feeders, branch circuits, disconnecting means, motor controllers, and overload protective equipment, shall be required to comply with all applicable provisions of this *Code*.

(C) Electrolytic Cell Lines. Electrolytic cell lines shall comply with the provisions of Chapters 1, 2, 3, and 4 except as amended in 668.3(C)(1), (C)(2), (C)(3), or (C)(4).

(1) Conductors. The electrolytic cell line conductors shall not be required to comply with the provisions of Articles 110, 210, 215, 220, and 225. See 668.11.

(2) Overcurrent Protection. Overcurrent protection of electrolytic cell dc process power circuits shall not be required to comply with the requirements of Article 240.

(3) Grounding. Equipment located or used within the electrolytic cell line working zone or associated with the cell line dc power circuits shall not be required to comply with the provisions of Article 250.

(4) Working Zone. The electrolytic cells, cell line attachments, and the wiring of auxiliary equipment and devices within the cell line working zone shall not be required to comply with the provisions of Articles 110, 210, 215, 220, and 225. See 668.30.

FPN: See 668.15 for equipment, apparatus, and structural component grounding.

668.10 Cell Line Working Zone.

(A) Area Covered. The space envelope of the cell line working zone shall encompass spaces that meet any of the following conditions:

(1) Is within 2.5 m (96 in.) above energized surfaces of electrolytic cell lines or their energized attachments

(2) Is below energized surfaces of electrolytic cell lines or their energized attachments, provided the headroom in the space beneath is less than 2.5 m (96 in.)

(3) Is within 1.0 m (42 in.) horizontally from energized surfaces of electrolytic cell lines or their energized attachments or from the space envelope described in 668.10(A)(1) or (A)(2)

(B) Area Not Covered. The cell line working zone shall not be required to extend through or beyond walls, floors, roofs, partitions, barriers, or the like.

668.11 Direct-Current Cell Line Process Power Supply.

(A) Not Grounded. The dc cell line process power-supply conductors shall not be required to be grounded.

(B) Metal Enclosures Grounded. All metal enclosures of dc cell line process power-supply apparatus operating at a power-supply potential between terminals of over 50 volts shall be grounded by either of the following means:

(1) Through protective relaying equipment

(2) By a minimum 2/0 AWG copper grounding conductor or a conductor of equal or greater conductance

(C) Grounding Requirements. The grounding connections required by 668.11(B) shall be installed in accordance with 250.8, 250.10, 250.12, 250.68, and 250.70.

668.12 Cell Line Conductors.

(A) Insulation and Material. Cell line conductors shall be either bare, covered, or insulated and of copper, aluminum, copper-clad aluminum, steel, or other suitable material.

(B) Size. Cell line conductors shall be of such cross-sectional area that the temperature rise under maximum load conditions

and at maximum ambient shall not exceed the safe operating temperature of the conductor insulation or the material of the conductor supports.

(C) Connections. Cell line conductors shall be joined by bolted, welded, clamped, or compression connectors.

668.13 Disconnecting Means.

(A) More Than One Process Power Supply. Where more than one dc cell line process power supply serves the same cell line, a disconnecting means shall be provided on the cell line circuit side of each power supply to disconnect it from the cell line circuit.

(B) Removable Links or Conductors. Removable links or removable conductors shall be permitted to be used as the disconnecting means.

668.14 Shunting Means.

(A) Partial or Total Shunting. Partial or total shunting of cell line circuit current around one or more cells shall be permitted.

(B) Shunting One or More Cells. The conductors, switches, or combination of conductors and switches used for shunting one or more cells shall comply with the applicable requirements of 668.12.

668.15 Grounding. For equipment, apparatus, and structural components that are required to be grounded by provisions of Article 668, the provisions of Article 250 shall apply, except a water pipe electrode shall not be required to be used. Any electrode or combination of electrodes described in 250.52 shall be permitted.

668.20 Portable Electrical Equipment.

(A) Portable Electrical Equipment Not to Be Grounded. The frames and enclosures of portable electrical equipment used within the cell line working zone shall not be grounded.

Exception No. 1: Where the cell line voltage does not exceed 200 volts dc, these frames and enclosures shall be permitted to be grounded.

Exception No. 2: These frames and enclosures shall be permitted to be grounded where guarded.

(B) Isolating Transformers. Electrically powered, hand-held, cord-connected portable equipment with ungrounded frames or enclosures used within the cell line working zone shall be connected to receptacle circuits that have only ungrounded conductors such as a branch circuit supplied by an isolating transformer with an ungrounded secondary.

(C) Marking. Ungrounded portable electrical equipment shall be distinctively marked and shall employ plugs and receptacles of a configuration that prevents connection of this equipment to grounding receptacles and that prevents inadvertent interchange of ungrounded and grounded portable electrical equipments.

668.21 Power Supply Circuits and Receptacles for Portable Electrical Equipment.

(A) Isolated Circuits. Circuits supplying power to ungrounded receptacles for hand-held, cord-connected equipments shall be electrically isolated from any distribution system supplying areas other than the cell line working zone and shall be ungrounded. Power for these circuits shall be supplied through isolating transformers. Primaries of such transformers shall operate at not more than 600 volts between conductors and shall be provided with proper overcurrent protection. The secondary voltage of such transformers shall not exceed 300 volts between conductors, and all circuits supplied from such secondaries shall be ungrounded and shall have an approved overcurrent device of proper rating in each conductor.

(B) Noninterchangeability. Receptacles and their mating plugs for ungrounded equipment shall not have provision for a grounding conductor and shall be of a configuration that prevents their use for equipment required to be grounded.

(C) Marking. Receptacles on circuits supplied by an isolating transformer with an ungrounded secondary shall be a distinctive configuration, distinctively marked, and shall not be used in any other location in the plant.

668.30 Fixed and Portable Electrical Equipment.

(A) Electrical Equipment Not Required to Be Grounded. Alternating-current systems supplying fixed and portable electrical equipment within the cell line working zone shall not be required to be grounded.

(B) Exposed Conductive Surfaces Not Required to Be Grounded. Exposed conductive surfaces, such as electrical equipment housings, cabinets, boxes, motors, raceways, and the like, that are within the cell line working zone shall not be required to be grounded.

(C) Wiring Methods. Auxiliary electrical equipment such as motors, transducers, sensors, control devices, and alarms, mounted on an electrolytic cell or other energized surface, shall be connected to premises wiring systems by any of the following means:

(1) Multiconductor hard usage cord.
(2) Wire or cable in suitable raceways or metal or nonmetallic cable trays. If metal conduit, cable tray, armored cable, or similar metallic systems are used, they shall be installed with insulating breaks such that they do not cause a potentially hazardous electrical condition.

(D) Circuit Protection. Circuit protection shall not be required for control and instrumentation that are totally within the cell line working zone.

(E) Bonding. Bonding of fixed electrical equipment to the energized conductive surfaces of the cell line, its attachments, or auxiliaries shall be permitted. Where fixed electrical equipment is mounted on an energized conductive surface, it shall be bonded to that surface.

668.31 Auxiliary Nonelectric Connections. Auxiliary nonelectric connections, such as air hoses, water hoses, and the like, to an electrolytic cell, its attachments, or auxiliary equipments shall not have continuous conductive reinforcing wire, armor, braids, and the like. Hoses shall be of a nonconductive material.

668.32 Cranes and Hoists.

(A) Conductive Surfaces to Be Insulated from Ground. The conductive surfaces of cranes and hoists that enter the cell line working zone shall not be required to be grounded. The portion of an overhead crane or hoist that contacts an energized electrolytic cell or energized attachments shall be insulated from ground.

(B) Hazardous Electrical Conditions. Remote crane or hoist controls that could introduce hazardous electrical conditions into the cell line working zone shall employ one or more of the following systems:

(1) Isolated and ungrounded control circuit in accordance with 668.21(A)
(2) Nonconductive rope operator
(3) Pendant pushbutton with nonconductive supporting means and having nonconductive surfaces or ungrounded exposed conductive surfaces
(4) Radio

668.40 Enclosures. General-purpose electrical equipment enclosures shall be permitted where a natural draft ventilation system prevents the accumulation of gases.

ARTICLE 669
Electroplating

669.1 Scope. The provisions of this article apply to the installation of the electrical components and accessory equipment that supply the power and controls for electroplating, anodizing, electropolishing, and electrostripping. For purposes of this article, the term *electroplating* shall be used to identify any or all of these processes.

669.3 General. Equipment for use in electroplating processes shall be identified for such service.

669.5 Branch-Circuit Conductors. Branch-circuit conductors supplying one or more units of equipment shall have an ampacity of not less than 125 percent of the total connected load. The ampacities for busbars shall be in accordance with 366.10.

669.6 Wiring Methods. Conductors connecting the electrolyte tank equipment to the conversion equipment shall be in accordance with 669.6(A) and 669.6(B).

(A) Systems Not Exceeding 50 Volts Direct Current. Insulated conductors shall be permitted to be run without insulated support, provided they are protected from physical damage. Bare copper or aluminum conductors shall be permitted where supported on insulators.

(B) Systems Exceeding 50 Volts Direct Current. Insulated conductors shall be permitted to be run on insulated supports, provided they are protected from physical damage. Bare copper or aluminum conductors shall be permitted where supported on insulators and guarded against accidental contact up to the point of termination in accordance with 110.27.

669.7 Warning Signs. Warning signs shall be posted to indicate the presence of bare conductors.

669.8 Disconnecting Means.

(A) More Than One Power Supply. Where more than one power supply serves the same dc system, a disconnecting means shall be provided on the dc side of each power supply.

(B) Removable Links or Conductors. Removable links or removable conductors shall be permitted to be used as the disconnecting means.

669.9 Overcurrent Protection. Direct-current conductors shall be protected from overcurrent by one or more of the following:

(1) Fuses or circuit breakers

(2) A current-sensing device that operates a disconnecting means

(3) Other approved means

ARTICLE 670
Industrial Machinery

670.1 Scope. This article covers the definition of, the nameplate data for, and the size and overcurrent protection of supply conductors to industrial machinery.

FPN: For information on the workspace requirements for equipment containing supply conductor terminals, see 110.26. For information on the workspace requirements for machine power and control equipment, see NFPA 79–2002, *Electrical Standard for Industrial Machinery.*

670.2 Definitions.

Industrial Machinery (Machine). A power-driven machine (or a group of machines working together in a coordinated manner), not portable by hand while working, that is used to process material by cutting; forming; pressure; electrical, thermal, or optical techniques; lamination; or a combination of these processes. It can include associated equipment used to transfer material or tooling, including fixtures, to assemble/disassemble, to inspect or test, or to package. [The associated electrical equipment, including the logic controller(s) and associated software or logic together with the machine actuators and sensors, are considered as part of the industrial machine.]

Industrial Manufacturing System. A systematic array of one or more industrial machines that is not portable by hand and includes any associated material handling, manipulating, gauging, measuring, or inspection equipment.

670.3 Machine Nameplate Data.

(A) Permanent Nameplate. A permanent nameplate shall be attached to the control equipment enclosure or machine and shall be plainly visible after installation. The nameplate shall include the following information:

(1) Supply voltage, phase, frequency, and full-load current

(2) Maximum ampere rating of the short-circuit and ground-fault protective device

(3) Ampere rating of largest motor, from the motor nameplate, or load

(4) Short circuit current rating of the machine industrial control panel based on one of the following:

    a. Short circuit current rating of a listed and labeled machine control enclosure or assembly

    b. Short circuit current rating established utilizing an approved method

FPN: UL 508A-2001, Supplement SB, is an example of an approved method.

(5) Electrical diagram number(s) or the number of the index to the electrical drawings

The full-load current shown on the nameplate shall not be less than the sum of the full-load currents required for all motors and other equipment that may be in operation at the same time under normal conditions of use. Where unusual type loads, duty cycles, and so forth require oversized conductors or permit reduced-size conductors, the required capacity shall be included in the marked "full-load current." Where more than one incoming supply circuit is to be provided, the nameplate shall state the preceding information for each circuit.

FPN: See 430.22(E) and 430.26 for duty cycle requirements.

(B) Overcurrent Protection. Where overcurrent protection is provided in accordance with 670.4(B), the machine shall be marked "overcurrent protection provided at machine supply terminals."

670.4 Supply Conductors and Overcurrent Protection.

(A) Size. The size of the supply conductor shall be such as to have an ampacity not less than 125 percent of the full-load current rating of all resistance heating loads plus 125 percent of the full-load current rating of the highest rated motor plus the sum of the full-load current ratings of all other connected motors and apparatus based on their duty cycle that may be in operation at the same time.

> FPN No. 1: See the 0–2000-volt ampacity tables of Article 310 for ampacity of conductors rated 600 volts and below.

> FPN No. 2: See 430.22(E) and 430.26 for duty cycle requirements.

(B) Disconnecting Means. A machine shall be considered as an individual unit and therefore shall be provided with disconnecting means. The disconnecting means shall be permitted to be supplied by branch circuits protected by either fuses or circuit breakers. The disconnecting means shall not be required to incorporate overcurrent protection.

(C) Overcurrent Protection. Where furnished as part of the machine, overcurrent protection for each supply circuit shall consist of a single circuit breaker or set of fuses, the machine shall bear the marking required in 670.3 and the supply conductors shall be considered either as feeders or taps as covered by 240.21.

The rating or setting of the overcurrent protective device for the circuit supplying the machine shall not be greater than the sum of the largest rating or setting of the branch-circuit short-circuit and ground-fault protective device provided with the machine, plus 125 percent of the full-load current rating of all resistance heating loads, plus the sum of the full-load currents of all other motors and apparatus that could be in operation at the same time.

Exception: Where one or more instantaneous trip circuit breakers or motor short-circuit protectors are used for motor branch-circuit short-circuit and ground-fault protection as permitted by 430.52(C), the procedure specified above for determining the maximum rating of the protective device for the circuit supplying the machine shall apply with the following provision: For the purpose of the calculation, each instantaneous trip circuit breaker or motor short-circuit protector shall be assumed to have a rating not exceeding the maximum percentage of motor full-load current permitted by Table 430.52 for the type of machine supply circuit protective device employed.

Where no branch-circuit short-circuit and ground-fault protective device is provided with the machine, the rating or setting of the overcurrent protective device shall be based on 430.52 and 430.53, as applicable.

ARTICLE 675
Electrically Driven or Controlled Irrigation Machines

I. General

675.1 Scope. The provisions of this article apply to electrically driven or controlled irrigation machines, and to the branch circuits and controllers for such equipment.

675.2 Definitions.

Center Pivot Irrigation Machine. A multimotored irrigation machine that revolves around a central pivot and employs alignment switches or similar devices to control individual motors.

Collector Rings. An assembly of slip rings for transferring electrical energy from a stationary to a rotating member.

Irrigation Machine. An electrically driven or controlled machine, with one or more motors, not hand portable, and used primarily to transport and distribute water for agricultural purposes.

675.3 Other Articles. These provisions are in addition to, or amendatory of, the provisions of Article 430 and other articles in this *Code* that apply except as modified in this article.

675.4 Irrigation Cable.

(A) Construction. The cable used to interconnect enclosures on the structure of an irrigation machine shall be an assembly of stranded, insulated conductors with nonhygroscopic and nonwicking filler in a core of moisture- and flame-resistant nonmetallic material overlaid with a metallic covering and jacketed with a moisture-, corrosion-, and sunlight-resistant nonmetallic material.

The conductor insulation shall be of a type listed in Table 310.13 for an operating temperature of 75°C (167°F) and for use in wet locations. The core insulating material thickness shall not be less than 0.76 mm (30 mils), and the metallic overlay thickness shall not be less than 0.20 mm (8 mils). The jacketing material thickness shall not be less than 1.27 mm (50 mils).

A composite of power, control, and grounding conductors in the cable shall be permitted.

(B) Alternate Wiring Methods. Installation of other listed cables complying with the construction requirements of 675.4(A) shall be permitted.

(C) Supports. Irrigation cable shall be secured by straps, hangers, or similar fittings identified for the purpose and so installed as not to damage the cable. Cable shall be supported at intervals not exceeding 1.2 m (4 ft).

(D) Fittings. Fittings shall be used at all points where irrigation cable terminates. The fittings shall be designed for use with the cable and shall be suitable for the conditions of service.

675.5 More Than Three Conductors in a Raceway or Cable. The signal and control conductors of a raceway or cable shall not be counted for the purpose of derating the conductors as required in 310.15(B)(2)(a).

675.6 Marking on Main Control Panel. The main control panel shall be provided with a nameplate that shall give the following information:

(1) The manufacturer's name, the rated voltage, the phase, and the frequency

(2) The current rating of the machine

(3) The rating of the main disconnecting means and size of overcurrent protection required

675.7 Equivalent Current Ratings. Where intermittent duty is not involved, the provisions of Article 430 shall be used for determining ratings for controllers, disconnecting means, conductors, and the like. Where irrigation machines have inherent intermittent duty, the determinations of equivalent current ratings in 675.7(A) and 675.7(B) shall be used.

(A) Continuous-Current Rating. The equivalent continuous-current rating for the selection of branch-circuit conductors and overcurrent protection shall be equal to 125 percent of the motor nameplate full-load current rating of the largest motor, plus a quantity equal to the sum of each of the motor nameplate full-load current ratings of all remaining motors on the circuit, multiplied by the maximum percent duty cycle at which they can continuously operate.

(B) Locked-Rotor Current. The equivalent locked-rotor current rating shall be equal to the numerical sum of the locked-rotor current of the two largest motors plus 100 percent of the sum of the motor nameplate full-load current ratings of all the remaining motors on the circuit.

675.8 Disconnecting Means.

(A) Main Controller. A controller that is used to start and stop the complete machine shall meet all of the following requirements:

(1) An equivalent continuous current rating not less than specified in 675.7(A) or 675.22(A)

(2) A horsepower rating not less than the value from Table 430.251(A) and Table 430.251(B), based on the equivalent locked-rotor current specified in 675.7(B) or 675.22(B)

Exception: A listed molded case switch shall not require a horsepower rating.

(B) Main Disconnecting Means. The main disconnecting means for the machine shall provide overcurrent protection, shall be at the point of connection of electrical power to the machine or shall be visible and not more than 15 m (50 ft) from the machine, and shall be readily accessible and capable of being locked in the open position. This disconnecting means shall have a horsepower and current rating not less than required for the main controller.

Exception No. 1: Circuit breakers without marked horsepower ratings shall be permitted in accordance with 430.109.

Exception No. 2: A listed fusible molded case switch without marked horsepower ratings shall be permitted.

(C) Disconnecting Means for Individual Motors and Controllers. A disconnecting means shall be provided to simultaneously disconnect all ungrounded conductors for each motor and controller and shall be located as required by Article 430, Part IX. The disconnecting means shall not be required to be readily accessible.

675.9 Branch-Circuit Conductors. The branch-circuit conductors shall have an ampacity not less than specified in 675.7(A) or 675.22(A).

675.10 Several Motors on One Branch Circuit.

(A) Protection Required. Several motors, each not exceeding 2 hp rating, shall be permitted to be used on an irrigation machine circuit protected at not more than 30 amperes at 600 volts, nominal, or less, provided all of the following conditions are met:

(1) The full-load rating of any motor in the circuit shall not exceed 6 amperes.

(2) Each motor in the circuit shall have individual overload protection in accordance with 430.32.

(3) Taps to individual motors shall not be smaller than 14 AWG copper and not more than 7.5 m (25 ft) in length.

(B) Individual Protection Not Required. Individual branch-circuit short-circuit protection for motors and motor controllers shall not be required where the requirements of 675.10(A) are met.

675.11 Collector Rings.

(A) Transmitting Current for Power Purposes. Collector rings shall have a current rating not less than 125 percent of the full-load current of the largest device served plus the full-load current of all other devices served, or as determined from 675.7(A) or 675.22(A).

(B) Control and Signal Purposes. Collector rings for control and signal purposes shall have a current rating not less than 125 percent of the full-load current of the largest device served plus the full-load current of all other devices served.

(C) Grounding. The collector ring used for grounding shall have a current rating not less than that sized in accordance with 675.11(A).

(D) Protection. Collector rings shall be protected from the expected environment and from accidental contact by means of a suitable enclosure.

675.12 Grounding. The following equipment shall be grounded:

(1) All electrical equipment on the irrigation machine
(2) All electrical equipment associated with the irrigation machine
(3) Metal junction boxes and enclosures
(4) Control panels or control equipment that supplies or controls electrical equipment to the irrigation machine

Exception: Grounding shall not be required on machines where all of the following provisions are met:

(a) The machine is electrically controlled but not electrically driven.
(b) The control voltage is 30 volts or less.
(c) The control or signal circuits are current limited as specified in Chapter 9, Tables 11(A) and 11(B).

675.13 Methods of Grounding. Machines that require grounding shall have a non–current-carrying equipment grounding conductor provided as an integral part of each cord, cable, or raceway. This grounding conductor shall be sized not less than the largest supply conductor in each cord, cable, or raceway. Feeder circuits supplying power to irrigation machines shall have an equipment grounding conductor sized according to Table 250.122.

675.14 Bonding. Where electrical grounding is required on an irrigation machine, the metallic structure of the machine, metallic conduit, or metallic sheath of cable shall be bonded to the grounding conductor. Metal-to-metal contact with a part that is bonded to the grounding conductor and the non–current-carrying parts of the machine shall be considered as an acceptable bonding path.

675.15 Lightning Protection. If an irrigation machine has a stationary point, a grounding electrode system in accordance with Article 250, Part III, shall be connected to the machine at the stationary point for lightning protection.

675.16 Energy from More Than One Source. Equipment within an enclosure receiving electrical energy from more than one source shall not be required to have

a disconnecting means for the additional source, provided that its voltage is 30 volts or less and it meets the requirements of Part III of Article 725.

675.17 Connectors. External plugs and connectors on the equipment shall be of the weatherproof type.

Unless provided solely for the connection of circuits meeting the requirements of Part III of Article 725, external plugs and connectors shall be constructed as specified in 250.124(A).

II. Center Pivot Irrigation Machines

675.21 General. The provisions of Part II are intended to cover additional special requirements that are peculiar to center pivot irrigation machines. See 675.2 for the definition of *Center Pivot Irrigation Machine.*

675.22 Equivalent Current Ratings. To establish ratings of controllers, disconnecting means, conductors, and the like, for the inherent intermittent duty of center pivot irrigation machines, the determinations in 675.22(A) and 675.22(B) shall be used.

(A) Continuous-Current Rating. The equivalent continuous-current rating for the selection of branch-circuit conductors and branch-circuit devices shall be equal to 125 percent of the motor nameplate full-load current rating of the largest motor plus 60 percent of the sum of the motor nameplate full-load current ratings of all remaining motors on the circuit.

(B) Locked-Rotor Current. The equivalent locked-rotor current rating shall be equal to the numerical sum of two times the locked-rotor current of the largest motor plus 80 percent of the sum of the motor nameplate full-load current ratings of all the remaining motors on the circuit.

ARTICLE 680
Swimming Pools, Fountains, and Similar Installations

I. General

680.1 Scope. The provisions of this article apply to the construction and installation of electrical wiring for and equipment in or adjacent to all swimming, wading, therapeutic, and decorative pools; fountains; hot tubs; spas; and hydromassage bathtubs, whether permanently installed or storable, and to metallic auxiliary equipment, such as pumps, filters, and similar equipment. The term *body of water* used throughout Part I applies to all bodies of water covered in this scope unless otherwise amended.

680.2 Definitions.

Cord-and-Plug-Connected Lighting Assembly. A lighting assembly consisting of a luminaire (lighting fixture) intended for installation in the wall of a spa, hot tub, or storable pool, and a cord-and-plug-connected transformer.

Dry-Niche Luminaire (Lighting Fixture). A luminaire (lighting fixture) intended for installation in the wall of a pool or fountain in a niche that is sealed against the entry of pool water.

Equipment, Fixed. Equipment that is fastened or otherwise secured at a specific location.

Equipment, Portable. Equipment that is actually moved or can easily be moved from one place to another in normal use.

Equipment, Stationary. Equipment that is not easily moved from one place to another in normal use.

Forming Shell. A structure designed to support a wet-niche luminaire (lighting fixture) assembly and intended for mounting in a pool or fountain structure.

Fountain. Fountains, ornamental pools, display pools, and reflection pools. The definition does not include drinking fountains.

Hydromassage Bathtub. A permanently installed bathtub equipped with a recirculating piping system, pump, and associated equipment. It is designed so it can accept, circulate, and discharge water upon each use.

Maximum Water Level. The highest level that water can reach before it spills out.

No-Niche Luminaire (Lighting Fixture). A luminaire (lighting fixture) intended for installation above or below the water without a niche.

Packaged Spa or Hot Tub Equipment Assembly. A factory-fabricated unit consisting of water-circulating, heating, and control equipment mounted on a common base, intended to operate a spa or hot tub. Equipment can include pumps, air blowers, heaters, lights, controls, sanitizer generators, and so forth.

Packaged Therapeutic Tub or Hydrotherapeutic Tank Equipment Assembly. A factory-fabricated unit consisting of water-circulating, heating, and control equipment mounted on a common base, intended to operate a therapeutic tub or hydrotherapeutic tank. Equipment can include pumps, air blowers, heaters, lights, controls, sanitizer generators, and so forth.

Permanently Installed Decorative Fountains and Reflection Pools. Those that are constructed in the ground, on the ground, or in a building in such a manner that the fountain cannot be readily disassembled for storage, whether or not served by electrical circuits of any nature. These units are primarily constructed for their aesthetic value and are not intended for swimming or wading.

Permanently Installed Swimming, Wading, and Therapeutic Pools. Those that are constructed in the ground or partially in the ground, and all others capable of holding water in a depth greater than 1.0 m (42 in.), and all pools installed inside of a building, regardless of water depth, whether or not served by electrical circuits of any nature.

Pool. Manufactured or field-constructed equipment designed to contain water on a permanent or semipermanent basis and used for swimming, wading, or other purposes.

Pool Cover, Electrically Operated. Motor-driven equipment designed to cover and uncover the water surface of a pool by means of a flexible sheet or rigid frame.

Self-Contained Spa or Hot Tub. Factory-fabricated unit consisting of a spa or hot tub vessel with all water-circulating, heating, and control equipment integral to the unit. Equipment can include pumps, air blowers, heaters, lights, controls, sanitizer generators, and so forth.

Self-Contained Therapeutic Tubs or Hydrotherapeutic Tanks. A factory-fabricated unit consisting of a therapeutic tub or hydrotherapeutic tank with all water-circulating, heating, and control equipment integral to the unit. Equipment may include pumps, air blowers, heaters, light controls, sanitizer generators, and so forth.

Spa or Hot Tub. A hydromassage pool, or tub for recreational or therapeutic use, not located in health care facilities, designed for immersion of users, and usually having a filter, heater, and motor-driven blower. It may be installed indoors or outdoors, on the ground or supporting structure, or in the ground or supporting structure. Generally, a spa or hot tub is not designed or intended to have its contents drained or discharged after each use.

Storable Swimming or Wading Pool. Those that are constructed on or above the ground and are capable of holding water to a maximum depth of 1.0 m (42 in.), or a pool with nonmetallic, molded polymeric walls or inflatable fabric walls regardless of dimension.

Through-Wall Lighting Assembly. A lighting assembly intended for installation above grade, on or through the wall of a pool, consisting of two interconnected groups of components separated by the pool wall.

Wet-Niche Luminaire (Lighting Fixture). A luminaire (lighting fixture) intended for installation in a forming shell mounted in a pool or fountain structure where the luminaire (fixture) will be completely surrounded by water.

680.3 Other Articles. Except as modified by this article, wiring and equipment in or adjacent to pools and fountains shall comply with other applicable provisions of this *Code*, including those provisions identified in Table 680.3.

Table 680.3 Other Articles

Topic	Section or Article
Wiring	Chapters 1–4
Junction box support	314.23
Rigid nonmetallic conduit	352.12
Audio Equipment	Article 640, Parts I and II
Adjacent to pools and fountains	640.10
Underwater speakers*	

*Underwater loudspeakers shall be installed in accordance with 680.27(A).

680.4 Approval of Equipment. All electrical equipment installed in the water, walls, or decks of pools, fountains, and similar installations shall comply with the provisions of this article.

680.5 Ground-Fault Circuit Interrupters. Ground-fault circuit interrupters (GFCIs) shall be self-contained units, circuit-breaker or receptacle types, or other listed types.

680.6 Grounding. Electrical equipment shall be grounded in accordance with Parts V, VI, and VII of Article 250 and connected by wiring methods of Chapter 3, except as modified by this article. The following equipment shall be grounded:

(1) Through-wall lighting assemblies and underwater luminaires (lighting fixtures), other than those low-voltage systems listed for the application without a grounding conductor

(2) All electrical equipment located within 1.5 m (5 ft) of the inside wall of the specified body of water

(3) All electrical equipment associated with the recirculating system of the specified body of water

(4) Junction boxes

(5) Transformer enclosures

(6) Ground-fault circuit interrupters

(7) Panelboards that are not part of the service equipment and that supply any electrical equipment associated with the specified body of water

680.7 Cord-and-Plug-Connected Equipment. Fixed or stationary equipment other than an underwater luminaire (lighting fixture) for a permanently installed pool shall be permitted to be connected with a flexible cord to facilitate the removal or disconnection for maintenance or repair.

(A) Length. For other than storable pools, the flexible cord shall not exceed 900 mm (3 ft) in length.

(B) Equipment Grounding. The flexible cord shall have a copper equipment grounding conductor sized in accordance with 250.122 but not smaller than 12 AWG. The cord shall terminate in a grounding-type attachment plug.

(C) Construction. The equipment grounding conductors shall be connected to a fixed metal part of the assembly. The removable part shall be mounted on or bonded to the fixed metal part.

680.8 Overhead Conductor Clearances. Overhead conductors shall meet the clearance requirements in this section. Where a minimum clearance from the water level is given, the measurement shall be taken from the maximum water level of the specified body of water.

(A) Power. With respect to service drop conductors and open overhead wiring, swimming pool and similar installations shall comply with the minimum clearances given in Table 680.8 and illustrated in Figure 680.8.

FPN: Open overhead wiring as used in this article typically refers to conductor(s) not in an enclosed raceway.

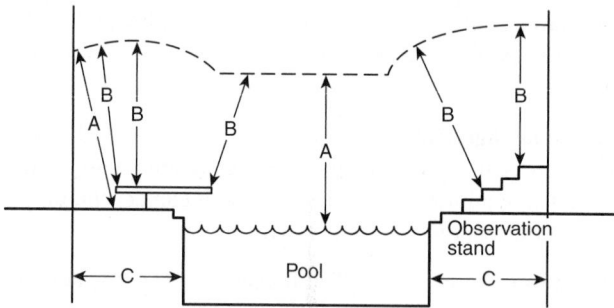

Figure 680.8 Clearances from Pool Structures.

(B) Communications Systems. Communication, radio, and television coaxial cables within the scope of Articles 800 through 820 shall be permitted at a height of not less than 3.0 m (10 ft) above swimming and wading pools, diving structures, and observation stands, towers, or platforms.

(C) Network-Powered Broadband Communications Systems. The minimum clearances for overhead network-powered broadband communications systems conductors from pools or fountains shall comply with the provisions in Table 680.8 for conductors operating at 0 to 750 volts to ground.

680.9 Electric Pool Water Heaters. All electric pool water heaters shall have the heating elements subdivided into loads not exceeding 48 amperes and protected at not over 60 amperes. The ampacity of the branch-circuit conductors and the rating or setting of overcurrent protective devices shall not be less than 125 percent of the total nameplate-rated load.

Table 680.8 Overhead Conductor Clearances

| | Clearance Parameters | Insulated Cables, 0–750 Volts to Ground, Supported on and Cabled Together with an Effectively Grounded Bare Messenger or Effectively Grounded Neutral Conductor | | All Other Conductors Voltage to Ground | | | |
| | | | | 0 through 15 kV | | Over 15 through 50 kV | |
		m	ft	m	ft	m	ft
A.	Clearance in any direction to the water level, edge of water surface, base of diving platform, or permanently anchored raft	6.9	22.5	7.5	25	8.0	27
B.	Clearance in any direction to the observation stand, tower, or diving platform	4.4	14.5	5.2	17	5.5	18
C.	Horizontal limit of clearance measured from inside wall of the pool	This limit shall extend to the outer edge of the structures listed in A and B of this table but not to less than 3 m (10 ft).					

680.10 Underground Wiring Location. Underground wiring shall not be permitted under the pool or within the area extending 1.5 m (5 ft) horizontally from the inside wall of the pool unless this wiring is necessary to supply pool equipment permitted by this article. Where space limitations prevent wiring from being routed a distance 1.5 m (5 ft) or more from the pool, such wiring shall be permitted where installed in rigid metal conduit, intermediate metal conduit, or a nonmetallic raceway system. All metal conduit shall be corrosion resistant and suitable for the location. The minimum burial depth shall be as given in Table 680.10.

Table 680.10 Minimum Burial Depths

| Wiring Method | Minimum Burial | |
	mm	in.
Rigid metal conduit	150	6
Intermediate metal conduit	150	6
Nonmetallic raceways listed for direct burial without concrete encasement	450	18
Other approved raceways*	450	18

*Raceways approved for burial only where concrete encased shall require a concrete envelope not less than 50 mm (2 in.) thick.

680.11 Equipment Rooms and Pits. Electric equipment shall not be installed in rooms or pits that do not have drainage that adequately prevents water accumulation during normal operation or filter maintenance.

680.12 Maintenance Disconnecting Means. One or more means to disconnect all ungrounded conductors shall be provided for all utilization equipment other than lighting. Each means shall be readily accessible and within sight from its equipment.

II. Permanently Installed Pools

680.20 General. Electrical installations at permanently installed pools shall comply with the provisions of Part I and Part II of this article.

680.21 Motors.

(A) Wiring Methods.

(1) General. The branch circuits for pool-associated motors shall be installed in rigid metal conduit, intermediate metal conduit, rigid nonmetallic conduit, or Type MC cable listed for the location. Other wiring methods and materials shall be permitted in specific locations or applications as covered in this section. Any wiring method employed shall contain an insulated copper equipment grounding conductor sized in accordance with 250.122 but not smaller than 12 AWG.

(2) On or Within Buildings. Where installed on or within buildings, electrical metallic tubing shall be permitted.

(3) Flexible Connections. Where necessary to employ flexible connections at or adjacent to the motor, liquidtight flexible metal or nonmetallic conduit with approved fittings shall be permitted.

(4) One-Family Dwellings. In the interior of one-family dwellings, or in the interior of accessory buildings associated with a one-family dwelling, any of the wiring methods recognized in Chapter 3 of this *Code* that comply with the provisions of this paragraph shall be permitted. Where run in a cable assembly, the equipment grounding conductor shall be permitted to be uninsulated, but it shall be enclosed within the outer sheath of the cable assembly.

(5) Cord-and-Plug Connections. Pool-associated motors shall be permitted to employ cord-and-plug connections. The flexible cord shall not exceed 900 mm (3 ft) in length. The flexible cord shall include an equipment grounding conductor sized in accordance with 250.122 and shall terminate in a grounding-type attachment plug.

(B) Double Insulated Pool Pumps. A listed cord-and-plug-connected pool pump incorporating an approved system of double insulation that provides a means for grounding only the internal and nonaccessible, non–current-carrying metal parts of the pump shall be connected to any wiring method recognized in Chapter 3 that is suitable for the location. Where the bonding grid is connected to the equipment grounding conductor of the motor circuit in accordance with the second paragraph of 680.26(B)(4), the branch circuit wiring shall comply with 680.21(A).

680.22 Area Lighting, Receptacles, and Equipment.

(A) Receptacles.

(1) Circulation and Sanitation System, Location. Receptacles that provide power for water-pump motors or for other loads directly related to the circulation and sanitation system shall be located at least 3.0 m (10 ft) from the inside walls of the pool, or not less than 1.5 m (5 ft) from the inside walls of the pool if they meet all of the following conditions:

(1) Consist of single receptacles
(2) Employ a locking configuration
(3) Are of the grounding type
(4) Have GFCI protection

(2) Other Receptacles, Location. Other receptacles shall be not less than 3.0 m (10 ft) from the inside walls of a pool.

(3) Dwelling Unit(s). Where a permanently installed pool is installed at a dwelling unit(s), no fewer than one 125-volt 15- or 20-ampere receptacle on a general-purpose branch circuit

shall be located not less than 3.0 m (10 ft) from, and not more than 6.0 m (20 ft) from, the inside wall of the pool. This receptacle shall be located not more than 2.0 m (6 ft 6 in.) above the floor, platform, or grade level serving the pool.

(4) Restricted Space. Where a pool is within 3.0 m (10 ft) of a dwelling and the dimensions of the lot preclude meeting the required clearances, not more than one receptacle outlet shall be permitted if not less than 1.5 m (5 ft) measured horizontally from the inside wall of the pool.

(5) GFCI Protection. All 15- and 20-ampere, single-phase, 125-volt receptacles located within 6.0 m (20 ft) of the inside walls of a pool shall be protected by a ground-fault circuit interrupter. Receptacles that supply pool pump motors and that are rated 15 or 20 amperes, 125 volts through 250 volts, single phase, shall be provided with GFCI protection.

(6) Measurements. In determining the dimensions in this section addressing receptacle spacings, the distance to be measured shall be the shortest path the supply cord of an appliance connected to the receptacle would follow without piercing a floor, wall, ceiling, doorway with hinged or sliding door, window opening, or other effective permanent barrier.

(B) Luminaires (Lighting Fixtures), Lighting Outlets, and Ceiling-Suspended (Paddle) Fans.

(1) New Outdoor Installation Clearances. In outdoor pool areas, luminaires (lighting fixtures), lighting outlets, and ceiling-suspended (paddle) fans installed above the pool or the area extending 1.5 m (5 ft) horizontally from the inside walls of the pool shall be installed at a height not less than 3.7 m (12 ft) above the maximum water level of the pool.

(2) Indoor Clearances. For installations in indoor pool areas, the clearances shall be the same as for outdoor areas unless modified as provided in this paragraph. If the branch circuit supplying the equipment is protected by a ground-fault circuit interrupter, the following equipment shall be permitted at a height not less than 2.3 m (7 ft 6 in.) above the maximum pool water level:

(1) Totally enclosed luminaires (fixtures)
(2) Ceiling-suspended (paddle) fans identified for use beneath ceiling structures such as provided on porches or patios

(3) Existing Installations. Existing luminaires (lighting fixtures) and lighting outlets located less than 1.5 m (5 ft) measured horizontally from the inside walls of a pool shall be not less than 1.5 m (5 ft) above the surface of the maximum water level, shall be rigidly attached to the existing structure, and shall be protected by a ground-fault circuit interrupter.

(4) GFCI Protection in Adjacent Areas. Luminaires (lighting fixtures), lighting outlets, and ceiling-suspended (paddle) fans installed in the area extending between 1.5 m (5 ft) and 3.0 m (10 ft) horizontally from the inside walls of a pool shall be protected by a ground-fault circuit interrupter unless installed not less than 1.5 m (5 ft) above the maximum water level and rigidly attached to the structure adjacent to or enclosing the pool.

(5) Cord-and-Plug-Connected Luminaires (Lighting Fixtures). Cord-and-plug-connected luminaires (lighting fixtures) shall comply with the requirements of 680.7 where installed within 4.9 m (16 ft) of any point on the water surface, measured radially.

(C) Switching Devices. Switching devices shall be located at least 1.5 m (5 ft) horizontally from the inside walls of a pool unless separated from the pool by a solid fence, wall, or other permanent barrier. Alternatively, a switch that is listed as being acceptable for use within 1.5 m (5 ft) shall be permitted.

680.23 Underwater Luminaires (Lighting Fixtures). This section covers all luminaires (lighting fixtures) installed below the normal water level of the pool.

(A) General.

(1) Luminaire (Fixture) Design, Normal Operation. The design of an underwater luminaire (lighting fixture) supplied from a branch circuit either directly or by way of a transformer meeting the requirements of this section shall be such that, where the luminaire (fixture) is properly installed without a ground-fault circuit interrupter, there is no shock hazard with any likely combination of fault conditions during normal use (not relamping).

(2) Transformers. Transformers used for the supply of underwater luminaires (fixtures), together with the transformer enclosure, shall be listed as a swimming pool and spa transformer. The transformer shall be an isolated winding type with an ungrounded secondary that has a grounded metal barrier between the primary and secondary windings.

(3) GFCI Protection, Relamping. A ground-fault circuit interrupter shall be installed in the branch circuit supplying luminaires (fixtures) operating at more than 15 volts such that there is no shock hazard during relamping. The installation of the ground-fault circuit interrupter shall be such that there is no shock hazard with any likely fault-condition combination that involves a person in a conductive path from any ungrounded part of the branch circuit or the luminaire (fixture) to ground.

(4) Voltage Limitation. No luminaires (lighting fixtures) shall be installed for operation on supply circuits over 150 volts between conductors.

(5) Location, Wall-Mounted Luminaires (Fixtures). Luminaires (lighting fixtures) mounted in walls shall be installed with the top of the luminaire (fixture) lens not less than 450 mm (18 in.) below the normal water level of the

pool, unless the luminaire (lighting fixture) is listed and identified for use at lesser depths. No luminaire (fixture) shall be installed less than 100 mm (4 in.) below the normal water level of the pool.

(6) Bottom-Mounted Luminaires (Fixtures). A luminaire (lighting fixture) facing upward shall have the lens adequately guarded to prevent contact by any person.

(7) Dependence on Submersion. Luminaires (fixtures) that depend on submersion for safe operation shall be inherently protected against the hazards of overheating when not submerged.

(8) Compliance. Compliance with these requirements shall be obtained by the use of a listed underwater luminaire (lighting fixture) and by installation of a listed ground-fault circuit interrupter in the branch circuit or a listed transformer for luminaires (fixtures) operating at not more than 15 volts.

(B) Wet-Niche Luminaires (Fixtures).

(1) Forming Shells. Forming shells shall be installed for the mounting of all wet-niche underwater luminaires (fixtures) and shall be equipped with provisions for conduit entries. Metal parts of the luminaire (fixture) and forming shell in contact with the pool water shall be of brass or other approved corrosion-resistant metal. All forming shells used with nonmetallic conduit systems, other than those that are part of a listed low-voltage lighting system not requiring grounding, shall include provisions for terminating an 8 AWG copper conductor.

(2) Wiring Extending Directly to the Forming Shell. Conduit shall be installed from the forming shell to a junction box or other enclosure conforming to the requirements in 680.24. Conduit shall be rigid metal, intermediate metal, liquidtight flexible nonmetallic, or rigid nonmetallic.

(a) Metal Conduit. Metal conduit shall be approved and shall be of brass or other approved corrosion-resistant metal.

(b) Nonmetallic Conduit. Where a nonmetallic conduit is used, an 8 AWG insulated solid or stranded copper bonding jumper shall be installed in this conduit unless a listed low-voltage lighting system not requiring grounding is used. The bonding jumper shall be terminated in the forming shell, junction box or transformer enclosure, or ground-fault circuit-interrupter enclosure. The termination of the 8 AWG bonding jumper in the forming shell shall be covered with, or encapsulated in, a listed potting compound to protect the connection from the possible deteriorating effect of pool water.

(3) Equipment Grounding Provisions for Cords. Wet-niche luminaires (lighting fixtures) that are supplied by a flexible cord or cable shall have all exposed non–current-carrying metal parts grounded by an insulated copper equipment grounding conductor that is an integral part of the cord or cable. This grounding conductor shall be connected to a grounding terminal in the supply junction box, transformer enclosure, or other enclosure. The grounding conductor shall not be smaller than the supply conductors and not smaller than 16 AWG.

(4) Luminaire (Fixture) Grounding Terminations. The end of the flexible-cord jacket and the flexible-cord conductor terminations within a luminaire (fixture) shall be covered with, or encapsulated in, a suitable potting compound to prevent the entry of water into the luminaire (fixture) through the cord or its conductors. In addition, the grounding connection within a luminaire (fixture) shall be similarly treated to protect such connection from the deteriorating effect of pool water in the event of water entry into the luminaire (fixture).

(5) Luminaire (Fixture) Bonding. The luminaire (fixture) shall be bonded to and secured to the forming shell by a positive locking device that ensures a low-resistance contact and requires a tool to remove the luminaire (fixture) from the forming shell. Bonding shall not be required for luminaires (fixtures) that are listed for the application and have no non–current-carrying metal parts.

(6) Servicing. All luminaires shall be removable from the water for relamping or normal maintenance. Luminaires shall be installed in such a manner that personnel can reach the luminaire for relamping, maintenance, or inspection while on the deck or equivalently dry location.

(C) Dry-Niche Luminaires (Fixtures).

(1) Construction. A dry-niche luminaire (lighting fixture) shall be provided with a provision for drainage of water and a means for accommodating one equipment grounding conductor for each conduit entry.

(2) Junction Box. A junction box shall not be required but, if used, shall not be required to be elevated or located as specified in 680.24(A)(2) if the luminaire (fixture) is specifically identified for the purpose.

(D) No-Niche Luminaires (Fixtures). A no-niche luminaire (fixture) shall meet the construction requirements of 680.23(B)(3) and be installed in accordance with the requirements of 680.23(B). Where connection to a forming shell is specified, the connection shall be to the mounting bracket.

(E) Through-Wall Lighting Assembly. A through-wall lighting assembly shall be equipped with a threaded entry or hub, or a nonmetallic hub, for the purpose of accommodating the termination of the supply conduit. A through-wall lighting assembly shall meet the construction requirements of 680.23(B)(3) and be installed in accordance with the requirements of 680.23. Where connection to a forming shell is specified, the connection shall be to the conduit termination point.

(F) Branch-Circuit Wiring.

(1) Wiring Methods. Branch-circuit wiring on the supply side of enclosures and junction boxes connected to conduits run to wet-niche and no-niche luminaires (fixtures), and the field wiring compartments of dry-niche luminaires (fixtures), shall be installed using rigid metal conduit, intermediate metal conduit, liquidtight flexible nonmetallic conduit, or rigid nonmetallic conduit. Where installed on buildings, electrical metallic tubing shall be permitted, and where installed within buildings, electrical nonmetallic tubing, Type MC cable, or electrical metallic tubing shall be permitted.

Exception: Where connecting to transformers for pool lights, liquidtight flexible metal conduit or liquidtight flexible nonmetallic conduit shall be permitted. The length shall not exceed 1.8 m (6 ft) for any one length or exceed 3.0 m (10 ft) in total length used. Liquidtight flexible nonmetallic conduit, Type B (LFNC-B), shall be permitted in lengths longer than 1.8 m (6 ft).

(2) Equipment Grounding. Through-wall lighting assemblies, wet-niche, dry-niche, or no-niche luminaires (lighting fixtures) shall be connected to an insulated copper equipment grounding conductor installed with the circuit conductors. The equipment grounding conductor shall be installed without joint or splice except as permitted in (F)(2)(a) and (F)(2)(b). The equipment grounding conductor shall be sized in accordance with Table 250.122 but shall not be smaller than 12 AWG.

Exception: An equipment grounding conductor between the wiring chamber of the secondary winding of a transformer and a junction box shall be sized in accordance with the overcurrent device in this circuit.

    (a) If more than one underwater luminaire (lighting fixture) is supplied by the same branch circuit, the equipment grounding conductor, installed between the junction boxes, transformer enclosures, or other enclosures in the supply circuit to wet-niche luminaires (fixtures), or between the field-wiring compartments of dry-niche luminaires (fixtures), shall be permitted to be terminated on grounding terminals.

    (b) If the underwater luminaire (lighting fixture) is supplied from a transformer, ground-fault circuit interrupter, clock-operated switch, or a manual snap switch that is located between the panelboard and a junction box connected to the conduit that extends directly to the underwater luminaire (lighting fixture), the equipment grounding conductor shall be permitted to terminate on grounding terminals on the transformer, ground-fault circuit interrupter, clock-operated switch enclosure, or an outlet box used to enclose a snap switch.

(3) Conductors. Conductors on the load side of a ground-fault circuit interrupter or of a transformer, used to comply with the provisions of 680.23(A)(8), shall not occupy raceways, boxes, or enclosures containing other conductors unless one of the following conditions applies:

(1) The other conductors are protected by ground-fault circuit interrupters.

(2) The other conductors are grounding conductors.

(3) The other conductors are supply conductors to a feed-through type ground-fault circuit interrupter.

(4) Ground-fault circuit interrupters shall be permitted in a panelboard that contains circuits protected by other than ground-fault circuit interrupters.

680.24 Junction Boxes and Enclosures for Transformers or Ground-Fault Circuit Interrupters.

(A) Junction Boxes. A junction box connected to a conduit that extends directly to a forming shell or mounting bracket of a no-niche luminaire (fixture) shall meet the requirements of this section.

(1) Construction. The junction box shall be listed as a swimming pool junction box and shall comply with the following conditions:

(1) Be equipped with threaded entries or hubs or a nonmetallic hub

(2) Be comprised of copper, brass, suitable plastic, or other approved corrosion-resistant material

(3) Be provided with electrical continuity between every connected metal conduit and the grounding terminals by means of copper, brass, or other approved corrosion-resistant metal that is integral with the box

(2) Installation. Where the luminaire (fixture) operates over 15 volts, the junction box location shall comply with (A)(2)(a) and (A)(2)(b). Where the luminaire (fixture) operates at less than 15 volts, the junction box location shall be permitted to comply with (A)(2)(c).

(a) Vertical Spacing. The junction box shall be located not less than 100 mm (4 in.), measured from the inside of the bottom of the box, above the ground level, or pool deck, or not less than 200 mm (8 in.) above the maximum pool water level, whichever provides the greater elevation.

(b) Horizontal Spacing. The junction box shall be located not less than 1.2 m (4 ft) from the inside wall of the pool, unless separated from the pool by a solid fence, wall, or other permanent barrier.

(c) Flush Deck Box. If used on a lighting system operating at 15 volts or less, a flush deck box shall be permitted if both of the following apply:

(1) An approved potting compound is used to fill the box to prevent the entrance of moisture.

(2) The flush deck box is located not less than 1.2 m (4 ft) from the inside wall of the pool.

(B) Other Enclosures. An enclosure for a transformer, ground-fault circuit interrupter, or a similar device connected to a conduit that extends directly to a forming shell or mounting bracket of a no-niche luminaire (fixture) shall meet the requirements of this section.

(1) Construction. The enclosure shall be listed and labeled for the purpose and meet the following requirements:

(1) Equipped with threaded entries or hubs or a nonmetallic hub

(2) Comprised of copper, brass, suitable plastic, or other approved corrosion-resistant material

(3) Provided with an approved seal, such as duct seal at the conduit connection, that prevents circulation of air between the conduit and the enclosures

(4) Provided with electrical continuity between every connected metal conduit and the grounding terminals by means of copper, brass, or other approved corrosion-resistant metal that is integral with the box

(2) Installation.

(a) Vertical Spacing. The enclosure shall be located not less than 100 mm (4 in.), measured from the inside of the bottom of the box, above the ground level, or pool deck, or not less than 200 mm (8 in.) above the maximum pool water level, whichever provides the greater elevation.

(b) Horizontal Spacing. The enclosure shall be located not less than 1.2 m (4 ft) from the inside wall of the pool, unless separated from the pool by a solid fence, wall, or other permanent barrier.

(C) Protection. Junction boxes and enclosures mounted above the grade of the finished walkway around the pool shall not be located in the walkway unless afforded additional protection, such as by location under diving boards, adjacent to fixed structures, and the like.

(D) Grounding Terminals. Junction boxes, transformer enclosures, and ground-fault circuit-interrupter enclosures connected to a conduit that extends directly to a forming shell or mounting bracket of a no-niche luminaire (fixture) shall be provided with a number of grounding terminals that shall be no fewer than one more than the number of conduit entries.

(E) Strain Relief. The termination of a flexible cord of an underwater luminaire (lighting fixture) within a junction box, transformer enclosure, ground-fault circuit interrupter, or other enclosure shall be provided with a strain relief.

(F) Grounding. The junction box, transformer enclosure, or other enclosure in the supply circuit to a wet-niche or no-niche luminaire (lighting fixture) and the field-wiring chamber of a dry-niche luminaire (lighting fixture) shall be grounded to the equipment grounding terminal of the panelboard. This terminal shall be directly connected to the panelboard enclosure.

680.25 Feeders. These provisions shall apply to any feeder on the supply side of panelboards supplying branch circuits for pool equipment covered in Part II of this article and on the load side of the service equipment or the source of a separately derived system.

(A) Wiring Methods. Feeders shall be installed in rigid metal conduit, intermediate metal conduit, liquidtight flexible nonmetallic conduit, or rigid nonmetallic conduit. Electrical metallic tubing shall be permitted where installed on or within a building, and electrical nonmetallic tubing shall be permitted where installed within a building.

Exception: An existing feeder between an existing remote panelboard and service equipment shall be permitted to run in flexible metal conduit or an approved cable assembly that includes an equipment grounding conductor within its outer sheath. The equipment grounding conductor shall comply with 250.24(A)(5).

(B) Grounding. An equipment grounding conductor shall be installed with the feeder conductors between the grounding terminal of the pool equipment panelboard and the grounding terminal of the applicable service equipment or source of a separately derived system. For other than (1) existing feeders covered in 680.25(A), Exception, or (2) feeders to separate buildings that do not utilize an insulated equipment grounding conductor in accordance with 680.25(B)(2), this equipment grounding conductor shall be insulated.

(1) Size. This conductor shall be sized in accordance with 250.122 but not smaller than 12 AWG. On separately derived systems, this conductor shall be sized in accordance with Table 250.66 but not smaller than 8 AWG.

(2) Separate Buildings. A feeder to a separate building or structure shall be permitted to supply swimming pool equipment branch circuits, or feeders supplying swimming pool equipment branch circuits, if the grounding arrangements in the separate building meet the requirements in 250.32(B)(1). Where installed in other than existing feeders covered in 680.25(A), Exception, a separate equipment grounding conductor shall be an insulated conductor.

680.26 Equipotential Bonding.

(A) Performance. The equipotential bonding required by this section shall be installed to eliminate voltage gradients in the pool area as prescribed.

FPN: The 8 AWG or larger solid copper bonding conductor shall not be required to be extended or attached to any remote panelboard, service equipment, or any electrode.

(B) Bonded Parts. The parts specified in 680.26(B)(1) through (B)(5) shall be bonded together.

(1) Metallic Structural Components. All metallic parts of the pool structure, including the reinforcing metal of the pool shell, coping stones, and deck, shall be bonded. The usual steel tie wires shall be considered suitable for bonding the reinforcing steel together, and welding or special clamping shall not be required. These tie wires shall be made tight. If reinforcing steel is effectively insulated by an encapsulating nonconductive compound at the time of manufacture and installation, it shall not be required to be bonded. Where reinforcing steel of the pool shell or the reinforcing steel of coping stones and deck is encapsulated with a nonconductive compound or another conductive material is not available, provisions shall be made for an alternative means to eliminate voltage gradients that would otherwise be provided by unencapsulated, bonded reinforcing steel.

(2) Underwater Lighting. All metal forming shells and mounting brackets of no-niche luminaires (fixtures) shall be bonded unless a listed low-voltage lighting system with nonmetallic forming shells not requiring bonding is used.

(3) Metal Fittings. All metal fittings within or attached to the pool structure shall be bonded. Isolated parts that are not over 100 mm (4 in.) in any dimension and do not penetrate into the pool structure more than 25 mm (1 in.) shall not require bonding.

(4) Electrical Equipment. Metal parts of electrical equipment associated with the pool water circulating system, including pump motors and metal parts of equipment associated with pool covers, including electric motors, shall be bonded. Accessible metal parts of listed equipment incorporating an approved system of double insulation and providing a means for grounding internal nonaccessible, non–current-carrying metal parts shall not be bonded by a direct connection to the equipotential bonding grid. The means for grounding internal nonaccessible, non–current carrying metal parts shall be an equipment grounding conductor run with the power-supply conductors in the case of motors supplied with a flexible cord, or a grounding terminal in the case of motors intended for permanent connection.

Where a double-insulated water-pump motor is installed under the provisions of this rule, a solid 8 AWG copper conductor that is of sufficient length to make a bonding connection to a replacement motor shall be extended from the bonding grid to an accessible point in the motor vicinity. Where there is no connection between the swimming pool bonding grid and the equipment grounding system for the premises, this bonding conductor shall be connected to the equipment grounding conductor of the motor circuit.

(5) Metal Wiring Methods and Equipment. Metal-sheathed cables and raceways, metal piping, and all fixed metal parts that are within the following distances of the pool, except those separated from the pool by a permanent barrier, shall be bonded.

(1) Within 1.5 m (5 ft) horizontally of the inside walls of the pool

(2) Within 3.7 m (12 ft) measured vertically above the maximum water level of the pool, or any observation stands, towers, or platforms, or any diving structures

(C) Equipotential Bonding Grid. The parts specified in 680.26(B) shall be connected to an equipotential bonding grid with a solid copper conductor, insulated, covered, or bare, not smaller than 8 AWG or rigid metal conduit of brass or other identified corrosion-resistant metal conduit. Connection shall be made by exothermic welding or by listed pressure connectors or clamps that are labeled as being suitable for the purpose and are of stainless steel, brass, copper, or copper alloy. The equipotential bonding grid shall extend under paved walking surfaces for 1 m (3 ft) horizontally beyond the inside walls of the pool and shall be permitted to be any of the following:

(1) Structural Reinforcing Steel. The structural reinforcing steel of a concrete pool where the reinforcing rods are bonded together by the usual steel tie wires or the equivalent

(2) Bolted or Welded Metal Pools. The wall of a bolted or welded metal pool

(3) Alternate Means. This system shall be permitted to be constructed as specified in (a) through (c):

   a. Materials and Connections. The grid shall be constructed of minimum 8 AWG bare solid copper conductors. Conductors shall be bonded to each other at all points of crossing. Connections shall be made as required by 680.26(D).

   b. Grid Structure. The equipotential bonding grid shall cover the contour of the pool and the pool deck extending 1 m (3 ft) horizontally from the inside walls of the pool. The equipotential bonding grid shall be arranged in a 300 mm (12 in.) by 300 mm (12 in.) network of conductors in a uniformly spaced perpendicular grid pattern with tolerance of 100 mm (4 in.).

   c. Securing. The below-grade grid shall be secured within or under the pool and deck media.

> A tentative interim amendment (TIA) to 680.26(C) and 680.26(C)(1) was issued by the Standards Council on July 29, 2005. See page 773.

(D) Connections. Where structural reinforcing steel or the walls of bolted or welded metal pool structures are used as an equipotential bonding grid for nonelectrical parts, the connections shall be made in accordance with 250.8.

(E) Pool Water Heaters. For pool water heaters rated at more than 50 amperes and having specific instructions regarding bonding and grounding, only those parts designated to be bonded shall be bonded and only those parts designated to be grounded shall be grounded.

680.27 Specialized Pool Equipment.

(A) Underwater Audio Equipment. All underwater audio equipment shall be identified for the purpose.

(1) Speakers. Each speaker shall be mounted in an approved metal forming shell, the front of which is enclosed by a captive metal screen, or equivalent, that is bonded to, and secured to, the forming shell by a positive locking device that ensures a low-resistance contact and requires a tool to open for installation or servicing of the speaker. The forming shell shall be installed in a recess in the wall or floor of the pool.

(2) Wiring Methods. Rigid metal conduit or intermediate metal conduit of brass or other identified corrosion-resistant metal, liquidtight flexible nonmetallic conduit (LFNC-B), or rigid nonmetallic conduit shall extend from the forming shell to a listed junction box or other enclosure as provided in 680.24. Where rigid nonmetallic conduit or liquidtight flexible nonmetallic conduit is used, an 8 AWG insulated solid or stranded copper bonding jumper shall be installed in this conduit. The bonding jumper shall be terminated in the forming shell and the junction box. The termination of the 8 AWG bonding jumper in the forming shell shall be covered with, or encapsulated in, a listed potting compound to protect such connection from the possible deteriorating effect of pool water.

(3) Forming Shell and Metal Screen. The forming shell and metal screen shall be of brass or other approved corrosion-resistant metal. All forming shells shall include provisions for terminating an 8 AWG copper conductor.

(B) Electrically Operated Pool Covers.

(1) Motors and Controllers. The electric motors, controllers, and wiring shall be located not less than 1.5 m (5 ft) from the inside wall of the pool unless separated from the pool by a wall, cover, or other permanent barrier. Electric motors installed below grade level shall be of the totally enclosed type. The device that controls the operation of the motor for an electrically operated pool cover shall be located such that the operator has full view of the pool.

> FPN No. 1: For cabinets installed in damp and wet locations, see 312.2(A).
>
> FPN No. 2: For switches or circuit breakers installed in wet locations, see 404.4.
>
> FPN No. 3: For protection against liquids, see 430.11.

(2) Protection. The electric motor and controller shall be connected to a circuit protected by a ground-fault circuit interrupter.

(C) Deck Area Heating. These provisions of this section shall apply to all pool deck areas, including a covered pool, where electrically operated comfort heating units are installed within 6.0 m (20 ft) of the inside wall of the pool.

(1) Unit Heaters. Unit heaters shall be rigidly mounted to the structure and shall be of the totally enclosed or guarded types. Unit heaters shall not be mounted over the pool or within the area extending 1.5 m (5 ft) horizontally from the inside walls of a pool.

(2) Permanently Wired Radiant Heaters. Radiant electric heaters shall be suitably guarded and securely fastened to their mounting device(s). Heaters shall not be installed over a pool or within the area extending 1.5 m (5 ft) horizontally from the inside walls of the pool and shall be mounted at least 3.7 m (12 ft) vertically above the pool deck unless otherwise approved.

(3) Radiant Heating Cables Not Permitted. Radiant heating cables embedded in or below the deck shall not be permitted.

III. Storable Pools

680.30 General. Electrical installations at storable pools shall comply with the provisions of Part I and Part III of this article.

680.31 Pumps. A cord-connected pool filter pump shall incorporate an approved system of double insulation or its equivalent and shall be provided with means for grounding only the internal and nonaccessible non–current-carrying metal parts of the appliance.

The means for grounding shall be an equipment grounding conductor run with the power-supply conductors in the flexible cord that is properly terminated in a grounding-type attachment plug having a fixed grounding contact member.

680.32 Ground-Fault Circuit Interrupters Required. All electrical equipment, including power-supply cords, used with storable pools shall be protected by ground-fault circuit interrupters.

All 125-volt receptacles located within 6.0 m (20 ft) of the inside walls of a storable pool shall be protected by a ground-fault circuit interrupter. In determining these dimensions, the distance to be measured shall be the shortest path the supply cord of an appliance connected to the receptacle would follow without piercing a floor, wall, ceiling, doorway with hinged or sliding door, window opening, or other effective permanent barrier.

FPN: For flexible cord usage, see 400.4.

680.33 Luminaires (Lighting Fixtures). An underwater luminaire (lighting fixture), if installed, shall be installed in or on the wall of the storable pool. It shall comply with either 680.33(A) or 680.33(B).

(A) 15 Volts or Less. A luminaire (lighting fixture) shall be part of a cord-and-plug-connected lighting assembly.

This assembly shall be listed as an assembly for the purpose and have the following construction features:

(1) No exposed metal parts

(2) A luminaire (fixture) lamp that operates at 15 volts or less

(3) An impact-resistant polymeric lens, luminaire (fixture) body, and transformer enclosure

(4) A transformer meeting the requirements of 680.23(A)(2) with a primary rating not over 150 volts

(B) Over 15 Volts But Not Over 150 Volts. A lighting assembly without a transformer and with the luminaire (fixture) lamp(s) operating at not over 150 volts shall be permitted to be cord-and-plug connected where the assembly is listed as an assembly for the purpose. The installation shall comply with 680.23(A)(5), and the assembly shall have the following construction features:

(1) No exposed metal parts

(2) An impact-resistant polymeric lens and luminaire (fixture) body

(3) A ground-fault circuit interrupter with open neutral protection as an integral part of the assembly

(4) The luminaire (fixture) lamp permanently connected to the ground-fault circuit interrupter with open-neutral protection

(5) Compliance with the requirements of 680.23(A)

680.34 Receptacle Locations. Receptacles shall not be less than 3.0 m (10 ft) from the inside walls of a pool. In determining these dimensions, the distance to be measured shall be the shortest path the supply cord of an appliance connected to the receptacle would follow without piercing a floor, wall, ceiling, doorway with hinged or sliding door, window opening, or other effective permanent barrier.

IV. Spas and Hot Tubs

680.40 General. Electrical installations at spas and hot tubs shall comply with the provisions of Part I and Part IV of this article.

680.41 Emergency Switch for Spas and Hot Tubs. A clearly labeled emergency shutoff or control switch for the purpose of stopping the motor(s) that provide power to the recirculation system and jet system shall be installed at a point readily accessible to the users and not less than 1.5 m (5 ft) away, adjacent to, and within sight of the spa or hot tub. This requirement shall not apply to single-family dwellings.

680.42 Outdoor Installations. A spa or hot tub installed outdoors shall comply with the provisions of Parts I and II of this article, except as permitted in 680.42(A) and 680.42(B), that would otherwise apply to pools installed outdoors.

(A) Flexible Connections. Listed packaged spa or hot tub equipment assemblies or self-contained spas or hot tubs utilizing a factory-installed or assembled control panel or panelboard shall be permitted to use flexible connections as covered in 680.42(A)(1) and (A)(2).

(1) Flexible Conduit. Liquidtight flexible metal conduit or liquidtight flexible nonmetallic conduit shall be permitted in lengths of not more than 1.8 m (6 ft).

(2) Cord-and-Plug Connections. Cord-and-plug connections with a cord not longer than 4.6 m (15 ft) shall be permitted where protected by a ground-fault circuit interrupter.

(B) Bonding. Bonding by metal-to-metal mounting on a common frame or base shall be permitted. The metal bands or hoops used to secure wooden staves shall not be required to be bonded as required in 680.26.

(C) Interior Wiring to Outdoor Installations. In the interior of a one-family dwelling or in the interior of another building or structure associated with a one-family dwelling, any of the wiring methods recognized in Chapter 3 of this *Code* that contain a copper equipment grounding conductor that is insulated or enclosed within the outer sheath of the wiring method and not smaller than 12 AWG shall be permitted to be used for the connection to motor, heating, and control loads that are part of a self-contained spa or hot tub or a packaged spa or hot tub equipment assembly. Wiring to an underwater light shall comply with 680.23 or 680.33.

680.43 Indoor Installations. A spa or hot tub installed indoors shall comply with the provisions of Parts I and II of this article except as modified by this section and shall be connected by the wiring methods of Chapter 3.

Exception: Listed spa and hot tub packaged units rated 20 amperes or less shall be permitted to be cord-and-plug connected to facilitate the removal or disconnection of the unit for maintenance and repair.

(A) Receptacles. At least one 125-volt, 15- or 20-ampere receptacle on a general-purpose branch circuit shall be located not less than 1.5 m (5 ft) from, and not exceeding 3.0 m (10 ft) from, the inside wall of the spa or hot tub.

(1) Location. Receptacles shall be located at least 1.5 m (5 ft) measured horizontally from the inside walls of the spa or hot tub.

(2) Protection, General. Receptacles rated 125 volts and 30 amperes or less and located within 3.0 m (10 ft) of the inside walls of a spa or hot tub shall be protected by a ground-fault circuit interrupter.

(3) Protection, Spa or Hot Tub Supply Receptacle. Receptacles that provide power for a spa or hot tub shall be ground-fault circuit-interrupter protected.

(4) Measurements. In determining the dimensions in this section addressing receptacle spacings, the distance to be measured shall be the shortest path the supply cord of an appliance connected to the receptacle would follow without piercing a floor, wall, ceiling, doorway with hinged or sliding door, window opening, or other effective permanent barrier.

(B) Installation of Luminaires (Lighting Fixtures), Lighting Outlets, and Ceiling-Suspended (Paddle) Fans.

(1) Elevation. Luminaires (lighting fixtures), except as covered in 680.43(B)(2), lighting outlets, and ceiling-suspended (paddle) fans located over the spa or hot tub or within 1.5 m (5 ft) from the inside walls of the spa or hot tub shall comply with the clearances specified in (B)(1)(a), (B)(1)(b), and (B)(1)(c) above the maximum water level.

(a) Without GFCI. Where no GFCI protection is provided, the mounting height shall be not less than 3.7 m (12 ft).

(b) With GFCI. Where GFCI protection is provided, the mounting height shall be permitted to be not less than 2.3 m (7 ft 6 in.).

(c) Below 2.3 m (7 ft 6 in.). Luminaires (lighting fixtures) meeting the requirements of item (1) or (2) and protected by a ground-fault circuit interrupter shall be permitted to be installed less than 2.3 m (7 ft 6 in.) over a spa or hot tub:

(1) Recessed luminaires (fixtures) with a glass or plastic lens, nonmetallic or electrically isolated metal trim, and suitable for use in damp locations

(2) Surface-mounted luminaires (fixtures) with a glass or plastic globe, a nonmetallic body, or a metallic body isolated from contact, and suitable for use in damp locations

(2) Underwater Applications. Underwater luminaires (lighting fixtures) shall comply with the provisions of 680.23 or 680.33.

(C) Wall Switches. Switches shall be located at least 1.5 m (5 ft), measured horizontally, from the inside walls of the spa or hot tub.

(D) Bonding. The following parts shall be bonded together:

(1) All metal fittings within or attached to the spa or hot tub structure

(2) Metal parts of electrical equipment associated with the spa or hot tub water circulating system, including pump motors

(3) Metal conduit and metal piping that are within 1.5 m (5 ft) of the inside walls of the spa or hot tub and that are not separated from the spa or hot tub by a permanent barrier

(4) All metal surfaces that are within 1.5 m (5 ft) of the inside walls of the spa or hot tub and that are not separated from the spa or hot tub area by a permanent barrier

Exception: Small conductive surfaces not likely to become energized, such as air and water jets and drain fittings, where not connected to metallic piping, towel bars, mirror frames, and similar nonelectrical equipment, shall not be required to be bonded.

(5) Electrical devices and controls that are not associated with the spas or hot tubs and that are located not less than 1.5 m (5 ft) from such units; otherwise they shall be bonded to the spa or hot tub system

(E) Methods of Bonding. All metal parts associated with the spa or hot tub shall be bonded by any of the following methods:

(1) The interconnection of threaded metal piping and fittings

(2) Metal-to-metal mounting on a common frame or base

(3) The provisions of a copper bonding jumper, insulated, covered, or bare, not smaller than 8 AWG solid.

(F) Grounding. The following equipment shall be grounded:

(1) All electric equipment located within 1.5 m (5 ft) of the inside wall of the spa or hot tub

(2) All electric equipment associated with the circulating system of the spa or hot tub

(G) Underwater Audio Equipment. Underwater audio equipment shall comply with the provisions of Part II of this article.

680.44 Protection. Except as otherwise provided in this section, the outlet(s) that supplies a self-contained spa or hot tub, a packaged spa or hot tub equipment assembly, or a field-assembled spa or hot tub shall be protected by a ground-fault circuit interrupter.

(A) Listed Units. If so marked, a listed self-contained unit or listed packaged equipment assembly that includes integral ground-fault circuit-interrupter protection for all electrical parts within the unit or assembly (pumps, air blowers, heaters, lights, controls, sanitizer generators, wiring, and so forth) shall be permitted without additional GFCI protection.

(B) Other Units. A field assembled spa or hot tub rated 3 phase or rated over 250 volts or with a heater load of more than 50 amperes shall not require the supply to be protected by a ground-fault circuit interrupter.

(C) Combination Pool and Spa or Hot Tub. A combination pool/hot tub or spa assembly commonly bonded need not be protected by a ground-fault circuit interrupter.

> FPN: See 680.2 for definitions of *self-contained spa or hot tub* and for *packaged spa or hot tub equipment assembly.*

V. Fountains

680.50 General. The provisions of Part I and Part V of this article shall apply to all permanently installed fountains as defined in 680.2. Fountains that have water common to a pool shall additionally comply with the requirements in Part II of this article. Part V does not cover self-contained, portable fountains not larger than 1.5 m (5 ft) in any dimension. Portable fountains shall comply with Parts II and III of Article 422.

680.51 Luminaires (Lighting Fixtures), Submersible Pumps, and Other Submersible Equipment.

(A) Ground-Fault Circuit Interrupter. Luminaires (lighting fixtures), submersible pumps, and other submersible equipment, unless listed for operation at 15 volts or less and supplied by a transformer that complies with 680.23(A)(2), shall be protected by a ground-fault circuit interrupter.

(B) Operating Voltage. No luminaires (lighting fixtures) shall be installed for operation on supply circuits over 150 volts between conductors. Submersible pumps and other submersible equipment shall operate at 300 volts or less between conductors.

(C) Luminaire (Lighting Fixture) Lenses. Luminaires (lighting fixtures) shall be installed with the top of the luminaire (fixture) lens below the normal water level of the fountain unless listed for above-water locations. A luminaire (lighting fixture) facing upward shall have the lens adequately guarded to prevent contact by any person.

(D) Overheating Protection. Electrical equipment that depends on submersion for safe operation shall be protected against overheating by a low-water cutoff or other approved means when not submerged.

(E) Wiring. Equipment shall be equipped with provisions for threaded conduit entries or be provided with a suitable flexible cord. The maximum length of exposed cord in the fountain shall be limited to 3.0 m (10 ft). Cords extending beyond the fountain perimeter shall be enclosed in approved wiring enclosures. Metal parts of equipment in contact with water shall be of brass or other approved corrosion-resistant metal.

(F) Servicing. All equipment shall be removable from the water for relamping or normal maintenance. Luminaires (fixtures) shall not be permanently embedded into the fountain structure such that the water level must be reduced or the fountain drained for relamping, maintenance, or inspection.

(G) Stability. Equipment shall be inherently stable or be securely fastened in place.

680.52 Junction Boxes and Other Enclosures.

(A) General. Junction boxes and other enclosures used for other than underwater installation shall comply with 680.24.

(B) Underwater Junction Boxes and Other Underwater Enclosures. Junction boxes and other underwater enclosures shall meet the requirements of 680.52(B)(1) and (B)(2).

(1) Construction.

(a) Underwater enclosures shall be equipped with provisions for threaded conduit entries or compression glands or seals for cord entry.

(b) Underwater enclosures shall be submersible and made of copper, brass, or other approved corrosion-resistant material.

(2) Installation. Underwater enclosure installations shall comply with (a) and (b).

(a) Underwater enclosures shall be filled with an approved potting compound to prevent the entry of moisture.

(b) Underwater enclosures shall be firmly attached to the supports or directly to the fountain surface and bonded as required. Where the junction box is supported only by the conduit, the conduit shall be of copper, brass, stainless steel, or other approved corrosion-resistant metal. Where the box is fed by nonmetallic conduit, it shall have additional supports and fasteners of copper, brass, or other approved corrosion-resistant material.

FPN: See 314.23 for support of enclosures.

680.53 Bonding. All metal piping systems associated with the fountain shall be bonded to the equipment grounding conductor of the branch circuit supplying the fountain.

FPN: See 250.122 for sizing of these conductors.

680.54 Grounding. The following equipment shall be grounded:

(1) All electrical equipment located within the fountain or within 1.5 m (5 ft) of the inside wall of the fountain

(2) All electrical equipment associated with the recirculating system of the fountain

(3) Panelboards that are not part of the service equipment and that supply any electrical equipment associated with the fountain

680.55 Methods of Grounding.

(A) Applied Provisions. The provisions of 680.21(A), 680.23(B)(3), 680.23(F)(1) and (F)(2), 680.24(F), and 680.25 shall apply.

(B) Supplied by a Flexible Cord. Electrical equipment that is supplied by a flexible cord shall have all exposed non–current-carrying metal parts grounded by an insulated copper equipment grounding conductor that is an integral part of this cord. The grounding conductor shall be connected to a grounding terminal in the supply junction box, transformer enclosure, or other enclosure.

680.56 Cord-and-Plug-Connected Equipment.

(A) Ground-Fault Circuit Interrupter. All electrical equipment, including power-supply cords, shall be protected by ground-fault circuit interrupters.

(B) Cord Type. Flexible cord immersed in or exposed to water shall be of a type for extra-hard usage, as designated in Table 400.4, and shall be a listed type with a "W" suffix.

(C) Sealing. The end of the flexible cord jacket and the flexible cord conductor termination within equipment shall be covered with, or encapsulated in, a suitable potting compound to prevent the entry of water into the equipment through the cord or its conductors. In addition, the ground connection within equipment shall be similarly treated to protect such connections from the deteriorating effect of water that may enter into the equipment.

(D) Terminations. Connections with flexible cord shall be permanent, except that grounding-type attachment plugs and receptacles shall be permitted to facilitate removal or disconnection for maintenance, repair, or storage of fixed or stationary equipment not located in any water-containing part of a fountain.

680.57 Signs.

(A) General. This section covers electric signs installed within a fountain or within 3.0 m (10 ft) of the fountain edge.

(B) Ground-Fault Circuit-Interrupter Protection for Personnel. All circuits supplying the sign shall have ground-fault circuit-interrupter protection for personnel.

(C) Location.

(1) Fixed or Stationary. A fixed or stationary electric sign installed within a fountain shall be not less than 1.5 m (5 ft) inside the fountain measured from the outside edges of the fountain.

(2) Portable. A portable electric sign shall not be placed within a pool or fountain or within 1.5 m (5 ft) measured horizontally from the inside walls of the fountain.

(D) Disconnect. A sign shall have a local disconnecting means in accordance with 600.6 and 680.12.

(E) Bonding and Grounding. A sign shall be grounded and bonded in accordance with 600.7.

680.58 GFCI Protection for Adjacent Receptacle Outlets. All 15- or 20-ampere, single-phase 125-volt through 250-volt receptacles located within 6.0 m (20 ft) of a fountain edge shall be provided with GFCI protection.

VI. Pools and Tubs for Therapeutic Use

680.60 General. The provisions of Part I and Part VI of this article shall apply to pools and tubs for therapeutic use in health care facilities, gymnasiums, athletic training rooms, and similar areas. Portable therapeutic appliances shall comply with Parts II and III of Article 422.

FPN: See 517.2 for definition of health care facilities.

680.61 Permanently Installed Therapeutic Pools. Therapeutic pools that are constructed in the ground, on the ground, or in a building in such a manner that the pool cannot be readily disassembled shall comply with Parts I and II of this article.

Exception: The limitations of 680.22(B)(1) through (B)(4) shall not apply where all luminaires (lighting fixtures) are of the totally enclosed type.

680.62 Therapeutic Tubs (Hydrotherapeutic Tanks). Therapeutic tubs, used for the submersion and treatment of patients, that are not easily moved from one place to another in normal use or that are fastened or otherwise secured at a specific location, including associated piping systems, shall conform to this part.

(A) Protection. Except as otherwise provided in this section, the outlet(s) that supplies a self-contained therapeutic tub or hydrotherapeutic tank, a packaged therapeutic tub or hydrotherapeutic tank, or a field-assembled therapeutic tub or hydrotherapeutic tank shall be protected by a ground-fault circuit interrupter.

(1) Listed Units. If so marked, a listed self-contained unit or listed packaged equipment assembly that includes integral ground-fault circuit-interrupter protection for all electrical parts within the unit or assembly (pumps, air blowers, heaters, lights, controls, sanitizer generators, wiring, and so forth) shall be permitted without additional GFCI protection.

(2) Other Units. A therapeutic tub or hydrotherapeutic tank rated 3 phase or rated over 250 volts or with a heater load of more than 50 amperes shall not require the supply to be protected by a ground-fault circuit interrupter.

(B) Bonding. The following parts shall be bonded together:

(1) All metal fittings within or attached to the tub structure
(2) Metal parts of electrical equipment associated with the tub water circulating system, including pump motors
(3) Metal-sheathed cables and raceways and metal piping that are within 1.5 m (5 ft) of the inside walls of the tub and not separated from the tub by a permanent barrier
(4) All metal surfaces that are within 1.5 m (5 ft) of the inside walls of the tub and not separated from the tub area by a permanent barrier

(5) Electrical devices and controls that are not associated with the therapeutic tubs and located within 1.5 m (5 ft) from such units.

(C) Methods of Bonding. All metal parts required to be bonded by this section shall be bonded by any of the following methods:

(1) The interconnection of threaded metal piping and fittings
(2) Metal-to-metal mounting on a common frame or base
(3) Connections by suitable metal clamps
(4) By the provisions of a solid copper bonding jumper, insulated, covered, or bare, not smaller than 8 AWG

(D) Grounding.

(1) Fixed or Stationary Equipment. The equipment specified in (D)(1)(a) and (D)(1)(b) shall be grounded.

(a) Location. All electrical equipment located within 1.5 m (5 ft) of the inside wall of the tub shall be grounded
(b) Circulation System. All electrical equipment associated with the circulating system of the tub shall be grounded.

(2) Portable Equipment. Portable therapeutic appliances shall meet the grounding requirements in 250.114.

(E) Receptacles. All receptacles within 1.5 m (5 ft) of a therapeutic tub shall be protected by a ground-fault circuit interrupter.

(F) Luminaires (Lighting Fixtures). All luminaires (lighting fixtures) used in therapeutic tub areas shall be of the totally enclosed type.

VII. Hydromassage Bathtubs

680.70 General. Hydromassage bathtubs as defined in 680.2 shall comply with Part VII of this article. They shall not be required to comply with other parts of this article.

680.71 Protection. Hydromassage bathtubs and their associated electrical components shall be protected by a ground-fault circuit interrupter. All 125-volt, single-phase receptacles not exceeding 30 amperes and located within 1.5 m (5 ft) measured horizontally of the inside walls of a hydromassage tub shall be protected by a ground-fault circuit interrupter(s).

680.72 Other Electrical Equipment. Luminaires (lighting fixtures), switches, receptacles, and other electrical equipment located in the same room, and not directly associated with a hydromassage bathtub, shall be installed in accordance with the requirements of Chapters 1 through 4 in this *Code* covering the installation of that equipment in bathrooms.

680.73 Accessibility. Hydromassage bathtub electrical equipment shall be accessible without damaging the building structure or building finish.

680.74 Bonding. All metal piping systems and all grounded metal parts in contact with the circulating water shall be bonded together using a copper bonding jumper, insulated, covered, or bare, not smaller than 8 AWG solid.

ARTICLE 682
Natural and Artificially Made Bodies of Water

I. General

682.1 Scope. This article applies to the installation of electrical wiring for, and equipment in and adjacent to, natural or artificially made bodies of water not covered by other articles in this *Code*, such as but not limited to aeration ponds, fish farm ponds, storm retention basins, treatment ponds, irrigation (channels) facilities.

682.2 Definitions.

Artificially Made Bodies of Water. Bodies of water that have been constructed or modified to fit some decorative or commercial purpose such as, but not limited to, aeration ponds, fish farm ponds, storm retention basins, treatment ponds, irrigation (channel) facilities. Water depths may vary seasonally or be controlled.

Electrical Datum Plane. The electrical datum plane as used in this article is defined as follows:

(1) In land areas subject to tidal fluctuation, the electrical datum plane is a horizontal plane 600 mm (2 ft) above the highest tide level for the area occurring under normal circumstances, that is, highest high tide.

(2) In land areas not subject to tidal fluctuation, the electrical datum plane is a horizontal plane 600 mm (2 ft) above the highest water level for the area occurring under normal circumstances.

(3) In land areas subject to flooding, the electrical datum plane based on (1) or (2) above is a horizontal plane 600 mm (2 ft) above the point identified as the prevailing high water mark or an equivalent benchmark based on seasonal or storm-driven flooding from the authority having jurisdiction.

(4) The electrical datum plane for floating structures and landing stages that are (1) installed to permit rise and fall response to water level, without lateral movement,

and (2) that are so equipped that they can rise to the datum plane established for (1) or (2) above, is a horizontal plane 750 mm (30 in.) above the water level at the floating structure or landing stage and a minimum of 300 mm (12 in.) above the level of the deck.

Equipotential Plane. An area where wire mesh or other conductive elements are on, embedded in, or placed under the walk surface within 75 mm (3 in.), bonded to all metal structures and fixed nonelectrical equipment that may become energized, and connected to the electrical grounding system to prevent a difference in voltage from developing within the plane.

Natural Bodies of Water. Bodies of water such as lakes, streams, ponds, rivers, and other naturally occurring bodies of water, which may vary in depth throughout the year.

Shoreline. The farthest extent of standing water under the applicable conditions that determine the electrical datum plane for the specified body of water.

682.3 Other Articles. Wiring and equipment in or adjacent to natural or artificially made bodies of water shall comply with the applicable provisions of other articles of this *Code*, except as modified by this article. If the water is subject to boat traffic, the wiring shall comply with 555.13(B).

II. Installation

682.10 Electrical Equipment and Transformers. Electrical equipment and transformers, including their enclosures, shall be specifically approved for the intended location. No portion of an enclosure for electrical equipment not identified for operation while submerged shall be located below the electrical datum plane.

682.11 Location of Service Equipment. On land, the service equipment for floating structures and submersible electrical equipment shall be located no closer than 1.5 m (5 ft) horizontally from the shoreline and live parts elevated a minimum of 300 mm (12 in.) above the electrical datum plane. Service equipment shall disconnect when the water level reaches the height of the established electrical datum plane.

682.12 Electrical Connections. All electrical connections not intended for operation while submerged shall be located at least 300 mm (12 in.) above the deck of a floating or fixed structure, but not below the electrical datum plane.

682.13 Wiring Methods and Installation. Wiring methods and installations of Chapter 3 and Articles 553, 555, and 590 shall be permitted where identified for use in wet locations.

682.14 Disconnecting Means for Floating Structures or Submersible Electrical Equipment.

(A) Type. The disconnecting means shall be permitted to consist of a circuit breaker, switch, or both and shall be properly identified as to which structure or equipment it controls.

(B) Location. The disconnecting means shall be readily accessible on land and shall be located in the supply circuit ahead of the structure or the equipment connection. The disconnecting means shall be located not more than 750 mm (30 in.) from the structure or equipment connection. The disconnecting means shall be within sight of, but not closer than, 1.5 m (5 ft) horizontally from the edge of the shoreline and live parts elevated a minimum of 300 mm (12 in.) above the electrical datum plane.

682.15 Ground Fault Circuit Interrupter (GFCI) Protection. Fifteen- and 20-ampere single-phase, 125-volt through 250-volt receptacles installed outdoors and in or on floating buildings or structures within the electrical datum plane area that are used for storage, maintenance, or repair where portable electric hand tools, electrical diagnostic equipment, or portable lighting equipment are to be used shall be provided with GFCI protection. The GFCI protection device shall be located not less than 300 mm (12 in.) above the established electrical datum plane.

III. Grounding and Bonding

682.30 Grounding. Wiring and equipment within the scope of this article shall be grounded as specified in Articles 250, 553, and 555 and with the requirements in Part III.

682.31 Equipment Grounding Conductors.

(A) Type. Equipment grounding conductors shall be insulated copper conductors sized in accordance with 250.122 but not smaller than 12 AWG.

(B) Feeders. Where a feeder supplies a remote panelboard, an insulated equipment grounded conductor shall extend from a grounding terminal in the service to a grounding terminal and busbar in the remote panelboard.

(C) Branch Circuits. The insulated equipment grounding conductor for branch circuits shall terminate at a grounding terminal in a remote panelboard or the grounding terminal in the main service equipment.

(D) Cord-and-Plug-Connected Appliances. Where required to be grounded, cord-and-plug-connected appliances shall be grounded by means of an equipment grounding conductor in the cord and a grounding-type attachment plug.

682.32 Bonding of Non–Current-Carrying Metal Parts. All metal parts in contact with the water, all metal piping, tanks, and all non–current-carrying metal parts that may become energized shall be bonded to the grounding bus in the panelboard.

682.33 Equipotential Planes and Bonding of Equipment Planes. An equipotential plane shall be installed where required in this section to mitigate step and touch voltages at electrical equipment.

(A) Areas Requiring Equipotential Planes. Equipotential planes shall be installed adjacent to all outdoor service equipment or disconnecting means that control equipment in or on water, that have a metallic enclosure and controls accessible to personnel, and that are likely to become energized. The equipotential plane shall encompass the area around the equipment and shall extend from the area directly below the equipment out not less than 900 mm (36 in.) in all directions from which a person would be able to stand and come in contact with the equipment.

(B) Areas Not Requiring Equipotential Planes. Equipotential planes shall not be required for the controlled equipment supplied by the service equipment or disconnecting means. All circuits rated not more than 60 amperes at 120 through 250 volts, single phase, shall have GFCI protection.

(C) Bonding. Equipotential planes shall be bonded to the electrical grounding system. The bonding conductor shall be solid copper, insulated, covered or bare, and not smaller than 8 AWG. Connections shall be made by exothermic welding or by listed pressure connectors or clamps that are labeled as being suitable for the purpose and are of stainless steel, brass, copper, or copper alloy.

ARTICLE 685
Integrated Electrical Systems

I. General

685.1 Scope. This article covers integrated electrical systems, other than unit equipment, in which orderly shutdown is necessary to ensure safe operation. An *integrated electrical system* as used in this article is a unitized segment of an industrial wiring system where all of the following conditions are met:

(1) An orderly shutdown is required to minimize personnel hazard and equipment damage.

(2) The conditions of maintenance and supervision ensure that qualified persons service the system. The name(s)

of the qualified person(s) shall be kept in a permanent record at the office of the establishment in charge of the completed installation.

A person designated as a qualified person shall possess the skills and knowledge related to the construction and operation of the electrical equipment and installation and shall have received documented safety training on the hazards involved. Documentation of their qualifications shall be on file with the office of the establishment in charge of the completed installation.

(3) Effective safeguards acceptable to the authority having jurisdiction are established and maintained.

685.3 Application of Other Articles. The articles/sections in Table 685.3 apply to particular cases of installation of conductors and equipment, where there are orderly shutdown requirements that are in addition to those of this article or are modifications of them.

Table 685.3 Application of Other Articles

Conductor/Equipment	Section
More than one building or other structure	225, Part II
Ground-fault protection of equipment	230.95, Exception No. 1
Protection of conductors	240.4
Electrical system coordination	240.12
Ground-fault protection of equipment	240.13(1)
Grounding ac systems of 50 volts to 1000 volts	250.21
Equipment protection	427.22
Orderly shutdown	430.44
Disconnection	430.74, Exception Nos. 1 and 2
Disconnecting means in sight from controller	430.102(A), Exception No. 2
Energy from more than one source	430.113, Exception Nos. 1 and 2
Disconnecting means	645.10, Exception
Uninterruptible power supplies (UPS)	645.11(1)
Point of connection	705.12(A)

II. Orderly Shutdown

685.10 Location of Overcurrent Devices in or on Premises. Location of overcurrent devices that are critical to integrated electrical systems shall be permitted to be accessible, with mounting heights permitted to ensure security from operation by unqualified personnel.

685.12 Direct-Current System Grounding. Two-wire dc circuits shall be permitted to be ungrounded.

685.14 Ungrounded Control Circuits. Where operational continuity is required, control circuits of 150 volts or less from separately derived systems shall be permitted to be ungrounded.

ARTICLE 690
Solar Photovoltaic Systems

I. General

690.1 Scope. The provisions of this article apply to solar photovoltaic electrical energy systems, including the array circuit(s), inverter(s), and controller(s) for such systems. [See Figure 690.1(A) and Figure 690.1(B).] Solar photovoltaic systems covered by this article may be interactive with other electrical power production sources or stand-alone, with or without electrical energy storage such as batteries. These systems may have ac or dc output for utilization.

Notes:
1. These diagrams are intended to be a means of identification for photovoltaic system components, circuits, and connections.
2. Disconnecting means required by Article 690, Part III, are not shown.
3. System grounding and equipment grounding are not shown. See Article 690, Part V.

Figure 690.1(A) Identification of Solar Photovoltaic System Components.

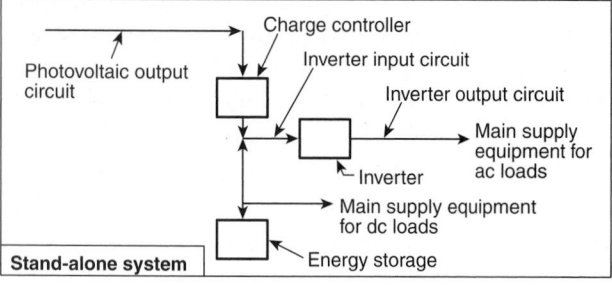

Notes:
1. These diagrams are intended to be a means of identification for photovoltaic system components, circuits, and connections.
2. Disconnecting means and overcurrent protection required by Article 690 are not shown.
3. System grounding and equipment grounding are not shown. See Article 690, Part V.
4. Custom designs occur in each configuration, and some components are optional.

Figure 690.1(B) Identification of Solar Photovoltaic System Components in Common System Configurations.

690.2 Definitions.

Alternating-Current (ac) Module (Alternating-Current Photovoltaic Module). A complete, environmentally protected unit consisting of solar cells, optics, inverter, and other components, exclusive of tracker, designed to generate ac power when exposed to sunlight.

Array. A mechanically integrated assembly of modules or panels with a support structure and foundation, tracker, and other components, as required, to form a direct-current power-producing unit.

Bipolar Photovoltaic Array. A photovoltaic array that has two outputs, each having opposite polarity to a common reference point or center tap.

Blocking Diode. A diode used to block reverse flow of current into a photovoltaic source circuit.

Building Integrated Photovoltaics. Photovoltaic cells, devices, modules, or modular materials that are integrated

into the outer surface or structure of a building and serve as the outer protective surface of that building.

Charge Controller. Equipment that controls dc voltage or dc current, or both, used to charge a battery.

Diversion Charge Controller. Equipment that regulates the charging process of a battery by diverting power from energy storage to direct-current or alternating-current loads or to an interconnected utility service.

Electrical Production and Distribution Network. A power production, distribution, and utilization system, such as a utility system and connected loads, that is external to and not controlled by the photovoltaic power system.

Hybrid System. A system comprised of multiple power sources. These power sources may include photovoltaic, wind, micro-hydro generators, engine-driven generators, and others, but do not include electrical production and distribution network systems. Energy storage systems, such as batteries, do not constitute a power source for the purpose of this definition.

Interactive System. A solar photovoltaic system that operates in parallel with and may deliver power to an electrical production and distribution network. For the purpose of this definition, an energy storage subsystem of a solar photovoltaic system, such as a battery, is not another electrical production source.

Inverter. Equipment that is used to change voltage level or waveform, or both, of electrical energy. Commonly, an inverter [also known as a power conditioning unit (PCU) or power conversion system (PCS)] is a device that changes dc input to an ac output. Inverters may also function as battery chargers that use alternating current from another source and convert it into direct current for charging batteries.

Inverter Input Circuit. Conductors between the inverter and the battery in stand-alone systems or the conductors between the inverter and the photovoltaic output circuits for electrical production and distribution network.

Inverter Output Circuit. Conductors between the inverter and an ac panelboard for stand-alone systems or the conductors between the inverter and the service equipment or another electric power production source, such as a utility, for electrical production and distribution network.

Module. A complete, environmentally protected unit consisting of solar cells, optics, and other components, exclusive of tracker, designed to generate dc power when exposed to sunlight.

Panel. A collection of modules mechanically fastened together, wired, and designed to provide a field-installable unit.

Photovoltaic Output Circuit. Circuit conductors between the photovoltaic source circuit(s) and the inverter or dc utilization equipment.

Photovoltaic Power Source. An array or aggregate of arrays that generates dc power at system voltage and current.

Photovoltaic Source Circuit. Circuits between modules and from modules to the common connection point(s) of the dc system.

Photovoltaic System Voltage. The direct current (dc) voltage of any photovoltaic source or photovoltaic output circuit. For multiwire installations, the photovoltaic system voltage is the highest voltage between any two dc conductors.

Solar Cell. The basic photovoltaic device that generates electricity when exposed to light.

Solar Photovoltaic System. The total components and subsystems that, in combination, convert solar energy into electrical energy suitable for connection to a utilization load.

Stand-Alone System. A solar photovoltaic system that supplies power independently of an electrical production and distribution network.

690.3 Other Articles. Wherever the requirements of other articles of this *Code* and Article 690 differ, the requirements of Article 690 shall apply and, if the system is operated in parallel with a primary source(s) of electricity, the requirements in 705.14, 705.16, 705.32, and 705.43 shall apply.

Exception: Solar photovoltaic systems, equipment, or wiring installed in a hazardous (classified) location shall also comply with 500.1, 505.1, and 510.1.

690.4 Installation.

(A) Solar Photovoltaic System. A solar photovoltaic system shall be permitted to supply a building or other structure in addition to any service(s) of another electricity supply system(s).

(B) Conductors of Different Systems. Photovoltaic source circuits and photovoltaic output circuits shall not be contained in the same raceway, cable tray, cable, outlet box, junction box, or similar fitting as feeders or branch circuits of other systems, unless the conductors of the different systems are separated by a partition or are connected together.

(C) Module Connection Arrangement. The connections to a module or panel shall be arranged so that removal of a module or panel from a photovoltaic source circuit does not interrupt a grounded conductor to another photovoltaic source circuit. Sets of modules interconnected as systems rated at 50 volts or less, with or without blocking diodes, and having a single overcurrent device shall be considered as a single-source circuit. Supplementary overcurrent devices used for the exclusive protection of the photovoltaic modules are not considered as overcurrent devices for the purpose of this section.

(D) Equipment. Inverters or motor generators shall be identified for use in solar photovoltaic systems.

690.5 Ground-Fault Protection. Roof-mounted dc photovoltaic arrays located on dwellings shall be provided with dc ground-fault protection to reduce fire hazards.

(A) Ground-Fault Detection and Interruption. The ground-fault protection device or system shall be capable of detecting a ground fault, interrupting the flow of fault current, and providing an indication of the fault.

(B) Disconnection of Conductors. The ungrounded conductors of the faulted source circuit shall be automatically disconnected. If the grounded conductors of the faulted source circuit are disconnected to comply with the requirements of 690.5(A), all conductors of the faulted source circuit shall be opened automatically and simultaneously. Opening the grounded conductor of the array or opening the faulted sections of the array shall be permitted to interrupt the ground-fault current path.

(C) Labels and Markings. Labels and markings shall be applied near the ground-fault indicator at a visible location, stating that, if a ground fault is indicated, the normally grounded conductors may be energized and ungrounded.

690.6 Alternating-Current (ac) Modules.

(A) Photovoltaic Source Circuits. The requirements of Article 690 pertaining to photovoltaic source circuits shall not apply to ac modules. The photovoltaic source circuit, conductors, and inverters shall be considered as internal wiring of an ac module.

(B) Inverter Output Circuit. The output of an ac module shall be considered an inverter output circuit.

(C) Disconnecting Means. A single disconnecting means, in accordance with 690.15 and 690.17, shall be permitted for the combined ac output of one or more ac modules. Additionally, each ac module in a multiple ac-module system shall be provided with a connector, bolted, or terminal-type disconnecting means.

(D) Ground-Fault Detection. Alternating-current-module systems shall be permitted to use a single detection device to detect only ac ground faults and to disable the array by removing ac power to the ac module(s).

(E) Overcurrent Protection. The output circuits of ac modules shall be permitted to have overcurrent protection and conductor sizing in accordance with 240.5(B)(2).

II. Circuit Requirements

690.7 Maximum Voltage.

(A) Maximum Photovoltaic System Voltage. In a dc photovoltaic source circuit or output circuit, the maximum photovoltaic system voltage for that circuit shall be calculated as the sum of the rated open-circuit voltage of the series-connected photovoltaic modules corrected for the lowest expected ambient temperature. For crystalline and multi-crystalline silicon modules, the rated open-circuit voltage shall be multiplied by the correction factor provided in Table 690.7. This voltage shall be used to determine the voltage rating of cables, disconnects, overcurrent devices, and other equipment. Where the lowest expected ambient temperature is below −40°C (−40°F), or where other than crystalline or multicrystalline silicon photovoltaic modules are used, the system voltage adjustment shall be made in accordance with the manufacturer's instructions.

Table 690.7 Voltage Correction Factors for Crystalline and Multicrystalline Silicon Modules

Ambient Temperature (°C)	Correction Factors for Ambient Temperatures Below 25°C (77°F) (Multiply the rated open-circuit voltage by the appropriate correction factor shown below.)	Ambient Temperature (°F)
25 to 10	1.06	77 to 50
9 to 0	1.10	49 to 32
−1 to −10	1.13	31 to 14
−11 to −20	1.17	13 to −4
−21 to −40	1.25	−5 to −40

(B) Direct-Current Utilization Circuits. The voltage of dc utilization circuits shall conform with 210.6.

(C) Photovoltaic Source and Output Circuits. In one- and two-family dwellings, photovoltaic source circuits and photovoltaic output circuits that do not include lampholders, fixtures, or receptacles shall be permitted to have a maximum photovoltaic system voltage up to 600 volts. Other installations with a maximum photovoltaic system voltage over 600 volts shall comply with Article 690, Part I.

(D) Circuits Over 150 Volts to Ground. In one- and two-family dwellings, live parts in photovoltaic source circuits and photovoltaic output circuits over 150 volts to ground shall not be accessible to other than qualified persons while energized.

> FPN: See 110.27 for guarding of live parts, and 210.6 for voltage to ground and between conductors.

(E) Bipolar Source and Output Circuits. For 2-wire circuits connected to bipolar systems, the maximum system voltage shall be the highest voltage between the conductors of the 2-wire circuit if all of the following conditions apply:

(1) One conductor of each circuit is solidly grounded.

(2) Each circuit is connected to a separate subarray.

(3) The equipment is clearly marked with a label as follows:

WARNING
BIPOLAR PHOTOVOLTAIC ARRAY.
DISCONNECTION OF NEUTRAL OR
GROUNDED CONDUCTORS MAY RESULT IN
OVERVOLTAGE ON ARRAY OR INVERTER.

690.8 Circuit Sizing and Current.

(A) Calculation of Maximum Circuit Current. The maximum current for the specific circuit shall be calculated in accordance with 690.8(A)(1) through (A)(4).

(1) Photovoltaic Source Circuit Currents. The maximum current shall be the sum of parallel module rated short-circuit currents multiplied by 125 percent.

(2) Photovoltaic Output Circuit Currents. The maximum current shall be the sum of parallel source circuit maximum currents as calculated in 690.8(A)(1).

(3) Inverter Output Circuit Current. The maximum current shall be the inverter continuous output current rating.

(4) Stand-Alone Inverter Input Circuit Current. The maximum current shall be the stand-alone continuous inverter input current rating when the inverter is producing rated power at the lowest input voltage.

(B) Ampacity and Overcurrent Device Ratings. Photovoltaic system currents shall be considered to be continuous.

(1) Sizing of Conductors and Overcurrent Devices. The circuit conductors and overcurrent devices shall be sized to carry not less than 125 percent of the maximum currents as calculated in 690.8(A). The rating or setting of overcurrent devices shall be permitted in accordance with 240.4(B) and (C).

Exception: Circuits containing an assembly, together with its overcurrent device(s), that is listed for continuous operation at 100 percent of its rating shall be permitted to be utilized at 100 percent of its rating.

(2) Internal Current Limitation. Overcurrent protection for photovoltaic output circuits with devices that internally limit the current from the photovoltaic output circuit shall be permitted to be rated at less than the value calculated in 690.8(B)(1). This reduced rating shall be at least 125 percent of the limited current value. Photovoltaic output circuit conductors shall be sized in accordance with 690.8(B)(1).

Exception: An overcurrent device in an assembly listed for continuous operation at 100 percent of its rating shall be permitted to be utilized at 100 percent of its rating.

(C) Systems with Multiple Direct-Current Voltages. For a photovoltaic power source that has multiple output circuit voltages and employs a common-return conductor, the ampacity of the common-return conductor shall not be less than the sum of the ampere ratings of the overcurrent devices of the individual output circuits.

(D) Sizing of Module Interconnection Conductors. Where a single overcurrent device is used to protect a set of two or more parallel-connected module circuits, the ampacity of each of the module interconnection conductors shall not be less than the sum of the rating of the single fuse plus 125 percent of the short-circuit current from the other parallel-connected modules.

690.9 Overcurrent Protection.

(A) Circuits and Equipment. Photovoltaic source circuit, photovoltaic output circuit, inverter output circuit, and storage battery circuit conductors and equipment shall be protected in accordance with the requirements of Article 240. Circuits connected to more than one electrical source shall have overcurrent devices located so as to provide overcurrent protection from all sources.

Exception: An overcurrent device shall not be required for circuit conductors sized in accordance with 690.8(B) and located where one of the following apply:

(a) There are no external sources such as parallel-connected source circuits, batteries, or backfeed from inverters.

(b) The short-circuit currents from all sources do not exceed the ampacity of the conductors.

FPN: Possible backfeed of current from any source of supply, including a supply through an inverter into the photovoltaic output circuit and photovoltaic source circuits, is a consideration in determining whether adequate overcurrent protection from all sources is provided for conductors and modules.

(B) Power Transformers. Overcurrent protection for a transformer with a source(s) on each side shall be provided in accordance with 450.3 by considering first one side of the transformer, then the other side of the transformer, as the primary.

Exception: A power transformer with a current rating on the side connected toward the photovoltaic power source, not less than the short-circuit output current rating of the inverter, shall be permitted without overcurrent protection from that source.

(C) Photovoltaic Source Circuits. Branch-circuit or supplementary-type overcurrent devices shall be permitted to provide overcurrent protection in photovoltaic source circuits. The overcurrent devices shall be accessible but shall not be required to be readily accessible.

Standard values of supplementary overcurrent devices allowed by this section shall be in one ampere size increments, starting at one ampere up to and including 15 amperes. Higher standard values above 15 amperes for supplementary overcurrent devices shall be based on the standard sizes provided in 240.6(A).

(D) Direct-Current Rating. Overcurrent devices, either fuses or circuit breakers, used in any dc portion of a photovoltaic power system shall be listed for use in dc circuits and shall have the appropriate voltage, current, and interrupt ratings.

(E) Series Overcurrent Protection. In series-connected strings of two or more modules, a single overcurrent protection device shall be permitted.

690.10 Stand-Alone Systems. The premises wiring system shall be adequate to meet the requirements of this *Code* for a similar installation connected to a service. The wiring on the supply side of the building or structure disconnecting means shall comply with this *Code* except as modified by 690.10(A), (B), and (C).

(A) Inverter Output. The ac inverter output from a stand-alone system shall be permitted to supply ac power to the building or structure disconnecting means at current levels below the rating of that disconnecting means.

(B) Sizing and Protection. The circuit conductors between the inverter output and the building or structure disconnecting means shall be sized based on the output rating of the inverter. These conductors shall be protected from overcurrents in accordance with Article 240. The overcurrent protection shall be located at the output of the inverter.

(C) Single 120-Volt Supply. The inverter output of a stand-alone solar photovoltaic system shall be permitted to supply 120 volts to single-phase, 3-wire, 120/240-volt service equipment or distribution panels where there are no 240-volt outlets and where there are no multiwire branch circuits. In all installations, the rating of the overcurrent device connected to the output of the inverter shall be less than the rating of the neutral bus in the service equipment. This equipment shall be marked with the following words or equivalent:

WARNING
SINGLE 120-VOLT SUPPLY. DO NOT CONNECT
MULTIWIRE BRANCH CIRCUITS!

III. Disconnecting Means

690.13 All Conductors. Means shall be provided to disconnect all current-carrying conductors of a photovoltaic power source from all other conductors in a building or other structure. A switch or circuit breaker shall not be installed in a grounded conductor unless that switch or circuit breaker is part of a ground-fault detection system required by 690.5 and that switch or circuit breaker is automatically opened and indicated as a normal function of the device in responding to ground faults.

> FPN: The grounded conductor may have a bolted or terminal disconnecting means to allow maintenance or troubleshooting by qualified personnel.

690.14 Additional Provisions. Photovoltaic disconnecting means shall comply with 690.14(A) through 690.14(D).

(A) Disconnecting Means. The disconnecting means shall not be required to be suitable as service equipment and shall be rated in accordance with 690.17.

(B) Equipment. Equipment such as photovoltaic source circuit isolating switches, overcurrent devices, and blocking diodes shall be permitted on the photovoltaic side of the photovoltaic disconnecting means.

(C) Requirements for Disconnecting Means. Means shall be provided to disconnect all conductors in a building or other structure from the photovoltaic system conductors.

(1) Location. The photovoltaic disconnecting means shall be installed at a readily accessible location either on the outside of a building or structure or inside nearest the point of entrance of the system conductors.

Exception: Installations that comply with 690.31(E) shall be permitted to have the disconnecting means located remote from the point of entry of the system conductors.

The photovoltaic system disconnecting means shall not be installed in bathrooms.

(2) Marking. Each photovoltaic system disconnecting means shall be permanently marked to identify it as a photovoltaic system disconnect.

(3) Suitable for Use. Each photovoltaic system disconnecting means shall be suitable for the prevailing conditions. Equipment installed in hazardous (classified) locations shall comply with the requirements of Articles 500 through 517.

(4) Maximum Number of Disconnects. The photovoltaic system disconnecting means shall consist of not more than six switches or six circuit breakers mounted in a single enclosure, in a group of separate enclosures, or in or on a switchboard.

(5) Grouping. The photovoltaic system disconnecting means shall be grouped with other disconnecting means for the system to comply with 690.14(C)(4). A photovoltaic disconnecting means shall not be required at the photovoltaic module or array location.

(D) Utility-Interactive Inverters Mounted in Not-Readily-Accessible Locations. Utility-interactive inverters shall be permitted to be mounted on roofs or other exterior areas that are not readily accessible. These installations shall comply with (1) through (4):

(1) A direct-current photovoltaic disconnecting means shall be mounted within sight of or in the inverter.

(2) An alternating-current disconnecting means shall be mounted within sight of or in the inverter.

(3) The alternating-current output conductors from the inverter and an additional alternating-current disconnecting means for the inverter shall comply with 690.14(C)(1).

(4) A plaque shall be installed in accordance with 705.10.

690.15 Disconnection of Photovoltaic Equipment. Means shall be provided to disconnect equipment, such as inverters, batteries, charge controllers, and the like, from all ungrounded conductors of all sources. If the equipment is energized from more than one source, the disconnecting means shall be grouped and identified.

A single disconnecting means in accordance with 690.17 shall be permitted for the combined ac output of one or more inverters or ac modules in an interactive system.

690.16 Fuses. Disconnecting means shall be provided to disconnect a fuse from all sources of supply if the fuse is energized from both directions and is accessible to other than qualified persons. Such a fuse in a photovoltaic source circuit shall be capable of being disconnected independently of fuses in other photovoltaic source circuits.

690.17 Switch or Circuit Breaker. The disconnecting means for ungrounded conductors shall consist of a manually operable switch(es) or circuit breaker(s) complying with all of the following requirements:

(1) Located where readily accessible

(2) Externally operable without exposing the operator to contact with live parts

(3) Plainly indicating whether in the open or closed position

(4) Having an interrupting rating sufficient for the nominal circuit voltage and the current that is available at the line terminals of the equipment

Where all terminals of the disconnecting means may be energized in the open position, a warning sign shall be mounted on or adjacent to the disconnecting means. The sign shall be clearly legible and have the following words or equivalent:

WARNING
ELECTRIC SHOCK HAZARD.
DO NOT TOUCH TERMINALS. TERMINALS
ON BOTH THE LINE AND
LOAD SIDES MAY BE ENERGIZED
IN THE OPEN POSITION.

Exception: A connector shall be permitted to be used as an ac or a dc disconnecting means, provided that it complies with the requirements of 690.33 and is listed and identified for the use.

690.18 Installation and Service of an Array. Open circuiting, short circuiting, or opaque covering shall be used to disable an array or portions of an array for installation and service.

FPN: Photovoltaic modules are energized while exposed to light. Installation, replacement, or servicing of array components while a module(s) is irradiated may expose persons to electric shock.

IV. Wiring Methods

690.31 Methods Permitted.

(A) Wiring Systems. All raceway and cable wiring methods included in this *Code* and other wiring systems and fittings specifically intended and identified for use on photovoltaic arrays shall be permitted. Where wiring devices with integral enclosures are used, sufficient length of cable shall be provided to facilitate replacement.

FPN: Photovoltaic modules operate at elevated temperatures when exposed to high ambient temperatures and to bright sunlight. These temperatures may routinely exceed 70°C (158°F) in many locations. Module interconnection conductors are available with insulation rated for wet locations and a temperature rating of 90°C (194°F) or greater.

(B) Single-Conductor Cable. Types SE, UF, USE, and USE-2 single-conductor cable shall be permitted in photovoltaic source circuits where installed in the same manner as a Type UF multiconductor cable in accordance with Part II of Article 340. Where exposed to sunlight, Type UF cable identified as sunlight-resistant shall be used.

(C) Flexible Cords and Cables. Flexible cords and cables, where used to connect the moving parts of tracking PV modules, shall comply with Article 400 and shall be of a type identified as a hard-service cord or portable power cable; they shall be suitable for extra-hard usage, listed for outdoor use, water resistant, and sunlight resistant. Allowable ampacities shall be in accordance with 400.5. For ambient temperatures exceeding 30°C (86°F), the ampacities shall be derated by the appropriate factors given in Table 690.31(C).

(D) Small-Conductor Cables. Single-conductor cables listed for outdoor use that are sunlight resistant and moisture resistant in sizes 16 AWG and 18 AWG shall be permitted for module interconnections where such cables meet the ampacity requirements of 690.8. Section 310.15 shall be used to determine the cable ampacity and temperature derating factors.

(E) Direct-Current Photovoltaic Source and Output Circuits Inside a Building. Where direct current photovoltaic source or output circuits of a utility-interactive inverter from a building-integrated or other photovoltaic system are run inside a building or structure, they shall be contained in metallic raceways or enclosures from the point of penetration of the surface of the building or structure to the first readily accessible disconnecting means. The disconnecting means shall comply with 690.14(A) through 690.14(D).

690.32 Component Interconnections. Fittings and connectors that are intended to be concealed at the time of on-site assembly, where listed for such use, shall be permitted for on-site interconnection of modules or other array components. Such fittings and connectors shall be equal to the wiring method employed in insulation, temperature rise, and fault-current withstand, and shall be capable of resisting the effects of the environment in which they are used.

690.33 Connectors. The connectors permitted by Article 690 shall comply with 690.33(A) through 690.33(E).

(A) Configuration. The connectors shall be polarized and shall have a configuration that is noninterchangeable with receptacles in other electrical systems on the premises.

Table 690.31(C) Correction Factors

Ambient Temperature (°C)	Temperature Rating of Conductor				Ambient Temperature (°F)
	60°C (140°F)	75°C (167°F)	90°C (194°F)	105°C (221°F)	
30	1.00	1.00	1.00	1.00	86
31–35	0.91	0.94	0.96	0.97	87–95
36–40	0.82	0.88	0.91	0.93	96–104
41–45	0.71	0.82	0.87	0.89	105–113
46–50	0.58	0.75	0.82	0.86	114–122
51–55	0.41	0.67	0.76	0.82	123–131
56–60	—	0.58	0.71	0.77	132–140
61–70	—	0.33	0.58	0.68	141–158
71–80	—	—	0.41	0.58	159–176

(B) Guarding. The connectors shall be constructed and installed so as to guard against inadvertent contact with live parts by persons.

(C) Type. The connectors shall be of the latching or locking type.

(D) Grounding Member. The grounding member shall be the first to make and the last to break contact with the mating connector.

(E) Interruption of Circuit. The connectors shall be capable of interrupting the circuit current without hazard to the operator.

690.34 Access to Boxes. Junction, pull, and outlet boxes located behind modules or panels shall be so installed that the wiring contained in them can be rendered accessible directly or by displacement of a module(s) or panel(s) secured by removable fasteners and connected by a flexible wiring system.

690.35 Ungrounded Photovoltaic Power Systems. Photovoltaic power systems shall be permitted to operate with ungrounded photovoltaic source and output circuits where the system complies with 690.35(A) through 690.35(G).

(A) Disconnects. All photovoltaic source and output circuit conductors shall have disconnects complying with 690, Part III.

(B) Overcurrent Protection. All photovoltaic source and output circuit conductors shall have overcurrent protection complying with 690.9.

(C) Ground-Fault Protection. All photovoltaic source and output circuits shall be provided with a ground-fault protection device or system that complies with (1) through (3):

(1) Detects a ground fault.

(2) Indicates that a ground fault has occurred

(3) Automatically disconnects the conductors and/or shuts off the utility-interactive inverter or charge controller for that portion of the faulted array

(D) The photovoltaic source and output conductors shall consist of sheathed (jacketed) multi-conductor cables or shall be installed in a raceway.

(E) The photovoltaic power system direct-current circuits shall be permitted to be used with ungrounded battery systems complying with 690.71(G).

(F) The photovoltaic power source shall be labeled with the following warning at each junction box, combiner box, disconnect, and device where the ungrounded circuits may be exposed during service:

WARNING
ELECTRIC SHOCK HAZARD. THE DIRECT
CURRENT CIRCUIT CONDUCTORS OF THIS
PHOTOVOLTAIC POWER SYSTEM ARE
UNGROUNDED BUT MAY BE ENERGIZED
WITH RESPECT TO GROUND DUE TO
LEAKAGE PATHS AND/OR GROUND FAULTS.

(G) The inverters or charge controllers used in systems with ungrounded photovoltaic source and output circuits shall be listed for the purpose.

V. Grounding

690.41 System Grounding. For a photovoltaic power source, one conductor of a two-wire system with a photovoltaic system voltage over 50 volts and the reference (center tap) conductor of a bipolar system shall be solidly grounded or shall use other methods that accomplish equivalent system protection in accordance with 250.4(A) and that utilize equipment listed and identified for the use.

Exception: Systems complying with 690.35.

690.42 Point of System Grounding Connection. The dc circuit grounding connection shall be made at any single point on the photovoltaic output circuit.

> FPN: Locating the grounding connection point as close as practicable to the photovoltaic source better protects the system from voltage surges due to lightning.

690.43 Equipment Grounding. Exposed non–current-carrying metal parts of module frames, equipment, and conductor enclosures shall be grounded in accordance with 250.134 or 250.136(A) regardless of voltage.

690.45 Size of Equipment Grounding Conductor. Where not protected by the ground-fault protection equipment required by 690.5, the equipment-grounding conductor for photovoltaic source and photovoltaic output circuits shall be sized for 125 percent of the photovoltaic-originated short-circuit currents in that circuit. Where protected by the ground-fault protection equipment required by 690.5, the equipment-grounding conductors for photovoltaic source and photovoltaic output circuits shall be sized in accordance with 250.122.

690.47 Grounding Electrode System.

(A) Alternating-Current Systems. If installing an ac system, a grounding electrode system shall be provided in accordance with 250.50 through 250.60. The grounding electrode conductor shall be installed in accordance with 250.64.

(B) Direct-Current Systems. If installing a dc system, a grounding electrode system shall be provided in accordance with 250.166 for grounded systems or 250.169 for ungrounded systems. The grounding electrode conductor shall be installed in accordance with 250.64.

(C) Systems with Alternating-Current and Direct-Current Grounding Requirements. Photovoltaic power systems with both alternating-current and direct-current (dc) grounding requirements shall be permitted to be grounded as described in (1) or (2):

(1) A grounding-electrode conductor shall be connected between the identified dc grounding point to a separate dc grounding electrode. The dc grounding-electrode conductor shall be sized according to 250.166. The dc grounding electrode shall be bonded to the ac-grounding electrode to make a grounding electrode system according to 250.52 and 250.53. The bonding conductor shall be no smaller than the largest grounding electrode conductor, either ac or dc.

(2) The dc grounding electrode conductor and ac grounding electrode conductor shall be connected to a single grounding electrode. The separate grounding electrode conductors shall be sized as required by 250.66 (ac) and 250.166 (dc).

690.48 Continuity of Equipment Grounding Systems. Where the removal of equipment disconnects the bonding connection between the grounding electrode conductor and exposed conducting surfaces in the photovoltaic source or output circuit equipment, a bonding jumper shall be installed while the equipment is removed.

690.49 Continuity of Photovoltaic Source and Output Circuit Grounded Conductors. Where the removal of the utility-interactive inverter or other equipment disconnects the bonding connection between the grounding electrode conductor and the photovoltaic source and/or photovoltaic output circuit grounded conductor, a bonding jumper shall be installed to maintain the system grounding while the inverter or other equipment is removed.

VI. Marking

690.51 Modules. Modules shall be marked with identification of terminals or leads as to polarity, maximum overcurrent device rating for module protection, and with the following ratings:

(1) Open-circuit voltage
(2) Operating voltage
(3) Maximum permissible system voltage
(4) Operating current
(5) Short-circuit current
(6) Maximum power

690.52 Alternating-Current Photovoltaic Modules. Alternating-current modules shall be marked with identifi-

cation of terminals or leads and with identification of the following ratings:

(1) Nominal operating ac voltage
(2) Nominal operating ac frequency
(3) Maximum ac power
(4) Maximum ac current
(5) Maximum overcurrent device rating for ac module protection

690.53 Direct-Current Photovoltaic Power Source. A marking for the direct-current photovoltaic power source indicating items (1) through (4) shall be provided by the installer at an accessible location at the disconnecting means for this power source:

(1) Operating current
(2) Operating voltage
(3) Maximum system voltage
(4) Short-circuit current

> FPN: Reflecting systems used for irradiance enhancement may result in increased levels of output current and power.

690.54 Interactive System Point of Interconnection. All interactive system(s) points of interconnection with other sources shall be marked at an accessible location at the disconnecting means as a power source with the maximum ac output operating current and the operating ac voltage.

690.55 Photovoltaic Power Systems Employing Energy Storage. Photovoltaic power systems employing energy storage shall also be marked with the maximum operating voltage, including any equalization voltage and the polarity of the grounded circuit conductor.

690.56 Identification of Power Sources.

(A) Facilities with Stand-Alone Systems. Any structure or building with a photovoltaic power system that is not connected to a utility service source and is a stand-alone system shall have a permanent plaque or directory installed on the exterior of the building or structure at a readily visible location acceptable to the authority having jurisdiction. The plaque or directory shall indicate the location of system disconnecting means and that the structure contains a stand-alone electrical power system.

(B) Facilities with Utility Services and PV Systems. Buildings or structures with both utility service and a photovoltaic system shall have a permanent plaque or directory providing the location of the service disconnecting means and the photovoltaic system disconnecting means, if not located at the same location.

VII. Connection to Other Sources

690.60 Identified Interactive Equipment. Only inverters and ac modules listed and identified as interactive shall be permitted in interactive systems.

690.61 Loss of Interactive System Power. An inverter or an ac module in an interactive solar photovoltaic system shall automatically de-energize its output to the connected electrical production and distribution network upon loss of voltage in that system and shall remain in that state until the electrical production and distribution network voltage has been restored.

A normally interactive solar photovoltaic system shall be permitted to operate as a stand-alone system to supply loads that have been disconnected from electrical production and distribution network sources.

690.62 Ampacity of Neutral Conductor. If a single-phase, 2-wire inverter output is connected to the neutral and one ungrounded conductor (only) of a 3-wire system or of a 3-phase, 4-wire wye-connected system, the maximum load connected between the neutral and any one ungrounded conductor plus the inverter output rating shall not exceed the ampacity of the neutral conductor.

690.63 Unbalanced Interconnections.

(A) Single Phase. Single-phase inverters for photovoltaic systems and ac modules in interactive solar photovoltaic systems shall not be connected to 3-phase power systems unless the interconnected system is designed so that significant unbalanced voltages cannot result.

(B) Three Phase. Three-phase inverters and 3-phase ac modules in interactive systems shall have all phases automatically de-energized upon loss of, or unbalanced, voltage in one or more phases unless the interconnected system is designed so that significant unbalanced voltages will not result.

690.64 Point of Connection. The output of a photovoltaic power source shall be connected as specified in 690.64(A) or 690.64(B).

(A) Supply Side. A photovoltaic power source shall be permitted to be connected to the supply side of the service disconnecting means as permitted in 230.82(6).

(B) Load Side. A photovoltaic power source shall be permitted to be connected to the load side of the service disconnecting means of the other source(s) at any distribution equipment on the premises, provided that all of the following conditions are met:

(1) Each source interconnection shall be made at a dedicated circuit breaker or fusible disconnecting means.

(2) The sum of the ampere ratings of overcurrent devices in circuits supplying power to a busbar or conductor shall not exceed the rating of the busbar or conductor.

Exception: For a dwelling unit, the sum of the ampere ratings of the overcurrent devices shall not exceed 120 percent of the rating of the busbar or conductor.

(3) The interconnection point shall be on the line side of all ground-fault protection equipment.

Exception: Connection shall be permitted to be made to the load side of ground-fault protection, provided that there is ground-fault protection for equipment from all ground-fault current sources.

(4) Equipment containing overcurrent devices in circuits supplying power to a busbar or conductor shall be marked to indicate the presence of all sources.

Exception: Equipment with power supplied from a single point of connection.

(5) Circuit breakers, if backfed, shall be identified for such operation. Dedicated circuit breakers backfed from listed utility-interactive inverters complying with 690.60 shall not be required to be individually clamped to the panelboard bus bars. A front panel shall clamp all circuit breakers to the panelboard bus bars. Main circuit breakers connected directly to energized feeders shall also be individually clamped.

VIII. Storage Batteries

690.71 Installation.

(A) General. Storage batteries in a solar photovoltaic system shall be installed in accordance with the provisions of Article 480. The interconnected battery cells shall be considered grounded where the photovoltaic power source is installed in accordance with 690.41.

(B) Dwellings.

(1) Operating Voltage. Storage batteries for dwellings shall have the cells connected so as to operate at less than 50 volts nominal. Lead-acid storage batteries for dwellings shall have no more than twenty-four 2-volt cells connected in series (48-volts nominal).

Exception: Where live parts are not accessible during routine battery maintenance, a battery system voltage in accordance with 690.7 shall be permitted.

(2) Guarding of Live Parts. Live parts of battery systems for dwellings shall be guarded to prevent accidental contact by persons or objects, regardless of voltage or battery type.

FPN: Batteries in solar photovoltaic systems are subject to extensive charge–discharge cycles and typically require frequent maintenance, such as checking electrolyte and cleaning connections.

(C) Current Limiting. A listed, current-limiting, overcurrent device shall be installed in each circuit adjacent to the batteries where the available short-circuit current from a battery or battery bank exceeds the interrupting or withstand ratings of other equipment in that circuit. The installation of current-limiting fuses shall comply with 690.16.

(D) Battery Nonconductive Cases and Conductive Racks. Flooded, vented, lead-acid batteries with more than twenty-four 2-volt cells connected in series (48 volts, nominal) shall not use conductive cases or shall not be installed in conductive cases. Conductive racks used to support the nonconductive cases shall be permitted where no rack material is located within 150 mm (6 in.) of the tops of the nonconductive cases.

This requirement shall not apply to any type of valve-regulated lead-acid (VRLA) battery or any other types of sealed batteries that may require steel cases for proper operation.

(E) Disconnection of Series Battery Circuits. Battery circuits subject to field servicing, where more than twenty-four 2-volt cells are connected in series (48 volts, nominal), shall have provisions to disconnect the series-connected strings into segments of 24 cells or less for maintenance by qualified persons. Non–load-break bolted or plug-in disconnects shall be permitted.

(F) Battery Maintenance Disconnecting Means. Battery installations, where there are more than twenty-four 2-volt cells connected in series (48 volts, nominal), shall have a disconnecting means, accessible only to qualified persons, that disconnects the grounded circuit conductor(s) in the battery electrical system for maintenance. This disconnecting means shall not disconnect the grounded circuit conductor(s) for the remainder of the photovoltaic electrical system. A non–load-break-rated switch shall be permitted to be used as the disconnecting means.

(G) Battery Systems of More Than 48 Volts. On photovoltaic systems where the battery system consists of more than twenty-four 2-volt cells connected in series (more than 48 volts, nominal), the battery system shall be permitted to operate with ungrounded conductors, provided the following conditions are met:

(1) The photovoltaic array source and output circuits shall comply with 690.41.

(2) The dc and ac load circuits shall be solidly grounded.

(3) All main ungrounded battery input/output circuit conductors shall be provided with switched disconnects and overcurrent protection.

(4) A ground-fault detector and indicator shall be installed to monitor for ground faults in the battery bank.

690.72 Charge Control.

(A) General. Equipment shall be provided to control the charging process of the battery. Charge control shall not be required where the design of the photovoltaic source circuit is matched to the voltage rating and charge current requirements of the interconnected battery cells and the maximum charging current multiplied by 1 hour is less than 3 percent of the rated battery capacity expressed in ampere-hours or as recommended by the battery manufacturer.

All adjusting means for control of the charging process shall be accessible only to qualified persons.

> FPN: Certain battery types such as valve-regulated lead acid or nickel cadmium can experience thermal failure when overcharged.

(B) Diversion Charge Controller.

(1) Sole Means of Regulating Charging. A photovoltaic power system employing a diversion charge controller as the sole means of regulating the charging of a battery shall be equipped with a second independent means to prevent overcharging of the battery.

(2) Circuits with Direct-Current Diversion Charge Controller and Diversion Load. Circuits containing a dc diversion charge controller and a dc diversion load shall comply with the following:

(1) The current rating of the diversion load shall be less than or equal to the current rating of the diversion load charge controller. The voltage rating of the diversion load shall be greater than the maximum battery voltage. The power rating of the diversion load shall be at least 150 percent of the power rating of the photovoltaic array.

(2) The conductor ampacity and the rating of the overcurrent device for this circuit shall be at least 150 percent of the maximum current rating of the diversion charge controller.

(3) PV Systems Using Utility-Interactive Inverters. Photovoltaic power systems using utility-interactive inverters to control battery state-of-charge by diverting excess power into the utility system shall comply with (1) and (2):

(1) These systems shall not be required to comply with 690.72(B)(2). The charge regulation circuits used shall comply with the requirements of 690.8.

(2) These systems shall have a second, independent means of controlling the battery charging process for use when the utility is not present or when the primary charge controller fails or is disabled.

690.74 Battery Interconnections. Flexible cables, as identified in Article 400, in sizes 2/0 AWG and larger shall be permitted within the battery enclosure from battery terminals to a nearby junction box where they shall be connected to an approved wiring method. Flexible battery cables shall also be permitted between batteries and cells within the battery enclosure. Such cables shall be listed for hard-service use and identified as moisture resistant.

IX. Systems Over 600 Volts

690.80 General. Solar photovoltaic systems with a maximum system voltage over 600 volts dc shall comply with Article 490 and other requirements applicable to installations rated over 600 volts.

690.85 Definitions. For the purposes of Part IX of this article, the voltages used to determine cable and equipment ratings are as follows.

Battery Circuits. In battery circuits, the highest voltage experienced under charging or equalizing conditions.

Photovoltaic Circuits. In dc photovoltaic source circuits and photovoltaic output circuits, the maximum system voltage.

ARTICLE 692
Fuel Cell Systems

I. General

692.1 Scope. This article identifies the requirements for the installation of fuel cell power systems, which may be stand-alone or interactive with other electrical power production sources and may be with or without electrical energy storage such as batteries. These systems may have ac or dc output for utilization.

692.2 Definitions.

Fuel Cell. An electrochemical system that consumes fuel to produce an electric current. The main chemical reaction used in a fuel cell for producing electric power is not combustion. However, there may be sources of combustion used within the overall fuel cell system such as reformers/fuel processors.

Fuel Cell System. The complete aggregate of equipment used to convert chemical fuel into usable electricity. A fuel cell system typically consists of a reformer, stack, power inverter, and auxiliary equipment.

Interactive System. A fuel cell system that operates in parallel with and may deliver power to an electrical production and distribution network. For the purpose of this definition, an energy storage subsystem of a fuel cell system, such as a battery, is not another electrical production source.

Maximum System Voltage. The highest fuel cell inverter output voltage between any ungrounded conductors present at accessible output terminals.

Output Circuit. The conductors used to connect the fuel cell system to its electrical point of delivery. In the case of sites that have series- or parallel-connected multiple units, the term *output circuit* also refers to the conductors used to electrically interconnect the fuel cell system(s).

Point of Common Coupling. The point at which the power production and distribution network and the customer interface occurs in an interactive system. Typically, this is the load side of the power network meter.

Stand-Alone System. A fuel cell system that supplies power independently of an electrical production and distribution network.

692.3 Other Articles. Wherever the requirements of other articles of this *Code* and Article 692 differ, the requirements of Article 692 shall apply, and, if the system is operated in parallel with a primary source(s) of electricity, the requirements in 705.14, 705.16, 705.32, and 705.43 shall apply.

692.4 Installation.

(A) Fuel Cell System. A fuel cell system shall be permitted to supply a building or other structure in addition to any service(s) of another electricity supply system(s).

(B) Identification. A permanent plaque or directory, denoting all electrical power sources on or in the premises, shall be installed at each service equipment location.

692.6 Listing Requirement. The fuel cell system shall be evaluated and listed for its intended application prior to installation.

II. Circuit Requirements

692.8 Circuit Sizing and Current.

(A) Nameplate Rated Circuit Current. The nameplate(s) rated circuit current shall be the rated current indicated on the fuel cell nameplate(s).

(B) Conductor Ampacity and Overcurrent Device Ratings. The ampacity of the feeder circuit conductors from the fuel cell system(s) to the premises wiring system shall not be less than the greater of (1) nameplate(s) rated circuit current or (2) the rating of the fuel cell system(s) overcurrent protective device(s).

(C) Ampacity of Grounded or Neutral Conductor. If an interactive single-phase, 2-wire fuel cell output(s) is connected to the grounded or neutral conductor and a single ungrounded conductor of a 3-wire system or of a 3-phase,

4-wire wye-connected system, the maximum unbalanced neutral load current plus the fuel cell system(s) output rating shall not exceed the ampacity of the grounded or neutral conductor.

692.9 Overcurrent Protection.

(A) Circuits and Equipment. If the fuel cell system is provided with overcurrent protection sufficient to protect the circuit conductors that supply the load, additional circuit overcurrent devices shall not be required. Equipment and conductors connected to more than one electrical source shall be protected.

(B) Accessibility. Overcurrent devices shall be readily accessible.

692.10 Stand-Alone Systems. The premises wiring system shall meet the requirements of this *Code* except as modified by 692.10(A), (B), and (C).

(A) Fuel Cell System Output. The fuel cell system output from a stand-alone system shall be permitted to supply ac power to the building or structure disconnecting means at current levels below the rating of that disconnecting means.

(B) Sizing and Protection. The circuit conductors between the fuel cell system(s) output and the building or structure disconnecting means shall be sized based on the output rating of the fuel cell system(s). These conductors shall be protected from overcurrents in accordance with 240.4. The overcurrent protection shall be located at the output of the fuel cell system(s).

(C) Single 120-Volt Nominal Supply. The inverter output of a stand-alone fuel cell system shall be permitted to supply 120 volts, nominal, to single-phase, 3-wire 120/240-volt service equipment or distribution panels where there are no 240-volt loads and where there are no multiwire branch circuits. In all installations, the rating of the overcurrent device connected to the output of the fuel cell system(s) shall be less than the rating of the service equipment. This equipment shall be marked as follows:

WARNING
SINGLE 120-VOLT SUPPLY.
DO NOT CONNECT MULTIWIRE
BRANCH CIRCUITS!

III. Disconnecting Means

692.13 All Conductors. Means shall be provided to disconnect all current-carrying conductors of a fuel cell system power source from all other conductors in a building or other structure.

692.14 Provisions. The provisions of 225.31 and 225.33 through 225.40 shall apply to the fuel cell source disconnecting means. The disconnecting means shall not be required to be suitable as service equipment and shall be rated in accordance with 692.17.

692.17 Switch or Circuit Breaker. The disconnecting means for ungrounded conductors shall consist of readily accessible, manually operable switch(es) or circuit breaker(s).

Where all terminals of the disconnecting means may be energized in the open position, a warning sign shall be mounted on or adjacent to the disconnecting means. The sign shall be clearly legible and shall have the following words or equivalent:

DANGER
ELECTRIC SHOCK HAZARD.
DO NOT TOUCH TERMINALS.
TERMINALS ON BOTH THE LINE AND
LOAD SIDES MAY BE ENERGIZED
IN THE OPEN POSITION.

IV. Wiring Methods

692.31 Wiring Systems. All raceway and cable wiring methods included in Chapter 3 of this *Code* and other wiring systems and fittings specifically intended and identified for use with fuel cell systems shall be permitted. Where wiring devices with integral enclosures are used, sufficient length of cable shall be provided to facilitate replacement.

V. Grounding

692.41 System Grounding. For a fuel cell system output circuit, one conductor of a 2-wire system rated over 50 volts and a neutral conductor of a 3-wire system shall be solidly grounded by either 692.41(A) or 692.41(B).

(A) Stand-Alone Systems. Grounding and bonding shall be in accordance with 250.30.

(B) Other Than Stand-Alone Systems.

(1) Two-Wire Systems. One conductor shall be terminated at the grounded circuit conductor terminal of the premises wiring system.

(2) Three-Wire Systems. The neutral conductor shall be terminated at the grounded circuit conductor terminal of the premises wiring system.

692.44 Equipment Grounding Conductor. A separate equipment grounding conductor shall be installed.

692.45 Size of Equipment Grounding Conductor. The equipment grounding conductor shall be sized in accordance with 250.122.

692.47 Grounding Electrode System. Any supplementary grounding electrode(s) required by the manufacturer shall be connected to the equipment grounding conductor specified in 250.118.

VI. Marking

692.53 Fuel Cell Power Sources. A marking specifying the fuel cell system, output voltage, output power rating, and continuous output current rating shall be provided at the disconnecting means for the fuel cell power source at an accessible location on the site.

692.54 Fuel Shut-Off. The location of the manual fuel shut-off valve shall be marked at the location of the primary disconnecting means of the building or circuits supplied.

692.56 Stored Energy. A fuel cell system that stores electrical energy shall require the following warning sign, or equivalent, at the location of the service disconnecting means of the premises:

WARNING
FUEL CELL POWER SYSTEM CONTAINS
ELECTRICAL ENERGY STORAGE DEVICES.

VII. Connection to Other Circuits

692.59 Transfer Switch. A transfer switch shall be required in non–grid-interactive systems that use utility grid backup. The transfer switch shall maintain isolation between the electrical production and distribution network and the fuel cell system. The transfer switch shall be permitted to be located externally or internally to the fuel cell system unit. When the utility service conductors of the structure are connected to the transfer switch, the switch shall comply with Article 230, Part V.

692.60 Identified Interactive Equipment. Only fuel cell systems listed and identified as interactive shall be permitted in interactive systems.

692.61 Output Characteristics. The output of a fuel cell system operating in parallel with an electric supply system shall be compatible with the voltage, wave shape, and frequency of the system to which it is connected.

FPN: The term *compatible* does not necessarily mean matching the primary source wave shape.

692.62 Loss of Interactive System Power. The fuel cell system shall be provided with a means of detecting when the electrical production and distribution network has become de-energized and shall not feed the electrical production and distribution network side of the point of common coupling during this condition. The fuel cell system shall remain in that state until the electrical production and distribution network voltage has been restored.

A normally interactive fuel cell system shall be permitted to operate as a stand-alone system to supply loads that have been disconnected from electrical production and distribution network sources.

692.64 Unbalanced Interconnections.

(A) Single Phase. Single-phase interactive fuel cell systems shall not be connected to a 3-phase power system unless the interactive system is so designed that significant unbalanced voltages cannot result.

(B) Three Phase. Three-phase interactive fuel cell systems shall have all phases automatically de-energized upon loss of voltage, or upon unbalance of voltage in one or more phases, unless the interactive system is designed so that significant unbalanced voltages will not result.

692.65 Point of Connection. The output of a fuel cell system power source shall be connected as specified in 692.65(A) or 692.65(B).

(A) Supply Side. A fuel cell system power source shall be permitted to be connected to the supply side of the service disconnecting means as permitted in 230.82(6).

(B) Load Side. A fuel cell system power source shall be permitted to be connected to the load side of the service disconnecting means of the other source(s) at any distribution equipment on the premises, provided that all of the following conditions are met:

(1) Each source interconnection shall be made at a dedicated circuit breaker or fusible disconnecting means.

(2) The sum of the ampere ratings of overcurrent devices in circuits supplying power to a busbar or conductor shall not exceed the rating of the busbar or conductor.

Exception: For a dwelling unit, the sum of the ampere ratings of the overcurrent devices shall not exceed 120 percent of the rating of the busbar or conductor.

(3) The interconnection point shall be on the line side of all ground-fault protection equipment.

(4) Equipment containing overcurrent devices in circuits supplying power to a busbar or conductor shall be marked to indicate the presence of all sources.

(5) Equipment such as circuit breakers, if backfed, shall be identified for such operation.

(6) The circuit breaker on the dedicated output of a utility-interactive inverter shall be positioned in the distribution equipment at the opposite (load) end from the input feeder connection or main circuit location. A permanent warning label shall be applied to the distribution equipment with the following, or equivalent:

WARNING
FUEL CELL POWER SYSTEM OUTPUT.
DO NOT RELOCATE THIS CIRCUIT BREAKER.

VIII. Outputs Over 600 Volts

692.80 General. Fuel cell systems with a maximum output voltage over 600 volts ac shall comply with the requirements of other articles applicable to such installations.

ARTICLE 695
Fire Pumps

FPN: Rules that are followed by a reference in brackets contain text that has been extracted from NFPA 20-2003, *Standard for the Installation of Stationary Pumps for Fire Protection.* Only editorial changes were made to the extracted text to make it consistent with this *Code.*

695.1 Scope.

(A) Covered. This article covers the installation of the following:

(1) Electric power sources and interconnecting circuits

(2) Switching and control equipment dedicated to fire pump drivers

(B) Not Covered. This article does not cover the following:

(1) The performance, maintenance, and acceptance testing of the fire pump system, and the internal wiring of the components of the system

(2) Pressure maintenance (jockey or makeup) pumps

FPN: See NFPA 20-2003, *Standard for the Installation of Stationary Pumps for Fire Protection,* for further information.

695.2 Definitions.

Fault Tolerant External Control Circuits. Those control circuits either entering or leaving the fire pump controller enclosure, which if broken, disconnected, or shorted will not prevent the controller from starting the fire pump from all other internal or external means and may cause the controller to start the pump under these conditions.

On-Site Power Production Facility. The normal supply of electric power for the site that is expected to be constantly producing power.

On-Site Standby Generator. A facility producing electric power on site as the alternate supply of electric power. It differs from an on-site power production facility, in that it is not constantly producing power.

695.3 Power Source(s) for Electric Motor-Driven Fire Pumps. Electric motor-driven fire pumps shall have a reliable source of power.

(A) Individual Sources. Where reliable, and where capable of carrying indefinitely the sum of the locked-rotor current of the fire pump motor(s) and the pressure maintenance pump motor(s) and the full-load current of the associated fire pump accessory equipment when connected to this power supply, the power source for an electric motor-driven fire pump shall be one or more of the following.

(1) Electric Utility Service Connection. A fire pump shall be permitted to be supplied by a separate service, or from a connection located ahead of and not within the same cabinet, enclosure, or vertical switchboard section as the service disconnecting means. The connection shall be located and arranged so as to minimize the possibility of damage by fire from within the premises and from exposing hazards. A tap ahead of the service disconnecting means shall comply with 230.82(5). The service equipment shall comply with the labeling requirements in 230.2 and the location requirements in 230.72(B). [NFPA 20:9.2.2]

(2) On-Site Power Production Facility. A fire pump shall be permitted to be supplied by an on-site power production facility. The source facility shall be located and protected to minimize the possibility of damage by fire. [NFPA 20:9.2.3]

(B) Multiple Sources. Where reliable power cannot be obtained from a source described in 695.3(A), power shall be supplied from an approved combination of two or more of either of such sources, or from an approved combination of feeders constituting two or more power sources as covered in 695.3(B)(2), or from an approved combination of one or more of such power sources in combination with an on-site standby generator complying with 695.3(B)(1) and (B)(3).

(1) Generator Capacity. An on-site generator(s) used to comply with this section shall be of sufficient capacity to allow normal starting and running of the motor(s) driving the fire pump(s) while supplying all other simultaneously operated load. Automatic shedding of one or more optional standby loads in order to comply with this capacity requirement shall be permitted. A tap ahead of the on-site generator disconnecting means shall not be required. The requirements of 430.113 shall not apply. [NFPA 20:9.6.1]

(2) Feeder Sources. This section applies to multibuilding campus-style complexes with fire pumps at one or more buildings. Where sources in 695.3(A) are not practicable, and with the approval of the authority having jurisdiction, two or more feeder sources shall be permitted as one power source or as more than one power source where such feeders are connected to or derived from separate utility services. The connection(s), overcurrent protective device(s), and disconnecting means for such feeders shall meet the requirements of 695.4(B). [NFPA 20:9.2.5.3]

(3) Arrangement. The power sources shall be arranged so that a fire at one source will not cause an interruption at the other source. [NFPA 20:9.2.5.1]

695.4 Continuity of Power. Circuits that supply electric motor-driven fire pumps shall be supervised from inadvertent disconnection as covered in 695.4(A) or 695.4(B).

(A) Direct Connection. The supply conductors shall directly connect the power source to either a listed fire pump controller or listed combination fire pump controller and power transfer switch. [NFPA 20:9.3.2.2.2]

(B) Supervised Connection. A single disconnecting means and associated overcurrent protective device(s) shall be permitted to be installed between a remote power source and one of the following:

(1) A listed fire pump controller

(2) A listed fire pump power transfer switch

(3) A listed combination fire pump controller and power transfer switch

For systems installed under the provisions of 695.3(B)(2) only, such additional disconnecting means and associated overcurrent protective device(s) shall be permitted as required to comply with other provisions of this *Code*. Overcurrent protective devices between an on-site standby generator and a fire pump controller shall be selected and sized according to 430.62 to provide short-circuit protection only. All disconnecting devices and overcurrent protective devices that are unique to the fire pump loads shall comply with 695.4(B)(1) through (B)(5).

(1) Overcurrent Device Selection. The overcurrent protective device(s) shall be selected or set to carry indefinitely the sum of the locked-rotor current of the fire pump motor(s) and the pressure maintenance pump motor(s) and the full-load current of the associated fire pump accessory equipment when connected to this power supply. The requirement to carry the locked-rotor currents indefinitely shall not apply to conductors or devices other than overcurrent devices in the fire pump motor circuit(s).

(2) Disconnecting Means. The disconnecting means shall comply with all of the following:

(1) Be identified as suitable for use as service equipment

(2) Be lockable in the closed position

(3) Not be located within equipment that feeds loads other than the fire pump

(4) Be located sufficiently remote from other building or other fire pump source disconnecting means such that inadvertent contemporaneous operation would be unlikely

(3) Disconnect Marking. The disconnecting means shall be marked "Fire Pump Disconnecting Means." The letters shall be at least 25 mm (1 in.) in height, and they shall be visible without opening enclosure doors or covers.

(4) Controller Marking. A placard shall be placed adjacent to the fire pump controller, stating the location of this disconnecting means and the location of the key (if the disconnecting means is locked).

(5) Supervision. The disconnecting means shall be supervised in the closed position by one of the following methods:

(1) Central station, proprietary, or remote station signal device

(2) Local signaling service that causes the sounding of an audible signal at a constantly attended point

(3) Locking the disconnecting means in the closed position

(4) Sealing of disconnecting means and approved weekly recorded inspections when the disconnecting means are located within fenced enclosures or in buildings under the control of the owner [NFPA 20:9.3.2.2.3]

695.5 Transformers. Where the service or system voltage is different from the utilization voltage of the fire pump motor, transformer(s) protected by disconnecting means and overcurrent protective devices shall be permitted to be installed between the system supply and the fire pump controller in accordance with 695.5(A) and (B), or (C). Only transformers covered in 695.5(C) shall be permitted to supply loads not directly associated with the fire pump system.

(A) Size. Where a transformer supplies an electric motor-driven fire pump, it shall be rated at a minimum of 125 percent of the sum of the fire pump motor(s) and pressure maintenance pump(s) motor loads, and 100 percent of the associated fire pump accessory equipment supplied by the transformer.

(B) Overcurrent Protection. The primary overcurrent protective device(s) shall be selected or set to carry indefinitely the sum of the locked-rotor current of the fire pump motor(s) and the pressure maintenance pump motor(s) and the full-load current of the associated fire pump accessory equipment when connected to this power supply. Secondary overcurrent protection shall not be permitted. The requirement to carry the locked-rotor currents indefinitely shall not apply to conductors or devices other than overcurrent devices in the fire pump motor circuit(s).

(C) Feeder Source. Where a feeder source is provided in accordance with 695.3(B)(2), transformers supplying the fire pump system shall be permitted to supply other loads. All other loads shall be calculated in accordance with Article 220, including demand factors as applicable.

(1) Size. Transformers shall be rated at a minimum of 125 percent of the sum of the fire pump motor(s) and pressure maintenance pump(s) motor loads, and 100 percent of the remaining load supplied by the transformer.

(2) Overcurrent Protection. The transformer size, the feeder size, and the overcurrent protective device(s) shall be coordinated such that overcurrent protection is provided for the transformer in accordance with 450.3 and for the feeder in accordance with 215.3, and such that the overcurrent protective device(s) is selected or set to carry indefinitely the sum of the locked-rotor current of the fire pump motor(s), the pressure maintenance pump motor(s), the full-load current of the associated fire pump accessory equipment, and 100 percent of the remaining loads supplied by the transformer. The requirement to carry the locked-rotor currents indefinitely shall not apply to conductors or devices other than overcurrent devices in the fire pump motor circuit(s).

695.6 Power Wiring. Power circuits and wiring methods shall comply with the requirements in 695.6(A) through (H), and as permitted in 230.90(A), Exception No. 4; 230.94, Exception No. 4; 230.95, Exception No. 2; 240.13; 230.208; 240.4(A); and 430.31.

(A) Service Conductors. Supply conductors shall be physically routed outside a building(s) and shall be installed as service entrance conductors in accordance with Article 230. Where supply conductors cannot be physically routed outside buildings, they shall be permitted to be routed through buildings where installed in accordance with 230.6(1) or 230.6(2). Where a fire pump is wired under the provisions of 695.3(B)(2), this requirement shall apply to all supply conductors on the load side of the service disconnecting means that constitute the normal source of supply to that fire pump.

Exception: Where there are multiple sources of supply with means for automatic connection from one source to the other, the requirement shall apply only to those conductors on the load side of that point of automatic connection between sources.

(B) Circuit Conductors. Fire pump supply conductors on the load side of the final disconnecting means and overcurrent device(s) permitted by 695.4(B) shall be kept entirely independent of all other wiring. They shall supply only loads that are directly associated with the fire pump system, and they shall be protected to resist potential damage by fire, structural failure, or operational accident. They shall be permitted to be routed through a building(s) using one of the following methods:

(1) Be encased in a minimum 50 mm (2 in.) of concrete

(2) Be within an enclosed construction dedicated to the fire pump circuit(s) and having a minimum of a 1-hour fire resistive rating

(3) Be a listed electrical circuit protective system with a minimum 1-hour fire rating

Exception: The supply conductors located in the electrical equipment room where they originate and in the fire pump room shall not be required to have the minimum 1-hour fire separation or fire resistance rating, unless otherwise required by 700.9(D) of this Code.

(C) Conductor Size.

(1) Fire Pump Motors and Other Equipment. Conductors supplying a fire pump motor(s), pressure maintenance pumps, and associated fire pump accessory equipment shall have a rating not less than 125 percent of the sum of the fire pump motor(s) and pressure maintenance motor(s) full-load current(s), and 100 percent of the associated fire pump accessory equipment.

(2) Fire Pump Motors Only. Conductors supplying only a fire pump motor shall have a minimum ampacity in accordance with 430.22 and shall comply with the voltage drop requirements in 695.7.

(D) Overload Protection. Power circuits shall not have automatic protection against overloads. Branch-circuit and feeder conductors shall be protected against short circuit only. Where a tap is made to supply a fire pump, the wiring shall be treated as service conductors in accordance with 230.6. The applicable distance and size restrictions in 240.21 shall not apply.

Exception No. 1: Conductors between storage batteries and the engine shall not require overcurrent protection or disconnecting means.

Exception No. 2: For on-site standby generator(s) rated to produce continuous current in excess of 225 percent of the full-load amperes of the fire pump motor, the conductors between the on-site generator(s) and the combination fire pump transfer switch controller or separately mounted transfer switch shall be installed in accordance with 695.6(B) or protected in accordance with 430.52.

The protection provided shall be in accordance with the short-circuit current rating of the combination fire pump transfer switch controller or separately mounted transfer switch.

(E) Pump Wiring. All wiring from the controllers to the pump motors shall be in rigid metal conduit, intermediate metal conduit, liquidtight flexible metal conduit, or liquidtight flexible nonmetallic conduit Type LFNC-B, listed Type MC cable with an impervious covering, or Type MI cable.

(F) Junction Points. Where wire connectors are used in the fire pump circuit, the connectors shall be listed. A fire pump controller or fire pump power transfer switch, where provided, shall not be used as a junction box to supply other equipment, including a pressure maintenance (jockey) pump(s). A fire pump controller and fire pump power transfer switch, where provided, shall not serve any load other than the fire pump for which it is intended.

(G) Mechanical Protection. All wiring from engine controllers and batteries shall be protected against physical damage and shall be installed in accordance with the controller and engine manufacturer's instructions.

(H) Ground Fault Protection of Equipment. Ground fault protection of equipment shall not be permitted for fire pumps.

695.7 Voltage Drop. The voltage at the controller line terminals shall not drop more than 15 percent below normal (controller-rated voltage) under motor starting conditions. The voltage at the motor terminals shall not drop more than 5 percent below the voltage rating of the motor when the motor is operating at 115 percent of the full-load current rating of the motor.

Exception: This limitation shall not apply for emergency run mechanical starting. [NFPA 20:9.4]

695.10 Listed Equipment. Diesel engine fire pump controllers, electric fire pump controllers, electric motors, fire pump power transfer switches, foam pump controllers, and limited service controllers shall be listed for fire pump service. [NFPA 20:9.5.1.1, 10.1.2.1, 12.1.3.1]

695.12 Equipment Location.

(A) Controllers and Transfer Switches. Electric motor-driven fire pump controllers and power transfer switches shall be located as close as practicable to, and within sight of, the motors that they control.

(B) Engine-Drive Controllers. Engine-drive fire pump controllers shall be located as close as is practical to, and within sight of, the engines that they control.

(C) Storage Batteries. Storage batteries for fire pump engine drives shall be supported above the floor, secured against displacement, and located where they are not subject to physical damage, flooding with water, excessive temperature, or excessive vibration.

(D) Energized Equipment. All energized equipment parts shall be located at least 300 mm (12 in.) above the floor level.

(E) Protection Against Pump Water. Fire pump controllers and power transfer switches shall be located or protected so that they are not damaged by water escaping from pumps or pump connections.

(F) Mounting. All fire pump control equipment shall be mounted in a substantial manner on noncombustible supporting structures.

695.14 Control Wiring.

(A) Control Circuit Failures. External control circuits that extend outside the fire pump room shall be arranged so that failure of any external circuit (open or short circuit) shall not prevent the operation of a pump(s) from all other internal or external means. Breakage, disconnecting, shorting of the wires, or loss of power to these circuits could cause continuous running of the fire pump but shall not prevent the controller(s) from starting the fire pump(s) due to causes other than these external control circuits. All control conductors within the fire pump room that are not fault tolerant shall be protected against physical damage. [NFPA 20:10.5.2.6, 12.5.2.5]

(B) Sensor Functioning. No undervoltage, phase-loss, frequency-sensitive, or other sensor(s) shall be installed that automatically or manually prohibit actuation of the motor contactor. [NFPA 20:10.4.5.6]

Exception: A phase loss sensor(s) shall be permitted only as a part of a listed fire pump controller.

(C) Remote Device(s). No remote device(s) shall be installed that will prevent automatic operation of the transfer switch. [NFPA 20:10.8.1.3]

(D) Engine-Drive Control Wiring. All wiring between the controller and the diesel engine shall be stranded and sized to continuously carry the charging or control currents as required by the controller manufacturer. Such wiring shall be protected against physical damage. Controller manufacturer's specifications for distance and wire size shall be followed. [NFPA 20:12.3.5.1]

(E) Electric Fire Pump Control Wiring Methods. All electric motor-driven fire pump control wiring shall be in rigid metal conduit, intermediate metal conduit, liquidtight flexible metal conduit, liquidtight flexible nonmetallic conduit Type B (LFNC-B), listed Type MC cable with an impervious covering, or Type MI cable.

(F) Generator Control Wiring Methods. Control conductors installed between the fire pump power transfer switch and the standby generator supplying the fire pump during normal power loss shall be kept entirely independent of all other wiring. They shall be protected to resist potential damage by fire or structural failure. They shall be permitted to be routed through a building(s) encased in 50 mm (2 in.) of concrete or within enclosed construction dedicated to the fire pump circuits and having a minimum 1-hour fire resistance rating, or circuit protective systems with a minimum of 1-hour fire resistance. The installation shall comply with any restrictions provided in the listing of the electrical circuit protective system used.

Chapter 7 Special Conditions

ARTICLE 700
Emergency Systems

I. General

700.1 Scope. The provisions of this article apply to the electrical safety of the installation, operation, and maintenance of emergency systems consisting of circuits and equipment intended to supply, distribute, and control electricity for illumination, power, or both, to required facilities when the normal electrical supply or system is interrupted.

Emergency systems are those systems legally required and classed as emergency by municipal, state, federal, or other codes, or by any governmental agency having jurisdiction. These systems are intended to automatically supply illumination, power, or both, to designated areas and equipment in the event of failure of the normal supply or in the event of accident to elements of a system intended to supply, distribute, and control power and illumination essential for safety to human life.

FPN No. 1: For further information regarding wiring and installation of emergency systems in health care facilities, see Article 517.

FPN No. 2: For further information regarding performance and maintenance of emergency systems in health care facilities, see NFPA 99-2002, *Standard for Health Care Facilities.*

FPN No. 3: Emergency systems are generally installed in places of assembly where artificial illumination is required for safe exiting and for panic control in buildings subject to occupancy by large numbers of persons, such as hotels, theaters, sports arenas, health care facilities, and similar institutions. Emergency systems may also provide power for such functions as ventilation where essential to maintain life, fire detection and alarm systems, elevators, fire pumps, public safety communications systems, industrial processes where current interruption would produce serious life safety or health hazards, and similar functions.

FPN No. 4: For specification of locations where emergency lighting is considered essential to life safety, see NFPA *101*®-2003, *Life Safety Code*®.

FPN No. 5: For further information regarding performance of emergency and standby power systems, see NFPA 110-2002, *Standard for Emergency and Standby Power Systems.*

700.2 Application of Other Articles. Except as modified by this article, all applicable articles of this *Code* shall apply.

700.3 Equipment Approval. All equipment shall be approved for use on emergency systems.

700.4 Tests and Maintenance.

(A) Conduct or Witness Test. The authority having jurisdiction shall conduct or witness a test of the complete system upon installation and periodically afterward.

(B) Tested Periodically. Systems shall be tested periodically on a schedule acceptable to the authority having jurisdiction to ensure the systems are maintained in proper operating condition.

(C) Battery Systems Maintenance. Where battery systems or unit equipments are involved, including batteries used for starting, control, or ignition in auxiliary engines, the authority having jurisdiction shall require periodic maintenance.

(D) Written Record. A written record shall be kept of such tests and maintenance.

(E) Testing Under Load. Means for testing all emergency lighting and power systems during maximum anticipated load conditions shall be provided.

FPN: For testing and maintenance procedures of emergency power supply systems (EPSSs), see NFPA 110-2002, *Standard for Emergency and Standby Power Systems.*

700.5 Capacity.

(A) Capacity and Rating. An emergency system shall have adequate capacity and rating for all loads to be operated simultaneously. The emergency system equipment shall be suitable for the maximum available fault current at its terminals.

(B) Selective Load Pickup, Load Shedding, and Peak Load Shaving. The alternate power source shall be permitted to supply emergency, legally required standby, and optional standby system loads where the source has adequate capacity or where automatic selective load pickup and load shedding is provided as needed to ensure adequate power to (1) the emergency circuits, (2) the legally required standby circuits, and (3) the optional standby circuits, in that order of priority. The alternate power source shall be permitted to be used for peak load shaving, provided these conditions are met.

Peak load-shaving operation shall be permitted for satisfying the test requirement of 700.4(B), provided all other conditions of 700.4 are met.

A portable or temporary alternate source shall be available whenever the emergency generator is out of service for major maintenance or repair.

700.6 Transfer Equipment.

(A) General. Transfer equipment, including automatic transfer switches, shall be automatic, identified for emergency use, and approved by the authority having jurisdiction. Transfer equipment shall be designed and installed to prevent the inadvertent interconnection of normal and emergency sources of supply in any operation of the transfer equipment. Transfer equipment and electric power production systems installed to permit operation in parallel with the normal source shall meet the requirements of Article 705.

(B) Bypass Isolation Switches. Means shall be permitted to bypass and isolate the transfer equipment. Where bypass isolation switches are used, inadvertent parallel operation shall be avoided.

(C) Automatic Transfer Switches. Automatic transfer switches shall be electrically operated and mechanically held.

(D) Use. Transfer equipment shall supply only emergency loads.

700.7 Signals. Audible and visual signal devices shall be provided, where practicable, for the purpose described in 700.7(A) through 700.7(D).

(A) Derangement. To indicate derangement of the emergency source.

(B) Carrying Load. To indicate that the battery is carrying load.

(C) Not Functioning. To indicate that the battery charger is not functioning.

(D) Ground Fault. To indicate a ground fault in solidly grounded wye emergency systems of more than 150 volts to ground and circuit-protective devices rated 1000 amperes or more. The sensor for the ground-fault signal devices shall be located at, or ahead of, the main system disconnecting means for the emergency source, and the maximum setting of the signal devices shall be for a ground-fault current of 1200 amperes. Instructions on the course of action to be taken in event of indicated ground fault shall be located at or near the sensor location.

FPN: For signals for generator sets, see NFPA 110-2002, *Standard for Emergency and Standby Power Systems.*

700.8 Signs.

(A) Emergency Sources. A sign shall be placed at the service entrance equipment, indicating type and location of on-site emergency power sources.

Exception: A sign shall not be required for individual unit equipment as specified in 700.12(F).

(B) Grounding. Where the grounded circuit conductor connected to the emergency source is connected to a grounding electrode conductor at a location remote from

the emergency source, there shall be a sign at the grounding location that shall identify all emergency and normal sources connected at that location.

II. Circuit Wiring

700.9 Wiring, Emergency System.

(A) Identification. All boxes and enclosures (including transfer switches, generators, and power panels) for emergency circuits shall be permanently marked so they will be readily identified as a component of an emergency circuit or system.

(B) Wiring. Wiring of two or more emergency circuits supplied from the same source shall be permitted in the same raceway, cable, box, or cabinet. Wiring from an emergency source or emergency source distribution overcurrent protection to emergency loads shall be kept entirely independent of all other wiring and equipment, unless otherwise permitted in (1) through (4):

(1) Wiring from the normal power source located in transfer equipment enclosures

(2) Wiring supplied from two sources in exit or emergency luminaires (lighting fixtures)

(3) Wiring from two sources in a common junction box, attached to exit or emergency luminaires (lighting fixtures)

(4) Wiring within a common junction box attached to unit equipment, containing only the branch circuit supplying the unit equipment and the emergency circuit supplied by the unit equipment

(C) Wiring Design and Location. Emergency wiring circuits shall be designed and located so as to minimize the hazards that might cause failure due to flooding, fire, icing, vandalism, and other adverse conditions.

(D) Fire Protection. Emergency systems shall meet the additional requirements in 700.9(D)(1) and (D)(2) assembly occupancies for not less than 1000 persons or in buildings above 23 m (75 ft) in height with any of the following occupancy classes: assembly, educational, residential, detention and correctional, business, and mercantile.

(1) Feeder-Circuit Wiring. Feeder-circuit wiring shall meet one of the following conditions:

(1) Be installed in spaces or areas that are fully protected by an approved automatic fire suppression system

(2) Be a listed electrical circuit protective system with a minimum 1-hour fire rating

(3) Be protected by a listed thermal barrier system for electrical system components

(4) Be protected by a fire-rated assembly listed to achieve a minimum fire rating of 1 hour

(5) Be embedded in not less than 50 mm (2 in.) of concrete

(6) Be a cable listed to maintain circuit integrity for not less than 1 hour when installed in accordance with the listing requirements

(2) Feeder-Circuit Equipment. Equipment for feeder circuits (including transfer switches, transformers, and panelboards) shall be located either in spaces fully protected by approved automatic fire suppression systems (including sprinklers, carbon dioxide systems) or in spaces with a 1-hour fire resistance rating.

> FPN: For the definition of *occupancy classification*, see Section 6.1 of NFPA *101*-2003, *Life Safety Code*.

III. Sources of Power

700.12 General Requirements. Current supply shall be such that, in the event of failure of the normal supply to, or within, the building or group of buildings concerned, emergency lighting, emergency power, or both shall be available within the time required for the application but not to exceed 10 seconds. The supply system for emergency purposes, in addition to the normal services to the building and meeting the general requirements of this section, shall be one or more of the types of systems described in 700.12(A) through 700.12(E). Unit equipment in accordance with 700.12(F) shall satisfy the applicable requirements of this article.

In selecting an emergency source of power, consideration shall be given to the occupancy and the type of service to be rendered, whether of minimum duration, as for evacuation of a theater, or longer duration, as for supplying emergency power and lighting due to an indefinite period of current failure from trouble either inside or outside the building.

Equipment shall be designed and located so as to minimize the hazards that might cause complete failure due to flooding, fires, icing, and vandalism.

Equipment for sources of power as described in 700.12(A) through 700.12(E) where located within assembly occupancies for greater than 1000 persons or in buildings above 23 m (75 ft) in height with any of the following occupancy classes — assembly, educational, residential, detention and correctional, business, and mercantile — shall be installed either in spaces fully protected by approved automatic fire suppression systems (sprinklers, carbon dioxide systems, and so forth) or in spaces with a 1-hour fire rating.

> FPN No. 1: For the definition of occupancy classification, see Section 6.1 of NFPA *101*-2003, *Life Safety Code*.
>
> FPN No. 2: Assignment of degree of reliability of the recognized emergency supply system depends on the careful evaluation of the variables at each particular installation.

(A) Storage Battery. Storage batteries used as a source of power for emergency systems shall be of suitable rating and capacity to supply and maintain the total load for a minimum period of 1½ hours, without the voltage applied to the load falling below 87½ percent of normal.

Batteries, whether of the acid or alkali type, shall be designed and constructed to meet the requirements of emergency service and shall be compatible with the charger for that particular installation.

For a sealed battery, the container shall not be required to be transparent. However, for the lead acid battery that requires water additions, transparent or translucent jars shall be furnished. Automotive-type batteries shall not be used.

An automatic battery charging means shall be provided.

(B) Generator Set.

(1) Prime Mover-Driven. For a generator set driven by a prime mover acceptable to the authority having jurisdiction and sized in accordance with 700.5, means shall be provided for automatically starting the prime mover on failure of the normal service and for automatic transfer and operation of all required electrical circuits. A time-delay feature permitting a 15-minute setting shall be provided to avoid retransfer in case of short-time reestablishment of the normal source.

(2) Internal Combustion as Prime Movers. Where internal combustion engines are used as the prime mover, an on-site fuel supply shall be provided with an on-premise fuel supply sufficient for not less than 2 hours' full-demand operation of the system. Where power is needed for the operation of the fuel transfer pumps to deliver fuel to a generator set day tank, this pump shall be connected to the emergency power system.

(3) Dual Supplies. Prime movers shall not be solely dependent on a public utility gas system for their fuel supply or municipal water supply for their cooling systems. Means shall be provided for automatically transferring from one fuel supply to another where dual fuel supplies are used.

Exception: Where acceptable to the authority having jurisdiction, the use of other than on-site fuels shall be permitted where there is a low probability of a simultaneous failure of both the off-site fuel delivery system and power from the outside electrical utility company.

(4) Battery Power and Dampers. Where a storage battery is used for control or signal power or as the means of starting the prime mover, it shall be suitable for the purpose and shall be equipped with an automatic charging means independent of the generator set. Where the battery charger is required for the operation of the generator set, it shall be connected to the emergency system. Where power is required for the operation of dampers used to ventilate the generator set, the dampers shall be connected to the emergency system.

(5) Auxiliary Power Supply. Generator sets that require more than 10 seconds to develop power shall be permitted if an auxiliary power supply energizes the emergency system until the generator can pick up the load.

(6) Outdoor Generator Sets. Where an outdoor housed generator set is equipped with a readily accessible disconnecting means located within sight of the building or structure supplied, an additional disconnecting means shall not be required where ungrounded conductors serve or pass through the building or structure.

(C) Uninterruptible Power Supplies. Uninterruptible power supplies used to provide power for emergency systems shall comply with the applicable provisions of 700.12(A) and 700.12(B).

(D) Separate Service. Where acceptable to the authority having jurisdiction as suitable for use as an emergency source of power, an additional service shall be permitted. This service shall be in accordance with the applicable provisions of Article 230 and the following additional requirements:

(1) Separate service drop or service lateral

(2) Service conductors sufficiently remote electrically and physically from any other service conductors to minimize the possibility of simultaneous interruption of supply

(E) Fuel Cell System. Fuel cell systems used as a source of power for emergency systems shall be of suitable rating and capacity to supply and maintain the total load for not less than 2 hours of full-demand operation.

Installation of a fuel cell system shall meet the requirements of Parts II through VIII of Article 692.

Where a single fuel cell system serves as the normal supply for the building or group of buildings concerned, it shall not serve as the sole source of power for the emergency standby system.

(F) Unit Equipment. Individual unit equipment for emergency illumination shall consist of the following:

(1) A rechargeable battery

(2) A battery charging means

(3) Provisions for one or more lamps mounted on the equipment, or shall be permitted to have terminals for remote lamps, or both

(4) A relaying device arranged to energize the lamps automatically upon failure of the supply to the unit equipment

The batteries shall be of suitable rating and capacity to supply and maintain at not less than 87½ percent of the nominal battery voltage for the total lamp load associated with the unit for a period of at least 1½ hours, or the unit equipment shall supply and maintain not less than 60 percent of the initial emergency illumination for a period of at least 1½ hours. Storage batteries, whether of the acid or alkali type, shall be designed and constructed to meet the requirements of emergency service.

Unit equipment shall be permanently fixed in place (i.e., not portable) and shall have all wiring to each unit installed in accordance with the requirements of any of the wiring methods in Chapter 3. Flexible cord-and-plug connection shall be permitted, provided that the cord does not exceed 900 mm (3 ft) in length. The branch circuit feeding the unit equipment shall be the same branch circuit as that serving the normal lighting in the area and connected ahead of any local switches. The branch circuit that feeds unit equipment shall be clearly identified at the distribution panel. Emergency luminaires (illumination fixtures) that obtain power from a unit equipment and are not part of the unit equipment shall be wired to the unit equipment as required by 700.9 and by one of the wiring methods of Chapter 3.

Exception: In a separate and uninterrupted area supplied by a minimum of three normal lighting circuits, a separate branch circuit for unit equipment shall be permitted if it originates from the same panelboard as that of the normal lighting circuits and is provided with a lock-on feature.

IV. Emergency System Circuits for Lighting and Power

700.15 Loads on Emergency Branch Circuits. No appliances and no lamps, other than those specified as required for emergency use, shall be supplied by emergency lighting circuits.

700.16 Emergency Illumination. Emergency illumination shall include all required means of egress lighting, illuminated exit signs, and all other lights specified as necessary to provide required illumination.

Emergency lighting systems shall be designed and installed so that the failure of any individual lighting element, such as the burning out of a light bulb, cannot leave in total darkness any space that requires emergency illumination.

Where high-intensity discharge lighting such as high- and low-pressure sodium, mercury vapor, and metal halide is used as the sole source of normal illumination, the emergency lighting system shall be required to operate until normal illumination has been restored.

Exception: Alternative means that ensure emergency lighting illumination level is maintained shall be permitted.

700.17 Circuits for Emergency Lighting. Branch circuits that supply emergency lighting shall be installed to provide service from a source complying with 700.12 when the normal supply for lighting is interrupted. Such installations shall provide either of the following:

(1) An emergency lighting supply, independent of the general lighting supply, with provisions for automatically transferring the emergency lights upon the event of failure of the general lighting system supply

(2) Two or more separate and complete systems with independent power supply, each system providing sufficient current for emergency lighting purposes

Unless both systems are used for regular lighting purposes and are both kept lighted, means shall be provided for automatically energizing either system upon failure of the other. Either or both systems shall be permitted to be a part of the general lighting system of the protected occupancy if circuits supplying lights for emergency illumination are installed in accordance with other sections of this article.

700.18 Circuits for Emergency Power. For branch circuits that supply equipment classed as emergency, there shall be an emergency supply source to which the load will be transferred automatically upon the failure of the normal supply.

V. Control — Emergency Lighting Circuits

700.20 Switch Requirements. The switch or switches installed in emergency lighting circuits shall be arranged so that only authorized persons have control of emergency lighting.

Exception No. 1: Where two or more single-throw switches are connected in parallel to control a single circuit, at least one of these switches shall be accessible only to authorized persons.

Exception No. 2: Additional switches that act only to put emergency lights into operation but not disconnect them shall be permissible.

Switches connected in series or 3- and 4-way switches shall not be used.

700.21 Switch Location. All manual switches for controlling emergency circuits shall be in locations convenient to authorized persons responsible for their actuation. In facilities covered by Articles 518 and 520, a switch for controlling emergency lighting systems shall be located in the lobby or at a place conveniently accessible thereto.

In no case shall a control switch for emergency lighting be placed in a motion-picture projection booth or on a stage or platform.

Exception: Where multiple switches are provided, one such switch shall be permitted in such locations where arranged so that it can only energize the circuit, but cannot de-energize the circuit.

700.22 Exterior Lights. Those lights on the exterior of a building that are not required for illumination when there is sufficient daylight shall be permitted to be controlled by an automatic light-actuated device.

VI. Overcurrent Protection

700.25 Accessibility. The branch-circuit overcurrent devices in emergency circuits shall be accessible to authorized persons only.

700.26 Ground-Fault Protection of Equipment. The alternate source for emergency systems shall not be required to have ground-fault protection of equipment with automatic disconnecting means. Ground-fault indication of the emergency source shall be provided per 700.7(D).

700.27 Coordination. Emergency system(s) overcurrent devices shall be selectively coordinated with all supply side overcurrent protective devices.

ARTICLE 701
Legally Required Standby Systems

I. General

701.1 Scope. The provisions of this article apply to the electrical safety of the installation, operation, and maintenance of legally required standby systems consisting of circuits and equipment intended to supply, distribute, and control electricity to required facilities for illumination or power, or both, when the normal electrical supply or system is interrupted.

The systems covered by this article consist only of those that are permanently installed in their entirety, including the power source.

> FPN No. 1: For additional information, see NFPA 99-2002, *Standard for Health Care Facilities*.
>
> FPN No. 2: For further information regarding performance of emergency and standby power systems, see NFPA 110-2002, *Standard for Emergency and Standby Power Systems*.
>
> FPN No. 3: For further information, see ANSI/IEEE 446-1995, *Recommended Practice for Emergency and Standby Power Systems for Industrial and Commercial Applications*.

701.2 Definition.

Legally Required Standby Systems. Those systems required and so classed as legally required standby by municipal, state, federal, or other codes or by any governmental agency having jurisdiction. These systems are intended to automatically supply power to selected loads (other than those classed as emergency systems) in the event of failure of the normal source.

FPN: Legally required standby systems are typically installed to serve loads, such as heating and refrigeration systems, communications systems, ventilation and smoke removal systems, sewage disposal, lighting systems, and industrial processes, that, when stopped during any interruption of the normal electrical supply, could create hazards or hamper rescue or fire-fighting operations.

701.3 Application of Other Articles. Except as modified by this article, all applicable articles of this *Code* shall apply.

701.4 Equipment Approval. All equipment shall be approved for the intended use.

701.5 Tests and Maintenance for Legally Required Standby Systems.

(A) Conduct or Witness Test. The authority having jurisdiction shall conduct or witness a test of the complete system upon installation.

(B) Tested Periodically. Systems shall be tested periodically on a schedule and in a manner acceptable to the authority having jurisdiction to ensure the systems are maintained in proper operating condition.

(C) Battery Systems Maintenance. Where batteries are used for control, starting, or ignition of prime movers, the authority having jurisdiction shall require periodic maintenance.

(D) Written Record. A written record shall be kept on such tests and maintenance.

(E) Testing Under Load. Means for testing legally required standby systems under load shall be provided.

FPN: For testing and maintenance procedures of emergency power supply systems (EPSSs), see NFPA 110-2002, *Standard for Emergency and Standby Power Systems.*

701.6 Capacity and Rating. A legally required standby system shall have adequate capacity and rating for the supply of all equipment intended to be operated at one time. Legally required standby system equipment shall be suitable for the maximum available fault current at its terminals.

The legally required standby alternate power source shall be permitted to supply both legally required standby and optional standby system loads under either of the following conditions:

(1) Where the alternate source has adequate capacity to handle all connected loads

(2) Where automatic selective load pickup and load shedding is provided that will ensure adequate power to the legally required standby circuits

701.7 Transfer Equipment.

(A) General. Transfer equipment, including automatic transfer switches, shall be automatic and identified for standby use and approved by the authority having jurisdiction. Transfer equipment shall be designed and installed to prevent the inadvertent interconnection of normal and alternate sources of supply in any operation of the transfer equipment. Transfer equipment and electric power production systems installed to permit operation in parallel with the normal source shall meet the requirements of Article 705.

(B) Bypass Isolation Switches. Means to bypass and isolate the transfer switch equipment shall be permitted. Where bypass isolation switches are used, inadvertent parallel operation shall be avoided.

(C) Automatic Transfer Switches. Automatic transfer switches shall be electrically operated and mechanically held.

701.8 Signals. Audible and visual signal devices shall be provided, where practicable, for the purposes described in 701.8(A), (B), and (C).

(A) Derangement. To indicate derangement of the standby source.

(B) Carrying Load. To indicate that the standby source is carrying load.

(C) Not Functioning. To indicate that the battery charger is not functioning.

FPN: For signals for generator sets, see NFPA 110-2002, *Standard for Emergency and Standby Power Systems.*

701.9 Signs.

(A) Mandated Standby. A sign shall be placed at the service entrance indicating type and location of on-site legally required standby power sources.

Exception: A sign shall not be required for individual unit equipment as specified in 701.11(G).

(B) Grounding. Where the grounded circuit conductor connected to the legally required standby power source is connected to a grounding electrode conductor at a location remote from the legally required standby power source, there shall be a sign at the grounding location that shall identify all legally required standby power and normal sources connected at that location.

II. Circuit Wiring

701.10 Wiring Legally Required Standby Systems. The legally required standby system wiring shall be permitted to occupy the same raceways, cables, boxes, and cabinets with other general wiring.

III. Sources of Power

701.11 Legally Required Standby Systems. Current supply shall be such that, in the event of failure of the normal supply to, or within, the building or group of buildings concerned, legally required standby power will be available within the time required for the application but not to exceed 60 seconds. The supply system for legally required standby purposes, in addition to the normal services to the building, shall be permitted to comprise one or more of the types of systems described in 701.11(A) through 701.11(F). Unit equipment in accordance with 701.11(G) shall satisfy the applicable requirements of this article.

In selecting a legally required standby source of power, consideration shall be given to the type of service to be rendered, whether of short-time duration or long duration.

Consideration shall be given to the location or design, or both, of all equipment to minimize the hazards that might cause complete failure due to floods, fires, icing, and vandalism.

> FPN: Assignment of degree of reliability of the recognized legally required standby supply system depends on the careful evaluation of the variables at each particular installation.

(A) Storage Battery. A storage battery shall be of suitable rating and capacity to supply and maintain at not less than 87½ percent of system voltage the total load of the circuits supplying legally required standby power for a period of at least 1½ hours.

Batteries, whether of the acid or alkali type, shall be designed and constructed to meet the service requirements of emergency service and shall be compatible with the charger for that particular installation.

For a sealed battery, the container shall not be required to be transparent. However, for the lead acid battery that requires water additions, transparent or translucent jars shall be furnished. Automotive-type batteries shall not be used.

An automatic battery charging means shall be provided.

(B) Generator Set.

(1) Prime Mover-Driven. For a generator set driven by a prime mover acceptable to the authority having jurisdiction and sized in accordance with 701.6, means shall be provided for automatically starting the prime mover upon failure of the normal service and for automatic transfer and operation of all required electrical circuits. A time-delay feature permitting a 15-minute setting shall be provided to avoid retransfer in case of short-time re-establishment of the normal source.

(2) Internal Combustion Engines as Prime Mover. Where internal combustion engines are used as the prime mover, an on-site fuel supply shall be provided with an on-premise fuel supply sufficient for not less than 2 hours' full-demand operation of the system.

(3) Dual Fuel Supplies. Prime movers shall not be solely dependent on a public utility gas system for their fuel supply or municipal water supply for their cooling systems. Means shall be provided for automatically transferring one fuel supply to another where dual fuel supplies are used.

Exception: Where acceptable to the authority having jurisdiction, the use of other than on-site fuels shall be permitted where there is a low probability of a simultaneous failure of both the off-site fuel delivery system and power from the outside electrical utility company.

(4) Battery Power. Where a storage battery is used for control or signal power or as the means of starting the prime mover, it shall be suitable for the purpose and shall be equipped with an automatic charging means independent of the generator set.

(5) Outdoor Generator Sets. Where an outdoor housed generator set is equipped with a readily accessible disconnecting means located within sight of the building or structure supplied, an additional disconnecting means shall not be required where ungrounded conductors serve or pass through the building or structure.

(C) Uninterruptible Power Supplies. Uninterruptible power supplies used to provide power for legally required standby systems shall comply with the applicable provisions of 701.11(A) and 701.11(B).

(D) Separate Service. Where acceptable to the authority having jurisdiction as a source of power, an additional service shall be permitted. This service shall be in accordance with the applicable provisions of Article 230, with separate service drop or lateral sufficiently remote electrically and physically from any other service to minimize the possibility of simultaneous interruption of supply from an occurrence in another service.

(E) Connection Ahead of Service Disconnecting Means. Where acceptable to the authority having jurisdiction, connections located ahead of and not within the same cabinet, enclosure, or vertical switchboard section as the service disconnecting means shall be permitted. The legally required standby service shall be sufficiently separated from the normal main service disconnecting means to prevent simultaneous interruption of supply through an occurrence within the building or groups of buildings served.

> FPN: See 230.82 for equipment permitted on the supply side of a service disconnecting means.

(F) Fuel Cell System. Fuel cell systems used as a source of power for legally required standby systems shall be of suitable rating and capacity to supply and maintain the total load for not less than 2 hours of full-demand operation.

Installation of a fuel cell system shall meet the requirements of Parts II through VIII of Article 692.

Where a single fuel cell system serves as the normal supply for the building or group of buildings concerned, it shall not serve as the sole source of power for the legally required standby system.

(G) Unit Equipment. Individual unit equipment for legally required standby illumination shall consist of the following:

(1) A rechargeable battery

(2) A battery charging means

(3) Provisions for one or more lamps mounted on the equipment and shall be permitted to have terminals for remote lamps

(4) A relaying device arranged to energize the lamps automatically upon failure of the supply to the unit equipment

The batteries shall be of suitable rating and capacity to supply and maintain at not less than 87½ percent of the nominal battery voltage for the total lamp load associated with the unit for a period of at least 1½ hours, or the unit equipment shall supply and maintain not less than 60 percent of the initial legally required standby illumination for a period of at least 1½ hours. Storage batteries, whether of the acid or alkali type, shall be designed and constructed to meet the requirements of emergency service.

Unit equipment shall be permanently fixed in place (i.e., not portable) and shall have all wiring to each unit installed in accordance with the requirements of any of the wiring methods in Chapter 3. Flexible cord-and-plug connection shall be permitted, provided that the cord does not exceed 900 mm (3 ft) in length. The branch circuit feeding the unit equipment shall be the same branch circuit as that serving the normal lighting in the area and connected ahead of any local switches. Legally required standby luminaires (illumination fixtures) that obtain power from a unit equipment and are not part of the unit equipment shall be wired to the unit equipment by one of the wiring methods of Chapter 3.

Exception: In a separate and uninterrupted area supplied by a minimum of three normal lighting circuits, a separate branch circuit for unit equipment shall be permitted if it originates from the same panelboard as that of the normal lighting circuits and is provided with a lock-on feature.

IV. Overcurrent Protection

701.15 Accessibility. The branch-circuit overcurrent devices in legally required standby circuits shall be accessible to authorized persons only.

701.17 Ground-Fault Protection of Equipment. The alternate source for legally required standby systems shall not be required to have ground-fault protection of equipment.

701.18 Coordination. Legally required standby system(s) overcurrent devices shall be selectively coordinated with all supply side overcurrent protective devices.

ARTICLE 702
Optional Standby Systems

I. General

702.1 Scope. The provisions of this article apply to the installation and operation of optional standby systems.

The systems covered by this article consist of those that are permanently installed in their entirety, including prime movers, and those that are arranged for a connection to a premises wiring system from a portable alternate power supply.

702.2 Definition.

Optional Standby Systems. Those systems intended to supply power to public or private facilities or property where life safety does not depend on the performance of the system. Optional standby systems are intended to supply on-site generated power to selected loads either automatically or manually.

> FPN: Optional standby systems are typically installed to provide an alternate source of electric power for such facilities as industrial and commercial buildings, farms, and residences and to serve loads such as heating and refrigeration systems, data processing and communications systems, and industrial processes that, when stopped during any power outage, could cause discomfort, serious interruption of the process, damage to the product or process, or the like.

702.3 Application of Other Articles. Except as modified by this article, all applicable articles of this *Code* shall apply.

702.4 Equipment Approval. All equipment shall be approved for the intended use.

702.5 Capacity and Rating. An optional standby system shall have adequate capacity and rating for the supply of all equipment intended to be operated at one time. Optional standby system equipment shall be suitable for the maximum available fault current at its terminals. The user of the optional standby system shall be permitted to select the load connected to the system.

702.6 Transfer Equipment. Transfer equipment shall be suitable for the intended use and designed and installed so as to prevent the inadvertent interconnection of normal and alternate sources of supply in any operation of the transfer equipment. Transfer equipment and electric power production systems installed to permit operation in parallel with the normal source shall meet the requirements of Article 705.

Transfer equipment, located on the load side of branch circuit protection, shall be permitted to contain supplementary overcurrent protection having an interrupting rating sufficient for the available fault current that the generator can deliver. The supplementary overcurrent protection devices shall be part of a listed transfer equipment.

Transfer equipment shall be required for all standby systems subject to the provisions of this article and for which an electric-utility supply is either the normal or standby source.

Exception: Temporary connection of a portable generator without transfer equipment shall be permitted where conditions of maintenance and supervision ensure that only qualified persons service the installation and where the normal supply is physically isolated by a lockable disconnect means or by disconnection of the normal supply conductors.

702.7 Signals. Audible and visual signal devices shall be provided, where practicable, for the following purposes.

(1) Derangement. To indicate derangement of the optional standby source.

(2) Carrying Load. To indicate that the optional standby source is carrying load.

Exception: Signals shall not be required for portable standby power sources.

702.8 Signs.

(A) Standby. A sign shall be placed at the service-entrance equipment that indicates the type and location of on-site optional standby power sources. A sign shall not be required for individual unit equipment for standby illumination.

(B) Grounding. Where the grounded circuit conductor connected to the optional standby power source is connected to a grounding electrode conductor at a location remote from the optional standby power source, there shall be a sign at the grounding location that shall identify all optional standby power and normal sources connected at that location.

II. Circuit Wiring

702.9 Wiring Optional Standby Systems. The optional standby system wiring shall be permitted to occupy the same raceways, cables, boxes, and cabinets with other general wiring.

III. Grounding

702.10 Portable Generator Grounding.

(A) Separately Derived System. Where a portable optional standby source is used as a separately derived system, it shall be grounded to a grounding electrode in accordance with 250.30.

(B) Nonseparately Derived System. Where a portable optional standby source is used as a nonseparately derived system, the equipment grounding conductor shall be bonded to the system grounding electrode.

IV. Sources of Power

702.11 Outdoor Generator Sets. Where an outdoor housed generator set is equipped with a readily accessible disconnecting means located within sight of the building or structure supplied, an additional disconnecting means shall not be required where ungrounded conductors serve or pass through the building or structure.

ARTICLE 705
Interconnected Electric Power Production Sources

705.1 Scope. This article covers installation of one or more electric power production sources operating in parallel with a primary source(s) of electricity.

FPN: Examples of the types of primary sources are a utility supply, on-site electric power source(s), or other sources.

705.2 Definition.

Interactive System. An electric power production system that is operating in parallel with and capable of delivering energy to an electric primary source supply system.

705.3 Other Articles. Interconnected electric power production sources shall comply with this article and also with the applicable requirements of the articles in Table 705.3.

Table 705.3 Other Articles

Equipment/System	Article
Generators	445
Emergency systems	700
Legally required standby systems	701
Optional standby systems	702

Exception No. 1: Installation of solar photovoltaic systems operated as interconnected power sources shall be in accordance with Article 690.

Exception No. 2: Installation of fuel cell systems operated as interconnected power sources shall be in accordance with Article 692.

705.10 Directory. A permanent plaque or directory, denoting all electrical power sources on or in the premises, shall be installed at each service equipment location and at locations of all electric power production sources capable of being interconnected.

Exception: Installations with large numbers of power production sources shall be permitted to be designated by groups.

705.12 Point of Connection. The outputs of electric power production systems shall be interconnected at the premises service disconnecting means.

(A) Integrated Electric System. The outputs shall be permitted to be interconnected at a point or points elsewhere on the premises where the system qualifies as an integrated electric system and incorporates protective equipment in accordance with all applicable sections of Article 685.

(B) General. The outputs shall be permitted to be interconnected at a point or points elsewhere on the premises where all of the following conditions are met:

(1) The aggregate of nonutility sources of electricity has a capacity in excess of 100 kW, or the service is above 1000 volts.

(2) The conditions of maintenance and supervision ensure that qualified persons service and operate the system.

(3) Safeguards and protective equipment are established and maintained.

705.14 Output Characteristics. The output of a generator or other electric power production source operating in parallel with an electric supply system shall be compatible with the voltage, wave shape, and frequency of the system to which it is connected.

> FPN: The term *compatible* does not necessarily mean matching the primary source wave shape.

705.16 Interrupting and Short-Circuit Current Rating. Consideration shall be given to the contribution of fault currents from all interconnected power sources for the interrupting and short-circuit current ratings of equipment on interactive systems.

705.20 Disconnecting Means, Sources. Means shall be provided to disconnect all ungrounded conductors of an electric power production source(s) from all other conductors.

705.21 Disconnecting Means, Equipment. Means shall be provided to disconnect equipment, such as inverters or transformers associated with a power production source, from all ungrounded conductors of all sources of supply. Equipment intended to be operated and maintained as an integral part of a power production source exceeding 1000 volts shall not be required to have a disconnecting means.

705.22 Disconnect Device. The disconnecting means for ungrounded conductors shall consist of a manually or power operable switch(es) or circuit breaker(s) with the following features:

(1) Located where accessible

(2) Externally operable without exposing the operator to contact with live parts and, if power operable, of a type that can be opened by hand in the event of a power supply failure

(3) Plainly indicating whether in the open or closed position

(4) Having ratings not less than the load to be carried and the fault current to be interrupted

For disconnect equipment energized from both sides, a marking shall be provided to indicate that all contacts of the disconnect equipment may be energized.

> FPN No. 1: In parallel generation systems, some equipment, including knife blade switches and fuses, is likely to be energized from both directions. See 240.40.

> FPN No. 2: Interconnection to an off-premises primary source could require a visibly verifiable disconnecting device.

705.30 Overcurrent Protection. Conductors shall be protected in accordance with Article 240. Equipment and conductors connected to more than one electrical source shall have a sufficient number of overcurrent devices located so as to provide protection from all sources.

(A) Generators. Generators shall be protected in accordance with 445.12.

(B) Solar Photovoltaic Systems. Solar photovoltaic systems shall be protected in accordance with Article 690.

(C) Transformers. Overcurrent protection for a transformer with a source(s) on each side shall be provided in accordance with 450.3 by considering first one side of the transformer, then the other side of the transformer, as the primary.

(D) Fuel Cell Systems. Fuel cell systems shall be protected in accordance with Article 692.

705.32 Ground-Fault Protection. Where ground-fault protection is used, the output of an interactive system shall be connected to the supply side of the ground-fault protection.

Exception: Connection shall be permitted to be made to the load side of ground-fault protection, provided that there is ground-fault protection for equipment from all ground-fault current sources.

705.40 Loss of Primary Source. Upon loss of primary source, an electric power production source shall be automatically disconnected from all ungrounded conductors of the primary source and shall not be reconnected until the primary source is restored.

> FPN No. 1: Risks to personnel and equipment associated with the primary source could occur if an interactive electric power production source can operate as an island. Special detection methods can be required to determine that a primary source supply system outage has occurred and whether there should be automatic disconnection. When the primary source supply system is restored, special detection methods can be required to limit exposure of power production sources to out-of-phase reconnection.

> FPN No. 2: Induction-generating equipment on systems with significant capacitance can become self-excited upon loss of primary source and experience severe overvoltage as a result.

705.42 Unbalanced Interconnections. A 3-phase electric power production source shall be automatically disconnected from all ungrounded conductors of the interconnected systems when one of the phases of that source opens. This requirement shall not be applicable to an electric power production source providing power for an emergency or legally required standby system.

705.43 Synchronous Generators. Synchronous generators in a parallel system shall be provided with the necessary equipment to establish and maintain a synchronous condition.

705.50 Grounding. Interconnected electric power production sources shall be grounded in accordance with Article 250.

Exception: For direct-current systems connected through an inverter directly to a grounded service, other methods that accomplish equivalent system protection and that utilize equipment listed and identified for the use shall be permitted.

ARTICLE 720
Circuits and Equipment Operating at Less Than 50 Volts

720.1 Scope. This article covers installations operating at less than 50 volts, direct current or alternating current.

720.2 Other Articles. Installations operating at less than 50 volts, direct current or alternating current, as covered in Articles 411, 517, 550, 551, 552, 650, 669, 690, 725, and 760 shall not be required to comply with this article.

720.3 Hazardous (Classified) Locations. Installations coming within the scope of this article and installed in hazardous (classified) locations shall also comply with the appropriate provisions of Articles 500 through 517.

720.4 Conductors. Conductors shall not be smaller than 12 AWG copper or equivalent. Conductors for appliance branch circuits supplying more than one appliance or appliance receptacle shall not be smaller than 10 AWG copper or equivalent.

720.5 Lampholders. Standard lampholders that have a rating of not less than 660 watts shall be used.

720.6 Receptacle Rating. Receptacles shall have a rating of not less than 15 amperes.

720.7 Receptacles Required. Receptacles of not less than 20-ampere rating shall be provided in kitchens, laundries, and other locations where portable appliances are likely to be used.

720.8 Overcurrent Protection. Overcurrent protection shall comply with Article 240.

720.9 Batteries. Installations of storage batteries shall comply with Article 480.

720.10 Grounding. Grounding shall be as provided in Article 250.

720.11 Mechanical Execution of Work. Circuits operating at less than 50 volts shall be installed in a neat and workmanlike manner. Cables shall be supported by the building structure in such a manner that the cable will not be damaged by normal building use.

ARTICLE 725
Class 1, Class 2, and Class 3 Remote-Control, Signaling, and Power-Limited Circuits

I. General

725.1 Scope. This article covers remote-control, signaling, and power-limited circuits that are not an integral part of a device or appliance.

> FPN: The circuits described herein are characterized by usage and electrical power limitations that differentiate them from electric light and power circuits; therefore, alternative requirements to those of Chapters 1 through 4 are given with regard to minimum wire sizes, derating factors, overcurrent protection, insulation requirements, and wiring methods and materials.

725.2 Definitions.

Abandoned Class 2, Class 3, and PLTC Cable. Installed Class 2, Class 3, and PLTC cable that is not terminated at equipment and not identified for future use with a tag.

Circuit Integrity (CI) Cable. Cable(s) used for remote control, signaling, or power-limited systems that supply critical circuits to ensure survivability for continued circuit operation for a specified time under fire conditions.

Class 1 Circuit. The portion of the wiring system between the load side of the overcurrent device or power-limited supply and the connected equipment. The voltage and power limitations of the source are in accordance with 725.21.

Class 2 Circuit. The portion of the wiring system between the load side of a Class 2 power source and the connected equipment. Due to its power limitations, a Class 2 circuit considers safety from a fire initiation standpoint and provides acceptable protection from electric shock.

Class 3 Circuit. The portion of the wiring system between the load side of a Class 3 power source and the connected equipment. Due to its power limitations, a Class 3 circuit considers safety from a fire initiation standpoint. Since higher levels of voltage and current than for Class 2 are permitted, additional safeguards are specified to provide protection from an electric shock hazard that could be encountered.

725.3 Other Articles. Circuits and equipment shall comply with the articles or sections listed in 725.3(A) through 725.3(G). Only those sections of Article 300 referenced in this article shall apply to Class 1, Class 2, and Class 3 circuits.

(A) Number and Size of Conductors in Raceway. Section 300.17.

(B) Spread of Fire or Products of Combustion. Section 300.21. The accessible portion of abandoned Class 2, Class 3, and PLTC cables shall be removed.

(C) Ducts, Plenums, and Other Air-Handling Spaces. Class 1, Class 2, and Class 3 circuits installed in ducts, plenums, or other space used for environmental air shall comply with 300.22. Type CL2P or CL3P cables and plenum signaling raceways shall be permitted for Class 2 and Class 3 circuits installed in other spaces used for environmental air.

(D) Hazardous (Classified) Locations. Articles 500 through 516 and Article 517, Part IV, where installed in hazardous (classified) locations.

(E) Cable Trays. Article 392, where installed in cable tray.

(F) Motor Control Circuits. Article 430, Part VI, where tapped from the load side of the motor branch-circuit protective device(s) as specified in 430.72(A).

(G) Instrumentation Tray Cable. See Article 727.

725.7 Access to Electrical Equipment Behind Panels Designed to Allow Access. Access to electrical equipment shall not be denied by an accumulation of wires and cables that prevents removal of panels, including suspended ceiling panels.

725.8 Mechanical Execution of Work. Class 1, Class 2, and Class 3 circuits shall be installed in a neat and workmanlike manner. Cables and conductors installed exposed on the surface of ceilings and sidewalls shall be supported by the building structure in such a manner that the cable will not be damaged by normal building use. Such cables shall be supported by straps, staples, hangers, or similar fittings designed and installed so as not to damage the cable. The installation shall also conform with 300.4(D).

725.10 Class 1, Class 2, and Class 3 Circuit Identification. Class 1, Class 2, and Class 3 circuits shall be identified at terminal and junction locations, in a manner that prevents unintentional interference with other circuits during testing and servicing.

725.11 Safety-Control Equipment.

(A) Remote-Control Circuits. Remote-control circuits for safety-control equipment shall be classified as Class 1 if the failure of the equipment to operate introduces a direct fire or life hazard. Room thermostats, water temperature regulating devices, and similar controls used in conjunction with electrically controlled household heating and air conditioning shall not be considered safety-control equipment.

(B) Physical Protection. Where damage to remote-control circuits of safety control equipment would introduce a hazard, as covered in 725.11(A), all conductors of such remote-control circuits shall be installed in rigid metal conduit, intermediate metal conduit, rigid nonmetallic conduit, electrical metallic tubing, Type MI cable, Type MC cable, or be otherwise suitably protected from physical damage.

725.15 Class 1, Class 2, and Class 3 Circuit Requirements. A remote-control, signaling, or power-limited circuit shall comply with the following parts of this article:

(1) Class 1 Circuits: Parts I and II

(2) Class 2 and Class 3 Circuits: Parts I and III

II. Class 1 Circuits

725.21 Class 1 Circuit Classifications and Power Source Requirements. Class 1 circuits shall be classified as either Class 1 power-limited circuits where they comply with the power limitations of 725.21(A) or as Class 1 remote-control and signaling circuits where they are used for remote-control or signaling purposes and comply with the power limitations of 725.21(B).

(A) Class 1 Power-Limited Circuits. These circuits shall be supplied from a source that has a rated output of not more than 30 volts and 1000 volt-amperes.

(1) Class 1 Transformers. Transformers used to supply power-limited Class 1 circuits shall comply with the applicable sections within Parts I and II of Article 450.

(2) Other Class 1 Power Sources. Power sources other than transformers shall be protected by overcurrent devices rated at not more than 167 percent of the volt-ampere rating of the source divided by the rated voltage. The overcurrent devices shall not be interchangeable with overcurrent devices of higher ratings. The overcurrent device shall be permitted to be an integral part of the power supply.

To comply with the 1000 volt-ampere limitation of 725.21(A), the maximum output (VA_{max}) of power sources other than transformers shall be limited to 2500 volt-amperes, and the product of the maximum current (I_{max}) and maximum voltage (V_{max}) shall not exceed 10,000 volt-amperes. These ratings shall be determined with any overcurrent-protective device bypassed.

VA_{max} is the maximum volt-ampere output after one minute of operation regardless of load and with overcurrent protection bypassed, if used. Current-limiting impedance shall not be bypassed when determining VA_{max}.

I_{max} is the maximum output current under any noncapacitive load, including short circuit, and with overcurrent protection bypassed, if used. Current-limiting impedance should not be bypassed when determining I_{max}. Where a current-limiting impedance, listed for the purpose or as part of a listed product, is used in combination with a stored energy source, for example, storage battery, to limit the output current, I_{max} limits apply after 5 seconds.

V_{max} is the maximum output voltage regardless of load with rated input applied.

(B) Class 1 Remote-Control and Signaling Circuits. These circuits shall not exceed 600 volts. The power output of the source shall not be required to be limited.

725.23 Class 1 Circuit Overcurrent Protection. Overcurrent protection for conductors 14 AWG and larger shall be provided in accordance with the conductor ampacity, without applying the derating factors of 310.15 to the ampacity calculation. Overcurrent protection shall not exceed 7 amperes for 18 AWG conductors and 10 amperes for 16 AWG.

Exception: Where other articles of this Code permit or require other overcurrent protection.

> FPN: For example, see 430.72 for motors, 610.53 for cranes and hoists, and 517.74(B) and 660.9 for X-ray equipment.

725.24 Class 1 Circuit Overcurrent Device Location. Overcurrent devices shall be located as specified in 725.24(A), (B), (C), (D), or (E).

(A) Point of Supply. Overcurrent devices shall be located at the point where the conductor to be protected receives its supply.

(B) Feeder Taps. Class 1 circuit conductors shall be permitted to be tapped, without overcurrent protection at the tap, where the overcurrent device protecting the circuit conductor is sized to protect the tap conductor.

(C) Branch Circuit Taps. Class 1 circuit conductors 14 AWG and larger that are tapped from the load side of the overcurrent-protective device(s) of a controlled light and power circuit shall require only short-circuit and ground-fault protection and shall be permitted to be protected by the branch-circuit overcurrent protective device(s) where the rating of the protective device(s) is not more than 300 percent of the ampacity of the Class 1 circuit conductor.

(D) Primary Side of Transformer. Class 1 circuit conductors supplied by the secondary of a single-phase transformer having only a 2-wire (single-voltage) secondary shall be permitted to be protected by overcurrent protection provided on the primary side of the transformer, provided this protection is in accordance with 450.3 and does not exceed the value determined by multiplying the secondary conductor ampacity by the secondary-to-primary transformer voltage ratio. Transformer secondary conductors other than 2 wire shall not be considered to be protected by the primary overcurrent protection.

(E) Input Side of Electronic Power Source. Class 1 circuit conductors supplied by the output of a single-phase, listed electronic power source, other than a transformer, having only a 2-wire (single voltage) output for connection to Class 1 circuits shall be permitted to be protected by overcurrent protection provided on the input side of the electronic power source, provided this protection does not exceed the value determined by multiplying the Class 1 circuit conductor ampacity by the output-to-input voltage ratio. Electronic power source outputs, other than 2 wire (single voltage), shall not be considered to be protected by the primary overcurrent protection.

725.25 Class 1 Circuit Wiring Methods. Class 1 circuits shall be installed in accordance with Part I of Article 300 and with the wiring methods from the appropriate articles in Chapter 3.

Exception No. 1: The provisions of 725.26 through 725.28 shall be permitted to apply in installations of Class 1 circuits.

Exception No. 2: Methods permitted or required by other articles of this Code shall apply to installations of Class 1 circuits.

725.26 Conductors of Different Circuits in the Same Cable, Cable Tray, Enclosure, or Raceway. Class 1 circuits shall be permitted to be installed with other circuits as specified in 725.26(A) and 725.26(B).

(A) Two or More Class 1 Circuits. Class 1 circuits shall be permitted to occupy the same cable, cable tray, enclosure, or raceway without regard to whether the individual circuits are alternating current or direct current, provided all conductors are insulated for the maximum voltage of any conductor in the cable, cable tray, enclosure, or raceway.

(B) Class 1 Circuits with Power Supply Circuits. Class 1 circuits shall be permitted to be installed with power supply conductors as specified in 725.26(B)(1) through (B)(4).

(1) In a Cable, Enclosure, or Raceway. Class 1 circuits and power supply circuits shall be permitted to occupy the same cable, enclosure, or raceway only where the equipment powered is functionally associated.

(2) In Factory- or Field-Assembled Control Centers. Class 1 circuits and power supply circuits shall be permitted to be installed in factory- or field-assembled control centers.

(3) In a Manhole. Class 1 circuits and power supply circuits shall be permitted to be installed as underground conductors in a manhole in accordance with one of the following:

(1) The power-supply or Class 1 circuit conductors are in a metal-enclosed cable or Type UF cable.

(2) The conductors are permanently separated from the power-supply conductors by a continuous firmly fixed nonconductor, such as flexible tubing, in addition to the insulation on the wire.

(3) The conductors are permanently and effectively separated from the power supply conductors and securely fastened to racks, insulators, or other approved supports.

(4) In Cable Trays. In cable trays, where the Class 1 circuit conductors and power-supply conductors not functionally associated with them are separated by a solid fixed barrier of a material compatible with the cable tray, or where the power-supply or Class 1 circuit conductors are in a metal-enclosed cable.

725.27 Class 1 Circuit Conductors.

(A) Sizes and Use. Conductors of sizes 18 AWG and 16 AWG shall be permitted to be used, provided they supply loads that do not exceed the ampacities given in 402.5 and are installed in a raceway, an approved enclosure, or a listed cable. Conductors larger than 16 AWG shall not supply loads greater than the ampacities given in 310.15. Flexible cords shall comply with Article 400.

(B) Insulation. Insulation on conductors shall be suitable for 600 volts. Conductors larger than 16 AWG shall comply with Article 310. Conductors in sizes 18 AWG and 16 AWG shall be Type FFH-2, KF-2, KFF-2, PAF, PAFF, PF, PFF, PGF, PGFF, PTF, PTFF, RFH-2, RFHH-2, RFHH-3, SF-2, SFF-2, TF, TFF, TFFN, TFN, ZF, or ZFF. Conductors with other types and thicknesses of insulation shall be permitted if listed for Class 1 circuit use.

725.28 Number of Conductors in Cable Trays and Raceway, and Derating.

(A) Class 1 Circuit Conductors. Where only Class 1 circuit conductors are in a raceway, the number of conductors shall be determined in accordance with 300.17. The derating factors given in 310.15(B)(2)(a) shall apply only if such conductors carry continuous loads in excess of 10 percent of the ampacity of each conductor.

(B) Power-Supply Conductors and Class 1 Circuit Conductors. Where power-supply conductors and Class 1 circuit conductors are permitted in a raceway in accordance with 725.26, the number of conductors shall be determined in accordance with 300.17. The derating factors given in 310.15(B)(2)(a) shall apply as follows:

(1) To all conductors where the Class 1 circuit conductors carry continuous loads in excess of 10 percent of the ampacity of each conductor and where the total number of conductors is more than three

(2) To the power-supply conductors only, where the Class 1 circuit conductors do not carry continuous loads in excess of 10 percent of the ampacity of each conductor and where the number of power-supply conductors is more than three

(C) Class 1 Circuit Conductors in Cable Trays. Where Class 1 circuit conductors are installed in cable trays, they shall comply with the provisions of 392.9 through 392.11.

725.29 Circuits Extending Beyond One Building. Class 1 circuits that extend aerially beyond one building shall also meet the requirements of Article 225.

III. Class 2 and Class 3 Circuits

725.41 Power Sources for Class 2 and Class 3 Circuits.

(A) Power Source. The power source for a Class 2 or a Class 3 circuit shall be as specified in 725.41(A)(1), (A)(2), (A)(3), (A)(4), or (A)(5):

FPN No. 1: Figure 725.41 illustrates the relationships between Class 2 or Class 3 power sources, their supply, and the Class 2 or Class 3 circuits.

FPN No. 2: Table 11(A) and Table 11(B) in Chapter 9 provide the requirements for listed Class 2 and Class 3 power sources.

(1) A listed Class 2 or Class 3 transformer

(2) A listed Class 2 or Class 3 power supply

(3) Other listed equipment marked to identify the Class 2 or Class 3 power source

Exception No. 1: Thermocouples shall not require listing as a Class 2 power source.

Exception No. 2: Limited power circuits of listed equipment where these circuits have energy levels rated at or below the limits established in Chapter 9, Table 11(A) and Table 11(B).

FPN: Examples of other listed equipment are as follows:

(1) A circuit card listed for use as a Class 2 or Class 3 power source where used as part of a listed assembly

(2) A current-limiting impedance, listed for the purpose, or part of a listed product, used in conjunction with a non–power-limited transformer or a stored energy source, for example, storage battery, to limit the output current

(3) A thermocouple

(4) Limited voltage/current or limited impedance secondary communications circuits of listed industrial control equipment

(4) Listed information technology (computer) equipment limited power circuits.

FPN: One way to determine applicable requirements for listing of information technology (computer) equipment is to refer to UL 1950-1995, *Standard for Safety of Information Technology Equipment, Including Electrical Business Equipment.* Typically such circuits are used to interconnect information technology equipment for the purpose of exchanging information (data).

(5) A dry cell battery shall be considered an inherently limited Class 2 power source, provided the voltage is 30 volts or less and the capacity is equal to or less than that available from series connected No. 6 carbon zinc cells.

(B) Interconnection of Power Sources. Class 2 or Class 3 power sources shall not have the output connections paralleled or otherwise interconnected unless listed for such interconnection.

725.42 Circuit Marking. The equipment supplying the circuits shall be durably marked where plainly visible to indicate each circuit that is a Class 2 or Class 3 circuit.

Figure 725.41 Class 2 and Class 3 Circuits.

725.51 Wiring Methods on Supply Side of the Class 2 or Class 3 Power Source. Conductors and equipment on the supply side of the power source shall be installed in accordance with the appropriate requirements of Chapters 1 through 4. Transformers or other devices supplied from electric light or power circuits shall be protected by an overcurrent device rated not over 20 amperes.

Exception: The input leads of a transformer or other power source supplying Class 2 and Class 3 circuits shall be permitted to be smaller than 14 AWG, but not smaller than 18 AWG if they are not over 12 in. (305 mm) long and if they have insulation that complies with 725.27(B).

725.52 Wiring Methods and Materials on Load Side of the Class 2 or Class 3 Power Source. Class 2 and Class 3 circuits on the load side of the power source shall be permitted to be installed using wiring methods and materials in accordance with either 725.52(A) or 725.52(B).

(A) Class 1 Wiring Methods and Materials. Installation shall be in accordance with 725.25.

Exception No. 1: The derating factors given in 310.15(B)(2)(a) shall not apply.

Exception No. 2: Class 2 and Class 3 circuits shall be permitted to be reclassified and installed as Class 1 circuits if the Class 2 and Class 3 markings required in 725.42 are eliminated and the entire circuit is installed using the wiring methods and materials in accordance with Part II, Class 1 circuits.

FPN: Class 2 and Class 3 circuits reclassified and installed as Class 1 circuits are no longer Class 2 or Class 3 circuits, regardless of the continued connection to a Class 2 or Class 3 power source.

(B) Class 2 and Class 3 Wiring Methods. Conductors on the load side of the power source shall be insulated at not less than the requirements of 725.82 and shall be installed in accordance with 725.54 and 725.61.

Exception No. 1: As provided for in 620.21 for elevators and similar equipment.

Exception No. 2: Other wiring methods and materials installed in accordance with the requirements of 725.3 shall be permitted to extend or replace the conductors and cables described in 725.82 and permitted by 725.52(B).

725.54 Installation of Conductors and Equipment in Cables, Compartments, Cable Trays, Enclosures, Manholes, Outlet Boxes, Device Boxes, and Raceways for Class 2 and Class 3 Circuits. Conductors and equipment for Class 2 and Class 3 circuits shall be installed in accordance with 725.55 through 725.58.

725.55 Separation from Electric Light, Power, Class 1, Non–Power-Limited Fire Alarm Circuit Conductors, and Medium Power Network-Powered Broadband Communications Cables.

(A) General. Cables and conductors of Class 2 and Class 3 circuits shall not be placed in any cable, cable tray, compartment, enclosure, manhole, outlet box, device box, raceway, or similar fitting with conductors of electric light, power, Class 1, non–power-limited fire alarm circuits, and medium power network-powered broadband communications circuits unless permitted by 725.55(B) through 725.55(J).

(B) Separated by Barriers. Class 2 and Class 3 circuits shall be permitted to be installed together with the conductors of electric light, power, Class 1, non–power-limited fire alarm and medium power network-powered broadband communications circuits where they are separated by a barrier.

(C) Raceways Within Enclosures. In enclosures, Class 2 and Class 3 circuits shall be permitted to be installed in a raceway to separate them from Class 1, non–power-limited fire alarm and medium power network-powered broadband communications circuits.

(D) Associated Systems Within Enclosures. Class 2 and Class 3 circuit conductors in compartments, enclosures, device boxes, outlet boxes, or similar fittings shall be permitted to be installed with electric light, power, Class 1, non–power-limited fire alarm, and medium power network-powered broadband communications circuits where they are introduced solely to connect the equipment connected to Class 2 and Class 3 circuits, and where (1) or (2) applies:

(1) The electric light, power, Class 1, non–power-limited fire alarm, and medium power network-powered broadband communications circuit conductors are routed to maintain a minimum of 6 mm (0.25 in.) separation from the conductors and cables of Class 2 and Class 3 circuits.

(2) The circuit conductors operate at 150 volts or less to ground and also comply with one of the following:

a. The Class 2 and Class 3 circuits are installed using Type CL3, CL3R, or CL3P or permitted substitute cables, provided these Class 3 cable conductors extending beyond the jacket are separated by a minimum of 6 mm (0.25 in.) or by a nonconductive sleeve or nonconductive barrier from all other conductors.

b. The Class 2 and Class 3 circuit conductors are installed as a Class 1 circuit in accordance with 725.21.

(E) Enclosures with Single Opening. Class 2 and Class 3 circuit conductors entering compartments, enclosures, device boxes, outlet boxes, or similar fittings shall be permitted to be installed with Class 1, non–power-limited fire alarm and medium power network-powered broadband communications circuits where they are introduced solely to connect the equipment connected to Class 2 and Class 3 circuits. Where Class 2 and Class 3 circuit conductors must enter an enclosure that is provided with a single opening, they shall be permitted to enter through a single fitting (such as a tee), provided the conductors are separated from the conductors of the other circuits by a continuous and firmly fixed nonconductor, such as flexible tubing.

(F) Manholes. Underground Class 2 and Class 3 circuit conductors in a manhole shall be permitted to be installed with Class 1, non–power-limited fire alarm and medium power network-powered broadband communications circuits where one of the following conditions is met:

(1) The electric light, power, Class 1, non–power-limited fire alarm and medium power network-powered broadband communications circuit conductors are in a metal-enclosed cable or Type UF cable.

(2) The Class 2 and Class 3 circuit conductors are permanently and effectively separated from the conductors of other circuits by a continuous and firmly fixed nonconductor, such as flexible tubing, in addition to the insulation or covering on the wire.

(3) The Class 2 and Class 3 circuit conductors are permanently and effectively separated from conductors of the other circuits and securely fastened to racks, insulators, or other approved supports.

(G) Closed-Loop and Programmed Power Distribution. Class 2 and Class 3 conductors shall be permitted to be installed in accordance with 780.6.

(H) Cable Trays. Class 2 and Class 3 circuit conductors shall be permitted to be installed in cable trays, where the conductors of the electric light, Class 1, and non–power-limited fire alarm circuits are separated by a solid fixed barrier of a material compatible with the cable tray or where the Class 2 or Class 3 circuits are installed in Type MC cable.

(I) In Hoistways. In hoistways, Class 2 or Class 3 circuit conductors shall be installed in rigid metal conduit, rigid nonmetallic conduit, intermediate metal conduit, liquidtight flexible nonmetallic conduit, or electrical metallic tubing. For elevators or similar equipment, these conductors shall be permitted to be installed as provided in 620.21.

(J) Other Applications. For other applications, conductors of Class 2 and Class 3 circuits shall be separated by at least 50 mm (2 in.) from conductors of any electric light, power, Class 1 non–power-limited fire alarm or medium power network-powered broadband communications circuits unless one of the following conditions is met:

(1) Either (a) all of the electric light, power, Class 1, non–power-limited fire alarm and medium power network-powered broadband communications circuit conductors or (b) all of the Class 2 and Class 3 circuit conductors are in a raceway or in metal-sheathed, metal-clad, non–metallic-sheathed, or Type UF cables.

(2) All of the electric light, power, Class 1 non–power-limited fire alarm, and medium power network-powered broadband communications circuit conductors are permanently separated from all of the Class 2 and Class 3 circuit conductors by a continuous and firmly fixed nonconductor, such as porcelain tubes or flexible tubing, in addition to the insulation on the conductors.

725.56 Installation of Conductors of Different Circuits in the Same Cable, Enclosure, or Raceway.

(A) Two or More Class 2 Circuits. Conductors of two or more Class 2 circuits shall be permitted within the same cable, enclosure, or raceway.

(B) Two or More Class 3 Circuits. Conductors of two or more Class 3 circuits shall be permitted within the same cable, enclosure, or raceway.

(C) Class 2 Circuits with Class 3 Circuits. Conductors of one or more Class 2 circuits shall be permitted within the same cable, enclosure, or raceway with conductors of Class 3 circuits, provided that the insulation of the Class 2 circuit conductors in the cable, enclosure, or raceway is at least that required for Class 3 circuits.

(D) Class 2 and Class 3 Circuits with Communications Circuits.

(1) Classified as Communications Circuits. Class 2 and Class 3 circuit conductors shall be permitted in the same cable with communications circuits, in which case the Class 2 and Class 3 circuits shall be classified as communications circuits and shall be installed in accordance with the requirements of Article 800. The cables shall be listed as communications cables or multipurpose cables.

(2) Composite Cables. Cables constructed of individually listed Class 2, Class 3, and communications cables under a common jacket shall be permitted to be classified as com-

munications cables. The fire resistance rating of the composite cable shall be determined by the performance of the composite cable.

(E) Class 2 or Class 3 Cables with Other Circuit Cables. Jacketed cables of Class 2 or Class 3 circuits shall be permitted in the same enclosure or raceway with jacketed cables of any of the following:

(1) Power-limited fire alarm systems in compliance with Article 760

(2) Nonconductive and conductive optical fiber cables in compliance with Article 770

(3) Communications circuits in compliance with Article 800

(4) Community antenna television and radio distribution systems in compliance with Article 820

(5) Low-power, network-powered broadband communications in compliance with Article 830

(F) Class 2 or Class 3 Conductors or Cables and Audio System Circuits. Audio system circuits described in 640.9(C), and installed using Class 2 or Class 3 wiring methods in compliance with Sections 725.54 and 725.61, shall not be permitted to be installed in the same cable or raceway with Class 2 or Class 3 conductors or cables.

725.57 Installation of Circuit Conductors Extending Beyond One Building.
Where Class 2 or Class 3 circuit conductors extend beyond one building and are run so as to be subject to accidental contact with electric light or power conductors operating over 300 volts to ground, or are exposed to lightning on interbuilding circuits on the same premises, the requirements of the following shall also apply:

(1) Sections 800.44, 800.50, 800.53, 800.93, 800.100, 800.170(A), and 800.170(B) for other than coaxial conductors

(2) Sections 820.44, 820.93, and 820.100 for coaxial conductors

725.58 Support of Conductors.
Class 2 or Class 3 circuit conductors shall not be strapped, taped, or attached by any means to the exterior of any conduit or other raceway as a means of support. These conductors shall be permitted to be installed as permitted by 300.11(B)(2).

725.61 Applications of Listed Class 2, Class 3, and PLTC Cables.
Class 2, Class 3, and PLTC cables shall comply with any of the requirements described in 725.61(A) through 725.61(H).

(A) Plenums. Cables installed in ducts, plenums, and other spaces used for environmental air shall be Type CL2P or CL3P. Listed wires and cables installed in compliance with 300.22 shall be permitted. Listed plenum signaling raceways shall be permitted to be installed in other spaces used for environmental air as described in 300.22(C). Only Type CL2P or CL3P cable shall be permitted to be installed in these raceways.

(B) Riser. Cables installed in risers shall be as described in any of (B)(1), (B)(2), or (B)(3):

(1) Cables installed in vertical runs and penetrating more than one floor, or cables installed in vertical runs in a shaft, shall be Type CL2R or CL3R. Floor penetrations requiring Type CL2R or CL3R shall contain only cables suitable for riser or plenum use. Listed riser signaling raceways shall be permitted to be installed in vertical riser runs in a shaft from floor to floor. Only Type CL2R, CL3R, CL2P, or CL3P cables shall be permitted to be installed in these raceways.

(2) Other cables as covered in Table 725.61 and other listed wiring methods as covered in Chapter 3 shall be installed in metal raceways, or located in a fireproof shaft having firestops at each floor.

(3) Type CL2, CL3, CL2X, and CL3X cables shall be permitted in one- and two-family dwellings. Listed general purpose signaling raceways shall be permitted for use with Type CL2, CL3, CL2X and CL3X cables.

FPN: See 300.21 for firestop requirements for floor penetrations.

(C) Cable Trays. Cables installed in cable trays outdoors shall be Type PLTC. Cables installed in cable trays indoors shall be Types PLTC, CL3P, CL3R, CL3, CL2P, CL2R, and CL2.

Listed signaling raceways shall be permitted for use with cable trays.

FPN: See 800.133(B) for cables permitted in cable trays.

(D) Hazardous (Classified) Locations. Cables installed in hazardous locations shall be as described in 725.61(D)(1) through (D)(4).

(1) Type PLTC. Cables installed in hazardous (classified) locations shall be Type PLTC. Where the use of Type PLTC cable is permitted by 501.10(B), 502.10(B), and 504.20, the cable shall be installed in cable trays, in raceways, supported by messenger wire, or otherwise adequately supported and mechanically protected by angles, struts, channels, or other mechanical means. The cable shall be permitted to be directly buried where the cable is listed for this use.

(2) Intrinsically Safe Circuits and Nonincendive Field Wiring. Wiring for nonincendive circuits as permitted by 501.10(B)(3), and wiring for intrinsically safe circuits as permitted by 504.20, shall be permitted for circuits derived from Class 2 sources.

(3) Thermocouple Circuits. Conductors in Type PLTC cables used for Class 2 thermocouple circuits shall be per-

mitted to be any of the materials used for thermocouple extension wire.

(4) In Industrial Establishments. In industrial establishments where the conditions of maintenance and supervision ensure that only qualified persons service the installation, and where the cable is not subject to physical damage, Type PLTC cable that complies with the crush and impact requirements of Type MC cable and is identified for such use shall be permitted to be exposed between the cable tray and utilization equipment or device. The cable shall be continuously supported and protected against physical damage using mechanical protection such as dedicated struts, angles, or channels. The cable shall be secured at intervals not exceeding 1.8 m (6 ft).

(E) Other Wiring Within Buildings. Cables installed in building locations other than those covered in 725.61(A) through 725.61(D) shall be as described in any of (1) through (7).

(1) Type CL2 or CL3 shall be permitted.

(2) Type CL2X or CL3X shall be permitted to be installed in a raceway or in accordance with other wiring methods covered in Chapter 3.

(3) Cables shall be permitted to be installed in nonconcealed spaces where the exposed length of cable does not exceed 3 m (10 ft).

(4) Listed Type CL2X cables less than 6 mm (0.25 in.) in diameter and listed Type CL3X cables less than 6 mm (0.25 in.) in diameter shall be permitted to be installed in one- and two-family dwellings.

(5) Listed Type CL2X cables less than 6 mm (0.25 in.) in diameter and listed Type CL3X cables less than 6 mm (0.25 in.) in diameter shall be permitted to be installed in nonconcealed spaces in multifamily dwellings.

(6) Type CMUC undercarpet communications wires and cables shall be permitted to be installed under carpet.

(7) In industrial establishments where the conditions of maintenance and supervision ensure that only qualified persons service the installation, and where the cable is not subject to physical damage, Type PLTC cable that complies with the crush and impact requirements of Type MC cable and is identified for such use shall be permitted to be exposed between the cable tray and the utilization equipment or device. The cable shall be continuously supported and protected against physical damage using mechanical protection such as dedicated struts, angles, or channels. The cable shall be supported and secured at intervals not exceeding 1.8 m (6 ft).

(F) Cross-Connect Arrays. Type CL2 or CL3 conductors or cables shall be used for cross-connect arrays.

(G) Class 2 and Class 3 Cable Substitutions. The substitutions for Class 2 and Class 3 cables listed in Table 725.61

shall be permitted. Where substitute cables are installed, the wiring requirements of Article 725, Parts I and III, shall apply.

FPN: For information on Types CMP, CMR, CM, and CMX cables, see 800.179.

Table 725.61 Cable Substitutions

Cable Type	Permitted Substitutions
CL3P	CMP
CL2P	CMP, CL3P
CL3R	CMP, CL3P, CMR
CL2R	CMP, CL3P, CL2P, CMR, CL3R
PLTC	
CL3	CMP, CL3P, CMR, CL3R, CMG, CM, PLTC
CL2	CMP, CL3P, CL2P, CMR, CL3R, CL2R, CMG, CM, PLTC, CL3
CL3X	CMP, CL3P, CMR, CL3R, CMG, CM, PLTC, CL3, CMX
CL2X	CMP, CL3P, CL2P, CMR, CL3R, CL2R, CMG, CM, PLTC, CL3, CL2, CMX, CL3X

Type CM—Communications wires and cables
Type CL2 and CL3—Class 2 and Class 3 remote-control, signaling, and power-limited cables
Type PLTC—Power-limited tray cable

[A]▶[B] Cable A shall be permitted to be used in place of Cable B.

Figure 725.61 Cable Substitution Hierarchy

(H) Class 2, Class 3, PLTC Circuit Integrity (CI) Cable or Electrical Circuit Protective System. Circuit integrity (CI) cable or a listed electrical circuit protective system shall be permitted for use in remote control, signaling, or power limited systems that supply critical circuits to ensure survivability for continued circuit operation for a specified time under fire conditions.

IV. Listing Requirements

725.82 Listing and Marking of Class 2, Class 3, and Type PLTC Cables. Class 2, Class 3, and Type PLTC cables and nonmetallic signaling raceways installed as wiring methods within buildings shall be listed as being resistant to the spread of fire and other criteria in accordance with 725.82(A) through 725.82(K) and shall be marked in accordance with 725.82(L).

(A) Types CL2P and CL3P. Types CL2P and CL3P plenum cable shall be listed as being suitable for use in ducts, plenums, and other space for environmental air and shall also be listed as having adequate fire-resistant and low smoke-producing characteristics.

FPN: One method of defining low smoke-producing cable is by establishing an acceptable value of the smoke produced when tested in accordance with NFPA 262-2002, *Standard Method of Test for Flame Travel and Smoke of Wires and Cables for Use in Air-Handling Spaces*, to a maximum peak optical density of 0.5 and a maximum average optical density of 0.15. Similarly, one method of defining fire-resistant cables is by establishing a maximum allowable flame travel distance of 1.52 m (5 ft) when tested in accordance with the same test.

(B) Types CL2R and CL3R. Types CL2R and CL3R riser cables shall be marked as Type CL2R or CL3R, respectively, and be listed as suitable for use in a vertical run in a shaft or from floor to floor and shall also be listed as having fire-resistant characteristics capable of preventing the carrying of fire from floor to floor.

FPN: One method of defining fire-resistant characteristics capable of preventing the carrying of fire from floor to floor is that the cables pass the requirements of ANSI/UL 1666-2002, *Test for Flame Propagation Height of Electrical and Optical-Fiber Cable Installed Vertically in Shafts.*

(C) Types CL2 and CL3. Types CL2 and CL3 cables shall be marked as Type CL2 or CL3, respectively, and be listed as suitable for general-purpose use, with the exception of risers, ducts, plenums, and other space used for environmental air, and shall also be listed as being resistant to the spread of fire.

FPN: One method of defining *resistant to the spread of fire* is that the cables do not spread fire to the top of the tray in the vertical tray flame test in ANSI/UL 1581-1991, *Reference Standard for Electrical Wires, Cables and Flexible Cords.*

Another method of defining *resistant to the spread of fire* is for the damage (char length) not to exceed 1.5 m (4 ft 11 in.) when performing the CSA vertical flame test for cables in cable trays, as described in CSA C22.2 No. 0.3-M-1985, *Test Methods for Electrical Wires and Cables.*

(D) Types CL2X and CL3X. Types CL2X and CL3X limited-use cables shall be marked as Type CL2X or CL3X respectively, and be listed as being suitable for use in dwellings and for use in raceway and shall also be listed as being resistant to flame spread.

FPN: One method of determining that cable is resistant to flame spread is by testing the cable to the VW-1 (vertical wire) flame test in ANSI/UL 1581-1991, *Reference Standard for Electrical Wires, Cables and Flexible Cords.*

(E) Type PLTC. Type PLTC nonmetallic-sheathed, power-limited tray cable shall be listed as being suitable for cable trays and shall consist of a factory assembly of two or more insulated conductors under a nonmetallic jacket. The insulated conductors shall be 22 AWG through 12 AWG. The conductor material shall be copper (solid or stranded). Insulation on conductors shall be suitable for 300 volts. The cable core shall be either (1) two or more parallel conductors, (2) one or more group assemblies of twisted or parallel conductors, or (3) a combination thereof. A metallic shield or a metallized foil shield with drain wire(s) shall be permitted to be applied either over the cable core, over groups of conductors, or both. The cable shall be listed as being resistant to the spread of fire. The outer jacket shall be a sunlight- and moisture-resistant nonmetallic material.

Exception No. 1: Where a smooth metallic sheath, continuous corrugated metallic sheath, or interlocking tape armor is applied over the nonmetallic jacket, an overall nonmetallic jacket shall not be required. On metallic-sheathed cable without an overall nonmetallic jacket, the information required in 310.11 shall be located on the nonmetallic jacket under the sheath.

Exception No. 2: Conductors in PLTC cables used for Class 2 thermocouple circuits shall be permitted to be any of the materials used for thermocouple extension wire.

FPN: One method of defining *resistant to the spread of fire* is that the cables do not spread fire to the top of the tray in the vertical tray flame test in ANSI/UL 1581-1991, *Reference Standard for Electrical Wires, Cables and Flexible Cords.*

Another method of defining *resistant to the spread of fire* is for the damage (char length) not to exceed 1.5 m (4 ft 11 in.) when performing the CSA vertical flame test for cables in cable trays, as described in CSA C22.2 No. 0.3-M-1985, *Test Methods for Electrical Wires and Cables.*

(F) Circuit Integrity (CI) Cable or Electrical Circuit Protective System. Cables used for survivability of critical circuits shall be listed as circuit integrity (CI) cable. Cables specified in 725.61(A), (B), (D)(1), and (E), and used for circuit integrity, shall have the additional classification using the suffix "-CI". Cables that are part of a listed electrical circuit protective system shall be considered to meet the requirements of survivability.

FPN: One method of defining circuit integrity is by establishing a minimum 2-hour fire resistance rating when tested in accordance with UL 2196-2002, *Standard for Tests of Fire Resistive Cables.*

(G) Class 2 and Class 3 Cable Voltage Ratings. Class 2 cables shall have a voltage rating of not less than 150 volts. Class 3 cables shall have a voltage rating of not less than 300 volts.

(H) Class 3 Single Conductors. Class 3 single conductors used as other wiring within buildings shall not be smaller than 18 AWG and shall be Type CL3. Conductor types described in 725.27(B) that are also listed as Type CL3 shall be permitted.

FPN: One method of defining *resistant to the spread of fire* is that the cables do not spread fire to the top of the tray in the vertical tray flame test in ANSI/UL 1581-1991, *Reference Standard for Electrical Wires, Cables and Flexible Cords.*

Another method of defining *resistant to the spread of fire* is for the damage (char length) not to exceed 1.5 m (4 ft 11 in.) when performing the CSA vertical flame test for cables in cable trays as described in CSA C22.2 No. 0.3-M-1985, *Test Methods for Electrical Wires and Cables.*

(I) Plenum Signaling Raceways. Plenum signaling raceways shall be listed as having adequate fire-resistant and low smoke-producing characteristics.

(J) Riser Signaling Raceways. Riser signaling raceways shall be listed as having adequate fire-resistant characteristics capable of preventing the carrying of fire from floor to floor.

FPN: One method of defining fire-resistant characteristics capable of preventing the carrying of fire from floor to floor is that the raceways pass the requirements of the Test for Flame Propagation (Riser) in UL 2024, *Standard for Optical Fiber Cable Raceway.*

(K) General-Purpose Signaling Raceways. General-purpose signaling raceways shall be listed as being resistant to the spread of fire.

FPN: One method of defining resistance to the spread of fire is that the raceways pass the requirements of the Vertical-Tray Flame Test (General use) in UL 2024, *Standard for Optical Fiber Cable Raceway.*

(L) Marking. Cables shall be marked in accordance with 310.11(A)(2), (A)(3), (A)(4), and (A)(5) and Table 725.82. Voltage ratings shall not be marked on the cables.

FPN: Voltage markings on cables may be misinterpreted to suggest that the cables may be suitable for Class 1 electric light and power applications.

Exception: Voltage markings shall be permitted where the cable has multiple listings and a voltage marking is required for one or more of the listings.

Table 725.82 Cable Marking

Cable Marking	Type
CL3P	Class 3 plenum cable
CL2P	Class 2 plenum cable
CL3R	Class 3 riser cable
CL2R	Class 2 riser cable
PLTC	Power-limited tray cable
CL3	Class 3 cable
CL2	Class 2 cable
CL3X	Class 3 cable, limited use
CL2X	Class 2 cable, limited use

FPN: Class 2 and Class 3 cable types are listed in descending order of fire resistance rating, and Class 3 cables are listed above Class 2 cables because Class 3 cables can substitute for Class 2 cables.

ARTICLE 727
Instrumentation Tray Cable: Type ITC

727.1 Scope. This article covers the use, installation, and construction specifications of instrumentation tray cable for application to instrumentation and control circuits operating at 150 volts or less and 5 amperes or less.

727.2 Definition.

Type ITC Instrumentation Tray Cable. A factory assembly of two or more insulated conductors, with or without a grounding conductor(s), enclosed in a nonmetallic sheath.

727.3 Other Articles. In addition to the provisions of this article, installation of Type ITC cable shall comply with other applicable articles of this *Code*, such as Articles 240, 250, 300, and 392.

727.4 Uses Permitted. Type ITC cable shall be permitted to be used as follows in industrial establishments where the conditions of maintenance and supervision ensure that only qualified persons service the installation:

(1) In cable trays.

(2) In raceways.

(3) In hazardous locations as permitted in 501.10, 502.10, 503.10, 504.20, 504.30, 504.80, and 505.15.

(4) Enclosed in a smooth metallic sheath, continuous corrugated metallic sheath, or interlocking tape armor applied over the nonmetallic sheath in accordance with 727.6. The cable shall be supported and secured at intervals not exceeding 1.8 m (6 ft).

(5) Without a metallic sheath or armor between cable tray and equipment in lengths not to exceed 15 m (50 ft),

where the cable is supported and protected against physical damage using mechanical protection, such as struts, angles, or channels. The cable shall be supported and secured at intervals not exceeding 1.8 m (6 ft).

(6) Between cable tray and equipment in lengths not to exceed 15 m (50 ft), where the cable complies with the crush and impact requirements of Type MC cable and is identified for such use. The cable shall be supported and secured at intervals not exceeding 1.8 m (6 ft).

(7) As aerial cable on a messenger.

(8) Direct buried where identified for the use.

(9) Under raised floors in rooms containing industrial process control equipment and rack rooms where arranged to prevent damage to the cable.

(10) Under raised floors in information technology equipment rooms in accordance with 645.5(D)(5)(c).

727.5 Uses Not Permitted. Type ITC cable shall not be installed on circuits operating at more than 150 volts or more than 5 amperes.

Installation of Type ITC cable with other cables shall be subject to the stated provisions of the specific articles for the other cables. Where the governing articles do not contain stated provisions for installation with Type ITC cable, the installation of Type ITC cable with the other cables shall not be permitted.

Type ITC cable shall not be installed with power, lighting, Class 1, or non–power-limited circuits.

Exception No. 1: Where terminated within equipment or junction boxes and separations are maintained by insulating barriers or other means.

Exception No. 2: Where a metallic sheath or armor is applied over the nonmetallic sheath of the Type ITC cable.

727.6 Construction. The insulated conductors of Type ITC cable shall be in sizes 22 AWG through 12 AWG. The conductor material shall be copper or thermocouple alloy. Insulation on the conductors shall be rated for 300 volts. Shielding shall be permitted.

The cable shall be listed as being resistant to the spread of fire. The outer jacket shall be sunlight and moisture resistant.

Where a smooth metallic sheath, continuous corrugated metallic sheath, or interlocking tape armor is applied over the nonmetallic sheath, an overall nonmetallic jacket shall not be required.

727.7 Marking. The cable shall be marked in accordance with 310.11(A)(2), (A)(3), (A)(4), and (A)(5). Voltage ratings shall not be marked on the cable.

727.8 Allowable Ampacity. The allowable ampacity of the conductors shall be 5 amperes, except for 22 AWG conductors, which shall have an allowable ampacity of 3 amperes.

727.9 Overcurrent Protection. Overcurrent protection shall not exceed 5 amperes for 20 AWG and larger conductors, and 3 amperes for 22 AWG conductors.

727.10 Bends. Bends in Type ITC cables shall be made so as not to damage the cable.

ARTICLE 760
Fire Alarm Systems

I. General

760.1 Scope. This article covers the installation of wiring and equipment of fire alarm systems including all circuits controlled and powered by the fire alarm system.

> FPN No. 1: Fire alarm systems include fire detection and alarm notification, guard's tour, sprinkler waterflow, and sprinkler supervisory systems. Circuits controlled and powered by the fire alarm system include circuits for the control of building systems safety functions, elevator capture, elevator shutdown, door release, smoke doors and damper control, fire doors and damper control and fan shutdown, but only where these circuits are powered by and controlled by the fire alarm system. For further information on the installation and monitoring for integrity requirements for fire alarm systems, refer to the *NFPA 72®-2002, National Fire Alarm Code®.*

> FPN No. 2: Class 1, 2, and 3 circuits are defined in Article 725.

760.2 Definitions.

Abandoned Fire Alarm Cable. Installed fire alarm cable that is not terminated at equipment other than a connector and not identified for future use with a tag.

Fire Alarm Circuit. The portion of the wiring system between the load side of the overcurrent device or the power-limited supply and the connected equipment of all circuits powered and controlled by the fire alarm system. Fire alarm circuits are classified as either non–power-limited or power-limited.

Fire Alarm Circuit Integrity (CI) Cable. Cable used in fire alarm systems to ensure continued operation of critical circuits during a specified time under fire conditions.

Non–Power-Limited Fire Alarm Circuit (NPLFA). A fire alarm circuit powered by a source that complies with 760.21 and 760.23.

Power-Limited Fire Alarm Circuit (PLFA). A fire alarm circuit powered by a source that complies with 760.41.

760.3 Other Articles. Circuits and equipment shall comply with 760.3(A) through 760.3(F). Only those sections of Article 300 referenced in this article shall apply to fire alarm systems.

(A) Spread of Fire or Products of Combustion. Section 300.21. The accessible portion of abandoned fire alarm cables shall be removed.

(B) Ducts, Plenums, and Other Air-Handling Spaces. Section 300.22, where installed in ducts or plenums or other spaces used for environmental air.

Exception: As permitted in 760.30(B)(1) and (B)(2) and 760.61(A).

(C) Hazardous (Classified) Locations. Articles 500 through 516 and Article 517, Part IV, where installed in hazardous (classified) locations.

(D) Corrosive, Damp, or Wet Locations. Sections 110.11, 300.6, and 310.9 where installed in corrosive, damp, or wet locations.

(E) Building Control Circuits. Article 725 where building control circuits (e.g., elevator capture, fan shutdown) are associated with the fire alarm system.

(F) Optical Fiber Cables. Where optical fiber cables are utilized for fire alarm circuits, the cables shall be installed in accordance with Article 770.

760.7 Access to Electrical Equipment Behind Panels Designed to Allow Access. Access to electrical equipment shall not be denied by an accumulation of conductors and cables that prevents removal of panels, including suspended ceiling panels.

760.8 Mechanical Execution of Work. Fire alarm circuits shall be installed in a neat workmanlike manner. Cables and conductors installed exposed on the surface of ceilings and sidewalls shall be supported by the building structure in such a manner that the cable will not be damaged by normal building use. Such cables shall be supported by straps, staples, hangers, or similar fittings designed and installed so as not to damage the cable. The installation shall also conform with 300.4(D).

> FPN: One source of information describing industry practices is ANCI/NECA 305-2001, *Standard for Fire Alarm System Job Practice.*

760.9 Fire Alarm Circuit and Equipment Grounding. Fire alarm circuits and equipment shall be grounded in accordance with Article 250.

760.10 Fire Alarm Circuit Identification. Fire alarm circuits shall be identified at terminal and junction locations in a manner that will prevent unintentional interference with the signaling circuit during testing and servicing.

760.11 Fire Alarm Circuits Extending Beyond One Building. Power-limited fire alarm circuits that extend beyond one building and run outdoors either shall meet the installation requirements of Parts II, III, and IV of Article 800 or shall meet the installation requirements of Part I of Article 300. Non–power-limited fire alarm circuits that extend beyond one building and run outdoors shall meet the installation requirements of Part I of Article 300 and the applicable sections of Part I of Article 225.

760.15 Fire Alarm Circuit Requirements. Fire alarm circuits shall comply with 760.15(A) and 760.15(B).

(A) Non–Power-Limited Fire Alarm (NPLFA) Circuits. See Parts I and II.

(B) Power-Limited Fire Alarm (PLFA) Circuits. See Parts I and III.

II. Non–Power-Limited Fire Alarm (NPLFA) Circuits

760.21 NPLFA Circuit Power Source Requirements. The power source of non–power-limited fire alarm circuits shall comply with Chapters 1 through 4, and the output voltage shall not be more than 600 volts, nominal. These circuits shall not be supplied through ground-fault circuit interrupters or arc-fault circuit interrupters.

> FPN: See 210.8(A)(5), Exception No. 3, for receptacles in dwelling-unit unfinished basements that supply power for fire alarm systems.

760.23 NPLFA Circuit Overcurrent Protection. Overcurrent protection for conductors 14 AWG and larger shall be provided in accordance with the conductor ampacity without applying the derating factors of 310.15 to the ampacity calculation. Overcurrent protection shall not exceed 7 amperes for 18 AWG conductors and 10 amperes for 16 AWG conductors.

Exception: Where other articles of this Code permit or require other overcurrent protection.

760.24 NPLFA Circuit Overcurrent Device Location. Overcurrent devices shall be located at the point where the conductor to be protected receives its supply.

Exception No. 1: Where the overcurrent device protecting the larger conductor also protects the smaller conductor.

Exception No. 2: Transformer secondary conductors. Non–power-limited fire alarm circuit conductors supplied by the secondary of a single-phase transformer that has only a 2-wire (single-voltage) secondary shall be permitted to be protected by overcurrent protection provided by the primary (supply) side of the transformer, provided the protection is in accordance with 450.3 and does not exceed the value determined by multiplying the secondary conductor ampacity by the secondary-to-primary transformer voltage ratio. Transformer secondary conductors other than 2-wire shall not be considered to be protected by the primary overcurrent protection.

Exception No. 3: Electronic power source output conductors. Non–power-limited circuit conductors supplied by the output of a single-phase, listed electronic power source, other than a transformer, having only a 2-wire (single-voltage) output for connection to non–power-limited circuits shall be permitted to be protected by overcurrent protection provided on the input side of the electronic power source, provided this protection does not exceed the value determined by multiplying the non–power-limited circuit conductor ampacity by the output-to-input voltage ratio. Electronic power source outputs, other than 2-wire (single voltage), connected to non–power-limited circuits shall not be considered to be protected by overcurrent protection on the input of the electronic power source.

> FPN: A single-phase, listed electronic power supply whose output supplies a 2-wire (single-voltage) circuit is an example of a non–power-limited power source that meets the requirements of 760.21.

760.25 NPLFA Circuit Wiring Methods. Installation of non–power-limited fire alarm circuits shall be in accordance with 110.3(B), 300.11, 300.15, 300.17, and other appropriate articles of Chapter 3.

Exception No. 1: As provided in 760.26 through 760.30.

Exception No. 2: Where other articles of this Code require other methods.

760.26 Conductors of Different Circuits in Same Cable, Enclosure, or Raceway.

(A) Class 1 with NPLFA Circuits. Class 1 and non–power-limited fire alarm circuits shall be permitted to occupy the same cable, enclosure, or raceway without regard to whether the individual circuits are alternating current or direct current, provided all conductors are insulated for the maximum voltage of any conductor in the enclosure or raceway.

(B) Fire Alarm with Power-Supply Circuits. Power-supply and fire alarm circuit conductors shall be permitted in the same cable, enclosure, or raceway only where connected to the same equipment.

760.27 NPLFA Circuit Conductors.

(A) Sizes and Use. Only copper conductors shall be permitted to be used for fire alarm systems. Size 18 AWG and

16 AWG conductors shall be permitted to be used, provided they supply loads that do not exceed the ampacities given in Table 402.5 and are installed in a raceway, an approved enclosure, or a listed cable. Conductors larger than 16 AWG shall not supply loads greater than the ampacities given in 310.15, as applicable.

(B) Insulation. Insulation on conductors shall be suitable for 600 volts. Conductors larger than 16 AWG shall comply with Article 310. Conductors 18 AWG and 16 AWG shall be Type KF-2, KFF-2, PAFF, PTFF, PF, PFF, PGF, PGFF, RFH-2, RFHH-2, RFHH-3, SF-2, SFF-2, TF, TFF, TFN, TFFN, ZF, or ZFF. Conductors with other types and thickness of insulation shall be permitted if listed for non–power-limited fire alarm circuit use.

FPN: For application provisions, see Table 402.3.

(C) Conductor Materials. Conductors shall be solid or stranded copper.

Exception to (B) and (C): Wire Types PAF and PTF shall be permitted only for high-temperature applications between 90°C (194°F) and 250°C (482°F).

760.28 Number of Conductors in Cable Trays and Raceways, and Derating.

(A) NPLFA Circuits and Class 1 Circuits. Where only non–power-limited fire alarm circuit and Class 1 circuit conductors are in a raceway, the number of conductors shall be determined in accordance with 300.17. The derating factors given in 310.15(B)(2)(a) shall apply if such conductors carry continuous load in excess of 10 percent of the ampacity of each conductor.

(B) Power-Supply Conductors and Fire Alarm Circuit Conductors. Where power-supply conductors and fire alarm circuit conductors are permitted in a raceway in accordance with 760.26, the number of conductors shall be determined in accordance with 300.17. The derating factors given in 310.15(B)(2)(a) shall apply as follows:

(1) To all conductors where the fire alarm circuit conductors carry continuous loads in excess of 10 percent of the ampacity of each conductor and where the total number of conductors is more than three

(2) To the power-supply conductors only, where the fire alarm circuit conductors do not carry continuous loads in excess of 10 percent of the ampacity of each conductor and where the number of power-supply conductors is more than three

(C) Cable Trays. Where fire alarm circuit conductors are installed in cable trays, they shall comply with 392.9 through 392.11.

760.30 Multiconductor NPLFA Cables. Multiconductor non–power-limited fire alarm cables that meet the require-

ments of 760.81 shall be permitted to be used on fire alarm circuits operating at 150 volts or less and shall be installed in accordance with 760.30(A) and 760.30(B).

(A) NPLFA Wiring Method. Multiconductor non–power-limited fire alarm circuit cables shall be installed in accordance with 760.30(A)(1), (A)(2), and (A)(3).

(1) Exposed or Fished in Concealed Spaces. In raceway or exposed on surface of ceiling and sidewalls or fished in concealed spaces. Cable splices or terminations shall be made in listed fittings, boxes, enclosures, fire alarm devices, or utilization equipment. Where installed exposed, cables shall be adequately supported and installed in such a way that maximum protection against physical damage is afforded by building construction such as baseboards, door frames, ledges, and so forth. Where located within 2.1 m (7 ft) of the floor, cables shall be securely fastened in an approved manner at intervals of not more than 450 mm (18 in.).

(2) Passing Through a Floor or Wall. In metal raceway or rigid nonmetallic conduit where passing through a floor or wall to a height of 2.1 m (7 ft) above the floor unless adequate protection can be afforded by building construction such as detailed in 760.30(A)(1) or unless an equivalent solid guard is provided.

(3) In Hoistways. In rigid metal conduit, rigid nonmetallic conduit, intermediate metal conduit, liquidtight flexible nonmetallic conduit, or electrical metallic tubing where installed in hoistways.

Exception: As provided for in 620.21 for elevators and similar equipment.

(B) Applications of Listed NPLFA Cables. The use of non–power-limited fire alarm circuit cables shall comply with 760.30(B)(1) through (B)(4).

(1) Ducts and Plenums. Multiconductor non–power-limited fire alarm circuit cables, Types NPLFP, NPLFR, and NPLF, shall not be installed exposed in ducts or plenums.

FPN: See 300.22(B).

(2) Other Spaces Used for Environmental Air. Cables installed in other spaces used for environmental air shall be Type NPLFP.

Exception No. 1: Types NPLFR and NPLF cables installed in compliance with 300.22(C).

Exception No. 2: Other wiring methods in accordance with 300.22(C) and conductors in compliance with 760.27(C).

Exception No. 3: Type NPLFP-CI cable shall be permitted to be installed to provide a 2-hour circuit integrity rated cable.

(3) Riser. Cables installed in vertical runs and penetrating more than one floor or cables installed in vertical runs in a shaft shall be Type NPLFR. Floor penetrations requiring Type NPLFR shall contain only cables suitable for riser or plenum use.

Exception No. 1: Type NPLF or other cables that are specified in Chapter 3 and are in compliance with 760.27(C) and encased in metal raceway.

Exception No. 2: Type NPLF cables located in a fireproof shaft having firestops at each floor.

> FPN: See 300.21 for firestop requirements for floor penetrations.

Exception No. 3: Type NPLFR-CI cable shall be permitted to be installed to provide a 2-hour circuit integrity rated cable.

(4) Other Wiring Within Buildings. Cables installed in building locations other than the locations covered in 760.30(B)(1), (B)(2), and (B)(3) shall be Type NPLF.

Exception No. 1: Chapter 3 wiring methods with conductors in compliance with 760.27(C).

Exception No. 2: Type NPLFP or Type NPLFR cables shall be permitted.

Exception No. 3: Type NPLF-CI cable shall be permitted to be installed to provide a 2-hour circuit integrity rated cable.

III. Power-Limited Fire Alarm (PLFA) Circuits

760.41 Power Sources for PLFA Circuits. The power source for a power-limited fire alarm circuit shall be as specified in 760.41(A), (B), or (C). These circuits shall not be supplied through ground-fault circuit interrupters or arc-fault circuit interrupters.

> FPN No. 1: Tables 12(A) and 12(B) in Chapter 9 provide the listing requirements for power-limited fire alarm circuit sources.

> FPN No. 2: See 210.8(A)(5), Exception No. 3, for receptacles in dwelling-unit unfinished basements that supply power for fire alarm systems.

(A) Transformers. A listed PLFA or Class 3 transformer.

(B) Power Supplies. A listed PLFA or Class 3 power supply.

(C) Listed Equipment. Listed equipment marked to identify the PLFA power source.

> FPN: Examples of listed equipment are a fire alarm control panel with integral power source; a circuit card listed for use as a PLFA source, where used as part of a listed assembly; a current-limiting impedance, listed for the purpose or part of a listed product, used in conjunction with a non–power-limited transformer or a stored energy source, for example, storage battery, to limit the output current.

760.42 Circuit Marking. The equipment supplying PLFA circuits shall be durably marked where plainly visible to indicate each circuit that is a power-limited fire alarm circuit.

> FPN: See 760.52(A), Exception No. 3, where a power-limited circuit is to be reclassified as a non–power-limited circuit.

760.51 Wiring Methods on Supply Side of the PLFA Power Source. Conductors and equipment on the supply side of the power source shall be installed in accordance with the appropriate requirements of Part II and Chapters 1 through 4. Transformers or other devices supplied from power-supply conductors shall be protected by an overcurrent device rated not over 20 amperes.

Exception: The input leads of a transformer or other power source supplying power-limited fire alarm circuits shall be permitted to be smaller than 14 AWG, but not smaller than 18 AWG, if they are not over 300 mm (12 in.) long and if they have insulation that complies with 760.27(B).

760.52 Wiring Methods and Materials on Load Side of the PLFA Power Source. Fire alarm circuits on the load side of the power source shall be permitted to be installed using wiring methods and materials in accordance with 760.52(A), 760.52(B), or a combination of (A) and (B).

(A) NPLFA Wiring Methods and Materials. Installation shall be in accordance with 760.25, and conductors shall be solid or stranded copper.

Exception No. 1: The derating factors given in 310.15(B)(2)(a) shall not apply.

Exception No. 2: Conductors and multiconductor cables described in and installed in accordance with 760.27 and 760.30 shall be permitted.

Exception No. 3: Power-limited circuits shall be permitted to be reclassified and installed as non–power-limited circuits if the power-limited fire alarm circuit markings required by 760.42 are eliminated and the entire circuit is installed using the wiring methods and materials in accordance with Part II, Non–Power-Limited Fire Alarm Circuits.

> FPN: Power-limited circuits reclassified and installed as non–power-limited circuits are no longer power-limited circuits, regardless of the continued connection to a power-limited source.

(B) PLFA Wiring Methods and Materials. Power-limited fire alarm conductors and cables described in 760.82 shall be installed as detailed in 760.52(B)(1), (B)(2), or (B)(3) of this section. Devices shall be installed in accordance with 110.3(B), 300.11(A), and 300.15.

(1) Exposed or Fished in Concealed Spaces. In raceway or exposed on the surface of ceiling and sidewalls or fished in concealed spaces. Cable splices or terminations shall be made in listed fittings, boxes, enclosures, fire alarm devices, or utilization equipment. Where installed exposed, cables shall be adequately supported and installed in such a way that maximum protection against physical damage is afforded by building construction such as baseboards, door frames, ledges, and so forth. Where located within 2.1 m (7 ft) of the floor, cables shall be securely fastened in an approved manner at intervals of not more than 450 mm (18 in.).

(2) Passing Through a Floor or Wall. In metal raceways or rigid nonmetallic conduit where passing through a floor or wall to a height of 2.1 m (7 ft) above the floor, unless adequate protection can be afforded by building construction such as detailed in 760.52(B)(1) or unless an equivalent solid guard is provided.

(3) In Hoistways. In rigid metal conduit, rigid nonmetallic conduit, intermediate metal conduit, or electrical metallic tubing where installed in hoistways.

Exception: As provided for in 620.21 for elevators and similar equipment.

760.54 Installation of Conductors and Equipment in Cables, Compartments, Cable Trays, Enclosures, Manholes, Outlet Boxes, Device Boxes, and Raceways for Power-Limited Circuits. Conductors and equipment for power-limited fire alarm circuits shall be installed in accordance with 760.55 through 760.58.

760.55 Separation from Electric Light, Power, Class 1, NPLFA, and Medium Power Network-Powered Broadband Communications Circuit Conductors.

(A) General. Power-limited fire alarm circuit cables and conductors shall not be placed in any cable, cable tray, compartment, enclosure, manhole, outlet box, device box, raceway, or similar fitting with conductors of electric light, power, Class 1, non–power-limited fire alarm circuits, and medium power network-powered broadband communications circuits unless permitted by 760.55(B) through 760.55(G).

(B) Separated by Barriers. Power-limited fire alarm circuit cables shall be permitted to be installed together with Class 1, non–power-limited fire alarm, and medium power network-powered broadband communications circuits where they are separated by a barrier.

(C) Raceways Within Enclosures. In enclosures, power-limited fire alarm circuits shall be permitted to be installed in a raceway within the enclosure to separate them from Class 1, non–power-limited fire alarm, and medium power network-powered broadband communications circuits.

(D) Associated Systems Within Enclosures. Power-limited fire alarm conductors in compartments, enclosures, device boxes, outlet boxes, or similar fittings shall be permitted to be

installed with electric light, power, Class 1, non–power-limited fire alarm, and medium power network-powered broadband communications circuits where they are introduced solely to connect the equipment connected to power-limited fire alarm circuits, and comply with either of the following conditions:

(1) The electric light, power, Class 1, non–power-limited fire alarm, and medium power network-powered broadband communications circuit conductors are routed to maintain a minimum of 6 mm (0.25 in.) separation from the conductors and cables of power-limited fire alarm circuits.

(2) The circuit conductors operate at 150 volts or less to ground and also comply with one of the following:

　a. The fire alarm power-limited circuits are installed using Type FPL, FPLR, FPLP, or permitted substitute cables, provided these power-limited cable conductors extending beyond the jacket are separated by a minimum of 6 mm (0.25 in.) or by a nonconductive sleeve or nonconductive barrier from all other conductors.

　b. The power-limited fire alarm circuit conductors are installed as non–power-limited circuits in accordance with 760.25.

(E) Enclosures with Single Opening. Power-limited fire alarm circuit conductors entering compartments, enclosures, device boxes, outlet boxes, or similar fittings shall be permitted to be installed with electric light, power, Class 1, non–power-limited fire alarm, and medium power network-powered broadband communications circuits where they are introduced solely to connect the equipment connected to power-limited fire alarm circuits or to other circuits controlled by the fire alarm system to which the other conductors in the enclosure are connected. Where power-limited fire alarm circuit conductors must enter an enclosure that is provided with a single opening, they shall be permitted to enter through a single fitting (such as a tee), provided the conductors are separated from the conductors of the other circuits by a continuous and firmly fixed nonconductor, such as flexible tubing.

(F) In Hoistways. In hoistways, power-limited fire alarm circuit conductors shall be installed in rigid metal conduit, rigid nonmetallic conduit, intermediate metal conduit, liquidtight flexible nonmetallic conduit, or electrical metallic tubing. For elevators or similar equipment, these conductors shall be permitted to be installed as provided in 620.21.

(G) Other Applications. For other applications, power-limited fire alarm circuit conductors shall be separated by at least 50 mm (2 in.) from conductors of any electric light, power, Class 1, non–power-limited fire alarm, or medium power network-powered broadband communications circuits unless one of the following conditions is met:

(1) Either (a) all of the electric light, power, Class 1, non–power-limited fire alarm, and medium power network-powered broadband communications circuit conductors or (b) all of the power-limited fire alarm circuit conductors are in a raceway or in metal-sheathed, metal-clad, nonmetallic-sheathed, or Type UF cables.

(2) All of the electric light, power, Class 1, non–power-limited fire alarm, and medium power network-powered broadband communications circuit conductors are permanently separated from all of the power-limited fire alarm circuit conductors by a continuous and firmly fixed nonconductor, such as porcelain tubes or flexible tubing, in addition to the insulation on the conductors.

760.56 Installation of Conductors of Different PLFA Circuits, Class 2, Class 3, and Communications Circuits in the Same Cable, Enclosure, or Raceway.

(A) Two or More PLFA Circuits. Cable and conductors of two or more power-limited fire alarm circuits, communications circuits, or Class 3 circuits shall be permitted within the same cable, enclosure, or raceway.

(B) Class 2 Circuits with PLFA Circuits. Conductors of one or more Class 2 circuits shall be permitted within the same cable, enclosure, or raceway with conductors of power-limited fire alarm circuits, provided that the insulation of the Class 2 circuit conductors in the cable, enclosure, or raceway is at least that required by the power-limited fire alarm circuits.

(C) Low-Power Network-Powered Broadband Communications Cables and PLFA Cables. Low-power network-powered broadband communications circuits shall be permitted in the same enclosure or raceway with PLFA cables.

(D) Audio System Circuits and PLFA Circuits. Audio system circuits described in 640.9(C) and installed using Class 2 or Class 3 wiring methods in compliance with 725.54 and 725.61 shall not be permitted to be installed in the same cable or raceway with power-limited conductors or cables.

760.57 Conductor Size. Conductors of 26 AWG shall be permitted only where spliced with a connector listed as suitable for 26 AWG to 24 AWG or larger conductors that are terminated on equipment or where the 26 AWG conductors are terminated on equipment listed as suitable for 26 AWG conductors. Single conductors shall not be smaller than 18 AWG.

760.58 Support of Conductors. Power-limited fire alarm circuit conductors shall not be strapped, taped, or attached by any means to the exterior of any conduit or other raceway as a means of support.

760.59 Current-Carrying Continuous Line-Type Fire Detectors.

(A) Application. Listed continuous line-type fire detectors, including insulated copper tubing of pneumatically operated detectors, employed for both detection and carrying signaling currents shall be permitted to be used in power-limited circuits.

(B) Installation. Continuous line-type fire detectors shall be installed in accordance with 760.42 through 760.52 and 760.54.

760.61 Applications of Listed PLFA Cables. PLFA cables shall comply with the requirements described in either 760.61(A), (B), or (C) or where cable substitutions are made as shown in 760.61(D).

(A) Plenum. Cables installed in ducts, plenums, and other spaces used for environmental air shall be Type FPLP. Types FPLP, FPLR, and FPL cables installed in compliance with 300.22 shall be permitted. Type FPLP-CI cable shall be permitted to be installed to provide a 2-hour circuit integrity rated cable.

(B) Riser. Cables installed in risers shall be as described in either (1), (2), or (3):

(1) Cables installed in vertical runs and penetrating more than one floor, or cables installed in vertical runs in a shaft, shall be Type FPLR. Floor penetrations requiring Type FPLR shall contain only cables suitable for riser or plenum use. Type FPLR-CI cable shall be permitted to be installed to provide a 2-hour circuit integrity rated cable.

(2) Other cables shall be installed in metal raceways or located in a fireproof shaft having firestops at each floor.

(3) Type FPL cable shall be permitted in one- and two-family dwellings.

FPN: See 300.21 for firestop requirements for floor penetrations.

(C) Other Wiring Within Buildings. Cables installed in building locations other than those covered in 760.61(A) or 760.61(B) shall be as described in either (1), (2), (3), or (4). Type FPL-CI cable shall be permitted to be installed as described in either (1), (2), (3), or (4) to provide a 2-hour circuit integrity rated cable.

(1) Type FPL shall be permitted.

(2) Cables shall be permitted to be installed in raceways.

(3) Cables specified in Chapter 3 and meeting the requirements of 760.82(A) and 760.82(B) shall be permitted to be installed in nonconcealed spaces where the exposed length of cable does not exceed 3 m (10 ft).

(4) A portable fire alarm system provided to protect a stage or set when not in use shall be permitted to use wiring methods in accordance with 530.12.

(D) Fire Alarm Cable Substitutions. The substitutions for fire alarm cables listed in Table 760.61 shall be permitted. Where substitute cables are installed, the wiring requirements of Article 760, Parts I and III shall apply.

FPN: For information on communications cables (CMP, CMR, CMG, CM), see 800.179.

Type CM—Communications wires and cables
Type FPL—Power-limited fire alarm cables

A ▶ B Cable A shall be permitted to be used in place of Cable B.
26 AWG minimum

Figure 760.61 Cable Substitution Hierarchy.

Table 760.61 Cable Substitutions

Cable Type	References	Permitted Substitutions
FPLP	760.61(A)	CMP
FPLR	760.61(B)	CMP, FPLP, CMR
FPL	760.61(C)	CMP, FPLP, CMR, FPLR, CMG, CM

IV. Listing Requirements

760.81 Listing and Marking of NPLFA Cables. Non–power-limited fire alarm cables installed as wiring within buildings shall be listed in accordance with 760.81(A) and 760.81(B) and as being resistant to the spread of fire in accordance with 760.81(C) through 760.81(F), and shall be marked in accordance with 760.81(G).

(A) NPLFA Conductor Materials. Conductors shall be 18 AWG or larger solid or stranded copper.

(B) Insulated Conductors. Insulated conductors shall be suitable for 600 volts. Insulated conductors 14 AWG and larger shall be one of the types listed in Table 310.13 or one that is identified for this use. Insulated conductors 18 AWG and 16 AWG shall be in accordance with 760.27.

(C) Type NPLFP. Type NPLFP non–power-limited fire alarm cable for use in other space used for environmental air shall be listed as being suitable for use in other space used for environmental air as described in 300.22(C) and shall also be listed as having adequate fire-resistant and low smoke-producing characteristics.

FPN: One method of defining low smoke-producing cable is by establishing an acceptable value of the smoke produced when tested in accordance with NFPA 262-2002, *Standard Method of Test for Flame Travel and Smoke of Wires and Cables for Use in Air-Handling Spaces*, to a maximum peak optical density of 0.5 and a maximum average optical density of 0.15. Similarly, one method of defining fire-resistant cables is by establishing a maximum allowable flame travel distance of 1.52 m (5 ft) when tested in accordance with the same test.

(D) Type NPLFR. Type NPLFR non–power-limited fire alarm riser cable shall be listed as being suitable for use in a vertical run in a shaft or from floor to floor and shall also be listed as having fire-resistant characteristics capable of preventing the carrying of fire from floor to floor.

FPN: One method of defining fire-resistant characteristics capable of preventing the carrying of fire from floor to floor is that the cables pass ANSI/UL 1666-2002, *Test for Flame Propagation Height of Electrical and Optical-Fiber Cables Installed Vertically in Shafts*.

(E) Type NPLF. Type NPLF non–power-limited fire alarm cable shall be listed as being suitable for general-purpose fire alarm use, with the exception of risers, ducts, plenums, and other space used for environmental air, and shall also be listed as being resistant to the spread of fire.

FPN No. 1: One method of defining *resistant to the spread of fire* is that the cables do not spread fire to the top of the tray in the vertical-tray flame test in ANSI/UL 1581-1991, *Reference Standard for Electrical Wires, Cables and Flexible Cords*.

FPN No. 2: Another method of defining *resistant to the spread of fire* is for the damage (char length) not to exceed 1.5 m (4 ft 11 in.) when performing the CSA vertical flame test for cables in cable trays, as described in CSA C22.2 No. 0.3-M-1985, *Test Methods for Electrical Wires and Cables*.

(F) Fire Alarm Circuit Integrity (CI) Cable or Electrical Circuit Protective System. Cables used for survivability of critical circuits shall be listed as circuit integrity (CI) cable. Cables specified in 760.81(C), (D), and (E), and used for circuit integrity shall have the additional classification using the suffix "-CI." Cables that are part of a listed electrical circuit protective system shall be considered to meet the requirements of survivability.

FPN No. 1: Fire alarm circuit integrity (CI) cable and electrical circuit protective systems may be used for fire alarm circuits to comply with the survivability requirements of *NFPA 72®*-2002, *National Fire Alarm Code®*, 6.9.4.3 and 6.9.4.6, that the circuit maintain its electrical function during fire conditions for a defined period of time.

FPN No. 2: One method of defining circuit integrity (CI) cable is by establishing a minimum 2-hour fire resistance rating for the cable when tested in accordance with UL 2196-1995, *Standard for Tests of Fire Resistive Cables*.

(G) NPLFA Cable Markings. Multiconductor non–power-limited fire alarm cables shall be marked in accordance with Table 760.81(G). Non–power-limited fire alarm circuit cables shall be permitted to be marked with a maximum usage voltage rating of 150 volts. Cables that are listed for circuit integrity shall be identified with the suffix "CI" as defined in 760.81(F).

Table 760.81(G) NPLFA Cable Markings

Cable Marking	Type	Reference
NPLFP	Non–power-limited fire alarm circuit cable for use in "other space used for environmental air"	760.81(C) and (G)
NPLFR	Non–power-limited fire alarm circuit riser cable	760.81(D) and (G)
NPLF	Non–power-limited fire alarm circuit cable	760.81(E) and (G)

Note: Cables identified in 760.81(C), (D), and (E) and meeting the requirements for circuit integrity shall have the additional classification using the suffix "CI" (for example, NPLFP-CI, NPLFR-CI, and NPLF-CI).

FPN: Cable types are listed in descending order of fire resistance rating.

760.82 Listing and Marking of PLFA Cables and Insulated Continuous Line-Type Fire Detectors. Type FPL cables installed as wiring within buildings shall be listed as being resistant to the spread of fire and other criteria in accordance with 760.82(A) through 760.82(H) and shall be marked in accordance with 760.82(I). Insulated continuous line-type fire detectors shall be listed in accordance with 760.82(J).

(A) Conductor Materials. Conductors shall be solid or stranded copper.

(B) Conductor Size. The size of conductors in a multiconductor cable shall not be smaller than 26 AWG. Single conductors shall not be smaller than 18 AWG.

(C) Ratings. The cable shall have a voltage rating of not less than 300 volts.

(D) Type FPLP. Type FPLP power-limited fire alarm plenum cable shall be listed as being suitable for use in ducts, plenums, and other space used for environmental air and shall also be listed as having adequate fire-resistant and low smoke-producing characteristics.

FPN: One method of defining low smoke-producing cable is by establishing an acceptable value of the smoke produced when tested in accordance with NFPA 262-2002, *Standard Method of Test for Flame Travel and Smoke of Wires and Cables for Use in Air-Handling Spaces*, to a maximum peak optical density of 0.5 and a maximum average optical density of 0.15. Similarly, one method of defining fire-resistant cables is by establishing a maximum allowable flame travel distance of 1.52 m (5 ft) when tested in accordance with the same test.

(E) Type FPLR. Type FPLR power-limited fire alarm riser cable shall be listed as being suitable for use in a vertical run in a shaft or from floor to floor and shall also be listed as having fire-resistant characteristics capable of preventing the carrying of fire from floor to floor.

FPN: One method of defining fire-resistant characteristics capable of preventing the carrying of fire from floor to floor is that the cables pass the requirements of ANSI/UL 1666-2002, *Standard Test for Flame Propagation Height of Electrical and Optical-Fiber Cable Installed Vertically in Shafts*.

(F) Type FPL. Type FPL power-limited fire alarm cable shall be listed as being suitable for general-purpose fire alarm use, with the exception of risers, ducts, plenums, and other spaces used for environmental air, and shall also be listed as being resistant to the spread of fire.

FPN: One method of defining *resistant to the spread of fire* is that the cables do not spread fire to the top of the tray in the vertical-tray flame test in ANSI/UL 1581-1991, *Reference Standard for Electrical Wires, Cables and Flexible Cords*.

Another method of defining *resistant to the spread of fire* is for the damage (char length) not to exceed 1.5 m (4 ft 11 in.) when performing the CSA vertical flame test for cables in cable trays, as described in CSA C22.2 No. 0.3-M-1985, *Test Methods for Electrical Wires and Cables*.

(G) Fire Alarm Circuit Integrity (CI) Cable or Electrical Circuit Protective System. Cables used for survivability of critical circuits shall be listed as circuit integrity (CI) cable. Cables specified in 760.82(D), (E), (F), and (H) and used for circuit integrity shall have the additional classification using the suffix "-CI." Cables that are part of a listed electrical circuit protective system shall be considered to meet the requirements of survivability.

FPN No. 1: Fire alarm circuit integrity (CI) cable and electrical circuit protective systems may be used for fire alarm circuits to comply with the survivability requirements of *NFPA 72®*-2002, *National Fire Alarm Code®*, 6.9.4.3 and 6.9.4.6, that the circuit maintain its electrical function during fire conditions for a defined period of time.

FPN No. 2: One method of defining circuit integrity (CI) cable is by establishing a minimum 2-hour fire resistance rating for the cable when tested in accordance with UL 2196-1995, *Standard for Tests of Fire Resistive Cables*.

(H) Coaxial Cables. Coaxial cables shall be permitted to use 30 percent conductivity copper-covered steel center conductor wire and shall be listed as Type FPLP, FPLR, or FPL cable.

(I) Cable Marking. The cable shall be marked in accordance with Table 760.82(I). The voltage rating shall not be marked on the cable. Cables that are listed for circuit integrity shall be identified with the suffix CI as defined in 760.82(G).

> FPN: Voltage ratings on cables may be misinterpreted to suggest that the cables may be suitable for Class 1, electric light, and power applications.

Exception: Voltage markings shall be permitted where the cable has multiple listings and voltage marking is required for one or more of the listings.

Table 760.82(I) Cable Markings

Cable Marking	Type
FPLP	Power-limited fire alarm plenum cable
FPLR	Power-limited fire alarm riser cable
FPL	Power-limited fire alarm cable

Note: Cables identified in 760.82(D), (E), and (F) as meeting the requirements for circuit integrity shall have the additional classification using the suffix "CI" (for example, FPLP-CI, FPLR-CI, and FPL-CI).

> FPN: Cable types are listed in descending order of fire-resistance rating.

(J) Insulated Continuous Line-Type Fire Detectors. Insulated continuous line-type fire detectors shall be rated in accordance with 760.82(C), listed as being resistant to the spread of fire in accordance with 760.82(D) through 760.82(F), marked in accordance with 760.82(I), and the jacket compound shall have a high degree of abrasion resistance.

ARTICLE 770
Optical Fiber Cables and Raceways

I. General

770.1 Scope. The provisions of this article apply to the installation of optical fiber cables and raceways. This article does not cover the construction of optical fiber cables and raceways.

770.2 Definitions.

Abandoned Optical Fiber Cable. Installed optical fiber cable that is not terminated at equipment other than a connector and not identified for future use with a tag.

Exposed. The circuit is in such a position that, in case of failure of supports and insulation, contact with another circuit may result.

> FPN: See Article 100 for two other definitions of *Exposed*.

Optical Fiber Raceway. A raceway designed for enclosing and routing listed optical fiber cables.

Point of Entrance. The point at which the cable emerges from an external wall, from a concrete floor slab, or from a rigid metal conduit or an intermediate metal conduit grounded to an electrode in accordance with 800.100(B).

770.3 Other Articles. Circuits and equipment shall comply with 770.3(A) and 770.3(B). Only those sections of Article 300 referenced in this article shall apply to optical fiber cables and raceways.

(A) Spread of Fire or Products of Combustion. The requirements of 300.21 for electrical installations shall also apply to installations of optical fiber cables and raceways. The accessible portion of abandoned optical fiber cables shall be removed.

(B) Ducts, Plenums, and Other Air-Handling Spaces. The requirements of 300.22 for electric wiring shall also apply to installations of optical fiber cables and raceways where they are installed in ducts or plenums or other space used for environmental air.

Exception: As permitted in 770.154(A).

770.6 Optical Fiber Cables. Optical fiber cables transmit light for control, signaling, and communications through an optical fiber.

770.9 Types. Optical fiber cables can be grouped into three types.

(A) Nonconductive. These cables contain no metallic members and no other electrically conductive materials.

(B) Conductive. These cables contain non–current-carrying conductive members such as metallic strength members, metallic vapor barriers, and metallic armor or sheath.

(C) Composite. These cables contain optical fibers and current-carrying electrical conductors, and shall be permitted to contain non–current-carrying conductive members such as metallic strength members and metallic vapor barriers. Composite optical fiber cables shall be classified as electrical cables in accordance with the type of electrical conductors.

770.12 Raceways for Optical Fiber Cables. Installations of raceways shall comply with 770.12(A) through 770.12(D).

(A) Listed Chapter 3 Raceways. Listed optical fiber cable shall be permitted to be installed in any type of listed raceway permitted in Chapter 3 where that listed raceway is installed in accordance with Chapter 3. Where optical fiber cables are installed within raceway without current-carrying conductors, the raceway fill tables of Chapter 3 and Chapter 9 shall not apply. Where nonconductive optical fiber cables are installed with electric conductors in a raceway, the raceway fill tables of Chapter 3 and Chapter 9 shall apply.

(B) Optical Fiber Raceways. Listed optical fiber cable shall be permitted to be installed in listed plenum optical fiber raceway, listed riser optical fiber raceway, or listed general-purpose optical fiber raceway installed in accordance with 770.154 and 362.24 through 362.56, where the requirements applicable to electrical nonmetallic tubing shall apply.

(C) Innerduct. Listed plenum optical fiber raceway, listed riser optical fiber raceway, or listed general-purpose optical fiber raceway installed in accordance with 770.154 shall be permitted to be installed as innerduct in any type of listed raceway permitted in Chapter 3.

(D) Entering Buildings. Unlisted underground or outside plant construction plastic innerduct entering the building from the outside shall be terminated and firestopped at the point of entrance.

770.21 Access to Electrical Equipment Behind Panels Designed to Allow Access. Access to electrical equipment shall not be denied by an accumulation of cables that prevents removal of panels, including suspended ceiling panels.

770.24 Mechanical Execution of Work. Optical fiber cables shall be installed in a neat and workmanlike manner. Cables installed exposed on the surface of ceilings and sidewalls shall be supported by the building structure in such a manner that the cable will not be damaged by normal building use. Such cables shall be secured by straps, staples, hangers, or similar fittings designed and installed so as not to damage the cable. The installation shall also conform with 300.4(D) and 300.11.

> FPN: Accepted industry practices are described in ANSI/NECA/BICSI 568-2001, *Standard for Installing Commercial Building Telecommunications Cabling*, and other ANSI-approved installation standards.

II. Protection

770.93 Grounding of Entrance Cables. Where exposed to contact with electric light or power conductors, the non–current-carrying metallic members of optical fiber cables entering buildings shall be grounded as close to the point of entrance as practicable or shall be interrupted as close to the point of entrance as practicable by an insulating joint or equivalent device.

III. Cables Within Buildings

770.113 Installation and Marking of Listed Optical Fiber Cables. Listed optical fiber cables shall be installed as wiring within buildings. Optical fiber cables shall be marked in accordance with Table 770.113.

Exception No. 1: Optical fiber cables shall not be required to be listed and marked where the length of the cable within the building, measured from its point of entrance, does not exceed 15 m (50 ft) and the cable enters the building from the outside and is terminated in an enclosure.

> FPN: Splice cases or terminal boxes, both metallic and plastic types, typically are used as enclosures for splicing or terminating optical fiber cables.

Exception No. 2: Nonconductive optical fiber cables shall not be required to be listed and marked where the cable enters the building from the outside and is run in raceway systems installed in compliance with any of the following articles in Chapter 3: Article 342, Intermediate Metal Conduit: Type IMC; Article 344, Rigid Metal Conduit: Type RMC; Article 352, Rigid Nonmetallic Conduit: Type RNC; and Article 358, Electrical Metallic Tubing: Type EMT.

770.133 Installation of Optical Fibers and Electrical Conductors.

(A) With Conductors for Electric Light, Power, Class 1, Non–Power-Limited Fire Alarm, or Medium Power Network-Powered Broadband Communications Circuits. Optical fibers shall be permitted within the same composite cable for electric light, power, Class 1, non–power-limited fire alarm, or medium power network-powered broadband communications circuits operating at 600 volts or less only where the functions of the optical fibers and the electrical conductors are associated.

Nonconductive optical fiber cables shall be permitted to occupy the same cable tray or raceway with conductors for electric light, power, Class 1, non–power-limited fire alarm, Type ITC, or medium power network-powered broadband communications circuits, operating at 600 volts or less. Conductive optical fiber cables shall not be permitted to occupy the same cable tray or raceway with conductors for electric light, power, Class 1, non–power-limited fire alarm, Type ITC, or medium power network-powered broadband communications circuits.

Table 770.113 Cable Markings

Cable Marking	Type	Reference
OFNP	Nonconductive optical fiber plenum cable	770.179(A) and 770.154
OFCP	Conductive optical fiber plenum cable	770.179(A) and 770.154(A)
OFNR	Nonconductive optical fiber riser cable	770.179(B) and 770.154(B)
OFCR	Conductive optical fiber riser cable	770.179(B) and 770.154(B)
OFNG	Nonconductive optical fiber general-purpose cable	770.179(C) and 770.154(C)
OFCG	Conductive optical fiber general-purpose cable	770.179(C) and 770.154(C)
OFN	Nonconductive optical fiber general-purpose cable	770.179(D) and 770.154(C)
OFC	Conductive optical fiber general-purpose cable	770.179(D) and 770.154(C)

FPN No. 1: Cables types are listed in descending order of fire resistance rating. Within each fire resistance rating, nonconductive cable is listed first because it may substitute for the conductive cable.

FPN No. 2: See the referenced sections for requirements and permitted uses.

Composite optical fiber cables containing only current-carrying conductors for electric light, power, Class 1 circuits rated 600 volts or less shall be permitted to occupy the same cabinet, cable tray, outlet box, panel, raceway, or other termination enclosure with conductors for electric light, power, or Class 1 circuits operating at 600 volts or less.

Nonconductive optical fiber cables shall not be permitted to occupy the same cabinet, outlet box, panel, or similar enclosure housing the electrical terminations of an electric light, power, Class 1, non–power-limited fire alarm, or medium power network-powered broadband communications circuit.

Exception No. 1: Occupancy of the same cabinet, outlet box, panel, or similar enclosure shall be permitted where nonconductive optical fiber cable is functionally associated with the electric light, power, Class 1, non–power-limited fire alarm, or medium power network-powered broadband communications circuit.

Exception No. 2: Occupancy of the same cabinet, outlet box, panel, or similar enclosure shall be permitted where nonconductive optical fiber cables are installed in factory- or field-assembled control centers.

Exception No. 3: In industrial establishments only, where conditions of maintenance and supervision ensure that only

qualified persons service the installation, nonconductive optical fiber cables shall be permitted with circuits exceeding 600 volts.

Exception No. 4: In industrial establishments only, where conditions of maintenance and supervision ensure that only qualified persons service the installation, composite optical fiber cables shall be permitted to contain current-carrying conductors operating over 600 volts.

(B) With Other Conductors. Optical fibers shall be permitted in the same cable, and conductive and nonconductive optical fiber cables shall be permitted in the same cable tray, enclosure, or raceway with conductors of any of the following:

(1) Class 2 and Class 3 remote-control, signaling, and power-limited circuits in compliance with Article 725

(2) Power-limited fire alarm systems in compliance with Article 760

(3) Communications circuits in compliance with Article 800

(4) Community antenna television and radio distribution systems in compliance with Article 820

(5) Low-power network-powered broadband communications circuits in compliance with Article 830

(C) Grounding. Non–current-carrying conductive members of optical fiber cables shall be grounded in accordance with Article 250.

770.154 Applications of Listed Optical Fiber Cables and Raceways. Nonconductive and conductive optical fiber cables shall comply with any of the requirements given in 770.154(A) through 770.154(E) or where cable substitutions are made as shown in 770.154(F).

(A) Plenums. Cables installed in ducts, plenums, and other spaces used for environmental air shall be Type OFNP or OFCP. Abandoned cables shall not be permitted to remain. Types OFNR, OFCR, OFNG, OFN, OFCG, and OFC cables installed in compliance with 300.22 shall be permitted. Listed plenum optical fiber raceways shall be permitted to be installed in ducts and plenums as described in 300.22(B) and in other spaces used for environmental air as described in 300.22(C). Only type OFNP and OFCP cables shall be permitted to be installed in these raceways.

FPN: See 8.14.1 of NFPA 13 (2002), *Installation of Sprinkler Systems,* for requirements for sprinklers in concealed spaces containing exposed combustibles.

(B) Riser. Cables installed in risers shall be as described in any of the following:

(1) Cables installed in vertical runs and penetrating more than one floor, or cables installed in vertical runs in a shaft, shall be Type OFNR or OFCR. Floor penetrations requiring Type OFNR or OFCR shall contain only cables suitable for riser or plenum use. Abandoned cables shall not be permitted to remain. Listed riser

optical fiber raceways shall be permitted to be installed in vertical riser runs in a shaft from floor to floor. Only Type OFNP, OFCP, OFNR, and OFCR cables shall be permitted to be installed in these raceways.

(2) Type OFNG, OFN, OFCG, and OFC cables shall be permitted to be encased in a metal raceway or located in a fireproof shaft having firestops at each floor.

(3) Type OFNG, OFN, OFCG, and OFC cables shall be permitted in one- and two-family dwellings.

FPN: See 300.21 for firestop requirements for floor penetrations.

(C) Other Wiring Within Buildings. Cables installed in building locations other than the locations covered in 770.154(A) and 770.154(B) shall be Type OFNG, OFN, OFCG, or OFC. Such cables shall be permitted to be installed in listed general-purpose optical fiber raceways.

(D) Hazardous (Classified) Locations. Cables installed in hazardous (classified) locations shall be any type indicated in Table 770.154.

(E) Cable Trays. Optical fiber cables of the types listed in Table 770.113 shall be permitted to be installed in cable trays.

FPN: It is not the intent to require that these optical fiber cables be listed specifically for use in cable trays.

(F) Cable Substitutions. The substitutions for optical fiber cables listed in Table 770.154 shall be permitted.

Table 770.154 Cable Substitutions

Cable Type	Permitted Substitutions
OFNP	None
OFCP	OFNP
OFNR	OFNP
OFCR	OFNP, OFCP, OFNR
OFNG, OFN	OFNP, OFNR
OFCG, OFC	OFNP, OFCP, OFNR, OFCR, OFNG, OFN

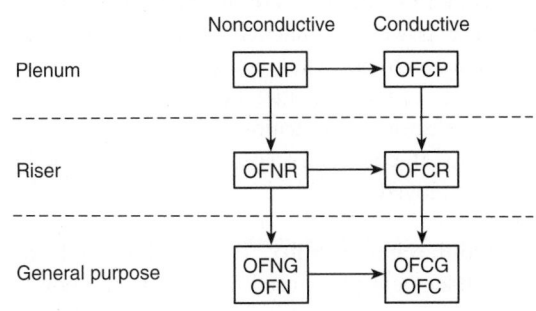

A → B   Cable A may be used in place of cable B.

Figure 770.154 Cable Substitution Hierarchy.

IV. Listing Requirements

770.179 Optical Fiber Cables. Optical fiber cables shall be listed in accordance with 770.179(A) through 770.179(D).

(A) Types OFNP and OFCP. Types OFNP and OFCP nonconductive and conductive optical fiber plenum cables shall be listed as being suitable for use in ducts, plenums, and other space used for environmental air and shall also be listed as having adequate fire resistant and low smoke producing characteristics.

FPN: One method of defining a cable that is low smoke producing cable and fire-resistant cable is that the cable exhibits a maximum peak optical density of 0.5 or less, an average optical density of 0.15 or less, and a maximum flame spread distance of 1.52 m (5 ft) or less when tested in accordance with NFPA 262–2002, *Standard Method of Test for Flame Travel and Smoke of Wires and Cables for Use in Air-Handling Spaces.*

(B) Types OFNR and OFCR. Types OFNR and OFCR nonconductive and conductive optical fiber riser cables shall be listed as being suitable for use in a vertical run in a shaft or from floor to floor and shall also be listed as having the fire-resistant characteristics capable of preventing the carrying of fire from floor to floor.

FPN: One method of defining fire-resistant characteristics capable of preventing the carrying of fire from floor to floor is that the cables pass the requirements of ANSI/UL 1666-2002, *Standard Test for Flame Propagation Height of Electrical and Optical-Fiber Cable Installed Vertically in Shafts.*

(C) Types OFNG and OFCG. Types OFNG and OFCG nonconductive and conductive general-purpose optical fiber cables shall be listed as being suitable for general-purpose use, with the exception of risers and plenums, and shall also be listed as being resistant to the spread of fire.

FPN: One method of defining *resistance to the spread of fire* is for the damage (char length) not to exceed 1.5 m (4 ft 11 in.) when performing the vertical flame test for cables in cable trays, as described in CSA C22.2 No. 0.3-M-1985, *Test Methods for Electrical Wires and Cables.*

(D) Types OFN and OFC. Types OFN and OFC nonconductive and conductive optical fiber cables shall be listed as being suitable for general-purpose use, with the exception of risers, plenums, and other spaces used for environmental air, and shall also be listed as being resistant to the spread of fire.

FPN: One method of defining *resistant to the spread of fire* is that the cables do not spread fire to the top of the tray in the vertical-tray flame test in ANSI/UL 1581-1991, *Reference Standard for Electrical Wires, Cables, and Flexible Cords.*

Another method of defining *resistant to the spread of fire* is for the damage (char length) not to exceed 1.5 m (4 ft 11 in.) when performing the vertical flame test for cables in cable trays, as described in CSA C22.2 No. 0.3-M-1985, *Test Methods for Electrical Wires and Cables.*

770.182 Optical Fiber Raceways. Optical fiber raceways shall be listed in accordance with 770.182(A) through 770.182(C).

(A) Plenum Optical Fiber Raceway. Plenum optical fiber raceways shall be listed as having adequate fire-resistant and low smoke-producing characteristics.

> FPN: One method of defining that an optical fiber raceway is a low smoke producing raceway and a fire-resistant raceway is that the raceway exhibits a maximum peak optical density of 0.5 or less, an average optical density of 0.15 or less, and a maximum flame spread distance of 1.52 m (5 ft) or less when tested in accordance with the plenum test in UL 2024, *Standard for Optical Fiber Cable Raceway.*

(B) Riser Optical Fiber Raceway. Riser optical fiber raceways shall be listed as having fire-resistant characteristics capable of preventing the carrying of fire from floor to floor.

> FPN: One method of defining fire-resistant characteristics capable of preventing the carrying of fire from floor to floor is that the raceways pass the requirements of the test for Flame Propagation (riser) in UL 2024, *Standard for Optical Fiber Cable Raceway.*

(C) General-Purpose Optical Fiber Cable Raceway. General-purpose optical fiber cable raceway shall be listed as being resistant to the spread of fire.

> FPN: One method of defining resistance to the spread of fire is that the raceways pass the requirements of the Vertical-Tray Flame Test (General Use) in UL 2024, *Standard for Optical Fiber Cable Raceway.*

ARTICLE 780
Closed-Loop and Programmed Power Distribution

780.1 Scope. The provisions of this article apply to premise power distribution systems jointly controlled by a signaling between the energy controlling equipment and utilization equipment.

780.2 General.

(A) Other Articles. Except as modified by the requirements of this article, all other applicable articles of this *Code* shall apply.

(B) Component Parts. All equipment and conductors shall be listed and identified.

780.3 Control. The control equipment and all power switching devices operated by the control equipment shall be listed and identified. The system shall operate in accordance with 780.3(A) through 780.3(D).

(A) Characteristic Electrical Identification Required. Outlets shall not be energized unless the utilization equipment first exhibits a characteristic electrical identification.

(B) Conditions for De-Energization. Outlets shall be de-energized when any of the following conditions occur:

(1) A nominal-operation acknowledgment signal is not being received from the utilization equipment connected to the outlet.

(2) A ground-fault condition exists.

(3) An overcurrent condition exists.

(C) Additional Conditions for De-Energization When an Alternate Source of Power Is Used. In addition to the requirements in 780.3(B), outlets shall be de-energized when any of the following conditions occur:

(1) The grounded conductor is not properly grounded.

(2) Any ungrounded conductor is not at nominal voltage.

(D) Controller Malfunction. In the event of a controller malfunction, all associated outlets shall be de-energized.

780.5 Power Limitation in Signaling Circuits. For signaling circuits not exceeding 24 volts, the current required shall not exceed 1 ampere where protected by an overcurrent device or an inherently limited power source.

780.6 Cables and Conductors.

(A) Hybrid Cable. Listed hybrid cable consisting of power, communications, and signaling conductors shall be permitted under a common jacket. The jacket shall be applied so as to separate the power conductors from the communications and signaling conductors. An optional outer jacket shall be permitted to be applied. The individual conductors of a hybrid cable shall conform to the *Code* provisions applicable to their current, voltage, and insulation rating. The signaling conductors shall not be smaller than 24 AWG copper.

(B) Cables and Conductors in the Same Cabinet, Panel, or Box. The power, communications, and signaling conductors of listed hybrid cable are permitted to occupy the same cabinet, panel, or outlet box (or similar enclosure housing the electrical terminations of electric light or power circuits) only if connectors specifically listed for hybrid cable are employed.

780.7 Noninterchangeability. Receptacles, cord connectors, and attachment plugs used on closed-loop power distribution systems shall be constructed so that they are not interchangeable with other receptacles, cord connectors, and attachment plugs.

Chapter 8 Communications Systems

ARTICLE 800
Communications Circuits

FPN: Rules that are followed by a reference in brackets contain text that has been extracted from NFPA 97–2003, *Standard Glossary of Terms Relating to Chimneys, Vents, and Heat-Producing Appliances.* Only editorial changes were made to the extracted text to make it consistent with this *Code.*

I. General

800.1 Scope. This article covers telephone, telegraph (except radio), outside wiring for fire alarm and burglar alarm, and similar central station systems; and telephone systems not connected to a central station system but using similar types of equipment, methods of installation, and maintenance.

> FPN No. 1: For further information for fire alarm, sprinkler waterflow, and sprinkler supervisory systems, see Article 760.

> FPN No. 2: For installation requirements of optical fiber cables, see Article 770.

> FPN No. 3: For installation requirements for network-powered broadband communications circuits, see Article 830.

800.2 Definitions. See Article 100. For purposes of this article, the following additional definitions apply.

Abandoned Communications Cable. Installed communications cable that is not terminated at both ends at a connector or other equipment and not identified for future use with a tag.

Air Duct. A conduit or passageway for conveying air to or from heating, cooling, air conditioning, or ventilating equipment, but not including the plenum. [NFPA 97:1.2.6]

Block. A square or portion of a city, town, or village enclosed by streets and including the alleys so enclosed, but not any street.

Cable. A factory assembly of two or more conductors having an overall covering.

Cable Sheath. A covering over the conductor assembly that may include one or more metallic members, strength members, or jackets.

Communications Circuit Integrity (CI) Cable. Cable used in communications systems to ensure continued operation of critical circuits during a specified time under fire conditions.

Communications Equipment. The electronic equipment that performs the telecommunications operations for the transmission of audio, video, and data, and including power equipment (e.g., dc converters, inverters and batteries) and technical support equipment (e.g., computers).

Exposed. A circuit that is in such a position that, in case of failure of supports and insulation, contact with another circuit may result.

> FPN: See Article 100 for two other definitions of *Exposed.*

Point of Entrance. Within a building, the point at which the wire or cable emerges from an external wall, from a concrete floor slab, or from a rigid metal conduit or an intermediate metal conduit grounded to an electrode in accordance with 800.100(B).

Premises. The land and buildings of a user located on the user side of the utility-user network point of demarcation.

Wire. A factory assembly of one or more insulated conductors without an overall covering.

800.3 Other Articles.

(A) Hybrid Power and Communications Cables. The provisions of 780.6 shall apply for listed hybrid power and communications cables in closed-loop and programmed power distribution.

> FPN: See 800.179(J) for hybrid power and communications cable in other applications.

(B) Hazardous (Classified) Locations. Communications circuits and equipment installed in a location that is classified in accordance with Article 500 shall comply with the applicable requirements of Chapter 5.

(C) Spread of Fire or Products of Combustion. Section 300.21 shall apply. The accessible portion of abandoned communications cables shall not be permitted to remain.

(D) Equipment in Other Space Used for Environmental Air. Section 300.22(C) shall apply.

800.18 Installation of Equipment. Equipment electrically connected to a telecommunications network shall be listed in accordance with 800.170. Installation of equipment shall also comply with 110.3(B).

Exception: This listing requirement shall not apply to test equipment that is intended for temporary connection to a telecommunications network by qualified persons during the course of installation, maintenance, or repair of telecommunications equipment or systems.

800.21 Access to Electrical Equipment Behind Panels Designed to Allow Access. Access to electrical equipment shall not be denied by an accumulation of wires and cables that prevents removal of panels, including suspended ceiling panels.

800.24 Mechanical Execution of Work. Communications circuits and equipment shall be installed in a neat and workmanlike manner. Cables installed exposed on the surface of ceilings and sidewalls shall be supported by the building structure in such a manner that the cable will not be damaged by normal building use. Such cables shall be secured by straps, staples, hangers, or similar fittings designed and installed so as not to damage the cable. The installation shall also conform with 300.4(D) and 300.11.

> FPN: Accepted industry practices are described in ANSI/NECA/BICSI 568-2001, *Standard for Installing Commercial Building Telecommunications Cabling,* and other ANSI-approved installation standards.

II. Wires and Cables Outside and Entering Buildings

800.44 Overhead Communications Wires and Cables. Overhead communications wires and cables entering buildings shall comply with 800.44(A) and 800.44(B).

(A) On Poles and In-Span. Where communications wires and cables and electric light or power conductors are supported by the same pole or run parallel to each other in-span, the conditions described in 800.44(A)(1) through (A)(4) shall be met.

(1) Relative Location. Where practicable, the communications wires and cables shall be located below the electric light or power conductors.

(2) Attachment to Crossarms. Communications wires and cables shall not be attached to a cross-arm that carries electric light or power conductors.

(3) Climbing Space. The climbing space through communications wires and cables shall comply with the requirements of 225.14(D).

(4) Clearance. Supply service drops of 0–750 volts running above and parallel to communications service drops shall have a minimum separation of 300 mm (12 in.) at any point in the span, including the point of and at their attachment to the building, provided the nongrounded conductors are insulated and that a clearance of not less than 1.0 m (40 in.) is maintained between the two services at the pole.

(B) Above Roofs. Communications wires and cables shall have a vertical clearance of not less than 2.5 m (8 ft) from all points of roofs above which they pass.

Exception No. 1: Auxiliary buildings, such as garages and the like.

Exception No. 2: A reduction in clearance above only the overhanging portion of the roof to not less than 450 mm (18 in.) shall be permitted if (a) not more than 1.2 m (4 ft) of communications service-drop conductors pass above the roof overhang and (b) they are terminated at a through- or above-the-roof raceway or approved support.

Exception No. 3: Where the roof has a slope of not less than 100 mm in 300 mm (4 in. in 12 in.), a reduction in clearance to not less than 900 mm (3 ft) shall be permitted.

> FPN: For additional information regarding overhead wires and cables, see ANSI C2-2002, *National Electric Safety Code*, Part 2, Safety Rules for Overhead Lines.

800.47 Underground Circuits Entering Buildings. Underground communications wires and cables entering buildings shall comply with 800.47(A) and 800.47(B).

(A) With Electric Light or Power Conductors. Underground communications wires and cables in a raceway, handhole enclosure, or manhole containing electric light, power, Class 1, or non–power-limited fire alarm circuit conductors shall be in a section separated from such conductors by means of brick, concrete, or tile partitions or by means of a suitable barrier.

(B) Underground Block Distribution. Where the entire street circuit is run underground and the circuit within the block is placed so as to be free from the likelihood of accidental contact with electric light or power circuits of over 300 volts to ground, the insulation requirements of 800.50(A) and 800.50(C) shall not apply, insulating supports shall not be required for the conductors, and bushings shall not be required where the conductors enter the building.

800.50 Circuits Requiring Primary Protectors. Circuits that require primary protectors as provided in 800.90 shall comply with 800.50(A), (B), and (C).

(A) Insulation, Wires, and Cables. Communications wires and cables without a metallic shield, running from the last outdoor support to the primary protector, shall be listed.

(B) On Buildings. Communications wires and cables in accordance with 800.50(A) shall be separated at least 100 mm (4 in.) from electric light or power conductors not in a raceway or cable or be permanently separated from conductors of the other system by a continuous and firmly fixed nonconductor in addition to the insulation on the wires, such as porcelain tubes or flexible tubing. Communications wires and cables in accordance with 800.50(A) exposed to accidental contact with electric light and power conductors operating at over 300 volts to ground and attached to buildings shall be separated from woodwork by being supported on glass, porcelain, or other insulating material.

Exception: Separation from woodwork shall not be required where fuses are omitted as provided for in 800.90(A)(1), or where conductors are used to extend circuits to a building from a cable having a grounded metal sheath.

(C) Entering Buildings. Where a primary protector is installed inside the building, the communications wires and cables shall enter the building either through a noncombustible, nonabsorbent insulating bushing or through a metal raceway. The insulating bushing shall not be required where the entering communications wires and cables (1) are in metal-sheathed cable, (2) pass through masonry, (3) meet the requirements of 800.50(A) and fuses are omitted as provided in 800.90(A)(1), or (A)(4) meet the requirements of 800.50(A) and are used to extend circuits to a building from a cable having a grounded metallic sheath. Raceways or bushings shall slope upward from the outside or, where this cannot be done, drip loops shall be formed in the communications wires and cables immediately before they enter the building.

Raceways shall be equipped with an approved service head. More than one communications wire and cable shall be permitted to enter through a single raceway or bushing. Conduits or other metal raceways located ahead of the primary protector shall be grounded.

800.53 Lightning Conductors. Where practicable, a separation of at least 1.8 m (6 ft) shall be maintained between communications wires and cables on buildings and lightning conductors.

III. Protection

800.90 Protective Devices.

(A) Application. A listed primary protector shall be provided on each circuit run partly or entirely in aerial wire or aerial cable not confined within a block. Also, a listed primary protector shall be provided on each circuit, aerial or underground, located within the block containing the building served so as to be exposed to accidental contact with electric light or power conductors operating at over 300 volts to ground. In addition, where there exists a lightning exposure, each interbuilding circuit on a premises shall be protected by a listed primary protector at each end of the interbuilding circuit. Installation of primary protectors shall also comply with 110.3(B).

> FPN No. 1: On a circuit not exposed to accidental contact with power conductors, providing a listed primary protector in accordance with this article helps protect against other hazards, such as lightning and above-normal voltages induced by fault currents on power circuits in proximity to the communications circuit.

> FPN No. 2: Interbuilding circuits are considered to have a lightning exposure unless one or more of the following conditions exist:
>
> (1) Circuits in large metropolitan areas where buildings are close together and sufficiently high to intercept lightning.
> (2) Interbuilding cable runs of 42 m (140 ft) or less, directly buried or in underground conduit, where a continuous metallic cable shield or a continuous metallic conduit containing the cable is bonded to each building grounding electrode system.
> (3) Areas having an average of five or fewer thunderstorm days per year and earth resistivity of less than 100 ohmmeters. Such areas are found along the Pacific coast.

(1) Fuseless Primary Protectors. Fuseless-type primary protectors shall be permitted under any of the conditions given in (A)(1)(a) through (A)(1)(e).

(a) Where conductors enter a building through a cable with grounded metallic sheath member(s) and where the conductors in the cable safely fuse on all currents greater than the current-carrying capacity of the primary protector and of the primary protector grounding conductor

(b) Where insulated conductors in accordance with 800.50(A) are used to extend circuits to a building from a cable with an effectively grounded metallic sheath member(s) and where the conductors in the cable or cable stub, or the connections between the insulated conductors and the exposed plant, safely fuse on all currents greater than the current-carrying capacity of the primary protector, or the associated insulated conductors and of the primary protector grounding conductor

(c) Where insulated conductors in accordance with 800.50(A) or 800.50(B) are used to extend circuits to a building from other than a cable with metallic sheath member(s), where (1) the primary protector is listed as being suitable for this purpose for application with circuits extending from other than a cable with metallic sheath members, and (2) the connections of the insulated conductors to the exposed plant or the conductors of the exposed plant safely fuse on all currents greater than the current-carrying capacity of the primary protector, or associated insulated conductors and of the primary protector grounding conductor

(d) Where insulated conductors in accordance with 800.50(A) are used to extend circuits aerially to a building from an unexposed buried or underground circuit

(e) Where insulated conductors in accordance with 800.50(A) are used to extend circuits to a building from cable with an effectively grounded metallic sheath member(s), and where (1) the combination of the primary protector and insulated conductors is listed as being suitable for this purpose for application with circuits extending from a cable with an effectively grounded metallic sheath member(s), and (2) the insulated conductors safely fuse on all currents greater than the current-carrying capacity of the primary protector and of the primary protector grounding conductor

(2) Fused Primary Protectors. Where the requirements listed under 800.90(A)(1)(a) through (A)(1)(e) are not met, fused-type primary protectors shall be used. Fused-type primary protectors shall consist of an arrester connected between each line conductor and ground, a fuse in series with each line conductor, and an appropriate mounting arrangement. Primary protector terminals shall be marked to indicate line, instrument, and ground, as applicable.

(B) Location. The primary protector shall be located in, on, or immediately adjacent to the structure or building served and as close as practicable to the point of entrance.

FPN: See 800.2 for the definition of *point of entrance*.

For purposes of this section, primary protectors located at mobile home service equipment located in sight from and not more than 9.0 m (30 ft) from the exterior wall of the mobile home it serves, or at a mobile home disconnecting means grounded in accordance with 250.32 and located in sight from and not more than 9.0 m (30 ft) from the exterior wall of the mobile home it serves, shall be considered to meet the requirements of this section.

FPN: Selecting a primary protector location to achieve the shortest practicable primary protector grounding conductor helps limit potential differences between communications circuits and other metallic systems.

(C) Hazardous (Classified) Locations. The primary protector shall not be located in any hazardous (classified) location as defined in Article 500 or in the vicinity of easily ignitible material.

Exception: As permitted in 501.150, 502.150, and 503.150.

(D) Secondary Protectors. Where a secondary protector is installed in series with the indoor communications wire and cable between the primary protector and the equipment, it shall be listed for the purpose in accordance with 800.170(B).

FPN: Secondary protectors on exposed circuits are not intended for use without primary protectors.

800.93 Cable Grounding. The metallic sheath of communications cables entering buildings shall be grounded as close as practicable to the point of entrance or shall be interrupted as close to the point of entrance as practicable by an insulating joint or equivalent device.

FPN: See 800.2 for the definition of *point of entrance*.

IV. Grounding Methods

800.100 Cable and Primary Protector Grounding. The metallic member(s) of the cable sheath, where required to be grounded by 800.93, and primary protectors shall be grounded as specified in 800.100(A) through 800.100(D).

(A) Grounding Conductor.

(1) Insulation. The grounding conductor shall be insulated and shall be listed as suitable for the purpose.

(2) Material. The grounding conductor shall be copper or other corrosion-resistant conductive material, stranded or solid.

(3) Size. The grounding conductor shall not be smaller than 14 AWG.

(4) Length. The primary protector grounding conductor shall be as short as practicable. In one- and two-family dwellings, the primary protector grounding conductor shall be as short as practicable, not to exceed 6.0 m (20 ft) in length.

FPN: Similar grounding conductor length limitations applied at apartment buildings and commercial buildings help to reduce voltages that may be developed between the building's power and communications systems during lightning events.

Exception: In one- and two-family dwellings where it is not practicable to achieve an overall maximum primary protector grounding conductor length of 6.0 m (20 ft), a separate communications ground rod meeting the minimum dimensional criteria of 800.100(B)(2)(2) shall be driven, the primary protector shall be grounded to the communications ground rod in accordance with 800.100(C), and the communications ground rod shall be bonded to the power grounding electrode system in accordance with 800.100(D).

(5) Run in Straight Line. The grounding conductor shall be run to the grounding electrode in as straight a line as practicable.

(6) Physical Damage. Where necessary, the grounding conductor shall be guarded from physical damage. Where the grounding conductor is run in a metal raceway, both ends of the raceway shall be bonded to the grounding conductor or the same terminal or electrode to which the grounding conductor is connected.

(B) Electrode. The grounding conductor shall be connected in accordance with 800.100(B)(1) and (B)(2).

(1) In Buildings or Structures with Grounding Means. To the nearest accessible location on the following:

(1) The building or structure grounding electrode system as covered in 250.50

(2) The grounded interior metal water piping system, within 1.5 m (5 ft) from its point of entrance to the building, as covered in 250.52

(3) The power service accessible means external to enclosures as covered in 250.94

(4) The metallic power service raceway

(5) The service equipment enclosure

(6) The grounding electrode conductor or the grounding electrode conductor metal enclosure

(7) The grounding conductor or the grounding electrode of a building or structure disconnecting means that is grounded to an electrode as covered in 250.32

For purposes of this section, the mobile home service equipment or the mobile home disconnecting means, as described in 800.90(B), shall be considered accessible.

(2) In Buildings or Structures Without Grounding Means. If the building or structure served has no grounding means, as described in 800.100(B)(1), the grounding conductor shall be connected to either of the following:

(1) To any one of the individual electrodes described in 250.52(A)(1), (A)(2), (A)(3), or (A)(4)

(2) If the building or structure served has no grounding means, as described in 800.100(B)(1) or (B)(2)(1), to an effectively grounded metal structure or to a ground rod or pipe not less than 1.5 m (5 ft) in length and 12.7 mm (½ in.) in diameter, driven, where practicable, into permanently damp earth and separated from lightning conductors as covered in 800.53 and at least 1.8 m (6 ft) from electrodes of other systems. Steam or hot water pipes or air terminal conductors (lightning-rod conductors) shall not be employed as electrodes for protectors.

(C) Electrode Connection. Connections to grounding electrodes shall comply with 250.70.

(D) Bonding of Electrodes. A bonding jumper not smaller than 6 AWG copper or equivalent shall be connected between the communications grounding electrode and power grounding electrode system at the building or structure served where separate electrodes are used.

Exception: At mobile homes as covered in 800.106.

FPN No. 1:   See 250.60 for use of air terminals (lightning rods).

FPN No. 2:   Bonding together of all separate electrodes limits potential differences between them and between their associated wiring systems.

800.106 Primary Protector Grounding and Bonding at Mobile Homes.

(A) Grounding. Where there is no mobile home service equipment located in sight from, and not more than 9.0 m (30 ft) from, the exterior wall of the mobile home it serves, or there is no mobile home disconnecting means grounded in accordance with 250.32 and located within sight from, and not more than 9.0 m (30 ft) from, the exterior wall of the mobile home it serves, the primary protector ground shall be in accordance with 800.100(B)(2).

(B) Bonding. The primary protector grounding terminal or grounding electrode shall be bonded to the metal frame or available grounding terminal of the mobile home with a copper grounding conductor not smaller than 12 AWG under either of the following conditions:

(1) Where there is no mobile home service equipment or disconnecting means as in 800.106(A)

(2) Where the mobile home is supplied by cord and plug

V.   Communications Wires and Cables Within Buildings

800.110 Raceways for Communications Wires and Cables. Where communications wires and cables are installed in a raceway, the raceway shall be either of a type permitted in Chapter 3 and installed in accordance with Chapter 3 or a listed nonmetallic raceway complying with 800.182, and installed in accordance with 362.24 through 362.56, where the requirements applicable to electrical nonmetallic tubing apply.

Exception: Conduit fill restrictions shall not apply.

800.113 Installation and Marking of Communications Wires and Cables. Listed communications wires and cables and listed multipurpose cables shall be installed as wiring within buildings. Communications cables and undercarpet communications wires shall be marked in accordance with Table 800.113. The cable voltage rating shall not be marked on the cable or on the undercarpet communications wire.

FPN: Voltage markings on cables may be misinterpreted to suggest that the cables may be suitable for Class 1, electric light, and power applications.

Exception No. 1: Voltage markings shall be permitted where the cable has multiple listings and voltage marking is required for one or more of the listings.

Exception No. 2: Listing and marking shall not be required where the length of the cable within the building, measured from its point of entrance, does not exceed 15 m (50 ft) and the cable enters the building from the outside and is terminated in an enclosure or on a listed primary protector.

FPN No. 1 to Exception No. 2: Splice cases or terminal boxes, both metallic and plastic types, are typically used as enclosures for splicing or terminating telephone cables.

FPN No. 2 to Exception No. 2: This exception limits the length of unlisted outside plant cable to 15 m (50 ft), while 800.90(B) requires that the primary protector be located as close as practicable to the point at which the cable enters the building. Therefore, in installations requiring a primary protector, the outside plant cable may not be permitted to extend 15 m (50 ft) into the building if it is practicable to place the primary protector closer than 15 m (50 ft) to the entrance point.

Table 800.113   Cable Markings

Cable Marking	Type	Reference
CMP	Communications plenum cable	800.179(A) and 800.154(A)
CMR	Communications riser cable	800.179(B) and 800.154(B)
CMG	Communications general-purpose cable	800.179(C) and 800.154(D) and (E)(1)
CM	Communications general-purpose cable	800.179(D) and 800.154(D) and (E)(1)
CMX	Communications cable, limited use	800.179(E) and 800.154(E)(2), (3), (4), and (5)
CMUC	Undercarpet communications wire and cable	800.179(F) and 800.154(E)(6)

FPN No. 1: Cable types are listed in descending order of fire resistance rating.

FPN No. 2: See the referenced sections for permitted uses.

800.133 Installation of Communications Wires, Cables, and Equipment. Communications wires and cables from the protector to the equipment or, where no protector is required, communications wires and cables attached to the outside or inside of the building shall comply with 800.133(A) through 800.133(D).

(A) Separation from Other Conductors.

(1) In Raceways, Boxes, and Cables.

(a) Other Power-Limited Circuits. Communications cables shall be permitted in the same raceway or enclosure with cables of any of the following:

(1) Class 2 and Class 3 remote-control, signaling, and power-limited circuits in compliance with Article 725

(2) Power-limited fire alarm systems in compliance with Article 760

(3) Nonconductive and conductive optical fiber cables in compliance with Article 770

(4) Community antenna television and radio distribution systems in compliance with Article 820

(5) Low-power network-powered broadband communications circuits in compliance with Article 830

(b) Class 2 and Class 3 Circuits. Class 1 circuits shall not be run in the same cable with communications circuits. Class 2 and Class 3 circuit conductors shall be permitted in the same cable with communications circuits, in which case the Class 2 and Class 3 circuits shall be classified as communications circuits and shall meet the requirements of this article. The cables shall be listed as communications cables or multipurpose cables.

Exception: Cables constructed of individually listed Class 2, Class 3, and communications cables under a common jacket shall not be required to be classified as communications cable. The fire-resistance rating of the composite cable shall be determined by the performance of the composite cable.

(c) Electric Light, Power, Class 1, Non–Power-Limited Fire Alarm, and Medium Power Network-Powered Broadband Communications Circuits in Raceways, Compartments, and Boxes. Communications conductors shall not be placed in any raceway, compartment, outlet box, junction box, or similar fitting with conductors of electric light, power, Class 1, non–power-limited fire alarm, or medium power network-powered broadband communications circuits.

Exception No. 1: Where all of the conductors of electric light, power, Class 1, non–power-limited fire alarm, and medium power network-powered broadband communications circuits are separated from all of the conductors of communications circuits by a permanent barrier or listed divider.

Exception No. 2: Power conductors in outlet boxes, junction boxes, or similar fittings or compartments where such conductors are introduced solely for power supply to communications equipment. The power circuit conductors shall be routed within the enclosure to maintain a minimum of 6 mm (0.25 in.) separation from the communications circuit conductors.

Exception No. 3: As permitted by 620.36.

(2) Other Applications. Communications wires and cables shall be separated at least 50 mm (2 in.) from conductors of any electric light, power, Class 1, non–power-limited fire alarm, or medium power network-powered broadband communications circuits.

Exception No. 1: Where either (1) all of the conductors of the electric light, power, Class 1, non–power-limited fire alarm, and medium power network-powered broadband communications circuits are in a raceway or in metal-sheathed, metal-clad, nonmetallic-sheathed, Type AC, or Type UF cables, or (2) all of the conductors of communications circuits are encased in raceway.

Exception No. 2: Where the communications wires and cables are permanently separated from the conductors of electric light, power, Class 1, non–power-limited fire alarm, and medium power network-powered broadband communications circuits by a continuous and firmly fixed nonconductor, such as porcelain tubes or flexible tubing, in addition to the insulation on the wire.

(B) Cable Trays. Types CMP, CMR, CMG, and CM communications cables shall be permitted to be installed in cable trays. Communications raceways, as described in 800.179, shall be permitted to be installed in cable trays.

(C) Support of Conductors. Raceways shall be used for their intended purpose. Communications cables or wires shall not be strapped, taped, or attached by any means to the exterior of any conduit or raceway as a means of support.

Exception: Overhead (aerial) spans of communications cables or wires shall be permitted to be attached to the exterior of a raceway-type mast intended for the attachment and support of such conductors.

(D) Wiring in Ducts for Dust, Loose Stock, or Vapor Removal. Section 300.22(A) shall apply.

800.154 Applications of Listed Communications Wires and Cables and Communications Raceways. Communications wires and cables shall comply with the requirements of 800.154(A) through 800.154(F) or where cable substitutions are made in accordance with 800.154(G)

(A) Plenum. Cables installed in ducts, plenums, and other spaces used for environmental air shall be Type CMP. Abandoned cables shall not be permitted to remain. Types CMP, CMR, CMG, CM, and CMX and communications wire installed in compliance with 300.22 shall be permitted. Listed plenum communications raceways shall be permitted to be installed in ducts and plenums as described in 300.22(B) and in other spaces used for environmental air as described in 300.22(C). Only Type CMP cable shall be permitted to be installed in raceways.

> FPN: See 8.14.1 of NFPA 13-2002, *Installation of Sprinkler Systems,* for requirements for sprinklers in concealed spaces containing exposed combustibles.

(B) Riser. Cables installed in risers shall comply with 800.154(B)(1), (B)(2), or (B)(3).

(1) Cables in Vertical Runs. Cables installed in vertical runs and penetrating more than one floor, or cables installed in vertical runs in a shaft, shall be Type CMR. Floor penetrations requiring Type CMR shall contain only cables suitable for riser or plenum use. Abandoned cables shall not be permitted to remain. Listed riser communications raceways shall be permitted to be installed in vertical riser runs in a shaft from floor to floor. Only Type CMR and CMP cables shall be permitted to be installed in these raceways.

(2) Metal Raceways or Fireproof Shafts. Listed communications cables shall be encased in a metal raceway or located in a fireproof shaft having firestops at each floor.

(3) One- and Two-Family Dwellings. Type CM and CMX cable shall be permitted in one- and two-family dwellings.

> FPN: See 800.3(C) for firestop requirements for floor penetrations.

(C) Distributing Frames and Cross-Connect Arrays. Listed communications wire and Types CMP, CMR, CMG, and CM communications cables shall be used in distributing frames and cross-connect arrays.

(D) Cable Trays. Types CMP, CMR, CMG, and CM communications cables shall be permitted to be installed in cable trays.

(E) Other Wiring Within Buildings. Cables installed in building locations other than the locations covered in 800.154(A) through 800.154(D) shall be in accordance with 800.154(E)(1) through (E)(6).

(1) General. Cables shall be Type CMG or Type CM. Listed communications general-purpose raceways shall be permitted. Only Types CMG, CM, CMR, or CMP cables shall be permitted to be installed in general-purpose communications raceways.

(2) In Raceways. Listed communications wires that are enclosed in a raceway of a type included in Chapter 3 shall be permitted.

(3) Nonconcealed Spaces. Type CMX communications cable shall be permitted to be installed in nonconcealed spaces where the exposed length of cable does not exceed 3 m (10 ft).

(4) One- and Two-Family Dwellings. Type CMX communications cable less than 6 mm (0.25 in.) in diameter shall be permitted to be installed in one- and two-family dwellings.

(5) Multi-Family Dwellings. Type CMX communications cable less than 6 mm (0.25 in.) in diameter shall be permitted to be installed in nonconcealed spaces in multi-family dwellings.

(6) Under Carpets. Type CMUC undercarpet communications wires and cables shall be permitted to be installed under carpet.

(F) Hybrid Power and Communications Cable. Hybrid power and communications cable listed in accordance with 800.179(I) shall be permitted to be installed in one- and two-family dwellings.

(G) Cable Substitutions. The uses and permitted substitutions for communications cables listed in Table 800.154 shall be considered suitable for the purpose and shall be permitted.

> FPN: For information on Types CMP, CMR, CMG, CM, and CMX cables, see 800.179.

VI. Listing Requirements

800.170 Equipment. Communications equipment shall be listed as being suitable for electrical connection to a telecommunications network.

Table 800.154 Cable Substitutions

Cable Type	Use	References	Permitted Substitutions
CMR	Communications riser cable	800.154(B)	CMP
CMG, CM	Communications general-purpose cable	800.154(E)(1)	CMP, CMR
CMX	Communications cable, limited use	800.154(E)	CMP, CMR, CMG, CM

FPN: See Figure 800.154, Cable Substitution Hierarchy.

Figure 800.154 Cable Substitution Hierarchy.

FPN: One way to determine applicable requirements is to refer to UL 1950-1993, *Standard for Safety of Information Technology Equipment, Including Electrical Business Equipment*, third edition; UL 1459-1995, *Standard for Safety, Telephone Equipment*, third edition; or UL 1863-1995, *Standard for Safety, Communications Circuit Accessories*, second edition. For information on listing requirements for communications raceways, see UL 2024-1995, *Standard for Optical Fiber Raceways.*

(A) Primary Protectors. The primary protector shall consist of an arrester connected between each line conductor and ground in an appropriate mounting. Primary protector terminals shall be marked to indicate line and ground as applicable.

FPN: One way to determine applicable requirements for a listed primary protector is to refer to ANSI/UL 497-1995, *Standard for Protectors for Paired Conductor Communications Circuits.*

(B) Secondary Protectors. The secondary protector shall be listed as suitable to provide means to safely limit currents to less than the current-carrying capacity of listed indoor communications wire and cable, listed telephone set line cords, and listed communications terminal equipment having ports for external wire line communications circuits. Any overvoltage protection, arresters, or grounding connection shall be connected on the equipment terminals side of the secondary protector current-limiting means.

FPN: One way to determine applicable requirements for a listed secondary protector is to refer to UL 497A-1996, *Standard for Secondary Protectors for Communications Circuits.*

800.173 Drop Wire and Cable. Communications wires and cables without a metallic shield, running from the last outdoor support to the primary protector, shall be listed as being suitable for the purpose and shall have current-carrying capacity as specified in 800.90(A)(1)(b) or (A)(1)(c).

800.179 Communications Wires and Cables. Communications wires and cables shall have a voltage rating of not less than 300 volts and shall be listed in accordance with 800.179(A) through 800.179(J). Conductors in communications cables, other than in a coaxial cable, shall be copper.

FPN: See 800.170 for listing requirement for equipment.

(A) Type CMP. Type CMP communications plenum cable shall be listed as being suitable for use in ducts, plenums, and other spaces used for environmental air and shall also be listed as having adequate fire-resistant and low smoke-producing characteristics.

FPN: One method of defining a cable that is low smoke-producing cable and fire-resistant cable is that the cable exhibits a maximum peak optical density of 0.5 or less, an average optical density of 0.15 or less, and a maximum flame spread distance of 1.52 m (5 ft) or less when tested in accordance with NFPA 262-2002, *Standard Method of Test for Flame Travel and Smoke of Wires and Cables for Use in Air-Handling Spaces.*

(B) Type CMR. Type CMR communications riser cable shall be listed as being suitable for use in a vertical run in a shaft or from floor to floor and shall also be listed as having fire-resistant characteristics capable of preventing the carrying of fire from floor to floor.

FPN: One method of defining fire-resistant characteristics capable of preventing the carrying of fire from floor to floor is that the cables pass the requirements of ANSI/UL 1666-2002, *Standard Test for Flame Propagation Height of Electrical and Optical-Fiber Cable Installed Vertically in Shafts.*

(C) Type CMG. Type CMG general-purpose communications cable shall be listed as being suitable for general-purpose communications use, with the exception of risers and plenums, and shall also be listed as being resistant to the spread of fire.

FPN: One method of defining *resistant to the spread of fire* is for the damage (char length) not to exceed 1.5 m (4 ft 11 in.) when performing the vertical flame test for cables in cable trays, as described in CSA C22.2 No. 0.3-M-1985, *Test Methods for Electrical Wires and Cables.*

(D) Type CM. Type CM communications cable shall be listed as being suitable for general-purpose communications use, with the exception of risers and plenums, and shall also be listed as being resistant to the spread of fire.

FPN: One method of defining *resistant to the spread of fire* is that the cables do not spread fire to the top of the tray in the vertical-tray flame test in ANSI/UL 1581-1991, *Reference Standard for Electrical Wires, Cables and Flexible Cords.* Another method of defining *resistant to the spread of fire* is for the damage (char length) not to exceed 1.5 m (4 ft 11 in.) when performing the vertical flame test for cables in cable trays, as described in CSA C22.2 No. 0.3-M-1985, *Test Method for Electrical Wires and Cables.*

(E) Type CMX. Type CMX limited-use communications cable shall be listed as being suitable for use in dwellings and for use in raceway and shall also be listed as being resistant to flame spread.

FPN: One method of determining that cable is resistant to flame spread is by testing the cable to the VW-1 (vertical-wire) flame test in ANSI/UL 1581-1991, *Reference Standard for Electrical Wires, Cables and Flexible Cords.*

(F) Type CMUC Undercarpet Wire and Cable. Type CMUC undercarpet communications wire and cable shall be listed as being suitable for undercarpet use and shall also be listed as being resistant to flame spread.

FPN: One method of determining that cable is resistant to flame spread is by testing the cable to the VW-1 (vertical-wire) flame test in ANSI/UL 1581-1991, *Reference Standard for Electrical Wires, Cables and Flexible Cords.*

(G) Multipurpose (MP) Cables. Until July 1, 2003, cables that meet the requirements for Types CMP, CMR, CMG, and CM and also satisfy the requirements of 760.82(B) for multiconductor cables and 760.82(H) for coaxial cables shall be permitted to be listed and marked as multipurpose cable Types MPP, MPR, MPG, and MP, respectively.

(H) Communications Circuit Integrity (CI) Cable. Cables suitable for use in communications systems to ensure survivability of critical circuits during a specified time under fire conditions shall be listed as circuit integrity (CI) cable. Cables identified in 800.179(A), (B), (C), (D), and (E) that meet the requirements for circuit integrity shall have the additional classification using the suffix "CI."

FPN: One method of defining circuit integrity (CI) cable is by establishing a minimum 2-hour fire resistance rating for the cable when tested in accordance with UL 2196-1995, *Standard for Tests of Fire Resistive Cables.*

(I) Communications Wires. Communications wires, such as distributing frame wire and jumper wire, shall be listed as being resistant to the spread of fire.

FPN: One method of defining *resistant to the spread of fire* is that the cables do not spread fire to the top of the tray in the vertical-tray flame test in ANSI/UL 1581-1991, *Reference Standard for Electrical Wires, Cables and Flexible Cords.* Another method of defining *resistant to the spread of fire* is for the damage (char length) not to exceed 1.5 m (4 ft 11 in.) when performing the vertical flame test for cables in cable trays, as described in CSA C22.2 No. 0.3-M-1985, *Test Methods for Electrical Wires and Cables.*

(J) Hybrid Power and Communications Cable. Listed hybrid power and communications cable shall be permitted where the power cable is a listed Type NM or NM-B conforming to the provisions of Article 334, and the communications cable is a listed Type CM, the jackets on the listed NM or NM-B and listed CM cables are rated for 600 volts minimum, and the hybrid cable is listed as being resistant to the spread of fire.

FPN: One method of defining *resistant to the spread of fire* is that the cables do not spread fire to the top of the tray in the vertical-tray flame test in ANSI/UL 1581-1991, *Reference Standard for Electrical Wires, Cables and Flexible Cords.* Another method of defining *resistant to the spread of fire* is for the damage (char length) not to exceed 1.5 m (4 ft 11 in.) when performing the vertical flame test for cables in cable trays, as described in CSA C22.2 No. 0.3-M-1985, *Test Methods for Electrical Wires and Cables.*

800.182 Communications Raceways. Communications raceways shall be listed in accordance with 800.182(A) through 800.182(C).

(A) Plenum Communications Raceways. Plenum communications raceways listed as plenum optical fiber raceways shall be permitted for use in ducts, plenums, and other spaces used for environmental air and shall also be listed as having adequate fire-resistant and low smoke-producing characteristics.

FPN: One method of defining that an optical fiber raceway is a low smoke producing raceway and a fire-resistant raceway is that the raceway exhibits a maximum peak optical density of 0.5 or less, an average optical density of 0.15 or less, and a maximum flame spread distance of 1.52 m (5 ft) or less when tested in accordance with the plenum test in UL 2024, *Standard for Optical Fiber Cable Raceway.*

(B) Riser Communications Raceways. Riser communications raceways shall be listed as having adequate fire-resistant characteristics capable of preventing the carrying of fire from floor to floor.

FPN: One method of defining fire-resistant characteristics capable of preventing the carrying of fire from floor to floor is that the raceways pass the requirements of the test for Flame Propagation (riser) in UL 2024, *Standard for Optical Fiber Cable Raceway.*

(C) General-Purpose Communications Raceways. General-purpose communications raceways shall be listed as being resistant to the spread of fire.

> FPN: One method of defining *resistance to the spread of fire* is that the raceways pass the requirements of the Vertical-Tray Flame Test (General Use) in UL 2024, *Standard for Optical Fiber Cable Raceway.*

ARTICLE 810
Radio and Television Equipment

I. General

810.1 Scope. This article covers antenna systems for radio and television receiving equipment, amateur radio transmitting and receiving equipment, and certain features of transmitter safety. This article covers antennas such as multi-element, vertical rod, and dish, and also covers the wiring and cabling that connects them to equipment. This article does not cover equipment and antennas used for coupling carrier current to power line conductors.

810.2 Definitions. For definitions applicable to this article, see Article 100.

810.3 Other Articles. Wiring from the source of power to and between devices connected to the interior wiring system shall comply with Chapters 1 through 4 other than as modified by Parts I and II of Article 640. Wiring for audio signal processing, amplification, and reproduction equipment shall comply with Article 640. Coaxial cables that connect antennas to equipment shall comply with Article 820.

810.4 Community Television Antenna. The antenna shall comply with this article. The distribution system shall comply with Article 820.

810.5 Radio Noise Suppressors. Radio interference eliminators, interference capacitors, or noise suppressors connected to power-supply leads shall be of a listed type. They shall not be exposed to physical damage.

II. Receiving Equipment — Antenna Systems

810.11 Material. Antennas and lead-in conductors shall be of hard-drawn copper, bronze, aluminum alloy, copper-clad steel, or other high-strength, corrosion-resistant material.

Exception: Soft-drawn or medium-drawn copper shall be permitted for lead-in conductors where the maximum span between points of support is less than 11 m (35 ft).

810.12 Supports. Outdoor antennas and lead-in conductors shall be securely supported. The antennas or lead-in conductors shall not be attached to the electric service mast. They shall not be attached to poles or similar structures carrying open electric light or power wires or trolley wires of over 250 volts between conductors. Insulators supporting the antenna conductors shall have sufficient mechanical strength to safely support the conductors. Lead-in conductors shall be securely attached to the antennas.

810.13 Avoidance of Contacts with Conductors of Other Systems. Outdoor antennas and lead-in conductors from an antenna to a building shall not cross over open conductors of electric light or power circuits and shall be kept well away from all such circuits so as to avoid the possibility of accidental contact. Where proximity to open electric light or power service conductors of less than 250 volts between conductors cannot be avoided, the installation shall be such as to provide a clearance of at least 600 mm (2 ft).

Where practicable, antenna conductors shall be installed so as not to cross under open electric light or power conductors.

810.14 Splices. Splices and joints in antenna spans shall be made mechanically secure with approved splicing devices or by such other means as will not appreciably weaken the conductors.

810.15 Grounding. Masts and metal structures supporting antennas shall be grounded in accordance with 810.21.

810.16 Size of Wire-Strung Antenna — Receiving Station.

(A) Size of Antenna Conductors. Outdoor antenna conductors for receiving stations shall be of a size not less than given in Table 810.16(A).

Table 810.16(A) Size of Receiving Station Outdoor Antenna Conductors

Material	Minimum Size of Conductors (AWG) Where Maximum Open Span Length Is		
	Less Than 11 m (35 ft)	11 m to 45 m (35 ft to 150 ft)	Over 45 m (150 ft)
Aluminum alloy, hard-drawn copper	19	14	12
Copper-clad steel, bronze, or other high-strength material	20	17	14

(B) Self-Supporting Antennas. Outdoor antennas, such as vertical rods, dishes, or dipole structures, shall be of corrosion-resistant materials and of strength suitable to withstand ice and wind loading conditions and shall be located well away from overhead conductors of electric light and power circuits of over 150 volts to ground, so as to avoid the possibility of the antenna or structure falling into or making accidental contact with such circuits.

810.17 Size of Lead-in — Receiving Station. Lead-in conductors from outside antennas for receiving stations shall, for various maximum open span lengths, be of such size as to have a tensile strength at least as great as that of the conductors for antennas as specified in 810.16. Where the lead-in consists of two or more conductors that are twisted together, are enclosed in the same covering, or are concentric, the conductor size shall, for various maximum open span lengths, be such that the tensile strength of the combination is at least as great as that of the conductors for antennas as specified in 810.16.

810.18 Clearances — Receiving Stations.

(A) Outside of Buildings. Lead-in conductors attached to buildings shall be installed so that they cannot swing closer than 600 mm (2 ft) to the conductors of circuits of 250 volts or less between conductors, or 3.0 m (10 ft) to the conductors of circuits of over 250 volts between conductors, except that in the case of circuits not over 150 volts between conductors, where all conductors involved are supported so as to ensure permanent separation, the clearance shall be permitted to be reduced but shall not be less than 100 mm (4 in.). The clearance between lead-in conductors and any conductor forming a part of a lightning rod system shall not be less than 1.8 m (6 ft) unless the bonding referred to in 250.60 is accomplished. Underground conductors shall be separated at least 300 mm (12 in.) from conductors of any light or power circuits or Class 1 circuits.

Exception: Where the electric light or power conductors, Class 1 conductors, or lead-in conductors are installed in raceways or metal cable armor.

(B) Antennas and Lead-ins — Indoors. Indoor antennas and indoor lead-ins shall not be run nearer than 50 mm (2 in.) to conductors of other wiring systems in the premises.

Exception No. 1: Where such other conductors are in metal raceways or cable armor.

Exception No. 2: Where permanently separated from such other conductors by a continuous and firmly fixed nonconductor, such as porcelain tubes or flexible tubing.

(C) In Boxes or Other Enclosures. Indoor antennas and indoor lead-ins shall be permitted to occupy the same box or enclosure with conductors of other wiring systems where separated from such other conductors by an effective permanently installed barrier.

810.19 Electric Supply Circuits Used in Lieu of Antenna — Receiving Stations. Where an electric supply circuit is used in lieu of an antenna, the device by which the radio receiving set is connected to the supply circuit shall be listed.

810.20 Antenna Discharge Units — Receiving Stations.

(A) Where Required. Each conductor of a lead-in from an outdoor antenna shall be provided with a listed antenna discharge unit.

Exception: Where the lead-in conductors are enclosed in a continuous metallic shield that either is permanently and effectively grounded or is protected by an antenna discharge unit.

(B) Location. Antenna discharge units shall be located outside the building or inside the building between the point of entrance of the lead-in and the radio set or transformers and as near as practicable to the entrance of the conductors to the building. The antenna discharge unit shall not be located near combustible material or in a hazardous (classified) location as defined in Article 500.

(C) Grounding. The antenna discharge unit shall be grounded in accordance with 810.21.

810.21 Grounding Conductors — Receiving Stations. Grounding conductors shall comply with 810.21(A) through 810.21(K).

(A) Material. The grounding conductor shall be of copper, aluminum, copper-clad steel, bronze, or similar corrosion-resistant material. Aluminum or copper-clad aluminum grounding conductors shall not be used where in direct contact with masonry or the earth or where subject to corrosive conditions. Where used outside, aluminum or copper-clad aluminum shall not be installed within 450 mm (18 in.) of the earth.

(B) Insulation. Insulation on grounding conductors shall not be required.

(C) Supports. The grounding conductors shall be securely fastened in place and shall be permitted to be directly attached to the surface wired over without the use of insulating supports.

Exception: Where proper support cannot be provided, the size of the grounding conductors shall be increased proportionately.

(D) Mechanical Protection. The grounding conductor shall be protected where exposed to physical damage, or the size of the grounding conductors shall be increased proportionately to compensate for the lack of protection. Where the grounding conductor is run in a metal raceway, both ends of the raceway shall be bonded to the grounding conductor or to the same terminal or electrode to which the grounding conductor is connected.

(E) Run in Straight Line. The grounding conductor for an antenna mast or antenna discharge unit shall be run in as straight a line as practicable from the mast or discharge unit to the grounding electrode.

(F) Electrode. The grounding conductor shall be connected as follows:

(1) To the nearest accessible location on the following:

   a. The building or structure grounding electrode system as covered in 250.50

   b. The grounded interior metal water piping systems, within 1.52 m (5 ft) from its point of entrance to the building, as covered in 250.52

   c. The power service accessible means external to the building, as covered in 250.94

   d. The metallic power service raceway

   e. The service equipment enclosure, or

   f. The grounding electrode conductor or the grounding electrode conductor metal enclosures; or

(2) If the building or structure served has no grounding means, as described in 810.21(F)(1), to any one of the individual electrodes described in 250.52; or

(3) If the building or structure served has no grounding means, as described in 810.21(F)(1) or (F)(2), to an effectively grounded metal structure or to any of the individual electrodes described in 250.52

(G) Inside or Outside Building. The grounding conductor shall be permitted to be run either inside or outside the building.

(H) Size. The grounding conductor shall not be smaller than 10 AWG copper, 8 AWG aluminum, or 17 AWG copper-clad steel or bronze.

(I) Common Ground. A single grounding conductor shall be permitted for both protective and operating purposes.

(J) Bonding of Electrodes. A bonding jumper not smaller than 6 AWG copper or equivalent shall be connected between the radio and television equipment grounding electrode and the power grounding electrode system at the building or structure served where separate electrodes are used.

(K) Electrode Connection. Connections to grounding electrodes shall comply with 250.70.

III. Amateur Transmitting and Receiving Stations — Antenna Systems

810.51 Other Sections. In addition to complying with Part III, antenna systems for amateur transmitting and receiving stations shall also comply with 810.11 through 810.15.

810.52 Size of Antenna. Antenna conductors for transmitting and receiving stations shall be of a size not less than given in Table 810.52.

Table 810.52 Size of Amateur Station Outdoor Antenna Conductors

Material	Minimum Size of Conductors (AWG) Where Maximum Open Span Length Is	
	Less Than 45 m (150 ft)	Over 45 m (150 ft)
Hard-drawn copper	14	10
Copper-clad steel, bronze, or other high-strength material	14	12

810.53 Size of Lead-in Conductors. Lead-in conductors for transmitting stations shall, for various maximum span lengths, be of a size at least as great as that of conductors for antennas as specified in 810.52.

810.54 Clearance on Building. Antenna conductors for transmitting stations, attached to buildings, shall be firmly mounted at least 75 mm (3 in.) clear of the surface of the building on nonabsorbent insulating supports, such as treated pins or brackets equipped with insulators having not less than 75-mm (3-in.) creepage and airgap distances. Lead-in conductors attached to buildings shall also comply with these requirements.

Exception: Where the lead-in conductors are enclosed in a continuous metallic shield that is permanently and effectively grounded, they shall not be required to comply with these requirements. Where grounded, the metallic shield shall also be permitted to be used as a conductor.

810.55 Entrance to Building. Except where protected with a continuous metallic shield that is permanently and effectively grounded, lead-in conductors for transmitting stations shall enter buildings by one of the following methods:

(1) Through a rigid, noncombustible, nonabsorbent insulating tube or bushing

(2) Through an opening provided for the purpose in which the entrance conductors are firmly secured so as to provide a clearance of at least 50 mm (2 in.)

(3) Through a drilled window pane

810.56 Protection Against Accidental Contact. Lead-in conductors to radio transmitters shall be located or installed so as to make accidental contact with them difficult.

810.57 Antenna Discharge Units — Transmitting Stations. Each conductor of a lead-in for outdoor antennas shall be provided with an antenna discharge unit or other suitable means that drain static charges from the antenna system.

Exception No. 1: Where protected by a continuous metallic shield that is permanently and effectively grounded.

Exception No. 2: Where the antenna is permanently and effectively grounded.

810.58 Grounding Conductors — Amateur Transmitting and Receiving Stations. Grounding conductors shall comply with 810.58(A) through 810.58(C).

(A) Other Sections. All grounding conductors for amateur transmitting and receiving stations shall comply with 810.21(A) through 810.21(K).

(B) Size of Protective Grounding Conductor. The protective grounding conductor for transmitting stations shall be as large as the lead-in but not smaller than 10 AWG copper, bronze, or copper-clad steel.

(C) Size of Operating Grounding Conductor. The operating grounding conductor for transmitting stations shall not be less than 14 AWG copper or its equivalent.

IV. Interior Installation — Transmitting Stations

810.70 Clearance from Other Conductors. All conductors inside the building shall be separated at least 100 mm (4 in.) from the conductors of any electric light, power, or signaling circuit.

Exception No. 1: As provided in Article 640.

Exception No. 2: Where separated from other conductors by raceway or some firmly fixed nonconductor, such as porcelain tubes or flexible tubing.

810.71 General. Transmitters shall comply with 810.71(A) through 810.71(C).

(A) Enclosing. The transmitter shall be enclosed in a metal frame or grille, or separated from the operating space by a barrier or other equivalent means, all metallic parts of which are effectively connected to ground.

(B) Grounding of Controls. All external metal handles and controls accessible to the operating personnel shall be effectively grounded.

(C) Interlocks on Doors. All access doors shall be provided with interlocks that disconnect all voltages of over 350 volts between conductors when any access door is opened.

ARTICLE 820
Community Antenna Television and Radio Distribution Systems

FPN: Rules that are followed by a reference in brackets contain text that has been extracted from NFPA 97-2003, *Standard Glossary of Terms Relating to Chimneys, Vents, and Heat-Producing Appliances.* Only editorial changes were made to the extracted text to make it consistent with this *Code.*

I. General

820.1 Scope. This article covers coaxial cable distribution of radio frequency signals typically employed in community antenna television (CATV) systems.

820.2 Definitions. See Article 100. For the purposes of this article, the following additional definitions apply.

Abandoned Coaxial Cable. Installed coaxial cable that is not terminated at equipment other than a coaxial connector and not identified for future use with a tag.

Air Duct. A conduit or passageway for conveying air to or from heating, cooling, air conditioning, or ventilating equipment, but not including the plenum. [NFPA 97:1.2.6]

Exposed. An exposed cable is one that is in such a position that, in case of failure of supports and insulation, contact with another circuit could result.

FPN: See Article 100 for two other definitions of *exposed.*

Point of Entrance. The point within a building at which the cable emerges from an external wall, from a concrete floor slab, or from a rigid metal conduit or an intermediate metal conduit grounded to an electrode in accordance with 820.100(B).

Premises. The land and buildings of a user located on the user side of utility-user network point of demarcation.

820.3 Other Articles. Circuits and equipment shall comply with 820.3(A) through 820.3(G).

(A) Spread of Fire or Products of Combustion. Section 300.21 shall apply. The accessible portion of abandoned coaxial cables shall be removed.

(B) Ducts, Plenums, and Other Air-Handling Spaces. Section 300.22, where installed in ducts, plenums, or other spaces used for environmental air, shall apply.

Exception: As permitted in 820.154(A).

(C) Installation and Use. Section 110.3 shall apply.

(D) Installations of Conductive and Nonconductive Optical Fiber Cables. Article 770 shall apply.

(E) Communications Circuits. Article 800 shall apply.

(F) Network-Powered Broadband Communications Systems. Article 830 shall apply.

(G) Alternate Wiring Methods. The wiring methods of Article 830 shall be permitted to substitute for the wiring methods of Article 820.

> FPN: Use of Article 830 wiring methods will facilitate the upgrading of Article 820 installations to network-powered broadband applications.

820.15 Energy Limitations. Coaxial cable shall be permitted to deliver low-energy power to equipment that is directly associated with the radio frequency distribution system if the voltage is not over 60 volts and if the current supply is from a transformer or other device that has energy-limiting characteristics.

820.21 Access to Electrical Equipment Behind Panels Designed to Allow Access. Access to electrical equipment shall not be denied by an accumulation of wires and cables that prevents removal of panels, including suspended ceiling panels.

820.24 Mechanical Execution of Work. Community antenna television and radio distribution systems shall be installed in a neat and workmanlike manner. Cables installed exposed on the surface of ceiling and sidewalls shall be supported by the building structure in such a manner that the cable will not be damaged by normal building use. Such cables shall be secured by straps, staples, hangers, or similar fittings designed and installed so as not to damage the cable. The installation shall also conform with 300.4(D) and 300.11.

> FPN: Accepted industry practices are described in ANSI/NECA/BICSI 568–2001, *Standard for Installing Commercial Building Telecommunications Cabling,* and other ANSI-approved installation standards.

II. Cables Outside and Entering Buildings

820.44 Overhead Cables. Coaxial cables, prior to the point of grounding, as defined in 820.93, shall comply with 820.44(A) through 820.44(F).

(A) On Poles. Where practicable, conductors on poles shall be located below the electric light, power, Class 1, or non–power-limited fire alarm circuit conductors and shall not be attached to a crossarm that carries electric light or power conductors.

(B) Lead-in Clearance. Lead-in or aerial-drop cables from a pole or other support, including the point of initial attachment to a building or structure, shall be kept away from electric light, power, Class 1, or non–power-limited fire alarm circuit conductors so as to avoid the possibility of accidental contact.

Exception: Where proximity to electric light, power, Class 1, or non–power-limited fire alarm circuit service conductors cannot be avoided, the installation shall be such as to provide clearances of not less than 300 mm (12 in.) from light, power, Class 1, or non–power-limited fire alarm circuit service drops. The clearance requirement shall apply at all points along the drop, and it shall increase to 1.02 m (40 in.) at the pole.

(C) On Masts. Aerial cable shall be permitted to be attached to an above-the-roof raceway mast that does not enclose or support conductors of electric light or power circuits.

(D) Above Roofs. Cables shall have a vertical clearance of not less than 2.5 m (8 ft) from all points of roofs above which they pass.

Exception No. 1: Auxiliary buildings such as garages and the like.

Exception No. 2: A reduction in clearance above only the overhanging portion of the roof to not less than 450 mm (18 in.) shall be permitted if (1) not more than 1.2 m (4 ft) of communications service drop conductors pass above the roof overhang, and (2) they are terminated at a raceway mast or other approved support.

Exception No. 3: Where the roof has a slope of not less than 100 mm in 300 mm (4 in. in 12 in.), a reduction in clearance to not less than 900 mm (3 ft) shall be permitted.

(E) Between Buildings. Cables extending between buildings and also the supports or attachment fixtures shall be acceptable for the purpose and shall have sufficient strength to withstand the loads to which they may be subjected.

Exception: Where a cable does not have sufficient strength to be self-supporting, it shall be attached to a supporting messenger cable that, together with the attachment fixtures or supports, shall be acceptable for the purpose and shall have sufficient strength to withstand the loads to which they may be subjected.

(F) On Buildings. Where attached to buildings, cables shall be securely fastened in such a manner that they will be separated from other conductors in accordance with 820.44(F)(1), (F)(2), and (F)(3).

(1) Electric Light or Power. The coaxial cable shall have a separation of at least 100 mm (4 in.) from electric light, power, Class 1, or non–power-limited fire alarm circuit conductors not in raceway or cable, or shall be permanently separated from conductors of the other system by a continuous and firmly fixed nonconductor in addition to the insulation on the wires.

(2) Other Communications Systems. Coaxial cable shall be installed so that there will be no unnecessary interference in the maintenance of the separate systems. In no case shall the conductors, cables, messenger strand, or equipment of one system cause abrasion to the conductors, cable, messenger strand, or equipment of any other system.

(3) Lightning Conductors. Where practicable, a separation of at least 1.8 m (6 ft) shall be maintained between any coaxial cable and lightning conductors.

> FPN: For additional information regarding overhead wires and cables, see ANSI C2-2002, *National Electric Safety Code*, Part 2, Safety Rules for Overhead Lines.

820.47 Underground Circuits Entering Buildings.

(A) Underground Systems. Underground coaxial cables in a duct, pedestal, handhole enclosure, or manhole that contains electric light or power conductors or Class 1 circuits shall be in a section permanently separated from such conductors by means of a suitable barrier.

(B) Direct-Buried Cables and Raceways. Direct-buried coaxial cable shall be separated at least 300 mm (12 in.) from conductors of any light or power or Class 1 circuit.

Exception No. 1: Where electric service conductors or co-axial cables are installed in raceways or have metal cable armor.

Exception No. 2: Where electric light or power branch-circuit or feeder conductors or Class 1 circuit conductors are installed in a raceway or in metal-sheathed, metal-clad, or Type UF or Type USE cables; or the coaxial cables have metal cable armor or are installed in a raceway.

III. Protection

820.93 Grounding of Outer Conductive Shield of a Coaxial Cable. The outer conductive shield of the coaxial cable shall be grounded at the building premises as close to the point of cable entrance or attachment as practicable.

For purposes of this section, grounding located at mobile home service equipment located in sight from, and not more than 9.0 m (30 ft) from, the exterior wall of the mobile home it serves, or at a mobile home disconnecting means grounded in accordance with 250.32 and located in sight from and not more than 9.0 m (30 ft) from the exterior

wall of the mobile home it serves, shall be considered to meet the requirements of this section.

> FPN: Selecting a grounding location to achieve the shortest practicable grounding conductor helps limit potential differences between CATV and other metallic systems.

(A) Shield Grounding. Where the outer conductive shield of a coaxial cable is grounded, no other protective devices shall be required.

(B) Shield Protection Devices. Grounding of a coaxial drop cable shield by means of a protective device that does not interrupt the grounding system within the premises shall be permitted.

IV. Grounding Methods

820.100 Cable Grounding. Where required by 820.93, the shield of the coaxial cable shall be grounded as specified in 820.100(A) through 820.100(D).

(A) Grounding Conductor.

(1) Insulation. The grounding conductor shall be insulated and shall be listed as suitable for the purpose.

(2) Material. The grounding conductor shall be copper or other corrosion-resistant conductive material, stranded or solid.

(3) Size. The grounding conductor shall not be smaller than 14 AWG. It shall have a current-carrying capacity approximately equal to that of the outer conductor of the coaxial cable. The grounding conductor shall not be required to exceed 6 AWG.

(4) Length. The grounding conductor shall be as short as practicable. In one- and two-family dwellings, the grounding conductor shall be as short as practicable, not to exceed 6.0 m (20 ft) in length.

> FPN: Similar grounding conductor length limitations applied at apartment buildings and commercial buildings will help to reduce voltages that may be developed between the building's power and communications systems during lightning events.

Exception: In one- and two-family dwellings where it is not practicable to achieve an overall maximum grounding conductor length of 6.0 m (20 ft), a separate ground as specified in 250.52(A)(5), (A)(6), or (A)(7) shall be used, the grounding conductor shall be grounded to the separate ground in accordance with 250.70, and the separate ground bonded to the power grounding electrode system in accordance with 820.100(D).

(5) Run in Straight Line. The grounding conductor shall be run to the grounding electrode in as straight a line as practicable.

(6) Physical Protection. Where subject to physical damage, the grounding conductor shall be adequately protected. Where the grounding conductor is run in a metal raceway, both ends of the raceway shall be bonded to the grounding conductor or the same terminal or electrode to which the grounding conductor is connected.

(B) Electrode. The grounding conductor shall be connected in accordance with 820.100(B)(1) and (B)(2).

(1) In Buildings or Structures with Grounding Means. To the nearest accessible location on the following:

(1) The building or structure grounding electrode system as covered in 250.50

(2) The grounded interior metal water piping system, within 1.52 m (5 ft) from its point of entrance to the building, as covered in 250.52

(3) The power service accessible means external to enclosures as covered in 250.94

(4) The metallic power service raceway

(5) The service equipment enclosure

(6) The grounding electrode conductor or the grounding electrode conductor metal enclosure, or

(7) The grounding conductor or the grounding electrode of a building or structure disconnecting means that is grounded to an electrode as covered in 250.32

(2) In Buildings or Structures Without Grounding Means. If the building or structure served has no grounding means, as described in 820.100(B)(1):

(1) To any one of the individual electrodes described in 250.52(A)(1), (A)(2), (A)(3), (A)(4); or,

(2) If the building or structure served has no grounding means, as described in 820.100(B)(1) or (B)(2)(1), to an effectively grounded metal structure or to any one of the individual electrodes described in 250.52(A)(5), (A)(6), and (A)(7).

(C) Electrode Connection. Connections to grounding electrodes shall comply with 250.70.

(D) Bonding of Electrodes. A bonding jumper not smaller than 6 AWG copper or equivalent shall be connected between the community antenna television system's grounding electrode and the power grounding electrode system at the building or structure served where separate electrodes are used.

Exception: At mobile homes as covered in 820.106.

FPN No. 1: See 250.60 for use of air terminals (lightning rods).

FPN No. 2: Bonding together of all separate electrodes limits potential differences between them and between their associated wiring systems.

820.103 Equipment Grounding. Unpowered equipment and enclosures or equipment powered by the coaxial cable shall be considered grounded where connected to the metallic cable shield.

820.106 Bonding and Grounding at Mobile Homes.

(A) Grounding. Where there is no mobile home service equipment located in sight from, and not more than 9.0 m (30 ft) from, the exterior wall of the mobile home it serves or there is no mobile home disconnecting means grounded in accordance with 250.32 and located within sight from, and not more than 9.0 m (30 ft) from, the exterior wall of the mobile home it serves, the coaxial cable shield ground, or surge arrester ground, shall be in accordance with 820.100(B)(2).

(B) Bonding. The coaxial cable shield grounding terminal, surge arrester grounding terminal, or grounding electrode shall be bonded to the metal frame or available grounding terminal of the mobile home with a copper grounding conductor not smaller than 12 AWG under any of the following conditions:

(1) Where there is no mobile home service equipment or disconnecting means as in 820.106(A)

(2) Where the mobile home is supplied by cord and plug

V. Cables Within Buildings

820.110 Raceways for Coaxial Cables. Where coaxial cables are installed in a raceway, the raceway shall be either of a type permitted in Chapter 3 and installed in accordance with Chapter 3 or a listed nonmetallic raceway complying with 820.182(A), (B), or (C), as applicable, and installed in accordance with 362.24 through 362.56, where the requirements applicable to electrical nonmetallic tubing apply.

Exception: Conduit fill restrictions shall not apply.

820.113 Installation and Marking of Coaxial Cables. Listed coaxial cables shall be installed as wiring within buildings. Coaxial cables shall be marked in accordance with Table 820.113. The cable voltage rating shall not be marked on the cable.

FPN: Voltage markings on cables could be misinterpreted to suggest that the cables may be suitable for Class 1, electric light, and power applications.

Exception No. 1: Voltage markings shall be permitted where the cable has multiple listings and voltage marking is required for one or more of the listings.

Exception No. 2: Listing and marking shall not be required where the length of the cable within the building, measured from its point of entrance, does not exceed 15 m (50 ft) and the cable enters the building from the outside and is terminated at a grounding block.

Table 820.113 Cable Markings

Cable Marking	Type	Reference
CATVP	CATV plenum cable	820.179(A) and 820.154(A)
CATVR	CATV riser cable	820.179(B) and 820.154(B)
CATV	CATV cable	820.179(C) and 820.154(D)
CATVX	CATV cable, limited use	820.179(D) and 820.154(D)

FPN No. 1: Cable types are listed in descending order of fire-resistance rating.

FPN No. 2: See the referenced sections for listing requirements and permitted uses.

820.133 Installation of Cables and Equipment. Beyond the point of grounding, as defined in 820.93, the cable installation shall comply with 820.133(A) through 820.133(C).

(A) Separation from Other Conductors.

(1) In Raceways and Boxes.

(1) Other Circuits. Coaxial cables shall be permitted in the same raceway or enclosure with jacketed cables of any of the following:

   a. Class 2 and Class 3 remote-control, signaling, and power-limited circuits in compliance with Article 725

   b. Power-limited fire alarm systems in compliance with Article 760

   c. Nonconductive and conductive optical fiber cables in compliance with Article 770

   d. Communications circuits in compliance with Article 800

   e. Low-power network-powered broadband communications circuits in compliance with Article 830

(2) Electric Light, Power, Class 1, Non–Power-Limited Fire Alarm, and Medium Power Network-Powered Broadband Communications Circuits. Coaxial cable shall not be placed in any raceway, compartment, outlet box, junction box, or other enclosures with conductors of electric light, power, Class 1, non–power-limited fire alarm, or medium power network-powered broadband communications circuits.

Exception No. 1: Where all of the conductors of electric light, power, Class 1, non–power-limited fire alarm, and medium power network-powered broadband communications circuits are separated from all of the coaxial cables by a permanent barrier or listed divider.

Exception No. 2: Power circuit conductors in outlet boxes, junction boxes, or similar fittings or compartments where such conductors are introduced solely for power supply to

the coaxial cable system distribution equipment. The power circuit conductors shall be routed within the enclosure to maintain a minimum 6-mm (0.25-in.) separation from co-axial cables.

(2) Other Applications. Coaxial cable shall be separated at least 50 mm (2 in.) from conductors of any electric light, power, Class 1, non–power-limited fire alarm, or medium power network-powered broadband communications circuits.

Exception No. 1: Where either (1) all of the conductors of electric light, power, Class 1, non–power-limited fire alarm, and medium power network-powered broadband communications circuits are in a raceway, or in metal-sheathed, metal-clad, nonmetallic-sheathed, Type AC or Type UF cables, or (2) all of the coaxial cables are encased in raceway.

Exception No. 2: Where the coaxial cables are permanently separated from the conductors of electric light, power, Class 1, non–power-limited fire alarm, and medium power network-powered broadband communications circuits by a continuous and firmly fixed nonconductor, such as porcelain tubes or flexible tubing, in addition to the insulation on the wire.

(B) Hybrid Power and Coaxial Cabling. The provisions of 780.6 shall apply for listed hybrid power and coaxial cabling in closed-loop and programmed power distribution.

(C) Support of Cables. Raceways shall be used for their intended purpose. Coaxial cables shall not be strapped, taped, or attached by any means to the exterior of any conduit or raceway as a means of support.

Exception: Overhead (aerial) spans of coaxial cables shall be permitted to be attached to the exterior of a raceway-type mast intended for the attachment and support of such cables.

820.154 Applications of Listed CATV Cables and CATV Raceways. CATV cables shall comply with the requirements of 820.154(A) through 820.154(D) or where cable substitutions are made as shown in Table 820.154.

(A) Plenums. Cables installed in ducts, plenums, and other spaces used for environmental air shall be Type CATVP. Abandoned cables shall not be permitted to remain. Types CATVP, CATVR, CATV, and CATVX cables installed in compliance with 300.22 shall be permitted. Listed plenum CATV raceways shall be permitted to be installed in ducts and plenums as described in 300.22(B) and in other spaces used for environmental air as described in 300.22(C). Only Type CATVP cable shall be permitted to be installed in these raceways.

   FPN: See 8.14.1 of NFPA 13-2002, *Installation of Sprinkler Systems,* for requirements for sprinklers in concealed spaces containing exposed combustibles.

(B) Riser. Cables installed in risers shall comply with any of the requirements of 820.154(B)(1) through (B)(3).

(1) Cables in Vertical Runs. Cables installed in vertical runs and penetrating more than one floor, or cables installed in vertical runs in a shaft, shall be Type CATVR. Floor penetrations requiring Type CATVR shall contain only cables suitable for riser or plenum use. Abandoned cables shall not be permitted to remain. Listed riser CATV raceways shall be permitted to be installed in vertical riser runs in a shaft from floor to floor. Only Type CATVR and CATVP cables shall be permitted to be installed in these raceways.

(2) Metal Raceways or Fireproof Shafts. Types CATV and CATVX cables shall be permitted to be encased in a metal raceway or located in a fireproof shaft having fire-stops at each floor.

(3) One- and Two-Family Dwellings. Types CATV and CATVX cables shall be permitted in one- and two-family dwellings.

> FPN: See 820.3(A) for the firestop requirements for floor penetrations.

(C) Cable Trays. Cables installed in cable trays shall be Types CATVP, CATVR, and CATV.

(D) Other Wiring Within Buildings. Cables installed in building locations other than the locations covered in 820.154(A) and 820.154(B) shall be with any of the requirements in 820.154(D)(1) through (D)(5). Abandoned cables in hollow spaces shall not be permitted to remain.

(1) General. Type CATV shall be permitted. Listed CATV general-purpose raceways shall be permitted. Only Types CATV, CATVX, CATVR, or CATVP cables shall be permitted to be installed in general-purpose communications raceways.

(2) In Raceways. Type CATVX shall be permitted to be installed in a raceway.

(3) Nonconcealed Spaces. Type CATVX shall be permitted to be installed in nonconcealed spaces where the exposed length of cable does not exceed 3 m (10 ft).

(4) One- and Two-Family Dwellings. Type CATVX cables less than 10 mm (0.375 in.) in diameter shall be permitted to be installed in one- and two-family dwellings.

(5) Multifamily Dwellings. Type CATVX cables less than 10 mm (0.375 in.) in diameter shall be permitted to be installed in multifamily dwellings.

> FPN No. 1: See Figure 820.154, Cable Substitution Hierarchy.
>
> FPN No. 2: The substitute cables in Table 820.154 are only coaxial-type cables.

VI. Listing Requirements

820.179 Coaxial Cables. Cables shall be listed in accordance with 820.179(A) through 820.179(D).

Table 820.154 Coaxial Cable Uses and Permitted Substitutions

Cable Type	Permitted Substitutions
CATVP	CMP, BLP
CATVR	CATVP, CMP, CMR, BMR, BLP, BLR
CATV	CATVP, CMP, CATVR, CMR, CMG, CM, BMR, BM, BLP, BLR, BL
CATVX	CATVP, CMP, CATVR, CMR, CATV, CMG, CM, BMR, BM, BLP, BLR, BL, BLX

Type CATV — Community antenna television cables
Type CM — Communications cables

A ▶ B   Coaxial cable A shall be permitted to be used in place of coaxial cable B.

Figure 820.154 Cable Substitution Hierarchy.

(A) Type CATVP. Type CATVP community antenna television plenum cable shall be listed as being suitable for use in ducts, plenums, and other spaces used for environmental air and shall also be listed as having adequate fire-resistant and low smoke-producing characteristics.

> FPN: One method of defining a cable that is low smoke-producing cable and fire-resistant cable is that the cable exhibits a maximum peak optical density of 0.5 or less, an average optical density of 0.15 or less, and a maximum flame spread distance of 1.52 m (5 ft) or less when tested in accordance with NFPA 262, *Standard Method of Test for Flame Travel and Smoke of Wires and Cables for Use in Air Handling Spaces.*

(B) Type CATVR. Type CATVR community antenna television riser cable shall be listed as being suitable for use in a vertical run in a shaft or from floor to floor and shall also be listed as having fire-resistant characteristics capable of preventing the carrying of fire from floor to floor.

FPN: One method of defining fire-resistant characteristics capable of preventing the carrying of fire from floor to floor is that the cables pass the requirements of ANSI/UL 1666-2002, *Standard Test for Flame Propagation Height of Electrical and Optical-Fiber Cable Installed Vertically in Shafts.*

(C) Type CATV. Type CATV community antenna television cable shall be listed as being suitable for general-purpose CATV use, with the exception of risers and plenums, and shall also be listed as being resistant to the spread of fire.

FPN: One method of defining *resistant to the spread of fire* is that the cables do not spread fire to the top of the tray in the vertical-tray flame test in ANSI/UL 1581-1991, *Reference Standard for Electrical Wires, Cables and Flexible Cords.*

Another method of defining *resistant to the spread of fire* is for the damage (char length) not to exceed 1.5 m (4 ft 11 in.) when performing the vertical flame test for cables in cable trays, as described in CSA C22.2 No. 0.3-M-1985, *Test Methods for Electrical Wires and Cables.*

(D) Type CATVX. Type CATVX limited-use community antenna television cable shall be listed as being suitable for use in dwellings and for use in raceway and shall also be listed as being resistant to flame spread.

FPN: One method of determining that cable is resistant to flame spread is by testing the cable to the VW-1 (vertical-wire) flame test in ANSI/UL 1581-1991, *Reference Standard for Electrical Wires, Cables and Flexible Cords.*

820.182 CATV Raceways. CATV raceways shall be listed in accordance with 820.182(A) through 820.182(C).

(A) Plenum CATV Raceways. Plenum CATV raceways shall be listed for use in other spaces used for environmental air and shall also be listed as having adequate fire-resistant and low smoke-producing characteristics.

FPN: One method of defining that an optical fiber raceway is a low smoke producing raceway and a fire-resistant raceway is that the raceway exhibits a maximum peak optical density of 0.5 or less, an average optical density of 0.15 or less, and a maximum flame spread distance of 1.52 m (5 ft) or less when tested in accordance with the plenum test in UL 2024, *Standard for Optical-Fiber Cable Raceway.*

(B) Riser CATV Raceways. Riser CATV raceways shall be listed for use in risers and shall also be listed as having adequate fire-resistant characteristics capable of preventing the carrying of fire from floor to floor.

FPN: One method of defining fire-resistant characteristics capable of preventing the carrying of fire from floor to floor is that the raceways pass the requirements of the Test for Flame Propagation (Riser) in UL 2024, *Standard for Optical-Fiber Cable Raceway.*

(C) General-Purpose CATV Raceways. General purpose CATV raceways shall be listed suitable for general-purpose use and shall also be listed as being resistant to the spread of fire.

FPN: One method of defining resistance to the spread of fire is that the raceway pass the requirements of the Vertical-Tray Flame Test (General Use) in UL 2024, *Standard for Optical-Fiber Cable Raceway.*

ARTICLE 830
Network-Powered Broadband Communications Systems

I. General

830.1 Scope. This article covers network-powered broadband communications systems that provide any combination of voice, audio, video, data, and interactive services through a network interface unit.

FPN No. 1: A typical basic system configuration includes a cable supplying power and broadband signal to a network interface unit that converts the broadband signal to the component signals. Typical cables are coaxial cable with both broadband signal and power on the center conductor, composite metallic cable with a coaxial member for the broadband signal and a twisted pair for power, and composite optical fiber cable with a pair of conductors for power. Larger systems may also include network components such as amplifiers that require network power.

FPN No. 2: See 90.2(B)(4) for installations of broadband communications systems that are not covered.

830.2 Definitions. See Article 100. For purposes of this article, the following additional definitions apply.

Abandoned Network-Powered Broadband Communications Cable. Installed network-powered broadband communications cable that is not terminated at equipment other than a connector and not identified for future use with a tag.

Block. A square or portion of a city, town, or village enclosed by streets, including the alleys so enclosed but not any street.

Exposed to Accidental Contact with Electrical Light or Power Conductors. A circuit in such a position that, in case of failure of supports or insulation, contact with another circuit may result.

Fault Protection Device. An electronic device that is intended for the protection of personnel and functions under fault conditions, such as network-powered broadband communications cable short or open circuit, to limit the current or voltage, or both, for a low-power network-powered broadband communications circuit and provide acceptable protection from electric shock.

Network Interface Unit (NIU). A device that converts a broadband signal into component voice, audio, video, data, and interactive services signals. The NIU provides isolation between the network power and the premises signal circuits. The NIU may also contain primary and secondary protectors.

Network-Powered Broadband Communications Circuit. The circuit extending from the communications utility's serving terminal or tap up to and including the NIU.

> FPN: A typical single-family network-powered communications circuit consists of a communications drop or communications service cable and an NIU and includes the communications utility's serving terminal or tap where it is not under the exclusive control of the communications utility.

Point of Entrance. The point within a building at which the cable emerges from an external wall, from a concrete floor slab, or from a rigid metal conduit or an intermediate metal conduit grounded to an electrode in accordance with 830.100(B).

Premises Wiring. The circuits located on the user side of the network interface unit.

830.3 Other Articles. Circuits and equipment shall comply with 830.3(A) through 830.3(E).

(A) Spread of Fire or Products of Combustion. Section 300.21 shall apply. The accessible portion of abandoned network-powered broadband communications cables shall be removed.

(B) Ducts, Plenums, and Other Air-Handling Spaces. Section 300.22 shall apply where installed in ducts, plenums, or other spaces used for environmental air.

Exception: As permitted in 830.154(B).

(C) Equipment in Other Space Used for Environmental Air. Section 300.22(C) shall apply.

(D) Output Circuits. As appropriate for the services provided, the output circuits derived from the network interface unit shall comply with the requirements of the following:

(1) Installations of communications circuits — Article 800

(2) Installations of community antenna television and radio distribution circuits — Article 820

Exception: 830.90(B)(3) shall apply where protection is provided in the output of the NIU.

(3) Installations of optical fiber cables — Article 770

(4) Installations of Class 2 and Class 3 circuits — Article 725

(5) Installations of power-limited fire alarm circuits — Article 760

(E) Hazardous (Classified) Locations. Network-powered broadband communications circuits and equipment installed in a location that is classified in accordance with Article 500 shall comply with the applicable requirements of Chapter 5.

830.15 Power Limitations. Network-powered broadband communications systems shall be classified as having low or medium power sources as defined in Table 830.15.

Table 830.15 Limitations for Network-Powered Broadband Communications Systems

Network Power Source	Low	Medium
Circuit voltage, V_{max} (volts)[1]	0–100	0–150
Power limitation, VA_{max} (volt-amperes)[1]	250	250
Current limitation, I_{max} (amperes)[1]	$1000/V_{max}$	$1000/V_{max}$
Maximum power rating (volt-amperes)	100	100
Maximum voltage rating (volts)	100	150
Maximum overcurrent protection (amperes)[2]	$100/V_{max}$	NA

[1]V_{max}, I_{max}, and VA_{max} are determined with the current-limiting impedance in the circuit (not bypassed) as follows:

V_{max}—Maximum system voltage regardless of load with rated input applied.

I_{max}—Maximum system current under any noncapacitive load, including short circuit, and with overcurrent protection bypassed if used. I_{max} limits apply after 1 minute of operation.

VA_{max}—Maximum volt-ampere output after 1 minute of operation regardless of load and overcurrent protection bypassed if used.

[2]Overcurrent protection is not required where the current-limiting device provides equivalent current limitation and the current-limiting device does not reset until power or the load is removed.

830.21 Access to Electrical Equipment Behind Panels Designed to Allow Access. Access to electrical equipment shall not be denied by an accumulation of wires and cables that prevents removal of panels, including suspended ceiling panels.

830.24 Mechanical Execution of Work. Network-powered broadband communications circuits and equipment shall be installed in a neat and workmanlike manner. Cables installed exposed on the surface of ceilings and sidewalls shall be supported by the building structure in such a manner that the cable will not be damaged by normal building use. Such cables shall be secured by straps, staples, hangers, or similar fittings designed and installed so as not to damage the cable. The installation shall also conform with 300.4(D) and 300.11.

> FPN: Accepted industry practices are described in ANSI/NECA/BICSI 568–2001, *Standard for Installing Commercial Building Telecommunications Cabling*, and other ANSI-approved installation standards.

II. Cables Outside and Entering Buildings

830.40 Entrance Cables. Network-powered broadband communications cables located outside and entering buildings shall comply with 830.40(A) and 830.40(B).

(A) Medium Power Circuits. Medium power network-powered broadband communications circuits located outside and entering buildings shall be installed using Type BMU, Type BM, or Type BMR network-powered broadband communications medium power cables.

(B) Low-Power Circuits. Low-power network-powered broadband communications circuits located outside and entering buildings shall be installed using Type BLU or Type BLX low-power network-powered broadband communications cables. Cables shown in Table 830.133 shall be permitted to substitute.

Exception: Outdoor community antenna television and radio distribution system coaxial cables installed prior to January 1, 2000, and installed in accordance with Article 820, shall be permitted for low-power-type, network-powered broadband communications circuits.

830.44 Aerial Cables. Aerial network-powered broadband communications cables shall comply with 830.44(A) through 830.44(I).

> FPN: For additional information regarding overhead wires and cables, see ANSI C2-2002, *National Electric Safety Code*, Part 2, Safety Rules For Overhead Lines.

(A) On Poles. Where practicable, network-powered broadband communications cables on poles shall be located below the electric light, power, Class 1, or non–power-limited fire alarm circuit conductors and shall not be attached to a crossarm that carries electric light or power conductors.

(B) Climbing Space. The climbing space through network-powered broadband communications cables shall comply with the requirements of 225.14(D).

(C) Lead-in Clearance. Lead-in or aerial-drop network-powered broadband communications cables from a pole or other support, including the point of initial attachment to a building or structure, shall be kept away from electric light, power, Class 1, or non–power-limited fire alarm circuit conductors so as to avoid the possibility of accidental contact.

Exception: Where proximity to electric light, power, Class 1, or non–power-limited fire alarm circuit service conductors cannot be avoided, the installation shall be such as to provide clearances of not less than 300 mm (12 in.) from light, power, Class 1, or non–power-limited fire alarm circuit service drops. The clearance requirement shall apply to all points along the drop, and it shall increase to 1.02 m (40 in.) at the pole.

(D) Clearance from Ground. Overhead spans of network-powered broadband communication cables shall conform to not less than the following:

(1) 2.9 m (9.5 ft) — above finished grade, sidewalks, or from any platform or projection from which they might be reached and accessible to pedestrians only

(2) 3.5 m (11.5 ft) — over residential property and driveways, and those commercial areas not subject to truck traffic

(3) 4.7 m (15.5 ft) — over public streets, alleys, roads, parking areas subject to truck traffic, driveways on other than residential property, and other land traversed by vehicles such as cultivated, grazing, forest, and orchard

> FPN: These clearances have been specifically chosen to correlate with ANSI C2-2002, *National Electrical Safety Code*, Table 232-1, which provides for clearances of wires, conductors, and cables above ground and roadways, rather than using the clearances referenced in 225.18. Because Article 800 and Article 820 have had no required clearances, the communications industry has used the clearances from the NESC for their installed cable plant.

(E) Over Pools. Clearance of network-powered broadband communications cable in any direction from the water level, edge of pool, base of diving platform, or anchored raft shall comply with those clearances in 680.8.

(F) Above Roofs. Network-powered broadband communications cables shall have a vertical clearance of not less than 2.5 m (8 ft) from all points of roofs above which they pass.

Exception No. 1: Auxiliary buildings such as garages and the like.

Exception No. 2: A reduction in clearance above only the overhanging portion of the roof to not less than 450 mm (18 in.) shall be permitted if (1) not more than 1.2 m (4 ft) of the broadband communications drop cables pass above the roof overhang, and (2) they are terminated at a through-the-roof raceway or support.

Exception No. 3: Where the roof has a slope of not less than 100 mm in 300 mm (4 in. in 12 in.), a reduction in clearance to not less than 900 mm (3 ft) shall be permitted.

(G) Final Spans. Final spans of network-powered broadband communications cables without an outer jacket shall be permitted to be attached to the building, but they shall be kept not less than 900 mm (3 ft) from windows that are designed to be opened, doors, porches, balconies, ladders, stairs, fire escapes, or similar locations.

Exception: Conductors run above the top level of a window shall be permitted to be less than the 900-mm (3-ft) requirement above.

Overhead network-powered broadband communications cables shall not be installed beneath openings through which materials may be moved, such as openings in farm and commercial buildings, and shall not be installed where they will obstruct entrance to these building openings.

(H) Between Buildings. Network-powered broadband communications cables extending between buildings and also the supports or attachment fixtures shall be acceptable for the purpose and shall have sufficient strength to withstand the loads to which they may be subjected.

Exception: Where a network-powered broadband communications cable does not have sufficient strength to be self-supporting, it shall be attached to a supporting messenger cable that, together with the attachment fixtures or supports, shall be acceptable for the purpose and shall have sufficient strength to withstand the loads to which they may be subjected.

(I) On Buildings. Where attached to buildings, network-powered broadband communications cables shall be securely fastened in such a manner that they are separated from other conductors in accordance with 830.44(I)(1) through (I)(4).

(1) Electric Light or Power. The network-powered broadband communications cable shall have a separation of at least 100 mm (4 in.) from electric light, power, Class 1, or non–power-limited fire alarm circuit conductors not in raceway or cable, or be permanently separated from conductors of the other system by a continuous and firmly fixed nonconductor in addition to the insulation on the wires.

(2) Other Communications Systems. Network-powered broadband communications cables shall be installed so that there will be no unnecessary interference in the maintenance of the separate systems. In no case shall the conductors, cables, messenger strand, or equipment of one system cause abrasion to the conductors, cables, messenger strand, or equipment of any other system.

(3) Lightning Conductors. Where practicable, a separation of at least 1.8 m (6 ft) shall be maintained between any network-powered broadband communications cable and lightning conductors.

(4) Protection from Damage. Network-powered broadband communications cables attached to buildings and located within 2.5 m (8 ft) of finished grade shall be protected by enclosures, raceways, or other approved means.

Exception: A low-power network-powered broadband communications circuit that is equipped with a listed fault protection device, appropriate to the network-powered broadband communications cable used, and located on the network side of the network-powered broadband communications cable being protected.

830.47 Underground Circuits Entering Buildings.

(A) Underground Systems. Underground network-powered broadband communications cables in a duct, pedestal, handhole enclosure, or manhole that contains electric light, power conductors, non–power-limited fire alarm circuit conductors, or Class 1 circuits shall be in a section permanently separated from such conductors by means of a suitable barrier.

(B) Direct-Buried Cables and Raceways. Direct-buried network-powered broadband communications cables shall be separated at least 300 mm (12 in.) from conductors of any light, power, non–power-limited fire alarm circuit conductors or Class 1 circuit.

Exception No. 1: Where electric service conductors or network-powered broadband communications cables are installed in raceways or have metal cable armor.

Exception No. 2: Where electric light or power branch-circuit or feeder conductors, non–power-limited fire alarm circuit conductors, or Class 1 circuit conductors are installed in a raceway or in metal-sheathed, metal-clad, or Type UF or Type USE cables; or the network-powered broadband communications cables have metal cable armor or are installed in a raceway.

(C) Mechanical Protection. Direct-buried cable, conduit, or other raceways shall be installed to meet the minimum cover requirements of Table 830.47. In addition, direct-buried cables emerging from the ground shall be protected by enclosures, raceways, or other approved means extending from the minimum cover distance required by Table 830.47 below grade to a point at least 2.5 m (8 ft) above finished grade. In no case shall the protection be required to exceed 450 mm (18 in.) below finished grade. Type BMU and BLU direct-buried cables emerging from the ground shall be installed in rigid metal conduit, intermediate metal conduit, rigid nonmetallic conduit, or other approved means extending from the minimum cover distance required by Table 830.47 below grade to the point of entrance.

Exception: A low-power network-powered broadband communications circuit that is equipped with a listed fault protection device, appropriate to the network-powered broadband communications cable used, and located on the network side of the network-powered broadband communications cable being protected.

(D) Pools. Cables located under the pool or within the area extending 1.5 m (5 ft) horizontally from the inside wall of the pool shall meet those clearances and requirements specified in 680.10.

Table 830.47 Network-Powered Broadband Communications Systems Minimum Cover Requirements (*Cover* is the shortest distance measured between a point on the top surface of any direct-buried cable, conduit, or other raceway and the top surface of finished grade, concrete, or similar cover.)

Location of Wiring Method or Circuit	Direct Burial Cables		Rigid Metal Conduit or Intermediate Metal Conduit		Nonmetallic Raceways Listed for Direct Burial; Without Concrete Encasement or Other Approved Raceways	
	mm	in.	mm	in.	mm	in.
All locations not specified below	450	18	150	6	300	12
In trench below 50-mm (2-in.) thick concrete or equivalent	300	12	150	6	150	6
Under a building (in raceway only)	0	0	0	0	0	0
Under minimum of 100-mm (4-in.) thick concrete exterior slab with no vehicular traffic and the slab extending not less than 150 mm (6 in.) beyond the underground installation	300	12	100	4	100	4
One- and two-family dwelling driveways and outdoor parking areas and used only for dwelling-related purposes	300	12	300	12	300	12

Notes:
1. Raceways approved for burial only where concrete encased shall require a concrete envelope not less than 50 mm (2 in.) thick.
2. Lesser depths shall be permitted where cables rise for terminations or splices or where access is otherwise required.
3. Where solid rock is encountered, all wiring shall be installed in metal or nonmetallic raceway permitted for direct burial. The raceways shall be covered by a minimum of 50 mm (2 in.) of concrete extending down to rock.
4. Low-power network-powered broadband communications circuits using directly buried community antenna television and radio distribution system coaxial cables that were installed outside and entering buildings prior to January 1, 2000, in accordance with Article 820 shall be permitted where buried to a minimum depth of 300 mm (12 in.).

III. Protection

830.90 Primary Electrical Protection.

(A) Application. Primary electrical protection shall be provided on all network-powered broadband communications conductors that are neither grounded nor interrupted and are run partly or entirely in aerial cable not confined within a block. Also, primary electrical protection shall be provided on all aerial or underground network-powered broadband communications conductors that are neither grounded nor interrupted and are located within the block containing the building served so as to be exposed to lightning or accidental contact with electric light or power conductors operating at over 300 volts to ground.

Exception: Where electrical protection is provided on the derived circuit(s) (output side of the NIU) in accordance with 830.90(B)(3).

FPN No. 1: On network-powered broadband communications conductors not exposed to lightning or accidental contact with power conductors, providing primary electrical protection in accordance with this article helps protect against other hazards, such as ground potential rise caused by power fault currents, and above-normal voltages induced by fault currents on power circuits in proximity to the network-powered broadband communications conductors.

FPN No. 2: Network-powered broadband communications circuits are considered to have a lightning exposure unless one or more of the following conditions exist:

(1) Circuits in large metropolitan areas where buildings are close together and sufficiently high to intercept lightning.

(2) Areas having an average of five or fewer thunderstorm days per year and earth resistivity of less than 100 ohm-meters. Such areas are found along the Pacific coast.

(1) Fuseless Primary Protectors. Fuseless-type primary protectors shall be permitted where power fault currents on all protected conductors in the cable are safely limited to a value no greater than the current-carrying capacity of the primary protector and of the primary protector grounding conductor.

(2) Fused Primary Protectors. Where the requirements listed in 830.90(A)(1) are not met, fused-type primary protectors shall be used. Fused-type primary protectors shall consist of an arrester connected between each conductor to be protected and ground, a fuse in series with each conductor to be protected, and an appropriate mounting arrangement. Fused primary protector terminals shall be marked to indicate line, instrument, and ground, as applicable.

(B) Location. The location of the primary protector, where required, shall comply with (B)(1), (B)(2), or (B)(3):

(1) A listed primary protector shall be applied on each network-powered broadband communications cable external to and on the network side of the network interface unit.

(2) The primary protector function shall be an integral part of and contained in the network interface unit. The network interface unit shall be listed as being suitable for application with network-powered broadband communications systems and shall have an external marking indicating that it contains primary electrical protection.

(3) The primary protector(s) shall be provided on the derived circuit(s) (output side of the NIU), and the combination of the NIU and the protector(s) shall be listed as being suitable for application with network-powered broadband communications systems.

A primary protector, whether provided integrally or external to the network interface unit, shall be located as close as practicable to the point of entrance.

For purposes of this section, a network interface unit and any externally provided primary protectors located at mobile home service equipment located in sight from and not more than 9.0 m (30 ft) from the exterior wall of the mobile home it serves, or at a mobile home disconnecting means grounded in accordance with 250.32 and located in sight from and not more than 9.0 m (30 ft) from the exterior wall of the mobile home it serves, shall be considered to meet the requirements of this section.

FPN: Selecting a network interface unit and primary protector location to achieve the shortest practicable primary protector grounding conductor helps limit potential differences between communications circuits and other metallic systems.

(C) Hazardous (Classified) Locations. The primary protector or equipment providing the primary protection function shall not be located in any hazardous (classified) location as defined in Article 500 or in the vicinity of easily ignitible material.

Exception: As permitted in 501.150, 502.150, and 503.150.

830.93 Grounding or Interruption of Metallic Members of Network-Powered Broadband Communications Cables. The shields of network-powered broadband communications cables used for communications or powering shall be grounded at the building as close as practicable to the point of entrance or attachment of the NIU. Metallic cable members not used for communications or powering shall be grounded or interrupted by an insulating joint or equivalent device as close as practicable to the point of entrance or attachment of the NIU.

For purposes of this section, grounding or interruption of network-powered broadband communications cable metallic

members installed at mobile home service equipment located in sight from and no more than 9.0 m (30 ft) from the exterior wall of the mobile home it serves, or at a mobile home disconnecting means grounded in accordance with 250.32 and located in sight from and not more than 9.0 m (30 ft) from the exterior wall of the mobile home it serves, shall be considered to meet the requirements of this section.

FPN: Selecting a grounding location to achieve the shortest practicable grounding conductor helps limit potential differences between the network-powered broadband communications circuits and other metallic systems.

IV. Grounding Methods

830.100 Cable, Network Interface Unit, and Primary Protector Grounding. Network interface units containing protectors, NIUs with metallic enclosures, primary protectors, and the metallic members of the network-powered broadband communications cable that are intended to be grounded shall be grounded as specified in 830.100(A) through 830.100(D).

(A) Grounding Conductor.

(1) Insulation. The grounding conductor shall be insulated and shall be listed as suitable for the purpose.

(2) Material. The grounding conductor shall be copper or other corrosion-resistant conductive material, stranded or solid.

(3) Size. The grounding conductor shall not be smaller than 14 AWG and shall have a current-carrying capacity approximately equal to that of the grounded metallic member(s) and protected conductor(s) of the network-powered broadband communications cable. The grounding conductor shall not be required to exceed 6 AWG.

(4) Length. The grounding conductor shall be as short as practicable. In one-family and multifamily dwellings, the grounding conductor shall be as short as permissible, not to exceed 6.0 m (20 ft) in length.

FPN: Similar grounding conductor length limitations applied at apartment buildings and commercial buildings will help to reduce voltages that may be developed between the building's power and communications systems during lightning events.

Exception: In one- and two-family dwellings where it is not practicable to achieve an overall maximum grounding conductor length of 6.0 m (20 ft), a separate communications ground rod meeting the minimum dimensional criteria of 830.100(B)(2)(2) shall be driven, and the grounding conductor shall be connected to the communications ground rod in accordance with 830.100(C). The communications ground rod shall be bonded to the power grounding electrode system in accordance with 830.100(D).

(5) Run in Straight Line. The grounding conductor shall be run to the grounding electrode in as straight a line as practicable.

(6) Physical Protection. Where subject to physical damage, the grounding conductor shall be adequately protected. Where the grounding conductor is run in a metal raceway, both ends of the raceway shall be bonded to the grounding conductor or the same terminal or electrode to which the grounding conductor is connected.

(B) Electrode. The grounding conductor shall be connected as follows.

(1) In Buildings or Structures with Grounding Means. To the nearest accessible location on the following:

(1) The building or structure grounding electrode system as covered in 250.50

(2) The grounded interior metal water piping system, within 1.5 m (5 ft) from its point of entrance to the building, as covered in 250.52

(3) The power service accessible means external to enclosures as covered in 250.94

(4) The metallic power service raceway

(5) The service equipment enclosure

(6) The grounding electrode conductor or the grounding electrode metal enclosure, or

(7) The grounding conductor or the grounding electrode of a building or structure disconnecting means that is grounded to an electrode as covered in 250.32

For purposes of this section, the mobile home service equipment or the mobile home disconnecting means, as described in 830.93, shall be considered accessible.

(2) In Buildings or Structures Without Grounding Means. If the building or structure served has no grounding means, as described in (B)(1), the grounding conductor shall be connected to either of the following:

(1) To any one of the individual electrodes described in 250.52(A)(1), (A)(2), (A)(3), or (A)(4)

(2) If the building or structure served has no grounding means, as described in 830.100(B)(1) or (B)(2)(1), to an effectively grounded metal structure or to a ground rod or pipe not less than 1.5 m (5 ft) in length and 12.7 mm (½ in.) in diameter, driven, where practicable, into permanently damp earth and separated from lightning conductors as covered in 800.53 and at least 1.8 m (6 ft) from electrodes of other systems. Steam or hot water pipes or lightning-rod conductors shall not be employed as electrodes for protectors, NIUs with integral protection, grounded metallic members, NIUs with metallic enclosures, and other equipment.

(C) Electrode Connection. Connections to grounding electrodes shall comply with 250.70.

(D) Bonding of Electrodes. A bonding jumper not smaller than 6 AWG copper or equivalent shall be connected between the network-powered broadband communications system grounding electrode and the power grounding electrode system at the building or structure served where separate electrodes are used.

Exception: At mobile homes as covered in 830.106.

FPN No. 1: See 250.60 for use of lightning rods.

FPN No. 2: Bonding together of all separate electrodes limits potential differences between them and between their associated wiring systems.

830.106 Bonding and Grounding at Mobile Homes.

(A) Grounding. Where there is no mobile home service equipment located in sight from and not more than 9.0 m (30 ft) from the exterior wall of the mobile home it serves, or there is no mobile home disconnecting means grounded in accordance with 250.32 and located within sight from and not more than 9.0 m (30 ft) from the exterior wall of the mobile home it serves, the network-powered broadband communications cable, network interface unit, and primary protector ground shall be installed in accordance with 830.100(B)(2).

(B) Bonding. The network-powered broadband communications cable grounding terminal, network interface unit grounding terminal, if present, and primary protector grounding terminal shall be bonded together with a copper bonding conductor not smaller than 12 AWG. The network-powered broadband communications cable grounding terminal, network interface unit grounding terminal, primary protector grounding terminal, or the grounding electrode shall be bonded to the metal frame or available grounding terminal of the mobile home with a copper bonding conductor not smaller than 12 AWG under any of the following conditions:

(1) Where there is no mobile home service equipment or disconnecting means as in 830.106(A)

(2) Where the mobile home is supplied by cord and plug

V. Wiring Methods Within Buildings

830.133 Installation of Network-Powered Broadband Communications Cables and Equipment. Cable and equipment installations within buildings shall comply with 830.133(A) through 830.133(D), as applicable.

(A) Separation of Conductors.

(1) In Raceways and Enclosures.

(a) Low and Medium Power Network-Powered Broadband Communications Circuit Cables. Low and medium power network-powered broadband communications cables shall be permitted in the same raceway or enclosure.

(b) Low-Power Network-Powered Broadband Communications Circuit Cables. Low-power network-powered broadband communications cables shall be permitted in the same raceway or enclosure with jacketed cables of any of the following circuits:

(1) Class 2 and Class 3 remote-control, signaling, and power-limited circuits in compliance with Article 725

(2) Power-limited fire alarm systems in compliance with Article 760

(3) Communications circuits in compliance with Article 800

(4) Nonconductive and conductive optical fiber cables in compliance with Article 770

(5) Community antenna television and radio distribution systems in compliance with Article 820

(c) Medium Power Network-Powered Broadband Communications Circuit Cables. Medium power network-powered broadband communications cables shall not be permitted in the same raceway or enclosure with conductors of any of the following circuits:

(1) Class 2 and Class 3 remote-control, signaling, and power-limited circuits in compliance with Article 725

(2) Power-limited fire alarm systems in compliance with Article 760

(3) Communications circuits in compliance with Article 800

(4) Conductive optical fiber cables in compliance with Article 770

(5) Community antenna television and radio distribution systems in compliance with Article 820

(d) Electric Light, Power, Class 1, Non–Powered Broadband Communications Circuit Cables. Network-powered broadband communications cable shall not be placed in any raceway, compartment, outlet box, junction box, or similar fittings with conductors of electric light, power, Class 1, or non–power-limited fire alarm circuit cables.

Exception No. 1: Where all of the conductors of electric light, power, Class 1, non–power-limited fire alarm circuits are separated from all of the network-powered broadband communications cables by a permanent barrier or listed divider.

Exception No. 2: Power circuit conductors in outlet boxes, junction boxes, or similar fittings or compartments where such conductors are introduced solely for power supply to the network-powered broadband communications system distribution equipment. The power circuit conductors shall be routed within the enclosure to maintain a minimum 6-mm (0.25-in.) separation from network-powered broadband communications cables.

(2) Other Applications. Network-powered broadband communications cable shall be separated at least 50 mm (2 in.) from conductors of any electric light, power, Class 1, and non–power-limited fire alarm circuits.

Exception No. 1: Where either (1) all of the conductors of electric light, power, Class 1, and non–power-limited fire alarm circuits are in a raceway, or in metal-sheathed, metal-clad, nonmetallic-sheathed, Type AC, or Type UF cables, or (2) all of the network-powered broadband communications cables are encased in raceway.

Exception No. 2: Where the network-powered broadband communications cables are permanently separated from the conductors of electric light, power, Class 1, and non-power-limited fire alarm circuits by a continuous and firmly fixed nonconductor, such as porcelain tubes or flexible tubing, in addition to the insulation on the wire.

(B) Support of Conductors. Raceways shall be used for their intended purpose. Network-powered broadband communications cables shall not be strapped, taped, or attached by any means to the exterior of any conduit or raceway as a means of support.

(C) Cable Substitutions. The substitutions for network-powered broadband cables listed in Table 830.133 shall be permitted. All cables in Table 830.133, other than network-powered broadband cables, shall be coaxial cables.

Table 830.133 Cable Substitutions

Cable Type	Permitted Cable Substitutions
BM	BMR
BLP	CMP, CL3P
BLR	CMP, CL3P, CMR, CL3R, BLP, BMR
BL	CMP, CMR, CM, CMG, CL3P, CL3R, CL3, BMR, BM, BLP, BLR
BLX	CMP, CMR, CM, CMG, CMX, CL3P, CL3R, CL3, CL3X, BMR, BM, BLP, BRP, BL

(D) Installation and Use. Section 110.3(B) shall apply.

830.151 Medium Power Network-Powered Broadband Communications System Wiring Methods. Medium power network-powered broadband communications systems shall be installed within buildings using listed Type BM or Type BMR, network-powered broadband communications medium power cables.

(A) Ducts, Plenums, and Other Air-Handling Spaces. Section 300.22 shall apply.

(B) Riser. Cables installed in vertical runs and penetrating more than one floor, or cables installed in vertical runs in a shaft, shall be Type BMR. Floor penetrations requiring Type BMR shall contain only cables suitable for riser or plenum use.

Exception No. 1: Type BM cables encased in metal raceway or located in a fireproof shaft that has firestops at each floor.

Exception No. 2: Type BM cables in one- and two-family dwellings.

(C) Other Wiring. Cables installed in locations other than the locations covered in 830.151(A) and 830.151(B) shall be Type BM.

Exception: Type BMU cable where the cable enters the building from the outside and is run in rigid metal conduit or intermediate metal conduit, and such conduits are grounded to an electrode in accordance with 830.100(B).

830.154 Low-Power Network-Powered Broadband Communications System Wiring Methods. Low-power network-powered broadband communications systems shall comply with any of the requirements of 830.154(A) through 830.154(D).

(A) In Buildings. Low-power network-powered broadband communications systems shall be installed within buildings using listed Type BLX, Type BL, Type BLR, or Type BLP network-powered broadband communications low-power cables.

(B) Ducts, Plenums, and Other Air-Handling Spaces. Cables installed in ducts, plenums, and other spaces used for environmental air shall be Type BLP. Type BLX cable installed in compliance with 300.22 shall be permitted.

(C) Riser. Cables installed in risers shall comply with any of the requirements in 830.154(C)(1), (C)(2), or (C)(3).

(1) Cables in Vertical Runs. Cables installed in vertical runs and penetrating more than one floor, or cables installed in vertical runs in a shaft, shall be Type BLP, BLR, or BMR. Floor penetrations requiring Type BMR or BLR shall contain only cables suitable for riser or plenum use.

(2) Metal Raceways or Fireproof Shafts. Type BLX cables shall be permitted to be encased in a metal raceway or located in a fireproof shaft having firestops at each floor.

(3) One- and Two-Family Dwellings. Type BLX or BL cables less than 10 mm (0.375 in.) in diameter shall be permitted in one- and two-family dwellings.

(D) Other Wiring. Cables installed in locations other than those covered in 830.154(A), (B), and (C) shall comply with the requirements of 830.154(D)(1) through (D)(5).

(1) General. Type BLP, BL, or BM shall be permitted.

(2) In Raceways. Type BLX shall be permitted to be installed in a raceway.

(3) Type BLU Cable. Type BLU cable entering the building from outside shall be permitted to be run in rigid metal conduit or intermediate metal conduit. Such conduits shall be grounded to an electrode in accordance with 830.100(B)

(4) One- and Two-Family Dwellings. Type BLX or BL cables less than 10 mm (0.375 in.) in diameter shall be permitted to be installed in one- and two-family dwellings.

(5) Type BLX Cable. Type BLX cable entering the building from outside and terminated at a grounding block or a primary protection location shall be permitted to be installed, provided that the length of cable within the building does not exceed 15 m (50 ft).

> FPN: This provision limits the length of Type BLX cable to 15 m (50 ft), while 830.90(B) requires that the primary protector, or NIU with integral protection, be located as close as practicable to the point at which the cable enters the building. Therefore, in installations requiring a primary protector, or NIU with integral protection, Type BLX cable may not be permitted to extend 15 m (50 ft) into the building if it is practicable to place the primary protector closer than 15 m (50 ft) to the entrance point.

830.157 Protection Against Physical Damage. Section 300.4 shall apply.

830.160 Bends. Bends in network broadband cable shall be made so as not to damage the cable.

VI. Listing Requirements

830.179 Network-Powered Broadband Communications Equipment and Cables. Network-powered broadband communications equipment and cables shall be listed as suitable for the purpose.

Exception No. 1: This listing requirement shall not apply to community antenna television and radio distribution system coaxial cables that were installed prior to January 1, 2000, in accordance with Article 820 and are used for low-power network-powered broadband communications circuits.

Exception No. 2: Substitute cables for network-powered broadband communications cables shall be permitted as shown in Table 830.133.

(A) Listing and Marking. Listing and marking of network-powered broadband communications cables shall comply with 830.179(A)(1) or (A)(2).

(1) Type BMU, Type BM, and Type BMR Cables. Network-powered broadband communications medium power underground cable, Type BMU; network-powered broadband communications medium power cable, Type BM; and network-powered broadband communications medium power riser cable, Type BMR, shall be factory-assembled cables consisting of a jacketed coaxial cable, a jacketed combination of coaxial cable and multiple individual conductors, or a jacketed combination of an optical fiber cable and multiple individual conductors. The insulation for the individual conductors shall be rated for 300 volts minimum. Cables intended for outdoor use shall be listed as suitable for the application. Cables shall be marked in accordance with 310.11. Type BMU cables shall be jacketed and listed as being suitable for outdoor underground use. Type BM cables shall be listed as being suitable for general-purpose use, with the exception of risers and plenums, and shall also be listed as being resistant to the spread of fire. Type BMR cables shall be listed as being suitable for use in a vertical run in a shaft or from floor to floor and shall also be listed as having fire-resistant characteristics capable of preventing the carrying of fire from floor to floor.

FPN No. 1: One method of defining *resistant to spread of fire* is that the cables do not spread fire to the top of the tray in the vertical tray flame test in ANSI/UL 1581-1991, *Reference Standard for Electrical Wires, Cables and Flexible Cords.* Another method of defining *resistant to the spread of fire* is for the damage (char length) not to exceed 1.5 m (4 ft 11 in.) when performing the CSA vertical flame test for cables in cable trays, as described in CSA C22.2 No. 0.3-M-1985, *Test Methods for Electrical Wires and Cables.*

FPN No. 2: One method of defining fire-resistant characteristics capable of preventing the carrying of fire from floor to floor is that the cables pass the requirements of ANSI/UL 1666-2002, *Standard Test for Flame Propagation Height of Electrical and Optical-Fiber Cable Installed Vertically in Shafts.*

(2) Type BLU, Type BLX, Type BL, and Type BLP Cables. Network-powered broadband communications low-power underground cable, Type BLU; limited use network-powered broadband communications low-power cable, Type BLX; network-powered broadband communications low-power cable, Type BL; network-powered broadband communications low-power riser cable, Type BLR; and network-powered broadband communications low-power plenum cable, Type BLP, shall be factory-assembled cables consisting of a jacketed coaxial cable, a jacketed combination of coaxial cable and multiple individual conductors, or a jacketed combination of an optical fiber cable and multiple individual conductors. The insulation for the individual conductors shall be rated for 300 volts minimum. Cables intended for outdoor use shall be listed as suitable for the application. Cables shall be marked in accordance with 310.11. Type BLU cables shall be jacketed and listed as being suitable for outdoor underground use. Type BLX limited-use cables shall be listed as being suitable for use outside, for use in dwellings, and for use in raceways and shall also be listed as being resistant to flame spread. Type BL cables shall be listed as being suitable for general-purpose use, with the exception of risers and plenums, and shall also be listed as being resistant to the spread of fire. Type BLR cables shall be listed as being suitable for use in a vertical run in a shaft or from floor to floor and shall also be listed as having fire-resistant characteristics capable of preventing the carrying of fire from floor to floor. Type BLP cables shall be listed as being suitable for use in ducts, plenums, and other spaces used for environmental air and shall also be listed as having adequate fire-resistant and low smoke-producing characteristics.

FPN No. 1: One method of determining that cable is resistant to flame spread is by testing the cable to VW-1 (vertical-wire) flame test in ANSI/UL 1581-1991, *Reference Standard for Electrical Wires, Cables and Flexible Cords.*

FPN No. 2: One method of defining *resistant to spread of fire* is that the cables do not spread fire to the top of the tray in the vertical tray flame test in ANSI/UL 1584-1991, *Reference Standard for Electrical Wires, Cables and Flexible Cords.*

FPN No. 3: One method of defining fire-resistant characteristics capable of preventing the carrying of fire from floor to floor is that the cables pass the requirements of ANSI/UL 1666-1997, *Standard Test for Flame Propagation Height of Electrical and Optical-Fiber Cable Installed Vertically in Shafts.*

FPN No. 4: One method of defining a cable that is low smoke-producing cable and fire-resistant cable is that the cable exhibits a maximum peak optical density of 0.5 or less, an average optical density of 0.15 or less, and a maximum flame spread distance of 1.52 m (5 ft) or less when tested in accordance with NFPA 262-1999, *Standard Method of Test for Flame Travel and Smoke of Wires and Cables for Use in Air Handling Spaces.*

Chapter 9 Tables

Table 1 Percent of Cross Section of Conduit and Tubing for Conductors

Number of Conductors	All Conductor Types
1	53
2	31
Over 2	40

FPN No. 1: Table 1 is based on common conditions of proper cabling and alignment of conductors where the length of the pull and the number of bends are within reasonable limits. It should be recognized that, for certain conditions, a larger size conduit or a lesser conduit fill should be considered.

FPN No. 2: When pulling three conductors or cables into a raceway, if the ratio of the raceway (inside diameter) to the conductor or cable (outside diameter) is between 2.8 and 3.2, jamming can occur. While jamming can occur when pulling four or more conductors or cables into a raceway, the probability is very low.

Notes to Tables

(1) See Annex C for the maximum number of conductors and fixture wires, all of the same size (total cross-sectional area including insulation) permitted in trade sizes of the applicable conduit or tubing.

(2) Table 1 applies only to complete conduit or tubing systems and is not intended to apply to sections of conduit or tubing used to protect exposed wiring from physical damage.

(3) Equipment grounding or bonding conductors, where installed, shall be included when calculating conduit or tubing fill. The actual dimensions of the equipment grounding or bonding conductor (insulated or bare) shall be used in the calculation.

(4) Where conduit or tubing nipples having a maximum length not to exceed 600 mm (24 in.) are installed between boxes, cabinets, and similar enclosures, the nipples shall be permitted to be filled to 60 percent of their total cross-sectional area, and 310.15(B)(2)(a) adjustment factors need not apply to this condition.

(5) For conductors not included in Chapter 9, such as multiconductor cables, the actual dimensions shall be used.

(6) For combinations of conductors of different sizes, use Table 5 and Table 5A for dimensions of conductors and Table 4 for the applicable conduit or tubing dimensions.

(7) When calculating the maximum number of conductors permitted in a conduit or tubing, all of the same size (total cross-sectional area including insulation), the next higher whole number shall be used to determine the maximum number of conductors permitted when the calculation results in a decimal of 0.8 or larger.

(8) Where bare conductors are permitted by other sections of this *Code*, the dimensions for bare conductors in Table 8 shall be permitted.

(9) A multiconductor cable of two or more conductors shall be treated as a single conductor for calculating percentage conduit fill area. For cables that have elliptical cross sections, the cross-sectional area calculation shall be based on using the major diameter of the ellipse as a circle diameter.

Table 2 Radius of Conduit and Tubing Bends

Conduit or Tubing Size		One Shot and Full Shoe Benders		Other Bends	
Metric Designator	Trade Size	mm	in.	mm	in.
16	½	101.6	4	101.6	4
21	¾	114.3	4½	127	5
27	1	146.05	5¾	152.4	6
35	1¼	184.15	7¼	203.2	8
41	1½	209.55	8¼	254	10
53	2	241.3	9½	304.8	12
63	2½	266.7	10½	381	15
78	3	330.2	13	457.2	18
91	3½	381	15	533.4	21
103	4	406.4	16	609.6	24
129	5	609.6	24	762	30
155	6	762	30	914.4	36

Table 4 Dimensions and Percent Area of Conduit and Tubing (Areas of Conduit or Tubing for the Combinations of Wires Permitted in Table 1, Chapter 9)

Article 358 — Electrical Metallic Tubing (EMT)

Metric Designator	Trade Size	Nominal Internal Diameter		Total Area 100%		60%		1 Wire 53%		2 Wires 31%		Over 2 Wires 40%	
		mm	in.	mm²	in.²	mm²	in.²	mm²	in.²	mm²	in.²	mm²	in.²
16	½	15.8	0.622	196	0.304	118	0.182	104	0.161	61	0.094	78	0.122
21	¾	20.9	0.824	343	0.533	206	0.320	182	0.283	106	0.165	137	0.213
27	1	26.6	1.049	556	0.864	333	0.519	295	0.458	172	0.268	222	0.346
35	1¼	35.1	1.380	968	1.496	581	0.897	513	0.793	300	0.464	387	0.598
41	1½	40.9	1.610	1314	2.036	788	1.221	696	1.079	407	0.631	526	0.814
53	2	52.5	2.067	2165	3.356	1299	2.013	1147	1.778	671	1.040	866	1.342
63	2½	69.4	2.731	3783	5.858	2270	3.515	2005	3.105	1173	1.816	1513	2.343
78	3	85.2	3.356	5701	8.846	3421	5.307	3022	4.688	1767	2.742	2280	3.538
91	3½	97.4	3.834	7451	11.545	4471	6.927	3949	6.119	2310	3.579	2980	4.618
103	4	110.1	4.334	9521	14.753	5712	8.852	5046	7.819	2951	4.573	3808	5.901

Article 362 — Electrical Nonmetallic Tubing (ENT)

Metric Designator	Trade Size	Nominal Internal Diameter		Total Area 100%		60%		1 Wire 53%		2 Wires 31%		Over 2 Wires 40%	
		mm	in.	mm²	in.²	mm²	in.²	mm²	in.²	mm²	in.²	mm²	in.²
16	½	14.2	0.560	158	0.246	95	0.148	84	0.131	49	0.076	63	0.099
21	¾	19.3	0.760	293	0.454	176	0.272	155	0.240	91	0.141	117	0.181
27	1	25.4	1.000	507	0.785	304	0.471	269	0.416	157	0.243	203	0.314
35	1¼	34.0	1.340	908	1.410	545	0.846	481	0.747	281	0.437	363	0.564
41	1½	39.9	1.570	1250	1.936	750	1.162	663	1.026	388	0.600	500	0.774
53	2	51.3	2.020	2067	3.205	1240	1.923	1095	1.699	641	0.993	827	1.282
63	2½	—	—	—	—	—	—	—	—	—	—	—	—
78	3	—	—	—	—	—	—	—	—	—	—	—	—
91	3½	—	—	—	—	—	—	—	—	—	—	—	—

Article 348 — Flexible Metal Conduit (FMC)

Metric Designator	Trade Size	Nominal Internal Diameter		Total Area 100%		60%		1 Wire 53%		2 Wires 31%		Over 2 Wires 40%	
		mm	in.	mm²	in.²	mm²	in.²	mm²	in.²	mm²	in.²	mm²	in.²
12	⅜	9.7	0.384	74	0.116	44	0.069	39	0.061	23	0.036	30	0.046
16	½	16.1	0.635	204	0.317	122	0.190	108	0.168	63	0.098	81	0.127
21	¾	20.9	0.824	343	0.533	206	0.320	182	0.283	106	0.165	137	0.213
27	1	25.9	1.020	527	0.817	316	0.490	279	0.433	163	0.253	211	0.327
35	1¼	32.4	1.275	824	1.277	495	0.766	437	0.677	256	0.396	330	0.511
41	1½	39.1	1.538	1201	1.858	720	1.115	636	0.985	372	0.576	480	0.743
53	2	51.8	2.040	2107	3.269	1264	1.961	1117	1.732	653	1.013	843	1.307
63	2½	63.5	2.500	3167	4.909	1900	2.945	1678	2.602	982	1.522	1267	1.963
78	3	76.2	3.000	4560	7.069	2736	4.241	2417	3.746	1414	2.191	1824	2.827
91	3½	88.9	3.500	6207	9.621	3724	5.773	3290	5.099	1924	2.983	2483	3.848
103	4	101.6	4.000	8107	12.566	4864	7.540	4297	6.660	2513	3.896	3243	5.027

Table 4 *Continued*

Article 342 — Intermediate Metal Conduit (IMC)

Metric Designator	Trade Size	Nominal Internal Diameter		Total Area 100%		60%		1 Wire 53%		2 Wires 31%		Over 2 Wires 40%	
		mm	in.	mm²	in.²	mm²	in.²	mm²	in.²	mm²	in.²	mm²	in.²
12	⅜	—	—	—	—	—	—	—	—	—	—	—	—
16	½	16.8	0.660	222	0.342	133	0.205	117	0.181	69	0.106	89	0.137
21	¾	21.9	0.864	377	0.586	226	0.352	200	0.311	117	0.182	151	0.235
27	1	28.1	1.105	620	0.959	372	0.575	329	0.508	192	0.297	248	0.384
35	1¼	36.8	1.448	1064	1.647	638	0.988	564	0.873	330	0.510	425	0.659
41	1½	42.7	1.683	1432	2.225	859	1.335	759	1.179	444	0.690	573	0.890
53	2	54.6	2.150	2341	3.630	1405	2.178	1241	1.924	726	1.125	937	1.452
63	2½	64.9	2.557	3308	5.135	1985	3.081	1753	2.722	1026	1.592	1323	2.054
78	3	80.7	3.176	5115	7.922	3069	4.753	2711	4.199	1586	2.456	2046	3.169
91	3½	93.2	3.671	6822	10.584	4093	6.351	3616	5.610	2115	3.281	2729	4.234
103	4	105.4	4.166	8725	13.631	5235	8.179	4624	7.224	2705	4.226	3490	5.452

Article 356— Liquidtight Flexible Nonmetallic Conduit (LFNC-B*)

Metric Designator	Trade Size	Nominal Internal Diameter		Total Area 100%		60%		1 Wire 53%		2 Wires 31%		Over 2 Wires 40%	
		mm	in.	mm²	in.²	mm²	in.²	mm²	in.²	mm²	in.²	mm²	in.²
12	⅜	12.5	0.494	123	0.192	74	0.115	65	0.102	38	0.059	49	0.077
16	½	16.1	0.632	204	0.314	122	0.188	108	0.166	63	0.097	81	0.125
21	¾	21.1	0.830	350	0.541	210	0.325	185	0.287	108	0.168	140	0.216
27	1	26.8	1.054	564	0.873	338	0.524	299	0.462	175	0.270	226	0.349
35	1¼	35.4	1.395	984	1.528	591	0.917	522	0.810	305	0.474	394	0.611
41	1½	40.3	1.588	1276	1.981	765	1.188	676	1.050	395	0.614	510	0.792
53	2	51.6	2.033	2091	3.246	1255	1.948	1108	1.720	648	1.006	836	1.298

*Corresponds to 356.2(2)

Article 356 — Liquidtight Flexible Nonmetallic Conduit (LFNC-A*)

Metric Designator	Trade Size	Nominal Internal Diameter		Total Area 100%		60%		1 Wire 53%		2 Wires 31%		Over 2 Wires 40%	
		mm	in.	mm²	in.²	mm²	in.²	mm²	in.²	mm²	in.²	mm²	in.²
12	⅜	12.6	0.495	125	0.192	75	0.115	66	0.102	39	0.060	50	0.077
16	½	16.0	0.630	201	0.312	121	0.187	107	0.165	62	0.097	80	0.125
21	¾	21.0	0.825	346	0.535	208	0.321	184	0.283	107	0.166	139	0.214
27	1	26.5	1.043	552	0.854	331	0.513	292	0.453	171	0.265	221	0.342
35	1¼	35.1	1.383	968	1.502	581	0.901	513	0.796	300	0.466	387	0.601
41	1½	40.7	1.603	1301	2.018	781	1.211	690	1.070	403	0.626	520	0.807
53	2	52.4	2.063	2157	3.343	1294	2.006	1143	1.772	669	1.036	863	1.337

*Corresponds to 356.2(1)

(Continues)

Table 4   *Continued*

Article 350 — Liquidtight Flexible Metal Conduit (LFMC)

Metric Designator	Trade Size	Nominal Internal Diameter		Total Area 100%		60%		1 Wire 53%		2 Wires 31%		Over 2 Wires 40%	
		mm	in.	mm²	in.²	mm²	in.²	mm²	in.²	mm²	in.²	mm²	in.²
12	3/8	12.5	0.494	123	0.192	74	0.115	65	0.102	38	0.059	49	0.077
16	1/2	16.1	0.632	204	0.314	122	0.188	108	0.166	63	0.097	81	0.125
21	3/4	21.1	0.830	350	0.541	210	0.325	185	0.287	108	0.168	140	0.216
27	1	26.8	1.054	564	0.873	338	0.524	299	0.462	175	0.270	226	0.349
35	1 1/4	35.4	1.395	984	1.528	591	0.917	522	0.810	305	0.474	394	0.611
41	1 1/2	40.3	1.588	1276	1.981	765	1.188	676	1.050	395	0.614	510	0.792
53	2	51.6	2.033	2091	3.246	1255	1.948	1108	1.720	648	1.006	836	1.298
63	2 1/2	63.3	2.493	3147	4.881	1888	2.929	1668	2.587	976	1.513	1259	1.953
78	3	78.4	3.085	4827	7.475	2896	4.485	2559	3.962	1497	2.317	1931	2.990
91	3 1/2	89.4	3.520	6277	9.731	3766	5.839	3327	5.158	1946	3.017	2511	3.893
103	4	102.1	4.020	8187	12.692	4912	7.615	4339	6.727	2538	3.935	3275	5.077
129	5	—	—	—	—	—	—	—	—	—	—	—	—
155	6	—	—	—	—	—	—	—	—	—	—	—	—

Article 344 — Rigid Metal Conduit (RMC)

Metric Designator	Trade Size	Nominal Internal Diameter		Total Area 100%		60%		1 Wire 53%		2 Wires 31%		Over 2 Wires 40%	
		mm	in.	mm²	in.²	mm²	in.²	mm²	in.²	mm²	in.²	mm²	in.²
12	3/8	—	—	—	—	—	—	—	—	—	—	—	—
16	1/2	16.1	0.632	204	0.314	122	0.188	108	0.166	63	0.097	81	0.125
21	3/4	21.2	0.836	353	0.549	212	0.329	187	0.291	109	0.170	141	0.220
27	1	27.0	1.063	573	0.887	344	0.532	303	0.470	177	0.275	229	0.355
35	1 1/4	35.4	1.394	984	1.526	591	0.916	522	0.809	305	0.473	394	0.610
41	1 1/2	41.2	1.624	1333	2.071	800	1.243	707	1.098	413	0.642	533	0.829
53	2	52.9	2.083	2198	3.408	1319	2.045	1165	1.806	681	1.056	879	1.363
63	2 1/2	63.2	2.489	3137	4.866	1882	2.919	1663	2.579	972	1.508	1255	1.946
78	3	78.5	3.090	4840	7.499	2904	4.499	2565	3.974	1500	2.325	1936	3.000
91	3 1/2	90.7	3.570	6461	10.010	3877	6.006	3424	5.305	2003	3.103	2584	4.004
103	4	102.9	4.050	8316	12.882	4990	7.729	4408	6.828	2578	3.994	3326	5.153
129	5	128.9	5.073	13050	20.212	7830	12.127	6916	10.713	4045	6.266	5220	8.085
155	6	154.8	6.093	18821	29.158	11292	17.495	9975	15.454	5834	9.039	7528	11.663

Article 352 — Rigid PVC Conduit (RNC), Schedule 80

Metric Designator	Trade Size	Nominal Internal Diameter		Total Area 100%		60%		1 Wire 53%		2 Wires 31%		Over 2 Wires 40%	
		mm	in.	mm²	in.²	mm²	in.²	mm²	in.²	mm²	in.²	mm²	in.²
12	3/8	—	—	—	—	—	—	—	—	—	—	—	—
16	1/2	13.4	0.526	141	0.217	85	0.130	75	0.115	44	0.067	56	0.087
21	3/4	18.3	0.722	263	0.409	158	0.246	139	0.217	82	0.127	105	0.164
27	1	23.8	0.936	445	0.688	267	0.413	236	0.365	138	0.213	178	0.275
35	1 1/4	31.9	1.255	799	1.237	480	0.742	424	0.656	248	0.383	320	0.495
41	1 1/2	37.5	1.476	1104	1.711	663	1.027	585	0.907	342	0.530	442	0.684
53	2	48.6	1.913	1855	2.874	1113	1.725	983	1.523	575	0.891	742	1.150
63	2 1/2	58.2	2.290	2660	4.119	1596	2.471	1410	2.183	825	1.277	1064	1.647
78	3	72.7	2.864	4151	6.442	2491	3.865	2200	3.414	1287	1.997	1660	2.577
91	3 1/2	84.5	3.326	5608	8.688	3365	5.213	2972	4.605	1738	2.693	2243	3.475
103	4	96.2	3.786	7268	11.258	4361	6.755	3852	5.967	2253	3.490	2907	4.503
129	5	121.1	4.768	11518	17.855	6911	10.713	6105	9.463	3571	5.535	4607	7.142
155	6	145.0	5.709	16513	25.598	9908	15.359	8752	13.567	5119	7.935	6605	10.239

Table 4 *Continued*

Articles 352 and 353 — Rigid PVC Conduit (RNC), Schedule 40, and HDPE Conduit

Metric Designator	Trade Size	Nominal Internal Diameter		Total Area 100%		60%		1 Wire 53%		2 Wires 31%		Over 2 Wires 40%	
		mm	in.	mm^2	in.^{2}	mm^2	in.^{2}	mm^2	in.^{2}	mm^2	in.^{2}	mm^2	in.^{2}
12	³⁄₈	—	—	—	—	—	—	—	—	—	—	—	—
16	½	15.3	0.602	184	0.285	110	0.171	97	0.151	57	0.088	74	0.114
21	¾	20.4	0.804	327	0.508	196	0.305	173	0.269	101	0.157	131	0.203
27	1	26.1	1.029	535	0.832	321	0.499	284	0.441	166	0.258	214	0.333
35	1¼	34.5	1.360	935	1.453	561	0.872	495	0.770	290	0.450	374	0.581
41	1½	40.4	1.590	1282	1.986	769	1.191	679	1.052	397	0.616	513	0.794
53	2	52.0	2.047	2124	3.291	1274	1.975	1126	1.744	658	1.020	849	1.316
63	2½	62.1	2.445	3029	4.695	1817	2.817	1605	2.488	939	1.455	1212	1.878
78	3	77.3	3.042	4693	7.268	2816	4.361	2487	3.852	1455	2.253	1877	2.907
91	3½	89.4	3.521	6277	9.737	3766	5.842	3327	5.161	1946	3.018	2511	3.895
103	4	101.5	3.998	8091	12.554	4855	7.532	4288	6.654	2508	3.892	3237	5.022
129	5	127.4	5.016	12748	19.761	7649	11.856	6756	10.473	3952	6.126	5099	7.904
155	6	153.2	6.031	18433	28.567	11060	17.140	9770	15.141	5714	8.856	7373	11.427

Article 352 — Type A, Rigid PVC Conduit (RNC)

Metric Designator	Trade Size	Nominal Internal Diameter		Total Area 100%		60%		1 Wire 53%		2 Wires 31%		Over 2 Wires 40%	
		mm	in.	mm^2	in.^{2}	mm^2	in.^{2}	mm^2	in.^{2}	mm^2	in.^{2}	mm^2	in.^{2}
16	½	17.8	0.700	249	0.385	149	0.231	132	0.204	77	0.119	100	0.154
21	¾	23.1	0.910	419	0.650	251	0.390	222	0.345	130	0.202	168	0.260
27	1	29.8	1.175	697	1.084	418	0.651	370	0.575	216	0.336	279	0.434
35	1¼	38.1	1.500	1140	1.767	684	1.060	604	0.937	353	0.548	456	0.707
41	1½	43.7	1.720	1500	2.324	900	1.394	795	1.231	465	0.720	600	0.929
53	2	54.7	2.155	2350	3.647	1410	2.188	1245	1.933	728	1.131	940	1.459
63	2½	66.9	2.635	3515	5.453	2109	3.272	1863	2.890	1090	1.690	1406	2.181
78	3	82.0	3.230	5281	8.194	3169	4.916	2799	4.343	1637	2.540	2112	3.278
91	3½	93.7	3.690	6896	10.694	4137	6.416	3655	5.668	2138	3.315	2758	4.278
103	4	106.2	4.180	8858	13.723	5315	8.234	4695	7.273	2746	4.254	3543	5.489
129	5	—	—	—	—	—	—	—	—	—	—	—	—
155	6	—	—	—	—	—	—	—	—	—	—	—	—

Article 352 — Type EB, PVC Conduit (RNC)

Metric Designator	Trade Size	Nominal Internal Diameter		Total Area 100%		60%		1 Wire 53%		2 Wires 31%		Over 2 Wires 40%	
		mm	in.	mm^2	in.^{2}	mm^2	in.^{2}	mm^2	in.^{2}	mm^2	in.^{2}	mm^2	in.^{2}
16	½	—	—	—	—	—	—	—	—	—	—	—	—
21	¾	—	—	—	—	—	—	—	—	—	—	—	—
27	1	—	—	—	—	—	—	—	—	—	—	—	—
35	1¼	—	—	—	—	—	—	—	—	—	—	—	—
41	1½	—	—	—	—	—	—	—	—	—	—	—	—
53	2	56.4	2.221	2498	3.874	1499	2.325	1324	2.053	774	1.201	999	1.550
63	2½	—	—	—	—	—	—	—	—	—	—	—	—
78	3	84.6	3.330	5621	8.709	3373	5.226	2979	4.616	1743	2.700	2248	3.484
91	3½	96.6	3.804	7329	11.365	4397	6.819	3884	6.023	2272	3.523	2932	4.546
103	4	108.9	4.289	9314	14.448	5589	8.669	4937	7.657	2887	4.479	3726	5.779
129	5	135.0	5.316	14314	22.195	8588	13.317	7586	11.763	4437	6.881	5726	8.878
155	6	160.9	6.336	20333	31.530	12200	18.918	10776	16.711	6303	9.774	8133	12.612

Table 5 Dimensions of Insulated Conductors and Fixture Wires

Type	Size (AWG or kcmil)	Approximate Diameter		Approximate Area	
		mm	in.	mm²	in.²
Type: FFH-2, RFH-1, RFH-2, RHH*, RHW*, RHW-2*, RHH, RHW, RHW-2, SF-1, SF-2, SFF-1, SFF-2, TF, TFF, THHW, THW, THW-2, TW, XF, XFF					
RFH-2, FFH-2	18	3.454	0.136	9.355	0.0145
	16	3.759	0.148	11.10	0.0172
RHH, RHW, RHW-2	14	4.902	0.193	18.90	0.0293
	12	5.385	0.212	22.77	0.0353
	10	5.994	0.236	28.19	0.0437
	8	8.280	0.326	53.87	0.0835
	6	9.246	0.364	67.16	0.1041
	4	10.46	0.412	86.00	0.1333
	3	11.18	0.440	98.13	0.1521
	2	11.99	0.472	112.9	0.1750
	1	14.78	0.582	171.6	0.2660
	1/0	15.80	0.622	196.1	0.3039
	2/0	16.97	0.668	226.1	0.3505
	3/0	18.29	0.720	262.7	0.4072
	4/0	19.76	0.778	306.7	0.4754
	250	22.73	0.895	405.9	0.6291
	300	24.13	0.950	457.3	0.7088
	350	25.43	1.001	507.7	0.7870
	400	26.62	1.048	556.5	0.8626
	500	28.78	1.133	650.5	1.0082
	600	31.57	1.243	782.9	1.2135
	700	33.38	1.314	874.9	1.3561
	750	34.24	1.348	920.8	1.4272
	800	35.05	1.380	965.0	1.4957
	900	36.68	1.444	1057	1.6377
	1000	38.15	1.502	1143	1.7719
	1250	43.92	1.729	1515	2.3479
	1500	47.04	1.852	1738	2.6938
	1750	49.94	1.966	1959	3.0357
	2000	52.63	2.072	2175	3.3719
SF-2, SFF-2	18	3.073	0.121	7.419	0.0115
	16	3.378	0.133	8.968	0.0139
	14	3.759	0.148	11.10	0.0172
SF-1, SFF-1	18	2.311	0.091	4.194	0.0065
RFH-1, XF, XFF	18	2.692	0.106	5.161	0.0080
TF, TFF, XF, XFF	16	2.997	0.118	7.032	0.0109
TW, XF, XFF, THHW, THW, THW-2	14	3.378	0.133	8.968	0.0139

Table 5 *Continued*

Type	Size (AWG or kcmil)	Approximate Diameter		Approximate Area	
		mm	in.	mm²	in.²
TW, THHW, THW, THW-2	12	3.861	0.152	11.68	0.0181
	10	4.470	0.176	15.68	0.0243
	8	5.994	0.236	28.19	0.0437
RHH*, RHW*, RHW-2*	14	4.140	0.163	13.48	0.0209
RHH*, RHW*, RHW-2*, XF, XFF	12	4.623	0.182	16.77	0.0260
Type: RHH*, RHW*, RHW-2*, THHN, THHW, THW, THW-2, TFN, TFFN, THWN, THWN-2, XF, XFF					
RHH,* RHW,* RHW-2,* XF, XFF	10	5.232	0.206	21.48	0.0333
RHH*, RHW*, RHW-2*	8	6.756	0.266	35.87	0.0556
TW, THW, THHW, THW-2, RHH*, RHW*, RHW-2*	6	7.722	0.304	46.84	0.0726
	4	8.941	0.352	62.77	0.0973
	3	9.652	0.380	73.16	0.1134
	2	10.46	0.412	86.00	0.1333
	1	12.50	0.492	122.6	0.1901
	1/0	13.51	0.532	143.4	0.2223
	2/0	14.68	0.578	169.3	0.2624
	3/0	16.00	0.630	201.1	0.3117
	4/0	17.48	0.688	239.9	0.3718
	250	19.43	0.765	296.5	0.4596
	300	20.83	0.820	340.7	0.5281
	350	22.12	0.871	384.4	0.5958
	400	23.32	0.918	427.0	0.6619
	500	25.48	1.003	509.7	0.7901
	600	28.27	1.113	627.7	0.9729
	700	30.07	1.184	710.3	1.1010
	750	30.94	1.218	751.7	1.1652
	800	31.75	1.250	791.7	1.2272
	900	33.38	1.314	874.9	1.3561
	1000	34.85	1.372	953.8	1.4784
	1250	39.09	1.539	1200	1.8602
	1500	42.21	1.662	1400	2.1695
	1750	45.11	1.776	1598	2.4773
	2000	47.80	1.882	1795	2.7818
TFN, TFFN	18	2.134	0.084	3.548	0.0055
	16	2.438	0.096	4.645	0.0072

(Continues)

Table 5 *Continued*

Type	Size (AWG or kcmil)	Approximate Diameter		Approximate Area	
		mm	in.	mm²	in.²
THHN, THWN, THWN-2	14	2.819	0.111	6.258	0.0097
	12	3.302	0.130	8.581	0.0133
	10	4.166	0.164	13.61	0.0211
	8	5.486	0.216	23.61	0.0366
	6	6.452	0.254	32.71	0.0507
	4	8.230	0.324	53.16	0.0824
	3	8.941	0.352	62.77	0.0973
	2	9.754	0.384	74.71	0.1158
	1	11.33	0.446	100.8	0.1562
	1/0	12.34	0.486	119.7	0.1855
	2/0	13.51	0.532	143.4	0.2223
	3/0	14.83	0.584	172.8	0.2679
	4/0	16.31	0.642	208.8	0.3237
	250	18.06	0.711	256.1	0.3970
	300	19.46	0.766	297.3	0.4608

Type: FEP, FEPB, PAF, PAFF, PF, PFA, PFAH, PFF, PGF, PGFF, PTF, PTFF, TFE, THHN, THWN, THWN-2, Z, ZF, ZFF

Type	Size (AWG or kcmil)	Approximate Diameter		Approximate Area	
		mm	in.	mm²	in.²
THHN, THWN, THWN-2	350	20.75	0.817	338.2	0.5242
	400	21.95	0.864	378.3	0.5863
	500	24.10	0.949	456.3	0.7073
	600	26.70	1.051	559.7	0.8676
	700	28.50	1.122	637.9	0.9887
	750	29.36	1.156	677.2	1.0496
	800	30.18	1.188	715.2	1.1085
	900	31.80	1.252	794.3	1.2311
	1000	33.27	1.310	869.5	1.3478
PF, PGFF, PGF, PFF, PTF, PAF, PTFF, PAFF	18	2.184	0.086	3.742	0.0058
	16	2.489	0.098	4.839	0.0075
PF, PGFF, PGF, PFF, PTF, PAF, PTFF, PAFF, TFE, FEP, PFA, FEPB, PFAH	14	2.870	0.113	6.452	0.0100
TFE, FEP, PFA, FEPB, PFAH	12	3.353	0.132	8.839	0.0137
	10	3.962	0.156	12.32	0.0191
	8	5.232	0.206	21.48	0.0333
	6	6.198	0.244	30.19	0.0468
	4	7.417	0.292	43.23	0.0670
	3	8.128	0.320	51.87	0.0804
	2	8.941	0.352	62.77	0.0973
TFE, PFAH	1	10.72	0.422	90.26	0.1399
TFE, PFA, PFAH, Z	1/0	11.73	0.462	108.1	0.1676
	2/0	12.90	0.508	130.8	0.2027
	3/0	14.22	0.560	158.9	0.2463
	4/0	15.70	0.618	193.5	0.3000
ZF, ZFF	18	1.930	0.076	2.903	0.0045
	16	2.235	0.088	3.935	0.0061

Table 5 *Continued*

Type	Size (AWG or kcmil)	Approximate Diameter		Approximate Area	
		mm	in.	mm²	in.²
Z, ZF, ZFF	14	2.616	0.103	5.355	0.0083
Z	12	3.099	0.122	7.548	0.0117
	10	3.962	0.156	12.32	0.0191
	8	4.978	0.196	19.48	0.0302
	6	5.944	0.234	27.74	0.0430
	4	7.163	0.282	40.32	0.0625
	3	8.382	0.330	55.16	0.0855
	2	9.195	0.362	66.39	0.1029
	1	10.21	0.402	81.87	0.1269
Type: KF-1, KF-2, KFF-1, KFF-2, XHH, XHHW, XHHW-2, ZW					
XHHW, ZW, XHHW-2, XHH	14	3.378	0.133	8.968	0.0139
	12	3.861	0.152	11.68	0.0181
	10	4.470	0.176	15.68	0.0243
	8	5.994	0.236	28.19	0.0437
	6	6.960	0.274	38.06	0.0590
	4	8.179	0.322	52.52	0.0814
	3	8.890	0.350	62.06	0.0962
	2	9.703	0.382	73.94	0.1146
XHHW, XHHW-2, XHH	1	11.23	0.442	98.97	0.1534
	1/0	12.24	0.482	117.7	0.1825
	2/0	13.41	0.528	141.3	0.2190
	3/0	14.73	0.58	170.5	0.2642
	4/0	16.21	0.638	206.3	0.3197
	250	17.91	0.705	251.9	0.3904
	300	19.30	0.76	292.6	0.4536
	350	20.60	0.811	333.3	0.5166
	400	21.79	0.858	373.0	0.5782
	500	23.95	0.943	450.6	0.6984
	600	26.75	1.053	561.9	0.8709
	700	28.55	1.124	640.2	0.9923
	750	29.41	1.158	679.5	1.0532
	800	30.23	1.190	717.5	1.1122
	900	31.85	1.254	796.8	1.2351
	1000	33.32	1.312	872.2	1.3519
	1250	37.57	1.479	1108	1.7180
	1500	40.69	1.602	1300	2.0157
	1750	43.59	1.716	1492	2.3127
	2000	46.28	1.822	1682	2.6073
KF-2, KFF-2	18	1.600	0.063	2.000	0.0031
	16	1.905	0.075	2.839	0.0044
	14	2.286	0.090	4.129	0.0064
	12	2.769	0.109	6.000	0.0093
	10	3.378	0.133	8.968	0.0139
KF-1, KFF-1	18	1.448	0.057	1.677	0.0026
	16	1.753	0.069	2.387	0.0037
	14	2.134	0.084	3.548	0.0055
	12	2.616	0.103	5.355	0.0083
	10	3.226	0.127	8.194	0.0127

*Types RHH, RHW, and RHW-2 without outer covering.

Table 5A Compact Aluminum Building Wire Nominal Dimensions* and Areas

Size (AWG or kcmil)	Bare Conductor Diameter		Types THW and THHW				Type THHN				Type XHHW				Size (AWG or kcmil)
			Approximate Diameter		Approximate Area		Approximate Diameter		Approximate Area		Approximate Diameter		Approximate Area		
	mm	in.	mm	in.	mm²	in.²	mm	in.	mm²	in.²	mm	in.	mm²	in.²	
8	3.404	0.134	6.477	0.255	32.90	0.0510	—	—	29.16	0.0452	5.690	0.224	25.42	0.0394	8
6	4.293	0.169	7.366	0.290	42.58	0.0660	6.096	0.240	29.16	0.0452	6.604	0.260	34.19	0.0530	6
4	5.410	0.213	8.509	0.335	56.84	0.0881	7.747	0.305	47.10	0.0730	7.747	0.305	47.10	0.0730	4
2	6.807	0.268	9.906	0.390	77.03	0.1194	9.144	0.360	65.61	0.1017	9.144	0.360	65.61	0.1017	2
1	7.595	0.299	11.81	0.465	109.5	0.1698	10.54	0.415	87.23	0.1352	10.54	0.415	87.23	0.1352	1
1/0	8.534	0.336	12.70	0.500	126.6	0.1963	11.43	0.450	102.6	0.1590	11.43	0.450	102.6	0.1590	1/0
2/0	9.550	0.376	13.84	0.545	150.5	0.2332	12.57	0.495	124.1	0.1924	12.45	0.490	121.6	0.1885	2/0
3/0	10.74	0.423	14.99	0.590	176.3	0.2733	13.72	0.540	147.7	0.2290	13.72	0.540	147.7	0.2290	3/0
4/0	12.07	0.475	16.38	0.645	210.8	0.3267	15.11	0.595	179.4	0.2780	14.99	0.590	176.3	0.2733	4/0
250	13.21	0.520	18.42	0.725	266.3	0.4128	17.02	0.670	227.4	0.3525	16.76	0.660	220.7	0.3421	250
300	14.48	0.570	19.69	0.775	304.3	0.4717	18.29	0.720	262.6	0.4071	18.16	0.715	259.0	0.4015	300
350	15.65	0.616	20.83	0.820	340.7	0.5281	19.56	0.770	300.4	0.4656	19.30	0.760	292.6	0.4536	350
400	16.74	0.659	21.97	0.865	379.1	0.5876	20.70	0.815	336.5	0.5216	20.32	0.800	324.3	0.5026	400
500	18.69	0.736	23.88	0.940	447.7	0.6939	22.48	0.885	396.8	0.6151	22.35	0.880	392.4	0.6082	500
600	20.65	0.813	26.67	1.050	558.6	0.8659	25.02	0.985	491.6	0.7620	24.89	0.980	486.6	0.7542	600
700	22.28	0.877	28.19	1.110	624.3	0.9676	26.67	1.050	558.6	0.8659	26.67	1.050	558.6	0.8659	700
750	23.06	0.908	29.21	1.150	670.1	1.0386	27.31	1.075	585.5	0.9076	27.69	1.090	602.0	0.9331	750
900	25.37	0.999	31.09	1.224	759.1	1.1766	30.33	1.194	722.5	1.1196	29.69	1.169	692.3	1.0733	900
1000	26.92	1.060	32.64	1.285	836.6	1.2968	31.88	1.255	798.1	1.2370	31.24	1.230	766.6	1.1882	1000

*Dimensions are from industry sources.

Table 8 Conductor Properties

Size (AWG or kcmil)	Area mm²	Circular mils	Stranding Quantity	Stranding Diameter mm	Stranding Diameter in.	Overall Diameter mm	Overall Diameter in.	Overall Area mm²	Overall Area in.²	Uncoated ohm/km	Uncoated ohm/kFT	Coated ohm/km	Coated ohm/kFT	Aluminum ohm/km	Aluminum ohm/kFT
18	0.823	1620	1	—	—	1.02	0.040	0.823	0.001	25.5	7.77	26.5	8.08	42.0	12.8
18	0.823	1620	7	0.39	0.015	1.16	0.046	1.06	0.002	26.1	7.95	27.7	8.45	42.8	13.1
16	1.31	2580	1	—	—	1.29	0.051	1.31	0.002	16.0	4.89	16.7	5.08	26.4	8.05
16	1.31	2580	7	0.49	0.019	1.46	0.058	1.68	0.003	16.4	4.99	17.3	5.29	26.9	8.21
14	2.08	4110	1	—	—	1.63	0.064	2.08	0.003	10.1	3.07	10.4	3.19	16.6	5.06
14	2.08	4110	7	0.62	0.024	1.85	0.073	2.68	0.004	10.3	3.14	10.7	3.26	16.9	5.17
12	3.31	6530	1	—	—	2.05	0.081	3.31	0.005	6.34	1.93	6.57	2.01	10.45	3.18
12	3.31	6530	7	0.78	0.030	2.32	0.092	4.25	0.006	6.50	1.98	6.73	2.05	10.69	3.25
10	5.261	10380	1	—	—	2.588	0.102	5.26	0.008	3.984	1.21	4.148	1.26	6.561	2.00
10	5.261	10380	7	0.98	0.038	2.95	0.116	6.76	0.011	4.070	1.24	4.226	1.29	6.679	2.04
8	8.367	16510	1	—	—	3.264	0.128	8.37	0.013	2.506	0.764	2.579	0.786	4.125	1.26
8	8.367	16510	7	1.23	0.049	3.71	0.146	10.76	0.017	2.551	0.778	2.653	0.809	4.204	1.28
6	13.30	26240	7	1.56	0.061	4.67	0.184	17.09	0.027	1.608	0.491	1.671	0.510	2.652	0.808
4	21.15	41740	7	1.96	0.077	5.89	0.232	27.19	0.042	1.010	0.308	1.053	0.321	1.666	0.508
3	26.67	52620	7	2.20	0.087	6.60	0.260	34.28	0.053	0.802	0.245	0.833	0.254	1.320	0.403
2	33.62	66360	7	2.47	0.097	7.42	0.292	43.23	0.067	0.634	0.194	0.661	0.201	1.045	0.319
1	42.41	83690	19	1.69	0.066	8.43	0.332	55.80	0.087	0.505	0.154	0.524	0.160	0.829	0.253
1/0	53.49	105600	19	1.89	0.074	9.45	0.372	70.41	0.109	0.399	0.122	0.415	0.127	0.660	0.201
2/0	67.43	133100	19	2.13	0.084	10.62	0.418	88.74	0.137	0.3170	0.0967	0.329	0.101	0.523	0.159
3/0	85.01	167800	19	2.39	0.094	11.94	0.470	111.9	0.173	0.2512	0.0766	0.2610	0.0797	0.413	0.126
4/0	107.2	211600	19	2.68	0.106	13.41	0.528	141.1	0.219	0.1996	0.0608	0.2050	0.0626	0.328	0.100
250	127	—	37	2.09	0.082	14.61	0.575	168	0.260	0.1687	0.0515	0.1753	0.0535	0.2778	0.0847
300	152	—	37	2.29	0.090	16.00	0.630	201	0.312	0.1409	0.0429	0.1463	0.0446	0.2318	0.0707
350	177	—	37	2.47	0.097	17.30	0.681	235	0.364	0.1205	0.0367	0.1252	0.0382	0.1984	0.0605
400	203	—	37	2.64	0.104	18.49	0.728	268	0.416	0.1053	0.0321	0.1084	0.0331	0.1737	0.0529
500	253	—	37	2.95	0.116	20.65	0.813	336	0.519	0.0845	0.0258	0.0869	0.0265	0.1391	0.0424
600	304	—	61	2.52	0.099	22.68	0.893	404	0.626	0.0704	0.0214	0.0732	0.0223	0.1159	0.0353
700	355	—	61	2.72	0.107	24.49	0.964	471	0.730	0.0603	0.0184	0.0622	0.0189	0.0994	0.0303
750	380	—	61	2.82	0.111	25.35	0.998	505	0.782	0.0563	0.0171	0.0579	0.0176	0.0927	0.0282
800	405	—	61	2.91	0.114	26.16	1.030	538	0.834	0.0528	0.0161	0.0544	0.0166	0.0868	0.0265
900	456	—	61	3.09	0.122	27.79	1.094	606	0.940	0.0470	0.0143	0.0481	0.0147	0.0770	0.0235
1000	507	—	61	3.25	0.128	29.26	1.152	673	1.042	0.0423	0.0129	0.0434	0.0132	0.0695	0.0212
1250	633	—	91	2.98	0.117	32.74	1.289	842	1.305	0.0338	0.0103	0.0347	0.0106	0.0554	0.0169
1500	760	—	91	3.26	0.128	35.86	1.412	1011	1.566	0.02814	0.00858	0.02814	0.00883	0.0464	0.0141
1750	887	—	127	2.98	0.117	38.76	1.526	1180	1.829	0.02410	0.00735	0.02410	0.00756	0.0397	0.0121
2000	1013	—	127	3.19	0.126	41.45	1.632	1349	2.092	0.02109	0.00643	0.02109	0.00662	0.0348	0.0106

Notes:

1. These resistance values are valid **only** for the parameters as given. Using conductors having coated strands, different stranding type, and, especially, other temperatures changes the resistance.

2. Formula for temperature change: $R_2 = R_1 [1 + \alpha (T_2 - 75)]$ where $\alpha_{cu} = 0.00323$, $\alpha_{AL} = 0.00330$ at 75°C.

3. Conductors with compact and compressed stranding have about 9 percent and 3 percent, respectively, smaller bare conductor diameters than those shown. See Table 5A for actual compact cable dimensions.

4. The IACS conductivities used: bare copper = 100%, aluminum = 61%.

5. Class B stranding is listed as well as solid for some sizes. Its overall diameter and area is that of its circumscribing circle.

FPN: The construction information is per NEMA WC8-1992 or ANSI/UL 1581-1998. The resistance is calculated per National Bureau of Standards Handbook 100, dated 1966, and Handbook 109, dated 1972.

Table 9 Alternating-Current Resistance and Reactance for 600-Volt Cables, 3-Phase, 60 Hz, 75°C (167°F) — Three Single Conductors in Conduit

	Ohms to Neutral per Kilometer Ohms to Neutral per 1000 Feet														
Size (AWG or kcmil)	X_L (Reactance) for All Wires		Alternating-Current Resistance for Uncoated Copper Wires			Alternating-Current Resistance for Aluminum Wires			Effective Z at 0.85 *PF* for Uncoated Copper Wires			Effective Z at 0.85 *PF* for Aluminum Wires			Size (AWG or kcmil)
	PVC, Aluminum Conduits	Steel Conduit	PVC Conduit	Aluminum Conduit	Steel Conduit	PVC Conduit	Aluminum Conduit	Steel Conduit	PVC Conduit	Aluminum Conduit	Steel Conduit	PVC Conduit	Aluminum Conduit	Steel Conduit	
14	0.190 0.058	0.240 0.073	10.2 3.1	10.2 3.1	10.2 3.1	— —	— —	— —	8.9 2.7	8.9 2.7	8.9 2.7	— —	— —	— —	14
12	0.177 0.054	0.223 0.068	6.6 2.0	6.6 2.0	6.6 2.0	10.5 3.2	10.5 3.2	10.5 3.2	5.6 1.7	5.6 1.7	5.6 1.7	9.2 2.8	9.2 2.8	9.2 2.8	12
10	0.164 0.050	0.207 0.063	3.9 1.2	3.9 1.2	3.9 1.2	6.6 2.0	6.6 2.0	6.6 2.0	3.6 1.1	3.6 1.1	3.6 1.1	5.9 1.8	5.9 1.8	5.9 1.8	10
8	0.171 0.052	0.213 0.065	2.56 0.78	2.56 0.78	2.56 0.78	4.3 1.3	4.3 1.3	4.3 1.3	2.26 0.69	2.26 0.69	2.30 0.70	3.6 1.1	3.6 1.1	3.6 1.1	8
6	0.167 0.051	0.210 0.064	1.61 0.49	1.61 0.49	1.61 0.49	2.66 0.81	2.66 0.81	2.66 0.81	1.44 0.44	1.48 0.45	1.48 0.45	2.33 0.71	2.36 0.72	2.36 0.72	6
4	0.157 0.048	0.197 0.060	1.02 0.31	1.02 0.31	1.02 0.31	1.67 0.51	1.67 0.51	1.67 0.51	0.95 0.29	0.95 0.29	0.98 0.30	1.51 0.46	1.51 0.46	1.51 0.46	4
3	0.154 0.047	0.194 0.059	0.82 0.25	0.82 0.25	0.82 0.25	1.31 0.40	1.35 0.41	1.31 0.40	0.75 0.23	0.79 0.24	0.79 0.24	1.21 0.37	1.21 0.37	1.21 0.37	3
2	0.148 0.045	0.187 0.057	0.62 0.19	0.66 0.20	0.66 0.20	1.05 0.32	1.05 0.32	1.05 0.32	0.62 0.19	0.62 0.19	0.66 0.20	0.98 0.30	0.98 0.30	0.98 0.30	2
1	0.151 0.046	0.187 0.057	0.49 0.15	0.52 0.16	0.52 0.16	0.82 0.25	0.85 0.26	0.82 0.25	0.52 0.16	0.52 0.16	0.52 0.16	0.79 0.24	0.79 0.24	0.82 0.25	1
1/0	0.144 0.044	0.180 0.055	0.39 0.12	0.43 0.13	0.39 0.12	0.66 0.20	0.69 0.21	0.66 0.20	0.43 0.13	0.43 0.13	0.43 0.13	0.62 0.19	0.66 0.20	0.66 0.20	1/0
2/0	0.141 0.043	0.177 0.054	0.33 0.10	0.33 0.10	0.33 0.10	0.52 0.16	0.52 0.16	0.52 0.16	0.36 0.11	0.36 0.11	0.36 0.11	0.52 0.16	0.52 0.16	0.52 0.16	2/0
3/0	0.138 0.042	0.171 0.052	0.253 0.077	0.269 0.082	0.259 0.079	0.43 0.13	0.43 0.13	0.43 0.13	0.289 0.088	0.302 0.092	0.308 0.094	0.43 0.13	0.43 0.13	0.46 0.14	3/0
4/0	0.135 0.041	0.167 0.051	0.203 0.062	0.220 0.067	0.207 0.063	0.33 0.10	0.36 0.11	0.33 0.10	0.243 0.074	0.256 0.078	0.262 0.080	0.36 0.11	0.36 0.11	0.36 0.11	4/0
250	0.135 0.041	0.171 0.052	0.171 0.052	0.187 0.057	0.177 0.054	0.279 0.085	0.295 0.090	0.282 0.086	0.217 0.066	0.230 0.070	0.240 0.073	0.308 0.094	0.322 0.098	0.33 0.10	250
300	0.135 0.041	0.167 0.051	0.144 0.044	0.161 0.049	0.148 0.045	0.233 0.071	0.249 0.076	0.236 0.072	0.194 0.059	0.207 0.063	0.213 0.065	0.269 0.082	0.282 0.086	0.289 0.088	300
350	0.131 0.040	0.164 0.050	0.125 0.038	0.141 0.043	0.128 0.039	0.200 0.061	0.217 0.066	0.207 0.063	0.174 0.053	0.190 0.058	0.197 0.060	0.240 0.073	0.253 0.077	0.262 0.080	350
400	0.131 0.040	0.161 0.049	0.108 0.033	0.125 0.038	0.115 0.035	0.177 0.054	0.194 0.059	0.180 0.055	0.161 0.049	0.174 0.053	0.184 0.056	0.217 0.066	0.233 0.071	0.240 0.073	400

Table 9 *Continued*

	Ohms to Neutral per Kilometer / Ohms to Neutral per 1000 Feet														
	X_L (Reactance) for All Wires		Alternating-Current Resistance for Uncoated Copper Wires			Alternating-Current Resistance for Aluminum Wires			Effective Z at 0.85 PF for Uncoated Copper Wires			Effective Z at 0.85 PF for Aluminum Wires			
Size (AWG or kcmil)	PVC, Aluminum Conduits	Steel Conduit	PVC Conduit	Aluminum Conduit	Steel Conduit	PVC Conduit	Aluminum Conduit	Steel Conduit	PVC Conduit	Aluminum Conduit	Steel Conduit	PVC Conduit	Aluminum Conduit	Steel Conduit	Size (AWG or kcmil)
500	0.128 0.039	0.157 0.048	0.089 0.027	0.105 0.032	0.095 0.029	0.141 0.043	0.157 0.048	0.148 0.045	0.141 0.043	0.157 0.048	0.164 0.050	0.187 0.057	0.200 0.061	0.210 0.064	500
600	0.128 0.039	0.157 0.048	0.075 0.023	0.092 0.028	0.082 0.025	0.118 0.036	0.135 0.041	0.125 0.038	0.131 0.040	0.144 0.044	0.154 0.047	0.167 0.051	0.180 0.055	0.190 0.058	600
750	0.125 0.038	0.157 0.048	0.062 0.019	0.079 0.024	0.069 0.021	0.095 0.029	0.112 0.034	0.102 0.031	0.118 0.036	0.131 0.040	0.141 0.043	0.148 0.045	0.161 0.049	0.171 0.052	750
1000	0.121 0.037	0.151 0.046	0.049 0.015	0.062 0.019	0.059 0.018	0.075 0.023	0.089 0.027	0.082 0.025	0.105 0.032	0.118 0.036	0.131 0.040	0.128 0.039	0.138 0.042	0.151 0.046	1000

Notes:

1. These values are based on the following constants: UL-Type RHH wires with Class B stranding, in cradled configuration. Wire conductivities are 100 percent IACS copper and 61 percent IACS aluminum, and aluminum conduit is 45 percent IACS. Capacitive reactance is ignored, since it is negligible at these voltages. These resistance values are valid only at 75°C (167°F) and for the parameters as given, but are representative for 600-volt wire types operating at 60 Hz.

2. *Effective Z* is defined as $R \cos(\theta) + X \sin(\theta)$, where θ is the power factor angle of the circuit. Multiplying current by effective impedance gives a good approximation for line-to-neutral voltage drop. Effective impedance values shown in this table are valid only at 0.85 power factor. For another circuit power factor (*PF*), effective impedance (*Ze*) can be calculated from R and X_L values given in this table as follows: $Ze = R \times PF + X_L \sin[\arccos(PF)]$.

Tables 11(A) and 11(B)

For listing purposes, Table 11(A) and Table 11(B) provide the required power source limitations for Class 2 and Class 3 power sources. Table 11(A) applies for alternating-current sources, and Table 11(B) applies for direct-current sources.

The power for Class 2 and Class 3 circuits shall be either (1) inherently limited, requiring no overcurrent protection, or (2) not inherently limited, requiring a combination of power source and overcurrent protection. Power sources designed for interconnection shall be listed for the purpose.

As part of the listing, the Class 2 or Class 3 power source shall be durably marked where plainly visible to indicate the class of supply and its electrical rating. A Class 2 power source not suitable for wet location use shall be so marked.

Exception: Limited power circuits used by listed information technology equipment.

Overcurrent devices, where required, shall be located at the point where the conductor to be protected receives its supply and shall not be interchangeable with devices of higher ratings. The overcurrent device shall be permitted as an integral part of the power source.

Table 11(A) Class 2 and Class 3 Alternating-Current Power Source Limitations

Power Source		Inherently Limited Power Source (Overcurrent Protection Not Required)				Not Inherently Limited Power Source (Overcurrent Protection Required)			
		Class 2			Class 3	Class 2			Class 3
Source voltage V_{max} (volts) (see Note 1)		0 through 20*	Over 20 and through 30*	Over 30 and through 150	Over 30 and through 100	0 through 20*	Over 20 and through 30*	Over 30 and through 100	Over 100 and through 150
Power limitations VA_{max} (volt-amperes) (see Note 1)		—	—	—	—	250 (see Note 3)	250	250	N.A.
Current limitations I_{max} (amperes) (see Note 1)		8.0	8.0	0.005	$150/V_{max}$	$1000/V_{max}$	$1000/V_{max}$	$1000/V_{max}$	1.0
Maximum overcurrent protection (amperes)		—	—	—	—	5.0	$100/V_{max}$	$100/V_{max}$	1.0
Power source maximum nameplate rating	VA (volt-amperes)	$5.0 \times V_{max}$	100	$0.005 \times V_{max}$	100	$5.0 \times V_{max}$	100	100	100
	Current (amperes)	5.0	$100/V_{max}$	0.005	$100/V_{max}$	5.0	$100/V_{max}$	$100/V_{max}$	$100/V_{max}$

*Voltage ranges shown are for sinusoidal ac in indoor locations or where wet contact is not likely to occur. For nonsinusoidal or wet contact conditions, see Note 2.

Table 11(B) Class 2 and Class 3 Direct-Current Power Source Limitations

Power Source		Inherently Limited Power Source (Overcurrent Protection Not Required)					Not Inherently Limited Power Source (Overcurrent Protection Required)			
		Class 2				Class 3	Class 2		Class 3	
Source voltage V_{max} (volts) (see Note 1)		0 through 20*	Over 20 and through 30*	Over 30 and through 60*	Over 60 and through 150	Over 60 and through 100	0 through 20*	Over 20 and through 60*	Over 60 and through 100	Over 100 and through 150
Power limitations VA_{max} (volt-amperes) (see Note 1)		—	—	—	—	—	250 (see Note 3)	250	250	N.A.
Current limitations I_{max} (amperes) (see Note 1)		8.0	8.0	$150/V_{max}$	0.005	$150/V_{max}$	$1000/V_{max}$	$1000/V_{max}$	$1000/V_{max}$	1.0
Maximum overcurrent protection (amperes)		—	—	—	—	—	5.0	$100/V_{max}$	$100/V_{max}$	1.0
Power source maximum nameplate rating	VA (volt-amperes)	$5.0 \times V_{max}$	100	100	$0.005 \times V_{max}$	100	$5.0 \times V_{max}$	100	100	100
	Current (amperes)	5.0	$100/V_{max}$	$100/V_{max}$	0.005	$100/V_{max}$	5.0	$100/V_{max}$	$100/V_{max}$	$100/V_{max}$

*Voltage ranges shown are for continuous dc in indoor locations or where wet contact is not likely to occur. For interrupted dc or wet contact conditions, see Note 4.

Notes for Tables 11(A) and 11(B)

1. V_{max}, I_{max}, and VA_{max} are determined with the current-limiting impedance in the circuit (not bypassed) as follows:

V_{max}: Maximum output voltage regardless of load with rated input applied.

I_{max}: Maximum output current under any noncapacitive load, including short circuit, and with overcurrent protection bypassed if used. Where a transformer limits the output current, I_{max} limits apply after 1 minute of operation. Where a current-limiting impedance, listed for the purpose, or as part of a listed product, is used in combination with a nonpower-limited transformer or a stored energy source, e.g., storage battery, to limit the output current, I_{max} limits apply after 5 seconds.

VA_{max}: Maximum volt-ampere output after 1 minute of operation regardless of load and overcurrent protection bypassed if used.

2. For nonsinusoidal ac, V_{max} shall not be greater than 42.4 volts peak. Where wet contact (immersion not included) is likely to occur, Class 3 wiring methods shall be used or V_{max} shall not be greater than 15 volts for sinusoidal ac and 21.2 volts peak for nonsinusoidal ac.

3. If the power source is a transformer, VA_{max} is 350 or less when V_{max} is 15 or less.

4. For dc interrupted at a rate of 10 to 200 Hz, V_{max} shall not be greater than 24.8 volts peak. Where wet contact (immersion not included) is likely to occur, Class 3 wiring methods shall be used, or V_{max} shall not be greater than 30 volts for continuous dc; 12.4 volts peak for dc that is interrupted at a rate of 10 to 200 Hz.

Tables 12(A) and 12(B)

For listing purposes, Tables 12(A) and 12(B) provide the required power source limitations for power-limited fire alarm sources. Table 12(A) applies for alternating-current sources, and Table 12(B) applies for direct-current sources.

The power for power-limited fire alarm circuits shall be either (1) inherently limited, requiring no overcurrent protection, or (2) not inherently limited, requiring the power to be limited by a combination of power source and overcurrent protection.

As part of the listing, the PLFA power source shall be durably marked where plainly visible to indicate that it is a power-limited fire alarm power source. The overcurrent device, where required, shall be located at the point where the conductor to be protected receives its supply and shall not be interchangeable with devices of higher ratings. The overcurrent device shall be permitted as an integral part of the power source.

Table 12(A) PLFA Alternating-Current Power Source Limitations

Power Source		Inherently Limited Power Source (Overcurrent Protection Not Required)			Not Inherently Limited Power Source (Overcurrent Protection Required)		
Circuit voltage V_{max} (volts) (see Note 1)		0 through 20	Over 20 and through 30	Over 30 and through 100	0 through 20	Over 20 and through 100	Over 100 and through 150
Power limitations VA_{max} (volt-amperes) (see Note 1)		—	—	—	250 (see Note 2)	250	N.A.
Current limitations I_{max} (amperes) (see Note 1)		8.0	8.0	$150/V_{max}$	$1000/V_{max}$	$1000/V_{max}$	1.0
Maximum overcurrent protection (amperes)		—	—	—	5.0	$100/V_{max}$	1.0
Power source maximum nameplate ratings	VA (volt-amperes)	$5.0 \times V_{max}$	100	100	$5.0 \times V_{max}$	100	100
	Current (amperes)	5.0	$100/V_{max}$	$100/V_{max}$	5.0	$100/V_{max}$	$100/V_{max}$

Table 12(B) PLFA Direct-Current Power Source Limitations

Power Source		Inherently Limited Power Source (Overcurrent Protection Not Required)			Not Inherently Limited Power Source (Overcurrent Protection Required)		
Circuit voltage V_{max} (volts) (see Note 1)		0 through 20	Over 20 and through 30	Over 30 and through 100	0 through 20	Over 20 and through 100	Over 100 and through 150
Power limitations VA_{max} (volt-amperes) (see Note 1)		—	—	—	250 (see Note 2)	250	N.A.
Current limitations I_{max} (amperes) (see Note 1)		8.0	8.0	$150/V_{max}$	$1000/V_{max}$	$1000/V_{max}$	1.0
Maximum overcurrent protection (amperes)		—	—	—	5.0	$100/V_{max}$	1.0
Power source maximum nameplate ratings	VA (volt-amperes)	$5.0 \times V_{max}$	100	100	$5.0 \times V_{max}$	100	100
	Current (amperes)	5.0	$100/V_{max}$	$100/V_{max}$	5.0	$100/V_{max}$	$100/V_{max}$

Notes for Tables 12(A) and 12(B)

1. V_{max}, I_{max}, and VA_{max} are determined as follows:

V_{max}: Maximum output voltage regardless of load with rated input applied.

I_{max}: Maximum output current under any noncapacitive load, including short circuit, and with overcurrent protection bypassed if used. Where a transformer limits the output current, I_{max} limits apply after 1 minute of operation. Where a current-limiting impedance, listed for the purpose, is used in combination with a nonpower-limited transformer or a stored energy source, e.g., storage battery, to limit the output current, I_{max} limits apply after 5 seconds.

VA_{max}: Maximum volt-ampere output after 1 minute of operation regardless of load and overcurrent protection bypassed if used. Current limiting impedance shall not be bypassed when determining I_{max} and VA_{max}.

2. If the power source is a transformer, VA_{max} is 350 or less when V_{max} is 15 or less.

Annex A Product Safety Standards

Annex A is not a part of the requirements of this NFPA document but is included for informational purposes only.

This informational annex provides a list of product safety standards used for product listing where that listing is required by this *Code*. It is recognized that this list is current at the time of publication but that new standards or modifications to existing standards can occur at any time while this edition of the *Code* is in effect.

This annex does not form a mandatory part of the requirements of this *Code* but is intended only to provide *Code* users with informational guidance about the product characteristics about which *Code* requirements have been based.

Product Standard Name	Product Standard Number
Antenna-Discharge Units	UL 452
Arc-Fault Circuit-Interrupters	UL 1699
Armored Cable	UL 4
Attachment Plugs and Receptacles	UL 498
Audio/Video and Musical Instrument Apparatus for Household, Commercial, and Similar General Use	UL 60065
Audio-Video Products and Accessories	UL 1492
Busways	UL 857
Cables — Thermoplastic-Insulated Underground Feeder and Branch-Circuit Cables	UL 493
Cables — Thermoplastic-Insulated Wires and Cables	UL 83
Cables — Thermoset-Insulated Wires and Cables	UL 44
Cables for Non–Power-Limited Fire-Alarm Circuits	UL 1425
Cables for Power-Limited Fire-Alarm Circuits	UL 1424
Capacitors	UL 810
Cellular Metal Floor Raceways and Fittings	UL 209
Class 2 and Class 3 Transformers	UL 1585
Class 2 Power Units	UL 1310
Commercial Audio Equipment	UL 813
Communication Circuit Accessories	UL 1863
Communications Cables	UL 444
Community-Antenna Television Cables	UL 1655
Conduit — Type EB and A Rigid PVC Conduit and HDPE Conduit	UL 651A
Continuous Length HDPE Conduit	UL 651B HDPE
Control Centers for Changing Message Type Electric Signs	UL 1433
Cord Sets and Power-Supply Cords	UL 817
Data-Processing Cable	UL 1690
Dead-Front Switchboards	UL 891
Electric Motors	UL 1004
Electric Signs	UL 48
Electric Spas, Equipment Assemblies, and Associated Equipment	UL 1563
Electric Vehicle (EV) Charging System Equipment	UL 2202
Electric Water Heaters for Pools and Tubs	UL 1261
Electrical Apparatus for Explosive Gas Atmospheres	(UL 60079 Series)
Electrical Apparatus for Use in Class I, Zone 1 Hazardous (Classified) Locations Type of Protection — Encapsulation "m"	ISA S12.23.01
Electrical Apparatus for Use in Class I, Zones O & 1 Hazardous (Classified) Locations: General Requirements	ISA 12.0.01
Electrical Apparatus for Use in Class I, Zone 1 Hazardous (Classified) Locations: Type of Protection — Increased Safety "e"	ISA S12.16.01
Electrical Apparatus for Use in Class I, Zone 1 Hazardous (Classified) Locations: Type of Protection — Flameproof "d"	ISA S12.22.01
Electrical Apparatus for Use in Class I, Zone 1 Hazardous (Classified) Locations: Type of Protection — Powder Filling "q"	ISA S12.25.01
Electrical Apparatus for Use in Class I, Zone 1 Hazardous (Classified) Locations: Type of Protection — Oil-Immersion "O"	ISA S12.26.01
Electrical Heating Appliances	UL 499
Electrical Metallic Tubing — Aluminum	UL 797A
Electrical Metallic Tubing — Steel	UL 797
Electrical Nonmetallic Tubing	UL 1653
Electric-Battery-Powered Industrial Trucks	UL 583
Electrode Receptacles for Gas-Tube Signs	UL 879
Emergency Lighting and Power Equipment	UL 924
Enclosed and Dead-Front Switches	UL 98
Enclosures for Electrical Equipment	UL 50
Energy Management Equipment	UL 916
Fire Pump Controllers	UL 218

Product Standard Name	Product Standard Number
Fittings for Cable and Conduit	UL 514B
Flat-Plate Photovoltaic Modules and Panels	UL 1703
Flexible Cord and Fixture Wire	UL 62
Flexible Lighting Products	UL 2388
Flexible Metal Conduit	UL 1
Fluorescent-Lamp Ballasts	UL 935
Gas-Burning Heating Appliances for Manufactured Homes and Recreational Vehicles	UL 307B
Gas-Fired Cooking Appliances for Recreational Vehicles	UL 1075
Gas-Tube-Sign and Ignition Cable	UL 814
General-Use Snap Switches	UL 20
Ground-Fault Circuit-Interrupters	UL 943
Ground-Fault Sensing and Relaying Equipment	UL 1053
Grounding and Bonding Equipment	UL 467
Heating and Cooling Equipment	UL 1995
High-Intensity-Discharge Lamp Ballasts	UL 1029
High Voltage Industrial Control Equipment	UL 347
Household Refrigerators and Freezers	UL 250
Industrial Battery Chargers	UL 1564
Industrial Control Equipment	UL 508
Industrial Control Panels	UL 508A
Instrumentation Tray Cable	UL 2250
Insulated Wire Connector Systems for Underground Use or in Damp or Wet Locations	UL 486D
Intermediate Metal Conduit — Steel	UL 1242
Inverters, Converters, and Controllers for Use in Independent Power Systems	UL 1741
Isolated Power Systems Equipment	UL 1047
Junction Boxes for Swimming Pool Luminaires	UL 1241
Liquid Fuel-Burning Heating Appliances for Manufactured Homes and Recreational Vehicles	UL 307A
Liquid-Tight Flexible Nonmetallic Conduit	UL 1660
Liquid-Tight Flexible Steel Conduit	UL 360
Low Voltage Landscape Lighting Systems	UL 1838
Low-Voltage Fuses — Part 1: General Requirements	UL 248-1
Low-Voltage Fuses — Part 2: Class C Fuses	UL 248-2
Low-Voltage Fuses — Part 3: Class CA and CB Fuses	UL 248-3
Low-Voltage Fuses — Part 4: Class CC Fuses	UL 248-4
Low-Voltage Fuses — Part 5: Class G Fuses	UL 248-5
Low-Voltage Fuses — Part 6: Class H Non-Renewable Fuses	UL 248-6
Low-Voltage Fuses — Part 7: Class H Renewable Fuses	UL 248-7
Low-Voltage Fuses — Part 8: Class J Fuses	UL 248-8
Low-Voltage Fuses — Part 9: Class K Fuses	UL 248-9
Low-Voltage Fuses — Part 10: Class L Fuses	UL 249-10
Low-Voltage Fuses — Part 11: Plug Fuses	UL 248-11
Low-Voltage Fuses — Part 12: Class R Fuses	UL 248-12
Low-Voltage Fuses — Part 13: Semiconductor Fuses	UL 248–13
Low-Voltage Fuses — Part 14: Supplemental Fuses	UL 248–14
Low-Voltage Fuses — Part 15: Class T Fuses	UL 248-15
Low-Voltage Fuses — Part 16: Test Limiters	UL 248-16
Low-Voltage Lighting Fixtures for Use in Recreational Vehicles	UL 234
Luminaire Reflector Kits for Installation on Previously Installed Fluorescent Luminaires, Supplemental Requirements	UL 1598
Machine-Tool Wires and Cables	UL 1063
Manufactured Wiring Systems	UL 183
Medical Electrical Equipment — Part 1: General Requirements	UL 60601–1
Medium-Voltage Power Cables	UL 1072
Metal-Clad Cables	UL 1569
Metal-Clad Cables and Cable-Sealing Fittings for Use in Hazardous (Classified) Locations	UL 2225
Metallic Outlet Boxes	UL 514A
Mobile Home Pipe Heating Cable	UL 1462
Molded-Case Circuit Breakers, Molded-Case Switches, and Circuit-Breaker Enclosures	UL 489
Motor Control Centers	UL 845
Motor-Operated Appliances	UL 73
Neon Transformers and Power Supplies	UL 2161
Nonincendive Electrical Equipment for Use in Class I and II, Division 2 and Class III, Divisions 1 and 2 Hazardous (Classified) Locations	ISA S12.12
Nonmetallic Outlet Boxes, Flush-Device Boxes, and Covers	UL 514C
Nonmetallic Surface Raceways and Fittings	UL 5A
Nonmetallic Underground Conduit with Conductors	UL 1990
Office Furnishings	UL 1286
Optical Fiber Cable	UL 1651
Optical Fiber Cable Raceway	UL 2024
Panelboards	UL 67
Personal Protection Systems for Electric Vehicle Supply Circuits: General Requirements	UL 2231–1
Personal Protection Systems for Electric Vehicle Supply Circuits: Particular Requirements for Protection Devices for Use in Charging Systems	UL 2231–2
Plugs, Receptacles and Couplers for Electrical Vehicles	UL 2251
Portable Electric Luminaires	UL 153

(Continues)

Product Standard Name	Product Standard Number
Potting Compounds for Swimming Pool, Fountain, and Spa Equipment	UL 676A
Power Conversion Equipment	UL 508C
Power Outlets	UL 231
Power Units Other Than Class 2	UL 1012
Power-Limited Circuit Cables	UL 13
Professional Video and Audio Equipment	UL 1419
Protectors for Coaxial Communications Circuits	UL 497C
Protectors for Data Communication and Fire Alarm Circuits	UL 497B
Protectors for Paired Conductor Communications Circuits	UL 497
Reference Standard for Electrical Wires, Cables, and Flexible Cords	UL 1581
Reinforced Thermosetting Resin Conduit (RTRC) and Fittings	UL 1684
Residential Pipe Heating Cable	UL 2049
Rigid Metal Conduit — Steel	UL 6
Roof and Gutter De-Icing Cable Units	UL 1588
Room Air Conditioners	UL 484
Safety of Information Technology Equipment, Part 1: General Requirements	UL 60950–1
Schedule 40 and 80 Rigid PVC Conduit	UL 651
Seasonal and Holiday Decorative Products	UL 588
Secondary Protectors for Communications Circuits	UL 497A
Service-Entrance Cables	UL 854
Smoke Detectors for Fire Alarm Signaling Systems	UL 268
Specialty Transformers	UL 506
Splicing Wire Connectors	UL 486C
Stationary Engine Generator Assemblies	UL 2200
Strut-Type Channel Raceways and Fittings	UL 5B
Surface Metal Raceways and Fittings	UL 5
Surface Raceways and Fittings for Use with Data, Signal and Control Circuits	UL 5C
Surge Arresters — Gapped Silicon-Carbide Surge Arresters for AC Power Circuits	IEEE C62.1
Surge Arresters — Metal-Oxide Surge Arresters for AC Power Circuits	IEEE C62.11
Swimming Pool Pumps, Filters, and Chlorinators	UL 1081
Transfer Switch Equipment	UL 1008
Transient Voltage Surge Suppressors	UL 1449
Underfloor Raceways and Fittings	UL 884
Underwater Luminaires and Submersible Junction Boxes	UL 676
Uninterruptible Power Systems	UL 1778
Vacuum Cleaners, Blower Cleaners, and Household Floor Finishing Machines	UL 1017
Waste Disposers	UL 430
Wire Connectors and Soldering Lugs for Use with Copper Conductors	UL 486A
Wire Connectors for Use with Aluminum Conductors	UL 486B
Wireways, Auxiliary Gutters, and Associated Fittings	UL 870

Annex B   Application Information for Ampacity Calculation

This annex is not a part of the requirements of this NFPA document but is included for informational purposes only.

B.310.15(B)(1) Formula Application Information. This annex provides application information for ampacities calculated under engineering supervision.

B.310.15(B)(2) Typical Applications Covered by Tables. Typical ampacities for conductors rated 0 through 2000 volts are shown in Table B.310.1 through Table B.310.10. Underground electrical duct bank configurations, as detailed in Figure B.310.3, Figure B.310.4, and Figure B.310.5, are utilized for conductors rated 0 through 5000 volts. In Figure B.310.2 through Figure B.310.5, where adjacent duct banks are used, a separation of 1.5 m (5 ft) between the centerlines of the closest ducts in each bank or 1.2 m (4 ft) between the extremities of the concrete envelopes is sufficient to prevent derating of the conductors due to mutual heating. These ampacities were calculated as detailed in the basic ampacity paper, AIEE Paper 57-660, *The Calculation of the Temperature Rise and Load Capability of Cable Systems,* by J. H. Neher and M. H. McGrath. For additional information concerning the application of these ampacities, see IEEE/ICEA Standard S-135/P-46-426, *Power Cable Ampacities,* and IEEE Standard 835-1994, *Standard Power Cable Ampacity Tables.*

Typical values of thermal resistivity (Rho) are as follows:

Average soil (90 percent of USA) = 90
Concrete = 55
Damp soil (coastal areas, high water table) = 60
Paper insulation = 550
Polyethylene (PE) = 450
Polyvinyl chloride (PVC) = 650
Rubber and rubber-like = 500
Very dry soil (rocky or sandy) = 120

Thermal resistivity, as used in this annex, refers to the heat transfer capability through a substance by conduction. It is the reciprocal of thermal conductivity and is normally expressed in the units °C-cm/watt. For additional information on determining soil thermal resistivity (Rho), see ANSI/IEEE Standard 442-1996, *Guide for Soil Thermal Resistivity Measurements.*

B.310.15(B)(3) Criteria Modifications. Where values of load factor and Rho are known for a particular electrical duct bank installation and they are different from those shown in a specific table or figure, the ampacities shown in the table or figure can be modified by the application of factors derived from the use of Figure B.310.1.

Where two different ampacities apply to adjacent portions of a circuit, the higher ampacity can be used beyond the point of transition, a distance equal to 3 m (10 ft) or 10 percent of the circuit length figured at the higher ampacity, whichever is less.

Where the burial depth of direct burial or electrical duct bank circuits are modified from the values shown in a figure or table, ampacities can be modified as shown in (a) and (b) as follows.

(a)   Where burial depths are increased in part(s) of an electrical duct run to avoid underground obstructions, no decrease in ampacity of the conductors is needed, provided the total length of parts of the duct run increased in depth to avoid obstructions is less than 25 percent of the total run length.

(b)   Where burial depths are deeper than shown in a specific underground ampacity table or figure, an ampacity derating factor of 6 percent per increased 300 mm (foot) of depth for all values of Rho can be utilized. No rating change is needed where the burial depth is decreased.

B.310.15(B)(4) Electrical Ducts. The term *electrical duct(s)* is defined in 310.60.

B.310.15(B)(5) Tables B.310.6 and B.310.7.

(a)   To obtain the ampacity of cables installed in two electrical ducts in one horizontal row with 190-mm (7.5-in.) center-to-center spacing between electrical ducts, similar to Figure B.310.2, Detail 1, multiply the ampacity shown for one duct in Table B.310.6 and Table B.310.7 by 0.88.

(b)   To obtain the ampacity of cables installed in four electrical ducts in one horizontal row with 190-mm (7.5-in.) center-to-center spacing between electrical ducts, similar to Figure B.310.2, Detail 2, multiply the ampacity shown for three electrical ducts in Table B.310.6 and Table B.310.7 by 0.94.

B.310.15(B)(6) Electrical Ducts Used in Figure B.310.2. If spacing between electrical ducts, as shown in Figure B.310.2, is less than specified in Figure B.310.2, where electrical ducts enter equipment enclosures from underground, the ampacity of conductors contained within such electrical ducts need not be reduced.

B.310.15(B)(7) Examples Showing Use of Figure B.310.1 for Electrical Duct Bank Ampacity Modifications. Figure B.310.1 is used for interpolation or extrapolation for values of Rho and load factor for cables installed in electrical ducts. The upper family of curves shows the variation in ampacity and Rho at unity load factor in terms of I_1, the ampacity for Rho = 60, and 50 percent load factor. Each curve is designated for a particular ratio I_2/I_1, where I_2 is the ampacity at Rho = 120 and 100 percent load factor.

The lower family of curves shows the relationship between Rho and load factor that will give substantially the same ampacity as the indicated value of Rho at 100 percent load factor.

As an example, to find the ampacity of a 500 kcmil copper cable circuit for six electrical ducts as shown in Table B.310.5: At the Rho = 60, LF = 50, I_1 = 583; for Rho = 120 and LF = 100, I_2 = 400. The ratio I_2/I_1 = 0.686. Locate Rho = 90 at the bottom of the chart and follow the 90 Rho line to the intersection with 100 percent load factor where the equivalent Rho = 90. Then

follow the 90 Rho line to I_2/I_1 ratio of 0.686 where F = 0.74. The desired ampacity = 0.74 × 583 = 431, which agrees with the table for Rho = 90, LF = 100.

To determine the ampacity for the same circuit where Rho = 80 and LF = 75, using Figure B.310.1, the equivalent Rho = 43, F = 0.855, and the desired ampacity = 0.855 × 583 = 498 amperes. Values for using Figure B.310.1 are found in the electrical duct bank ampacity tables of this annex.

Where the load factor is less than 100 percent and can be verified by measurement or calculation, the ampacity of electrical duct bank installations can be modified as shown. Different values of Rho can be accommodated in the same manner.

Table B.310.1 Ampacities of Two or Three Insulated Conductors, Rated 0 Through 2000 Volts, Within an Overall Covering (Multiconductor Cable), in Raceway in Free Air Based on Ambient Air Temperature of 30°C (86°F)

Size (AWG or kcmil)	Temperature Rating of Conductor. (See Table 310.13.)						Size (AWG or kcmil)
	60°C (140°F)	75°C (167°F)	90°C (194°F)	60°C (140°F)	75°C (167°F)	90°C (194°F)	
	Types TW, UF	Types RHW, THHW, THW, THWN, XHHW, ZW	Types THHN, THHW, THW-2, THWN-2, RHH, RWH-2, USE-2, XHHW, XHHW-2, ZW-2	Type TW	Types RHW, THHW, THW, THWN, XHHW	Types THHN, THHW, THW-2, THWN-2, RHH, RWH-2,USE-2, XHHW, XHHW-2, ZW-2	
	COPPER			ALUMINUM OR COPPER-CLAD ALUMINUM			
14	16*	18*	21*	—	—	—	14
12	20*	24*	27*	16*	18*	21*	12
10	27*	33*	36*	21*	25*	28*	10
8	36	43	48	28	33	37	8
6	48	58	65	38	45	51	6
4	66	79	89	51	61	69	4
3	76	90	102	59	70	79	3
2	88	105	119	69	83	93	2
1	102	121	137	80	95	106	1
1/0	121	145	163	94	113	127	1/0
2/0	138	166	186	108	129	146	2/0
3/0	158	189	214	124	147	167	3/0
4/0	187	223	253	147	176	197	4/0
250	205	245	276	160	192	217	250
300	234	281	317	185	221	250	300
350	255	305	345	202	242	273	350
400	274	328	371	218	261	295	400
500	315	378	427	254	303	342	500

Table B.310.1 *Continued*

	Temperature Rating of Conductor. (See Table 310.13.)						
	60°C (140°F)	75°C (167°F)	90°C (194°F)	60°C (140°F)	75°C (167°F)	90°C (194°F)	
	Types TW, UF	Types RHW, THHW, THW, THWN, XHHW, ZW	Types THHN, THHW, THW-2, THWN-2, RHH, RWH-2, USE-2, XHHW, XHHW-2, ZW-2	Type TW	Types RHW, THHW, THW, THWN, XHHW	Types THHN, THHW, THW-2, THWN-2, RHH, RWH-2,USE-2, XHHW, XHHW-2, ZW-2	
Size (AWG or kcmil)	COPPER			ALUMINUM OR COPPER-CLAD ALUMINUM			Size (AWG or kcmil)
600	343	413	468	279	335	378	600
700	376	452	514	310	371	420	700
750	387	466	529	321	384	435	750
800	397	479	543	331	397	450	800
900	415	500	570	350	421	477	900
1000	448	542	617	382	460	521	1000

Correction Factors

Ambient Temp. (°C)	For ambient temperatures other than 30°C (86°F), multiply the ampacities shown above by the appropriate factor shown below.						Ambient Temp. (°F)
21–25	1.08	1.05	1.04	1.08	1.05	1.04	70–77
26–30	1.00	1.00	1.00	1.00	1.00	1.00	79–86
31–35	0.91	0.94	0.96	0.91	0.94	0.96	88–95
36–40	0.82	0.88	0.91	0.82	0.88	0.91	97–104
41–45	0.71	0.82	0.87	0.71	0.82	0.87	106–113
46–50	0.58	0.75	0.82	0.58	0.75	0.82	115–122
51–55	0.41	0.67	0.76	0.41	0.67	0.76	124–131
56–60	—	0.58	0.71	—	0.58	0.71	133–140
61–70	—	0.33	0.58	—	0.33	0.58	142–158
71–80	—	—	0.41	—	—	0.41	160–176

*Unless otherwise specifically permitted elsewhere in this *Code*, the overcurrent protection for these conductor types shall not exceed 15 amperes for 14 AWG, 20 amperes for 12 AWG, and 30 amperes for 10 AWG copper; or 15 amperes for 12 AWG and 25 AWG amperes for 10 AWG aluminum and copper-clad aluminum.

Table B.310.3 Ampacities of Multiconductor Cables with Not More Than Three Insulated Conductors, Rated 0 Through 2000 Volts, in Free Air Based on Ambient Air Temperature of 40°C (104°F) (For Types TC, MC, MI, UF, and USE Cables)

| Size (AWG or kcmil) | Temperature Rating of Conductor. (See Table 310.13.) | | | | | | | | Size (AWG or kcmil) |
| | 60°C (140°F) | 75°C (167°F) | 85°C (185°F) | 90°C (194°F) | 60°C (140°F) | 75°C (167°F) | 85°C (185°F) | 90°C (194°F) | |
	COPPER				ALUMINUM OR COPPER-CLAD ALUMINUM				
18	—	—	—	11*	—	—	—	—	18
16	—	—	—	16*	—	—	—	—	16
14	18*	21*	24*	25*	—	—	—	—	14
12	21*	28*	30*	32*	18*	21*	24*	25*	12
10	28*	36*	41*	43*	21*	28*	30*	32*	10
8	39	50	56	59	30	39	44	46	8
6	52	68	75	79	41	53	59	61	6
4	69	89	100	104	54	70	78	81	4
3	81	104	116	121	63	81	91	95	3
2	92	118	132	138	72	92	103	108	2
1	107	138	154	161	84	108	120	126	1
1/0	124	160	178	186	97	125	139	145	1/0
2/0	143	184	206	215	111	144	160	168	2/0
3/0	165	213	238	249	129	166	185	194	3/0
4/0	190	245	274	287	149	192	214	224	4/0
250	212	274	305	320	166	214	239	250	250
300	237	306	341	357	186	240	268	280	300
350	261	337	377	394	205	265	296	309	350
400	281	363	406	425	222	287	317	334	400
500	321	416	465	487	255	330	368	385	500
600	354	459	513	538	284	368	410	429	600
700	387	502	562	589	306	405	462	473	700
750	404	523	586	615	328	424	473	495	750
800	415	539	604	633	339	439	490	513	800
900	438	570	639	670	362	469	514	548	900
1000	461	601	674	707	385	499	558	584	1000

Correction Factors

Ambient Temp. (°C)	For ambient temperatures other than 40°C (104°F), multiply the ampacities shown above by the appropriate factor shown below.								Ambient Temp. (°F)
21–25	1.32	1.20	1.15	1.14	1.32	1.20	1.15	1.14	70–77
26–30	1.22	1.13	1.11	1.10	1.22	1.13	1.11	1.10	79–86
31–35	1.12	1.07	1.05	1.05	1.12	1.07	1.05	1.05	88–95
36–40	1.00	1.00	1.00	1.00	1.00	1.00	1.00	1.00	97–104
41–45	0.87	0.93	0.94	0.95	0.87	0.93	0.94	0.95	106–113
46–50	0.71	0.85	0.88	0.89	0.71	0.85	0.88	0.89	115–122
51–55	0.50	0.76	0.82	0.84	0.50	0.76	0.82	0.84	124–131
56–60	—	0.65	0.75	0.77	—	0.65	0.75	0.77	133–140
61–70	—	0.38	0.58	0.63	—	0.38	0.58	0.63	142–158
71–80	—	—	0.33	0.44	—	—	0.33	0.44	160–176

*Unless otherwise specifically permitted elsewhere in this *Code*, the overcurrent protection for these conductor types shall not exceed 15 amperes for 14 AWG, 20 amperes for 12 AWG, and 30 amperes for 10 AWG copper; or 15 amperes for 12 AWG and 25 amperes for 10 AWG aluminum and copper-clad aluminum.

Table B.310.5 Ampacities of Single Insulated Conductors, Rated 0 through 2000 Volts, in Nonmagnetic Underground Electrical Ducts (One Conductor per Electrical Duct), Based on Ambient Earth Temperature of 20°C (68°F), Electrical Duct Arrangement per Figure B.310.2, Conductor Temperature 75°C (167°F)

Size (kcmil)	3 Electrical Ducts (Fig. B.310.2, Detail 2) Types RHW, THHW, THW, THWN, XHHW, USE			6 Electrical Ducts (Fig. B.310.2, Detail 3) Types RHW, THHW, THW, THWN, XHHW, USE			9 Electrical Ducts (Fig. B.310.2, Detail 4) Types RHW, THHW, THW, THWN, XHHW, USE			3 Electrical Ducts (Fig. B.310.2, Detail 2) Types RHW, THHW, THW, THWN, XHHW, USE			6 Electrical Ducts (Fig. B.310.2, Detail 3) Types RHW, THHW, THW, THWN, XHHW, USE			9 Electrical Ducts (Fig. B.310.2, Detail 4) Types RHW, THHW, THW, THWN, XHHW, USE			Size (kcmil)
	COPPER									ALUMINUM OR COPPER-CLAD ALUMINUM									
	RHO 60 LF 50	RHO 90 LF 100	RHO 120 LF 100	RHO 60 LF 50	RHO 90 LF 100	RHO 120 LF 100	RHO 60 LF 50	RHO 90 LF 100	RHO 120 LF 100	RHO 60 LF 50	RHO 90 LF 100	RHO 120 LF 100	RHO 60 LF 50	RHO 90 LF 100	RHO 120 LF 100	RHO 60 LF 50	RHO 90 LF 100	RHO 120 LF 100	
250	410	344	327	386	295	275	369	270	252	320	269	256	302	230	214	288	211	197	250
350	503	418	396	472	355	330	446	322	299	393	327	310	369	277	258	350	252	235	350
500	624	511	484	583	431	400	545	387	360	489	401	379	457	337	313	430	305	284	500
750	794	640	603	736	534	494	674	469	434	626	505	475	581	421	389	538	375	347	750
1000	936	745	700	864	617	570	776	533	493	744	593	557	687	491	453	629	432	399	1000
1250	1055	832	781	970	686	632	854	581	536	848	668	627	779	551	508	703	478	441	1250
1500	1160	907	849	1063	744	685	918	619	571	941	736	689	863	604	556	767	517	477	1500
1750	1250	970	907	1142	793	729	975	651	599	1026	796	745	937	651	598	823	550	507	1750
2000	1332	1027	959	1213	836	768	1030	683	628	1103	850	794	1005	693	636	877	581	535	2000

Ambient Temp. (°C)	Correction Factors						Ambient Temp. (°F)
6–10	1.09	1.09	1.09	1.09	1.09	1.09	43–50
11–15	1.04	1.04	1.04	1.04	1.04	1.04	52–59
16–20	1.00	1.00	1.00	1.00	1.00	1.00	61–68
21–25	0.95	0.95	0.95	0.95	0.95	0.95	70–77
26–30	0.90	0.90	0.90	0.90	0.90	0.90	79–86

Table B.310.6 Ampacities of Three Insulated Conductors, Rated 0 through 2000 Volts, Within an Overall Covering (Three-Conductor Cable) in Underground Electrical Ducts (One Cable per Electrical Duct) Based on Ambient Earth Temperature of 20°C (68°F), Electrical Duct Arrangement per Figure B.310.2, Conductor Temperature 75°C (167°F)

Size (AWG or kcmil)	1 Electrical Duct (Fig. B.310.2, Detail 1) Types RHW, THHW, THW, THWN, XHHW, USE			3 Electrical Ducts (Fig. B.310.2, Detail 2) Types RHW, THHW, THW, THWN, XHHW, USE			6 Electrical Ducts (Fig. B.310.2, Detail 3) Types RHW, THHW, THW, THWN, XHHW, USE			1 Electrical Duct (Fig. B.310.2, Detail 1) Types RHW, THHW, THW, THWN, XHHW, USE			3 Electrical Ducts (Fig. B.310.2, Detail 2) Types RHW, THHW, THW, THWN, XHHW, USE			6 Electrical Ducts (Fig. B.310.2, Detail 3) Types RHW, THHW, THW, THWN, XHHW, USE			Size (AWG or kcmil)
	COPPER									ALUMINUM OR COPPER-CLAD ALUMINUM									
	RHO 60 LF 50	RHO 90 LF 100	RHO 120 LF 100	RHO 60 LF 50	RHO 90 LF 100	RHO 120 LF 100	RHO 60 LF 50	RHO 90 LF 100	RHO 120 LF 100	RHO 60 LF 50	RHO 90 LF 100	RHO 120 LF 100	RHO 60 LF 50	RHO 90 LF 100	RHO 120 LF 100	RHO 60 LF 50	RHO 90 LF 100	RHO 120 LF 100	
8	58	54	53	56	48	46	53	42	39	45	42	41	43	37	36	41	32	30	8
6	77	71	69	74	63	60	70	54	51	60	55	54	57	49	47	54	42	39	6
4	101	93	91	96	81	77	91	69	65	78	72	71	75	63	60	71	54	51	4
2	132	121	118	126	105	100	119	89	83	103	94	92	98	82	78	92	70	65	2
1	154	140	136	146	121	114	137	102	95	120	109	106	114	94	89	107	79	74	1
1/0	177	160	156	168	137	130	157	116	107	138	125	122	131	107	101	122	90	84	1/0
2/0	203	183	178	192	156	147	179	131	121	158	143	139	150	122	115	140	102	95	2/0
3/0	233	210	204	221	178	158	205	148	137	182	164	159	172	139	131	160	116	107	3/0
4/0	268	240	232	253	202	190	234	168	155	209	187	182	198	158	149	183	131	121	4/0
250	297	265	256	280	222	209	258	184	169	233	207	201	219	174	163	202	144	132	250
350	363	321	310	340	267	250	312	219	202	285	252	244	267	209	196	245	172	158	350
500	444	389	375	414	320	299	377	261	240	352	308	297	328	254	237	299	207	190	500
750	552	478	459	511	388	362	462	314	288	446	386	372	413	314	293	374	254	233	750
1000	628	539	518	579	435	405	522	351	321	521	447	430	480	361	336	433	291	266	1000

Ambient Temp. (°C)	Correction Factors																		Ambient Temp. (°F)
6–10	1.09			1.09			1.09			1.09			1.09			1.09			43–50
11–15	1.04			1.04			1.04			1.04			1.04			1.04			52–59
16–20	1.00			1.00			1.00			1.00			1.00			1.00			61–68
21–25	0.95			0.95			0.95			0.95			0.95			0.95			70–77
26–30	0.90			0.90			0.90			0.90			0.90			0.90			79–86

Table B.310.7 Ampacities of Three Single Insulated Conductors, Rated 0 Through 2000 Volts, in Underground Electrical Ducts (Three Conductors per Electrical Duct) Based on Ambient Earth Temperature of 20°C (68°F), Electrical Duct Arrangement per Figure B.310.2, Conductor Temperature 75°C (167°F)

Size (AWG or kcmil)	1 Electrical Duct (Fig. B.310.2, Detail 1) Types RHW, THHW, THW, THWN, XHHW, USE			3 Electrical Ducts (Fig. B.310.2, Detail 2) Types RHW, THHW, THW, THWN, XHHW, USE			6 Electrical Ducts (Fig. B.310.2, Detail 3) Types RHW, THHW, THW, THWN, XHHW, USE			1 Electrical Duct (Fig. B.310.2, Detail 1) Types RHW, THHW, THW, THWN, XHHW, USE			3 Electrical Ducts (Fig. B.310.2, Detail 2) Types RHW, THHW, THW, THWN, XHHW, USE			6 Electrical Ducts (Fig. B.310.2, Detail 3) Types RHW, THHW, THW, THWN, XHHW, USE			Size (AWG or kcmil)
	COPPER									ALUMINUM OR COPPER-CLAD ALUMINUM									
	RHO 60 LF 50	RHO 90 LF 100	RHO 120 LF 100	RHO 60 LF 50	RHO 90 LF 100	RHO 120 LF 100	RHO 60 LF 50	RHO 90 LF 100	RHO 120 LF 100	RHO 60 LF 50	RHO 90 LF 100	RHO 120 LF 100	RHO 60 LF 50	RHO 90 LF 100	RHO 120 LF 100	RHO 60 LF 50	RHO 90 LF 100	RHO 120 LF 100	
8	63	58	57	61	51	49	57	44	41	49	45	44	47	40	38	45	34	32	8
6	84	77	75	80	67	63	75	56	53	66	60	58	63	52	49	59	44	41	6
4	111	100	98	105	86	81	98	73	67	86	78	76	79	67	63	77	57	52	4
3	129	116	113	122	99	94	113	83	77	101	91	89	83	77	73	84	65	60	3
2	147	132	128	139	112	106	129	93	86	115	103	100	108	87	82	101	73	67	2
1	171	153	148	161	128	121	149	106	98	133	119	115	126	100	94	116	83	77	1
1/0	197	175	169	185	146	137	170	121	111	153	136	132	144	114	107	133	94	87	1/0
2/0	226	200	193	212	166	156	194	136	126	176	156	151	165	130	121	151	106	98	2/0
3/0	260	228	220	243	189	177	222	154	142	203	178	172	189	147	138	173	121	111	3/0
4/0	301	263	253	280	215	201	255	175	161	235	205	198	219	168	157	199	137	126	4/0
250	334	290	279	310	236	220	281	192	176	261	227	218	242	185	172	220	150	137	250
300	373	321	308	344	260	242	310	210	192	293	252	242	272	204	190	245	165	151	300
350	409	351	337	377	283	264	340	228	209	321	276	265	296	222	207	266	179	164	350
400	442	376	361	394	302	280	368	243	223	349	297	284	321	238	220	288	191	174	400
500	503	427	409	460	341	316	412	273	249	397	338	323	364	270	250	326	216	197	500
600	552	468	447	511	371	343	457	296	270	446	373	356	408	296	274	365	236	215	600
700	602	509	486	553	402	371	492	319	291	488	408	389	443	321	297	394	255	232	700
750	632	529	505	574	417	385	509	330	301	508	425	405	461	334	309	409	265	241	750
800	654	544	520	597	428	395	527	338	308	530	439	418	481	344	318	427	273	247	800
900	692	575	549	628	450	415	554	355	323	563	466	444	510	365	337	450	288	261	900
1000	730	605	576	659	472	435	581	372	338	597	494	471	538	385	355	475	304	276	1000

Ambient Temp. (°C)	Correction Factors																		Ambient Temp. (°F)
6–10	1.09			1.09			1.09			1.09			1.09			1.09			43–50
11–15	1.04			1.04			1.04			1.04			1.04			1.04			52–59
16–20	1.00			1.00			1.00			1.00			1.00			1.00			61–68
21–25	0.95			0.95			0.95			0.95			0.95			0.95			70–77
26–30	0.90			0.90			0.90			0.90			0.90			0.90			79–86

Table B.310.8 Ampacities of Two or Three Insulated Conductors, Rated 0 Through 2000 Volts, Cabled Within an Overall (Two- or Three-Conductor) Covering, Directly Buried in Earth, Based on Ambient Earth Temperature of 20°C (68°F), Arrangement per Figure B.310.2, 100 Percent Load Factor, Thermal Resistance (Rho) of 90

Size (AWG or kcmil)	1 Cable (Fig. B.310.2, Detail 5)		2 Cables (Fig. B.310.2, Detail 6)		1 Cable (Fig. B.310.2, Detail 5)		2 Cables (Fig. B.310.2, Detail 6)		Size (AWG or kcmil)
	60°C (140°F)	75°C (167°F)	60°C (140°F)	75°C (167°F)	60°C (140°F)	75°C (167°F)	60°C (140°F)	75°C (167°F)	
	TYPES				TYPES				
	UF	RHW, THHW, THW, THWN, XHHW, USE	UF	RHW, THHW, THW, THWN, XHHW, USE	UF	RHW, THHW, THW, THWN, XHHW, USE	UF	RHW, THHW, THW, THWN, XHHW, USE	
	COPPER				ALUMINUM OR COPPER-CLAD ALUMINUM				
8	64	75	60	70	51	59	47	55	8
6	85	100	81	95	68	75	60	70	6
4	107	125	100	117	83	97	78	91	4
2	137	161	128	150	107	126	110	117	2
1	155	182	145	170	121	142	113	132	1
1/0	177	208	165	193	138	162	129	151	1/0
2/0	201	236	188	220	157	184	146	171	2/0
3/0	229	269	213	250	179	210	166	195	3/0
4/0	259	304	241	282	203	238	188	220	4/0
250	—	333	—	308	—	261	—	241	250
350	—	401	—	370	—	315	—	290	350
500	—	481	—	442	—	381	—	350	500
750	—	585	—	535	—	473	—	433	750
1000	—	657	—	600	—	545	—	497	1000
Ambient Temp. (°C)	Correction Factors								Ambient Temp. (°F)
6–10	1.12	1.09	1.12	1.09	1.12	1.09	1.12	1.09	43–50
11–15	1.06	1.04	1.06	1.04	1.06	1.04	1.06	1.04	52–59
16–20	1.00	1.00	1.00	1.00	1.00	1.00	1.00	1.00	61–68
21–25	0.94	0.95	0.94	0.95	0.94	0.95	0.94	0.95	70–77
26–30	0.87	0.90	0.87	0.90	0.87	0.90	0.87	0.90	79–86

Note: For ampacities of Type UF cable in underground electrical ducts, multiply the ampacities shown in the table by 0.74.

Table B.310.9 Ampacities of Three Triplexed Single Insulated Conductors, Rated 0 Through 2000 Volts, Directly Buried in Earth Based on Ambient Earth Temperature of 20°C (68°F), Arrangement per Figure B.310.2, 100 Percent Load Factor, Thermal Resistance (Rho) of 90

Size (AWG or kcmil)	See Fig. B.310.2, Detail 7		See Fig. B.310.2, Detail 8		See Fig. B.310.2, Detail 7		See Fig. B.310.2, Detail 8		Size (AWG or kcmil)
	60°C (140°F)	75°C (167°F)	60°C (140°F)	75°C (167°F)	60°C (140°F)	75°C (167°F)	60°C (140°F)	75°C (167°F)	
	TYPES				TYPES				
	UF	USE	UF	USE	UF	USE	UF	USE	
	COPPER				ALUMINUM OR COPPER-CLAD ALUMINUM				
8	72	84	66	77	55	65	51	60	8
6	91	107	84	99	72	84	66	77	6
4	119	139	109	128	92	108	85	100	4
2	153	179	140	164	119	139	109	128	2
1	173	203	159	186	135	158	124	145	1
1/0	197	231	181	212	154	180	141	165	1/0
2/0	223	262	205	240	175	205	159	187	2/0
3/0	254	298	232	272	199	233	181	212	3/0
4/0	289	339	263	308	226	265	206	241	4/0
250	—	370	—	336	—	289	—	263	250
350	—	445	—	403	—	349	—	316	350
500	—	536	—	483	—	424	—	382	500
750	—	654	—	587	—	525	—	471	750
1000	—	744	—	665	—	608	—	544	1000
Ambient Temp. (°C)	Correction Factors								Ambient Temp. (°F)
6–10	1.12	1.09	1.12	1.09	1.12	1.09	1.12	1.09	43–50
11–15	1.06	1.04	1.06	1.04	1.06	1.04	1.06	1.04	52–59
16–20	1.00	1.00	1.00	1.00	1.00	1.00	1.00	1.00	61–68
21–25	0.94	0.95	0.94	0.95	0.94	0.95	0.94	0.95	70–77
26–30	0.87	0.90	0.87	0.90	0.87	0.90	0.87	0.90	79–86

Table B.310.10 Ampacities of Three Single Insulated Conductors, Rated 0 Through 2000 Volts, Directly Buried in Earth Based on Ambient Earth Temperature of 20°C (68°F), Arrangement per Figure B.310.2, 100 Percent Load Factor, Thermal Resistance (Rho) of 90

Size (AWG or kcmil)	See Fig. B.310.2, Detail 9		See Fig. B.310.2, Detail 10		See Fig. B.310.2, Detail 9		See Fig. B.310.2, Detail 10		Size (AWG or kcmil)
	60°C (140°F)	75°C (167°F)	60°C (140°F)	75°C (167°F)	60°C (140°F)	75°C (167°F)	60°C (140°F)	75°C (167°F)	
	TYPES				TYPES				
	UF	USE	UF	USE	UF	USE	UF	USE	
	COPPER				ALUMINUM OR COPPER-CLAD ALUMINUM				
8	84	98	78	92	66	77	61	72	8
6	107	126	101	118	84	98	78	92	6
4	139	163	130	152	108	127	101	118	4
2	178	209	165	194	139	163	129	151	2
1	201	236	187	219	157	184	146	171	1
1/0	230	270	212	249	179	210	165	194	1/0
2/0	261	306	241	283	204	239	188	220	2/0
3/0	297	348	274	321	232	272	213	250	3/0
4/0	336	394	309	362	262	307	241	283	4/0
250	—	429	—	394	—	335	—	308	250
350	—	516	—	474	—	403	—	370	350
500	—	626	—	572	—	490	—	448	500
750	—	767	—	700	—	605	—	552	750
1000	—	887	—	808	—	706	—	642	1000
1250	—	979	—	891	—	787	—	716	1250
1500	—	1063	—	965	—	862	—	783	1500
1750	—	1133	—	1027	—	930	—	843	1750
2000	—	1195	—	1082	—	990	—	897	2000
Ambient Temp.(°C)	Correction Factors								Ambient Temp.(°F)
6–10	1.12	1.09	1.12	1.09	1.12	1.09	1.12	1.09	43–50
11–15	1.06	1.04	1.06	1.04	1.06	1.04	1.06	1.04	52–59
16–20	1.00	1.00	1.00	1.00	1.00	1.00	1.00	1.00	61–68
21–25	0.94	0.95	0.94	0.95	0.94	0.95	0.94	0.95	70–77
26–30	0.87	0.90	0.87	0.90	0.87	0.90	0.87	0.90	79–86

Figure B.310.1 Interpolation Chart for Cables in a Duct Bank I_1 = ampacity for Rho = 60, 50 LF; I_2 = ampacity for Rho = 120, 100 LF (load factor); desired ampacity = F × I_1.

Detail 1
290 mm × 290 mm
(11.5 in. × 11.5 in.)
Electrical duct bank
One electrical duct

Detail 2
475 mm × 475 mm
(19 in. × 19 in.)
Electrical duct bank
Three electrical ducts
or

675 mm × 290 mm
(27 in. × 11.5 in.)
Electrical duct bank
Three electrical ducts

Detail 3
475 mm × 675 mm
(19 in. × 27 in.)
Electrical duct bank
Six electrical ducts
or

675 mm × 475 mm
(27 in. × 19 in.)
Electrical duct bank

Detail 4
675 mm × 675 mm
(27 in. × 27 in.)
Electrical duct bank
Nine electrical ducts

Detail 5
Buried 3
conductor
cable

Detail 6
Buried 3
conductor
cables

Detail 7
Buried triplexed
cables (1 circuit)

Detail 8
Buried triplexed
cables (2 circuits)

Detail 9
Buried single-conductor
cables (1 circuit)

Detail 10
Buried single-conductor
cables (2 circuits)

Note 1: Minimum burial depths to top electrical ducts or cables shall be in accordance with 300.5. Maximum depth to the top of electrical duct banks shall be 750 mm (30 in.) and maximum depth to the top of direct buried cables shall be 900 mm (36 in.).

Note 2: For two and four electrical duct installations with electrical ducts installed in a single row, see B.310.15(B)(5).

Legend

⬚ Backfill (earth or concrete)

◯ Electrical duct

● Cable or cables

Figure B.310.2 Cable Installation Dimensions for Use with Table B.310.5 through Table B.310.10.

Design Criteria
Neutral and Equipment
  Grounding conductor (EGC)
  Duct = 150 mm (6 in.)
Phase Ducts = 75 to 125 mm (3 to 5 in.)
Conductor Material = Copper
Number of Cables per Duct = 3

Number of Cables per Phase = 9
Rho concrete = Rho Earth − 5

Rho PVC Duct = 650
Rho Cable Insulation = 500
Rho Cable Jacket = 650

Notes:
1. Neutral configuration per 300.5(I), Exception No. 2, for isolated phase installations in nonmagnetic ducts.
2. Phasing is A, B, C in rows or columns. Where magnetic electrical ducts are used, conductors are installed A, B, C per electrical duct with the neutral and all equipment grounding conductors in the same electrical duct. In this case, the 6-in. trade size neutral duct is eliminated.
3. Maximum harmonic loading on the neutral conductor cannot exceed 50 percent of the phase current for the ampacities shown in the table.
4. Metallic shields of Type MV-90 cable shall be grounded at one point only where using A, B, C phasing in rows or columns.

Size kcmil	TYPES RHW, THHW, THW, THWN, XHHW, USE, OR MV-90*			Size kcmil
	Total per Phase Ampere Rating			
	RHO EARTH 60 LF 50	RHO EARTH 90 LF 100	RHO EARTH 120 LF 100	
250	2340 (260A/Cable)	1530 (170A/Cable)	1395 (155A/Cable)	250
350	2790 (310A/Cable)	1800 (200A/Cable)	1665 (185A/Cable)	350
500	3375 (375A/Cable)	2160 (240A/Cable)	1980 (220A/Cable)	500

Ambient Temp. (°C)	For ambient temperatures other than 20°C (68°F), multiply the ampacities shown above by the appropriate factor shown below.					Ambient Temp. (°F)
6–10	1.09	1.09	1.09	1.09	1.09	43–50
11–15	1.04	1.04	1.04	1.04	1.04	52–59
16–20	1.00	1.00	1.00	1.00	1.00	61–68
21–25	0.95	0.95	0.95	0.95	0.95	70–77
26–30	0.90	0.90	0.90	0.90	0.90	79–86

*Limited to 75°C conductor temperature.

FPN Figure B.310.3 Ampacities of Single Insulated Conductors Rated 0 through 5000 Volts in Underground Electrical Ducts (Three Conductors per Electrical Duct), Nine Single-Conductor Cables per Phase Based on Ambient Earth Temperature of 20°C (68°F), Conductor Temperature 75°C (167°F).

Design Criteria
Neutral and Equipment
  Grounding Conductor (EGC)
  Duct = 150 mm (6 in.)
Phase Ducts = 75 mm (3 in.)
Conductor Material = Copper
Number of Cables per Duct = 1

Number of Cables per Phase = 4
Rho Concrete = Rho Earth − 5
Rho PVC Duct = 650

Rho Cable Insulation = 500
Rho Cable Jacket = 650

Notes:
1. Neutral configuration per 300.5(I), Exception No. 2.
2. Maximum harmonic loading on the neutral conductor cannot exceed 50 percent of the phase current for the ampacities shown in the table.
3. Metallic shields of Type MV-90 cable shall be grounded at one point only.

Size kcmil	TYPES RHW, THHW, THW, THWN, XHHW, USE, OR MV-90*			Size kcmil
	Total per Phase Ampere Rating			
	RHO EARTH 60 LF 50	RHO EARTH 90 LF 100	RHO EARTH 120 LF 100	
750	2820 (705A/Cable)	1860 (465A/Cable)	1680 (420A/Cable)	750
1000	3300 (825A/Cable)	2140 (535A/Cable)	1920 (480A/Cable)	1000
1250	3700 (925A/Cable)	2380 (595A/Cable)	2120 (530A/Cable)	1250
1500	4060 (1015A/Cable)	2580 (645A/Cable)	2300 (575A/Cable)	1500
1750	4360 (1090A/Cable)	2740 (685A/Cable)	2460 (615A/Cable)	1750

Ambient Temp. (°C)	For ambient temperatures other than 20°C (68°F), multiply the ampacities shown above by the appropriate factor shown below.					Ambient Temp. (°F)
6–10	1.09	1.09	1.09	1.09	1.09	43–50
11–15	1.04	1.04	1.04	1.04	1.04	52–59
16–20	1.00	1.00	1.00	1.00	1.00	61–68
21–25	0.95	0.95	0.95	0.95	0.95	70–77
26–30	0.90	0.90	0.90	0.90	0.90	79–86

*Limited to 75°C conductor temperature.

FPN Figure B.310.4 Ampacities of Single Insulated Conductors Rated 0 through 5000 Volts in Nonmagnetic Underground Electrical Ducts (One Conductor per Electrical Duct), Four Single-Conductor Cables per Phase Based on Ambient Earth Temperature of 20°C (68°F), Conductor Temperature 75°C (167°F).

Design Criteria

Neutral and Equipment
   Grounding Conductor (EGC)
   Duct = 150 mm (6 in.)
Phase Ducts = 75 mm (3 in.)
Conductor Material = Copper
Number of Cables per Duct = 1

Number of Cables per Phase = 5
Rho Earth = Rho Earth – 5
Rho PVC Duct = 650

Rho Cable Insulation = 500
Rho Cable Jacket = 650

Notes:
1. Neutral configuration per 300.5(I), Exception No. 2.
2. Maximum harmonic loading on the neutral conductor cannot exceed 50 percent of the phase current for the ampacities shown in the table.
3. Metallic shields of Type MV-90 cable shall be grounded at one point only.

Size kcmil	TYPES RHW, THHW, THW, THWN, XHHW, USE, OR MV-90*			Size kcmil
	Total per Phase Ampere Rating			
	RHO EARTH 60 LF 50	RHO EARTH 90 LF 100	RHO EARTH 120 LF 100	
2000	5575 (1115A/Cable)	3375 (675A/Cable)	3000 (600A/Cable)	2000

Ambient Temp. (°C)	For ambient temperatures other than 20°C (68°F), multiply the ampacities shown above by the appropriate factor shown below.					Ambient Temp. (°F)
6–10	1.09	1.09	1.09	1.09	1.09	43–50
11–15	1.04	1.04	1.04	1.04	1.04	52–59
16–20	1.00	1.00	1.00	1.00	1.00	61–68
21–25	0.95	0.95	0.95	0.95	0.95	70–77
26–30	0.90	0.90	0.90	0.90	0.90	79–86

*Limited to 75°C conductor temperature.

FPN Figure B.310.5 Ampacities of Single Insulated Conductors Rated 0 through 5000 Volts in Nonmagnetic Underground Electrical Ducts (One Conductor per Electrical Duct), Five Single-Conductor Cables per Phase Based on Ambient Earth Temperature of 20°C (68°F), Conductor Temperature 75°C (167°F).

Table B.310.11 Adjustment Factors for More Than Three Current-Carrying Conductors in a Raceway or Cable with Load Diversity

Number of Current-Carrying Conductors	Percent of Values in Tables as Adjusted for Ambient Temperature if Necessary
4 – 6	80
7 – 9	70
10 – 24	70*
25 – 42	60*
43 – 85	50*

*These factors include the effects of a load diversity of 50 percent.

FPN: The ampacity limit for the number of current-carrying conductors in 10 through 85 is based on the following formula. For greater than 85 conductors, special calculations are required that are beyond the scope of this table.

$$A_2 = \sqrt{\frac{0.5N}{E}} \times (A_1) \text{ or } A_1, \text{ whichever is less}$$

where:
A_1 = ampacity from Table 310.16; Table 310.18; Table B.310.1; Table B.310.6; and Table B.310.7 multiplied by the appropriate factor from Table B.310.11.

N = total number of conductors used to obtain multiplying factor from Table B.310.11

E = desired number of current-carrying conductors in the raceway or cable

A_2 = ampacity limit for the current-carrying conductors in the raceway or cable

Example 1

Calculate the ampacity limit for twelve 14 AWG THWN current-carrying conductors (75°C) in a raceway that contains 24 conductors.

$$A_2 = \sqrt{\frac{(0.5)(24)}{12}} \times 20(0.7)$$

$$= 14 \text{ amperes (i.e., 50 percent diversity)}$$

Example 2

Calculate the ampacity limit for eighteen 14 AWG THWN current-carrying conductors (75°C) in a raceway that contains 24 conductors.

$$A_2 = \sqrt{\frac{(0.5)(24)}{18}} \times 20(0.7) = 11.5 \text{ amperes}$$

Annex C   Conduit and Tubing Fill Tables for Conductors and Fixture Wires of the Same Size

This annex is not a part of the requirements of this NFPA document but is included for informational purposes only.

*Where this table is used in conjunction with Tables C.1 through C.12, the conductors installed must be of the compact type.

Table C.1 Maximum Number of Conductors or Fixture Wires in Electrical Metallic Tubing (EMT) (*Based on Table 1, Chapter 9*)

| | | CONDUCTORS | | | | | | | | | |
| | Conductor Size (AWG kcmil) | Metric Designator (Trade Size) | | | | | | | | | |
Type		16 (½)	21 (¾)	27 (1)	35 (1¼)	41 (1½)	53 (2)	63 (2½)	78 (3)	91 (3½)	103 (4)
RHH, RHW, RHW-2	14	4	7	11	20	27	46	80	120	157	201
	12	3	6	9	17	23	38	66	100	131	167
	10	2	5	8	13	18	30	53	81	105	135
	8	1	2	4	7	9	16	28	42	55	70
	6	1	1	3	5	8	13	22	34	44	56
	4	1	1	2	4	6	10	17	26	34	44
	3	1	1	1	4	5	9	15	23	30	38
	2	1	1	1	3	4	7	13	20	26	33
	1	0	1	1	1	3	5	9	13	17	22
	1/0	0	1	1	1	2	4	7	11	15	19
	2/0	0	1	1	1	2	4	6	10	13	17
	3/0	0	0	1	1	1	3	5	8	11	14
	4/0	0	0	1	1	1	3	5	7	9	12
	250	0	0	0	1	1	1	3	5	7	9
	300	0	0	0	1	1	1	3	5	6	8
	350	0	0	0	1	1	1	3	4	6	7
	400	0	0	0	1	1	1	2	4	5	7
	500	0	0	0	0	1	1	2	3	4	6
	600	0	0	0	0	1	1	1	3	4	5
	700	0	0	0	0	0	1	1	2	3	4
	750	0	0	0	0	0	1	1	2	3	4
	800	0	0	0	0	0	1	1	2	3	4
	900	0	0	0	0	0	1	1	1	3	3
	1000	0	0	0	0	0	1	1	1	2	3
	1250	0	0	0	0	0	0	1	1	1	2
	1500	0	0	0	0	0	0	1	1	1	1
	1750	0	0	0	0	0	0	1	1	1	1
	2000	0	0	0	0	0	0	1	1	1	1
TW	14	8	15	25	43	58	96	168	254	332	424
	12	6	11	19	33	45	74	129	195	255	326
	10	5	8	14	24	33	55	96	145	190	243
	8	2	5	8	13	18	30	53	81	105	135
RHH*, RHW*, RHW-2*, THHW, THW, THW-2	14	6	10	16	28	39	64	112	169	221	282
RHH*, RHW*, RHW-2*, THHW, THW	12	4	8	13	23	31	51	90	136	177	227
	10	3	6	10	18	24	40	70	106	138	177
RHH*, RHW*, RHW-2*, THHW, THW, THW-2	8	1	4	6	10	14	24	42	63	83	106

Table C.1 *Continued*

	Conductor Size (AWG kcmil)	Metric Designator (Trade Size)									
Type		16 (½)	21 (¾)	27 (1)	35 (1¼)	41 (1½)	53 (2)	63 (2½)	78 (3)	91 (3½)	103 (4)
RHH*, RHW*, RHW-2*, TW, THW, THHW, THW-2	6	1	3	4	8	11	18	32	48	63	81
	4	1	1	3	6	8	13	24	36	47	60
	3	1	1	3	5	7	12	20	31	40	52
	2	1	1	2	4	6	10	17	26	34	44
	1	1	1	1	3	4	7	12	18	24	31
	1/0	0	1	1	2	3	6	10	16	20	26
	2/0	0	1	1	1	3	5	9	13	17	22
	3/0	0	1	1	1	2	4	7	11	15	19
	4/0	0	0	1	1	1	3	6	9	12	16
	250	0	0	1	1	1	3	5	7	10	13
	300	0	0	1	1	1	2	4	6	8	11
	350	0	0	0	1	1	1	4	6	7	10
	400	0	0	0	1	1	1	3	5	7	9
	500	0	0	0	1	1	1	3	4	6	7
	600	0	0	0	1	1	1	2	3	4	6
	700	0	0	0	0	1	1	1	3	4	5
	750	0	0	0	0	1	1	1	3	4	5
	800	0	0	0	0	1	1	1	3	3	5
	900	0	0	0	0	0	1	1	2	3	4
	1000	0	0	0	0	0	1	1	2	3	4
	1250	0	0	0	0	0	1	1	1	2	3
	1500	0	0	0	0	0	1	1	1	1	2
	1750	0	0	0	0	0	0	1	1	1	2
	2000	0	0	0	0	0	0	1	1	1	1
THHN, THWN, THWN-2	14	12	22	35	61	84	138	241	364	476	608
	12	9	16	26	45	61	101	176	266	347	443
	10	5	10	16	28	38	63	111	167	219	279
	8	3	6	9	16	22	36	64	96	126	161
	6	2	4	7	12	16	26	46	69	91	116
	4	1	2	4	7	10	16	28	43	56	71
	3	1	1	3	6	8	13	24	36	47	60
	2	1	1	3	5	7	11	20	30	40	51
	1	1	1	1	4	5	8	15	22	29	37
	1/0	1	1	1	3	4	7	12	19	25	32
	2/0	0	1	1	2	3	6	10	16	20	26
	3/0	0	1	1	1	3	5	8	13	17	22
	4/0	0	1	1	1	2	4	7	11	14	18
	250	0	0	1	1	1	3	6	9	11	15
	300	0	0	1	1	1	3	5	7	10	13
	350	0	0	1	1	1	2	4	6	9	11
	400	0	0	0	1	1	1	4	6	8	10
	500	0	0	0	1	1	1	3	5	6	8
	600	0	0	0	1	1	1	2	4	5	7
	700	0	0	0	1	1	1	2	3	4	6
	750	0	0	0	0	1	1	1	3	4	5
	800	0	0	0	0	1	1	1	3	4	5
	900	0	0	0	0	1	1	1	3	3	4
	1000	0	0	0	0	1	1	1	2	3	4
FEP, FEPB, PFA, PFAH, TFE	14	12	21	34	60	81	134	234	354	462	590
	12	9	15	25	43	59	98	171	258	337	430
	10	6	11	18	31	42	70	122	185	241	309
	8	3	6	10	18	24	40	70	106	138	177
	6	2	4	7	12	17	28	50	75	98	126
	4	1	3	5	9	12	20	35	53	69	88
	3	1	2	4	7	10	16	29	44	57	73
	2	1	1	3	6	8	13	24	36	47	60

(Continues)

Table C.1 *Continued*

		CONDUCTORS									
	Conductor Size (AWG kcmil)	Metric Designator (Trade Size)									
Type		16 (½)	21 (¾)	27 (1)	35 (1¼)	41 (1½)	53 (2)	63 (2½)	78 (3)	91 (3½)	103 (4)
PFA, PFAH, TFE	1	1	1	2	4	6	9	16	25	33	42
PFAH, TFE PFA, PFAH, TFE, Z	1/0	1	1	1	3	5	8	14	21	27	35
	2/0	0	1	1	3	4	6	11	17	22	29
	3/0	0	1	1	2	3	5	9	14	18	24
	4/0	0	1	1	1	2	4	8	11	15	19
Z	14	14	25	41	72	98	161	282	426	556	711
	12	10	18	29	51	69	114	200	302	394	504
	10	6	11	18	31	42	70	122	185	241	309
	8	4	7	11	20	27	44	77	117	153	195
	6	3	5	8	14	19	31	54	82	107	137
	4	1	3	5	9	13	21	37	56	74	94
	3	1	2	4	7	9	15	27	41	54	69
	2	1	1	3	6	8	13	22	34	45	57
	1	1	1	2	4	6	10	18	28	36	46
XHH, XHHW, XHHW-2, ZW	14	8	15	25	43	58	96	168	254	332	424
	12	6	11	19	33	45	74	129	195	255	326
	10	5	8	14	24	33	55	96	145	190	243
	8	2	5	8	13	18	30	53	81	105	135
	6	1	3	6	10	14	22	39	60	78	100
	4	1	2	4	7	10	16	28	43	56	72
	3	1	1	3	6	8	14	24	36	48	61
	2	1	1	3	5	7	11	20	31	40	51
XHH, XHHW, XHHW-2	1	1	1	1	4	5	8	15	23	30	38
	1/0	1	1	1	3	4	7	13	19	25	32
	2/0	0	1	1	2	3	6	10	16	21	27
	3/0	0	1	1	1	3	5	9	13	17	22
	4/0	0	1	1	1	2	4	7	11	14	18
	250	0	0	1	1	1	3	6	9	12	15
	300	0	0	1	1	1	3	5	8	10	13
	350	0	0	1	1	1	2	4	7	9	11
	400	0	0	0	1	1	1	4	6	8	10
	500	0	0	0	1	1	1	3	5	6	8
	600	0	0	0	1	1	1	2	4	5	6
	700	0	0	0	0	1	1	2	3	4	6
	750	0	0	0	0	1	1	1	3	4	5
	800	0	0	0	0	1	1	1	3	4	5
	900	0	0	0	0	1	1	1	3	3	4
	1000	0	0	0	0	0	1	1	2	3	4
	1250	0	0	0	0	0	1	1	1	2	3
	1500	0	0	0	0	0	1	1	1	1	3
	1750	0	0	0	0	0	0	1	1	1	2
	2000	0	0	0	0	0	0	1	1	1	1

Table C.1 *Continued*

	Conductor Size (AWG/ kcmil)	Metric Designator (Trade Size)					
Type		16 (½)	21 (¾)	27 (1)	35 (1¼)	41 (1½)	53 (2)
FFH-2, RFH-2, RFHH-3	18	8	14	24	41	56	92
	16	7	12	20	34	47	78
SF-2, SFF-2	18	10	18	30	52	71	116
	16	8	15	25	43	58	96
	14	7	12	20	34	47	78
SF-1, SFF-1	18	18	33	53	92	125	206
RFH-1, RFHH-2, TF, TFF, XF, XFF	18	14	24	39	68	92	152
RFHH-2, TF, TFF, XF, XFF	16	11	19	31	55	74	123
XF, XFF	14	8	15	25	43	58	96
TFN, TFFN	18	22	38	63	108	148	244
	16	17	29	48	83	113	186
PF, PFF, PGF, PGFF, PAF, PTF, PTFF, PAFF	18	21	36	59	103	140	231
	16	16	28	46	79	108	179
	14	12	21	34	60	81	134
ZF, ZFF, ZHF, HF, HFF	18	27	47	77	133	181	298
	16	20	35	56	98	133	220
	14	14	25	41	72	98	161
KF-2, KFF-2	18	39	69	111	193	262	433
	16	27	48	78	136	185	305
	14	19	33	54	93	127	209
	12	13	23	37	64	87	144
	10	8	15	25	43	58	96
KF-1, KFF-1	18	46	82	133	230	313	516
	16	33	57	93	161	220	362
	14	22	38	63	108	148	244
	12	14	25	41	72	98	161
	10	9	16	27	47	64	105
XF, XFF	12	4	8	13	23	31	51
	10	3	6	10	18	24	40

Notes:

1. This table is for concentric stranded conductors only. For compact stranded conductors, Table C.1(A) should be used.

2. Two-hour fire-rated RHH cable has ceramifiable insulation which has much larger diameters than other RHH wires. Consult manufacturer's conduit fill tables.

*Types RHH, RHW, and RHW-2 without outer covering.

Table C.1(A) Maximum Number of Compact Conductors in Electrical Metallic Tubing (EMT)
(*Based on Table 1, Chapter 9*)

		COMPACT CONDUCTORS									
	Conductor Size	Metric Designator (Trade Size)									
Type	(AWG/ kcmil)	16 (½)	21 (¾)	27 (1)	35 (1¼)	41 (1½)	53 (2)	63 (2½)	78 (3)	91 (3½)	103 (4)
THW,	8	2	4	6	11	16	26	46	69	90	115
THW-2,	6	1	3	5	9	12	20	35	53	70	89
THHW	4	1	2	4	6	9	15	26	40	52	67
	2	1	1	3	5	7	11	19	29	38	49
	1	1	1	1	3	4	8	13	21	27	34
	1/0	1	1	1	3	4	7	12	18	23	30
	2/0	0	1	1	2	3	5	10	15	20	25
	3/0	0	1	1	1	3	5	8	13	17	21
	4/0	0	1	1	1	2	4	7	11	14	18
	250	0	0	1	1	1	3	5	8	11	14
	300	0	0	1	1	1	3	5	7	9	12
	350	0	0	1	1	1	2	4	6	8	11
	400	0	0	0	1	1	1	4	6	8	10
	500	0	0	0	1	1	1	3	5	6	8
	600	0	0	0	1	1	1	2	4	5	7
	700	0	0	0	1	1	1	2	3	4	6
	750	0	0	0	0	1	1	1	3	4	5
	900	0	0	0	0	1	1	2	3	4	5
	1000	0	0	0	0	1	1	1	2	3	4
THHN,	8	—	—	—	—	—	—	—	—	—	—
THWN,	6	2	4	7	13	18	29	52	78	102	130
THWN-2	4	1	3	4	8	11	18	32	48	63	81
	2	1	1	3	6	8	13	23	34	45	58
	1	1	1	2	4	6	10	17	26	34	43
	1/0	1	1	1	3	5	8	14	22	29	37
	2/0	1	1	1	3	4	7	12	18	24	30
	3/0	0	1	1	2	3	6	10	15	20	25
	4/0	0	1	1	1	3	5	8	12	16	21
	250	0	1	1	1	1	4	6	10	13	16
	300	0	0	1	1	1	3	5	8	11	14
	350	0	0	1	1	1	3	5	7	10	12
	400	0	0	1	1	1	2	4	6	9	11
	500	0	0	0	1	1	1	4	5	7	9
	600	0	0	0	1	1	1	3	4	6	7
	700	0	0	0	1	1	1	2	4	5	7
	750	0	0	0	1	1	1	2	4	5	6
	900	0	0	0	0	1	1	2	3	4	5
	1000	0	0	0	0	1	1	1	3	3	4
XHHW,	8	3	5	8	15	20	34	59	90	117	149
XHHW-2	6	1	4	6	11	15	25	44	66	87	111
	4	1	3	4	8	11	18	32	48	63	81
	2	1	1	3	6	8	13	23	34	45	58
	1	1	1	2	4	6	10	17	26	34	43
	1/0	1	1	1	3	5	8	14	22	29	37
	2/0	1	1	1	3	4	7	12	18	24	31
	3/0	0	1	1	2	3	6	10	15	20	25
	4/0	0	1	1	1	3	5	8	13	17	21
	250	0	1	1	1	2	4	7	10	13	17
	300	0	0	1	1	1	3	6	9	11	14
	350	0	0	1	1	1	3	5	8	10	13
	400	0	0	1	1	1	2	4	7	9	11
	500	0	0	0	1	1	1	4	6	7	9
	600	0	0	0	1	1	1	3	4	6	8
	700	0	0	0	1	1	1	2	4	5	7
	750	0	0	0	1	1	1	2	3	5	6
	900	0	0	0	0	1	1	2	3	4	5
	1000	0	0	0	0	1	1	1	3	4	5

Definition: *Compact stranding* is the result of a manufacturing process where the standard conductor is compressed to the extent that the interstices (voids between strand wires) are virtually eliminated.

Table C.2 Maximum Number of Conductors or Fixture Wires in Electrical Nonmetallic Tubing (ENT) (*Based on Table 1, Chapter 9*)

		CONDUCTORS					
	Conductor Size (AWG/ kcmil)	Metric Designator (Trade Size)					
Type		16 (½)	21 (¾)	27 (1)	35 (1¼)	41 (1½)	53 (2)
RHH, RHW, RHW-2	14	3	6	10	19	26	43
	12	2	5	9	16	22	36
	10	1	4	7	13	17	29
	8	1	1	3	6	9	15
	6	1	1	3	5	7	12
	4	1	1	2	4	6	9
	3	1	1	1	3	5	8
	2	0	1	1	3	4	7
	1	0	1	1	1	3	5
	1/0	0	0	1	1	2	4
	2/0	0	0	1	1	1	3
	3/0	0	0	1	1	1	3
	4/0	0	0	1	1	1	2
	250	0	0	0	1	1	1
	300	0	0	0	1	1	1
	350	0	0	0	1	1	1
	400	0	0	0	1	1	1
	500	0	0	0	0	1	1
	600	0	0	0	0	1	1
	700	0	0	0	0	0	1
	750	0	0	0	0	0	1
	800	0	0	0	0	0	1
	900	0	0	0	0	0	1
	1000	0	0	0	0	0	1
	1250	0	0	0	0	0	0
	1500	0	0	0	0	0	0
	1750	0	0	0	0	0	0
	2000	0	0	0	0	0	0
TW	14	7	13	22	40	55	92
	12	5	10	17	31	42	71
	10	4	7	13	23	32	52
	8	1	4	7	13	17	29
RHH*, RHW*, RHW-2*, THHW, THW, THW-2	14	4	8	15	27	37	61
RHH*, RHW*, RHW-2*, THHW, THW	12	3	7	12	21	29	49
	10	3	5	9	17	23	38
RHH*, RHW*, RHW-2*, THHW, THW, THW-2	8	1	3	5	10	14	23

(*Continues*)

Table C.2 *Continued*

	Conductor Size (AWG/ kcmil)	CONDUCTORS					
		Metric Designator (Trade Size)					
Type		16 (½)	21 (¾)	27 (1)	35 (1¼)	41 (1½)	53 (2)
RHH*,	6	1	2	4	7	10	17
RHW*,	4	1	1	3	5	8	13
RHW-2*,	3	1	1	2	5	7	11
TW, THW,	2	1	1	2	4	6	9
THHW,	1	0	1	1	3	4	6
THW-2	1/0	0	1	1	2	3	5
	2/0	0	1	1	1	3	5
	3/0	0	0	1	1	2	4
	4/0	0	0	1	1	1	3
	250	0	0	1	1	1	2
	300	0	0	0	1	1	2
	350	0	0	0	1	1	1
	400	0	0	0	1	1	1
	500	0	0	0	1	1	1
	600	0	0	0	0	1	1
	700	0	0	0	0	1	1
	750	0	0	0	0	1	1
	800	0	0	0	0	1	1
	900	0	0	0	0	0	1
	1000	0	0	0	0	0	1
	1250	0	0	0	0	0	1
	1500	0	0	0	0	0	0
	1750	0	0	0	0	0	0
	2000	0	0	0	0	0	0
THHN,	14	10	18	32	58	80	132
THWN,	12	7	13	23	42	58	96
THWN-2	10	4	8	15	26	36	60
	8	2	5	8	15	21	35
	6	1	3	6	11	15	25
	4	1	1	4	7	9	15
	3	1	1	3	5	8	13
	2	1	1	2	5	6	11
	1	1	1	1	3	5	8
	1/0	0	1	1	3	4	7
	2/0	0	1	1	2	3	5
	3/0	0	1	1	1	3	4
	4/0	0	0	1	1	2	4
	250	0	0	1	1	1	3
	300	0	0	1	1	1	2
	350	0	0	0	1	1	2
	400	0	0	0	1	1	1
	500	0	0	0	1	1	1
	600	0	0	0	1	1	1
	700	0	0	0	0	1	1
	750	0	0	0	0	1	1
	800	0	0	0	0	1	1
	900	0	0	0	0	1	1
	1000	0	0	0	0	0	1
FEP, FEPB,	14	10	18	31	56	77	128
PFA, PFAH,	12	7	13	23	41	56	93
TFE	10	5	9	16	29	40	67
	8	3	5	9	17	23	38
	6	1	4	6	12	16	27
	4	1	2	4	8	11	19
	3	1	1	4	7	9	16
	2	1	1	3	5	8	13

Table C.2 *Continued*

	Conductor Size (AWG/ kcmil)	Metric Designator (Trade Size)					
Type		16 (½)	21 (¾)	27 (1)	35 (1¼)	41 (1½)	53 (2)
PFA, PFAH, TFE	1	1	1	1	4	5	9
PFA, PFAH, TFE, Z	1/0	0	1	1	3	4	7
	2/0	0	1	1	2	4	6
	3/0	0	1	1	1	3	5
	4/0	0	1	1	1	2	4
Z	14	12	22	38	68	93	154
	12	8	15	27	48	66	109
	10	5	9	16	29	40	67
	8	3	6	10	18	25	42
	6	1	4	7	13	18	30
	4	1	3	5	9	12	20
	3	1	1	3	6	9	15
	2	1	1	3	5	7	12
	1	1	1	2	4	6	10
XHH, XHHW, XHHW-2, ZW	14	7	13	22	40	55	92
	12	5	10	17	31	42	71
	10	4	7	13	23	32	52
	8	1	4	7	13	17	29
	6	1	3	5	9	13	21
	4	1	1	4	7	9	15
	3	1	1	3	6	8	13
	2	1	1	2	5	6	11
XHH, XHHW, XHHW-2	1	1	1	1	3	5	8
	1/0	0	1	1	3	4	7
	2/0	0	1	1	2	3	6
	3/0	0	1	1	1	3	5
	4/0	0	0	1	1	2	4
	250	0	0	1	1	1	3
	300	0	0	1	1	1	3
	350	0	0	1	1	1	2
	400	0	0	0	1	1	1
	500	0	0	0	1	1	1
	600	0	0	0	1	1	1
	700	0	0	0	0	1	1
	750	0	0	0	0	1	1
	800	0	0	0	0	1	1
	900	0	0	0	0	1	1
	1000	0	0	0	0	0	1
	1250	0	0	0	0	0	1
	1500	0	0	0	0	0	1
	1750	0	0	0	0	0	0
	2000	0	0	0	0	0	0

Table C.2 *Continued*

	Conductor Size (AWG/ kcmil)	Metric Designator (Trade Size)					
Type		**16** (½)	**21** (¾)	**27** (1)	**35** (1¼)	**41** (1½)	**53** (2)
FFH-2, RFH-2,	18	6	12	21	39	53	88
	16	5	10	18	32	45	74
RFHH-3 SF-2, SFF-2	18	8	15	27	49	67	111
	16	7	13	22	40	55	92
	14	5	10	18	32	45	74
SF-1, SFF-1	18	15	28	48	86	119	197
RFH-1, RFHH-2, TF, TFF, XF, XFF	18	11	20	35	64	88	145
RFHH-2, TF, TFF, XF, XFF	16	9	16	29	51	71	117
XF, XFF	14	7	13	22	40	55	92
TFN, TFFN	18	18	33	57	102	141	233
	16	13	25	43	78	107	178
PF, PFF, PGF, PGFF, PAF, PTF, PTFF, PAFF	18	17	31	54	97	133	221
	16	13	24	42	75	103	171
	14	10	18	31	56	77	128
ZF, ZFF, ZHF, HF, HFF	18	22	40	70	125	172	285
	16	16	29	51	92	127	210
	14	12	22	38	68	93	154
KF-2, KFF-2	18	31	58	101	182	250	413
	16	22	41	71	128	176	291
	14	15	28	49	88	121	200
	12	10	19	33	60	83	138
	10	7	13	22	40	55	92
KF-1, KFF-1	18	38	69	121	217	298	493
	16	26	49	85	152	209	346
	14	18	33	57	102	141	233
	12	12	22	38	68	93	154
	10	7	14	24	44	61	101
XF, XFF	12	3	7	12	21	29	49
	10	3	5	9	17	23	38

Notes:

1. This table is for concentric stranded conductors only. For compact stranded conductors, Table C.2(A) should be used.

2. Two-hour fire-rated RHH cable has ceramifiable insulation which has much larger diameters than other RHH wires.

Consult manufacturer's conduit fill tables.

*Types RHH, RHW, and RHW-2 without outer covering.

Table C.2(A) Maximum Number of Compact Conductors in Electrical Nonmetallic Tubing (ENT) (*Based on Table 1, Chapter 9*)

	Conductor Size (AWG/ kcmil)	COMPACT CONDUCTORS					
		Metric Designator (Trade Size)					
Type		16 (½)	21 (¾)	27 (1)	35 (1¼)	41 (1½)	53 (2)
THW,	8	1	3	6	11	15	25
THW-2,	6	1	2	4	8	11	19
THHW	4	1	1	3	6	8	14
	2	1	1	2	4	6	10
	1	0	1	1	3	4	7
	1/0	0	1	1	3	4	6
	2/0	0	1	1	2	3	5
	3/0	0	1	1	1	3	4
	4/0	0	0	1	1	2	4
	250	0	0	1	1	1	3
	300	0	0	1	1	1	2
	350	0	0	0	1	1	2
	400	0	0	0	1	1	1
	500	0	0	0	1	1	1
	600	0	0	0	1	1	1
	700	0	0	0	0	1	1
	750	0	0	0	0	1	1
	900	0	0	0	0	1	1
	1000	0	0	0	0	0	1
THHN,	8	—	—	—	—	—	—
THWN,	6	1	4	7	12	17	28
THWN-2	4	1	2	4	7	10	17
	2	1	1	3	5	7	12
	1	1	1	2	4	5	9
	1/0	1	1	1	3	5	8
	2/0	0	1	1	3	4	6
	3/0	0	1	1	2	3	5
	4/0	0	1	1	1	2	4
	250	0	0	1	1	1	3
	300	0	0	1	1	1	3
	350	0	0	1	1	1	2
	400	0	0	0	1	1	2
	500	0	0	0	1	1	1
	600	0	0	0	1	1	1
	700	0	0	0	1	1	1
	750	0	0	0	1	1	1
	900	0	0	0	0	1	1
	1000	0	0	0	0	1	1
XHHW,	8	2	4	8	14	19	32
XHHW-2	6	1	3	6	10	14	24
	4	1	2	4	7	10	17
	2	1	1	3	5	7	12
	1	1	1	2	4	5	9
	1/0	1	1	1	3	5	8
	2/0	0	1	1	3	4	7
	3/0	0	1	1	2	3	5
	4/0	0	1	1	1	3	4
	250	0	0	1	1	1	3
	300	0	0	1	1	1	3
	350	0	0	1	1	1	3
	400	0	0	1	1	1	2
	500	0	0	0	1	1	1
	600	0	0	0	1	1	1
	700	0	0	0	1	1	1
	750	0	0	0	1	1	1
	900	0	0	0	0	1	1
	1000	0	0	0	0	1	1

Definition: *Compact stranding* is the result of a manufacturing process where the standard conductor is compressed to the extent that the interstices (voids between strand wires) are virtually eliminated.

Table C.3 Maximum Number of Conductors or Fixture Wires in Flexible Metal Conduit (FMC) (*Based on Table 1, Chapter 9*)

		CONDUCTORS									
	Conductor Size (AWG/ kcmil)	Metric Designator (Trade Size)									
Type		16 (½)	21 (¾)	27 (1)	35 (1¼)	41 (1½)	53 (2)	63 (2½)	78 (3)	91 (3½)	103 (4)
RHH, RHW, RHW-2	14	4	7	11	17	25	44	67	96	131	171
	12	3	6	9	14	21	37	55	80	109	142
	10	3	5	7	11	17	30	45	64	88	115
	8	1	2	4	6	9	15	23	34	46	60
	6	1	1	3	5	7	12	19	27	37	48
	4	1	1	2	4	5	10	14	21	29	37
	3	1	1	1	3	5	8	13	18	25	33
	2	1	1	1	3	4	7	11	16	22	28
	1	0	1	1	1	2	5	7	10	14	19
	1/0	0	1	1	1	2	4	6	9	12	16
	2/0	0	1	1	1	1	3	5	8	11	14
	3/0	0	0	1	1	1	3	5	7	9	12
	4/0	0	0	1	1	1	2	4	6	8	10
	250	0	0	0	1	1	1	3	4	6	8
	300	0	0	0	1	1	1	2	4	5	7
	350	0	0	0	1	1	1	2	3	5	6
	400	0	0	0	0	1	1	1	3	4	6
	500	0	0	0	0	1	1	1	3	4	5
	600	0	0	0	0	1	1	1	2	3	4
	700	0	0	0	0	0	1	1	1	3	3
	750	0	0	0	0	0	1	1	1	2	3
	800	0	0	0	0	0	1	1	1	2	3
	900	0	0	0	0	0	1	1	1	2	3
	1000	0	0	0	0	0	1	1	1	1	3
	1250	0	0	0	0	0	0	1	1	1	1
	1500	0	0	0	0	0	0	1	1	1	1
	1750	0	0	0	0	0	0	1	1	1	1
	2000	0	0	0	0	0	0	0	1	1	1
TW	14	9	15	23	36	53	94	141	203	277	361
	12	7	11	18	28	41	72	108	156	212	277
	10	5	8	13	21	30	54	81	116	158	207
	8	3	5	7	11	17	30	45	64	88	115
RHH*, RHW*, RHW-2* THHW, THW, THW-2	14	6	10	15	24	35	62	94	135	184	240
RHH*, RHW*, RHW-2*, THHW, THW	12	5	8	12	19	28	50	75	108	148	193
	10	4	6	10	15	22	39	59	85	115	151
RHH*, RHW*, RHW-2*, THHW, THW, THW-2	8	1	4	6	9	13	23	35	51	69	90

Table C.3 *Continued*

	Conductor Size (AWG/ kcmil)	Metric Designator (Trade Size)									
Type		16 (½)	21 (¾)	27 (1)	35 (1¼)	41 (1½)	53 (2)	63 (2½)	78 (3)	91 (3½)	103 (4)
RHH*, RHW*, RHW-2*, TW, THW, THHW, THW-2	6	1	3	4	7	10	18	27	39	53	69
	4	1	1	3	5	7	13	20	29	39	51
	3	1	1	3	4	6	11	17	25	34	44
	2	1	1	2	4	5	10	14	21	29	37
	1	1	1	1	2	4	7	10	15	20	26
	1/0	0	1	1	1	3	6	9	12	17	22
	2/0	0	1	1	1	3	5	7	10	14	19
	3/0	0	1	1	1	2	4	6	9	12	16
	4/0	0	0	1	1	1	3	5	7	10	13
	250	0	0	1	1	1	3	4	6	8	11
	300	0	0	1	1	1	2	3	5	7	9
	350	0	0	0	1	1	1	3	4	6	8
	400	0	0	0	1	1	1	3	4	6	7
	500	0	0	0	1	1	1	2	3	5	6
	600	0	0	0	0	1	1	1	3	4	5
	700	0	0	0	0	1	1	1	2	3	4
	750	0	0	0	0	1	1	1	2	3	4
	800	0	0	0	0	1	1	1	1	3	4
	900	0	0	0	0	0	1	1	1	3	3
	1000	0	0	0	0	0	1	1	1	2	3
	1250	0	0	0	0	0	1	1	1	1	2
	1500	0	0	0	0	0	0	1	1	1	1
	1750	0	0	0	0	0	0	1	1	1	1
	2000	0	0	0	0	0	0	1	1	1	1
THHN, THWN, THWN-2	14	13	22	33	52	76	134	202	291	396	518
	12	9	16	24	38	56	98	147	212	289	378
	10	6	10	15	24	35	62	93	134	182	238
	8	3	6	9	14	20	35	53	77	105	137
	6	2	4	6	10	14	25	38	55	76	99
	4	1	2	4	6	9	16	24	34	46	61
	3	1	1	3	5	7	13	20	29	39	51
	2	1	1	3	4	6	11	17	24	33	43
	1	1	1	1	3	4	8	12	18	24	32
	1/0	1	1	1	2	4	7	10	15	20	27
	2/0	0	1	1	1	3	6	9	12	17	22
	3/0	0	1	1	1	2	5	7	10	14	18
	4/0	0	1	1	1	1	4	6	8	12	15
	250	0	0	1	1	1	3	5	7	9	12
	300	0	0	1	1	1	3	4	6	8	11
	350	0	0	1	1	1	2	3	5	7	9
	400	0	0	0	1	1	1	3	5	6	8
	500	0	0	0	1	1	1	2	4	5	7
	600	0	0	0	0	1	1	1	3	4	5
	700	0	0	0	0	1	1	1	3	4	5
	750	0	0	0	0	1	1	1	2	3	4
	800	0	0	0	0	1	1	1	2	3	4
	900	0	0	0	0	0	1	1	1	3	4
	1000	0	0	0	0	0	1	1	1	3	3
FEP, FEPB, PFA, PFAH, TFE	14	12	21	32	51	74	130	196	282	385	502
	12	9	15	24	37	54	95	143	206	281	367
	10	6	11	17	26	39	68	103	148	201	263
	8	4	6	10	15	22	39	59	85	115	151
	6	2	4	7	11	16	28	42	60	82	107
	4	1	3	5	7	11	19	29	42	57	75
	3	1	2	4	6	9	16	24	35	48	62
	2	1	1	3	5	7	13	20	29	39	51

(Continues)

Table C.3 *Continued*

	Conductor Size (AWG/ kcmil)	CONDUCTORS									
		Metric Designator (Trade Size)									
Type		16 (½)	21 (¾)	27 (1)	35 (1¼)	41 (1½)	53 (2)	63 (2½)	78 (3)	91 (3½)	103 (4)
PFA, PFAH, TFE	1	1	1	2	3	5	9	14	20	27	36
PFA, PFAH, TFE, Z	1/0	1	1	1	3	4	8	11	17	23	30
	2/0	1	1	1	2	3	6	9	14	19	24
	3/0	0	1	1	1	3	5	8	11	15	20
	4/0	0	1	1	1	2	4	6	9	13	16
Z	14	15	25	39	61	89	157	236	340	463	605
	12	11	18	28	43	63	111	168	241	329	429
	10	6	11	17	26	39	68	103	148	201	263
	8	4	7	11	17	24	43	65	93	127	166
	6	3	5	7	12	17	30	45	65	89	117
	4	1	3	5	8	12	21	31	45	61	80
	3	1	2	4	6	8	15	23	33	45	58
	2	1	1	3	5	7	12	19	27	37	49
	1	1	1	2	4	6	10	15	22	30	39
XHH, XHHW, XHHW-2, ZW	14	9	15	23	36	53	94	141	203	277	361
	12	7	11	18	28	41	72	108	156	212	277
	10	5	8	13	21	30	54	81	116	158	207
	8	3	5	7	11	17	30	45	64	88	115
	6	1	3	5	8	12	22	33	48	65	85
	4	1	2	4	6	9	16	24	34	47	61
	3	1	1	3	5	7	13	20	29	40	52
	2	1	1	3	4	6	11	17	24	33	44
XHH, XHHW, XHHW-2	1	1	1	1	3	5	8	13	18	25	32
	1/0	1	1	1	2	4	7	10	15	21	27
	2/0	0	1	1	2	3	6	9	13	17	23
	3/0	0	1	1	1	3	5	7	10	14	19
	4/0	0	1	1	1	2	4	6	9	12	15
	250	0	0	1	1	1	3	5	7	10	13
	300	0	0	1	1	1	3	4	6	8	11
	350	0	0	1	1	1	2	4	5	7	9
	400	0	0	0	1	1	1	3	5	6	8
	500	0	0	0	1	1	1	3	4	5	7
	600	0	0	0	0	1	1	1	3	4	5
	700	0	0	0	0	1	1	1	3	4	5
	750	0	0	0	0	1	1	1	2	3	4
	800	0	0	0	0	1	1	1	2	3	4
	900	0	0	0	0	0	1	1	1	3	4
	1000	0	0	0	0	0	1	1	1	3	3
	1250	0	0	0	0	0	1	1	1	1	3
	1500	0	0	0	0	0	1	1	1	1	2
	1750	0	0	0	0	0	0	1	1	1	1
	2000	0	0	0	0	0	0	1	1	1	1

Table C.3 *Continued*

Type	Conductor Size (AWG/ kcmil)	Metric Designator (Trade Size)					
		16 (½)	21 (¾)	27 (1)	35 (1¼)	41 (1½)	53 (2)
FFH-2, RFH-2, RFHH-3	18	8	14	22	35	51	90
	16	7	12	19	29	43	76
SF-2, SFF-2	18	11	18	28	44	64	113
	16	9	15	23	36	53	94
	14	7	12	19	29	43	76
SF-1, SFF-1	18	19	32	50	78	114	201
RFH-1, RFHH-2, TF, TFF, XF, XFF	18	14	24	37	58	84	148
RFHH-2, TF, TFF, XF, XFF	16	11	19	30	47	68	120
XF, XFF	14	9	15	23	36	53	94
TFN, TFFN	18	23	38	59	93	135	237
	16	17	29	45	71	103	181
PF, PFF, PGF, PGFF, PAF, PTF, PTFF, PAFF	18	22	36	56	88	128	225
	16	17	28	43	68	99	174
	14	12	21	32	51	74	130
ZF, ZFF, ZHF, HF, HFF	18	28	47	72	113	165	290
	16	20	35	53	83	121	214
	14	15	25	39	61	89	157
KF-2, KFF-2	18	41	68	105	164	239	421
	16	28	48	74	116	168	297
	14	19	33	51	80	116	204
	12	13	23	35	55	80	140
	10	9	15	23	36	53	94
KF-1, KFF-1	18	48	82	125	196	285	503
	16	34	57	88	138	200	353
	14	23	38	59	93	135	237
	12	15	25	39	61	89	157
	10	10	16	25	40	58	103
XF, XFF	12	5	8	12	19	28	50
	10	4	6	10	15	22	39

Notes:

1. This table is for concentric stranded conductors only. For compact stranded conductors, Table C.3(A) should be used.

2. Two-hour fire-rated RHH cable has ceramifiable insulation which has much larger diameters than other RHH wires.

Consult manufacturer's conduit fill tables.

*Types RHH, RHW, and RHW-2 without outer covering.

Table C.3(A) Maximum Number of Compact Conductors in Flexible Metal Conduit (FMC)
(*Based on Table 1, Chapter 9*)

		COMPACT CONDUCTORS									
	Conductor Size	Metric Designator (Trade Size)									
Type	(AWG/ kcmil)	16 (½)	21 (¾)	27 (1)	35 (1¼)	41 (1½)	53 (2)	63 (2½)	78 (3)	91 (3½)	103 (4)
THW,	8	2	4	6	10	14	25	38	55	75	98
THHW,	6	1	3	5	7	11	20	29	43	58	76
THW-2	4	1	2	3	5	8	15	22	32	43	57
	2	1	1	2	4	6	11	16	23	32	42
	1	1	1	1	3	4	7	11	16	22	29
	1/0	1	1	1	2	3	6	10	14	19	25
	2/0	0	1	1	1	3	5	8	12	16	21
	3/0	0	1	1	1	2	4	7	10	14	18
	4/0	0	1	1	1	1	4	6	8	11	15
	250	0	0	1	1	1	3	4	7	9	12
	300	0	0	1	1	1	2	4	6	8	10
	350	0	0	1	1	1	2	3	5	7	9
	400	0	0	0	1	1	1	3	5	6	8
	500	0	0	0	1	1	1	3	4	5	7
	600	0	0	0	0	1	1	1	3	4	6
	700	0	0	0	0	1	1	1	3	4	5
	750	0	0	0	0	1	1	1	2	3	5
	900	0	0	0	0	1	1	1	2	3	4
	1000	0	0	0	0	0	1	1	1	3	4
THHN,	8	—	—	—	—	—	—	—	—	—	—
THWN,	6	3	4	7	11	16	29	43	62	85	111
THWN-2	4	1	3	4	7	10	18	27	38	52	69
	2	1	1	3	5	7	13	19	28	38	49
	1	1	1	2	3	5	9	14	21	28	37
	1/0	1	1	1	3	4	8	12	17	24	31
	2/0	1	1	1	2	4	6	10	14	20	26
	3/0	0	1	1	1	3	5	8	12	17	22
	4/0	0	1	1	1	2	4	7	10	14	18
	250	0	1	1	1	1	3	5	8	11	14
	300	0	0	1	1	1	3	5	7	9	12
	350	0	0	1	1	1	3	4	6	8	10
	400	0	0	1	1	1	2	3	5	7	9
	500	0	0	0	1	1	1	3	4	6	8
	600	0	0	0	1	1	1	2	3	5	6
	700	0	0	0	0	1	1	1	3	4	6
	750	0	0	0	0	1	1	1	3	4	5
	900	0	0	0	0	1	1	1	2	3	4
	1000	0	0	0	0	0	1	1	1	3	4
XHHW,	8	3	5	8	13	19	33	50	71	97	127
XHHW-2	6	2	4	6	9	14	24	37	53	72	95
	4	1	3	4	7	10	18	27	38	52	69
	2	1	1	3	5	7	13	19	28	38	49
	1	1	1	2	3	5	9	14	21	28	37
	1/0	1	1	1	3	4	8	12	17	24	31
	2/0	1	1	1	2	4	7	10	15	20	26
	3/0	0	1	1	1	3	5	8	12	17	22
	4/0	0	1	1	1	2	4	7	10	14	18
	250	0	1	1	1	1	4	5	8	11	14
	300	0	0	1	1	1	3	5	7	9	12
	350	0	0	1	1	1	3	4	6	8	11
	400	0	0	1	1	1	2	4	5	7	10
	500	0	0	0	1	1	1	3	4	6	8
	600	0	0	0	1	1	1	2	3	5	6
	700	0	0	0	0	1	1	1	3	4	6
	750	0	0	0	0	1	1	1	3	4	5
	900	0	0	0	0	1	1	2	2	3	4
	1000	0	0	0	0	1	1	1	2	3	4

Definition: *Compact stranding* is the result of a manufacturing process where the standard conductor is compressed to the extent that the interstices (voids between strand wires) are virtually eliminated.

Table C.4 Maximum Number of Conductors or Fixture Wires in Intermediate Metal Conduit (IMC) (*Based on Table 1, Chapter 9*)

		CONDUCTORS									
	Conductor Size (AWG/ kcmil)	Metric Designator (Trade Size)									
Type		16 (½)	21 (¾)	27 (1)	35 (1¼)	41 (1½)	53 (2)	63 (2½)	78 (3)	91 (3½)	103 (4)
RHH, RHW, RHW-2	14	4	8	13	22	30	49	70	108	144	186
	12	4	6	11	18	25	41	58	89	120	154
RHH, RHW, RHW-2	10	3	5	8	15	20	33	47	72	97	124
	8	1	3	4	8	10	17	24	38	50	65
	6	1	1	3	6	8	14	19	30	40	52
	4	1	1	3	5	6	11	15	23	31	41
	3	1	1	2	4	6	9	13	21	28	36
	2	1	1	1	3	5	8	11	18	24	31
	1	0	1	1	2	3	5	7	12	16	20
	1/0	0	1	1	1	3	4	6	10	14	18
	2/0	0	1	1	1	2	4	6	9	12	15
	3/0	0	0	1	1	1	3	5	7	10	13
	4/0	0	0	1	1	1	3	4	6	9	11
	250	0	0	1	1	1	1	3	5	6	8
	300	0	0	0	1	1	1	3	4	6	7
	350	0	0	0	1	1	1	2	4	5	7
	400	0	0	0	1	1	1	2	3	5	6
	500	0	0	0	1	1	1	1	3	4	5
	600	0	0	0	0	1	1	1	2	3	4
	700	0	0	0	0	1	1	1	2	3	4
	750	0	0	0	0	1	1	1	1	3	4
	800	0	0	0	0	0	1	1	1	3	3
	900	0	0	0	0	0	1	1	1	2	3
	1000	0	0	0	0	0	1	1	1	2	3
	1250	0	0	0	0	0	1	1	1	1	2
	1500	0	0	0	0	0	0	1	1	1	1
	1750	0	0	0	0	0	0	1	1	1	1
	2000	0	0	0	0	0	0	1	1	1	1
TW	14	10	17	27	47	64	104	147	228	304	392
	12	7	13	21	36	49	80	113	175	234	301
	10	5	9	15	27	36	59	84	130	174	224
	8	3	5	8	15	20	33	47	72	97	124
RHH*, RHW*, RHW-2*, THHW, THW, THW-2	14	6	11	18	31	42	69	98	151	202	261
RHH*, RHW*, RHW-2*, THHW, THW	12	5	9	14	25	34	56	79	122	163	209
	10	4	7	11	19	26	43	61	95	127	163
RHH*, RHW*, RHW-2*, THHW, THW, THW-2	8	2	4	7	12	16	26	37	57	76	98
RHH*, RHW*, RHW-2*, TW, THHW, THW, THW-2	6	1	3	5	9	12	20	28	43	58	75
	4	1	2	4	6	9	15	21	32	43	56

(Continues)

Table C.4 *Continued*

		CONDUCTORS									
	Conductor Size (AWG/ kcmil)	Metric Designator (Trade Size)									
Type		16 (½)	21 (¾)	27 (1)	35 (1¼)	41 (1½)	53 (2)	63 (2½)	78 (3)	91 (3½)	103 (4)
RHH*, RHW*, RHW-2*, TW, THW, THHW, THW-2	3	1	1	3	6	8	13	18	28	37	48
	2	1	1	3	5	6	11	15	23	31	41
	1	1	1	1	3	4	7	11	16	22	28
	1/0	1	1	1	3	4	6	9	14	19	24
	2/0	0	1	1	2	3	5	8	12	16	20
	3/0	0	1	1	1	3	4	6	10	13	17
	4/0	0	1	1	1	2	4	5	8	11	14
	250	0	0	1	1	1	3	4	7	9	12
	300	0	0	1	1	1	2	4	6	8	10
	350	0	0	1	1	1	2	3	5	7	9
	400	0	0	0	1	1	1	3	4	6	8
	500	0	0	0	1	1	1	2	4	5	7
	600	0	0	0	1	1	1	1	3	4	5
	700	0	0	0	0	1	1	1	3	4	5
	750	0	0	0	0	1	1	1	2	3	4
	800	0	0	0	0	1	1	1	2	3	4
	900	0	0	0	0	1	1	1	2	3	4
	1000	0	0	0	0	0	1	1	1	3	3
	1250	0	0	0	0	0	1	1	1	1	3
	1500	0	0	0	0	0	1	1	1	1	2
	1750	0	0	0	0	0	0	1	1	1	1
	2000	0	0	0	0	0	0	1	1	1	1
THHN, THWN, THWN-2	14	14	24	39	68	91	149	211	326	436	562
	12	10	17	29	49	67	109	154	238	318	410
	10	6	11	18	31	42	68	97	150	200	258
	8	3	6	10	18	24	39	56	86	115	149
	6	2	4	7	13	17	28	40	62	83	107
	4	1	3	4	8	10	17	25	38	51	66
	3	1	2	4	6	9	15	21	32	43	56
	2	1	1	3	5	7	12	17	27	36	47
	1	1	1	2	4	5	9	13	20	27	35
	1/0	1	1	1	3	4	8	11	17	23	29
	2/0	1	1	1	3	4	6	9	14	19	24
	3/0	0	1	1	2	3	5	7	12	16	20
	4/0	0	1	1	1	2	4	6	9	13	17
	250	0	0	1	1	1	3	5	8	10	13
	300	0	0	1	1	1	3	4	7	9	12
	350	0	0	1	1	1	2	4	6	8	10
	400	0	0	1	1	1	2	3	5	7	9
	500	0	0	0	1	1	1	3	4	6	7
	600	0	0	0	1	1	1	2	3	5	6
	700	0	0	0	1	1	1	1	3	4	5
	750	0	0	0	1	1	1	1	3	4	5
	800	0	0	0	0	1	1	1	3	4	5
	900	0	0	0	0	1	1	1	2	3	4
	1000	0	0	0	0	1	1	1	2	3	4
FEP, FEPB, PFA, PFAH, TFE	14	13	23	38	66	89	145	205	317	423	545
	12	10	17	28	48	65	106	150	231	309	398
	10	7	12	20	34	46	76	107	166	221	285
	8	4	7	11	19	26	43	61	95	127	163
	6	3	5	8	14	19	31	44	67	90	116
	4	1	3	5	10	13	21	30	47	63	81
	3	1	3	4	8	11	18	25	39	52	68
	2	1	2	4	6	9	15	21	32	43	56

Table C.4 *Continued*

		CONDUCTORS									
	Conductor Size (AWG/ kcmil)	Metric Designator (Trade Size)									
Type		16 (½)	21 (¾)	27 (1)	35 (1¼)	41 (1½)	53 (2)	63 (2½)	78 (3)	91 (3½)	103 (4)
PFA, PFAH, TFE	1	1	1	2	4	6	10	14	22	30	39
PFA, PFAH, TFE, Z	1/0	1	1	1	4	5	8	12	19	25	32
	2/0	1	1	1	3	4	7	10	15	21	27
	3/0	0	1	1	2	3	6	8	13	17	22
	4/0	0	1	1	1	3	5	7	10	14	18
Z	14	16	28	46	79	107	175	247	381	510	657
	12	11	20	32	56	76	124	175	271	362	466
	10	7	12	20	34	46	76	107	166	221	285
	8	4	7	12	21	29	48	68	105	140	180
	6	3	5	9	15	20	33	47	73	98	127
	4	1	3	6	10	14	23	33	50	67	87
	3	1	2	4	7	10	17	24	37	49	63
	2	1	1	3	6	8	14	20	30	41	53
	1	1	1	3	5	7	11	16	25	33	43
XHH, XHHW, XHHW-2, ZW	14	10	17	27	47	64	104	147	228	304	392
	12	7	13	21	36	49	80	113	175	234	301
	10	5	9	15	27	36	59	84	130	174	224
	8	3	5	8	15	20	33	47	72	97	124
	6	1	4	6	11	15	24	35	53	71	92
	4	1	3	4	8	11	18	25	39	52	67
	3	1	2	4	7	9	15	21	33	44	56
	2	1	1	3	5	7	12	18	27	37	47
XHH, XHHW, XHHW-2	1	1	1	2	4	5	9	13	20	27	35
	1/0	1	1	1	3	5	8	11	17	23	30
	2/0	1	1	1	3	4	6	9	14	19	25
	3/0	0	1	1	2	3	5	7	12	16	20
	4/0	0	1	1	1	2	4	6	10	13	17
	250	0	0	1	1	1	3	5	8	11	14
	300	0	0	1	1	1	3	4	7	9	12
	350	0	0	1	1	1	3	4	6	8	10
	400	0	0	1	1	1	3	3	5	7	9
	500	0	0	0	1	1	1	3	4	6	8
	600	0	0	0	1	1	1	2	3	5	6
	700	0	0	0	1	1	1	1	3	4	5
	750	0	0	0	1	1	1	1	3	4	5
	800	0	0	0	0	1	1	1	3	4	5
	900	0	0	0	0	1	1	1	2	3	4
	1000	0	0	0	0	1	1	1	2	3	4
	1250	0	0	0	0	0	1	1	1	2	3
	1500	0	0	0	0	0	1	1	1	1	2
	1750	0	0	0	0	0	1	1	1	1	2
	2000	0	0	0	0	0	0	1	1	1	1

(Continues)

Table C.4 *Continued*

	Conductor Size (AWG/ kcmil)	Metric Designator (Trade Size)					
		FIXTURE WIRES					
Type		**16** **(½)**	**21** **(¾)**	**27** **(1)**	**35** **(1¼)**	**41** **(1½)**	**53** **(2)**
FHH-2, RFH-2, RFHH-3	18	9	16	26	45	61	100
	16	8	13	22	38	51	84
SF-2, SFF-2	18	12	20	33	57	77	126
	16	10	17	27	47	64	104
	14	8	13	22	38	51	84
SF-1, SFF-1	18	21	36	59	101	137	223
RFH-1, RFHH-2, TF, TFF, XF, XFF	18	15	26	43	75	101	165
RFH-2, TF, TFF, XF, XFF	16	12	21	35	60	81	133
XF, XFF	14	10	17	27	47	64	104
TFN, TFFN	18	25	42	69	119	161	264
	16	19	32	53	91	123	201
PF, PFF, PGF, PGFF, PAF, PTF, PTFF, PAFF	18	23	40	66	113	153	250
	16	18	31	51	87	118	193
	14	13	23	38	66	89	145
ZF, ZFF, ZHF, HF, HFF	18	30	52	85	146	197	322
	16	22	38	63	108	145	238
	14	16	28	46	79	107	175
KF-2, KFF-2	18	44	75	123	212	287	468
	16	31	53	87	149	202	330
	14	21	36	60	103	139	227
	12	14	25	41	70	95	156
	10	10	17	27	47	64	104
KF-1, KFF-1	18	52	90	147	253	342	558
	16	37	63	103	178	240	392
	14	25	42	69	119	161	264
	12	16	28	46	79	107	175
	10	10	18	30	52	70	114
XF, XFF	12	5	9	14	25	34	56
	10	4	7	11	19	26	43

Notes:

1. This table is for concentric stranded conductors only. For compact stranded conductors, Table C.4(A) should be used.

2. Two-hour fire-rated RHH cable has ceramifiable insulation which has much larger diameters than other RHH wires.

Consult manufacturer's conduit fill tables.

*Types RHH, RHW, and RHW-2 without outer covering.

Table C.4(A) Maximum Number of Compact Conductors in Intermediate Metal Conduit (IMC) (*Based on Table 1, Chapter 9*)

		COMPACT CONDUCTORS									
	Conductor Size (AWG/ kcmil)	Metric Designator (Trade Size)									
Type		16 (½)	21 (¾)	27 (1)	35 (1¼)	41 (1½)	53 (2)	63 (2½)	78 (3)	91 (3½)	103 (4)
THW,	8	2	4	7	13	17	28	40	62	83	107
THW-2,	6	1	3	6	10	13	22	31	48	64	82
THHW	4	1	2	4	7	10	16	23	36	48	62
	2	1	1	3	5	7	12	17	26	35	45
	1	1	1	1	4	5	8	12	18	25	32
	1/0	1	1	1	3	4	7	10	16	21	27
	2/0	0	1	1	3	4	6	9	13	18	23
	3/0	0	1	1	2	3	5	7	11	15	20
	4/0	0	1	1	1	2	4	6	9	13	16
	250	0	0	1	1	1	3	5	7	10	13
	300	0	0	1	1	1	3	4	6	9	11
	350	0	0	1	1	1	2	4	6	8	10
	400	0	0	1	1	1	2	3	5	7	9
	500	0	0	0	1	1	1	3	4	6	8
	600	0	0	0	1	1	1	2	3	5	6
	700	0	0	0	1	1	1	1	3	4	5
	750	0	0	0	1	1	1	1	3	4	5
	900	0	0	0	0	1	1	1	2	3	4
	1000	0	0	0	0	1	1	1	2	3	4
THHN,	8	—	—	—	—	—	—	—	—	—	—
THWN,	6	3	5	8	14	19	32	45	70	93	120
THWN-2	4	1	3	5	9	12	20	28	43	58	74
	2	1	1	3	6	8	14	20	31	41	53
	1	1	1	3	5	6	10	15	23	31	40
	1/0	1	1	2	4	5	9	13	20	26	34
	2/0	1	1	1	3	4	7	10	16	22	28
	3/0	0	1	1	3	4	6	9	14	18	24
	4/0	0	1	1	2	3	5	7	11	15	19
	250	0	1	1	1	2	4	6	9	12	15
	300	0	0	1	1	1	3	5	7	10	13
	350	0	0	1	1	1	3	4	7	9	11
	400	0	0	1	1	1	2	4	6	8	10
	500	0	0	1	1	1	2	3	5	7	9
	600	0	0	0	1	1	1	2	4	5	7
	700	0	0	0	1	1	1	2	3	5	6
	750	0	0	0	1	1	1	1	3	4	6
	900	0	0	0	0	1	1	2	3	3	5
	1000	0	0	0	0	1	1	1	2	3	4
XHHW,	8	3	6	9	16	22	37	52	80	107	138
XHHW-2	6	2	4	7	12	16	27	38	59	80	103
	4	1	3	5	9	12	20	28	43	58	74
	2	1	1	3	6	8	14	20	31	41	53
	1	1	1	3	5	6	10	15	23	31	40
	1/0	1	1	2	4	5	9	13	20	26	34
	2/0	1	1	1	3	4	7	11	17	22	29
	3/0	0	1	1	3	4	6	9	14	18	24
	4/0	0	1	1	2	3	5	7	11	15	20
	250	0	1	1	1	2	4	6	9	12	16
	300	0	0	1	1	1	3	5	8	10	13
	350	0	0	1	1	1	3	4	7	9	12
	400	0	0	1	1	1	3	4	6	8	11
	500	0	0	1	1	1	2	3	5	7	9
	600	0	0	0	1	1	1	2	4	5	7
	700	0	0	0	1	1	1	2	3	5	6
	750	0	0	0	1	1	1	1	3	4	6
	900	0	0	0	0	1	1	2	3	4	5
	1000	0	0	0	0	1	1	1	2	3	4

Definition: *Compact stranding* is the result of a manufacturing process where the standard conductor is compressed to the extent that interstices (voids between strand wires) are virtually eliminated.

Table C.5 Maximum Number of Conductors or Fixture Wires in Liquidtight Flexible Nonmetallic Conduit (Type LFNC-B*) (*Based on Table 1, Chapter 9*)

		CONDUCTORS						
	Conductor Size (AWG/ kcmil)	Metric Designator (Trade Size)						
Type		12 (⅜)	16 (½)	21 (¾)	27 (1)	35 (1¼)	41 (1½)	53 (2)
RHH, RHW, RHW-2	14	2	4	7	12	21	27	44
	12	1	3	6	10	17	22	36
	10	1	3	5	8	14	18	29
	8	1	1	2	4	7	9	15
	6	1	1	1	3	6	7	12
	4	0	1	1	2	4	6	9
	3	0	1	1	1	4	5	8
	2	0	1	1	1	3	4	7
	1	0	0	1	1	1	3	5
	1/0	0	0	1	1	1	2	4
	2/0	0	0	1	1	1	1	3
	3/0	0	0	0	1	1	1	3
	4/0	0	0	0	1	1	1	2
	250	0	0	0	0	1	1	1
	300	0	0	0	0	1	1	1
	350	0	0	0	0	1	1	1
	400	0	0	0	0	1	1	1
	500	0	0	0	0	1	1	1
	600	0	0	0	0	0	1	1
	700	0	0	0	0	0	0	1
	750	0	0	0	0	0	0	1
	800	0	0	0	0	0	0	1
	900	0	0	0	0	0	0	1
	1000	0	0	0	0	0	0	1
	1250	0	0	0	0	0	0	0
	1500	0	0	0	0	0	0	0
	1750	0	0	0	0	0	0	0
	2000	0	0	0	0	0	0	0
TW	14	5	9	15	25	44	57	93
	12	4	7	12	19	33	43	71
	10	3	5	9	14	25	32	53
	8	1	3	5	8	14	18	29
RHH†, RHW†, RHW-2†, THHW, THW, THW-2	14	3	6	10	16	29	38	62
RHH†, RHW†, RHW-2†, THHW, THW	12	3	5	8	13	23	30	50
	10	1	3	6	10	18	23	39
RHH†, RHW†, RHW-2†, THHW, THW, THW-2	8	1	1	4	6	11	14	23
RHH†, RHW†, RHW-2†, TW, THW, THHW, THW-2	6	1	1	3	5	8	11	18
	4	1	1	1	3	6	8	13
	3	1	1	1	3	5	7	11

Table C.5 *Continued*

	Conductor Size (AWG/ kcmil)	Metric Designator (Trade Size)						
Type		12 (³⁄₈)	16 (½)	21 (¾)	27 (1)	35 (1¼)	41 (1½)	53 (2)
RHH†,	2	0	1	1	2	4	6	9
RHW†,	1	0	1	1	1	3	4	7
RHW-2†,	1/0	0	0	1	1	2	3	6
TW, THW,	2/0	0	0	1	1	2	3	5
THHW,	3/0	0	0	1	1	1	2	4
THW-2	4/0	0	0	0	1	1	1	3
	250	0	0	0	1	1	1	3
	300	0	0	0	1	1	1	2
	350	0	0	0	0	1	1	1
	400	0	0	0	0	1	1	1
	500	0	0	0	0	1	1	1
	600	0	0	0	0	1	1	1
	700	0	0	0	0	0	1	1
	750	0	0	0	0	0	1	1
	800	0	0	0	0	0	1	1
	900	0	0	0	0	0	0	1
	1000	0	0	0	0	0	0	1
	1250	0	0	0	0	0	0	1
	1500	0	0	0	0	0	0	0
	1750	0	0	0	0	0	0	0
	2000	0	0	0	0	0	0	0
THHN,	14	8	13	22	36	63	81	133
THWN,	12	5	9	16	26	46	59	97
THWN-2	10	3	6	10	16	29	37	61
	8	1	3	6	9	16	21	35
	6	1	2	4	7	12	15	25
	4	1	1	2	4	7	9	15
	3	1	1	1	3	6	8	13
	2	1	1	1	3	5	7	11
	1	0	1	1	1	4	5	8
	1/0	0	1	1	1	3	4	7
	2/0	0	0	1	1	2	3	6
	3/0	0	0	1	1	1	3	5
	4/0	0	0	1	1	1	2	4
	250	0	0	0	1	1	1	3
	300	0	0	0	1	1	1	3
	350	0	0	0	1	1	1	2
	400	0	0	0	0	1	1	1
	500	0	0	0	0	1	1	1
	600	0	0	0	0	1	1	1
	700	0	0	0	0	1	1	1
	750	0	0	0	0	0	1	1
	800	0	0	0	0	0	1	1
	900	0	0	0	0	0	1	1
	1000	0	0	0	0	0	0	1
FEP,	14	7	12	21	35	61	79	129
FEPB,	12	5	9	15	25	44	57	94
PFA,	10	4	6	11	18	32	41	68
PFAH,	8	1	3	6	10	18	23	39
TFE	6	1	2	4	7	13	17	27
	4	1	1	3	5	9	12	19
	3	1	1	2	4	7	10	16
	2	1	1	1	3	6	8	13
PFA, PFAH, TFE	1	0	1	1	2	4	5	9
PFA, PFAH	1/0	0	1	1	1	3	4	7

(Continues)

Table C.5 *Continued*

		CONDUCTORS						
	Conductor Size (AWG/ kcmil)	Metric Designator (Trade Size)						
Type		12 (⅜)	16 (½)	21 (¾)	27 (1)	35 (1¼)	41 (1½)	53 (2)
TFE, Z	2/0	0	1	1	1	3	4	6
	3/0	0	0	1	1	2	3	5
	4/0	0	0	1	1	1	2	4
Z	14	9	15	26	42	73	95	156
	12	6	10	18	30	52	67	111
	10	4	6	11	18	32	41	68
	8	2	4	7	11	20	26	43
	6	1	3	5	8	14	18	30
	4	1	1	3	5	9	12	20
	3	1	1	2	4	7	9	15
	2	0	1	1	3	6	7	12
	1	0	1	1	2	5	6	10
XHH, XHHW, XHHW-2, ZW	14	5	9	15	25	44	57	93
	12	4	7	12	19	33	43	71
	10	3	5	9	14	25	32	53
	8	1	3	5	8	14	18	29
	6	1	1	3	6	10	13	22
	4	1	1	2	4	7	9	16
	3	1	1	1	3	6	8	13
	2	1	1	1	3	5	7	11
XHH, XHHW, XHHW-2	1	0	1	1	1	4	5	8
	1/0	0	1	1	1	3	4	7
	2/0	0	0	1	1	2	3	6
	3/0	0	0	1	1	1	3	5
	4/0	0	0	1	1	1	2	4
	250	0	0	0	1	1	1	3
	300	0	0	0	1	1	1	3
	350	0	0	0	1	1	1	2
	400	0	0	0	0	1	1	1
	500	0	0	0	0	1	1	1
	600	0	0	0	0	1	1	1
	700	0	0	0	0	1	1	1
	750	0	0	0	0	0	1	1
	800	0	0	0	0	0	1	1
	900	0	0	0	0	0	1	1
	1000	0	0	0	0	0	0	1
	1250	0	0	0	0	0	0	1
	1500	0	0	0	0	0	0	1
	1750	0	0	0	0	0	0	0
	2000	0	0	0	0	0	0	0
		FIXTURE WIRES						
FFH-2, RFH-2	18	5	8	15	24	42	54	89
	16	4	7	12	20	35	46	75
SF-2, SFF-2	18	6	11	19	30	53	69	113
	16	5	9	15	25	44	57	93
	14	4	7	12	20	35	46	75
SF-1, SFF-1	18	11	19	33	53	94	122	199
RFH-1, RFHH-2, TF, TFF, XF, XFF	18	8	14	24	39	69	90	147
RFHH-2, TF, TFF, XF, XFF	16	7	11	20	32	56	72	119
XF, XFF	14	5	9	15	25	44	57	93
TFN, TFFN	18	14	23	39	63	111	144	236
	16	10	17	30	48	85	110	180

Table C.5 *Continued*

		FIXTURE WIRES						
	Conductor Size (AWG/ kcmil)	Metric Designator (Trade Size)						
Type		12 (⅜)	16 (½)	21 (¾)	27 (1)	35 (1¼)	41 (1½)	53 (2)
PF, PFF, PGF, PGFF, PAF, PTF, PTFF, PAFF	18	13	21	37	60	105	136	223
	16	10	16	29	46	81	105	173
	14	7	12	21	35	61	79	129
HF, HFF, ZF, ZFF, ZHF	18	17	28	48	77	136	176	288
	16	12	20	35	57	100	129	212
	14	9	15	26	42	73	95	156
KF-2, KFF-2	18	24	40	70	112	197	255	418
	16	17	28	49	79	139	180	295
	14	12	19	34	54	95	123	202
	12	8	13	23	37	65	85	139
	10	5	9	15	25	44	57	93
KF-1, KFF-1	18	29	48	83	134	235	304	499
	16	20	34	58	94	165	214	350
	14	14	23	39	63	111	144	236
	12	9	15	26	42	73	95	156
	10	6	10	17	27	48	62	102
XF, XFF	12	3	5	8	13	23	30	50
	10	1	3	6	10	18	23	39

Notes:

1. This table is for concentric stranded conductors only. For compact stranded conductors, Table C.5(A) should be used.

2. Two-hour fire-rated RHH cable has ceramifiable insulation which has much larger diameters than other RHH wires.

Consult manufacturer's conduit fill tables.

*Corresponds to 356.2(2).

†Types RHH, RHW, and RHW-2 without outer covering.

Table C.5(A) Maximum Number of Compact Conductors in Liquidtight Flexible Nonmetallic Conduit (Type LFNC-B*) (*Based on Table 1, Chapter 9*)

		COMPACT CONDUCTORS						
	Conductor Size	Metric Designator (Trade Size)						
Type	(AWG/ kcmil)	12 (⅜)	16 (½)	21 (¾)	27 (1)	35 (1¼)	41 (1½)	53 (2)
THW,	8	1	2	4	7	12	15	25
THW-2,	6	1	1	3	5	9	12	19
THHW	4	1	1	2	4	7	9	14
	2	1	1	1	3	5	6	11
	1	0	1	1	1	3	4	7
	1/0	0	1	1	1	3	4	6
	2/0	0	0	1	1	2	3	5
	3/0	0	0	1	1	1	3	4
	4/0	0	0	1	1	1	2	4
	250	0	0	0	1	1	1	3
	300	0	0	0	1	1	1	2
	350	0	0	0	1	1	1	2
	400	0	0	0	0	1	1	1
	500	0	0	0	0	1	1	1
	600	0	0	0	0	1	1	1
	700	0	0	0	0	1	1	1
	750	0	0	0	0	0	1	1
	900	—	0	0	0	0	1	1
	1000	0	0	0	0	0	1	1
THHN,	8	—	—	—	—	—	—	—
THWN,	6	1	2	4	7	13	17	28
THWN-2	4	1	1	3	4	8	11	17
	2	1	1	1	3	6	7	12
	1	0	1	1	2	4	6	9
	1/0	0	1	1	1	4	5	8
	2/0	0	1	1	1	3	4	6
	3/0	0	0	1	1	2	3	5
	4/0	0	0	1	1	1	3	4
	250	0	0	1	1	1	1	3
	300	0	0	0	1	1	1	3
	350	0	0	0	1	1	1	2
	400	0	0	0	1	1	1	2
	500	0	0	0	0	1	1	1
	600	0	0	0	0	1	1	1
	700	0	0	0	0	1	1	1
	750	0	0	0	0	1	1	1
	900	—	0	0	0	0	1	1
	1000	0	0	0	0	0	1	1
XHHW,	8	1	3	5	9	15	20	33
XHHW-2	6	1	2	4	6	11	15	24
	4	1	1	3	4	8	11	17
	2	1	1	1	3	6	7	12
	1	0	1	1	2	4	6	9
	1/0	0	1	1	1	4	5	8
	2/0	0	1	1	1	3	4	7
	3/0	0	0	1	1	2	3	5
	4/0	0	0	1	1	1	3	4
	250	0	0	1	1	1	1	3
	300	0	0	0	1	1	1	3
	350	0	0	0	1	1	1	3
	400	0	0	0	1	1	1	2
	500	0	0	0	0	1	1	1
	600	0	0	0	0	1	1	1
	700	0	0	0	0	1	1	1
	750	0	0	0	0	1	1	1
	900	—	0	0	0	0	1	1
	1000	0	0	0	0	0	1	1

*Corresponds to 356.2(2).

Definition: *Compact stranding* is the result of a manufacturing process where the standard conductor is compressed to the extent that the interstices (voids between strand wires) are virtually eliminated.

Table C.6 Maximum Number of Conductors or Fixture Wires in Liquidtight Flexible Nonmetallic Conduit (Type LFNC-A*) (*Based on Table 1, Chapter 9*)

		CONDUCTORS						
	Conductor Size (AWG/ kcmil)	Metric Designator (Trade Size)						
Type		12 (⅜)	16 (½)	21 (¾)	27 (1)	35 (1¼)	41 (1½)	53 (2)
RHH,	14	2	4	7	11	20	27	45
RHW,	12	1	3	6	9	17	23	38
RHW-2	10	1	3	5	8	13	18	30
	8	1	1	2	4	7	9	16
	6	1	1	1	3	5	7	13
	4	0	1	1	2	4	6	10
	3	0	1	1	1	4	5	8
	2	0	1	1	1	3	4	7
	1	0	0	1	1	1	3	5
	1/0	0	0	1	1	1	2	4
	2/0	0	0	1	1	1	1	4
	3/0	0	0	0	1	1	1	3
	4/0	0	0	0	1	1	1	3
	250	0	0	0	0	1	1	1
	300	0	0	0	0	1	1	1
	350	0	0	0	0	1	1	1
	400	0	0	0	0	1	1	1
	500	0	0	0	0	0	1	1
	600	0	0	0	0	0	1	1
	700	0	0	0	0	0	0	1
	750	0	0	0	0	0	0	1
	800	0	0	0	0	0	0	1
	900	0	0	0	0	0	0	1
	1000	0	0	0	0	0	0	1
	1250	0	0	0	0	0	0	0
	1500	0	0	0	0	0	0	0
	1750	0	0	0	0	0	0	0
	2000	0	0	0	0	0	0	0
TW	14	5	9	15	24	43	58	96
	12	4	7	12	19	33	44	74
	10	3	5	9	14	24	33	55
	8	1	3	5	8	13	18	30
RHH[†], RHW[†], RHW-2[†], THHW, THW, THW-2	14	3	6	10	16	28	38	64
RHH[†], RHW[†], RHW-2[†], THHW, THW	12	3	4	8	13	23	31	51
	10	1	3	6	10	18	24	40
RHH[†], RHW[†], RHW-2[†], THHW, THW, THW-2	8	1	1	4	6	10	14	24

(Continues)

Table C.6 *Continued*

		CONDUCTORS						
	Conductor Size (AWG/ kcmil)	Metric Designator (Trade Size)						
Type		12 (⅜)	16 (½)	21 (¾)	27 (1)	35 (1¼)	41 (1½)	53 (2)
RHH†,	6	1	1	3	4	8	11	18
RHW†,	4	1	1	1	3	6	8	13
RHW-2†,	3	1	1	1	3	5	7	11
TW,	2	0	1	1	2	4	6	10
THW, THHW,	1	0	1	1	1	3	4	7
THW-2	1/0	0	0	1	1	2	3	6
	2/0	0	0	1	1	1	3	5
	3/0	0	0	1	1	1	2	4
	4/0	0	0	0	1	1	1	3
	250	0	0	0	1	1	1	3
	300	0	0	0	1	1	1	2
	350	0	0	0	0	1	1	1
	400	0	0	0	0	1	1	1
	500	0	0	0	0	1	1	1
	600	0	0	0	0	1	1	1
	700	0	0	0	0	0	1	1
	750	0	0	0	0	0	1	1
	800	0	0	0	0	0	1	1
	900	0	0	0	0	0	0	1
	1000	0	0	0	0	0	0	1
	1250	0	0	0	0	0	0	1
	1500	0	0	0	0	0	0	1
	1750	0	0	0	0	0	0	0
	2000	0	0	0	0	0	0	0
THHN,	14	8	13	22	35	62	83	137
THWN,	12	5	9	16	25	45	60	100
THWN-2	10	3	6	10	16	28	38	63
	8	1	3	6	9	16	22	36
	6	1	2	4	6	12	16	26
	4	1	1	2	4	7	9	16
	3	1	1	1	3	6	8	13
	2	1	1	1	3	5	7	11
	1	0	1	1	1	4	5	8
	1/0	0	1	1	1	3	4	7
	2/0	0	0	1	1	2	3	6
	3/0	0	0	1	1	1	3	5
	4/0	0	0	1	1	1	2	4
	250	0	0	0	1	1	1	3
	300	0	0	0	1	1	1	3
	350	0	0	0	1	1	1	2
	400	0	0	0	0	1	1	1
	500	0	0	0	0	1	1	1
	600	0	0	0	0	1	1	1
	700	0	0	0	0	1	1	1
	750	0	0	0	0	0	1	1
	800	0	0	0	0	0	1	1
	900	0	0	0	0	0	1	1
	1000	0	0	0	0	0	0	1
FEP,	14	7	12	21	34	60	80	133
FEPB,	12	5	9	15	25	44	59	97
PFA,	10	4	6	11	18	31	42	70
PFAH,	8	1	3	6	10	18	24	40
TFE	6	1	2	4	7	13	17	28
	4	1	1	3	5	9	12	20
	3	1	1	2	4	7	10	16
	2	1	1	1	3	6	8	13
PFA, PFAH, TFE	1	0	1	1	2	4	5	9

Table C.6 *Continued*

		CONDUCTORS						
	Conductor Size (AWG/ kcmil)	Metric Designator (Trade Size)						
Type		12 (⅜)	16 (½)	21 (¾)	27 (1)	35 (1¼)	41 (1½)	53 (2)
PFA,	1/0	0	1	1	1	3	5	8
PFAH,	2/0	0	1	1	1	3	4	6
TFE, Z	3/0	0	0	1	1	2	3	5
	4/0	0	0	1	1	1	2	4
Z	14	9	15	25	41	72	97	161
	12	6	10	18	29	51	69	114
	10	4	6	11	18	31	42	70
	8	2	4	7	11	20	26	44
	6	1	3	5	8	14	18	31
	4	1	1	3	5	9	13	21
	3	1	1	2	4	7	9	15
	2	1	1	1	3	6	8	13
	1	1	1	1	2	4	6	10
XHH,	14	5	9	15	24	43	58	96
XHHW,	12	4	7	12	19	33	44	74
XHHW-2,	10	3	5	9	14	24	33	55
ZW	8	1	3	5	8	13	18	30
	6	1	1	3	5	10	13	22
	4	1	1	2	4	7	10	16
	3	1	1	1	3	6	8	14
	2	1	1	1	3	5	7	11
XHH,	1	0	1	1	1	4	5	8
XHHW,	1/0	0	1	1	1	3	4	7
XHHW-2	2/0	0	0	1	1	2	3	6
	3/0	0	0	1	1	1	3	5
	4/0	0	0	1	1	1	2	4
	250	0	0	0	1	1	1	3
	300	0	0	0	1	1	1	3
	350	0	0	0	1	1	1	2
	400	0	0	0	0	1	1	1
	500	0	0	0	0	1	1	1
	600	0	0	0	0	1	1	1
	700	0	0	0	0	1	1	1
	750	0	0	0	0	0	1	1
	800	0	0	0	0	0	1	1
	900	0	0	0	0	0	1	1
	1000	0	0	0	0	0	0	1
	1250	0	0	0	0	0	0	1
	1500	0	0	0	0	0	0	1
	1750	0	0	0	0	0	0	0
	2000	0	0	0	0	0	0	0
		FIXTURE WIRES						
FFH-2,	18	5	8	14	23	41	55	92
RFH-2, RFHH-3	16	4	7	12	20	35	47	77
SF-2,	18	6	11	18	29	52	70	116
SFF-2	16	5	9	15	24	43	58	96
	14	4	7	12	20	35	47	77
SF-1, SFF-1	18	12	19	33	52	92	124	205
RFH-1, RFHH-2, TF, TFF, XF, XFF	18	8	14	24	39	68	91	152
RFHH-2, TF, TFF, XF, XFF	16	7	11	19	31	55	74	122
XF, XFF	14	5	9	15	24	43	58	96

(Continues)

Table C.6 *Continued*

		FIXTURE WIRES						
	Conductor Size	Metric Designator (Trade Size)						
Type	(AWG/ kcmil)	12 (⅜)	16 (½)	21 (¾)	27 (1)	35 (1¼)	41 (1½)	53 (2)
TFN,	18	14	22	39	62	109	146	243
TFFN	16	10	17	29	47	83	112	185
PF, PFF, PGF,	18	13	21	37	59	103	139	230
PGFF, PAF, PTF,	16	10	16	28	45	80	107	178
PTFF, PAFF	14	7	12	21	34	60	80	133
HF, HFF,	18	17	27	47	76	133	179	297
ZF, ZFF,	16	12	20	35	56	98	132	219
ZHF	14	9	15	25	41	72	97	161
KF-2,	18	25	40	69	110	193	260	431
KFF-2	16	17	28	48	77	136	183	303
	14	12	19	33	53	94	126	209
	12	8	13	23	36	64	86	143
	10	5	9	15	24	43	58	96
KF-1,	18	29	48	82	131	231	310	514
KFF-1	16	21	33	57	92	162	218	361
	14	14	22	39	62	109	146	243
	12	9	15	25	41	72	97	161
	10	6	10	17	27	47	63	105
XF, XFF	12	3	4	8	13	23	31	51
	10	1	3	6	10	18	24	40

Notes:

1. This table is for concentric stranded conductors only. For compact stranded conductors, Table C.6(A) should be used.

2. Two-hour fire-rated RHH cable has ceramifiable insulation which has much larger diameters than other RHH wires.

Consult manufacturer's conduit fill tables.

*Corresponds to 356.2(1).

†Types RHH, RHW, and RHW-2 without outer covering.

Table C.6(A) Maximum Number of Compact Conductors in Liquidtight Flexible Nonmetallic Conduit (Type LFNC-A*) (*Based on Table 1, Chapter 9*)

		COMPACT CONDUCTORS						
	Conductor Size	Metric Designator (Trade Size)						
Type	(AWG/ kcmil)	12 (⅜)	16 (½)	21 (¾)	27 (1)	35 (1¼)	41 (1½)	53 (2)
THW,	8	1	2	4	6	11	16	26
THW-2,	6	1	1	3	5	9	12	20
THHW	4	1	1	2	4	7	9	15
	2	1	1	1	3	5	6	11
	1	0	1	1	1	3	4	8
	1/0	0	1	1	1	3	4	7
	2/0	0	0	1	1	2	3	5
	3/0	0	0	1	1	1	3	5
	4/0	0	0	1	1	1	2	4
	250	0	0	0	1	1	1	3
	300	0	0	0	1	1	1	3
	350	0	0	0	1	1	1	2
	400	0	0	0	0	1	1	1
	500	0	0	0	0	1	1	1
	600	0	0	0	0	1	1	1
	700	0	0	0	0	1	1	1
	750	0	0	0	0	0	1	1
	900	—	0	0	0	0	1	1
	1000	0	0	0	0	0	1	1
THHN,	8	—	—	—	—	—	—	—
THWN,	6	1	2	4	7	13	18	29
THWN-2	4	1	1	3	4	8	11	18
	2	1	1	1	3	6	8	13
	1	0	1	1	2	4	6	10
	1/0	0	1	1	1	3	5	8
	2/0	0	1	1	1	3	4	7
	3/0	0	0	1	1	2	3	6
	4/0	0	0	1	1	1	3	5
	250	0	0	1	1	1	1	3
	300	0	0	0	1	1	1	3
	350	0	0	0	1	1	1	3
	400	0	0	0	1	1	1	2
	500	0	0	0	0	1	1	1
	600	0	0	0	0	1	1	1
	700	0	0	0	0	1	1	1
	750	0	0	0	0	1	1	1
	900	—	0	0	0	0	1	1
	1000	0	0	0	0	0	1	1
XHHW,	8	1	3	5	8	15	20	34
XHHW-2	6	1	2	4	6	11	15	25
	4	1	1	3	4	8	11	18
	2	1	1	1	3	6	8	13
	1	0	1	1	2	4	6	10
	1/0	0	1	1	1	3	5	8
	2/0	0	1	1	1	3	4	7
	3/0	0	0	1	1	2	3	6
	4/0	0	0	1	1	1	3	5
	250	0	0	1	1	1	2	4
	300	0	0	0	1	1	1	3
	350	0	0	0	1	1	1	3
	400	0	0	0	1	1	1	2
	500	0	0	0	0	1	1	1
	600	0	0	0	0	1	1	1
	700	0	0	0	0	1	1	1
	750	0	0	0	0	1	1	1
	900	—	0	0	0	0	1	1
	1000	0	0	0	0	0	1	1

*Corresponds to 356.2(1).

Definition: *Compact stranding* is the result of a manufacturing process where the standard conductor is compressed to the extent that the interstices (voids between strand wires) are virtually eliminated.

Table C.7 Maximum Number of Conductors or Fixture Wires in Liquidtight Flexible Metal Conduit (LFMC) (*Based on Table 1, Chapter 9*)

Type	Conductor Size (AWG/ kcmil)	CONDUCTORS Metric Designator (Trade Size)									
		16 (½)	21 (¾)	27 (1)	35 (1¼)	41 (1½)	53 (2)	63 (2½)	78 (3)	91 (3½)	103 (4)
RHH, RHW, RHW-2	14	4	7	12	21	27	44	66	102	133	173
	12	3	6	10	17	22	36	55	84	110	144
	10	3	5	8	14	18	29	44	68	89	116
	8	1	2	4	7	9	15	23	36	46	61
	6	1	1	3	6	7	12	18	28	37	48
	4	1	1	2	4	6	9	14	22	29	38
	3	1	1	1	4	5	8	13	19	25	33
	2	1	1	1	3	4	7	11	17	22	29
	1	0	1	1	1	3	5	7	11	14	19
	1/0	0	1	1	1	2	4	6	10	13	16
	2/0	0	1	1	1	1	3	5	8	11	14
	3/0	0	0	1	1	1	3	4	7	9	12
	4/0	0	0	1	1	1	2	4	6	8	10
	250	0	0	0	1	1	1	3	4	6	8
	300	0	0	0	1	1	1	2	4	5	7
	350	0	0	0	1	1	1	2	3	5	6
	400	0	0	0	1	1	1	1	3	4	6
	500	0	0	0	1	1	1	1	3	4	5
	600	0	0	0	0	1	1	1	2	3	4
	700	0	0	0	0	0	1	1	1	3	3
	750	0	0	0	0	0	1	1	1	2	3
	800	0	0	0	0	0	1	1	1	2	3
	900	0	0	0	0	0	1	1	1	2	3
	1000	0	0	0	0	0	1	1	1	1	3
	1250	0	0	0	0	0	0	1	1	1	1
	1500	0	0	0	0	0	0	1	1	1	1
	1750	0	0	0	0	0	0	1	1	1	1
	2000	0	0	0	0	0	0	0	1	1	1
TW	14	9	15	25	44	57	93	140	215	280	365
	12	7	12	19	33	43	71	108	165	215	280
	10	5	9	14	25	32	53	80	123	160	209
	8	3	5	8	14	18	29	44	68	89	116
RHH*, RHW*, RHW-2*, THHW, THW, THW-2	14	6	10	16	29	38	62	93	143	186	243
RHH*, RHW*, RHW-2*, THHW, THW	12	5	8	13	23	30	50	75	115	149	195
	10	3	6	10	18	23	39	58	89	117	152
RHH*, RHW*, RHW-2*, THHW, THW, THW-2	8	1	4	6	11	14	23	35	53	70	91

Table C.7 *Continued*

	CONDUCTORS										
	Conductor Size (AWG/ kcmil)	Metric Designator (Trade Size)									
Type		16 (½)	21 (¾)	27 (1)	35 (1¼)	41 (1½)	53 (2)	63 (2½)	78 (3)	91 (3½)	103 (4)
RHH*,	6	1	3	5	8	11	18	27	41	53	70
RHW*,	4	1	1	3	6	8	13	20	30	40	52
RHW-2*,	3	1	1	3	5	7	11	17	26	34	44
TW,	2	1	1	2	4	6	9	14	22	29	38
THW,	1	1	1	1	3	4	7	10	15	20	26
THHW,	1/0	0	1	1	2	3	6	8	13	17	23
THW-2	2/0	0	1	1	2	3	5	7	11	15	19
	3/0	0	1	1	1	2	4	6	9	12	16
	4/0	0	0	1	1	1	3	5	8	10	13
	250	0	0	1	1	1	3	4	6	8	11
	300	0	0	1	1	1	2	3	5	7	9
	350	0	0	0	1	1	1	3	5	6	8
	400	0	0	0	1	1	1	3	4	6	7
	500	0	0	0	1	1	1	2	3	5	6
	600	0	0	0	1	1	1	1	3	4	5
	700	0	0	0	0	1	1	1	2	3	4
	750	0	0	0	0	1	1	1	2	3	4
	800	0	0	0	0	1	1	1	2	3	4
	900	0	0	0	0	0	1	1	1	3	3
	1000	0	0	0	0	0	1	1	1	2	3
	1250	0	0	0	0	0	1	1	1	1	2
	1500	0	0	0	0	0	0	1	1	1	2
	1750	0	0	0	0	0	0	1	1	1	1
	2000	0	0	0	0	0	0	1	1	1	1
THHN,	14	13	22	36	63	81	133	201	308	401	523
THWN,	12	9	16	26	46	59	97	146	225	292	381
THWN-2	10	6	10	16	29	37	61	92	141	184	240
	8	3	6	9	16	21	35	53	81	106	138
	6	2	4	7	12	15	25	38	59	76	100
	4	1	2	4	7	9	15	23	36	47	61
	3	1	1	3	6	8	13	20	30	40	52
	2	1	1	3	5	7	11	17	26	33	44
	1	1	1	1	4	5	8	12	19	25	32
	1/0	1	1	1	3	4	7	10	16	21	27
	2/0	0	1	1	2	3	6	8	13	17	23
	3/0	0	1	1	1	3	5	7	11	14	19
	4/0	0	1	1	1	2	4	6	9	12	15
	250	0	0	1	1	1	3	5	7	10	12
	300	0	0	1	1	1	3	4	6	8	11
	350	0	0	1	1	1	2	3	5	7	9
	400	0	0	0	1	1	1	3	5	6	8
	500	0	0	0	1	1	1	2	4	5	7
	600	0	0	0	1	1	1	1	3	4	6
	700	0	0	0	1	1	1	1	3	4	5
	750	0	0	0	0	1	1	1	3	3	5
	800	0	0	0	0	1	1	1	2	3	4
	900	0	0	0	0	1	1	1	2	3	4
	1000	0	0	0	0	0	1	1	1	3	3
FEP,	14	12	21	35	61	79	129	195	299	389	507
FEPB,	12	9	15	25	44	57	94	142	218	284	370
PFA,	10	6	11	18	32	41	68	102	156	203	266
PFAH,	8	3	6	10	18	23	39	58	89	117	152
TFE	6	2	4	7	13	17	27	41	64	83	108
	4	1	3	5	9	12	19	29	44	58	75
	3	1	2	4	7	10	16	24	37	48	63
	2	1	1	3	6	8	13	20	30	40	52

(Continues)

Table C.7 *Continued*

		CONDUCTORS									
	Conductor Size (AWG/ kcmil)	Metric Designator (Trade Size)									
Type		16 (½)	21 (¾)	27 (1)	35 (1¼)	41 (1½)	53 (2)	63 (2½)	78 (3)	91 (3½)	103 (4)
PFA, PFAH, TFE	1	1	1	2	4	5	9	14	21	28	36
PFA, PFAH, TFE, Z	1/0	1	1	1	3	4	7	11	18	23	30
	2/0	1	1	1	3	4	6	9	14	19	25
	3/0	0	1	1	2	3	5	8	12	16	20
	4/0	0	1	1	1	2	4	6	10	13	17
Z	14	20	26	42	73	95	156	235	360	469	611
	12	14	18	30	52	67	111	167	255	332	434
	10	8	11	18	32	41	68	102	156	203	266
	8	5	7	11	20	26	43	64	99	129	168
	6	4	5	8	14	18	30	45	69	90	118
	4	2	3	5	9	12	20	31	48	62	81
	3	2	2	4	7	9	15	23	35	45	59
	2	1	1	3	6	7	12	19	29	38	49
	1	1	1	2	5	6	10	15	23	30	40
XHH, XHHW, XHHW-2, ZW	14	9	15	25	44	57	93	140	215	280	365
	12	7	12	19	33	43	71	108	165	215	280
	10	5	9	14	25	32	53	80	123	160	209
	8	3	5	8	14	18	29	44	68	89	116
	6	1	3	6	10	13	22	33	50	66	86
	4	1	2	4	7	9	16	24	36	48	62
	3	1	1	3	6	8	13	20	31	40	52
	2	1	1	3	5	7	11	17	26	34	44
	1	1	1	1	4	5	8	12	19	25	33
XHH, XHHW, XHHW-2	1/0	1	1	1	3	4	7	10	16	21	28
	2/0	0	1	1	2	3	6	9	13	17	23
	3/0	0	1	1	1	3	5	7	11	14	19
	4/0	0	1	1	1	2	4	6	9	12	16
	250	0	0	1	1	1	3	5	7	10	13
	300	0	0	1	1	1	3	4	6	8	11
	350	0	0	1	1	1	2	3	5	7	10
	400	0	0	0	1	1	1	3	5	6	8
	500	0	0	0	1	1	1	2	4	5	7
	600	0	0	0	1	1	1	1	3	4	6
	700	0	0	0	1	1	1	1	3	4	5
	750	0	0	0	0	1	1	1	3	3	5
	800	0	0	0	0	1	1	1	2	3	4
	900	0	0	0	0	1	1	1	2	3	4
	1000	0	0	0	0	0	1	1	1	3	3
	1250	0	0	0	0	0	1	1	1	1	3
	1500	0	0	0	0	0	1	1	1	1	2
	1750	0	0	0	0	0	0	1	1	1	2
	2000	0	0	0	0	0	0	1	1	1	2

Table C.7 *Continued*

FIXTURE WIRES

Type	Conductor Size (AWG/ kcmil)	Metric Designator (Trade Size)					
		16 (½)	21 (¾)	27 (1)	35 (1¼)	41 (1½)	53 (2)
FFH-2, RFH-2, RFHH-3	18	8	15	24	42	54	89
	16	7	12	20	35	46	75
SF-2, SFF-2	18	11	19	30	53	69	113
	16	9	15	25	44	57	93
	14	7	12	20	35	46	75
SF-1, SFF-1	18	19	33	53	94	122	199
RFH-1, RFHH-2, TF, TFF, XF, XFF	18	14	24	39	69	90	147
RFHH-2, TF, TFF, XF, XFF	16	11	20	32	56	72	119
XF, XFF	14	9	15	25	44	57	93
TFN, TFFN	18	23	39	63	111	144	236
	16	17	30	48	85	110	180
PF, PFF, PGF, PGFF, PAF, PTF, PTFF, PAFF	18	21	37	60	105	136	223
	16	16	29	46	81	105	173
	14	12	21	35	61	79	129
HF, HFF, ZF, ZFF, ZHF	18	28	48	77	136	176	288
	16	20	35	57	100	129	212
	14	15	26	42	73	95	156
KF-2, KFF-2	18	40	70	112	197	255	418
	16	28	49	79	139	180	295
	14	19	34	54	95	123	202
	12	13	23	37	65	85	139
	10	9	15	25	44	57	93
KF-1, KFF-1	18	48	83	134	235	304	499
	16	34	58	94	165	214	350
	14	23	39	63	111	144	236
	12	15	26	42	73	95	156
	10	10	17	27	48	62	102
XF, XFF	12	5	8	13	23	30	50
	10	3	6	10	18	23	39

Notes:

1. This table is for concentric stranded conductors only. For compact stranded conductors, Table C.7(A) should be used.

2. Two-hour fire-rated RHH cable has ceramifiable insulation which has much larger diameters than other RHH wires.

Consult manufacturer's conduit fill tables.

*Types RHH, RHW, and RHW-2 without outer covering.

Table C.7(A) Maximum Number of Compact Conductors in Liquidtight Flexible Metal Conduit (LFMC) (*Based on Table 1, Chapter 9*)

		COMPACT CONDUCTORS										
	Conductor Size	Metric Designator (Trade Size)										
Type	(AWG/ kcmil)	12 (⅜)	16 (½)	21 (¾)	27 (1)	35 (1¼)	41 (1½)	53 (2)	63 (2½)	78 (3)	91 (3½)	103 (4)
THW,	8	1	2	4	7	12	15	25	38	58	76	99
THW-2,	6	1	1	3	5	9	12	19	29	45	59	77
THHW	4	1	1	2	4	7	9	14	22	34	44	57
	2	1	1	1	3	5	6	11	16	25	32	42
	1	0	1	1	1	3	4	7	11	17	23	30
	1/0	0	1	1	1	3	4	6	10	15	20	26
	2/0	0	0	1	1	2	3	5	8	13	16	21
	3/0	0	0	1	1	1	3	4	7	11	14	18
	4/0	0	0	1	1	1	2	4	6	9	12	15
	250	0	0	0	1	1	1	3	4	7	9	12
	300	0	0	0	1	1	1	2	4	6	8	10
	350	0	0	0	1	1	1	2	3	5	7	9
	400	0	0	0	0	1	1	1	3	5	6	8
	500	0	0	0	0	1	1	1	3	4	5	7
	600	0	0	0	0	1	1	1	1	3	4	6
	700	0	0	0	0	1	1	1	1	3	4	5
	750	0	0	0	0	0	1	1	1	3	3	5
	900	—	0	0	0	0	1	1	1	2	3	4
	1000	0	0	0	0	0	1	1	1	1	3	4
THHN,	8	—	—	—	—	—	—	—	—	—	—	—
THWN,	6	1	2	4	7	13	17	28	43	66	86	112
THWN-2	4	1	1	3	4	8	11	17	26	41	53	69
	2	1	1	1	3	6	7	12	19	29	38	50
	1	0	1	1	2	4	6	9	14	22	28	37
	1/0	0	1	1	1	4	5	8	12	19	24	32
	2/0	0	1	1	1	3	4	6	10	15	20	26
	3/0	0	0	1	1	2	3	5	8	13	17	22
	4/0	0	0	1	1	1	3	4	7	10	14	18
	250	0	0	1	1	1	1	3	5	8	11	14
	300	0	0	0	1	1	1	3	4	7	9	12
	350	0	0	0	1	1	1	2	4	6	8	11
	400	0	0	0	1	1	1	2	3	5	7	9
	500	0	0	0	0	1	1	1	3	5	6	8
	600	0	0	0	0	1	1	1	2	4	5	6
	700	0	0	0	0	1	1	1	1	3	4	6
	750	0	0	0	0	1	1	1	1	3	4	5
	900	—	0	0	0	0	1	1	1	2	3	4
	1000	0	0	0	0	0	1	1	1	2	3	4
XHHW,	8	1	3	5	9	15	20	33	49	76	98	129
XHHW-2	6	1	2	4	6	11	15	24	37	56	73	95
	4	1	1	3	4	8	11	17	26	41	53	69
	2	1	1	1	3	6	7	12	19	29	38	50
	1	0	1	1	2	4	6	9	14	22	28	37
	1/0	0	1	1	1	4	5	8	12	19	24	32
	2/0	0	1	1	1	3	4	7	10	16	20	27
	3/0	0	0	1	1	2	3	5	8	13	17	22
	4/0	0	0	1	1	1	3	4	7	11	14	18
	250	0	0	1	1	1	1	3	5	8	11	15
	300	0	0	0	1	1	1	3	5	7	9	12
	350	0	0	0	1	1	1	3	4	6	8	11
	400	0	0	0	1	1	1	2	4	6	7	10
	500	0	0	0	0	1	1	1	3	5	6	8
	600	0	0	0	0	1	1	1	2	4	5	6
	700	0	0	0	0	1	1	1	1	3	4	6
	750	0	0	0	0	1	1	1	1	3	4	5
	900	—	0	0	0	0	1	1	2	2	3	4
	1000	0	0	0	0	0	1	1	1	2	3	4

Definition: *Compact stranding* is the result of a manufacturing process where the standard conductor is compressed to the extent that the interstices (voids between strand wires) are virtually eliminated.

Table C.8 Maximum Number of Conductors or Fixture Wires in Rigid Metal Conduit (RMC)
(*Based on Table 1, Chapter 9*)

| | | CONDUCTORS | | | | | | | | | | | |
| | Conductor Size (AWG/ kcmil) | Metric Designator (Trade Size) | | | | | | | | | | | |
Type		16 (½)	21 (¾)	27 (1)	35 (1¼)	41 (1½)	53 (2)	63 (2½)	78 (3)	91 (3½)	103 (4)	129 (5)	155 (6)
RHH, RHW, RHW-2	14	4	7	12	21	28	46	66	102	136	176	276	398
	12	3	6	10	17	23	38	55	85	113	146	229	330
	10	3	5	8	14	19	31	44	68	91	118	185	267
	8	1	2	4	7	10	16	23	36	48	61	97	139
	6	1	1	3	6	8	13	18	29	38	49	77	112
	4	1	1	2	4	6	10	14	22	30	38	60	87
	3	1	1	2	4	5	9	12	19	26	34	53	76
	2	1	1	1	3	4	7	11	17	23	29	46	66
	1	0	1	1	1	3	5	7	11	15	19	30	44
	1/0	0	1	1	1	2	4	6	10	13	17	26	38
	2/0	0	1	1	1	2	4	5	8	11	14	23	33
	3/0	0	0	1	1	1	3	4	7	10	12	20	28
	4/0	0	0	1	1	1	3	4	6	8	11	17	24
	250	0	0	0	1	1	1	3	4	6	8	13	18
	300	0	0	0	1	1	1	2	4	5	7	11	16
	350	0	0	0	1	1	1	2	4	5	6	10	15
	400	0	0	0	1	1	1	1	3	4	6	9	13
	500	0	0	0	1	1	1	1	3	4	5	8	11
	600	0	0	0	0	1	1	1	2	3	4	6	9
	700	0	0	0	0	1	1	1	1	3	4	6	8
	750	0	0	0	0	0	1	1	1	3	3	5	8
	800	0	0	0	0	0	1	1	1	2	3	5	7
	900	0	0	0	0	0	1	1	1	2	3	5	7
	1000	0	0	0	0	0	1	1	1	1	3	4	6
	1250	0	0	0	0	0	0	1	1	1	1	3	5
	1500	0	0	0	0	0	0	1	1	1	1	3	4
	1750	0	0	0	0	0	0	1	1	1	1	2	4
	2000	0	0	0	0	0	0	0	1	1	1	2	3
TW	14	9	15	25	44	59	98	140	216	288	370	581	839
	12	7	12	19	33	45	75	107	165	221	284	446	644
	10	5	9	14	25	34	56	80	123	164	212	332	480
	8	3	5	8	14	19	31	44	68	91	118	185	267
RHH*, RHW*, RHW-2*, THHW, THW, THW-2	14	6	10	17	29	39	65	93	143	191	246	387	558
RHH*, RHW*, RHW-2*, THHW, THW	12	5	8	13	23	32	52	75	115	154	198	311	448
	10	3	6	10	18	25	41	58	90	120	154	242	350
RHH*, RHW*, RHW-2*, THHW, THW, THW-2	8	1	4	6	11	15	24	35	54	72	92	145	209

(Continues)

Table C.8 *Continued*

		CONDUCTORS											
	Conductor Size	**Metric Designator (Trade Size)**											
	(AWG/	**16**	**21**	**27**	**35**	**41**	**53**	**63**	**78**	**91**	**103**	**129**	**155**
Type	kcmil)	**(½)**	**(¾)**	**(1)**	**(1¼)**	**(1½)**	**(2)**	**(2½)**	**(3)**	**(3½)**	**(4)**	**(5)**	**(6)**
RHH*,	6	1	3	5	8	11	18	27	41	55	71	111	160
RHW*,	4	1	1	3	6	8	14	20	31	41	53	83	120
RHW-2*,	3	1	1	3	5	7	12	17	26	35	45	71	103
TW,	2	1	1	2	4	6	10	14	22	30	38	60	87
THW,	1	1	1	1	3	4	7	10	15	21	27	42	61
THHW,	1/0	0	1	1	2	3	6	8	13	18	23	36	52
THW-2	2/0	0	1	1	2	3	5	7	11	15	19	31	44
	3/0	0	1	1	1	2	4	6	9	13	16	26	37
	4/0	0	0	1	1	1	3	5	8	10	14	21	31
	250	0	0	1	1	1	3	4	6	8	11	17	25
	300	0	0	1	1	1	2	3	5	7	9	15	22
	350	0	0	0	1	1	1	3	5	6	8	13	19
	400	0	0	0	1	1	1	3	4	6	7	12	17
	500	0	0	0	1	1	1	2	3	5	6	10	14
	600	0	0	0	1	1	1	1	3	4	5	8	12
	700	0	0	0	0	1	1	1	2	3	4	7	10
	750	0	0	0	0	1	1	1	2	3	4	7	10
	800	0	0	0	0	1	1	1	2	3	4	6	9
	900	0	0	0	0	1	1	1	1	3	4	6	8
	1000	0	0	0	0	0	1	1	1	2	3	5	8
	1250	0	0	0	0	0	1	1	1	1	2	4	6
	1500	0	0	0	0	0	1	1	1	1	2	3	5
	1750	0	0	0	0	0	0	1	1	1	1	3	4
	2000	0	0	0	0	0	0	1	1	1	1	3	4
THHN,	14	13	22	36	63	85	140	200	309	412	531	833	1202
THWN,	12	9	16	26	46	62	102	146	225	301	387	608	877
THWN-2	10	6	10	17	29	39	64	92	142	189	244	383	552
	8	3	6	9	16	22	37	53	82	109	140	221	318
	6	2	4	7	12	16	27	38	59	79	101	159	230
	4	1	2	4	7	10	16	23	36	48	62	98	141
	3	1	1	3	6	8	14	20	31	41	53	83	120
	2	1	1	3	5	7	11	17	26	34	44	70	100
	1	1	1	1	4	5	8	12	19	25	33	51	74
	1/0	1	1	1	3	4	7	10	16	21	27	43	63
	2/0	0	1	1	2	3	6	8	13	18	23	36	52
	3/0	0	1	1	1	3	5	7	11	15	19	30	43
	4/0	0	1	1	1	2	4	6	9	12	16	25	36
	250	0	0	1	1	1	3	5	7	10	13	20	29
	300	0	0	1	1	1	3	4	6	8	11	17	25
	350	0	0	1	1	1	2	3	5	7	10	15	22
	400	0	0	1	1	1	2	3	5	7	8	13	20
	500	0	0	0	1	1	1	2	4	5	7	11	16
	600	0	0	0	1	1	1	1	3	4	6	9	13
	700	0	0	0	1	1	1	1	3	4	5	8	11
	750	0	0	0	0	1	1	1	3	4	5	7	11
	800	0	0	0	0	1	1	1	2	3	4	7	10
	900	0	0	0	0	1	1	1	2	3	4	6	9
	1000	0	0	0	0	1	1	1	1	3	4	6	8
FEP,	14	12	22	35	61	83	136	194	300	400	515	808	1166
FEPB,	12	9	16	26	44	60	99	142	219	292	376	590	851
PFA,	10	6	11	18	32	43	71	102	157	209	269	423	610
PFAH,	8	3	6	10	18	25	41	58	90	120	154	242	350
TFE	6	2	4	7	13	17	29	41	64	85	110	172	249
	4	1	3	5	9	12	20	29	44	59	77	120	174
	3	1	2	4	7	10	17	24	37	50	64	100	145
	2	1	1	3	6	8	14	20	31	41	53	83	120

Table C.8 *Continued*

		CONDUCTORS											
	Conductor Size	Metric Designator (Trade Size)											
Type	(AWG/ kcmil)	16 (½)	21 (¾)	27 (1)	35 (1¼)	41 (1½)	53 (2)	63 (2½)	78 (3)	91 (3½)	103 (4)	129 (5)	155 (6)
PFA, PFAH, TFE	1	1	1	2	4	6	9	14	21	28	37	57	83
PFA, PFAH, TFE, Z	1/0	1	1	1	3	5	8	11	18	24	30	48	69
	2/0	1	1	1	3	4	6	9	14	19	25	40	57
	3/0	0	1	1	2	3	5	8	12	16	21	33	47
	4/0	0	1	1	1	2	4	6	10	13	17	27	39
Z	14	15	26	42	73	100	164	234	361	482	621	974	1405
	12	10	18	30	52	71	116	166	256	342	440	691	997
	10	6	11	18	32	43	71	102	157	209	269	423	610
	8	4	7	11	20	27	45	64	99	132	170	267	386
	6	3	5	8	14	19	31	45	69	93	120	188	271
	4	1	3	5	9	13	22	31	48	64	82	129	186
	3	1	2	4	7	9	16	22	35	47	60	94	136
	2	1	1	3	6	8	13	19	29	39	50	78	113
	1	1	1	2	5	6	10	15	23	31	40	63	92
XHH, XHHW, XHHW-2, ZW	14	9	15	25	44	59	98	140	216	288	370	581	839
	12	7	12	19	33	45	75	107	165	221	284	446	644
	10	5	9	14	25	34	56	80	123	164	212	332	480
	8	3	5	8	14	19	31	44	68	91	118	185	267
	6	1	3	6	10	14	23	33	51	68	87	137	197
	4	1	2	4	7	10	16	24	37	49	63	99	143
	3	1	1	3	6	8	14	20	31	41	53	84	121
	2	1	1	3	5	7	12	17	26	35	45	70	101
	1	1	1	1	4	5	9	12	19	26	33	52	76
XHH, XHHW, XHHW-2	1/0	1	1	1	3	4	7	10	16	22	28	44	64
	2/0	0	1	1	2	3	6	9	13	18	23	37	53
	3/0	0	1	1	1	3	5	7	11	15	19	30	44
	4/0	0	1	1	1	2	4	6	9	12	16	25	36
	250	0	0	1	1	1	3	5	7	10	13	20	30
	300	0	0	1	1	1	3	4	6	9	11	18	25
	350	0	0	1	1	1	2	3	6	7	10	15	22
	400	0	0	1	1	1	2	3	5	7	9	14	20
	500	0	0	0	1	1	1	2	4	5	7	11	16
	600	0	0	0	1	1	1	1	3	4	6	9	13
	700	0	0	0	1	1	1	1	3	4	5	8	11
	750	0	0	0	0	1	1	1	3	4	5	7	11
	800	0	0	0	0	1	1	1	2	3	4	7	10
	900	0	0	0	0	1	1	1	2	3	4	6	9
	1000	0	0	0	0	1	1	1	1	3	4	6	8
	1250	0	0	0	0	0	1	1	1	2	3	4	6
	1500	0	0	0	0	0	1	1	1	1	2	4	5
	1750	0	0	0	0	0	0	1	1	1	1	3	5
	2000	0	0	0	0	0	0	1	1	1	1	3	4

(Continues)

Table C.8 *Continued*

		FIXTURE WIRES					
	Conductor Size (AWG/ kcmil)	**Metric Designator (Trade Size)**					
Type		**16** (½)	**21** (¾)	**27** (1)	**35** (1¼)	**41** (1½)	**53** (2)
FFH-2, RFH-2, RFHH-3	18	8	15	24	42	57	94
	16	7	12	20	35	48	79
SF-2, SFF-2	18	11	19	31	53	72	118
	16	9	15	25	44	59	98
	14	7	12	20	35	48	79
SF-1, SFF-1	18	19	33	54	94	127	209
RFH-1, RFHH-2, TF, TFF, XF, XFF	18	14	25	40	69	94	155
RFHH-2, TF, TFF, XF, XFF	16	11	20	32	56	76	125
XF, XFF	14	9	15	25	44	59	98
TFN, TFFN	18	23	40	64	111	150	248
	16	17	30	49	84	115	189
PF, PFF, PGF, PGFF, PAF, PTF, PTFF, PAFF	18	21	38	61	105	143	235
	16	16	29	47	81	110	181
	14	12	22	35	61	83	136
HF, HFF, ZF, ZFF, ZHF	18	28	48	79	135	184	303
	16	20	36	58	100	136	223
	14	15	26	42	73	100	164
KF-2, KFF-2	18	40	71	114	197	267	439
	16	28	50	80	138	188	310
	14	19	34	55	95	129	213
	12	13	23	38	65	89	146
	10	9	15	25	44	59	98
KF-1, KFF-1	18	48	84	136	235	318	524
	16	34	59	96	165	224	368
	14	23	40	64	111	150	248
	12	15	26	42	73	100	164
	10	10	17	28	48	65	107
XF, XFF	12	5	8	13	23	32	52
	10	3	6	10	18	25	41

Notes:

1. This table is for concentric stranded conductors only. For compact stranded conductors, Table C.8(A) should be used.

2. Two-hour fire-rated RHH cable has ceramifiable insulation which has much larger diameters than other RHH wires. Consult manufacturer's conduit fill tables.

*Types RHH, RHW, and RHW-2 without outer covering.

Table C.8(A) Maximum Number of Compact Conductors in Rigid Metal Conduit (RMC)
(*Based on Table 1, Chapter 9*)

		COMPACT CONDUCTORS											
	Conductor Size	Metric Designator (Trade Size)											
Type	(AWG/ kcmil)	16 (½)	21 (¾)	27 (1)	35 (1¼)	41 (1½)	53 (2)	63 (2½)	78 (3)	91 (3½)	103 (4)	129 (5)	155 (6)
THW,	8	2	4	7	12	16	26	38	59	78	101	158	228
THW-2,	6	1	3	5	9	12	20	29	45	60	78	122	176
THHW	4	1	2	4	7	9	15	22	34	45	58	91	132
	2	1	1	3	5	7	11	16	25	33	43	67	97
	1	1	1	1	3	5	8	11	17	23	30	47	68
	1/0	1	1	1	3	4	7	10	15	20	26	41	59
	2/0	0	1	1	2	3	6	8	13	17	22	34	50
	3/0	0	1	1	1	3	5	7	11	14	19	29	42
	4/0	0	1	1	1	2	4	6	9	12	15	24	35
	250	0	0	1	1	1	3	4	7	9	12	19	28
	300	0	0	1	1	1	3	4	6	8	11	17	24
	350	0	0	1	1	1	2	3	5	7	9	15	22
	400	0	0	1	1	1	1	3	5	7	8	13	20
	500	0	0	0	1	1	1	3	4	5	7	11	17
	600	0	0	0	1	1	1	1	3	4	6	9	13
	700	0	0	0	1	1	1	1	3	4	5	8	12
	750	0	0	0	0	1	1	1	3	4	5	7	11
	900	0	0	0	0	1	1	1	2	3	4	6	9
	1000	0	0	0	0	1	1	1	1	3	4	6	9
THHN,	8	—	—	—	—	—	—	—	—	—	—	—	—
THWN,	6	2	5	8	13	18	30	43	66	88	114	179	258
THWN-2	4	1	3	5	8	11	18	26	41	55	70	110	159
	2	1	1	3	6	8	13	19	29	39	50	79	114
	1	1	1	2	4	6	10	14	22	29	38	60	86
	1/0	1	1	1	4	5	8	12	19	25	32	51	73
	2/0	1	1	1	3	4	7	10	15	21	26	42	60
	3/0	0	1	1	2	3	6	8	13	17	22	35	51
	4/0	0	1	1	1	3	5	7	10	14	18	29	42
	250	0	1	1	1	2	4	5	8	11	14	23	33
	300	0	0	1	1	1	3	4	7	10	12	20	28
	350	0	0	1	1	1	3	4	6	8	11	17	25
	400	0	0	1	1	1	2	3	5	7	10	15	22
	500	0	0	0	1	1	1	3	5	6	8	13	19
	600	0	0	0	1	1	1	2	4	5	6	10	15
	700	0	0	0	1	1	1	1	3	4	6	9	13
	750	0	0	0	1	1	1	1	3	4	5	9	13
	900	0	0	0	0	1	1	1	2	3	4	6	9
	1000	0	0	0	0	1	1	1	2	3	4	6	9
XHHW,	8	3	5	9	15	21	34	49	76	101	130	205	296
XHHW-2	6	2	4	6	11	15	25	36	56	75	97	152	220
	4	1	3	5	8	11	18	26	41	55	70	110	159
	2	1	1	3	6	8	13	19	29	39	50	79	114
	1	1	1	2	4	6	10	14	22	29	38	60	86
	1/0	1	1	1	4	5	8	12	19	25	32	51	73
	2/0	1	1	1	3	4	7	10	16	21	27	43	62
	3/0	0	1	1	2	3	6	8	13	17	22	35	51
	4/0	0	1	1	1	3	5	7	11	14	19	29	42
	250	0	1	1	1	2	4	5	8	11	15	23	34
	300	0	0	1	1	1	3	5	7	10	13	20	29
	350	0	0	1	1	1	3	4	6	9	11	18	25
	400	0	0	1	1	1	2	4	6	8	10	16	23
	500	0	0	0	1	1	1	3	5	6	8	13	19
	600	0	0	0	1	1	1	2	4	5	7	10	15
	700	0	0	0	1	1	1	1	3	4	6	9	13
	750	0	0	0	1	1	1	1	3	4	5	8	12
	900	0	0	0	0	1	1	2	2	3	5	7	10
	1000	0	0	0	0	1	1	1	2	3	4	7	10

Definition: *Compact stranding* is the result of a manufacturing process where the standard conductor is compressed to the extent that the interstices (voids between strand wires) are virtually eliminated.

Table C.9 Maximum Number of Conductors or Fixture Wires in Rigid PVC Conduit, Schedule 80 (*Based on Table 1, Chapter 9*)

		CONDUCTORS											
	Conductor Size	Metric Designator (Trade Size)											
Type	(AWG/ kcmil)	16 (½)	21 (¾)	27 (1)	35 (1¼)	41 (1½)	53 (2)	63 (2½)	78 (3)	91 (3½)	103 (4)	129 (5)	155 (6)
RHH, RHW, RHW-2	14	3	5	9	17	23	39	56	88	118	153	243	349
	12	2	4	7	14	19	32	46	73	98	127	202	290
	10	1	3	6	11	15	26	37	59	79	103	163	234
	8	1	1	3	6	8	13	19	31	41	54	85	122
	6	1	1	2	4	6	11	16	24	33	43	68	98
	4	1	1	1	3	5	8	12	19	26	33	53	77
	3	0	1	1	3	4	7	11	17	23	29	47	67
	2	0	1	1	3	4	6	9	14	20	25	41	58
	1	0	1	1	1	2	4	6	9	13	17	27	38
	1/0	0	0	1	1	1	3	5	8	11	15	23	33
	2/0	0	0	1	1	1	3	4	7	10	13	20	29
	3/0	0	0	1	1	1	3	4	6	8	11	17	25
	4/0	0	0	0	1	1	2	3	5	7	9	15	21
	250	0	0	0	1	1	1	2	4	5	7	11	16
	300	0	0	0	1	1	1	2	3	5	6	10	14
	350	0	0	0	1	1	1	1	3	4	5	9	13
	400	0	0	0	0	1	1	1	3	4	5	8	12
	500	0	0	0	0	1	1	1	2	3	4	7	10
	600	0	0	0	0	0	1	1	1	3	3	6	8
	700	0	0	0	0	0	1	1	1	2	3	5	7
	750	0	0	0	0	0	1	1	1	2	3	5	7
	800	0	0	0	0	0	1	1	1	2	3	4	7
	1000	0	0	0	0	0	1	1	1	1	2	4	5
	1250	0	0	0	0	0	0	1	1	1	1	3	4
	1500	0	0	0	0	0	0	1	1	1	1	2	4
	1750	0	0	0	0	0	0	0	1	1	1	2	3
	2000	0	0	0	0	0	0	0	1	1	1	1	3
TW	14	6	11	20	35	49	82	118	185	250	324	514	736
	12	5	9	15	27	38	63	91	142	192	248	394	565
	10	3	6	11	20	28	47	67	106	143	185	294	421
	8	1	3	6	11	15	26	37	59	79	103	163	234
RHH*, RHW*, RHW-2*, THHW, THW, THW-2	14	4	8	13	23	32	55	79	123	166	215	341	490
RHH*, RHW*, RHW-2*, THHW, THW	12	3	6	10	19	26	44	63	99	133	173	274	394
	10	2	5	8	15	20	34	49	77	104	135	214	307
RHH*, RHW*, RHW-2*, THHW, THW, THW-2	8	1	3	5	9	12	20	29	46	62	81	128	184

Table C.9 *Continued*

		CONDUCTORS											
	Conductor Size (AWG/ kcmil)	Metric Designator (Trade Size)											
Type		16 (½)	21 (¾)	27 (1)	35 (1¼)	41 (1½)	53 (2)	63 (2½)	78 (3)	91 (3½)	103 (4)	129 (5)	155 (6)
RHH*,	6	1	1	3	7	9	16	22	35	48	62	98	141
RHW*,	4	1	1	3	5	7	12	17	26	35	46	73	105
RHW-2*,	3	1	1	2	4	6	10	14	22	30	39	63	90
TW,	2	1	1	1	3	5	8	12	19	26	33	53	77
THW,	1	0	1	1	2	3	6	8	13	18	23	37	54
THHW,	1/0	0	1	1	1	3	5	7	11	15	20	32	46
THW-2	2/0	0	1	1	1	2	4	6	10	13	17	27	39
	3/0	0	0	1	1	1	3	5	8	11	14	23	33
	4/0	0	0	1	1	1	3	4	7	9	12	19	27
	250	0	0	0	1	1	2	3	5	7	9	15	22
	300	0	0	0	1	1	1	3	5	6	8	13	19
	350	0	0	0	1	1	1	2	4	6	7	12	17
	400	0	0	0	1	1	1	2	4	5	7	10	15
	500	0	0	0	1	1	1	1	3	4	5	9	13
	600	0	0	0	0	1	1	1	2	3	4	7	10
	700	0	0	0	0	1	1	1	2	3	4	6	9
	750	0	0	0	0	0	1	1	1	3	4	6	8
	800	0	0	0	0	0	1	1	1	3	3	6	8
	900	0	0	0	0	0	1	1	1	2	3	5	7
	1000	0	0	0	0	0	1	1	1	2	3	5	7
	1250	0	0	0	0	0	1	1	1	1	2	4	5
	1500	0	0	0	0	0	0	1	1	1	1	3	4
	1750	0	0	0	0	0	0	1	1	1	1	3	4
	2000	0	0	0	0	0	0	0	1	1	1	2	3
THHN,	14	9	17	28	51	70	118	170	265	358	464	736	1055
THWN,	12	6	12	20	37	51	86	124	193	261	338	537	770
THWN-2	10	4	7	13	23	32	54	78	122	164	213	338	485
	8	2	4	7	13	18	31	45	70	95	123	195	279
	6	1	3	5	9	13	22	32	51	68	89	141	202
	4	1	1	3	6	8	14	20	31	42	54	86	124
	3	1	1	3	5	7	12	17	26	35	46	73	105
	2	1	1	2	4	6	10	14	22	30	39	61	88
	1	0	1	1	3	4	7	10	16	22	29	45	65
	1/0	0	1	1	2	3	6	9	14	18	24	38	55
	2/0	0	1	1	1	3	5	7	11	15	20	32	46
	3/0	0	1	1	1	2	4	6	9	13	17	26	38
	4/0	0	0	1	1	1	3	5	8	10	14	22	31
	250	0	0	1	1	1	3	4	6	8	11	18	25
	300	0	0	0	1	1	2	3	5	7	9	15	22
	350	0	0	0	1	1	1	3	5	6	8	13	19
	400	0	0	0	1	1	1	3	4	6	7	12	17
	500	0	0	0	1	1	1	2	3	5	6	10	14
	600	0	0	0	0	1	1	1	3	4	5	8	12
	700	0	0	0	0	1	1	1	2	3	4	7	10
	750	0	0	0	0	1	1	1	2	3	4	7	9
	800	0	0	0	0	1	1	1	2	3	4	6	9
	900	0	0	0	0	0	1	1	1	3	3	6	8
	1000	0	0	0	0	0	1	1	1	2	3	5	7
FEP,	14	8	16	27	49	68	115	164	257	347	450	714	1024
FEPB,	12	6	12	20	36	50	84	120	188	253	328	521	747
PFA,	10	4	8	14	26	36	60	86	135	182	235	374	536
PFAH,	8	2	5	8	15	20	34	49	77	104	135	214	307
TFE	6	1	3	6	10	14	24	35	55	74	96	152	218
	4	1	2	4	7	10	17	24	38	52	67	106	153
	3	1	1	3	6	8	14	20	32	43	56	89	127
	2	1	1	3	5	7	12	17	26	35	46	73	105

(Continues)

Table C.9 *Continued*

	Conductor Size (AWG/ kcmil)	CONDUCTORS											
		Metric Designator (Trade Size)											
Type		16 (½)	21 (¾)	27 (1)	35 (1¼)	41 (1½)	53 (2)	63 (2½)	78 (3)	91 (3½)	103 (4)	129 (5)	155 (6)
PFA, PFAH, TFE	1	1	1	1	3	5	8	11	18	25	32	51	73
PFA, PFAH, TFE, Z	1/0	0	1	1	3	4	7	10	15	20	27	42	61
	2/0	0	1	1	2	3	5	8	12	17	22	35	50
	3/0	0	1	1	1	2	4	6	10	14	18	29	41
	4/0	0	0	1	1	1	4	5	8	11	15	24	34
Z	14	10	19	33	59	82	138	198	310	418	542	860	1233
	12	7	14	23	42	58	98	141	220	297	385	610	875
	10	4	8	14	26	36	60	86	135	182	235	374	536
	8	3	5	9	16	22	38	54	85	115	149	236	339
	6	2	4	6	11	16	26	38	60	81	104	166	238
	4	1	2	4	8	11	18	26	41	55	72	114	164
	3	1	2	3	5	8	13	19	30	40	52	83	119
	2	1	1	2	5	6	11	16	25	33	43	69	99
	1	0	1	2	4	5	9	13	20	27	35	56	80
XHH, XHHW, XHHW-2, ZW	14	6	11	20	35	49	82	118	185	250	324	514	736
	12	5	9	15	27	38	63	91	142	192	248	394	565
	10	3	6	11	20	28	47	67	106	143	185	294	421
	8	1	3	6	11	15	26	37	59	79	103	163	234
	6	1	2	4	8	11	19	28	43	59	76	121	173
	4	1	1	3	6	8	14	20	31	42	55	87	125
	3	1	1	3	5	7	12	17	26	36	47	74	106
	2	1	1	2	4	6	10	14	22	30	39	62	89
XHH, XHHW, XHHW-2	1	0	1	1	3	4	7	10	16	22	29	46	66
	1/0	0	1	1	2	3	6	9	14	19	24	39	56
	2/0	0	1	1	1	3	5	7	11	16	20	32	46
	3/0	0	1	1	1	2	4	6	9	13	17	27	38
	4/0	0	0	1	1	1	3	5	8	11	14	22	32
	250	0	0	1	1	1	3	4	6	9	11	18	26
	300	0	0	1	1	1	2	3	5	7	10	15	22
	350	0	0	0	1	1	1	3	5	6	8	14	20
	400	0	0	0	1	1	1	3	4	6	7	12	17
	500	0	0	0	1	1	1	2	3	5	6	10	14
	600	0	0	0	0	1	1	1	3	4	5	8	11
	700	0	0	0	0	1	1	1	2	3	4	7	10
	750	0	0	0	0	1	1	1	2	3	4	6	9
	800	0	0	0	0	1	1	1	1	3	4	6	9
	900	0	0	0	0	0	1	1	—	3	3	5	8
	1000	0	0	0	0	0	1	1	1	2	3	5	7
	1250	0	0	0	0	0	1	1	1	1	2	4	6
	1500	0	0	0	0	0	0	1	1	1	1	3	5
	1750	0	0	0	0	0	0	1	1	1	1	3	4
	2000	0	0	0	0	0	0	1	1	1	1	2	4

Table C.9 *Continued*

FIXTURE WIRES

Type	Conductor Size (AWG/ kcmil)	Metric Designator (Trade Size)					
		16 (½)	21 (¾)	27 (1)	35 (1¼)	41 (1½)	53 (2)
FFH-2, RFH-2, RFHH-3	18	6	11	19	34	47	79
	16	5	9	16	28	39	67
SF-2, SFF-2	18	7	14	24	43	59	100
	16	6	11	20	35	49	82
	14	5	9	16	28	39	67
SF-1, SFF-1	18	13	25	42	76	105	177
RFH-1, RFHH-2, TF, TFF, XF, XFF	18	10	18	31	56	77	130
RFHH-2, TF, TFF, XF, XFF	16	8	15	25	45	62	105
XF, XFF	14	6	11	20	35	49	82
TFN, TFFN	18	16	29	50	90	124	209
	16	12	22	38	68	95	159
PF, PFF, PGF, PGFF, PAF, PTF, PTFF, PAFF	18	15	28	47	85	118	198
	16	11	22	36	66	91	153
	14	8	16	27	49	68	115
HF, HFF, ZF, ZFF, ZHF	18	19	36	61	110	152	255
	16	14	27	45	81	112	188
	14	10	19	33	59	82	138
KF-2, KFF-2	18	28	53	88	159	220	371
	16	19	37	62	112	155	261
	14	13	25	43	77	107	179
	12	9	17	29	53	73	123
	10	6	11	20	35	49	82
KF-1, KFF-1	18	33	63	106	190	263	442
	16	23	44	74	133	185	310
	14	16	29	50	90	124	209
	12	10	19	33	59	82	138
	10	7	13	21	39	54	90
XF, XFF	12	3	6	10	19	26	44
	10	2	5	8	15	20	34

Notes:

1. This table is for concentric stranded conductors only. For compact stranded conductors, Table C.9(A) should be used.

2. Two-hour fire-rated RHH cable has ceramifiable insulation which has much larger diameters than other RHH wires.

Consult manufacturer's conduit fill tables.

*Types RHH, RHW, and RHW-2 without outer covering.

Table C.9(A) Maximum Number of Compact Conductors in Rigid PVC Conduit, Schedule 80
(*Based on Table 1, Chapter 9*)

		COMPACT CONDUCTORS											
	Conductor Size	Metric Designator (Trade Size)											
Type	(AWG/ kcmil)	16 (½)	21 (¾)	27 (1)	35 (1¼)	41 (1½)	53 (2)	63 (2½)	78 (3)	91 (3½)	103 (4)	129 (5)	155 (6)
THW,	8	1	3	5	9	13	22	32	50	68	88	140	200
THW-2,	6	1	2	4	7	10	17	25	39	52	68	108	155
THHW	4	1	1	3	5	7	13	18	29	39	51	81	116
	2	1	1	1	4	5	9	13	21	29	37	60	85
	1	0	1	1	3	4	6	9	15	20	26	42	60
	1/0	0	1	1	2	3	6	8	13	17	23	36	52
	2/0	0	1	1	1	3	5	7	11	15	19	30	44
	3/0	0	0	1	1	2	4	6	9	12	16	26	37
	4/0	0	0	1	1	1	3	5	8	10	13	22	31
	250	0	0	1	1	1	2	4	6	8	11	17	25
	300	0	0	0	1	1	2	3	5	7	9	15	21
	350	0	0	0	1	1	1	3	5	6	8	13	19
	400	0	0	0	1	1	1	3	4	6	7	12	17
	500	0	0	0	1	1	1	2	3	5	6	10	14
	600	0	0	0	0	1	1	1	3	4	5	8	12
	700	0	0	0	0	1	1	1	2	3	4	7	10
	750	0	0	0	0	1	1	1	2	3	4	7	10
	900	0	0	0	0	0	1	1	2	3	4	6	8
	1000	0	0	0	0	0	1	1	1	2	3	5	8
THHN,	8	—	—	—	—	—	—	—	—	—	—	—	—
THWN,	6	1	3	6	11	15	25	36	57	77	99	158	226
THWN-2	4	1	1	3	6	9	15	22	35	47	61	98	140
	2	1	1	2	5	6	11	16	25	34	44	70	100
	1	1	1	1	3	5	8	12	19	25	33	53	75
	1/0	0	1	1	3	4	7	10	16	22	28	45	64
	2/0	0	1	1	2	3	6	8	13	18	23	37	53
	3/0	0	1	1	1	3	5	7	11	15	19	31	44
	4/0	0	0	1	1	2	4	6	9	12	16	25	37
	250	0	0	1	1	1	3	4	7	10	12	20	29
	300	0	0	1	1	1	3	4	6	8	11	17	25
	350	0	0	0	1	1	2	3	5	7	9	15	22
	400	0	0	0	1	1	1	3	5	6	8	13	19
	500	0	0	0	1	1	1	2	4	5	7	11	16
	600	0	0	0	1	1	1	1	3	4	6	9	13
	700	0	0	0	0	1	1	1	3	4	5	8	12
	750	0	0	0	0	1	1	1	3	4	5	8	11
	900	0	0	0	0	0	1	1	2	3	4	6	8
	1000	0	0	0	0	0	1	1	1	3	3	5	8
XHHW,	8	1	4	7	12	17	29	42	65	88	114	181	260
XHHW-2	6	1	3	5	9	13	21	31	48	65	85	134	193
	4	1	1	3	6	9	15	22	35	47	61	98	140
	2	1	1	2	5	6	11	16	25	34	44	70	100
	1	1	1	1	3	5	8	12	19	25	33	53	75
	1/0	0	1	1	3	4	7	10	16	22	28	45	64
	2/0	0	1	1	2	3	6	8	13	18	24	38	54
	3/0	0	1	1	1	3	5	7	11	15	19	31	44
	4/0	0	0	1	1	2	4	6	9	12	16	26	37
	250	0	0	1	1	1	3	5	7	10	13	21	30
	300	0	0	1	1	1	3	4	6	8	11	17	25
	350	0	0	1	1	1	2	3	5	7	10	15	22
	400	0	0	0	1	1	1	3	5	7	9	14	20
	500	0	0	0	1	1	1	2	4	5	7	11	17
	600	0	0	0	1	1	1	1	3	4	6	9	13
	700	0	0	0	0	1	1	1	3	4	5	8	12
	750	0	0	0	0	1	1	1	2	3	5	7	11
	900	0	0	0	0	1	1	1	2	3	4	6	8
	1000	0	0	0	0	0	1	1	1	3	3	6	8

Definition: *Compact stranding* is the result of a manufacturing process where the standard conductor is compressed to the extent that the interstices (voids between strand wires) are virtually eliminated.

Table C.10 Maximum Number of Conductors or Fixture Wires in Rigid PVC Conduit, Schedule 40 and HDPE Conduit (*Based on Table 1, Chapter 9*)

		CONDUCTORS											
	Conductor Size (AWG/ kcmil)	Metric Designator (Trade Size)											
Type		16 (½)	21 (¾)	27 (1)	35 (1¼)	41 (1½)	53 (2)	63 (2½)	78 (3)	91 (3½)	103 (4)	129 (5)	155 (6)
RHH, RHW, RHW-2	14	4	7	11	20	27	45	64	99	133	171	269	390
	12	3	5	9	16	22	37	53	82	110	142	224	323
	10	2	4	7	13	18	30	43	66	89	115	181	261
	8	1	2	4	7	9	15	22	35	46	60	94	137
	6	1	1	3	5	7	12	18	28	37	48	76	109
	4	1	1	2	4	6	10	14	22	29	37	59	85
	3	1	1	1	4	5	8	12	19	25	33	52	75
	2	1	1	1	3	4	7	10	16	22	28	45	65
	1	0	1	1	1	3	5	7	11	14	19	29	43
	1/0	0	1	1	1	2	4	6	9	13	16	26	37
	2/0	0	0	1	1	1	3	5	8	11	14	22	32
	3/0	0	0	1	1	1	3	4	7	9	12	19	28
	4/0	0	0	1	1	1	2	4	6	8	10	16	24
	250	0	0	0	1	1	1	3	4	6	8	12	18
	300	0	0	0	1	1	1	2	4	5	7	11	16
	350	0	0	0	1	1	1	2	3	5	6	10	14
	400	0	0	0	1	1	1	1	3	4	6	9	13
	500	0	0	0	0	1	1	1	3	4	5	8	11
	600	0	0	0	0	1	1	1	2	3	4	6	9
	700	0	0	0	0	0	1	1	1	3	3	6	8
	750	0	0	0	0	0	1	1	1	2	3	5	8
	800	0	0	0	0	0	1	1	1	2	3	5	7
	900	0	0	0	0	0	1	1	1	2	3	5	7
	1000	0	0	0	0	0	1	1	1	1	3	4	6
	1250	0	0	0	0	0	0	1	1	1	1	3	5
	1500	0	0	0	0	0	0	1	1	1	1	3	4
	1750	0	0	0	0	0	0	1	1	1	1	2	3
	2000	0	0	0	0	0	0	0	1	1	1	2	3
TW	14	8	14	24	42	57	94	135	209	280	361	568	822
	12	6	11	18	32	44	72	103	160	215	277	436	631
	10	4	8	13	24	32	54	77	119	160	206	325	470
	8	2	4	7	13	18	30	43	66	89	115	181	261
RHH*, RHW*, RHW-2*, THHW, THW, THW-2	14	5	9	16	28	38	63	90	139	186	240	378	546
RHH*, RHW*, RHW-2*, THHW, THW	12	4	8	12	22	30	50	72	112	150	193	304	439
	10	3	6	10	17	24	39	56	87	117	150	237	343
RHH*, RHW*, RHW-2*, THHW, THW, THW-2	8	1	3	6	10	14	23	33	52	70	90	142	205

(Continues)

Table C.10 *Continued*

	CONDUCTORS											
Type	Conductor Size (AWG/ kcmil)	Metric Designator (Trade Size)										
		16 (½)	21 (¾)	27 (1)	35 (1¼)	41 (1½)	53 (2)	63 (2½)	78 (3)	91 (3½)	103 (4)	129 (5)	155 (6)
RHH*, RHW*, RHW-2*, TW, THW, THHW, THW-2	6	1	2	4	8	11	18	26	40	53	69	109	157
	4	1	1	3	6	8	13	19	30	40	51	81	117
	3	1	1	3	5	7	11	16	25	34	44	69	100
	2	1	1	2	4	6	10	14	22	29	37	59	85
	1	0	1	1	3	4	7	10	15	20	26	41	60
	1/0	0	1	1	2	3	6	8	13	17	22	35	51
	2/0	0	1	1	1	3	5	7	11	15	19	30	43
	3/0	0	1	1	1	2	4	6	9	12	16	25	36
	4/0	0	0	1	1	1	3	5	8	10	13	21	30
	250	0	0	1	1	1	3	4	6	8	11	17	25
	300	0	0	1	1	1	2	3	5	7	9	15	21
	350	0	0	0	1	1	1	3	5	6	8	13	19
	400	0	0	0	1	1	1	3	4	6	7	12	17
	500	0	0	0	1	1	1	2	3	5	6	10	14
	600	0	0	0	0	1	1	1	3	4	5	8	11
	700	0	0	0	0	1	1	1	2	3	4	7	10
	750	0	0	0	0	1	1	1	2	3	4	6	10
	800	0	0	0	0	1	1	1	2	3	4	6	9
	900	0	0	0	0	0	1	1	1	3	3	6	8
	1000	0	0	0	0	0	1	1	1	2	3	5	7
	1250	0	0	0	0	0	1	1	1	1	2	4	6
	1500	0	0	0	0	0	1	1	1	1	1	3	5
	1750	0	0	0	0	0	0	1	1	1	1	3	4
	2000	0	0	0	0	0	0	1	1	1	1	3	4
THHN, THWN, THWN-2	14	11	21	34	60	82	135	193	299	401	517	815	1178
	12	8	15	25	43	59	99	141	218	293	377	594	859
	10	5	9	15	27	37	62	89	137	184	238	374	541
	8	3	5	9	16	21	36	51	79	106	137	216	312
	6	1	4	6	11	15	26	37	57	77	99	156	225
	4	1	2	4	7	9	16	22	35	47	61	96	138
	3	1	1	3	6	8	13	19	30	40	51	81	117
	2	1	1	3	5	7	11	16	25	33	43	68	98
	1	1	1	1	3	5	8	12	18	25	32	50	73
	1/0	1	1	1	3	4	7	10	15	21	27	42	61
	2/0	0	1	1	2	3	6	8	13	17	22	35	51
	3/0	0	1	1	1	3	5	7	11	14	18	29	42
	4/0	0	1	1	1	2	4	6	9	12	15	24	35
	250	0	0	1	1	1	3	4	7	10	12	20	28
	300	0	0	1	1	1	3	4	6	8	11	17	24
	350	0	0	1	1	1	2	3	5	7	9	15	21
	400	0	0	0	1	1	1	3	5	6	8	13	19
	500	0	0	0	1	1	1	2	4	5	7	11	16
	600	0	0	0	1	1	1	1	3	4	5	9	13
	700	0	0	0	0	1	1	1	3	4	5	8	11
	750	0	0	0	0	1	1	1	2	3	4	7	11
	800	0	0	0	0	1	1	1	2	3	4	7	10
	900	0	0	0	0	1	1	1	2	3	4	6	9
	1000	0	0	0	0	0	1	1	1	3	3	6	8
FEP, FEPB, PFA, PFAH, TFE	14	11	20	33	58	79	131	188	290	389	502	790	1142
	12	8	15	24	42	58	96	137	212	284	366	577	834
	10	6	10	17	30	41	69	98	152	204	263	414	598
	8	3	6	10	17	24	39	56	87	117	150	237	343
	6	2	4	7	12	17	28	40	62	83	107	169	244
	4	1	3	5	8	12	19	28	43	58	75	118	170
	3	1	2	4	7	10	16	23	36	48	62	98	142
	2	1	1	3	6	8	13	19	30	40	51	81	117

Table C.10 *Continued*

		CONDUCTORS											
	Conductor Size	Metric Designator (Trade Size)											
Type	(AWG/ kcmil)	16 (½)	21 (¾)	27 (1)	35 (1¼)	41 (1½)	53 (2)	63 (2½)	78 (3)	91 (3½)	103 (4)	129 (5)	155 (6)
PFA, PFAH, TFE	1	1	1	2	4	5	9	13	20	28	36	56	81
PFA, PFAH, TFE, Z	1/0	1	1	1	3	4	8	11	17	23	30	47	68
	2/0	0	1	1	3	4	6	9	14	19	24	39	56
	3/0	0	1	1	2	3	5	7	12	16	20	32	46
	4/0	0	1	1	1	2	4	6	9	13	16	26	38
Z	14	13	24	40	70	95	158	226	350	469	605	952	1376
	12	9	17	28	49	68	112	160	248	333	429	675	976
	10	6	10	17	30	41	69	98	152	204	263	414	598
	8	3	6	11	19	26	43	62	96	129	166	261	378
	6	2	4	7	13	18	30	43	67	90	116	184	265
	4	1	3	5	9	12	21	30	46	62	80	126	183
	3	1	2	4	6	9	15	22	34	45	58	92	133
	2	1	1	3	5	7	12	18	28	38	49	77	111
	1	1	1	2	4	6	10	14	23	30	39	62	90
XHH, XHHW, XHHW-2, ZW	14	8	14	24	42	57	94	135	209	280	361	568	822
	12	6	11	18	32	44	72	103	160	215	277	436	631
	10	4	8	13	24	32	54	77	119	160	206	325	470
	8	2	4	7	13	18	30	43	66	89	115	181	261
	6	1	3	5	10	13	22	32	49	66	85	134	193
	4	1	2	4	7	9	16	23	35	48	61	97	140
	3	1	1	3	6	8	13	19	30	40	52	82	118
	2	1	1	3	5	7	11	16	25	34	44	69	99
XHH, XHHW, XHHW-2	1	1	1	1	3	5	8	12	19	25	32	51	74
	1/0	1	1	1	3	4	7	10	16	21	27	43	62
	2/0	0	1	1	2	3	6	8	13	17	23	36	52
	3/0	0	1	1	1	3	5	7	11	14	19	30	43
	4/0	0	1	1	1	2	4	6	9	12	15	24	35
	250	0	0	1	1	1	3	5	7	10	13	20	29
	300	0	0	1	1	1	3	4	6	8	11	17	25
	350	0	0	1	1	1	2	3	5	7	9	15	22
	400	0	0	0	1	1	1	3	5	6	8	13	19
	500	0	0	0	1	1	1	2	4	5	7	11	16
	600	0	0	0	1	1	1	1	3	4	5	9	13
	700	0	0	0	0	1	1	1	3	4	5	8	11
	750	0	0	0	0	1	1	1	2	3	4	7	11
	800	0	0	0	0	1	1	1	2	3	4	7	10
	900	0	0	0	0	1	1	1	2	3	4	6	9
	1000	0	0	0	0	0	1	1	1	3	3	6	8
	1250	0	0	0	0	0	1	1	1	1	3	4	6
	1500	0	0	0	0	0	1	1	1	1	2	4	5
	1750	0	0	0	0	0	0	1	1	1	1	3	5
	2000	0	0	0	0	0	0	1	1	1	1	3	4

(Continues)

Table C.10 *Continued*

	Conductor Size (AWG/ kcmil)	Metric Designator (Trade Size)					
Type		16 (½)	21 (¾)	27 (1)	35 (1¼)	41 (1½)	53 (2)
FFH-2, RFH-2, RFHH-3	18	8	14	23	40	54	90
	16	6	12	19	33	46	76
SF-2, SFF-2	18	10	17	29	50	69	114
	16	8	14	24	42	57	94
	14	6	12	19	33	46	76
SF-1, SFF-1	18	17	31	51	89	122	202
RFHH-2, TF, TFF, XF, XFF RFH-1,	18	13	23	38	66	90	149
RFHH-2, TF, TFF, XF, XFF	16	10	18	30	53	73	120
XF, XFF	14	8	14	24	42	57	94
TFN, TFFN	18	20	37	60	105	144	239
	16	16	28	46	80	110	183
PF, PFF, PGF, PGFF, PAF, PTF, PTFF, PAFF	18	19	35	57	100	137	227
	16	15	27	44	77	106	175
	14	11	20	33	58	79	131
HF, HFF, ZF, ZFF, ZHF	18	25	45	74	129	176	292
	16	18	33	54	95	130	216
	14	13	24	40	70	95	158
KF-2, KFF-2	18	36	65	107	187	256	424
	16	26	46	75	132	180	299
	14	17	31	52	90	124	205
	12	12	22	35	62	85	141
	10	8	14	24	42	57	94
KF-1, KFF-1	18	43	78	128	223	305	506
	16	30	55	90	157	214	355
	14	20	37	60	105	144	239
	12	13	24	40	70	95	158
	10	9	16	26	45	62	103
XF, XFF	12	4	8	12	22	30	50
	10	3	6	10	17	24	39

Notes:

1. This table is for concentric stranded conductors only. For compact stranded conductors, Table C.10(A) should be used.

2. Two-hour fire-rated RHH cable has ceramifiable insulation which has much larger diameters than other RHH wires.
Consult manufacturer's conduit fill tables.

*Types RHH, RHW, and RHW-2 without outer covering.

Table C.10(A) Maximum Number of Compact Conductors in Rigid PVC Conduit, Schedule 40 and HDPE Conduit (*Based on Table 1, Chapter 9*)

		COMPACT CONDUCTORS											
	Conductor Size	Metric Designator (Trade Size)											
Type	(AWG/ kcmil)	16 (½)	21 (¾)	27 (1)	35 (1¼)	41 (1½)	53 (2)	63 (2½)	78 (3)	91 (3½)	103 (4)	129 (5)	155 (6)
THW,	8	1	4	6	11	15	26	37	57	76	98	155	224
THW-2,	6	1	3	5	9	12	20	28	44	59	76	119	173
THHW	4	1	1	3	6	9	15	21	33	44	57	89	129
	2	1	1	2	5	6	11	15	24	32	42	66	95
	1	1	1	1	3	4	7	11	17	23	29	46	67
	1/0	0	1	1	3	4	6	9	15	20	25	40	58
	2/0	0	1	1	2	3	5	8	12	16	21	34	49
	3/0	0	1	1	1	3	5	7	10	14	18	29	42
	4/0	0	1	1	1	2	4	5	9	12	15	24	35
	250	0	0	1	1	1	3	4	7	9	12	19	27
	300	0	0	1	1	1	2	4	6	8	10	16	24
	350	0	0	1	1	1	2	3	5	7	9	15	21
	400	0	0	0	1	1	1	3	5	6	8	13	19
	500	0	0	0	1	1	1	2	4	5	7	11	16
	600	0	0	0	1	1	1	1	3	4	5	9	13
	700	0	0	0	0	1	1	1	3	4	5	8	12
	750	0	0	0	0	1	1	1	2	3	5	7	11
	900	0	0	0	0	1	1	1	2	3	4	6	9
	1000	0	0	0	0	1	1	1	1	3	4	6	9
THHN,	8	—	—	—	—	—	—	—	—	—	—	—	—
THWN,	6	2	4	7	13	17	29	41	64	86	111	175	253
THWN-2	4	1	2	4	8	11	18	25	40	53	68	108	156
	2	1	1	3	5	8	13	18	28	38	49	77	112
	1	1	1	2	4	6	9	14	21	29	37	58	84
	1/0	1	1	1	3	5	8	12	18	24	31	49	72
	2/0	0	1	1	3	4	7	9	15	20	26	41	59
	3/0	0	1	1	2	3	5	8	12	17	22	34	50
	4/0	0	1	1	1	3	4	6	10	14	18	28	41
	250	0	0	1	1	1	3	5	8	11	14	22	32
	300	0	0	1	1	1	3	4	7	9	12	19	28
	350	0	0	1	1	1	3	4	6	8	10	17	24
	400	0	0	1	1	1	2	3	5	7	9	15	22
	500	0	0	0	1	1	1	3	4	6	8	13	18
	600	0	0	0	1	1	1	2	4	5	6	10	15
	700	0	0	0	1	1	1	1	3	4	5	9	13
	750	0	0	0	1	1	1	1	3	4	5	8	12
	900	0	0	0	0	1	1	1	2	3	4	6	9
	1000	0	0	0	0	1	1	1	2	3	4	6	9
XHHW,	8	3	5	8	14	20	33	47	73	99	127	200	290
XHHW-2	6	1	4	6	11	15	25	35	55	73	94	149	215
	4	1	2	4	8	11	18	25	40	53	68	108	156
	2	1	1	3	5	8	13	18	28	38	49	77	112
	1	1	1	2	4	6	9	14	21	29	37	58	84
	1/0	1	1	1	3	5	8	12	18	24	31	49	72
	2/0	1	1	1	3	4	7	10	15	20	26	42	60
	3/0	0	1	1	2	3	5	8	12	17	22	34	50
	4/0	0	1	1	1	3	5	7	10	14	18	29	42
	250	0	0	1	1	1	4	5	8	11	14	23	33
	300	0	0	1	1	1	3	4	7	9	12	19	28
	350	0	0	1	1	1	3	4	6	8	11	17	25
	400	0	0	1	1	1	2	3	5	7	10	15	22
	500	0	0	0	1	1	1	3	4	6	8	13	18
	600	0	0	0	1	1	1	2	4	5	6	10	15
	700	0	0	0	1	1	1	1	3	4	5	9	13
	750	0	0	0	1	1	1	1	3	4	5	8	12
	900	0	0	0	0	1	1	1	2	3	4	6	9
	1000	0	0	0	0	1	1	1	2	3	4	6	9

Definition: *Compact stranding* is the result of a manufacturing process where the standard conductor is compressed to the extent that the interstices (voids between strand wires) are virtually eliminated.

Table C.11 Maximum Number of Conductors or Fixture Wires in Type A, Rigid PVC Conduit
(Based on Table 1, Chapter 9)

		CONDUCTORS									
	Conductor Size	Metric Designator (Trade Size)									
Type	(AWG/ kcmil)	16 (½)	21 (¾)	27 (1)	35 (1¼)	41 (1½)	53 (2)	63 (2½)	78 (3)	91 (3½)	103 (4)
RHH, RHW, RHW-2	14	5	9	15	24	31	49	74	112	146	187
	12	4	7	12	20	26	41	61	93	121	155
	10	3	6	10	16	21	33	50	75	98	125
	8	1	3	5	8	11	17	26	39	51	65
	6	1	2	4	6	9	14	21	31	41	52
	4	1	1	3	5	7	11	16	24	32	41
	3	1	1	3	4	6	9	14	21	28	36
	2	1	1	2	4	5	8	12	18	24	31
	1	0	1	1	2	3	5	8	12	16	20
	1/0	0	1	1	2	3	5	7	10	14	18
	2/0	0	1	1	1	2	4	6	9	12	15
	3/0	0	1	1	1	1	3	5	8	10	13
	4/0	0	0	1	1	1	3	4	7	9	11
	250	0	0	1	1	1	1	3	5	7	8
	300	0	0	1	1	1	1	3	4	6	7
	350	0	0	0	1	1	1	2	4	5	7
	400	0	0	0	1	1	1	2	4	5	6
	500	0	0	0	1	1	1	1	3	4	5
	600	0	0	0	0	1	1	1	2	3	4
	700	0	0	0	0	1	1	1	2	3	4
	750	0	0	0	0	1	1	1	1	3	4
	800	0	0	0	0	1	1	1	1	3	3
	900	0	0	0	0	0	1	1	1	2	3
	1000	0	0	0	0	0	1	1	1	2	3
	1250	0	0	0	0	0	1	1	1	1	2
	1500	0	0	0	0	0	0	1	1	1	1
	1750	0	0	0	0	0	0	1	1	1	1
	2000	0	0	0	0	0	0	1	1	1	1
TW	14	11	18	31	51	67	105	157	235	307	395
	12	8	14	24	39	51	80	120	181	236	303
	10	6	10	18	29	38	60	89	135	176	226
	8	3	6	10	16	21	33	50	75	98	125
RHH*, RHW*, RHW-2*, THHW, THW, THW-2	14	7	12	20	34	44	70	104	157	204	262
RHH*, RHW*, RHW-2*, THHW, THW	12	6	10	16	27	35	56	84	126	164	211
	10	4	8	13	21	28	44	65	98	128	165
RHH*, RHW*, RHW-2*, THHW, THW, THW-2	8	2	4	8	12	16	26	39	59	77	98
RHH*, RHW*, RHW-2*, TW, THHW, THW, THW-2	6	1	3	6	9	13	20	30	45	59	75

Table C.11   *Continued*

	Conductor Size (AWG/ kcmil)	\multicolumn{10}{c}{CONDUCTORS}

Type	Conductor Size (AWG/ kcmil)	\multicolumn{10}{c}{Metric Designator (Trade Size)}

Type	Conductor Size (AWG/ kcmil)	16 (½)	21 (¾)	27 (1)	35 (1¼)	41 (1½)	53 (2)	63 (2½)	78 (3)	91 (3½)	103 (4)
RHH*,	4	1	2	4	7	9	15	22	33	44	56
RHW*,	3	1	1	4	6	8	13	19	29	37	48
RHW-2*,	2	1	1	3	5	7	11	16	24	32	41
TW,	1	1	1	1	3	5	7	11	17	22	29
THW,	1/0	1	1	1	3	4	6	10	14	19	24
THHW,	2/0	0	1	1	2	3	5	8	12	16	21
THW-2	3/0	0	1	1	1	3	4	7	10	13	17
	4/0	0	1	1	1	2	4	6	9	11	14
	250	0	0	1	1	1	3	4	7	9	12
	300	0	0	1	1	1	2	4	6	8	10
	350	0	0	1	1	1	2	3	5	7	9
	400	0	0	1	1	1	1	3	5	6	8
	500	0	0	0	1	1	1	2	4	5	7
	600	0	0	0	1	1	1	1	3	4	5
	700	0	0	0	1	1	1	1	3	4	5
	750	0	0	0	1	1	1	1	3	3	4
	800	0	0	0	0	1	1	1	2	3	4
	900	0	0	0	0	1	1	1	2	3	4
	1000	0	0	0	0	1	1	1	1	3	3
	1250	0	0	0	0	0	1	1	1	1	3
	1500	0	0	0	0	0	1	1	1	1	2
	1750	0	0	0	0	0	0	1	1	1	1
	2000	0	0	0	0	0	0	1	1	1	1
THHN,	14	16	27	44	73	96	150	225	338	441	566
THWN,	12	11	19	32	53	70	109	164	246	321	412
THWN-2	10	7	12	20	33	44	69	103	155	202	260
	8	4	7	12	19	25	40	59	89	117	150
	6	3	5	8	14	18	28	43	64	84	108
	4	1	3	5	8	11	17	26	39	52	66
	3	1	2	4	7	9	15	22	33	44	56
	2	1	1	3	6	8	12	19	28	37	47
	1	1	1	2	4	6	9	14	21	27	35
	1/0	1	1	2	4	5	8	11	17	23	29
	2/0	1	1	1	3	4	6	10	14	19	24
	3/0	0	1	1	2	3	5	8	12	16	20
	4/0	0	1	1	1	3	4	6	10	13	17
	250	0	1	1	1	2	3	5	8	10	14
	300	0	0	1	1	1	3	4	7	9	12
	350	0	0	1	1	1	2	4	6	8	10
	400	0	0	1	1	1	2	3	5	7	9
	500	0	0	1	1	1	1	3	4	6	7
	600	0	0	0	1	1	1	2	3	5	6
	700	0	0	0	1	1	1	1	3	4	5
	750	0	0	0	1	1	1	1	3	4	5
	800	0	0	0	1	1	1	1	3	4	5
	900	0	0	0	0	1	1	1	2	3	4
	1000	0	0	0	0	1	1	1	2	3	4
FEP,	14	15	26	43	70	93	146	218	327	427	549
FEPB,	12	11	19	31	51	68	106	159	239	312	400
PFA,	10	8	13	22	37	48	76	114	171	224	287
PFAH,	8	4	8	13	21	28	44	65	98	128	165
TFE	6	3	5	9	15	20	31	46	70	91	117
	4	1	4	6	10	14	21	32	49	64	82
	3	1	3	5	8	11	18	27	40	53	68
	2	1	2	4	7	9	15	22	33	44	56

(Cotinues)

Table C.11 *Continued*

Type	Conductor Size (AWG/ kcmil)	Metric Designator (Trade Size)									
		16 (½)	21 (¾)	27 (1)	35 (1¼)	41 (1½)	53 (2)	63 (2½)	78 (3)	91 (3½)	103 (4)
PFA, PFAH, TFE	1	1	1	3	5	6	10	15	23	30	39
PFA, PFAH, TFE, Z	1/0	1	1	2	4	5	8	13	19	25	32
	2/0	1	1	1	3	4	7	10	16	21	27
	3/0	1	1	1	3	3	6	9	13	17	22
	4/0	0	1	1	2	3	5	7	11	14	18
Z	14	18	31	52	85	112	175	263	395	515	661
	12	13	22	37	60	79	124	186	280	365	469
	10	8	13	22	37	48	76	114	171	224	287
	8	5	8	14	23	30	48	72	108	141	181
	6	3	6	10	16	21	34	50	76	99	127
	4	2	4	7	11	15	23	35	52	68	88
	3	1	3	5	8	11	17	25	38	50	64
	2	1	2	4	7	9	14	21	32	41	53
	1	1	1	3	5	7	11	17	26	33	43
XHH, XHHW, XHHW-2, ZW	14	11	18	31	51	67	105	157	235	307	395
	12	8	14	24	39	51	80	120	181	236	303
	10	6	10	18	29	38	60	89	135	176	226
	8	3	6	10	16	21	33	50	75	98	125
	6	2	4	7	12	15	24	37	55	72	93
	4	1	3	5	8	11	18	26	40	52	67
	3	1	2	4	7	9	15	22	34	44	57
	2	1	1	3	6	8	12	19	28	37	48
XHH, XHHW, XHHW-2	1	1	1	3	4	6	9	14	21	28	35
	1/0	1	1	2	4	5	8	12	18	23	30
	2/0	1	1	1	3	4	6	10	15	19	25
	3/0	0	1	1	2	3	5	8	12	16	20
	4/0	0	1	1	1	3	4	7	10	13	17
	250	0	1	1	1	2	3	5	8	11	14
	300	0	0	1	1	1	3	5	7	9	12
	350	0	0	1	1	1	3	4	6	8	10
	400	0	0	1	1	1	2	3	5	7	9
	500	0	0	1	1	1	1	3	4	6	8
	600	0	0	0	1	1	1	2	3	5	6
	700	0	0	0	1	1	1	1	3	4	5
	750	0	0	0	1	1	1	1	3	4	5
	800	0	0	0	1	1	1	1	3	4	5
	900	0	0	0	0	1	1	1	2	3	4
	1000	0	0	0	0	1	1	1	2	3	4
	1250	0	0	0	0	0	1	1	1	2	3
	1500	0	0	0	0	0	1	1	1	1	2
	1750	0	0	0	0	0	1	1	1	1	2
	2000	0	0	0	0	0	0	1	1	1	1

Table C.11 *Continued*

	Conductor Size (AWG/ kcmil)	Metric Designator (Trade Size)					
Type		**16** **(½)**	**21** **(¾)**	**27** **(1)**	**35** **(1¼)**	**41** **(1½)**	**53** **(2)**
FFH-2, RFH-2, RFHH-3	18	10	18	30	48	64	100
	16	9	15	25	41	54	85
SF-2, SFF-2	18	13	22	37	61	81	127
	16	11	18	31	51	67	105
	14	9	15	25	41	54	85
SF-1, SFF-1	18	23	40	66	108	143	224
RFH-1, RFHH-2, TF, TFF, XF, XFF	18	17	29	49	80	105	165
RFHH-2, TF, TFF, XF, XFF	16	14	24	39	65	85	134
XF, XFF	14	11	18	31	51	67	105
TFN, TFFN	18	28	47	79	128	169	265
	16	21	36	60	98	129	202
PF, PFF, PGF, PGFF, PAF, PTF, PTFF, PAFF	18	26	45	74	122	160	251
	16	20	34	58	94	124	194
	14	15	26	43	70	93	146
HF, HFF, ZF, ZFF, ZHF	18	34	58	96	157	206	324
	16	25	42	71	116	152	239
	14	18	31	52	85	112	175
KF-2, KFF-2	18	49	84	140	228	300	470
	16	35	59	98	160	211	331
	14	24	40	67	110	145	228
	12	16	28	46	76	100	157
	10	11	18	31	51	67	105
KF-1, KFF-1	18	59	100	167	272	357	561
	16	41	70	117	191	251	394
	14	28	47	79	128	169	265
	12	18	31	52	85	112	175
	10	12	20	34	55	73	115
XF, XFF	12	6	10	16	27	35	56
	10	4	8	13	21	28	44

Notes:

1. This table is for concentric stranded conductors only. For compact stranded conductors, Table C.11(A) should be used.

2. Two-hour fire-rated RHH cable has ceramifiable insulation which has much larger diameters than other RHH wires.

Consult manufacturer's conduit fill tables.

*Types RHH, RHW, and RWH-2 without outer covering.

Table C.11(A) Maximum Number of Compact Conductors in Type A, Rigid PVC Conduit
(*Based on Table 1, Chapter 9*)

COMPACT CONDUCTORS

Type	Conductor Size (AWG/ kcmil)	Metric Designator (Trade Size)									
		16 (½)	21 (¾)	27 (1)	35 (1¼)	41 (1½)	53 (2)	63 (2½)	78 (3)	91 (3½)	103 (4)
THW,	8	3	5	8	14	18	28	42	64	84	107
THW-2,	6	2	4	6	10	14	22	33	49	65	83
THHW	4	1	3	5	8	10	16	24	37	48	62
	2	1	1	3	6	7	12	18	27	36	46
	1	1	1	2	4	5	8	13	19	25	32
	1/0	1	1	1	3	4	7	11	16	21	28
	2/0	1	1	1	3	4	6	9	14	18	23
	3/0	0	1	1	2	3	5	8	12	15	20
	4/0	0	1	1	1	3	4	6	10	13	17
	250	0	1	1	1	1	3	5	8	10	13
	300	0	0	1	1	1	3	4	7	9	11
	350	0	0	1	1	1	2	4	6	8	10
	400	0	0	1	1	1	2	3	5	7	9
	500	0	0	1	1	1	1	3	4	6	8
	600	0	0	0	1	1	1	2	3	5	6
	700	0	0	0	1	1	1	1	3	4	5
	750	0	0	0	1	1	1	1	3	4	5
	900	0	0	0	0	1	1	2	2	3	4
	1000	0	0	0	0	1	1	1	2	3	4
THHN,	8	—	—	—	—	—	—	—	—	—	—
THWN,	6	3	5	9	15	20	32	48	72	94	121
THWN-2	4	1	3	6	9	12	20	30	45	58	75
	2	1	2	4	7	9	14	21	32	42	54
	1	1	1	3	5	7	10	16	24	31	40
	1/0	1	1	2	4	6	9	13	20	27	34
	2/0	1	1	1	3	5	7	11	17	22	28
	3/0	1	1	1	3	4	6	9	14	18	24
	4/0	0	1	1	2	3	5	8	11	15	19
	250	0	1	1	1	2	4	6	9	12	15
	300	0	1	1	1	1	3	5	8	10	13
	350	0	0	1	1	1	3	4	7	9	11
	400	0	0	1	1	1	2	4	6	8	10
	500	0	0	1	1	1	2	3	5	7	9
	600	0	0	0	1	1	1	3	4	5	7
	700	0	0	0	1	1	1	2	3	5	6
	750	0	0	0	1	1	1	2	3	4	6
	900	0	0	0	1	1	1	2	3	4	5
	1000	0	0	0	0	1	1	1	2	3	4
XHHW,	8	4	6	11	18	23	37	55	83	108	139
XHHW-2	6	3	5	8	13	17	27	41	62	80	103
	4	1	3	6	9	12	20	30	45	58	75
	2	1	2	4	7	9	14	21	32	42	54
	1	1	1	3	5	7	10	16	24	31	40
	1/0	1	1	2	4	6	9	13	20	27	34
	2/0	1	1	1	3	5	7	11	17	22	29
	3/0	1	1	1	3	4	6	9	14	18	24
	4/0	0	1	1	2	3	5	8	12	15	20
	250	0	1	1	1	2	4	6	9	12	16
	300	0	1	1	1	1	3	5	8	10	13
	350	0	0	1	1	1	3	5	7	9	12
	400	0	0	1	1	1	3	4	6	8	11
	500	0	0	1	1	1	2	3	5	7	9
	600	0	0	0	1	1	1	3	4	5	7
	700	0	0	0	1	1	1	2	3	5	6
	750	0	0	0	1	1	1	2	3	4	6
	900	0	0	0	1	1	1	2	3	4	5
	1000	0	0	0	0	1	1	1	2	3	4

Definition: *Compact stranding* is the result of a manufacturing process where the standard conductor is compressed to the extent that the interstices (voids between strand wires) are virtually eliminated.

Table C.12 Maximum Number of Conductors in Type EB, PVC Conduit
(Based on Table 1, Chapter 9)

		CONDUCTORS					
	Conductor Size (AWG/ kcmil)	Metric Designator (Trade Size)					
Type		53 (2)	78 (3)	91 (3½)	103 (4)	129 (5)	155 (6)
RHH, RHW, RHW-2	14	53	119	155	197	303	430
	12	44	98	128	163	251	357
	10	35	79	104	132	203	288
	8	18	41	54	69	106	151
	6	15	33	43	55	85	121
	4	11	26	34	43	66	94
	3	10	23	30	38	58	83
	2	9	20	26	33	50	72
	1	6	13	17	21	33	47
	1/0	5	11	15	19	29	41
	2/0	4	10	13	16	25	36
	3/0	4	8	11	14	22	31
	4/0	3	7	9	12	18	26
	250	2	5	7	9	14	20
	300	1	5	6	8	12	17
	350	1	4	5	7	11	16
	400	1	4	5	6	10	14
	500	1	3	4	5	9	12
	600	1	3	3	4	7	10
	700	1	2	3	4	6	9
	750	1	2	3	4	6	9
	800	1	2	3	4	6	8
	900	1	1	2	3	5	7
	1000	1	1	2	3	5	7
	1250	1	1	1	2	3	5
	1500	0	1	1	1	3	4
	1750	0	1	1	1	3	4
	2000	0	1	1	1	2	3
TW	14	111	250	327	415	638	907
	12	85	192	251	319	490	696
	10	63	143	187	238	365	519
	8	35	79	104	132	203	288
RHH*, RHW*, RHW-2*, THHW, THW, THW-2	14	74	166	217	276	424	603
RHH*, RHW*, RHW-2*, THHW, THW	12	59	134	175	222	341	485
	10	46	104	136	173	266	378
RHH*, RHW*, RHW-2*, THHW, THW, THW-2	8	28	62	81	104	159	227

(Continues)

Table C.12 *Continued*

	Conductor Size (AWG/ kcmil)	Metric Designator (Trade Size)					
Type		53 (2)	78 (3)	91 (3½)	103 (4)	129 (5)	155 (6)
RHH*,	6	21	48	62	79	122	173
RHW*,	4	16	36	46	59	91	129
RHW-2*,	3	13	30	40	51	78	111
TW, THW,	2	11	26	34	43	66	94
THHW,	1	8	18	24	30	46	66
THW-2	1/0	7	15	20	26	40	56
	2/0	6	13	17	22	34	48
	3/0	5	11	14	18	28	40
	4/0	4	9	12	15	24	34
	250	3	7	10	12	19	27
	300	3	6	8	11	17	24
	350	2	6	7	9	15	21
	400	2	5	7	8	13	19
	500	1	4	5	7	11	16
	600	1	3	4	6	9	13
	700	1	3	4	5	8	11
	750	1	3	4	5	7	11
	800	1	3	3	4	7	10
	900	1	2	3	4	6	9
	1000	1	2	3	4	6	8
	1250	1	1	2	3	4	6
	1500	1	1	1	2	4	6
	1750	1	1	1	2	3	5
	2000	0	1	1	1	3	4
THHN,	14	159	359	468	595	915	1300
THWN,	12	116	262	342	434	667	948
THWN-2	10	73	165	215	274	420	597
	8	42	95	124	158	242	344
	6	30	68	89	114	175	248
	4	19	42	55	70	107	153
	3	16	36	46	59	91	129
	2	13	30	39	50	76	109
	1	10	22	29	37	57	80
	1/0	8	18	24	31	48	68
	2/0	7	15	20	26	40	56
	3/0	5	13	17	21	33	47
	4/0	4	10	14	18	27	39
	250	4	8	11	14	22	31
	300	3	7	10	12	19	27
	350	3	6	8	11	17	24
	400	2	6	7	10	15	21
	500	1	5	6	8	12	18
	600	1	4	5	6	10	14
	700	1	3	4	6	9	12
	750	1	3	4	5	8	12
	800	1	3	4	5	8	11
	900	1	3	3	4	7	10
	1000	1	2	3	4	6	9
FEP, FEPB,	14	155	348	454	578	888	1261
PFA, PFAH,	12	113	254	332	422	648	920
TFE	10	81	182	238	302	465	660
	8	46	104	136	173	266	378
	6	33	74	97	123	189	269
	4	23	52	68	86	132	188
	3	19	43	56	72	110	157
	2	16	36	46	59	91	129

Table C.12 *Continued*

	Conductor Size (AWG/kcmil)	CONDUCTORS					
		Metric Designator (Trade Size)					
Type		53 (2)	78 (3)	91 (3½)	103 (4)	129 (5)	155 (6)
PFA, PFAH, TFE	1	11	25	32	41	63	90
PFA, PFAH, TFE, Z	1/0	9	20	27	34	53	75
	2/0	7	17	22	28	43	62
	3/0	6	14	18	23	36	51
	4/0	5	11	15	19	29	42
Z	14	186	419	547	696	1069	1519
	12	132	297	388	494	759	1078
	10	81	182	238	302	465	660
	8	51	115	150	191	294	417
	6	36	81	105	134	206	293
	4	24	55	72	92	142	201
	3	18	40	53	67	104	147
	2	15	34	44	56	86	122
	1	12	27	36	45	70	99
XHH, XHHW, XHHW-2, ZW	14	111	250	327	415	638	907
	12	85	192	251	319	490	696
	10	63	143	187	238	365	519
	8	35	79	104	132	203	288
	6	26	59	77	98	150	213
	4	19	42	56	71	109	155
	3	16	36	47	60	92	131
	2	13	30	39	50	77	110
XHH, XHHW, XHHW-2	1	10	22	29	37	58	82
	1/0	8	19	25	31	48	69
	2/0	7	16	20	26	40	57
	3/0	6	13	17	22	33	47
	4/0	5	11	14	18	27	39
	250	4	9	11	15	22	32
	300	3	7	10	12	19	28
	350	3	6	9	11	17	24
	400	2	6	8	10	15	22
	500	1	5	6	8	12	18
	600	1	4	5	6	10	14
	700	1	3	4	6	9	12
	750	1	3	4	5	8	12
	800	1	3	4	5	8	11
	900	1	3	3	4	7	10
	1000	1	2	3	4	6	9
	1250	1	1	2	3	5	7
	1500	1	1	1	3	4	6
	1750	1	1	1	2	4	5
	2000	0	1	1	1	3	5

Notes:

1. This table is for concentric stranded conductors only. For compact stranded conductors, Table C.12(A) should be used.

2. Two-hour fire-rated RHH cable has ceramifiable insulation which has much larger diameters than other RHH wires.

Consult manufacturer's conduit fill tables.

*Types RHH, RHW, and RHW-2 without outer covering.

Table C.12(A) Maximum Number of Compact Conductors in Type EB, PVC Conduit
(Based on Table 1, Chapter 9)

		COMPACT CONDUCTORS					
	Conductor Size	Metric Designator (Trade Size)					
Type	(AWG/ kcmil)	53 (2)	78 (3)	91 (3½)	103 (4)	129 (5)	155 (6)
THW,	8	30	68	89	113	174	247
THW-2,	6	23	52	69	87	134	191
THHW	4	17	39	51	65	100	143
	2	13	29	38	48	74	105
	1	9	20	26	34	52	74
	1/0	8	17	23	29	45	64
	2/0	6	15	19	24	38	54
	3/0	5	12	16	21	32	46
	4/0	4	10	14	17	27	38
	250	3	8	11	14	21	30
	300	3	7	9	12	19	26
	350	3	6	8	11	17	24
	400	2	6	7	10	15	21
	500	1	5	6	8	12	18
	600	1	4	5	6	10	14
	700	1	3	4	6	9	13
	750	1	3	4	5	8	12
	900	1	3	4	5	7	10
	1000	1	2	3	4	7	9
THHN,	8	—	—	—	—	—	—
THWN,	6	34	77	100	128	196	279
THWN-2	4	21	47	62	79	121	172
	2	15	34	44	57	87	124
	1	11	25	33	42	65	93
	1/0	9	22	28	36	56	79
	2/0	8	18	23	30	46	65
	3/0	6	15	20	25	38	55
	4/0	5	12	16	20	32	45
	250	4	10	13	16	25	35
	300	4	8	11	14	22	31
	350	3	7	9	12	19	27
	400	3	6	8	11	17	24
	500	2	5	7	9	14	20
	600	1	4	6	7	11	16
	700	1	4	5	6	10	14
	750	1	4	5	6	9	14
	900	1	3	4	5	7	10
	1000	1	3	3	4	7	10
XHHW,	8	39	88	115	146	225	320
XHHW-2	6	29	65	85	109	167	238
	4	21	47	62	79	121	172
	2	15	34	44	57	87	124
	1	11	25	33	42	65	93
	1/0	9	22	28	36	56	79
	2/0	8	18	24	30	47	67
	3/0	6	15	20	25	38	55
	4/0	5	12	16	21	32	46
	250	4	10	13	17	26	37
	300	4	8	11	14	22	31
	350	3	7	10	12	19	28
	400	3	7	9	11	17	25
	500	2	5	7	9	14	20
	600	1	4	6	7	11	16
	700	1	4	5	6	10	14
	750	1	3	5	6	9	13
	900	1	3	4	5	7	10
	1000	1	3	4	5	7	10

Definition: *Compact stranding* is the result of a manufacturing process where the standard conductor is compressed to the extent that the interstices (voids between strand wires) are virtually eliminated.

Annex D   Examples

This annex is not a part of the requirements of this NFPA document but is included for informational purposes only.

Selection of Conductors. In the following examples, the results are generally expressed in amperes (A). To select conductor sizes, refer to the 0 through 2000 volt (V) ampacity tables of Article 310 and the rules of 310.15 that pertain to these tables.

Voltage. For uniform application of Articles 210, 215, and 220, a nominal voltage of 120, 120/240, 240, and 208Y/120 V is used in calculating the ampere load on the conductor.

Fractions of an Ampere. Except where the calculations result in a major fraction of an ampere (0.5 or larger), such fractions are permitted to be dropped.

Power Factor. Calculations in the following examples are based, for convenience, on the assumption that all loads have the same power factor (PF).

Ranges. For the calculation of the range loads in these examples, Column C of Table 220.55 has been used. For optional methods, see Columns A and B of Table 220.55. Except where the calculations result in a major fraction of a kilowatt (0.5 or larger), such fractions are permitted to be dropped.

SI Units. For metric conversions, 0.093 m^2 = 1 ft^2 and 0.3048 m = 1 ft.

Example D1(a) One-Family Dwelling

The dwelling has a floor area of 1500 ft^2, exclusive of an unfinished cellar not adaptable for future use, unfinished attic, and open porches. Appliances are a 12-kW range and a 5.5-kW, 240-V dryer. Assume range and dryer kW ratings equivalent to kVA ratings in accordance with 220.54 and 220.55.

Calculated Load *[see 220.40]*

General Lighting Load: 1500 ft^2 at 3 VA per ft^2 = 4500 VA

Minimum Number of Branch Circuits Required *[see 210.11(A)]*

General Lighting Load: 4500 VA ÷ 120 V = 37.5 A
This requires three 15-A, 2-wire or two 20-A, 2-wire circuits.
Small Appliance Load: Two 2-wire, 20-A circuits *[see 210.11(C)(1)]*
Laundry Load: One 2-wire, 20-A circuit *[see 210.11(C)(2)]*
Bathroom Branch Circuit: One 2-wire, 20-A circuit (no additional load calculation is required for this circuit) *[see 210.11(C)(3)]*

Minimum Size Feeder Required *[see 220.40]*

General Lighting		4,500 VA
Small Appliance		3,000 VA
Laundry		1,500 VA
	Total	9,000 VA
3000 VA at 100%		3,000 VA
9000 VA – 3000 VA = 6000 VA at 35%		2,100 VA
	Net Load	5,100 VA
Range (*see Table 220.55*)		8,000 VA
Dryer Load (*see Table 220.54*)		5,500 VA
Net Calculated Load		**18,600 VA**

Net Calculated Load for 120/240-V, 3-wire, single-phase service or feeder

$$18,600 \text{ VA} \div 240 \text{ V} = 77.5 \text{ A}$$

Sections 230.42(B) and 230.79 require service conductors and disconnecting means rated not less than 100 amperes.

Calculation for Neutral for Feeder and Service

Lighting and Small Appliance Load	5,100 VA
Range: 8000 VA at 70% (*see 220.61*)	5,600 VA
Dryer: 5500 VA at 70% (*see 220.61*)	3,850 VA
Total	14,550 VA

Calculated Load for Neutral

$$14,550 \text{ VA} \div 240 \text{ V} = 60.6 \text{ A}$$

Example D1(b) One-Family Dwelling

Assume same conditions as Example No. D1(a), plus addition of one 6-A, 230-V, room air-conditioning unit and one 12-A, 115-V, room air-conditioning unit,* one 8-A, 115-V, rated waste disposer, and one 10-A, 120-V, rated dishwasher. See Article 430 for general motors and Article 440, Part VII, for air-conditioning equipment. Motors have nameplate ratings of 115 V and 230 V for use on 120-V and 240-V nominal voltage systems.

*(For feeder neutral, use larger of the two appliances for unbalance.)
From Example D1(a), feeder current is 78 A (3-wire, 240 V).

	Line A	Neutral	Line B
Amperes from Example D1(a)	78	61	78
One 230-V air conditioner	6	—	6
One 115-V air conditioner and 120-V dishwasher	12	12	10
One 115-V disposer	—	8	8
25% of largest motor (*see 430.24*)	3	3	2
Total amperes per line	99	84	104

Therefore, the service would be rated 110 A.

Example D2(a) Optional Calculation for One-Family Dwelling, Heating Larger Than Air Conditioning
[see 220.82]

The dwelling has a floor area of 1500 ft^2, exclusive of an unfinished cellar not adaptable for future use, unfinished attic, and open porches. It has a 12-kW range, a 2.5-kW water heater, a 1.2-kW dishwasher, 9 kW of electric space heating installed in five rooms, a 5-kW clothes dryer, and a 6-A, 230-V, room air-conditioning unit. Assume range, water heater, dishwasher, space heating, and clothes dryer kW ratings equivalent to kVA.

Air Conditioner kVA Calculation

$$6 \text{ A} \times 230 \text{ V} \div 1000 = 1.38 \text{ kVA}$$

This 1.38 kVA [item 1 from 220.82(C)] is less than 40% of 9 kVA of separately controlled electric heat [item 6 from 220.82(C)], so the 1.38 kVA need not be included in the service calculation.

General Load

1500 ft^2 at 3 VA	4,500 VA
Two 20-A appliance outlet circuits at 1500 VA each	3,000 VA
Laundry circuit	1,500 VA
Range (at nameplate rating)	12,000 VA
Water heater	2,500 VA
Dishwasher	1,200 VA
Clothes dryer	5,000 VA
Total	29,700 VA

Application of Demand Factor *[see 220.82(B)]*

First 10 kVA of general load at 100%	10,000 VA
Remainder of general load at 40% (19.7 kVA × 0.4)	7,880 VA
Total of general load	17,880 VA
9 kVA of heat at 40% (9000 VA × 0.4) =	3,600 VA
Total	21,480 VA

Calculated Load for Service Size

$$21.48 \text{ kVA} = 21,480 \text{ VA}$$
$$21,480 \text{ VA} \div 240 \text{ V} = 89.5 \text{ A}$$

Therefore, the minimum service rating would be 100 A in accordance with 230.42 and 230.79.

Feeder Neutral Load, per 220.61

1500 ft² at 3 VA		4,500 VA
Three 20-A circuits at 1500 VA		4,500 VA
	Total	9,000 VA
3000 VA at 100%		3,000 VA
9000 VA − 3000 VA = 6000 VA at 35%		2,100 VA
	Subtotal	5,100 VA
Range: 8 kVA at 70%		5,600 VA
Clothes dryer: 5 kVA at 70%		3,500 VA
Dishwasher		1,200 VA
	Total	15,400 VA

Calculated Load for Neutral

$$15,400 \text{ VA} \div 240 \text{ V} = 64.2 \text{ A}$$

Example D2(b) Optional Calculation for One-Family Dwelling, Air Conditioning Larger Than Heating
[see 220.82(A) and 220.82(C)]

The dwelling has a floor area of 1500 ft², exclusive of an unfinished cellar not adaptable for future use, unfinished attic, and open porches. It has two 20-A small appliance circuits, one 20-A laundry circuit, two 4-kW wall-mounted ovens, one 5.1-kW counter-mounted cooking unit, a 4.5-kW water heater, a 1.2-kW dishwasher, a 5-kW combination clothes washer and dryer, six 7-A, 230-V room air-conditioning units, and a 1.5-kW permanently installed bathroom space heater. Assume wall-mounted ovens, counter-mounted cooking unit, water heater, dishwasher, and combination clothes washer and dryer kW ratings equivalent to kVA.

Air Conditioning kVA Calculation

$$\text{Total amperes} = 6 \text{ units} \times 7 \text{ A} = 42 \text{ A}$$
$$42 \text{ A} \times 240 \text{ V} \div 1000 = 10.08 \text{ kVA (assume PF} = 1.0)$$

Load Included at 100%

Air Conditioning: Included below *[see item 1 in 220.82(C)]*
Space Heater: Omit *[see item 5 in 220.82(C)]*

General Load

1500 ft² at 3 VA		4,500 VA
Two 20-A small appliance circuits at 1500 VA each		3,000 VA
Laundry circuit		1,500 VA
Two ovens		8,000 VA
One cooking unit		5,100 VA
Water heater		4,500 VA
Dishwasher		1,200 VA
Washer/dryer		5,000 VA
	Total general load	32,800 VA
First 10 kVA at 100%		10,000 VA
Remainder at 40% (22.8 kVA × 0.4 × 1000)		9,120 VA
	Subtotal general load	19,120 VA
Air conditioning		10,080 VA
	Total	29,200 VA

Calculated Load for Service

$$29,200 \text{ VA} \div 240 \text{ V} = 122 \text{ A (service rating)}$$

Feeder Neutral Load, per 220.61

Assume that the two 4-kVA wall-mounted ovens are supplied by one branch circuit, the 5.1-kVA counter-mounted cooking unit by a separate circuit.

1500 ft² at 3 VA		4,500 VA
Three 20-A circuits at 1500 VA		4,500 VA
	Subtotal	9,000 VA
3000 VA at 100%		3,000 VA
9000 VA − 3000 VA = 6000 VA at 35%		2,100 VA
	Subtotal	5,100 VA

Two 4-kVA ovens plus one 5.1-kVA cooking unit = 13.1 kVA. Table 220.55 permits 55% demand factor or 13.1 kVA × 0.55 = 7.2 kVA feeder capacity.

	Subtotal from above	5,100 VA
Ovens and cooking unit: 7200 VA × 70% for neutral load		5,040 VA
Clothes washer/dryer: 5 kVA × 70% for neutral load		3,500 VA
Dishwasher		1,200 VA
	Total	14,840 VA

Calculated Load for Neutral

$$14,840 \text{ VA} \div 240 \text{ V} = 61.83 \text{ A (use 62 A)}$$

Example D2(c) Optional Calculation for One-Family Dwelling with Heat Pump (Single-Phase, 240/120-Volt Service) *(see 220.82)*

The dwelling has a floor area of 2000 ft², exclusive of an unfinished cellar not adaptable for future use, unfinished attic, and open porches. It has a 12-kW range, a 4.5-kW water heater, a 1.2-kW dishwasher, a 5-kW clothes dryer, and a 2½-ton (24-A) heat pump with 15 kW of backup heat.

Heat Pump kVA Calculation

$$24 \text{ A} \times 240 \text{ V} \div 1000 = 5.76 \text{ kVA}$$

This 5.76 kVA is less than 15 kVA of the backup heat; therefore, the heat pump load need not be included in the service calculation *[see 220.82(C)]*.

General Load

2000 ft² at 3 VA		6,000 VA
Two 20-A appliance outlet circuits at 1500 VA each		3,000 VA
Laundry circuit		1,500 VA
Range (at nameplate rating)		12,000 VA
Water heater		4,500 VA
Dishwasher		1,200 VA
Clothes dryer		5,000 VA
	Subtotal general load	33,200 VA
First 10 kVA at 100%		10,000 VA
Remainder of general load at 40% 23,200 VA × 0.4)		9,280 VA
	Total net general load	19,280 VA

Heat Pump and Supplementary Heat*

$$240 \text{ V} \times 24 \text{ A} = 5760 \text{ VA}$$

15 kW Electric Heat:

$$5760 \text{ VA} + (15,000 \text{ VA} \times 65\%) = 5.76 \text{ kVA} + 9.75 \text{ kVA} = 15.51 \text{ kVA}$$

*If supplementary heat is not on at same time as heat pump, heat pump kVA need not be added to total.

Totals

Net general load	19,280 VA
Heat pump and supplementary heat	15,510 VA
Total	34,790 VA

Calculated Load for Service

$$34.79 \text{ kVA} \times 1000 \div 240 \text{ V} = 144.96 \text{ A}$$

Therefore, this dwelling unit would be permitted to be served by a 150-A service.

Example D3 Store Building

A store 50 ft by 60 ft, or 3000 ft^2, has 30 ft of show window. There are a total of 80 duplex receptacles. The service is 120/240 V, single phase 3-wire service. Actual connected lighting load is 8500 VA.

Calculated Load *(see 220.40)*

Noncontinuous Loads
Receptacle Load *(see 220.44)*

80 receptacles at 180 VA	14,400 VA
10,000 VA at 100%	10,000 VA
14,400 VA − 10,000 VA = 4400 at 50%	2,200 VA
Subtotal	12,200 VA

Continuous Loads
General Lighting*

3000 ft^2 at 3 VA per ft^2	9,000 VA
Show Window Lighting Load	
30 ft at 200 VA per ft	6,000 VA
Outside Sign Circuit *[see 220.14(F)]*	1,200 VA
Subtotal	16,200 VA
Subtotal from noncontinuous	12,200 VA
Total noncontinuous loads + continuous loads =	28,400 VA

*In the example, 125% of the actual connected lighting load (8500 VA × 1.25 = 10,625 VA) is less than 125% of the load from Table 220.12, so the minimum lighting load from Table 220.12 is used in the calculation. Had the actual lighting load been greater than the value calculated from Table 220.12, 125% of the actual connected lighting load would have been used.

Minimum Number of Branch Circuits Required

General Lighting: Branch circuits need only be installed to supply the actual connected load *[see 210.11(B)]*.

$$8500 \text{ VA} \times 1.25 = 10,625 \text{ VA}$$
$$10,625 \text{ VA} \div 240 \text{ V} = 44 \text{ A for 3-wire, 120/240 V}$$

The lighting load would be permitted to be served by 2-wire or 3-wire, 15- or 20-A circuits with combined capacity equal to 44 A or greater for 3-wire circuits or 88 A or greater for 2-wire circuits. The feeder capacity as well as the number of branch-circuit positions available for lighting circuits in the panelboard must reflect the full calculated load of 9000 VA × 1.25 = 11,250 VA.

Show Window

$$6000 \text{ VA} \times 1.25 = 7500 \text{ VA}$$
$$7500 \text{ VA} \div 240 \text{ V} = 31 \text{ A for 3-wire, 120/240 V}$$

The show window lighting is permitted to be served by 2-wire or 3-wire circuits with a capacity equal to 31 A or greater for 3-wire circuits or 62 A or greater for 2-wire circuits.

Receptacles required by 210.62 are assumed to be included in the receptacle load above if these receptacles do not supply the show window lighting load.

Receptacles

Receptacle Load:14,400 VA ÷ 240 V = 60 A for 3-wire, 120/240 V

The receptacle load would be permitted to be served by 2-wire or 3-wire circuits with a capacity equal to 60 A or greater for 3-wire circuits or 120 A or greater for 2-wire circuits.

Minimum Size Feeder (or Service) Overcurrent Protection
[see 215.3 or 230.90]

Subtotal noncontinuous loads	12,200 VA
Subtotal continuous load at 125%	
(16,200 VA × 1.25)	20,250 VA
Total	32,450 VA

$$32,450 \text{ VA} \div 240 \text{ V} = 135 \text{ A}$$

The next higher standard size is 150 A *(see 240.6)*.

Minimum Size Feeders (or Service Conductors) Required
[see 215.2, 230.42(A)]

For 120/240 V, 3-wire system,

$$32,450 \text{ VA} \div 240 \text{ V} = 135 \text{ A}$$

Service or feeder conductor is 1/0 Cu per 215.3 and Table 310.16 (with 75°C terminations).

Example D3(a) Industrial Feeders in a Common Raceway

An industrial multi-building facility has its service at the rear of its main building, and then provides 480Y/277-volt feeders to additional buildings behind the main building in order to segregate certain processes. The facility supplies its remote buildings through a partially enclosed access corridor that extends from the main switchboard rearward along a path that provides convenient access to services within 15 m (50 ft) of each additional building supplied. Two building feeders share a common raceway for approximately 45 m (150 ft) and run in the access corridor along with process steam and control and communications cabling. The steam raises the ambient temperature around the power raceway to as much as 35°C. At a tee fitting, the individual building feeders then run to each of the two buildings involved. The feeder neutrals are not connected to the equipment grounding conductors in the remote buildings. All distribution equipment terminations are listed as being suitable for 75°C connections.

Each of the two buildings has the following loads:

Lighting, 11,600 VA, comprised of electric-discharge luminaires connected at 277 V

Receptacles, 22 125-volt, 20 ampere receptacles on general-purpose branch circuits, supplied by separately derived systems in each of the buildings

1-Air compressor, 460 volt, three phase, 7.5 hp

1-Grinder, 460 volt, three phase,1.5 hp

3-Welders, AC transformer type (nameplate: 23 amperes, 480 volts, 60 percent duty cycle)

3-Industrial Process Dryers, 480 volt, three phase,15 kW each (assume continuous use throughout certain shifts)

Determine the overcurrent protection and conductor size for the feeders in the common raceway, assuming the use of XHHW-2 insulation (90°C):

Calculated Load {Note: For reasonable precision, volt-ampere calculations are carried to three significant figures only; where loads are converted to amperes, the results are rounded to the nearest ampere *[see 220.5(B)]*}.

Noncontinuous Loads
Receptacle Load (see 220.44)

22 receptacles at 180 VA	3,960 VA
Welder Load [see 630.11(A), Table 630.11(A)]	
Each welder: 480V × 23A × 0.78 = 8,610 VA	
All 3 welders: [see 630.11(B)] (demand factors 100%, 100%, 85% respectively)	
8,610 VA + 8,610 VA + 7,320 VA =	24,500 VA
Subtotal, Noncontinuous Loads	**28,500 VA**

Motor Loads (see 430.24, Table 430.250)

Air compressor: 11 A × 480 V × √3 =	9,150 VA
Grinder: 3 A × 480 V × √3 =	2,490 VA
Largest motor, additional 25%:	2,290 VA
Subtotal, Motor Loads	**13,900 VA**

By using 430.24, the motor loads and the noncontinuous loads can be combined for the remaining calculation.

Subtotal for load calculations, Noncontinuous Loads	**42,400 VA**

Continuous Loads

General Lighting		11,600 VA
3 Industrial Process Dryers	15 kW each	45,000 VA
Subtotal, Continuous Loads:		**56,600 VA**

Overcurrent protection *(see 215.3)*

The overcurrent protective device must accommodate 125% of the continuous load, plus the noncontinuous load:

Continuous load	56,600 VA
Noncontinuous load	42,400 VA
Subtotal, actual load [actual load in amperes]	**99,000 VA**
99,000 VA ÷ (480V × √3) = 119 A]	
(25% of 56,600 VA) *(See 215.3)*	**14,200 VA**
Total VA	**113,200 VA**

Conversion to amperes using three significant figures:
113,200 VA / (480V × √3) = 136 A
Minimum size overcurrent protective device: 136 A
Minimum standard size overcurrent protective
device *(see 240.6)*: 150 amperes

Where the overcurrent protective device and its assembly are listed for operation at 100 percent of its rating, a 125 ampere overcurrent protective device would be permitted. However, overcurrent protective device assemblies listed for 100 percent of their rating are typically not available at the 125-ampere rating. *(See 215.3 Exception.)*

Ungrounded Feeder Conductors

The conductors must independently meet requirements for (1) terminations, and (2) conditions of use throughout the raceway run.

Minimum size conductor at the overcurrent device termination *[see 110.14(C) and 215.2(A)(1), using 75°C ampacity column in Table 310.16]:* 1/0 AWG.

Minimum size conductors in the raceway based on actual load *[see Article 100, Ampacity, and 310.15(B)(2)(a) and correction factors to Table Table 310.16]:*

99,000 VA / 0.7 / 0.96 = 147,000 VA

(70% = 310.15(B)(2)(a)) & (0.96 = Correction factors to Table 310.16)

Conversion to amperes:

147,000 VA / (480V × √3) = 177 A

Note that the neutral conductors are counted as current-carrying conductors *[see 310.15(B)(4)(c)]* in this example because the discharge lighting has substantial nonlinear content. This requires a 2/0 AWG conductor based on the 90°C column of Table 310.16 Therefore, the worst case is given by the raceway conditions, and 2/0 AWG conductors must be used. If the utility corridor was at normal temperatures [(30°C (86°F)], and if the lighting at each building were supplied from the local separately derived system (thus requiring no neutrals in the supply feeders) the raceway result (99,000 VA / 0.8 = 124,000 VA; 124,000 VA / (480V × √3) = 149 A, or a 1 AWG conductor @ 90°C) could not be used because the termination result (1/0 AWG based on the 75°C column of) would become the worst case, requiring the larger conductor.

In every case, the overcurrent protective device shall provide overcurrent protection for the feeder conductors in accordance with their ampacity as provided by this *Code (see 240.4)*. A 90°C 2/0 AWG conductor has a Table 310.16 ampacity of 195 amperes. Adjusting for the conditions of use (35°C ambient temperature, 8 current-carrying conductors in the common raceway),

195 amperes × 0.96 × 0.7 = 131 A

The 150-ampere circuit breaker protects the 2/0 AWG feeder conductors, because 240.4(B) permits the use of the next higher standard size overcurrent protective device. Note that the feeder layout precludes the application of 310.15(A)(2) Exception.

Feeder Neutral Conductor *(see 220.61)*

Because 210.11(B) does not apply to these buildings, the load cannot be assumed to be evenly distributed across phases. Therefore the maximum imbalance must be assumed to be the full lighting load in this case, or 11,600 VA. (11,600 VA / 277V = 42 amperes.) The ability of the neutral to return fault current *[see 250.32(B)(2)(2)]* is not a factor in this calculation.

Although the neutral runs between the main switchboard and the building panelboard, likely terminating on a busbar at both locations, the busbar connections are part of listed devices and are not "separately installed pressure devices." Therefore 110.14(C)(2) does not apply, and the normal termination temperature limits apply. In addition, the listing requirement to gain exemption from the additional sizing allowance under continuous loading *(see 215.3Exception)* covers not just the overcurrent protective device, but its entire assembly as well. Therefore, since the lighting load is continuous, the minimum conductor size is based on 1.25 × (11,600 VA / 277V) = 52 amperes, to be evaluated under the 75°C column of Table 310.16. The minimum size of the neutral is 6 AWG. This size is also the minimum size required by 215.2(A)(1), because the minimum size equipment grounding conductor for a 150 ampere circuit, as covered in Table 250.122, is 6 AWG.

Example D4(a) Multifamily Dwelling

A multifamily dwelling has 40 dwelling units.

Meters are in two banks of 20 each with individual feeders to each dwelling unit.

One-half of the dwelling units are equipped with electric ranges not exceeding 12 kW each. Assume range kW rating equivalent to kVA rating in accordance with 220.55. Other half of ranges are gas ranges.

Area of each dwelling unit is 840 ft².

Laundry facilities on premises are available to all tenants. Add no circuit to individual dwelling unit.

Calculated Load for Each Dwelling Unit *(see Article 220)*

General Lighting: 840 ft² at 3 VA per ft² = 2520 VA

Special Appliance: Electric range *(see 220.55)* = 8000 VA

Minimum Number of Branch Circuits Required for Each Dwelling Unit *[see 210.11(A)]*

General Lighting Load: 2520 VA ÷ 120 V = 21 A or two 15-A, 2-wire circuits; or two 20-A, 2-wire circuits

Small Appliance Load: Two 2-wire circuits of 12 AWG wire *[see 210.11(C)(1)]*

Range Circuit: 8000 VA ÷ 240 V = 33 A or a circuit of two 8 AWG conductors and one 10 AWG conductor per 210.19(A)(3)

Minimum Size Feeder Required for Each Dwelling Unit *(see 215.2)*

Calculated Load *(see Article 220)*:	
General Lighting	2,520 VA
Small Appliance (two 20-ampere circuits)	3,000 VA
Subtotal Calculated Load (without ranges)	5,520 VA

Application of Demand Factor *(see Table 220.42)*

First 3000 VA at 100%	3,000 VA
5520 VA − 3000 VA = 2520 VA at 35%	882 VA
Net Calculated Load (without ranges)	3,882 VA
Range Load	8,000 VA
Net Calculated Load (with ranges)	11,882 VA

Size of Each Feeder *(see 215.2)*

For 120/240-V, 3-wire system (without ranges)
Net calculated load of 3882 VA ÷ 240 V = 16.2 A

For 120/240-V, 3-wire system (with ranges)
Net calculated load, 11,882 VA ÷ 240 V = 49.5 A

Feeder Neutral

Lighting and Small Appliance Load	3,882 VA
Range Load: 8000 VA at 70% *(see 220.61)*	5,600 VA
(only for apartments with electric range)	5,600 VA
Net Calculated Load (neutral)	9,482 VA

Calculated Load for Neutral

9482 VA ÷ 240 V= 39.5 A

Minimum Size Feeders Required from Service Equipment to Meter Bank (For 20 Dwelling Units — 10 with Ranges)

Total Calculated Load:	
Lighting and Small Appliance	
20 units × 5520 VA	110,400 VA

Application of Demand Factor	
First 3000 VA at 100%	3,000 VA
110,400 VA − 3000 VA = 107,400 VA at 35%	37,590 VA

Net Calculated Load	40,590 VA
Range Load: 10 ranges (less than 12 kVA) *(see Col. C, Table 220.55)*	25,000 VA

Net Calculated Load (with ranges)	65,590 VA

Net calculated load for 120/240-V, 3-wire system,

$$65{,}590 \text{ VA} \div 240 \text{ V} = 273 \text{ A}$$

Feeder Neutral

Lighting and Small Appliance Load	40,590 VA
Range Load: 25,000 VA at 70% *[see 220.61(B)]*	17,500 VA

Calculated Load (neutral)	58,090 VA

Calculated Load for Neutral

$$58{,}090 \text{ VA} \div 240 \text{ V} = 242 \text{ A}$$

Further Demand Factor *[220.61(B)]*

200 A at 100%	200 A
242 A − 200 A = 42 A at 70%	29 A

Net Calculated Load (neutral)	229 A

Minimum Size Main Feeders (or Service Conductors) Required (Less House Load) (For 40 Dwelling Units — 20 with Ranges)

Total Calculated Load:	
Lighting and Small Appliance Load	
40 units × 5520 VA	220,800 VA

Application of Demand Factor

(from Table 220.42)

First 3000 VA at 100%	3,000 VA
Next 120,000 VA − 3000 VA = 117,000 VA at 35%	40,950 VA
Remainder 220,800 VA − 120,000 VA =	25,200 VA
100,800 VA at 25%	

Net Calculated Load	69,150 VA
Range Load: 20 ranges (less than 12 kVA) *(see Col. C, Table 220.55)*	35,000 VA

Net Calculated Load	104,150 VA
For 120/240-V, 3-wire system	

$$\text{Net calculated load of } 104{,}150 \text{ VA} \div 240 \text{ V} = 434 \text{ A}$$

Feeder Neutral

Lighting and Small Appliance Load	69,150 VA
Range: 35,000 VA at 70%	24,500 VA
[see 220.61(B)]	

Calculated Load (neutral)	93,650 VA

$$93{,}650 \text{ VA} \div 240 \text{ V} = 390 \text{ A}$$

Further Demand Factor *[see 220.61(B)]*

200 A at 100%	200 A
390 A − 200 A = 190 A at 70%	133 A

Net Calculated Load (neutral)	333 A

[See Table 310.16 through Table 310.21, and 310.15(B)(2) and (B)(4).]

Example D4(b) Optional Calculation for Multifamily Dwelling

A multifamily dwelling equipped with electric cooking and space heating or air conditioning has 40 dwelling units.

Meters are in two banks of 20 each plus house metering and individual feeders to each dwelling unit.

Each dwelling unit is equipped with an electric range of 8-kW nameplate rating, four 1.5-kW separately controlled 240-V electric space heaters, and a 2.5-kW, 240-V electric water heater. Assume range, space heater, and water heater kW ratings equivalent to kVA.

A common laundry facility is available to all tenants *[see 210.52(F), Exception No. 1]*.

Area of each dwelling unit is 840 ft².

Calculated Load for Each Dwelling Unit *(see Article 220)*

General Lighting Load:	
840 ft² at 3 VA per ft²	2,520 VA
Electric range	8,000 VA
Electric heat: 6 kVA (or air conditioning if larger)	6,000 VA
Electric water heater	2,500 VA

Minimum Number of Branch Circuits Required for Each Dwelling Unit

General Lighting Load: 2520 VA ÷ 120 V = 21 A or two 15-A, 2-wire circuits, or two 20-A, 2-wire circuits

Small Appliance Load: Two 2-wire circuits of 12 AWG *[see 210.11(C)(1)]*

Range Circuit *(See Table 220.55, Column B)*:

8000 VA × 80% ÷ 240 V = 27 A on a circuit of three 10 AWG conductors per 210.19(A)(3)

Space Heating: 6000 VA ÷ 240 V = 25 A

Number of circuits *(see 210.11)*

Minimum Size Feeder Required for Each Dwelling Unit *(see 215.2)*

Calculated Load *(see Article 220)*:	
General Lighting	2,520 VA
Small Appliance (two 20-A circuits)	3,000 VA

Subtotal Calculated Load (without range and space heating)	5,520 VA

Application of Demand Factor

First 3000 VA at 100%	3,000 VA
5520 VA − 3000 VA = 2520 VA at 35%	882 VA

Net Calculated Load (without range and space heating)	3,882 VA
Range	6,400 VA
Space Heating *(see 220.51)*	6,000 VA
Water Heater	2,500 VA

Net Calculated Load (for individual dwelling unit)	18,782 VA

Size of Each Feeder

For 120/240-V, 3-wire system,
Net calculated load of 18,782 VA ÷ 240 V = 78 A

Feeder Neutral *(see 220.61)*

Lighting and Small Appliance	3,882 VA
Range Load: 6400 VA at 70% *[see 220.61(B)]*	4,480 VA
Space and Water Heating (no neutral): 240 V	0 VA
Net Calculated Load (neutral)	8,362 VA

Calculated Load for Neutral

8362 VA ÷ 240 V = 35 A

Minimum Size Feeder Required from Service Equipment to Meter Bank (For 20 Dwelling Units)

Total Calculated Load:

Lighting and Small Appliance Load 20 units × 5520 VA	110,400 VA
Water and Space Heating Load 20 units × 8500 VA	170,000 VA
Range Load: 20 × 8000 VA	160,000 VA
Net Calculated Load (20 dwelling units)	440,400 VA
Net Calculated Load Using Optional Calculation *(see Table 220.84)* 440,400 VA × 0.38	167,352 VA

167,352 VA ÷ 240 V = 697 A

Minimum Size Main Feeder Required (Less House Load) (For 40 Dwelling Units)

Calculated Load:

Lighting and Small Appliance Load 40 units × 5520 VA	220,800 VA
Water and Space Heating Load 40 units × 8500 VA	340,000 VA
Range: 40 ranges × 8000 VA	320,000 VA
Net Calculated Load (40 dwelling units)	880,800 VA

Net Calculated Load Using Optional Calculation *(see Table 220.84)*

880,800 VA × 0.28 = 246,624 VA
246,624 VA ÷ 240 V = 1028 A

Feeder Neutral Load for Feeder from Service Equipment to Meter Bank (For 20 Dwelling Units)

Lighting and Small Appliance Load 20 units × 5520 VA	110,400 VA
First 3000 VA at 100%	3,000 VA
110,400 VA − 3000 VA = 107,400 VA at 35%	37,590 VA
Net Calculated Load	40,590 VA
20 ranges: 35,000 VA at 70% *[see Table 220.55 and Section 220.61(B)]*	24,500 VA
Total	65,090 VA

65,090 VA ÷ 240 V = 271 A

Further Demand Factor *[see 220.61(B)]*

First 200 A at 100%	200 A
Balance: 271 A − 200 A = 71 A at 70%	50 A
Total	250 amperes

Feeder Neutral Load of Main Feeder (Less House Load) (For 40 Dwelling Units)

Lighting and Small Appliance Load 40 units × 5520 VA	220,800 VA
First 3000 VA at 100%	3,000 VA
Next 120,000 VA − 3000 VA = 117,000 VA at 35%	40,950 VA
Remainder 220,800 VA − 120,000 VA = 100,800 VA at 25%	25,200 VA
Net Calculated Load	69,150 VA
40 ranges: 55,000 VA at 70% *[see Table 220.55 and Section 220.61(B)]*	38,500 VA
Total	107,650 VA

107,650 VA ÷ 240 V = 449 A

Further Demand Factor *[see 220.61(B)]*

First 200 A at 100%	200 A
Balance: 449 − 200 A = 249 A at 70%	174 A
Total	374 A

Example D5(a) Multifamily Dwelling Served at 208Y/120 Volts, Three Phase

All conditions and calculations are the same as for the multifamily dwelling [Example D4(a)] served at 120/240 V, single phase except as follows:
Service to each dwelling unit would be two phase legs and neutral.

Minimum Number of Branch Circuits Required for Each Dwelling Unit *(see 210.11)*

Range Circuit: 8000 VA ÷ 208 V = 38 A or a circuit of two 8 AWG conductors and one 10 AWG conductor per 210.19(A)(3)

Minimum Size Feeder Required for Each Dwelling Unit *(see 215.2)*

For 120/208-V, 3-wire system (without ranges),
Net calculated load of 3882 VA ÷ 2 legs ÷ 120 V/leg = 16.2 A
For 120/208-V, 3-wire system (with ranges),
Net calculated load (range) of 8000 VA ÷ 208 V = 38.5 A
Total load (range + lighting) = 38.5 A + 16.2 A = 54.7 A
Feeder neutral: (range) of 8000 VA × 70% = 5600 VA ÷ 208 V = 26.9 A
Total load: (range + lighting) = 26.9 A + 16.2 A = 43.1 A

Minimum Size Feeders Required from Service Equipment to Meter Bank (For 20 Dwelling Units — 10 with Ranges)

For 208Y/120-V, 3-phase, 4-wire system,
Ranges: Maximum number between any two phase legs = 4
2 × 4 = 8.
Table 220.55 demand = 23,000 VA
Per phase demand = 23,000 VA ÷ 2 = 11,500 VA
Equivalent 3-phase load = 34,500 VA
Net Calculated Load (total):

40,590 VA + 34,500 VA = 75,090 VA
75,090 VA ÷ (208 V)(1.732) = 208.4 A

Feeder Neutral Size

Net Calculated Lighting and Appliance Load & Equivalent Range Load:

40,590 VA + (34,500 VA at 70%) = 64,700 VA

Net Calculated Neutral Load:

64,700 VA ÷ (208 V)(1.732) = 179.7 A

Minimum Size Main Feeder (Less House Load)
(For 40 Dwelling Units — 20 with Ranges)

For 208Y/120-V, 3-phase, 4-wire system,
Ranges:

    Maximum number between any two phase legs = 7
       2 × 7 = 14.
    Table 220.55 demand = 29,000 VA
    Per phase demand = 29,000 VA ÷ 2 = 14,500 VA
    Equivalent 3-phase load = 43,500 VA
    Net Calculated Load (total):

          69,150 VA + 43,500 VA = 112,650 VA
          112,650 VA ÷ (208 V)(1.732) = 312.7 A

Main Feeder Neutral Size:

          69,150 VA + (43,500 VA at 70%) = 99,600 VA
          99,600 VA ÷ (208 V)(1.732) = 276.5 A

Further Demand Factor *(see 220.61)*

200 A at 100%	200.0 A
276.5 A – 200 A = 76.5 A at 70%	53.6 A
Net Calculated Load (neutral)	253.6 A

Example D5(b) Optional Calculation for Multifamily Dwelling Served at 208Y/120 Volts, Three Phase

All conditions and calculations are the same as for Optional Calculation for the Multifamily Dwelling [Example D4(b)] served at 120/240 V, single phase except as follows:

    Service to each dwelling unit would be two phase legs and neutral.

Minimum Number of Branch Circuits Required for Each Dwelling Unit *(see 210.11)*

Range Circuit *(see Table 220.55 Column B):* 8000 VA at 80% ÷ 208 V = 30.7 A or a circuit of two 8 AWG conductors and one 10 AWG conductor per 210.19(A)(3)
Space Heating: 6000 VA ÷ 208 V = 28.8 A
Two 20-ampere, 2-pole circuits required, 12 AWG conductors

Minimum Size Feeder Required for Each Dwelling Unit

120/208-V, 3-wire circuit
    Net calculated load of 18,782 VA ÷ 208 V = 90.3 A
    Net calculated load (lighting line to neutral):

        3882 VA ÷ 2 legs ÷ 120 V per leg = 16.2 amperes

    Line to line = 14,900 VA ÷ 208 V = 71.6 A
    Total load = 16.2 A + 71.6 A = 87.8 A

Minimum Size Feeder Required for Service Equipment to Meter Bank
(For 20 Dwelling Units)

Net Calculated Load

        167,352 VA ÷ (208 V)(1.732) = 464.9 A

Feeder Neutral Load

        65,080 VA ÷ (208 V)(1.732) = 180.65 A

Minimum Size Main Feeder Required (Less House Load)
(For 40 Dwelling Units)

Net Calculated Load

        246,624 VA ÷ (208 V)(1.732) = 684.6 A

Main Feeder Neutral Load

        107,650 VA ÷ (208 V)(1.732) = 298.8 A

Further Demand Factor *[see 220.61(B)]*

200 A at 100%	200.0 A
298.8 A – 200 A = 98.8 A at 70%	69.2 A
Net Calculated Load (neutral)	269.2 A

Example D6 Maximum Demand for Range Loads

Table 220.55, Column C applies to ranges not over 12 kW. The application of Note 1 to ranges over 12 kW (and not over 27 kW) and Note 2 to ranges over 8¾ kW (and not over 27 kW) is illustrated in the following two examples.

A. Ranges All the Same Rating *(see Table 220.55, Note 1)*
Assume 24 ranges, each rated 16 kW.
From Table 220.55, Column C, the maximum demand for 24 ranges of 12-kW rating is 39 kW. 16 kW exceeds 12 kW by 4.
5% × 4 = 20% (5% increase for each kW in excess of 12)
39 kW × 20% = 7.8 kW increase
39 + 7.8 = 46.8 kW (value to be used in selection of feeders)

B. Ranges of Unequal Rating *(see Table 220.55, Note 2)*
Assume 5 ranges, each rated 11 kW; 2 ranges, each rated 12 kW; 20 ranges, each rated 13.5 kW; 3 ranges, each rated 18 kW.

5 ranges × 12 kW =	60 kW	(use 12 kW for range rated less than 12)
2 ranges × 12 kW =	24 kW	
20 ranges × 13.5 kW =	270 kW	
3 ranges × 18 kW =	54 kW	
30 ranges, Total kW =	408 kW	

    408 ÷ 30 ranges = 13.6 kW (average to be used for calculation)

From Table 220.55, Column C, the demand for 30 ranges of 12-kW rating is 15 kW + 30 (1 kW × 30 ranges) = 45 kW. 13.6 kW exceeds 12 kW by 1.6 kW (use 2 kW).

    5% × 2 = 10% (5% increase for each kW in excess of 12 kW)
        45 kW × 10% = 4.5 kW increase
    45 kW + 4.5 kW = 49.5 kW (value to be used in selection of feeders)

Example D8 Motor Circuit Conductors, Overload Protection, and Short-Circuit and Ground-Fault Protection *(see 240.6, 430.6, 430.22, 430.23, 430.24, 430.32, 430.52, and 430.62, Table 430.52 and Table 430.250)*

Determine the minimum required conductor ampacity, the motor overload protection, the branch-circuit short-circuit and ground-fault protection, and the feeder protection, for three induction-type motors on a 480-V, 3-phase feeder, as follows:

    (a) One 25-hp, 460-V, 3-phase, squirrel-cage motor, nameplate full-load current 32 A, Design B, Service Factor 1.15
    (b) Two 30-hp, 460-V, 3-phase, wound-rotor motors, nameplate primary full-load current 38 A, nameplate secondary full-load current 65 A, 40°C rise.

Conductor Ampacity

The full-load current value used to determine the minimum required conductor ampacity is obtained from Table 430.250 *[see 430.6(A)]* for the squirrel-cage motor and the primary of the wound-rotor motors. To obtain the minimum required conductor ampacity, the full-load current is multiplied by 1.25 *[see 430.22 and 430.23(A)]*.

For the 25-hp motor,

$$34 \text{ A} \times 1.25 = 42.5 \text{ A}$$

For the 30-horsepower motors,

$$40 \text{ A} \times 1.25 = 50 \text{ A}$$

$$65 \text{ A} \times 1.25 = 81.25 \text{ A}$$

Motor Overload Protection

Where protected by a separate overload device, the motors are required to have overload protection rated or set to trip at not more than 125% of the nameplate full-load current *[see 430.6(A) and 430.32(A)(1)]*.

For the 25-hp motor,

$$32 \text{ A} \times 1.25 = 40.0 \text{ A}$$

For the 30-hp motors,

$$38 \text{ A} \times 1.25 = 47.5 \text{ A}$$

Where the separate overload device is an overload relay (not a fuse or circuit breaker), and the overload device selected at 125% is not sufficient to start the motor or carry the load, the trip setting is permitted to be increased in accordance with 430.32(C).

Branch-Circuit Short-Circuit and Ground-Fault Protection

The selection of the rating of the protective device depends on the type of protective device selected, in accordance with 430.52 and Table 430.52. The following is for the 25-hp motor.

(a) Nontime-Delay Fuse: The fuse rating is 300% × 34 A = 102 A. The next larger standard fuse is 110 A *[see 240.6 and 430.52(C)(1), Exception No. 1]*. If the motor will not start with a 110-A nontime-delay fuse, the fuse rating is permitted to be increased to 125 A because this rating does not exceed 400% *[see 430.52(C)(1), Exception No. 2(a)]*.

(b) Time-Delay Fuse: The fuse rating is 175% × 34 A = 59.5 A. The next larger standard fuse is 60 A *[see 240.6 and 430.52(C)(1), Exception No. 1]*. If the motor will not start with a 60-A time-delay fuse, the fuse rating is permitted to be increased to 70 A because this rating does not exceed 225% *[see 430.52(C)(1), Exception No. 2(b)]*.

Feeder Short-Circuit and Ground-Fault Protection

The rating of the feeder protective device is based on the sum of the largest branch-circuit protective device (example is 110 A) plus the sum of the full-load currents of the other motors, or 110 A + 40 A + 40 A = 190 A. The nearest standard fuse that does not exceed this value is 175 A *[see 240.6 and 430.62(A)]*.

Example D9 Feeder Ampacity Determination for Generator Field Control *[see 215.2, 430.24, 430.24 Exception No. 1, 620.13, 620.14, 620.61, and Table 430.22(E) and 620.14]*

Determine the conductor ampacity for a 460-V 3-phase, 60-Hz ac feeder supplying a group of six elevators. The 460-V ac drive motor nameplate rating of the largest MG set for one elevator is 40 hp and 52 A, and the remaining elevators each have a 30-hp, 40-A, ac drive motor rating for their MG sets. In addition to a motor controller, each elevator has a separate motion/operation controller rated 10 A continuous to operate microprocessors, relays, power supplies, and the elevator car door operator. The MG sets are rated continuous.

Conductor Ampacity. Conductor ampacity is determined as follows:

(a) Per 620.13(D) and 620.61(B)(1), use Table 430.22(E), for intermittent duty (elevators). For intermittent duty using a continuous rated motor, the percentage of nameplate current rating to be used is 140%.

(b) For the 30-hp ac drive motor,

$$140\% \times 40 \text{ A} = 56 \text{ A}.$$

(c) For the 40-hp ac drive motor,

$$140\% \times 52 \text{ A} = 73 \text{ A}.$$

(d) The total conductor ampacity is the sum of all the motor currents:

$$(1 \text{ motor} \times 73 \text{ A}) + (5 \text{ motors} \times 56 \text{ A}) = 353 \text{ A}$$

(e) Per 620.14 and Table 620.14, the conductor (feeder) ampacity would be permitted to be reduced by the use of a demand factor. Constant loads are not included *(see 620.14, FPN)*. For six elevators, the demand factor is 0.79. The feeder diverse ampacity is, therefore, 0.79 × 353 A = 279 A.

(f) Per 430.24 and 215.3, the controller continuous current is 125% × 10 A = 12.5 A

(g) The total feeder ampacity is the sum of the diverse current and all the controller continuous current.

$$I_{\text{total}} = 279 \text{ A} + (6 \text{ elevators} \times 12.5 \text{ A}) = 354 \text{ A}$$

(h) This ampacity would be permitted to be used to select the wire size. See Figure D9.

Figure D9 Generator Field Control.

Example D10 Feeder Ampacity Determination for Adjustable Speed Drive Control *[see 215.2, 430.24, 620.13, 620.14, 620.61, and Table 430.22(E)*

Determine the conductor ampacity for a 460-V, 3-phase, 60-Hz ac feeder supplying a group of six identical elevators. The system is adjustable-speed SCR dc drive. The power transformers are external to the drive (motor controller) cabinet. Each elevator has a separate motion/operation controller connected to the load side of the main line disconnect switch rated 10 A continuous to operate microprocessors, relays, power supplies, and the elevator car door operator. Each transformer is rated 95 kVA with an efficiency of 90%.

Conductor Ampacity

Conductor ampacity is determined as follows:

(a) Calculate the nameplate rating of the transformer:

$$I = \frac{95 \text{ kVA} \times 1000}{\sqrt{3} \times 460 \text{ V} \times 0.90_{\text{eff.}}} = 133 \text{ A}$$

(b) Per 620.13(D), for six elevators, the total conductor ampacity is the sum of all the currents.

$$6 \text{ elevators} \times 133 \text{ A} = 798 \text{ A}$$

(c) Per 620.14 and Table 620.14, the conductor (feeder) ampacity would be permitted to be reduced by the use of a demand factor. Constant loads are not included *(see 620.13, FPN No. 2)*. For six elevators, the demand factor is 0.79. The feeder diverse ampacity is, therefore, $0.79 \times 798\ A = 630\ A$.

(d) Per 430.24 and 215.3, the controller continuous current is $125\% \times 10\ A = 12.5\ A$.

(e) The total feeder ampacity is the sum of the diverse current and all the controller constant current.

$$I_{total} = 630\ A + (6\ \text{elevators} \times 12.5\ A) = 705\ A$$

(f) This ampacity would be permitted to be used to select the wire size.

See Figure D10.

Figure D10 Adjustable Speed Drive Control.

Example D11 Mobile Home *(see 550.18)*

A mobile home floor is 70 ft by 10 ft and has two small appliance circuits; a 1000-VA, 240-V heater; a 200-VA, 120-V exhaust fan; a 400-VA, 120-V dishwasher; and a 7000-VA electric range.

Lighting and Small Appliance Load

Lighting (70 ft × 10 ft × 3 VA per ft²)	2,100 VA
Small appliance (1500 VA × 2 circuits)	3,000 VA
Laundry (1500 VA × 1 circuit)	1,500 VA
Subtotal	6,600 VA
First 3000 VA at 100%	3,000 VA
Remainder (6600 VA – 3000 VA = 3600 VA) × 35%	1,260 VA
Total	4,260 VA

$$4260\ VA \div 240\ V = 17.75\ A\ \text{per leg}$$

Amperes per Leg	Leg A	Leg B
Lighting and appliances	17.75	17.75
Heater (1000 VA ÷ 240 V)	4.20	4.20
Fan (200 VA × 125% ÷ 120 V)	2.08	—
Dishwasher (400 VA ÷ 120 V)	—	3.30
Range (7000 VA × 0.8 ÷ 240 V)	23.30	23.30
Total amperes per leg	47.33	48.55

Based on the higher current calculated for either leg, a minimum 50-A supply cord would be required.

For SI units, 0.093 m² = 1 ft² and 0.3048 m = 1 ft.

Example D12 Park Trailer *(see 552.47)*

A park trailer floor is 40 ft by 10 ft and has two small appliance circuits, a 1000-VA, 240-V heater, a 200-VA, 120-V exhaust fan, a 400-VA, 120-V dishwasher, and a 7000-VA electric range.

Lighting and Small Appliance Load

Lighting (40 ft × 10 ft × 3 VA per ft²)	1,200 VA
Small appliance (1500 VA × 2 circuits)	3,000 VA
Laundry (1500 VA × 1 circuit)	1,500 VA
Subtotal	5,700 VA
First 3000 VA at 100%	3,000 VA
Remainder (5700 VA – 3000 VA = 2700 VA) × 35%	945 VA
Total	3,945 VA

$$3945\ VA \div 240\ V = 16.44\ A\ \text{per leg}$$

Amperes per Leg	Leg A	Leg B
Lighting and appliances	16.44	16.44
Heater (1000 VA ÷ 240 V)	4.20	4.20
Fan (200 VA × 125% ÷ 120 V)	2.08	—
Dishwasher (400 VA ÷ 120 V)	—	3.3
Range (7000 VA × 0.8 ÷ 240 V)	23.30	23.30
Totals	46.02	47.24

Based on the higher current calculated for either leg, a minimum 50-A supply cord would be required.

For SI units, 0.093 m² = 1 ft² and 0.3048 m = 1 ft.

Annex E   Types of Construction

This annex is not a part of the requirements of this NFPA document but is included for informational purposes only.

The five different types of construction can be summarized briefly as follows (see also Table E.2):

Type I is a Fire-Resistive construction type. All structural elements and most interior elements are required to be noncombustible. Interior, nonbearing partitions are permitted to be 1 or 2 hour rated. For nearly all occupancy types, Type I construction can be of unlimited height.

Type II construction has 3 categories, Fire-Resistive, One-Hour Rated and Non-Rated. The number of stories permitted for multifamily dwellings varies from 2 for Non-Rated and 4 for One-Hour Rated to 12 for Fire-Resistive construction.

Type III construction has two categories, One-Hour Rated and Non-Rated. Both categories require the structural framework and exterior walls to be of noncombustible material. One-Hour Rated construction requires all interior partitions to be one-hour rated. Non-Rated construction allows nonbearing interior partitions to be of non-rated construction. The maximum permitted number of stories for multifamily dwellings and other structures is 2 for Non-Rated and 4 for One-Hour Rated.

Type IV is a single construction category which provides for heavy timber construction. Both the structural

Table E.1 Fire Resistance Ratings (in hours) for Type I through Type V Construction

	Type I		Type II			Type III		Type IV	Type V	
	443	332	222	111	000	211	200	2HH	111	000
Exterior Bearing Walls –										
Supporting more than one floor, columns, or other bearing walls......	4	3	2	1	0^1	2	2	2	1	0^1
Supporting one floor only....................	4	3	2	1	0^1	2	2	2	1	0^1
Supporting a roof only..........................	4	3	1	1	0^1	2	2	2	1	0^1
Interior Bearing Walls –										
Supporting more than one floor, columns, or other bearing walls......	4	3	2	1	0	1	0	2	1	0
Supporting one floor only....................	3	2	2	1	0	1	0	1	1	0
Supporting roofs only..........................	3	2	1	1	0	1	0	1	1	0
Columns –										
Supporting more than one floor, columns, or other bearing walls......	4	3	2	1	0	1	0	H^2	1	0
Supporting one floor only....................	3	2	2	1	0	1	0	H^2	1	0
Supporting roofs only..........................	3	2	1	1	0	1	0	H^2	1	0
Beams, Girders, Trusses & Arches –										
Supporting more than one floor, columns, or other bearing walls......	4	3	2	1	0	1	0	H^2	1	0
Supporting one floor only....................	3	2	2	1	0	1	0	H^2	1	0
Supporting roofs only..........................	3	2	1	1	0	1	0	H^2	1	0
Floor Construction	3	2	2	1	0	1	0	H^2	1	0
Roof Construction	2	$1^1/_2$	1	1	0	1	0	H^2	1	0
Exterior Nonbearing Walls[3]	0^1	0^1	0^1	0^1	0^1	0^1	0^1	0^1	0^1	0^1

        Those members that shall be permitted to be of approved combustible material.

Source: Table 3.1 from NFPA 220, *Standard on Building Construction,* 1999.
[1] See A-3-1 in NFPA 220.
[2] "H" indicates heavy timber members; see text for requirements.
[3] Exterior nonbearing walls meeting the conditions of acceptance of NFPA 285, *Standard Method of Test for the Evaluation of Flammability Characteristics of Exterior Non-Load-Bearing Wall Assemblies Containing Combustible Components Using the Intermediate-Scale, Multistory Test Apparatus,* shall be permitted to be used.

Table E.2 Maximum Number of Stories for Types V, IV, and III Construction

Construction Type	Maximum Number of Stories Permitted
V Non-Rated	2
V Non-Rated, Sprinklered	3
V One-Hour Rated	3
V One-Hour Rated, Sprinklered	4
IV Heavy Timber	4
IV Heavy Timber, Sprinklered	5
III Non-Rated	2
III Non-Rated, Sprinklered	3
III One-Hour Rated	4
III One-Hour Rated, Sprinklered	5

framework and the exterior walls are required to be noncombustible except that wood members of certain minimum sizes are allowed. This construction type is seldom used for multifamily dwellings but, if used, would be permitted to be 4 stories high.

Type V construction has two categories, One-Hour Rated and Non-Rated. One-Hour Rated construction requires a minimum of one-hour rated construction throughout the building. Non-rated construction allows non rated interior partitions with certain restrictions. The maximum permitted number of stories for multifamily dwellings and other structures is 2 for Non-Rated and 3 for One-Hour Rated.

Annex F   Cross-Reference Tables

This annex is not a part of the requirements of this NFPA document but is included for informational purposes only.

Table F.1 Chapter 3 Cross-Reference from the 2005 *NEC* to the 2002 *NEC* to the 1999 *NEC*

2005 *NEC*	2002 *NEC*	1999 *NEC*	Article Title
300	300	300	Wiring Methods
310	310	310	Conductors for General Wiring
312	312	373	Cabinets, Cutout Boxes, and Meter Socket Enclosures
314	314	370	Outlet, Device, Pull, and Junction Boxes; Conduit Bodies; Fittings; and Manholes
320	320	333	Armored Cable: Type AC
322	322	363	Flat Cable Assemblies: Type FC
324	324	328	Flat Conductor Cable: Type FCC
326	326	325	Integrated Gas Spacer Cable: Type IGS
328	328	326	Medium Voltage Cable: Type MV
330	330	334	Metal-Clad Cable: Type MC
332	332	330	Mineral-Insulated, Metal-Sheathed Cable: Type MI
334	334	336	Nonmetallic-Sheathed Cable: Types NM, NMC, and NMS
336	336	340	Power and Control Tray Cable: Type TC
338	338	338	Service-Entrance Cable: Types SE and USE
340	340	339	Underground Feeder and Branch-Circuit Cable: Type UF
342	342	345	Intermediate Metal Conduit: Type IMC
344	344	346	Rigid Metal Conduit: Type RMC
348	348	350	Flexible Metal Conduit: Type FMC
350	350	351 (Part A)	Liquidtight Flexible Metal Conduit: Type LFMC
352	352	347	Rigid Nonmetallic Conduit: Type RNC
353 (New)	—	—	High Density Polyethylene Conduit: Type HDPE Conduit
354	354	343	Nonmetallic Underground Conduit with Conductors: Type NUCC
356	356	351 (Part B)	Liquidtight Flexible Nonmetallic Conduit: Type LFNC
358	358	348	Electrical Metallic Tubing: Type EMT
360	360	349	Flexible Metallic Tubing: Type FMT
362	362	331	Electrical Nonmetallic Tubing: Type ENT
366	366	374	Auxiliary Gutters
368	368	364	Busways
370	370	365	Cablebus
372	372	358	Cellular Concrete Floor Raceways
374	374	356	Cellular Metal Floor Raceways
376	376	362 (Part A)	Metal Wireways
378	378	362 (Part B)	Nonmetallic Wireways
380	380	353	Multioutlet Assembly
382	382	342	Nonmetallic Extensions
384	384	352 (Part C)	Strut-Type Channel Raceway
386	386	352 (Part A)	Surface Metal Raceways
388	388	352 (Part B)	Surface Nonmetallic Raceways
390	390	354	Underfloor Raceways
392	392	318	Cable Trays
394	394	324	Concealed Knob-and-Tube Wiring
396	396	321	Messenger Supported Wiring
398	398	320	Open Wiring on Insulators
404	404	380	Switches
408	408	384	Switchboards and Panelboards
590	527	305	Temporary Installations

Table F.2 Chapter 3 Cross-Reference, 1999 – 2002 – 2005 *NEC*

1999 *NEC*	2002 *NEC*	2005 *NEC*	Article Title
300	300	300	Wiring Methods
305	527	590	Temporary Installations
310	310	310	Conductors for General Wiring
318	392	392	Cable Trays
320	398	398	Open Wiring on Insulators
321	396	396	Messenger Supported Wiring
324	394	394	Concealed Knob-and-Tube Wiring
325	326	326	Integrated Gas Spacer Cable: Type IGS
326	328	328	Medium Voltage Cable: Type MV
328	324	324	Flat Conductor Cable: Type FCC
330	332	332	Mineral-Insulated, Metal-Sheathed Cable: Type MI
331	362	362	Electrical Nonmetallic Tubing: Type ENT
333	320	320	Armored Cable: Type AC
334	330	330	Metal-Clad Cable: Type MC
336	334	334	Nonmetallic-Sheathed Cable: Types NM, NMC, and NMS
338	338	338	Service-Entrance Cable: Types SE and USE
339	340	340	Underground Feeder and Branch-Circuit Cable: Type UF
340	336	336	Power and Control Tray Cable: Type TC
342	382	382	Nonmetallic Extensions
343	354	354	Nonmetallic Underground Conduit with Conductors: Type NUCC
345	342	342	Intermediate Metal Conduit: Type IMC
346	344	344	Rigid Metal Conduit: Type RMC
347	352	352	Rigid Nonmetallic Conduit: Type RNC
348	358	358	Electrical Metallic Tubing: Type EMT
349	360	360	Flexible Metallic Tubing: Type FMT
350	348	348	Flexible Metal Conduit: Type FMC
351 (Part A)	350	350	Liquidtight Flexible Metal Conduit: Type LFMC
351 (Part B)	356	356	Liquidtight Flexible Nonmetallic Conduit: Type LFNC
352 (Part C)	384	384	Strut-Type Channel Raceway
352 (Part A)	386	386	Surface Metal Raceways
352 (Part B)	388	388	Surface Nonmetallic Raceways
353	380	380	Multioutlet Assembly
—	—	353 (New)	High Density Polyethylene Conduit: Type HDPE Conduit
354	390	390	Underfloor Raceways
356	374	374	Cellular Metal Floor Raceways
358	372	372	Cellular Concrete Floor Raceways
362 (Part A)	376	376	Metal Wireways
362 (Part B)	378	378	Nonmetallic Wireways
363	322	322	Flat Cable Assemblies: Type FC
364	368	368	Busways
365	370	370	Cablebus
370	314	314	Outlet, Device, Pull, and Junction Boxes; Conduit Bodies; Fittings; and Manholes
373	312	312	Cabinets, Cutout Boxes, and Meter Socket Enclosures
374	366	366	Auxiliary Gutters
380	404	404	Switches
384	408	408	Switchboards and Panelboards

Table F.3 Chapter 3 Alphabetical Cross-Reference, 2005 – 2002 – 1999 *NEC*

Article Title	2005 *NEC*	2002 *NEC*	1999 *NEC*
Armored Cable: Type 320 AC	320	320	333
Auxiliary Gutters	366	366	374
Busways	368	368	364
Cabinets, Cutout Boxes, and Meter Socket Enclosures	312	312	373
Cable Trays	392	392	318
Cablebus	370	370	365
Cellular Concrete Floor Raceways	372	372	358
Cellular Metal Floor Raceways	374	374	356
Concealed Knob-and-Tube Wiring	394	394	324
Conductors for General Wiring	310	310	310
Electrical Metallic Tubing: Type EMT	358	358	348
Electrical Nonmetallic Tubing: Type ENT	362	362	331
Flat Cable Assemblies: Type FC	322	322	363
Flat Conductor Cable: Type FCC	324	324	328
Flexible Metal Conduit: Type FMC	348	348	350
Flexible Metallic Tubing: Type FMT	360	360	349
High Density Polyethylene Conduit: Type HDPE Conduit	353 (New)	—	—
Integrated Gas Spacer Cable: Type IGS	326	326	325
Intermediate Metal Conduit: Type IMC	342	342	345
Liquidtight Flexible Metal Conduit: Type LFMC	350	350	351 (Part A)
Liquidtight Flexible Nonmetallic Conduit: Type LFNC	356	356	351 (Part B)
Medium Voltage Cable: Type MV	328	328	326
Messenger Supported Wiring	396	396	321
Metal Wireways	376	376	362 (Part A)
Metal-Clad Cable: Type MC	330	330	334
Mineral-Insulated, Metal-Sheathed Cable: Type MI	332	332	330
Multioutlet Assembly	380	380	353
Nonmetallic Extensions	382	382	342
Nonmetallic Underground Conduit with Conductors: Type NUCC	354	354	343
Nonmetallic Wireways	378	378	362 (Part B)
Nonmetallic-Sheathed Cable: Types NM, NMC, and NMS	334	334	336
Open Wiring on Insulators	398	398	320
Outlet, Device, Pull, and Junction Boxes; Conduit Bodies; Fittings; and Manholes	314	314	370
Power and Control Tray Cable: Type TC	336	336	340
Rigid Metal Conduit: Type RMC	344	344	346
Rigid Nonmetallic Conduit: Type RNC	352	352	347
Service-Entrance Cable: Types SE and USE	338	338	338
Strut-Type Channel Raceway	384	384	352 (Part C)
Surface Metal Raceways	386	386	352 (Part A)
Surface Nonmetallic Raceways	388	388	352 (Part B)
Switchboards and Panelboards	408	408	384
Switches	404	404	380
Temporary Installations	590	527	305
Underfloor Raceways	390	390	354
Underground Feeder and Branch-Circuit Cable: Type UF	340	340	339
Wiring Methods	300	300	300

Annex G   Administration and Enforcement

Annex G is not a part of the requirements of this NFPA document and is included for informational purposes only. This annex is informative unless specifically adopted by the local jurisdiction adopting the National Electrical Code®.

80.1 Scope. The following functions are covered:

(1) The inspection of electrical installations as covered by 90.2

(2) The investigation of fires caused by electrical installations

(3) The review of construction plans, drawings, and specifications for electrical systems

(4) The design, alteration, modification, construction, maintenance, and testing of electrical systems and equipment

(5) The regulation and control of electrical installations at special events including but not limited to exhibits, trade shows, amusement parks, and other similar special occupancies

80.2 Definitions.

Authority Having Jurisdiction. The organization, office, or individual responsible for approving equipment, materials, an installation, or a procedure.

Chief Electrical Inspector. An electrical inspector who either is the authority having jurisdiction or is designated by the authority having jurisdiction and is responsible for administering the requirements of this *Code.*

Electrical Inspector. An individual meeting the requirements of 80.27 and authorized to perform electrical inspections.

80.3 Purpose. The purpose of this article shall be to provide requirements for administration and enforcement of the *National Electrical Code.*

80.5 Adoption. Article 80 shall not apply unless specifically adopted by the local jurisdiction adopting the *National Electrical Code.*

80.7 Title. The title of this *Code* shall be NFPA 70, *National Electrical Code®*, of the National Fire Protection Association. The short title of this *Code* shall be the *NEC®.*

80.9 Application.

(A) New Installations. This *Code* applies to new installations. Buildings with construction permits dated after adoption of this *Code* shall comply with its requirements.

(B) Existing Installations. Existing electrical installations that do not comply with the provisions of this *Code* shall be permitted to be continued in use unless the authority having jurisdiction determines that the lack of conformity with this *Code* presents an imminent danger to occupants. Where changes are required for correction of hazards, a reasonable amount of time shall be given for compliance, depending on the degree of the hazard.

(C) Additions, Alterations, or Repairs. Additions, alterations, or repairs to any building, structure, or premises shall conform to that required of a new building without requiring the existing building to comply with all the requirements of this *Code.* Additions, alterations, installations, or repairs shall not cause an existing building to become unsafe or to adversely affect the performance of the building as determined by the authority having jurisdiction. Electrical wiring added to an existing service, feeder, or branch circuit shall not result in an installation that violates the provisions of the *Code* in force at the time the additions are made.

80.11 Occupancy of Building or Structure.

(A) New Construction. No newly constructed building shall be occupied in whole or in part in violation of the provisions of this *Code.*

(B) Existing Buildings. Existing buildings that are occupied at the time of adoption of this *Code* shall be permitted to remain in use provided the following conditions apply:

(1) The occupancy classification remains unchanged

(2) There exists no condition deemed hazardous to life or property that would constitute an imminent danger

80.13 Authority. Where used in this article, the term *authority having jurisdiction* shall include the chief electrical inspector or other individuals designated by the governing body. This *Code* shall be administered and enforced by the authority having jurisdiction designated by the governing authority as follows.

(1) The authority having jurisdiction shall be permitted to render interpretations of this *Code* in order to provide clarification to its requirements, as permitted by 90.4.

(2) When the use of any electrical equipment or its installations is found to be dangerous to human life or property, the authority having jurisdiction shall be empowered to have the premises disconnected from its source of electric supply, as established by the Board. When such equipment or installation has been so condemned or disconnected, a notice shall be placed thereon listing the

causes for the condemnation, the disconnection, or both and the penalty under 80.23 for the unlawful use thereof. Written notice of such condemnation or disconnection and the causes therefor shall be given within 24 hours to the owners, the occupant, or both, of such building, structure, or premises. It shall be unlawful for any person to remove said notice, to reconnect the electric equipment to its source of electric supply, or to use or permit to be used electric power in any such electric equipment until such causes for the condemnation or disconnection have been remedied to the satisfaction of the inspection authorities.

(3) The authority having jurisdiction shall be permitted to delegate to other qualified individuals such powers as necessary for the proper administration and enforcement of this *Code*.

(4) Police, fire, and other enforcement agencies shall have authority to render necessary assistance in the enforcement of this *Code* when requested to do so by the authority having jurisdiction.

(5) The authority having jurisdiction shall be authorized to inspect, at all reasonable times, any building or premises for dangerous or hazardous conditions or equipment as set forth in this *Code*. The authority having jurisdiction shall be permitted to order any person(s) to remove or remedy such dangerous or hazardous condition or equipment. Any person(s) failing to comply with such order shall be in violation of this *Code*.

(6) Where the authority having jurisdiction deems that conditions hazardous to life and property exist, he or she shall be permitted to require that such hazardous conditions in violation of this *Code* be corrected.

(7) To the full extent permitted by law, any authority having jurisdiction engaged in inspection work shall be authorized at all reasonable times to enter and examine any building, structure, or premises for the purpose of making electrical inspections. Before entering a premises, the authority having jurisdiction shall obtain the consent of the occupant thereof or obtain a court warrant authorizing entry for the purpose of inspection except in those instances where an emergency exists. As used in this section, *emergency* means circumstances that the authority having jurisdiction knows, or has reason to believe, exist and that reasonably can constitute immediate danger to persons or property.

(8) Persons authorized to enter and inspect buildings, structures, and premises as herein set forth shall be identified by proper credentials issued by this governing authority.

(9) Persons shall not interfere with an authority having jurisdiction carrying out any duties or functions prescribed by this *Code*.

(10) Persons shall not use a badge, uniform, or other credentials to impersonate the authority having jurisdiction.

(11) The authority having jurisdiction shall be permitted to investigate the cause, origin, and circumstances of any fire, explosion, or other hazardous condition.

(12) The authority having jurisdiction shall be permitted to require plans and specifications to ensure compliance with this *Code*.

(13) Whenever any installation subject to inspection prior to use is covered or concealed without having first been inspected, the authority having jurisdiction shall be permitted to require that such work be exposed for inspection. The authority having jurisdiction shall be notified when the installation is ready for inspection and shall conduct the inspection within ___ days.

(14) The authority having jurisdiction shall be permitted to order the immediate evacuation of any occupied building deemed unsafe when such building has hazardous conditions that present imminent danger to building occupants.

(15) The authority having jurisdiction shall be permitted to waive specific requirements in this *Code* or permit alternative methods where it is assured that equivalent objectives can be achieved by establishing and maintaining effective safety. Technical documentation shall be submitted to the authority having jurisdiction to demonstrate equivalency and that the system, method, or device is approved for the intended purpose.

(16) Each application for a waiver of a specific electrical requirement shall be filed with the authority having jurisdiction and shall be accompanied by such evidence, letters, statements, results of tests, or other supporting information as required to justify the request. The authority having jurisdiction shall keep a record of actions on such applications, and a signed copy of the authority having jurisdiction's decision shall be provided for the applicant.

80.15 Electrical Board.

(A) Creation of the Electrical Board. There is hereby created the Electrical Board of the _____ of _____, hereinafter designated as the Board.

(B) Appointments. Board members shall be appointed by the Governor with the advice and consent of the Senate (or by the Mayor with the advice and consent of the Council, or the equivalent).

(1) Members of the Board shall be chosen in a manner to reflect a balanced representation of individuals or organizations. The Chair of the Board shall be elected by the Board membership.

(2) The Chief Electrical Inspector in the jurisdiction adopting this Article authorized in (B)(3)(a) shall be the non-voting secretary of the Board. Where the Chief Electrical Inspector of a local municipality serves a Board at a state level, he or she shall be permitted to serve as a voting member of the Board.

(3) The board shall consist of not fewer than five voting members. Board members shall be selected from the following:

   a. Chief Electrical Inspector from a local government (for State Board only)
   b. An electrical contractor operating in the jurisdiction
   c. A licensed professional engineer engaged primarily in the design or maintenance of electrical installations
   d. A journeyman electrician

(4) Additional membership shall be selected from the following:

   a. A master (supervising) electrician
   b. The Fire Marshal (or Fire Chief)
   c. A representative of the property/casualty insurance industry
   d. A representative of an electric power utility operating in the jurisdiction
   e. A representative of electrical manufacturers primarily and actively engaged in producing materials, fittings, devices, appliances, luminaires (fixtures), or apparatus used as part of or in connection with electrical installations
   f. A member of the labor organization that represents the primary electrical workforce
   g. A member from the public who is not affiliated with any other designated group
   h. A representative of a telecommunications utility operating in the jurisdiction

(C) Terms. Of the members first appointed, _____ shall be appointed for a term of 1 year, _____ for a term of 2 years, _____ for a term of 3 years, and _____ for a term of 4 years, and thereafter each appointment shall be for a term of 4 years or until a successor is appointed. The Chair of the Board shall be appointed for a term not to exceed _____ years.

(D) Compensation. Each appointed member shall receive the sum of _____dollars ($_____) for each day during which the member attends a meeting of the Board and, in addition thereto, shall be reimbursed for direct lodging, travel, and meal expenses as covered by policies and procedures established by the jurisdiction.

(E) Quorum. A quorum as established by the Board operating procedures shall be required to conduct Board business. The Board shall hold such meetings as necessary to carry out the purposes of Article 80. The Chair or a majority of the members of the Board shall have the authority to call meetings of the Board.

(F) Duties. It shall be the duty of the Board to:

(1) Adopt the necessary rules and regulations to administer and enforce Article 80.

(2) Establish qualifications of electrical inspectors.

(3) Revoke or suspend the recognition of any inspector's certificate for the jurisdiction.

(4) After advance notice of the public hearings and the execution of such hearings, as established by law, the Board is authorized to establish and update the provisions for the safety of electrical installations to conform with the current edition of the *National Electrical Code* (NFPA 70) and other nationally recognized safety standards for electrical installations.

(5) Establish procedures for recognition of electrical safety standards and acceptance of equipment conforming to these standards.

(G) Appeals.

(1) Review of Decisions. Any person, firm, or corporation may register an appeal with the Board for a review of any decision of the Chief Electrical Inspector or of any Electrical Inspector, provided that such appeal is made in writing within fifteen (15) days after such person, firm, or corporation shall have been notified. Upon receipt of such appeal, said Board shall, if requested by the person making the appeal, hold a public hearing and proceed to determine whether the action of the Board, or of the Chief Electrical Inspector, or of the Electrical Inspector complies with this law and, within fifteen (15) days after receipt of the appeal or after holding the hearing, shall make a decision in accordance with its findings.

(2) Conditions. Any person shall be permitted to appeal a decision of the authority having jurisdiction to the Board when it is claimed that any one or more of the following conditions exist:

   a. The true intent of the codes or ordinances described in this *Code* has been incorrectly interpreted.
   b. The provisions of the codes or ordinances do not fully apply.
   c. A decision is unreasonable or arbitrary as it applies to alternatives or new materials.

(3) Submission of Appeals. A written appeal, outlining the *Code* provision from which relief is sought and the remedy proposed, shall be submitted to the authority having jurisdiction within 15 calendar days of notification of violation.

(H) Meetings and Records. Meetings and records of the Board shall conform to the following:

(1) Meetings of the Board shall be open to the public as required by law.

(2) Records of meetings of the Board shall be available for review during normal business hours, as required by law.

80.17 Records and Reports. The authority having jurisdiction shall retain records in accordance with (A) and (B).

(A) Retention. The authority having jurisdiction shall keep a record of all electrical inspections, including the date of such inspections and a summary of any violations found to exist, the date of the services of notices, and a record of the final disposition of all violations. All required records shall be maintained until their usefulness has been served or as otherwise required by law.

(B) Availability. A record of examinations, approvals, and variances granted shall be maintained by the authority having jurisdiction and shall be available for public review as prescribed by law during normal business hours.

80.19 Permits and Approvals. Permits and approvals shall conform to (A) through (H).

(A) Application.

(1) Activity authorized by a permit issued under this *Code* shall be conducted by the permittee or the permittee's agents or employees in compliance with all requirements of this *Code* applicable thereto and in accordance with the approved plans and specifications. No permit issued under this *Code* shall be interpreted to justify a violation of any provision of this *Code* or any other applicable law or regulation. Any addition or alteration of approved plans or specifications shall be approved in advance by the authority having jurisdiction, as evidenced by the issuance of a new or amended permit.

(2) A copy of the permit shall be posted or otherwise readily accessible at each work site or carried by the permit holder as specified by the authority having jurisdiction.

(B) Content. Permits shall be issued by the authority having jurisdiction and shall bear the name and signature of the authority having jurisdiction or that of the authority having jurisdiction's designated representative. In addition, the permit shall indicate the following:

(1) Operation or activities for which the permit is issued

(2) Address or location where the operation or activity is to be conducted

(3) Name and address of the permittee

(4) Permit number and date of issuance

(5) Period of validity of the permit

(6) Inspection requirements

(C) Issuance of Permits. The authority having jurisdiction shall be authorized to establish and issue permits, certificates, notices, and approvals, or orders pertaining to electrical safety hazards pursuant to 80.23, except that no permit shall be required to execute any of the classes of electrical work specified in the following:

(1) Installation or replacement of equipment such as lamps and of electric utilization equipment approved for connection to suitable permanently installed receptacles. Replacement of flush or snap switches, fuses, lamp sockets, and receptacles, and other minor maintenance and repair work, such as replacing worn cords and tightening connections on a wiring device

(2) The process of manufacturing, testing, servicing, or repairing electric equipment or apparatus

(D) Annual Permits. In lieu of an individual permit for each installation or alteration, an annual permit shall, upon application, be issued to any person, firm, or corporation regularly employing one or more employees for the installation, alteration, and maintenance of electric equipment in or on buildings or premises owned or occupied by the applicant for the permit. Upon application, an electrical contractor as agent for the owner or tenant shall be issued an annual permit. The applicant shall keep records of all work done, and such records shall be transmitted periodically to the Electrical Inspector.

(E) Fees. Any political subdivision that has been provided for electrical inspection in accordance with the provisions of Article 80 may establish fees that shall be paid by the applicant for a permit before the permit is issued.

(F) Inspection and Approvals.

(1) Upon the completion of any installation of electrical equipment that has been made under a permit other than an annual permit, it shall be the duty of the person, firm, or corporation making the installation to notify the Electrical Inspector having jurisdiction, who shall inspect the work within a reasonable time.

(2) Where the Inspector finds the installation to be in conformity with the statutes of all applicable local ordinances and all rules and regulations, the Inspector shall issue to the person, firm, or corporation making the installation a certificate of approval, with duplicate copy for delivery to the owner, authorizing the connection to the supply of electricity and shall send written notice of such authorization to the supplier of electric service. When a certificate of temporary approval is issued authorizing the connection of an installation, such certificates shall be issued to expire at a time to be stated therein and shall be revocable by the Electrical Inspector for cause.

(3) When any portion of the electrical installation within the jurisdiction of an Electrical Inspector is to be hidden from view by the permanent placement of parts of the building, the person, firm, or corporation installing the equipment shall notify the Electrical Inspector, and such equipment shall not be concealed until it has been approved by the Electrical Inspector or until _____ days have elapsed from the time of such notification, provided that on large installations, where the concealment of equipment proceeds continuously, the person, firm, or corporation installing the equipment shall give the Electrical Inspector due notice in advance, and inspections shall be made periodically during the progress of the work.

(4) At regular intervals, the Electrical Inspector having jurisdiction shall visit all buildings and premises where work may be done under annual permits and shall inspect all electric equipment installed under such permits since the date of the previous inspection. The Electrical Inspector shall issue a certificate of approval for such work as is found to be in conformity with the provisions of Article 80 and all applicable ordinances, orders, rules, and regulations, after payments of all required fees.

(5) If, upon inspection, any installation is found not to be fully in conformity with the provisions of Article 80, and all applicable ordinances, rules, and regulations, the Inspector making the inspection shall at once forward to the person, firm, or corporation making the installation a written notice stating the defects that have been found to exist.

(G) Revocation of Permits. Revocation of permits shall conform to the following:

(1) The authority having jurisdiction shall be permitted to revoke a permit or approval issued if any violation of this *Code* is found upon inspection or in case there have been any false statements or misrepresentations submitted in the application or plans on which the permit or approval was based.

(2) Any attempt to defraud or otherwise deliberately or knowingly design, install, service, maintain, operate, sell, represent for sale, falsify records, reports, or applications, or other related activity in violation of the requirements prescribed by this *Code* shall be a violation of this *Code*. Such violations shall be cause for immediate suspension or revocation of any related licenses, certificates, or permits issued by this jurisdiction. In addition, any such violation shall be subject to any other criminal or civil penalties as available by the laws of this jurisdiction.

(3) Revocation shall be constituted when the permittee is duly notified by the authority having jurisdiction.

(4) Any person who engages in any business, operation, or occupation, or uses any premises, after the permit issued therefor has been suspended or revoked pursuant to the provisions of this *Code*, and before such suspended permit has been reinstated or a new permit issued, shall be in violation of this *Code*.

(5) A permit shall be predicated upon compliance with the requirements of this *Code* and shall constitute written authority issued by the authority having jurisdiction to install electrical equipment. Any permit issued under this *Code* shall not take the place of any other license or permit required by other regulations or laws of this jurisdiction.

(6) The authority having jurisdiction shall be permitted to require an inspection prior to the issuance of a permit.

(7) A permit issued under this *Code* shall continue until revoked or for the period of time designated on the permit. The permit shall be issued to one person or business only and for the location or purpose described in the permit. Any change that affects any of the conditions of the permit shall require a new or amended permit.

(H) Applications and Extensions. Applications and extensions of permits shall conform to the following:

(1) The authority having jurisdiction shall be permitted to grant an extension of the permit time period upon presentation by the permittee of a satisfactory reason for failure to start or complete the work or activity authorized by the permit.

(2) Applications for permits shall be made to the authority having jurisdiction on forms provided by the jurisdiction and shall include the applicant's answers in full to inquiries set forth on such forms. Applications for permits shall be accompanied by such data as required by the authority having jurisdiction, such as plans and specifications, location, and so forth. Fees shall be determined as required by local laws.

(3) The authority having jurisdiction shall review all applications submitted and issue permits as required. If an application for a permit is rejected by the authority having jurisdiction, the applicant shall be advised of the reasons for such rejection. Permits for activities requiring evidence of financial responsibility by the jurisdiction shall not be issued unless proof of required financial responsibility is furnished.

80.21 Plans Review. Review of plans and specifications shall conform to (A) through (C).

(A) Authority. For new construction, modification, or rehabilitation, the authority having jurisdiction shall be permitted to review construction documents and drawings.

(B) Responsibility of the Applicant. It shall be the responsibility of the applicant to ensure the following:

(1) The construction documents include all of the electrical requirements.

(2) The construction documents and drawings are correct and in compliance with the applicable codes and standards.

(C) Responsibility of the Authority Having Jurisdiction. It shall be the responsibility of the authority having jurisdiction to promulgate rules that cover the following:

(1) Review of construction documents and drawings within established time frames for the purpose of acceptance or to provide reasons for nonacceptance

(2) Review and approval by the authority having jurisdiction shall not relieve the applicant of the responsibility of compliance with this *Code*.

(3) Where field conditions necessitate any substantial change from the approved plan, the authority having jurisdiction shall be permitted to require that the corrected plans be submitted for approval.

80.23 Notice of Violations, Penalties. Notice of violations and penalties shall conform to (A) and (B).

(A) Violations.

(1) Whenever the authority having jurisdiction determines that there are violations of this *Code*, a written notice shall be issued to confirm such findings.

(2) Any order or notice issued pursuant to this *Code* shall be served upon the owner, operator, occupant, or other person responsible for the condition or violation, either by personal service or mail or by delivering the same to, and leaving it with, some person of responsibility upon the premises. For unattended or abandoned locations, a copy of such order or notice shall be posted on the premises in a conspicuous place at or near the entrance to such premises and the order or notice shall be mailed by registered or certified mail, with return receipt requested, to the last known address of the owner, occupant, or both.

(B) Penalties.

(1) Any person who fails to comply with the provisions of this *Code* or who fails to carry out an order made pursuant to this *Code* or violates any condition attached to a permit, approval, or certificate shall be subject to the penalties established by this jurisdiction.

(2) Failure to comply with the time limits of an abatement notice or other corrective notice issued by the authority having jurisdiction shall result in each day that such violation continues being regarded as a new and separate offense.

(3) Any person, firm, or corporation who shall willfully violate any of the applicable provisions of this article shall be guilty of a misdemeanor and, upon conviction thereof, shall be punished by a fine of not less than _____dollars ($_____) or more than _____dollars ($_____) for each offense, together with the costs of prosecution, imprisonment, or both, for not less than _____ (_____) days or more than _____ (_____) days.

80.25 Connection to Electricity Supply. Connections to the electric supply shall conform to (A) through (E).

(A) Authorization. Except where work is done under an annual permit and except as otherwise provided in 80.25, it shall be unlawful for any person, firm, or corporation to make connection to a supply of electricity or to supply electricity to any electric equipment installation for which a permit is required or that has been disconnected or ordered to be disconnected.

(B) Special Consideration. By special permission of the authority having jurisdiction, temporary power shall be permitted to be supplied to the premises for specific needs of the construction project. The Board shall determine what needs are permitted under this provision.

(C) Notification. If, within _____ business days after the Electrical Inspector is notified of the completion of an installation of electric equipment, other than a temporary approval installation, the Electrical Inspector has neither authorized connection nor disapproved the installation, the supplier of electricity is authorized to make connections and supply electricity to such installation.

(D) Other Territories. If an installation or electric equipment is located in any territory where an Electrical Inspector has not been authorized or is not required to make inspections, the supplier of electricity is authorized to make connections and supply electricity to such installations.

(E) Disconnection. Where a connection is made to an installation that has not been inspected, as outlined in the preceding paragraphs of this section, the supplier of electricity shall immediately report such connection to the Chief Electrical Inspector. If, upon subsequent inspection, it is found that the installation is not in conformity with the provisions of Article 80, the Chief Electrical Inspector shall notify the person, firm, or corporation making the installation to rectify the defects and, if such work is not completed within fifteen (15) business days or a longer period as may be specified by the Board, the Board shall have the authority to cause the disconnection of that portion of the installation that is not in conformity.

80.27 Inspector's Qualifications.

(A) Certificate. All electrical inspectors shall be certified by a nationally recognized inspector certification program accepted by the Board. The certification program shall specifically qualify the inspector in electrical inspections. No person shall be employed as an Electrical Inspector unless that person is the holder of an Electrical Inspector's certificate of qualification issued by the Board, except that any person who on the date on which this law went into effect was serving as a legally appointed Electrical Inspector of _____ shall, upon application and payment of the prescribed fee and without examination, be issued a special certificate permitting him or her to continue to serve as an Electrical Inspector in the same territory.

(B) Experience. Electrical inspector applicants shall demonstrate the following:

(1) Have a demonstrated knowledge of the standard materials and methods used in the installation of electric equipment

(2) Be well versed in the approved methods of construction for safety to persons and property

(3) Be well versed in the statutes of _____ relating to electrical work and the *National Electrical Code*, as approved by the American National Standards Institute

(4) Have had at least ____ years' experience as an Electrical Inspector or ____ years in the installation of electrical equipment. In lieu of such experience, the applicant shall be a graduate in electrical engineering or of a similar curriculum of a college or university considered by the Board as having suitable requirements for graduation and shall have had two years' practical electrical experience.

(C) Recertification. Electrical inspectors shall be recertified as established by provisions of the applicable certification program.

(D) Revocation and Suspension of Authority. The Board shall have the authority to revoke an inspector's authority to conduct inspections within a jurisdiction.

80.29 Liability for Damages. Article 80 shall not be construed to affect the responsibility or liability of any party owning, designing, operating, controlling, or installing any electric equipment for damages to persons or property caused by a defect therein, nor shall the _____ or any of its employees be held as assuming any such liability by reason of the inspection, reinspection, or other examination authorized.

80.31 Validity. If any section, subsection, sentence, clause, or phrase of Article 80 is for any reason held to be unconstitutional, such decision shall not affect the validity of the remaining portions of Article 80.

80.33 Repeal of Conflicting Acts. All acts or parts of acts in conflict with the provisions of Article 80 are hereby repealed.

80.35 Effective Date. Article 80 shall take effect _____ (_____) days after its passage and publication.

Index

NFPA 70

National Electrical Code®

2005 Edition

Reference: 680.26
TIA 05-2 (NFPA 70)
(SC 05-7-15)/Log No. 821)

Pursuant to Section 5 of the NFPA Regulations Governing Committee Projects, the National Fire Protection Association has issued the following Tentative Interim Amendment to NFPA 70, *National Electrical Code®*, 2005 edition. The TIA was processed by the National Electrical Code® Committee, and was issued by the Standards Council on July 29, 2005, with an effective date of August 18, 2005.

A Tentative Interim Amendment is tentative because it has not been processed through the entire standards-making procedures. It is interim because it is effective only between editions of the standard. A TIA automatically becomes a proposal of the proponent for the next edition of the standard; as such, it then is subject to all of the procedures of the standards-making process.

1. Revise 680.26 (C) & 680.26 (C)(1) as follows:

(C) Equipotential Bonding Grid. The parts specified in 680.26(B) shall be connected to an equipotential bonding grid with a solid copper conductor, insulated, covered, or bare, not smaller than 8 AWG or rigid metal conduit of brass or other identified corrosion-resistant metal conduit. Connection shall be made by exothermic welding or by listed pressure connectors or clamps that are labeled as being suitable for the purpose and are of stainless steel, brass, copper, or copper alloy. The equipotential bonding grid shall conform to the contours of the pool and shall extend within or under paved walking surfaces for 1 m (3 ft) horizontally beyond the inside walls of the pool and shall be permitted to be any of the following:

Exception: The equipotential bonding grid shall not be required to be installed under the bottom of or vertically along the walls of vinyl lined polymer wall, fiberglass composite, or other pools constructed of nonconductive materials. Any metal parts of the pool, including metal structural supports, shall be bonded in accordance with 680.26(B). For the purposes of this section, poured concrete, pneumatically applied (sprayed) concrete, and concrete block, with painted or plastered coatings, shall be considered conductive material.

(1) Structural Reinforcing Steel. The structural reinforcing steel of a concrete pool or deck where the reinforcing rods are bonded together by the usual steel tie wires or the equivalent. Where deck reinforcing steel is not an integral part of the pool, the deck reinforcing steel shall be bonded to other parts of the bonding grid using a minimum 8 AWG solid copper conductor. Connection shall be per 680.26(D).

Sequence of Events Leading to Publication of an NFPA Committee Document

Call goes out for proposals to amend existing document or for recommendations on new document.

▼

Committee meets to act on proposals, to develop its own proposals, and to prepare its report.

▼

Committee votes on proposals by letter ballot. If two-thirds approve, report goes forward. Lacking two-thirds approval, report returns to committee.

▼

Report — *Report on Proposals* (ROP) — is published for public review and comment.

▼

Committee meets to act on each public comment received.

▼

Committee votes on comments by letter ballot. If two-thirds approve, supplementary report goes forward. Lacking two-thirds approval, supplementary report returns to committee.

▼

Supplementary report — *Report on Comments* (ROC) — is published for public review.

▼

NFPA membership meets (Annual or Fall Meeting) and acts on committee report (ROP or ROC).

▼

Committee votes on any amendments to report approved at NFPA Annual or Fall Meeting.

▼

Appeals to Standards Council on Association action must be filed within 20 days of the NFPA Annual or Fall Meeting.

▼

Standards Council decides, based on all evidence, whether or not to issue standard or to take other action, including upholding any appeals.

Committee Membership Classifications

The following classifications apply to Technical Committee members and represent their principal interest in the activity of the committee.

M   *Manufacturer:* A representative of a maker or marketer of a product, assembly, or system, or portion thereof, that is affected by the standard.

U   *User:* A representative of an entity that is subject to the provisions of the standard or that voluntarily uses the standard.

I/M   *Installer/Maintainer:* A representative of an entity that is in the business of installing or maintaining a product, assembly, or system affected by the standard.

L   *Labor:* A labor representative or employee concerned with safety in the workplace.

R/T   *Applied Research/Testing Laboratory:* A representative of an independent testing laboratory or independent applied research organization that promulgates and/or enforces standards.

E   *Enforcing Authority:* A representative of an agency or an organization that promulgates and/or enforces standards.

I   *Insurance:* A representative of an insurance company, broker, agent, bureau, or inspection agency.

C   *Consumer:* A person who is, or represents, the ultimate purchaser of a product, system, or service affected by the standard, but who is not included in the *User* classification.

SE   *Special Expert:* A person not representing any of the previous classifications, but who has a special expertise in the scope of the standard or portion thereof.

NOTES:

1. "Standard" connotes code, standard, recommended practice, or guide.

2. A representative includes an employee.

3. While these classifications will be used by the Standards Council to achieve a balance for Technical Committees, the Standards Council may determine that new classifications of members or unique interests need representation in order to foster the best possible committee deliberations on any project. In this connection, the Standards Council may make such appointments as it seems appropriate in the public interest, such as the classification of "Utilities" in the National Electrical Code Committee.

4. Representatives of subsidiaries of any group are generally considered to have the same classification as the parent organization.

2008 *National Electrical Code*® Schedule
(2007 *World Safety Congress and Exposition*®)

Date	Event
November 4, 2005 (5:00 PM EST)	Receipt of Proposals
January 9–21, 2006	Code-Making Panel Meetings (ROP)
April 24–28, 2006	Correlating Committee Meeting
July 14, 2006	ROP to Mailing House
October 20, 2006 (5:00 EST)	Receipt of Comments
November 28–December 9, 2006	Code-Making Panel Meetings (ROC)
February 19–23, 2007	Correlating Committee Meeting
March 23, 2007	ROC to Mailing House
June 3–7, 2007	*NFPA World Safety Congress and Exposition*® (Location TBD)
July 2007	Standards Council Issuance

Anyone may submit proposals to amend the 2005 *Code*. A sample form for this purpose may be obtained from the Secretary of the Standards Council at NFPA headquarters, and a copy is included in this *Code*.

Method of Submitting a Proposal to Revise the *National Electrical Code*®

The following is based on the NFPA Regulations Governing Committee Projects, adopted by the Board of Directors in October 1996 (last amended in March 2004).

A proposal to revise the 2005 edition of the *National Electrical Code* must be submitted so that the proposal is received at NFPA headquarters by November 4, 2005, as indicated in the time schedule for the 2008 *National Electrical Code*. A proposal received after this date will be returned to the submitter. The proposal is to be sent to the Secretary of the Standards Council at NFPA Headquarters, 1 Batterymarch Park, P.O. Box 9101, Quincy, MA 02169-7471.

Each proposal must include the following:

1. Identification of the submitter (the person's name) and his or her affiliation (i.e., committee, organization, company), where appropriate
2. An indication that the proposal is for revision of the 2005 *National Electrical Code* and identification of the specific section number, table number (or equivalent identification) of the section, etc., to be revised
3. A statement of the problem and substantiation for the proposal
4. The proposed text of the proposal, including the wording to be added, revised (and how revised), or deleted

Proposals that do not include all of the above information may not be acted on by the National Electrical Code Committee.

It is preferred that the forms available from NFPA for submittal of proposals be used. A separate proposal form should be used for revision of each section of the *Code*.

A proposal form appears on the following page.

FORM FOR PROPOSALS FOR 2008 *NATIONAL ELECTRICAL CODE*®

Mail to: Secretary, Standards Council
National Fire Protection Association
1 Batterymarch Park, P.O. Box 9101
Quincy, Massachusetts 02169-7471

Fax to: (617) 770-3500

Notes: 1. All proposals must be received by 5:00 p.m. EST on Friday, November 4, 2005.
Proposals received after 5:00 p.m. EST, Friday, November 4, 2005, will be returned to the submitter.
2. Type or print legibly in black ink. Limit each proposal to a SINGLE section. Use a separate copy for each proposal.
3. If supplementary material (photographs, diagrams, reports, etc.) is included, you may be required to submit sufficient copies for all members and alternates of the technical committee.

Please indicate in which format you wish to receive your ROP/ROC: ❏ electronic   ❏ paper   ❏ download

Date _____ Name _____ Tel. No.: _____

Company _____

Street Address _____

Organization Represented (if any) _____

1. Section/Paragraph _____

2. Proposal Recommends (check one)   ❏ new text   ❏ revised text   ❏ deleted text

3. Proposal (include proposed new or revised wording or identify wording to be deleted). Note: Proposed text should be in a legislative format: i.e., use underscore to denote wording to be inserted (<u>inserted wording</u>) and strike-through to denote wording to be deleted (~~deleted wording~~).

4. Statement of Problem and Substantiation for Proposal. Note: State the problem that will be resolved by your recommendation; give the specific reason for your proposal and include copies of the tests, research papers, fire experience, etc. If more than 200 words, it may be abstracted for publication.

5. ❏ **This Proposal is original material.** Note: Original material is considered to be the submitter's own idea based on or as a result of his/her own experience, thought, or research and, to the best of his/her knowledge, is not copied from another source.

❏ **This Proposal is not original material; its source (if known) is as follows:** _____

**If you need further information on the standards-making process, please contact the
Standards Administration Department at (617) 984-7249.
For technical assistance, please call NFPA at (617) 770-3000.**

I hereby grant the NFPA all and full rights in copyright, in this proposal, and I understand that I acquire no rights in any publication of NFPA in which this proposal in this or another similar or analogous form is used.

_____
Signature (required)

PLEASE USE SEPARATE FORM FOR EACH PROPOSAL

FORM FOR PROPOSALS FOR 2008 *NATIONAL ELECTRICAL CODE®*

Mail to: Secretary, Standards Council
National Fire Protection Association
1 Batterymarch Park, P.O. Box 9101
Quincy, Massachusetts 02169-7471

Fax to: (617) 770-3500

FOR OFFICE USE ONLY
Log # _____
Date Rec'd _____

Notes:
1. All proposals must be received by 5:00 p.m. EST on Friday, November 4, 2005.
   Proposals received after 5:00 p.m. EST, Friday, November 4, 2005, will be returned to the submitter.
2. Type or print legibly in black ink. Limit each proposal to a SINGLE section. Use a separate copy for each proposal.
3. If supplementary material (photographs, diagrams, reports, etc.) is included, you may be required to submit sufficient copies for all members and alternates of the technical committee.

Please indicate in which format you wish to receive your ROP/ROC: ❏ electronic   ❏ paper   ❏ download

Date _____ Name _____ Tel. No.: _____

Company _____

Street Address _____

Organization Represented (if any) _____

1. Section/Paragraph _____

2. **Proposal Recommends** (check one)   ❏ new text   ❏ revised text   ❏ deleted text

3. **Proposal (include proposed new or revised wording or identify wording to be deleted).** Note: Proposed text should be in a legislative format: i.e., use underscore to denote wording to be inserted (inserted wording) and strike-through to denote wording to be deleted (deleted wording).

4. **Statement of Problem and Substantiation for Proposal.** Note: State the problem that will be resolved by your recommendation; give the specific reason for your proposal and include copies of the tests, research papers, fire experience, etc. If more than 200 words, it may be abstracted for publication.

5. ❏ **This Proposal is original material.** Note: Original material is considered to be the submitter's own idea based on or as a result of his/her own experience, thought, or research and, to the best of his/her knowledge, is not copied from another source.

   ❏ **This Proposal is not original material; its source (if known) is as follows:** _____

**If you need further information on the standards-making process, please contact the
Standards Administration Department at (617) 984-7249.
For technical assistance, please call NFPA at (617) 770-3000.**

I hereby grant the NFPA all and full rights in copyright, in this proposal, and I understand that I acquire no rights in any publication of NFPA in which this proposal in this or another similar or analogous form is used.

_____
Signature (required)

PLEASE USE SEPARATE FORM FOR EACH PROPOSAL

FORM FOR PROPOSALS FOR 2008 *NATIONAL ELECTRICAL CODE*®

Mail to: Secretary, Standards Council
National Fire Protection Association
1 Batterymarch Park, P.O. Box 9101
Quincy, Massachusetts 02169-7471

Fax to: (617) 770-3500

Notes:
1. All proposals must be received by 5:00 p.m. EST on Friday, November 4, 2005.
   Proposals received after 5:00 p.m. EST, Friday, November 4, 2005, will be returned to the submitter.
2. Type or print legibly in black ink. Limit each proposal to a SINGLE section. Use a separate copy for each proposal.
3. If supplementary material (photographs, diagrams, reports, etc.) is included, you may be required to submit sufficient copies for all members and alternates of the technical committee.

Please indicate in which format you wish to receive your ROP/ROC: ❏ electronic ❏ paper ❏ download

Date _____ Name _____ Tel. No.: _____

Company _____

Street Address _____

Organization Represented (if any) _____

1. Section/Paragraph _____

2. **Proposal Recommends** (check one) ❏ new text ❏ revised text ❏ deleted text

3. **Proposal (include proposed new or revised wording or identify wording to be deleted).** Note: Proposed text should be in a legislative format: i.e., use underscore to denote wording to be inserted (<u>inserted wording</u>) and strike-through to denote wording to be deleted (~~deleted wording~~).

4. **Statement of Problem and Substantiation for Proposal.** Note: State the problem that will be resolved by your recommendation; give the specific reason for your proposal and include copies of the tests, research papers, fire experience, etc. If more than 200 words, it may be abstracted for publication.

5. ❏ **This Proposal is original material.** Note: Original material is considered to be the submitter's own idea based on or as a result of his/her own experience, thought, or research and, to the best of his/her knowledge, is not copied from another source.

   ❏ **This Proposal is not original material; its source (if known) is as follows:** _____

**If you need further information on the standards-making process, please contact the
Standards Administration Department at (617) 984-7249.
For technical assistance, please call NFPA at (617) 770-3000.**

I hereby grant the NFPA all and full rights in copyright, in this proposal, and I understand that I acquire no rights in any publication of NFPA in which this proposal in this or another similar or analogous form is used.

_____
Signature (required)

PLEASE USE SEPARATE FORM FOR EACH PROPOSAL

FORM FOR PROPOSALS FOR 2008 *NATIONAL ELECTRICAL CODE*®

Mail to: Secretary, Standards Council
National Fire Protection Association
1 Batterymarch Park, P.O. Box 9101
Quincy, Massachusetts 02169-7471

Fax to: (617) 770-3500

<table>
<tr><td>FOR OFFICE USE ONLY
Log # _____
Date Rec'd _____</td></tr>
</table>

Notes:
1. All proposals must be received by 5:00 p.m. EST on Friday, November 4, 2005.
   Proposals received after 5:00 p.m. EST, Friday, November 4, 2005, will be returned to the submitter.
2. Type or print legibly in black ink. Limit each proposal to a SINGLE section. Use a separate copy for each proposal.
3. If supplementary material (photographs, diagrams, reports, etc.) is included, you may be required to submit sufficient copies for all members and alternates of the technical committee.

Please indicate in which format you wish to receive your ROP/ROC: ❏ electronic ❏ paper ❏ download

Date _____ Name _____ Tel. No.:_____

Company _____

Street Address _____

Organization Represented (if any) _____

1. Section/Paragraph _____

2. Proposal Recommends (check one) ❏ new text ❏ revised text ❏ deleted text

3. Proposal (include proposed new or revised wording or identify wording to be deleted). Note: Proposed text should be in a legislative format: i.e., use underscore to denote wording to be inserted (<u>inserted wording</u>) and strike-through to denote wording to be deleted (~~deleted wording~~).

4. Statement of Problem and Substantiation for Proposal. Note: State the problem that will be resolved by your recommendation; give the specific reason for your proposal and include copies of the tests, research papers, fire experience, etc. If more than 200 words, it may be abstracted for publication.

5. ❏ **This Proposal is original material.** Note: Original material is considered to be the submitter's own idea based on or as a result of his/her own experience, thought, or research and, to the best of his/her knowledge, is not copied from another source.

❏ **This Proposal is not original material; its source (if known) is as follows:** _____

<table>
<tr><td>If you need further information on the standards-making process, please contact the
Standards Administration Department at (617) 984-7249.
For technical assistance, please call NFPA at (617) 770-3000.</td></tr>
</table>

I hereby grant the NFPA all and full rights in copyright, in this proposal, and I understand that I acquire no rights in any publication of NFPA in which this proposal in this or another similar or analogous form is used.

_____
Signature (required)

PLEASE USE SEPARATE FORM FOR EACH PROPOSAL

Use This Code Better

NFPA membership puts the code information you need for your job in your hands faster. Join NFPA today and get:

- FREE answers to your code questions as often as you want from an NFPA expert via email or over the phone to save you time and money [arrow/burst by this: Not available to the general public!]
- Voting privileges on proposed changes to all NFPA codes and standards
- NFPA Journal magazine subscription for the latest in building, fire, electrical and life safety developments around the world
- Timely alerts regarding changes to NFPA codes and standards
- Members-only access to code information and reports at www.nfpa.org
- 10% across-the-board discount on all NFPA publications, products, seminars and services

"As an NFPA member, you have faster, easy access to valuable code information and contacts you can go to for specific help. Those connections save you time and money on the job. I can't imagine doing my job without belonging to NFPA."

Raymond A. Grill, P.E., Sr., Vice President
Rolf Jensen & Associates, Inc., Fairfax, VA

✓ YES! I want to join NFPA for faster access to the code information and resources I need in my job.

1. Please Complete:

Name_____

Title_____

Organization_____

Address_____

City_____ State_____ Zip_____

Country_____

Day Phone_____ Fax_____

Email_____

Your Job Title: (please check one)
- ☐ Architect, Engineer, Consultant, Contractor (C17)
- ☐ Owner, President, Manager, Administrator (C10)
- ☐ Fire Chief, Other Fire Service (A11)
- ☐ Facilities Safety Officer (F14)
- ☐ Inspector, Building Official, Fire Marshal (F03)
- ☐ Loss Control, Risk Manager (L11)
- ☐ Other:_____ (G11)

Type of Organization: (please check one)
- ☐ Architecture, Engineering, Contracting (A14)
- ☐ Government (C12)
- ☐ Fire Service, Public and Private (AA1)
- ☐ Industrial Firm (Factory, Warehouse) (C11)
- ☐ Commercial Firm (Office, Retail, Lodging, Restaurant) (G13)
- ☐ Institutional (Health Care, Education, Detention, Museums) (B11)
- ☐ Electrical Services, Installation (J11)
- ☐ Insurance, Risk Management (B12)
- ☐ Utilities (G12)
- ☐ Other:_____ (G11)

2. Please choose your method of payment:

Annual Dues: $135
- ☐ Bill me later ☐ Payment enclosed (payable to: NFPA)
- ☐ Purchase Order #:_____ (Please attach this form to your Purchase Order)

Charge my: ☐ AMEX® ☐ VISA® ☐ MasterCard® ☐ Discover®

Card #:_____ Exp:____ /____

Signature:**X**_____

Regular membership in NFPA is individual and non-transferable. Voting privileges begin after 180 days of membership. Annual membership dues include a $40.50 subscription to NFPA Journal®.

Send it now!

Detach and Mail this page to:
NFPA
11 Tracy Drive
Avon, MA 02322-9908

OR

Fax Toll Free 1-800-593-6372

For Fastest Service:
Call Toll Free 1-800-344-3555
(M–F, 8:30 am – 8:00 pm ET)
or visit www.nfpa.org

For international orders:
please call 1-617-770-3000
or fax 1-508-895-8301

Want More From Your NFPA Membership? Get it for FREE!

As an NFPA member, you can enroll in your industry-specific Section now for free and get direct access to the information that impacts your job the most, including:

- Insight from your industry peers on code use in action
- Free information and publications on the latest building, fire, electrical and life safety news in your industry
- Opportunities to directly impact code changes and development you want to see
- Credentials to build your career and professional recognition

Section membership is FREE to all NFPA members!
Enroll in your industry-specific Section online at www.nfpa.org ...
or look for more information and a free Section enrollment form in your NFPA New Member Kit.

Dues amount subject to change.   9H-MBR-12